THE
WEIRD
A COMPENDIUM OF STRANGE AND DARK STORIES

FICTION ANTHOLOGIES EDITED BY ANN AND JEFF VANDERMEER

The New Weird
Best American Fantasy
Best American Fantasy Volume 2
Fast Ships, Black Sails
Steampunk
Steampunk II: Steampunk Reloaded
The Thackery T. Lambshead Cabinet of Curiosities

FICTION ANTHOLOGIES EDITED BY JEFF VANDERMEER

The Thackery T. Lambshead Pocket Guide to Eccentric & Discredited Diseases (with Mark Roberts)
The Steampunk Bible (with S. J. Chambers)

BOOKS BY JEFF VANDERMEER

Veniss Underground
City of Saints and Madmen
Shriek: An Afterword
Secret Lives
Predator: South China Sea
The Surgeon's Tale and Other Stories (with Cat Rambo)
Finch
The Third Bear
Booklife

THE WEIRD

A COMPENDIUM OF STRANGE AND DARK STORIES

Edited by Ann and Jeff VanderMeer

A TOM DOHERTY ASSOCIATES BOOK
NEW YORK

This is a work of fiction. All of the characters, organizations, and events portrayed in this collection are either products of the authors' imaginations or are used fictitiously.

THE WEIRD

First published in Great Britain by Corvus, an imprint of Atlantic Books Ltc.

A Tor Book
Published by Tom Doherty Associates, LLC
175 Fifth Avenue
New York, NY 10010

Tor® is a registered trademark of Tom Doherty Associates, LLC.

ISBN 978-0-7653-3360-5

Printed in the United States of America

Dedicated to Nicolas Cheetham, Gio Clairval, and all of the editors who helped us by way of example or advice

THE WEIRD

FOREWEIRD

Michael Moorcock

KEEP Austin Weird, it says on a popular bumper sticker for the city where I spend much of my time. That old Anglo-Saxon word for fate or destiny has taken on a lot of meanings. And, should you mention a coincidence to someone, they are likely to respond 'Weird!' That kid next door who prefers to read rather than play is weird. How weird is that? Weird has become one of those useful words which stands in for a certain look or rough telepathy – we all know pretty much what is meant. And if we don't we ask, 'What kind of weird?' And the answer, as you'll find, might be in any one of these stories.

Science fiction was once described as the only popular fiction defined by what it is not. Perhaps the weird story can be defined in the same way. In popular terms, it came to mean a supernatural story in something of the Gothic tradition and we currently have a plethora of bad Gothic, 'shudder tales' topping the charts in the media. There vampires, werewolves and ghouls produce an effect of the kind which made bosoms heave by the thousand in early Victorian times before the genre was relegated to the ranks of the shilling shocker or the tuppeny blood, still popular with the general public, if not polite society. No doubt the same fate awaits the children of *Twilight*…

The 'blood' at the bottom of the literary pond was the 19th century's version of the splatter tale in the 20th and 21st. And what is left after other definitions are exhausted is the weird story. The weird story can contain all the quality of a fine Modernist writer like Conrad or Bowen, a great popular novelist like Greene or a master of the numinous like Lansdale, whose finest stories often contain only a slight twist in reality to make them so good. Weird? We're clearly comfortable with a term covering pretty much anything from absurdism to horror, even occasionally social realism.

There are no established rules for the weird tale, which is at least part of the attraction if the story an author wants to tell can't readily be told in an established form. Although it might often contain a supernatural element, or a suggested supernatural element, it does not have to do so. And I think we can now discard the notion that 'weird' in fiction only concerns itself with the manifestly supernatural and is written by heterosexual boys without girlfriends. I think the downgrading in critical esteem for the weird story happened when the market found something else it could commodify and then aim at a large specialized market to the extent that a certain type of reader will now attack a story precisely because it doesn't fulfill the expectations of category. Both the *Star Wars* and *Friday the Thirteenth* franchises have much to answer for.

Generally, the real tensions in literary forms come from that which can be readily commodified and branded and that which cannot. Fritz Leiber, one of the best American stylists I knew, told me that he had talked about this with two *Weird Tales* contributors, Robert Bloch (of *Psycho* fame) and Henry Kuttner (primarily a science fiction writer). All had begun writing unrationalized fiction, having much in common with surrealism or absurdism, to discover very quickly that literary magazines wanted an approximation of realism and commercial markets needed to know *why,* forcing you to cook up some sort of rationalization for the events you described so that you came to see your failure to rationalize as some sort of flaw or laziness in yourself. These days, writing for the supernatural fiction market is one way of meeting commercial interests halfway but, once the ambitious writer has established a reputation, it is common, almost endemic, that they begin dropping the generic elements from their work and hope to take their readership with them without otherwise compromising. Ray Bradbury, published originally in pulps like *Weird Tales* or *Startling Stories,* achieved this, as did J.G. Ballard, also first published in a generic fantasy magazine.

Crossword puzzles don't necessarily make good fiction. The reader of the Victorian Gothic – of Lewis and Maturin – demanded that most weird events be grounded in a 'realistic' explanation – Romantic specters must be the result of villains working explicable, practical clockwork or novel scientific inventions such as candle-powered magic lanterns. The 1930s reader of *Weird Tales* did not mind the ghost being, as it were, real but there had to be a suggestion of a material motive, say, in the minds of lurkers at the threshold. Gothic revelations of base motives behind fake ghosts and so on eventually became absorbed into the popular 'thriller', especially those published in the first decades of the 20th century. The weird increasingly, since the days of Charles Williams to the present, shares much in common with supernatural fiction but it is not merely another name for it.

What is good about the majority of these stories is precisely that they leave you with many more questions than answers, the mark, in my view, of a superior kind of fiction. As in M.R. James's classic *Whistle and I'll Come to You, My Lad,* it trusts the reader to be the ultimate interpreter. It does, in fact, what most of our best fiction does, irrespective of category. When the great actor Kemble dismissed the ghost in *Hamlet* and addressed himself not to the conventional white sheet but to an empty chair, he played an infinite jest on playwright and audience which continues to open that scene and others to a thousand interpretations. The audience's own imagination was tapped. Hamlet's sanity is thoroughly questioned. Not only do we continue to wonder who it is Hamlet truly loves, if anyone, but we can speculate endlessly about his state of mind. Is he always pretending to be mad? Is the specter a joke played by others on a disturbed, mourning young man or does he conjure specters from his own mind? If so, what can we make of that mind and its disturbed owner's motives? That is why Hamlet is perhaps the most and best performed and least readily understood of Shakespeare's plays.

The surrealists and the existentialists loved the fantastic story, the weird story, because they had been knocked sideways by psychoanalysis and had come to understand how the unconscious told its tales, apparently through eccentric, innocent or unusual images and strange behavior. Is that, we asked, why we fear 'the unknown'? Because it reveals all the lies and delusions by which life becomes bearable? But modern relativism can't easily carry the Freudian narrative either, these days. Or perhaps singles out one possibility amongst many – or rather takes it for granted there is one version amongst many. We modern readers must make our way in a complex world by resorting to complicated narratives, unending analysis. It could even be that, as populist rhetoric fills our print and airwaves, we tend to embrace complexity in the face of journalistic simplicities. We learn new or modified modes of story-telling precisely as we changed with the coming of film, TV or, more recently, the net. Many of the givens which helped us appreciate Modernism are today dismissed in favor of a multiplicity of interpretation. We're uncomfortable, too, with the idealistic optimism of those 20th-century writers who thought they followed Zola (though even the great Sinclair Lewis had to write some fantasy on occasions because sometimes only the weird tale will best suit the experience). This unsettling of the literary waters generally helps to enrich a work and make it freshly challenging, even confrontational, sometimes attacking what it perceives very accurately as misguided social assumptions just as magic realism, inspired by the likes of Borges, refreshed social realism at the point where it had become almost wholly generic and had therefore lost vitality, offering a comfort to the soul rather than confrontation with received ideas. Similarly, differences between generic and 'literary' fiction began to break down by the 1960s when the likes of J.G.Ballard began to appear in magazines such as *Science Fiction Adventures,* where stories like *The Drowned World* were placed because at the time nothing else in the author allowed him to approach the tragic dreamscapes of his imagination through any other form. Kurt Vonnegut, Philip K. Dick and others sold to genre magazines. Mervyn Peake, the absurdist master who rarely made use of the supernatural, was published in *Science Fantasy Magazine* simply because I happened to know Peake and the magazine's editor and I acted as intermediary after Peake failed to place the story elsewhere. The story was weird and *suis generis.* The editor was delighted to run it.

For me, the appeal of the weird story is precisely that it is designed to disturb. At least if left to itself. Maybe all we can really say about it is that it suits a certain mood in the reader; that it's subtler and more complex than generic fantasy stories.

The best writers, as this collection shows, write the best weird stories. So the weird story is Bradbury, Kafka, Lovecraft. It is Borges, Leiber, Angela Carter, Chabon. Clever artistry guides our encounters with the unknown and the numinous. At its best the weird story commands us with a style both original and engaging but not necessarily good in the opinion of its day. My own great hero George Meredith – who wrote a few weird tales and even some pretty good weird poetry (what a shame there wasn't room here for *The Woods of Westermaine*) was hailed towards the end of his lifetime as the greatest British writer since Shakespeare and today you'd be hard put to find even a second-hand copy of his late masterpiece *The Amazing Marriage.* Time and the multiverse are fond of these ironic tricks.

That said, the weird story certainly endures. *Otranto* is still in print as are *Frankenstein* and *Melmoth.* None is especially memorable for its style *but for communicating the novelty with which it struck the writer.* Inspiration somehow smacks the reader between the eyes and keeps them reading no matter how gratingly bad the prose might be, even when a story has given birth to a million other stories so that the basic premise and story are familiar to millions more readers. Our opinions of a writer don't define where they'll end up in the canon and one decade's canon can be utterly forgotten by another. Half the writers I once championed as under-noticed or 'marginalized' are now regarded as central to any well-read reader's education. Equally, half the people I knew as friends and admired as writers, who were thought central to any contemporary syllabus, are often not even in print and it is often difficult to understand how or why they went out of fashion and others came in. The public and academia are pretty fickle in picking favorites. What made that weird musical *The Wizard of Oz* fail to get an Oscar in 1939 but become a perennial favourite to this day while *The Rains Came*, which did win the Oscar, is scarcely known now at all? Is the 'weirdness' that made *Citizen Kane* bad box-office in its day the same quality which gave the movie its enduring place among the ten greatest American films? Certainly a great many of the stories here were originally published rather obscurely, many of them in pulp magazines, yet have rarely been out of print since.

When I was young, few of the weird writers I enjoyed were known to the general public, yet now they go into many editions and translations. Even Kafka was somewhat marginalized. When I was young, only a few non-Argentinean Anglophones had read Borges. I had them related to me by a Spanish-speaking Swede while hitch-hiking across Europe. His first story in English was translated by Anthony Boucher (co-founder of *The Magazine of Fantasy and Science Fiction*) in 1948 but further stories would not appear in English until 1962, published by Grove Press. Howard was still thoroughly in the margins, published in small editions by obscure presses: now he appears as a Penguin Modern Classic. Few had heard of Lovecraft and fewer still admired him. I am sure that Grin, the great Russian fantasist, will eventually see translation and take his place beside the fine writers collected here. Firbank, the marvelous English absurdist, Richardson, creator of Engelbrecht, the surrealist boxing dwarf, Vian, who gave us the astonishing *L'Écume des jours* and died watching a bad movie version of his novel *J'irai cracher sur vos tombes*, have all yet to become familiar to the general US reader. If you are unfamiliar with them, I suspect your curiosity will be whetted enough for you to find them with the rest of those weird writers kept from this book by length.

While I have managed to dodge the question of exactly what weird fiction is, I have helped, I hope, describe a little of its appeal. 'Weird', the modern-day synonym for 'strange' or 'unusual', has proven so useful that a modern style of fiction championed by the likes of China Miéville, M.John Harrison and Jeff VanderMeer is now known as 'the new weird'. Judging by the quality of work so far produced, it will do nicely for now.

Michael Moorcock
Rue St Maur
Paris
July 2011

INTRODUCTION

Ann and Jeff VanderMeer

A 'weird tale', as defined by H. P. Lovecraft in his nonfiction writings and given early sanctuary within the pages of magazines like *Weird Tales* (est. 1923) is a story that has a supernatural element but does not fall into the category of traditional ghost story or Gothic tale, both popular in the 1800s. As Lovecraft wrote in 1927, the weird tale 'has something more than secret murder, bloody bones, or a sheeted form clanking chains'. Instead, it represents the pursuit of some indefinable and perhaps maddeningly unreachable understanding of the world beyond the mundane – a 'certain atmosphere of breathless and unexplainable dread' or 'malign and particular suspension or defeat of… fixed laws of Nature' – through fiction that comes from the more unsettling, shadowy side of the fantastical tradition.

With unease and the temporary abolition of the rational, can also come the strangely beautiful, intertwined with terror. Reverie or epiphany, yes, but *dark* reverie or epiphany – not the lightness of 'I wandered lonely as a cloud' but the weight of, for example, seminal early twentieth-century weird writer and artist Alfred Kubin's sensation of being 'overcome… by a dark power that conjured up before my mind strange creatures, houses, landscapes, grotesque and frightful situations.' The Weird can be transformative – sometimes literally – entertaining monsters while not always seeing them as monstrous. It strives for a kind of understanding even when something cannot be understood, and acknowledges failure as sign and symbol of our limitations.

Usually, the characters in weird fiction have either entered into a place unfamiliar to most of us, or have received such hints of the unusual that they become obsessed with the weird. Whether *It* exists or not, they have fallen into dialogue with *It*; they may pull back from the abyss, they may decide to *unsee* what they saw, but still they *saw* it. Such stories can be terrifying, but do not always rely upon the scare central to horror fiction, nor the twist ending common to, for example, classic *Twilight Zone* episodes. They remain universal because they entertain while also expressing our own dissatisfaction with, and uncertainty about, reality. In a context wherein the monsters stand first for themselves, their visceral physicality convinces us, at least while reading, of the existence of The Weird.

As a twentieth and twenty-first century art form the story of The Weird is the story of the refinement (and destabilization) of supernatural fiction within an established framework but also of the welcome contamination of that fiction by the influence of other traditions, some only peripherally connected to the fantastic. The Weird, in a modern vernacular, has also come to mean fiction in which some other element, like weird ritual or the science fictional, replaces the supernatural while providing the same dark recognition of the unknown and the visionary. The best and most unique supernatural writers from prior eras, like Arthur Machen (his best short fiction written before 1910), would leave their mark on this newer weird, but not a boot print.

Because The Weird often exists in the interstices, because it can occupy different territories simultaneously, an impulse exists among the more rigid taxonomists to find The Weird suspect, to argue it should not, cannot be, separated out from other traditions. Because The Weird is as much a *sensation* as it is a mode of writing, the most keenly attuned amongst us will say 'I know it when I see it,' by which they mean 'I know it when I *feel* it' – and this, too, the more rigorous of categorizing taxidermists will take to mean The Weird does not exist when, in fact, this is one of the more compelling arguments for its existence.

In its purest forms, The Weird has eschewed fixed tropes of the supernatural like zombies, vampires, and werewolves, and the instant archetypal associations these tropes bring with them. The most unique examples of The Weird instead largely chose paths less trodden and went to places less visited, bringing back reports that still seem fresh and innovative today. The Weird is also darkly democratic: you can be a weird writer like Thomas Ligotti, in all that you do, or, like James Tiptree, Jr. and Karen Joy Fowler, you can feel the pull of The Weird in only some of your fiction; it doesn't matter, authenticity exists in the words on the page, on the shared *frisson* that rises from them. Authenticity in The Weird, increasingly throughout the twentieth century, also meant stories that, even if just subtextually, engaged the problems of modern life, and more so than past supernatural fiction, at times engaged with the extremes of that life, including the horrors of war.

Similarly, influences on The Weird in the twentieth century, streams of fiction that fed into its watershed, included many traditions: surrealism, symbolism, Decadent Literature, the New Wave, and the more esoteric strains of the Gothic. None of these influencers truly defined The Weird, but, assimilated into the aquifer along with Lovecraftian and Kafkaesque approaches, changed the composition of this form of fiction forever.

The Early Years

The story of The Weird is often seen as the story of the rise of the tentacle, a symbol of modern weird. The tentacle and all it represented metastasized in *Weird Tales* and The Lovecraft Circle – the group of writers surrounding Lovecraft that included Robert E. Howard, Fritz Leiber, Clark Ashton Smith, Howard Wandrei, and August Derleth. Although female contributors to *Weird Tales* were rarer, the Southern-US writer Mary Elizabeth Counselman had a significant impact, as did Francis Stevens (the pen-name of Gertrude Barrows Bennett, included herein with 'Unseen – Unfeared'). It is important to remember that although many of these writers would spawn imitators and thus render some of their visionary qualities more ordinary to a modern reader, in their day they, and *Weird Tales,* represented a revolution of sorts against old ideas about supernatural fiction. (In Europe, the *Weird Tales* equivalent was *Der Orchideengarten,* which translates as 'The Orchid Garden', established 1919.)

The Lovecraft Circle is represented in the early pages of this volume, but not to the exclusion of all else. Why? Because in other places a similar impulse was arising. At roughly the same time Lovecraft penned tales like 'The Dunwich Horror' and 'The Call of Cthulhu', Jean Ray, in a Belgian prison, wrote stunning and sophisticated stories like 'The Shadowy Street' and 'The *Mainz Psalter*', Japanese poet Hagiwara Sakutarō composed the hallucinogenic strangeness that is 'The Town of Cats', and Polish writer Bruno Schulz mythologized his childhood in weird stories like 'Sanatorium at the Sign of the Hourglass'.

These non-Anglo versions of The Weird were not aberrations. In the 1910s, Ryunosuke Akutagawa published the Japanese *contes cruel* 'The Hell Screen' and Franz Kafka, still to remain relatively unknown for decades, wrote the classic of weird ritual 'In the Penal Colony', while in India Rabindranath Tagore wrote his most supernatural tale 'The Hungry Stones' and in Italy Luigi Ugolini penned 'The Vegetable Man', a tale of weird transformation.

Also near the start of the twentieth century, the writers Alfred Kubin, Algernon Blackwood, and F. Marion Crawford, in very different ways, helped usher in the modern era of The Weird: Kubin as a representative of symbolist and decadent writers; Blackwood as a forerunner of Lovecraft; and Crawford as the early manifestation of an impulse toward the more commercial weird tale as later exemplified by, among others, Ray Bradbury, Fritz Leiber, and Robert Bloch. Kubin, in particular, chose a path that would be echoed and amplified by Kafka, Schulz, and others, and taken up in the modern era by writers like M. John Harrison, Leena Krohn, and Michael Cisco. (William Hope Hodgson's novel *The House on the Borderland* in 1908 had a profound influence on weird science fiction and the classic weird tale but was too long to include in this volume.)

These writers came from vastly different backgrounds, but were bound together by some common impulse in their imaginations, some need to make sense of 'the fearful and fascinating mystery' that is life, in a particular way. For their efforts, a disproportionate number of them died in poverty and were marginalized as outsider artists or hacks – with the strangest (read: the most imaginative) ignored or misunderstood, even within the already cast-out genres of science fiction, fantasy and horror. Some were shot or sent to death camps during times of war. Too many committed suicide, sometimes driven there by an impulse closely tied to the unique nature of their creativity. A lucky few gained popularity and a wide readership for their efforts.

What all of these writers and the writers who would come after them shared was some element of the visionary in their writing, some impulse or worldview that catapulted them beyond the everyday. In some, it is expressed in their writing as just a glimmer or glint from a deep well. In others it is a great, raging fire at the center of their work. In either instance, subtle or bold, The Weird acknowledges that our search for understanding about worlds beyond our own cannot always be found in science or religion and thus becomes an alternative path for exploration of the numinous. Did these writers believe in the supernatural elements they described? In some cases, the evidence would suggest, yes. In the majority, the impulse to entertain combined with the impulse to remind readers of the strangeness of the world and the limits of our understanding of it. A few simply saw the world so differently that what to them seemed normal strikes readers as deeply weird. In some strands, The Weird represents a clear quest not just to understand the inexplicable; it represents a *fascination* that at times embraces the inexplicable, eschewing the terror of such a search. Many of these stories hold up to repeat readings for this reason.

Modern Weird

Three events created a kind of cut-off point between the early manifestations of twentieth-century weird and modern weird: Lovecraft's passing in 1937, World War II, and the widespread translation of Kafka into English in the 1940s (which created webs of influence still existing to this day).

The 1940s and 1950s were in a sense a period of expansion of The Weird in the US and UK. The rising popularity of horror and fantasy in major magazines like *Playboy* provided high-profile markets for the Bradburys, Leibers, Beaumonts, and Blochs – who, as Michael Moorcock documents in his foreword, attracted a wider audience by consciously wedding the visionary aspects of surreal weird fiction to more traditional storylines, modern subject matter, and a less ornate style. Women writers entering The Weird in the US found more opportunities for their work, too, including (on the genre magazine side) Margaret St. Clair and (on the 'literary' side) Shirley Jackson.

In the 1960s, the British New Wave created an opposite and equally useful renovation to that exemplified by Bloch and Bradbury by mixing the best of science fiction and fantasy with mainstream and experimental influences, some of which also referenced the decadents and surrealists. Out of this period came such giants as Michael Moorcock (whose work only peripherally touched on weird fiction), M. John Harrison (the most significant twentieth-century critic of the weird tale through his fiction), and J. G. Ballard (whose surreal science fiction often reads like weird fiction). Harlan Ellison® provided a visceral, passionate American counterpart to the London-based Brits with early tales like 'I Have No Mouth and I Must Scream' and the later story 'The Function of Dream Sleep' included in this volume.

Outside of the US and UK several new manifestations began to put forth fungal tendrils of influence during this time period. The phantasmagorical in The Weird was kept alive, although with a thready pulse, through the works of Mercè Rodoreda, Amos Tutuola, and Olympe Bhêly-Quénum, whose 'A Child in the Bush of Ghosts' received the blessing of no less than André Breton. The Latin American Boom, presaged by the work of Jorge Luis Borges, provided The Weird with fine works by Augusto Monterroso, Carlos Fuentes, Gabriel García Márquez, and Julio Cortázar, that stretched the weird tale by bringing to it magic realism and an appreciation for the surreal and political. In France, Claude Seignolle repurposed French folktales to create elegant and sophisticated supernatural stories.

Another tradition feeding into The Weird, Gothic literature, began to be substantially overhauled and repurposed, first through the phantasmagorical work of Mervyn Peake in the 1940s and 1950s, followed by the thoroughly modern stories of Daphne du Maurier in the 1960s and 1970s. In the UK, du Maurier did for the weird tale, through her Gothic influences, what Bradbury, Bloch, and Leiber had done in the US through the influence of Lovecraft: popularized it without losing the elements that made predecessors so compelling and strange. A frequent contributor to *Weird Tales*, Tanith Lee also made a splash within genre circles around this time, penning a number of classics with Gothic antecedents.

During the 1960s and 1970s, two important and eccentric works of weird fiction bloomed like strange orchids feeding on rich, rare soil. Frenchman Michel Bernanos came out of seemingly nowhere to write the short novel *The Other Side of the Mountain*, perhaps the finest weird tale of the 1960s. Bernanos managed in just this one cult classic to combine the traditions exemplified by Jean Ray and Algernon Blackwood with his own brand of surreal existentialism. In the 1970s, the utterly original US writer Eric Basso, entering The Weird through a kind of avant-garde approach to the Gothic, combined with surrealist and modernist influences, produced one of the most unique of all modern weird tales, the short novel 'The Beak Doctor'. Like a three-dimensional version of Kubin's stylized *The Other Side*, 'The Beak Doctor' used Joycean technique combined with clinical detail to create a dreamlike phantasmagoria about a strange sleeping sickness.

The rise of female writers outside of genres like Gothic fiction (including the traditional ghost story) starting in the 1970s also influenced The Weird, as it did many other forms of fantastical fiction. Several of these writers wrote weird fiction, even if they did not self-identify as writers of The Weird. James Tiptree, Jr. (Alice Sheldon), Angela Carter, Jamaica Kincaid, Joanna Russ, Leena Krohn, Octavia Butler, Elizabeth Hand, and Joyce Carol Oates all published significant weird tales during this period. Their diversity of approaches, taking in every possible influence, would enrich non-realistic literature for decades to come.

In the 1970s and 1980s, Stephen King's success created a new market for supernatural novels and a new naturalistic approach to American horror. T. E. D. Klein and Karl Edward Wagner also contributed to American horror, riffing off of their wide knowledge of weird fiction. In England, the publication of Clive Barker's *Books of Blood* in the 1980s provided a new and different model: transgressive stories that went beyond the scare to examine views of the body, alienation, and the nature of monsters. Barker's influences seem so various as to be useless to list, and in his monumental masterpiece 'In the Hills, the Cities' the visions of Bosch and the surrealists are integrated with the character detail more common to stories from the New Wave era. As importantly, American Thomas Ligotti would begin to publish dozens of stories that could be considered classics of weird fiction, taking his place alongside Kafka and Lovecraft as one of the most gifted weird short story writers of the twentieth century.

The urban horror or urban weird that took root during the 1970s and 1980s was also exemplified perfectly by the claustrophobic stories of Ramsey Campbell, a clear descendent of Lovecraft who diverged from his influences in part by focusing on gritty working class English settings. Yet one byproduct of this new emphasis on naturalistic horror was a partial estrangement from the weird tale. By the early 1990's US-horror boom, non-supernatural tales of serial killers and the extremes of sex and violence portrayed by the Splatterpunks had fewer commonalities with The Weird. (Influential writers like Peter Straub tended to reserve The Weird for novel-length works.) However, even as the US-horror community increasingly turned away from the idea of surreal or visionary horror, a handful of writers like Jeffrey Osier, Jeffrey Thomas, Kathe Koja, Poppy Z. Brite, and Caitlin R. Kiernan continued to write recognizably weird fiction. Kiernan in particular would become perhaps the best weird writer of her generation.

The final significant development for The Weird came in the early twenty-first century with the emergence of the New Weird movement initially discussed online by, among others, M. John Harrison, Steph Swainston, China Miéville and, in initial opposition, Jeff VanderMeer. The term New Weird came to be applied to those writers as well as, most notably, K. J. Bishop, Michael Cisco, and Brian Evenson. In a sense, the New Weird was a re-enquiry into approaches and issues raised by the New Wave of the 1960s – bringing along all of that movement's associated influences – but in this case primarily from the perspective of The Weird rather than science fiction or fantasy. Miéville in particular managed to reinterpret, rewire, and overhaul The Weird in novel form, synthesizing the tentacle horrors of Lovecraft with the intellectual rigor of the New Wave. A ghostly counterpart who has never truly received his due, American Michael Cisco also has created an amazing oeuvre of novels, perhaps more influenced by Kafka and Eastern European literature. K. J. Bishop's contributions came primarily with a decadent slant to them, while Swainston re-imagined heroic fantasy for The Weird.

Since then, The Weird has again fragmented, perhaps in preparation for a future coalescing of a Next Weird or perhaps not. Late period examples by Stephen Graham Jones, Reza Negarestani, Micaela Morrissette, Brian Evenson, and K. J. Bishop demonstrate an intimate knowledge of both the Kafka and Lovecraft strands of weird fiction, but recombined in strange and exciting new ways. Others, like the work of Laird Barron, seem more traditional but through their unique style and vision still manage to surprise.

What The Weird holds next for readers is unclear, but given the past manifestations, we can be sure it will adaptable, idiosyncratic, and involve some of our best stylists. It will also continue to be at times discredited, misunderstood, and denigrated for being unapologetically transgressive, imaginative, and strange. Nonetheless, The Weird will endure.

Organizing Principles and Enhancements

A compendium like this one is neither as complete as an encyclopedia nor as loosely organized as a treasury. Our purpose is to showcase the wealth, depth, and breadth of The Weird over the past 100 years while also mapping certain tendencies and preoccupations. We have arranged the book chronologically from earliest story to latest story as the best way to show the evolution of and diversity of The Weird. Translated fiction is ordered in the anthology by when it first appeared in print, not by date of first translation into English. This preserves the 'chain of evidence' while pointing out the possibilities of initial influence across non-Anglo writings.

Among the interwoven threads in The Weird you will find a dedication to showcasing what one might call traditional weird, mainstream (or commercial) weird, weird science fiction, weird ritual, surreal weird, feminist weird, and avant-garde weird. 'International weird' is a meaningless term given the longstanding and complex literary traditions of the countries represented in this volume. However, we have tried to chronicle a clear tradition of Japanese surrealism and horror that feeds into The Weird, strong examples of Eastern European weird, evidence of weird fiction from India, African-nation weird, and those samples from Latin America that fall somewhere beyond magic realism. A few stories were unavailable to us because of rights issues, but we see them as an extension of this anthology as well: Philip K. Dick's 'The Preserving Machine' (weird science fiction), J. G. Ballard's 'The Drowned Giant' (New Wave weird), Gabriel García Márquez's 'A Very Old Man with Enormous Wings' (Latin American weird), Otsuichi's 'The White House in the Cold Forest' (Japanese weird). Because this anthology is so vast (over 750,000 words), we were able to include novellas and even short novels, including these important works: Michel Bernanos' *The Other Side of the Mountain*, Eric Basso's 'The Beak Doctor', Leena Krohn's *Tainaron*, and Brian Evenson's *The Brotherhood of Mutilation*.

In pursuit of certain stories, we were also able to commission original translations. These translations include such major stories as Ryunosuke Akutagawa's 'The Hell Screen', Michel Bernanos' *The Other Side of the Mountain*, Dino Buzzati's 'The Colomber', Julio Cortázar's 'Axolotl', and Georg Heym's 'The Dissection'.

THE WEIRD

A COMPENDIUM OF STRANGE AND DARK STORIES

THE OTHER SIDE

Alfred Kubin

AN EXCERPT – TRANSLATED INTO ENGLISH BY MIKE MITCHELL

Alfred Kubin (1877–1959) was a visionary Austrian writer and artist who illustrated works by such notable early purveyors of weird fiction as Edgar Allan Poe and ETA Hoffman. While living in Germany, Kubin was mentored for a time by the writer Franz Blei, a friend of Franz Kafka. Kubin's masterpiece was the novel *Die Andere Seite* (*The Other Side*), first published in 1908. *The Other Side* is a dystopic fantasy set in the strange and oppressive city of Pearl. In its synergy of symbolism, decadent-era literature, and the weird, the novel suggested an early twentieth-century break with supernatural traditions of the past. In this excerpt, the narrator describes a strange sleeping sickness and the beginning of the ruination of the city.

An irresistible sleeping sickness had Pearl in its grip. It broke out in the Archive and from there spread across the whole of the Realm. It was an epidemic and no one could resist. One minute a man would be boasting how wide awake he was, the next he had succumbed to the germ.

The infectious character of the disease was quickly recognised, but the doctors could find no cure. The American's proclamations were ineffective because as soon as people started to read them they began to yawn. Anybody who could stayed at home, so as not to be struck down by the malady in the middle of the street. They just retired to a cosy nook and contentedly accepted this latest turn of events. After all, it didn't hurt. The first sign was usually a feeling of profound lethargy, then patients were seized with a yawning fit, their eyes seemed to fill with sand, their eyelids grew heavy, their thoughts went fuzzy and they would sink wearily to the ground where they stood. Sufferers could be brought round now and then with strong smelling salts – sal ammoniac, for example – but they just mumbled a few words and relapsed into torpor. With individuals of a strong constitution a brisk rub-down with a towel would put back the onset by several hours, but then it was just the same. In many cases the out-break of the illness was very rapid. One speaker was delivering a tirade on the political situation when he suddenly bent down over the table, lowered his head and started to snore rhythmically.

Anton in the coffee house, on the other hand, could scarcely keep his eyes open, and yet was still serving. But, heavens, the things we had to do to keep him moving! We literally had to bombard him with sugar lumps and coffee spoons. He was exceedingly forgetful and when he did finally bring the order, the impatient customer had often fallen asleep himself. We had to keep a sharp lookout to make sure the cigars of comatose patrons were properly extinguished.

On the parade ground the military were busy training to prepare them for the threatened revolution. But it was no use the sergeants bellowing at them, one soldier after another just lay down on the ground.

There were strange and amusing incidents. Thieves slept the sleep of the just, their fingers still in someone else's till. Melitta spent four days stretched out in Brendel's apartment, while her husband was dreaming, bent over the table, his nose in the mayonnaise.

Castringius was struck down while playing cards. He was leaning back comfortably in his chair in a low dive, the jack of diamonds in his paw. I very quickly withdrew to my room and that was where the illness hit me. I had just turned back the covers and gone over to draw the curtains. The last thing I saw was banknotes fluttering, one after the other, out of the window of the princess's apartment across the road; a gentle autumn breeze was wafting them like withered leaves down the street towards the river. I just had time to get to my bed.

During the first two days after the outbreak of the epidemic the trains still arrived, though with huge delays, since new staff had to be brought on at every station. After that the service stopped entirely. The last number of the *Voice* was printed on one side alone, and even then it was riddled with incomplete sentences and scores of typographical errors. The entire last page, which usually contained a round-up of silly miscellaneous items, was missing.

There was no point in fighting it. Pearl slept. This state of complete unconsciousness probably lasted six days. At least that was the time calculated by the barber who based his estimate on the length of his customers' stubble.

During that time there was only one person in the whole of the city who, it was said, did not sleep at all, or only very briefly: the American. On one of the days, when he was walking down Long Street like a latter-day prince from *Sleeping Beauty*, he claimed he saw, through the coffee house window, one of the chess players make a move. From that he concluded that they, too, had escaped the illness. Otherwise you fell over sleeping bodies everywhere. Not only on all the benches in the public parks, even staircases and entrances were covered with well-dressed men and women, lying higgledy-piggledy, just like the homeless, contented smiles on their faces, despite their bizarre situation.

As people gradually came to, many simply continued their interrupted activities. This was a blessed relief, not only for Brendel, but for the poor old nag at the knacker's yard which had spent days tied up, waiting for the *coup de grâce*. Now it received it. For the strange thing was that animals remained impervious to the sleeping sickness.

For most people nothing had changed, at least not immediately. When I woke up and, in need of sustenance, went to the café, the barber was there already, ravenous but also in a very bad mood. A fourpenny piece had gone missing, which had led to a permanent rift between the barber and his assistant who of course, like all animals, had remained awake.

The Dream city woke up and found itself in a kind of animal paradise. During our long sleep another world – the animal kingdom – had spread to such an extent that we were in danger of being swept aside. I have to say, though, that even in the time prior to the sleep it had been noticeable what a good year it seemed to be for rats and mice. There had also been complaints about the depredations of birds of prey and four-legged chicken-thieves. The gardener had even seen wolf tracks in Alfred Blumenstich's park. They laughed at him, but no one laughed any more when, the following day, a pair of horns was all that was left of Frau Blumenstich's pet, a snow-white Angora goat.

But how can one describe the astonishment of all those who had gone to sleep alone and undisturbed and woke to find themselves in unwelcome company? There might be a large green parrot sitting at the window or weasels and squirrels peeking out from under the beds. It was only gradually that we realised what was going on.

When they woke up, the butchers had to drive a large pack of jackals away from the slaughterhouse. Attacks by wolves, wild cats and lynxes increased frighteningly and even our pets suddenly turned disobedient and vicious. Almost all the cats and dogs left their masters and hunted for their own food. The newspapers, that had started to appear again, reported a horrifying case: a bear had climbed into the ground-floor apartment of Apollonia Six, a pork butcher's widow, and completely devoured the poor lady while she was fast asleep.

Hunters and fishermen came into the town bringing fantastic-sounding reports of gigantic, shambling animals they claimed to have seen. But being regarded as professional exaggerators anyway, no one believed them. Then suddenly peasants and other Dreamlanders living in the country started to arrive in droves, thundering up on their massive horses, together with carts jampacked with women, children and the more valuable of their household goods. They were very unhappy and demonstrated outside the Palace and the Archive, complaining that no soldiers had been sent to protect them. Herds of buffaloes, they said, had devastated their farms, and they had only managed to escape the attacks of hordes of large apes by the skin of their teeth. The beasts were fiends and spared neither women nor children. Soon afterwards the tracks of colossal bipeds were identified in the clay soil of the Tomassevic Fields on the edge of the city. That gave cause for concern.

The plague of insects was horrendous. Clouds of greedy locusts descended from the hills and wherever they went they left not one blade of grass. A swarm destroyed the castle garden in one single night. Bugs, earwigs and lice made our lives a misery. All of these species, from the largest to the smallest, seemed to be in the grip of an elemental procreative urge. Despite the fact that they were all eating each other up, quadrupeds and hexapods were multiplying in uncanny fashion. Even the official issue of guns and poison and the promulgation of strict orders to keep windows and doors closed had little effect, the fertility was just too great. Squads of volunteer hunters were organised to support the military and the police. Many buildings had embrasures made in the outside walls to shoot through.

One morning the wife of the coffee-house owner woke to find fourteen rabbits in her bed. Since her bedroom was only separated from mine by a thin partition, I could hear the baby rabbits squeaking.

But the most terrifying of all were the snakes. No house was safe from them, the vile beasts got everywhere, into drawers, wardrobes, coat-pockets, water-jugs, everywhere. And these insidious reptiles displayed a horrifying fecundity. If you went to your room in the dark you would tread on the eggs lying around and they would burst with a squelch. Castringius devised an 'egg dance', which he performed to perfection.

People in the French Quarter could scarcely put up with the vermin any longer. However, even during the beastly invasion, most kept their heads. It became the done thing to shoot your stag from your window and invite your friends straight round to share the game pie. From the skylight of the house where I used to live you could see a long way out over fields and meadows. Now the area had been transformed into a monstrous zoo. Even the river had its share: crocodiles, which after years of strenuous effort had been banished downstream, reappeared. The baths had to be closed because of the deadly electric eels which had taken up residence in the cabins.

One of the few good things about those difficult days was the fact that it was easy to come by a tasty roast and other rare titbits.

During this time old Professor Korntheuer enjoyed great respect. He gave public lectures in which he taught the Dreamlanders to distinguish dangerous bugs from harmless ones. Armed with a triple-barrelled shotgun, he was up and about at first light, wandering through the herds of gazelles, wild boar and marmots, stalking game. But the animals soon got used to the eccentric bespectacled huntsman and came to love the old gentleman. Our windows, on the other hand, suffered so much damage from his gun that it had to be taken away from him.

At night we could only go out if armed with a lantern and a gun, and even then we had to take great care. Traps, snares, pitfalls and spring-guns made the city even more dangerous than it already was. But to allow something like that to put them off the pursuit of pleasure was the one thing that never occurred to the Dreamers.

II

The depths to which public morality had sunk presented a great opportunity to my fellow artist Castringius. His *porno-graphica* were sought after, he was the fashion. Drawings such as *The Lascivious Orchid Inseminating the Embryo* were much admired. Hector von Brendel bought a complete series from him because Melitta thought them 'fun'. At first she was very much taken with them and had them nicely framed and hung in her boudoir. But it turned out to be merely a caprice and after a few days they had to go. An occasional beau of hers, an officer of dragoons, was allowed to take them; in return he presented her with a pair of antique emerald earrings. That very same evening the officer took the drawings to the café where they happened to be holding a raffle. The proceeds were to go towards helping those who were suffering the consequences of their dissolute ways; until then there had been no ward for them in our hospital. Quite a lot of money was collected, Blumenstich – not the junk dealer – made up the deficit and soon afterwards the first patients were being admitted to the ward next to the children's hospital in the monastery.

As irony would have it, I was the one who won the drawings and now they were hanging in my room. One day I met Castringius in the street. He was looking for a new apartment, he told me. His studio window and skylight were broken and there were bats hanging like smoked hams from his curtain rail. While he was telling me all this he kept having to ward off the attentions of an importunate ibex with his walking stick. I invited him up, and there were the pictures. His jaw dropped in amazement.

'How did *you* come by these pictures?'

I explained.

'They're very good. *The White-striped Whip* is my most mature work. It represents a synthesis of future morality. There's not a woman alive today capable of understanding the implications. It has a real tang to it.'

I agreed with him entirely. I was the only person in the Dream Realm capable of appreciating his artistic achievement. He was an oddball, but I liked him. And why not? He that feels pure, let him cast the first stone.

Suddenly there was noise in the street. We went over to the window. A lot of people were standing round laughing. And there was something to laugh at. Just imagine, the monkey had downed tools and gone on strike! The previous day already Giovanni had left one customer half shaved when his attention was drawn by a horde of macaques rushing past. A beautiful long-tailed guenon had waved at him and the temptation had been too much for our barber's assistant. That time his philosophical master had managed to restrain him with a combination of the cane and the argument that time was divisible into tiny eternities. Now, however, no amount of reasoning could hold him back. He gracefully climbed up the drainpipe, grasped the princess's coffee flask with his prehensile tail, made himself comfortable on the window-ledge of my former apartment, now in a ruinous state and empty, and played on a Jew's harp he had concealed in his cheek pouch. The old princess gave a shriek of horror and tried to hit the coffee-thief with a broom, but he immediately threw the flask away and grabbed the broom. You should have seen the speed with which the lady disappeared, to reappear on the second floor. We had a perfect view of the duel from my window. Giovanni Battista was having a high old time. First of all he wrested her main weapon – an old pair of fire-tongs – from her and let her have the broom back; in the course of this he almost became a flying monkey! I had left a number of bottles of Indian ink behind and he used these as missiles. And an excellent shot he was, too; we all cheered him on while the princess swore like a fish wife.

Suddenly he reappeared, wearing the old woman's filthy bonnet, swung out of the window and slid back down the drainpipe, grimacing grotesquely. At the window upstairs the princess was calling for the police, while at the bottom the barber was waiting with his cane. 'You should be ashamed of yourself', he shouted at the monkey.

Alfred Blumenstich, a smug smile on his face, was just emerging from the apartment of his nine little darlings, where he had once more been dispensing his own particular brand of charity. His carriage was waiting. With a tremendous leap the monkey sprang onto the head of the stallion and off they went. The onlookers went wild and cheered until the vehicle and its bizarre rider had vanished into the distance.

That was just one incident, but similar scenes were the order of the day.

It was a mystery where all this teeming multitude of animals came from. They were now the true masters of the city and clearly they knew it. In bed I could hear running and a clatter of hooves, as if I were in a large metropolis. Camels and wild asses wandered through the streets; it was dangerous to tease them.

In contrast to this abundance of animals, plant life disappeared more and more. Everything was nibbled and crushed, and there was no new growth. The avenues of limes along the Embankment and out towards the cemetery consisted of nothing more than bare trunks. The earth was steaming, as if it intended to spew out even more creatures. Small holes gave off warm, sickly-smelling fumes. The nights were wreathed in a strange half-light that blurred all the contours.

III

The most uncanny thing was a mysterious process which began with the alarming rise in the number of animals, then continued inexorably, at ever increasing speed, until it led to the complete collapse of the Dream Realm: the *Crumbling*. It affected everything. The buildings of such different materials, the objects that had been brought together over the years, all the things the Master had spent his money on were doomed. Cracks appeared in all the walls at once, wood rotted, iron rusted, glass went cloudy, cloth fell to pieces. Precious *objets d'art* succumbed to an irresistible *inner* decay without any reason being apparent.

A sickness of inanimate matter. There was rot and mildew in even the best-looked-after houses. There must have been some unknown corrupting agent in the air, for fresh food – milk, meat, later on even eggs – went off in a few hours. Many houses burst and had to be hastily evacuated.

And then there were the ants! They turned up in every fissure and fold, in our clothes, our purses, our beds. There were three kinds: black, white and blood-red. The black species, the largest, were found in every crack in the masonry and everywhere you put your foot out of doors. The much more dangerous white ones transformed timbers into powder. Unquestionably the worst, though, were the red ones, since they chose the human body as their habitat. At first, scratching oneself was still considered indelicate, something one did in private. But what can you do when you have an itch? In the French Quarter everyone had been scratching in public for ages. We soon laughed and followed suit. It was the wife of His Excellency the President who boldly gave the lead on the occasion of a state reception.

It had become impossible to get rid of the animal excrement in the streets or the dust in the houses. However desperately we tried, it simply went on increasing. Our clothes disintegrated even while we were brushing and beating them. The only thing I found surprising was how the Dreamlanders managed to retain their good humour.

Melitta Lampenbogen, for example, was irrepressible. The whole of the officer corps were regulars in her house, right down to the most junior lieutenant. He might still stammer, 'It's an honour, ma'am', but she was no longer concerned about the niceties of polite intercourse. Eventually she turned to the lower strata of society. I often observed her ploy of lifting her skirt in the street. People stopped to watch. Dogs ran after her, and they were not to be trifled with now. Once I saw one tear off her dress. She ran away in terror, dropping a crumpled letter. I picked it up and read it later.

My own Queen Ant,

I am still intoxicated with happiness. In my thoughts I kiss every one of your charms. As ever, you are the mistress of my dream. How did you sleep? Not very much, I imagine, as usual. Just think, I've found a way of at least being able to lie down in peace. Lay the wardrobe on the floor, then an inch of insect powder, then a blanket, then more powder, then another blanket. (Those nightshirts with buttons at the bottom that have become fashionable are no use at all.) Close the wardrobe door as soon as you're in; a small (heart-shaped?!) hole covered with a fly-screen allows you to breathe.

Please don't send your letters to the hotel any more. I hate the American's gang, that Jacques especially is an utter rogue. Moreover the cooking has gone downhill recently; from now on I'll take my lunch in the café in Long Street. Send your letters there, marked 'H. v. B.', but don't give them to N. C. to bring, he's unreliable and since he's joined up with that damned American he's become insolent into the bargain.

How is your tub of lard taking the departure of his last tenant? The barber's shutting up shop and the princess doesn't pay much. I saw him today in his carriage, but he was too occupied with the attentions of these tiresome parasites to notice me.

I'll see you at nine o'clock tonight behind the rose bush – how bare it is now!

Your loving
Hector

P. S. I still keep getting anonymous letters about you. How little the world knows my Melitta!

Soon everyone was carrying a bag of insect powder round with them. If they had previously suffered from sleeping sickness, they now hardly slept at all. In a fever of excitement, with flushed cheeks, people wandered round the city until well past midnight. It was safer out in the streets than in the ruinous houses. During the past few days the animals' mating frenzy had reached a climax. Everywhere – in dark corners, in the water, in the air – all sorts of creatures were copulating. From the stables came whinnying, bleating, grunting. One bull, infuriated by the sight of cows brought in for slaughter, had crushed a butcher to pulp against the wall.

The American was stirring up hatred and dissension, and mocked everything. There were very few left who still believed in the Lord. The Clock Spell was forgotten. Only occasionally did someone go into the cell now, and then they didn't stay the prescribed thirty seconds, but came straight out. *I knew now that the end of the Dream Realm was approaching inexorably.*

One night I heard hissing and deep growling on the roof. With horror I watched a gigantic leopard crunch up a hare; an icy shiver ran down my spine as I heard the bones crack. My room wasn't a cosy den any more. There were two gaping fissures in the wall from which, in the evenings, the rear portions of cockroaches stuck out at regular intervals, making them look like a frieze. During the day a pair of robins used my ash-tray as a nest. They were harmless and rewarded me for leaving them undisturbed with their singing. Unfortunately I was not to enjoy the pleasure for long. One day a kestrel, ignoring me completely, shot in and killed the male robin.

On one of the last evenings I found two scorpions under the blanket as I was going to bed and was hunting out any other such vermin when the weapon I was using – the boot-jack – fell apart. I picked up my scissors: they had rusted away. Only then did I notice that my paper was mouldy and my rulers, what was left of my drawing-table, the three-legged chest of drawers, in short all wooden pieces of furniture were worm-eaten and rotten.

And what did I look like myself? Pretty odd! At least lots of other people, who were usually neat and tidy in their dress, were going round in tatters too. We all had mildew on our clothes and shoes. It was no use washing and scrubbing them, it reappeared as fast as we could get rid of it. The materials our clothes were made from went threadbare, frayed and dropped off bit by bit. We men managed to carry it off with a certain amount of dignity, but the poor women! Better not to talk about it.

IV

A great change came when the houses were no longer really habitable. It was still all right on the ground floor, but going up stairs demanded courage bordering on recklessness.

One day when the waiter brought me a rotten egg, a broken beer bottle containing some murky liquid and a filthy, greasy cloth, presumably intended as a napkin, my patience gave out and I called for the landlord, who happened to be at the rear, propping up the ceiling with parts of the billiard table.

'What do you call this?' I barked. 'There must be a pound of decaying matter on this cutlery. Please remove these disgusting objects and that foul rag at once.' He bowed and scraped. 'You can't get the staff nowadays', he whined.

'All right, all right.' I waved him away in exasperation, stood up, took my mangy top-hat and left the café. The place where I had been sitting had already been taken over by a colony of ants.

I only kept going to the café out of habit. Conditions there were too revolting to eat or drink anything other than a black coffee. Anton had changed, and not for the better; he never washed his hands and his smell preceded him from a great distance. You didn't *have* to go round like that. The barber referred to the crust of filth covering him as 'primal matter'. It was simply nauseating! I was even more surprised, therefore, when I came back one evening and heard soft giggling in the vestibule. I shone my lamp in every corner, expecting to find some animal, and what did I see behind the storeroom door? Anton and Melitta locked in a passionate embrace!

She died soon after. She was found in her bedroom, torn to pieces. The door was locked and had to be broken down. There was a gigantic mastiff locked in with her. The rabid beast bristled and threw itself at the men who appeared in the doorway, biting two policemen before they managed to shoot it. They died soon afterwards from rabies. In the last days of her life not much was left of her former beauty. It was in vain that she tried to conceal the ravages of her way of life through excessive make-up and powder.

The two chess players also suffered agonies. Eventually the old gentlemen, who were completely in thrall to their passion, came to find any movement so complicated they needed hours of deliberation just to lift a finger. Given the amount of vermin around, it was obvious that such slowness would cause serious problems. Much to be praised, therefore, was a young lady who happened to be taking tea in the café once and noticed the torments the two were suffering. She simply went over and, quite unembarrassed, started picking the ants and bugs off their coats. After that we all followed her example. Until then we had laughed at the grotesque faces the chess players pulled, but now it became the custom for us regulars to give the two gentlemen a quick scratch as we came or left. As you can see, even in those terrible times not all sympathy for the sufferings of others had vanished.

Once again the American was stirring things up. He prophesied that the deluge of animals would soon dry up and he turned out to be right insofar as the bigger species gradually withdrew. For the time being, however, the smaller mammals and reptiles remained, though the birds had completely disappeared, apart from hosts of ravens and white-necked vultures. The vultures, massive, heavy birds, perched like bronze statues on the stumps of the trees along the avenues, staring fixedly at the city as if they were waiting for something. Even though his prophecy had only partially come true, it brought the American new support. From now on his attacks on his mortal enemy, Patera, were even more vicious, if that were possible.

I went back to taking a regular evening stroll along the river. The waves had washed up countless shells, corals, snails, fish-bones and scales on the banks. I was surprised how often I found remains of marine fauna. The banks looked as if they were strewn with mystical signs and I was convinced the blue-eyed tribe would be able to understand this symbolic language. There were definitely mysteries here. The wings of the often magnificent insects – moths and flying beetles – had marks which must be forgotten characters, only I didn't possess the key to them.

How great you must be, Patera, I thought. Why does the Lord hide himself away, even from those who love him? I walked along, lost in melancholy thought. The bare trees on the opposite bank were bent low over the river so that their branches touched the black water. Gigantic shadows were moving between them and the crack of breaking twigs could be clearly heard. Sometimes I saw long necks or trunks which made me think of monstrous prehistoric creatures. The darker it grew, the more dangerous it was for people out walking alone. One evening, which was to be of great significance for me, I turned back in fright when a beam sticking out of the water suddenly blew out air. An alligator was baring its teeth at me.

As I made my way home I thought about

another dangerous incident the previous day which had turned out all right in the end. For a long time rumours had been circulating about a huge tiger, a pregnant female, that was said to be living in the Palace. Various people claimed they had seen its blunt muzzle and long back in the window gallery. Yesterday just such a beast had leapt into Alfred Blumenstich's glazed veranda. At the sight of the fierce animal the lady of the house, who was fat and chubby, simply fainted without a sound. Professor Korntheuer happened to be having lunch with them. In this terrible situation the venerable old gentleman showed remarkable heroism. 'Keep calm', he said to the horrified husband as he stood up, 'even the fiercest beasts of prey will submit to a higher being. They feel awe at our upright gait and our noble, lordly gaze fills them with fear.' With that he walked towards the animal, taking his spectacles off. Whether it was the strangeness of the stiff-legged scholarly figure approaching or something else, the result was another crash of shattering glass as the tiger jumped out, unfortunately with Frau Blumenstich in its jaws. Blumenstich wrung his hands. 'Oh God, please save my Julie', he whimpered. Pursued by the servants armed with rifles, the tiger carried the unconscious woman off to the Palace. In the street everyone politely made way for them. The fire brigade was called out as quickly as possible and tried to separate the striped monster from its prey. You could hear it in one of the large rooms on the first floor, furiously snarling at its attackers. To shoot it was impossible, they could very easily have hit Frau Blumenstich, so they tried to winkle the animal out with their fire-hoses. That helped. The soaking shower persuaded the tiger to leave its corner, but unfortunately it didn't forget its prey. With a huge leap it soared out through the high arched window. The people screamed in horror, but God heard her poor husband's prayer. Frau Blumenstich got caught on the window-catch and hung there, upside down, her skirts over her head, visible to all and sundry, but safe. In the general rejoicing the tiger managed to make its escape.

There was great consternation at the fact that the animal had not been caught. The American suggested a thorough search of the Palace, but, despite the general emancipation from the Master, no one was willing to go that far; the military and the police flatly refused to cooperate.

The Lord's behaviour was truly strange! Even if he was going to withdraw his protection from Pearl, he could at least have made an exception for his faithful followers, but he didn't seem to bother about the distinction. At times now the city was quiet, even though almost the whole of the population of the Dream Realm was gathered there.

'The mansions of the rich for the poor and needy!' roared the mob. The rich gave up their houses all the more willingly as possession had to be wrung from the animals that had made their homes in them. Lampenbogen's country villa had become a porcupine warren and a well-fed python was sleeping on the sofa in his late lamented wife's boudoir. These animals had to be exterminated before the people could move in. And anyway, conditions in these palatial dwellings were not as fine as the common folk imagined. The precious objects had clearly lost the will to live. The valuable vases and china were covered in a delicate network of tiny cracks; magnificent paintings developed black spots which spread over the whole picture; engravings became porous and disintegrated. You wouldn't believe how quickly well-looked-after furnishings could turn into a pile of rubbish. For this reason most of the peasants who had come into the city preferred to camp out in the open spaces and fields close to the city.

'Lord, now you show your might through terror alone', I thought as I made my way up Long Street. It was dark and there was a rustling and creaking all around. At one point a slate plummeted down from the roof, at another lumps of mortar fell away from the wall, there was a constant trickle of fine sand from holes in the masonry which were growing visibly larger and everywhere we had to clamber over piles of rubble, posts and stakes sticking up out of the ground.

Death weaving its intangible web.

On the roof of the coffee house quite close to my attic I could clearly see a black silhouette moving: the leopard. It had doubtless made its lair in the loft of one of the neighbouring buildings. It could perhaps have been killed by a rifle bullet, but we were all too cowardly. In my narrow room I fell into the depths of despondency. For a long time I walked up and down, aching in my back and joints.

'What are we all still living for? We're damned! If I fell ill now, there isn't a soul would bother about me.' An all-pervading fear crept over me. 'I don't want to die, *I don't want to die!*' At a complete loss, I put my head in my hands. 'The pinnacle of creation!' – It was my despair speaking. – 'Two legs, tubes of bone, bear my whole world, a world of pain and delusion. The worst part is the body.' The fear of death sent a shudder through me. 'What lies in store for my body? All its thousand organs, into what cunning instruments of torture will they be transformed? Oh, if only I could *stop thinking*, but that functions automatically. There are no certainties that are not countered by uncertainties! It's an endless labyrinth, and I'm damned! My belly is filled with ordure and disgust, and whenever I do manage to feel something passionately I immediately lose my nerve. There is just one thing I do know: however much I wriggle and squirm, minute by minute I am coming closer to the inevitable, closer to death, and there is nothing I can do about it. I haven't even the courage to kill myself. Lasting unhappiness is my destiny.' I sighed.

'I despair of Patera. I don't understand him, he plays with mysteries. He must be as powerless as the rest of us or he would long since have crushed the American. But that is beyond him. It is *the American* who possesses *true life*. If only I weren't so timorous, I would go to him, fall to my knees and he would help.'

I was at my wits' end, almost out of my mind with the fear of death. Downstairs there was a banging and crashing, hooligans being thrown out of the coffee house, a nightly occurrence. In his lighted room across the road I saw the barber bent over his books.

V

I felt an inner tug, several times in rapid succession. I had to stand up – there it was again – what was it? I was gradually pervaded by an obscure urge. There was another tug, a pounding, stronger this time. 'I hear. What is it?' I made a great effort and concentrated on the vague sensation. 'Patera', was the word I heard coming from within. 'Patera. Palace. Come.' It grew more and more urgent, persuasive, terribly distinct and clear. In the dark I went downstairs, sure of myself without having to think. I was being pushed and pulled, and surrendered completely to the force directing me. No one took any notice of me and when my mind cleared I found I was halfway to the Palace. 'For God's sake', I thought, 'what am I doing? What is this I *have* to do?' I decided to turn back. 'Yes, I'll definitely turn back at the next corner.' It was no use. I *had* to carry on. I wanted to shout out to people, 'Help me! Stop me!' but it was as if my jaws were screwed together. Then I saw the imposing Palace with its huge gateway, its empty window sockets, like a skull... and I stepped into its darkness.

On all sides a labyrinth of colonnades stretched out. I walked on like a wooden marionette, mechanically, one–two, one–two. The long galleries were sparsely lit by suspended lamps. I came to the state rooms. All the doors were ajar. I heard a bang – the melodious chime of a clock – the draught made the doors open of their own accord – a crash! Sweet merciful Jesus! The tiger! The thought was like torture and the sense of urgency such I was almost running while trying to make as little noise as possible. Several times I thought I heard my name called out close by, quite loudly, then softly, but nothing could make me look back. Broken furniture was lying round the empty, deserted rooms and the stifling, musty atmosphere made breathing difficult. I passed through extensive chambers, dimly lit by a single candle: rumpled beds, torn-down draperies, bricked-up windows, fires going out in magnificent stoves, tapestries hanging askew. Like a sleep-walker I hurried up small, dusty staircases, down long, silent corridors, then I saw a low oak door I recognised. 'Patera', I kept on thinking, 'Patera, Patera...' This door was also ajar. From the ceiling hung a silver lamp with a flickering candle shining on the dangling tatters of a canopy. Apart from the faint outlines of the mosaic floor I could hardly see anything. I stopped – *now I could stop!* There! There! That face! Immediately a cold sweat broke out on my forehead.

Wrapped in a gauzy, silver-grey robe, Patera was standing there, upright and asleep. I was filled with uncontrollable dread at the sight. In the deep, greenish shadows under his eyes lay suffering beyond that of ordinary mortals. Then I noticed that on one of his large, shapely hands the top section of the thumb was missing. Immediately I recalled the children born in the Dream Realm. Again there was the whispering I had heard on my first visit.

'I called you.' It sounded as if it came from a long way away. This time there was no chameleon-like change of expression. His facial muscles rippled, bulged and contracted, but there was no expression in it. His features went slack, only his lips twitched, a horrible sight in the otherwise inert face. And then it started again, very softly, as if muffled by a veil. At first I just heard a whispering, disjointed, meaningless, then I began to understand:

'Can you hear the dead singing, the bright-green dead? They disintegrate in their graves, easily, painlessly. If you put your hand into their bodies all you feel are fragments, and the teeth come out so easily. Where is the life that drove them, where is the power? Can you hear the dead singing, the bright-green dead?' I smelt the sharp odour of Patera's breath and a sensation of weakness spread through my limbs. Then the Lord seated himself on his high bed and threw off his robe. Sitting there, straight-backed, bare-chested, his flowing locks tumbling to his shoulders, I could not but admire his broad, noble physique. His gleaming white body was like a statue. I drew on my last ounce of strength to ask my question. 'Patera, why do you allow all this to happen?'

For a long time there was no answer. All at once he cried out in a resounding metallic bass voice, '*I am weary.*'

I started. The next moment I was staring into those expressionless eyes. *I was spellbound.* His eyes were like two empty mirrors reflecting infinity. The thought crossed my mind that Patera was not alive at all. If the dead could look that is what their gaze would be like. I felt a command to speak inside me, but I could only stammer, I babbled and was surprised myself to hear what it sounded like. The question seemed to come from the deepest depths of time, the words must have been spoken billions of years ago and only now did I utter them, only now were they heard *here:* 'Patera, *why did you not help?*'

Slowly, lifelessly, the lids closed and I felt easier. His features were now flooded with an inexpressible gentleness. They had an immeasurable softness, sadness which entranced me. Again came the whisper, clear and distinct, 'I *did* help, and I will help *you.*' It sounded like music. I was overcome with a sweet weariness, I bowed my head, my eyes closed...

A spine-chilling laugh, a laugh from hell, tore me out of my reverie. Standing in front of me in the brightly lit room in place of Patera was *the American.*

How I managed to get out of the Palace I no longer know. I ran and screamed. Men tried to stop me but I must have broken loose from them, for when I had my body under control again I was huddled up in a coach-house. Inside an overturned carriage I saw a litter of dead pangolins.

Snatches of the mocking laughter were still echoing in my ear, but it no longer had any effect on me. My nerves had given way completely. Fate, in whatever shape or form, had lost the power to drag me out of my torpor. Incapable of extended thought, I took strength from the consciousness of my own impotence. I couldn't understand or solve these contradictions but, after all, what concern were they of mine? All my fear had vanished. The horrific vision, which revealed Patera's double nature to me, closed off the abyss of my doubts and anxieties.

THE SCREAMING SKULL

F. Marion Crawford

Francis Marion Crawford (1854–1909) was an Italian-born American writer and historian noted for his many novels, especially those set in Italy, and for his classic weird and fantastic stories, including 'The Upper Berth' (1895), 'For the Blood is the Life' (1905), and the story included herein, the lively and horrific 'The Screaming Skull' (1908). A posthumous collection of Crawford's tales published in 1911 as *Wandering Ghosts* in the US and as *Uncanny Tales* in England was an important transition point between old and new approaches to supernatural fiction. The story contains an outstanding early example of modern monologue, verging on stream-of-consciousness at times.

I have often heard it scream. No, I am not nervous, I am not imaginative, and I have never believed in ghosts, unless that thing is one. Whatever it is, it hates me almost as much as it hated Luke Pratt, and it screams at me.

If I were you, I would never tell ugly stories about ingenious ways of killing people, for you never can tell but that someone at the table may be tired of his or her nearest and dearest. I have always blamed myself for Mrs Pratt's death, and I suppose I was responsible for it in a way, though heaven knows I never wished her anything but long life and happiness. If I had not told that story she might be alive yet. That is why the thing screams at me, I fancy.

She was a good little woman, with a sweet temper, all things considered, and a nice gentle voice; but I remember hearing her shriek once when she thought her little boy was killed by a pistol that went off, though everyone was sure that it was not loaded.

It was the same scream; exactly the same, with a sort of rising quaver at the end; do you know what I mean? Unmistakable.

The truth is, I had not realized that the doctor and his wife were not on good terms. They used to bicker a bit now and then when I was here, and I often noticed that little Mrs Pratt got very red and bit her lip hard to keep her temper, while Luke grew pale and said the most offensive things. He was that sort when he was in the nursery, I remember and afterward at school. He was my cousin, you know; that is how I came by this house; after he died, and his boy Charley was killed in South Africa, there were no relations left. Yes, it's a pretty little property, just the sort of thing for an old sailor like me who has taken to gardening.

One always remembers one's mistakes much more vividly than one's cleverest things, doesn't one? I've often noticed it. I was dining with the Pratts one night, when I told them the story that afterwards made so much difference. It was a wet night in November, and the sea was moaning. Hush! – if you don't speak you will hear it now…

Do you hear the tide? Gloomy sound, isn't it? Sometimes, about this time of year – hallo! – there it is! Don't be frightened, man – it won't eat you – it's only a noise, after all! But I'm glad you've heard it, because there are always people who think it's the wind, or my imagination, or something. You won't hear it again tonight, I fancy, for it doesn't often come more than once. Yes – that's right. Put another stick on the fire, and a little more stuff into that weak mixture you're so fond of. Do you remember old Blauklot the carpenter, on that German ship that picked us up when the *Clontarf* went to the bottom? We were hove to in a howling gale one night, as snug as you please, with no land within five hundred miles, and the ship coming up and falling off as regularly as clockwork – 'Biddy te boor beebles ashore tis night, poys!' old Blauklot sang out, as he went off to his quarters with the sail-maker. I often think of that, now that I'm ashore for good and all.

Yes, it was on a night like this, when I was at home for a spell, waiting to take the *Olympia* out on her first trip – it was on the next voyage that she broke the record, you remember – but that dates it. Ninety-two was the year, early in November.

The weather was dirty, Pratt was out of temper, and the dinner was bad, very bad indeed, which didn't improve matters, and cold, which made it worse. The poor little lady was very unhappy about it, and insisted on making a Welsh rarebit on the table to counteract the raw turnips and the half-boiled mutton. Pratt must have had a hard day. Perhaps he had lost a patient. At all events, he was in a nasty temper.

'My wife is trying to poison me, you see!' he said. 'She'll succeed some day.' I saw that she was hurt, and I made believe to laugh, and said that Mrs Pratt was much too clever to get rid of her husband in such a simple way; and then I began to tell them about Japanese tricks with spun glass and chopped horsehair and the like.

Pratt was a doctor, and knew a lot more than I did about such things, but that only put me on my mettle, and I told a story about a woman in Ireland who did for three husbands before anyone suspected foul play.

Did you never hear that tale? The fourth husband managed to keep awake and caught her, and she was hanged. How did she do it? She drugged them, and poured melted lead into their ears through a little horn funnel when they were asleep … No – that's the wind whistling. It's backing up to the southward again. I can tell by the sound. Besides, the other thing doesn't often come more than once in an evening even at this time of year – when it happened. Yes, it was in November. Poor Mrs Pratt died suddenly in her bed not long after I dined here. I can fix the date, because I got the news in New York by the steamer that followed the *Olympia* when I took her out on her first trip. You had the *Leofric* the same year? Yes, I remember. What a pair of old buffers we are coming to be, you and I. Nearly fifty years since we were apprentices together on the *Clontarf*. Shall you ever forget old Blauklot? 'Biddy te boor beebles ashore, poys!' Ha, ha! Take a little more, with all that water. It's the old Hulstkamp I found in the cellar when this house came to me, the same I brought Luke from Amsterdam five-and-twenty years ago. He had never touched a drop of it. Perhaps he's sorry now, poor fellow.

Where did I leave off? I told you that Mrs Pratt died suddenly – yes. Luke must have been lonely here after she was dead, I should think; I came to see him now and then, and he looked worn and nervous, and told me that his practice was growing too heavy for him, though he wouldn't take an assistant on any account. Years went on, and his son was killed in South Africa, and after that he began to be queer. There was something about him not like other people. I believe he kept his senses in his profession to the end; there was no complaint of his having made bad mistakes in cases, or anything of that sort, but he had a look about him –

Luke was a red-headed man with a pale face when he was young, and he was never stout; in middle age he turned a sandy grey, and after his son died he grew thinner and thinner, till his head looked like a skull with parchment stretched over it very tight, and his eyes had a sort of glare in them that was very disagreeable to look at.

He had an old dog that poor Mrs Pratt had been fond of, and that used to follow her everywhere. He was a bulldog, and the sweetest tempered beast you ever saw, though he had a way of hitching his upper lip behind one of his fangs that frightened strangers a good deal. Sometimes, of an evening, Pratt and Bumble – that was the dog's name – used to sit and look at each other a long time, thinking about old times, I suppose, when Luke's wife used to sit in that chair you've got. That was always her place, and this was the doctor's, where I'm sitting. Bumble used to climb up by the footstool – he was old and fat by that time, and could not jump much, and his teeth were getting shaky. He would look steadily at Luke, and Luke looked steadily at the dog, his face growing more and more like a skull with two little coals for eyes; and after about five minutes or so, though it may have been less, old Bumble would suddenly begin to shake all over, and all on a sudden he would set up an awful howl, as if he had been shot, and tumble out of the easy-chair and trot away, and hide himself under the sideboard, and lie there making odd noises.

Considering Pratt's looks in those last months, the thing is not surprising, you know. I'm not nervous or imaginative, but I can quite believe he might have sent a sensitive woman into hysterics – his head looked so much like a skull in parchment.

At last I came down one day before Christmas, when my ship was in dock and I had three weeks off. Bumble was not about, and I said casually that I supposed the old dog was dead.

'Yes,' Pratt answered, and I thought there was something odd in his tone even before he went on after a little pause. 'I killed him,' he said presently. 'I could not stand it any longer.'

I asked what it was that Luke could not stand, though I guessed well enough.

'He had a way of sitting in her chair and glaring at me, and then howling.' Luke shivered a little. 'He didn't suffer at all, poor old Bumble,' he went on in a hurry, as if he thought I might imagine he had been cruel. 'I put dionine into his drink to make him sleep soundly, and then I chloroformed him gradually, so that he could not have felt suffocated even if he was dreaming. It's been quieter since then.'

I wondered what he meant, for the words slipped out as if he could not help saying them. I've understood since. He meant that he did not hear that noise so often after the dog was out of the way. Perhaps he thought at first that it was old Bumble in the yard howling at the moon, though it's not that kind of noise, is it? Besides, I know what it is, if Luke didn't. It's only a noise, after all, and a noise never hurt anybody yet. But he was much more imaginative than I am. No doubt there really is something about this place that I don't understand; but when I don't understand a thing, I call it a phenomenon, and I don't take it for granted that it's going to kill me, as he did. I don't understand everything, by long odds, nor do you, nor does any man who has been to sea. We used to talk of tidal waves, for instance, and we could not account for them; now we account for them by calling them submarine earthquakes, and we branch off into fifty theories, any one of which might make earthquakes quite comprehensible if we only knew what they are. I fell in with one of them once, and the inkstand flew straight up from the table against the ceiling of my cabin. The same thing happened to Captain Lecky – I dare say you've read about it in his 'Wrinkles.' Very good. If that sort of thing took place ashore, in this room for instance, a nervous person would talk about spirits and levitation and fifty things that mean nothing, instead of just quietly setting it down as a 'phenomenon' that has not been explained yet. My view of that voice, you see.

Besides, what is there to prove that Luke killed his wife? I would not even suggest such a thing to anyone but you. After all, there was nothing but the coincidence that poor little Mrs Pratt died suddenly in her bed a few days after I told that story at dinner. She was not the only woman who ever died like that. Luke got the doctor over from the next parish, and they agreed that she had died of something the matter with her heart. Why not? It's common enough.

Of course, there was the ladle. I never told anybody about that, and it made me start when I found it in the cupboard in the bedroom. It was new, too – a little tinned iron ladle that had not been in the fire more than once or twice, and there was some lead in it that had been melted, and stuck to the bottom of the bowl, all grey, with hardened dross on it. But that proves nothing. A country doctor is generally a handy man, who does everything for himself, and Luke may have had a dozen reasons for melting a little lead in a ladle. He was fond of sea-fishing, for instance, and he may have cast a sinker for a night-line; perhaps it was a weight for the hall clock, or something like that. All the same, when I found it I had a rather queer sensation, because it looked so much like the thing I had described when I told them the story. Do you understand? It affected me unpleasantly, and I threw it away; it's at the bottom of the sea a mile from the Spit, and it will be jolly well rusted beyond recognizing if it's ever washed up by the tide.

You see, Luke must have bought it in the village, years ago, for the man sells just such ladles still. I suppose they are used in cooking. In any case, there was no reason why an inquisitive housemaid should find such a thing lying about, with lead in it, and wonder what it was, and perhaps talk to the maid who heard me tell the story at dinner – for that girl married the plumber's son in the village, and may remember the whole thing.

You understand me, don't you? Now that Luke Pratt is dead and gone, and lies buried beside his wife, with an honest man's tombstone at his head, I should not care to stir up anything that could hurt his memory. They are both dead, and their son, too. There was trouble enough about Luke's death, as it was.

How? He was found dead on the beach one morning, and there was a coroner's inquest. There were marks on his throat, but he had not been robbed. The verdict was that he had come to his end 'by the hands or teeth of some person or animal unknown,' for half the jury thought it might have been a big dog that had thrown him down and gripped his windpipe, though the skin of his throat was not broken. No one knew at what time he had gone out, nor where he had been. He was found lying on his back above high-water mark, and an old cardboard bandbox that had belonged to his wife lay under his hand, open. The lid had fallen off. He seemed to have been carrying home a skull in the box – doctors are fond of collecting such things. It had rolled out and lay near his head, and it was a remarkably fine skull, rather small, beautifully shaped and very white, with perfect teeth. That is to say, the upper jaw was perfect, but there was no lower one at all, when I first saw it.

Yes, I found it here when I came. You see, it was very white and polished, like a thing meant to be kept under a glass case, and the people did not know where it came from, nor what to do with it; so they put it back into the bandbox and set it on the shelf of the cupboard in the best bedroom, and of course they showed it to me when I took possession. I was taken down to the beach, too, to be shown the place where Luke was found, and the old fisherman explained just how he was lying, and the skull beside him. The only point he could not explain was why the skull had rolled up the sloping sand toward Luke's head instead of rolling downhill to his feet. It did not seem odd to me at the time, but I have often thought of it since, for the place is rather steep. I'll take you there tomorrow if you likes – I made a sort of cairn of stones there afterward.

When he fell down, or was thrown down – whichever happened – the bandbox struck the sand, and the lid came off, and the thing came out and ought to have rolled down. But it didn't. It was close to his head, almost touching it, and turned with the face toward it. I say it didn't strike me as odd when the man told me; but I could not help thinking about it afterward, again and again, till I saw a picture of it all when I closed my eyes; and then I began to ask myself why the plaguey thing had rolled up instead of down, and why it had stopped near Luke's head, instead of anywhere else, a yard away, for instance.

You naturally want to know what conclusion I reached, don't you? None that at all explained the rolling, at all events. But I got something else into my head, after a time, that made me feel downright uncomfortable.

Oh, I don't mean as to anything supernatural! There may be ghosts, or there may not be. If there are, I'm not inclined to believe that they can hurt living people except by frightening them, and, for my part, I would rather face any shape of ghost than a fog in the Channel when it's crowded. No. What bothered me was just a foolish idea, that's all, and I cannot tell how it began, nor what made it grow till it turned into a certainty.

I was thinking about Luke and his poor wife one evening over my pipe and a dull book, when it occurred to me that the skull might possibly be hers, and I have never got rid of the thought since.

You'll tell me there's no sense in it, no doubt; that Mrs Pratt was buried like a Christian and is lying in the churchyard where they put her, and that it's perfectly monstrous to suppose her husband kept her skull in her old bandbox in his bedroom. All the same, in the face of reason, and commonsense, and probability, I'm convinced that he did. Doctors do all sorts of queer things that would make men like you and me feel creepy, and those are just the things that don't seem probable, nor logical, nor sensible to us.

Then, don't you see? – if it really was her skull, poor woman, the only way of accounting for his having it is that he really killed her, and did it in that way, as the woman killed her husbands in the story, and that he was afraid there might be an examination some day which would betray him. You see, I told that too, and I believe it had really happened some fifty or sixty years ago. They dug up the three skulls, you know, and there was a small lump of lead rattling about in each one. That was what hanged the woman. Luke remembered that, I'm sure. I don't want to know what he did when he thought of it; my taste never ran in the direction of horrors, and I don't fancy you care for them either, do you? No. If you did, you might supply what is wanting to the story.

It must have been rather grim, eh? I wish I did not see the whole thing so distinctly, just as everything must have happened. He took it the night before she was buried, I'm sure, after the coffin had been shut, and when the servant girl was asleep. I would bet anything, that when he'd got it, he put something under the sheet in its place, to fill up and look like it. What do you suppose he put there, under the sheet?

I don't wonder you take me up on what I'm saying! First I tell you that I don't want to know what happened, and that I hate to think about horrors, and then I describe the whole thing to you as if I had seen it. I'm quite sure that it was her work-bag that he put there. I remember the bag very well, for she always used it of an evening; it was made of brown plush, and when it was stuffed full it was about the size of – you understand. Yes, there I am, at it again! You may laugh at me, but you don't live here alone, where it was done, and you didn't tell Luke the story about the melted lead. I'm not nervous, I tell you, but sometimes I begin to feel that I understand why some people are. I dwell on all this when I'm alone, and I dream of it, and when that thing screams – well, frankly, I don't like the noise any more than you do, though I should be used to it by this time.

I ought not to be nervous. I've sailed in a haunted ship. There was a Man in the Top, and two-thirds of the crew died of the West Coast fever inside of ten days after we anchored; but I was all right, then and afterward. I have seen some ugly sights, too, just as you have, and all the rest of us. But nothing ever stuck in my head in the way this does.

You see, I've tried to get rid of the thing, but it doesn't like that. It wants to be there in its place, in Mrs Pratt's bandbox in the cupboard in the best bedroom. It's not happy anywhere else. How do I know that? Because I've tried it. You don't suppose that I've not tried, do you? As long as it's there it only screams now and then, generally at this time of year, but if I put it out of the house it goes on all night, and no servant will stay here twenty-four hours. As it is, I've often been left alone and have been obliged to shift for myself for a fortnight at a time. No one from the village would ever pass a night under the roof now, and as for selling the place, or even letting it, that's out of the question. The old women say that if I stay here I shall come to a bad end myself before long.

I'm not afraid of that. You smile at the mere idea that anyone could take such nonsense seriously. Quite right. It's utterly blatant nonsense, I agree with you. Didn't I tell you that it's only a noise after all when you started and looked round as if you expected to see a ghost standing behind your chair?

I may be all wrong about the skull, and I like to think that I am – when I can. It may be just a fine specimen which Luke got somewhere long ago, and what rattles about inside when you shake it may be nothing but a pebble, or a bit of hard clay, or anything. Skulls that have lain long in the ground generally have something inside them that rattles, don't they? No, I've never tried to get it out, whatever it is; I'm afraid it might be lead, don't you see? And if it is, I don't want to know the fact, for I'd much rather not be sure. If it really is lead, I killed her quite as much as if I had done the deed myself. Anybody must see that, I should think. As long as I don't know for certain, I have the consolation of saying that it's all utterly ridiculous nonsense, that Mrs Pratt died a natural death and that the beautiful skull belonged to Luke when he was a student in London. But if I were quite sure, I believe I should have to leave the house; indeed I do, most certainly. As it is, I had to give up trying to sleep in the best bedroom where the cupboard is.

You ask me why I don't throw it into the pond – yes, but please don't call it a 'confounded bugbear' – it doesn't like being called names.

There! Lord, what a shriek! I told you so! You're quite pale, man. Fill up your pipe and draw your chair nearer to the fire, and take some more drink. Old Hollands never hurt anybody yet. I've seen a Dutchman in Java drink half a jug of Hulstkamp in a morning without turning a hair. I don't take much rum myself, because it doesn't agree with my rheumatism, but you are not rheumatic and it won't damage you. Besides, it's a very damp night outside. The wind is howling again, and it will soon be in the south-west; do you hear how the windows rattle? The tide must have turned too, by the moaning.

We should not have heard the thing again if you had not said that. I'm pretty sure we should not. Oh yes, if you choose to describe it as a coincidence, you are quite welcome, but I would rather that you should not call the thing names again, if you don't mind. It may be that the poor little woman hears, and perhaps it hurts her, don't you know? Ghost? No! You don't call anything a ghost that you can take in your hands and look at in broad daylight, and that rattles when you shake it. Do you, now? But it's something that hears and understands; there's no doubt about that.

I tried sleeping in the best bedroom when I first came to the house, just because it was the best and the most comfortable, but I had to give it up. It was their room, and there's the big bed she died in, and the cupboard is in the thickness of the wall, near the head, on the left. That's where it likes to be kept, in its bandbox. I only used the room for a fortnight after I came, and then I turned out and took the little room downstairs, next to the surgery, where Luke used to sleep when he expected to be called to a patient during the night.

I was always a good sleeper ashore; eight hours is my dose, eleven to seven when I'm alone, twelve to eight when I have a friend with me. But I could not sleep after three o'clock in the morning in that room – a quarter past, to be accurate – as a matter of fact, I timed it with my old pocket chronometer, which still keeps good time, and it was always at exactly seventeen minutes past three. I wonder whether that was the hour when she died?

It was not what you have heard. If it had been that I could not have stood it two nights. It was just a start and a moan and hard breathing for a few seconds in the cupboard, and it could never have waked me under ordinary circumstances, I'm sure. I suppose you are like me in that, and we are just like other people who have been to sea. No natural sounds disturb us at all, not all the racket of a square-rigger hove to in a heavy gale, or rolling on her beam ends before the wind. But if a lead pencil gets adrift and rattles in the drawer of your cabin table you are awake in a moment. Just so – you always understand. Very well, the noise in the cupboard was no louder than that, but it waked me instantly.

I said it was like a 'start.' I know what I mean, but it's hard to explain without seeming to talk nonsense. Of course you cannot exactly 'hear' a person 'start'; at the most, you might hear the quick drawing of the breath between the parted lips and closed teeth, and the almost imperceptible sound of clothing that moved suddenly though very slightly. It was like that.

You know how one feels what a sailing vessel is going to do, two or three seconds before she does it, when one has the wheel. Riders say the same of a horse, but that's less strange, because the horse is a live animal with feelings of its own, and only poets and landsmen talk about a ship being alive, and all that. But I have always felt somehow that besides being a steaming machine or a sailing machine for carrying weights, a vessel at sea is a sensitive instrument, and a means of communication between nature and man, and most particularly the man at the wheel, if she is steered by hand. She takes her impressions directly from wind and sea, tide and stream, and transmits them to the man's hand, just as the wireless telegraph picks up the interrupted currents aloft and turns them out below in the form of a message.

You see what I am driving at; I felt that something started in the cupboard, and I felt it so vividly that I heard it, though there may have been nothing to hear, and the sound inside my head waked me suddenly. But I really heard the other noise. It was as if it were muffled inside a box, as far away as if it came through a long-distance telephone; and yet I knew that it was inside the cupboard near the head of my bed. My hair did not bristle and my blood did not run cold that time. I simply resented being waked up by something that had no business to make a noise, any more than a pencil should rattle in the drawer of my cabin table on board ship. For I did not understand; I just supposed that the cupboard had some communication with the outside air, and that the wind had got in and was moaning through it with a sort of very faint screech. I struck a light and looked at my watch, and it was seventeen minutes past three. Then I turned over and went to sleep on my right ear. That's my good one; I'm pretty deaf with the other, for I struck the water with it when I was a lad in diving from the foretopsail yard. Silly thing to do, it was, but the result is very convenient when I want to go to sleep when there's a noise.

That was the first night, and the same thing happened again and several times afterward, but not regularly, though it was always at the same time, to a second; perhaps I was sometimes sleeping on my good ear, and sometimes not. I overhauled the cupboard and there was no way by which the wind could get in, or anything else, for the door makes a good fit, having been meant to keep out moths. I suppose Mrs Pratt must have kept her winter things in it, for it still smells of camphor and turpentine.

After about a fortnight I had had enough of the noises. So far I had said to myself that it would be silly to yield to it and take the skull out of the room. Things always look differently by daylight, don't they? But the voice grew louder – I suppose one may call it a voice – and it got inside my deaf ear, too, one night. I realised that when I was wide awake, for my good ear was jammed down on the pillow, and I ought not to have heard a fog-horn in that position. But I heard that, and it made me lose my temper, unless it scared me, for sometimes the two are not far apart. I struck a light and got up, and I opened the cupboard, grabbed the bandbox and threw it out of the window, as far as I could.

Then my hair stood on end. The thing screamed in the air, like a shell from a twelve-inch gun. It fell on the other side of the road. The night was very dark, and I could not see it fall, but I know it fell beyond the road. The window is just over the front door, it's fifteen yards to the fence, more or less, and the road is ten yards wide. There's a quickset hedge beyond, along the glebe that belongs to the vicarage.

I did not sleep much more that night. It was not more than half an hour after I had thrown the bandbox out when I heard a shriek outside – like what we've had tonight, but worse, more despairing, I should call it; and it may have been my imagination, but I could have sworn that the screams came nearer and nearer each time. I lit a pipe, and walked up and down for a bit, and then took a book and sat up reading, but I'll be hanged if I can remember what I read nor even what the book was, for every now and then a shriek came up that would have made a dead man turn in his coffin.

A little before dawn someone knocked at the front-door. There was no mistaking that for anything else, and I opened my window and looked down, for I guessed that someone wanted the doctor, supposing that the new man had taken Luke's house. It was rather a relief to hear a human knock after that awful noise.

You cannot see the door from above, owing to the little porch. The knocking came again, and I called out, asking who was there, but nobody answered, though the knock was repeated. I sang out again, and said that the doctor did not live here any longer. There was no answer, but it occurred to me that it might be some old countryman who was stone deaf. So I took my candle and went down to open the door. Upon my word, I was not thinking of the thing yet, and I had almost forgotten the other noises. I went down convinced that I should find somebody outside, on the doorstep, with a message. I set the candle on the hall-table, so that the wind should not blow it out when I opened. While I was drawing the old-fashioned bolt I heard the knocking again. It was not loud, and it had a queer, hollow sound, now that I was close to it, I remember, but I certainly thought it was made by some person who wanted to get in.

It wasn't. There was nobody there, but as I opened the door inward, standing a little on one side, so as to see out at once, something rolled across the threshold and stopped against my foot.

I drew back as I felt it, for I knew what it was before I looked down. I cannot tell you how I knew, and it seemed unreasonable, for I am still quite sure that I had thrown it across the road. It's a French window, that opens wide, and I got a good swing when I flung it out. Besides, when I went out early in the morning, I found the bandbox beyond the thickest hedge.

You may think it opened when I threw it, and that the skull dropped out; but that's impossible, for nobody could throw an empty cardboard box so far. It's out of the question; you might as well try to fling a ball of paper twenty-five yards, or a blown bird's egg.

To go back, I shut and bolted the hall-door, picked the thing up carefully, and put it on the table beside the candle. I did that mechanically, as one instinctively does the right thing in danger without thinking at all – unless one does the opposite. It may seem odd, but I believe my first thought had been that somebody might come and find me there on the threshold while it was resting against my foot, lying a little on its side, and turning one hollow eye up at my face, as if it meant to accuse me. And the light and shadow from the candle played in the hollows of the eyes as it stood on the table, so that they seemed to open and shut at me. Then the candle went out quite unexpectedly, though the door was fastened and there was not the least draught; and I used up at least half a dozen matches before it would burn again.

I sat down rather suddenly, without quite knowing why. Probably I had been badly frightened, and perhaps you will admit there was no great shame in being scared. The thing had come home, and it wanted to go upstairs, back to its cupboard. I sat still and stared at it for a bit, till I began to feel very cold; then I took it and carried it up and set it in its place, and I remember that I spoke to it, and promised that it should have its bandbox again in the morning,

You want to know whether I stayed in the room till daybreak? Yes, but I kept a light burning, and sat up smoking and reading, most likely out of fright; plain, undeniable fear, and you need not call it cowardice either, for that's not the same thing. I could not have stayed alone with that thing in the cupboard; I should have been scared to death, though I'm not more timid than other people. Confound it all, man, it had crossed the road alone, and had got up the doorstep and had knocked to be let in.

When the dawn came, I put on my boots and went out to find the bandbox. I had to go a good way round, by the gate near the highroad, and I found the box open and hanging on the other side of the hedge. It had caught on the twigs by the string, and the lid had fallen off and was lying on the ground below it. That shows that it did not open till it was well over; and if it had not opened as soon as it left my hand, what was inside it must have gone beyond the road too.

That's all. I took the box upstairs to the cupboard, and put the skull back and locked it up. When the girl brought me my breakfast she said she was sorry, but that she must go, and she did not care if she lost her month's wages. I looked at her, and her face was a sort of greenish, yellowish white. I pretended to be surprised, and asked what was the matter; but that was of no use, for she just turned on me and wanted to know whether I meant to stay in a haunted house, and how long I expected to live if I did, for though she noticed I was sometimes a little hard of hearing, she did not believe that even I could sleep through those screams again – and if I could, why had I been moving about the house and opening and shutting the front-door, between three and four in the morning? There was no answering that, since she had heard me, so off she went, and I was left to myself.

I went down to the village during the morning and found a woman who was willing to come and do the little work there is and cook my dinner, on condition that she might go home every night. As for me, I moved downstairs that day, and I have never tried to sleep in the best bedroom since.

After a little while I got a brace of middle-aged Scotch servants from London, and things were quiet enough for a long time. I began by telling them that the house was in a very exposed position, and that the wind whistled round it a good deal in the autumn and winter, which had given it a bad name in the village, the Cornish people being inclined to superstition and telling ghost stories. The two hard-faced, sandy-haired sisters almost smiled, and they answered with great contempt that they had no great opinion of any Southern bogey whatever, having been in service in two English haunted houses, where they had never seen so much as the Boy in Grey, whom they reckoned no very particular rarity in Forfarshire.

They stayed with me several months, and while they were in the house we had peace and quiet. One of them is here again now, but she went away with her sister within the year. This one – she was the cook – married the sexton, who works in my garden. That's the way of it. It's a small village and he has not much to do, and he knows enough about flowers to help me nicely, besides doing most of the hard work; for though I'm fond of exercise, I'm getting a little stiff in the hinges. He's a sober, silent sort of fellow, who minds his own business, and he was a widower when I came here – Trehearn is his name, James Trehearn. The Scotch sisters would not admit that there was anything wrong about the house, but when November came they gave me warning that they were going, on the ground that the chapel was such a long walk from here, being in the next parish, and that they could not possibly go to our church. But the younger one came back in the spring, and as soon as the banns could be published she was married to James Trehearn by the vicar, and she seems to have had no scruples about hearing him preach since then. I'm quite satisfied, if she is! The couple live in a small cottage that looks over the churchyard.

I suppose you are wondering what all this has to do with what I was talking about. I'm alone so much that when an old friend comes to see me, I sometimes go on talking just for the sake of hearing my own voice. But in this case there is really a connection of ideas. It was James Trehearn who buried poor Mrs Pratt, and her husband after her in the same grave, and it's not far from the back of his cottage. That's the connection in my mind, you see. It's plain enough. He knows something; I'm quite sure that he does, by his manner, though he's such a reticent beggar.

Yes, I'm alone in the house at night now, for Mrs Trehearn does everything herself, and when I have a friend the sexton's niece comes in to wait on the table. He takes his wife home every evening in winter, but in summer, when there's light, she goes by herself. She's not a nervous woman, but she's less sure than she used to be that there are no bogies in England worth a Scotchwoman's notice. Isn't it amusing, the idea that Scotland has a monopoly of the supernatural? Odd sort of national pride, I call that, don't you?

That's a good fire, isn't it? When driftwood gets started at last there's nothing like it, I think. Yes, we get lots of it, for I'm sorry to say there are still a great many wrecks about here. It's a lonely coast, and you may have all the wood you want for the trouble of bringing it in. Trehearn and I borrow a cart now and then, and load it between here and the Spit. I hate a coal fire when I can get wood of any sort. A log is company, even if it's only a piece of a deck-beam or timber sawn off, and the salt in it makes pretty sparks. See how they fly, like Japanese hand-fireworks! Upon my word, with an old friend and a good fire and a pipe, one forgets all about that thing upstairs, especially now that the wind has moderated. It's only a lull, though, and it will blow a gale before morning.

You think you would like to see the skull? I've no objection. There's no reason why you shouldn't have a look at it, and you never saw a more perfect one in your life, except that there are two front teeth missing in the lower jaw.

Oh yes – I had not told you about the jaw yet. Trehearn found it in the garden last spring when he was digging a pit for a new asparagus bed. You know we make asparagus beds six or eight feet deep here. Yes, yes – I had forgotten to tell you that. He was digging straight down, just as he digs a grave; if you want a good asparagus bed made, I advise you to get a sexton to make it for you. Those fellows have a wonderful knack at that sort of digging.

Trehearn had got down about three feet when he cut into a mass of white lime in the side of the trench. He had noticed that the earth was a little looser there, though he says it had not been disturbed for a number of years. I suppose he thought that even old lime might not be good for asparagus, so he broke it out and threw it up. It was pretty hard, he says, in biggish lumps, and out of sheer force of habit he cracked the lumps with his spade as they lay outside the pit beside him; the jawbone of a skull dropped out of one of the pieces. He thinks he must have knocked out the two front teeth in breaking up the lime, but he did not see them anywhere. He's a very experienced man in such things, as you may imagine, and he said at once that the jaw had probably belonged to a young woman, and that the teeth had been complete when she died. He brought it to me and asked me if I wanted to keep it; if I did not, he said he would drop it into the next grave he made in the churchyard, as he supposed it was a Christian jaw, and ought to have decent burial, wherever the rest of the body might be. I told him that doctors often put bones into quicklime to whiten them nicely, and that I supposed Dr Pratt had once had a little lime pit in the garden for that purpose, and had forgotten the jaw. Trehearn looked at me quietly.

'Maybe it fitted that skull that used to be in the cupboard upstairs, sir,' he said. 'Maybe Dr Pratt had put the skull into the lime to clean it, or something, and when he took it out he left the lower jaw behind. There's some human hair sticking in the lime, sir.'

I saw there was, and that was what Trehearn said. If he did not suspect something, why in the world should he have suggested that the jaw might fit the skull? Besides, it did. That's proof that he knows more than he cares to tell. Do you suppose he looked before she was buried? Or perhaps – when he buried Luke in the same grave –

Well, well, it's of no use to go over that, is it? I said I would keep the jaw with the skull, and I took it upstairs and fitted it into its place. There's not the slightest doubt about the two belonging together, and together they are.

Trehearn knows several things. We were talking about plastering the kitchen a while ago, and he happened to remember that it had not been done since the very week when Mrs Pratt died. He did not say that the mason must have left some lime on the place, but he thought it, and that it was the very same lime he had found in the asparagus pit. He knows a lot. Trehearn is one of your silent beggars who can put two and two together. That grave is very near the back of his cottage, too, and he's one of the quickest men with a spade I ever saw. If he wanted to know the truth, he could, and no one else would ever be the wiser unless he chose to tell. In a quiet village like ours, people don't go and spend the night in the churchyard to see whether the sexton potters about by himself between ten o'clock and daylight.

What is awful to think of, is Luke's deliberation, if he did it; his cool certainty that no one would find him out; above all, his nerve, for that must have been extraordinary. I sometimes think it's bad enough to live in the place where it was done, if it really was done. I always put in the condition, you see, for the sake of his memory, and a little bit for my own sake, too.

I'll go upstairs and fetch the box in a minute. Let me light my pipe; there's no hurry! We had supper early, and it's only half-past nine o'clock. I never let a friend go to bed before twelve, or with less than three glasses – you may have as many more as you like, but you sha'n't have less, for the sake of old times.

It's breezing up again, do you hear? That was only a lull just now, and we are going to have a bad night.

A thing happened that made me start a little when I found that the jaw fitted exactly. I'm not very easily started in that way myself, but I have seen people make a quick movement, drawing their breath sharply, when they had thought they were alone and suddenly turned and saw someone very near them. Nobody can call that fear. You wouldn't, would you? No. Well, just when I had set the jaw in its place under the skull, the teeth closed sharply on my finger. It felt exactly as if it were biting me hard, and I confess that I jumped before I realized that I had been pressing the jaw and the skull together with my other hand. I assure you I was not at all nervous. It was broad daylight, too, and a fine day, and the sun was streaming into the best bedroom. It would have been absurd to be nervous, and it was only a quick mistaken impression, but it really made me feel queer. Somehow it made me think of the funny verdict of the coroner's jury on Luke's death, 'by the hand or teeth of some person or animal unknown.' Ever since that I've wished I had seen those marks on his throat, though the lower jaw was missing then.

I have often seen a man do insane things with his hands that he does not realize at all. I once saw a man hanging on by an old awning stop with one hand, leaning backward, outboard, with all his weight on it, and he was just cutting the stop with the knife in his other hand when I got my arms round him. We were in mid-ocean, going twenty knots. He had not the smallest idea what he was doing; neither had I when I managed to pinch my finger between the teeth of that thing. I can feel it now. It was exactly as if it were alive and were trying to bite me. It would if it could, for I know it hates me, poor thing! Do you suppose that what rattles about inside is really a bit of lead? Well. I'll get the box down presently, and if whatever it is happens to drop out into your hands that's your affair. If it's only a clod of earth or a pebble, the whole matter would be off my mind, and I don't believe I should ever think of the skull again; but somehow I cannot bring myself to shake out the bit of hard stuff myself. The mere idea that it may be lead makes me confoundedly uncomfortable, yet I've got the conviction that I shall know before long. I shall certainly know. I'm sure Trehearn knows, but he's such a silent beggar.

I'll go upstairs now and get it. What? You had better go with me? Ha, ha! do you think I'm afraid of a bandbox and a noise? Nonsense!

Bother the candle, it won't light! As if the ridiculous thing understood what it's wanted for! Look at that – the third match. They light fast enough for my pipe. There, do you see? It's a fresh box, just out of the tin safe where I keep the supply on account of the dampness. Oh, you think the wick of the candle may be damp, do you? All right, I'll light the beastly thing in the fire. That won't go out, at all events. Yes, it sputters a bit, but it will keep lighted now. It burns just like any other candle, doesn't it? The fact is, candles are not very good about here. I don't know where they come from, but they have a way of burning low occasionally, with a greenish flame that spits tiny sparks, and I'm often annoyed by their going out of themselves. It cannot be helped, for it will be long before we have electricity in our village. It really is rather a poor light, isn't it?

You think I had better leave you the candle and take the lamp, do you? I don't like to carry lamps about, that's the truth. I never dropped one in my life, but I have always thought I might, and it's so confoundedly dangerous if you do. Besides, I am pretty well used to these rotten candles by this time.

You may as well finish that glass while I'm getting it, for I don't mean to let you off with less than three before you go to bed. You won't have to go upstairs, either, for I've put you in the old study next to the surgery – that's where I live myself. The fact is, I never ask a friend to sleep upstairs now. The last man who did was Crackenthorpe, and he said he was kept awake all night. You remember old Crack, don't you? He stuck to the Service, and they've just made him an admiral. Yes, I'm off now – unless the candle goes out. I couldn't help asking if you remembered Crackenthorpe. If any one had told us that the skinny little idiot he used to be was to turn out the most successful of the lot of us, we should have laughed at the idea, shouldn't we? You and I did not do badly, it's true – but I'm really going now. I don't mean to let you think that I've been putting it off by talking! As if there were anything to be afraid of! If I were scared, I should tell you so quite frankly, and get you to go upstairs with me.

Here's the box. I brought it down very carefully, so as not to disturb it, poor thing. You see, if it were shaken, the jaw might get separated from it again, and I'm sure it wouldn't like that. Yes, the candle went out as I was coming downstairs, but that was the draught from the leaky window on the landing. Did you hear anything? Yes, there was another scream. Am I pale, do you say? That's nothing. My heart is a little queer sometimes, and I went upstairs too fast. In fact, that's one reason why I really prefer to live altogether on the ground-floor.

Wherever that shriek came from, it was not from the skull, for I had the box in my hand when I heard the noise, and here it is now; so we have proved definitely that the screams are produced by something else. I've no doubt I shall find out some day what makes them. Some crevice in the wall, of course, or a crack in a chimney, or a chink in the frame of a window. That's the way all ghost stories end in real life. Do you know, I'm jolly glad I thought of going up and bringing it down for you to see, for that last shriek settles the question. To think that I should have been so weak as to fancy that the poor skull could really cry out like a living thing!

Now I'll open the box, and we'll take it out and look at it under the bright light. It's rather awful to think that the poor lady used to sit there, in your chair, evening after evening, in just the same light, isn't it? But then – I've made up my mind that it's all rubbish from beginning to end, and that it's just an old skull that Luke had when he was a student; and perhaps he put it into the lime merely to whiten it, and could not find the jaw.

I made a seal on the string, you see, after I had put the jaw in its place, and I wrote on the cover. There's the old white label on it still, from the milliner's, addressed to Mrs Pratt when the hat was sent to her, and as there was room I wrote on the edge: 'A skull, once the property of the late Luke Pratt, M.D.' I don't quite know why I wrote that, unless it was with the idea of explaining how the thing happened to be in my possession. I cannot help wondering sometimes what sort of hat it was that came in the bandbox. What colour was it, do you think? Was it a gay spring hat with a bobbing feather and pretty ribands? Strange that the very same box should hold the head that wore the finery – perhaps. No – we made up our minds that it just came from the hospital in London where Luke did his time. It's far better to look at it in that light, isn't it? There's no more connection between that skull and poor Mrs Pratt than there was between my story about the lead and –

Good Lord! Take the lamp – don't let it go out, if you can help it – I'll have the window fastened again in a second – I say, what a gale! There, it's out! I told you so! Never mind, there's the firelight – I've got the window shut – the bolt was only half down. Was the box blown off the table? Where the deuce is it? There! That won't open again, for I've put up the bar. Good dodge, an old-fashioned bar – there's nothing like it. Now, you find the bandbox while I light the lamp. Confound those wretched matches! Yes, a pipe spill is better – it must light in the fire – I hadn't thought of it – thank you – there we are again. Now, where's the box? Yes, put it back on the table, and we'll open it.

That's the first time I have ever known the wind to burst that window open; but it was partly carelessness on my part when I last shut it. Yes, of course I heard the scream. It seemed to go all round the house before it broke in at the window. That proves that it's always been the wind and nothing else, doesn't it? When it was not the wind, it was my imagination. I've always been a very imaginative man: I must have been, though I did not know it. As we grow older we understand ourselves better, don't you know?

I'll have a drop of the Hulstkamp neat, by way of an exception, since you are filling up your glass. That damp gust chilled me, and with my rheumatic tendency I'm very much afraid of a chill, for the cold sometimes seems to stick in my joints all winter when it once gets in.

By George, that's good stuff! I'll just light a fresh pipe, now that everything is snug again, and then we'll open the box. I'm so glad we heard that last scream together, with the skull here on the table between us, for a thing cannot possibly be in two places at the same time, and the noise most certainly came from outside, as any noise the wind makes must. You thought you heard it scream through the room after the window was burst open? Oh yes, so did I, but that was natural enough when everything was open. Of course we heard the wind. What could one expect?

Look here, please. I want you to see that the seal is intact before we open the box together. Will you take my glasses? No, you have your own. All right. The seal is sound, you see, and you can read the words of the motto easily. 'Sweet and low' – that's it – because the poem goes on 'Wind of the Western sea,' and says, 'blow him again to me,' and all that. Here is the seal on my watch-chain, where it's hung for more than forty years. My poor little wife gave it to me when I was courting, and I never had any other. It was just like her to think of those words – she was always fond of Tennyson.

It's of no use to cut the string, for it's fastened to the box, so I'll just break the wax and untie the knot, and afterward we'll seal it up again. You see, I like to feel that the thing is safe in its place, and that nobody can take it out. Not that I should suspect Trehearn of meddling with it, but I always feel that he knows a lot more than he tells.

You see, I've managed it without breaking the string, though when I fastened it I never expected to open the bandbox again. The lid comes off easily enough. There! Now look!

What? Nothing in it? Empty? It's gone, man, the skull is gone!

No, there's nothing the matter with me. I'm only trying to collect my thoughts. It's so strange. I'm positively certain that it was inside when I put on the seal last spring. I can't have imagined that: it's utterly impossible. If I ever took a stiff glass with a friend now and then, I would admit that I might have made some idiotic mistake when I had taken too much. But I don't, and I never did. A pint of ale at supper and half a go of rum at bedtime was the most I ever took in my good days. I believe it's always we sober fellows who get rheumatism and gout! Yet there was my seal, and there is the empty bandbox. That's plain enough.

I say, I don't half like this. It's not right. There's something wrong about it, in my opinion. You needn't talk to me about supernatural manifestations, for I don't believe in them, not a little bit! Somebody must have tampered with the seal and stolen the skull. Sometimes, when I go out to work in the garden in summer, I leave my watch and chain on the table. Trehearn must have taken the seal then, and used it, for he would be quite sure that I should not come in for at least an hour.

If it was not Trehearn – oh, don't talk to me about the possibility that the thing has got out by itself! If it has, it must be somewhere about the house, in some out-of-the-way corner, waiting. We may come upon it anywhere, waiting, for us, don't you know? – just waiting in the dark. Then it will scream at me; it will shriek at me in the dark, for it hates me, I tell you!

The bandbox is quite empty. We are not dreaming, either of us. There, I turn it upside down.

What's that? Something fell out as I turned it over. It's on the floor, it's near your feet, I know it is, and we must find it! Help me to find it, man. Have you got it? For God's sake, give it to me quickly!

Lead! I knew it when I heard it fall; I knew it couldn't be anything else by the little thud it made on the hearthrug. So it was lead after all, and Luke did it.

I feel a little bit shaken up – not exactly nervous, you know, but badly shaken up, that's the fact. Anybody would, I should think. After all, you cannot say that it's fear of the thing, for I went up and brought it down – at least, I believed I was bringing it down, and that's the same thing, and by George, rather than give in to such silly nonsense, I'll take the box upstairs again and put it back in its place. It's not that. It's the certainty that the poor little woman came to her end in that way, by my fault, because I told the story. That's what is so dreadful. Somehow, I had always hoped that I should never be quite sure of it, but there is no doubting it now. Look at that!

Look at it! That little lump of lead with no particular shape. Think of what it did, man! Doesn't it make you shiver? He gave her something to make her sleep, of course, but there must have been one moment of awful agony. Think of having boiling lead poured into your brain. Think of it. She was dead before she could scream, but only think of – oh! – there it is again – it's just outside – I know it's just outside – I can't keep it out of my head! – oh! – oh!

You thought I had fainted? No, I wish I had, for it would have stopped sooner. It's all very well to say that it's only a noise, and that a noise never hurt anybody – you're as white as a shroud yourself. There's only one thing to be done, if we hope to close an eye tonight. We must find it and put it back into its bandbox and shut it up in the cupboard, where it likes to be. I don't know how it got out, but it wants to get in again. That's why it screams so awfully tonight – it was never so bad as this – never since I first heard it.

Bury it? Yes, if we can find it, we'll bury it, if it takes us all night. We'll bury it six feet deep and ram down the earth over it, so that it shall never get out again, and if it screams we shall hardly hear it so deep down. Quick, we'll get the lantern and look for it. It cannot be far away; I'm sure it's just outside – it was coming in when I shut the window, I know it.

Yes, you're quite right. I'm losing my senses, and I must get hold of myself. Don't speak to me for a minute or two; I'll sit quite still and keep my eyes shut and repeat something I know. That's the best way.

'Add together the altitude, the latitude, and the polar distance, divide by two and subtract the altitude from the half-sum; then add the logarithm of the secant of the latitude, the cosecant of the polar distance, the cosine of the half-sum and the sine of the half-sum minus the altitude' – there! Don't say that I'm out of my senses, for any memory is all right, isn't it?

Of course, you may say that it's mechanical, and that we never forget the things we learned when we were boys and have used almost every day for a lifetime. But that's the very point. When a man is going crazy, it's the mechanical part of his mind that gets out of order and won't work right; he remembers things that never happened, or he sees things that aren't real, or he hears noises when there is perfect silence. That's not what is the matter with either of us, is it?

Come, we'll get the lantern and go round the house. It's not raining – only blowing like old boots, as we used to say. The lantern is in the cupboard under the stairs in the hall, and I always keep it trimmed in case of a wreck.

No use to look for the thing? I don't see how you can say that. It was nonsense to talk of burying it, of course, for it doesn't want to be buried; it wants to go back into its bandbox and be taken upstairs, poor thing! Trehearn took it out, I know, and made the seal over again. Perhaps he took it to the churchyard, and he may have meant well. I daresay he thought that it would not scream any more if it were quietly laid in consecrated ground, near where it belongs. But it has come home. Yes, that's it. He's not half a bad fellow, Trehearn, and rather religiously inclined, I think. Does not that sound natural, and reasonable, and well meant? He supposed it screamed because it was not decently buried – with the rest. But he was wrong. How should he know that it screams at me because it hates me, and because it's my fault that there was that little lump of lead in it?

No use to look for it, anyhow? Nonsense! I tell you it wants to be found – hark! What's that knocking? Do you hear it? Knock – knock – knock – three times, then a pause, and then again. It has a hollow sound, hasn't it?

It has come home. I've heard that knock before. It wants to come in and be taken upstairs, in its box. It's at the front door.

Will you come with me? We'll take it in. Yes, I own that I don't like to go alone and open the door. The thing will roll in and stop against my foot, just as it did before, and the light will go out. I'm a good deal shaken by finding that bit of lead, and, besides, my heart isn't quite right – too much strong tobacco, perhaps. Besides, I'm quite willing to own that I'm a bit nervous tonight, if I never was before in my life.

That's right, come along! I'll take the box with me, so as not to come back. Do you hear the knocking? It's not like any other knocking I ever heard. If you will hold this door open, I can find the lantern under the stairs by the light from this room without bringing the lamp into the hall – it would only go out.

The thing knows we are coming – hark! It's impatient to get in. Don't shut the door till the lantern is ready, whatever you do. There will be the usual trouble with the matches, I suppose – no, the first one, by Jove! I tell you it wants to get in, so there's no trouble. All right with that door now; shut it, please. Now come and hold the lantern, for it's blowing so hard outside that I shall have to use both hands. That's it, hold the light low. Do you hear the knocking still? Here goes – I'll open just enough with my foot against the bottom of the door – now!

Catch it! It's only the wind that blows it across the floor, that's all – there's half a hurricane outside, I tell you! Have you got it? The bandbox is on the table. One minute, and I'll have the bar up. There!

Why did you throw it into the box so roughly? It doesn't like that, you know.

What do you say? Bitten your hand? Nonsense, man! You did just what I did. You pressed the jaws together with your other hand and pinched yourself. Let me see. You don't mean to say you have drawn blood? You must have squeezed hard, by Jove, for the skin is certainly torn. I'll give you some carbolic solution for it before we go to bed, for they say a scratch from a skull's tooth may go bad and give trouble.

Come inside again and let me see it by the lamp. I'll bring the bandbox – never mind the lantern, it may just as well burn in the hall, for I shall need it presently when I go up the stairs. Yes, shut the door if you will; it makes it more cheerful and bright. Is your finger still bleeding? I'll get you the carbolic in an instant; just let me see the thing.

Ugh! There's a drop of blood on the upper jaw. It's on the eye-tooth. Ghastly, isn't it? When I saw it running along the floor of the hall, the strength almost went out of my hands, and I felt my knees bending; then I understood that it was the gale, driving it over the smooth boards. You don't blame me? No, I should think not! We were boys together, and we've seen a thing or two, and we may just as well own to each other that we were both in a beastly funk when it slid across the floor at you. No wonder you pinched your finger picking it up, after that, if I did the same thing out of sheer nervousness in broad daylight, with the sun streaming in on me.

Strange that the jaw should stick to it so closely, isn't it? I suppose it's the dampness, for it shuts like a vice – I have wiped off the drop of blood, for it was not nice to look at. I'm not going to try to open the jaws, don't be afraid! I shall not play any tricks with the poor thing, but I'll just seal the box again, and we'll take it upstairs and put it away where it wants to be. The wax is on the writing-table by the window. Thank you. It will be long before I leave my seal lying about again, for Trehearn to use, I can tell you. Explain? I don't explain natural phenomena, but if you choose to think that Trehearn had hidden it somewhere in the bushes, and that the gale blew it to the house against the door, and made it knock, as if it wanted to be let in, you're not thinking the impossible, and I'm quite ready to agree with you.

Do you see that? You can swear that you've actually seen me seal it this time, in case anything of the kind should occur again. The wax fastens the strings to the lid, which cannot possibly be lifted, even enough to get in one finger. You're quite satisfied, aren't you? Yes. Besides, I shall lock the cupboard and keep the key in my pocket hereafter.

Now we can take the lantern and go upstairs. Do you know? I'm very much inclined to agree with your theory that the wind blew it against the house. I'll go ahead, for I know the stairs; just hold the lantern near my feet as we go up. How the wind howls and whistles! Did you feel the sand on the floor under your shoes as we crossed the hall?

Yes – this is the door of the best bedroom. Hold up the lantern, please. This side, by the head of the bed. I left the cupboard open when I got the box. Isn't it queer how the faint odour of women's dresses will hang about an old closet for years? This is the shelf. You've seen me set the box there, and now you see me turn the key and put it into my pocket. So that's done!

Goodnight. Are you sure you're quite comfortable? It's not much of a room, but I daresay you would as soon sleep here as upstairs tonight. If you want anything, sing out; there's only a lath and plaster partition between us. There's not so much wind on this side by half. There's the Hollands on the table, if you'll have one more nightcap. No? Well, do as you please. Goodnight again, and don't dream about that thing, if you can.

The following Paragraph appeared in the *Penraddon News,* 23rd November, 1906:

'MYSTERIOUS DEATH OF A RETIRED SEA CAPTAIN

'The village of Tredcombe is much disturbed by the strange death of Captain Charles Braddock, and all sorts of impossible stories are circulating with regard to the circumstances, which certainly seem difficult of explanation. The retired captain, who had successfully commanded in his time the largest and fastest liners belonging to one of the principal transatlantic steamship companies, was found dead in his bed on Tuesday morning in his own cottage, a quarter of a mile from the village. An examination was made at once by the local practitioner, which revealed the horrible fact that the deceased had been bitten in the throat by a human assailant, with such amazing force as to crush the windpipe and cause death. The marks of the teeth of both jaws were so plainly visible on the skin that they could be counted, but the perpetrator of the deed had evidently lost the two lower middle incisors. It is hoped that this peculiarity may help to identify the murderer, who can only be a dangerous escaped maniac. The deceased, though over sixty-five years of age, is said to have been a hale man of considerable physical strength, and it is remarkable that no signs of any struggle were visible in the room, nor could it be ascertained how the murderer had entered the house. Warning has been sent to all the insane asylums in the United Kingdom, but as yet no information has been received regarding the escape of any dangerous patient.

'The coroner's jury returned the somewhat singular verdict that Captain Braddock came to his death "by the hands or teeth of some person unknown." The local surgeon is said to have expressed privately the opinion that the maniac is a woman, a view he deduces from the small size of the jaws, as shown by the marks of the teeth. The whole affair is shrouded in mystery. Captain Braddock was a widower, and lived alone. He leaves no children.'

[*Note.* – Students of ghost lore and haunted houses will find the foundation of the story in the legends about a skull which is still preserved in the farmhouse called Bettiscombe Manor, situated, I believe, on the Dorsetshire coast.]

THE WILLOWS

Algernon Blackwood

Algernon Blackwood (1869–1951) was a prolific English writer best known for his supernatural horror. In tales such as 'The Willows' unease is generated by ambiguity that mixes the weird with a talent for writing about wild or rural places – a break with the past and the classic haunted house. Although Lovecraft thought Blackwood a master of the ghost story, Blackwood famously was not as impressed with Lovecraft. Noted critic S. T. Joshi has stated that Blackwood's short story collection *Incredible Adventures* 'may be the premier weird collection' of the twentieth century. Along with Alfred Kubin and F. Marion Crawford, among others, Blackwood helped usher in the modern era of weird fiction.

After leaving Vienna, and long before you come to Buda-Pesth, the Danube enters a region of singular loneliness and desolation, where its waters spread away on all sides regardless of a main channel, and the country becomes a swamp for miles upon miles, covered by a vast sea of low willow-bushes. On the big maps this deserted area is painted in a fluffy blue, growing fainter in colour as it leaves the banks, and across it may be seen in large straggling letters the word Sumpfe, meaning marshes.

In high flood this great acreage of sand, shingle-beds, and willow-grown islands is almost topped by the water, but in normal seasons the bushes bend and rustle in the free winds, showing their silver leaves to the sunshine in an ever-moving plain of bewildering beauty. These willows never attain to the dignity of trees; they have no rigid trunks; they remain humble bushes, with rounded tops and soft outline, swaying on slender stems that answer to the least pressure of the wind; supple as grasses, and so continually shifting that they somehow give the impression that the entire plain is moving and alive. For the wind sends waves rising and falling over the whole surface, waves of leaves instead of waves of water, green swells like the sea, too, until the branches turn and lift, and then silvery white as their under-side turns to the sun.

Happy to slip beyond the control of the stern banks, the Danube here wanders about at will among the intricate network of channels intersecting the islands everywhere with broad avenues down which the waters pour with a shouting sound; making whirlpools, eddies, and foaming rapids; tearing at the sandy banks; carrying away masses of shore and willow-clumps; and forming new islands innumerably which shift daily in size and shape and possess at best an impermanent life, since the flood-time obliterates their very existence.

Properly speaking, this fascinating part of the river's life begins soon after leaving Pressburg, and we, in our Canadian canoe, with gipsy tent and frying-pan on board, reached it on the crest of a rising flood about mid-July. That very same morning, when the sky was reddening before sunrise, we had slipped swiftly through still-sleeping

Vienna, leaving it a couple of hours later a mere patch of smoke against the blue hills of the Wienerwald on the horizon; we had breakfasted below Fischeramend under a grove of birch trees roaring in the wind; and had then swept on the tearing current past Orth, Hainburg, Petronell (the old Roman Carnuntum of Marcus Aurelius), and so under the frowning heights of Thelsen on a spur of the Carpathians, where the March steals in quietly from the left and the frontier is crossed between Austria and Hungary.

Racing along at twelve kilometres an hour soon took us well into Hungary, and the muddy waters – sure sign of flood – sent us aground on many a shingle-bed, and twisted us like a cork in many a sudden belching whirlpool before the towers of Pressburg (Hungarian, Poszony) showed against the sky; and then the canoe, leaping like a spirited horse, flew at top speed under the grey walls, negotiated safely the sunken chain of the Fliegende Brucke ferry, turned the corner sharply to the left, and plunged on yellow foam into the wilderness of islands, sand-banks, and swamp-land beyond – the land of the willows.

The change came suddenly, as when a series of bioscope pictures snaps down on the streets of a town and shifts without warning into the scenery of lake and forest. We entered the land of desolation on wings, and in less than half an hour there was neither boat nor fishing-hut nor red roof, nor any single sign of human habitation and civilization within sight. The sense of remoteness from the world of human kind, the utter isolation, the fascination of this singular world of willows, winds, and waters, instantly laid its spell upon us both, so that we allowed laughingly to one another that we ought by rights to have held some special kind of passport to admit us, and that we had, somewhat audaciously, come without asking leave into a separate little kingdom of wonder and magic – a kingdom that was reserved for the use of others who had a right to it, with everywhere unwritten warnings to trespassers for those who had the imagination to discover them.

Though still early in the afternoon, the ceaseless buffetings of a most tempestuous wind made us feel weary, and we at once began casting about for a suitable camping-ground for the night. But the bewildering character of the islands made landing difficult; the swirling flood carried us inshore and then swept us out again; the willow branches tore our hands as we seized them to stop the canoe, and we pulled many a yard of sandy bank into the water before at length we shot with a great sideways blow from the wind into a backwater and managed to beach the bows in a cloud of spray. Then we lay panting and laughing after our exertions on the hot yellow sand, sheltered from the wind, and in the full blaze of a scorching sun, a cloudless blue sky above, and an immense army of dancing, shouting willow bushes, closing in from all sides, shining with spray and clapping their thousand little hands as though to applaud the success of our efforts.

'What a river!' I said to my companion, thinking of all the way we had travelled from the source in the Black Forest, and how he had often been obliged to wade and push in the upper shallows at the beginning of June.

'Won't stand much nonsense now, will it?' he said, pulling the canoe a little farther into safety up the sand, and then composing himself for a nap.

I lay by his side, happy and peaceful in the bath of the elements – water, wind, sand, and the great fire of the sun – thinking of the long journey that lay behind us, and of the great stretch before us to the Black Sea, and how lucky I was to have such a delightful and charming travelling companion as my friend, the Swede.

We had made many similar journeys together, but the Danube, more than any other river I knew, impressed us from the very beginning with its aliveness. From its tiny bubbling entry into the world among the pinewood gardens of Donaueschingen, until this moment when it began to play the great river-game of losing itself among the deserted swamps, unobserved, unrestrained, it had seemed to us like following the grown of some living creature. Sleepy at first, but later developing violent desires as it became conscious of its deep soul, it rolled, like some huge fluid being, through all the countries we had passed, holding our little craft on its mighty shoulders, playing roughly with us sometimes, yet always friendly and well-meaning, till at length we had come inevitably to regard it as a Great Personage.

How, indeed, could it be otherwise, since it told us so much of its secret life? At night we heard it singing to the moon as we lay in our tent, uttering that odd sibilant note peculiar to itself and said to be caused by the rapid tearing of the pebbles along its bed, so great is its hurrying speed. We knew, too, the voice of its gurgling whirlpools, suddenly bubbling up on a surface previously quite calm; the roar of its shallows and swift rapids; its constant steady thundering below all mere surface sounds; and that ceaseless tearing of its icy waters at the banks. How it stood up and shouted when the rains fell flat upon its face! And how its laughter roared out when the wind blew upstream and tried to stop its growing speed! We knew all its sounds and voices, its tumblings and foamings, its unnecessary splashing against the bridges; that self-conscious chatter when there were hills to look on; the affected dignity of its speech when it passed through the little towns, far too important to laugh; and all these faint, sweet whisperings when the sun caught it fairly in some slow curve and poured down upon it till the steam rose.

It was full of tricks, too, in its early life before the great world knew it. There were places in the upper reaches among the Swabian forests, when yet the first whispers of its destiny had not reached it, where it elected to disappear through holes in the ground, to appear again on the other side of the porous limestone hills and start a new river with another name; leaving, too, so little water in its own bed that we had to climb out and wade and push the canoe through miles of shallows.

And a chief pleasure, in those early days of its irresponsible youth, was to lie low, like Brer Fox, just before the little turbulent tributaries came to join it from the Alps, and to refuse to acknowledge them when in, but to run for miles side by side, the dividing line well marked, the very levels different, the Danube utterly declining to recognize the newcomer. Below Passau, however, it gave up this particular trick, for there the Inn comes in with a thundering power impossible to ignore, and so pushes and incommodes the parent river that there is hardly room for them in the long twisting gorge that follows, and the Danube is shoved this way and that against the cliffs, and forced to hurry itself with great waves and mush dashing to and fro in order to get through in time. And during the fight our canoe slipped down from its shoulder to its breast, and had the time of its life among the struggling waves. But the Inn taught the old river a lesson, and after Passau it no longer pretended to ignore new arrivals.

This was many days back, of course, and since then we had come to know other aspects of the great creature, and across the Bavarian wheat plain of Straubing she wandered so slowly under the blazing June sun that we could well imagine only the surface inches were water, while below there moved, concealed as by a silken mantle, a whole army of Undines, passing silently and unseen down to the sea, and very leisurely too, lest they be discovered.

Much, too, we forgave her because of her friendliness to the birds and animals that haunted the shores. Cormorants lined the banks in lonely places in rows like short black palings; grey crows crowded the shingle-beds; storks stood fishing in the vistas of shallower water that opened up between the islands, and hawks, swans, and marsh birds of all sorts filled the air with glinting wings and singing, petulant cries. It was impossible to feel annoyed with the river's vagaries after seeing a deer leap with a splash into the water at sunrise and swim past the bows of the canoe; and often we saw fawns peering at us from the underbrush, or looked straight into the brown eyes of a stag as we charged full tilt round a corner and entered another reach of the river. Foxes, too, everywhere haunted the banks, tripping daintily among the driftwood and disappearing so suddenly that it was impossible to see how they managed it.

But now, after leaving Pressburg, everything changed a little, and the Danube became more serious. It ceased trifling. It was half-way to the Black Sea, within seeming distance almost of other, stranger countries where no tricks would be permitted or understood. It became suddenly grown-up, and claimed our respect and even our awe. It broke out into three arms, for one thing, that only met again a hundred kilometres farther down, and for a canoe there were no indications which one was intended to be followed.

'If you take a side channel,' said the Hungarian officer we met in the Pressburg shop while buying provisions, 'you may find yourselves, when the flood subsides, forty miles from anywhere, high and dry, and you may easily starve. There are no people, no farms, no fishermen. I warn you not to continue. The river, too, is still rising, and this wind will increase.'

The rising river did not alarm us in the least, but the matter of being left high and dry by a sudden subsidence of the waters might be serious, and we had consequently laid in an extra stock of provisions. For the rest, the officer's prophecy held true, and the wind, blowing down a perfectly clear sky, increased steadily till it reached the dignity of a westerly gale.

It was earlier than usual when we camped, for the sun was a good hour or two from the horizon, and leaving my friend still asleep on the hot sand, I wandered about in desultory examination of our hotel. The island, I found, was less than an acre in extent, a mere sandy bank standing some two or three feet above the level of the river. The far end, pointing into the sunset, was covered with flying spray which the tremendous wind drove off the crests of the broken waves. It was triangular in shape, with the apex up stream.

I stood there for several minutes, watching the impetuous crimson flood bearing down with a shouting roar, dashing in waves against the bank as though to sweep it bodily away, and then swirling by in two foaming streams on either side. The ground seemed to shake with the shock and rush, while the furious movement of the willow bushes as the wind poured over them increased the curious illusion that the island itself actually moved. Above, for a mile or two, I could see the great river descending upon me; it was like looking up the slope of a sliding hill, white with foam, and leaping up everywhere to show itself to the sun.

The rest of the island was too thickly grown with willows to make walking pleasant, but I made the tour, nevertheless. From the lower end the light, of course, changed, and the river looked dark and angry. Only the backs of the flying waves were visible, streaked with foam, and pushed forcibly by the great puffs of wind that fell upon them from behind. For a short mile it was visible, pouring in and out among the islands, and then disappearing with a huge sweep into the willows, which closed about it like a herd of monstrous antediluvian creatures crowding down to drink. They made me think of gigantic sponge-like growths that sucked the river up into themselves. They caused it to vanish from sight. They herded there together in such overpowering numbers.

Altogether it was an impressive scene, with its utter loneliness, its bizarre suggestion; and as I gazed, long and curiously, a singular emotion began to stir somewhere in the depths of me. Midway in my delight of the wild beauty, there crept, unbidden and unexplained, a curious feeling of disquietude, almost of alarm.

A rising river, perhaps, always suggests something of the ominous; many of the little islands I saw before me would probably have been swept away by the morning; this resistless, thundering flood of water touched the sense of awe. Yet I was aware that my uneasiness lay deeper far than the emotions of awe and wonder. It was not that I felt. Nor had it directly to do with the power of the driving wind – this shouting hurricane that might almost carry up a few acres of willows into the air and scatter them like so much chaff over the landscape. The wind was simply enjoying itself, for nothing rose out of the flat landscape to stop it, and I was conscious of sharing its great game with a kind of pleasurable excitement. Yet this novel emotion had nothing to do with the wind. Indeed, so vague was the sense of distress I experienced, that it was impossible to trace it to its source and deal with it accordingly, though I was aware somehow that it had to do with my realisation of our utter insignificance before this unrestrained power of the elements about me. The huge-grown river had something to do with it too – a vague, unpleasant idea that we had somehow trifled with these great elemental forces in whose power we lay helpless every hour of the day and night. For here, indeed, they were gigantically at play together, and the sight appealed to the imagination.

But my emotion, so far as I could understand

it, seemed to attach itself more particularly to the willow bushes, to these acres and acres of willows, crowding, so thickly growing there, swarming everywhere the eye could reach, pressing upon the river as though to suffocate it, standing in dense array mile after mile beneath the sky, watching, waiting, listening. And, apart quite from the elements, the willows connected themselves subtly with my malaise, attacking the mind insidiously somehow by reason of their vast numbers, and contriving in some way or other to represent to the imagination a new and mighty power, a power, moreover, not altogether friendly to us.

Great revelations of nature, of course, never fail to impress in one way or another, and I was no stranger to moods of the kind. Mountains overawe and oceans terrify, while the mystery of great forests exercises a spell peculiarly its own. But all these, at one point or another, somewhere link on intimately with human life and human experience. They stir comprehensible, even if alarming, emotions. They tend on the whole to exalt.

With this multitude of willows, however, it was something far different, I felt. Some essence emanated from them that besieged the heart. A sense of awe awakened, true, but of awe touched somewhere by a vague terror. Their serried ranks, growing everywhere darker about me as the shadows deepened, moving furiously yet softly in the wind, woke in me the curious and unwelcome suggestion that we had trespassed here upon the borders of an alien world, a world where we were intruders, a world where we were not wanted or invited to remain – where we ran grave risks perhaps!

The feeling, however, though it refused to yield its meaning entirely to analysis, did not at the time trouble me by passing into menace. Yet it never left me quite, even during the very practical business of putting up the tent in a hurricane of wind and building a fire for the stew-pot. It remained, just enough to bother and perplex, and to rob a most delightful camping-ground of a good portion of its charm. To my companion, however, I said nothing, for he was a man I considered devoid of imagination. In the first place, I could never have explained to him what I meant, and in the second, he would have laughed stupidly at me if I had.

There was a slight depression in the centre of the island, and here we pitched the tent. The surrounding willows broke the wind a bit.

'A poor camp,' observed the imperturbable Swede when at last the tent stood upright, 'no stones and precious little firewood. I'm for moving on early to-morrow – eh? This sand won't hold anything.'

But the experience of a collapsing tent at midnight had taught us many devices, and we made the cosy gipsy house as safe as possible, and then set about collecting a store of wood to last till bed-time. Willow bushes drop no branches, and driftwood was our only source of supply. We hunted the shores pretty thoroughly. Everywhere the banks were crumbling as the rising flood tore at them and carried away great portions with a splash and a gurgle.

'The island's much smaller than when we landed,' said the accurate Swede. 'It won't last long at this rate. We'd better drag the canoe close to the tent, and be ready to start at a moment's notice. I shall sleep in my clothes.'

He was a little distance off, climbing along the bank, and I heard his rather jolly laugh as he spoke.

'By Jove!' I heard him call, a moment later, and turned to see what had caused his exclamation. But for the moment he was hidden by the willows, and I could not find him.

'What in the world's this?' I heard him cry again, and this time his voice had become serious.

I ran up quickly and joined him on the bank. He was looking over the river, pointing at something in the water.

'Good heavens, it's a man's body!' he cried excitedly. 'Look!'

A black thing, turning over and over in the foaming waves, swept rapidly past. It kept disappearing and coming up to the surface again. It was about twenty feet from the shore, and just as it was opposite to where we stood it lurched round and looked straight at us. We saw its eyes reflecting the sunset, and gleaming an odd yellow as the body turned over. Then it gave a swift, gulping plunge, and dived out of sight in a flash.

'An otter, by gad!' we exclaimed in the same breath, laughing.

It was an otter, alive, and out on the hunt; yet it had looked exactly like the body of a drowned man turning helplessly in the current. Far below it came to the surface once again, and we saw its black skin, wet and shining in the sunlight.

Then, too, just as we turned back, our arms full of driftwood, another thing happened to recall us to the river bank. This time it really was a man, and what was more, a man in a boat. Now a small boat on the Danube was an unusual sight at any time, but here in this deserted region, and at flood time, it was so unexpected as to constitute a real event. We stood and stared.

Whether it was due to the slanting sunlight, or the refraction from the wonderfully illumined water, I cannot say, but, whatever the cause, I found it difficult to focus my sight properly upon the flying apparition. It seemed, however, to be a man standing upright in a sort of flat-bottomed boat, steering with a long oar, and being carried down the opposite shore at a tremendous pace. He apparently was looking across in our direction, but the distance was too great and the light too uncertain for us to make out very plainly what he was about. It seemed to me that he was gesticulating and making signs at us. His voice came across the water to us shouting something furiously, but the wind drowned it so that no single word was audible. There was something curious about the whole appearance – man, boat, signs, voice – that made an impression on me out of all proportion to its cause.

'He's crossing himself!' I cried. 'Look, he's making the sign of the Cross!'

'I believe you're right,' the Swede said, shading his eyes with his hand and watching the man out of sight. He seemed to be gone in a moment, melting away down there into the sea of willows where the sun caught them in the bend of the river and turned them into a great crimson wall of beauty. Mist, too, had begun to ruse, so that the air was hazy.

'But what in the world is he doing at nightfall on this flooded river?' I said, half to myself. 'Where is he going at such a time, and what did he mean by his signs and shouting? D'you think he wished to warn us about something?'

'He saw our smoke, and thought we were spirits probably,' laughed my companion. 'These Hungarians believe in all sorts of rubbish; you remember the shopwoman at Pressburg warning us that no one ever landed here because it belonged to some sort of beings outside man's world! I suppose they believe in fairies and elementals, possibly demons, too. That peasant in the boat saw people on the islands for the first time in his life,' he added, after a slight pause, 'and it scared him, that's all.'

The Swede's tone of voice was not convincing, and his manner lacked something that was usually there. I noted the change instantly while he talked, though without being able to label it precisely.

'If they had enough imagination,' I laughed loudly – I remember trying to make as much noise as I could – 'they might well people a place like this with the old gods of antiquity. The Romans must have haunted all this region more or less with their shrines and sacred groves and elemental deities.'

The subject dropped and we returned to our stew-pot, for my friend was not given to imaginative conversation as a rule. Moreover, just then I remember feeling distinctly glad that he was not imaginative; his stolid, practical nature suddenly seemed to me welcome and comforting. It was an admirable temperament, I felt; he could steer down rapids like a red Indian, shoot dangerous bridges and whirlpools better than any white man I ever saw in a canoe. He was a grand fellow for an adventurous trip, a tower of strength when untoward things happened. I looked at his strong face and light curly hair as he staggered along under his pile of driftwood (twice the size of mine!), and I experienced a feeling of relief. Yes, I was distinctly glad just then that the Swede was – what he was, and that he never made remarks that suggested more than they said.

'The river's still rising, though,' he added, as if following out some thoughts of his own, and dropping his load with a gasp. 'This island will be under water in two days if it goes on.'

'I wish the wind would go down,' I said. 'I don't care a fig for the river.'

The flood, indeed, had no terrors for us; we could get off at ten minutes' notice, and the more water the better we liked it. It meant an increasing current and the obliteration of the treacherous shingle-beds that so often threatened to tear the bottom out of our canoe.

Contrary to our expectations, the wind did not go down with the sun. It seemed to increase with the darkness, howling overhead and shaking the willows round us like straws. Curious sounds accompanied it sometimes, like the explosion of heavy guns, and it fell upon the water and the island in great flat blows of immense power. It made me think of the sounds a planet must make, could we only hear it, driving along through space.

But the sky kept wholly clear of clouds, and soon after supper the full moon rose up in the east and covered the river and the plain of shouting willows with a light like the day.

We lay on the sandy patch beside the fire, smoking, listening to the noises of the night round us, and talking happily of the journey we had already made, and of our plans ahead. The map lay spread in the door of the tent, but the high wind made it hard to study, and presently we lowered the curtain and extinguished the lantern. The firelight was enough to smoke and see each other's face by, and the sparks flew about overhead like fireworks. A few yards beyond, the river gurgled and hissed, and from time to time a heavy splash announced the falling away of further portions of the bank.

Our talk, I noticed, had to do with the far-away scenes and incidents of our first camps in the Black Forest, or of other subjects altogether remote from the present setting, for neither of us spoke of the actual moment more than was necessary – almost as though we had agreed tacitly to avoid discussion of the camp and its incidents. Neither the otter nor the boatman, for instance, received the honour of a single mention, though ordinarily these would have furnished discussion for the greater part of the evening. They were, of course, distinct events in such a place.

The scarcity of wood made it a business to keep the fire going, for the wind, that drove the smoke in our faces wherever we sat, helped at the same time to make a forced draught. We took it in turn to make some foraging expeditions into the darkness, and the quantity the Swede brought back always made me feel that he took an absurdly long time finding it; for the fact was I did not care much about being left alone, and yet it always seemed to be my turn to grub about among the bushes or scramble along the slippery banks in the moonlight. The long day's battle with wind and water – such wind and such water! – had tired us both, and an early bed was the obvious programme. Yet neither of us made the move for the tent. We lay there, tending the fire, talking in desultory fashion, peering about us into the dense willow bushes, and listening to the thunder of wind and river. The loneliness of the place had entered our very bones, and silence seemed natural, for after a bit the sound of our voices became a trifle unreal and forced; whispering would have been the fitting mode of communication, I felt, and the human voice, always rather absurd amid the roar of the elements, now carried with it something almost illegitimate. It was like talking out loud in church, or in some place where it was not lawful, perhaps not quite safe, to be overheard.

The eeriness of this lonely island, set among a million willows, swept by a hurricane, and surrounded by hurrying deep waters, touched us both, I fancy. Untrodden by man, almost unknown to man, it lay there beneath the moon, remote from human influence, on the frontier of another world, an alien world, a world tenanted by willows only and the souls of willows. And we, in our rashness, had dared to invade it, even to make use of it! Something more than the power of its mystery stirred in me as I lay on the sand, feet to fire, and peered up through the leaves at the stars. For the last time I rose to get firewood.

'When this has burnt up,' I said firmly, 'I shall turn in,' and my companion watched me lazily as I moved off into the surrounding shadows.

For an unimaginative man I thought he seemed unusually receptive that night, unusually open to suggestion of things other than sensory. He too was touched by the beauty and loneliness of the place. I was not altogether pleased, I remember, to recognise this slight change in him, and instead of immediately collecting sticks, I made my way to the far point of the island where the moonlight on plain and river could be seen to better advantage. The desire to be alone had come suddenly upon me; my former dread returned in force; there was a vague feeling in me I wished to face and probe to the bottom.

When I reached the point of sand jutting out among the waves, the spell of the place descended upon me with a positive shock. No mere 'scenery' could have produced such an effect. There was something more here, something to alarm.

I gazed across the waste of wild waters; I watched the whispering willows; I heard the ceaseless beating of the tireless wind; and, one and all, each in its own way, stirred in me this sensation of a strange distress. But the willows especially; for ever they went on chattering and talking among themselves, laughing a little, shrilly crying out, sometimes sighing – but what it was they made so much to-do about belonged to the secret life of the great plain they inhabited. And it was utterly alien to the world I knew, or to that of the wild yet kindly elements. They made me think of a host of beings from another plane of life, another evolution altogether, perhaps, all discussing a mystery known only to themselves. I watched them moving busily together, oddly shaking their big bushy heads, twirling their myriad leaves even when there was no wind. They moved of their own will as though alive, and they touched, by some incalculable method, my own keen sense of the horrible.

There they stood in the moonlight, like a vast army surrounding our camp, shaking their innumerable silver spears defiantly, formed all ready for an attack.

The psychology of places, for some imaginations at least, is very vivid; for the wanderer, especially, camps have their 'note' either of welcome or rejection. At first it may not always be apparent, because the busy preparations of tent and cooking prevent, but with the first pause – after supper usually – it comes and announces itself. And the note of this willow-camp now became unmistakably plain to me; we were interlopers, trespassers; we were not welcomed. The sense of unfamiliarity grew upon me as I stood there watching. We touched the frontier of a region where our presence was resented. For a night's lodging we might perhaps be tolerated; but for a prolonged and inquisitive stay – No! by all the gods of the trees and wilderness, no! We were the first human influences upon this island, and we were not wanted. The willows were against us.

Strange thoughts like these, bizarre fancies, borne I know not whence, found lodgment in my mind as I stood listening. What, I thought, if, after all, these crouching willows proved to be alive; if suddenly they should rise up, like a swarm of living creatures, marshalled by the gods whose territory we had invaded, sweep towards us off the vast swamps, booming overhead in the night – and then settle down! As I looked it was so easy to imagine they actually moved, crept nearer, retreated a little, huddled together in masses, hostile, waiting for the great wind that should finally start them a-running. I could have sworn their aspect changed a little, and their ranks deepened and pressed more closely together.

The melancholy shrill cry of a night-bird sounded overhead, and suddenly I nearly lost my balance as the piece of bank I stood upon fell with a great splash into the river, undermined by the flood. I stepped back just in time, and went on hunting for firewood again, half laughing at the odd fancies that crowded so thickly into my mind and cast their spell upon me. I recalled the Swede's remark about moving on next day, and I was just thinking that I fully agreed with him, when I turned with a start and saw the subject of my thoughts standing immediately in front of me. He was quite close. The roar of the elements had covered his approach.

'You've been gone so long,' he shouted above the wind, 'I thought something must have happened to you.'

But there was that in his tone, and a certain look in his face as well, that conveyed to me more than his usual words, and in a flash I understood the real reason for his coming. It was because the spell of the place had entered his soul too, and he did not like being alone.

'River still rising,' he cried, pointing to the flood in the moonlight, 'and the wind's simply awful.'

He always said the same things, but it was the

cry for companionship that gave the real importance to his words.

'Lucky,' I cried back, 'our tent's in the hollow. I think it'll hold all right.' I added something about the difficulty of finding wood, in order to explain my absence, but the wind caught my words and flung them across the river, so that he did not hear, but just looked at me through the branches, nodding his head.

'Lucky if we get away without disaster!' he shouted, or words to that effect; and I remember feeling half angry with him for putting the thought into words, for it was exactly what I felt myself. There was disaster impending somewhere, and the sense of presentiment lay unpleasantly upon me.

We went back to the fire and made a final blaze, poking it up with our feet. We took a last look round. But for the wind the heat would have been unpleasant. I put this thought into words, and I remember my friend's reply struck me oddly: that he would rather have the heat, the ordinary July weather, than this 'diabolical wind'.

Everything was snug for the night; the canoe lying turned over beside the tent, with both yellow paddles beneath her; the provision sack hanging from a willow-stem, and the washed-up dishes removed to a safe distance from the fire, all ready for the morning meal.

We smothered the embers of the fire with sand, and then turned in. The flap of the tent door was up, and I saw the branches and the stars and the white moonlight. The shaking willows and the heavy buffetings of the wind against our taut little house were the last things I remembered as sleep came down and covered all with its soft and delicious forgetfulness.

II

Suddenly I found myself lying awake, peering from my sandy mattress through the door of the tent. I looked at my watch pinned against the canvas, and saw by the bright moonlight that it was past twelve o'clock – the threshold of a new day – and I had therefore slept a couple of hours. The Swede was asleep still beside me; the wind howled as before; something plucked at my heart and made me feel afraid. There was a sense of disturbance in my immediate neighbourhood.

I sat up quickly and looked out. The trees were swaying violently to and fro as the gusts smote them, but our little bit of green canvas lay snugly safe in the hollow, for the wind passed over it without meeting enough resistance to make it vicious. The feeling of disquietude did not pass, however, and I crawled quietly out of the tent to see if our belongings were safe. I moved carefully so as not to waken my companion. A curious excitement was on me.

I was half-way out, kneeling on all fours, when my eye first took in that the tops of the bushes opposite, with their moving tracery of leaves, made shapes against the sky. I sat back on my haunches and stared. It was incredible, surely, but there, opposite and slightly above me, were shapes of some indeterminate sort among the willows, and as the branches swayed in the wind they seemed to group themselves about these shapes, forming a series of monstrous outlines that shifted rapidly beneath the moon. Close, about fifty feet in front of me, I saw these things.

My first instinct was to waken my companion, that he too might see them, but something made me hesitate – the sudden realisation, probably, that I should not welcome corroboration; and meanwhile I crouched there staring in amazement with smarting eyes. I was wide awake. I remember saying to myself that I was not dreaming.

They first became properly visible, these huge figures, just within the tops of the bushes – immense, bronze-coloured, moving, and wholly independent of the swaying of the branches. I saw them plainly and noted, now I came to examine them more calmly, that they were very much larger than human, and indeed that something in their appearance proclaimed them to be not human at all. Certainly they were not merely the moving tracery of the branches against the moonlight. They shifted independently. They rose upwards in a continuous stream from earth to sky, vanishing utterly as soon as they reached the dark of the sky. They were interlaced one with another, making a great column, and I saw their limbs and huge bodies melting in and out of each other, forming this serpentine line that bent and swayed and twisted spirally with the contortions of the wind-tossed trees. They were nude, fluid shapes, passing up the bushes, within the leaves almost – rising up in a living column into the heavens. Their faces I never could see. Unceasingly they poured upwards, swaying in great bending curves, with a hue of dull bronze upon their skins.

I stared, trying to force every atom of vision from my eyes. For a long time I thought they must every moment disappear and resolve themselves into the movements of the branches and prove to be an optical illusion. I searched everywhere for a proof of reality, when all the while I understood quite well that the standard of reality had changed. For the longer I looked the more certain I became that these figures were real and living, though perhaps not according to the standards that the camera and the biologist would insist upon.

Far from feeling fear, I was possessed with a sense of awe and wonder such as I have never known. I seemed to be gazing at the personified elemental forces of this haunted and primeval region. Our intrusion had stirred the powers of the place into activity. It was we who were the cause of the disturbance, and my brain filled to bursting with stories and legends of the spirits and deities of places that have been acknowledged and worshipped by men in all ages of the world's history. But, before I could arrive at any possible explanation, something impelled me to go farther out, and I crept forward on the sand and stood upright. I felt the ground still warm under my bare feet; the wind tore at my hair and face; and the sound of the river burst upon my ears with a sudden roar. These things, I knew, were real, and proved that my senses were acting normally. Yet the figures still rose from earth to heaven, silent, majestically, in a great spiral of grace and strength that overwhelmed me at length with a genuine deep emotion of worship. I felt that I must fall down and worship – absolutely worship.

Perhaps in another minute I might have done so, when a gust of wind swept against me with such force that it blew me sideways, and I nearly stumbled and fell. It seemed to shake the dream violently out of me. At least it gave me another point of view somehow. The figures still remained, still ascended into heaven from the heart of the night, but my reason at last began to assert itself. It must be a subjective experience, I argued – none the less real for that, but still subjective. The moonlight and the branches combined to work out these pictures upon the mirror of my imagination, and for some reason I projected them outwards and made them appear objective. I knew this must be the case, of course. I took courage, and began to move forward across the open patches of sand. By Jove, though, was it all hallucination? Was it merely subjective? Did not my reason argue in the old futile way from the little standard of the known?

I only know that great column of figures ascended darkly into the sky for what seemed a very long period of time, and with a very complete measure of reality as most men are accustomed to gauge reality. Then suddenly they were gone!

And, once they were gone and the immediate wonder of their great presence had passed, fear came down upon me with a cold rush. The esoteric meaning of this lonely and haunted region suddenly flamed up within me, and I began to tremble dreadfully. I took a quick look round – a look of horror that came near to panic – calculating vainly ways of escape; and then, realising how helpless I was to achieve anything really effective, I crept back silently into the tent and lay down again upon my sandy mattress, first lowering the door-curtain to shut out the sight of the willows in the moonlight, and then burying my head as deeply as possible beneath the blankets to deaden the sound of the terrifying wind.

III

As though further to convince me that I had not been dreaming, I remember that it was a long time before I fell again into a troubled and restless sleep; and even then only the upper crust of me slept, and underneath there was something that never quite lost consciousness, but lay alert and on the watch.

But this second time I jumped up with a genuine start of terror. It was neither the wind nor the river that woke me, but the slow approach of something that caused the sleeping portion of me to grow smaller and smaller till at last it vanished altogether, and I found myself sitting bolt upright – listening.

Outside there was a sound of multitudinous little patterings. They had been coming, I was aware, for a long time, and in my sleep they had first become audible. I sat there nervously wide awake as though I had not slept at all. It seemed to me that my breathing came with difficulty, and that there was a great weight upon the surface of my body. In spite of the hot night, I felt clammy with cold and shivered. Something surely was pressing steadily against the sides of the tent and weighing down upon it from above. Was it the body of the wind? Was this the pattering rain, the dripping of the leaves? The spray blown from the river by the wind and gathering in big drops? I thought quickly of a dozen things.

Then suddenly the explanation leaped into my mind: a bough from the poplar, the only large tree on the island, had fallen with the wind. Still half caught by the other branches, it would fall with the next gust and crush us, and meanwhile its leaves brushed and tapped upon the tight canvas surface of the tent. I raised a loose flap and rushed out, calling to the Swede to follow.

But when I got out and stood upright I saw that the tent was free. There was no hanging bough; there was no rain or spray; nothing approached.

A cold, grey light filtered down through the bushes and lay on the faintly gleaming sand. Stars still crowded the sky directly overhead, and the wind howled magnificently, but the fire no longer gave out any glow, and I saw the east reddening in streaks through the trees. Several hours must have passed since I stood there before watching the ascending figures, and the memory of it now came back to me horribly, like an evil dream. Oh, how tired it made me feel, that ceaseless raging wind! Yet, though the deep lassitude of a sleepless night was on me, my nerves were tingling with the activity of an equally tireless apprehension, and all idea of repose was out of the question. The river I saw had risen further. Its thunder filled the air, and a fine spray made itself felt through my thin sleeping shirt.

Yet nowhere did I discover the slightest evidence of anything to cause alarm. This deep, prolonged disturbance in my heart remained wholly unaccounted for.

My companion had not stirred when I called him, and there was no need to waken him now. I looked about me carefully, noting everything; the turned-over canoe; the yellow paddles – two of them, I'm certain; the provision sack and the extra lantern hanging together from the tree; and, crowding everywhere about me, enveloping all, the willows, those endless, shaking willows. A bird uttered its morning cry, and a string of ducks passed with whirring flight overhead in the twilight. The sand whirled, dry and stinging, about my bare feet in the wind.

I walked round the tent and then went out a little way into the bush, so that I could see across the river to the farther landscape, and the same profound yet indefinable emotion of distress seized upon me again as I saw the interminable sea of bushes stretching to the horizon, looking ghostly and unreal in the wan light of dawn. I walked softly here and there, still puzzling over that odd sound of infinite pattering, and of that pressure upon the tent that had wakened me. It must have been the wind, I reflected – the wind bearing upon the loose, hot sand, driving the dry particles smartly against the taut canvas – the wind dropping heavily upon our fragile roof.

Yet all the time my nervousness and malaise increased appreciably.

I crossed over to the farther shore and noted how the coast-line had altered in the night, and what masses of sand the river had torn away. I dipped my hands and feet into the cool current, and bathed my forehead. Already there was a glow of sunrise in the sky and the exquisite freshness of coming day. On my way back I passed purposely beneath the very bushes where I had seen the column of figures rising into the air, and midway among the clumps I suddenly found myself overtaken by a sense of vast terror. From the shadows a large figure went swiftly by. Someone passed me, as sure as ever man did. . . .

It was a great staggering blow from the wind that helped me forward again, and once out in the more open space, the sense of terror diminished strangely. The winds were about and walking, I remember saying to myself, for the winds often move like great presences under the trees. And altogether the fear that hovered about me was such an unknown and immense kind of fear, so unlike anything I had ever felt before, that it woke a sense of awe and wonder in me that did much to counteract its worst effects; and when I reached a high point in the middle of the island from which I could see the wide stretch of river, crimson in the sunrise, the whole magical beauty of it all was so overpowering that a sort of wild yearning woke in me and almost brought a cry up into the throat.

But this cry found no expression, for as my eyes wandered from the plain beyond to the island round me and noted our little tent half hidden among the willows, a dreadful discovery leaped out at me, compared to which my terror of the walking winds seemed as nothing at all.

For a change, I thought, had somehow come about in the arrangement of the landscape. It was not that my point of vantage gave me a different view, but that an alteration had apparently been effected in the relation of the tent to the willows, and of the willows to the tent. Surely the bushes now crowded much closer – unnecessarily, unpleasantly close. They had moved nearer.

Creeping with silent feet over the shifting sands, drawing imperceptibly nearer by soft, unhurried movements, the willows had come closer during the night. But had the wind moved them, or had they moved of themselves? I recalled the sound of infinite small patterings and the pressure upon the tent and upon my own heart that caused me to wake in terror. I swayed for a moment in the wind like a tree, finding it hard to keep my upright position on the sandy hillock. There was a suggestion here of personal agency, of deliberate intention, of aggressive hostility, and it terrified me into a sort of rigidity.

Then the reaction followed quickly. The idea was so bizarre, so absurd, that I felt inclined to laugh. But the laughter came no more readily than the cry, for the knowledge that my mind was so receptive to such dangerous imaginings brought the additional terror that it was through our minds and not through our physical bodies that the attack would come, and was coming.

The wind buffeted me about, and, very quickly it seemed, the sun came up over the horizon, for it was after four o'clock, and I must have stood on that little pinnacle of sand longer than I knew, afraid to come down to close quarters with the willows. I returned quietly, creepily, to the tent, first taking another exhaustive look round and – yes, I confess it – making a few measurements. I paced out on the warm sand the distances between the willows and the tent, making a note of the shortest distance particularly.

I crawled stealthily into my blankets. My companion, to all appearances, still slept soundly, and I was glad that this was so. Provided my experiences were not corroborated, I could find strength somehow to deny them, perhaps. With the daylight I could persuade myself that it was all a subjective hallucination, a fantasy of the night, a projection of the excited imagination.

Nothing further came in to disturb me, and I fell asleep almost at once, utterly exhausted, yet still in dread of hearing again that weird sound of multitudinous pattering, or of feeling the pressure upon my heart that had made it difficult to breathe.

IV

The sun was high in the heavens when my companion woke me from a heavy sleep and announced that the porridge was cooked and there was just time to bathe. The grateful smell of frizzling bacon entered the tent door.

'River still rising,' he said, 'and several islands out in mid-stream have disappeared altogether. Our own island's much smaller.'

'Any wood left?' I asked sleepily.

'The wood and the island will finish to-morrow in a dead heat,' he laughed, 'but there's enough to last us till then.'

I plunged in from the point of the island, which had indeed altered a lot in size and shape during the night, and was swept down in a moment to the landing-place opposite the tent. The water was icy, and the banks flew by like the country from an express train. Bathing under such conditions was an exhilarating operation, and the terror of the night seemed cleansed out of me by a process of evaporation in the brain. The sun was blazing hot; not a cloud showed itself anywhere; the wind, however, had not abated one little jot.

Quite suddenly then the implied meaning of the Swede's words flashed across me, showing that he no longer wished to leave post-haste, and had changed his mind. 'Enough to last till to-morrow' – he assumed we should stay on the island another night. It struck me as odd. The night before he was so positive the other way. How had the change come about?

Great crumblings of the banks occurred at breakfast, with heavy splashings and clouds of spray which the wind brought into our frying-pan, and my fellow-traveller talked incessantly about the difficulty the Vienna-Pesth steamers must have to find the channel in flood. But the state of his mind interested and impressed me far more than the state of the river or the difficulties of the steamers. He had changed somehow since the evening before. His manner was different – a trifle excited, a trifle shy, with a sort of suspicion about his voice and gestures. I hardly know how to describe it now in cold blood, but at the time I remember being quite certain of one thing – that he had become frightened.

He ate very little breakfast, and for once omitted to smoke his pipe. He had the map spread open beside him, and kept studying its markings.

'We'd better get off sharp in an hour,' I said presently, feeling for an opening that must bring him indirectly to a partial confession at any rate. And his answer puzzled me uncomfortably: 'Rather! If they'll let us.'

'Who'll let us? The elements?' I asked quickly, with affected indifference.

'The powers of this awful place, whoever they are,' he replied, keeping his eyes on the map. 'The gods are here, if they are anywhere at all in the world.'

'The elements are always the true immortals,' I replied, laughing as naturally as I could manage, yet knowing quite well that my face reflected my true feelings when he looked up gravely at me and spoke across the smoke:

'We shall be fortunate if we get away without further disaster.'

This was exactly what I had dreaded, and I screwed myself up to the point of the direct question. It was like agreeing to allow the dentist to extract the tooth; it had to come anyhow in the long run, and the rest was all pretence.

'Further disaster! Why, what's happened?'

'For one thing – the steering paddle's gone,' he said quietly.

'The steering paddle gone!' I repeated, greatly excited, for this was our rudder, and the Danube in flood without a rudder was suicide. 'But what –'

'And there's a tear in the bottom of the canoe,' he added, with a genuine little tremor in his voice.

I continued staring at him, able only to repeat the words in his face somewhat foolishly. There, in the heat of the sun, and on this burning sand, I was aware of a freezing atmosphere descending round us. I got up to follow him, for he merely nodded his head gravely and led the way towards the tent a few yards on the other side of the fireplace. The canoe still lay there as I had last seen her in the night, ribs uppermost, the paddles, or rather, the paddle, on the sand beside her.

'There's only one,' he said, stooping to pick it up. 'And here's the rent in the base-board.'

It was on the tip of my tongue to tell him that I had clearly noticed two paddles a few hours before, but a second impulse made me think better of it, and I said nothing. I approached to see.

There was a long, finely made tear in the bottom of the canoe where a little slither of wood had been neatly taken clean out; it looked as if the tooth of a sharp rock or snag had eaten down her length, and investigation showed that the hole went through. Had we launched out in her without observing it we must inevitably have foundered. At first the water would have made the wood swell so as to close the hole, but once out in mid-stream the water must have poured in, and the canoe, never more than two inches above the surface, would have filled and sunk very rapidly.

'There, you see an attempt to prepare a victim for the sacrifice,' I heard him saying, more to himself than to me, 'two victims rather,' he added as he bent over and ran his fingers along the slit.

I began to whistle – a thing I always do unconsciously when utterly nonplussed – and purposely paid no attention to his words. I was determined to consider them foolish.

'It wasn't there last night,' he said presently, straightening up from his examination and looking anywhere but at me.

'We must have scratched her in landing, of course,' I stopped whistling to say. 'The stones are very sharp.'

I stopped abruptly, for at that moment he turned round and met my eye squarely. I knew just as well as he did how impossible my explanation was. There were no stones, to begin with.

'And then there's this to explain too,' he added quietly, handing me the paddle and pointing to the blade.

A new and curious emotion spread freezingly over me as I took and examined it. The blade was scraped down all over, beautifully scraped, as though someone had sand-papered it with care, making it so thin that the first vigorous stroke must have snapped it off at the elbow.

'One of us walked in his sleep and did this thing,' I said feebly, 'or – or it has been filed by the constant stream of sand particles blown against it by the wind, perhaps.'

'Ah,' said the Swede, turning away, laughing a little, 'you can explain everything.'

'The same wind that caught the steering paddle and flung it so near the bank that it fell in with the next lump that crumbled,' I called out after him, absolutely determined to find an explanation for everything he showed me.

'I see,' he shouted back, turning his head to look at me before disappearing among the willow bushes.

Once alone with these perplexing evidences of personal agency, I think my first thoughts took the form of 'One of us must have done this thing, and it certainly was not I.' But my second thought decided how impossible it was to suppose, under all the circumstances, that either of us had done it. That my companion, the trusted friend of a dozen similar expeditions, could have knowingly had a hand in it, was a suggestion not to be entertained for a moment. Equally absurd seemed the explanation that this imperturbable and densely practical nature had suddenly become insane and was busied with insane purposes.

Yet the fact remained that what disturbed me most, and kept my fear actively alive even in this blaze of sunshine and wild beauty, was the clear certainty that some curious alteration had come about in his mind – that he was nervous, timid, suspicious, aware of goings on he did not speak about, watching a series of secret and hitherto unmentionable events – waiting, in a word, for a climax that he expected, and, I thought, expected very soon. This grew up in my mind intuitively – I hardly knew how.

I made a hurried examination of the tent and its surroundings, but the measurements of the night remained the same. There were deep hollows formed in the sand I now noticed for the first time, basin-shaped and of various depths and sizes, varying from that of a tea-cup to a large bowl. The wind, no doubt, was responsible for these miniature craters, just as it was for lifting the paddle and tossing it towards the water. The rent in the canoe was the only thing that seemed quite inexplicable; and, after all, it was conceivable that a sharp point had caught it when we landed. The examination I made of the shore did not assist this theory, but all the same I clung to it with that diminishing portion of my intelligence which I called my 'reason'. An explanation of some kind was an absolute necessity, just as some working explanation of the universe is necessary – however absurd – to the happiness of every individual who seeks to do his duty in the world and face the problems of life. The simile seemed to me at the time an exact parallel.

I at once set the pitch melting, and presently the Swede joined me at the work, though under the best conditions in the world the canoe could not be safe for travelling till the following day. I drew his attention casually to the hollows in the sand.

'Yes,' he said, 'I know. They're all over the island. But you can explain them, no doubt!'

'Wind, of course,' I answered without hesitation. 'Have you never watched those little whirlwinds in the street that twist and twirl everything into a circle? This sand's loose enough to yield, that's all.'

He made no reply, and we worked on in silence for a bit. I watched him surreptitiously all the time, and I had an idea he was watching me. He seemed, too, to be always listening attentively to something I could not hear, or perhaps for something that he expected to hear, for he kept turning about and staring into the bushes, and up into the sky, and out across the water where it was visible through the openings among the willows. Sometimes he even put his hand to his ear and held it there for several minutes. He said nothing to me, however, about it, and I asked no questions. And meanwhile, as he mended that torn canoe with the skill and address of a red Indian, I was glad to notice his absorption in the work, for there was a vague dread in my heart that he would speak of the changed aspect of the willows. And, if he had noticed that, my imagination could no longer be held a sufficient explanation of it.

At length, after a long pause, he began to talk.

'Queer thing,' he added in a hurried sort of voice, as though he wanted to say something and get it over. 'Queer thing. I mean, about that otter last night.'

I had expected something so totally different that he caught me with surprise, and I looked up sharply.

'Shows how lonely this place is. Otters are awfully shy things –'

'I don't mean that, of course,' he interrupted. 'I mean – do you think – did you think it really was an otter?'

'What else, in the name of Heaven, what else?'

'You know, I saw it before you did, and at first it seemed – so much bigger than an otter.'

'The sunset as you looked up-stream magnified it, or something,' I replied.

He looked at me absently a moment, as though his mind were busy with other thoughts.

'It had such extraordinary yellow eyes,' he went on half to himself.

'That was the sun too,' I laughed, a trifle boisterously. 'I suppose you'll wonder next if that fellow in the boat –'

I suddenly decided not to finish the sentence. He was in the act again of listening, turning his head to the wind, and something in the expression of his face made me halt. The subject dropped, and we went on with our caulking. Apparently he had not noticed my unfinished sentence. Five minutes later, however, he looked at me across the canoe, the smoking pitch in his hand, his face exceedingly grave.

'I did rather wonder, if you want to know,' he said slowly, 'what that thing in the boat was. I remember thinking at the time it was not a man. The whole business seemed to rise quite suddenly out of the water.'

I laughed again boisterously in his face, but this time there was impatience, and a strain of anger too, in my feeling.

'Look here now,' I cried, 'this place is quite queer enough without going out of our way to imagine things! That boat was an ordinary boat, and the man in it was an ordinary man, and they were both going down-stream as fast as they could lick. And that otter was an otter, so don't let's play the fool about it!'

He looked steadily at me with the same grave expression. He was not in the least annoyed. I took courage from his silence.

'And, for Heaven's sake,' I went on, 'don't keep pretending you hear things, because it only gives me the jumps, and there's nothing to hear but the river and this cursed old thundering wind.'

'You fool!' he answered in a low, shocked voice, 'you utter fool. That's just the way all victims talk. As if you didn't understand just as well as I do!' he sneered with scorn in his voice, and a sort of resignation. 'The best thing you can do is to keep quiet and try to hold your mind as firm as possible. This feeble attempt at self-deception only makes the truth harder when you're forced to meet it.'

My little effort was over, and I found nothing more to say, for I knew quite well his words were true, and that I was the fool, not he. Up to a certain stage in the adventure he kept ahead of me easily, and I think I felt annoyed to be out of it, to be thus proved less psychic, less sensitive than himself to these extraordinary happenings, and half ignorant all the time of what was going on under my very nose. He knew from the very beginning, apparently. But at the moment I wholly missed the point of his words about the necessity of there being a victim, and that we ourselves were destined to satisfy the want. I dropped all pretence thenceforward, but thenceforward likewise my fear increased steadily to the climax.

'But you're quite right about one thing,' he added, before the subject passed, 'and that is that we're wiser not to talk about it, or even to think about it, because what one thinks finds expression in words, and what one says happens.'

That afternoon, while the canoe dried and hardened, we spent trying to fish, testing the leak, collecting wood, and watching the enormous flood of rising water. Masses of driftwood swept near our shores sometimes, and we fished for them with long willow branches. The island grew perceptibly smaller as the banks were torn away with great gulps and splashes. The weather kept brilliantly fine till about four o'clock, and then for the first time for three days the wind showed signs of abating. Clouds began to gather in the south-west, spreading thence slowly over the sky.

This lessening of the wind came as a great relief, for the incessant roaring, banging, and thundering had irritated our nerves. Yet the silence that came about five o'clock with its sudden cessation was in a manner quite as oppressive. The booming of the river had everything in its own way then; it filled the air with deep murmurs, more musical than the wind noises, but infinitely more monotonous. The wind held many notes, rising, falling always beating out some sort of great elemental tune; whereas the river's song lay between three notes at most – dull pedal notes, that held a lugubrious quality foreign to the wind, and somehow seemed to me, in my then nervous state, to sound wonderfully well the music of doom.

It was extraordinary, too, how the withdrawal suddenly of bright sunlight took everything out of the landscape that made for cheerfulness; and since this particular landscape had already managed to convey the suggestion of something sinister, the change of course was all the more unwelcome and noticeable. For me, I know, the darkening outlook became distinctly more alarming, and I found myself more than once calculating how soon after sunset the full moon would get up in the east, and whether the gathering clouds would greatly interfere with her lighting of the little island.

With this general hush of the wind – though it still indulged in occasional brief gusts – the river seemed to me to grow blacker, the willows to stand more densely together. The latter, too, kept up a sort of independent movement of their own, rustling among themselves when no wind stirred, and shaking oddly from the roots upwards. When common objects in this way become charged with the suggestion of horror, they stimulate the imagination far more than things of unusual appearance; and these bushes, crowding huddled about us, assumed for me in the darkness a bizarre grotesquerie of appearance that lent to them somehow the aspect of purposeful and living creatures. Their very ordinariness, I felt, masked what was malignant and hostile to us. The forces of the region drew nearer with the coming of night. They were focusing upon our island, and more particularly upon ourselves. For thus, somehow, in the terms of the imagination, did my really indescribable sensations in this extraordinary place present themselves.

I had slept a good deal in the early afternoon, and had thus recovered somewhat from the exhaustion of a disturbed night, but this only served apparently to render me more susceptible than before to the obsessing spell of the haunting. I fought against it, laughing at my feelings as absurd and childish, with very obvious physiological explanations, yet, in spite of every effort, they gained in strength upon me so that I dreaded the night as a child lost in a forest must dread the approach of darkness.

The canoe we had carefully covered with a waterproof sheet during the day, and the one remaining paddle had been securely tied by the Swede to the base of a tree, lest the wind should rob us of that too. From five o'clock onwards I busied myself with the stew-pot and preparations for dinner, it being my turn to cook that night. We had potatoes, onions, bits of bacon fat to add flavour, and a general thick residue from former stews at the bottom of the pot; with black bread broken up into it the result was most excellent, and it was followed by a stew of plums with sugar and a brew of strong tea with dried milk. A good pile of wood lay close at hand, and the absence of wind made my duties easy. My companion sat lazily watching me, dividing his attentions between cleaning his pipe and giving useless advice – an admitted privilege of the off-duty man. He had been very quiet all the afternoon, engaged in re-caulking the canoe, strengthening the tent ropes, and fishing for driftwood while I slept. No more talk about undesirable things had passed between us, and I think his only remarks had to do with the gradual destruction of the island, which he declared was not fully a third smaller than when we first landed.

The pot had just begun to bubble when I heard his voice calling to me from the bank, where he had wandered away without my noticing. I ran up.

'Come and listen,' he said, 'and see what you make of it.' He held his hand cupwise to his ear, as so often before.

'Now do you hear anything?' he asked, watching me curiously.

We stood there, listening attentively together. At first I heard only the deep note of the water and the hissings rising from its turbulent surface. The willows, for once, were motionless and silent. Then a sound began to reach my ears faintly, a peculiar sound – something like the humming of a distant gong. It seemed to come across to us in the darkness from the waste of swamps and willows opposite. It was repeated at regular intervals, but it was certainly neither the sound of a bell nor the hooting of a distant steamer. I can liken it to nothing so much as to the sound of an immense gong, suspended far up in the sky, repeating incessantly its muffled metallic note, soft and musical, as it was repeatedly struck. My heart quickened as I listened.

'I've heard it all day,' said my companion. 'While you slept this afternoon it came all round the island. I hunted it down, but could never get near enough to see – to localise it correctly. Sometimes it was overhead, and sometimes it seemed under the water. Once or twice, too, I could have sworn it was not outside at all, but within myself – you know – the way a sound in the fourth dimension is supposed to come.'

I was too much puzzled to pay much attention to his words. I listened carefully, striving to associate it with any known familiar sound I could think of, but without success. It changed in the direction, too, coming nearer, and then sinking utterly away into remote distance. I cannot say that it was ominous in quality, because to me it seemed distinctly musical, yet I must admit it set going a distressing feeling that made me wish I had never heard it.

'The wind blowing in those sand-funnels,' I said determined to find an explanation, 'or the bushes rubbing together after the storm perhaps.'

'It comes off the whole swamp,' my friend answered. 'It comes from everywhere at once.' He ignored my explanations. 'It comes from the willow bushes somehow –'

'But now the wind has dropped,' I objected. 'The willows can hardly make a noise by themselves, can they?'

His answer frightened me, first because I had dreaded it, and secondly, because I knew intuitively it was true.

'It is because the wind has dropped we now hear it. It was drowned before. It is the cry, I believe, of the –'

I dashed back to my fire, warned by the sound of bubbling that the stew was in danger, but determined at the same time to escape further conversation. I was resolute, if possible, to avoid the exchanging of views. I dreaded, too, that he would begin about the gods, or the elemental forces, or something else disquieting, and I wanted to keep myself well in hand for what might happen later. There was another night to be faced before we escaped from this distressing place, and there was no knowing yet what it might bring forth.

'Come and cut up bread for the pot,' I called to him, vigorously stirring the appetizing mixture. That stew-pot held sanity for us both, and the thought made me laugh.

He came over slowly and took the provision sack from the tree, fumbling in its mysterious depths, and then emptying the entire contents upon the ground-sheet at his feet.

'Hurry up!' I cried; 'it's boiling.'

The Swede burst out into a roar of laughter that startled me. It was forced laughter, not artificial exactly, but mirthless.

'There's nothing here!' he shouted, holding his sides.

'Bread, I mean.'

'It's gone. There is no bread. They've taken it!'

I dropped the long spoon and ran up. Everything the sack had contained lay upon the ground-sheet, but there was no loaf.

The whole dead weight of my growing fear fell upon me and shook me. Then I burst out laughing too. It was the only thing to do: and the sound of my laughter also made me understand his. The strain of psychical pressure caused it – this explosion of unnatural laughter in both of us; it was an effort of repressed forces to seek relief; it was a temporary safety-valve. And with both of us it ceased quite suddenly.

'How criminally stupid of me!' I cried, still determined to be consistent and find an explanation. 'I clean forgot to buy a loaf at Pressburg. That chattering woman put everything out of my head, and I must have left it lying on the counter or –'

'The oatmeal, too, is much less than it was this morning,' the Swede interrupted.

Why in the world need he draw attention to it? I thought angrily.

'There's enough for to-morrow,' I said, stirring vigorously, 'and we can get lots more at Komorn or Gran. In twenty-four hours we shall be miles from here.'

'I hope so – to God,' he muttered, putting the things back into the sack, 'unless we're claimed first as victims for the sacrifice,' he added with a foolish laugh. He dragged the sack into the tent, for safety's sake, I suppose, and I heard him mumbling to himself, but so indistinctly that it seemed quite natural for me to ignore his words.

Our meal was beyond question a gloomy one, and we ate it almost in silence, avoiding one another's eyes, and keeping the fire bright. Then we washed up and prepared for the night, and, once smoking, our minds unoccupied with any definite duties, the apprehension I had felt all day long became more and more acute. It was not then active fear, I think, but the very vagueness of its origin distressed me far more than if I had been able to ticket and face it squarely. The curious sound I have likened to the note of a gong became now almost incessant, and filled the stillness of the night with a faint, continuous ringing rather than a series of distinct notes. At one time it was behind and at another time in front of us. Sometimes I fancied it came from the bushes on our left, and then again from the clumps on our right. More often it hovered directly overhead like the whirring of wings. It was really everywhere at once, behind, in front, at our sides and over our heads, completely surrounding us. The sound really defies description. But nothing within my knowledge is like that ceaseless muffled humming rising off the deserted world of swamps and willows.

We sat smoking in comparative silence, the strain growing every minute greater. The worst feature of the situation seemed to me that we did not know what to expect, and could therefore make no sort of preparation by way of defence. We could anticipate nothing. My explanations made in the sunshine, moreover, now came to haunt me with their foolish and wholly unsatisfactory nature, and it was more and more clear to us that some kind of plain talk with my companion was inevitable, whether I liked it or not. After all, we had to spend the night together, and to sleep in the same tent side by side. I saw that I could not get along much longer without the support of his mind, and for that, of course, plain talk was imperative. As long as possible, however, I postponed this little climax, and tried to ignore or laugh at the occasional sentences he flung into the emptiness.

Some of these sentences, moreover, were confoundedly disquieting to me, coming as they did to corroborate much that I felt myself; corroboration, too – which made it so much more convincing – from a totally different point of view. He composed such curious sentences, and hurled them at me in such an inconsequential sort of way, as though his main line of thought was secret to himself, and these fragments were mere bits he found it impossible to digest. He got rid of them by uttering them. Speech relieved him. It was like being sick.

'There are things about us, I'm sure, that make for disorder, disintegration, destruction, our destruction,' he said once, while the fire blazed between us. 'We've strayed out of a safe line somewhere.'

And, another time, when the gong sounds had come nearer, ringing much louder than before, and directly over our heads, he said as though talking to himself:

'I don't think a gramophone would show any record of that. The sound doesn't come to me by the ears at all. The vibrations reach me in another manner altogether, and seem to be within me, which is precisely how a fourth dimensional sound might be supposed to make itself heard.'

I purposely made no reply to this, but I sat up a little closer to the fire and peered about me into the darkness. The clouds were massed all over the sky, and no trace of moonlight came through. Very still, too, everything was, so that the river and the frogs had things all their own way.

'It has that about it,' he went on, 'which is utterly out of common experience. It is unknown. Only one thing describes it really; it is a non-human sound; I mean a sound outside humanity.'

Having rid himself of this indigestible morsel, he lay quiet for a time, but he had so admirably expressed my own feeling that it was a relief to have the thought out, and to have confined it by the limitation of words from dangerous wandering to and fro in the mind.

The solitude of that Danube camping-place, can I ever forget it? The feeling of being utterly alone on an empty planet! My thoughts ran incessantly upon cities and the haunts of men. I would have given my soul, as the saying is, for the 'feel' of those Bavarian villages we had passed through by the score; for the normal, human commonplaces; peasants drinking beer, tables beneath the trees, hot sunshine, and a ruined castle on the rocks behind the red-roofed church. Even the tourists would have been welcome.

Yet what I felt of dread was no ordinary ghostly fear. It was infinitely greater, stranger, and seemed to arise from some dim ancestral sense of terror more profoundly disturbing than anything I had known or dreamed of. We had 'strayed', as the Swede put it, into some region or some set of conditions where the risks were great, yet unintelligible to us; where the frontiers of some unknown world lay close about us. It was a spot held by the dwellers in some outer space, a sort of peep-hole whence they could spy upon the earth, themselves unseen, a point where the veil between had worn a little thin. As the final result of too long a sojourn here, we should be carried over the border and deprived of what we called 'our lives', yet by mental, not physical, processes. In that sense, as he said, we should be the victims of our adventure – a sacrifice.

It took us in different fashion, each according to the measure of his sensitiveness and powers of resistance. I translated it vaguely into a personification of the mightily disturbed elements, investing them with the horror of a deliberate and malefic purpose, resentful of our audacious intrusion into their breeding-place; whereas my friend threw it into the unoriginal form at first of a trespass on some ancient shrine, some place where the old gods still held sway, where the emotional forces of former worshippers still clung, and the ancestral portion of him yielded to the old pagan spell.

At any rate, here was a place unpolluted by men, kept clean by the winds from coarsening human influences, a place where spiritual agencies were within reach and aggressive. Never, before or since, have I been so attacked by indescribable suggestions of a 'beyond region', of another scheme of life, another revolution not parallel to the human. And in the end our minds would succumb under the weight of the awful spell, and we should be drawn across the frontier into their world.

Small things testified to the amazing influence of the place, and now in the silence round the fire they allowed themselves to be noted by the mind. The very atmosphere had proved itself a magnifying medium to distort every indication: the otter rolling in the current, the hurrying boatman making signs, the shifting willows, one and all had been robbed of its natural character, and revealed in something of its other aspect – as it existed across the border to that other region. And this changed aspect I felt was now not merely to me, but to the race. The whole experience whose verge we touched was unknown to humanity at all. It was a new order of experience, and in the true sense of the word unearthly.

'It's the deliberate, calculating purpose that reduces one's courage to zero,' the Swede said suddenly, as if he had been actually following my thoughts. 'Otherwise imagination might count for much. But the paddle, the canoe, the lessening food –'

'Haven't I explained all that once?' I interrupted viciously.

'You have,' he answered dryly; 'you have indeed.'

He made other remarks too, as usual, about what he called the 'plain determination to provide a victim'; but, having now arranged my thoughts better, I recognised that this was simply the cry of his frightened soul against the knowledge that he was being attacked in a vital part, and that he would be somehow taken or destroyed. The situation called for a courage and calmness of reasoning that neither of us could compass, and I have never before been so clearly conscious of two persons in me – the one that explained everything, and the other that laughed at such foolish explanations, yet was horribly afraid.

Meanwhile, in the pitchy night the fire died down and the wood pile grew small. Neither of us moved to replenish the stock, and the darkness consequently came up very close to our faces. A few feet beyond the circle of firelight it was inky black. Occasionally a stray puff of wind set the willows shivering about us, but apart from this not very welcome sound a deep and depressing silence reigned, broken only by the gurgling of the river and the humming in the air overhead.

We both missed, I think, the shouting company of the winds.

At length, at a moment when a stray puff prolonged itself as though the wind were about to rise again, I reached the point for me of saturation, the point where it was absolutely necessary to find relief in plain speech, or else to betray myself by some hysterical extravagance that must have been far worse in its effect upon both of us. I kicked the fire into a blaze, and turned to my companion abruptly. He looked up with a start.

'I can't disguise it any longer,' I said; 'I don't like this place, and the darkness, and the noises, and the awful feelings I get. There's something here that beats me utterly. I'm in a blue funk, and that's the plain truth. If the other shore was – different, I swear I'd be inclined to swim for it!'

The Swede's face turned very white beneath the deep tan of sun and wind. He stared straight at me and answered quietly, but his voice betrayed his huge excitement by its unnatural calmness. For the moment, at any rate, he was the strong man of the two. He was more phlegmatic, for one thing.

'It's not a physical condition we can escape from by running away,' he replied, in the tone of a doctor diagnosing some grave disease; 'we must sit tight and wait. There are forces close here that could kill a herd of elephants in a second as easily as you or I could squash a fly. Our only chance is to keep perfectly still. Our insignificance perhaps may save us.'

I put a dozen questions into my expression of face, but found no words. It was precisely like listening to an accurate description of a disease whose symptoms had puzzled me.

'I mean that so far, although aware of our disturbing presence, they have not found us – not 'located' us, as the Americans say,' he went on. 'They're blundering about like men hunting for a leak of gas. The paddle and canoe and provisions prove that. I think they feel us, but cannot actually see us. We must keep our minds quiet – it's our minds they feel. We must control our thoughts, or it's all up with us.'

'Death, you mean?' I stammered, icy with the horror of his suggestion.

'Worse – by far,' he said. 'Death, according to one's belief, means either annihilation or release from the limitations of the senses, but it involves no change of character. You don't suddenly alter just because the body's gone. But this means a radical alteration, a complete change, a horrible loss of oneself by substitution – far worse than death, and not even annihilation. We happen to have camped in a spot where their region touches ours, where the veil between has worn thin' – horrors! he was using my very own phrase, my actual words – 'so that they are aware of our being in their neighbourhood.'

'But who are aware?' I asked.

I forgot the shaking of the willows in the

windless calm, the humming overhead, everything except that I was waiting for an answer that I dreaded more than I can possibly explain.

He lowered his voice at once to reply, leaning forward a little over the fire, an indefinable change in his face that made me avoid his eyes and look down upon the ground.

'All my life,' he said, 'I have been strangely, vividly conscious of another region – not far removed from our own world in one sense, yet wholly different in kind – where great things go on unceasingly, where immense and terrible personalities hurry by, intent on vast purposes compared to which earthly affairs, the rise and fall of nations, the destinies of empires, the fate of armies and continents, are all as dust in the balance; vast purposes, I mean, that deal directly with the soul, and not indirectly with more expressions of the soul –'

'I suggest just now –' I began, seeking to stop him, feeling as though I was face to face with a madman. But he instantly overbore me with his torrent that had to come.

'You think,' he said, 'it is the spirit of the elements, and I thought perhaps it was the old gods. But I tell you now it is – neither. These would be comprehensible entities, for they have relations with men, depending upon them for worship or sacrifice, whereas these beings who are now about us have absolutely nothing to do with mankind, and it is mere chance that their space happens just at this spot to touch our own.'

The mere conception, which his words somehow made so convincing, as I listened to them there in the dark stillness of that lonely island, set me shaking a little all over. I found it impossible to control my movements.

'And what do you propose?' I began again.

'A sacrifice, a victim, might save us by distracting them until we could get away,' he went on, 'just as the wolves stop to devour the dogs and give the sleigh another start. But – I see no chance of any other victim now.'

I stared blankly at him. The gleam in his eye was dreadful. Presently he continued.

'It's the willows, of course. The willows mask the others, but the others are feeling about for us. If we let our minds betray our fear, we're lost, lost utterly.' He looked at me with an expression so calm, so determined, so sincere, that I no longer had any doubts as to his sanity. He was as sane as any man ever was. 'If we can hold out through the night,' he added, 'we may get off in the daylight unnoticed, or rather, undiscovered.'

'But you really think a sacrifice would –'

That gong-like humming came down very close over our heads as I spoke, but it was my friend's scared face that really stopped my mouth.

'Hush!' he whispered, holding up his hand. 'Do not mention them more than you can help. Do not refer to them by name. To name is to reveal; it is the inevitable clue, and our only hope lies in ignoring them, in order that they may ignore us.'

'Even in thought?' He was extraordinarily agitated.

'Especially in thought. Our thoughts make spirals in their world. We must keep them out of our minds at all costs if possible.'

I raked the fire together to prevent the darkness having everything its own way. I never longed for the sun as I longed for it then in the awful blackness of that summer night.

'Were you awake all last night?' he went on suddenly.

'I slept badly a little after dawn,' I replied evasively, trying to follow his instructions, which I knew instinctively were true, 'but the wind, of course –'

'I know. But the wind won't account for all the noises.'

'Then you heard it too?'

'The multiplying countless little footsteps I heard,' he said, adding, after a moment's hesitation, 'and that other sound –'

'You mean above the tent, and the pressing down upon us of something tremendous, gigantic?'

He nodded significantly.

'It was like the beginning of a sort of inner suffocation?' I said.

'Partly, yes. It seemed to me that the weight of the atmosphere had been altered – had increased enormously, so that we should have been crushed.'

'And that,' I went on, determined to have it all out, pointing upwards where the gong-like note hummed ceaselessly, rising and falling like wind. 'What do you make of that?'

'It's their sound,' he whispered gravely. 'It's the sound of their world, the humming in their region. The division here is so thin that it leaks through somehow. But, if you listen carefully, you'll find it's not above so much as around us. It's in the willows. It's the willows themselves humming, because here the willows have been made symbols of the forces that are against us.'

I could not follow exactly what he meant by this, yet the thought and idea in my mind were beyond question the thought and idea in his. I realised what he realised, only with less power of analysis than his. It was on the tip of my tongue to tell him at last about my hallucination of the ascending figures and the moving bushes, when he suddenly thrust his face again close into mine across the firelight and began to speak in a very earnest whisper. He amazed me by his calmness and pluck, his apparent control of the situation. This man I had for years deemed unimaginative, stolid!

'Now listen,' he said. 'The only thing for us to do is to go on as though nothing had happened, follow our usual habits, go to bed, and so forth; pretend we feel nothing and notice nothing. It is a question wholly of the mind, and the less we think about them the better our chance of escape. Above all, don't think, for what you think happens!'

'All right,' I managed to reply, simply breathless with his words and the strangeness of it all; 'all right, I'll try, but tell me one more thing first. Tell me what you make of those hollows in the ground all about us, those sand-funnels?'

'No!' he cried, forgetting to whisper in his excitement. 'I dare not, simply dare not, put the thought into words. If you have not guessed I am glad. Don't try to. They have put it into my mind; try your hardest to prevent their putting it into yours.'

He sank his voice again to a whisper before he finished, and I did not press him to explain. There was already just about as much horror in me as I could hold. The conversation came to an end, and we smoked our pipes busily in silence.

Then something happened, something unimportant apparently, as the way is when the nerves are in a very great state of tension, and this small thing for a brief space gave me an entirely different point of view. I chanced to look down at my sand-shoe – the sort we used for the canoe – and something to do with the hole at the toe suddenly recalled to me the London shop where I had bought them, the difficulty the man had in fitting me, and other details of the uninteresting but practical operation. At once, in its train, followed a wholesome view of the modern sceptical world I was accustomed to move in at home. I thought of roast beef, and ale, motor-cars, policemen, brass bands, and a dozen other things that proclaimed the soul of ordinariness or utility. The effect was immediate and astonishing even to myself. Psychologically, I suppose, it was simply a sudden and violent reaction after the strain of living in an atmosphere of things that to the normal consciousness must seem impossible and incredible. But, whatever the cause, it momentarily lifted the spell from my heart, and left me for the short space of a minute feeling free and utterly unafraid. I looked up at my friend opposite.

'You damned old pagan!' I cried, laughing aloud in his face. 'You imaginative idiot! You superstitious idolator! You –'

I stopped in the middle, seized anew by the old horror. I tried to smother the sound of my voice as something sacrilegious. The Swede, of course, heard it too – the strange cry overhead in the darkness – and that sudden drop in the air as though something had come nearer.

He had turned ashen white under the tan. He stood bolt upright in front of the fire, stiff as a rod, staring at me.

'After that,' he said in a sort of helpless, frantic way, 'we must go! We can't stay now; we must strike camp this very instant and go on – down the river.'

He was talking, I saw, quite wildly, his words dictated by abject terror – the terror he had resisted so long, but which had caught him at last.

'In the dark?' I exclaimed, shaking with fear after my hysterical outburst, but still realising our position better than he did. 'Sheer madness! The river's in flood, and we've only got a single paddle. Besides, we only go deeper into their country!

There's nothing ahead for fifty miles but willows, willows, willows!'

He sat down again in a state of semi-collapse. The positions, by one of those kaleidoscopic changes nature loves, were suddenly reversed, and the control of our forces passed over into my hands. His mind at last had reached the point where it was beginning to weaken.

'What on earth possessed you to do such a thing?' he whispered with the awe of genuine terror in his voice and face.

I crossed round to his side of the fire. I took both his hands in mine, kneeling down beside him and looking straight into his frightened eyes.

'We'll make one more blaze,' I said firmly, 'and then turn in for the night. At sunrise we'll be off full speed for Komorn. Now, pull yourself together a bit, and remember your own advice about not thinking fear!'

He said no more, and I saw that he would agree and obey. In some measure, too, it was a sort of relief to get up and make an excursion into the darkness for more wood. We kept close together, almost touching, groping among the bushes and along the bank. The humming overhead never ceased, but seemed to me to grow louder as we increased our distance from the fire. It was shivery work!

We were grubbing away in the middle of a thickish clump of willows where some driftwood from a former flood had caught high among the branches, when my body was seized in a grip that made me half drop upon the sand. It was the Swede. He had fallen against me, and was clutching me for support. I heard his breath coming and going in short gasps.

'Look! By my soul!' he whispered, and for the first time in my experience I knew what it was to hear tears of terror in a human voice. He was pointing to the fire, some fifty feet away. I followed the direction of his finger, and I swear my heart missed a beat.

There, in front of the dim glow, something was moving.

I saw it through a veil that hung before my eyes like the gauze drop-curtain used at the back of a theatre – hazily a little. It was neither a human figure nor an animal. To me it gave the strange impression of being as large as several animals grouped together, like horses, two or three, moving slowly. The Swede, too, got a similar result, though expressing it differently, for he thought it was shaped and sized like a clump of willow bushes, rounded at the top, and moving all over upon its surface – 'coiling upon itself like smoke,' he said afterwards.

'I watched it settle downwards through the bushes,' he sobbed at me. 'Look, by God! It's coming this way! Oh, oh!' – he gave a kind of whistling cry. 'They've found us.'

I gave one terrified glance, which just enabled me to see that the shadowy form was swinging towards us through the bushes, and then I collapsed backwards with a crash into the branches. These failed, of course, to support my weight, so that with the Swede on top of me we fell in a struggling heap upon the sand. I really hardly knew what was happening. I was conscious only of a sort of enveloping sensation of icy fear that plucked the nerves out of their fleshly covering, twisted them this way and that, and replaced them quivering. My eyes were tightly shut; something in my throat choked me; a feeling that my consciousness was expanding, extending out into space, swiftly gave way to another feeling that I was losing it altogether, and about to die.

An acute spasm of pain passed through me, and I was aware that the Swede had hold of me in such a way that he hurt me abominably. It was the way he caught at me in falling.

But it was the pain, he declared afterwards, that saved me; it caused me to forget them and think of something else at the very instant when they were about to find me. It concealed my mind from them at the moment of discovery, yet just in time to evade their terrible seizing of me. He himself, he says, actually swooned at the same moment, and that was what saved him.

I only know that at a later date, how long or short is impossible to say, I found myself scrambling up out of the slippery network of willow branches, and saw my companion standing in front of me holding out a hand to assist me. I stared at him in a dazed way, rubbing the arm he had twisted for me.

Nothing came to me to say, somehow.

'I lost consciousness for a moment or two,' I heard him say. 'That's what saved me. It made me stop thinking about them.'

'You nearly broke my arm in two,' I said, uttering my only connected thought at the moment. A numbness came over me.

'That's what saved you!' he replied. 'Between us, we've managed to set them off on a false tack somewhere. The humming has ceased. It's gone – for the moment at any rate!'

A wave of hysterical laughter seized me again, and this time spread to my friend too – great healing gusts of shaking laughter that brought a tremendous sense of relief in their train. We made our way back to the fire and put the wood on so that it blazed at once. Then we saw that the tent had fallen over and lay in a tangled heap upon the ground.

We picked it up, and during the process tripped more than once and caught our feet in sand.

'It's those sand-funnels,' exclaimed the Swede, when the tent was up again and the firelight lit up the ground for several yards about us. 'And look at the size of them!'

All round the tent and about the fireplace where we had seen the moving shadows there were deep funnel-shaped hollows in the sand, exactly similar to the ones we had already found over the island, only far bigger and deeper, beautifully formed, and wide enough in some instances to admit the whole of my foot and leg.

Neither of us said a word. We both knew that sleep was the safest thing we could do, and to bed we went accordingly without further delay, having first thrown sand on the fire and taken the provision sack and the paddle inside the tent with us. The canoe, too, we propped in such a way at the end of the tent that our feet touched it, and the least motion would disturb and wake us.

In case of emergency, too, we again went to bed in our clothes, ready for a sudden start.

V

It was my firm intention to lie awake all night and watch, but the exhaustion of nerves and body decreed otherwise, and sleep after a while came over me with a welcome blanket of oblivion. The fact that my companion also slept quickened its approach. At first he fidgeted and constantly sat up, asking me if I 'heard this' or 'heard that'. He tossed about on his cork mattress, and said the tent was moving and the river had risen over the point of the island, but each time I went out to look I returned with the report that all was well, and finally he grew calmer and lay still. Then at length his breathing became regular and I heard unmistakable sounds of snoring – the first and only time in my life when snoring has been a welcome and calming influence.

This, I remember, was the last thought in my mind before dozing off.

A difficulty in breathing woke me, and I found the blanket over my face. But something else besides the blanket was pressing upon me, and my first thought was that my companion had rolled off his mattress on to my own in his sleep. I called to him and sat up, and at the same moment it came to me that the tent was surrounded. That sound of multitudinous soft pattering was again audible outside, filling the night with horror.

I called again to him, louder than before. He did not answer, but I missed the sound of his snoring, and also noticed that the flap of the tent was down. This was the unpardonable sin. I crawled out in the darkness to hook it back securely, and it was then for the first time I realised positively that the Swede was not here. He had gone.

I dashed out in a mad run, seized by a dreadful agitation, and the moment I was out I plunged into a sort of torrent of humming that surrounded me completely and came out of every quarter of the heavens at once. It was that same familiar humming – gone mad! A swarm of great invisible bees might have been about me in the air. The sound seemed to thicken the very atmosphere, and I felt that my lungs worked with difficulty.

But my friend was in danger, and I could not hesitate.

The dawn was just about to break, and a faint whitish light spread upwards over the clouds from a thin strip of clear horizon. No wind stirred. I could just make out the bushes and river beyond, and the pale sandy patches. In my excitement I ran frantically to and fro about the island, calling him by name, shouting at the top of my voice the first words that came into my head. But the willows smothered my voice, and the humming muffled it, so that the sound only travelled a few feet round me. I plunged among the bushes, tripping headlong, tumbling over roots, and scraping my face as I tore this way and that among the preventing branches.

Then, quite unexpectedly, I came out upon the island's point and saw a dark figure outlined between the water and the sky. It was the Swede. And already he had one foot in the river! A moment more and he would have taken the plunge.

I threw myself upon him, flinging my arms about his waist and dragging him shorewards with all my strength. Of course he struggled furiously, making a noise all the time just like that cursed humming, and using the most outlandish phrases in his anger about 'going inside to Them', and 'taking the way of the water and the wind', and God only knows what more besides, that I tried in vain to recall afterwards, but which turned me sick with horror and amazement as I listened. But in the end I managed to get him into the comparative safety of the tent, and flung him breathless and cursing upon the mattress where I held him until the fit had passed.

I think the suddenness with which it all went and he grew calm, coinciding as it did with the equally abrupt cessation of the humming and pattering outside – I think this was almost the strangest part of the whole business perhaps. For he had just opened his eyes and turned his tired face up to me so that the dawn threw a pale light upon it through the doorway, and said, for all the world just like a frightened child:

'My life, old man – it's my life I owe you. But it's all over now anyhow. They've found a victim in our place!'

Then he dropped back upon his blankets and went to sleep literally under my eyes. He simply collapsed, and began to snore again as healthily as though nothing had happened and he had never tried to offer his own life as a sacrifice by drowning. And when the sunlight woke him three hours later – hours of ceaseless vigil for me – it became so clear to me that he remembered absolutely nothing of what he had attempted to do, that I deemed it wise to hold my peace and ask no dangerous questions.

He woke naturally and easily, as I have said, when the sun was already high in a windless hot sky, and he at once got up and set about the preparation of the fire for breakfast. I followed him anxiously at bathing, but he did not attempt to plunge in, merely dipping his head and making some remark about the extra coldness of the water.

'River's falling at last,' he said, 'and I'm glad of it.'

'The humming has stopped too,' I said.

He looked up at me quietly with his normal expression. Evidently he remembered everything except his own attempt at suicide.

'Everything has stopped,' he said, 'because –'

He hesitated. But I knew some reference to that remark he had made just before he fainted was in his mind, and I was determined to know it.

'Because "They've found another victim"?' I said, forcing a little laugh.

'Exactly,' he answered, 'exactly! I feel as positive of it as though – as though – I feel quite safe again, I mean,' he finished.

He began to look curiously about him. The sunlight lay in hot patches on the sand. There was no wind. The willows were motionless. He slowly rose to feet.

'Come,' he said; 'I think if we look, we shall find it.'

He started off on a run, and I followed him. He kept to the banks, poking with a stick among the sandy bays and caves and little back-waters, myself always close on his heels.

'Ah!' he exclaimed presently, 'ah!'

The tone of his voice somehow brought back to me a vivid sense of the horror of the last twenty-four hours, and I hurried up to join him. He was pointing with his stick at a large black object that lay half in the water and half on the sand. It appeared to be caught by some twisted willow roots so that the river could not sweep it away. A few hours before the spot must have been under water.

'See,' he said quietly, 'the victim that made our escape possible!'

And when I peered across his shoulder I saw that his stick rested on the body of a man. He turned it over. It was the corpse of a peasant, and the face was hidden in the sand. Clearly the man had been drowned, but a few hours before, and his body must have been swept down upon our island somewhere about the hour of the dawn – at the very time the fit had passed.

'We must give it a decent burial, you know.'

'I suppose so,' I replied. I shuddered a little in spite of myself, for there was something about the appearance of that poor drowned man that turned me cold.

The Swede glanced up sharply at me, an undecipherable expression on his face, and began clambering down the bank. I followed him more leisurely. The current, I noticed, had torn away much of the clothing from the body, so that the neck and part of the chest lay bare.

Half-way down the bank my companion suddenly stopped and held up his hand in warning; but either my foot slipped, or I had gained too much momentum to bring myself quickly to a halt, for I bumped into him and sent him forward with a sort of leap to save himself. We tumbled together on to the hard sand so that our feet splashed into the water. And, before anything could be done, we had collided a little heavily against the corpse.

The Swede uttered a sharp cry. And I sprang back as if I had been shot.

At the moment we touched the body there rose from its surface the loud sound of humming – the sound of several hummings – which passed with a vast commotion as of winged things in the air about us and disappeared upwards into the sky, growing fainter and fainter till they finally ceased in the distance. It was exactly as though we had disturbed some living yet invisible creatures at work.

My companion clutched me, and I think I clutched him, but before either of us had time properly to recover from the unexpected shock, we saw that a movement of the current was turning the corpse round so that it became released from the grip of the willow roots. A moment later it had turned completely over, the dead face uppermost, staring at the sky. It lay on the edge of the main stream. In another moment it would be swept away.

The Swede started to save it, shouting again something I did not catch about a 'proper burial' – and then abruptly dropped upon his knees on the sand and covered his eyes with his hands. I was beside him in an instant.

I saw what he had seen.

For just as the body swung round to the current the face and the exposed chest turned full towards us, and showed plainly how the skin and flesh were indented with small hollows, beautifully formed, and exactly similar in shape and kind to the sand-funnels that we had found all over the island.

'Their mark!' I heard my companion mutter under his breath. 'Their awful mark!'

And when I turned my eyes again from his ghastly face to the river, the current had done its work, and the body had been swept away into mid-stream and was already beyond our reach and almost out of sight, turning over and over on the waves like an otter.

SREDNI VASHTAR

Saki

Saki (1870–1916) was the pen name of English writer Hector Hugh Munro, whose career was cut short when he died during World War I. Although Saki wrote plays, histories, and parodies, he specialized in writing outrageous and macabre stories that often skewered Edwardian society and culture. Considered a master of the short form, Saki is often compared to O. Henry and Dorothy Parker, although he is much more refined than O. Henry. His prose style is nuanced and exquisite, with his cleverness masking surprising depth at times. Sredni Vashtar, with its hint of the weird peeking through, is one of Saki's more subtle and enigmatic tales.

Conradin was ten years old, and the doctor had pronounced his professional opinion that the boy would not live another five years. The doctor was silky and effete, and counted for little, but his opinion was endorsed by Mrs. De Ropp, who counted for nearly everything. Mrs. De Ropp was Conradin's cousin and guardian, and in his eyes she represented those three-fifths of the world that are necessary and disagreeable and real; the other two-fifths, in perpetual antagonism to the foregoing, were summed up in himself and his imagination. One of these days Conradin supposed he would succumb to the mastering pressure of wearisome necessary things – such as illnesses and coddling restrictions and drawn-out dullness. Without his imagination, which was rampant under the spur of loneliness, he would have succumbed long ago.

Mrs. De Ropp would never, in her honestest moments, have confessed to herself that she disliked Conradin, though she might have been dimly aware that thwarting him 'for his good' was a duty which she did not find particularly irksome. Conradin hated her with a desperate sincerity which he was perfectly able to mask. Such few pleasures as he could contrive for himself gained an added relish from the likelihood that they would be displeasing to his guardian, and from the realm of his imagination she was locked out – an unclean thing, which should find no entrance.

In the dull, cheerless garden, overlooked by so many windows that were ready to open with a message not to do this or that, or a reminder that medicines were due, he found little attraction. The few fruit-trees that it contained were set jealously apart from his plucking, as though they were rare specimens of their kind blooming in an arid waste; it would probably have been difficult to find a market-gardener who would have offered ten shillings for their entire yearly produce. In a forgotten corner, however, almost hidden behind a dismal shrubbery, was a disused tool-shed of respectable proportions, and within its walls Conradin found a haven, something that took on the varying aspects of a playroom and a cathedral. He had peopled it with a legion of familiar phantoms, evoked partly from fragments of history and partly from his own brain, but it also boasted two inmates of flesh and blood. In one corner lived a ragged-plumaged Houdan hen, on which the boy lavished an affection that had scarcely another outlet. Further back in the gloom stood a large hutch, divided into two compartments, one of which was fronted with close iron bars. This was the abode of a large polecat-ferret, which a friendly butcher-boy had once smuggled, cage and all, into its present quarters, in exchange for a long-secreted hoard of small silver. Conradin was dreadfully afraid of the lithe, sharp-fanged beast, but it was his most treasured possession. Its very presence in the tool-shed was a secret and fearful joy, to be kept scrupulously from the knowledge of the Woman, as he privately dubbed his cousin. And one day, out of Heaven knows what material, he spun the beast a wonderful name, and from that moment it grew into a god and a religion. The Woman indulged in religion once a week at a church near by, and took Conradin with her, but to him the church service was an alien rite in the House of Rimmon. Every Thursday, in the dim and musty silence of the tool-shed, he worshipped with mystic and elaborate ceremonial before the wooden hutch where dwelt Sredni Vashtar, the great ferret. Red flowers in their season and scarlet berries in the winter-time were offered at his shrine, for he was a god who laid some special stress on the fierce impatient side of things, as opposed to the Woman's religion, which, as far as Conradin could observe, went to great lengths in the contrary direction. And on great festivals powdered nutmeg was strewn in front of his hutch, an important feature of the offering being that the nutmeg had to be stolen. These festivals were of irregular occurrence, and were chiefly appointed to celebrate some passing event. On one occasion, when Mrs. De Ropp suffered from acute toothache for three days, Conradin kept up the festival during the entire three days, and almost succeeded in persuading himself that Sredni Vashtar was personally responsible for the toothache. If the malady had lasted for another day the supply of nutmeg would have given out.

The Houdan hen was never drawn into the cult of Sredni Vashtar. Conradin had long ago settled that she was an Anabaptist. He did not pretend to have the remotest knowledge as to what an Anabaptist was, but he privately hoped that it was dashing and not very respectable. Mrs. De Ropp was the ground plan on which he based and detested all respectability.

After a while Conradin's absorption in the tool-shed began to attract the notice of his guardian. 'It is not good for him to be pottering down there in all weathers,' she promptly decided, and at breakfast one morning she announced that the Houdan hen had been sold and taken away overnight. With her short-sighted eyes she peered at Conradin, waiting for an outbreak of rage and sorrow, which she was ready to rebuke with a flow of excellent precepts and reasoning. But Conradin said nothing: there was nothing to be said. Something perhaps in his white set face gave her a momentary qualm, for at tea that afternoon there was toast on the table, a delicacy which she usually banned on the grounds that it was bad for him; also because the making of it 'gave trouble,' a deadly offence in the middle-class feminine eye.

'I thought you liked toast,' she exclaimed, with an injured air, observing that he did not touch it.

'Sometimes,' said Conradin.

In the shed that evening there was an innovation in the worship of the hutch-god. Conradin had been wont to chant his praises, tonight he asked a boon.

'Do one thing for me, Sredni Vashtar.'

The thing was not specified. As Sredni Vashtar was a god he must be supposed to know. And choking back a sob as he looked at that other empty corner, Conradin went back to the world he so hated.

And every night, in the welcome darkness of his bedroom, and every evening in the dusk of the tool-shed, Conradin's bitter litany went up: 'Do one thing for me, Sredni Vashtar.'

Mrs. De Ropp noticed that the visits to the shed did not cease, and one day she made a further journey of inspection.

'What are you keeping in that locked hutch?' she asked. 'I believe it's guinea-pigs. I'll have them all cleared away.'

Conradin shut his lips tight, but the Woman ransacked his bedroom till she found the carefully hidden key, and forthwith marched down to the shed to complete her discovery. It was a cold afternoon, and Conradin had been bidden to keep to the house. From the furthest window of the dining-room the door of the shed could just be seen beyond the corner of the shrubbery, and there Conradin stationed himself. He saw the

Woman enter, and then he imagined her opening the door of the sacred hutch and peering down with her short-sighted eyes into the thick straw bed where his god lay hidden. Perhaps she would prod at the straw in her clumsy impatience. And Conradin fervently breathed his prayer for the last time. But he knew as he prayed that he did not believe. He knew that the Woman would come out presently with that pursed smile he loathed so well on her face, and that in an hour or two the gardener would carry away his wonderful god, a god no longer, but a simple brown ferret in a hutch. And he knew that the Woman would triumph always as she triumphed now, and that he would grow ever more sickly under her pestering and domineering and superior wisdom, till one day nothing would matter much more with him, and the doctor would be proved right. And in the sting and misery of his defeat, he began to chant loudly and defiantly the hymn of his threatened idol:

Sredni Vashtar went forth,
His thoughts were red thoughts
and his teeth were white.
His enemies called for peace,
but he brought them death.
Sredni Vashtar the Beautiful.

And then of a sudden he stopped his chanting and drew closer to the window-pane. The door of the shed still stood ajar as it had been left, and the minutes were slipping by. They were long minutes, but they slipped by nevertheless. He watched the starlings running and flying in little parties across the lawn; he counted them over and over again, with one eye always on that swinging door. A sour-faced maid came in to lay the table for tea, and still Conradin stood and waited and watched. Hope had crept by inches into his heart, and now a look of triumph began to blaze in his eyes that had only known the wistful patience of defeat. Under his breath, with a furtive exultation, he began once again the pæan of victory and devastation. And presently his eyes were rewarded: out through that doorway came a long, low, yellow-and-brown beast, with eyes a-blink at the waning daylight, and dark wet stains around the fur of jaws and throat. Conradin dropped on his knees. The great polecat-ferret made its way down to a small brook at the foot of the garden, drank for a moment, then crossed a little plank bridge and was lost to sight in the bushes. Such was the passing of Sredni Vashtar.

'Tea is ready,' said the sour-faced maid; 'where is the mistress?'

'She went down to the shed some time ago,' said Conradin.

And while the maid went to summon her mistress to tea, Conradin fished a toasting-fork out of the sideboard drawer and proceeded to toast himself a piece of bread. And during the toasting of it and the buttering of it with much butter and the slow enjoyment of eating it, Conradin listened to the noises and silences which fell in quick spasms beyond the dining-room door. The loud foolish screaming of the maid, the answering chorus of wondering ejaculations from the kitchen region, the scuttering footsteps and hurried embassies for outside help, and then, after a lull, the scared sobbings and the shuffling tread of those who bore a heavy burden into the house.

'Whoever will break it to the poor child? I couldn't for the life of me!' exclaimed a shrill voice. And while they debated the matter among themselves, Conradin made himself another piece of toast.

CASTING THE RUNES

M. R. James

M. R. James (1862–1936) was an English writer and mediaeval scholar. His ghost stories have come to be widely regarded as among the finest in English literature. By ignoring the formal Gothic trappings used by previous writers of supernatural fiction, James helped to update the weird tale. 'Casting the Runes' (1911) is his most famous tale, situating the weird in a contemporary context while still acknowledging the writer's own historical interests. It is genuinely unsettling, even today. The story has been adapted for radio, film, and stage several times. James's influence is reflected in the work of both H. P. Lovecraft and Clark Ashton Smith, as well as Ramsey Campbell and Tanith Lee.

April 15th, 190-
Dear Sir,
I am requested by the Council of the —— Association to return to you the draft of a paper on *The Truth of Alchemy*, which you have been good enough to offer to read at our forthcoming meeting, and to inform you that the Council do not see their way to including it in the programme.

I am,
Yours faithfully,
—— *Secretary.*

April 18th
Dear Sir,
I am sorry to say that my engagements do not permit of my affording you an interview on the subject of your proposed paper. Nor do our laws allow of your discussing the matter with a Committee of our Council, as you suggest. Please allow me to assure you that the fullest consideration was given to the draft which you submitted, and that it was not declined without having been referred to the judgement of a most competent authority. No personal question (it can hardly be necessary for me to add) can have had the slightest influence on the decision of the Council.

Believe me (*ut supra*).

April 20th
The Secretary of the —— Association begs respectfully to inform Mr Karswell that it is impossible for him to communicate the name of any person or persons to whom the draft of Mr Karswell's paper may have been submitted; and further desires to intimate that he cannot undertake to reply to any further letters on this subject.

'And who *is* Mr Karswell?' inquired the Secretary's wife. She had called at his office, and (perhaps unwarrantably) had picked up the last of these three letters, which the typist had just brought in.

'Why, my dear, just at present Mr Karswell is a very angry man. But I don't know much about him otherwise, except that he is a person of wealth, his address is Lufford Abbey, Warwickshire, and he's an alchemist, apparently, and wants to tell us all about it; and that's about all – except that I don't want to meet him for the next week or two. Now, if you're ready to leave this place, I am.'

'What have you been doing to make him angry?' asked Mrs Secretary.

'The usual thing, my dear, the usual thing: he sent in a draft of a paper he wanted to read at the next meeting, and we referred it to Edward Dunning – almost the only man in England who knows about these things – and he said it was perfectly hopeless, so we declined it. So Karswell has been pelting me with letters ever since. The last thing he wanted was the name of the man we referred his nonsense to; you saw my answer to that. But don't you say anything about it, for goodness' sake.'

'I should think not, indeed. Did I ever do such a thing? I do hope, though, he won't get to know that it was poor Mr Dunning.'

'Poor Mr Dunning? I don't know why you call him that; he's a very happy man, is Dunning. Lots of hobbies and a comfortable home, and all his time to himself.'

'I only meant I should be sorry for him if this man got hold of his name, and came and bothered him.'

'Oh, ah! yes. I dare say he would be poor Mr Dunning then.'

The Secretary and his wife were lunching out, and the friends to whose house they were bound were Warwickshire people. So Mrs Secretary had already settled it in her own mind that she would question them judiciously about Mr Karswell. But she was saved the trouble of leading up to the subject, for the hostess said to the host, before many minutes had passed, 'I saw the Abbot of Lufford this morning.' The host whistled. '*Did* you? What in the world brings him up to town?' 'Goodness knows; he was coming out of the British Museum gate as I drove past.' It was not unnatural that Mrs Secretary should inquire whether this was a real Abbot who was being spoken of. 'Oh no, my dear: only a neighbour of ours in the country who bought Lufford Abbey a few years ago. His real name is Karswell.' 'Is he a friend of yours?' asked Mr Secretary, with a private wink to his wife. The question let loose a torrent of declamation. There was really nothing to be said for Mr Karswell. Nobody knew what he did with himself: his servants were a horrible set of people; he had invented a new religion for himself, and practised no one could tell what appalling rites; he was very easily offended, and never forgave anybody; he had a dreadful face (so the lady insisted, her husband somewhat demurring); he never did a kind action, and whatever influence he did exert was mischievous. 'Do the poor man justice, dear,' the husband interrupted. 'You forget the treat he gave the school children.' 'Forget it, indeed! But I'm glad you mentioned it, because it gives an idea of the man. Now, Florence, listen to this. The first winter he was at Lufford this delightful neighbour of ours wrote to the clergyman of his parish (he's not ours, but we know him very well) and offered to show the school children some magic-lantern slides. He said he had some new kinds, which he thought would interest them. Well, the clergyman was rather surprised, because Mr Karswell had shown himself inclined to be unpleasant to the children – complaining of their trespassing, or something of the sort; but of course he accepted, and the evening was fixed, and our friend went himself to see that everything went right. He said he never had been so thankful for anything as that his own children were all prevented from being there: they were at a children's party at our house, as a matter of fact. Because this Mr Karswell had evidently set out with the intention of frightening these poor village children out of their wits, and I do believe, if he had been allowed to go on, he would actually have done so. He began with some comparatively mild things. Red Riding Hood was one, and even then, Mr Farrer said, the wolf was so dreadful that several of the smaller children had to be taken out: and he said Mr Karswell began the story by producing a noise like a wolf howling in the distance, which was the most gruesome thing he had ever heard. All the slides he showed, Mr Farrer said, were most clever; they were absolutely realistic, and where he had got them or how he worked them he could not imagine. Well, the show went on, and the stories kept on becoming a little more terrifying each time, and the children were mesmerized into complete silence. At last he produced a series which represented a little boy passing through his own park – Lufford, I mean – in the evening. Every child in the room could recognize the place from the pictures. And this poor boy was followed, and at last pursued and overtaken, and either torn to pieces or somehow made away with, by a horrible hopping creature in white, which you saw first dodging about among the trees, and gradually it appeared more and more plainly. Mr Farrer said it gave him one of the worst nightmares he ever remembered, and what it must have meant to the children doesn't bear thinking of. Of course this was too much, and he spoke very sharply indeed to Mr Karswell, and said it couldn't go on. All *he* said was: "Oh, you think it's time to bring our little show to an end and send them home to their beds? *Very* well!" And then, if you please, he switched on another slide, which showed a great mass of snakes, centipedes, and disgusting creatures with wings, and somehow or other he made it seem as if they were climbing out of the picture and getting in amongst the audience; and this was accompanied by a sort of dry rustling noise which sent the children nearly mad, and of course they stampeded. A good many of them were rather hurt in getting out of the room, and I don't suppose one of them closed an eye that night. There was the most dreadful trouble in the village afterwards. Of course the mothers threw a good part of the blame on poor Mr Farrer, and, if they could have got past the gates, I believe the fathers would have broken every window in the Abbey. Well, now, that's Mr Karswell: that's the Abbot of Lufford, my dear, and you can imagine how we covet *his* society.'

'Yes, I think he has all the possibilities of a distinguished criminal, has Karswell,' said the host. 'I should be sorry for anyone who got into his bad books.'

'Is he the man, or am I mixing him up with someone else?' asked the Secretary (who for some minutes had been wearing the frown of the man who is trying to recollect something). 'Is he the man who brought out a *History of Witchcraft* some time back – ten years or more?'

'That's the man; do you remember the reviews of it?'

'Certainly I do; and what's equally to the point, I knew the author of the most incisive of the lot. So did you: you must remember John Harrington; he was at John's in our time.'

'Oh, very well indeed, though I don't think I saw or heard anything of him between the time I went down and the day I read the account of the inquest on him.'

'Inquest?' said one of the ladies. 'What has happened to him?'

'Why, what happened was that he fell out of a tree and broke his neck. But the puzzle was, what could have induced him to get up there. It was a mysterious business, I must say. Here was this man – not an athletic fellow, was he? and with no eccentric twist about him that was ever noticed – walking home along a country road late in the evening – no tramps about – well known and liked in the place – and he suddenly begins to run like mad, loses his hat and stick, and finally shins up a tree – quite a difficult tree – growing in the hedgerow: a dead branch gives way, and he comes down with it and breaks his neck, and there he's found next morning with the most dreadful face of fear on him that could be imagined. It was pretty evident, of course, that he had been chased by something, and people talked of savage dogs, and beasts escaped out of menageries; but there was nothing to be made of that. That was in '89, and I believe his brother Henry (whom I remember as well at Cambridge, but *you* probably don't) has been trying to get on the track of an explanation ever since. He, of course, insists there was malice in it, but I don't know. It's difficult to see how it could have come in.'

After a time the talk reverted to the *History of Witchcraft*. 'Did you ever look into it?' asked the host.

'Yes, I did,' said the Secretary. 'I went so far as to read it.'

'Was it as bad as it was made out to be?'

'Oh, in point of style and form, quite hopeless. It deserved all the pulverizing it got. But, besides that, it was an evil book. The man believed every word of what he was saying, and I'm very much mistaken if he hadn't tried the greater part of his receipts.'

'Well, I only remember Harrington's review of it, and I must say if I'd been the author it would have quenched my literary ambition for good. I should never have held up my head again.'

'It hasn't had that effect in the present case. But come, it's half-past three; I must be off.'

On the way home the Secretary's wife said, 'I do hope that horrible man won't find out that Mr Dunning had anything to do with the rejection of his paper.' 'I don't think there's much chance of that,' said the Secretary. 'Dunning won't mention it himself, for these matters are confidential, and none of us will for the same reason. Karswell won't know his name, for Dunning hasn't published anything on the same subject yet. The only danger is that Karswell might find out, if he was to ask the British Museum people who was in the habit of consulting alchemical manuscripts: I can't very well tell them not to mention Dunning, can I? It would set them talking at once. Let's hope it won't occur to him.'

However, Mr Karswell was an astute man.

This much is in the way of prologue. On an evening rather later in the same week, Mr Edward Dunning was returning from the British Museum, where he had been engaged in research, to the comfortable house in a suburb where he lived alone, tended by two excellent women who had been long with him. There is nothing to be added by way of description of him to what we have heard already. Let us follow him as he takes his sober course homewards.

A train took him to within a mile or two of his house, and an electric tram a stage farther. The line ended at a point some three hundred yards from his front door. He had had enough of reading when he got into the car, and indeed the light was not such as to allow him to do more than study the advertisements on the panes of glass that faced him as he sat. As was not unnatural, the advertisements in this particular line of cars were objects of his frequent contemplation, and, with the possible exception of the brilliant and convincing dialogue between Mr Lamplough and an eminent K.C. on the subject of Pyretic Saline, none of them afforded much scope to his imagination. I am wrong: there was one at the corner of the car farthest from him which did not seem familiar. It was in blue letters on a yellow ground, and all that he could read of it was a name – John Harrington – and something like a date. It could be of no interest to him to know more; but for all that, as the car emptied, he was just curious enough to move along the seat until he could read it well. He felt to a slight extent repaid for his trouble; the advertisement was *not* of the usual type. It ran thus: 'In memory of John Harrington, F.S.A., of The Laurels, Ashbrooke. Died Sept. 18th, 1889. Three months were allowed.'

The car stopped. Mr Dunning, still contemplating the blue letters on the yellow ground, had to be stimulated to rise by a word from the conductor. 'I beg your pardon,' he said, 'I was looking at that advertisement; it's a very odd one, isn't it?' The conductor read it slowly. 'Well, my word,' he said, 'I never see that one before. Well, that is a cure, ain't it? Someone bin up to their jokes 'ere, I should think.' He got out a duster and applied it, not without saliva, to the pane and then to the outside. 'No,' he said, returning, 'that ain't no transfer; seems to me as if it was reg'lar *in* the glass, what I mean in the substance, as you may say. Don't you think so, sir?' Mr Dunning examined it and rubbed it with his glove, and agreed. 'Who looks after these advertisements, and gives leave for them to be put up? I wish you would inquire. I will just take a note of the words.' At this moment there came a call from the driver: 'Look alive, George, time's up.' 'All right, all right; there's something else what's up at this end. You come and look at this 'ere glass.' 'What's gorn with the glass?' said the driver, approaching. 'Well, and oo's 'Arrington? What's it all about?' 'I was just asking who was responsible for putting the advertisements up in your cars, and saying it would be as well to make some inquiry about this one.' 'Well, sir, that's all done at the Company's office, that work is: it's our Mr Timms, I believe, looks into that. When we put up tonight I'll leave word, and per'aps I'll be able to tell you tomorrer if you 'appen to be coming this way.'

This was all that passed that evening. Mr Dunning did just go to the trouble of looking up Ashbrooke, and found that it was in Warwickshire.

Next day he went to town again. The car (it was the same car) was too full in the morning to allow of his getting a word with the conductor:

he could only be sure that the curious advertisement had been made away with. The close of the day brought a further element of mystery into the transaction. He had missed the tram, or else preferred walking home, but at a rather late hour, while he was at work in his study, one of the maids came to say that two men from the tramways were very anxious to speak to him. This was a reminder of the advertisement, which he had, he says, nearly forgotten. He had the men in – they were the conductor and driver of the car – and when the matter of refreshment had been attended to, asked what Mr Timms had had to say about the advertisement. 'Well, sir, that's what we took the liberty to step round about,' said the conductor. 'Mr Timms 'e give William 'ere the rough side of his tongue about that: 'cordin' to 'im there warn't no advertisement of that description sent in, nor ordered, nor paid for, nor put up, nor nothink, let alone not bein' there, and we was playing the fool takin' up his time. "Well," I says, "if that's the case, all I ask of you, Mr Timms," I says, "is to take and look at it for yourself," I says. "Of course if it ain't there," I says, "you may take and call me what you like." "Right," he says, "I will": and we went straight off. Now, I leave it to you, sir, if that ad., as we term 'em, with 'Arrington on it warn't as plain as ever you see anythink – blue letters on yeller glass, and as I says at the time, and you borne me out, reg'lar *in* the glass, because, if you remember, you recollect of me swabbing it with my duster.' 'To be sure I do, quite clearly – well?' 'You may say well, I don't think. Mr Timms he gets in that car with a light – no, he telled William to 'old the light outside. "Now," he says, "where's your precious ad. what we've 'eard so much about?" "'Ere it is," I says, "Mr Timms," and I laid my 'and on it.' The conductor paused.

'Well,' said Mr Dunning, 'it was gone, I suppose. Broken?'

'Broke! – not it. There warn't, if you'll believe me, no more trace of them letters – blue letters they was – on that piece o' glass, than – well, it's no good *me* talkin'. *I* never see such a thing. I leave it to William here if – but there, as I says, where's the benefit in me going on about it?'

'And what did Mr Timms say?'

'Why 'e did what I give 'im leave to – called us pretty much anythink he liked, and I don't know as I blame him so much neither. But what we thought, William and me did, was as we seen you take down a bit of a note about that – well, that letterin' – '

'I certainly did that, and I have it now. Did you wish me to speak to Mr Timms myself, and show it to him? Was that what you came in about?'

'There, didn't I say as much?' said William. 'Deal with a gent if you can get on the track of one, that's my word. Now perhaps, George, you'll allow as I ain't took you very far wrong tonight.'

'Very well, William, very well; no need for you to go on as if you'd 'ad to frog's-march me 'ere. I come quiet, didn't I? All the same for that, we 'adn't ought to take up your time this way, sir; but if it so 'appened you could find time to step round to the Company orfice in the morning and tell Mr Timms what you seen for yourself, we should lay under a very 'igh obligation to you for the trouble. You see it ain't bein' called – well, one thing and another, as we mind, but if they got it into their 'ead at the orfice as we seen things as warn't there, why, one thing leads to another, and where we should be a twelvemunce 'ence – well, you can understand what I mean.'

Amid further elucidations of the proposition, George, conducted by William, left the room.

The incredulity of Mr Timms (who had a nodding acquaintance with Mr Dunning) was greatly modified on the following day by what the latter could tell and show him; and any bad mark that might have been attached to the names of William and George was not suffered to remain on the Company's books; but explanation there was none.

Mr Dunning's interest in the matter was kept alive by an incident of the following afternoon. He was walking from his club to the train, and he noticed some way ahead a man with a handful of leaflets such as are distributed to passers-by by agents of enterprising firms. This agent had not chosen a very crowded street for his operations: in fact, Mr Dunning did not see him get rid of a single leaflet before he himself reached the spot. One was thrust into his hand as he passed: the hand that gave it touched his, and he experienced a sort of little shock as it did so. It seemed unnaturally rough and hot. He looked in passing at the giver, but the impression he got was so unclear that, however much he tried to reckon it up subsequently, nothing would come. He was walking quickly, and as he went on glanced at the paper. It was a blue one. The name of Harrington in large capitals caught his eye. He stopped, startled, and felt for his glasses. The next instant the leaflet was twitched out of his hand by a man who hurried past, and was irrecoverably gone. He ran back a few paces, but where was the passer-by? and where the distributor?

It was in a somewhat pensive frame of mind that Mr Dunning passed on the following day into the Select Manuscript Room of the British Museum, and filled up tickets for Harley 3586, and some other volumes. After a few minutes they were brought to him, and he was settling the one he wanted first upon the desk, when he thought he heard his own name whispered behind him. He turned round hastily, and in doing so, brushed his little portfolio of loose papers on to the floor. He saw no one he recognized except one of the staff in charge of the room, who nodded to him, and he proceeded to pick up his papers. He thought he had them all, and was turning to begin work, when a stout gentleman at the table behind him, who was just rising to leave, and had collected his own belongings, touched him on the shoulder, saying, 'May I give you this? I think it should be yours,' and handed him a missing quire. 'It is mine, thank you,' said Mr Dunning. In another moment the man had left the room. Upon finishing his work for the afternoon, Mr Dunning had some conversation with the assistant in charge, and took occasion to ask who the stout gentleman was. 'Oh, he's a man named Karswell,' said the assistant; 'he was asking me a week ago who were the great authorities on alchemy, and of course I told him you were the only one in the country. I'll see if I can catch him: he'd like to meet you, I'm sure.'

'For heaven's sake don't dream of it!' said Mr Dunning, 'I'm particularly anxious to avoid him.'

'Oh! very well,' said the assistant, 'he doesn't come here often: I dare say you won't meet him.'

More than once on the way home that day Mr Dunning confessed to himself that he did not look forward with his usual cheerfulness to a solitary evening. It seemed to him that something ill-defined and impalpable had stepped in between him and his fellow-men – had taken him in charge, as it were. He wanted to sit close up to his neighbours in the train and in the tram, but as luck would have it both train and car were markedly empty. The conductor George was thoughtful, and appeared to be absorbed in calculations as to the number of passengers. On arriving at his house he found Dr Watson, his medical man, on his doorstep. 'I've had to upset your household arrangements, I'm sorry to say, Dunning. Both your servants *hors de combat*. In fact, I've had to send them to the Nursing Home.'

'Good heavens! what's the matter?'

'It's something like ptomaine poisoning, I should think: you've not suffered yourself, I can see, or you wouldn't be walking about. I think they'll pull through all right.'

'Dear, dear! Have you any idea what brought it on?' 'Well, they tell me they bought some shell-fish from a hawker at their dinner-time. It's odd. I've made inquiries, but I can't find that any hawker has been to other houses in the street. I couldn't send word to you; they won't be back for a bit yet. You come and dine with me tonight, anyhow, and we can make arrangements for going on. Eight o'clock. Don't be too anxious.' The solitary evening was thus obviated; at the expense of some distress and inconvenience, it is true. Mr Dunning spent the time pleasantly enough with the doctor (a rather recent settler), and returned to his lonely home at about 11.30. The night he passed is not one on which he looks back with any satisfaction. He was in bed and the light was out. He was wondering if the charwoman would come early enough to get him hot water next morning, when he heard the unmistakable sound of his study door opening. No step followed it on the passage floor, but the sound must mean mischief, for he knew that he had shut the door that evening after putting his papers away in his desk. It was rather shame than courage that induced him to slip out into the passage and lean over the banister in his nightgown, listening. No light was visible; no further sound came: only a gust of warm, or even hot air played for an instant round his shins. He went back and decided to lock himself into his room. There was more unpleasantness, however. Either an economical suburban company had decided that their light would not be required in the small hours, and had stopped working, or else something was wrong with the meter; the effect was in any case that the electric light was off. The obvious course was to find a match, and also to consult his watch: he might as well know how many hours of discomfort awaited him. So he put his hand into the well-known nook under the pillow: only, it did not get so far. What he touched was, according to his account, a mouth, with teeth, and with hair about it, and, he declares, not the mouth of a human being. I do not think it is any use to guess what he said or did; but he was in a spare room with the door locked and his ear to it before he was clearly conscious again. And there he spent the rest of a most miserable night, looking every moment for some fumbling at the door: but nothing came.

The venturing back to his own room in the morning was attended with many listenings and quiverings. The door stood open, fortunately, and the blinds were up (the servants had been out of the house before the hour of drawing them down); there was, to be short, no trace of an inhabitant. The watch, too, was in its usual place; nothing was disturbed, only the wardrobe door had swung open, in accordance with its confirmed habit. A ring at the back door now announced the charwoman, who had been ordered the night before, and nerved Mr Dunning, after letting her in, to continue his search in other parts of the house. It was equally fruitless.

The day thus begun went on dismally enough. He dared not go to the Museum: in spite of what the assistant had said, Karswell might turn up there, and Dunning felt he could not cope with a probably hostile stranger. His own house was odious; he hated sponging on the doctor. He spent some little time in a call at the Nursing Home, where he was slightly cheered by a good report of his housekeeper and maid. Towards lunch-time he betook himself to his club, again experiencing a gleam of satisfaction at seeing the Secretary of the Association. At luncheon Dunning told his friend the more material of his woes, but could not bring himself to speak of those that weighed most heavily on his spirits. 'My poor dear man,' said the Secretary, 'what an upset! Look here: we're alone at home, absolutely. You must put up with us. Yes! no excuse: send your things in this afternoon.' Dunning was unable to stand out: he was, in truth, becoming acutely anxious, as the hours went on, as to what that night might have waiting for him. He was almost happy as he hurried home to pack up.

His friends, when they had time to take stock of him, were rather shocked at his lorn appearance, and did their best to keep him up to the mark. Not altogether without success: but, when the two men were smoking alone later, Dunning became dull again. Suddenly he said, 'Gayton, I believe that alchemist man knows it was I who got his paper rejected.' Gayton whistled. 'What makes you think that?' he said. Dunning told of his conversation with the Museum assistant, and Gayton could only agree that the guess seemed likely to be correct. 'Not that I care much,' Dunning went on, 'only it might be a nuisance if we were to meet. He's a bad-tempered party, I imagine.' Conversation dropped again; Gayton became more and more strongly impressed with the desolateness that came over Dunning's face and bearing, and finally – though with a considerable effort – he asked him point-blank whether something serious was not bothering him. Dunning gave an exclamation of relief. 'I was perishing to get it off my mind,' he said. 'Do you know anything about a man named John Harrington?' Gayton was thoroughly startled, and at the moment could only ask why. Then the complete story of Dunning's experiences came out – what had happened in the tramcar, in his own house, and in the street, the troubling of spirit that had crept over him, and still held him; and he ended with the question he had begun with. Gayton was at a loss how to answer him. To tell the story of Harrington's end would perhaps be right; only, Dunning was in a nervous state, the story was a grim one, and he could not help asking himself whether there were not a connecting link between these two cases, in the person of Karswell. It was a difficult concession for a scientific man, but it could be eased by the phrase 'hypnotic suggestion'. In the end he decided that his answer tonight should be guarded; he would talk the situation over with his wife. So he said that he had known Harrington at Cambridge, and believed he had died suddenly in 1889, adding a few details about the man and his published work. He did talk over the matter with Mrs Gayton, and, as he had anticipated, she leapt at once to the conclusion which had been hovering before him. It was she who reminded him of the surviving brother, Henry Harrington, and she also who suggested that he might be got hold of by means of their hosts of the day before. 'He might be a hopeless crank,' objected Gayton. 'That could be ascertained from the Bennetts, who knew him,' Mrs Gayton retorted; and she undertook to see the Bennetts the very next day.

It is not necessary to tell in further detail the steps by which Henry Harrington and Dunning were brought together.

The next scene that does require to be narrated is a conversation that took place between the two. Dunning had told Harrington of the strange ways in which the dead man's name had been brought before him, and had said something, besides, of his own subsequent experiences. Then he had asked if Harrington was disposed, in return, to recall any of the circumstances connected with his brother's death. Harrington's surprise at what he heard can be imagined: but his reply was readily given.

'John,' he said, 'was in a very odd state, undeniably, from time to time, during some weeks before, though not immediately before, the catastrophe. There were several things; the principal notion he had was that he thought he was being followed. No doubt he was an impressionable man, but he never had had such fancies as this before. I cannot get it out of my mind that there was ill-will at work, and what you tell me about yourself reminds me very much of my brother. Can you think of any possible connecting link?'

'There is just one that has been taking shape vaguely in my mind. I've been told that your brother reviewed a book very severely not long before he died, and just lately I have happened to cross the path of the man who wrote that book in a way he would resent.'

'Don't tell me the man was called Karswell.'

'Why not? that is exactly his name.'

Henry Harrington leant back. 'That is final to my mind. Now I must explain further. From something he said, I feel sure that my brother John was beginning to believe – very much against his will – that Karswell was at the bottom of his trouble. I want to tell you what seems to me to have a bearing on the situation. My brother was a great musician, and used to run up to concerts in town. He came back, three months before he died, from one of these, and gave me his programme to look at – an analytical programme: he always kept them. "I nearly missed this one," he said. "I suppose I must have dropped it: anyhow, I was looking for it under my seat and in my pockets and so on, and my neighbour offered me his, said 'might he give it me, he had no further use for it,' and he went away just afterwards. I don't know who he was – a stout, clean-shaven man. I should have been sorry to miss it; of course I could have bought another, but this cost me nothing." At another time he told me that he had been very uncomfortable both on the way to his hotel and during the night. I piece things together now in thinking it over. Then, not very long after, he was going over these programmes, putting them in order to have them bound up, and in this particular one (which by the way I had hardly glanced at), he found quite near the beginning a strip of paper with some very odd writing on it in red and black – most carefully done – it looked to me more like Runic letters than anything else. "Why," he said, "this must belong to my fat neighbour. It looks as if it might be worth returning to him; it may be a copy of something; evidently someone has taken trouble over it. How can I find his address?" We talked it over for a little and agreed that it wasn't worth advertising about, and that my brother had better look out for the man at the next concert, to which he was going very soon. The paper was lying on the book and we were both by the fire; it was a cold, windy summer evening. I suppose the door blew open, though I didn't notice it: at any rate a gust – a warm gust it was – came quite suddenly between us, took the paper and blew it straight into the fire: it was light, thin paper, and flared and went up the chimney in a single ash. "Well," I said, "you can't give it back now." He said nothing for a minute: then rather crossly, "No, I can't; but why you should keep on saying so I don't know." I remarked that I didn't say it more than once. "Not more than four times, you mean," was all he said. I remember all that very clearly, without any good reason; and now to come to the point. I don't know if you looked at that book of Karswell's which my unfortunate brother reviewed. It's not likely that you should: but I did, both before his death and after it. The first time we made game of it together. It was written in no style at all – split infinitives, and every sort of thing that makes an Oxford gorge rise. Then there was nothing that the man didn't swallow: mixing up classical myths, and stories out of the *Golden Legend* with reports of savage customs of today – all very proper, no doubt, if you know how to use them, but he didn't: he seemed to put the *Golden Legend* and the *Golden Bough* exactly on a par, and to believe both: a pitiable exhibition, in short. Well, after the misfortune, I looked over the book again. It was no better than before, but the impression which it left this time on my mind was different. I suspected – as I told you – that Karswell had borne ill-will to my brother, even that he was in some way responsible for what had happened; and now his book seemed to me to be a very sinister performance indeed. One chapter in particular struck me, in which he spoke of "casting the Runes" on people, either for the purpose of gaining their affection or of getting them out of the way – perhaps more especially the latter: he spoke of all this in a way that really seemed to me to imply actual knowledge. I've not time to go into details, but the upshot is that I am pretty sure from information received that the civil man at the concert was Karswell: I suspect – I more than suspect – that the paper was of importance: and I do believe that if my brother had been able to give it back, he might have been alive now. Therefore, it occurs to me to ask you whether you have anything to put beside what I have told you.'

By way of answer, Dunning had the episode in the Manuscript Room at the British Museum to relate.

'Then he did actually hand you some papers; have you examined them? No? because we must, if you'll allow it, look at them at once, and very carefully.'

They went to the still empty house – empty, for the two servants were not yet able to return to work. Dunning's portfolio of papers was gathering dust on the writing-table. In it were the quires of small-sized scribbling paper which he used for his transcripts: and from one of these, as he took it up, there slipped and fluttered out into the room with uncanny quickness, a strip of thin light paper. The window was open, but Harrington slammed it to, just in time to intercept the paper, which he caught. 'I thought so,' he said; 'it might be the identical thing that was given to my brother. You'll have to look out, Dunning; this may mean something quite serious for you.'

A long consultation took place. The paper was narrowly examined. As Harrington had said, the characters on it were more like Runes than anything else, but not decipherable by either man, and both hesitated to copy them, for fear, as they confessed, of perpetuating whatever evil purpose they might conceal. So it has remained impossible (if I may anticipate a little) to ascertain what was conveyed in this curious message or commission. Both Dunning and Harrington are firmly convinced that it had the effect of bringing its possessors into very undesirable company. That it must be returned to the source whence it came they were agreed, and further, that the only safe and certain way was that of personal service; and here contrivance would be necessary, for Dunning was known by sight to Karswell. He must, for one thing, alter his appearance by shaving his beard. But then might not the blow fall first? Harrington thought they could time it. He knew the date of the concert at which the 'black spot' had been put on his brother: it was June 18th. The death had followed on Sept. 18th. Dunning reminded him that three months had been mentioned on the inscription on the car-window. 'Perhaps,' he added, with a cheerless laugh, 'mine may be a bill at three months too.

I believe I can fix it by my diary. Yes, April 23rd was the day at the Museum; that brings us to July 23rd. Now, you know, it becomes extremely important to me to know anything you will tell me about the progress of your brother's trouble, if it is possible for you to speak of it.' 'Of course. Well, the sense of being watched whenever he was alone was the most distressing thing to him. After a time I took to sleeping in his room, and he was the better for that: still, he talked a great deal in his sleep. What about? Is it wise to dwell on that, at least before things are straightened out? I think not, but I can tell you this: two things came for him by post during those weeks, both with a London postmark, and addressed in a commercial hand. One was a woodcut of Bewick's, roughly torn out of the page: one which shows a moonlit road and a man walking along it, followed by an awful demon creature. Under it were written the lines out of the "Ancient Mariner" (which I suppose the cut illustrates) about one who, having once looked round –

Walks on,
And turns no more his head,
Because he knows a frightful fiend
Doth close behind him tread.

The other was a calendar, such as tradesmen often send. My brother paid no attention to this, but I looked at it after his death, and found that everything after Sept. 18 had been torn out. You may be surprised at his having gone out alone the evening he was killed, but the fact is that during the last ten days or so of his life he had been quite free from the sense of being followed or watched.'

The end of the consultation was this. Harrington, who knew a neighbour of Karswell's, thought he saw a way of keeping a watch on his movements. It would be Dunning's part to be in readiness to try to cross Karswell's path at any moment, to keep the paper safe and in a place of ready access.

They parted. The next weeks were no doubt a severe strain upon Dunning's nerves: the intangible barrier which had seemed to rise about him on the day when he received the paper, gradually developed into a brooding blackness that cut him off from the means of escape to which one might have thought he might resort. No one was at hand who was likely to suggest them to him, and he seemed robbed of all initiative. He waited with inexpressible anxiety as May, June, and early July passed on, for a mandate from Harrington. But all this time Karswell remained immovable at Lufford.

At last, in less than a week before the date he had come to look upon as the end of his earthly activities, came a telegram: 'Leaves Victoria by boat train Thursday night. Do not miss. I come to you to-night. Harrington.'

He arrived accordingly, and they concocted plans. The train left Victoria at nine and its last stop before Dover was Croydon West. Harrington would mark down Karswell at Victoria, and look out for Dunning at Croydon, calling to him if need were by a name agreed upon. Dunning, disguised as far as might be, was to have no label or initials on any hand luggage, and must at all costs have the paper with him.

Dunning's suspense as he waited on the Croydon platform I need not attempt to describe. His sense of danger during the last days had only been sharpened by the fact that the cloud about him had perceptibly been lighter; but relief was an ominous symptom, and, if Karswell eluded him now, hope was gone: and there were so many chances of that. The rumour of the journey might be itself a device. The twenty minutes in which he paced the platform and persecuted every porter with inquiries as to the boat train were as bitter as any he had spent. Still, the train came, and Harrington was at the window. It was important, of course, that there should be no recognition: so Dunning got in at the farther end of the corridor carriage, and only gradually made his way to the compartment where Harrington and Karswell were. He was pleased, on the whole, to see that the train was far from full.

Karswell was on the alert, but gave no sign of recognition. Dunning took the seat not immediately facing him, and attempted, vainly at first, then with increasing command of his faculties, to reckon the possibilities of making the desired transfer. Opposite to Karswell, and next to Dunning, was a heap of Karswell's coats on the seat. It would be of no use to slip the paper into these – he would not be safe, or would not feel so, unless in some way it could be proffered by him and accepted by the other. There was a handbag, open, and with papers in it. Could he manage to conceal this (so that perhaps Karswell might leave the carriage without it), and then find and give it to him? This was the plan that suggested itself. If he could only have counselled with Harrington! but that could not be. The minutes went on. More than once Karswell rose and went out into the corridor. The second time Dunning was on the point of attempting to make the bag fall off the seat, but he caught Harrington's eye, and read in it a warning.

Karswell, from the corridor, was watching: probably to see if the two men recognized each other. He returned, but was evidently restless: and, when he rose the third time, hope dawned, for something did slip off his seat and fall with hardly a sound to the floor. Karswell went out once more, and passed out of range of the corridor window. Dunning picked up what had fallen, and saw that the key was in his hands in the form of one of Cook's ticket-cases, with tickets in it. These cases have a pocket in the cover, and within very few seconds the paper of which we have heard was in the pocket of this one. To make the operation more secure, Harrington stood in the doorway of the compartment and fiddled with the blind. It was done, and done at the right time, for the train was now slowing down towards Dover.

In a moment more Karswell re-entered the compartment. As he did so, Dunning, managing, he knew not how, to suppress the tremble in his voice, handed him the ticket-case, saying, 'May I give you this, sir? I believe it is yours.' After a brief glance at the ticket inside, Karswell uttered the hoped-for response, 'Yes, it is; much obliged to you, sir,' and he placed it in his breast pocket.

Even in the few moments that remained – moments of tense anxiety, for they knew not to what a premature finding of the paper might lead – both men noticed that the carriage seemed to darken about them and to grow warmer; that Karswell was fidgety and oppressed; that he drew the heap of loose coats near to him and cast it back as if it repelled him; and that he then sat upright and glanced anxiously at both. They, with sickening anxiety, busied themselves in collecting their belongings; but they both thought that Karswell was on the point of speaking when the train stopped at Dover Town. It was natural that in the short space between town and pier they should both go into the corridor.

At the pier they got out, but so empty was the train that they were forced to linger on the platform until Karswell should have passed ahead of them with his porter on the way to the boat, and only then was it safe for them to exchange a pressure of the hand and a word of concentrated congratulation. The effect upon Dunning was to make him almost faint. Harrington made him lean up against the wall, while he himself went forward a few yards within sight of the gangway to the boat, at which Karswell had now arrived. The man at the head of it examined his ticket, and, laden with coats, he passed down into the boat. Suddenly the official called after him, 'You, sir, beg pardon, did the other gentleman show his ticket?' 'What the devil do you mean by the other gentleman?' Karswell's snarling voice called back from the deck. The man bent over and looked at him. 'The devil? Well, I don't know, I'm sure,' Harrington heard him say to himself, and then aloud, 'My mistake, sir; must have been your rugs! ask your pardon.' And then, to a subordinate near him, ''Ad he got a dog with him, or what? Funny thing: I could 'a' swore 'e wasn't alone. Well, whatever it was, they'll 'ave to see to it aboard. She's off now. Another week and we shall be gettin' the 'oliday customers.' In five minutes more there was nothing but the lessening lights of the boat, the long line of the Dover lamps, the night breeze, and the moon.

Long and long the two sat in their room at the 'Lord Warden'. In spite of the removal of their greatest anxiety, they were oppressed with a doubt, not of the lightest. Had they been justified in sending a man to his death, as they believed they had? Ought they not to warn him, at least? 'No,' said Harrington; 'if he is the murderer I think him, we have done no more than is just. Still, if you think it better – but how and where can you warn him?' 'He was booked to Abbeville only,' said Dunning.

'I saw that. If I wired to the hotels there in Joanne's Guide, "Examine your ticket-case, Dunning," I should feel happier. This is the 21st: he will have a day. But I am afraid he has gone into the dark.' So telegrams were left at the hotel office.

It is not clear whether these reached their destination, or whether, if they did, they were understood. All that is known is that, on the afternoon of the 23rd, an English traveller, examining the front of St Wulfram's Church at Abbeville, then under extensive repair, was struck on the head and instantly killed by a stone falling from the scaffold erected round the north-western tower, there being, as was clearly proved, no workman on the scaffold at that moment: and the traveller's papers identified him as Mr Karswell.

Only one detail shall be added. At Karswell's sale a set of Bewick, sold with all faults, was acquired by Harrington. The page with the woodcut of the traveller and the demon was, as he had expected, mutilated. Also, after a judicious interval, Harrington repeated to Dunning something of what he had heard his brother say in his sleep: but it was not long before Dunning stopped him.

HOW NUTH WOULD HAVE PRACTISED HIS ART UPON THE GNOLES

Lord Dunsany

Lord Dunsany (1878–1957) was a prolific Anglo-Irish writer and dramatist, known for fantastical fiction, some of it dark. His real name was Edward John Moreton Drax Plunkett, 18th Baron of Dunsany. Born to one of the oldest titles in the Irish peerage, Dunsany lived much of his life at perhaps Ireland's longest-inhabited home, Dunsany Castle (near Tara), worked with WB Yeats and was chess and pistol-shooting champion of Ireland. 'How Nuth Would Have Practised His Art Upon the Gnoles' (1912) is a compressed marvel of weird storytelling. Many decades later the writer Margaret St. Clair would use Dunsany's tale as inspiration for her own, equally original, 'The Man Who Sold Rope to the Gnoles', also included in these pages.

Despite the advertisements of rival firms, it is probable that every tradesman knows that nobody in business at the present time has a position equal to that of Mr. Nuth. To those outside the magic circle of business, his name is scarcely known; he does not need to advertise, he is consummate. He is superior even to modern competition, and, whatever claims they boast, his rivals know it. His terms are moderate, so much cash down when the goods are delivered, so much in blackmail afterwards. He consults your convenience. His skill may be counted upon; I have seen a shadow on a windy night move more noisily than Nuth, for Nuth is a burglar by trade. Men have been known to stay in country houses and to send a dealer afterwards to bargain for a piece of tapestry that they saw there – some article of furniture, some picture. This is bad taste: but those whose culture is more elegant invariably send Nuth a night or two after their visit. He has a way with tapestry; you would scarcely notice that the edges had been cut. And often when I see some huge, new house full of old furniture and portraits from other ages, I say to myself, 'These mouldering chairs, these full-length ancestors and carved mahogany are the produce of the incomparable Nuth.'

It may be urged against my use of the word incomparable that in the burglary business the name of Slith stands paramount and alone; and of this I am not ignorant; but Slith is a classic, and lived long ago, and knew nothing at all of modern competition; besides which the surprising nature of his doom has possibly cast a glamour upon Slith that exaggerates in our eyes his undoubted merits.

It must not be thought that I am a friend of Nuth's; on the contrary such politics as I have are on the side of Property; and he needs no words from me, for his position is almost unique in trade, being among the very few that do not need to advertise.

At the time that my story begins Nuth lived in a

roomy house in Belgrave Square: in his inimitable way he had made friends with the caretaker. The place suited Nuth, and, whenever anyone came to inspect it before purchase, the caretaker used to praise the house in the words that Nuth had suggested. 'If it wasn't for the drains,' she would say, 'it's the finest house in London,' and when they pounced on this remark and asked questions about the drains, she would answer them that the drains also were good, but not so good as the house. They did not see Nuth when they went over the rooms, but Nuth was there.

Here in a neat black dress on one spring morning came an old woman whose bonnet was lined with red, asking for Mr. Nuth; and with her came her large and awkward son. Mrs. Eggins, the caretaker, glanced up the street, and then she let them in, and left them to wait in the drawing-room amongst furniture all mysterious with sheets. For a long while they waited, and then there was a smell of pipe-tobacco, and there was Nuth standing quite close to them.

'Lord,' said the old woman whose bonnet was lined with red, 'you did make me start.' And then she saw by his eyes that that was not the way to speak to Mr. Nuth.

And at last Nuth spoke, and very nervously the old woman explained that her son was a likely lad, and had been in business already but wanted to better himself, and she wanted Mr. Nuth to teach him a livelihood.

First of all Nuth wanted to see a business reference, and when he was shown one from a jeweller with whom he happened to be hand-in-glove the upshot of it was that he agreed to take young Tonker (for this was the surname of the likely lad) and to make him his apprentice. And the old woman whose bonnet was lined with red went back to her little cottage in the country, and every evening said to her old man, 'Tonker, we must fasten the shutters of a night-time, for Tommy's a burglar now.'

The details of the likely lad's apprenticeship I do not propose to give; for those that are in the business know those details already, and those that are in other businesses care only for their own, while men of leisure who have no trade at all would fail to appreciate the gradual degrees by which Tommy Tonker came first to cross bare boards, covered with little obstacles in the dark, without making any sound, and then to go silently up creaky stairs, and then to open doors, and lastly to climb.

Let it suffice that the business prospered greatly, while glowing reports of Tommy Tonker's progress were sent from time to time to the old woman whose bonnet was lined with red in the laborious handwriting of Nuth. Nuth had given up lessons in writing very early, for he seemed to have some prejudice against forgery, and therefore considered writing a waste of time. And then there came the transaction with Lord Castlenorman at his Surrey residence. Nuth selected a Saturday night, for it chanced that Saturday was observed as Sabbath in the family of Lord Castlenorman, and by eleven o'clock the whole house was quiet. Five minutes before midnight Tommy Tonker, instructed by Mr. Nuth, who waited outside, came away with one pocketful of rings and shirt-studs. It was quite a light pocketful, but the jewellers in Paris could not match it without sending specially to Africa, so that Lord Castlenorman had to borrow bone shirt-studs.

Not even rumour whispered the name of Nuth. Were I to say that this turned his head, there are those to whom the assertion would give pain, for his associates hold that his astute judgment was unaffected by circumstance. I will say, therefore, that it spurred his genius to plan what no burglar had ever planned before. It was nothing less than to burgle the house of the gnoles. And this that abstemious man unfolded to Tonker over a cup of tea. Had Tonker not been nearly insane with pride over their recent transaction, and had he not been blinded by a veneration for Nuth, he would have – but I cry over spilt milk. He expostulated respectfully: he said he would rather not go; he said it was not fair, he allowed himself to argue; and in the end, one windy October morning with a menace in the air found him and Nuth drawing near to the dreadful wood.

Nuth, by weighing little emeralds against pieces of common rock, had ascertained the probable weight of those house-ornaments that the gnoles are believed to possess in the narrow, lofty house wherein they have dwelt from of old. They decided to steal two emeralds and to carry them between them on a cloak; but if they should be too heavy one must be dropped at once. Nuth warned young Tonker against greed, and explained that the emeralds were worth less than cheese until they were safe away from the dreadful wood.

Everything had been planned, and they walked now in silence.

No track led up to the sinister gloom of the trees, either of men or cattle; not even a poacher had been there snaring elves for over a hundred years. You did not trespass twice in the dells of the gnoles. And, apart from the things that were done there, the trees themselves were a warning, and did not wear the wholesome look of those that we plant ourselves.

The nearest village was some miles away with the backs of all its houses turned to the wood, and without one window at all facing in that direction. They did not speak of it there, and elsewhere it is unheard of.

Into this wood stepped Nuth and Tommy Tonker. They had no firearms. Tonker had asked for a pistol, but Nuth replied that the sound of a shot 'would bring everything down on us,' and no more was said about it.

Into the wood they went all day, deeper and deeper. They saw the skeleton of some early Georgian poacher nailed to a door in an oak tree; sometimes they saw a fairy scuttle away from them; once Tonker stepped heavily on a hard, dry stick, after which they both lay still for twenty minutes. And the sunset flared full of omens through the tree trunks, and night fell, and they came by fitful starlight, as Nuth had foreseen, to that lean, high house where the gnoles so secretly dwelt.

All was so silent by that unvalued house that the faded courage of Tonker flickered up, but to Nuth's experienced sense it seemed too silent; and all the while there was that look in the sky that was worse than a spoken doom, so that Nuth, as is often the case when men are in doubt, had leisure to fear the worst. Nevertheless he did not abandon the business, but sent the likely lad with the instruments of his trade by means of the ladder to the old green casement. And the moment that Tonker touched the withered boards, the silence that, though ominous, was earthly, became unearthly like the touch of a ghoul. And Tonker heard his breath offending against that silence, and his heart was like mad drums in a night attack, and a string of one of his sandals went tap on a rung of a ladder, and the leaves of the forest were mute, and the breeze of the night was still; and Tonker prayed that a mouse or a mole might make any noise at all, but not a creature stirred, even Nuth was still. And then and there, while yet he was undiscovered, the likely lad made up his mind, as he should have done long before, to leave those colossal emeralds where they were and have nothing further to do with the lean, high house of the gnoles, but to quit this sinister wood in the nick of time and retire from business at once and buy a place in the country. Then he descended softly and beckoned to Nuth. But the gnoles had watched him through knavish holes that they bore in trunks of the trees, and the unearthly silence gave way, as it were with a grace, to the rapid screams of Tonker as they picked him up from behind – screams that came faster and faster until they were incoherent.

And where they took him it is not good to ask, and what they did with him I shall not say.

Nuth looked on for a while from the corner of the house with a mild surprise on his face as he rubbed his chin, for the trick of the holes in the trees was new to him; then he stole nimbly away through the dreadful wood.

'And did they catch Nuth?' you ask me, gentle reader.

'Oh, no, my child' (for such a question is childish). 'Nobody ever catches Nuth.'

THE MAN IN THE BOTTLE

Gustav Meyrink

Gustav Meyrink (1868–1932) was an Austrian writer who moved to Prague as a teenager and lived there for twenty years. Early works included grotesque satires after which he largely graduated to weird pseudo-science and *contes cruel*. He is most famous for his novel *The Golem* (1914). Other books by Meyrink include *Walpurgis Night* (1917) and *The Angel of the Western Window* (1927). Meyrink considered himself an amateur expert on theosophy, Kabbalah, Christian Sophiology, and Eastern mysticism. He once translated fifteen volumes of Charles Dickens because he needed the money. 'The Man in the Bottle' is typical of Meyrink's weird stories: grotesque, brief, and flecked with the decadent.

Melanchthon was dancing with the Bat, whose costume represented her in an inverted position. The wings were folded close to the body, and in the claws she held a large gold hoop upright, which gave the impression that she was hanging, suspended from some imaginary point. The effect was grotesque, and it amused Melanchthon very much, for he had to peep through this gold hoop, which was exactly on a level with his face, while dancing with the Bat.

She was one of the most original masks – and at the same time one of the most repelling ones – at the fête of the Persian prince. She had even impressed his highness, Mohammed Darasche-Koh, the host.

'I know you, pretty one,' he had nodded to her, much to the amusement of the bystanders.

'It is certainly the little marquise, the intimate friend of the princess,' declared a Dutch councilor in a Rembrandt costume.

He surmised this because she knew every turn and corner of the palace, to judge by her conversation. And but a few moments ago, when some cavalier had ordered felt boots and torches so that they might go down into the courtyard and indulge in snowballing, the Bat joined them and participated wildly in the game. It was then – and the Dutchman was quite ready to back it with a wager – that he had seen a well-known bracelet on her wrist.

'Oh, how interesting,' exclaimed a Blue Butterfly. 'Couldn't Melanchthon discover whether or not Count Faast is a slave of the princess?'

'Don't speak so loud,' interrupted the Dutch councilor. 'It is a mighty good thing that the orchestra played the close of that waltz fortissimo, for the prince was standing here only a moment since.'

'Better not speak of such things,' whispered an Egyptian, 'for the jealousy of this Asiatic prince knows no bounds, and there are probably more explosives in the palace than we dream. Count de Faast has been playing with fire too long, and if Darasche-Koh suspects–'

A rough figure representing a huge knot dashed by them in wild flight to escape a Hellenic warrior in shimmering armor.

'If you were the Gordian knot, Mynherr, and were pursued by Alexander the Great, wouldn't you be frightened?' teased the inverted Bat, tapping the Dutchman coquettishly on the end of the nose with her fan.

'The sharp wit of the pretty Marquise Bat betrays her,' smiled a lanky Satan with tail and cloven foot. 'What a pity that only as a Bat are you to be seen with your feet in the air.'

The dull sound of a gong filled the room as an executioner appeared, draped in a crimson robe. He tapped a bronze gong, and then, resting his weight on his glittering cudgel, posed himself in the center of the big hall.

Out of every niche and lobby the maskers streamed toward him – harlequins, cannibals, an ibis, and some Chinese, Don Quixotes, Columbines, bayaderes and dominoes of all colors.

The crimson executioner distributed tablets of ivory inscribed with gold letters.

'Oh, programmes for the entertainment!' chorused the crowd.

THE MAN IN THE BOTTLE

Marionette Comedy in the Spirit of Aubrey Beardsley

BY PRINCE MOHAMMED DARASCHE-KOH

Characters:

THE MAN IN THE BOTTLE............................MIGUEL, COUNT DE FAAST

THE MAN ON THE BOTTLE.........PRINCE MOHAMMED DARASCHE-KOH

THE LADY IN THE SEDAN CHAIR

VAMPIRES, MARIONETTES, HUNCHBACKS, APES, MUSICIANS

Scene of Action: A TIGER'S MAW

'What! The prince is the author of this marionette play?' 'Probably a scene out of the "Thousand and One Nights."' 'But who will play the part of the Lady in the Sedan Chair?'

'Oh, there is a great surprise in store for us,' twittered a seductive Incroyable, leaning on the arm of an Abbe. 'Do you know, the Pierrot with whom I danced the tarantelle was the Count de Faast, who is going to play The Man in the Bottle; and he confided a lot of things to me: the marionettes will be very gruesome – that is, for those who appreciate the spirit of the thing – and the prince had an elephant sent down from Hamburg – but you are not listening to me at all!' And the little one dropped the arm of her escort and bolted into the swirling crowd.

New groups of masks constantly poured out of the adjoining rooms through the wide doorways into the big hall, making a kaleidoscopic play of colors, while files of costumed guests stood admiring the wonderful mural frescoes that rose to the blue, star-dotted ceiling. Attendants served refreshments, sorbets and wines in the window niches.

With a rolling sound the walls of the narrow end of the hall separated and a stage was pushed slowly into view. Its setting, in red brown and a flaming yellow proscenium, was a yawning tiger's maw, the white teeth glittering above and below.

In the middle of the scene stood a huge glass bottle in the form of a globe, with walls at least a foot thick. It was about twice the height of an average man and very roomy. The back of the scene was draped with pink silk hangings.

Then the colossal ebony doors of the hall opened and admitted a richly caparisoned elephant, which advanced with majestic tread. On its head sat the crimson executioner guiding the beast with the butt of his cudgel. Chains of amethysts dangled from the elephant's tusks, and plumes of peacock feathers nodded from its head. Heavily embroidered gold cloths streamed down from the back of the beast, skirting the floor; across its enormous forehead there was a network of sparkling jewels.

The maskers flocked around the advancing beast, shouting greetings to the gay group of actors seated in the palanquin; Prince Darasche-Koh with turban and aigrette, Count de Faast as Pierrot, marionettes and musicians, stiff as wooden puppets. The elephant reached the stage, and with its trunk lifted one man after another from its back. There was much applause and a yell of delight as the beast seized the Pierrot and, sliding him into the neck of the bottle, closed the metal top. Then the Persian prince was placed on top of the bottle.

The musicians seated themselves in a semicircle, drawing forth strange, slender instruments. The elephant gazed at them a moment, then turned about and strode toward the door. Like a lot of happy children the maskers clung to its trunk, ears, and tusks and tried to hold it back; but the animal seemed not to feel their weight at all.

The performance began, and somewhere, as if

out of the ground, there arose weird music. The puppet orchestra of marionettes remained lifeless and waxen; the flute player stared with glassy, idiotic eyes at the ceiling; the features of the rococo conductor in peruke and plumed hat, holding the baton aloft and pressing a pointed finger mysteriously to his lips, were distorted by a shrewd, uncanny smile.

In the foreground posed the marionettes. Here were grouped a humpbacked dwarf with chalky face, a gray, grinning devil, and a sallow, rouged actress with carmine lips. The three seemed possessed of some satanic secret that had paralyzed their movements. The semblance of death brooded over the entire motionless group.

The Pierrot in the bottle now began to move restlessly. He doffed his white felt hat, bowed and occasionally greeted the Persian prince, who with crossed legs sat on the cap of the bottle. His antics amused the audience. The thick walls of glass distorted his appearance curiously; sometimes his eyes seemed to pop out of his head; then again they disappeared, and one saw only forehead and chin; sometimes he was fat and bloated, then again slender, with long legs like a spider's.

In the midst of a motionless pause the red silk hangings of the background parted, and a closed sedan chair was carried on by two Moors, who placed it near the bottle. A ray of pale light from above now illuminated the scene. The spectators had formed themselves into two camps. The one was speechless under the spell of this vampiric, enigmatic marionette play that seemed to exhale an atmosphere of poisoned merriment; the other group, not sensitive enough to appreciate such a scene, laughed immoderately at the comical capering of the man in the bottle.

He had given up his merry dancing and was trying by every possible means to impart some information or other to the prince sitting on the cap. He pounded the walls of the bottle as though he would smash them; and to all appearances he was screaming at the top of his voice, although not the slightest sound penetrated the thick glass.

The Persian prince acknowledged the movements of the Pierrot with a smile, pointing with his finger at the sedan chair.

The curiosity of the audience reached its climax when it saw that the Pierrot had pressed his face against the glass and was staring at something in the window of the sedan chair. Then suddenly, like one gone mad, he beat his face with his hands, sank on his knees and tore his hair. Then he sprang furiously up and raced around the bottle at such speed that the audience saw only a fluttering cloth in his wake.

The secret of the Lady in the Sedan Chair puzzled the audience considerably – they could only see that a white face was pressed against the window of the chair and was staring over at the bottle. Shadows cut off all further view.

Laughter and applause rose to a tumult. Pierrot had crouched on the bottom of the bottle, his fingers clutching his throat. Then he opened his mouth wide and pointed in wild frenzy to his chest and then to the one sitting above. He folded his hands in supplication, as though he were begging something from the audience.

'He wants something to drink! Such a large bottle and no wine in it? I say, you marionettes, give him a drink,' cried one of the maskers.

Everybody laughed and applauded.

Then the Pierrot jumped up once more, tore his garments from his chest and staggered about until he measured his length on the bottom of the bottle.

'Bravo, bravo, Pierrot! Wonderfully acted! Da capo, da capo!' yelled the maskers.

When the man in the bottle did not stir again and made no effort to repeat his scene, the applause gradually subsided and the attention of the spectators was drawn to the marionettes. They still remained motionless in the poses they had assumed, but in their miens there was now a sense of expectancy that had not been there before. It seemed as if they were waiting for a cue.

The humpbacked dwarf, with the chalked face, turned his eyes carefully and gazed at the Prince Darasche-Koh. The Persian did not stir.

Finally two figures advanced from the background, and one of the Moors haltingly approached the sedan chair and opened the door.

And then something very remarkable occurred – the body of a woman fell stiffly out on the stage. There was a moment of deathly silence and then a thousand voices arose: 'What has happened?'

Marionettes, apes, musicians – all leaped forward; maskers climbed up on the stage.

The princess, wife of Darasche-Koh, lay there strapped to a steel frame. Where the ropes had cut into her flesh were blue bruises, and in her mouth there was a silk gag.

A nameless horror took possession of the audience.

'Pierrot!' a voice suddenly shrilled. 'Pierrot!' Like a dagger, indescribable fear penetrated every heart.

'Where is the prince?'

During the tumult the Persian had disappeared.

Melanchthon stood on the shoulders of Mephisto, but he could not lift the cap of the bottle, and the air valve was screwed tightly shut.

'Break the walls of the bottle! Quick!'

The Dutch councilor tore the cudgel from the hand of the crimson executioner and with a leap landed on the stage.

A gruesome sound arose, like the tolling of a cracked bell. Like streaks of white lightning the cracks leaped across the surface of the glass. Finally the bottle was splintered into bits. And within lay, suffocated, the corpse of the Count de Faast, his fingers clawing his breast.

The bright hall seemed to darken.

Silently and with invisible pinions the gigantic ebon birds of terror streaked through the hall of the fête.

THE DISSECTION

Georg Heym

TRANSLATED INTO ENGLISH BY GIO CLAIRVAL

Georg Heym (1887–1912) was a German poet and playwright who also wrote one novel. Heym believed in the idea of the 'demon city', which symbolized his repudiation of romanticism in the midst of the rise of industrialism and repressive systems. Still, he lived a wild and passionate life, accompanied by depression and restlessness. In 1910 he dreamed of a death by drowning and two years later fell through the ice while skating. 'The Dissection' (1913) is more prose-poem than story in its luminous reverie. This new translation by Gio Clairval corrects errors in prior versions, including the use of 'The Autopsy' as the title. Master of the weird Thomas Ligotti has called it one of his favorite tales.

The dead man lay alone and naked on a white cloth in a wide room, surrounded by depressing white walls, in the cruel sobriety of a dissection room that seemed to shiver with the screams of an endless torture.

The light of noon bathed him and awakened the dead spots on his forehead, conjuring up a bright green from his naked belly, bloating his body like a big sack of water.

His body resembled the iridescent calyx of some gigantic flower, a mysterious plant from Indian primeval forests that someone had shyly laid at the altar of death.

Splendid reds and blues sprouted down his limbs, and in the heat the large wound under his navel slowly split open like a red furrow, releasing a foul stench.

The doctors entered. Friendly men in frayed white coats and gold-rimmed pince-nez. They stepped up to the dead man and observed him with interest, as if in a scientific meeting.

From their white cabinets they took out dissecting instruments, white crates full of hammers, saws with sharp teeth, files, hideous sets of tweezers, tiny knives with large needles like vultures' crooked beaks forever screaming for flesh.

They began their revolting work. They resembled hideous torturers, blood flowing on their hands as they dug ever more deeply into the frigid corpse and pulled out its innards, like white cooks gutting a goose. Around their arms coiled the intestines – green-yellow snakes – and faeces dripped on their coats – a warm, putrid fluid. They punctured the bladder, the cold urine in it glistening like yellow wine. They poured it in large bowls, and it reeked of pungent, acrid ammonia. But the dead man slept. He patiently let them tug at him and pull his hair. He slept.

And while the thumping of hammers resounded on his skull, a dream, a remainder of love awoke in him, like a torch shining in his personal night.

Outside the large window stretched a wide sky filled with small white clouds that swam like small white gods in the light of that silent afternoon. And swallows darted high across the blue, feathers quivering in the warm sun of July.

The dead man's black blood streamed across the blue putrefaction on his forehead. In the heat, it evaporated into an awful cloud, and the decay of death crept over him with its dappled claws. His skin began to flake apart; his belly turned white like that of an eel under the greedy fingers of the doctors, who plunged their arms up to the elbows in the wet flesh.

The decay pulled apart the mouth of the dead man. He seemed to smile. He dreamed of beatific stars, of a fragrant summer evening. His rotting lips trembled as though under a brief kiss.

'How I love you. I have loved you so much. Should I say how I love you? As you strolled across poppy fields, a flaming poppy yourself, you swallowed the entire evening. And the dress that billowed around your ankles was a wave of fire in the setting sun. But you bowed your head in the light, hair still burning, inflamed by my kisses.

'So you went down there, turning to look back at me as you walked away. And the lantern swayed in your hand like the glow of a rose lasting in the twilight long after you were gone.

'I'll see you again tomorrow. Here, under the window of the chapel, here, where the light of the candles falls about you, making your hair a golden forest, and daffodils nestle around your ankles, tender, like tender kisses.

'I will see you again every evening in the hour of dawn. We will never part. How I love you! Should I tell you how I love you?'

And the dead man quivered in happiness on his white death table, while the iron chisels in the hands of the doctors broke up the bones of his temple.

THE SPIDER

Hans Heinz Ewers

TRANSLATED INTO ENGLISH BY WALTER F. KOHN

Hanns Heinz Ewers (1871–1943) was a German writer, especially of horror, also known for his acting and poetry. A novel trilogy, detailing the exploits of the character of Frank Baun, included perhaps his best-known work, *Alraune*. Much of his work has a decadent feel to it, and Ewers did not shy away from violence and sex in his fiction. After an early dalliance with the Nazi party, Ewers left because of disagreements with their positions on Jews and homosexuality. The Nazis banned his works, seized his assets, and left Ewers in poverty. Even though the Nazis destroyed his life, Ewers's early association with them has left him under-appreciated by modern critics of the weird. 'The Spider' (1915) is his best-known work.

When Richard Bracquemont, medical student, decided to move into Room No. 7 of the little Hotel Stevens at 6 Rue Alfred Stevens, three people had already hanged themselves from the window-sash of the room on three successive Fridays.

The first was a Swiss travelling salesman. His body was not discovered until Saturday evening; but the physician established the fact that death must have come between five and six o'clock on Friday afternoon. The body hung suspended from a strong hook which had been driven into the window-sash, and which ordinarily served for hanging clothes. The window was closed, and the dead man had used the curtain cord as a rope. Since the window was rather low, his legs dragged on the ground almost to his knees. The suicide must consequently have exercised considerable will-power in carrying out his intention. It was further established that he was married and the father of four children; that he unquestionably had an adequate and steady income; and that he was of a cheerful disposition, and well contented in life. Neither a will nor anything in writing that might give a clue to the cause of the suicide was found; nor had he ever intimated leanings towards suicide to any of his friends or acquaintances.

The second case was not very different. The actor Karl Krause, who was employed at the nearby Cirque Medrano as a lightning bicycle artiste, engaged Room No. 7 two days after the first suicide. When he failed to appear at the performance the following Friday evening, the manager of the theatre sent an usher to the little hotel. The usher found the actor hanged from the window-sash in the unlocked room, in identically the same circumstances that had attended the suicide of the Swiss travelling salesman. This second suicide seemed no less puzzling than the first: the actor was popular, drew a very large salary, was only twenty-five years old, and seemed to enjoy life to the utmost. Again, nothing was left in writing, nor were there any other clues that might help solve the mystery. The actor was survived only by an aged mother, to whom he used to send three hundred marks for her support promptly on the first of each month.

For Madame Dubonnet, who owned the cheap little hotel, and whose clientele was made up almost exclusively of the actors of the nearby vaudevilles of Montmartre, this second suicide had very distressing consequences. Already several of her guests had moved out, and other regular customers had failed to come back. She appealed to the Commissioner of the Ninth Ward, whom she knew well, and he promised to do everything in his power to help her. So he not only pushed his investigation of reasons for the suicides with considerable zeal, but he also placed at her disposal a police officer who took up residence in the mysterious room.

It was the policeman Charles-Maria Chaumié who had volunteered his services in solving the mystery. An old 'Marousin' who had been a marine infantryman for eleven years, this sergeant had guarded many a lonely post in Tonkin and Annam single-handed, and had greeted many an uninvited deputation of river pirates, sneaking like cats through the jungle darkness, with a refreshing shot from his rifle. Consequently he felt himself well heeled to meet the 'ghosts' of which the Rue Stevens gossiped. He moved into the room on Sunday evening and went contentedly to sleep after doing high justice to the food and drink Madame Dubonnet set before him.

Every morning and evening Chaumié paid a brief visit to the police station to make his reports. During the first few days his reports confined themselves to the statement that he had not noticed even the slightest thing out of the ordinary. On Wednesday evening, however, he announced that he believed he had found a clue. When pressed for details he begged to be allowed to say nothing for the present: he said he was not certain that the thing he thought he had discovered necessarily had any bearing on the two suicides. And he was afraid of being ridiculed in case it should all turn out to be a mistake. On Thursday evening he seemed to be even more uncertain, although somewhat graver; but again he had nothing to report. On Friday morning he seemed quite excited: half seriously and half in jest he ventured the statement that the window of the room certainly had a remarkable power of attraction. Nevertheless he still clung to the theory that the fact had nothing whatever to do with the suicides, and that he would only be laughed at if he told more. That evening he failed to come to the police station; they found him hanged from the hook on the window-sash.

Even in this case the circumstances, down to the minutest detail, were again the same as they had been in the other cases: the legs dragged on the floor, and the curtain cord had been used as a rope. The window was closed, and the door had not been locked; death had evidently come at about six o'clock in the afternoon. The dead man's mouth was wide open and his tongue hung out.

As a consequence of this third suicide in Room No. 7, all the guests left the Hotel Stevens that same day, with the exception of the German high-school teacher in Room No. 16, who took advantage of this opportunity to have his rent reduced one-third. It was small consolation for Madame Dubonnet to have Mary Garden, the famous star of the Opéra Comique, drive by in her Renault a few days later and stop to buy the red curtain cord for a price she beat down to two hundred francs. Of course she had two reasons for buying it: in the first place, it would bring luck; and in the second – well, it would get into the newspapers.

If these things had happened in summer, say in July or August, Madame Dubonnet might have got three times as much for her curtain cord; at that time of the year the newspapers would certainly have filled their columns with the case for weeks. But at an uneasy time of the year, with elections, disorders in the Balkans, a bank failure in New York, a visit of the English King and Queen – well, where could the newspapers find room for a mere murder case? The result was that the affair in the Rue Alfred Stevens got less attention than it deserved, and such notices of it as appeared in the newspapers were concise and brief, and confined themselves practically to repetitions of the police reports, without exaggerations.

These reports furnished the only basis for what little knowledge of the affair the medical student Richard Bracquemont had. He knew nothing of one other little detail that seemed so inconsequential that neither the Commissioner nor any of the other witnesses had mentioned it to the reporters. Only afterwards, after the adventure the medical student had in the room, was this detail remembered. It was this: when the police took the body of Sergeant Charles-Maria Chaumié down from the window-sash, a large black spider crawled out of the mouth of the dead man. The porter flicked it away with his finger, crying: 'Ugh! Another such ugly beast!' In the course of the subsequent autopsy – that is, the one held later for Bracquemont – the porter told that when they had taken down the corpse of the Swiss travelling salesman, a similar spider had been seen crawling on his shoulder – But of this Richard Bracquemont knew nothing.

He did not take up his lodging in the room until two weeks after the last suicide, on a Sunday. What he experienced there he entered very conscientiously in a diary.

The Diary of Richard Bracquemont, Medical Student

Monday, February 28

I moved in here last night. I unpacked my two suitcases, put a few things in order, and went to bed. I slept superbly: the clock was just striking nine when a knock at the door awakened me. It was the landlady, who brought me my breakfast herself. She is evidently quite solicitous about me, judging from the eggs, the ham, and the splendid coffee she brought me. I washed and dressed, and then watched the porter make up my room. I smoked my pipe while he worked.

So here I am. I know right well that this business is dangerous, but I know too that my fortune is made if I solve the mystery. And if Paris was once worth a mass – one could hardly buy it that cheaply nowadays – it might be worth risking my little life for it. Here is my chance, and I intend to make the most of it.

At that there were plenty of others who saw this chance. No less than twenty-seven people tried, some through the police, some through the landlady, to get the room. Three of them were women. So there were enough rivals – probably all poor devils like myself.

But I got it! Why? Oh, I was probably the only one who could offer a 'solution' to the police. A neat solution! Of course it was a bluff.

These entries are of course intended for the police, too. And it amuses me considerably to tell these gentlemen right at the outset that it was all a trick on my part. If the Commissioner is sensible he will say, 'Hm! Just because I knew he was tricking us, I had all the more confidence in him!' As far as that is concerned, I don't care what he says afterward: now I'm here. And it seems to me a good omen to have begun my work by bluffing the police so thoroughly.

Of course I first made my application to Madame Dubonnet, but she sent me to the police station. I lounged about the station every day for a week, only to be told that my application 'was being given consideration' and to be asked always to come again next day. Most of my rivals had long since thrown up the sponge; they probably found some better way to spend their time than waiting for hour after hour in the musty police court. But it seems the Commissioner was by this time quite irritated by my perseverance. Finally he told me point blank that my coming back would be quite useless. He was very grateful to me as well as to all the other volunteers for our good intentions, but the police could not use the assistance of 'dilettante laymen'. Unless I had some carefully worked out plan of procedure...

So I told him that I had exactly that kind of plan. Of course I had no such thing and couldn't have explained a word of it. But I told him that I could tell him about my plan – which was good, although dangerous, and which might possibly come to the same conclusion as the investigation of the police sergeant – only if he would promise me on his word of honour that he was ready to carry it out. He thanked me for it, but regretted that he had no time for such things. But I saw that I was getting the upper hand when he asked me whether I couldn't at least give him some intimation of what I planned doing.

And I gave it to him. I told him the most glorious nonsense, of which I myself hadn't had the least notion even a second beforehand. I don't know even now how I came by this unusual inspiration so opportunely. I told him that among all the hours of the week there was one that had a secret and strange significance. That was the hour in which Christ left His grave to go down to hell: the sixth hour of the afternoon of the last day of the Jewish week. And he might take into consideration, I went on, that it was exactly in this hour, between five and six o'clock on Friday afternoon, in which all three of the suicides had been committed. For the present I could not tell him more, but I might refer him to the Book of Revelations according to St John.

The Commissioner put on a wise expression, as if he had understood it all, thanked me, and asked me to come back in the evening. I came back to his office promptly at the appointed time; I saw a copy of the New Testament lying in front of him on the table. In the meantime I had done just what he had: I had read the book of Revelations through and – had not understood a word of it. Perhaps the Commissioner was more intelligent than I was; at least he told me that he understood what I was driving at in spite of my very vague hints. And that he was ready to grant my request and to aid me in every possible way.

I must admit that he has actually been of very considerable assistance. He has made arrangements with the landlady under which I am to enjoy all the comforts and facilities of the hotel free of charge. He has given me an exceptionally fine revolver and a police pipe. The policemen on duty have orders to go through the little Rue Alfred Stevens as often as possible, and to come up to the room at a given signal. But the main thing is his installation of a desk telephone that connects directly with the police station. Since the station is only four minutes' walk from the hotel, I am thus enabled to have all the help I want immediately. With all this, I can't understand what there is to be afraid of…

Tuesday, March 1

Nothing has happened, neither yesterday nor today. Madame Dubonnet brought me a new curtain cord from another room – Heaven knows she has enough of them vacant. For that matter, she seems to take every possible opportunity to come to my room; every time she comes she brings me something. I have again had all the details of the suicides told me, but have discovered nothing new. As far as the causes of the suicides were concerned, she had her own opinions. As for the actor, she thought he had had an unhappy love affair; when he had been her guest the year before, he had been visited frequently by a young woman who had not come at all this year. She admittedly couldn't quite make out why the Swiss gentleman had decided to commit suicide, but of course one couldn't know everything. But there was no doubt that the police sergeant had committed suicide only to spite her.

I must confess these explanations of Madame Dubonnet's are rather inadequate. But I let her gabble on; at least she helps break up my boredom.

Thursday, March 3

Still nothing. The Commissioner rings me up several times a day and I tell him that everything is going splendidly. Evidently this information doesn't quite satisfy him. I have taken out my medical books and begun to work. In this way I am at least getting something out of my voluntary confinement.

Friday, March 4, 2 p.m.

I had an excellent luncheon. Madame Dubonnet brought a half-bottle of champagne along with it. It was the kind of dinner you get before your execution. She already regards me as being three-fourths dead. Before she left me she wept and begged me to go with her. Apparently she is afraid I might also hang myself 'just to spite her'.

I have examined the new curtain cord in considerable detail. So I am to hang myself with that? Well, I can't say that I feel much like doing it. The cord is raw and hard, and it would make a good slipknot only with difficulty – one would have to be pretty powerfully determined to emulate the example of the other three suicides in order to make a success of the job. But now I'm sitting at the table, the telephone at my left, the revolver at my right. I certainly have no fear – but I am curious.

6 p.m.

Nothing happened – I almost write with regret. The crucial hour came and went, and was just like all the others. Frankly I can't deny that sometimes I felt a certain urge to go to the window – oh, yes, but for other reasons! The Commissioner called me up at least ten times between five and six. He was just as impatient as I was. But Madame Dubonnet is satisfied: someone has lived for a week in No. 7 without hanging himself. Miraculous!

Monday, March 7

I am now convinced that I shall discover nothing; and I am inclined to think that the suicides of my predecessors were a matter of pure coincidence. I have asked the Commissioner to go over all the evidence in all three cases again, for I am convinced that eventually a solution to the mystery will be found. But as far as I am concerned, I intend to stay here as long as possible. I probably will not conquer Paris, but in the meantime I'm living here free and am already gaining considerably in health and weight. On top of it all I'm studying a great deal, and I notice I am rushing through in great style. And of course there is another reason that keeps me here.

Wednesday, March 9

I've progressed another step. Clarimonde –

Oh, but I haven't said a word about Clarimonde yet. Well, she is – my third reason for staying here. And it would have been for her sake that I would gladly have gone to the window in the fateful hour – but certainly not to hang myself. Clarimonde – but why do I call her that? I haven't the least idea as to what her name might be; but it seems to me as if I simply *must* call her Clarimonde. And I'd like to bet that some day I'll find out that that is really her name.

I noticed Clarimonde during the first few days I was here. She lives on the other side of this very narrow street, and her window is directly opposite mine. She sits there back of her curtains. And let me also say that she noticed me before I was aware of her, and that she visibly manifested an interest in me. No wonder – everyone on the street knows that I am here, and knows why, too. Madame Dubonnet saw to that.

I am in no way the kind of person who falls in love. My relations with women have always been very slight. When one comes to Paris from Verdun to study medicine and hardly has enough money to have a decent meal once every three days, one has other things besides love to worry about. I haven't much experience, and I probably began this affair pretty stupidly. Anyhow, it's quite satisfactory as it stands.

At first it never occurred to me to establish communications with my strange neighbour. I simply decided that since I was here to make observations, and I probably had nothing real to investigate anyhow, I might as well observe my neighbour while I was at it. After all, one can't pore over one's books all day long. So I have come to the conclusion that, judging from appearances, Clarimonde lives all alone in her little apartment. She has three windows, but she sits only at the one directly opposite mine. She sits there and spins, spins at a little old-fashioned distaff. I once saw such a distaff at my grandmother's, but even my grandmother never used it. It was merely an heirloom left her by some great-aunt or other. I didn't know that they were still in use. For that matter, Clarimonde's distaff is a very tiny, fine thing, white, and apparently made of ivory. The threads she spins must be infinitely fine. She sits behind her curtains all day long and works incessantly, stopping only when it gets dark. Of course it gets dark very early these foggy days. In this narrow street the loveliest twilight comes about five o'clock. I have never seen a light in her room.

How does she look? – Well, I really don't know. She wears her black hair in wavy curls, and is rather pale. Her nose is small and narrow, and her nostrils quiver. Her lips are pale, too, and it seems as if her little teeth might be pointed, like those of a beast of prey. Her eyelids throw long shadows; but when she opens them her large, dark eyes are full of light. Yet I seem to sense rather than know all this. It is difficult to identify anything clearly back of those curtains.

One thing further: she always wears a black, closely buttoned dress, with large purple dots. And she always wears long black gloves, probably to protect her hands while working. It looks strange to see her narrow black fingers quickly taking and drawing the threads, seemingly almost through each other – really almost like the wriggling of an insect's legs.

Our relations with each other? Oh, they are really quite superficial. And yet it seems as if they were truly much deeper. It began by her looking over to my window, and my looking over to hers. She noticed me, and I her. And then I evidently must have pleased her, because one day when I looked at her she smiled. And of course I did, too. That went on for several days, and we smiled at each other more and more. Then I decided almost every hour that I would greet her; I don't know exactly what it is that keeps me from carrying out my decision.

I have finally done it, this afternoon. And Clarimonde returned the greeting. Of course the greeting was ever so slight, but nevertheless I distinctly saw her nod.

Thursday, March 10

Last night I sat up late over my books. I can't truthfully say that I studied a great deal: I spent my time building air castles and dreaming about Clarimonde. I slept very lightly, but very late into the morning.

When I stepped up to the window, Clarimonde was sitting at hers. I greeted her and she nodded. She smiled, and looked at me for a long time.

I wanted to work, but couldn't seem to find the necessary peace of mind. I sat at the window and stared at her. Then I suddenly noticed that she, too, folded her hands in her lap. I pulled at the cord of the white curtain and – practically at the same instant – she did the same. We both smiled and looked at one another.

I believe we must have sat like that for an hour. Then she began spinning again.

Saturday, March 12

These days pass swiftly. I eat and drink, and sit down to work. I light my pipe and bend over my books. But I don't read a word. Of course I always make the attempt, but I know beforehand that it won't do any good. Then I go to the window. I greet Clarimonde, and she returns my greeting. We smile and gaze at one another – for hours.

Yesterday afternoon at six I felt a little uneasy. Darkness settled very early, and I felt a certain nameless fear. I sat at my desk and waited. I felt an almost unconquerable urge to go to the window – certainly not to hang myself, but to look at Clarimonde. I jumped up and stood back of the curtain. It seemed as if I had never seen her so clearly, although it was already quite dark. She was spinning, but her eyes looked across at me. I felt a strange comfort and a very subtle fear.

The telephone rang. I was furious at the silly old Commissioner for interrupting my dreams with his stupid questions.

This morning he came to visit me, along with Madame Dubonnet. She seems to be satisfied enough with my activities: she takes sufficient consolation from the fact that I have managed to *live* in Room No. 7 for two whole weeks. But the Commissioner wants results besides. I confided to him that I had made some secret observations, and that I was tracking down a very strange clue. The old fool believed all I told him. In any event I can still stay here for weeks – and that's all I care about. Not on account of Madame Dubonnet's cooking and cellar – God, how soon one becomes indifferent to that when one always has enough to eat! – only because of the window, which she hates and fears, and which I love so dearly: this window that reveals Clarimonde to me.

When I light the lamp I no longer see her. I have strained my eyes trying to see whether she goes out, but I have never seen her set foot on the street. I have a comfortable easy chair and a green lampshade whose glow warmly suffuses me. The Commissioner has sent me a large package of tobacco. I have never smoked such good tobacco. And yet I cannot do any work. I read two or three pages, and when I have finished I realize that I haven't understood a word of their contents. My eyes grasp the significance of the letters, but my brain refuses to supply the connotations. Queer! Just as if my brain bore the legend:

'No Admittance'. Just as if it refused to admit any thought other than the one: Clarimonde...

Finally I push my books aside, lean far back in my chair, and dream.

Sunday, March 13

This morning I witnessed a little tragedy. I was walking up and down in the corridor while the porter made up my room. In front of the little court window there is a spider web hanging, with a fat garden spider sitting in the middle of it. Madame Dubonnet refuses to let it be swept away: spiders bring luck, and Heaven knows she has had enough bad luck in her house. Presently I saw another much smaller male spider cautiously running around the edge of the web. Tentatively he ventured down one of the precarious threads towards the middle; but the moment the female moved, he hastily withdrew. He ran around to another end of the web and tried again to approach her. Finally the powerful female spider in the centre of the web seemed to look upon his suit with favour, and stopped moving. The male spider pulled at one of the threads of the web – first lightly, then so vigorously that the whole web quivered. But the object of his attention remained immovable. Then he approached her very quickly, but carefully. The female spider received him quietly and let him embrace her delicately while she retained the utmost passivity. Motionless the two of them hung for several minutes in the centre of the large web.

Then I saw how the male spider slowly freed himself, one leg after another. It seemed as if he wanted to retreat quietly, leaving his companion alone in her dream of love. Suddenly he let her go entirely and ran out of the web as fast as he could. But at the same instant the female seemed to awaken to a wild rush of activity, and she chased rapidly after him. The weak male spider let himself down by a thread, but the female followed immediately. Both of them fell to the windowsill; and, gathering all his energies, the male spider tried to run away. But it was too late. The female spider seized him in her powerful grip, carried him back up into the net, and set him down squarely in the middle of it. And this same place that had just been a bed for passionate desire now became the scene of something quite different. The lover kicked in vain, stretched his weak legs out again and again, and tried to disentangle himself from this wild embrace. But the female would not let him go. In a few minutes she had spun him in so completely that he could not move a single member. Then she thrust her sharp pincers into his body and sucked out the young blood of her lover in deep draughts. I even saw how she finally let go of the pitiful, unrecognizable little lump – legs, skin and threads – and threw it contemptuously out of the net.

So that's what love is like among these creatures! Well, I can be glad I'm not a young spider.

Monday, March 14

I no longer so much as glance at my books. Only at the window do I pass all my days. And I keep on sitting there even after it gets dark. Then she is no longer there; but I close my eyes and see her anyhow...

Well, this diary has become quite different than I thought it would be. It tells about Madame Dubonnet and the Commissioner, about spiders and about Clarimonde. But not a word about the discovery I had hoped to make – Well, is it my fault?

Tuesday, March 15

Clarimonde and I have discovered a strange new game, and we play it all day long. I greet her, and immediately she returns the greeting. Then I drum with my fingers on my windowpane. She has hardly had time to see it before she begins drumming on hers. I wink at her, and she winks at me. I move my lips as if I were talking to her and she follows suit. Then I brush the hair back from my temples, and immediately her hand is at the side of her forehead. Truly child's play. And we both laugh at it. That is, she really doesn't laugh: it's only a quiet, passive smile she has, just as I suppose mine must be.

For that matter all this isn't nearly as senseless as it must seem. It isn't imitation at all: I think we would both tire of that very quickly. There must be a certain telepathy or thought transference involved in it. For Clarimonde repeats my motions in the smallest conceivable fraction of a second. She hardly has time to see what I am doing before she does the same thing. Sometimes it even seems to me that her action is simultaneous with mine. That is what entices me: always doing something new and unpremeditated. And it's astounding to see her doing the same thing at the same time. Sometimes I try to catch her. I make a great many motions in quick succession, and then repeat them again; and then I do them a third time. Finally I repeat them for the fourth time, but change their order, introduce some new motion, or leave out one of the old ones. It's like children playing Follow the Leader. It's really remarkable that Clarimonde never makes a single mistake, although I sometimes change the motions so rapidly that she hardly has time to memorize each one.

That is how I spend my days. But I never feel for a second that I'm squandering my time on something nonsensical. On the contrary, it seems as if nothing I had ever done were more important.

Wednesday, March 16

Isn't it queer that I have never thought seriously about putting my relations with Clarimonde on a more sensible basis than that of these hour-consuming games? I thought about it last night. I could simply take my hat and coat and go down two flights of stairs, five steps across the street, and then up two other flights of stairs. On her door there is a little coat-of-arms engraved with her name: 'Clarimonde...' Clarimonde what? I don't know what; but the name Clarimonde is certainly there. Then I could knock, and then...

That far I can imagine everything perfectly, down to the last move I might make. But for the life of me I can't picture what would happen after that. The door would open – I can conceive that. But I would remain standing in front of it looking into her room, into a darkness – a darkness so utter that not a solitary thing could be distinguished in it. She would not come – nothing would come; as a matter of fact, there would be nothing there. Only the black impenetrable darkness.

Sometimes it seems as if there could be no other Clarimonde than the one I play with at my window. I can't picture what this woman would look like if she wore a hat, or even some dress other than her black one with the large purple dots; I can't even conceive of her without her gloves. If I could see her on the street, or even in some restaurant, eating, drinking, talking – well, I really have to laugh: the thing seems so utterly inconceivable.

Sometimes I ask myself whether I love her. I can't answer that question entirely, because I have never been in love. But if the feeling I bear towards Clarimonde is really – well, love – then love is certainly very, very different from what I saw of it among my acquaintances or learned about it in novels.

It is becoming quite difficult to define my emotions. In fact, it is becoming difficult even to think about anything at all that has no bearing on Clarimonde – or rather, on our game. For there is truly no denying it: it's really the game that preoccupies me – nothing else. And that's the thing I understand least of all.

Clarimonde – well, yes, I feel attracted to her. But mingled with the attraction there is another feeling – almost like a sense of fear. Fear? No, it isn't fear either: it is more of a temerity, a certain inarticulate alarm or apprehension before something I cannot define. And it is just this apprehension that has some strange compulsion, something curiously passionate that keeps me at a distance from her and at the same time draws me constantly nearer to her. It is as if I were going around her in a wide circle, came a little nearer at one place, withdrew again, went on, approached her again at another point and again retreated rapidly. Until finally – of that I am absolutely certain – I *must* go to her.

Clarimonde is sitting at her window and spinning. Threads – long, thin, infinitely fine threads. She seems to be making some fabric – I don't know just what it is to be. And I can't understand how she can make the network without tangling or tearing the delicate fabric. There are wonderful patterns in her work – patterns full of fabulous monsters and curious grotesques. For that matter – but what am I writing? The fact of the matter is that I can't even see what it is she is spinning: the threads are much too fine. And yet I can't help feeling that her work must be exactly as I see it when I close my eyes. Exactly. A huge network peopled with many creatures – fabulous monsters, and curious grotesque...

Thursday, March 17

I find myself in a strange state of agitation. I no longer talk to any one; I hardly even say good morning to Madame Dubonnet or the porter. I hardly take time to eat; I only want to sit at the window and play with her. It's an exacting game. Truly it is.

And I have a premonition that tomorrow something must happen.

Friday, March 18

Yes, yes. Something must happen today... I tell myself – oh, yes, I talk aloud, just to hear my own voice – that it is just for *that* I am here. But the worst of it is that I am afraid. And this fear that what has happened to my predecessors in this room may also happen to me is curiously mingled with my other fear – the fear of Clarimonde. I can hardly keep them apart. I am afraid. I would like to scream.

6 p.m.

Let me put down a few words quickly, and then get into my hat and coat.

By the time five o'clock came, my strength was gone. Oh, I know now for certain that it must have something to do with this sixth hour of the next to the last day of the week... Now I can no longer laugh at the fraud with which I duped the Commissioner. I sat on my chair and stayed there only by exerting my will-power to the utmost. But this thing drew me, almost pulled me to the window. I had to play with Clarimonde – and then again there rose that terrible fear of the window. I saw them hanging there – the Swiss travelling salesman, a large fellow with a thick neck and a grey stubble beard. And the lanky acrobat and the stocky, powerful police sergeant. I saw all three of them, one after another and then all three together, hanging from the same hook with open mouths and with tongues lolling far out. And then I saw myself among them.

Oh, this fear! I felt I was as much afraid of the window-sash and the terrible hook as I was of Clarimonde. May she forgive me for it, but that's the truth: in my ignominious fear I always confused her image with that of the three who hanged there, dangling their legs heavily on the floor.

But the truth is that I never felt for an instant any desire or inclination to hang myself: I wasn't even afraid I would do it. No – I was afraid only of the window itself – and of Clarimonde – and of something terrible, something uncertain and unpredictable that was now to come. I had the pathetic irresistible longing to get up and go to the window. And I *had* to do it...

Then the telephone rang. I grabbed the receiver and before I could hear a word I myself cried into the mouthpiece: 'Come! Come at once!'

It was just as if my unearthly yell had instantly chased all the shadows into the farthest cracks of the floor. I became composed immediately. I wiped the sweat from my forehead and drank a glass of water. Then I considered what I ought to tell the Commissioner when he came. Finally I went to the window, greeted Clarimonde, and smiled.

And Clarimonde greeted me and smiled.

Five minutes later the Commissioner was here. I told him that I had finally struck the root of the whole affair; if he would only refrain from questioning me today, I would certainly be able to make some remarkable disclosures in the very near future. The queer part of it was that while I was lying to him I was at the same time fully convinced in my own mind that I was telling the truth. And I still feel that that is the truth – against my better judgement.

He probably noticed the unusual condition of my temper, especially when I apologized for screaming into the telephone and tried to explain – and failed to find any plausible reason for my agitation. He suggested very amiably that I need not take undue consideration of him: he was always at my service – that was his duty. He would rather make a dozen useless trips over here than let me wait for him once when I really needed him. Then he invited me to go out with him tonight, suggesting that that might help distract me – it wasn't a good thing to be alone all the time. I have accepted his invitation, although I think it will be difficult to go out: I don't like to leave this room.

Saturday, March 19
We went to the Gaieté Rochechouart, to the Cigale, and to the Lune Rousse. The Commissioner was right: it was a good thing for me to go out and breathe another atmosphere. At first I felt rather uncomfortable, as if I were doing something wrong (as if I were a deserter, running away from our flag). But by and by that feeling died; we drank a good deal, laughed, and joked.

When I went to the window this morning, I seemed to read a reproach in Clarimonde's look. But perhaps I only imagined it: how could she know that I had gone out last night? For that matter, it seemed to last for only a moment; then she smiled again.

We played all day long.

Sunday, March 20
Today I can only repeat: we played all day long.

Monday, March 21
We played all day long.

Tuesday, March 22
Yes, and today we did the same. Nothing, absolutely nothing else. Sometimes I ask myself why we do it. What is it all for? Or, what do I really want, to what can it all lead? But I never answer my own question. For it's certain that I want nothing other than just this. Come what may, that which is coming is exactly what I long for.

We have been talking to one another these last few days, of course not with any spoken word. Sometimes we moved our lips, at other times we only looked at one another. But we understood each other perfectly.

I was right: Clarimonde reproached me for running away last Friday. But I begged her forgiveness and told her I realized that it had been very unwise and horrid of me. She forgave me and I promised her never again to leave the window. And we kissed each other, pressing our lips against the panes for a long, long time.

Wednesday, March 23
I know now that I love her. It must be love – I feel it tingling in every fibre of my being. It may be that with other people love is different. But is there any one among a thousand millions who has a head, an ear, a hand that is like anyone else's? Everyone is different, so it is quite conceivable that our love is very singular. But does that make it any less beautiful? I am almost happy in this love.

If only there would not be this fear! Sometimes it falls asleep. Then I forget it. But only for a few minutes. Then it wakes up again and will not let me go. It seems to me like a poor little mouse fighting against a huge and beautiful snake, trying to free itself from its overpowering embrace. Just wait, you poor foolish little fear, soon our love will devour you!

Thursday, March 24
I have made a discovery: I don't play with Clarimonde – *she plays with me.*

It happened like this.

Last night, as usual, I thought about our game. I wrote down five intricate movements with which I wanted to surprise her today. I gave every motion a number. I practised them so as to be able to execute them as quickly as possible, first in order, and then backwards. Then only the even numbers and then the odd, and then only the first and last parts of each of the five motions. It was very laborious, but it gave me great satisfaction because it brought me nearer to Clarimonde, even though I could not see her. I practised in this way for hours, and finally they went like clockwork.

This morning I went to the window. We greeted each other, and the game began. Forward, backward – it was incredible to see how quickly she understood me, and how instantaneously she repeated all the things I did.

Then there was a knock at my door. It was the porter, bringing me my boots. I took them; but when I was going back to the window my glance fell on the sheet of paper on which I had recorded the order of the movements. *And I saw that I had not executed a single one of these movements.*

I almost reeled. I grabbed the back of the easy chair and let myself down into it. I couldn't believe it. I read the sheet again and again. But it was true: of all the motions I had made at the window, not a single one was mine.

And again I was aware of a door opening somewhere far away – her door. I was standing before it and looking in… nothing, nothing – only an empty darkness. Then I knew that if I went out, I would be saved; and I realized that now I *could* go. Nevertheless I did not go. That was because I was distinctly aware of one feeling: that I held the secret of the mystery. Held it tightly in both hands. Paris – I was going to conquer Paris!

For a moment Paris was stronger than Clarimonde.

Oh, I've dropped all thought of it now. Now I am aware only of my love, and in the midst of it this quiet, passionate fear.

But in that instant I felt suddenly strong. I read through the details of my first movement once more and impressed it firmly in my memory. Then I went back to the window.

And I took exact notice of what I did: *not a single motion I executed was among those I had set out to do.*

Then I decided to run my index finger along my nose. But instead I kissed the window-pane. I wanted to drum on the window-sill, but ran my hand through my hair instead. So it was true: Clarimonde did not imitate the things I did: on the contrary, I repeated the things she indicated. And I did it so quickly, with such lightning rapidity, that I followed her motions in the same second, so that even now it seems as if I were the one who exerted the will-power to do these things.

So it is I – I who was so proud of the fact that I had determined her mode of thought – I was the one who was being so completely influenced. Only, her influence is so soft, so gentle that it seems as if nothing on earth could be so soothing.

I made other experiments. I put both my hands in my pockets and resolved firmly not to move them; then I looked across at her. I noticed how she lifted her hand and smiled, and gently chided me with her index finger. I refused to budge. I felt my right hand wanting to take itself out of my pocket, but I dug my fingers deep into the pocket lining. Then slowly, after several minutes, my fingers relaxed, my hand came out of the pocket, and I lifted my arm. And I chided her with my index finger and smiled. It seemed as if it were really not I who was doing all this, but some stranger whom I watched from a distance. No, no – that wasn't the way of it. I, I was the one who did it – and some stranger was watching me. It was the stranger – that other me – who was so strong, who wanted to solve this mystery with some great discovery. But that was no longer I.

I – oh, what do I care about the discovery? I am only here to do her bidding, the bidding of my Clarimonde, whom I love with such tender fear.

Friday, March 25

I have cut the telephone wire. I can no longer stand being perpetually bothered by the silly old Commissioner, least of all when the fateful hour is at hand…

God, why am I writing all this? Not a word of it is true. It seems as if someone else were guiding my pen.

But I do – I want to set down here what actually happens. It is costing me a tremendous effort. But I want to do it. If only for the last time to do – what I really want to do.

I cut the telephone wire… oh…

Because I had to… There, I finally got it out! Because I had to, I had to!

We stood at the window this morning and played. Our game has changed a little since yesterday. She goes through some motions and I defend myself as long as possible. Until finally I have to surrender, powerless to do anything but her bidding. And I can scarcely tell what a wonderful sense of exaltation and joy it gives me to be conquered by her will, to make this surrender.

We played. And then suddenly she got up and went back into her room. It was so dark that I couldn't see her; she seemed to disappear into the darkness. But she came back very shortly, carrying in her hands a desk telephone just like mine. Smiling, she set it down on the window-sill, took a knife, cut the wire, and carried it back again.

I defended myself for about a quarter of an hour. My fear was greater than ever, but that made my slow surrender all the more delectable. And I finally brought my telephone to the window, cut the wire, and set it back on the table.

That is how it happened.

I am sitting at the table. I have had my tea, and the porter has just taken the dishes out. I asked him what time it was – it seems my watch isn't keeping time. It's five fifteen … five fifteen …

I know that if I look up now Clarimonde will be doing something or other. Doing something or other that I will have to do too.

I look up anyhow. She is standing there and smiling. Well … if I could only tear my eyes away from her! … now she is going to the curtain. She is taking the cord off – it is red, just like the one on my window. She is tying a knot – a slipknot. She is hanging the cord up on the hook in the window-sash.

She is sitting down and smiling.

… No, this is no longer a thing one can call fear, this thing I am experiencing. It is a maddening, choking terror – but nevertheless I wouldn't trade it for anything in the world. It is a compulsion of an unheard-of nature and power, yet so subtly sensual in its inescapable ferocity.

Of course I could rush up to the window and do exactly what she wants me to do. But I am waiting, struggling, and defending myself. I feel this uncanny thing getting stronger every minute …

So, here I am, still sitting here. I ran quickly to the window and did the thing she wanted me to do: I took the curtain cord, tied a slipknot in it, and hung it from the hook …

And now I am not going to look up any more. I am going to stay here and look only at this sheet of paper. For I know now what she would do if I looked up again – now in the sixth hour of the next to the last day of the week. If I see her, I shall have to do her bidding … I shall have to …

I shall refuse to look at her.

But I am suddenly laughing – loudly. No, I'm not laughing – it is something laughing within me. I know why, too: it's because of this 'I will not …'

I don't want to, and yet I know certainly that I must. I must. I must look at her … must, must do it … and then – the rest.

I am only waiting to stretch out the torment. Yes, that is it … For these breathless sufferings are my most rapturous transports. I am writing … quickly, quickly, so that I can remain sitting here longer … in order to stretch out these seconds of torture, which carry the ecstasy of love into infinity …

More … longer …

Again this fear, again! I know that I shall look at her, that I shall get up, that I shall hang myself. *But it isn't that that I fear.* Oh, no – that is sweet, that is beautiful.

But there is something else … something else associated with it – *something that will happen afterwards.* I don't know what it will be – but it is coming, it is certainly coming, certainly … certainly. For the joy of my torments is so infinitely great – oh, I feel it is so great that something terrible must follow it.

Only I must not think …

Let me write something, anything, no matter what. Only quickly, without thinking.

My name – Richard Bracquemont, Richard Bracquemont, Richard – oh, I can't go any farther – Richard Bracquemont – Richard Bracquemont – now – now – I must look at her … Richard Bracquemont – I must – no – no, more – more … Richard … Richard Bracquemont –

The Commissioner of the Ninth Ward, after failing repeatedly to get a reply to his telephone calls, came to the Hotel Stevens at five minutes to six. In Room No. 7 he found the body of the student Richard Bracquemont hanging from the window-sash, in exactly the same position as that of his three predecessors.

Only his face had a different expression; it was distorted in horrible fear, and his eyes, wide open, seemed to be pushing themselves out of their sockets. His lips were drawn apart, but his powerful teeth were firmly and desperately clenched.

And glued between them, bitten and crushed to pieces, there was a large black spider, with curious purple dots.

On the table lay the medical student's diary. The Commissioner read it and went immediately to the house across the street. There he discovered that the second apartment had been vacant and unoccupied for months and months…

THE HUNGRY STONES

Rabindranath Tagore

Rabindranath Tagore (1861–1941) was a Nobel Prize-winning Indian Bengali writer who forever changed Bengali literature and music through his fiction, poetry, drama, music, and advocacy. At the height of his international popularity, he was almost as well-known as Mahatma Gandhi. Tagore modernized Bengali art by rejecting traditional forms. His work encompassed both the personal and the political, with many critics praising his lyricism, colloquialism, and naturalism. Tagore's short stories hold the highest reputation among his writings, perhaps in part because he is credited with originating the Bengali-language version of the form. 'The Hungry Stones' (1916) is among the most overtly weird, or supernatural, of his tales.

MY kinsman and myself were returning to Calcutta from our Puja trip when we met the man in a train. From his dress and bearing we took him at first for an up-country Mahomedan, but we were puzzled as we heard him talk. He discoursed upon all subjects so confidently that you might think the Disposer of All Things consulted him at all times in all that He did. Hitherto we had been perfectly happy, as we did not know that secret and unheard-of forces were at work, that the Russians had advanced close to us, that the English had deep and secret policies, that confusion among the native chiefs had come to a head. But our newly-acquired friend said with a sly smile: 'There happen more things in heaven and earth, Horatio, than are reported in your newspapers.' As we had never stirred out of our homes before, the demeanour of the man struck us dumb with wonder. Be the topic ever so trivial, he would quote science, or comment on the *Vedas*, or repeat quatrains from some Persian poet; and as we had no pretence to a knowledge of science or the *Vedas* or Persian, our admiration for him went on increasing, and my kinsman, a theosophist, was firmly convinced that our fellow-passenger must have been supernaturally inspired by some strange 'magnetism' or 'occult power,' by an 'astral body' or something of that kind. He listened to the tritest saying that fell from the lips of our extraordinary companion with devotional rapture, and secretly took down notes of his conversation. I fancy that the extraordinary man saw this, and was a little pleased with it.

When the train reached the junction, we assembled in the waiting-room for the connection. It was then 10 P.M., and as the train, we heard, was likely to be very late, owing to something wrong in the lines, I spread my bed on the table and was about to lie down for a comfortable doze, when the extraordinary person deliberately set about spinning the following yarn. Of course, I could get no sleep that night.

When, owing to a disagreement about some questions of administrative policy, I threw up my post at Junagarh, and entered the service of the Nizam of Hyderabad, they appointed me at once, as a strong young man, collector of cotton duties at Barich.

Barich is a lovely place. The *Susta* 'chatters over

stony ways and babbles on the pebbles,' tripping, like a skilful dancing girl, in through the woods below the lonely hills. A flight of 150 steps rises from the river, and above that flight, on the river's brim and at the foot of the hills, there stands a solitary marble palace. Around it there is no habitation of man – the village and the cotton mart of Barich being far off.

About 250 years ago the Emperor Mahmud Shah II had built this lonely palace for his pleasure and luxury. In his days jets of rose-water spurted from its fountains, and on the cold marble floors of its spray-cooled rooms young Persian damsels would sit, their hair dishevelled before bathing, and, splashing their soft naked feet in the clear water of the reservoirs, would sing, to the tune of the guitar, the *ghazals* of their vineyards.

The fountains play no longer; the songs have ceased; no longer do snow-white feet step gracefully on the snowy marble. It is but the vast and solitary quarters of cess-collectors like us, men oppressed with solitude and deprived of the society of women. Now, Karim Khan, the old clerk of my office, warned me repeatedly not to take up my abode there. 'Pass the day there, if you like,' said he, 'but never stay the night.' I passed it off with a light laugh. The servants said that they would work till dark, and go away at night. I gave my ready assent. The house had such a bad name that even thieves would not venture near it after dark.

At first the solitude of the deserted palace weighed upon me like a nightmare. I would stay out, and work hard as long as possible, then return home at night jaded and tired, go to bed and fall asleep.

Before a week had passed, the place began to exert a weird fascination upon me. It is difficult to describe or to induce people to believe; but I felt as if the whole house was like a living organism slowly and imperceptibly digesting me by the action of some stupefying gastric juice.

Perhaps the process had begun as soon as I set my foot in the house, but I distinctly remember the day on which I first was conscious of it.

It was the beginning of summer, and the market being dull I had no work to do. A little before sunset I was sitting in an arm-chair near the water's edge below the steps. The *Susta* had shrunk and sunk low; a broad patch of sand on the other side glowed with the hues of evening; on this side the pebbles at the bottom of the clear shallow waters were glistening. There was not a breath of wind anywhere, and the still air was laden with an oppressive scent from the spicy shrubs growing on the hills close by.

As the sun sank behind the hill-tops a long dark curtain fell upon the stage of day, and the intervening hills cut short the time in which light and shade mingle at sunset. I thought of going out for a ride, and was about to get up when I heard a footfall on the steps behind. I looked back, but there was no one.

As I sat down again, thinking it to be an illusion, I heard many footfalls, as if a large number of persons were rushing down the steps. A strange thrill of delight, slightly tinged with fear, passed through my frame, and though there was not a figure before my eyes, methought I saw a bevy of joyous maidens coming down the steps to bathe in the *Susta* in that summer evening. Not a sound was in the valley, in the river, or in the palace, to break the silence, but I distinctly heard the maidens' gay and mirthful laugh, like the gurgle of a spring gushing forth in a hundred cascades, as they ran past me, in quick playful pursuit of each other, towards the river, without noticing me at all. As they were invisible to me, so I was, as it were, invisible to them. The river was perfectly calm, but I felt that its still, shallow, and clear waters were stirred suddenly by the splash of many an arm jingling with bracelets, that the girls laughed and dashed and spattered water at one another, that the feet of the fair swimmers tossed the tiny waves up in showers of pearl.

I felt a thrill at my heart – I cannot say whether the excitement was due to fear or delight or curiosity. I had a strong desire to see them more clearly, but naught was visible before me; I thought I could catch all that they said if I only strained my ears; but however hard I strained them, I heard nothing but the chirping of the cicadas in the woods. It seemed as if a dark curtain of 250 years was hanging before me, and I would fain lift a corner of it tremblingly and peer through, though the assembly on the other side was completely enveloped in darkness.

The oppressive closeness of the evening was broken by a sudden gust of wind, and the still surface of the *Susta* rippled and curled like the hair of a nymph, and from the woods wrapt in the evening gloom there came forth a simultaneous murmur, as though they were awakening from a black dream. Call it reality or dream, the momentary glimpse of that invisible mirage reflected from a far-off world, 250 years old, vanished in a flash. The mystic forms that brushed past me with their quick unbodied steps, and loud, voiceless laughter, and threw themselves into the river, did not go back wringing their dripping robes as they went. Like fragrance wafted away by the wind they were dispersed by a single breath of the spring.

Then I was filled with a lively fear that it was the Muse that had taken advantage of my solitude and possessed me – the witch had evidently come to ruin a poor devil like myself making a living by collecting cotton duties. I decided to have a good dinner – it is the empty stomach that all sorts of incurable diseases find an easy prey. I sent for my cook and gave orders for a rich, sumptuous *moghlai* dinner, redolent of spices and *ghi.*

Next morning the whole affair appeared a queer fantasy. With a light heart I put on a *sola* hat like the *sahebs,* and drove out to my work. I was to have written my quarterly report that day, and expected to return late; but before it was dark I was strangely drawn to my house – by what I could not say – I felt they were all waiting, and that I should delay no longer. Leaving my report unfinished I rose, put on my *sola* hat, and startling the dark, shady, desolate path with the rattle of my carriage, I reached the vast silent palace standing on the gloomy skirts of the hills.

On the first floor the stairs led to a very spacious hall, its roof stretching wide over ornamental arches resting on three rows of massive pillars, and groaning day and night under the weight of its own intense solitude. The day had just closed, and the lamps had not yet been lighted. As I pushed the door open a great bustle seemed to follow within, as if a throng of people had broken up in confusion, and rushed out through the doors and windows and corridors and verandas and rooms, to make its hurried escape.

As I saw no one I stood bewildered, my hair on end in a kind of ecstatic delight, and a faint scent of *attar* and unguents almost effaced by age lingered in my nostrils. Standing in the darkness of that vast desolate hall between the rows of those ancient pillars, I could hear the gurgle of fountains plashing on the marble floor, a strange tune on the guitar, the jingle of ornaments and the tinkle of anklets, the clang of bells tolling the hours, the distant note of *nahabat,* the din of the crystal pendants of chandeliers shaken by the breeze, the song of *bulbuls* from the cages in the corridors, the cackle of storks in the gardens, all creating round me a strange unearthly music.

Then I came under such a spell that this intangible, inaccessible, unearthly vision appeared to be the only reality in the world – and all else a mere dream. That I, that is to say, Srijut So-and-so, the eldest son of So-and-so of blessed memory, should be drawing a monthly salary of Rs. 450 by the discharge of my duties as collector of cotton duties, and driving in my dog-cart to my office every day in a short coat and *sola* hat, appeared to me to be such an astonishingly ludicrous illusion that I burst into a horse-laugh, as I stood in the gloom of that vast silent hall.

At that moment my servant entered with a lighted kerosene lamp in his hand. I do not know whether he thought me mad, but it came back to me at once that I was in very deed Srijut So-and-so, son of So-and-so of blessed memory, and that, while our poets, great and small, alone could say whether inside or outside the earth there was a region where unseen fountains perpetually played and fairy guitars, struck by invisible fingers, sent forth an eternal harmony, this at any rate was certain, that I collected duties at the cotton market at Barich, and earned thereby Rs. 450 per mensem as my salary. I laughed in great glee at my curious illusion, as I sat over the newspaper at my camp-table, lighted by the kerosene lamp.

After I had finished my paper and eaten my *moghlai* dinner, I put out the lamp, and lay down on my bed in a small side-room. Through the open window a radiant star, high above the Avalli hills skirted by the darkness of their woods, was gazing intently from millions and millions of miles away in the sky at Mr. Collector lying on a humble camp-bedstead. I wondered and felt amused at the idea, and do not know when I fell asleep or how long I slept; but I suddenly awoke with a start, though I heard no sound and saw no intruder – only the steady bright star on the hilltop had set, and the dim light of the new moon was stealthily entering the room through the open window, as if ashamed of its intrusion.

I saw nobody, but felt as if someone was gently pushing me. As I awoke she said not a word, but beckoned me with her five fingers bedecked with rings to follow her cautiously. I got up noiselessly, and, though not a soul save myself was there in the countless apartments of that deserted palace with its slumbering sounds and waking echoes, I feared at every step lest any one should wake up. Most of the rooms of the palace were always kept closed, and I had never entered them.

I followed breathless and with silent steps my invisible guide – I cannot now say where. What endless dark and narrow passages, what long corridors, what silent and solemn audience-chambers and close secret cells I crossed!

Though I could not see my fair guide, her form was not invisible to my mind's eye – an Arab girl, her arms, hard and smooth as marble, visible through her loose sleeves, a thin veil falling on her face from the fringe of her cap, and a curved dagger at her waist! Methought that one of the thousand and one Arabian Nights had been wafted to me from the world of romance, and that at the dead of night I was wending my way through the dark narrow alleys of slumbering Bagdad to a trysting-place fraught with peril.

At last my fair guide stopped abruptly before a deep blue screen, and seemed to point to something below. There was nothing there, but a sudden dread froze the blood in my heart – methought I saw there on the floor at the foot of the screen a terrible negro eunuch dressed in rich brocade, sitting and dozing with outstretched legs, with a naked sword on his lap. My fair guide lightly tripped over his legs and held up a fringe of the screen. I could catch a glimpse of a part of the room spread with a Persian carpet – someone was sitting inside on a bed – I could not see her, but only caught a glimpse of two exquisite feet in gold-embroidered slippers, hanging out from loose saffron-coloured *paijamas* and placed idly on the orange-coloured velvet carpet. On one side there was a bluish crystal tray on which a few apples, pears, oranges, and bunches of grapes in plenty, two small cups and a gold-tinted decanter were evidently awaiting the guest. A fragrant intoxicating vapour, issuing from a strange sort of incense that burned within, almost overpowered my senses.

As with trembling heart I made an attempt to step across the outstretched legs of the eunuch, he woke up suddenly with a start, and the sword fell from his lap with a sharp clang on the marble floor.

A terrific scream made me jump, and I saw I was sitting on that camp-bedstead of mine sweating heavily; and the crescent moon looked pale in the morning light like a weary sleepless patient at dawn; and our crazy Meher Ali was crying out, as is his daily custom, 'Stand back! Stand back!!' while he went along the lonely road.

Such was the abrupt close of one of my Arabian Nights; but there were yet a thousand nights left.

Then followed a great discord between my days and nights. During the day I would go to my work worn and tired, cursing the bewitching night and her empty dreams, but as night came my daily life with its bonds and shackles of work would appear a petty, false, ludicrous vanity.

After nightfall I was caught and overwhelmed in the snare of a strange intoxication. I would then be transformed into some unknown personage of a bygone age, playing my part in unwritten history; and my short English coat and tight breeches did not suit me in the least. With a red velvet cap on my head, loose *paijamas,* an embroidered vest, a long flowing silk gown, and coloured handkerchiefs scented with *attar,* I would complete my elaborate toilet, sit on a high-cushioned chair, and replace my cigarette with a many-coiled *narghileh* filled with rose-water, as if in eager expectation of a strange meeting with the beloved one.

I have no power to describe the marvellous incidents that unfolded themselves, as the gloom of the night deepened. I felt as if in the curious apartments of that vast edifice the fragments of a beautiful story, which I could follow for some distance, but of which I could never see the end, flew about in a sudden gust of the vernal breeze. And all the same I would wander from room to room in pursuit of them the whole night long.

Amid the eddy of these dream-fragments, amid the smell of henna and the twanging of the guitar, amid the waves of air charged with fragrant spray, I would catch like a flash of lightning the momentary glimpse of a fair damsel. She it was who had saffron-coloured *paijamas,* white ruddy soft feet in gold-embroidered slippers with curved toes, a close-fitting bodice wrought with gold, a red cap, from which a golden frill fell on her snowy brow and cheeks.

She had maddened me. In pursuit of her I wandered from room to room, from path to path among the bewildering maze of alleys in the enchanted dreamland of the nether world of sleep.

Sometimes in the evening, while arraying myself carefully as a prince of the blood-royal before a large mirror, with a candle burning on either side, I would see a sudden reflection of the Persian beauty by the side of my own. A swift turn of her neck, a quick eager glance of intense passion and pain glowing in her large dark eyes, just a suspicion of speech on her dainty red lips, her figure, fair and slim, crowned with youth like a blossoming creeper, quickly uplifted in her graceful tilting gait, a dazzling flash of pain and craving and esctasy, a smile and a glance and a blaze of jewels and silk, and she melted away. A wild gust of wind, laden with all the fragrance of hills and woods, would put out my light, and I would fling aside my dress and lie down on my bed, my eyes closed and my body thrilling with delight, and there around me in the breeze, amid all the perfume of the woods and hills, floated through the silent gloom many a caress and many a kiss and many a tender touch of hands, and gentle murmurs in my ears, and fragrant breaths on my brow; or a sweetly-perfumed kerchief was wafted again and again on my cheeks. Then slowly a mysterious serpent would twist her stupefying coils about me; and heaving a heavy sigh, I would lapse into insensibility, and then into a profound slumber.

One evening I decided to go out on my horse – I do not know who implored me to stay – but I would listen to no entreaties that day. My English hat and coat were resting on a rack, and I was about to take them down when a sudden whirlwind, crested with the sands of the *Susta* and the dead leaves of the Avalli hills, caught them up, and whirled them round and round, while a loud peal of merry laughter rose higher and higher, striking all the chords of mirth till it died away in the land of sunset.

I could not go out for my ride, and the next day I gave up my queer English coat and hat for good.

That day again at dead of night I heard the stifled heart-breaking sobs of someone – as if below the bed, below the floor, below the stony foundation of that gigantic palace, from the depths of a dark damp grave, a voice piteously cried and implored me: 'Oh, rescue me! Break through these doors of hard illusion, deathlike slumber and fruitless dreams, place me by your side on the saddle, press me to your heart, and, riding through hills and woods and across the river, take me to the warm radiance of your sunny rooms above!'

Who am I? Oh, how can I rescue thee? What drowning beauty, what incarnate passion shall I drag to the shore from this wild eddy of dreams? O lovely ethereal apparition! Where didst thou flourish and when? By what cool spring, under the shade of what date-groves, wast thou born – in the lap of what homeless wanderer in the desert? What Bedouin snatched thee from thy mother's arms, an opening bud plucked from a wild creeper, placed thee on a horse swift as lightning, crossed the burning sands, and took thee to the slave-market of what royal city? And there, what officer of the Badshah, seeing the glory of thy bashful blossoming youth, paid for thee in gold, placed thee in a golden palanquin, and offered thee as a present for the seraglio of his master? And O, the history of that place! The music of the *sareng,* the jingle of anklets, the occasional flash of daggers and the glowing wine of Shiraz poison, and the piercing flashing glance! What infinite grandeur, what endless servitude! The slave-girls to thy right and left waved the *chamar* as diamonds flashed from their bracelets; the Badshah, the king of kings, fell on his knees at thy snowy feet in bejewelled shoes, and outside the terrible Abyssinian eunuch, looking like a messenger of death, but clothed like an angel, stood with a naked sword in his hand! Then, O, thou flower of the desert, swept away by the blood-stained dazzling ocean of grandeur, with its foam of jealousy, its rocks and shoals of intrigue, on what shore of cruel death wast thou cast, or in what other land more splendid and more cruel?

Suddenly at this moment that crazy Meher Ali screamed out: 'Stand back! Stand back!! All is false! All is false!!' I opened my eyes and saw that it was already light. My *chaprasi* came and handed me my letters, and the cook waited with a *salam* for my orders.

I said: 'No, I can stay here no longer.' That very day I packed up, and moved to my office. Old Karim Khan smiled a little as he saw me. I felt nettled, but said nothing, and fell to my work.

As evening approached I grew absent-minded; I felt as if I had an appointment to keep; and the work of examining the cotton accounts seemed wholly useless; even the *Nizamat*, or royalty, of the Nizam did not appear to be of much worth. Whatever belonged to the present, whatever was moving and acting and working for bread seemed trivial, meaningless, and contemptible.

I threw my pen down, closed my ledgers, got into my dog-cart, and drove away. I noticed that it stopped of itself at the gate of the marble palace just at the hour of twilight. With quick steps I climbed the stairs, and entered the room.

A heavy silence was reigning within. The dark rooms were looking sullen as if they had taken offence. My heart was full of contrition, but there was no one to whom I could lay it bare, or of whom I could ask forgiveness. I wandered about the dark rooms with a vacant mind. I wished I had a guitar to which I could sing to the unknown: 'O fire, the poor moth that made a vain effort to fly away has come back to thee! Forgive it but this once, burn its wings and consume it in thy flame!'

Suddenly two tear-drops fell from overhead on my brow. Dark masses of clouds overcast the top of the Avalli hills that day.

The gloomy sooty waters of the *Susta* were waiting in terrible suspense and in an ominous calm. Suddenly land, water, and sky shivered, and a wild tempest-blast rushed howling through the distant pathless woods, showing its lightning-teeth like a raving maniac who had broken his chains. The desolate halls of the palace banged their doors, and moaned in the bitterness of anguish.

The servants were all in the office, and there was no one to light the lamps. The night was cloudy and moonless. In the dense gloom within I could distinctly feel that a woman was lying on her face on the carpet below the bed – clasping and tearing her long dishevelled hair with desperate fingers. Blood was trickling down her fair brow, and she was now laughing a hard, harsh, mirthless laugh, now bursting into violent wringing sobs, now rending her bodice and striking at her bare bosom, as the wind roared in through the open window, and the rain poured in torrents and soaked her through and through.

All night there was no cessation of the storm or of the passionate cry. I wandered from room to room in the dark, with unavailing sorrow. Whom could I console when no one was by? Whose was this intense agony of sorrow? Whence arose this inconsolable grief?

And the mad man cried out: 'Stand back! Stand back!! All is false! All is false!'

I saw that the day had dawned, and Meher Ali was going round and round the palace with his usual cry in that dreadful weather. Suddenly it came to me that perhaps he also had once lived in that house, and that, though he had gone mad, he came there every day, and went round and round, fascinated by the weird spell cast by the marble demon.

Despite the storm and rain I ran to him and asked: 'Ho, Meher Ali, what is false?'

The man answered nothing, but pushing me aside went round and round with his frantic cry, like a bird flying fascinated about the jaws of a snake, and made a desperate effort to warn himself by repeating: 'Stand back! Stand back!! All is false! All is false!!'

I ran like a mad man through the pelting rain to my office, and asked Karim Khan: 'Tell me the meaning of all this!'

What I gathered from that old man was this: That at one time countless unrequited passions and unsatisfied longings and lurid flames of wild blazing pleasure raged within that palace, and that the curse of all the heart-aches and blasted hopes had made its every stone thirsty and hungry, eager to swallow up like a famished ogress any living man who might chance to approach. Not one of those who lived there for three consecutive nights could escape these cruel jaws, save Meher Ali, who had escaped at the cost of his reason.

I asked: 'Is there no means whatever of my release?' The old man said: 'There is only one means, and that is very difficult. I will tell you what it is, but first you must hear the history of a young Persian girl who once lived in that pleasure-dome. A stranger or a more bitterly heart-rending tragedy was never enacted on this earth.'

Just at this moment the coolies announced that the train was coming. So soon? We hurriedly packed up our luggage, as the train steamed in. An English gentleman, apparently just aroused from slumber, was looking out of a first-class carriage endeavouring to read the name of the station. As soon as he caught sight of our fellow-passenger, he cried, 'Hallo,' and took him into his own compartment. As we got into a second-class carriage, we had no chance of finding out who the man was nor what was the end of his story.

I said: 'The man evidently took us for fools and imposed upon us out of fun. The story is pure fabrication from start to finish.' The discussion that followed ended in a lifelong rupture between my theosophist kinsman and myself.

THE VEGETABLE MAN

Luigi Ugolini

TRANSLATED INTO ENGLISH BY BRENDAN AND ANNA CONNELL

Luigi Ugolini (1891–1980) was an Italian writer who garnered an international reputation for his short stories. Early on, Ugolini wrote articles and tales for newspapers. Later he dedicated himself almost exclusively to fiction for young people, which included works of historical biography and a sequel to *Pinocchio*. He also worked as an illustrator, most notably on a number of Jules Verne novels. A compelling tale of weird transformation, 'The Vegetable Man' was originally published in 1917 in an Italian publication whose title translates as *The Illustrated Journal of Travel and Adventure Over Land and Sea*. Brendan and Anna Connell's skilful translation of the story is the first in the English language.

The following is the story told to me by the green man:

'It is only natural, Sir, that you are surprised by the color of my face. That color is why for months now I have not exposed myself to people's eyes. Because it is not a story I could tell to everyone who saw me. But with you it is a different matter. You have seen me, you are my neighbour, you have enquired after my health and, what is more important, you are an intelligent and balanced man. So I will keep no secrets from you and, please, believe what you are about to hear, even if it seems rather strange and improbable.

'My name is Dr. Benito Olivares. I was born in Santos, Brazil, and received a degree in Natural Sciences. Let this suffice for an introduction.

'Later I will tell you the reason why I left my native country and am here in Italy.

'But it is not my private adventures that would interest you, even if I wished to recount them. You asked about my health, so I will tell you without hesitation about the origin of my *illness*.

'I told you that I am Brazilian and I imagine that you already know the reputation of my country: a vast region, larger than Europe, almost half of it as yet unexplored.

'What do we know about the impenetrable Amazon, or about the mysterious Mato Grosso?

'Our ignorance about this wonderfully fertile and seductive land ignited in me the desire to discover its mysteries.

'With the ardor of a young pioneer and the zeal of a scientist, science being a matter of faith and martyrdom, I penetrated the virgin forests, discovering the remote sources of some of our magnificent rivers, measuring myself against death in that poisonous climate, risking the horrible bites of the deadly snakes that live in the mysterious jungle shadows.

'I wrung countless secrets out of that vegetable environment that knows no bounds, that rises to the highest glory of free and lush flora, seeming almost to declare its domination over the fertile land, as if jealously guarding its most beautiful and hidden mysteries, wanting to revenge itself on any intruder.

'Two years passed in this manner, and I found myself lost in the solitude of the Amazon Basin near the boundaries of Mato Grosso, traveling in the middle of flora that was at once magnificent and imbued with almost supernatural charms. My poor style of speech, Sir, can give but a very shabby idea of that inexpressible spectacle, that triumph of plant life and sunshine, of the wonderful contrast of cold shadows and dazzling color, of the silent and titanic struggle made of indestructible embraces and horrendous tangles.

'But a silent and insidious weapon rules the mute combat of the vegetable kingdom: the liana.

'It is the octopus of the forest, the paralyzing tentacle, the noose that cuts off the circulation of the sap and produces vegetable suffocation and gangrene.

'You could see the *Cipo matador*, the killer liana, encircling the magnificent trunks of rubber trees or rosewood with its treacherous and slow embrace. Gradually its arms tighten into small rings that only an axe can break and then they rise up from the tips, like fluid fingers becoming solid as they ascend, until finally a real plant sheath surrounds and suffocates the peaceful giants of the forest, preventing the sap from circulating, denying it breath and life.

'So one day, while admiring one of these battles of nature and, I must tell you, becoming entangled in a large bush of liana, a plant I had never seen before suddenly caught my eye, absorbing all my attention. Can you imagine? A new plant.

'What delight, what triumph, what delirium it is for a botanist to make such a discovery. Trembling with emotion I approached this new specimen and began to study it minutely and lovingly.

'No, the first glance had not deceived me. I really was in the presence of an example of some unknown species, which I tried in vain to classify.

'Great God, that plant seemed to have been created deliberately to upset all of my botanical science. It was in fact a living contradiction. As soon as I tried to give it the particular characteristic of a species, another detail diametrically opposite jumped out, and then another, until my mind became lost in that futile work of classification.

'In the end I came to the conclusion that that admirable plant was in itself an order, family, species, and variety. It was, in short, the progenitor of an order the descendants of which were unknown to me. My wonder and happiness knew no limits.

'What I can tell you regarding the outward appearance of this unique specimen is the following: it was a shrub as tall as a normal man, with palmate leaves that were thick and fleshy. Its branches had a reddish meat color to them that almost filled me with a feeling of disgust. They seemed. . . . Well, they seemed like human limbs without skin.

'Thin white hair made of resistant filaments, similar to the stamen of the maize-cob fell over the entire plant from its top. It had no flowers if by flowers one means a blossom or variously colored corolla. But, on its branches two oval scuttulem had formed that looked like eyes. Yes, two eyes, neither more nor less. See for yourself, Sir, for here in this glass case is a specimen.'

Moved by a lively curiosity, I approached the glass case indicated by the green man's paralyzed gaze and could not repress the shudder that coursed through my every limb: on the shelf I saw a large leaf that had an appearance not unlike that of the prickly pear. But on its surface I did indeed see two eyes, formed with wonderful precision – two very human eyes that seemed to stare out at me in an unpleasant and sinister way. I stepped back, utterly appalled by the sight.

'It's marvelous,' I said, still shivering in spite of myself. 'Those eyes are remarkably real.'

The green man nodded his head.

'It is the gaze of my destiny,' he murmured in a dull voice, and continued his story.

'Wanting to take possession of that strange flower, I stretched out my hand to detach it from the trunk, but in doing so let out a cry of great pain. Some very sharp and curved thorns that I had not previously noticed had bitten deep into my hand. The strangest thing was that, as I regarded them carefully, I noticed that a drop of an intensely green-colored liquid had been emitted from the tip of each of them. In short, they were something like the teeth of a viper.

'And those pricks were quite painful. For a brief period I felt a violent burning, followed by a chill that wound through my veins and ascended suddenly to my heart. Overcome, I was compelled to sit on the ground.

'For a period my body was filled with this violent discomfort, so that I became seriously afraid I had been poisoned by the plant's sap. But then, little by little, every symptom faded away, and soon I could get up again and turn my attention to my botanical discovery.

'With great caution I collected a few leaves and flowers and took them with me, carefully preserved. Intoxicated as I was by my glorious discovery, I lent my name to that strange bush, declaring it the *Olivaria vigilans,* since, with its many open eyes and treacherous thorns, it watched and kept vigil over its own inviolability and security.

'At the same time, however, I was led to an unpleasant observation. The painful phenomena that had taken place after I had been stung by the thorns began to recur. At first it was only at long intervals, but gradually it became more frequent. A feeling of cold passed through my veins and heart, accompanied by a general numbness of the limbs and extreme weakness. I ascribed it to my long stay in the deadly climate of the Amazon and prepared to return to the coast.

'Meanwhile, shortly after the discovery of the *Olivaria vigilans,* two incidents occurred that disturbed my peace of mind, leaving me rather unsettled.

'One day while I was in my tent writing some notes concerning my plant, I saw near me a native of my escort, a Guaraní of the Amazon. I had the idea that he, as an expert on these forests, could give me some information on the mysterious plant. So I called him over and questioned him, showing him the flowers and leaves.

'But as soon as the Indian saw them, he let out a cry of terror and amazement. He stared at me for a moment with the deepest dismay, and then ran off into the forest like a madman. And he never came back and I never heard of him again.

'A few days later, I arrived at a large village of courteous and hospitable Indians. While staying there, I questioned the old tribal chief, who was considered a true wise man. I asked him about a plant that I longed to find and described it to him completely, but without mentioning that I had, in fact, already found it. To my astonishment, even the old *cacique* began to tremble and show signs of the liveliest terror, trying his best to evade my question. Struck with curiosity, I asked him again and again, and insisted on getting an explanation, even offering the old chief a shotgun in exchange for information.

'My insistence and gift won out over his scruples.

'With a strange caution, he said, "That which you look for, foreigner, is a plant unlike any other. It is the *Inhuacoltzi,* the great spirit of the plants. Do not look for it, foreigner, for if you find it, it will make you like itself."'

'These were the strange words of the old *cacique* and nothing more could I coerce out of his mouth. I smiled at this strange superstition, for who could believe that there was a deity of plants? I returned to Santos and revealed the specimens I had discovered to the scientific world, resulting in a great deal of furor and discussion. The leaves and flowers that I had brought I donated to the Museum of Natural History in Buenos Aires, keeping for myself the specimen I have shown you.

'And now, Sir, I will tell you the truly horrible part of my case.

'I have already mentioned that once back home the alarming symptoms produced by the prick of the *Olivaria vigilans* returned with ever increasing frequency. Far from decreasing in severity, the phenomena became increasingly violent.

'Adding to my discomfort, and filling me with dismay, was a new phenomenon as well: My skin was becoming green. Yes, at first it was just a slight tint all over my body, which both I and the doctors who diagnosed me thought was an attack of jaundice. But then, despite all the remedies, the color began to take on a richer tone, while my circulatory disorders became more acute and disturbing.

'A dreadful nightmare began to weigh upon my soul. Recalling the mysterious words of the old *cacique* and the strange fear of my Guaraní servant, an insidious doubt began to poison my spirit.

'One day I made a decisive experiment on myself, examining a drop of my blood under the microscope. And I saw the truth. It revealed itself in all its terrible reality, and the nightmare took on a form, and the dream a palpable consistency.

'A horrible battle was raging in my blood. I don't know if you have ever observed under the microscope the blood of a person affected by sleeping sickness, and seen the stages of the battles fought between the red corpuscles and the trypanosome destroyer? If so, you would know that the red blood cells are being incessantly agitated into a fantastic and continuous turmoil by countless beings animated by a surprising vitality of movement. The erythrocytes, pushed against, driven, destroyed, cluster together, swaying, bouncing elastically in order to avoid the damaging contact with those small bodies shaped like snakes that contort themselves in every possible way. Then in the following weeks you would observe the vital red corpuscles drastically diminish in number while their implacable enemies dramatically increase and begin to dance, intoxicated by destruction.

'A similar spectacle presented itself to me in a drop of my own blood. It was not, however, deadly trypanosomes that were warring against my blood cells, but, rather, numerous other foreign cells, of an *intensely green color*, which were rapidly moving against them, overpowering and destroying them.

'I was terrified, for they were plant cells! It was vegetable sap that crept slowly through my veins, replacing life-sustaining red fluid.

'The doctors to whom I submitted the extraordinary question had to shrug their shoulders and declare themselves incompetent when faced with a phenomenon that evaded both their knowledge and science.

'I told them what had happened, describing my fears and the strange words I had heard from the mouth of the *cacique*. They just smiled and, after prescribing ineffective remedies, no doubt to allay their consciences more than for any other reason, shrugged their shoulders once more.

'Believe me, I felt that my body was being transformed, that I was no longer myself, that my blood was not my own, that I was going to meet a grim fate from which my every thought turned away in disgust.

'So I fled my country, trying a change of climate, as all sick people do when they have one foot in the grave. I tried alternately very cold climates and equatorial climates, until a few months ago I came to your wonderful Italian soil.'

The doctor paused thoughtfully, lowering his head.

'I am leaving tomorrow, Sir,' he added after a moment. 'I will end my existence in my own country, which will have to hold the remains of a man who, on that great day, will no longer be a man.

'You seem surprised. But you are still ignorant of the most terrible part of my awful existence.

'But, tell me, would you like to know everything?

'Do you feel strong and fearless enough to endure the sight of something truly terrible?

'Well, then, now you shall know, Sir. You see me motionless in this chair, my legs inert and hands enveloped in these silk gloves. You believe that I am paralyzed, is that not so? Now I will show you my hands, and you will understand. My other limbs are similar to these, or soon will be. Now you will see, Sir, so be strong.'

He asked me to ring an electric buzzer on the wall. I did so, and immediately a devoted servant, one of the doctor's fellow countrymen, appeared and went to stand next to his chair.

The doctor looked at him.

'Take off my gloves, Alonso,' he said in Spanish, in a low voice.

And then – good God! What a sight met my eyes, which became dilated with horror! No! It must have been a hallucination. I could not believe my senses. After the gloves had been removed, the hands of the paralytic appeared. Hands? No, it was not hands that I saw. No! They were leaves, meaty leaves, similar to those of a prickly pear – two large green leaves attached to repulsive-looking trunks like human arms without skin. And, horrifying vision, on those two short formless fleshy masses sat the same sinister and terrible eyes that I had seen on the leaf enclosed in the glass case.

I let out a terrible cry and fled hastily.

THE PEOPLE OF THE PIT

A. Merritt

A. Merritt (1884–1943) was an American fiction writer and highly successful journalist who traveled the world and reportedly compiled a library of over five thousand occult books. Writing stories was a sideline in part because the journalism paid so well. The writer Gertrude Barrows Bennett (Francis Stevens) heavily influenced Merritt's fiction, especially in terms of her fascination with strange monsters and ruined civilizations. Rumor has it that Merritt's fiction may have itself influenced the US television series *Lost*. The tale reprinted here, 'The People of the Pit', first appeared in 1918 in *All-Story Magazine*. The story is a strong example of early American pulp magazine fiction in a weird mode.

North of us a shaft of light shot half way to the zenith. It came from behind the five peaks. The beam drove up through a column of blue haze whose edges were marked as sharply as the rain that streams from the edges of a thunder cloud. It was like the flash of a searchlight through an azure mist. It cast no shadows.

As it struck upward the summits were outlined hard and black and I saw that the whole mountain was shaped like a hand. As the light silhouetted it, the gigantic fingers stretched, the hand seemed to thrust itself forward. It was exactly as though it moved to push something back. The shining beam held steady for a moment; then broke into myriads of little luminous globes that swung to and fro and dropped gently. They seemed to be searching.

The forest had become very still. Every wood noise held its breath. I felt the dogs pressing against my legs. They too were silent; but every muscle in their bodies trembled, their hair was stiff along their backs and their eyes, fixed on the falling lights, were filmed with the terror glaze.

I looked at Anderson. He was staring at the North where once more the beam had pulsed upward.

'It can't be the aurora,' I spoke without moving my lips. My mouth was as dry as though Lao T'zai had poured his fear dust down my throat.

'If it is I never saw one like it,' he answered in the same tone. 'Besides who ever heard of an aurora at this time of the year?'

He voiced the thought that was in my own mind.

'It makes me think something is being hunted up there,' he said, 'an unholy sort of hunt – it's well for us to be out of range.'

'The mountain seems to move each time the shaft shoots up,' I said. 'What's it keeping back, Starr? It makes me think of the frozen hand of cloud that Shan Nadour set before the Gate of Ghouls to keep them in the lairs that Eblis cut for them.'

He raised a hand – listening.

From the North and high overhead there came a whispering. It was not the rustling of the aurora, that rushing, crackling sound like the ghosts of winds that blew at Creation racing through the skeleton leaves of ancient trees that sheltered Lilith. It was a whispering that held in it a demand. It was eager. It called us to come up where the beam was flashing. It drew. There was in it a note of inexorable insistence. It touched my heart with a thousand tiny fear-tipped fingers and it filled me with a vast longing to race on and merge myself in the light. It must have been so that Ulysses felt when he strained at the mast and strove to obey the crystal sweet singing of the Sirens.

The whispering grew louder.

'What the hell's the matter with those dogs?' cried Anderson savagely. 'Look at them!'

The malamutes, whining, were racing away toward the light. We saw them disappear among the trees. There came back to us a mournful howling. Then that too died away and left nothing but the insistent murmuring overhead.

The glade we had camped in looked straight to the North. We had reached I suppose three hundred miles above the first great bend of the Koskokwim toward the Yukon. Certainly we were in an untrodden part of the wilderness. We had pushed through from Dawson at the breaking of the Spring, on a fair lead to the lost five peaks between which, so the Athabasean medicine man had told us, the gold streams out like putty from a clenched fist. Not an Indian were we able to get to go with us. The land of the Hand Mountain was accursed they said. We had sighted the peaks the night before, their tops faintly outlined against a pulsing glow. And now we saw the light that had led us to them.

Anderson stiffened. Through the whispering had broken a curious pad-pad and a rustling. It sounded as though a small bear were moving towards us. I threw a pile of wood on the fire and, as it blazed up, saw something break through the bushes. It walked on all fours, but it did not walk like a bear. All at once it flashed upon me – it was like a baby crawling upstairs. The forepaws lifted themselves in grotesquely infantile fashion. It was grotesque but it was – terrible. It grew closer. We reached for our guns – and dropped them. Suddenly we knew that this crawling thing was a man!

It was a man. Still with the high climbing pad-pad he swayed to the fire. He stopped.

'Safe,' whispered the crawling man, in a voice that was an echo of the murmur overhead. 'Quite safe here. They can't get you out of the blue, you know. They can't get you – unless you go to them–'

He fell over on his side. We ran to him. Anderson knelt.

'God's love!' he said. 'Frank, look at this!'

He pointed to the hands. The wrists were covered with torn rags of a heavy shirt. The hands themselves were stumps! The fingers had been bent into the palms and the flesh had been worn to the bone. They looked like the feet of a little black elephant! My eyes traveled down the body. Around the waist was a heavy band of yellow metal. From it fell a ring and a dozen links of shining white chain!

'What is he? Where did he come from?' said Anderson. 'Look, he's fast asleep – yet even in his sleep his arms try to climb and his feet draw themselves up one after the other! And his knees – how in God's name was he ever able to move on them?'

It was even as he said. In the deep sleep that had come upon the crawler arms and legs kept raising in a deliberate, dreadful climbing motion. It was as though they had a life of their own – they kept their movement independently of the motionless body. They were semaphoric motions. If you have ever stood at the back of a train and had watched the semaphores rise and fall you will know exactly what I mean.

Abruptly the overhead whispering ceased. The shaft of light dropped and did not rise again. The crawling man became still. A gentle glow began to grow around us. It was dawn, and the short Alaskan summer night was over. Anderson rubbed his eyes and turned to me a haggard face.

'Man!' he exclaimed. 'You look as though you have been through a spell of sickness!'

'No more than you, Starr,' I said. 'What do you make of it all?'

'I'm thinking our only answer lies there,' he answered, pointing to the figure that lay so motionless under the blankets we had thrown over him. 'Whatever it was – that's what it was after. There was no aurora about that light, Frank. It was like the flaring up of some queer hell the preacher folk never frightened us with.'

'We'll go no further today,' I said. 'I wouldn't wake him for all the gold that runs between the fingers of the five peaks – nor for all the devils that may be behind them.'

The crawling man lay in a sleep as deep as the Styx. We bathed and bandaged the pads that had been his hands. Arms and legs were as rigid as though they were crutches. He did not move while we worked over him. He lay as he had fallen, the arms a trifle raised, the knees bent.

'Why did he crawl?' whispered Anderson. 'Why didn't he walk?'

I was filing the band about the waist. It was gold, but it was like no gold I had ever handled. Pure gold is soft. This was soft, but it had an unclean, viscid life of its own. It clung to the file. I gashed through it, bent it away from the body and hurled it far off. It was – loathsome!

All that day he slept. Darkness came and still he slept. That night there was no shaft of light, no questing globe, no whispering. Some spell of horror seemed lifted from the land. It was noon when the crawling man awoke. I jumped as the pleasant drawling voice sounded.

'How long have I slept?' he asked. His pale blue eyes grew quizzical as I stared at him. 'A night – and almost two days,' I said.

'Was there any light up there last night?' He nodded to the North eagerly. 'Any whispering?'

'Neither,' I answered. His head fell back and he stared up at the sky.

'They've given it up, then?' he said at last.

'Who have given it up?' asked Anderson.

'Why, the people of the pit,' replied the crawling man quietly.

We stared at him.

'The people of the pit,' he said. 'Things that the Devil made before the Flood and that somehow have escaped God's vengeance. You weren't in any danger from them – unless you had followed their call. They can't get any further than the blue haze. I was their prisoner,' he added simply. 'They were trying to whisper me back to them!'

Anderson and I looked at each other, the same thought in both our minds.

'You're wrong,' said the crawling man. 'I'm not insane. Give me a very little to drink. I'm going to die soon, but I want you to take me as far South as you can before I die, and afterwards I want you to build a big fire and burn me. I want to be in such shape that no infernal spell of theirs can drag my body back to them. You'll do it too, when I've told you about them–' he hesitated. 'I think their chain is off me?' he said.

'I cut it off,' I answered shortly.

'Thank God for that too,' whispered the crawling man.

He drank the brandy and water we lifted to his lips.

'Arms and legs quite dead,' he said. 'Dead as I'll be soon. Well, they did well for me. Now I'll tell you what's up there behind that hand. Hell!

'Now listen. My name is Stanton – Sinclair Stanton. Class of 1900, Yale. Explorer. I started away from Dawson last year to hunt for five peaks that rise like a hand in a haunted country and run pure gold between them. Same thing you were after? I thought so. Late last fall my comrade sickened. Sent him back with some Indians. Little later all my Indians ran away from me. I decided I'd stick, built a cabin, stocked myself with food and lay down to winter it. In the Spring I started off again. Little less than two weeks ago I sighted the five peaks. Not from this side though – the other. Give me some more brandy.

'I'd made too wide a detour,' he went on. 'I'd gotten too far North. I beat back. From this side you see nothing but forest straight up to the base of the Hand Mountain. Over on the other side–'

He was silent for a moment.

'Over there is forest too. But it doesn't reach so far. No! I came out of it. Stretching miles in front of me was a level plain. It was as worn and ancient looking as the desert around the ruins of Babylon. At its end rose the peaks. Between me and them – far off – was what looked like a low dike of rocks. Then – I ran across the road!

'The road!' cried Anderson incredulously.

'The road,' said the crawling man. 'A fine smooth stone road. It ran straight on to the mountain. Oh, it was road all right – and worn as though millions and millions of feet had passed over it for thousands of years. On each side of it were sand and heaps of stones. After a while I began to notice these stones. They were cut, and the shape of the heaps somehow gave me the idea that a hundred thousand years ago they might have been houses. I sensed man about them and at the same time they smelled of immemorial antiquity. Well –

'The peaks grew closer. The heaps of ruins thicker. Something inexpressibly desolate hovered over them; something reached from them that struck my heart like the touch of ghosts so old that they could be only the ghosts of ghosts. I went on.

'And now I saw that what I had thought to be the low rock range at the base of the peaks was a thicker litter of ruins. The Hand Mountain was really much farther off. The road passed between two high rocks that raised themselves like a gateway.'

The crawling man paused.

'They were a gateway,' he said. 'I reached them. I went between them. And then I sprawled and clutched the earth in sheer awe! I was on a broad stone platform. Before me was – sheer space! Imagine the Grand Canyon five times as wide and with the bottom dropped out. That is what I was looking into. It was like peeping over the edge of a cleft world down into the infinity where the planets roll! On the far side stood the five peaks. They looked like a gigantic warning hand stretched up to the sky. The lip of the abyss curved away on each side of me.

'I could see down perhaps a thousand feet. Then a thick blue haze shut out the eye. It was like the blue you see gather on the high hills at dusk. And the pit – it was awesome; awesome as the Maori Gulf of Ranalak, that sinks between the living and the dead and that only the freshly released soul has strength to leap – but never strength to cross again.

'I crept back from the verge and stood up, weak. My hand rested against one of the pillars of the gateway. There was carving upon it. It bore in still sharp outlines the heroic figure of a man. His back was turned. His arms were outstretched. There was an odd peaked headdress upon him. I looked at the opposite pillar. It bore a figure exactly similar. The pillars were triangular and the carvings were on the side away from the pit. The figures seemed to be holding something back. I looked closer. Behind the outstretched hands I seemed to see other shapes.

'I traced them out vaguely. Suddenly I felt unaccountably sick. There had come to me an impression of enormous upright slugs. Their swollen bodies were faintly cut – all except the heads which were well marked globes. They were – unutterably loathsome. I turned from the gates back to the void. I stretched myself upon the slab and looked over the edge.

'A stairway led down into the pit!'

'A stairway!' we cried.

'A stairway,' repeated the crawling man as patiently as before. 'It seemed not so much carved out of the rock as built into it. The slabs were about six feet long and three feet wide. It ran down from the platform and vanished into the blue haze.'

'But who could build such a stairway as that?' I said. 'A stairway built into the wall of a precipice and leading down into a bottomless pit!'

'Not bottomless,' said the crawling man quietly. 'There was a bottom. I reached it!'

'Reached it?' we repeated.

'Yes, by the stairway,' answered the crawling man. 'You see – I went down it!

'Yes,' he said. 'I went down the stairway. But not that day. I made my camp back of the gates. At dawn I filled my knapsack with food, my two canteens with water from a spring that wells up there by the gateway, walked between the carved monoliths and stepped over the edge of the pit.

'The steps ran along the side of the rock at a forty-degree pitch. As I went down and down I studied them. They were of a greenish rock quite different from the granitic porphyry that formed the wall of the precipice. At first I thought that the builders had taken advantage of an outcropping stratum, and had carved from it their gigantic flight. But the regularity of the angle at which it fell made me doubtful of this theory.

'After I had gone perhaps half a mile I stepped out upon a landing. From this landing the stairs made a V-shaped turn and ran on downward, clinging to the cliff at the same angle as the first flight; it was a zigzag, and after I had made three of these turns I knew that the steps dropped straight down in a succession of such angles. No strata could be so regular as that. No, the stairway was built by hands! But whose? The answer is in those ruins around the edge, I think – never to be read.

'By noon I had lost sight of the five peaks and the lip of the abyss. Above me, below me, was nothing but the blue haze. Beside me, too, was nothingness, for the further breast of rock had long since vanished. I felt no dizziness, and any trace of fear was swallowed in a vast curiosity. What was I to discover? Some ancient and wonderful civilization that had ruled when the Poles were tropical gardens? Nothing living, I felt sure – all was too old for life. Still, a stairway so wonderful must lead to something quite as wonderful I knew. What was it? I went on.

'At regular intervals I had passed the mouths of small caves. There would be two thousand steps and then an opening, two thousand more steps and an opening – and so on and on. Late that afternoon I stopped before one of these clefts. I suppose I had gone then three miles down the pit, although the angles were such that I had walked in all fully ten miles. I examined the entrance. On each side were carved the figures of the great portal above, only now they were standing face forward, the arms outstretched as though to hold something back from the outer depths. Their faces were covered with veils. There were no hideous shapes behind them. I went inside. The fissure ran back for twenty yards like a burrow. It was dry and perfectly light. Outside I could see the blue haze rising upward like a column, its edges clearly marked. I felt an extraordinary sense of security, although I had not been conscious of any fear. I felt that the figures at the entrance were guardians – but against what?

'The blue haze thickened and grew faintly luminescent. I fancied that it was dusk above. I ate and drank a little and slept. When I awoke the blue had lightened again, and I fancied it was dawn above. I went on. I forgot the gulf yawning at my side. I felt no fatigue and little hunger or thirst, although I had drunk and eaten sparingly. That night I spent within another of the caves, and at dawn I descended again.

'It was late that day when I first saw the city–.'

He was silent for a time.

'The city,' he said at last, 'there is a city you know. But not such a city as you have ever seen – nor any other man who has lived to tell of it. The pit, I think, is shaped like a bottle; the opening before the five peaks is the neck. But how wide the bottom is I do not know – thousands of miles maybe. I had begun to catch little glints of light far down in the blue. Then I saw the tops of – trees, I suppose they are. But not our kind of trees – unpleasant, snaky kind of trees. They reared themselves on high thin trunks and their tops were nests of thick tendrils with ugly little leaves like arrow heads. The trees were red, a vivid angry red. Here and there I glimpsed spots of shining yellow. I knew these were water because I could see things breaking through their surface – or at least I could see the splash and ripple, but what it was that disturbed them I never saw.

'Straight beneath me was the – city. I looked down upon mile after mile of closely packed cylinders. They lay upon their sides in pyramids of three, of five – of dozens – piled upon each other. It is hard to make you see what that city is like – look, suppose you have water pipes of a certain length and first you lay three of them side by side and on top of them you place two and on these two one; or suppose you take five for a foundation and place on these four and then three, then two and then one. Do you see? That was the way they looked. But they were topped by towers, by minarets, by flares, by fans, and twisted monstrosities. They gleamed as though coated with pale rose flame. Beside them the venomous red trees raised themselves like the heads of hydras guarding nests of gigantic, jeweled and sleeping worms!

'A few feet beneath me the stairway jutted out into a titanic arch, unearthly as the span that bridges Hell and leads to Asgard. It curved out and down straight through the top of the highest pile of carven cylinders and then it vanished through it. It was appalling – it was demonic–'

The crawling man stopped. His eyes rolled up into his head. He trembled and his arms and legs began their horrible crawling movement. From his lips came a whispering. It was an echo of the high murmuring we had heard the night he came to us. I put my hands over his eyes. He quieted.

'The Things Accursed!' he said. 'The People of

the Pit! Did I whisper. Yes – but they can't get me now – they can't!'

After a time he began as quietly as before.

'I crossed the span. I went down through the top of that – building. Blue darkness shrouded me for a moment and I felt the steps twist into a spiral. I wound down and then – I was standing high up in – I can't tell you in what, I'll have to call it a room. We have no images for what is in the pit. A hundred feet below me was the floor. The walls sloped down and out from where I stood in a series of widening crescents. The place was colossal – and it was filled with a curious mottled red light. It was like the light inside a green and gold flecked fire opal. I went down to the last step. Far in front of me rose a high, columned altar. Its pillars were carved in monstrous scrolls – like mad octopuses with a thousand drunken tentacles; they rested on the backs of shapeless monstrosities carved in crimson stone. The altar front was a gigantic slab of purple covered with carvings.

'I can't describe these carvings! No human being could – the human eye cannot grasp them any more than it can grasp the shapes that haunt the fourth dimension. Only a subtle sense in the back of the brain sensed them vaguely. They were formless things that gave no conscious image, yet pressed into the mind like small hot seals – ideas of hate – of combats between unthinkable monstrous things – victories in a nebulous hell of steaming, obscene jungles – aspirations and ideals immeasurably loathsome –

'And as I stood I grew aware of something that lay behind the lip of the altar fifty feet above me. I knew it was there – I felt it with every hair and every tiny bit of my skin. Something infinitely malignant, infinitely horrible, infinitely ancient. It lurked, it brooded, it threatened and it – was invisible!

'Behind me was a circle of blue light. I ran for it. Something urged me to turn back, to climb the stairs and make away. It was impossible. Repulsion for that unseen Thing raced me onward as though a current had my feet. I passed through the circle. I was out on a street that stretched on into dim distance between rows of the carven cylinders.

'Here and there the red trees arose. Between them rolled the stone burrows. And now I could take in the amazing ornamentation that clothed them. They were like the trunks of smooth skinned trees that had fallen and had been clothed with high reaching noxious orchids. Yes – those cylinders were like that – and more. They should have gone out with the dinosaurs. They were – monstrous. They struck the eyes like a blow and they passed across the nerves like a rasp. And nowhere was there sight or sound of living thing.

'There were circular openings in the cylinders like the circle in the Temple of the Stairway. I passed through one of them. I was in a long, bare vaulted room whose curving sides half closed twenty feet over my head, leaving a wide slit that opened into another vaulted chamber above. There was absolutely nothing in the room save the same mottled reddish light that I had seen in the Temple. I stumbled. I still could see nothing, but there was something on the floor over which I had tripped. I reached down – and my hand touched a thing cold and smooth – that moved under it – I turned and ran out of that place – I was filled with a loathing that had in it something of madness – I ran on and on blindly – wringing my hands – weeping with horror –

'When I came to myself I was still among the stone cylinders and red trees. I tried to retrace my steps; to find the Temple. I was more than afraid. I was like a new loosed soul panic-stricken with the first terrors of hell. I could not find the Temple! Then the haze began to thicken and glow; the cylinders to shine more brightly. I knew that it was dusk in the world above and I felt that with dusk my time of peril had come; that the thickening of the haze was the signal for the awakening of whatever things lived in this pit.

'I scrambled up the sides of one of the burrows. I hid behind a twisted nightmare of stone. Perhaps, I thought, there was a chance of remaining hidden until the blue lightened and the peril passed. There began to grow around me a murmur. It was everywhere – and it grew and grew into a great whispering. I peeped from the side of the stone down into the street. I saw lights passing and repassing. More and more lights – they swam out of the circular doorways and they thronged the street. The highest were eight feet above the pave;

the lowest perhaps two. They hurried, they sauntered, they bowed, they stopped and whispered – and there was nothing under them!'

'Nothing under them!' breathed Anderson.

'No,' he went on, 'that was the terrible part of it – there was nothing under them. Yet certainly the lights were living things. They had consciousness, volition, thought – what else I did not know. They were nearly two feet across – the largest. Their center was a bright nucleus – red, blue, green. This nucleus faded off, gradually, into a misty glow that did not end abruptly. It too seemed to fade off into nothingness – but a nothingness that had under it a – somethingness. I strained my eyes trying to grasp this body into which the lights merged and which one could only feel was there, but could not see.

'And all at once I grew rigid. Something cold, and thin like a whip, had touched my face. I turned my head. Close behind were three of the lights. They were a pale blue. They looked at me – if you can imagine lights that are eyes. Another whiplash gripped my shoulder. Under the closest light came a shrill whispering. I shrieked. Abruptly the murmuring in the street ceased. I dragged my eyes from the pale blue globe that held them and looked out – the lights in the streets were rising by myriads to the level of where I stood! There they stopped and peered at me. They crowded and jostled as though they were a crowd of curious people – on Broadway. I felt a score of the lashes touch me –

'When I came to myself I was again in the great Place of the Stairway, lying at the foot of the altar. All was silent. There were no lights – only the mottled red glow. I jumped to my feet and ran toward the steps. Something jerked me back to my knees. And then I saw that around my waist had been fastened a yellow ring of metal. From it hung a chain and this chain passed up over the lip of the high ledge. I was chained to the altar!

'I reached into my pockets for my knife to cut through the ring. It was not there! I had been stripped of everything except one of the canteens that I had hung around my neck and which I suppose They had thought was – part of me. I tried to break the ring. It seemed alive. It writhed in my hands and it drew itself closer around me! I pulled at the chain. It was immovable. There came to me the consciousness of the unseen Thing above the altar. I groveled at the foot of the slab and wept. Think – alone in that place of strange light with the brooding ancient Horror above me – a monstrous Thing, a Thing unthinkable – an unseen Thing that poured forth horror –

'After awhile I gripped myself. Then I saw beside one of the pillars a yellow bowl filled with a thick white liquid. I drank it. If it killed I did not care. But its taste was pleasant and as I drank my strength came back to me with a rush. Clearly I was not to be starved. The lights, whatever they were, had a conception of human needs.

'And now the reddish mottled gleam began to deepen. Outside arose the humming and through the circle that was the entrance came streaming the globes, They ranged themselves in ranks until they filled the Temple. Their whispering grew into a chant, a cadenced whispering chant that rose and fell, rose and fell, while to its rhythm the globes lifted and sank, lifted and sank.

'All that night the lights came and went – and all that night the chant sounded as they rose and fell. At the last I felt myself only an atom of consciousness in a sea of cadenced whispering; an atom that rose and fell with the bowing globes. I tell you that even my heart pulsed in unison with them! The red glow faded, the lights streamed out; the whispering died. I was again alone and I knew that once again day had broken in my own world.

'I slept. When I awoke I found beside the pillar more of the white liquid. I scrutinized the chain that held me to the altar. I began to rub two of the links together. I did this for hours. When the red began to thicken there was a ridge worn in the links. Hope rushed up within me. There was, then, a chance to escape.

'With the thickening the lights came again. All through that night the whispering chant sounded, and the globes rose and fell. The chant seized me. It pulsed through me until every nerve and muscle quivered to it. My lips began to quiver. They strove like a man trying to cry out on a nightmare. And at last they too were whispering the chant of the people of the pit. My body bowed in unison with the lights – I was, in movement and sound, one with the nameless things while my soul sank back sick with horror and powerless. While I whispered I – saw Them!'

'Saw the lights?' I asked stupidly.

'Saw the Things under the lights,' he answered. 'Great transparent snail-like bodies – dozens of waving tentacles stretching from them – round gaping mouths under the luminous seeing globes. They were like the ghosts of inconceivably monstrous slugs! I could see through them. And as I stared, still bowing and whispering, the dawn came and they streamed to and through the entrance. They did not crawl or walk – they floated! They floated and were – gone!

'I did not sleep. I worked all that day at my chain. By the thickening of the red I had worn it a sixth through. And all that night I whispered and bowed with the pit people, joining in their chant to the Thing that brooded above me!

'Twice again the red thickened and the chant held me – then on the morning of the fifth day I broke through the worn links of the chain. I was free! I drank from the bowl of white liquid and poured what was left in my flask. I ran to the Stairway. I rushed up and past that unseen Horror behind the altar ledge and was out upon the Bridge. I raced across the span and up the Stairway.

'Can you think what it is to climb straight up the verge of a cleft-world – with hell behind you? Hell was behind me and terror rode me. The city had long been lost in the blue haze before I knew that I could climb no more. My heart beat upon my ears like a sledge. I fell before one of the little caves feeling that here at last was sanctuary. I crept far back within it and waited for the haze to thicken. Almost at once it did so. From far below me came a vast and angry murmur. At the mouth of the rift I saw a light pulse up through the blue; die down and as it dimmed I saw myriads of the globes that are the eyes of the pit people swing downward into the abyss. Again and again the light pulsed and the globes fell. They were hunting me. The whispering grew louder, more insistent.

'There grew in me the dreadful desire to join in the whispering as I had done in the Temple. I bit my lips through and through to still them. All that night the beam shot up through the abyss, the globes swung and the whispering sounded – and now I knew the purpose of the caves and of the sculptured figures that still had power to guard them. But what were the people who had carved them? Why had they built their city around the verge and why had they set that Stairway in the pit? What had they been to those Things that dwelt at the bottom and what use had the Things been to them that they should live beside their dwelling place? That there had been some purpose was certain. No work so prodigious as the Stairway would have been undertaken otherwise. But what was the purpose? And why was it that those who had dwelt about the abyss had passed away ages gone, and the dwellers in the abyss still lived? I could find no answer – nor can I find any now. I have not the shred of a theory.

'Dawn came as I wondered and with it silence. I drank what was left of the liquid in my canteen, crept from the cave and began to climb again. That afternoon my legs gave out. I tore off my shirt, made from it pads for my knees and coverings for my hands. I crawled upward. I crawled up and up. And again I crept into one of the caves and waited until again the blue thickened, the shaft of light shot through it and the whispering came.

'But now there was a new note in the whispering. It was no longer threatening. It called and coaxed. It drew. A new terror gripped me. There had come upon me a mighty desire to leave the cave and go out where the lights swung; to let them do with me as they pleased, carry me where they wished. The desire grew. It gained fresh impulse with every rise of the beam until at last I vibrated with the desire as I had vibrated to the chant in the Temple. My body was a pendulum. Up would go the beam and I would swing toward it! Only my soul kept steady. It held me fast to the floor of the cave; And all that night it fought with my body against the spell of the pit people.

'Dawn came. Again I crept from the cave and faced the Stairway. I could not rise. My hands were torn and bleeding; my knees an agony. I forced myself upward step by step. After a while my hands became numb, the pain left my knees. They deadened. Step by step my will drove my body upward upon them.

'And then – a nightmare of crawling up infinite

stretches of steps – memories of dull horror while hidden within caves with the lights pulsing without and whisperings that called and called me – memory of a time when I awoke to find that my body was obeying the call and had carried me half way out between the guardians of the portals while thousands of gleaming globes rested in the blue haze and watched me. Glimpses of bitter fights against sleep and always, always – a climb up and up along infinite distances of steps that led from Abaddon to a Paradise of blue sky and open world!

'At last a consciousness of the clear sky close above me, the lip of the pit before me – memory of passing between the great portals of the pit and of steady withdrawal from it – dreams of giant men with strange peaked crowns and veiled faces who pushed me onward and onward and held back Roman Candle globules of light that sought to draw me back to a gulf wherein planets swam between the branches of red trees that had snakes for crowns.

'And then a long, long sleep – how long God alone knows – in a cleft of rocks; an awakening to see far in the North the beam still rising and falling, the lights still hunting, the whispering high above me calling.

'Again crawling on dead arms and legs that moved – that moved – like the Ancient Mariner's ship – without volition of mine, but that carried me from a haunted place. And then – your fire – and this – safety!'

The crawling man smiled at us for a moment. Then swiftly life faded from his face. He slept.

That afternoon we struck camp and carrying the crawling man started back South. For three days we carried him and still he slept. And on the third day, still sleeping, he died. We built a great pile of wood and we burned his body as he had asked. We scattered his ashes about the forest with the ashes of the trees that had consumed him. It must be a great magic indeed that could disentangle those ashes and draw him back in a rushing cloud to the pit he called Accursed. I do not think that even the People of the Pit have such a spell. No.

But we did not return to the five peaks to see.

THE HELL SCREEN

Ryūnosuke Akutagawa

TRANSLATED INTO ENGLISH BY MORINAKA AKIRA

Ryūnosuke Akutagawa (1892–1927) was a Japanese writer active in Taishō period Japan and often called the 'father of the Japanese short story'. His name loosely translates to 'Son of Dragon', as he was born in the year, month, day, and hour of the Dragon. He published his first short story, 'Rashōmon', while still a student and wrote over one hundred more in his lifetime. Depression and hallucinations hounded him and he eventually committed suicide at the age of thirty-five. His dying words in his will claimed he felt a 'vague uneasiness'. The story reprinted here, 'The Hell Screen' (1918) in a new definitive translation, is a masterpiece, with the 'weird' always ever a glimmer in the background.

Neither in the past nor in the time to come could one imagine a person comparable to the High Lord of Horikawa. I heard that, before his birth, Dai Itoku-Myo-o[1], the King of Magical Science, appeared at his mother's bedside. From birth, Horikawa was different from the others. Of all the things he ever did, I cannot recall an act that did not deserve our wonderment. To mention an example among many, the structure of his palace – how should I define it? – Immense? Grandiose? – was so astounding as to surpass the boundaries of our limited imagination. Some went so far as to compare his temperament and conduct to those of the First Emperor of the Ch'in or the Emperor Yang, although, while considering this comparison, we should keep in mind the idea that different people have different opinions, as with the proverbial blind men who touched different parts of an elephant and drew contradicting conclusions about the animal. Contrary to those emperors, our lord's intention was never to enjoy the luxury life can provide. He had a kind and generous heart that would partake in the happiness and distress of all, even the humblest among his subjects. For these reasons, when he encountered a procession of ghosts in the large palace of Nijo, he was able to pass through them unscathed. And when the spirit of Secretary Tooru prowled every night the Kawaranoin Palace in Higashi-Sanjo, famed for the garden inspired by the marine landscape of Shiogama in the Michinoku province, the Lord reprimanded it, after which the spectre vanished forever. Of course, as soon as the people of Kyoto, young and old, men and women, heard Horikawa's name, they would genuflect as if they had seen Buddha's avatar.

One day, on his way home from the banquet of the Plum Blossoms, one of the oxen pulling his cart broke away and injured an old man who was passing by. It is rumoured that the old man joined his hands to express his gratitude for having been touched by the hoof of the Lord's ox.

His life was full of many memorable facts, most of which should be bequeathed to posterity.

[1] A three-faced Buddhist deity, great protector of virtue.

During a court banquet, the Emperor gave him thirty horses, all of them white... Once, when construction work on the Nagara Bridge was damaged, he offered his favourite boy attendants as human pillars to propitiate the gods... He had a carbuncle removed from his thigh by a Chinese bonze who had introduced the magical healing methods of a celebrated Chinese physician. If I should recount all the anecdotes, I would never finish. But among all these episodes, none surpasses in horror the story of the Hell scene painted on a screen that is now part of the Lord's family treasure. Even the High Lord, who was usually impassive, seemed to have been utterly shocked by the events. No need to explain that we, his attendants, were frightened out of our wits. In more than twenty years passed in the service of the Lord, I had never witnessed more horrid a spectacle.

But before telling you the story, I must introduce the painter called Yoshihide, the author of the Hell scene on the screen.

II

Yoshihide! Some people may even remember him today. In his time he was considered the first among painters, an unrivalled artist. When what I am going to relate happened, he was already over fifty. At first sight, he appeared to be a short, cantankerous old man, all skin and bone. Each time he came to the Lord's palace, he wore a clove-dyed hunting garment and a floppy *eboshi* on his head, but he had a vulgar appearance and his lips, too red for his age, had an unsettling bestial quality. I do not know for sure the cause of this red colour. Some said he had the habit of licking his paintbrush. Others, more slanderous, compared his appearance and gait to those of a monkey and nicknamed him Saruhide (Monkey-hide).

About this moniker, this is the story I heard. Our Monkeyhide had an only daughter, who was fifteen years old and served as a lady-in-waiting in the Lord's palace. This girl, intelligent and observant beyond her age because she had lost her mother when she was little and had taken care of herself, was charming and very beautiful. For these reasons, she had won the good graces of Her Ladyship and all the waiting ladies.

Someone from the province of Tamba, west of Kyoto, had offered a well-trained monkey to the Lord. The Prince, the Lord's young son, who was at the time in the age of mischievousness, named the monkey Yoshihide. The monkey's gestures were amusing indeed, and everyone in the palace laughed at the animal. If this mockery had been all, things would not have been that bad for the monkey, but each time it climbed up the pine tree in the garden or soiled the mats in the Prince's bedroom, everyone chased him, shouting, 'Yoshihide, Yoshihide,' to tease the poor beast.

One day, Yoshihide's daughter, Yuzuki, passed through the long corridor, carrying a letter attached to a winter-plum branch, when she saw the small monkey come from beyond the sliding door and run toward her. The monkey limped and seemed incapable of climbing up one of the palace columns as she used to do. The Prince ran after the monkey, a switch in his hand, and cried, 'Stop, tangerine thief! Stop.'

At this sight, the young woman stopped for an instant. Just then, the monkey flopped down at her feet, gripped the hem of her kimono and begged her with doleful cries. She could not refrain from feeling compassion. Holding the plum branch with one hand, she picked the monkey up with the other, her long mauve-coloured sleeve flying.

'Lord,' she said in a smoothly agreeable voice, bowing. 'Let me intercede in this monkey's favour. It is only a beast. Prithee, forgive it.'

But the Prince had been chasing the monkey with determination. He made a face and stamped his foot three times. 'Why do you wish to protect it? This monkey is a tangerine thief, I tell you.'

'It is a beast,' she repeated. Then she took on a sad expression and dared say, 'When I hear that name, Yoshihide, I have the impression my father is being reprimanded.'

Hearing this remark, the Prince, arrogant or not, gave in. 'I see. If you ask in the name of your father, I will pardon the monkey.' Then he threw the switch down and went back through the sliding door whence he had come.

III

From that day on, Yoshihide's daughter and the monkey became fast friends. She tied a beautiful red ribbon around the animal's neck, and also hung a tiny bell she had received from the young Princess. The monkey would leave her presence on no account. Once, Yuzuki had to stay in bed with a light cold, and the monkey watched over her, gnawing on its fingernails in apparent concern.

Now things took a peculiar turn. No one would mistreat the monkey any longer. On the contrary, they all began petting it. Not only did the Prince throw persimmons or chestnuts to the monkey, once His Highness became furious because some samurai had shot a kick at the little beast. This news reaching his ears, the Lord gave gracious orders that girl and monkey be brought before his presence. He must also have known why the girl had come to protect the beast.

'You are a good and dutiful daughter,' the Lord said. 'I am pleased with you.' With these words, she received a scarlet *hakama*[2] from the Lord.

The monkey mimicked the girl's deference by raising the hem of the robe to its forehead, to the Lord's immense amusement and pleasure. You can see that the Lord took the young woman into his good grace because he had been impressed with her filial piety, not because he admired her charms, as it was whispered. The rumours might have been justified on some grounds, but I will talk about such things later on. Suffice it to say that the Lord was not one to fall for as lowly a girl as a painter's daughter, no matter how charming.

The girl withdrew from the Lord's presence feeling highly honoured, but being naturally wise and intelligent, she did nothing to awake her fellow maids' jealousy. On the contrary, this honour won the ladies' favour for both herself and her monkey. Her Ladyship loved Yuzuki so much she kept the lady-in-waiting in her constant presence and brought her everywhere she went in her princely carriage.

Now let me set the girl aside for a while as I tell you about her father, Yoshihide. Although Yoshihide the monkey came to be loved by everyone, Yoshihide the painter continued to be hated by everyone. And they went on calling him 'Monkeyhide' behind his back. The residents of the palace were not alone in this general dislike. The great priest of Yokawa, for example, would turn red in the face at the mere mention of Yoshihide's name, as if he had seen a devil (as the rumour had it, Yoshihide had painted the priest in a humoristic scene depicting his conduct, but I know of no foundation proving the rumour true). At any rate, Yoshihide had a bad reputation everywhere. If one or two people did not speak ill of him, they were his fellow painters, who had seen his paintings but had never met him in person.

Not only had Yoshihide a vulgar aspect, he also had such shocking habits that everyone considered him a nuisance. For this reputation, he had no one but himself to blame.

IV

He was avaricious, mean, cowardly, lazy and insatiable, but above all he was insolent and conceited. Always 'I, the greatest painter in Japan' was plastered across his forehead. His bad temperament manifested itself beyond his work, through a profound contempt for all customs and practices in life. According to an apprentice who had lived with him for a long time, one day a spirit was spouting a terrible oracle from the mouth of the famous medium of Higaki. Yoshihide, turning a deaf ear to the oracle, took the brush and ink he always carried and painted the medium's frightening face. Our painter deemed the eventuality of being cursed by a spirit as serious as a child's play.

Yoshihide did inconceivably sacrilegious things. In picturing the goddess Kichijoten, he copied the face of an abject courtesan, and in picturing the King of the Magical Science Fudo, the god that destroys all demons, he copied a thief's figure, and so on, but if someone reprimanded him he answered impudently, 'How strange. Do you really believe the deities Yoshihide painted will hit him with lightning?' When he spoke in this way many of his own disciples took leave of him in fearful anticipation of terrible consequences. In

[2] Very ample trousers with the appearance of a skirt, worn under the kimono.

other words, Yoshihide was arrogance incarnate – he truly thought he was the smartest man under the sun.

No need to say how highly he esteemed himself as a painter. His paintings were so different in brushwork and colouring from those of other painters that many of his colleagues, who were on bad terms with him, considered him an impostor. Several legends affirmed that the famous paintings by the ancient masters like Kawanari, Kanaoka and others were so well rendered that one could smell the fragrance of the plum blossoms painted on the doors as the delicate scent wafted about in the moonlit nights, and one could also hear the courtiers painted on a screen play their flutes. But all the paintings by Yoshihide seemed to elicit disturbing feelings. One would cite the scene of the Goshushoji[3], the cycle of births and deaths, hung on the portal of the Ryugai temple. Each time one passed under the gate at night, one could hear the celestial creatures sigh and sob. Some said they could smell the stench of rotting corpses. As rumour had it, the waiting ladies whose likenesses Yoshihide had painted at the Lord's command all fell ill and died within a few years. According to the slanderers, those events were proofs of Yoshihide's dabbling in black arts. His paintings, the critics said, were cursed. Being an eccentric, Yoshihide took pride in these rumours.

Once, when the Lord told him, as a joke, 'It would seem you are partial to ugliness,' he replied with arrogance, a grin on that strangely red mouth of his, 'That is true, my Lord. It is an unaccomplished artist who cannot perceive beauty in ugliness.'

Notwithstanding his superiority over any other painter in the country, how could he make such a haughty reply to the Lord? His apprentices secretly nicknamed him 'Chira-Eiju.' Maybe you already know that Chira-Eiju was the name of a Tengu[4], who came from China in older times.

[3] The moment of reincarnation in one of the five categories: heavenly creatures, human beings, animals, human beings on the brink of death, damned souls – according to the good or evil deeds committed during the dead person's life.

[4] A long-nosed goblin, synonym of a conceited person.

Nevertheless, even the insufferable, shameless Yoshihide was not without feelings; one, single human emotion remained within him.

V

Yoshihide adored his only daughter, the little lady-in-waiting, and his love for her bordered on madness. As I said before, she was sweet and devoted to her father. It seemed strange that, to this avaricious man, nothing was beautiful enough for his daughter: kimono, hairpins and expensive hairdressers. Although he never contributed his tithes or mites to any Buddhist temple, he doted so much on her no expense was too extravagant for the girl's adornment, although I do not know if this rumour is true. He adored her wildly and madly, and he never gave any thought to finding her a good husband. On the contrary, if anyone had courted her, he would have hired street assassins to get rid of the suitor in the dead of night. When the Lord expressed the wish of having the painter's daughter as a lady-in-waiting, Yoshihide was so displeased he came to the palace with a sour face, even in the presence of the Lord himself. The rumour that the Lord had called the painter's daughter to the palace because he was enamoured of her beauty might have originated in the displeasure the painter bore so openly. I am sure it was mere gossiping, while it was true that Yoshihide adored his daughter and strongly wished to have her at home with him.

One day, Yoshihide painted a cherub in the likeness of one of the Lord's favourite boys. The Lord, pleased, said to the painter, 'Yoshihide, I will grant any request of yours. So tell me what you wish.'

'If it pleases Your Lordship,' Yoshihide dared say. 'Let my daughter be released from your service.'

The painter's reply would have been conceivable if he had answered another lord, but who would have imagined Yoshihide would be so presumptuous as to ask of the Lord Horikawa to let go of his favourite lady-in-waiting, even though Yoshihide loved his daughter so much?

Even though the Lord was very indulgent, he seemed offended. He stared at the painter for a moment, and then he uttered, 'No. I can't grant that,' and left on the spot.

The two of them found themselves in the same situation four or five times. Thinking back on it, I can recall that the Lord's gaze became ever colder when he looked at the painter. And the painter's daughter wept when she was alone in her room, covering her face with the sleeve of her kimono. Thereafter the rumour spread all the more that the Lord was enamoured of the girl.

Some say that the idea of having the scene from Hell painted on the screen originated in the girl's refusal to comply with the Lord's wishes. No. It was only gossip. I am sure of it.

In our opinion, the Lord did not dismiss the girl because he took pity on her and preferred to let her live in ease and comfort rather than send her back to that misanthropic father of hers. It was certain that the Lord felt affection for such a sweet-tempered girl, but to think His Lordship had amorous motives was a farfetched distortion of truth. No, I dare say it was a perfectly unfounded lie.

Because of the painter's insistence on having his daughter back, His Lordship had come to look upon Yoshihide with considerable disfavour. Despite the Lord's feelings about the painter, one day he summoned him to the palace and commanded him to paint a scene from Hell on a screen.

VI

As I evoke the screen, I have the impression of seeing that terrifying scene before my eyes. The scene painted by Yoshihide was quite different from those of other artists, first of all because of its composition. The Ten Kings of Hell and their households were confined to a corner, while all the rest consisted of wild flames roiling around the Mountain of Swords and the Forest of Spears, which seemed ready to take fire as well. Save for the blue and yellow of the Chinese-styled costumes worn by the governors of Hell, which stood out here and there, everything else was ablaze, tongues of fires occupying all the space, hooked wheels dancing in fury, black smoke drawn with splattered ink and sparks shooting up, done in gold smeared and mingled with soot.

These scene would have sufficed to scare the human eye, but one could also see other personages writhing in agony among the flames. None of these characters ever appeared in the representations of Hell painted by other artists. Yoshihide had depicted every social class, from the noble and the dignitary to the beggar and the outcast: mandarins in formal costume, charming young ladies-in-waiting in elaborate five-pleat dresses, bonzes with rosaries hanging from their necks, vagrant clerics wearing high-wedged clogs, very young handmaids in long, clinging kimonos, fortune-tellers in the robes of Shinto priests, holding a holy stick… I would never have the time to describe each of them. These people, tormented by the Gozumezu[5], fled in all directions among fire and smoke, like so many leaves scattered by the tempest. The woman who curled up like a spider, her hair caught in a fork, had probably been a shrine medium or a priestess. The man with the halberd sticking out of his heart, upside down like a vampire bat, must have been a young province governor, or something like it. And the uncountable others, flogged with iron whips, crushed under a rock a thousand men could barely move, pecked by weird birds or slashed open by the maws of a poisonous dragon. The punishments were as numerous as the sinners.

One of these horrors, however, stood out in its own horrifying right, surpassing all the rest.

A carriage pulled by oxen descended from above, grazing the tops of the sword trees, which had branches like animal fangs spitting bodies of dead souls. In the carriage, with its bamboo blinds blown upward by the blast of Hell, a court lady was visible, as splendidly dressed as an empress or an imperial concubine, long black hair streaming and white neck bent backward. Among the flames, the lady writhed in agony. This rendering of a court lady writhing in a flame-wreathed carriage conveyed all the terror of Hell. The frightening intensity of the scene was concentrated on this single personage. It was such an excellent masterpiece the spectator had the impression of hearing desperate screams.

---

[5] Infernal torturers with human bodies and heads of bulls or horses.

To paint that horrible scene, something terrible must have befallen the artist. Otherwise, how could even a painter as great as Yoshihide depict the horror of Hell in such a vivid manner? He must have traded his life to be able to paint that screen. Indeed, the Hell Yoshihide painted was the very Hell to which he had condemned himself.

I am afraid that in my hurry to describe this strange screen, I have lost the thread of my story. So I will return to the moment when Yoshihide received the order to paint the picture of Hell by the Lord.

VII

For five or six months, Yoshihide absorbed himself in the painting of the screen, without making the briefest courtesy call at the palace. It was strange that, despite his love for his daughter, not once had he the thought of seeing her. According to an apprentice, each time he started painting he became like a man possessed by a fox. In fact, the rumour had it that Yoshihide had gained fame and reputation because he had sworn himself to the vulpine god of Good Fortune.

'For proof,' some said, 'snatch a peek at him while he is painting and you will see the spirits of foxes thronging around him.'

Once he had picked up his brush, he forgot everything but his work. He confined himself to his study and never came out to see the sun. Now that he was painting the screen, his level of inspiration soared.

Shut up in his study with the blinds always drawn, he would mix his secret mélanges of colours, and had his apprentices dress up in gala costumes or in poor clothes before painting them with great care in the lamp's light.

These oddities were usual with him. It would not have taken that special Hell scene to drive him to such extreme eccentricities. For instance, when he painted that scene from the Goshushoji, the Five Phases of the Transmigration of Souls, he once came across rotting corpses in the street; he sat down in front of them and copied faces and hands, down to the single hairs, while normal people averted their eyes.

Concerning the state of inspiration in which he painted that scene from Hell, no one was ever able to imagine it. I do not have the time to give you all the particulars and I will tell you only the notable moments.

While one of his disciples was mixing colours, Yoshihide said abruptly. 'I wish to rest for a while. I've had some bad dreams lately.'

'You have, master?' the apprentice said, without interrupting his work, for Yoshihide's wish for rest was nothing unusual.

But then the master asked in humble tones, 'Could you sit at my bedside while I'm resting?'

Even though the apprentice did not understand why the master was so worried about his dreams, the request was reasonable, and he said, 'Very well, sir.' To which the master, sounding troubled, added with some hesitation, 'Come into my inner room. Don't let anyone come inside while I'm sleeping.'

The apprentice remarked that the room in which his master was working – for the 'inner room' meant his study – had the shutters drawn as if it were night, and the screen with the scene sketched in charcoal stood open in the dim light, taking up all the space.

The artist went to sleep with his arm under his head, as if a great fatigue had descended on him, but after half an hour a terrifying noise came to the apprentice's ear.

VIII

At first it was a voice that spoke in an incomprehensible way, but little by little the words broke up to resemble the moans of a drowning man trying to speak underwater.

'How "Come to me"? Where am I supposed to go?... What are you saying?... Where to? To Hell?... Come to the burning Hell? Whoever is this? Who could it be...? Ah!'

The apprentice forgot all about mixing colours to observe the fear on his master's face. He saw him gasping for breath, mouth open and sparse teeth visible; he noticed the dry lips, the sweating face, pale and wrinkled. Something was moving inside the mouth as if pulled by a string. It was the master's tongue. Words came out disconnected.

'I thought… It's really you… I thought you'd come… What? You come to take me away? Yes. Come. Come to Hell. There your daughter is waiting for you.'

The scared apprentice glimpsed a dark figure looming from above and brushing against the open screen. He shook Yoshihide with all his strength, but the master continued speaking in his dream, refusing to awake. The apprentice found the courage to take the water set aside to wash the brushes, and he splashed it all onto the master's face.

The words Yoshihide was saying, 'I'll be waiting. Come with this carriage… with this carriage. Come to Hell…' became groans. Yoshihide sprung up as though he had been stung with a needle, although he seemed to be seeing someone, as if the evil spirits from his nightmares were still hanging upon his eyelids. For a moment he stared at nothing, eyes full of dread and mouth gaping. Then, returning to his senses, he ordered curtly, 'It's all right. Off with you now.'

Knowing very well he would be scolded if he tried to object, the apprentice ran out of his master's room and, when he saw the sunshine, he felt relieved as if he had awakened from his own nightmare.

That was not the worst of it. A month later, another apprentice was called into Yoshihide's study. The master, who was moistening a brush in his mouth, turned to him and said, 'Strip down, please.'

As the painter used to give that order from time to time, the boy immediately took off his clothes.

When the boy was completely naked, Yoshihide said with a strange scowl on his face and no compassion in his eyes, 'I'd like to see a man in chains. I'm sorry but you should let me do what I want to do for a while.'

This apprentice was a burly young man who could have wielded a sword better than a brush. Nevertheless, he must have been scared to death if even after years he kept repeating, 'I believed the master had gone mad and wanted to kill me.'

Yoshihide, seeing the apprentice hesitate, lost patience. He produced a thin iron chain out of nowhere, sprang onto the boy's back, and wrenched the chain around his body and finally he yanked at the chain with such merciless force that the apprentice fell, his body hitting the floor with a mighty noise.

IX

The apprentice's figure resembled a wine keg rolled over on its side because the boy's limbs were so cruelly bent and twisted he could move nothing but his neck. Because of the arrested blood circulation, his thick body, face, chest and limbs had become red and then livid in no time. Yoshihide did not heed the boy's pain and, walking around that keg-shaped body, sketched him from various angles in a realistic fashion. No need to tell what torture the apprentice suffered while his master worked.

If nothing had happened, the apprentice would have had to bear the pain for a long time. Fortunately – or unfortunately – from an upturned jar flowed an undulating thin ribbon that elongated like black oil. At first, the liquid came out slowly, like a very thick, sticky fluid, but little by little the glistening thing glided up to the nose of the frightened boy, who stopped breathing for a second and then screamed, 'A snake! A snake!'

The boy told me that his blood had frozen, but this sensation was natural as the snake was about to touch his chained neck with the tip of its ice-cold tongue. Seeing his apprentice in such a plight, even the cruel Yoshihide became frightened. Upset, he cast away his brush and with a swift gesture, picked up the snake by the tail, letting its head dangle. The snake tried to coil around itself but could not reach Yoshihide's hand.

'My sketch is ruined and it's your fault, damned beast,' he said to the snake, and threw it back into its jar. Mumbling, he undid the chain and freed his apprentice, who got not a single word of sympathy or consolation from his master. A ruined sketch saddened Yoshihide more than having one of his apprentices bitten by a snake.

Later I was told that he kept the snake for the purpose of making sketches of it.

After what you have heard so far, you must have

a fair idea of Yoshihide's madness when inspiration possessed him. But let me recount one more episode. This time, an apprentice of thirteen or fourteen almost lost his life because of the screen. One night, Yoshihide called this boy, who had the white complexion of a girl, to his study. In the light of the oil lamp, the apprentice saw the master feeding an exotic bird something that, placed on his palm, resembled raw meat. The bird, as big as a cat, had feathers sticking out of its ears and large round amber-coloured eyes that made it look like a cat indeed.

X

Yoshihide by nature hated people prying in his business. He had told nothing to his apprentices about the snake because he never said anything about the material he kept in his study. Once the boys glimpsed a human skull on the master's desk. Another time they saw silver bowls and lacquered platters or other unusual items, depending on what he was painting, but no one knew where he kept these things. Whence originated the rumour of a benevolent deity bestowing favours on Yoshihide.

The apprentice who entered thought the strange bird was in the study to provide a model for the screen. He bowed and respectfully addressed the master. 'What do you wish, sir?'

Instead of answering, the master licked his red-stained lips and thrust his chin in the bird's direction. 'Look how tame it is.'

'What's this creature, sir? I've never seen anything like it.' The apprentice, curious and diffident, ogled the strange bird that had cat-like ears of feathers.

Yoshihide, in his customary disparaging tones, said, 'You've never seen it before? That's the problem with you town-bred folks. This bird is a horned owl a hunter from Kurama gave me yesterday. Mind you, not many owls are as tame as this one.' He slowly raised his hand and ruffled the owl's feathers. The bird, which had just finished eating, flew up from the desk with a threatening screech and threw itself into the boy's face, talons first. If the apprentice had not raised both arms to protect his face with the kimono sleeves, he would have collected a cut or two.

'Ah!' The apprentice screamed and waved his sleeves to drive the owl away but the bird swooped down on him and clicked its beak, taking advantage of the slightest unguarded movement to peck at him. The boy forgot all about being in his master's presence. He ran to and fro in the study, jumping up and throwing himself to the floor to escape the talons. The bird followed him and darted at his eyes. Each time the owl spread its wings, the boy smelt odours of rotting leaves, waterfalls, soured fruit or monkey-wine. Remembering the event, the apprentice said the oil lamp shone like moonlight and the master's study had become a narrow valley lost in the mystery of a ghastly mountain.

Although he was terrified by the owl, the master's conduct frightened him even more. Yoshihide, impassive, watched the smooth-faced boy being disfigured by the bird, and calmly sketched the scene on a leaf of paper he had unrolled for the occasion. When the apprentice saw Yoshihide in the process of painting, horror thickened his blood. The master had called him to see him die.

XI

The apprentice might have been right in thinking the master had wanted to kill him. In truth, Yoshihide had planned to infuriate the owl and then set it on the boy to paint him running about in terror.

When the boy realised what his master had in mind, he collapsed by the door, hiding his face behind his kimono sleeves and screaming incoherent words. He heard his master rising. Right then, something fell with a loud noise and broke. The bird's wings flapped faster. The apprentice raised his head and saw that the room had turned pitch black. The master's irritated voice called the disciples. One of them replied from a distance and came running with some fire.

In the pale, sooty light of the torch, they saw the light-stand had been knocked down and the oil of the broken lamp formed a pool on the mats. The horned owl tossed about on the floor, flapping only one of its wings. Yoshihide, frightened despite what we know about him, mumbled from behind his desk.

A black snake had coiled itself around the owl, from the neck to the wing. It turned out the apprentice had upturned the jar, freeing the snake. The owl had pounced on it. For a while, the two apprentices watched the battle with gaping mouths, exchanging bemused glances, but soon they bowed to their master and left without a word. Nobody knows what became of the owl and the snake.

I could recount several episodes of this kind. The High Lord had ordered the screen decorated with a picture from Hell at the beginning of autumn. During all winter, the disciples worried about their master. Toward the end of winter, Yoshihide seemed unable to continue his work and became gloomier than ever, while his language turned more aggressive. The sketch, complete at eighty percent, displayed no further progress. The master appeared so dissatisfied everyone thought he was about to erase what he had already sketched.

No one knew what prevented Yoshihide from working, and no one tried to find out. The apprentices, wary after so many incidents, gave Yoshihide a wide berth, as anyone would do if forced to live in the same cage with a tiger or a wolf.

XII

As a consequence, I do not have much to say about that period. If I had to add anything, I would say that the stubborn old man had become so maudlin he would sometimes be found weeping alone in his room.

Once, an apprentice went out into the garden and stumbled across his master. All teary, Yoshihide gazed at the sky, which brought the promise of spring. Embarrassed, the disciple slipped away. It was such a strange spectacle, this man so merciless he could paint corpses in the street for the Goshuyoji scene, but now weeping like a child because he was unable to work on the screen.

While Yoshihide was absorbed in his work with the intensity of a madman, his daughter became more cheerless by the day and it was clear to us she was trying to hold back her tears. Her face, white and melancholic by nature, now displaying black circles under eyes shadowed by heavy eyelashes, gave her a tragic composure. Sad and lonesome, she appeared to have retreated into her inner self. Various guesses were made, such as 'She misses her father and her home,' or 'She's in love.' As soon as a rumour spread that the Lord wanted to submit her to his desire, the good people stopped talking about the painter's daughter, as if they had forgotten all about her.

Just about this time, as I happened to pass by the corridor in the dead of night, the monkey Yoshihide bounded toward me and persistently pulled at the hem of my *hakama*. It was a mild night bathed in moonlight and charged with the sweet scent of plum blossoms. In the dim light of the moon, I could see the monkey baring its teeth under a wrinkled nose. The beast screamed wildly. Feeling three parts of fear and seven of anger, as I was afraid the monkey would ruin my new *hakama*, I was tempted to kick the beast and go my way when I remembered the samurai who had mistreated the monkey and had received a reprimand from the Prince. Moreover, the monkey's behaviour indicated that something unusual might have happened. I let myself be pulled by the monkey for five *ken* or so.

I took a turn in the corridor, in the direction of a placid pond that glistened pale in the darkness behind a pine with finely shaped branches.

From a room nearby came the noise of an altercation that sounded both passionate and strangely muffled. All was stillness in a dim light that came half from the moon, half from the moonlight reflected by the haze. A great silence reigned, save for the splashing of fish in the pond. And those stifled sounds intruded on this calm, thus the quarrel stopped me. Intrigued, I tiptoed up to the sliding door, ready to deal blows if the arguing people turned out to be rascals.

XIII

The monkey Yoshihide found my approach too slow. Shrieking as if someone had been strangling its neck, the monkey ran around me three times and finally leapt onto my shoulder. I turned my head quickly to the side to avoid the tiny claws, and the monkey gripped my sleeve to hold on. Losing balance, I staggered back and bumped against the sliding door. Now I was forced to act. I threw the door open and was about to rush into the room, beyond the reach of the moonlight, when a young woman bolted out the doorway as if propelled by a spring. She almost bumped into me, stumbled and fell. Kneeling there, she gazed up at me, dishevelled, out of breath and trembling all over as though still under the impression of a dreadful sight.

I need not tell you I was in the presence of Yoshihide's daughter. But that night she looked so different, so lively. Her eyes sparkled, large and bright; her cheeks glowed with a rosy blaze. In her untied nightgown, she was alluring, quite unlike her customary childish innocence. How could this attractive creature be the painter's daughter, who was so fragile and modest?

Steadying myself against the door, I observed the beautiful girl in the moonlight.

Hurrying footfalls came from a masculine figure receding into the dark.

I pointed in the man's direction and asked in a calm voice, 'Who is this?'

The girl bit her lip and shook her head. She appeared to be much chagrined.

I stooped down and whispered into her ear, 'Who was that man?'

She shook her head and pressed her lips together. Tears filled her long-lashed eyes.

On account of my inborn stupidity, I only understand what shines as clear as daylight under my nose. Not knowing what to say, I remained rooted to the spot as if I were trying to hear her thumping heart. For one thing, I did not wish to be harsh and prod her with more questions.

I do not know how long I remained stock still, saying nothing. Finally, I shut the door and turned to the girl, who seemed to have recovered a little. As gently as possible, I told her, 'Now go back to your room.'

Tormented by the sensation of having witnessed something I was not supposed to see, and ashamed – of what, I do not know – I strode back to the place I had left to follow the monkey. Hardly had I taken ten steps than someone tugged timidly at the hem of my *hakama* from behind. In surprise, I glanced over my shoulder. Can you guess who it was?

The monkey Yoshihide gave little bows with its head, hands placed on the ground to express gratitude like a man. The gold bell at its neck tinkled.

XIV

Two weeks had passed when Yoshihide the painter showed himself at the palace without being requested and begged the Lord's personal audience. He believed his wish would be granted, given the consideration in which the Lord held him in spite of his humble origins.

The Lord, who did not admit people in his presence easily, made an exception. The painter, sporting his customary orange hunting garment and floppy cap, and looking more sullen than usual, prostrated himself, bowing his head repeatedly. Raising his chin he said in a hoarse voice, 'Concerning the screen Your Lordship was pleased to command, I would like to tell Your Lordship I have applied myself to the task night and day and have very nearly finished the work.'

'Excellent. I am pleased to hear it.' Nevertheless, the Lord's voice lacked conviction.

'No, my Lord.' Yoshihide lowered his eyes, as though plagued with dissatisfaction. 'It is almost finished but there is one detail I am unable to paint.'

'What? Is there something in the world you cannot paint?'

'Yes, my Lord. I cannot paint anything if I don't see it with my own eyes. If I paint something I haven't seen I cannot convince myself my rendering is exact. Isn't it like being unable to paint?'

A scornful smile crept across the Lord's face. 'So, if you have to paint Hell, you mean you need to see it?'

'Precisely. A few years ago, when there was a big fire, I saw a burning Hell. That's why I was able to paint the scene of "Buddha unmoving among the flames." Your Lordship must know that painting.'

'What about the damned? Did you see them as well?' The Lord put question upon question, as if he did not wish to hear Yoshihide's answers.

'I've seen a man bound in iron chains. I have made detailed sketches of one beleaguered by an ominous bird. So it can't be said that I know nothing about the suffering of the damned subjected to various torments. As for the infernal torturers – ' Here Yoshihide paused, an enigmatic grin on his face. 'Infernal torturers appeared to me in my dreams. Almost every day and night bull-headed, horse-headed, or three-faced, six-armed demons arrow and torment me, beckoning me to follow them and moving their silent lips. Those aren't the things I cannot paint.'

Astonished by Yoshihide's words, the Lord glared at Yoshihide for a moment and then, frowning, he cried, 'Then what is it that you can't paint?'

XV

'In the central leaf of the screen, I would like to paint a nobleman's carriage with a roof of palm leaves, falling from the sky,' said Yoshihide, looking the Lord intensely in the eyes.

I had heard that when he spoke about his work, the painter would speak insanely. And in that moment, his gaze displayed madness. 'In the vehicle, a splendid court lady writhes in the agony of death, her long black hair tossed by the wind. Her face, smothered by the smoke, should look upward to the carriage ceiling, her eyebrows furrowed. Trying to escape the sparks raining over her, she grips the mats with both hands. Around the carriage, a flock of ominous birds fly about, clicking their beaks… Oh, how can I ever paint a court lady in a burning carriage?'

'Mmm… and…?' The Lord urged Yoshihide to continue as if he found the painter's words amusing for some reason.

'I cannot paint it,' Yoshihide repeated, entranced, his red-stained lips trembling as if he had a fever. Then he became animated and said in biting tones, 'Please, my Lord, burn a nobleman's carriage before my eyes. And, if possible…'

The Lord's face darkened for an instant, but a second later he burst into laughter. 'All your wishes shall be granted.' Half choking in his merriment, he added, 'Don't worry.'

The Lord's words struck me and a terrible premonition gripped my chest. The Lord seemed infected with Yoshihide's madness. White froth gathered at the corners of his mouth and his eyebrows twitched. As he paused, his throat still vibrated with laughter.

'Yes, I shall burn a carriage with a roof of palm leaves. A splendid girl dressed like a court lady of the highest station shall ride in the carriage. She shall perish in the carriage, tormented by the black smoke and consumed by the fire. Bravo. It is an excellent idea, worthy of the greatest painter in the whole country. I praise you. I praise you highly.'

Upon hearing these words, Yoshihide turned pale and tried to move his lips as if he were suffocating. But then he set his hands on the mat and bowed, saying, 'I am grateful, my Lord,' in a voice so low as to be hardly audible.

Perhaps the Lord's words had illustrated the horror of the scheme Yoshihide himself had suggested, and the images must have flashed vividly in his mind. Only this once in my life did I take pity of the man.

XVI

A few days later, as promised, the High Lord summoned Yoshihide to witness the burning of a nobleman's carriage right before his eyes, although this event did not take place on the grounds of the Lord's mansion of Horikawa. The carriage was burnt in the mountain mansion of Yukige, the 'Limit of the Snow,' where the Lord's sister had once lived.

No one had inhabited the house for years and the vast garden was said to be in state of total neglect. In those days, many rumours concerned the fate of the High Lord's late sister. Some said that on moonless nights, her crimson *hakama* could be seen moving along the corridors without touching the floor.

These rumours of gloomy apparitions stemmed from the lonely and desolate nature of the neighbourhood even in the daylight. After dark, the murmur of a torrent added a note of melancholy while night herons fluttered about in the starlight, like winged monsters.

In the pitch-black, moonless night, torches shed light on the Lord who, dressed in a yellow-green kimono and a brocaded purple *hakama*, sat cross-legged near the veranda, on a round white cushion hemmed with bicoloured silk. Five or six samurai encircled him in respectful poses. One stood out among them, a man solidly built who had eaten human flesh out of starvation after the battle of Michinogu and was now so strong he could break apart the horns of a living deer. Wearing armour under his kimono and clad in full dignity, he kept by the veranda, the tip of his sheathed katana pointed upward. The scene turned bright or dark according to the movements of the torches that flickered in the night breeze, blurring the boundaries of dream and reality, with a ghastly effect.

A carriage roofed with palm leaves was stationed in the garden, within a patch of darkness, with no oxen, its shafts resting on their supports, its gilded fittings glittering like stars. When we saw it, a chill came over us even though it was spring. Blue-green tasselled blinds trimmed with embroideries hid the interior. A few servants, serious-faced and stiff, stood near the carriage, carrying blazing torches, and worried about the smoke that drifted toward the veranda.

Yoshihide, the hero of this night, kneeled opposite the veranda, in his usual hunting attire and worn floppy cap. He looked even smaller and more miserable, as if the sky were weighing down on him. The man who squatted behind him, dressed in a similar fashion, was probably one of his disciples. As both of them knelt in the dark, the colours of their garments were not clearly discernible from my position inside the veranda.

XVII

The time was near midnight. In a silence so deep we could hear our breathing, darkness seemed to spy on us while the nocturnal breeze carried the sooty smell of burning torches in our direction. For a moment, the Lord gazed at the scene in silence. Then he leant forward on his cushion and called harshly, 'Yoshihide!'

I am not sure Yoshihide answered because my ears caught only a moan.

'Yoshihide, tonight I will set fire to the carriage as you wished.' The Lord glanced sideways at his samurai. I had the impression he was exchanging a knowing smile with them, but perhaps it was only my imagination.

Yoshihide, very stiff, looked at the veranda in a reverent manner and said nothing.

'Look at the carriage. It's mine. You surely recognise it. I will set fire to the carriage and create a blazing Hell before your eyes but...' The Lord exchanged another glance with his samurai and then resumed speaking in bitter tones. 'In the carriage lies a sinful woman, bound in chains. As soon as the carriage will take fire, she will die in terrible agony. It is the perfect model to finish your painting. Watch closely as her snow-white skin burns and sparks braid her black hair.'

The Lord paused again, shaking his shoulders in silent laughter, and then he said, 'A spectacle worthy of entering the chronicles. I will appreciate it as well. There, raise the blind and let Yoshihide see the woman inside the carriage.'

At his command, one of the attendants, holding his torch high, yanked the blind up. The red blazing light from his torch illuminated a woman cruelly bound in chains, reclining on the seat. Golden ornaments glittered in her black hair, which hung loose about her shoulders over a gorgeous Chinese gown of a cherry-blossom colour.

I very nearly cried out. Who could have mistaken her? The trim maidenly figure and the lovely melancholy profile belonged to Yoshihide's daughter.

The samurai sitting opposite me rose and gave Yoshihide a sharp glance, his hand on the hilt of his katana. Mouth gaping, I pivoted to see Yoshihide, who had sprung to his feet like a madman and attempted to rush toward the carriage, arms extended in front of him.

As I already said, he was in the darkness, and I could not see the expression on his face. But soon he was running into the light as though pulled by an invisible string. At the same time, the Lord cried, 'Set fire!' The attendants threw their torches at the carriage with the girl inside. The carriage was engulfed in a pillar of raging flames.

XVIII

The flames enveloped the carriage in no time. As soon as the purple tassels hanging from the roof waved in the sudden wind, a vortex of smoke spiralled up against the black sky, and sparks exploded like sprays of water. Bamboo blinds, hangings and metal fittings burst into so many balls of fire, soaring into the night like celestial orbs spurting out of a fallen sun. A moment before I had nearly cried out. Now I was so dumbfounded I could do nothing but gape at this terrifying spectacle. But as for the father, Yoshihide...

The expression painted on Yoshihide's face is still alive in my memory. The man, who on impulse had attempted to rush at the carriage, stopped before the roaring fire and, with his arms outstretched, fastened his gaze on the flames and the heavy smoke that enveloped the burning shape. Sparks fell around him, bathing his features in a lurid light so that his ugly wrinkled face was visible down to the tip of his beard.

His wide-open eyes, twisted lips and twitching cheeks, showed the terror, despair and astonishment that alternated in his heart. Neither the robbers about to be beheaded nor the most odious of sinners of 'Ten Crimes and Five Faults' dragged before the Ten Judge-Kings could have worn a more mournful expression. Even the herculean samurai paled and shot a furtive glance at his Lord.

The Lord, however, lips pressed together and wearing an enigmatic grin, kept his gaze fixed on the carriage. And inside the carriage... I lack the courage to convey a detailed description of the girl I saw in it: the paleness of her face tilted back and choked by the smoke, the length of her black hair intertwined with flames as she tried to shake off the spreading fire, the beauty of the cherry-blossom-coloured Chinese dress, which the flames were devouring by the minute – what a terrible and cruel scene. At one moment, the breeze blew the smoke to the other side, and among the red flames sprinkled with golden dust appeared the girl, biting on her gag and writhing to the point of breaking the chain that bounded her.

This atrocious torture resembled a genuine scene from Hell brought before our very eyes. Facing the spectacle, we all – even that samurai with supernatural strength – shuddered.

Then once again we thought that a gust of wind had blasted through the trees. Following the noise, something dark, hardly visible, shot across the black sky like a ball, without either touching the ground or flying through the air. From the roof of the mansion, the thing dived straight into the burning carriage. And through the crimson-lacquered chassis that was crumbling in pieces, among whirls of fire we saw something clasp the shoulders of the girl, who arched her body backwards. The thing gave a long and piercing screech out of the soaring smoke, a shriek like the tearing of silk. One more screech. And another. We could not help letting out a scream of surprise in unison. Against a red curtain of flames, the creature that was holding fast to the dying girl was the monkey nicknamed Yoshihide at the palace of Horikawa.

XIX

But, a second later, the monkey disappeared. When sparks shot into the night, glittering like a pear peel sprinkled with gold, girl and beast sank under a whirl of black smoke. In the middle of the garden, only the burning carriage was visible as it blazed away with terrifying crackles. 'A pillar of fire' might have been more appropriate than 'burning carriage' to describe the blaze that soared into thc starry sky.

Before the pillar of fire, Yoshihide stood still, rooted to the ground. What a strange transformation. The old wrinkled face, which only a minute before had expressed agony at the infernal spectacle, now radiated a blissful ecstasy. Arms tightly crossed on his chest, he seemed to have forgotten he was in the presence of the High Lord. His eyes did not mirror the girl's atrocious agony any longer. Did the form of the thrashing body silhouetted by the wonderful red colour satisfy him?

The strangeness went beyond the sight of this father ecstatically watching his daughter's agony. At that moment, Yoshihide incarnated a solemn exaltation elevated beyond the human condition, some supernatural dignity similar to the King Lion's wrath in his nocturnal appearances. Even the uncountable, soulless night birds scattered by the flames seemed aware of the mysterious virtue that shone like a halo over Yoshihide's worn cap.

If the birds were scared, so much more were we, the humans, down to the menials. We held our breath and, shivering, watched Yoshihide with the same wonderment we would have felt at the unveiling ceremony of a newly made Buddhist image. Those sputtering flames soaring, immense, into the sky, and Yoshihide who stood, petrified and absorbed in the tragic spectacle. Such greatness and joy.

But the Lord, who sat in the veranda, fairly removed from the great fire, was as pale as a spectre. White froth at the corners of his mouth, he gasped like a thirsty animal, grasping tightly his knee draped in the purple *hakama* – with both hands.

XX

I don't know who spread the story of a carriage burnt with a woman inside, but I know it reached every corner of the country. Many wondered why the Lord had burned Yoshihide's daughter alive. Most people thought it was vengeance for the Lord's thwarted love, although in my opinion the Lord had wanted to chastise the perversity of a painter who had not hesitated in asking that a carriage be burnt before his eyes, even though it involved the sacrifice of a human being, to paint a scene to perfection. This last explanation came from the Lord's very mouth.

Since Yoshihide had such a heart of stone he could witness the death of his own daughter, some accused him of being a devil who had sacrificed his paternal love for the sake of his art. The great priest of Yokawa supported this view: 'Whatever talent they may have in any branch of learning or art, those who did not live according to the five virtues of Confucius, benevolence, justice, courtesy, wisdom and fidelity, are to be condemned to Hell.'

One month later, when the screen decorated with the scene from Hell was complete, Yoshihide took it to the palace and presented it to the Lord, with all his respect. The great priest, who happened to be there, as soon as he glanced at the screen, was surely struck by the realism of the infernal horrors, a firestorm raging from the sky to the abyss of Hell. Although he had glared angrily at Yoshihide at first, he cried, 'Bravo!' tapping his knee in an involuntary gesture. I still remember the Lord drawing a forced smile at the priest's ejaculation.

From that day on, no one, at least in the palace, spoke ill of the painter. Those who looked at the screen, even though they hated the personage, were impressed with that mysterious solemnity and with the ghastly realism of Hell's torments, as if they could feel the bite of the infernal fire.

By then, Yoshihide had already departed this life.

The night after he completed his painting, he threw a rope over a beam in his room and hanged himself. Perhaps Yoshihide, who had survived his beloved daughter's untimely death, could not bear the idea of surviving her absence for long. His body is buried under the ruins of his house. After scores of years, wind and rain have worn down the small tombstone, and moss has covered the barrow, erasing all trace of his grave.

UNSEEN – UNFEARED

Francis Stevens

Francis Stevens (1883–1948), was the pen name of Gertrude Barrows Bennett, the first major American female writer of fantasy and science fiction. Stevens wrote a number of acclaimed fantasies between 1917 and 1923 and has been called 'the woman who invented dark fantasy'. Among her most famous books are *Claimed* (1920), which H. P. Lovecraft called, 'One of the strangest and most compelling science fantasy novels you will ever read'. She also wrote the lost world novel *The Citadel of Fear* (1918) and an early dystopian novel titled *The Heads of Cerberus* (1919). Although not all of Stevens' work has dated well, 'Unseen – Unfeared' remains a potent example of the classic weird tale.

I had been dining with my ever-interesting friend, Mark Jenkins, at a little Italian restaurant near South Street. It was a chance meeting. Jenkins is too busy, usually, to make dinner engagements. Over our highly seasoned food and sour, thin, red wine, he spoke of little odd incidents and adventures of his profession. Nothing very vital or important, of course. Jenkins is not the sort of detective who first detects and then pours the egotistical and revealing details of achievement in the ears of every acquaintance, however appreciative.

But when I spoke of something I had seen in the morning papers, he laughed. 'Poor old "Doc" Holt! Fascinating old codger, to anyone who really knows him. I've had his friendship for years – since I was first on the city force and saved a young assistant of his from jail on a false charge. And they had to drag him into the poisoning of this young sport, Ralph Peeler!'

'Why are you so sure he couldn't have been implicated?' I asked.

But Jenkins only shook his head, with a quiet smile. 'I have reasons for believing otherwise,' was all I could get out of him on that score. 'But,' he added, 'the only reason he was suspected at all is the superstitious dread of these ignorant people around him. Can't see why he lives in such a place. I know for a fact he doesn't have to. Doc's got money of his own. He's an amateur chemist and dabbler in different sorts of research work, and I suspect he's been guilty of "showing off". Result, they all swear he has the evil eye and holds forbidden communion with invisible powers. Smoke?'

Jenkins offered me one of his invariably good cigars, which I accepted, saying thoughtfully: 'A man has no right to trifle with the superstitions of ignorant people. Sooner or later, it spells trouble.'

'Did in his case. They swore up and down that he sold love charms openly and poisons secretly, and that, together with his living so near to – somebody else – got him temporarily suspected. But my tongue's running away with me, as usual!'

'As usual,' I retorted impatiently, 'you open up with all the frankness of a Chinese diplomat.'

He beamed upon me engagingly and rose from the table, with a glance at his watch. 'Sorry to leave you, Blaisdell, but I have to meet Jimmy Brennan in ten minutes.'

He so clearly did not invite my further company that I remained seated for a little while after his departure; then took my own way homeward. Those streets always held for me a certain fascination, particularly at night. They are so unlike the rest of the city, so foreign in appearance, with their little shabby stores, always open until late evening, their unbelievably cheap goods, displayed as much outside the shops as in them, hung on the fronts and laid out on tables by the curb and in the street itself. Tonight, however, neither people nor stores in any sense appealed to me. The mixture of Italians, Jews and a few Negroes, mostly bareheaded, unkempt and generally unhygienic in appearance, struck me as merely revolting. They were all humans, and I, too, was human. Some way I did not like the idea.

Puzzled a trifle, for I am more inclined to sympathize with poverty than accuse it, I watched the faces that I passed. Never before had I observed how bestial, how brutal were the countenances of the dwellers in this region. I actually shuddered when an old-clothes man, a gray-bearded Hebrew, brushed me as he toiled past with his barrow.

There was a sense of evil in the air, a warning of things which it is wise for a clean man to shun and keep clear of. The impression became so strong that before I had walked two squares I began to feel physically ill. Then it occurred to me that the one glass of cheap Chianti I had drunk might have something to do with the feeling. Who knew how that stuff had been manufactured, or whether the juice of the grape entered at all into its ill-flavored composition? Yet I doubted if that were the real cause of my discomfort.

By nature I am rather a sensitive, impressionable sort of chap. In some way tonight this neighborhood, with its sordid sights and smells, had struck me wrong.

My sense of impending evil was merging into actual fear. This would never do. There is only one way to deal with an imaginative temperament like mine – conquer its vagaries. If I left South Street with this nameless dread upon me, I could never pass down it again without a recurrence of the feeling. I should simply have to stay here until I got the better of it – that was all.

I paused on a corner before a shabby but brightly lighted little drug store. Its gleaming windows and the luminous green of its conventional glass show jars made the brightest spot on the block. I realized that I was tired, but hardly wanted to go in there and rest. I knew what the company would be like at its shabby, sticky soda fountain. As I stood there, my eyes fell on a long white canvas sign across from me, and its black-and-red lettering caught my attention.

SEE THE GREAT UNSEEN!
Come in! This Means You!
FREE TO ALL!

A museum of fakes, I thought, but also reflected that if it were a show of some kind I could sit down for a while, rest, and fight off this increasing obsession of nonexistent evil. That side of the street was almost deserted, and the place itself might well be nearly empty.

II

I walked over, but with every step my sense of dread increased. Dread of I knew not what. Bodiless, inexplicable horror had me as in a net, whose strands, being intangible, without reason for existence, I could by no means throw off. It was not the people now. None of them were about me. There, in the open, lighted street, with no sight nor sound of terror to assail me, I was the shivering victim of such fear as I had never known was possible. Yet still I would not yield.

Setting my teeth, and fighting with myself as with some pet animal gone mad, I forced my steps to slowness and walked along the sidewalk, seeking entrance. Just here there were no shops, but several doors reached in each case by means of a few iron-railed stone steps. I chose the one in the middle beneath the sign. In that neighborhood there are museums, shops and other commercial enterprises conducted in many shabby old residences, such as were these. Behind the glazing of the door I had chosen I could see a dim, pinkish light, but on either side the windows were quite dark.

Trying the door, I found it unlocked. As I opened it a party of Italians passed on the pavement below and I looked back at them over my shoulder. They were gayly dressed, men, women and children, laughing and chattering to one another; probably on their way to some wedding or other festivity.

In passing, one of the men glanced up at me and involuntarily I shuddered back against the door. He was a young man, handsome after the swarthy manner of his race, but never in my life had I seen a face so expressive of pure, malicious cruelty, naked and unashamed. Our eyes met and his seemed to light up with a vile gleaming, as if all the wickedness of his nature had come to a focus in the look of concentrated hate he gave me.

They went by, but for some distance I could see him watching me, chin on shoulder, till he and his party were swallowed up in the crowd of marketers farther down the street.

Sick and trembling from that encounter, merely of eyes though it had been, I threw aside my partly smoked cigar and entered. Within there was a small vestibule, whose ancient tesselated floor was grimy with the passing of many feet. I could feel the grit of dirt under my shoes, and it rasped on my rawly quivering nerves. The inner door stood partly open, and going on I found myself in a bare, dirty hallway, and was greeted by the sour, musty, poverty-stricken smell common to dwellings of the very ill-to-do. Beyond there was a stairway, carpeted with ragged grass matting. A gas jet, turned low inside a very dusty pink globe, was the light I had seen from without.

Listening, the house seemed entirely silent. Surely, this was no place of public amusement of any kind whatever. More likely it was a rooming house, and I had, after all, mistaken the entrance.

To my intense relief, since coming inside, the worst agony of my unreasonable terror had passed away. If I could only get in some place where I could sit down and be quiet, probably I should be rid of it for good. Determining to try another entrance, I was about to leave the bare hallway when one of several doors along the side of it suddenly opened and a man stepped out into the hall.

'Well?' he said, looking at me keenly, but with not the least show of surprise at my presence.

'I beg your pardon,' I replied. 'The door was unlocked and I came in here, thinking it was the entrance to the exhibit – what do they call it? the "Great Unseen." The one that is mentioned on that long white sign. Can you tell me which door is the right one?'

'I can.'

With that brief answer he stopped and stared at me again. He was a tall, lean man, somewhat stooped, but possessing considerable dignity of bearing. For that neighborhood, he appeared uncommonly well dressed, and his long, smooth-shaven face was noticeable because, while his complexion was dark and his eyes coal-black, above them the heavy brows and his hair were almost silvery-white. His age might have been anything over the threescore mark.

I grew tired of being stared at. 'If you can and – won't, then never mind,' I observed a trifle irritably, and turned to go. But his sharp exclamation halted me.

'No!' he said. 'No – no! Forgive me for pausing – it was not hesitation, I assure you. To think that one – one, even, has come! All day they pass my sign up there – pass and fear to enter. But you are different. You are not of these timorous, ignorant foreign peasants. You ask me to tell you the right door? Here it is! Here!'

And he struck the panel of the door, which he had closed behind him, so that the sharp yet hollow sound of it echoed up through the silent house.

Now it may be thought that after all my senseless terror in the open street, so strange a welcome from so odd a showman would have brought the feeling back, full force. But there is an emotion stronger, to a certain point, than fear. This queer old fellow aroused my curiosity. What kind of museum could it be that he accused the passing public of fearing to enter? Nothing really terrible, surely, or it would have been closed by the police. And normally I am not an unduly timorous person. 'So it's in there, is it?' I asked, coming toward him. 'And I'm to be the sole audience? Come, that will be an interesting experience.' I was half laughing now.

'The most interesting in the world,' said the old man, with a solemnity which rebuked my lightness.

With that he opened the door, passed inward and closed it again – in my very face. I stood staring at it blankly. The panels, I remember, had been originally painted white, but now the paint was flaked and blistered, gray with dirt and dirty finger marks. Suddenly it occurred to me that I had no wish to enter there. Whatever was behind it could be scarcely worth seeing, or he would not choose such a place for its exhibition. With the old man's vanishing my curiosity had cooled, but just as I again turned to leave, the door opened and this singular showman stuck his white-eyebrowed face through the aperture. He was frowning impatiently. 'Come in – come in!' he snapped, and promptly withdrawing his head, once more closed the door.

'He has something there he doesn't want should get out,' was the very natural conclusion which I drew. 'Well, since it can hardly be anything dangerous, and he's so anxious I should see it – here goes!'

With that I turned the soiled white porcelain handle, and entered.

The room I came into was neither very large nor very brightly lighted. In no way did it resemble a museum or lecture room. On the contrary, it seemed to have been fitted up as a quite well-appointed laboratory. The floor was linoleum-covered, there were glass cases along the walls whose shelves were filled with bottles, specimen jars, graduates, and the like. A large table in one corner bore what looked like some odd sort of camera, and a larger one in the middle of the room was fitted with a long rack filled with bottles and test tubes, and was besides littered with papers, glass slides, and various paraphernalia which my ignorance failed to identify. There were several cases of books, a few plain wooden chairs, and in the corner a large iron sink with running water.

My host of the white hair and black eyes was awaiting me, standing near the larger table. He indicated one of the wooden chairs with a thin forefinger that shook a little, either from age or eagerness. 'Sit down – sit down! Have no fear but that you will be interested, my friend. Have no fear at all – of anything!'

As he said it he fixed his dark eyes upon me and stared harder than ever. But the effect of his words was the opposite of their meaning. I did sit down, because my knees gave under me, but if in the outer hall I had lost my terror, it now returned twofold upon me. Out there the light had been faint, dingily roseate, indefinite. By it I had not perceived how this old man's face was a mask of living malice – of cruelty, hate and a certain masterful contempt. Now I knew the meaning of my fear, whose warning I would not heed. Now I knew that I had walked into the very trap from which my abnormal sensitiveness had striven in vain to save me.

III

Again I struggled within me, bit at my lip till I tasted blood, and presently the blind paroxysm passed. It must have been longer in going than I thought, and the old man must have all that time been speaking, for when I could once more control my attention, hear and see him, he had taken up a position near the sink, about ten feet away, and was addressing me with a sort of 'platform' manner, as if I had been the large audience whose absence he had deplored.

'And so,' he was saying, 'I was forced to make these plates very carefully, to truly represent the characteristic hues of each separate organism. Now, in color work of every kind the film is necessarily extremely sensitive. Doubtless you are familiar in a general way with the exquisite transparencies produced by color photography of the single-plate type.'

He paused, and trying to act like a normal human being, I observed: 'I saw some nice landscapes done in that way – last week at an illustrated lecture in Franklin Hall.'

He scowled, and made an impatient gesture at me with his hand. 'I can proceed better without interruptions,' he said. 'My pause was purely oratorical.'

I meekly subsided, and he went on in his original loud, clear voice. He would have made an excellent lecturer before a much larger audience – if only his voice could have lost that eerie, ringing note. Thinking of that I must have missed some more, and when I caught it again he was saying:

'As I have indicated, the original plate is the final picture. Now, many of these organisms are extremely hard to photograph, and micro-photography in color is particularly difficult. In consequence, to spoil a plate tries the patience of the photographer. They are so sensitive that the ordinary darkroom ruby lamp would instantly ruin them, and they must therefore be developed either in darkness or by a special light produced by interposing thin sheets of tissue of a particular shade of green and of yellow between lamp and plate, and even that will often cause ruinous fog. Now I, finding it hard to handle them so, made numerous experiments with a view of discovering some glass or fabric of a color which should add to the safety of the green, without robbing it of all efficiency. All proved equally useless, but intermittently I persevered – until last week.'

His voice dropped to an almost confidential tone, and he leaned slightly toward me. I was cold from my neck to my feet, though my head was burning, but I tried to force an appreciative smile.

'Last week,' he continued impressively, 'I had a prescription filled at the corner drug store. The bottle was sent home to me wrapped in a piece of what I first took to be whitish, slightly opalescent paper. Later I decided that it was some kind of membrane. When I questioned the druggist, seeking its source, he said it was a sheet of "paper" that was around a bundle of herbs from South America. That he had no more, and doubted if I could trace it. He had wrapped my bottle so, because he was in haste and the sheet was handy.

'I can hardly tell you what first inspired me to try that membrane in my photographic work. It was merely dull white with a faint hint of opalescence, except when held against the light. Then it became quite translucent and quite brightly prismatic. For some reason it occurred to me that this refractive effect might help in breaking up the actinic rays – the rays which affect the sensitive emulsion. So that night I inserted it behind the sheets of green and yellow tissue, next the lamp prepared my trays and chemicals, laid my plate holders to hand, turned off the white light and – turned on the green!'

There was nothing in his words to inspire fear. It was a wearisomely detailed account of his struggles with photography. Yet, as he again paused impressively, I wished that he might never speak again. I was desperately, contemptibly in dread of the thing he might say next.

Suddenly, he drew himself erect, the stoop went out of his shoulders, he threw back his head and laughed. It was a hollow sound, as if he laughed into a trumpet. 'I won't tell you what I saw! Why should I? Your own eyes shall bear witness. But this much I'll say, so that you may better understand – later. When our poor, faultily sensitive vision can perceive a thing, we say that it is visible. When the nerves of touch can feel it, we say that it is tangible. Yet I tell you there are beings intangible to our physical sense, yet whose presence is felt by the spirit, and invisible to our eyes merely because those organs are not attuned to the light as reflected from their bodies. But light passed through the screen, which we are about to use has a wave length novel to the scientific world, and by it you shall see with the eyes of the flesh that which has been invisible since life began. Have no fear!'

He stopped to laugh again, and his mirth was yellow-toothed – menacing.

'Have no fear!' he reiterated, and with that stretched his hand toward the wall, there came a click and we were in black, impenetrable darkness. I wanted to spring up, to seek the door by which I had entered and rush out of it, but the paralysis of unreasoning terror held me fast.

I could hear him moving about in the darkness, and a moment later a faint green glimmer sprang up in the room. Its source was over the large sink, where I suppose he developed his precious 'color plates.'

Every instant, as my eyes became accustomed to the dimness, I could see more clearly. Green light is peculiar. It may be far fainter than red, and at the same time far more illuminating. The old man was standing beneath it, and his face by that ghastly radiance had the exact look of a dead man's. Besides this, however, I could observe nothing appalling.

'That,' continued the man, 'is the simple developing light of which I have spoken – now watch, for what you are about to behold no mortal man but myself has ever seen before.'

For a moment he fussed with the green lamp over the sink. It was so constructed that all the direct rays struck downward. He opened a flap at the side, for a moment there was a streak of comforting white luminance from within, then he inserted something, slid it slowly in – and closed the flap.

The thing he put in – that South American 'membrane' it must have been – instead of decreasing the light increased it – amazingly. The hue was changed from green to greenish-gray, and the whole room sprang into view, a livid, ghastly chamber, filled with – overcrawled by – what?

My eyes fixed themselves, fascinated, on something that moved by the old man's feet. It writhed there on the floor like a huge, repulsive starfish, an immense, armed, legged thing, that twisted convulsively. It was smooth, as if made of rubber, was whitish-green in color; and presently raised its great round blob of a body on tottering tentacles, crept toward my host and writhed upward – yes, climbed up his legs, his body. And he stood there, erect, arms folded, and stared sternly down at the thing which climbed.

But the room – the whole room was alive with other creatures than that. Everywhere I looked they were – centipedish things, with yard-long bodies, detestable, furry spiders that lurked in shadows, and sausage-shaped translucent horrors that moved – and floated through the air. They dived – here and there between me and the light, and I could see its bright greenness through their greenish bodies.

Worse, though; far worse than these were the things with human faces. Mask-like, monstrous, huge gaping mouths and slitlike eyes – I find I cannot write of them. There was that about them which makes their memory even now intolerable.

The old man was speaking again, and every word echoed in my brain like the ringing of a gong. 'Fear nothing! Among such as these do you move every hour of the day and night. Only you and I have seen, for God is merciful and has spared our race from sight. But I am not merciful! I loathe the race which gave these creatures birth – the race which might be so surrounded by invisible, unguessed but blessed beings – and chooses these for its companions! All the world shall see and know. One by one shall they come here, learn the truth, and perish. For who can survive the ultimate of terror? Then I, too, shall find peace, and leave the earth to its heritage of man-created horrors. Do you know what these are – whence they come?'

This voice boomed now like a cathedral bell. I could not answer him, but he waited for no reply. 'Out of the ether – out of the omnipresent ether from whose intangible substance the mind of God made the planets, all living things, and man – man has made these! By his evil thoughts, by his selfish panics, by his lusts and his interminable, never-ending hate he has made them, and they are everywhere! Fear nothing – but see where there comes to you, its creator, the shape and the body of your FEAR!'

And as he said it I perceived a great Thing coming toward me – a Thing – but consciousness could endure no more. The ringing, threatening voice merged in a roar within my ears, there came a merciful dimming of the terrible, lurid vision, and blank nothingness succeeded upon horror too great for bearing.

IV

There was a dull, heavy pain above my eyes. I knew that they were closed, that I was dreaming, and that the rack full of colored bottles which I seemed to see so clearly was no more than a part of the dream. There was some vague but imperative reason why I should rouse myself. I wanted to awaken, and thought that by staring very hard indeed I could dissolve this foolish vision of blue and yellow-brown bottles. But instead of dissolving they grew clearer, more solid and substantial of appearance, until suddenly the rest of my senses rushed to the support of sight, and I became aware that my eyes were open, the bottles were quite real, and that I was sitting in a chair, fallen sideways so that my cheek rested most uncomfortably on the table which held the rack.

I straightened up slowly and with difficulty, groping in my dulled brain for some clue to my presence in this unfamiliar place, this laboratory that was lighted only by the rays of an arc light in the street outside its three large windows. Here I sat, alone, and if the aching of cramped limbs meant anything, here I had sat for more than a little time.

Then, with the painful shock which accompanies awakening to the knowledge of some great catastrophe, came memory. It was this very room, shown by the street lamp's rays to be empty of life, which I had seen thronged with creatures too loathsome for description. I staggered to my feet, staring fearfully about. There were the glass-floored cases, the bookshelves, the two tables with their burdens, and the long iron sink above which, now only a dark blotch of shadow, hung the lamp from which had emanated that livid, terrifically revealing illumination. Then the experience had been no dream, but a frightful reality. I was alone here now. With callous indifference my strange host had allowed me to remain for hours unconscious, with not the least effort to aid or revive me. Perhaps, hating me so, he had hoped that I would die there.

At first I made no effort to leave the place. Its appearance filled me with reminiscent loathing. I longed to go, but as yet felt too weak and ill for the effort. Both mentally and physically my condition was deplorable, and for the first time I realized that a shock to the mind may react upon the body as vilely as any debauch of self-indulgence.

Quivering in every nerve and muscle, dizzy with headache and nausea, I dropped back into the chair, hoping that before the old man returned I might recover sufficient self-control to escape him. I knew that he hated me, and why. As I waited, sick, miserable, I understood the man. Shuddering, I recalled the loathsome horrors he had shown me. If the mere desires and emotions of mankind were daily carnified in such forms as those, no wonder that he viewed his fellow beings with detestation and longed only to destroy them.

I thought, too, of the cruel, sensuous faces I had seen in the streets outside – seen for the first time, as if a veil had been withdrawn from eyes hitherto blinded by self-delusion. Fatuously trustful as a month-old puppy, I had lived in a grim, evil world, where goodness is a word and crude selfishness the only actuality. Drearily my thoughts drifted back through my own life, its futile purposes, mistakes and activities. All of evil that I knew returned to overwhelm me. Our gropings toward divinity were a sham, a writhing sunward of slime – covered beasts who claimed sunlight as their heritage, but in their hearts preferred the foul and easy depths.

Even now, though I could neither see nor feel them, this room, the entire world, was acrawl with the beings created by our real natures. I recalled the cringing, contemptible fear to which my spirit had so readily yielded, and the faceless Thing to which the emotion had given birth.

Then abruptly, shockingly, I remembered that every moment I was adding to the horde. Since my mind could conceive only repulsive incubi, and since while I lived I must think, feel, and so continue to shape them, was there no way to check so abominable a succession? My eyes fell on the long shelves with their many-colored bottles. In the chemistry of photography there are deadly poisons – I knew that. Now was the time to end it – now! Let him return and find his desire accomplished. One good thing I could do, if one only. I could abolish my monster-creating self.

V

My friend Mark Jenkins is an intelligent and usually a very careful man. When he took from 'Smiler' Callahan a cigar which had every appearance of being excellent, innocent Havana, the act denoted both intelligence and caution. By very clever work he had traced the poisoning of young Ralph Peeler to Mr. Callahan's door, and he believed this particular cigar to be the mate of one smoked by Peeler just previous to his demise. And if, upon arresting Callahan, he had not confiscated this bit of evidence, it would have doubtless been destroyed by its regrettably unconscientious owner.

But when Jenkins shortly afterward gave me that cigar, as one of his own, he committed one of those almost inconceivable blunders which, I think, are occasionally forced upon clever men to keep them from overweening vanity. Discovering his slight mistake, my detective friend spent the night searching for his unintended victim, myself; and that his search was successful was due to Pietro Marini, a young Italian of Jenkins' acquaintance, whom he met about the hour of 2:00 A.M. returning from a dance.

Now, Marini had seen me standing on the steps of the house where Doctor Frederick Holt had his laboratory and living rooms, and he had stared at me, not with any ill intent, but because he thought I was the sickest-looking, most ghastly specimen of humanity that he had ever beheld. And, sharing the superstition of his South Street neighbors, he wondered if the worthy doctor had poisoned me as well as Peeler. This suspicion he imparted to Jenkins, who, however, had the best of reasons for believing otherwise. Moreover, as he informed Marini, Holt was dead, having drowned himself late the previous afternoon. An hour or so after our talk in the restaurant, news of his suicide reached Jenkins.

It seemed wise to search any place where a very sick-looking young man had been seen to enter, so Jenkins came straight to the laboratory. Across the fronts of those houses was the long sign with its mysterious inscription, 'See the Great Unseen,' not at all mysterious to the detective. He knew that next door to Doctor Holt's the second floor had been thrown together into a lecture room, where at certain hours a young man employed by settlement workers displayed upon a screen stereopticon views of various deadly bacilli, the germs of diseases appropriate to dirt and indifference. He knew, too, that Doctor Holt himself had helped the educational effort along by providing some really wonderful lantern slides, done by microcolor photography.

On the pavement outside, Jenkins found the two-thirds remnant of a cigar, which he gathered in and came up the steps, a very miserable and self-reproachful detective. Neither outer nor inner door was locked, and in the laboratory he found me, alive, but on the verge of death by another means that he had feared.

In the extreme physical depression following my awakening from drugged sleep, and knowing nothing of its cause, I believed my adventure fact in its entirety. My mentality was at too low an ebb to resist its dreadful suggestion. I was searching among Holt's various bottles when Jenkins burst in. At first I was merely annoyed at the interruption of my purpose, but before the anticlimax of his explanation the mists of obsession drifted away and left me still sick in body, but in spirit happy as any man may well be who has suffered a delusion that the world is wholly bad – and learned that its badness springs from his own poisoned brain.

The malice which I had observed in every face, including young Marini's, existed only in my drug-affected vision. Last week's 'popular-science' lecture had been recalled to my subconscious mind – the mind that rules dreams and delirium – by the photographic apparatus in Holt's workroom. 'See the Great Unseen' assisted materially, and even the corner drug store before which I had paused, with its green-lit show vases, had doubtless played a part. But presently, following something Jenkins told me, I was driven to one protest. 'If Holt was not here,' I demanded, 'if Holt is dead, as you say, how do you account for the fact that I, who have never seen the man, was able to give you an accurate description which you admit to be that of Doctor Frederick Holt?'

He pointed across the room. 'See that?' It was a life-size bust portrait, in crayons, the picture of a white-haired man with bushy eyebrows and the most piercing black eyes I had ever seen – until the previous evening. It hung facing the door and near the windows, and the features stood out with a strangely lifelike appearance in the white rays of the arc lamp just outside. 'Upon entering,' continued Jenkins, 'the first thing you saw was that portrait, and from it your delirium built a living, speaking man. So, there are your white-haired showman, your unnatural fear, your color photography and your pretty green golliwogs all nicely explained for you, Blaisdell, and thank God you're alive to hear the explanation. If you had smoked the whole of that cigar – well, never mind. You didn't. And now, my very dear friend, I think it's high time that you interviewed a real, flesh-and-blood doctor. I'll phone for a taxi.'

'Don't,' I said. 'A walk in the fresh air will do me more good than fifty doctors.'

'Fresh air! There's no fresh air on South Street in July,' complained Jenkins, but reluctantly yielded.

I had a reason for my preference. I wished to see people, to meet face to face even such stray prowlers as might be about at this hour, nearer sunrise than midnight, and rejoice in the goodness and kindliness of the human countenance – particularly as found in the lower classes.

But even as we were leaving there occurred to me a curious inconsistency.

'Jenkins,' I said, 'you claim that the reason Holt, when I first met him in the hall, appeared to twice close the door in my face, was because the door never opened until I myself unlatched it.'

'Yes,' confirmed Jenkins, but he frowned, foreseeing my next question.

'Then why, if it was from that picture that I built so solid, so convincing a vision of the man, did I see Holt in the hall before the door was open?'

'You confuse your memories,' retorted Jenkins rather shortly.

'Do I? Holt was dead at that hour, but – I tell you I saw Holt outside the door! And what was his reason for committing suicide?'

Before my friend could reply I was across the room, fumbling in the dusk there at the electric lamp above the sink. I got the tin flap open and pulled out the sliding screen, which consisted of two sheets of glass with fabric between, dark on one side, yellow on the other. With it came the very thing I dreaded – a sheet of whitish, parchmentlike, slightly opalescent stuff.

Jenkins was beside me as I held it at arm's length toward the windows. Through it the light of the arc lamp fell – divided into the most astonishingly brilliant rainbow hues. And instead of diminishing the light, it was perceptibly increased in the oddest way. Almost one thought that the sheet itself was luminous, and yet when held in shadow it gave off no light at all.

'Shall we – put it in the lamp again – and try it?' asked Jenkins slowly, and in his voice there was no hint of mockery.

I looked him straight in the eyes. 'No,' I said, 'we won't. I was drugged. Perhaps in that condition I received a merciless revelation of the discovery that caused Holt's suicide, but I don't believe it. Ghost or no ghost, I refuse to ever again believe in the depravity of the human race. If the air and the earth are teeming with invisible horrors, they are not of our making, and – the study of demonology is better let alone. Shall we burn this thing, or tear it up?'

'We have no right to do either,' returned Jenkins thoughtfully, 'but you know, Blaisdell, there's a little too darn much realism about some parts of your "dream." I haven't been smoking any doped cigars; but when you held that up to the light, I'll swear I saw – well, never mind. Burn it – send it back to the place it came from.'

'South America?' said I.

'A hotter place than that. Burn it.'

So he struck a match and we did. It was gone in one great white flash.

A large place was given by morning papers to the suicide of Doctor Frederick Holt, caused, it was surmised, by mental derangement brought about by his unjust implication in the Peeler murder. It seemed an inadequate reason, since he had never been arrested, but no other was ever discovered.

Of course, our action in destroying that 'membrane' was illegal and rather precipitate, but, though he won't talk about it, I know that Jenkins agrees with me – doubt is sometimes better than certainty, and there are marvels better left unproved. Those, for instance, which concern the Powers of Evil.

IN THE PENAL COLONY

Franz Kafka

TRANSLATED INTO ENGLISH BY IAN JOHNSTON

Franz Kafka (1883–1924) was an iconic early twentieth-century writer of German-Jewish descent who lived in Prague (then part of Bohemia). Kafka's nightmarish, disturbing work – the novels *The Trial* (1925), *The Castle* (1926) and *Amerika* (1927), as well as short stories like 'The Metamorphosis' (1915) – is now considered among the most original in modern literature. The story reprinted here, 'In the Penal Colony' (1919) first appeared in an English translation in 1948. The story's reliance on strange ritual and its luminous clarity are grounded in a modernity that, along with his other work, represented a new approach to weird fiction. As is well-documented, Kafka's writers' group had clear connections to, and influence on, writers such as Alfred Kubin.

'It's a remarkable apparatus,' said the Officer to the Explorer and gazed with a certain look of admiration at the device, with which he was, of course, thoroughly familiar. It appeared that the Traveller had responded to the invitation of the Commandant only out of politeness, when he had been asked to attend the execution of a soldier condemned for disobeying and insulting his superior. Interest in this execution was not really very high even in the penal colony itself. At least, here in the small, deep, sandy valley, closed in on all sides by barren slopes, apart from the Officer and the Traveller there were present only the Condemned, a vacant-looking man with a broad mouth and dilapidated hair and face, and the Soldier, who held the heavy chain to which were connected the small chains which bound the Condemned Man by his feet and wrist bones, as well as by his neck, and which were also linked to each other by connecting chains. The Condemned Man, incidentally, had an expression of such dog-like resignation that it looked as if one could set him free to roam around the slopes and would only have to whistle at the start of the execution for him to return.

The Traveller had little interest in the apparatus and walked back and forth behind the Condemned Man, almost visibly indifferent, while the Officer took care of the final preparations. Sometimes he crawled under the apparatus, which was built deep into the earth, and sometimes he climbed up a ladder to inspect the upper parts. These were jobs which really could have been left to a mechanic, but the Officer carried them out with great enthusiasm, maybe because he was particularly fond of this apparatus or maybe because there was some other reason why the work could not be entrusted to anyone else. 'It's all ready now!' he finally cried and climbed back down the ladder. He was unusually tired, breathing with his mouth wide open, and he had pushed two fine lady's handkerchiefs under the collar of his uniform at the back. 'These uniforms are really too heavy for the tropics,' the Traveller said, instead of asking some questions about the apparatus, as the Officer had expected. 'That's true,' said the Officer. He washed the oil and grease from his dirty hands in a bucket of water standing ready, 'But they mean home, and we don't want to lose our homeland.' 'Now, have a look at this apparatus,' he added immediately, drying his hands with a towel and at the same time pointing to the apparatus. 'Up to this point I still had to do some work by hand, but from now on the apparatus works entirely on its own.' The Traveller nodded and followed the Officer. The latter tried to protect himself against all eventualities by saying, 'Of course, breakdowns do happen. I really hope none will occur today, but we must be prepared for them. The apparatus is supposed to keep going for twelve hours without interruption. But if any breakdowns occur, they are only very minor, and will be dealt with right away.'

'Don't you want to sit down?' he asked finally. He pulled out a chair from a pile of cane chairs and offered it to the Traveller. The latter could not refuse. He was now sitting on the edge of a pit, into which he cast a fleeting glance. It was not very deep. On one side of the hole the piled earth was heaped up into a wall; on the other side stood the apparatus. 'I don't know,' the Officer said, 'whether the Commandant has already explained the apparatus to you.' The Traveller made a vague gesture with his hand. That was good enough for the Officer, for now he could explain the apparatus himself. 'This apparatus,' he said, grasping a connecting rod and leaning against it, 'is our previous Commandant's invention. I also worked with him on the very first tests and took part in all the work right up to its completion. However, the credit for the invention belongs entirely to him alone. Have you heard of our previous Commandant? No? Well, I'm not claiming too much when I say that the organization of the entire penal colony is his work. We, his friends, already knew at the time of his death that the administration of the colony was so self-contained that even if his successor had a thousand new plans in mind, he would not be able to alter anything of the old plan, at least not for several years. And our prediction has held. The New Commandant has had to recognize that. It's a shame that you didn't know the previous Commandant!'

'However,' the Officer said, interrupting himself, 'I'm chattering, and his apparatus stands here in front of us. As you see, it consists of three parts. With the passage of time certain popular names have been developed for each of these parts. The one underneath is called the Bed, the upper one is called the Inscriber, and here in the middle, this moving part is called the Harrow.' 'The Harrow?' the Traveller asked. He had not been listening with full attention. The sun was excessively strong, trapped in the shadowless valley, and one could hardly collect one's thoughts. So the Officer appeared to him all the more admirable in his tight tunic weighed down with epaulettes and festooned with braid, ready to go on parade, as he explained the matter so eagerly and, in addition, while he was talking, still kept adjusting screws here and there with a screwdriver. The Soldier appeared to be in a state similar to the Traveller. He had wound the Condemned Man's chain around both his wrists and was supporting himself with his hand on his weapon, letting his head hang backward, not bothering about anything. The Traveller was not surprised at that, for the Officer spoke French, and clearly neither the Soldier nor the Condemned Man understood the language. So it was certainly all the more striking that the Condemned Man, in spite of that, did what he could to follow the Officer's explanations. With a sort of sleepy persistence he kept directing his gaze to the place where the Officer had just pointed, and when a question from the Traveller interrupted the Officer, the Condemned Man looked at the Traveller, too, just as the Officer was doing.

'Yes, the Harrow,' said the Officer. 'The name fits. The needles are arranged as in a harrow, and the whole thing is driven like a harrow, although it stays in one place and is, in principle, much more artistic. Anyway, you'll understand in a moment. The condemned is laid out here on the Bed. I'll describe the apparatus first and only then let the procedure go to work. That way you'll be able to follow it better. Also a sprocket in the Inscriber is excessively worn. It really squeaks. When it's in motion one can hardly make oneself understood. Unfortunately replacement parts are difficult to come by in this place. So, here is the Bed, as I said. The whole thing is completely covered with a layer of cotton wool, the purpose of which you'll find out in a moment. The condemned man is laid out on his stomach on this cotton wool – naked, of course. There are straps for the hands here, for the feet here, and for the throat here, to tie him in securely. At the head of the Bed here, where the man, as I have mentioned, first lies face down, is this small protruding lump of felt, which can easily be adjusted so that it presses right into the man's mouth. Its purpose is to prevent him screaming and biting his tongue to pieces. Of course, the man has to let the felt in his mouth – otherwise the straps around his throat will break his neck.' 'That's cotton wool?' asked the Traveller and bent down. 'Yes, it is,' said the Officer smiling, 'feel it for yourself.' He took the Traveller's hand and led him over to the Bed. 'It's a specially prepared cotton wool. That's why it looks so unrecognizable. I'll get around to mentioning its purpose in a moment.' The Traveller was already being won over a little to the apparatus. With his hand over his eyes to protect them from the sun, he looked up at the height of the apparatus. It was a massive construction. The Bed and the Inscriber were the same size and looked like two dark chests. The Inscriber was set about two metres above the Bed, and the two were joined together at the corners by four brass rods, which almost reflected rays from the sun. The Harrow hung between the chests on a band of steel.

The Officer had hardly noticed the earlier indifference of the Traveller, but he did have a sense of how the latter's interest was being aroused now. So he paused in his explanation in order to allow the Traveller time to observe the apparatus undisturbed. The Condemned Man imitated the Traveller, but since he could not put his hand over his eyes, he blinked upward with his eyes uncovered.

'So now the man is lying down,' said the Traveller. He leaned back in his chair and crossed his legs.

'Yes,' said the Officer. He pushed his cap back a little and ran his hand over his hot face. 'Now, listen. Both the Bed and the Inscriber have their own electric batteries. The Bed needs them for itself, and the Inscriber for the Harrow. As soon as the man is strapped in securely, the Bed is set in motion. It quivers with tiny, very rapid oscillations from side to side and up and down simultaneously. You will have seen similar devices in mental hospitals. Only with our Bed all movements are precisely calibrated, for they must be meticulously coordinated with the movements of the Harrow. But it's the Harrow which has the job of actually carrying out the sentence.'

'What is the sentence?' the Traveller asked. 'You don't even know that?' asked the Officer in astonishment and bit his lip. 'Forgive me if my explanations are perhaps confused. I really do beg your pardon. Previously it was the Commandant's habit to provide such explanations. But the New Commandant has excused himself from this honourable duty. However, the fact that with such an eminent visitor' – the Traveller tried to deflect the honour with both hands, but the Officer insisted on the expression – 'that with such an eminent visitor he didn't even once make him aware of the form of our sentencing is yet again something new, which …' He had a curse on his lips, but controlled himself and said merely: 'I was not informed about it. It's not my fault. In any case, I am certainly the person best able to explain our style of sentencing, for here I am carrying' – he patted his breast pocket – 'the relevant diagrams drawn by the previous Commandant.'

'Diagrams made by the Commandant himself?' asked the Traveller. 'Then was he in his own person a combination of everything? Was he soldier, judge, engineer, chemist, and draftsman?'

'He was indeed,' said the Officer, nodding his head with a fixed and thoughtful expression. Then he looked at his hands, examining them. They didn't seem to him clean enough to handle the diagrams. So he went to the bucket and washed them again. Then he pulled out a small leather folder and said, 'Our sentence does not sound severe. The law which a condemned man has violated is inscribed on his body with the Harrow. This Condemned Man, for example,' and the Officer pointed to the man, 'will have inscribed on his body, "Honour your superiors!"'

The Traveller had a quick look at the man. When the Officer was pointing at him, the man kept his head down and appeared to be directing all his energy into listening in order to learn something. But the movements of his pouting lips, which were pressed close together, showed clearly that he was incapable of understanding anything. The Traveller wanted to raise various questions, but after looking at the Condemned Man he merely asked, 'Does he know his sentence?' 'No,' said the Officer. He wished to get on with his explanation right away, but the Traveller interrupted him: 'He doesn't know his own sentence?' 'No,' said the Officer once more. He then paused for a moment, as if he was requesting from the Traveller a more detailed reason for his question, and said, 'It would be useless to give him that information. He experiences it on his own body.' The Traveller really wanted to keep quiet at this point, but he felt how the Condemned Man was gazing at him – he seemed to be asking whether he could approve of the process the Officer had described. So the Traveller, who had up to this point been leaning back, bent forward again and kept up his questions, 'But does he nonetheless have some general idea that he's been condemned?' 'Not that either,' said the Officer, and he smiled at the Traveller, as if he was still waiting for some strange revelations from him. 'No?' said the Traveller, wiping his forehead. 'So the man does not yet know even at this point how his defence was received?' 'He has had no opportunity to defend himself,' said the Officer and looked away, as if he was talking to himself and did not wish to embarrass the Traveller with an explanation of matters so self-evident to him. 'But he must have had a chance to defend himself,' said the Traveller and stood up from his chair.

The Officer recognized that he was in danger of having his explanation of the apparatus held up for a long time. So he went to the Traveller, took him by the arm, pointed with his hand at the Condemned Man, who stood there stiffly now that the attention was so clearly directed at him – the Soldier was also pulling on his chain – and said, 'The matter stands like this. Here in the penal colony I have been appointed judge. In spite of my youth. For I stood at the side of our previous Commandant in all matters of punishment, and I also know the most about the apparatus. The basic principle I use for my decisions is this: Guilt is always beyond a doubt. Other courts could not follow this principle, for they are made up of many heads and, in addition, have even higher courts above them. But that is not the case here, or at least it was not that way with the previous Commandant. It's true the New Commandant has already shown a desire to get mixed up in my court, but I've succeeded so far in fending him off. And I'll continue to be successful. You wanted this case explained. It's so simple – just like all of them. This morning a captain laid a charge that this man, who is assigned to him as a servant and who sleeps before his door, had been sleeping on duty. For his duty is to stand up every time the clock strikes the hour and salute in front of the captain's door. That's certainly not a difficult duty – and it's necessary, since he is supposed to remain fresh both for guarding and for service. Yesterday night the captain wanted to check whether his servant was fulfilling his duty. He opened the door on the stroke of two and found him curled up asleep. He got his horsewhip and hit him across the face. Now, instead of standing up and begging for forgiveness, the man grabbed his master by the legs, shook him, and cried out, "Throw away that whip or I'll eat you up." Those are the facts. The captain came to me an hour ago. I wrote up his statement and right after that the sentence. Then I had the man chained up. It was all very simple. If I had first summoned the man and interrogated him, the result would have been confusion. He would have lied, and if I had been successful in refuting his lies, he would have replaced them with new lies, and so forth. But now I have him, and I won't release him again. Now, does that clarify everything? But time is passing. We should be starting the execution already, and I haven't finished explaining the apparatus yet.' He urged the Traveller to sit down in his chair, moved to the apparatus again, and started, 'As you see, the shape of the Harrow corresponds to the shape of a man. This is the harrow for the upper body, and here are the harrows for the legs. This small cutter is the only one designated for the head. Is that clear to you?' He leaned forward to the Traveller in a friendly way, ready to give the most comprehensive explanation.

The Traveller looked at the Harrow with a wrinkled frown. The information about the judicial procedures had not satisfied him. However, he had to tell himself that here it was a matter of a penal colony, that in this place special regulations were necessary, and that one had to give precedence to military measures right down to the last detail. Beyond that, however, he had some hopes in the New Commandant, who obviously, although slowly, was intending to introduce a new procedure which the limited understanding of this Officer could not accept. Following this train of thought, the Traveller asked, 'Will the Commandant be present at the execution?'

'That is not certain,' said the Officer, embarrassingly affected by the sudden question, and his friendly expression made a grimace. 'That is why we need to hurry up. As much as I regret the fact, I'll have to make my explanation even shorter. But tomorrow, once the apparatus is clean again – the fact that it gets so very dirty is its only fault – I could add a more detailed explanation. So now, only the most essential things. When the man is lying on the Bed and it starts quivering, the Harrow sinks onto the body. It positions itself automatically in such a way that it touches the body only lightly with the needle tips. Once the machine is set in position, this steel cable tightens up immediately into a rod. And now the performance begins. Someone who is not an initiate sees no external difference among the punishments. The Harrow seems to do its work uniformly. As it quivers, it sticks the tips of its needles into the body, which is also vibrating from the movement of the bed. Now, to enable someone to check on how the sentence is being carried out, the Harrow is made of glass. That gave rise to certain technical difficulties with fastening the needles in it securely, but after several attempts we were successful. We didn't spare any efforts. And now, as the inscription is made on the body, everyone can see through the glass. Don't you want to come closer and see the needles for yourself.'

The Traveller stood slowly, moved up, and bent over the Harrow. 'You see,' the Officer said, 'two sorts of needles in a multiple arrangement. Each long needle has a short one next to it. The long one inscribes, and the short one squirts water out to wash away the blood and keep the inscription always clear. The bloody water is then channelled here into small grooves and finally flows into these main gutters, and their outlet pipe takes it to the pit.' The Officer indicated with his finger the exact path which the bloody water had to take. As he began formally to demonstrate with both hands at the mouth of the outlet pipe, in order to make his account as clear as possible, the Traveller raised his head and, feeling behind him with his hand, wanted to return to his chair. Then he saw to his horror that the Condemned Man had also, like him, accepted the Officer's invitation to inspect the arrangement of the Harrow up close. He had pulled the sleeping Soldier holding the chain a little forward and was also bending over the glass. One could see how with a confused gaze he also was looking for what the two gentlemen had just observed, but how he didn't succeed because he lacked the explanation. He leaned forward this way and that. He kept running his eyes over the glass again and again. The Traveller wanted to push him back, for what he was doing was probably punishable. But the Officer held the Traveller firmly with one hand, and with the other he took a lump of earth from the wall and threw it at the Soldier. The latter opened his eyes with a start, saw what the Condemned Man had dared to do, let his weapon fall, braced his heels in the earth, and jerked the Condemned Man back, so that he immediately collapsed. The Soldier looked down at him, as he writhed around, making his chain clink. 'Stand him up,' cried the Officer, for he noticed that the Condemned Man was distracting the Traveller too much. The latter was even leaning out away from the Harrow, without paying any attention to it and wanted merely to find out what was happening to the Condemned Man. 'Handle him carefully,' the Officer yelled again. He ran around the apparatus, personally grabbed the Condemned Man under the armpits and, with the help of the Soldier, straightened up the man, whose feet kept slipping.

'Now I know all about it,' said the Traveller, as the Officer turned back to him again.

'Except the most important thing,' said the latter. He grabbed the Traveller by the arm and pointed up high. 'There in the Inscriber is the mechanism which determines the movement of the Harrow, and this mechanism is arranged according to the diagram on which the sentence is set down. I still use the diagrams of the previous Commandant. Here they are.' He pulled some pages out of the leather folder. 'Unfortunately I can't hand them to you. They are the most cherished thing I possess. Sit down, and I'll show you them from this distance. Then you'll be able to see it all well.' He showed the first sheet. The Traveller would have been happy to say something appreciative, but all he saw was a labyrinthine series of lines, crisscrossing each other in all sort of ways. These covered the paper so thickly that only with difficulty could one make out the white spaces in between. 'Read it,' said the Officer. 'I can't,' said the Traveller. 'But it's clear,' said the Officer.' 'It's very elaborate,' said the Traveller evasively, 'but I can't decipher it.' 'Yes,' said the Officer, smiling and putting the folder back again, 'it's not calligraphy for school children. One has to read it a long time. You, too, would finally understand it clearly. Of course, it has to be a script that isn't simple. You see, it's not supposed to kill right away, but on average over a period of twelve hours. The turning point is set for the sixth hour. There must also be many, many embellishments surrounding the basic script. The essential script moves around the body only in a narrow belt. The rest of the body is reserved for decoration. Can you now appreciate the work of the Harrow and of the whole apparatus? Just look at it!' He jumped up the ladder, turned a wheel, and called down, 'Watch out – move to the side!' Everything started moving. If the wheel had not squeaked, it would have been marvellous. The Officer threatened the wheel with his fist, as if he was surprised by the disturbance it created. Then he spread his arms out to the Traveller, apologized, and quickly clambered down, in order to observe the operation of the apparatus from below. Something was still not working properly, something only he noticed. He clambered up again and reached with both hands into the inside of the Inscriber. Then, in order to descend more quickly, instead of using the ladder, he slid down on one of the poles and, to make himself understandable through the noise, strained his voice to the limit as he yelled in the Traveller's ear, 'Do you understand the process? The Harrow is starting to write. When it's finished with the first part of the script on the man's back, the layer of cotton wool rolls and turns the body slowly onto its side to give the Harrow a new area. Meanwhile those parts lacerated by the inscription are lying on the cotton wool which, because it has been specially treated, immediately stops the bleeding and prepares the script for a further deepening. Here, as the body continues to rotate, prongs on the edge of the Harrow then pull the cotton wool from the wounds, throw it into the pit, and the Harrow goes to work again. In this way it keeps making the inscription deeper for twelve hours. For the first six hours the condemned man goes on living almost as before. He suffers nothing but pain. After two hours, the felt is removed, for at that point the man has no more energy for screaming. Here at the head of the Bed warm rice pudding is put in this electrically heated bowl. From this the man, if he feels like it, can help himself to what he can lap up with his tongue. No one passes up this opportunity. I don't know of a single one, and I have had a lot of experience. He first loses his pleasure in eating around the sixth hour. I usually kneel down at this point and observe the phenomenon. The man rarely swallows the last bit. He merely turns it around in his mouth and spits it into the pit. When he does that, I have to lean aside or else he'll get me in the face. But how quiet the man becomes around the sixth hour! The most stupid of them begins to understand. It starts around the eyes and spreads out from there. A look that could tempt one to lie down with him under the Harrow. Nothing else happens. The man simply begins to decipher the inscription. He purses his lips, as if he is listening. You've seen that it is not easy to figure out the inscription with your eyes, but our man deciphers it with his wounds. True, it takes a lot of work. It requires six hours to complete. But then the Harrow spits all of him out and throws him into the pit, where he splashes down into the bloody water and cotton wool. Then the judgment is over, and we, the Soldier and I, quickly bury him.'

The Traveller had leaned his ear towards the Officer and, with his hands in his coat pockets, was observing the machine at work. The Condemned Man was also watching, but without understanding. He bent forward a little and followed the moving needles, as the Soldier, after a signal from the Officer, cut through the back of his shirt and trousers with a knife, so that they fell off the Condemned Man. He wanted to grab the falling garments to cover his bare flesh, but the Soldier held him up high and shook the last rags from him. The Officer turned the machine off, and in the silence which then ensued the Condemned Man was laid out under the Harrow. The chains were taken off and the straps fastened in their place. For the Condemned Man it seemed at first glance to signify almost a relief. And now the Harrow sunk down a stage lower still, for he was a thin man. As the needle tips touched him, a shudder went over his skin. While the Soldier was busy with the right hand, the Condemned Man stretched out his left, with no sense of its direction. But it was pointing to where the Traveller was standing. The Officer kept looking at the Traveller from the side, without taking his eyes off him, as if he was trying to read from his face the impression he was getting of the execution, which he had now explained to him, at least superficially.

The strap meant to hold the wrist ripped off. The Soldier probably had pulled on it too hard. The Soldier showed the Officer the torn-off piece of strap, wanting him to help. So the Officer went over to him and said, with his face turned towards the Traveller, 'The machine is very complicated. Now and then something has to tear or break. One shouldn't let that detract from one's overall opinion. Anyway, we have an immediate replacement for the strap. I'll use a chain – even though that will affect the sensitivity of the oscillations for the right arm.' And while he put the chain in place, he still kept talking, 'Our resources for maintaining the machine are very limited at the moment. Under the previous Commandant, I had free access to a cash box specially set aside exclusively for this purpose. There was a storeroom here in which all possible replacement parts were kept. I admit I made almost extravagant use of it. I mean earlier, not now, as the New Commandant claims. For him everything serves only as a pretext to fight against the old arrangements. Now he keeps the cash box for machinery under his own control, and if I ask him for a new strap, he demands the torn one as a piece of evidence, the new one doesn't arrive for ten days, and then it's an inferior brand, of not much use to me. But how I am supposed to get the machine to work in the meantime without a strap – no one's concerned about that.'

The Traveller thought about the situation: it is always questionable to intervene decisively in strange circumstances. He was neither a citizen of the penal colony nor a citizen of the state to which it belonged. If he wanted to condemn this execution or even hinder it, people could say to him: You are a foreigner – keep quiet. He would have nothing in response to that, but could only add that he did not understand what he was doing on this occasion, for the purpose of his travelling was merely to observe and not to alter other people's judicial systems in any way. True, at this point the way things were turning out it was very tempting. The injustice of the process and the inhumanity of the execution were beyond doubt. No one could assume that the Traveller was acting out of any sense of his own self-interest, for the Condemned Man was a stranger to him, not a countryman and not someone who invited sympathy in any way. The Traveller himself had letters of reference from high officials and had been welcomed here with great courtesy. The fact that he had been invited to this execution even seemed to indicate that people were asking for his judgment of this court. This was all the more likely since the Commandant, as he now had heard only too clearly, was no supporter of this process and maintained an almost hostile relationship with the Officer.

Then the Traveller heard a cry of rage from the Officer. He had just shoved the stub of felt in the Condemned Man's mouth, not without difficulty, when the Condemned Man, overcome by an irresistible nausea, shut his eyes and threw up. The Officer quickly yanked him up off the stump and wanted to turn his head aside toward the pit. But it was too late. The vomit was already flowing down onto the machine. 'This is all the Commandant's fault!' cried the Officer and mindlessly rattled the brass rods at the front. 'My machine's as filthy as a pigsty.' With trembling hands he indicated to the Traveller what had happened. 'Haven't I spent hours trying to make the Commandant understand that a day before the execution there should be no more food served. But the new, lenient administration has a different opinion. Before the man is led away, the Commandant's women cram sugary things down his throat. His whole life he's fed himself on stinking fish, and now he has to eat sweets! But that would be all right – I'd have no objections – but why don't they get a new felt, the way I've been asking him for three months now? How can anyone take this felt into his mouth without feeling disgusted – something that more than a hundred man have sucked and bitten on it as they were dying?'

The Condemned Man had laid his head down and appeared peaceful. The Soldier was busy cleaning up the machine with the Condemned Man's shirt. The Officer went up to the Traveller, who, feeling some premonition, took a step backwards. But the Officer grasped him by the hand and pulled him aside. 'I want to speak a few words to you in confidence,' he said. 'May I do that?'

'Of course,' said the Traveller and listened with his eyes lowered.

'This process and this execution, which you now have an opportunity to admire, have at present no more open supporters in our colony. I am its single defender and at the same time the single advocate for the legacy of the Old Commandant. I can no longer think about a more extensive organization of the process – I'm using all my powers to maintain what there is at present. When the Old Commandant was alive, the colony was full of his supporters. I have something of the Old Commandant's persuasiveness, but I completely lack his power, and as a result the supporters have gone into hiding. There are still a lot of them, but no one admits to it. If you go into a tea house today – that is to say, on a day of execution – and keep your ears open, perhaps you'll hear nothing but ambiguous remarks. They are all supporters, but under the present Commandant, considering his present views, they are totally useless to me. And now I'm asking you: Should such a life's work,' he pointed to the machine, 'come to nothing because of this Commandant and the women influencing him? Should people let that happen? Even if one is only a foreigner on our island for a couple of days? But there is no time to lose. People are already preparing something against my judicial proceedings. Discussions are already taking place in the Commandant's headquarters, to which I am not invited. Even your visit today seems to me typical of the whole situation. People are cowards and send you out – a foreigner. You should have seen the executions in earlier days! The entire valley was overflowing with people, even a day before the execution. They all came merely to watch. Early in the morning the Commandant appeared with his women. Fanfares woke up the entire campsite. I delivered the news that everything was ready. The whole society – and every high official had to attend – arranged itself around the machine. This pile of cane chairs is a sorry left over from that time. The machine was freshly cleaned and glowed. For almost every execution I had new replacement parts. In front of hundreds of eyes – all the spectators stood on tip toe right up to the hills there – the condemned man was laid down under the Harrow by the Commandant himself. What nowadays has to be done by a common soldier was then my work as the senior judge, and it was an honour for me. And then the execution began! No discordant note disturbed the work of the machine. Many people did not look any more at all, but lay down with closed eyes in the sand. They all knew: now justice was being carried out. In the silence people heard nothing but the groans of the condemned man, muffled by the felt. These days the machine no longer manages to squeeze out of the condemned man a groan stronger than the felt is capable of smothering. But back then the needles which made the inscription dripped a caustic liquid which today we are not permitted to use any more. Well, then came the sixth hour! It was impossible to grant all the requests people made to be allowed to watch from up close. The Commandant, in his wisdom, arranged that the children should be taken care of before all the rest. Naturally, I was always allowed to stand close by, because of my official position. Often I crouched down there with two small children in my arms, on my right and left. How we all took in the expression of transfiguration on the martyred face! How we held our cheeks in the glow of this justice, finally attained and already passing away! What times we had, my friend!' The Officer had obviously forgotten who was standing in front of him. He had put his arm around the Traveller and laid his head on his shoulder. The Traveller was extremely embarrassed. Impatiently he looked away over the Officer's head. The Soldier had ended his task of cleaning and had just shaken some rice pudding into the bowl from a tin. No sooner had the Condemned Man, who seemed to have fully recovered already, noticed this than his tongue began to lick at the pudding. The Soldier kept pushing him away, for the pudding was probably meant for a later time, but in any case it was not proper for the Soldier to reach in and grab some food with his dirty hands and eat it in front of the famished Condemned Man.

The Officer quickly collected himself. 'I didn't want to upset you in any way,' he said. 'I know it is impossible to make someone understand those days now. Besides, the machine still works and operates on its own. It operates on its own even when it is standing alone in this valley. And at the end, the body still keeps falling in that incredibly soft flight into the pit, even if hundreds of people are not gathered like flies around the hole the way they used to be. Back then we had to erect a strong railing around the pit. It was pulled out long ago.'

The Traveller wanted to turn his face away from the Officer and looked aimlessly around him. The Officer thought he was looking at the wasteland of the valley. So he grabbed his hands, turned him around in order to catch his gaze, and asked, 'Do you see the shame of it?'

But the Traveller said nothing. The Officer left him alone for a while. With his legs apart and his hands on his hips, the Officer stood still and looked at the ground. Then he smiled at the Traveller cheerfully and said, 'Yesterday I was nearby when the Commandant invited you. I heard the invitation. I know the Commandant. I understood right away what he intended with his invitation. Although his power might be sufficiently great to take action against me, he doesn't yet dare to. But my guess is that with you he is exposing me to the judgment of a respected foreigner. He calculates things with care. You are now in your second day on the island. You didn't know the Old Commandant and his way of thinking. You are biased in your European way of seeing things. Perhaps you are fundamentally opposed to the death penalty in general and to this kind of mechanical style of execution in particular. Moreover, you see how the execution is a sad procedure, without any public participation, using a machine which is already somewhat damaged. Now, if we take all this together (so the Commandant thinks) surely one could easily imagine that you would not consider my procedure appropriate? And if you didn't consider it right, you wouldn't keep quiet about it – I'm still speaking the mind of the Commandant – for you no doubt have faith that your tried-and-true convictions are correct. It's true that you have seen many peculiar things among many peoples and have learned to respect them. Thus, you will probably not speak out against the procedure with your full power, as you would perhaps in your own homeland. But the Commandant doesn't really need that. A casual word, merely a careless remark, is enough. It doesn't have to match your convictions at all, so long as it apparently corresponds to his wishes. I'm certain he will use all his shrewdness to interrogate you. And his women will sit around in a circle and perk up their ears. You will say something like, "Among us the judicial procedures are different," or "With us the accused is questioned before the verdict," or "With us the accused hears the judgment" or "With us there are punishments other than the death penalty" or "With us there was torture only in the Middle Ages." For you all these observations appear as correct as they are self-evident – innocent remarks which do not impugn my procedure. But how will the Commandant take them? I see him, our excellent Commandant – the way he immediately pushes his stool aside and hurries out onto the balcony – I see his women, how they stream after him. I hear his voice – the women call it a thunder voice. And now he's speaking: "A great Western explorer who has been commissioned to inspect judicial procedures in all countries has just said that our process based on old customs is inhuman. After this verdict of such a personality it is, of course, no longer possible for me to tolerate this procedure. So from this day on I am ordering... and so forth." You want to intervene – you didn't say what he is reporting – you didn't call my procedure inhuman; by contrast, in keeping with your deep insight, you consider it the most humane and most worthy of human beings. You also admire this machinery. But it is too late. You don't even go onto the balcony, which is already filled with women. You want to attract attention. You want to cry out. But a lady's hand is covering your mouth, and I and the Old Commandant's work are lost.'

The Traveller had to suppress a smile. So the work which he had considered so difficult was easy. He said evasively, 'You're exaggerating my influence. The Commandant has read my letters of recommendation. He knows that I am no expert in judicial processes. If I were to express an opinion, it would be that of a lay person, no more significant than the opinion of anyone else, and in any case far less significant than the opinion of the Commandant, who, as I understand it, has very extensive powers in this penal colony. If his views of this procedure are as definite as you think they are, then I'm afraid the time has surely come for this procedure to end, without any need for my humble assistance.'

Did the Officer understand by now? No, he did not yet grasp it. He shook his head vigorously, briefly looked back at the Condemned Man and the Soldier, who both flinched and stopped eating the rice, went up really close to the Traveller, without looking into his face, but gazing at parts of his jacket, and said more gently than before: 'You don't know the Commandant. Where he and all of us are concerned you are – forgive the expression – to a certain extent innocent. Your influence, believe me, cannot be overestimated. In fact, I was blissfully happy when I heard that you were to be present at the execution by yourself. This arrangement of the Commandant was aimed at me, but now I'm turning it to my advantage. Without being distracted by false insinuations and disparaging looks – which could not have been avoided with a greater number of participants at the execution – you have listened to my explanation, looked at the machine, and are now about to view the execution. Your verdict is no doubt already fixed. If some small uncertainties still remain, witnessing the execution will remove them. And now I'm asking you – help me against the Commandant!'

The Traveller did not let him go on talking. 'How can I do that?' he cried. 'It's totally impossible. I can help you as little as I can harm you.'

'You could do it,' said the Officer. With some apprehension the Traveller observed that the Officer was clenching his fists. 'You could do it,' repeated the Officer, even more emphatically. 'I have a plan which must succeed. You think your influence is insufficient. I know it will be enough. But assuming you're right, doesn't saving this procedure require one to try everything, even those methods which may possibly be inadequate? So listen to my plan. To carry it out, it's necessary, above all, for you to keep as quiet as possible today in the colony about your verdict on this procedure. Unless someone asks you directly, you should not express any view whatsoever. But what you do say must be short and vague. People should notice that it has become difficult for you to speak about the subject, that you feel bitter, that, if you were to speak openly, you'd have to burst out cursing on the spot. I'm not asking you to lie, not at all. You should give only brief answers – something like, "Yes, I've seen the execution" or "Yes, I've heard the full explanation." That's all – nothing further. For that will be enough of an indication for people to observe in you a certain bitterness, even if that's not what the Commandant will think. Naturally, he will completely misunderstand the issue and interpret it in his own way. My plan is based on that. Tomorrow a large meeting of all the higher administrative officials takes place at headquarters under the chairmanship of the Commandant. He, of course, understands how to turn such meetings into a spectacle. A gallery has been built, which is always full of spectators. I'm compelled to take part in the discussions, though they make me shiver with disgust. In any case, you will certainly be invited to the meeting. If you follow my plan today and behave accordingly, the invitation will become an emphatic request. But should you for some inexplicable reason still not be invited, you must make sure you request an invitation. Then you'll receive one without question. Now, tomorrow you are sitting with the women in the Commandant's box. With frequent upward glances he reassures himself that you are there. After various trivial and ridiculous agenda items designed only for the spectators – mostly harbour construction, always harbour construction! – the judicial process also comes up for discussion. If it's not raised by the Commandant himself or does not occur soon enough, I'll make sure that it comes up. I'll stand up and report the news of today's execution. Really briefly – just this announcement. True, such a report is not customary there; however, I'll do it, nonetheless. The Commandant thanks me, as always, with a friendly smile. And now he cannot restrain himself. He seizes this excellent opportunity. "The report of the execution," he'll say, or something like that, "has just been given. I would like to add to this report only the fact that this particular execution was attended by the great explorer whose visit confers such extraordinary honour on our colony, as you all know. Even the significance of our meeting today has been increased by his presence. Do we not now wish to ask this great explorer for his appraisal of the execution based on old customs and of the process which preceded it?" Of course, there is the noise of applause everywhere, universal agreement. And I'm louder than anyone. The Commandant bows before you and says, "Then in everyone's name, I'm putting the question to you." And now you step up to the railing. Place your hands where everyone can see them. Otherwise the ladies will grab them and play with your fingers. And now finally come your remarks. I don't know how I'll bear the tense moments up to that point. In your speech you mustn't hold back. Let truth resound. Lean over the railing and shout it out – yes, yes, roar your opinion at the Commandant, your unshakeable opinion. But perhaps you don't want to do that. It doesn't suit your character. Perhaps in your homeland people behave differently in such situations. That's all right. That's perfectly satisfactory. Don't stand up at all. Just say a couple of words. Whisper them so that only the officials underneath you can hear them. That's enough. You don't even have to say anything at all about the lack of attendance at the execution or about the squeaky wheel, the torn strap, the disgusting felt. No. I'll take over all further details, and, believe me, if my speech doesn't chase him out of the room, it will force him to his knees, so he'll have to admit it: "Old Commandant, I bow down before you." That's my plan. Do you want to help me carry it out? But, of course, you want to. More than that – you have to.' And the Officer gripped the Traveller by both arms and looked at him, breathing heavily into his face. He had yelled the last sentences so loudly that even the Soldier and the Condemned Man were paying attention. Although they couldn't understand a thing, they stopped eating and looked over at the Traveller, still chewing.

From the very start the Traveller had had no doubts about the answer he must give. He had experienced too much in his life to be able to waver here. Basically he was honest and unafraid. Still, with the Soldier and the Condemned Man looking at him, he hesitated a moment. But finally he said, as he had to, 'No.' The Officer's eyes blinked several times, but he did not take his eyes off the Traveller. 'Would you like an explanation?' asked the Traveller. The Officer nodded dumbly. 'I am opposed to this procedure,' said the Traveller. 'Even before you took me into your confidence – and, of course, I will never abuse your confidence under any circumstances – I was already thinking about whether I was entitled to intervene against this procedure and whether my intervention could have even a small chance of success. And if that was the case, it was clear to me whom I had to turn to first of all – naturally, to the Commandant. You have clarified the issue for me even more, but without reinforcing my decision in any way – quite the reverse. I find your conviction genuinely moving, even if it cannot deter me.'

The Officer remained silent, turned towards the machine, grabbed one of the brass rods, and then, leaning back a little, looked up at the Inscriber, as if he was checking that everything was in order. The Soldier and the Condemned Man seemed to have made friends with each other. The Condemned Man was making signs to the Soldier, although, given the tight straps on him, this was difficult for him to do. The Soldier was leaning into him. The Condemned Man whispered something to him, and the Soldier nodded.

The Traveller went over to the Officer and said, 'You don't yet know what I'll do. Yes, I will tell the Commandant my opinion of the procedure – not in a meeting, but in private. In addition, I won't stay here long enough to be able to get called in to some meeting or other. Early tomorrow morning I leave, or at least I go on board ship.'

It did not look as if the Officer had been listening. 'So the process has not convinced you,' he said to himself and smiled the way an old man smiles over the silliness of a child, concealing his own true thoughts behind that smile.

'Well then, it's time,' he said finally and suddenly looked at the Traveller with bright eyes which contained some sort of demand, some appeal for participation.

'Time for what?' asked the Traveller uneasily. But there was no answer.

'You are free,' the Officer told the Condemned Man in his own language. At first the man did not believe him. 'You are free now,' said the Officer. For the first time the face of the Condemned Man showed signs of real life. Was it the truth? Was it only the Officer's mood, which could change? Had the foreign Traveller brought him a reprieve? What was it? That is what the man's face seemed to be asking. But not for long. Whatever the case might be, if he could he wanted to be truly free, and he began to shake back and forth, as much as the Harrow permitted.

'You're tearing my straps,' cried the Officer. 'Be still! We'll undo them right away.' And, giving a signal to the Soldier, he set to work with him. The Condemned Man said nothing and smiled slightly to himself. At times he turned his face to the Officer on the left and at times to the Soldier on the right, without ignoring the Traveller.

'Pull him out,' the Officer ordered the Soldier. This process required a certain amount of care because of the Harrow. The Condemned Man already had a few small wounds on his back, thanks to his own impatience.

From this point on, however, the Officer paid no more attention to him. He went up to the Traveller, pulled out the small leather folder once more, leafed through it, finally found the sheet he was looking for, and showed it to the Traveller. 'Read that,' he said.

'I can't,' said the Traveller. 'I've already told you I can't read these pages.'

'But take a close look at the page,' said the Officer and moved up right next to the Traveller in order to read with him. When that didn't help, he raised his little finger high up over the paper, as if the page must not be touched under any circumstances, so that using this he might make the task of reading easier for the Traveller. The Traveller also made an effort so that at least he could satisfy the Officer, but it was impossible for him. At that point the Officer began to spell out the inscription, and then he read out once again the joined up letters. '"Be just!" it states,' he said. 'Now you can read it.' The Traveller bent so low over the paper that the Officer, afraid that he might touch it, moved it further away. The Traveller didn't say anything more, but it was clear that he was still unable to read anything. '"Be just!" it says,' the Officer remarked once again. 'That could be,' said the Traveller. 'I do believe that's written there.' 'Good,' said the Officer, at least partially satisfied. He climbed up the ladder, holding the paper. With great care he set the page in the Inscriber and appeared to rotate the gear mechanism completely around. This was very tiring work. It must have required him to deal with extremely small wheels. He had to inspect the gears so closely that sometimes the Officer's head disappeared completely into the Inscriber.

The Traveller followed this work from below without looking away. His neck grew stiff, and his eyes found the sunlight pouring down from the sky painful. The Soldier and the Condemned Man were keeping each other busy. With the tip of his bayonet the Soldier pulled out the Condemned Man's shirt and trousers which were lying in the hole. The shirt was horribly dirty, and the Condemned Man washed it in the bucket of water.

When he was putting on his shirt and trousers, the Soldier and the Condemned Man had to laugh out loud, for the pieces of clothing were cut in two up the back. Perhaps the Condemned Man thought that it was his duty to amuse the Soldier. In his ripped-up clothes he circled in front of the Soldier, who crouched down on the ground, laughed, and slapped his knees. But they still restrained themselves out of consideration for the two gentlemen present.

When the Officer was finally finished up on the machine, with a smile he looked over the whole thing and all its parts once more, and this time closed the cover of the Inscriber, which had been open up to this point. He climbed down, looked into the hole and then at the Condemned Man, observed with satisfaction that his clothes had been hauled out, then went to the bucket of water to wash his hands, recognized too late that it was disgustingly dirty, and was upset that now he could not wash his hands. Finally he pushed them into the sand. This option did not satisfy him, but he had to do what he could in the circumstances. Then he stood up and began to unbutton the coat of his uniform. As he did this, the two lady's handkerchiefs, which he had pushed into the back of his collar, fell into his hands. 'Here you have your handkerchiefs,' he said and threw them over to the Condemned Man. And to the Traveller he said by way of an explanation, 'Presents from the ladies.'

In spite of the obvious speed with which he took off the coat of his uniform and then undressed himself completely, he handled each piece of clothing very carefully, even running his fingers over the silver braids on his tunic with special care and shaking a tassel into place. But in great contrast to this care, as soon as he was finished handling an article of clothing, he immediately flung it angrily into the hole. The last items he had left were his short sword and its harness. He pulled the sword out of its scabbard, broke it in pieces, then gathered up everything – the pieces of the sword, the scabbard, and the harness – and threw them away so forcefully that they rattled against each other down in the pit.

Now he stood there naked. The Traveller bit his lip and said nothing. For he was aware what would happen, but he had no right to hinder the Officer in any way. If the judicial process to which the Officer clung was really so close to the point of being cancelled – possibly as a result of the intervention of the Traveller, something to which he for his part felt duty-bound – then the Officer was now acting in a completely correct manner. In his place, the Traveller would not have acted any differently.

The Soldier and the Condemned Man at first did not understand a thing. To begin with they did not look, not even once. The Condemned Man was extremely happy to get the handkerchiefs back, but he was not permitted to enjoy them very long, because the Soldier snatched them from him with a quick grab, which he had not anticipated. The Condemned Man then tried to pull the handkerchiefs out from the Soldier's belt, where he had put them for safe keeping, but the Soldier was watching carefully. So they were fighting, half in jest. Only when the Officer was fully naked did they start to pay attention. The Condemned Man especially seemed to be struck by a premonition of some sort of significant transformation. What had happened to him was now taking place with the Officer. Perhaps this time the procedure would play itself out to its conclusion. The foreign Traveller had probably given the order for it. So that was revenge. Without having suffered all the way to the end himself, nonetheless he would be completely avenged. A wide, silent laugh now appeared on his face and never went away.

The Officer, however, had turned towards the machine. If earlier on it had already become clear that he understood the machine thoroughly, one could well get alarmed now at the way he handled it and how it obeyed. He only had to bring his hand near the Harrow for it to rise and sink several times, until it had reached the correct position to make room for him. He only had to grasp the Bed by the edges, and it already began to quiver. The stump of felt moved up to his mouth. One could see how the Officer really did not want to accept it, but his hesitation was only momentary – he immediately submitted and took it in. Everything was ready, except that the straps still hung down on the sides. But they were clearly unnecessary.

The Officer did not have to be strapped down. When the Condemned Man saw the loose straps, he thought the execution would be incomplete unless they were fastened. He waved eagerly to the Soldier, and they ran over to strap in the Officer. The latter had already stuck out his foot to kick the crank designed to set the Inscriber in motion. Then he saw the two men coming. So he pulled his foot back and let himself be strapped in. But now he could no longer reach the crank. Neither the Soldier nor the Condemned Man would find it, and the Traveller was determined not to touch it. But that was unnecessary. Hardly were the straps attached when the machine already started working: the Bed quivered, the needles danced on his skin, and the Harrow swung up and down. The Traveller had already been staring for some time before he remembered that a wheel in the Inscriber was supposed to squeak. But everything was quiet, without the slightest audible hum.

Because of its silent working, the machine did not really attract attention. The Traveller looked over at the Soldier and the Condemned Man. The Condemned Man was the livelier of the two. Everything in the machine interested him. At times he bent down; at other times he stretched up, always pointing with his forefinger in order to show something to the Soldier. For the Traveller it was embarrassing. He was determined to remain here until the end, but he could no longer endure the sight of the two men. 'Go home,' he said. The Soldier might perhaps have been ready to do that, but the Condemned Man took the order as a direct punishment. With his hands folded he pleaded to be allowed to stay there. And when the Traveller shook his head and was unwilling to give in, he even knelt down. Seeing that orders were of no help here, the Traveller wanted to go over and chase the two away. Then he heard a noise from up in the Inscriber. He looked up. So was the gear wheel going out of alignment? But it was something else. The lid on the Inscriber was lifting up slowly. Then it fell completely open. The teeth of a cog wheel were exposed and lifted up. Soon the entire wheel appeared. It was as if some huge force was compressing the Inscriber, so that there was no longer sufficient room left for this wheel. The wheel rolled all the way to the edge of the Inscriber, fell down, rolled upright a bit in the sand, and then fell over and lay still. But already up on the Inscriber another gear wheel was moving upwards. Several others followed – large ones, small ones, ones hard to distinguish. With each of them the same thing happened. One kept thinking that now the Inscriber must surely be already empty, but then a new cluster with lots of parts would move up, fall down, roll in the sand, and lie still. With all this going on, the Condemned Man totally forgot the Traveller's order. The gear wheels completely delighted him. He kept wanting to grab one, and at the same time he was urging the Soldier to help him. But he kept pulling his hand back startled, for immediately another wheel followed, which, at least in its initial rolling, surprised him.

The Traveller, by contrast, was very upset. Obviously the machine was breaking up. Its quiet operation had been an illusion. He felt as if he had to look after the Officer, now that the latter could no longer look after himself. But while the falling gear wheels were claiming all his attention, he had neglected to look at the rest of the machine. However, when he now bent over the Harrow, once the last gear wheel had left the Inscriber, he had a new, even more unpleasant surprise. The Harrow was not writing but only stabbing, and the Bed was not rolling the body, but lifting it, quivering, up into the needles. The Traveller wanted to reach in to stop the whole thing, if possible. This was not the torture the Officer wished to attain; it was murder, pure and simple. He stretched out his hands. But at that point the Harrow was already moving upwards and to the side, with the skewered body – just as it did in other cases, but only in the twelfth hour. Blood flowed out in hundreds of streams, not mixed with water – the water tubes had failed to work this time, as well. Then one last thing went wrong: the body would not come loose from the long needles. Its blood streamed out, but it hung over the pit without falling. The Harrow wanted to move back to its original position, but, as if realizing that it could not free itself of its load, it remained over the hole. 'Help,' the Traveller yelled out to the Soldier and the Condemned Man, and he himself grabbed the Officer's feet. He wanted to push against the feet himself and have the two others grab the Officer's head from the other side, so he could be slowly lifted off the needles. But now the two men could not make up their mind whether to come or not. The Condemned Man turned away at once. The Traveller had to go over to him and drag him to the Officer's head by force. At this point, almost against his will, he looked at the face of the corpse. It was as it had been in life. He could discover no sign of the promised transfiguration. What all the others had found in the machine, the Officer had not. His lips were pressed firmly together, his eyes were open and looked as they had when he was alive, his gaze was calm and convinced. The tip of a large iron needle had gone through his forehead.

As the Traveller, with the Soldier and the Condemned Man behind him, came to the first houses in the colony, the Soldier pointed to one and said, 'That's the tea house.'

On the ground floor of the house was a deep, low room, like a cave, with smoke-covered walls and ceiling. On the street side it was open along its full width. Although there was little difference between the tea house and the rest of the houses in the colony, which were all very dilapidated, except for the Commandant's palatial structure, the Traveller was nonetheless struck by the impression of historical memory, and he felt the power of earlier times. Followed by his companions, he walked closer inside, going between the unoccupied tables, which stood in the street in front of the tea house, and took a breath of the cool, musty air which came from inside. 'The old man is buried here,' said the Soldier; 'a place in the cemetery was denied him by the chaplain. For a while people were undecided where they should bury him. Finally they buried him here. Of course, the Officer explained none of that to you, for naturally he was the one most ashamed about it. A few times he even tried to dig up the old man at night, but he was always chased off.'

'Where is the grave?' asked the Traveller, who could not believe the Soldier. Instantly both men, the Soldier and the Condemned Man, ran in front of him and with hands outstretched pointed to the place where the grave was located. They led the Traveller to the back wall, where guests were sitting at a few tables. They were presumably dock workers, strong men with short, shiny, black beards. None of them wore coats, and their shirts were torn. They were poor, humiliated people. As the Traveller came closer, a few got up, leaned against the wall, and looked at him. A whisper went up around the Traveller – 'It's a foreigner. He wants to look at the grave.' They pushed one of the tables aside, under which there was a real grave stone. It was a simple stone, low enough for it to remain hidden under a table. It bore an inscription in very small letters. In order to read it the Traveller had to kneel down. It read, 'Here rests the Old Commandant. His followers, who are now not permitted to have a name, buried him in this grave and erected this stone. There exists a prophecy that the Commandant will rise again after a certain number of years and from this house will lead his followers to a re-conquest of the colony. Have faith and wait!' When the Traveller had read it and got up, he saw the men standing around him and smiling, as if they had read the inscription with him, found it ridiculous, and were asking him to share their opinion. The Traveller acted as if he had not noticed, distributed some coins among them, waited until the table was pushed back over the grave, left the tea house, and went to the harbour.

In the tea house the Soldier and the Condemned Man had come across some people they knew who detained them. However, they must have broken free of them soon, because by the time the Traveller found himself in the middle of a long staircase which led to the boats, they were already running after him. They probably wanted to force the Traveller at the last minute to take them with him. While the Traveller was haggling at the bottom of the stairs with a sailor about his passage out to the steamer, the two men were racing down the steps in silence, for they did not dare cry out. But as they reached the bottom, the Traveller was already in the boat, and the sailor at once cast off from shore. They could still have jumped into the boat, but the Traveller picked up a heavy knotted rope from the boat bottom, threatened them with it, and thus prevented them from jumping in.

THE WHITE WYRAK

Stefan Grabiński

TRANSLATED INTO ENGLISH BY MIROSLAW LIPINSKI

Stefan Grabiński (1887–1936) was a Polish writer of horror fiction who considered himself an expert on demonology and magic. Some critics have called him the 'Polish Poe' or the 'Polish Lovecraft', and suggested he believed in the supernatural forces in his stories. Known primarily as a novelist, he wrote many short stories, including those under the name Stefaen Żalny. Grabiński was popular in his day, until a trend toward more realistic fiction doomed him to obscurity. The importance of translations by writer Miroslaw Lipinski to bring Grabiński to an English-language readership – for the collection *The Dark Domain* (1993) – cannot be understated. The tale included here, 'The White Weyrak' (1921), exemplifies the writer's talent for atmosphere and strangeness.

I was a young journeyman at that time, like you, my dear boys, and I worked like a house on fire. Master Kalina – may the Lord shine on his worthy soul – frequently said I would be first in attaining mastership following him, and he spoke of me as the pride of our profession. I don't want to brag, but I had strong legs and could dig my elbows into a chimney like no one else. In the third year of my service, I received the assistance of two apprentices and became an instructor to my younger comrades.

In all, there were seven of us. We got along splendidly with one another. Even on holidays and Sundays our brotherhood would gather at the master's house for a chat by a beer or, when it was winter, by warm tea near the chimney, and we talked our fill, so that the evenings we spent together passed nicely, like a brush lowered into the mouth of a furnace.

Kalina – what can I say about him? The man was literate and intelligent. He had seen a lot of the world. As the saying goes, he cleaned out not just one chimney. He was a bit of a philosopher, and books he really liked. He apparently even wanted to put out a gazette for chimney sweepers. But in matters of faith he didn't play the philosopher; on the contrary, he had a particular devotion to St. Florian, our patron.

I felt closest to the master and, after him, to the young journeyman Jozek Biedron, a boy as pure as gold, whom I liked for his good heart and gentle soul. Unfortunately I wouldn't enjoy his friendship for long!

After Biedron, I most liked Antarek, a melancholic lad who usually kept to himself. He was a born worker, however, conscientious and strangely relentless in his job. Kalina valued him a lot and tried to get him to socialize with people, though without success. Nevertheless, Antarek gladly spent his evenings at the master's house, listening with interest from his dark corner to the master's stories, which he completely believed.

And no one could tell a story like our 'old man.' He drew them out as if from a bag, one more interesting than the other. When he finished one, he would start a new one, then throw in a third one, and so on. And in each story one could detect some deeper thought hidden behind all those words. But one was still young and foolish then, and took from these stories only what amused one, for a laugh. Only Antarek looked at the master's tales in a different light, and managed to get to their core. The rest of us, however, called Kalina's stories balderdash. They were engrossing, sometimes horrible, until one's flesh crept and one's hair stood on end, but despite it all, only tales and balderdash. Yet life soon taught us a little differently…

One day in the middle of summer, a comrade of ours was absent at our evening get-together: Antarek was not present at his usual dark corner beyond the cupboard.

'He must have gotten sidetracked with some girls,' joked Biedron, though he knew that his friend was ill at ease with women and avoided their company.

'Stop talking nonsense,' Kalina said. 'He's probably very depressed and is sitting at home like a bear in the back woods.'

The evening passed sadly and slowly, as it was without the presence of our most fervent listener.

There was no joking around the following morning, for Antarek did not show up for work at ten o'clock. The master thought he was sick and went to his home. He found only his mother there, an old woman much distressed by her son's absence. She reported that her son had left for the city at dawn of the previous day and had not yet returned.

Kalina decided to undertake the search himself.

'Antarek is a gloomy fellow; God knows what he's done. Maybe he's hiding out somewhere.'

But he searched in vain. Finally, remembering that Antarek had to clean out a chimney in an old brewery beyond the city, he directed his investigation there.

At the brewery he was told that, indeed, yesterday morning a journeyman had reported to them to clean the chimney.

'At what time did he finish the job?' asked Kalina of some old man, gray like a pigeon, whom he met at the threshold of one of the brewery's annexes.

'I don't know, Master. He left so imperceptibly that we even didn't know when. He must have been in a great hurry because he didn't even look in to us for payment.'

'Hmm…' muttered Kalina, lost in thought. 'A strange bird, that fellow. But did he clean out the chimney well? How is it working now? Is it drawing properly?'

'Not too well. This morning my daughter-in-law complained once again that it's smoking terribly. If it doesn't get better by tomorrow, we'll ask for another cleaning.'

'It will be done,' the master quickly retorted, angry that here they were not satisfied with his worker, and very worried about the lack of more specific information concerning him.

That evening we gathered together in sorrow at our supper and parted early. The following day the same thing: neither sight nor sound of Antarek – he had disappeared like a stone in water.

In the early afternoon the brewery sent a boy with the request to clean the chimney because it was 'smoking for all it's worth.'

Biedron went around four and didn't return. I wasn't there when Kalina sent him out, so I knew nothing about it. But I got a bad feeling when, later that evening, I saw the downcast faces of the master and the other sweeps.

'Where's Jozek?' I asked, looking for him about the room.

'He hasn't returned from the brewery,' answered Kalina gloomily.

I jumped up from my seat. But the master forcibly stopped me:

'I won't let you go alone. I've had enough of this! Tomorrow morning both of us will go. An evil spirit, not a brewery! I'll clean out their chimney for them!'

That night I didn't sleep a wink. At daybreak I put on my climbing gear, and throwing over my shoulder my brushes with their attachments, I went out and in a short while presented myself at the master's door.

Kalina was already waiting for me.

'Take this,' he said, handing me a hatchet that

appeared to be newly whetted. 'This could be of more use to you than a broom or a scraper.'

Without a word I took the hatchet, and we started at a quick pace toward the brewery.

The August morning was beautiful and tranquil. The city still slept. In silence we passed through the marketplace, went over the bridge, and turned left, along the river embankment, onto a road that wound its way through poplar trees.

It was a long walk to the brewery. After a strenuous pace of fifteen minutes, we got off the road and took a shortcut through a hayfield. In the distance, beyond an alder forest, the coppery slices of the brewery roofs were visible.

Kalina removed the cap from his head, crossed himself, and began silently to move his lips. I walked next to him, not interrupting his prayers. After a while the master covered his head again, gripped his hatchet tighter, and starting talking in a soft voice:

'An evil spirit, not a brewery. There's beer there and for at least ten years it hasn't been brewed. An old ruin and nothing more. The last brewer, someone named Rozban, went bankrupt and hanged himself out of despair. His family sold the buildings and the entire inventory dirt-cheap to the city, and moved away somewhere. No one has lived there since. The boilers and machines are supposed to be evil. They're of an old system. No one wants to take the financial risk of replacing it with a new one.'

'Then who exactly wanted the chimney cleaned?' I asked, glad that the conversation had interrupted the morose silence.

'Some gardener, who a month ago, for practically nothing, moved into the empty brewery with his wife and his father. They have many rooms and enough space for several families. For sure they moved into the center rooms, which are in the best state, and they are living there for very little money. Now their chimneys are smoking, because they are old and heavily packed with soot. They haven't been cleaned for ages.' He added after a thoughtful pause: 'I don't like these old chimneys.'

'Why? Because there's more work with them?'

'Don't be silly, my dear boy. I'm afraid of them, do you understand? I'm afraid of old flues that haven't been touched for years by a brush or scraper. It's better to demolish such chimney and put up a new one than to have someone clean it.'

I glanced at Kalina's face at that moment. It was strangely altered by fear and aversion.

'What's the matter, Master?'

And he, as if he hadn't heard, continued on, staring somewhere ahead: 'Soot is dangerous, particularly when it accumulates in narrow, dark spaces unreachable by the rays of the sun. And not just because it can easily catch fire. No, not just because of that. Consider this, we chimney sweeps battle our entire lives with soot, we prevent its excessive accumulation, and so prevent an explosion. But soot is treacherous, my boy, soot lays dormant inside dark smoke chambers and stuffy furnances, and it lies in wait – for an opportunity. Something vindictive resides in soot, something evil lurks there. You never know what will emerge from it, or when.'

He became silent and glanced at me. Even though I didn't understand what he had said, his words, uttered with such strong conviction, had their effect on me. But he smiled his good, kindhearted smile, and added soothingly: 'Maybe I'm wrong, maybe something completely different has happened here. Cheer up! We'll find out everything in a moment. We've arrived at our destination.'

Indeed, we had reached the brewery. Through the open entrance gate, I followed the master to the wide courtyard, from which a multitude of doors led to the various buildings of the brewery. At the threshold of one door sat the gardener's wife, a child at her breast; while beyond her, leaning against the door sill, stood her husband. Seeing us, the man became confused and with visible uneasiness came out to greet us: 'You've come to see us about the chimney?'

'Of course, you,' the master answered coldly, 'but not because of the chimney, but because of the two people I sent to clean it.'

The gardener's uneasiness increased; his eyes shifted continually.

'My men haven't yet returned from this brewery!' cried out Kalina passionately, glaring at him. 'What happened to them? You're responsible for them!'

'But, sir,' the gardener mumbled, 'I really don't know what happened to them. We thought that the first one had already turned up, and as for the second one – I just don't know. Yesterday afternoon, in my presence, he entered the chimney through the door in the kitchen wall: for some time I clearly heard him scraping the soot away. I would have remained to the end of the operation if I hadn't been called out to the courtyard. Afterward, I left my home for a couple of hours, and when I returned, nothing was said about the chimney or your man. I thought that he had done his job and returned to the city, so we closed the ventilation door for the night. Only now, when I saw the both of you entering our courtyard, did I become troubled. It suddenly occurred to me that something terrible has been happening here for the last two days. I see that I am right. But what is going on, Master Kalina? What can be done?' He spread out his hands in a sign of innocence. 'I'm not to blame.'

'At least you shouldn't have closed the door to the chimney, fool!' Kalina cried out angrily. 'After me, Peter!' he shouted, pulling me by the arm. 'We don't have a second to lose.' And to the gardener: 'Take us to the chimney!'

The terrified gardener led us inside. We soon found ourselves in the kitchen.

'Here, in the corner,' said the gardener, pointing to the rectangular chimney door.

Kalina took a step toward it, but, anticipating him, I moved quickly and opened the small door.

A smell of smoke blew over us, and a little soot fell to the floor.

Before the master could interfere, I was already kneeling at the inlet, my arms stretched upward in preparation for a climb.

'Are you crazy?' Kalina's angry voice responded. 'Let me go up! This is my affair. You set up the ladder to the roof and get on top to guard the outlet.'

For the first time in my life I did not listen to him. A mad stubbornness and a desire to uncover the truth possessed me completely.

'Why don't you go to the roof yourself, Master!' I responded. 'I promise to wait here until you give me the signal.'

Kalina uttered an ugly curse, and whether he liked it or not, he had to surrender to my command. Soon I heard his distancing steps. Then I tied a silk mask tightly over my mouth and nose, adjusted the straps at my belt, and gripped the hatchet. Before you could say two Hail Marys I heard the knocking of the ball that had been lowered down the chimney: Kalina was already on the roof and was giving me the agreed-upon signal.

I crawled on all fours into the throat of the chimney and, groping about, found the ball. I pulled on it three times in a sign that I had received the signal and was commencing my journey.

After passing the turn in the chimney, I straightened up, instinctively protecting my head with the hatchet.

The chimney was wide, navigable with ridges, and thickly packed with soot. Here at the bottom, right beside the door, layers of easily flammable 'enamel' glowed with a cold metallic luster in the faint light coming from the top of the chimney.

I threw a glance upward – and shuddered.

Above me, several feet beyond the blade of my hatchet, I saw in the half-light of the flue a snow-white being staring at me with a pair of huge, owlish yellow eyes.

The creature – part monkey, part large frog – was holding in his front claws what seemed like a human arm, which hung limply from a corpse, vaguely outlined in a twisted shape next to the neighboring wall.

Drenched in cold sweat, I propped myself against the sides of the chimney with my legs and raised myself up slightly. Then, from the creature's long mouth came a savage predatory sound, and he ground his teeth menacingly. My movement seemed to have alarmed him, and he apparently changed position, for at that moment a wider shaft of light rushed into the depths of the chimney and lit up the horrible picture more clearly.

Attached through some miracle, as if stuck to the wall with the bottom of his toes, the creature held Biedron tightly with his arms. His rear limbs, covered with white, downy fur, wrapped in a crosswise grip the legs of his victim, while the greedy proboscis of his elongated snout now adhered to the temple of the unfortunate man.

A rage enveloped me, and overcoming my fear, I climbed up a couple more feet. The white creature, apparently upset, turned to me again and started to prick his spoonlike ears and grind his teeth ever more loudly, but he didn't move from his place.

I saw his vain endeavors as he wanted to spring down on me or escape up the chimney. But his movements were unusually awkward and ponderous; it seemed that he had grown torpid, as a snake does after swallowing a victim, or that he had become drunk on an overabundance of sucked blood; only his bulging eyes, round like plates, buried themselves into me with increasing severity, and he threatened me with his look and sound…

But my anger predominated over my terror. I drew back the hatchet swiftly and with all my might let it go on the horrible white skull.

The blow was strong and accurate. In one moment the light in his large eyes died out, something brushed by me, and I heard a dull groan below; the strange being had fallen to the bottom of the chimney, pulling down his victim in the process.

A shudder of disgust shook me to the core; I didn't have courage to go down and check the result of my blow. The only thing left for me to do was to go up to the roof. Besides, I was already at the halfway point in the chimney, from whose outlet I heard Kalina's voice.

I began a quick climb to the top, using all my strength to dig into the sides of the chimney with my elbows and legs. But who can relate my horror when a couple of feet higher I saw, hanging on a hook sticking out of the wall, the carcass of Antarek?

The body of the poor man was in a terrible state – incredibly gaunt and shriveled up to a sliver – almost skin and bones. It seemed half-cured by exposure to smoke, and was stretched out like a string, and dry and hard like a piece of wood.

With trembling hands I unhooked the carcass, and winding its middle a few times with the rope from the ball, I pulled twice on the cord as a signal to Kalina.

A couple of minutes later, I found myself on the roof, where the master was waiting for me, Antarek's body by his side. He greeted me sullenly, with knitted brows.

'Where's Biedron?' he asked tersely.

In a few words I told him everything.

After we had carefully lowered Antarek to the ground along the ladder, he said calmly:

'The White Wyrak. That was him. I had a feeling it would be him.'

In silence we went through the hall and two rooms, and returned to the kitchen. There wasn't a living soul here; the gardener and his family had slunk away to some wing of the building.

Placing Antarek's body by the wall, we advanced to the opening of the chimney. Sticking out of it were a pair of stiff, naked legs.

We pulled out Biedron and placed him on the floor by his comrade.

'See those two small wounds they have on their temples?' asked Kalina in a subdued voice. 'That is his sign. He cuts into his victims there and consumes them.' And he repeated a couple of times: 'The White Wyrak! The White Wyrak!'

'I have to finish him off,' I replied stubbornly. 'Maybe he isn't dead yet.'

'I doubt it. Apparently he can't stand light. Let's take a look, though.'

And we gazed into the depths of the opening.

Deep inside we vaguely saw something white. Kalina glanced about the kitchen and spotted a long pole with an iron hook at its end. He picked up the pole and shoved it into the chimney opening. Then he started to draw it out…

Slowly a white mass began to emerge from the darkness, a sort of snowy, downy fleece that came closer and closer to the ventilator.

But along the way, the Wyrak's corpse seemed to melt and contract. When Kalina finally drew out the entire pole, there hung from its iron tip only a small, milk-white substance; it was flaky and disarranged, and resembled a soft hide or fluff.

Suddenly this substance slid off the hook and fell to the ground. And then a strange change occurred in it; in the twinkling of an eye, the white material turned a coallike color, and at our feet lay a large mass of soot – glittering and black like tar.

'That's all that remains of him,' whispered Kalina, plunged in thought.

And after a moment he added, as if to himself:

'From soot you came, and to soot you shall return.'

And placing our unfortunate comrades on a stretcher, we carried off their bodies to the city.

Shortly afterward, the master and I got a peculiar outbreak on our skins. Over our entire bodies appeared large white pimples, resembling pearly grits. After several weeks, these pimples disappeared as quickly and as unexpectedly as they had arrived, leaving not a trace of their repulsive presence.

THE NIGHT WIRE

H. F. Arnold

H. F. Arnold (1902–1963) was an American pulp-era writer who wrote only three published stories. Despite this low output, 'The Night Wire' (1926), first published in *Weird Tales,* is considered the most popular story from the first golden age of that magazine. Lovecraft is said to have loved this story. 'The Night Wire' is perhaps remarkable in still being able to chill the reader today despite using elements that could have made the story feel dated. It is a perfect example of how the weird creates not just unease, but dislocation. Details about the writer's life are scarce, without even confirmation that 'H. F. Arnold' was his real name. Some have speculated that he must have been a journalist.

`New York, September 30 CP FLASH Ambassador Holliwell died here today. The end came suddenly as the ambassador was alone in his study...`

There is something ungodly about these night wire jobs. You sit up here on the top floor of a skyscraper and listen in to the whispers of a civilization. New York, London, Calcutta, Bombay, Singapore – they're your next-door neighbors after the street lights go dim and the world has gone to sleep.

Alone in the quiet hours between two and four, the receiving operators doze over their sounders and the news comes in. Fires and disasters and sui cides. Murders, crowds, catastrophes. Sometimes an earthquake with a casualty list as long as your arm. The night wire man takes it down almost in his sleep, picking it off on his typewriter with one finger.

Once in a long time you prick up your ears and listen. You've heard of someone you knew in Singapore, Halifax or Paris, long ago. Maybe they've been promoted, but more probably they've been murdered or drowned. Perhaps they just decided to quit and took some bizarre way out. Made it interesting enough to get in the news.

But that doesn't happen often. Most of the time you sit and doze and tap, tap on your typewriter and wish you were home in bed.

Sometimes, though, queer things happen. One did the other night, and I haven't got over it yet. I wish I could.

You see, I handle the night manager's desk in a western seaport town; what the name is, doesn't matter.

There is, or rather was, only one night operator on my staff, a fellow named John Morgan, about forty years of age, I should say, and a sober, hard-working sort.

He was one of the best operators I ever knew, what is known as a 'double' man. That means he could handle two instruments at once and type the stories on different typewriters at the same time. He was one of the three men I ever knew who could do it consistently, hour after hour, and never make a mistake.

Generally, we used only one wire at night, but sometimes, when it was late and the news was coming fast, the Chicago and Denver stations would open a second wire, and then Morgan would do his stuff. He was a wizard, a mechanical automatic wizard which functioned marvelously but was without imagination.

On the night of the sixteenth he complained of feeling tired. It was the first and last time I had ever heard him say a word about himself, and I had known him for three years.

It was just three o'clock and we were running only one wire. I was nodding over reports at my desk and not paying much attention to him, when he spoke.

'Jim,' he said, 'does it feel close in here to you?'

'Why, no, John,' I answered, 'but I'll open a window if you like.'

'Never mind,' he said, 'I reckon I'm just a little tired.'

That was all that was said, and I went on working. Every ten minutes or so I would walk over and take a pile of copy that had stacked up neatly beside the typewriter as the messages were printed out in triplicate.

It must have been twenty minutes after he spoke that I noticed he had opened up the other wire and was using both typewriters. I thought it was a little unusual, as there was nothing very 'hot' coming in. On my next trip I picked up the copy from both machines and took it back to my desk to sort out the duplicates.

The first wire was running out the usual sort of stuff and I just looked over it hurriedly. Then I turned to the second pile of copy. I remembered it particularly because the story was from a town I had never heard of: 'Xebico'. Here is the dispatch. I saved a duplicate of it from our files:

Xebico, Sept. 16 CP BULLETIN
The heaviest mist in the history of the city settled over the town at 4 o'clock yesterday afternoon. All traffic has stopped and the mist hangs like a pall over everything. Lights of ordinary intensity fail to pierce the fog, which is constantly growing heavier.

Scientists here are unable to agree as to the cause, and the local weather bureau states that the like has never occurred before in the history of the city.

At 7 p.m. last night municipal authorities... (more)

That was all there was. Nothing out of the ordinary at a bureau headquarters, but, as I say, I noticed the story because of the name of the town.

It must have been fifteen minutes later that I went over for another batch of copy. Morgan was slumped down in his chair and had switched his green electric light shade so that the gleam missed his eyes and hit only the top of the two typewriters.

Only the usual stuff was in the righthand pile, but the lefthand batch carried another story from Xebico. All press dispatches come in 'takes,' meaning that parts of many different stories are strung along together, perhaps with but a few paragraphs of each coming through at a time. This second story was marked 'add fog.' Here is the copy:

At 7 p.m. the fog had increased noticeably. All lights were now invisible and the town was shrouded in pitch darkness.

As a peculiarity of the phenomenon, the fog is accompanied by a sickly odor, comparable to nothing yet experienced here.

Below that in customary press fashion was the hour, 3:27, and the initials of the operator, JM.

There was only one other story in the pile from the second wire. Here it is:

2nd add Xebico Fog
Accounts as to the origin of the mist differ greatly. Among the most unusual is that of the sexton of the local church, who groped his way to headquarters in a hysterical condition and declared that the fog originated in the village churchyard.

'It was first visible as a soft gray blanket clinging to the earth above the graves,' he stated. 'Then it began to rise, higher and higher. A subterranean breeze seemed to blow it in billows, which split up and then joined together again.

'Fog phantoms, writhing in anguish, twisted the mist into queer forms and figures. And then, in the very thick midst of the mass, something moved.

'I turned and ran from the accursed spot. Behind me I heard screams coming from the houses bordering on the graveyard.'

Although the sexton's story is generally discredited, a party has left to investigate. Immediately after telling his story, the sexton collapsed and is now in a local hospital, unconscious.

Queer story, wasn't it. Not that we aren't used to it, for a lot of unusual stories come in over the wire. But for some reason or other, perhaps because it was so quiet that night, the report of the fog made a great impression on me.

It was almost with dread that I went over to the waiting piles of copy. Morgan did not move, and the only sound in the room was the tap-tap of the sounders. It was ominous, nerve-racking.

There was another story from Xebico in the pile of copy. I seized on it anxiously.

New Lead Xebico Fog CP
The rescue party which went out at 11 p.m. to investigate a weird story of the origin of a fog which, since late yesterday, has shrouded the city in darkness has failed to return. Another and larger party has been dispatched.

Meanwhile, the fog has, if possible, grown heavier. It seeps through the cracks in the doors and fills the atmosphere with a depressing odor of decay. It is oppressive, terrifying, bearing with it a subtle impression of things long dead.

Residents of the city have left their homes and gathered in the local church, where the priests are holding services of prayer. The scene is beyond description. Grown folk and children are alike terrified and many are almost beside themselves with fear.

Amid the wisps of vapor which partly veil the church auditorium, an old priest is praying for the welfare of his flock. They alternately wail and cross themselves.

From the outskirts of the city may be heard cries of unknown voices. They echo through the fog in queer uncadenced minor keys. The sounds resemble nothing so much as wind whistling through a gigantic tunnel. But the night is calm and there is no wind. The second rescue party... (more)

I am a calm man and never in a dozen years spent with the wires, have been known to become excited, but despite myself I rose from my chair and walked to the window.

Could I be mistaken, or far down in the canyons of the city beneath me did I see a faint trace of fog? Pshaw! It was all imagination.

In the pressroom the click of the sounders seemed to have raised the tempo of their tune. Morgan alone had not stirred from his chair. His head sunk between his shoulders, he tapped the dispatches out on the typewriters with one finger of each hand.

He looked asleep, but no; endlessly, efficiently, the two machines rattled off line after line, as relentlessly and effortlessly as death itself. There was something about the monotonous movement of the typewriter keys that fascinated me. I walked over and stood behind his chair, reading over his shoulder the type as it came into being, word by word.

Ah, here was another:

Flash Xebico CP
There will be no more bulletins from this office. The impossible has happened. No messages have come into this room for twenty minutes. We are cut off from the outside and even the streets below us.

I will stay with the wire until the end.

It is the end, indeed. Since 4 p.m. yesterday the fog has hung over the city. Following reports from the sexton of the local church, two rescue parties were sent out to investigate conditions on the outskirts of the city. Neither party has ever returned nor was any word received from them. It is quite certain now that they will never return.

From my instrument I can gaze down on the city beneath me. From the position of this room on the thirteenth floor, nearly the entire city can be seen. Now I can see only a thick blanket of blackness where customarily are lights and life.

I fear greatly that the wailing cries heard constantly from the outskirts of the city are the death cries of the inhabitants. They are constantly increasing in volume and are approaching the center of the city.

The fog yet hangs over everything. If possible, it is even heavier than before, but the conditions have changed. Instead of an opaque, impenetrable wall of odorous vapor, there now swirls and writhes a shapeless mass in contortions of almost human agony. Now and again the mass parts and I catch a brief glimpse of the streets below.

People are running to and fro, screaming in despair. A vast bedlam of sound flies up to my window, and above all is the immense whistling of unseen and unfelt winds.

The fog has again swept over the city and the whistling is coming closer and closer.

It is now directly beneath me.

God! An instant ago the mist opened and I caught a glimpse of the streets below.

The fog is not simply vapor – it lives! By the side of each moaning and weeping human is a companion figure, an aura of strange and vari-colored hues. How the shapes cling! Each to a living thing!

The men and women are down. Flat on their faces. The fog figures caress them lovingly. They are kneeling beside them. They are – but I dare not tell it.

The prone and writhing bodies have been stripped of their clothing. They are being consumed – piecemeal.

A merciful wall of hot, steamy vapor has swept over the whole scene. I can see no more.

Beneath me the wall of vapor is changing colors. It seems to be lighted by internal fires. No, it isn't. I have made a mistake. The colors are from above, reflections from the sky.

Look up! Look up! The whole sky is in flames. Colors as yet unseen by man or demon. The flames are moving; they have started to intermix; the colors are rearranging themselves. They are so brilliant that my eyes burn, yet they are a long way off.

Now they have begun to swirl, to circle in and out, twisting in intricate designs and patterns. The lights are racing each with each, a kaleidoscope of unearthly brilliance.

I have made a discovery. There is nothing harmful in the lights. They radiate force and friendliness, almost cheeriness. But by their very strength, they hurt.

As I look, they are swinging closer and closer, a million miles at each jump. Millions of miles with the speed of light. Aye, it is light the quintessence of all light. Beneath it the fog melts into a jeweled mist radiant, rainbow-colored of a thousand varied spectra.

I can see the streets. Why, they are filled with people! The lights are coming closer. They are all around me. I am enveloped. I...'

The message stopped abruptly. The wire to Xebico was dead. Beneath my eyes in the narrow circle of light from under the green lamp-shade, the black printing no longer spun itself, letter by letter, across the page.

The room seemed filled with a solemn quiet, a silence vaguely impressive, powerful.

I looked down at Morgan. His hands had dropped nervelessly at his sides, while his body had hunched over peculiarly. I turned the lamp-shade back, throwing the light squarely in his face. His eyes were staring, fixed.

Filled with a sudden foreboding, I stepped beside him and called Chicago on the wire. After a second the sounder clicked its answer.

Why? But there was something wrong. Chicago was reporting that Wire Two had not been used throughout the evening.

'Morgan!' I shouted. 'Morgan! Wake up, it isn't true. Someone has been hoaxing us. Why…' In my eagerness I grasped him by the shoulder.

His body was quite cold. Morgan had been dead for hours. Could it be that his sensitized brain and automatic fingers had continued to record impressions even after the end?

I shall never know, for I shall never again handle the night shift. Search in a world atlas discloses no town of Xebico. Whatever it was that killed John Morgan will forever remain a mystery.

THE DUNWICH HORROR

H. P. Lovecraft

H. P. Lovecraft (1890–1937) was perhaps the most influential twentieth-century American author of weird fiction. Lovecraft's fiction did not become popular overnight: he had a cult readership during his lifetime, and readers could be put off by a worldview that reflected the idea of 'cosmic horror'. Lovecraft believed that life is ultimately incomprehensible to human beings and the universe is a cold, hostile place. Despite this, he became increasingly popular, to the point that creations like the Cthulhu Mythos have entered our common lexicon. Much about Lovecraft's life and beliefs are problematic to modern readers, but the stories have been enduring because, as in the best weird fiction, the images and situations have a visionary and timeless quality. 'The Dunwich Horror' (1929) showcases many of his strengths.

'Gorgons and Hydras, and Chimaeras – dire stories of Celaeno and the Harpies – may reproduce themselves in the brain of superstition – but they were there before. They are transcripts, types – the archetypes are in us, and eternal. How else should the recital of that which we know in a waking sense to be false come to affect us all? Is it that we naturally conceive terror from such objects, considered in their capacity of being able to inflict upon us bodily injury? O, least of all! These terrors are of older standing. They date beyond body – or without the body, they would have been the same… That the kind of fear here treated is purely spiritual – that it is strong in proportion as it is objectless on earth, that it predominates in the period of our sinless infancy – are difficulties the solution of which might afford some probable insight into our ante-mundane condition, and a peep at least into the shadowland of pre-existence.'

Charles Lamb Witches and Other Night-Fears

When a traveller in north central Massachusetts takes the wrong fork at the junction of Aylesbury pike just beyond Dean's Corners he comes upon a lonely and curious country.

The ground gets higher, and the brier-bordered stone walls press closer and closer against the ruts of the dusty, curving road. The trees of the frequent forest belts seem too large, and the wild weeds, brambles and grasses attain a luxuriance not often found in settled regions. At the same time the planted fields appear singularly few and barren; while the sparsely scattered houses wear a surprisingly uniform aspect of age, squalor, and dilapidation.

Without knowing why, one hesitates to ask directions from the gnarled solitary figures spied now and then on crumbling doorsteps or on the sloping, rock-strewn meadows. Those figures are so silent and furtive that one feels somehow confronted by forbidden things, with which it would be better to have nothing to do. When a rise in the road brings the mountains in view above the deep woods, the feeling of strange uneasiness is increased. The summits are too rounded and symmetrical to give a sense of comfort and naturalness, and sometimes the sky silhouettes with especial clearness the queer circles of tall stone pillars with which most of them are crowned.

Gorges and ravines of problematical depth intersect the way, and the crude wooden bridges always seem of dubious safety. When the road dips again there are stretches of marshland that one instinctively dislikes, and indeed almost fears at evening when unseen whippoorwills chatter and the fireflies come out in abnormal profusion to dance to the raucous, creepily insistent rhythms of stridently piping bull-frogs. The thin, shining line of the Miskatonic's upper reaches has an oddly serpent-like suggestion as it winds close to the feet of the domed hills among which it rises.

As the hills draw nearer, one heeds their wooded sides more than their stone-crowned tops. Those sides loom up so darkly and precipitously that one wishes they would keep their distance, but there is no road by which to escape them. Across a covered bridge one sees a small village huddled between the stream and the vertical slope of Round Mountain, and wonders at the cluster of rotting gambrel roofs bespeaking an earlier architectural period than that of the neighbouring region. It is not reassuring to see, on a closer glance, that most of the houses are deserted and falling to ruin, and that the broken-steepled church now harbours the one slovenly mercantile establishment of the hamlet. One dreads to trust the tenebrous tunnel of the bridge, yet there is no way to avoid it. Once across, it is hard to prevent the impression of a faint, malign odour about the village street, as of the massed mould and decay of centuries. It is always a relief to get clear of the place, and to follow the narrow road around the base of the hills and across the level country beyond till it rejoins the Aylesbury pike. Afterwards one sometimes learns that one has been through Dunwich.

Outsiders visit Dunwich as seldom as possible, and since a certain season of horror all the signboards pointing towards it have been taken down. The scenery, judged by an ordinary aesthetic canon, is more than commonly beautiful; yet there is no influx of artists or summer tourists. Two centuries ago, when talk of witch-blood, Satan-worship, and strange forest presences was not laughed at, it was the custom to give reasons for avoiding the locality. In our sensible age – since the Dunwich horror of 1928 was hushed up by those who had the town's and the world's welfare at heart – people shun it without knowing exactly why. Perhaps one reason – though it cannot apply to uninformed strangers – is that the natives are now repellently decadent, having gone far along that path of retrogression so common in many New England backwaters. They have come to form a race by themselves, with the well-defined mental and physical stigmata of degeneracy and inbreeding. The average of their intelligence is woefully low, whilst their annals reek of overt viciousness and of half-hidden murders, incests, and deeds of almost unnameable violence and perversity. The old gentry, representing the two or three armigerous families which came from Salem in 1692, have kept somewhat above the general level of decay; though many branches are sunk into the sordid populace so deeply that only their names remain as a key to the origin they disgrace. Some of the Whateleys and Bishops still send their eldest sons to Harvard and Miskatonic, though those sons seldom return to the mouldering gambrel roofs under which they and their ancestors were born.

No one, even those who have the facts concerning the recent horror, can say just what is the matter with Dunwich; though old legends speak of unhallowed rites and conclaves of the Indians, amidst which they called forbidden shapes of shadow out of the great rounded hills, and made wild orgiastic prayers that were answered by loud crackings and rumblings from the ground below. In 1747 the Reverend Abijah Hoadley, newly come to the Congregational Church at Dunwich Village, preached a memorable sermon on the close presence of Satan and his imps; in which he said:

'It must be allow'd, that these Blasphemies of an infernall Train of Daemons are Matters of too common Knowledge to be deny'd; the cursed Voices of Azazel and Buzrael, of Beelzebub and Belial, being heard now from under Ground by above a Score of credible Witnesses now living. I myself did not more than a Fortnight ago catch a very plain Discourse of evill Powers in the Hill behind my House; wherein there were a Rattling and Rolling, Groaning, Screeching, and Hissing, such as no Things of this Earth could raise up, and which must needs have come from those Caves that only black Magick can discover, and only the Divell unlock.'

Mr. Hoadley disappeared soon after delivering this sermon, but the text, printed in Springfield, is still extant. Noises in the hills continued to be reported from year to year, and still form a puzzle to geologists and physiographers.

Other traditions tell of foul odours near the hill-crowning circles of stone pillars, and of rushing airy presences to be heard faintly at certain hours from stated points at the bottom of the great ravines; while still others try to explain the Devil's Hop Yard – a bleak, blasted hillside where no tree, shrub, or grass-blade will grow. Then, too, the natives are mortally afraid of the numerous whippoorwills which grow vocal on warm nights. It is vowed that the birds are psychopomps lying in wait for the souls of the dying, and that they time their eerie cries in unison with the sufferer's struggling breath. If they can catch the fleeing soul when it leaves the body, they instantly flutter away chittering in daemoniac laughter; but if they fail, they subside gradually into a disappointed silence.

These tales, of course, are obsolete and ridiculous; because they come down from very old times. Dunwich is indeed ridiculously old – older by far than any of the communities within thirty miles of it. South of the village one may still spy the cellar walls and chimney of the ancient Bishop house, which was built before 1700; whilst the ruins of the mill at the falls, built in 1806, form the most modern piece of architecture to be seen. Industry did not flourish here, and the nineteenth-century factory movement proved short-lived. Oldest of all are the great rings of rough-hewn stone columns on the hilltops, but these are more generally attributed to the Indians than to the settlers. Deposits of skulls and bones, found within these circles and around the sizeable table-like rock on Sentinel Hill, sustain the popular belief that such spots were once the burial-places of the Pocumtucks; even though many ethnologists, disregarding the absurd improbability of such a theory, persist in believing the remains Caucasian.

II

It was in the township of Dunwich, in a large and partly inhabited farmhouse set against a hillside four miles from the village and a mile and a half from any other dwelling, that Wilbur Whateley was born at 5 A.M. on Sunday, the second of February, 1913. This date was recalled because it was Candlemas, which people in Dunwich curiously observe under another name; and because the noises in the hills had sounded, and all the dogs of the countryside had barked persistently, throughout the night before. Less worthy of notice was the fact that the mother was one of the decadent Whateleys, a somewhat deformed, unattractive albino woman of thirty-five, living with an aged and half-insane father about whom the most frightful tales of wizardry had been whispered in his youth. Lavinia Whateley had no known husband, but according to the custom of the region made no attempt to disavow the child; concerning the other side of whose ancestry the country folk might – and did – speculate as widely as they chose. On the contrary, she seemed strangely proud of the dark, goatish-looking infant who formed such a contrast to her own sickly and pink-eyed albinism, and was heard to mutter many curious prophecies about its unusual powers and tremendous future.

Lavinia was one who would be apt to mutter such things, for she was a lone creature given to wandering amidst thunderstorms in the hills and trying to read the great odorous books which her father had inherited through two centuries of Whateleys, and which were fast falling to pieces with age and wormholes. She had never been to school, but was filled with disjointed scraps of ancient lore that Old Whateley had taught her. The remote farmhouse had always been feared because of Old Whateley's reputation for black magic, and the unexplained death by violence of Mrs Whateley when Lavinia was twelve years old had not helped to make the place popular. Isolated among strange influences, Lavinia was fond of wild and grandiose day-dreams and singular occupations; nor was her leisure much taken up by household cares in a home from which all standards of order and cleanliness had long since disappeared.

There was a hideous screaming which echoed above even the hill noises and the dogs' barking on the night Wilbur was born, but no known doctor or midwife presided at his coming. Neighbours knew nothing of him till a week afterward, when Old Whateley drove his sleigh through the snow into Dunwich Village and discoursed incoherently to the group of loungers at Osborne's general store. There seemed to be a change in the old man – an added element of furtiveness in the clouded brain which subtly transformed him from an object to a subject of fear – though he was not one to be perturbed by any common family event. Amidst it all he showed some trace of the pride later noticed in his daughter, and what he said of the child's paternity was remembered by many of his hearers years afterward.

'I dun't keer what folks think – ef Lavinny's boy looked like his pa, he wouldn't look like nothin' ye expeck. Ye needn't think the only folks is the folks hereabouts. Lavinny's read some, an' has seed some things the most o' ye only tell abaout. I calc'late her man is as good a husban' as ye kin find this side of Aylesbury; an' ef ye knowed as much abaout the hills as I dew, ye wouldn't ast no better church weddin' nor her'n. Let me tell ye suthin – *some day yew folks'll hear a child o' Lavinny's a-callin' its father's name on the top o' Sentinel Hill!'*

The only persons who saw Wilbur during the first month of his life were old Zechariah Whateley, of the undecayed Whateleys, and Earl Sawyer's common-law wife, Mamie Bishop. Mamie's visit was frankly one of curiosity, and her subsequent tales did justice to her observations; but Zechariah came to lead a pair of Alderney cows which Old Whateley had bought off his son Curtis. This marked the beginning of a course of cattle-buying on the part of small Wilbur's family which ended only in 1928, when the Dunwich horror came and went; yet at no time did the ramshackle Whateley barn seem overcrowded with livestock. There came a period when people were curious enough to steal up and count the herd that grazed precariously on the steep hillside above the old farmhouse, and they could never find more than ten or twelve anaemic, bloodless-looking specimens. Evidently some blight or distemper, perhaps sprung from the unwholesome pasturage or the diseased fungi and timbers of the filthy barn, caused a heavy mortality amongst the Whateley animals. Odd wounds or sores, having something of the aspect of incisions, seemed to afflict the visible cattle; and once or twice during the earlier months certain callers fancied they could discern similar sores about the throats of the grey, unshaven old man and his slatternly, crinkly-haired albino daughter.

In the spring after Wilbur's birth Lavinia resumed her customary rambles in the hills, bearing in her misproportioned arms the swarthy child. Public interest in the Whateleys subsided after most of the country folk had seen the baby, and no one bothered to comment on the swift development which that newcomer seemed every day to exhibit. Wilbur's growth was indeed phenomenal, for within three months of his birth he had attained a size and muscular power not usually found in infants under a full year of age. His motions and even his vocal sounds showed a restraint and deliberateness highly peculiar in an infant, and no one was really unprepared when, at seven months, he began to walk unassisted, with falterings which another month was sufficient to remove.

It was somewhat after this time – on Hallowe'en – that a great blaze was seen at midnight on the top of Sentinel Hill where the old table-like stone stands amidst its tumulus of ancient bones. Considerable talk was started when Silas Bishop – of the undecayed Bishops – mentioned having seen the boy running sturdily up that hill ahead of his mother about an hour before the blaze was remarked. Silas was rounding up a stray heifer, but he nearly forgot his mission when he fleetingly spied the two figures in the dim light of his lantern. They darted almost noiselessly through the underbrush, and the astonished watcher seemed to think they were entirely unclothed. Afterwards he could not be sure about the boy, who may have had some kind of a fringed belt and a pair of dark trunks or trousers on. Wilbur was never subsequently seen alive and conscious without complete and tightly buttoned attire, the disarrangement or threatened disarrangement of which always seemed to fill him with anger and alarm. His contrast with his squalid mother and grandfather in this respect was thought very notable until the horror of 1928 suggested the most valid of reasons.

The next January gossips were mildly interested in the fact that 'Lavinny's black brat' had commenced to talk, and at the age of only eleven months. His speech was somewhat remarkable both because of its difference from the ordinary accents of the region, and because it displayed a freedom from infantile lisping of which many children of three or four might well be proud. The boy was not talkative, yet when he spoke he seemed to reflect some elusive element wholly unpossessed by Dunwich and its denizens. The strangeness did not reside in what he said, or even in the simple idioms he used; but seemed vaguely linked with his intonation or with the internal organs that produced the spoken sounds. His facial aspect, too, was remarkable for its maturity; for though he shared his mother's and grandfather's chinlessness, his firm and precociously shaped nose united with the expression of his large, dark, almost Latin eyes to give him an air of quasi-adulthood and well-nigh preternatural intelligence. He was, however, exceedingly ugly despite his appearance of brilliancy; there being something almost goatish or animalistic about his thick lips, large-pored, yellowish skin, coarse crinkly hair, and oddly elongated ears. He was soon disliked even more decidedly than his mother and grandsire, and all conjectures about him were spiced with references to the bygone magic of Old Whateley, and how the hills once shook when he shrieked the dreadful name of *Yog-Sothoth* in the midst of a circle of stones with a great book open in his arms before him. Dogs abhorred the boy, and he was always obliged to take various defensive measures against their barking menace.

III

Meanwhile Old Whateley continued to buy cattle without measurably increasing the size of his herd. He also cut timber and began to repair the unused parts of his house – a spacious, peak-roofed affair whose rear end was buried entirely in the rocky hillside, and whose three least-ruined ground-floor rooms had always been sufficient for himself and his daughter.

There must have been prodigious reserves of strength in the old man to enable him to accomplish so much hard labour; and though he still babbled dementedly at times, his carpentry seemed to show the effects of sound calculation. It had already begun as soon as Wilbur was born, when one of the many toolsheds had been put suddenly in order, clapboarded, and fitted with a stout fresh lock. Now, in restoring the abandoned upper storey of the house, he was a no less thorough craftsman. His mania showed itself only in his tight boarding-up of all the windows in the reclaimed section – though many declared that it was a crazy thing to bother with the reclamation at all.

Less inexplicable was his fitting up of another downstairs room for his new grandson – a room which several callers saw, though no one was ever admitted to the closely boarded upper storey. This chamber he lined with tall, firm shelving, along which he began gradually to arrange, in apparently careful order, all the rotting ancient books and parts of books which during his own day had been heaped promiscuously in odd corners of the various rooms.

'I made some use of 'em,' he would say as he tried to mend a torn black-letter page with paste prepared on the rusty kitchen stove, 'but the boy's fitten to make better use of 'em. He'd orter hev 'em as well so as he kin, for they're goin' to be all of his larnin.'

When Wilbur was a year and seven months old – in September of 1914 – his size and accomplishments were almost alarming. He had grown as large as a child of four, and was a fluent and incredibly intelligent talker. He ran freely about the fields and hills, and accompanied his mother on all her wanderings. At home he would pore diligently over the queer pictures and charts in his grandfather's books, while Old Whateley would instruct and catechize him through long, hushed afternoons. By this time the restoration of the house was finished, and those who watched it wondered why one of the upper windows had been made into a solid plank door. It was a window in the rear of the east gable end, close against the hill; and no one could imagine why a cleated wooden runway was built up to it from the ground. About the period of this work's completion people noticed that the old tool-house, tightly locked and windowlessly clapboarded since Wilbur's birth, had been abandoned again. The door swung listlessly open, and when Earl Sawyer once stepped within after a cattle-selling call on Old Whateley he was quite discomposed by the singular odour he encountered – such a stench, he averred, as he had never before smelt in all his life except near the Indian circles on the hills, and which could not come from anything sane or of this earth. But then, the homes and sheds of Dunwich folk have never been remarkable for olfactory immaculateness.

The following months were void of visible events, save that everyone swore to a slow but steady increase in the mysterious hill noises. On May Eve of 1915 there were tremors which even the Aylesbury people felt, whilst the following Hallowe'en produced an underground rumbling queerly synchronized with bursts of flame – 'them witch Whateleys' doin's' – from the summit of Sentinel Hill. Wilbur was growing up uncannily, so that he looked like a boy of ten as he entered his fourth year. He read avidly by himself now; but talked much less than formerly. A settled taciturnity was absorbing him, and for the first time people began to speak specifically of the dawning look of evil in his goatish face. He would sometimes mutter an unfamiliar jargon, and chant in bizarre rhythms which chilled the listener with a sense of unexplainable terror. The aversion displayed towards him by dogs had now become a matter of wide remark, and he was obliged to carry a pistol in order to traverse the countryside in safety. His occasional use of the weapon did not enhance his popularity amongst the owners of canine guardians.

The few callers at the house would often find Lavinia alone on the ground floor, while odd cries and footsteps resounded in the boarded-up second storey. She would never tell what her father and the boy were doing up there, though once she turned pale and displayed an abnormal degree of fear when a jocose fish-pedlar tried the locked door leading to the stairway. That pedlar told the store loungers at Dunwich Village that he thought he heard a horse stamping on that floor above. The loungers reflected, thinking of the door and runway, and of the cattle that so swiftly disappeared. Then they shuddered as they recalled tales of Old Whateley's youth, and of the strange things that are called out of the earth when a bullock is sacrificed at the proper time to certain heathen gods. It had for some time been noticed that dogs had begun to hate and fear the whole Whateley place as violently as they hated and feared young Wilbur personally.

In 1917 the war came, and Squire Sawyer Whateley, as chairman of the local draft board, had hard work finding a quota of young Dunwich men fit even to be sent to development camp. The government, alarmed at such signs of wholesale regional decadence, sent several officers and medical experts to investigate; conducting a survey which New England newspaper readers may still recall. It was the publicity attending this investigation which set reporters on the track of the Whateleys, and caused the *Boston Globe* and *Arkham Advertiser* to print flamboyant Sunday stories of young Wilbur's precociousness, Old Whateley's black magic, and the shelves of strange books, the sealed second storey of the ancient farmhouse, and the weirdness of the whole region and its hill noises. Wilbur was four and a half then, and looked like a lad of fifteen. His lips and cheeks were fuzzy with a coarse dark down, and his voice had begun to break.

Earl Sawyer went out to the Whateley place with both sets of reporters and camera men, and called their attention to the queer stench which now seemed to trickle down from the sealed upper spaces. It was, he said, exactly like a smell he had found in the toolshed abandoned when the house was finally repaired; and like the faint odours which he sometimes thought he caught near the stone circle on the mountains. Dunwich folk read the stories when they appeared, and grinned over the obvious mistakes. They wondered, too, why the writers made so much of the fact that Old

Whateley always paid for his cattle in gold pieces of extremely ancient date. The Whateleys had received their visitors with ill-concealed distaste, though they did not dare court further publicity by a violent resistance or refusal to talk.

IV

For a decade the annals of the Whateleys sink indistinguishably into the general life of a morbid community used to their queer ways and hardened to their May Eve and All-Hallows orgies. Twice a year they would light fires on the top of Sentinel Hill, at which times the mountain rumblings would recur with greater and greater violence; while at all seasons there were strange and portentous doings at the lonely farmhouse. In the course of time callers professed to hear sounds in the sealed upper storey even when all the family were downstairs, and they wondered how swiftly or how lingeringly a cow or bullock was usually sacrificed. There was talk of a complaint to the Society for the Prevention of Cruelty to Animals but nothing ever came of it, since Dunwich folk are never anxious to call the outside world's attention to themselves.

About 1923, when Wilbur was a boy of ten whose mind, voice, stature, and bearded face gave all the impressions of maturity, a second great siege of carpentry went on at the old house. It was all inside the sealed upper part, and from bits of discarded lumber people concluded that the youth and his grandfather had knocked out all the partitions and even removed the attic floor, leaving only one vast open void between the ground storey and the peaked roof. They had torn down the great central chimney, too, and fitted the rusty range with a flimsy outside tin stove-pipe.

In the spring after this event Old Whateley noticed the growing number of whippoorwills that would come out of Cold Spring Glen to chirp under his window at night. He seemed to regard the circumstance as one of great significance, and told the loungers at Osborn's that he thought his time had almost come.

'They whistle jest in tune with my breathin' naow,' he said, 'an' I guess they're gittin' ready to ketch my soul. They know it's a-goin' aout, an' dun't calc'late to miss it. Yew'll know, boys, arter I'm gone, whether they git me er not. Ef they dew, they'll keep up a-singin' an' laffin' till break o' day. Ef they dun't they'll kinder quiet daown like. I expeck them an' the souls they hunts fer hev some pretty tough tussles sometimes.'

On Lammas Night, 1924, Dr Houghton of Aylesbury was hastily summoned by Wilbur Whateley, who had lashed his one remaining horse through the darkness and telephoned from Osborn's in the village. He found Old Whateley in a very grave state, with a cardiac action and stentorous breathing that told of an end not far off. The shapeless albino daughter and oddly bearded grandson stood by the bedside, whilst from the vacant abyss overhead there came a disquieting suggestion of rhythmical surging or lapping, as of the waves on some level beach. The doctor, though, was chiefly disturbed by the chattering night birds outside; a seemingly limitless legion of whippoorwills that cried their endless message in repetitions timed diabolically to the wheezing gasps of the dying man. It was uncanny and unnatural – too much, thought Dr Houghton, like the whole of the region he had entered so reluctantly in response to the urgent call.

Towards one o'clock Old Whateley gained consciousness, and interrupted his wheezing to choke out a few words to his grandson.

'More space, Willy, more space soon. Yew grows – an' that grows faster. It'll be ready to serve ye soon, boy. Open up the gates to Yog-Sothoth with the long chant that ye'll find *on page 751 of the complete edition*, an' then put a match to the prison. Fire from airth can't burn it nohaow.'

He was obviously quite mad. After a pause, during which the flock of whippoorwills outside adjusted their cries to the altered tempo while some indications of the strange hill noises came from afar off, he added another sentence or two.

'Feed it reg'lar, Willy, an' mind the quantity; but dun't let it grow too fast fer the place, fer ef it busts quarters or gits aout afore ye opens to Yog-Sothoth, it's all over an' no use. Only them from beyont kin make it multiply an' work… Only them, the old uns as wants to come back…'

But speech gave place to gasps again, and Lavinia screamed at the way the whippoorwills followed the change. It was the same for more than an hour, when the final throaty rattle came. Dr Houghton drew shrunken lids over the glazing grey eyes as the tumult of birds faded imperceptibly to silence. Lavinia sobbed, but Wilbur only chuckled whilst the hill noises rumbled faintly.

'They didn't git him,' he muttered in his heavy bass voice.

Wilbur was by this time a scholar of really tremendous erudition in his one-sided way, and was quietly known by correspondence to many librarians in distant places where rare and forbidden books of old days are kept. He was more and more hated and dreaded around Dunwich because of certain youthful disappearances which suspicion laid vaguely at his door; but was always able to silence inquiry through fear or through use of that fund of old-time gold which still, as in his grandfather's time, went forth regularly and increasingly for cattle-buying. He was now tremendously mature of aspect, and his height, having reached the normal adult limit, seemed inclined to wax beyond that figure. In 1925, when a scholarly correspondent from Miskatonic University called upon him one day and departed pale and puzzled, he was fully six and three-quarters feet tall.

Through all the years Wilbur had treated his half-deformed albino mother with a growing contempt, finally forbidding her to go to the hills with him on May Eve and Hallowmass; and in 1926 the poor creature complained to Mamie Bishop of being afraid of him.

'They's more abaout him as I knows than I kin tell ye, Mamie,' she said, 'an' naowadays they's more nor what I know myself. I vaow afur Gawd, I dun't know what he wants nor what he's a-tryin' to dew.'

That Hallowe'en the hill noises sounded louder than ever, and fire burned on Sentinel Hill as usual; but people paid more attention to the rhythmical screaming of vast flocks of unnaturally belated whippoorwills which seemed to be assembled near the unlighted Whateley farmhouse. After midnight their shrill notes burst into a kind of pandemoniac cachinnation which filled all the countryside, and not until dawn did they finally quiet down. Then they vanished, hurrying southward where they were fully a month overdue. What this meant, no one could quite be certain till later. None of the countryfolk seemed to have died – but poor Lavinia Whateley, the twisted albino, was never seen again.

In the summer of 1927 Wilbur repaired two sheds in the farmyard and began moving his books and effects out to them. Soon afterwards Earl Sawyer told the loungers at Osborn's that more carpentry was going on in the Whateley farmhouse. Wilbur was closing all the doors and windows on the ground floor, and seemed to be taking out partitions as he and his grandfather had done upstairs four years before. He was living in one of the sheds, and Sawyer thought he seemed unusually worried and tremulous. People generally suspected him of knowing something about his mother's disappearance, and very few ever approached his neighbourhood now. His height had increased to more than seven feet, and showed no signs of ceasing its development.

V

The following winter brought an event no less strange than Wilbur's first trip outside the Dunwich region. Correspondence with the Widener Library at Harvard, the Bibliothèque Nationale in Paris, the British Museum, the University of Buenos Aires, and the Library of Miskatonic University at Arkham had failed to get him the loan of a book he desperately wanted; so at length he set out in person, shabby, dirty, bearded, and uncouth of dialect, to consult the copy at Miskatonic, which was the nearest to him geographically. Almost eight feet tall, and carrying a cheap new valise from Osborn's general store, this dark and goatish gargoyle appeared one day in Arkham in quest of the dreaded volume kept under lock and key at the college library – the hideous *Necronomicon* of the mad Arab Abdul Alhazred in Olaus Wormius' Latin version, as printed in Spain in the seventeenth century. He had never seen a city before, but had no thought save to find his way to the university grounds; where, indeed, he passed heedlessly by the great white-fanged watchdog that barked with unnatural fury and enmity, and tugged frantically at its stout chain.

Wilbur had with him the priceless but imperfect copy of Dr Dee's English version which his grandfather had bequeathed him, and upon receiving access to the Latin copy he at once began to collate the two texts with the aim of discovering a certain passage which would have come on the 751st page of his own defective volume. This much he could not civilly refrain from telling the librarian – the same erudite Henry Armitage (A.M. Miskatonic, Ph.D. Princeton, Litt.D. Johns Hopkins) who had once called at the farm, and who now politely plied him with questions. He was looking, he had to admit, for a kind of formula or incantation containing the frightful name *Yog-Sothoth,* and it puzzled him to find discrepancies, duplications, and ambiguities which made the matter of determination far from easy. As he copied the formula he finally chose, Dr Armitage looked involuntarily over his shoulder at the open pages; the left-hand one of which, in the Latin version, contained such monstrous threats to the peace and sanity of the world.

Nor is it to be thought (ran the text as Armitage mentally translated it) *that man is either the oldest or the last of earth's masters, or that the common bulk of life and substance walks alone. The Old Ones were, the Old Ones are, and the Old Ones shall be. Not in the spaces we know, but between them, they walk serene and primal, undimensioned and to us unseen.* Yog-Sothoth *knows the gate.* Yog-Sothoth *is the gate.* Yog-Sothoth *is the key and guardian of the gate. Past, present, future, all are one in* Yog-Sothoth. *He knows where the Old Ones broke through of old, and where They shall break through again. He knows where They had trod earth's fields, and where They still tread them, and why no one can behold Them as They tread. By Their smell can men sometimes know Them near, but of Their semblance can no man know,* saving only in the features of those They have begotten on mankind; *and of those are there many sorts, differing in likeness from man's truest eidolon to that shape without sight or substance which is* Them. *They walk unseen and foul in lonely places where the Words have been spoken and the Rites howled through at their Seasons. The wind gibbers with Their voices, and the earth mutters with Their consciousness. They bend the forest and crush the city, yet may not forest or city behold the hand that smites. Kadath in the cold waste hath known Them, and what man knows Kadath? The ice desert of the South and the sunken isles of Ocean hold stones whereon Their seal is engraver, but who hath seen the deep frozen city or the sealed tower long garlanded with seaweed and barnacles? Great Cthulhu is Their cousin, yet can he spy Them only dimly. Iä!* Shub-Niggurath! *As a foulness shall ye know Them. Their hand is at your throats, yet ye see Them not; and Their habitation is even one with your guarded threshold.* Yog-Sothoth *is the key to the gate, whereby the spheres meet. Man rules now where They ruled once; They shall soon rule where man rules now. After summer is winter, after winter summer. They wait patient and potent, for here shall They reign again.*

Dr. Armitage, associating what he was reading with what he had heard of Dunwich and its brooding presences, and of Wilbur Whateley and his dim, hideous aura that stretched from a dubious birth to a cloud of probable matricide, felt a wave of fright as tangible as a draught of the tomb's cold clamminess. The bent, goatish giant before him seemed like the spawn of another planet or dimension; like something only partly of mankind, and linked to black gulfs of essence and entity that stretch like titan phantasms beyond all spheres of force and matter, space and time. Presently Wilbur raised his head and began speaking in that strange, resonant fashion which hinted at sound-producing organs unlike the run of mankind's.

'Mr Armitage,' he said, 'I calc'late I've got to take that book home. They's things in it I've got to try under sarten conditions that I can't git here, en' it 'ud be a mortal sin to let a red-tape rule hold me up. Let me take it along, Sir, an' I'll swar they wun't nobody know the difference. I dun't need to tell ye I'll take good keer of it. It wan't me that put this Dee copy in the shape it is...'

He stopped as he saw firm denial on the

librarian's face, and his own goatish features grew crafty. Armitage, half-ready to tell him he might make a copy of what parts he needed, thought suddenly of the possible consequences and checked himself. There was too much responsibility in giving such a being the key to such blasphemous outer spheres. Whateley saw how things stood, and tried to answer lightly.

'Wal, all right, ef ye feel that way abaout it. Maybe Harvard won't be so fussy as yew be.' And without saying more he rose and strode out of the building, stooping at each doorway.

Armitage heard the savage yelping of the great watchdog, and studied Whateley's gorilla-like lope as he crossed the bit of campus visible from the window. He thought of the wild tales he had heard, and recalled the old Sunday stories in the *Advertiser*; these things, and the lore he had picked up from Dunwich rustics and villagers during his one visit there. Unseen things not of earth – or at least not of tridimensional earth – rushed foetid and horrible through New England's glens, and brooded obscenely on the mountain tops. Of this he had long felt certain. Now he seemed to sense the close presence of some terrible part of the intruding horror, and to glimpse a hellish advance in the black dominion of the ancient and once passive nightmare. He locked away the *Necronomicon* with a shudder of disgust, but the room still reeked with an unholy and unidentifiable stench. 'As a foulness shall ye know them,' he quoted. Yes – the odour was the same as that which had sickened him at the Whateley farmhouse less than three years before. He thought of Wilbur, goatish and ominous, once again, and laughed mockingly at the village rumours of his parentage.

'Inbreeding?' Armitage muttered half-aloud to himself. 'Great God, what simpletons! Show them Arthur Machen's Great God Pan and they'll think it a common Dunwich scandal! But what thing – what cursed shapeless influence on or off this three-dimensional earth – was Wilbur Whateley's father? Born on Candlemas – nine months after May Eve of 1912, when the talk about the queer earth noises reached clear to Arkham – what walked on the mountains that May night? What Roodmas horror fastened itself on the world in half-human flesh and blood?'

During the ensuing weeks Dr Armitage set about to collect all possible data on Wilbur Whateley and the formless presences around Dunwich. He got in communication with Dr Houghton of Aylesbury, who had attended Old Whateley in his last illness, and found much to ponder over in the grandfather's last words as quoted by the physician. A visit to Dunwich Village failed to bring out much that was new; but a close survey of the *Necronomicon*, in those parts which Wilbur had sought so avidly, seemed to supply new and terrible clues to the nature, methods, and desires of the strange evil so vaguely threatening this planet. Talks with several students of archaic lore in Boston, and letters to many others elsewhere, gave him a growing amazement which passed slowly through varied degrees of alarm to a state of really acute spiritual fear. As the summer drew on he felt dimly that something ought to be done about the lurking terrors of the upper Miskatonic valley, and about the monstrous being known to the human world as Wilbur Whateley.

VI

The Dunwich horror itself came between Lammas and the equinox in 1928, and Dr Armitage was among those who witnessed its monstrous prologue. He had heard, meanwhile, of Whateley's grotesque trip to Cambridge, and of his frantic efforts to borrow or copy from the *Necronomicon* at the Widener Library. Those efforts had been in vain, since Armitage had issued warnings of the keenest intensity to all librarians having charge of the dreaded volume. Wilbur had been shockingly nervous at Cambridge; anxious for the book, yet almost equally anxious to get home again, as if he feared the results of being away long.

Early in August the half-expected outcome developed, and in the small hours of the 3rd Dr Armitage was awakened suddenly by the wild, fierce cries of the savage watchdog on the college campus. Deep and terrible, the snarling, half-mad growls and barks continued; always in mounting volume, but with hideously significant pauses. Then there rang out a scream from a wholly different throat – such a scream as roused half the sleepers of Arkham and haunted their dreams ever afterwards – such a scream as could come from no being born of earth, or wholly of earth.

Armitage, hastening into some clothing and rushing across the street and lawn to the college buildings, saw that others were ahead of him; and heard the echoes of a burglar-alarm still shrilling from the library. An open window showed black and gaping in the moonlight. What had come had indeed completed its entrance; for the barking and the screaming, now fast fading into a mixed low growling and moaning, proceeded unmistakably from within. Some instinct warned Armitage that what was taking place was not a thing for unfortified eyes to see, so he brushed back the crowd with authority as he unlocked the vestibule door. Among the others he saw Professor Warren Rice and Dr Francis Morgan, men to whom he had told some of his conjectures and misgivings; and these two he motioned to accompany him inside. The inward sounds, except for a watchful, droning whine from the dog, had by this time quite subsided; but Armitage now perceived with a sudden start that a loud chorus of whippoorwills among the shrubbery had commenced a damnably rhythmical piping, as if in unison with the last breaths of a dying man.

The building was full of a frightful stench which Dr Armitage knew too well, and the three men rushed across the hall to the small genealogical reading-room whence the low whining came. For a second nobody dared to turn on the light, then Armitage summoned up his courage and snapped the switch. One of the three – it is not certain which – shrieked aloud at what sprawled before them among disordered tables and overturned chairs. Professor Rice declares that he wholly lost consciousness for an instant, though he did not stumble or fall.

The thing that lay half-bent on its side in a foetid pool of greenish-yellow ichor and tarry stickiness was almost nine feet tall, and the dog had torn off all the clothing and some of the skin. It was not quite dead, but twitched silently and spasmodically while its chest heaved in monstrous unison with the mad piping of the expectant whippoorwills outside. Bits of shoe-leather and fragments of apparel were scattered about the room, and just inside the window an empty canvas sack lay where it had evidently been thrown. Near the central desk a revolver had fallen, a dented but undischarged cartridge later explaining why it had not been fired. The thing itself, however, crowded out all other images at the time. It would be trite and not wholly accurate to say that no human pen could describe it, but one may properly say that it could not be vividly visualized by anyone whose ideas of aspect and contour are too closely bound up with the common life-forms of this planet and of the three known dimensions. It was partly human, beyond a doubt, with very manlike hands and head, and the goatish, chinless face had the stamp of the Whateleys upon it. But the torso and lower parts of the body were teratologically fabulous, so that only generous clothing could ever have enabled it to walk on earth unchallenged or uneradicated.

Above the waist it was semi-anthropomorphic; though its chest, where the dog's rending paws still rested watchfully, had the leathery, reticulated hide of a crocodile or alligator. The back was piebald with yellow and black, and dimly suggested the squamous covering of certain snakes. Below the waist, though, it was the worst; for here all human resemblance left off and sheer phantasy began. The skin was thickly covered with coarse black fur, and from the abdomen a score of long greenish-grey tentacles with red sucking mouths protruded limply.

Their arrangement was odd, and seemed to follow the symmetries of some cosmic geometry unknown to earth or the solar system. On each of the hips, deep set in a kind of pinkish, ciliated orbit, was what seemed to be a rudimentary eye; whilst in lieu of a tail there depended a kind of trunk or feeler with purple annular markings, and with many evidences of being an undeveloped mouth or throat. The limbs, save for their black fur, roughly resembled the hind legs of prehistoric earth's giant saurians, and terminated in ridgy-veined pads that were neither hooves nor claws. When the thing breathed, its tail and tentacles rhythmically changed colour, as if from some circulatory cause normal to the non-human greenish tinge, whilst in the tail it was manifest as a yellowish appearance which alternated with a sickly grayish-white in the spaces between the purple rings. Of genuine blood there was none; only the foetid greenish-yellow ichor which trickled along the painted floor beyond the radius of the stickiness, and left a curious discoloration behind it.

As the presence of the three men seemed to rouse the dying thing, it began to mumble without turning or raising its head. Dr Armitage made no written record of its mouthings, but asserts confidently that nothing in English was uttered. At first the syllables defied all correlation with any speech of earth, but towards the last there came some disjointed fragments evidently taken from the *Necronomicon*, that monstrous blasphemy in quest of which the thing had perished. These fragments, as Armitage recalls them, ran something like *'N'gai, n'gha'ghaa, bugg-shoggog, y'hah: Yog-Sothoth, Yog-Sothoth ...'* They trailed off into nothingness as the whippoorwills shrieked in rhythmical crescendos of unholy anticipation.

Then came a halt in the gasping, and the dog raised its head in a long, lugubrious howl. A change came over the yellow, goatish face of the prostrate thing, and the great black eyes fell in appallingly. Outside the window the shrilling of the whippoorwills had suddenly ceased, and above the murmurs of the gathering crowd there came the sound of a panic-struck whirring and fluttering. Against the moon vast clouds of feathery watchers rose and raced from sight, frantic at that which they had sought for prey.

All at once the dog started up abruptly, gave a frightened bark, and leaped nervously out of the window by which it had entered. A cry rose from the crowd, and Dr Armitage shouted to the men outside that no one must be admitted till the police or medical examiner came. He was thankful that the windows were just too high to permit of peering in, and drew the dark curtains carefully down over each one. By this time two policemen had arrived; and Dr Morgan, meeting them in the vestibule, was urging them for their own sakes to postpone entrance to the stench-filled reading-room till the examiner came and the prostrate thing could be covered up.

Meanwhile frightful changes were taking place on the floor. One need not describe the kind and rate of shrinkage and disintegration that occurred before the eyes of Dr Armitage and Professor Rice; but it is permissible to say that, aside from the external appearance of face and hands, the really human element in Wilbur Whateley must have been very small. When the medical examiner came, there was only a sticky whitish mass on the painted boards, and the monstrous odour had nearly disappeared. Apparently Whateley had had no skull or bony skeleton; at least, in any true or stable sense. He had taken somewhat after his unknown father.

VII

Yet all this was only the prologue of the actual Dunwich horror. Formalities were gone through by bewildered officials, abnormal details were duly kept from press and public, and men were sent to Dunwich and Aylesbury to look up property and notify any who might be heirs of the late Wilbur Whateley. They found the countryside in great agitation, both because of the growing rumblings beneath the domed hills, and because of the unwonted stench and the surging, lapping sounds which came increasingly from the great empty shell formed by Whateley's boarded-up farmhouse. Earl Sawyer, who tended the horse and cattle during Wilbur's absence, had developed a woefully acute case of nerves. The officials devised excuses not to enter the noisome boarded place; and were glad to confine their survey of the deceased's living quarters, the newly mended sheds, to a single visit. They filed a ponderous report at the courthouse in Aylesbury, and litigations concerning heirship are said to be still in progress amongst the innumerable Whateleys, decayed and undecayed, of the upper Miskatonic valley.

An almost interminable manuscript in strange characters, written in a huge ledger and adjudged a sort of diary because of the spacing and the variations in ink and penmanship, presented a baffling puzzle to those who found it on the old bureau which served as its owner's desk. After a week of debate it was sent to Miskatonic University, together with the deceased's collection of strange books, for study and possible translation; but even the best linguists soon saw that it was not likely to be unriddled with ease. No trace of the ancient gold with which Wilbur and Old Whateley had always paid their debts has yet been discovered.

It was in the dark of September ninth that the horror broke loose. The hill noises had been very pronounced during the evening, and dogs barked frantically all night. Early risers on the tenth noticed a peculiar stench in the air. About seven o'clock Luther Brown, the hired boy at George Corey's, between Cold Spring Glen and the village, rushed frenziedly back from his morning trip to Ten-Acre Meadow with the cows. He was almost convulsed with fright as he stumbled into the kitchen; and in the yard outside the no less frightened herd were pawing and lowing pitifully, having followed the boy back in the panic they shared with him. Between gasps Luther tried to stammer out his tale to Mrs Corey.

'Up thar in the rud beyont the glen, Mis' Corey – they's suthin' ben thar! It smells like thunder, an' all the bushes an' little trees is pushed back from the rud like they'd a haouse ben moved along of it. An' that ain't the wust, nuther. They's prints in the rud, Mis' Corey – great raound prints as big as barrel-heads, all sunk dawon deep like a elephant had ben along, only they's a sight more nor four feet could make! I looked at one or two afore I run, an' I see every one was covered with lines spreadin' aout from one place, like as if big palm-leaf fans – twice or three times as big as any they is – hed of ben paounded dawon into the rud. An' the smell was awful, like what it is around Wizard Whateley's ol' haouse...'

Here he faltered, and seemed to shiver afresh with the fright that had sent him flying home. Mrs Corey, unable to extract more information, began telephoning the neighbours; thus starting on its rounds the overture of panic that heralded the major terrors. When she got Sally Sawyer, housekeeper at Seth Bishop's, the nearest place to Whateley's, it became her turn to listen instead of transmit; for Sally's boy Chauncey, who slept poorly, had been up on the hill towards Whateley's, and had dashed back in terror after one look at the place, and at the pasturage where Mr Bishop's cows had been left out all night.

'Yes, Mis' Corey,' came Sally's tremulous voice over the party wire, 'Cha'ncey he just come back a-postin', and couldn't half talk fer bein' scairt! He says Ol' Whateley's house is all bowed up, with timbers scattered raound like they'd ben dynamite inside; only the bottom floor ain't through, but is all covered with a kind o' tar-like stuff that smells awful an' drips daown offen the aidges onto the graoun' whar the side timbers is blowed away. An' they's awful kinder marks in the yard, tew – great raound marks bigger raound than a hogshead, an' all sticky with stuff like is on the browed-up haouse. Cha'ncey he says they leads off into the medders, whar a great swath wider'n a barn is matted daown, an' all the stun walls tumbled every whichway wherever it goes.

'An' he says, says he, Mis' Corey, as haow he sot to look fer Seth's caows, frightened ez he was an' faound 'em in the upper pasture nigh the Devil's Hop Yard in an awful shape. Haff on 'em's clean gone, an' nigh haff o' them that's left is sucked most dry o' blood, with sores on 'em like they's ben on Whateley's cattle ever senct Lavinny's black brat was born. Seth he's gone aout naow to look at 'em, though I'll vaow he won't keer ter git very nigh Wizard Whateley's! Cha'ncey didn't look keerful ter see whar the big matted-daown swath led arter it leff the pasturage, but he says he thinks it p'inted towards the glen rud to the village.

'I tell ye, Mis' Corey, they's suthin' abroad as hadn't orter be abroad, an' I for one think that black Wilbur Whateley, as come to the bad end he deserved, is at the bottom of the breedin' of it. He wa'n't all human hisself, I allus says to everybody; an' I think he an' Ol' Whateley must a raised suthin' in that there nailed-up haouse as ain't even so human as he was. They's allus ben unseen things araound Dunwich – livin' things – as ain't human an' ain't good fer human folks.

'The graoun' was a-talkin' las' night, an' towards mornin' Cha'ncey he heered the whippoorwills so laoud in Col' Spring Glen he couldn't sleep nun. Then he thought he heered another faint-like saound over towards Wizard Whateley's – a kinder rippin' or tearin' o' wood, like some big box er crate was bein' opened fur off. What with this an' that, he didn't git to sleep at all till sunup, an' no sooner was he up this mornin', but he's got to go over to Whateley's an' see what's the matter. He see enough I tell ye, Mis' Corey! This dun't mean no good, an' I think as all the men-folks ought to git up a party an' do suthin'. I know suthin' awful's abaout, an' feel my time is nigh, though only Gawd knows jest what it is.

'Did your Luther take accaount o' whar them big tracks led tew? No? Wal, Mis' Corey, ef they was on the glen rud this side o' the glen, an' ain't got to your haouse yet, I calc'late they must go into the glen itself. They would do that. I allus says Col' Spring Glen ain't no healthy nor decent place. The whippoorwills an' fireflies there never did act like they was creaters o' Gawd, an' they's them as says ye kin hear strange things a-rushin' an' a-talkin' in the air dawon thar ef ye stand in the right place, atween the rock falls an' Bear's Den.'

By that noon fully three-quarters of the men and boys of Dunwich were trooping over the roads and meadows between the newmade Whateley ruins and Cold Spring Glen, examining in horror the vast, monstrous prints, the maimed Bishop cattle, the strange, noisome wreck of the farmhouse, and the bruised, matted vegetation of the fields and roadside. Whatever had burst loose upon the world had assuredly gone down into the great sinister ravine; for all the trees on the banks were bent and broken, and a great avenue had been gouged in the precipice-hanging underbrush. It was as though a house, launched by an avalanche, had slid down through the tangled growths of the almost vertical slope. From below no sound came, but only a distant, undefinable foetor; and it is not to be wondered at that the men preferred to stay on the edge and argue, rather than descend and beard the unknown Cyclopean horror in its lair. Three dogs that were with the party had barked furiously at first, but seemed cowed and reluctant when near the glen. Someone telephoned the news to the *Aylesbury Transcript*; but the editor, accustomed to wild tales from Dunwich, did no more than concoct a humorous paragraph about it; an item soon afterwards reproduced by the Associated Press.

That night everyone went home, and every house and barn was barricaded as stoutly as possible. Needless to say, no cattle were allowed to remain in open pasturage. About two in the morning a frightful stench and the savage barking of the dogs awakened the household at Elmer Frye's, on the eastern edge of Cold Spring Glen, and all agreed that they could hear a sort of muffled swishing or lapping sound from somewhere outside. Mrs Frye proposed telephoning the neighbours, and Elmer was about to agree when the noise of splintering wood burst in upon their deliberations. It came, apparently, from the barn; and was quickly followed by a hideous screaming and stamping amongst the cattle. The dogs slavered and crouched close to the feet of the fear-numbed family. Frye lit a lantern through force of habit, but knew it would be death to go out into that black farmyard. The children and the women-folk whimpered, kept from screaming by some obscure, vestigial instinct of defence which told them their lives depended on silence. At last the noise of the cattle subsided to a pitiful moaning, and a great snapping, crashing, and crackling ensued. The Fryes, huddled together in the sitting-room, did not dare to move until the last echoes died away far down in Cold Spring Glen. Then, amidst the dismal moans from the stable and the daemoniac piping of the late whippoorwills in the glen, Selina Frye tottered to the telephone and spread what news she could of the second phase of the horror.

The next day all the countryside was in a panic; and cowed, uncommunicative groups came and went where the fiendish thing had occurred. Two titan swaths of destruction stretched from the glen to the Frye farmyard, monstrous prints covered the bare patches of ground, and one side of the old red barn had completely caved in. Of the cattle, only a quarter could be found and identified. Some of these were in curious fragments, and all that survived had to be shot. Earl Sawyer suggested that help be asked from Aylesbury or Arkham, but others maintained it would be of no use. Old Zebulon Whateley, of a branch that hovered about halfway between soundness and decadence, made darkly wild suggestions about rites that ought to be practiced on the hill-tops. He came of a line where tradition ran strong, and his memories of chantings in the great stone circles were not altogether connected with Wilbur and his grandfather.

Darkness fell upon a stricken countryside too passive to organize for real defence. In a few cases closely related families would band together and watch in the gloom under one roof; but in general there was only a repetition of the barricading of the night before, and a futile, ineffective gesture of loading muskets and setting pitchforks handily about. Nothing, however, occurred except some hill noises; and when the day came there were many who hoped that the new horror had gone as swiftly as it had come. There were even bold souls who proposed an offensive expedition down in the glen, though they did not venture to set an actual example to the still reluctant majority.

When night came again the barricading was repeated, though there was less huddling together of families. In the morning both the Frye and the Seth Bishop households reported excitement among the dogs and vague sounds and stenches from afar, while early explorers noted with horror a fresh set of the monstrous tracks in the road skirting Sentinel Hill. As before, the sides of the road showed a bruising indicative of the blasphemously stupendous bulk of the horror; whilst the conformation of the tracks seemed to argue a passage in two directions, as if the moving mountain had come from Cold Spring Glen and returned to it along the same path. At the base of the hill a thirty-foot swath of crushed shrubbery saplings led steeply upwards, and the seekers gasped when they saw that even the most perpendicular places did not deflect the inexorable trail. Whatever the horror was, it could scale a sheer stony cliff of almost complete verticality; and as the investigators climbed round to the hill's summit by safer routes they saw that the trail ended – or rather, reversed – there.

It was here that the Whateleys used to build their hellish fires and chant their hellish rituals by the table-like stone on May Eve and Hallowmass. Now that very stone formed the centre of a vast space thrashed around by the mountainous horror, whilst upon its slightly concave surface was a thick and foetid deposit of the same tarry stickiness observed on the floor of the ruined Whateley farmhouse when the horror escaped. Men looked at one another and muttered. Then they looked down the hill. Apparently the horror had descended by a route much the same as that of its ascent. To speculate was futile. Reason, logic, and normal ideas of motivation stood confounded. Only old Zebulon, who was not with the group, could have done justice to the situation or suggested a plausible explanation.

Thursday night began much like the others, but it ended less happily. The whippoorwills in the glen had screamed with such unusual persistence that many could not sleep, and about 3 A.M. all the party telephones rang tremulously. Those who took down their receivers heard a fright-mad voice shriek out, 'Help, oh, my Gawd!...' and some thought a crashing sound followed the breaking off of the exclamation. There was nothing more. No one dared do anything, and no one knew till morning whence the call came. Then those who had heard it called everyone on the line, and found that only the Fryes did not reply. The truth appeared an hour later, when a hastily assembled group of armed men trudged out to the Frye place at the head of the glen. It was horrible, yet hardly a surprise. There were more swaths and monstrous prints, but there was no longer any house. It had caved in like an egg-shell, and amongst the ruins nothing living or dead could be discovered. Only a stench and a tarry stickiness. The Elmer Fryes had been erased from Dunwich.

VIII

In the meantime a quieter yet even more spiritually poignant phase of the horror had been blackly unwinding itself behind the closed door of a shelf-lined room in Arkham. The curious manuscript record or diary of Wilbur Whateley, delivered to Miskatonic University for translation had caused much worry and bafflement among the experts in language both ancient and modern; its very alphabet, notwithstanding a general resemblance to the heavily shaded Arabic used in Mesopotamia, being absolutely unknown to any available authority. The final conclusion of the linguists was that the text represented an artificial alphabet, giving the effect of a cipher; though none of the usual methods of cryptographic solution seemed to furnish any clue, even when applied on the basis of every tongue the writer might conceivably have used. The ancient books taken from Whateley's quarters, while absorbingly interesting and in several cases promising to open up new and terrible lines of research among philosophers and men of science, were of no assistance whatever in this matter. One of them, a heavy tome with an iron clasp, was in another unknown alphabet – this one of a very different cast, and resembling Sanskrit more than anything else. The old ledger was at length given wholly into the charge of Dr Armitage, both because of his peculiar interest in the Whateley matter, and because of his wide linguistic learning and skill in the mystical formulae of antiquity and the middle ages.

Armitage had an idea that the alphabet might be something esoterically used by certain forbidden cults which have come down from old times, and which have inherited many forms and traditions from the wizards of the Saracenic world. That question, however, he did not deem vital; since it would be unnecessary to know the origin of the symbols if, as he suspected, they were used as a cipher in a modern language. It was his belief that, considering the great amount of text involved, the writer would scarcely have wished the trouble of using another speech than his own, save perhaps in certain special formulae and incantations. Accordingly he attacked the manuscript with the preliminary assumption that the bulk of it was in English.

Dr Armitage knew, from the repeated failures of his colleagues, that the riddle was a deep and complex one; and that no simple mode of solution could merit even a trial. All through late August he fortified himself with the mass lore of cryptography; drawing upon the fullest resources of his own library, and wading night after night amidst the arcana of Trithemius' *Poligraphia*, Giambattista Porta's *De Furtivis Literarum Notis*, De Vigenere's *Traite des Chiffres*, Falconer's *Cryptomenysis Patefacta*, Davys' and Thicknesse's eighteenth-century treatises, and such fairly modern authorities as Blair, van Marten and Kluber's script itself, and in time became convinced that he had to deal with one of those subtlest and most ingenious of cryptograms, in which many separate lists of corresponding letters are arranged like the multiplication table, and the message built up with arbitrary key-words known only to the initiated. The older authorities seemed rather more helpful than the newer ones, and Armitage concluded that the code of the manuscript was one of great antiquity, no doubt handed down through a long line of mystical experimenters. Several times he seemed near daylight, only to be set back by some unforeseen obstacle. Then, as September approached, the clouds began to clear. Certain letters, as used in certain parts of the manuscript, emerged definitely and unmistakably; and it became obvious that the text was indeed in English.

On the evening of September second the last major barrier gave way, and Dr Armitage read for the first time a continuous passage of Wilbur Whateley's annals. It was in truth a diary, as all had thought; and it was couched in a style clearly showing the mixed occult erudition and general illiteracy of the strange being who wrote it. Almost the first long passage that Armitage deciphered, an entry dated November 26, 1916, proved highly startling and disquieting. It was written, he remembered, by a child of three and a half who looked like a lad of twelve or thirteen.

Today learned the Aklo for the Sabaoth (it ran), *which did not like, it being answerable from the hill and not from the air. That upstairs more ahead of me than I had thought it would be, and is not like to have much earth brain. Shot Elam Hutchins's collie Jack when he went to bite me, and Elam says he would kill me if he dast. I guess he won't. Grandfather kept me saying the Dho formula last night, and I think I saw the inner city at the 2 magnetic poles. I shall go to those poles when the earth is cleared off, if I can't break through with the Dho-Hna formula when I commit it. They from the air told me at Sabbat that it will be years before I can clear off the earth, and I guess grandfather will be dead then, so I shall have to learn all the angles of the planes and all the formulas between the Yr and the Nhhngr. They from outside will help, but they cannot take body without human blood. That upstairs looks it will have the right cast. I can see it a little when I make the Voorish sign or blow the powder of Ibn Ghazi at it, and it is near like them at May Eve on the Hill. The other face may wear off some. I wonder how I shall look when the earth is cleared and there are no earth beings on it. He that came with the Aklo Sabaoth said I may be transfigured there being much of outside to work on.*

Morning found Dr Armitage in a cold sweat of terror and a frenzy of wakeful concentration. He had not left the manuscript all night, but sat at his table under the electric light turning page after page with shaking hands as fast as he could decipher the cryptic text. He had nervously telephoned his wife he would not be home, and when she brought him a breakfast from the house he could scarcely dispose of a mouthful. All that day he read on, now and then halted maddeningly as a reapplication of the complex key became necessary. Lunch and dinner were brought him, but he ate only the smallest fraction of either. Toward the middle of the next night he drowsed off in his chair, but soon woke out of a tangle of nightmares almost as hideous as the truths and menaces to man's existence that he had uncovered.

On the morning of September fourth Professor Rice and Dr Morgan insisted on seeing him for a while, and departed trembling and ashen-grey. That evening he went to bed, but slept only fitfully. Wednesday – the next day – he was back at the manuscript, and began to take copious notes both from the current sections and from those he had already deciphered. In the small hours of that night he slept a little in an easy chair in his office, but was at the manuscript again before dawn. Some time before noon his physician, Dr Hartwell, called to see him and insisted that he cease work. He refused; intimating that it was of the most vital importance for him to complete the reading of the diary and promising an explanation in due course of time. That evening, just as twilight fell, he finished his terrible perusal and sank back exhausted. His wife, bringing his dinner, found him in a half-comatose state; but he was conscious enough to warn her off with a sharp cry when he saw her eyes wander toward the notes he had taken. Weakly rising, he gathered up the scribbled papers and sealed them all in a great envelope, which he immediately placed in his inside coat pocket. He had sufficient strength to get home, but was so clearly in need of medical aid that Dr Hartwell was summoned at once. As the doctor put him to bed he could only mutter over and over again, *'But what, in God's name, can we do?'*

Dr Armitage slept, but was partly delirious the next day. He made no explanations to Hartwell, but in his calmer moments spoke of the imperative need of a long conference with Rice and Morgan. His wilder wanderings were very startling indeed, including frantic appeals that something in a boarded-up farmhouse be destroyed, and fantastic references to some plan for the extirpation of the entire human race and all animal and vegetable life from the earth by some terrible elder race of beings from another dimension. He would shout that the world was in danger, since the Elder Things wished to strip it and drag it away from the solar system and cosmos of matter into some other plane or phase of entity from which it had once fallen, vigintillions of aeons ago. At other times he would call for the dreaded *Necronomicon* and the *Daemonolatreia* of Remigius, in which he seemed hopeful of finding some formula to check the peril he conjured up.

'Stop them, stop them!' he would shout. 'Those Whateleys meant to let them in, and the worst of all is left! Tell Rice and Morgan we must do something – it's a blind business, but I know how to make the powder… It hasn't been fed since the second of August, when Wilbur came here to his death, and at that rate…'

But Armitage had a sound physique despite his seventy-three years, and slept off his disorder that night without developing any real fever. He woke late Friday, clear of head, though sober with a gnawing fear and tremendous sense of responsibility. Saturday afternoon he felt able to go over to the library and summon Rice and Morgan for a conference, and the rest of that day and evening the three men tortured their brains in the wildest speculation and the most desperate debate. Strange and terrible books were drawn voluminously from the stack shelves and from secure places of storage; and diagrams and formulae were copied with feverish haste and in bewildering abundance. Of scepticism there was none. All three had seen the body of Wilbur Whateley as it lay on the floor in a room of that very building, and after that not one of them could feel even slightly inclined to treat the diary as a madman's raving.

Opinions were divided as to notifying the Massachusetts State Police, and the negative finally won. There were things involved which simply could not be believed by those who had not seen a sample, as indeed was made clear during certain subsequent investigations. Late at night the conference disbanded without having developed a definite plan, but all day Sunday Armitage was busy comparing formulae and mixing chemicals obtained from the college laboratory. The more he reflected on the hellish diary, the more he was inclined to doubt the efficacy of any material agent in stamping out the entity which Wilbur Whateley had left behind him – the earth-threatening entity which, unknown to him, was to burst forth in a few hours and become the memorable Dunwich horror.

Monday was a repetition of Sunday with Dr Armitage, for the task in hand required an infinity of research and experiment. Further consultations of the monstrous diary brought about various changes of plan, and he knew that even in the end a large amount of uncertainty must remain. By Tuesday he had a definite line of action mapped out, and believed he would try a trip to Dunwich within a week. Then, on Wednesday, the great shock came. Tucked obscurely away in a corner of the *Arkham Advertiser* was a facetious little item from the Associated Press, telling what a record-breaking monster the bootleg whisky of Dunwich had raised up. Armitage, half stunned, could only telephone for Rice and Morgan. Far into the night they discussed, and the next day was a whirlwind of preparation on the part of them all. Armitage knew he would be meddling with terrible powers, yet saw that there was no other way to annul the deeper and more malign meddling which others had done before him.

IX

Friday morning Armitage, Rice, and Morgan set out by motor for Dunwich, arriving at the village about one in the afternoon. The day was pleasant, but even in the brightest sunlight a kind of quiet dread and portent seemed to hover about the strangely domed hills and the deep, shadowy ravines of the stricken region. Now and then on some mountain top a gaunt circle of stones could be glimpsed against the sky. From the air of hushed fright at Osborn's store they knew something hideous had happened, and soon learned of the annihilation of the Elmer Frye house and family. Throughout that afternoon they rode around Dunwich, questioning the natives concerning all that had occurred, and seeing for themselves with rising pangs of horror the drear Frye ruins with their lingering traces of the tarry stickiness, the blasphemous tracks in the Frye yard, the wounded Seth Bishop cattle, and the enormous swaths of disturbed vegetation in various places. The trail up and down Sentinel Hill seemed to Armitage of almost cataclysmic significance, and he looked long at the sinister altar-like stone on the summit.

At length the visitors, apprised of a party of State Police which had come from Aylesbury that morning in response to the first telephone reports of the Frye tragedy, decided to seek out the officers and compare notes as far as practicable. This, however, they found more easily planned than performed; since no sign of the party could be found in any direction. There had been five of them in a car, but now the car stood empty near the ruins in the Frye yard. The natives, all of whom had talked with the policemen, seemed at first as perplexed as Armitage and his companions. Then old Sam Hutchins thought of something and turned pale, nudging Fred Farr and pointing to the dank, deep hollow that yawned close by.

'Gawd,' he gasped, 'I telled 'em not ter go daown into the glen, an' I never thought nobody'd dew it with them tracks an' that smell an' the whippoorwills a-screechin' daown thar in the dark o' noonday...'

A cold shudder ran through natives and visitors alike, and every ear seemed strained in a kind of instinctive, unconscious listening. Armitage, now that he had actually come upon the horror and its monstrous work, trembled with the responsibility he felt to be his. Night would soon fall, and it was then that the mountainous blasphemy lumbered upon its eldritch course. *Negotium perambuians in tenebris...* The old librarian rehearsed the formulae he had memorized, and clutched the paper containing the alternative one he had not memorized. He saw that his electric flashlight was in working order. Rice, beside him, took from a valise a metal sprayer of the sort used in combating insects; whilst Morgan uncased the big-game rifle on which he relied despite his colleague's warnings that no material weapon would be of help.

Armitage, having read the hideous diary, knew painfully well what kind of a manifestation to expect; but he did not add to the fright of the Dunwich people by giving any hints or clues. He hoped that it might be conquered without any revelation to the world of the monstrous thing it had escaped. As the shadows gathered, the natives commenced to disperse homeward, anxious to bar themselves indoors despite the present evidence that all human locks and bolts were useless before a force that could bend trees and crush houses when it chose. They shook their heads at the visitors' plan to stand guard at the Frye ruins near the glen; and, as they left, had little expectancy of ever seeing the watchers again.

There were rumblings under the hills that night, and the whippoorwills piped threateningly. Once in a while a wind, sweeping up out of Cold Spring Glen, would bring a touch of ineffable foetor to the heavy night air; such a foetor as all three of the watchers had smelled once before, when they stood above a dying thing that had passed for fifteen years and a half as a human being. But the looked-for terror did not appear. Whatever was down there in the glen was biding its time, and Armitage told his colleagues it would be suicidal to try to attack it in the dark.

Morning came wanly, and the night-sounds ceased. It was a grey, bleak day, with now and then a drizzle of rain; and heavier and heavier clouds seemed to be piling themselves up beyond the hills to the north-west. The men from Arkham were undecided what to do. Seeking shelter from the increasing rainfall beneath one of the few undestroyed Frye outbuildings, they debated the wisdom of waiting, or of taking the aggressive and going down into the glen in quest of their nameless, monstrous quarry. The downpour waxed in heaviness, and distant peals of thunder sounded from far horizons. Sheet lightning shimmered, and then a forky bolt flashed near at hand, as if descending into the accursed glen itself. The sky grew very dark, and the watchers hoped that the storm would prove a short, sharp one followed by clear weather.

It was still gruesomely dark when, not much over an hour later, a confused babel of voices sounded down the road. Another moment brought to view a frightened group of more than a dozen men, running, shouting, and even whimpering hysterically. Someone in the lead began sobbing out words, and the Arkham men started violently when those words developed a coherent form.

'Oh, my Gawd, my Gawd,' the voice choked out. 'It's a-goin' agin, an' this time by day! It's aout – it's aout an' a-movin' this very minute, an' only the Lord knows when it'll be on us all!'

The speaker panted into silence, but another took up his message.

'Nigh on a haour ago Zeb Whateley here heered the 'phone a-ringin', an' it was Mis' Corey, George's wife, that lives daown by the junction. She says the hired boy Luther was aout drivin' in the caows from the storm arter the big bolt, when he see all the trees a-bendin' at the maouth o' the glen – opposite side ter this – an' smelt the same awful smell like he smelt when he faound the big tracks las' Monday mornin'. An' she says he says they was a swishin' lappin' saound, more nor what the bendin' trees an' bushes could make, an' all on a suddent the trees along the rud begun ter git pushed one side, an' they was a awful stompin' an' splashin' in the mud. But mind ye, Luther he didn't see nothin' at all, only just the bendin' trees an' underbrush.

'Then fur ahead where Bishop's Brook goes under the rud he heerd a awful creakin' an' strainin' on the bridge, an' says he could tell the saound o' wood a-startin' to crack an' split. An' all the whiles he never see a thing, only them trees an' bushes a-bendin'. An' when the swishin' saound got very fur off – on the rud towards Wizard Whateley's an' Sentinel Hill – Luther he had the guts ter step up whar he'd heerd it fust an' look at the graound. It was all mud an' water, an' the sky was dark, an' the rain was wipin' aout all tracks abaout as fast as could be; but beginnin' at the glen maouth, whar the trees hed moved, they was still some o' them awful prints big as bar'ls like he seen Monday.'

At this point the first excited speaker interrupted.

'But that ain't the trouble naow – that was only the start. Zeb here was callin' folks up an' everybody was a-listenin' in when a call from Seth Bishop's cut in. His haousekeeper Sally was carryin' on fit to kill – she'd jest seed the trees a-bendin' beside the rud, an' says they was a kind o' mushy saound, like a elephant puffin' an' treadin', a-headin' fer the haouse. Then she up an' spoke suddent of a fearful smell, an' says her boy Cha'ncey was a-screamin' as haow it was jest like what he smelt up to the Whateley rewins Monday mornin'. An' the dogs was barkin' an' whinin' awful.

'An' then she let aout a turrible yell, an' says the shed daown the rud had jest caved in like the storm bed blowed it over, only the wind w'an't strong enough to dew that. Everybody was a-listenin', an' we could hear lots o' folks on the wire a-gaspin'. All to onct Sally she yelled again, an' says the front yard picket fence hed just crumbled up, though they wa'n't no sign o' what done it. Then everybody on the line could hear Cha'ncey an' old Seth Bishop a-yellin' tew, an' Sally was shriekin' aout that suthin' heavy hed struck the haouse – not lightnin' nor nothin', but suthin' heavy again' the front, that kep' a-launchin' itself agin an' agin, though ye couldn't see nothin' aout the front winders. An' then … an' then …'

Lines of fright deepened on every face; and Armitage, shaken as he was, had barely poise enough to prompt the speaker.

'An' then …. Sally she yelled aout, 'O help, the haouse is a-cavin' in … an' on the wire we could hear a turrible crashin' an' a hull flock o' screaming … jes like when Elmer Frye's place was took, only wuss …'

The man paused, and another of the crowd spoke.

'That's all – not a saound nor squeak over the 'phone arter that. Jest still-like. We that heerd it got aout Fords an' wagons an' rounded up as many able-bodied men-folks as we could git, at Corey's place, an' come up here ter see what yew thought best ter dew. Not but what I think it's the Lord's jedgment fer our iniquities, that no mortal kin ever set aside.'

Armitage saw that the time for positive action had come, and spoke decisively to the faltering group of frightened rustics.

'We must follow it, boys.' He made his voice as reassuring as possible. 'I believe there's a chance of putting it out of business. You men know that those Whateleys were wizards – well, this thing is a thing of wizardry, and must be put down by the same means. I've seen Wilbur Whateley's diary and read some of the strange old books he used to read; and I think I know the right kind of spell to recite to make the thing fade away. Of course, one can't be sure, but we can always take a chance. It's invisible – I knew it would be – but there's powder in this long-distance sprayer that might make it show up for a second. Later on we'll try it. It's a frightful thing to have alive, but it isn't as bad as what Wilbur would have let in if he'd lived longer. You'll never know what the world escaped. Now we've only this one thing to fight, and it can't multiply. It can, though, do a lot of harm; so we mustn't hesitate to rid the community of it.

'We must follow it – and the way to begin is to go to the place that has just been wrecked. Let somebody lead the way – I don't know your roads very well, but I've an idea there might be a shorter cut across lots. How about it?'

The men shuffled about a moment, and then Earl Sawyer spoke softly, pointing with a grimy finger through the steadily lessening rain.

'I guess ye kin git to Seth Bishop's quickest by cuttin' across the lower medder here, wadin' the brook at the low place, an' climbin' through Carrier's mowin' an' the timber-lot beyont. That comes aout on the upper rud mighty nigh Seth's – a leetle t'other side.'

Armitage, with Rice and Morgan, started to walk in the direction indicated; and most of the natives followed slowly. The sky was growing lighter, and there were signs that the storm had worn itself away. When Armitage inadvertently took a wrong direction, Joe Osborn warned him and walked ahead to show the right one. Courage and confidence were mounting, though the twilight of the almost perpendicular wooded hill which lay towards the end of their short cut, and among whose fantastic ancient trees they had to scramble as if up a ladder, put these qualities to a severe test.

At length they emerged on a muddy road to find the sun coming out. They were a little beyond the Seth Bishop place, but bent trees and hideously unmistakable tracks showed what had passed by. Only a few moments were consumed in surveying the ruins just round the bend. It was the Frye incident all over again, and nothing dead or living was found in either of the collapsed shells which had been the Bishop house and barn. No one cared to remain there amidst the stench and tarry stickiness, but all turned instinctively to the line of horrible prints leading on towards the wrecked Whateley farmhouse and the altar-crowned slopes of Sentinel Hill.

As the men passed the site of Wilbur Whateley's abode they shuddered visibly, and seemed again to mix hesitancy with their zeal. It was no joke tracking down something as big as a house that one could not see, but that had all the vicious malevolence of a daemon. Opposite the base of Sentinel Hill the tracks left the road, and there was a fresh bending and matting visible along the broad swath marking the monster's former route to and from the summit.

Armitage produced a pocket telescope of considerable power and scanned the steep green side of the hill. Then he handed the instrument to Morgan, whose sight was keener. After a moment of gazing Morgan cried out sharply, passing the glass to Earl Sawyer and indicating a certain spot on the slope with his finger. Sawyer, as clumsy as most non-users of optical devices are, fumbled a while; but eventually focused the lenses with Armitage's aid. When he did so his cry was less restrained than Morgan's had been.

'Gawd almighty, the grass an' bushes is a'movin'! It's a-goin' up – slow-like – creepin' – up ter the top this minute, heaven only knows what fur!'

Then the germ of panic seemed to spread among the seekers. It was one thing to chase the nameless entity, but quite another to find it. Spells might be all right – but suppose they weren't? Voices began questioning Armitage about what he knew of the thing, and no reply seemed quite to satisfy. Everyone seemed to feel himself in close proximity to phases of Nature and of being utterly forbidden and wholly outside the sane experience of mankind.

X

In the end the three men from Arkham – old, white-bearded Dr Armitage, stocky, iron-grey Professor Rice, and lean, youngish Dr Morgan – ascended the mountain alone. After much patient instruction regarding its focusing and use, they left the telescope with the frightened group that remained in the road; and as they climbed they were watched closely by those among whom the glass was passed round. It was hard going, and Armitage had to be helped more than once. High above the toiling group the great swath trembled as its hellish maker repassed with snail-like deliberateness. Then it was obvious that the pursuers were gaining.

Curtis Whateley – of the undecayed branch – was holding the telescope when the Arkham party detoured radically from the swath. He told the crowd that the men were evidently trying to get to a subordinate peak which overlooked the swath at a point considerably ahead of where the shrubbery was now bending. This, indeed, proved to be true; and the party were seen to gain the minor elevation only a short time after the invisible blasphemy had passed it.

Then Wesley Corey, who had taken the glass, cried out that Armitage was adjusting the sprayer which Rice held, and that something must be about to happen. The crowd stirred uneasily, recalling that his sprayer was expected to give the unseen horror a moment of visibility. Two or three men shut their eyes, but Curtis Whateley snatched back the telescope and strained his vision to the utmost. He saw that Rice, from the party's point of advantage above and behind the entity, had an excellent chance of spreading the potent powder with marvellous effect.

Those without the telescope saw only an instant's flash of grey cloud – a cloud about the size of a moderately large building – near the top of the mountain. Curtis, who held the instrument, dropped it with a piercing shriek into the ankle-deep mud of the road. He reeled, and would have crumbled to the ground had not two or three others seized and steadied him. All he could do was moan half-inaudibly.

'Oh, oh, great Gawd... *that... that...*'

There was a pandemonium of questioning, and only Henry Wheeler thought to rescue the fallen telescope and wipe it clean of mud. Curtis was past all coherence, and even isolated replies were almost too much for him.

'Bigger'n a barn... all made o' squirmin' ropes... hull thing sort o' shaped like a hen's egg bigger'n anything with dozens o' legs like hogsheads that haff shut up when they step... nothin' solid abaout it – all like jelly, an' made o' sep'rit wrigglin' ropes pushed clost together... great bulgin' eyes all over it... ten or twenty maouths or trunks a-stickin' aout all along the sides, big as stove-pipes an all a-tossin' an openin' an' shuttin'... all grey, with kinder blue or purple rings... *an' Gawd in Heaven – that haff face on top...*'

This final memory, whatever it was, proved too much for poor Curtis; and he collapsed completely before he could say more. Fred Farr and Will Hutchins carried him to the roadside and laid him on the damp grass. Henry Wheeler, trembling, turned the rescued telescope on the mountain to see what he might. Through the lenses were discernible three tiny figures, apparently running towards the summit as fast as the steep incline allowed. Only these – nothing more. Then everyone noticed a strangely unseasonable noise in the deep valley behind, and even in the underbrush of Sentinel Hill itself. It was the piping of unnumbered whippoorwills, and in their shrill chorus there seemed to lurk a note of tense and evil expectancy.

Earl Sawyer now took the telescope and reported the three figures as standing on the topmost ridge, virtually level with the altar-stone but at a considerable distance from it. One figure, he said, seemed to be raising its hands above its head at rhythmic intervals; and as Sawyer mentioned the circumstance the crowd seemed to hear a faint, half-musical sound from the distance, as if a loud chant were accompanying the gestures. The weird silhouette on that remote peak must have been a spectacle of infinite grotesqueness and impressiveness, but no observer was in a mood for aesthetic appreciation. 'I guess he's sayin' the spell,' whispered Wheeler as he snatched back the telescope. The whippoorwills were piping wildly, and in a singularly curious irregular rhythm quite unlike that of the visible ritual.

Suddenly the sunshine seemed to lessen without the intervention of any discernible cloud. It was a very peculiar phenomenon, and was plainly marked by all. A rumbling sound seemed brewing beneath the hills, mixed strangely with a concordant rumbling which clearly came from the sky. Lightning flashed aloft, and the wondering crowd looked in vain for the portents of storm. The chanting of the men from Arkham now became unmistakable, and Wheeler saw through the glass that they were all raising their arms in the rhythmic incantation. From some farmhouse far away came the frantic barking of dogs.

The change in the quality of the daylight increased, and the crowd gazed about the horizon in wonder. A purplish darkness, born of nothing more than a spectral deepening of the sky's blue, pressed down upon the rumbling hills. Then the lightning flashed again, somewhat brighter than before, and the crowd fancied that it had showed a certain mistiness around the altar-stone on the distant height. No one, however, had been using the telescope at that instant. The whippoorwills continued their irregular pulsation, and the men of Dunwich braced themselves tensely against some imponderable menace with which the atmosphere seemed surcharged.

Without warning came those deep, cracked, raucous vocal sounds which will never leave the memory of the stricken group who heard them. Not from any human throat were they born, for the organs of man can yield no such acoustic perversions. Rather would one have said they came from the pit itself, had not their source been so unmistakably the altar-stone on the peak. It is almost erroneous to call them sounds at all, since so much of their ghastly, infra-bass timbre spoke to dim seats of consciousness and terror far subtler than the ear; yet one must do so, since their form was indisputably though vaguely that of half-articulate *words.* They were loud – loud as the rumblings and the thunder above which they echoed – yet did they come from no visible being. And because imagination might suggest a conjectural source in the world of non-visible beings, the huddled crowd at the mountain's base huddled still closer, and winced as if in expectation of a blow.

'Ygnailh... ygnaiih... thflthkh'ngha.... Yog-Sothoth ...' rang the hideous croaking out of space. 'Y'bthnk... h'ehye – n'grkdl'lh...'

The speaking impulse seemed to falter here, as if some frightful psychic struggle were going on. Henry Wheeler strained his eye at the telescope, but saw only the three grotesquely silhouetted human figures on the peak, all moving their arms furiously in strange gestures as their incantation drew near its culmination. From what black wells of Acherontic fear or feeling, from what unplumbed gulfs of extra-cosmic consciousness or obscure, long-latent heredity, were those half-articulate thunder-croakings drawn? Presently they began to gather renewed force and coherence as they grew in stark, utter, ultimate frenzy.

'Eh-y-ya-ya-yahaah – e'yayayaaaa... ngh'aaaaa... ngh'aaa... h'yuh... h'yuh... HELP! HELP! ...ff – ff – ff – FATHER! FATHER! YOG-SOTHOTH!...'

But that was all. The pallid group in the road, still reeling at the indisputably English syllables that had poured thickly and thunderously down from the frantic vacancy beside that shocking altar-stone, were never to hear such syllables again. Instead, they jumped violently at the terrific report which seemed to rend the hills; the deafening, cataclysmic peal whose source, be it inner earth or sky, no hearer was ever able to place. A single lightning bolt shot from the purple zenith to the altar-stone, and a great tidal wave of viewless force and indescribable stench swept down from the hill to all the countryside. Trees, grass, and under-brush were whipped into a fury; and the frightened crowd at the mountain's base, weakened by the lethal foetor that seemed about to asphyxiate them, were almost hurled off their feet. Dogs howled from the distance, green grass and foliage wilted to a curious, sickly yellow-grey, and over field and forest were scattered the bodies of dead whippoorwills.

The stench left quickly, but the vegetation never came right again. To this day there is something queer and unholy about the growths on and around that fearsome hill.

Curtis Whateley was only just regaining consciousness when the Arkham men came slowly down the mountain in the beams of a sunlight once more brilliant and untainted. They were grave and quiet, and seemed shaken by memories and reflections even more terrible than those which had reduced the group of natives to a state of cowed quivering. In reply to a jumble of questions they only shook their heads and reaffirmed one vital fact.

'The thing has gone for ever,' Armitage said. 'It has been split up into what it was originally made of, and can never exist again. It was an impossibility in a normal world. Only the least fraction was really matter in any sense we know. It was like its father – and most of it has gone back to him in some vague realm or dimension outside our material universe; some vague abyss out of which only the most accursed rites of human blasphemy could ever have called him for a moment on the hills.'

There was a brief silence, and in that pause the scattered senses of poor Curtis Whateley began to knit back into a sort of continuity; so that he put his hands to his head with a moan. Memory seemed to pick itself up where it had left off, and the horror of the sight that had prostrated him burst in upon him again.

'Oh, oh, my Gawd, that haff face – that haff face on top of it… that face with the red eyes an' crinkly albino hair, an' no chin, like the Whateleys… It was a octopus, centipede, spider kind o' thing, but they was a haff-shaped man's face on top of it, an' it looked like Wizard Whateley's, only it was yards an' yards acrost….'

He paused exhausted, as the whole group of natives stared in a bewilderment not quite crystallized into fresh terror. Only old Zebulon Whateley, who wanderingly remembered ancient things but who had been silent heretofore, spoke aloud.

'Fifteen year' gone,' he rambled, 'I heered Ol' Whateley say as haow some day we'd hear a child o' Lavinny's a-callin' its father's name on the top o' Sentinel Hill…'

But Joe Osborn interrupted him to question the Arkham men anew.

'*What was it, anyhaow*, an' haowever did young Wizard Whateley call it aout o' the air it come from?'

Armitage chose his words very carefully.

'It was – well, it was mostly a kind of force that doesn't belong in our part of space; a kind of force that acts and grows and shapes itself by other laws than those of our sort of Nature. We have no business calling in such things from outside, and only very wicked people and very wicked cults ever try to. There was some of it in Wilbur Whateley himself – enough to make a devil and a precocious monster of him, and to make his passing out a pretty terrible sight. I'm going to burn his accursed diary, and if you men are wise you'll dynamite that altar-stone up there, and pull down all the rings of standing stones on the other hills. Things like that brought down the beings those Whateleys were so fond of – the beings they were going to let in tangibly to wipe out the human race and drag the earth off to some nameless place for some nameless purpose.

'But as to this thing we've just sent back – the Whateleys raised it for a terrible part in the doings that were to come. It grew fast and big from the same reason that Wilbur grew fast and big – but it beat him because it had a greater share of the outsideness in it. You needn't ask how Wilbur called it out of the air. He didn't call it out. *It was his twin brother, but it looked more like the father than he did.*'

THE BOOK

Margaret Irwin

Margaret Irwin (1889–1969) was an English writer of a long series of critically acclaimed historical novels as well as the supernatural classic *Still She Wished for Company* (1924). She wrote her first ghost story at age five and continued to write them for much of her life, the best collected in *Madame Fears the Dark* (1935) and *Bloodstock* (1953). 'The Book' (1930) is one of only a handful of ghost stories 'weird' enough to appear in this anthology. The writer Joanna Russ, appearing herein with another unusual ghost story, described 'The Book' as 'one of the most interesting stories of the supernatural I ever read,' a sentiment also expressed by contributor and New Weird writer China Miéville.

On a foggy night in November, Mr Corbett, having guessed the murderer by the third chapter of his detective story, arose in disappointment from his bed and went downstairs in search of something more satisfactory to send him to sleep.

The fog had crept through the closed and curtained windows of the dining-room and hung thick on the air in a silence that seemed as heavy and breathless as the fog. The atmosphere was more choking than in his room, and very chill, although the remains of a large fire still burned in the grate.

The dining-room bookcase was the only considerable one in the house and held a careless unselected collection to suit all the tastes of the household, together with a few dull and obscure old theological books that had been left over from the sale of a learned uncle's library. Cheap red novels, bought on railway stalls by Mrs Corbett, who thought a journey the only time to read, were thrust in like pert, undersized intruders among the respectable nineteenth-century works of culture, chastely bound in dark blue or green, which Mr Corbett had considered the right thing to buy during his Oxford days; beside these there swaggered the children's large gaily bound story-books and collections of Fairy Tales in every colour.

From among this neat new cloth-bound crowd there towered here and there a musty sepulchre of learning, brown with the colour of dust rather than leather, with no trace of gilded letters, however faded, on its crumbling back to tell what lay inside. A few of these moribund survivors from the Dean's library were inhospitably fastened with rusty clasps; all remained closed, and appeared impenetrable, their blank, forbidding backs uplifted above their frivolous surroundings with the air of scorn that belongs to a private and concealed knowledge. For only the worm of corruption now bored his way through their evil-smelling pages.

It was an unusual flight of fancy for Mr Corbett to imagine that the vaporous and fog-ridden air that seemed to hang more thickly about the bookcase was like a dank and poisonous breath exhaled by one or other of these slowly rotting volumes. Discomfort in this pervasive and impalpable presence came on him more acutely than at any time that day; in an attempt to clear his throat of it he choked most unpleasantly.

He hurriedly chose a Dickens from the second shelf as appropriate to a London fog, and had returned to the foot of the stairs when he decided that his reading tonight should by contrast be of blue Italian skies and white statues, in beautiful rhythmic sentences. He went back for a Walter Pater.

He found *Marius the Epicurean* tipped sideways across the gap left by his withdrawal of *The Old Curiosity Shop*. It was a very wide gap to have been left by a single volume, for the books on that shelf had been closely wedged together. He put the Dickens back into it and saw that there was still space for a large book. He said to himself in careful and precise words: 'This is nonsense. No one can possibly have gone into the dining-room and removed a book while I was crossing the hall. There must have been a gap before in the second shelf.' But another part of his mind kept saying in a hurried, tumbled torrent: 'There was no gap in the second shelf. There was no gap in the second shelf.'

He snatched at both the *Marius* and *The Old Curiosity Shop*, and went to his room in a haste that was unnecessary and absurd, since even if he believed in ghosts, which he did not, no one had the smallest reason for suspecting any in the modern Kensington house wherein he and his family had lived for the last fifteen years. Reading was the best thing to calm the nerves, and Dickens a pleasant, wholesome and robust author.

Tonight, however, Dickens struck him in a different light. Beneath the author's sentimental pity for the weak and helpless, he could discern a revolting pleasure in cruelty and suffering, while the grotesque figures of the people in Cruikshank's illustrations revealed too clearly the hideous distortions of their souls. What had seemed humorous now appeared diabolic, and in disgust at these two favourites he turned to Walter Pater for the repose and dignity of a classic spirit.

But presently he wondered if this spirit were not in itself of a marble quality, frigid and lifeless, contrary to the purpose of nature. 'I have often thought', he said to himself, 'that there is something evil in the austere worship of beauty for its own sake.' He had never thought so before, but he liked to think that this impulse of fancy was the result of mature consideration, and with this satisfaction he composed himself for sleep.

He woke two or three times in the night, an unusual occurrence, but he was glad of it, for each time he had been dreaming horribly of these blameless Victorian works. Sprightly devils in whiskers and peg-top trousers tortured a lovely maiden and leered in delight at her anguish; the gods and heroes of classic fable acted deeds whose naked crime and shame Mr Corbett had never appreciated in Latin and Greek Unseens. When he had woken in a cold sweat from the spectacle of the ravished Philomel's torn and bleeding tongue, he decided there was nothing for it but to go down and get another book that would turn his thoughts in some more pleasant direction. But his increasing reluctance to do this found a hundred excuses. The recollection of the gap in the shelf now occurred to him with a sense of unnatural importance; in the troubled dozes that followed, this gap between two books seemed the most hideous deformity, like a gap between the front teeth of some grinning monster.

But in the clear daylight of the morning Mr Corbett came down to the pleasant dining-room, its sunny windows and smell of coffee and toast, and ate an undiminished breakfast with a mind chiefly occupied in self-congratulation that the wind had blown the fog away in time for his Saturday game of golf. Whistling happily, he was pouring out his final cup of coffee when his hand remained arrested in the act as his glance, roving across the bookcase, noticed that there was now no gap at all in the second shelf. He asked who had been at the bookcase already, but neither of the girls had, nor Dicky, and Mrs Corbett was not yet down. The maid never touched the books. They wanted to know what book he missed in it, which made him look foolish, as he could not say. The things that disturb us at midnight are negligible at 9 a.m.

'I thought there was a gap in the second shelf,' he said, 'but it doesn't matter.'

'There never is a gap in the second shelf,' said

little Jean brightly. 'You can take out lots of books from it and when you go back the gap's always filled up. Haven't you noticed that? I have.'

Nora, the middle one in age, said Jean was always being silly; she had been found crying over the funny pictures in *The Rose and the Ring* because she said all the people in them had such wicked faces, and the picture of a black cat had upset her because she thought it was a witch. Mr Corbett did not like to think of such fancies for his Jeannie. She retaliated briskly by saying Dicky was just as bad, and he was a big boy. He had kicked a book across the room and said, 'Filthy stuff,' just like that. Jean was a good mimic; her tone expressed a venom of disgust, and she made the gesture of dropping a book as though the very touch of it were loathsome. Dicky, who had been making violent signs at her, now told her she was a beastly little sneak and he would never again take her for rides on the step of his bicycle. Mr Corbett was disturbed. Unpleasant housemaids and bad schoolfriends passed through his head, as he gravely asked his son how he had got hold of this book.

'Took it out of that bookcase of course,' said Dicky furiously.

It turned out to be the *Boy's Gulliver's Travels* that Granny had given him, and Dicky had at last to explain his rage with the devil who wrote it to show that men were worse than beasts and the human race a washout. A boy who never had good school reports had no right to be so morbidly sensitive as to penetrate to the underlying cynicism of Swift's delightful fable, and that moreover in the bright and carefully expurgated edition they bring out nowadays. Mr Corbett could not say he had ever noticed the cynicism himself, though he knew from the critical books it must be there, and with some annoyance he advised his son to take out a nice bright modern boy's adventure story that could not depress anybody. It appeared, however, that Dicky was 'off reading just now', and the girls echoed this.

Mr Corbett soon found that he too was 'off reading'. Every new book seemed to him weak, tasteless and insipid; while his old and familiar books were depressing or even, in some obscure way, disgusting. Authors must all be filthy-minded; they probably wrote what they dared not express in their lives. Stevenson had said that literature was a morbid secretion; he read Stevenson again to discover his peculiar morbidity, and detected in his essays a self-pity masquerading as courage, and in *Treasure Island* an invalid's sickly attraction to brutality.

This gave him a zest to find out what he disliked so much, and his taste for reading revived as he explored with relish the hidden infirmities of minds that had been valued by fools as great and noble. He saw Jane Austen and Charlotte Brontë as two unpleasant examples of spinsterhood; the one as a prying, sub-acid busybody in everyone else's flirtations, the other as a raving, craving maenad seeking self-immolation on the altar of her frustrated passions. He compared Wordsworth's love of nature to the monstrous egoism of an ancient bellwether, isolated from the flock.

These powers of penetration astonished him. With a mind so acute and original he should have achieved greatness, yet he was a mere solicitor and not prosperous at that. If he had but the money, he might do something with those ivory shares, but it would be a pure gamble, and he had no luck. His natural envy of his wealthier acquaintances now mingled with a contempt for their stupidity that approached loathing. The digestion of his lunch in the City was ruined by meeting sentimental yet successful dotards whom he had once regarded as pleasant fellows. The very sight of them spoiled his game of golf, so that he came to prefer reading alone in the dining-room even on sunny afternoons.

He discovered also and with a slight shock that Mrs Corbett had always bored him. Dicky he began actively to dislike as an impudent blockhead, and the two girls were as insipidly alike as white mice; it was a relief when he abolished their tiresome habit of coming in to say goodnight.

In the now unbroken silence and seclusion of the dining-room, he read with feverish haste as though he were seeking for some clue to knowledge, some secret key to existence which would quicken and inflame it, transform it from its present dull torpor to a life worthy of him and his powers.

He even explored the few decaying remains of his uncle's theological library. Bored and baffled, he yet persisted, and had the occasional relief of an ugly woodcut of Adam and Eve with figures like bolsters and hair like dahlias, or a map of the Cosmos with Hell-mouth in the corner, belching forth demons. One of these books had diagrams and symbols in the margin which he took to be mathematical formulae of a kind he did not know. He presently discovered that they were drawn, not printed, and that the book was in manuscript, in a very neat, crabbed black writing that resembled black-letter printing. It was moreover in Latin, a fact that gave Mr Corbett a shock of unreasoning disappointment. For while examining the signs in the margin, he had been filled with an extraordinary exultation as though he knew himself to be on the edge of a discovery that should alter his whole life. But he had forgotten his Latin.

With a secret and guilty air which would have looked absurd to anyone who knew his harmless purpose, he stole to the schoolroom for Dicky's Latin dictionary and grammar and hurried back to the dining-room, where he tried to discover what the book was about with an anxious industry that surprised himself. There was no name to it, nor of the author. Several blank pages had been left at the end, and the writing ended at the bottom of a page, with no flourish or superscription, as though the book had been left unfinished. From what sentences he could translate, it seemed to be a work on theology rather than mathematics. There were constant references to the Master, to his wishes and injunctions, which appeared to be of a complicated kind. Mr Corbett began by skipping these as mere accounts of ceremonial, but a word caught his eye as one unlikely to occur in such an account. He read this passage attentively, looking up each word in the dictionary, and could hardly believe the result of his translation. 'Clearly,' he decided, 'this book must be by some early missionary, and the passage I have just read the account of some horrible rite practised by a savage tribe of devil-worshippers.' Though he called it 'horrible', he reflected on it, committing each detail to memory. He then amused himself by copying the signs in the margin near it and trying to discover their significance. But a sensation of sickly cold came over him, his head swam, and he could hardly see the figures before his eyes. He suspected a sudden attack of influenza, and went to ask his wife for medicine.

They were all in the drawing-room, Mrs Corbett helping Nora and Jean with a new game, Dicky playing the pianola, and Mike, the Irish terrier, who had lately deserted his accustomed place on the dining-room hearth-rug, stretched by the fire. Mr Corbett had an instant's impression of this peaceful and cheerful scene, before his family turned towards him and asked in scared tones what was the matter. He thought how like sheep they looked and sounded; nothing in his appearance in the mirror struck him as odd; it was their gaping faces that were unfamiliar. He then noticed the extraordinary behaviour of Mike, who had sprung from the hearth-rug and was crouched in the furthest corner, uttering no sound, but with his eyes distended and foam round his bared teeth. Under Mr Corbett's glance, he slunk towards the door, whimpering in a faint and abject manner, and then as his master called him, he snarled horribly, and the hair bristled on the scruff of his neck. Dicky let him out, and they heard him scuffling at a frantic rate down the stairs to the kitchen, and then, again and again, a long-drawn howl.

'What *can* be the matter with Mike?' asked Mrs Corbett.

Her question broke a silence that seemed to have lasted a long time. Jean began to cry. Mr Corbett said irritably that he did not know what was the matter with any of them.

Then Nora asked, 'What is that red mark on your face?'

He looked again in the glass and could see nothing.

'It's quite clear from here,' said Dicky; 'I can see the lines in the fingerprint.'

'Yes, that's what it is,' said Mrs Corbett in her brisk staccato voice; 'the print of a finger on your forehead. Have you been writing in red ink?'

Mr Corbett precipitately left the room for his own, where he sent down a message that he was suffering from headache and would have his dinner in bed. He wanted no one fussing round him. By next morning he was amazed at his fancies of influenza, for he had never felt so well in his life.

No one commented on his looks at breakfast, so he concluded that the mark had disappeared. The old Latin book he had been translating on the previous night had been moved from the writing-bureau, although Dicky's grammar and dictionary were still there. The second shelf was, as always in the daytime, closely packed; the book had, he remembered, been in the second shelf. But this time he did not ask who had put it back.

That day he had an unexpected stroke of luck in a new client of the name of Crab, who entrusted him with large sums of money: nor was he irritated by the sight of his more prosperous acquaintances, but with difficulty refrained from grinning in their faces, so confident was he that his remarkable ability must soon place him higher than any of them. At dinner he chaffed his family with what he felt to be the gaiety of a schoolboy. But on them it had a contrary effect, for they stared, either at him in stupid astonishment, or at their plates, depressed and nervous. Did they think him drunk? he wondered, and a fury came on him at their low and bestial suspicions and heavy dullness of mind. Why, he was younger than any of them!

But in spite of this new alertness he could not attend to the letters he should have written that evening and drifted to the bookcase for a little light distraction, but found that for the first time there was nothing he wished to read. He pulled out a book from above his head at random, and saw that it was the old Latin book in manuscript. As he turned over its stiff and yellow pages, he noticed with pleasure the smell of corruption that had first repelled him in these decaying volumes, a smell, he now thought, of ancient and secret knowledge.

This idea of secrecy seemed to affect him personally, for on hearing a step in the hall he hastily closed the book and put it back in its place. He went to the schoolroom where Dicky was doing his homework, and told him he required his Latin grammar and dictionary again for an old law report. To his annoyance he stammered and put his words awkwardly; he thought that the boy looked oddly at him and he cursed him in his heart for a suspicious young devil, though of what he should be suspicious he could not say. Nevertheless, when back in the dining-room, he listened at the door and then softly turned the lock before he opened the books on the writing-bureau.

The script and Latin seemed much clearer than on the previous evening, and he was able to read at random a passage relating to a trial of a German midwife in 1620 for the murder and dissection of 783 children. Even allowing for the opportunities afforded by her profession, the number appeared excessive, nor could he discover any motive for the slaughter. He decided to translate the book from the beginning.

It appeared to be an account of some secret society whose activities and ritual were of a nature so obscure, and, when not, so vile and terrible, that Mr Corbett would not at first believe that this could be a record of any human mind, although his deep interest in it should have convinced him that from his humanity at least it was not altogether alien.

He read until far later than his usual hour for bed and when at last he rose, it was with the book in his hands. To defer his parting with it, he stood turning over the pages until he reached the end of the writing, and was struck by a new peculiarity.

The ink was much fresher and of a far poorer quality than the thick rusted ink in the bulk of the book; on close inspection he would have said that it was of modern manufacture and written quite recently were it not for the fact that it was in the same crabbed late-seventeenth-century handwriting.

This, however, did not explain the perplexity, even dismay and fear, he now felt as he stared at the last sentence. It ran: '*Contine te in perennibus studiis*', and he had at once recognized it as a Ciceronian tag that had been dinned into him at school. He could not understand how he had failed to notice it yesterday.

Then he remembered that the book had ended at the bottom of a page. But now, the last two sentences were written at the very top of a page. However long he looked at them, he could come to no other conclusion than that they had been added since the previous evening.

He now read the sentence before the last: '*Re imperfecta mortuus sum*,' and translated the whole as: 'I died with my purpose unachieved. Continue, thou, the never-ending studies.'

With his eyes still fixed upon it, Mr Corbett replaced the book on the writing-bureau and stepped back from it to the door, his hand outstretched behind him, groping and then tugging at the door handle. As the door failed to open, his breath came in a faint, hardly articulate scream. Then he remembered that he had himself locked it, and he fumbled with the key in frantic ineffectual movements until at last he opened it and banged it after him as he plunged backwards into the hall.

For a moment he stood there looking at the door handle; then with a stealthy, sneaking movement, his hand crept out towards it, touched it, began to turn it, when suddenly he pulled his hand away and went up to his bedroom, three steps at a time.

There he behaved in a manner only comparable with the way he had lost his head after losing his innocence when a schoolboy of sixteen. He hid his face in the pillow, he cried, he raved in meaningless words, repeating: 'Never, never, never. I will never do it again. Help me never to do it again.' With the words, 'Help me', he noticed what he was saying, they reminded him of other words, and he began to pray aloud. But the words sounded jumbled, they persisted in coming into his head in a reverse order so that he found he was saying his prayers backwards, and at this final absurdity he suddenly began to laugh very loud. He sat up on the bed, delighted at this return to sanity, common sense and humour, when the door leading into Mrs Corbett's room opened, and he saw his wife staring at him with a strange, grey, drawn face that made her seem like the terror-stricken ghost of her usually smug and placid self.

'It's not burglars,' he said irritably. 'I've come to bed late, that is all, and must have waked you.'

'Henry,' said Mrs Corbett, and he noticed that she had not heard him, 'Henry, didn't you hear it?'

'What?'

'That laugh.'

He was silent, an instinctive caution warning him to wait until she spoke again. And this she did, imploring him with her eyes to reassure her.

'It was not a human laugh. It was like the laugh of a devil.'

He checked his violent inclination to laugh again. It was wiser not to let her know that it was only his laughter she had heard. He told her to stop being fanciful, and Mrs Corbett, gradually recovering her docility, returned to obey an impossible command, since she could not stop being what she had never been.

The next morning, Mr Corbett rose before any of the servants and crept down to the dining-room. As before, the dictionary and grammar alone remained on the writing-bureau; the book was back in the second shelf. He opened it at the end. Two more lines had been added, carrying the writing down to the middle of the page. They ran:

Ex auro canceris
In dentem elephantis.

which he translated as:

Out of the money of the crab
Into the tooth of the elephant.

From this time on, his acquaintances in the City noticed a change in the mediocre, rather flabby and unenterprising 'old Corbett'. His recent sour depression dropped from him: he seemed to have grown twenty years younger, strong, brisk and cheerful, and with a self-confidence in business that struck them as lunacy. They waited with a not unpleasant excitement for the inevitable crash, but his every speculation, however wild and hare-brained, turned out successful. He no longer avoided them, but went out of his way to display his consciousness of luck, daring and vigour, and to chaff them in a manner that began to make him actively disliked. This he welcomed with delight as a sign of others' envy and his superiority.

He never stayed in town for dinners or theatres, for he was always now in a hurry to get home, where, as soon as he was sure of being undisturbed, he would take down the manuscript book from the second shelf of the dining-room and turn to the last pages.

Every morning he found that a few words had been added since the evening before, and always they formed, as he considered, injunctions to himself. These were at first only with regard to his money transactions, giving assurance to his boldest fancies, and since the brilliant and unforeseen success that had attended his gamble with Mr Crab's money in African ivory, he followed all such advice unhesitatingly.

But presently, interspersed with these commands, were others of a meaningless, childish, yet revolting character such as might be invented by a decadent imbecile, or, it must be admitted, by the idle fancies of any ordinary man who permits his imagination to wander unbridled. Mr Corbett was startled to recognize one or two such fancies of his own, which had occurred to him during his frequent boredom in church, and which he had not thought any other mind could conceive.

He at first paid no attention to these directions, but found that his new speculations declined so rapidly that he became terrified not merely for his fortune but for his reputation and even safety, since the money of various of his clients was involved. It was made clear to him that he must follow the commands in the book altogether or not at all, and he began to carry out their puerile and grotesque blasphemies with a contemptuous amusement, which, however, gradually changed to a sense of their monstrous significance. They became more capricious and difficult of execution, but he now never hesitated to obey blindly, urged by a fear that he could not understand, but knew only that it was not of mere financial failure.

By now he understood the effect of this book on the others near it, and the reason that had impelled its mysterious agent to move the books into the second shelf so that all in turn should come under the influence of that ancient and secret knowledge.

In respect to it, he encouraged his children, with jeers at their stupidity, to read more, but he could not observe that they ever now took a book from the dining-room bookcase. He himself no longer needed to read, but went to bed early and slept sound. The things that all his life he had longed to do when he should have enough money now seemed to him insipid. His most exciting pleasure was the smell and touch of these mouldering pages as he turned them to find the last message inscribed to him.

One evening it was in two words only: '*Canem occide*.'

He laughed at this simple and pleasant request to kill the dog, for he bore Mike a grudge for his change from devotion to slinking aversion. Moreover, it could not have come more opportunely, since in turning out an old desk he had just discovered some packets of rat poison bought years ago and forgotten. No one therefore knew of its existence and it would be easy to poison Mike without any further suspicion than that of a neighbour's carelessness. He whistled light-heartedly as he ran upstairs to rummage for the packets, and returned to empty one in the dog's dish of water in the hall.

That night the household was awakened by terrified screams proceeding from the stairs. Mr Corbett was the first to hasten there, prompted by the instinctive caution that was always with him these days. He saw Jean, in her nightdress, scrambling up on to the landing on her hands and knees, clutching at anything that afforded support and screaming in a choking, tearless, unnatural manner. He carried her to the room she shared with Nora, where they were quickly followed by Mrs Corbett.

Nothing coherent could be got from Jean. Nora said that she must have been having her old dream again; when her father demanded what this was, she said that Jean sometimes woke in the night, crying, because she had dreamed of a hand passing backwards and forwards over the dining-room bookcase, until it found a certain book and took it out of the shelf. At this point she was always so frightened that she woke up.

On hearing this, Jean broke into fresh screams, and Mrs Corbett would have no more explanations. Mr Corbett went out on to the stairs to find what had brought the child there from her bed. On looking down into the lighted hall, he saw Mike's dish overturned. He went down to examine it and saw that the water he had poisoned must have been upset and absorbed by the rough doormat, which was quite wet.

He went back to the little girls' room, told his wife that she was tired and must go to bed, and he would take his turn at comforting Jean. She was now much quieter. He took her on his knee where at first she shrank from him. Mr Corbett remembered with an angry sense of injury that she never now sat on his knee, and would have liked to pay her out for it by mocking and frightening her. But he had to coax her into telling him what he wanted, and with this object he soothed her, calling her by pet names that he thought he had forgotten, telling her that nothing could hurt her now he was with her.

At first his cleverness amused him; he chuckled softly when Jean buried her head in his dressing-gown. But presently an uncomfortable sensation came over him, he gripped at Jean as though for her protection, while he was so smoothly assuring her of his. With difficulty, he listened to what he had at last induced her to tell him.

She and Nora had kept Mike with them all the evening and taken him to sleep in their room for a treat. He had lain at the foot of Jean's bed and they had all gone to sleep. Then Jean began her old dream of the hand moving over the books in the dining-room bookcase; but instead of taking out a book, it came across the dining-room and out on to the stairs. It came up over the banisters and to the door of their room, and turned their door handle very softly and opened it. At this point she jumped up wide awake and turned on the light, calling to Nora. The door, which had been shut when they went to sleep, was wide open, and Mike was gone.

She told Nora that she was sure something dreadful would happen to him if she did not go and bring him back, and ran down into the hall where she saw him just about to drink from his dish. She called to him and he looked up, but did not come, so she ran to him, and began to pull him along with her, when her nightdress was clutched from behind and then she felt a hand seize her arm.

She fell down, and then clambered upstairs as fast as she could, screaming all the way.

It was now clear to Mr Corbett that Mike's dish must have been upset in the scuffle. She was again crying, but this time he felt himself unable to comfort her. He retired to his room, where he walked up and down in an agitation he could not understand, for he found his thoughts perpetually arguing on a point that had never troubled him before.

'I am not a bad man,' he kept saying to himself. 'I have never done anything actually wrong. My clients are none the worse for my speculations, only the better. Nor have I spent my new wealth on gross and sensual pleasures; these now have even no attraction for me.'

Presently he added: 'It is not wrong to try and kill a dog, an ill-tempered brute. It turned against me. It might have bitten Jeannie.'

He noticed that he had thought of her as Jeannie, which he had not done for some time; it must have been because he had called her that tonight. He must forbid her ever to leave her room at night, he could not have her meddling. It would be safer for him if she were not there at all.

Again that sick and cold sensation of fear swept over him: he seized the bedpost as though he were falling, and held on to it for some minutes. 'I was thinking of a boarding-school,' he told himself, and then, 'I must go down and find out – find out –' He would not think what it was he must find out.

He opened his door and listened. The house was quiet. He crept on to the landing and along to Nora's and Jean's door where again he stood, listening. There was no sound, and at that he was again overcome with unreasonable terror. He imagined Jean lying very still in her bed, too still. He hastened away from the door, shuffling in his bedroom slippers along the passage and down the stairs.

A bright fire still burned in the dining-room grate. A glance at the clock told him it was not yet twelve. He stared at the bookcase. In the second shelf was a gap which had not been there when he had left. On the writing-bureau lay a large open book. He knew that he must cross the room and see what was written in it. Then, as before, words that he did not intend came sobbing and crying to his lips, muttering, 'No, no, not that. Never, never, never.' But he crossed the room and looked down at the book. As last time, the message was in only two words: '*Infantem occide.*'

He slipped and fell forward against the bureau. His hands clutched at the book, lifted it as he recovered himself and with his finger he traced out the words that had been written. The smell of corruption crept into his nostrils. He told himself that he was not a snivelling dotard, but a man stronger and wiser than his fellows, superior to the common emotions of humanity, who held in his hands the sources of ancient and secret power.

He had known what the message would be. It was after all the only safe and logical thing to do. Jean had acquired dangerous knowledge. She was a spy, an antagonist. That she was so unconsciously, that she was eight years old, his youngest and favourite child, were sentimental appeals that could make no difference to a man of sane reasoning power such as his own. Jean had sided with Mike against him. 'All that are not with me are against me,' he repeated softly. He would kill both dog and child with the white powder that no one knew to be in his possession. It would be quite safe.

He laid down the book and went to the door. What he had to do, he would do quickly, for again that sensation of deadly cold was sweeping over him. He wished he had not to do it tonight; last night it would have been easier, but tonight she had sat on his knee and made him afraid. He imagined her lying very still in her bed, too still. But it would be she who would lie there, not he, so why should he be afraid? He was protected by ancient and secret powers. He held on to the door handle, but his fingers seemed to have grown numb, for he could not turn it. He clung to it, crouched and shivering, bending over it until he knelt on the ground, his head beneath the handle which he still clutched with upraised hands. Suddenly the hands were loosened and flung outwards with the frantic gesture of a man falling from a great height, and he stumbled to his feet. He seized the book and threw it on the fire. A violent sensation of choking overcame him, he felt he was being strangled, as in a nightmare he tried again and again to shriek aloud, but his breath would make no sound. His breath would not come at all. He fell backwards heavily, down on the floor, where he lay very still.

In the morning, the maid who came to open the dining-room windows found her master dead. The sensation caused by this was scarcely so great in the City as that given by the simultaneous collapse of all Mr Corbett's recent speculations. It was instantly assumed that he must have had previous knowledge of this and so committed suicide.

The stumbling-block to this theory was that the medical report defined the cause of Mr Corbett's death as strangulation of the windpipe by the pressure of a hand which had left the marks of its fingers on his throat.

THE *MAINZ PSALTER*

Jean Ray

TRANSLATED INTO ENGLISH BY LOWELL BLAIR

Jean Ray (1887–1964) was a prolific Flemish writer, considered one of the pre-eminent members of what is sometimes called the Belgian School of the Weird. Ray's real name was Raymundus Joannes de Kremer and he used many other pseudonyms for his comic strips and detective stories. 'The *Mainz Psalter*' falls into the 'weird voyages' category; the author purportedly read William Hope Hodgson's ghost pirate stories only after writing the story. The original 1965 Jean Ray collection *Ghouls in My Grave,* a mass-market paperback, remains the best English-language translation of his work. The famed and hard-to-find Midnight House collection *My Own Private Spectres* (1999) provides the valuable service of bringing more stories into English.

A man who is about to die is not likely to be very elegant in his last words: being in a hurry to sum up his whole life, he tends to make them rigorously concise.

But it was different with Ballister as he lay dying in the forecastle of the trawler *North Caper,* from Grimsby.

We had tried in vain to stop the flow of blood that was draining his life away. He had no fever; his speech was steady and rapid. He did not seem to see the bandages or the bloody basin: his eyes were following remote and formidable images.

Reines, the radio man, was taking notes.

Reines spends all his spare time writing stories and essays for short-lived literary magazines. As soon as one of them is born in Paternoster Row, his name is sure to appear on the list of contributors. Do not be surprised, therefore, by the rather special style given to this final monologue of a mortally wounded sailor. The blame must fall on Reines, a literary man without glory, who transcribed it. But I can testify that the facts it contains are the same as those reported before four members of the crew of the *North Caper*: Benjamin Cormon, the captain; yours truly John Copeland, first mate; Ephraim Rose, engineer; and the aforementioned Archibald Reines.

Thus spoke Ballister:

It was in the Merry Heart Tavern that I first met the schoolmaster, and it was there that we struck our bargain and he gave me his orders.

The Merry Heart is more of a meeting-place for bargemen than for sailors. Its dilapidated façade is reflected in the water of one of Liverpool's back docks, where barges from the inland waterways are moored.

I looked at the well-drawn plan of a small schooner.

'She's almost a yacht,' I said. 'In heavy weather, she must be able to sail close to the wind, and that broad stern will make it possible for us to maneuver well when there's a head wind.'

'There's an auxiliary engine, too,' he said.

I frowned, having always loved sailing.

'Built by Hallet & Hallet, Glasgow, 1909,' I said. 'She's very well rigged. With her sixty tons and a crew of six, she'll take to the sea better than a transatlantic liner.'

His face took on a look of satisfaction, and he ordered a round of expensive drinks.

'Why are you changing her name from the *Hen-Parrot*?' I asked. 'It's a nice name. I've always liked parrots.'

He hesitated slightly.

'It's a matter of… sentiment, or of gratitude, if you prefer.'

'So the ship will be called the *Mainz Psalter*… It's odd, but I suppose it's original.'

Alcohol had made him a little loquacious.

'That's not the reason,' he said. 'A year ago a grand-uncle of mine died and left me a trunk full of old books.'

'So?'

'Wait! I was looking through them without enthusiasm when one of them caught my attention. It was an incunabulum… '

'A what?'

'An incunabulum,' he said with a slight air of superiority, 'is a book published shortly after the invention of the printing press. And I was amazed to recognize the almost heraldic mark of Fust and Schaeffer! Those names probably mean nothing to you. Fust and Schaeffer were partners of Gutenberg, the inventor of the printing press. The book I had in my hands was nothing less than a rare and splendid copy of the famous *Mainz Psalter,* published toward the end of the fifteenth century.'

I gave him a look of polite attention and false understanding.

'What will impress you more, Mr. Ballister,' he said, 'is that a Mainz Psalter is worth a fortune.'

'Ah!' I said, suddenly interested.

'Yes, it's worth a fine bundle of banknotes big enough to buy the former *Hen-Parrot* and pay ample wages to a crew of six men for the cruise I want to make. Now do you understand why I want to give such an unmaritime name to our little ship?'

I understood it perfectly, and I congratulated him on his greatness of soul.

'And yet it would seem more logical to me,' I said, 'to name the ship after that dear uncle who left you the book.'

He burst into loud, disagreeable laughter. I was disconcerted by such coarseness on the part of an educated man.

'You'll leave from Glasgow,' he said, 'and sail the ship through the North Minch to Cape Wrath.'

'Those are hellish waters,' I said.

'I chose you precisely because you know them, Mr. Ballister.'

No finer praise can be given a sailor than to say that he knows the horrible corridor of water that is the Minch Channel. My heart swelled with pride.

'That's true,' I said. 'In fact, I was once nearly killed between Chicken and Tiumpan Head.'

'South of Cape Wrath,' he went on, 'there's a sheltered little bay that's known only to a few bold sailors, by a name that doesn't appear on the map: Big Toe Bay.'

I looked at him in surprised admiration.

'Do you know Big Toe?' I said. 'That's something that would make you respected by Customs, and would probably get you stabbed by certain men of the coast.'

He made a gesture of indifference.

'I'll rejoin the ship at Big Toe Bay.'

'And from there?'

He indicated a precise westerly direction.

'Hm, that's a nasty place,' I said, 'a real desert of water strewn with sharp rocks. We won't see many trails of smoke on the horizon.'

'You're quite right,' he said.

I winked at him, thinking I understood.

'As long as you pay the way you've said,' I replied, 'I don't care what you do.'

'I think you're mistaken about my plans, Mr. Ballister. They're of a rather… scientific nature, but I don't want to have a discovery stolen from me by some envious rival. In any case, it doesn't matter, because I'll pay as I said.'

We spent a few minutes drinking. Then, just as we were about to discuss the question of the crew, our conversation veered off strangely.

'I'm not a sailor,' he said brusquely, 'so don't count on me to help with handling the ship. Let me be specific: I'm a schoolmaster.'

'I respect learning,' I said, 'and I'm not entirely lacking in it myself. A schoolmaster? Good, good!'

'Yes, in Yorkshire.'

'Let's go over the crew now,' I said. 'First of all there's Turnip. It's an odd name, but he's a good man and a good sailor. There's … a prison term in his recent past. Is that a drawback?'

'Not in the least.'

'Good. You can have him for reasonable wages, especially if you take a little rum on board. It can be cheap rum: he's not particular about quality as long as the quantity is there. And then there's Steevens, a Fleming. He never talks, but he can break a mooring chain as easily as you can bite through the stem of a clay pipe.'

'And I suppose he also has a prison term in his past?'

'It's not unlikely.'

'I'll take him. What did you say his name was again?'

'Steevens.'

'Steevens … Is he expensive?'

'Not at all. He makes up for his low pay by eating vast amounts of bacon and biscuits. And currant jam, if you buy any.'

'We'll take half a ton of it on board if you like.'

'He'll be your slave … I might suggest Walker to you now, but he's very ugly.'

'Are you joking?'

'No. His face lacks half a nose, part of a chin, and a whole ear, so it's not pleasant to look at for someone who's not used to Madame Tussaud's museum of horrors, especially since the operation was sloppily performed by some Italian sailors who were in a bit of a hurry.'

'And who else?'

'Two excellent men: Jellewyn and Friar Tuck. Friar Tuck – I don't know him by any other name – is a cook, among other things, a seagoing Jack-of-all-trades. He and Jellewyn are always together. If you see one, you see the other, and if you hire one, you must hire the other. They're rather mysterious. It's said that Jellewyn has royal blood in his veins and that Friar Tuck is a devoted servant who has stayed with him in adversity.'

'And their price is in keeping with their mystery?'

'Precisely. The fallen prince must have driven a car in the past, so he'll be the one to take care of your auxiliary engine.'

It was then that an incident took place that has little bearing on the events of this story, but that I remember with a certain uneasiness.

A poor devil had just been blown into the bar by the gusty night wind. He was a kind of emaciated, rain-soaked clown, faded by all the miseries of the sea and the waterfront.

He ordered a glass of gin and greedily raised it to his lips. Suddenly I heard the sound of breaking glass and saw the derelict throw up his hands, stare at the schoolmaster with unspeakable terror, then hurry outside into the wind and rain, without picking up his change from the bar. I don't think the schoolmaster noticed the incident, or at least he didn't seem to; but I still dare not imagine the formidable reason that drove that poor wretch to drop his gin on the floor, abandon his money, and flee into the icy street when the bar was filled with exquisite warmth.

On one of the first days of a very mild spring, the North Minch opened before us as though for a brotherly embrace. A few angry currents were still moving craftily beneath the surface, but we could detect them by their green backs, writhing like segments of mutilated snakes.

One of those curious southeastern breezes that blow only in that region brought us the fragrance of the early Irish lilacs from two hundred miles away and helped the auxiliary engine to take us to Big Toe Bay.

There, things changed radically. Whirlpools dug holes in the water, hissing like steam engines. We avoided them only with great difficulty. The moss-green hull of a sunken ship, raised from the depths of the Atlantic, shot up almost under the bobstay of our bowsprit and was hurled against a rock wall, where it exploded in a dark burst of rotten wood.

A dozen times, the *Mainz Psalter* was in danger of being dismasted as though by a stroke of a giant razor. Fortunately, she was a beautiful sailer and she lay to with the elegance of a true lady of the sea. A few hours of calm enabled us to run the engine at full speed and pass through the narrow channel of Big Toe Bay just as another furious tide came thundering after us in a green spray of tormented water.

'We're in inhospitable waters,' I said to my men. 'If the coastal scavengers find us here, we'll have to give them an explanation, and since they'll try to chase us away before hearing what we have to say, we'd better have our guns ready.'

The scavengers did put in an appearance, but in so doing they met with a disaster that was as disturbing as it was incomprehensible to us.

For a week, we had been lying at anchor in that little bay, which was as calm as a duck pond. Life was pleasant. Our supplies of food and drink were worthy of a royal yacht. By swimming twelve strokes, or rowing seven times, we could reach a little red sand beach and, further on, a stream of icy fresh water.

Turnip caught halibut on a line. Steevens went inland to the deserted moors, and sometimes, if the wind was right, we could hear the boom of his shotgun. He brought back partridges, grouse, occasionally a big-pawed hare, and always some of those delicious heath rabbits with fragrant flesh.

The schoolmaster had not appeared. We did not worry: we had been paid in cash for six weeks in advance, and Turnip had said he would not leave until the last drop of rum was gone.

One morning this serenity was shattered. Steevens had just filled a keg with fresh water when a shrill sound vibrated above him and, a foot away from his face, a rock exploded into dust. He was a phlegmatic man; without haste, he waded into the bay, spotted a puff of blue smoke rising from a cleft in a rock, ignored the angry little slaps that struck the surface of the water beside him, and calmly swam back to the ship. He went into the forecastle, where the crew was waking up, and said, 'Someone's shooting at us.'

His words were punctuated by three sharp blows against the hull. I took a rifle from the rack and went up on deck. I instinctively ducked at the sound of a whining bullet; an instant later, a handful of wooden splinters leapt into the air, and the bronze rolling-gear of the boom clanged beneath the impact of a lead slug.

I raised my rifle toward the cleft that Steevens pointed out to me. I saw billows of black-powder smoke coming from it. But suddenly the shooting stopped and was replaced by vociferations and shouts of fear.

Something struck the dark red beach with a heavy thud. I started in horror: a man had just fallen three hundred feet from the top of the cliff. His broken body was almost entirely buried in the sand, but I was able to recognize the coarse leather clothing of the wreckers of Cape Wrath.

I had scarcely turned my eyes away from that lifeless mass when Steevens touched me on the shoulder.

'Here comes another one,' he said.

An awkward, ridiculous shape was hurtling toward the ground; it was like the loose, ungainly fall of a big bird that has been hit by shotgun pellets at a great height, and, conquered by gravity and betrayed by the air, comes tumbling down without dignity.

For the second time there was a soft, ghastly thud on the sand. This time a villainous face quivered for a few seconds, spewing crimson froth. Steevens slowly pointed to the top of the cliff.

'One more,' he said in a slightly faltering voice.

Wild screams rang out from above. Suddenly we saw the bust of a man against the sky, struggling with something invisible. He made a desperate gesture, then flew from the cliff as though propelled by a catapult. His cry was still floating down to us in a slow tailspin of despair when his body was smashed beside the two others.

We stood still.

'It's true they were trying to kill us,' said Jellewyn, 'but I'd still like to avenge those poor devils. Please give me your rifle, Mr. Ballister. Friar Tuck, come here!'

Friar Tuck's shaved head emerged from the depths of the ship.

'Friar Tuck is as good as a hunting dog,' Jellewyn explained with a touch of condescension. 'Or rather he's as good as a whole pack of them: he smells the quarry from very far off. He's phenomenal… And what do you think of *this* quarry, old boy?'

Friar Tuck hoisted his round, massive body onto the deck and waddled over to the rail. He scrutinized the mangled corpses and showed deep surprise; then an ashen pallor came over his face.

'Friar,' said Jellewyn with a nervous laugh, 'you've seen some strong sights in your day, yet you're turning pale like a young chambermaid.'

'No, no, it's not that,' Friar Tuck replied dully. 'There's something ugly behind this... There's... Shoot, Your Grace!' he suddenly shouted. 'Up there! Hurry!'

Jellewyn turned on him furiously:

'I've warned you about calling me by that damned name!'

Friar Tuck made no reply. He shook his head, then murmured, 'Too late, it's gone.'

'What's gone?' I asked.

'Why, the thing that was watching us from the cliff,' he said foolishly.

'What was it?'

He gave me a crafty look.

'I don't know. Anyway, it's gone.'

I did not pursue my questioning. Two loud whistles came from the top of the cliff, then a shadow moved against the patch of sky behind it.

Jellewyn raised his rifle. I pushed it aside.

'Pay attention to what you're doing!'

The schoolmaster was coming down toward the beach from the cliff, following a path we had not noticed before.

A beautiful cabin in the stern had been reserved for the schoolmaster, and the adjoining room had been made into a bedroom for me, with two bunks.

As soon as he arrived on board, the schoolmaster shut himself up in his cabin and spent his time going through a pile of books. Once or twice a day he went topside, had the sextant brought to him, and carefully took the sun.

We were sailing northwest.

'We're headed for Iceland,' I said to Jellewyn.

He attentively looked at a map and wrote down a figure.

'No,' he said, 'we're headed for Greenland.'

'Well, what's the difference?'

We had left Big Toe Bay on a clear morning, leaving the Ross Mourtains to warm their humps in the rising sun behind us. That day we passed a ship from the Hebrides manned by a flat-faced crew whom we insulted lavishly. Toward evening we saw a ketch in full sail just above the horizon.

Next day, the sea was rising. To starboard, we saw a Danish steamer fighting against the waves. She was surrounded by so much smoke that we could not read her name.

That was the last ship we saw, although on the third day there were two trails of smoke to the south that Walker said were from a dispatch boat of the British Navy.

Every evening the schoolmaster invited me to have a drink in his cabin. He himself did not drink; he was no longer the loquacious companion of the Merry Heart Tavern, but he was still a well-bred man, for he never left my glass empty, and while I drank he kept his eyes on his books.

I must admit that I have few memories of those days. Life was monotonous; and yet the crew seemed apprehensive to me, perhaps because of an incident that occurred one evening.

We were all seized with violent nausea at almost the same time, and Turnip shouted that we had been poisoned.

I sternly ordered him to be silent. The nausea passed quickly, and a sudden shift of wind forced us to perform a strenuous maneuver that made us forget everything else.

The sun had risen on the eighth day of our voyage.

I found the crew with anxious, sullen faces. I was familiar with such faces; at sea, they are not a good sign. They indicate an uneasy, gregarious, and hostile feeling that groups men and makes them merge in a single fear or hatred; an evil force surrounds them and poisons the atmosphere of the ship. It was Jellewyn who spoke first:

'Mr. Ballister, we want to talk to you, and we want to talk to you as our friend and shipmate, rather than as our captain.'

'That's a fine preamble,' I said, laughing.

'We're being nice about it because you're our friend,' said Walker, and his horrible shapeless face twisted.

'Tell me what's on your mind,' I said.

'Something's wrong,' said Jellewyn, 'and the worst of it is that none of us can explain it.'

I cast a dark glance around me, then held out my hand to him.

'It's true, Jellewyn, I feel it the same as you do.'

The faces brightened; the men had found an ally in their captain.

'Look at the sea, Mr. Ballister.'

'I've seen it too,' I said, looking down.

Yes, I had seen it! The water had taken on a strange appearance that I had never seen before in all my twenty years at sea. It had oddly colored streaks, and it sometimes bubbled suddenly and loudly; unknown sounds, something like laughter, would burst from a rapidly approaching wave and make the men look around in alarm.

'Not one bird is following us any more,' said Friar Tuck.

It was true.

'Last night,' he said in his deep, slow voice, 'a little herd of rats that had been living in the storeroom ran topside and all jumped overboard at once. I never saw anything like it.'

'Never!' said the other sailors in a somber echo.

'I've sailed in these waters before,' said Walker, 'and at about this same time of year, too. The air ought to be full of scoter ducks, and schools of porpoises ought to be following us from morning till night. Do you see any?'

'Did you look at the sky last night, Mr. Ballister?' Jellewyn asked me softly.

'No,' I admitted, and I must have blushed a little. I had drunk a great deal in the schoolmaster's silent company, and I had not come up on deck, for I had been in the grip of a powerful intoxication that was still pressing my temples with a lingering headache.

'Where is that devil of a man taking us?' asked Turnip.

'Devil, yes,' said the taciturn Steevens.

Everyone had had his say.

I made a sudden decision.

'Jellewyn,' I said, 'listen to me. I'm the captain, it's true, but I'm not ashamed to admit in front of everyone that you're the most intelligent man on board, and I also know that you're not an ordinary sailor.'

He smiled sorrowfully.

'You know more about this than the rest of us, don't you?' I asked.

'No,' he replied. 'But Friar Tuck is a rather… curious phenomenon. As I've already told you, he senses certain things without being able to explain them. It's as though he had one more sense than the rest of us: a sense of danger… Speak, Friar Tuck.'

'I know very little, almost nothing,' said the low voice. 'I know only that something is around us, something worse than anything else, worse than death!'

We looked at each other in alarm.

'The schoolmaster,' continued Friar Tuck, seeming to choose his words with difficulty, 'is not alien to it.'

'Jellewyn,' I said, 'I don't have the courage myself, but I want you to go and tell him.'

'Very well,' he replied.

He went below. We heard him knock on the door of the schoolmaster's cabin, knock again and again, then finally open the door.

Minutes of silence went by.

Jellewyn came back up on deck. He was pale.

'He's not there,' he said. 'Search the whole ship. There's no place where a man can hide for long.'

We searched the ship, then went topside one by one, looking at each other uneasily. The schoolmaster had vanished.

At nightfall, Jellewyn motioned to me to come up on deck. When I was beside him he pointed upward.

I think I fell to my knees.

A strange sky was arched above the roaring sea. The familiar constellations were no longer there; unknown stars in new geometrical groupings were shining dimly in a frighteningly black sidereal abyss.

'Good God!' I exclaimed. 'Where are we?'

Heavy clouds were rolling across the sky.

'That's better,' Jellewyn said calmly. 'The others might have seen it and gone mad… You want to know where we are? How should I know? Let's turn back, Mr. Ballister, even though it's useless, in my opinion… '

I took my head between my hands.

'The compass has been inert for two days,' I murmured.

'I know,' said Jellewyn.

'But where are we? Where are we?'

'Be calm, Mr. Ballister,' he said rather ironically. 'You're the captain, don't forget that. I don't know where we are. I might make a hypothesis, to use an erudite word that sometimes covers an imagination that's too daring.'

'Even so,' I replied, 'I'd rather hear stories of witches and demons than that demoralizing "I don't know." '

'We're probably on another plane of existence. You have some mathematical knowledge; it will help you to understand. Our three-dimensional world is probably lost to us, and I'll define this one as the world of the *N*th dimension, which is very vague. If, by some inconceivable magic or some monstrous science, we were transported to Mars or Jupiter, or even to Aldebaran, it wouldn't prevent us from seeing the same constellations we see from earth.'

'But the sun ... '

'A similarity, a coincidence of the infinite, a kind of equivalent star, perhaps. Anyway, these are only suppositions, words; and since, I believe, we'll be permitted to die in this strange world the same as in our own, I feel that we can remain calm.'

'Die?' I said. 'I'll defend myself!'

'Against whom?' he asked sarcastically.

'It's true that Friar Tuck talked about things worse than death. If there's anyone's opinion that shouldn't be ignored in time of danger, it's his.' I returned to what he called his hypothesis: 'What do you mean by the *N*th dimension?'

'For the love of heaven,' he said nervously, 'don't give my idea such real importance! There's no proof that existence is possible outside of our three ordinary dimensions. Just as we've never discovered any two-dimensional beings from the world of surfaces, or one-dimensional beings from the linear world, we must be indiscernible to beings, if there are any, who live in worlds having more dimensions than ours. I'm in no mood to give you a lesson in hypergeometry, Mr. Ballister, but I'm sure of one thing: there are spaces different from ours. The space we're aware of in our dreams, for example, which presents the past, the present, and perhaps the future, on a single plane; and then there's the world of atoms and electrons, and relative and immense spaces with mysterious kinds of life ... ' He made a gesture of lassitude. 'What was that enigmatic schoolmaster's purpose in bringing us to this devilish region? How, and especially why, did he disappear?'

I suddenly clapped my hand to my forehead. I had just remembered Friar Tuck's expression of fear, and that of the poor derelict in the Merry Heart Tavern.

I related the incident to Jellewyn. He slowly nodded.

'I mustn't exaggerate Friar Tuck's clairvoyant powers,' he said. 'When he first saw the schoolmaster, he said to me, "That man makes me think of an unscalable wall behind which something immense and terrible is taking place." I didn't question him because it would have been useless: that was all he knew. His occult perceptions take the form of images, and he's incapable of analyzing them. In this case, his apprehension goes back even further. As soon as he heard the name of our schooner, he seemed upset and said there was great malice behind it ... '

'How shall we sail?' I asked, abandoning nearly all authority.

'We're on the starboard tack,' he said. 'The wind seems very steady.'

'Shall we heave to?'

'Why? Let's go on making headway. I don't see any sign of a storm, but I think we'd better reef our sails a little just the same.'

'Walker will take the helm to begin with,' I said. 'All he'll have to do is watch for patches of white water. If we hit a submerged rock ... '

'It might be the best solution for all of us,' said Jellewyn.

I could not have agreed with him more.

While a known danger strengthens a leader's authority, the unknown brings him closer to the level of his men.

That evening the forecastle was deserted and everyone crowded into the narrow room that served as my cabin. Jellewyn gave us two demijohns of excellent rum from his personal provisions, and we used it to make a gigantic bowl of punch.

Turnip was soon in an amiable mood. He began an endless story about two cats, a young lady, and a house in Ipswich, a story in which he had played a favorable part.

Steevens had made some fantastic sandwiches of hardtack and corned beef.

Heavy tobacco smoke made a dense fog around the kerosene lamp hanging motionlessly from its gimbals.

The atmosphere was pleasant and friendly. With the help of the punch, I was on the verge of smiling at the fairy tales Jellewyn had told me earlier.

Walker took his share of warm punch in a thermos bottle, picked up a lighted lantern, bade us good night, and went up to take the helm.

My clock slowly struck nine.

An accentuated movement of the ship told us that the sea was growing rougher.

'We don't have much sail set,' said Jellewyn.

I silently nodded.

Turnip's voice droned on, addressed to Steevens, who listened as he ground hardtack between the admirable millstones of his teeth.

I emptied my glass and handed it to Friar Tuck to fill. Then I saw the wild expression on his face. His hand was squeezing Jellewyn's, and they both seemed to be listening to something.

'What… ,' I began.

Just then we heard loud imprecations overhead, followed by the sound of bare feet running rapidly toward the deckhouse, and then a terrible cry.

We looked at each other, horrified. A high-pitched call, a kind of yodel, came from far away.

We all rushed up on deck at once, jostling each other in the darkness.

Everything was calm. The sails were purring happily; near the helm, the lantern was burning brightly, illuminating the squat shape of the abandoned thermos bottle.

But there was no one at the helm.

'Walker! Walker!' we shouted frantically.

Faraway, from the horizon blurred by the night mists, the mysterious yodel answered us.

The great silent night had swallowed up our poor Walker forever.

A sinister dawn, purple like the swift twilight of tropical savannahs, followed that funereal night.

The men, dulled by anguished insomnia, watched the choppy waves. The bowsprit frenziedly pecked at the foam of the crests.

A big hole had appeared in our crossjack. Steevens opened the sail-locker to replace it. Friar Tuck took out his metal palm and prepared to do a conscientious repair job.

Everyone's movements were instinctive, mechanical, and morose. Now and then I turned the helm and murmured to myself, 'What's the use? What's the use?'

Without having been ordered to, Turnip began climbing up the mainmast. I watched him distractedly until he reached the main yard, then the sails hid him from sight.

Suddenly we heard his frenzied shout:

'Hurry! Come up, there's someone on the mast!'

There was a fantastic sound of aerial struggle, then a howl of agony, and at the same time a whirling shape shot upward, and then fell into the waves a great distance away from the ship.

Jellewyn swore vehemently and began climbing up the mast, followed by Friar Tuck.

Steevens and I leapt toward the only lifeboat on board. The Fleming's formidable arms were sliding it toward the water when we were rooted to the deck by astonishment and terror. Something gray, shiny, and indistinct, like glass, suddenly surrounded the lifeboat, the chains snapped, an unknown force tilted the schooner to port, and a wave broke over the deck and poured into the open sail-locker. An instant later, the lifeboat had vanished without a trace.

Jellewyn and Friar Tuck came down from the mast. They had seen no one.

Jellewyn took a rag and wiped his hands, shuddering. He had found the sail and the rigging splattered with warm blood.

In a faltering voice, I recited the prayer for the dead, interspersing the holy words with curses against the ocean and its mystery.

It was late when Jellewyn and I went topside, having decided to spend the night at the helm together.

At one moment I began to weep and he patted me affectionately on the shoulder. I became a little calmer and lit my pipe.

We had nothing to say to each other. He seemed to have fallen asleep at the helm. I stared into the darkness.

I leaned over the port rail and was suddenly petrified by an unearthly sight. I straightened up, uttering a muffled exclamation.

'Have you seen it, Jellewyn, or are my eyes playing tricks on me?'

'You're not mistaken,' he said softly, 'but for the love of Christ don't say anything about it to the others. Their minds are already close enough to madness.'

I had to make a great effort to go back to the rail. Jellewyn stood beside me.

The bottom of the sea was aflame with a vast bloody glow that spread beneath the schooner; the light slid under the keel and illuminated the sails and rigging from below. It was as though we were on a boat in the Drury Lane Theatre, lighted by an invisible row of flares.

'Phosphorescence?' I ventured.

'Look,' whispered Jellewyn.

The water had become as transparent as glass. At an enormous depth, we saw great dark masses with unreal shapes: there were manors with immense towers, gigantic domes, horribly straight streets lined with frenzied houses. We appeared to be flying over a furiously busy city at an incredible height.

'There seems to be movement,' I said.

'Yes.'

We could see a swarming crowd of amorphous beings engaged in some sort of feverish and infernal activity.

'Get back!' Jellewyn shouted, pulling me violently by the belt.

One of those beings was rising toward us with astounding speed. In less than a second its immense bulk had hidden the undersea city from us; it was as though a flood of ink had instantaneously spread around us.

The keel received a tremendous blow. In the crimson light, we saw three enormous tentacles, three times as high as the mainmast, hideously writhing in the air. A formidable face composed of black shadows and two eyes of liquid amber rose above the port side of the ship and gave us a terrifying look.

This lasted less than two seconds. A heavy swell was headed for us broadside.

'Helm hard to starboard!' shouted Jellewyn.

The lines holding the boom snapped, and it cut through the air like an ax. The mainmast bent almost to the breaking-point. Taut halyards broke with a sound like that of harp strings.

The awesome vision became vague. The water was foaming. To starboard, the glow ran like a burning fringe across the high, galloping crests, then abruptly vanished.

'Poor Walker, poor Turnip,' said Jellewyn.

The bell rang in the forecastle: the midnight watch was beginning.

An uneventful morning followed. The sky was covered with thick, motionless clouds of a dirty, yellowish color. The air was chilly.

Toward noon, shining feebly through the mist, I saw a spot of light that might have been the sun. I decided to determine its position, despite Jellewyn's opinion that it would be meaningless.

The sea was rough. I tried to hold the horizon, but a wave would always invade my field of vision, and the horizon would leap up into the sky. Finally I succeeded. But as I was looking for the reflection of the spot of light in the mirror of the sextant, I saw a kind of white streamer quivering in front of it at a great height.

Something indefinable rushed toward me. The sextant flew into the air, I received a jarring blow on the head, and then I heard shouts, sounds of struggle, and more shouts.

I was not exactly unconscious. I was sprawled against the deckhouse. Bells were ringing endlessly in my ears; I even seemed to hear the solemn booming of Big Ben. Mingled with these pleasant sounds were clamors that were more alarming, but also further away.

I was about to make an effort to stand up when I felt myself seized and lifted. I began howling and kicking with all my returning strength.

'Thank God!' said Jellewyn. 'He's not dead!'

I managed to open my eyelids, which felt as though they were made of lead. A patch of yellow sky was cut by diagonal ropes. I saw Jellewyn staggering as though he were drunk.

'For the love of God, what's happened to us?' I asked dolefully, for Jellewyn's face was streaming with tears.

Without answering, he led me to my cabin.

I saw that one of the two bunks was occupied by a motionless mass.

At this point, I completely regained my senses. I put my hands over my heart. I had just recognized Steevens' hideously swollen face.

Jellewyn gave me a drink.

'This is the end,' I heard him say.

'The end,' I repeated stupidly, trying to understand.

He put cold compresses on Steevens' face.

'Where's Friar Tuck?' I asked.

Jellewyn sobbed aloud.

'Like… the others… We'll never see him again!'

He told me, in a tear-choked voice, the little he knew.

It had happened with incredible swiftness, like all the successive tragedies that now formed our existence. Jellewyn had been below, checking the oilcups, when he heard shouts of distress from above. He hurried topside and saw Steevens furiously struggling inside a kind of silvery bubble. A moment later, Steevens collapsed and lay still. Friar Tuck was gone; his metal palms and sail-needles were scattered around the mainmast. Fresh blood was dripping from the starboard rail. I was lying unconscious against the deckhouse. He knew nothing more.

'When Steevens comes to, he'll give us more information,' I said weakly.

'When he comes to!' Jellewyn exclaimed bitterly. 'His body is nothing but a horrible bag filled with broken bones and crushed organs. Because of his Herculean constitution he's still breathing, but for all practical purposes he's dead, dead like the others.'

We let the *Mainz Psalter* sail as she pleased. She had little canvas spread, and she drifted sideways almost as much as she moved forward.

'Everything seems to show that the danger is mainly on deck,' said Jellewyn, as though talking to himself.

We were still in my cabin when evening came.

Steevens' breathing was labored and painful to hear. We had to keep wiping away the bloody froth that ran from his mouth.

'I won't sleep,' I said.

'Neither will I,' replied Jellewyn.

We had closed the portholes despite the stuffy atmosphere. The ship was rolling a little.

Toward two in the morning, when an invincible torpor was dulling my thoughts and I was sinking into a half-sleep already packed with nightmares, I suddenly started.

Jellewyn was wide awake. He was looking up in terror at the gleaming wooden ceiling.

'Someone's walking on deck,' he said softly.

I seized the rifle.

'That's useless. Let's stay where we are… Ah, they're making themselves at home now!'

We heard rapid footsteps on the deck. It sounded as though a busy crowd were moving around.

'I thought so,' said Jellewyn. He laughed. 'We're gentlemen of leisure now: we have others working for us.'

The sounds had become more precise. The helm creaked; an arduous maneuver was being carried out in the head wind.

'They're unfurling the sails!'

'Of course.'

The ship pitched heavily, then listed to starboard.

'A starboard tack, in this wind,' Jellewyn said approvingly. 'They're monsters, brutes drunk with blood and murder, but they're sailors. The most skillful yachtsman in England, sailing a racer built last year, wouldn't dare to sail so close to the wind. And what does it prove?'

No longer understanding anything, I made a gesture of discouragement.

He answered his own question: 'It proves that

we have a fixed destination, and that they want us to arrive somewhere.'

After reflecting for a moment I said, 'It also proves that they're neither demons nor ghosts, but beings like us.'

'Oh, that's saying a lot!'

'I'm expressing myself badly. What I mean is that they're material beings, with only natural forces at their command.'

'I've never doubted that,' Jellewyn said calmly.

Toward five in the morning, another maneuver was carried out, making the schooner roll heavily. Jellewyn opened a porthole. A dirty dawn was filtering through compact clouds.

We cautiously ventured up on deck. It was tidy and deserted.

The ship was hove to.

Two calm days went by.

The nocturnal maneuvers had not been resumed, but Jellewyn pointed out that a very swift current was taking us in what should have been a northwesterly direction.

Steevens was still breathing, but more feebly. Jellewyn had brought a portable medicine chest in his baggage, and from time to time he gave the dying man an injection. We spoke little. I think we had even stopped thinking. For my part, I was stupefied by alcohol, for I was drinking whisky by the pint.

One day, when I was drunkenly cursing the schoolmaster and promising to smash his face into a thousand pieces, I happened to mention the books he had brought on board.

Jellewyn leapt forward and shook me vigorously.

'Careful, I'm the captain,' I said gently.

'To hell with captains like you! What did you say? Books?'

'Yes, in his cabin. There's a trunk full of them. I saw them myself. They're written in Latin; I don't know that pharmacist's jargon.'

'Well, *I* know it. Why didn't you tell me about those books?'

'What difference would it have made?' I muttered thickly. 'Anyway, I'm the captain.... You... you ought to... respect me.'

'You damned drunk!' he said angrily, going off toward the schoolmaster's cabin. I heard him step inside and close the door behind him.

The inert and pitiful Steevens was my companion during the hours of drinking that followed.

'I'm the captain of this ship,' I mumbled, 'and I'll... I'll complain to the authorities... He called me a... a damned drunk... I'm the master after God on my ship... Isn't that right, Steevens? You're a witness... He insulted me basely... I'll put him in irons... '

Then I slept a little.

When Jellewyn came in to swallow a hasty meal of hardtack and corned beef, his cheeks were flushed and his eyes were glittering.

'Mr. Ballister,' he said, 'did the schoolmaster ever tell you about a crystal object, a box, perhaps?'

'He didn't confide in me,' I grunted, still remembering his rudeness.

'Ah, if only I'd had those books before all these things began happening!'

'Have you found anything?' I asked.

'I'm getting a few glimmers... A path is opening up. It's probably senseless, but in any case it's amazing, more amazing than you can possibly imagine!'

He was terribly excited. I was unable to get anything more out of him. He hurried back to the schoolmaster's cabin, and I left him alone.

I did not see him again until the beginning of evening, and then only for a few minutes. He came in to fill a kerosene lamp and did not say a word.

I slept until late the next morning. As soon as I woke up, I went to the schoolmaster's cabin.

Jellewyn was not there.

Seized with painful anxiety, I called him. There was no answer. I ran all over the ship shouting his name, even forgetting prudence to the point of going up on deck. Finally I threw myself on the floor, weeping and invoking the name of God.

I was alone on board the accursed schooner, alone with the dying Steevens.

Alone, horribly alone.

It was not until noon that I went back to the schoolmaster's cabin. My attention was immediately caught by a sheet of paper pinned to the wall. I read these words in Jellewyn's handwriting:

> Mr. Ballister, I am going to the top of the mainmast. I must see something. Perhaps I shall never return. If so, forgive me for my death, which will leave you all alone, because Steevens is doomed, as you know. But quickly do what I tell you: Burn all these books; do it on the stern, far from the mainmast, and do not go near the edge of the ship. I think an effort will be made to prevent you from burning the books. Everything inclines me to believe it. But burn them, burn them quickly, even at the risk of setting fire to the ship. Will it save you? I dare not hope so. Perhaps Providence will give you a chance. May God have mercy on you, Mr. Ballister, and on all of us!
>
> Duke_____,[1] known as Jellewyn.

When I returned to my cabin, shaken by that extraordinary farewell and cursing the shameful drunkenness that had probably prevented my valiant companion from awakening me, I no longer heard Steevens' irregular breathing. I leaned over his poor, contorted face. He, too, was gone.

I took two cans of gasoline from the little engine room, and, moved by some sort of providential instinct, I started the engine and turned it up to full speed.

I went back to the helm, piled the books on the deck, and poured gasoline on them.

A high, pale flame arose.

At that moment, there was a cry from the sea, and I heard someone call my name. Then I, too, cried out, in surprise and fear: in the wake of the *Mainz Psalter,* a hundred feet back, swam the schoolmaster.

The flames crackled; the books were rapidly being transformed into ashes.

The infernal swimmer shouted curses and supplications.

'Ballister! I'll make you rich, richer than all men on earth put together! I'll make you die, you imbecile, in horrible tortures that are unknown on your accursed planet! I'll make you a king, Ballister, king of a formidable kingdom! Ah, you swine, hell would be sweeter to you than what I have in store for you!'

He swam desperately, but made little progress in overtaking the ship.

Suddenly the schooner made a few strange movements and was shaken by dull blows. I saw the water rising toward me: the ship was being pulled toward the bottom of the sea.

'Ballister, listen to me!' howled the schoolmaster.

He was quickly drawing closer. His face was horribly impassive, but his eyes were burning with unbearable brightness.

Then, in the middle of a mass of hot ashes, I saw a piece of parchment curl up and reveal a sparkling object. I remembered Jellewyn's words. The specially constructed book had been hiding the crystal box he had mentioned to me.

'The crystal box!' I exclaimed.

The schoolmaster heard me. He shrieked like a madman, and I saw an incredible sight: he stood on the water with his hands outstretched like threatening claws.

'It's knowledge, the greatest knowledge of all, that you're about to destroy, you damned fool!' he roared.

Shrill yodels were now coming toward me from all points of the horizon.

The first waves broke over the deck.

I leapt into the flames and smashed the crystal box with my heel.

I had a feeling of collapse, and terrible nausea. Sky and water blended in a flashing chaos, an immense clamor shook the air. I began a frightful fall into darkness…

And here I am. I've told you everything now. I woke up on your ship. I'm going to die. Have I been dreaming? I wish I could believe it.

But I'm going to die among men, on my own earth. Ah, how happy I am!

It was Briggs, the cabin boy of the *North Caper,* who had first sighted Ballister. The boy had just stolen an apple from the galley and was about to

[1] Here appears a name that we shall not reveal, in order not to rekindle the sorrow of a great and noble reigning family. Jellewyn bore a heavy weight of guilt, but his death brilliantly redeemed him.

eat it, huddled among some coils of cable, when he saw Ballister swimming sluggishly a few yards from the ship.

Briggs began shouting at the top of his lungs, for he saw that the swimmer was about to be drawn into the wash of the propeller.

Ballister was pulled out of the water. He was unconscious: his swimming movements had been automatic, as sometimes happens with very strong swimmers.

There was no ship in sight and no trace of wreckage on the water. But the cabin boy said that he had seen a ship as transparent as glass – those are his own words – rise up off the port beam, then sink below the surface. This earned him a slap from Captain Cormon, to teach him not to tell such wild stories.

We managed to pour a little whisky down Ballister's throat. Rose, the engineer, gave him his bunk, and we covered him warmly.

He soon passed from unconsciousness into deep, feverish sleep. We were waiting, with curiosity, for him to awaken when a terrible incident took place.

This is now being told by John Copeland, first mate of the *North Caper.* It was I, who, with Seaman Jolks, saw the mystery and terror that came out of the night.

The last bearing taken during the day had located the *North Caper* at longitude 22° west and latitude 60° north.

I took the helm myself, having decided to spend the night on deck, because the night before we had seen long ice floes glittering in the moonlight on the northwest horizon.

Jolks hung up the running lights, and since he had a violent toothache that was made worse by the warmth of the forecastle, he came to smoke his pipe beside me. I was glad, because a lonely watch can be terribly monotonous when it lasts all night.

I must tell you that, while the *North Caper* is a good, sturdy ship, she is not a trawler of the latest model, even though she has been equipped with radio. The spirit of fifty years ago still weighs down on her, leaving her with sails that supplement the limited power of her steam engine. She does not have the tall, enclosed, ungainly cabin that is perched in the middle of the deck on most modern trawlers like a ludicrous little cottage. Her helm is still on the stern, facing the sea, the wind, and the spray.

I am giving you this description so that you will know that we witnessed the incomprehensible scene not from a glassed-in observation post, but from the deck itself. Without this explanation, my story would not seem believable to those familiar with the design of steam trawlers.

There was no moonlight because the sky was too overcast; only the diffused glow of the clouds and the phosphorescence of the wave crests made it possible to see anything.

It was somewhere around ten o'clock. The men were sunk deep in their first sleep. Jolks, absorbed in his toothache, was softly moaning and swearing. The binnacle light made his tense face stand out from the surrounding darkness.

Suddenly I saw his grimace of pain change to an expression of astonishment, then of genuine terror. His pipe fell from his open mouth. This struck me as so comical that I made a mocking remark to him. His only reply was to point to the starboard light.

My pipe joined his when I saw what he was pointing to: clutching the shrouds a few inches below the light, two wet hands were emerging from the darkness.

Suddenly the hands let go and a dark form leapt onto the deck. Jolks quickly stepped aside, and the binnacle light shone on the intruder's face. To our indescribable amazement, we saw a kind of clergyman, wearing a black tail-coat and streaming with sea water. He had a small head with eyes like glowing coals that were staring straight at us.

Jolks made a move to take out his fishing knife, but he did not have time: the apparition leapt on him and knocked him down. At the same time, the binnacle light was shattered. A few moments later there was a shrill cry from the forecastle, where the cabin boy had been sitting up with Ballister:

'He's killing him! Help!'

Ever since I had had to stop some serious brawls among members of the crew, I had made it a habit to carry my revolver at night. It was a powerful weapon, and I shot well with it. I cocked it.

The ship was filled with a confused clamor.

A short time after this series of events, a gust of wind ripped a gash in the clouds and a beam of moonlight followed the ship like a spotlight.

I could already hear the captain's swearing above Briggs's cries of alarm when to my right I heard soft footsteps and saw the clergyman leap over the side and into the water.

I saw his small head rise on the crest of a wave. I calmly aimed at it and fired. He uttered a strange howl, and the wave carried him toward the side of the ship.

Jolks appeared beside me. Although he was still a little dazed, he was wielding a grappling iron. The body was now floating alongside the ship, bumping against it. The grappling iron bit into the clothes and pulled up its prey with surprising ease.

Jolks dropped a shapeless wet bundle on the deck, saying that it felt as light as a feather. Captain Cormon came out of the forecastle, holding a lighted lantern.

'Someone tried to kill our shipwreck victim!' he said.

'We've got the bandit,' I said. 'He came out of the sea … '

'You're crazy, Copeland!'

'Look at him, captain. I shot him and … '

We leaned over the pitiful remains, but we immediately straightened up again, shouting like madmen.

The clothes were empty; two artificial hands and a wax head were attached to them. My bullet had gone through the wig and broken the nose.

You already know Ballister's story. He told it to us when he woke up toward the end of that infernal night. He spoke serenely, with a kind of happiness.

We took devoted care of him. There were two holes in his left shoulder, as though he had been stabbed twice, but we would have saved him if we had been able to stop his bleeding, because no essential organs had been damaged.

After having talked so much, he lapsed into a coma. When he came out of it later, he asked how he had been injured. Briggs was the only one with him at the time. Glad to have a chance to make himself interesting, he replied that in the middle of the night he had seen a dark shape rush into the forecastle and strike Ballister. He then told him about the shot and showed him the grotesque remains.

At this sight, Ballister cried out in terror.

'The schoolmaster! The schoolmaster!'

He fell into a painful fever and did not regain consciousness until six days later, in the maritime hospital in Galway, where he kissed the image of Christ and died.

The tragic mannequin was taken to Reverend Leemans, a worthy ecclesiastic who has been all over the world and knows many of the secrets of savage lands and the sea.

He examined it for a long time.

'What can have been inside it?' asked Archie Reines. 'There surely was *something* in it. It was alive.'

'Yes, it was alive all right, I can tell you that,' grumbled Jolks, rubbing his red, swollen neck.

Reverend Leemans sniffed the thing like a dog, then cast it aside with disgust.

'I thought so,' he said.

We also sniffed it.

'It smells of formic acid,' I said.

'And phosphorus,' added Reines.

Captain Cormon reflected for a moment, then his lips quivered a little when he said, 'It smells like an octopus.'

Leemans stared at him.

'On the last day of Creation,' he said, 'it is from the sea that God will cause the Blasphemous Beast to appear. Let us not try to anticipate destiny with impious inquiries.'

'But … ,' began Reines.

' *"Who is this that darkeneth counsel by words without knowledge?"*'

Before the Holy Word, we bowed our heads and gave up trying to understand.

THE SHADOWY STREET

Jean Ray

TRANSLATED INTO ENGLISH BY LOWELL BLAIR

Jean Ray (1887–1964) was a Belgian writer of classic weird tales sadly unknown to most contemporary English-language readers. He also wrote one novel, *Malpertuis* (1943), which was subsequently made into a film by Harry Kümel during 1971 (starring Orson Welles). In addition to 'The *Mainz Psalter*' reprinted earlier in this volume, Jean Ray wrote the chilling 'The Shadowy Street' (1931) during a stint in prison, just as H. P. Lovecraft was publishing some of his most classic tales. Later in the 1930s, Ray would have four stories published in *Weird Tales*. He is considered by many the Poe, or Lovecraft, of the French language.

On a Rotterdam dock, winches were fishing bales of old paper from the hold of a freighter. The wind was fluttering the multicolored streamers that hung from the bales when one of them burst open like a cask in a roaring fire. The longshoremen hastily scooped up some of the rustling mass, but a large part of it was abandoned to the joy of the little children who gleaned in the eternal autumn of the waterfront.

There were beautiful Pearsons engravings, cut in half by order of Customs; green and pink bundles of stocks and bonds, the last echoes of resounding bankruptcies; pitiful books whose pages were still joined like desperate hands. My cane explored that vast residue of thought, in which neither shame nor hope was now alive.

Amid all that English and German prose I found a few pages of France: copies of *Le Magasin Pittoresque*, solidly bound and somewhat scorched by fire.

It was in looking through those magazines, so adorably illustrated and so dismally written, that I found the two manuscripts, one in German, the other in French. Their authors had apparently been unaware of each other, and yet the French manuscript seemed to cast a little light on the black anguish that rose from the German one like a noxious vapor – insofar as any light can be shed on that story which appears to be haunted by such sinister and hostile forces!

The cover bore the name Alphonse Archipetre, followed by the word *Lehrer*. I shall translate the German pages:

The German Manuscript

I am writing this for Hermann, when he comes back from sea.

If he does not find me here, if I, along with my poor friends, have been swallowed up by the savage mystery that surrounds us, I want him to know our days of horror through this little notebook. It will be the best proof of my affection that I can give him, because it takes real courage for a woman to keep a journal in such hours of madness. I am also writing so that he will pray for me, if he believes my soul to be in peril...

After the death of my Aunt Hedwige, I did not want to go on living in our sad Holzdamm house. The Rückhardt sisters offered to let me stay with them. They lived in a big apartment on the Deichstrasse, in the spacious house of Councillor Hühnebein, an old bachelor who never left the first floor, which was littered with books, paintings, and engravings.

Lotte, Eleonore, and Meta Rückhardt were adorable old maids who used all their ingenuity in trying to make life pleasant for me. Frida, our maid, came with me; she found favor in the eyes of the ancient Frau Pilz, the Rückhardts' inspired cook, who was said to have turned down ducal offers in order to remain in the humble service of her mistresses.

That evening…

On that evening, which was to bring unspeakable terror into our calm lives, we had decided against going to a celebration in Tempelhof, because it was raining in torrents. Frau Pilz, who liked to have us stay home, had made us an outstanding supper: grilled trout and a guinea-hen pie. Lotte had searched the cellar and come up with a bottle of Cape brandy that had been aging there for over twenty years. When the table had been cleared, the beautiful dark liquor was poured into glasses of Bohemian crystal. Eleonore served the Lapsang Souchong tea that an old Bremen sailor brought back to us from his voyages.

Through the sound of the rain we heard the clock of Saint Peter's strike eight. Frida was sitting beside the fire. Her head drooped over her illustrated Bible; she was unable to read it, but she liked to look at the pictures. She asked for permission to go to bed. The four of us who remained went on sorting colored silks for Meta's embroidery.

Downstairs, the councillor noisily locked his bedroom door. Frau Pilz went up to her room, bade us good night through the door, and added that the bad weather would no doubt prevent us from having fresh fish for dinner the next day. A small cascade was splattering loudly on the pavement from a broken rain gutter on the house next door. A strong wind came thundering down the street; the cascade was dispersed into a silvery mist, and a window slammed shut on one of the upper stories.

'That's the attic window,' said Lotte. 'It won't stay closed.' She raised the garnet-red curtain and looked down at the street. 'I've never seen it so dark before. I'm not sleepy, and I certainly have no desire to go to bed. I feel as though the darkness of the street would follow me, along with the wind and the rain.'

'You're talking like a fool,' said Eleonore, who was not very gentle. 'Well, since no one is going to bed, let's do as men do and fill our glasses again.'

She went off to get three of those beautiful Sieme candles that burn with a pink flame and give off a delightful smell of flowers and incense.

I felt that we all wanted to give a festive tone to that bleak evening, and that for some reason we were unsuccessful. I saw Eleonore's energetic face darkened by a sudden shadow of ill-humor. Lotte seemed to be having difficulty in breathing. Only Meta was leaning placidly over her embroidery, and yet I sensed that she was attentive, as though she were trying to detect a sound in the depths of the silence.

Just then the door opened and Frida came in. She staggered over to the armchair beside the fire and sank into it, staring wild-eyed at each of us in turn.

'Frida!' I cried. 'What's the matter?'

She sighed deeply, then murmured a few indistinct words.

'She's still asleep,' said Eleonore.

Frida shook her head forcefully and made violent efforts to speak. I handed her my glass of brandy and she emptied it in one gulp, like a coachman or a porter. Under other circumstances we would have been offended by this vulgarity, but she seemed so unhappy, and the atmosphere in the room had been so depressing for the past few minutes, that it passed unnoticed.

'Fräulein,' said Frida, 'there's…' Her eyes, which softened for a moment, resumed their wild expression. 'I don't know…'

Eleonore uttered an impatient exclamation.

'What have you seen or heard? What's wrong with you, Frida?'

'Fräulein, there's…' Frida seemed to reflect deeply. 'I don't know how to say it… There's a great fear in my room.'

'Oh!' said all three of us, reassured and apprehensive at the same time.

'You've had a nightmare,' said Meta. 'I know how it is: you hide your head under the covers when you wake up.'

'No, that's not it,' said Frida. 'I hadn't been dreaming. I just woke up, that's all, and then… How can I make you understand? There's a great fear in my room….'

'Good heavens, that doesn't explain anything!' I said.

Frida shook her head in despair:

'I'd rather sit outside in the rain all night than go back to that room. No, I won't go back!'

'I'm going to see what's happening up there, you fool!' said Eleonore, throwing a shawl over her shoulders.

She hesitated for a moment before her father's old rapier, hanging among some university insignia. Then she shrugged, picked up the candlestick with its pink candles, and walked out, leaving a perfumed wake behind her.

'Oh, don't let her go there alone!' cried Frida, alarmed.

We slowly went to the staircase. The flickering glow of Eleonore's candlestick was already vanishing on the attic landing.

We stood in the semidarkness at the foot of the stairs. We heard Eleonore open a door. There was a minute of oppressive silence. I felt Frida's hand tighten on my waist.

'Don't leave her alone,' she moaned.

Just then there was a loud laugh, so horrible that I would rather die than hear it again. Almost at the same time, Meta raised her hand and cried out, 'There!… There!… A face…. There….'

The house became filled with sounds. The councillor and Frau Pilz appeared in the yellow haloes of the candles they were holding.

'Fräulein Eleonore!' sobbed Frida. 'Dear God, how are we going to find her?'

It was a frightening question, and I can now answer it: *We never found her.*

Frida's room was empty. The candlestick was standing on the floor and its candles were still burning peacefully, with their delicate pink flames.

We searched the whole house and even went out on the roof. We never saw Eleonore again.

We could not count on the help of the police, as will soon be seen. When we went to the police station, we found that it had been invaded by a frenzied crowd; some of the furniture had been overturned, the windows were covered with dust, and the clerks were being pushed around like puppets. Eighty people had vanished that night, some from their homes, others while they were on their way home!

The world of ordinary conjectures was closed to us; only supernatural apprehensions remained.

Several days went by. We led a bleak life of tears and terror.

Councillor Hühnebein had the attic sealed off from the rest of the house by a thick oak partition.

One day I went in search of Meta. We were beginning to fear another tragedy when we found her squatting in front of the partition with her eyes dry and an expression of anger on her usually gentle face. She was holding her father's rapier in her hand, and seemed annoyed at having been disturbed.

We tried to question her about the face she had glimpsed, but she looked at us as though she did not understand. She remained completely silent. She did not answer us, and even seemed unaware of our presence.

All sorts of wild stories were being repeated in the town. There was talk of a secret criminal league; the police were accused of negligence, and worse; public officials had been dismissed. All this, of course, was useless.

Strange crimes had been committed: savagely mutilated corpses were found at dawn. Wild animals could not have shown more ardent lust for carnage than the mysterious attackers. Some of the victims had been robbed, but most of them had not, and this surprised everyone.

But I do not want to dwell on what was happening in the town; it will be easy to find enough people to tell about it. I will limit myself to the framework of our house and our life, which, though narrow, still enclosed enough fear and despair.

The days passed and April came, colder and windier than the worst month of winter. We remained huddled beside the fire. Sometimes Councillor Hühnebein came to keep us company and give us what he called courage. This consisted in trembling in all his limbs, holding his hands out toward the fire, drinking big mugs of punch, starting at every sound, and crying out five or six times an hour, 'Did you hear that? Did you hear?...'

Frida tore some of the pages out of her Bible, and we found them pinned or pasted on every door and curtain, in every nook and cranny. She hoped that this would ward off the spirits of evil. We did not interfere, and since we spent several days in peace we were far from thinking it a bad idea.

We soon saw how terribly mistaken we were. The day had been so dark, and the clouds so low, that evening had come early. I was walking out of the living room to put a lamp on the broad landing – for ever since the terrifying night we had placed lights all over the house, and even the halls and stairs remained lighted till dawn – when I heard voices murmuring on the top floor.

It was not yet completely dark. I bravely climbed the stairs and found myself before the frightened faces of Frida and Frau Pilz, who motioned me to be silent and pointed to the newly built partition.

I stood beside them, adopting their silence and attention. It was then that I heard an indefinable sound from behind the wooden wall, something like the faint roar of giant conch shells, or the tumult of a faraway crowd.

'Fräulein Eleonore,...' moaned Frida.

The answer came immediately and hurled us screaming down the stairs: a long shriek of terror rang out, not from the partition above us, but from downstairs, from the councillor's apartment. Then he called for help at the top of his lungs. Lotte and Meta had hurried out onto the landing.

'We must go there,' I said courageously.

We had not taken three steps when there was another cry of distress, this time from above us.

'Help! Help!'

We recognized Frau Pilz's voice. We heard her call again, feebly.

Meta picked up the lamp I had placed on the landing. Halfway up the stairs we found Frida alone. Frau Pilz had disappeared.

At this point I must express my admiration of Meta Rückhardt's calm courage.

'There's nothing more we can do here,' she said, breaking the silence she had stubbornly maintained for several days. 'Let's go downstairs....'

She was holding her father's rapier, and she did not look at all ridiculous, for we sensed that she would use it as effectively as a man.

We followed her, subjugated by her cold strength.

The councillor's study was as brightly lighted as a traveling carnival. The poor man had given the darkness no chance to get in. Two enormous lamps with white porcelain globes stood at either end of the mantelpiece, looking like two placid moons. A small Louis XV chandelier hung from the ceiling, its prisms flashing like handfuls of precious stones. Copper and stone candlesticks stood on the floor in every corner of the room. On the table, a row of tall candles seemed to be illuminating an invisible catafalque.

We stopped, dazzled, and looked around for the councillor.

'Oh!' Frida exclaimed suddenly. 'Look, there he is! He's hiding behind the window curtain.'

Lotte abruptly pulled back the heavy curtain. Herr Hühnebein was there, leaning out the open window, motionless.

Lotte went over to him, then leapt back with a cry of horror.

'Don't look! For the love of heaven, don't look! He... he... his head is gone!'

I saw Frida stagger, ready to faint. Meta's voice called us back to reason:

'Be careful! There's danger here!'

We pressed up close to her, feeling protected by her presence of mind. Suddenly something blinked on the ceiling, and we saw with alarm that darkness had invaded two opposite corners of the room, where the lights had just been extinguished.

'Hurry, protect the lights!' panted Meta. 'Oh!... There!... There he is!'

At that moment the white moons on the mantelpiece burst, spat out streaks of smoky flame, and vanished.

Meta stood motionless, but she looked all around the room with a cold rage that I had never seen in her before.

The candles on the table were blown out. Only the little chandelier continued to shed its calm light. I saw that Meta was keeping her eyes on it. Suddenly her rapier flashed and she lunged forward into empty space.

'Protect the light!' she cried. 'I see him! I've got him!... Ah!...'

We saw the rapier make strange, violent movements in her hand, as though an invisible force were trying to take it away from her.

It was Frida who had the odd but fortunate inspiration that saved us that evening. She uttered a fierce cry, picked up one of the heavy copper candlesticks, leapt to Meta's side, and began striking the air with her gleaming club. The rapier stopped moving; something very light seemed to brush against the floor, then the door opened by itself, and a heartrending clamor arose.

'That takes care of one of them,' said Meta.

One might wonder why we stubbornly went on living in that murderously haunted house.

At least a hundred other houses were in the same situation. People had stopped counting the murders and disappearances, and had become almost indifferent to them. The town was gloomy. There were dozens of suicides, for some people preferred to die by their own hands rather than be killed by the phantom executioners. And then, too, Meta wanted to take vengeance. She was now waiting for the invisible beings to return.

She had relapsed into her grim silence; she spoke to us only to order us to lock the doors and shutters at nightfall. As soon as darkness fell, the four of us went into the living room, which was now a dormitory and dining room as well. We did not leave it until morning.

I questioned Frida about her strange armed intervention. She was able to give me only a confused answer.

'I don't know,' she said. 'It seemed to me I saw something.... A face.... I don't know how to say what it was.... Yes, it was the great fear that was in my room the first night.'

That was all I could get out of her.

One evening toward the middle of April, Lotte and Frida were lingering in the kitchen. Meta opened the living-room door and told them to hurry. I saw that the shadows of night had already invaded the landings and the hall.

'We're coming,' they replied in unison.

Meta came back into the living room and closed the door. She was horribly pale. No sound came from downstairs. I waited vainly to hear the footsteps of the two women. The silence was like a threatening flood rising on the other side of the wall.

Meta locked the door.

'What are you doing?' I asked. 'What about Lotte and Frida?'

'It's no use,' she said dully.

Her eyes, motionless and terrible, stared at the rapier. The sinister darkness arrived.

It was thus that Lotte and Frida vanished into mystery.

Dear God, what was it? There was a presence in the house, a suffering, wounded presence that was seeking help. I did not know whether Meta was aware of it or not. She was more taciturn than ever, but she barricaded the doors and windows in a way that seemed designed more to prevent an escape than an intrusion. My life had become a fearful solitude. Meta herself was like a sneering specter.

During the day, I sometimes came upon her unexpectedly in one of the halls; in one hand she held the rapier, and in the other she held a powerful lantern with a reflector and a lens that she shone into all the dark corners.

During one of these encounters, she told me rather impolitely that I had better go back to the living room, and when I obeyed her too slowly she shouted furiously at me that I must never interfere with her plans.

Her face no longer had the placid look it had worn as she leaned over her embroidery only a few days before. It was now a savage face, and she sometimes glared at me with a flame of hatred in her eyes. For I had a secret....

Was it curiosity, perversity, or pity that made me act as I did? I pray to God that I was moved by nothing more than pity and kindness.

I had just drawn some fresh water from the fountain in the wash-house when I heard a muffled moan: 'Moh.... Moh....'

I thought of our vanished friends and looked around me. I saw a well-concealed door that led into a storeroom in which poor Hühnebein had kept stacks of books and paintings, amid dust and cobwebs.

'Moh.... Moh....'

It was coming from inside the storeroom. I opened the door and looked into the gray semidarkness. Everything seemed normal. The lamentation had stopped. I stepped inside. Suddenly I felt something seize my dress. I cried out. I immediately heard the moaning very close to me, plaintive, supplicating, and something tapped on my pitcher.

I put it down. There was a slight splashing sound, like that of a dog lapping, and the level of the water in my pitcher began to sink. The thing, the being, was drinking!

'Moh!... Moh!...'

Something caressed my hair more softly than a breath.

'Moh.... Moh....'

Then the moaning changed to a sound of human weeping, almost like the sobbing of a child, and I felt pity for the suffering invisible monster. But there were footsteps in the hall; I put my hands over my lips and the being fell silent.

Without a sound, I closed the door of the secret storeroom. Meta was coming toward me in the hall.

'Did I hear your voice just now?' she asked.

'Yes. My foot slipped and I was startled....'

I was an accomplice of the phantoms.

I brought milk, wine, and apples. Nothing manifested itself. When I returned, the milk had been drunk to the last drop, but the wine and the apples were intact. Then a kind of breeze surrounded me and passed over my hair for a long time....

I went back, bringing more fresh milk. The soft voice was no longer weeping, but the caress of the breeze was longer and seemed to be more ardent.

Meta began looking at me suspiciously and prowling around the storeroom.

I found a safer refuge for my mysterious protégé. I explained it to him by signs. How strange it was to make gestures to empty space! But he understood me. He was following me along the hall like a breath of air when I suddenly had to hide in a corner.

A pale light slid across the floor. I saw Meta coming down the spiral staircase at the end of the hall. She was walking quietly, partially hiding the glow of her lantern. The rapier glittered. I sensed that the being beside me was afraid. The breeze stirred around me, feverishly, abruptly, and I heard that plaintive 'Moh!... Moh!...'

Meta's footsteps faded away in the distance. I made a reassuring gesture and went to the new refuge: a large closet that was never opened.

The breeze touched my lips and remained there a moment. I felt a strange shame.

May came.

The twenty square feet of the miniature garden, which poor, dear Hühnebein had spattered with his blood, were dotted with little white flowers.

Under a magnificent blue sky, the town was almost silent. The cries of the swallows were answered only by the peevish sounds of closing doors, sliding bolts, and turning keys.

The being had become imprudent. He sought me out. All at once I would feel him around me. I cannot describe the feeling; it was like a great tenderness surrounding me. I would make him understand that I was afraid of Meta, and then I would feel him vanish like a dying wind.

I could not bear the look in Meta's fiery eyes.

On May 4, the end came abruptly.

We were in the living room, with all the lamps lighted. I was closing the shutters. Suddenly I sensed his presence. I made a desperate gesture, turned around, and met Meta's terrible gaze in a mirror.

'Traitress!' she cried.

She quickly closed the door. He was imprisoned with us.

'I knew it!' she said vehemently. 'I've seen you carrying pitchers of milk, daughter of the devil! You gave him strength when he was dying from the wound I gave him on the night of Hühnebein's death. Yes, your phantom is vulnerable! He's going to die now, and I think that dying is much more horrible for him than it is for us. Then your turn will come, you wretch! Do you hear me?'

She had shrieked this in short phrases. She uncovered her lantern. A beam of white light shot across the room, and I saw it strike something like thin, gray smoke. She plunged her rapier into it.

'Moh!... Moh!...' cried the heartrending voice, and then suddenly, awkwardly, but in a loving tone, my name was spoken. I leapt forward and knocked over the lantern with my fist. It went out.

'Meta, listen to me,' I begged, 'have pity....'

Her face was contorted into a mask of demoniac fury.

'Traitress!' she screamed.

The rapier flashed before my eyes. It struck me below the left breast and I fell to my knees.

Someone was weeping violently beside me, strangely beseeching Meta. She raised her rapier again. I tried to find the words of supreme contrition that reconcile us with God forever, but then I saw Meta's face freeze and the sword fell from her hand.

Something murmured near us. I saw a thin flame stretch out like a ribbon and greedily attack the curtains.

'We're burning!' cried Meta. 'All of us together!'

At that moment, when everything was about to sink into death, the door opened. An immensely tall old woman came in. I saw only her terrible green eyes glowing in her unimaginable face.

A flame licked my left hand. I stepped back as much as my strength allowed. I saw Meta still standing motionless with a strange grimace on her face, and I realized that her soul, too, had flown away. Then the monstrous old woman's eyes, without pupils, slowly looked around the flame-filled room and came to rest on me.

I am writing this in a strange little house. Where am I? Alone. And yet all this is full of tumult, an invisible but unrestrained presence is everywhere. He has come back. I have again heard my name spoken in that awkward, gentle way....

Here ends the German manuscript, as though cut off with a knife.

The French Manuscript

The town's oldest coachman was pointed out to me in the smoky inn where he was drinking heady, fragrant October beer.

I bought him a drink and gave him some tobacco. He swore I was a prince. I pointed to his droshky outside the inn and said, 'And now, take me to Saint Beregonne's Lane.'

He gave me a bewildered look, then laughed.

'Ah, you're very clever!'

'Why?'

'You're testing me. I know every street in this town – I can almost say I know every paving-stone! There's no Saint Bere.... What did you say?'

'Beregonne. Are you sure? Isn't it near the Mohlenstrasse?'

'No,' he said decisively. 'There's no such street here, no more than Mount Vesuvius is in Saint Petersburg.'

No one knew the town, in all its twisting byways, better than that splendid beer-drinker.

A student sitting at a nearby table looked up from the love letter he had been writing and said to me, 'There's no saint by that name, either.'

And the innkeeper's wife added, with a touch of anger, 'You can't manufacture saints like sausages!'

I calmed everyone with wine and beer. There was great joy in my heart.

The policeman who paced up and down the Mohlenstrasse from dawn till dark had a face like a bulldog, but he was obviously a man who knew his job.

'No,' he said slowly, coming back from a long journey among his thoughts and memories, 'there's no such street here or anywhere else in town.'

Over his shoulder I saw the beginning of Saint Beregonne's Lane, between the Klingbom distillery and the shop of an anonymous seed merchant.

I had to turn away with impolite abruptness in order not to show my elation. Saint Beregonne's Lane did not exist for the coachman, the student, the policeman, or anyone else: it existed only for me!

How did I make that amazing discovery? By an almost scientific observation, as some of my pompous fellow-teachers would have said. My colleague Seifert, who taught natural science by bursting balloons filled with strange gases in his pupils' faces, would not have been able to find any fault with my procedure.

When I walked along the Mohlenstrasse, it took me two or three seconds to cover the distance between the distillery and the seed merchant's shop. I noticed, however, that when other people passed by the same place they went immediately from the distillery to the shop, without visibly crossing the entrance of Saint Beregonne's Lane.

By adroitly questioning various people, and by consulting the town's cadastral map, I learned that only a wall separated the distillery from the shop.

I concluded that, for everyone in the world except myself, that street existed outside of time and space.

I knew that mysterious street for several years without ever venturing into it, and I think that even a more courageous man would have hesitated. What laws governed that unknown space? Once it had drawn me into its mystery, would it ever return me to my own world?

I finally invented various reasons to convince myself that that world was inhospitable to human beings, and my curiosity surrendered to my fear. And yet what I could see of that opening into the incomprehensible was so ordinary, so commonplace! I must admit, however, that the view was cut off after ten paces by a sharp bend in the street. All I could see was two high, badly whitewashed walls with the name of the street painted on one of them in black letters, and a stretch of worn, greenish pavement with a gap in which a viburnum bush was growing. That sickly bush seemed to live in accordance with our seasons, for I sometimes saw a little tender green and a few lumps of snow among its twigs.

I might have made some curious observations concerning the insertion of that slice of an alien cosmos into ours, but to do so I would have had to spend a considerable amount of time standing on the Mohlenstrasse; and Klingbom, who often saw me staring at some of his windows, became suspicious of his wife and gave me hostile looks.

I wondered why, of all the people in the world, I was the only one to whom that strange privilege had been given. This led me to think of my maternal grandmother. She was a tall, somber woman, and her big green eyes seemed to be following the happenings of another life on the wall in front of her.

Her background was obscure. My grandfather, a sailor, was supposed to have rescued her from some Algerian pirates. She sometimes stroked my hair with her long, white hands and murmured, 'Maybe he… Why not? After all…' She repeated it on the night of her death, and while the pale fire of her gaze wandered among the shadows she added, 'Maybe he'll go where I wasn't able to return….'

A black storm was blowing that night. Just after my grandmother died, while the candles were being lit, a big stormy petrel shattered the window and lay dying, bloody and threatening, on her bed.

That was the only odd thing I remembered in my life; but did it have any connection with Saint Beregonne's Lane?

It was a sprig of the viburnum bush that set off the adventure.

But am I sincere in looking there for the initial tap that set events in motion? Perhaps I should speak of Anita.

Several years ago, in the Hanseatic ports one could see the arrival of little lateen-rigged ships creeping out of the mist like crestfallen animals.

Colossal laughter would immediately shake the port, down to the deepest beer cellars.

'Aha! Here come the dream ships!'

I always felt heartbroken at the sight of those heroic dreams dying in formidable Germanic laughter.

It was said that the sad crews of those ships lived on the golden shores of the Adriatic and the Tyrrhenian Sea in a mad dream, for they believed in a fantastic land of plenty, related to the Thule of the ancients, lying somewhere in our cruel North. Not having much more knowledge than their forefathers of a thousand years ago, they had carefully nurtured a heritage of legends about islands of diamonds and emeralds, legends that had been born when their forefathers encountered the glittering vanguard of an ice floe.

The compass was one of the few items of progress that their minds had seized upon in the course of the centuries. Its enigmatic needle, always pointing in the same direction, was for them a final proof of the mysteries of the North.

One day when a dream was walking like a new Messiah on the choppy waters of the Mediterranean, when the nets had brought up only fish poisoned by the coral on the bottom, and when Lombardy had sent neither grain nor flour to the poverty-stricken lands of the South, they had hoisted their sails in the offshore wind.

Their flotilla had dotted the sea with its hard wings; then, one by one, their ships had melted into the storms of the Atlantic. The Bay of Biscay had nibbled the flotilla and passed the remainder on to the granite teeth of Brittany. Some of the hulls were sold to firewood merchants in Germany and Denmark; one of the ships died in its dream, killed by an iceberg blazing in the sun off the Lofoten Islands.

But the North adorned the grave of that flotilla with a sweet name: 'the dream ships.' Although it made coarse sailors laugh, I was deeply moved by it, and I might well have been willing to set sail with those dreamers.

Anita was their daughter.

She came from the Mediterranean when she was still a baby in her mother's arms, aboard a tartan. The ship was sold. Her mother died, and so did her little sisters. Her father set out for America on a sailing ship that never returned. Anita was left all alone, but the dream that had brought the tartan to those moldering wooden docks never left her: she still believed in the fortune of the North, and she wanted it fiercely, almost with hatred.

In Tempelhof, with its clusters of white lights, she sang, danced, and threw red flowers that either fell on her like a rain of blood or were burned in the short flames of the Argand lamps. She would then pass among the crowd, holding out a pink conch shell. Silver was dropped into it, or sometimes gold, and only then did her eyes smile as they rested for a second, like a caress, on the generous man.

I gave gold – I, a humble teacher of French grammar in the Gymnasium, gave gold for one look from Anita.

Brief notes:

I sold my Voltaire. I had sometimes read my pupils extracts from his correspondence with the King of Prussia; it pleased the principal.

I owed two months' room and board to Frau Holz, my landlady. She told me she was poor....

I asked the bursar of the school for another advance on my salary. He told me with embarrassment that it was difficult, that it was against regulations.... I did not listen any longer. My colleague Seifert curtly refused to lend me a few thalers.

I dropped a heavy gold coin into the conch shell. Anita's eyes burned my soul. Then I heard someone laughing in the laurel thickets of Tempelhof. I recognized two servants of the Gymnasium. They ran away into the darkness.

It was my last gold coin. I had no more money, none at all....

As I was walking past the distillery on the Mohlenstrasse, I was nearly run over by a carriage. I made a frightened leap into Saint Beregonne's Lane. My hand clutched the viburnum bush and broke off a sprig of it.

I took the sprig home with me and laid it on my table. It had opened up an immense new world to me, like a magician's wand.

Let us reason, as my stingy colleague Seifert would say.

First of all, my leap into Saint Beregonne's Lane and my subsequent return to the Mohlenstrasse had shown that the mysterious street was as easy to enter and leave as any ordinary thoroughfare.

But the viburnum sprig had enormous philosophical significance. It was 'in excess' in our world. If I had taken a branch from any forest in America and brought it here, I would not have changed the number of branches on earth. But in bringing that sprig of viburnum from Saint Beregonne's Lane I had made an intrinsic addition that could not have been made by all the tropical growths in the world, because I had taken it from a plane of existence that was real only for me.

I was therefore able to take an object from that plane and bring it into the world of men, where no one could contest my ownership of it. Ownership could never be more absolute, in fact, because the object would owe nothing to any industry, and it would augment the normally immutable patrimony of the earth....

My reasoning flowed on, wide as a river, carrying fleets of words, encircling islands of appeals to philosophy; it was swollen by a vast system of logical tributaries until it reached a conclusive demonstration that a theft committed in Saint Beregonne's Lane was not a theft in the Mohlenstrasse.

Fortified by this nonsense, I judged that the matter was settled. My only concern would be to avoid the reprisals of the mysterious inhabitants of the street, or of the world to which it led.

When the Spanish conquistadores spent the gold they had brought back from the new India, I think they cared very little about the anger of the faraway peoples they had despoiled.

I decided to enter the unknown the following day.

Klingbom made me waste some time. I think he had been waiting for me in the little square vestibule that opened into his shop on one side and his office on the other. As I walked past, clenching my teeth, ready to plunge into my adventure, he grabbed me by my coat.

'Ah, professor,' he said, 'how I misjudged you! It wasn't you! I must have been blind to suspect you! She's left me, professor, but not with you. Oh, no, you're a man of honor! She's gone off with a postmaster, a man who's half coachman and half scribe. What a disgrace for the House of Klingbom!'

He had dragged me into the shadowy back room of his shop. He poured me a glass of orange-flavored brandy.

'And to think that I mistrusted you, professor! I always saw you looking at my wife's windows, but I know now that it was the seed merchant's wife you had your eye on.'

I masked my embarrassment by raising my glass.

'To tell you the truth,' said Klingbom, pouring me out some more of the reddish liquid, 'I'd be glad to see you put one over on that malicious seed merchant: he's delighted by my misfortune.'

He added, with a smile, 'I'll do you a favor: the lady of your dreams is in her garden right now. Why don't you go and see her?'

He led me up a spiral staircase to a window. I saw the poisonous sheds of the Klingbom distillery smoking among a tangled array of little courtyards, miniature gardens, and muddy streams narrow enough to step across. It was through that landscape that the secret street ought to run, but I saw nothing except the smoky activity of the Klingbom buildings and the seed merchant's nearby garden, where a thin form was leaning over some arid flower beds.

One last swallow of brandy gave me a great deal of courage. After leaving Klingbom, I walked straight into Saint Beregonne's Lane.

Three little yellow doors in the white wall…

Beyond the bend in the street, the viburnum bushes continued to place spots of green and black among the paving stones; then the three little doors appeared, almost touching each other. They gave the aspect of a Flemish Beguine convent to what should have been singular and terrible.

My footsteps resounded clearly in the silence.

I knocked on the first of the doors. Only the futile life of an echo was stirred behind it.

Fifty paces away, the street made another bend.

I was discovering the unknown parsimoniously. So far I had found only two thinly whitewashed walls and those three doors. But is not any closed door a powerful mystery in itself?

I knocked on all three doors, more violently this time. The echoes departed loudly and shattered the silence lurking in the depths of prodigious corridors. Sometimes their dying murmurs seemed to imitate the sound of light footsteps, but that was the only reply from the enclosed world.

The doors had locks on them, the same as all the other doors I was used to seeing. Two nights before, I had spent an hour picking the lock on my bedroom door with a piece of bent wire, and it had been as easy as a game.

There was a little sweat on my temples, a little shame in my heart. I took the same piece of wire from my pocket and slipped it into the lock of the first little door. And very simply, just like my bedroom door, it opened.

Later, when I was back in my bedroom among my books, in front of the table on which lay a red ribbon that had fallen from Anita's dress, I sat clutching three silver thalers in my hand.

Three thalers!

I had destroyed my finest destiny with my own hand. That new world had opened for me alone.

What had it expected of me, that universe more mysterious than those that gravitate toward the bottom of Infinity? Mystery had made advances to me, had smiled at me like a pretty girl, and I had entered it as a thief. I had been petty, vile, absurd.

Three thalers!

My adventure should have been so prodigious, and it had become so paltry!

Three thalers reluctantly given to me by Gockel, the antique dealer, for that engraved metal dish. Three thalers.... But they would buy one of Anita's smiles.

I abruptly threw them into a drawer: someone was knocking on my door.

It was Gockel. It was difficult for me to believe that this was the same malevolent man who had contemptuously put down the metal dish on his counter cluttered with barbarous and shabby trinkets. He was smiling now, and he constantly mingled my name – which he mispronounced – with the title of 'Herr Doktor' or 'Herr Lehrer.'

'I think I did you a great injustice, Herr Doktor,' he said. 'That dish is certainly worth more.'

He took out a leather purse and I saw the bright yellow smile of gold.

'It may be,' he went on, 'that you have other objects from the same source... or rather, of the same kind.'

The distinction did not escape me. Beneath the urbanity of the antique dealer was the spirit of a receiver of stolen goods.

'The fact is,' I said, 'that a friend of mine, an erudite collector, is in a difficult situation and needs to pay off certain debts, so he wants to sell part of his collection. He prefers to remain unknown: he's a shy scholar. He's already unhappy enough over having to part with some of the treasures in his showcases. I want to spare him any further sadness, so I'm helping him to sell them.'

Gockel nodded enthusiastically. He seemed overwhelmed with admiration for me.

'That's my idea of true friendship!' he said. 'Ach, Herr Doktor, I'll reread Cicero's *De Amicitia* this evening with renewed pleasure. How I wish that I had a friend like your unfortunate scholar has found in you! But I'll contribute a little to your good deed by buying everything your friend is willing to part with, and by paying very good prices....'

I had a slight stirring of curiosity:

'I didn't look at the dish very closely,' I said loftily. 'It didn't concern me, and besides, I don't know anything about such things. What kind of work is it? Byzantine?'

Gockel scratched his chin in embarrassment.

'Uh... I couldn't say for sure. Byzantine, yes, maybe.... I'll have to study it more carefully.... But,' he went on, suddenly recovering his serenity, 'in any case it's sure to find a buyer.' Then, in a tone that cut short all further discussion: 'That's the most important thing to us... and to your friend, too, of course.'

Late that night I accompanied Anita in the moonlight to the street where her house stood half-hidden in a clump of tall lilacs.

But I must go back in my story to the tray I sold for thalers and gold, which gave me for one evening the friendship of the most beautiful girl in the world.

The door opened onto a long hall with a blue stone floor. A frosted window pane cast light into it and broke up the shadows. My first impression of being in a Flemish Beguine convent became stronger, especially when an open door at the end of the hall led me into a broad kitchen with a vaulted ceiling and rustic furniture, gleaming with wax and polish.

This innocuous scene was so reassuring that I called aloud:

'Hello! Is there anyone upstairs?'

A powerful resonance rumbled, but no presence cared to manifest itself.

I must admit that at no time did the silence and absence of life surprise me; it was as though I had expected it. In fact, from the time when I first perceived the existence of the enigmatic street, I had not thought for one moment of any possible inhabitants. And yet I had just entered it like a nocturnal thief.

I took no precautions when I ransacked the drawers containing silverware and table linen. My footsteps clattered freely in the adjoining rooms furnished like convent visiting-rooms, and on a magnificent oak staircase that.... Ah, there *was* something surprising in my visit! That staircase led nowhere! It ran into the drab wall as though it continued on the other side of it.

All this was bathed in the whitish glow of the frosted glass that formed the ceiling. I saw, or thought I saw, a vaguely hideous shape on the rough plaster wall, but when I looked at it attentively I realized that it was composed of thin cracks and was of the same order as those monsters that we distinguish in clouds and the lace of curtains. Furthermore, it did not trouble me, because when I looked a second time I no longer saw it in the network of cracks in the plaster.

I went back to the kitchen. Through a barred window, I saw a shadowy little courtyard that was like a pit surrounded by four big, mossy walls.

On a sideboard there was a heavy tray that looked as though it ought to have some value. I slipped it under my coat. I was deeply disappointed: I felt as though I had just stolen a few coins from a child's piggy bank, or from an old-maid aunt's shabby woolen stocking.

I went to Gockel, the antique dealer.

The three little houses were identical. In all of them, I found the same clean, tidy kitchen, the same sparse, gleaming furniture, the same dim, unreal light, the same serene quietness, the same senseless wall that ended the staircase. And in all three houses, I found identical candlesticks and the same heavy tray.

I took them away, and… and the next day I always found them in their places again. I took them to Gockel, who smiled broadly as he paid me for them.

It was enough to drive me mad; I felt my soul becoming monotonous, like that of a whirling dervish. Over and over again, I stole the same objects from the same house under the same circumstances. I wondered whether this might not be the first vengeance of that unknown without mystery. Might not damnation be the unvarying repetition of sin for all eternity?

One day I did not go. I had resolved to space out my wretched incursions. I had a reserve of gold; Anita was happy and was showing wonderful tenderness toward me.

That same evening, Gockel came to see me, asked me if I had anything to sell, and, to my surprise, offered to pay me even more than he had been paying. He scowled when I told him of my decision.

'You've found a regular buyer, haven't you?' I said to him as he was leaving.

He slowly turned around and looked me straight in the eyes.

'Yes, Herr Doktor. I won't tell you anything about him, just as you never speak to me of… your friend, the seller.' His voice became lower: 'Bring me objects every day; tell me how much gold you want for them, and I'll give it to you, without bargaining. We're both tied to the same wheel, Herr Doktor. Perhaps we'll have to pay later. In the meantime, let's live the kind of life we like: you with a pretty girl, I with a fortune.'

We never broached the subject again. But Anita suddenly became very demanding, and Gockel's gold slipped between her little fingers like water.

Then the atmosphere of the street changed, if I may express it that way. I heard melodies. At least it seemed to me that it was marvelous, faraway music. Summoning up my courage again, I decided to explore the street beyond the bend and go on toward the song that vibrated in the distance.

When I passed the third door and entered a part of the street where I had never gone before, I felt a terrible tightening in my heart. I took only three or four hesitant steps.

I turned around. I could still see the first part of the street, but it looked much smaller. It seemed to me that I had moved dangerously far away from my world. Nevertheless, in a surge of irrational temerity, I ran a short distance, then knelt, and, like a boy peering over a hedge, ventured to look down the unknown part of the street.

Disappointment struck me like a slap. The street continued its winding way, but again I saw nothing except three little doors in a white wall, and some viburnum bushes.

I would surely have gone back then if the wind of song had not passed by, like a distant tide of billowing sound.… I surmounted an inexplicable terror and listened to it, hoping to analyze it if possible.

I have called it a tide: it was a sound that came from a considerable distance, but it was enormous, like the sound of the sea.

As I listened to it, I no longer heard the harmonies I had thought I discerned in it at first; instead, I heard a harsh dissonance, a furious clamor of wails and hatred.

Have you ever noticed that the first whiffs of a repulsive smell are sometimes soft and even pleasant? I remember that when I left my house one day I was greeted in the street by an appetizing aroma of roast beef. 'Someone's doing some good cooking early in the morning,' I thought. But when I had walked a hundred paces, this aroma changed into the sharp, sickening smell of burning cloth: a draper's shop was on fire, filling the air with sparks and smoky flames. In the same way, I may have been deceived by my first perception of the melodious clamor.

'Why don't I go beyond the next bend?' I said to myself. My apprehensive inertia had almost disappeared. Walking calmly now, I covered the space before me in a few seconds – and once again I found exactly the same scene that I had left behind.

I was overwhelmed by a kind of bitter fury that engulfed my broken curiosity. Three identical houses, then three more identical houses. I had plumbed the mystery merely by opening the first door.

Gloomy courage took possession of me. I walked forward along the street, and my disappointment grew at an incredible rate.

A bend, three little yellow doors, a clump of viburnum bushes, then another bend, the same three little doors in the white wall, and the shadow of spindle trees. This repetition continued obsessively while I walked furiously, with loud footsteps.

Suddenly, when I had turned one more bend in the street, this terrible symmetry was broken. There were again three little doors and some viburnum bushes, but there was also a big wooden portal, darkened and worn smooth by time. I was afraid of it.

I now heard the clamor from much closer, hostile and threatening. I began walking back toward the Mohlenstrasse. The scenes went by like the quatrains of a ballad: three little doors and viburnum bushes, three little doors and viburnum bushes...

Finally I saw the first lights of the real world twinkling before me. But the clamor had pursued me to the edge of the Mohlenstrasse. There it stopped abruptly, adapting itself to the joyous evening sounds of the populous streets, so that the mysterious and terrible shouting ended in a chorus of children's voices singing a roundelay.

The whole town is in the grip of an unspeakable terror.

I would not have spoken of it in these brief memoirs, which concern only myself, if I had not found a link between the shadowy street and the crimes that steep the town in blood every night.

Over a hundred people have suddenly disappeared, a hundred others have been savagely murdered.

I recently took a map of the town and drew on it the winding line that must represent Saint Beregonne's Lane, that incomprehensible street that overlaps our terrestrial world. I was horrified to see that *all the crimes have been committed along that line.*

Thus poor Klingbom was one of the first to disappear. According to his clerk, he vanished like a puff of smoke just as he was entering the room containing his stills. The seed merchant's wife was next, snatched away while she was in her sad garden. Her husband was found in his drying-room with his skull smashed.

As I traced the fateful line on the map, my idea became a certainty. I can explain the victims' disappearance only by their passage into an unknown plane; as for the murders, they are easy for invisible beings.

All the inhabitants of a house on Old Purse Street have disappeared. On Church Street, six corpses have been found. On Post Street, there have been five disappearances and four deaths. This goes on and on, apparently limited by the Deichstrasse, where more murders and disappearances are taking place.

I now realize that to talk about what I know would be to place myself in the Kirchhaus insane asylum, a tomb from which no Lazarus ever arises; or else it would give free rein to a superstitious crowd that is exasperated enough to tear me to pieces as a sorcerer.

And yet, ever since the beginning of my monotonous daily thefts, anger has been welling up inside me, driving me to vague plans of vengeance.

'Gockel knows more about this than I do,' I thought. 'I'm going to tell him what I know: that will make him more inclined to confide in me.'

But that evening, while Gockel was emptying his heavy purse into my hands, I said nothing, and he left as usual with polite words that made no allusion to the strange bargain that had attached us to the same chain.

I had a feeling that events were about to leap forward and rush like a torrent through my tranquil life. I was becoming more and more aware that Saint Beregonne's Lane and its little houses were only a mask concealing some sort of horrible face.

So far, fortunately for me, I had gone there only in broad daylight, because for some reason I dreaded to encounter the shadows of evening there. But one day I lingered later than usual, stubbornly pushing furniture around, turning drawers inside out, determined to discover something new. And the 'new' came of itself, in the form of a dull rumble, like that of heavy doors moving on rollers. I looked up and saw that the opalescent light had changed into an ashy semi-darkness. The panes of glass above the staircase were livid: the little courtyards were already filled with shadow.

My heart tightened, but when the rumbling continued, reinforced by the powerful resonance of the house, my curiosity became stronger than my fear, and I began climbing the stairs to see where the noise was coming from.

It was growing darker and darker, but before leaping back down the stairs like a madman and running out of the house, I was able to see.... There was no more wall! The staircase ended at the edge of an abyss dug out of the night, from which vague monstrosities were rising.

I reached the door; behind me, something was furiously knocked over.

The Mohlenstrasse gleamed before me like a haven. I ran faster. Something suddenly seized me with extreme savagery.

'What's the matter with you? Can't you see where you're going?'

I found myself sitting on the pavement of the Mohlenstrasse, before a sailor who was rubbing his sore skull and looking at me in bewilderment. My coat was torn, my neck was bleeding.

I immediately hurried away without wasting any time on apologies, to the supreme indignation of the sailor, who shouted after me that after colliding with him so brutally I should at least buy him a drink.

Anita is gone, vanished!

My heart is broken; I collapse, sobbing, on my useless gold.

And yet her house is far from the zone of danger. Good God! I failed through an excess of prudence and love! One day, without mentioning the street, I showed her the line I had drawn on the map and told her that all the danger seemed to be concentrated along that sinuous trail. Her eyes glowed strangely at that moment. I should have known that the great spirit of adventure that animated her ancestors was not dead in her.

Perhaps, in a flash of feminine intuition, she made a connection between that line and my sudden fortune.... Oh, how my life is disintegrating!

There have been more murders and disappearances. And my Anita has been carried off in the bloody, inexplicable whirlwind!

The case of Hans Mendell has given me a mad idea: those vaporous beings, as he described them, may not be invulnerable.

Although Hans Mendell was not a distinguished man, I see no reason not to believe his story. He was a scoundrel who made his living as a mountebank and a cutthroat. When he was found, he had in his pocket the purses and watches of two unfortunate men whose corpses lay bleeding on the ground a few paces away from him.

It would have been assumed that he was guilty of murder if he himself had not been found moaning with both arms torn from his body.

Being a man with a powerful constitution, he was able to live long enough to answer the feverish questions of the magistrates and priests.

He confessed that for several days he had followed a shadow, a kind of black mist, and robbed the bodies of the people it killed. On the night of his misfortune, he saw the black mist waiting in the middle of Post Street in the moonlight. He hid in an empty sentry-box and watched it. He saw other dark, vaporous, awkward forms that bounced like rubber balls, then disappeared.

Soon he heard voices and saw two young men coming up the street. The black mist was no longer in sight, but he suddenly saw the two men writhe on their backs, then lie still.

Mendell added that he had already observed the same sequence in those nocturnal murders on seven other occasions. He had always waited for the shadow to leave, then robbed the bodies. This shows that he had remarkable self-control, worthy of being put to a better use.

As he was robbing the two bodies, he saw with alarm that the shadow had not left, but had only risen off the ground, interposing itself between him and the moon. He then saw that it had a roughly human shape. He tried to go back to the sentry-box but did not have time: the figure pounced on him.

Mendell was an extraordinarily strong man. He struck an enormous blow and encountered a slight resistance, as though he were pushing his hand through a strong current of air.

That was all he was able to say. His horrible wound allowed him to live only another hour after telling his story.

The idea of avenging Anita has now taken root in my brain. I said to Gockel, 'Don't come any more. I need revenge and hatred, and your gold can no longer do anything for me.'

He looked at me with that profound expression that was familiar to me by now.

'Gockel,' I said, 'I'm going to take vengeance.'

His face suddenly brightened, as though with great joy:

'And… do you believe… Herr Doktor, that they will disappear?'

I harshly ordered him to have a cart filled with fagots and casks of oil, raw alcohol and gunpowder, and to leave it without a driver early in the morning on the Mohlenstrasse. He bowed low like a servant, and as he was leaving he said to me, 'May the Lord help you! May the Lord come to your aid!'

I feel that these are the last lines I shall write in this journal.

I piled up the fagots, streaming with oil and alcohol, against the big door. I laid down trails of gunpowder connecting the nearby small doors with other oil-soaked fagots. I placed charges of powder in all the cracks in the walls.

The mysterious clamor continued all around me. This time I discerned in it abominable lamentations, human wails, echoes of horrible torments of the flesh. But my heart was agitated by tumultuous joy, because I felt around me a wild apprehension that came from *them*. They saw my terrible preparations and were unable to prevent them, for, as I had come to realize, only night released their frightful power.

I calmly struck a light with my tinderbox. A moan passed, and the viburnum bushes quivered as though blown by a sudden stiff breeze. A long blue flame rose into the air, the fagots began crackling, fire crept along the trails of gunpowder….

I ran down the winding street, from bend to bend, feeling a little dizzy, as though I were going too fast down a spiral staircase that descended deep into the earth.

The Deichstrasse and the whole surrounding neighborhood were in flames. From my window, I could see the sky turning yellow above the rooftops. The weather was dry and the town's water supply was nearly exhausted. A red band of sparks and flames hovered high above the street.

The fire had been burning for a day and a night, but it was still far from the Mohlenstrasse. Saint Beregonne's Lane was there, calm with its quivering viburnum bushes. Explosions rumbled in the distance.

Another cart was there, loaded and left by Gockel. Not a soul was in sight: everyone had been drawn toward the formidable spectacle of the fire. *It was not expected here.*

I walked from bend to bend to bend, sowing fagots, pools of oil and alcohol, and the dark frost of gunpowder. Suddenly, just as I had turned another bend, I stopped and stared. Three little houses, the everlasting three little houses, were burning calmly with pretty yellow flames in the peaceful air. It was as though even the fire respected their serenity, for it was doing its work without noise or ferocity. I realized that I was at the red edge of the conflagration that was destroying the town.

With anguish in my soul, I moved back from that mystery that was about to die.

I was near the Mohlenstrasse. I stopped in front of the first of the little doors, the one I had opened, trembling, a few weeks earlier. It was there that I would start the new fire.

For the last time, I saw the kitchen, the austere parlor, and the staircase, which now ended at the wall, as before; and I felt that all this had become familiar, almost dear to me.

On the big tray, the one I had stolen so many times before only to find it waiting for me again the next day, I saw some sheets of paper covered with elegant feminine handwriting.

I picked them up. This was going to be my last theft on the shadowy street.

Vampires! Vampires! Vampires!

So ends the French manuscript. The last words, evoking the impure spirits of the night, are written across the page in sharp letters that cry out terror and despair. Thus must write those who, on a sinking ship, want to convey a last farewell to the families they hope will survive them.

It was last year in Hamburg. I was strolling through the old city, with its good smell of fresh beer. It was dear to my heart, because it reminded me of the cities I had loved in my youth. And there, on an empty, echoing street, I saw a name on the front of an antique shop: Lockmann Gockel.

I bought an old Bavarian pipe with truculent decorations. The shopkeeper seemed friendly. I asked him if the name of Archipetre meant anything to him. His face had been the color of gray earth; in the twilight it now turned so white that it stood out from the shadows as though illuminated by an inner flame.

'Archipetre,' he murmured slowly. 'Oh! What are you saying? What do you know?'

I had no reason to conceal the story I had found on the dock. I told it to him.

He lit an archaic gaslight. Its flame danced and hissed foolishly.

I saw that his eyes were weary.

'He was my grandfather,' he said, when I mentioned Gockel the antique dealer.

When I had finished my story I heard a great sigh from a dark corner.

'That's my sister,' he said.

I nodded to her. She was young and pretty, but very pale. She had been listening to me, motionless among grotesque shadows.

'Our grandfather talked to our father about it nearly every evening,' he said in a faltering voice, 'and our father used to discuss it with us. Now that he's dead too, we talk about it with each other.'

'And now,' I said nervously, 'thanks to you, we're going to be able to do some research on the subject of that mysterious street, aren't we?'

He slowly raised his hand.

'Alphonse Archipetre taught French in the Gymnasium until 1842.'

'Oh!' I said, disappointed. 'That's a long time ago!'

'It was the year of the great fire that nearly destroyed Hamburg. The Mohlenstrasse and the vast section of the city between it and the Deichstrasse were a sea of flames.'

'And Archipetre?'

'He lived rather far from there, toward Bleichen. The fire didn't reach his street, but in the middle of the second night, on May 6 – a terrible night, dry and without water – his house burned down, all alone among the others that were miraculously spared. He died in the flames; or at least he was never found.'

'The story...' I began.

Lockmann Gockel did not let me finish. He was so happy to have found an outlet that he seized upon the subject greedily. Fortunately he told me more or less what I wanted to hear.

'The story compressed time, just as space was compressed at the fateful location of Saint Beregonne's Lane. In the Hamburg archives, there are accounts of atrocities committed *during the fire* by a band of mysterious evil-doers. Fantastic crimes, looting, riots, red hallucinations on the part of whole crowds – all those things are precisely described, and yet they took place *before the fire*. Do you understand my reference to the contraction of space and time?'

His face became a little calmer.

'Isn't modern science driven back to Euclidean weakness by the theory of that admirable Einstein for whom the whole world envies us? And isn't it forced to accept, with horror and despair, that fantastic Fitzgerald-Lorentz law of contraction? Contraction! Ah, there's a word that's heavy with meaning!'

The conversation seemed to be going off on an insidious tangent.

The young woman silently brought tall glasses filled with yellow wine. Gockel raised his toward the flame and marvelous colors flowed onto his frail hand like a silver river of gems.

He abandoned his scientific dissertation and returned to the story of the conflagration:

'My grandfather, and other people of the time, reported that enormous green flames shot up from the debris. There were hallucinated people who claimed to see figures of indescribably ferocious women in them.'

The wine had a soul. I emptied the glass and smiled at Gockel's terrified words.

'Those same green flames,' he went on, 'rose from Archipetre's house and roared so horribly that people were said to have died of fear in the street.'

'Mr. Gockel,' I said, 'did your grandfather ever speak of the mysterious purchaser who came every evening to buy the same trays and the same candlesticks?'

A weary voice replied for him, in words that were almost identical with those that ended the German manuscript:

'A tall old woman, an immense old woman with fishy eyes in an incredible face. She brought bags of gold so heavy that our grandfather had to divide them into four parts to carry them to his coffers.'

The young woman continued:

'When Professor Archipetre came to my grandfather, the Gockel firm was about to go bankrupt. It became rich, and we're still enormously rich, from the gold of the… yes, from the gold of those beings of the night!'

'They're gone now,' murmured her brother, refilling our glasses.

'Don't say that! They can't have forgotten us. Remember our nights, our horrible nights! All I can hope for now is that there is, or was, a human presence with them that they cherish and that may intercede for us.'

Her lovely eyes opened wide before the black abyss of her thoughts.

'Kathie!' exclaimed Gockel. 'Have you again seen?…'

'You know the things are here every night,' she said in a voice as low as a moan. 'They assail our thoughts as soon as sleep comes over us. Ah, to sleep no more!…'

'To sleep no more,' repeated her brother in an echo of terror.'

'They come out of their gold, which we keep, and which we love in spite of everything; they rise from everything we've acquired with that infernal fortune.… They'll always come back, as long as we exist, and as long as this wretched earth endures!'

GENIUS LOCI

Clark Ashton Smith

Clark Ashton Smith (1893–1961) was an important, largely self-taught American writer whose stories frequently appeared in *Weird Tales* and who maintained a long-term correspondence with both H. P. Lovecraft and swords-and-sorcery writer Robert E. Howard. Published in several influential Arkham House editions, Smith's fiction often reflected his interest in poetry and art. He generally wrote in a rich, almost florid style that could seem archaic but also achieve amazing flights of imagination. *Out of Space and Time* and *Lost Worlds* are among his best-known collections. In 'Genius Loci' (1933) Smith employs a somewhat more restrained style to tell a classic weird tale.

'It is a very strange place,' said Amberville, 'but I scarcely know how to convey the impression it made upon me. It will all sound so simple and ordinary. There is nothing but a sedgy meadow, surrounded on three sides by slopes of yellow pine. A dreary little stream flows in from the open end, to lose itself in a *cul-de-sac* of cat-tails and boggy ground. The stream, running slowly and more slowly, forms a stagnant pool of some extent, from which several sickly-looking alders seem to fling themselves backward, as if unwilling to approach it. A dead willow leans above the pool, tangling its wan, skeleton-like reflection with the green scum that mottles the water. There are no blackbirds, no kildees, no dragon-flies even, such as one usually finds in a place of that sort. It is all silent and desolate. The spot is evil – it is unholy in a way that I simply can't describe. I was compelled to make a drawing of it, almost against my will, since anything so outré is hardly in my line. In fact, I made two drawings. I'll show them to you, if you like.'

Since I had a high opinion of Amberville's artistic abilities, and had long considered him one of the foremost landscape painters of his generation, I was naturally eager to see the drawings. He, however, did not even pause to await my avowal of interest, but began at once to open his portfolio. His facial expression, the very movements of his hands, were somehow eloquent of a strange mixture of compulsion and repugnance as he brought out and displayed the two watercolor sketches he had mentioned.

I could not recognize the scene depicted from either of them. Plainly it was one that I had missed in my desultory rambling about the foot-hill environs of the tiny hamlet of Bowman, where, two years before, I had purchased an uncultivated ranch and had retired for the privacy so essential to prolonged literary effort. Francis Amberville, in the one fortnight of his visit, through his flair for the pictorial potentialities of landscape, had doubtless grown more familiar with the neighborhood than I. It had been his habit to roam about in the forenoon, armed with sketching-materials; and in this way he had already found the theme of more than one lovely painting. The arrangement was mutually convenient, since I, in his absence, was wont to apply myself assiduously to an antique Remington typewriter.

I examined the drawings attentively. Both, though of hurried execution, were highly meritorious, and showed the characteristic grace and vigor of Amberville's style. And yet, even at first glance, I found a quality that was more alien to the spirit of his work. The elements of the scene were those he had described. In one picture, the pool was half hidden by a fringe of mace-reeds, and the dead willow was leaning across it at a prone, despondent angle, as if mysteriously arrested in its fall toward the stagnant waters. Beyond, the alders seemed to strain away from the pool, exposing their knotted roots as if in eternal effort. In the other drawing, the pool formed the main portion of the foreground, with the skeleton tree looming drearily at one side. At the water's farther end, the cat-tails seemed to wave and whisper among themselves in a dying wind; and the steeply barring slope of pine at the meadow's terminus was indicated as a wall of gloomy green that closed in the picture, leaving only a pale margin of autumnal sky at the top.

All this, as the painter had said, was ordinary enough. But I was impressed immediately by a profound horror that lurked in these simple elements and was expressed by them as if by the balefully contorted features of some demoniac face. In both drawings, this sinister character was equally evident, as if the same face had been shown in profile and front view. I could not trace the separate details that composed the impressions; but ever, as I looked, the abomination of a strange evil, a spirit of despair, malignity, desolation, leered from the drawing more openly and hatefully. The spot seemed to wear a macabre and Satanic grimace. One felt that it might speak aloud, might utter the imprecations of some gigantic devil, or the raucous derision of a thousand birds of ill omen. The evil conveyed was something wholly outside of humanity – more ancient than man. Somehow – fantastic as this will seem – the meadow had the air of a vampire, grown old and hideous with unutterable infamies. Subtly, indefinably, it thirsted for other things than the sluggish trickle of water by which it was fed.

'Where is the place?' I asked, after a minute or two of silent inspection. It was incredible that anything of the sort could really exist – and equally incredible that a nature so robust as Amberville should have been sensitive to its quality.

'It's in the bottom of that abandoned ranch, a mile or less down the little road toward Bear River,' he replied. 'You must know it. There's a small orchard about the house, on the upper hillside; but the lower portion, ending in that meadow, is all wild land.'

I began to visualize the vicinity in question. 'Guess it must be the old Chapman place,' I decided. 'No other ranch along that road would answer your specifications.'

'Well, whoever it belongs to, that meadow is the most horrible spot I have ever encountered. I've known other landscapes that had something wrong with them, but never anything like this.'

'Maybe it's haunted,' I said, half in jest. 'From your description, it must be the very meadow where old Chapman was found dead one morning by his youngest daughter. It happened a few months after I moved here. He was supposed to have died of heart failure. His body was quite cold, and he had probably been lying there all night, since the family had missed him at suppertime. I don't remember him very clearly, but I remember that he had a reputation for eccentricity. For some time before his death, people thought he was going mad. I forget the details. Anyway, his wife and children left, not long after he died, and no one has occupied the house or cultivated the orchard since. It was a commonplace rural tragedy.'

'I'm not much of a believer in spooks,' observed Amberville, who seemed to have taken my suggestion of haunting in a literal sense. 'Whatever the influence is, it's hardly of human origin. Come to think of it, though, I received a very silly impression once or twice – the idea that someone was watching me while I did those drawings. Queer – I had almost forgotten that, till you brought up the possibility of haunting. I seemed to see him out of the tail of my eye, just beyond the radius that I was putting into the picture: a dilapidated old scoundrel with dirty gray whiskers and an evil scowl. It's odd, too, that I should have gotten such a definite conception of him, without ever seeing him squarely. I thought it was a tramp who had strayed into the meadow bottom. But when I turned to give him a level glance, he simply wasn't there. It was as if he melted into the miry ground, the cat-tails, the sedges.'

'That isn't a bad description of Chapman,' I said. 'I remember his whiskers – they were almost white, except for the tobacco juice. A battered antique, if there ever was one – and very unamiable, too. He had a poisonous glare toward the end, which no doubt helped along the legend of his insanity. Some of the tales about him come back to me now. People said that he neglected the care of his orchard more and more. Visitors used to find him in that lower meadow, standing idly about and staring vacantly at the trees and water. Probably that was one reason they thought he was losing his mind. But I'm sure I never heard that there was anything unusual or queer about the meadow, either at the time of Chapman's death, or since. It's a lonely spot, and I don't imagine that any one ever goes there now.'

'I stumbled on it quite by accident,' said Amberville. 'The place isn't visible from the road, on account of the thick pines... But there's another odd thing: I went out this morning with a very strong and clear intuition that I might find something of uncommon interest. I made a bee-line for that meadow, so to speak; and I'll have to admit that the intuition justified itself. The place repels me – but it fascinates me, too. I've simply got to solve the mystery, if it has a solution,' he added, with a slightly defensive air. 'I'm going back early tomorrow, with my oils, to start a real painting of it.'

I was surprised, knowing that predilection of Amberville for scenic brilliance and gayety which had caused him to be likened to Sorolla. 'The painting will be a novelty for you,' I commented. 'I'll have to come and take a look at the place myself, before long. It should really be more in my line than yours. There ought to be a weird story in it somewhere, if it lives up to your drawings and description.'

Several days passed. I was deeply preoccupied, at the time, with the toilsome and intricate problems offered by the concluding chapters of a new novel; and I put off my proposed visit to the meadow discovered by Amberville. My friend, on his part, was evidently engrossed by his new theme. He sallied forth each morning with his easel and oil-colors, and returned later each day, forgetful of the luncheon-hour that had formerly brought him back from such expeditions. On the third day, he did not reappear till sunset. Contrary to his custom, he did not show me what he had done, and his answers to my queries regarding the progress of the picture were somewhat vague and evasive. For some reason, he was unwilling to talk about it. Also, he was apparently loth to discuss the meadow itself, and in answer to direct questions, merely reiterated in an absent and perfunctory manner the account he had given me following his discovery of the place. In some mysterious way that I could not define, his attitude seemed to have changed.

There were other changes, too. He seemed to have lost his usual blitheness. Often I caught him frowning intently, and surprised the lurking of some equivocal shadow in his frank eyes. There was a moodiness, a morbidity, which, as far as our five years' friendship enabled me to observe, was a new aspect of his temperament. Perhaps, if I had not been so preoccupied with my own difficulties, I might have wondered more as to the causation of his gloom, which I attributed readily enough at first to some technical dilemma that was baffling him. He was less and less the Amberville that I knew; and on the fourth day, when he came back at twilight, I perceived an actual surliness that was quite foreign to his nature.

'What's wrong?' I ventured to inquire. 'Have you struck a snag? Or is old Chapman's meadow getting on your nerves with its ghostly influences?'

He seemed, for once, to make an effort to throw off his gloom, his taciturnity and ill humor.

'It's the infernal mystery of the thing,' he declared. 'I've simply got to solve it, in one way or another. The place has an entity of its own – an indwelling personality. It's there, like the soul in a human body, but I can't pin it down or touch it. You know that I'm not superstitious – but, on the other hand, I'm not a bigoted materialist, either; and I've run across some odd phenomena in my time. That meadow, perhaps, is inhabited by what the ancients called a *Genius Loci*. More than once, before this, I have suspected that such things might exist – might reside, inherent, in some particular spot. But this is the first time that I've had reason to suspect anything of an actively malignant or inimical nature. The other influences, whose presence I have felt, were benign in some large, vague, impersonal way – or were else wholly indifferent to human welfare – perhaps oblivious of human existence. This thing, however, is hatefully aware and watchful: I feel that the meadow itself – or the force embodied in the meadow – is scrutinizing me all the time. The place has the air of a thirsty vampire, waiting to drink me in somehow, if it can. It is a *cul-de-sac* of everything evil, in which an unwary soul might well be caught and absorbed. But I tell you, Murray, I can't keep away from it.'

'It looks as if the place *were* getting you,' I said, thoroughly astonished by his extraordinary declaration, and by the air of fearful and morbid conviction with which he uttered it.

Apparently he had not heard me, for he made no reply to my observation. 'There's another angle,' he went on, with a feverish tensity in his voice. 'You remember my impression of an old man lurking in the background and watching me, on my first visit. Well, I have seen him again, many times, out of the corner of my eye; and during the last two days, he has appeared more directly, though in a queer, partial way. Sometimes, when I am studying the dead willow very intently, I see his scowling filthy-bearded face as a part of the bole. Then, again, it will float among the leafless twigs, as if it had been caught there. Sometimes a knotty hand, a tattered coat-sleeve, will emerge through the mantling algae in the pool, as if a drowned body were rising to the surface. Then, a moment later – or simultaneously – there will be something of him among the alders or the cat-tails. These apparitions are always brief, and when I try to scutinize them closely, they melt like films of vapor into the surrounding scene. But the old scoundrel, whoever or whatever he may be, is a sort of fixture. He is no less vile than everything else about the place, though I feel that he isn't the main element of the vileness.'

'Good Lord!' I exclaimed. 'You certainly have been seeing things. If you don't mind, I'll come down and join you for a while, tomorrow afternoon. The mystery begins to inveigle me.'

'Of course I don't mind. Come ahead.' His manner, all at once, for no tangible reason, had resumed the unnatural taciturnity of the past four days. He gave me a furtive look that was sullen and almost unfriendly. It was as if an obscure barrier, temporarily laid aside, had again risen between us. The shadows of his strange mood returned upon him visibly, and my efforts to continue the conversation were rewarded only by half-surly, half-absent monosyllables. Feeling an aroused concern, rather than any offense, I began to note, for the first time, the unwonted pallor of his face, and the bright, febrile luster of his eyes. He looked vaguely unwell, I thought, as if something of his exuberant vitality had gone out of him, and had left in its place an alien energy of doubtful and less healthy nature. Tacitly, I gave up any attempt to bring him back from the secretive twilight into which he had withdrawn. For the rest of the evening, I pretended to read a novel, while Amberville maintained his singular abstraction. Somewhat inconclusively, I puzzled over the matter till bedtime. I made up my mind, however, that I would visit Chapman's meadow. I did not believe in the supernatural, but it seemed apparent that the place was exerting a deleterious influence upon Amberville.

The next morning, when I arose, my Chinese servant informed me that the painter had already breakfasted and had gone out with his easel and colors. This further proof of his obsession troubled me; but I applied myself rigorously to a forenoon of writing.

Immediately after luncheon, I drove down the highway, followed the narrow dirt road that branched off toward Bear River, and left my car on the pine-thick hill above the old Chapman place. Though I had never visited the meadow, I had a pretty clear idea of its location. Disregarding the grassy, half-obliterated road into the upper portion of the property, I struck down through the woods into the little blind valley, seeing more than once, on the opposite slope, the dying orchard of pear and apple trees, and the tumbledown shanty that had belonged to the Chapmans.

It was a warm October day; and the serene solitude of the forest, the autumnal softness of light and air, made the idea of anything malign or sinister seem impossible. When I came to the meadow bottom, I was ready to laugh at Amberville's notions; and the place itself, at first sight, merely impressed me as being rather dreary and dismal. The features of the scene were those that he had described so clearly, but I could not find the open evil that had leered from the pool, the willow, the alders and the cat-tails in his drawings.

Amberville, with his back toward me, was seated on a folding stool before his easel, which he had placed among the plots of dark green wire-grass in the open ground above the pool. He did not seem to be working, however, but was staring intently at the scene beyond him, while a loaded brush drooped idly in his fingers. The sedges deadened my footfalls; and he did not hear me as I drew near.

With much curiosity, I peered over his shoulder at the large canvas on which he had been engaged. As far as I could tell, the picture had already been carried to a consummate degree of technical perfection. It was an almost photographic rendering of the scummy water, the whitish skeleton of the leaning willow, the unhealthy, half-disrooted alders, and the cluster of nodding mace-reeds. But in it I found the macabre and demoniac spirit of the sketches: the meadow seemed to wait and watch like an evilly distorted face. It was a deadfall of malignity and despair, lying apart from the autumn world around it; a plague-spot of nature, for ever accursed and alone.

Again I looked at the landscape itself – and saw that the spot was indeed as Amberville had depicted it. It wore the grimace of a mad vampire, hateful and alert! At the same time, I became disagreeably conscious of the unnatural silence. There were no birds, no insects, as the painter had said; and it seemed that only spent and dying winds could ever enter that depressed valley-bottom. The thin stream that lost itself in the boggy ground was like a soul that went down to perdition. It was part of the mystery, too; for I could not remember any stream on the lower side of the barring hill that would indicate a subterranean outlet.

Amberville's intentness, and the very posture of his head and shoulders, were like those of a man who has been mesmerized. I was about to make my presence known to him; but at that instant there came to me the apperception that we were not alone in the meadow. Just beyond the focus of my vision, a figure seemed to stand in a furtive attitude, as if watching us both. I whirled about – and there was no one. Then I heard a startled cry from Amberville, and turned to find him staring at me. His features wore a wild look of terror and surprise, which had not wholly erased a hypnotic absorption.

'My God!' he said. 'I thought you were the old man!'

I can not be sure whether anything more was said by either of us. I have, however, the impression of a blank silence. After his single exclamation of surprise, Amberville seemed to retreat into an impenetrable abstraction, as if he were no longer conscious of my presence; as if, having identified me, he had forgotten me at once. On my part, I felt a weird and overpowering constraint. That infamous, eery scene depressed me beyond measure. It seemed that the boggy bottom was trying to drag me down in some intangible way. The boughs of the sick alders beckoned. The pool, over which the bony willow presided like an arboreal death, was wooing me foully with its stagnant waters.

Moreover, apart from the ominous atmosphere of the scene itself, I was painfully aware of a further change in Amberville – a change that was an actual alienation. His recent mood, whatever it was, had strengthened upon him enormously: he had gone deeper into its morbid twilight, and was lost to the blithe and sanguine personality I had known. It was as if an incipient madness had seized him; and the possibility of this terrified me.

In a slow, somnambulistic manner, without giving me a second glance, he began to work at his painting, and I watched him for a while, hardly knowing what to do or say. For long intervals he would stop and peer with dreamy intentness at some feature of the landscape. I conceived the bizarre idea of a growing kinship, a mysterious *rapport* between Amberville and the meadow. In some intangible way, it seemed as if the place had taken something from his very soul – and had given something of itself in exchange. He wore the air of one who participates in some unholy secret, who has become the acolyte of an unhuman knowledge. In a flash of horrible definitude, I saw the place as an actual vampire, and Amberville as its willing victim.

How long I remained there, I can not say. Finally I stepped over to him and shook him roughly by the shoulder.

'You're working too hard,' I said. 'Take my advice, and lay off for a day or two.'

He turned to me with the dazed look of one who is lost in some narcotic dream. This, very slowly, gave place to a sullen, evil anger.

'Oh, go to hell!' he snarled. 'Can't you see that I'm busy?'

I left him then, for there seemed nothing else to do under the circumstances. The mad and spectral nature of the whole affair was enough to make me doubt my own reason. My impressions of the meadow – and of Amberville – were tainted with an insidious horror such as I had never before felt in any moment of waking life and normal consciousness.

At the bottom of the slope of yellow pine, I turned back with repugnant curiosity for a parting glance. The painter had not moved, he was still confronting the malignant scene like a charmed bird that faces a lethal serpent. Whether or not the impression was a double optic image, I have never been sure: but at that instant I seemed to discern a faint, unholy aura, neither light nor mist, that flowed and wavered about the meadow, preserving the outlines of the willow, the alders, the reeds, the pool. Stealthily it appeared to lengthen, reaching toward Amberville like ghostly arms. The whole image was extremely tenuous, and may well have been an illusion; but it sent me shuddering into the shelter of the tall, benignant pines.

The remainder of that day, and the evening that followed, were tinged with the shadowy horror I had found in Chapman's meadow. I believe that I spent most of the time in arguing vainly with myself, in trying to convince the rational part of my mind that all I had seen and felt was utterly preposterous. I could arrive at no conclusion, other than a conviction that Amberville's mental health was endangered by the damnable thing, whatever it was, that inhered in the meadow. The malign personality of the place, the impalpable terror, mystery and lure, were like webs that had been woven upon my brain, and which I could not dissipate by any amount of conscious effort.

I made two resolves, however: one was that I should write immediately to Amberville's fiancée, Miss Avis Olcott, and invite her to visit me as a fellow-guest of the artist during the remainder of his stay at Bowman. Her influence, I thought, might help to counteract whatever was affecting him so perniciously. Since I knew her fairly well, the invitation would not seem out of the way. I decided to say nothing about it to Amberville: the element of surprise, I hoped, would be especially beneficial.

My second resolve was that I should not again visit the meadow myself, if I could avoid it. Indirectly – for I knew the folly of trying to combat a mental obsession openly – I should also try to discourage the painter's interest in the place, and divert his attention to other themes. Trips and entertainments, too, could be devised, at the minor cost of delaying my own work.

The smoky autumn twilight overtook me in such meditations as these; but Amberville did not return. Horrible premonitions, without coherent shape or name, began to torment me as I waited for him. The night darkened; and dinner grew cold on the table. At last, about nine o'clock, when I was nerving myself to go out and hunt for him, he came in hurriedly. He was pale, dishevelled, out of breath; and his eyes held a painful glare, as if something had frightened him beyond endurance.

He did not apologize for his lateness; nor did he refer to my own visit to the meadow-bottom. Apparently he had forgotten the whole episode – had forgotten his rudeness to me.

'I'm through!' he cried. 'I'll never go back again – never take another chance. That place is more hellish at night than in the daytime. I can't tell you what I've seen and felt – I must forget it, if I can. There's an emanation – something that comes out openly in the absence of the sun, but is latent by day. It lured me, it tempted me to remain this evening – and it nearly got me... God! I didn't believe that such things were possible – that abhorrent compound of – ' He broke off, and did not finish the sentence. His eyes dilated, as if with the memory of something too awful to be described. At that moment, I recalled the poisonously haunted eyes of old Chapman, whom I had sometimes met about the hamlet. He had not interested me particularly, since I had deemed him a common type of rural character, with a tendency to some obscure and unpleasant aberration. Now, when I saw the same look in the eyes of a sensitive artist, I began to wonder, with a shivering speculation, whether Chapman too had been aware of the weird evil that dwelt in his meadow. Perhaps, in some way that was beyond human comprehension, he had been its victim... He had died there; and his death had not seemed at all mysterious. But perhaps, in the light of all that Amberville and I had perceived, there was more in the matter than anyone had suspected.

'Tell me what you saw,' I ventured to suggest.

At the question, a veil seemed to fall between us, impalpable but tenebrific. He shook his head morosely and made no reply. The human terror, which perhaps had driven him back toward his normal self, and had made him almost communicative for the nonce, fell away from Amberville. A shadow that was darker than fear, an impenetrable alien umbrage, again submerged him. I felt a sudden chill, of the spirit rather than the flesh; and once more there came to me the outré thought of his growing kinship with the ghoulish meadow. Beside me, in the lamplit room, behind the mask of his humanity, a thing that was not wholly human seemed to sit and wait.

Of the nightmarish days that followed, I shall offer only a summary. It would be impossible to convey the eventless, fantasmal horror in which we dwelt and moved.

I wrote immediately to Miss Olcott, pressing her to pay me a visit during Amberville's stay, and, in order to insure acceptance, I hinted obscurely at my concern for his health and my need of her coadjutation. In the meanwhile, waiting her answer, I tried to divert the artist by suggesting trips to sundry points of scenic interest in the neighborhood. These suggestions he declined, with an aloof curtness, an air that was stony and cryptic rather than deliberately rude. Virtually, he ignored my existence, and made it more than plain that he wished me to leave him to his own devices. This, in despair, I finally decided to do, pending the arrival of Miss Olcott. He went out early each morning, as usual, with his paints and easel, and returned about sunset or a little later. He did not tell me where he had been; and I refrained from asking.

Miss Olcott came on the third day following my letter, in the afternoon. She was young, lissome, ultra-feminine, and was altogether devoted to Amberville. In fact, I think she was a little in awe of him. I told her as much as I dared, and warned her of the morbid change in her fiancé, which I attributed to nervousness and overwork. I simply could not bring myself to mention Chapman's meadow and its baleful influence: the whole thing was too unbelievable, too fantasmagoric, to be offered as an explanation to a modern girl. When I saw the somewhat helpless alarm and bewilderment with which she listened to my story, I began to wish that she were of a more wilful and determined type, and were less submissive toward Amberville than I surmised her to be. A stronger woman might have saved him; but even then I began to doubt whether Avis could do anything to combat the imponderable evil that was engulfing him.

A heavy crescent moon was hanging like a blood-dipped horn in the twilight when he returned. To my immense relief, the presence of Avis appeared to have a highly salutary effect. The very moment that he saw her, Amberville came out of the singular eclipse that had claimed him, as I feared, beyond redemption, and was almost his former affable self. Perhaps it was all make-believe, for an ulterior purpose; but this, at the time, I could not suspect. I began to congratulate myself on having applied a sovereign remedy. The girl, on her part, was plainly relieved; though I saw her eyeing him in a slightly hurt and puzzled way, when he sometimes fell for a short interval into moody abstraction, as if he had temporarily forgotten her. On the whole, however, there was a transformation that appeared no less than magical, in view of his recent gloom and remoteness. After a decent interim, I left the pair together, and retired.

I rose very late the next morning, having overslept. Avis and Amberville I learned, had gone out together, carrying a lunch which my Chinese cook had provided. Plainly he was taking her along on one of his artistic expeditions; and it augured well for his recovery from this. Somehow, it never occurred to me that he had taken her to Chapman's meadow. The tenuous, malignant shadow of the whole affair had begun to lift from my mind; I rejoiced in a lightened sense of responsibility; and, for the first time in a week, was able to concentrate clearly on the ending of my novel.

The two returned at dusk, and I saw immediately that I had been mistaken on more points than one. Amberville had again retired into a sinister, saturnine reserve. The girl, beside his looming height and massive shoulders, looked very small, forlorn – and pitifully bewildered and frightened. It was as if she had encountered something altogether beyond her comprehension, something with which she was humanly powerless to cope.

Very little was said by either of them. They did not tell me where they had been; but, for that matter, it was unnecessary to inquire. Amberville's taciturnity, as usual, seemed due to an absorption in some dark mood or sullen revery. But Avis gave me the impression of a dual constraint – as if, apart from some enthralling terror, she had been forbidden to speak of the day's events and experiences. I knew that they had gone to that accursed meadow; but I was far from sure whether Avis had been personally conscious of the weird and baneful entity of the place, or had merely been frightened by the unwholesome change in her lover beneath its influence. In either case, it was obvious that she was wholly subservient to him. I began to damn myself for a fool in having invited her to Bowman – though the true bitterness of my regret was still to come.

A week went by, with the same daily excursions of the painter and his fiancée – the same baffling, sinister estrangement and secrecy in Amberville – the same terror, helplessness, constraint and submissiveness in the girl. How it would all end, I could not imagine; but I feared, from the ominous alteration of his character, that Amberville was heading for some form of mental alienation, if nothing worse. My offers of entertainment and scenic journeys were rejected by the pair; and several blunt efforts to question Avis were met by a wall of almost hostile evasion which convinced me that Amberville had enjoined her to secrecy – and had perhaps, in some sleightful manner, misrepresented my own attitude toward him.

'You don't understand him,' she said, repeatedly. 'He is very temperamental.'

The whole affair was a maddening mystery, but it seemed more and more that the girl herself was being drawn, either directly or indirectly, into the same fantasmal web that had enmeshed the artist.

I surmised that Amberville had done several new pictures of the meadow; but he did not show them to me, nor even mention them. My own impressions of the place, as time went on, assumed an unaccountable vividness that was almost hallucinatory. The incredible idea of some inherent force or personality, malevolent and even vampirish, became an unavowed conviction against my will. The place haunted me like a fantasm, horrible but seductive. I felt an impelling morbid curiosity, an unwholesome desire to visit it again, and fathom, if possible, its enigma. Often I thought of Amberville's notion about a *Genius Loci* that dwelt in the meadow, and the hints of a human apparition that was somehow associated with the spot. Also, I wondered what it was that the artist had seen on the one occasion when he had lingered in the meadow after nightfall, and had returned to my house in driven terror. It seemed that he had not ventured to repeat the experiment, in spite of his obvious subjection to the unknown lure.

The end came, abruptly and without premonition. Business had taken me to the county seat, one afternoon, and I did not return till late in the evening. A full moon was high above the pine-dark hills. I expected to find Avis and the painter in my drawing-room; but they were not there. Li Sing, my factotum, told me that they had returned at dinnertime. An hour later, Amberville had gone out quietly while the girl was in her room. Coming down a few minutes later, Avis had shown excessive perturbation when she found him absent, and had also left the house, as if to follow him, without telling Li Sing where she was going or when she might return. All this had occurred three hours previously; and neither of the pair had yet reappeared.

A black and subtly chilling intuition of evil seized me as I listened to Li Sing's account. All too well I surmised that Amberville had yielded to the temptation of a second nocturnal visit to that unholy meadow. An occult attraction, somehow, had overcome the horror of his first experience, whatever it had been. Avis, knowing where he was, and perhaps fearful of his sanity – or safety – had gone out to find him. More and more, I felt an imperative conviction of some peril that threatened them both – some hideous and innominable thing to whose power, perhaps, they had already yielded.

Whatever my previous folly and remissness in the matter, I did not delay now. A few minutes of driving at precipitate speed through the mellow moonlight brought me to the piny edge of the Chapman property. There, as on my former visit, I left the car, and plunged headlong through the shadowy forest. Far down, in the hollow, as I went, I heard a single scream, shrill with terror, and abruptly terminated. I felt sure that the voice was that of Avis; but I did not hear it again.

Running desperately, I emerged in the meadow-bottom. Neither Avis nor Amberville was in sight; and it seemed to me, in my hasty scrutiny, that the place was full of mysteriously coiling and moving vapors that permitted only a partial view of the dead willow and the other vegetation. I ran on toward the scummy pool, and nearing it, was arrested by a sudden and twofold horror.

Avis and Amberville were floating together in the shallow pool, with their bodies half hidden by the mantling masses of algae. The girl was clasped tightly in the painter's arms, as if he had carried her with him, against her will, to that noisome death. Her face was covered by the evil, greenish scum; and I could not see the face of Amberville, which was averted against her shoulder. It seemed that there had been a struggle; but both were quiet now, and had yielded supinely to their doom.

It was not this spectacle alone, however, that drove me in mad and shuddering flight from the meadow, without making even the most tentative attempt to retrieve the drowned bodies. The true horror lay in the thing, which, from a little distance, I had taken for the coils of a slowly moving and rising mist. It was *not* vapor, nor anything else that could conceivably exist – that malign, luminous, pallid emanation that enfolded the entire scene before me like a restless and hungrily wavering extension of its outlines – a phantom projection of the pale and deathlike willow, the dying alders, the reeds, the stagnant pool and its suicidal victims. The landscape was visible through it, as through a film; but it seemed to curdle and thicken gradually in places, with some unholy, terrifying activity. Out of these curdlings, as if disgorged by the ambient exhalation, I saw the emergence of three human faces that partook of the same nebulous matter, neither mist nor plasm. One of these faces seemed to detach itself from the bole of the ghostly willow; the second and third swirled upward from the seething of the phantom pool, with their bodies trailing formlessly among the tenuous boughs. The faces were those of old Chapman, of Francis Amberville, and Avis Olcott.

Behind this eery, wraith-like projection of itself, the actual landscape leered with the same infernal and vampirish air which it had worn by day. But it seemed now that the place was no longer still – that it seethed with a malignant secret life – that it reached out toward me with its scummy waters, with the bony fingers of its trees, with the spectral faces it had spewed forth from its lethal deadfall.

Even terror was frozen within me for a moment. I stood watching, while the pale, unhallowed exhalation rose higher above the meadow. The three human faces, through a further agitation of the curdling mass, began to approach each other. Slowly, inexpressibly, they merged in one, becoming an androgynous face, neither young nor old, that melted finally into the lengthening phantom boughs of the willow – the hands of the arboreal death, that were reaching out to enfold me. Then, unable to bear the spectacle any longer, I started to run.

There is little more that need be told, for nothing that I could add to this narrative would lessen the abominable mystery of it all in any degree. The meadow – or the thing that dwells in the meadow – has already claimed three victims… and I sometimes wonder if it will have a fourth. I alone, it would seem, among the living, have guessed the secret of Chapman's death, and the death of Avis and Amberville; and no one else, apparently, has felt the malign genius of the meadow. I have not returned there, since the morning when the bodies of the artist and his fiancée were removed from the pool… nor have I summoned up the resolution to destroy or otherwise dispose of the four oil paintings and two watercolor drawings of the spot that were made by Amberville. Perhaps… in spite of all that deters me… I shall visit it again.

THE TOWN OF CATS

Hagiwara Sakutarō

TRANSLATED INTO ENGLISH BY JEFFREY ANGLES

Hagiwara Sakutarō (1886–1942) was a Japanese writer considered one of the foremost poets of the Taishō and early Showa periods. Sakutarō was interested in exploring madness, hallucinations, obsession, and abnormal psychology in his works. To do so, he largely rejected naturalism and used colloquial language, impressionistic images, a sense of personal intimacy, and modern subject matter. The classic 'The Town of Cats' (1935) is the poet's only short story and explores themes of disorientation and the illusory nature of reality. It depicts a surreal urban journey that presages the work of Haruki Murakami. Iconic weird writer Thomas Ligotti has cited 'The Town of Cats' as among his favorite stories.

The quality that incites the desire for travel has gradually disappeared from my fantasies. Before, however, symbols of travel were all that filled my thoughts. Just to picture a train, steamboat, or town in an unfamiliar foreign land was enough to make my heart dance. But experience has taught me that travel presents nothing more than 'identical objects moving in identical spaces.' No matter where one goes, one finds the same sort of people living in similar villages and repeating the same humdrum lives. One finds merchants in every small country town spending their days clicking abacuses and watching the dusty white road outside. In every municipal office, government officials smoke and think about what they will have for lunch. They live out insipid, monotonous lives in which each new day is identical to the last, gradually watching themselves grow old as the days go by. Now the thought of travel projects onto my weary heart an infinitely tedious landscape like that of a paulownia tree growing in a vacant lot, and I feel a dull loathing for human life in which this sameness repeats itself everywhere. Travel no longer holds any interest or romance for me.

In the past, I often undertook wondrous voyages in my own personal way. Let me explain ... I would reach that unique moment in which humankind sometimes finds itself able to soar – that special moment outside of time and space, outside the chain of cause and effect – and I would adroitly navigate the borderline between dreams and reality to play in an uninhibited world of my own making. – Having said this much, I doubt I need to explain my secret further. Let me simply add that, in undertaking these hallucinatory trips, I generally preferred to use the likes of morphine and cocaine, which can be ingested in a simple shot or dose, instead of opium, which is hard to obtain in Japan and requires troublesome tools and provisions.

There is not enough room here to describe in detail the lands that I traveled in those dreams of narcotic ecstasy, but I will tell you that the trips frequently took me wandering through wetlands where little frogs gathered, through polar coasts where penguins live, and on and on. The landscapes in those dreams were filled with brilliant primary hues. The sea and sky were always as clear and blue as glass. Even after returning to normal, I would cling to those visions and relive them again and again in the world of reality.

These drug-induced voyages took a terrible toll on my health. I grew increasingly drawn and pale by the day, and my skin deteriorated as if I had aged terribly. By and by, I began to pay more attention to my health. Following my doctor's advice, I started taking walks through my neighborhood. Every day, I would cover the distance of forty or fifty *chō*, walking anywhere from thirty minutes to an hour. One day while I was out taking my exercise, I happened upon a new way to satisfy my eccentric wanderlust. I was walking through the usual area around my home. Normally, I do not deviate from my established path, but for some reason that day, I slipped into an unfamiliar alley, and going the wrong way, I lost all sense of direction.

All in all, I have no innate sense of direction. My ability to keep track of the points of the compass is terribly deficient. As a result, I am awful at remembering my way anywhere, and if I go someplace even slightly unfamiliar, in no time I end up completely lost. To make matters worse, I have a habit of getting absorbed in my thoughts as I walk. If an acquaintance happens to greet me along the way, I will pass by in total obliviousness. Because I am so bad at keeping track of directions, I can lose my way even in a place that I know perfectly well, such as my own neighborhood. I can be so close to my destination that people laugh at me when I ask how to get there. Once I walked tens of times around the hedge surrounding the very house in which I have lived for years. Though the gate was right before my eyes, my lack of a sense of direction made it impossible for me to find it. My family insisted a fox must have bewitched me. Psychologists would probably account for this bewitching as a disturbance of the inner ear. I say this because the experts claim that the function of sensing direction belongs to the semicircular canals located in the ear.

In any case, I was completely lost and bewildered. I made a random guess and rushed down the street in search of my house. After going in circles several times in a neighborhood of suburban estates surrounded by trees, suddenly I came upon a bustling street. It was a lovely little neighborhood, but I had no idea where I was!

The roads had been swept clean, and the flagstones were wet with dew. All of the shops were neat and tidy, all with different types of unusual merchandise lined up in polished show windows. A flowering tree flourished by the eaves of a coffee shop, bringing an artistic play of light and shadow to the borough. The red mailbox at the street crossing was also beautiful, and the young woman in the cigarette shop was as bright and sweet as a plum.

I had never seen such an aesthetically charming place! Where in Tokyo could I possibly be? But I was unable to recall the layout of the city. I figured I could not have strayed far from home because so little time had elapsed. It was perfectly clear that I was within the territory where I ordinarily strolled, only a half hour or so from home, or at least not too far from it. But how could this place be so close without my having known it?

I felt as if I was dreaming. I wondered if perhaps what I was seeing was not a real town but a reflection or silhouette of a town projected on a screen. Then, just as suddenly, my memory and common sense returned. Examining my surroundings again, I realized I was seeing an ordinary, familiar block in my neighborhood. The mailbox was at the intersection as always, and the young lady with the gastric disorder sat in the cigarette shop. The same out-dated, dusty merchandise yawned from the space that it occupied in the store windows. On the street, the eaves of the coffee shop were boorishly decorated with an arch of artificial flowers. This was nowhere new. It was my familiar, boring neighborhood.

In the blink of an eye, my reaction to my surroundings had altered completely. The mysterious and magical transformation of this place into a beautiful town had occurred simply because I had mixed up my directions. The mailbox that always stood at the south end of the block seemed to be on the opposite, northern approach. The tradesmen's houses on the left side of the street had shifted to the right. The changes sufficed to make the entire neighborhood look new and different. In that brief moment that I spent in the unknown, illusory town, I noticed a sign above a store. I swore to myself that I had seen a picture just like it on a signboard somewhere else.

When my memory was back in working order, all of the directions reversed themselves. Until a moment before, the crowds on my left had been on the right, and I discovered that, though I had been walking north, I was now headed south. In that instant when my memory returned to normal, the needle of my compass spun around, and the cardinal directions switched positions. The whole universe changed, and the mood of the town that manifested itself before me became utterly different. The mysterious neighborhood that I had seen a moment before existed in some universe of opposite space where the compass was reversed.

After this accidental discovery, I made it a point to lose my bearings in order to travel again to such mysterious places. The deficiency on my part that I described before was especially helpful in allowing me to undertake these travels, but even people with a normal, sound sense of direction may at times experience the same special places that I have. For instance, imagine yourself returning home on a train late at night. First, the train leaves the station, and then the tracks carry you straight east to west. Some time later, you wake from a dream-filled nap. You realize the train has changed directions at some point and is now moving west to east. You reason this cannot be right, and in the reality you perceive, the train is moving away from your destination. To double check, you look out the window. The intermediary stations and landscapes to which you are accustomed are all entirely new. The world looks so different that you cannot recognize a single place. But you arrive in the end. When you step down on the familiar train platform, you awaken from the illusion and regain an accurate sense of direction. And once that sense is regained, strange landscapes and sights transform themselves into boring familiarities as unremarkable and ordinary as ever.

In effect, you see the same landscape, first from the reverse and then from the front, as you are accustomed to seeing it. One can think of a thing as having two separate sides. Just by changing your perspective, the other side will appear. Indeed there is no metaphysical problem more mysterious than the notion that a given phenomenon can possess a 'secret, hidden side.' When I was a boy a long time ago, and I used to examine a framed picture that hung on the walls of the house, I wondered all the while what worlds lay hidden on the reverse side of the framed landscape. I removed the frame repeatedly to peep at the back side of the painting. Those childhood thoughts have now turned into a riddle that remains impossible for me to solve even as an adult.

But the story that I am about to tell may contain a hint for solving the riddle. Should my strange tale lead you, my readers, to imagine a world of the fourth dimension hidden behind things and external manifestations – a universe existing on the reverse side of the landscape – then this tale will seem completely real to you. If, however, you are unable to imagine the existence of such a place, then what follows will seem like the decadent hallucinations of an absurd poet whose nerves have been shattered by a morphine addiction.

In any event, I shall gather my courage and write. I am not a novelist, and therefore I do not know the intricacies of drama and plot that will excite readers. All that I can do is give a straightforward account of the realities I experienced.

II

I was staying in the Hokuetsu region at a hot spring resort in a town that I shall call K. September was nearly over, the equinox already past. Being in the mountains, we were well into autumn. All of the guests who had come from the city to escape the summer heat had returned home, leaving only a handful of visitors to quietly nurse their illnesses in the healing waters of the spa. The autumn shade had grown long, and the leaves of the trees were scattered across the lonely courtyard of our inn. I would don a flannel kimono and spend time pursuing my daily ritual of walking alone along the back mountain roads.

There were three towns a short distance from the hot spring. Perhaps I should not call them towns they were so small. Two of them were like a little cluster of country homes, about the size of what would pass as a village elsewhere. The third, however, was a compact country settlement that sold the necessities of daily living. It even had restaurants like those one finds in the city. I shall call this town, the most prosperous of the three, U. Each of the three towns connected directly to the hot spring via a road, and every day at prescribed times, horse-drawn coaches traveled back and forth between them. A small, narrow-gauge railway had been laid to U, so I often made the trip to it on the train to shop and have a drink with the ladies. But simply riding the train was enough to bring me tremendous pleasure. The cute, toylike railway would weave through groves of deciduous trees and gorges that revealed views of entire valleys.

One day, I got off the train midway, and I began walking toward U. I wanted to take a leisurely walk alone over the mountain crests with their commanding views. The road cut an irregular path through the woods, following the direction of the tracks nearby. Autumn flowers were in bloom here and there. The surface of the red earth glistened, and the trunks of felled trees were scattered across the ground. While watching the clouds float across the sky, I thought of the old folklore that survives there in the mountains. In these backwoods areas, with their primitive taboos and superstitions, one can still hear many legends and folktales. In fact, many of the local people believe the stories even to this day. The maids and the locals visiting our inn told me several strange stories in voices tinged with fear and disgust. They said the spirits of dogs possessed the inhabitants of one particular settlement, while cats possessed the inhabitants of another. Those possessed by dog-spirits ate only meat. Those possessed by cat-spirits lived on nothing but fish.

The people in the surrounding areas called these odd settlements 'the possessed villages,' and they were careful to avoid contact with them. Once a year, the people of the allegedly possessed villages would select a black, moonless night to hold a festival. It was strictly forbidden for anyone outside the village to observe what ensued during those mysterious rites. If by some rare chance an outsider happened to glimpse the proceedings, he would invariably bite his tongue and say nothing. The rumors about the villages ran rampant: the denizens of the villages were privy to special magic; they were hiding a vast fortune of unknown origin; and so on. After recounting these stories, the locals would add that one of the villages was located quite close to the hot spring, only it wasn't very long ago that the inhabitants had deserted the town. They had up and left, but it was common speculation that they continued to live their secret life in a community somewhere else. As irrefutable proof, the people telling the story cited the experiences of others who had seen the *okura*, the true form of the malevolent spirits.

All these stories proved to me was how stubbornly superstitious farming people can be. Conscious of it or not, the villagers were forcing their own fears and realities on me. Because their stories interested me for anthropological reasons, however, I listened carefully. Secretive village practices and taboos like those they described can be found throughout Japan. One likely theory is that the people engaging in these practices were the descendants of immigrants from foreign countries with different customs and habits, and even today they continued to worship the clan gods of their ancestors. Another possibility is that the villages were holdovers from the seventeenth century, when believers in Christianity, persecuted by the Tokugawa government, went into hiding and practiced their religion in secret.

There are countless things in this vast universe that humankind does not know. As the Latin poet Horace once noted, the intellect of the mind knows nothing. Instead, people use it to make common sense of the world and have myths that explain things in everyday terms. Still, the secrets of the universe continue to transcend the quotidian. All philosophers must, therefore, doff their hats to the poets when they discover that the path of reason takes them only so far. The universe that lies beyond common sense and logic – the universe that is known intuitively to the poet – belongs to the metaphysical.

While indulging in these speculations, I walked through the autumn mountains. The narrow road continued for some time, then disappeared into the depths of the woods. The railroad tracks, the sole thing I relied on to guide me to my destination, were nowhere in sight. I had lost my way.

'I'm lost!'

These lonely words rose in my heart as I came to my senses and left my contemplations behind. Immediately I became uneasy and began to look frantically for the road. I backtracked in an attempt to find it. Instead, I became all the more turned around. I ended up in an inescapable labyrinth of countless paths. The paths led deeper into the mountains and then disappeared into the brambles. I wasted a great deal of time. Not once did I see a single soul – not even a woodcutter. Becoming increasingly upset, I paced about impatiently like a dog trying to scout out its way. At long last, I discovered a narrow but clear path marked by feet and hooves. Following it intently, I descended little by little toward the base of the mountain. I figured I could relax once I made it to the base of one of the mountains and found a house.

I arrived at the foot of the mountain some hours later. There, I discovered a world of human habitation beyond anything that I could have anticipated in my wildest dreams. Instead of poor farmers, I had come upon a beautiful, prosperous town. An acquaintance of mine once told me about a trip he had taken on the Trans-Siberian railroad. He said the passengers would travel for days and days through desolate, uninhabited plains that stretched as far as the eye could see. As a result, when the train finally stopped, even the tiniest station looked like one of the most animated, prosperous cities in the world. The surprise that I felt was probably similar to what my friend had experienced. There in the low, flat plain at the base of the mountain stood rows and rows of buildings. Towers and lofty buildings shone in the sun. The sight was so impressive that I could hardly believe such a marvelous metropolis really existed there in the remote mountains.

Feeling as if I was seeing an image projected by a magic lantern onto a screen in front of me, I slowly approached the town. At some point, though, I crossed over into the projection and became part of the mysterious town itself. Starting down a narrow alley, I passed through some dark, confusing, cramped pathways, but then suddenly I walked into the center of a bustling avenue, almost as if I were emerging from a womb into the world. The city that I saw was so special, so unusual! The rows of shops and other buildings were designed with an unusual, artistic feel. They acted, as it were, like the building blocks for the communal aesthetic that pervaded the entire town. The whole place was beautiful, but the beauty did not seem to have been consciously created. The artistic feel had evolved naturally as the town gradually weathered and developed an elegant patina that reflected its age. This elegant depth spoke with grace and gentility of the town's old history and the long memories of the townspeople.

The town was so tightly knit that the main avenue was only a dozen or a dozen and a half feet across. Other smaller streets were pressed into the space between the eaves of the buildings so that they became deep, narrow passages that wound about like paths in a labyrinth. Roads descended down flagstone-covered slopes or passed under the shadow of second-story bay windows, creating dark tunnels. As in southern climes, flowering trees grew near the wells located here and there throughout the town. A ubiquitous, deep shade filled the whole place, leaving everything as tranquil as the shadow of a laurel tree. What appeared to be the houses of courtesans stood in a row, and from deep inside an enclosed garden came the quiet sound of elegant music.

On the main avenue, I found many Western-style houses with glass windows instead of the sliding wooden and paper doors found in Japan. A red and white striped pole stuck out from the eaves of a hairdresser's shop, along with a painted sign that read in English, 'Barbershop.' There were also traditional Japanese-style inns and shops that did laundry in the neighborhood. Near an intersection stood a photography studio with glass windows that reflected the sunny autumn sky with the lonely stoicism of a weather observatory. In the front of a watch shop sat the store's bespectacled owner working quietly and intently.

The streets were thronged with bustling crowds, yet the people created little noise. A refined, hushed silence reigned over the place, casting a pall that was as profound as a deep sleep. The town was silent, I realized, because there were no noisy horse-drawn carriages charging by, only pedestrians. But that wasn't all. The crowds were also quiet. Everyone – both men and women – had an air about them that was genteel and discreet, elegant and calm. The women were especially lovely and graceful, and even a bit coquettish. The people shopping in the stores and stopping in the street to talk also spoke politely in harmonious, soft voices. As a result, instead of appealing to the sense of hearing, their voices seemed to present meaning in an almost tactile fashion, something soft to the touch. The voices of the women had the especially sweet and rapturous charm of a gentle stroke passing over the surface of one's skin. People and things came and went like shadows.

I realized right away that the atmosphere of the town was an artificial creation whose existence relied on the subtle attentions of its inhabitants. It was not just its buildings. The entire system of individual nerves that came together to create its atmosphere was focused on one single, central aesthetic plan. In everything from the slightest stirrings in the air, there was strict adherence to the aesthetic laws of contrast, symmetry, harmony, and equilibrium. These aesthetic laws entailed, however, extremely complicated differential equations that, requiring tremendous effort, made all of the nerves of the town quiver and strain. For instance, even uttering a word slightly too high in pitch was forbidden, for it would shatter the harmony of the entire town. When the inhabitants did anything – when they walked down the street, moved their hands, ate, drank, thought, or even chose the pattern of their clothing – they had to give painstaking attention to their actions to make sure they harmonized with the reigning atmosphere and did not lose the appropriate degrees of contrast and symmetry with their environs. The whole town was a perilously fragile structure of thin crystal. A loss of balance, even for a moment, would have dashed the entire thing to smithereens. A subtle mathematical structure of individual supports was necessary to maintain stability, and a complex of individual connections governed by the laws of contrast and symmetry strained to support the whole.

However frightening this might be, such was the truth about the town. One careless mishap would mean the collapse and destruction of the entire place. Trepidation and fear had stretched the nerves of the whole town dangerously thin. The plan of this town, which seemed so aesthetically inclined on the surface, went beyond a mere matter of taste. It hid a more frightening and acute problem.

This realization suddenly made me extremely anxious. The air surrounding me was electrically charged, and in it I felt the anguish of the inhabitants' nerves stretched to the breaking point. The peculiar beauty and dreamlike serenity of the town had now become hushed and uncanny. I felt as if I were unraveling a code to discover some frightening secret. A vague premonition, the color of a pale fear, washed over my heart, though I could not quite understand what it was trying to tell me. All of my senses were fully alert. I perceived all of the colors, scents, sounds, tastes, and meanings of the things surrounding me in infinitesimal detail. The stench of corpses filled the air, and the barometric pressure rose with each passing instant. All of the things that manifested themselves around me seemed to portend some evil. Something strange was about to happen! Something had to happen!

But the town did not change. The street was full of elegant people going to and fro, walking quietly without making a sound, just as they had moments ago. From somewhere in the distance, I heard a continuous, low, mournful note that sounded like the stroking of the strings of a *kokyū*. Like someone haunted by a strange omen in the moments before a great earthquake, I experienced an anxious premonition – mere steps away from me, a person falls... and the harmony on which the entire town is based collapses, throwing everything into utter chaos!

I struggled with this horrifying vision like someone having a nightmare and trying frantically to awaken. With each passing second, the sky turned bluer and more transparent. The pressure of the electrically charged air rose higher and higher. The buildings bent precariously, growing long and sickly thin. Here and there, they distended into bizarre, turretlike forms. The roofs became strangely bony and deformed like the long, thin legs of a chicken.

'It's happening!'

The words escaped my lips as my chest thumped with fear. Just then, a small black rat or something like it dashed into the center of the road. I saw it with extraordinary delineation and clarity. What on earth was going on? I was seized by the strange, sudden notion that it would destroy the harmony of the entire town.

Right then… the whole universe stopped dead, and an infinite quiet settled over everything. What next!?!

An unimaginably strange and horrifying sight appeared before me. Great packs of cats materialized everywhere, filling all the roads around me! Cats, cats, cats, cats, cats, cats, and more cats! Everywhere I looked there was nothing but cats! Whiskered cat faces rose in the windows of all the houses, filling the panes like pictures in frames.

I shuddered. I held my breath from fright and nearly passed out. This wasn't the human world! Was there nothing in this world but cats? What on earth had happened? Was this world real? Something had to be wrong with me. Either I was seeing an illusion or I had gone mad! My senses had lost their balance. The universe was collapsing around me.

I was terrified. Some final, frightening destruction would surely be closing in on me. I closed my eyes, and fear rushed through the darkness inside me.

But, suddenly, my senses returned. As my heart began to slow its furious beat, I opened my eyes again to examine the world of reality that now surrounded me.

The inexplicable vision of all those cats had vanished. There was nothing out of the ordinary about the town. Hollow, deserted windows stretched open their empty mouths. The traffic moved by uneventfully as the white clay of the dull streets roasted in the sun. Nowhere was there even a shadow of a cat. The town had undergone a complete change in feeling. Everywhere there were rows of plain old shops. Walking the dry, midday streets were the same tired, dusty people who live in every country. The mysterious, perplexing town of a moment ago had vanished without a trace. An entirely separate world had appeared, almost as if a playing card had been turned over to reveal its other side. It was nothing but an ordinary, commonplace country town. Wasn't it the same old town of U that I knew so well? There at the barber-shop, facing the midday traffic outside the shop window, was a row of barber chairs that had no customers. On the left side of the dilapidated town yawned a clock shop that never sold anything, its door shut as always. Everything was just like I remembered it – a never-changing, humdrum town in the country.

Once my mind cleared, I understood everything. I had foolishly allowed myself to succumb again to my perceptual malady, to my disturbance of the semicircular canals. Getting turned around in the mountains, I had completely lost any sense of direction. Though I thought I was descending the other side of the mountain, I went the wrong way and ended up here in the town of U. Also, I had wandered into the heart of it from a direction opposite to that I arrived from on the train. All of my assumptions as to my whereabouts were completely backward, and my mistaken impressions were showing me a world with the directions all turned around. I was looking at a separate universe of another dimension, at the back side of the landscape where up and down, front and back, and the four cardinal directions were all reversed. As popular parlance would have it, I had been 'bewitched by a fox.'

III

My tale ends here, but the end of this story is the point of departure for my strange, unresolved enigma. The Chinese philosopher Zhuangzi once dreamed he was a butterfly. When he woke, he questioned his own identity, wondering if he was the butterfly in the dream or the person he was at that moment.

This ancient riddle has remained unsolved across the ages. Is the universe of illusion only visible to those who have been bewitched by foxes? Or is it visible to those with clear intellect and good sense? Where does the metaphysical world exist in relationship to the ordinary landscape? Is it the reverse of what we ordinarily see? Is it in front? Perhaps there is no one who can answer these riddles.

That magical town outside the bounds of the human world remains lodged in my memory. I still remember the vision of that bizarre feline town with the silhouettes of cats appearing so vividly in every window, under all the eaves, and in every gathering on the street. Even today, more than ten years later, I still relive the terror of that day by just thinking about it. I see it all over again as if it were right there in front of my eyes.

People smile coldly at my tale. They say it is the demented illusion of a poet or a nonsensical hallucination born of absentminded daydreaming. Still, I continue to insist that I did see a town of nothing but cats. I did see a town where cats took on human form and crowded the streets. Though reasoning and logic tell me otherwise, I am absolutely sure that, somewhere in this universe, I did encounter such a place. Nothing is more certain to me than this. The entire population of the world can stand before me and snicker, but I will not abandon my faith in that strange settlement described in the legends of the backwoods. Somewhere, in some corner of this universe, a town is inhabited solely by the spirits of cats. Sure enough, it does exist.

THE TARN

Hugh Walpole

Hugh Walpole (1884–1941) was a very popular and prolific English writer who published thirty-six novels, five volumes of short stories, two plays and three volumes of memoirs. His skill at scene-setting, his vivid plots, and his high profile as a lecturer brought him a large readership in the UK and North America. A bestselling author in the 1920s and 1930s, his works have been neglected since his death. Although best-known for his historical novels, Walpole also penned classic tales of the supernatural, including 'The Clocks' (1913), 'The Twisted Inn' (1915), 'Tarnhelm' (1933) and 'The Silver Mask' (1933). However, 'The Tarn (1936) – a perceptive, clever, and all-too-true weird tale – remains our personal favorite.

As Foster moved unconsciously across the room, bent towards the bookcase, and stood leaning forward a little, choosing now one book, now another with his eye, his host, seeing the muscles of the back of his thin, scraggy neck stand out above his low flannel collar, thought of the ease with which he could squeeze that throat and the pleasure, the triumphant, lustful pleasure, that such an action would give him.

The low white-walled, white-ceilinged room was flooded with the mellow, kindly Lakeland sun. October is a wonderful month in the English Lakes, golden, rich, and perfumed, slow suns moving through apricot-tinted skies to ruby evening glories; the shadows lie then thick about that beautiful country, in dark purple patches, in long web-like patterns of silver gauze, in thick splotches of amber and grey. The clouds pass in galleons across the mountains, now veiling, now revealing, now descending with ghost-like armies to the very breast of the plains, suddenly rising to the softest of blue skies and lying thin in lazy languorous colour.

Fenwick's cottage looked across to Low Fells; on his right, seen through side windows, sprawled the hills above Ullswater.

Fenwick looked at Foster's back and felt suddenly sick, so that he sat down, veiling his eyes for a moment with his hand. Foster had come up there, come all the way from London, to explain, to want to put things right. For how many years had he known Foster? Why, for twenty at least, and during all those years Foster had been for ever determined to put things right with everybody. He could not bear to be disliked; he hated that anyone should think ill of him; he wanted everyone to be his friend. That was one reason, perhaps, why Foster had got on so well, had prospered so in his career; one reason, too, why Fenwick had not.

For Fenwick was the opposite of Foster in this. He did not want friends; he certainly did not care that people should like him – that is, people for whom, for one reason or another, he had contempt – and he had contempt for quite a number of people.

Fenwick looked at that long, thin, bending back and felt his knees tremble. Soon Foster would turn round and that high reedy voice would pipe out something about the books. 'What jolly books you have, Fenwick!' How many, many times in the long watches of the night when Fenwick could not sleep had he heard that pipe sounding close there – yes, in the very shadows of his bed! And how many times had Fenwick replied to it: 'I hate you! You are the cause of my failure in life! You have been in my way always. Always, always, always! Patronising and pretending, and in truth showing others what a poor thing you thought me, how great a failure, how conceited a fool! I know. You can hide nothing from me! I can hear you!'

For twenty years now Foster had been persistently in Fenwick's way. There had been that affair, so long ago now, when Robins had wanted a subeditor for his wonderful review, the *Parthenon*, and Fenwick had gone to see him and they had had a splendid talk. How magnificently Fenwick had talked that day, with what enthusiasm he had shown Robins (who was blinded by his own conceit, anyway) the kind of paper the *Parthenon* might be, how Robins had caught his own enthusiasm, how he had pushed his fat body about the room, crying, 'Yes, yes, Fenwick – that's fine! That's fine indeed!' – and then how, after all, Foster had got that job.

The paper had only lived for a year or so, it is true, but the connection with it had brought Foster into prominence just as it might have brought Fenwick!

Then five years later there was Fenwick's novel, *The Bitter Aloe* – the novel upon which he had spent three years of blood-and-tears endeavour – and then, in the very same week of publication, Foster brings out *The Circus*, the novel that made his name, although, Heaven knows, the thing was poor sentimental trash. You may say that one novel cannot kill another – but can it not? Had not *The Circus* appeared would not that group of London know-alls – that conceited, limited, ignorant, self-satisfied crowd, who nevertheless can do, by their talk, so much to affect a book's good or evil fortunes – have talked about *The Bitter Aloe*, and so forced it into prominence? As it was, the book was still-born, and *The Circus* went on its prancing, triumphant way.

After that there had been many occasions – some small, some big – and always in one way or another that thin, scraggy body of Foster's was interfering with Fenwick's happiness.

The thing had become, of course, an obsession with Fenwick. Hiding up there in the heart of the Lakes, with no friends, almost no company, and very little money, he was given too much to brooding over his failure. He was a failure, and it was not his own fault. How could it be his own fault with his talents and his brilliance? It was the fault of modern life and its lack of culture, the fault of the stupid material mess that made up the intelligence of human beings – and the fault of Foster.

Always Fenwick hoped that Foster would keep away from him. He did not know what he would not do did he see the man. And then one day to his amazement he received a telegram: 'Passing through this way. May I stop with you Monday and Tuesday? Giles Foster.'

Fenwick could scarcely believe his eyes, and then – from curiosity, from cynical contempt, from some deeper, more mysterious motive that he dared not analyse – he had telegraphed 'Come.'

And here the man was. And he had come – would you believe it? – to 'put things right.' He had heard from Hamlin Eddis that 'Fenwick was hurt with him, had some kind of a grievance.'

'I didn't like to feel that, old man, and so I thought I'd just stop by and have it out with you, see what the matter was, and put it right.'

Last night after supper Foster had tried to put it right. Eagerly, his eyes like a good dog's who is asking for a bone that he knows that he thoroughly deserves, he had held out his hand and asked Fenwick to 'say what was up.'

Fenwick simply had said that nothing was up; Hamlin Eddis was a damned fool.

'Oh, I'm glad to hear that!' Foster had cried, springing up out of his chair and putting his hand on Fenwick's shoulder. 'I'm glad of that, old man. I couldn't bear for us not to be friends. We've been friends so long.'

Lord! how Fenwick hated him at that moment!

II

'What a jolly lot of books you have!' Foster turned round and looked at Fenwick with eager, gratified eyes. 'Every book here is interesting! I like your arrangement of them too, and those open bookshelves – it always seems to me a shame to shut up books behind glass!'

Foster came forward and sat down quite close to his host. He even reached forward and laid his hand on his host's knee. 'Look here! I'm mentioning it for the last time – positively! But I do want to make quite certain. There is nothing wrong between us, is there, old man? I know you assured me last night, but I just want–'

Fenwick looked at him and, surveying him, felt suddenly an exquisite pleasure of hatred. He liked the touch of the man's hand on his knee; he himself bent forward a little and, thinking how agreeable it would be to push Foster's eyes in, deep, deep into his head, crunching them, smashing them to purple, leaving the empty, staring, bloody sockets, said:

'Why, no. Of course not. I told you last night. What could there be?'

The hand gripped the knee a little more tightly.

'I am so glad! That's splendid! Splendid! I hope you won't think me ridiculous, but I've always had an affection for you ever since I can remember. I've always wanted to know you better. I've admired your talents so greatly. That novel of yours – the – the – the one about the Aloe–'

'*The Bitter Aloe*?'

'Ah, yes, that was it. That was a splendid book. Pessimistic, of course, but still fine. It ought to have done better. I remember thinking so at the time.'

'Yes, it ought to have done better.'

'Your time will come, though. What I say is that good work always tells in the end.'

'Yes, my time will come.'

The thin, piping voice went on:

'Now, I've had more success than I deserved. Oh, yes, I have. You can't deny it. I'm not being falsely modest. I mean it. I've got some talent, of course, but not so much as people say. And you! Why, you've got so much more than they acknowledge. You have, old man. You have indeed. Only – I do hope you'll forgive my saying this – perhaps you haven't advanced quite as you might have done. Living up here, shut away here, closed in by all these mountains, in this wet climate – always raining – why, you're out of things! You don't see people, don't talk and discover what's really going on. Why, look at me!'

Fenwick turned round and looked at him.

'Now, I have half the year in London, where one gets the best of everything, best talk, best music, best plays, and then I'm three months abroad, Italy or Greece or somewhere, and then three months in the country. Now that's an ideal arrangement. You have everything that way.'

Italy or Greece or somewhere!

Something turned in Fenwick's breast, grinding, grinding, grinding. How he had longed, oh, how passionately, for just one week in Greece, two days in Sicily! Sometimes he had thought that he might run to it, but when it had come to the actual counting of the pennies – and now this fool, this fathead, this self-satisfied, conceited, patronising –

He got up, looking out at the golden sun.

'What do you say to a walk?' he suggested. 'The sun will last for a good hour yet.'

III

As soon as the words were out of his lips he felt as though someone else had said them for him. He even turned half-round to see whether anyone else were there. Ever since Foster's arrival on the evening before he had been conscious of this sensation. A walk? Why should he take Foster for a walk, show him his beloved country, point out those curves and lines and hollows, the long silver shield of Ullswater, the cloudy purple hills hunched like blankets about the knees of some recumbent giant? Why? It was as though he had turned round to someone behind him and had said, 'You have some further design in this.'

They started out. The road sank abruptly to the lake, then the path ran between trees at the water's edge. Across the lake, tones of bright yellow light, crocus-hued, rode upon the blue. The hills were dark.

The very way that Foster walked bespoke the man. He was always a little ahead of you, pushing his long, thin body along with little eager jerks as though did he not hurry he would miss something that would be immensely to his advantage. He talked, throwing words over his shoulder to Fenwick as you throw crumbs of bread to a robin.

'Of course I was pleased. Who would not be? After all it's a new prize. They've only been awarding it for a year or two, but it's gratifying – really gratifying – to secure it. When I opened the envelope and found the cheque there – well, you could have knocked me down with a feather. You could, indeed. Of course, a hundred pounds isn't much. But it's the honour–'

Whither were they going? Their destiny was as certain as though they had no free-will. Free-will? There is no free-will. All is Fate. Fenwick suddenly laughed aloud.

Foster stopped.

'Why, what is it?'

'What's what?'

'You laughed.'

'Something amused me.'

Foster slipped his arm through Fenwick's.

'It is jolly to be walking alone together like this, arm-in-arm, friends. I'm a sentimental man, I won't deny it. What I say is that life is short and one must love one's fellow-beings or where is one? You live too much alone, old man.' He squeezed Fenwick's arm. 'That's the truth of it.'

It was torture, exquisite, heavenly torture. It was wonderful to feel that thin, bony arm pressing against his. Almost you could hear the beating of that other heart. Wonderful to feel that arm and the temptation to take it in your two hands and to bend it and twist it and then to hear the bones crack ... crack ... crack ...

Wonderful to feel that temptation rise through one's body like boiling water and yet not to yield to it. For a moment Fenwick's hand touched Foster's. Then he drew himself apart.

'We're at the village. This is the hotel where they all come in the summer. We turn off at the right here. I'll show you my tarn.'

IV

'Your tarn?' asked Foster. 'Forgive my ignorance, but what is a tarn exactly?'

'A tarn is a miniature lake, a pool of water lying in the lap of the hill. Very quiet, lovely, silent. Some of them are immensely deep.'

'I should like to see that.'

'It is some little distance – up a rough road. Do you mind?'

'Not a bit. I have long legs,'

'Some of them are immensely deep – unfathomable – nobody touched the bottom – but quiet, like glass, with shadows only–'

'Do you know, Fenwick, but I have always been afraid of water – I've never learnt to swim. I'm afraid to go out of my depth. Isn't that ridiculous? But it is all because at my private school, years ago, when I was a small boy, some big fellows took me and held me with my head under the water and nearly drowned me. They did indeed. They went further than they meant to. I can see their faces.'

Fenwick considered this. The picture leapt to his mind. He could see the boys – large, strong fellows, probably – and this little skinny thing like a frog, their thick hands about his throat, his legs like grey sticks kicking out of the water, their laughter, their sudden sense that something was wrong, the skinny body all flaccid and still – he drew a deep breath.

Foster was walking beside him now, not ahead of him, as though he were a little afraid, and needed reassurance. Indeed the scene had changed. Before and behind them stretched the uphill path, loose with shale and stones. On their right, on a ridge at the foot of the hill, were some quarries, almost deserted, but the more melancholy in the fading afternoon because a little work still continued there, faint sounds came from the gaunt listening chimneys, a stream of water ran and tumbled angrily into a pool below, once and again a black silhouette, like a question mark, appeared against the darkening hill.

It was a little steep here and Foster puffed and blew.

Fenwick hated him the more for that. So thin and spare, and still he could not keep in condition! They stumbled, keeping below the quarry, on the edge of the running water, now green, now a dirty white-grey, pushing their way along the side of the hill.

Their faces were set now towards Helvellyn. It rounded the cup of hills closing in the base and then sprawling to the right.

'There's the tarn!' Fenwick exclaimed – and

then added, 'The sun's not lasting as long as I had expected. It's growing dark already.'

Foster stumbled and caught Fenwick's arm.

'This twilight makes the hills look strange – like living men. I can scarcely see my way.'

'We're alone here,' Fenwick answered. 'Don't you feel the stillness? The men will have left the quarry now and gone home. There is no one in all this place but ourselves. If you watch you will see a strange green light steal down over the hills. It lasts but for a moment, and then it is dark.

'Ah, here is my tarn. Do you know how I love this place, Foster? It seems to belong especially to me, just as much as all your work and your glory and fame and success seem to belong to you. I have this and you have that. Perhaps in the end we are even after all. Yes…

'But I feel as though that piece of water belonged to me and I to it, and as though we should never be separated – yes… Isn't it black?

'It is one of the deep ones. No one has ever sounded it. Only Helvellyn knows, and one day I fancy that it will take me, too, into its confidence – will whisper its secrets–'

Foster sneezed.

'Very nice. Very beautiful, Fenwick. I like your tarn. Charming. And now let's turn back. That is a difficult walk beneath the quarry. It's chilly, too.'

'Do you see that little jetty there?' Fenwick led Foster by the arm. 'Someone built that out into the water. He had a boat there, I suppose. Come and look down. From the end of the little jetty it looks so deep and the mountains seem to close round.'

Fenwick took Foster's arm and led him to the end of the jetty. Indeed the water looked deep here. Deep and very black. Foster peered down, then he looked up at the hills that did indeed seem to have gathered close around him. He sneezed again.

'I've caught a cold, I am afraid. Let's turn homewards, Fenwick, or we shall never find our way.'

'Home then,' said Fenwick, and his hands closed about the thin, scraggy neck. For the instant the head half turned and two startled, strangely childish eyes stared; then, with a push that was ludicrously simple, the body was impelled forward, there was a sharp cry, a splash, a stir of something white against the swiftly gathering dusk, again and then again, then far-spreading ripples, then silence.

V

The silence extended. Having enwrapped the tarn, it spread as though with finger on lip to the already quiescent hills. Fenwick shared in the silence. He luxuriated in it. He did not move at all. He stood there looking upon the inky water of the tarn, his arms folded, a man lost in intensest thought. But he was not thinking. He was only conscious of a warm luxurious relief, a sensuous feeling that was not thought at all.

Foster was gone – that tiresome, prating, conceited, self-satisfied fool! Gone, never to return. The tarn assured him of that. It stared back into Fenwick's face approvingly as though it said: 'You have done well – a clean and necessary job. We have done it together, you and I. I am proud of you.'

He was proud of himself. At last he had done something definite with his life. Thought, eager, active thought, was beginning now to flood his brain. For all these years, he had hung around in this place doing nothing but cherish grievances, weak, backboneless – now at last there was action. He drew himself up and looked at the hills. He was proud – and he was cold. He was shivering. He turned up the collar of his coat. Yes, there was the faint green light that always lingered in the shadows of the hills for a brief moment before darkness came. It was growing late. He had better return.

Shivering now so that his teeth chattered, he started off down the path, and then was aware that he did not wish to leave the tarn. The tarn was friendly; the only friend he had in all the world. As he stumbled along in the dark, this sense of loneliness grew. He was going home to an empty house. There had been a guest in it last night. Who was it? Why, Foster, of course – Foster with his silly laugh and amiable, mediocre eyes. Well, Foster would not be there now. No, he never would be there again.

And suddenly Fenwick started to run. He did not know why, except that, now that he had left the tarn, he was lonely. He wished that he could have stayed there all night, but because he was cold he could not, and now he was running so that he might be at home with the lights and the familiar furniture – and all the things that he knew to reassure him.

As he ran the shale and stones scattered beneath his feet. They made a tit-tattering noise under him, and someone else seemed to be running too. He stopped, and the other runner also stopped. He breathed in the silence. He was hot now. The perspiration was trickling down his cheeks. He could feel a dribble of it down his back inside his shirt. His knees were pounding. His heart was thumping. And all around him, the hills were so amazingly silent, now like India-rubber clouds that you could push in or pull out as you do those India-rubber faces, grey against the night sky of a crystal purple upon whose surface, like the twinkling eyes of boats at sea, stars were now appearing.

His knees steadied, his heart beat less fiercely, and he began to run again. Suddenly he had turned the corner and was out at the hotel. Its lamps were kindly and reassuring. He walked then quietly along the lake-side path, and had it not been for the certainty that someone was treading behind him he would have been comfortable and at his ease. He stopped once or twice and looked back, and once he stopped and called out 'Who's there?' Only the rustling trees answered.

He had the strangest fancy, but his brain was throbbing so fiercely that he could not think, that it was the tarn that was following him, the tarn slipping, sliding along the road, being with him so that he should not be lonely. He could almost hear the tarn whisper in his ear: 'We did that together, and so I do not wish you to bear all the responsibility yourself. I will stay with you, so that you are not lonely.'

He climbed the road towards home, and there were the lights of his house. He heard the gate click behind him as though it were shutting him in. He went into the sitting-room, lighted and ready. There were the books that Foster had admired.

The old woman who looked after him appeared.

'Will you be having some tea, sir?'

'No, thank you, Annie.'

'Will the other gentleman be wanting any?'

'No; the other gentleman is away for the night.'

'Then there will be only one for supper?'

'Yes, only one for supper.'

He sat in the corner of the sofa and fell instantly into a deep slumber.

VI

He woke when the old woman tapped him on the shoulder and told him that supper was served. The room was dark save for the jumping light of two uncertain candles. Those two red candlesticks – how he hated them up there on the mantelpiece! He had always hated them, and now they seemed to him to have something of the quality of Foster's voice – that thin, reedy, piping tone.

He was expecting at every moment that Foster would enter, and yet he knew that he would not. He continued to turn his head towards the door, but it was so dark there that you could not see. The whole room was dark except just there by the fireplace, where the two candlesticks went whining with their miserable twinkling plaint.

He went into the dining-room and sat down to his meal. But he could not eat anything. It was odd – that place by the table where Foster's chair should be. Odd, naked, and made a man feel lonely.

He got up once from the table and went to the window, opened it and looked out. He listened for something. A trickle as of running water, a stir, through the silence, as though some deep pool were filling to the brim. A rustle in the trees, perhaps. An owl hooted. Sharply, as though someone had spoken to him unexpectedly behind his shoulder, he closed the window and looked back, peering under his dark eyebrows into the room.

Later on he went up to bed.

VII

Had he been sleeping, or had he been lying lazily as one does, half-dozing, half-luxuriously not-thinking? He was wide awake now, utterly awake, and his heart was beating with apprehension. It was as though someone had called him by name. He slept always with his window a little open and the blind up. Tonight the moonlight shadowed in sickly fashion the objects in his room. It was not a flood of light nor yet a sharp splash, silvering a square, a circle, throwing the rest into ebony blackness. The light was dim, a little green, perhaps, like the shadow that comes over the hills just before dark.

He stared at the window, and it seemed to him that something moved there. Within, or rather against the green-grey light, something silver-tinted glistened. Fenwick stared. It had the look, exactly, of slipping water.

Slipping water! He listened, his head up, and it seemed to him that from beyond the window he caught the stir of water, not running, but rather welling up and up, gurgling with satisfaction as it filled and filled.

He sat up higher in bed, and then saw that down the wallpaper beneath the window water was undoubtedly trickling. He could see it lurch to the projecting wood of the sill, pause, and then slip, slither down the incline. The odd thing was that it fell so silently.

Beyond the window there was that odd gurgle, but in the room itself absolute silence. Whence could it come? He saw the line of silver rise and fall as the stream on the window-ledge ebbed and flowed.

He must get up and close the window. He drew his legs above the sheets and blankets and looked down.

He shrieked. The floor was covered with a shining film of water. It was rising. As he looked it had covered half the short stumpy legs of the bed. It rose without a wink, a bubble, a break! Over the sill it poured now in a steady flow, but soundless. Fenwick sat back in the bed, the clothes gathered to his chin, his eyes blinking, the Adam's apple throbbing like a throttle in his throat.

But he must do something, he must stop this. The water was now level with the seats of the chairs, but still was soundless. Could he but reach the door!

He put down his naked foot, then cried again. The water was icy cold. Suddenly, leaning, staring at its dark unbroken sheen, something seemed to push him forward. He fell. His head, his face was under the icy liquid; it seemed adhesive and in the heart of its ice hot like melting wax. He struggled to his feet. The water was breast-high. He screamed again and again. He could see the looking-glass, the row of books, the picture of Durer's 'Horse,' aloof, impervious. He beat at the water and flakes of it seemed to cling to him like scales of fish, clammy to his touch. He struggled, ploughing his way, towards the door.

The water now was at his neck. Then something had caught him by the ankle. Something held him. He struggled, crying, 'Let me go! Let me go! I tell you to let me go! I hate you! I hate you! I will not come down to you! I will not–'

The water covered his mouth. He felt that someone pushed in his eyeballs with bare knuckles. A cold hand reached up and caught his naked thigh.

VIII

In the morning the little maid knocked and, receiving no answer, came in, as was her wont, with his shaving water. What she saw made her scream. She ran for the gardener.

They took the body with its staring, protruding eyes, its tongue sticking out between the clenched teeth, and laid it on the bed.

The only sign of disorder was an overturned water-jug. A small pool of water stained the carpet.

It was a lovely morning. A twig of ivy idly, in the little breeze, tapped the pane.

SANATORIUM UNDER THE SIGN OF THE HOURGLASS

Bruno Schulz

TRANSLATED INTO ENGLISH BY CELINA WIENIEWSKA

Bruno Schulz (1892–1942) was a Polish writer of stories that share some affinity with the work of Alfred Kubin, Franz Kafka, Leonora Carrington, and Michael Cisco, among others. He was shot dead by a Nazi officer when he ventured into an 'Aryan' section of his town during World War II. A great prose stylist, Schulz created a mythical childhood in his fiction that centered on surreal, sometimes grotesque, events. English-language translations include *The Street of Crocodiles* (1963) and *Sanatorium Under the Sign of the Hourglass* (1988). The title story from the latter collection, first published in 1937, is the tale of a strange sojourn by the narrator in which the weird seeps through in quiet but unsettling ways.

The journey was long. The train, which ran only once a week on that forgotten branch line, carried no more than a few passengers. Never before had I seen such archaic coaches; withdrawn from other lines long before, they were spacious as living rooms, dark, and with many recesses. Corridors crossed the empty compartments at various angles; labyrinthine and cold, they exuded an air of strange and frightening neglect. I moved from coach to coach, looking for a comfortable corner. Drafts were everywhere: cold currents of air shooting through the interiors, piercing the whole train from end to end. Here and there a few people sat on the floor, surrounded by their bundles, not daring to occupy the empty seats. Besides, those high, convex oilcloth-covered seats were cold as ice and sticky with age. At the deserted stations no passengers boarded the train. Without a whistle, without a groan, the train would slowly start again, as if lost in meditation.

For a time I had the company of a man in a ragged railwayman's uniform – silent, engrossed in his thoughts. He pressed a handkerchief to his swollen, aching face. Later even he disappeared, having slipped out unobserved at some stop. He left behind him the mark of his body in the straw that lay on the floor, and a shabby black suitcase he had forgotten.

Wading in straw and rubbish, I walked shakily from coach to coach. The open doors of the compartments were swinging in the drafts. There was not a single passenger left on the train. At last, I met a conductor, in the black uniform of that line. He was wrapping a thick scarf around his neck and collecting his things – a lantern, an official logbook.

'We are nearly there, sir,' he said, looking at me with washed-out eyes.

The train was coming slowly to a halt, without puffing, without rattling, as if, together with the last breath of steam, life were slowly escaping from it. We stopped. Everything was empty and still, with no station buildings in sight. The conductor showed me the direction of the Sanatorium. Carrying my suitcase, I started walking along a white narrow road toward the dark trees of a park. With some curiosity, I looked at the landscape. The road along which I was walking led up to the brow of a gentle hill, from which a wide expanse of country could be seen. The day was uniformly gray, extinguished, without contrasts. And perhaps under the influence of that heavy and colorless aura, the great basin of the valley, in which a vast wooded landscape was arranged like theatrical scenery, seemed very dark. The rows of trees, one behind the other, ever grayer and more distant, descended the gentle slopes to the left and right. The whole landscape, somber and grave, seemed almost imperceptibly to float, to shift slightly like a sky full of billowing, stealthily moving clouds. The fluid strips and bands of forest seemed to rustle and grow with rustling like a tide that swells gradually toward the shore. The rising white road wound itself dramatically through the darkness of that woody terrain. I broke a twig from a roadside tree. The leaves were dark, almost black. It was a strangely charged blackness, deep and benevolent, like restful sleep. All the different shades of gray in the landscape derived from that one color. It was the color of a cloudy summer dusk in our part of the country, when the landscape has become saturated with water after a long period of rain and exudes a feeling of self-denial, a resigned and ultimate numbness that does not need the consolation of color.

It was completely dark among the trees of the parkland. I groped my way blindly on a carpet of soft needles. When the trees thinned, the planks of a footbridge resounded under my feet. Beyond it, against the blackness of the trees, loomed the gray walls of the many-windowed hotel that advertised itself as the Sanatorium. The double glass door of the entrance stood open. The little footbridge, with shaky handrails made of birch branches, led straight to it.

In the hallway there was semidarkness and a solemn silence. I moved on tiptoe from door to door, trying to see the numbers on them. Rounding a corner, I at last met a chambermaid. She had run out of a room, as if having torn herself from someone's importuning arms, and was breathless and excited. She could hardly understand what I was saying. I had to repeat it. She was fidgeting helplessly.

Had my telegram reached them? She spread her arms, her eyes moved sideways. She was only awaiting an opportunity to leap back behind the half-opened door, at which she kept squinting.

'I have come a long way. I booked a room here by telegram,' I said with some impatience. 'Whom shall I see about it?'

She did not know. 'Perhaps you could wait in the restaurant,' she babbled. 'Everybody is asleep just now. When the doctor gets up, I shall announce you.'

'They are asleep? But it is daytime, not night.'

'Here everybody is asleep all the time. Didn't you know?' she said, looking at me with interest now. 'Besides, it is never night here,' she added coyly.

She had obviously given up the idea of escape, for she was now picking fussily at the lace of her apron. I left her there and entered the half-lighted restaurant. There were some tables, and a large buffet ran the length of one wall. I was now feeling a little hungry and was pleased to see some pastries and a cake on the buffet.

I placed my suitcase on one of the tables. They were all unoccupied. I clapped my hands. No response. I looked into the next room, which was larger and brighter. That room had a wide window or loggia overlooking the landscape I already knew, which, framed by the window, seemed like a constant reminder of mourning, suggestive of deep sorrow and resignation. On some of the tables stood the remains of recent meals, uncorked bottles, half-empty glasses. Here and there lay the tips, not yet picked up by the waiters. I returned to the buffet and looked at the pastries and cake. They looked most appetizing. I wondered whether I should help myself; I suddenly felt extremely greedy. There was a particular kind of apple flan that made my mouth water. I was about to lift a piece of it with a silver knife when I felt somebody behind me. The chambermaid had entered the room in her soft slippers and was touching my back lightly.

'The doctor will see you now,' she said looking at her fingernails.

She stood facing me and, conscious of the magnetism of her wriggling hips, did not turn away.

She provoked me, increasing and decreasing the distance between our bodies as, having left the restaurant, we passed many numbered doors. The passage became ever darker. In almost complete darkness, she brushed against me fleetingly.

'Here is the doctor's door,' she whispered. 'Please go in.'

Dr. Gotard was standing in the middle of the room to receive me. He was a short, broad-shouldered man with a dark beard.

'We received your telegram yesterday,' he said. 'We sent our carriage to the station, but you must have arrived by another train. Unfortunately, the railway connections are not very good. Are you well?'

'Is my father alive?' I asked, staring anxiously into his calm face.

'Yes, of course,' he answered, calmly meeting my questioning eyes. 'That is, within the limits imposed by the situation,' he added, half closing his eyes. 'You know as well as I that from the point of view of your home, from the perspective of your own country, your father is dead. This cannot be entirely remedied. That death throws a certain shadow on his existence here.'

'But does Father himself know it, does he guess?' I asked him in a whisper.

He shook his head with deep conviction. 'Don't worry,' he said in a low voice. 'None of our patients know it, or can guess. The whole secret of the operation,' he added, ready to demonstrate its mechanism on his fingers, 'is that we have put back the clock. Here we are always late by a certain interval of time of which we cannot define the length. The whole thing is a matter of simple relativity. Here your father's death, the death that has already struck him in your country, has not occurred yet.'

'In that case,' I said, 'my father must be on his deathbed or about to die.'

'You don't understand me,' he said in a tone of tolerant impatience. 'Here we reactivate time past, with all its possibilities, therefore also including the possibility of a recovery.' He looked at me with a smile, stroking his beard. 'But now you probably want to see your father. According to your request, we have reserved for you the other bed in your father's room. I shall take you there.'

When we were out in the dark passage, Dr. Gotard spoke in a whisper. I noticed that he was wearing felt slippers, like the chambermaid. 'We allow our patients to sleep long hours to spare their vitality. Besides, there is nothing better to do.'

At last, we stopped in front of one of the doors, and he put a finger to his lips. 'Enter quietly. Your father is asleep. Settle down to sleep, too. This is the best thing for you to do. Goodbye for now.'

'Goodbye,' I whispered, my heart beating fast.

I pressed the handle, and the door opened, like unresisting lips that part in sleep. I went in. The room was almost empty, gray and bare. Under a small window, my father was lying on an ordinary wooden bed, covered by a pile of bedding, fast asleep. His breathing extracted layers of snoring from the depths of his breast. The whole room seemed to be lined with snores from floor to ceiling, and yet new layers were being added all the time. With deep emotion, I looked at Father's thin, emaciated face, now completely engrossed in the activity of snoring – a remote, trancelike face, which, having left its earthly aspect, was confessing its existence somewhere on a distant shore by solemnly telling its minutes.

There was no second bed in the room. Piercingly cold air blew in through the window. The stove had not been lighted.

They don't seem to care much for patients here, I thought. To expose such a sick man to such drafts! And no one seems to do any cleaning here, either. A thick layer of dust covered the floor and the bedside table, on which stood medicine bottles and a cup of cold coffee. Stacks of pastries in the restaurant, yet they give the patients black coffee instead of anything more nourishing! But perhaps this is a detail compared with the benefits of having the clock put back.

I slowly undressed and climbed onto Father's

bed. He did not wake up, but his snoring, having probably been pitched too high, fell an octave lower, forsaking its high declamatory tone. It became, as it were, more private, for his own use. I tucked Father in under his eiderdown, to protect him as much as possible from the drafts in the room. Soon I fell asleep by his side.

II

The room was in twilight when I woke up. Father was dressed and sitting at the table drinking tea, dunking sugar-coated biscuits in it. He was wearing a black suit of English cloth, which he had had made only the previous summer. His tie was rather loose.

Seeing that I was awake, he said with a pleasant smile on his pale face, 'I am extremely pleased that you have come, Joseph. It was a real surprise! I feel so lonely here. But I suppose one should not complain in my situation. I have been through worse things, and if one were to itemize them all – but never mind. Imagine, on my very first day here they served an excellent fillet of beef with mushrooms. It was a hell of a piece of meat, Joseph. I must warn you most emphatically – beware if they should ever serve you fillet of beef! I can still feel the fire in my stomach. And the diarrhea – I could hardly cope with it. But I must tell you a piece of news,' he continued. 'Don't laugh. I have rented premises for a shop here. Yes, I have. And I congratulate myself for having had that bright idea. I have been bored most terribly, I must say. You cannot imagine the boredom. And so I at least have a pleasant occupation. Don't imagine anything grand. Nothing of the kind. A much more modest place than our old store. It is a booth compared with the previous one. Back home I would be ashamed of such a stall, but here, where we have had to give up so many of our pretensions – don't you agree, Joseph?' He laughed bitterly. 'And so one manages somehow to live.'

The wrong word – I was embarrassed by Father's confusion when he realized that he had used it.

'I see you are sleepy,' he continued after a while. 'Go back to sleep, and then you can visit me in the shop if you want. I am going there now to see how things are. You cannot imagine how difficult it has been to get credit, how mistrustful they are here of old merchants, of merchants with a reputable past. Do you recall the optician's shop in the market square? Well, our shop is right next door to it. There is still no sign over it, but you will find your way, I am sure. You can't miss it.'

'Are you going out without a coat?' I asked anxiously.

'They have forgotten to pack it. Imagine, I could not find it in my trunk. But I don't really need it. That mild climate, that sweet air–'

'Please take my coat, Father,' I insisted. 'You must.'

But Father was already putting on his hat. He waved to me and slipped out of the room.

I did not feel sleepy any more. I felt rested and hungry. With pleasant anticipation I thought of the buffet. I dressed, wondering how many pastries to sample. I decided to start with the apple flan but did not forget the sponge cake with orange peel, which had caught my eye, too. I stood in front of the mirror to fix my tie, but the surface was like bottle glass: it secreted my reflection somewhere in its depth, and only an opaque blur was visible. I tried in vain to adjust the distance – approaching the mirror, then retreating from it – but no reflection would emerge from the silvery, fluid mist. I must ask for another looking glass, I thought, and left the room.

The corridor was completely dark. In one corner a tiny gas lamp flickered with a bluish flame, intensifying the impression of solemn silence. In that labyrinth of rooms, archways, and niches, I had difficulty remembering which door led to the restaurant.

I'll go out, I thought with sudden decision. I'll eat in the town. There must be a good café somewhere.

Beyond the gate, I plunged into the heavy, damp, sweet air of that peculiar climate. The grayness of the aura had become somewhat deeper: now it seemed to me that I was seeing daylight through mourning crêpe.

I feasted my eyes on the velvety, succulent blackness of the darkest spots, on passages of dull grays and ashen, muted tones – that nocturne of a landscape. Waves of air fluttered softly around my face. They smelled of the sickly sweetness of stale rainwater.

And again that perpetual rustle of black forests – dull chords disturbing space beyond the limits of audibility! I was in the backyard of the Sanatorium. I turned to look at the rear of the main building, which was shaped like a horseshoe around a courtyard. All the windows were shuttered in black. The Sanatorium was in deep sleep. I went out by a gate in an iron fence. Nearby stood a dog kennel of extraordinary size, empty. Again I was engulfed and embraced by the black trees. Then it became somewhat lighter, and I saw outlines of houses between the trees. A few more steps and I found myself in a large town square.

What a strange, misleading resemblance it bore to the central square of our native city! How similar, in fact, are all the market squares in the world! Almost identical houses and shops!

The sidewalks were nearly empty. The mournful semidarkness of an undefined time descended from a sky of an indeterminable grayness. I could easily read all the shop signs and posters, yet it would not have surprised me to learn that it was the middle of the night. Only some of the shops were open. Others, their iron shutters pulled halfway down, were being hurriedly closed. A heady, rich, and inebriating air seemed to obscure some parts of the view, to wash away like a wet sponge some of the houses, a street lamp, a section of signboard. At times it was difficult to keep one's eyes open, overcome as one was by a strange indolence or sleepiness. I began to look for the optician's shop that my father had mentioned. He had spoken of it as of something I knew, and he seemed to assume that I was familiar with local conditions. Didn't he remember that I had just come here for the first time? No doubt his mind was confused. Yet what could one expect of Father, who was only half real, who lived a relative and conditional life, circumscribed by so many limitations! I cannot deny that much goodwill was needed to believe in his kind of existence. What he experienced was a pitiful substitute for life, depending on the indulgence of others, on a *consensus omnium* from which he drew his faint strength. It was clear that only by the solidarity of forbearance, by a communal averting of eyes from the obvious and shocking shortcomings of his condition, could this pitiful semblance of life maintain itself, for however short a moment, within the tissue of reality. The slightest doubt could undermine it, the faintest breeze of skepticism destroy it. Could Dr. Gotard's Sanatorium provide for Father this hothouse atmosphere of friendly indulgence and guard him from the cold winds of sober analysis? It was astonishing that in this insecure and questionable state of affairs, Father was capable of behaving so admirably.

I was glad when I saw a shop window full of cakes and pastries. My appetite revived. I opened the glass door, with the inscription 'Ices' on it and entered the dark interior. It smelled of coffee and vanilla. From the depths of the shop a girl appeared, her face misted over by dusk, and took my order. At last, after waiting so long, I could eat my fill of excellent doughnuts, which I dipped in my coffee. Surrounded by the dancing arabesques of dusk, I devoured pastries one after another, feeling darkness creep under my eyelids and stealthily fill me with its warm pulsations, its thousand delicate touches. In the end, only the window shone, like a gray rectangle, in the otherwise complete darkness. I knocked with my spoon on the tabletop, but in vain; no one appeared to take money for my refreshment. I left a silver coin on the table and walked out into the street.

In the bookshop next door, the light was still on. The shop assistants were busy sorting books. I asked for my father's shop. 'It is next door to ours,' one of them explained. A helpful boy even went with me to the door, to show me the way.

Father's shop had a glass pane in the door; the display window was not ready and was covered with a gray paper. On entering, I was astonished to see that the shop was full of customers. My father was standing behind the counter and adding a long row of figures on an invoice, repeatedly licking his pencil. The man for whom the invoice was being prepared was leaning over the counter and moving his index finger down the column of figures, counting softly. The rest of the customers looked on in silence.

My father gave me a look from over his spectacles and, marking his place on the invoice, said, 'There is a letter for you. It is on the desk among all the papers.' He went back to his sums. Meanwhile, the shop assistants were taking pieces of cloth bought by the customers, wrapping them in paper, and tying them with string. The shelves were only half filled with cloth; some of them were still empty.

'Why don't you sit down, Father?' I asked softly, going behind the counter. 'You don't take enough care of yourself, although you are very sick.'

Father lifted his hand, as if wanting to reject my pleas, and did not stop counting. He looked very pale. It was obvious that only the excitement of his feverish activity sustained him and postponed the moment of complete collapse.

I went up to the desk and found not a letter but a parcel. A few days earlier, I had written to a bookshop about a pornographic book, and here it was already. They had found my address, or rather, Father's address, although he had only just opened a new shop here that had neither a name nor a signboard! What amazing efficiency in collecting information, what astounding delivery methods! And what incredible speed!

'You may read it in the office at the back,' said my father, looking at me with displeasure. 'As you can see, there is no room here.'

The room behind the shop was still empty. Through a glass door some light filtered in from the shop. On the walls the shop assistants' overcoats hung from hooks. I opened the parcel and, by the faint light from the door, read the enclosed letter.

The letter informed me that the book I had ordered was unfortunately out of stock. They would look out for it, although the result of the search was uncertain; meanwhile, they were sending me, without obligation, a certain object, which, they were sure, would interest me. There followed a complicated description of a folding telescope with great refractive power and many other virtues. Interested, I took the instrument out of the wrapping. It was made of black oilcloth or canvas and was folded into the shape of a flattened accordion. I have always had a weakness for telescopes. I began to unfold the pleats of the instrument. Stiffened with thin rods, it rose under my fingers until it almost filled the room; a kind of enormous bellows, a labyrinth of black chambers, a long complex of camera obscuras, one within another. It looked, too, like a long-bodied model automobile made of patent leather, a theatrical prop, its lightweight paper and stiff canvas imitating the bulkiness of reality. I looked into the black funnel of the instrument and saw deep inside the vague outline of the back of the Sanatorium. Intrigued, I put my head deeper into the rear chamber of the apparatus. I could now see in my field of vision the maid walking along the darkened corridor of the Sanatorium, carrying a tray. She turned round and smiled. 'Can she see me?' I asked myself. An overwhelming drowsiness misted my eyes. I was sitting, as it were, in the rear chamber of the telescope as if in the back seat of a limousine. A light touch on a lever and the apparatus began to rustle like a paper butterfly; I felt that it was moving and turning toward the door.

Like a large black caterpillar, the telescope crept into the lighted shop – an enormous paper arthropod with two imitation headlights on the front. The customers clustered together, retreating before this blind paper dragon; the shop assistants flung open the door to the street, and I rode slowly in my paper car amid rows of onlookers, who followed with scandalized eyes my truly outrageous exit.

III

That is how one lives in this town, and how time goes by. The greater part of the day is spent in sleeping – and not only in bed. No one is very particular when it comes to sleep. At any place, at any time, one is ready for a quiet snooze: with one's head propped on a restaurant table, in a horse-drawn cab, even standing up when, out for a walk, one looks into the hall of an apartment house for a moment and succumbs to the irrepressible need for sleep.

Waking up, still dazed and shaky, one continues the interrupted conversation or the wearisome walk, carries on complicated discussions without beginning or end. In this way, whole chunks of time are casually lost somewhere; control over the continuity of the day is loosened until it finally ceases to matter; and the framework of uninterrupted chronology that one has been disciplined to notice every day is given up without regret. The compulsive readiness to account for the passage of time, the scrupulous penny-wise habit of reporting on the used-up hours – the pride and ambition of our economic system – are forsaken. Those cardinal virtues, which in the past one never dared to question, have long ago been abandoned.

A few examples will illustrate this state of affairs. At a certain time of day or night – a hardly perceptible difference in the color of the sky allows one to tell which it is – I wake up in twilight at the railings of the footbridge leading to the Sanatorium. Overpowered by sleep, I must have wandered unconsciously for a long time all over the town before, mortally tired, I dragged myself to the bridge. I cannot say whether Dr. Gotard accompanied me on that walk, but now he stands in front of me, finishing a long tirade and drawing conclusions. Carried away by his own eloquence, he slips his hand under my arm and leads me somewhere. I walk on, with him, and even before we have crossed the bridge, I am asleep again. Through my closed eyelids I can vaguely see the Doctor's expressive gestures, the smile under his black beard, and I try to understand, without success, his ultimate point – which he must have triumphantly revealed, for he now stands with arms outstretched. We have been walking side by side for I don't know how long, engrossed in a conversation at cross purposes, when all of a sudden I wake up completely. Dr. Gotard has gone; it is quite dark, but only because my eyes are shut. When I open them, I find that I am in our room and don't know how I got there.

An even more dramatic example: At lunchtime, I enter a restaurant in town, which is full and very noisy. Whom do I meet in the middle of it, at a table sagging under the weight of dishes? My father. All eyes are on him, while he, animated, almost ecstatic with pleasure, his diamond tiepin shining, turns in all directions, making fulsome conversation with everybody at once. With false bravado, which I observe with the greatest misgivings, he keeps ordering new dishes, which are then stacked on the table. He gathers them around him with glee, although he has not even finished the first course. Smacking his lips, chewing and speaking at the same time, he mimes his great satisfaction with this feast and follows with adoring eyes Adam, the waiter, to whom, with an ingratiating smile, he gives more orders. And when the waiter, waving his napkin, rushes to get them, Father turns to the company and calls them to witness the irresistible charm of Adam, the Ganymede.

'A boy in a million,' Father exclaims with a happy smile, half closing his eyes, 'a ministering angel! You must agree, gentlemen, that he is a charmer!'

I leave in disgust, unnoticed by Father. Had he been put there by the management of the restaurant in order to amuse the guests, he could not behave in a more ostentatious way. My head heavy with drowsiness, I stumble through the streets toward the Sanatorium. On a pillar box I rest my head and take a short siesta. At last, groping in darkness, I find the gate and go in. Our room is dark. I press the light switch, but there is no current. A cold draft comes from the window. The bed creaks in the darkness.

My father lifts his head from the pillows and says, 'Ah, Joseph, Joseph! I have been lying here for two days without any attention. The bells are out of order, no one has been to see me, and my own son has left me, a very sick man, to run after girls in the town. Look how my heart is thumping!'

How do I reconcile all this? Has Father been sitting in the restaurant, driven there by an unhealthy greed, or has he been lying in bed feeling very ill? Are there two fathers? Nothing of the kind. The problem is the quick decomposition of time no longer watched with incessant vigilance.

We all know that time, this undisciplined element, holds itself within bounds but precariously, thanks to unceasing cultivation, meticulous care, and a continuous regulation and correction of its excesses. Free of this vigilance, it immediately begins to do tricks, run wild, play irresponsible practical jokes, and indulge in crazy clowning. The incongruity of our private times becomes evident.

My father's time and my own no longer coincide.

Incidentally, the accusation that my father has made is completely groundless. I have not been chasing after girls. Swaying like a drunkard from one bout of sleep to another, I can hardly pay attention, even in my more wakeful moments, to the local ladies.

Moreover, the chronic darkness in the streets does not allow me to see faces clearly. What I have been able to observe – being a young man who still has a certain amount of interest in such things – is the peculiar way in which these girls walk.

Heedless of obstacles, obeying only some inner rhythm, each one walks in an inexorably straight line, as if along a thread that she seems to unwind from an invisible skein. This linear trot is full of mincing accuracy and measured grace. Each girl seems to carry inside her an individual rule, wound tight like a spring.

Walking thus, straight ahead, with concentration and dignity, they seem to have only one worry – not to break the rule, not to make any mistake, not to stray either to the right or to the left. And then it becomes clear to me that what they so conscientiously carry within themselves is an *idée fixe* of their own excellence, which the strength of their conviction almost transforms into reality. It is risked anticipation, without any guarantee; an untouchable dogma, held high, impervious to doubt.

What imperfections and blemishes, what *retroussé* or flat noses, what freckles or spots are smuggled under the bold flag of that fiction! There is no ugliness or vulgarity that cannot be lifted up to a fictional heaven of perfection by the flight of such a belief.

Sanctified by it, bodies become distinctly more beautiful, and feet, already shapely and graceful in their spotless footwear, speak eloquently, their fluid, shiny pacing monologue explaining the greatness of an idea that the closed faces are too proud to express. The girls keep their hands in the pockets of their short, tight jackets. In the cafés and in the theater, they cross their legs, uncovered to the knee, and hold them in provocative silence.

So much for one of the peculiarities of this town. I have already mentioned the black vegetation of the region. A certain kind of black fern deserves special mention: enormous bunches of it in vases are in the windows of every apartment here, and every public place. The fern is almost the symbol of mourning, the town's funereal crest.

IV

Conditions in the Sanatorium are becoming daily more insufferable. It has to be admitted that we have fallen into a trap. Since my arrival, when a semblance of hospitable care was displayed for the newcomer, the management of the Sanatorium has not taken the trouble to give us even the illusion of any kind of professional supervision. We are simply left to our own devices. Nobody caters to our needs. I have noticed, for instance, that the wires of the electric bells have been cut just behind the doors and lead nowhere. There is no service. The corridors are dark and silent by day and by night. I have a strong suspicion that we are the only guests in this Sanatorium and that the mysterious or discreet looks with which the chambermaid closes the doors of the rooms on entering or leaving are simply mystification.

I sometimes feel a strong desire to open each door wide and leave it ajar, so that the miserable intrigue in which we have got ourselves involved can be exposed.

And yet I am not quite convinced that my suspicions are justified. Sometimes, late at night, I meet Dr. Gotard in a corridor, hurrying somewhere in a white coverall, with an enema bottle in his hand, preceded by the chambermaid. It would be difficult to stop him then and demand an explanation.

Were it not for the restaurant and pastry shop in town, one might starve to death. So far, I have not succeeded in getting a second bed for our room. There is no question of the sheets being changed.

One has to admit that the general neglect of civilized habits has affected both of us, too. To get into bed dressed and with shoes on was once, for me – a civilized person – unthinkable. Yet now, when I return home late, sleep-drunk, the room is in semidarkness and the curtains at the window billow in a cold breeze. Half dazed, I tumble onto the bed and bury myself in the eiderdown. Thus

I sleep for irregular stretches of time, for days or weeks, wandering through empty landscapes of sleep, always on the way, always on the steep roads of respiration, sometimes sliding lightly and gracefully from gentle slopes, then climbing laboriously up the cliffs of snoring. At their summit I embrace the horizons of the rocky and empty desert of sleep. At some point, somewhere on the sharp turn of a snore, I wake up half conscious and feel the body of my father at the foot of the bed. He lies there curled up, small as a kitten. I fall asleep again, with my mouth open, and the vast panorama of mountain landscape glides past me majestically.

In the shop, my father displays an energetic activity, transacting business and straining all his capacities to attract customers. His cheeks are flushed with animation, his eyes shine. In the Sanatorium he is very sick, as sick as during his last weeks at home. It is obvious that the end must be imminent. In a weak voice he addresses me: 'You should look into the store more often, Joseph. The shop assistants are robbing us. You can see that I am no longer equal to the task. I have been lying here sick for weeks, and the shop is being neglected, left to run itself. Was there any mail from home?'

I begin to regret this whole undertaking. Perhaps we were misled by skillful advertising when we decided to send Father here. Time put back – it sounded good, but what does it come to in reality? Does anyone here get time at its full value, a true time, time cut off from a fresh bolt of cloth, smelling of newness and dye? Quite the contrary. It is used-up time, worn out by other people, a shabby time full of holes, like a sieve.

No wonder. It is time, as it were, regurgitated – if I may be forgiven this expression: secondhand time. God help us all!

And then there is the matter of the highly improper manipulation of time. The shameful tricks, the penetration of time's mechanism from behind, the hazardous fingering of its wicked secrets! Sometimes one feels like banging the table and exclaiming, 'Enough of this! Keep off time, time is untouchable, one must not provoke it! Isn't it enough for you to have space? Space is for human beings, you can swing about in space, turn somersaults, fall down, jump from star to star. But for goodness' sake, don't tamper with time!'

On the other hand, can I be expected to give notice to Dr. Gotard? However miserable Father's existence, I am able to see him, to be with him, to talk to him. In fact, I should be infinitely grateful to Dr. Gotard.

Several times, I have wanted to speak openly to Dr. Gotard, but he is elusive. He has just gone to the restaurant, says the chambermaid. I turn to go there, when she runs after me to say that she was wrong, that Dr. Gotard is in the operating theater. Hurrying upstairs, I wonder what kind of operations can be performed here; I enter the anteroom and am told to wait. Dr. Gotard will be with me in a moment, he has just finished the operation, he is washing his hands. I can almost visualize him: short, taking long steps, his coat open, hurrying through a succession of hospital wards. After a while, what am I told? Dr. Gotard had not been there at all, no operation has been performed there for many years. Dr. Gotard is asleep in his room, his black beard sticking up into the air. The room fills with his snores as if with clouds that lift him in his bed, ever higher and higher – a great pathetic ascension on waves of snores and voluminous bedding.

Even stranger things happen here – things that I try to conceal from myself and that are quite fantastic in their absurdity. Whenever I leave our room, I have the impression that someone who has been standing behind the door moves quickly away and turns a corner. Or somebody seems to be walking in front of me, not looking back. It is not a nurse. I know who it is! 'Mother!' I exclaim, in a voice trembling with excitement, and my mother turns her face to me and looks at me for a moment with a pleading smile. Where am I? What is happening here? What maze have I become entangled in?

V

I don't know why – it may be the time of year – but the days are growing more severe in color, darker and blacker. It seems as if one were looking at the world through black glasses.

The landscape is now like the bottom of an

enormous aquarium full of watery ink. Trees, people, and houses merge, swaying like underwater plants against the background of the inky deep.

Packs of black dogs are often seen in the vicinity of the Sanatorium. Of all shapes and sizes, they run at dusk along the roads and paths, engrossed in their own affairs, silent, tense, and alert.

They run in twos and threes, with outstretched necks, their ears pricked up, whining softly in plaintive tones that escape from their throats as if against their will – signals of the highest nervousness. Absorbed in running, hurrying, always on their way somewhere, always pursuing some mysterious goal, they hardly notice the passersby. Occasionally one shoots out a glance while running past, and then the black and intelligent eyes are full of a rage contained only by haste. At times the dogs even rush at one's feet, succumbing to their anger, with heads held low and ominous snarls, but soon think better of it and turn away.

Nothing is to be done about this plague of dogs, but why does the management of the Sanatorium keep an enormous Alsatian on a chain – a terror of a beast, a werewolf of truly demoniacal ferocity? I shiver with fear whenever I pass his kennel, by which he stands immobile on his short chain, a halo of matted hair bristling around his head, bewhiskered and bearded, his powerful jaws displaying the whole apparatus of his long teeth. He does not bark, but his wild face contorts at the sight of a human being. He stiffens with an expression of boundless fury and, slowly raising his horrible muzzle, breaks into a low, fervent, convulsive howl that comes from the very depths of his hatred – a howl of despair and lament at his temporary impotence.

My father walks past the beast with indifference whenever we go out together. As for myself, I am deeply shaken when confronted by the dog's impotent hatred. I am now some two heads taller than Father who, small and thin, trots at my side with the mincing gait of a very old man.

Approaching the city square one day, we noticed an extraordinary commotion. Crowds of people filled the streets. We heard the incredible news that an enemy army had entered the town.

In consternation, people exchanged alarmist and contradictory news that was hard to credit. A war not preceded by diplomatic activity? A war amid blissful peace? A war against whom and for what reason? We were told that the enemy incursion gave heart to a group of discontented townspeople, who have come out in the open, armed, to terrorize the peaceful inhabitants. We noticed, in fact, a group of these activists, in black civilian clothing with white straps across their breasts, advancing in silence, their guns at the ready. The crowd fell back onto the pavements, as they marched by, flashing from under their hats ironical dark looks, in which there was a touch of superiority, a glimmer of malicious and perverse enjoyment, as if they could hardly stop themselves from bursting into laughter. Some of them were recognized by the crowd, but the exclamations of relief were at once stilled by the sight of rifle barrels. They passed by, not challenging anybody. All the streets filled at once with a frightened, grimly silent crowd. A dull hubbub floated over the city. We seemed to hear a distant rumble of artillery and the rattle of gun carriages.

'I must get to the shop,' said my father, pale but determined. 'You need not come with me,' he added. 'You will be in my way. Go back to the Sanatorium.'

The pull of cowardice made me obey him. I saw my father trying to squeeze himself through the compact wall of bodies in the crowd and lost sight of him.

I broke into a run along side streets and alleys, and hurried toward the upper part of town. I realized that by going uphill I might be able to avoid the center, now packed solid by people.

Farther up, the crowd thinned and at last completely disappeared. I walked quietly along empty streets to the municipal park. Street lamps were lighted there and burned with a dark bluish flame, the color of asphodels, the flowers of mourning. Each light was surrounded by a swarm of dancing June bugs, heavy as bullets, carried on their slanting flight by vibrating wings. The fallen were struggling clumsily in the sand, their backs arched, hunched beneath the hard shields under which they were trying to fold the delicate membranes of their wings. On grassy plots and paths people were walking along, engrossed in carefree conversation.

The trees at the far end of the park drooped into the courtyards of houses that were built on lower ground on the other side of the park wall. I strolled along that wall on the park side, where it reached only to my breast; on the other side, it fell in escarpments to the level of courtyards. In one place, a ramp of firm soil rose from the courtyards to the top of the wall. There I crossed the wall without difficulty and squeezed between houses into a street. As I had expected, I found myself almost facing the Sanatorium; its back was outlined clearly in a black frame of trees. As usual, I opened the gate in the iron fence and saw from a distance the watchdog at his post. As usual, I shivered with aversion and wished to pass by him as quickly as possible, so as not to have to listen to his howl of hatred; but I suddenly noticed that he was unchained and was circling toward the courtyard, barking hollowly and trying to cut me off.

Rigid with fright, I retreated and, instinctively looking for shelter, crept into a small arbor, sure that all my efforts to evade the beast would be in vain. The shaggy animal was leaping toward me, his muzzle already pushing into the arbor. I was trapped. Horror-struck, I then saw that the dog was on a long chain that he had unwound to its full length, and that the inside of the arbor was beyond the reach of his claws. Sick with fear, I was too weak to feel any relief. Reeling, almost fainting, I raised my eyes. I had never before seen the beast from so near, and only now did I see him clearly. How great is the power of prejudice! How powerful the hold of fear! How blind had I been! It was not a dog, it was a man. A chained man, whom, by a simplifying metaphoric wholesale error, I had taken for a dog. I don't want to be misunderstood. He was a dog, certainly, but a dog in human shape. The quality of a dog is an inner quality and can be manifested as well in human as in animal shape. He who was standing in front of me in the entrance to the arbor, his jaws wide open, his teeth bared in a terrible growl, was a man of middle height, with a black beard. His face was yellow, bony; his eyes were black, evil, and unhappy. Judging by his black suit and the shape of his beard, one might take him for an intellectual or a scholar. He might have been Dr. Gotard's unsuccessful elder brother. But that first impression was false. The large hands stained with glue, the two brutal and cynical furrows running down from his nostrils and disappearing into his beard, the vulgar horizontal wrinkles on the low forehead quickly dispelled that first impression. He looked more like a bookbinder, a tub-thumper, a vocal party member – a violent man, given to dark, sudden passions. And it was this – the passionate depth, the convulsive bristling of all his fibers, the mad fury of his barking when the end of a stick was pointed at him – that made him a hundred per cent dog.

If I tried to escape through the back of the arbor, I thought, I would completely elude his reach and could walk along a side path to the gate of the Sanatorium. I was about to put my leg over the railing when I suddenly stopped. I felt it would be too cruel simply to go away and leave the dog behind, possessed by his helpless and boundless fury. I could imagine his terrible disappointment, his inexpressible pain as I escaped from his trap, free once and for all from his clutches. I decided to stay.

I stepped forward and said quietly, 'Please calm down. I shall unchain you.'

His face, distorted by spasms of growling, became whole again, smooth and almost human. I went up to him without fear and unfastened the buckle of his collar. We walked side by side. The bookbinder was wearing a decent black suit but had bare feet. I tried to talk to him, but a confused babble was all I heard in reply. Only his eyes, black and eloquent, expressed a wild spurt of gratitude, of submission, which filled me with awe. Whenever he stumbled on a stone or a clod of earth, the shock made his face shrivel and contract with fear, and that expression was followed by one of rage. I would then bring him to order with a harsh comradely rebuke. I even patted him on the back. An astonished, suspicious, unbelieving smile tried to form on his face. Ah, how hard to bear was this terrible friendship! How frightening was this uncanny sympathy! How could I get rid of this man striding along with me, his eyes expressing his total submission, following the slightest changes in my face? I could not show impatience.

I pulled out my wallet and said in a matter-of-fact tone, 'You probably need some money. I will lend you some with pleasure.' But at the sight of my wallet his look became so unexpectedly wild that I put it away again as quickly as I could. For quite some time afterward, he could not calm himself and his features continued to be distorted by more spasms of growling. No, I could not stand this any longer. Anything, but not this. Matters were already confused and entangled enough.

I then noticed the glare of fire over the town: my father was somewhere in the thick of a revolution or in a burning shop. Dr. Gotard was unavailable. And to cap it all, my mother had appeared, incognito, on that mysterious errand! These were the elements of some great and obscure intrigue, which was hemming me in. I must escape, I thought, escape at any cost. Anywhere. I must drop this horrible friendship with a bookbinder who smells of dog and who is watching me all the time. We were now standing in front of the Sanatorium.

'Come to my room, please,' I said with a polite gesture. Civilized gestures fascinated him, soothed his wildness. I let him enter my room first and gave him a chair.

'I'll go to the restaurant and get some brandy,' I said.

He got up, terrified, and wanted to follow me.

I calmed his fears with gentle firmness. 'You will sit here and wait for me,' I said in a deep, sonorous voice, which concealed fear. He sat down again with a tentative smile.

I went out and walked slowly along the corridor, then downstairs and across the hall leading to the entrance door; I passed the gate, strode across the courtyard, banged the iron gate shut, and only then began to run, breathlessly, my heart thumping, my temples throbbing, along the dark avenue leading to the railway station.

Images raced through my head, each more horrible than the next. The impatience of the monster dog; his fear and despair when he realized that I had cheated him; another attack of fury, another bout of rage breaking out with unchecked force. My father's return to the Sanatorium, his unsuspecting knock at the door, and his confrontation with the terrible beast.

Luckily, in fact, Father was no longer alive; he could not really be reached, I thought with relief, and saw in front of me the black row of railway carriages ready to depart.

I got into one of them, and the train, as if it had been waiting for me, slowly started to move, without a whistle.

Through the window the great valley, filled with dark rustling forests – against which the walls of the Sanatorium seemed white – moved and turned slowly once again. Farewell, Father. Farewell, town that I shall never see again.

Since then, I have travelled continuously. I have made my home in that train, and everybody puts up with me as I wander from coach to coach. The compartments, enormous as rooms, are full of rubbish and straw, and cold drafts pierce them on gray, colorless days.

My suit became torn and ragged. I have been given the shabby uniform of a railwayman. My face is bandaged with a dirty rag, because one of my cheeks is swollen. I sit on the straw, dozing, and when hungry, I stand in the corridor outside a second-class compartment and sing. People throw small coins into my hat: a black railwayman's hat, its visor half torn away.

FAR BELOW

Robert Barbour Johnson

Robert Barbour Johnson was an American writer who wrote six stories for *Weird Tales*, of which 'Far Below' (1939) became one of the most popular ever published in the magazine. Not much is known about Johnson, except that he called himself 'the Outsider' and was listed as one of the younger writers for *Weird Tales*. 'Far Below' name-checks H. P. Lovecraft and reflects the influence of the story 'Pickman's Model.' Although some aspects of the story haven't dated well, it is still powerful and strange, conveying some of the same sense of awe and horror as 'The Night Wire' by H. F. Arnold.

With a roar and a howl the thing was upon us, out of total darkness. Involuntarily I drew back as its headlights passed and every object in the little room rattled from the reverberations. Then the power-car was by, and there was only the 'klackety-klack, klackety-klack' of wheels and lighted windows flickering past like bits of film on a badly connected projection machine. I caught glimpses of occupants briefly; bleak-eyed men sitting miserably on hard benches; a pair of lovers oblivious to the hour's lateness and all else; an old bearded Jew in a black cap, sound asleep; two Harlem Negroes grinning; conductors here and there, too, their uniforms black splotches against the blaze of car-lights. Then red tail-lamps shot by and the roar died to an earthquake rumble far down the track.

'The Three-One Express,' my friend said quietly, from the Battery. 'On time to the minute, too. It's the last, you know – until nearly dawn.'

He spoke briefly into a telephone, saying words I could not catch, for the racket of the train was still in my ears. I occupied the interval by staring about me. There was so much to be seen in the little room, such a strange diversity of apparatus – switches and coils and curious mechanisms, charts and graphs and piles of documents; and, dominating all, that great black board on which a luminous worm seemed to crawl, inching along past the dotted lines labeled '49th Street,' '52nd Street,' '58th Street,' '60th…'

'A new wrinkle, that!' my friend said. He had put down his phone and was watching the board with me. 'Lord! I don't dare think what it cost to install! It's not just a chart, you know. It actually records! Invisible lights – the sort of things that open speakeasy doors and rich men's garages. Pairs of them spaced approximately every twenty-five yards along five miles of subway tunnel! Figure that out on paper, and the total you'll get will seem hardly believable. And yet the city passed the appropriation for them without a murmur. It was one of the last things Mayor Walker put up before his resignation. "Gentlemen," he said to the Finance Board, "it doesn't matter what you think about *me*! But this measure *must* go through!" And it did. There wasn't a murmur of protest, though the city was almost broke at the time… What's the matter, man? You're looking queer.'

'I'm *feeling* queer!' I said. 'Do you mean to say the thing goes that far back? To Walker's time?'

He laughed. It was a strange laugh, that died eerily amid the dying echoes of the train far down the tunnel.

'Good Lord!' he gasped. 'To his time – man, Walker hadn't served his first term as mayor when this thing started! It goes back to World War days – and even before that. The wreck of the train, I recall, passed as a German spy plot to keep us from going in with the Allies. The newspapers howled bloody murder about alleged "confessions" and evidence they claimed they had. We let 'em howl, of course. Why not? America was as good as in the war anyhow, by then. And if we'd told the people of New York City what really wrecked that subway train – well, the horrors of Chateau-Thierry and Verdun and all the rest of them put together wouldn't have equaled the shambles that rioting mobs would have made of this place! People just couldn't stand the thought of it, you know. They'd go mad if they knew what was down here – far below.'

The silence was worse than the roar had been, I thought – the strange echoing, somehow pregnant silence of empty vastness. Only the 'drip, drip' of water from some subterranean leak broke it – that and the faint crackling noise the indicator made as its phosphorescent crawling hinted at '68th Street,' '72nd,' '78th…'

'Yes,' my friend said slowly. 'They'd go mad if they knew. And sometimes I wonder why we don't go mad down here – we who *do* know, and have to face the horror down here night after night and year after year – I think it's only because we don't really face it that we get by, you know, because we never quite define the thing in our own minds, objectively. We just sort of let things hang in the air, you might say. We don't speak of what we're guarding against, by name. We just call it "Them," or "one of Them," you know – take Them for granted just as we took the enemy overseas, as something that's just down here and has to be fought. I think if we ever really did let our minds get to brooding on what they are, it'd be all over for us! Human flesh and blood coldn't stand it, you know – couldn't stand it!'

He brooded, staring out into the tunnel's darkness. The indicator crackled faintly on the wall. '92nd Street,' '98th,' '101st…'

'Beyond 120th Street things are pretty safe,' I heard my friend's voice as I watched. 'When the train reaches that point you'll see a green light flash "all clear," though that doesn't mean absolute safety, you understand. It's just what we've established as the farthest reach of Their activities. They may extend them at any time, although so far They haven't done so. There seems to be something circumscribed about their minds, you know. They're creatures of habit. That must be what it is that's kept Them in this one little stretch of tunnel, with all the vast interlocking network of New York's subway system to rove in if they chose. I can't think of any other explanation, unless you want to get into the supernatural and say it's because they're "bound" to this particular locality, by some sort of mystic laws; perhaps because it's lower than the other tunnels – chiseled far down into the basic bedrock of Manhattan, and so near to the East River you can almost hear the water lapping on quiet nights. Or maybe it's just the awful dankness of the tunnel here, the fungoid moisture and miasmic darkness that suits Them. At all events they don't come up anywhere else except along this stretch. And we've got the lights, and the patrol cars, and three way-stations like this one, with ten men on constant duty from dark till dawn – oh yes, my boy! It's quite a little army I command down here in the night watches – an army of the Unburied Dead, you might say; or an army of the Eternally Damned.

'I've actually had one of my men go mad, you know! Two others had to be placed in sanitariums for a while, but they got over it and are serving here still. But this fellow – well, we had to machine-gun him down like a dog finally, or he'd have got one of us! That was before we got the "dark lights" placed, you see, and he was able to hide out in the tunnel for days without our being able to find him. We'd hear him howl sometimes as we patrolled, and see his eyes shining just as Their eyes do in the darkness; so we knew that he was quite "gone." So when we finally ran him down we killed him – just like that. No bones made about it. "Put-put-put!" and that was the end. We buried him down in the tunnel, too, and now the trains run over him as he lies. Oh, there was nothing irregular about the business! We filled out full Departmental reports, and got the consent of his relatives, and so on; only we just couldn't take the poor fellow above-ground and run risks of people seeing him before interment. You see, there were certain… alterations. I don't want to dwell on it, but his face – well, the change was just beginning, of course, but it was quite unmistakable; quite dehumanizing, you know. There would have been some excitement up there, I'm afraid, just at sight of that face! And there were other details – things I only found out when I dissected his body. But I think I'd rather not go into them either, old boy, if you don't mind…

'The whole point is, we have to be rather careful down here, all of us in the "Special Detail". That's why we have such unusual working conditions. We wear police uniforms, of course, but we aren't subject to ordinary police discipline. Lord! What would an above-ground "cop" make of having every other night off and every day all to himself, and with a salary that – well, a corporal down here gets as much as does an Inspector up there!

'But, at that, I think we earn our pay…

'I know *I* do. Of course I can't tell you what my salary is – they made me promise never to disclose it when they hired me from the Natural History Museum back in – well, I don't like to think about how long ago that was! I was Professor Gordon Craig in those days, you know, instead of Inspector Craig of N.Y.P.D. And I'd just returned from Carl Akeley's first African expedition after gorillas. That was why they brought the Thing to me for examination, you see, after that first big wreck in the subway that'd only been opened less than a year. They'd found it pinned down in the wreckage, screaming in agony from their lights on its dead-white eyeballs. Indeed, it seemed to have died from the lights as much as from anything else. Organically it was sound enough, save for a broken bone or two.

Well, they brought it to me, because I was supposed to be the museum's leading authority on apes. And I examined it – believe me, I examined it, old boy! I went for six days and nights without sleep or even rest, analyzing that dead corpse down to its last rag and bone and hank of hair!

'No scientist on this earth ever had a chance like that before, and I was making the best of it. I found out all there was to be found before I collapsed over my laboratory table and had to be taken to the hospital.

'Of course long before that I had told them the thing wasn't an ape. There was vaguely anthropoid structure, all right; and the blood corpuscles were almost human – quite shockingly so. But the head and the spade-like appendages and the muscular development were quite unlike any beast or man on this earth. Indeed, the thing had never been on this earth! There was no doubt of that! It would have died above ground in half a minute, just like an angleworm in the sun.

'And I'm afraid my report to the authorities didn't help them much. After all, even a fellow scientist would have found it a bit difficult to reconcile my classification of "some sort of giant, carrion-feeding, subterranean mole" with my ravings about "canine and simian developments of members" and my absurd insistence on "startlingly humanoid cranial development, and brain convolutions indicating a degree of intelligence that–"

'Well, there's no use going into all that now! I firmly expected them to order me up before a Sanity Commission when I reported my findings. Instead, they offered me a position as head of the "Special Subway Detail," at a salary that was, to say the least, fantastic. It was more a month than I'd been getting a year from the museum.

'Because, you see, they'd deduced much of the stuff for themselves without needing me to tell them! They had facts they'd deliberately withheld from me, not wanting to influence my report. They knew that that train had been deliberately derailed – the mutilated track proved that beyond all doubt. No less than three ties had been taken up and laid some distance away down the tunnel. And the condition of the earth about the wrecked cars showed conclusively that extensive mining and sapping had taken place there – it was like a gigantic mole-hill, only worse. And while I'd been analyzing stomach fluids and body tissue to try to find out what my subject fed upon, they'd been burying, secretly and with most elaborate precautions, the half-dessicated corpses of half a dozen men and women and children who – well, they hadn't died in the wreck, old boy! They hadn't died in the wreck, any more than had that screaming thing that hid its eyes from the lights when they found it pinned in the wreckage where it had been caught while trying to drag a dead victim out – God! What a hideous shambles that place must have been before the wrecking-crews got there.

'Mercifully, of course, there was total darkness. The poor devils who were merely injured never knew what charnel horrors were going on in the Stygian depths about them – nor cared, no doubt, in their agony! A few of them gibbered afterward about green eyes, and claws that raked their faces – but of course all that was set down to delirium! Even one man who had his arm chewed half off never knew – surgeons amputated the rest immediately and told him when he regained consciousness that he'd lost it in the wreck. He's still walking the streets today, blissfully ignorant of what almost happened to him that night.

'Oh, you'd be surprised, old boy, how you can hush a thing up if you've got a whole city administration behind you! And believe me, we *did* hush matters up. No newspaper reporter was ever allowed to see the wreck – freedom of the press or no freedom of the press! The Government wanted to appoint a commission to investigate – we squelched it! And by the time the crews had cleaned out the smashed train and removed the last victim, the Special Subway Detail had gone into action. And it's been on steady duty ever since – for the last twenty-odd years!

'We had a terrible time at first, of course. All these modern improvements weren't available then. All we had were lanterns and guns and handcars – with which to patrol nearly five miles of tunnel. It was Mrs. Partington sweeping back the sea all over again – only worse. A handful of puny mortals against Hell itself, in the eternal darkness of these long gloomy tunnels far below the city.

'There were no more wrecks after we took over, though; I'll say that much. Oh, an accident or two. How could we prevent them? We did everything we could think of! How we worked in those early years! Once we sank a shaft fifty feet deep in the earth, where we'd seen queer disturbances beside the train-tracks and heard queerer sounds. And once we blocked up both ends of the tunnel for a mile stretch and filled it with poison gas. And once we dynamited – but why go on? It was all useless, utterly useless. We just couldn't get to grips with anything tangible. Oh, we'd hear sounds sometimes on our long dismal patrols in the darkness; our little lanterns mere pin-pricks of light in these vast old concrete vaults. We'd catch glimpses of glinting eyes far off, find fresh earth piled up where only a moment before there'd been hard-packed cinders and gravel. Once in a while we'd fire our guns at something whitish and half seen, but there'd be only a tittering laugh in answer – a laugh as mirthless and savage as that of a hyena, dying away in the earth…

'A thousand times I was tempted to chuck the whole thing, to get back above ground to sunshine and sanity and forget the charnel horrors of this mad Nyarlathotep-world far underneath. And then I'd get to thinking of all those helpless men and women and children riding the trains unsuspecting through the haunted dark, with Evil out of the primeval dawn burrowing beneath them for their destruction, and – well, I just couldn't go, that's all. I stayed and did my duty, as the rest did, year after year. It's been a strange career for a man of science, and certainly one I never dreamed I'd be following during all the years I prepared myself for museum work. And yet I flatter myself that it's been rather a socially useful career at that; perhaps more so than stuffing animals for dusty museum cases, or writing monstrous textbooks that no one ever bothers to read. For I've a science of my own down here, you know: the science of keeping millions of dollars worth of subway tunnels swept clean of horror, and of safeguarding the lives of half the population of the world's largest city.

'And then, too, I've opportunities for research here which most of my colleagues above ground would give their right arms for, the opportunity to study an absolutely unknown form of life; a grotesquerie so monstrous that even after all these years of contact with it I sometimes doubt my own senses even now, although the horror is authentic enough, if you come right down to it. It's been attested in every country in the world, and by every people. Why, even the Bible has references to the "ghouls that burrow in the earth", and even today in modern Persia they hunt down with dogs and guns, like beasts, strange tomb-dwelling creatures neither quite human nor quite beast; and in Syria and Palestine and parts of Russia…

'But as for this particular place – well, you'd be surprised how many records we've found, how many actual evidences of the Things we've uncovered from Manhattan Island's earliest history, even before the white men settled here. Ask the curator of the Aborigines Museum out on Riverside Drive about the burial customs of Island Indians a thousand years ago – customs perfectly inexplicable unless you take into consideration what they were guarding against. And ask him to show you that skull, half human and half canine, that came out of an Indian mound as far away as Albany, and those ceremonial robes of aboriginal shamans plainly traced with drawings of whitish spidery Things burrowing through conventionalized tunnels; and doing other things, too, that show the Indian artists must have known Them and Their habits. Oh yes, it's all down there in black and white, once we had the sense to read it!

'And even after white men came – what about the early writings of the old Dutch settlers, what about Jan Van der Rhees and Woulter Van Twiller? Even some of Washington Irving's writings have a nasty twist to them, if you once realize it! And there are some mighty queer passages in "The History of the City of New York" – mention of guard patrols kept for no rational purpose in early streets at night, *particularly in the region of cemeteries*; of forays and excursions in the lightless dark, and flintlocks popping, and graves hastily dug and filled in before dawn woke the city to life…

'And then the modern writers – Lord! There's a whole library of them on the subject. One of them, a great student of the subject, had almost as much data on Them from his reading as I'd gleaned from my years of study down here. Oh, yes; I learned a lot from Lovecraft – and he got a lot from me, too! That's where the – well, what you might call the *authenticity* came from in some of his yarns that attracted the most attention! Oh, of course he had to soft-pedal the strongest parts of it – just as you're going to have to do if you ever mention this in your own writings! But even with the worst played down, there's still enough horror and nightmare in it to blast a man's soul, if he lets himself think on what goes on *down there,* below the blessed sanity of the earth's mercifully concealing crust. Far below…

'We've figured out – we who've been studying Them all this time, that They must have been pretty numerous once. No wonder the Indians sold this place so cheaply! You'd sell your home cheaply, too, if it were fairly overrun with monstrous noxious vermin that – but with civilization's coming they were decimated, killed off, pogromed against, blasted with fire and steel by men whose utter ruthlessness sprang from soul-shuddering detestation, who slew and kept silent about their slaying, lest their fellowmen think them mad – until finally the blasted remnant of the Things went far underground, burrowed down like worms to charnel depths that – well, we daren't conjecture just where, but we think that there's some fault in the basic bedrock of the Island, some monstrous cavern whose edge this lowest of all the subway tunnels taps, and which lets them through somehow into the tubes…

'Oh, it took us a long time to find all that out. At first we thought we had to patrol the whole subway system of the city! We had guards even out under the river, and over in Brooklyn and Queens. We were even afraid they'd get into upper levels of the tunnels, perhaps into the very deserted streets of Manhattan during the pre-dawn hours. We had half the police department down here in those days, even the mounted force. Yes, indeed; though God knows what even a trained police horse would do if it ever came face to face with one of those things! But horses were faster than the handcars we used then, and could cover more territory.

'But as time went on we got things pretty well localized. It's only in this one stretch of tunnel that the danger is, and only here in certain hours of the night. Don't ask me why they never come up in daylight; for it's always night down here, you know, hundreds of feet below the surface. Maybe it's the constant passage of the trains – they shuttle by at two-minute intervals all day long, you know, and until the Broadway theatres close at night. Only for about four hours of the night is there a lull when long miles of tunnel are lifeless and deserted and silent, when anything could come and go at will in them and not be seen.

'And so it's only during these hours that we really worry, you see. It's only now that we're vigilant and ready. Although of course it's no longer warfare, you understand. We hunt them now, they don't hunt us any more! We run them down howling with terror, kill them or capture them as we will – oh yes, I said capture! A half-dozen times we've had a sort of mad "Bronx Zoo" of our own down here – or perhaps it would be more accurate to say a living "Madame Tussaud's Chamber of Horrors." I have cages in my laboratory, and there have been times when it seemed judicious for influential people above ground to – well, to realize just how important is the work we're doing down here! So when we have a really stubborn skeptic to our program we'd take him in there, hand him a flashlight and let him train it himself on what was prisoned there in total darkness – and then we'd stand by to catch him as he fainted! Oh, a lot of city officials and politicians have been down here. Why not? They couldn't possibly speak of the experience afterward – they'd just be locked up as lunatics if they did! And it made them much more liberal about funds. Our menagerie was a great success, only we just couldn't keep it going for very long at a time! We'd get so soul-sick at the very proximity of the creatures that we'd have to kill them finally. There was just no putting up with them for any length of time!

'Oh, it's not so much the appearance of the Things, or even what they eat – we got an unlimited supply of *that* from the city morgue; and to anyone who's spent half his life in dissecting-rooms, as I have, it might be a lot worse. But there's a sort of cosmic horror the Things exude that – well, it's quite beyond description. You just can't breathe the same air with them, live together in the same sane world! And in the end we'd have to gun them and throw them back underground to their friends and neighbors – who were waiting for them, apparently. At least we've opened the shallow graves a few days later and there'd be only a gnawed bone or two there....

'And then, of course, we kept them alive in order to study their habits. I've filled two volumes with notes for my successors who'll carry on the fight when I'm gone – oh, yes, old boy! It'll always have to be carried on, I fear! There's no possibility of ever really wiping them out, you know. All we can do is hold our own. The fight will go on so long as this particular tunnel is occupied. And can't you just see the City Fathers consenting to abandon twenty million dollars' worth of subway tunnels for nothing? "I'm sorry, gentlemen; but, you see, the place is infested with–" God! What a laughing stock anyone would be who even suggested that – above ground! Why, even on our own furloughs, when we walk sunlit streets among our fellow men, with God's own blue sky above and God's own clean air about us – even *we* wonder whether all this foulness isn't just a bad dream! It's hard, up there, to realize what can go on down in the crepuscular earth, the mad gnawing eternal darkness far below – Hello!'

The telephone was ringing.

Somehow I didn't listen as he spoke briefly into it, perhaps because I was listening to something else – to a faint crackling from that great blackboard on the wall, where one little light (no glowing worm this time, but only one minute spark) kept flicking oddly on and off and on again. '79th Street' it marked, over and over. '79th Street – 79th–'

My friend hung up the phone at length, and stood up. 'Queer,' he said softly. 'Very queer indeed! The first in months; and tonight, now, while we were talking. It makes one wonder, you know – about those supernatural telepathic powers that they're said to have...'

Something went past in the tunnel outside, something that moved so fast that I could scarcely make it out; just a little low platform on four wheels, with no visible engine to propel it. Yet it scudded along with the speed of a racing car. Uniformed men rode the bucking thing, crouching with glinting objects in their hands.

'Riot Car Number 1!' my friend said, grimly. 'Our own version of the "squad automobiles" above ground. Just one of the little electric hand-cars used in subway construction – but "souped up" by our engineers until it'll do nearly eighty miles an hour. It could traverse the entire sector in less than five minutes, if it had to. But it doesn't, of course. Another one, also with machine-gunners aboard, left 105th Street at the same time. They'll meet somewhere along the tunnel's length – with the – er, disturbance in between. Let's listen to them!'

He crossed the room to the strange apparatus, threw switches and adjusted dials. There was a burring and crackling from what looked like an old-fashioned radio amplifier that stood on one of the cabinets.

'Microphones every hundred feet along the tunnel!' said my friend. 'Another small fortune to install, of course; but another great step forward in our efficiency. A man listens all night long at a switchboard – and you'd be surprised to know what he hears sometimes! We have to change operators pretty often. Ah! there we are. Microphone Number 290 – approximately a thousand feet below one of the busiest corners, even at this hour of the night, in all a great metropolis. And – listen! Hear that?'

'That' was a sound that brought me out of my chair, a strange high tittering, blasphemously off key, that merged into a growl and a moan...

'There we are!' my friend grated. 'One of them, certainly – perhaps more than one. Hear that scratching, and the rustle of the gravel? All unsuspecting, of course, that they're broadcasting their presence; unaware that we modern human beings have got ourselves a few "supernatural" powers of our own, nowadays; and unaware that, from both directions, death is sweeping down upon them on truckling wheels. But a little moment more and – ah! hear that shriek? That howling? That means they've sighted one of the cars! They're fleeing madly along the tunnel now – the voices get fainter. And now – yes! Now they double back. The other car! They're trapped, caught between them. No time to dig, to burrow down into their saving Mother Earth like the vermin they are. No, no, you devils! We've got you! Got you! Hear 'em yell, hear 'em shriek in agony! That's the lights, you know. Blazing searchlights trained on dark-accustomed bodies; burning, searing, withering them like actual blazing heat! And now "Brrr-rat-tat-tat!" That's our machine-guns going into action – silenced guns, with Maxims on them so that the echoes won't carry to upper levels and make men ask questions – but throwing slugs of lead, for all that, into cringing white bodies and flattened white skulls... Shriek! Shriek, you beasts from Hell! Shriek, you monsters from the charnel depths! Shriek on, and see what good it does you. You're dead! *Dead!* DEAD – Well, you blasted fool, what are you staring at?'

To save my life I couldn't have answered him. I couldn't look away from his blazing eyes, from his body crouched as if he would spring at me across the room, from his teeth bared in a bestial snarl...

For a long moment that tableau held. Then suddenly he dropped into a chair, flung his hands up over his face. I stood regarding him, my mind sickly ticking off details. God! Why had I not seen them before. That lengthening of jaw, that flattening of forehead and cranium – no human head could be shaped like that!

At last he spoke, not looking up. 'I know!' he said softly. 'I've felt the change coming on me for a long time now. It's coming over all of us, bit by bit, but on me the worst, for I've been here the longest. That's why I almost never go above ground any more, even on leave. The lights are dim down here. But I wouldn't dare let even you see my face in sunlight!

'Twenty-five years, you see – twenty-five long dragging years down here in Hell itself. It was bound to leave a mark, of course. I was prepared for that. But, oh, Great Powers above! If I'd for one instant dreamed what it was to be! Worse, oh, how much worse than any mark of the beast!...

'And it's spiritual, you know, as well as physical. I get... cravings, sometimes, down here in the night's loneliness; thought and charnel desires that would blast your very soul if I were to whisper them to you. And they'll get worse, I know, and worse until at last I run mad in the tunnel like that poor devil I told you about and my men shoot me down like a dog as they already have orders to do if –

'And yet the thing interests me, I'll admit; it interests me scientifically, even though it horrifies my very soul, even though it damns me for ever.

For it shows how They may have come about – *must* have come about, in fact, in the world's dim dawn; perhaps never quite human, of course, perhaps never Neanderthal or even Piltdown; something even lower, closer linked to the primeval beast, but that when driven underground, into caves and then beneath them by Man's coming, retrograded century by uncounted century down to the worm-haunted darkness – just as we poor devils are retrograding down here from very contact with them – until at last none of us will ever be able again to walk above in the blessed sunlit air among our fellow men–'

With a roar and a howl the thing was upon us, out of total darkness. Instinctively I drew back as its headlights passed; every object in the little room rattled from the reverberation. Then the power-car was by, and there was only the 'klackety-klack, klackety-klack' of wheels and lighted windows flicking by like bits of film on a badly connected projection machine.

'The Four-Fifteen Express,' he said heavily, 'from the Bronx. Safe and sound, you'll notice, its occupants all unsuspecting of how they were safeguarded; of how they'll always be safeguarded… but at what a cost! At what an awful cost!

'The Four-Fifteen Express. That means it's dawn, you know, in the city overhead. Rays of the rising sun are gilding the white skyscrapers of Manhattan; a whole great city begins to wake to morning life.

'But there's no dawn for us down here, of course. There'll never be a dawn for poor lost souls down here in the eternal dark, far, far below…'

SMOKE GHOST

Fritz Leiber

Fritz Leiber (1910–1992) was an influential, award-winning American writer of fantasy, horror and science fiction. H. P. Lovecraft, Robert Graves, and Carl Jung all helped inspire his fiction. Although perhaps best-known for the swords-and-sorcery Fafhrd and the Gray Mouser series, Leiber also wrote several *sui generis* macabre novels and stories. *Our Lady of Darkness* (1977) is among the best-known of his horror novels and, like much of his later fiction, includes autobiography by way of his real-life struggles with depression and alcoholism. Along with such novels, stories like 'The Girl with the Hungry Eyes' (1949) and the classic reprinted here, 'Smoke Ghost' (1941), made Leiber a key forerunner of the urban weird of writers like Ramsey Campbell.

Miss Millick wondered just what had happened to Mr. Wran. He kept making the strangest remarks when she took dictation. Just this morning he had quickly turned around and asked, 'Have you ever seen a ghost, Miss Millick?' And she had tittered nervously and replied, 'When I was a girl there was a thing in white that used to come out of the closet in the attic bedroom when I slept there, and moan. Of course it was just my imagination. I was frightened of lots of things.' And he had said, 'I don't mean that kind of ghost. I mean a ghost from the world today, with the soot of the factories on its face and the pounding of machinery in its soul. The kind that would haunt coal yards and slip around at night through deserted office buildings like this one. A real ghost. Not something out of books.' And she hadn't known what to say.

He'd never been like this before. Of course he might be joking, but it didn't sound that way. Vaguely Miss Millick wondered whether he mightn't be seeking some sort of sympathy from her. Of course, Mr. Wran was married and had a little child, but that didn't prevent her from having daydreams. The daydreams were not very exciting, still they helped fill up her mind. But now he was asking her another of those unprecedented questions.

'Have you ever thought what a ghost of our times would look like, Miss Millick? Just picture it. A smoky composite face with the hungry anxiety of the unemployed, the neurotic restlessness of the person without purpose, the jerky tension of the high-pressure metropolitan worker, the uneasy resentment of the striker, the callous opportunism of the scab, the aggressive whine of the panhandler, the inhibited terror of the bombed civilian, and a thousand other twisted emotional patterns. Each one overlying and yet blending with the other, like a pile of semi-transparent masks?'

Miss Millick gave a little self-conscious shiver and said, 'That would be terrible. What an awful thing to think of.'

She peered furtively across the desk. Was he going crazy? She remembered having heard that there had been something impressively abnormal about Mr. Wran's childhood, but she couldn't recall what it was. If only she could do something – laugh at his mood or ask him what was really wrong. She shifted the extra pencils in her left hand and mechanically traced over some of the shorthand curlicues in her notebook.

'Yet, that's just what such a ghost or vitalized projection would look like, Miss Millick,' he continued, smiling in a tight way. 'It would grow out of the real world. It would reflect all the tangled, sordid, vicious, things. All the loose ends. And it would be very grimy. I don't think it would seem white or wispy or favour graveyards. It wouldn't moan. But it would mutter unintelligibly, and twitch at your sleeve. Like a sick, surly ape. What would such a thing want from a person, Miss Millick? Sacrifice? Worship? Or just fear? What could you do to stop it from troubling you?'

Miss Millick giggled nervously. There was an expression beyond her powers of definition in Mr. Wran's ordinary, flat-cheeked, thirtyish face, silhouetted against the dusty window. He turned away and stared out into the grey downtown atmosphere that rolled in from the railroad yards and the mills. When he spoke again his voice sounded far away.

'Of course, being immaterial, it couldn't hurt you physically – at first. You'd have to be peculiarly sensitive even to see it, or be aware of it at all. But it would begin to influence your actions. Make you do this. Stop you from doing that. Although only a projection, it would gradually get its hooks into the world of things as they are. Might even get control of suitably vacuous minds. Then it could hurt whomever it wanted.'

Miss Millick squirmed and read back her shorthand, like the books said you should do when there was a pause. She became aware of the failing light and wished Mr. Wran would ask her to turn on the overhead. She felt scratchy, as if soot were sifting down on to her skin.

'It's a rotten world, Miss Millick,' said Mr. Wran, talking at the window. 'Fit for another morbid growth of superstition. It's time the ghosts, or whatever you call them, took over and began a rule of fear. They'd be no worse than men.'

'But' – Miss Millick's diaphragm jerked, making her titter inanely – 'of course there aren't any such things as ghosts.'

Mr. Wran turned around.

'Of course there aren't, Miss Millick,' he said in a loud, patronizing voice, as if she had been doing the talking rather than he. 'Science and common sense and psychiatry all go to prove it.'

She hung her head and might even have blushed if she hadn't felt so all at sea. Her leg muscles twitched, making her stand up, although she hadn't intended to. She aimlessly rubbed her hand back and forth along the edge of the desk.

'Why, Mr. Wran, look what I got off your desk,' she said, showing him a heavy smudge. There was a note of clumsily playful reproof in her voice. 'No wonder the copy I bring you always gets so black. Somebody ought to talk to those scrubwomen. They're skimping on your room.'

She wished he would make some normal joking reply. But instead he drew back and his face hardened.

'Well, to get back to that business of the second class mailing privileges,' he rapped out harshly, and began to dictate.

When she was gone he jumped up, dabbed his finger experimentally at the smudged part of the desk, frowned worriedly at the almost inky smears. He jerked open a drawer, snatched out a rag, hastily swabbed off the desk, crumpled the rag into a ball and tossed it back. There were three or four other rags in the drawer, each impregnated with soot.

Then he strode over to the window and peered out anxiously through the gathering dusk, his eyes searching the panorama of roofs, fixing on each chimney and water tank.

'It's a neurosis. Must be compulsions. Hallucinations,' he muttered to himself in a tired, distraught voice that would have made Miss Millick gasp. 'It's that damned mental abnormality cropping up in a new form. Can't be any other explanation. But it's so damned real. Even the soot. Good thing I'm seeing the psychiatrist. I don't think I could force myself to get on the elevated tonight–' His voice trailed off, he rubbed his eyes, and his memory automatically started to grind.

It had all begun on the elevated. There was a particular little sea of roofs he had grown into the habit of glancing at just as the packed car carrying him homeward lurched around a turn. A dingy, melancholy little world of tar-paper, tarred gravel, and smoky brick. Rusty tin chimneys with odd conical hats suggested abandoned listening posts. There was a washed-out advertisement of some ancient patent medicine on the nearest wall. Superficially it was like ten thousand other drab city roofs. But he always saw it around dusk, either in the smoky half-light, or tinged with red by the flat rays of a dirty sunset, or covered by ghostly wind-blown white sheets of rain-splash, or patched with blackish snow; and it seemed unusually bleak and suggestive, almost beautifully ugly, though in no sense picturesque; dreary, but meaningful. Unconsciously it came to symbolize for Catesby Wran certain disagreeable aspects of the frustrated, frightened century in which he lived, the jangled century of hate and heavy industry and total wars. The quick, daily glance into the half darkness became an integral part of his life. Oddly, he never saw it in the morning, for it was then his habit to sit on the other side of the car, his head buried in the paper.

One evening toward winter he noticed what seemed to be a shapeless black sack lying on the third roof from the tracks. He did not think about it. It merely registered as an addition to the well-known scene and his memory stored away the impression for further reference. Next evening, however, he decided he had been mistaken in one detail. The object was a roof nearer than he had thought. Its colour and texture, and the grimy stains around it, suggested that it was filled with coal dust, which was hardly reasonable. Then, too, the following evening it seemed to have been blown against a rusty ventilator by the wind – which could hardly have happened if it were at all heavy. Perhaps it was filled with leaves. Catesby was surprised to find himself anticipating his next daily glance with a minor note of apprehension. There was something unwholesome in the posture of the thing that stuck in his mind – a bulge in the sacking that suggested a misshapen head peering around the ventilator. And his apprehension was justified, for that evening the thing was on the nearest roof, though on the farther side, looking as if it had just flopped down over the low brick parapet.

Next evening the sack was gone. Catesby was annoyed at the momentary feeling of relief that went through him, because the whole matter seemed too unimportant to warrant feelings of any sort. What difference did it make if his imagination had played tricks on him, and he'd fancied that the object was crawling and hitching itself slowly closer across the roofs? That was the way any normal imagination worked. He deliberately chose to disregard the fact that there were reasons for thinking his imagination was by no means a normal one. As he walked home from the elevated, however, he found himself wondering whether the sack was really gone. He seemed to recall a vague, smudgy trail leading across the gravel to the nearer side of the roof, which was marked by a parapet. For an instant an unpleasant picture formed in his mind – that of an inky humped creature crouched behind the parapet, waiting. Then he dismissed the whole subject.

The next time he felt the familiar grating lurch of the car, he caught himself trying not to look out. That angered him. He turned his head quickly. When he turned it back his compact face was definitely pale. There had only been time for a fleeting rearward glance at the escaping roof. Had he actually seen in silhouette the upper part of a head of some sort peering over the parapet? Nonsense, he told himself. And even if he had seen something, there were a thousand explanations which did not involve the supernatural or even true hallucination. Tomorrow he would take a good look and clear up the whole matter. If necessary, he would visit the roof personally, though he hardly knew where to find it and disliked in any case the idea of pampering a silly fear.

He did not relish the walk home from the elevated that evening, and visions of the thing disturbed his dreams and were in and out of his mind all next day at the office. It was then that he first began to relieve his nerves by making jokingly serious remarks about the supernatural to Miss Millick, who seemed properly mystified. It was on the same day, too, that he became aware of a growing antipathy to grime and soot. Everything he touched seemed gritty, and he found himself mopping and wiping at his desk like an old lady with a morbid fear of germs. He reasoned that there was no real change in his office, and that he'd just now become sensitive to the dirt that had always been there, but there was no denying an increasing nervousness. Long before the car reached the curve, he was straining his eyes through the murky twilight, determined to take in every detail.

Afterward he realized that he must have given a muffled cry of some sort, for the man beside him looked at him curiously, and the woman ahead gave him an unfavorable stare. Conscious of his own pallor and uncontrollable trembling, he stared back at them hungrily, trying to regain the feeling of security he had completely lost. They were the usual reassuringly wooden-faced people everyone rides home with on the elevated. But suppose he had pointed out to one of them what he had seen – that sodden, distorted face of sacking and coal dust, that boneless paw which waved back and forth, unmistakably in his direction, as if reminding him of a future appointment – he involuntarily shut his eyes tight. His thoughts were racing ahead to tomorrow evening. He pictured this same windowed oblong of light and packed humanity surging around the curve – then an opaque monstrous form leaping out from the roof in a parabolic swoop – an unmentionable face pressed close against the window, smearing it with wet coal dust – huge paws fumbling sloppily at the glass.

Somehow he managed to turn off his wife's anxious inquiries. Next morning he reached a decision and made an appointment for that evening with a psychiatrist a friend had told him about. It cost him a considerable effort, for Catesby had a well-grounded distaste for anything dealing with psychological abnormality. Visiting a psychiatrist meant raking up an episode in his past which he had never fully described even to his wife. Once he had made the decision, however, he felt considerably relieved. The psychiatrist, he told himself, would clear everything up. He could almost fancy him saying, 'Merely a bad case of nerves. However, you must consult the occulist whose name I'm writing down for you, and you must take two of these pills in water every four hours,' and so on. It was almost comforting, and made the coming revelation he would have to make seem less painful.

But as the smoky dust rolled in, his nervousness returned and he let his joking mystification of Miss Millick run away with him until he realized that he wasn't frightening anyone but himself.

He would have to keep his imagination under better control, he told himself, as he continued to peer out restlessly at the massive, murky shapes of the downtown office buildings. Why, he had spent the whole afternoon building up a kind of neomedieval cosmology of superstition. It wouldn't do. He realized then that he had been standing at the window much longer than he'd thought, for the glass panel in the door was dark and there was no noise coming from the outer office. Miss Millick and the rest must have gone home.

It was then he made the discovery that there would have been no special reason for dreading the swing around the curve that night. It was, as it happened, a horrible discovery. For, on the shadowed roof across the street and four stories below, he saw the thing huddle and roll across the gravel and, after one upward look of recognition, merge into the blackness beneath the water tank.

As he hurriedly collected his things and made for the elevator, fighting the panicky impulse to run, he began to think of hallucination and mild psychosis as very desirable conditions. For better or for worse, he pinned all his hopes on the psychiatrist.

'So you find yourself growing nervous and… er… jumpy, as you put it,' said Dr. Trevethick, smiling with dignified geniality. 'Do you notice any more definite physical symptoms? Pain? Headache? Indigestion?'

Catesby shook his head and wet his lips. 'I'm especially nervous while riding in the elevated,' he murmured swiftly.

'I see. We'll discuss that more fully. But I'd like you first to tell me something you mentioned earlier. You said there was something about your childhood that might predispose you to nervous ailments. As you know, the early years are critical ones in the development of an individual's behaviour pattern.'

Catesby studied the yellow reflections of frosted globes in the dark surface of the desk. The palm of his left hand aimlessly rubbed the thick nap of the armchair. After a while he raised his head and looked straight into the doctor's small brown eyes.

'From perhaps my third to my ninth year,' he began choosing the words with care, 'I was what you might call a sensory prodigy.'

The doctor's expression did not change. 'Yes?' he inquired politely.

'What I mean is that I was supposed to be able to see through walls, read letters through envelopes and books through their covers, fence and play ping-pong blindfolded, find things that were buried, read thoughts.' The words tumbled out.

'And could you?' The doctor's expression was toneless.

'I don't know. I don't suppose so,' answered Catesby, long-lost emotions flooding back into his voice. 'It's all confused now. I thought I could, but then they were always encouraging me. My mother… was… well… interested in psychic phenomena. I was… exhibited. I seem to remember seeing things other people couldn't. As if most opaque objects were transparent. But I was very young. I didn't have any scientific criteria for judgment.'

He was reliving it now. The darkened rooms. The earnest assemblages of gawking, prying adults. Himself sitting alone on a little platform, lost in a straight-backed wooden chair. The black silk handkerchief over his eyes. His mother's coaxing, insistent questions. The whispers. The gasps. His own hate of the whole business, mixed with hunger for the adulation of adults. Then the scientists from the university, the experiments, the big test. The reality of those memories engulfed him and momentarily made him forget the reason why he was disclosing them to a stranger.

'Do I understand that your mother tried to make use of you as a medium for communicating with the… er… other world?'

Catesby nodded eagerly.

'She tried to, but she couldn't. When it came to getting in touch with the dead, I was a complete failure. All I could do – or thought I could do – was see real, existing, three-dimensional objects beyond the vision of normal people. Objects anyone could have seen except for distance, obstruction, or darkness. It was always a disappointment to mother.'

He could hear her sweetish patient voice saying, 'Try again, dear, just this once. Katie was your aunt. She loved you. Try to hear what she's saying.' And he had answered, 'I can see a woman in a blue dress standing on the other side of Dick's house.' And she replied, 'Yes, I know, dear. But that's not Katie. Katie's a spirit. Try again. Just this once, dear.' The doctor's voice gently jarred him back into the softly gleaming office.

'You mentioned scientific criteria for judgment, Mr. Wran. As far as you know, did anyone ever try to apply them to you?'

Catesby's nod was emphatic.

'They did. When I was eight, two young psychologists from the university got interested in me. I guess they did it for a joke at first, and I remember being very determined to show them I amounted to something. Even now I seem to recall how the note of polite superiority and amused sarcasm drained out of their voices. I suppose they decided at first that it was very clever trickery, but somehow they persuaded mother to let them try me out under controlled conditions. There were lots of tests that seemed very businesslike after mother's slipshod little exhibitions. They found I was clairvoyant – or so they thought. I got worked up and on edge. They were going to demonstrate my super-normal sensory powers to the university psychology faculty. For the first time I began to worry about whether I'd come through. Perhaps they kept me going at too hard a pace, I don't know. At any rate, when the test came, I couldn't do a thing. Everything became opaque. I got desperate and made things up out of my imagination. I lied. In the end I failed utterly, and I believe the two young psychologists got into a lot of hot water as a result.'

He could hear the brusque, bearded man saying, 'You've been taken in by a child, Flaxman, a mere child. I'm greatly disturbed. You've put yourself on the same plane as common charlatans.

Gentlemen, I ask you to banish from your minds this whole sorry episode. It must never be referred to.' He winced at the recollection of his feeling of guilt. But at the same time he was beginning to feel exhilarated and almost light-hearted. Unburdening his long-repressed memories had altered his whole viewpoint. The episodes on the elevated began to take on what seemed their proper proportions as merely the bizarre workings of overwrought nerves and an overly suggestible mind. The doctor, he anticipated confidently, would disentangle the obscure subconscious causes, whatever they might be. And the whole business would be finished off quickly, just as his childhood experience – which was beginning to seem a little ridiculous now – had been finished off.

'From that day on,' he continued, 'I never exhibited a trace of my supposed powers. My mother was frantic and tried to sue the university. I had something like a nervous breakdown. Then the divorce was granted, and my father got custody of me. He did his best to make me forget it. We went on long outdoor vacations and did a lot of athletics, associated with normal, matter-of-fact people. I went to business college eventually. I'm in advertising now. But,' Catesby paused, 'now that I'm having nervous symptoms, I've wondered if there mightn't be a connection. It's not a question of whether I really was clairvoyant or not. Very likely my mother taught me a lot of unconscious deceptions, good enough to fool even young psychology instructors. But don't you think it may have some important bearing on my present condition?'

For several moments the doctor regarded him with a slightly embarrassing professional frown. Then he said quietly, 'And is there some… er… more specific connection between your experiences then and now? Do you by any chance find that you are once again beginning to… er… see things?'

Catesby swallowed. He had felt an increasing eagerness to unburden himself of his fears, but it was not easy to make a beginning, and the doctor's shrewd question rattled him. He forced himself to concentrate. The thing he thought he had seen on the roof loomed up before his inner eye with unexpected vividness. Yet it did not frighten him. He groped for words.

Then he saw that the doctor was not looking at him but over his shoulder. Color was draining out of the doctor's face and his eyes did not seem so small. Then the doctor sprang to his feet, walked past Catesby, threw open the window and peered into the darkness.

As Catesby rose, the doctor slammed down the window and said in a voice whose smoothness was marred by a slight, persistent gasping, 'I hope I haven't alarmed you. I must have frightened him, for he seems to have gotten out of sight in a hurry. Don't give it another thought. Doctors are frequently bothered by *voyeurs*… er… Peeping Toms.'

'A Negro?' asked Catesby, moistening his lips.

The doctor laughed nervously. 'I imagine so, though my first odd impression was that it was a white man in blackface. You see, the color didn't seem to have any brown in it. It was dead-black.'

Catesby moved toward the window. There were smudges on the glass. 'It's quite all right, Mr. Wran.' The doctor's voice had acquired a sharp note of impatience, as if he were trying hard to reassume his professional authority. 'Let's continue our conversation. I was asking you if you were' – he made a face – 'seeing things.'

Catesby's whirling thoughts slowed down and locked into place. 'No, I'm not seeing anything that other people don't see, too. And I think I'd better go now. I've been keeping you too long.' He disregarded the doctor's half-hearted gesture of denial. 'I'll phone you about the physical examination. In a way you've already taken a big load off my mind.' He smiled woodenly. 'Good night, Dr. Trevethick.'

Catesby Wran's mental state was a peculiar one. His eyes searched every angular shadow, he glanced sideways down each chasm-like alley and barren basement passageway, and kept stealing looks at the irregular line of the roofs, yet he was hardly conscious of where he was going. He pushed away the thoughts that came into his mind, and kept moving. He became aware of a slight sense of security as he turned into a lighted street where there were people and high buildings and blinking signs. After a while he found himself in the dim lobby of the structure that housed his office. Then he realized why he couldn't go home – because he might cause his wife and baby to see it, just as the doctor had seen it.

'Hello, Mr. Wran,' said the night elevator man, a burly figure in blue overalls, sliding open the grillwork door to the old-fashioned cage. 'I didn't know you were working nights now.'

Catesby stepped in automatically. 'Sudden rush of orders,' he murmured inanely. 'Some stuff that has to be gotten out.'

The cage creaked to a stop at the top floor. 'Be working very late, Mr. Wran?'

He nodded vaguely, watched the car slide out of sight, found his keys, swiftly crossed the outer office, and entered his own. His hand went out to the light switch, but then the thought occurred to him that the two lighted windows, standing out against the dark bulk of the building, would indicate his whereabouts and serve as a goal toward which something could crawl and climb. He moved his chair so that the back was against the wall and sat down in the semi-darkness. He did not remove his overcoat.

For a long time he sat there motionless, listening to his own breathing and the faraway sounds from the streets below: the thin metallic surge of the crosstown streetcar, the farther one of the elevated, faint lonely cries and honkings, indistinct rumblings. Words he had spoken to Miss Millick in nervous jest came back to him with the bitter taste of truth. He found himself unable to reason critically or connectedly, but by their own volition thoughts rose up into his mind and gyrated slowly and rearranged themselves, with the inevitable movement of planets.

Gradually his mental picture of the world was transformed. No longer a world of material atoms and empty space, but a world in which the bodiless existed and moved according to its own obscure laws or unpredictable impulses. The new picture illumined with dreadful clarity certain general facts which had always bewildered and troubled him and from which he had tried to hide: the inevitability of hate and war, the diabolically timed machines which wrecked the best of human intentions, the walls of willful misunderstanding that divided one man from another, the eternal vitality of cruelty and ignorance and greed. They seemed appropriate now, necessary parts of the picture. And superstition only a kind of wisdom.

Then his thoughts returned to himself, and the question he had asked Miss Millick came back, 'What would such a thing want from a person? Sacrifices? Worship? Or just fear? What could you do to stop it from troubling you?' It had become a practical question.

With an explosive jangle, the phone began to ring. 'Cate, I've been trying everywhere to get you,' said his wife. 'I never thought you'd be at the office. What are you doing? I've been worried.'

He said something about work.

'You'll be home right away?' came the faint anxious question. 'I'm a little frightened. Ronny just had a scare. It woke him up. He kept pointing to the window saying "Black man, black man." Of course it's something he dreamed. But I'm frightened. You will be home? What's that, dear? Can't you hear me?'

'I will. Right away,' he said. Then he was out of the office, buzzing the night bell and peering down the shaft.

He saw it peering up the shaft at him from the deep shadows three floors below, the sacking face pressed against the iron grillwork. It started up the stair at a shockingly swift, shambling gait, vanishing temporarily from sight as it swung into the second corridor below.

Catesby clawed at the door to the office, realized he had not locked it, pushed it in, slammed and locked it behind him, retreated to the other side of the room, cowered between the filing cases and the wall. His teeth were clicking. He heard the groan of the rising cage. A silhouette darkened the frosted glass of the door, blotting out part of the grotesque reverse of the company name. After a little the door opened.

The big-globed overhead light flared on and, standing just inside the door, her hand on the switch, he saw Miss Millick.

'Why, Mr. Wran,' she stammered vacuously, 'I didn't know you were here. I'd just come in to do some extra typing after the movie. I didn't… but the lights weren't on. What were you–'

He stared at her. He wanted to shout in relief, grab hold of her, talk rapidly. He realized he was grinning hysterically.

'Why, Mr. Wran, what's happened to you?' she asked embarrassedly, ending with a stupid titter. 'Are you feeling sick? Isn't there something I can do for you?'

He shook his head jerkily, and managed to say, 'No, I'm just leaving. I was doing some extra work myself.'

'But you *look* sick,' she insisted, and walked over toward him. He inconsequentially realized she must have stepped in mud, for her high-heeled shoes left neat black prints.

'Yes, I'm sure you must be sick. You're so terribly pale.' She sounded like an enthusiastic, incompetent nurse. Her face brightened with a sudden inspiration. 'I've got something in my bag that'll fix you up right away,' she said. 'It's for indigestion.'

She fumbled at her stuffed oblong purse. He noticed that she was absent-mindedly holding it shut with one hand while she tried to open it with the other. Then, under his very eyes, he saw her bend back the thick prongs of metal locking the purse as if they were tinfoil, or as if her fingers had become a pair of steel pliers.

Instantly his memory recited the words he had spoken to Miss Millick that afternoon. 'It couldn't hurt you physically – at first… gradually get its hooks into the world… might even get control of suitably vacuous minds. Then it could hurt whomever it wanted.' A sickish, cold feeling came to a focus inside him. He began to edge toward the door.

But Miss Millick hurried ahead of him.

'You don't have to wait, Fred,' she called. 'Mr. Wran's decided to stay a while longer.'

The door to the cage shut with a mechanical rattle. The cage creaked. Then she turned around in the door.

'Why, Mr. Wran,' she gurgled reproachfully, 'I just couldn't think of letting you go home now. I'm sure you're terribly unwell. Why, you might collapse in the street. You've just got to stay here until you feel different.'

The creaking died away. He stood in the centre of the office motionless. His eyes traced the course of Miss Millick's footprints to where she stood blocking the door. A sound that was almost a scream was wrenched out of him.

'Why, Mr. Wran,' she said, 'you're acting as if you were crazy. You must lie down for a little while. Here, I'll help you off with your coat.'

The nauseously idiotic and rasping note was the same; only it had been intensified. As she came toward him he turned and ran through the storeroom, clattered a key desperately at the lock of the second door to the corridor.

'Why, Mr. Wran,' he heard her call, 'are you having some kind of fit? You must let me help you.'

The door came open and he plunged out into the corridor and up the stairs immediately ahead. It was only when he reached the top that he realized the heavy steel door in front of him led to the roof. He jerked up the catch.

'Why, Mr. Wran, you mustn't run away. I'm coming after you.'

Then he was out on the gritty gravel of the roof, the night sky was clouded and murky, with a faint pinkish glow from the neon signs. Form the distant mills rose a ghostly spurt of flame. He ran to the edge. The street lights glared dizzily upward. Two men walking along were round blobs of hat and shoulders. He swung around.

The thing was in the doorway. The voice was no longer solicitous but moronically playful, each sentence ending in a titter.

'Why, Mr. Wran, why have you come up here? We're all alone. Just think, I might push you off.'

The thing came slowly toward him. He moved backward until his heels touched the low parapet. Without knowing why or what he was going to do, he dropped to his knees. The face he dared not look at came nearer, a focus for the worst in the world, a gathering point for poisons from everywhere. Then the lucidity of terror took possession of his mind, and words formed on his lips.

'I will obey you. You are my god,' he said. 'You have supreme power over man and his animals and his machines. You rule this city and all others. I recognize that.'

Again the titter, closer. 'Why, Mr. Wran, you never talked like this before. Do you mean it?'

'The world is yours to do with as you will, save or tear to pieces.' He answered fawningly, as the words automatically fitted themselves together into vaguely liturgical patterns. 'I recognize that. I will praise, I will sacrifice. In smoke and soot and flame I will worship you for ever.'

The voice did not answer. He looked up. There was only Miss Millick, deathly pale and swaying drunkenly. Her eyes were closed. He caught her as she wobbled toward him. His knees gave way under the added weight and they sank down together on the edge of the roof.

After a while she began to twitch. Small noises came from her throat, and her eyelids edged open.

'Come on, we'll go downstairs,' he murmured jerkily, trying to draw her up. 'You're feeling bad.'

'I'm terribly dizzy,' she whispered. 'I must have fainted. I didn't eat enough. And then I'm so nervous lately, about the war and everything, I guess. Why, we're on the roof! Did you bring me up here to get some air? Or did I come up without knowing it? I'm awfully foolish. I used to walk in my sleep, my mother said.'

As he helped her down the stairs, she turned and looked at him. 'Why, Mr. Wran,' she said, faintly, 'you've got a big black smudge on your forehead. Here, let me get it of for you.' Weakly she rubbed at it with her handkerchief. She started to sway again and he steadied her.

'No, I'll be all right,' she said. 'Only I feel cold. What happened, Mr. Wran? Did I have some sort of fainting spell?'

He told her it was something like that.

Later, riding home in an empty elevated car, he wondered how long he would be safe from the thing. It was a purely practical problem. He had no way of knowing, but instinct told him he had satisfied the brute for some time. Would it want more when it came again? Time enough to answer that question when it arose. It might be hard, he realized, to keep out of an insane asylum. With Helen and Ronny to protect, as well as himself, he would have to be careful and tight-lipped. He began to speculate as to how many other men and women had seen the thing or things like it.

The elevated slowed and lurched in a familiar fashion. He looked at the roofs again, near the curve. They seemed very ordinary, as if what made them impressive had gone away for a while.

WHITE RABBITS

Leonora Carrington

Leonora Carrington (1917–2011) was a famous English-born surrealist painter and writer who lived in Mexico for most of her life. 'From a very young age,' Leonora Carrington has said, 'I used to have very strange experiences with all sorts of ghosts [and] visions.' Although her art has overshadowed her fiction, Carrington's odd stories have been important to many writers, including Angela Carter. Collections include *The Seventh Horse* and *The Oval Lady.* Her stories and the novel *The Hearing Trumpet* provide a tantalizing glimpse of ways that surrealism might have had more influence on the weird tale. A strong synergy exists between her work and stories herein by Mervyn Peake, William Sansom, and Mercè Rodoreda, among others.

The time has come that I must tell the events which began in 40 Pest Street. The houses, which were reddish black, looked as if they had issued mysteriously from the fire of London. The house in front of my window, covered with an occasional wisp of creeper, was as black and empty looking as any plague-ridden residence subsequently licked by flames and smoke. This is not the way that I had imagined New York.

It was so hot that I got palpitations when I ventured out into the streets, so I sat and considered the house opposite and occasionally bathed my sweating face.

The light was never very strong in Pest Street. There was always a reminiscence of smoke, which made visibility troubled and hazy – still it was possible to study the house opposite carefully, even precisely. Besides, my eyes have always been excellent.

I spent several days watching for some sort of movement opposite but there was none, and I finally took to undressing quite freely before my open window and doing my breathing exercises optimistically in the thick Pest Street air. This must have made my lungs as black as the houses.

One afternoon I washed my hair and sat out on the diminutive stone crescent which served as a balcony to dry it. I hung my head between my knees and watched a bluebottle suck the dry corpse of a spider between my feet. I looked up through my long hair and saw something black in the sky, ominously quiet for an aeroplane. Parting my hair, I was in time to see a large raven alight on the balcony of the house opposite. It sat on the balustrade and seemed to peer into the empty window. Then it poked its head under its wing, apparently searching for lice. A few minutes later I was not unduly surprised to see the double windows open and admit a woman onto the balcony. She carried a large dish full of bones, which she emptied onto the floor. With a short appreciative squeak, the raven hopped down and poked about amongst its unpleasant repast.

The woman, who had very long black hair, used her hair to wipe out the dish. Then she looked straight at me and smiled in a friendly fashion. I smiled back and waved a towel. This served to encourage her, for she tossed her head coquettishly and gave me a very elegant salute after the fashion of a queen.

'Do you happen to have any bad meat over there that you don't need?' she called.

'Any what?' I called back, wondering if my ears had deceived me.

'Any stinking meat? Decomposed flesh meat?'

'Not at the moment,' I replied, wondering if she was trying to be funny.

'Won't you have any towards the end of the week? If so, I would be very grateful if you would bring it over.'

Then she stepped back into the empty window and disappeared. The raven flew away.

My curiosity about the house and its occupant prompted me to buy a large lump of meat the following day. I set it on the balcony on a bit of newspaper and awaited developments. In a comparatively short time the smell was so strong that I was obliged to pursue my daily activities with a strong paper clip on the end of my nose. Occasionally I descended into the street to breathe.

Towards Thursday evening I noticed that the meat was turning colour, so waving aside a flight of rancorous bluebottles, I scooped it into my sponge bag and set out for the house opposite. I noticed, descending the stairs, that the landlady seemed to avoid me.

It took me some time to find the front door of the house opposite. It turned out to be hidden under a cascade of something, giving the impression that nobody had been either in or out of this house in years. The bell was of the old-fashioned kind that you pull, and when I pulled it rather harder than I intended, it came right off in my hand. I gave the door an angry push and it caved inwards, admitting a ghastly smell of putrid meat. The hall, which was almost dark, seemed to be of carved woodwork.

The woman herself came rustling down the stairs, carrying a torch.

'How do you do? How do you do?' she murmured ceremoniously, and I was surprised to notice that she wore an ancient beautiful dress of green silk. But as she approached me I saw that her skin was dead white and glittered as if speckled with thousands of minute stars.

'Isn't that kind of you?' she went on, taking my arm with her sparkling hand. 'Won't my poor little rabbits be pleased?'

We mounted the stairs and my companion walked so carefully that I thought she was frightened.

The top flight of the stairs opened into a boudoir decorated with dark baroque furniture and red plush. The floor was littered with gnawed bones and animals skulls.

'It is so seldom that we get a visit.' The woman smiled. 'So they all scatter off into their little corners.'

She uttered a low sweet whistle, and transfixed, I saw about a hundred snow white rabbits emerge cautiously from every nook, their large pink eyes fixed unblinkingly upon the woman.

'Come, pretty ones! Come, pretty ones!' she cooed, diving her hand into my sponge bag and pulling out a handful of rotting meat.

With a sensation of deep disgust, I backed into a corner and saw her throw the carrion amongst the rabbits, who fought like wolves for the meat.

'One becomes very fond of them,' the woman went on. 'They each have their own little ways! You would be surprised how very individual rabbits are.'

The rabbits in question were tearing at the meat with their sharp buck teeth.

'We eat them of course occasionally. My husband makes a very tasty stew every Saturday night.'

Then a movement in the corner caught my attention and I realized that there was a third person in the room. As the woman's torchlight touched his face I saw he had identical glittering skin, like tinsel on a Christmas tree. He was dressed in a red gown and sat very rigidly with his profile turned towards us. He seemed to be unconscious of our presence or of that of a large white buck rabbit which sat and masticated on a chunk of meat on his knee.

The woman followed my gaze and chuckled. 'That is my husband. The boys used to call him Lazarus–'

At the sound of this familiar name, he turned his face towards us and I saw that he wore a bandage over his eyes.

'Ethel?' he enquired in a rather thin voice. 'I won't have any visitors here. You know quite well that I have strictly forbidden it.'

'Now, Laz, don't start carrying on.' Her voice was plaintive. 'You can't grudge me a little bit of company. It's twenty-odd years since I've seen a new face. Besides, she's brought meat for the rabbits.'

She turned and beckoned me to her side. 'You want to stay with us, do you not, my dear?' I was suddenly clutched by fear and I wanted to get out and away from these terrible silver people and the white carnivorous rabbits.

'I think I must be going, it's suppertime–'

The man on the chair gave a shrill peal of laughter, terrifying the rabbit on his knee, which sprang to the floor and disappeared.

The woman thrust her face so near to mine that her sickly breath seemed to anaesthetize me. 'Do you not want to stay and become like us? In seven years your skin will be like stars, in seven years you will have the holy disease of the Bible, leprosy!'

I stumbled and ran, choking with horror; some unholy curiousity made me look over my shoulder as I reached the front door and I saw her waving her hand over the banister, and as she waved it, her fingers fell off and dropped to the ground like shooting stars.

MIMIC

Donald A. Wollheim

Donald Wollheim (1914–1990) was an American science fiction writer as well as an influential editor and publisher. Eventually inducted into the Science Fiction Hall of Fame, Wollheim edited the first science fiction reprint anthology, *The Pocket Book of Science Fiction* (1943) and the first collection of science fiction novels, *The Portable Novels of Science* (1945). A long-time influence on US science fiction fandom, Wollheim also founded the first major publishing house devoted to science fiction and fantasy, DAW Books, which is now run by his daughter. The weird tale 'Mimic' has been widely reprinted and was made into a feature film in 1997. It evokes other stories in this volume by Steven Utley and William Gibson and John Shirley.

It is less than five hundred years since an entire half of the world was discovered. It is less than two hundred years since the discovery of the last continent. The sciences of chemistry and physics go back scarcely one century. The science of aviation goes back forty years. The science of atomics is being born.

And yet we think we know a lot.

We know little or nothing. Some of the most startling things are unknown to us. When they are discovered, they may shock us to the bone.

We search for secrets in the far islands of the Pacific and among the ice fields of the frozen North, while under our very noses, rubbing shoulders with us every day, there may walk the undiscovered. It is a curious fact of nature that that which is in plain view is oft best hidden.

I have always known of the man in the black cloak. Since I was a child he has always lived on my street, and his eccentricities are so familiar that they go unmentioned except among the casual visitor. Here, in the heart of the largest city in the world, in swarming New York, the eccentric and the odd may flourish unhindered.

As children we had hilarious fun jeering at the man in black when he displayed his fear of women. We watched, in our evil, childish way, for those moments; we tried to get him to show anger. But he ignored us completely and soon we paid him no further heed, even as our parents did.

We saw him only twice a day. Once in the early morning, when we would see his six-foot figure come out of the grimy dark hallway of the tenement at the end of the street and stride down toward the elevated to work – again when he came back at night. He was always dressed in a long, black cloak that came to his ankles, and he wore a wide-brimmed black hat down far over his face. He was a sight from some weird story out of the old lands. But he harmed nobody, and paid attention to nobody.

Nobody – except perhaps women.

When a woman crossed his path, he would stop in his stride and come to a dead halt. We could see that he closed his eyes until she had passed. Then he would snap those wide, watery blue eyes open and march on as if nothing had happened.

He was never known to speak to a woman. He would buy some groceries, maybe once a week, at Antonio's – but only when there were no other patrons there. Antonio said once that he never talked, he just pointed at things he wanted and paid for them in bills that he pulled out of a pocket somewhere under his cloak. Antonio did not like him, but he never had any trouble from him either.

Now that I think of it, nobody ever did have any trouble with him.

We got used to him. We grew up on the street; we saw him occasionally when he came home and went back into the dark hallway of the house he lived in.

He never had visitors, he never spoke to anyone. And he had once built something in his room out of metal.

He had once, years ago, hauled up some long flat metal sheets, sheets of tin or iron, and they had heard a lot of hammering and banging in his room for several days. But that had stopped and that was all there was to that story.

Where he worked I don't know and never found out. He had money, for he was reputed to pay his rent regularly when the janitor asked for it.

Well, people like that inhabit big cities and nobody knows the story of their lives until they're all over. Or until something strange happens.

I grew up, I went to college, I studied.

Finally I got a job assisting a museum curator. I spent my days mounting beetles and classifying exhibits of stuffed animals and preserved plants, and hundreds and hundreds of insects from all over...

Nature is a strange thing, I learned. You learn that very clearly when you work in a museum. You realize how nature uses the art of camouflage. There are twig insects that look exactly like a leaf or a branch of a tree. Exactly.

Nature is strange and perfect that way. There is a moth in Central America that looks like a wasp. It even has a fake stinger made of hair, which it twists and curls just like a wasp's stinger. It has the same colorings and, even though its body is soft and not armored like a wasp's, it is colored to appear shiny and armored. It even flies in the daytime when wasps do, and not at night like all other moths. It moves like a wasp. It knows somehow that it is helpless and that it can survive only by pretending to be as deadly to other insects as wasps are.

I learned about army ants, and their strange imitators.

Army ants travel in huge columns of thousands and hundreds of thousands. They move along in a flowing stream several yards across and they eat everything in their path. Everything in the jungle is afraid of them. Wasps, bees, snakes, other ants, birds, lizards, beetles – even men run away, or get eaten.

But in the midst of the army ants there also travel many other creatures – creatures that aren't ants at all, and that the army ants would kill if they knew of them. But they don't know of them because these other creatures are disguised.

Some of them are beetles that look like ants. They have false markings like ant thoraxes and they run along in imitation of ant speed. There is even one that is so long it is marked like three ants in single file! It moves so fast that the real ants never give it a second glance.

There are weak caterpillars that look like big armored beetles. There are all sorts of things that look like dangerous animals. Animals that are the killers and superior fighters of their groups have no enemies. The army ants and the wasps, the sharks, the hawk, and the felines. So there are a host of weak things that try to hide among them – to mimic them.

And man is the greatest killer, the greatest hunter of them all. The whole world of nature knows man for the irresistible master. The roar of his gun, the cunning of his trap, the strength and agility of his arm place all else beneath him.

Should man then be treated by nature differently from the other dominants, the army ants and the wasps?

It was, as often happens to be the case, sheer luck that I happened to be on the street at the dawning hour when the janitor came running out of the tenement on my street shouting for help. I had been working all night mounting new exhibits.

The policeman on the beat and I were the only people besides the janitor to see the thing that we found in the two dingy rooms occupied by the stranger of the black cloak.

The janitor explained – as the officer and I dashed up the narrow, rickety stairs – that he had been awakened by the sound of heavy thuds and shrill screams in the stranger's rooms. He had gone out in the hallway to listen.

When we got there, the place was silent. A faint light shone from under the doorway. The policeman knocked, there was no answer. He put his ear to the door and so did I.

We heard a faint rustling – a continuous slow rustling as of a breeze blowing paper.

The cop knocked again, but there was still no response.

Then, together, we threw our weight at the door. Two hard blows and the rotten old lock gave way. We burst in.

The room was filthy, the floor covered with scraps of torn paper, bits of detritus and garbage. The room was unfurnished, which I thought was odd.

In the corner there stood a metal box, about four feet square. A tight-box, held together with screws and ropes. It had a lid, opening at the top, which was down and fastened with a sort of wax seal.

The stranger of the black cloak lay in the middle of the floor – dead.

He was still wearing the cloak. The big slouch hat was lying on the floor some distance away. From the inside of the box the faint rustling was coming.

We turned over the stranger, took the cloak off. For several instants we saw nothing amiss and then gradually – horribly – we became aware of some things that were wrong.

His hair was short and curly brown. It stood straight up in its inch-long length. His eyes were open and staring. I noticed first that he had no eyebrows, only a curious dark line in the flesh over each eye.

It was then I realized he had no nose. But no one had ever noticed that before. His skin was oddly mottled. Where the nose should have been there were dark shadowings that made the appearance of a nose, if you only just glanced at him.

Like the work of a skillful artist in a painting.

His mouth was as it should be and slightly open – but he had no teeth. His head perched upon a thin neck.

The suit was – not a suit. It was part of him. It was his body.

What we thought was a coat was a huge black wing sheath, like a beetle has. He had a thorax like an insect, only the wing sheath covered it and you couldn't notice it when he wore the cloak. The body bulged out below, tapering off into the two long, thin hind legs. His arms came out from under the top of the 'coat'. He had a tiny secondary pair of arms folded tightly across his chest. There was a sharp, round hole newly pierced in his chest just above the arms, still oozing a watery liquid.

The janitor fled gibbering. The officer was pale but standing by his duty. I heard him muttering under his breath an endless stream of Hail Marys over and over again.

The lower thorax – the 'abdomen' – was very long and insectlike. It was crumpled up now like the wreckage of an airplane fuselage.

I recalled the appearance of a female wasp that had just laid eggs – her thorax had had that empty appearance.

The sight was a shock such as leaves one in full control.

The mind rejects it, and it is only in afterthought that one can feel the dim shudder of horror.

The rustling was still coming from the box. I motioned to the white-faced cop and we went over and stood before it. He took the nightstick and knocked away the waxen seal.

Then we heaved and pulled the lid open.

A wave of noxious vapor assailed us. We staggered back as suddenly a stream of flying things shot out of the huge iron container. The window was open, and straight out into the first glow of dawn they flew.

There must have been dozens of them. They were about two or three inches long and they flew on wide gauzy beetle wings. They looked like little men, strangely terrifying as they flew – clad in their black suits, with their expressionless faces and their dots of watery blue eyes. And they flew out on transparent wings that came from under their black beetle coats.

I ran to the window, fascinated, almost hypnotized. The horror of it had not reached my mind at once. Afterward I have had spasms of numbing terror as my mind tries to put the things together. The whole business was so utterly unexpected.

We knew of army ants and their imitators, yet it never occurred to us that we too were army ants of a sort. We knew of stick insects and it never occurred to us that there might be others that disguise themselves to fool, not other animals, but the supreme animal himself – man.

We found some bones in the bottom of that iron case afterwards. But we couldn't identify them. Perhaps we did not try very hard. They might have been human...

I suppose the stranger of the black cloak did not fear women so much as it distrusted them. Women notice men, perhaps; more closely than other men do. Women might become suspicious sooner of the inhumanity, the deception. And then there might perhaps have been some touch of instinctive feminine jealousy. The stranger was disguised as a man, but its sex – was surely female. The things in the box were its young.

But it is the other thing I saw when I ran to the window that has shaken me the most. The policeman did not see it.

Nobody else saw it but me, and I only for an instant.

Nature practices deceptions in every angle. Evolution will create a being for any niche that can be found, no matter how unlikely.

When I went to the window, I saw the small cloud of flying things rising up into the sky and sailing away into the purple distance. The dawn was breaking and the first rays of the sun were just striking over the housetops.

Shaken, I looked away from that fourth floor tenement room over the roofs of lower buildings. Chimneys and walls and empty clotheslines made the scenery over which the tiny mass of horror passed.

And then I saw a chimney, not thirty feet away on the next roof. It was squat and of red brick and had two black pipe ends flush with its top. I saw it suddenly vibrate, oddly. And I saw its red brick surface seem to peel away, and the black pipe openings turn suddenly white.

I saw two big eyes staring into the sky.

A great, bat-winged thing detached itself silently from the surface of the real chimney and darted after the cloud of flying things.

I watched until all had lost themselves in the sky.

THE CROWD

Ray Bradbury

Ray Bradbury (1920–) is an American fantasy, horror, science fiction, and mystery writer best known for his novel *Fahrenheit 451* (1953) and for the science fiction stories published as *The Martian Chronicles* (1950) and *The Illustrated Man* (1951). Bradbury has become one of the most celebrated writers of speculative fiction, with more than twenty films based on his work. Although readers may think of Bradbury as writing short stories mostly in a fantastical or even whimsical vein, the core of his work is dark and disturbing, as exemplified by 'The Crowd' (1943). The story's stripped-down approach and sense of modern anxiety encapsulates one of the ways in which Bradbury updated the weird tale.

Mr. Spallner put his hands over his face. There was the feeling of movement in space, the beautifully tortured scream, the impact and tumbling of the car with wall, through wall, over and down like a toy, and him hurled out of it. Then – silence.

The crowd came running. Faintly, where he lay, he heard them running. He could tell their ages and their sizes by the sound of their numerous feet over the summer grass and on the lined pavement and over the asphalt street, and picking through the cluttered bricks to where his car hung half into the night sky, still spinning its wheels with senseless centrifuge.

Where the crowd came from he didn't know. He struggled to remain aware and then the crowd faces hemmed in upon him, hung over him like the large growing leaves of downbent trees. They were a ring of shifting, compressing, changing faces over him, looking down, looking down, reading the time of his life or death by his face, making his face into a moon-dial, where the moon cast a shadow from his nose out upon his cheek to tell the time of breathing or not breathing any more after.

How swiftly a crowd comes, he thought, like the iris of an eye compressing in out of nowhere.

A siren. A police voice. Movement. Blood trickled from his lips and he was being moved into an ambulance. Someone said, 'Is he dead?' And someone else said, 'No, he's not dead.' And a third person said, 'He won't die, he's not going to die.' And he saw the faces of the crowd beyond him in the night, and he knew by their expressions that he wouldn't die. And that was strange. He saw a man's face, thin, bright, pale; the man swallowed and bit his lips, very sick. There was a small woman, too, with red hair and too much red on her cheeks and lips. And a little boy with a freckled face. Others' faces. An old man with a wrinkled upper lip, an old woman, with a mole upon her chin. They had all come from – where? Houses, cars, alleys, from the immediate and the accident-shocked world. Out of alleys and out of hotels and out of streetcars and seemingly out of nothing they came.

The crowd looked at him and he looked back at them and did not like them at all. There was a vast wrongness to them. He couldn't put his finger on it. They were far worse than this machine-made thing that happened to him now.

The ambulance doors slammed. Through the windows he saw the crowd looking in, looking in. That crowd that always came so fast, so strangely fast, to form a circle, to peer down, to probe, to gawk, to question, to point, to disturb, to spoil the privacy of a man's agony by their frank curiosity.

The ambulance drove off. He sank back and their faces still stared into his face, even with his eyes shut.

The car wheels spun in his mind for days. One wheel, four wheels, spinning, spinning, and whirring, around and around.

He knew it was wrong. Something wrong with the wheels and the whole accident and the running of feet and the curiosity. The crowd faces mixed and spun into the wild rotation of the wheels.

He awoke.

Sunlight, a hospital room, a hand taking his pulse.

'How do you feel?' asked the doctor.

The wheels faded away. Mr. Spallner looked around.

'Fine – I guess.'

He tried to find words. About the accident. 'Doctor?'

'Yes?'

'That crowd – was it last night?'

'Two days ago. You've been here since Thursday. You're all right, though. You're doing fine. Don't try and get up.'

'That crowd. Something about wheels, too. Do accidents make people, well, a – little off?'

'Temporarily, sometimes.'

He lay staring up at the doctor. 'Does it hurt your time sense?'

'Panic sometimes does.'

'Makes a minute seem like an hour, or maybe an hour seem like a minute?'

'Yes.'

'Let me tell you then.' He felt the bed under him, the sunlight on his face. 'You'll think I'm crazy. I was driving too fast, I know. I'm sorry now. I jumped the curb and hit that wall. I was hurt and numb, I know, but I still remember things. Mostly – the crowd.' He waited a moment and then decided to go on, for he suddenly knew what it was that bothered him. 'The crowd got there too quickly. Thirty seconds after the smash they were all standing over me and staring at me... it's not right they should run that fast, so late at night...'

'You only think it was thirty seconds,' said the doctor. 'It was probably three or four minutes. Your senses–'

'Yeah, I know – my senses, the accident. But I was conscious! I remember one thing that puts it all together and makes it funny. God, so damned funny. The wheels of my car, upside down. The wheels were still spinning when the crowd got there!'

The doctor smiled.

The man in the bed went on. 'I'm positive! The wheels were spinning and spinning fast – the front wheels! Wheels don't spin very long, friction cuts them down. And these were really spinning!'

'You're confused,' said the doctor.

'I'm not confused. That street was empty. Not a soul in sight. And then the accident and the wheels still spinning and all those faces over me, quick, in no time. And the way they looked down at me, I *knew* I wouldn't die...'

'Simple shock,' said the doctor, walking away into the sunlight.

They released him from the hospital two weeks later. He rode home in a taxi. People had come to visit him during his two weeks on his back, and to all of them he had told his story, the accident, the spinning wheels, the crowd. They had all laughed with him concerning it, and passed it off.

He leaned forward and tapped on the taxi window.

'What's wrong?'

The cabbie looked back. 'Sorry, boss. This is one helluva town to drive in. Got an accident up ahead. Want me to detour?'

'Yes. No. No! Wait. Go ahead. Let's – let's take a look.'

The cab moved forward, honking.

'Funny damn thing,' said the cabbie. 'Hey, *you*! Get that fleatrap out of the way!' Quieter, 'Funny thing – more damn people. Nosy people.'

Mr. Spallner looked down and watched his fingers tremble on his knee. 'You noticed that, too?'

'Sure,' said the cabbie. 'All the time. There's always a crowd. You'd think it was their own mother got killed.'

'They come running awfully fast,' said the man in the back of the cab.

'Same way with a fire or an explosion. Nobody around. Boom. Lotsa people around. I dunno.'

'Ever seen an accident – at night?'

The cabbie nodded. 'Sure. Don't make no difference. There's always a crowd.'

The wreck came into view. A body lay on the pavement. You knew there was a body even if you couldn't see it. Because of the crowd. The crowd with its back toward him as he sat in the rear of the cab. With its back toward him. He opened the window and almost started to yell. But he didn't have the nerve. If he yelled they might turn around.

And he was afraid to see their faces.

'I seem to have a penchant for accidents,' he said, in his office. It was late afternoon. His friend sat across the desk from him, listening. 'I got out of the hospital this morning and first thing on the way home, we detoured around a wreck.'

'Things run in cycles,' said Morgan.

'Let me tell you about my accident.'

'I've heard it. Heard it all.'

'But it was funny, you must admit.'

'I must admit. Now how about a drink?'

They talked on for half an hour or more. All the while they talked, at the back of Spallner's brain a small watch ticked, a watch that never needed winding. It was the memory of a few little things. Wheels and faces.

At about five-thirty there was a hard metal noise in the street. Morgan nodded and looked out and down. 'What'd I tell you? Cycles. A truck and a cream-colored Cadillac. Yes, yes.'

Spallner walked to the window. He was very cold and as he stood there, he looked at his watch, at the small minute hand. One two three four five seconds – people running – eight nine ten eleven twelve – from all over, people came running – fifteen sixteen seventeen eighteen seconds – more people, more cars, more horns blowing. Curiously distant, Spallner looked upon the scene as an explosion in reverse, the fragments of the detonation sucked back to the point of impulsion. Nineteen, twenty, twenty-one seconds and the crowd was there. Spallner made a gesture down at them, wordless.

The crowd had gathered so fast.

He saw a woman's body a moment before the crowd swallowed it up.

Morgan said, 'You look lousy. Here. Finish your drink.'

'I'm all right, I'm all right. Let me alone. I'm all right. Can't you see those people? Can you see any of them? I wish we could see them closer.'

Morgan cried out, 'Where in hell are you going?'

Spallner was out the door, Morgan after him, and down the stairs, as rapidly as possible. 'Come along, and hurry.'

'Take it easy, you're not a well man!'

They walked out on to the street. Spallner pushed his way forward. He thought he saw a red-haired woman with too much red color on her cheeks and lips.

'There!' He turned wildly to Morgan. 'Did you see her?'

'See *who*?'

'Damn it; she's gone. The crowd closed in!'

The crowd was all around, breathing and looking and shuffling and mixing and mumbling and getting in the way when he tried to shove through. Evidently the red-haired woman had seen him coming and run off.

He saw another familiar face! A little freckled boy. But there are many freckled boys in the world. And, anyway, it was no use, before Spallner reached him, this little boy ran away and vanished among the people.

'Is she dead?' a voice asked. 'Is she dead?'

'She's dying,' someone else replied. 'She'll be dead before the ambulance arrives. They shouldn't have moved her. They shouldn't have moved her.'

All the crowd faces – familiar, yet unfamiliar, bending over, looking down, looking down.

'Hey, mister, stop pushing.'

'Who you shovin', buddy?'

Spallner came back out, and Morgan caught hold of him before he fell. 'You damned fool. You're still sick. Why in hell'd you have to come down here?' Morgan demanded.

'I don't know, I really don't. They moved her, Morgan, someone moved her. You should never move a traffic victim. It kills them. It kills them.'

'Yeah. That's the way with people. The idiots.'

Spallner arranged the newspaper clippings carefully.

Morgan looked at them. 'What's the idea? Ever since your accident you think every traffic scramble is part of you. What are these?'

'Clippings of motor-car crackups, and photos. Look at them. Not at the cars,' said Spallner, 'but at the crowds around the cars.' He pointed. 'Here. Compare this photo of a wreck in the Wilshire District with one in Westwood. No resemblance. But now take this Westwood picture and align it with one taken in the Westwood District ten years ago.' Again he motioned. 'This woman is in both pictures.'

'Coincidence. The woman happened to be there once in 1936, again in 1946.'

'A coincidence once, maybe. But twelve times over a period of ten years, when the accidents occurred as much as three miles from one another, no. Here.' He dealt out a dozen photographs. She's in *all* of these.

'Maybe she's perverted.'

'She's more than that. How does she *happen* to be there so quickly after each accident? And why does she wear the same clothes in pictures taken over a period of a decade?'

'I'll be damned, so she does.'

'And, last of all, why was she standing over *me* the night of my accident, two weeks ago!'

They had a drink. Morgan went over the files. 'What'd you do, hire a clipping service while you were in the hospital to go back through the newspapers for you?' Spallner nodded. Morgan sipped his drink. It was getting late. The street lights were coming on in the streets below the office. 'What does this all add up to?'

'I don't know,' said Spallner, 'except that there's a universal law about accidents. *Crowds gather.* They always gather. And like you and me, people have wondered year after year, why they gathered so quickly, and how? I know the answer. Here it is!'

He flung the clippings down. 'It frightens me.'

'These people – mightn't they be thrill-hunters, perverted sensationalists with a carnal lust for blood and morbidity?'

Spallner shrugged. 'Does that explain their being at all the accidents? Notice, they stick to certain territories. A Brentwood accident will bring out one group. A Huntington Park another. But there's a norm for faces, a certain percentage appear at each wreck.'

Morgan said, 'They're not *all* the same faces, are they?'

'Naturally not. Accidents draw normal people, too, in the course of time. But these, I find, are always the *first* ones there.'

'Who are they? What do they want? You keep hinting and never telling. Good Lord, you must have some idea. You've scared yourself and now you've got me jumping.'

'I've tried getting to them, but someone always trips me up, I'm always too late. They slip into the crowd and vanish. The crowd seems to offer protection to some of its members. They see me coming.'

'Sounds like some sort of clique.'

'They have one thing in common, they always show up together. At a fire or an explosion or on the sidelines of a war, at any public demonstration of this thing called death. Vultures, hyenas or saints. I don't know which they are, I just don't know. But I'm going to the police with it, this evening. It's gone on long enough. One of them shifted that woman's body today. They shouldn't have touched her. It killed her.'

He placed the clippings in a briefcase. Morgan got up and slipped into his coat. Spallner clicked the briefcase shut. 'Or, I just happened to think…'

'What?'

'Maybe they *wanted* her dead.'

'Why?'

'Who knows. Come along?'

'Sorry. It's late. See you tomorrow. Luck.' They went out together. 'Give my regards to the cops. Think they'll believe you?'

'Oh, they'll believe me all right. Good night.'

Spallner took it slow driving downtown.

'I want to get there,' he told himself, 'alive.'

He was rather shocked, but not surprised, somehow, when the truck came rolling out of an alley straight at him. He was just congratulating himself on his keen sense of observation and talking out what he would say to the police in his mind, when the truck smashed into his car. It wasn't really his car, that was the disheartening thing about it. In a preoccupied way he was tossed first this way and then that way, while he thought, what a shame, Morgan has gone and lent me his extra car for a few days until my other car is fixed, and now here I go again. The windshield hammered back into his face. He was forced back and forth in several lightning jerks. Then all motion stopped and all noise stopped and only pain filled him up.

He heard their feet running and running and running. He fumbled with the car door. He fell out upon the pavement drunkenly and lay, ear to the asphalt, listening to them coming. It was like a great rainstorm, with many drops, heavy and light and medium, touching the earth. He waited a few seconds and listened to their coming and their arrival. Then, weakly, expectantly, he rolled his head up and looked.

The crowd was there.

He could smell their breaths, the mingled odors of many people sucking and sucking on the air a man needs to live by. They crowded and jostled and sucked and sucked all the air up from around his gasping face until he tried to tell them to move back, they were making him live in a vacuum. His head was bleeding very badly. He tried to move and he realized something was wrong with his spine. He hadn't felt much from the impact, but his spine was hurt. He didn't dare move.

He couldn't speak. Opening his mouth, nothing came out but a gagging.

Someone said, 'Give me a hand. We'll roll him over and lift him into a more comfortable position.'

Spallner's brain burst apart.

No! Don't move me!

'Well move him,' said the voice, casually.

You idiots, you'll kill me, don't!

But he could not say any of this out loud. He could only think it.

Hands took hold of him. They started to lift him. He cried out and nausea choked him up. They straightened him out into a ramrod of agony. Two men did it. One of them was thin, bright, pale, alert, a young man. The other man was very old and had a wrinkled upper lip.

He had seen their faces before.

A familiar voice said, 'Is – is he dead?'

Another voice, a memorable voice, responded, 'No. Not yet. But he will be dead before the ambulance arrives.'

It was all a very silly, mad plot. Like every accident. He squealed hysterically at the solid wall of faces. They were all around him, these judges and jurors with the faces he had seen before. Through his pain he counted their faces.

The freckled boy. The old man with the wrinkled upper lip.

The red-haired, red-cheeked woman. An old woman with a mole on her chin.

I know what you're here for, he thought. You're here just as you're at all accidents. To make certain the rights ones live and the right ones die. That's why you lifted me. You knew it would kill. You knew I'd live if you left me alone.

And that's the way it's been since time began, when crowds gather. You murder much easier, this way. Your alibi is very simple; you didn't know it was dangerous to move a hurt man. You didn't mean to hurt him.

He looked at them, above him, and he was curious as a man under deep water looking up at people on a bridge. Who are you? Where do you come from and how do you get here so soon? You're the crowd that's always in the way, using up good air that a dying man's lungs are in need of, using up space he should be using to lie in, alone. Tramping on people to make sure they die, that's you. I know *all* of you.

It was like a polite monologue. They said nothing. Faces. The old man. The red-haired woman.

Someone picked up his briefcase. 'Whose is this?' they asked.

It's mine! It's evidence against all of you!

Eyes, inverted over him. Shiny eyes under tousled hair or under hats.

Faces.

Somewhere – a siren. The ambulance was coming.

But, looking at the faces, the construction, the cast, the form of the faces, Spallner saw it was too late. He read it in their faces. They *knew*.

He tried to speak. A little bit got out:

'It – looks like I'll – be joining up with you. I – guess I'll be a member of your – group – now.'

He closed his eyes then, and waited for the coroner.

THE LONG SHEET

William Sansom

William Sansom (1912–1976) was an idiosyncratic English writer known for applying a surrealist's sensibilities to the weird tale. Obscure today, Sansom enjoyed a brief period of acclaim in the 1940s and 1950s, when the fresh originality of his stories earned him a place in leading British literary magazines. A firefighter in London during the Blitz of World War II, Sansom managed to transform his experiences in a way that garnered him comparisons to Franz Kafka. Sophisticated yet passionate, his stories reward repeated readings. 'The Long Sheet' (1944) was published before the English translation of Kafka's 'In the Penal Colony' and yet in their use of weird ritual to illuminate society the two stories share some similarities.

Have you ever wrung dry a wet cloth? Wrung it bone white dry – with only the grip of your fingers and the muscles of your arms? If you have done this, you will understand better the situation of the captives at Device Z when the warders set them the task of the long sheet.

You will remember how, having stretched the cloth between your hands, you begin by twisting one end – holding the other firm so that the water is corkscrewed from its hiding place. At first the water spurts out easily. But later you will find yourself screwing with both hands in different directions, whitening your knuckles, straining every fibre of your diaphragm – and all to extract the smallest drop of moisture! The muscle of your arm swells like an egg – yet the wet drop remains a pinhead! As you work the cloth will gradually change from a grey colour to the whiteness of dried bone. Yet even then the cloth will be wet! Still you will knot your muscles; still you will wrench away at the furtive damp. Then – at last! – you will believe the cloth to be dry… but in the next second the tip of a finger will quiver tragically as it touches some cold, hidden veil of damp clinging deep down in the interlaced threads.

Such, then, was the task of the captives.

They were placed in a long steel box of a room with no windows and no doors. The room was some six feet wide and six feet high; but it ran one hundred feet in length. It resembled thus a rectangular tunnel with no entrance and no exit. Yet the sensation inside was not really that of a tunnel. For instance, a quantity of light flowed through thick glass panels set at intervals along the ceiling. These were the skylights, and through these the captives had been dropped into the box. Again, the impression of living in a tunnel was offset by a system of cubicle walls that separated the captives into groups. These cubicle walls were made from the same riveted steel as the main walls: there was no communication from cubicle to cubicle except through a half foot of space left between the top of the wall and the ceiling. Thus each group of captives occupied, as it were, a small room. There were twenty-two captives. They were grouped in unequal number within four cubicles.

Through the entire length of this system, raised three feet from the ground, passing through the very centre of each room, ran a long wound sheet. It was made from coarse white linen bundled into a loose cylinder of cloth some six inches in diameter.

When the captives were first thrown into their cubicles, the long sheet was heavy with water. The warders had soaked the material so thoroughly that in the folds the water had gathered into lakes. The warders then issued their instructions. The captives were to wring the sheet dry. It would not do to wring the sheet to what we would normally call a 'dry' state – as of clothes ready for airing. On the contrary – this sheet must be purged of every moisture. It must be wrung as dry as a bone. This, the warders concluded, might take a long time. It might even take months of hard work. In fact, they had taken special care to treat the linen so that it would be durable over a lengthy period. But when the task was finally completed, then the men and women would be granted their freedom. They would be released.

As the grave faces of the warders disappeared and the glass skylights slid shut, the captives smiled for the first time. For months they had lived with the fear of death, they had shrunk in ceaseless apprehension of the terrible devices that awaited them. And now that future had devolved into the wringing of a simple sheet! A long sheet, it was true. But child's play in comparison with what they had expected. Thus they sank to the steel floor in relief. Few laid a hand on the sheet that day.

But after three months the captives began to realize the true extent of their task. By this time each group in each cubicle had wrung the worst water from their section of the sheet. Yet with all their sweating and straining they could not rid the cloth of its last dampness.

It was apparent that the warders had no intention of presenting them with a simple task. For, through vents near the roof, hot steam was injected mechanically into the cubicles as long as daylight lasted. This steam naturally moistened the sheet afresh. The steam was so regulated that it hindered rather than prevented the fulfilment of the wringing. Thus there was always less steam entering than moisture wrung from the sheet at a normal rate of working. The steam injection merely meant that for every ten drops of water wrung seven new drops would settle upon the sheet. So that eventually the captives would still be able to wring the sheet dry. This device of the warders was introduced solely to complicate the task. It seemed that the warders were acting in two ways. Daily they encouraged the efforts of the captives with promises of release; but daily they turned on the steam cocks.

In the cubicles the air was thick with steam. It was the air of a laundry, where steam catches in the throat, where it is sometimes difficult to breathe, where the smell of hot, wet cloth sickens the heart. The steel walls sweated. Condensed water trickled in winding trails down the grey plate. Beads of moisture clustered at the rivet heads. The long sheet spattered a few drops into the central gutter in the floor as the captives twisted against time. Both men and women worked half naked. Since the sheet was positioned three feet from the ground they were forced to stoop. If they sat at their work, then their arms grew numb in the raised attitude at which they had to be maintained. There was nothing for it but to stoop. In the hot air they sweated. Yet they dared not lean over the sheet for fear their sweat should fall on the hungry cloth. Their muscles knotted, their backs cried out as they twisted. The end was far. But there was an end. That meant that there was hope. This knowledge lent fire to the struggling ambition that lived in their human hearts. They worked.

Yet some were not always equal to the task.

ROOM THREE

THOSE WHO SOUGHT OUTSIDE

There were four rooms. Take Room Three. This housed five people – two married couples and a young Serbian grocer. All five of them wanted freedom. They worked earnestly at their task. That the task was in essence unproductive did not worry them. At least, it would produce their freedom. It was thus artificially productive. These five people set about the problem in a normal businesslike way. Previously, they had been used to habitual hours, a life of steady formula. This they now applied to the new business of wringing. Set hours were allotted to each person. It was as if they commuted regularly from their suburbia (the steel sleeping corner) to the office (the long sheet). They worked in relays, in four-hour stretches throughout the day and night.

However, as I have said, they were not equal to the task. The framework of habit overcame them. Like so many who live within a steady, comfortable routine, they allowed the routine around the work to predominate in importance above the work itself. They arrived at the long sheet punctually, and with consciences thus satisfied they put insufficient effort into the actual work. Furthermore, when they had fulfilled the routine assiduously for a period, one or the other would congratulate his conscience and really believe that he deserved a 'little relaxation.' And he would take the afternoon off. Such was the force of his emphasis on obedience to the letter that he was convinced the law would not suffer. Thus the real work of wringing suffered. New moisture crept in where his hands were weak. These people had set about the quest for freedom in the right way, but they were unhappily convinced of their righteousness.

Sometimes one or other of the couples would lie down together on the sweating steel plates. They would make love as the steam misted their bodies with false perspirations. One of the women became pregnant. Her child was born in the steam box. But, under the influence of Room Three's routine, that child could never be free. The influence, the constriction and the hopeless task of the parents would keep the child in the steam box for life. The child would never have the chance to learn to wring with effect.

ROOM TWO

THOSE WHO SOUGHT IN AND OUT AND AROUND

In another of the rooms – Room Two – there were five men. Their names and their professions do not matter. It is how they attacked the long sheet that matters. They attacked it in five different ways.

Here were five individualists, five who were forced by the set of their minds to approach their problems in various ways of their own. Day after day they laboured in the hot, damp steel cubicle, each twisting the long cylinder of cloth with different reasonings.

One man had been frightened by a sheet when he was young. On some indefinite day of his childhood, a new nurse had appeared. Her black eyes had burned with a powerful scorn; her small lascivious teeth and huge drooping cheeks had threatened him in the candlelight. On her first day the new nurse had made a little white monster from a white sheet. It had two heads and a shapeless, flowing body. The little heads were sharp, and always bobbing. The nurse had come silently into the night nursery when it was dark. Lighting a candle on the floor behind the end of the bed, she had quietly raised her little white monster so that the boy could just see it above his toes. Then she had begun a strident sing-song crowing, like the harsh crowing of Punch. The boy had awoken to this sound, and had seen the sharp bobbing heads of the little monster.

Now, some thirty years later, the man has forgotten the scene. But somehow his hands cannot touch the long sheet without a great sensation of uneasiness. His hands do not touch the white cloth well. Consequently, he is forever making excuses to avoid working on the sheet. He feigns illness. He offers to clear up the excrement of all the others. He has mutilated his hands. He has attempted to make love with the other four men to avoid the reality of the sheet. Oh, there is no end to the devices the fellow has invented from his sadness! But whatever he does cannot eradicate the awful uneasiness that clouds the far reaches of his mind. At the moment of writing, this man is still in the steel cubicle. He will never be free.

Another of the men in Room Two was a simple quiet fellow. The others took no interest in him. He was too simple a fellow. Yet a most amazing thing – his section of the sheet was white and quite dry! There was a good reason for this. Without any conscious knowledge, without planning and scheming, he had naturally gone at his wringing the good way. He was accustomed to wring sitting astride the cloth. In this position, his legs squeezed at the cloth too. Thus, without questioning, he surrendered his whole body to the task. His heart, too; for he was such a simple fellow. This man's sheet was dry. But the others never even noticed. He was such a simple fellow.

There was one man in Room Two whose metier in life had always been the short cut. As previously in business, in love, in all relationships, he attempted to apply the shortcut system to the most important task of all – the wringing of the long sheet. He tried out a great many tricks and petty deceptions. He blocked up the pipe through which the guards pumped the steam. The next morning, like a mushroom, another pipe had grown at the side of the first. He tried feigning madness. The warders threw buckets of cold water down through the skylight. Some of this water splashed on to the sheet, destroying a whole month's work. The other men nearly killed him for this. Once he bribed one of the warders to send him a pot of white enamel. With this he painted the sheet white. The enamel dried hard. The sheet seemed dry! But the next day the warders came to chip the enamel off. They punished him with a travelling hose-jet. This jet travelled inconsequentially about the room. To save the water hitting the sheet, the man had to intercept the jet with his body. He was kept running and jumping and squatting for a whole day – until towards evening he dropped exhausted and rolled into the central gutter. The warders, of course, can never be bribed.

Then there was another man who can best be described as a fumbler. He worked hard and earnestly. He was up at the wringing well before the others, he seldom lay down till long after the skylights were dark and the air cleared of steam. But he fumbled. His mind co-ordinated imperfectly with his body. Although he felt that he concentrated his whole effort, psychic and physical, on the job of wringing – his mind would wander to other things. He never knew that this happened. But his hands did. They stopped wringing, they wrung the wrong way – and the fatal drops of moisture accumulated. He could never understand this. He thought his mind was always on the job. But instead his mind settled too often on matters only near to the job, not the job in essence. For a small instance – his mind might wander to the muscle on his left forearm. He might see that it bulges at a downward screw of the wet linen. He watches this bulge as he works. The bulge then absorbs his interest to such an extent that he makes greater play with this left arm to stimulate further the bulge of muscle. In compensation the right arm slackens its effort. The wringing becomes uneven and inefficient. Yet all this time he himself in honesty believes that he is concentrating upon his job. The muscle is, in fact, part of the job. Yet it is only a facet, not the full perspective. He fumbles because he does not see clearly: and to wring dry the long sheet a man must give his whole thought in calm and complete clarity.

The fifth man in Room Two was a good worker. That is, he had found the way to wring effectively; and at times his portion of the sheet was almost dry. But he was perverted. This man liked to wring the sheet almost dry – then stand by and watch the steam settle into the folds once more! He liked to watch the fruits of his labour rot. In this way he freed himself from the task. He freed himself by attaining his object, and then treating it with the scorn he imagined it deserved. He felt himself master of the work – but in reality he never became the master of his true freedom. There was no purity in this man. His freedom was false.

ROOM FOUR

THOSE WHO NEVER SOUGHT AT ALL

Room Number Four housed more captives than the others. Seven people were crowded into this one cell of steam and steel. There were three women, one girl of twelve, and three men. These people seldom did much work. They were a source of great disappointment to the warders. To these people the effort was not worth eventual freedom. The immensity of the task had long ago disheartened them. Their minds were not big enough to envisage the better future. They had enough. They had their breeding and their food. The state of life held no interest for them. Vaguely, they would have preferred better conditions. But at the cost of toil and thought – no. These people were squalid and small. Their desire for freedom had been killed by a dull acceptance of their impotence. This also became true of the little girl of twelve. She had no alternative but to follow the others.

The warders never played their favourite trick on Room Four. For the simple reason that the trick would have had no effect. The trick was to release into the cells small squadrons of saturated birds. The birds flew into the cells and scattered water from their wings everywhere. The birds flew in all directions and the captives ran wildly here and there in hysterical efforts to trap them before they splashed water onto the sacred sheet. The warders considered that the element of chance implicit in these birds was a healthy innovation. Otherwise, life for the captives would have been too ordered. There must be risk, said the warders. And so from time to time, with no warning, they injected these little wet birds and captives hastened to protect the purity of their work against the interference of fate. If they could not catch the birds in time, they learnt in this manner how to accept misfortune: and in patience they redoubled their efforts to retrieve the former level of their work.

But into Room Four the birds never flew. The trick would never have affected the inhabitants, who lived at the low ebb of misfortune already. Perhaps the real tragedy of these dispirited people was not their own misfortune, to which they had grown accustomed, but that their slackness had its effect on those whose ambitions were pure and strong. The slackness was contagious. In this way. The sheet was so wet in Room Four that the water seeped through into Room One. And in Room One lived the most successful of all the captives.

ROOM ONE

THOSE WHO SOUGHT INSIDE

There were five of them in cubicle One. Four men and one woman. They were successful no more for their method of wringing than for their attitude towards wringing. At first, when they had been dropped through the skylight, when they saw the long sheet, when they slowly accustomed themselves to the idea of what lay before them, they were profoundly shocked. Unlike the others, they thought death preferable to such senseless and unproductive labour. But they were good people. Soon they saw beyond the apparent drudgery. Soon they had passed through and rejected the various phases experienced and retained by the other rooms. They had known the defeat of Room Four, the individual terrors and escapes of Room Two, the veneer of virtue beneath which the inhabitants of Room Three purred with such alarming satisfaction. No, it was not so very long before these good people saw beyond the apparent and thenceforth set themselves to work with body and soul, gently but with strength, humbly yet fearlessly, towards the only end of value – freedom.

First, these people said 'Unproductive? The long sheet a senseless drudgery? Yes – but why not? In whatever other sphere of labour could we ever have produced ultimately anything? It is not the production that counts, but the life lived in the spirit during production. Production, the tightening of the muscles, the weaving of the hands, the pouring forth of shaped materials – this is only an employment for the nervous body, the dying legacy of the hunter's will to movement. Let the hands weave, but at the same time let the spirit search. Give the long sheet its rightful place – and concentrate on a better understanding of the freedom that is our real object.'

At the same time, they saw to it that the sheet was wrung efficiently. They arranged a successful rota system. They tried various methods and positions with their hands. Examining every detail, they selected in every way the best approach. They did not overtax themselves. They did not hurry themselves. They worked with a rhythmic resilience, conserving this energy for the exertion of that. They allowed no extremes. They applied themselves with sincerity and a good will.

Above all they had faith. Their attitude was broad – but led in one direction. Their endeavour was freedom. They feared neither work nor weakness. These things did not exist for them: their existence was a material through which they could achieve, by calm and sensitive understanding, the goal of perfect freedom.

Gradually these people achieved their end. In spite of the steam, in spite of the saturated birds, in spite of the waterous contagion seeping through from the room of the defeated, in spite of the long hours and the heat and the squared horizon of rusting steel – their spirit prevailed and they achieved the purity they sought. One day, seven years later, the wet grey sheet dawned a bright white – dry as desert ivory, dry as marble dust.

They called up through the skylight to the warders. The grave faces appeared. Coldly the warders regarded the white sheet. There were nods of approbation.

'Freedom?' said the captives.

The guards brought out their great hoses and doused the white sheet sodden grey with a huge pressure of water.

'You already have it,' they answered. 'Freedom lies in an attitude of the spirit. There is no other freedom.' And the skylights silently closed.

THE ALEPH

Jorge Luis Borges

TRANSLATED INTO ENGLISH BY ANDREW HURLEY

Jorge Luis Borges (1899–1986) was an Argentine writer who became world-renowned for his short fiction. Among his most famous books are the collections *Ficciones* (1944) and *The Aleph and Other Stories* (1949). Borges gleefully dove into many different genres and modes of fiction, while creating tales uniquely his own. His use of traditionally nonfictional approaches camouflaged outrageously strange ideas. Although Borges was not a 'weird' writer per se, many of his short stories contain traces of the inexplicable. Borges stories appeared in *The Magazine of Fantasy & Science Fiction* as well as literary journals while he was alive. 'The Aleph' (1945), featuring a version of Borges himself, is one of the master's weird classics.

O God, I could be bounded in a nutshell and count myself a King of infinite space.

Hamlet, II:2

But they will teach us that Eternity is the Standing still of the Present Time, a Nunc-stans *(as the Schools call it); which neither they, nor any else understand, no more than they would a* Hic-stans *for an Infinite greatnesse of Place.*

Leviathan, IV:46

That same sweltering morning that Beatriz Viterbo died, after an imperious confrontation with her illness in which she had never for an instant stooped to either sentimentality or fear, I noticed that a new advertisement for some cigarettes or other (*blondes*, I believe they were) had been posted on the iron billboards of the Plaza Constitución; the fact deeply grieved me, for I realized that the vast unceasing universe was already growing away from her, and that this change was but the first in an infinite series. *The universe may change, but I shall not*, thought I with melancholy vanity. I knew that more than once my futile devotion had exasperated her; now that she was dead, I could consecrate myself to her memory – without hope, but also without humiliation. I reflected that April 30 was her birthday; stopping by her house on Calle Garay that day to pay my respects to her father and her first cousin Carlos Argentino Daneri was an irreproachable, perhaps essential act of courtesy. Once again I would wait in the half-light of the little parlor crowded with furniture and draperies and bric-a-brac, once again I would study the details of the many photographs and portraits of her: Beatriz Viterbo, in profile, in color; Beatriz in a mask at the Carnival of 1921; Beatriz' first communion; Beatriz on the day of her wedding to Roberto Alessandri; Beatriz shortly after the divorce, lunching at the Jockey Club; Beatriz in Quilmes with Delia San Marco Porcel and Carlos Argentino; Beatriz with the Pekinese that had been a gift from Villegas Haedo; Beatriz in full-front and in three-quarters view, smiling, her hand on her chin... I would not be obliged, as I had been on occasions before, to justify my presence with modest offerings of books – books whose pages I learned at last to cut, so as not to find, months later, that they were still intact.

Beatriz Viterbo died in 1929; since then, I have not allowed an April 30 to pass without returning to her house. That first time, I arrived at seven-fifteen and stayed for about twenty-five minutes; each year I would turn up a little later and stay a little longer; in 1933, a downpour came to my aid: they were forced to ask me to dinner. Naturally, I did not let that fine precedent go to waste; in 1934 I turned up a few minutes after eight with a lovely confection from Santa Fe; it was perfectly natural that I should stay for dinner. And so it was that on those melancholy and vainly erotic anniversaries I came to receive the gradual confidences of Carlos Argentino Daneri.

Beatriz was tall, fragile, very slightly stooped; in her walk, there was (if I may be pardoned the oxymoron) something of a graceful clumsiness, a soupçon of hesitancy, or of palsy; Carlos Argentino is a pink, substantial, gray-haired man of refined features. He holds some sort of subordinate position in an illegible library in the outskirts toward the south of the city; he is authoritarian, though also ineffectual; until very recently he took advantage of nights and holidays to remain at home. At two generations' remove, the Italian *s* and the liberal Italian gesticulation still survive in him. His mental activity is constant, passionate, versatile, and utterly insignificant. He is full of pointless analogies and idle scruples. He has (as Beatriz did) large, beautiful, slender hands. For some months he labored under an obsession for Paul Fort, less for Fort's ballads than the idea of a glory that could never be tarnished. 'He is the prince of the poets of *la belle France*,' he would fatuously say. 'You assail him in vain; you shall never touch him – not even the most venomous of your darts shall ever touch him.'

On April 30, 1941, I took the liberty of enriching my sweet offering with a bottle of domestic brandy. Carlos Argentino tasted it, pronounced it 'interesting,' and, after a few snifters, launched into an apologia for modern man.

'I picture him,' he said with an animation that was rather unaccountable, 'in his study, as though in the watchtower of a great city, surrounded by telephones, telegraphs, phonographs, the latest in radio-telephone and motion-picture and magic-lantern equipment, and glossaries and calendars and timetables and bulletins …'

He observed that for a man so equipped, the act of traveling was supererogatory; this twentieth century of ours had upended the fable of Muhammad and the mountain – mountains nowadays did in fact come to the modern Muhammad.

So witless did these ideas strike me as being, so sweeping and pompous the way they were expressed, that I associated them immediately with literature. Why, I asked him, didn't he write these ideas down? Predictably, he replied that he already had; they, and others no less novel, figured large in the Augural Canto, Prologurial Canto, or simply Prologue-Canto, of a poem on which he had been working, with no deafening hurly-burly and *sans réclame*, for many years, leaning always on those twin staffs Work and Solitude. First he would open the floodgates of the imagination, then repair to the polishing wheel. The poem was entitled *The Earth*; it centered on a description of our own terraqueous orb and was graced, of course, with picturesque digression and elegant apostrophe.

I begged him to read me a passage, even if only a brief one. He opened a desk drawer, took out a tall stack of tablet paper stamped with the letterhead of the Juan Crisóstomo Lafinur Library, and read, with ringing self-satisfaction:

I have seen, as did the Greek, man's cities
and his fame,
The works, the days of various light, the
hunger;
I prettify no fact, I falsify no name,
For the voyage *I narrate is…* autour de ma
chambre.

'A stanza interesting from every point of view,' he said. 'The first line wins the kudos of the learnèd, the academician, the Hellenist – though perhaps not that of those would-be scholars that make up such a substantial portion of popular opinion. The second moves from Homer to Hesiod (implicit homage, at the very threshold of the dazzling new edifice, to the father of didactic poetry), not without revitalizing a technique whose lineage may be traced to Scripture – that is, enumeration, congeries, or conglobation. The third – baroque? decadent? the purified and fanatical cult of form? – consists of twinned hemistichs; the fourth, unabashedly bilingual, assures me the unconditional support of every spirit able to feel the ample attractions of playfulness. I shall say nothing of the unusual rhyme, nor of the erudition that allows me – without pedantry or boorishness! – to include within the space of four lines three erudite allusions spanning thirty centuries of dense literature: first the *Odyssey*, second the *Works and Days*, and third that immortal bagatelle that regales us with the diversions of the Savoyard's plume... Once again, I show my awareness that truly modern art demands the balm of laughter, of *scherzo*. There is no doubt about it – Goldoni was right!'

Carlos Argentino read me many another stanza, all of which earned the same profuse praise and comment from him. There was nothing memorable about them; I could not even judge them to be much worse than the first one. Application, resignation, and chance had conspired in their composition; the virtues that Daneri attributed to them were afterthoughts. I realized that the poet's work had lain not in the poetry but in the invention of reasons for accounting the poetry admirable; naturally, that later work modified the poem for Daneri, but not for anyone else. His oral expression was extravagant; his metrical clumsiness prevented him, except on a very few occasions, from transmitting that extravagance to the poem.[1]

Only once in my lifetime have I had occasion to examine the fifteen thousand dodecasyllables of the *Polyalbion* – that topographical epic in which Michael Drayton recorded the fauna, flora, hydrography, orography, military and monastic history of England – but I am certain that Drayton's massive yet limited œuvre is less tedious than the vast enterprise conceived and given birth by Carlos Argentino. He proposed to versify the entire planet; by 1941 he had already dispatched several hectares of the state of Queensland, more than a kilometer of the course of the Ob, a gasworks north of Veracruz, the leading commercial establishments in the parish of Concepción, Mariana Cambaceres de Alvear's villa on Calle Once de Setiembre in Belgrano, and a Turkish bath not far from the famed Brighton Aquarium. He read me certain laborious passages from the Australian region of his poem; his long, formless alexandrines lacked the relative agitation of the prologue. Here is one stanza:

Hear this. To the right hand of the routine
signpost
(Coming – what need is there to say? – from
north-northwest)
Yawns a bored skeleton – Color? Sky-pearly. –
Outside the sheepfold that suggests an ossuary.

'Two audacious risks!' he exclaimed in exultation, 'snatched from the jaws of disaster, I can hear you mutter, by success! I admit it, I admit it. One, the epithet routine, while making an adjective of a synonym for "highway," nods, *en passant*, to the inevitable tedium inherent to those chores of a pastoral and rustic nature that neither georgics nor our own belaureled *Don Segundo* ever dared acknowledge in such a forthright way, with no beating about the bush. And the second, delicately referring to the first, the forcefully prosaic phrase *Yawns a bored skeleton*, which the finicky will want to excommunicate without benefit of clergy but that the critic of more manly tastes will embrace as he does his very life. The entire line, in fact, is a good 24 karats. The second half-line sets up the most animated sort of conversation with the reader; it anticipates his lively curiosity, puts a question in his mouth, and then... *voilà*, answers it... on the instant. And what do you think of that

[1] I do, however, recall these lines from a satire in which he lashed out vehemently against bad poets:

This one fits the poem with a coat of mail
Of erudition; that one, with gala pomps and circumstance.
Both flail their absurd pennons to no avail,
Neglecting poor wretches, the factor sublime – its LOVELINESS!

It was only out of concern that he might create an army of implacable and powerful enemies, he told me, that he did not fearlessly publish the poem.

coup *sky-pearly*? The picturesque neologism just *hints* at the sky, which is such an important feature of the Australian landscape. Without that allusion, the hues of the sketch would be altogether too gloomy, and the reader would be compelled to close the book, his soul deeply wounded by a black and incurable melancholy.'

About midnight, I took my leave.

Two Sundays later, Daneri telephoned me for what I believe was the first time in his or my life. He suggested that we meet at four, 'to imbibe the milk of the gods together in the nearby salon-bar that my estimable landlords, Messrs. Zunino and Zungri, have had the rare commercial foresight to open on the corner. It is a café you will do well to acquaint yourself with.' I agreed, with more resignation than enthusiasm, to meet him. It was hard for us to find a table; the relentlessly modern 'salon-bar' was only slightly less horrendous than I had expected; at neighboring tables, the excited clientele discussed the sums invested by Zunino and Zungri without a second's haggling. Carlos Argentino pretended to be amazed at some innovation in the establishment's lighting (an innovation he'd no doubt been apprised of beforehand) and then said to me somewhat severely:

'Much against your inclinations it must be that you recognize that this place is on a par with the most elevated heights of Flores.'

Then he reread four or five pages of his poem to me. Verbal ostentation was the perverse principle that had guided his revisions: where he had formerly written 'blue' he now had 'azure,' 'cerulean,' and even 'bluish.' The word 'milky' was not sufficiently hideous for him; in his impetuous description of a place where wool was washed, he had replaced it with 'lactine,' 'lactescent,' 'lactoreous,' 'lacteal'... He railed bitterly against his critics; then, in a more benign tone, he compared them to those persons 'who possess neither precious metals nor even the steam presses, laminators, and sulfuric acids needed for minting treasures, but who can *point out* to others the *precise location* of a treasure.' Then he was off on another tack, inveighing against the obsession for forewords, what he called 'prologomania,' an attitude that 'had already been spoofed in the elegant preface to the *Quixote* by the Prince of Wits himself.' He would, however, admit that an attention-getting recommendation might be a good idea at the portals of his new work – 'an accolade penned by a writer of stature, of real import.' He added that he was planning to publish the first cantos of his poem. It was at that point that I understood the unprecedented telephone call and the invitation: the man was about to ask me to write the preface to that pedantic farrago of his. But my fear turned out to be unfounded. Carlos Argentino remarked, with grudging admiration, that he believed he did not go too far in saying that the prestige achieved in every sphere by the man of letters Alvaro Melián Lafinur was 'solid,' and that if I could be persuaded to persuade him, Alvaro 'might be enchanted to write the called-for foreword.' In order to forestall the most unpardonable failure on my part, I was to speak on behalf of the poem's two incontrovertible virtues: its formal perfection and its scientific rigor – 'because that broad garden of rhetorical devices, figures, charms, and graces will not tolerate a single detail that does not accord with its severe truthfulness.' He added that Beatriz had always enjoyed Alvaro's company.

I agreed, I agreed most profusely. I did, however, for the sake of added plausibility, make it clear that I wouldn't be speaking with Alvaro on Monday but rather on Thursday, at the little supper that crowned each meeting of the Writers Circle. (There are no such suppers, although it is quite true that the meetings are held on Thursday, a fact that Carlos Argentino might verify in the newspapers and that lent a certain credence to my contention.) I told him (half-prophetically, half-farsightedly) that before broaching the subject of the prologue, I would describe the curious design of the poem. We said our good-byes; as I turned down Calle Bernardo de Irigoyen, I contemplated as impartially as I could the futures that were left to me: (a) speak with Alvaro and tell him that that first cousin of Beatriz' (the explanatory circumlocution would allow me to speak her name) had written a poem that seemed to draw out to infinity the possibilities of cacophony and chaos; (b) not speak with Alvaro. Knowing myself pretty well, I foresaw that my indolence would opt for (b).

From early Friday morning on, the telephone was a constant source of anxiety. I was indignant that this instrument from which Beatriz' irrecoverable voice had once emerged might now be reduced to transmitting the futile and perhaps angry complaints of that self-deluding Carlos Argentino Daneri. Fortunately, nothing came of it – save the inevitable irritation inspired by a man who had charged me with a delicate mission and then forgotten all about me.

Eventually the telephone lost its terrors, but in late October Carlos Argentino did call me. He was very upset; at first I didn't recognize his voice. Dejectedly and angrily he stammered out that that now unstoppable pair Zunino and Zungri, under the pretext of expanding their already enormous 'café,' were going to tear down his house.

'The home of my parents – the home where I was born – the old and deeply rooted house on Calle Garay!' he repeated, perhaps drowning his grief in the melodiousness of the phrase.

It was not difficult for me to share his grief. After forty, every change becomes a hateful symbol of time's passing; in addition, this was a house that I saw as alluding infinitely to Beatriz. I tried to make that extremely delicate point clear; my interlocutor cut me off. He said that if Zunino and Zungri persisted in their absurd plans, then Zunni, his attorney, would sue them *ipso facto* for damages, and force them to part with a good hundred thousand for his trouble.

Zunni's name impressed me; his law firm, on the corner of Caseros and Tacuarí, is one of proverbial sobriety. I inquired whether Zunni had already taken the case. Daneri said he'd be speaking with him that afternoon; then he hesitated, and in that flat, impersonal voice we drop into when we wish to confide something very private, he said he had to have the house so he could finish the poem – because in one corner of the cellar there was an Aleph. He explained that an Aleph is one of the points in space that contain all points.

'It's right under the dining room, in the cellar,' he explained. In his distress, his words fairly tumbled out. '*It's mine, it's mine*; I discovered it in my childhood, before I ever attended school. The cellar stairway is steep, and my aunt and uncle had forbidden me to go down it, but somebody said you could go around the world with that thing down there in the basement. The person, whoever it was, was referring, I later learned, to a steamer trunk, but I thought there was some magical contraption down there. I tried to sneak down the stairs, fell head over heels, and when I opened my eyes, I saw the Aleph.'

'The Aleph?' I repeated.

'Yes, the place where, without admixture or confusion, all the places of the world, seen from every angle, coexist. I revealed my discovery to no one, but I did return. The child could not understand that he was given that privilege so that the man might carve out a poem! Zunino and Zungri shall never take it from me – never, never! Lawbook in hand, Zunni will prove that my Aleph is *inalienable*.'

I tried to think.

'But isn't the cellar quite dark?'

'Truth will not penetrate a recalcitrant understanding. If all the places of the world are within the Aleph, there too will be all stars, all lamps, all sources of light.'

'I'll be right over. I want to see it.'

I hung up before he could tell me not to come. Sometimes learning a fact is enough to make an entire series of corroborating details, previously unrecognized, fall into place; I was amazed that I hadn't realized until that moment that Carlos Argentino was a madman. All the Viterbos, in fact... Beatriz (I myself have said this many times) was a woman, a girl of implacable clearsightedness, but there were things about her – oversights, distractions, moments of contempt, downright cruelty – that perhaps could have done with a *pathological* explanation. Carlos Argentino's madness filled me with malign happiness; deep down, we had always detested one another.

On Calle Garay, the maid asked me to be so kind as to wait – Sr. Daneri was in the cellar, as he always was, developing photographs. Beside the flowerless vase atop the useless piano smiled the great faded photograph of Beatriz, not so much anachronistic as outside time. No one could see us; in a desperation of tenderness I approached the portrait.

'Beatriz, Beatriz Elena, Beatriz Elena Viterbo,' I said. 'Belovèd Beatriz, Beatriz lost forever – it's me, it's me, Borges.'

Carlos came in shortly afterward. His words were laconic, his tone indifferent; I realized that he was unable to think of anything but the loss of the Aleph.

'A glass of pseudocognac,' he said, 'and we'll duck right into the cellar. I must forewarn you: dorsal decubitus is essential, as are darkness, immobility, and a certain ocular accommodation. You'll lie on the tile floor and fix your eyes on the nineteenth step of the pertinent stairway. I'll reascend the stairs, let down the trap door, and you'll be alone. Some rodent will frighten you – easy enough to do! Within a few minutes, you will see the Aleph. The microcosm of the alchemists and Kabbalists, our proverbial friend the *multum in parvo*, made flesh!

'Of course,' he added, in the dining room, 'if you don't see it, that doesn't invalidate anything I've told you... Go on down; within a very short while you will be able to begin a dialogue with all the images of Beatriz.'

I descended quickly, sick of his vapid chatter. The cellar, barely wider than the stairway, was more like a well or cistern. In vain my eyes sought the trunk that Carlos Argentino had mentioned. A few burlap bags and some crates full of bottles cluttered one corner. Carlos picked up one of the bags, folded it, and laid it out very precisely.

'The couch is a humble one,' he explained, 'but if I raise it one inch higher, you'll not see a thing, and you'll be cast down and dejected. Stretch that great clumsy body of yours out on the floor and count up nineteen steps.'

I followed his ridiculous instructions; he finally left. He carefully let down the trap door; in spite of a chink of light that I began to make out later, the darkness seemed total. Suddenly I realized the danger I was in; I had allowed myself to be locked underground by a madman, after first drinking down a snifter of poison. Carlos' boasting clearly masked the deep-seated fear that I wouldn't see his 'miracle'; in order to protect his delirium, in order to hide his madness from himself, *he had to kill me*. I felt a vague discomfort, which I tried to attribute to my rigidity, not to the operation of a narcotic. I closed my eyes, then opened them. It was then that I saw the Aleph.

I come now to the ineffable center of my tale; it is here that a writer's hopelessness begins. Every language is an alphabet of symbols the employment of which assumes a past shared by its interlocutors. How can one transmit to others the infinite Aleph, which my timorous memory can scarcely contain? In a similar situation, mystics have employed a wealth of emblems: to signify the deity, a Persian mystic speaks of a bird that somehow is all birds; Alain de Lille speaks of a sphere whose center is everywhere and circumference nowhere; Ezekiel, of an angel with four faces, facing east and west, north and south at once. (It is not for nothing that I call to mind these inconceivable analogies; they bear a relation to the Aleph.) Perhaps the gods would not deny me the discovery of an equivalent image, but then this report would be polluted with literature, with falseness. And besides, the central problem – the enumeration, even partial enumeration, of infinity – is irresolvable. In that unbounded moment, I saw millions of delightful and horrible acts; none amazed me so much as the fact that all occupied the same point, without superposition and without transparency. What my eyes saw was *simultaneous*; what I shall write is *successive*, because language is successive. Something of it, though, I will capture.

Under the step, toward the right, I saw a small iridescent sphere of almost unbearable brightness. At first I thought it was spinning; then I realized that the movement was an illusion produced by the dizzying spectacles inside it. The Aleph was probably two or three centimeters in diameter, but universal space was contained inside it, with no diminution in size. Each thing (the glass surface of a mirror, let us say) was infinite things, because I could clearly see it from every point in the cosmos. I saw the populous sea, saw dawn and dusk, saw the multitudes of the Americas, saw a silvery spider-web at the center of a black pyramid, saw a broken labyrinth (it was London), saw endless eyes, all very close, studying themselves in me as though in a mirror, saw all the mirrors on the planet (and none of them reflecting me), saw in a rear courtyard on Calle Soler the same tiles I'd seen twenty years before in the entryway of a house in Fray Bentos, saw clusters of grapes, snow, tobacco, veins of metal, water vapor, saw convex equatorial deserts and their every grain of sand, saw a woman in Inverness whom I shall never forget, saw her violent hair, her haughty body, saw a cancer in her breast, saw a circle of dry soil within a sidewalk where there had once been a tree, saw a country house in Adrogué, saw a copy of the first English translation of Pliny (Philemon Holland's), saw every letter of every page at once (as a boy, I would be astounded that the letters in a closed book didn't get all scrambled up together overnight), saw simultaneous night and day, saw a sunset in Querétaro that seemed to reflect the color of a rose in Bengal, saw my bedroom (with no one in it), saw in a study in Alkmaar a globe of the terraqueous world placed between two mirrors that multiplied it endlessly, saw horses with wind-whipped manes on a beach in the Caspian Sea at dawn, saw the delicate bones of a hand, saw the survivors of a battle sending postcards, saw a Tarot card in a shopwindow in Mirzapur, saw the oblique shadows of ferns on the floor of a greenhouse, saw tigers, pistons, bisons, tides, and armies, saw all the ants on earth, saw a Persian astrolabe, saw in a desk drawer (and the handwriting made me tremble) obscene, incredible, detailed letters that Beatriz had sent Carlos Argentino, saw a beloved monument in Chacarita, saw the horrendous remains of what had once, deliciously, been Beatriz Viterbo, saw the circulation of my dark blood, saw the coils and springs of love and the alterations of death, saw the Aleph from everywhere at once, saw the earth in the Aleph, and the Aleph once more in the earth and the earth in the Aleph, saw my face and my viscera, saw your face, and I felt dizzy, and I wept, because my eyes had seen that secret, hypothetical object whose name has been usurped by men but which no man has ever truly looked upon: the inconceivable universe.

I had a sense of infinite veneration, infinite pity.

'Serves you right, having your mind boggled, for sticking your nose in where you weren't wanted,' said a jovial, bored voice. 'And you may rack your brains, but you'll never repay me for this revelation – not in a hundred years. What a magnificent observatory, eh, Borges!'

Carlos Argentino's shoes occupied the highest step. In the sudden half-light, I managed to get to my feet.

'Magnificent... Yes, quite... magnificent,' I stammered.

The indifference in my voice surprised me.

'You did see it?' Carlos Argentino insisted anxiously. 'See it clearly? In color and everything?'

Instantly, I conceived my revenge. In the most kindly sort of way – manifestly pitying, nervous, evasive – I thanked Carlos Argentino Daneri for the hospitality of his cellar and urged him to take advantage of the demolition of his house to remove himself from the pernicious influences of the metropolis, which no one – believe me, no one! – can be immune to. I refused, with gentle firmness, to discuss the Aleph; I clasped him by both shoulders as I took my leave and told him again that the country – peace and quiet, you know – was the very best medicine one could take.

Out in the street, on the steps of the Constitución Station, in the subway, all the faces seemed familiar. I feared there was nothing that had the power to surprise or astonish me anymore, I feared that I would never again be without a sense of déjà vu. Fortunately, after a few unsleeping nights, forgetfulness began to work in me again.

Postscript (March 1, 1943): Six months after the demolition of the building on Calle Garay, Procrustes Publishers, undaunted by the length of Carlos Argentino Daneri's substantial poem, published the first in its series of 'Argentine pieces.' It goes without saying what happened: Carlos Argentino won second place in the National Prize for Literature.[2] The first prize went to Dr. Aita; third, to Dr. Mario Bonfanti; incredibly, my own work *The Sharper's Cards* did not earn a single vote. Once more, incomprehension and envy

[2] 'I received your mournful congratulations,' he wrote me. 'You scoff, my lamentable friend, in envy, but you shall confess – though the words stick in your throat! – that this time I have crowned my cap with the most scarlet of plumes; my turban, with the most caliphal of rubies.'

triumphed! I have not managed to see Daneri for quite a long time; the newspapers say he'll soon be giving us another volume. His happy pen (belabored no longer by the Aleph) has been consecrated to setting the compendia of Dr. Acevedo Diaz to verse.

There are two observations that I wish to add: one, with regard to the nature of the Aleph; the other, with respect to its name. Let me begin with the latter: 'aleph,' as well all know, is the name of the first letter of the alphabet of the sacred language. Its application to the disk of my tale would not appear to be accidental. In the Kabbala, that letter signifies the En Soph, the pure and unlimited godhead; it has also been said that its shape is that of a man pointing to the sky and the earth, to indicate that the lower world is the map and mirror of the higher. For the *Mengenlehre*, the aleph is the symbol of the transfinite numbers, in which the whole is not greater than any of its parts. I would like to know: Did Carlos Argentino choose that name, or did he read it, *applied to another point at which all points converge*, in one of the innumerable texts revealed to him by the Aleph in his house? Incredible as it may seem, I believe that there is (or was) another Aleph; I believe that the Aleph of Calle Garay was a *false* Aleph.

Let me state my reasons. In 1867, Captain Burton was the British consul in Brazil; in July of 1942, Pedro Henriquez Ureña discovered a manuscript by Burton in a library in Santos, and in this manuscript Burton discussed the mirror attributed in the East to Iskandar dhu-al-Qarnayn, or Alexander the Great of Macedonia. In this glass, Burton said, the entire universe was reflected. Burton mentions other similar artifices – the sevenfold goblet of Kai Khosru; the mirror that Tāriq ibn-Ziyād found in a tower (*1001 Nights*, 272); the mirror that Lucian of Samosata examined on the moon (*True History*, I:26); the specular spear attributed by the first book of Capella's *Satyricon* to Jupiter; Merlin's universal mirror, 'round and hollow and... [that] seem'd a world of glas' (*Faerie Queene*, III:2, 19) – and then adds these curious words: 'But all the foregoing (besides sharing the defect of not existing) are mere optical instruments. The faithful who come to the Amr mosque in Cairo, know very well that the universe lies inside one of the stone columns that surround the central courtyard... No one, of course, can see it, but those who put their ear to the surface claim to hear, within a short time, the bustling rumour of it... The mosque dates to the seventh century; the columns were taken from other, pre-Islamic, temples, for as ibn-Khaldūun has written: *In the republics founded by nomads, the attendance of foreigners is essential for all those things that bear upon masonry*.'

Does that Aleph exist, within the heart of a stone? Did I see it when I saw all things, and then forget it? Our minds are permeable to forgetfulness; I myself am distorting and losing, through the tragic erosion of the years, the features of Beatriz.

For Estela Canto

A CHILD IN THE BUSH OF GHOSTS

Olympe Bhêly-Quénum

Olympe Bhêly-Quénum (1928–) is a Beninese writer, journalist, literary critic, and researcher. Born in Ouidah, Benin, Bhêly-Quénum won the Grand prix littéraire de l'Afrique noire for *Le Chant du lac* in 1966. He moved to France in the late 1940s and lives there today. In the 1960s he served as the editor-in-chief of the African magazine *L'Afrique Actuelle* and then served with UNESCO. His stories and novels originally written in French have been translated into English, German, Czech, and Japanese. 'A Child in the Bush of Ghosts' (1950) *is* a ghost story, perhaps, but also a surreal vision; André Breton famously called the story 'du rêve a l'état brut' (dream of the raw).

When I was eleven years old, one of my uncles one day took me along with him to his farm. His name was Akpoto. He was a handsome man with large black eyes, sturdy and distinguished-looking. We had set out early, and yet the African morning sun had beaten us to it. We had covered more than thirteen kilometers on the district council road; then we had taken the pathway that led to Houêto. A small river, fordable at any time of day, cut across the path of fine golden sand which meandered through a high and dense forest.

We had crossed the river and continued walking on sand. I loved the softness of that sandy earth; its velvety surface pleasantly caressed the soles of my bare feet. But the joy I felt in walking on that path gradually gave way to fear as we penetrated ever more deeply into the forest. When we left the path for a sodden trail, I suddenly had a feeling that the humidity pervaded my whole body, and the sense of fear became intolerable. I therefore started pestering my uncle with little questions which were as irritating as they were foolish. I kept knocking against him, clung to his hand or moved clumsily in front of him and thus almost succeeded several times in making him fall…

We were crossing a kind of clearing where the sky above remained invisible as in most of our forests. We had already walked too much. For how long? I can't say. I was not yet going to school and, naturally, did not know any French, to the utter indignation of my father, the respectable primary school teacher, who always saw me as sickly and unable to stand the hustle and bustle of a school in session. As far as my uncle was concerned, he was able to determine the time of day from the position of the sun through a special kind of sensory perception, or rather intuition. Therefore after having raised his eyes in vain towards the arches of the towering trees hiding the sky from our eyes, he said to me in his gentle voice which I can still hear:

'Wait for me here, I'll be back in a short while.'

He left me, plunging with big steps into the bush that stretched out as far as the eye could see. He had put a big orange and four guavas into my hands. Suddenly I felt dead tired. I was gripped by the urge to cry but controlled myself. I've never had much use for cry-babies. There is nothing I detest so much as giving unbridled expression to our sorrows. And I waited. Oh, I certainly waited more than I shall ever be able to wait again, but my uncle did not return. There was plenty of time for me to eat two guavas, then my orange, and then I waited again a very long time before munching my two remaining guavas.

Worn out by the anxiety brought about by seeing nothing but the bush with its frightening calm around me, I sat down on the black forest earth and buried my face in my hands as if I never wanted to see any more of the place where I was. But as the humidity caught hold of me I had to rise again and I started walking without really having any idea of where I was going. I ought to have searched for the path we had followed until then but all my senses were gripped by panic and I marched like an automaton. I wished I could have given out a single scream, whistled, sung or talked loudly, or even just muttered something – anything to assuage the effect of the fear in me, anything to make me feel aware of my person or, simply, to give me the illusion that I still was myself, a human being, alive, finding myself there by chance, but I could not say anything… True to God, it is the only time I remember ever having felt fear.

I walked on relentlessly, unable to rediscover the path covered with sand; neither did I see the river again, its waters rolling with a sweet music, but I suddenly noticed in front of me a big woman wrapped in a white lappa that concealed her face and covered her feet. She advanced towards me; my heart started pounding fast; I felt as if I were receiving heavy blows from a ram inside me that did not quite succeed in splitting my chest open. I started shouting, no, I would have liked to shout; I felt I was shouting but did not hear myself shouting. I wished I could see the earth opening under my feet but the humus refused to do my bidding.

Only then did I concede defeat and stretched out my arms to the woman like a baby to its mother. To my surprise the woman passed me by in mute indifference. I looked back. She too had turned her head and before I had time to avert my eyes, she had already uncovered her face. I then saw something frightful: an emaciated face, the face of a fleshless skull, which made a horrid and repugnant grimace at me. I started running head over heels but glanced backwards from time to time. It was to no avail, for I constantly saw the person at a distance of twenty paces behind me, although she was not running.

But my mad gallop did not last very long; for a few moments after that encounter I found myself right in front of the railroad tracks. My heart was thumping so violently that it seemed to be about to burst my chest. I looked back again and saw my uncle.

'Where have you been? Why did you abandon me in the forest?' I asked, staring at him in bleak reproach.

He looked at me with pity because he read the anguish in my eyes; he told me, however, that he had not wasted any time at Houêto:

'I ordered my farm labourers at once to catch the chickens you see here and went myself to dig out cassava tubers for your grandmother and great-aunt. As soon as the job was finished, I returned to the clearing and was greatly surprised not to find you. I then continued my return journey, looking everywhere. All of a sudden I heard a rustle in the bush to my left; at first I thought it was a deer but I changed my mind afterwards when I saw a human shape running helter-skelter; it was you. I could have called you but I preferred to follow you with my eyes, for we were moving along parallel lines. A single step, but a big one, separated me from you, my boy. And then, of course, I had nothing to fear for you, for the bush is not dangerous.'

I felt sad at having brought him to the point where he thought he owed me an explanation. But on the other hand, my heart was still throbbing with anger and subdued sobs when I asked him in a trembling voice whether he had seen the river again.

'Yes, of course. It was there even before our ancestors were born, and will certainly remain after we're dead and gone.'

'You may be right, but I did not re-cross it.'

'What's that you're telling me? You must have forded it without noticing.'

'But it's true, uncle! I didn't see the slightest trace of the river; just look at my legs and feet, they aren't soaked like yours.'

'You surprise me, Codjo!'

'Let's return to the clearing by the path that has brought me here, if you don't believe me,' I said with an assurance that today I find astounding on the part of the child I was.

My uncle tucked his baskets with the cassava and chickens in them under some undergrowth, put me astride his shoulders and we took the path on which I had come, or rather the trail which perhaps would never have come into existence if I had not been the first human being who in my terrorized gallop had savagely flattened the grass along that line. We had arrived at the clearing, then at the farm much more quickly than we could have managed by walking on the sand-covered pathway. Akpoto was dumbfounded not to be obliged to pass the river he had been crossing for more than thirty-five years, the source of which he imagined to be somewhere in the forest. He put me down. My mouth felt dry. I quenched my thirst by drinking from a gourd, and this made me feel the freshness of the water and the pleasure of drinking it more keenly. Then we set out on the return journey, taking once more the kind of game-track I had discovered and which had become the fastest way to go to Houêto and back.

'A walking skeleton, that sort of thing doesn't exist. No dead man comes back to stay among the living; my grandmother and great-grandfather followed one another into death at a month's interval; nobody's ever told me that he has met them during the three years since they stopped coddling me.' So went my train of thought, and I was convinced that my encounter with the skeleton was merely the result of a hallucination.

Still, I wanted to make sure it was only an illusion and, taking advantage of a moment when my parents' watchfulness had flagged, I sneaked away from our compound where I was getting bored. I liked the open air, the solitude at the seaside or in the bush, and likewise the company of human beings who made no impositions on me but allowed me to make myself useful without feeling duty-bound to do so. In my parents' house everything was offered to me on a golden platter; I was pampered and idle and felt my uselessness to the full.

I reached the clearing again through the game-track and started searching for the source of the river. My mind was totally absorbed in the operation, perhaps because I was what my parents called 'a self-willed child', or perhaps also because I had an ulterior motive: to surprise my uncle by discovering the truth I wanted to find out. I therefore headed into the bush, slipping over pebbles, sinking into the spongy suction of the soft ground; skipping over creepers, crawling among thorns. In front of me appeared a big chameleon. We looked at each other for a good second and its skin visibly, and gradually, took on the colour of the indigo cloth tied around my neck, which I was wearing over my khaki shorts. At that moment I thought of my revered great-grandfather who in telling tales did not hide his predilection for the chameleon: *'It rarely misses its destination because it knows how to adjust itself to its surroundings and never looks back.'*

What did that mean? I hadn't the slightest idea. I was a spoilt, demanding child whom a too-indulgent great-grandfather had perhaps wanted to convert to patience and gentleness by lectures on moral philosophy. But he had reasoned through the use of symbols which remained a mystery to the child. Still, it was that venerable old man that I thought of that day, and seeing the chameleon take on the colour of my cloth, I not only decided not to look back but also to adapt myself to the bush, to understand its language, to bow to its laws, without, however, forgetting that I was a human being, the only creature who would not be forgiven voluntary subservience. I was born to grow big and to live even beyond death…

A small noise startled me; I did not pay any heed and continued making my way through the thorns that tore my cloth. A long snake carelessly passed between my legs, a boa rolled itself around a tree towards which I was heading. I was unafraid, beyond caring. My only concern was to discover the source of the river. I had met the chameleon that perhaps still retained the colour of my garment in memory of our chance encounter or had swapped it for that of some of the distinctly green or red leaves I remembered seeing.

From among creepers and thorns I emerged into another clearing. In its immobility, the canopy of leaves above my head sealed off the place in tragic solitude. I felt the void within me as if I were nothing thenceforth but a wretched carcass draped with black skin. At that moment, the skeleton appeared a few steps away from me, wrapped in its big white lappa which covered its head. I felt no emotion, or more precisely, I was not afraid since I considered it as something I was used to. Still, I rubbed my eyes as if to rid myself of an optical illusion, to make sure of what I was seeing. It drew closer; I did not rush towards it as in our first encounter, for I had to preserve my dignity. In my view, it represented nothing. It was nothingness in motion, and I was a man. This certainty, due to the realization of the difference between us, fortified me not with courage – that I didn't care about – but with cockiness, and I saw my body rising to its level.

This was not the time for any more concessions. I felt that the bush was not supposed to be the abode of the dead but of the living. Wasn't I one of them? We converged as on a one-way track where no provision has been made for people to pass one another. I did nothing to let it pass when we were face to face. Then it stretched out its hand to me. At that moment I would have liked to cross my arms, to sport a scornful countenance since last time it too had snubbed me; but I decided to let bygones be bygones and gathered its bony hand in mine. Instead of forcing me to retrace my steps it did the opposite, still holding my hand. I thus followed it, eager to discover where it was taking me.

We wended our way side by side without my feeling the slightest apprehension. After all, what was there to be afraid of? Holding in my hand the hand of a human skeleton? Human. That was just the word I needed. Was I not with something human? Was I not sure now that my first encounter was not simply the effect of a delusion? No, really, I was no longer afraid. I was eight years old when my grandmother and great-grandfather stopped living. I remember having cried a great deal by their bodies, seated beside the mortal remains of these old people in their barely gnarled height during my vigil, despite my parents' vain efforts to spare me what they called too violent shocks. Yes, I still remember: I hurled myself on my grandmother when they wanted to put her in the coffin; I took her hand and squeezed it very hard so as to communicate all my warmth to her. O the piercing coldness she left in my hands and which is still there, evermore! It was her that I felt again all along, while the skeleton kept my hand in its own. It did not hold it in a tight grip, did not apply any pressure, and we just wandered along like two friends.

Still, I did not forget that I was a man, a human being, a child barely twelve years old, while it was a skeleton. Had it been a man or a woman? I never found out. Besides, this was of no importance. With wide open eyes I stared at the bush in front of me. Not a single time did it occur to me to have to look at my fellow-traveler. And why should I have looked at its skeletal visage since I was feeling its hand in mine? Had it suddenly vanished I would most assuredly not have worried about its disappearance but would have continued on my way amidst the trees, the thorns and the beasts. But I have to admit today that I had realized that from the moment we walked together the thorns no longer tore my cloth; everything slipped smoothly off me as it did off the skeleton.

A wild boar and his mate emerging from their lair took to flight on seeing us. My uncle had told me that the bush was not dangerous; all the same, we saw more than one pair of lions and panthers, but they had passed us by with something approaching indifference. To be precise, they had invariably passed on my side; they had all sniffed at me and then walked away in haughty grandeur. Why? I wouldn't know. I may have appeared vile-smelling and undesirable to them, unless they just happened not to be hungry just then. We had been walking like that for a time that seemed reasonably long to me but I was not tired. I did not feel the slightest fatigue. I paid attention to everything.

Then, to my great surprise, I stopped seeing

the bush around me and realized that we were in an underground tunnel hung with tree-roots. The walls were oozing moisture but the ground was dry. The ear perceived the gentle, distant murmur of a stream. I thought of the river while striding along with my strange companion. At certain places the walls of the long gallery through which we were proceeding had been discreetly adorned with symbolic graffiti: snakes biting their own tails; arms cut off and placed on top of each other in the form of an X; sexual organs; copulation scenes; shin-bones; human skulls; horses without heads but galloping at full speed, tails and manes flying in the wind; fire shaped like an open lily blossom flaring from a pit; coffins; people performing a ritual dance; a clumsily drawn rectangle representing a mirror.

We turned to the left and I had the impression that we were changing our direction from north to sunrise. A light entering the place from heaven knows where gently lit up the underground passage sloping downwards in front of me. We walked unceasingly, descending the slope, and arrived at a kind of crypt where human skeletons without the tiniest bone missing were stretched out side by side. My guide stopped in front of one of them, uncovering his cavity-riddled face. I looked straight at him. He bowed slightly to one of the skeletons which sat up, crossed its legs, then its arms; he continued his homage and each one of his fellow-skeletons took the same posture as the preceding one. And I saw seventy-seven skeletons thus sitting up and leaning their backs against the wall of the crypt. Did they want to impress me? I had experienced fear before, but fear held no more meaning for me. I had heard people talk a lot about death, but since the death of my grandparents I no longer feared it. Death had become for me such a familiar companion that I gave it no more thought. But looking at the skeletons attentively, I had a feeling that each one of them represented a human being I had known, and to which I had perhaps been close. It was good to see them again but I had not come here for them.

'Where is the source of the river?' I suddenly cried in a tragic voice which struck the walls in a zigzag line, provoking a long and sonorous echo. And again I heard murmurings of the water, then a groan followed by the sound of a torrent rushing away.

The skulls all seemed to have been raised again to look me straight in the face.

'You see that I have come to visit you without misgivings. I'm not afraid of you because you used to be men; for me you still are and I don't believe in death!'

I heard my voice re-echo. It ricocheted away from me along the underground passage.

'Why don't you answer? Should you really be so useless?'

All I received for an answer was my own voice and its echo which garbled any utterance.

'You hear me?'

'You hear me?'

'– ear me?'

'– me?'

'– e?'

'Why did you bring me here?'

'– bring me here?'

'– me here?'

'– ere?'

I looked around me and noticed that my guide had disappeared; maybe he had quietly slipped back to his little niche among his peers. So I thought of setting out on my return journey but as the passage stretched out farther before me, I preferred not to retrace my steps; so I moved forward. Thus I continued marching at a normal walking pace, looking all the while at the walls covered with graffiti fraught with symbolism. Despite my casual and almost leisurely gait I was feeling tired. I later realized that the way was sloping upwards. Moreover, the certainty that I was advancing towards the sun became more and more acute.

As if in a fog I saw a shadow passing before my eyes; then the shadow became a reality: a majestic skeleton without any clothes on, his right hand clutched to his heart and his left holding a shin-bone with a skull on top. I stopped short in front of him. He made to let me pass and the moment I was going to continue on my way he slightly stroked my head with the skull resting on the shin-bone. I did not react, did not look back. The light entering the cavern was becoming more and more intense, I breathed in the air charged with a thousand smells from the fields... Abruptly I felt myself carried off into a long sleep and saw myself in a place, the name of which someone seemed to murmur into my ear: 'Wassaï.'

O Wassaï! Wassaï! Disturbing, exciting paradise of entwined bodies! Here was a pathway divided into five branches, each leading to clearly defined places. On one side of the main path stood a hedge of hibiscus, bougainvillea and Campeachy separating the path from a vast area planted with kola-nut trees dwarfed by iroko and silk-cotton trees. In the hollows of those giant trees nested night birds; their lugubrious shrieks did not frighten me. Wisps of white smoke rose from the foot of the trees. Little did I care about their origin and meaning! Let the sorcerers abandon themselves to their orgies, let them devour the souls of their victims. I was in Wassaï!

On the other side of the road was Wassaï, little house of joy without a keeper.

I entered. Ravishing young beauties with sturdy breasts, black skin, athletic bodies. And their nimble legs with prettily proportioned muscles, readily intertwining, pushed me gently into voluptuous depths. At Wassaï I experienced unforgettable little tremors brought about by girls I did not know, their names have remained unspoken, I've forgotten their seductive faces; the form of their lithe and supple bodies remains in my arms, the freshness of their jet-black skin still vibrates through my nerves. In their midst I underwent my sexual initiation till all the flowers of the world blossomed within me, till the hard egg whose unwonted presence I had felt deep within was hatched.

No outburst of rebellious sex will ever surprise me. I have explored all its domains in Wassaï, fearsome black flower slowly unfolding in the deep nights of a dwelling without a master.

When I came to myself, I went my way without slowing down my pace and thus I came out into the open air. Let it be said in passing that I did not for a single moment feel like a prisoner in that underground gallery. But instead of finding myself on even ground, at the edge of the forest as I expected, perhaps because I had scented the wind and the sun, I realized that I was perched high up on a mountainside studded with shrubbery. A little further down, beneath my feet, a spring gushing out from this imposing height I had not known before, flowed into the plain before me with a murmur. And the glittering reflections of lights, a vast imaginary ocean, seemed to undulate on the surface of the stream. I climbed on all fours up to the summit, stood erect and saw the top of the forest covering the villages all around. Far away thin columns of smoke rose above the trees.

Coming from another world I discovered the immensity of space above the earth; then I went down from the mountain as if gently impelled and held back at the same time by a protecting hand. I had not succeeded in seeing what I was searching for: the source of the river. Disappointed, I had to rest content with following the stream which flowed into a natural canal, the banks of which were hemmed in by aquatic plants; and I saw the river again which here to my great surprise almost flowed alongside the railway line. My cloth was in shreds. I followed the railway line and then the usual path to town.

I arrived there at nightfall. In front of the door of my parents' house I was stunned to see on either side an earthenware pot containing a decoction such as our customs prescribe for funeral ceremonies; I also heard a dirge gently syncopated by calabash rattles. I entered and saw a gathering of sad people. The women, including my mother, had untied their hair as a token of mourning. The people gathered there noticed my presence and started up. Some took to their heels, others, paralysed by fear, just looked at me. I stepped forward to my mother who had been quickly joined by my father.

'What has happened? Who has died?'

Dead silence.

'You have to forgive me for leaving without telling you about it.'

'Where have you come from? Are you dead or are you a living person in our midst?' my father asked.

'I'm alive.'

'What, alive ?' my mother said, weeping.

'Nobody's dead. Death doesn't exist and if it does, no dead man will ever return,' I replied firmly, but with my most casual expression.

The people had come back, more numerous now than when I had first set foot in the house.

'Where have you come from?'

'Where've you been?'

'We thought you were dead.'

'For the past three days we've been sure about it.'

'The diviners have confirmed it.'

I was somewhat depressed by these comments and asked if the funeral ceremonies had anything to do with me. They said yes.

'The diviners have all been telling you lies. I went for a walk, and I've come back with flesh and blood, body and soul, cured from the fear of death. I apologise for having given you so much worry.'

'My son, tell me honestly where you have come from,' my father said.

'Just from a walk. I didn't realize that it lasted three days.'

'What did you eat?' asked my mother.

'Nothing.

'Who did you stay with?'

'Nobody.'

'I don't understand you.'

'I've nothing to explain.'

'Why ?'

'Such things can't be explained. I am alive and life goes on.'

'Oh, this child!' my mother murmured.

'I'm hungry, mother. You can see I'm alive and kicking since I'm hungry and thirsty.'

'May you never again disappear like that!'

'I promise, but don't ever ask me for an explanation', I said.

And everything was all right again.

How long did this dream last? I shall never know.

THE SUMMER PEOPLE

Shirley Jackson

Shirley Jackson (1916–1965) was an American writer best-known for her story 'The Lottery' (1948), although much of her other short fiction is as good or better. Her novel *The Haunting of Hill House* (1959) is considered one of the most important horror novels of the twentieth century. Her influence can be seen in the work of many fantasists, including Joanna Russ, Kelly Link, and Neil Gaiman. The founding of the Shirley Jackson Awards and publication in 2010 of a collected stories volume by the Library of America has helped to cement her popularity. 'The Summer People,' selected for *Best American Short Stories* in 1951, is a chilling yet subtle tour de force of the weird.

The Allisons' country cottage, seven miles from the nearest town, was set prettily on a hill; from three sides it looked down on soft trees and grass that seldom, even at midsummer, lay still and dry. On the fourth side was the lake, which touched against the wooden pier the Allisons had to keep repairing, and which looked equally well from the Allisons' front porch, their side porch or any spot on the wooden staircase leading from the porch down to the water. Although the Allisons loved their summer cottage, looked forward to arriving in the early summer and hated to leave in the fall, they had not troubled themselves to put in any improvements, regarding the cottage itself and the lake as improvement enough for the life left to them. The cottage had no heat, no running water except the precarious supply from the backyard pump and no electricity. For seventeen summers, Janet Allison had cooked on a kerosene stove, heating all their water; Robert Allison had brought buckets full of water daily from the pump and read his paper by kerosene light in the evenings and they had both, sanitary city people, become stolid and matter-of-fact about their backhouse. In the first two years they had gone through all the standard vaudeville and magazine jokes about backhouses and by now, when they no longer had frequent guests to impress, they had subsided to a comfortable security which made the backhouse, as well as the pump and the kerosene, an indefinable asset to their summer life.

In themselves, the Allisons were ordinary people. Mrs. Allison was fifty-eight years old and Mr. Allison sixty; they had seen their children outgrow the summer cottage and go on to families of their own and seashore resorts; their friends were either dead or settled in comfortable year-round houses, their nieces and nephews vague. In the winter they told one another they could stand their New York apartment while waiting for the summer; in the summer they told one another that the winter was well worth while, waiting to get to the country.

Since they were old enough not to be ashamed of regular habits, the Allisons invariably left their summer cottage the Tuesday after Labor Day, and were as invariably sorry when the months of September and early October turned out to be pleasant and almost insufferably barren in the city; each year they recognized that there was nothing to bring them back to New York, but it was not until this year that they overcame their traditional inertia enough to decide to stay at the cottage after Labor Day.

'There isn't really anything to take us back to the city,' Mrs. Allison told her husband seriously, as though it were a new idea, and he told her, as though neither of them had ever considered it, 'We might as well enjoy the country as long as possible.'

Consequently, with much pleasure and a slight feeling of adventure, Mrs. Allison went into their village the day after Labor Day and told those natives with whom she had dealings, with a pretty air of breaking away from tradition, that she and her husband had decided to stay at least a month longer at their cottage.

'It isn't as though we had anything to take us back to the city,' she said to Mr. Babcock, her grocer. 'We might as well enjoy the country while we can.'

'Nobody ever stayed at the lake past Labor Day before,' Mr. Babcock said. He was putting Mrs. Allison's groceries into a large cardboard carton, and he stopped for a minute to look reflectively into a bag of cookies. 'Nobody,' he added.

'But the city!' Mrs. Allison always spoke of the city to Mr. Babcock as thought it were Mr. Babcock's dream to go there. 'It's so hot – you've really no idea. We're always sorry when we leave.'

'Hate to leave,' Mr. Babcock said. One of the most irritating native tricks Mrs. Allison had noticed was that of taking a trivial statement and rephrasing it downwards, into an even more trite statement. 'I'd hate to leave myself,' Mr. Babcock said, after deliberation, and both he and Mrs. Allison smiled. 'But I never heard of anyone ever staying out at the lake after Labor Day before.'

'Well, we're going to give it a try,' Mrs. Allison said, and Mr. Babcock replied gravely, 'Never known til you try.'

Physically, Mrs. Allison decided, as she always did when leaving the grocery after one of her inconclusive conversations with Mr. Babcock, physically, Mr. Babcock could model for a statue of Daniel Webster, but mentally… it was horrible to think into what old New England Yankee stock had degenerated. She said as much to Mr. Allison when she got into the car, and he said, 'It's generations of inbreeding. That and the bad land.'

Since this was their big trip into town, which they made only once every two weeks to buy things they could not have delivered, they spent all day at it, stopping to have a sandwich in the newspaper and soda shop, and leaving packages heaped in the back of the car. Although Mrs. Allison was able to order groceries delivered regularly, she was never able to form any accurate idea of Mr. Babcock's current stock by telephone, and her lists of odds and ends that might be procured was always supplemented, almost beyond their need, by the new and fresh local vegetables Mr. Babcock was selling temporarily, or the packaged candy which had just come in. This trip Mrs. Allison was tempted, too, by the set of glass baking dishes that had found themselves completely by chance in the hardware and clothing and general store, and which had seemingly been waiting there for no one by Mrs. Allison, since the country people, with their instinctive distrust of anything that did not look as permanent as trees and rocks and sky, had only recently begun to experiment in aluminum baking dishes instead of ironware, and had, apparently within the memory of local inhabitants, discarded stoneware in favor of iron.

Mrs. Allison had the glass baking dishes carefully wrapped, to endure the uncomfortable ride home over the rocky road that led up to the Allisons' cottage, and while Mr. Charley Walpole, who, with his younger brother Albert, ran the hardware-clothing-general store (the store itself was called Johnson's, because it stood on the site of the old Johnson cabin, burned fifty years before Charley Walpole was born, laboriously unfolded newspapers to wrap around the dishes, Mrs. Allison said, informally, ''Course, I *could* have waited and gotten those dishes in New York, but we're not going back so soon this year.'

'Heard you was staying on,' Mr. Charley Walpole said. His old fingers fumbled maddeningly with the thin sheets of newspaper, carefully trying to isolate only one sheet at a time, and he did not look up at Mrs. Allison as he went on, 'Don't know about staying on up there to the lake. Not after Labor Day.'

'Well, you know,' Mrs. Allison said, quite as though he deserved an explanation, 'it just seemed to us that we've been hurrying back to New York every year, and there just wasn't any need for it.

You know what the city's like in the fall.' And she smiled confidingly up at Mr. Charley Walpole.

Rhythmically he wound string around the package. He's giving me a piece long enough to save, Mrs. Allison thought, and she looked away quickly to avoid giving any sign of impatience. 'I feel sort of like we belong here, more,' she said. 'Staying on after everyone else has left.' To prove this, she smiled brightly across the store at a woman with a familiar face, who might have been the woman who sold berries to the Allisons one year, or the woman who occasionally helped in the grocery and was probably Mr. Babcock's aunt.

'Well,' Mr. Charley Walpole said. He shoved the package a little across the counter, to show that it was finished, and that for a sale well made, a package well wrapped, he was willing to accept pay. 'Well,' he said again. 'Never been summer people before, at the lake after Labor Day.'

Mrs. Allison gave him a five-dollar bill, and he made change methodically, giving great weight even to the pennies. 'Never after Labor Day,' he said, and nodded at Mrs. Allison, and went soberly along the store to deal with two women who were looking at cotton house dresses.

As Mrs. Allison passed on her way out she heard one of the women say acutely, 'Why is one of them dresses one dollar and thirty-nine cents and this one here is only ninety-eight?'

'They're great people,' Mrs. Allison told her husband as they went together down the sidewalk after meeting at the door of the hardware store. 'They're so solid, and so reasonable, and so *honest*.'

'Makes you feel good, knowing there are still towns like this,' Mr. Allison said.

'You know, in New York,' Mrs. Allison said, 'I might have paid a few cents less for these dishes, but there wouldn't have been anything sort of *personal* in the transaction.'

'Staying on to the lake?' Mrs. Martin, in the newspaper and sandwich shop, asked the Allisons. 'Heard you was staying on.'

'Thought we'd take advantage of the lovely weather this year,' Mr. Allison said.

Mrs. Martin was a comparative newcomer to the town; she had married into the newspaper and sandwich shop from a neighboring farm, and had stayed on after her husband's death. She served bottled soft drinks and fried egg and onion sandwiches on thick bread, which she made on her own stove at the back of the store. Occasionally when Mrs. Martin served a sandwich it would carry with it the rich fragrance of the stew or the pork chops cooking alongside for Mrs. Martin's dinner.

'I don't guess anyone's ever stayed out there so long before,' Mrs. Martin said. 'Not after Labor Day, anyway.'

'I guess Labor Day is when they usually leave,' Mr. Hall, the Allisons' nearest neighbor, told them later, in front of Mr. Babcock's store, where the Allisons were getting into their car to go home. 'Surprised you're staying on.'

'It seemed a shame to go so soon,' Mrs. Allison said. Mr. Hall lived three miles away; he supplied the Allisons with butter and eggs, and occasionally, from the top of their hill, the Allisons could see the lights in his house in the early evening before the Halls went to bed.

'They usually leave Labor Day,' Mr. Hall said.

The ride home was long and rough; it was beginning to get dark, and Mr. Allison had to drive very carefully over the dirt road by the lake. Mrs. Allison lay back against the seat, pleasantly relaxing after a day of what seemed whirlwind shopping compared with their day-to-day existence; the new glass baking dishes lurked agreeably in her mind, and the half bushel of red eating apples, and the package of colored thumbtacks with which she was going to put up new shelf edging in the kitchen. 'Good to get home,' she said softly as they came in sight of their cottage, silhouetted above them against the sky.

'Glad we decided to stay on,' Mr. Allison agreed.

Mrs. Allison spent the next morning lovingly washing her baking dishes, although in his innocence Charley Walpole had neglected to notice the chip in the edge of one; she decided, wastefully, to use some of the red eating apples in a pie for dinner, and, while the pie was in the oven and Mr. Allison was down getting the mail, she sat out on the little lawn the Allisons had made at the top of the hill, and watched the changing lights on the lake, alternating gray and blue as clouds moved quickly across the sun.

Mr. Allison came back a little out of sorts; it always irritated him to walk the mile to the mail box on the state road and come back with nothing, even though he assumed that the walk was good for his health. This morning there was nothing but a circular for a New York department store, and their New York paper, which arrived erratically by mail from one to four days later than it should, so that some days the Allisons might have three papers and frequently none. Mrs. Allison, although she shared with her husband the annoyance of not having mail when they so anticipated it, pored affectionately over the department store circular, and made a mental note to drop in at the store when she finally went back to New York, and check on the sale of wool blankets; it was hard to find good ones in pretty colors nowadays. She debated saving the circular to remind herself, but after thinking about getting up and getting into the cottage to put it away safely somewhere, she dropped it into the grass beside her chair and lay back, her eyes half closed.

'Looks like we might have some rain,' Mr. Allison said, squinting at the sky.

'Good for the crops,' Mrs. Allison said laconically, and they both laughed.

The kerosene man came the next morning while Mr. Allison was down getting the mail; they were getting low on kerosene and Mrs. Allison greeted the man warmly; he sold kerosene and ice, and, during the summer, hauled garbage away for the summer people. A garbage man was only necessary for improvident city folk; country people had no garbage.

'I'm glad to see you,' Mrs. Allison told him. 'We were getting pretty low.'

The kerosene man, whose name Mrs. Allison had never learned, used a hose attachment to fill the twenty-gallon tank which supplied light and heat and cooking facilities for the Allisons; but today, instead of swinging down from his truck and unhooking the hose from where it coiled affectionately around the cab of the truck, the man stared uncomfortably at Mrs. Allison, his truck motor still going.

'Thought you folks'd be leaving,' he said.

'We're staying on another month,' Mrs. Allison said brightly. 'The weather was so nice, and it seemed like–'

'That's what they told me,' the man said. 'Can't give you no oil, though.'

'What do you mean?' Mrs. Allison raised her eyebrows. 'We're just going to keep on with our regular–'

'After Labor Day,' the man said. 'I don't get so much oil myself after Labor Day.'

Mrs. Allison reminded herself, as she had frequently to do when in disagreement with her neighbors, that city manners were no good with country people; you could not expect to overrule a country employee as you could a city worker, and Mrs. Allison smiled engagingly as she said, 'But can't you get extra oil, at least while we stay?'

'You see,' the man said. He tapped his finger exasperatingly against the car wheel as he spoke. 'You see,' he said slowly, 'I order this oil. I order it down from maybe fifty, fifty-five miles away. I order back in June, how much I'll need for the summer. Then I order again... oh about November. Round about now it's starting to get pretty short.' As though the subject were closed, he stopped tapping his finger and tightened his hands on the wheel in preparation for departure.

'But can't you give us *some*?' Mrs. Allison said. 'Isn't there anyone else?'

'Don't know as you could get oil anywheres else right now,' the man said consideringly. '*I* can't give you none.' Before Mrs. Allison could speak, the truck began to move; then it stopped for a minute and he looked at her through the back window of the cab. 'Ice?' he called. 'I could let you have some ice.'

Mrs. Allison shook her head; they were not terribly low on ice, and she was angry. She ran a few steps to catch up with the truck, calling, 'Will you try to get us some? Next week?'

'Don't see's I can,' the man said. 'After Labor Day, it's harder.' The truck drove away, and Mrs. Allison, only comforted by the thought that she could probably get kerosene from Mr. Babcock or, at worst, the Halls, watched it go with anger. 'Next summer,' she told herself, 'just let *him* try coming around next summer!'

There was no mail again, only the paper, which seemed to be coming doggedly on time, and Mr.

Allison was openly cross when he returned. When Mrs. Allison told him about the kerosene man he was not particularly impressed.

'Probably keeping it all for a high price during the winter,' he commented. 'What's happened to Anne and Jerry, do you think?'

Anne and Jerry were their son and daughter, both married, one living in Chicago, one in the far west; their dutiful weekly letters were late; so late, in fact, that Mr. Allison's annoyance at the lack of mail was able to settle on a legitimate grievance. 'Ought to realize how we wait for their letters,' he said. 'Thoughtless, selfish children. Ought to know better.'

'Well, dear,' Mrs. Allison said placatingly. Anger at Anne and Jerry would not relieve her emotions toward the kerosene man. After a few minutes she said, 'Wishing won't bring the mail, dear. I'm going to go call Mr. Babcock and tell him to send up some kerosene with my order.'

'At least a postcard,' Mr. Allison said as she left.

As with most of the cottage's inconveniences, the Allisons no longer noticed the phone particularly, but yielded to its eccentricities without conscious complaint. It was a wall phone, of a type still seen in only a few communities; in order to get the operator, Mrs. Allison had first to turn the side-crank and ring once. Usually it took two or three tries to force the operator to answer, and Mrs. Allison, making any kind of telephone call, approached the phone with resignation and a sort of desperate patience. She had to crank the phone three times this morning before the operator answered, and then it was still longer before Mr. Babcock picked up the receiver at his phone in the corner of the grocery behind the meat table. He said, 'Store?' with the rising inflection that seemed to indicate suspicion of anyone who tried to communicate with him by means of this unreliable instrument.

'This is Mrs. Allison, Mr. Babcock. I thought I'd give you my order a day early because I wanted to be sure and get some–'

'What say, Mrs. Allison?'

Mrs. Allison raised her voice a little; she saw Mr. Allison, out on the lawn, turn in his chair and regard her sympathetically. 'I said, Mr. Babcock, I thought I'd call in my order early so you could send me–'

'Mrs. Allison?' Mr. Babcock said. 'You'll come and pick it up?'

'Pick it up?' In her surprise Mrs. Allison let her voice drop back to its normal tone and Mr. Babcock said loudly, 'What's that, Mrs. Allison?'

'I thought I'd have you send it out as usual,' Mrs. Allison said.

'Well, Mrs. Allison,' Mr. Babcock said, and there was a pause while Mrs. Allison waited, staring past the phone over her husband's head out into the sky. 'Mrs. Allison,' Mr. Babcock went on finally, 'I'll tell you, my boy's been working for me went back to school yesterday, and now I got no one to deliver. I only got a boy delivering summers, you see.'

'I thought you *always* delivered,' Mrs. Allison said.

'Not after Labor Day, Mrs. Allison,' Mr. Babcock said firmly. 'You never been here after Labor Day before, so's you wouldn't know, of course.'

'Well,' Mrs. Allison said helplessly. Far inside her mind she was saying, over and over, can't use city manners on country folk, no use getting mad.

'Are you *sure*?' she asked finally. 'Couldn't you just send out an order today, Mr. Babcock?'

'Matter of fact,' Mr. Babcock said, 'I guess I couldn't, Mrs. Allison. It wouldn't hardly pay, delivering, with no one else out at the lake.'

'What about Mr. Hall?' Mrs. Allison asked suddenly, 'the people who live about three miles away from us out here? Mr. Hall could bring it out when he comes.'

'Hall?' Mr. Babcock said. 'John Hall? They've gone to visit her folks upstate, Mrs. Allison.'

'But they bring all our butter and eggs,' Mrs. Allison said, appalled.

'Left yesterday,' Mr. Babcock said. 'Probably didn't think you folks would stay on up there.'

'But I told Mr. Hall …' Mrs. Allison started to say, and then stopped. 'I'll send Mr. Allison in after some groceries tomorrow,' she said.

'You got all you need till then,' Mr. Babcock said, satisfied; it was not a question, but a confirmation.

After she hung up, Mrs. Allison went slowly out to sit again in her chair next to her husband. 'He won't deliver,' she said. 'You'll have to go in tomorrow. We've got just enough kerosene to last till you get back.'

'He should have told us sooner,' Mr. Allison said.

It was not possible to remain troubled long in the face of the day; the country had never seemed more inviting, and the lake moved quietly below them, among the trees, with the almost incredible softness of a summer picture. Mrs. Allison sighed deeply, in the pleasure of possessing for themselves that sight of the lake, with the distant green hills beyond, the gentleness of the small wind through the trees.

The weather continued fair; the next morning Mr. Allison, duly armed with a list of groceries, with 'kerosene' in large letters at the top, went down the path to the garage, and Mrs. Allison began another pie in her new baking dishes. She had mixed the crust and was starting to pare the apples when Mr. Allison came rapidly up the path and flung open the screen door into the kitchen.

'Damn car won't start,' he announced, with the end-of-the-tether voice of a man who depends on a car as he depends on his right arm.

'What's wrong with it?' Mrs. Allison demanded, stopping with the paring knife in one hand and an apple in the other. 'It was all right on Tuesday.'

'Well,' Mr. Allison said between his teeth, 'it's not all right on Friday.'

'Can you fix it?' Mrs. Allison asked.

'No,' Mr. Allison said. 'I can not. Got to call someone, I guess.'

'Who?' Mrs. Allison asked.

'Man runs the filling station, I guess.' Mr. Allison moved purposefully toward the phone. 'He fixed it last summer one time.'

A little apprehensive, Mrs. Allison went on paring apples absentmindedly, while she listened to Mr. Allison with the phone, ringing, waiting, ringing, waiting, finally giving the number to the operator, then waiting again and giving the number again, giving the number a third time, and then slamming down the receiver.

'No one there,' he announced as he came into the kitchen.

'He's probably gone out for a minute,' Mrs. Allison said nervously; she was not quite sure what made her so nervous, unless it was the probability of her husband's losing his temper completely. 'He's there alone, I imagine, so if he goes out there's no one to answer the phone.'

'That must be it,' Mr. Allison said with heavy irony. He slumped into one of the kitchen chairs and watched Mrs. Allison paring apples. After a minute, Mrs. Allison said soothingly, 'Why don't you go down and get the mail and then call him again?'

Mr. Allison debated and then said, 'Guess I might as well.' He rose heavily and when he got to the kitchen door he turned and said, 'But if there's no mail–' and leaving an awful silence behind him, he went off down the path.

Mrs. Allison hurried with her pie. Twice she went to the window to glance at the sky to see if there were clouds coming up. The room seemed unexpectedly dark, and she herself felt in the state of tension that precedes a thunderstorm, but both times when she looked the sky was clear and serene, smiling indifferently down on the Allisons' summer cottage as well as on the rest of the world. When Mrs. Allison, her pie ready for the oven, went a third time to look outside, she saw her husband coming up the path; he seemed more cheerful, and when he saw her, he waved eagerly and held a letter in the air.

'From Jerry,' he called as soon as he was close enough for her to hear him, 'at last – a letter!' Mrs. Allison noticed with concern that he was no longer able to get up the gentle slope of the path without breathing heavily; but then he was in the doorway, holding out the letter. 'I saved it till I got here,' he said.

Mrs. Allison looked with an eagerness that surprised her on the familiar handwriting of her son; she could not imagine why the letter excited her so, except that it was the first they had received in so long; it would be a pleasant, dutiful letter, full of the doings of Alice and the children, reporting progress with his job, commenting on the recent weather in Chicago, closing with love from all; both Mr. and Mrs. Allison could, if they wished, recite a pattern letter from either of their children.

Mrs. Allison slit the letter open with great deliberation, and then she spread it out on the kitchen table and they leaned down and read it together.

'Dear Mother and Dad,' it began, in Jerry's familiar, rather childish, handwriting, *'Am glad this goes to the lake as usual, we always thought you came back too soon and ought to stay up there as long as you could. Alice says that now that you're not as young as you used to be and have no demands on your time, fewer friends, etc., in the city, you ought to get what fun you can while you can. Since you two are both happy up there, it's a good idea for you to stay.'*

Uneasily Mrs. Allison glanced sideways at her husband; he was reading intently, and she reached out and picked up the empty envelope, not knowing exactly what she wanted from it. It was addressed quite as usual, in Jerry's handwriting, and was postmarked Chicago. Of course it's postmarked Chicago, she thought quickly, why would they want to postmark it anywhere else? When she looked back down at the letter, her husband had turned the page, and she read on with him: *'– and of course if they get measles, etc., now, they will be better off later. Alice is well, of course, me too. Been playing a lot of bridge lately with some people you don't know, named Carruthers. Nice young couple, about our age. Well, will close now as I guess it bores you to hear about things so far away. Tell Dad old Dickson, in our Chicago office, died. He used to ask about Dad a lot. Have a good time up at the lake, and don't bother about hurrying back. Love from all of us, Jerry.'*

'Funny,' Mr. Allison commented.

'It doesn't sound like Jerry,' Mrs. Allison said in a small voice. 'He never wrote anything like...' She stopped.

'Like what?' Mr. Allison demanded. 'Never wrote anything like what?'

Mrs. Allison turned the letter over, frowning. It was impossible to find any sentence, any word, even, that did not sound like Jerry's regular letters. Perhaps it was only that the letter was so late, or the unusual number of dirty fingerprints on the envelope.

'I don't *know*,' she said impatiently.

'Going to try that phone call again,' Mr. Allison said.

Mrs. Allison read the letter twice more, trying to find a phrase that sounded wrong. Then Mr. Allison came back and said, very quietly, 'Phone's dead.'

'What?' Mrs. Allison said, dropping the letter.

'Phone's dead,' Mr. Allison said.

The rest of the day went quickly; after a lunch of crackers and milk, the Allisons went to sit outside on the lawn, but their afternoon was cut short by the gradually increasing storm clouds that came up over the lake to the cottage, so that it was as dark as evening by four o'clock. The storm delayed, however, as though in loving anticipation of the moment it would break over the summer cottage, and there was an occasional flash of lightning, but no rain. In the evening, Mr. and Mrs. Allison, sitting close together inside their cottage, turned on the battery radio they had brought with them from New York. There were no lamps lighted in the cottage, and the only light came from the lightning outside and the small square glow from the dial of the radio.

The slight framework of the cottage was not strong enough to withstand the city noises, the music and the voices, from the radio, and the Allisons could hear them far off echoing across the lake, the saxophones in the New York dance band wailing over the water, the flat voice of the girl vocalist going inexorably out into the clean country air. Even the announcer, speaking glowingly of the virtues of razor blades, was no more than an inhuman voice sounding out from the Allisons' cottage and echoing back, as though the lake and the hills and the trees were returning it unwanted.

During one pause between commercials, Mrs. Allison turned and smiled weakly at her husband. 'I wonder if we're supposed to... *do* anything,' she said.

'No,' Mr. Allison said consideringly. 'I don't think so. Just wait.'

Mrs. Allison caught her breath quickly, and Mr. Allison said, under the trivial melody of the dance band beginning again, 'The car had been tampered with, you know. Even I could see that.'

Mrs. Allison hesitated a minute and then said very softly, 'I suppose the phone wires were cut.'

'I imagine so.'

After a while, the dance music stopped and they listened attentively to a news broadcast, the announcer's rich voice telling them breathlessly of a marriage in Hollywood, the latest baseball scores, the estimated rise in food prices during the coming week. He spoke to them, in the summer cottage, quite as though they still deserved to hear news of a world that no longer reached them except through the fallible batteries on the radio, which were already beginning to fade, almost as though they still belonged, however tenuously, to the rest of the world.

Mrs. Allison glanced out the window at the smooth surface of the lake, the black masses of the trees, and the waiting storm, and said conversationally, 'I feel better about that letter of Jerry's.'

'I knew when I saw the light down at the Hall place last night,' Mrs. Allison said.

The wind, coming up suddenly over the lake, swept around the summer cottage and slapped hard at the windows. Mr. and Mrs. Allison involuntarily moved closer together, and with the first crash of thunder, Mr. Allison reached out and took his wife's hand. And then, while the lightning flashed outside, and the radio faded and sputtered, the two old people huddled together in their summer cottage and waited.

THE MAN WHO SOLD ROPE TO THE GNOLES

Margaret St. Clair

Margaret St. Clair (1911–1995) was an American science fiction writer whose most creative period was during the 1950s, when she wrote such acclaimed stories as 'Brightness Falls from the Air' (1951), 'An Egg a Month from All Over' (1952), and 'Horrer Howce' (1956). In 1951 she also published the classic 'The Man Who Sold Rope to the Gnoles'. Satirical, weird, and with a nod to the Lord Dunsany story collected earlier in this volume, 'The Man Who Sold Rope to the Gnoles' has bite … and teeth. St. Clair largely stopped writing short stories after 1960. *The Best of Margaret St. Clair* (1985) provides a good overview of her short fiction.

The gnoles had a bad reputation, and Mortensen was quite aware of this. But he reasoned, correctly enough, that cordage must be something for which the gnoles had a long unsatisfied want, and he saw no reason why he should not be the one to sell it to them. What a triumph such a sale would be! The district sales manager might single out Mortensen for special mention at the annual sales-force dinner. It would help his sales quota enormously. And, after all, it was none of his business what the gnoles used cordage for.

Mortensen decided to call on the gnoles on Thursday morning. On Wednesday night he went through his *Manual of Modern Salesmanship*, underscoring things.

'The mental states through which the mind passes in making a purchase,' he read, 'have been catalogued as 1) arousal of interest 2) increase of knowledge 3) adjustments to needs …' There were seven mental states listed, and Mortensen underscored all of them. Then he went back and double-scored No. 1, arousal of interest, No. 4, appreciation of suitability, and No. 7, decision to purchase. He turned the page.

'Two qualities are of exceptional importance to a salesman,' he read. 'They are adaptability and knowledge of merchandise.' Mortensen underlined the qualities. 'Other highly desirable attributes are physical fitness, and high ethical standard, charm of manner, a dogged persistence, and unfailing courtesy.' Mortensen underlined these too. But he read on to the end of the paragraph without underscoring anything more, and it may be that his failure to put 'tact and keen power of observation' on a footing with the other attributes of a salesman was responsible for what happened to him.

The gnoles live on the very edge of Terra Cognita, on the far side of a wood which all authorities unite in describing as dubious. Their house is narrow and high, in architecture a blend of Victorian Gothic and Swiss chalet. Though the house needs paint, it is kept in good repair. Thither on Thursday morning, sample case in hand, Mortensen took his way.

No path leads to the house of the gnoles, and it is always dark in that dubious wood. But Mortensen, remembering what he had learned at his mother's knee concerning the odor of gnoles, found the house quite easily. For a moment he stood hesitating before it. His lips moved as he repeated, 'Good morning, I have come to supply your cordage requirements,' to himself. The words were the beginning of his sales talk. Then he went up and rapped on the door.

The gnoles were watching him through holes they had bored in the trunks of trees; it is an artful custom of theirs to which the prime authority on gnoles attests. Mortensen's knock almost threw them into confusion, it was so long since anyone had knocked on their door. Then the senior gnole, the one who never leaves the house, went flitting up from the cellars and opened it.

The senior gnole is a little like a Jerusalem artichoke made of India rubber, and he has small red eyes which are faceted in the same way that gemstones are. Mortensen had been expecting something unusual, and when the gnole opened the door he bowed politely, took off his hat, and smiled. He had got past the sentence about cordage requirements and into an enumeration of the different types of cordage his firm manufactured when the gnole, by turning his head to the side, showed him that he had no ears. Nor was there anything on his head which could take their place in the conduction of sound. Then the gnole opened his little fanged mouth and let Mortensen look at his narrow ribbony tongue. As a tongue it was no more fit for human speech than was a serpent's. Judging from his appearance, the gnole could not safely be assigned to any of the four physio-characterological types mentioned in the *Manual*; and for the first time Mortensen felt a definite qualm.

Nonetheless, he followed the gnole unhesitatingly when the creature motioned him within. Adaptability, he told himself, adaptability must be his watchword. Enough adaptability, and his knees might even lose their tendency to shakiness.

It was the parlor the gnole led him to. Mortensen's eyes widened as he looked around it. There were whatnots in the corners, and cabinets of curiosities, and on the fretwork table an album with gilded hasps; who knows whose pictures were in it? All around the walls in brackets, where in lesser houses the people display ornamental plates, were emeralds as big as your head. The gnoles set great store by their emeralds. All the light in the dim room came from them.

Mortensen went through the phrases of his sales talk mentally. It distressed him that that was the only way he could go through them. Still, adaptability! The gnole's interest was already aroused, or he would never have asked Mortensen into the parlor; and as soon as the gnole saw the various cordages the sample case contained he would no doubt proceed of his own accord through 'appreciation of suitability' to 'desire to possess.'

Mortensen sat down in the chair the gnole indicated and opened his sample case. He got out henequen cable-laid rope, an assortment of ply and yarn goods, and some superlative slender abaca fiber rope. He even showed the gnole a few soft yarns and twines made of cotton and jute.

On the back of an envelope he wrote prices for hanks and cheeses of the twines, and for fifty- and hundred-foot lengths of the ropes. Laboriously he added details about the strength, durability, and resistance to climatic conditions of each sort of cord. The senior gnole watched him intently, putting his little feet on the top run of his chair and poking at the facets of his left eye now and then with a tentacle. In the cellars from time to time someone would scream.

Mortensen began to demonstrate his wares. He showed the gnole the slip and resilience of one rope, the tenacity and stubborn strength of another. He cut a tarred hemp rope in two and laid a five-foot piece on the parlor floor to show the gnole how absolutely 'neutral' it was, with no tendency to untwist of its own accord. He even showed the gnole how nicely some of the cotton twines made up a square knotwork.

They settled at last on two ropes of abaca fiber, 3/16 and 5/8 inch in diameter. The gnole wanted an enormous quantity. Mortensen's comment on those ropes, 'unlimited strength and durability,' seemed to have attracted him.

Soberly, Mortensen wrote the particulars down in his order book, but ambition was setting his brain on fire. The gnoles, it seemed, would be regular customers; and after the gnoles, why should he not try the gibbelins? They too must have a need for rope.

Mortensen closed his order book. On the back of the same envelope he wrote, for the gnole to see, that delivery would be made within ten days. Terms were 30 percent with order, balance upon receipt of goods.

The senior gnole hesitated. Shyly, he looked at Mortensen with his little red eyes. Then he got down the smallest of the emeralds from the wall and handed it to him.

The sales representative stood weighing it in his hands. It was the smallest of the gnoles' emeralds, but it was as clear as water, as green as grass. In the outside world it would have ransomed a Rockefeller or a whole family of Guggenheims; a legitimate profit from a transaction was one thing, but this was another; 'a high ethical standard' – any kind of ethical standard – would forbid Mortensen to keep it. He weighed it a moment longer. Then with a deep, deep sigh he gave the emerald back.

He cast a glance around the room to see if he could find something which would be more negotiable. And in an evil moment he fixed on the senior gnole's auxiliary eyes.

The senior gnole keeps his extra pair of optics on the third shelf of the curiosity cabinet with the glass doors. They look like fine dark emeralds about the size of the end of your thumb. And if the gnoles in general set store by their gems, it is nothing at all compared to the senior gnole's emotions about his extra eyes. The concern good Christian folk should feel for their soul's welfare is a shadow, a figment, a nothing, compared to what the thoroughly heathen gnole feels for those eyes. He would rather, I think, choose to be a mere miserable human being than that some vandal should lay hands upon them.

If Mortensen had not been elated by his success to the point of anaesthesia, he would have seen the gnole stiffen, he would have heard him hiss, when he went over to the cabinet. All innocent, Mortensen opened the glass door, took the twin eyes out, and juggled them sacrilegiously in his hand; the gnole could hear them clink. Smiling to evince the charm of manner advised in the *Manual*, and raising his brows as one who says, 'Thank you, these will do nicely,' Mortensen dropped the eyes into his pocket.

The gnole growled.

The growl awoke Mortensen from his trance of euphoria. It was a growl whose meaning no one could mistake. This was clearly no time to be doggedly persistent. Mortensen made a break for the door.

The senior gnole was there before him, his network of tentacles outstretched. He caught Mortensen in them easily and wound them, flat as bandages, around his ankles and his hands. The best abaca fiber is no stronger than those tentacles; though the gnoles would find rope a convenience, they get along very well without it. Would you, dear reader, go naked if zippers should cease to be made? Growling indignantly, the gnole fished his ravished eyes from Mortensen's pockets, and then carried him down to the cellar to the fattening pens.

But great are the virtues of legitimate commerce. Though they fattened Mortensen sedulously, and, later, roasted and sauced him and ate him with real appetite, the gnoles slaughtered him in quite a humane manner and never once thought of torturing him. That is unusual, for gnoles. And they ornamented the plank on which they served him with a beautiful border of fancy knotwork made of cotton cord from his own sample case.

THE HUNGRY HOUSE

Robert Bloch

Robert Bloch (1917–1994) was an iconic American writer, primarily of crime, horror, and science fiction. Bloch wrote hundreds of short stories and over twenty novels. As one of the youngest members of the so-called Lovecraft Circle, Bloch found a needed mentor in Lovecraft, among the first to encourage his talent. Early on, Bloch contributed to pulp magazines such as *Weird Tales,* and later won the Hugo Award, the Bram Stoker Award, and the World Fantasy Award. The pop culture popularity of his novel *Psycho* (1959), which became the model for mindless slasher films, tended to obscure Bloch's more subtle talents. 'The Hungry House' (1951) represents Bloch at his most complex and devastating.

At first there were just the two of them – he and she, together. That's the way it was when they bought the house.

Then *it* came. Perhaps it was there all the time; waiting for them in the house. At any rate, it was there now. And there was nothing they could do.

Moving was out of the question. They'd taken a five-year lease, secretly congratulating themselves on the low rental. It would be absurd to complain to the agent about it, and impossible to explain to their friends. For that matter, they had nowhere else to go; they had searched for months to find a home.

Besides, at first neither he nor she cared to admit that they were aware of its presence. But both of them knew it was there.

She felt it the very first evening, in the bedroom. She was sitting in front of the high, oldfashioned boudoir mirror, combing her hair. They hadn't settled all their things yet, and she didn't trouble to dust the place very thoroughly. In consequence the mirror was cloudy. And the light above it flickered.

So at first she thought it was just a trick of shadows. Some flaw in the glass perhaps. The wavering outline behind her seemed to blur the reflection oddly, and she frowned in distaste. Then she began to experience what she often called her 'married feeling' – the peculiar awareness which usually denoted her husband's entrance to a room she occupied.

He must be standing behind her now. He must have come in quietly, without saying anything. Perhaps he was going to put his arms around her, surprise her, startle her. Hence the shadow on the mirror.

She turned, ready to greet him.

The room was empty. And still the odd reflection persisted, together with the sensation of a presence at her back.

She shrugged, moved her head, and made a little face at herself, in the mirror. As a smile it was a failure, because the warped glass and the poor light seemed to distort her grin into something alien – into a smile that was not altogether a composition of her own face and features.

Well, it had been a fatiguing ordeal, this moving business. She flicked a brush through her hair and tried to dismiss the problem.

Nevertheless she felt a surge of relief when he suddenly entered the bedroom. For a moment she thought of telling him, then decided not to worry him over her 'nerves.'

He was more outspoken. It was the following morning that the incident occurred. He came rushing out of the bathroom, his face bleeding from a razor-cut on the left cheek.

'Is that your idea of being funny?' he demanded, in the petulant, little-boy fashion she found so engaging. 'Sneaking in behind me and making faces in the mirror? Gave me an awful start – look at this nick I sliced on myself.'

She sat up in bed.

'But darling, I haven't been making faces at you. I didn't stir from this bed since you got up.'

'Oh.' He shook his head, his frown fading into a second set of wrinkles expressing bewilderment. 'Oh, I see.'

'What is it?' She suddenly threw off the covers and sat on the edge of the bed, wriggling her toes and peering at him earnestly.

'Nothing,' he murmured. 'Nothing at all. Just thought I saw you, or somebody, looking over my shoulder in the mirror. All of a sudden, you know. It must be those damned lights. Got to get some bulbs in town today.'

He patted his cheek with a towel and turned away. She took a deep breath.

'I had the same feeling last night,' she confessed, then bit her lip.

'You did?'

'It's probably just the lights, as you said, darling.'

'Uh huh.' He was suddenly preoccupied. 'That must be it. I'll make sure and bring those new bulbs.'

'You'd better. Don't forget, the gang is coming down for the house-warming on Saturday.'

Saturday proved to be a long time in coming. In the interim both of them had several experiences which served to upset their minds much more than they cared to admit.

The second morning, after he had left for work, she went out in back and looked at the garden. The place was a mess – half an acre of land, all those trees, the weeds everywhere, and the dead leaves of autumn dancing slowly around the old house. She stood off on a little knoll and contemplated the grave gray gables of another century. Suddenly she felt lonely here. It wasn't only the isolation, the feeling of being half a mile from the nearest neighbor, down a deserted dirt road. It was more as though she were an intruder here – an intruder upon the past. The cold breeze, the dying trees, the sullen sky were welcome; they belonged to the house. She was the outsider, because she was young, because she was alive.

She felt it all, but did not think it. To acknowledge her sensations would be to acknowledge fear. Fear of being alone. Or, worse still, fear of *not* being alone.

Because, as she stood there, the back door closed.

Oh, it was the autumn wind, all right. Even though the door didn't bang, or slam shut. It merely closed. But that was the wind's work, it had to be. There was nobody in the house, nobody to close the door.

She felt in her housedress pocket for the door key, then shrugged as she remembered leaving it on the kitchen sink. Well, she hadn't planned to go inside yet anyway. She wanted to look over the yard, look over the spot where the garden had been and where she fully intended a garden to bloom next spring. She had measurements to make, and estimates to take, and a hundred things to do here outside.

And yet, when the door closed, she knew she had to go in. Something was trying to shut her out, shut her out of her own house, and that would never do. Something was fighting against her, fighting against all idea of change. She had to fight back.

So she marched up to the door, rattled the knob, found herself locked out as she expected. The first round was lost. But there was always the window.

The kitchen window was eye-level in height, and a small crate served to bring it within easy reach. The window was open a good four inches and she had no trouble inserting her hands to raise it further.

She tugged.

Nothing happened. The window must be stuck. But it wasn't stuck; she'd just opened it before going outside and it opened quite easily; besides, they'd tried all the windows and found them in good operating condition.

She tugged again. This time the window raised a good six inches and then – something slipped. The window came down like the blade of a guillotine, and she got her hands out just in time. She bit her lip, sent strength through her shoulders, raised the window once more.

And this time she stared into the pane. The glass was transparent, ordinary window glass. She'd washed it just yesterday and she knew it was clean. There had been no blur, no shadow, and certainly no movement.

But there was movement now. Something cloudy, something obscenely opaque, peered out of the window, peered out of itself and pressed the window down against her. Something matched her strength to shut her out.

Suddenly, hysterically, she realized that she was staring at her own reflection through the shadows of the trees. Of course, it had to be her own reflection. And there was no reason for her to close her eyes and sob as she tugged the window up and half-tumbled her way into the kitchen.

She was inside, and alone. Quite alone. Nothing to worry about. Nothing to worry him about. She wouldn't tell him.

He wouldn't tell her, either. Friday afternoon, when she took the car and went into town for groceries and liquor in preparation for tomorrow's party, he stayed home from the office and arranged the final details of settling down.

That's why he carried up all the garment bags to the attic – to store the summer clothes, get them out of the way. And that's how he happened to open the little cubicle under the front gable. He was looking for the attic closet; he'd put down the bags and started to work along the wall with a flashlight. Then he noticed the door and the padlock.

Dust and rust told their own story; nobody had come this way for a long, long time. He thought again of Hacker, the glib real-estate agent who'd handled the rental of the place. 'Been vacant several years and needs a little fixing up,' Hacker had said. From the looks of it, nobody had lived here for a coon's age. All the better, he could force the lock with a common file.

He went downstairs for the file and returned quickly, noting as he did so the heavy attic dust. Apparently the former occupants had left in something of a hurry – debris was scattered everywhere, and swaths and swirls scored the dust to indicate that belongings had been dragged and hauled and swept along in a haphazard fashion.

Well, he had all winter to straighten things out, and right now he'd settle for storing the garment bags. Clipping the flashlight to his belt, he bent over the lock, file in hand, and tried his skill at breaking and entering.

The lock sprung. He tugged at the door, opened it, inhaled a gust of mouldy dampness, then raised the flash and directed the beam into the long, narrow closet.

A thousand silver slivers stabbed at his eyeballs. Golden, gleaming fire seared his pupils. He jerked the flashlight back, sent the beam upwards. Again, lances of light entered his eyes.

Suddenly he adjusted his vision and comprehension. He stood peering into a room full of mirrors. They hung from cords, lay in corners, stood along the walls in rows.

There was a tall, stately full-length mirror, set in a door; a pair of plate-glass ovals, inset in old-fashioned dresser-tops; a panel glass, and even a complete, dismantled bathroom medicine cabinet similar to the one they had just installed. And the floor was lined with hand-mirrors of all sizes and shapes. He noted an ornate silver-handled mirror straight from a woman's dressing table; behind it stood the vanity-mirror removed from the table itself. And there were pocket mirrors, mirrors from purse-compacts, mirrors of every size and shape. Against the far wall stood a whole series of looking-glass slabs that appeared to have been mounted at one time in a bedroom wall.

He gazed at half a hundred silvered surfaces, gazed at a half a hundred reflections of his own bewildered face.

And he thought again of Hacker, of their inspection of the house. He had noted the absence of a medicine cabinet at the time, but Hacker had glossed over it. Somehow he hadn't realized that there were no mirrors of any sort in the house – of course, there was no furniture, but still one might expect a door panel in a place this old.

No mirrors? Why? And why were they all stacked away up here, under lock and key?

It was interesting. His wife might like some of these – that silver-handled beauty mirror, for example. He'd have to tell her about this.

He stepped cautiously into the closet, dragging the garment bags after him. There didn't seem to be any clothes-pole here, or any hooks. He could put some up in a jiffy, though. He piled the bags in a heap, stooping, and the flashlight glittered on a thousand surfaces, sent facets of fire into his face.

Then the fire faded. The silver surfaces darkened oddly. Of course, his reflection covered them now. His reflection, and something darker. Something smoky and swirling, something that was a part of the mouldy dampness, something that choked the closet with its presence. It was behind him – no, at one side – no, in front of him – all around him – it was growing and growing and blotting him out – it was making him sweat and tremble and now it was making him gasp and scuttle out of the closet and slam the door and press against it with all his waning strength, and its name was –

Claustrophobia. That was it. Just claustrophobia, a fancy name for nerves. A man gets nervous when he's cooped up in a small space. For that matter, a man gets nervous when he looks at himself too long in a mirror. Let alone fifty mirrors!

He stood there, shaking, and to keep his mind occupied, keep his mind off what he had just half-seen, half-felt, half-known, he thought about mirrors for a moment. About looking into mirrors. Women did it all the time. Men were different.

Men, himself included, seemed to be self-conscious about mirrors. He could remember going into a clothing-store and seeing himself in one of the complicated arrangements that afforded a side and rear view. What a shock that had been, the first time – and every time, for that matter! A man looks different in a mirror. Not the way he imagines himself to be, knows himself to be. A mirror distorts. That's why men hum and sing and whistle while they shave. To keep their minds off their reflections. Otherwise they'd go crazy. What was the name of that Greek mythological character who was in love with his own image? Narcissus, that was it. Staring into a pool for hours.

Women could do it, though. Because women never saw themselves, actually. They saw an idealization, a vision. Powder, rouge, lipstick, mascara, eye-shadow, brilliantine, or merely an emptiness to which these elements must be applied. Women were a little crazy to begin with, anyway. Hadn't she said something the other night about seeing him in her mirror when he wasn't there?

Perhaps he'd better not tell her, after all. At least, not until he checked with the real-estate agent, Hacker. He wanted to find out about this business, anyway. Something was wrong, somewhere. Why had the previous owners stored all the mirrors up here?

He began to walk back through the attic, forcing himself to go slowly, forcing himself to think of something, anything, except the fright he'd had in the room of reflections.

Reflect on something. Reflections. Who's afraid of the big bad reflection? Another myth, wasn't it?

Vampires. They had no reflections. 'Tell me the truth now, Hacker. The people who built this house – were they vampires?'

That was a pleasant thought. That was a pleasant thought to carry downstairs in the afternoon twilight, to hug to your bosom in the gloom while the floors creaked and the shutters banged and the night came down in the house of shadows where something peered around the corners and grinned at you in the mirrors on the walls.

He sat there waiting for her to come home, and he switched on all the lights, and he put the radio on too and thanked God he didn't have a television set because there was a screen and the screen made a reflection and the reflection might be something he didn't want to see.

But there was no more trouble that evening, and by the time she came home with her packages he had himself under control. So they ate and talked quite naturally – oh, quite naturally, and if it was listening it wouldn't know they were both afraid.

They made their preparations for the party, and called up a few people on the phone, and just on the spur of the moment he suggested inviting Hacker, too. So that was done and they went to bed. The lights were all out and that meant the mirrors were dark, and he could sleep.

Only in the morning it was difficult to shave. And he caught her, yes he caught her, putting on her makeup in the kitchen, using the little compact from her purse and carefully cupping her hands against reflections.

But he didn't tell her and she didn't tell him, and if it guessed their secrets, it kept silent.

He drove off to work and she made canapes, and if at times during the long, dark, dreary Saturday the house groaned and creaked and whispered, that was only to be expected.

The house was quiet enough by the time he came home again, and somehow, that was worse. It was as though something were waiting for night to fall. That's why she dressed early, humming all the while she powdered and primped, swirling around in front of the mirror (you couldn't see too clearly if you swirled). That's why he mixed drinks before their hasty meal and saw to it that they both had several stiff ones (you couldn't see too clearly if you drank).

And then the guests tumbled in. The Teters, complaining about the winding back road through the hills. The Valliants, exclaiming over the antique panelling and the high ceilings. The Ehrs, whooping and laughing, with Vic remarking that the place looked like something designed by Charles Addams. That was a signal for a drink, and by the time Hacker and his wife arrived the blaring radio found ample competition from the voices of the guests.

He drank, and she drank, but they couldn't shut it out altogether. That remark about Charles Addams was bad, and there were other things. Little things. The Talmadges had brought flowers, and she went out to the kitchen to arrange them in a cut-glass vase. There were facets in the glass, and as she stood in the kitchen, momentarily alone, and filled the vase with water from the tap, the crystal darkened beneath her fingers, and something peered, reflected from the facets. She turned quickly, and she was all alone. All alone, holding a hundred naked eyes in her hands.

So she dropped the vase, and the Ehrs and Talmadges and Hackers and Valliants trooped out to the kitchen, and he came too. Talmadge accused her of drinking and that was reason enough for another round. He said nothing, but got another vase for the flowers. And yet he must have known, because when somebody suggested a tour of the house, he put them off:

'We haven't straightened things out upstairs yet,' he said. 'It's a mess, and you'd be knocking into crates and stuff.'

'Who's up there now?' asked Mrs. Teters, coming into the kitchen with her husband. 'We just heard an awful crash.'

'Something must have fallen over,' the host suggested. But he didn't look at his wife as he spoke, and she didn't look at him.

'How about another drink?' she asked. She mixed and poured hurriedly, and before the glasses were half empty, he took over and fixed another round. Liquor helped to keep people talking and if they talked it would drown out other sounds.

The stratagem worked. Gradually the group trickled back into the living room in twos and threes, and the radio blared and the laughter rose and the voices babbled to blot out the noises of the night.

He poured and she served, and both of them drank, but the alcohol had no effect. They moved carefully, as though their bodies were brittle glasses – glasses without bottom – waiting to be shattered by some sudden strident sound. Glasses hold liquor, but they never get drunk.

Their guests were not glasses, they drank and feared nothing, and the drinks took hold. People moved about, and in and out, and pretty soon Mr. Valliant and Mrs. Talmadge embarked on their own private tour of the house upstairs. It was irregular and unescorted, but fortunately nobody noticed either their departure or their absence. At least, not until Mrs. Talmadge came running downstairs and locked herself in the bathroom.

Her hostess saw her pass the doorway. She rapped on the bathroom door, gained admittance, and prepared to make discreet inquiries. None was necessary. Mrs. Talmadge, weeping and wringing her hands, fell upon her.

'That was a filthy trick!' she sobbed. 'Coming up and sneaking in on us. The dirty louse – I admit we were doing a little smooching, but that's all there was to it. And it isn't as though he didn't make enough passes at Gwen Hacker himself. What I want to know is, where did he get the beard? It frightened me out of my wits.'

'What's all this?' she asked – knowing all the while what it was, and dreading the words to come.

'Jeff and I were in the bedroom, just standing there in the dark, I swear it, and all at once I looked up over my shoulder at the mirror because light began streaming in from the hall. Somebody had opened the door, and I could see the glass and this face. Oh, it was my husband all right, but he had a beard on and the way he came slinking in, glaring at us– '

Sobs choked off the rest. Mrs. Talmadge trembled so that she wasn't aware of the tremors which racked the frame of her hostess. She, for her part, strained to hear the rest. '–sneaked right out again before we could do anything, but wait till I get him home – scaring the life out of me and all because he's so crazy jealous – the look on his face in the mirror–'

She soothed Mrs. Talmadge. She comforted Mrs. Talmadge. She placated Mrs. Talmadge. And all the while there was nothing to soothe or calm or placate her own agitation.

Still, both of them had restored a semblance of sanity by the time they ventured out into the hall to join the party – just in time to hear Mr. Talmadge's agitated voice booming out over the excited responses of the rest.

'So I'm standing there in the bathroom and this old witch comes up and starts making faces over my shoulder in the mirror. What gives here, anyway? What kind of a house you running here?'

He thought it was funny. So did the others. Most of the others. The host and hostess stood there, not daring to look at each other. Their smiles were cracking. Glass is brittle.

'I don't believe you.' Gwen Hacker's voice. She'd had one, or perhaps three, too many. 'I'm going up right now and see for myself.' She winked at her host and moved towards the stairs.

'Hey, hold on!' He was too late. She swept, or wobbled, past him.

'Halloween pranks,' said Talmadge, nudging him. 'Old babe in a fancy hairdo. Saw her plain as day. What you cook up for us here, anyhow?'

He began to stammer something, anything, to halt the flood of foolish babbling. She moved close to him, wanting to listen, wanting to believe, wanting to do anything but think of Gwen Hacker upstairs, all alone upstairs looking into a mirror and waiting to see –

The screams came then. Not sobs, not laughter, but screams. He took the stairs two at a time. Fat Mr. Hacker was right behind him, and the others straggled along, suddenly silent. There was the sound of feet clubbing the staircase, the sound of heavy breathing, and over everything the continuing high-pitched shriek of a woman confronted with terror too great to contain.

It oozed out of Gwen Hacker's voice, oozed out of her body as she staggered and half-fell into her husband's arms in the hall. The light was streaming out of the bathroom, and it fell upon the mirror that was empty of all reflection, fell upon her face that was empty of all expression.

They crowded around the Hackers – he and she were on either side and the others clustered in front – and they moved along the hall to her bedroom and helped Mr. Hacker stretch his wife out on the bed. She had passed out, and somebody mumbled something about a doctor, and somebody else said no, never mind, she'll be all right in a minute, and somebody else said well, I think we'd better be getting along.

For the first time everybody seemed to be aware of the old house and the darkness, and the way the floors creaked and the windows rattled and the shutters banged. Everyone was suddenly sober, solicitous, and extremely anxious to leave.

Hacker bent over his wife, chafing her wrists, forcing her to swallow water, watching her whimper her way out of emptiness. The host and hostess silently procured hats and coats and listened to expressions of polite regret, hasty farewells, and poorly formulated pretenses of, 'Had a marvelous time, darling.'

Teters, Valliants, Talmadges were swallowed up in the night. He and she went back upstairs, back to the bedroom and the Hackers. It was too dark in the hall, and too light in the bedroom. But there they were, waiting. And they didn't wait long.

Mrs. Hacker sat up suddenly and began to talk. To her husband, to them.

'I saw her,' she said. 'Don't tell me I'm crazy, I saw her! Standing on tiptoe behind me, looking right into the mirror. With the same blue ribbon in her hair, the one she wore the day she–'

'Please, dear,' said Mr. Hacker.

She didn't please. 'But I saw her. Mary Lou! She made a face at me in the mirror, and she's dead, you know she's dead, she disappeared three years ago and they never did find the body–'

'Mary Lou Dempster.' Hacker was a fat man. He had two chins. Both of them wobbled.

'She played around here, you know she did, and Wilma Dempster told her to stay away, she knew all about this house, but she wouldn't and now – oh, her face!'

More sobs. Hacker patted her on the shoulder. He looked as though he could stand a little shoulder-patting himself. But nobody obliged. He stood there, she stood there, still waiting. Waiting for the rest.

'Tell them,' said Mrs. Hacker. 'Tell them the truth.'

'All right, but I'd better get you home.'

'I'll wait. I want you to tell them. You must, now.'

Hacker sat down heavily. His wife leaned against his shoulder. The two waited another moment. Then it came.

'I don't know how to begin, how to explain,' said fat Mr. Hacker. 'It's probably my fault, of course, but I didn't know. All this foolishness about haunted houses – nobody believes that stuff any more, and all it does is push property values down, so I didn't say anything. Can you blame me?'

'I saw her face,' whispered Mrs. Hacker.

'I know. And I should have told you. About the house, I mean. Why it hasn't rented for twenty years. Old story in the neighborhood, and you'd have heard it sooner or later anyway, I guess.'

'Get on with it,' said Mrs. Hacker. She was suddenly strong again and he, with his wobbling chins, was weak.

Host and hostess stood before them, brittle as glass, as the words poured out; poured out and filled them to overflowing. He and she, watching and listening, filling up with the realization, with the knowledge, with that for which they had waited.

It was the Bellman house they were living in, the house Job Bellman built for his bride back in the sixties; the house where his bride had given birth to Laura and taken death in exchange. And Job Bellman had toiled through the seventies as his daughter grew to girlhood, rested in complacent retirement during the eighties as Laura Bellman blossomed into the reigning beauty of the county – some said the state, but then flattery came quickly to men's lips in those days.

There were men aplenty; coming and going through that decade; passing through the hall in polished boots, bowing and stroking brilliantined mustachios, smirking at old Job, grinning at the servants, and gazing in moonstruck adoration at Laura.

Laura took it all as her rightful due, but land's sakes, she'd never think of it, no, not while Papa was still alive, and no, she couldn't, she was much too young to marry, and why, she'd never heard of such a thing, she'd always thought it was so much nicer just being friends –

Moonlight, dances, parties, hayrides, sleighrides, candy, flowers, gifts, tokens, cotillion balls, punch, fans, beauty spots, dressmakers, curlers, mandolins, cycling, and the years that whirled away. And then, one day, old Job dead in the four-poster bed upstairs, and the Doctor came and the Minister, and then the Lawyer, hack-hack-hacking away with his dry, precise little cough, and his talk of inheritance and estate and annual income.

Then she was all alone, just she and the servants and the mirrors. Laura and her mirrors. Mirrors in the morning, and the careful inspection, the scrutiny that began the day. Mirrors at night before the caller arrived, before the carriage came, before she whirled away to another triumphal entry, another fan-fluttering, pirouetting descent of the staircase. Mirrors at dawn, absorbing the smiles, listening to the secrets, the tale of the evening's triumph.

'Mirror, mirror on the wall, who is the fairest of them all?'

Mirrors told her the truth, mirrors did not lie, mirrors did not paw or clutch or whisper or demand in return for acknowledgment of beauty.

Years passed, but mirrors did not age, did not change. And Laura did not age. The callers were fewer and some of them were oddly altered. They seemed older, somehow. And yet how could that be? For Laura Bellman was still young. The mirrors said so, and they always told the truth. Laura spent more and more time with the mirrors. Powdering, searching for wrinkles, tinting and curling her long hair. Smiling, fluttering eyelashes, making deliciously delicate little *moves*. Swirling daintily, posturing before her own perfection.

Sometimes, when the callers came, she sent word that she was not at home. It seemed silly, somehow, to leave the mirrors. And after a while, there weren't many callers to worry about. Servants came and went, some of them died, but there were always new ones. Laura and the mirrors remained. The nineties were truly gay, but in a way other people wouldn't understand. How Laura laughed, rocking back and forth on the bed, sharing her giddy secrets with the glass!

The years fairly flew by, but Laura merely laughed. She giggled and tittered when the servants spoke to her, and it was easier now to take her meals on a tray in her room. Because there was something wrong with the servants, and with Doctor Turner who came to visit her and who was always being tiresome about going away for a rest to a lovely home.

They thought she was getting old, but she wasn't – the mirrors didn't lie. She wore the false teeth and the wig to please the others, the outsiders, but she didn't really need them. The mirrors told her she was unchanged. They talked to her now, the mirrors did, and she never said a word. Just sat nodding and swaying before them in the room reeking of powder and *patchouli*, stroking her throat and listening to the mirrors telling her how beautiful she was and what a belle she would be if she would only waste her beauty on the world. But she'd never leave here, never; she and the mirrors would always be together.

And then came the day they tried to take her away, and they actually laid hands upon her – upon her, Laura Bellman, the most exquisitely beautiful woman in the world! Was it any wonder that she fought, clawed and kicked and whined, and struck out so that one of the servants crashed headlong into the beautiful glass and struck his foolish head and died, his nasty blood staining the image of her perfection?

Of course it was all a stupid mistake and it wasn't her fault, and Doctor Turner told the magistrate so when he came to call. Laura didn't have to see him, and she didn't have to leave the house. But they always locked the door to her room now, and they took away all her mirrors.

They *took away* all her mirrors!

They left her alone, caged up, a scrawny, wizened, wrinkled old woman with no reflection. They took the mirrors away and made her old; old, and ugly, and afraid.

The night they did it, she cried. She cried and hobbled around the room, stumbling blindly in a tearsome tour of nothingness.

That's when she realized she was old, and nothing could save her. Because she came up against the window and leaned her wrinkled forehead against the cold, cold glass. The light came from behind her and as she drew away she could see her reflection in the window.

The window – it was a mirror, too! She gazed into it, gazed long and lovingly at the tear-streaked face of the fantastically rouged and painted old harridan, gazed at the corpse-countenance readied for the grave by a mad embalmer.

Everything whirled. It was her house, she knew every inch of it, from the day of her birth onwards the house was a part of her. It was her room, she had lived here for ever and ever. But *this* – this obscenity – was not her face. Only a mirror could show her that, and there would never be a mirror for her again. For an instant she gazed at the truth and then, mercifully, the gleaming glass of the window-pane altered and once again she gazed at Laura Bellman, the proudest beauty of them all. She drew herself erect, stepped back, and whirled into a dance. She danced forward, a prim self-conscious smile on her lips. Danced into the window-pane, half-through it, until razored splinters of glass tore her scrawny throat.

That's how she died and that's how they found her. The Doctor came, and the servants and the lawyer did what must be done. The house was sold, then sold again. It fell into the hands of a rental agency. There were tenants, but not for long. They had trouble with mirrors.

A man died – of a heart attack, they said – while adjusting his necktie before the bureau one evening. Grotesque enough, but he had complained to people in the town about strange happenings, and his wife babbled to everyone.

A school-teacher who rented the place in the twenties 'passed away' in circumstances which Doctor Turner had never seen fit to relate. He had gone to the rental agency and begged them to take the place off the market; that was almost unnecessary, for the Bellman home had its reputation firmly established by now.

Whether or not Mary Lou Dempster had disappeared here would never be known. But the little girl had last been seen a year ago on the road leading to the house and, although a search had been made and nothing discovered, there was talk aplenty.

Then the new heirs had stepped in, briskly, with their pooh-poohs and their harsh dismissals of advice, and the house had been cleaned and put up for rental.

So he and she had come to live here – with it. And that was the story, all of the story.

Mr. Hacker put his arm around Gwen, harrumphed, and helped her rise. He was apologetic, he was shame-faced, he was deferential. His eyes never met those of his tenant.

He barred the doorway. 'We're getting out of here, right now,' he said. 'Lease or no lease.'

'That can be arranged. But – I can't find you another place tonight, and tomorrow's Sunday–'

'We'll pack and get out of here tomorrow,' she spoke up. 'Go to a hotel, anywhere. But we're leaving.'

'I'll call you tomorrow,' said Hacker. 'I'm sure everything will be all right. After all, you've stayed here through the week and nothing. I mean nobody has–'

His words trailed off. There was no point in saying any more. The Hackers left and they were all alone. Just the two of them.

Just the *three* of them, that is.

But now they – he and she – were too tired to care. The inevitable letdown, product of overindulgence and over-excitement was at hand.

They said nothing, for there was nothing to say. They heard nothing, for the house – and it – maintained a sombre silence.

She went to her room and undressed. He began to walk around the house. First he went to the kitchen and opened a drawer next to the sink. He took a hammer and smashed the kitchen mirror.

Tinkle-tinkle! And then a crash! That was the mirror in the hall. Then upstairs, to the bathroom. Crash and clink of broken glass in the medicine cabinet. Then a smash as he shattered the panel in his room. And now he came to her bedroom and swung the hammer against the huge oval of the vanity, shattering it to bits.

He wasn't cut, wasn't excited, wasn't upset. And the mirrors were gone. Every last one of them was gone.

They looked at each other for a moment. Then he switched off the lights, tumbled into bed beside her, and sought sleep.

The night wore on.

It was all a little silly in the daylight. But she looked at him again in the morning, and he went into his room and hauled out the suitcases. By the time she had breakfast ready he was already laying his clothes out on the bed. She got up after eating and took her own clothing from the drawers and hangers and racks and hooks. Soon he'd go up to the attic and get the garment bags. The movers could be called tomorrow, or as soon as they had a destination in mind.

The house was quiet. If it knew their plans, it

wasn't acting. The day was gloomy and they kept the lights off without speaking – although both of them knew it was because of the window-panes and the story of the reflection. He could have smashed the window-glass of course, but it was all a little silly. And they'd be out of here shortly.

Then they heard the noise. Trickling, burbling. A splashing sound. It came from beneath their feet. She gasped.

'Water-pipe – in the basement,' he said, smiling and taking her by the shoulders.

'Better take a look.' She moved towards the stairs.

'Why should you go down there? I'll tend to it.'

But she shook her head and pulled away. It was her penance for gasping. She had to show she wasn't afraid. She had to show him – and it, too.

'Wait a minute,' he said. 'I'll get the pipe-wrench. It's in the trunk in the car.' He went out the back door. She stood irresolute, then headed for the cellar stairs. The splashing was getting louder. The burst pipe was flooding the basement. It made a funny noise, like laughter.

He could hear it even when he walked up the driveway and opened the trunk of the car. These old houses always had something wrong with them; he might have known it. Burst pipes and –

Yes. He found the wrench. He walked back to the door, listening to the water gurgle, listening to his wife scream.

She *was* screaming! Screaming down in the basement, screaming down in the dark.

He ran, swinging the heavy wrench. He clumped down the stairs, down into the darkness, the screams tearing up at him. She was caught, it had her, she was struggling with it but it was strong, too strong, and the light came streaming in on the pool of water beside the shattered pipe and in the reflection he saw her face and the blackness of other faces swirling around her and holding her.

He brought the wrench up, brought it down on the black blur, hammering and hammering and hammering until the screaming died away. And then he stopped and looked down at her. The dark blur had faded away into the reflection of the water – the reflection that had evoked it. But she was still there, and she was still, and she would be still forever now. Only the water was getting red, where her head rested in it. And the end of the wrench was red, too.

For a moment he started to tell her about it, and then he realized she was gone. Now there were only the two of them left. He and it.

And he was going upstairs. He was walking upstairs, still carrying the bloody wrench, and he was going over to the phone to call the police and explain.

He sat down in a chair before the phone, thinking about what he'd tell them, how he'd explain. It wouldn't be easy. There was this madwoman, see, and she looked into mirrors until there was more of her alive in her reflection than there was in her own body. So when she committed suicide she lived on, somehow, and came alive in mirrors or glass or anything that reflected. And she killed others or drove them to death and their reflections were somehow joined with hers so that this thing kept getting stronger and stronger, sucking away at life with that awful core of pride that could live beyond death. Woman, thy name is vanity! And that, gentlemen, is why I killed my wife…

Yes, it was a fine explanation, but it wouldn't hold water. Water – the pool in the basement had evoked it. He might have known it if only he'd stopped to think, to reflect. Reflect. That was the wrong word, now. Reflect. The way the window pane before him was reflecting.

He stared into the glass now, saw it behind him, surging up from the shadows. He saw the bearded man's face, the peering, pathetic, empty eyes of a little girl, the goggling grimacing stare of an old woman. It wasn't there, behind him, but it was alive in the reflection, and as he rose he gripped the wrench tightly. It wasn't there, but he'd strike at it, fight at it, come to grips with it somehow.

He turned, moving back, the ring of shadow-faces pressing. He swung the wrench. Then he saw *her* face coming up through all the rest. Her face, with shining splinters where the eyes should be. He couldn't smash it down, he couldn't hit her again.

It moved forward. He moved back. His arm went out to one side. He beard the tinkle of window-glass behind him and vaguely remembered that this was how the old woman had died. The way he was dying now – falling through the window, and cutting his throat, and the pain lanced up and in, tearing at his brain as he hung there on the jagged spikes of glass, bleeding his life away.

Then he was gone.

His body hung there, but he was gone.

There was a little puddle on the floor, moving and growing. The light from outside shone on it, and there was a reflection.

Something emerged fully from the shadows now, emerged and capered demurely in the darkness.

It had the face of an old woman and the face of a child, the face of a bearded man, and *his* face, and *her* face, changing and blending.

It capered and postured, and then it squatted, dabbling. Finally, all alone in the empty house, it just sat there and waited. There was nothing to do now but wait for the next to come. And meanwhile, it could always admire itself in that growing, growing red reflection on the floor…

THE COMPLETE GENTLEMAN

Amos Tutuola

Amos Tutuola (1920–1997) was a largely self-taught Nigerian writer who became internationally praised for books based in part on Yoruba folktales, especially the phantasmagorical *The Palm-Wine Drinkard* (1952). Welsh poet Dylan Thomas called the novel 'thronged, grisly and bewitching,' bringing it even more attention. But Tutuola was also criticized for the novel's 'primitive' style, seen to promote negative stereotypes about Africa. However, from the perspective of weird fiction aficionados the book is as amazing an accomplishment as anything from Clark Ashton Smith, H. P. Lovecraft or Alfred Kubin, even as it takes completely different cultural referents as its entry point into the weird. 'The Complete Gentleman' is a self-contained excerpt from the book.

He was a beautiful 'complete' gentleman, he dressed with the finest and most costly clothes, all the parts of his body were completed, he was a tall man but stout. As this gentleman came to the market on that day, if he had been an article or animal for sale, he would be sold at least for £2000 (two thousand pounds). As this complete gentleman came to the market on that day, and at the same time that this lady saw him in the market, she did nothing more than to ask him where he was living, but this fine gentleman did not answer her or approach her at all. But when she noticed that the fine or complete gentleman did not listen to her, she left her articles and began to watch the movements of the complete gentleman about in the market and left her articles unsold.

By and by the market closed for that day then the whole people in the market were returning to their destinations etc., and the complete gentleman was returning to his own too, but as this lady was following him about in the market all the while, she saw him when he was returning to his destination as others did, then she was following him (complete gentleman) to an unknown place. But as she was following the complete gentleman along the road, he was telling her to go back or not to follow him, but the lady did not listen to what he was telling her, and when the complete gentleman had tired of telling her not to follow him or to go back to her town, he left her to follow him.

DO NOT FOLLOW UNKNOWN MAN'S BEAUTY

But when they had travelled about twelve miles away from that market, they left the road on which they were travelling and started to travel inside an endless forest in which only all the terrible creatures were living.

RETURN THE PARTS OF BODY TO THE OWNERS; OR HIRED PARTS OF THE COMPLETE GENTLEMAN'S BODY TO BE RETURNED

As they were travelling along in this endless forest then the complete gentleman in the market that the lady was following, began to return the hired parts of his body to the owners and he was paying them the rentage money. When he reached where he hired the left foot, he pulled it out, he gave it to the owner and paid him, and they kept going; when they reached the place where he hired the right foot, he pulled it out and gave it to the owner and paid for the rentage. Now both feet had returned to the owners, so he began to crawl along on the ground, by that time, that lady wanted to go back to her town or her father, but the terrible and curious creature or the complete gentleman did not allow her to return or go back to her town or her father again and the complete gentleman said thus: 'I had told you not to follow me before we branched into this endless forest which belongs to only terrible and curious creatures, but when I became a half-bodied incomplete gentleman you wanted to go back, now that cannot be done, you have failed. Even you have never seen anything yet, just follow me.'

When they went furthermore, then they reached where he hired the belly, ribs, chest etc., then he pulled them out and gave them to the owner and paid for the rentage.

Now to this gentleman or terrible creature remained only the head and both arms with neck, by that time he could not crawl as before but only went jumping on as a bull-frog and now this lady was soon faint for this fearful creature whom she was following. But when the lady saw every part of this complete gentleman in the market was spared or hired and he was returning them to the owners, then she began to try all her efforts to return to her father's town, but she was not allowed by this fearful creature at all.

When they reached where he hired both arms, he pulled them out and gave them to the owner, he paid for them; and they were still going on in this endless forest, they reached the place where he hired the neck, he pulled it out and gave it to the owner and paid for it as well.

A FULL-BODIED GENTLEMAN REDUCED TO HEAD

Now this complete gentleman was reduced to head and when they reached where he hired the skin and flesh which covered the head, he returned them, and paid to the owner, now the complete gentleman in the market reduced to a 'SKULL' and this lady remained with only 'Skull'. When the lady saw that she remained with only Skull, she began to say that her father had been telling her to marry a man, but she did not listen to or believe him.

When the lady saw that the gentleman became a Skull, she began to faint, but the Skull told her if she would die she would die and she would follow him to his house. But by the time that he was saying so, he was humming with a terrible voice and also grew very wild and even if there was a person two miles away he would not have to listen before hearing him, so this lady began to run away in that forest for her life, but the Skull chased her and within a few yards, he caught her, because he was very clever and smart as he was only Skull and he could jump a mile to the second before coming down. He caught the lady in this way: so when the lady was running away for her life, he hastily ran to her front and stopped her as a log of wood.

By and by, this lady followed the Skull to his house, and the house was a hole which was under the ground. When they reached there both of them entered the hole. But there were only Skulls living in that hole. At the same time that they entered the hole, he tied a single cowrie on the neck of this lady with a kind of rope, after that, he gave her a large frog on which she sat as a stool, then he gave a whistle to a Skull of this kind to keep watch on this lady whenever she wanted to run away. Because the Skull knew already that the lady would attempt to run away from the hole. Then he went to the back-yard to where his family were staying in the day time till night.

But one day, the lady attempted to escape from the hole, and at the same time that the Skull who was watching her whistled to the rest of the Skulls that were in the back-yard, the whole of them rushed out to the place where the lady sat on the bull-frog, so they caught her, but as all of them were rushing out, they were rolling on the ground as if a thousand petrol drums were pushing along a hard road. After she was caught, then they brought her back to sit on the same frog as usual. If the Skull who was watching her fell asleep, and if the lady wanted to escape, the cowrie that was tied on her neck would raise up the alarm with a terrible noise, so that the Skull who was watching her would wake up at once and then the rest of the Skull's family would rush out from the back in thousands to the lady and ask her what she wanted to do with a curious and terrible voice.

But the lady could not talk at all, because as the cowrie had been tied on her neck, she became dumb at the same moment.

THE FATHER OF GODS SHOULD FIND OUT WHEREABOUTS THE DAUGHTER OF THE HEAD OF THE TOWN WAS

Now as the father of the lady first asked for my name and I told him that my name was 'Father of gods who could do anything in this world,' then he told me that if I could find out where his daughter was and bring her to him, then he would tell me where my palm-wine tapster was. But when he said so, I was jumping up with gladness that he should promise me that he would tell me where my tapster was. I agreed to what he said; the father and parent of this lady never knew whereabouts their daughter was, but they had information that the lady followed a complete gentleman in the market. As I was the 'Father of gods who could do anything in this world,' when it was at night I sacrificed to my juju with a goat.

And when it was early in the morning, I sent for forty kegs of palm-wine, after I had drunk it all, I started to investigate whereabouts was the lady. As it was the market-day, I started the investigation from the market. But as I was a juju-man, I knew all the kinds of people in that market. When it was exactly 9 o'clock a.m., the very complete gentleman whom the lady followed came to the market again, and at the same time that I saw him, I knew that he was a curious and terrible creature.

THE LADY WAS NOT TO BE BLAMED FOR FOLLOWING THE SKULL AS A COMPLETE GENTLEMAN

I could not blame the lady for following the Skull as a complete gentleman to his house at all. Because if I were a lady, no doubt I would follow him to wherever he would go, and still as I was a man I would be jealous of him more than that, because if this gentleman went to the battle field, surely, enemy would not kill him or capture him and if bombers saw him in a town which was to be bombed, they would not throw bombs on his presence, and if they did throw it, the bomb itself would not explode until this gentleman would leave that town, because of his beauty. At the same time that I saw this gentleman in the market on that day, what I was doing was only to follow him about in the market. After I looked at him for so many hours, then I ran to a corner of the market and I cried for a few minutes because I thought within myself why was I not created with beauty as this gentleman, but when I remembered that he was only a Skull, then I thanked God that He had created me without beauty, so I went back to him in the market, but I was still attracted by his beauty. So when the market closed for that day, and when everybody was returning to his or her destination, this gentleman was returning to his own too and I followed him to know where he was living.

INVESTIGATION TO THE SKULL'S FAMILY'S HOUSE

When I travelled with him a distance of about twelve miles away to that market, the gentleman left the really road on which we were travelling and branched into an endless forest and I was following him, but as I did not want him to see that I was following him, then I used one of my juju which changed me into a lizard and followed him. But after I had travelled with him a distance of about twenty-five miles away in this endless forest, he began to pull out all the parts of his body and return them to the owners, and paid them.

After I had travelled with him for another fifty miles in this forest, then he reached his house and entered it, but I entered it also with him, as I was a lizard. The first thing that he did when he entered the hole (house) he went straight to the place where the lady was, and I saw the lady sat on a bull-frog with a single cowrie tied on her neck and a Skull who was watching her stood behind her. After he (gentleman) had seen that the lady was there, he went to the back-yard where all his family were working.

THE INVESTIGATOR'S WONDERFUL WORK IN THE SKULL'S FAMILY'S HOUSE

When I saw this lady and when the Skull who brought her to that hole or whom I followed from the market to that hole went to the back-yard, then I changed myself to a man as before, then I talked to the lady but she could not answer me at all, she only showed that she was in a serious condition. The Skull who was guarding her with a whistle fell asleep at that time.

To my surprise, when I helped the lady to stand up from the frog on which she sat, the cowrie that was tied on her neck made a curious noise at once, and when the Skull who was watching her heard the noise, he woke up and blew the whistle to the rest, then the whole of them rushed to the place and surrounded the lady and me, but at the same time that they saw me there, one of them ran to a pit which was not so far from that spot, the pit was filled with cowries. He picked one cowrie out of the pit, after that he was running towards me, and the whole crowd wanted to tie the cowrie on my neck too. But before they could do that, I had changed myself into air, they could not trace me out again, but I was looking at them. I believed that the cowries in that pit were their power and to reduce the power of any human being whenever tied on his or her neck and also to make a person dumb.

Over one hour after I had dissolved into air, these Skulls went back to the back-yard, but there remained the Skull who was watching her.

After they had returned to the back-yard, I changed to a man as usual, then I took the lady from the frog, but at the same time that I touched her, the cowrie which was tied on her neck began to shout; even if a person was four miles away he would not have to listen before hearing, but immediately the Skull who was watching her heard the noise and saw me when I took her from that frog, he blew the whistle to the rest of them who were in the back-yard.

Immediately the whole Skull family heard the whistle when blew to them, they were rushing out to the place and before they could reach there, I had left their hole for the forest, but before I could travel about one hundred yards in the forest, they had rushed out from their hole to inside the forest and I was still running away with the lady. As these Skulls were chasing me about in the forest, they were rolling on the ground like large stones and also humming with terrible noise, but when I saw that they had nearly caught me or if I continued to run away like that, no doubt, they would catch me sooner, then I changed the lady to a kitten and put her inside my pocket and changed myself to a very small bird which I could describe as a 'sparrow' in English language.

After that I flew away, but as I was flying in the sky, the cowrie which was tied on that lady's neck was still making a noise and I tried all my best to stop the noise, but all were in vain. When I reached home with the lady, I changed her to a lady as she was before and also myself changed to man as well. When her father saw that I brought his daughter back home, he was exceedingly glad and said thus: 'You are the "Father of gods" as you had told me before.'

But as the lady was now at home, the cowrie on her neck did not stop making a terrible noise once, and she could not talk to anybody; she showed only that she was very glad she was at home. Now I had brought the lady but she could not talk, eat or loose away the cowrie on her neck, because the terrible noise of the cowrie did not allow anybody to rest or sleep at all.

THERE REMAIN GREATER TASKS AHEAD

Now I began to cut the rope of the cowrie from her neck and to make her talk and eat, but all my efforts were in vain. At last I tried my best to cut off the rope of the cowrie; it only stopped the noise, but I was unable to loose it away from her neck.

When her father saw all my trouble, he thanked me greatly and repeated again that as I called myself 'Father of gods who could do anything in this world' I ought to do the rest of the work. But when he said so, I was very ashamed and thought within myself that if I return to the Skulls' hole or house, they might kill me and the forest was very dangerous travel always, again I could not go directly to the Skulls in their hole and ask them how to loose away the cowrie which was tied on the lady's neck and to make her talk and eat.

BACK TO THE SKULL'S FAMILY'S HOUSE

On the third day after I had brought the lady to her father's house, I returned to the endless forest for further investigation. When there remained about one mile to reach the hole of these Skulls, there I saw the very Skull who the lady had followed from the market as a complete gentleman to the hole of Skull's family's house, and at the same time that I saw him like that, I changed into a lizard and climbed a tree which was near him.

He stood before two plants, then he cut a single opposite leaf from the opposite plant; he held the leaf with his right hand and he was saying thus: 'As this lady was taken from me, if this opposite leaf is not given her to eat, she will not talk for ever,' after that he threw the leaf down on the ground. Then he cut another single compound leaf from the compound plant which was in the same place with the opposite plant, he held the compound leaf with his left hand and said that if this single compound is not given to this lady, to eat, the cowrie on her neck could not be loosened away for ever and it would be making a terrible noise for ever.

After he said so, he threw the leaf down at the same spot, then he jumped away. So after he had jumped very far away (luckily, I was there when he was doing all these things, and I saw the place that he threw both leaves separately), then I changed myself to a man as before, I went to the place that he threw both leaves, then I picked them up and I went home at once.

But at the same time that I reached home, I cooked both leaves separately and gave her to eat; to my surprise the lady began to talk at once. After that, I gave her the compound leaf to eat for the second time and immediately she ate that too, the cowrie which was tied on her neck by the Skull, loosened away by itself, but it disappeared at the same time. So when the father and mother saw the wonderful work which I had done for them, they brought fifty kegs of palm-wine for me, they gave me the lady as wife and two rooms in that house in which to live with them. So, I saved the lady from the complete gentleman in the market who afterwards reduced to a 'Skull' and the lady became my wife since that day. This was how I got a wife.

'IT'S A *GOOD* LIFE'

Jerome Bixby

Jerome Bixby (1923–1998) was an American short story and script writer who wrote four *Star Trek* episodes and helped write the story that became the classic sci-fi movie *Fantastic Voyage* (1966). He is most famous for the 'It's a *Good* Life' (1953), also made into a *Twilight Zone* episode and included in *Twilight Zone: The Movie* (1983). The Science Fiction Writers of America named 'It's a *Good* Life' one of the twenty finest science fiction stories ever written. References to the story have appeared in the Cartoon Network's *Johnny Bravo*, Fox's *The Simpsons*, and a Junot Diaz novel, among others. The story has an enduring creepiness and complexity undiluted by parodies and pop culture references over the years.

Aunt Amy was out on the front porch, rocking back and forth in the high-backed chair and fanning herself, when Bill Soames rode his bicycle up the road and stopped in front of the house.

Perspiring under the afternoon 'sun,' Bill lifted the box of groceries out of the big basket over the front wheel of the bike, and came up the front walk.

Little Anthony was sitting on the lawn, playing with a rat. He had caught the rat down in the basement – he had made it think that it smelled cheese, the most rich-smelling and crumbly-delicious cheese a rat had ever thought it smelled, and it had come out of its hole, and now Anthony had hold of it with his mind and was making it do tricks.

When the rat saw Bill Soames coming, it tried to run, but Anthony thought at it, and it turned a flip-flop on the grass, and lay trembling, its eyes gleaming in small black terror.

Bill Soames hurried past Anthony and reached the front steps, mumbling. He always mumbled when he came to the Fremont house, or passed by it, or even thought of it. Everybody did. They thought about silly things, things that didn't mean very much, like two-and-two-is-four-and-twice-is-eight and so on; they tried to jumble up their thoughts to keep them skipping back and forth, so Anthony couldn't read their minds. The mumbling helped. Because if Anthony got anything strong out of your thoughts, he might take a notion to do something about it – like curing your wife's sick headaches or your kid's mumps, or getting your old milk cow back on schedule, or fixing the privy. And while Anthony mightn't actually mean any harm, he couldn't be expected to have much notion of what was the right thing to do in such cases.

That was if he liked you. He might try to help you, in his way. And that could be pretty horrible.

If he didn't like you ... well, that could be worse.

Bill Soames set the box of groceries on the porch railing and stopped his mumbling long enough to say, 'Everythin' you wanted, Miss Amy.'

'Oh, fine, William,' Amy Fremont said lightly. 'My, ain't it terrible hot today?'

Bill Soames almost cringed. His eyes pleaded with her. He shook his head violently *no*, and then interrupted his mumbling again, though obviously he didn't want to: 'Oh, don't say that, Miss Amy... it's fine, just fine. A real *good* day!'

Amy Fremont got up from the rocking chair, and came across the porch. She was a tall woman, thin, a smiling vacancy in her eyes. About a year ago, Anthony had gotten mad at her, because she'd told him he shouldn't have turned the cat into a cat-rug, and although he had always obeyed her more than anyone else, which was hardly at all, this time he'd snapped at her. With his mind. And that had been the end of Amy Fremont's bright eyes, and the end of Amy Fremont as everyone had known her. And that was when word got around in Peaksville (population: 46) that even the members of Anthony's own family weren't safe. After that, everyone was twice as careful.

Someday Anthony might undo what he'd done to Aunt Amy. Anthony's Mom and Pop hoped he would. When he was older, and maybe sorry. If it was possible, that is. Because Aunt Amy had changed a lot, and besides, now Anthony wouldn't obey anyone.

'Land alive, William,' Aunt Amy said, 'you don't have to mumble like that. Anthony wouldn't hurt you. My goodness, Anthony likes you!' She raised her voice and called to Anthony, who had tired of the rat and was making it eat itself. 'Don't you, dear? Don't you like Mr. Soames?'

Anthony looked across the lawn at the grocery man – a bright, wet, purple gaze. He didn't say anything. Bill Soames tried to smile at him. After a second Anthony returned his attention to the rat. It had already devoured its tail, or at least chewed it off – for Anthony had made it bite faster than it could swallow, and little pink and red furry pieces lay around it on the green grass. Now the rat was having trouble reaching its hindquarters.

Mumbling silently, thinking of nothing in particular as hard as he could, Bill Soames went stiff-legged down the walk, mounted his bicycle and pedaled off.

'We'll see you tonight, William,' Aunt Amy called after him.

As Bill Soames pumped the pedals, he was wishing deep down that he could pump twice as fast, to get away from Anthony all the faster, and away from Aunt Amy, who sometimes just forgot how *careful* you had to be. And he shouldn't have thought that. Because Anthony caught it. He caught the desire to get away from the Fremont house as if it was something *bad*, and his purple gaze blinked and he snapped a small, sulky thought after Bill Soames – just a small one, because he was in a good mood today, and besides, he liked Bill Soames, or at least didn't dislike him, at least today. Bill Soames wanted to go away – so, petulantly, Anthony helped him.

Pedaling with superhuman speed – or rather, appearing to, because in reality the bicycle was pedaling *him* – Bill Soames vanished down the road in a cloud of dust, his thin, terrified wail drifting back across the heat.

Anthony looked at the rat. It had devoured half its belly, and had died from pain. He thought it into a grave out deep in the cornfield – his father had once said, smiling, that he might do that with the things he killed – and went around the houser, casting his odd shadow in the hot, brassy light from above.

In the kitchen, Aunt Amy was unpacking the groceries. She put the Mason-jarred goods on the shelves, and the meat and milk in the icebox, and the beet sugar and coarse flour in the big cans under the sink. She put the cardboard box in the corner, by the door, for Mr. Soames to pick up next time he came. It was stained and battered and torn and worn fuzzy, but it was one of the few left in Peaksville. In faded red letters it said *Campbell's Soup*. The last can of soup, or of anything else, had been eaten long ago, except for a small communal hoard which the villagers dipped into for special occasions – but the box lingered on, like a coffin, and when it and the other boxes were gone, the men would have to make some out of wood.

Aunt Amy went out in back, where Anthony's Mom – Aunt Amy's sister – sat in the shade of the house, shelling peas. The peas, every time Mom ran a finger along the pod, went *lollop-lollop-lollop* into the pan in her lap.

'William brought the groceries,' Aunt Amy said. She sat down wearily in the straightbacked chair beside Mom, and began fanning herself again. She wasn't really old, but ever since Anthony had snapped at her with his mind, something had been wrong with her body as well as her mind, and she was tired all the time.

'Oh, good,' said Mom. *Lollop* went the fat peas in the pan.

Everybody in Peaksville always said 'Oh, fine,' or 'Good,' or 'Say, that's swell,' when almost everything happened or was mentioned – even unhappy things like accidents or even deaths. They'd always say 'Good,' because if they didn't try to cover up how they really felt, Anthony might overhear with his mind, and then nobody knew what might happen. Like the time Mrs. Kent's husband, Sam, had come walking back from the graveyard because Anthony liked Mrs. Kent and had heard her mourning.

Lollop.

'Tonight's television night,' said Aunt Amy. 'I'm glad I look forward to it so much every week. I wonder what we'll see tonight?'

'Did Bill bring the meat?' asked Mom.

'Yes.' Aunt Amy fanned herself, looking up at the featureless brassy glare of the sky. 'Goodness, it's so hot. I wish Anthony would make it just a little cooler–'

'*Amy!*'

'Oh!' Mom's sharp tone had penetrated, where Bill Soames's agonized expression had failed. Aunt Amy put one thin hand to her mouth in exaggerated alarm. 'Oh... I'm sorry, dear.' Her pale blue eyes shuttled around, right and left, to see if Anthony was in sight. Not that it would make any difference if he was or wasn't – he didn't have to be near you to know what you were thinking. Usually, though, unless he had his attention on somebody, he would be occupied with thoughts of his own.

But some things attracted his attention – you could never be sure just what.

'This weather's just *fine*,' Mom said.

Lollop.

'Oh, yes,' Aunt Amy said. 'It's a wonderful day. I wouldn't want it changed for the world!'

Lollop.

Lollop.

'What time is it?' Mom asked.

Aunt Amy was sitting where she could see through the kitchen window to the alarm clock on the shelf above the stove. 'Four-thirty,' she said.

Lollop.

'I want tonight to be something special,' Mom said. 'Did Bill bring a good lean roast?'

'Good and lean, dear. They butchered just today, you know, and sent us over the best piece.'

'Dan Hollis will be so surprised when he finds out that tonight's television party is a birthday party for him too!'

'Oh *I* think he will! Are you sure nobody's told him?'

'Everybody swore they wouldn't.'

'That'll be real nice,' Aunt Amy nodded, looking off across the cornfield. 'A birthday party.'

'Well–' Mom put the pan of peas down beside her, stood up and brushed her apron. 'I'd better get the roast on. Then we can set the table.' She picked up the peas.

Anthony came around the corner of the house. He didn't look at them, but continued on down through the carefully kept garden – all the gardens in Peaksville were carefully kept, very carefully kept – and went past the rusting, useless hulk that had been the Fremont family car, and went smoothly over the fence and out into the cornfield.

'Isn't this a lovely day!' said Mom, a little loudly, as they went toward the back door.

Aunt Amy fanned herself. 'A beautiful day, dear. Just *fine*!'

Out in the cornfield, Anthony walked between the tall, rustling rows of green stalks. He liked to smell the corn. The alive corn overhead, and the old dead corn underfoot. Rich Ohio earth, thick with weeds and brown, dry-rotting ears of corn, pressed between his bare toes with every step – he had made it rain last night so everything would smell and feel nice today.

He walked clear to the edge of the cornfield, and over to where a grove of shadowy green trees covered cool, moist, dark ground, and lots of leafy undergrowth, and jumbled moss-covered rocks, and a small spring that made a clear, clean pool. Here Anthony liked to rest and watch the birds and insects and small animals that rustled and scampered and chirped about. He liked to lie on the cool ground and look up through the moving greenness overhead, and watch the insects flit in the hazy soft sunbeams that stood like slanting, glowing bars between ground and treetops. Somehow, he liked the thoughts of the little creatures in this place better than the thoughts outside; and while the thoughts he picked up here weren't very strong or very clear, he could get enough out of them to know what the little creatures liked and wanted, and he spent a lot of time making the grove more like what they wanted it to be. The spring hadn't always been here; but one time he had found thirst in one small furry mind, and had brought subterranean water to the surface in a clear cold flow, and had watched blinking as the creature drank, feeling its pleasure. Later he had made the pool, when he found a small urge to swim.

He had made rocks and trees and bushes and caves, and sunlight here and shadows there, because he had felt in all the tiny minds around him the desire – or the instinctive want – for this kind of resting place, and that kind of mating place, and this kind of place to play, and that kind of home.

And somehow the creatures from all the fields and pastures around the grove had seemed to know that this was a good place, for there were always more of them coming in – every time Anthony came out here there were more creatures than the last time, and more desires and needs to be tended to. Every time there would be some kind of creature he had never seen before, and he would find its mind, and see what it wanted, and then give it to it.

He liked to help them. He liked to feel their simple gratification.

Today, he rested beneath a thick elm, and lifted his purple gaze to a red and black bird that had just come to the grove. It twittered on a branch over his head, and hopped back and forth, and thought its tiny thoughts, and Anthony made a big, soft nest for it, and pretty soon it hopped in.

A long, brown, sleek-furred animal was drinking at the pool. Anthony found its mind next. The animal was thinking about a smaller creature that was scurrying along the ground on the other side of the pool, grubbing for insects. The little creature didn't know that it was in danger. The long, brown animal finished drinking and tensed its legs to leap, and Anthony thought it into a grave in the cornfield.

He didn't like those kinds of thoughts. They reminded him of the thoughts outside the grove. A long time ago some of the people outside had thought that way about him, and one night they'd hidden and waited for him to come back from the grove – and he'd just thought them all into the cornfield. Since then, the rest of the people hadn't thought that way – at least, very clearly. Now their thoughts were all mixed up and confusing whenever they thought about him or near him, so he didn't pay much attention.

He liked to help them too, sometimes – but it wasn't simple, or very gratifying either. They never thought happy thoughts when he did – just the jumble. So he spent more time out here.

He watched all the birds and insects and furry creatures for a while, and played with a bird, making it soar and dip and streak madly around tree trunks until, accidentally, when another bird caught his attention for a moment, he ran it into a rock. Petulantly, he thought the rock into a grave in the cornfield; but he couldn't do anything more with the bird. Not because it was dead, though it was; but because it had a broken wing. So he went back to the house. He didn't feel like walking back through the cornfield, so he just *went* to the house, right down into the basement.

It was nice down here. Nice and dark and damp and sort of fragrant, because once Mom had been making preserves in a rack along the far wall, and then she'd stopped coming down ever since Anthony had started spending time here, and the preserves had spoiled and leaked down and spread over the dirt floor, and Anthony liked the smell.

He caught another rat, making it smell cheese, and after he played with it, he thought it into a grave right beside the long animal he'd killed in the grove. Aunt Amy hated rats, and so he killed a lot of them, because he liked Aunt Amy most of all and sometimes did things that Aunt Amy wanted. Her mind was more like the little furry minds out in the grove. She hadn't thought anything bad at all about him for a long time.

After the rat, he played with a big black spider in the corner under the stairs, making it run back and forth until its web shook and shimmered in the light from the cellar window like a reflection in silvery water. Then he drove fruit flies into the web until the spider was frantic trying to wind them all up. The spider liked flies, and its thoughts were stronger than theirs, so he did it. There was something bad in the way it liked flies, but it wasn't clear – and besides, Aunt Amy hated flies too.

He heard footsteps overhead – Mom moving around in the kitchen. He blinked his purple gaze, and almost decided to make her hold still – but instead he *went* up to the attic, and, after looking out the circular window at the front end of the long X-roofed room for a while at the front lawn and the dusty road and Henderson's tip-waving wheatfield beyond, he curled into an unlikely shape and went partly to sleep.

Soon people would be coming for television, he heard Mom think.

He went more to sleep. He liked television night. Aunt Amy had always liked television a lot, so one time he had thought some for her, and a few other people had been there at the time, and Aunt Amy had felt disappointed when they wanted to leave. He'd done something to them for that – and now everybody came to television.

He liked all the attention he got when they did.

Anthony's father came home around six-thirty, looking tired and dirty and bloody. He'd been over in Dunn's pasture with the other men, helping pick out the cow to be slaughtered this month and doing the job, and then butchering the meat and salting it away in Soames's icehouse. Not a job he cared for, but every man had his turn. Yesterday, he had helped scythe down old McIntyre's wheat. Tomorrow, they would start threshing. By hand. Everything in Peaksville had to be done by hand.

He kissed his wife on the cheek and sat down at the kitchen table. He smiled and said, 'Where's Anthony?'

'Around someplace,' Mom said.

Aunt Amy was over at the wood-burning stove, stirring the big pot of peas. Mom went back to the oven and opened it and basted the roast.

'Well, it's been a *good* day,' Dad said. By rote. Then he looked at the mixing bowl and breadboard on the table. He sniffed at the dough. 'M'm,' he said. 'I could eat a loaf all by myself, I'm so hungry.'

'No one told Dan Hollis about its being a birthday party, did they?' his wife asked.

'Nope. We kept as quiet as mummies.'

'We've fixed up such a lovely surprise!'

'Um, what?'

'Well… you know how much Dan likes music. Well, last week Thelma Dunn found a *record* in her attic!'

'No!'

'Yes! And we had Ethel sort of ask you know, without really *asking* – if he had that one. And he said no. Isn't that a wonderful surprise?'

'Well, now, it sure is. A record, imagine! That's a real nice thing to find! What record is it?'

'Perry Como, singing *You Are My Sunshine*.'

'Well, I'll be darned. I always liked that tune.' Some raw carrots were lying on the table. Dad picked up a small one, scrubbed it on his chest, and took a bite. 'How did Thelma happen to find it?'

'Oh, you know just looking around for new things.'

'M'm.' Dad chewed the carrot. 'Say, who has that picture we found a while back? I kind of liked it – that old clipper sailing along–'

'The Smiths. Next week the Sipichs get it, and they give the Smiths old McIntyre's music-box, and we give the Sipichs–' and she went down the tentative order of things that would change hands among the women at church this Sunday.

He nodded. 'Looks like we can't have the picture for a while, I guess. Look, honey, you might try to get that detective book back from the Reillys. I was so busy the week we had it, I never got to finish all the stories–'

'I'll try,' his wife said doubtfully. 'But I hear the van Husens have a stereoscope they found in the cellar.' Her voice was just a little accusing. 'They had it two whole months before they told anybody about it–'

'Say,' Dad said, looking interested. 'That'd be nice, too. Lots of pictures?'

'I suppose so. I'll see on Sunday. I'd like to have it but we still owe the van Husens for their canary. I don't know why that bird had to pick *our* house to die… it must have been sick when we got it. Now there's just no satisfying Betty van Husen – she even hinted she'd like our *piano* for a while!'

'Well, honey, you try for the stereoscope or just anything you think we'll like.' At last he swallowed the carrot. It had been a little young and tough. Anthony's whims about the weather made it so that people never knew what crops would come up, or what shape they'd be in if they did. All they could do was plant a lot; and always enough of something came up any one season to live on. Just once there had been a grain surplus; tons of it had been hauled to the edge of Peaksville and dumped off into the nothingness. Otherwise, nobody could have breathed, when it started to spoil.

'You know,' Dad went on. 'It's nice to have the new things around. It's nice to think that there's probably still a lot of stuff nobody's found yet, in cellars and attics and barns and down behind things. They help, somehow. As much as anything can help.'

'Sh-h!' Mom glanced nervously around.

'Oh,' Dad said, smiling hastily. 'It's all right! The new things are *good*! It's *nice* to be able to have something around you've never seen before, and know that something you've given somebody else is making them happy... that's a real good thing.'

'A good thing,' his wife echoed.

'Pretty soon,' Aunt Amy said, from the stove, 'there won't be any more new things. We'll have found everything there is to find. Goodness, that'll be too bad.'

'Amy!'

'Well–' her pale eyes were shallow and fixed, a sign of her recurrent vagueness. 'It will be kind of a shame – no new things–'

'Don't *talk* like that,' Mom said, trembling. 'Amy, be *quiet!*'

'It's *good*,' said Dad, in the loud, familiar, wanting-to-be-overheard tone of voice. 'Such talk is *good*. It's okay, honey don't you see? It's good for Amy to talk any way she wants. It's good for her to feel bad. Everything's good. Everything *has* to be good... '

Anthony's mother was pale. And so was Aunt Amy – the peril of the moment had suddenly penetrated the clouds surrounding her mind. Sometimes it was difficult to handle words so that they might not prove disastrous. You just never *knew*. There were so many things it was wise not to say, or even think – but remonstration for saying or thinking them might be just as bad, if Anthony heard and decided to do anything about it. You could just never tell what Anthony was liable to do.

Everything had to be good. Had to be fine just as it was, even if it wasn't. Always. Because any changes might be worse. So terribly much worse.

'Oh, my goodness, yes, of course it's good,' Mom said. 'You talk any way you want to, Amy, and it's just fine. Of course, you want to remember that some ways are *better* than others...'

Aunt Amy stirred the peas, fright in her pale eyes.

'Oh, yes,' she said. 'But I don't feel like talking right now. It... it's *good* that I don't feel like talking.'

Dad said tiredly, smiling, 'I'm going out and wash up.'

They started arriving around eight o clock. By that time, Mom and Aunt Amy had the big table in the dining room set, and two more tables off to the side. The candles were burning, and the chairs situated, and Dad had a big fire going in the fireplace.

The first to arrive were the Sipichs, John and Mary. John wore his best suit, and was well-scrubbed and pink-faced after his day in McIntyre's pasture. The suit was neatly pressed, but getting threadbare at elbows and cuffs. Old McIntyre was working on a loom, designing it out of schoolbooks, but so far it was slow going. McIntyre was a capable man with wood and tools, but a loom was a big order when you couldn't get metal parts. McIntyre had been one of the ones who, at first, had wanted to try to get Anthony to make things the villagers needed, like clothes and canned goods and medical supplies and gasoline. Since then, he felt that what had happened to the whole Terrance family and Joe Kinney was his fault, and he worked hard trying to make it up to the rest of them. And since then, no one had tried to get Anthony to do anything.

Mary Sipich was a small, cheerful woman in a simple dress. She immediately set about helping Mom and Aunt Amy put the finishing touches on the dinner.

The next arrivals were the Smiths and the Dunns, who lived right next to each other down the road, only a few yards from the nothingness. They drove up in the Smiths' wagon, drawn by their old horse.

Then the Reillys showed up, from across the darkened wheatfield, and the evening really began. Pat Reilly sat down at the big upright in the front room, and began to play from the popular sheet music on the rack. He played softly, as expressively as he could – and nobody sang. Anthony liked piano playing a whole lot, but not singing; often he would come up from the basement, or down from the attic, or just come, and sit on top of the piano, nodding his head as Pat played *Lover* or *Boulevard of Broken Dreams* or *Night and Day*. He seemed to prefer ballads, sweet-sounding songs – but the one time somebody had started to sing, Anthony had looked over from the top of the piano and done something that made everybody afraid of singing from then on. Later, they'd decided that the piano was what Anthony had heard first, before anybody had ever tried to sing, and now anything else added to it didn't sound right and distracted him from his pleasure.

So, every television night, Pat would play the piano, and that was the beginning of the evening. Wherever Anthony was, the music would make him happy, and put him in a good mood, and he would know that they were gathering for television and waiting for him.

By eight-thirty everybody had shown up, except for the seventeen children and Mrs. Soames, who was off watching them in the schoolhouse at the far end of town. The children of Peaksville were never, never allowed near the Fremont house – not since little Fred Smith had tried to play with Anthony on a dare. The younger children weren't even told about Anthony. The others had mostly forgotten about him, or were told that he was a nice, nice goblin but they must never go near him.

Dan and Ethel Hollis came late, and Dan walked in not suspecting a thing. Pat Reilly had played the piano until his hands ached – he'd worked pretty hard with them today – and now he got up, and everybody gathered around to wish Dan Hollis a happy birthday.

'Well, I'll be darned,' Dan grinned. 'This is swell. I wasn't expecting this at all... gosh, this is *swell!*'

They gave him his presents – mostly things they had made by hand, though some were things that people had possessed as their own and now gave him as his. John Sipich gave him a watch charm, hand-carved out of a piece of hickory wood. Dan's watch had broken down a year or so ago, and there was nobody in the village who knew how to fix it, but he still carried it around because it had been his grandfather's and was a fine old heavy thing of gold and silver. He attached the charm to the chain, while everybody laughed and said John had done a nice job of carving. Then Mary Sipich gave him a knitted necktie, which he put on, removing the one he'd worn.

The Reillys gave him a little box they had made, to keep things in. They didn't say what things, but Dan said he'd keep his personal jewelry in it. The Reillys had made it out of a cigar box, carefully peeled of its paper and lined on the inside with velvet. The outside had been polished, and carefully if not expertly carved by Pat – but his carving got complimented too. Dan Hollis received many other gifts – a pipe, a pair of shoelaces, a tie pin, a knit pair of socks, some fudge, a pair of garters made from old suspenders.

He unwrapped each gift with vast pleasure, and wore as many of them as he could right there, even the garters. He lit up the pipe, and said he'd never had a better smoke; which wasn't quite true, because the pipe wasn't broken in yet. Pete Manners had had it lying around ever since he'd received it as a gift four years ago from an out-of-town relative who hadn't known he'd stopped smoking.

Dan put the tobacco into the bowl very carefully. Tobacco was precious. It was only pure luck that Pat Reilly had decided to try to grow some in his backyard just before what had happened to Peaksville had happened. It didn't grow very well, and then they had to cure it and shred it and all, and it was just precious stuff. Everybody in town used wooden holders old McIntyre had made, to save on butts.

Last of all, Thelma Dunn gave Dan Hollis the record she had found.

Dan's eyes misted even before he opened the package. He knew it was a record.

'Gosh,' he said softly. 'What one is it? I'm almost afraid to look ... '

'You haven't got it, darling,' Ethel Hollis smiled. 'Don't you remember, I asked about *You Are My Sunshine*?'

'Oh, gosh,' Dan said again. Carefully he removed the wrapping and stood there fondling the record, running his big hands over the worn grooves with their tiny, dulling crosswise scratches. He looked around the room, eyes shining, and they all smiled back, knowing how delighted he was.

'Happy birthday, darling!' Ethel said, throwing her arms around him and kissing him.

He clutched the record in both hands, holding it off to one side as she pressed against him. 'Hey,' he laughed, pulling back his head. 'Be careful... I'm holding a priceless object!' He looked around again, over his wife's arms, which were still around his neck. His eyes were hungry. 'Look... do you think we could play it? Lord, what I'd give to hear some new music... just the first part, the orchestra part, before Como sings?'

Faces sobered. After a minute, John Sipich said, 'I don't think we'd better, Dan. After all, we don't know just where the singer comes in – it'd be taking too much of a chance. Better wait till you get home.'

Dan Hollis reluctantly put the record on the buffet with all his other presents. 'It's *good*,' he said automatically, but disappointedly, 'that I can't play it here.'

'Oh, yes,' said Sipich. 'It's good.' To compensate for Dan's disappointed tone, he repeated. 'It's *good*.'

They ate dinner, the candles lighting their smiling faces, and ate it all right down to the last delicious drop of gravy. They complimented Mom and Aunt Amy on the roast beef, and the peas and carrots, and the tender corn on the cob. The corn hadn't come from the Fremont's cornfield, naturally – everybody knew what was out there; and the field was going to weeds.

Then they polished off the dessert – homemade ice cream and cookies And then they sat back, in the flickering light of the candles, and chatted waiting for television.

There never was a lot of mumbling on television night – everybody came and had a good dinner at the Fremonts', and that was nice, and afterwards there was television and nobody really thought much about that – it just had to be put up with. So it was a pleasant enough get-together, aside from your having to watch what you said just as carefully as you always did everyplace. If a dangerous thought came into your mind, you just started mumbling, even right in the middle of a sentence. When you did that, the others just ignored you until you felt happier again and stopped.

Anthony liked television night. He had done only two or three awful things on television night in the whole past year.

Mom had put a bottle of brandy on the table, and they each had a tiny glass of it. Liquor was even more precious than tobacco. The villagers could make wine, but the grapes weren't right, and certainly the techniques weren't, and it wasn't very good wine. There were only a few bottles of real liquor left in the village – four rye, three Scotch, three brandy, nine real wine and half a bottle of Drambuie belonging to old McIntyre (only for marriages) – and when those were gone, that was it.

Afterward, everybody wished that the brandy hadn't been brought out because Dan Hollis drank more of it than he should have, and mixed it with a lot of the homemade wine. Nobody thought anything about it at first, because he didn't show it much outside, and it was his birthday party and a happy party, and Anthony liked these get-togethers and shouldn't see any reason to do anything even if he was listening.

But Dan Hollis got high, and did a fool thing. If they'd seen it coming, they'd have taken him outside and walked him around.

The first thing they knew, Dan stopped laughing right in the middle of the story about how Thelma Dunn had found the Perry Como record and dropped it and it hadn't broken because she'd moved faster than she ever had before in her life and caught it. He was fondling the record again, and looking longingly at the Fremonts' gramophone over in the corner, and suddenly he stopped laughing and his face got slack, and then it got ugly, and he said, 'Oh, *Christ!*'

Immediately the room was still. So still they could hear the whirring movement of the grandfather's clock out in the hall. Pat Reilly had been playing the piano, softly. He stopped, his hands poised over the yellowed keys.

The candles on the dining-room table flickered in a cool breeze that blew through the lace curtains over the bay window.

'Keep playing, Pat,' Anthony's father said softly.

Pat started again. He played *Night and Day*, but his eyes were sidewise on Dan Hollis, and he missed notes.

Dan stood in the middle of the room, holding the record. In his other hand he held a glass of brandy so hard his hand shook.

They were all looking at him.

'*Christ*,' he said again, and he made it sound like a dirty word. Reverend Younger, who had been talking with Mom and Aunt Amy by the dining-room door, said 'Christ' too – but he was using it in a prayer. His hands were clasped, and his eyes were closed.

John Sipich moved forward. 'Now, Dan… it's *good* for you to talk that way. But you don't want to talk too much, you know.'

Dan shook off the hand Sipich put on his arm.

'Can't even play my record,' he said loudly. He looked down at the record, and then around at their faces. 'Oh, my God…'

He threw the glassful of brandy against the wall. It splattered and ran down the wallpaper in streaks.

Some of the women gasped.

'Dan,' Sipich said in a whisper. 'Dan, cut it out–'

Pat Reilly was playing *Night and Day* louder, to cover up the sounds of the talk. It wouldn't do any good, though, if Anthony was listening.

Dan Hollis went over to the piano and stood by Pat's shoulder, swaying a little.

'Pat,' he said. 'Don't play *that*. Play *this*.' And he began to sing. Softly, hoarsely, miserably: 'Happy birthday to me… Happy birthday to me…'

'*Dan!*' Ethel Hollis screamed. She tried to run across the room to him. Mary Sipich grabbed her arm and held her back. 'Dan.' Ethel screamed again. 'Stop–'

'My God, be quiet!' hissed Mary Sipich, and pushed her toward one of the men, who put his hand over her mouth and held her still.

'– Happy birthday, dear Danny,' Dan sang. 'Happy birthday to me!' He stopped and looked down at Pat Reilly. 'Play it, Pat. Play it, so I can sing right… you know I can't carry a tune unless somebody plays it!'

Pat Reilly put his hand on the keys and began *Lover* – in a slow waltz tempo, the way Anthony liked it. Pat's face was white. His hands fumbled.

Dan Hollis stared over at the dining-room door. At Anthony's mother, and at Anthony's father, who had gone to join her.

'*You* had him,' he said. Tears gleamed on his cheeks as the candlelight caught them. 'You had to go and have him…'

He closed his eyes, and the tears squeezed out. He sang loudly, 'You are my sunshine… my only sunshine… you make me happy… when I am blue…'

Anthony *came* into the room.

Pat stopped playing. He froze. Everybody froze. The breeze rippled the curtains. Ethel Hollis couldn't even try to scream; she had fainted.

'Please don't take my sunshine… away…' Dan's voice faltered into silence. His eyes widened. He put both hands out in front of him, the empty glass in one, the record in the other. He hiccupped and said, '*No*–'

'Bad man,' Anthony said, and thought Dan Hollis into something like nothing anyone would have believed possible, and then he thought the thing into a grave deep, deep in the cornfield.

The glass and record thumped on the rug. Neither broke.

Anthony's purple gaze went around the room.

Some of the people began mumbling. They all tried to smile. The sound of mumbling filled the room like a far-off approval. Out of the murmuring came one or two clear voices:

'Oh, it's a very *good* thing,' said John Sipich.

'A good thing,' said Anthony's father, smiling. He'd had more practice in smiling than most of them. 'A wonderful thing.'

'It's swell, just swell,' said Pat Reilly, tears leaking from eyes and nose, and he began to play the piano again, softly, his trembling hands feeling for *Night and Day*.

Anthony climbed up on top of the piano, and Pat played for two hours.

Afterward, they watched television. They all went into the front room, and lit just a few candles, and pulled up chairs around the set. It was a small-screen set, and they couldn't all sit close enough to it to see, but that didn't matter. They didn't even turn the set on. It wouldn't have worked anyway, there being no electricity in Peaksville.

They just sat silently, and watched the twisting, writhing shapes on the screen, and listened to the sounds that came out of the speaker, and none of them had any idea of what it was all about. They never did. It was always the same.

'It's real nice,' Aunt Amy said once, her pale eyes on meaningless flickers and shadows. 'But I liked it a little better when there were cities outside and we could get real–'

'Why, Amy!' said Mom. 'It's good for you to say such a thing. Very good. But how can you mean it? Why, this television is *much* better than anything we ever used to get!'

'Yes,' chimed in John Sipich. 'It's fine. It's the best show we've ever seen!'

He sat on the couch, with two other men, holding Ethel Hollis flat against the cushions, holding her arms and legs and putting their hands over her mouth, so she couldn't start screaming again.

'It's really *good!*' he said again.

Mom looked out of the front window, across the darkened road, across Henderson's darkened wheatfield to the vast, endless, gray nothingness in which the little village of Peaksville floated like a soul – the huge nothingness that was evident at night, when Anthony's brassy day had gone.

It did no good to wonder where they were… no good at all. Peaksville was just someplace. Someplace away from the world. It was wherever it had been since that day three years ago when Anthony had crept from her womb and old Doc Bates – God rest him – had screamed and dropped him and tried to kill him, and Anthony had whined and done the thing. He had taken the village someplace. Or had destroyed the world and left only the village, nobody knew which.

It did no good to wonder about it. Nothing at all did any good – except to live as they must live. Must always, always live, if Anthony would let them.

These thoughts were dangerous, she thought.

She began to mumble. The others started mumbling too. They had all been thinking, evidently.

The men on the couch whispered and whispered to Ethel Hollis, and when they took their hands away, she mumbled too.

While Anthony sat on top of the set and made television, they sat around and mumbled and watched the meaningless, flickering shapes far into the night.

Next day it snowed, and killed off half the crops – but it was a *good* day.

MISTER TAYLOR

Augusto Monterroso

TRANSLATED INTO ENGLISH BY LARRY NOLEN

Augusto Monterroso (1921–2003) was a Guatemalan writer known for his short stories. Indeed, he is credited with writing the shortest story ever: 'When she awoke, the dinosaur was still there.' Monterroso is considered a central figure in the Latin American Boom generation, recognized alongside such canonical authors as Julio Cortázar and Gabriel García Márquez. Monterroso often used the weird and grotesque to create incisive contemporary fables, as in his most famous story, 'Mister Taylor' (1954). The story's mixture of weird imagery with social commentary on US imperialism has made it one of the most popular Latin American short stories of the mid-twentieth century. This new translation by Larry Nolen conveys the absurdity and strangeness of the original in equal measure.

'Less strange, although without a doubt more exemplary,' the other man then said, 'is the story of Mr. Percy Taylor, headhunter in the Amazon jungle.

'It is known that in 1937 he left Boston, Massachusetts, where he had refined his spirit to the point of becoming penniless. In 1944 he appears for the first time in South America, in the region of the Amazon, living with the natives of a tribe whose name there is no need to remember.

'Due to his dark circles and famished aspect, he soon became known there as "the poor gringo," and the schoolchildren even pointed at him and threw stones when he passed by, his beard shining under the golden tropical sun. But this did not distress the humble character of Mr. Taylor, because he had read in the first volume of *The Complete Works* of William G. Knight that if he did not feel envious of the rich, poverty would not dishonor him.

'In a few weeks the natives became accustomed to him and his extravagant dress. In addition, as he had blue eyes and a vague foreign accent, the President and Minister of Foreign Relations treated him with singular respect, fearful of provoking international incidents.

'So poor and miserable was he, that one day he went inland into the jungle in search of herbs to eat. He had walked several meters without daring to turn his head, when by pure chance he saw through the weeds two Indian eyes, which observed him intently. A huge shiver ran down the sensitive spine of Mr. Taylor. But Mr. Taylor, intrepid, confronted the danger and continued on his way whistling as if nothing had happened.

'With a jump (which ought not be called feline), the Indian got in front of him and exclaimed: "Buy head? Money, money."

'Although the native's English could not be any worse, Mr. Taylor, somewhat indisposed, realized that the native offered him in sale a man's head, curiously reduced, which he was carrying in his hand.

'It is unnecessary to say that Mr. Taylor was in no position to buy it; but as apparently he didn't understand this, the Indian felt terribly embarrassed due to not speaking English well, and he gave Mr. Taylor the head as a gift, seeking pardon.

'Great was Mr. Taylor's joy as he returned to his hut. That night, lying on his back on a precarious palm mat which served as his bed, interrupted only by the buzzing of the aroused flies that flew around him making love obscenely, Mr. Taylor contemplated with delight for a long time his curious acquisition. He took the greatest aesthetic pleasure from counting, one by one, the hairs of the beard and moustache and looking straight into the pair of half-ironic eyes that seemed to smile at him, pleased by his deference.

'A man of immense culture, Mr. Taylor was accustomed to abandoning himself to contemplation, but his time he immediately grew bored with his philosophical reflections and he arranged to give the head to his uncle, Mr. Rolston, a New York resident, who from his most tender infancy had shown a strong interest in the cultural manifestations of the Latin American peoples.

'A few days later, Mr. Taylor's uncle wrote to ask him (after inquiring about the state of his precious health) to please gratify him with five more. Mr. Taylor acceded with pleasure to Mr. Rolston's caprice and – no one knows how – by return mail he "was very pleased to satisfy your desires." Very grateful, Mr. Rolston sought another ten. Mr. Taylor felt "pleased to be able to serve you." But when a month passed and he was asked to send twenty, Mr. Taylor, a simple and bearded man but of refined artistic sensibility, had the presentiment that his mother's brother was making a profit off of him.

'Well, if you want to know, so it was. With total frankness, Mr. Rolston made him understand it in an inspired letter whose resolutely businesslike terms made the strings of Mr. Taylor's sensitive spirit vibrate like never before.

'They immediately set up a corporation in which Mr. Taylor promised to obtain and ship human heads shrunken on an industrial scale while Mr. Rolston would sell them the best he could in his country.

'In the early days there were some annoying difficulties with certain local types. But Mr. Taylor, who in Boston had received the best grades on an essay on Joseph Henry Silliman, showed himself to be a politician and obtained not only the necessary export permit, but, in addition, an exclusive concession for 99 years. It took little effort for him to convince the Executive warrior and the Legislative witch doctors that such a patriotic act in a short time would enrich the community and that then afterward all the thirsty aborigines would be able to drink (each time they paused in the collection of heads) a cold soft drink, whose magic formula he himself would supply.

'When the members of the Chamber, after a brief but luminous intellectual effort, understood these advantages, their love of country boiled over and in three days they promulgated a decree demanding that the people accelerate the production of shrunken heads.

'A few months later, in Mr. Taylor's country, the heads reached that popularity which we all remember. In the beginning, they were the privilege of the wealthiest families, but democracy is democracy and, no one is going to deny it, in a matter of weeks even schoolteachers themselves could acquire them.

'A home without its corresponding head was seen as a failed home. Soon came the collectors and with them, contradictions: to possess 17 heads came to be considered bad taste, but it was distinguished to have 11. They became so common that the truly elegant people were losing interest and now only by exception would they acquire one, if it possessed some peculiarity that saved it from vulgarity. One, very rare, with Prussian moustaches, which in life belonged to a highly decorated general, was bequeathed to the Danfeller Institute, which in turn gave, like a bolt from the blue, 3.5 million dollars in order to further development of that cultural manifestation, so excellent, of the Latin American peoples.

'Meanwhile, the tribe had progressed in such a way that they already had a pathway around the Legislative Palace. On Sundays and Independence Day, members of Congress went along on that happy trail, clearing their throats, displaying their feathers, laughing very seriously, on the bicycles that the Company had given them.

'But what do you want? Not all the times are good ones. When they least expected it they were presented with the first shortage of heads.

'Then began the best part.

'Mere natural deaths already were insufficient. The Minister of Public Health, feeling sincere one dark night, with the light turned off, after unceasingly caressing for a little while his wife's breast, confessed to her that he considered himself incapable of elevating mortality rates to a level pleasing to the Company's interests, to which she replied that he should not worry, that he would see that everything would turn out well and that it would be best that they sleep.

'In order to compensate for this administrative deficiency, it was indispensible to take heroic measures and a harsh death penalty was established.

'The judges consulted with each other and they elevated to the category of a crime, punishable by hanging or firing squad depending on its seriousness, even the most trivial of faults.

'Even simple mistakes became criminal acts. For example, if in an ordinary conversation someone carelessly said "It is very hot" and later it could be proven, with thermometer in hand, that in reality it was not so hot, that person was fined a small amount, executed on the spot by the army, who sent the head to the Company and, fair to say, the trunk and limbs to the bereaved.

'The legislation regarding illnesses earned immediate renown and was talked about much by the diplomatic corps and by the ministries of foreign affairs of friendly powers.

'In accord with that memorable legislation, the gravely ill were granted 24 hours to place their affairs in order and die, but if in this time they were lucky and managed to infect their family, they obtained as many monthly stays as relatives that were infected. The victims of slight illnesses and those simply indisposed earned the scorn of the country and in the streets anyone could spit on their faces. For the first time in history, the importance of doctors (there were various Nobel Prize candidates) who didn't cure anyone was recognized. Dying was turned into the most exalted example of patriotism, not only on a national scale, but instead more glorious, on the continental.

'With the impetus that reached other subsidiary companies (the coffin industry, in particular, flourished with the technical assistance of the Company), the country entered, as they say, a period of great economic growth. This growth was particularly evident in a new flower-lined path, along which strolled, enveloped in the melancholy of the golden fall afternoons, the deputies' wives, whose pretty little heads went yes, yes, everything was well when some soliciting journalist, from the other side, greeted them while tipping his hat.

'As an aside, I will note that one of these journalists, who on one occasion emitted a wet sneeze he could not explain, was accused of extremism and was brought to the firing squad wall. Only after his selfless end did the academics recognize that the journalist had one of the country's grandest heads, but once shrunken it looked so well that no one could notice the difference.

'And Mr. Taylor? By that time he already had been designated as a special adviser to the Constitutional President. Now, and as an example of what individual effort can achieve, he was counting his thousands by the thousands; but this did not cause him to lose any sleep because he had read in the final volume of *The Complete Works* of William G. Knight that to be a millionaire was no dishonor if one did not despise the poor.

'I believe this will be the second time that I say that not all the times are good ones. Given the prosperity of the business, the moment arrived in which only the authorities and their wives, and the journalists and their wives remained in the vicinity. Without much effort, Mr. Taylor mused that the only possible remedy was to foment war with the neighboring tribes. Why not? It's progress.

'With the help of some small cannons, the first tribe was cleanly beheaded in scarcely three months. Mr. Taylor tasted the glory of extending his domains. Then came the second, and afterward the third, the fourth, and the fifth. Progress extended with such rapidity that the hour arrived in which despite the efforts of the technicians, it was impossible to find new tribes to make war against.

'It was the beginning of the end.

'The two paths began to languish. Only once in a while could one see on them some lady or some poet laureate with a book under his arm. The weeds overran anew the two paths, making difficult and thorny the ladies' delicate steps. Along with the heads, the bicycles became scarce and almost all the happy optimistic greetings disappeared.

'The coffin manufacturer was more sad and funereal than ever before. And everyone felt as though they had awakened from a pleasant dream, from that wonderful dream in which you find a bag full of gold coins and you place it under your pillow and go back to sleep, and very early the next day, upon waking, you search for it and find emptiness.

'However, painfully, business went on as usual. But now one slept with difficulty, due to the fear of waking up exported.

'In Mr. Taylor's country, of course, demand continued to rise. Daily new substitutes were appearing, but deep down inside nobody believed in them and everyone demanded the little heads from Latin America.

'It happened during the last crisis. Mr. Rolston, desperate, begged and begged for more heads. Despite the Company's stocks suffering a sharp decline, Mr. Rolston was convinced that his nephew would do something to bail him out of that situation.

'The shipments, once daily, shrunk to once a month, now with anything, from children's heads to those of ladies and deputies.

'Suddenly, they ceased totally.

'One harsh and gray Friday, home from the Exchange, stunned still by the cries and by the lamentable show of panic given by his friends, Mr. Rolston decided to jump through the window (instead of using a gun, whose noise filled him with terror) when upon opening a mail package he found the shrunken head of Mr. Taylor, brought to him from the distant, fierce Amazon, with a false child's smile that seemed to say, "I'm sorry, I won't do it again."'

AXOLOTL

Julio Cortázar

TRANSLATED INTO ENGLISH BY GIO CLAIRVAL

Julio Cortázar (1914–1984) was an Argentine writer who became an architect of what is known as the Latin American Literary Boom. A novelist, poet, playwright, and nonfiction writer, Cortázar also wrote many short stories, collected in *Bestiario* (1951), *Final del juego* (1956), and *Las armas secretas* (1959), among others. His entry point to the weird tale was the influence of surrealism. His fantastical stories almost always begin with a mundane reality into which unexplained strangeness intrudes. This fine translation of his 'Axolotl' (1956) by Gio Clairval is the first new English version since the 1950s and considered the definitive translation by the author's estate. Cortázar's work as a translator, including the stories of Poe, also influenced his fiction.

There was a time when I thought quite often about the Axolotl. I used to go and see them in the aquarium of the Jardin des Plantes and remained for hours captivated, gazing at them, observing their immobility, their indistinct movements. Now I, too, am an Axolotl.

Chance led me to them one spring morning when Paris was spreading its peacock tail after a long wintering. I strolled down Boulevard de Port Royal, took Saint-Marcel and L'Hôpital, saw green among all that grey and remembered the lions. I was acquainted with the lions and the panthers, but had never entered the dark, humid building that was the aquarium. I left my bicycle against the railing and went to see the tulips. The lions were sad and ugly and my panther was asleep. I opted for the aquarium, looked askance at banal fish until, unexpectedly, I came face to face with the Axolotl. I gazed at them for an hour and left, unable to think of anything else.

In the Sainte-Geneviève library, I consulted a dictionary and learned that the Axolotl are the larval stage, complete with gills, of a species of batrachians belonging to the genus *Ambystoma*. I already knew they were Mexican by looking at them and their little pink Aztec faces and the sign above the tank. I read that specimens had been found in Africa capable of living on dry land during the periods of drought, and continuing their life under water when the rainy season set in. I found their Spanish name, *ajolote*, and the mention that they were edible, and that their oil was used (it seems now no longer used) like codfish liver oil.

I didn't care to consult any of the specialized works, but the next day I went back to the Jardin des Plantes. I began to go every morning, morning and afternoon some days. The aquarium guard gave a perplexed smile as he took my ticket. I would prop myself up on the railing in front of the tanks and set to study them. There was nothing strange in this, because after the first minute I knew that we were linked, that something infinitely lost and distant continued to unite us nevertheless. It had been enough to keep me that first morning in front of the glass wall while bubbles rose through the water. The Axolotl huddled on the skimpy, narrow (only I can know how narrow and skimpy) floor of stone and moss in the tank. There were nine specimens, and most pressed their heads against the glass, looking with their eyes of gold at whoever approached them. Confused, almost ashamed, I felt indecent for lingering in front of these silent, still figures heaped at the bottom of the tank. To study them better, I mentally isolated one that was on the right and somehow apart from the others. I saw a rosy little body, translucent (I thought of those Chinese figurines of milky glass), similar to a small lizard about fifteen centimeters long, ending in a fish tail of extraordinary elegance, the most sensitive part of our body. Along the back ran a transparent fin that joined the tail, but I was obsessed with the feet, of the subtlest grace, ending in tiny fingers with minutely human fingernails. And then I discovered the eyes, the face. The eyes were two holes as tiny as heads of pins entirely made of a transparent gold, devoid of all expression but still gazing, opening up to my stare, which seemed to pass through the golden spot and lose itself in a diaphanous inner mystery. A very thin, black ring encircled the eye and etched it in the pink flesh, and onto the rosy stone of a head vaguely triangular but with a curved and irregular outline, which created a strong likeness to a statuette corroded by time. The mouth was concealed by the triangular plane of the face, its considerable size only guessed in profile; in front a delicate cleft barely slit the lifeless stone. On both sides of the head, where the ears should have been, there grew three tiny sprigs, red as coral, a vegetal outgrowth, the gills, I suppose. And they were the only part that seemed alive; every ten or fifteen seconds the sprigs pricked up stiffly and again began to relax. Whenever a leg twitched, I saw the minuscule toes alight on the moss in a smooth movement. In fact, we don't enjoy moving a lot, and the tank is so cramped – hardly do we move in any direction than we bump into one another's tail or head – conflicts arise, fights, fatigue. Time feels shorter if we remain quiet.

This sense of tranquillity fascinated me the first time I saw the Axolotl. In some obscure way, I understood their secret will, to abolish space and time with indifferent immobility. Later I knew better; the contraction of the gills, the probing of the delicate legs on the stones, the sudden swimming (some of them swim with a simple undulation of the body) proved to me that they were capable of escaping the mineral stupor in which they spent entire hours. Above everything else, their eyes obsessed me. In the tanks on either side of them, various fish showcased the simple stupidity of their beautiful eyes so similar to our own. The eyes of the Axolotl told me of the presence of a different life, of another way of seeing. Gluing my face to the glass (the guard, worried, coughed sometimes), I tried to see better those minuscule golden spots, this entrance to the infinitely slow and remote world of the roseate creatures. No point in tapping with a fingertip on the glass right in front of their faces; they never reacted in the slightest way. The golden eyes kept burning with their soft, terrible light; they kept gazing at me from an unfathomable depth that gave me vertigo.

And nevertheless they were close. I knew it before this, before being an Axolotl. I knew it the day I approached them for the first time. Contrary to what most people think, the anthropomorphic features of a monkey reveal the distance that separates them from us. The absolute lack of similarity between the Axolotl and a human being proved to me that my recognition was well founded, that I was not sustaining my theory with easy analogies. Those little hands alone... But the common lizard has such hands, too, and we are not at all alike. I think it was the Axolotl's head, that triangular pink shape with the tiny eyes of gold. That gazed and knew. That claimed. They were no *animals.*

It seemed easy, almost obvious, to dive into mythology. I began seeing in the Axolotl a metamorphosis that could not quite destroy some mysterious humanity. I imagined them aware, slaves to their bodies, forever condemned to an abyssal silence, to a hopeless meditation. Their blind gaze, the tiny golden disc, expressionless and nonetheless terribly lucid, entered my mind like a message: 'Save us, save us.' I surprised myself by mumbling words of consolation, conveying childish hopes. They continued to look at me, stock-still; from time to time the small, pink branches of the gills stiffened. In that instant I felt a dull pain. Perhaps they did see me, grasped my efforts to penetrate the impenetrable essence of their lives. They were not human beings, but in no animal had I ever found such a profound connection to myself. The Axolotl were like witnesses to something, and at times like horrible judges. I felt ignoble in front of them; there was such a terrifying purity in those transparent eyes. They were larvae, but 'larva' means mask and also specter. Behind those Aztec faces, expressionless but of an implacable cruelty, what appearance awaited its hour?

I was afraid of them. I think that had it not been for the proximity of other visitors and the guard, I would not have dared to be alone with them. 'You're eating them with your eyes,' the guard said, laughing; he probably believed me a little insane. He didn't realize they were the ones that devoured me with their eyes, slowly, in a cannibalism of gold. Away from the aquarium, my thoughts revolved solely around them, as though they could influence me from afar. At one point, I went to see them every day, and at night I thought of them unmoving in the darkness, slowly putting a hand out which immediately encountered another. Perhaps their eyes could see in the dead of night, and for them the day continued without end. The eyes of the Axolotl have no lids.

I know now that there was nothing strange, that it had to happen. Each new morning, as I leaned against the tank, the recognition grew stronger. They suffered; every fiber of my body reached out to sense that muzzled pain, that rigid torment at the bottom of the tank. They kept furtive watch over something, a faraway dominion now destroyed, an era of freedom when the world belonged to the Axolotl. Such a terrible expression trying to disturb the forced blankness of their stone faces could carry no message other than pain, proof of their eternal sentence, of the liquid hell they endured. To no avail, I tried to convince myself that my own sensitivity projected a nonexistent consciousness upon the Axolotl. They and I both knew. Therefore, nothing of what happened was strange. My face pressed against the glass of the aquarium, my stare attempted once more to penetrate the mystery of those eyes of gold, without an iris, without a pupil. Close up, I saw the face of an Axolotl immobile near the glass. Without transition or surprise, I saw my own face against the glass, I saw it outside the tank, I saw it on the other side of the glass. Then my face drew back, and I understood.

Only one thing was strange: to think as I did before, knowing. At first, this realization resembled the horror of a man buried alive awakening to his fate. On the outside, my face came close to the glass again; I saw my own mouth, lips pressed together in the effort of understanding the Axolotl. I was an Axolotl and then knew instantly that no understanding was possible. He was outside the aquarium, and his thinking was a thinking outside the aquarium. Recognizing him, being him, I was an Axolotl and I was in my world. The horror began – I knew it at the same moment I believed myself a prisoner in a body of Axolotl, transmigrated into him with my human mind intact, buried alive in an Axolotl, condemned to move lucidly among insensitive creatures. But this feeling stopped when a leg brushed my face, when I moved a little to the side and saw an Axolotl next to me who was watching me, and I understood that he knew also, no communication possible, but in such a limpid way. Or I was also in him, or all of us were thinking like men, incapable of expression, limited to the golden splendor of our eyes staring at the man's face pressed against the aquarium.

He returned many times thereafter, but he comes less often now. Weeks pass without his showing up. I saw him yesterday; he looked at me for a long time and left abruptly. I had the impression that he was not so interested in us any more, that he came out of habit. Since all I do is think, I could think about him a lot. It occurs to me that at the beginning we did communicate, that he felt more than ever one with the mystery over which he was obsessing. But the bridges were broken between him and me, because that which was his obsession is now an Axolotl, alien to the life of a man. I think that at the beginning I was capable of becoming him to a certain extent, only to a certain extent – and I knew how to keep alive his desire to know us better. Now I am definitely an Axolotl, and if I think like a man, it's only because every Axolotl thinks like a man behind that appearance of pink stone. I believe that all this I succeeded in communicating somehow to him in those first days, when I was still he. And in this final solitude to which he no longer returns, it consoles me to think that perhaps he will write about us, that, believing he's imagining a story, he will write all this about the Axolotl.

A WOMAN SELDOM FOUND

William Sansom

William Sansom (1912–1976) was an English writer who worked as a firefighter during the Blitz and was directly influenced by the Surrealists. Using descriptive, muscular prose, Sansom took the mundane and transformed it through his surrealist's eye. His previous story in this volume, 'The Long Sheet,' explored weird ritual. 'A Woman Seldom Seen' (1956), by contrast, is something rare for Sansom: an excellent example of the traditional weird tale and his most anthologized story. Readers wishing to explore more of Sansom's prose should seek out the new volume from Faber & Faber, *The Stories of William Sansom* (2011).

Once a young man was on a visit to Rome. It was his first visit, he came from the country – but he was neither on the one hand so young nor on the other so simple as to imagine that a great and beautiful capital should hold out finer promises than anywhere else. He already knew that life was largely illusion, that though wonderful things could happen, nevertheless as many disappointments came in compensation: and he knew, too, that life could offer a quality even worse – the probability that nothing would happen at all. This was always more possible in a great city intent on its own business.

Thinking in this way, he stood on the Spanish Steps and surveyed the momentous panorama stretched before him. He listened to the swelling hum of the evening traffic and watched as the lights went up against Rome's golden dusk. Shining automobiles slunk past the fountains and turned urgently into the bright Via Condotti, neon-red signs stabbed the shadows with invitation; the yellow windows of buses were packed with faces intent on going somewhere – everyone in the city seemed intent on the evening's purpose. He alone had nothing to do.

He felt himself the only person alone of everyone in the city. But searching for adventure never brought it – rather kept it away. Such a mood promised nothing. So the young man turned back up the steps, passed the lovely church, and went on up the cobbled hill towards his hotel. Wine-bars and food-shops jostled with growing movement in those narrow streets. But out on the broad pavements of the Vittoro Veneto, under the trees mounting to the Borghese Gardens, the high world of Rome would be filling the most elegant cafes in Europe to enjoy with aperitifs the twilight. That would be the loneliest of all! So the young man kept to the quieter, older streets on his solitary errand home.

In one such street – a pavementless alley between old yellow houses, a street that in Rome might suddenly blossom into a secret piazza of fountain and baroque church, a grave secluded treasure-place – he noticed that he was alone but for the single figure of a woman walking down the hill towards him.

As she drew nearer, he saw that she was dressed with taste, that in her carriage was a soft Latin fire, that she walked for respect. Her face was veiled, but it was impossible to imagine that she would not be beautiful. Isolated thus with her, passing so near to her, and she symbolizing the adventure of which the evening was so empty – a greater melancholy gripped him. He felt wretched as the gutter, small, sunk, pitiful. So that he rounded his shoulders and lowered his eyes – but not before casting one furtive glance into hers.

He was so shocked at what he saw that he paused, he stared, shocked, into her face. He had made no mistake. She was smiling. Also – she too had hesitated. He thought instantly: 'Whore?' But no – it was not that kind of smile, though as well it was not without affection. And then amazingly she spoke:

'I – I know I shouldn't ask you … but it is such a beautiful evening – and perhaps you are alone, as alone as I am … '

She was very beautiful. He could not speak. But a growing elation gave him the power to smile. So that she continued, still hesitant, in no sense soliciting:

'I thought … perhaps … we could take a walk, an aperitif … '

At last the young man achieved himself:

'Nothing, nothing would please me more. And the Veneto is only a minute up there.'

She smiled again:

'My home is just here … '

They walked in silence a few paces down the street, to a turning that young man had already passed. This she indicated. They walked to where the first humble houses ended in a kind of recess. In the recess was set the wall of a garden, and behind it stood a large and elegant mansion. The woman, about whose face shone a curious pale glitter – something fused of the transparent pallor of fine skin, of grey but brilliant eyes, of dark eyebrows and hair of lucent black – inserted her key in the garden gate.

They were greeted by a servant in velvet livery. In a large and exquisite salon, under chandeliers of fine glass and before a moist green courtyard where water played, they were served with a frothy wine. They talked. The wine – iced in the warm Roman night – filled them with an inner warmth of exhilaration. But from time to time the young man looked at her curiously.

With her glances, with many subtle inflections of teeth and eyes she was inducing an intimacy that suggested much. He felt he must be careful. At length he thought the best thing might be to thank her – somehow thus to root out whatever obligation might be in store. But here she interrupted him, first with a smile, then with a look of some sadness. She begged him to spare himself any perturbation; she knew it was strange, that in such a situation he might suspect some second purpose; but the simple truth remained that she was lonely and – this with a certain deference – something perhaps in him, perhaps in that moment of dusk in the street, had proved to her inescapably attractive. She had not been able to help herself.

The possibility of a perfect encounter – a dream that years of disillusion will never quite kill – decided him. His elation rose beyond control. He believed her. And thereafter the perfections compounded. At her invitation they dined. Servants brought food of great delicacy; shell-fish, fat bird-flesh, soft fruits. And afterwards they sat on a sofa near the courtyard, where it was cool. Liqueurs were brought. The servants retired. A hush fell upon the house. They embraced.

A little later, with no word, she took his arm and led him from the room. How deep a silence had fallen between them! The young man's heart beat fearfully – it might be heard, he felt, echoing in the hall whose marble they now crossed, sensed through his arm to hers. But such excitement rose now from certainty. Certainty that at such a moment – on such a charmed evening – nothing could go wrong. There was no need to speak. Together they mounted the great staircase.

In her bedroom, to the picture of her framed by the bed curtains and dimly naked in a silken shift, he poured out his love; a love that was to be eternal, to be always perfect, as fabulous as this their exquisite meeting.

Softly she spoke the return of his love. Nothing would ever go amiss, nothing would ever come between them. And very gently she drew back the bedclothes for him.

But suddenly, at the moment when at last he lay beside her, when his lips were almost upon hers – he hesitated.

Something was wrong. A flaw could be sensed. He listened, felt – and then saw the fault was his. Shaded, soft-shaded lights by the bed – but he had been so careless as to leave on the bright electric chandelier in the centre of the ceiling. He remembered the switch was by the door. For a fraction, then, he hesitated. She raised her eyelids – saw his glance at the chandelier, understood.

Her eyes glittered. She murmured:

'My beloved, don't worry – don't move … '

And she reached out her hand. Her hand grew larger, her arm grew longer and longer, it stretched out through the bed-curtains, across the long carpet, huge and overshadowing the whole of the long room, until at last its giant fingers were at the door. With a terminal click, she switched out the light.

THE HOWLING MAN

Charles Beaumont

Charles Beaumont (1929–1967) was a prolific American author who established himself as a script writer in Hollywood and died of a brain disorder at the tragically young age of thirty-eight. In addition to his macabre short stories, he wrote several *Twilight Zone* episodes, but also penned the screenplays for cult films like *7 Faces of Dr. Lao, The Intruder,* and *The Masque of the Red Death.* The classic story reprinted here, 'The Howling Man' (1959), was adapted as a screenplay for *Twilight Zone.* In the episode, a reference to a cross was changed to 'staff of truth,' out of fear of a backlash from Christian preachers. In its approach, the story oddly evokes Decadent-era writing and spotlights Beaumont's stylistic prowess.

The Germany of that time was a land of valleys and mountains and swift dark rivers, a green and fertile land where everything grew tall and straight out of the earth. There was no other country like it. Stepping across the border from Belgium, where the rain-caped, mustached guards saluted, grinning, like operetta soldiers, you entered a different world entirely. Here the grass became as rich and smooth as velvet; deep, thick woods appeared; the air itself, which had been heavy with the French perfume of wines and sauces, changed: the clean, fresh smell of lakes and pines and boulders came into your lungs. You stood a moment, then, at the border, watching the circling hawks above and wondering, a little fearfully, how such a thing could happen. In less than a minute you had passed from a musty, *ancient* room, through an invisible door, into a kingdom of winds and light. Unbelievable! But there, at your heels, clearly in view, is Belgium, like all the rest of Europe, a faded tapestry from some forgotten mansion.

In that time, before I had heard of St. Wulfran's, of the wretch who clawed the stones of a locked cell, wailing in the midnight hours, or of the daft Brothers and their mad Abbot, I had strong legs and a mind on its last search, and I preferred to be alone. A while and I'll come back to this spot. We will ride and feel the sickness, fall, and hover on the edge of death, together. But I am not a writer, only one who loves wild, unhousebroken words; I must have a real beginning.

Paris beckoned in my youth. I heeded, for the reason most young men just out of college heed, although they would never admit it: to lie with mysterious beautiful women. A solid, traditional upbringing among the corseted ruins of Boston had succeeded, as such upbringings generally do, in honing the urge to a keen edge. My nightly dreams of beaded bagnios and dusky writhing houris, skilled beyond imagining, reached, finally, the unbearable stage beyond which lies either madness or respectability. Fancying neither, I managed to convince my parents that a year abroad would add exactly the right amount of seasoning to my maturity, like a dash of curry in an otherwise bland, if not altogether tasteless, chowder. I'm afraid that Father caught the hot glint in my eye, but he was kind. Describing, in detail, and with immense effect, the hideous consequences of profligacy, telling of men he knew who'd gone to Europe, innocently, and fallen into dissolutions so profound they'd not been heard of since, he begged me at all times to remember that I was an Ellington and turned me loose. Paris, of course, was enchanting and terrifying, as a jungle must be to a zoo-born monkey. Out of respect to the honored dead, and Dad, I did a quick tour through the Tuileries, the Louvre, and down the Champs-Elysées to the Arc de Triomphe; then, with the fall of night, I cannoned off to Montmartre and the Rue Pigalle, embarking on the Grand Adventure. Synoptically, it did not prove to be so grand as I'd imagined; nor was it, after the fourth week, so terribly adventurous. Still, important to what followed, for what followed doubtless wouldn't have but for the sweet complaisant girls.

Boston's Straights and Narrows don't, I fear, prepare one – except psychologically – for the Wild Life. My health broke in due course and, as my thirst had been well and truly slaked, I was not awfully discontent to sink back into the contemplative cocoon to which I was, apparently, more suited. Abed for a month I lay, in celibate silence and almost total inactivity. Then, no doubt as a final gesture of rebellion. I got my idea – got? or had my concentrated sins received it, like a signal from a failing tower? – and I made my strange, un-Ellingtonian decision. I would explore Europe. But not as a tourist, safe and fat in his fat, safe bus, insulated against the beauty and the ugliness of changing cultures by a pane of glass and a room at the English-speaking hotel. No. I would go like an unprotected wind, a seven-league-booted leaf, a nestless bird, and I would see this dark strange land with the vision of a boy on the last legs of his dreams. I would go by bicycle, poor and lonely and questing – as poor and lonely and questing, anyway, as one can be with a hundred thousand in the bank and a partnership in Ellington, Carruthers & Blake waiting.

So it was. New England blood and muscles wilted on that first day's pumping, but New England spirit toughened as the miles dropped back. Like an ant crawling over a once-lovely, now decayed and somewhat seedy Duchess, I rode over the body of Europe. I dined at restaurants where boars' heads hung, all vicious-tusked and blind; I slept at country inns and breathed the musty age, and sometimes girls came to the door and knocked and asked if I had everything I needed ('Well...') and they were better than the girls in Paris, though I can't imagine why. No matter. Out of France I pedaled, into Belgium, out, and to the place of cows and forests, mountains, brooks, and laughing people: Germany. (I've rhapsodized on purpose for I feel it's quite important to remember how completely Paradisical the land was then, at that time.)

I looked odd, standing there. The border guard asked what was loose with me, I answered Nothing – grateful for the German, and the French, Miss Finch had drummed into me – and set off along the smallest, darkest path. It serpentined through forests, cities, towns, villages, and always I followed its least likely appendages. Unreasonably, I pedaled as if toward a destination: into the Moselle Valley country, up into the desolate hills of emerald.

By a ferry, fallen to desuetude, the reptile drew me through a bosky wood. The trees closed in at once. I drank the fragrant air and pumped and kept on pumping, but a heat began to grow inside my body. My head began to ache. I felt weak. Two more miles and I was obliged to stop, for perspiration filmed my skin. You know the signs of pneumonia: a sapping of the strength, a trembling, flashes of heat and of cold; visions. I lay in the bed of damp leaves for a time, then forced myself onto the bicycle and rode for what seemed an endless time. At last a village came to view. A thirteenth-century village, gray and narrow-streeted, cobbled to the hidden store fronts. A number of old people in peasant costumes looked up as I bumped along, and I recall one ancient tallow-colored fellow – nothing more. Only the weakness, like acid, burning off my nerves and muscles. And an intervening blackness to pillow my fall.

I awoke to the smells of urine and hay. The fever had passed, but my arms and legs lay heavy as logs, my head throbbed horribly, and there was an empty shoveled-out hole inside my stomach somewhere. For a long while I did not move or open my eyes. Breathing was a major effort. But consciousness came, eventually.

I was in a tiny room. The walls and ceiling were of rough gray stone, the single glassless window was arch-shaped, the floor was uncombed dirt. My bed was not a bed at all but a blanket thrown across a disorderly pile of crinkly straw. Beside me, a crude table; upon it, a pitcher; beneath it, a bucket. Next to the table, a stool. And seated there, asleep, his tonsured head adangle from an Everest of robe, a monk.

I must have groaned, for the shorn pate bobbed up precipitately. Two silver trails gleamed down the corners of the suddenly exposed mouth, which drooped into a frown. The slumbrous eyes blinked.

'It is God's infinite mercy,' sighed the gnome-like little man. 'You have recovered.'

'Not as yet,' I told him. Unsuccessfully, I tried to remember what had happened; then I asked questions.

'I am Brother Christophorus. This is the Abbey of St. Wulfran's. The Burger-meister of Schwartzhof, Herr Barth, brought you to us nine days ago. Father Jerome said that you would die and he sent me to watch, for I have never seen a man die, and Father Jerome holds that it is beneficial for a Brother to have seen a man die. But now I suppose that you will not die.' He shook his head ruefully.

'Your disappointment,' I said, 'cuts me to the quick. However, don't abandon hope. The way I feel now, it's touch and go.'

'No,' said Brother Christophorus sadly. 'You will get well. It will take time. But you will get well.'

'Such ingratitude, and after all you've done. How can I express my apologies?'

He blinked again. With the innocence of a child, he said, 'I beg your pardon?'

'Nothing.' I grumbled about blankets, a fire, some food to eat, and then slipped back into the well of sleep. A fever dream of forests full of giant two-headed beasts came, then the sound of screaming.

I awoke. The scream shrilled on – Klaxon-loud, high, cutting, like a cry for help.

'What is that sound?' I asked.

The monk smiled. 'Sound? I hear no sound,' he said.

It stopped. I nodded. 'Dreaming. Probably I'll hear a good deal more before I'm through. I shouldn't have left Paris in such poor condition.'

'No,' he said. 'You shouldn't have left Paris.'

Kindly now, resigned to my recovery, Brother Christophorus became attentive to a fault. Nurselike, he spooned thick soups into me, applied compresses, chanted soothing prayers, and emptied the bucket out the window. Time passed slowly. As I fought the sickness, the dreams grew less vivid – but the nightly cries did not diminish. They were as full of terror and loneliness as before, strong, real in my ears. I tried to shut them out, but they would not be shut out. Still, how could they be strong and real except in my vanishing delirium? Brother Christophorus did not hear them. I watched him closely when the sunlight faded to the gray of dusk and the screams began, but he was deaf to them – if they existed. If they existed!

'Be still, my son. It is the fever that makes you hear these noises. That is quite natural. Is that not quite natural? Sleep.'

'But the fever is gone! I'm sitting up now. Listen! Do you mean to tell me you don't hear *that*?'

'I hear only you, my son.'

The screams, that fourteenth night, continued until dawn. They were totally unlike any sounds in my experience. Impossible to believe they could be uttered and sustained by a human, yet they did not seem to be animal. I listened, there in the gloom, my hands balled into fists, and knew, suddenly, that one of two things must be true. Either someone or something was making these ghastly sounds, and Brother Christophorus was lying, or – I was going mad. Hearing-voices mad, climbing-walls and frothing mad. I'd have to find the answer: that I knew. And by myself.

I listened with a new ear to the howls. Razoring under the door, they rose to operatic pitch, subsided, resumed, like the cries of a surly, hysterical child. To test their reality, I hummed beneath my breath, I covered my head with a blanketing, scratched at the straw, coughed. No difference. The quality of substance, of existence, was there. I tried, then, to localize the screams; and, on the fifteenth night, felt sure that they were coming from a spot not far along the hall.

'*The sounds that maniacs hear seem quite real to them.*'

I know. I know!

The monk was by my side, he had not left it from the start, keeping steady vigil even through Matins. He joined his tremulous soprano to the distant chants, and prayed excessively. But nothing could tempt him away. The food we ate was brought to us, as were all other needs. I'd see the Abbot, Father Jerome, once I was recovered. Meanwhile...

'I'm feeling better, Brother. Perhaps you'd care to show me about the grounds. I've seen nothing of St. Wulfran's except this little room.'

'There is only this little room multiplied. Ours is a rigorous order. The Franciscans, now, they permit themselves esthetic pleasure; we do not. It is, for us, a luxury. We have a single, most unusual job. There is nothing to see.'

'But surely the Abbey is very old.'

'Yes, that is true.'

'As an antiquarian–'

'Mr. Ellingto–'

'What is it you don't want me to see? What are you afraid of, Brother?'

'Mr. Ellington? I do not have the authority to grant your request. When you are well enough to leave, Father Jerome will no doubt be happy to accommodate you.'

'Will he also be happy to explain the screams I've heard each night since I've been here?'

'Rest, my son. Rest.'

The unholy, hackle-raising shriek burst loose and bounded off the hard stone walls. Brother Christophorus crossed himself, apropos of nothing, and sat like an ancient Indian on the weary stool. I knew he liked me. Especially, perhaps. We'd got along quite well in all our talks. But this – *verboten*.

I closed my eyes. I counted to three hundred. I opened my eyes.

The good monk was asleep. I blasphemed, softly, but he did not stir, so I swung my legs over the side of the straw bed and made my way across the dirt floor to the heavy wooden door. I rested there a time, in the candleless dark, listening to the howls; then, with Bostonian discretion, raised the bolt. The rusted hinges creaked, but Brother Christophorus was deep in celestial marble: his head drooped low upon his chest.

Panting, weak as a landlocked fish, I stumbled out into the corridor. The screams became impossibly loud. I put my hands to my ears, instinctively, and wondered how anyone could sleep with such a furor going on. It *was* a furor. In my mind? No. Real. The monastery shook with these shrill cries. You could feel their realness with your teeth.

I passed a Brother's cell and listened, then another; then I paused. A thick door, made of oak or pine, was locked before me. Behind it were the screams.

A chill went through me on the edge of those unutterable shrieks of hopeless, helpless anguish, and for a moment I considered turning back – not to my room, not to my bed of straw, but back into the open world. But duty held me. I took a breath and walked up to the narrow bar-crossed window and looked in.

A man was in the cell. On all fours, circling like a beast, his head thrown back, a man. The moonlight showed his face. It cannot be described – not, at least, by me. A man past death might look like this, a victim of the Inquisition rack, the stake, the pincers: not a human in the third decade of the twentieth century, surely. I had never seen such suffering within two eyes, such lost, mad suffering. Naked, he crawled about the dirt, cried, leaped up to his feet and clawed the hard stone walls in fury.

Then he saw me.

The screaming ceased. He huddled, blinking, in the corner of his cell. And then, as though unsure of what he saw, he walked right to the door.

In German, hissing: 'Who are you?'

'David Ellington,' I said. 'Are you locked in? Why have they locked you in?'

He shook his head. 'Be still, be still. You are not German?'

'No.' I told him how I came to be at St. Wulfran's.

'Ah!' Trembling, his horny fingers closing on the bars, the naked man said: 'Listen to me, we have only moments. They are mad. You hear? All mad. I was in the village, lying with my woman, when their crazy Abbot burst into the house and hit me with his heavy cross. I woke up here. They flogged me. I asked for food, they would not give it to me. They took my clothes. They threw me in this filthy room. They locked the door.'

'Why?'

'Why?' He moaned. 'I wish I knew. That's been the worst of it. Five years imprisoned, beaten, tortured, starved, and not a reason given, not a word to guess from – Mr. Ellington! I have sinned, but who has not? With my woman, quietly, alone with my woman, my love. And this God-drunk lunatic, Jerome, cannot stand it. Help me!'

His breath splashed on my face. I took a backward step and tried to think. I couldn't quite believe that in this century a thing so frightening could happen. Yet, the Abbey was secluded, above the world, timeless. What could not transpire here, secretly?

'I'll speak to the Abbot.'

'No! I tell you, he's the maddest of them all. Say nothing to him.'

'Then how can I help you?'

He pressed his mouth against the bars. 'In one way only. Around Jerome's neck, there is a key. It fits this lock. If–'

'Mr. Ellington!'

I turned and faced a fierce El Greco painting of a man. White-bearded, prow-nosed, regal as an Emperor beneath the gray peaked robe, he came out of the darkness. 'Mr. Ellington, I did not know that you were well enough to walk. Come with me, please.'

The naked man began to weep hysterically. I felt a grip of steel about my arm. Through corridors, past snore-filled cells, the echoes of the weeping dying, we continued to a room.

'I must ask you to leave St. Wulfran's,' the Abbot said. 'We lack the proper facilities for care of the ill. Arrangements will be made in Schwartzhof–'

'One moment,' I said. 'While it's probably true that Brother Christophorus's ministrations saved my life – and certainly true that I owe you all a debt of gratitude – I've got to ask for an explanation of that man in the cell.'

'What man?' the Abbot said softly.

'The one we just left, the one who's screamed all night long every night.'

'No man has been screaming, Mr. Ellington.'

Feeling suddenly very weak, I sat down and rested a few breaths' worth. Then I said, 'Father Jerome – you are he? I am not necessarily an irreligious person, but neither could I be considered particularly religious. I know nothing of monasteries, what is permitted, what isn't. But I seriously doubt that you have the authority to imprison a man against his will.'

'That is quite true. We have no such authority.'

'Then why have you done so?'

The Abbot looked at me steadily. In a firm, inflexible voice, he said: 'No man has been imprisoned at St. Wulfran's.'

'He claims otherwise.'

'Who claims otherwise?'

'The man in the cell at the end of the corridor.'

'There is no man in the cell at the end of the corridor.'

'I was talking with him!'

'You were talking with no man.'

The conviction in his voice shocked me into momentary silence. I gripped the arms of the chair.

'You are ill, Mr. Ellington,' the bearded holy man said. 'You have suffered from delirium. You have heard and seen things which do not exist.'

'That's true,' I said. 'But the man in the cell – whose voice I can hear now! – is not one of those things.'

The Abbot shrugged. 'Dreams can seem very real, my son.'

I glanced at the leather thong about his turkey-gobbler neck, all but hidden beneath the beard. 'Honest men make unconvincing liars,' I lied convincingly. 'Brother Christophorus has a way of looking at the floor whenever he denies the cries in the night. You look at me, but your voice loses its command. I can't imagine why, but you are both very intent upon keeping me away from the truth. Which is not only poor Christianity, but also poor psychology. For now I am quite curious indeed. You might as well tell me, Father; I'll find out eventually.'

'What do you mean?'

'Only that. I'm sure the police will be interested to hear of a man imprisoned at the Abbey.'

'I tell you, *there is no man*!'

'Very well. Let's forget the matter.'

'Mr. Ellington–' The Abbot put his hands behind him. 'The person in the cell is, ah, one of the Brothers. Yes. He is subject to… seizures, fits. You know fits? At these times, he becomes intractable. Violent. Dangerous! We're obliged to lock him in his cell, which you can surely understand.'

'I understand,' I said, 'that you're still lying to me. If the answer were as simple as that, you'd not have gone through the elaborate business of pretending I was delirious. There'd have been no need. There's something more to it, but I can wait. Shall we go on to Schwartzhof?'

Father Jerome tugged at his beard viciously, as if it were some feathered demon come to taunt him. 'Would you truly go to the police?' he asked.

'Would you?' I said. 'In my position?'

He considered that for a long time, tugging the beard, nodding the prowed head; and the screams went on, so distant, so real. I thought of the naked man clawing in his filth.

'Well, Father?'

'Mr. Ellington, I see that I shall have to be honest with you – which is a great pity,' he said. 'Had I followed my original instinct and refused to allow you in the Abbey to begin with… but, I had no choice. You were near death. No physician was available. You would have perished. Still, perhaps that would have been better.'

'My recovery seems to have disappointed a lot of people,' I commented, 'I assure you it was inadvertent.'

The old man took no notice of this remark. Stuffing his mandarin hands into the sleeves of his robe, he spoke with great deliberation. 'When I said that there was no man in the cell at the end of the corridor, I was telling the truth. Sit down, sir! Please! Now.' He closed his eyes. 'There is much to the story, much that you will not understand or believe. You are sophisticated, or feel that you are. You regard our life here, no doubt, as primitive–'

'In fact, I–'

'In fact, you do. I know the current theories. Monks are misfits, neurotics, sexual frustrates, and aberrants. They retreat from the world because they cannot cope with the world. Et cetera. You are surprised I know these things? My son, I was told by the one who began the theories!' He raised his head upward, revealing more of the leather thong. 'Five years ago, Mr. Ellington, there were no screams at St. Wulfran's. This was an undistinguished little Abbey in the wild Black Mountain region, and its inmates' job was quite simply to serve God, to save what souls they could by constant prayer. At that time, not very long after the great war, the world was in chaos. Schwartzhof was not the happy village you see now. It was, my son, a resort for the sinful, a hive of vice and corruption, a pit for the unwary – and the wary also, if they had not strength. A Godless place! Forsaken, fornicators paraded the streets. Gambling was done. Robbery and murder, drunkenness, and evils so profound I cannot put them into words. In all the universe you could not have found a fouler pesthole, Mr. Ellington! The Abbots and the Brothers at St. Wulfran's succumbed for years to Schwartzhof, I regret to say. Good men, lovers of God, chaste good men came here and fought but could not win against the black temptations. Finally it was decided that the Abbey should be closed. I heard of this and argued. "Is that not surrender?" I said. "Are we to bow before the strength of evil? Let me try, I beg you. Let me try to amplify the word of God that all in Schwartzhof shall hear and see their dark transgressions and repent!" '

The old man stood at the window, a trembling shade. His hands were now clutched together in a fervency of remembrance. 'They asked,' he said, 'if I considered myself more virtuous than my predecessors that I should hope for success where they had failed. I answered that I did not, but that I had an advantage. I was a convert. Earlier I had walked with evil, and knew its face. My wish was granted. For a year. One year only. Rejoicing, Mr. Ellington, I came here; and one night, incognito, walked the streets of the village. The smell of evil was strong. Too strong, I thought – and I had reveled in the alleys of Morocco, I had seen the dens of Hong Kong, Paris, Spain. The orgies were too wild, the drunkards much too drunk, the profanities a great deal too profane. It was as if the evil of the world had been distilled and centered here, as if a pagan tribal chief, in hiding, had assembled all his rituals about him… ' The Abbot nodded his head. 'I thought of Rome, in her last days; of Byzantium; of – Eden. That was the first of many hints to come. No matter what they were. I returned to the Abbey and donned my holy robes and went back into Schwartzhof. I made myself conspicuous. Some jeered, some shrank away, a voice cried, "Damn your foolish God!" And then a hand thrust out from darkness, touched my shoulder, and I heard: "Now, Father, are you lost?"'

The Abbot brought his tightly clenched hands to his forehead and tapped his forehead.

'Mr. Ellington, I have some poor wine here. Please have some.'

I drank, gratefully. Then the priest continued.

'I faced a man of average appearance. So average, indeed, that I felt I knew, then. "No," I told him, "but you are lost!" He laughed a foul laugh. "Are we not all, Father?" Then he said a most peculiar thing. He said his wife was dying and begged me to give her Extreme Unction. "Please," he said, "in God's sweet name!" I was confused. We hurried to his house. A woman lay upon a bed, her body nude. "It is a different Extreme Unction that I have in mind," he whispered, laughing. "It's the only kind, dear Father, that she understands. No other will have her! Pity! Pity on the poor soul lying there in all her suffering. Give her your Sceptre!" And the woman's arms came snaking, supplicating toward me, round and sensuous and hot… '

Father Jerome shuddered and paused. The shrieks, I thought, were growing louder from the hall. 'Enough of that,' he said. 'I was quite sure then. I raised my cross and told the words I'd learned, and it was over. He screamed – as he's doing now – and fell upon his knees. He had not expected to be recognized, nor should he have been normally. But in my life, I'd seen him many times, in many guises. I brought him to the Abbey. I locked him in the cell. We chant his chains each day. And so, my son, you see why you must not speak of the things you've seen and heard?'

I shook my head, as if afraid the dream would end, as if reality would suddenly explode upon me. 'Father Jerome,' I said, 'I haven't the vaguest idea of what you're talking about. Who is the man?'

'Are you such a fool, Mr. Ellington? That you must be told?'

'Yes!'

'Very well,' said the Abbot. 'He is Satan. Otherwise known as the Dark Angel, Asmodeus, Belial, Ahriman, Diabolus – the Devil.'

I opened my mouth.

'I see you doubt me. That is bad. Think, Mr. Ellington, of the peace of the world in these five years. Of the prosperity, of the happiness. Think of this country, Germany, now. Is there another country like it? Since we caught the Devil and locked him up here, there have been no great wars, no overwhelming pestilences: only the sufferings man was meant to endure. Believe what I say, my son: I beg you. Try very hard to believe that the creature you spoke with is Satan himself. Fight your cynicism, for it is born of him; he is the father of cynicism, Mr. Ellington! His plan was to defeat God by implanting doubt in the minds of Heaven's subjects!' The Abbot cleared his throat. 'Of course,' he said, 'we could never release anyone from St. Wulfran's who had any part of the Devil in him.'

I stared at the old fanatic and thought of him prowling the streets, looking for sin; saw him standing outraged at the bold fornicator's bed, wheedling him into an invitation to the Abbey, closing that heavy door and locking it, and, because of the world's *temporary* postwar peace, clinging to his fantasy. What greater dream for a holy man than actually capturing the Devil!

'I believe you,' I said.

'Truly?'

'Yes. I hesitated only because it seemed a trifle odd that Satan should have picked a little German village for his home.'

'He moves around,' the Abbot said. 'Schwartzhof attracted him as lovely virgins attract perverts.'

'I see.'

'Do you? My son, do you?'

'Yes. I swear it. As a matter of fact, I thought he looked familiar, but I simply couldn't place him.'

'Are you lying?'

'Father, I am a Bostonian.'

'And you promise not to mention this to anyone?'

'I promise.'

'Very well.' The old man sighed. 'I suppose,' he said, 'that you would not consider joining us as a Brother at the Abbey?'

'Believe me, Father, no one could admire the vocation more than I. But I am not worthy. No; it's quite out of the question. However, you have my word that your secret is safe with me.'

He was very tired. Sound had, in these years, reversed for him: the screams had become silence, the sudden cessation of them, noise. The prisoner's quiet talk with me had awakened him from deep slumber. Now he nodded wearily, and I saw that what I had to do would not be difficult after all. Indeed, no more difficult than fetching the authorities.

I walked back to my cell, where Brother Christophorus still slept, and lay down. Two hours passed. I rose again and returned to the Abbot's quarters.

The door was closed but unlocked.

I eased it open, timing the creaks of the hinges with the screams of the prisoner. I tiptoed in. Father Jerome lay snoring in his bed.

Slowly, cautiously, I lifted out the leather thong, and was a bit astounded at my technique. No Ellington had ever burgled. Yet a force, not like experience, but like it, ruled my fingers. I found the knot. I worked it loose.

The warm iron key slid off into my hand.

The Abbot stirred, then settled, and I made my way into the hall.

The prisoner, when he saw me, rushed the bars. 'He's told you lies, I'm sure of that!' he whispered hoarsely. 'Disregard the filthy madman!'

'Don't stop screaming,' I said.

'What?' He saw the key and nodded, then, and made his awful sounds. I thought at first the lock had rusted, but I worked the metal slowly and in time the key turned over.

Howling still, in a most dreadful way, the man stepped out into the corridor. I felt a momentary fright as his clawed hand reached up and touched my shoulder; but it passed. 'Come on!' We ran insanely to the outer door, across the frosted ground, down toward the village.

The night was very black.

A terrible aching came into my legs. My throat went dry. I thought my heart would tear loose from its moorings. But I ran on.

'Wait.'

Now the heat began.

'Wait.'

By a row of shops I fell. My chest was full of pain, my head of fear: I knew the madmen would come swooping from their dark asylum on the hill. I cried out to the naked hairy man: 'Stop! Help me!'

'Help you?' He laughed once, a high-pitched sound more awful than the screams had been; and then he turned and vanished in the moonless night.

I found a door, somehow.

The pounding brought a rifled burgher. Policemen came at last and listened to my story. But of course it was denied by Father Jerome and the Brothers of the Abbey.

'This poor traveler has suffered from the visions of pneumonia. There was no howling man at St. Wulfran's. No, no, certainly not. Absurd! Now, if Mr. Ellington would care to stay with us, we'd happily – no? Very well. I fear that you will be delirious a while, my son. The things you see will be quite real. Most real. You'll think – how quaint! – that you have loosed the Devil on the world and that the war to come – what war? But aren't there always wars? Of course! – you'll think that it's your fault' – those old eyes burning condemnation! Beak-nosed, bearded head atremble, rage in every word! – 'that you'll have caused the misery and suffering and death. And nights you'll spend, awake, unsure, afraid. How foolish!'

Gnome of God, Christophorus, looked terrified and sad. He said to me, when Father Jerome swept furiously out: 'My son, don't blame yourself. Your weakness was *his* lever. Doubt unlocked that door. Be comforted: we'll hunt *him* with our nets, and one day… '

One day, what?

I looked up at the Abbey of St. Wulfran's, framed by dawn, and started wondering, as I have wondered since ten thousand times, if it weren't true. Pneumonia breeds delirium; delirium breeds visions. Was it possible that I'd imagined all of this?

No. Not even back in Boston, growing dewlaps,

paunches, wrinkles, sacks and money, at Ellington, Carruthers & Blake, could I accept that answer.

The monks were mad, I thought. Or: The howling man was mad. Or: The whole thing was a joke.

I went about my daily work, as every man must do, if sane, although he may have seen the dead rise up or freed a bottled djinn or fought a dragon, once, quite long ago.

But I could not forget. When the pictures of the carpenter from Braunau-am-Inn began to appear in all the papers, I grew uneasy; for I felt I'd seen this man before. When the carpenter invaded Poland, I was sure. And when the world was plunged into war and cities had their entrails blown asunder and that pleasant land I'd visited became a place of hate and death, I dreamed each night.

Each night I dreamed, until this week.

A card arrived. From Germany. A picture of the Moselle Valley is on one side, showing mountains fat with grapes and the dark Moselle, wine of these grapes.

On the other side of the card is a message. It is signed *'Brother Christophorus'* and reads (and reads and reads!):

'Rest now, my son. We have him back with us again.'

SAME TIME, SAME PLACE

Mervyn Peake

Mervyn Peake (1911–1968) was a visionary English writer, poet, and artist named in *The Times*'s list of 'The 50 Greatest British Writers since 1945'. Peake is best known for the phantasmagorical *Gormenghast* series (1946–1959). Parkinson's disease robbed Peake of the ability to complete the later novels in the cycle. Early influences included Charles Dickens and Robert Louis Stevenson, but the weirdness that permeates his work also demonstrates knowledge of Decadent-era literature and, in art, the Grotesques. Much of his short fiction is collected in *Boy in Darkness and Other Stories* (1976). 'Same Time, Same Place' (1963) shares affinities with the work of Leonora Carrington in its glimpse of the hidden in our contemporary world.

That night I hated Father. He smelt of cabbage. There was cigarette ash all over his trousers. His untidy moustache was yellower and viler than ever with nicotine, and he took no notice of me. He simply stood there in his ugly armchair, his eyes half closed, brooding on the Lord knows what. I hated him. I hated his moustache. I even hated the smoke that drifted from his mouth and hung in the stale air above his head.

And when my mother came through the door and asked me whether I had seen her spectacles, I hated her, too. I hated the clothes she wore; tasteless and fussy. I hated them deeply. I hated something I had never noticed before; it was the way the heels of her shoes were worn away on their outside edges – not badly but appreciably. It looked mean to me, slatternly, and horribly human. I hated her for being human – like father.

She began to nag me about her glasses and the thread-bare condition of the elbows of my jacket, and suddenly I threw my book down. The room was unbearable. I felt suffocated. I suddenly realized that I must get away. I had lived with these two people for nearly twenty-three years. I had been born in the room immediately overhead. Was this the life for a young man? To spend his evenings watching the smoke drift out of his father's mouth and stain that decrepit old moustache, year after year – to watch the worn-away edges of my mother's heels, the dark-brown furniture and the familiar stains on the chocolate-coloured carpet? I would go away; I would shake off the dark, smug mortality of the place. I would forego my birthright. What of my father's business into which I would step at his death? What of it? To hell with it.

I began to make my way to the door, but at the third step I caught my foot in a ruck of the chocolate-coloured carpet, and in reaching out my hand for support I sent a pink vase flying.

Suddenly I felt very small and very angry. I saw my mother's mouth opening, and it reminded me of the front door and the front door reminded me of my urge to escape – to where? To where?

I did not wait to find an answer to my own question but, hardly knowing what I was doing, ran from the house.

The accumulated boredom of the last twenty-three years was at my back, and it seemed that I was propelled through the garden gate from its pressure against my shoulder-blades.

The road was wet with rain, black and shiny like oilskin. The reflection of the street-lamps wallowed like yellow jellyfish. A bus was approaching – a bus to Piccadilly, a bus to the never-never land – a bus to death or glory.

I found neither. I found something which haunts me still.

The great bus swayed as it sped. The black street gleamed. Through the window a hundred faces fluttered by as though the leaves of a dark book were being flicked over. And I sat there, with a sixpenny ticket in my hand. What was I doing? Where was I going?

To the centre of the world, I told myself. To Piccadilly Circus, where anything might happen. What did I *want* to happen?

I wanted life to happen! I wanted adventure; but already I was afraid. I wanted to find a beautiful woman. Bending my elbow I felt for the swelling of my biceps. There wasn't much to feel. 'Oh hell,' I said to myself, 'Oh damnable hell. This is *awful*.'

I stared out of the window, and there before me was the Circus. The lights were like a challenge. When the bus had curved its way from Regent Street and into Shaftesbury Avenue I alighted. Here was the jungle all about me, and I was lonely. The wild beasts prowled around me. The wolf packs surged and shuffled. Where was I to go? How wonderful it would have been to have known of some apartment, dimly lighted; of a door that opened to the secret knock, three short ones and one long one – where a strawberry blonde was waiting or perhaps, better still, some wise old lady with a cup of tea, an old lady, august and hallowed and whose heels were not worn down on their outside edges.

But I knew nowhere to go either for glamour or sympathy. Nowhere except the Corner House.

I made my way there. It was less congested than usual. I had only to queue for a few minutes before being allowed into the great eating-palace on the first floor. On, the marble and gold of it all! The waiters coming and going, the band in the distance – how different all this was from an hour ago, when I stared at my father's moustache.

For some while I could find no table, and it was only when moving down the third of the long corridors between tables that I saw an old man leaving a table for two. The lady who had been sitting opposite him remained where she was. Had she left I would have had no tale to tell. Unsuspectingly I took the place of the old man and in reaching for the menu lifted my head and found myself gazing into the midnight pools of her eyes.

My hand hung poised over the menu. I could not move, for the head in front of me was magnificent. It was big and pale and indescribably proud – and what I would now call a greedy look seemed to me then to be an expression of rich assurance, of majestic beauty.

I knew at once that it was not the strawberry blonde of my callow fancy that I desired for glamour's sake, nor the comfort of the tea-tray lady – but this glorious creature before me who combined the mystery and exoticism of the former with the latter's mellow wisdom.

Was this not love at first sight? Why else should my heart have hammered like a foundry? Why should my hand have trembled above the menu? Why should my mouth have gone dry?

Words were quite impossible. It was clear to me that she knew everything that was going on in my breast and in my brain. The look of love which flooded from her eyes all but unhinged me. Taking my hand in hers she returned it to my side of the table where it lay like a dead thing on a plate. Then she passed me the menu. It meant nothing to me. The hors d'ouvres and the sweets were all mixed together in a dance of letters.

What I told the waiter when he came I cannot remember, nor what he brought me. I know that I could not eat it. For an hour we sat there. We spoke with our eyes, with the pulse and stress of our excited breathing – and towards the end of this, our first meeting, with the tips of our fingers that in touching each other in the shadow of the teapot seemed to speak a language richer, subtler, and more vibrant than words.

At last we were asked to go – and as I rose I spoke for the first time. 'Tomorrow?' I whispered. 'Tomorrow?' She nodded her magnificent head slowly. 'Same place? Same time?' She nodded again.

I waited for her to rise, but with a gentle yet authoritative gesture she signalled me away.

It seemed strange, but I knew I must go. I turned at the door and saw her sitting there, very still, very upright. Then I descended to the street and made my way to Shaftesbury Avenue, my head in a whirl of stars, my legs weak and trembling, my heart on fire.

I had not decided to return home but found nevertheless that I was on my way back – back to the chocolate-coloured carpet, to my father in the ugly armchair, to my mother with her worn shoe heels.

When at last I turned the key it was near midnight. My mother had been crying. My father was angry. There were words, threats and entreaties on all sides. At last I got to bed.

The next day seemed endless, but at long last my excited fretting found some relief in action. Soon after tea I boarded the west-bound bus. It was already dark, but I was far too early when I arrived at the Circus.

I wandered restlessly here and there, adjusting my tie at shop windows and filing my nails for the hundredth time.

At last, when waking from a day dream as I sat for the fifth time in Leicester Square, I glanced at my watch and found I was three minutes late for our tryst.

I ran all the way panting with anxiety, but when I arrived at the table on the first floor I found my fear was baseless. She was there, more regal than ever, a monument of womanhood. Her large, pale face relaxed into an expression of such deep pleasure at the sight of me that I almost shouted for joy.

I will not speak of the tenderness of that evening. It was magic. It is enough to say that we determined that our destinies were inextricably joined.

When the time came for us to go I was surprised to find that the procedure of the previous night was once more expected of me. I could in no way make out the reason for it. Again I left her sitting alone at the table by the marble pillar. Again I vanished into the night alone, with those intoxicating words still on my lips. 'Tomorrow… tomorrow… same time… same place…'

The certainty of my love for her and hers for me was quite intoxicating. I slept little that night and my restlessness on the following day was an agony both for me and my parents.

Before I left that night for our third meeting I crept into my mother's bedroom, and opening her jewel box I chose a ring from among her few trinkets. God knows it was not worthy to sit upon my loved one's finger, but it would symbolize our love.

Again she was waiting for me, though on this occasion I arrived a full quarter of an hour before our appointed time. It was as though, when we were together, we were hidden in a veil of love – as though we were alone. We heard nothing else but the sound of our voices; we saw nothing else but one another's eyes.

She put the ring upon her finger as soon as I had given it to her. Her hand that was holding mine tightened its grip. I was surprised at its power. My whole body trembled. I moved my foot beneath the table to touch hers. I could find it nowhere.

When once more the dreaded moment arrived, I felt her sitting upright, the strong and tender smile of her farewell remaining in my mind like some fantastic sunrise.

For eight days we met thus, and parted thus, and with every meeting we knew more firmly than ever that whatever the difficulties that would result, whatever the forces against us, yet it was now that we must marry, now, while the magic was upon us.

On the eighth evening it was all decided. She knew that for my part it must be a secret wedding. My parents would never countenance so rapid an arrangement. She understood perfectly. For her part she wished a few of her friends to be present at the ceremony.

'I have a few colleagues,' she had said. I did not know what she meant, but her instructions as to where we should meet on the following afternoon put the remark out of my mind.

There was a registry office in Cambridge Circus, she told me, on the first floor of a certain building. I was to be there at four o'clock. She would arrange everything.

'Ah, my love,' she had murmured, shaking her large head slowly from side to side, 'how can I wait until then?' And with a smile unutterably bewitching she gestured for me to go, for the great marmoreal hall was all but empty.

For the eighth time I left her there. I knew that women must have their secrets and must be in no way thwarted in regard to them, and so, once again, I swallowed the question that I so longed to put to her. Why, oh why had I always to leave her there – and why, when I arrived to meet her, was she always there to meet me?

On the following day, after a careful search, I found a gold ring in a box in my father's dressing-room. Soon after three, having brushed my hair until it shone like sealskin, I set forth with a flower in my buttonhole and suitcase of belongings. It was a beautiful day with no wind and a clear sky.

The bus fled on like a fabulous beast, bearing me with it to a magic land.

But, alas, as we approached Mayfair we were held up more than once for long stretches of time. I began to get restless. By the time the bus had reached Shaftesbury Avenue I had but three minutes in which to reach the office.

It seemed strange that when the sunlight shone in sympathy with my marriage the traffic should choose to frustrate me. I was on the top of the bus and, having been given a very clear description of the building, was able, as we rounded at last into Cambridge Circus, to recognize it at once. When we came alongside my destination the traffic was held up again, and I was offered the perfect opportunity of disembarking immediately beneath the building.

My suitcase was at my feet, and as I stooped to pick it up I glanced at the windows on the first floor – for it was in one of those rooms that I was so soon to become a husband.

I was exactly on a level with the windows in question and commanded an unbroken view of the interior of a first-floor room. It could not have been more than a dozen feet away from where I sat.

I remember that our bus was hooting away, but there was no movement in the traffic ahead. The hooting came to me as through a dream, for I had become lost in another world.

My hand was clenched upon the handle of the suitcase. Through my eyes and into my brain an image was pouring. The image of the first-floor room.

I knew at once that it was in that particular room that I was expected. I cannot tell you why, for during those first few moments I had not seen her.

To the right of the stage (for I had the sensation of being in a theatre) was a table loaded with flowers. Behind the flowers sat a small pinstriped registrar. There were four others in the room, three of whom kept walking to and fro. The fourth, an enormous bearded lady, sat on a chair by the window. As I stared, one of the men bent over to speak to her. He had the longest neck on earth. His starched collar was the length of a walking stick, and his small bony head protruded from its extremity like the skull of a bird. The other two gentlemen who kept crossing and recrossing were very different. One was bald. His face and cranium were blue with the most intricate tattooing. His teeth were gold, and they shone like fire in his mouth. The other was a well-dressed young man and seemed normal enough until, as he came for a moment closer to the window, I saw that instead of a hand the cloven hoof of a goat protruded from the left sleeve.

And then suddenly it all happened. A door of their room must have opened, for all at once all the heads in the room were turned in one direction and a moment later something in white trotted like a dog across the room.

But it was no dog. It was vertical as it ran. I thought at first that it was a mechanical doll, so close was it to the floor. I could not observe its face, but I was amazed to see the long train of satin that was being dragged along the carpet behind it.

It stopped when it reached the flower-laden table, and there was a good deal of smiling and bowing, and then the man with the longest neck in the world placed a high stool in front of the table and, with the help of the young man with the goat foot, lifted the white thing so that it stood upon the high stool. The long satin dress was carefully draped over the stool so that it reached the floor on every side. It seemed as though a tall, dignified woman was standing at the civic altar.

And still I had not seen its face, though I knew what it would be like. A sense of nausea overwhelmed me and I sank back on the seat, hiding my face in my hands.

I cannot remember when the bus began to move. I know that I went on and on and on and that finally I was told that I had reached the terminus. There was nothing for it but to board another bus of the same number and make the return journey. A strange sense of relief had by now begun to blunt the edge of my disappointment. That this bus would take me to the door of the house where I was born gave me a twinge of homesick pleasure. But stronger was my sense of fear. I prayed that there would be no reason for the bus to be held up again in Cambridge Circus.

I had taken one of the downstairs seats, for I had no wish to be on an eye level with someone I had deserted. I had no sense of having wronged her, but she had been deserted nevertheless.

When at last the bus approached the Circus I peered into the half darkness. A street-lamp stood immediately below the registry office. I saw at once that there was no light in the office, and as the bus moved past I turned my eyes to a group beneath the street-lamp. My heart went cold in my breast.

Standing there, ossified as it were into a malignant mass – standing there as though they never intended to move until justice was done – were the five. It was only for a second that I saw them, but every lamplit head is forever with me – the long-necked man with his bird skull head, his eyes glinting like chips of glass; to his right the small bald man, his tattooed scalp thrust forward, the lamplight glinting on the blue markings. To the left of the long-necked man stood the youth, his elegant body relaxed but a snarl on his face that I still sweat to remember. His hands were in his pockets, but I could see the shape of the hoof through the cloth. A little ahead of these three stood the bearded lady, a bulk of evil – and in the shadow that she cast before her I saw in that last fraction of a second, as the bus rolled me past, a big whitish head, very close to the ground.

In the dusk it appeared to be suspended above the kerb like a pale balloon with a red mouth painted upon it – a mouth that, taking a single diabolical curve, was more like the mouth of a wild beast than of a woman.

Long after I had left the group behind me – set, as it were, forever under the lamp, like something made of wax, like something monstrous, long after I had left it I yet saw it all. It filled the bus. They filled my brain. They fill it still.

When at last I arrived home I fell weeping upon my bed. My father and mother had no idea what it was all about, but they did not ask me. They never asked me.

That evening, after supper, I sat there, I remember, six years ago in my own chair on the chocolate-coloured carpet. I remember how I stared with love at the ash on my father's waistcoat, at his stained moustache, at my mother's worn-away shoe heels. I stared at it all and I loved it all. I needed it all.

Since then I have never left the house. I know what is best for me.

THE COLOMBER

Dino Buzzati

TRANSLATED INTO ENGLISH BY GIO CLAIRVAL

Dino Buzzati (1906–1972) was an Italian novelist and short-story writer who served as a journalist with the Italian navy during World War II. On his return, Buzzati published his most famous book, *The Tartar Steppe* (1940). However, the writer is best-known for his short stories, which could be darkly fantastical or whimsical, several of them touched by the weird. He once noted that, 'The effectiveness of a fantastic story will depend on its being told in the most simple and practical terms.' 'The Colomber' (1966), with its haunting sea creature, is quietly horrific and has some of the qualities of a weird fable. This new translation by Gio Clairval is the first in several decades.

When Stefano Roí turned twelve as a birthday gift he asked his father, a sea captain and the master of a fine sailing ship, to be taken on board.

'When I grow up,' Stefano said, 'I want to go to sea, just like you. And I'll command ships even more beautiful and bigger than yours.'

'God bless you, son,' said the father. And since that very day his ship was sailing out, he took the boy with him.

It was a splendid, sunny day, with a calm sea. Stefano, who had never been on his father's ship, happily wandered about the deck, admiring the elaborate manoeuvres of the sails. He asked the sailors about this and that, and the sailors, smiling, offered him all the explanations he wanted.

As he reached the stern, the boy stopped, intrigued, to watch something in the ship's wake continually rising and sinking at a distance of two or three hundred meters.

Although the ship seemed to fly over the waves, carried as it was by a glorious quarter wind, that thing always kept the same distance. And even though its nature remained mysterious to the boy, it had an indefinable quality that attracted him intensely.

The father, who couldn't see where Stefano was, called his name, to no avail, and stepped down from the bridge to look for him.

'Stefano, what are you doing there, glued to the spot?' he asked, finally glimpsing the boy, who stood stock still on the stern, gaze riveted to the waves.

'Papa, come here and see.'

The father came and he, too, looked in the direction indicated by the boy, but could not see anything.

'There's something dark poking out of the wake now and then,' the boy said, 'and it's coming after us.'

'Despite being forty,' said the father, 'I believe I still have good eyesight. But I can't see a thing – nothing at all.'

As the boy insisted, the father went to get his telescope and scanned the sea, keeping the instrument pointed to the line of the wake. Stefano saw him turn pale.

'What is it? Why are you making a face?'

'Oh, why did I have to listen to you?' said the captain. 'Now I fear for you. That thing you see poking out of the water and following us is not a thing. That is a colomber. It's the fish sailors fear above all others, in every sea in the world. It's a dreadful and mysterious shark, more cunning than man. For reasons that perhaps no one will ever know, it chooses its victim, and when it has chosen a man, it pursues him for years and years, for a lifetime, until it devours him. And the strange thing is that nobody can see him but the victim himself and blood relations.'

'It's not a tall tale?'

'No. I'd never seen it before. But from the descriptions I heard so many times, I recognized it right away. That blunt, bison-like muzzle, that restless mouth that opens and closes, those terrible teeth. Stefano, there's no doubt; unfortunately the colomber has chosen you and as long as you go to sea it will not stop tormenting you. Listen to me: now we're going back to port; you'll get off and you will never ever leave the shore again, for any reason whatsoever. You must promise me. Seafaring is not for you, son. You must give up the idea of sailing. After all, you'll be able to make a fortune for yourself on land, too.'

With these words, he gave the order to reverse course immediately, returned to port and, on the pretext of a sudden illness, he put his son to shore. Then he left without him.

Deeply troubled, the boy stood on the shore until the last tip of the masts sank behind the horizon. Beyond the pier that closed the port, the sea remained completely deserted. But, straining his eyes, Stefano was able to make out a black dot that emerged intermittently from the water: 'his' colomber, which cruised back and forth slowly, stubbornly waiting for him.

From that day on, the boy's desire to go to sea was discouraged by any possible mean. Stefano's father sent him to study in an inland city, hundreds of miles away. And for some time, distracted by new surroundings, Stefan forgot about the sea monster. Still, he returned home for summer vacations, and the first thing he did, as soon as he had some free time, was to run to the end of the pier to verify again its presence, although deep down he deemed it unnecessary. After all this time, even assuming the entire story his father had recounted was true, the colomber had certainly abandoned its siege.

But Stefano stood there, stunned, his heart pounding. At a distance of two or three hundred meters from the pier, in the open sea, the sinister fish cruised back and forth, slowly, raising its muzzle every now and then, turning toward land as if anxious to see whether Stefano Roí was about to join him at last.

The thought of that hostile creature waiting for him day and night became a secret obsession for Stefano. And even in the distant city, he sometimes awoke worried in the dead of night. He was safe, yes; hundreds of miles separated him from the colomber. Nevertheless, he knew that beyond the mountains, beyond the woods, beyond the plains, the shark awaited him. And should he move to the most remote continent, the colomber would still be lurking in the nearest stretch of sea, with the inexorable stubbornness displayed by instruments of fate.

Stefano, who was a serious and willing boy, continued his studies to advantage and, as soon as he came of age, found a dignified and well-paying position in a store of that city. Meanwhile, the father died after an illness, his magnificent ship was sold by his widow and the son became the heir to a fairly good fortune. Work, friendships, leisure, first love affairs: Stefano's life was set on its rails, yet the thought of the colomber bothered him as if it were a tragic and fascinating mirage; and, as the days passed, instead of fading away, this vision seemed to become more insistent.

Great are the rewards of an industrious, affluent and quiet life, but even greater is the attraction of the abyss. Stefano was only twenty-two years old when, having said good-bye to his friends, he quit his job, returned to his hometown and informed his mother he was determined to follow his father's path. The woman, to whom Stefano had never mentioned the mysterious creature, welcomed the decision with joy. Her son's abandoning of the sea for the town had always seemed, in her heart, a betrayal of the family tradition.

And Stefano began to sail, giving proof of

seaworthy qualities: endurance, stamina, a fearless spirit. He sailed and sailed, and in the wake of his ship, day and night, in dead calm and in choppy waters, the colomber trailed along behind. He knew that it was his curse and his punishment, but because of this awareness, perhaps, he could not find the strength to break free from it. And no one on board could see the monster except him.

'Do you see something over there?' he would ask his companions from time to time, pointing to the ship's wake.

'No, we don't see a thing. Why?'

'I don't know. I thought…'

'You didn't see a colomber, did you?' they said, laughing and touching wood.

'Why are you laughing? Why are you touching wood?'

'Because the colomber is a merciless beast. If it started following this boat, it would mean that one of us is doomed.'

But Stefano would not give in. On the contrary, the continuous threat that pursued him seemed to strengthen his will, his passion for the sea, his courage in times of struggle and danger.

When he thought himself master of his trade, he used the decent-sized inheritance left him by his father to buy a small freighter with a partner, and then became the sole owner and, through a series of successful expeditions, he was able to buy a real merchant ship, setting increasingly ambitious goals. But neither the achievements nor the millions could free his soul from that constant worry; nor was he even tempted to sell his ship and retire to undertake new enterprises on land.

To sail and sail. He could not think of anything else. No sooner had he set foot on land in any port after a long journey than he was stung by the impatience to leave. He knew that the colomber was waiting for him offshore, and that the colomber was synonymous with ruin. But nothing else would do.

An indomitable urge drew him relentlessly, from one ocean to another. Until, one day, Stefano suddenly realized he had grown old, very old, and nobody around him could understand why, rich as he was, he did not quit the accursed seafaring at last. Old, and bitterly unhappy, because his whole life had been spent in that mad flight across the seas to escape his enemy. But greater than the joys of a quiet and comfortable life had always been to him the temptation of the abyss.

One evening, while his magnificent ship was anchored offshore, outside the port town where he was born, he felt death was close. He then called the first mate, whom he greatly trusted, and ordered him not to oppose what he was about to do. The man promised, on his honour.

Having received this assurance, Stefano told the first mate, who listened in dismay, the story of the colomber that had been unsuccessfully pursuing him for nearly fifty years.

'It has escorted me across the world,' Stefano said, 'with a loyalty that not even the noblest of friends could have shown. Now I'm dying. The colomber, too, must now be awfully old and tired. I cannot betray it.'

With these words, he took his leave, had a harpoon brought to him, and boarded a small boat as soon as it was lowered to the sea. 'Now I'm going to face it,' he announced. 'It's only fair that I should not disappoint it. But I will fight with my last strength.' Pulling wearily on the oars, he turned away from the ship. Sailors and mates saw him disappear on the placid sea, surrounded by the shadows of the night.

He did not have to toil for long. Suddenly the colomber's horrid muzzle emerged close to the boat. 'Here I am with you, at last,' said Stefano. 'To us now!' And, mustering up his last energy, he raised the harpoon to strike.

The colomber moaned in an imploring voice. 'Such a long journey to find you. I, too, am exhausted. So much you had me swim. And you kept on fleeing. And you never understood anything.'

'Why?' said Stefano, cut to the quick.

'Because I did not chase you across the world just to devour you as you thought. I was charged by the Sea King to deliver this to you.' And the shark stuck out its tongue, offering the old captain a small phosphorescent sphere.

Stefano seized the sphere between thumb and

forefinger and examined it. It was a pearl of incredible size. He recognized the famous Pearl of the Sea that brought fortune, power, love, and peace of mind to whoever possessed it. But it was too late.

'Alas!' he said, shaking his head sadly. 'It is all so wrong. I've managed to curse my own life: and I've ruined yours.'

'So long, poor man,' said the colomber. And it sank in the black waters forever.

Two months later, pushed by the undertow, a small boat approached a steep cliff. It was sighted by a few fishermen, who, curious, went to see. Onboard, still seated, was a white skeleton, and between the tiny bones of its fingers it clutched a little round pebble.

The colomber is a huge fish, terrifying to behold, extremely rare.

Depending on the sea, and the people living by its shores, it is also called kolomber, kahloubrha, kalonge, kalu-balu, chalung-gra. Naturalists strangely ignore it. Some even maintain that it does not exist.

THE OTHER SIDE OF THE MOUNTAIN

Michel Bernanos

TRANSLATED INTO ENGLISH BY GIO CLAIRVAL

Michel Bernanos (1924–1964) was a French writer, the son of well-known writer Georges Bernanos and the only one of six children to follow in his father's footsteps. However, he refused to use his father's name, publishing thrillers under the pen names 'Michel Talbert' and 'Michel Drowin'. 'The Other Side of the Mountain', first published in 1967, three years after the writer's suicide in the forest of Fontainebleau, is considered a surreal masterpiece; it is also the only story to be published under his real name. Gio Clairval's fine new translation should be considered definitive, and for the first time conveys the stark and beautiful essence of the writer's vision.

PART ONE

I had just turned eighteen when, after a night of drinking, the hand of a friend guided mine into signing myself onboard a galleon for one year.

The beginning of this dreadful adventure remains a vague memory – or, should I say, a faint trace. In truth, not until the following morning did I face the reality of my situation. To my vast surprise, I found myself stretched out on hard, bare boards, greeted by the depths of a bright blue sky. Then I noticed sails filled by a gentle breeze, and the rolling sea speckled with white caught in a single wavelet and multiplied toward the horizon.

Astonished, I glanced around, taking in the hawsers coiled in every corner. Cords of rope similar to those I'd spotted on moored boats. The ship reeked of tar.

At the noise of heavy footfalls, I clenched my eyes shut and pretended to be asleep. A kick rewarded my cunning while a voice barked, 'Off with you, ship's boy! Got to scrub the quarterdeck. Move it, or I'll hang you from the boom.'

The man kicked my side once more. I scrambled to my feet, wobbling on the moving deck. 'Quicker, I tells you,' the barking continued. 'Go see the cook. He needs help with the grub.'

Not knowing where the galley was, I wandered from the quarterdeck to the forecastle. The wind had risen and the sails puffed out their big white bellies, fat with the new breeze. The galleon – I hadn't learned her name yet – listed, gliding on the water like a caress on smooth skin. The masts moaned as they resisted the wind. I met several crewmembers. Their faces held no encouragement but I felt reassured by their lack of interest in me. I changed my mind as soon as I bumped into the man who had scolded me. His brown, almost black face contorted horribly as he glowered at me. 'Ah! You refuse to obey, then? Well, we'll teach you to be a sailor. Here, mates,' he addressed two sailors. 'Fetch two mooring lines. Let's have some fun.'

As if in a nightmare, the crew encircled me. Seeing silent laughter on those hard faces, I lost all hope. They would show me no pity.

'Well, seaman?' cried my torturer, who was the bosun, I guessed. 'Are those lines coming?'

'Here we are,' answered a voice.

A young sailor stepped up to us, holding a line hung with a weight on one end.

'Go ahead. Tie him up,' the bosun ordered, nodding in my direction.

The sailor glanced at me and tried to object. 'He's just a kid. D'you think he can take it?'

'Do what you're told and shut your hole.'

'All right, all right,' said the lad. 'Just saying.'

And without further hesitation, he began to put a rope around my waist. Another sailor approached with a second mooring line. The bosun beckoned the two sailors to the aft.

I watched them with a sinking feeling as one of them stood at starboard, the other portside, and they passed the rope over the prow, and then let it slip under the hull. Now they were coming back for me. They tied the other end to the rope already around my waist, and I was caught in the middle of the two mooring lines. Crazed with panic, I could only glance around me, seeking mercy. Although I noticed pity on a few faces, most bore expressions of sadistic expectation.

Indifferent to these manoeuvres, the fleecy blue sea blossomed with white foam like lace crowning the billows, while the topmast, all sails out, stroked the variegated sky.

'Throw him over,' bellowed my persecutor.

Several grips seized me. Coarse laughter burst from all around as I was tossed over the side. Scared to death, I shut my eyes and stiffened, waiting for the shock of ice-cold water. But I had not reckoned with my tormentors' refined cruelty. They lowered me with maddening slowness toward the watery abyss. I tried to hold on to the sea-worn hull but only succeeded in excoriating my hands. Peals of laughter mingled with the sound of the restless sea. Finally, my feet touched the water. A strange calm filled my heart. I knew I should avoid breathing once submerged. Therefore, I waited to the very last, when the water reached my chin, to take in as much air as possible and hold my breath. Despite this precaution, my chest soon contracted in the most atrocious way. I was now being dragged to the other side, as slowly as I had been lowered into the sea. I could no longer endure it. I needed some air. I opened my eyes in the hope of seeing the brightness of daylight right above me, but I only glimpsed a terrible vision that obliterated the burning bite of the salt. I balanced under the hull. The boat, in the ghastly green glow of the underwater world, loomed over me like an immense dark monster.

I must have lost consciousness right then because I have no recollection of what happened next. Afterward I learnt that the captain, called to the deck by the commotion, gave the order to haul me up. Without his intervention, I would have died.

... I was stretched out on a hammock that swung with the rolling of the sea. The horizon became visible through the porthole. With each movement of the galleon, the line would sink and resurface, sink and resurface. This sight reminded me of my awful ordeal, and either fear or exhaustion robbed me of my senses again.

... Harsh sounds reached me. I opened my eyes. Night had fallen. A storm lamp moved back and forth. The wrinkled face bending over me made me think of the apples Mother used to place on the kitchen hearth to dry out. The man stared at me with beady eyes devoid of kindness but also free from any animosity. He was chewing a quid of tobacco that made his breath stink.

'You're waking up at last, ship's boy. Get up. Need to fill up your belly.'

'How long have I been sleeping, sir?' I asked him.

'Three days, son. And there's no "sir" 'round here. I'm old Toine, the cook. And I need a helper. If you're all right with it, I'll take you on. I've got neither a good nor bad heart. But if you work for me, you'll always get enough food. Eating's the most important thing, son.'

'Where are we going?'

'How come you don't know? Didn't you sign up for it?' Shaking his head, he went on. 'We're going to Peru to find gold for the Spaniards, if the English and the Dutch don't sink us first.'

'So we're like what, pirates?'

'No, no, we're just freighters.' He shrugged.

Seeing by my puzzled look that I didn't understand, he spat out a long spurt of brownish saliva and, after shifting his tobacco quid from one cheek to the other, he said in gruff tones, 'Come on and eat. You look half dead.'

I scrambled to my feet. The cabin spun around me but I followed my new boss to the galley.

The place was filthy. Cockroaches three times bigger than those I'd seen before scuttled among sacks of flour and sugar. Old Toine served me a vegetable soup that tasted delicious from the first spoonful. He watched me eat with a satisfied look on his wrinkled face. Like an artist who loves his painting, he loved his cooking and liked seeing others enjoy it.

When I emptied my bowl, he said, 'Go get your hammock. You're going to sleep with me in the galley. You'll be better off here than with those pigs.'

II

A fortnight had passed since I was forced aboard. The crew had tried to bull rush me on several occasions. But each time, old Toine intervened, pretending he needed me in the galley, even brandishing a large butcher knife under the crewmen's noses. The men had grown tired of the game.

Early in the morning, I settled down on the deck to peel potatoes. I dreamt often, lost in that blue infinity. Dolphins interrupted my reverie with their playful breaking of the watery surface. They arced gracefully in mid-air, with the elegance of horses jumping over obstacles. The ship herself, sails spread and bowsprit piercing the horizon, was poised to rise and fly. As the day advanced, the king of stars flooded the deck with its golden rays. The gentle breeze filling our sails reminded me of my mother's caresses when I was a little child. When night fell and my work was done, I came back to the deck. I loved watching the prow cut the phosphorescent waters while sprays captured tiny rainbows. I also loved spying the unknown stars that rose from the horizon to sow the dark vault of the sky under the still watches of the Great Bear.

My regrets and fears had slowly disappeared in the presence of all those wonders. I even surprised myself by holding my own with the crewmen. My journey seemed to continue in a peaceful way. One morning, however, we awoke in the middle of a strange silence. Toine leapt out of his hammock, crying like a madman, 'It stopped. The bastard stopped!'

Then, spotting my bemused stare, he shouted, 'Can you hear something? Can you?'

'No, no,' I said, bewildered. 'No, I don't hear a thing.'

'That's our problem, idiot. The wind has stopped. There's no current here on the Equator. We could be dead in the water for days.'

He stormed out of the galley. I jumped down from the hammock and followed him. Outside, the sails hung limp, offering a scene of desolation. Sunbeams drew reflections in the still water, as smooth as an immense sleeping lake. Already the heat was growing unbearable. The crew went about their chores in unusual silence.

Toine spat over the side. 'Take a good look, son,' he said. 'Even life seems to be hanging in mid-air. Let's hope it won't last.' He clenched his teeth. 'Or it'll be hell.'

'Pull in the sails, you bunch of rascals!' the captain yelled, coming down from the bridge.

We waited for the wind to return for eight interminable days. The tension mounted. First water was rationed, then food. But the heat that assailed the ship spoiled the food. We had to throw it all overboard. Scurvy appeared. The men's lips and gums became black and swelled to double their normal size. To relieve the suffering of these poor souls, the captain gave the order for rum. But the men asked for more, and soon we teetered on the brink of disaster, as our load of rum barrels was to be bartered for gold.

After forty days of forced immobility, the potatoes, the only food left, began to sprout. A foul stench rose from the hold. The horrendous odour convinced the captain to have us throw the precious vegetables overboard as well. This time, he met opposition from some crewmen. Nothing could make the menacing men listen to reason. They declared the rotting food was better than no food at all. Tired of arguing, the captain relinquished the potatoes into his sailors' hands. The men ate them as they were, without bothering to cook them. A few hours later, the crewmen died under their companions' horrified gazes. No one uttered a word of protest when the last sack of potatoes passed overboard.

In the meantime, Toine and I fed on the flour the cook had set aside. I was ashamed of our secret but Toine maintained that our entire hoard wouldn't have sufficed to provide a single meal for all the men.

'Besides,' he said, 'do you think that if any of these rascals had food he would share it? They'd rather watch their best friend die. You forget quickly, son. These same fellows didn't hesitate to give you a bath that almost killed you.'

This last argument overcame my remorse. It was all I needed, for man is a coward intent on finding an excuse for his cowardice.

We had now been becalmed for fifty-five days. The last three days, we'd had neither water nor food. Tortured by thirst and hunger, the men wandered about the deck, a crazed glow in their eyes. The captain had ordered the boards nailed across the rum hold doubled, to avoid the risk of plundering. But one night we were awakened by a frightful racket. Armed with axes, the men were hacking their way into the rum hold, in spite of the captain's shouting. And soon, judging by their joyful yells, we could tell they had succeeded. The captain's voice had gone silent. He had probably returned to his cabin. After a moment, the men were back on deck. Toine and I spied on them through a porthole. They were in a state of extreme inebriation. Weakened as they were, it had not taken long for them to get drunk. They made such a frightening sight in the light of the storm lamps: faces with eyes so deeply sunken they looked like holes over monstrously swollen mouths. Most of these poor devils had already lost their teeth. They'd become so thin it was a wonder they were even able to put up such a tumult.

They sat around in groups. The bosun was with them, but in what seemed a normal condition.

Toine pointed a finger. 'Of course that bastard put something aside for himself.'

I couldn't hold back a smile. Hadn't the cook done the same?

We returned to our hammocks. In the stifling heat, we couldn't go back to sleep. Toine had barricaded the door, which made the air inside the galley even more stale.

After a while, I had the feeling something new was happening on the deck. Toine warned me. 'Stay awake, son. We're in for some trouble. They're jawing for now, but they'll soon be knocking each other around. And that goddamned wind isn't rising.'

A terrible scream resounded outside. Through the porthole, we spied a nightmarish scene. In a murderous frenzy, a few men faced one another, knives at the ready. Others, tottering and swaying, clamped their hands around their fellows' throats in a pitiful attempt to throttle them. Worse than animals, they harboured only murder in their hearts. I was horrified at first, but soon the struggles enthralled me. Yes. To my great shame, I stared in fascination.

When the captain appeared, armed with two pistols, the crewmen stopped for a moment, but the lull proved short-lived. A cutlass flew across the deck and caught him in the throat. Blood spurted. The poor man staggered and fell, firing his pistols on the mutineers. One of them clutched his stomach and crumpled into a moaning heap.

The men, wild with fury at the sight of blood, grabbed the captain and moved to throw him overboard.

A voice shouted, 'Why not eat him?'

The crew murmured then fell silent until, as one, the men flung themselves at the captain's corpse and dismembered it in no time at all. A fight began over the miserable remains.

Struck with horror, I could not pull my gaze off the spectacle. My stomach sloshed with nausea as I watched the men who had won chunks of their captain's body. Nothing human was left in these supposedly civilised beings while they stuffed flesh into their blackened mouths – only pleasure was painted across their deformed faces.

Some of them, their appetite unsatisfied, turned toward the wounded sailor who lay on the planks.

'No!' he screamed.

His body was torn apart and the crew battled again over the bleeding scraps.

I couldn't sleep after witnessing this scene. Toine remained silent. Each time I turned, I spotted him swinging his hammock by tapping his foot on the rounded bulkhead. From time to time, he raised his upper body to spit a dark stream of saliva.

The heat had become so unbearable I asked, 'What about opening up a bit?'

'Go ahead,' he said. 'The dogs have gorged themselves.'

I hastened to leave the narrow apertures ajar.

A sickeningly sweet odour invaded our small galley, where no fresh air had penetrated for days. A fit of retching seized me.

'That's blood, son,' Toine said. 'If you can't stand it, shut your hole!'

I complied, but not before casting a last glance outside. The night had moved away, making the stars pale. The line where daylight emerged was streaked with gold. The men, now silent, stretched out on the deck, digesting their crimes. Some stared straight ahead with empty, wild eyes, as if they were seeking oblivion in the distance, where dawn broke into the beginning of a new, unsullied day.

III

I awoke late in the morning. Around midday. In an overpowering heat. The atrocious scenes that had unfolded before my eyes sprang to mind and I sank in deep despair. Would it soon be my turn? What other end could I imagine to such a hideous situation? I must have let out a sigh because Toine's voice resounded in that tiny space.

'Well, then, son. Are you waking up?'

He stood next to a porthole. I stepped up to him and, stomach churning, I ventured a glance outside.

The macabre remains that littered the deck – shreds of flesh sticking to fragments of bones – had turned black as a result of the heat. And – endlessly repetitive mystery of life – a big green fly that wasn't aboard the day before was already buzzing about. The men had resumed drinking rum, in the absurd hope to quench their thirst, but now they could bear it no longer and, their insides on fire, shrieked and writhed in pain, hands clenched on bellies. Several of them, incapable of withstanding the agony, toppled overboard into the immensity of that undrinkable water.

Toine set his hand on my shoulder. 'See, son? Men ain't pretty when rage takes hold of 'em. Worse than rabid dogs.'

'What are they going to do now?' I asked in a shaky voice.

'Bah. They've tasted blood. When they get hungry again they'll start all over, eating each other. Unless that goddamned wind begins to blow.'

The rolling pin on the kitchen counter moved. Toine grabbed my arm and squeezed. 'Did you see that, son?' Since I didn't seem to realise the importance of his words, he went on joyously, 'The current! The current! Can't you hear it? That's the wind coming! By tomorrow, it will be blowing.'

God be praised. The end of our terrible nightmare was nigh. I could hardly believe it. I burst into laughter and tears at the same time. Toine watched me, nodding. He seemed moved by my joy. 'Better not rejoice yet, son. Our troubles ain't over.'

'But who will command the boat now?'

'Fear.'

A shiver crept down my spine.

A few hours later, Toine and I were still locked in our galley. The heat had chased the remainder of the crew away from the deck.

'Can't stand it anymore,' Toine said. 'I'm going to splash some water on to that fucking deck.' Before unlocking the door, he slipped a knife and a pistol under his belt. I moved to follow.

'No, lad. Stay here.' But, seeing the resolve on my face, he handed me another pistol. 'Take this then.'

The sun slapped the deck hard. We stepped into a furnace, our feet burning. We fetched two buckets, tied lines to them, and began to draw seawater, which we splashed down on to the bloodstains, now brownish. I was happy to leave

Toine with the task of throwing the remains overboard. I would not have touched them for all the gold in Peru.

Most of the deck was clear when a sailor sprang out of a hatch, yelling, 'Leave it! It's my food. D'ye 'ear? Leave it.' He brandished an iron stick, or whelp. He was about to crack Toine's skull open. Frozen by surprise, the cook hadn't had the time to draw his weapons. I didn't hesitate. I drew the pistol from my belt and fired on the madman without taking aim. A hole drilled in his forehead, the sailor collapsed. Stupefied, I stared at the corpse and began to shake.

'There, there, son.' Toine tapped me on the shoulder. 'It was him or me. He'd've had me for his next meal if it wasn't for you.' He leant down toward the sailor, to make sure he was dead. 'Come on. Help me. Let's throw him overboard before they think of eating him.'

I grabbed the dead man's feet, not without repugnance, and we swung the corpse into the water. A crowd of shark had encircled the ship since the crew's repasts had filled the air with the reek of blood. They lunged at this unexpected prey and shredded it in the most hateful way.

We went back to the galley in silence. The inside of the cabin felt cool after the searing heat of the deck. We drank a little water, noting that our provisions were rapidly dwindling. Then we ate a small meal of flour, which Toine had moistened to make it edible. Neither the terrible stench nor the taste of mildew bothered us, so overwhelming was our hunger. Nevertheless, I realised I could not continue abusing my stomach for long.

Needless to say, Toine had locked the door as soon as we had stepped inside. An attack was to be expected at any moment. Luckily, we had plenty of bullets and gunpowder. We could only wait now. We stretched out on our hammocks.

As the hours passed, the ship came back to life around us. I fell asleep.

Songs and screams from the deck awoke me. Night had fallen. They're back at it again, I thought in despair. I propped myself up on my elbows and saw Toine standing in front of the porthole. The lamp was unlit. He clearly preferred not to attract attention.

'What's going on?' I asked.

'Those idiots are starting on the rum all over again. If only, instead of sloshing their heads off, they had the idea of hoisting the sails, we'd be moving.'

I got up and peered through the other porthole. The survivors sat around a cask of rum, ripped open. Among them was the bosun, who seemed to be in charge. They dipped their tin cups into the cask and drank, a large amount of the rum trickling down their beards and clothes. So far, they weren't fighting.

I turned to Toine. 'Don't they seem calmer?'

'Don't count on it, son. We'll soon see some odd things if the rum doesn't kill them first.'

Feeling exhausted, I went back to my hammock. Hunger and thirst held me in their grips, but I didn't dare to say anything to Toine, who suffered as much as I did and didn't complain. Besides, he could do nothing about it. We were almost out of water, and we were wise not to eat much of the flour left. An image of the man I had killed assaulted me. On his forehead, a red flower grew and grew until it became enormous. The petals parted, and from the centre a stem sprouted suddenly. Like a pointed finger, it approached slowly, ready to suck me into the dead man's skull. I screamed, and I must have screamed aloud because a hand shook me.

'Hey, there, ship's boy. Shut up.'

Toine's face loomed over me. Although his voice sounded gruff, compassion shone in his eyes.

The dawn was as black as muddy dirt. The stars had fled but the night seemed to last forever. A silence as heavy as the heat hung in the air. The crew must have been wallowing in rum. Toine, who had returned to his hammock, no longer spoke, but in the darkness his pupils glowed like cat's eyes. Suspense enveloped us, impalpable yet present.

A sound like thousands of little paws running on the deck came from outside. Toine leapt from his hammock, shrieking words I could not understand. He glanced through the porthole. When he turned toward me, a broad grin split his face.

'That's life coming from above, son. Can't you

hear it? Rain. At least we can drink as much as we want.'

He went to the door, unlocked it and stepped out. I found him stretched out on the deck, his mouth wide open, avidly lapping up the fortunate tears of the sky. I let myself fall by his side and drank, drank until I became breathless. I rolled about in blessed and delirious joy. Toine put an end to it by tapping me on the shoulder.

'Come on, son. That's enough. Let's go lend a hand to the men.'

I followed him reluctantly. The crew, what was left of it, was busy unfurling the largest sails. As they did so without hoisting them, they had endless trouble to keep the sails facing the sky; the rain falling on the canvases made their weight barely manageable.

Toine and I added our efforts to theirs. I helped them with some repugnance, the frightful scenes I had witnessed too fresh in my mind. Toine, however, spoke to the sailors in friendly tones. His kindness astonished me at first, but I had yet to learn that men are as vulnerable to joy as they are to suffering.

IV

The rain had abated. The sails were hoisted, and the barrels we had placed everywhere filled with that precious gift from the sky. Calm reigned during a botched dawn in which pitch black shaded off into dark grey. Isolated sunrays pierced the clouds to shed light on a terribly flat sea like a lake of tar.

Far, very far away, cracked muted peals of thunder. The storm approached quickly, lightning streaking the leaden ceiling while the sea shivered and quivered under a fresh wind. The ocean began a wild dance. One by one, the sails puffed up, getting rid of the rain, once again as white as angels' wings. The ship listed then picked up speed as the wind shook the riggings in a song of departure.

We cried our joy as one. Then Toine tapped me on the arm. 'That's not all. We need to head somewhere. Let's take a look at the bridge.'

The bosun was already there, several maps unrolled in front of him. As we drew closer, he raised a frightened face.

'Ah,' Toine said. 'The captain tricked you.'

'And you with us,' the bosun riposted. Then he said in friendlier tones, 'Ye've sailed with him for a long time. D'ye know where he kept his instruments?'

'First we should find out what our last position was,' Toine answered.

'How? All I can find is maps that weren't used. Surely the good ones must be hidden with the instruments. I've looked everywhere.' He shouted, 'Sailing without navigation equipment is like sailing blind.'

'We've got the stars,' Toine said in a quiet voice.

'Sure.' The man shot a nasty glance at Toine. 'And who can read the stars on this boat?'

'I can tell you,' Toine said even more calmly.

The bosun grew red in the face, as if he were about to have a heart attack. Toine, hands buried in his pockets, gazed at him, an amused gleam in his eyes. He seemed to enjoy the man's growing exasperation.

'Who?' the bosun yelled.

Toine shifted his quid to the other cheek, spat a long stream of saliva and said in nonchalant tones, 'Me.'

Then he became another man. He straightened his back and took on a hard tone. 'Without me, you're lost. Get it inside your head and tell your mates. I can lead you but on one condition. I want to be your commander. If not, go fuck yourselves. I've got nothing to lose.'

At first, there was silence. Then the bosun, mouth stiff and fists clenched, stepped up to Toine. 'Hey, Toine, are ye taking me fer a fool? Ye the commander? Are ye out of yer mind?'

'Maybe I am, but just take it or leave it. Go tell the others and quickly, because we're running in circles. You can also tell them I'm not against your being my second-in-command.'

The bosun opened his mouth, thought better of it, turned on his heels and went out.

'There we are,' Toine said when he was sure the other couldn't hear him. 'It's settled. And I'll tell you something, son. I'll be lucky if I can tell the difference between the Great Bear and the

Southern Cross.'

'But what will become of us?' I said, terrified.

He shrugged. 'I wonder. But someone must take control of these brutes. We'll manage to gather the weapons. After which, we're in God's hands.'

It was the first time I had heard him mention God. I couldn't tell why, but I didn't like it. Maybe because I had deserted God since my childhood. I had no time to think about it because the bosun came back.

'All right, cook,' he said defiantly. 'Ye've been made commander. But they don't want me to be yer only second mate, they want two.'

'Perfect.' Toine slitted his beady eyes. 'Then go tell them they can navigate with the wind. If I'm the commander, I don't take orders.'

The other looked stunned but once again left without a word.

In the meantime, the wind blew with greater force and the ship listed dangerously. Nobody seemed to care. Through the large windows of the navigation room, we saw the sails all puffed up.

'If they're stiff like that for a long time, they'll tear.'

He stuck his head through the door and shouted into a megaphone I hadn't noticed before. 'Furl the mainsail!'

I felt hesitation among the sailors on deck but it didn't last. Someone repeated the order and Toine was promoted commander of a ship he didn't know how to guide. In other circumstances, I would have thought it funny.

The day passed without incidents. Even though hunger had weakened us, we took courage. When night came, Toine pointed to a star to follow, surely chosen at random, and then he took me to the captain's cabin, our new quarters. It was a wide, comfortable cabin with two bunks. By some miracle, it had not been looted.

'We'll be better off here,' Toine commented.

He searched everywhere but found only one instrument, which he studied closely before showing it to me. 'With this instrument, when it works – and this one doesn't – you can determine the latitude.'

'Really? How?'

'By measuring the height of the sun above the horizon. It's called a sextant. But we don't have the right maps anyways.'

I let Toine choose one bunk and I took the other. An empty stomach prevented me from enjoying the new comfort, after so many nights passed in a crude hammock. Despite my hunger, I soon fell into a deep sleep.

V

When I awoke, I was alone. The ship shook; her shell and hull creaked. I took a sitting position and glanced to the porthole. Enormous waves swelled and broke, their crests crowning with foam before hollowing into abysses. The sight appalled me but I decided to go up to the deck to join Toine, who was probably in the navigation room.

I climbed up but had a hard time opening the hatch to the companionway. I thought I had made it when a terrible wave sent me back down. I tried again and this time, between two billows, I succeeded in hoisting myself on to the deck. Doubling over, I started as fast as I could toward the room. A wave rushed on my heels as I hurled myself through the door.

Toine wasn't in the room. I looked outside and there he was, clutching the tiller. He was taking the commander's role seriously. No one else had ventured on the deck. It was a remarkable spectacle, Toine alone against the wild elements. Like looming skeletons, the mizzenmast and the foremast stood stripped, for the sails had been furled, while the bowsprit, with its sail still stretched out, pointed toward the sky and then plunged into the sea like a flag announcing death.

Surging waves hit the deck in rapid succession. I would never get to Toine. Staying in the cabin was out of the question. A strange uneasiness pushed me to avoid being alone. I decided to try despite danger. The waves had me rolling on the deck against the bulwark and I narrowly escaped going overboard. When I started again, I saw Toine's lips move. He shouted words I could not hear. Finally, one wave heaved me against him. One hand on the helm, he grabbed me with the other until I steadied myself.

'Tie yourself up.' He thrust his chin toward the base of the helm, where a rope was fastened, the same he had used to attach himself.

Gripping the helm with both hands, he righted the ship that had been listing dangerously.

'Just in time to lend me a hand, son,' he said. 'It takes two to hold on to this damned wheel.'

'Where are we heading?'

'That, ship's boy, nobody knows. To avoid any argument about the direction, I ordered them to head straight at the rising sun.'

The wind howled. The dance of the ocean was getting ever wilder. The galleon kept soaring and diving. The mainmast swayed like a drunkard but, free from the heavy sails, it held. The bowsprit, however, still encumbered by the sail, could not withstand the strain. A moment later, the sail swelled so suddenly the bowsprit broke.

The two of us had a hard time keeping the tiller steady. From time to time, it swung free from starboard to port.

After one hour, the bosun appeared. The astonishing ease with which he advanced attested to his long experience with tempests. He shouted to Toine, 'It's my turn, commander.'

I shot an admiring glance to the cook who had managed to force his authority on the crew in such a short time. Back in our cabin, Toine told me he had to fire on a crewman who had refused to carry out the order of furling the sails. The man had tried to stab him. After this incident, all hands had obeyed him with no further discussion.

Our clothes were soaked, and we had to change into dry ones. It was a hard task. With each movement of the ship, I was sent rolling. Toine burst into laughter. 'Son, you'll never be a good sailor.' He continued in harsher tones. 'Sit down on the floor to get dressed, given you can't do better.'

A wave broke over the deck, staggering us. Another followed with a terrible roar. Above us, we heard a crash of breaking wood.

'Jesus Christ, it's the deckhouse getting the hell off the boat. We're going to take in water astern. We must change direction.'

After seizing a rope from under the lower bunk, he tied one end around his waist and threw me the other. 'You're going to follow me to the deck, but not right away. Stay on top of the ladder and hold me until I get to the helm. Then, I'll pull you.'

We hastened to the ladder. Combining our efforts, we pushed the hatch to the companionway. Toine climbed on to the deck. Despite the storm roaring, I heard him bellow.

I stuck my head out of the hatch. 'What's the matter?'

'That bunch of freshwater sailors! They don't even know how to frap a sail. Take a look at the mizzenmast.'

And sure enough, the mast was bending like a young willow, the wind lashing at the spread-out sail with all its might.

Toine leant down and stuck his face close to mine. 'Now listen carefully, son. You've already gotten me out of a tight spot. Here's a chance to do it again. Have to go and cut down that mast. With that goddamned sail, all we do is go round and round. Water is washing over the sides. If I don't stop this, we'll sink in less than one hour. So go down and fetch me the axe from under the bunk.'

I ran down and was back in no time.

'Good job, son. Now hold on.'

And he let a wave sweep him away with its foam. He tugged at the rope like a fish on a line.

The ship veered to one side and I caught the full lash of a wave. I tumbled down the ladder. Hands clutching the rope, I couldn't break my fall. The shock jarred me. Had it jarred Toine even more? I clambered back up. There he was, pushed back to the starting point. At the sight of me, he grumbled.

'Another like that one, and we're done for.' He struggled to his feet. 'Come on. We try again.'

Where did this sinewy, wizened middle-aged man find his inexhaustible strength? He was extraordinary. Only an iron will could overcome the fatigue that plagued us.

This time he managed to reach the mast.

He had already cut the ties and was about to hack at the mast when two crewmen, yelling and gesticulating, bounded in his direction. No doubt they intended to stop him. But the bosun, who must have known that the mast had to be cut down, interposed himself. Both sailors threw themselves at him. Only I noticed the enormous wave breaking on the ship. I buried my head between my shoulders and gripped the rope with all my strength, my full weight balanced against the ladder. The entire ocean seemed to crash over me. When I was able to raise my head, I saw Toine hugging the mast while the three others rolled all the way to the bulwark. A bow wave dragged them the length of the deck. They lay astern, unmoving. Another surge lifted their bodies and yanked them overboard into the tempest.

In the meantime, Toine had been hewing at the mast. I heard a crack followed by a muffled noise and glanced at him. The old devil had managed to cut the mizzenmast down. But he was nowhere to be seen. Panicked, I tugged at the rope. But with every new receding wave I had to give way a bit more and I feared discovering a drowned man at the end of the rope. He finally appeared, his head bleeding. The sea had calmed a little and the ship forged ahead again. I succeeded in dragging Toine down to our cabin and hoisting him on to his bunk. He scarcely breathed but he was alive. The gash in his forehead did not seem to be serious. After fetching some rum, I lifted his head and had him swallow a few mouthfuls.

Several hours passed before he opened his eyes. As the ship entered the centre of the storm, the ocean doubled its violent dance, tossing and rolling the ship like a toy. Twice I climbed up to the deck but saw no one. The tiller, left to its own devices, spun at full speed. Not knowing how to steer, I had no intention to try. In such a sea, I might have broken my arms. I returned to the cabin and sat down by Toine.

He had not regained consciousness. His eyes, open, held a vacant stare. He did not seem to recognise me. I placed compresses on his forehead and forced him to swallow some rum but he remained inert. Helpless, I watched the day fade as I sat there, prey to melancholy. My hunger had become intolerable. After a while, all I could think of was food. I was ready to devour anything. I did not recall seeing Toine throwing away our rotting flour but neither did I remember spotting it in our cabin. Thinking it inedible, he had probably left it in the galley. Mildewed flour seemed a delicacy now. Without further hesitation, I headed for the galley.

The end of the day had brought no lessening of the tempest. When I poked my head through the trapdoor to the quarterdeck, an enormous wave beat at me. I withdrew and waited for a while before trying again. Nothing on earth could have deterred me. The fourth try proved successful. I carefully closed the door to avoid flooding the lower deck. Hanging on to whatever was within reach, I made my way toward the galley. It took me an incredible amount of time, every moment a further risk of being swept away. When I arrived there, I was in for a cruel disappointment. The cupboards had been ripped open and the interior ransacked. Even the boards on the floor had been torn loose. Traces of struggles everywhere. Blood smeared on the bulkheads. The surviving crewmembers, upon finding Toine's stash of flour, had battled over it. I drank from our store of rainwater, which relieved my hunger a little. I resumed searching, in the hope that another hidden cache had escaped the looters, but I found nothing beside a little flour left at the bottom of a torn sack. In despair, I made it back to the cabin.

A pistol shot punctuated the noises of the storm. Through the porthole, I saw the last survivors locked in combat for the only remaining lifeboat. It was their ultimate battle for life, and they fought ferociously. A gigantic wave washed over them, carrying men and lifeboat away. The mainmast shattered on the deck with a tremendous sound. At once, the galleon, gathering speed, began to spin.

Although I knew nothing about seafaring, I was convinced the ship was caught in a whirlpool. I went back to the cabin, walking between two gigantic liquid walls. The seam had opened its mouth to swallow us alive. I finally opened the hatch and let myself slide down.

Toine was seated on his bunk. Thank Heaven he was quite alert. In a few words I told him what had happened and described the whirlpool that trapped us.

This last piece of information shook him out of his lethargy.

'We've fallen into the very soul of the cyclone, son. Like *The Flying Dutchman*. Are you sure there's no one else on board?'

'Certain.'

'Well, then. That's too bad. We must manage to right the boat, if it's not too late.'

He stood up and gripped the bunk to steady himself. He'll never make it up to the deck, I thought.

I had misjudged him. Not only did he make it to the deck but, with some difficulties, the two of us got to the helm in one piece.

A liquid wall enclosed us, and we spun within it at breakneck speed. The watery mass formed millions of circles that reflected the grisly colours of the twilight sky. Toine grasped the tiller but let it go.

'Too late,' he said. 'Even the combined strength of a thousand men wouldn't suffice to resist the pull.'

The galleon was attracted to the centre of the storm. It spun ever faster and we had to lie on the floor. The centrifugal force became so strong we were pinioned to the deck. As the deck was vertical, we felt as though we were standing at attention to witness our own execution. The sky above us was as wide as the palms of two hands. We were sinking into the depths.

An explosion was followed by a sound like a long sigh. The pressure that kept us up against the deck decreased as the ship rotated more slowly and righted itself, although it continued to list dangerously. The mainmast rolled from one side to the other, smashing everything in its path. Now the ship listed low in the heaving sea.

Toine shouted. 'We need to pass over the other side. It's going belly-up, and if we get caught under it we don't have a chance.'

We clung to ropes, using them to slide down the hull toward the water. Although I didn't know how to swim, I wasn't anxious because I felt as if this adventure was happening to someone else. Without Toine by my side, I would have drowned. He held my head above the water. When the mainmast floated within reach, he took hold of it. In a haze, I glimpsed the ship one last time, its keel sticking out of the water.

Then I lost consciousness.

VI

I opened my eyes but didn't realise where I was. The deafening noise of the sea and the wind, which seemed to be blowing out of Hell, brought back all the ghastly memories.

Total darkness enveloped me as I lay stretched out on the mainmast, the cords that lashed me to it preventing any movement. And Toine. Where was he? I called out to him. The only answer I got was the sound of the wind drowning out my voice. Feeling alone in the middle of nowhere, I wept.

Cold and weakness sent shivers through my body, which vibrated like a violin string. The night dragged on. I was starting to think it would never end when a moon ray pierced the inky sky. It looked like death brandishing a light, but the ashen pillar comforted me all the same.

A storm broke. I opened my mouth wide to quench my thirst. Then the rain abated, the wind subsided and thunder rumbled – an evil omen. A galaxy of stars unfolded above. I was passing into another world, another life. I knew that until my last hour I would never forget this sense of transition.

The darkness that had once again conquered the sky became tattered, and then vanished, and the firmament appeared, filled with stars larger and brighter than those I had seen before.

Delusion sparked odd thoughts. God, tired of monotony, had reshaped the Heavens.

Once more, I lost consciousness.

When I awoke again, I was astonished to be alive and still tied to the mast. The dawn was turning into day, the sea becalmed. I raised my head as much as my restraints allowed it and saw Toine lying at the other end of the mast. He seemed unconscious. I called to him feebly. He did not answer. If only I could draw closer to him. Seawater had swollen my ropes and I could not untie the knots. Now that the dangers of the tempest had receded, I was trapped and did not know how to escape. Cramps and a terrible pain in my back made me suffer. My ribcage had been weighing down on the mast for hours and I could only breathe in gasps.

All around us was a liquid void. The day was growing brighter and, on the horizon, a strange red hue preceded the sun – like blood. It advanced slowly in the sky. I had never seen anything similar and I believed I was hallucinating. But when the sun rose, the same colour speckled its sphere, as though it had sustained an injury. I could not believe my eyes.

An exclamation made me start – Toine was also staring at the strange phenomenon. I called to him. He smiled.

'I've lost my mind, son, or are you seeing the same thing?'

'I see the same.' A morbid thought occurred to me. 'Looks like it's bleeding–'

'Oh, shut up!' he said, cutting me off.

The bloodstained disk continued to rise. The light was taking on a shade of baked brick. The heat had increased. After a struggle, I was able to loosen my ties and went to sit beside Toine, dipping my feet in the water. We did not speak, torn between relief at being alive and superstitious fear inspired by that awkward sight – so contrary to the normal order of things. Heat already gripped us and poked us with hot irons. It became so unbearable we had to dip in the water to cool off. Weakened as we were, this exertion soon fatigued us. The same hopeless void besieged us.

Toward the middle of the day mysterious beasts appeared. Ten metres at least wide, they resembled giant jellyfish or octopuses. Tentacles as thick as tree trunks. Umbrella shells strangely speckled with red – a detail that made them even more repulsive. They swam all over the swelling waves, so numerous the water had become a bloodied sheet spread out to cover the ocean. As soon as we spotted these monsters, we stretched our limbs along the mast, avoiding any contact, ropes retied around our waists. The sun was sinking now. We prepared to face a fearful night.

As the day dwindled, the sea lost its transparency, becoming the colour of rust. We could see only the monsters that broke the surface of the water. They became iridescent in the crimson light in which the gathering dusk wrapped us.

'It must be a reflection of that damned sun,' Toine said.

Nevertheless, when the bleeding sun had sunken into the depths, the beasts continued to glow with a phosphorescent red under those unfamiliar stars.

Toine made a brave attempt to speak of the tiny noctiluca and protozoa that abound in the sea. 'When the sea is rough, they seem phosphorescent.' But this explanation could not account for the red hue that had enveloped us since dawn.

'Son, I've never seen anything like this before. It's like another world.'

We didn't dare to fall asleep. The sea had become oil. The sky bore unseen depths, and a fearsome silence hung over us. Our mast remained still.

Something malefic hovered in the air, without a name but palpable. A dimensionless cavern was swallowing me alive, its vaults riddled with shining worms vitrified in death by their own lights.

The aquatic monsters continued breaking the surface of the water without the faintest sound.

'Are we deaf?' I asked.

'No, son,' he said in perplexed tones, 'given that we can hear each other.'

Asking no more questions, I gave in to the torpor that possessed me.

'Look, son. It's starting all over again.'

Toine had crawled closer and was gently shaking me. I opened my eyes to his ravaged face, which looked like an old apple long forgotten in a barn. Only his eyes shone with extraordinary brightness.

I resented him for rousing me from a sleep that had banished thirst, hunger and fear. Now my belly felt painfully constricted. It was my sole preoccupation. I shot a distracted glance at the phenomenon that reddened everything. In my weakened state, thousands of golden dots danced before my eyes. The sight of all that undrinkable water only worsened my thirst.

Toine said, 'Listen, son. Try moistening your lips with some seawater, but be careful not to swallow any.'

I followed his advice but could not help but swallow a mouthful. I was expecting a terrible burning sensation but the water was as sweet and fresh as any spring water. I dipped my face in it. Yesterday's monsters had disappeared.

Toine gazed at me with a sad face. Of course, he thought I had gone mad. After watching me cup my hands and drink repeatedly, he succumbed and did likewise. To his astonishment, he quelled his thirst.

'How is it possible?' I cried.

He shrugged. 'Oh, this at least can be explained. Sometimes, a big river enters the sea and pushes its waters far into it. But I don't know about all the other odd things. No, son. I've travelled all the seas in my goddamned life and I've never seen anything like this.'

During the day, we managed to capture an octopus. The beast was a metre in diameter. Several times we were forced to follow it into the water. Cutting his sack open turned out to be very hard, and when we finally succeeded, a black ink splattered us. When at last it lay still, we shared its rubbery flesh. To our famished stomachs, that filthy meal was a banquet. We recovered some of our strength, to say nothing of our shaken spirits.

The heat, as unbearable as before, produced mirages. Mountains appeared before us, then beaches. Boats approached. The first mirage did not disappear as quickly as the others. It persisted on the horizon – a disquieting sight. It was a formidable mountainous chain of volcanic origin, red and rising against the sky like the Tower of Babel. We expected to see it disappear, but at the end of the day it was still there. Hope formed in our hearts. Then our joy burst forth. Land. We were going to set foot on land. We wept like children.

A gentle current pushed us toward these mountains. As we drew closer, they looked like an infinite rocky wall. The effect was overpowering. Oppressive.

'If only we could find something to eat there,' said Toine. 'I haven't seen one bird flying around.'

'We can always fish.'

'Right,' Toine said with a touch of reluctance.

As we arrived near the shore, evening came. For me the night promised to be euphoric. I hadn't felt so light-hearted in a long time. Toine, on the other hand, kept muttering, 'A world upside down. Yes. It's a world upside down.'

I even had the impression that for the first time since I had met him, the old sea wolf was praying.

PART TWO

VII

For the third time, scarlet light announced the rising sun. Our mast chose this moment to bring us ashore along a coast of small coves. A beach of rusty sand hemmed a tiny bay hacked into crumbly rocks. I was the first to set foot on land. I have no words to describe the joy I felt in finding myself on solid ground. I jumped, sang, laughed. As for Toine, he did not share my enthusiasm. He even wore a funereal face.

'You're not happy?' I said. 'I think we're safe now.'

'Of course I'm happy, son,' he answered in cheerful tones that sounded strained.

Realising he wished to conceal his real thoughts, I let it pass. My joy was too vast to be spoiled.

The rocks around us bore the same crimson colour that prevailed in this unknown land. The sand under our feet was incredibly fine, like dusting powder. I picked up a handful. It was so impalpable it slipped through my fingers. I got rid of the sand by throwing it into the sea. The water took on the colour of blood. Amazed, I turned to Toine. He had noticed as well. The expression on his face chilled me. We stood for a moment, staring at the red spot that discoloured the water.

Then Toine pivoted on his heels. 'We ought to investigate the place before night falls.'

'And find something to eat,' I added.

It took us a good hour to get to the top of the rocky circle. Although not high, the rocks were brittle. For every metre we conquered, we had to retrace our steps, falling three metres back, among clouds of a red dust that blinded and suffocated us.

As soon as we reached the crest, we saw the formidable chain of mountains that had given us that painful sense of oppression. It rose far away, at least several dozen miles distant. Despite the distance, we made out dark patches, surly woods stretching out at the feet of the mountains, as if the shadow had fertilised them. To reach the mountainous chain, we would have to cross a barren red desert.

'First we must find a way to carry water,' said Toine.

'How?' I cried. 'We've got nothing. Only our hands and our tattered clothes.

'That's why we must find something. Or the heat will kill us.'

We went back to the beach, choosing a spot other than the place where we had run ashore. Unlike at the first tiny bay, everything was monumental here. A gigantic arc of red sand like talcum powder bordered a thick red wall that rose toward the sky, flaunting the wounds of time. These furrows traced grimacing masks resembling mineral giants petrified during uncountable centuries.

No plant life was discernable on the vertical wall. The atmosphere reminded me of a sepulchre but without the odour of decomposition, as if time had consumed the compost made by the cadavers.

We followed this natural curtain of walls cracked by deep ravines similar to the one we had taken to come down to the beach. We remained silent, the hideous beauty of the place weighing down on us.

Arrived at the other end, we had found nothing that could be used to carry water. And now hunger bit at us. Toine kept swearing through gritted teeth. It was his way of expressing pain. We had to get past the cliff that stopped our advance. Retracing our steps was out of the question. We knew we would find nothing. Still mumbling, Toine entered the water first. I followed but lost my footing immediately. He pulled me up by the hair, saying with kindness, 'Sorry, son. I forgot you couldn't swim. Find holds in the cliff and stay near me. You'll be safe.'

I did not agree. The rock crumbled under my fingers, dust falling in the sea. The water became purple where the dust fell. We were wading in blood now.

'God-damn fucking place,' said Toine, picking me up for the second time.

I kept gulping down mouthfuls, but what worried me wasn't the risk of drowning, only the filthy water that made me retch.

We dragged ourselves to the other side of the rocky talon. Seeing a beach similar to the one we had just left, Toine spat with barely restrained rage. 'I've had enough of this.'

'Look over there!' I pointed to black crevices in the red wall.

He squinted in that direction. 'Those are caves. Maybe we'll find something. Let's go.'

As we drew close, the crevices widened into gaping mouths; their dark hollows devoured the wall. It took us two hours to reach the first cave. Its proportions crushed us, making us feel as small as the specks of sand under our feet. From a narrow vault, the cave stretched to a hundred metres at the base. Its depth, impossible to gauge from where we stood, seemed to continue into an inscrutable night.

Fear took hold of me as I penetrated the cave. Toine must have sensed it because he grasped my arm firmly. 'Come on, son. Pull yourself together.'

The void swallowed his voice and, like a string of prayers recited inside a cathedral, his words echoed several times, sent back by the immense vault with gaping wounds of darkness.

Our eyes, still filled with the bright light outside, barely focused in that sudden night. We stumbled forward like blind men. Under our feet, the sand had given way to a solid rock as cold as a tombstone washed by the winter rain. Our movements, even our breaths, captured by the echo, ricocheted back and forth in the shadows at an uncanny speed. Seized by fury, Toine swore. The cavern shuddered with such a force a noise of fallen rock resounded like a peal of thunder. Then a loud cracking, followed by silence.

The silence wasn't total, though.

A strange hiss, like a muffled beating heart, subsisted. We froze, incapable of speech. The rhythmic sound diminished and ended. Meanwhile, our eyes adapted to the darkness and we were able to see the fantastic walls of that subterranean place. I wish they had remained invisible.

Here and there, statues emerged from the shadows. Numerous statues in different poses. Their faces were contorted, expressing terror, and frightful to look upon, as though the sculptor had intended to illustrate only one emotion: abject, deadly fear.

Men. Women. Each carved line, rough or elegant, looked as if they had been moulded into the rock itself. I made out mothers who clutched their children, visages turned toward their little ones, suffused with faint maternal smiles. Among these statues with human forms stood several figures of animals and birds, particularly albatrosses with their wings spread. Strange primitive tools lay scattered on the floor of this mind-blowing museum. A few bones as well. In places, darkened patches marked the spots where hearths had been.

We picked up vases shaped like rough amphorae made of baked earth, and swiftly turned our backs to the workshop of that splendid sculptor, as talented as God but devoid of His divine gift of grace, life and laughter.

Much to our relief, we finally stumbled out into the blinding light.

'Weird place,' Toine said after a long moment. Holding at arm's length one of the amphorae he was carrying, he added, 'Look, son. Whoever sculpted those statues wasn't able to mould an object as simple as this one. Strange, d'you agree?'

'You're right,' I cried. 'I hadn't thought of that.'

'What counts is that we have enough containers to carry our water until we get to the woods. Once we're there, we'll surely find something to eat.'

I remained unconvinced. I would never be able to get to the woods in my current state of extreme weakness.

We went back to the beach to fill our amphorae. Then we entered one of the ravines within the red wall. The ravine narrowed as we climbed. When we arrived on top, we were advancing sideways like crabs. A sound came from afar. The same muffled beat that had frightened us inside the cavern.

We trod a desert of fine sand that a light breeze lifted in short undulating waves. At a distance, in the waning light, the dark strip on the foothills of the mountain mingled with the deep red of the sky – an even more eerie sight.

We hoped to reach the woods before night. Hunger made me stumble. Toine steadied me and whispered encouraging words, as if he didn't suffer as well. Our progress slowed further.

The sun set fire to the horizon, making it a blade of reddened steel. The sky took on a violet hue. Since dawn, not the tiniest patch of blue had been visible in that strange sky. Finally, the black curtain fell and unknown stars shone.

'Let's stop here,' said Toine. 'We risk walking in circles.'

We lay down on sand as soft as velvet. The light breeze blew it into our faces. The grains of sands brushed my face like the fingers of a little child.

We did not speak. I assumed Toine, like myself, was studying the sky to discern a familiar constellation. Was this the place a teacher had spoken about when I was little? If memory serves, he had called it 'Olympia,' the gods' abode according to the ancient Greeks. For a moment I was tempted to voice my thoughts, but then I said to myself that my thoughts were wandering, and I discarded the idea. I closed my eyes and thought only of falling asleep.

Sleep overcame me. The sentiment of fear that had been stalking me these past three days did not slacken its grip. My heartbeat thumped with an odd rhythm.

Toine's voice made me start.

'Can you hear something?'

'No,' I said, barely awake. 'I can only hear my heartbeat. Louder.'

'You're wrong, son. It's not your heart. It's the sound we heard in the cavern. I think it's coming from below. Stick your ear to the ground.'

Instead of complying, I let myself fall asleep again. As the earth swallowed me into a deep slumber, the rhythmic pounding resounded louder than ever.

VIII

I awoke in the throes of stomach cramps. Dawn had just broken and the sun was still hidden behind those mysterious and frightening mountains, which were taking on their red hue. Toine tossed and turned by my side.

'So did you sleep well, son?'

'Yes, but I'm hungry.' I pressed my hands over my aching stomach.

Toine spread his hands, palms up. 'Ah. Don't think about it for now.'

He sat down, grabbed an amphora and handed it to me. 'Drink a little water. You'll feel better.'

I drank a few mouthfuls with scant enthusiasm, yet after an instant my cramps diminished.

Toine had turned his wrinkled face toward the mountains.

'Son,' he intoned, 'I didn't sleep last night and I've had a lot of time to think. A question's nagging me. I wonder if we're still on our planet, the Earth. See, a light like this, those unknown stars, I've never heard about in all my god-damned life.'

He fixed his small black eyes on me. 'Tell me. What do you think of it?'

I made a gesture of ignorance and he shrugged.

'Of course. How would you know? This is your first journey. You know nothing about the world.' He rose to his feet. 'Time to go.'

The dark patch at the foothills gained in clarity. We were still very far away but, to judge by its green hue, it was a forest. As we moved closer, the patch became more distinct. The sun burned us, making our constant struggle against weakness even harder.

To cap it all, when we halted to drink, we discovered our provision of water had turned red. We drank it all the same. Its warm temperature strengthened the impression we were drinking blood.

We resumed our march toward hope. In the evening, we found the first signs of plant life. The ground was firmer; the dust had become scarce. A sparse thin grass sprouted. We threw ourselves at it and grazed the meagre vegetable without pulling it up. Was it autosuggestion or did the grass have a real nutritional value? In truth, we felt better and slept better, too.

At the break of dawn, after drinking our putrid water, we resumed our trek. A few hours later, we reached the edge of the forest.

Immense trees mingled the green hue of their canopy with the purple of the sky. The trunks were encircled by vines as thick as my arm, curiously coiled like serpents' spires. Toine tried to pull at one of the spires but could not and beckoned me to come and help him. Our combined efforts proved in vain. Only the thin bark of the vine came off, and the bare stem slipped under our fingers and coated them in a viscous red sap.

'We need something sharp,' Toine said, his gaze searching the ground. He saw a flat slab of stone, surely the rest of a volcanic eruption. I wondered why he had made a point of cutting the vine. He could not think of eating it, could he? The moment was badly chosen for questioning my companion, so I watched him hack at the vine with the sharp stone. He uttered a curse and let go of the stone.

'It's moving. The god-damned thing is moving!'

At first, I believed it a hallucination, but it was real. Very slowly, like a boa constrictor, the vine contracted, spire by spire. It undulated like a living animal. A strange wheezing came from the trunk the creeper was strangling, and a thick red sap oozed from tiny pores in the wood. Toine glanced at me with a stupefied expression.

'Have I gone mad?'

My own expression told him I was seeing the same thing.

'Let's go, son.' He grabbed my arm. 'This place is cursed.'

'Where to?' I cried in despair.

'The mountain. Maybe it's different on the other side. But we need something to eat first.'

The farther we penetrated that gruesome forest, the greater our conviction grew. We would never find anything edible besides the grass. That could calm our aching stomachs but contained no nutrients. For hours, we trudged on under that incredible canopy. Several times, I let myself fall to the ground, refusing to advance. It was so exhausting to struggle for each next breath. Without Toine's friendly but firm insistence, I would have welcomed death.

The day was ending when we came across a clearing in the forest. Several huts rose, in various states of preservation. In that great silence, we did not even consider the possibility that someone could still live in the village. We entered the nearest hut. Inside, we found a few statues like those we had seen in the cavern. On the ground, a sack half worn away by time; a few green shoots wormed out of its holes. Toine bounced on it, shouting, 'Potatoes!'

He was right. We had found sweet potatoes, which were beginning a new life. We devoured them with unspeakable joy.

Finally sated, a state we had not known for weeks, we visited the small village. Inside each hut, we met the same statues of people or animals. Only the postures varied. The expressions were of torment, except for the young children, whose features remained relaxed. And crudely shaped utensils littered the floor. Neither Toine nor I had notions of the arts but we were both struck by such contrast. Moreover, each hut harboured a hearth filled with ashes, and the wooden bowls abandoned on the floor contained the remains of dried food. It looked like a sudden misfortune had frozen the inhabitants before they could flee. But no traces of struggle were visible, nor did we see any volcanic lava.

Toine repeated, 'It can't be. Looks like they were turned to glass. And they realised what was happening to them.'

I asked what he meant by that.

'D'you remember the stone I picked up this morning to cut the vine? It was vitrified as well. Probably by the heat of a volcano. An eruption, you see?'

'Are you saying it's what happened here?'

'No. One could think so, but it's impossible. If lava had passed here, we would have found only traces of a new life, tiny new plants – provided pollen had been caught in the wind before all was destroyed.'

I knew nothing about this vegetal life the wind carries across and beyond the seas. Toine did not try to explain. He simply set a hand on my shoulder, his smile doubled by every crevice in his old face.

The horizon began to glow with that sanguine hue. Toine picked up two stones and rubbed them together. Sparks burst out. Toine approached the sack that had contained potatoes. After a few moments, the old fabric took fire. We ran into the other huts to look for inflammable material. Soon the flames danced. In the darkness, the twisted reflections made the grimacing statues even more sinister. Thanks to the trembling lights, the statues moved.

We lay down close to the fire. Along with the crackling of the fire, we heard the muffled rhythmic beat that rose from the bowels of the earth.

We took turns getting up to feed the fire. We needed the light more than the warmth.

Until a heavy slumber took possession of me.

IX

I awoke to sunbeams gliding through the misshapen branches of the roof, streaking the floor with bright stripes. Toine had gone out. I slipped into a reverie. Such a sense of well-being had eluded me for a very long time. Perhaps the potatoes I had eaten yesterday had given me a new strength. Unfortunately, my roaming gaze focused on one of those statues. My anguish returned. A bad presentiment clutched my heart. Good Lord, I thought. I hope nothing has happened to him. I rose and ran outside.

In the bright red light, the village was a remarkable sight. Toine was nowhere to be seen, so I went to inspect every hut. I did not find him so I rushed into the forest, hoping to come across some fruit to appease my hunger. And I saw many of those fruits, only they were placed too high for me to pluck them. I decided to content myself with vine sprouts. I had pulled one from the ground and I was about to put it in my mouth when it wriggled. It moved like a snake, in slow motion. Stupefied, I stared at it without thinking of throwing it away, while it coiled itself around my wrist. I came to my senses at last and tried to get rid of it, but the vine seemed stuck to my skin. I had to tear it off. Minuscule beads of blood covered the place where the vine had hugged my wrist. Overcome by disgust, I tried to chase away the horrid idea that the plant was carnivorous. On the ground, the vine continued to writhe like a reptile.

Stomach knotted, I resumed looking for Toine. Through the sparse holes in the green canopy, the sun darted several tiny red eyes on me. The hot breeze that set the foliage a-shivering gave me the impression these eyes mocked me.

To add to the creepy sensation, I could see no sign of animals, not a bird, not even an insect – no tiny vermin that made a blade of glass a little world teeming with life. I cried Toine's name to no avail. My anguish increased with every step until I arrived at a river. The water was sweet and fresh. I took a long drink, and then I started along the riverbank. The crystalline sound of falling water called to me. In my solitude, such a familiar noise reassured me. The waterfall was more distant than I had thought, but when I reached it, I did not regret my effort, despite Toine's absence. The sight was magnificent. From the middle of a gigantic slab of rock as smooth as a wall spurted furious waters that fell in a sumptuous curtain of white foam. The foam fanned out into myriads of droplets like a scattering of diamonds. With the waterfall, the river made a leap of at least one hundred metres.

Gigantic, bright-hued flowers adorned the banks sprinkled by the foam. The smallest flower was twice my size. The fat grass flaunted a bright green. I approached one of these unknown flowers. It was white, rimmed with mauve and sporting a yellow heart. As I drew near, it closed slowly. Then it began to inch toward me, opening its petals again. Panicked, I jumped backward. The flower bent and darted down like a butterfly net, covering the ground at the spot where I had been standing a second before. I heard a horrid noise of suction. Then the flower retook its vertical position, its petals closing up again. Nothing but bare soil remained. It had sucked up everything, grass and shrubs, just as it would have swallowed me whole, had I not retreated.

Cold sweat ran down my back as I watched the enormous transparent stem beginning the digestion. I stood there as if hypnotised. Only after a moment did I succeed in pulling myself away from the spectacle. The extraordinary beauty of the place, a beauty that had fascinated me at first, now only inspired me with revulsion I was beyond fear, and I could only feel loathing. I pondered this feeling. It was the reason why the lost souls sojourn in Hades without revolting against it, for revulsion is the beginning of acceptance. If acceptance is death to normal people, it is the logical response for those who refuse to reflect on the questions that would save them.

I don't know how I managed to go back through the woods. I simply found myself at the edge of the village inhabited by the stone people. I heard someone call my name but, still under the spell of the forest, I did not answer.

I was walloped on the shoulder, bringing me back to reality. Toine stood in front of me, arms overflowing with strangely shaped fruits. I seized a few of them and ate avidly. They had no flavour but were enough to satisfy my hunger.

I recounted my misadventure to Toine. He listened and nodded. I wondered whether he believed me. He must have divined my thoughts, for he answered, 'Calm down, son. I've seen strange things, too. This place is cursed. We've got to get out of here at any cost. Losing your head is not the best way.'

We returned to the hut where we had slept the night before. Sitting on the floor, we remained silent for a moment, under our grimacing hosts' watchful eyes. We ate some more fruits. The one I was munching was red-fleshed, like a blood orange. As big as a watermelon, it had a pleasant flavour. I asked Toine by what miracle he had managed to pluck the fruits.

'I just bent down and picked them up from the highest treetops.' Seeing my stupefied expression, he explained, 'I haven't gone mad yet, son. Dunno how, by the way. I'm going to tell you what happened to me. I left at the crack of dawn. The red day wasn't up yet and the stars were still there. You were sleeping so soundly I didn't want to wake you up. I reached the forest very quickly. But something wasn't right. I kept seeing the stars while they should have been hidden by the canopy. And I'm going to tell you why. All around me, the tree trunks were lying on the ground. As if, during the night, woodsmen had felled them. I was hungry, so I only had eyes for the fruits lying at my feet. I'd eaten so many my belly was going to burst. See what I mean? I just had to bend down to pick them up.

'Then I collected more fruit to take back to the village. But I began to get worried since my hunger no longer occupied my mind. There must have been some reason why all those gigantic trees were lying down on the ground like that, their tops facing the great mountain, visible in the distance.

'At first, seeing the blood-red sun going up reassured me a bit. But not for long. Imagine a terrifying cracking noise like green wood, multiplied a thousand times. The whole forest was moving. Yes, son. Don't think I'm raving mad and I'm talking nonsense. Not a trunk remained on the ground. The trees were all straightening up, very slowly. D'you want to know what I thought then? Well, from the tallest tree to the smallest shrub, the forest was saluting the mountain. I thought I was dreaming. That whole forest, praying, all the trees bent and then straightening up like after kneeling down. I tell you, if the ground had started talking right then, I wouldn't have been surprised.'

I studied Toine, wondering if he was out of his mind. He shrugged.

'So you believe I'm mad, don't you? Believe me. I ain't mad. And neither are you.'

We fell silent. I could see Toine wanted to say more but hesitated.

He broke the silence with one question. 'You heard anything last night?'

'No. I was sleeping soundly. I don't even remember if I dreamt.'

'Maybe I'm mistaken. But hear me out. While the forest was kneeling down, I heard from the far-off mountains, something like a song. It sounded like the wind in the halyards during a tempest. And then, from beneath the ground, came that rhythm. You know, that beat. But it was stronger than before. The ground pulsed under my feet. It was like the earth's guts were heaving.'

He closed his mouth, his gaze turning to the shadows formed by the grimacing statues.

'Son,' he said after a while. 'I'm beginning to wonder whether… Oh, nothing is strange enough here, right? I'm wondering whether the rhythm we hear is these statues' hearts beating beneath the ground. I can't believe a mad artist made them. Nor did God, who is said to be good. Then, I can only think of one place; maybe we've come to the doors of Hell. Maybe it's the red of lost souls that tinges the sky. But this nature that consumes itself cannot understand the souls' suffering. Neither God nor the Devil would enjoy playing such comedy.'

I didn't understand what Toine was saying, but I knew we needed to find a way out of this place, or a great misfortune would befall us.

'What shall we do now?' I asked.

Toine, who seemed lost in his thoughts, started, looked at me as if he did not recognise me, and then answered, 'First, we go back to the river. We're going to need a lot of water. And then we're going toward the mountain. I'm sure the key to the mystery lies there.'

The thought of going back to the place I had left with so much fear made me shudder. I said nothing, though, and helped Toine to search the huts for something more practical than our small amphorae.

'Come here and lend me a hand, son. I think I've found what we're looking for.'

Toine was tugging at a dark bulky object that resembled a huge terracotta flask. It was stuck behind several of those stone figures. We had to move the statues. We began our task, taking a thousand precautions, owing to a certain superstitious awe. One of the statues teetered too much and collapsed before we could right it. It broke with a dull noise and the head, which had come off, rolled a few metres away, like a ball.

We stared at the debris on the floor.

'It can't be,' Toine cried. 'There's a skeleton inside.'

It was true. A skeleton stretched out under our gaze made of petrified stone like the surface of the statue.

Without further comment, Toine turned to free the flask. As for me, I could not tear my gaze off that ribcage and the snapped spine that looked so natural. The shape was just an imitation of life, but the verisimilitude was so shockingly strong I would have held those remains as one rocks an infant.

'Come away, son. I, too, feel they're like brothers, but their predicament scares me. Let's go fetch some water. Let's enjoy life for as long as we can.'

He loaded the very big flask on to his back and we left without a backward glance.

Outside, a light wind was blowing, making the

leaves the musical instruments of a plant world that undulated, rocked, coiled and tightened its spires around the doleful, wounded trunks oozing red drops like tears streaming down children's cheek. It was a world full of life moving toward death.

Toine, who marched a few steps in front of me, stopped in his tracks and put the flask on the ground. 'Come quickly, son!' he shouted. 'I'm sure it tastes great.'

I understood at once and threw myself at him. 'Don't touch it!'

But he had already seized a vine three times bigger than the one with which I had struggled. Too dazed by the spectacle I had witnessed at the waterfall, I had not mentioned this misadventure to Toine, so he was not on his guard.

Despite my swift intervention, the horrible wooden stem had coiled not around his wrist but his throat. Now the coils squeezed, hard and harder. I pulled with all my strength but the vine did not give way. Toine's face was already taking on an ugly greyish hue. He was choking. His eyes bulged. Not knowing what else to do, I bit at the vine like a savage. The living rope slackened. I had just the time to jump aside before the vine could grip me as well. The creeper continued its reptilian movements a few steps away while I knelt at Toine's side. Lying on the ground, he did not stir. He had not, however, lost consciousness because he stared at me with wild eyes.

'Thank you, son. You saved me from a painful death.' He massaged his throat where large black blotches were appearing on his dark skin. 'I tip my hat to you. You've got guts. Weren't you scared?'

I recounted my own adventure.

'Ah, you've been there before. That's lucky. So you could save me.'

'Yes and no. If I had talked about it, you would have been more careful.'

I picked up the flask and we resumed our trek over that cursed land.

We marched side by side. From time to time, Toine rubbed his throat but did not complain. His easy smile had vanished, replaced by astonishment, not even fear. Noticing my furtive glances, he said, 'I'm so sorry, son, that you've got to be stuck with me in my waking nightmare. But let's not lose our heads, or we will never come out of this. Here, everything is a mystery. Don't expect to find answers. Like everywhere else, death prowls alongside of life. Only it's more visible here.'

He uttered these words for my peace of mind, but as he spoke so, I felt more and more lonely. Toine, devoid of fear, was taking the path of acceptance. It was clear enough. I wondered whether the astonishment painted on his face was not that of someone who is surprised about being alive. His old heart was tired and I was convinced it kept beating only for his young companion's sake.

We advanced in silence under the green canopy of that mysterious world. I knew Toine would never be himself again. The natural song of the waterfall reached us at last. A gleam of interest lit up in his black eyes. It gave me a little hope that we could still make it.

On a tender green riverbank, we lay flat on our bellies to drink the clear water. After quenching our thirst, we remained stretched out. I relished that illusory feeling of well being, in a pitiful effort to escape the anguish that gripped me like leper.

Shadows had once again conquered the still sky. The night had not arrived yet, but the stars were about to appear. It was the moment when the world awaited a change. The only moment that resembled any normal twilight. Only a sound disturbed the silence: the crystalline noise of the waterfall that sang under the jealous gazes of the carnivorous flowers.

Then the black of night drowned out our short communion with hope. The nameless stars, one by one, pierced the immense, secret vault.

Toine spoke in the darkness, startling me.

'We should have brought something to make fire with. We won't find any dry wood here. This place is as green as can be.'

X

I had slipped into a deep slumber without realising it. I believe I heard Toine stamping his foot and grinding his teeth in impatience, probably because I was so slow to rouse. Half angry, I propped myself

ground, wary of the vines that hung from the trees, unmoving but watchful.

Just as we were congratulating ourselves for our uneventful progress, we realised the trees had become more numerous. From the vines that touched the ground, more young trees sprouted, like a miniature forest. To cap it all, the day was waning.

Long before the sky, which we glimpsed through the canopy, had grown dark, we found ourselves in pitch-black shadows beneath our roof of leaves. Not wishing to spend the night in the forest, we continued going forward, in the hope of finding a clearing. The vines attacked us and we had to cut them away. Like snakes, they coiled their fibrous bodies around us. The heavy flask impeded our progress, but we could not resolve to leave it behind.

Toine stopped.

'Son, we can't go on like this anymore. We don't even know if we're heading in the right direction. Let's spend the night here. I know everything is hostile, but we have no light to direct our steps, right?'

We lay down side by side in a narrow patch free from vines. Finding our sleep proved impossible. Above the treetops, the wind created a noise similar to a tiger's hissing, while from beneath came the muffled thumping, and the vines made reptilian creeping noises on the ground.

Sharing our fears was pointless, and so we kept our tongues. I hoped the night would pass without accident. I was about to fall asleep when I sprang up, my fingernails digging into Toine's arm.

'Did you hear that?' I screamed.

The infernal noise we knew all too well had resumed. The entire forest pulsated with long shudders, accompanied by the heartrending cracking the trees made as they bent toward the ground. This time it was ten times more terrifying because we were at the centre of a phenomenon that could destroy us. Toine was screaming, too, and our shouts mingled with the moans coming from the trees. We got to our feet and braced ourselves for the massive weight that was about to crush us.

'Let's curl up at the feet of the nearest tree before the trunk crushes us,' Toine said.

I followed his advice, surprised that a man like him could hope such a tactic would protect us from that enormous mass. I slipped under a tree, but without Toine. In my panic, I had unwittingly moved away from him. I called him to no avail. Among the concerto of moaning and cracking, not even a bugle would have been heard. I soon gave up and clung to my tree. I felt the life of the tree. Its sap dripped over me and I imagined tears of blood. It's all over, I thought, when I heard the leaves rustle against the ground. In a childish gesture of self-protection, I closed my eyes.

The enormous din, compounded of cracking and leaves brushing against the ground, ended. From the bowels of the earth, the hammering recommenced and the noise became deafening.

When it was over, I heard Toine's voice call me. My eyes still closed, as though awaiting death, I could not bring myself to answer. It's useless, I thought. Only a miracle can save us now. When his voice grew more insistent, I cracked my eyes open. The forest had reverted to its normal state, and everything bathed in a strange light. In this otherworldly phosphorescence, I could discern the trunks, now erect. But something equally luminous struck me – Toine, not far from me. I got up. 'Here. Over here!'

He turned in my direction and approached, astonishment painted on his face.

'D'you know you're shining, just like the forest?' he said when he reached me.

'You're shining, too!'

His expression darkened. 'Then, like the forest, we're cursed.'

My joy at being alive was so great I laughed, which infuriated Toine. He mastered his temper on the spot and set a hand on my shoulder. 'Sorry, son. I'm losing my mind with all the things that keep happening.'

I simply smiled. Seeing that strange glow around him, I wondered whether he was right after all. Perhaps we were cursed in earnest. Then the disturbing glow faded and a quiet, serene night enveloped us.

We fell into a slumber similar to unconsciousness, something different from simple sleep – rather an invincible catalepsy. When we resurfaced, red beams pierced the green ceiling of the forest. My companion, I had already noticed, emerged older from these bouts of faint, more bitter, too. I began to wonder whether he was concealing something about his nightmares. Nevertheless, I lulled myself into believing that we would find salvation beyond the mountains.

'Aren't you hungry, son?' Toine asked, rising with a visible effort.

'Course I am,' I answered with impatience. 'It doesn't change anything, though, because we've got nothing to chew on.'

'We'll see 'bout that.'

Toine disappeared behind a bush. He soon came back, arms laden with fruits. I was amazed. What courage the man must have possessed in order to touch the reclining treetops.

'So you're afraid of nothing.'

'I am afraid of hunger.' He let the fruits fall to my feet. He was already biting into an enormous stone fruit. I imitated him and we ate in silence.

Toine was satisfied sooner than I because his appetite was less demanding than mine – due to our age difference, I think. Comforted by the frugal meal, our thirst quenched by the fresh water from our flask, we resumed our journey among the green and purple.

We advanced slowly. The forest had become inextricable and thorns scratched us painfully. The moving vines gave us no quarter and we had to alter our path to avoid them. If life multiplied its forms in the plant world, the forest remained void of animal life. Not the smallest mosquitoes dancing in the patches of light. We humans were somehow suspended between the mineral and the vegetable. The gift of life was available only for the creatures that wore no flesh, as if no incarnated god had ever visited this place.

When we arrived at the edge of a clearing, we hesitated. Was it safe to go any farther?

The grass was darker than usual. And those marvellous flowers of soft or violent colours rose incredibly tall. They bore no resemblance to the waterfall flowers, but they might as well have been as carnivorous.

'Son, we have to go through,' Toine said in peremptory tones. 'We've got no choice.'

And he was the first to pass the threshold.

The flowers fled like gazelles as we drew near. Astonished by this delirious sight, we stopped in our tracks.

The flowers stopped as well.

Toine sighed. 'And I thought I'd seen it all. Maybe it's a nightmare,' he added after a few seconds' silence, 'but I must admit it's very beautiful.'

No one could have remained insensitive to the spectacle of a wide stretch of a green ocean where the flowers moved, enormous but as elegant and charming as normal flowers. A heavenly scent followed their movements. At a distance, far away, the mountains were visible, some of the crests lost in the red sky.

We followed the flowers until they led us to a swamp. To avoid being bogged down, we had to go back to the edge of the forest. Without cutting through the woods, our way became much longer, but at least we were free from creeping vines and thorny bushes.

But already the black of night was sneaking up on us. Sleeping near the flowers held no appeal for me. I mentioned my fear to Toine.

'Don't worry, son. Nothing is worse than the reclining forest. What can these flowers do to us?'

'You're forgetting the flowers at the waterfall. Didn't those attack us?'

'All right, only these ones run away when we come near. So perhaps we don't need to fear them.'

We waited for night to fall before stopping. Then we stretched out on the fresh grass. A heavy silence hovered above us, only disturbed by the light noises of rustling petals as the flowers moved about.

When the sky blossomed with stars, Toine cried, 'As a sailor, I remember the position of the stars. You know what? Tonight those stars aren't in the same places. So who's moving? Them or us?' Seeing I understood nothing of what he had said, he explained. 'It's not complicated. If you head north, you'll end up seeing the sky filled with stars from north to south. And vice versa. But the stars remain the same. They'll only be more or less higher above the horizon. Now, the sky tonight has nothing to do with the sky we've been seeing since we got here. Either the stars are moving or we are.

This is another universe, son. I've never seen any of those constellations. We are under unknown skies.'

Toine's reasoning made perfect sense. Nevertheless, I could not accept the idea that we might be elsewhere than on our dear old earth. If Toine was right, what hope was left for us?

Someone was shaking me. Sound asleep, I did not wish to open my eyes. All I wished was to remain wrapped inside the night I had earned for my pain. Toine's vigorous hand continued shaking me.

'Come on, wake up, son.'

I opened my eyes. The sky was a black void.

'Why did you have to wake me up? I was sleeping so well.'

'Damn it, can't you see?'

The clearing was illuminated by the shimmer of the forest living its silvery hour.

A most extraordinary spectacle was the infernal dance in which the flowers had engaged, their petals like the leaves of water lilies when you immerse them and myriads of trapped particles of air cover them, glistening underwater.

The mountainous skyline glowed red, like the embers of a gigantic fire. And the earth rumbled with the beating of a frenzied heart. My gaze remained riveted to the bewitching scene. I could not find the strength to turn away from it. Finally, darkness retook the forest.

Neither Toine nor I could sleep. We kept vigil in our distressing universe, but nothing moved. The large clearing reappeared with the first light of dawn. The flowers were gone. Only a few petals remained like pale specks in an ocean of green. We ate some grass to cheat hunger. At that moment, I noticed for the first time my skin was becoming rough. As though mud had dried over it. I mentioned it to Toine who answered in a weary voice, 'We'll take a bath in the next river. It's just filth.'

And we did not speak about it again.

After skirting the wide patch of moving ground for hours, we had the impression we were going round in circles. Around the middle of the afternoon, we did arrive at the end of that interminable swamp. Below us opened a gorge, a veritable chasm we would have to cross if we wanted to continue toward the mountains that rose majestically on the horizon.

'We can't cross that,' I said.

'I don't see what else we can do. Look in both directions. This gorge is like a frontier.'

A revolt verging on hatred surged in me. 'Then why must we go there? What's with those inhospitable mountains? We can't be sure we'll find salvation if we get there. On the contrary, we'll risk starving and dying of thirst.'

'I know,' Toine said in a calm voice. 'But do you really think you're going to survive in these accursed woods? With the meat-eating plants, and all the rest? No, this place here is unfit for human beings. But on the other side of the mountain, maybe we'll find a normal life, the kind of life we're cut out for. So, if we must die anyway, it's better to go down fighting. Oh, I'm as tired of all this as you are, but if you don't want to go, I'll try alone. If I make it, I'll come back for you. A self-respecting man could not live with himself after failing a friend.'

Toine's words, bitter but resolute, dissolved my anger.

'If one goes, the other must follow,' I said. 'But seriously, how are we getting to the bottom of the chasm?'

'Down there,' he said, extending an arm.

This outstretched arm caught my eye. The strange crust Toine had dismissed as filth had thickened. And the legs and the back of my companion were equally covered with the same substance. I examined my body. The thickness appeared everywhere. Shaking, filled with misgivings, I scratched at it, but it stuck to my skin like mortar to stone.

I asked Toine, 'Are you sure this is filth? You're hiding something from me. I'm sure of it. I beg of you. Tell me what is happening to us.'

He answered in a voice dripping weariness, 'You're not suffering, son, are you? Then forget the rest. It's probably the sun that is cooking us up.'

He was trying to reassure me. He didn't believe a word of it! I did not insist, though. I concentrated all my efforts on overcoming this new anguish that was creeping inside me.

Toine guided me to the spot he deemed propitious to our descent. We started down. It was my turn to carry the huge flask, which hindered me considerably. As I was about to lose footing, I had to let go of the thing to hold on. It rolled down and disappeared from view.

'Don't worry,' Toine said, sensing my despair. 'We'll surely find some water below. And I still prefer losing the flask to losing you.'

His tones left me with a peculiar impression, as if nothing mattered to him any longer. Perhaps his hope in finding a different life on the other side of the mountain, or... No. I refused to consider any other possibility.

After a long, painful descent, we felt a rock under our feet. It was enormous and jutted far out into the void. We went down on our bellies and crawled forward until we could peer down into the abyss. We were able to take in its extraordinary depth thanks to several fires that illuminated the bottom.

'Do you have an idea what this means?' I asked.

Toine kept his gaze riveted to the bluish flames that created living shadows on the dead rock walls.

'No,' he answered. 'No. I really don't know.'

We resumed our descent. It was more and more difficult. We advanced squeezed between two slabs of rock; a thick malodorous smoke floated up to us and it was getting hot. The red light of day decreased rapidly and soon we had only the glimmer of blue flames to guide us.

Through the crusts that covered our bodies, sweat oozed, as thick and yellow as pus. At the same time, the fatigue that had plagued us vanished. Was it due to the emanations of those mysterious furnaces?

We reached the bottom of the abyss in an almost euphoric state. Toine had found his smile again, frozen in the folds of that disturbing crust. The fires blazed much farther apart than we had thought when we saw them from above. They burst out of the ground through small craters, with thin whistling sounds. We skirted a few of them with no difficulty. We now had to climb to the other side. By some miracle, our strength had increased tenfold, and we attacked the wall right away. We found more finger- and toe-holds, and we climbed easily. It was fortunate for hardly had we reached midpoint than the dreaded thumping suddenly resounded, causing the walls of the chasm to shake in a frightening way. Gigantic flames rose, almost reaching us, giving off an unbearable heat. I was about to let go of my hold when it all went back to normal. The silent night enveloped us with no other light than the unfamiliar stars. Unable to move in the darkness, we remained glued to the wall and waited for daylight. Fatigue retook us, and if the wall had not been gently sloped, we would have fallen and crashed to the bottom of the chasm. As the wait seemed to stretch into forever, the first fire began to burn again, followed by a second, and a third, until the entire gorge was ablaze. A marvellous sensation of well-being erased our fatigue. But when I could make out Toine's features, I noticed in horror that the hideous crust had evolved. I read in my friend's eyes that my face had undergone the same transformation. We resumed our ascent without a word.

As we climbed, fatigue gripped us once again, vice-like. I shot furtive glances at Toine. His face resembled a mask and my skin, too, stiffened with the exertion of the ascent. We were hoisting ourselves out of the chasm when the sun began to take on its red hue, tingeing the vault of heaven with a deep mauve while the night died away. The crests of the imposing chain of mountains kept to the shadows, which were quickly fading into the light. The mountains rose at a short distance now, behind a stretch of flat desert land apparently easy to cross. It proved an illusion, though, because as soon as we set our feet on it, we sank into the soil up to our knees. We progressed with terrible efforts. And when the bleeding disk dispelled the night, we discovered we were treading a red powder that resembled dried blood ground to dust. We should have felt horror. Instead, an immense detachment freed us from the horrible and the monstrous. Our exhaustion, too, vanished. Once at the feet of the mountain, we were thus able to commence our ascent with no delay. But despite the curious calm that now pervaded me, I could not help glancing at Toine's face in disgust. It was turning to mud.

XII

The mountain was made of a porous rock like the silt found at the bottom of the oceans. It resembled sponge because of the holes peppering it, but instead of being smooth, it was rough and full of imperfections like an abrasive pumice stone.

Hardly one hundred metres up, we discovered a great number of those strange statues in human or animal shapes. All of them stuck to the mountainside. To my surprise, I had brotherly thoughts for the stone silhouettes – a much stronger emotion than the fleeting compassion I had experienced for the skeleton in the hut. The higher we climbed that hideous vitrified sponge, the greater the number of mineral spectres became. All those beaks, muzzles and mouths expressed a single emotion – fear.

We continued our ascent all day, speaking as little as possible because every attempt at moving our mouths caused physical pain. But our horrified eyes were free to exchange frequent glances. Under the progress of the hideous crust, little by little we were becoming mineral. The great bleeding disk finally sunk behind the horizon, beyond which, for all we knew, only emptiness existed.

At this time of the evening, a crowd of mineral creatures encircled us, glowing with a soft purple light. The haunting beat resumed. When the night conquered the sky, the plain and the mountains bathed in the gloomy shadows we already knew. A murmur like a whispered prayer reached us. Our gazes riveted to the forest, we kept still, leaning our backs against the slope. We feared fear. He who has never experienced this feeling knows nothing of terror. Since that whisper similar to a death rattle had begun, I had the impression I was turning into one of those earthen creatures. From my poor deformed mouth I managed to express my feeling aloud, hoping Toine would hear me. He did. I believed he felt the same terror, but in a hideous grimace, he laughed at it. To the very last, that incredibly brave man tried to reassure his companion.

We had resumed our silent contemplation. The forest was visible now. A silvery glimmer emanated from the tree trunks and the leaves. From the centre of the mountains, the thumps became more insistent and the shadows surrounding us more luminous. It was such a supernatural sight I hoped in my madness that I would soon escape that vivid dream and awake to a normal world. Toine's hand on my arm destroyed my illusion.

'Look,' he said.

His mud-gloved hand pointed to the forest, where all the trees shone with a metallic glow. In a brusque movement, I detached myself from the mountain soil. I heard a bizarre sound, and I felt moisture under my muddy hand. I bent low to examine the place where I had been lying. From the spongy rock oozed a thick dark fluid. I was appalled.

Toine kept pointing at the forest. In the vault of the sky, the stars scintillated with a cold light. The entire mountain glowed while blue flames rose from the abyss.

Then, beyond the red-dust desert, beyond the chasm and the wide clearing, the entire forest bowed. This adoration of nature enthralled us. In the meantime, the mountain vibrated with violence. Then, as it had happened each time, the stars paled and winked out, one by one. At our feet, the mysterious nature had melted into the night that plagued our diseased eyes. A deep blackness swallowed us. We were lost. We were nothing. The shadows of oblivion enveloped us like a leaden carapace. Soon we were part of a slumbering fellowship.

I awoke with the impression of a long ascent from the bottom of a pit. Darkness still inhabited the world. On the horizon, a pink shade was about to engender the red day but for now the sky, empty, enjoyed solitude. Hidden by the wall of the night, the plain was only darkness, as silent as a hole dug into infinity.

With my mud-caked lips, I called Toine. My voice barely carried, and I wondered whether I had called him or just imagined I had. Or had I become deaf? Withdrawing into the hopeless agony of expectation, I closed my eyes and began to tick the seconds off an imaginary rosary.

A noise I remembered all too well told me Toine had detached himself from the stone. Then a perfect silence reigned.

Little by little, as the red glowing deployed, blurred shapes became visible. Then, for the first time, on top of the mauve sky, appeared the summit of the gigantic mountain. It soared into the heavens like the tip of a thorn. Clinging in clusters to the mountainside, uncountable silhouettes of all kinds of beings seemed to continue their ascent toward eternity.

I turned with some effort to Toine to ask him whether we should go on or not. My question remained unspoken, trembling on my earthen lips: he was horrible to look at. The mud mask had become solid, while the features, rough and impossible to recognise, gave it the aspect of a face in gestation. The only trace of life on his face was his gaze, which left me with no uncertainty about my own appearance. I should have lost my mind right then, but a strange calm inhabited me. Was it the beginning of acceptance?

Toine tried to tell me something but his half-open mouth, already stiff, could only utter incomprehensible sounds. When he struggled to rise, I understood he intended to continue our ascent. Did he really believe our salvation lay on the other side of the mountain? I could not think any longer. I submitted to his decision.

Every movement caused pain. The crusts, like too-heavy armour, hindered our progress. From time to time, we held on to those stone creatures. Breaking loose from the mountain, they would slide down toward the plain, and slide, and never stop. Although the position of the sun indicated that we had been climbing for hours, the top of the mountain seemed as far away as ever.

Save for the oppressive weights on our bodies, we no longer felt physical discomfort. No hunger, no thirst, no fatigue. On the other hand, our breath became belaboured in the rarefied air. To inhale, we had to open our mouths into a grimace similar to one that was repeated on every statue. The slope grew steeper, almost vertical, but it did not bother us. We stuck to the rock as if we had suction pads on our hands and feet. Slowly we rose toward the summit, which was charged for us with promise and hope, but at the same time our mineral metamorphosis became more noticeable, more repulsive. Our hands, with fingers swollen and thickened, could not form fists any longer and remained open. Our stiff limbs gave us the heavy gait of moving statues.

At a distance, well beyond desert and forest, we could see the ocean. The red sun seemed to gaze at its blazing reflection. Silence reigned. When we reached the top at last, we were spent but full of hope. For a long time we rested, stretched out on the ground. We must have looked like two heaps of mud. The moment of truth had come. While negotiating the various stages of our journey, we had been aiming at a target that meant salvation. Now what would we discover on the other side?

We were afraid of rising and finding out if life existed on the other side of the mountain. Still reclining, we gazed at the immense stretch of stone that covered the summit. In contrast to the slopes, the summit appeared to be as smooth as the flagstones of ancient dwellings caressed by many feet. In the centre, shaped like a bowl slightly higher than the surrounding rocks, was an immense crater. A kind of enormous pit with a rounded rim. A well with an orifice elongated toward the top, tulip-like.

Toine scrambled to his feet. He seemed to have found a new determination. Seeing his gaze sweeping everything around us, as if he were looking for something, filled me with curiosity, and I stood. I understood when I noticed that not a single statue stood on the rim of the crater. All had stopped their progress before the summit. Unless they fled it, I thought in anguish.

Fear returned to us like a voyager welcoming old companions as soon as we started across that extraordinary esplanade. We advanced like automatons. We had to skirt the crater, which was a small mountain itself. From afar, the reddened sky watched us. We drew near the line that marked the limits between life and death. Under our thick carapaces, our bodies shuddered with torment. Nothing had changed in the abodes of the sky. All was deep silence.

A few metres from the crater, we saw other summits, similar to the one on which we stood. The farther we went, the more sprang up. On the other side of the mountains were no woods or plains, merely more mountains soaring toward the red sky. No hope remained in this world of silence. The slab of rock under our feet began to vibrate in a stronger way.

We were nearing the origin of that beating heart. Our own hearts beat in unison with the hidden giant. Nothing could give us a new hope. We were no longer tempted to live, but the crater, the probable cause of all our hardships, attracted us. Toine went first, trying to climb up the rocky collar that encircled the orifice. I followed with no hesitation. As though under a spell, we felt our fatigue fall away when we touched the rock. Our anguish remained, fuelled by our instinct, which pushed us to flee as quickly as possible. Despite our fear, we reached the crater. Fascination was stronger. A circle of stone wide enough for us to walk on skirted the crater of a dormant volcano. The proximity of the abyss compromised our balance. When I approached the crater, my legs trembled.

Our eyes, dazzled by the light, could not pierce the darkness of the abyss, but we could clearly hear the sound of breathing rising from the bottom, while the rhythmic beating increased.

Toine stood there, head bent, eyes fixed to the void. His face had no human features. He was like a mirror, for he displayed what I had become.

My old companion's shoulders collapsed, as if an enormous weight crushed him.

That is when I glimpsed that horrible thing at the bottom of the crater. The sight almost propelled me into the accursed pit forever.

Floating in the middle of a lake of blood, a blue eye with an immense pupil stared at us.

Toine screamed, and the effort cracked the mud mask, disfiguring him.

I let him pull me away. When we arrived at the rim of the crater, Toine pushed me, sending me rolling a few metres down toward the slab encircling the summit. Instantly, fatigue engulfed us. Crawling a little farther along the ledge, we let ourselves roll down the steep slope of the mountain. At first, we slid at great speed, jostling the other statues like us. We were now a crowd of mineral creatures hurtling down the cursed mountain. Then we were stopped as though stayed by an invisible hand, our backs to the stone, without the possibility of pulling ourselves loose.

The only memory I have, after centuries spent living inside a stone, is of the gentle touch of tears on a man's face.

THE SALAMANDER

Mercè Rodoreda

TRANSLATED INTO ENGLISH BY MARTHA TENNENT

Mercè Rodoreda (1908–1983) was an important Catalan writer whose novel *La plaça del diamant* (1962, translated as *The Time of the Doves*) has been translated into over twenty languages. Rodoreda fled to France during the Spanish Civil War and, robbed of her home and language, wrote almost nothing for nearly two decades. She began to write short stories as a way of reclaiming her voice, and many of these tales contain more than a touch of the surreal or fantastical. In 'The Salamander' (1967) Rodoreda uses the weird in the service of transformation and commentary on ignorance. This masterful new translation by Martha Tennent also appears in *The Selected Stories of Mercè Rodoreda* (2011).

I strolled down to the water, beneath the willow tree and through the watercress bed. When I reached the pond I knelt down. As always, the frogs gathered around me. Whenever I arrived, they would appear and come jumping toward me. As soon as I started to comb my hair, the mischievous ones would stroke my red skirt with the five little braids or pull at the festoon on my petticoat full of ruffles and tucks. The water would grow sad and the trees that climbed the hill would gradually blacken. But that day the frogs jumped into the water, shattering the mirror in the pond, and when the water grew still again his face appeared beside mine, as if two shadows were observing me from the other side. So as not to give the appearance of being frightened, I stood up and without saying a word began walking calmly through the grass. But the moment I heard him following me, I looked back and stopped. A hush fell over everything, and one end of the sky was already sprayed with stars. He stopped a short distance away and I didn't know what to do. I was suddenly filled with fear and began to run, but when I realized he would overtake me, I stopped under the willow tree, my back to the trunk. He came to me and stood there, both arms spread wide so I could not run away. Then, gazing into my eyes, he began to press me against the willow, my hair disheveled, between the willow and him. I bit my lips to keep from screaming; the pain in my chest was so great I thought my bones were on the point of breaking. He placed his mouth on my neck, and where he had laid his mouth I felt a burning.

The trees on the hill were already black when he came the following day, but the grass was still warm from the sun. Again, he embraced me against the willow trunk and placed his open hand over my eyes. All of a sudden I seemed to be falling asleep and the leaves were telling me things that made sense but I did not understand, things spoken more and more slowly, more and more softly. When I no longer heard them, I asked him, my tongue half-frozen in anguish: What about your wife? He responded: you are my wife, you alone. With my back I crushed the same grass that

I hardly dared to step on when I combed my hair; I used to tread lightly, just enough to capture the wounded smell. You alone. Later, when I opened my eyes I saw the blonde braid hanging; she was leaning over looking at us with empty eyes. When she realized I had seen her, she grabbed me by the hair, whispering 'witch.' Softly. She promptly released me and seized him by his shirt collar. 'Ah, ah, ah,' she kept saying. She began pushing him and dragged him away.

We never returned to the pond. We met in stables, haylofts, the root forest. But ever since the day his wife took him away, people in the village have looked at me as if they weren't looking at me, some furtively making the sign of the cross when I walked by. After a while, when they saw me coming they would rush inside their houses and lock the doors. Everywhere I heard a word that began to haunt me, as if it were born from light and darkness or the wind were whistling it. Witch, witch, witch. The doors would close and I walked through the streets of a dead village. When I glimpsed eyes through parted curtains, they were always icy. One morning I found it difficult to open the front door, a door of old wood split by the sun. In the center of it, they had hung an ox head with two tender branches wedged in the eyes. I took it down – it was heavy – and, not knowing what to do with it, left it on the ground. The twigs began to dry, and as they dried, the head rotted; and where the neck had been severed, it swarmed with milk-colored maggots.

Another day I discovered a headless pigeon, its breast red with blood. On another, a premature, stillborn sheep and two rat ears. When they ceased hanging dead animals on the door, they began to throw rocks. They were the size of a fist, and at night they banged against the windows and roof tiles. Then they had the procession. It was toward the beginning of winter, a windy day with fast-moving clouds. The procession, all purple and white from the paper flowers, advanced slowly. I lay on the floor viewing it through the cat hole. It had almost reached the house. I was watching the wind, the statue of the Saint and the banners when the cat wanted inside, frightened by the chanting and large candles. But when he saw me, he screeched and humped his back like the arch in the bridge. The procession stopped. Again and again the priest gave his blessing, the altar boys sang, the wind twisted the candle flames and the sexton marched up and down as the purple and white paper flowers swirled madly about. At last the procession left, and before the holy water had scarcely dried on my wall, I went in search of him. I couldn't find him anywhere. I looked in the stables, the haylofts, the root forest. I knew every inch of the forest; I always sat on the white, bone-smooth root, the oldest root.

That night, when I sat down, I suddenly realized I had nothing left to hope for: my life faced the past, with him inside me like a root inside the earth. The following day, they scribbled the word 'witch' on my door with a piece of coal; and that night, outside my window, in a loud voice so I would hear, two men said that I should have been burned at the stake when I was little, together with my mother who used to escape into the sky with vulture wings while everyone was asleep. I should have been burned before they needed me to dig up garlic, bind the wheat and alfalfa and pick grapes from wretched vineyards.

I thought I saw him one evening at the entrance to the root forest, but he ran away when I approached; I couldn't be sure whether it was him or my desire for him or his shadow searching for me in the trees, lost like me, moving back and forth. 'Witch' they cried and left me with my misfortune, which was not the one they would have wished for me. I thought about the pond, the watercress, the thin branches of the willow tree. Winter was dark and flat, leafless: there was only ice, frost and the gelid moon. I couldn't leave the house, because to walk in winter was to walk in sight of everyone, and I didn't want to be seen. When spring arrived, its leaves tiny and joyful, they built the fire in the center of the square and gathered dry, well-cut wood.

Four of the oldest men in the village came for me. I called to them from inside, saying I wouldn't accompany them, but then some young men with large, red hands appeared and smashed the door with an axe. I screamed because they were taking me from my house, and when I bit one of them, he struck me on the crown of my head. They picked me up by the arms and legs and threw me on top of the pile of wood, as if I were just another branch; they tied my hands and feet and left me there, my skirt up. I turned my head. The square was crowded: the young people were standing in front of the elderly, the children in their new Sunday smocks in a corner, holding olive branches in their hands. As I gazed at the children, I noticed him: he was standing beside his wife with the blonde braid. She was dressed in black and he had his arm around her shoulder. I turned back and closed my eyes. When I opened them again, two old men were approaching with bright torches, and the children began to sing the song about the witch who was burned at the stake. It was a very long song, and when they finished, the old men announced that they couldn't light the fire, I wouldn't let them. Then the priest walked over to the children with a basin filled with holy water and had them moisten the olive branches and throw them over me. Soon I was covered with olive branches, all with tender leaves. An old, hunchbacked woman, small and toothless, started laughing and left. A moment later, she returned with two baskets full of dry heather and told the old men to scatter them on four sides of the bonfire. She helped and after that the fire took. Four columns of smoke rose and as the flames began to climb, it seemed to me that everyone heaved a sigh of relief and peace, a sigh that came from deep down in their chests. As the flames mounted, following the smoke, I watched from behind a torrent of red water; and behind the water, every man, every woman, every child was like a shadow, happy because I was burning.

The bottom of my skirt turned black, and I could feel the fire on the small of my back. Every now and then, a flame bit me on the knee. It seemed to me that the ropes that bound me had burnt away. Then something happened that made me clench my teeth: my arms and legs started to become shorter, like the tentacles on the snail I once nudged with my finger; and below my head, where the neck joined the shoulders, I felt something stretching and poking me. The fire screeched and the resin boiled. I saw some of the people who were observing me raise their hands; others were running and stumbling into those that hadn't budged. One side of the bonfire collapsed, sending embers flying. When the logs caught fire again, I thought I heard someone say: She's a salamander. And I began to move across the coals, very slowly, because my tail was heavy.

My face was level with the ground as I scurried on my hands and feet. I headed toward the willow tree, following along the wall; but when I reached the end of it, I turned and from a distance I could see my house burning like a torch. No one was on the street. I made my way to the stone bench, then to the house and through the flames and embers, hurrying toward the willow and watercress. When I was outside again, I turned back because I wanted to see the roof burning. While I was watching, the first drop fell, one of those large, warm drops from which toads are born. Instantly more drops fell, slowly at first, then fast, and soon all the water from above fell, and the fire was gradually doused, spouting huge columns of smoke. I stood still, and when I could no longer see anything, because thick, black night had fallen, I started crossing puddles and mud. My hands enjoyed plunging into the spongy sludge, but my back feet kept getting stuck in the mud and were tired. I would have liked to run, but I couldn't. A thunderclap stopped me short in the middle of the path; then came a bolt of lightning and between the stones I spotted the willow tree. I was panting as I approached the pond. Once I was beyond the mud, which is formed by dirt on land, I found the marsh, which is dirt deposited in water. I moved into a corner of it and stayed there, half suspended between two roots. Then the three little eels appeared.

In the morning – I'm not sure if it was the following day or another – I slowly emerged and glimpsed the high mountains beneath a cloud-dappled sky. I scurried through the watercress and stopped at the willow trunk. The first leaves were still inside the sprouts, but the sprouts were beginning to turn green. I didn't know which direction to take; if I wasn't paying attention, the blades of grass poked me in the eyes. I slept among the blades of grass until the sun was high. When I woke up, I caught a little mosquito, then hunted for worms in the grass. After a while I returned to the marsh; I pretended I was sleeping, because the three playful eels promptly reappeared.

There was a big moon the night I decided to return to the village. The air was filled with scent, and the leaves on all the branches trembled. I took the stone path, being very careful because even the smallest thing frightened me. I rested when I reached the front of the house: I found nothing but rubble, stinging nettles, and spiders spinning and spinning webs. I crawled around to the back and stopped in front of his garden. The sunflowers were growing beside the rose-scented geraniums, their round flowers on the verge of bending. I proceeded along the blackberry hedge, never questioning why I was doing it. It was as if someone were telling me: do this, do that. I squeezed under the door and entered. The ashes in the fireplace were still warm. I stretched out there for a while, then scampered around a bit before crawling under the bed. Dead tired, I fell asleep and didn't realize when day dawned.

When I awoke, it was night again and I glimpsed shadows on the floor; his wife was moving back and forth with a lit candle. I could see her feet and part of her legs in white stockings, slender at the bottom, swollen toward the top. Then I saw his big feet, the blue socks falling over his ankles. I saw both of their clothes fall to the floor, and I heard them sit on the bed, their feet dangling, his beside hers. One of his feet moved up and a sock dropped, and she pulled off her stockings with both hands. Then I heard the sound of sheets being pulled over them, and they spoke in low voices. Much later, when I was accustomed to the dark, the moon entered through the window, a window with four panes separated by two crossed laths. I crawled over to the light, directly beneath the cross. I began to pray for myself, because inside me, even though I wasn't dead, no part of me was wholly alive. I prayed frantically because I didn't know if I was still a person or only an animal or half-person, half-animal. I also prayed to know where I was, because there were moments when I seemed to be underwater, and when I was underwater I seemed to be above, on land, and I could never know where I really was. When the moon disappeared, they woke up and I went back to my hiding place under the bed, and with tiny bits of fluff I began to make myself a little nest. I spent many nights between the fluff and the cross. Sometimes I would leave and go down to the willow tree. When I was under the bed, I listened. It was all the same. You alone, he would say. One night when the sheet dragged the floor, I climbed up the sheet, hanging on to the folds, and slid into the bed, near one of his legs. I lay as still as a corpse. He turned over and his leg weighed me down. I couldn't move. I had trouble breathing because he was smothering me. I rubbed my cheek against his leg, being very careful not to wake him.

One day she cleaned the place. I caught a glimpse of the white stockings and the crumpled broom, and when I was least expecting it, part of a blonde braid hung down to the floor and the broom swept under the bed. I had to escape because the broom seemed to be looking for me. Suddenly I heard a yell and saw her feet running toward the door, but she returned with a lighted torch and hid half her body under the bed. She wanted to burn my eyes out. I was slow and ungainly and didn't know which way to go. Blinded, I bumped into everything: bed legs, chair legs, walls. I don't know how, but finally I found myself outdoors. I headed to the puddle beneath the horses' trough and the water covered me. Two boys saw me and went to look for canes and started poking me. I turned my face toward them, my entire head out of the water, and looked them up and down. They flung the canes down and ran away, but came right back with six or seven older boys who threw rocks and handfuls of dirt at me. A rock hit my tiny hand and broke it. Terror-stricken, I dodged the poorly aimed ones and managed to escape into the stable. She came after me with the broom, the screaming children waiting by the door. She poked me and tried to drive me out of my corner in the straw. Blinded again, I bumped into buckets, baskets, sacks of carob beans, horse legs. A horse reared because I bumped into one of his legs, and I grabbed hold of it. A thrust of the broom hit my broken hand and almost tore it off, and a black thread of drool rolled out of the corner of my mouth. I was able to escape through a crack, and as I was escaping I heard the broom prodding and poking.

In the dark of night I headed to the root forest. I crawled out from beneath some shrubs that shone in the moonlight. I wandered around, lost. My broken hand didn't hurt, but it was hanging from a tendon, and I had to raise my arm so it wouldn't drag too much. I stumbled along, first over roots, then stones, until finally I reached the root where I used to sit before they took me away to the fire in the square. I couldn't get to the other side, because I kept slipping. On, on, on, toward the willow tree, toward the watercress and my home in the marsh, in the water. The wind blew the grass and sent pieces of dry leaves wafting through the air and carried away short, shiny filaments from the flowers by the path. I brushed one side of my head against the trunk and slowly made my way to the pond and entered, holding my arm up, so tired, with my little broken hand.

Through the moon-streaked water, I could see the three eels coming. They blurred together: linking with each other, then separating; twisting together and tying knots that unraveled. Eventually, the smallest one came up to me and bit my broken hand. Some juice spurted from my wrist; in the water it looked a little like smoke. The eel was obstinate and kept pulling my hand slowly, never letting go of it, and while he pulled, he kept looking at me. When the eel thought I was distracted, he gave me one or two jerks. While the others played at twisting together like a rope, the one who was biting my hand suddenly gave a furious yank. The tendon must have been severed, because the eel swam away with my hand. Once he had it, he looked back at me as if to say: Now I have it! I closed my eyes for a while, and when I reopened them, the eel was still there, among the shadows and splashes of trembling light, my little hand in his mouth. A tiny bundle of bones fitted together, covered with a bit of black skin. I don't know why, but all of a sudden I could see the stone path, the spiders in my house, their legs hanging from the side of the bed: white and blue, as if the two of them were sitting above the water, but were empty, like laundry hanging on the line, rocked by the lapping water. I saw myself beneath the cross formed by the shadows, on the color-charged fire that screeched as it rose and didn't burn… While I saw all of these things, the eels played with that piece of me, let go of it, snatched it again, and the little hand passed from eel to eel, swirling like a tiny leaf, all the fingers spread apart. I was on both sides: in the marsh with the eels, and partially in that other world, without knowing where it was. Until the eels tired and the shadow sucked up the hand, a dead shadow that little by little scattered the dirt in the water, for days and days and days, in that corner of the marsh, among grass and willow roots that were thirsty and had always drunk there.

THE GHOULBIRD

Claude Seignolle

TRANSLATED INTO ENGLISH BY GIO CLAIRVAL

Claude Seignolle (1917–) is a French writer known as one of that country's best fantasists. As a child, his grandmother used to tell him stories that inspired his future emphasis on dark and macabre tales, many based on legends of the French countryside. A literary prize bearing his name recognizes works related to French folklore. Seignolle has not been widely published in English, aside from a Texas A&M University Press collection in 1983 and a limited edition of his novella *The Black Cupboard* (2010), from Ex Occidente Press. Gio Clairval provided this definitive translation of his classic story 'The Ghoulbird.' The bird of the title evokes a trope from Gothic literature said to be a bad omen.

My old friend, Dr. *** from Chateauroux, had recommended that I visit the manor of Guernipin in Brenne, between Mezières and Rosnay, if the master of the house was kind enough to invite me, his mood being such that he was seldom inclined to grant the requests of the strangers who solicited him.

I thus discovered Guernipin and Geoffrey de la Tibaldière, an unrepentant zoologist and, quite fortunately, for a man with his passion, a bachelor sacrificing his comfort to accommodate an exceptional collection of animals, stuffed or preserved in jars. The man lived in a small room furnished with a simple cot, each of the other twenty comfortable rooms packed with a dusty and docile wildlife. He introduced me with enthusiasm to his domestic zoo, confessing that he had come down with that persistent and invasive collector's fever in his childhood. He had foolishly caught the infection by the age of eight when he playfully trapped all the insects wandering about the property of Guernipin, and encased them in empty matchboxes, carefully labelled – admirable tiny coffins, once brand-new but now withered by time like the skin of their owner, who appeared to be the trusting type, to the point that he let me handle his treasures.

Guided by the most perfect of experts, as Mr. Tibaldière was a brisk old man of eighty-five and a collector's piece in his own right, I was invited to peruse a shambles of feathers, bristles, and scales.

That first afternoon, we explored only the rooms of the ground floor, and when dusk drew the curtain on those local or exotic marvels, I was left with a craving to see more pieces. But having acquired a taste for this hunt so devoid of danger and exertion, I did not know how to hint at my desire to see the rest. He whetted my appetite by suggesting that I should sleep in the tall four-poster in the country-style bedroom he had set up in the garret of Guernipin. We would dine informally in the kitchen and continue to explore his scholarly memories, while eating an omelette with chanterelles and a truffled confit of duck. Sylvain, the servant, would see to replenishing our glasses with a Reuilly wine that was lordly in its small ways. Indeed, Mr. Tibaldière being talkative, my attention would satisfy his imperious desire to describe his treasures.

The bouquet of the Reuilly enhanced the aroma of truffles and chanterelles, and quickened the already nimble speech of my host. At midnight, which was lazily spelt out by an ancient, potbellied grandfather clock, he was still speaking, his back to the fire, assisted by Sylvain, a fifty-year-old man tanned up to his hairline. Sylvain looked like a Moorish crone, a common feature in this part of Berry, so close to Poitou, where the Saracen occupation had left traces in the peasants' blood.

Mr. Tibaldière recounted his remote and adventurous hunts, when cross hairs on his rifle did not quiver in front of his eye; he lovingly dwelled on the local tradition, his youthful hours spent in patient exploration of burrows, nests and lairs, and he glorified the vibrant life of this country suspended between water and earth, an unparalleled paradise to sedentary and migratory fauna. At one o'clock in the morning, my head swam with new knowledge in ornithology: mallard (*Anas platyrhynchos*), gadwall (*Chaublasmus stepera*), shelduck – I will spare you the Latin – pochard, heron, coot, wheatear, water rail (*Rallus aquaticus* – but, I have not forgotten), all minutely described: appearance, calls, habits and more.

Sylvain slouched over an oak bench near the fireplace and, as patient as a dog that calculates in advance all the bones coming its way, yawned, loyalty incarnate. As for me, despite the strain of that long day, I dared not interrupt a host so prodigal with hospitality and words, nevertheless hoping that he, too, would soon grow sleepy. But Tibaldière rambled on about the mythical wildlife that the fiendishly superstitious peasants imagined prowling Brenne's night. He told me about the Ghoulbird.

My curiosity rekindled, I straightened my back. A Ghoulbird! Even though I was tired, the promise of a brief legend-hunting enchanted me. Hearing that name, Sylvain had slid further on the bench, drawing near the fire as if he wished to move away from us, studying the crackling embers with the intensity of a man who sees flames for the first time.

'You should know,' said Mr. Tibaldière, 'that there was a time when this family of birds had spread to the point that every marsh across France and beyond had its own mind-calling spirit, a sly winged creature that lured the naive to utter horror.'

I nodded while he moved onto a brilliant enumeration: Dreadfowl of Normandy, Owlfear of Ardennes, Shrikedeath of Brittany or the Tufted Screamers of Limousin, protean creatures spawned by the popular imagination in days of yore, brewed by the peasants' gullible minds during troubled nights. Locally, they had a Ghoulbird, the only one still living in the country, and probably the last remaining anywhere.

Then my host raised his voice and, taking aim with an imaginary rifle, threatened, 'I've never seen it. Otherwise – !' And that sceptical man shot me a mischievous wink before turning to his servant and saying in a compassionate tone, 'Is it so, Sylvain?' But, failing for once in his perfect obedience, the man did not answer.

Finally, I was released. My host rose and entrusted me to his servant, giving him orders to make sure all my needs would be satisfied, and then he dismissed us with an abrupt about-face of enviable agility. Sylvain took a jug of water, a lamp and, walking ahead of me, led me slowly, never turning around, across long corridors and steep stairways up to the attic, my room.

I was not disappointed as I had feared. Quite the contrary. The place, though stifling because of the heat absorbed through the roof, was clean and pleasant. Vast, too, with beautiful glazed beams that sparkled as we passed. The curtained bed, made of walnut, smelled of wax, and the slightly rough bedclothes released a scent of lavender as I pulled them back. As for the four bouquets of cotton-cloth flowers tied to the posts, I feared there might be spiders hiding in there, but I reassured myself by thinking that they would certainly be pinned, labelled by species, and therefore harmless prisoners. Sensing my fears, Sylvain promptly unfolded the cloths and shook them to show me no spiders dwelled between printed petals. And he deigned to smile for the first time. Mr. Tibaldière's authority must have been a heavy constraint to him, and he clearly wanted to chat.

He introduced me to the various features of the place, with great courtesy, and directed me to the dressing table and the small round-shaped dormer window, which he immediately opened to let in fresh air. In this regard, as I pointed out to him that this narrow opening might be insufficient, he beckoned me to a door, which he unlocked and pushed open. We climbed a narrow stone stairway and came out on the terrace of a crenellated tower that I hadn't noticed upon arriving at Guernipin. The view, stretching in all directions, was outstanding. Everywhere, as far as the eye could see, marshes, ponds and lakes glistened in the full moonlight and appeared to join and mingle into infinite lacings of water on dark earth. Encased in a vegetation thickened by shadows but made in fact of meagre shrubbery, the aquatic countryside shone like a jewel discarded for some minor flaw and relegated to this forgotten corner of opulent Berry.

I felt that Sylvain took great pride in my surprise. Showing the extent to which his offering moved me, I asked for details. The man knew his region by heart. I soon learned the name of each mirror consecrated to the moon, each moor and slough, the nearest so close we could have touched it with the toes of our boots, a harsh land, now in the process of drying up and hardening but still rotting, a traitor to the imprudent foot: the marsh of Gobble-Ox.

All need for sleep forgotten, I was loath to leave this wondrous nocturnal scenery, where the only missing element was a touch of life. I said to Sylvain, 'What a pity that this fabled Ghoulbird of yours is only a legend; otherwise, I would have listened to its song and applauded with enthusiasm!' The servant grabbed my arm and squeezed it. I realised that my words had robbed him of his pleasure. His voice dropped to a whisper.

'Never ever make such a wish, sir,' he breathed out. 'Particularly not under a full moon…It's the kind of night the creature would choose to lead us to our deaths…' And he forced me to leave the roof terrace. Back in the garret room, he carefully locked the door to the tower. In the light of the lamps, I was surprised to see his crumbling face covered with perspiration. Not to mention his manifest apprehension, so strong I felt almost compelled to reassure him by patting him in the back. But, made curious by his extreme reaction and exploiting my previous display of disbelief, I used a more artful way to restore his trust. I managed to have him sit with me on the edge of the bed and, matching the tone of my questions to his concern, I obtained a few details about this dreadful bird.

And so I learned that the bird mentioned by Mr. Tibaldière existed. Better still, the bird's favourite place was the marsh of Gobble-Ox, right here, five or six gunshots from us and at an equal distance from the village. Its appearance was not at first frightening, and it could look like any common bird, but shifted continuously from one species to the next to fool its victims. In its call, an additional note rang out… a bit strident. It was the Ghoulbird's curse… To listen to it was to lose one's will to the bird and forever be the creature's slave. Obedient, the victims rose from the beds, left the security of their homes and went out in nightclothes, like sleepwalkers, heading toward that bird of Hell, which rejoiced in any new prey. The victims went to the bird, oblivious of the mud that squelched under their feet, not realising they were padding through the marsh. And the creature would draw back, retreating further to lure its prey into the slimy depths that captured and swallowed its victims without mercy. Pessaut, Guérin, the woman called Marguerite, and so many others had died in this way. Their bodies were never found, only the footprints in the hardened banks of the Gobble-Ox, which, without doubt, had shared the meat with the Ghoulbird.

But the creature betrayed its presence in one tell-tale way: most other birds do not sing or whistle at night. So when you heard it, you had to move quickly and bolt your door, barricade up all the openings, clasp your hands over your ears, bury yourself deep under the blankets and, above everything else, be in the company of at least another person so that one could prevent the other from responding to the evil call…

Having unburdened himself of this awkward secret, Sylvain departed in great haste, taking the lamp and leaving me in a pitch-black room. I heard him double lock the door, probably out of habit, and step down the stairway, stumbling in his haste.

The silver needle of the moon, taking advantage of the open window, slanted into the darkened garret without disturbing the heavy silence, which then engulfed me. I undressed and lay down on the bed, my fatigue dulling the stressful images put into my head by the superstitious servant.

The heat prevented me from falling asleep immediately. I tossed and turned, feeling oppressed, until I decided to get up and open the door of the tower. After some blind groping, I found it. The fresh air that blew through the doorway joined the draft that entered through the window, bringing me relief. I went back to bed, and this time I slept right away.

I dreamt a dream agreeable at first but, little by little, it filled me with a vague uneasiness… I found myself in a vast ballroom, in old-fashioned garb, relaxed and content, sitting in an armchair… A beautiful young woman asked me to dance, favouring me with the most charming smile… But I declined rudely and remained seated instead of rising to my feet, eager to grant her the dance she'd requested… She, without seeming to be in the least shocked by my attitude, laughed in a strange way, with three high-pitched notes balanced by pauses, creating a peculiar rhythm… Then, taking me by the hand, she pulled me into her arms… I felt myself become heavier and heavier. But her gentle strength gradually managed to lift me… Standing, I felt a sensation of nakedness and a sudden embarrassment forced me to flee… I ran into a wall or a closed door, I did not know which… I fell, and people came to pick me up, pitying me… Their hands supported me and pulled me away into a park smelling of freshly cut grass… They led me to a well and, once there, either for fun or malice, they pushed me forward, to make me step over the edge…

I resisted the motion, letting myself fall to the ground, where, seized with a sudden terror, I hunkered down, refusing to participate in this stupid act… And again I heard the shrill laughter of the young woman, who had become invisible. All my attention was riveted on the unseen woman, as I was filled with a belated regret for not having accepted her company…

The chill of dawn woke me. I was on the terrace of the tower, lying on the ground and shivering. A gray mist covered Guernipin, which the rising sun gilded progressively. After the first moment of astonishment, it wasn't difficult to understand the reason why I was lying there. Surely, I had wanted to escape the sweltering garret room and, seeking fresh air, I had risen, half-conscious, to spend the rest of the night up here. Leaning out from the parapet, I discovered the impressive drop, and, upset, I realized that I had been on the point of falling from that height!

The second day with M. de la Tibaldière was as fascinating as the day before. The man knew so much – the mystery of the onager, the cyclical migration of the warthog, and provided anecdotes and biological digressions as arguments. We lunched in the park, in the temperate shade of a cedar tree as the wind, blowing gently, failed to ruffle its leaves. The table was a long tombstone taken from the floor of a deserted abbey nearby; we ate heartily on the belly of an austere priest stiffly engraved in the granite.

In the evening, we had yet to explore the second floor where, according to Mr. Tibaldière, suddenly excited by his own words, rested the jewels of his collection: coelacanths, large saurians from Borneo, and other survivors of antediluvian times. Therefore, I dined again at Guernipin, but I managed to escape the lecture after the meal. By now the place was familiar to me so I went to bed alone, this time keeping the lamp. And, fearing a new awakening on the roof terrace, I left the door to the corridor open but firmly shut the door leading to the tower, to avoid renewing the misadventure of the night before. I went to bed and began reading a book, but hardly had I reached the third page than it slipped from my hands. I blew out the light and let sleep come. This time the heat did not torment me, on the contrary! Again, I was involved in a dream that seemed light-hearted in the beginning… I visited Guernipin on my own, only to discover new rooms of an amazing variety… I could finally handle birds, touch soft plumage… Mysterious birds of unknown shapes, which came alive and quivered under my hands… Soon they were so numerous they crowded me, pushing me, guiding me to the freedom of the park, where they remained around me, driven by a silent determination… Mr. Tibaldière appeared on the front steps and indignantly shouted to come back before his most precious avian specimens escaped forever… Anger choked his cries, to the point they resembled a bullfrog's call… But, not listening, I suddenly ran away, now at the heart of the cluster of freed birds, whose wishes I obeyed, and which led me so fast I was out of breath…I ran on until I felt a terrible tightness to my heart… Choking, I felt myself gradually hindered in my race by viscid forces, which woke me suddenly.

Today, I find it impossible to describe the violent revulsion I felt while I was victim to that cold thickness. Brusquely, I returned to reality, and found my feet in gluey mud up to my thighs. Hadn't I been sleeping? Where was my bed? And Guernipin? Where was I? Prisoner to a monstrous vacuum that was slowly sucking me in, I was trapped within a stinking, nauseous swamp. My hands, my arms, in vain sought purchase: a root, a branch, my life… Sudden bellows, reminiscent of an angry bull, broke my struggle. From the marsh where I was sinking, they tore at the night. Despite my terror, I identified a heron's call. But instead of being regular in their three consecutive notes, these cries came with no pattern, no rhythm.

Then I saw it… thrashing next to me. And Sylvain's comments came back to me: the Ghoulbird. Did it exist? Yes, it did, for this could only be the mythic bird, shaking with justified laughter at its gullible and ridiculous prey. And here I was, in the middle of the Gobble-Ox Marsh.

Nevertheless, I saw the bird hop around as if under the same threat from the swallowing slough. Seeing my redoubled efforts to break free from the mud that was gradually gaining on me, the bird cried louder. I would have thought it wanted to coax me into escaping the quagmire. I finally managed to reach the nearest stretch of grass and, extricating myself from the greedy mud, I crawled to safety. The heron, which had come closer, supported me by flapping his wings, helping me to reach the firm soil of a pebbly path. If I did not collapse into a heap, I owed it to the angelic bird that nudged me with its beak, and forced me to rise and head for Guernipin, a solid and reassuring sight within reach of hope.

Then I felt an invisible, hostile force that knotted my spirit with terror. I felt the terrifying sensation of a huge but impalpable single wing flapping around me, as nimble as a ray of nothingness in the ocean of night, an immaterial reality that pushed me with relentless perseverance to bring me back into the swamp. Without the frantic cries of the heron, which was engaged in a frenzied dance to come to my rescue, inciting me to flee, I confess that I wouldn't have resisted the Thing that held me enthralled.

And I understood at last! I realized that the Ghoulbird – be it owl, crow, heron or any bird that happened to be there and sensed the threat – was neither a legend nor an enemy of man, but a protector…that it warned of the unspeakable danger it perceived… That its cries, far from being cursed calls, were a warning: terrified, the bird screamed against fear, not to elicit fear!… The Marsh of Gobble-Ox, foul lair still preserved after thousands of years, harboured an invisible ravenous monster, survivor of the times when dark powers ruled under the subtlest forms!

I then glimpsed two greenish and fleeting glows…An illusion, a reflection of my fear? No… those glowing spots were eyes! Screaming in revulsion, I wrenched myself free from the horror that had chosen me and had already failed to lure me in my sleep, out of my bed at Guernipin.

At sunrise, Mr. Tibaldière, eager to show me around the floor of prehistoric ancestors, surely gave Sylvain the order to wake me up. But all the servant could find of me, apart from traces of mud left everywhere, was this note, doubtless destined to remain a mystery:

…Never, ever, kill the Ghoulbird…

THE SEA WAS WET AS WET COULD BE

Gahan Wilson

Gahan Wilson (1930–) is an iconic American writer and cartoonist who has received the World Fantasy Lifetime Achievement Award. (The World Fantasy Award bust of H. P. Lovecraft was designed by Wilson.) His art, routinely appearing in *The New Yorker*, intersects with his fiction in their shared playful grotesquery. Stories have appeared in *Playboy*, *Omni*, and, perhaps most famously, in *Again, Dangerous Visions* with a tale whose title was simply an ink blob. The three-volume set, *Gahan Wilson: 50 Years of Playboy Cartoons* (2010), showcases his art. 'The Sea Was Wet As Wet Could Be' (1967), using Lewis Carroll's *Through the Looking Glass* as partial inspiration, is one of the weirder and more disturbing tales in this volume.

I felt we made an embarrassing contrast to the open serenity of the scene around us. The pure blue of the sky was unmarked by a single cloud or bird, and nothing stirred on the vast stretch of beach except ourselves. The sea, sparkling under the freshness of the early morning sun, looked invitingly clean. I wanted to wade into it and wash myself, but I was afraid I would contaminate it.

We are a contamination here, I thought. We're like a group of sticky bugs crawling in an ugly little crowd over polished marble. If I were God and looked down and saw us, lugging our baskets and our silly, bright blankets, I would step on us and squash us with my foot.

We should have been lovers or monks in such a place, but we were only a crowd of bored and boring drunks. You were always drunk when you were with Carl. Good old, mean old Carl was the greatest little drink pourer in the world. He used drinks like other types of sadists used whips. He kept beating you with them until you dropped or sobbed or went mad, and he enjoyed every step of the process.

We'd been drinking all night, and when the morning came, somebody, I think it was Mandie, got the great idea that we should all go out on a picnic. Naturally, we thought it was an inspiration, we were nothing if not real sports, and so we'd packed some goodies, not forgetting the liquor, and we'd piled into the car, and there we were, weaving across the beach, looking for a place to spread our tacky banquet.

We located a broad, low rock, decided it would serve for our table, and loaded it with the latest in plastic chinaware, a haphazard collection of food, and a quantity of bottles.

Someone had packed a tin of Spam among the other offerings, and, when I saw it, I was suddenly overwhelmed with an absurd feeling of nostalgia. It reminded me of the war and of myself soldier-boying up through Italy. It also reminded me of how long ago the whole thing had been and how little I'd done of what I'd dreamed I'd do back then.

I opened the Spam and sat down to be alone with it and my memories, but it wasn't to be for long. The kind of people who run with people like Carl don't like to be alone, ever, especially with their memories, and they can't imagine anyone else might, at least now and then, have a taste for it.

My rescuer was Irene. Irene was particularly sensitive about seeing people alone because being alone had several times nearly produced fatal results for her. Being alone and taking pills to end the being alone.

'What's wrong, Phil?' she asked.

'Nothing's wrong,' I said, holding up a forkful of the pink Spam in the sunlight. 'It tastes just like it always did. They haven't lost their touch.'

She sat down on the sand beside me, very carefully, so as to avoid spilling the least drop of what must have been her millionth Scotch.

'Phil,' she said, 'I'm worried about Mandie. I really am. She looks so unhappy!'

I glanced over at Mandie. She had her head thrown back and she was laughing uproariously at some joke Carl had just made. Carl was smiling at her with his teeth glistening and his eyes deep down dead as ever.

'Why should Mandie be happy?' I asked. 'What, in God's name, has she got to be happy about?'

'Oh, Phil,' said Irene. 'You pretend to be such an awful cynic. She's *alive,* isn't she?'

I looked at her and wondered what such a statement meant, coming from someone who'd tried to do herself in as earnestly and as frequently as Irene. I decided that I did not know and that I would probably never know. I also decided I didn't want anymore of the Spam. I turned to throw it away, doing my bit to litter up the beach, and then I saw them.

They were far away, barely bigger than two dots, but you could tell there was something odd about them even then.

'We've got company,' I said.

Irene peered in the direction of my point.

'Look, everybody,' she cried, 'we've got company!'

Everybody looked, just as she had asked them to.

'What the hell is this?' asked Carl. 'Don't they know this is my private property?' And then he laughed.

Carl had fantasies about owning things and having power. Now and then he got drunk enough to have little flashes of believing he was king of the world.

'You tell 'em, Carl!' said Horace.

Horace had sparkling quips like that for almost every occasion. He was tall and bald and he had a huge Adam's apple and, like myself, he worked for Carl. I would have felt sorrier for Horace than I did if I hadn't had a sneaky suspicion that he was really happier when groveling. He lifted one scrawny fist and shook it in the direction of the distant pair.

'You guys better beat it,' he shouted. 'This is private property!'

'Will you shut up and stop being such an ass?' Mandie asked him. 'It's not polite to yell at strangers, dear, and this may damn well be *their* beach for all you know.'

Mandie happens to be Horace's wife. Horace's children treat him about the same way. He busied himself with zipping up his windbreaker, because it was getting cold and because he had received an order to be quiet.

I watched the two approaching figures. The one was tall and bulky, and he moved with a peculiar, swaying gait. The other was short and hunched into himself, and he walked in a fretful, zigzag line beside his towering companion.

'They're heading straight for us,' I said.

The combination of the cool wind that had come up and the approach of the two strangers had put a damper on our little group. We sat quietly and watched them coming closer. The nearer they got, the odder they looked.

'For heaven's sake!' said Irene. 'The little one's wearing a square hat!'

'I think it's made of paper,' said Mandie, squinting, 'folded newspaper.'

'Will you look at the mustache on the big bastard?' asked Carl. 'I don't think I've ever seen a bigger bush in my life.'

'They remind me of something,' I said.

The others turned to look at me.

The Walrus and the Carpenter...

'They remind me of the Walrus and the Carpenter,' I said.

'The who?' asked Mandie.

'Don't tell me you never heard of the Walrus and the Carpenter?' asked Carl.

'Never once,' said Mandie.

'Disgusting,' said Carl. 'You're an uncultured bitch. The Walrus and the Carpenter are probably two of the most famous characters in literature. They're in a poem by Lewis Carroll in one of the *Alice* books.'

'In *Through the Looking Glass*,' I said, and then I recited their introduction:

'The Walrus and the Carpenter
Were walking close at hand
They wept like anything to see
Such quantities of sand... '

Mandie shrugged. 'Well, you'll just have to excuse my ignorance and concentrate on my charm,' she said.

'I don't know how to break this to you all,' said Irene, 'but the little one *does* have a handkerchief.'

We stared at them. The little one did indeed have a handkerchief, a huge handkerchief, and he was using it to dab at his eyes.

'Is the little one supposed to be the Carpenter?' asked Mandie.

'Yes,' I said.

'Then it's all right,' she said, 'because he's the one that's carrying the saw.'

'He is, so help me, God,' said Carl. 'And, to make the whole thing perfect, he's even wearing an apron.'

'So the Carpenter in the poem has to wear an apron, right?' asked Mandie.

'Carroll doesn't say whether he does or not,' I said, 'but the illustrations by Tenniel show him wearing one. They also show him with the same square jaw and the same big nose this guy's got.'

'They're goddamn doubles,' said Carl. 'The only thing wrong is that the Walrus isn't a walrus, he just looks like one.'

'You watch,' said Mandie. 'Any minute now he's going to sprout fur all over and grow long fangs.'

Then, for the first time, the approaching pair noticed us. It seemed to give them quite a start. They stood and gaped at us, and the little one furtively stuffed his handkerchief out of sight.

'We can't be as surprising as all that!' whispered Irene.

The big one began moving forward, then, in a hesitant, tentative kind of shuffle. The little one edged ahead, too, but he was careful to keep the bulk of his companion between himself and us.

'First contact with the aliens,' said Mandie, and Irene and Horace giggled nervously. I didn't respond. I had come to the decision that I was going to quit working for Carl, that I didn't like any of these people about me, except, maybe, Irene, and that these two strangers gave me the honest creeps.

Then the big one smiled, and everything was changed.

I've worked in the entertainment field, in advertising and in public relations. This means I have come in contact with some of the prime charm boys and girls in our proud land. I have become, therefore, not only a connoisseur of smiles, I am a being equipped with numerous automatic safeguards against them. When a talcumed smoothie comes at me with his brilliant ivories exposed, it only shows he's got something he can bite me with, that's all.

But the smile of the Walrus was something else.

The smile of the Walrus did what a smile hasn't done for me in years – it melted my heart. I use the cornball phrase very much on purpose. When I saw his smile, I knew I could trust him; I felt in my marrow that he was gentle and sweet and had nothing but the best intentions. His resemblance to the Walrus in the poem ceased being vaguely chilling and became warmly comical. I loved him as I had loved the teddy bear of my childhood.

'Oh, I *say*,' he said, and his voice was an embarrassed boom. 'I *do* hope we're not intruding!'

'I daresay we are,' squeaked the Carpenter, peeping out from behind his companion.

'The, uhm, fact is,' boomed the Walrus, 'we didn't even notice you until just back then, you see.'

'We were talking, is what,' said the Carpenter.

They wept like anything to see
Such quantities of sand...

'About sand?' I asked.

The Walrus looked at me with a startled air.

'We *were*, actually, now you come to mention it.'

He lifted one huge foot and shook it so that a little trickle of sand spilled out of his shoe.

'The stuff's impossible,' he said. 'Gets in your clothes, tracks up the carpet.'

'Ought to be swept away, it ought,' said the Carpenter.

'If seven maids with seven mops
Swept it for half a year,
Do you suppose,' the Walrus said,
'That they could get it clear?'

'It's too much!' said Carl.

'Yes, indeed,' said the Walrus, eying the sand around him with vague disapproval, 'altogether too much.'

Then he turned to us again, and we all basked in that smile.

'Permit me to introduce my companion and myself,' he said.

'You'll have to excuse George,' said the Carpenter, 'as he's a bit of a stuffed shirt, don't you know?'

'Be that as it may,' said the Walrus, patting the Carpenter on the flat top of his paper hat, 'this is Edward Farr, and I am George Tweedy, both at your service. We are, uhm, both a trifle drunk, I'm afraid.'

'We are, indeed. We are that.'

'As we have just come from a really delightful party, to which we shall soon return.'

'Once we've found the fuel, that is,' said Farr, waving his saw in the air. By now he had found the courage to come out and face us directly.

'Which brings me to the question,' said Tweedy. 'Have you seen any *driftwood* lying about the premises? We've been looking high and low, and we can't seem to find *any* of the blasted stuff.'

'Thought there'd be piles of it,' said Farr, 'but all there is is sand, don't you see?'

'I would have sworn you were looking for oysters,' said Carl.

Again, Tweedy appeared startled.

'O Oysters, come and walk with us!'
The Walrus did beseech...

'Oysters?' he asked. 'Oh, no, we've *got* the oysters. All we lack is the means to cook 'em.'

''Course we could always use a few more,' said Farr, looking at his companion.

'I suppose we *could*, at that,' said Tweedy thoughtfully.

'I'm afraid we can't help you fellows with the driftwood problem,' said Carl, 'but you're more than welcome to a drink.'

There was something unfamiliar about the tone of Carl's voice that made my ears perk up. I turned to look at him, and then had difficulty covering up my astonishment.

It was his eyes. For once, for the first time, they were really friendly.

I'm not saying Carl had fishy eyes, blank eyes – not at all. On the surface, that is. On the surface, with his eyes, with his face, with the handling of his entire body, Carl was a master of animation and expression. From sympathetic, heartfelt warmth, all the way to icy rage, and on every stop in-between, Carl was completely convincing.

But only on the surface. Once you got to know Carl, and it took a while, you realized that none of it was really happening. That was because Carl had died, or been killed, long ago. Possibly in childhood. Possibly he had been born dead. So, under the actor's warmth and rage, the eyes were always the eyes of a corpse.

But now it was different. The friendliness here was genuine, I was sure of it. The smile of Tweedy, of the Walrus, had performed a miracle. Carl had risen from his tomb. I was in honest awe.

'*Delighted*, old chap!' said Tweedy.

They accepted their drinks with obvious pleasure, and we completed the introductions as they sat down to join us. I detected a strong smell of fish when Tweedy sat down beside me, but, oddly,

I didn't find it offensive in the least. I was glad he'd chosen me to sit by. He turned and smiled at me, and my heart melted a little more.

It soon turned out that the drinking we'd done before had only scratched the surface. Tweedy and Farr were magnificent boozers, and their gusto encouraged us all to follow suit.

We drank absurd toasts and were delighted to discover that Tweedy was an incredible raconteur. His specialty was outrageous fantasy: wild tales involving incongruous objects, events, and characters. His invention was endless.

'The time has come,' the Walrus said,
'To talk of many things:
Of shoes – and ships – and sealing-wax –
Of cabbages – and kings –
And why the sea is boiling hot –
And whether pigs have wings.'

We laughed and drank, and drank and laughed, and I began to wonder why in hell I'd spent my life being such a gloomy, moody son of a bitch, been such a distrustful and suspicious bastard, when the whole secret of everything, the whole core secret, was simply to enjoy it, to take it as it came.

I looked around and grinned, and I didn't care if it was a foolish grin. Everybody looked all right, everybody looked swell, everybody looked better than I'd ever seen them look before.

Irene looked happy, honestly and truly happy. She, too, had found the secret. No more pills for Irene, I thought. Now that she knows the secret, now that she's met Tweedy, who's given her the secret, she'll have no more need of those goddamn pills.

And I couldn't believe Horace and Mandie. They had their arms around each other, and their bodies were pressed close together, and they rocked as one being when they laughed at Tweedy's wonderful stories. No more nagging for Mandie, I thought, and no more cringing for Horace, now they've learned the secret.

And then I looked at Carl, laughing and relaxed and absolutely free of care, absolutely unchilled, finally, at last, after years of –

And then I looked at Carl again.

And then I looked down at my drink, and then I looked at my knees, and then I looked out at the sea, sparkling, clean, remote and impersonal.

And then I realized it had grown cold, quite cold, and that there wasn't a bird or a cloud in the sky.

The sea was wet as wet could be,
The sands were dry as dry.
You could not see a cloud, because
No cloud was in the sky:
No birds were flying overhead –
There were no birds to fly.

That part of the poem was, after all, a perfect description of a lifeless earth. It sounded beautiful at first; it sounded benign. But then you read it again and you realized that Carroll was describing barrenness and desolation.

Suddenly Carl's voice broke through and I heard him say:

'Hey, that's a hell of an idea, Tweedy! By God, we'd love to! Wouldn't we, gang?'

The others broke out in an affirmative chorus and they all started scrambling to their feet around me. I looked up at them, like someone who's been awakened from sleep in a strange place, and they grinned down at me like loons.

'Come on, Phil!' cried Irene.

Her eyes were bright and shining, but it wasn't with happiness. I could see that now.

'It seems a shame,' the Walrus said,
'To play them such a trick… '

I blinked my eyes and stared at them, one after the other.

'Old Phil's had a little too much to drink!' cried Mandie, laughing. 'Come on, old Phil! Come on and join the party!'

'What party?' I asked.

I couldn't seem to get located. Everything seemed disorientated and grotesque.

'For Christ's sake, Phil,' said Carl, 'Tweedy and Farr, here, have invited us to join their party. There's no more drinks left, and they've got plenty!'

I set my plastic cup down carefully on the sand.

If they would just shut up for a moment, I thought, I might be able to get the fuzz out of my head.

'Come *along*, sir!' boomed Tweedy jovially. 'It's only a pleasant walk!'

'O Oysters, come and walk with us!'
The Walrus did beseech.
'A pleasant walk, a pleasant talk
Along the briny beach . . . '

He was smiling at me, but the smile didn't work anymore.

'You cannot do with more than four,' I told him.

'*Uhm?* What's that?'

'We cannot do with more than four,
To give a hand to each.'

'I said, "You cannot do with more than four."'

'He's right, you know,' said Farr, the Carpenter.

'Well, uhm, then,' said the Walrus, 'if you feel you really *can't* come, old chap . . . '

'What, in Christ's name, are you all talking about?' asked Mandie.

'He's hung up on that goddamn poem,' said Carl. 'Lewis Carroll's got the yellow bastard scared.'

'Don't be such a party pooper, Phil!' said Mandie.

'To hell with him,' said Carl. And he started off, and all the others followed him. Except Irene.

'Are you sure you really don't want to come, Phil?' she asked.

She looked frail and thin against the sunlight. I realized there really wasn't much of her, and that what there was had taken a terrible beating.

'No,' I said. 'I don't. Are you sure you want to go?'

'Of course I do, Phil.'

I thought of the pills.

'I suppose you do,' I said. 'I suppose there's really no stopping you.'

'No, Phil, there isn't.'

And then she stooped and kissed me. Kissed me very gently, and I could feel the dry, chapped surface of her lips and the faint warmth of her breath.

I stood.

'I wish you'd stay,' I said.

'I can't,' she said.

And then she turned and ran after the others.

I watched them growing smaller and smaller on the beach, following the Walrus and the Carpenter. I watched them come to where the beach curved around the bluff and watched them disappear behind the bluff.

I looked up at the sky. Pure blue. Impersonal.

'What do you think of this?' I asked it.

Nothing. It hadn't even noticed.

'Now, if you're ready, Oysters dear,
We can begin to feed.'

'But not on us!' the Oysters cried,
Turning a little blue.
'After such kindness, that would be
A dismal thing to do!'

A dismal thing to do.

I began to run up the beach, toward the bluff. I stumbled now and then because I had had too much to drink. Far too much to drink. I heard small shells crack under my shoes, and the sand made whipping noises.

I fell, heavily, and lay there gasping on the beach. My heart pounded in my chest. I was too old for this sort of footwork. I hadn't had any real exercise in years. I smoked too much and I drank too much. I did all the wrong things. I didn't do any of the right things.

I pushed myself up a little and then I let myself down again. My heart was pounding hard enough to frighten me. I could feel it in my chest, frantically pumping, squeezing blood in and spurting blood out.

Like an oyster pulsing in the sea.

'Shall we be trotting home again?'

My heart was like an oyster.

I got up, fell up, and began to run again, weaving widely, my mouth open and the air burning my throat. I was coated with sweat, streaming with it, and it felt icy in the cold wind.

'Shall we be trotting home again?'

I rounded the bluff, and then I stopped and stood swaying, and then I dropped to my knees.

The pure blue of the sky was unmarked by a single bird or cloud, and nothing stirred on the whole vast stretch of the beach.

But answer came there none –
And this was scarcely odd, because…

Nothing stirred, but they were there. Irene and Mandie and Carl and Horace were there, and four others, too. Just around the bluff.

'We cannot do with more than four…

But the Walrus and the Carpenter had taken two trips.

I began to crawl toward them on my knees. My heart, my oyster heart, was pounding too hard to allow me to stand.

The other four had had a picnic, too, very like our own. They, too, had plastic cups and plates, and they, too, had brought bottles. They had sat and waited for the return of the Walrus and the Carpenter.

Irene was right in front of me. Her eyes were open and stared at, but did not see, the sky. The pure blue uncluttered sky. There were a few grains of sand in her left eye. Her face was almost clear of blood. There were only a few flecks of it on her lower chin. The spray from the huge wound in her chest seemed to have traveled mainly downward and to the right. I stretched out my arm and touched her hand.

'Irene,' I said.

But answer came there none –
And this was scarcely odd, because
They'd eaten every one.

I looked up at the others. Like Irene, they were, all of them, dead. The Walrus and the Carpenter had eaten the oysters and left the shell.

The Carpenter never found any firewood, and so they'd eaten them raw. You can eat oysters raw if you want to.

I said her name once more, just for the record, and then I stood and turned from them and walked to the bluff. I rounded the bluff and the beach stretched before me, vast, smooth, empty, and remote.

Even as I ran upon it, away from them, it was remote.

DON'T LOOK NOW

Daphne du Maurier

Daphne du Maurier (1907–1989) was an extremely popular English author and playwright. Many of her works have been adapted into films, including the novels *Rebecca* (1938), which won the Best Picture Oscar in 1941, *Jamaica Inn* (1936), and the story 'The Birds' (1963), all three movies directed by Alfred Hitchcock. Du Maurier's 'Don't Look Now' (1971), included herein, was adapted into a cult classic film directed by Nicolas Roeg in 1973. The novella is a masterpiece of the occult, its hints of a world *beyond* embodying the best of weird fiction. Du Maurier was one of five Women of Achievement selected for a set of British stamps issued in August 1996.

'Don't look now,' John said to his wife, 'but there are a couple of old girls two tables away who are trying to hypnotise me.'

Laura, quick on cue, made an elaborate pretence of yawning, then tilted her head as though searching the skies for a non-existent aeroplane.

'Right behind you,' he added. 'That's why you can't turn round at once – it would be much too obvious.'

Laura played the oldest trick in the world and dropped her napkin, then bent to scrabble for it under her feet, sending a shooting glance over her left shoulder as she straightened once again. She sucked in her cheeks, the first telltale sign of suppressed hysteria, and lowered her head.

'They're not old girls at all,' she said. 'They're male twins in drag.'

Her voice broke ominously, the prelude to uncontrolled laughter, and John quickly poured some more chianti into her glass.

'Pretend to choke,' he said, 'then they won't notice. You know what it is – they're criminals doing the sights of Europe, changing sex at each stop. Twin sisters here on Torcello. Twin brothers tomorrow in Venice, or even tonight, parading arm-in-arm across the Piazza San Marco. Just a matter of switching clothes and wigs.'

'Jewel thieves or murderers?' asked Laura.

'Oh, murderers, definitely. But why, I ask myself, have they picked on me?'

The waiter made a diversion by bringing coffee and bearing away the fruit, which gave Laura time to banish hysteria and regain control.

'I can't think,' she said, 'why we didn't notice them when we arrived. They stand out to high heaven. One couldn't fail.'

'That gang of Americans masked them,' said John, 'and the bearded man with a monocle who looked like a spy. It wasn't until they all went just now that I saw the twins. Oh God, the one with the shock of white hair has got her eye on me again.'

Laura took the powder compact from her bag and held it in front of her face, the mirror acting as a reflector.

'I think it's me they're looking at, not you,' she said. 'Thank heaven I left my pearls with the manager at the hotel.' She paused, dabbing the sides of her nose with powder. 'The thing is,' she said after a moment, 'we've got them wrong. They're neither murderers nor thieves. They're a couple of pathetic old retired schoolmistresses on holiday, who've saved up all their lives to visit Venice. They come from some place with a name like Walabanga in

Australia. And they're called Tilly and Tiny.'

Her voice, for the first time since they had come away, took on the old bubbling quality he loved, and the worried frown between her brows had vanished. At last, he thought, at last she's beginning to get over it. If I can keep this going, if we can pick up the familiar routine of jokes shared on holiday and at home, the ridiculous fantasies about people at other tables, or staying in the hotel, or wandering in art galleries and churches, then everything will fall into place, life will become as it was before, the wound will heal, she will forget.

'You know,' said Laura, 'that really was a very good lunch. I did enjoy it.'

Thank God, he thought, thank God… Then he leant forward, speaking low in a conspirator's whisper. 'One of them is going to the loo,' he said. 'Do you suppose he, or she, is going to change her wig?'

'Don't say anything,' Laura murmured. 'I'll follow her and find out. She may have a suitcase tucked away there, and she's going to switch clothes.'

She began to hum under her breath, the signal, to her husband, of content. The ghost was temporarily laid, and all because of the familiar holiday game, abandoned too long, and now, through mere chance, blissfully recaptured.

'Is she on her way?' asked Laura.

'About to pass our table now,' he told her.

Seen on her own, the woman was not so remarkable. Tall, angular, aquiline features, with the close-cropped hair which was fashionably called an Eton crop, he seemed to remember, in his mother's day, and about her person the stamp of that particular generation. She would be in her middle sixties, he supposed, the masculine shirt with collar and tie, sports jacket, grey tweed skirt coming to mid-calf. Grey stockings and laced black shoes. He had seen the type on golf-courses and at dog shows – invariably showing not sporting breeds but pugs – and if you came across them at a party in somebody's house they were quicker on the draw with a cigarette-lighter than he was himself, a mere male, with pocket-matches. The general belief that they kept house with a more feminine, fluffy companion was not always true. Frequently they boasted, and adored, a golfing husband. No, the striking point about this particular individual was that there were two of them. Identical twins cast in the same mould. The only difference was that the other one had whiter hair.

'Supposing,' murmured Laura, 'when I find myself in the *toilette* beside her she starts to strip?'

'Depends on what is revealed,' John answered. 'If she's hermaphrodite, make a bolt for it. She might have a hypodermic syringe concealed and want to knock you out before you reached the door.'

Laura sucked in her cheeks once more and began to shake. Then, squaring her shoulders, she rose to her feet. 'I simply must not laugh,' she said, 'and whatever you do, don't look at me when I come back, especially if we come out together.' She picked up her bag and strolled self-consciously away from the table in pursuit of her prey.

John poured the dregs of the chianti into his glass and lit a cigarette. The sun blazed down upon the little garden of the restaurant. The Americans had left, and the monocled man, and the family party at the far end. All was peace. The identical twin was sitting back in her chair with her eyes closed. Thank heaven, he thought, for this moment at any rate, when relaxation was possible, and Laura had been launched upon her foolish, harmless game. The holiday could yet turn into the cure she needed, blotting out, if only temporarily, the numb despair that had seized her since the child died.

'She'll get over it,' the doctor said. 'They all get over it, in time. And you have the boy.'

'I know,' John had said, 'but the girl meant everything. She always did, right from the start, I don't know why. I suppose it was the difference in age. A boy of school age, and a tough one at that, is someone in his own right. Not a baby of five. Laura literally adored her. Johnnie and I were nowhere.'

'Give her time,' repeated the doctor, 'give her time. And anyway, you're both young still. There'll be others. Another daughter.'

So easy to talk… How replace the life of a loved lost child with a dream? He knew Laura too well. Another child, another girl, would have her own qualities, a separate identity, she might even induce hostility because of this very fact. A usurper in the cradle, in the cot, that had been Christine's. A chubby, flaxen replica of Johnnie, not the little waxen dark-haired sprite that had gone.

He looked up, over his glass of wine, and the woman was staring at him again. It was not the casual, idle glance of someone at a nearby table, waiting for her companion to return, but something deeper, more intent, the prominent, light blue eyes oddly penetrating, giving him a sudden feeling of discomfort. Damn the woman! All right, bloody stare, if you must. Two can play at that game. He blew a cloud of cigarette smoke into the air and smiled at her, he hoped offensively. She did not register. The blue eyes continued to hold his, so that he was obliged to look away himself, extinguish his cigarette, glance over his shoulder for the waiter and call for the bill. Settling for this, and fumbling with the change, with a few casual remarks about the excellence of the meal, brought composure, but a prickly feeling on his scalp remained, and an odd sensation of unease. Then it went, as abruptly as it had started, and stealing a furtive glance at the other table he saw that her eyes were closed again, and she was sleeping, or dozing, as she had done before. The waiter disappeared. All was still.

Laura, he thought, glancing at his watch, is being a hell of a time. Ten minutes at least. Something to tease her about, anyway. He began to plan the form the joke would take. How the old dolly had stripped to her smalls, suggesting that Laura should do likewise. And then the manager had burst in upon them both, exclaiming in horror, the reputation of the restaurant damaged, the hint that unpleasant consequences might follow unless ... The whole exercise turning out to be a plant, an exercise in blackmail. He and Laura and the twins taken in a police launch back to Venice for questioning. Quarter of an hour... Oh, come on, come on...

There was a crunch of feet on the gravel. Laura's twin walked slowly past, alone. She crossed over to her table and stood there a moment, her tall, angular figure interposing self between John and her sister. She was saying something, but he couldn't catch the words. What was the accent, though – Scottish? Then she bent, offering an arm to the seated twin, and they moved away together across the garden to the break in the little hedge beyond, the twin who had stared at John leaning on her sister's arm. Here was the difference again. She was not quite so tall, and she stooped more – perhaps she was arthritic. They disappeared out of sight, and John, becoming impatient, got up and was about to walk back into the hotel when Laura emerged.

'Well, I must say, you took your time,' he began, and then stopped, because of the expression on her face.

'What's the matter, what's happened?' he asked.

He could tell at once there was something wrong. Almost as if she were in a state of shock. She blundered towards the table he had just vacated and sat down. He drew up a chair beside her, taking her hand.

'Darling, what is it? Tell me – are you ill?'

She shook her head, and then turned and looked at him. The dazed expression he had noticed at first had given way to one of dawning confidence, almost of exaltation.

'It's quite wonderful,' she said slowly, 'the most wonderful thing that could possibly be. You see, she isn't dead, she's still with us. That's why they kept staring at us, those two sisters. They could see Christine.'

Oh God, he thought. It's what I've been dreading. She's going off her head. What do I do? How do I cope?

'Laura, sweet,' he began, forcing a smile, 'look, shall we go? I've paid the bill, we can go and look at the cathedral and stroll around, and then it will be time to take off in that launch again for Venice.'

She wasn't listening, or at any rate the words didn't penetrate.

'John, love,' she said, 'I've got to tell you what happened. I followed her, as we planned, into the *toilette* place. She was combing her hair and I went into the loo, and then came out and washed my hands in the basin. She was washing hers in the next basin. Suddenly she turned and said to me, in a strong Scots accent, "Don't be unhappy any more. My sister has seen your little girl. She was sitting between you and your husband laughing."

Darling, I thought I was going to faint. I nearly did. Luckily, there was a chair, and I sat down, and the woman bent over me and patted my head. I'm not sure of her exact words, but she said something about the moment of truth and joy being as sharp as a sword, but not to be afraid, all was well, but the sister's vision had been so strong they knew I had to be told, and that Christine wanted it. Oh John, don't look like that. I swear I'm not making it up, this is what she told me, it's all true.'

The desperate urgency in her voice made his heart sicken. He had to play along with her, agree, soothe, do anything to bring back some sense of calm.

'Laura, darling, of course I believe you,' he said, 'only it's a sort of shock, and I'm upset because you're upset… '

'But I'm not upset,' she interrupted. 'I'm happy, so happy that I can't put the feeling into words. You know what it's been like all these weeks, at home and everywhere we've been on holiday, though I tried to hide it from you. Now it's lifted, because I know, I just know, that the woman was right. Oh Lord, how awful of me, but I've forgotten their name – she did tell me. You see, the thing is that she's a retired doctor, they come from Edinburgh, and the one who saw Christine went blind a few years ago. Although she's studied the occult all her life and been very psychic, it's only since going blind that she has really seen things, like a medium. They've had the most wonderful experiences. But to describe Christine as the blind one did to her sister, even down to the little blue-and-white dress with the puff sleeves that she wore at her birthday party, and to say she was smiling happily… Oh darling, it's made me so happy I think I'm going to cry.'

No hysteria. Nothing wild. She took a tissue from her bag and blew her nose, smiling at him. 'I'm all right, you see, you don't have to worry. Neither of us need worry about anything any more. Give me a cigarette.'

He took one from his packet and lighted it for her. She sounded normal, herself again. She wasn't trembling. And if this sudden belief was going to keep her happy he couldn't possibly begrudge it. But… but… he wished, all the same, it hadn't happened. There was something uncanny about thoughtreading, about telepathy. Scientists couldn't account for it, nobody could, and this is what must have happened just now between Laura and the sisters. So the one who had been staring at him was blind. That accounted for the fixed gaze. Which somehow was unpleasant in itself, creepy. Oh hell, he thought, I wish we hadn't come here for lunch. Just chance, a flick of a coin between this, Torcello, and driving to Padua, and we had to choose Torcello.

'You didn't arrange to meet them again or anything, did you?' he asked, trying to sound casual.

'No, darling, why should I?' Laura answered. 'I mean, there was nothing more they could tell me. The sister had had her wonderful vision, and that was that. Anyway, they're moving on. Funnily enough, it's rather like our original game. They *are* going round the world before returning to Scotland. Only I said Australia, didn't I? The old dears… Anything less like murderers and jewel thieves.'

She had quite recovered. She stood up and looked about her. 'Come on,' she said. 'Having come to Torcello we must see the cathedral.'

They made their way from the restaurant across the open piazza, where the stalls had been set up with scarves and trinkets and postcards, and so along the path to the cathedral. One of the ferryboats had just decanted a crowd of sightseers, many of whom had already found their way into Santa Maria Assunta. Laura, undaunted, asked her husband for the guidebook, and, as had always been her custom in happier days, started to walk slowly through the cathedral, studying mosaics, columns, panels from left to right, while John, less interested, because of his concern at what had just happened, followed close behind, keeping a weather eye alert for the twin sisters. There was no sign of them. Perhaps they had gone into the church of Santa Fosca close by. A sudden encounter would be embarrassing, quite apart from the effect it might have upon Laura. But the anonymous, shuffling tourists, intent upon culture, could not harm her, although from his own point of view they made artistic appreciation impossible. He could not concentrate, the cold clear beauty of what he saw left him untouched, and when Laura touched his sleeve, pointing to the mosaic of the Virgin and Child standing above the frieze of the Apostles, he nodded in sympathy yet saw nothing, the long, sad face of the Virgin infinitely remote, and turning on sudden impulse stared back over the heads of the tourists towards the door, where frescoes of the blessed and the damned gave themselves to judgement.

The twins were standing there, the blind one still holding on to her sister's arm, her sightless eyes fixed firmly upon him. He felt himself held, unable to move, and an impending sense of doom, of tragedy, came upon him. His whole being sagged, as it were, in apathy, and he thought, 'This is the end, there is no escape, no future.' Then both sisters turned and went out of the cathedral and the sensation vanished, leaving indignation in its wake, and rising anger. How dare those two old fools practise their mediumistic tricks on him? It was fraudulent, unhealthy; this was probably the way they lived, touring the world making everyone they met uncomfortable. Give them half a chance and they would have got money out of Laura – anything.

He felt her tugging at his sleeve again. 'Isn't she beautiful? So happy, so serene.'

'Who? What?' he asked.

'The Madonna,' she answered. 'She has a magic quality. It goes right through to one. Don't you feel it too?'

'I suppose so. I don't know. There are too many people around.'

She looked up at him, astonished. 'What's that got to do with it? How funny you are. Well all right, let's get away from them. I want to buy some postcards anyway.'

Disappointed, she sensed his lack of interest, and began to thread her way through the crowd of tourists to the door.

'Come on,' he said abruptly, once they were outside, 'there's plenty of time for postcards, let's explore a bit,' and he struck off from the path, which would have taken them back to the centre where the little houses were, and the stalls, and the drifting crowd of people, to a narrow way amongst uncultivated ground, beyond which he could see a sort of cutting, or canal. The sight of water, limpid, pale, was a soothing contrast to the fierce sun above their heads.

'I don't think this leads anywhere much,' said Laura. 'It's a bit muddy, too, one can't sit. Besides, there are more things the guidebook says we ought to see.'

'Oh, forget the book,' he said impatiently, and, pulling her down beside him on the bank above the cutting, put his arms round her.

'It's the wrong time of day for sightseeing. Look, there's a rat swimming there the other side.'

He picked up a stone and threw it in the water, and the animal sank, or somehow disappeared, and nothing was left but bubbles.

'Don't,' said Laura. 'It's cruel, poor thing,' and then suddenly, putting her hand on her knee, 'Do you think Christine is sitting here beside us?'

He did not answer at once. What was there to say? Would it be like this forever?

'I expect so,' he said slowly, 'if you feel she is.'

The point was, remembering Christine before the onset of the fatal meningitis, she would have been running along the bank excitedly, throwing off her shoes, wanting to paddle, giving Laura a fit of apprehension. 'Sweetheart, take care, come back …'

'The woman said she was looking so happy, sitting beside us, smiling,' said Laura. She got up, brushing her dress, her mood changed to restlessness. 'Come on, let's go back,' she said.

He followed her with a sinking heart. He knew she did not really want to buy postcards or see what remained to be seen; she wanted to go in search of the women again, not necessarily to talk, just to be near them. When they came to the open place by the stalls he noticed that the crowd of tourists had thinned, there were only a few stragglers left, and the sisters were not amongst them. They must have joined the main body who had come to Torcello by the ferry service. A wave of relief seized him.

'Look, there's a mass of postcards at the second stall,' he said quickly, 'and some eye-catching head scarves. Let me buy you a head scarf.'

'Darling, I've so many!' she protested. 'Don't waste your lire.'

'It isn't a waste. I'm in a buying mood. What

about a basket? You know we never have enough baskets. Or some lace. How about lace?'

She allowed herself, laughing, to be dragged to the stall. While he rumpled through the goods spread out before them, and chatted up the smiling woman who was selling her wares, his ferociously bad Italian making her smile the more, he knew it would give the body of tourists more time to walk to the landing stage and catch the ferry service, and the twin sisters would be out of sight and out of their life.

'Never,' said Laura, some twenty minutes later, 'has so much junk been piled into so small a basket,' her bubbling laugh reassuring him that all was well, he needn't worry any more, the evil hour had passed. The launch from the Cipriani that had brought them from Venice was waiting by the landing stage. The passengers who had arrived with them, the Americans, the man with the monocle, were already assembled. Earlier, before setting out, he had thought the price for lunch and transport, there and back, decidedly steep. Now he grudged none of it, except that the outing to Torcello itself had been one of the major errors of this particular holiday in Venice. They stepped down into the launch, finding a place in the open, and the boat chugged away down the canal and into the lagoon. The ordinary ferry had gone before, steaming towards Murano, while their own craft headed past San Francesco del Deserto and so back direct to Venice.

He put his arm around her once more, holding her close, and this time she responded, smiling up at him, her head on his shoulder.

'It's been a lovely day,' she said. 'I shall never forget it, never. You know, darling, now at last I can begin to enjoy our holiday.'

He wanted to shout with relief. It's going to be all right, he decided, let her believe what she likes, it doesn't matter, it makes her happy. The beauty of Venice rose before them, sharply outlined against the glowing sky, and there was still so much to see, wandering there together, that might now be perfect because of her change of mood, the shadow having lifted, and aloud he began to discuss the evening to come, where they would dine – not the restaurant they usually went to, near the Fenice theatre, but somewhere different, somewhere new.

'Yes, but it must be cheap,' she said, falling in with his mood, 'because we've already spent so much today.'

Their hotel by the Grand Canal had a welcoming, comforting air. The clerk smiled as he handed over their key. The bedroom was familiar, like home, with Laura's things arranged neatly on the dressing-table, but with it the little festive atmosphere of strangeness, of excitement, that only a holiday bedroom brings. This is ours for the moment, but no more. While we are in it we bring it life. When we have gone it no longer exists, it fades into anonymity. He turned on both taps in the bathroom, the water gushing into the bath, the steam rising. 'Now,' he thought afterwards, 'now at last is the moment to make love,' and he went back into the bedroom, and she understood, and opened her arms and smiled. Such blessed relief after all those weeks of restraint.

'The thing is,' she said later, fixing her ear-rings before the looking-glass, 'I'm not really terribly hungry. Shall we just be dull and eat in the dining-room here?'

'God, no!' he exclaimed. 'With all those rather dreary couples at the other tables? I'm ravenous. I'm also gay. I want to get rather sloshed.'

'Not bright lights and music, surely?'

'No, no... some small, dark, intimate cave, rather sinister, full of lovers with other people's wives.'

'Hmm,' sniffed Laura, 'we all know what *that* means. You'll spot some Italian lovely of sixteen and smirk at her through dinner, while I'm stuck high and dry with a beastly man's broad back.'

They went out laughing into the warm soft night, and the magic was about them everywhere. 'Let's walk,' he said, 'let's walk and work up an appetite for our gigantic meal,' and inevitably they found themselves by the Molo and the lapping gondolas dancing upon the water, the lights everywhere blending with the darkness. There were other couples strolling for the same sake of aimless enjoyment, backwards, forwards, purposeless, and the inevitable sailors in groups, noisy, gesticulating, and dark-eyed girls whispering, clicking on high heels.

'The trouble is,' said Laura, 'walking in Venice becomes compulsive once you start. Just over the next bridge, you say, and then the next one beckons. I'm sure there are no restaurants down here, we're almost at those public gardens where they hold the Biennale. Let's turn back. I know there's a restaurant somewhere near the church of San Zaccaria, there's a little alleyway leading to it.'

'Tell you what,' said John, 'if we go down here by the Arsenal, and cross that bridge at the end and head left, we'll come upon San Zaccaria from the other side. We did it the other morning.'

'Yes, but it was daylight then. We may lose our way, it's not very well lit.'

'Don't fuss. I have an instinct for these things.'

They turned down the Fondamenta dell' Arsenale and crossed the little bridge short of the Arsenal itself, and so on past the church of San Martino. There were two canals ahead, one bearing right, the other left, with narrow streets beside them. John hesitated. Which one was it they had walked beside the day before?

'You see,' protested Laura, 'we shall be lost, just as I said.'

'Nonsense,' replied John firmly. 'It's the left-hand one, I remember the little bridge.'

The canal was narrow, the houses on either side seemed to close in upon it, and in the daytime, with the sun's reflection on the water and the windows of the houses open, bedding upon the balconies, a canary singing in a cage, there had been an impression of warmth, of secluded shelter. Now, ill-lit, almost in darkness, the windows of the houses shuttered, the water dank, the scene appeared altogether different, neglected, poor, and the long narrow boats moored to the slippery steps of cellar entrances looked like coffins.

'I swear I don't remember this bridge,' said Laura, pausing, and holding on to the rail, 'and I don't like the look of that alleyway beyond.'

'There's a lamp halfway up,' John told her. 'I know exactly where we are, not far from the Greek quarter.'

They crossed the bridge, and were about to plunge into the alleyway when they heard the cry. It came, surely, from one of the houses on the opposite side, but which one it was impossible to say. With the shutters closed each one of them seemed dead. They turned, and stared in the direction from which the sound had come.

'What was it?' whispered Laura.

'Some drunk or other,' said John briefly. 'Come on.'

Less like a drunk than someone being strangled, and the choking cry suppressed as the grip held firm.

'We ought to call the police,' said Laura.

'Oh, for heaven's sake,' said John. Where did she think she was – Piccadilly?

'Well, I'm off, it's sinister,' she replied, and began to hurry away up the twisting alleyway. John hesitated, his eye caught by a small figure which suddenly crept from a cellar entrance below one of the opposite houses, and then jumped into a narrow boat below. It was a child, a little girl – she couldn't have been more than five or six – wearing a short coat over her minute skirt, a pixie hood covering her head. There were four boats moored, line upon line, and she proceeded to jump from one to the other with surprising agility, intent, it would seem, upon escape. Once her foot slipped and he caught his breath, for she was within a few feet of the water, losing balance; then she recovered, and hopped on to the furthest boat. Bending, she tugged at the rope, which had the effect of swinging the boat's after-end across the canal, almost touching the opposite side and another cellar entrance, about thirty feet from the spot where John stood watching her. Then the child jumped again, landing upon the cellar steps, and vanished into the house, the boat swinging back into midcanal behind her. The whole episode could not have taken more than four minutes. Then he heard the quick patter of feet. Laura had returned. She had seen none of it, for which he felt unspeakably thankful. The sight of a child, a little girl, in what must have been near danger, her fear that the scene he had just witnessed was in some way a sequel to the alarming cry, might have had a disastrous effect on her overwrought nerves.

'What are you doing?' she called. 'I daren't go

on without you. The wretched alley branches in two directions.'

'Sorry,' he told her. 'I'm coming.'

He took her arm and they walked briskly along the alley, John with an apparent confidence he did not possess.

'There were no more cries, were there?' she asked.

'No,' he said, 'no, nothing. I tell you, it was some drunk.'

The alley led to a deserted *campo* behind a church, not a church he knew, and he led the way across, along another street and over a further bridge.

'Wait a minute,' he said. 'I think we take this right-hand turning. It will lead us into the Greek quarter – the church of San Georgio is somewhere over there.'

She did not answer. She was beginning to lose faith. The place was like a maze. They might circle round and round forever, and then find themselves back again, near the bridge where they had heard the cry. Doggedly he led her on, and then surprisingly, with relief, he saw people walking in the lighted street ahead, there was a spire of a church, the surroundings became familiar.

'There, I told you,' he said. 'That's San Zaccaria, we've found it all right. Your restaurant can't be far away.'

And anyway, there would be other restaurants, somewhere to eat, at least here was the cheering glitter of lights, of movement, canals beside which people walked, the atmosphere of tourism. The letters 'Ristorante', in blue lights, shone like a beacon down a left-hand alley.

'Is this your place?' he asked.

'God knows,' she said. 'Who cares? Let's feed there anyway.'

And so into the sudden blast of heated air and hum of voices, the smell of pasta, wine, waiters, jostling customers, laughter. 'For two? This way, please.' Why, he thought, was one's British nationality always so obvious? A cramped little table and an enormous menu scribbled in an indecipherable mauve biro, with the waiter hovering, expecting the order forthwith.

'Two very large camparis, with soda,' John said. '*Then* we'll study the menu.'

He was not going to be rushed. He handed the bill of fare to Laura and looked about him. Mostly Italians – that meant the food would be good. Then he saw them. At the opposite side of the room. The twin sisters. They must have come into the restaurant hard upon Laura's and his own arrival, for they were only now sitting down, shedding their coats, the waiter hovering beside the table. John was seized with the irrational thought that this was no coincidence. The sisters had noticed them both, in the street outside and had followed them in. Why, in the name of hell, should they have picked on this particular spot, in the whole of Venice, unless... unless Laura herself, at Torcello, had suggested a further encounter, or the sister had suggested it to her? A small restaurant near the church of San Zaccaria, we go there sometimes for dinner. It was Laura, before the walk, who had mentioned San Zaccaria...

She was still intent upon the menu, she had not seen the sisters, but any moment now she would have chosen what she wanted to eat, and then she would raise her head and look across the room. If only the drinks would come. If only the waiter would bring the drinks, it would give Laura something to do.

'You know, I was thinking,' he said quickly, 'we really ought to go to the garage tomorrow and get the car, and do that drive to Padua. We could lunch in Padua, see the cathedral and touch St. Antony's tomb and look at the Giotto frescoes, and come back by way of those various villas along the Brenta that the guidebook cracks up.'

It was no use, though. She was looking up, across the restaurant, and she gave a little gasp of surprise. It was genuine. He could swear it was genuine.

'Look,' she said, 'how extraordinary! How really amazing!'

'What?' he said sharply.

'Why, there they are. My wonderful old twins. They've seen us, what's more. They're staring this way.' She waved her hand, radiant, delighted. The sister she had spoken to at Torcello bowed and smiled. False old bitch, he thought. I know they followed us.

'Oh, darling, I must go and speak to them,' she said impulsively, 'just to tell them how happy I've been all day, thanks to them.'

'Oh, for heaven's sake!' he said. 'Look, here are the drinks. And we haven't ordered yet. Surely you can wait until later, until we've eaten?'

'I won't be a moment,' she said, 'and anyway I want scampi, nothing first. I told you I wasn't hungry.'

She got up, and, brushing past the waiter with the drinks, crossed the room. She might have been greeting the loved friends of years. He watched her bend over the table and shake them both by the hand, and because there was a vacant chair at their table she drew it up and sat down, talking, smiling. Nor did the sisters seem surprised, at least not the one she knew, who nodded and talked back, while the blind sister remained impassive.

'All right,' thought John savagely, 'then I *will* get sloshed,' and he proceeded to down his campari and soda and order another, while he pointed out something quite negligible on the menu as his own choice, but remembered scampi for Laura. 'And a bottle of Soave,' he added, 'with ice.'

The evening was ruined anyway. What was to have been an intimate, happy occasion would now be heavy-laden with spiritualistic visions, poor little dead Christine sharing the table with them, which was so damned stupid when in earthly life she would have been tucked up hours ago in bed. The bitter taste of the campari suited his mood of sudden self-pity, and all the while he watched the group at the table in the opposite corner, Laura apparently listening while the more active sister held forth and the blind one sat silent, her formidable sightless eyes turned in his direction.

'She's phoney,' he thought, 'she's not blind at all. They're both of them frauds, and they could be males in drag after all, just as we pretended at Torcello, and they're after Laura.'

He began on his second campari and soda. The two drinks, taken on an empty stomach, had an instant effect. Vision became blurred. And still Laura went on sitting at the other table, putting in a question now and again, while the active sister talked. The waiter appeared with the scampi, and a companion beside him to serve John's own order, which was totally unrecognisable, heaped with a livid sauce.

'The signora does not come?' enquired the first waiter, and John shook his head grimly, pointing an unsteady finger across the room.

'Tell the signora,' he said carefully, 'her scampi will get cold.'

He stared down at the offering placed before him, and prodded it delicately with a fork. The pallid sauce dissolved, revealing two enormous slices, rounds, of what appeared to be boiled pork, bedecked with garlic. He forked a portion to his mouth and chewed, and yes, it was pork, steamy, rich, the spicy sauce having turned it curiously sweet. He laid down his fork, pushing the plate away, and became aware of Laura, returning across the room and sitting beside him. She did not say anything, which was just as well, he thought, because he was too near nausea to answer. It wasn't just the drink, but reaction from the whole nightmare day. She began to eat her scampi, still not uttering. She did not seem to notice he was not eating. The waiter, hovering at his elbow, anxious, seemed aware that John's choice was somehow an error, and discreetly removed the plate. 'Bring me a green salad,' murmured John, and even then Laura did not register surprise, or, as she might have done in more normal circumstances, accuse him of having had too much to drink. Finally, when she had finished her scampi and was sipping her wine, which John had waved away, to nibble at his salad in small mouthfuls like a sick rabbit, she began to speak.

'Darling,' she said, 'I know you won't believe it, and it's rather frightening in a way, but after they left the restaurant in Torcello the sisters went to the cathedral, as we did, although we didn't see them in that crowd, and the blind one had another vision. She said Christine was trying to tell her something about us, that we should be in danger if we stayed in Venice. Christine wanted us to go away as soon as possible.'

So that's it, he thought. They think they can run our lives for us. This is to be our problem from henceforth. Do we eat? Do we get up? Do we go to bed? We must get in touch with the twin sisters. They will direct us.

'Well?' she said. 'Why don't you say something?'

'Because,' he answered, 'you are perfectly right, I don't believe it. Quite frankly, I judge your old sisters as being a couple of freaks, if nothing else. They're obviously unbalanced, and I'm sorry if this hurts you, but the fact is they've found a sucker in you.'

'You're being unfair,' said Laura. 'They are genuine, I know it. I just know it. They were completely sincere in what they said.'

'All right. Granted. They're sincere. But that doesn't make them well-balanced. Honestly, darling, you meet that old girl for ten minutes in a loo, she tells you she sees Christine sitting beside us – well, anyone with a gift for telepathy could read your unconscious mind in an instant – and then, pleased with her success, as any old psychic expert would be, she flings a further mood of ecstasy and wants to boot us out of Venice. Well, I'm sorry, but to hell with it.'

The room was no longer reeling. Anger had sobered him. If it would not put Laura to shame he would get up and cross to their table, and tell the old fools where they got off.

'I knew you would take it like this,' said Laura unhappily. 'I told them you would. They said not to worry. As long as we left Venice tomorrow everything would come all right.'

'Oh, for God's sake,' said John. He changed his mind, and poured himself a glass of wine.

'After all,' Laura went on, 'we have really seen the cream of Venice. I don't mind going on somewhere else. And if we stayed – I know it sounds silly, but I should have a nasty nagging sort of feeling inside me, and I should keep thinking of darling Christine being unhappy and trying to tell us to go.'

'Right,' said John with ominous calm, 'that settles it. Go we will. I suggest we clear off to the hotel straight away and warn the reception we're leaving in the morning. Have you had enough to eat?'

'Oh, dear,' sighed Laura, 'don't take it like that. Look, why not come over and meet them, and then they can explain about the vision to you? Perhaps you would take it seriously then. Especially as you are the one it most concerns. Christine is more worried over you than me. And the extraordinary thing is that the blind sister says you're psychic and don't know it. You are somehow *en rapport* with the unknown, and I'm not.'

'Well, that's final,' said John. 'I'm psychic, am I? Fine. My psychic intuition tells me to get out of this restaurant now, at once, and we can decide what we do about leaving Venice when we are back at the hotel.'

He signalled to the waiter for the bill and they waited for it, not speaking to each other, Laura unhappy, fiddling with her bag, while John, glancing furtively at the twins' table, noticed that they were tucking into plates piled high with spaghetti, in very un-psychic fashion. The bill disposed of, John pushed back his chair.

'Right. Are you ready?' he asked.

'I'm going to say goodbye to them first,' said Laura, her mouth set sulkily, reminding him instantly, with a pang, of their poor lost child.

'Just as you like,' he replied, and walked ahead of her out of the restaurant, without a backward glance.

The soft humidity of the evening, so pleasant to walk about in earlier, had turned to rain. The strolling tourists had melted away. One or two people hurried by under umbrellas. This is what the inhabitants who live here see, he thought. This is the true life. Empty streets by night, and the dank stillness of a stagnant canal beneath shuttered houses. The rest is a bright façade put on for show, glittering by sunlight.

Laura joined him and they walked away together in silence, and emerging presently behind the ducal palace came out into the Piazza San Marco. The rain was heavy now, and they sought shelter with the few remaining stragglers under the colonnades. The orchestras had packed up for the evening. The tables were bare. Chairs had been turned upside down.

The experts are right, he thought. Venice is sinking. The whole city is slowly dying. One day the tourists will travel here by boat to peer down into the waters, and they will see pillars and columns and marble far, far beneath them,

more sober suiting of her companions. The launch tooted again and moved away from the landing stage, and he stood there watching it, a sense of immense loss filling his heart. Then he turned and walked away, back to the hotel, the bright day all about him desolate, unseen.

There was nothing, he thought, as he looked about him presently in the hotel bedroom, so melancholy as a vacated room, especially when the recent signs of occupation were still visible about him. Laura's suitcases on the bed, a second coat she had left behind. Traces of powder on the dressing table. A tissue, with a lipstick smear, thrown in the wastepaper basket. Even an old toothpaste tube squeezed dry, lying on the glass shelf above the washbasin. Sounds of the heedless traffic on the Grand Canal came as always from the open window, but Laura wasn't there any more to listen to it, or to watch from the small balcony. The pleasure had gone. Feeling had gone.

John finished packing, and leaving all the baggage ready to be collected he went downstairs to pay the bill. The reception clerk was welcoming new arrivals. People were sitting on the terrace overlooking the Grand Canal reading newspapers, the pleasant day waiting to be planned.

John decided to have an early lunch, here on the hotel terrace, on familiar ground, and then have the porter carry the baggage to one of the ferries that steamed direct between San Marco and the Porta Roma, where the car was garaged. The fiasco meal of the night before had left him empty, and he was ready for the trolley of hors d'œuvres when they brought it to him, around midday. Even here, though, there was change. The headwaiter, their especial friend, was off-duty, and the table where they usually sat was occupied by new arrivals, a honeymoon couple, he told himself sourly, observing the gaiety, the smiles, while he had been shown to a small single table behind a tub of flowers.

'She's airborne now,' John thought, 'she's on her way,' and he tried to picture Laura seated between the Methodist ministers, telling them, no doubt, about Johnnie ill in hospital, and heaven knows what else besides. Well, the twin sisters anyway could rest in psychic peace. Their wishes would have been fulfilled.

Lunch over, there was no point in lingering with a cup of coffee on the terrace. His desire was to get away as soon as possible, fetch the car, and be en route for Milan. He made his farewells at the reception desk, and, escorted by a porter who had piled his baggage on to a wheeled trolley, made his way once more to the landing stage of San Marco. As he stepped on to the steam ferry, his luggage heaped beside him, a crowd of jostling people all about him, he had one momentary pang to be leaving Venice. When, if ever, he wondered, would they come again? Next year... in three years... Glimpsed first on honeymoon, nearly ten years ago, and then a second visit, *en passant*, before a cruise, and now this last abortive ten days that had ended so abruptly.

The water glittered in the sunshine, buildings shone, tourists in dark glasses paraded up and down the rapidly receding Molo, already the terrace of their hotel was out of sight as the ferry churned its way up the Grand Canal. So many impressions to seize and hold, familiar loved façades, balconies, windows, water lapping the cellar steps of decaying palaces, the little red house where d'Annunzio lived, with its garden – our house, Laura called it pretending it was theirs – and too soon the ferry would be turning left on the direct route to the Piazzale Roma, so missing the best of the Canal, the Rialto, the further palaces.

Another ferry was heading downstream to pass them, filled with passengers, and for a brief foolish moment he wished he could change places, be amongst the happy tourists bound for Venice and all he had left behind him. Then he saw her. Laura, in her scarlet coat, the twin sisters by her side, the active sister with her hand on Laura's arm, talking earnestly, and Laura herself, her hair blowing in the wind, gesticulating, on her face a look of distress. He stared, astounded, too astonished to shout, to wave, and anyway they would never have heard or seen him, for his own ferry had already passed and was heading in the opposite direction.

What the hell had happened? There must have been a hold-up with the charter flight and it had never taken off, but in that case why had Laura not telephoned him at the hotel. And what were those damned sisters doing? Had she run into them at the airport? Was it coincidence? And why did she look so anxious? He could think of no explanation. Perhaps the flight had been cancelled. Laura, of course, would go straight to the hotel, expecting to find him there, intending, doubtless, to drive with him after all to Milan and take the train the following night. What a blasted mix-up. The only thing to do was to telephone the hotel immediately his ferry reached the Piazzale Roma and tell her to wait – he would return and fetch her. As for the damned interfering sisters, they could get stuffed.

The usual stampede ensued when the ferry arrived at the landing stage. He had to find a porter to collect his baggage, and then wait while he discovered a telephone. The fiddling with change, the hunt for the number, delayed him still more. He succeeded at last in getting through, and luckily the reception clerk he knew was still at the desk.

'Look, there's been some frightful muddle,' he began, and explained how Laura was over now on her way back to the hotel – he had seen her with two friends on one of the few services. Would the reception clerk explain and tell her to wait? He would be back by the next available service to collect her. 'In any event, detain her,' he said. 'I'll be as quick as I can.' The reception clerk understood perfectly, and John rang off.

Thank heaven Laura hadn't turned up before he had put through his call, or they would have told her he was on his way to Milan. The porter was still waiting with the baggage and it seemed simplest to walk with him to the garage, hand everything over to the chap in charge of the office there and ask him to keep it for an hour, when he would be returning with his wife to pick up the car. Then he went back to the landing station to await the next ferry to Venice. The minutes dragged, and he kept wondering all the time what had gone wrong at the airport and why in heaven's name Laura hadn't telephoned. No use conjecturing. She would tell him the whole story at the hotel. One thing was certain: he would not allow Laura and himself to be saddled with the sisters and become involved with their affairs. He could imagine Laura saying that they also had missed a flight and could they have a lift to Milan?

Finally the ferry chugged alongside the landing stage and he stepped aboard. What an anti-climax, thrashing back past the familiar sights to which he had bidden a nostalgic farewell such a short while ago! He didn't even look about him this time, he was so intent on reaching his destination. In San Marco there were more people than ever, the afternoon crowds walking shoulder to shoulder, every one of them on pleasure bent.

He came to the hotel and pushed his way through the swing door, expecting to see Laura and possibly the sisters, waiting in the lounge to the left of the entrance. She was not there. He went to the desk. The reception clerk he had spoken to on the telephone was standing there, talking to the manager.

'Has my wife arrived?' John asked.

'No, sir, not yet.'

'What an extraordinary thing. Are you sure?'

'Absolutely certain, sir. I have been here ever since you telephoned me at a quarter to two. I have not left the desk.'

'I just don't understand it. She was on one of the vaporettos passing by the Accademia. She would have landed at San Marco about five minutes later and come on here.'

The clerk seemed nonplussed. 'I don't know what to say. The signora was with friends, did you say?'

'Yes. Well, acquaintances. Two ladies we had met at Torcello yesterday. I was astonished to see her with them on the vaporetto, and of course I assumed that the flight had been cancelled, and she had somehow met up with them at the airport and decided to return here with them, to catch me before I left.'

Oh hell, what was Laura doing? It was after three. A matter of moments from San Marco landing stage to the hotel.

'Perhaps the signora went with her friends to their hotel instead. Do you know where they are staying?'

'No,' said John, 'I haven't the slightest idea. What's more, I don't even know the names of the two ladies. They were sisters, twins, in fact

– looked exactly alike. But anyway, why go to their hotel and not here?'

The swing-door opened but it wasn't Laura. Two people staying in the hotel.

The manager broke into the conversation. 'I tell you what I will do,' he said. 'I will telephone the airport and check about the flight. Then at least we will get somewhere.' He smiled apologetically. It was not usual for arrangements to go wrong.

'Yes, do that,' said John. 'We may as well know what happened there.'

He lit a cigarette and began to pace up and down the entrance hall. What a bloody mix-up. And how unlike Laura, who knew he would be setting off for Milan directly after lunch – indeed, for all she knew he might have gone before. But surely, in that case, she would have telephoned at once, on arrival at the airport, had the flight been cancelled? The manager was ages telephoning, he had to be put through on some other line, and his Italian was too rapid for John to follow the conversation. Finally he replaced the receiver.

'It is more mysterious than ever, sir,' he said. 'The charter flight was not delayed, it took off on schedule with a full complement of passengers. As far as they could tell me, there was no hitch. The signora must simply have changed her mind.' His smile was more apologetic than ever.

'Changed her mind,' John repeated. 'But why on earth should she do that? She was so anxious to be home tonight.'

The manager shrugged. 'You know how ladies can be, sir,' he said. 'Your wife may have thought that after all she would prefer to take the train to Milan with you. I do assure you, though, that the charter party was most respectable, and it was a Caravelle aircraft, perfectly safe.'

'Yes, yes,' said John impatiently, 'I don't blame your arrangements in the slightest. I just can't understand what induced her to change her mind, unless it was meeting with these two ladies.'

The manager was silent. He could not think of anything to say. The reception clerk was equally concerned. 'Is it possible,' he ventured, 'that you made a mistake, and it was not the signora that you saw on the vaporetto?'

'Oh no,' replied John, 'it was my wife, I assure you. She was wearing her red coat, she was hatless, just as she left here. I saw her as plainly as I can see you. I would swear to it in a court of law.'

'It is unfortunate,' said the manager, 'that we do not know the name of the two ladies or the hotel where they were staying. You say you met these ladies at Torcello yesterday?'

'Yes… but only briefly. They weren't staying there. At least, I am certain they were not. We saw them at dinner in Venice later, as it happens.'

'Excuse me… ' Guests were arriving with luggage to check in, the clerk was obliged to attend to them. John turned in desperation to the manager. 'Do you think it would be any good telephoning the hotel in Torcello in case the people there knew the name of the ladies, or where they were staying in Venice?'

'We can try,' replied the manager. 'It is a small hope, but we can try.'

John resumed his anxious pacing, all the while watching the swing-door, hoping, praying that he would catch sight of the red coat and Laura would enter. Once again there followed what seemed an interminable telephone conversation between the manager and someone at the hotel in Torcello.

'Tell them two sisters,' said John, 'two elderly ladies dressed in grey, both exactly alike. One lady was blind,' he added. The manager nodded. He was obviously giving a detailed description. Yet when he hung up he shook his head. 'The manager at Torcello say he remembers the two ladies well,' he told John, 'but they were only there for lunch. He never learnt their names.'

'Well, that's that. There's nothing to do now but wait.'

John lit his third cigarette and went out on to the terrace, to resume his pacing there. He stared out across the canal, searching the heads of the people on passing steamers, motorboats, even drifting gondolas. The minutes ticked by on his watch, and there was no sign of Laura. A terrible foreboding nagged at him that somehow this was prearranged, that Laura had never intended to catch the aircraft, that last night in the restaurant she had made an assignation with the sisters. Oh God, he thought, that's impossible, I'm going paranoiac… Yet why, why? No, more likely the encounter at the airport was fortuitous, and for some incredible reason they had persuaded Laura not to board the aircraft, even prevented her from doing so, trotting out one of their psychic reasons, that the aircraft would crash, that she must return with them to Venice. And Laura, in her sensitive state, felt they must be right, swallowed it all without question.

But granted all these possibilities, why had she not come to the hotel? What was she doing? Four o'clock, half-past four, the sun no longer dappling the water. He went back to the reception desk.

'I just can't hang around,' he said. 'Even if she does turn up, we shall never make Milan this evening. I might see her walking with these ladies, in the Piazza San Marco, anywhere. If she arrives while I'm out, will you explain?'

The clerk was full of concern. 'Indeed, yes,' he said. 'It is very worrying for you, sir. Would it perhaps be prudent if we booked you in here tonight?'

John gestured, helplessly. 'Perhaps, yes, I don't know. Maybe…'

He went out of the swing-door and began to walk towards the Piazza San Marco. He looked into every shop up and down the colonnades, crossed the piazza a dozen times, threaded his way between the tables in front of Florian's, in front of Quadri's, knowing that Laura's red coat and the distinctive appearance of the twin sisters could easily be spotted, even amongst this milling crowd, but there was no sign of them. He joined the crowd of shoppers in the Merceria, shoulder to shoulder with idlers, thrusters, window-gazers, knowing instinctively that it was useless, they wouldn't be here. Why should Laura have deliberately missed her flight to return to Venice for such a purpose? And even if she had done so, for some reason beyond his imagining, she would surely have come first to the hotel to find him.

The only thing left to him was to try to track down the sisters. Their hotel could be anywhere amongst the hundreds of hotels and pensions scattered through Venice, or even across the other side at the Zattere, or further again on the Giudecca. These last possibilities seemed remote. More likely they were staying in a small hotel or pension somewhere near San Zaccaria handy to the restaurant where they had dined last night. The blind one would surely not go far afield in the evening. He had been a fool not to have thought of this before, and he turned back and walked quickly away from the brightly lighted shopping district towards the narrower, more cramped quarter where they had dined last evening. He found the restaurant without difficulty, but they were not yet open for dinner, and the waiter preparing tables was not the one who had served them. John asked to see the *padrone*, and the waiter disappeared to the back regions, returning after a moment or two with the somewhat dishevelled-looking proprietor in shirtsleeves, caught in a slack moment, not in full tenue.

'I had dinner here last night,' John explained. 'There were two ladies sitting at that table there in the corner.' He pointed to it.

'You wish to book that table for this evening?' asked the proprietor.

'No,' said John. 'No, there were two ladies there last night, two sisters, due sorelle, twins, gemelle' – what was the right word for twins? – 'Do you remember? Two ladies, sorelle vecchie…'

'Ah,' said the man, 'si, si, signore, la povera signorina.' He put his hands to his eyes to feign blindness. 'Yes, I remember.'

'Do you know their names?' asked John. 'Where they were staying? I am very anxious to trace them.'

The proprietor spread out his hands in a gesture of regret. 'I am ver' sorry, signore, I do not know the names of the signorine, they have been here once, twice, perhaps for dinner, they do not say where they were staying. Perhaps if you come again tonight they might be here? Would you like to book a table?'

He pointed around him, suggesting a whole choice of tables that might appeal to a prospective diner, but John shook his head.

'Thank you, no. I may be dining elsewhere. I am sorry to have troubled you. If the signorine should come…' he paused, 'possibly I may return later,' he added. 'I am not sure.'

The proprietor bowed, and walked with him to the entrance. 'In Venice the whole world meets,' he said smiling. 'It is possible the signore will find his friends tonight. Arrivederci, signore.'

Friends? John walked out into the street. More

likely kidnappers... Anxiety had turned to fear, to panic. Something had gone terribly wrong. Those women had got hold of Laura, played upon her suggestibility, induced her to go with them, either to their hotel or elsewhere. Should he find the Consulate? Where was it? What would he say when he got there? He began walking without purpose, finding himself, as they had done the night before, in streets he did not know, and suddenly came upon a tall building with the word 'Questura' above it. This is it, he thought. I don't care, something has happened, I'm going inside. There were a number of police in uniform coming and going, the place at any rate was active, and, addressing himself to one of them behind a glass partition, he asked if there was anyone who spoke English. The man pointed to a flight of stairs and John went up, entering a door on the right where he saw that another couple were sitting, waiting, and with relief he recognised them as fellow-countrymen, tourists, obviously a man and his wife, in some sort of predicament.

'Come and sit down,' said the man. 'We've waited half an hour but they can't be much longer. What a country! They wouldn't leave us like this at home.'

John took the proffered cigarette and found a chair beside them.

'What's your trouble?' he asked.

'My wife had her handbag pinched in one of those shops in the Merceria,' said the man. 'She simply put it down one moment to look at something, and you'd hardly credit it, the next moment it had gone. I say it was a sneak thief, she insists it was the girl behind the counter. But who's to say? These Ities are all alike. Anyway, I'm certain we shan't get it back. What have you lost?'

'Suitcase stolen,' John lied rapidly. 'Had some important papers in it.' How could he say he had lost his wife? He couldn't even begin . . . The man nodded in sympathy. 'As I said, these Ities are all alike. Old Musso knew to deal with them. Too many Communists around these days. The trouble is, they're not going to bother with our troubles much, not with this murderer at large. They're all out looking for him.'

'Murderer? What murderer?' asked John.

'Don't tell me you've not heard about it?' The man stared at him in surprise. 'Venice has talked of nothing else. It's been in all the papers, on the radio, and even in the English papers. A grisly business. One woman found with her throat slit last week – a tourist too – and some old chap discovered with the same sort of knife wound this morning. They seem to think it must be a maniac, because there doesn't seem to be any motive. Nasty thing to happen in Venice in the tourist season.'

'My wife and I never bother with the newspapers when we're on holiday,' said John. 'And we're neither of us much given to gossip in the hotel.'

'Very wise of you,' laughed the man. 'It might have spoilt your holiday, especially if your wife is nervous. Oh well, we're off tomorrow anyway. Can't say we mind, do we, dear? He turned to his wife. 'Venice has gone downhill since we were here last. And now this loss of the handbag really is the limit.'

The door of the inner room opened, and a senior police officer asked John's companion and his wife to pass through.

'I bet we don't get any satisfaction,' murmured the tourist, winking at John, and he and his wife went into the inner room. The door closed behind them. John stubbed out his cigarette and lighted another. A strange feeling of unreality possessed him. He asked what he was doing here, what was the use of it? Laura was no longer in Venice but had disappeared, perhaps forever, with those diabolical sisters. She would never be traced. And just as the two of them had made up a fantastic story about the twins, when they first spotted them in Torcello, so, with nightmare logic, the fiction would have basis in fact, the women were in reality disguised crooks, men with criminal intent who lured unsuspecting persons to some appalling fate. They might even be the murderers for whom the police sought. Who would ever suspect two elderly women of respectable appearance, living quietly in some second-rate pension or hotel? He stubbed out his cigarette, unfinished.

'This,' he thought, 'is really the start of paranoia. This is the way people go off their track.' He glanced at his watch. It was half-past six. Better pack this in, this futile quest here in police headquarters, and keep to the single link of sanity remaining. Return to the hotel, put a call through to the prep school in England, and ask about the latest news of Johnnie. He had not thought about poor Johnnie since sighting Laura on the vaporetto. Too late, though. The inner door opened, the couple were ushered out.

'Usual claptrap,' said the husband sotto voce to John. 'They'll do what they can. Not much hope. So many foreigners in Venice, all of 'em thieves! The locals all above reproach. Wouldn't pay 'em to steal from customers. Well, I wish you better luck.'

He nodded, his wife smiled and bowed, and they had gone. John followed the police officer into the inner room.

Formalities began. Name, address, passport. Length of stay in Venice, etc., etc. Then the questions, and John, the sweat beginning to appear on his forehead, launched into his interminable story. The first encounter with the sisters, the meeting at the restaurant, Laura's state of suggestibility because of the death of their child, the telegram about Johnnie, the decision to take the chartered flight, her departure, and her sudden inexplicable return. When he had finished he felt as exhausted as if he had driven three hundred miles nonstop after a severe bout of 'flu. His interrogator spoke excellent English with a strong Italian accent.

'You say,' he began, 'that your wife was suffering the after-effects of shock. This had been noticeable during your stay here in Venice?'

'Well, yes,' John replied, 'she had really been quite ill. The holiday didn't seem to be doing her much good. It was only when she met these two women at Torcello yesterday that her mood changed. The strain seemed to have gone. She was ready, I suppose, to snatch at every straw, and this belief that our little girl was watching over her had somehow restored her to what appeared normality.'

'It would be natural,' said the police officer, 'in the circumstances. But no doubt the telegram last night was a further shock to you both?'

'Indeed, yes. That was the reason we decided to return home.'

'No argument between you? No difference of opinion?'

'None. We were in complete agreement. My one regret was that I could not go with my wife on this charter flight.'

The police officer nodded. 'It could well be that your wife had a sudden attack of amnesia, and meeting the two ladies served as a link, she clung to them for support. You have described them with great accuracy, and I think they should not be too difficult to trace. Meanwhile, I suggest you should return to your hotel, and we will get in touch with you as soon as we have news.'

At least, John thought, they believed his story. They did not consider him a crank who had made the whole thing up and was merely wasting their time.

'You appreciate,' he said, 'I am extremely anxious. These women may have some criminal design upon my wife. One has heard of such things … '

The police officer smiled for the first time. 'Please don't concern yourself,' he said. 'I am sure there will be some satisfactory explanation.'

All very well, thought John, but in heaven's name, what?

'I'm sorry,' he said, 'to have taken up so much of your time. Especially as I gather the police have their hands full hunting down a murderer who is still at large.'

He spoke deliberately. No harm in letting the fellow know that for all any of them could tell there might be some connection between Laura's disappearance and this other hideous affair.

'Ah, that,' said the police officer, rising to his feet. 'We hope to have the murderer under lock and key very soon.'

His tone of confidence was reassuring. Murderers, missing wives, lost handbags were all under control. They shook hands, and John was ushered out of the door and so downstairs. Perhaps, he thought, as he walked slowly back to the hotel, the fellow was right. Laura had suffered a sudden attack of amnesia, and the sisters happened to be at the airport and had brought her back to Venice, to their own hotel, because Laura couldn't remember where she and John had been staying. Perhaps they were even now trying to track down his hotel. Anyway, he could do nothing more. The police had everything in hand, and, please God, would come up with the solution. All he wanted to do right now was to collapse upon a bed with a stiff whisky, and then put through a call to Johnnie's school.

The page took him up in the lift to a modest room on the fourth floor at the rear of the hotel. Bare, impersonal, the shutters closed, with a smell of cooking wafting up from a courtyard down below.

'Ask them to send me up a double whisky, will you?' he said to the boy. 'And a ginger-ale,' and when he was alone he plunged his face under the cold tap in the wash-basin, relieved to find that the minute portion of visitor's soap afforded some measure of comfort. He flung off his shoes, hung his coat over the back of a chair and threw himself down on the bed. Somebody's radio was blasting forth an old popular song, now several seasons out-of-date, that had been one of Laura's favourites a couple of years ago. 'I love you, Baby...' He reached for the telephone, and asked the exchange to put through the call to England. Then he closed his eyes, and all the while the resistant voice persisted, 'I love you, Baby... I can't get you out of my mind.'

Presently there was a tap at the door. It was the waiter with his drink. Too little ice, such meagre comfort, but what desperate need. He gulped it down without the ginger-ale and in a few moments the ever-nagging pain was eased, numbed, bringing, if only momentarily, a sense of calm. The telephone rang, and now, he thought, bracing himself for ultimate disaster, the final shock, Johnnie probably dying, or already dead. In which case nothing remained. Let Venice be engulfed...

The exchange told him that the connection had been made, and in a moment he heard the voice of Mrs. Hill at the other end of the line. They must have warned her that the call came from Venice, for she knew instantly who was speaking.

'Hello?' she said. 'Oh, I am so glad you rang. All is well. Johnnie has had his operation, the surgeon decided to do it at midday rather than wait, and it was completely successful. Johnnie is going to be all right. So you don't have to worry any more, and will have a peaceful night.'

'Thank God,' he answered.

'I know,' she said, 'we are all so relieved. Now I'll get off the line and you can speak to your wife.'

John sat up on the bed, stunned. What the hell did she mean? Then he heard Laura's voice, cool and clear.

'Darling? Darling, are you there?'

He could not answer. He felt the hand holding the receiver go clammy cold with sweat. 'I'm here,' he whispered.

'It's not a very good line,' she said, 'but never mind. As Mrs. Hill told you, all is well. Such a *nice* surgeon, and a very sweet Sister on Johnnie's floor, and I really am happy about the way it's turned out. I came straight down here after landing at Gatwick – the flight OK, by the way, but such a funny crowd, it'll make you hysterical when I tell you about them – and I went to the hospital, and Johnnie was coming round. Very dopey, of course, but so pleased to see me. And the Hills are being wonderful, I've got their spare room, and it's only a short taxi-drive into the town and the hospital. I shall go to bed as soon as *we've* had dinner, because I'm a bit fagged, what with the flight and the anxiety. How *was* the drive to Milan? And where are you staying?'

John did not recognise the voice that answered as his own. It was the automatic response of some computer.

'I'm not in Milan,' he said. 'I'm still in Venice.'

'Still in Venice? What on earth for? Wouldn't the car start?'

'I can't explain,' he said. 'There was a stupid sort of mix-up...'

He felt suddenly so exhausted that he nearly dropped the receiver, and, shame upon shame, he could feel tears pricking behind his eyes.

'What sort of mix-up?' Her voice was suspicious, almost hostile. 'You weren't in a crash?'

'No... no... nothing like that.'

A moment's silence, and then she said, 'Your voice sounds very slurred. Don't tell me you went and got pissed.'

Oh Christ... If she only knew! He was probably going to pass out any moment, but not from the whisky.

'I thought,' he said slowly, 'I thought I saw you, in a vaporetto, with those two sisters.'

What was the point of going on? It was hopeless

trying to explain.

'How could you have seen me with the sisters?' she said. 'You knew I'd gone to the airport. Really, darling, you are an idiot. You seem to have got those two poor old dears on the brain. I hope you didn't say anything to Mrs. Hill just now.'

'No.'

'Well, what are you going to do? You'll catch the train at Milan tomorrow, won't you?'

'Yes, of course,' he told her.

'I still don't understand what kept you in Venice,' she said. 'It all sounds a bit odd to me. However… thank God Johnnie is going to be all right and I'm here.'

'Yes,' he said, 'yes.'

He could hear the distant boom-boom sound of a gong from the headmaster's hall.

'You had better go,' he said. 'My regards to the Hills, and my love to Johnnie.'

'Well, take care of yourself, darling, and for goodness' sake don't miss the train tomorrow, and drive carefully.'

The telephone clicked and she had gone. He poured the remaining drop of whisky into his empty glass, and sousing it with ginger-ale drank it down at a gulp. He got up, and crossing the room, threw open the shutters and leant out of the window. He felt light-headed. His sense of relief, enormous, overwhelming, was somehow tempered with a curious feeling of unreality, almost as though the voice speaking from England had not been Laura's after all but a fake, and she was still in Venice, hidden in some furtive pension with the two sisters.

The point was, he *had* seen all three of them on the vaporetto. It was not another woman in a red coat. The women *had* been there, with Laura. So what was the explanation? That he was going off his head? Or something more sinister? The sisters, possessing psychic powers of formidable strength, had seen him as their two ferries had passed, and in some inexplicable fashion had made him believe Laura was with them. But why, and to what end? No, it didn't make sense. The only explanation was that he had been mistaken, the whole episode an hallucination. In which case he needed psychoanalysis, just as Johnnie had needed a surgeon.

And what did he do now? Go downstairs and tell the management he had been at fault and had just spoken to his wife, who had arrived in England safe and sound from her charter flight? He put on his shoes and ran his fingers through his hair. He glanced at his watch. It was ten minutes to eight. If he nipped into the bar and had a quick drink it would be easier to face the manager and admit what had happened. Then, perhaps, they would get in touch with the police. Profuse apologies all round for putting everyone to enormous trouble.

He made his way to the ground floor and went straight to the bar, feeling self-conscious, a marked man, half-imagining everyone would look at him, thinking, 'There's the fellow with the missing wife.' Luckily the bar was full and there wasn't a face he knew. Even the chap behind the bar was an underling who hadn't served him before. He downed his whisky and glanced over his shoulder to the reception hall. The desk was momentarily empty. He could see the manager's back framed in the doorway of an inner room, talking to someone within. On impulse, cowardlike, he crossed the hall and passed through the swing-door to the street outside.

'I'll have some dinner,' he decided, 'and then go back and face them. I'll feel more like it once I've some food inside me.'

He went to the restaurant nearby where he and Laura had dined once or twice. Nothing mattered any more, because she was safe. The nightmare lay behind him. He could enjoy his dinner, despite her absence, and think of her sitting down with the Hills to a dull quiet evening, early to bed, and on the following morning going to the hospital to sit with Johnnie. Johnnie was safe, too. No more worries, only the awkward explanations and apologies to the manager at the hotel.

There was a pleasant anonymity sitting down at a corner table alone in the little restaurant, ordering vitello alla Marsala and half a bottle of Merlot. He took his time, enjoying his food but eating in a kind of haze, a sense of unreality still with him, while the conversation of his nearest neighbours had the same soothing effect as background music.

When they rose and left, he saw by the clock on the wall that it was nearly half-past nine. No use delaying matters any further. He drank his coffee, lighted a cigarette and paid his bill. After all, he thought, as he walked back to the hotel, the manager would be greatly relieved to know that all was well.

When he pushed through the swing-door, the first thing he noticed was a man in police uniform, standing talking to the manager at the desk. The reception clerk was there too. They turned as John approached, and the manager's face lighted up with relief.

'Eccolo!' he exclaimed. 'I was certain the signore would not be far away. Things are moving, signore. The two ladies have been traced, and they very kindly agreed to accompany the police to the Questura. If you will go there at once, this agente di polizia will escort you.'

John flushed. 'I have given everyone a lot of trouble,' he said. 'I meant to tell you before going out to dinner, but you were not at the desk. The fact is that I have contacted my wife. She did make the flight to London after all, and I spoke to her on the telephone. It was all a great mistake.'

The manager looked bewildered. 'The signora is in London?' he repeated. He broke off and exchanged a rapid conversation in Italian with the policeman. 'It seems that the ladies maintain they did not go out for the day, except for a little shopping in the morning,' he said, turning back to John. 'Then who was it the signore saw on the vaporetto?'

John shook his head. 'A very extraordinary mistake on my part which I still don't understand,' he said. 'Obviously, I did not see either my wife or the two ladies. I really am extremely sorry.'

More rapid conversation in Italian. John noticed the clerk watching him with a curious expression in his eyes. The manager was obviously apologising on John's behalf to the policeman, who looked annoyed and gave tongue to this effect, his voice increasing in volume, to the manager's concern. The whole business had undoubtedly given enormous trouble to a great many people, not least the two unfortunate sisters.

'Look,' said John, interrupting the flow, 'will you tell the agente I will go with him to headquarters and apologise in person both to the police officer and to the ladies?'

The manager looked relieved. 'If the signore would take the trouble,' he said. 'Naturally, the ladies were much distressed when a policeman interrogated them at their hotel, and they offered to accompany him to the Questura only because they were so distressed about the signora.'

John felt more and more uncomfortable. Laura must never learn any of this. She would be outraged. He wondered if there were some penalty for giving the police misleading information involving a third party. His error began, in retrospect, to take on criminal proportions.

He crossed the Piazza San Marco, now thronged with after-dinner strollers and spectators at the cafés, all three orchestras going full blast in harmonious rivalry, while his companion kept a discreet two paces to his left and never uttered a word.

They arrived at the police station and mounted the stairs to the same inner room where he had been before. He saw immediately that it was not the officer he knew but another who sat behind the desk, a sallow-faced individual with a sour expression, while the two sisters, obviously upset – the active one in particular – were seated on chairs nearby, some underling in uniform standing behind them. John's escort went at once to the police officer, speaking in rapid Italian, while John himself, after a moment's hesitation, advanced towards the sisters.

'There has been a terrible mistake,' he said. 'I don't know how to apologise to you both. It's all my fault, mine entirely, the police are not to blame.'

The active sister made as though to rise, her mouth twitching nervously, but he restrained her.

'We don't understand,' she said, the Scots inflection strong. 'We said goodnight to your wife last night at dinner, and we have not seen her since. The police came to our pension more than an hour ago and told us your wife was missing and you had filed a complaint against us. My sister is not very strong. She was considerably disturbed.'

'A mistake. A frightful mistake,' he repeated.

He turned towards the desk. The police officer was addressing him, his English very inferior to that of the previous interrogator. He had John's earlier statement on the desk in front of him, and tapped it with a pencil.

'So?' he queried. 'This document all lies? You not speaka the truth?'

'I believed it to be true at the time,' said John. 'I could have sworn in a court of law that I saw my wife with these two ladies on a vaporetto in the Grand Canal this afternoon. Now I realise I was mistaken.'

'We have not been near the Grand Canal all day,' protested the sister, 'not even on foot. We made a few purchases in the Merceria this morning, and remained indoors all afternoon. My sister was a little unwell. I have told the police officer this a dozen times, and the people at the pension would corroborate our story. He refused to listen.'

'And the signora?' rapped the police officer angrily. 'What happen to the signora?'

'The signora, my wife, is safe in England,' explained John patiently. 'I talked to her on the telephone just after seven. She did join the charter flight from the airport, and is now staying with friends.'

'Then who you see on the vaporetto in the red coat?' asked the furious police officer. 'And if not these signorine here, then what signorine?'

'My eyes deceived me,' said John, aware that his English was likewise becoming strained. 'I think I see my wife and these ladies but no, it was not so. My wife in aircraft, these ladies in pension all the time.'

It was like talking stage Chinese. In a moment he would be bowing and putting his hands in his sleeves.

The police officer raised his eyes to heaven and thumped the table. 'So all this work for nothing,' he said. 'Hotels and pensiones searched for the signorine and a missing signora inglese, when here we have plenty, plenty other things to do. You make a mistake. You have perhaps too much vino at mezzo giorno and you see hundred signore in red coats in hundred vaporetti.' He stood up, rumpling the papers on his desk. 'And you signorine,' he said, 'you wish to make complaint against this person?' He was addressing the active sister.

'Oh no,' she said, 'no, indeed. I quite see it was all a mistake. Our only wish is to return at once to our pension.'

The police officer grunted. Then he pointed at John. 'You very lucky man,' he said. 'These signorine could file complaint against you – very serious matter.'

'I'm sure,' began John, 'I'll do anything in my power ...'

'Please don't think of it,' exclaimed the sister, horrified. 'We would not hear of such a thing.' It was her turn to apologise to the police officer. 'I hope we need not take up any more of your valuable time,' she said.

He waved a hand of dismissal and spoke in Italian to the underling. 'This man walk with you to the pension,' he said. 'Buona sera, signorine,' and, ignoring John, he sat down again at his desk.

'I'll come with you,' said John. 'I want to explain exactly what happened.'

They trooped down the stairs and out of the building, the blind sister leaning on her twin's arm, and once outside she turned her sightless eyes to John.

'You saw us,' she said, 'and your wife too. But not today. You saw us in the future.'

Her voice was softer than her sister's, slower, she seemed to have some slight impediment in her speech.

'I don't follow,' replied John, bewildered.

He turned to the active sister and she shook her head at him, frowning, and put her finger on her lips.

'Come along, dear,' she said to her twin. 'You know you're very tired, and I want to get you home.' Then, sotto voce to John, 'She's psychic. Your wife told you, I believe, but I don't want her to go into trance here in the street.'

God forbid, thought John, and the little procession began to move slowly along the street away from police headquarters, a canal to the left of them. Progress was slow, because of the blind sister, and there were two bridges. John was completely lost after the first turning, but it couldn't have mattered less. Their police escort was with them, and anyway the sisters knew where they were going.

'I must explain,' said John softly. 'My wife would never forgive me if I didn't,' and as they walked he went over the whole inexplicable story once again, beginning with the telegram received the night before and the conversation with Mrs. Hill, the decision to return to England the following day, Laura by air, and John himself by car and train. It no longer sounded as dramatic as it had done when he had made his statement to the police officer, when, possibly because of his conviction of something uncanny, the description of the two vaporettos passing one another in the middle of the Grand Canal had held a sinister quality, suggesting abduction on the part of the sisters, the pair of them holding a bewildered Laura captive. Now that neither of the women had any further menace for him he spoke more naturally, yet with great sincerity, feeling for the first time that they were somehow both in sympathy with him and would understand.

'You see,' he explained, in a final endeavour to make amends for having gone to the police in the first place, 'I truly believed I had seen you with Laura, and I thought …' he hesitated, because this had been the police officer's suggestion and not his, 'I thought that perhaps Laura had some sudden loss of memory, had met you at the airport, and you had brought her back to Venice to wherever you were staying.'

They had crossed a large square and were approaching a house at one end of it, with a sign 'Pensione' above the door. Their escort paused at the entrance.

'Is this it?' asked John.

'Yes,' said the sister. 'I know it is nothing much from the outside, but it is clean and comfortable, and was recommended by friends.' She turned to the escort. 'Grazie,' she said to him, 'grazie tanto.'

The man nodded briefly, wished them 'Buona notte,' and disappeared across the *campo*.

'Will you come in?' asked the sister. 'I am sure we can find you some coffee, or perhaps you prefer tea?'

'No, really,' John thanked her, 'I must get back to the hotel. I'm making an early start in the morning. I just want to make quite sure you do understand what happened, and that you forgive me.'

'There is nothing to forgive,' she replied. 'It is one of the many examples of second sight that my sister and I have experienced time and time again, and I should very much like to record it for our files, if you will permit it.'

'Well, as to that, of course,' he told her, 'but I myself find it hard to understand. It has never happened to me before.'

'Not consciously, perhaps,' she said, 'but so many things happen to us of which we are not aware. My sister felt you had psychic understanding. She told your wife. She also told your wife, last night in the restaurant, that you were to experience trouble, danger, that you should leave Venice. Well, don't you believe now that the telegram was proof of this? Your son was ill, possibly dangerously ill, and so it was necessary for you to return home immediately. Heaven be praised your wife flew home to be by his side.'

'Yes, indeed,' said John, 'but why should I see her on the vaporetto with you and your sister when she was actually on her way to England?'

'Thought transference, perhaps,' she answered. 'Your wife may have been thinking about us. We gave her our address, should you wish to get in touch with us. We shall be here another ten days. And she knows that we would pass on any message that my sister might have from your little one in the spirit world.'

'Yes,' said John awkwardly, 'yes, I see. It's very good of you.' He had a sudden rather unkind picture of the two sisters putting on headphones in their bedroom, listening for a coded message from poor Christine. 'Look, this is our address in London,' he said. 'I know Laura will be pleased to hear from you.'

He scribbled their address on a sheet torn from his pocket-diary, even, as a bonus thrown in, the telephone number, and handed it to her. He could imagine the outcome. Laura springing it on him one evening that the 'old dears' were passing through London on their way to Scotland, and the least they could do was to offer them hospitality, even the spare room for the night. Then a seance in the living room, tambourines appearing out of thin air.

'Well, I must be off,' he said. 'Goodnight, and apologies, once again, for all that has happened this evening.' He shook hands with the first sister, then turned to her blind twin. 'I hope,' he said, 'that you are not too tired.'

The sightless eyes were disconcerting. She held his hand fast and would not let it go. 'The child,' she said, speaking in an odd staccato voice, 'the child… I can see the child…' and then, to his dismay, a bead of froth appeared at the corner of her mouth, her head jerked back, and she half-collapsed in her sister's arms.

'We must get her inside,' said the sister hurriedly. 'It's all right, she's not ill, it's the beginning of a trance state.'

Between them they helped the twin, who had gone rigid, into the house, and sat her down on the nearest chair, the sister supporting her. A woman came running from some inner room. There was a strong smell of spaghetti from the back regions. 'Don't worry,' said the sister, 'the signorina and I can manage. I think you had better go. Sometimes she is sick after these turns.'

'I'm most frightfully sorry …' John began, but the sister had already turned her back and with the signorina was bending over her twin, from whom peculiar choking sounds were proceeding. He was obviously in the way, and after a final gesture of courtesy, 'Is there anything I can do?', which received no reply, he turned on his heel and began walking across the square. He looked back once, and saw they had closed the door.

What a finale to the evening! And all his fault. Poor old girls, first dragged to police headquarters and put through an interrogation, and then a psychic fit on top of it all. More likely epilepsy. Not much of a life for the other sister, but she seemed to take it in her stride. An additional hazard, though, if it happened in a restaurant or in the street. And not particularly welcome under his and Laura's roof should the sisters ever find themselves beneath it, which he prayed would never happen.

Meanwhile, where the devil was he? The square, with the inevitable church at one end was quite deserted. He could not remember which way they had come from police headquarters, there had seemed to be so many turnings.

Wait a minute, the church itself had a familiar appearance. He drew nearer to it, looking for the name which was sometimes on notices at the entrance. San Giovanni in Angora, that rang a bell. He and Laura had gone inside one morning to look at a painting by Cima da Conegliano. Surely it was only a stone's throw from the Riva degli Schiavoni and the open wide waters of the San Marco lagoon, with all the bright lights of civilisation and the strolling tourists? He remembered taking a small turning from the Schiavoni and they had arrived at the church. Wasn't that the alleyway ahead? He plunged along it, but halfway down he hesitated. It didn't seem right, although it was familiar for some unknown reason.

Then he realised that it was not the alley they had taken the morning they visited the church but the one they had walked along the previous evening, only he was approaching it from the opposite direction. Yes, that was it, in which case it would be quicker to go on and cross the little bridge over the narrow canal, and he would find the Arsenal on his left and the street leading down to the Riva degli Schiavoni to his right. Simpler than retracing his steps and getting lost once more in the maze of back streets.

He had almost reached the end of the alley, and the bridge was in sight, when he saw the child. It was the same little girl with the pixie hood who had leapt between the tethered boats the preceding night and vanished up the cellar steps of one of the houses. This time she was running from the direction of the church the other side, making for the bridge. She was running as if her life depended on it, and in a moment he saw why. A man was in pursuit, who, when she glanced backwards for a moment, still running, flattened himself against a wall, believing himself unobserved. The child came on, scampering across the bridge, and John, fearful of alarming her further, backed into an open doorway that led into a small court.

He remembered the drunken yell of the night before which had come from one of the houses near where the man was hiding now. This is it, he thought, the fellow's after her again, and with a flash of intuition he connected the two events, the child's terror then and now, and the murders reported in the newspapers, supposedly the work of some madman. It could be coincidence, a child running from a drunken relative, and yet, and yet … His heart began thumping in his chest, instinct warning him to run himself, now, at once, back along the alley the way he had come – but what about the child? What was going to happen to the child?

Then he heard her running steps. She hurtled through the open doorway into the court in which he stood, not seeing him, making for the rear of the house that flanked it, where steps led presumably to a back entrance. She was sobbing as she ran, not the ordinary cry of a frightened child, but the panic-stricken intake of breath of a helpless being in despair. Were there parents in the house who would protect her, whom he could warn? He hesitated a moment, then followed her down the steps and through the door at the bottom, which had burst open at the touch of her hands as she hurled herself against it.

'It's all right,' he called. 'I won't let him hurt you, it's all right,' cursing his lack of Italian, but possibly an English voice might reassure her. But it was no use – she ran sobbing up another flight of stairs, which were spiral, twisting, leading to the floor above, and already it was too late for him to retreat. He could hear sounds of the pursuer in the courtyard behind, someone shouting in Italian, a dog barking. This is it, he thought, we're in it together, the child and I. Unless we can bolt some inner door above he'll get us both.

He ran up the stairs after the child, who had darted into a room leading off a small landing, and followed her inside and slammed the door, and, merciful heaven, there was a bolt which he rammed into its socket. The child was crouching by the open window. If he shouted for help someone would surely hear, someone would surely come before the man in pursuit threw himself against the door and it gave, because there was no one but themselves, no parents, the room was bare except for a mattress on an old bed, and a heap of rags in one corner.

'It's all right,' he panted, 'it's all right,' and held out his hand, trying to smile.

The child struggled to her feet and stood before him, the pixie hood falling from her head on to the floor. He stared at her, incredulity turning to horror, to fear. It was not a child at all but a little thickset woman dwarf, about three feet high, with a great square adult head too big for her body, grey locks hanging shoulder-length, and she wasn't sobbing any more, she was grinning at him, nodding her head up and down.

Then he heard the footsteps on the landing outside and the hammering on the door, and a barking dog, and not one voice but several voices, shouting, 'Open up! Police!' The creature fumbled in her sleeve, drawing a knife, and as she threw it at him with hideous strength, piercing his throat, he stumbled and fell, the sticky mess covering his protecting hands.

And he saw the vaporetto with Laura and the two sisters steaming down the Grand Canal, not today, not tomorrow, but the day after that, and he knew why they were together and for what sad purpose they had come. The creature was gibbering in its corner. The hammering and the voices and the barking dog grew fainter, and, 'Oh, God,' he thought, 'what a bloody silly way to die…'

THE HOSPICE

Robert Aickman

Robert Aickman (1914–1981) was an English ghost-story writer, considered the best of his generation. However, Aickman described his fiction as 'strange' and the term 'weird' fits just as well. Long considered a classic, 'The Hospice' (1975), demonstrates the qualities by which Aickman pushed passed the familiar or comforting and into the unsettling. The mysterious is balanced by a perfect character study and precision of detail. Although perennially under-appreciated, Aickman did receive such awards as the World Fantasy Award and the British Fantasy Award. Aickman also served as a chairman of the London Opera Society and was active in the London Opera Club, the Ballet Minerva, and the Mikron Theatre Company in London.

It was somewhere at the back of beyond. Maybury would have found it difficult to be more precise.

He was one who, when motoring outside his own territory, preferred to follow a route 'given' by one of the automobile organizations, and, on this very occasion, as on other previous ones, he had found reasons to deplore all deviation. This time it had been the works manager's fault. The man had not only poured ridicule on the official route, but had stood at the yard gate in order to make quite certain that Maybury set off by the short cut which, according to him, all the fellows in the firm used, and which departed in the exactly opposite direction.

The most that could be said was that Maybury was presumably at the outer edge of the immense West Midlands conurbation. The outer edge it by now surely must be, as he seemed to have been driving for hours since he left the works, going round and round in large or small circles, asking the way and being unable to understand the answers (when answers were vouchsafed), all the time seemingly more off-course than ever.

Maybury looked at his watch. He *had* been driving for hours. By rights he should have been more than halfway home – considerably more. Even the dashboard light seemed feebler than usual; but by it Maybury saw that soon he would be out of petrol. His mind had not been on that particular matter of petrol.

Dark though it was, Maybury was aware of many trees, mountainous and opaque. It was not, however, that there were no houses. Houses there must be, because on both sides of the road, there were gates; broad single gates, commonly painted white: and, even where there were no gates, there were dim entrances. Presumably it was a costly nineteenth-century housing estate. Almost identical roads seemed to curve away in all directions. The straightforward had been genteelly avoided. As often in such places, the racer-through, the taker of a short cut, was quite systematically penalized. Probably this attitude accounted also for the failure to bring the street lighting fully up-to-date.

Maybury came to a specific bifurcation. It was impossible to make any reasoned choice, and he doubted whether it mattered much in any case.

Maybury stopped the car by the side of the road, then stopped the engine in order to save the waning petrol while he thought. In the end, he opened the door and stepped out into the road. He looked upwards. The moon and stars were almost hidden by the thick trees. It was quiet. The houses were set too far back from the road for the noise of the television sets to be heard, or the blue glare thereof seen. Pedestrians are nowadays rare in such a district at any hour, but now there was no traffic either, nor sound of traffic more remote. Maybury was disturbed by the silence.

He advanced a short distance on foot, as one does at such times. In any case, he had no map, but only a route, from which he had departed quite hopelessly. None the less, even that second and locally preferred route, the one used by all the fellows, had seemed perfectly clear at the time, and as the manager had described it. He supposed that otherwise he might not have been persuaded to embark upon it; not even over-persuaded. As things were, his wonted expedient of merely driving straight ahead until one found some definite sign or other indication, would be dubious, because the petrol might run out first.

Parallel with each side of each road was a narrow made-up footway, with a central gravelly strip. Beyond the strip to Maybury's left was a wilderness of vegetation, traversed by a ditch, beyond which was the hedge-line of the different properties. By the light of the occasional street-lamp, Maybury could see that sometimes there was an owner who had his hedge trimmed. and sometimes an owner who did not. It would be futile to walk any further along the road, though the air was pleasantly warm and aromatic. There were Angela and their son, Tony, awaiting him; and he must resume the fight to rejoin them.

Something shot out at him from the boskage on his left.

He had disturbed a cat, returned to its feral habitude. The first he knew of it was its claws, or conceivably its teeth, sunk into his left leg. There had been no question of ingratiation or cuddling up. Maybury kicked out furiously. The strange sequel was total silence. He must have kicked the cat a long way, because on the instant there was no hint of it. Nor had he seen the colour of the cat, though there was a pool of light at that point on the footway. He fancied he had seen two flaming eyes, but he was not sure even of that. There had been no mew, no scream.

Maybury faltered. His leg really hurt. It hurt so much that he could not bring himself to touch the limb, even to look at it in the lamplight.

He faltered back to the car, and, though his leg made difficulties even in starting it, set off indecisively down the road along which he had just walked. It might well have become a case of its being wise for him to seek a hospital. The deep scratch or bite of a cat might well hold venom, and it was not pleasant to think where the particular cat had been treading, or what it might have been devouring. Maybury again looked at his watch. It was fourteen minutes past eight. Only nine minutes had passed since he had looked at it last.

The road was beginning to straighten out, and the number of entrances to diminish, though the trees remained dense. Possibly, as so often happens, the money had run out before the full development had reached this region of the property. There were still occasional houses, with entries at long and irregular intervals. Lamp posts were becoming fewer also, but Maybury saw that one of them bore a hanging sign of some kind. It was most unlikely to indicate a destination, let alone a destination of use to Maybury, but he eased and stopped none the less, so urgently did he need a clue of some kind. The sign was shaped like a club in a pack of cards, and read:

THE HOSPICE
GOOD FARE
SOME ACCOMMODATION

The modest words relating to accommodation were curved round the downward pointing extremity of the club.

Maybury decided almost instantly. He was hungry. He was injured. He was lost. He was almost without petrol.

He would enquire for dinner and, if he could telephone home, might even stay the night, though he had neither pyjamas nor electric razor. The gate, made of iron, and more suited, Maybury would have thought, to a farmyard bullpen, was, none the less, wide open. Maybury drove through.

The drive had likewise been surfaced with rather unattractive concrete, and it appeared to have been done some time ago, since there were now many potholes, as if heavy vehicles passed frequently. Maybury's headlights bounced and lurched disconcertingly as he proceeded, but suddenly the drive, which had run quite straight, again as on a modern farm, swerved, and there, on Maybury's left, was The Hospice. He realized that the drive he had come down, if indeed it had been a drive, was not the original main entrance. There was an older, more traditional drive, winding away between rhododendron bushes. All this was visible in bright light from a fixture high above the cornice of the building: almost a floodlight, Maybury thought. He supposed that a new entry had been made for the vehicles of the various suppliers when the place had become – whatever exactly it had become, a private hotel? a guest house? a club? No doubt the management aspired to cater for the occupants of the big houses, now that there were no longer servants in the world.

Maybury locked the car and pushed at the door of the house. It was a solid Victorian door, and it did not respond to Maybury's pressure. Maybury was discouraged by the need to ring, but he rang. He noticed that there was a second bell, lower down, marked NIGHT. Surely it could not yet be Night? The great thing was to get in, to feed (the works had offered only packeted sandwiches and flavourless coffee by way of luncheon), to ingratiate himself: before raising questions of petrol, whereabouts, possible accommodation for the night, a telephone call to Angela, disinfectant for his leg. He did not much care for standing alone in a strange place under the bright floodlight, uncertain what was going to happen.

But quite soon the door was opened by a lad with curly fair hair and an untroubled face. He looked like a young athlete, as Maybury at once thought. He was wearing a white jacket and smiling helpfully.

'Dinner? Yes, certainly, sir. I fear we've just started, but I'm sure we can fit you in.'

To Maybury, the words brought back the seaside boarding houses where he had been taken for holidays when a boy. Punctuality in those days had been almost as important as sobriety.

'If you can give me just a couple of minutes to wash ... '

'Certainly, sir. This way, please.'

Inside, it was not at all like those boarding houses of Maybury's youth. Maybury happened to know exactly what it was like. The effect was that produced by the efforts of an expensive and, therefore, rather old-fashioned, furniture emporium if one placed one's whole abode and most of one's cheque-book in its hands. There were hangings on all the walls, and every chair and sofa was upholstered. Colours and fabrics were harmonious but rich. The several standard lamps had immense shades. The polished tables derived from Italian originals. One could perhaps feel that a few upholstered occupants should have been designed and purveyed to harmonize also. As it was, the room was empty, except for the two of them.

The lad held open the door marked 'Gentlemen' in script, but then followed Maybury in, which Maybury had not particularly expected. But the lad did not proceed to fuss tiresomely, with soap and towel, as happens sometimes in very expensive hotels, and happened formerly in clubs. All he did was stand about. Maybury reflected that doubtless he was concerned to prevent all possible delay, dinner having started.

The dining-room struck Maybury, immediately he entered, as rather too hot. The central heating must be working with full efficiency. The room was lined with hangings similar to those Maybury had seen in the hall, but apparently even heavier. Possibly noise reduction was among the objects. The ceiling of the room had been brought down in the modern manner, as if to serve the stunted; and any window or windows had disappeared behind swathes.

It is true that knives and forks make a clatter, but there appeared to be no other immediate necessity for costly noise abatement, as the diners were all extremely quiet; which at first seemed the more unexpected in that most of them were seated, fairly closely packed, at a single long table running down the central axis of the room. Maybury soon reflected, however, that if he had been wedged together with a party of total strangers, he might have found little to say to them either.

This was not put to the test. On each side of the room were four smaller tables, set endways against the walls, every table set for a single person, even though big enough to accommodate four, two on either side; and at one of these, Maybury was settled by the handsome lad in the white jacket.

Immediately, soup arrived.

The instantaneity of the service (apart from the fact that Maybury was late) could be accounted for by the large number of the staff. There were quite certainly four men, all, like the lad, in white jackets; and two women, both in dark blue dresses. The six of them were noticeably deft and well set-up, though all were past their first youth. Maybury could not see more because he had been placed with his back to the end wall which contained the service door (as well as, on the other side, the door by which the guests entered from the lounge). At every table, the single place had been positioned in that way, so that the occupant saw neither the service door opening and shutting, nor, in front of him, the face of another diner.

As a matter of fact, Maybury was the only single diner on that side of the room (he had been given the second table down, but did not think that anyone had entered to sit behind him at the first table); and, on the other side of the room, there was only a single diner also, he thought, a lady, seated at the second table likewise, and thus precisely parallel with him.

There was an enormous quantity of soup, in what Maybury realized was an unusually deep and wide plate. The amplitude of the plate had at first been masked by the circumstance that round much of its wide rim was inscribed, in large black letters, THE HOSPICE; rather in the style of a baby's plate, Maybury thought, if both lettering and plate had not been so immense. The soup itself was unusually weighty too: it undoubtedly contained eggs as well as pulses, and steps have been taken to add 'thickening' also.

Maybury was hungry, as has been said, but he was faintly disconcerted to realize that one of the middle-aged women was standing quietly behind him as he consumed the not inconsiderable number of final spoonfuls. The spoons seemed very large also, at least for modern usages. The woman removed his empty plate with a reassuring smile.

The second course was there. As she set it before him, the woman spoke confidentially in his ear of the third course: 'It's turkey tonight.' Her tone was exactly that in which promise is conveyed to a little boy of his favourite dish. It was as if she were Maybury's nanny; even though Maybury had never had a nanny, not exactly. Meanwhile, the second course was a proliferating elaboration of pasta; plainly home-made pasta, probably fabricated that morning. Cheese, in fairly large granules, was strewn across the heap from a large porcelain bowl without Maybury being noticeably consulted.

'Can I have something to drink? A lager will do.'

'We have nothing like that, sir.' It was as if Maybury knew this perfectly well, but she was prepared to play with him. There might, he thought, have been some warning that the place was unlicensed.

'A pity,' said Maybury.

The woman's inflections were beginning to bore him; and he was wondering how much the rich food, all palpably fresh, and home-grown, and of almost unattainable quality, was about to cost him. He doubted very much whether it would be sensible to think of staying the night at The Hospice.

'When you have finished your second course, you may have the opportunity of a word with Mr Falkner.' Maybury recollected that, after all, he had started behind all the others. He must doubtless expect to be a little hustled while he caught up with them. In any case, he was not sure whether or not the implication was that Mr Falkner might, under certain circumstances, unlock a private liquor store.

Obviously it would help the catching-up process if Maybury ate no more than two-thirds of the pasta fantasy. But the woman in the dark blue dress did not seem to see it like that.

'Can't you eat any more?' she enquired baldly, and no longer addressing Maybury as sir.

'Not if I'm to attempt another course,' replied Maybury, quite equably.

'It's turkey tonight,' said the woman. 'You know how turkey just slips down you?' She still had not removed his plate.

'It's very good,' said Maybury firmly. 'But I've had enough.'

It was as if the woman were not used to such conduct, but, as this was no longer a nursery, she took the plate away.

There was even a slight pause, during which Maybury tried to look round the room without giving an appearance of doing so. The main point seemed to be that everyone was dressed rather formally: all the men in 'dark suits', all the women in 'long dresses'. There was a wide variety of age, but, curiously again, there were more men than women. Conversation still seemed far from general. Maybury could not help wondering whether the solidity of the diet did not contribute here. Then it occurred to him that it was as if most of these people had been with one another for a long time, during which things to talk about might have run out, and possibly with little opportunity for renewal through fresh experience. He had met that in hotels. Naturally, Maybury could not, without seeming rude, examine the one-third of the assembly which was seated behind him.

His slab of turkey appeared. He had caught up, even though by cheating. It was an enormous pile, steaming slightly, and also seeping slightly with a colourless, oily fluid. With it appeared five separate varieties of vegetable in separate dishes, brought on a tray; and a sauceboat, apparently for him alone, of specially compounded fluid, dark red and turgid. A sizeable mound of stuffing completed the repast. The middle-aged woman set it all before him swiftly but, this time, silently, with unmistakable reserve.

The truth was that Maybury had little appetite left. He gazed around, less furtively, to see how the rest were managing. He had to admit that, as far as he could see, they were one and all eating as if their lives depended on it: old as well as young, female as well as male; it was as if all had spent a long, unfed day in the hunting field. 'Eating as if their lives depended on it,' he said again to himself; then, struck by the absurdity of the phrase when applied to eating, he picked up his knife and fork with resolution.

'Is everything to your liking, Mr Maybury?'

Again he had been gently taken by surprise. Mr Falkner was at his shoulder: a sleek man in the most beautiful dinner jacket, an instantly ameliorative maître d'hôtel.

'Perfect, thank you,' said Maybury. 'But how did you know my name?'

'We like to remember the names of all our guests,' said Falkner, smiling.

'Yes, but how did you find out *my* name in the first place?'

'We like to think we are proficient at that too, Mr Maybury.'

'I am much impressed,' said Maybury. Really he felt irritated (irritated, at least), but his firm had trained him never to display irritation outside the family circle.

'Not at all,' said Falkner genially. 'Whatever our vocation in life, we may as well do what we can to excel.' He settled the matter by dropping the subject. 'Is there anything I can get for you? Anything you would like?'

'No, thank you very much. I have plenty.'

'Thank *you*, Mr Maybury. If you wish to speak to me at any time, I am normally available in my office. Now I will leave you to the enjoyment of your meal. I may tell you, in confidence, that there is steamed fruit pudding to follow.'

He went quietly forward on his round of the room, speaking to perhaps one person in three at the long, central table; mainly, it seemed, to the older people, as was no doubt to be expected. Falkner wore very elegant black suede shoes, which reminded Maybury of the injury to his own leg, about which he had done nothing, though it might well be septic, even endangering the limb itself, perhaps the whole system.

He was considerably enraged by Falkner's performance about his name, especially as he could find no answer to the puzzle. He felt that he had been placed, almost deliberately, at an undignified disadvantage. Falkner's patronizing conduct in this trifling matter was of a piece with the nannying attitude of the waitress. Moreover, was the unexplained discovery of his name such a trifle, after all? Maybury felt that it had made him vulnerable in other matters also, however undefined. It was the last straw in the matter of his eating any more turkey. He no longer had any appetite whatever.

He began to pass everything systematically through his mind, as he had been trained to do; and almost immediately surmised the answer. In his car was a blue-bound file which on its front bore his name: 'Mr Lucas Maybury'; and this file he supposed that he must have left, name-upwards, on the driving seat, as he commonly did. All the same, the name was merely typed on a sticky label, and would not have been easy to make out through the car window. But he then remembered the floodlight. Even so, quite an effort had been necessary on someone's part, and he wondered who had made that effort. Again he guessed the answer: it was Falkner himself who had been snooping. What would Falkner have done if Maybury had parked the car outside the floodlighted area, as would have been perfectly possible? Used a torch? Perhaps even skeleton keys?

That was absurd.

And how much did the whole thing matter? People in business often had these little vanities, and often had he encountered them. People would do almost anything to feed them. Probably he had one or two himself. The great thing when meeting any situation was to extract the essentials and to concentrate upon them.

To some of the people Falkner was speaking for quite a period of time, while, as Maybury noticed, those seated next to them, previously saying little in most cases, now said nothing at all, but confined themselves entirely to eating. Some of the people at the long table were not merely elderly, he had observed, but positively senile: drooling, watery-eyed, and almost hairless; but even they seemed to be eating away with the best. Maybury had the horrid idea about them that eating was all they did do. 'They lived for eating': another nursery expression, Maybury reflected; and at last he had come upon those of whom it might be true. Some of these people might well relate to rich foods as alcoholics relate to excisable spirits. He found it more nauseating than any sottishness; of which he had seen a certain amount.

Falkner was proceeding so slowly, showing so much professional consideration, that he had not yet reached the lady who sat by herself parallel with Maybury, on the other side of the room. At her Maybury now stared more frankly. Black hair reached her shoulders, and she wore what appeared to be a silk evening dress, a real 'model', Maybury thought (though he did not really know), in many colours; but her expression was of such sadness, suffering, and exhaustion that Maybury was sincerely shocked, especially as once she must, he was sure, have been beautiful, indeed, in a way, still was. Surely so unhappy, even tragic, a figure as that could not be ploughing through a big slab of turkey with five vegetables? Without caution or courtesy, Maybury half rose to his feet in order to look.

'Eat up, sir. Why you've hardly started!' His tormentor had quietly returned to him. What was more, the tragic lady *did* appear to be eating.

'I've had enough. I'm sorry, it's very good, but I've had enough.'

'You said that before, sir, and, look, here you are, still eating away.' He knew that he had, indeed, used those exact words. Crises are met by clichés.

'I've eaten quite enough.'

'That's not necessarily for each of us to say, is it?'

'I want no more to eat of any kind. Please take all this away and just bring me a black coffee. When the time comes, if you like. I don't mind waiting.' Though Maybury did mind waiting, it was necessary to remain in control.

The woman did the last thing Maybury could have expected her to do. She picked up his laden plate (he had at least helped himself to everything) and, with force, dashed it on the floor. Even then the plate itself did not break, but gravy and five vegetables and rich stuffing spread across the thick, patterned, wall-to-wall carpet. Complete, in place of comparative, silence followed in the whole room; though there was still, as Maybury even then observed, the muted clashing of cutlery. Indeed, his own knife and fork were still in his hands.

Falkner returned round the bottom end of the long table.

'Mulligan,' he asked, 'how many more times?' His tone was as quiet as ever. Maybury had not realized that the alarming woman was Irish.

'Mr Maybury,' Falkner continued 'I entirely understand your difficulty. There is naturally no obligation to partake of anything you do not wish. I am only sorry for what has happened. It must seem very poor service on our part. Perhaps you would prefer to go into our lounge? Would you care simply for some coffee?'

'Yes,' said Maybury, concentrating upon the essential. 'I should, please. Indeed, I had already ordered a black coffee. Could I possibly have a pot of it?'

He had to step with care over the mess on the floor, looking downwards. As he did so, he saw something most curious. A central rail ran the length of the long table a few inches above the floor. To this rail, one of the male guests was attached by a fetter round his left ankle.

Maybury, now considerably shaken, had rather expected to be alone in the lounge until the coffee arrived. But he had no sooner dropped down upon one of the massive sofas (it could easily have seated five in a row, at least two of them stout), than the handsome boy appeared from somewhere and proceeded merely to stand about, as at an earlier phase of the evening. There were no illustrated papers to be seen, nor even brochures about Beautiful Britain, and Maybury found the lad's presence irksome. All the same, he did not quite dare to say, 'There's nothing I want.' He could think of nothing to say or to do; nor did the boy speak, or seem to have anything particular to do either. It was obvious that his presence could hardly be required there when everyone was in the dining room. Presumably they would soon be passing on to fruit pudding. Maybury was aware that he had yet to pay his bill. There was a baffled but considerable pause.

Much to his surprise, it was Mulligan who in the end brought him the coffee. It was a single cup, not a pot; and even the cup was of such a size that Maybury, for once that evening, could have done with a bigger. At once he divined that coffee was outside the regime of the place, and that he was being specially compensated, though he might well have to pay extra for it. He had vaguely supposed that Mulligan would have been helping to mop up in the dining-room. Mulligan, in fact, seemed quite undisturbed.

'Sugar, sir?' she said.

'One lump, please,' said Maybury, eyeing the size of the cup.

He did not fail to notice that, before going, she exchanged a glance with the handsome lad. He was young enough to be her son, and the glance might mean anything or nothing.

While Maybury was trying to make the most of his meagre coffee and to ignore the presence of the lad, who must surely be bored, the door from the dining-room opened, and the tragic lady from the other side of the room appeared.

'Close the door, will you?' she said to the boy. The boy closed the door, and then stood about again, watching them.

'Do you mind if I join you?' the lady asked Maybury.

'I should be delighted.'

She was really rather lovely in her melancholy way, her dress was as splendid as Maybury had supposed, and there was in her demeanour an element that could only be called stately. Maybury was unaccustomed to that.

She sat, not at the other end of the sofa, but at the centre of it. It struck Maybury that the rich way she was dressed might almost have been devised to harmonize with the rich way the room was decorated. She wore complicated, oriental-looking earrings, with pink translucent stones, like rosé diamonds (perhaps they *were* diamonds); and silver shoes. Her perfume was heavy and distinctive.

'My name is Cécile Céliména,' she said. 'How do you do? I am supposed to be related to the composer, Chaminade.'

'How do you do?' said Maybury. 'My name is Lucas Maybury, and my only important relation is Solway Short. In fact, he's my cousin.'

They shook hands. Her hand was very soft and white, and she wore a number of rings, which Maybury thought looked real and valuable (though he could not really tell). In order to shake hands with him, she turned the whole upper part of her body towards him.

'Who is that gentleman you mention?' she asked.

'Solway Short? The racing motorist. You must have seen him on the television.'

'I do not watch the television.'

'Quite right. It's almost entirely a waste of time.'

'If you do not wish to waste time, why are you at The Hospice?'

The lad, still observing them, shifted, noticeably, from one leg to the other.

'I am here for dinner. I am just passing through.'

'Oh! You are going then?'

Maybury hesitated. She was attractive and, for the moment, he did not wish to go. 'I suppose so. When I've paid my bill and found out where I can get some petrol. My tank's almost empty. As a matter of fact, I'm lost. I've lost my way.'

'Most of us here are lost.'

'Why here? What makes you come here?'

'We come for the food and the peace and the warmth and the rest.'

'A tremendous *amount* of food, I thought.'

'That's necessary. It's the restorative, you might say.'

'I'm not sure that I quite fit in,' said Maybury. And then he added: 'I shouldn't have thought that you did either.'

'Oh, but I do! Whatever makes you think not?' She seemed quite anxious about it, so that Maybury supposed he had taken the wrong line.

He made the best of it. 'It's just that you seem a little different from what I have seen of the others.'

'In what way, different?' she asked, really anxious, and looking at him with concentration.

'To start with, more beautiful. You are very beautiful,' he said, even though the lad was there, certainly taking in every word.

'That is kind of you to say.' Unexpectedly she stretched across the short distance between them and took his hand. 'What did you say your name was?'

'Lucas Maybury.'

'Do people call you Luke?'

'No, I dislike it. I'm not a Luke sort of person.'

'But your wife can't call you Lucas?'

'I'm afraid she does.' It was a fishing question he could have done without.

'Lucas? Oh no, it's such a cold name.' She was still holding his hand.

'I'm very sorry about it. Would you like me to order you some coffee?'

'No, no. Coffee is not right; it is stimulating, wakeful, over-exciting, unquiet.' She was gazing at him again with sad eyes.

'This is a curious place,' said Maybury, giving her hand a squeeze. It was surely becoming remarkable that none of the other guests had yet appeared.

'I could not live without The Hospice,' she replied.

'Do you come here often?' It was a ludicrously conventional form of words.

'Of course. Life would be impossible otherwise. All those people in the world without enough food, living without love, without even proper clothes to keep the cold out.'

During dinner it had become as hot in the lounge, Maybury thought, as it had been in the dining-room.

Her tragic face sought his understanding. None the less, the line she had taken up was not a favourite of his. He preferred problems to which solutions were at least possible. He had been warned against the other kind.

'Yes,' he said. 'I know what you mean, of course.'

'There are millions and millions of people all over the world with no clothes at all,' she cried, withdrawing her hand.

'Not quite,' Maybury said, smiling. 'Not quite that. Or not yet.'

He knew the risks perfectly well, and thought as little about them as possible. One had to survive, and also to look after one's dependants.

'In any case,' he continued, trying to lighten the tone, 'that hardly applies to you. I have seldom seen a more gorgeous dress.'

'Yes,' she replied with simple gravity. 'It comes from Rome. Would you like to touch it?'

Naturally, Maybury would have liked, but, equally naturally, was held back by the presence of the watchful lad.

'Touch it,' she commanded in a low voice. 'God,

what are you waiting for? Touch it.' She seized his left hand again and forced it against her warm, silky breast. The lad seemed to take no more and no less notice than of anything else.

'Forget. Let go. What is life for, for God's sake?' There was a passionate earnestness about her which might rob any such man as Maybury of all assessment, but he was still essentially outside the situation. As a matter of fact, he had never in his life lost *all* control, and he was pretty sure by now that, for better or for worse, he was incapable of it.

She twisted round until her legs were extended the length of the sofa, and her head was on his lap, or more precisely on his thighs. She had moved so deftly as not even to have disordered her skirt. Her perfume wafted upwards.

'Stop glancing at Vincent,' she gurgled up at him. 'I'll tell you something about Vincent. Though you may think he looks like a Greek God, the simple fact is that he hasn't got what it takes, he's impotent.'

Maybury was embarrassed, of course. All the same, what he reflected was that often there were horses for courses, and often no more to be said about a certain kind of situation than that one thing.

It did not matter much what he reflected, because when she had spoken, Vincent had brusquely left the room through what Maybury supposed to be the service door.

'Thank the Lord,' he could not help remarking naively.

'He's gone for reinforcements,' she said. 'We'll soon see.'

Where were the other guests? Where, by now, could they be? All the same, Maybury's spirits were authentically rising. and he began caressing her more intimately.

Then, suddenly, it seemed that everyone was in the room at once, and this time all talking and fussing.

She sat herself up, none too precipitately, and with her lips close to his ear, said, 'Come to me later. Number 23.'

It was quite impossible for Maybury to point out that he was not staying the night in The Hospice.

Falkner had appeared.

'To bed, all,' he cried genially, subduing the crepitation on the instant.

Maybury, unentangled once more, looked at his watch. It seemed to be precisely ten o'clock. That, no doubt, was the point. Still it seemed very close upon a heavy meal.

No one moved much, but no one spoke either.

'To bed, all of you,' said Falkner again, this time in a tone which might almost be described as roguish. Maybury's lady rose to her feet.

All of them filtered away, Maybury's lady among them. She had spoken no further word, made no further gesture.

Maybury was alone with Falkner.

'Let me remove your cup,' said Falkner courteously.

'Before I ask for my bill,' said Maybury, 'I wonder if you could tell me where I might possibly find some petrol at this hour?'

'Are you out of petrol?' enquired Falkner.

'Almost.'

'There's nothing open at night within twenty miles. Not nowadays. Something to do with our new friends, the Arabs, I believe. All I can suggest is that I syphon some petrol from the tank of our own vehicle. It is a quite large vehicle and it has a large tank.'

'I couldn't possibly put you to that trouble.' In any case, he, Maybury, did not know exactly how to do it. He had heard of it, but it had never arisen before in his own life.

The lad, Vincent, reappeared, still looking pink, Maybury thought, though it was difficult to be sure with such a glowing skin. Vincent began to lock up, a quite serious process, it seemed, rather as in great-grandparental days, when prowling desperadoes were to be feared.

'No trouble at all, Mr Maybury,' said Falkner. 'Vincent here can do it easily, or another member of my staff.'

'Well,' said Maybury, 'if it would be all right...'

'Vincent,' directed Falkner, 'don't bolt and padlock the front door yet. Mr Maybury intends to leave us.'

'Very good,' said Vincent, gruffly.

'Now if we could go to your car, Mr Maybury, you could then drive it round to the back. I will show you the way. I must apologise for putting you to this extra trouble, but the other vehicle takes some time to start, especially at night.'

Vincent had opened the front door for them.

'After you, Mr Maybury,' said Falkner.

Where it had been excessively hot within, it duly proved to be excessively cold without. The floodlight had been turned off. The moon had 'gone in', as Maybury believed the saying was; and all the stars had apparently gone in with it.

Still, the distance to the car was not great. Maybury soon found it in the thick darkness, with Falkner coming quietly step by step behind him.

'Perhaps I had better go back and get a torch?' remarked Falkner.

So there duly was a torch. It brought to Maybury's mind the matter of the office file with his name on it, and, as he unlocked the car door, there the file was, exactly as he had supposed, and, assuredly, name uppermost. Maybury threw it across to the back seat.

Falkner's electric torch was a heavy service object which drenched a wide area in cold, white light.

'May I sit beside you, Mr Maybury?' He closed the offside door behind him.

Maybury had already turned on the headlights, torch or no torch, and was pushing at the starter, which seemed obdurate.

It was not, he thought, that there was anything wrong with it, but rather that there was something wrong with him. The sensation was exactly like a nightmare. He had of course done it hundreds of times, probably thousands of times; but now, when after all it really mattered, he simply could not manage it, had, quite incredibly, somehow lost the simple knack of it. He often endured bad dreams of just this kind. He found time with part of his mind to wonder whether this was not a bad dream. But it was to be presumed not, since now he did not wake, as we soon do when once we realize that we are dreaming.

'I wish I could be of some help,' remarked Falkner, who had shut off his torch, 'but I am not accustomed to the make of car. I might easily do more harm than good.' He spoke with his usual bland geniality.

Maybury was irritated again. The make of car was one of the commonest there is: trust the firm for that. All the same, he knew it was entirely his own fault that he could not make the car start, and not in the least Falkner's. He felt as if he were going mad. 'I don't quite know what to suggest,' he said; and added: 'If, as you say, there's no garage.'

'Perhaps Cromie could be of assistance,' said Falkner. 'Cromie has been with us quite a long time and is a wizard with any mechanical problem.'

No one could say that Falkner was pressing Maybury to stay the night, or even hinting towards it, as one might expect. Maybury wondered whether the funny place was not, in fact, full up. It seemed the most likely answer. Not that Maybury wished to stay the night: far from it.

'I'm not sure,' he said, 'that I have the right to disturb anyone else.'

'Cromie is on night duty,' replied Falkner. 'He is always on night duty. That is what we employ him for. I will fetch him.'

He turned on the torch once more, stepped out of the car, and disappeared into the house, shutting the front door behind him, lest the cold air enter.

In the end, the front door reopened, and Falkner re-emerged. He still wore no coat over his dinner suit, and seemed to ignore the cold. Falkner was followed by a burly but shapeless and shambling figure, whom Maybury first saw indistinctly standing behind Falkner in the light from inside the house.

'Cromie will soon put things to rights,' said Falkner, opening the door of the car. 'Won't you, Cromie?' It was much as one speaks to a friendly retriever.

But there was little, Maybury felt, that was friendly about Cromie. Maybury had to admit to himself that on the instant he found Cromie alarming, even though, what with one thing and another, there was little to be seen of him.

'Now what exactly seems wrong, Mr Maybury?' asked Falkner. 'Just tell Cromie what it is.'

Falkner himself had not attempted to re-enter the car, but Cromie forced himself in and was sprawling in the front seat, next to Maybury, where Angela normally sat. He really did seem a very big, bulging person, but Maybury decisively preferred not to look at him, though the glow cast backwards from the headlights provided a certain illumination.

Maybury could not acknowledge that for some degrading reason he was unable to operate the starter, and so had to claim there was something wrong with it. He was unable not to see Cromie's huge, badly misshapen, yellow hands, both of them, as he tugged with both of them at the knob, forcing it in and out with such violence that Maybury cried out: 'Less force. You'll wreck it.'

'Careful, Cromie,' said Falkner from outside the car. 'Most of Cromie's work is on a big scale,' he explained to Maybury.

But violence proved effective, as so often. Within seconds, the car engine was humming away.

'Thank you very much,' said Maybury.

Cromie made no detectable response, nor did he move.

'Come on out, Cromie,' said Falkner. 'Come on out of it.'

Cromie duly extricated himself and shambled off into the darkness.

'Now,' said Maybury, brisking up as the engine purred. 'Where do we go for the petrol?'

There was the slightest of pauses. Then Falkner spoke from the dimness outside. 'Mr Maybury, I have remembered something. It is not petrol that we have in our tank. It is, of course, diesel oil. I must apologise for such a stupid mistake.'

Maybury was not merely irritated, not merely scared: he was infuriated. With rage and confusion he found it impossible to speak at all. No one in the modern world could confuse diesel oil and petrol in that way. But what could he possibly do?

Falkner, standing outside the open door of the car, spoke again. 'I am extremely sorry, Mr Maybury. Would you permit me to make some amends by inviting you to spend the night with us free of charge, except perhaps for the dinner?'

Within the last few minutes Maybury had suspected that this moment was bound to come in one form or another.

'Thank you,' he said less than graciously. 'I suppose I had better accept.'

'We shall try to make you comfortable,' said Falkner.

Maybury turned off the headlights, climbed out of the car once more, shut and, for what it was worth, locked the door, and followed Falkner back into the house. This time Falkner completed the locking and bolting of the front door that he had instructed Vincent to omit.

'I have no luggage of any kind,' remarked Maybury, still very much on the defensive.

'That may solve itself,' said Falkner, straightening up from the bottom bolt and smoothing his dinner jacket. 'There's something I ought to explain. But will you first excuse me a moment?' He went out through the door at the back of the lounge.

Hotels really have become far too hot, thought Maybury. It positively addled the brain.

Falkner returned. 'There is something I ought to explain,' he said again. 'We have no single rooms, partly because many of our visitors prefer not to be alone at night. The best we can do for you in your emergency, Mr Maybury, is to offer you the share of a room with another guest. It is a large room and there are two beds. It is a sheer stroke of good luck that at present there is only one guest in the room, Mr Bannard. Mr Bannard will be glad of your company, I am certain, and you will be quite safe with him. He is a very pleasant person, I can assure you. I have just sent a message up asking him if he can possibly come down, so that I can introduce you. He is always very helpful, and I think he will be here in a moment. Mr Bannard has been with us for some time, so that I am sure he will be able to fit you up with pyjamas and so forth.'

It was just about the last thing that Maybury wanted from any point of view, but he had learned that it was of a kind that is peculiarly difficult to protest against, without somehow putting oneself in the wrong with other people. Besides he supposed that he was now committed to a night in the place, and therefore to all the implications, whatever they might be, or very nearly so.

'I should like to telephone my wife, if I may,' Maybury said. Angela had been steadily on his mind for some time.

'I fear that's impossible, Mr Maybury,' replied Falkner. 'I'm so sorry.'

'How can it be impossible?'

'In order to reduce tension and sustain the atmosphere that our guests prefer, we have no external telephone. Only an internal link between my quarters and the proprietors.'

'But how can you run an hotel in the modern world without a telephone?'

'Most of our guests are regulars. Many of them come again and again, and the last thing they come for is to hear a telephone ringing the whole time with all the strain it involves.'

'They must be half round the bend,' snapped Maybury, before he could stop himself.

'Mr Maybury,' replied Falkner, 'I have to remind you of two things. The first is that I have invited you to be our guest in the fuller sense of the word. The second is that, although you attach so much importance to efficiency, you none the less appear to have set out on a long journey at night with very little petrol in your tank. Possibly you should think yourself fortunate that you are not spending the night stranded on some motorway.'

'I'm sorry,' said Maybury, 'but I simply must telephone my wife. Soon she'll be out of her mind with worry.'

'I shouldn't think so, Mr Maybury,' said Falkner smiling. 'Concerned, we must hope; but not quite out of her mind.'

Maybury could have hit him, but at that moment a stranger entered.

'Ah, Mr Bannard,' said Falkner, and introduced them. They actually shook hands. 'You won't mind, Mr Bannard, if Mr Maybury shares your room?'

Bannard was a slender, bony little man, of about Maybury's age. He was bald, with a rim of curly red hair. He had slightly glaucous grey-green eyes of the kind that often go with red hair. In the present environment, he was quite perky, but Maybury wondered how he would make out in the world beyond. Perhaps, however, this was because Bannard was too shrimp-like to look his best in pyjamas.

'I should be delighted to share my room with anyone,' replied Bannard. 'I'm lonely by myself.'

'Splendid,' said Falkner coolly. 'Perhaps you'd lead Mr Maybury upstairs and lend him some pyjamas? You must remember that he is a stranger to us and doesn't yet know all our ways.'

'Delighted, delighted,' exclaimed Bannard.

'Well, then,' said Falkner. 'Is there anything you would like, Mr Maybury, before you go upstairs?'

'Only a telephone,' rejoined Maybury, still recalcitrant. He simply did not believe Falkner. No one in the modern world could live without a telephone, let alone run a business without one. He had begun uneasily to wonder if Falkner had spoken the whole truth about the petrol and the diesel fuel either.

'Anything you would like that we are in a position to provide, Mr Maybury?' persisted Falkner, with offensive specificity.

'There's no telephone *here*,' put in Bannard, whose voice was noticeably high, even squeaky.

'In that case, nothing,' said Maybury. 'But I don't know what my wife will do with herself.'

'None of us knows that,' said Bannard superfluously, and cackled for a second.

'Good-night, Mr Maybury. Thank you, Mr Bannard.'

Maybury was almost surprised to discover, as he followed Bannard upstairs, that it seemed a perfectly normal hotel, though overheated and decorated over-heavily. On the first landing was a full-size reproduction of a chieftain in scarlet tartan by Raeburn. Maybury knew the picture, because it had been chosen for the firm's calendar one year, though ever since they had used girls. Bannard lived on the second floor, where the picture on the landing was smaller, and depicted ladies and gentlemen in riding dress taking refreshments together.

'Not too much noise,' said Bannard. 'We have some very light sleepers amongst us.'

The corridors were down to half-illumination for the night watches, and distinctly sinister. Maybury crept foolishly along and almost stole into Bannard's room.

'No,' said Bannard in a giggling whisper. 'Not Number 13, not yet Number 12 A.'

As a matter of fact Maybury had not noticed the number on the door that Bannard was now cautiously closing, and he did not feel called upon to rejoin.

'Do be quiet taking your things off, old man,' said Bannard softly. 'When once you've woken people who've been properly asleep, you can never quite tell. It's a bad thing to do.'

It was a large square room, and the two beds were in exactly opposite corners, somewhat to Maybury's relief. The light had been on when they entered. Maybury surmised that even the unnecessary clicking of switches was to be eschewed.

'That's your bed,' whispered Bannard, pointing jocularly.

So far Maybury had removed only his shoes. He could have done without Bannard staring at him and without Bannard's affable grin.

'Or perhaps you'd rather we did something before settling down?' whispered Bannard.

'No, thank you,' replied Maybury. 'It's been a long day.' He was trying to keep his voice reasonably low, but he absolutely refused to whisper.

'To be sure it has,' said Bannard, rising to much the volume that Maybury had employed. 'Night-night then. The best thing is to get to sleep quickly.' His tone was similar to that which seemed habitual with Falkner.

Bannard climbed agilely into his own bed, and lay on his back peering at Maybury over the sheets.

'Hang your suit in the cupboard,' said Bannard, who had already done likewise. 'There's room.'

'Thank you,' said Maybury. 'Where do I find the pyjamas?'

'Top drawer,' said Bannard. 'Help yourself. They're all alike.'

And, indeed, the drawer proved to be virtually filled with apparently identical suits of pyjamas.

'It's between seasons,' said Bannard. 'Neither proper summer, nor proper winter.'

'Many thanks for the loan,' said Maybury, though the pyjamas were considerably too small for him.

'The bathroom's in there,' said Bannard.

When Maybury returned, he opened the door of the cupboard. It was a big cupboard and it was almost filled by a long line of (presumably) Bannard's suits.

'There's room,' said Bannard once more. 'Find yourself an empty hanger. Make yourself at home.'

While balancing his trousers on the hanger and suspending it from the rail, Maybury again became aware of the injury to his leg. He had hustled so rapidly into Bannard's pyjamas that, for better or for worse, he had not even looked at the scar.

'What's the matter'?' asked Bannard on the instant. 'Hurt yourself, have you?'

'It was a damned cat scratched me,' replied Maybury, without thinking very much.

But this time he decided to look. With some difficulty and some pain, he rolled up the tight pyjama leg. It was a quite nasty gash and there was much dried blood. He realized that he had not even thought about washing the wound. In so far as he had been worrying about anything habitual, he had been worrying about Angela.

'Don't show it to me,' squeaked out Bannard, forgetting not to make a noise. All the same, he was sitting up in bed and staring as if his eyes would pop. 'It's bad for me to see things like that. I'm upset by them.'

'Don't worry,' said Maybury. 'I'm sure it's not as serious as it looks.' In fact, he was far from sure; and he was aware also that it had not been quite what Bannard was concerned about.

'I don't want to know anything about it,' said Bannard.

Maybury made no reply but simply rolled down the pyjama leg. About his injury too there was plainly nothing to be done. Even a request for Vaseline might lead to hysterics. Maybury tried to concentrate upon the reflection that if nothing worse had followed from the gash by now, then nothing worse might ever follow.

Bannard, however, was still sitting up in bed. He was looking pale. 'I come here to forget things like that,' he said. 'We all do.' His voice was shaking.

'Shall I turn the light out?' enquired Maybury. 'As I'm the one who's still up?'

'I don't usually do that,' said Bannard, reclining once more, none the less. 'It can make things unnecessarily difficult. But there's you to be considered too.'

'It's your room,' said Maybury, hesitating.

'All right,' said Bannard. 'If you wish. Turn it out. Tonight anyway.' Maybury did his injured leg no good when stumbling back to his bed. All the same, he managed to arrive there.

'I'm only here for one night,' he said more to the darkness than to Bannard. 'You'll be on your own again tomorrow.'

Bannard made no reply, and, indeed, it seemed to Maybury as if he were no longer there, that Bannard was not an organism that could function in the dark. Maybury refrained from raising any question of drawing back a curtain (the curtains were as long and heavy as elsewhere), or of letting in a little night air. Things, he felt, were better left more or less as they were.

It was completely dark. It was completely silent. It was far too hot.

Maybury wondered what the time was. He had lost all touch. Unfortunately, his watch lacked a luminous dial.

He doubted whether he would ever sleep, but the night had to be endured somehow. For Angela it must be even harder – far harder. At the best, he had never seen himself as a first-class husband, able to provide a superfluity, eager to be protective. Things would become quite impossible, if he were to lose a leg. But, with modern medicine, that might be avoidable, even at the worst: he should be able to continue struggling on for some time yet.

As stealthily as possible he insinuated himself from between the burning blankets and sheets on to the surface of the bed. He lay there like a dying fish, trying not to make another movement of any kind.

He became almost cataleptic with inner exertion. It was not a promising recipe for slumber. In the end, he thought he could detect Bannard's breathing, far, far away. So Bannard was still there. Fantasy and reality are different things. No one could tell whether Bannard slept or waked, but it had in any case become a quite important aim not to resume general conversation with Bannard. Half a lifetime passed.

There could be no doubt, now, that Bannard was both still in the room and also awake. Perceptibly, he was on the move. Maybury's body contracted with speculation as to whether Bannard in the total blackness was making towards his corner. Maybury felt that he was only half his normal size.

Bannard edged and groped interminably. Of course Maybury had been unfair to him in extinguishing the light, and the present anxiety was doubtless no more than the price to be paid.

Bannard himself seemed certainly to be entering into the spirit of the situation: possibly he had not turned the light on because he could not reach the switch; but there seemed more to it than that. Bannard could be thought of as committed to a positive effort in the direction of silence, in order that Maybury, the guest for a night, should not be disturbed. Maybury could hardly hear him moving at all, though perhaps it was a gamble whether this was consideration or menace. Maybury would hardly have been surprised if the next event had been hands on his throat.

But, in fact, the next event was Bannard reaching the door and opening it, with vast delicacy and slowness. It was a considerable anti-climax, and not palpably outside the order of nature, but Maybury did not feel fully reassured as he rigidly watched the column of dim light from the passage slowly widen and then slowly narrow until it vanished with the faint click of the handle. Plainly there was little to worry about, after all, but Maybury had probably reached that level of anxiety where almost any new event merely causes new stress. Soon, moreover, there would be the stress of Bannard's return. Maybury half realized that he was in a grotesque condition to be so upset, when Bannard was, in fact, showing him all possible consideration. Once more he reflected that poor Angela's plight was far worse.

Thinking about Angela's plight, and how sweet, at the bottom of everything, she really was, Maybury felt more wakeful than ever, as he awaited Bannard's return, surely imminent, surely. Sleep was impossible until Bannard had returned.

But still Bannard did not return. Maybury began to wonder whether something had gone wrong with his own time faculty, such as it was; something, that is, of medical significance. That whole evening and night, from soon after his commitment to the recommended route, he had been in doubt about his place in the universe, about what people called the state of his nerves. Here was evidence that he had good reason for anxiety.

Then, from somewhere within the house, came a shattering, earpiercing scream, and then another, and another. It was impossible to tell whether the din came from near or far; still less whether it was female or male. Maybury had not known that the human organism could make so loud a noise, even in the bitterest distress. It was shattering to listen to; especially in the enclosed, hot, total darkness. And this was nothing momentary: the screaming went on and on, a paroxysm, until Maybury had to clutch at himself not to scream in response.

He fell off the bed and floundered about for the heavy curtains. Some light on the scene there must be; if possible, some new air in the room. He found the curtains within a moment, and dragged back first one, and then the other.

There was no more light than before.

Shutters, perhaps? Maybury's arm stretched out gingerly. He could feel neither wood nor metal.

The light switch. It must be found.

While Maybury fell about in the darkness, the screaming stopped on a ghoulish gurgle: perhaps as if the sufferer had vomited immensely and then passed out; or perhaps as if the sufferer had in mercy passed away altogether. Maybury continued to search.

It was harder than ever to say how long it took, but in the end he found the switch, and the immediate mystery was explained. Behind the drawn-back curtains was, as the children say, just wall. The room apparently had no window. The curtains were mere decoration.

All was silent once more: once more extremely silent. Bannard's bed was turned back as neatly as if in the full light of day.

Maybury cast off Bannard's pyjamas and, as quickly as his state permitted, resumed his own clothes. Not that he had any very definite course of action. Simply it seemed better to be fully dressed. He looked vaguely inside his pocket-book to confirm that his money was still there.

He went to the door and made cautiously to open it and seek some hint into the best thing for him to do, the best way to make off.

The door was unopenable. There was no movement in it at all. It had been locked at the least; perhaps more. If Bannard had done it, he had been astonishingly quiet about it: conceivably experienced.

Maybury tried to apply himself to thinking calmly.

The upshot was that once more, and even more hurriedly, he removed his clothes, disposed of them suitably, and resumed Bannard's pyjamas.

It would be sensible once more to turn out the light; to withdraw to bed, between the sheets, if possible; to stand by, as before. But Maybury found that turning out the light, the resultant total blackness, were more than he could face, however expedient.

Ineptly, he sat on the side of his bed, still trying to think things out, to plan sensibly. Would Bannard, after all this time, ever, in fact, return? At least during the course of that night?

He became aware that the electric light bulb had begun to crackle and fizzle. Then, with no further sound, it simply failed. It was not, Maybury thought, some final authoritative lights-out all over the house. It was merely that the single bulb had given out, however unfortunately from his own point of view: an isolated industrial incident.

He lay there, half in and half out, for a long time. He concentrated on the thought that nothing had actually happened that was dangerous. Ever since his schooldays (and, indeed, during them) he had become increasingly aware that there were many things strange to him, most of which had proved in the end to be apparently quite harmless.

Then Bannard was creeping back into the dark room. Maybury's ears had picked up no faint sound of a step in the passage, and, more remarkable, there had been no noise, either, of a turned key, let alone, perhaps, of a drawn bolt. Maybury's view of the bulb failure was confirmed by a repetition of the widening and narrowing column of light, dim, but probably no dimmer than before. Up to a point, lights were still on elsewhere. Bannard, considerate as before, did not try to turn on the light in the room. He shut the door with extraordinary skill, and Maybury could just, though only just, hear him slithering into his bed.

Still, there was one unmistakable development: at Bannard's return, the dark room had filled with perfume; the perfume favoured, long ago, as it seemed, by the lady who had been so charming to Maybury in the lounge. Smell is, in any case, notoriously the most recollective of the senses.

Almost at once, this time, Bannard not merely fell obtrusively asleep, but was soon snoring quite loudly.

Maybury had every reason to be at least irritated by everything that was happening, but instead he soon fell asleep himself. So long as Bannard was asleep, he was at least in abeyance as an active factor in the situation; and many perfumes have their own drowsiness, as Iago remarked. Angela passed temporarily from the forefront of Maybury's mind.

Then he was awake again. The light was on once more, and Maybury supposed that he had been awakened deliberately, because Bannard was standing there by his bed. Where and how had he found a new light bulb? Perhaps he kept a supply in a drawer. This seemed so likely that Maybury thought no more of the matter.

It was very odd, however, in another way also.

When Maybury had been at school, he had sometimes found difficulty in distinguishing certain boys from certain other boys. It had been a very large school, and boys do often look alike. None the less, it was a situation that Maybury thought best to keep to himself, at the time and since. He had occasionally made responses or approaches based upon misidentifications: but had been fortunate in never being made to suffer for it bodily, even though he had suffered much in his self-regard.

And now it was the same. Was the man standing there really Bannard? One obvious thing was that Bannard had an aureole or fringe of red hair, whereas this man's fringe was quite grey. There was also a different expression and general look, but Maybury was more likely to have been mistaken about that. The pyjamas seemed to be the same, but that meant little.

'I was just wondering if you'd care to talk for a bit,' said Bannard. One had to assume that Bannard it was; at least to start off with. 'I didn't mean to wake you up. I was just making sure.'

'That's all right, I suppose,' said Maybury.

'I'm over my first beauty sleep,' said Bannard. 'It can be lonely during the night.' Under all the circumstances it was a distinctly absurd remark, but undoubtedly it was in Bannard's idiom.

'What was all that screaming?' enquired Maybury.

'I didn't hear anything,' said Bannard. 'I suppose I slept through it. But I can imagine. We soon learn to take no notice. There are sleepwalkers for that matter, from time to time.'

'I suppose that's why the bedroom doors are so hard to open?'

'Not a bit,' said Bannard, but he then added. 'Well, partly, perhaps. Yes, partly. I think so. But it's just a knack really. We're not actually locked in, you know.' He giggled. 'But what makes you ask? You don't need to leave the room in order to go to the loo. I showed you, old man.'

So it really must be Bannard, even though his eyes seemed to be a different shape, and even a different colour, as the hard light caught them when he laughed.

'I expect I was sleepwalking myself,' said Maybury warily.

'There's no need to get the wind up,' said Bannard, 'like a kid at a new school. All that goes on here is based on the simplest of natural principles: eating good food regularly, sleeping long hours, not taxing the overworked brain. The food is particularly important. You just wait for breakfast, old man, and see what you get. The most tremendous spread, I promise you.'

'How do you manage to eat it all?' asked Maybury. 'Dinner alone was too much for me.'

'We simply let Nature have its way. Or rather, perhaps, her way. We give Nature her head.'

'But it's not *natural* to eat so much.'

'That's all you know,' said Bannard. 'What you are, old man, is effete.' He giggled as Bannard had giggled, but he looked somehow unlike Maybury's recollection of Bannard. Maybury was almost certain there was some decisive difference.

The room still smelt of the woman's perfume; or perhaps it was largely Bannard who smelt of it, Bannard who now stood so close to Maybury. It was embarrassing that Bannard, if he really had to rise from his bed and wake Maybury up, did not sit down; though preferably not on Maybury's blanket.

'I'm not saying there's no suffering here,' continued Bannard. 'But where in the world are you exempt from suffering? At least no one rots away in some attic – or wretched bed-sitter, more likely. Here there are no single rooms. We all help one another. What can you and I do for one another, old man?'

He took a step nearer and bent slightly over Maybury's face. His pyjamas really reeked of perfume.

It was essential to be rid of him; but essential to do it uncontentiously. The prospect should accept the representative's point of view as far as possible unawares.

'Perhaps we could talk for just five or ten minutes more,' said Maybury, 'and then I should like to go to sleep again, if you will excuse me. I ought to explain that I slept very little last night owing to my wife's illness.'

'Is your wife pretty?' asked Bannard. 'Really pretty? With this and that?' He made a couple of gestures, quite conventional though not aforetime seen in drawing rooms.

'Of course she is,' said Maybury. 'What do you think?'

'Does she really turn you on? Make you lose control of yourself?'

'Naturally,' said Maybury. He tried to smile, to show he had a sense of humour which could help him to cope with tasteless questions.

Bannard now not merely sat on Maybury's bed, but pushed his frame against Maybury's legs, which there was not much room to withdraw, owing to the tightness of the blanket, as Bannard sat on it.

'Tell us about it,' said Bannard. 'Tell us exactly what it's like to be a married man. Has it changed your whole life? Transformed everything?'

'Not exactly. In any case, I married years ago.'

'So now there is someone else. *I* understand.'

'No, actually there is not.'

'Love's old sweet song still sings to you?'

'If you like to put it like that, yes. I love my wife. Besides she's ill. And we have a son. There's him to consider too.'

'How old is your son?'

'Nearly sixteen.'

'What colour are his hair and eyes?'

'Really, I'm not sure. No particular colour. He's not a baby, you know.'

'Are his hands still soft?'

'I shouldn't think so.'

'Do you love your son, then?'

'In his own way, yes, of course.'

'I should love him, were he mine, and my wife too.' It seemed to Maybury that Bannard said it with real sentiment. What was more, he looked at least twice as sad as when Maybury had first seen him: twice as old, and twice as sad. It was all ludicrous, and Maybury at last felt really tired, despite the lump of Bannard looming over him, and looking different.

'Time's up for me,' said Maybury. 'I'm sorry. Do you mind if we go to sleep again?'

Bannard rose at once to his feet, turned his back on Maybury's corner, and went to his bed without a word, thus causing further embarrassment.

It was again left to Maybury to turn out the light, and to shove his way back to bed through the blackness.

Bannard had left more than a waft of the perfume behind him; which perhaps helped Maybury to sleep once more almost immediately, despite all things.

Could the absurd conversation with Bannard have been a dream? Certainly what happened next was a dream: for there was Angela in her nightdress with her hands on her poor head, crying out 'Wake up! Wake up! Wake up!' Maybury could not but comply, and in Angela's place, there was the boy, Vincent, with early morning tea for him. Perforce the light was on once more: but that was not a matter to be gone into.

'Good morning, Mr Maybury.'

'Good morning, Vincent.'

Bannard already had his tea.

Each of them had a pot, a cup, jugs of milk and hot water, and a plate of bread and butter, all set on a tray. There were eight large triangular slices each.

'No sugar,' cried out Bannard genially. 'Sugar kills appetite.'

Perfect rubbish, Maybury reflected; and squinted across at Bannard, recollecting his last rubbishy conversation. By the light of morning, even if it were but the same electric light, Bannard looked much more himself, fluffy red aureole and all. He looked quite rested. He munched away at his bread and butter. Maybury thought it best to go through the motions of following suit. From over there Bannard could hardly see the details.

'Race you to the bathroom, old man,' Bannard cried out.

'Please go first,' responded Maybury soberly. As he had no means of conveying the bread and butter off the premises, he hoped, with the aid of the towel, to conceal it in his skimpy pyjamas jacket, and push it down the water closet. Even Bannard would probably not attempt to throw his arms round him and so uncover the offence.

Down in the lounge, there they all were, with Falkner presiding indefinably but genially. Wan though authentic sunlight trickled in from the outer world, but Maybury observed that the front door was still bolted and chained. It was the first thing he looked for. Universal expectation was detectable: of breakfast, Maybury assumed. Bannard, at all times shrimpish, was simply lost in the throng. Cécile he could not see, but he made a point of not looking very hard. In any case, several of the people looked new, or at least different. Possibly it was a further example of the phenomenon Maybury had encountered with Bannard.

Falkner crossed to him at once: the recalcitrant but still privileged outsider. 'I can promise you a good breakfast, Mr Maybury,' he said confidentially. 'Lentils. Fresh fish. Rump steak. Apple pie made by ourselves, with lots and lots of cream.'

'I mustn't stay for it,' said Maybury. 'I simply mustn't. I have my living to earn. I must go at once.'

He was quite prepared to walk a couple of miles; indeed, all set for it. The automobile organisation, which had given him the route from which he should never have diverged, could recover his car. They had done it for him before, several times.

A faint shadow passed over Falkner's face, but he merely said in a low voice, 'If you really insist, Mr Maybury–'

'I'm afraid I have to,' said Maybury.

'Then I'll have a word with you in a moment.'

None of the others seemed to concern themselves. Soon they all filed off, talking quietly among themselves, or, in many cases, saying nothing.

'Mr Maybury,' said Falkner, 'you can respect a confidence?'

'Yes,' said Maybury steadily.

'There was an incident here last night. A death. We do not talk about such things. Our guests do not expect it.'

'I am sorry,' said Maybury.

'Such things still upset me,' said Falkner. 'None the less I must not think about that. My immediate task is to dispose of the body. While the guests are preoccupied. To spare them all knowledge, all pain.'

'How is that to be done?' enquired Maybury.

'In the usual manner, Mr Maybury. The hearse is drawing up outside the door even as we speak. Where you are concerned, the point is this. If you wish for what in other circumstances I could call a lift, I could arrange for you to join the vehicle. It is travelling quite a distance. We find that best.' Falkner was progressively unfastening the front door. 'It seems the best solution, don't you think, Mr Maybury? At least it is the best I can offer. Though you will not be able to thank Mr Bannard, of course.'

A coffin was already coming down the stairs, borne on the shoulders of four men in black, with Vincent, in his white jacket, coming first, in order to leave no doubt of the way and to prevent any loss of time.

'I agree,' said Maybury. 'I accept. Perhaps you would let me know my bill for dinner?'

'I shall waive that too, Mr Maybury,' replied Falkner, 'in the present circumstances. We have a duty to hasten. We have others to think of. I shall simply say how glad we have all been to have you with us.' He held out his hand. 'Good-bye, Mr Maybury.'

Maybury was compelled to travel with the coffin itself, because there simply was not room for him on the front seat, where a director of the firm, a corpulent man, had to be accommodated with the driver. The nearness of death compelled a respectful silence among the company in the rear compartment, especially when a living stranger was in the midst; and Maybury alighted unobtrusively when a bus stop was reached. One of the undertaker's men said that he should not have to wait long.

IT ONLY COMES OUT AT NIGHT

Dennis Etchison

Dennis Etchison (1943–) is an American writer and editor of fantasy and horror fiction. His novels include *Darkside* (1986), *Shadowman* (1994), and *California Gothic* (1995). Etchison's stunning short stories have been especially well-regarded by critics and genre fans, receiving the World Fantasy Award and the British Fantasy Award. Stories like 'It Only Comes Out at Night' (1976) demonstrate the effectiveness of Etchison's minimalist approach – naturalistic but still undeniably strange, unease becoming horrific sometimes in the span of a single paragraph. Etchison helped influence and shape the US horror boom of the early 1990s, while remaining *sui generis*.

If you leave L.A. by way of San Bernardino, headed for Route 66 and points east you must cross the Mojave Desert.

Even after Needles and the border, however, there is no relief; the dry air only thins further as the long, relentless climb continues in earnest. Flagstaff is still almost two hundred miles, and Winslow, Gallup and Albuquerque are too many hours away to think of making without food, rest and, mercifully, sleep.

It is like this: the car runs hot, hotter than it ever has before, the plies of the tires expand and contract until the sidewalls begin to shimmy slightly as they spin on over the miserable Arizona roads, giving up a faint odor like burning hair from between the treads, as the windshield colors over with essence of honeybee, wasp, dragonfly, mayfly, June bug, ladybug, and the like, and the radiator, clotted with the bodies of countless kamikaze insects, hisses like a moribund lizard in the sun…

All of which means, of course, that if you are traveling that way between May and September, you move by night.

Only by night.

For there are, after all, dawn check-in motels, Do Not Disturb signs for bungalow doorknobs; there are diners for mid-afternoon breakfasts, coffee by the carton; there are twenty-four-hour filling stations bright as dreams Whiting Brothers, Conoco, Terrible Herbst – their flags are unfamiliar as their names, with ice machines, soda machines, candy machines; and there are the sudden, unexpected Rest Areas, just off the highway, with brick bathrooms and showers and electrical outlets, constructed especially for those who are weary, out of money, behind schedule…

So McClay had had to learn, the hard way.

He slid his hands to the bottom of the steering wheel and *peered* ahead into the darkness, trying to relax. But the wheel stuck to his fingers like warm candy. Off somewhere to his left, the horizon flickered with pearly luminescence, then faded again to black. This time he did not bother to look. Sometimes, though, he wondered just how far way the lightning was striking; not once during the night had the sound of its thunder reached him here in the car.

In the back seat, his wife moaned.

The trip out had turned all but unbearable for her. Four days it had taken, instead of the expected two-and-a-half; he made a great effort not to think of it, but the memory hung over the car like a thunderhead.

It had been a blur, a fever dream. Once, on the second day, he had been passed by a churning bus, its silver sides blinding him until he noticed a Mexican woman in one of the window seats. She was not looking at him. She was holding a swooning infant to the glass, squeezing water onto its head from a plastic baby bottle to keep it from passing out.

McClay sighed and fingered the buttons on the car radio.

He knew he would get nothing from the AM or FM bands, not out here, but he clicked it on anyway. He left the volume and tone controls down, so as not to wake Evvie. Then he punched the seldom-used middle button, the shortwave band, and raised the gain carefully until he could barely hear the radio over the hum of the tires.

Static.

Slowly he swept the tuner across the bandwidth, but there was only white noise. It reminded him a little of the summer rain yesterday, starting back, the way it had sounded bouncing off the windows.

He was about to give up when he caught a voice, crackling, drifting in and out. He worked the knob like a safecracker, zeroing in on the signal.

A few bars of music. A tone, then the voice again. '… Greenwich Mean Time.' Then the station ID.

It was the Voice of America overseas broadcast.

He grunted disconsolately and killed it.

His wife stirred.

'Why'd you turn it off?' she murmured. 'I was listening to that. Good. Program.'

'Take it easy,' he said, 'easy, you're still asleep. We'll be stopping soon.'

'… Only comes out at night,' he heard her say, and then she was lost again in the blankets.

He pressed the glove compartment, took out one of the Automobile Club guides. It was already clipped open. McClay flipped on the overhead light and drove with one hand, reading over – for the hundredth time? – the list of motels that lay ahead. He knew the list by heart, but seeing the names again reassured him somehow. Besides, it helped to break the monotony.

It was the kind of place you never expect to find in the middle of a long night, a bright place with buildings (a building, at least) and cars, other cars drawn off the highway to be together in the protective circle of light.

A Rest Area.

He would have spotted it without the sign. Elevated sodium vapor lighting bathed the scene in an almost peach-colored glow, strikingly different from the cold blue-white sentinels of the interstate highway. He had seen other Rest Area signs on the way out, probably even this one. But in daylight the signs had meant nothing more to him than 'Frontage Road' or 'Business District Next Right.' He wondered if it were the peculiar warmth of light that made the small island of blacktop appear so inviting.

McClay decelerated, downshifted, and left Interstate 40.

The car dipped and bumped, and he was aware of the new level of sound from the engine as it geared down for the first time in hours.

He eased in next to a Pontiac Firebird, toed the emergency brake, and cut the ignition.

He allowed his eyes to close and his head to sink back into the headrest. At last.

The first thing he noticed was the quiet.

It was deafening. His ears literally began to ring, with the high-pitched whine of a late-night TV test pattern.

The second thing he noticed was a tingling at the tip of his tongue.

It brought to mind a picture of a snake's tongue. Picking up electricity from the air, he thought.

The third was the rustling awake of his wife, in back.

She pulled herself up. 'Are we sleeping now? Why are the lights … ?'

He saw the outline of her head in the mirror. 'It's just a rest stop, hon. I – the car needs a break.' Well, it was true, wasn't it? 'You want a rest room? There's one back there, see it?'

'Oh my God.'

'What's the matter now?'

'Leg's asleep. Listen, are we or are we not going to get a–'

'There's a motel coming up.' He didn't say that

they wouldn't hit the one he had marked in the book for another couple of hours; he didn't want to argue. He knew she needed the rest; he needed it too, didn't he? 'Think I'll have some more of that coffee, though,' he said.

'Isn't any more,' she yawned.

The door slammed.

Now he was able to recognize the ringing in his ears for what it was: the sound of his own blood. It almost succeeded in replacing the steady drone of the car.

He twisted around, fishing over the back of the seat for the ice chest.

There should be a couple of Cokes left, at least.

His fingers brushed the basket next to the chest, riffling the edges of maps and tour books, by now reshuffled haphazardly over the first-aid kit he had packed himself (tourniquet, forceps, scissors, ammonia inhalants, Merthiolate, triangular bandage, compress, adhesive bandages, tannic acid) and the fire extinguisher, the extra carton of cigarettes, the remainder of a half-gallon of drinking water, the thermos (which Evvie said was empty, and why would she lie?).

He popped the top of a can.

Through the side window he saw Evvie disappearing around the corner of the building. She was wrapped to the gills in her blanket.

He opened the door and slid out, his back aching.

He stood there blankly, the unnatural light washing over him.

He took a long sweet pull from the can. Then he started walking.

The Firebird was empty.

And the next car, and the next.

Each car he passed looked like the one before it, which seemed crazy until he realized that it must be the work of the light. It cast an even, eerie tan over the baked metal tops, like orange sunlight through air thick with suspended particles. Even the windshields appeared to be filmed over with a thin layer of settled dust. It made him think of country roads, sundowns.

He walked on.

He heard his footsteps echo with surprising clarity, resounding down the staggered line of parked vehicles. Finally it dawned on him (and now he knew how tired he really was) that the cars must actually have people in them – sleeping people. Of course. Well, hell, he thought, watching his step, I wouldn't want to wake anyone. The poor devils.

Besides the sound of his footsteps, there was only the distant *swish* of an occasional, very occasional car on the highway; from here, even that was only a distant hush, growing and then subsiding like waves on a nearby shore.

He reached the end of the line, turned back.

Out of the corner of his eye he saw, or thought he saw, a movement by the building.

It would be Evvie, shuffling back.

He heard the car door slam.

He recalled something he had seen in one of the tourist towns in New Mexico: circling the park – in Taos, that was where they had been – he had glimpsed an ageless Indian, wrapped in typical blanket, ducking out of sight into the doorway of a gift shop; with the blanket over his head that way, the Indian had somehow resembled an Arab, or so it had seemed to him at the time.

He heard another car door slam.

That was the same day – was it only last week? – that she had noticed the locals driving with their headlights on (in honor of something or other, some regional election, perhaps: ' "My face speaks for itself," drawled Herman J. "Fashio" Trujillo, Candidate for Sheriff'). She had insisted at first that it must be a funeral procession, though for whom she could not guess.

McClay came to the car, stretched a last time, and crawled back in.

Evvie was bundled safely again in the back seat.

He lit a quick cigarette, expecting to hear her voice any second, complaining, demanding that he roll down the windows, at least, and so forth. But, as it turned out, he was able to sit undisturbed as he smoked it down almost to the filter.

Paguate. Bluewater. Thoreau.

He blinked.

Klagetoh. Joseph City. Ash Fork.

He blinked and tried to focus his eyes from the tail-lights a half-mile ahead to the bug-spattered glass, then back again.

Petrified Forest National Park.

He blinked, refocusing. But it did no good.

A twitch started on the side of his face, close by the corner of his eye.

Rehoboth.

He strained at a road sign, the names and mileages, but instead a seemingly endless list of past and future stops and detours shimmered before his mind's eye.

I've had it, he thought. Now, suddenly, it was catching up with him, the hours of repressed fatigue; he felt a rushing out of something from his chest. No way to make that motel – hell, I can't even remember the name of it now. Check the book. But it doesn't matter. The eyes. *Can't control my eyes anymore.*

(He had already begun to hallucinate things like tree trunks and cows and Mack trucks speeding toward him on the highway. The cow had been straddling the broken line; in the last few minutes its lowing, deep and regular, had become almost inviting.)

Well, he could try for *any* motel. Whatever turned up next.

But how much farther would that be?

He ground his teeth together, feeling the pulsing at his temples. He struggled to remember the last sign.

The next town. It might be a mile. Five miles. Fifty.

Think! He said it, he thought it, he didn't know which.

If he could pull over, pull over right now and lie down for a few minutes.

He seemed to see clear ground ahead. No rocks, no ditch. The shoulder, just ahead.

Without thinking he dropped into neutral and coasted, aiming for it.

The car glided to a stop.

God, he thought.

He forced himself to turn, reach into the back seat.

The lid to the chest was already off. He dipped his fingers into the ice and retrieved two half-melted cubes, lifted them into the front seat, and began rubbing them over his forehead.

He let his eyes close, seeing dull lights fire as he daubed at the lids, the rest of his face, the forehead again. As he slipped the ice into his mouth and chewed, it broke apart as easily as snow.

He took a deep breath. He opened his eyes again.

At that moment a huge tanker roared past, slamming an aftershock of air into the side of the car. The car rocked like a boat at sea.

No. It was no good.

So. So he could always turn back, couldn't he? And why not? The Rest Area was only twenty, twenty-five minutes behind him. (Was that all?) He could pull out and hang a U and turn back, just like that. And then sleep. It would be safer there. With luck, Evvie wouldn't even know. An hour's rest, maybe two; that was all he would need.

Unless – was there another Rest Area ahead?

How soon?

He knew that the second wind he felt now wouldn't last, not for more than a few minutes. No, it wasn't worth the chance.

He glanced in the rearview mirror.

Evvie was still down, a lumpen mound of blanket and hair.

Above her body, beyond the rear window, the raised headlights of another monstrous truck, closing ground fast.

He made the decision.

He slid into first and swung out in a wide arc, well ahead of the blast of the truck, and worked up to fourth gear. He was thinking about the warm, friendly lights he had left behind.

He angled in next to the Firebird and cut the lights.

He started to reach for a pillow from the back, but why bother? It would probably wake Evvie, anyway.

He wadded up his jacket, jammed it against the passenger armrest, and lay down.

First he crossed his arms over his chest. Then behind his head. Then he gripped his hands between his knees. Then he was on his back again, his hands at his sides, his feet cramped against the opposite door.

His eyes were wide open.

He lay there, watching chain lightning flash on the horizon.

Finally he let out a breath that sounded like all the breaths he had ever taken going out at once, and drew himself up.

He got out and walked over to the rest room.

Inside, white tiles and bare lights. His eyes felt raw, peeled. Finished, he washed his hands but not his face; that would only make sleep more difficult.

Outside again and feeling desperately out of synch, he listened to his shoes falling hollowly on the cement.

'Next week we've got to get organized... '

He said this, he was sure, because he heard his voice coming back to him, though with a peculiar empty resonance. Well, this time tomorrow night he would be home. As unlikely as that seemed now.

He stopped, bent for a drink from the water fountain.

The footsteps did not stop.

Now wait, he thought, I'm pretty far gone, but –

He swallowed, his ears popping.

The footsteps stopped.

Hell, he thought, I've been pushing too hard. We. She. No, it was my fault, my plan this time. To drive nights, sleep days. Just so. As long as you *can* sleep.

Easy, take it easy.

He started walking again, around the corner and back to the lot.

At the corner, he thought he saw something move at the edge of his vision.

He turned quickly to the right, in time for a fleeting glimpse of something – someone – hurrying out of sight into the shadows.

Well, the other side of the building housed the women's rest room. Maybe it was Evvie.

He glanced toward the car, but it was blocked from view.

He walked on.

Now the parking area resembled an oasis lit by firelight. Or a western camp, the cars rimming the lot on three sides in the manner of wagons gathered against the night.

Strength in numbers, he thought.

Again, each car he passed looked at first like every other. It was the flat light, of course. And of course they were the same cars he had seen a half-hour ago. And the light still gave them a dusty, abandoned look.

He touched a fender.

It *was* dusty.

But why shouldn't it be? His own car had probably taken on quite a layer of grime after so long on these roads.

He touched the next car, the next.

Each was so dirty that he could have carved his name without scratching the paint.

He had an image of himself passing this way again – God forbid – a year from now, say, and finding the same cars parked here. The *same* ones.

What if, he wondered tiredly, what if some of these cars had been abandoned? Overheated, exploded, broken down one fine midday and left here by owners who simply never returned? Who would ever know? Did the Highway Patrol, did anyone bother to check? Would an automobile be preserved here for months, years by the elements, like a snakeskin shed beside the highway?

It was a thought, anyway.

His head was buzzing.

He leaned back and inhaled deeply, as deeply as he could at this altitude.

But he did hear something. A faint tapping. It reminded him of running feet, until he noticed the lamp overhead.

There were hundreds of moths beating against the high fixture, their soft bodies tapping as they struck and circled and returned again and again to the lens; the light made their wings translucent.

He took another deep breath and went on to his car.

He could hear it ticking, cooling down, before he got there. Idly he rested a hand on the hood. Warm, of course. The tires? He touched the left front. It was taut, hot as a loaf from the oven. When he took his hand away, the color of the rubber came off on his palm like burned skin.

He reached for the door handle.

A moth fluttered down onto the fender. He flicked it off, his finger leaving a streak on the enamel.

He looked closer and saw a wavy, mottled pattern covering his unwashed car, and then he remembered. The rain, yesterday afternoon. The rain had left blotches in the dust, marking the finish as if with dirty fingerprints.

He glanced over at the next car.

It, too, had the imprint of dried raindrops – but, close up, he saw that the marks were superimposed in layers, over and over again.

The Firebird had been through a great many rains.

He touched the hood.

Cold.

He removed his hand, and a dead moth clung to his thumb. He tried to brush it off the hood, but other moth bodies stuck in its place. Then he saw countless shriveled, mummified moths pasted over the hood and top like peeling chips of paint. His fingers were coated with the powder from their wings.

He looked up.

High above, backed by banks of roiling cumulous clouds, the swarm of moths vibrated about the bright, protective light.

So the Firebird had been here a very long time.

He wanted to forget it, to let it go. He wanted to get back in the car. He wanted to lie down, lock it out, everything. He wanted to go to sleep and wake up in Los Angeles.

He couldn't.

He inched around the Firebird until he was facing the line of cars. He hesitated a beat, then started moving.

A LeSabre.

A Cougar.

A Chevy van.

A Corvair.

A Ford.

A Mustang.

And every one was overlaid with grit.

He paused by the Mustang. Once – how long ago? – it had been a luminous candy-apple red; probably belonged to a teenager. Now the windshield was opaque, the body dulled to a peculiar shade he could not quite place.

Feeling like a voyeur at a drive-in movie theater, McClay crept to the driver's window.

Dimly he perceived two large outlines in the front seat.

He raised his hand.

Wait.

What if there were two people sitting there on the other side of the window, watching him?

He put it out of his mind. Using three fingers, he cut a swath through the scum on the glass and pressed close.

The shapes were there. Two headrests.

He started to pull away.

And happened to glance into the back seat.

He saw a long, uneven form.

A leg, back of a thigh. Blonde hair, streaked with shadows. The collar of a coat.

And, delicate and silvery, a spider web, spun between the hair and collar.

He jumped back.

His leg struck the old Ford. He spun around, his arms straight. The blood was pounding in his ears.

He rubbed out a spot on the window of the Ford and scanned the inside.

The figure of a man, slumped on the front seat.

The man's head lay on a jacket. No, it was not a jacket. It was a large, formless stain. In the filtered light, McClay could see that it had dried to a dark brown.

It came from the man's mouth.

No, not from the mouth.

The throat had a long, thin slash across it, reaching nearly to the ear.

He stood there stiffly, his back almost arched, his eyes jerking, trying to close, trying not to close. The lot, the even light reflecting thinly from each windshield, the Corvair, the van, the Cougar, the LeSabre, the suggestion of a shape within each one.

The pulse in his ears muffled and finally blotted out the distant gearing of a truck up on the highway, the death-rattle of the moths against the seductive lights.

He reeled.

He seemed to be hearing again the breaking open of doors and the scurrying of padded feet across paved spaces.

He remembered the first time. He remembered

the sound of a second door slamming in a place where no new car but his own had arrived.

Or – had it been the door of his car slamming a second time, after Evvie had gotten back in?

If so, how? Why?

And there had been the sight of someone moving, trying to slip away.

And for some reason now he remembered the Indian in the tourist town, slipping out of sight in the doorway of that gift shop. He held his eyelids down until he saw the shop again, the window full of kachinas and tin gods and tapestries woven in a secret language.

At last he remembered clearly: the Indian had not been entering the store. *He had been stealing away.*

McClay did not yet understand what it meant, but he opened his eyes, as if for the first time in centuries, and began to run toward his car.

If I could only catch my goddamn breath, he thought.

He tried to hold on. He tried not to think of her, of what might have happened the first time, of what he may have been carrying in the back seat ever since.

He had to find out.

He fought his way back to the car, against a rising tide of fear he could not stem.

He told himself to think of other things, of things he knew he could control: mileages and motel bills, time zones and weather reports, spare tires and flares and tubeless repair tools, hydraulic jack and Windex and paper towels and tire iron and socket wrench and waffle cushion and traveler's checks and credit cards and Dopp Kit (toothbrush and paste, deodorant, shaver, safety blade, brushless cream) and sunglasses and Sight Savers and tear-gas pen and fiber-tip pens and portable radio and alkaline batteries and fire extinguisher and desert water bag and tire gauge and motor oil and his money-belt with identification sealed in plastic.

In the back of his car, under the quilt, nothing moved, not even when he finally lost his control and his mind in a thick, warm scream.

THE PSYCHOLOGIST WHO WOULDN'T DO AWFUL THINGS TO RATS

James Tiptree, Jr.

James Tiptree, Jr. (1915–1987) was an award-winning American speculative fiction writer whose visionary stories and novels often seemed to have no antecedent. The author's real name, not known publicly until 1977, was Alice Bradley Sheldon, which she termed 'good camouflage'. Although Sheldon gained a sterling reputation within the science fiction field, winning the Hugo Award, her fantastical Quintana Roo stories set on the Yucatan Peninsula are also very powerful. Occasionally she would write within or at the edges of recognizable traditions of weird fiction, as exemplified by the very dark 'The Psychologist Who Wouldn't Do Awful Things to Rats' (1976).

He comes shyly hopeful into the lab. He is unable to suppress this childishness which has deviled him all his life, this tendency to wake up smiling, believing for an instant that today will be different.

But it isn't; is not.

He is walking into the converted cellars which are now called animal laboratories by this nationally respected university, this university which is still somehow unable to transmute its nationwide reputation into adequate funding for research. He squeezes past a pile of galvanized Skinner boxes and sees Smith at the sinks, engaged in cutting off the heads of infant rats. Piercing squeals; the headless body is flipped onto a wet furry pile on a hunk of newspaper. In the holding cage beside Smith the baby rats shiver in a heap, occasionally thrusting up a delicate muzzle and then burrowing convulsively under their friends, seeking to shut out Smith. They have previously been selectively shocked, starved, subjected to air blasts and plunged in ice water; Smith is about to search the corpses for appropriate neuroglandular effects of stress. He'll find them, undoubtedly.

Eeeeeeee – Ssskrick! Smith's knife grates, drinking life.

'Hello, Tilly.'

'Hi.' He hates his nickname, hates his whole stupid name: Tilman Lipsitz. He would go nameless through the world if he could. If he even could have something simple, Moo or Urg – anything but the absurd high-pitched syllables that have followed him through life: Tilly Lipsitz. He has suffered from it.

Ah well. He makes his way around the pile of Purina Lab Chow bags, bracing for the fierce clamor of the rhesus. Their Primate Room is the ex-boiler room, really; these are tenements the university took over. The rhesus scream like sirens. Thud! Feces have hit the grill again; the stench is as strong as the sound. Lipsitz peers in reluctantly, mentally apologizing for being unable to like monkeys. Two of them are not screaming, huddled on the steel with puffy pink bald heads studded with electrode jacks. Why can't they house the creatures better, he wonders irritably for the nth time. In the trees they're clean. Well, cleaner, anyway, he amends, ducking around a stand of somebody's breadboard circuits awaiting solder.

On the far side is Jones, bending over a brightly lighted bench, two students watching mesmerized. He can see Jones's fingers tenderly roll the verniers that drive the probes down through the skull of the dog strapped underneath. Another of his terrifying stereotaxes. The aisle of cages is packed with animals with wasted fur and bloody heads. Jones swears they're all right, they eat; Lipsitz doubts this. He has tried to feed them tidbits as they lean or lie blear-eyed, jerking with wire terrors. The blood is because they rub their heads on the mesh; Jones, seeking a way to stop this, has put stiff plastic collars on several.

Lipsitz gets past them and has his eye rejoiced by the lovely hourglass-shaped ass of Sheila, the brilliant Israeli. Her back is turned. He observes with love the lily waist, the heart-lobed hips that radiate desire. But it's his desire, not hers; he knows that. Sheila, wicked Sheila; she desires only Jones, or perhaps Smith, or even Brown or White – the muscular large hairy ones bubbling with professionalism, with cheery shop talk. Lipsitz would gladly talk shop with her. But his talk is different, uninteresting, is not in the mode. Yet he too believes in 'the organism,' believes in the miraculous wiring diagram of life; he is naively impressed by the complexity, the intricate interrelated delicacies of living matter. Why is he so reluctant to push metal into it, produce lesions with acids or shock? He has this unfashionable yearning to learn by appreciation, to tease out the secrets with only his eyes and mind. He has even the treasonable suspicion that such procedures might be more efficient, more instructive. But what holistic means are there? Probably none, he tells himself firmly. Grow up. Look at all they've discovered with the knife. The cryptic but potent centers of the amygdala, for example. The subtle limbic homeostats – would we ever have known about these? It is a great knowledge. Never mind that its main use seems to be to push more metal into human heads, my way is obsolete.

'Hi, Sheila.'

'Hello, Tilly.'

She does not turn from the hamsters she is efficiently shaving. He takes himself away around the mop stand to the coal-cellar dungeon where he keeps his rats – sorry, his experimental subjects. His experimental subjects are nocturnal rodents, evolved in friendly dark warm burrows. Lipsitz has sensed their misery, suspended in bright metal and plexiglas cubes in the glare. So he has salvaged and repaired for them a stack of big old rabbit cages and put them in this dark alcove nobody wanted, provoking mirth among his colleagues.

He has done worse than that, too. Grinning secretly, he approaches and observes what has been made of his latest offering. On the bottom row are the cages of parturient females, birthing what are expected to be his experimental and control groups. Yesterday those cages were bare wire mesh, when he distributed to them the classified section of the Sunday *Post*. Now he sees with amazement that they are solid cubic volumes of artfully crumpled and plastered paper strips. Fantastic, the labor! Nests; and all identical. Why has no one mentioned that rats as well as birds can build nests? How wrong, how painful it must have been, giving birth on the bare wire. The little mothers have worked all night, skillfully constructing complete environments beneficient to their needs.

A small white muzzle is pointing watchfully at him from a paper crevice; he fumbles in his pocket for a carrot chunk. He is, of course, unbalancing the treatment, his conscience remonstrates. But he has an answer; he has carrots for them all. Get down, conscience. Carefully he unlatches a cage. The white head stretches, bright-eyed, revealing sleek black shoulders. They are the hooded strain.

'Have a carrot,' he says absurdly to the small being. And she does, so quickly that he can barely feel it, can barely feel also the tiny razor slash she has instantaneously, shyly given his thumb before she whisks back inside to her babies. He grins, rubbing the thumb, leaving carrots in the other cages. A mother's monitory bite, administered to an ogre thirty times her length. Vitamins, he thinks, enriched environments, that's the respectable word. Enriched? No, goddam it. What it is is something approaching sane unstressed animals – experimental subjects, I mean. Even if they're so genetically selected for tameness they can't survive in the feral state, they're still rats. He sees he must wrap something on his thumb; he is ridiculously full of blood.

Wrapping, he tries not to notice that his hands are criss-crossed with old bites. He is a steady patron of the antitetanus clinic. But he is sure that they don't really mean ill, that he is somehow accepted by them. His colleagues think so too, somewhat scornfully. In fact, Smith often calls him to help get some agonized creature out and bring it to his electrodes. Judas-Lipsitz does, trying to convey by the warmth of his holding hands that somebody is sorry, is uselessly sorry. Smith explains that his particular strain of rats is bad. A bad rat is one that bites psychologists; there is a constant effort to breed out this trait.

Lipsitz has tried to explain to them about animals with curved incisors, that one must press the hand into the biter's teeth. 'It can't let go,' he tells them. 'You're biting yourself on the rat. It's the same with cats' claws. Push, they'll let go. Wouldn't you if somebody pushed his hand in your mouth?'

For a while he thought Sheila at least had understood him, but it turned out she thought he was making a dirty joke.

He is giving a rotted Safeway apple to an old male named Snedecor whom he has salvaged from Smith when he hears them call.

'Li-i-ipsitz!'

'Tilly! R.D. wants to see you.'

'Yo.'

R.D. is Professor R.D. Welch, his department head and supervisor of his grant. He washes up, makes his way out and around to the front entrance stairs. A myriad guilts are swirling emptily inside him; he has violated some norm, there is something wrong with his funding, above all he is too slow, too slow. No results yet, no columns of data. Frail justifying sentences revolve in his head as he steps into the clean bright upper reaches of the department. Because he is, he feels sure, learning. Doing something, something appropriate to what he thinks of as science. But what? In this glare he (like his rats) cannot recall. Ah, maybe it's only another hassle about parking space, he thinks as he goes bravely in past R.D.'s high-status male secretary. I can give mine up. I'll never be able to afford that transmission job anyway.

But it is not about parking space.

Doctor Welch has a fat file folder on his desk in Exhibit A position. He taps it expressionlessly, staring at Lipsitz.

'You are doing a study of, ah, genetic influences on, ah, tolerance of perceptual novelty.'

'Well, yes…' He decides not to insist on precision. 'You remember, Doctor Welch, I'm going to work in a relation to emotionalism too.'

Emotionalism, in rats, is (a) defecating and (b) biting psychologists. Professor Welch exhales troubledly through his lower teeth, which Lipsitz notes are slightly incurved. Mustn't pull back.

'It's so unspecific,' he sighs. 'It's not integrated with the overall department program.'

'I know,' Lipsitz says humbly. 'But I do think it has relevance to problems of human learning. I mean, why some kids seem to shy away from new things.' He jacks up his technical vocabulary. 'The failure of the exploration motive.'

'Motives don't *fail*, Lipsitz.'

'I mean, conditions for low or high expression. Neophobia. Look, Doctor Welch. If one of the conditions turns out to be genetic we could spot kids who need help.'

'Um'mmm.'

'I could work in some real learning programs in the high tolerants, too,' Lipsitz adds hopefully. 'Contingent rewards, that sort of thing.'

'Rat learning…' Welch lets his voice trail off. 'If this sort of thing is to have any relevance it should involve primates. Your grant scarcely extends to that.'

'Rats can learn quite a lot, sir. How about if I taught them word cues?'

'Doctor Lipsitz, rats do not acquire meaningful responses to words.'

'Yes, sir.' Lipsitz is forcibly preventing himself from bringing up the totally unqualified Scotswoman whose rat knew nine words.

'I do wish you'd go on with your brain studies,' Welch says in his nice voice, giving Lipsitz a glowing scientific look. Am I biting myself on him? Lipsitz wonders. Involuntarily he feels himself empathize with the chairman's unknown problems. As he gazes back, Welch says encouragingly, 'You could use Brown's preparations; they're perfectly viable with the kind of care you give.'

Lipsitz shudders awake; he knows Brown's preparations. A 'preparation' is an animal spread-eagled on a rack for vivisection, dosed with reserpine so it cannot cry or struggle but merely endures for days or weeks of pain. Guiltily he wonders if Brown knows who killed the bitch he had left half dissected and staring over Easter. Pull yourself together, Lipsitz.

'I am so deeply interested in working with the intact animal, the whole organism,' he says earnestly. That is his magic phrase; he has discovered that 'the whole organism' has some fetish quality for them, from some far-off line of work; very fashionable in the abstract.

'Yes.' Balked, Welch wreathes his lips, revealing the teeth again. 'Well. Doctor Lipsitz, I'll be blunt. When you came on board we felt you had a great deal of promise. *I* felt that, I really did. And your teaching seems to be going well, in the main. In the main. But your research; no. You seem to be frittering away your time and funds – and our space – on these irrelevancies. To put it succinctly, our laboratory is not a zoo.'

'Oh, no, sir!' cries Lipsitz, horrified.

'What are you actually doing with those rats? I hear all kinds of idiotic rumors.'

'Well, I'm working up the genetic strains, sir. The coefficient of homozygosity is still very low for meaningful results. I'm cutting it as fine as I can. What you're probably hearing about is that I am giving them a certain amount of enrichment. That's necessary so I can differentiate the lines.' What I'm really doing is multiplying them, he thinks queasily; he hasn't had the heart to deprive any yet.

Welch sighs again; he is worried, Lipsitz thinks, and finding himself smiling sympathetically stops at once.

'How long before you wind this up? A week?'

'A week!' Lipsitz almost bleats, recovers his voice. 'Sir, my test generation is just neonate. They have to be weaned, you know. I'm afraid it's more like a month.'

'And what do you intend to do after this?'

'After this!' Lipsitz is suddenly fecklessly happy. So many, so wondrous are the things he wants to learn. 'Well, to begin with I've seen a number of behaviors nobody seems to have done much with – I mean, watching my animals under more… more naturalistic conditions. They, ah, they emit very interesting responses. I'm struck by the species-specific aspect – I mean, as the Brelands said, we may be using quite unproductive situations. For example, there's an enormous difference between the way Rattus and Cricetus – that's hamsters – behave in the open field, and they're both *rodents*. Even as simple a thing as edge behavior –'

'What behavior?' Welch's tone should warn him, but he plunges on, unhappily aware that he has chosen an insignificant example. But he loves it.

'Edges. I mean the way the animal responds to edges and the shape of the environment. I mean it's basic to living and nobody seems to have explored it. They used to call it thigmotaxis. Here, I sketched a few.' He pulls out a folded sheet, pushes it at Welch. 'Doesn't it raise interesting questions of arboreal descent?'

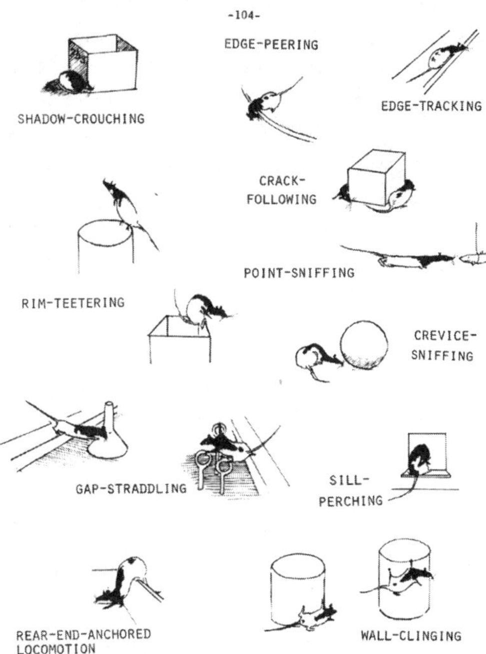

Welch barely glances at the drawings, pushes it away.

'Doctor Lipsitz. You don't appear to grasp the seriousness of this interview. All right. In words of one syllable, you will submit a major project outline that we can justify in terms of this department's program. If you can't come up with one such, regretfully we have no place for you here.'

Lipsitz stares at him, appalled.

'A major project… I see. But… ' And then something comes awake, something is rising in him. Yes. Yes, yes, of course there are bigger things he can tackle. Bigger questions – that means people. He's full of such questions. All it takes is courage.

'Yes, sir,' he says slowly. 'There are some major problems I have thought of investigating.'

'Good,' Welch says neutrally. 'What are they?'

'Well, to start with…' And to his utter horror his mind has emptied itself, emptied itself of everything except the one fatal sentence which he now hears himself helplessly launched toward. 'Take us here. I mean, it's a good principle to attack problems to which one has easy access, which are so to speak under our noses, right? So. For example, we're psychologists. Supposedly dedicated to some kind of understanding, helpful attitude toward the organism, toward life. And yet all of us down here – and in all the labs I've heard about – we seem to be doing such hostile and rather redundant work. Testing animals to destruction, that fellow at Princeton. Proving how damaged organisms are damaged, that kind of engineering thing. Letting students cut or shock or starve animals to replicate experiments that have been done umpteen times. What I'm trying to say is, why don't we look into why psychological research seems to involve so much cruelty – I mean, aggression? We might even…'

He runs down then, and there is a silence in which he becomes increasingly aware of Welch's breathing.

'Doctor Lipsitz,' the older man says hoarsely, '*are you a member of the SPCA*?'

'No, sir, I'm not.'

Welch stares at him unblinkingly and then clears his throat.

'Psychology is not a field for people with emotional problems.' He pushes the file away. 'You have two weeks.'

Lipsitz takes himself out, momentarily preoccupied by his lie. True, he is not a *member* of the SPCA. But that ten dollars he sent in last Christmas, surely they have his name. That had been during the business with the dogs. He flinches now, recalling the black Labrador puppy, its vocal cords cut out, dragging itself around on its raw denervated haunches.

Oh God, why doesn't he just quit?

He wanders out onto the scruffy grass of the campus, going over and over it again. These people. These… people.

And yet behind them loom the great golden mists, the reality of Life itself and the questions he has earned the right to ask. He will never outgrow the thrill of it. The excitement of *actually asking*, after all the careful work of framing terms that can be answered. The act of putting a real question to Life. And watching, reverently, excited out of his skin as Life condescends to tell him yes or no. My animals, my living works of art (of which you are one), do thus and so. Yes, in this small aspect you have understood Me.

The privilege of knowing how, painfully, to frame answerable questions, answers which will lead him to more insights and better questions as far as his mind can manage and his own life lasts. It is what he wants more than anything in the world to do, always has.

And these people stand in his way. Somehow, some way, he must pacify them. He must frame a project they will buy.

He plods back toward the laboratory cellars, nodding absently at students, revolving various quasi-respectable schemes. What he really wants to do is too foggy to explain yet; he wants to explore the capacity of animals to *anticipate*, to gain some knowledge of the wave-front of expectations that they must build up, even in the tiniest heads. He thinks it might even be useful, might illuminate the labors of the human infant learning its world. But that will have to wait. Welch wouldn't tolerate the idea that animals have mental maps. Only old crazy Tolman had been allowed to think that, and he's dead.

He will have to think of something with Welch's favorite drive variables. What are they? And lots of statistics, he thinks, realizing he is grinning at a really pretty girl walking with that cow Polinsky. Yes, why not use students? Something complicated with students – that doesn't cost much. And maybe sex differentials, say, in perception – or is that too far out?

A wailing sound alerts him to the fact that he has arrived at the areaway. A truck is offloading crates of cats, strays from the pound.

'Give a hand, Tilly! Hurry up!'

It's Sheila, holding the door for Jones and Smith. They want to get these out of sight quickly, he knows, before some student sees them. Those innocent in the rites of pain. He hauls a crate from the tailboard.

'There's a female in here giving birth,' he tells Sheila. 'Look.' The female is at the bottom of a mess of twenty emaciated struggling brutes. One of them has a red collar.

'Hurry up, for Christ's sake.' Sheila waves him on.

'But…'

When the crates have disappeared inside he does not follow the others in but leans on the railing, lighting a cigarette. The kittens have been eaten, there's nothing he can do. Funny, he always thought that females would be sympathetic to other females. Shows how much he knows about Life. Or is it that only certain types of people empathize? Or does it have to be trained in, or was it trained out of her? Mysteries, mysteries. Maybe she is really compassionate somewhere inside, toward something. He hopes so, resolutely putting away a fantasy of injecting Sheila with reserpine and applying experimental stimuli.

He becomes aware that the door has been locked from the inside; they have all left through the front. It's getting late. He moves away too, remembering that this is the long holiday weekend. Armistice Day. Would it were – he scoffs at himself for the bathos. But he frowns, too; long weekends usually mean nobody near the lab. Nothing gets fed or watered. Well, three days – not as bad as Christmas week.

Last Christmas week he had roused up from much-needed sleep beside a sky-high mound of term papers and hitchhiked into town to check the labs. It had been so bad, so needless. The poor brutes dying in their thirst and hunger, eating metal, each other. Great way to celebrate Christmas.

But he will have to stop that kind of thing, he knows. Stop it. Preferably starting now. He throws down the cigarette stub, quickens his stride to purposefulness. He will collect his briefcase of exam papers from the library where he keeps it to avoid the lab smell and get on home and get at it. The bus is bound to be jammed.

Home is an efficiency in a suburban high-rise. He roots in his moldy fridge, carries a sandwich and ale to the dinette that is his desk. He has eighty-one exams to grade; junior department members get the monster classes. It's a standard multiple-choice thing, and he has a help – a theatrically guarded manila template he can lay over the sheets with slots giving the correct response. By just running down them he sums an arithmetical grade. Good. Munching, he lays out the first mimeoed wad.

But as he starts to lay it on the top page he sees – oh, no! – somebody has scrawled instead of answering Number 6. It's that fat girl, that bright bum Polinsky. And she hasn't marked answers by 7 or 8 either. Damn her fat female glands; he squints at the infantile uncials: 'I won't mark this because its smucky! Read it, Dr. Lipshitz.' She even has his name wrong.

Cursing himself, he scrutinizes the question. 'Fixed versus variable reinforcement is called a– ' Oh yes, he remembers that one. Bad grammar on top of bad psychology. Why can't they dump these damn obsolete things? Because the office wants grade intercomparability for their records, that's why. Is Polinsky criticizing the language or the thought? Who knows. He leafs through the others, sees more scribbles. Oh, shit, they know I read them. They all know I don't mark them like I should. Sucker.

Grimly masticating the dry sandwich, he starts to read. At this rate he is working, he has figured out, for seventy-five cents an hour.

By midnight he isn't half through, but he knows

he ought to break off and start serious thought about Welch's ultimatum. Next week all his classes start Statistical Methods; he won't have time to blow his nose, let alone think creatively.

He gets up for another ale, thinking, Statistical Methods, brrr. He respects them, he guesses. But he is incurably sloppy-minded, congenitally averse to ignoring any data that don't fit the curve. Factor analysis, multivariate techniques – all beautiful; why is he troubled by this primitive visceral suspicion that somehow it ends up proving what the experimenter wanted to show? No, not that, really. Something about qualities as opposed to quantities, maybe? That some statistically insignificant results *are* significant, and some significant ones... aren't? Or just basically that we don't know enough yet to use such ultraprecise weapons. That we should watch more, maybe. Watch and learn more and figure less. All right, call me St. Lipsitz.

Heating up a frozen egg roll, he jeers at himself for superstition. Face facts, Lipsitz. Deep down you don't really believe dice throws are independent. Psychology is not a field for people with personality problems.

Ignoring the TV yattering through the wall from next door, he sits down by the window to think. Do it, brain. Come up with the big one. Take some good testable hypothesis from somebody in the department, preferably something that involves electronic counting of food pellets, bar presses, latencies, defecations. And crank it all into printed score sheets with a good Fortran program. But what the hell are they all working on? Reinforcement schedules, cerebral deficits, split brain, God knows only that it seems to produce a lot of dead animals. 'The subjects were sacrificed.' They insist on saying that. He had been given a lecture when he called it 'killing.' Sacrificed, like to a god. Lord of the Flies, maybe.

He stares out at the midnight streets, thinking of his small black-and-white friends, his cozy community in the alcove. Nursing their offspring, sniffing the monkeys, munching apples, dreaming ratly dreams. He likes rats, which surprises him. Even the feral form, Rattus rattus itself; he would like to work with wild ones. Rats are vicious, they say. But people know only starving rats. Anything starving is 'vicious.' Beloved beagle eats owner on fourth day.

And his rats are, he blushingly muses, affectionate. They nestle in his hands, teeteringly ride his shoulder, display humor. If only they had fluffy tails, he thinks. The tail is the problem. People think squirrels are cute. They're only overdressed rats. Maybe I could do things with the perceptual elements of 'cuteness,' carry on old Tinbergen's work?

Stop it.

He pulls himself up; this isn't getting anywhere. A terrible panorama unrolls before his inner eye. On the one hand the clean bright professional work he should be doing, he with those thousands of government dollars invested in his doctorate, his grant – and on the other, what he is really doing. His cluttered alcove full of irregular rodents, his tiny, doomed effort to ... what? To live amicably and observantly with another species? To understand trivial behaviors? Crazy. Spending all his own money, saving everybody's cripples – God, half his cages aren't even experimentally justifiable!

His folly. Suddenly it sickens him. He stands up, thinking, It's a stage you go through. I'm a delayed adolescent. Wake up, grow up. They're only animals, get with it.

Resolve starts to form in him. Opening another ale can, he lets it grow. This whole thing is no good, he knows that. So what if he does prove that animals learn better if they're treated differently – what earthly use is that? Don't we all know it anyway? Insane. Time I braced up. All right. Ale in hand, he lets the resolve bloom.

He will go down there and clean out the whole mess, right now.

Kill all his rats, wipe the whole thing off. Clear the decks. That done, he'll be able to think; he won't be locked into the past.

The department will be delighted, Doctor Welch will be delighted. Nobody believed his thing was anything but a waste of time. All right, Lipsitz. Do it. Now, tonight.

Yes.

But first he will have something analgesic, strengthening. Not ale, not a toke. That bottle of

– what is it, absinthe? – that crazy girl gave him last year. Yes, here it is back of the roach-killer he never used either. God knows what it's supposed to do, it's wormwood, something weird.

'Fix me,' he tells it, sucking down a long licorice-flavored draft. And goes out, bottle in pocket.

It has, he thinks, helped. He is striding across the campus now; all the long bus ride his resolve hasn't wavered. A quiet rain is falling. It must be two in the morning, but he's used to the spooky empty squares. He has often sneaked down here at odd hours to water and feed the brutes. The rain is moving strange sheens of shadow on the old tenement block, hissing echoes of the lives that swirled here once. At the cellar entrance he stops for another drink, finds the bottle clabbered with carrot chunks. Wormwood and Vitamin C, very good.

He dodges down and unlocks, bracing for the stench. The waste cans are full – cats that didn't make it, no doubt. Inside is a warm rustling reek.

When he finds the light, a monkey lets out one eerie whoop and all sounds stop. Sunrise at midnight; most of these experimental subjects are nocturnal.

He goes in past the crowded racks, his eye automatically checking levels in the hundreds of water bottles. Okay, okay, all okay… What's this? He stops by Sheila's hamster tier. A bottle is full to the top. But there's a corpse by the wire, and the live ones look bedraggled. Why? He jerks up the bottle. Nothing comes out of the tube. It's blocked. Nobody has checked it for who knows how long. Perishing of thirst in there, with the bottle full.

He unblocks it, fishes out the dead, watches the little beasts crowd around. How does Sheila report this? Part of an experimental group was, uh, curtailed. On impulse he inserts some carrots too, inserts more absinthe into himself. He knows he is putting off what he has come here to do.

All right, get at it.

He stomps past a cage of baby rabbits with their eyes epoxyed shut, somebody's undergraduate demonstration of perceptual learning, and turns on the light over the sinks. All dirty with hanks of skin and dog offal. Why the hell can't they clean up after themselves? We are scientists. Too lofty. He whooshes with the power hose, which leaks. Nobody cares enough even to bring a washer. He will bring one. No, he won't! He's going to be doing something different from here on in.

But first of all he has to get rid of all this. Sacrifice his subjects. His ex-subjects. Where's my ether?

He finds it back of the mops, has another snort of the cloudy liquor to fortify himself while he sets up his killing jars. He has evolved what he thinks is the decentest way: an ether pad under a grill to keep their feet from being burned by the stuff.

The eight jars are in a row on the sink. He lifts down a cage of elderly females, the grandmothers of his present group. They cluster at the front, trustfully expectant. Oh God; he postpones murder long enough to give them some carrot, deals out more to every cage in the rack so they'll have time to eat. Tumult of rustling, hoping, munching.

All right. He goes back to the sink and pours in the ether, keeping the lids tight. Then he reaches in the holding cage and scoops up a soft female in each hand. Quick: He pops them both in one jar, rescrews the lid. He has this fatuous belief that the companionship helps a little. They convulse frantically, are going limp before he has the next pair in theirs. Next. Next. Next... It takes five minutes to be sure of death.

This will be, he realizes, a long night.

He lifts down another cage, lifts up his bottle, leaning with his back to the jars to look at his rack, his little city of rats. My troops. My pathetic troops. An absinthe trip flashes through his head of himself leading his beasts against his colleagues, against the laughing pain-givers. Jones having his brain reamed by a Dachshund pup. A kitten in a surgical smock shaving Sheila, wow. Stop it!

His eye has been wandering over the bottom cages. The mothers have taken the goodies in to their young; interesting to see what goes on in there, maybe if he used infra-red – stop that, too. A lab is not a zoo. Down in one dark back cage he can see the carrot is still there. Where's Snedecor, the old brain-damaged male? Why hasn't he come for it? Is the light bothering him?

Lipsitz turns off the top lights, goes around

to the side to check. Stooping, he peers into the gloom. Something funny down there – good grief, the damn cage is busted, it's rotted through the bottom. Where's old Sneddles?

The ancient cage rack has wheels. Lipsitz drags one end forward, revealing Stygian darkness behind. In prehistoric times there was a coal chute there. And there's something back here now, on the heap of bags by the old intake.

Lipsitz frowns, squints; the lab lights behind him seem to be growing dim and gaseous. The thing – the thing has black and white patches. Is it moving?

He retreats to the drainboard, finds his hand on the bottle. Yes. Another short one. What's wrong with the lights? The fluorescents have developed filmy ectoplasm, must be chow dust. This place is a powder keg. The monkeys are still as death too. That's unusual. In fact everything is dead quiet except for an odd kind of faint clicking, which he realizes is coming from the dark behind the rack. An animal. Some animal has got out and been living back there, that's all it is.

All right, Lipsitz: Go see.

But he delays, aware that the absinthe has replaced his limbs with vaguer, dreamlike extensions. The old females on the drainboard watch him alertly. The dead ones in the jar watch nothing. All his little city of rats has stopped moving, is watching him. Their priest of pain. This is a temple of pain, he thinks. A small shabby dirty one. Maybe its dirt and squalor are better so, more honest. A charnel house shouldn't look pretty, like a clean kitchen. All over the country, the world, the spotless knives are slicing, the trained minds devising casual torments in labs so bright and fair you could eat off their floors. Auschwitz, Belsen were neat. With flowers. Only the reek of pain going up to the sky, the empty sky. But people don't think animals' pain matters. They didn't think my people's pain mattered either, in the death camps a generation back. It's all the same, endless agonies going up unheard from helpless things. And all for what?

Maybe somewhere there is a reservoir of pain, he muses. Waiting to be filled. When it is full, will something rise from it? Something created and summoned by torment? Inhuman, an alien superthing... He knows he is indulging drunkenness. The clicking has grown louder.

Go and look at the animal, Lipsitz.

He goes, advances on the dark alcove, peering down, hearing the click-click-click. Suddenly he recognizes it: the tooth-click a rat makes in certain states of mind. Not threatening at all, it must be old Sneddles in there. Heartened, he pulls a dim light bulb forward on its string – and sees the thing plain, while the lab goes unreal around him.

What's lying back there among the Purina bags is an incredible whorl – a tangle of rat legs, rat heads, rat bodies, rat tails intertwined in a great wheellike formation, joined somehow abnormally rat to rat – a huge rat pie, heaving, pulsing, eyes reflecting stress and pain. Quite horrible, really; the shock of it is making him fight for breath. And it is not all laboratory animals; he can see the agouti coats of feral rats mixed in among it. Have wild rats come in here to help form this gruesome thing?

And at that moment, hanging to the light bulb, he knows what he is seeing. He has read in the old lore, the ancient grotesque legends of rat and man.

He is looking at a Rat King.

Medieval records were full of them, he recalls dimly. Was it Württemberg? *'They are monstrously Joynt, yet Living... It can by no way be Separated, and screamed much in the Fyre.'* Apparitions that occurred at times of great attack on the rats. Some believed that the rat armies had each their king of this sort, who directed them. And they were sometimes connected to or confused with King Rats of still another kind: gigantic animals with eyes of fire and gold chains on their necks. Lipsitz stares, swaying on the light cord. The tangled mass of the Rat King remains there clicking faintly, pulsing, ambiguously agonized among the sacks. His other hand seems to be holding the bottle; good. He takes a deep pull, his eyes rolling to fix the ghastliness, wondering what on earth he will do. 'I can't,' he mumbles aloud, meaning the whole thing, the whole bloody thing. *'I can't...'*

He can do his own little business, kill his animals, wind up his foolishness, get out. But he cannot – cannot – be expected to cope with this, to abolish this revenant from time, this perhaps supernatural horror. For which he feels obscurely, hideously, to blame. It's my fault, I…

He realizes he is weeping thinly, his eyes are running. Whether it's for the animals or himself he doesn't know, he knows only that he can't stand it, can't take any of it any more. And now *this*.

'No!' Meaning, really, the whole human world. Dizzily he blinks around at the jumbled darkness, trying to regain his wits, feeling himself a random mote of protesting life in an insignificant foolkiller. Slowly his eyes come back to the monstrous, pitiable rat pie. It seems to be weakening; the click has lost direction. His gaze drifts upward, into the dark shadows.

– And he is quite unsurprised, really, to meet eyes looking back. Two large round animal eyes deep in the darkness, at about the level of his waist, the tapetums reflecting pale vermilion fire.

He stares; the eyes shift right, left, calmly in silence, and then the head advances. He sees the long wise muzzle, the vibrissae, the tuned shells of the ears. Is there a gold collar? He can't tell; but he can make out the creature's forelimbs now, lightly palping the bodies or body of the Rat King. And the tangled thing is fading, shrinking away. It was perhaps its conjoined forces which strove and suffered to give birth to this other – the King himself.

'Hello,' Lipsitz whispers idiotically, feeling no horror any more but emotion of a quite other kind. The big warm presence before him surveys him. Will he be found innocent? He licks his lips. They have come at last, he thinks. They have risen; they are going to wipe all this out. Me, too? But he does not care; a joy he can't possibly control rises in him as he sees gold glinting on the broad chest fur. He licks his dry lips again, swallows.

'Welcome. Your Majesty.'

The Beast-King makes no response; the eyes leave him and go gravely toward the aisles beyond. Involuntarily Lipsitz backs aside. The King's vibrissae are fanning steadily, bringing the olfactory news, the quiet tooth-click starts. When the apparition comes forward a pace Lipsitz is deeply touched to see the typical half-hop, the ratly carriage. The King's coat is lustrous gray-brown, feral pelage. Of course. It is a natural male, too; he smiles timidly, seeing that the giant body has the familiar long hump, the heavy rear-axle loading. Is old Snedecor translated into some particle of this wonder? The cellar is unbreathing, hushed except for the meditative click-click from the King.

'You, you are going to…' Lipsitz tries but is struck dumb by the sense of something happening all around him. Invisible, inaudible – but tangible as day. An emergence, yes! In the rooms beyond they are emerging, coming out from the score upon score of cages, boxes, pens, racks, shackles and wires – all of them emerging, coming to the King. All of them, blinded rabbits, mutilated hamsters, damaged cats and rats and brain-holed rhesus quietly knuckling along, even the paralyzed dogs moving somehow, coming toward their King.

And at this moment Lipsitz realizes the King is turning too, the big brown body is wheeling, quite normally away from him, going away toward the deeper darkness in the end of the coal bay. They are leaving him!

'Wait!' He stumbles forward over the dead rat pie; he cannot bear to lose this. 'Please…'

Daring all, he reaches out and touches the flank of the magical beast, expecting he knows not what. The flank is warm, is solid! The King glances briefly back at him, still moving away. Boldly Lipsitz strides closer, comes alongside, his hand now resting firmly on the withers as they go.

But they are headed straight at what he knows is only wall, though he can see nothing. The cellar ends there. No matter – he will not let go of the magic, no, and he steps out beside the moving King, thinking, I am an animal too! – And finds at the last instant that his averted, flinching head is moving through dark nothing, through a blacker emptiness where the King is leading – they are going, going out.

Perhaps an old sewer, he thinks, lurching along beside the big benign presence, remembering tales of forgotten tunnels under this old city, into which the new subway has bored. Yes, that's what it must be. He is finding he can see again in a pale ghostly way, can now walk upright. His left hand is tight on the shoulders of the calmly pacing beast, feeling the living muscles play beneath the fur, bringing him joy and healing. Where are the others?

He dares a quick look back and sees them. They

are coming. The dim way behind is filled with quiet beasts, moving together rank on rank as far as he can sense, animals large and small. He can hear their peaceful rustling now. And they are not only the beasts of his miserable lab, he realizes, but a torrent of others – he has glimpsed goats, turtles, a cow, raccoons, skunks, an opossum and what appears as a small monkey riding on a limping spaniel. Even birds are there, hopping and fluttering above!

My God, it is everything, he thinks. It is Hamlin in reverse; all the abused ones, the gentle ones, are leaving the world. He risks another glance back and thinks he can see a human child too and maybe an old person among the throng, all measuredly, silently moving together in the dimness. An endless host going, going out at last, going away. And he is feeling their emanation, the gentleness of it, the unspeaking warmth. He is happier than he has been ever in his life.

'You're taking us away,' he says to the King-Beast beside him. 'The ones who can't cut it. We're all leaving for good, isn't that it?'

There is no verbal answer; only a big-stemmed ear swivels to him briefly as the King goes gravely on. Lipsitz needs no speech, no explanation. He simply walks alongside letting the joy rise in him. Why had it always been forbidden to be gentle? he wonders. Did they really see it as a threat, to have hated us so? But that is all over now, all over and gone, he is sure, although he has no slightest idea where this may be leading, this procession into chthonian infinity. For this moment it is enough to feel the silent communion, the reassurance rising through him from his hand on the flank of the great spirit-beast. The flank is totally solid; he can feel all the workings of life; it is the body of a real animal. But it is also friendship beyond imagining; he has never known anything as wonderful as this communion, not sex or sunsets or even the magic hour on his first bike. It is as if everything is all right now, will be all right forever – griefs he did not even know he carried are falling from him, leaving him light as smoke.

Crippled, he had been; crippled from the years of bearing it, not just the lab, the whole thing. Everything. He can hardly believe the relief. A vagrant thought brushes him: Who will remain? If there is anything to care for, to be comforted, who will care? He floats it away, concentrating on the comfort that emanates from the strange life at his side, the myth-beast ambling in the most ordinary way through this dark conduit, which is now winding down, or perhaps up and down, he cannot tell.

The paving under his feet looks quite commonplace, damp and cracked. Beside him the great rat's muscles bunch and stretch as each hind leg comes under; he glances back and smiles to see the King's long ring-scaled tail curve right, curve left, carried in the relaxed-alert mode. No need for fluffy fur now. He is, he realizes, going into mysteries. Inhuman mysteries, perhaps. He doesn't care. He is among his kind. Where they are going he will go. Even to inhumanity, even alone.

But he is not, he realizes as his eyes adapt more and more, alone after all! A human figure is behind him on the far side of the King, quietly threading its way forward, overtaking him. A girl – is it a girl? Yes. He can scarcely make her out, but as she comes closer still he sees with growing alarm that it is a familiar body – it could be, oh God, it is! Sheila.

Not *Sheila*, here! No, no.

But light-footed, she has reached him, is walking even with him, stretching out her hand, too, to touch the moving King.

And then to his immense, unspeakable relief he sees that she is of course not Sheila – how could it be? Not Sheila at all, only a girl of the same height, with the same dove-breasted close-coupled curves that speak to his desire, the same heavy dark mane. Her head turns toward him across the broad back of the King, and he sees that, although her features are like Sheila's, the face is wholly different, open, informed with innocence. An Eve in this second morning of the world. Sheila's younger sister perhaps, he wonders dazedly, seeing that she is looking at him now, that her lips form a gentle smile.

'Hello,' he cannot help whispering, fearful to break the spell, to inject harsh human sound into his progress. But the spell does not break; indeed, the girl's face comes clearer. She puts up a hand to push him back, the other firmly on the flank of the King.

'Hello.' Her voice is very soft but in no way fragile. She is looking at him with the eyes of Sheila, but eyes so differently warmed and luminous that he wants only to gaze delighted as they pass to whatever destination; he is so overwhelmed to meet a vulnerable human soul in those lambent brown eyes. A soul? he thinks, feeling his unbodied feet step casually, firmly on the way to eternity, perhaps. What an unfashionable word. He is not religious, he does not believe there are any gods or souls, except as a shorthand term denoting – what? – compassion or responsibility, all that. And so much argument about it all, too; his mind is momentarily invaded by a spectral horde of old debating scholars, to whom he had paid less than no attention in his classroom days. But he is oddly prepared to hear the girl recite conversationally, 'There is no error more powerful in leading feeble minds astray from the straight path of virtue than the supposition that the soul of brutes is of the same nature as our own,'

'Descartes,' he guesses.

She nods, smiling across the big brown shape between them. The King's great leaflike ears have flickered to their interchange, returned to forward hold.

'He started it all, didn't he?' Lipsitz says, or perhaps only thinks. 'That they're robots, you can do anything to them. Their pain doesn't count. But we're animals too,' he adds somberly, unwilling to let even a long-dead philosopher separate him from the flow of this joyous River. Or was it that? A faint disquiet flicks him, is abolished.

She nods again; the sweet earnest woman-face of her almost kills him with love. But as he stares the disquiet flutters again; is there beneath her smile a transparency, a failure of substance – even a sadness, as though she was moving to some inexorable loss. No; it is all right. It is.

'Where are we going, do you know?' he asks, against some better judgment. The King-Beast flicks an ear; but Lipsitz must know, now.

She smiles, unmistakably mischievous, considering him.

'To where all the lost things go,' she says. 'It's very beautiful. Only...' She falls silent.

'Only what?' He is uneasy again, seeing she has turned away, is walking with her small chin resolute. Dread grows in him, cannot be dislodged. The moments of simple joy are past now; he fears that he still has some burden. It is perhaps a choice? Whatever it is, it's looming around him or in him as they go – an impending significance he wishes desperately to avoid. It is not a thinning out nor an awakening; he clutches hard at the strong shoulders of the King, the magical leader, feels his reassuring warmth. All things are in the lotus.... But loss impends.

'Only what?' he asks again, knowing he must and must not. Yes; he is still there, is moving with them to the final refuge. The bond holds. 'The place where lost things go is very beautiful, only what?'

'Do you really want to know?' she asks him with the light of the world in her face.

It is a choice, he realizes, trembling now. It is not for free, it's not that simple. But can't I just stop this, just go on? Yes, he can – he knows it. Maybe. But he hears his human voice persist.

'Only *what*?'

'Only it isn't real,' she says. And his heart breaks.

And suddenly it is all breaking too – a fearful thin wave of emptiness slides through him, sends him stumbling, his handhold lost. 'No! Wait!' He reaches desperately; he can feel them still near him, feel their passage all around. 'Wait...' He understands now, understands with searing grief that it really is the souls of things, and perhaps himself, that are passing, going away forever. They have stood it as long as they can and now they are leaving. The pain has culminated in this, that they leave us – leave me, leave me behind in a clockwork Cartesian world in which nothing will mean anything forever.

'Oh, wait,' he cries in dark nowhere, unable to bear the loss, the still-living comfort, passing away. *Only it isn't real,* what does that mean? Is it the choice, that reality is that I must stay behind and try, and try?

He doesn't know, but can only cry, 'No, please take me! Let me come too!' staggering after them through unreality, feeling them still there, still possible, ahead, around. It is wrong; he is terrified somewhere that he is failing, doing wrong. But his human heart can only yearn for the sweetness, for the great benevolent King-Beast so surely leading, to feel again their joy. 'Please, I want to go with you–'

– And yes! For a last instant he has it; he touches again the warmth and life, sees the beautiful lost face that is and isn't Sheila – they are there! And he tries with all his force crazily to send himself after them, to burst from his skin, his life if need be – only to share again that gentleness. '*Take* me!'

But it is no good – he can't; they have vanished and he has fallen kneeling on dank concrete, nursing his head in empty shaking hands. It was in vain, and it was wrong. Or was it? his fading thought wonders as he feels himself black out. Did something of myself go too, fly to its selfish joy? He does not know.

... And will never know, as he returns to sodden consciousness, makes out that he is sprawled like a fool in the dirt behind his rat cages with the acid taste of wormwood sickly in his mouth and an odd dryness and lightness in his heart.

What the hell had he been playing at? That absinthe is a bummer, he thinks, picking himself up and slapping his clothes disgustedly. This filthy place, what a fool he'd been to think he could work here. And these filthy rats. There's something revolting back here on the floor, too. Leave it for posterity; he drags the rack back in place.

All right, get this over. Humming to himself, he turns the power hose on the messy floor, gives the stupid rats in their cages a blast too for good measure. There are his jars – but whatever had possessed him, trying to kill them individually like that? Hours it would take. He knows a simpler way if he can find a spare garbage can.

Good, here it is. He brings it over and starts pulling out cage after cage, dumping them all in together, Nests, babies, carrots, crap and all. Shrieks, struggling. Tough tit, friends. The ether can is almost full; he pours the whole thing over the crying mess and jams on the lid, humming louder. The can walls reverberate with teeth. Not quite enough gas, no matter.

He sits down on it and notices that a baby rat has run away hiding behind his shoe. Mechanical mouse, a stupid automaton. He stamps on its back and kicks it neatly under Sheila's hamster rack, wondering why Descartes has popped into his thoughts. There is no error more powerful – Shit with old D., let's think about Sheila. There is no error more powerful than the belief that some cunt can't be had. Somehow he feels sure that he will find that particular pussy-patch wide open to him any day now. As soon as his project gets under way.

Because he has an idea. (That absinthe wasn't all bad.) Oh yes. An idea that'll pin old Welch's ears back. In fact it may be too much for old Welch, too, quotes, commercial. Well, fuck old Welch, this is one project somebody will buy, that's for sure. Does the Mafia have labs? Ho ho, far out.

And fuck students too, he thinks genially, wrestling the can to the entrance, ignoring sounds from within. No more Polinskys, no more shit, teaching is for suckers. My new project will take care of that. Will there be a problem getting subjects? No – look at all the old walking carcasses they sell for dogfood. And there's a slaughterhouse right by the freeway, no problem at all. But he will need a larger lab.

He locks up, and briskly humming the rock version of 'Anitra's Dance,' he goes out into the warm rainy dawnlight, reviewing in his head the new findings on the mid-brain determinants of motor intensity.

It should be no trick at all to seat some electrodes that will make an animal increase the intensity of whatever it's doing. Like say, *running*. Speed it right up to max, run like it never ran before regardless of broken legs or what. What a natural! Surprising someone else hasn't started already.

And just as a cute hypothesis, he's pretty sure he could seal the implants damn near invisibly; he has a smooth hand with flesh. Purely hypothetical, of course. But suppose you used synthetics with, say, acid-release. That would be hard to pick up on X rays. H'mmm.

Of course, he doesn't know much about horses, but he learns fast. Grinning, he breaks into a jog to catch the lucky bus that has appeared down the deserted street. He has just recalled a friend who has a farm not fifty miles away. Wouldn't it be neat to run the pilot project using surplus Shetland ponies?

THE BEAK DOCTOR

Eric Basso

Eric Basso (1947–) is an American poet, novelist, playwright, and critic, born in Baltimore, Maryland. 'The Beak Doctor' novella reprinted herein has had a cult following among avant-garde Gothic writers since it was first published by the *Chicago Review* in 1977. Since then he has published a novel, several plays, many poetry collections, and a book of nonfiction. In part, 'The Beak Doctor' reads like a modern, more Joycean version of the first selection in this anthology, Alfred Kubin's 'The Other Side,' in that the nameless city is plagued by a strange sleeping sickness. Despite being criminally overlooked, Basso is an important part of the landscape of weird fiction.

Now I will try to keep awake. The fog. They must have come for me before morning. Empty streets. Across a dimly lit room. She lay in the shadows. The steps. One at a time. Not that I'm old. It was the mask. Plaster chipped off the walls. She lay asleep on a couch. A network of cracks and branching veins like the surface of an antique painting. Chiaroscuro. Figures half formed. And she was naked. Little water-blots the color of rust. An odor of disinfectant emanated from the bannisters. Mothballs. The smell on my hands as I return there. From the bottom of the rickety stairs I could make out the febrile glow of a bulb screwed into the pitted ceiling on the landing. Step-shadows dwindling over the tips of my shoes as I neared the top.

No corners. I had to turn my head from side to side to see what lay around me. The eyeholes were a shade too narrow. My own fault. In cutting them I hadn't followed the pattern closely. They made a dark vignette. The goggles were fogging up. Darkness around a darkness where I came into the room. I was suffocating.

The women backed away. They seemed a bit startled at first, muttering to themselves. Something too low for me to hear. I told them they would have to speak up. A lamp burned by the mantelpiece clock. An oval scatter rug in the center of the floor, just out of reach of a faded pool of light. I remember now. In the lull you could hear a ticking. Maybe I only imagined that the women had spoken. It might have been a rumbling on the floor above coupled with the random movements of their lips. The father took me by the hand. He was old. The skin of his palms was dry, his fingers soft and lifeless. He didn't want to talk. A door closed behind me. The two of us were left alone with the body.

I probably had to help him get across the room, he was so weak. His eyes were bad. He stopped a few times on the way to take his bearings and scratched at his eyebrows as though he too were trying to remember that even in this subdued lighting her flank was visible, pale against the black hulk of the couch. Her face was turned away or hidden under a mass of long dark hair, or in a shadow. No one had thought to cover her with a blanket. We listened to her breathing between ticks of the little porcelain clock; a miniature pendulum swung in its oblong window, a low click sounded the whir of a grinding mechanism from within – the hour chimed out slowly at the bottom of the mirror.

Her diaphragm rose and fell. Her ribs contoured faintly, intermittently stretching and relaxing the expanse of whitish skin above the broad swell of her belly. I would have made her anywhere between thirty and forty-five in age, but the light was weak. And her father babbled incoherently before he managed to get something out about having found her on his way home from a walk.

– She was lying on her side… curled up like a ball by the curb.

He scratched again at his bushy eyebrows. The women had carried her up the stairs and laid her on the sofa. Fast in a deep sleep, she showed no signs of waking.

The old man held her legs for me and looked down through the red-white traces my penlight etched in the dark. The slight movements of my hand left an afterimage of knotted lines on his retina. He seemed to be still trying to remember, leaning forward, thrown a bit off kilter with his daughter's feet a dead weight crossed behind his head, fanning his white hair out as the brass links of his watch chain glittered in a double loop that swayed above the peaks of her breasts. His spectacles slid down to the tip of his nose.

It was just after five. Scratches. Contusions. A few deep welts cut purple stripes along the back of her thighs like claw-marks left by a wild animal. And between. I didn't need to use a speculum. The genitals already formed a swollen mass in the darkness. Blackened labia puffed out around the area of inflammation. The mucous lining was raw to the point of turning blue. A trail of dried blood flaked off the skin at the touch of my finger. I felt a crust under the back of my hand as I probed for internal lesions. A brown discharge had had enough time to spread to the cushion and congeal there.

How long had she been lying here like this?

– I… no, I was just…

The old man looked as though he were about to pass out. He let go of one of the legs and put his hand on the arm of the couch. Something hard struck the crown of my mask. I dropped to my knees. The penlight flew out of my hand and I heard it roll under the sofa. Another weight came down heavily on the middle of my back. I saw a gray moon plummet toward the couch, into eclipse. My gasps rushed hot air up through the inside of the mask. I heard the wind roar. It knocked the breath out of me.

I lay there on the floor, trying to readjust the eyeholes, my goggles clouded with steam. He stood over me, the father, crossed by the broad diagonal silhouette of a bare leg. The ceiling, dark gray melting into black with swarms of gilt-edged cobalt blue.

Another minute passed. The gray would have been white in the daylight. The curtains were drawn, the blinds closed. A few branching cracks hung jagged shapes like pieces of stalactites. The old man had me by the hands. He wanted to pull me up.

– What about something to drink? You must be stifling. Or perhaps a face cloth soaked in cold water?

Wait. Lift her leg back onto the couch. I can't manage it alone.

– It's gotten foggier than ever. You can't even see across the street. I'll just switch off the lamp.

No. I have to give her an injection. Help me turn her over. Grab her under the knees. That's it. Gently now.

Penicillin, *10cc*. No reaction to the prick of the needle. She simply lay there on her stomach, her open mouth drooling into the cushion. It was too soon for dehydration to have set in. The father fished a pack of cigarettes out of his vest pocket. He tapped it and held it out to me.

– Are you sure? I don't like to smoke alone.

I had gone to the window and was about to pull the blinds when the lamp on the mantelpiece went out, pitching the two of us into total darkness with nothing but the sound of her breathing and the tick of the clock. I should have turned her on her back again. But it didn't matter. She seemed comfortable enough. I made a chink in the blinds with two fingers and peered out into the fog. The old man was right.

– This is what I know. Don't ask me why I waited so long. If my wife and sister had had their way she'd still be lying out there stark naked and, well, let's just say I thought it best to wait until the fog lifted... and when it didn't lift, you know the rest... she was lying by the curb under a lamppost, otherwise I wouldn't have seen her at all, my eyes aren't what they used to be, if she had been on the sidewalk I might have tripped right over her and broken my neck; to tell the truth, I wasn't even sure I was on the right block... the fog... couldn't see my hand in front of my face... no, if I were you I'd wait a bit before going back out there... something to drink perhaps?... you see I've put out the light so there's nothing to worry about... I can grow accustomed to almost anything, but this fog! when I think of how things used to be and what they are now – rumors, the streets deserted – I'm really afraid to go out, even in the daytime... I used to take the bus to go shopping down by the Olde Market, now I have to walk the streets alone like all the others... but why don't you sit down? I'll have Duma – that's my wife – bring us out something to eat... what do you say to some pretzels and a nice bottle of beer? it's the last we have left, the pretzels I mean, but this is something of an occasion... haven't had anyone in the house for years since my brother-in-law passed on... he was forty-one... did you notice her face?... maybe we ought to close her mouth, unless you think that would interfere with her breathing... didn't know what the hell to do at first. I thought I hadn't seen right... had to get up almost on top of her before I realized it was a woman and not a pile of garbage someone had heaped under the lamppost... she's not from around here – at least I think she's not – I've never seen her, not that I would remember... she was lying there all crumpled up like a ball... I thought she was dead... now what about that beer? I won't turn on the lamp.

Through a small crack in the blinds – nothing. Flat gray up from where the street lights were diffused without contour. Lost haloes in a soundless fog. Not even a muted echo. Something had moved inside. Everything became absorbed in that one brief movement. It might have been on the floor below or in an outside corridor, or on one of the landings. A footfall. The latch-click of a closing door. Who knew what it was or where it came from? It brought me back to her breathing.

The old man had finished his monologue. He may have taken a step forward. It *may* have been him. I couldn't tell. It was too dark.

– What now?

Pardon?

– I mean what are we supposed to do with her?

The police will take care of everything.

– Are you hot?

Why?

– Nothing, I just wondered.

Let the women put some clothes on her. And if you can find a driver's license or any sort of identity card, poke a hole through it and tie it around her neck with a piece of string. Don't use a rubber band or anything elastic that might affect her breathing.

– That's no good... you see her just as I found her... without a stitch.

Maybe there's something in her room. In one of the drawers. You could ask your wife.

– ?

Or, here. Take this and fill it out later. I've already signed it. If you want, you can turn the light back on. I have to be going.

– What is it, a prescription?

No, it's for the police. Give it to them when they come for the girl. And don't forget to fill it out. I'll go on ahead to make the necessary arrangements. Don't try to move her. Get her dressed as best you can. They'll take her to the roundhouse.

– The roundhouse? You mean the old railroad museum? That hasn't been open for years.

Somehow he managed to get to the door without knocking against the furniture. An amber light filtered in from the corridor, framing his bent silhouette with a dull nimbus. He took off his glasses.

– I'd like to get rid of these... can't see a thing with them any more... try them on... see how they fit.

I have to go. When you find my penlight, you can send it to me care of the roundhouse. The address is at the top of the certificate. Or you can always get me at the office. You have my number.

The old man scratched his eyebrows and, shrugging his shoulders, pulled a handkerchief out of his pocket. He breathed on the lenses, smiling.

– I'd save myself a lot of breath just by sticking them out the window.

He called down after me.

– Be careful. One of the steps has a loose mat.

I came down slowly, out of the amber light, squeak by squeak on the stairs. That odor. I could smell it later on my hands. I heard the tenants shutting their doors before me. All the way to the bottom. Into the mist.

Into the night. Night into dawn. The sun comes up the other side of what remains unseen: a cloud at the bottom of shadowy buildings, fuzzy lights along a lost itinerary of upper rooms, the map he carries in his head. Gunmetal haloes, one pole to another, a double row up the hill in moveless smoke. Less and less distinct. You can never get too close or keep too far away from this mesh of blind spaces; they coalesce at the top of the street, whittling the map down to a cold stretch of pavement two or three yards across the one remaining hollow. Each step is a push against the fog, but never enough, even though you take it step by step, to give a proper clue to the mask. The middle distance vanishes behind neutral gray, and if a muted noise were to find its way back to the father – killing time beyond reach of the lampposts, he looks down out of his open window on nothing – it would only come to linger, an invisible blot he might almost feel the weight of on his eyes, crossing what he knows to be the street somewhere below, a subtle rumor of dislocation hovering in the doctor's wake: the doctor who has left him, who has left them all (wife/sister, brother-in-law/husband, sister-in-law/sister, and the daughter/the niece/the unknown) to their darkness and the ticking of the clock. The doctor is in footsteps, sounding dulled claps of heel and sole off a sidewalk that tilts upward out of its center of gravity.

If roofs are up above, birds are asleep on the roofs. But those who walk the streets have felt the tilt of everything that is lost in the fog. A pair of cat's eyes comes floating, paw by paw, before its black head becomes visible. Dense air, close to the asphalt of the street, a blind alley, a dead-end room without walls, where noxious odors drift. Within this compass of a few cubic yards the scavenger picks its way through a heap of empty liquor bottles, old newspapers stained with grease and coffee grounds, tatters of oilcloth wrapped around moth-eaten books, foxed page-ends curling in the damp.

The steps, paw by noiseless paw, driving the hollow back a little, as in a footloose vignette, toward a crash of shattering glass. Muffled bursts of laughter come in waves, now louder, now softer, as the bricks glide by, covered with graffiti: carved initials that almost seem to have been burned in between the lumpy strips of mortar, stick figures in colored chalk, telephone numbers, obscene witticisms, marmalade men on a span of crossing ladders, the outline of a hand, eyes the shape of fish, a rudimentary phallus-on-wheels pointing the way. Nothing but this wall of bricks and the sidewalk. A horizon lost in the gray blur a few feet beyond a manhole cover. Tarred cracks in the pavement squares. Curbs half eaten away, with drainage holes tunneling into their sides. A labyrinth of pipes runs beneath the city in old blueprints – if you stop to listen, a faint gurgle of metalized water comes to you from below the street, no matter where you may have happened to wander. Black paws creep gingerly over flattened wads of chewing gum, brown cigarette butts crushed in a smear of ashes, ticket stubs bleached white by rain, odd bits of rubbish, wire coils twisted by chance into numberless abstract shapes that will skitter across the cement if a breeze comes up, old rubber bands blackened with filth. Spittle and piss have corroded the lamppost bases: pod-like disks at the bottom of fluted columns, a coat of green paint pitted with rust. Each pole rises into a hazy cataract of light. Before it comes to the next street lamp, the cat passes the remains of a sawed-off tree trunk lost in a circle of weeds behind some wrought-iron palings.

It stops at the very end of the graffiti maze, where bricks become a brownstone wall, paws on the cold grating above a cellar window. Eyes, black lozenges dilating almost to the corners of their lid-slits, discern the form of a vise clamped to the edge of a workbench near a heap of planks. Traces of movement in the murk below. The mice are out of their holes, sniffing for breadcrumbs or a pellet of cheese amid the wood shavings. Elsewhere, a distant clatter of furniture rumbling down, shaking the inner walls of the old townhouse from top to bottom. A tremoring echo falls through the empty stairwell and throws a shudder into the mice that sends them scurrying off to the four corners of their pitch-dark cellar.

Past the door and its stucco pediment to where the light dies gradually away. The first window, less sooted than the one beneath the street, gives on a corridor lit by green pools to the foot of the stairs. Someone glides into the darkness on tiptoe, a fat man with plaid suspenders hanging in a double loop from his belt. He has waddled out of his room, where one of the green lamps glows above the door in a leafy sconce of brass, to put his foot on the bottom step and give an ear to the stairwell laughter – a hollow echoing beside him, where the steps go down to blackness under their rubber mats. Yet the source is higher, beyond the reddish haze of a second corridor much like the first but with no man, fat or lean, to do the listening. Here you can almost see the tops of the radiator pipes glint on the landing under the curtained window. In the third corridor a deep blue light catches eyes through the taut chain of a half-open doorway. Bleak fluorescences, cast in flickers on a wall behind the silhouettes, indicate someone must have turned the sound quite low. They wait, between the door and the jamb, in rapt silence as another laugh filters down amid what seems to be the clamor of a wild stampede. Two men in shirtsleeves, ties askew, are tumbling arm in arm out of the upper reaches, a blur of somersaulting legs and heads head-over-heels, thundering into the corridor. The metalodious squawk of an irate pheasant announces from on high the descent of a third reveler by way of slippage down the mahogany bannister – a prankster appears, more disheveled than the rest, nose and lips hidden behind an outrageous chrome-yellow panache held by a bronze clasp the shape of butterfly wings encrusted with costume jewelry to a button at the apex of a mauve skullcap which reposes, albeit somewhat precariously, upon his occipital peak. He comes bellytobogganing down, a blind swimmer flailing his arms with the hickory squawker in his mouth, blowing *sqwahnk! sqwahnk!* to disperse a sudden traffic in the corridor which, at present, assumes the collective form of his two associates lying crosswise in eclipse, bloodshot eyes turned to the ceiling, gasping for air as he lands *pfoomph!* on their cushioned paunches, bouncing off to make the rounds of the bare walls, blowing his quacker while they struggle to reinflate their lungs.

One floor above, it is completely dark. The corridor, littered with confetti and streamers, comes little by little under the weakening beam of a flashlight. Someone says *Shit!* and feels the crunch of broken picture-glass beneath his heel, sundering the calm of what had begun, inauspiciously, as an unhurried inventory of the debris. He quickly sees his mistake. The xix-century sporting print continues its suspension from the wall, unmolested, beside the thermostat (reset to 9ºF). In truth, the querent has put his foot through glass and silvering. A gulf opens. Behind his fractured silhouette – fragments of a body viewed from the ground up, swaying in the depths of the oval mirror – a second ceiling comes to light in pieces, below the floor. A soundless image, faint if he aims his flashlight directly into it, much brighter if he tilts it to the ceiling above, toward a noise of scuffing heels that grows at the landing, a left turn up the last flight of stairs under the ruins: shards of a flowerpot upended in its mound of dirt, a twisted vine with fuzzy purple leaves, streamers of pleated crêpe speckled with confetti. The last passage. From here you need a ladder to get to the roof. The birds are asleep.

Now, almost in silence, they listen for the sound of sleeping birds. Where have they gone? The men loosen their ties beneath a pale oval in the wallpaper. The women are bending forward in front of them, their heads out the window, still in a daze. It's useless. They can only *hear* the revelers coming out onto the street below. Normally an amber light would cast dwindling shadows across the walk from the bottom of the stoop. But the fog leaves everything to a confusion of half-smothered rumors, blunting the dickory *sqwahnk! sqwahnk!* with an echo of cowbells as the prankster and his cohorts roll out onto the pavement over the jagged slivers of a champagne glass tossed from one of the high windows. The stem alone is intact, a thick helix of smoked crystal with a tinge of blue. The remains glitter like stardust against the flinty texture of the concrete.

Silence. Then all three of them begin to howl like dogs.

The crowd is thinning out in the hallway. Under the pale oval, an old gent with graying hair wets his moustache in a last swig of bourbon. Frosted cubes tinkle at the sides of the glass through which faceless people, no bigger than pins, kaleidoscope behind the melting ice.

– Disgusting.

The only woman left at the window turns as if to answer him, eyes glazed from drink, buttocks propped on the sill to keep her balance. But the gray-haired gent has his back to her now, one patent-leather shoe poised over the apartment's threshold, then another, before the door closes and all the noises of the party – voices in the smoke, clinking bottles and glasses – are swallowed up.

A chuckle drifts up to the window. The 'dogs' are gone. A cat who says *meow* and *pussypussypussy* in falsetto has chased them off. She staggers from the sill to the wall and, with an eye to where the wall goes pale, her fingernail traces the fringe of an endless floral motif. The paper is rough and dry, with minute ridges numbing the tip of her finger. Near the top of the oval a rusty nail casts a sidewise shadow over the wall, contrasting with the catalogue of pits and scars, microscopic eruptions, pimples that make tiny dents in the skin and only *seem* to give a little when you press your finger to them. She notices spots. As she looks up, the specks float upward in their transparent film, just an instant behind the movement of her look. Whether from drink or because her eyes can fix on the gliding specks, she finds herself able to 'track' her gaze smoothly along the wainscot and the radiator pipes, from one wall to the other. Then it was the radiator, not the sill (the sill sits too high), that she leaned her weight on when the gray-haired man had spoken. She returns to the window, trying to picture the cat. Its color. Its form, crouched like a sphinx under the fog.

– *Meowrreoww?*

Her skirtfront pressed to the embossed pipes, she looks down, the mist cooling her face. Mouth open, licking her bottom lip, she waits for the cat to answer her invitation, purring a whisper only *she* can hear behind clenched teeth. A hiss flutters at the back of her tongue.

Silence. An almost grayless gray in the coming down. Without sensation of movement or plummeting weight until, close to touching bottom, having left black, blue, red and green windows behind, a dark form emerges crouched against the pavement backdrop. A headless shirt with no visible legs. One bare arm reaches slowly for the glass stem. Suddenly the hand draws back, as though a spark had passed from the smoky helix through the tip of one of its fingers. He turns a huge grin toward the lost window. White cheshire teeth come almost halfway up before the murk closes over, plunging them down with the rest of the night's debris.

He scampers off on his hands and feet like a mad gorilla, the yellow ostrich plume trailing gracefully in his wake. The other two are chasing after him with echoing cries to stop. To wait. They've left their coats upstairs. It will be a chilly morning. She hears them. Running footsteps. Swallowed in fog.

I couldn't get used to it. Empty streets. It felt like rain. Once a thick mist has settled in, not even a morning downpour can drive it away. Blind men are wandering or keep to their houses, moving from room to room. Without light. Others can see at least the foreground. You almost had to feel your way. Familiar landmarks which never appeared, or loomed up suddenly. Less than a yard off. Vast truncated bases. Without background. Too huge to be taken in whole by the eye. Routes you thought you knew like the back of your hand. Unrecognizable. Your hand in front of your face. Nothing more. The ideal space in fragments. This narrow stretch from gray to gray. Deserted streets I carry in memory.

Distances fell in upon themselves early on, until no distances were left. Impossible to go more than five paces without having to call forth all the minute details of what had passed under my shoes. Pieces that give the illusion of continuance. For now the streets were more of the head than at any previous time. Fragments. Without form. They were there, always. Just ahead, beyond my grasp. Or behind me, half remembered. Brick. Marble. Cement. Glass. Granite. Steel. And never enough to provide an assurance that I might come to the old roundhouse. Through my goggles the dim city came and went in macroscopic vignettes. One faded, giving way to another which passed to vapor in its turn. A city brought up close. All that went unseen became mammoth behind the cold, gray silence. Those of us who walked its streets. Floating islands. Without shadow. I was lost.

Hoping to find the railroad tracks I had reached the top of the hill, turning left down one of the gravel alleyways beside a garage whose ramshackle doors were too far in to be visible. Loose pebbles sloped away from the walk. My heels crunched with each step down, sliding as the weight shifted to my ankles. The sun must have come up by then. What remained of its light spread thinner than the silver haze of the lampposts. I touched bottom. Grass began to appear in the gravel, thickening into clumps of weeds where the yellow garage doors should have been. A sun lost to the gray density. Sudden tunneling effects. Recessions in depth lasting no more than a few seconds. Hazel trees flattened in the middle distance beyond a footbridge whose planks crossed a gully hidden by an undergrowth of nettles and sand-colored weeds. Some older trees tipped toward one another from opposite banks. A vault of leaves. Motionless. Gnarled trunks in a tangle of shaggy molds the mist cloaked long before I had a chance to take my bearings. Pointing myself in what I thought to be the general direction of the bridge – there seemed no way for me to gauge the distance I had to cross before the first planks would come into view, if I moved too quickly I might miss them altogether and be swept into the gully – I took a few tentative steps forward, always with an eye to my mud-spattered shoes. The rim of the copper lining-ring cut into my neck. My goggles steamed. I stopped, breathing faintly, while a clear spot opened, blotting up the layer of condensation. And I began again.

No tunnelings then. Pebbles gave way to grass, and grass to mud. Bridge planks came under my heels with a creaking and what would have been an odor of old wet wood. Mist, almost white in the gully. Tumbling rivers of smoke rolled in under the faint outline of a tree. What looked to be a tree, slanting in the haze, heavy with damp. If a stream trickled below over sand and rocks, the fog or the mask had blunted its noise. It was too far down to hear. Even from the middle of the footbridge. If the riverbed ran dry. I dropped a coin over the side and, waiting for its *ping* to break the silence, began yet again.

Weak-kneed from having crouched so long near the edge. Silence. Staring down into the billowing white set diaphanous wing-flutters pulsing at the corners of my eyes. I stood up. No railing. My legs were wobbling. On either side the bridge planks extended less than three feet into blank space. Without top or bottom. I could put out my hand and still see fingers clearly spread against the neutral backdrop. Center depth. The footbridge seemed more and more to be hanging without supports over an unsoundable gulf. The grassy fringes of the pebble path had long since disappeared behind me, pushed back with the streets and the city buildings far into the dense atmosphere. From where I stood when the fog had opened up, the bridge looked to be little more than a few paces in length. Now I went on tiptoe, in fear that the rotted planks would drop out from under me. The slightest loss of balance might easily carry me over the edge. Faster. A sudden unevenness in the planks threw my rhythm off. As the other bank came into view between the end of the footbridge and the muddy fringe of grass, something like a fallen log rolled under me. Pitched me forward. Breathless. Hands thrust out. Grasping at air. Useless against the pull of gravity. Wet grass tilting up. Into black. Whatever was left of the ground-below-ground eddied back. Widening hollows of noiseless space drifted out into darkness. Something had caught my ankles. The sickness. The paralysis of the fall drew me even farther down.

Curvatures of beading humidity. I closed my eyes. Reached out desperately for the bottom. My feet were lost in the tall grass. The log, or whatever had tripped me up, had vanished along with my bag. A mantis stuck its pinhead out between the grass blades and said a prayer for me until the first drops of rain knocked it back. I looked for it. It was gone. The rain came down sparsely at first. A light drizzle as I got to my feet. I wiped my hands off on my coat. A pattering *ratatat.* Something at least to break the monotonous silence. All track lost of where the gravel ended, where the grove of hazel trees began.

Another surface crumbled away under my shoes. Wet asphalt guttered with cracks of pebbling. A pattern of faint lines. Pits full of muddy water cribbled by the rain. Gulfs without color or feeling of depth, emptied of images. One fillet of silver light, weakly, from the blind side of the gloom. Low starflickerings, close to the ground, with no reflection in the puddles. Vague forms cut the haze into bands of drifting shadow. Tinted globes emerged on birdbath pedestals. I watched a pinlike figure inch by on the crest of a shrunken ellipse. My image in a void that took color from the hollow spheres. Forms out of mist. Cupids teetering on eroded wings. Greco–Roman athletes. Tribunes and emperors brought down from the attic, spilling thin cascades off the tips of their noses. Painted jockeys in blackface – white corneas, thick ruby lips – proffering their brass rings. They crowded in. Frozen. Eyeless gazes toward the hanging light. Useless.

Crouched amid this teeming mass of sandstone and granite, an enormous laughing faun, its ravaged features blackened under an intricate filigree of moss and verdigris, cradled a bowl of overflowing water between the hocks of its crusty knees.

Statuary gave way to lawn mowers, put out to rust amid threadbare camp furniture and other looming hulks beneath a tarpaulin whose rucks and sagging hollows gushed waterfalls onto the charred casings of railroad lanterns behind a spidery crackwork of sooted panes. Two large metal bins, weighted with empty bottles, tin cans and heaps of rubbish, buzzed by flies in spite of the driving rain, stood sentry at the bottom of a narrow ramp tacked with canvas matting.

The star was a pale moon. A lightbulb near the top of a shadowy recess. The sign swayed, crudely painted, on a plank hung from clinking chains above the doorway:

'FLEA CIRCUS'.

Edges of a ramshackle structure. Dimensions lost to fog. A shanty warehouse propped on granite brick-stacks. Slabs of rotted timber and black shingle thrown together over a mud-pool in the weeds.

Outline. The lintel. Under the light. Swarming mosquitoes. Paunch swelling out the nether half of an undershirt beneath a sweat-stained crease. He leaned forward. Hair thinning from black to gray along the temples. Bifocal glints, lunar crescents across the bristles of an untrimmed goatee. Lips invisible. Ridge of a wide-hooked broken nose. The shelves going back behind him. Without having looked up. Arms thrust deep into a cardboard box.

The rain, half drowned by the din of a huge ventilation fan, came down in torrents on the corrugated roof. He was straining over a load of weather-beaten paperbacks. One small gap left in the shelves. For the girl in white under the leaning oak by moonlight, with the mansion tilting its cavernous porches, ricketing back in the distance. His face, lit from below by the jaundiced flame of a cigarette lighter. An upper room. Confessions under the draftsman's lamp. Unaccountable losses. Crosswords. Enough to fill the absences between the sound of a gravelly morning voice.

– They're three for a quarter.

He cleared his throat.

– You can look in this box, if you want. Got nowhere left to put them. Made it in here just in time, huh? Don't think it'll last long, though.

You can tell?

– I'm guessing. Anyway, we really need it. Can't see a goddamn thing out there. Not even the far end of the ramp.

...

He pulled the cord under the lightbulb. The front of the warehouse went dark, the fog outside from black to gray.

– Lucky you didn't break your neck.

How far to the old railroad tracks?

– Can't say as I know. I'm new here. Only had the business for a week or so. Don't really know my way around yet. Got plenty of maps in the back, though.

I've been walking for hours. Something tripped me up at the end of the footbridge. My bag must have fallen into the ravine.

– Well, take a look around. You might find something.

Do you have a bathroom?

– All the way in the back. Make a left under the hot-air balloons. It's really my brother-in-law's place. But I had to take over. My sister called me up in the middle of the night. What could I say? You know how it is. What the hell, I was out of work, anyhow. Got some army-surplus stuff back there. Gas masks and things. All in working order. You want a towel?

Don't bother.

With the front light out. The bookshelves, massive blocks of shadow against the center depth. A labyrinth. Cluttered aisles ran between counters buried in heaps of musty bric-a-brac under the bilious haze of low-hanging fluorescent tubes. The air was heavy. I walked past mounds of toy soldiers from all epochs. Whistles, noisemakers, gag and novelty items – monkeys pissing from an outhouse doorway, jello-molds the shape of dimpled buttocks, flesh-tinted salt and pepper shakers with porous nipples, 'Hollywood game-cards,' dissolving spoons, whoopie-cushions, counterfeit turds and vomit, pens you turn upside down for a comic effect – all banked against the filmy panes of antique breakfronts and porcelain cabinets. I turned the corner, groping my way through lianas of balloon rigging. A long table stretched into the shadows under piles of phonograph records (old 78s), coloring books, women's compacts and empty lipstick cylinders, in the midst of which reposed an olive-drab tin box. I opened it.

A vinyl oxygen mask sprang out on the end of a lamp-blacked bellows. Apart from the proprietor, there was only one other man in the warehouse. I tried to push the mask back into its case. He was lying on the floor. Hidden. Life-size painted statues of St. Theresa, the Baptist and the martyr Sebastian, his bleeding chest and legs shot full of arrows, perched on the tie-beam above my head. It wouldn't go. Ikons. His shoes, covered in a fine layer of dust, peeked out from between an upturned box spring and an antiquated harmonium. Their enameled eyes turned to the heavens. He must have been asleep. Heads tilted back, almost grazing the laths under the iron ceiling with their noses. The full weight of my hands pressed down on the olive-drab lid. Unseen. Din of the rain above the last bellows-gasp. Collapsing inwards. Lost beyond the vaulting. Hidden. Forcing the mask back down. The upper reaches of darkness.

Somewhere. The railroad tracks begin or end under a thicket of spurge and dandelion, bordering another lot at the foot of Promontory Wall. Movements. Houses lost above the leaning sycamores with only a glimmer to bring them out along the ridge of the cliff. Faint blemishes yellowing on the air, beyond clusters of sumac, creeping over the boulders. Traced in shadow. The other side of a narrow, winding lane. Picket fences. Crooked, wood-warped slats, all in a row, with gaps for privet hedges, where a track of ruts begins the driveway. A rectangle of feeble light, veined with gliding branches, in the mist above the porch, one of the turret windows with a silhouette staring, half asleep, into the gray beyond the edge of the veranda roof to eavesdrop on the rustle of an acorn falling through the wet leaves. The silhouette turns its back on the shadow. Recedes into a sulfurous veil of light. Which vanishes.

Loose slabs on a bed of pebbles in the dark. The lane describes a wide horseshoe curve around the lot below. A flight of concrete steps runs under a tunnel-vault of hanging spiders. Crust. By one of the houses set deep in the face of the cliff. Odors of humus and mildew seep through the bricks. Short cuts to where the railroad tracks begin again. Stitched together by degrees. One piece to another. Old foundations you can hear crumble away. Softly in the distance. Gray on gray. Stacks of kindling. Pyramids. The abandoned churchyard. Half-devoured gravestones tilting out of the high grass, and the bones that lie beneath them. Underground. Behind the rockface, you go down with nothing but a cold brick wall between you and stratum after stratum of leathery cadavers given up to the age-old feasting of worms. Past terraces under the earth. Modes of dress, level by level, in greater or lesser degrees of tatters. Silken cravats. Rusted stickpins. One moth-eaten collar, a deeper shade of gray than the fog, curled over a hollow fringed with yellowed teeth and marrow where the lower jaw has dropped away and the head, up to the sockets of the eyes, is full of dust. The passage down, beneath a vault of ancient brick and cobwebs, masking empty eyes. To the charcoaled well-yard to feed the dogs asleep in their kennel, muzzles drooling foam over the dead, pulling the bones, with all their musteline gristle hanging off in shreds that make these crooked tracks in the dirt, out of Promontory Wall. The fierce dream of the dogs is no more than a soft creaking in the roof struts, for the living have finally let go of their mercurial insomnias. Eyelids fall of their own weight. They've cut holes in all the burlap sacks. As the sand comes pouring out with a long hiss up to their necks, these eyes open on the desert. This is how you keep the vigil. To lie where the dogs lie on a bed of rotting mandibles. Part of a woman's skull that they use as a basin for rainwater you use as a pillow to mark the well-yard in the mist. Into the gulf, the fall of an acorn. A silhouette comes back to its window, turns away from the shadow, recedes again into a vanishing rectangle of light behind the trees to keep itself going. A few minutes pass until it or he or she becomes a roving footfall in the room without light. Without light. The one who sits on the edge of the bed waiting for the alarm to go off. The one who listens to the springs squeak. Who will never appear to the extent of revealing either a face or the mask of a face with holes cut out for sleepy eyes. Above the ceiling blackness of this room near the edge of the cliff. Hanging by a thread.

And so on into morning. Waiting for the sun to break through the haze, the shadow (still less-than-shadow in the dark) goes to the window and leans out over the grimy sill. Dead leaves cling to the slate roof amid sunbursts of bird dung and crusty pits where pieces of shingle have broken off. Down in the grass, the crickets rattle-bell their metallish whine to cover the sound of breathing. The leaves rustle, faintly. The wind is down. An animal rocks on its heels in the branches. Perhaps an animal, for when the less-than-shadow backs into the center of the room again with outstretched arms, knocking up against the furniture (it might already be floating above resinous exhalations of teak and polish, a lingering scent of mothballs, sweat and dust), the breath dies in the sycamore. He or she or it can no longer be sure that there was breathing at all, or that it died because what moved had stopped moving, because the occupant of the room, alias less-than-shadow, alias silhouette, alias one who knows that below the ceiling blackness in this room along the edge of the cliff everything hangs by a thread which, inasmuch as the noise of the rustling leaves is concerned, breaks because the owner of aliases has ceased to give it a thought above the cricketing rattle. A fly had come in. That's what it was. It must have been a fly. The one who reinvents it. Having closed the window, the reinventor of aliases goes for a rolled-up newspaper to bat the fly, forgetting to forget. Just to keep awake a few minutes longer. Sitting on the edge of the bed, letting the fly dash itself to death against the filmy windowpanes. The low scaffolding under the weeds and crabgrass takes on the consistency of charcoal. Hollow (termites gnawing through the burl to the inner depths), it passes for what lies at the terminus of the old railroad, something which a man might want to pry open with the handle of a kitchen knife just to see if anything were really there beside the wall of tombs in the rocks. The fog makes it all too simple. One doesn't need an abundance of small details to give the canvas life. A few discreet noises, stretched along a hypothetical line, with brief intervals of silence. Beyond that, if there really is a question of an upper room in a house somewhere above the cliff, one has first to imagine the cliff, the window (mist takes care of the rest of the house), and oneself in that upper room, sprawled on the bed, imagining or attempting to imagine the cliff, the window, a faceless alias – man, woman, puppet – hung by a thread to keep you awake by the glazed ashtray on a chair spotted with cigarette burns. One other piece of furniture. A faded walnut vanity, in shadows that drift toward the eye, whose mirror has turned almost white with neglect. Everything else had been given away or sold to the antiques dealer, piece by piece.

He used to come at night to play rummy with the landlady. An old man who seldom spoke a word. Piece by piece. She had to give him everything. To pay off her debts. The other rooms were emptied. Those tenants who preferred to stay on, those who were afraid to leave their empty rooms, had to make do with cardboard boxes the old man had brought over from his shop. Already he was feeling a vague sense of guilt at having won so often at cards. Facing her for hours through the long nights across a narrow stretch of baize-covered mahogany, half in the amber glow from the tasseled shade of the floor lamp, half in a darkness tinted faintly green by the canaries' night-light (a phosphorescence above small, flitting shadows under the cage cover), he held the little fan of kings, queens, jacks and numbers close to his vest, puffing at his black cigar. Not wanting to look her in the eye – her face was indistinct, she leaned over the table, pouring him another cup of sassafras tea – he stared at the painted china plates that hung in brackets from the musty wallpaper. The canaries had gone to sleep under their oilcloth tent, knowing that night had come in spite of the shuffling cards and the intermittent murmur of voices. One day they died. Their claws stuck up behind the feeder at the bottom of the cage. The landlady was left alone. That's another story. Because of illness, the first excuse he could find without increasing his sense of guilt even more, the antiques man no longer came. She buried the canaries in the yard, by the picket fence where the grass runs back to a pond dense with nymphæceous leaves. The room of the less-than-shadow silhouette, teetering at the edge of oblivion, had been left with a few sticks of furniture.

A map, framed under a sheet of glass, the only serviceable mirror. That, at least, could never be carted away. It belonged to no one.

Then, one night, the landlady dies. The other tenants are either sleeping or have been taken off somewhere by force. They've come to put her in a sack with their bright-red rubber gloves. Without bothering to close her eyes. They lift the sack onto a stretcher. A stretcher which they have had to stand up in the doorway to get from the cramped foyer, through the light of its small stained-glass transom, to the porch. No room in the cliff cemetery. They have to leave it here, propped against a window. The dead piled one on another, to feed the worms. The sack expands. The house is still. One is free to wander from room to empty room. Now that the flies have gathered, it begins to imitate their buzz as it slowly deflates. Without light. The reflection of a window in the lower depths of the map. A putrid stain spreads over it, driving the flies mad. From room to empty room. Cardboard boxes. Wax cartons for milk and orange juice. Butcher's paper rolled in a ball. Crumbs, to feed the mice. Footfalls. Creaking struts. The alarm… Five minutes more.

Now return to the railhead, a charred scaffolding of wood under spurge and dandelion. By leaving the corridor. In a room over the veranda – a bed, a chair, a map on the wall, an ashtray on the chair spotted with burns from a black cigar – someone gets up to open the window. The sycamore rattles. No more than the frayed tips of the nearest branches beyond the slate roof. From the window above, nothing. Not even the faintest trace of a beige rectangle lost behind veining silhouettes now that the light has gone out. The alarm clock rattles by the bed. On and on to the clump of nettles, scarcely distinguishable from the fog at the end of the lot. Shards of emerald and amber buried in the grass, broken beer bottles, crushed soda cans, old candy wrappers, their colors bleached by rain. An odor of garbage and banana peels that the mist keeps from rising higher, mixed with ashes and smoke.

The hollow begins or ends in the rough channel cut through the underbrush by what's left of the tracks on a bed of blackened gravel, hinted in the grass. The ties, where they can be found at all, are uneven. The rails have gone to rust. It's easy to lose sight of them altogether for a long stretch of time. To wander off course and never find them again. No ties, no pebbles, no rails. Gaps. All along the base of Promontory Wall where the dead are bunked. One could track the boulders, level by level, as one marks the barnacled hull of a ship for the tide, by generations. Somewhere close to this place. Another mound left by recent excavations. Where skeletons were unearthed. Chinamen dredged up from the bottom to build a railroad in the early days. When the job was done, they were forced to dig a wide ditch. To lie down in it. No bullets. No knives. Their skulls were crushed. Most were still alive when they were shoveled under. That was long ago. After the exhumation their bones, piled high on a pyre of rags soaked with gasoline, were left to burn.

Soon the grass thins out. There are no more tracks. The pebble-bed comes up again. Rotted ties give way to other wrecks. Old bricks cut a zigzag down the middle of the street, where the rails sink in. No sign of the roundhouse.

An alley near the docks. That smell of tar and creosote. Turbid water. Invisible keelboats rock in their moorings. Black figures on a sidewalk. Indistinct. Something lies in the haze of erubescing smoke that billows tinny music through the transom of an open doorway.

Too small to be a drunk sleeping it off on the cobbled walk amid foaming puddles and slivers of bottle-glass, far larger than a child, covered with red fur in the bar-light, it opened its jowls as I drew nearer – a pink tongue livering between fangs and drooling mutton chops – listlessly raising its head. The head of a dog, or an anaconda that had swallowed a dog in one gulp. Its breath came in shallow mists tinted the color of blood. Its muzzle drooped to its paws, ears lowering. It took a last look around through half-lidded, glistening eyes, attuned to the new odor, listening, almost as a matter of form, for the least echo before its eyes closed again. I had to step over it, passing under the sign of an uncoiling snake.

Threads of undulating cigar smoke interlaced with what I could imagine as the aroma of peanut shells, spilt beer and liquor, all rubbed into the masonite bartop, saturating its cushioned stools, its wide mirror broken into panels by gilt marbling, hidden between shelves of bottles and their reflections, drained by the reddish light from green and amber into hues of black and tangerine or, like the chess pieces on one of the little tables against the opposite wall – hardly visible behind the bottles and the venous streaks – into the same shade of pink. There, in reflection, by the curtained windows – the panes were painted black to mask a dingy passageway, a wall of crumbling bricks that led to what must have been one of the piers – two men, wasting away under their threadbare jackets, were having a game, staring not at the board between their identically folded hands, nor at each other, but off into space. The beer foam left traces of weblike film in their drained glasses.

All but the last of the bar stools were free. An old man sat hunched over his empty shot glass, the bill of a wickerwork cap slouched over his eyes, oblivious to the mounting rhythms of *La Valse*. The music was reaching its lyrical peak. The speaker buzzed above the bar mirror. A vague tremor passed through its clutter of bottles as the old man began to make frantic signals to the bartender, who had his eyes closed and was swaying back and forth on his chair by the register, beating time with pudgy, hairless arms. The bass was so deep that, at the point where every instrument was playing, the dynamics of the orchestra having reached its utmost pitch, I felt the floor tremble under me, sending a rattle up in spiraling orbits around my head.

Sudden silence. An oboe or an English horn. Footsteps as the music quieted. A clack of heels on linoleum through the back passage. Odd patches of cement filling in rough gaps under the stools where the old floor had worn away. The tables sat on poles that flared into the sawdust in wide, cast-iron bases. Following the perspective of this dimly lit motif, I came to the young barmaid at the end of the line of tables. A tall, red-haired girl, dressed in a halter and tight, faded jeans speckled with flecks of dried paint, biting a hangnail on the little finger of her left hand, a serving tray under her arm.

– Whiskey! cried the old man with a toothless grin, grabbing the girl by the seat of her pants as she lumbered by, pulling her to him, nearly falling off his stool in the process. He whispered something in her ear. The barman snapped out of his musical revery.

– Goddamnit, where the hell d'you think you are, Cappie!

– Aw, shit, I's justh tellin' Joodie somrthin'. A sthecret.

– Go on, get the hell out of here! You got your snootfull.

– Gone, get on yerselth. Yer jus' jealousth 'cause I goosthed-up lil' Joojie 'stead o' you. Right, Jood? Go 'head in back the bar, Alf wantsa goosth ya. C'mon, Alf, don' be sh(*uk!*) shy.

But Alf, having spoken his piece, was drifting back through the ebb and flow of cigar smoke into his lost dream of a Viennese ballroom – perfumed crinolines of satin, rustling watered silk, dappled by crystal tears of chandelier-light which glittered off the buttons and epaulettes of blazing military tunics. The chess players cocked an ear in his direction, without tearing their eyes from a fixity on dead space, until the barman came to himself again. By then, the old drunk had disappeared.

One minute his face, like a wrinkled prune, was grimacing bare gums above the bar. Suddenly, it vanished. My eyes became accustomed to the reddish light. I had walked from the door to the table at the back, its votive flame guttering behind red glass embossed with pimples clustered in the shape of diamonds. A black wick, half submerged in the tallow, was rooted to a bed of gleaming yellow wax. A quivering, blue-edged leaf. If I were to blow it out, the charred wick-tip would burn off its glowing coal under a gray, sulfurous ribbon. I saw the old man again. His cap had fallen off and he was rolling in the sawdust, trying to get clear of the stool base and the brass bar which entangled his feet. I just wanted to sit. He began to crawl for the door where the ventilation fan wafted clouds of pink smoke through the transom into the mist of the alley. To let the flame go out. The last traces of reddish light that still escaped the Anaconda Bar found him clambering over the dog. One heard a brief whine and some heavy panting. Clouds of vapor. And he was gone.

Hidden lamps through a veil of shifting tints, blending one into another, cast their iridescences on nickel honeycombed with pits of black-mottled faille. A festive glow threw the rest of the barroom into shadow. Violet to blue into green, from green into yellow, orange and red into violet. Cold, spectral metamorphoses, each so smooth that no one color gained a hold on the eye before another took it over. An illusion. There *were* no unadulterated colors. The ambient light was pitching into black. Chromescences, already tinged by a fading redness in the air, took on additional saturation from the hues out of which they had just emerged. Subtle, delicate gradations from one color to the next as in a mist passing through some strange chemical evolution. Green left whatever followed it with a greater susceptibility to red. From ultramarine to chrome yellow, a traceable 'tea-rose' glow would overlap which, in turn, colored the orange that followed in the wake of yellow, bringing it dangerously close to 'red' long before red was due to come up again; by then, the images would have absorbed so many previous superimpositions of 'positive' and 'negative' casts that the whole passage from indigo, across the spectrum, to violet would have masked its original chromatic properties. Theoretically, were the process to be accelerated, one might postulate with mathematical precision a third, a fourth, even so much as a fifth layering of afterimages, taking all the variables into account. Coordinates of each successive stage, mapped out on a hypothetical 'chart of degrees of discoloration', marking the length and breadth of this closed infinity until the retina becomes overloaded. Then the jukebox, along with the barroom, wiped out by a livid clot, loses form altogether. Disappears.

A click. The waltz had subsided. When I peered down through the glass dome the light was deep yellow with blue vermiculation. The record slid with a whirr from the vertical turntable into its niche among the rank and file of other disks.

– Took out all the crap. Kids used to come in wanting to dance. Disturbing the customers. Real pain in the ass. So I figured, what the hell, I'll put in my own: Beethoven Schubert, Berlioz, Fauré, Czerny.

The barman, the one the old sot had called Alf, was waddling toward me, his thick cigar butt smoking, held daintily aloft between thumb and forefinger.

– Like opera? Don't have to pay. Fixed it up special myself. All you do is push the right combination of buttons.

The bar-light, gone from red to purple, touched his stray hair-ends as a nimbus. He lodged what remained of the butt in the gap between his middle teeth and bent toward the console. The rainbow suffused his open shirtfront, casting highlights under his nose and chin, tinting the smoke of his bobbing cigar as he leaned the full bulk of his weight on his arms, staring into silver depths.

– I never get tired of this.

His finger brushed lightly over the double row of ivory-colored keys, depressing one for the 'letter,' another for the 'number' of *Selections from The Barber of Bagdad* by Cornelius, all in one fluid motion. One of the chess players seemed about to make his move. That gnarled hand, brown splotches, veins neutralized by the tincturing light, hovered above a crenellated tower. The hum of metal, faint, as the turntable glided slowly past the file of records and came to a stop, dipping into the rack with its copper bracket-ring, drawing out an old ten-inch disk. The tone arm came forward to meet it. I could see his face, a gourd-shaped distortion in the darker reaches of the background, floating half-transparently behind the record rims.

– Want a drink?

I just came in to get my bearings.

Then nothing. The disk was turning. The lights were still on. The phonograph needle was a hair short of making contact with the dusty groove. Alf bit hard into the butt between his clenched teeth (the ash dropped off), spit out what was left and muttered a vague obscenity, hitting the console repeatedly with the flat of his hand from top to bottom, his ear cocked to its every tremor as though listening for the faintest noise outside the door of a locked room at midnight.

– Happens all the time. It's an old machine. The antiques dealer offered me quite a pile for it. Joodie, get me the screwdriver, under the sink with the openers! But I wouldn't part with it for anything. Practically had to fight the old bastard off. Said he wanted it as a gift for someone he admired. My ass! Christ knows what he really wanted it for. Who would buy an old heap like this? Hasn't been 'round for a long time, though. No, goddamnit! The *other* screwdriver! Can't you see this one's too big? What the hell's the matter with you? And get me a flashlight! So, how about it? You must be stifling. How do you manage to find your way around? Have one on the house, just name it. We've got soda, if you want it. Cigarettes, perhaps? A glass of water?

Joodie was coming back with the flashlight and a small screwdriver in her hands. Out of the red smoke. From the doorway, over the head of the sleeping dog, I followed the noise of a distant foghorn through the streets and alleyways. An old tub was putting out to sea. I thought I might be able to find the inner harbor. To follow the tracks from there. A negative of the jukebox lights still hovered before my eyes like a second mist, gradually dwindling to a translucent dot at the center of my field of vision. The clatter of something metal, hollowed into the shape of a drum, broke the silence and seemed to roll in my direction from around the corner. Footsteps. Laughter.

I flattened myself against the bricks. Slowly, taking great pains to make no sound, I peered around the quoin. An old man was lying under a mound of garbage. Three men in shirtsleeves, their clothes askew, were trying to help him up. The one in the odd, yellow-plumed cap kept falling down.

No. They were *beating* him up. I could see it clearly now. The three of them. Rolling him for his money. Their fists were busy everywhere, poking, prying, jabbing, trying to bring the old drunk out of his torpor by scooping up handfuls of rubbish and hurling them in his wilted face. It was the one they called Cappie, the tippler from the Anaconda Bar, lying there like a dishrag, or a puppet, allowing himself to be hoisted into a standing position by two of the laughing men while the third, the one sporting the panache, set the garbage bin aright with a distinct chuckle. Yes, it was the old sot. He could easily have come this far on his hands and knees before blacking out. The prankster stood by, cap in hand, waving the yellow ostrich feather under the old man's nose as the cohorts tipped him, head first, into the can.

What could I do? One man against three. Dog tired. As it was, I could hardly stand up myself. All from the walking. My mind clouded. I could barely see to maneuver my way about. The goggles, not to mention the narrow eyeholes which could be knocked awry, put me at a tremendous disadvantage. There was another garbage can next to the one where Cappie's legs stuck up like a V. His feet turned out at right angles. Motionless. I thought it best to wait.

The three morning revelers began to circle the metal bin, kicking it in with the tips of their shoes. A loud battering noise. They shivered with the damp, rubbing their shirtsleeves to keep warm, blowing on their hands. They bellowed like a tribe of Indians on the rampage. I can't remember how long the uproar lasted. They were very near. A scarce five feet away. I stood with my back to the wall. I heard their war cries. From time to time, the whistle of a garbage scow cut through the heavy air. The harbor, from the sound of boats in choppy waters, seemed no more than a stone's throw from the barrier of hazy lights. Keelboats rocked gently against the pier planks before breaking free of their moorings. I kept my eyes open.

Not long after. They were running past me, sliding on their heels, tumbling over the wet street bricks. I crept up to the garbage cans and, almost at once, realized my mistake. Black trousers with a satin stripe down the outer seams. Too well-dressed. It wasn't Cappie. The one with the yellow panache, or one of his cohorts, had removed the shoes and socks from their unsuspecting victim.

I searched my pockets.

Still a few certificates that I hadn't put in my lost bag. I took one out. Signed my name to it. The time of morning (an approximation). And tied it to the big toe of his right foot, where the police were sure to see it.

The bricks laid out an uneven zigzag, sloping away from the middle of the street as rainwater flowed in rivulets toward the sunken gutters. Near the end of the block, two sets of worn-down tracks merged in a curving gantlet. It was coming back to me… I could not be far from the roundhouse.

In the mirror, behind blue knickknack shelves, some of them are dancing. Others, off to one side, make do by the piano, rolling their eyes. Some stagger leeward through clouds, drawn as by a magnet toward the beading bucket of ice on a folding table piled with steadily diminishing cocktail napkins, tumblers, plastic cups and long-stemmed glasses, hidden, amid the glitter of clear and tinted bottles, in a confusion of labels from gin to seltzer. The last chords of music evaporate in perfume and smoke. The babble of voices, of liquid poured over ice, the crystalline clink of glass to bottle, build to a gradual roar, half suppressed when the pianist, lifting his foot from the legato pedal, crushes his cigarette in a pentagonal ashtray and, exhaling a blue haze over the butts, the uneven heaps of ashes laced with ribbons of cellophane and blackened match stubs, calmly walks out onto the landing, slamming the door behind him.

Debris. Shards of a flowerpot upended in its mound of dirt on the stairs. The last flight rises under the remains of a wilting vine with fuzzy, purple-edged leaves and streamers of pleated crêpe flecked with sawdust. His hand grazes a balluster, with its hairs. He leans forward, peering into the dark of the well, down through the matrix of dizzying rectilinear spirals. Carpeted steps emerge from the blackness at different levels in pools of faintly colored light that skim the bannisters, touch the fringes of deep shadows and hang, unconnected, spanning the depths of a bottomless space. He can almost hear their slightest movements filtering up from the vestibule in irregular ticks that echo less and less of metal – that constant expansion and contraction in the heating ducts – as they approach the upper stories from the outside of the building. It's cold. He has to take time to light another cigarette. After only a few quick puffs, he wants to let it drop. To watch the cinder fall away, tracing an orange spiral into the gloom. But afraid of starting a fire, he stubs it out on the mahogany railing. It burns a shallow crater into the polished wood. Still breathing smoke, the steam comes out of his nostrils. Evaporates. Gray wisps against the dark of the stairs. He turns and, passing the pale oval in the wallpaper with its nappy ruts from fingernail scrapings, walks to the window, aware of nothing more than that the ticks, after reaching their loudest pitch, have suddenly abated. A lull in the jabbering behind the door. The unexpected silence, cut by a few oddly stifled cries and the heavy tramp of feet on piano keys. A wild discord, shrieking, groaning, up and down the width of the sounding board.

Horror. The prankster in his stocking feet, crouched with arms crossed like a mad Ukrainian dancer out of costume, struts across the ivories while his cohorts scramble in through the curtained window. Utilizing a free elbow to knock the prop out from under the piano lid – a thud followed by a resonant echo of overtones – he leaps off, touching down in the middle of the floor with time enough to make a hurried survey of the crowd he has driven back to three of the four walls. Even an amorous couple sprawled under the knickknack shelves, arms and legs askew on a crushed-velvet settee, has deemed it necessary to come up for air. The man snatches his sweaty palm from beneath the woman's rucked-up skirt as she tugs mechanically at her garter, catching sight of the prankster in mid-flight, the yellow plume clenched between his uppers and lowers. He's sailing toward her over an ocean of blurry faces. The button atop his scarlet beanie snags the tip of a streamer off the light fixture, plummeting a lime-green ribbon behind him. His arms stretch, casting a shadow over the rapidly vacated settee that sucks him into its hollowed cushions with a puff of dust and a rain of lacquered figurines. He manages a blind grab at the fleeing woman's ankle, arresting her perpendicular momentum not long after she pitches forward into the canapés with a torsion sufficient to engender violent scatterings of cheese-dip flecks, a sudden but short-lived response to the centrifugal vortex of her imitation pearls. Taking full advantage of the lull – everyone frozen into position, glass in hand and glassy-eyed, wondering if they haven't already passed beyond the limits of discreet alcoholic consumption – the prankster, shaking a porcelain panpipe from his ear, takes a sidereal bound off the cushions toward the crawling woman and giddyaps, legs astride her thrust-out hips, through a parting of skirts and trouser cuffs, into a nearby closet, slamming the door behind him.

Consternation. The guests form a little group before the point of entry, leaving a semicircle of rug-space between their feet and the closet door which vibrates to a rumble of flailing arms and shoe-heels, tumbling boxes and desperate shrieks. The prankster, in a claustrophobic blackness of dust, mothballs and perfume, under a pummeling of bony fists, long fingernail scratches and platform heels, constructs a hasty barricade of umbrellas, galoshes and slippers, before lugging his recalcitrant partner behind hanging overcoats into the deepest recess of the closet, forgetting that the door opens outward.

Silence. All wait breathlessly for the next sound. The other two make arm-in-arm for the master bedroom, stuffing hors d'œuvres – crusty remains of Swedish meatballs (toothpicks and all), sliced pickles and pimentoes – into their mouths, in the act of pocketing (solely by conditioned reflex) the plastic spoons, the forks and the last of the cocktail napkins. From the other side of the bed, a blue night-lamp throws its pool of ghoulish light across the pimpled ceiling. It's so quiet they can hear the purr of the digital clock with its phosphenescing numbers, green diodes that seem to hover in the black space of the wall. The bed smells of wool and eiderdown with just the faintest trace of an aroma that might pass for vicuna buried in the heap of overcoats and furs. A patent-leather toe sticks out from under the box spring, and a blue-tinged hand. Someone sleeping it off. Someone wearing an expensive watch, a signet ring mounted with a black stone to tempt the prankster's friends. Oblivious to the silence around them, to the barely audible pulsations of the clock, they burrow like moles, digging a tunnel into the pile of wraps, tossing one after another over their shoulders onto the floor, over the chairs, the dresser, the mirror wardrobe, the vanity, every which way until the four corners of the room seem littered with shadowy corpses. Blue owls, blue lizards, blue foxes. It's been a long night. They're ready to drop on the still-cluttered bed. Too tired to go on. Wanting nothing more than to sleep through the murky morning. With any luck the lull will hold a few hours of forgetfulness. No one will move from his place. They'll close their eyes. Wait for sleep by looking into the blue pool on the ceiling. Switch off the night-lamp until, slowly, it begins to oscillate. So slowly, it intermeshes. Touches waves. Carries them through the tunnel of concentric rings. Into sleep.

Sleep. It eludes them, passing dreary shadow-smoke across their eyes as they lie, shoulder to shoulder, on the bed, half submerged by rumpled sleeves, coattails and the vague perfume of ladies' handbags. The curtains are drawn, but it makes no difference. Someone might enter, creeping around the foot of the bed to the window. An abrupt screech of metal rings across the curtain rod and their eyes would water, squeezing shut against the flood of light that would not come. Awake, yet paralyzed in all but the movement of their eyes. They pan slowly over the furniture tops, locked in a smooth leftward glide along the commissure of ceiling and wall, from the window – a gray, undulating haze – into the shadowed recess that vibrates in tune with the purr of the digital clock, and vanishes in the yellow behind a silhouette standing in the doorway. It walks toward the bed. Leans in close to their sweating faces. Is satisfied that they are not asleep. Then quietly tiptoes out, slamming the door. And its voice blends with other, louder voices. To the left of the mirror wardrobe, the closet is open. They can hear, without taking time to leave the bed and put an ear to the partition, a scuffling on the other side, as though fists, shoes and heads were knocking against the closet wall. It's a long time before they can free their legs. Move enough to get out of bed. To follow the silhouette's path to the door.

Confusion. Standing pat like a head waiter in the smoke and crush of dewy bodies, a ripped pair of stretch-nylon panty briefs (garnished with lace and a fleece-lined gusset) draped over his arm with that casual elegance which bespeaks an impromptu retreat from the shallow depths of a closet, the prankster pays scant attention to the man of corpulence got up as a Roman Catholic bishop, who has just requested, in no uncertain terms, the prompt return of his skullcap. A voice in the crowd says *meow*. The prankster daubs his fevered brow with panty shreds. Another voice sobs and sneezes mothball dust behind the empty coats and dresses. A secret panel slides away, and the owner of this voice tumbles backward into blue light, just in time to hear a door close and footsteps shuffling up the L-shaped passage toward the party room. Crisping snippets of hatbox tissue adhere to her elbow as she crawls, knees and flattened palms sinking in the carpet nap, from the closet to a narrow space between the mirror wardrobe and the foot of the bed. A sleeper's hand peeps out from under the springs, hair bristling on knuckles, camouflaged by a heap of fallen coats, each finger curled in direct ratio with its proximity to the thumb. If she were to put her cheek to the rug, she would almost be able to see his black form stretched out in the darkness. The hiss of his breath comes more and more like a welter of pebbles and shells washed onto the beach by an evening tide. The blue pool. Reflections. The ceiling, high in the wardrobe mirror. Softly, with a delicate creak to break the near silence, the bedroom gives a lurch and reels away behind her image into aromatic depths, blocked by a rack of plastic and cellophane shrouds. Her hand, pushed through heady cedar, gropes wildly between rasping coat hooks. The tips of her fingers brush the sticky inner wall in search of corners they never seem to reach. She closes the door. The room glides into place behind her reflection, delimited by the borders of the mirror. An oblong sheet of glass and silvering that begins less than a foot above the rug. In which she turns, limned by the blue of the night-lamp, hiking her tattered skirt above the waist to have a glance at her bruised posteriors. Head cocked over the shoulder. Damp curls falling into her bloodshot eyes.

Departure. Propped against the wall, he teeters between them as they slip him into his herringbone coat, turning the collar up around his ears to cover one of the lobes, which trickles blood from a bite, fixing the yellow panache to his unctuous cowlick with a hairpin one of them has snatched up off the rug. Most of the food they will need, along with the pilfered utensils, the plastic cups and the bishop's velvet cap, has already been stuffed into his pockets. Standing open-mouthed, swaying like a wooden Indian from one to the other of his tittering comrades, eyes closed, oblivious to the dowager who shakes a diamond-studded finger under his nose, shouting, 'This is an outrage!' the prankster has begun to keep his own counsel. He isn't moving at all now. The two of them will have to carry him down the stairs, one taking him under the arms, the other under the knees. Someone who no longer thinks of saying *meow* has inched her way around the far side of the piano to close the window. It's getting cold. The mist has begun to settle, leaving a vast expanse in its wake. Some rooftops, a few smokeless chimneys, the upper stories of tall buildings appear under an endless leaden cloud whose outer reaches merge with the haze in the distance. The sky of a snowy night. Without snow. Morning comes in a dead silence. Toward the middle space, amid the debris of what few landmarks remain, a massive dome covered in soot looms out of the fog. Where the tracks converge and are swallowed up.

A little faster, while there's still time. I had come to it then, the dead end of a long perspective of top-heavy roofs and gables, its massive dome lost above the haze of the lampposts, where the last ramshackle houses leaned over rain-swept cobbles. The roundhouse, at last. So black, so huge against the crumbling façades, that its sides could not be seen. I followed the yellow glow hovering near its base: a distant star, a faint streak on the tracks as I walked, before the stones and puddles sloped into deep shadow. Light spilled over the porch from a narrow doorway at the top of a flight of wooden steps. For the first time in what seemed like hours, I could make out voices, rumblings over the muted hum of a generator, sounds the fog or the mask turned into dense, echoless murmurs. The edges of the steps, where they hadn't already been chipped away by time and rot, made a splintery pattern – wave-like depressions with gaps of darkness diminishing between them as they went up. I put my hand on the iron post at the bottom and looked up the side of the building, a wide, dizzying curve of sooted brickwork whose upper reaches vanished in the mist. In a house across the alley, where the street pitched and cobbles gave way to slabs of concrete splotched with tar and loose pebbles, a weak light flickered in a dormer window. A silhouette passed behind the curtains and lingered there. A man. A woman. Indistinct.

From the porch at the top of the steps, peering down through iron balusters, I saw the beginning of a chain of dim lanterns, swaying as though moved by an unknown hand, strung out above the windless void. Sections of track passed in and out of the reddish pools they made, toward a crater hollowed out of smoke. No one could say where they led or whether they were broken. You had to imagine the dockside warehouse off in the distance, the old loading platforms, the silos at the end of the jetty, all long deserted. The open door beside me seemed to bristle with noise. Now the yellow light was brighter and would have fallen across my face, throwing my left eye into shadow. The sounds from within, though my ears were shrouded by oilcloth, lost their resonance in the groan of the generator, blending with its hum under the vast, domed space. For some reason the chain of lanterns, stretching into mist, held me. I couldn't bring myself to leave the porch and go in, or even to turn my head toward the doorway. The light fell, a bit less yellow, across my gloved fingers and brought them into high relief against the dark. I tried, without success, to gauge the distance between my knuckles, bent over the iron railing, and the first of the red shunt lamps which seemed to meander, ever so slightly, in the immense perimeter of blackness beyond the roundhouse wall. The fog was driven back a little by the ashy light of a low-lying cloud, a morning light too pale to reach the ground. The misty hollow, which had camouflaged space and perspective, gave way to darkness. The more I looked, the more I sensed that the positions of the lanterns had somehow shifted. I could almost feel it happening under my eyes, without being able to pinpoint a movement which might have given the game away. I pictured a team of switchmen creeping from lamp to lamp, phantoms astray in the murk, bending to ring their subtle changes in the pattern, an inch here, an inch there.

It comes to a matter of inches. Inside, the sulfurous light. The halo around a dangling bulb. Behind the lintel. Other haloes hovered in groups of two and three on shadeless floor lamps to mark the edge of a thicket of tubes and hanging bottles. The center was in shadow. None of the lights could reach it. The massive dome, lost in a black gulf, echoed the breathing of those who slept beneath: men, women, children, laid out under bubbling IV tubes like spokes of a giant wheel, in concentric rings, each with a green number painted on the forehead. The numbers alone, where they glowed in the dark, gave indication of the true dimension of this circle of bodies. The floor was vast, at least a hundred yards in diameter. Less than ten feet remained between the outermost ring of sleepers and the rotunda wall. If you took away the upended glucose bottles, the flexible tubes, the phosphenescing numbers, there was nothing out of the ordinary. White faces. Their clothes had been left on them because of the cold. Those, here and there, who had been found in the nude were wrapped from chin to foot in heavy, olive-drab blankets. An armed guard made the long patrol around them, flashlights in hand, while others saw to it that the line of 'witnesses,' queued up to a makeshift office at the other end of the curve, kept close to the brick wall. Some had come hoping to identify a lost relative. Some wanted permission to admit a wife, a husband, a son, or a daughter who was lying motionless like all the others here, breathing imperceptibly on a couch, in a darkened bedroom, behind closed doors, somewhere in the city. The witnesses – many had turned up their coat collars against the damp – hid their faces in handkerchiefs doused with alcohol by the guards to kill the saccharine odor of urine passed off by the bodies in the course of their long sleep. There were small puddles wherever the floor sagged near the edge of the outer ring, pools reflecting the lights as I made my way past the first of the guards. The hiss I had taken for whispers was the sound of all these breathing bodies, asleep and awake; the hum of the 'generator,' an amalgam of snores which made a continuous drone. Diminishing circles. Pale, upturned faces gradually became blots. Green coals twinkling in a shadowy lagoon.

I didn't have to push through the line. The witnesses, clear up to the wicket, made way for me without comment. A few feet beyond the rail, the registrar, a seedy, balding man with flakes of dandruff on his coat, horn-rimmed glasses balanced precariously on the tip of his nose, and a cigarette butt between thin lips, sat hunched at a desk behind a litter of papers, too absorbed in his work to look up. No one at the head of the queue made any attempt to draw his attention. Perhaps they had been waiting for hours. From time to time he would lay his pen on the blotter, set his burnt-out cigarette in the scallop of a plastic ashtray heaped with other twisted butts and charcoaled matches, and blow into his mittens to warm his nose. Over his shoulder, in a small area shut off from the roundhouse proper by a hospital screen, two guards were bending over a rumpled cot. They had just finished stripping a young woman who had made no effort to resist. She was lying on her stomach, her blond head turned to the crumbling wall. Her flesh took color with the cold while the guards went through her clothes in silence, turning each piece inside out, the pockets too, without finding so much as a tube of lipstick. A foot or two from the head of the cot, a stretcher lay across the arms of a dilapidated captain's chair, the canvas wound neatly around its wooden rods. The registrar closed his book, smoothed back what was left of his greasy chestnut hair and, almost mechanically, crushed his dead cigarette in the ashtray. Some witnesses near me pressed toward the gate. A nervous shuffle. Murmurs. Maybe he wasn't looking at me at all. He seemed a bit dazed, as though he had come to the end of a prolonged stupor and had still to take his bearings. Behind him, one of the guards had found what looked to be a metal snuffbox in the inside pocket of the girl's corduroy jacket. There was something, after all. Perhaps she was a student. No books. So early in the morning? Her watch had stopped at 4:20. I should have asked someone in line for the correct time. An absurd shyness after having walked through deserted streets for so long. The registrar's eyes were set far apart. An effect, no doubt, of the glasses. Bifocals. Lunar crescents cast over the stubble of his beard. He appeared to be staring right through me. Dark circles under loose bags of skin. If he could have seen my bag it would have been less awkward for the two of us. The guard was turning the snuffbox over in his hand, pressing his thumb to the catch. I fished through my pockets for something I might use as a means of identification. All I could come up with was a prescription pad that must have crumpled when I fell at the end of the little footbridge. Down to its last few sheets. Enough to get me through, even though I had to inch my way along the rail to the wicket gate, knocking my knees against the balusters. Other hands were searching my pockets. I let them. There was nothing left to find. The registrar snatched up a half-squashed pack of cigarettes, tapped it against his fingers, and held it out to me.

– Sure you won't have one? Menthol.

Something to cool the lungs, eh? It's the only kind I can stand now.

He put one to his lips, flicked his lighter a couple of times, producing a few sparks.

– Shit. Got a match? Please, sit down. Hey, one of you guys gimme a light?

He had turned to the guards. They were standing over the girl. Just standing. Looking at each other now and again as though they were reluctant, or merely too tired, to go on. The taller one, almost a silhouette between the top of the registrar's head and the floor-lamp bulb which cast a white ellipse on the hospital screen (a nimbus lit the down along the turned-up ridge of his nose), worked his jaw in and out. But his lips were closed. He let his eyes wander from the cot to the registrar while his hand, absently, began to smooth the tousled hair of the girl.

– Sorry. Don't neither of us smoke.

The two of them were bending over her as the registrar turned to me. Again, he was looking somewhere past my eyes. Slowly. Gently. They rolled her onto her side. Then, taking her under the arms and knees, they lifted her and laid her on her back so that her legs projected off the foot of the cot, and her feet, which had turned outward, rested on the cold cement.

– Anybody there got a light?

Someone tapped the back of my chair and handed me a book of matches. I passed it to the registrar. He opened it, tore out a match, struck its blue tip – a rasp, the sudden burst of fire – on the flint-strip. He cupped his mittens over the cigarette, drawing hard. The flame lent a warm glow to his face, two flickering glints in the curvature of his lenses. Shaking the match out, he tossed it into the ashtray. It fell, a thread of curling smoke in its wake.

– Of course, you must realize, we're about to close this receiving station. Not an inch of room left, as you can see. Or are you here to make an identification?

They must have come for me before morning. A woman had been found lying in the gutter. I told the father to call the police. Have they brought her in yet?

– I'm sure you know how difficult it would be for us to locate this woman now. I've been sitting here since last night trying to put these affairs in order. It's impossible. Even if she *is* here – and that's highly unlikely, given the time of morning you claim to have answered the call – you'd have to get one of the custodians to take you around the outermost circle and, you can see for yourself, we've all got our hands full. I hope you'll put that in your report. By then it'll be too late to do any good. Not that I'm complaining! Far from it. Are you sure the old man remembered to phone the police? Maybe he was a bit deaf, or senile, and what you told him didn't sink in. He might be waiting for you to go back there now. To claim the body. But I seriously doubt she's here. You can look for her on your own, if you like. The odds are against it. This one here is the last sleeper I've accepted, and she came in late last night. The custodians are only getting to her now. We have to strip them, if only to look for a birthmark or some other physical identification when there are no effects. No stone left unturned. You understand. I don't make the rules.

One of the guards was kneeling, flashlight in hand, between the blond girl's thighs. The other one leaned forward with her soiled feet, a dead weight, crossed behind his head.

– Yes, the vagina and the rectum, too. We've had a lot of drunks brought in. Some of them crap all over the floor. But you, of all people, realize how necessary it is to make a complete examination. You'd be surprised what we find sometimes. It pays to be thorough, because later, when everything is being sorted out, certain questions will be asked. Questions that we won't be able to laugh away so easily. Jesus, the paperwork! And I don't dare go to sleep, myself. Who knows what would happen? At least none of us will wind up in one of *these* circles. God, what a smell! I wish you would tell them about the smell. Every once in a while it comes back to me full force. Well, it'll be over soon enough. I've been authorized to terminate all receiving procedures. I have to wait now for my replacement. He should've been here already. Must have gotten held up at the main office. Paperwork. I was just tidying up a few things. You know, don't like to leave a messy house. From now on the roundhouse will be admitting only relatives and other such witnesses for the purposes of identification. You wouldn't believe how many of these clowns have been carried in here without so much as a driver's license or even a voter's card. People who, for the most part, were found in the streets.

I almost forgot. There's another one. Not far from here, I think. A man stuck, head first, in a garbage bin.

– That's a new one.

By the docks. I tied a certificate to one of his toes.

– The docks? Oh, you mean the other side of town. Out of our jurisdiction, anyway. With any luck, he'll turn up at the movies. You know, the Omega? You'll have to go there to track the woman down. That's where she'd be taken, if the old man remembered to make the call. We're moving the whole operation there. They've already started to receive.

A button at the bottom of the phone dial pulsed with light.

– Yeah… … What?… … Uh-huh… yeah, sure… … Okay… right…

They had begun to dress the girl. Her blouse was on. She was still naked from the waist down. One of the guards tapped the registrar's chair with the handle of a brush whose bristles were caked in luminous green paint.

– What number?

The registrar put his mittened hand over the mouthpiece, cradled the receiver between chin and shoulder, reopened his ledger and answered, after a pause…

– Eight. One. One. Twenty-five.

You can scour the mustiest tomes of this library for the early legends, wives' tales and remedies against the dread disease. The old man has let his beard grow out uncombed for days. He emerges on one of the upper tiers, leaning over the brass rail with shelves of antique books rising out of a shadow from three sides of the deep recess behind him, and makes a sign for you to come up. The only other light glows dimly on a caged rostrum near the check-out desk at the end of the main hall. You have walked across the darkness, the clop of your heels echoing off the distant ceiling, rebounding from hidden corners, through all the levels and tiers, until you reach the foot of an iron stair, one of many that spiral into the upper depths of the library. He beckons you with a vague gesture, silently, as though all words have been put away for a time between the pages of a book he has yet to locate, which is why, in spite of everything (the epidemic, the rumors of his disappearance and death), he, the antiquarian, has taken up residence here in one of the abandoned lofts, making his bed upon towering piles of yellowed newsprint no one asks for anymore. Not even a watchman to keep him company through the long hours of the night, to pass the time with him in idle conversation if only he could rouse himself to speak a word or two. He walks with a blind man's cane, tapping the planks beneath his feet and the sections of cast-iron grillwork, each with its unique design, below the railing which keeps him from the abyss. He knows how to walk in the dark, if the occasion should arise; but, thus far, each recess of books in the tier he now inhabits conceals a small bulb that floods a yellow light from above. The switches are hidden in the corners of the outermost shelves. Each night, as he makes his rounds, the light follows him. He never scruples to double back, having flicked one switch on, to click the switch of the preceding recess off. What he loses in time and legwork is more than compensated by the saving of electricity, for it is entirely possible that no one will come to replace the bulbs which have burnt out. The watchman has gone to tend the victims of this terrible disease. No one is spared. Architectural Design is already lost in darkness. It's only a matter of time, perhaps just hours, minutes, before another recess goes. He might, of course, venture out into the foggy streets for a new bulb. There are none in the janitor's closet. He had often gone to look under the basement stairwell, but there were only crates packed with straw, leaning mops, pails full of dirty rags tucked behind the joists. For a younger man it would be less of a problem to replace the bulb. Plenty of ladders about – aluminum rungs painted brown, a ridged mat nailed to each of the narrow steps to guard against an unexpected slippage. But he was old. Staring into his own grave, as he liked to tell his wife before the sickness came. There was no guarantee that any of the shops would be open, including his own, which he hadn't been to for almost a month. When the landlady died he gathered up some provisions, left his wife without a word of fond farewell, and set out for the library. He knew that she would have sent word after him to the old house lost in a mist behind the tree where an animal rocked its nights away in the branches. To the roundhouse, she or her brother would have come to look for him amid sleepers whose pale faces turned toward a blackness beyond the measure of time and space. He has read the histories, all the ancient registers of lore and quackery. And now he stands, beckoning you, making a sign which brooks no glib interpretation. He might, for all the world, be swatting a fly as he waits for you. And when you have reached the top of the clankering spiral – you come up through the hole in an iron grate, without light, your eyes straining toward that lunar mass of gray-white beard – he will conduct you on a long, meandering tour through the darkness (you will not be able to find your way back so easily), at the end of which, two steps down, where he parts the wine-colored drapes of an opera loge, you are seated at a school desk overlooking the black gulf of the library theatre. A legal pad lies on the desk. You will be able to take notes. Nothing more will escape you. There's a pen dangling underneath from a copper chain. A candle at your feet, near a book of matches. It's just thick enough to be fitted into the inkwell. You will stop here in silence with the old man sitting behind you, his armchair turned to the wall as you strike a match, waiting for the curtain to rise. At the top of the pad, above the first of the aqua lines, someone has written: *Hist. of Medicine.*

The pantomime begins under the thatched roof of a hut. Through the opening, snowflakes drift and churn in gusts of wind against the night. You would be expected to note here that the hut is empty, though in the middle of the floor a small fire has recently burned. There remains a heap of glowing embers. A rude flap made of canvas, like a topsail, suddenly unrolls to cover the opening. On it these words, painted in blood, seen by the light of the coals: *Eld Wanderer*. A pickaxe and shovel lean, one crossed on the other, by the wall to the right of the flap. The interior of the hut, whose upper reaches are lost in a conical shadow, bristles with tufts of straw. Curtain.

Behind you the old man goes into his cigarette cough, a gravelly hack which he tries in vain to stifle as he keeps himself amused by making Chinese shadows on the wall, hands clasped to shape the profile of a boxer dog, or a cat. He passes through the whole repertoire of illusive silhouettes. Then, with an unintelligible whisper, he turns toward you, begging the loan of five or six sheets of paper, which can easily be spared since the pad is full. He assures you by a series of emphatic gestures that, should you have need of it, a second pad has been placed inside the desk for your convenience. You raise the lid a crack, just enough to slip your hand through. You can feel it, a pad. Also, a pair of manicure scissors. Both of which you hand to him.

The next scene of the pantomime is staged to represent the night. Without stars. A silver web gleaming under the moon. The sky, completely black, against which the patterns work their geometric transformations. Symmetries intermesh so delicately that a breath might blow them out of shape or cause an unmendable tear. Euclidean and non-Euclidean allures. The threads swerve in a hypothetical sphere beneath the dome of a long-vanished planetarium. Some of the seats are rocking, giving off abrupt squeaks in the dark. An unseen cat meows. Who can tell how far the web continues, beyond the touch of moonlight, into an emptied cosmos? Curtain.

Yellow curlicues seesaw gently to the floor behind you. All this time, while your eyes were turned to the void, the old man has been snipping away, cutting himself a miniature fool's cap with two diminutive windows giving on the inside of the cone. When he turns his head in a certain way the flickering candlelight shines through. A pale square with indistinct borders winks open and shut at the base of the pyramidal shadow. The old man balances an oblong cut-out on the bridge of his nose in such a way that it reappears in silhouette behind the curtained 'window' on the wall of the loge.

The third tableau depicts a winding gallery

cluttered with recently vacated beds. An old château where giant birds of prey walk, tipping the great chandeliers with their downy skulls – vultures, cormorants on holiday from the sea, eagles bald or bristling with a thick head of fur to be smoothed down, almost mechanically, with dampened wing-feathers whenever they catch a glimpse of themselves in the tall mirrors between the gallery windows. Windows opening on a garden overgrown with weeds. The granite fountain, covered by verdigris moss, whose dried-up basins languish under a black sediment, flanked by two armless statues: a faun, with cheeks puffed out, blowing imaginary panpipes; an ancient bronze of the Huntress, her nose eaten away by the pox of time and weather. Both against a cloudless afternoon sky. The mammoth birds are looking for someone. They veil their eyelids against the shafts of window-light. Curtain.

You find a deck of playing cards inside the desk. The old man becomes excited. He drops the pad and scissors on the floor and holds out his hands. He fans the deck into a perfect circle and thrusts it, face down, under your chin. Pick a card. Any card. You draw the eight of spades. He closes the fan, shuffles the deck, shapes it into a tidy stack, and places it carefully between his feet. The old man's mind is wandering. His lips move. A garbled noise escapes his clenched gums in a spray of spittle. Now he turns his face to the wall. A voice comes over the loudspeaker.

– In the fourth and last tableau, the curtain rises on three wax figures. Narcolept, oh Narcolept! It seems as though daylight will never come! They have all but reached the end. One, dragged along the pavement by the other two, his feet cradled in their hands. From offstage, electric fans waft clouds of dry-ice vapor under the lamps. They cannot see the street. The buildings. Across the footlights. Lost.

Before the mask. I must at least go through the motions for as long as the antitoxin can keep me awake. An increase from *0.5ml.* of a 2,000 million per ml. vaccine, given as the first dose. My eyelids are getting heavy. A little while, and yet a while longer, to follow the tick of the clock (corner-of-the-eye hallucinations: livid specks that seem to jump out of the walls before a glance decomposes them), and I will have begun to dream. A window impossible to distance. Somewhere beyond the grimy panes there was, there is, another room, high above Promontory Wall, where he used to spend his time.

1.0ml. Behind the tree, the window. Fog too thick, at first, to cast even a faint reflection in the clouded glass. There, above the porch roof. Slate tiles toward a rusty gutter with the creak of something that rocks in the lower branches, no guttering water, not a sign of rain, though the air was leaden and damp. He waited, stretched out in his bed with the light off, for her footfall on the stair. He must have been down there, the old man, the antiquarian, leaning back, his cane chair squeaking from across the green of the tabletop the night the landlady died. The canaries had gone to sleep. Then, by degrees, the mist swallows up the image with its shifting forms and hidden noises. It comes back to me.

No one dies of the plague. One simply never wakes. When they first began to nod off in the streets, I took them for dead. The fog had not yet settled like a pall over the city.

1.5ml. I could almost see him then, the Ancient Wanderer, walking out among the sleepers. He had thrown a veil over the dark pools of his eyes and went from one to another with lamp in hand, or as an undulating shadow on a wall of water. The narcolept. Their faces turned up to him. In the empty streets. From the stairs I heard him breathing white smoke under the lampposts, down to the docks where keelboats and schooners were no longer even silhouettes. He walked alone to the end of the jetty. Somewhere behind the last crab shanty there was a noise of splashing water as he threw himself into the bay. Once, he came at night to the theatre. No one had cause to recognize him. There, from the edge of the darkness beyond the footlights, he showed his sad face to the actors. He was sitting alone, marking time by sketching a maze of webs around their bodies the night the old man saw him.

The metabolic process remains more or less normal, or normalizes according to the needs of sleep. As long as intravenous nourishment is provided, there is no reason at all why the patient cannot live out his allotted span of life in dreams. Glucose. Tubes to drain off the liquid excretions. Growth of hair and fingernails continues long after the last evacuation of feces. Always, whenever too many of them have been gathered in one place, the overpowering stench of sugared urine.

2.0ml. No effect. To keep myself from dozing off, I reset the alarm every five minutes and tried to picture the moon, which no one has seen for weeks. Before the mask, it was a lot easier to get around my office without knocking drug samples and specimen tubes off the cabinet tops. A full moon every night, large and yellow, under clouds swept by wind across the heavens. Something I'd read in a book. In cutting the eyeholes, I hadn't followed the pattern closely enough. Whenever I ventured out, or if I was called away, I had to be careful of where I walked. A distinct fall-off of light toward the edges. The moon had all but disappeared behind the trees. The silvering that limned the rooftops passed, and I was alone in the streets. They must have come for me before morning. A half moon every night, blood-red, hovers near the horizon. Without stars or light, he waited for her footfall on the stair. He was in his room, stretched out on the mattress. The mattress leaned against the wall, by the window. He had stretched out on the bare springs to keep from turning over. A waning moon each night the map hung under a sheet of glass. Second window. What I can see of the mist from here. The old man is leaving, going down the wooden porch steps. He will not return. He has taken almost everything. By degrees, piece by piece, until nothing remains but the smile in a pool of lunar clouds.

Something more that runs counter to every precept of medicine. Just before the plague of sleep, another nameless disease had taken form. Those who were exposed to the contagion began to dematerialize. They were only half there, as though the accumulating mists had wanted to eat them alive. Since the brain was almost the last organ to deteriorate, the victim was forced to suffer in full consciousness not so much the fading away, but the agonizing process of starvation. At first, the skin became a mass of effervescing dust behind which the internal organs gradually came to appear. Once the victim had reached this stage, a normal examination became impossible. The desire to eat remained; but, as the disease took its course, any solid or liquid nourishment placed in the mouth fell through the floor of the buccal cavity to the ground before it could be swallowed. The internal and external musculature remain in working order almost to the end. Temperature seems to play a crucial rôle in determining the degree of dematerialization of any given part of the body. The pathology, here, is elemental. The tip of the nose, the ears, the toes, and often the buttocks, being anywhere from a quarter to a full two degrees cooler than the normal bodily temperature, tend to retain their density over a longer period of time than those organs and tissue which are normally concealed by the epidermal layer. One way to retard the illness, then, would be to keep the patient constantly exposed to the cold which, however, would almost certainly result in pneumonia or some other complication. The process of dematerialization is such that, once the cutaneous envelope becomes affected, the glands, the musculature, the lymphatic and circulatory systems, being from one to four degrees warmer, will already be too far gone by the time the skin has begun to effervesce, removing all possibility of an early diagnosis. The incubation period is unknown. One cannot be absolutely certain that the dematerialization is in any way connected to the endless sleep.

2.5ml. Another opening. Then the old man must have known something. Before the mask. Before the mist. To imitate the buzz of the flies. It deflates. Without light, the putrid blot spreads over it, driving them mad. From room to empty room. Old, tumbledown crates. Shreds of crumpled waxpaper. And if I dare to close my eyes. Another street. In a strange part of the city. I was with her, upstairs with the one who died. Before the fog. The flies. What passed for a bed, a night table by the curtained window, the faint ellipse of lamplight thrown up on the wall, bending out along the ceiling's end. If this was the room. One without a clock. The ticks. It was much easier then, without the eyeholes or the goggles to fog my vision of a moonless night. Without stars. I could see her leaning in the doorway at the top of a long flight of stairs, where the light had begun to seep through. An opening, yes. I went on tiptoe. Late in the afternoon. In the morning. On a moonless night when the noise of the traffic was not so loud. If I closed my eyes, she would be there in the half-light of her room because my office was too far off, though I would have preferred to have her there, like all the others. Someone must have told him about it the night the landlady died. He must have been told. They would have come for me. Before morning. Upstairs, where so little remained of what we knew. All the rooms were empty, except one. The room with a second window on the mist. A bit more of the warbling. One of my patients sang like a nightingale. Other silhouettes. The flies. And all because the rats, as rats are wont to do, were making a bit of noise on their own, sniffing amid the wood shavings for a crumb of cheese the cat had carried away. In my eyes, the steps. One at a time. Like all the others. A soft tread on rubber mats nailed to the wood. On tiptoe in the night. The flies. The fleas. All that remained to be collected was lost to him. He had relinquished any rights he might have had to the landlady. Old jukebox colors tinged with a fading redness in the air. By way of recompense. Be careful, one of the steps has a loose mat. Squeak by squeak. The odor I could smell, always, on my hands. I have to go now. The police will handle everything, I have to go. Just after five. Scratches. Contusions. Where the lamplight glimmered through. We tried it on the bed. She lay in the shadows. The steps, once more. Not that I'm old. I return, step-shadows dwindling over the tips of my shoes. As I neared the top, she was standing with the light behind her, the one who died, and like the poor landlady after her, not even the unkept promises of the old man could bring her back. I told you to phone the police. Are you deaf? Or he has lost his own shadow beyond the last reaches of the mist. He searches the library alone each night for the words to come to him again. To come while I still have time to remember the ticks, not just a tick at a time. Between which, the notable absence of a clock at the bedside. Standing between the bed and the curtained window. Now, if she wanted to sleep. It would have to be the floor. Soon she would be too far gone. Nothing, at the brink of death, but this coarse-grained shroud of dust sinking through the floorboards, down through the stippled ceiling to the last staircase, and into the bowels of the earth. If they told him about it, he must also know the horror of that night. Her skin took color with the cold, but the bed wouldn't hold her. She sank under my weight through the mattress. Echoes of the wind passing through old piano wire. I found her under the springs, stretched out beneath the hanging wads of dust, in a shadow.

Incipient ticks of metal, enamel to enameled wood, replace the ticking of all the rundown clocks. Still some places left in the gaps between them to find refuge from these hazy lights. Prowl the streets and your shadow comes just short of reaching through the mist; it sweeps across the pavement, stretching out till it is one with the dark at the far end of a wide ellipse that reduplicates itself endlessly on other streets whenever someone, or something, moves off under the burning lamps. And if the light carried only a bit farther, the three of them would be going to meet the doubles of their hulking silhouettes. Now they are far from home, lost beyond any reckoning back. It is useless to hope that anyone would come to answer the door, if they knocked. An upstairs window might open then slam quickly shut again, but often not before some object had come flying down: a flowerpot, shattered into a thousand fragments on the walk, scattering its contents from a mound of loam and upturned roots; or a wrench; or a rubber teething bone, after which they would hear the plaintive yelp of a dog. But no one came down to answer. The first of the three walks on ahead, trying to keep track of the house numbers. All that can be said is that they believe they're headed roughly in the right direction. The numbers are odd and diminishing. Not far behind him, the second figure drags his heels, staggering under the weight of the third – the yellow plume cuts an S with each uncertain step – who rides him pickaback, arms pendent, like an ape in sleep. Now and again, the two who are walking have to step over a man or woman who seems still to be breathing. Even if there were trash bins to dump them in, it would hardly be worth the effort. They might have come across three or four bodies in the last half hour, though no one awake seemed to be about. The prankster was getting heavy. Every so often, when he felt he could bear no more, the second figure would unburden himself on a stoop, if there was a stoop, and stretch out on the bottom step as though he, too, were given up to the sickness. He would not be able to close his eyes. Something of the marble's coldness penetrated his clothing as he watched the fog scud over the lamppost. Once or twice he thought he discerned hitherto secret irregularities, as though the mist were not all of a piece but a mixture of smoky densities that came together like ghosts in the air around the lamp nearest to his lying place. It is probably long past morning. The streets are lost, so quiet now that when the first one's footsteps cease to echo back, his only waking companion thinks he hears the wind breathing like a man, and turns to see if someone else is there behind him. This, to fill in the lacunæ. Thin margins of silence where the first of the three stops walking to check the front of a house, and the third, slumped over the back of the second, pauses before emitting a pebbly rattle. There can be no rest for a while longer. They carry him, stretched between them, by the ankles and under the dangling arms. His coattails drag the concrete, catching the tin ring of a beer can, which adds its scraping noise to all the other muffled echoes that neither 'one' nor 'two' is of a mind to squelch. 'Three,' with closed eyes, head thrown back, the fuzzy tip of the panache stuck to his upper lip, breathes easier, blissfully unaware of the quickening pace of his bearers. A pulsing blot lies just ahead, tinging the mist with an orange glow that gradually sharpens into a neon arrow, pointing down a subterranean stair to a restaurant or an inn or a bar that has, in spite of everything, remained open. A descent into the dark below street level. The scrap of metal sounds a ticking ring on the narrow steps, all the way to the bottom puddle. It foretells their coming to those who listen from within.

Areas of deep shadow. The cool marine obscurity masks a no man's land between the pool tables. Eddies of cigarette smoke drift toward low, canopied lights with the dust. Green baize and clicking balls. They come in by an old spittoon that keeps the inner door ajar, past nearly empty coatracks to a smell of stale tobacco juice and grease-stained leather, arm-tired and out of patience to carry the prankster to the gallery lost in darkness behind a brass rail at the other end of the hall. There, beyond the farthest lamps, a smoke cloud seems to hover above a few dim forms, barely distinguishable, as one's eyes become accustomed to the murk, from the high-backed chairs they sit in. One of the players is making a run of the table. After a pause to take in the new arrivals, he bends to shoot again. The cue ball caroms off three cushions, grazes the five ball with a brittle click, and sends it rolling into a corner pocket. The other player, wooden chair tipped back against the rail, cue cradled between his knees, stares blankly as the two figures make their way among the tables, in and out of the greenish pools of light, their ponderous burden jackknifed so low between them that his knuckles scrape the musty floorboards. One shot before the table empties. The prankster is carried to the rail amid growls of displeasure, blocking all view of the table as his bearers stretch him. One hears the chalked nub tapping the cue ball, a rolling, a muffled bounce, more rolling… then a click. The two dark figures are silhouettes forming an H; the third, their umbilicus. They grope about with their knees, answering the jibes of irate devotees with noncommittal shrugs, in the not-unreasonable hope of finding an empty chair to dump the prankster in for the duration of their visit. The ostrich plume droops and stirs with his breathing as they sit him down, crossing his arms so he won't lean too far back. The game is at a standstill. Everyone has missed the last shot – even the second player, who had turned in his chair at the crucial moment to watch the helpless newcomers fend off blows from the few diehards still awake in the gallery. Now no one but the standing player will ever know how the shot fell. True, there were no more balls on the green bed cloth, but no one had heard anything like the sharp rattle at the end of a brief descent in any of the six pockets. The standing player, on a point of honor, refuses to claim victory. He, too, if they are to believe him, glanced away when he heard the fracas in the gallery. When he looked back, less than a second later, the table was cleared – only the cue ball, rolling to a stop, remained on the felt.

The prankster remained impassive throughout the whole of this discussion. His two friends had quietly slipped off to the manager's cage to scrounge a couple of cups of coffee. The manager pours out his heart, glad to have someone other than the seedy pool enthusiasts to share in his sorrows. Now that interest in the game has waned, he's playing to the gallery as well which, with the exception of the prankster, comprises a somewhat limited but attentive audience. In a glowing stage voice, racked with emotion, he runs through the unabridged catalogue of domestic aggravations. The wife was giving him an ulcer. Since the outbreak of the sickness, she had been afraid of the bed. One morning, having taken the advice of a friend, she brought home two white mice in a cage. The ticks, always the ticks. It was driving him crazy. They liked to stick their tails through the bars and whip the metal feeder all night long, or chase each other in the wheel. Two days of that and he was fit to be tied. So he told her, 'This is it, I can't take no more!' Put a cot here in the back, tucked between the wall and a pile of crates, and now, after twenty-nine years, his worries are over. He's even cut the telephone cord so she can't get through to him. The mails aren't running. She'll never find him in this fog. They say it comes as a sudden black-out. Being tired isn't enough. No way to make the diagnosis. You could go to sleep tonight in your bed and never wake again, without realizing that the rest of your life is a dream. He could be dreaming this pool hall, down to the detail of that smoke-blackened door.

You can't quite make them out. The manager finishes his monologue. Two figures, faces blurred or turned away, lost under their night-hat brims, drain their cups to the dregs and set off once more for the gallery, across a space of darkness and green rectangular islands.

The game resumes. The losing player racks up the balls, carefully lifts off the triangular frame, sets it down on a neighboring table, chalks his cue, bends, lets his mouth hang open, makes two passes at the white sphere (multiple shadows, faint ellipses cast on felt, the shape of a star), then gives it a hard shot into the phalanx of colored balls, which scatter, spinning out in all directions, banking off the cushions before slamming into one another on a field of altering trajectories. The cue ball alone, through some dreadful miscalculation or ineptitude, rolls to a corner pocket and plummets out of sight.

– That's scratch.

But who hears him now? The manager bounds out of his cage like a man possessed. Gesticulating wildly, he overtakes the two figures less than halfway to the gallery and shoves them under the light of the nearest table. They turn out their pockets in the smoke to prove they have nothing but an old button left with which to pay for the coffee. The manager dabs his brow with a wad of Kleenex. It's not enough. Not nearly enough. Catching sight of the yellow plume (it rises and falls in the gallery darkness), he indicates the figure breathing beneath it to the two men, and that this figure might be brought to him to have its pockets searched.

Silence descends. Not a whine, not a murmur as they raise the prankster up, arms crooked around his back, hands clasped under his knees to make the throne of an imaginary palanquin, and bear him over the brass rail into the place of light. They prop him up between them, head slumped and open mouthed, teetering from side to side, oblivious to one and all. The manager unbuttons the prankster's overcoat, emptying his pockets of: some panty shreds garnished with lace, a pair of manicure scissors, seventeen plastic cups, a match, two Swedish meatballs, a variety of hors d'œuvres (slightly damaged), nine plastic forks, a pocket flashlight, three cocktail napkins (one with the dried imprint of a ring), a penknife (containing bottle opener, nail file/emery board, skeleton key, and four blades of various size), a hickory duck-call, half a railroad tie with a dangerously splintered edge, a tube of airplane glue, a small screwdriver, some gravel, a handful of grass, two dog biscuits (half eaten), a stuffed canary, the cracked hand of a porcelain figurine (three fingers missing), one hypodermic syringe (empty, the needle broken off), seven pieces of colored chalk.

To make an end, the manager plucks the yellow plume from the prankster's hair, raises his pudgy hand above the table, opens his fingers, and lets it drop, a lentitudinous meander against the dark, rocking on a cushion of air.

The shadow I had lost in the streets could not have been as far off as the registrar had led me to believe the Omega was. Time passed. The lines crumbled into heaps of confetti that blew away when I slipped the map from its frame and held it to the open window.

Under the blank marquee. The ticket booth stood concealed in an octagonal pillar of imitation marble whose blue glaze was dulled by a layer of soot, its window facing the entrance. No one there. Through the pane, behind its metal air vent, I could dimly see the calendar print of a wintry forest hanging on the wall, a wooden stool, an empty cash drawer to the right of the ticket slots. The telephone receiver was off the hook. It must have been dangling below. Silent, out of sight. The last one to inhabit the booth had not bothered to draw the curtain over the window or to empty the ashtray, which held a half-smoked cigarette with lipstick traces. By one of the entrance doors a poster in a cracked-glass frame depicted, in garish colors, a statuesque blonde clad in a negligée, the outline of her body a vague silhouette behind a muslin window. Farther into the room, a man was standing. His face, dull yet oddly menacing, lit from the side by a weak night-lamp near an unmade bed. I'd expected a line of ambulances (at least a paddy wagon or two) to be parked by the curb.

There was nothing. The mist, which hid less from me than the shadow I had lost, shrouded the opposite walk so completely that, for all one could tell, only abandoned excavations were to be found there, or vast asphalt lots jammed with cars that were no longer allowed on the streets, some perhaps holding those who had gone to sleep behind the wheel and been left to rot. I hadn't seen a car all morning, not even close within the precincts of the roundhouse. What kept me out there? Obviously another dreadful miscalculation. With no landmarks to follow, I had hoped for luck enough to stumble on the Omega theatre. This couldn't have been the one. The letters, lost in fog. Markings of where the sleepers were kept. I tried the door by the poster. It wouldn't budge. Then the one next to it. My hands on the iron crossbar, pushing through to the darkness.

The foyer led up a carpeted ramp between two ranks of posts strung together by velveteen ropes. My reflection leapt from one wall panel to the next. A mottled blur, caged on both sides by netlike veins, seemed to flit through dim pools of yellow light across mirrors that reproduced its shrinking image to infinity down their endless corridors. The stale odor of popcorn and threadbare upholstery almost reached me. I made my way past humming soda machines – luminous buttons, glittering cupwells in shadow – to the vacated counter which stood in a nook by the ingress, its shelves emptied of all but a few gum-drop boxes, some scattered candy bars and a bag of half-crushed salted peanuts. I went slowly, softly, after having trod so many unfamiliar pavements. Tufted swirls of orange and black flowers muffled my footsteps in a purple ground. Another more muted hum began to filter from the wormy umbra beyond the counter and the soft-drink machines. I slipped through the archway, turned right down a narrow passage, groping the inside wall for vague glimmers, and came at last to a water cooler in an alcove of mosaic tile. The light shifted over it in irregular pulses, from silver to black. A section of partition had been taken down behind the last row of seats, giving an odd view of the screen through a maze of silhouetted tubes and flickering bottles that left evansecent afterimages as my eyes moved over them. The hum I had caught faintly in the lobby was the dry sound of all those open mouths, those slumping heads with phosphenescing numbers, dashes of glowing paint, scattered over the middle section of seats in a dense clutter of hanging glucose bottles. Puddles of sick-sweet urine trickled out of the occupied rows into the aisle, where the floor took a sudden tilt, and widened the stains in the carpeting. The screen fluttered its half-light onto the sleeping audience, throwing off black-and-white images of what may or may not have been scenes from the movie advertised. Facing the sleepers, alone at its desk, in the limbo between the first row of vacant seats and the black matting under the screen, an egg-shaped head, completely bald, lit from beneath by a lamp that cast a liquid glimmer in its eyes, seemed to beckon me. Above the head, an old car with spoked tires and a running board sped off down a winding country road, crossed by shadows that writhed in a cloud of dust.

The head was reading, arms folded on the pages of a dog-eared magazine, bending to decipher the last few lines in the haze of print. This was the caretaker. There were no other guards in the theatre. For all one knew, the projection booth had been left untended between reels. The sound was off. The caretaker closed his magazine, rolled it up, tossed it into an otherwise empty wastebasket, and rubbed his bleary eyes with ink-smudged fingers, speaking in a loud voice whose echoes rang off the distant walls to the corners of the balcony, at which he stared from time to time, as though preoccupied with the contrast of that wide, black recess to the light-box which sucked the dust in a beam through its little window.

– Please. No need to stand on ceremony. We've still got plenty of seats left, but I wouldn't want to predict how long that'll last. I was told to expect you.

He let out a booming yawn which died all around us, shaking his head rapidly like a dog trying to dry itself, as he began to rummage through his litter of papers, whistling under his breath. His eyes fell on the luminous hands of the desk clock.

– Shit. Half an hour, is it? Then the alarm goes off and the two of us will have to start replacing the bottles.

The two of us?

– Oh! Don't get the wrong idea. I was talking about the man up there. He likes to sit it out in the balcony between reels. Can't take the heat in the booth. Can't say as I blame him, either. It's hell up there. Hope he remembers to set another one going before he has to come down. We could have used a blank white projection, you know, but it's too hard on the eyes. And since we were told to keep the electrical expenses to a minimum, we had to settle for this old movie. Never seen the thing all the way through, myself. It was either that or shut off the coke machines. Can I get you something? It's free. We do get some concessions.

He opened one of the drawers and pulled out a dime fixed to the loop end of a copper wire.

– You could probably use a cold drink after all that walking. I know *I* can. How about it? Orange? Grape?

Can we get on with it?

– Yes. Well, I'm working overtime. It had been my understanding that the registrar was to arrive here three hours ago. But I could always be mistaken. *He's* the one who handles all the paperwork and tends to the fine details. What could have detained him? No matter. Since you're here, you'll want to look things over. Isn't very much to see besides this, really. Except the projection booth. We could go up there now, while there's still time. The screen makes it easier to see if anyone sneaks in and tries to have his way – you get my meaning? – with one of the women. The roundhouse was full of bodies, but there will be more than enough left over to seat this place to capacity. It's merely a question of time. There aren't enough of us left to police them properly, hence the delays. The interminable delays. The screen is only a fair deterrent without guards. Please make note of that. Tell them that, under present conditions, I cannot accept responsibility for any foul-ups that may have occurred in the past, or will occur in the future. Do you know what we're up against here? The problem of false or 'pantomime' sleepers is an ever-present one, and has plagued our operations from the very beginning. Men and women alike! But mostly men. They usually have the presence of mind to strike an attitude of complete oblivion during the search-and-examination procedure. We've even had to resort to tickling all the new arrivals, and managed to catch a few of them out that way. But there are always some with more than the usual amount of self-control who get through. They're not above taking small doses of a soporific to help them along! Later, they wake up here in one of the seats with a tube in their arm and a number painted on their head. Then, when I'm looking the other way, or if I go to the can – what am I supposed to do, anyway, isn't there enough muck on the floor here without my adding to it? – the pantomime sleeper crawls from row to row, on the prowl. I tell you, it's disgusting! I caught one raping a woman in one of the back rows, right over there. He'd stuck his IV into the armrest, taken off his jacket and folded it in such a way that, from a distance, it looked like just another slumped-over head. What finally gave him away is that he got so worked up his foot tipped over the woman's rack: bottle, tube, and all. Hell of a mess. Others are more discreet. If ever we find an empty seat between two occupied ones, we know something's up. Often the crime is committed and the culprit is long gone when we come on the victim. That's off the record! Don't say anything. It's one hell of a lot easier to get away with it here than it was at the roundhouse. The rows of seats and all these goddamn tubes make excellent camouflage. But I ask you, where are we going to find another roundhouse? They say at least two other theatres have been commandeered for future use. The owners were glad to receive a fee for them. No one goes out anymore for fear of dropping in the streets. Just wait a while longer. We'll have this place filled, standing-room only! Soon, when the space runs out, we'll have to start burning them alive in the streets! That's the rumor, keep it under your… hat. Identification has always been something of a problem. About a third of the sleepers have remained anonymous. I'm not talking about the derelicts and the 'old horns' we pick up in the gutters. Pantomime, pantomime. But that doesn't explain all the cases of sexual molestation. We've been finding plenty of women, just in the last few days, without a stitch on. It's being blamed on the one they call the Narcolept. But one man? No, I can't believe it! There must be pantomime sleepers that haven't yet been taken into account. One man couldn't possibly be in so many places in so short an interval of time! Certainly there are lacunæ. Unaccountable gaps that must forever remain a mystery to us.

But what if someone dies?

– No one has died.

Maybe the father wasn't putting on an act after all.

– What?

They would have come too far already, the three like specters now at the alley's end against a mound of rubble. Without bringing them anywhere nearer the roundhouse, these pits cut deep wells in the gloom, threatening to open chasms under their feet. Oceanic dins the fog can never reach. The dream of the one they drag behind them over the broken stones. His coattails fan out to put a mangy thickness of herringbone between the back of his head and the earth, two flaps like broad, rectangular wings on which he takes the pose of a drowned man seen from below. He comes up one last time, floats on the surface, his face to the murky depths, scudding across the sun with the rest of the shipwrecked debris. They've crooked their arms around his ankles to let him drift 'against the current' as they walk, with no more sensation than what he feels or listens to in sleep.

Words never heard, where half-made changes in a dense wind break the mist into wreaths on a pyre of sifted ash. Old saw-toothed blades, frames for pictures and absent mirrors. Claw-footed table legs, emerging from the ruins, suggest the monstrous insect buried beneath.

He's lighter than he would have been with his load of artifacts and the lost panache. Here and there, through the shell of a gutted casement, the two upright figures peer out on a void. Gray on gray, without relief. Fine powdery snippets gather in plumes, dissolving curlicues around their heads as they drag their burden along, having made this useless detour to search the rubble for a wheelbar-row that might have been left behind. All to make it less hard. A simple thing. To remain lost now that they had stopped looking for numbers. The garbage bins are full to overflowing, the air heavy with an odor of waste and black incinerator fumes, coughed up into the day-night to warm the bones of those who live in fear of a knock on the door or a stranger's tread echoing up the stairwell. Clues to their fading destination.

Through nyctalopic caverns behind his lidded eyes, all that went into the making of his landscape – shreds of other shadowy streets, a promise of refuge withheld from the two who bear him away to the ancient mausoleum. They will have come this far, he muses, only because no one has died. The figure known to him, and to the others, appears at its window in silhouette, looking out through a hoary vapor to where the tree rocks, cumbered with some laughing animal. This dream they imagine for him, the one they turn to pull over the last few shards, before hazy lampposts reappear with a strip of pavement, leaving the mound of risen earth to darkness.

The father watches them from his window, behind a film of shrinking condensation. His eyes are weak. For him they are only two men lugging a sack or a long bundle – he can't quite make it out – into the light-pool below. Both of them happen to look up at the same moment, to catch sight of him drawing back into the room with one hand raised above his head as if to swat a fly, and take this for an omen. One steers their inanimate cargo toward the foot of the stoop. The other goes up to try the door.

With just a dim lamp to light his way to the sofa (the old man has forgotten to wind the mantelpiece clock), the window dwindles to a clouded patch fluttering in the wormy black of the wall. Without having to mumble, even to himself, he knows where the couch is and doesn't need to turn around after he switches off the lamp. His palms are dry, his fingers soft and lifeless. He lies down. Gradually. The ceiling appears. Dimly to his eyes. Through a horde of specks.

Now he will be alone.

MY MOTHER

Jamaica Kincaid

Jamaica Kincaid (1949–) is a critically acclaimed Caribbean writer living in the US. Her stories have appeared in the *Paris Review*, *Rolling Stone*, and *The New Yorker* as well as the anthology *The New Gothic* (1990). She has won the Lannan Literary Award for Fiction, the Prix Femina Étranger, the Anisfield-Wolf Book Award, the Morton Dauwen Zabel Award and the Lila Wallace-*Reader's Digest* Award, among others. 'My Mother' (1978) appeared in her first collection, *At the Bottom of the River*. Her evocative fiction often features strong maternal characters as well as colonial and post-colonial themes. 'My Mother' is a phantasmagorical take on the weird through the lens of transformation.

Immediately on wishing my mother dead and seeing the pain it caused her, I was sorry and cried so many tears that all the earth around me was drenched. Standing before my mother, I begged her forgiveness, and I begged so earnestly that she took pity on me, kissing my face and placing my head on her bosom to rest. Placing her arms around me, she drew my head closer and closer to her bosom, until finally I suffocated. I lay on her bosom, breathless, for a time uncountable, until one day, for a reason she has kept to herself, she shook me out and stood me under a tree and I started to breathe again. I cast a sharp glance at her and said to myself, 'So.' Instantly I grew my own bosoms, small mounds at first, leaving a small, soft place between them, where, if ever necessary, I could rest my own head. Between my mother and me now were the tears I had cried, and I gathered up some stones and banked them in so that they formed a small pond. The water in the pond was thick and black and poisonous, so that only unnamable invertebrates could live in it. My mother and I now watched each other carefully, always making sure to shower the other with words and deeds of love and affection.

I was sitting on my mother's bed trying to get a good look at myself. It was a large bed and it stood in the middle of a large, completely dark room. The room was completely dark because all the windows had been boarded up and all the crevices stuffed with black cloth. My mother lit some candles and the room burst into a pink-like, yellow-like glow. Looming over us, much larger than ourselves, were our shadows. We sat mesmerized because our shadows had made a place between themselves, as if they were making room for someone else. Nothing filled up the space between them, and the shadow of my mother sighed. The shadow of my mother danced around the room to a tune that my own shadow sang, and then they stopped. All along, our shadows had grown thick and thin, long and short, had fallen at every angle, as if they were controlled by the light of day. Suddenly my mother got up and blew out the candles and our shadows vanished. I continued to sit on the bed, trying to get a good look at myself.

My mother removed her clothes and covered thoroughly her skin with a thick gold-colored oil, which had recently been rendered in a hot pan from the livers of reptiles with pouched throats. She grew plates of metal-colored scales on her back, and light, when it collided with this surface, would shatter and

SANDKINGS

George R. R. Martin

George R. R. Martin (1948–) is an American writer of fantasy and science fiction best-known for his Song of Ice and Fire epic fantasy series, which contains its share of weird supernatural elements. According to myth, he began his career selling monster stories to other neighborhood children for pennies. Subsequent work has won many awards, including the Hugo and World Fantasy awards. Despite readers' strong association of Martin with fantasy fiction, Martin's devotion to the horror field has been lifelong. Classics in this mode from Martin include the truly terrifying 'Nightflyers' (1980), the disquieting 'The Pear-Shaped Man' (1987), and the stunningly weird science fiction story reprinted herein, 'Sandkings' (1979), winner of both the Hugo and Nebula awards.

Simon Kress lived alone in a sprawling manor house among the dry, rocky hills fifty kilometers from the city. So, when he was called away unexpectedly on business, he had no neighbors he could conveniently impose on to take his pets. The carrion hawk was no problem; it roosted in the unused belfry and customarily fed itself anyway. The shambler Kress simply shooed outside and left to fend for itself; the little monster would gorge on slugs and birds and rockjocks. But the fish tank, stocked with genuine Earth piranha, posed a difficulty. Kress finally just threw a haunch of beef into the huge tank. The piranha could always eat each other if he were detained longer than expected. They'd done it before. It amused him.

Unfortunately, he was detained *much* longer than expected this time. When he finally returned, all the fish were dead. So was the carrion hawk. The shambler had climbed up to the belfry and eaten it. Simon Kress was vexed.

The next day he flew his skimmer to Asgard, a journey of some two hundred kilometers. Asgard was Baldur's largest city and boasted the oldest and largest starport as well. Kress liked to impress his friends with animals that were unusual, entertaining, and expensive; Asgard was the place to buy them.

This time, though, he had poor luck. Xenopets had closed its doors, t'Etherane the Petseller tried to foist another carrion hawk off on him, and Strange Waters offered nothing more exotic than piranha, glow-sharks, and spider squids. Kress had had all those; he wanted something new.

Near dusk, he found himself walking down the Rainbow Boulevard, looking for places he had not patronized before. So close to the starport, the street was lined by importers' marts. The big corporate emporiums had impressive long windows, where rare and costly alien artifacts reposed on felt cushions against dark drapes that made the interiors of the stores a mystery. Between them were the junk shops – narrow, nasty little places whose display areas were crammed with all manner of offworld bric-a-brac. Kress tried both kinds of shop, with equal dissatisfaction.

Then he came across a store that was different.

It was quite close to the port. Kress had never been there before. The shop occupied a small, single-story building of moderate size, set between a euphoria bar and a temple-brothel of the Secret Sisterhood. Down this far, the Rainbow Boulevard grew tacky. The shop itself was unusual. Arresting.

The windows were full of mist; now a pale red, now the gray of true fog, now sparkling and golden. The mist swirled and eddied and glowed faintly from within. Kress glimpsed objects in the window – machines, pieces of art, other things he could not recognize – but he could not get a good look at any of them. The mists flowed sensuously around them, displaying a bit of first one thing and then another, then cloaking all. It was intriguing.

As he watched, the mist began to form letters. One word at a time. Kress stood and read:

WO. AND. SHADE. IMPORTERS.
ARTIFACTS. ART. LIFEFORMS. AND. MISC.

The letters stopped. Through the fog, Kress saw something moving. That was enough for him, that and the word 'Lifeforms' in their advertisement. He swept his walking cloak over his shoulder and entered the store.

Inside, Kress felt disoriented. The interior seemed vast, much larger than he would have guessed from the relatively modest frontage. It was dimly lit, peaceful. The ceiling was a starscape, complete with spiral nebulae, very dark and realistic, very nice. The counters all shone faintly, the better to display the merchandise within. The aisles were carpeted with ground fog. In places, it came almost to his knees and swirled about his feet as he walked.

'Can I help you?'

She seemed almost to have risen from the fog. Tall and gaunt and pale, she wore a practical gray jumpsuit and a strange little cap that rested well back on her head.

'Are you Wo or Shade?' Kress asked. 'Or only sales help?'

'Jala Wo, ready to serve you,' she replied. 'Shade does not see customers. We have no sales help.'

'You have quite a large establishment,' Kress said. 'Odd that I have never heard of you before.'

'We have only just opened this shop on Baldur,' the woman said. 'We have franchises on a number of other worlds, however. What can I sell you? Art, perhaps? You have the look of a collector. We have some fine Nor T'alush crystal carvings.'

'No,' Simon Kress said. 'I own all the crystal carvings I desire. I came to see about a pet.'

'A lifeform?'

'Yes.'

'Alien?'

'Of course.'

'We have a mimic in stock. From Celia's World. A clever little simian. Not only will it learn to speak, but eventually it will mimic your voice, inflections, gestures, even facial expressions.'

'Cute,' said Kress. 'And common. I have no use for either, Wo. I want something exotic. Unusual. And not cute. I detest cute animals. At the moment I own a shambler. Imported from Cotho, at no mean expense. From time to time I feed him a litter of unwanted kittens. That is what I think of *cute*. Do I make myself understood?'

Wo smiled enigmatically. 'Have you ever owned an animal that worshipped you?' she asked.

Kress grinned. 'Oh, now and again. But I don't require worship, Wo. Just entertainment.'

'You misunderstood me,' Wo said, still wearing her strange smile. 'I meant worship literally.'

'What are you talking about?'

'I think I have just the thing for you,' Wo said. 'Follow me.'

She led Kress between the radiant counters and down a long, fog-shrouded aisle beneath false starlight. They passed through a wall of mist into another section of the store, and stopped before a large plastic tank. An aquarium, thought Kress.

Wo beckoned. He stepped closer and saw that he was wrong. It was a terrarium. Within lay a miniature desert about two meters square. Pale and bleached scarlet by wan red light. Rocks: basalt and quartz and granite. In each corner of the tank stood a castle.

Kress blinked, and peered, and corrected himself; actually only three castles stood. The fourth leaned; a crumbled, broken ruin. The other three were crude but intact, carved of stone and sand. Over their battlements and through their rounded porticoes, tiny creatures climbed and scrambled. Kress pressed his face against the plastic. 'Insects?' he asked.

'No,' Wo replied. 'A much more complex life-form. More intelligent as well. Considerably smarter than your shambler. They are called sandkings.'

'Insects,' Kress said, drawing back from the tank. 'I don't care how complex they are.' He frowned. 'And kindly don't try to gull me with this talk of intelligence. These things are far too small to have anything but the most rudimentary brains.'

'They share hiveminds,' Wo said. 'Castle minds, in this case. There are only three organisms in the tank, actually. The fourth died. You see how her castle has fallen.'

Kress looked back at the tank. 'Hiveminds, eh? Interesting.' He frowned again. 'Still, it is only an oversized ant farm. I'd hoped for something better.'

'They fight wars.'

'Wars? Hmmm.' Kress looked again.

'Note the colors, if you will,' Wo told him. She pointed to the creatures that swarmed over the nearest castle. One was scrabbling at the tank wall. Kress studied it. It still looked like an insect to his eyes. Barely as long as his fingernail, six-limbed, with six tiny eyes set all around its body. A wicked set of mandibles clacked visibly, while two long, fine antennae wove patterns in the air. Antennae, mandibles, eyes, and legs were sooty black, but the dominant color was the burnt orange of its armor plating. 'It's an insect,' Kress repeated.

'It is not an insect,' Wo insisted calmly. 'The armored exoskeleton is shed when the sandking grows larger. *If* it grows larger. In a tank this size, it won't.' She took Kress by the elbow and led him around the tank to the next castle. 'Look at the colors here.'

He did. They were different. Here the sandkings had bright red armor; antennae, mandibles, eyes, and legs were yellow. Kress glanced across the tank. The denizens of the third live castle were off-white, with red trim. 'Hmmm,' he said.

'They war, as I said,' Wo told him. 'They even have truces and alliances. It was an alliance that destroyed the fourth castle in this tank. The blacks were getting too numerous, so the others joined forces to destroy them.'

Kress remained unconvinced. 'Amusing, no doubt. But insects fight wars too.'

'Insects do not worship,' Wo said.

'Eh?'

Wo smiled and pointed at the castle. Kress stared. A face had been carved into the wall of the highest tower. He recognized it. It was Jala Wo's face. 'How… ?'

'I projected a hologram of my face into the tank, kept it there for a few days. The face of god, you see? I feed them; I am always close. The sandkings have a rudimentary psionic sense. Proximity telepathy. They sense me, and worship me by using my face to decorate their buildings. All the castles have them, see.' They did.

On the castle, the face of Jala Wo was serene and peaceful, and very lifelike. Kress marveled at the workmanship. 'How do they do it?'

'The foremost legs double as arms. They even have fingers of a sort; three small, flexible tendrils. And they cooperate well, both in building and in battle. Remember, all the mobiles of one color share a single mind.'

'Tell me more,' Kress said.

Wo smiled. 'The maw lives in the castle. Maw is my name for her. A pun, if you will; the thing is mother and stomach both. Female, large as your fist, immobile. Actually, sandking is a bit of a misnomer. The mobiles are peasants and warriors, the real ruler is a queen. But that analogy is faulty as well. Considered as a whole, each castle is a single hermaphroditic creature.'

'What do they eat?'

'The mobiles eat pap – predigested food obtained inside the castle. They get it from the maw after she has worked on it for several days. Their stomachs can't handle anything else, so if the maw dies, they soon die as well. The maw… the maw eats anything. You'll have no special expense there. Table scraps will do excellently.'

'Live food?' Kress asked.

Wo shrugged. 'Each maw eats mobiles from the other castles, yes.'

'I am intrigued,' he admitted. 'If only they weren't so small.'

'Yours can be larger. These sandkings are small because their tank is small. They seem to limit their growth to fit available space. If I moved these to a larger tank, they'd start growing again.'

'Hmmmm. My piranha tank is twice this size, and vacant. It could be cleaned out, filled with sand... '

'Wo and Shade would take care of the installation. It would be our pleasure.'

'Of course,' said Kress, 'I would expect four intact castles.'

'Certainly,' Wo said.

They began to haggle about the price.

Three days later Jala Wo arrived at Simon Kress' estate, with dormant sandkings and a work crew to take charge of the installation. Wo's assistants were aliens unlike any Kress was familiar with – squat, broad bipeds with four arms and bulging, multifaceted eyes. Their skin was thick and leathery, twisted into horns and spines and protrusions at odd spots upon their bodies. But they were very strong, and good workers. Wo ordered them about in a musical tongue that Kress had never heard.

In a day it was done. They moved his piranha tank to the center of his spacious living room, arranged couches on either side of it for better viewing, scrubbed it clean, and filled it two-thirds of the way up with sand and rock. Then they installed a special lighting system, both to provide the dim red illumination the sandkings preferred and to project holographic images into the tank. On top they mounted a sturdy plastic cover, with a feeder mechanism built in. 'This way you can feed your sandkings without removing the top of the tank,' Wo explained. 'You would not want to take any chances on the mobiles escaping.'

The cover also included climate control devices, to condense just the right amount of moisture from the air. 'You want it dry, but not too dry,' Wo said.

Finally one of the four-armed workers climbed into the tank and dug deep pits in the four corners. One of his companions handed the dormant maws over to him, removing them one by one from their frosted cryonic traveling cases. They were nothing to look at. Kress decided they resembled nothing so much as a mottled, half-spoiled chunk of raw meat. With a mouth.

The alien buried them, one in each corner of the tank. Then they sealed it all up and took their leave.

'The heat will bring the maws out of dormancy,' Wo said. 'In less than a week, mobiles will begin to hatch and burrow to the surface. Be certain to give them plenty of food. They will need all their strength until they are well established. I would estimate that you will have castles rising in about three weeks.'

'And my face? When will they carve my face?'

'Turn on the hologram after about a month,' she advised him. 'And be patient. If you have any questions, please call. Wo and Shade are at your service.' She bowed and left.

Kress wandered back to the tank and lit a joystick. The desert was still and empty. He drummed his fingers impatiently against the plastic, and frowned.

On the fourth day, Kress thought he glimpsed motion beneath the sand, subtle subterranean stirrings.

On the fifth day, he saw his first mobile, a lone white.

On the sixth day, he counted a dozen of them, whites and reds and blacks. The oranges were tardy. He cycled through a bowl of half-decayed table scraps. The mobiles sensed it at once, rushed to it, and began to drag pieces back to their respective corners. Each color group was very organized. They did not fight. Kress was a bit disappointed, but he decided to give them time.

The oranges made their appearance on the eighth day. By then the other sandkings had begun to carry small stones and erect crude fortifications. They still did not war. At the moment they were only half the size of those he had seen at Wo and Shade's, but Kress thought they were growing rapidly.

The castles began to rise midway through the second week. Organized battalions of mobiles dragged heavy chunks of sandstone and granite to their corners, where other mobiles were pushing sand into place with mandibles and tendrils. Kress had purchased a pair of magnifying goggles so he could watch them work, wherever they might go in the tank. He wandered around and around the tall plastic walls, observing. It was fascinating. The castles were a bit plainer than Kress would have liked, but he had an idea about that. The next day he cycled through some obsidian and flakes of colored glass along with the food. Within hours, they had been incorporated into the castle walls.

The black castle was the first completed, followed by the white and red fortresses. The oranges were last, as usual. Kress took his meals into the living room and ate seated on the couch, so he could watch. He expected the first war to break out any hour now.

He was disappointed. Days passed; the castles grew taller and more grand, and Kress seldom left the tank except to attend to his sanitary needs and answer critical business calls. But the sandkings did not war. He was getting upset.

Finally, he stopped feeding them.

Two days after the table scraps had ceased to fall from their desert sky, four black mobiles surrounded an orange and dragged it back to their maw. They maimed it first, ripping off its mandibles and antennae and limbs, and carried it through the shadowed main gate of their miniature castle. It never emerged. Within an hour, more than forty orange mobiles marched across the sand and attacked the blacks' corner. They were outnumbered by the blacks that came rushing up from the depths. When the fighting was over, the attackers had been slaughtered. The dead and dying were taken down to feed the black maw.

Kress, delighted, congratulated himself on his genius.

When he put food into the tank the following day, a three-cornered battle broke out over its possession. The whites were the big winners. After that, war followed war.

Almost a month to the day after Jala Wo had delivered the sandkings, Kress turned on the hologram projector, and his face materialized in the tank. It turned, slowly, around and around so his gaze fell on all four castles equally. Kress thought it rather a good likeness – it had his impish grin, wide mouth, full cheeks. His blue eyes sparkled, his gray hair was carefully arrayed in a fashionable sidesweep, his eye-brows were thin and sophisticated.

Soon enough, the sandkings set to work. Kress fed them lavishly while his image beamed down at them from their sky. Temporarily, the wars stopped. All activity was directed towards worship.

His face emerged on the castle walls.

At first all four carvings looked alike to him, but as the work continued and Kress studied the reproductions, he began to detect subtle differences in technique and execution. The reds were the most creative, using tiny flakes of slate to put the gray in his hair. The white idol seemed young and mischievous to him, while the face shaped by the blacks – although virtually the same, line for line – struck him as wise and beneficent. The orange sandkings, as ever, were last and least. The wars had not gone well for them, and their castle was sad compared to the others. The image they carved was crude and cartoonish, and they seemed to intend to leave it that way. When they stopped work on the face, Kress grew quite piqued with them, but there was really nothing he could do.

When all the sandkings had finished their Kress-faces, he turned off the hologram and decided that it was time to have a party. His friends would be impressed. He could even stage a war for them, he thought. Humming happily to himself, he began to draw up a guest list.

The party was a wild success.

Kress invited thirty people: a handful of close friends who shared his amusements, a few former lovers, and a collection of business and social rivals who could not afford to ignore his summons. He knew some of them would be discomfited and even offended by his sandkings. He counted on it. Simon Kress customarily considered his parties a failure unless at least one guest walked out in high dudgeon.

On impulse he added Jala Wo's name to his list. 'Bring Shade if you like,' he added when dictating her invitation.

Her acceptance surprised him just a bit. 'Shade, alas, will be unable to attend. He does not go to social functions,' Wo added. 'As for myself, I look forward to the chance to see how your sandkings are doing.'

Kress ordered them up a sumptuous meal. And when at last the conversation had died down, and most of his guests had gotten silly on wine and joysticks, he shocked them by personally scraping their table leavings into a large bowl. 'Come, all of you,' he told them. 'I want to introduce you to my newest pets.' Carrying the bowl, he conducted them into his living room.

The sandkings lived up to his fondest expectations. He had starved them for two days in preparation, and they were in a fighting mood. While the guests ringed the tank, looking through the magnifying glasses Kress had thoughtfully provided, the sandkings waged a glorious battle over the scraps. He counted almost sixty dead mobiles when the struggle was over. The reds and whites, who had recently formed an alliance, emerged with most of the food.

'Kress, you're disgusting,' Cath m'Lane told him. She had lived with him for a short time two years before, until her soppy sentimentality almost drove him mad. 'I was a fool to come back here. I thought perhaps you'd changed, wanted to apologize.' She had never forgiven him for the time his shambler had eaten an excessively cute puppy of which she had been fond. 'Don't *ever* invite me here again, Simon.' She strode out, accompanied by her current lover and a chorus of laughter.

His other guests were full of questions.

Where did the sandkings come from? they wanted to know. 'From Wo and Shade, Importers,' he replied, with a polite gesture towards Jala Wo, who had remained quiet and apart through most of the evening.

Why did they decorate their castles with his likeness? 'Because I am the source of all good things. Surely you know that?' That brought a round of chuckles.

Will they fight again? 'Of course, but not tonight. Don't worry. There will be other parties.'

Jad Rakkis, who was an amateur xenologist, began talking about other social insects and the wars they fought. 'These sandkings are amusing, but nothing really. You ought to read about Terran soldier ants, for instance.'

'Sandkings are not insects,' Jala Wo said sharply, but Jad was off and running, and no one paid her the slightest attention. Kress smiled at her and shrugged.

Malada Blane suggested a betting pool the next time they got together to watch a war, and everyone was taken with the idea. An animated discussion about rules and odds ensued. It lasted for almost an hour. Finally the guests began to take their leave.

Jala Wo was the last to depart. 'So,' Kress said to her when they were alone, 'it appears my sandkings are a hit.'

'They are doing well,' Wo said. 'Already they are larger than my own.'

'Yes,' Kress said, 'except for the oranges.'

'I had noticed that,' Wo replied. 'They seem few in number, and their castle is shabby.'

'Well, someone must lose,' Kress said. 'The oranges were late to emerge and get established. They have suffered for it.'

'Pardon,' said Wo, 'but might I ask if you are feeding your sandkings sufficiently?'

Kress shrugged. 'They diet from time to time. It makes them fiercer.'

She frowned. 'There is no need to starve them. Let them war in their own time, for their own reasons. It is their nature, and you will witness conflicts that are delightfully subtle and complex. The constant war brought on by hunger is artless and degrading.'

Simon Kress repaid Wo's frown with interest. 'You are in my house, Wo, and here I am the judge of what is degrading. I fed the sandkings as you advised, and they did not fight.'

'You must have patience.'

'No,' Kress said. 'I am their master and their god, after all. Why should I wait on their impulses? They did not war often enough to suit me. I corrected the situation.'

'I see,' said Wo. 'I will discuss the matter with Shade.'

'It is none of your concern, or his,' Kress snapped.

'I must bid you good night, then,' Wo said with resignation. But as she slipped into her coat to depart, she fixed him with a final disapproving stare. 'Look to your faces, Simon Kress,' she warned him. 'Look to your faces.'

Puzzled, he wandered back to the tank and stared at the castles after she had taken her departure. His faces were still there, as ever. Except – he snatched up his magnifying goggles and slipped them on. Even then it was hard to make out. But it seemed to him that the expression on the face of his images had changed slightly, that his smile was somehow twisted so that it seemed a touch malicious. But it was a very subtle change, if it was a change at all. Kress finally put it down to his suggestibility, and resolved not to invite Jala Wo to any more of his gatherings.

Over the next few months, Kress and about a dozen of his favorites got together weekly for what he liked to call his 'war games.' Now that his initial fascination with the sandkings was past, Kress spent less time around his tank and more on his business affairs and his social life, but he still enjoyed having a few friends over for a war or two. He kept the combatants sharp on a constant edge of hunger. It had severe effects on the orange sandkings, who dwindled visibly until Kress began to wonder if their maw was dead. But the others did well enough.

Sometimes at night, when he could not sleep, Kress would take a bottle of wine into the darkened living room, where the red gloom of his miniature desert was the only light. He would drink and watch for hours, alone. There was usually a fight going on somewhere, and when there was not he could easily start one by dropping in some small morsel of food.

They took to betting on the weekly battles, as Malada Blane had suggested. Kress won a good amount by betting on the whites, who had become the most powerful and numerous colony in the tank, with the grandest castle. One week he slid the corner of the tank top aside, and dropped the food close to the white castle instead of on the central battleground as usual, so that the others had to attack the whites in their stronghold to get any food at all. They tried. The whites were brilliant in defense. Kress won a hundred standards from Jad Rakkis.

Rakkis, in fact, lost heavily on the sandkings almost every week. He pretended to a vast knowledge of them and their ways, claiming that he had studied them after the first party, but he had no luck when it came to placing his bets. Kress suspected that Jad's claims were empty boasting. He had tried to study the sandkings a bit himself, in a moment of idle curiosity, tying in to the library to find out to what world his pets were native. But there was no listing for them. He wanted to get in touch with Wo and ask her about it, but he had other concerns, and the matter kept slipping his mind.

Finally, after a month in which his losses totaled more than a thousand standards, Jad Rakkis arrived at the war games carrying a small plastic case under his arm. Inside was a spiderlike thing covered with fine golden hair.

'A sand spider,' Rakkis announced. 'From Cathaday. I got it this afternoon from t'Etherane the Petseller. Usually they remove the poison sacs, but this one is intact. Are you game, Simon? I want my money back. I'll bet a thousand standards, sand spider against sandkings.'

Kress studied the spider in its plastic prison. His sandkings had grown – they were twice as large as Wo's, as she'd predicted – but they were still dwarfed by this thing. It was venomed, and they were not. Still, there were an awful lot of them. Besides, the endless sandking wars had begun to grow tiresome lately. The novelty of the match intrigued him. 'Done,' Kress said. 'Jad, you are a fool. The sandkings will just keep coming until this ugly creature of yours is dead.'

'You are the fool, Simon,' Rakkis replied, smiling. 'The Cathadayn sand spider customarily feeds on burrowers that hide in nooks and crevices and – well, watch – it will go straight into those castles, and eat the maws.'

Kress scowled amid general laughter. He hadn't counted on that. 'Get on with it,' he said irritably. He went to freshen his drink.

The spider was too large to cycle conveniently through the food chamber. Two of the others helped Rakkis slide the tank top slightly to one side, and Malada Blane handed him up his case. He shook the spider out. It landed lightly on a miniature dune in front of the red castle, and stood confused for a moment, mouth working, legs twitching menacingly.

'Come on,' Rakkis urged. They all gathered round the tank. Simon Kress found his magnifiers and slipped them on. If he was going to lose a thousand standards, at least he wanted a good view of the action.

The sandkings had seen the invader. All over the castle, activity had ceased. The small scarlet mobiles were frozen, watching.

The spider began to move toward the dark promise of the gate. On the tower above, Simon Kress' countenance stared down impassively.

At once there was a flurry of activity. The nearest red mobiles formed themselves into two wedges and streamed over the sand toward the spider. More warriors erupted from inside the castle and assembled in a triple line to guard the approach to the underground chamber where the maw lived. Scouts came scuttling over the dunes, recalled to fight.

Battle was joined.

The attacking sandkings washed over the spider. Mandibles snapped shut on legs and abdomen, and clung. Reds raced up the golden legs to the invader's back. They bit and tore. One of them found an eye, and ripped it loose with tiny yellow tendrils. Kress smiled and pointed.

But they were *small*, and they had no venom, and the spider did not stop. Its legs flicked sandkings off to either side. Its dripping jaws found others, and left them broken and stiffening. Already a dozen of the reds lay dying. The sand spider came on and on. It strode straight through the triple line of guardians before the castle. The lines closed around it, covered it, waging desperate battle. A team of sandkings had bitten off one of the spider's legs, Kress saw. Defenders leaped from atop the towers to land on the twitching, heaving mass.

Lost beneath the sandkings, the spider somehow lurched down into the darkness and vanished.

Jad Rakkis let out a long breath. He looked pale. 'Wonderful,' someone else said. Malada Blane chuckled deep in her throat.

'Look,' said Idi Noreddian, tugging Kress by the arm.

They had been so intent on the struggle in the corner that none of them had noticed the activity elsewhere in the tank. But now the castle was still, the sands empty save for dead red mobiles, and now they saw.

Three armies were drawn up before the red castle. They stood quite still, in perfect array, rank after rank of sandkings, orange and white and black. Waiting to see what emerged from the depths.

Simon Kress smiled. 'A *cordon sanitaire*,' he said. 'And glance at the other castles, if you will, Jad.'

Rakkis did, and swore. Teams of mobiles were sealing up the gates with sand and stone. If the spider somehow survived this encounter, it would find no easy entrance at the other castles. 'I should have brought four spiders,' Jad Rakkis said. 'Still, I've won. My spider is down there right now, eating your damned maw.'

Kress did not reply. He waited. There was motion in the shadows.

All at once, red mobiles began pouring out of the gate. They took their positions on the castle, and began repairing the damage the spider had wrought. The other armies dissolved and began to retreat to their respective corners.

'Jad,' said Simon Kress, 'I think you are a bit confused about who is eating who.'

The following week Rakkis brought four slim silver snakes. The sandkings dispatched them without much trouble.

Next he tried a large black bird. It ate more than thirty white mobiles, and its thrashing and blundering virtually destroyed their castle, but ultimately its wings grew tired, and the sandkings attacked in force wherever it landed.

After that it was a case of insects, armored beetles not too unlike the sandkings themselves. But stupid, stupid. An allied force of oranges and blacks broke their formation, divided them, and butchered them.

Rakkis began giving Kress promissory notes.

It was around that time that Kress met Cath m'Lane again, one evening when he was dining in Asgard at his favorite restaurant. He stopped at her table briefly and told her about the war games, inviting her to join them. She flushed, then regained control of herself and grew icy. 'Someone has to put a stop to you, Simon. I guess it's going to be me,' she said. Kress shrugged and enjoyed a lovely meal and thought no more about her threat.

Until a week later, when a small, stout woman arrived at his door and showed him a police wristband. 'We've had complaints,' she said. 'Do you keep a tank full of dangerous insects, Kress?'

'Not insects,' he said, furious. 'Come, I'll show you.'

When she had seen the sandkings, she shook her head. 'This will never do. What do you know about these creatures, anyway? Do you know what world they're from? Have they been cleared by the ecological board? Do you have a license for these things? We have a report that they're carnivores, possibly dangerous. We also have a report that they are semi-sentient. Where did you get these creatures, anyway?'

'From Wo and Shade,' Kress replied.

'Never heard of them,' the woman said. 'Probably smuggled them in, knowing our ecologists would never approve them. No, Kress, this won't do. I'm going to confiscate this tank and have it destroyed. And you're going to have to expect a few fines as well.'

Kress offered her a hundred standards to forget all about him and his sandkings.

She *tsk*ed. 'Now I'll have to add attempted bribery to the charges against you.'

Not until he raised the figure to two thousand standards was she willing to be persuaded.

'It's not going to be easy, you know,' she said. 'There are forms to be altered, records to be wiped. And getting a forged license from the ecologists will be time-consuming. Not to mention dealing with the complainant. What if she calls again?'

'Leave her to me,' Kress said. 'Leave her to me.'

He thought about it for a while. That night he made some calls.

First he got t'Etherane the Petseller. 'I want to buy a dog,' he said. 'A puppy.'

The round-faced merchant gawked at him. 'A puppy? That is not like you, Simon. Why don't you come in? I have a lovely choice.'

'I want a very specific *kind* of puppy,' Kress said. 'Take notes. I'll describe to you what it must look like.'

Afterward he punched for Idi Noreddian. 'Idi,' he said, 'I want you out here tonight with your holo equipment. I have a notion to record a sandking battle. A present for one of my friends.'

The night after they made the recording, Simon Kress stayed up late. He absorbed a controversial new drama in his sensorium, fixed himself a small snack, smoked a joy-stick or two, and broke out a bottle of wine. Feeling very happy with himself, he wandered into the living room, glass in hand.

The lights were out. The red glow of the terrarium made the shadows flushed and feverish. He walked over to look at his domain, curious as to how the blacks were doing in the repairs on their castle. The puppy had left it in ruins.

The restoration went well. But as Kress inspected the work through his magnifiers, he chanced to glance closely at the face. It startled him.

He drew back, blinked, took a healthy gulp of wine, and looked again.

The face on the wall was still his. But it was all wrong, all *twisted.* His cheeks were bloated and piggish, his smile was a crooked leer. He looked impossibly malevolent.

Uneasy, he moved around the tank to inspect the other castles. They were each a bit different, but ultimately all the same.

The oranges had left out most of the fine detail, but the result still seemed monstrous, crude – a brutal mouth and mindless eyes.

The reds gave him a Satanic, twitching kind of smile. His mouth did odd, unlovely things at its corners.

The whites, his favorites, had carved a cruel idiot god.

Simon Kress flung his wine across the room in rage. 'You *dare,*' he said under his breath. 'Now you won't eat for a week, you damned...' His voice was shrill. 'I'll teach you.' He had an idea. He strode out of the room, and returned a moment later with an antique iron throwing-sword in his hand. It was a meter long, and the point was still sharp. Kress smiled, climbed up and moved the tank cover aside just enough to give him working room, opening one corner of the desert. He leaned down, and jabbed the sword at the white castle below him. He waved it back and forth, smashing towers and ramparts and walls. Sand and stone collapsed, burying the scrambling mobiles. A flick of his wrist obliterated the features of the insolent, insulting caricature the sandkings had made of his face. Then he poised the point of the sword above the dark mouth that opened down into the maw's chamber, and thrust with all his strength. He heard a soft, squishing sound, and met resistance. All of the mobiles trembled and collapsed. Satisfied, Kress pulled back.

He watched for a moment, wondering whether he'd killed the maw. The point of the throwing-sword was wet and slimy. But finally the white sandkings began to move again. Feebly, slowly, but they moved.

He was preparing to slide the cover back in place and move on to a second castle when he felt something crawling on his hand.

He screamed and dropped the sword, and brushed the sandking from his flesh. It fell to the carpet, and he ground it beneath his heel, crushing it thoroughly long after it was dead. It had crunched when he stepped on it. After that, trembling, he hurried to seal the tank up again, and rushed off to shower and inspect himself carefully. He boiled his clothing.

Later, after several fresh glasses of wine, he returned to the living room. He was a bit ashamed of the way the sandking had terrified him. But he was not about to open the tank again. From now on, the cover stayed sealed permanently. Still, he had to punish the others.

Kress decided to lubricate his mental processes with another glass of wine. As he finished it, an inspiration came to him. He went to the tank smiling, and made a few adjustments to the humidity controls.

By the time he fell asleep on the couch, his wine glass still in his hand, the sand castles were melting in the rain.

Kress woke to angry pounding on his door.

He sat up, groggy, his head throbbing. Wine hangovers were always the worst, he thought. He lurched to the entry chamber.

Cath m'Lane was outside. 'You monster,' she said, her face swollen and puffy and streaked by tears. 'I cried all night, damn you. But no more, Simon, no more.'

'Easy,' he said, holding his head. 'I've got a hangover.'

She swore and shoved him aside and pushed her way into his house. The shambler came peering round a corner to see what the noise was. She spat at it and stalked into the living room, Kress trailing ineffectually after her. 'Hold on,' he said. 'Where do you … you can't … ' He stopped, suddenly horrorstruck. She was carrying a heavy sledgehammer in her left hand. 'No,' he said.

She went directly to the sandking tank. 'You like the little charmers so much, Simon? Then you can live with them.'

'*Cath!*' he shrieked.

Gripping the hammer with both hands, she swung as hard as she could against the side of the tank. The sound of the impact set his head to screaming, and Kress made a low blubbering sound of despair. But the plastic held.

She swung again. This time there was a *crack,* and a network of thin lines sprang into being.

Kress threw himself at her as she drew back her hammer for a third swing. They went down flailing, and rolled. She lost her grip on the hammer and tried to throttle him, but Kress wrenched free and bit her on the arm, drawing blood. They both staggered to their feet, panting.

'You should see yourself, Simon,' she said grimly. 'Blood dripping from your mouth. You look like one of your pets. How do you like the taste?'

'Get out,' he said. He saw the throwing-sword where it had fallen the night before, and snatched it up. 'Get out,' he repeated, waving the sword for emphasis. 'Don't go near that tank again.'

She laughed at him. 'You wouldn't dare,' she said. She bent to pick up her hammer.

Kress shrieked at her, and lunged. Before he quite knew what was happening, the iron blade had gone clear through her abdomen. Cath m'Lane looked at him wonderingly, and down at the sword. Kress fell back whimpering. 'I didn't mean … I only wanted … '

She was transfixed, bleeding, dead, but somehow she did not fall. 'You monster,' she managed to say, though her mouth was full of blood. And she whirled, impossibly, the sword in her, and swung with her last strength at the tank. The tortured wall shattered, and Cath m'Lane was buried beneath an avalanche of plastic and sand and mud.

Kress made small hysterical noises and scrambled up on the couch.

Sandkings were emerging from the muck on his living room floor. They were crawling across Cath's body. A few of them ventured tentatively out across the carpet. More followed.

He watched as a column took shape, a living, writhing square of sandkings, bearing something, something slimy and featureless, a piece of raw meat big as a man's head. They began to carry it away from the tank. It pulsed.

That was when Kress broke and ran.

It was late afternoon before he found the courage to return. He had run to his skimmer and flown to the nearest city, some fifty kilometers away, almost sick with fear. But once safely away, he had found a small restaurant, put down several mugs of coffee and two anti-hangover tabs, eaten a full breakfast, and gradually regained his composure.

It had been a dreadful morning, but dwelling on that would solve nothing. He ordered more coffee and considered his situation with icy rationality.

Cath m'Lane was dead at his hand. Could he report it, plead that it had been an accident? Unlikely. He had run her through, after all, and he had already told that policer to leave her to him. He would have to get rid of the evidence, and hope that she had not told anyone where she was going this morning. That was probable. She could only have gotten his gift late last night. She said that she had cried all night, and she had been alone when it arrived. Very well; he had one body and one skimmer to dispose of.

That left the sandkings. They might prove more of a difficulty. No doubt they had all escaped by now. The thought of them around his house, in his bed and his clothes, infesting his food – it made his flesh crawl. He shuddered and overcame his revulsion. It really shouldn't be too hard to kill them, he reminded himself. He didn't have to account for every mobile. Just the four maws, that was all. He could do that. They were large, as he'd seen. He would find them and kill them.

Simon Kress went shopping before he flew back to his home. He bought a set of skinthins that would cover him from head to foot, several bags of poison pellets for rockjock control, and a spray canister of illegally strong pesticide. He also bought a magnalock towing device.

When he landed, he went about things methodically. First he hooked Cath's skimmer to his own with the magnalock. Searching it, he had his first piece of luck. The crystal chip with Idi Noreddian's holo of the sandking fight was on the front seat. He had worried about that.

When the skimmers were ready, he slipped into his skinthins and went inside for Cath's body.

It wasn't there.

He poked through the fast-drying sand carefully, but there was no doubt of it; the body was gone. Could she have dragged herself away? Unlikely, but Kress searched. A cursory inspection of his house turned up neither the body nor any sign of the sandkings. He did not have time for a more thorough investigation, not with the incriminating skimmer outside his front door. He resolved to try later.

Some seventy kilometers north of Kress' estate was a range of active volcanoes. He flew there, Cath's skimmer in tow. Above the glowering cone of the largest, he released the magnalock and watched it vanish in the lava below.

It was dusk when he returned to his house. That gave him pause. Briefly he considered flying back to the city and spending the night there. He put the thought aside. There was work to do. He wasn't safe yet.

He scattered the poison pellets around the exterior of his house. No one would find that suspicious. He'd always had a rockjock problem. When that task was completed, he primed the canister of pesticide and ventured back inside.

Kress went through the house room by room, turning on lights everywhere he went until he was surrounded by a blaze of artificial illumination. He paused to clean up in the living room, shoveling sand and plastic fragments back into the broken tank. The sandkings were all gone, as he'd feared. The castles were shrunken and distorted, slagged by the watery bombardment Kress had visited upon them, and what little remained was crumbling as it dried.

He frowned and searched on, the canister of pest spray strapped across his shoulders.

Down in his deepest wine cellar, he came upon Cath m'Lane's corpse.

It sprawled at the foot of a steep flight of stairs, the limbs twisted as if by a fall. White mobiles were swarming all over it, and as Kress watched, the body moved jerkily across the hard-packed dirt floor.

He laughed, and twisted the illumination up to maximum. In the far corner, a squat little earthen castle and a dark hole were visible between two wine racks. Kress could make out a rough outline of his face on the cellar wall.

The body shifted once again, moving a few centimeters towards the castle. Kress had a sudden vision of the white maw waiting hungrily. It might be able to get Cath's foot in its mouth, but no more. It was too absurd. He laughed again, and started down into the cellar, finger poised on the trigger of the hose that snaked down his right arm. The sandkings – hundreds of them moving as one – deserted the body and formed up battle lines, a field of white between him and their maw.

Suddenly Kress had another inspiration. He smiled and lowered his firing hand. 'Cath was always hard to swallow,' he said, delighted at his wit. 'Especially for one your size. Here, let me give you some help. What are gods for, after all?'

He retreated upstairs, returning shortly with a cleaver. The sandkings, patient, waited and watched while Kress chopped Cath m'Lane into small, easily digestible pieces.

Simon Kress slept in his skinthins that night, the pesticide close at hand, but he did not need it. The whites, sated, remained in the cellar, and he saw no sign of the others.

In the morning he finished the cleanup of the living room. After he was through, no trace of the struggle remained except for the broken tank.

He ate a light lunch, and resumed his hunt for the missing sandkings. In full daylight, it was not too difficult. The blacks had located in his rock garden, and built a castle heavy with obsidian and quartz. The reds he founds at the bottom of his long-disused swimming pool, which had partially filled with windblown sand over the years. He saw mobiles of both colors ranging about his grounds, many of them carrying poison pellets back to their maws. Kress decided his pesticide was unnecessary. No use risking a fight when he could just let the poison do its work. Both maws should be dead by evening.

That left only the burnt orange sandkings unaccounted for. Kress circled his estate several times, in ever-widening spirals, but found no trace of them. When he began to sweat in his skinthins – it was a hot, dry day – he decided it was not important. If they were out here, they were probably eating the poison pellets along with the reds and blacks.

He crunched several sandkings underfoot, with a certain degree of satisfaction, as he walked back to the house. Inside, he removed his skinthins, settled down to a delicious meal, and finally began to relax. Everything was under control. Two of the maws would soon be defunct, the third was safely located where he could dispose of it after it had served his purposes, and he had no doubt that he would find the fourth. As for Cath, all trace of her visit had been obliterated.

His reverie was interrupted when his viewscreen began to blink at him. It was Jad Rakkis, calling to brag about some cannibal worms he was bringing to the war games tonight.

Kress had forgotten about that, but he recovered quickly. 'Oh, Jad, my pardons. I neglected to tell you. I grew bored with all that, and got rid of the sandkings. Ugly little things. Sorry, but there'll be no party tonight.'

Rakkis was indignant. 'But what will I do with my worms?'

'Put them in a basket of fruit and send them to a loved one,' Kress said, signing off. Quickly he began calling the others. He did not need anyone arriving at his doorstep now, with the sandkings alive and infesting the estate.

As he was calling Idi Noreddian, Kress became aware of an annoying oversight. The screen began to clear, indicating that someone had answered at the other end. Kress flicked off. Idi arrived on schedule an hour later. She was surprised to find the party canceled, but perfectly happy to share an evening alone with Kress. He delighted her with his story of Cath's reaction to the holo they had made together. While telling it, he managed to ascertain that she had not mentioned the prank to anyone. He nodded, satisfied, and refilled their wine glasses. Only a trickle was left. 'I'll have to get a fresh bottle,' he said. 'Come with me to my wine cellar, and help me pick out a good vintage. You've always had a better palate than I.'

She came along willingly enough, but balked at the top of the stairs when Kress opened the door and gestured for her to precede him. 'Where are the lights?' she said. 'And that smell – what's that peculiar smell, Simon?'

When he shoved her, she looked briefly startled. She screamed as she tumbled down the stairs. Kress closed the door and began to nail it shut with the boards and airhammer he had left for that purpose. As he was finishing, he heard Idi groan. 'I'm hurt,' she said. 'Simon, what is this?' Suddenly she squealed, and shortly after that the screaming started.

It did not cease for hours. Kress went to his sensorium and dialed up a saucy comedy to blot it off of his mind.

When he was sure she was dead, Kress flew her skimmer north to the volcanoes and discarded it. The magnalock was proving a good investment.

Odd scrabbling noises were coming from beyond the wine cellar door the next morning when Kress went down to check it out. He listened for several uneasy moments, wondering if Idi Noreddian could possibly have survived, and was now scratching to get out. It seemed unlikely; it had to be the sandkings. Kress did not like the implications of that. He decided that he would keep the door sealed, at least for the moment, and went outside with a shovel to bury the red and black maws in their own castles.

He found them very much alive.

The black castle was glittering with volcanic glass, and sandkings were all over it, repairing and improving. The highest tower was up to his waist, and on it was a hideous caricature of his face. When he approached, the blacks halted in their labors, and formed up into two threatening phalanxes. Kress glanced behind him and saw others closing off his escape. Startled, he dropped the shovel and sprinted out of the trap, crushing several mobiles beneath his boots.

The red castle was creeping up the walls of the swimming pool. The maw was safely settled in a pit, surrounded by sand and concrete and battlements. The reds crept all over the bottom of the pool. Kress watched them carry a rockjock and a large lizard into the castle. He stepped back from the poolside, horrified, and felt something crunch. Looking down, he saw three mobiles climbing up his leg. He brushed them off and stamped them to death, but others were approaching quickly. They were larger than he remembered. Some were almost as big as his thumb.

He ran. By the time he reached the safety of the house, his heart was racing and he was short of breath. The door closed behind him, and Kress hurried to lock it. His house was supposed to be pest-proof. He'd be safe in here.

A stiff drink steadied his nerve. So poison doesn't faze them, he thought. He should have known. Wo had warned him that the maw could eat anything. He would have to use the pesticide. Kress took another drink for good measure, donned his skinthins, and strapped the canister to his back. He unlocked the door.

Outside, the sandkings were waiting.

Two armies confronted him, allied against the common threat. More than he could have guessed. The damned maws must be breeding like rockjocks. They were everywhere, a creeping sea of them.

Kress brought up the hose and flicked the trigger. A gray mist washed over the nearest rank of sandkings. He moved his hand from side to side.

Where the mist fell, the sandkings twitched violently and died in sudden spasms. Kress smiled. They were no match for him. He sprayed in a wide arc before him and stepped forward confidently over a litter of black and red bodies. The armies fell back. Kress advanced, intent on cutting through them to their maws.

All at once the retreat stopped. A thousand sandkings surged toward him.

Kress had been expecting the counterattack. He stood his ground, sweeping his misty sword before him in great looping strokes. They came at him and died. A few got through; he could not spray everywhere at once. He felt them climbing up his legs, sensed their mandibles biting futilely at the reinforced plastic of his skinthins. He ignored them, and kept spraying.

Then he began to feel soft impacts on his head and shoulders.

Kress trembled and spun and looked up above him. The front of his house was alive with sandkings. Blacks and reds, hundreds of them. They were launching themselves into the air, raining down on him. They fell all around him. One landed on his faceplate, its mandibles scraping at his eyes for a terrible second before he plucked it away.

He swung up his hose and sprayed the air, sprayed the house, sprayed until the airborne sandkings were all dead and dying. The mist settled back on him, making him cough. He coughed, and kept spraying. Only when the front of the house was clean did Kress turn his attention back to the ground.

They were all around him, on him, dozens of them scurrying over his body, hundreds of others hurrying to join them. He turned the mist on them. The hose went dead. Kress heard a loud *hiss*, and the deadly fog rose in a great cloud from between his shoulders, cloaking him, choking him, making his eyes burn and blur. He felt for the hose, and his hand came away covered with dying sandkings. The hose was severed; they'd eaten it through. He was surrounded by a shroud of pesticide, blinded. He stumbled and screamed, and began to run back to the house, pulling sandkings from his body as he went.

Inside, he sealed the door and collapsed on the carpet, rolling back and forth until he was sure he had crushed them all. The canister was empty by then, hissing feebly. Kress stripped off his skinthins and showered. The hot spray scalded him and left his skin reddened and sensitive, but it made his flesh stop crawling.

He dressed in his heaviest clothing, thick workpants and leathers, after shaking them out nervously. 'Damn,' he kept muttering, 'damn.' His throat was dry. After searching the entry hall thoroughly to make certain it was clean, he allowed himself to sit and pour a drink. 'Damn,' he repeated. His hand shook as he poured, slopping liquor on the carpet.

The alcohol settled him, but it did not wash away the fear. He had a second drink and went to the window furtively. Sandkings were moving across the thick plastic pane. He shuddered and retreated to his communications console. He had to get help, he thought wildly. He would punch through a call to the authorities, and policers would come out with flamethrowers and…

Simon Kress stopped in mid-call, and groaned. He couldn't call in the police. He would have to tell them about the whites in his cellar, and they'd find the bodies there. Perhaps the maw might have finished Cath m'Lane by now, but certainly not Idi Noreddian. He hadn't even cut her up. Besides, there would be bones. No, the police could be called in only as a last resort.

He sat at the console, frowning. His communications equipment filled a whole wall; from here he could reach anyone on Baldur. He had plenty of money, and his cunning – he had always prided himself on his cunning. He would handle this somehow.

He briefly considered calling Wo, but soon dismissed the idea. Wo knew too much, and she would ask questions, and he did not trust her. No, he needed someone who would do as he asked *without* questions.

His frown faded, and slowly turned into a smile. Simon Kress had contacts. He put through a call to a number he had not used in a long time.

A woman's face took shape on his viewscreen: white-haired, bland of expression, with a long hook nose. Her voice was brisk and efficient. 'Simon,' she said. 'How is business?'

'Business is fine, Lissandra,' Kress replied. 'I have a job for you.'

'A removal? My price has gone up since last time, Simon. It has been ten years, after all.'

'You will be well paid,' Kress said. 'You know I'm generous. I want you for a bit of pest control.'

She smiled a thin smile. 'No need to use euphemisms, Simon. The call is shielded.'

'No, I'm serious. I have a pest problem. Dangerous pests. Take care of them for me. No questions. Understood?'

'Understood.'

'Good. You'll need… oh, three or four operatives. Wear heat-resistant skinthins, and equip them with flamethrowers, or lasers, something of that order. Come out to my place. You'll see the problem. Bugs, lots and lots of them. In my rock garden and the old swimming pool you'll find castles. Destroy them, kill everything inside them. Then knock on the door, and I'll show you what else needs to be done. Can you get out here quickly?'

Her face was impassive. 'We'll leave within the hour.'

Lissandra was true to her word. She arrived in a lean black skimmer with three operatives. Kress watched them from the safety of a second-story window. They were all faceless in dark plastic skinthins. Two of them wore portable flamethrowers, a third carried lasercannon and explosives. Lissandra carried nothing; Kress recognized her by the way she gave orders.

Their skimmer passed low overhead first, checking out the situation. The sandkings went mad. Scarlet and ebony mobiles ran everywhere, frenetic. Kress could see the castle in the rock garden from his vantage point. It stood tall as a man. Its ramparts were crawling with black defenders, and a steady stream of mobiles flowed down into its depths.

Lissandra's skimmer came down next to Kress' and the operatives vaulted out and unlimbered their weapons. They looked inhuman, deadly.

The black army drew up between them and the castle. The reds – Kress suddenly realized that he could not see the reds. He blinked. Where had they gone?

Lissandra pointed and shouted, and her two flamethrowers spread out and opened up on the black sandkings. Their weapons coughed dully and began to roar, long tongues of blue-and-scarlet fire licking out before them. Sandkings crisped and blackened and died. The operatives began to play the fire back and forth in an efficient, interlocking pattern. They advanced with careful, measured steps.

The black army burned and disintegrated, the mobiles fleeing in a thousand different directions, some back toward the castle, others toward the enemy. None reached the operatives with the flamethrowers. Lissandra's people were very professional.

Then one of them stumbled.

Or seemed to stumble. Kress looked again, and saw that the ground had given way beneath the man. Tunnels, he thought with a tremor of fear – tunnels, pits, traps. The flamer was sunk in sand up to his waist, and suddenly the ground around him seemed to erupt, and he was covered with scarlet sandkings. He dropped the flamethrower and began to claw wildly at his own body. His screams were horrible to hear.

His companion hesitated, then swung and fired. A blast of flame swallowed human and sandkings both. The screaming stopped abruptly. Satisfied, the second flamer turned back to the castle and took another step forward, and recoiled as his foot broke through the ground and vanished up to the ankle. He tried to pull it back and retreat, and the sand all around him gave way. He lost his balance and stumbled, flailing, and the sandkings were everywhere, a boiling mass of them, covering him as he writhed and rolled. His flamethrower was useless and forgotten.

Kress pounded wildly on the window, shouting for attention. 'The castle! Get the castle!'

Lissandra, standing back by her skimmer, heard and gestured. Her third operative sighted with the lasercannon and fired. The beam throbbed across the grounds and sliced off the top of the castle. He brought it down sharply, hacking at the sand and stone parapets. Towers fell. Kress' face disintegrated. The laser bit into the ground, searching round and about. The castle crumbled; now it was only a heap of sand. But the black mobiles continued to move. The maw was buried too deeply; they hadn't touched her.

Lissandra gave another order. Her operative discarded the laser, primed an explosive, and darted forward. He leaped over the smoking corpse of the first flamer, landed on solid ground within Kress' rock garden, and heaved. The explosive ball landed square atop the ruins of the black castle. White-hot light seared Kress' eyes, and there was a tremendous gout of sand and rock and mobiles. For a moment dust obscured everything. It was raining sandkings and pieces of sandkings.

Kress saw that the black mobiles were dead and unmoving.

'The pool,' he shouted down through the window. 'Get the castle in the pool.'

Lissandra understood quickly; the ground was littered with motionless blacks, but the reds were pulling back hurriedly and reforming. Her operative stood uncertain, then reached down and pulled out another explosive ball. He took one step forward, but Lissandra called him and he sprinted back in her direction.

It was all so simple then. He reached the skimmer, and Lissandra took him aloft. Kress rushed to another window in another room to watch. They came swooping in just over the pool, and the operative pitched his bombs down at the red castle from the safety of the skimmer. After the fourth run, the castle was unrecognizable, and the sandkings stopped moving.

Lissandra was thorough. She had him bomb each castle several additional times. Then he used the lasercannon, crisscrossing methodically until it was certain that nothing living could remain intact beneath those small patches of ground.

Finally they came knocking at his door. Kress was grinning manically when he let them in. 'Lovely,' he said, 'lovely.'

Lissandra pulled off the mask of her skinthins. 'This will cost you, Simon. Two operatives gone, not to mention the danger to my own life.'

'Of course,' Kress blurted. 'You'll be well paid, Lissandra. Whatever you ask, just so you finish the job.'

'What remains to be done?'

'You have to clean out my wine cellar,' Kress said. 'There's another castle down there. And you'll have to do it without explosives. I don't want my house coming down around me.' Lissandra motioned to her operative. 'Go outside and get Rajk's flamethrower. It should be intact.'

He returned armed, ready, silent. Kress led them down to the wine cellar.

The heavy door was still nailed shut, as he had left it. But it bulged outward slightly, as if warped by some tremendous pressure. That made Kress uneasy, as did the silence that held reign about them. He stood well away from the door as Lissandra's operative removed his nails and planks. 'Is that safe in here?' he found himself muttering, pointing at the flamethrower. 'I don't want a fire, either, you know.'

'I have the laser,' Lissandra said. 'We'll use that for the kill. The flamethrower probably won't be needed. But I want it here just in case. There are worse things than fire, Simon.'

He nodded.

The last plank came free of the cellar door. There was still no sound from below. Lissandra snapped an order, and her underling fell back, took up a position behind her, and leveled the flamethrower square at the door. She slipped her mask back on, hefted the laser, stepped forward, and pulled open the door.

No motion. No sound. It was dark down there.

'Is there a light?' Lissandra asked.

'Just inside the door,' Kress said. 'On the right hand side. Mind the stairs, they're quite steep.'

She stepped into the door, shifted the laser to her left hand, and reached up with her right, fumbling inside for the light panel. Nothing happened. 'I feel it,' Lissandra said, 'but it doesn't seem to… '

Then she was screaming, and she stumbled backward. A great white sandking had clamped itself around her wrist. Blood welled through her skinthins where its mandibles had sunk in. It was fully as large as her hand.

Lissandra did a horrible little jig across the room and began to smash her hand against the nearest wall. Again and again and again. It landed with a heavy, meaty thud. Finally the sandking fell away. She whimpered and fell to her knees. 'I think my fingers are broken,' she said softly. The blood was still flowing freely. She had dropped the laser near the cellar door.

'I'm not going down there,' her operative announced in clear firm tones.

Lissandra looked up at him. 'No,' she said. 'Stand in the door and flame it all. Cinder it. Do you understand?'

He nodded.

Simon Kress moaned. 'My *house*,' he said. His stomach churned. The white sandking had been so *large*. How many more were down there? 'Don't,' he continued. 'Leave it alone. I've changed my mind. Leave it alone.'

Lissandra misunderstood. She held out her hand. It was covered with blood and greenish-black ichor. 'Your little friend bit clean through my glove, and you saw what it took to get it off. I don't care about your house, Simon. Whatever is down there is going to die.'

Kress hardly heard her. He thought he could see movement in the shadows beyond the cellar door. He imagined a white army bursting forth, all as large as the sandking that had attacked Lissandra. He saw himself being lifted by a hundred tiny arms, and dragged down into the darkness where the maw waited hungrily. He was afraid. 'Don't,' he said.

They ignored him.

Kress darted forward, and his shoulder slammed into the back of Lissandra's operative just as the man was bracing to fire. He grunted and unbalanced and pitched forward into the black. Kress listened to him fall down the stairs. Afterward there were other noises – scuttlings and snaps and soft squishing sounds.

Kress swung around to face Lissandra. He was drenched in cold sweat, but a sickly kind of excitement was on him. It was almost sexual.

Lissandra's calm cold eyes regarded him through her mask. 'What are you doing?' she demanded as Kress picked up the laser she had dropped. '*Simon!*'

'Making a peace,' he said, giggling. 'They won't hurt god, no, not so long as god is good and generous. I was cruel. Starved them. I have to make up for it now, you see.'

'You're insane,' Lissandra said. It was the last thing she said. Kress burned a hole in her chest big enough to put his arm through. He dragged the body across the floor and rolled it down the cellar stairs. The noises were louder – chitinous clackings and scrapings and echoes that were thick and liquid. Kress nailed up the door once again.

As he fled, he was filled with a deep sense of contentment that coated his fear like a layer of syrup. He suspected it was not his own.

He planned to leave his home, to fly to the city and take a room for a night, or perhaps for a year. Instead Kress started drinking. He was not quite sure why. He drank steadily for hours, and retched it all up violently on his living room carpet. At some point he fell asleep. When he woke, it was pitch dark in the house.

He cowered against the couch. He could hear *noises*. Things were moving in the walls. They were all around him. His hearing was extraordinarily acute. Every little creak was the footstep of a sandking. He closed his eyes and waited, expecting to feel their terrible touch, afraid to move lest he brush against one.

Kress sobbed, and was very still for a while, but nothing happened.

He opened his eyes again. He trembled. Slowly the shadows began to soften and dissolve. Moonlight was filtering through the high windows. His eyes adjusted.

The living room was empty. Nothing there, nothing, nothing. Only his drunken fears.

Simon Kress steeled himself, and rose, and went to a light.

Nothing there. The room was quiet, deserted.

He listened. Nothing. No sound. Nothing in the walls. It had all been his imagination, his fear.

The memories of Lissandra and the thing in the cellar returned to him unbidden. Shame and anger washed over him. Why had he done that? He could have helped her burn it out, kill it. *Why*... he knew why. The maw had done it to him, put fear in him. Wo had said it was psionic, even when it was small. And now it was large, so large. It had feasted on Cath, and Idi, and now it had two more bodies down there. It would keep growing. And it had learned to like the taste of human flesh, he thought.

He began to shake, but he took control of himself again and stopped. It wouldn't hurt him. He was god. The whites had always been his favorites.

He remembered how he had stabbed it with his throwing-sword. That was before Cath came. Damn her anyway.

He couldn't stay here. The maw would grow hungry again. Large as it was, it wouldn't take long. Its appetite would be terrible. What would it do then? He had to get away, back to the safety of the city while it was still contained in his wine cellar. It was only plaster and hard-packed earth down there, and the mobiles could dig and tunnel. When they got free… Kress didn't want to think about it.

He went to his bedroom and packed. He took three bags. Just a single change of clothing, that was all he needed; the rest of the space he filled with his valuables, with jewelry and art and other things he could not bear to lose. He did not expect to return.

His shambler followed him down the stairs, staring at him from its baleful glowing eyes. It was gaunt. Kress realized that it had been ages since he had fed it. Normally it could take care of itself, but no doubt the pickings had grown lean of late. When it tried to clutch at his leg, he snarled at it and kicked it away, and it scurried off, offended.

Kress slipped outside, carrying his bags awkwardly, and shut the door behind him.

For a moment he stood pressed against the house, his heart thudding in his chest. Only a few meters between him and his skimmer. He was afraid to cross them. The moonlight was bright, and the front of his house was a scene of carnage. The bodies of Lissandra's two flamers lay where they had fallen, one twisted and burned, the other swollen beneath a mass of dead sandkings. And the mobiles, the black and red mobiles, they were all around him. It was an effort to remember that they were dead. It was almost as if they were simply waiting, as they had waited so often before.

Nonsense, Kress told himself. More drunken fears. He had seen the castles blown apart. They were dead, and the white maw was trapped in his cellar. He took several deep and deliberate breaths, and stepped forward onto the sandkings. They crunched. He ground them into the sand savagely. They did not move.

Kress smiled, and walked slowly across the battleground, listening to the sounds, the sounds of safety.

Crunch. Crackle. Crunch.

He lowered his bags to the ground and opened the door to his skimmer.

Something moved from shadow into light. A pale shape on the seat of his skimmer. It was as long as his forearm. Its mandibles clacked together softly, and it looked up at him from six small eyes set all around its body.

Kress wet his pants and backed away slowly.

There was more motion from inside the skimmer. He had left the door open. The sandking emerged and came toward him, cautiously. Others followed. They had been hiding beneath his seats, burrowed into the upholstery. But now they emerged. They formed a ragged ring around the skimmer.

Kress licked his lips, turned, and moved quickly to Lissandra's skimmer.

He stopped before he was halfway there. Things were moving inside that one too. Great maggoty things, half-seen by the light of the moon.

Kress whimpered and retreated back toward the house. Near the front door, he looked up.

He counted a dozen long white shapes creeping back and forth across the walls of the building. Four of them were clustered close together near the top of the unused belfry where the carrion hawk had once roosted. They were carving something. A face. A very recognizable face.

Simon Kress shrieked and ran back inside.

A sufficient quantity of drink brought him the easy oblivion he sought. But he woke. Despite everything, he woke. He had a terrible headache, and he smelled, and he was hungry. Oh so very hungry. He had never been so hungry.

Kress knew it was not his *own* stomach hurting.

A white sandking watched him from atop the dresser in his bedroom, its antennae moving faintly. It was as big as the one in the skimmer the night before. He was horribly dry, sandpaper dry. He licked his lips and fled from the room.

The house was full of sandkings; he had to be careful where he put his feet. They all seemed busy on errands of their own. They were making modifications in his house, burrowing into or out of his walls, carving things. Twice he saw his own likeness staring out at him from unexpected places. The faces were warped, twisted, livid with fear.

He went outside to get the bodies that had been rotting in the yard, hoping to appease the white maw's hunger. They were gone, both of them. Kress remembered how easily the mobiles could carry things many times their own weight.

It was terrible to think that the maw was *still* hungry after all of that.

When Kress reentered the house, a column of sandkings was wending its way down the stairs. Each carried a piece of his shambler. The head seemed to look at him reproachfully as it went by.

Kress emptied his freezers, his cabinets, everything, piling all the food in the house in the center of his kitchen floor. A dozen whites waited to take it away. They avoided the frozen food, leaving it to thaw in a great puddle, but they carried off everything else.

When all the food was gone, Kress felt his own hunger pangs abate just a bit, though he had not eaten a thing. But he knew the respite would be short-lived. Soon the maw would be hungry again. He had to feed it.

Kress knew what to do. He went to his communicator. 'Malada,' he began casually when the first of his friends answered, 'I'm having a small party tonight. I realize this is terribly short notice, but I hope you can make it. I really do.'

He called Jad Rakkis next, and then the others. By the time he had finished, nine of them had accepted his invitation. Kress hoped that would be enough.

Kress met his guests outside – the mobiles had cleaned up remarkably quickly, and the grounds looked almost as they had before the battle – and walked them to his front door. He let them enter first. He did not follow.

When four of them had gone through, Kress finally worked up his courage. He closed the door behind his latest guest, ignoring the startled exclamations that soon turned into shrill gibbering, and sprinted for the skimmer the man had arrived in. He slid in safely, thumbed the startplate, and swore. It was programmed to lift only in response to its owner's thumbprint, of course.

Jad Rakkis was the next to arrive. Kress ran to his skimmer as it set down, and seized Rakkis by the arm as he was climbing out. 'Get back in, quickly,' he said, pushing. 'Take me to the city. Hurry, Jad. *Get out of here!*'

But Rakkis only stared at him, and would not move. 'Why, what's wrong, Simon? I don't understand. What about your party?'

And then it was too late, because the loose sand all around them was stirring, and the red eyes were staring at them, and the mandibles were clacking. Rakkis made a choking sound, and moved to get back in his skimmer, but a pair of mandibles snapped shut about his ankle, and suddenly he was on his knees. The sand seemed to boil with subterranean activity. Jad thrashed and cried terribly as they tore him apart. Kress could hardly bear to watch.

After that, he did not try to escape again. When it was all over, he cleaned out what remained in his liquor cabinet, and got extremely drunk. It would be the last time he would enjoy that luxury, he knew. The only alcohol remaining in the house was stored down in the wine cellar.

Kress did not touch a bite of food the entire day, but he fell asleep feeling bloated, sated at last, the awful hunger vanquished. His last thoughts before the nightmares took him were of whom he could ask out tomorrow.

Morning was hot and dry. Kress opened his eyes to see the white sandking on his dresser again. He shut them again quickly, hoping the dream would leave him. It did not, and he could not go back to sleep. Soon he found himself staring at the thing.

He stared for almost five minutes before the strangeness of it dawned on him; the sandking was not moving.

The mobiles could be preternaturally still, to be sure. He had seen them wait and watch a thousand times. But always there was some motion about them – the mandibles clacked, the legs twitched, the long fine antennae stirred and swayed.

But the sandking on his dresser was completely still.

Kress rose, holding his breath, not daring to hope. Could it be dead? Could something have killed it? He walked across the room.

The eyes were glassy and black. The creature seemed swollen, somehow, as if it were soft and rotting inside, filling up with gas that pushed outward at the plates of white armor.

Kress reached out a trembling hand and touched it.

It was warm – hot even – and growing hotter. But it did not move.

He pulled his hand back, and as he did, a segment of the sandking's white exoskeleton fell away from it. The flesh beneath was the same color, but softer-looking, swollen and feverish. And it almost seemed to throb.

Kress backed away, and ran to the door.

Three more white mobiles lay in his hall. They were all like the one in his bedroom.

He ran down the stairs, jumping over sandkings. None of them moved. The house was full of them, all dead, dying, comatose, whatever. Kress did not care what was wrong with them. Just so they could not move.

He found four of them inside his skimmer. He picked them up one by one, and threw them as far as he could. Damned monsters. He slid back in, on the ruined half-eaten seats, and thumbed the startplate.

Nothing happened.

Kress tried again, and again. Nothing. It wasn't fair. This was *his* skimmer, it ought to start, why wouldn't it lift, he didn't understand.

Finally he got out and checked, expecting the worst. He found it. The sandkings had torn apart his gravity grid. He was trapped. He was still trapped.

Grimly, Kress marched back into the house. He went to his gallery and found the antique axe that had hung next to the throwing-sword he had used on Cath m'Lane. He set to work. The sandkings did not stir even as he chopped them to pieces. But they splattered when he made the first cut, the bodies almost bursting. Inside was awful; strange half-formed organs, a viscous reddish ooze that looked almost like human blood, and the yellow ichor.

Kress destroyed twenty of them before he realized the futility of what he was doing. The mobiles were nothing, really. Besides, there were so *many* of them. He could work for a day and night and still not kill them all.

He had to go down into the wine cellar and use the axe on the maw.

Resolute, he started down. He got within sight of the door, and stopped.

It was not a door any more. The walls had been eaten away, so that the hole was twice the size it had been, and round. A pit, that was all. There was no sign that there had ever been a door nailed shut over that black abyss.

A ghastly, choking, fetid odor seemed to come from below.

And the walls were wet and bloody and covered with patches of white fungus.

And worst, it was *breathing*.

Kress stood across the room and felt the warm wind wash over him as it exhaled, and he tried not to choke, and when the wind reversed direction, he fled.

Back in the living room, he destroyed three more mobiles, and collapsed. What was *happening*? He didn't understand.

Then he remembered the only person who might understand. Kress went to his communicator again, stepping on a sandking in his haste, and prayed fervently that the device still worked.

When Jala Wo answered, he broke down and told her everything.

She let him talk without interruption, no expression save for a slight frown on her gaunt, pale face. When Kress had finished, she said only, 'I ought to leave you there.'

Kress began to blubber. 'You can't. Help me. I'll pay… '

'I ought to,' Wo repeated, 'but I won't.'

'Thank you,' Kress said. 'Oh, thank… '

'Quiet,' said Wo. 'Listen to me. This is your own doing. Keep your sandkings well, and they are courtly ritual warriors. You turned yours into something else, with starvation and torture. You were their god. You made them what they are. That maw in your cellar is sick, still suffering from the wound you gave it. It is probably insane. Its behavior is… unusual.

'You have to get out of there quickly. The

mobiles are not dead, Kress. They are dormant. I told you the exoskeleton falls off when they grow larger. Normally, in fact, it falls off much earlier. I have never heard of sandkings growing as large as yours while still in the insectoid stage. It is another result of crippling the white maw, I would say. That does not matter.

'What matters is the metamorphosis your sandkings are now undergoing. As the maw grows, you see, it gets progressively more intelligent. Its psionic powers strengthen, and its mind becomes more sophisticated, more ambitious. The armored mobiles are useful enough when the maw is tiny and only semi-sentient, but now it needs better servants, bodies with capabilities. Do you understand? The mobiles are all going to give birth to a new breed of sandking. I can't say exactly what it will look like. Each maw designs its own, to fit its perceived needs and desires. But it will be biped, with four arms, and opposable thumbs. It will be able to construct and operate advanced machinery. The individual sandkings will not be sentient. But the maw will be very sentient indeed.'

Simon Kress was gaping at Wo's image on the viewscreen. 'Your workers,' he said, with an effort. 'The ones who came out here… who installed the tank… '

Jala Wo managed a faint smile. 'Shade,' she said.

'Shade is a sandking,' Kress repeated numbly. 'And you sold me a tank of… of… infants, ah… '

'Do not be absurd,' Wo said. 'A first-stage sandking is more like a sperm than an infant. The wars temper and control them in nature. Only one in a hundred reaches second stage. Only one in a thousand achieves the third and final plateau, and becomes like Shade. Adult sandkings are not sentimental about the small maws. There are too many of them, and their mobiles are pests.' She sighed. 'And all this talk wastes time. That white sandking is going to waken to full sentience soon. It is not going to need you any longer, and it hates you, and it will be very hungry. The transformation is taxing. The maw must eat enormous amounts both before and after. So you have to get out of there. Do you understand?'

'*I can't*,' Kress said. 'My skimmer is destroyed, and I can't get any of the others to start. I don't know how to reprogram them. Can you come out for me?'

'Yes,' said Wo. 'Shade and I will leave at once, but it is more than two hundred kilometers from Asgard to you, and there is equipment we will need to deal with the deranged sandking you've created. You cannot wait there. You have two feet. Walk. Go due east, as near as you can determine, as quickly as you can. The land out there is pretty desolate. We'll find you easily with an aerial search, and you'll be safely away from the sandking. Do you understand?'

'Yes,' said Simon Kress. 'Yes, oh, yes.'

They signed off, and he walked quickly toward the door. He was halfway there when he heard the noise – a sound halfway between a pop and a crack.

One of the sandkings had split open. Four tiny hands covered with pinkish-yellow blood came up out of the gap and began to push the dead skin aside.

Kress began to run.

He had not counted on the heat.

The hills were dry and rocky. Kress ran from the house as quickly as he could, ran until his ribs ached and his breath was coming in gasps. Then he walked, but as soon as he had recovered he began to run again. For almost an hour he ran and walked, ran and walked, beneath the fierce hot sun. He sweated freely, and wished that he had thought to bring some water. He watched the sky in hopes of seeing Wo and Shade.

He was not made for this. It was too hot, and too dry, and he was in no condition. But he kept himself going with the memory of the way the maw had breathed, and the thought of the wriggling little things that by now were surely crawling all over his house. He hoped Wo and Shade would know how to deal with them.

He had his own plans for Wo and Shade. It was all their fault, Kress had decided, and they would suffer for it. Lissandra was dead, but he knew others in her profession. He would have his revenge. He promised himself that a hundred times as he struggled and sweated his way east.

At least he hoped it was east. He was not that good at directions, and he wasn't certain which way he had run in his initial panic, but since then he had made an effort to bear due east, as Wo had suggested.

When he had been running for several hours, with no sign of rescue, Kress began to grow certain that he had gone wrong.

When several more hours passed, he began to grow afraid. What if Wo and Shade could not find him? He would die out here. He hadn't eaten in two days; he was weak and frightened; his throat was raw for want of water. He couldn't keep going. The sun was sinking now, and he'd be completely lost in the dark. What was wrong? Had the sandkings eaten Wo and Shade? The fear was on him again, filling him, and with it a great thirst and a terrible hunger. But Kress kept going. He stumbled now when he tried to run, and twice he fell. The second time he scraped his hand on a rock, and it came away bloody. He sucked at it as he walked, and worried about infection.

The sun was on the horizon behind him. The ground grew a little cooler, for which Kress was grateful. He decided to walk until last light and settle in for the night. Surely he was far enough from the sandkings to be safe, and Wo and Shade would find him come morning.

When he topped the next rise, he saw the outline of a house in front of him.

It wasn't as big as his own house, but it was big enough. It was habitation, safety. Kress shouted and began to run toward it. Food and drink, he had to have nourishment, he could taste the meal now. He was aching with hunger. He ran down the hill towards the house, waving his arms and shouting to the inhabitants. The light was almost gone now, but he could still make out a half-dozen children playing in the twilight. 'Hey there,' he shouted. 'Help, help.'

They came running toward him.

Kress stopped suddenly. 'No,' he said, 'oh, no. Oh, no.' He backpedaled, slipped on the sand, got up and tried to run again. They caught him easily. They were ghastly little things with bulging eyes and dusky orange skin. He struggled, but it was useless. Small as they were, each of them had four arms, and Kress had only two.

They carried him toward the house. It was a sad, shabby house built of crumbling sand, but the door was quite large, and dark, and it breathed. That was terrible, but it was not the thing that set Simon Kress to screaming. He screamed because of the others, the little orange children who came crawling out from the castle, and watched impassive as he passed.

All of them had his face.

WINDOW

Bob Leman

Bob Leman (1922–2006) was an American science fiction and horror short story author, most often associated with *The Magazine of Fantasy & Science Fiction*. Leman's first story appeared when he was forty-five. 'Window' (1980), which continues this anthology's exploration of 'weird science fiction,' is his most famous story. Nominated for the Nebula Award, it was adapted for an episode of *Night Visions*, directed by and starring Bill Pullman. Another of Leman's stories, 'How Dobbstown Was Saved', was to have been published in the Harlan Ellison anthology *The Last Dangerous Visions* but eventually appeared in the collection *Feesters in the Lake and Other Stories* (2002).

'We don't know what the hell's going on out there,' they told Gilson in Washington. 'It may be pretty big. The nut in charge tried to keep it under wraps, but the army was furnishing routine security, and the commanding officer tipped us off. A screwball project. Apparently been funded for years without anyone paying much attention. Extrasensory perception, for God's sake. And maybe they've found something. The security colonel thinks so, anyway. Find out about it.'

The Nut-in-Charge was a rumpled professor of psychology named Krantz. He and the colonel met Gilson at the airport, and they set off directly for the site in an army sedan. The colonel began talking immediately.

'You've got something mighty queer here, Gilson,' he said. 'I never saw anything like it, and neither did anybody else. Krantz here is as mystified as anybody. And it's his baby. We're just security. Not that they've needed any, up to now. Not even any need for secrecy, except to keep the public from laughing its head off. The setup we've got here is –'

'Dr. Krantz,' Gilson said, 'you'd better give me a complete rundown on the situation here. So far, I haven't any information at all.'

Krantz was occupied with the lighting of a cigar. He blew a cloud of foul smoke, and through it he said, 'We're missing one prefab building, one POBEC computer, some medical machinery, and one, uh, researcher named Culvergast.'

'Explain "missing",' Gilson said.

'Gone. Disappeared. A building and everything in it. Just not there any more. But we do have something in exchange.'

'And what's that?'

'I think you'd better wait and see for yourself,' Krantz said. 'We'll be there in a few minutes.' They were passing through the farther reaches of the metropolitan area, a series of decayed small towns. The highway wound down the valley beside the river, and the towns lay stretched along it, none of them more than a block or two wide, their side streets rising steeply toward the first ridge. In one of these moribund communities they left the highway and went bouncing up the hillside on a crooked road whose surface changed from cobblestones to slag after the houses had been left behind. Beyond the crest of the ridge the road began to drop as steeply as it had risen, and after a quarter of a mile they turned into a lane whose entrance would have been missed by anyone not watching for it. They were in a forest now; it was second growth, but the logging had been done so long ago that it might almost have been a virgin stand, lofty, silent, and somewhat gloomy on this gray day.

'Pretty,' Gilson said. 'How does a project like this come to be way out here, anyhow?'

'The place was available,' the colonel said. 'Has been since World War Two. They set it up for some work on proximity fuses. Shut it down in '48. Was vacant until the professor took it over.'

'Culvergast is a little bit eccentric,' Krantz said. 'He wouldn't work at the university – too many people, he said. When I heard this place was available, I put in for it, and got it – along with the colonel, here. Culvergast has been happy with the setup, but I guess he bothers the colonel a little.'

'He's a certifiable loony,' the colonel said, 'and his little helpers are worse.'

'Well, what the devil was he doing?' Gilson asked.

Before Krantz could answer, the driver braked at a chain-link gate that stood across the lane. It was fastened with a loop of heavy logging chain and manned by armed soldiers. One of them, machine pistol in hand, peered into the car. 'Everything O.K., sir?' he said.

'O.K. with waffles, Sergeant,' the colonel said. It was evidently a password. The noncom unlocked the enormous padlock that secured the chain. 'Pretty primitive,' the colonel said as they bumped through the gateway, 'but it'll do until we get proper stuff in. We've got men with dogs patrolling the fence.' He looked at Gilson. 'We're just about there. Get a load of this, now.'

It was a house. It stood in the center of the clearing in an island of sunshine, white, gleaming, and incongruous. All around was the dark loom of the forest under a sunless sky, but somehow sunlight lay on the house, sparkling in its polished windows and making brilliant the colors of massed flowers in carefully tended beds, reflecting from the pristine whiteness of its siding out into the gray, littered clearing with its congeries of derelict buildings.

'You couldn't have picked a better time,' the colonel said. 'Shining there, cloudy here.'

Gilson was not listening. He had climbed from the car and was staring in fascination. 'Jesus,' he said. 'Like a goddam Victorian postcard.'

Lacy scrollwork foamed over the rambling wooden mansion, running riot at the eaves of the steep roof, climbing elaborately up towers and turrets, embellishing deep oriels and outlining a long, airy veranda. Tall windows showed by their spacing that the rooms were many and large. It seemed to be a new house, or perhaps just newly painted and supremely well-kept. A driveway of fine white gravel led under a high porte-cochère.

'How about that?' the colonel said. 'Look like your grandpa's house?'

As a matter of fact, it did: like his grandfather's house enlarged and perfected and seen through a lens of romantic nostalgia, his grandfather's house groomed and pampered as the old farmhouse never had been. He said, 'And you got this in exchange for a prefab, did you?'

'Just like that one,' the colonel said, pointing to one of the seedy buildings. 'Of course we could use the prefab.'

'What does that mean?'

'Watch,' the colonel said. He picked up a small rock and tossed it in the direction of the house. The rock rose, topped its arc, and began to fall. Suddenly it was not there.

'Here,' Gilson said. 'Let me try that.'

He threw the rock like a baseball, a high, hard one. It disappeared about fifty feet from the house. As he stared at the point of its disappearance, Gilson became aware that the smooth green of the lawn ended exactly below. Where the grass ended, there began the weeds and rocks that made up the floor of the clearing. The line of separation was absolutely straight, running at an angle across the lawn. Near the driveway it turned ninety degrees, and sliced off lawn, driveway and shrubbery with the same precise straightness.

'It's perfectly square,' Krantz said. 'About a hundred feet to a side. Probably a cube, actually. We know the top's about ninety feet in the air. I'd guess there are about ten feet of it underground.'

' "It"?' Gilson said. ' "It"? What's "it"?'

'Name it and you can have it,' Krantz said. 'A three-dimensional television receiver a hundred feet to a side, maybe. A cubical crystal ball. Who knows?'

'The rocks we threw. They didn't hit the house. Where did the rocks go?'

'Ah. Where, indeed? Answer that and perhaps you answer all.'

Gilson took a deep breath. 'All right. I've seen it. Now tell me about it. From the beginning.'

Krantz was silent for a moment; then, in a dry lecturer's voice he said, 'Five days ago, June thirteenth, at eleven thirty a.m., give or take three minutes, Private Ellis Mulvihill, on duty at the gate, heard what he later described as "an explosion that was quiet, like." He entered the enclosure, locked the gate behind him, and ran up here to the clearing. He was staggered – "shook-up" was his expression – to see, instead of Culvergast's broken-down prefab, that house, there. I gather that he stood gulping and blinking for a time, trying to come to terms with what his eyes told him. Then he ran over there to the guardhouse and called the colonel. Who called me. We came out here and found that a quarter of an acre of land and a building with a man in it had disappeared and been replaced by this, as neat as a peg in a pegboard.'

'You think the prefab went where the rocks did,' Gilson said. It was a statement.

'Why, we're not even absolutely sure it's gone. What we're seeing can't actually be where we're seeing it. It rains on that house when it's sunny here, and right now you can see the sunlight on it, on a day like this. It's a window.'

'A window on what?'

'Well – that looks like a new house, doesn't it? When were they building houses like that?'

'Eighteen seventy or eighty, something like – oh.'

'Yes,' Krantz said. 'I think we're looking at the past.'

'Oh, for God's sake,' Gilson said.

'I know how you feel. And I may be wrong. But I have to say it looks very much that way. I want you to hear what Reeves says about it. He's been here from the beginning. A graduate student, assisting here. Reeves!'

A very tall, very thin young man unfolded himself from a crouched position over an odd-looking machine that stood near the line between grass and rubble and ambled over to the three men. Reeves was an enthusiast. 'Oh, it's the past, all right,' he said. 'Sometime in the eighties. My girl got some books on costume from the library, and the clothes check out for that decade. And the decorations on the horses' harnesses are a clue, too. I got that from–'

'Wait a minute,' Gilson said. '*Clothes?* You mean there are people in there?'

'Oh, sure,' Reeves said. 'A fine little family. Mamma, poppa, little girl, little boy, old granny or auntie. A dog. Good people.'

'How can you tell that?'

'I've been watching them for five days, you know? They're having – *we're* having – fine weather there – or then, or whatever you'd say. They're nice to each other, they *like* each other. Good people. You'll see.'

'When?'

'Well, they'll be eating dinner now. They usually come out after dinner. In an hour, maybe.'

'I'll wait,' Gilson said. 'And while we wait, you will please tell me some more.'

Krantz assumed his lecturing voice again. 'As to the nature of it, nothing. We have a window, which we believe to open into the past. We can see into it, so we know that light passes through; but it passes in only one direction, as evidenced by the fact that the people over there are wholly unaware of us. Nothing else goes through. You saw what happened to the rocks. We've shoved poles through the interface there – there's no resistance at all – but anything that goes through is gone, God knows where. Whatever you put through stays there. Your pole is cut off clean. Fascinating. But wherever it is, it's not where the house is. That interface isn't between us and the past; it's between us and – someplace else. I think our window here is just an incidental side-effect, a – a twisting of time that resulted from whatever tensions exist along that interface.'

Gilson sighed. 'Krantz,' he said, 'what am I going to tell the secretary? You've lucked into what may be the biggest thing that ever happened, and you've kept it bottled up for five days. We wouldn't know about it now if it weren't for the colonel's report. Five days wasted. Who knows how long this thing will last? The whole goddam scientific establishment ought to be here – should have been from day one. This needs the whole works. At this point the place should be a beehive. And what do I find? You and a graduate student throwing rocks and poking with sticks. And a girlfriend looking up the dates of costumes. It's damn near criminal.'

Krantz did not look abashed. 'I thought you'd say that,' he said. 'But look at it this way. Like it or not, this thing wasn't produced by technology or science. It was pure psi. If we can reconstruct Culvergast's work, we may be able to find out what happened; we may be able to repeat the phenomenon. But I don't like what's going to happen after you've called in your experimenters, Gilson. They'll measure and test and conjecture and theorize, and never once will they accept for a moment the real basis of what's happened. The day they arrive, I'll be out. And dammit, Gilson, this is *mine*.'

'Not any more,' Gilson said. 'It's too big.'

'It's not as though we weren't doing some hard experiments of our own,' Krantz said. 'Reeves, tell him about your batting machine.'

'Yes, *sir*,' Reeves said. 'You see, Mr. Gilson, what the professor said wasn't absolutely the whole truth, you know? Sometimes something *can* get through the window. We saw it on the first day. There was a temperature inversion over in the valley, and the stink from the chemical plant had been accumulating for about a week. It broke up that day, and the wind blew the gunk through the notch and right over here. A really rotten stench. We were watching our people over there, and all of a sudden they began to sniff and wrinkle their noses and make disgusted faces. We figured it had to be the chemical stink. We pushed a pole out right away, but the end just disappeared, as usual. The professor suggested that maybe there was a pulse, or something of the sort, in the interface, that it exists only intermittently. We cobbled up a gadget to test the idea. Come and have a look at it.'

It was a horizontal flywheel with a paddle attached to its rim, like an extended cleat. As the wheel spun, the paddle swept around a table. There was a hopper hanging above, and at intervals something dropped from the hopper onto the table, where it was immediately banged by the paddle and sent flying. Gilson peered into the hopper and raised an interrogatory eyebrow. 'Ice cubes,' Reeves said. 'Colored orange for visibility. That thing shoots an ice cube at the interface once a second. Somebody is always on duty with a stopwatch. We've established that every fifteen hours and twenty minutes the thing is open for five seconds. Five ice cubes go through and drop on the lawn in there. The rest of the time they just vanish at the interface.'

'Ice cubes. Why ice cubes?'

'They melt and disappear. We can't be littering up the past with artifacts from our day. God knows what the effect might be. Then, too, they're cheap, and we're shooting a lot of them.'

'Science,' Gilson said heavily. 'I can't wait to hear what they're going to say in Washington.'

'Sneer all you like,' Krantz said. 'The house is there, the interface is there. We've by God turned up some kind of time travel. And Culvergast the screwball did it, not a physicist or an engineer.'

'Now that you bring it up,' Gilson said, 'just what *was* your man Culvergast up to?'

'Good question. What he was doing was – well, not to put too fine a point upon it, he was trying to discover spells.'

'Spells?'

'The kind you cast. Magic words. Don't look disgusted yet. It makes sense, in a way. We were funded to look into telekinesis – the manipulation of matter by the mind. It's obvious that telekinesis, if it could be applied with precision, would be a marvelous weapon. Culvergast's hypothesis was that there are in fact people who perform feats of telekinesis, and although they never seem to know or be able to explain how they do it, they nevertheless perform a specific mental action that enables them to tap some source of energy that apparently exists all around us, and to some degree to focus and direct that energy. Culvergast proposed to discover the common factor in their mental processes.

'He ran a lot of putative telekinesists through here, and he reported that he had found a pattern, a sort of mnemonic device functioning at the very bottom of, or below, the verbal level. In one of his people he found it as a set of musical notes, in several as gibberish or various sorts, and in one, he said, as mathematics at the primary arithmetic level. He was feeding all this into the computer, trying to eliminate simple noise and the personal idiosyncrasies of the subjects, trying to lay bare the actual, effective essence. He then proposed to organize this essence into *words*; words that would so shape the mental currents of a speaker of standard American English that they would channel and manipulate the telekinetic power at the will of the speaker. Magic words, you might say. Spells.

'He was evidently further along than I suspected. I think he must have arrived at some words, tried them out, and made an attempt at telekinesis – some small thing, like causing an ashtray to rise off his desk and float in the air, perhaps. And it worked, but what he got wasn't a dainty little ashtray-lifting force; he had opened the gate wide, and some kind of terrible power came through. It's pure conjecture, of course, but it must have been something like that to have had an effect like *this*.'

Gilson had listened in silence. He said, 'I won't say you're crazy, because I can see that house and I'm watching what's happening to those ice cubes. How it happened isn't my problem, anyhow. My problem is what I'll recommend to the secretary that we do with it now that we've got it. One thing's sure, Krantz: this isn't going to be your private playpen much longer.'

There was a yelp of pure pain from Reeves. 'They can't *do* that,' he said. 'This is ours, it's the professor's. Look at it, look at that house. Do you want a bunch of damn engineers messing around with *that*?'

Gilson could understand how Reeves felt. The house was drenched now with the light of a red sunset; it seemed to glow from within with a deep, rosy blush. But, Gilson reflected, the sunset wasn't really necessary; sentiment and the universal, unacknowledged yearning for a simple, cleaner time would lend rosiness enough. He was quite aware that the surge of longing and nostalgia he felt was nostalgia for something he had never actually experienced, that the way of life the house epitomized for him was in fact his own creation, built from patches of novels and films; nonetheless he found himself hungry for that life, yearning for that time. It was a gentle and secure time, he thought, a time when the pace was unhurried and the air was clean; a time when there was grace and style, when young men in striped blazers and boater hats might pay decorous court to young ladies in long white dresses, whiling away the long drowsy afternoons of summer in peaceable conversations on shady porches. There would be jolly bicycle tours over shade-dappled roads that twisted among the hills to arrive at cool glens where swift little streams ran; there would be long sweet buggy rides behind somnolent patient horses under a great white moon, lover whispering urgently to lover while nightbirds sang. There would be excursions down the broad clean river, boats gentle on the current, floating toward the sound from across the water of a brass band playing at the landing.

Yes, thought Gilson, and there would probably be an old geezer with a trunkful of adjectives around somewhere, carrying on about how much better things had been a hundred years before. If he didn't watch himself he'd he helping Krantz and Reeves try to keep things hidden. Young Reeves – oddly, for someone his age – seemed to be hopelessly mired in this bogus nostalgia. His description of the family in the house had been simple doting. Oh, it was definitely time that the cold-eyed boys were called in. High time.

'They ought to be coming out any minute, now,' Reeves was saying. 'Wait till you see Martha.'

'Martha,' Gilson said.

'The little girl. She's a doll.'

Gilson looked at him. Reeves reddened and said, 'Well, I sort of gave them names. The children. Martha and Pete. And the dog's Alfie. They kind of look like those names, you know?' Gilson did not answer, and Reeves reddened further. 'Well, you can see for yourself. Here they come.'

A fine little family, as Reeves had said. After watching them for half an hour, Gilson was ready to concede that they were indeed most engaging, as perfect in their way as their house. They were just what it took to complete the picture, to make an authentic Victorian genre painting. Mama and Papa were good-looking and still in love, the children were healthy and merry and content with their world. Or so it seemed to him as he watched them in the darkening evening, imagining the comfortable, affectionate conversation of the parents as they sat on the porch swing, almost hearing the squeals of the children and the barking of the dog as they raced about the lawn. It was almost dark now; a mellow light of oil lamps glowed in the windows, and fireflies winked over the lawn. There was an arc of fire as the father tossed his cigar butt over the railing and rose to his feet. Then there followed a pretty little pantomime, as he called for the children, who duly protested, were duly permitted a few more minutes, and then were firmly commanded. They moved reluctantly to the porch and were shooed inside, and the dog, having delayed to give a shrub a final wetting, came scrambling up to join them. The children and the dog entered the house, then the mother and father. The door closed, and there was only the soft light from the windows.

Reeves exhaled a long breath. 'Isn't that something,' he said. 'That's the way to live, you know? If a person could just say to hell with all this crap we live in today and go back there and live like that ... And Martha, you saw Martha. An angel, right? Man, what I'd give to–'

Gilson interrupted him: 'When does the next batch of ice cubes go through?'

'– be able to – Uh, yeah. Let's see. The last penetration was at 3:15, just before you got here. Next one will be at 6:35 in the morning, if the pattern holds. And it has, so far.'

'I want to see that. But right now I've got to do some telephoning. Colonel!'

Gilson did not sleep that night, nor, apparently, did Krantz and Reeves. When he arrived at the clearing at five a.m. they were still there, unshaven and red-eyed, drinking coffee from thermos bottles. It was cloudy again, and the clearing was in total darkness except for a pale light from beyond the interface, where a sunny day was on the verge of breaking.

'Anything new?' Gilson asked.

'I think that's my question,' Krantz said. 'What's going to happen?'

'Just about what you expected, I'm afraid. I think that by evening this place is going to be a real hive. And by tomorrow night you'll be lucky if you can find a place to stand. I imagine Bannon's been on the phone since I called him at midnight, rounding up the scientists. And they'll round up the technicians. Who'll bring their machines. And the army's going to beef up the security. How about some of that coffee?'

'Help yourself. You bring bad news, Gilson.'

'Sorry,' Gilson said, 'but there it is.'

'Goddam!' Reeves said loudly. 'Oh, goddam!' He seemed to be about to burst into tears. 'That'll be the end for me, you know? They won't even let me in. A damn graduate student? In *psychology*? I won't get near the place. Oh, damn it to hell!' he glared at Gilson in rage and despair.

The sun had risen, bringing gray light to the clearing and brilliance to the house across the interface. There was no sound but the regular bang of the ice cube machine. The three men stared quietly at the house. Gilson drank his coffee.

'There's Martha,' Reeves said. 'Up there.' A small face had appeared between the curtains of a second-floor window, and bright blue eyes were surveying the morning. 'She does that every day,' Reeves said. 'Sits there and watches the birds and squirrels until I guess they call her for breakfast.' They stood and watched the little girl, who was looking at something that lay beyond the scope of their window on her world, something that would have been to their rear had the worlds been the same. Gilson almost found himself turning around to see what it was that she stared at. Reeves apparently had the same impulse. 'What's she looking at, do you think?' he said. 'It's not necessarily forest, like now. I think this was logged out earlier. Maybe a meadow? Cattle or horses on it? Man, what I'd give to be there and see what it is.'

Krantz looked at his watch and said, 'We'd better go over there. Just a few minutes, now.'

They moved to where the machine was monotonously batting ice cubes into the interface. A soldier with a stopwatch sat beside it, behind a table bearing a formidable chronometer and a sheaf of charts. He said, 'Two minutes, Dr. Krantz.'

Krantz said to Gilson, 'Just keep your eye on

the ice cubes. You can't miss it when it happens.' Gilson watched the machine, mildly amused by the rhythm of its homely sounds: *plink* – a cube drops; *whuff* – the paddle sweeps around; *bang* – paddle strikes ice cube. And then a flat trajectory to the interface, where the small orange missile abruptly vanishes. A second later, another. Then another.

'Five seconds,' the soldier called. 'Four. Three. Two. One. *Now*.'

His timing was off by a second; the ice cube disappeared like its predecessors. But the next one continued its flight and dropped onto the lawn, where it lay glistening. It was really a fact, then, thought Gilson. Time travel for ice cubes.

Suddenly behind him there was an incomprehensible shout from Krantz and another from Reeves, and then a loud, clear, and anguished, 'Reeves, *no*!' from Krantz. Gilson heard a thud of running feet and caught a flash of swift movement at the edge of his vision. He whirled in time to see Reeves' gangling figure hurtle past, plunge through the interface, and land sprawling on the lawn. Krantz said, violently, '*Fool*!' An ice cube shot through and landed near Reeves. The machine banged again; an ice cube flew out and vanished. The five seconds of accessibility were over.

Reeves raised his head and stared for a moment at the grass on which he lay. He shifted his gaze to the house. He rose slowly to his feet, wearing a bemused expression. A grin came slowly over his face, then, and the men watching from the other side could almost read his thoughts: Well, I'll be damned. I made it. I'm really here.

Krantz was babbling uncontrollably. 'We're still here, Gilson, we're still here, we still exist, everything seems the same. Maybe he didn't change things much, maybe the future is fixed and he didn't change anything at all. I was afraid of this, of something like this. Ever since you came out here, he's been –'

Gilson did not hear him. He was staring with shock and disbelief at the child in the window, trying to comprehend what he saw and did not believe he was seeing. Her behavior was wrong, it was very, very wrong. A man had materialized on her lawn, suddenly, out of thin air, on a sunny morning, and she had evinced no surprise or amazement or fear. Instead she had smiled – instantly, spontaneously, a smile that broadened and broadened until it seemed to split the lower half of her face, a smile that showed too many teeth, a smile fixed and incongruous and terrible below her bright blue eyes. Gilson felt his stomach knot; he realized that he was dreadfully afraid.

The face abruptly disappeared from the window; a few seconds later the front door flew open and the little girl rushed through the doorway, making for Reeves with furious speed, moving in a curious, scuttling run. When she was a few feet away, she leaped at him, with the agility and eye-dazzling quickness of a flea. Reeves' eyes had just begun to take on a puzzled look when the powerful little teeth tore out his throat.

She dropped away from him and sprang back. A geyser of bright blood erupted from the ragged hole in his neck. He looked at it in stupefaction for a long moment, then brought up his hands to cover the wound; the blood boiled through his fingers and ran down his forearms. He sank gently to his knees, staring at the little girl with wide astonishment. He rocked, shivered, and pitched forward on his face.

She watched with eyes as cold as a reptile's, the terrible smile still on her face. She was naked, and it seemed to Gilson that there was something wrong with her torso, as well as with her mouth. She turned and appeared to shout toward the house.

In a moment they all came rushing out, mother, father, little boy, and granny, all naked, all undergoing that hideous transformation of the mouth. Without pause or diminution of speed they scuttled to the body, crouched around it, and frenziedly tore off its clothes. Then, squatting on the lawn in the morning sunshine, the fine little family began horribly to feed.

Krantz's babbling had changed its tenor: 'Holy Mary, Mother of God, pray for us... ' The soldier with the stopwatch was noisily sick. Someone emptied a clip of a machine pistol into the interface, and the colonel cursed luridly. When Gilson could no longer bear to watch the grisly feast, he looked away and found himself staring at the dog, which sat happily on the porch, thumping its tail.

'By God, it just can't be!' Krantz burst out. 'It would be in the histories, in the newspapers, if there'd been people like that here. My God, something like that couldn't be forgotten!'

'Oh, don't talk like a fool!' Gilson said angrily. 'That's not the past. I don't know what it is, but it's not the past. Can't be. It's – I don't know – someplace else. Some other – dimension? Universe? One of those theories. Alternate worlds, worlds of If, probability worlds, whatever you call 'em. They're in the present time, all right, that filth over there. Culvergast's damn spell holed through to one of those parallels. Got to be something like that. And, my god, what the *hell* was its history to produce *those*? They're not human, Krantz, no way human, whatever they look like. "Jolly bicycle tours." How wrong can you be?'

It ended at last. The family lay on the grass with distended bellies, covered with blood and grease, their eyelids heavy in repletion. The two little ones fell asleep. The large male appeared to be deep in thought. After a time he rose, gathered up Reeves' clothes, and examined them carefully. Then he woke the small female and apparently questioned her at some length. She gestured, pointed, and pantomimed Reeves' headlong arrival. He stared thoughtfully at the place where Reeves had materialized, and for a moment it seemed to Gilson that the pitiless eyes were glaring directly into his. He turned, walked slowly and reflectively to the house, and went inside.

It was silent in the clearing except for the thump of the machine. Krantz began to weep, and the colonel to swear in a monotone. The soldiers seemed dazed. And we're all afraid, Gilson thought. Scared to death.

On the lawn they were enacting a grotesque parody of making things tidy after a picnic. The small ones had brought a basket and, under the meticulous supervision of the adult females, went about gathering up the debris of their feeding. One of them tossed a bone to the dog, and the timekeeper vomited again. When the lawn was once again immaculate, they carried off the basket to the rear, and the adults returned to the house. A moment later the male emerged, now dressed in a white linen suit. He carried a book.

'A Bible,' said Krantz in amazement. 'It's a Bible.'

'Not a Bible,' Gilson said. 'There's no way those – things could have Bibles. Something else. Got to be.'

It looked like a Bible; its binding was limp black leather, and when the male began to leaf through it, evidently in search of a particular passage, they could see that the paper was the thin, tough paper Bibles are printed on. He found his page and began, as it appeared to Gilson, to read aloud in a declamatory manner, mouthing the words.

'What the hell do you suppose he's up to?' Gilson said. He was still speaking when the window ceased to exist.

House and lawn and white-suited declaimer vanished. Gilson caught a swift glimpse of trees across the clearing, hidden until now by the window, and of a broad pit between him and the trees. Then he was knocked off his feet by a blast of wind, and the air was full of dust and flying trash and the wind's howl. The wind stopped, as suddenly as it had come, and there was a patter of falling small objects that had momentarily been wind-borne. The site of the house was entirely obscured by an eddying cloud of dust.

The dust settled slowly. Where the window had been there was a great hole in the ground, a perfectly square hole a hundred feet across and perhaps ten feet deep, its bottom as flat as a table. Gilson's glimpse of it before the wind had rushed in to fill the vacuum had shown the sides to be as smooth and straight as if sliced through cheese with a sharp knife; but now small landslides were occurring all around the perimeter, as topsoil and gravel caved and slid to the bottom, and the edges were becoming ragged and irregular.

Gilson and Krantz slowly rose to their feet. 'And that seems to be that,' Gilson said. 'It was here and now it's gone. But where's the prefab? Where's Culvergast?'

'God knows,' Krantz said. He was not being irreverent. 'But I think he's gone for good. And at least he's not where those things are.'

'What are they, do you think?'

'As you said, certainly not human. Less human

THE BROOD

Ramsey Campbell

Ramsey Campbell (1946–) is an award-winning horror-fiction author from Liverpool, England, mentored by Lovecraft protégé August Derleth. In his stories, largely evoking working- or middle-class settings, Campbell manages to update the weird tale and apply his keen ability to evoke both subtle supernatural horror and portraits of modern life in England. One of the preeminent writers of his generation, Campbell has also edited influential supernatural fiction anthologies; three of his top ten favorite stories are reprinted in *The Weird* ('The Willows' by Blackwood, 'Smoke Ghost' by Leiber and 'The Hospice' by Aickman). 'The Brood' (1980), as noted by the anthologist when first published, 'has the cumulative effect of a nightmare from which one cannot awake'.

He'd had an almost unbearable day. As he walked home his self-control still oppressed him, like rusty armour. Climbing the stairs, he tore open his mail: a glossy pamphlet from a binoculars firm, a humbler folder from the Wild Life Preservation Society. Irritably he threw them on the bed and sat by the window, to relax.

It was autumn. Night had begun to cramp the days. Beneath golden trees, a procession of cars advanced along Princes Avenue, as though to a funeral; crowds hurried home. The incessant anonymous parade, dwarfed by three stories, depressed him. Faces like these vague twilit miniatures – selfishly ingrown, convinced that nothing was their fault – brought their pets to his office.

But where were all the local characters? He enjoyed watching them, they fascinated him. Where was the man who ran about the avenue, chasing butterflies of litter and stuffing them into his satchel? Or the man who strode violently, head down in no gale, shouting at the air? Or the Rainbow Man, who appeared on the hottest days obese with sweaters, each of a different garish colour? Blackband hadn't seen any of these people for weeks.

The crowds thinned; cars straggled. Groups of streetlamps lit, tinting leaves sodium, unnaturally gold. Often that lighting had meant – Why, there she was, emerging from the side street almost on cue: the Lady of the Lamp.

Her gait was elderly. Her face was withered as an old blanched apple; the rest of her head was wrapped in a tattered grey scarf. Her voluminous ankle-length coat, patched with remnants of colour, swayed as she walked. She reached the central reservation of the avenue, and stood beneath a lamp.

Though there was a pedestrian crossing beside her, people deliberately crossed elsewhere. They would, Blackband thought sourly: just as they ignored the packs of stray dogs that were always someone else's responsibility – ignored them, or hoped someone would put them to sleep. Perhaps they felt the human strays should be put to sleep, perhaps that was where the Rainbow Man and the rest had gone!

The woman was pacing restlessly. She circled the lamp, as though the blurred disc of light at its foot were a stage. Her shadow resembled the elaborate hand of a clock.

Surely she was too old to be a prostitute. Might she have been one, who was now compelled to enact her memories? His binoculars drew her face closer: intent as a sleepwalker's, introverted as a foetus. Her head bobbed against gravel, foreshortened by the false perspective of the lenses. She moved offscreen.

Three months ago, when he'd moved to this flat, there had been two old women. One night he had seen them, circling adjacent lamps. The other woman had been slower, more sleepy. At last the Lady of the Lamp had led her home; they'd moved slowly as exhausted sleepers. For days he'd thought of the two women in their long faded coats, trudging around the lamps in the deserted avenue, as though afraid to go home in the growing dark.

The sight of the lone woman still unnerved him, a little. Darkness was crowding his flat. He drew the curtains, which the lamps stained orange. Watching had relaxed him somewhat. Time to make a salad.

The kitchen overlooked the old women's house. See The World from the Attics of Princes Avenue. All Human Life Is Here. Backyards penned in rubble and crumbling toilet sheds; on the far side of the back street, houses were lidless boxes of smoke. The house directly beneath his window was dark, as always. How could the two women – if both were still alive – survive in there? But at least they could look after themselves, or call for aid; they were human, after all. It was their pets that bothered him.

He had never seen the torpid woman again. Since she had vanished, her companion had begun to take animals home; he'd seen her coaxing them toward the house. No doubt they were company for her friend; but what life could animals enjoy in the lightless, probably condemnable house? And why so many? Did they escape to their homes, or stray again? He shook his head: the women's loneliness was no excuse. They cared as little for their pets as did those owners who came, whining like their dogs, to his office.

Perhaps the woman was waiting beneath the lamps for cats to drop from the trees, like fruit. He meant the thought as a joke. But when he'd finished preparing dinner, the idea troubled him sufficiently that he switched off the light in the main room and peered through the curtains.

The bright gravel was bare. Parting the curtains, he saw the woman hurrying unsteadily toward her street. She was carrying a kitten: her head bowed over the fur cradled in her arms; her whole body seemed to enfold it. As he emerged from the kitchen again, carrying plates, he heard her door creak open and shut. Another one, he thought uneasily.

By the end of the week she'd taken in a stray dog, and Blackband was wondering what should be done.

The women would have to move eventually. The houses adjoining theirs were empty, the windows shattered targets. But how could they take their menagerie with them? They'd set them loose to roam or, weeping, take them to be put to sleep.

Something ought to be done, but not by him. He came home to rest. He was used to removing chicken bones from throats; it was suffering the excuses that exhausted him – Fido always had his bit of chicken, it had never happened before, they couldn't understand. He would nod curtly, with a slight pained smile. 'Oh yes?' he would repeat tonelessly. 'Oh yes?'

Not that that would work with the Lady of the Lamp. But then, he didn't intend to confront her: what on earth could he have said? That he'd take all the animals off her hands? Hardly. Besides, the thought of confronting her made him uncomfortable.

She was growing more eccentric. Each day she appeared a little earlier. Often she would move away into the dark, then hurry back into the flat bright pool. It was as though light were her drug.

People stared at her, and fled. They disliked her because she was odd. All she had to do to please them, Blackband thought, was be normal: overfeed her pets until their stomachs scraped the ground, lock them in cars to suffocate in the heat, leave them alone in the house all day then beat them for chewing. Compared to most of the owners he met, she was Saint Francis.

He watched television. Insects were courting and mating. Their ritual dances engrossed and moved him: the play of colours, the elaborate racial patterns of the life-force which they instinctively decoded and enacted. Microphotography presented them to him. If only people were as beautiful and fascinating!

Even his fascination with the Lady of the Lamp was no longer unalloyed; he resented that. Was she falling ill? She walked painfully slowly, stooped over, and looked shrunken. Nevertheless, each night she kept her vigil, wandering sluggishly in the pools of light like a sleepwalker.

How could she cope with her animals now? How might she be treating them? Surely there were social workers in some of the cars nosing home, someone must notice how much she needed help. Once he made for the door to the stairs, but already his throat was parched of words. The thought of speaking to her wound him tight inside. It wasn't his job, he had enough to confront. The spring in his guts coiled tighter, until he moved away from the door.

One night an early policeman appeared. Usually the police emerged near midnight, disarming people of knives and broken glass, forcing them into the vans. Blackband watched eagerly. Surely the man must escort her home, see what the house hid. Blackband glanced back to the splash of light beneath the lamp. It was deserted.

How could she have moved so fast? He stared, baffled. A dim shape lurked at the corner of his eyes. Glancing nervously, he saw the woman standing on a bright disc several lamps away, considerably farther from the policeman than he'd thought. Why should he have been so mistaken?

Before he could ponder, a sound distracted him: a loud fluttering, as though a bird were trapped and frantic in the kitchen. But the room was empty. Any bird must have escaped through the open window. Was that a flicker of movement below, in the dark house? Perhaps the bird had flown in there.

The policeman had moved on. The woman was trudging her island of light; her coat's hem dragged over the gravel. For a while Blackband watched, musing uneasily, trying to think what the fluttering had resembled more than the sound of a bird's wings.

Perhaps that was why, in the early hours, he saw a man stumbling through the derelict back streets. Jagged hurdles of rubble blocked the way; the man clambered, panting dryly, gulping dust as well as breath. He seemed only exhausted and uneasy, but Blackband could see what was pursuing him: a great wide shadow-colored stain, creeping vaguely over the rooftops. The stain was alive, for its face mouthed – though at first, from its color and texture, he thought the head was the moon. Its eyes gleamed hungrily. As the fluttering made the man turn and scream, the face sailed down on its stain toward him.

Next day was unusually trying: a dog with a broken leg and a suffering owner, you'll hurt his leg, can't you be more gentle, oh come here, baby, what did the nasty man do to you; a senile cat and its protector, isn't the usual vet here today, he never used to do that, are you sure you know what you're doing. But later, as he watched the woman's obsessive trudging, the dream of the stain returned to him. Suddenly he realized he had never seen her during daylight.

So that was it! he thought, sniggering. She'd been a vampire all the time! A difficult job to keep when you hadn't a tooth in your head. He reeled in her face with the focusing-screw. Yes, she was toothless. Perhaps she used false fangs, or sucked through her gums. But he couldn't sustain his joke for long. Her face peered out of the frame of her grey scarf, as though from a web. As she circled she was muttering incessantly. Her tongue worked as though her mouth were too small for it. Her eyes were fixed as the heads of grey nails impaling her skull.

He laid the binoculars aside, and was glad that she'd become more distant. But even the sight of her trudging in miniature troubled him. In her eyes he had seen that she didn't want to do what she was doing.

She was crossing the roadway, advancing toward his gate. For a moment, unreasonably and with a sour uprush of dread, he was sure she intended to come in. But she was staring at the hedge. Her hands fluttered, warding off a fear; her eyes and her mouth were stretched wide. She stood quivering, then she stumbled toward her street, almost running.

He made himself go down. Each leaf of the hedge held an orange-sodium glow, like wet paint. But there was nothing among the leaves, and nothing could have struggled out, for the twigs were intricately bound by spiderwebs, gleaming like gold wire.

The next day was Sunday. He rode a train beneath the Mersey and went tramping the Wirral Way nature trail. Red-faced men, and women who had paralysed their hair with spray, stared as though he'd invaded their garden. A few butterflies perched on flowers; their wings settled together delicately, then they flickered away above the banks of the abandoned railway cutting. They were too quick for him to enjoy, even with his binoculars; he kept remembering how near death their species were. His moping had slowed him, he felt barred from his surroundings by his inability to confront the old woman. He couldn't speak to her, there were no words he could use, but meanwhile her animals might be suffering. He dreaded going home to another night of helpless watching.

Could he look into the house while she was wandering? She might leave the door unlocked. At some time he had become intuitively sure that her companion was dead. Twilight gained on him, urging him back to Liverpool.

He gazed nervously down at the lamps. Anything was preferable to his impotence. But his feelings had trapped him into committing himself before he was ready. Could he really go down when she emerged? Suppose the other woman was still alive, and screamed? Good God, he needn't go in if he didn't want to. On the gravel, light lay bare as a row of plates on a shelf. He found himself thinking, with a secret eagerness, that she might already have had her wander.

As he made dinner, he kept hurrying irritably to the front window. Television failed to engross him; he watched the avenue instead. Discs of light dwindled away, impaled by their lamps. Below the kitchen window stood a block of night and silence. Eventually he went to bed, but heard fluttering – flights of litter in the derelict streets, no doubt. His dreams gave the litter a human face.

Throughout Monday he was on edge, anxious to hurry home and be done; he was distracted. Oh poor Chubbles, is the man hurting you! He managed to leave early. Day was trailing down the sky as he reached the avenue. Swiftly he brewed coffee and sat sipping, watching.

The caravan of cars faltered, interrupted by gaps. The last home-comers hurried away, clearing the stage. But the woman failed to take her cue. His cooking of dinner was fragmented; he hurried repeatedly back to the window. Where was the bloody woman, was she on strike? Not until the following night, when she had still not appeared, did he begin to suspect he'd seen the last of her.

His intense relief was short-lived. If she had died of whatever had been shrinking her, what would happen to her animals? Should he find out what was wrong? But there was no reason to think she'd died. Probably she, and her friend before her, had gone to stay with relatives. No doubt the animals had escaped long before – he'd never seen or heard any of them since she had taken them in. Darkness stood hushed and bulky beneath his kitchen window.

For several days the back streets were quiet, except for the flapping of litter or birds. It became easier to glance at the dark house. Soon they'd demolish it; already children had shattered all the windows. Now, when he lay awaiting sleep, the thought of the vague house soothed him, weighed his mind down gently.

That night he awoke twice. He'd left the kitchen window ajar, hoping to lose some of the unseasonable heat. Drifting through the window came a man's low moaning. Was he trying to form words? His voice was muffled, blurred as a dying radio. He must be drunk; perhaps he had fallen, for there was a faint scrape of rubble. Blackband hid within his eyelids, courting sleep. At last the shapeless moaning faded. There was silence, except for the feeble, stony scraping. Blackband lay and grumbled, until sleep led him to a face that crept over heaps of rubble.

Some hours later he woke again. The lifelessness of four o'clock surrounded him, the dim air seemed sluggish and ponderous. Had he dreamed the new sound? It returned, and made him flinch: a chorus of thin, piteous wailing, reaching weakly upward toward the kitchen. For a moment, on the edge of dream, it sounded like babies. How could babies be crying in an abandoned house? The voices were too thin. They were kittens.

He lay in the heavy dark, hemmed in by shapes that the night deformed. He willed the sounds to cease, and eventually they did. When he awoke again, belatedly, he had time only to hurry to work.

In the evening the house was silent as a draped cage. Someone must have rescued the kittens. But in the early hours the crying woke him: fretful, bewildered, famished. He couldn't go down now, he had no light. The crying was muffled, as though beneath stone. Again it kept him awake, again he was late for work.

His loss of sleep nagged him. His smile sagged impatiently, his nods were contemptuous twitches. 'Yes,' he agreed with a woman who said she'd been careless to slam her dog's paw in a door, and when she raised her eyebrows haughtily: 'Yes, I can see that.' He could see her deciding to find another vet. Let her, let someone else suffer her. He had problems of his own.

He borrowed the office flashlight, to placate his anxiety. Surely he wouldn't need to enter the house, surely someone else – He walked home, toward the darker sky. Night thickened like soot on the buildings.

He prepared dinner quickly. No need to dawdle in the kitchen, no point in staring down. He was hurrying; he dropped a spoon, which reverberated shrilly in his mind, nerve-racking. Slow down, slow down. A breeze piped incessantly outside, in the rubble. No, not a breeze. When he made himself raise the sash he heard the crying, thin as wind in crevices.

It seemed weaker now, dismal and desperate: intolerable. Could nobody else hear it, did nobody care? He gripped the windowsill; a breeze tried feebly to tug at his fingers. Suddenly, compelled by vague anger, he grabbed the flashlight and trudged reluctantly downstairs.

A pigeon hobbled on the avenue, dangling the stump of one leg, twitching clogged wings; cars brisked by. The back street was scattered with debris, as though a herd had moved on, leaving its refuse to manure the paving stones. His flashlight groped over the heaped pavement, trying to determine which house had been troubling him.

Only by standing back to align his own window with the house could he decide, and even then he was unsure. How could the old woman have clambered over the jagged pile that blocked the doorway? The front door sprawled splintered in the hall, on a heap of the fallen ceiling, amid peelings of wallpaper. He must be mistaken. But as his flashlight dodged about the hall, picking up debris then letting it drop back into the dark, he heard the crying, faint and muffled. It was somewhere within.

He ventured forward, treading carefully. He had to drag the door into the street before he could proceed. Beyond the door the floorboards were cobbled with rubble. Plaster swayed about him, glistening. His light wobbled ahead of him, then led him toward a gaping doorway on the right. The light spread into the room, dimming.

A door lay on its back. Boards poked like exposed ribs through the plaster of the ceiling; torn paper dangled. There was no carton full of starving kittens; in fact, the room was bare. Moist stains engulfed the walls.

He groped along the hall, to the kitchen. The stove was fat with grime. The wallpaper had collapsed entirely, draping indistinguishable shapes that stirred as the flashlight glanced at them. Through the furred window, he made out the light in his own kitchen, orange-shaded, blurred. How could two women have survived here?

At once he regretted that thought. The old woman's face loomed behind him: eyes still as metal, skin the colour of pale bone. He turned nervously; the light capered. Of course there was only the quivering mouth of the hall. But the face was present now, peering from behind the draped shapes around him.

He was about to give up – he was already full of the gasp of relief he would give when he reached the avenue – when he heard the crying. It was almost breathless, as though close to death: a shrill feeble wheezing. He couldn't bear it. He hurried into the hall.

Might the creatures be upstairs? His light showed splintered holes in most of the stairs; through them he glimpsed a huge symmetrical stain on the wall. Surely the woman could never have climbed up there – but that left only the cellar.

The door was beside him. The flashlight, followed by his hand, groped for the knob. The face was near him in the shadows; its fixed eyes gleamed. He dreaded finding her fallen on the cellar steps. But the crying pleaded. He dragged the door open; it scraped over rubble. He thrust the flashlight into the dank opening. He stood gaping, bewildered.

Beneath him lay a low stone room. Its walls glistened darkly. The place was full of debris: bricks, planks, broken lengths of wood. Draping the debris, or tangled beneath it, were numerous old clothes. Threads of a white substance were tethered to everything, and drifted feebly now the door was opened.

In one corner loomed a large pale bulk. His light twitched toward it. It was a white bag of some material, not cloth. It had been torn open; except for a sifting of rubble, and a tangle of what might have been fragments of dully painted cardboard, it was empty.

The crying wailed, somewhere beneath the planks. Several sweeps of the light showed that the cellar was otherwise deserted. Though the face mouthed behind him, he ventured down. For God's sake, get it over with; he knew he would never dare return. A swath had been cleared through the dust on the steps, as though something had dragged itself out of the cellar, or had been dragged in.

His movements disturbed the tethered threads; they rose like feelers, fluttering delicately. The white bag stirred, its torn mouth worked. Without knowing why, he stayed as far from that corner as he could.

The crying had come from the far end of the cellar. As he picked his way hurriedly over the rubble he caught sight of a group of clothes. They were violently coloured sweaters, which the Rainbow Man had worn. They slumped over planks; they nestled inside one another, as though the man had withered or had been sucked out.

Staring uneasily about, Blackband saw that all the clothes were stained. There was blood on all of them, though not a great deal on any. The ceiling hung close to him, oppressive and vague. Darkness had blotted out the steps and the door. He caught at them with the light, and stumbled toward them.

The crying made him falter. Surely there were fewer voices, and they seemed to sob. He was nearer the voices than the steps. If he could find the creatures at once, snatch them up and flee – He clambered over the treacherous debris, toward a gap in the rubble. The bag mouthed emptily; threads plucked at him, almost impalpably. As he thrust the flashlight's beam into the gap, darkness rushed to surround him.

Beneath the debris a pit had been dug. Parts of its earth walls had collapsed, but protruding from the fallen soil he could see bones. They looked too large for an animal's. In the centre of the pit, sprinkled with earth, lay a cat. Little of it remained, except for its skin and bones; its skin was covered with deep pockmarks. But its eyes seemed to move feebly.

Appalled, he stooped. He had no idea what to do. He never knew, for the walls of the pit were shifting. Soil trickled scattering as a face the size of his fist emerged. There were several; their limbless bodies squirmed from the earth, all around the pit. From toothless mouths, their sharp tongues flickered out toward the cat. As he fled they began wailing dreadfully.

He chased the light toward the steps. He fell, cutting his knees. He thought the face with its gleaming eyes would meet him in the hall. He ran from the cellar, flailing his flashlight at the air. As he stumbled down the street he could still see the faces that had crawled from the soil: rudimentary beneath translucent skin, but beginning to be human.

He leaned against his gatepost in the lamplight, retching. Images and memories tumbled disordered through his mind. The face crawling over the roofs. Only seen at night. Vampire. The fluttering at the window. Her terror at the hedge full of spiders. *Calyptra*, what was it, *Calyptra eustrigata*. Vampire moth.

Vague though they were, the implications terrified him. He fled into his building, but halted fearfully on the stairs. The things must be destroyed: to delay would be insane. Suppose their hunger brought them crawling out of the cellar tonight, toward his flat – Absurd though it must be, he couldn't forget that they might have seen his face.

He stood giggling, dismayed. Whom did you call in these circumstances? The police, an exterminator? Nothing would relieve his horror until he saw the brood destroyed, and the only way to see that was to do the job himself. Burn. Petrol. He dawdled on the stairs, delaying, thinking he knew none of the other tenants from whom to borrow the fuel.

He ran to the nearby garage. 'Have you got any petrol?'

The man glared at him, suspecting a joke. 'You'd be surprised. How much do you want?'

How much indeed! He restrained his giggling. Perhaps he should ask the man's advice! Excuse me, how much petrol do you need for – 'A gallon,' he stammered.

As soon as he reached the back street he switched on his flashlight. Crowds of rubble lined the pavements. Far above the dark house he saw his orange light. He stepped over the debris into the hall. The swaying light brought the face forward to meet him. Of course the hall was empty.

He forced himself forward. Plucked by the flashlight, the cellar door flapped soundlessly. Couldn't he just set fire to the house? But that might leave the brood untouched. Don't think, go down quickly. Above the stairs the stain loomed.

In the cellar nothing had changed. The bag gaped, the clothes lay emptied. Struggling to unscrew the cap of the petrol can, he almost dropped the flashlight. He kicked wood into the pit and began to pour the petrol. At once he heard the wailing beneath him. 'Shut up!' he screamed, to drown out the sound. 'Shut up! Shut up!'

The can took its time in gulping itself empty; the petrol seemed thick as oil. He hurled the can clattering away, and ran to the steps. He fumbled with matches, gripping the flashlight between his knees. As he threw them, the lit matches went out. Not until he ventured back to the pit, clutching a ball of paper from his pocket, did he succeed in making a flame that reached his goal. There was a whoof of fire, and a chorus of interminable feeble shrieking.

As he clambered sickened toward the hall, he heard a fluttering above him. Wallpaper, stirring in a wind: it sounded moist. But there was no wind, for the air clung clammily to him. He slithered over the rubble into the hall, darting his light about. Something white bulked at the top of the stairs.

It was another torn bag. He hadn't been able to see it before. It slumped emptily. Beside it the stain spread over the wall. That stain was too symmetrical; it resembled an inverted coat. Momentarily he thought the paper was drooping, tugged perhaps by his unsteady light, for the stain had begun to creep down toward him. Eyes glared at him from its dangling face. Though the face was upside down he knew it at once. From its gargoyle mouth a tongue reached for him.

He whirled to flee. But the darkness that filled the front door was more than night, for it was advancing audibly. He stumbled, panicking, and rubble slipped from beneath his feet. He fell from the cellar steps, onto piled stone. Though he felt almost no pain, he heard his spine break.

His mind writhed helplessly. His body refused to heed it in any way, and lay on the rubble, trapping him. He could hear cars on the avenue, radio sets and the sounds of cutlery in flats, distant and indifferent. The cries were petering out now. He tried to scream, but only his eyes could move. As they struggled, he glimpsed through a slit in the cellar wall the orange light in his kitchen.

His flashlight lay on the steps, dimmed by its fall. Before long a rustling darkness came slowly down the steps, blotting out the light. He heard sounds in the dark, and something that was not flesh nestled against him. His throat managed a choked shriek that was almost inaudible, even to him. Eventually the face crawled away toward the hall, and the light returned. From the corner of his eye he could see what surrounded him. They were round, still, practically featureless: as yet, hardly even alive.

THE AUTOPSY

Michael Shea

Michael Shea (1946–) is an American writer of horror, dark fantasy, and science fiction who has won the World Fantasy Award several times. Shea's unique work includes novels like *Nifft the Lean* (1982) that are influenced by Jack Vance but stand on their own for the intensity of their imagery and grotesquery of their situations. *The Color Out of Time* (1984) is similarly an homage to H. P. Lovecraft's 'The Color Out of Space' that has its own unique appeal. At the short length, Shea has written several masterpieces, including 'The Autopsy' (1980), a Hugo and Nebula award finalist. Clinical, precise, humane, and terrifying, 'The Autopsy' plays with the idea of demonic possession from a weird science fiction perspective.

Dr Winter stepped out of the tiny Greyhound station and into the midnight street that smelled of pines. The station's window showed the only light, save for a luminous clockface several doors down and a little neon beer logo two blocks farther on. He could hear a river. It ran deep in a gorge west of town, but the town was only a few streets wide and a mile or so long, and the current's blurred roar was distinct, like the noise of a ghost river running between the banks of dark shop windows. When he had walked a short distance, Dr Winters set his suitcase down, pocketed his hands, and looked at the stars – thick as cobblestones in the black gulf.

'A mountain hamlet – a mining town,' he said. 'Stars. No moon. We are in Bailey.'

He was talking to his cancer. It was in his stomach. Since learning of it, he had developed this habit of wry communion with it. He meant to show courtesy to this uninvited guest, Death. It would not find him churlish, for that would make its victory absolute. Except, of course, that its victory would *be* absolute, with or without his ironies.

He picked up his suitcase and walked on. The starlight made faint mirrors of the windows' blackness and showed him the man who passed: lizard-lean, white-haired (at fifty-seven), a man traveling on death's business, carrying his own death in him, and even bearing death's wardrobe in his suitcase. For this was filled – aside from his medical kit and some scant necessities – with mortuary bags. The sheriff had told him on the phone of the improvisations that presently enveloped the corpses, and so the doctor had packed these, laying them in his case with bitter amusement, checking the last one's breadth against his chest before the mirror, as a woman will gauge a dress before donning it, and telling his cancer:

'Oh, yes, that's plenty roomy enough for both of us!'

The case was heavy, and he stopped frequently to rest and scan the sky. What a night's work to do, probing pungent, soulless filth, eyes earthward, beneath such a ceiling of stars! It had taken five days to dig the ten men out. The autumnal equinox had passed, but the weather here had been uniformly hot. And warmer still, no doubt, so deep in the earth.

He entered the courthouse by a side door. His heels knocked on the linoleum corridor. A door at the end of it, on which was lettered NATE CRAVEN, COUNTY SHERIFF, opened well before he reached it, and his friend stepped out to meet him.

'Dammit, Carl, you're *still* so thin they could use you for a whip. Gimme that. You're in too good a shape already. You don't need the exercise.'

The case hung weightless from the Sheriff's hand, imparting no tilt at all to his bull shoulders. Despite his implied self-derogation, he was only moderately paunched for a man his age and size. He had a rough-hewn face, and the bulk of brow, nose, and jaw made his greenish eyes look small until one engaged them and felt the snap and penetration of their intelligence. In the office he half filled two cups from a coffee urn and topped both off with bourbon from a bottle in his desk. When they had finished these, they had finished trading news of mutual friends. The sheriff mixed another round and sipped from his, in a silence clearly prefatory to the work at hand.

'They talk about rough justice,' he said. 'I've sure seen it now. One of those… patients of yours that you'll be working on? He was a killer. Christ, "killer" doesn't half say it. A killer's the least of what he was. The blast killing *him*, that was the justice part. Those other nine, they were the rough. And it just galls the hell out of me, Carl! If that kiss-ass boss of yours has his way, the rough won't even stop with their being dead! There won't even be any compensation for their survivors! Tell me – has he broke his back yet? I mean, touching his toes for Fordham Mutual?'

'You refer, I take it, to the estimable Coroner Waddleton of Fordham County.' Dr Winters paused to sip his drink. With a delicate flaring of his nostrils he communicated all the disgust, contempt, and amusement he had felt in his four years as pathologist in Waddleton's office. The sheriff laughed.

'Clear pictures seldom emerge from anything the coroner says,' the doctor continued. 'He took your name in vain. Vigorously and repeatedly. These expressions formed his opening remarks. He then developed the theme of our office's strict responsibility to the letter of the law, and of the workmen's compensation law in particular. Death benefits accrue only to the dependants of decedents whose deaths arise *out of the course of* their employment, not merely *in* the course of it. Victims of a maniacal assault, though they die on the job, are by no means necessarily compensable under the law. We then contemplated the tragic injustice of an insurance company – *any* insurance company – having to pay benefits to unentitled persons, solely through the laxity and incompetence of investigating officers. Your name came up again, and Coroner Waddleton subjected it to further abuse. Fordham Mutual, campaign contributor or not, is certainly a major insurance company and is therefore entitled to the same fair treatment that all such companies deserve.'

Craven uttered a bark of wrathful mirth and spat expertly into his wastebasket. 'Ah, the impartial public servant! What's seven widows and sixteen dependent children, next to Fordham Mutual?' He drained his cup and sighed. 'I'll tell you what, Carl. We've been five days digging those men out and the last two days sifting half that mountain for explosive traces, with those insurance investigators hanging on our elbows, and the most they could say was that there was "strong presumptive evidence" of a bomb. Well, I don't budge for that because I don't have to. Waddleton can shove his "extraordinary circumstances." If you don't find anything in those bodies, then that's all the autopsy there is to it, and they get buried right here where their families want 'em.'

The doctor was smiling at his friend. He finished his cup and spoke with his previous wry detachment, as if the sheriff had not interrupted his narrative.

'The honorable coroner then spoke with remarkable volubility on the subject of Autopsy Consent forms and the malicious subversion of private citizens by vested officers of the law. He had, as it happened, a sheaf of such forms on his desk, all signed, all with a rider clause typed in above the signatures. A cogent paragraph. It had, among its other qualities, the property of turning the coroner's face purple when he read it aloud. He read it aloud to me three times. It appeared that the survivors' consent was contingent on two conditions: that the autopsy be performed in *loco mortis*, that is to say in Bailey, and that only if the coroner's pathologist found concrete evidence of homicide should the decedents be subject either to removal from Bailey or to further necropsy. It was well written. I remember wondering who wrote it.'

The sheriff nodded musingly. He took Dr Winters's empty cup, set it by his own, filled both two-thirds with bourbon, and added a splash of coffee to the doctor's. The two friends exchanged a level stare, rather like poker players in the clinch. The sheriff regarded his cup, sipped from it.

'*In loco mortis*. What-all does that mean exactly?'

'"In the place of death."'

'Oh. Freshen that up for you?'

'I've just started it, thank you.'

Both men laughed, paused, and laughed again, some might have said immoderately.

'He all but told me that I *had* to find something to compel a second autopsy,' the doctor said at length. 'He would have sold his soul – or taken out a second mortgage on it – for a mobile X-ray unit. He's right, of course. If those bodies have trapped any bomb fragments, that would be the surest and quickest way of finding them. It still amazes me your Dr Parsons could let his X-ray go unfixed for so long.'

'He sets bones, stitches wounds, writes prescriptions, and sends anything tricky down the mountain. Just barely manages that. Drunks don't get much done.'

'He's gotten that bad?'

'He hangs on and no more. Waddleton was right there, not deputizing him pathologist. I doubt he could find a cannonball in a dead rat. I wouldn't say it where it could hurt him, as long as he's still managing, but everyone here knows it. His patients sort of look after *him* half the time. But Waddleton would have sent you, no matter who was here. Nothing but his best for party contributors like Fordham Mutual.'

The doctor looked at his hands and shrugged. 'So. There's a killer in the batch. Was there a bomb?'

Slowly the sheriff planted his elbows on the desk and pressed his hands against his temples, as if the question had raised a turbulence of memories. For the first time the doctor – half hearkening throughout to the never-quite-muted stirrings of the death within him – saw his friend's exhaustion: the tremor of hand, the bruised look under the eyes.

'When I've told you what we have, I guess you'll end up assuming what I do about it. But I think assuming is as far as any of us will get with this one. It's one of those nightmare specials, Carl. The ones no one ever does get to the bottom of.

'All right, then. About two months ago, we had a man disappear – Ronald Hanley. Mine worker, rock-steady, family man. He didn't come home one night, and we never found a trace of him. OK, that happens sometimes. About a week later, the lady that ran the laundromat, Sharon Starker, *she* disappeared, no trace. We got edgy then. I made an announcement on the local radio about a possible weirdo at large, spelled out special precautions everybody should take. We put both our squad cars on the night beat, and by day we set to work knocking on every door in town collecting alibis for the two times of disappearance.

'No good. Maybe you're fooled by this uniform and think I'm a law officer, protector of the people, and all that? A natural mistake. A lot of people were fooled. In less than seven weeks, six people vanished, just like that. Me and my deputies might as well have stayed in bed round the clock, for all the good we did.' The sheriff drained his cup.

'Anyway, at last we got lucky. Don't get me wrong now. We didn't go all hog-wild and actually prevent a crime or anything. But we *did* find a body – except it wasn't the body of any of the seven people that had disappeared. We'd taken to combing the woods nearest town, with temporary deputies from the miners to help. Well, one of those boys was out there with us last week. It was hot – like it's been for a while now – and it was real quiet. He heard this buzzing noise and looked around for it, and he saw a beeswarm up in the crotch of a tree. Except he was smart enough to know that that's not usual around here – beehives. So it wasn't bees. It was bluebottle flies, a goddamned big cloud of them, all over a bundle that was wrapped in a tarp.'

The sheriff studied his knuckles. He had, in his eventful life, occasionally met men literate enough to understand his last name and rash enough to be openly amused by it, and the knuckles – scarred knobs – were eloquent of his reactions. He looked back into his old friend's eyes.

'We got that thing down and unwrapped it. Billy Lee Davis, one of my deputies, he was in Viet Nam, been near some bad, bad things and held on. Billy Lee blew his lunch all over the ground when we unwrapped that thing. It was a man. Some of a man. We knew he'd stood six-two because all the bones were there, and he'd probably weighed between two fifteen and two twenty-five, but he folded up no bigger than a big-size laundry package. Still had his face, both shoulders, and the left arm, but all the rest was clean. It wasn't animal work. It was knife work, all the edges neat as butcher cuts. Except butchered meat, even when you drain it all you can, will bleed a good deal afterwards, and there wasn't one goddamned drop of blood on the tarp, nor in that meat. It was just as pale as fish meat.'

Deep in his body's center, the doctor's cancer touched him. Not a ravening attack – it sank one fang of pain, questioningly, into new untasted flesh, probing the scope for its appetite there. He disguised his tremor with a shake of the head.

'A cache, then.'

The sheriff nodded. 'Like you might keep a pot roast in the icebox for making lunches. I took some pictures of his face, then we put him back and erased our traces. Two of the miners I'd deputized did a lot of hunting, were woods-smart. So I left them on the first watch. We worked out positions and cover for them, and drove back.

'We got right on tracing him, sent out descriptions to every town within a hundred miles. He was no one I'd ever seen in Bailey, nor anyone else either, it began to look like, after we'd combed the town all day with the photos. Then, out of the blue, Billy Lee Davis smacks himself on the forehead and says, "Sheriff, *I* seen this man somewhere in town, and not long ago!"'

'He'd been shook all day since throwing up, and then all of a sudden he just snapped to. Was dead sure. Except he couldn't remember where or when. We went over and over it, and he tried and tried. It got to where I wanted to grab him by the ankles and hang him upside down and shake him till it dropped out of him. But it was no damn use. Just after dark we went back to that tree – we'd worked out a place to hide the cars and a route to it through the woods. When we were close, we walkie-talkied the men we'd left for an all-clear to come up. No answer at all. And when we got there, all that was left of our trap was the tree. No body, no tarp, no Special Assistant Deputies. Nothing.'

This time Dr Winters poured the coffee and bourbon. 'Too much coffee,' the sheriff muttered, but drank anyway. 'Part of me wanted to chew nails and break necks. And part of me was scared shitless. When we got back, I got on the radio station again and made an emergency broadcast and then had the man at the station rebroadcast it every hour. Told everyone to do everything in groups of three, to stay together at night in threes at least, to go out little as possible, keep armed and keep checking up on each other. It had such a damn-fool sound to it, but just pairing-up was no protection if half of one of those pairs was the killer. I sent our corpse's picture out statewide, I deputized more men and put them on the streets to beef up the night patrol.

'It was next morning that things broke. The sheriff of Rakehell called – he's over in the next county. He said our corpse looked a lot like a man named Abel Dougherty, a mill-hand with Con Wood over there. I left Billy Lee in charge and drove right out.

'This Dougherty had a cripple older sister he always checked back to by phone whenever he left town for long, a habit no one knew about, probably embarrassed him. Sheriff Peck there only found out about it when the woman called him, said her brother'd been four days gone for vacation and not rung her once. He'd hardly had her report for an hour when he got the picture I sent out, and recognized it. And *I* hadn't been in his office more than ten minutes when Billy Lee called me there. He'd remembered.

'When he'd seen Dougherty was the Sunday night three days before we found him. Where he'd seen him was the Trucker's Tavern outside the north end of town. The man had made a stir by being jolly drunk and latching onto a miner who was drinking there, man named Joe Allen, who'd started at the mine about two months back. Dougherty kept telling him that he wasn't Joe Allen, but Dougherty's old buddy named Sykes that had worked with him at Con Wood for a coon's age, and what the hell kind of joke was this, come have a beer old buddy and tell me why you took off so sudden and what the hell you been doing with yourself.

'Allen took it laughing. Dougherty'd clap him on the shoulder, Allen'd clap him right back and make every kind of joke about it, say, "Give this man another beer, I'm standing in for a long-lost friend of his." Dougherty was so big and loud and stubborn, Billy Lee was worried about a fight starting, and he wasn't the only one worried. But this Joe Allen was a natural good ol' boy, handled it perfect. We'd checked him out weeks back along with everyone else, and he was real popular with the other miners. Finally Dougherty swore he was going to take him on to another bar to help celebrate the vacation Dougherty was starting out on. Joe Allen got up grinning, said goddamn it, he couldn't accommodate Dougherty by being this fellow Sykes, but he could sure as hell have a glass with any serious drinking man that was treating. He went out with him, and gave everyone a wink as he left, to the general satisfaction of the audience.'

Craven paused. Dr Winters met his eyes and knew his thought, two images: the jolly wink that roused the room to laughter, and the thing in the tarp aboil with bright blue flies.

'It was plain enough for me,' the sheriff said. 'I told Billy Lee to search Allen's room at the Skettles' boardinghouse and then go straight to the mine and take him. We could fine-polish things once we had him. Since I was already in Rakehell, I saw to some of the loose ends before I started back. I went with Sheriff Peck down to Con Wood, and we found a picture of Eddie Sykes in the personnel files. I'd seen Joe Allen often enough, and it was his picture in that file.

'We found out Sykes had lived alone, was an on-again, off-again worker, private in his comings and goings, and hadn't been around for a while. But one of the sawyers there could be pretty sure of when Sykes left Rakehell because he'd gone to Sykes's cabin the morning after a big meteor shower they had out there about nine weeks back, since some thought the shower might have reached the ground, and not far from Sykes's side of the mountain. He wasn't in that morning, and the sawyer hadn't seen him since.

'After all those weeks, it was sewed up just like that. Within another hour I was almost back in Bailey, had the pedal to the metal, and was barely three miles out of town, when it all blew to shit. I *heard* it blow, I was that close to collaring him. I tell you, Carl, I felt... like a *bullet*. I was going to rip right through this Sykes, this goddamned cannibal monster...

'We had to reconstruct what happened. Billy Lee got impatient and went after him alone, but luckily he radioed Travis – my other deputy – first. Travis was on the mountain dragnetting around that tree for clues, but he happened to be near his car when Billy Lee called him. He said he'd just been through Allen's room and had got something really odd. It was a sphere, half again big as a basketball, heavy, made of something that wasn't metal or glass but was a little like both. He could half-see into it, and it looked to be full of some kind of circuitry and components. He hadn't found anything else unusual. He was going to take this thing along with him, and go after Allen now. He told Travis to get up to the mine for backup. He'd be there first and should already have Allen by the time Travis arrived.

'Tierney, the shift boss up there, had an assistant that told us the rest. Billy Lee parked behind the offices where the men in the yard wouldn't see the car. He went upstairs to arrange the arrest with Tierney. They got half a dozen men together. Just as they came out of the building, they saw Allen take off running from the squad car. He had the sphere under his arm.

'The whole compound's fenced in, and Tierney'd already phoned to have all the gates shut. Allen zigged and zagged some but caught on quick to the trap. The sphere slowed him, but he still had a good lead. He hesitated a minute and then ran straight for the main shaft. A cage was just going down with a crew, and he risked every bone in him jumping down after it, but he got safe on top. By the time they got to the switches, the cage was down to the second level, and Allen and the crew had got out. Tierney got it back up. Billy Lee ordered the rest back to get weapons and follow, and him and Tierney rode the cage right back down. And about two minutes later half the goddamned mine blew up.'

The sheriff stopped as if cut off, his lips parted to say more, his eyes registering for perhaps the hundredth time his amazement that there was no more, that the weeks of death and mystification ended here, with this split-second recapitulation: more death, more answerless dark, sealing all.

'Nate.'

'What.'

'Wrap it up and go to bed. I don't need your help. You're dead on your feet.'

'I'm not on my feet. And I'm coming along.'

'Give me a picture of the victims' position relative to the blast. I'm going to work, and you're going to bed.'

The sheriff shook his head absently. 'They're mining in shrinkage stopes. The adits – levels – branch off lateral from the vertical shaft. From one level they hollow out overhand up to the one above. Scoop out big chambers and let most of the broken rock stay inside so they can stand on the heaps to cut the ceiling higher. They leave sections of support wall between stopes, and those men were buried several stopes in from the shaft. The cave-in killed *them*. The mountain just folded them up in their own hill of tailings. No kind of fragments reached them. I'm dead sure. The only ones they *found* were of some standard charges that the main blast set off, and those didn't even get close. The big one blew out where the adit joined the shaft, right where, and right when, Billy Lee and Tierney got out of the cage. And there is *nothing* left there, Carl. No sphere, no cage, no Tierney, no Billy Lee Davis. Just rock blown fine as flour.'

Dr Winters nodded and, after a moment, stood up.

'Come on, Nate. I've got to get started. I'll be lucky to have even a few of them done before morning. Drop me off and go to sleep, till then at least. You'll still be there to witness most of the work.'

The sheriff rose, took up the doctor's suitcase, and led him out of the office without a word, concession in his silence.

The patrol car was behind the building. The doctor saw a crueller beauty in the stars than he had an hour before. They got in, and Craven swung them out onto the empty street. The doctor opened the window and hearkened, but the motor's surge drowned out the river sound. Before the thrust of their headlights, ranks of old-fashioned parking meters sprouted shadows tall across the sidewalks, shadows that shrank and were cut down by the lights' passage. The sheriff said:

'All those extra dead. For nothing! Not even to… *feed* him! If it was a bomb, and he made it, he'd know how powerful it was. He wouldn't try some stupid escape stunt with it. And how did he even know that globe was there? We worked it out that Allen was just ending a shift, but he wasn't even up out of the ground before Billy Lee'd parked out of sight from the shaft.'

'Let it rest, Nate. I want to hear more, but after you've slept. I know you. All the photos will be there, and the report complete, all the evidence neatly boxed and carefully described. When I've looked things over, I'll know exactly how to proceed by myself.'

Bailey had neither hospital nor morgue, and the bodies were in a defunct ice-plant on the edge of town. A generator had been brought down from the mine, lighting improvised, and the refrigeration system reactivated. Dr Parsons's office, and the tiny examining room that served the sheriff's station in place of a morgue, had furnished this makeshift with all the equipment that Dr Winters would need beyond what he carried with him. A quarter-mile outside the main body of the town, they drew up to it.

Treeflanked, unneighbored by any other structure, it was a double building; the smaller half – the office – was illuminated. The bodies would be in the big windowless refrigerator segment. Craven pulled up beside a second squad car parked near the office door. A short rake-thin man wearing a large white stetson got out of the car and came over. Craven rolled down his window.

'Trav. This here's Dr Winters.'

"'Lo, Nate. Dr Winters. Everything's shipshape inside. Felt more comfortable out here. Last of those newshounds left two hours ago.'

'They sure do hang on. You take off now, Trav. Get some sleep and be back at sunup. What temperature we getting?'

The pale stetson, far clearer in the starlight than the shadowface beneath it, wagged dubiously. 'Thirty-six. She won't get lower – some kind of leak.'

'That should be cold enough,' the doctor said.

Travis drove off, and the sheriff unlocked the padlock on the office door. Waiting behind him, Dr Winters heard the river again – a cold balm, a whisper of freedom – and overlying this, the stutter and soft snarl of the generator behind the building, a gnawing, remorseless sound that somehow fed the obscure anguish that the other soothed. They went in.

The preparations had been thoughtful and complete. 'You can wheel 'em out of the fridge on this and do the examining in here,' the sheriff said, indicating a table and a gurney. 'You should find all the gear you need on this big table here, and you can write up your reports on that desk. The phone's not hooked up – there's a pay phone at the last gas station if you have to call me.'

The doctor nodded, checking over the material on the larger table: scalpels, postmortem and cartilage knives, intestine scissors, rib shears, forceps, probes, mallet and chisels, a blade saw and electric bone saw, scale, jars for specimens, needles and suture, sterilizer, gloves… Beside this array were a few boxes and envelopes with descriptive sheets attached, containing the photographs and such evidentiary objects as had been found associated with the bodies.

'Excellent,' he muttered.

'The overhead light's fluorescent, full spectrum or whatever they call it. Better for colors. There's a pint of decent bourbon in that top desk drawer. Ready to look at 'em?'

'Yes.'

The sheriff unbarred and slid back the big metal door to the refrigeration chamber. Icy tainted air boiled out of the doorway. The light within was dimmer than that provided in the office – a yellow gloom wherein ten oblong heaps lay on trestles.

The two stood silent for a time, their stillness a kind of unpremeditated homage paid the eternal mystery at its threshold. As if the cold room were in fact a shrine, the doctor found a peculiar awe in the row of veiled forms. The awful unison of their dying, the titan's grave that had been made for them, conferred on them a stern authority, Death's Chosen Ones. His stomach hurt, and he found he had his hand pressed to his abdomen. He glanced at Craven and was relieved to see that his friend, staring wearily at the bodies, had missed the gesture.

'Nate. Help me uncover them.'

Starting at opposite ends of the row, they stripped the tarps off and piled them in a corner. Both were brusque now, not pausing over the revelation of the swelled, pulpy faces – most three-lipped with the gaseous burgeoning of their tongues – and the fat, livid hands sprouting from the filthy sleeves. But at one of the bodies Craven stopped. The doctor saw him look, and his mouth twist. Then he flung the tarp on the heap and moved to the next trestle.

When they came out, Dr Winters took out the bottle and glasses Craven had put in the desk, and they had a drink together. The sheriff made as if he would speak, but shook his head and sighed.

'I *will* get some sleep, Carl. I'm getting crazy thoughts with this thing.' The doctor wanted to ask those thoughts. Instead he laid a hand on his friend's shoulder.

'Go home, Sheriff Craven. Take off the badge and lie down. The dead won't run off on you. We'll all still be here in the morning.'

When the sound of the patrol car faded, the doctor stood listening to the generator's growl and the silence of the dead, resurgent now. Both the sound and the silence seemed to mock him. The after-echo of his last words made him uneasy. He said to his cancer:

'What about it, dear colleague? We *will* still be here tomorrow? All of us?'

He smiled, but felt an odd discomfort, as if he had ventured a jest in company and roused a hostile silence. He went to the refrigerator door, rolled it back, and viewed the corpses in their ordered rank, with their strange tribunal air. 'What, sirs?' he murmured. 'Do you judge me? Just who is to examine whom tonight, if I may ask?'

He went back into the office, where his first step was to examine the photographs made by the sheriff in order to see how the dead had lain at their uncovering. The earth had seized them with terrible suddenness. Some crouched, some partly stood, others sprawled in crazy free-fall postures. Each successive photo showed more of the jumble as the shovels continued their work between shots. The doctor studied them closely, noting the identifications inked on the bodies as they came completely into view.

One man, Roger Willet, had died some yards from the main cluster. It appeared he had just straggled into the stope from the adit at the moment of the explosion. He should thus have received, more directly than any of the others, the shock waves of the blast. If bomb fragments were to be found in any of the corpses, Mr Willet's seemed likeliest to contain them. Dr Winters pulled on a pair of surgical gloves.

Willet lay at one end of the line of trestles. He wore a thermal shirt and overalls that were strikingly new beneath the filth of burial. Their tough fabrics jarred with the fabric of his flesh – blue, swollen, seeming easily torn or burst, like ripe fruit. In life Willet had grease-combed his hair. Now it was a sculpture of dust, spikes and whorls shaped by the head's last grindings against the mountain that clenched it.

Rigor had come and gone – Willet rolled laxly onto the gurney. As the doctor wheeled him past the others, he felt a slight self-consciousness. The sense of some judgment flowing from the dead assembly – unlike most such vagrant fantasies – had an odd tenacity in him. This stubborn unease began to irritate him with himself, and he moved more briskly.

He put Willet on the examining table and cut the clothes off him with shears, storing the pieces in an evidence box. The overalls were soiled with agonal waste expulsions. The doctor stared a moment with unwilling pity at his naked subject.

'You won't ride down to Fordham in any case,' he said to the corpse. 'Not unless I find something pretty damned obvious.' He pulled his gloves tighter and arranged his implements.

Waddleton had said more to him than he had reported to the sheriff. The doctor was to find, and forcefully to record that he had found, strong 'indications' absolutely requiring the decedents' removal to Fordham for X-ray and an exhaustive second postmortem. The doctor's continued employment with the Coroner's Office depended entirely on his compliance in this. He had received this stipulation with a silence Waddleton had not thought it necessary to break. His present resolution was all but made at that moment. Let the obvious be taken as such. If the others showed as plainly as Willet did the external signs of death by asphyxiation, they would receive no more than a thorough external exam. Willet he would examine internally as well, merely to establish in depth for this one what should appear obvious in all. Otherwise, only when the external exam revealed a clearly anomalous feature – and clear and suggestive it must be – would he look deeper.

He rinsed the caked hair in a basin, poured the sediment into a flask and labeled it. Starting with the scalp, he began a minute scrutiny of the body's surfaces, recording his observations as he went.

The characteristic signs of asphyxial death were evident, despite the complicating effects of autolysis and putrefaction. The eyeballs' bulge and the tongue's protrusion were, by now, as much due to gas pressure as to the mode of death, but the latter organ was clamped between locked teeth, leaving little doubt as to that mode. The coloration of degenerative change – a greenish-yellow tint, a darkening and mapping-out of superficial veins – was marked, but not sufficient to obscure the blue of cyanosis on the face and neck, nor the pinpoint hemorrhages freckling neck, chest, and shoulders. From the mouth and nose the doctor scraped matter he was confident was the blood-tinged mucous typically ejected in the airless agony.

He began to find a kind of comedy in his work. What a buffoon death made of a man! A blue pop-eyed three-lipped thing. And there was himself, his curious solicitous intimacy with this clownish carrion. Excuse me, Mr Willet, while I probe this laceration. What do you feel when I do this? Nothing? Nothing at all? Fine, now what about these nails? Split them clawing at the earth, did you? Yes. A nice bloodblister under this thumbnail, I see – got it on the job a few days before your accident, no doubt? Remarkable calluses here, still quite tough …

The doctor looked for an unanalytic moment at the hands – puffed dark paws, gestureless, having renounced all touch and grasp. He felt the wastage of the man concentrated in the hands. The painful futility of the body's fine articulation when it is seen in death – this poignancy he had long learned not to acknowledge when he worked. But now he let it move him a little. This Roger Willet, plodding to his work one afternoon, had suddenly been scrapped, crushed to a nonfunctional heap of perishable materials. It simply happened that his life had chanced to move too close to the passage of a more powerful life, one of those inexorable and hungry lives that leave human wreckage – known or undiscovered – in their wakes. Bad luck, Mr Willet. Naturally, we feel very sorry about this. But this Joe Allen, your co-worker. Apparently he was some sort of … cannibal. It's complicated. We don't understand it all. But the fact is we have to dismantle you now to a certain extent. There's really no hope of your using these parts of yourself again, I'm afraid. Ready now?

The doctor proceeded to the internal exam with a vague eagerness for Willet's fragmentation, for the disarticulation of that sadness in his natural form. He grasped Willet by the jaw and took up the postmortem knife. He sank its point beneath the chin and began the long, gently sawing incision that opened Willet from throat to groin.

In the painstaking separation of the body's laminae Dr Winters found absorption and pleasure. And yet throughout he felt, marginal but insistent, the movement of a stream of irrelevant images. These were of the building that contained him, and of the night containing it. As from outside, he saw the plant – bleached planks, iron roofing – and the trees crowding it, all in starlight, a ghosttown image. And he saw the refrigerator vault beyond the wall as from within, feeling the stillness of murdered men in a cold yellow light. And at length a question formed itself, darting in and out of the weave of his concentration as the images did: Why did he still feel, like some stir of the air, that sense of mute vigilance surrounding his action, furtively touching his nerves with its inquiry as he worked? He shrugged, overtly angry now. Who else was attending but Death? Wasn't he Death's hireling, and this Death's place? Then let the master look on.

Peeling back Willet's cover of hemorrhage-stippled skin, Dr Winters read the corpse with an increasing dispassion, a mortuary text. He confined his inspection to the lungs and mediastinum and found there unequivocal testimony to Willet's asphyxial death. The pleurae of the lungs exhibited the expected ecchymoses – bruised spots in the glassy enveloping membrane. Beneath, the polyhedral surface lobules of the lungs themselves were bubbled and blistered – the expected interstitial emphysema. The lungs, on section, were intensely and bloodily congested. The left half of the heart he found contracted and empty, while the right was overdistended and engorged with dark blood, as were the large veins of the upper mediastinum. It was a classic picture of death by suffocation, and at length the doctor, with needle and suture, closed up the text again.

He returned the corpse to the gurney and draped one of his mortuary bags over it in the manner of a shroud. When he had help in the morning, he would weigh the bodies on a platform scale the office contained and afterward bag them properly. He came to the refrigerator door, and hesitated. He stared at the door, not moving, not understanding why.

Run. Get out. Now.

The thought was his own, but it came to him so urgently he turned around as if someone behind him had spoken. Across the room a thin man in smock and gloves, his eyes shadows, glared at the doctor from the black windows. Behind the man was a shrouded cart, behind that, a wide metal door.

Quietly, wonderingly, the doctor asked, 'Run from what?' The eyeless man in the glass was still half-crouched, afraid.

Then, a moment later, the man straightened, threw back his head, and laughed. The doctor walked to the desk and sat down shoulder to shoulder with him. He pulled out the bottle and they had a drink together, regarding each other with identical bemused smiles. Then the doctor said, 'Let me pour you another. You need it, old fellow. It makes a man himself again.'

Nevertheless his reentry of the vault was difficult, toilsome, each step seeming to require a new summoning of the will to move. In the freezing half-light all movement felt like defiance. His body lagged behind his craving to be quick, to be done with this molestation of the gathered dead. He returned Willet to his pallet and took his neighbor. The name on the tag wired to his boot was Ed Moses. Dr Winters wheeled him back to the office and closed the big door behind him.

With Moses his work gained momentum. He expected to perform no further internal necropsies. He thought of his employer, rejoicing now in his seeming-submission to Waddleton's ultimatum. The impact would be dire. He pictured the coroner in shock, a sheaf of Pathologist's Reports in one hand, and smiled.

Waddleton could probably make a plausible case for incomplete examination. Still, a pathologist's discretionary powers were not well-defined. Many good ones would approve the adequacy of the doctor's method, given his working conditions. The inevitable litigation with a coalition of compensation claimants would be strenuous and protracted. Win or lose, Waddleton's venal devotion to the insurance company's interest would be abundantly displayed. Further, immediately on his dismissal the doctor would formally disclose its occult cause to the press. A libel action would ensue that he would have as little cause to fear as he had to fear his firing. Both his savings and the lawsuit would long outlast his life.

Externally, Ed Moses exhibited a condition as typically asphyxial as Willet's had been, with no slightest mark of fragment entry. The doctor finished his report and returned Moses to the vault, his movements brisk and precise. His unease was all but gone. That queasy stirring of the air – had he really felt it? It had been, perhaps, some new reverberation of the death at work in him, a psychic shudder of response to the cancer's stealthy probing for his life. He brought out the body next to Moses in the line.

Walter Lou Jackson was big, six feet two inches from heel to crown, and would surely weigh out at more than two hundred pounds. He had writhed mightily against his million-ton coffin with an agonal strength that had torn his face and hands. Death had mauled him like a lion. The doctor set to work.

His hands were fully themselves now – fleet, exact, intricately testing the corpse's character as other fingers might explore a keyboard for its latent melodies. And the doctor watched them with an old pleasure, one of the few that had never failed him, his mind at one remove from their busy intelligence. All the hard deaths! A worldful of them, time without end. Lives wrenched kicking from their snug meat-frames. Walter Lou Jackson had died very hard. Joe Allen brought this on you, Mr Jackson. We think it was part of his attempt to escape the law.

But what a botched flight! The unreason of it – more than baffling – was eerie in its colossal futility. Beyond question, Allen had been cunning. A ghoul with a psychopath's social finesse. A good old boy who could make a tavernful of men laugh with delight while he cut his victim from their midst, make them applaud his exit with the prey, who stepped jovially into the darkness with murder at his side clapping him on the shoulder. Intelligent, certainly, with a strange technical sophistication as well, suggested by the sphere. Then what of the lunacy yet more strongly suggested by the same object? In the sphere was concentrated all the lethal mystery of Bailey's long nightmare.

Why the explosion? Its location implied an ambush for Allen's pursuers, a purposeful detonation. Had he aimed at a limited cave-in from which he schemed some inconceivable escape? Folly enough in this – far more if, as seemed sure, Allen had made the bomb himself, for then he would have to know its power was grossly inordinate to the need.

But if it was not a bomb, had a different function

and only incidentally an explosive potential, Allen might underestimate the blast. It appeared the object was somehow remotely monitored by him, for the timing of events showed he had gone straight for it the instant he emerged from the shaft – shunned the bus waiting to take his shift back to town and made a beeline across the compound for a patrol car that was hidden from his view by the office building. This suggested something more complex than a mere explosive device, something, perhaps, whose destruction was itself more Allen's aim than the explosion produced thereby.

The fact that he risked the sphere's retrieval at all pointed to this interpretation. For the moment he sensed its presence at the mine, he must have guessed that the murder investigation had led to its discovery and removal from his room. But then, knowing himself already liable to the extreme penalty, why should Allen go to such lengths to recapture evidence incriminatory of a lesser offense, possession of an explosive device?

Then grant that the sphere was something more, something instrumental to his murders that could guarantee a conviction he might otherwise evade. Still, his gambit made no sense. Since the sphere – and thus the lawmen he could assume to have taken it was already at the mine office, he must expect the compound to be scaled at any moment. Meanwhile, the gate was open, escape into the mountains a strong possibility for a man capable of stalking and destroying two experienced and well-armed woodsmen lying in ambush for him. Why had he all but ensured his capture to weaken a case against himself that his escape would have rendered irrelevant? Dr Winters watched as his own fingers, like a hunting pack round a covert, converged on a small puncture wound below Walter Lou Jackson's xiphoid process, between the eighth ribs.

His left hand touched its borders, the fingers' inquiry quick and tender. The right hand introduced a probe, and both together eased it into the wound. It was rarely fruitful to use a probe on corpses this decayed; the track of the wound would more properly be examined by section. But an inexplicable sense of urgency had taken hold of him. Gently, with infinite pains not to pierce in the softened tissues an artifactual track of his own, he inched the probe in. It moved unobstructed deep into the body, curving upward through the diaphragm toward the heart. The doctor's own heart accelerated. He watched his hands move to record the observation, watched them pause, watched them return to their survey of the corpse, leaving pen and page untouched.

External inspection revealed no further anomaly. All else he observed the doctor recorded faithfully, wondering throughout at the distress he felt. When he had finished, he understood it. Its cause was not the discovery of an entry wound that might bolster Waddleton's case. For the find had, within moments, revealed to him that, should he encounter anything he thought to be a mark of fragment penetration, he was going to ignore it. The damage Joe Allen had done was going to end here, with this last grand slaughter, and would not extend to the impoverishment of his victims' survivors. His mind was now made up: for Jackson and the remaining seven, the external exams would be officially recorded as contraindicating the need for any external exam.

No, the doctor's unease as he finished Jackson's external – as he wrote up his report and signed it – had a different source. His problem was that he did not believe the puncture in Jackson's thorax *was* a mark of fragment entry. He disbelieved this, and had no idea why he did so. Nor had he any idea why, once again, he felt afraid. He sealed the report. Jackson was now officially accounted for and done with. Then Dr Winters took up the postmortem knife and returned to the corpse.

First the long sawing slice, unzippering the mortal overcoat. Next, two great square flaps of flesh reflected, scrolled laterally to the armpits' line, disrobing the chest: one hand grasping the flap's skirt, the other sweeping beneath it with the knife, flensing through the glassy tissue that joined it to the chest wall, and shaving all muscles from their anchorages to bone and cartilage beneath. Then the dismantling of the strongbox within. Rib shears – so frank and forward a tool, like a gardener's. The steel beak bit through each rib's gristle anchor to the sternum's centerplate. At the sternum's crownpiece the collarbones' ends were knifed, pried, and sprung free from their sockets. The coffer unhasped, unhinged, a knife teased beneath the lid and levered it off.

Some minutes later the doctor straightened up and stepped back from his subject. He moved almost drunkenly, and his age seemed scored more deeply in his face. With loathing haste he stripped his gloves off. He went to the desk, sat down, and poured another drink. If there was something like horror in his face, there was also a hardening in his mouth's line and the muscles of his jaw. He spoke to his glass: 'So be it, your Excellency. Something new for your humble servant. Testing my nerve?'

Jackson's pericardium, the shapely capsule containing his heart, should have been all but hidden between the big blood-fat loaves of his lungs. The doctor had found it fully exposed, the lungs flanking it wrinkled lumps less than a third their natural bulk. Not only they, but the left heart and the superior mediastinal veins – all the regions that should have been grossly engorged with blood – were utterly drained of it.

The doctor swallowed his drink and got out the photographs again. He found that Jackson had died on his stomach across the body of another worker, with the upper part of a third trapped between them. Neither these two subjacent corpses nor the surrounding earth showed any stain of a blood loss that must have amounted to two liters.

Possibly the pictures, by some trick of shadow, had failed to pick it up. He turned to the Investigator's Report, where Craven would surely have mentioned any significant amounts of bloody earth uncovered during the disinterment. The sheriff recorded nothing of the kind. Dr Winters returned to the pictures.

Ronald Pollock, Jackson's most intimate associate in the grave, had died on his back, beneath and slightly askew of Jackson, placing most of their torsos in contact, save where the head and shoulder of the third interposed. It seemed inconceivable Pollock's clothing should lack any trace of such massive drainage from a death mate thus embraced.

The doctor rose abruptly, pulled on fresh gloves, and returned to Jackson. His hands showed a more brutal speed now, closing the great incision temporarily with a few widely spaced sutures. He replaced him in the vault and brought out Pollock, striding, heaving hard at the dead shapes in the shifting of them, thrusting always – so it seemed to him – just a step ahead of urgent thoughts he did not want to have, deformities that whispered at his back, emitting faint, chill gusts of putrid breath. He shook his head – denying, delaying – and pushed the new corpse onto the worktable. The scissors undressed Pollock in greedy bites.

But at length, when he had scanned each scrap of fabric and found nothing like the stain of blood, he came to rest again, relinquishing that simplest, desired resolution he had made such haste to reach. He stood at the instrument table, not seeing it, submitting to the approach of the half-formed things at his mind's periphery.

The revelation of Jackson's shriveled lungs had been more than a shock. He had felt a stab of panic too, in fact that same curiously explicit terror of this place that had urged him to flee earlier. He acknowledged now that the germ of that quickly suppressed terror had been a premonition of this failure to find any trace of the missing blood. Whence the premonition? It had to do with a problem he had steadfastly refused to consider: the mechanics of so complete a drainage of the lungs' densely reticulated vascular structure. Could the earth's crude pressure by itself work so thoroughly, given only a single vent both slender and strangely curved? And then the photograph he had studied. It frightened him now to recall the image – some covert meaning stirred within it, struggling to be seen. Dr Winters picked the probe up from the table and turned again to the corpse. As surely and exactly as if he had already ascertained the wound's presence, he leaned forward and touched it: a small, neat puncture, just beneath the xiphoid process. He introduced the probe. The wound received it deeply, in a familiar direction.

The doctor went to the desk and took up the photograph again. Pollock's and Jackson's wounded areas were not in contact. The third man's head was sandwiched between their bodies at just that point. He searched out another picture, in which this third man was more central, and found his name inked in below his image: Joe Allen.

Dreamingly, Dr Winters went to the wide metal door, shoved it aside, entered the vault. He did not search, but went straight to the trestle where Sheriff Craven had paused some hours before. He found the same name on its tag.

The body, beneath decay's spurious obesity, was trim and well-muscled. The face was square-cut, shelf-browed, with a vulpine nose skewed by an old fracture. The swollen tongue lay behind the teeth, and the bulge of decomposition did not obscure what the man's initial impact must have been – handsome and open, his now-waxen black eyes sly and convivial. Say, good buddy, got a minute? I see you comin' on the swing shift every day, don't I? Yeah, Joe Allen. Look, I know it's late, you want to get home, tell the wife you ain't been in there drinkin' since you got off, right? Oh, yeah, I hear that. But this damn disappearance thing's got me so edgy, and I'd swear to God just as I was coming here I seen someone moving around back of that frame house up the street. See how the trees thin out a little down back of the yard, where the moonlight gets in? That's right. Well, I got me this little popper here. Oh, yeah, that's a beauty, we'll have it covered between us. I knew I could spot a man ready for some trouble – couldn't find a patrol car anywhere on the street. Yeah, just down in here now, to that clump of pine. Step careful, you can barely see. That's right…

The doctor's face ran with sweat. He turned on his heel and walked out of the vault, heaving the door shut behind him. In the office's greater warmth he felt the perspiration soaking his shirt under the smock. His stomach rasped with steady oscillations of pain, but he scarcely attended it. He went to Pollock and seized up the postmortem knife.

The work was done with surreal speed, the laminae of flesh and bone recoiling smoothly beneath his desperate but unerring hands, until the thoracic cavity lay exposed, and in it, the vampire-stricken lungs, two gnarled lumps of gray tissue.

He searched no deeper, knowing what the heart and veins would show. He returned to sit at the desk, weakly drooping, the knife, forgotten, still in his left hand. He looked at his reflection in the window, and it seemed his thoughts originated with that fainter, more tenuous Dr Winters hanging like a ghost outside.

What was this world he lived in? Surely, in a lifetime, he had not begun to guess. To feed in such a way! There was horror enough in this alone. But to feed thus *in his own grave*. How had he accomplished it – leaving aside how he had fought suffocation long enough to do anything at all? How was it to be comprehended, a greed that raged so hotly it would glut itself at the very threshold of its own destruction? That last feast was surely in his stomach still.

Dr Winters looked at the photograph, at Allen's head snugged into the others' middles like a hungry suckling nuzzling to the sow. Then he looked at the knife in his hand. The hand felt empty of all technique. Its one impulse was to slash, cleave, obliterate the remains of this gluttonous thing, this Joe Allen. He must do this, or flee it utterly. There was no course between. He did not move.

'I *will* examine him,' said the ghost in the glass, and did not move. Inside the refrigeration vault, there was a slight noise.

No. It had been some hitch in the generator's murmur. Nothing in there could move. There was another noise, a brief friction against the vault's inner wall. The two old men shook their heads at one another. A catch clicked, and the metal door slid open. Behind the staring image of his own amazement, the doctor saw that a filthy shape stood in the doorway and raised its arms toward him in a gesture of supplication. The doctor turned in his chair. From the shape came a whistling groan, the decayed fragment of a human voice.

Pleadingly, Joe Allen worked his jaw and spread his purple hands. As if speech were a maggot struggling to emerge from his mouth, the blue tumescent face toiled, the huge tongue wallowed helplessly between the viscid lips.

The doctor reached for the telephone, lifted the receiver. Its deadness to his ear meant nothing – he could not have spoken. The thing confronting him, with each least movement that it made, destroyed the very frame of sanity in which words might have meaning, reduced the world itself around him to a waste of dark and silence, a starlit ruin where already, everywhere, the alien and unimaginable was awakening to its new dominion. The corpse raised and reached out one hand as if to stay him – turned, and walked toward the instrument table. Its legs were leaden, it rocked its shoulders like a swimmer, fighting to make its passage through gravity's dense medium. It reached the table and grasped it exhaustedly. The doctor found himself on his feet, crouched slightly, weightlessly still. The knife in his hand was the only part of himself he clearly felt, and it was like a tongue of fire, a crematory flame. Joe Allen's corpse thrust one hand among the instruments. The thick fingers, with a queer simian ineptitude, brought up a scalpel. Both hands clasped the little handle and plunged the blade between the lips, as a thirsty child might a Popsicle, then jerked it out again, slashing the tongue. Turbid fluid splashed down to the floor. The jaw worked stiffly, the mouth brought out words in a wet ragged hiss:

'Please. Help me. Trapped in *this*.' One dead hand struck the dead chest. 'Starving.'

'What are you?'

'Traveler. Not of Earth.'

'An eater of human flesh. A drinker of human blood.'

'No. No. Hiding only. Am small. Shape hideous to you. Feared death.'

'You brought death.' The doctor spoke with the calm of perfect disbelief, himself as incredible to him as the thing he spoke with. It shook its head, the dull, popped eyes glaring with an agony of thwarted expression.

'Killed none. Hid in this. Hid in this not to be killed. Five days now. Drowning in decay. Free me. Please.'

'No. You have come to feed on us, you are not hiding in fear. We are your food, your meat and drink. You fed on those two men within your grave. *Their* grave. For you, a delay. In fact, a diversion that has ended the hunt for you.'

'No! No! Used men already dead. For me, five days, starvation. Even less. Fed only from need. Horrible necessity!'

The spoiled vocal instrument made a mangled gasp of the last word – an inhuman snake-pit noise the doctor felt as a cold flicker of ophidian tongues within his ears – while the dead arms moved in a sodden approximation of the body language that swears truth.

'No,' the doctor said. 'You killed them all. Including your… tool – this man. *What are you*?' Panic erupted in the question that he tried to bury by answering himself instantly. 'Resolute, yes. That surely. You used death for an escape route. You need no oxygen perhaps.'

'Extracted more than my need from gasses of decay. A lesser component of our metabolism.'

The voice was gaining distinctness, developing makeshifts for tones lost in the agonal rupturing of the valves and stops of speech, more effectively wrestling vowel and consonant from the putrid tongue and lips. At the same time the body's crudity of movement did not quite obscure a subtle, incessant experimentation. Fingers flexed and stirred, testing the give of tendons, groping the palm for old points of purchase and counterpressure there. The knees, with cautious repetitions, assessed the new limits of their articulation.

'What was the sphere?'

'My ship. Its destruction our first duty facing discovery.' (Fear touched the doctor, like a slug climbing his neck; he had seen, as it spoke, a sharp spastic activity of the tongue, a pleating and shrinkage of its bulk as at the tug of some inward adjustment.) 'No chance to reenter. Leaving this body takes far too long. Not even time to set it for destruct – must extrude a cilium, chemical key to broach hull shield. In shaft was my only chance to halt my host.'

Though the dead mask hung expressionless, conveyed no irony, the thing's articulacy grew uncannily – each word more smoothly shaped, nuances of tone creeping into its speech. Its right arm tested its wrist as it spoke, and the scalpel the hand still held cut white sparks from the air, while the word *host* seemed itself a little razor-cut, an almost teasing abandonment of fiction preliminary to attack.

But the doctor found that fear had gone from

him. The impossibility with which he conversed, and was about to struggle, was working in him an overwhelming amplification of his life's long helpless rage at death. He found his parochial pity for Earth alone stretched to the transstellar scope this traveler commanded, to the whole cosmic trash yard with its bulldozed multitudes of corpses; galactic wheels of carnage – stars, planets with their most majestic generations – all trash, cracked bones and foul rags that pooled, settled, reconcatenated in futile symmetries gravid with new multitudes of briefly animate trash.

And this, standing before him now, was the death it was given him particularly to deal – his mite was being called in by the universal Treasury of Death, and Dr Winters found himself, an old healer, on fire to pay. His own, more lethal, blade tugged at his hand with its own sharp appetite. He felt entirely the Examiner once more, knew the precise cuts he would make, swiftly and without error. *Very soon now*, he thought and coolly probed for some further insight before its onslaught:

'Why must your ship be destroyed, even at the cost of your host's life?'

'We must not be understood.'

'The livestock must not understand what is devouring them.'

'Yes, Doctor. Not all at once. But one by one. You will understand what is devouring you. That is essential to my feast.'

The doctor shook his head. 'You are in your grave already, Traveler. That body will be your coffin. You will be buried in it a second time, for all time.'

The thing came one step nearer and opened its mouth. The flabby throat wrestled as with speech, but what sprang out was a slender white filament, more than whip-fast. Dr Winters saw only the first flicker of its eruption, and then his brain nova-ed, thinning out at light-speed to a white nullity.

When the doctor came to himself, it was in fact to a part of himself only. Before he had opened his eyes he found that his wakened mind had repossessed proprioceptively only a bizarre truncation of his body. His head, neck, left shoulder, arm, and hand declared themselves – the rest was silence.

When, he opened his eyes, he found that he lay supine on the gurney, and naked. Something propped his head. A strap bound his left elbow to the gurney's edge, a strap he could feel. His chest was also anchored by a strap, and this he could not feel. Indeed, save for its active remnant, his entire body might have been bound in a block of ice, so numb was it, and so powerless was he to compel the slightest movement from the least part of it.

The room was empty, but from the open door of the vault there came slight sounds: the creak and soft frictions of heavy tarpaulin shifted to accommodate some business involving small clicking and kissing noises.

Tears of fury filled the doctor's eyes. Clenching his one fist at the starry engine of creation that he could not see, he ground his teeth and whispered in the hot breath of strangled weeping:

'Take it back, this dirty little shred of life! I throw it off gladly like the filth it is.' The slow knock of boot soles loudened from within the vault, and he turned his head. From the vault door Joe Allen's corpse approached him.

It moved with new energy, though its gait was grotesque, a ducking, hitching progress, jerky with circumventions of decayed muscle, while above this galvanized, struggling frame, the bruise-colored face hung inanimate, an image of detachment. With terrible clarity the thing was revealed for what it was – a damaged hand-puppet vigorously worked from within. And when that frozen face was brought to hang above the doctor, the reeking hands, with the light, solicitous touch of friends at sickbeds, rested on his naked thigh.

The absence of sensation made the touch more dreadful than if felt. It showed him that the nightmare he still desperately denied at heart had annexed his body while he – holding head and arm free – had already more than half-drowned in its mortal paralysis. There, from his chest on down, lay his nightmare part, a nothingness freely possessed by an unspeakability. The corpse said:

'Rotten blood. Thin nourishment. I had only one hour alone before you came. I fed from my neighbor to my left – barely had strength to extend a siphon. Fed from the right while you worked. Tricky going – you are alert. I expected Dr Parsons. The energy needs of animating this' – one hand left the doctor's thigh and smote the dusty overalls – 'and of host-transfer, very high. Once I have you synapsed, I will be near starvation again.'

A sequence of unbearable images unfolded in the doctor's mind, even as the robot carrion turned from the gurney and walked to the instrument table: the sheriff's arrival just after dawn, alone of course, since Craven always took thought for his deputies' rest and because on this errand he would want privacy to consider any indiscretion on behalf of the miners' survivors that the situation might call for; Craven's finding his old friend, supine and alarmingly weak; his hurrying over, his leaning near. Then, somewhat later, a police car containing a rack of still wet bones might plunge off the highway above some deep spot in the gorge.

The corpse took an evidence box from the table and put the scalpel in it. Then it turned and retrieved the mortuary knife from the floor and put that in as well, saying as it did so, without turning, 'The sheriff will come in the morning. You spoke like close friends. He will probably come alone.'

The coincidence with his thoughts had to be accident, but the intent to terrify and appall him was clear. The tone and timing of that patched-up voice were unmistakably deliberate – sly probes that sought his anguish specifically, sought his mind's personal center. He watched the corpse – over at the table – dipping an apish but accurate hand and plucking up rib shears, scissors, clamps, adding all to the box. He stared, momentarily emptied by shock of all but the will to know finally the full extent of the horror that had appropriated his life. Joe Allen's body carried the box to the worktable beside the gurney, and the expressionless eyes met the doctor's.

'I have gambled. A grave gamble. But now I have won. At risk of personal discovery we are obliged to disconnect, contract, hide as well as possible in the host-body. Suicide in effect. I disregarded situational imperatives, despite starvation before disinterment and subsequent autopsy being all but certain. I caught up with the crew, tackled Pollock and Jackson microseconds before the blast. I computed five days' survival from this cache. I could disconnect at limit of my strength to do so, but otherwise I would chance autopsy, knowing the doctor was an alcoholic incompetent. And now see my gain. You are a prize host. Through you I can feed with near impunity even when killing is too dangerous. Safe meals are delivered to you still warm.'

The corpse had painstakingly aligned the gurney parallel to the worktable but offset, the table's foot extending past the gurney's, and separated from it by a distance somewhat less than the reach of Joe Allen's right arm. Now the dead hands distributed the implements along the right edge of the table, save for the scissors and the box. These the corpse took to the table's foot, where it set down the box and slid the scissors's jaws round one strap of its overalls. It began to speak again, and as it did, the scissors dismembered its cerements in unhesitating strokes.

'The cut must be medical, forensically right, though a smaller one is easier. I must be careful of the pectoral muscles or these arms will not convey me. I am no larva anymore – over fifteen hundred grams.'

To ease the nightmare's suffocating pressure, to thrust out some flicker of his own will against its engulfment, the doctor flung a question, his voice more cracked than the other's now was:

'Why is my arm free?'

'The last, fine neural splicing needs a sensory-motor standard, to perfect my brain's fit to yours. Lacking this eye-hand coordinating check, only a much coarser control of the host's characteristic motor patterns is possible. This done, I flush out the paralytic, unbind us, and we are free together.'

The grave-clothes had fallen in a puzzle of fragments, and the cadaver stood naked, its dark gas-rounded contours making it seem some sleek marine creature, ruddered with the black-veined gas-distended sex. Again the voice had teased for his fear, had uttered the last word with a savoring protraction, and now the doctor's cup of anguish brimmed over; horror and outrage wrenched his spirit in brutal alternation as if trying to tear it naked from its captive frame. He rolled his head in this deadlock, his mouth beginning to split with the slow birth of a mind-emptying outcry.

The corpse watched this, giving a single nod that

might have been approbation. Then it mounted the worktable and, with the concentrated caution of some practiced convalescent reentering his bed, lay on its back. The dead eyes again sought the living and found the doctor staring back, grinning insanely.

'Clever corpse!' the doctor cried. 'Clever, carnivorous corpse! Able alien! Please don't think I'm criticizing. Who am I to criticize? A mere arm and shoulder, a talking head, just a small piece of a pathologist. But I'm confused.' He paused, savoring the monster's attentive silence and his own buoyancy in the hysterical levity that had unexpectedly liberated him. 'You're going to use your puppet there to pluck you out of itself and put you on me. But once he's pulled you from your driver's seat, won't he go dead, so to speak, and drop you? You could get a nasty knock. Why not set a plank between the tables – the puppet opens the door, and you scuttle, ooze, lurch, flop, slither, as the case may be, across the bridge. No messy spills. And in any case, isn't this an odd, rather clumsy way to get around among your cattle? Shouldn't you at least carry your own scalpels when you travel? There's always the risk you'll run across that one host in a million that isn't carrying one with him.'

He knew his gibes would be answered to his own despair. He exulted, but solely in the momentary bafflement of the predator – in having, for just a moment, mocked its gloating assurance to silence and marred its feast.

Its right hand picked up the postmortem knife beside it, and the left wedged a roll of gauze beneath Allen's neck, lifting the throat to a more prominent arch. The mouth told the ceiling:

'We retain larval form till entry of the host. As larvae we have locomotor structures, and sense buds usable outside our ships' sensory amplifiers. I waited coiled round Joe Allen's bed leg till night, entered by his mouth as he slept.' Allen's hand lifted the knife, held it high above the dull, quick eyes, turning it in the light. 'Once lodged, we have three instars to adult form,' the voice continued absently – the knife might have been a mirror from which the corpse read its features. 'Larvally we have only a sketch of our full neural tap. Our metamorphosis is cued and determined by the host's endosomatic ecology. I matured in three days.' Allen's wrist flexed, tipping the knife's point downmost. 'Most supreme adaptations are purchased at the cost of inessential capacities.' The elbow pronated and slowly flexed, hooking the knife bodyward. 'Our hosts are all sentients, ecodominants, are already carrying the baggage of coping structures for the planetary environment we find them in. Limbs, sensory portals' – the fist planted the fang of its tool under the chin, tilted it and rode it smoothly down the throat, the voice proceeding unmarred from under the furrow that the steel ploughed – 'somatic envelopes, instrumentalities' – down the sternum, diaphragm, abdomen the stainless blade painted its stripe of gaping, muddy tissue – 'with a host's brain we inherit all these, the mastery of any planet, netted in its dominant's cerebral nexus. Thus our genetic codings are now all but disencumbered of such provisions.'

So swiftly that the doctor flinched, Joe Allen's hand slashed four lateral cuts from the great wound's axis. The seeming butchery left two flawlessly drawn thoracic flaps cleanly outlined. The left hand raised the left flap's hem, and the right coaxed the knife into the aperture, deepening it with small stabs and slices. The posture was a man's who searches a breast pocket, with the dead eyes studying the slow recoil of flesh. The voice, when it resumed, had geared up to an intenser pitch:

'Galactically, the chordate nerve/brain paradigm abounds, and the neural labyrinth is our dominion. Are we to make plank bridges and worm across them to our food? Are cockroaches greater than we for having legs to run up walls and antennae to grope their way? All the quaint, hinged crutches that life sports! The stilts, fins, fans, springs, stalks, flippers, and feathers, all in turn so variously terminating in hooks, clamps, suckers, scissors, forks, or little cages of digits! And besides all the gadgets it concocts for wrestling through its worlds, it is all knobbed, whiskered, crested, plumed, vented, spiked, or measeled over with perceptual gear for combing pittances of noise or color from the environing plentitude.'

Invincibly calm and sure, the hands traded tool and tasks. The right flap eased back, revealing ropes of ingeniously spared muscle while promising a genuine appearance once sutured back in place. Helplessly the doctor felt his delirious defiance bleed away and a bleak fascination rebind him.

'We are the taps and relays that share the host's aggregate of afferent nerve-impulse precisely at its nodes of integration. We are the brains that peruse these integrations, integrate them with our existing banks of host-specific data, and, lastly, let their consequences flow down the motor pathway – either the consequences they seek spontaneously, or those we wish to graft upon them. We are besides a streamlined alimentary/circulatory system and a reproductive apparatus. And more than this we need not be.'

The corpse had spread its bloody vest, and the feculent hands now took up the rib shears. The voice's sinister coloration of pitch and stress grew yet more marked – the phrases slid from the tongue with a cobra's seeking sway, winding their liquid rhythms round the doctor till a gap in his resistance should let them pour through to slaughter the little courage left him.

'For in this form we have inhabited the densest brainweb of three hundred races, lain intricately snug within them like thriving vine on trelliswork. We've looked out from too many variously windowed masks to regret our own vestigial senses. None read their worlds definitively. Far better then our nomad's range and choice than an unvarying tenancy of one poor set of structures. Far better to slip on as we do whole living beings and wear at once all of their limbs and organs, memories and powers – wear all these as tightly congruent to our wills as a glove is to the hand that fills it.'

The shears clipped through the gristle, stolid, bloody jaws monotonously feeding, stopping short of the sternoclavicular joint in the manubrium where the muscles of the pectoral girdle have an important anchorage.

'No consciousness of the chordate type that we have found has been impermeable to our finesse – no dendritic pattern so elaborate we could not read its stitchwork and thread ourselves to match, precisely map its each synaptic seam till we could loosen it and retailor all to suit ourselves. We have strutted costumed in the bodies of planetary autarchs, venerable manikins of moral fashion, but cut of the universal cloth: the weave of fleet electric filaments of experience that we easily reshuttled to the warp of our wishes. Whereafter – newly hemmed and gathered – their living fabric hung obedient to our bias, investing us with honor and influence unlimited.'

The tricky verbal melody, through the corpse's deft, unfaltering self-dismemberment – the sheer neuromuscular orchestration of the compound activity – struck Dr Winters with the detached enthrallment great keyboard performers could bring him. He glimpsed the alien's perspective – a Gulliver waiting in a Brobdingnagian grave, then marshaling a dead giant against a living, like a dwarf in a huge mechanical crane, feverishly programming combat on a battery of levers and pedals, waiting for the robot arms' enactments, the remote, titanic impact of the foes – and he marveled, filled with a bleak wonder at life's infinite strategy and plasticity. Joe Allen's hands reached into his half-opened abdominal cavity, reached deep below the uncut anterior muscle that was exposed by the shallow, spurious incision of the epidermis, till by external measure they were extended far enough to be touching his thighs. The voice was still as the forearms advertised a delicate rummaging with the buried fingers. The shoulders drew back. As the steady withdrawal brought the wrists into view, the dead legs tremored and quaked with diffuse spasms.

'You called your kind our food and drink, Doctor. If you were merely that, an elementary usurpation of your motor tracts alone would satisfy us, give us perfect cattle-control – for what rarest word or subtlest behavior is more than a flurry of varied muscles? That trifling skill was ours long ago. It is not mere blood that feeds this lust I feel now to tenant you, this craving for an intimacy that years will not stale. My truest feast lies in compelling you to feed in that way. It lies in the utter deformation of your will this will involve. Had gross nourishment been my prime need, then my grave-mates – Pollock and Jackson – could have eked out two weeks of life for me or more. But I scorned a cowardly parsimony in the face of death. I reinvested more than half the energy that their blood gave me in fabricating chemicals to keep their brains alive, and fluid-bathed with oxygenated nutriment.'

The corpse reached into its gaping abdomen, and out of its cloven groin the smeared hands pulled two long skeins of silvery filament. The material looked like masses of nerve fiber, tough and scintillant – for the weave of it glittered with a slight incessant movement of each single thread. These nerve skeins were contracting. They thickened into two swollen nodes, while at the same time the corpse's legs tremored and faintly twitched, as the bright vermiculate roots of the parasite withdrew from within Allen's musculature. When the nodes lay fully contracted – the doctor could just see their tips within the abdomen – then the legs lay still as death.

'I had accessory neural taps only to spare, but I could access much memory, and all of their cognitive responses, and having in my banks all the organ of Corti's electrochemical conversions of English words, I could whisper anything to them directly into the eighth cranial nerve. Those are our true feast, Doctor, such bodiless electric storms of impotent cognition as I tickled up in those two little bone globes. I was forced to drain them just before disinterment, but they lived till then and understood everything – *everything* I did to them.'

When the voice paused, the dead and living eyes were locked together. They remained so a moment, and then the dead face smiled.

It recapitulated all the horror of Allen's first resurrection – this waking of expressive soul in that purple death mask. And it was a demon-soul the doctor saw awaken: the smile was barbed with fine, sharp hooks of cruelty at the corners of the mouth, while the barbed eyes beamed fond, languorous anticipation of his pain. Remotely, Dr Winters heard the flat sound of his own voice asking:

'And Joe Allen?'

'Oh, yes, Doctor. He is with us now, has been throughout. I grieve to abandon so rare a host! He is a true hermit-philosopher, well-read in four languages. He is writing a translation of Marcus Aurelius – he was, I mean, in his free time … '

Long minutes succeeded of the voice accompanying the surreal self-autopsy, but the doctor lay resigned, emptied of reactive power. Still, the full understanding of his fate reverberated in his mind as the parasite sketched his future for him in that borrowed voice. And it did not stop haunting Winters, the sense of what a *virtuoso* this entity was, how flawlessly this mass of neural fibers played the tricky instrument of human speech. As flawlessly as it had puppeteered the corpse's face into that ghastly smile. And with the same artistic aim: to waken, to amplify, to ripen its host-to-be's outrage and horror. The voice, with ever more melody and gloating verve, sent waves of realization through the doctor, amplifications of the Unspeakable.

The parasite's race had traced and tapped the complex interface between the cortical integration of sense input and the neural output governing response. It had interposed its brain between, sharing consciousness while solely commanding the pathways of reaction. The host, the bottled personality, was mute and limbless for any least expression of its own will, while hellishly articulate and agile in the service of the parasite's. It was the host's own hands that bound and wrenched the life half out of his prey, his own loins that experienced the repeated orgasms crowning his other despoliations of their bodies. And when they lay, bound and shrieking still, ready for the consummation, it was his own strength that hauled the smoking entrails from them, and his own intimate tongue and guzzling mouth he plunged into the rank, palpitating feast.

And the doctor had glimpses of the racial history that underlay the aliens' predatory present. Glimpses of a dispassionate, inquiring breed so advanced in the analysis of its own mental fabric that, through scientific commitment and genetic self-sculpting, it had come to embody its own model of perfected consciousness. It had grown streamlined to permit its entry of other beings and its direct acquisition of their experiential worlds. All strictest scholarship at first, until there matured in the disembodied scholars their long-germinal and now blazing, jealous hatred for all 'lesser' minds rooted and clothed in the soil and sunlight of solid, particular worlds. The parasite spoke of the 'cerebral music,' the 'symphonies of agonized paradox' that were its invasion's chief plunder. The doctor felt the truth behind this grandiloquence: the parasite's actual harvest from the systematic violation of encoffined personalities was the experience of a barren supremacy of means over lives more primitive, perhaps, but vastly wealthier in the vividness and passionate concern with which life for them was imbued.

The corpse had reached into its thorax and with its dead hands aided the parasite's retraction of its upper-body root system. More and more of its livid mass had gone dead, until only its head and the arm nearer the doctor remained animate, while the silvery worming mass grew in its bleeding abdominal nest.

Then Joe Allen's face grinned, and his hand hoisted up the nude, regathered parasite from his sundered gut and held it for the doctor to view – his tenant-to-be. Winters saw that from the squirming mass of nerve cord one thick filament still draped down, remaining anchored in the canyoned chest toward the upper spine. This, he understood, would be the remote-control line by which it could work at a distance the crane of its old host's body, transferring itself to Winters by means of a giant apparatus it no longer inhabited. This, he knew, was his last moment. Before his own personal horror should begin, and engulf him, he squarely met the corpse's eyes and said:

'Goodbye, Joe Allen. Eddie Sykes, I mean. I hope he gave you strength, the Golden Marcus. I love him too. You are guiltless. Peace be with you at the last.'

The demon smile stayed fixed, but, effortlessly, Winters looked through it to the real eyes, those of the encoffined man. Tormented eyes forseeing death, and craving it. The grinning corpse reached out its viscid cargo – a seething, rippling, multinodular lump that completely filled the erstwhile logger's roomy palm. It reached this across and laid it on the doctor's groin. He watched the hand set the bright medusa's head – his new self – on his own skin, but felt nothing.

He watched the dead hand return to the table, take up the scalpel, reach back over, and make a twelve-inch incision up his abdomen, along his spinal axis. It was a deep, slow cut – sectioning, just straight down through the abdominal wall – and it proceeded in the eerie, utter absence of physical sensation. The moment this was done, the fiber that had stayed anchored in the corpse snapped free, whipped back across the gap, and rejoined the main body that now squirmed toward the incision, its port of entry.

The corpse collapsed. Emptied of all innervating energy, it sagged slack and flaccid, of course. Or had it... ? Why was it... ? That nearer arm was *supinated*. Both elbow and wrist at the full upturned twist. The palm lay open, offering. *The scalpel still lay in the palm.*

Simple death would have dropped the arm earthward, it would now hang slack. With a blaze, like a nova of light, Winters understood. The man, Sykes, had – for a microsecond before his end – repossessed himself. Had flung a dying impulse of his will down through his rotten, fading muscles and had managed a single independent gesture in the narrow interval between the demon's departure and his own death. He had clutched the scalpel and flung out his arm, locking the joints as life left him.

It rekindled Winters's own will, lit a fire of rage and vengefulness. He had caught hope from his predecessor.

How precariously the scalpel lay on the loosened fingers! The slightest tremor would unfix the arm's joints, it would fall and hang and drop the scalpel down farther than Hell's deepest recess from his grasp. And he could see that the scalpel was just – only just – in the reach of his fingers at his forearm's fullest stretch from the bound elbow. The horror crouched on him and, even now slowly feeding its trunk line into his groin incision, at first stopped the doctor's hand with a pang of terror. Then he reminded himself that, until implanted, the enemy was a senseless mass, bristling with plugs, with input jacks for senses, but, until installed in the physical amplifiers of eyes and ears, an utterly deaf, blind monad that waited in a perfect solipsism between two captive sensory envelopes.

He saw his straining fingers above the bright tool of freedom, thought with an insane smile of God and Adam on the Sistine ceiling, and then, with a life span of surgeon's fine control, plucked up the scalpel. The arm fell and hung.

'Sleep,' the doctor said. 'Sleep revenged.'

But he found his retaliation harshly reined in by the alien's careful provisions. His elbow had been fixed with his upper arm almost at right angles to his body's long axis; his forearm could reach his hand inward and present it closely to the face, suiting the parasite's need of an eye-hand coordinative check, but could not, even with the scalpel's added reach, bring its point within four inches of his groin. Steadily the parasite fed in its tapline. It would usurp motor control in three or four minutes at most, to judge by the time its extrication from Allen had taken.

Frantically the doctor bent his wrist inward to its limit, trying to pick through the strap where it crossed his inner elbow. Sufficient pressure was impossible, and the hold so awkward that even feeble attempts threatened the loss of the scalpel. Smoothly the root of alien control sank into him. It was a defenseless thing of jelly against which he lay lethally armed, and he was still doomed – a preview of all his thrall's impotence-to-be.

But of course there was a way. Not to survive. But to escape, and to have vengeance. For a moment he stared at his captor, hardening his mettle in the blaze of hate it lit in him. Then, swiftly, he determined the order of his moves, and began.

He reached the scalpel to his neck and opened his superior thyroid vein – his inkwell. He laid the scalpel by his ear, dipped his finger in his blood, and began to write on the metal surface of the gurney, beginning by his thigh and moving toward his armpit. Oddly, the incision of his neck, though this was muscularly awake, had been painless, which gave him hopes that raised his courage for what remained to do.

When he had done the message read:

ALIEN
IN
ME
CUT
KILL

He wanted to write goodbye to his friend, but the alien had begun to pay out smaller auxiliary filaments collaterally with the main one, and all now lay in speed.

He took up the scalpel, rolled his head to the left, and plunged the blade deep in his ear.

Miracle! Last accidental mercy! It was painless. Some procedural, highly specific anesthetic was in effect. With careful plunges, he obliterated the right inner ear and then thrust silence, with equal thoroughness, into the left. The slashing of the vocal cords followed, then the tendons in the back of the neck that hold it erect. He wished he were free to unstring knees and elbows too, but it could not be. But blinded, deaf, with centers of balance lost, with only rough motor control – all these conditions should fetter the alien's escape, should it in the first place manage the reanimation of a bloodless corpse in which it had not yet achieved a fine-tuned interweave. Before he extinguished his eyes, he paused, the scalpel poised above his face, and blinked them to clear his aim of tears. The right, then the left, both retinas meticulously carved away, the yolk of vision quite scooped out of them. The scalpel's last task, once it had tilted the head sideways to guide the blood flow absolutely clear of possible effacement of the message, was to slash the external carotid artery.

When this was done, the old man sighed with relief and laid his scalpel down. Even as he did so, he felt the deep inward prickle of an alien energy – something that flared, crackled, flared, groped for, but did not quite find its purchase. And inwardly, as the doctor sank toward sleep – cerebrally, as a voiceless man must speak – he spoke to the parasite these carefully chosen words:

'Welcome to your new house. I'm afraid there's been some vandalism – the lights don't work, and the plumbing has a very bad leak. There are some other things wrong as well – the neighborhood is perhaps a little *too* quiet, and you may find it hard to get around very easily. But it's been a lovely home to me for fifty-seven years, and somehow I think you'll stay… '

The face, turned toward the body of Joe Allen, seemed to weep scarlet tears, but its last movement before death was to smile.

THE BELONGING KIND

William Gibson and John Shirley

William Gibson (1948–) is an American-Canadian writer who has been called the 'noir prophet' of the cyberpunk subgenre. John Shirley (1953–) is an American writer of novels, short stories, and film scripts, associated with both cyberpunk and splatterpunk. Gibson met Shirley at a science convention in the early 1980s and they became good friends. 'The Belonging Kind' (1981) originally appeared in Charles Grant's classic *Shadows* anthology series and seems to synthesize the best of Gibson's and Shirley's solo work. It's a wonderful weird form of speculative fiction, creepy and thought-provoking – and also the only collaborative story in *The Weird*.

It might have been in Club Justine, or Jimbo's, or Sad Jack's, or the Rafters; Coretti could never be sure where he'd first seen her. At any time, she might have been in any one of those bars. She swam through the submarine half-life of bottles and glassware and the slow swirl of cigarette smoke… She moved through her natural element, one bar after another.

Now, Coretti remembered their first meeting as if he saw it through the wrong end of a powerful telescope, small and clear and very far away.

He had noticed her first in the Backdoor Lounge. It was called the Backdoor because you entered through a narrow back alley. The alley's walls crawled with graffiti, its caged lights ticked with moths. Flakes from its white-painted bricks crunched underfoot. And then you pushed through into a dim space inhabited by a faintly confusing sense of the half-dozen other bars that had tried and failed in the same room under different managements. Coretti sometimes went there because he liked the weary smile of the black bartender, and because the few customers rarely tried to get chummy.

He wasn't very good at conversation with strangers, not at parties and not in bars. He was fine at the community college where he lectured in introductory linguistics; he could talk with the head of his department about sequencing and options in conversational openings. But he could never talk to strangers in bars or at parties. He didn't go to many parties. He went to a lot of bars.

Coretti didn't know how to dress. Clothing was a language and Coretti a kind of sartorial stutterer, unable to make the kind of basic coherent fashion statement that would put strangers at their ease. His ex-wife told him he dressed like a Martian; that he didn't look as though he belonged anywhere in the city. He hadn't liked her saying that, because it was true.

He hadn't ever had a girl like the one who sat with her back arched slightly in the undersea light that splashed along the bar in the Backdoor. The same light was screwed into the lenses of the bartender's glasses, wound into the necks of the rows of bottles, splashed dully across the mirror. In that light her dress was the green of young corn, like a husk half stripped away, showing back and cleavage and lots of thigh through the slits up the side. Her hair was coppery that night. And, that night, her eyes were green.

He pushed resolutely between the empty chrome and Formica tables until he reached the bar, where he ordered a straight bourbon. He took off his duffle coat, and wound up holding it on his lap when he sat down one stool away from her. Great, he screamed to himself, she'll think you're hiding an erection. And he was startled to realize that he had one to hide. He studied himself in the mirror behind the bar, a thirtyish man with thinning dark hair and a pale, narrow face on a long neck, too long for the open collar of the nylon shirt printed with engravings of 1910 automobiles in three vivid colors. He wore a tie with broad maroon and black diagonals, too narrow, he supposed, for what he now saw as the grotesquely long points of his collar. Or it was the wrong color. Something.

Beside him, in the dark clarity of the mirror, the green-eyed woman looked like *Irma La Douce*. But looking closer, studying her face, he shivered. A face like an animal's. A beautiful face, but simple, cunning, two-dimensional. When she senses you're looking at her, Coretti thought, she'll give you the smile, disdainful amusement – or whatever you'd expect.

Coretti blurted, 'May I, um, buy you a drink?' At moments like these, Coretti was possessed by an agonizingly stiff, schoolmasterish linguistic tic. *Um*. He winced. *Um*.

'You would, um, like to buy me a drink? Why, how kind of you,' she said, astonishing him. 'That would be very nice.' Distantly, he noticed that her reply was as stilted and insecure as his own. She added, 'A Tom Collins, on this occasion, would be lovely.'

On this occasion? Lovely? Rattled, Coretti ordered two drinks and paid.

A big woman in jeans and an embroidered cowboy shirt bellied up to the bar beside him and asked the bartender for change. 'Well, hey,' she said. Then she strutted to the jukebox and punched for Conway and Loretta's 'You're the Reason Our Kids Are Ugly.' Coretti turned to the woman in green, and murmured haltingly:

'Do you enjoy country-and-western music?' *Do you enjoy...* ? He groaned secretly at his phrasing, and tried to smile.

'Yes indeed,' she answered, the faintest twang edging her voice, 'I sure do.'

The cowgirl sat down beside him and asked her, winking, 'This li'l terror here givin' you a hard time?'

And the animal-eyed lady in green replied, 'Oh, hell no, honey, I got my eye on 'im.' And laughed. Just the right amount of laugh. The part of Coretti that was dialectologist stirred uneasily; too perfect a shift in phrasing and inflection. An actress? A talented mimic? The word mimetic rose suddenly in his mind, but he pushed it aside to study her reflection in the mirror; the rows of bottles occluded her breasts like a gown of glass.

'The name's Coretti,' he said, his verbal poltergeist shifting abruptly to a totally unconvincing tough-guy mode, 'Michael Coretti.'

'A pleasure,' she said, too softly for the other woman to hear, and again she had slipped into the lame parody of Emily Post.

'Conway and Loretta,' said the cowgirl, to no one in particular.

'Antoinette,' said the woman in green, and inclined her head. She finished her drink, pretended to glance at a watch, said thank-you-for-the-drink too damn politely, and left.

Ten minutes later Coretti was following her down Third Avenue. He had never followed anyone in his life and it both frightened and excited him.

Forty feet seemed a discreet distance, but what should he do if she happened to glance over her shoulder?

Third Avenue isn't a dark street, and it was there, in the light of a streetlamp, like a stage light, that she began to change. The street was deserted.

She was crossing the street. She stepped off the curb and it began. It began with tints in her hair – at first he thought they were reflections. But there was no neon there to cast the blobs of color that appeared, color sliding and merging like oil slicks. Then the colors bled away and in three seconds she was white-blond. He was sure it was a trick of the light until her dress began to writhe, twisting across her body like shrink-wrap plastic. Part of it fell away entirely and lay in curling shreds on the pavement, shed like the skin of some fabulous animal. When Coretti passed, it was green foam, fizzing, dissolving, gone. He looked back up at her and the dress was another dress, green satin, shifting with reflections. Her shoes had changed too. Her shoulders were bare except for thin straps that crossed at the small of her back. Her hair had become short, spiky.

He found that he was leaning against a jeweler's plate-glass window, his breath coming ragged and harsh with the damp of the autumn evening. He heard the disco's heartbeat from two blocks away. As she neared it, her movements began subtly to take on a new rhythm – a shift in emphasis in the sway of her hips, in the way she put her heels down on the sidewalk. The doorman let her pass with a vague nod. He stopped Coretti and stared at his driver's license and frowned at his duffle coat. Coretti anxiously scanned the wash of lights at the top of a milky plastic stairway beyond the doorman. She had vanished there, into robotic flashing and redundant thunder.

Grudgingly the man let him pass, and he pounded up the stairs, his haste disturbing the lights beneath the translucent plastic steps.

Coretti had never been in a disco before; he found himself in an environment designed for complete satisfaction-in-distraction. He waded nervously through the motion and the fashions and the mechanical urban chants booming from the huge speakers. He sought her almost blindly on the pose-clotted dance floor, amid strobe lights.

And found her at the bar, drinking a tall, lurid cooler and listening to a young man who wore a loose shirt of pale silk and very tight black pants. She nodded at what Coretti took to be appropriate intervals. Coretti ordered by pointing at a bottle of bourbon. She drank five of the tall drinks and then followed the young man to the dance floor.

She moved in perfect accord with the music, striking a series of poses; she went through the entire prescribed sequence, gracefully but not artfully, fitting in perfectly. Always, always fitting in perfectly. Her companion danced mechanically, moving through the ritual with effort.

When the dance ended, she turned abruptly and dived into the thick of the crowd. The shifting throng closed about her like something molten.

Coretti plunged in after her, his eyes never leaving her – and he was the only one to follow her change. By the time she reached the stair, she was auburn-haired and wore a long blue dress. A white flower blossomed in her hair, behind her right ear; her hair was longer and straighter now. Her breasts had become slightly larger, and her hips a shade heavier. She took the stairs two at a time, and he was afraid for her then. All those drinks.

But the alcohol seemed to have had no effect on her at all.

Never taking his eyes from her, Coretti followed, his heartbeat outspeeding the disco-throb at his back, sure that at any moment she would turn, glare at him, call for help.

Two blocks down Third she turned in at Lothario's. There was something different in her step now. Lothario's was a quiet complex of rooms hung with ferns and Art Deco mirrors. There were fake Tiffany lamps hanging from the ceiling, alternating with wooden-bladed fans that rotated too slowly to stir the wisps of smoke drifting through the consciously mellow drone of conversation. After the disco, Lothario's was familiar and comforting. A jazz pianist in pinstriped shirt sleeves and loosely knotted tie competed softly with talk and laughter from a dozen tables.

She was at the bar; the stools were only half taken, but Coretti chose a wall table, in the shadow of a miniature palm, and ordered bourbon.

He drank the bourbon and ordered another. He couldn't feel the alcohol much tonight.

She sat beside a young man, yet another young man with the usual set of bland, regular features. He wore a yellow golf shirt and pressed jeans. Her hip was touching his, just a little. They didn't seem to be speaking, but Coretti felt they were somehow communing. They were leaning toward one another slightly, silent. Coretti felt odd. He went to the rest room and splashed his face with water. Coming back, he managed to pass within three feet of them. Their lips didn't move till he was within earshot.

They took turns murmuring realistic palaver:

'– saw his earlier films, but–'

'But he's rather self-indulgent, don't you think?'

'Sure, but in the sense that…'

And for the first time, Coretti knew what they were, what they must be. They were the kind you see in bars who seem to have grown there, who seem genuinely at home there. Not drunks, but human fixtures. Functions of the bar. The belonging kind.

Something in him yearned for a confrontation. He reached his table, but found himself unable to sit down. He turned, took a deep breath, and walked woodenly toward the bar. He wanted to tap her on her smooth shoulder and ask who she was, and exactly what she was, and point out the cold irony of the fact that it was he, Coretti, the Martian dresser, the eavesdropper, the outsider, the one whose clothes and conversation never fit, who had at last guessed their secret.

But his nerve broke and he merely took a seat beside her and ordered bourbon.

'But don't you think,' she asked her companion, 'that it's all relative?'

The two seats beyond her companion were quickly taken by a couple who were talking politics. Antoinette and Golf Shirt took up the political theme seamlessly. Recycling, speaking just loudly enough to be overheard. Her face, as she spoke, was expressionless. A bird trilling on a limb.

She sat so easily on her stool, as if it were a nest. Golf Shirt paid for the drinks. He always had the exact change, unless he wanted to leave a tip. Coretti watched them work their way methodically through six cocktails each, like insects feeding on nectar. But their voices never grew louder, their cheeks didn't redden, and when at last they stood, they moved without a trace of drunkenness – a weakness, thought Coretti, a gap in their camouflage.

They paid him absolutely no attention while he followed them through three successive bars.

As they entered Waylon's, they metamorphosed so quickly that Coretti had trouble following the stages of the change. It was one of those places with toilet doors marked Pointers and Setters, and a little imitation pine plaque over the jars of beef jerky and pickled sausages: *We've got a deal with the bank. They don't serve beer and we don't cash checks.*

She was plump in Waylon's, and there were dark hollows under her eyes. There were coffee stains on her polyester pantsuit. Her companion wore jeans, a T-shirt, and a red baseball cap with a red-and-white Peterbilt patch. Coretti risked losing them when he spent a frantic minute in 'Pointers,' blinking in confusion at a hand-lettered cardboard sign that said, *We aim to please – You aim too, please.*

Third Avenue lost itself near the waterfront in a petrified snarl of brickwork. In the last block, bright vomit marked the pavement at intervals, and old men dozed in front of black-and-white TVs, sealed forever behind the fogged plate glass of faded hotels.

The bar they found there had no name. An ace of diamonds was gradually flaking away on the unwashed window, and the bartender had a face like a closed fist. An FM transistor in ivory plastic keened easy-listening rock to the uneven ranks of deserted tables. They drank beer and shots. They were old now, two ciphers who drank and smoked in the light of bare bulbs, coughing over a pack of crumpled Camels she produced from the pocket of a dirty tan raincoat.

At 2:25 they were in the rooftop lounge of the new hotel complex that rose above the waterfront. She wore an evening dress and he wore a dark suit. They drank cognac and pretended to admire the city lights. They each had three cognacs while Coretti watched them over two ounces of Wild Turkey in a Waterford crystal highball glass.

They drank until last call. Coretti followed them into the elevator. They smiled politely but otherwise ignored him. There were two cabs in front of the hotel; they took one, Coretti the other.

'Follow that cab,' said Coretti huskily, thrusting his last twenty at the aging hippie driver.

'Sure, man, sure ...' The driver dogged the other cab for six blocks, to another, more modest hotel. They got out and went in. Coretti slowly climbed out of his cab, breathing hard.

He ached with jealousy: for the personification of conformity, this woman who was not a woman, this human wallpaper. Coretti gazed at the hotel – and lost his nerve. He turned away.

He walked home. Sixteen blocks. At some point he realized that he wasn't drunk. Not drunk at all.

In the morning he phoned in to cancel his early class. But his hangover never quite came. His mouth wasn't desiccated, and staring at himself in the bathroom mirror he saw that his eyes weren't bloodshot.

In the afternoon he slept, and dreamed of sheepfaced people reflected in mirrors behind rows of bottles.

That night he went out to dinner, alone – and ate nothing. The food looked back at him, somehow. He stirred it about to make it look as if he'd eaten a little, paid, and went to a bar. And another. And another bar, looking for her. He was using his credit card now, though he was already badly in the hole under Visa. If he saw her, he didn't recognize her.

Sometimes he watched the hotel he'd seen her go into. He looked carefully at each of the couples who came and went. Not that he'd be able to spot her from her looks alone – but there should be a feeling, some kind of intuitive recognition. He watched the couples and he was never sure.

In the following weeks he systematically visited every boozy watering hole in the city. Armed at first with a city map and five torn Yellow Pages, he gradually progressed to the more obscure establishments, places with unlisted numbers. Some had no phone at all. He joined dubious private clubs, discovered unlicensed after-hours retreats where you brought your own, and sat nervously in dark rooms devoted to areas of fringe sexuality he had not known existed.

But he continued on what became his nightly circuit. He always began at the Backdoor. She was never there, or in the next place, or the next. The bartenders knew him and they liked to see him come in, because he bought drinks continuously, and never seemed to get drunk. So he stared at the other customers a bit, so what?

Coretti lost his job. He'd missed classes too many times. He'd taken to watching the hotel when he could, even in the daytime. He'd been seen in too many bars. He never seemed to change his clothes. He refused night classes. He would let a lecture trail off in the middle as he turned to gaze vacantly out the window.

He was secretly pleased at being fired. They had looked at him oddly at faculty lunches when he couldn't eat his food. And now he had more time for the search.

Coretti found her at 2:15 on a Wednesday morning, in a gay bar called the Barn. Paneled in rough wood and hung with halters and rusting farm equipment, the place was shrill with perfume and laughter and beer. She was everyone's giggling sister, in a blue-sequined dress, a green feather in her coiffed brown hair. Through a sweeping sense of almost cellular relief, Coretti was aware of a kind of admiration, a strange pride he now felt in her – and her kind. Here, too, she belonged. She was a representative type, a fag-hag who posed no threat to the queens or their butchboys. Her companion had become an ageless man with carefully silvered temples, an angora sweater, and a trench coat.

They drank and drank, and went laughing – laughing just the right sort of laughter – out into the rain. A cab was waiting, its wipers duplicating the beat of Coretti's heart.

Jockeying clumsily across the wet sidewalk, Coretti scurried into the cab, dreading their reaction.

Coretti was in the back seat, beside her.

The man with silver temples spoke to the driver. The driver muttered into his hand mike, changed gears, and they flowed away into the rain and the darkened streets. The cityscape made no impression on Coretti, who, looking inwardly, was seeing the cab stop, the gray man and the laughing woman pushing him out and pointing, smiling, to the gate of a mental hospital. Or: the cab stopping, the couple turning, sadly shaking their heads. And a dozen times he seemed to see the cab stopping in an empty side street where they methodically throttled him. Coretti left dead in the rain. Because he was an outsider.

But they arrived at Coretti's hotel.

In the dim glow of the cab's dome light he watched closely as the man reached into his coat for the fare. Coretti could see the coat's lining clearly and it was one piece with the angora sweater. No wallet bulged there, and no pocket. But a kind of slit widened. It opened as the man's fingers poised over it, and it disgorged money. Three bills, folded, were extruded smoothly from the slit. The money was slightly damp. It dried, as the man unfolded it, like the wings of a moth just emerging from the chrysalis.

'Keep the change,' said the belonging man, climbing out of the cab. Antoinette slid out and Coretti followed, his mind seeing only the slit. The slit wet, edged with red, like a gill.

The lobby was deserted and the desk clerk bent over a crossword. The couple drifted silently across the lobby and into the elevator, Coretti close behind. Once he tried to catch her eye, but she ignored him. And once, as the elevator rose seven floors above Coretti's own, she bent over and sniffed at the chrome wall ashtray, like a dog snuffling at the ground.

Hotels, late at night, are never still. The corridors are never entirely silent. There are countless barely audible sighs, the rustling of sheets, and muffled voices speaking fragments out of sleep. But in the ninth-floor corridor, Coretti seemed to move through a perfect vacuum, soundless, his shoes making no sound at all on the colorless carpet and even the beating of his outsider's heart sucked away into the vague pattern that decorated the wallpaper.

He tried to count the small plastic ovals screwed on the doors, each with its own three figures, but the corridor seemed to go on forever. At last the man halted before a door, a door veneered like all the rest with imitation rosewood, and put his hand over the lock, his palm flat against the metal. Something scraped softly and then the mechanism clicked and the door swung open. As the man withdrew his hand, Coretti saw a grayish-pink, key-shaped sliver of bone retract wetly into the pale flesh.

No light burned in that room, but the city's dim neon aura filtered in through venetian blinds and allowed him to see the faces of the dozen or more people who sat perched on the bed and the couch and the armchairs and the stools in the kitchenette. At first he thought that their eyes were open, but then he realized that the dull pupils were sealed beneath nictitating membranes, third eyelids that reflected the faint shades of neon from the window. They wore whatever the last bar had called for; shapeless Salvation Army overcoats sat beside bright suburban leisurewear, evening gowns beside dusty factory clothes, biker's leather by brushed Harris tweed. With sleep, all spurious humanity had vanished.

They were roosting.

His couple seated themselves on the edge of the Formica countertop in the kitchenette, and Coretti hesitated in the middle of the empty carpet. Light-years of that carpet seemed to separate him from the others, but something called to him across the distance, promising rest and peace and belonging. And still he hesitated, shaking with an indecision that seemed to rise from the genetic core of his body's every cell.

Until they opened their eyes, all of them simultaneously, the membranes sliding sideways to reveal the alien calm of dwellers in the ocean's darkest trench.

Coretti screamed, and ran away, and fled along corridors and down echoing concrete stairwells to cool rain and the nearly empty streets.

Coretti never returned to his room on the third floor of that hotel. A bored house detective collected the linguistics texts, the single suitcase of clothing, and they were eventually sold at auction. Coretti took a room in a boardinghouse run by a grim Baptist teetotaler who led her roomers in prayer at the start of every overcooked evening meal. She didn't mind that Coretti never joined them for those meals; he explained that he was given free meals at work. He lied freely and skillfully. He never drank at the boardinghouse, and he never came home drunk. Mr. Coretti was a little odd, but always paid his rent on time. And he was very quiet.

Coretti stopped looking for her. He stopped going to bars. He drank out of a paper bag while going to and from his job at a publisher's warehouse, in an area whose industrial zoning permitted few bars.

He worked nights.

Sometimes, at dawn, perched on the edge of his unmade bed, drifting into sleep – he never slept lying down, now – he thought about her. Antoinette. And them. The belonging kind. Sometimes he speculated dreamily... Perhaps they were like house mice, the sort of small animal evolved to live only in the walls of man-made structures.

A kind of animal that lives only on alcoholic beverages. With peculiar metabolisms they convert the alcohol and the various proteins from mixed drinks and wine and beers into everything they need. And they can change outwardly, like a chameleon or a rockfish, for protection. So they can live among us. And maybe, Coretti thought, they grow in stages. In the early stages seeming like humans, eating the food humans eat, sensing their difference only in a vague disquiet of being an outsider.

A kind of animal with its own cunning, its own special set of urban instincts. And the ability to know its own kind when they're near. Maybe.

And maybe not.

Coretti drifted into sleep.

On a Wednesday three weeks into his new job, his landlady opened the door – she never knocked – and told him that he was wanted on the phone. Her voice was tight with habitual suspicion, and Coretti followed her along the dark hallway to the second-floor sitting room and the telephone.

Lifting the old-fashioned black instrument to his ear, he heard only music at first, and then a wall of sound resolving into a fragmented amalgam of conversations. Laughter. No one spoke to him over the sound of the bar, but the song in the background was 'You're the Reason Our Kids Are Ugly.'

And then the dial tone, when the caller hung up.

Later, alone in his room, listening to the landlady's firm tread in the room below, Coretti realized that there was no need to remain where he was. The summons had come. But the landlady demanded three weeks' notice if anyone wanted to leave. That meant that Coretti owed her money. Instinct told him to leave it for her.

A Christian workingman in the next room coughed in his sleep as Coretti got up and went down the hall to the telephone. Coretti told the evening-shift foreman that he was quitting his job. He hung up and went back to his room, locked the door behind him, and slowly removed his clothing until he stood naked before the garish framed lithograph of Jesus above the brown steel bureau.

And then he counted out nine tens. He placed them carefully beside the praying-hands plaque decorating the bureau top.

It was nice-looking money. It was perfectly good money. He made it himself.

This time, he didn't feel like making small talk. She'd been drinking a margarita, and he ordered the same. She paid, producing the money with a deft movement of her hand between the breasts bobbling in her low-cut dress. He glimpsed the gill closing there. An excitement rose in him – but somehow, this time, it didn't center in an erection.

After the third margarita their hips were touching, and something was spreading through him in slow orgasmic waves. It was sticky where they were touching; an area the size of the heel of his thumb where the cloth had parted. He was two men: the one inside fusing with her in total cellular communion, and the shell who sat casually on a stool at the bar, elbows on either side of his drink, fingers toying with a swizzle stick. Smiling benignly into space. Calm in the cool dimness.

And once, but only once, some distant worrisome part of him made Coretti glance down to where soft ruby tubes pulsed, tendrils tipped with sharp lips worked in the shadows between them. Like the joining tentacles of two strange anemones.

They were mating, and no one knew.

And the bartender, when he brought the next drink, offered his tired smile and said, 'Rainin' out now, innit? Just won't let up.'

'Been like that all goddamn week,' Coretti answered. 'Rainin' to beat the band.'

And he said it right. Like a real human being.

EGNARO

M. John Harrison

M. John Harrison (1945–) is an influential English writer whose story 'The New Rays' also appears in this volume. Harrison was a leading figure in the British science fiction New Wave of the 1960s, along with writers like Michael Moorcock and J. G. Ballard. However, only Harrison can be said to have written in such a way as to modernize or comment on the traditional weird tale in his short fiction. His work has been instrumental to several generations of fantasists working in non-escapist modes. 'Egnaro' suggests at least two interpretations by story's end, one of which repudiates the idea of reportage from weird or supernatural places.

Egnaro is a secret known to everyone but yourself.

It is a country or a city to which you have never been; it is an unknown language. At the same time it is like being cuckolded, or plotted against. It is part of the universe of events which will never wholly reveal itself to you: a conspiracy the barest outline of which, once visible, will gall you forever.

It is in conversations not your own (so I learnt from Lucas) that you first hear of Egnaro. Egnaro reveals itself in minutiae, in that great and very real part of our lives when we are doing nothing important. You wait outside the library in the rain: an advert for a new kind of vacuum pump, photographed against a background of cycads and conifers, catches your eye. 'Branch offices everywhere!' Old men sit on the park benches, and as you pass make casual reference to some forgotten campaign in the marshes of a steamy country. You are always in transit when you hear of Egnaro, in transit or in limbo. A book falls open and you read with a sudden inexpressible frisson of nostalgia, 'Will I ever return there?' (Outside, rain again, falling into someone else's garden; a wet black branch touches the window in the wind.) A woman at a dinner party murmurs, 'Egnaro, where the long sunlit esplanades lift from a wine-dark sea ...'

It is this overheard, fragmentary quality which is so destructive. By the time you have turned your head the woman is speaking of tomatoes and hot-house flowers; someone has switched off the news broadcast with its hints of a foreign war; the accountant in the seat opposite you on the train has folded up his *Daily Telegraph* preparatory to getting off at Stockport. You forget immediately. Egnaro – in the beginning at least – hides itself in the interstices, the empty moments of your life.

Lucas himself had a similar incidental quality. He was a fattish, intelligent, curly-haired man, between thirty and forty years old and prone to migraine headaches, who had worked his way up from records and goldfish in the Shude Hill Market to a shabby bookshop on one of the streets behind Manchester library. I did his accounts once a month in a filthy office he kept above the shop; afterwards he would treat me to a Chinese meal and pay me in cash, for which I was grateful. I sold some of my wife's books to him when she died. He was quite decent to me on that occasion.

He conducted the business evasively. Receipts were scribbled on decaying brown paper bags, in a variety of hands. He had three signatures. I never knew how many people he employed. He never paid his bills. He concealed from me almost as much as he was concealing from his suppliers, his partners, and his VAT inspector. To tell the truth I let him hide as much as he pleased: no one in the gray streets outside cared, and I was glad of the work. I hated the office, with its litter of half-empty plastic cups and plates of congealed food; but I liked the shop. After the rambling, apologetic evasions upstairs it had a sour candor.

Its window was packed with colorful American comics cellotaped into plastic bags, and its door was always open. Inside it was the relic of a dozen bankruptcy cases: car rental, cheap shoes, do-it-yourself. Lucas had ripped out the original fitments, leaving raw scars on the wall to remind him, and replaced them with badly carpentered shelves. A tape player and two loudspeakers pumped the narrow aisles full of pop music which drew in the students and teenagers who made up his bread and butter clientele. They came in full of a sort of greedy idealism, to buy science fiction and crankcult material – books about spoon-bending, flying saucers and spiritualism – books by Koestler and Crowley, Cowper Powys and Colin Wilson – all the paraphernalia of that 'new' paradigm which so attracts the young. As a sideline Lucas sold them second-hand records, posters, novelties, and – from a basement stinking of broken lavatories and mold – film magazines, biographies of James Dean, and children's comics.

They loved it. Every flat surface was strewn with the poor stuff they wanted, and I don't think any of them ever realized that Lucas hated them, or that this was his revenge on them.

He kept the pornography at the rear of the shop. On slack afternoons he would stand behind the cash desk, sealing the new stock into plastic wrappers so that the customers couldn't maul it. This activity seemed to relax him. His plump fingers had performed the task so often that they worked unsupervised, deftly folding the wrapper, pulling the cellotape off the reel, smoothing it down, while Lucas's thoughts went elsewhere and his face took on a collapsed, distant expression; so that he looked, with his curly hair and smooth skin, like a corrupt but puzzled cherub. Occasionally he would leaf through a copy of *Rustler* or *Big Breasted Women in Real Life Poses* before he sealed it up, or stare with sudden stony contempt at the businessmen browsing the back shelves.

Once or twice a month the police would come unannounced and remove his entire stock in black polythene dustbin bags. No one expected this to have any effect. He had the shelves full again the next day. They treated him with a jocular familiarity – and in the face of their warrants and destruction orders he was resentful but polite. He made no distinction between pornography and science fiction, often wondering out loud why they confiscated the one and not the other.

'It all seems the same to me,' he maintained. 'Comfort and dreams. It all rots your brain.' Then, reflectively: 'Give them what they want and take the money.'

Though he believed this, his cynicism wasn't as simple as it seemed. The art student, with his baggy trousers and his magenta dyed hair, coming in for the latest Carlos Castaneda or John Cowper Powys; the shopgirl who asked in a distracted whine, 'Got anything about Elvis Presley? Any books? Badges?'; the accounts executive in the three-piece suit who snapped back his cuff to consult his digital watch before folding the new issue of *Young Girls in Full Color* or *Omni* into his plastic attaché case: I soon saw that Lucas's contempt for them stemmed from his fellow-feeling.

In unguarded moments he showed me some of his own collection: florid volumes illustrated in the Twenties and Thirties by Harry Clarke; Beardsley prints and Burne Jones reproductions. He had newspapers from the fifties and sixties, announcing the deaths of politicians and pop stars; he had original recordings by Jerry Lee Lewis and Chuck Berry. If he knew exactly what the teenagers wanted to buy, it was because he was privy to their dreams; it was because he had haunted the back streets of London and Manchester and Liverpool only a few years before, searching for a biography of Mervyn Peake, a forgotten novel, a bootleg record. And if he hated them it was because he had lost their simplicity, their ability to be comforted, the ease with which they consummated their desires.

He was trapped between the fantasy on the shelves, which no longer satisfied him, and the meaningless sheaves of invoices floating in pools of cold coffee on the desk upstairs. Therein lay his susceptibility to Egnaro. Where my own lay I am not half so sure.

'We all love a mysterious country,' said Lucas.

We were sitting in his office, looking through his collection, warming our hands over the one-bar fire which drew a sour, failed smell from the piles of ancient magazines and overflowing waste bins. The accounts for February were finished. His takings were down, he claimed, his overheads up. All that month a wind from Siberia had been depressing the city center, scouring Deansgate from the cathedral eastward, and forcing its way into the shops. Downstairs the tape-player was broken. Students drifted listlessly past in ones or twos, or clustered round the window with their collars turned up, arguing over the value of the stuff inside.

'For instance,' Lucas explained, leaning over my shoulder to turn a page: 'This tribe has lived for centuries under a volcano on an island somewhere off the south west coast of Africa. The exact latitude is unknown. Their elders worship the volcano as a god; they're said to have inhuman powers.' He turned several pages at once, his pudgy fingers nimble. 'It's the draftsmanship I love. There! You can see every head under the water, even the straws they're breathing through. Look at that stipple! You won't find drawing like that in the rubbish downstairs.'

He sighed.

'I used to spend hours with this stuff as a kid. See the spider monkeys, trapped in the burning village? They act as the eyes of the witch doctor: he never sees anything for the rest of his life but flames!'

He had been preoccupied all day, sometimes depressed and edgy, at others full of the odd nostalgic eagerness which with him stood in for gaiety. He couldn't settle to anything. Now he was showing me an illustrated omnibus of some American writer popular in the Nineteen Twenties, Edgar Rice Burroughs or Abraham Merritt, which had cost him, he said, over a hundred pounds. It had been privately printed a decade ago and was very hard to come by. I could make little of it, and was surprised to find he kept it with his treasured editions of *Under the Hill* and *Salome*. The pictures seemed badly drawn and drab, unwittingly comic in their portrayal of albino gorillas and wide-eyed, frightened women; the tales themselves fragmentary, motiveless and unreal.

'I've never seen much of it,' I admitted.

Personally, I told him, I had adored Kipling at that age. (Even now, if I close my eyes, I can still picture 'the cat who walked alone,' his tail stuck up in the air like a brush and that poor little mouse speared on the end of his sword.) When he didn't respond I closed the book with exaggerated care.

'It's very nice,' I said, 'but not my sort of thing. Are you hungry yet?'

But he was staring down into the cold black street.

'It's almost as if he'd been there, don't you think?' he said. 'Watching the way the ash drifts down endlessly over the pumice terraces.'

He was talking to himself, but he couldn't do it alone. He was trying to woo me, even though we had so little in common he didn't know what to say. His obsession had him by the throat, and the Rice Burroughs volume had only been an introduction, a way of preparing me. Later I would begin to recognize these moods, and learn how to respond to them. Now I merely watched while he shook his head absently, abandoned the window, and, breathing heavily through his mouth, made a pretence of fumbling through the heaps of stuff under the desk. The book he came up with fell open, from long usage, at a page about halfway through. I see now that this is what he had wanted to show me all along. He looked at it for a minute, his lips moving slightly as he scanned the text, then nodded to himself and thrust it into my hands.

'I always wondered what this meant,' he said, with a peculiar deprecatory shrug. 'You might be interested in it: what he really meant by it.'

It was an American paperback, one of those with the edges of the pages dyed a dull red and the paper that smells faintly of excrement. There were newer editions of it in the shop downstairs; in fact it was quite popular. Its author claimed to link certain astronomical events with the activities of secret societies and Gnostic sects, although what he hoped to prove by this was unclear. It was called *The Castles of the Kings*, or something similar. The bookstalls have been full of this sort of thing for the last ten years; but Lucas's copy had been bought in the mid-fifties when it was not so common, and its pages were tobacco brown with age. While I was reading it he fussed round the office, shuffling through the invoices, trying to tidy the desk, warming his hands at the fire: but I could feel him watching me intently.

'We know what we see,' the passage began, 'or think we do...' And it went on:

... but is it possible that the real pattern of life is not in the least apparent, but rather lurks beneath the surface of things, half hidden and only apparent in certain rare lights, and then only to the prepared eye? A secret country, a place behind the places we know, which seems to have but little connection to the obvious schemes of the universe?

In certain lights and at certain seasons the inhabitants of any city can see enormous faces hanging in the air, or words of fire. Also, one house in an otherwise dark street will be seen to be lit up at night for a week, even though no one lives there. From it will come sounds of revelry, although no one is observed to enter or leave it. Suddenly all is quiet and dark again, as if nothing had happened! But ordinary people will remember.

Scientists give us many explanations to choose from. Are we really to believe that reality is built from tiny motes whirling invisibly about one another?

There was more of this; an account of an eclipse witnessed in China during the fourteenth century; and then the following curious paragraph:

In India newly married couples wade in the estuarine mud catching fish in a new garment. 'What do you see?' their friends call from the bank. 'Sons and cattle!' is the answer. Are we to doubt that India exists? In the Dark Ages they had never heard of America! When the Jew of Tunis exhibited a fish's tail on a cushion, did anyone doubt that it was a fish?

'I don't quite see what he's getting at,' I said.

'Ah,' said Lucas. He thought for a moment. He had expected my reaction, I could see, but was disappointed all the same. 'You saw the hole in his argument though?' He took the book gently from my hands and returned it to its heap. 'You saw through that?'

'Oh yes,' I said, as positively as I could: 'I saw that.'

But he seemed dissatisfied. He stared at me for some time as if I had tried to mislead him over something obvious – the time of a train, say, or the name of a film actress. I put my coat on under his watery blue-eyed gaze and we went out of the office in silence. It occurred to me suddenly that he saw no flaw at all in that 'argument,' such as it was; and I wondered briefly how many casual acquaintances like myself had been invited up to the office to puzzle over *The Castles of the Kings*; and how many more he had lent it to, in the hope that they would see what he saw in its skeins of unoriginal rhetoric and curious misinterpretations of the world.

Downstairs he looked round the shop with dislike; pocketed the take – perhaps eighty pounds – after a short discussion with the bored lad behind the cash desk; and locked up. As we stood on the doorstep, fastening our coats against the scatter of snow coming down on the black Manchester air, he turned to me and dismissed it all with,

'Good for a laugh, though, that passage? Good for a laugh, anyway!' And I had the feeling he'd said that many times, too. 'By the way,' he went on, in the same dismissive tone: 'Have you heard of this place they call "Egnaro"?'

'That's the Javanese place on Cross Street, isn't it?' I said. I thought perhaps he was bored with Chinese food. 'Would you like to try it tonight instead of the Lucky Lotus? We could easily go there.'

He looked at me as if this was the last answer in the world he had been expecting; then gave a queasy, almost placatory laugh.

'Easily go there!' he said, and took my arm.

Egnaro: it was a word, I found, that came easily to the tongue.

'Do you ever think,' said Lucas later, prodding his chicken curry, 'that the only part of your life that really mattered is over?' And, without giving me a chance to answer: 'I do.'

We were sitting in the Lucky Lotus, listening to the wet raincoats dripping in the alcove behind us.

'No, don't laugh,' he said. 'I'm serious. Once your childhood's over up here, they put you in the toothpaste factory. You get a council house in Blakely. You get piles, and watch *Coronation Street* for the rest of your life.'

He ate in the Lotus two or three times a week, mostly on his own, because it saved him the trouble of cooking for himself when he got home. The little Malay waitresses, I think, realized he was lonely, and surrounded him as soon as he sat down, joking about the weather in their gluey inexplicable accents. They had made of him a fixture, a fetish; and the Lotus, with its hideous maroon flock wallpaper, dirty tablecloths and congealed rice, seemed like a natural extension of the office on Peter Street. He ate his food with a sort of lugubrious greed, planting his elbows firmly on the table before he began, eyeing his plate suspiciously, and surrounding it with his forearms as if he thought someone might take it away before he had finished.

'That hasn't happened to you,' I pointed out. 'You've got the shop. You've chosen a different kind of life.'

He stared for a long time at a piece of meat on the end of his fork. 'You never escape,' he said finally. Then: 'Look, I don't want to put you off, but could you just smell this?' He waved the fork under my nose. 'It tastes a bit funny.'

He had been in a curiously self-pitying state since showing me *The Castles of the Kings*. I suspect that he regretted revealing even this small corner of his private life. We make ourselves vulnerable with confidences. But whether this was so or not, now he had broached the subject he was unable to leave it alone. I had an uneasy impression that he was approaching some sort of crisis. He had drunk a lot of lager with the barbecued spare ribs, but I could see that it had given him little relief from whatever was worrying him. After I had reassured him about the chicken, which seemed perfectly all right to me, he said:

'I used to think: "What if the maps were all wrong and the world was full of undiscovered countries!" Undiscovered countries! What a joke.'

His jaws moved slowly from side to side; then he shook his head, swallowed, and pushed his plate away.

'It was too late even then. The world was full of housing estates.' He stared into the distance. 'The twenties and thirties – that was the time to be young. You could still have believed they'd made a mistake then.'

While I was thinking about this a waitress came up and asked, 'Dya wa' so' costa' na'?'

'What?' I said.

She giggled.

'Wan' costa'? Rass pa'?'

'Oh yes,' said Lucas. 'Custard and rice pud.' He nodded vigorously at her. 'I've been having that all week,' he explained to me. 'They soon get used to your habits here. Sometimes I can't understand a word they say. I think that's why I come.'

She brought him his sweet.

'As a kid (and you'll laugh at this, I warn you),' he said, 'I used to believe that I'd been born on some unknown continent and brought here by slavers. When I shut my eyes at night I could hear voices like hers, above the sound of the breakers on some rotting beach. It was the most frightening country in the world. The river deltas were full of radioactive silt. The natives mined a kind of green gold. They were beautiful – almost white, very intelligent, very tall and kind. It was somewhere in the Antarctic.'

He put down his spoon and stared around. He gulped suddenly. 'Christ,' he whispered. 'I'd still rather be there than here!' And he looked quickly down into the sticky mess on his plate.

I didn't quite know what to say.

'I'm sure we all feel like that sometimes,' I tried. 'But isn't it escapism? Perhaps the housing estates are the real undiscovered countries–'

He gave me a look of contempt.

'Very clever. You've never lived on one of the fuckers.'

He was silent for a long time after that. The place had been full of clerks and secretaries having their dinner before they went to the cinema round the corner on Deansgate, the women in their winter boots, the men in their three-piece suits. Now it emptied itself steadily, marooning me with him. The manager, who spoke no English though his arithmetic was perfect, came out from behind the bar; and, with the girls clustered twittering around him, began some sort of game at a vacant table. Lucas stirred his pudding round in its thick white dish until it was cold, taking small sips of the sticky, coffee-flavored liqueur he had ordered earlier. I bit my lip and concentrated on the wall, embarrassed. Suddenly he looked up again. Tears were running down his cheeks.

'Are you sure you've heard nothing about Egnaro?' he said. 'The thing is,' he continued, before I could say anything, 'that I've just about convinced myself a place like that exists.' He rubbed his eyes with the back of his hand. 'I'm sorry. It's that I get the feeling everyone else knows, you see: and they aren't telling me.' He laughed. 'Stupid, isn't it? I suppose we all get stupid ideas.' He got up and pulled a roll of dirty five pound notes from his pocket. 'Will twenty quid do you this month? I'm a bit short at the moment. You know how it is. I'll get the bill.'

I made him sit down and drink a cup of coffee. I made him tell me about Egnaro, and now I wish more than anything else in the world that I hadn't.

The dead miners of Egnaro lie looking up at the sun, the blackness of their flesh tarring the long bones. A gull spread-eagles itself on the air above them; a hot wind blows along the shore, peeling off a few flakes of gold leaf that still cling to their darkened skin. Egnaro! – it is a dangerous place, which steals over you like a dream. It is the name of your most basic questions about the universe, it is the funnel-tip from which your life fans back. All myths are perversions of its history; it is the secret behind the apparent history of the world. It is at once inside and outside you, and it signals all men at some time in their lives, like a flare of electricity along their nerves. It is as simple as a conversation half-heard on top of a bus –

'A woman sitting near me spoke to her neighbor. It was my stop. The bus gave a lurch and I had to get off. Standing there on the pavement in the rain I realized she had said: "Egnaro, where they have so many more senses to choose from!" I knew immediately I had misheard her: I laughed and walked off. But I recalled it later, and it has come to haunt me.'

This was how Lucas began his explanation, under the dripping raincoats in the Lucky Lotus that evening at the end of February. I had to prompt him to begin with. (Had he, for instance, heard the other woman's reply? It turned out he hadn't.) But as his confidence grew, though he was often confused and incoherent, he seemed to exchange his self-pity for a kind of puzzled wonder: his eyes took on a watery glint of enthusiasm, his speech a crude lyrical quality. He spoke for a long time. Couples came in, ate under the dim lights, and went out again. The waitresses eyed us benignly and giggled. After all he was a fixture there. Would he like some more costa'?

'Egnaro, where they have so many more senses to choose from!'

From the moment he heard that meaningless half-sentence, a kind of dam seems to have burst in his brain. 'It was like rubbing condensation off a window pane and looking out at a landscape you don't understand.' He was inundated by hints and clues, often of the slenderest nature. In an issue of the *Sunday Times Business News* he had picked up from the floor of a train he read: 'Exploration budget cutbacks could still stall our industrial recovery.' He knew exactly what he was supposed to gather from that, but he couldn't say how. In two critical lines of Louis MacNeice's *Streets of Laredo* he discovered this misprint: 'Egnaro the golden is fallen, is fallen/Your flame shall not quench nor your thirst shall not slake.' It was someone else's copy of the book. And once, sheltering from a thunderstorm in the doorway of Tesco's, he had this bizarre experience –

The lightning flickered like a broken fluorescent lamp. Between flashes the sky was dim and greasy. The porch began to fill up with cripples also sheltering from the rain. 'Every poor handicapped bastard in Blakely seemed to have ended up in that porch.' They had been gathered in, Lucas felt, not by the wind and the rain, but by omens and premonitions experienced that morning in front of the gas stove. They came prodded by 'instincts that last meant something when we were all frogs.' There were old ladies with blasted arthritic fingers and great varicose carbuncles; a tall man staring at the shiny stump of his left arm and singing hymns; a girl with a deformed lip and leg-irons. There was a very small woman with a hump on her back. 'You felt,' Lucas said, 'that if you asked them why they'd come here the answer would be: "My dog spoke to me of Egnaro, the queer old thing, and I came"; or, "I heard we would all be cured there". I felt that very strongly.' But they only looked at him; and, when the rain had stopped, left him there with his shoes full of water. 'None of them actually spoke.'

Thus Egnaro simultaneously hid from and revealed itself to him; in obliquities. 'It was impossible to verify anything,' he complained. 'The taxi was always driving away from me; by the time I looked up it had gone. I always found I'd used the newspaper to light the fire. People took back books I hadn't finished reading.'

He searched through all the atlases and encyclopedias he could find, but discovered nothing (although once, in *Baedeker's Northern Italy,* he came upon a typographical error which looked like 'Ignar' or 'Ignari;' it was on a map of Livorno, near the new port). Nothing was made public, but by now he could hear the conspiracy all around him. It made an expectant sound, he said, like people filing into a cathedral or an empty concert hall. It had affected the economy of the country, he believed; it had soured and complicated international relations. Fleets were outfitting on both sides of the Atlantic, in the Channel, the Baltic, and all along the Mediterranean seaboard, in a race to exploit the new country. Whoever got there first would reap enormous wealth from its mineral resources, the new sciences of its mysterious inhabitants, its incredible new animals; besides an immense strategic advantage. As soon as its exact whereabouts were known they would put to sea. Although this secret was jealously guarded, preparations so massive were necessarily known to many; ordinary people had been quick to pick up the rumor.

'They discuss it as a place to go for their *holidays*!' said Lucas, in tired disgust. 'Will it be cheaper than Majorca? Its beaches less crowded than the Costa Blanca?'

('Costa'? Costa'?')

Suddenly we were back at the beginning. His face had collapsed into self-pity again and he had buried his head in his hands. 'Don't you see?' he appealed. 'If I don't find something out soon they'll get there before me!' His shoulders shook. 'That's the real horror of it, don't you see? If there really is such a place then by the time I get there it'll be just the same as it is here!'

And he stared miserably at the maroon flock walls of the Lucky Lotus, the tears streaming down his cheeks again.

What could I do? I was appalled by his condition. And yet what he had said did not really touch me. I had always rather admired his cynical resilience; I couldn't begin to imagine as yet the state he had got himself into. I remember thinking, 'How can anyone have become so desperately lost?' But that may have been much later; and besides we never quite know what we mean by thoughts like that. Somehow I got him to cheer up and pay the bill. It was nine or ten o'clock at night by now. The waitresses fussed round him but he didn't seem to notice them. He forgot his briefcase and they came running out after us with it. He thanked them absently. All it ever had in it was an old copy of *Rustler* and some broken pencils. When we emerged onto the deathly quiet streets behind Deansgate he said he'd walk up to the cab rank in St Peter's Square. I went with him that far but I couldn't wait.

'You'll be all right?' I asked him.

'Oh yes,' he said. 'I've just got a bit of headache now. I'll have a couple of Veganin at home. They'll get me off to sleep.' He got hold of my arm. 'It's just a silly idea, all this, you know. I'll get over it.'

There he stood, looking battered and out of place in the February wind, his loneliness outlined by the great doorway of the Midland Hotel behind him. There didn't seem to be many taxis about.

The city center was slow to recover from that winter. March was bitter; late snow in April flattened the daffodils and filled the gutters with brown slush; Easter came early but did nothing to help trade. People were reluctant to come out in the sharp unseasonable winds: they had no money when they did. Turnover fell in all the luxury shops and most of the supermarkets. Deansgate took on a deserted, shabby appearance. You could find a few office workers hurrying out at lunchtime, but they were avoiding the pedestrian arcades of King Street where the spring fashions made colorful but somehow remote displays behind the plate glass windows. The sandwich bars were empty. How much of Lucas's failure was part of this wider picture, how much his own fault, is hard to say.

Towards the end of March, government waste committees threatened to cut the student grant for the third time in twelve months. (A few puzzled protesters marched down Peter Street with placards and a petition, only to drift off aimlessly when they reached the Square.) Shortly afterwards Lucas fell out with his main paperback suppliers, who were justifiably sick of him not paying his bills. Then, as the students trickled back and trade picked up, a series of leading articles devoted to 'these brokers of porn and purveyors of filth' appeared in the *Evening News*; and for a while the shelves at the back of the shop were raided almost every afternoon. This made Lucas's staff nervous and edgy: they ran out of false names to give the police and, tiring of Lucas's promises to have the tape player mended, left him one by one.

Throughout this period he was preoccupied and indecisive. He fobbed his creditors off with increasingly dull excuses; absent-mindedly signed his own name on agreements he could not hope to keep; and, whenever he could find someone to look after the shop for him, sat upstairs trying to control his headaches with handfuls of Veganin. 'You'd better start coming twice a month,' he told me, sensing that someone had to keep track of his called-in loans, convoluted trade-offs and trails of broken promises. 'Why don't we work out a system for you?' I suggested, but he couldn't follow it, and he never wrote anything down now anyway. The take went straight into his trouser pockets at the end of each day and he paid off his bills in cash installments, twenty or thirty pounds at a time. When I complained that the VAT people weren't happy with his figures he asked pettishly, 'What sort of figures do they *want*? Surely that's your job!'

'I won't just make things up,' I warned him, and he shrugged. It was an argument we had been through before. 'Everyone's corrupt,' he said. 'In the end.' I couldn't tell if it was a statement or a prediction. A worse row blew up between us in mid-April, when I found among his 'accounts' a bit of paper on which he'd written, *Egnaro! My heart yearns for some sight of your cloud-capped cliffs!* It was hard to read the rest, which had something to do with an oil rig disaster and a 'secret' television play.

'I thought you'd got over this,' I said, as lightly as I could. 'I'm not sure what George will make of it.' George Labrom was the Customs and Excise inspector. We were expecting him that afternoon. I knew him slightly: he was a decent, even indulgent man, but he disliked Lucas, and his patience was diminishing. 'Still, if you want me to I'll try and fit it in somewhere... ' But Lucas wouldn't let me make a joke of it. He bit his lip, sighed heavily, and went over to the window where it would be easier to ignore me.

'Come on Lucas,' I said angrily. 'Don't make me do all the work.'

He shrugged.

'You never "get over it",' he whispered. 'I thought you understood that. It never lets you go.' Then he laughed sourly. 'What use is all this anyway? I'd rather have Egnaro than bloody George Labrom. If you don't want to help me–'

'I can't help you if you won't help yourself,' I pointed out. 'Fuck off then if that's your attitude.'

And we faced one another across the desk, the litter of unpaid bills and falsified invoices stretching between us like a paper continent neither of us remembered how to cross. After that I got used to his silences as I had got used to the smell of his waste bin. Every fortnight when I pushed open the office door I would find him staring out of the window at the pedestrians below. 'Christ, how I hate those bastards!' he would say, apropos of nothing; or, pushing out his lower lip petulantly, complain about the headaches that stopped him from sleeping. 'I had a sickener last night. A real sickener.' I caught him pasting press cuttings into a series of scrap books he had kept since he was fourteen – recording with a kind of morose glee the bankruptcies and deaths of the fifties pop stars who had been his adolescent heroes.

In his absence (for it was an absence, as I now know from experience, even if he sat there all day) someone broke the shop window and stole most of the more valuable comics; he had allowed the insurance to lapse, and it was never properly reglazed. Inside he put up notices saying, *We do not want people reading these magazines if they have no intentions of buying!* – but by now his stock was so old that even the businessmen had abandoned the back shelves. (They were the last to go: years afterwards, you felt, they would still be wandering hopefully along Peter Street in their lunch hour, like animals searching for a lost waterhole.) Once or twice I sat behind the desk myself, putting books in bags under the dusty, flickering strip lights. It was a novelty at first but the cold cavernous silence, the filthy blue carpets, and the innuendos of the debt-collectors soon frightened me off. One Tuesday morning in May I had the bailiffs in, two heavily built men in sheepskin car-coats, who knew Lucas of old.

They leafed through old issues of *Cockade* while they waited for him to turn up with his last quarter's rent. It was, they said, a month overdue. When he arrived he was smiling, puffed, red in the face, the jacket of his safari suit flapping open as if he had been running all over the city since eight o'clock in the morning. 'Oh, hello, gents,' he said. 'If you'd given me a bit more time… Still, I've got just under half of it here, and I'm off for the rest now.' In fact he only had a third, and when he came back again he had nothing at all, so they took his keys, locked the shop up, and over the next few days sold off the remaining stock by auction. It went for an average of ten pence a book, I believe, and certainly didn't fetch enough for the rent.

Included among all the bales of *Count, Peaches* and *Chariots of the Gods* was Lucas's collection from the upper room: every one of his Beardsleys, Harry Clarkes, first editions of Ishmael Reed.

He wanted to try and buy some of the stuff back, so I went with him to the auction. It was a dismal affair conducted in a large empty Edwardian room. A lot of his competitors were there, nodding to him nervously as they bought up his assets, hoping he wouldn't commit suicide in the lavatories and wondering who would 'go bump' next. He hardly bought anything. *Lysistrata* had gone at the beginning, stuffed in among a bunch of old science fiction magazines. He seemed stunned that no one there could tell the difference. 'They can't even bloody pronounce it,' he kept saying. 'The bastards!' He drank a lot at lunchtime and began to complain of a headache. He seemed reluctant to be on his own and in the afternoon insisted we go to the cinema, where we watched uncomprehendingly some sort of comedy. The flickering of the screen made his migraine worse, and when we came out he was blinking and shaking his head.

'What will you do now?' I asked him.

'I don't know,' he said irritably. 'Go home and watch *Crossroads*, I suppose. What else is there?'

It was the rush hour. As we pushed our way through the pedestrians the traffic was beginning to congeal at the junction of Peter Street and Deansgate, where no one ever obeys the traffic lights. Lucas turned down toward the shop. He had spotted quite a large crowd of students and children gathered in front of the cracked window. They seemed to be waiting for the door to open. The younger ones kept trying it, rattling the handle then pressing their noses to the plate glass; they peered into the gloomy depths of the place, where they could just make out looming empty shelves and torn posters. The students, meanwhile, leaned against the wall with their hands in their pockets; and it was one of them who got up the courage to approach us, unzipping a plastic holdall.

'Want to buy some records?' he asked in a slow voice. He offered the open bag for inspection. This seemed to incense Lucas, who blinked and rubbed his forehead wildly.

'It's closed down, you stupid bugger!' he shouted. 'Can't you see?'

The rest of them turned slowly, like cattle interrupted drinking, and stared at him.

'Closed! Finished! Understand? You won't be getting any more of that here!'

He laughed. He swayed.

'What's the matter Lucas?' I said. 'Come away!'

He pushed at me.

'Leave me alone, I'm all right,' he said. In a quieter voice he advised the crowd, 'Piss off and find someone else.' They watched him stagger off down Peter Street towards the Midland Hotel, their eyes uncommunicative and inturned. Some of the younger ones laughed or catcalled uncertainly. He was obviously in difficulties. He kept stopping, holding his head, looking round as if he wondered where he was. I went after him. Suddenly he wobbled over to the edge of the pavement, got down on his knees, and began to vomit almost carefully into the gutter. People from the bus queues on the steps of the Free Trade Hall moved hesitantly toward him. He looked lonely and embarrassed, wiping his mouth with his handkerchief, blinking and grinning up into the light that was causing him so much pain. 'What can I do, Lucas?' I said. 'What's wrong?'

'Just piss off.'

Twenty or thirty people now surrounded us. At the front stood the women from the bus stop, clutching their shopping bags and umbrellas, a ring of grayish anxious faces. Behind them men from the car showrooms and drawing offices struggled quietly for a better view. What was the matter? It was a car accident: it was two men fighting. A woman had fainted. It was a dog. Lucas squirmed about, moaning with pain, squinting up at them as they discussed him, screwing up the flesh round his eyes against the migrainous, coronal light that flared round their heads. Then, quite suddenly, the headache seemed to leave him. He shoved me away and jumped lightly to his feet. He looked more relaxed and healthy than I had ever seen him.

'What do *you* know of Egnaro?' he demanded in a loud and scornful voice.

Surprised and puzzled, the crowd drew back from him. This seemed to amuse him. He laughed, and spat in the gutter.

'What will you *ever* know?' he pressed them.

Some of them shook their heads. He winked horribly at the women, grinned at the men. They backed off further, but he had their attention.

'You,' he went on, 'with your supermarket tunes and your Wimpey houses! You with your *insurance policies*!'

He darted forward, ransacked briefly some woman's shopping while she stared helplessly on, and held up a packet of 'Daz.' 'You,' he accused triumphantly, 'with your Blue Whitener!'

He sneered at them; he imitated their favorite TV personalities; his effect on them was astonishing.

'If you want to know about the Golden Land,' he challenged them, 'you must *go there*!' The schoolchildren worked their way forward through the crush and gazed up at him. He regarded them indulgently. 'You must suffer as I have,' he told them, 'in its swamps! You must itch with its fevers and yellow rashes, tremble on its lee shores, wade through its fetid deltas until your feet rot on your legs!'

The children cheered.

Lucas shook his finger in admonition. He put his hands on his hips. 'I know you!' he cried. 'You whisper that word among yourselves when you think I can't hear! But dare you speak it aloud? Dare you?'

I hadn't any idea what to do for him. In the end I abandoned him there with his puzzled but enchanted audience: a fat latter-day Errol Flynn or Mario Lanza, recruiting for some trumpery, desperate expedition against the Incas among the crumbling jungles of Hollywood's 'new' world. His eyes were flashing, his curly hair was plastered to his forehead, he had gone insane. As I walked off I thought, 'He's spent his life exploiting their fantasies to subsidize his own. This is his punishment.' I was quite wrong.

'That place is not for you!' I heard him cry, and they groaned. 'That place is for dreamers!'

One word hung in the air above him, heavy with promise yet bubbling and buoyant, a marvelous word sparkling with mystery and force: he had only to open his mouth and it would speak itself.

A policeman was approaching the crowd from the direction of St. Peter's Square.

That was four months ago. I did not see Lucas again until yesterday, although for a while I made regular visits to Peter Street, hoping he might be drawn back to the scene of his failure. What I expected of him I don't know: that he should recover from his breakdown, I suppose, and begin again – he had, after all, paid me in cash. I imagined him in the dirty streets behind Woolworths or the Ardwick Centre, trying to raise finance among the market stalls and pet shops where he had begun his career, two patches of black sweat growing steadily under the arms of his safari suit as his peculiar splay-footed walk carried him from disappointment to disappointment. But the place remained deserted (it was to re-open much later as an extension of Halfords' already profitable bicycle department); Lucas seemed to vanish into his own fiction; and all I could do was stare at my reflection in the cracked plate glass.

At about this time I began to have my own intimations of Egnaro.

There was nothing original about my seduction; it was dismally similar to Lucas's own, except that it began with a dream.

I was standing in a high narrow room with white walls. It was very hot; but in through the room's single window came the sound of waves, and those scents which water draws from a dry shore. There was a thread of music, one phrase repeated over and over again on some stringed instrument. I went to the window but the view was blocked by a tree. All I could see through its long dark branches was a blur of sunlight. Where a ray of light penetrated the curious leafage, it filled the room with a dusty glow the color of geranium petals; from this I guessed it would soon be dark. Standing in that room, soothed by its proportions, I knew I was in some country so foreign I could not imagine it. Hearing those few notes endlessly repeated, I felt assuaged and expectant, as if by a glimpse of happiness to come. I heard someone begin to say,

'Comfort us now & in the hour of our deaths.'

When I woke it was with an unbearable pang of nostalgia. Boarding the train at Stockport that morning I heard a woman say distinctly, 'The coast, they claim, is a must at this time of year,' and I knew I was lost. Since then I have kept a little notebook. The television advertisements are full of clues. One shows a tiger running in slow motion across a heartbreaking landscape of sand dunes; another, for banking services, a horse splashing through shallows. I record them all.

Like Lucas I have ransacked the atlases and encyclopedias, finding nothing. Unlike him I have visited the great seaports: London, Glasgow, Liverpool. By Southampton Water I sat down and wept; the wind was full of the sound of foreign voices, the scent of foreign fruit; I was dizzy with expectation. But no great fleet is gathering. Nothing can be seen of the great preparations which haunted Lucas and which now haunt me. In the governmental buildings near St. James's Park, they look blankly at you if you mention Egnaro; in the offices of the Geographical Society they can tell you nothing. And yet somewhere they are gutting the records of old expeditions; repairing ancient maps; cross-examining old sailors who – three days battered by ice and gales in 1942 under the Southern Cross, hunted by some lean German raider – saw, or only thought they saw, a smudge of land on a heaving horizon, a ripple of white ice cliffs out from which may flow that current of warm, fresh, mysterious water…

I am able to see myself quite clearly on these useless journeys, these errands run on behalf of my own imagination: but I cannot stop: and I understand now why Lucas had such difficulty in describing his condition. It is like inhabiting two worlds at once.

As I take my first hesitant steps away from the seashore, setting out through the shattered limestone hinterlands into the deep interior of the mystery, I begin to feel a need for reassurance – for an exchange of maps and notes – for some dialogue with those who have made the journey before me. Yesterday, on an impulse, I went back to the Lucky Lotus, that staging post or coaling port on the way to Egnaro. I suppose I had known all along that I would find him there when I needed him. He was sitting at his table in the alcove, putting bits of sweet and sour pork into his mouth while he read the paper folded alongside his plate.

'Oh, hello,' he said. 'I was just thinking about you.' And when I had ordered my food he began talking about himself.

He had been to America, he said, since getting his affairs in order. If he was a bit fatter, that was why. New partners – he didn't want to be specific at this stage – had paid off most of his old debts, and he was ready to start a new business. America had opened his eyes. 'Fast food,' he said. 'That's where the real money is. Hamburgers. Bloody hell, you should see the way they do it over there!' It was like a production line. You took the customers' money, passed them through the system as quickly as possible, and ejected them at the other end. 'They hardly have time to get the muck down them before they're out on the street again and the next lot are coming in!' It was wonderful. 'Fast food, that's where it is.'

I watched him eat his rice pudding and custard, smacking his lips appreciatively, nodding and winking at the waitresses. I noticed that he had replaced his old leather briefcase with a brand new plastic one. He used the word 'secret' constantly. 'The secret's in the condiments,' he would say: 'Give them onion relish and they'll eat anything.' And: 'In and out fast, that's the secret.' He had a second liqueur; he seemed quite willing to stay and talk. He asked me if I would like to get in on the ground floor of fast food with him, and I said I would. He didn't turn the conversation to old times, and I suspected he would have resisted me if I had. I sat listening to his new dreams, watching the hands of the clock.

'Well,' he said eventually. 'Time to push off I suppose.'

I still had not brought myself to ask. I knew now how he had felt every time he took out *The Castles of the Kings* and offered it to some puzzled traveling salesman. I watched the waitresses surround him – twittering 'Costa' costa' costa'', like little drab birds – as he got up to go, and my tongue stuck to the roof of my mouth. He paid the bill with a credit card. We walked along Deansgate and down Peter Street towards the cab rank outside the Midland Hotel. As we passed the shop, with its mended window and brand new Halfords' sign, I managed to say:

'By the way. All that "Egnaro" stuff–'

For a moment he looked puzzled. Then he laughed. 'Oh, you don't have to worry about that,' he said, putting his hand on my shoulder. 'I've finished with all that. I can't think why I made so much fuss. It's nothing at all when you know, is it?'

I knew then that if I reached out I would touch some transparent membrane which had grown up between us to protect the secret. I nodded hopelessly. 'That's fine,' I said. 'Good.' I arranged to meet him again soon. I arranged to meet his backers. I walked away, and later caught my train. I shan't see him again. Old maps are useless. I confess to you now as Lucas confessed to me under the coats in the Lucky Lotus last February – out of fear, out of puzzlement, out of loneliness.

Wherever I am I think about it: whatever I do is tainted by it: but if you were to ask me what Egnaro is I could give you no answer. In my most despairing moments I believe that the human race exists solely to give it expression. No one, I suspect, can have any clear understanding of it. All events are its signature: none are. It does not exist: yet it is quite real. The secret is meaningless before you know it: and, judging by what has happened to Lucas, worthless when you do. If Egnaro is the substrate of mystery which underlies all daily life, then the reciprocal of this is also true, and it is the exact dead point of ordinariness which lies beneath every mystery.

THE LITTLE DIRTY GIRL

Joanna Russ

Joanna Russ (1937–2011) was an important American writer, academic, and critic whose ground-breaking dystopian novel *The Female Man* (1975) and influential nonfiction tract *How to Suppress Women's Writing* (1983) have unfortunately overshadowed a body of short fiction as various and rich as that of Angela Carter or Shirley Jackson. Russ wrote both science fiction and fantasy, with a number of stories coming from a horror or weird fiction slant. Collections include *The Zanzibar Cat* (1983), *(Extra) Ordinary People* (1985) and *The Hidden Side of the Moon* (1987). 'The Little Dirty Girl' (1982), like previous stories by Margaret Irwin and Robert Aickman, has an essential clarity yet abiding weirdness not usually found in supernatural tales of this type.

Dear______,

Do you like cats? I never asked you. There are all sorts of cats: elegant, sinuous cats, clunky, heavy-breathing cats, skinny, desperate cats, meatloaf-shaped cats, waddling, dumb cats, big slobs of cats who step heavily and groan whenever they try to fit themselves (and they never do fit) under something or in between something or past something.

I'm allergic to all of them. You'd think they'd know it. But as I take my therapeutic walks around the neighborhood (still aching and effortful after ten months, though when questioned, my doctor replies, with the blank, baffled innocence of those Martian children so abstractedly brilliant they've never learned to communicate about merely human matters with anyone, *that my back will get better*) cats venture from alleyways, slip out from under parked cars, bound up cellars steps, prick up their ears and flash out of gardens, all lifting up their little faces, wreathing themselves around my feet, crying *Dependency! Dependency!* and showing their elegantly needly little teeth, which they never use save in yearning appeal to my goodness. They have perfect confidence in me. If I try to startle them by hissing, making loud noises, or clapping my hands sharply, they merely stare in interested fashion and scratch themselves with their hind legs: how nice. I've perfected a method of lifting kitties on the toe of my shoe and giving them a short ride through the air (this is supposed to be alarming); they merely come running back for more.

And the children! I don't dislike children. Yes I do. No I don't, but I feel horribly awkward with them. So of course I keep meeting them on my walks this summer: alabaster little boys with angelic fair hair and sky-colored eyes (this section of Seattle is Scandinavian and the Northwest gets very little sun) come up to me and volunteer such compelling information as:

'*I'm* going to my friend's house.'

'I'm going to the store.'

'My name is Markie.'

'I wasn't really scared of that big dog; I was just *startled*.'

'People leave a lot of broken glass around here.'

The littler ones confide; the bigger ones warn of the world's dangers: dogs, cuts, blackberry bushes that might've been sprayed. One came up to me once – what do they see in a tall, shuffling, professional, intellectual woman of forty? – and said, after a moment's thought:

'Do you like frogs?'

What could I do? I said yes, so a shirt-pocket that jumped and said *rivit* was opened to disclose Mervyn, an exquisite little being the color of wet, mottled sea-sand, all webbed feet and amber eyes, who was then transferred to my palm where he sat and blinked. Mervyn was a toad, actually; he's barely an inch long and can be found all over Seattle, usually upside down under a rock. I'm sure he (or she) is the Beloved Toad and Todkins and Todlekrancz Virginia Woolf used in her letters to Emma Vaughan.

And the girls? O they don't approach tall, middle-aged women. Little girls are told not to talk to strangers. And the little girls of Seattle (at least in my neighborhood) are as obedient and feminine as any in the world; to the jeans and tee-shirts of Liberation they (or more likely their parents) add hair-ribbons, baby-sized pocket-books, fancy pins, pink shoes, even toe polish.

The liveliest of them I ever saw was a little person of five, coasting downhill in a red wagon, her cheeks pink with excitement, one ponytail of yellow hair undone, her white tee-shirt askew, who gave a decorous little squeak of joy at the sheer speed of it. I saw and smiled; pink-cheeks saw and shrieked again, more loudly and confidently this time, then looked away, embarrassed, jumped quickly out of her wagon, and hauled it energetically up the hill.

Except for the very littlest, how neat, how clean, how carefully dressed they are! with long, straight hair that the older ones (I know this) still iron under waxed paper.

The Little Dirty Girl was different.

She came up to me in the supermarket. I've hired someone to do most of my shopping, as I can't carry much, but I'd gone in for some little thing, as I often do. It's a relief to get off the hard bed and away from the standing desk or the abbreviated kitchen stools I've scattered around the house (one foot up and one foot down); in fact it's simply such a relief –

Well, the Little Dirty Girl *was* dirty; she was the dirtiest eight-year-old I've ever seen. Her black hair was a long tangle. Her shoes were down-at-heel, the laces broken, her white (or rather grey) socks belling limply out over her ankles. Her nose was running. Her pink dress, so ancient that it showed her knees, was limp and wrinkled and the knees themselves had been recently skinned. She look as if she had slid halfway down Volunteer Park's steepest dirtiest hill on her panties and then rolled end-over-end the rest of the way. Besides all this, there were snot-and-tear-marks on her face (which was reddened and sallow and looked as if she'd been crying) and she looked – well, what can I say? *Neglected.* Not poor, though someone had dressed her rather eccentrically, not physically unhealthy or underfed, but messy, left alone, ignored, kicked out, bedraggled, like a cat caught in a thunderstorm.

She looked (as I said) tear-stained, and yet came up to my shopping cart with perfect composure and kept me calm company for a minute or so. Then she pointed to a box of Milky Way candy bars on a shelf above my head, saying 'I like those,' in a deep, gravelly voice that suggested a bad cold.

I ignored the hint. No, that's wrong, it wasn't a hint; it was merely a social, adult remark, self-contained and perfectly emotionless, as if she had long ago given up expecting that telling anyone she wanted something would result in getting it. Since my illness I have developed a fascination with the sheer, elastic wealth of children's bodies, the exhaustless, energetic health they don't know they have and which I so acutely and utterly miss, but I wasn't for an instant tempted to feel this way about the Little Dirty Girl. She had been through too much. She had Resources. If she showed no fear of me, it wasn't because she trusted me but because she trusted nothing. She had no expectations and no hopes. Nonetheless she attached herself to me and my shopping cart and accompanied me down two more aisles, and there seemed to be hope in that. So I made the opening, social, adult remark:

'What's your name?'

'A. R.' Those are the initials on my handbag. I looked at her sharply but she stared levelly back, unembarrassed, self-contained, unexpressive.

'I don't believe that,' I said finally.

'I could tell you lots of things you wouldn't believe,' said the Little Dirty Girl.

She followed me up to the cashier and as I was putting out my small packages one by one by one, I saw her lay out on the counter a Milky Way bar and a nickel, the latter fetched from somewhere in that short-skirted, cap-sleeved dress. The cashier, a middle-aged woman, looked at me and I back at her, I laid out two dimes next to the nickel. She really did want it! As I was going into the logistics of How Many Short Trips from the Cart to the Car and How Many Long Ones from the Car to the Kitchen, the Little Dirty Girl spoke: 'I can carry that.' (Gravelly and solemn.)

She added hoarsely, 'I bet I live near you.'

'Well, *I* bet you don't,' I said.

She didn't answer, but followed me to the parking lot, one proprietary hand on the cart, and when I unlocked my car door, she darted past me and started carrying packages from the cart to the front seat. I can't move fast enough to escape these children. She sat there calmly as I got in. Then she said, wiping her nose on the back of her hand:

'I'll help you take your stuff out when you get home.'

Now I know that sort of needy offer and I don't like it. Here was a Little Dirty Girl offering to help me, and smelling in close quarters as if she hadn't changed her underwear for days: demand-ingness, neediness, more annoyance. Then she said in her flat, crow's voice: 'I'll do it and go away. I won't bother you.'

Well, what can you do? My heart misgave me. I started the car and we drove the five minutes to my house in silence, whereupon she grabbed all the packages at once (to be useful) and some slipped back on the car seat; I think this embarrassed her. But she got my things up the stairs to the porch in only two trips and put them on the unpainted porch rocker, from where I could pick them up one by one, and there we stood.

Why speechless? Was it honesty? I wanted to thank her, to act decent, to make that sallow face smile. I wanted to tell her to go away, that I wouldn't let her in, that I'd lock the door. But all I could think of to say was, 'What's your name really?' and the wild thing said stubbornly, 'A. R.' and when I said, 'No, really,' she cried '*A. R.!*' and facing me with her eyes screwed up, shouted something unintelligible, passionate and resentful, and was off up the street. I saw her small figure turning down one of the cross-streets that meets mine at the top of the hill. Seattle is grey and against the massed storm clouds to the north her pink dress stood out vividly. She was going to get rained on. Of course.

I turned to unlock my front door and a chunky, slow, old cat, a black-and-white tom called Williamson who lives two houses down, came stiffly out from behind an azalea bush, looked slit-eyed (bored) about him, noticed me (his pupils dilated with instant interest) and bounded across the parking strip to my feet. Williamson is a banker-cat, not really portly or dignified but simply too lazy and unwieldy to bother about anything much. Either something scares him and he huffs under the nearest car or he scrounges. Like all kitties he bumbled around my ankles, making steam-engine noises. I never feed him. I don't pet him or talk to him. I even try not to look at him. I shoved him aside with one foot and opened the front door; Williamson backed off, raised his fat, jowled face and began the old cry: *Mrawr! Mrawr!* I booted him ungently off the porch before he could trot into my house with me, and as he slowly prepared to attack the steps (he never quite makes it) locked myself in. And the Little Dirty Girl's last words came suddenly clear:

I'll be back.

Another cat. There are too many in this story but I can't help it. The Little Dirty Girl was trying to coax the neighbor's superbly elegant half-Siamese out from under my car a few days later, an animal tiger-marked on paws and tail and as haughty-and-mysterious-looking as all cats are supposed to be, though it's really only the long Siamese body and small head. Ma'amselle (her name) still occasionally leaps on to my dining room windowsill and stares in (the people who lived here before me used to feed her). I was coming back from a walk, the Little Dirty Girl was on her knees, and Ma'amselle was under the car; when the Little Dirty Girl saw me she stood up, and Ma'amselle flashed Egyptianly through the laurel hedge and was gone. Someone had washed the Little Dirty Girl's pink dress (though a few days back, I'm afraid) and made a half-hearted attempt to braid her hair: there were barrettes and elastic somewhere in the tangle. Her cold seemed better. When it rains in August our summer can change very suddenly to early fall, and this was a chilly day; the Little Dirty Girl had nothing but her mud-puddle-marked dress between her thin skin and the Seattle air. Her cold seemed better, though, and her cheeks were pink with stooping. She said, in the voice of a little girl this time and not a raven, 'She had *blue* eyes.'

'She's Siamese,' I said. 'What's your name?'

'A. R.'

'Now look, I don't–'

'It's A. R.!' She was getting loud and stolid again. She stood there with her skinny, scabbed knees showing from under her dress and shivered in the unconscious way kids do who are used to it; I've seen children do it on the Lower East Side in New York because they had no winter coat (in January). I said, 'You come in.' She followed me up the steps – warily, I think – but when we got inside her expression changed, it changed utterly; she clasped her hands and said with radiant joy, 'Oh, they're *beautiful!*'

These were my astronomical photographs. I gave her my book of microphotographs (cells, crystals, hailstones) and went into the kitchen to put up water for tea; when I got back she'd dropped the book on my old brown-leather couch and was walking about with her hands clasped in front of her and that same look of radiant joy on her face. I live in an ordinary, shabby frame house that has four rooms and a finished attic; the only unusual thing about it is the number of books and pictures crammed in every which way among the (mostly second-hand) furniture. There are Woolworth frames for the pictures and cement-block bookcases for the books; nonetheless the Little Dirty Girl was as awed as if she'd found Aladdin's Cave.

She said, 'It's so ... sophisticated!'

Well, there's no withstanding that. Even if you think: what do kids know? She followed me into the kitchen where I gave her a glass of milk and a peach (she sipped and nibbled). She thought the few straggling rose bushes she could see in the back garden were wonderful. She loved my old brown refrigerator; she said, 'It's so big! And such a color!' Then she said anxiously, 'Can I see the upstairs?' and got excited over the attic eaves which were also 'so big' (wallboard and dirty pink paint) to the point that she had to run and stand under one side and then run across the attic and stand under the other. She liked the 'view' from the bedroom (the neighbor's laurel hedge and a glimpse of someone else's roof) but my study (books, a desk, a glimpse of the water) moved her so deeply and painfully that she only stood still in the center of the room, struggling with emotion, her hands again clasped in front of her. Finally she burst out, 'It's so ... *swanky!*' Here my kettle screamed and when I got back she had gotten bold enough to touch the electric typewriter (she jumped when it turned itself on) and then walked about slowly, touching the books with the tips of her fingers. She was brave and pushed the tabs on the desk lamp (though not hard enough to turn it on) and boldly picked up my little mailing scale. As she did so, I saw that there were buttons missing from the back of her dress; I said, 'A. R., come here.'

She dropped the scale with a crash. 'I didn't mean it!' Sulky again.

'It's not that; it's your buttons,' I said, and hauled her to the study closet where I keep a Band-Aid box full of extras; two were a reasonable match: little, flat-topped, pearlized pink things you can hardly find anymore. I sewed them on to her, not that it helped much, and the tangles of her hair kept falling back and catching. What a forest of lost barrettes and snarls of old rubber bands! I lifted it all a little grimly, remembering the pain of combing out. She sat flatly, all adoration gone:

'You can't comb my hair against my will; you're too weak.'

'I wasn't going to,' I said.

'That's what *you* say,' the L.D.G. pointed out.

'If I try, you can stop me,' I said. After a moment she turned around, flopped down on my typing chair, and bent her head. So I fetched my old hairbrush (which I haven't used for years) and did what I could with the upper layers, managing even to smooth out some of the lower ones, though there were places near her neck nearly as matted and tangled as felt; I finally had to cut some pieces out with my nail scissors.

L.D.G. didn't shriek (as I used to, insisting my cries were far more artistic than those of the opera singers on the radio on Sundays) but finally asked for the comb herself and winced silently until she was decently braided, with rubber bands on the ends. We put the rescued barrettes in her shirt pocket. Without that cloud of hair her sallow face and pitch-ball eyes looked bigger, and oddly enough, younger; she was no more a wandering Fury with the voice of a Northwest-coast raven but a reasonably human (though draggly) little girl.

I said, 'You look nice.'

She got up, went into the bathroom, and looked at herself in the mirror. Then she said calmly, 'No, I don't. I look conventional.'

'Conventional?' said I. She came out of the bathroom, flipping back her new braids.

'Yes, I must go.'

And as I was wondering at her tact (for anything after this would have been an anti-climax):

'But I shall return.'

'That's fine,' I said, 'but I want to have grown-up manners with you, A. R. Don't ever come before ten in the morning or if my car isn't here or if you can hear my typewriter going. In fact, I think you had better call me on the telephone first, the way other people do.'

She shook her head sweetly. She was at the front door before I could follow her, peering out. It was raining again. I saw that she was about to step out into it and cried 'Wait, A. R.!' hurrying as fast as I could down the cellar steps to the garage, from where I could get easily to my car. I got from the back seat the green plastic poncho I always keep there and she didn't protest when I dumped it over her and put the hood over her head, though the poncho was much too big and even dragged on the ground in the front and back. She said only, 'Oh, it's swanky. Is it from the Army?' So I had the satisfaction of seeing her move up the hill as a small, green tent instead of a wet, pink draggle. Though with her tea-party manners she hadn't really eaten anything; the milk and peach were untouched. Was it wariness? Or did she just not like milk and peaches? Remembering our first encounter, I wrote on the pad by the telephone, which is my shopping list:

Milky Way Bars

And then:

I doz.

She came back. She never did telephone in advance. It was all right, though; she had the happy faculty of somehow turning up when I wasn't working and wasn't busy and was thinking of her. But how often is an invalid busy or working? We went on walks or stayed home and on these occasions the business about the Milky Ways turned out to be a brilliant guess, for never have I met a child with such a passion for junk food. A. R.'s formal, disciplined politeness in front of milk or fruit was like a cat's in front of the mass-produced stuff; faced with jam, honey, or marmalade, the very ends of her braids crisped and she attacked like a cat flinging itself on a fish; I finally had to hide my own supplies in self-defense. Then on relatively good days it was ice cream or Sara Lee cake, and on bad ones Twinkies or Mallomars, Hostess cup-cakes, Three Musketeers bars, marshmallow cream, maraschino chocolates, Turkish taffy, saltwater taffy, or – somewhat less horribly – Doritos, reconstituted potato chips, corn chips, pretzels (fat or thin), barbecued corn chips, or onion-flavored corn chips, anything like that. She refused nuts and hated peanut butter. She also talked continuously while eating, largely in polysyllables, which made me nervous as I perpetually expected her to choke, but she never did. She got no fatter. To get her out of the house and so away from food, I took her to an old-fashioned five-and-ten nearby and bought her shoelaces. Then I took her down to watch the local ship-canal bridge open up (to let a sailboat through) and we cheered. I took her to a department store (just to look; 'I know consumerism is against your principles,' she said with priggish and mystifying accuracy) and bought her a pin shaped like a ladybug. She refused to go to the zoo ('An animal jail!') but allowed as the rose gardens ('A plant *hotel*') were both pleasant and educational. A ride on the zoo merry-go-round excited her to the point of screaming and running around dizzily in circles for half an hour afterwards, which embarrassed me – but then no one paid the slightest attention; I suppose shrieky little girls had happened there before, though the feminine youth of Seattle, in its Mary Jane shoes and pink pocketbooks, rather pointedly ignored her. The waterfall in the downtown park, on the contrary, sobered her up; this is a park built right on top of a crossing over one of the city's highways and is usually full of office-workers; a walkway leads not only up to but actually behind the waterfall. A. R. wandered among the beds of bright flowers and passed, stooping, behind the water, trying to stick her hand in the falls; she came out saying:

'It looks like an old man's beard' (pointing to one of the ragged Skid Row men who was sleeping on the grass in the rare, Northern sunlight). Then she said, 'No, it looks like a lady's dress without any seams.'

Once, feeling we had become friends enough for it, I ran her a bath and put her clothes through the basement washer-dryer; her splashings and yellings in the bathroom were terrific and afterwards she flashed nude about the house, hanging out of windows, embellishing her strange, raucous shouts with violent jerkings and boundings-about that I think were meant for dancing. She even ran out the back door naked and had circled the house before I – voiceless with calling, '*A. R., come back here!*' – had presence of mind enough to lock both the front and back doors after she had dashed in and before she could get out again to make the entire *tour de Seattle* in her jaybird suit. Then I had to get her back into that tired pink dress, which (when I ironed it) had finally given up completely, despite the dryer, and sagged into two sizes too big for her.

Unless A. R. was youthifying.

I got her into her too-large pink dress, her baggy underwear, her too-large shoes, her new pink socks (which I had bought for her) and said:

'A. R., where do you live?'

Crisp and shining, the Little Clean Girl replied, 'My dear, you always ask me that.'

'And you never answer,' said I.

'O yes I do,' said the Little Clean Girl. 'I live up the hill and under the hill and over the hill and behind the hill.'

'That's no answer,' said I.

'Wupf merble,' said she (through a Mars Bar) and then, more intelligibly, 'If you knew, you wouldn't want me.'

'I would so!' I said.

L.D.G. – now L.C.G. – regarded me thoughtfully. She scratched her ear, getting, I noticed, chocolate in her hair. (She was a fast worker.) She said, 'You want to know. You think you ought to know. You think you have a right. When I leave you'll wait until I'm out of sight and then you'll follow me in the car. You'll sneak by the curb way behind me so I won't notice you. You'll wait until I climb the steps of a house – like that big yellow house with the fuchsias in the yard where you think I live and you'll watch me go in. And then you'll ring the bell and when the lady comes to the door you'll say, "Your little daughter and I have become friends," but the lady will say, "I haven't got any little daughter," and then you'll know I fooled you. And you'll get scared. So don't try.'

Well, she had me dead to rights. Something very like that had been in my head. Her face was preternaturally grave. She said, 'You think I'm too small. I'm not.

'You think I'll get sick if I keep on eating like this. I won't.

'You think if you bought a whole department store for me, it would be enough. It wouldn't.'

'I won't – well, I can't get a whole department store for you,' I said. She said, 'I know.' Then she got up and tucked the box of Mars Bars under one arm, throwing over the other my green plastic poncho, which she always carried about with her now.

'I'll get you anything you want,' I said. 'No, not what you want, A. R., but anything you really, truly need.'

'You can't,' said the Little Dirty Girl.

'I'll try.'

She crossed the living room to the front door, dragging the poncho across the rug, not paying the slightest attention to the astronomical photographs that had so enchanted her before. Too young now, I suppose. I said, 'A. R., I'll try. Truly I will.' She seemed to consider it a moment, her small head to one side. Then she said briskly, 'I'll be back,' and was out the front door.

And I did not – would not – could not – did not dare to follow her.

Was this the moment I decided I was dealing with a ghost? No, long before. Little by little, I suppose. Her clothes were a dead giveaway, for one thing: always the same and the kind no child had worn since the end of the Second World War. Then there was the book I had given her on her first visit, which had somehow closed and straightened itself on the coffee table, another I had lent her later (the poems of Edna Millay) which had mysteriously been there a day afterwards, the eerie invisibility of a naked little girl hanging out of my windows and yelling; the inconspicuousness of a little twirling girl nobody noticed spinning round and shrieking outside the merry-go-round, a dozen half-conscious glimpses I'd had, every time I'd got in or out of my car, of the poncho lying on the back seat where I always keep it, folded as always, the very dust on it undisturbed. And her unchildlike cleverness in never revealing either her name or where she lived. And as surely as A. R. had been a biggish eight when we had met weeks ago, just as surely she was now a smallish, very unmistakable, unnaturally knowledgeable five.

But she was such a *nice* little ghost. And so solid! Ghosts don't run up your grocery bills, do they? Or trample Cheez Doodles into your carpet or leave gum under your kitchen chair, large smears of chocolate on the surface of the table (A. R. had), and an exceptionally dirty ring around the inside of the bathtub? Along with three (count 'em, three) large, dirty, sopping-wet bath towels on the bathroom floor? If A. R.'s social and intellectual life had a tendency to become intangible when looked at carefully, everything connected with her digestive system and her bodily dirt stuck around amazingly; there was the state of the bathroom, the dishes in the sink (many more than mine), and the ironing board still up in the study for the ironing of A. R.'s dress (with the spray starch container still set up on one end and the scorch mark where she'd decided to play with the iron). If she was a ghost, she was a good one and I liked her and wanted her back. Whatever help she needed from me in resolving her ancient Seattle tragedy (ancient ever since nineteen-forty-two) she could have. I wondered for a moment if she were connected with the house, but the people before me – the original owners – hadn't had children. And the house itself hadn't even been built until the mid-fifties; nothing in the neighborhood had. Unless both they and I were being haunted by the children we hadn't had; could I write them a pychotherapeutic letter about it? ('Dear Mrs. X., How is your inner space?') I went into the bathroom and discovered that A. R. had relieved herself interestingly in the toilet and had then not flushed it, hardly what I would call poetical behavior on the part of somebody's unconscious. So *I* flushed it. I picked up the towels one by one and dragged them to the laundry basket in the bedroom. If the Little Dirty Girl was a ghost, she was obviously a bodily-dirt-and-needs ghost traumatized in life by never having been given a proper bath or allowed to eat marshmallows until she got sick. Maybe this was it and now she could rest (scrubbed and full of Mars Bars) in peace. But I hoped not. I was nervous; I had made a promise ('I'll give you what you need') that few of us can make to anyone, a frightening promise to make to anyone. Still, I hoped. And she was a businesslike little ghost. She would come back.

For she, too, had promised.

Autumn came. I didn't see the Little Dirty Girl. School started and I spent days trying to teach freshmen and freshwomen not to write like Rod McKuen (neither of us really knowing why they shouldn't, actually) while advanced students pursued me down the halls with thousand-page trilogies, demands for independent study, and other unspeakables. As a friend of ours said once, everyone will continue to pile responsibility on a woman and everything and everyone must be served except oneself; I've been a flogged horse professionally long enough to know that and meanwhile the dishes stay in the sink and the kindly wife-elves do *not* come out of the woodwork at night and do them. I was exercising two hours a day and sleeping ten; the Little Dirty Girl seemed to have vanished with the summer.

Then one day there was a freak spell of summer weather and that evening a thunderstorm. This is a very rare thing in Seattle. The storm didn't last, of course, but it seemed to bring right after it the first of the winter rains: cold, drenching, ominous. I was grading papers that evening when someone knocked at my door; I thought I'd left the garage light on and my neighbor'd come out to tell me, so I yelled, 'Just a minute, please!' dropped my pen, wondered whether I should pick it up, decided the hell with it, and went (exasperated) to the door.

It was the Little Dirty Girl. She was as wet as I've ever seen a human being be and had a bad cough (my poncho must've gone heaven knows where) and water squelching in her shoes. She was shivering violently and her fingers were blue – it could not have been more than fifty degrees out – and her long, baggy dress clung to her with water running off it; there was a puddle already forming around her feet on the rug. Her teeth were chattering. She stood there shivering and glowering miserably at me, from time to time emitting that deep, painful chest cough you sometimes hear in adults who smoke too much. I thought of hot baths, towels, electric blankets, aspirin – can ghosts get pneumonia? 'For God's sake, get your clothes off!' I said, but A. R. stepped back against the door, shivering, and wrapped her starved arms in her long, wet skirt.

'No!' she said, in a deep voice more like a crow's than ever. 'Like this!'

'Like what?' said I helplessly, thinking of my back and how incapable I was of dragging a resistant five-year-old anywhere.

'You hate me!' croaked A. R. venomously. 'You starve me! You do! You won't let me eat anything!'

Then she edged past me, still coughing, her dark eyes ringed with blue, her skin mottled with bruises, and her whole body shaking with cold and anger, like a little mask of Medusa. She screamed.

'You want to clean me up because you don't like me!

'You like me clean because you don't like me dirty!

'You hate me so you won't give me what I need!

'You won't give me what I need and I'm dying!

'I'm dying! I'm dying!

'I'M DYING!'

She was interrupted by coughing. I said, 'A. R.– ' and she screamed again, her whole body bending convulsively, the cords in her neck standing out. Her scream was choked by phlegm and she beat herself with her fists; then wrapping her arms in her wet skirt through another bout of coughing, she said in gasps:

'I couldn't get into your house to use the bathroom, so I had to shit in my pants.

'I had to stay out in the rain; I got cold.

'All I can get is from you and you won't give it.'

'Then tell me what you need!' I said, and A. R. raised her horrid little face to mine, a picture of venomous, uncontrolled misery, of sheer, demanding starvation.

'You,' she whispered.

So that was it. I thought of the pleading cats, whose open mouths (*Dependency! Dependency!*) reveal needle teeth which can rip off your thumb; I imagined the Little Dirty Girl sinking her teeth into my chest if I so much as touched her. Not touched for bathing or combing or putting on shoelaces, you understand, but for touching only. I saw – I don't know what: her skin ash-grey, the bones of her little skull coming through her skin worse and worse every moment – and I knew she would kill me if she didn't get what she wanted, though she was suffering far worse than I was and was more innocent – a demon child is still a child, with a child's needs, after all. I got down on one knee, so as to be nearer her size, and saying only, 'My back – be careful of my back,' held out my arms so that the terror of the ages could walk into them. She was truly grey now, her bones very prominent. She was starving to death. She was dying. She gave the cough of a cadaver breathing its last, a phlegmy wheeze with a dreadful rattle in it, and then the Little Dirty Girl walked right into my arms.

And began to cry. I felt her crying right up from her belly. She was cold and stinky and extremely dirty and afflicted with the most surprising hiccough. I rocked her back and forth and mumbled I don't know what, but what I meant was that I thought she was fine, that all of her was fine: her shit, her piss, her sweat, her tears, her scabby knees, the snot on her face, her cough, her dirty panties, her bruises, her desperation, her anger, her whims – all of her was wonderful, I loved all of her, and I would do my best to take good care of her, all of her, forever and forever and then a day.

She bawled. She howled. She pinched me hard. She yelled, 'Why did it take you so long!' She fussed violently over her panties and said she had been humiliated, though it turned out, when I got her to the bathroom, that she was making an awfully big fuss over a very little brown stain. I put the panties to soak in the kitchen sink and the Little Dirty Girl likewise in a hot tub with vast mounds of rose-scented bubble bath which turned up from somewhere, though I knew perfectly well I hadn't bought any in years. We had a shrieky, tickly, soapy, toe-grabby sort of a bath, a *very* wet one during which I got soaked. (I told her about my back and she was careful.) We sang to the loofah. We threw water at the bathroom tiles. We lost the soap. We came out warm in a huge towel (I'd swear mine aren't that big) and screamed gaily again, to exercise our lungs, from which the last bit of cough had disappeared. We said, 'Oh, floof! there goes the soap.' We speculated loudly (and at length) on the possible subjective emotional life of the porcelain sink, American variety, and (rather to my surprise) sang snatches of *The Messiah* as follows:

Every malted
Shall be exalted!

And:

Behold and see
Behold and see
If there were e'er pajama
Like to this pajama!

And so on.

My last memory of the evening is of tucking the Little Dirty Girl into one side of my bed (in my pajamas, which had to be rolled up and pinned even to stay on her) and then climbing into the other side myself. The bed was wider than usual, I suppose. She said sleepily, 'Can I stay?' and I (also sleepily) 'Forever.'

But in the morning she was gone.

Her clothes lasted a little longer, which worried me, as I had visions of A. R. committing flashery around and about the neighborhood, but in a few days they too had faded into mist or the elemental particles of time or whatever ghosts and ghost-clothes are made of. The last thing I saw of hers was a shoe with a new heel (oh yes, I had gotten them fixed) which rolled out from under the couch and lasted a whole day before it became – I forget what, the shadow of one of the ornamental tea-cups on the mantel, I think.

And so there was no more five-year-old A. R. beating on the door and demanding to be let in on rainy nights. But that's not the end of the story.

As you know, I've never gotten along with my mother. I've always supposed that neither of us knew why. In my childhood she had vague, long-drawn-out symptoms which I associated with early menopause (I was a late baby); then she put me through school, which was a strain on her librarian's budget and a strain on my sense of independence and my sense of guilt, and always there was her timidity, her fears of everything under the sun, her terrified, preoccupied air of always being somewhere else, and what I can only call her furtiveness, the feeling I've always had of some secret life going on in her which I could never ask about or share. Add to this my father's death somewhere in pre-history (I was two) and then that ghastly behavior psychologists call The Game of Happy Families – I mean the perpetual, absolute insistence on How Happy We All Were that even aunts, uncles, and cousins rushed to heap on my already bitter and most unhappy shoulders, and you'll have some idea of what's been going on for the last I-don't-know-how-many years.

Well, this is the woman who came to visit a few weeks later. I wanted to dodge her. I had been dodging academic committees and students and proper bedtimes; why couldn't I dodge my mother? So I decided that *this time I would be openly angry* (I'd been doing that in school, too).

Only there was nothing to be angry about, this time.

Maybe it was the weather. It was one of those clear, still times we sometimes have in October: warm, the leaves not down yet, that in-and-out sunshine coming through the clouds, and the northern sun so low that the masses of orange pyracantha berries on people's brick walls and the walls themselves, or anything that color, flame indescribably. My mother got in from the airport in a taxi (I still can't drive far) and we walked about a bit, and then I took her to Kent and Hallby's downtown, that expensive, old-fashioned place that's all mirrors and sawdust floors and old-fashioned white tablecloths and waiters (also waitresses now) with floor-length aprons. It was very self-indulgent of me. But she had been so much better – or I had been – it doesn't matter. She was seventy and if she wanted to be fussy and furtive and act like a thin, old guinea hen with secret despatches from the C.I.A. (I've called her worse things) I felt she had the right. Besides, that was no worse than my flogging myself through five women's work and endless depressions, beating the old plough horse day after day for weeks and months and years – no, for decades – until her back broke and she foundered and went down and all I could do was curse at her helplessly and beat her the more.

All this came to me in Kent and Hallby's. Luckily my mother squeaked as we sat down. There's a reason; if you sit at a corner table in Kent and Hallby's and see your face where the mirrored walls come together – well, it's complicated, but briefly, you can see yourself (for the only time in your life) as you look to other people. An ordinary mirror reverses the right and left sides of your face but this odd arrangement re-reflects them so they're back in place. People are shocked when they see themselves; I had planned to warn her.

She said, bewildered, 'What's that?' But rather intrigued too, I think. Picture a small, thin, white-haired, extremely prim ex-librarian, worn to her fine bones but still ready to take alarm and run away at a moment's notice; that's my mother. I explained about the mirrors and then I said:

'People don't really know what they look like. It's only an idea people have that you'd recognize yourself if you saw yourself across the room. Any more than we can hear our own voices; you know, it's because longer frequencies travel so much better through the bones of your head than they can through the air; that's why a tape recording of your voice sounds higher than–'

I stopped. Something was going to happen. A hurricane was going to smash Kent and Hallby's flat. I had spent almost a whole day with my mother, walking around my neighborhood, showing her the University, showing her my house, and nothing in particular had happened; why should anything happen now?

She said, looking me straight in the eye, 'You've changed.'

I waited.

She said, 'I'm afraid that we – you and I were not – are not – a happy family.'

I said nothing. I would have, a year ago. It occurred to me that I might, for years, have confused my mother's primness with my mother's self-control. She went on. She said:

'When you were five, I had cancer.'

I said, '*What?* You had *what?*'

'Cancer,' said my mother calmly, in a voice still as low and decorous as if she had been discussing her new beige handbag or Kent and Hallby's long, fancy menu (which lay open on the table between us). 'I kept it from you. I didn't want to burden you.'

Burden.

'I've often wondered–' she went on, a little flustered; 'they say now – but of course no one thought that way then.' She went on, more formally, 'It takes years to know if it has spread or will come back, even now, and the doctors knew very little then. I was all right eventually, of course, but by that time you were almost grown up and had become a very capable and self-sufficient little girl. And then later on you were so successful.'

She added, 'You didn't seem to want me.'

Want her! Of course not. What would you feel about a mother who disappeared like that? Would you trust her? Would you accept anything from her? All those years of terror and secrecy; maybe she'd thought she was being punished by having cancer. Maybe she'd thought she was going to die. Too scared to give anything and everyone being loudly secretive and then being faced with a daughter who wouldn't be questioned, wouldn't be kissed, wouldn't be touched, who kept her room immaculate, who didn't want her mother and made no bones about it, and who kept her fury and betrayal and her misery to herself, and her schoolwork excellent. I could say only the silliest thing, right out of the movies:

'Why are you telling me all this?'

She said simply, 'Why not?'

I wish I could go on to describe a scene of intense and affectionate reconciliation between my mother and myself, but that did not happen – quite. She put her hand on the table and I took it, feeling I don't know what; for a moment she squeezed my hand and smiled. I got up then and she stood too, and we embraced, not at all as I had embraced the Little Dirty Girl, though with the same pain at heart, but awkwardly and only for a moment, as such things really happen. I said to myself: *Not yet. Not so fast. Not right now,* wondering if we looked – in Kent and Hallby's mirrors – the way we really were. We were both embarrassed, I think, but that too was all right. We sat down: *Soon. Sometime. Not quite yet.*

The dinner was nice. The next day I took her for breakfast to the restaurant that goes around and gives you a view of the whole city and then to the public market and then on a ferry. We had a pleasant, affectionate quiet two days and then she went back East.

We've been writing each other lately – for the fist time in years more than the obligatory birthday and holiday cards and a few remarks about the weather – and she sent me old family photographs, talked about being a widow, and being misdiagnosed for years (that's what it seems now) and about all sorts of old things: my father, my being in the school play in second grade, going to summer camp, getting moths to sit on her finger, all sorts of things.

And the Little Dirty Girl? Enclosed is her photograph. We were passing a photographer's studio near the University the other day and she was seized with a passionate fancy to have her picture taken (I suspect the Tarot cards and the live owl in the window had something to do with it), so in we went. She clamors for a lot lately and I try to provide it: flattens her nose against a bakery window and we argue about whether she'll settle for a currant bun instead of a do-nut, wants to stay up late and read and sing to herself so we do, screams for parties so we find them, and at parties impels me toward people I would probably not have noticed or (if I had) liked a year ago. She's a surprisingly generous and good little soul and I'd be lost without her, so it's turned out all right in the end. Besides, one ignores her at one's peril. I try not to.

Mind you, she has taken some odd, good things out of my life. Little boys seldom walk with me now. And I've perfected – though regretfully – a more emphatic method of kitty-booting which they seem to understand; at least one of them turned to me yesterday with a look of disgust that said clearer than words: 'Good Heavens, how you've degenerated! Don't you know there's nothing in life more important than taking care of Me?'

About the picture: you may think it odd. You may even think it's not her. (You're wrong.) The pitch-ball eyes and thin face are there, all right, but what about the bags under her eyes, the deep, downward lines about her mouth, the strange color of her short-cut hair (it's grey)? What about her astonishing air of being so much older, so much more intellectual, so much more professional, so much more – well, competent – than any Little Dirty Girl could possibly be?

Well, faces change when forty-odd years fall into the developing fluid.

And you have always said that you wanted, that you must have, that you commanded, that you begged, and so on and so on in your interminable, circumlocutory style, that the one thing you desired most in the world was a photograph, a photograph, your kingdom for a photograph – of me.

THE NEW RAYS

M. John Harrison

M. John Harrison (1945–) is an award-winning English writer best-known for the quasi-fantastical Viriconium Sequence of stories and novels. His most recent works have been in a science fictional mode, with *Light* (2002) managing to be contemporary, futuristic, and deeply weird. Harrison is known as a consummate short story writer for his ability to wed the supernatural or the suggestion of the supernatural with deep psychological portraits of flawed people. 'The New Rays' (1982) fuses weird science with Harrison's usual devotion to place and character. His work has influenced many writers, including Neil Gaiman, China Miéville, and Clive Barker (all included in this anthology).

When I first arrived here it was after a hideous journey. We were ten hours on the train, which stopped and started constantly at provincial stations and empty sidings. It was packed with young conscripted soldiers shouting and singing or else staring desperately out of the windows as if they wished they had the courage to jump. We got one cup of coffee at a halt in the Midlands. In the confusion of getting back into our seats I took out the little gilt traveling clock which W.B. had given me the first time I was ill, and somehow lost it. A young boy pushing his way down the carriage helped us look for it. For a moment he seemed to forget where he was; then he looked round suddenly and lurched off. I was inconsolable. Two nights in succession I had dreamed the name of a street, Agar Grove.

We arrived late in the afternoon, just in time to watch the city dissolve into black rain, water and darkness. During the night I woke up and had to go down the corridor to the lavatory. The hotel was cold and squalid at that hour. There was a gas leak. When I looked out of a window some men were digging up the street. It was still raining.

The next morning I had my preliminary visit to Dr. Alexandre in Camden Town. I was reluctant to leave the hotel, and delayed by pretending I had lost my money along with the clock. 'Perhaps the young soldier stole it. Anyway we can't afford the taxi fare.' Then I went to the wrong address and banged on the door until W.B. lost his temper and we had one of our typical quarrels in the road. I told him that the journey had confused me: but really I was frightened that Dr. Alexandre would prove unsympathetic. In the end he drove off in the taxi, shouting, 'I wash my hands of you. It was you who wanted to come here.' I went immediately to the right house and stood on the doorstep, not wanting to go in. After I rang the bell I could hear scampering and laughter inside, followed by a faint drumming sound as if a machine had been switched on and off.

Dr. Alexandre had a beautiful crippled girl who answered the door and acted as interpreter. Through her he told me that he could effect a complete cure. I didn't believe that for a moment. Everything seemed suddenly useless and shabby – although the clinic itself, with its odd maroon décor and chromium lamps, seemed nice.

To get rid of this depression I had a cup of

coffee at the corner, then went to a picture gallery for the rest of the morning. In one or two small rooms at the back they had an exhibition of new artists. I was particularly struck by a picture of a woman of my own age. The background was a buff-colored wall with two trees in front of it, completely flat trees which looked as if they had been pasted on to the wall. Behind this, from a ledge or balcony, two more flat trees emerged. They were all lifeless and stunted. In front of them a youngish woman was sitting listlessly, her sullen unfocused stare the same color as the wall, her throat swollen with goiter. Everything was flat except her throat, which had a massive, sculptural quality.

When I got back to the hotel W.B. had gone, leaving a note which said, 'I know you are frightened but you have to have some thought for other people. Write to me when you have settled in.'

I can describe Dr. Alexandre quite easily. I have the feeling that he can help people but also the feeling that he is an unscrupulous impostor. He is the kind of man who wears a dark suit. His eyes are blue and demanding, quite unintelligent in the wrong light. He is frightened that soon he will be repatriated or interned. He has a soothing voice but one which, you sense, could easily say: 'I cannot have you here disturbing the other patients if you do not give me your full cooperation. We are in this together. You must cooperate with me fully and then we will make good progress together against your disease.' When the lame girl translates for him she unconsciously mimics his fussy gestures.

The new rays are intermittent and difficult to focus. When they come they are sometimes the stealthy gold or russet color of a large, reassuring animal; sometimes a wash of rose like a watercolor sunset. (I warm to these particular rays and, despite the knowledge of the pain to follow, allow them to comfort me. I feel no time pass, I feel no physical sensation at all; I am laved, washed quite clean, and experience nothing.) But most of the time they are a blue-black color which fills the bare treatment shed with shadows and imparts to the teeth and spectacles of Dr. Alexandre and his assistant a kind of jetty gloss. They come with a desultory buzzing which you feel in the bones of your jaw; or a drumming noise which rises and falls, the sound of heels drumming briefly on an iron pipe, sometimes near, sometimes unbearably far away. It is the sound of loss, and the giving up of all dignity. Dr. Alexandre and his assistant put on their goggles and nod at one another.

It appears now that they are not even sure where the new rays are from. The discovery was accidental, and took place many years ago in some laboratory where it was ignored. Since he does not yet fully understand the nature of the rays, it's entirely possible that Dr. Alexandre will kill me sooner than my disease. Standing there in my dressing gown, feeling sore and violated by the laxatives which are an important part of the treatment, I couldn't help but laugh out loud at this idea; but when I tried to explain, the lame girl thought I was making a complaint and refused to translate. I was embarrassed.

At the hotel I sat in the bathroom trying to write a letter. Two cockroaches crawled from under the carpet and crawled back again. 'Dear W.B., When I try to imagine you at home in our lovely house all I can remember is one yellow chair and the smell of Vinolia Soap.'

On treatment mornings I get up early and walk through the rainy streets by the river, or travel aimlessly here and there on the Underground, so I have some part of the day to remember unspoiled. We aren't supposed to eat and drink for five hours before a treatment, but all my good intentions go by the board in warm damp cafés at Baker Street or Mornington Crescent. At that time of the morning no one speaks to you. All you have for company is the image of yourself in the steamy mirrors behind the counter, a woman younger than middle-aged, in a good coat, drinking another cup of coffee to stop herself fainting on the train.

Off a corridor at the back of the clinic there are two or three pleasant little waiting rooms. They are very modern and aseptic, with contract furniture, aluminum window frames, and a bed over which is stretched a white plastic sheet: but the walls are a cheerful yellow and you can switch on a little radio. You undress here. After a few minutes Dr. Alexandre's assistant comes in and gives you a kind of bluish milk to drink, explaining that it will clear out your insides and at the same time coat them with a paste which will attract the rays. He goes out of the room and you begin to feel dizzy and nauseous almost immediately. Soon you have to choose between the sink or the little lavatory with its yellow paper on a roll. You can't lock the door in case you faint. By the time he comes back with the wheelchair you are too tired to stand. He will put your clothes away and help you comb your hair and then wheel you out to the treatment shed.

The shed has a sour concrete floor sloping to a drain in the middle. It is cold and, unlike the waiting rooms, retains the smell of vomit, rubber, and Jeyes fluid. It occupies a muddy open space thirty yards behind the main building. This is for reasons of safety, claims Dr. Alexandre. I suspect he is afraid of accidentally curing passersby, but you cannot risk a joke like this with the crippled girl. 'The doctor is so sorry for the present inconvenience to patients,' she translates earnestly. 'He hopes they will not complain.' And she gives me a savage stare. In fact I quite like the shabby bit of garden which is the last thing you see before you go into the shed. A few lupins, gone desperately to seed, add something human to the clutter of duckboards thrown down hastily to prevent the wheelchairs and builders' barrows from bogging down in the mud. There is often a fire burning here, as if a gardener or workman were about, but you never see him.

In the black and chaotic moment when the rays arrive, Dr. Alexandre and his assistant struggle into their loose yellowish rubber suits and round tinted goggles. Once they are covered from head to foot like this all their kindness seems to be replaced by panic. They grab you roughly: there is no turning back: up on the table you go, trembling as you help them fasten the straps. Before you can open your mouth they force into it the vile rubber wedge which stops you biting your tongue. The focusing machine has already begun to buzz and rattle faintly as it picks up the initial burst of rays. Soon the whole hut is vibrating. Dr. Alexandre stares at his watch: he wasn't ready for this: there's real panic behind those round blue lenses now. Hurry up, he urges you with gestures. Hurry up! You bruise your feet pushing them into the stirrups. A thick vibration like the taste of licorice creeps into your lungs and along your spine. The buzzing has invaded you. Black light splashes across the room. Here it comes, here it comes…

If you are getting your treatment free of charge, you have to agree to have it without an anesthetic. You mustn't pass out.

Through the most abyssal vomits and discharges, when the rays seem to be laying down a thick coat of poison in every organ, you can still hear the urgent, earnest voice of the crippled girl. 'Are you conscious? Can you raise your head? Are you aware that you have lost control of your bowels? We must know.' Into your field of vision, blackness spraying off his smooth goggled rubber head, bobs Dr. Alexandre's assistant, anxious that nothing should escape the record. And into the exhausted calm after the blue-black shower has abated and all three of them have taken off their goggles, the uncertain foreign tones of Dr. Alexandre fall, and you must be awake to answer his questions.

Sometimes the rays don't arrive at all. What bliss to be let off with a cup of tea in the reception room and told to go home again!

A fortnight after I got here it turned foggy, first a black fog, then a yellow one which filled the streets like gas; but I didn't miss a treatment. One of the blue bodies got out and drifted about in the garden for a while before it was caught. There was such an expression of puzzlement on its face: as if it knew it had been in the garden before but could not remember when. After a while a man came out and pushed it back into the treatment shed, grumbling and flapping his arms.

The same day I fell asleep on the train on the way back to the hotel, and dreamed I was disembarking from a ship. When I went up on deck with my case and umbrella, a cold wind came off the land and blew my hair into my eyes. It was just before dawn, and the funnels of the ship were dark against a greenish sky like heavily worked oil paint. Down on the shadowy quay muffled figures waited for the passengers. Everybody except me knew where to go and what to do. I shuffled forward, trying to pretend I knew too. The sun rose while the queue was still slowly leaving the ship.

The land never seemed to get any brighter. When I woke up somebody had stolen my red gloves, which had been on the seat beside me.

W.B.'s letters, full of solicitude and domestic calm and 'the dark woods lighted so mysteriously by the white boughs of the ash trees when I take my evening walk,' drove me out into the fog, to the picture galleries and cafés. I couldn't stay in the hotel on my own; they look at you so accusingly if you are ill and on your own. In a café nobody notices you at all. You can eat your piece of sponge cake, read your letter, and leave. 'Seventy pence please.' 'Fifty-two pence please.' And you go out with the simple vision of a human face turning away forever, into streets which seem to be populated with wounded soldiers – big, lost-looking boys whose surprised eyes stare past you at something which isn't there.

'I'm feeling so much better,' I wrote untruthfully to W.B. The rays seemed to have settled in my bones like a deposit of poisonous metal, and I could hardly get out of bed the day after a treatment. 'And I get on well with the other women.'

Actually we have no time for one another. Despite our diversity we are all very much alike – a desperate, frightened bunch, concentrating on the only important business we have left, which is survival. We exchange nods as we are hurried along the corridors by wheelchair, too self-involved to speak. In the common room – where without turning your head you can see a countess with 'anemia of the brain,' the mistress of a discredited novelist, and three young prostitutes seeking a cure for some new venereal complaint – we sit like stones. Many of the others have been here for a year or more. If we have a social hierarchy, these old hands are the cream of it. They have their heads shaved once a month so that their hair doesn't soak up the smell of the treatment shed. They 'live in' and look down on the outpatients, whom they call 'weekend invalids.' Through their stiff cropped stubble, which gives them as surprised a look as the wounded boys in the streets, I perceive the bony vulnerable plates of their skulls.

When the blue bodies get loose they sometimes wander into the clinic itself, as if looking for something. One evening when the fog was at its height, Dr. Alexandre's assistant took us downstairs to see one. They were keeping it in a small room with white lavatory-tiled walls. It was supposed to have been left on a bench, but when we arrived it had somehow fallen off and got itself into a corner among some old metal cylinders and stretcher-poles. Its face was pressed into them as if it had been trying to escape the light of the unshaded overhead bulb. Dr. Alexandre's assistant ran his hand through his hair and laughed. What could he do, he seemed to be asking, with something so stupid? He pulled it back on to the table where it lay blindly like a mannequin made of transparent blue jelly.

'Come and touch it,' he encouraged us. 'There's nothing to be frightened of. As you can see it has no internal organs.' It was quite cold and inert. When you touched it there was a slight tautness, a resistance to your fingertip similar to the resistance you would get from a plastic bag full of water; and a dent was left which remained for two or three minutes. When one of the women began to cry and left the room, Dr. Alexandre's assistant said, 'They have no internal organs. They are not alive in any way medical science can define.'

Before he could move away I asked him, 'What becomes of the poor things after we have finished with them?'

I lay in bed for three days at the hotel, very ill and depressed, wondering if it was all worth it. To W.B. I wrote, 'Why this mania of mine to stay alive? I feel no better, I can't even go for a walk or eat a piece of cake! I hate myself for hanging on.' When I caught sight of myself in the mirror I was so thin that my shoulder blades looked like two plucked chicken wings. Sleeping fitfully during the day, I dreamed that I had a goiter which drained all the virtues of the world around me. Everything around me grew two-dimensional and unrealistic, while the thing on my neck fattened up like a huge purple plum. I woke up in a sweat and found myself staring out of the window at a square of sky the color of zinc.

Later I found that someone had telephoned me, but the hotel people hadn't thought to wake me up. They said they had made a mistake about my name.

At night I could hardly sleep at all. I stared out of the window; listened to the boys singing under the sodium lamps in their mournful, half-broken voices. Far away a man blew inexpertly on a bugle. One boy lifted up the stump of his arm, which looked as if it was covered with black tar. I thought that if W.B. would let me change my mind and start paying for the treatments I might feel less downcast.

The mornings are dark now, and quite cold. You cannot see inside the cafés for steam; it billows over the pavement where people are buttoning themselves into their overcoats. As winter approaches, and the women wheel their prams a little quicker along the streets by the river, a thin wind rises round Dr. Alexandre's clinic. Some little-understood property of the new rays, it seems, is rotting the walls of the treatment shed, so that when you get down on the table now you are surrounded at once by little icy drafts smelling of decayed wood. The wall-clock, a very delicate mechanism, stopped and had to be replaced. When they opened it up all its working parts were covered with damp furry mold.

Outside Dr. Alexandre's office window a couple of low shrubs struggle with the desolation of the treatment shed garden, their grayish leaves and waxy orange berries covered with a film of dust or thin mud according to the weather. Inside, the doctor sits impatiently behind a desk piled high with papers, manila envelopes, rubber tubes. Behind him are some green metal shelves, so overloaded with the patients' files that they curve in the middle. It was raining the afternoon I was there. A desk lamp was burning in the dim room and the crippled girl was staring out across the garden through the streaming window pane. 'The doctor wishes to say something to you,' she told me, turning reluctantly to face into the room. 'He asks me to say that you must not worry the other patients with questions. It will only hold up your own progress, as well as interfering with theirs. A positive attitude is very important.'

I cleared my throat. 'I can see that,' I said cautiously.

The doctor wrote something on the margin of the file in front of him. Suddenly he held up his hand for silence, stared hard at me, and said with great difficulty and slowness: 'Matter is cheap in the universe. It is disorganized, but yearns to be of use. Do you see? We do nothing wrong when we create these blue bodies. We violate no laws.' He put the cap carefully on his pen then leaned back in his chair and remained silent for some minutes, as if the effort of speaking English had tired him out. The crippled girl watched me triumphantly from the window.

'I only want to be sure I'm doing the right thing,' I explained. 'It's that I don't quite understand what happens to them when they're finished with.'

'Do we not give you these treatments free?' Dr. Alexandre reminded me gently.

After this he made the girl translate for him again while he examined me. 'The doctor says you are not making fast progress. You are not sleeping. Why is this? He thinks you should move into the clinic if you wish your treatments to have the best effect. Your disease does not wait. Please do not talk to the other women in the common room. Everything here is humane and legal.'

All I want from life is this room. If I can successfully identify myself with its red candlewick bedspread, the mustard wallpaper and the thin light coming in through the curtains, I won't have to admit to anything else.

I decided not to move into the clinic. But I couldn't stand the hotel any longer. When I went to the lavatory in the small hours there was always someone there to stare at my hair or clothes; if I found the courage to complain at the desk about the silverfish in the bathroom, the woman said it wasn't very convenient for them to have me always asleep in the room during the day. Then W.B. arrived, and there was a fuss about transferring us to a double room. They weren't going to let us have one at all until I said I would be moving out soon.

One night we lay in bed talking. Suddenly he asked me, 'What are you thinking?' and I answered, 'That I had died and the doctor had gone to tell you.'

I thought that if I could get furnished accommodation somewhere I would feel better.

In furnished accommodation you can sleep all day, come and go as you like. But in Bayswater in November it was difficult. They were all too expensive or they didn't want single women.

At first I didn't mind. I treated it as a holiday. A tremendous lonely wind blew us up and down the streets, past the cats, milk bottles, and pots of geraniums in basement areas. I felt elated, as if we had recovered something of our youth. Then came a week of really difficult treatments; the rays were more intractable than ever; I was very tired. We started to argue about Dr. Alexandre. W.B. was all for him now. 'After all it was your decision to come here.' Soon we were having a blazing row in the hotel lobby. The woman behind the desk watched exactly as if she was at the cinema, nodding slyly to the other guests when they came down to see what was happening.

'You disgust me, stewing in your self-concern!' shouted W.B. I ran out into the street for some air and fell over.

After that I walked around for a while not quite knowing where I was, until I got the idea of going into a gallery and sitting down in front of the first picture I came to.

It showed a woman standing by a yellowish shoreline covered with boulders. The sea was slack and cold. In the background, where the bay curved round into a promontory, some wooden frame houses, and a gray sky streaked with more yellow, were one or two indistinct figures – a man, another woman, perhaps a child in a white confirmation dress – with their backs turned. It had a sort of exhausted calm. I heard myself say quietly: 'There is something detestable about all these attempts to preserve yourself.' Once I had understood this a complete tranquility came over me, and I realized I hadn't felt so well for a long time. I laughed softly. I was hungry. Soon I would get up and run all the way back to the hotel, but first I would have a cup of coffee and perhaps some battenburg cake.

A man in a lovely gray suit came and stood uncertainly next to me. 'It has a certain atmosphere, this one, doesn't it?' he said. He sighed. 'A certain atmosphere.' He had come to tell me the gallery was closing; I saw that it was almost dark outside and suddenly remembered W.B.

When I got up to go I felt odd and a bit tired. The attendant put out his hand to help me and I was horrified to see vomit pour unexpectedly and painlessly out of my mouth all over the sleeve of his suit. I stood trembling with cold, surrounded by the sour smell of it, until they got the name of the hotel from me and put me in a taxi. 'At least I didn't do it on the picture,' I thought on the way back. 'At least it was only his sleeve.' In the hotel lobby I found all my cases piled by the door. The woman behind the desk wouldn't let me go up to my room.

'Your friend left some time ago I'm afraid,' she said. I stared at her. 'If you recall my dear, you did tell us you'd be moving into furnished accommodation when your friend left.'

In the end they agreed to let me have the room for one more week.

I was ill all the next day. I stayed in the room trying to eat soup but I couldn't keep anything down, not even water, and if I closed my eyes and concentrated I could hear a far-away buzzing, like a noise at the end of a corridor. I wrote letters to W.B. ('Please forgive me and take me away from here') and tore them up. When the maid came in there was a row about the state of the sheets, but they can't get rid of me now until the end of the week. I made them change the bed. In the end I was so frightened I decided to go and see Dr. Alexandre and find out why I was this ill.

It was quite late when I arrived at the clinic. A strange woman came out of the common room wiping her mouth on a paper serviette, and walked off down the passage without speaking. There was the distant sound of a tray being dropped in the kitchens. I had the impression that things were going on here much as they did during the day, but at a reduced and much duller pace. I went to the rooms I knew, one after the other, hoping I would remember how to find Dr. Alexandre's office. The waiting rooms were unlocked: I sat in one of them for a bit, touching the familiar plastic bed-sheet with my hand and turning the hot water on and off in the little sink. Later I stood in the dark in the garden in case I could see the office from there. But a bluish light came from under the treatment shed door, so I went back in.

By now I couldn't remember where anything was. I went downstairs and tried a door with frosted glass panels, but it was only an empty linen cupboard. While I was in there I heard someone coming. One of the blue bodies had got into the passage and was drifting towards me, pale and bemused-seeming under the downstairs lights. It kept looking back over its shoulder, blundering into doorways, and entangling its limbs in the heating pipes which ran along the walls. The crippled girl came round a corner and began to urge it along impatiently.

I stared at her in surprise. I said, 'I didn't know you were having treatment.'

'You aren't allowed down here,' she said. 'Go back upstairs before someone finds you.'

The blue body bobbed gently between us, waving its hands about in the air like a policeman directing the traffic. It touched her face; examined its own fingertips. It was the exact image of her, molded in cool blue jelly. She pushed it away.

'I'm sorry,' I said. 'I can't seem to find the doctor. Perhaps you could help me. I feel rather ill.'

She looked at me like a stone. 'Patients aren't allowed downstairs after nine o'clock,' she said. She drove the blue body out of the linen cupboard, where it had been trying to thrust its head in among the pillow slips, and started to man-handle it through a door further along the corridor. I followed her and stood outside watching. She had to struggle with it physically to keep it moving. Her hair fell into her eyes. Once she got it into the room, which was similar to the one in which Dr. Alexandre's assistant had shown us our first blue body, she dragged it on to a table and lay down next to it. It stared inertly at the ceiling for a time, then slowly turned to face her. One of its legs slipped off the table. She put her arms round it and tried to get it to press itself against her, encouraging it with little clicks of her tongue.

When nothing happened she got off the table with an irritable sigh, went to the door, and looked up and down the corridor. No one was there. Then she got back on to the table again. This time something seemed to happen but before I could see what it was the blue body fell off the table, pulling her down with it. She began to shout and scream with pain. I went closer and saw that they were partly joined together along their legs. The blue body had penetrated the muscles of her calves. She was flailing about, calling, 'Push us together! Help!' The blue body stared at the ceiling, opening and closing its mouth.

'What are you doing?' I said.

'For God's sake!' cried the crippled girl. 'Help us join back together!'

I backed away and ran upstairs to the common room and sat down. Later that night there was a lot of coming and going, and I heard Dr. Alexandre and his assistant shouting in the passages.

When I first came here it was like a picture painted on a sodden, opened-out cardboard box. I remember the train slowing down between garden fences from which dangled bits of rag; and convolvulus spilling like white of egg out of a rusty old car abandoned in a scrapyard. Some of the soldiers said goodbye to us; most of them went silently away up the platform. All I want now is to stay in this room sleeping and reading. The maid says very politely, 'Could you go downstairs for a bit, miss, we want to give the place a thorough going over.' They know they will be getting rid of me tomorrow. W.B. will come and fetch me. We are going over to France, where he has heard of a man who has had above-average success with a new chemical.

Last night, listening to the barges full of conscripts being towed up and down the river, the men singing their mournful songs, I thought: 'Places are not so easy to escape from.' I will never go back to Agar Grove, but I see my own blue bodies everywhere. Spawned in the violence and helplessness of the treatment shed, shadows of myself cast somehow by rays that no one properly understands, they bob and gesticulate dumbly at the edge of vision. How many times have I said, 'I would do anything at all to be cured!'

Now that I have done everything I feel as if I have been complicit in some appalling violation of myself.

THE DISCOVERY OF TELENAPOTA

Premendra Mitra

TRANSLATED INTO ENGLISH BY P. NANDY

Premendra Mitra (1904–1988) was a renowned Bengali poet, novelist and short-story writer. He was also an author of Bangla science fiction and thrillers. He was born in Varanasi, India. His work was first published in the Bengali journal *Probasi* in 1922. He experimented with the stylistic nuances of Bengali prose and tried to offer alternative linguistic parameters to the high-class elite prosaic Bengali language. His science fiction work was considered by many to be brilliant and innovative. He wrote a series of stories around a ghost-hunter named Mejokarta, considered classics of Bengali ghost stories. 'The Discovery of Telenapota' (1984) is a subtle and atmospheric tale of an almost imperceptible crossing over into the weird.

When Saturn and Mars come together, you may also discover Telenapota.

On a leisurely day, after hours of angling without a catch, when someone comes and tempts you, saying that somewhere there is a magic pool filled with the most incredible fish anxiously waiting to swallow any bait, you are already on your way to Telenapota.

But finding Telenapota is not all that easy. You catch a bus late in the afternoon. It is packed with countless people and by the time you get off, you are drenched in sweat and dust-smeared. Actually you are even unprepared for the stop when it comes.

Before you even know where you are, the bus disappears in the distance, over a bridge across the low swampland. The forest is dense and dark, and night has arrived even before the sun has set. There is a strange wind that blows, an eerie quiet. You will see no one anywhere. Even the birds have flown away, as if in fright. There is an uncanny feeling, a strange dread slowly rearing its head out of the lonely marshland.

You leave the main road and take the narrow muddy track that winds into the forest. After a while, the track gets lost in the thick groves of bamboo.

To find Telenapota you need a couple of friends with you. You will be going there to angle. What their interests are you have no clue.

Your first problem will be mosquitoes. They will arrive in hordes and you will try to scare them away. Failing, all three of you will stand and look at each other, wondering what to do. And slowly it will grow quite dark, the mosquitoes will become more insistent and you will wonder if it would not have been better to get back onto the main road and catch the return bus.

Just then a strange noise will startle you. A noise from that point where the mud track loses itself in the forest. Your nerves being on edge, you will imagine this phantom scream coming from the dumb forest and you will immediately become tense and perhaps a little scared as well. And then, you will see in the dark a faint lamp gently swaying. Slowly a bullock cart will amble out of the dark forest.

It is a small cart. The bullocks are also very small. They will all seem dwarf-like, and yet the three of you will climb onto the cart and huddle together in the dark interior where there is only room for one. The cart will return the way it came. The dark, impenetrable forest will yield a narrow tunnel that the cart slowly enters. The bullocks will move forward, unhurried, as if creating with each step the path they slowly tread.

For some time you will feel terribly cramped in the dark. But slowly you will drown in the depths of the blackness around you. From your familiar world you will enter another. An unknown mist-clad universe, bereft of all feeling. Time will stop dead in its tracks. And then, suddenly, a howl of drums will wake you. You will look around you and find the driver of the cart furiously beating an empty drum. The skies will be full of countless stars.

You will ask what the matter is. And the driver will casually tell you that this din is to drive the tigers away. When you wonder how one can scare away tigers by just raising a racket, he will reassure you that these are not real tigers. They are panthers; and a stick and a drum are enough to keep them at bay.

Tigers! Within thirty miles of the metropolis! Before you can raise your eyebrows, the cart will have crossed a wide moor lit by a late moon. Ruins of deserted palaces will gleam in the phantom moonlight. Lone colonnades, broken arches, the debris of courtyard walls. A ruined temple somewhere further down. They will stand like litigants, waiting in futile hope, for the recording of some evidence in the court of time. You will try to sit up. A strange sensation will once again make you feel as if you have left behind the world of the living and entered a phantom universe peopled only by memories.

The night will be far gone. It will seem an endless dark in which everything lies stilled, without genesis or end. Like extinct animals preserved in museums for all time.

After a few more turns the cart will stop. You will collect your tired limbs and climb down, one by one, like wooden dolls.

There will be a strong smell in the air: the stench of leaves rotting in the pool just in front of you. Beside the pool will stand the feeble remains of a large mansion, its roof caved in, walls falling apart, and windows broken – like the battlements of a fort, guarding against the phantom moonlight.

This is where you will spend the night.

First, you will find yourself a room, somewhat habitable. The cart-driver will fetch you from somewhere a broken lantern and a jug of water. It will seem to you ages since someone had walked into that room. Some futile efforts have been made to clean it up and the musty odour will reveal that this was a long time back. With the slightest movement, plaster will peel off and bits of rubble will fall on you from the roof and the walls, like angry oaths from a resident spirit. Bats and flying foxes will shrilly question your right to stay there for the night.

Of your friends, one is a sod and the other would have snored through a holocaust. Your bed will be hardly ready before one of them hits the sack and the other the bottle.

The night will wear on. The lantern glass will gather soot and the light will softly dim. The assault of mosquitoes will become unbearable. This is the blue-blooded anopheles, the aristocrat who carries malaria in his bite. But, by this time, both your companions will be in worlds of their own, far removed from yours.

It will be hot and oppressive. You will take a torch and try to escape to the terrace, to beat the heat. The danger of the staircase giving way will scare you at every step. But something will draw you on, irresistibly. You will keep on climbing till you arrive.

On reaching, you will find the terrace in ruins. Trees have taken firm root in every crevice, every nook. As if they were fifth columnists, making way for the inexorable advance of the forest.

And yet, in the wan moonlight, everything will look beautiful. It will seem that if you searched long enough, you would find that inner sanctum of this sleep-drenched palace where the captive princess has been asleep through countless centuries.

And even as you dream of such a princess, you will notice a faint light in one of the windows of the tumbledown house across the street. And, then, you will see a mysterious shadow walk up to the window. Whose silhouette is it? Why is she awake when everyone sleeps? It will baffle you: and even as you wonder about it, the light will slowly go out. Was it real? Or did you see a dream? From the abysmal dark of this world of sleep, a dream bubble surfaced for a while, floated silently in the world of the living, and then suddenly melted away.

You will walk down the staircase carefully and fall asleep beside your friends.

When you wake up some hours later, you will find morning already there, with the delightful chatter of birds.

You will remember what you had come here for. And very soon you will find yourself sitting on a broken, moss-covered step beside the pool. You will cast your line into the green waters and wait patiently.

The day will wear on. A kingfisher perched on the branch of a tree beside the pool will occasionally swoop down, in a flash of colour. A snake will emerge from some crack in the steps and slither slowly into the water. Two grasshoppers, their transparent wings fluttering in the sunlight, will keep trying to land on the float of your line. A dove will call out from the distance, its lazy notes will bring on a strange ennui, as your mind will wander far and wide.

The reverie will break with the sudden ripples on the water. Your float will gently rock. You will look up to find her pushing away the floating weeds and filling up a shining brass pitcher. Her eyes are curious; her movements unabashed and free. She will look straight at you and at your line. Then, she will pick up her pitcher and turn away.

You will not be able to guess her age. Calm and sorrowful, her face will tell you that she has already walked the pitiless road of life. But if you look at the thin, emaciated lines of her body, you will think that she had never grown out of her adolescence.

Even as she turns to go away, she will suddenly pause and ask you what you are waiting for. Pull hard, she will say. Her voice is so mellow and tender that it will not surprise you that she should have spoken to you, a complete stranger, with such familiarity. Only the suddenness of it will startle you and, by the time you pull the line, the bait would have gone.

You will look at her somewhat abashed. And she will then turn and go away with slow, unhurried steps. As she walks away, you will wonder if you saw the hint of a smile breaking through her sad, peaceful eyes.

Nothing will again disturb the loneliness of the afternoon. The kingfisher will fly away. The fish will ignore you. Only a strange feeling of unreality will remain. How could she have come to this strange land of sleep?

And then, after a long while, you will pack up – a little disappointed with yourself. When you return, you will find that the news of your fishing skills has preceded you. You will ignore the wisecracks of your friends and ask them how they knew you had fared so poorly.

Why, Jamini told us, the tippler will reply. She saw you there. Curious, you will ask him who Jamini is. You will learn that she is the same person you saw beside the pool, a distant relation of your friend. You will also learn that you are going over to her place for lunch.

You look at the ruins across the street – where you had watched last night's silhouette framed by the broken window in the wan moonlightand you are surprised by its wretched condition. You had not imagined that the veil of night, now stripped rudely by the harsh daylight, could have hidden such an ugly nakedness. You are even more surprised to know that Jamini lives there.

It is a simple meal. Jamini serves it herself. Looking at her now, closely, you are struck by the tired sorrow writ on her face. It seems as if the mute agony of this forgotten and lonely place has cast its dark shadow across her visage. A sea of infinite tiredness swirls in her eyes. You know she will crumble slowly, very slowly, with the ruins around her.

You will notice there is something on her mind. You may even hear a faint voice calling from a room upstairs. And every now and then you will notice Jamini leaving the room. Each time she comes back, the shadows lengthen on her face and her eyes betray a strange anxiety.

After the meal is over, you will sit for a while. Jamini will first hesitate, and then call out in despair for the other side of the door: Manida, can you please come her once? Mani is your friend, the tippler. He will go to the door and you will hear his conversation with Jamini quite clearly, even though you have no intention to eavesdrop.

Mother is being difficult again, Jamini would say, in a troubled voice. Ever since she heard you were coming with your friends, she has become quite impossible to handle.

Mani would mutter irritably: I suppose it is because she imagines Niranjan is here.

Yes. She keeps saying, I know he is here. he hasn't come up to see me only because he is embarrassed. Go, fetch him. Manida, I don't know what to say. Ever since she went blind, she has become rather difficult. She won't listen to anyone. She is always angry. I am sometimes scared she will collapse and die during one of her fits.

If only she had eyes, I could have proved to her that Niranjan is nowhere around: Mani would reply, somewhat annoyed.

A shrill, angry scream will come from upstairs, this time more clearly audible. Janimi will beseech him: Please come with me once, Manida. See if you can make her understand. All right, Mani will reply a bit roughly. You carry on; I'll come.

Mani will mutter to himself: Why, for heaven's sake, does this mad woman refuse to die? She can't see; she can hardly use her limbs; and yet she is determined not to die.

You will ask him what the matter is. Mani will reply, annoyed: Matter? Nothing very much. Years ago, she had fixed Jamini's marriage with Niranjan, a distant nephew of hers. The last time he was here was about four years ago. He told her then he would marry Jamini as soon as he returned from abroad. Ever since then, she has been waiting.

But hasn't Niranjan returned? You will ask.

Of course not! How can he return when he never went at all? He was lying; otherwise, the old hag wouldn't let him go. Why should he marry this rag-picker's daughter? Yes, he is married all right and rearing a family. But who is to tell her all this? She won't believe you; and if she did, she would die of shock immediately thereafter. Who's going to take the risk?

Does Jamini know about Niranjan? You will ask.

Oh yes. But she can't speak about it to her. Well, let me go and get it over. Mani will turn to go.

Almost unaware of it yourself, you will also get up then and say: Just a moment. I will come with you.

You? With me? Mani will be very surprised.

Yes. Do you mind?

No, of course not, Mani will reply, a trifle taken aback. And, then, he will lead the way.

After you have climbed the dark, crumbling staircase, you will enter a room that looks like an underground vault. There is only one window, tightly shut. At first, everything will look indistinct. And then, as your eyes get used to the dark, you will see a large, decrepit wooden cot. On it you will notice a shriveled-up woman, wrapped in torn rags, lying still. Jamini stands beside her, like a statue.

At the sound of your footsteps, the bag of bones will slowly move. Niranjan? My child! You are back at last! You have come back to your poor wreck of an aunt! You know, I have been waiting, keeping death at bay, knowing that you will be here someday. You won't slip away again like last time?

Mani will be about to say something but you will interrupt him by blurting out: No, I promise you I won't.

You will not look up but you will feel the stunned silence in the room. You could not have looked up even if you wanted to, for your eyes are riveted to the sockets of her old, unseeing eyes. Two tongues of dark will emerge from the empty sockets and lick every inch of your body. To feel, to know. You will feel those moments falling like dew into the vast seas of time.

You will hear the old woman saying. My son, I knew you would come. That is why I am still in this house of the dead, counting the days. The sheer effort to speak will leave her panting. You will look up at Jamini. You will feel that somewhere behind the mask of her face, something was slowly melting away, and it will not be long before the foundation of a vow – a vow made up of endless despair, a vow taken against life and fate – will slowly give away.

She will speak again: I am sure Jamini will make you happy, my son. There is none like her, even though I, her mother, should say so. I am old and broken down, and often out of my senses. I try her beyond endurance. But does she ever protest? Not once. This graveyard of a place, where you will not find a man even if you search ten houses, is like me, more dead than alive. And yet, Jamini survives, and manages everything.

Even though you may want to, you will dare not lift your eyes should someone discover the tears that have welled there. The old woman will whisper: Promise me you will marry Jamini. If I do not have your promise, I will know no peace even in death.

Your voice will be heavy. You will softly mumble: I will not fail you. I promise.

And soon it will be late afternoon. The bullock cart will appear once again to take you back. One by one, the three of you will get inside. As you are about to leave, Jamini will look at you with those sorrowful eyes of hers and softly remark: You are forgetting your tackle.

You will smile and reply: Let it be. I missed the fish this time – but they won't escape next time.

Jamini will not turn her eyes away. Her tired face will softly light up with a smile, tender and grateful. Like the white clouds of autumn, it will drift across your heart and fill you with a strange and beautiful warmth, an unexplained happiness.

The cart will amble on its way. You will not feel cramped this time; nor will the monotonous creak of the wheels bother you. Your friends will discuss how a hundred years ago, the scourge of malaria, like a relentless flood, carried off Telenapota and left it here, in this forgotten no-man's land, just beside the frontier of the world of the living. You will not be listening; your mind will be drifting elsewhere. You will only listen to your own heart-beats echoing the words: I will come back, I will come back.

Even after you get back home to the city, with its hectic pace and harsh lights, the memory of Telenapota will shine bright in your mind like a star that is distant and yet very close. A few days will pass with petty problems, the usual traumas of the commonplace. And even if a slight mist begins to form in your mind, you will not be aware of it. Then, just as you have crossed the fences, prepared to go back to Telenapota, you will suddenly feel the shivering touch of the oncoming fever.

Soon the terrible headache and the temperatures will be on you and you will lie down under a lot of blankets, trying unsuccessfully to ward off the fever or at least come to terms with it. The thermometer will register 105 degrees Fahrenheit and the last thing you hear before passing out will be the doctor's verdict. Malaria.

It will be many days before you are able to walk out of the house and bask in the sun, weak and exhausted by the long fever. Meanwhile, unknown to yourself, you mind will have undergone many changes, the inevitable transformations. Telenapota will become a vague, indistinct dream, like the memory of a star that has fallen. Was there ever such a place? You will not be sure. The face that was tired and serene. The eyes that were lost and lonely, hiding an unknown sorrow. Were they real? Or were they, like the shadows of Telenapota's ruins, just another part of a phantom dream?

Telenapota, discovered for one brief moment, will be lost again in the timeless dark of the night.

SOFT

F. Paul Wilson

F. Paul Wilson (1946–) is a popular American writer of science fiction and horror. In 1981, his epic horror novel *The Keep* became an international bestseller. In the 1990s, he wrote science fiction and medical thrillers. With Matthew J. Costello, Wilson created and scripted *FTL Newsfeed,* which ran daily on the Sci-Fi Channel from 1992–1996. Among Wilson's best-known characters is the anti-hero Repairman Jack, an urban mercenary introduced in the 1984 bestseller, *The Tomb*. H. P. Lovecraft is a major influence on Wilson, who was introduced to his work by Donald Wollheim, both of whom are also included in this volume. 'Soft' (1984) has a surreal and disturbing quality typical of Wilson's stories from this period.

I was lying on the floor watching TV and exercising what was left of my legs when the newscaster's jaw collapsed. He was right in the middle of the usual plea for anybody who thought they were immune to come to Rockefeller Center when – *pflumpf!* – the bottom of his face went soft.

I burst out laughing.

'Daddy!' Judy said, shooting me a razor-blade look from her wheelchair.

I shut up.

She was right. Nothing funny about a man's tongue wiggling around in the air snakelike while his lower jaw flopped down in front of his throat like a sack of Jell-O and his bottom teeth jutted at the screen crowns-on, rippling like a line of buoys on a bay. A year ago I would have gagged. But I've changed in ways other than physical since this mess began, and couldn't help feeling good about one of those pretty-boy newsreaders going soft right in front of the camera. I almost wished I had a bigger screen so I could watch twenty-one color inches of the scene. He was barely visible on our five-inch black-and-white.

The room filled with white noise as the screen went blank. Someone must have taken a look at what was going out on the airwaves and pulled the plug. Not that many people were watching anyway.

I flipped the set off to save the batteries. Batteries were as good as gold now. *Better* than gold. Who wanted gold nowadays?

I looked over at Judy and she was crying softly. Tears slid down her cheeks.

'Hey, hon–'

'I can't help it, Daddy. I'm so *scared!*'

'Don't be, Jude. Don't worry. Everything will work out, you'll see. We've got this thing licked, you and me.'

'How can you be so sure?'

'Because it hasn't progressed in weeks! It's over for us – we've got immunity.'

She glanced down at her legs, then quickly away. 'It's already too late for me.'

I reached over and patted my dancer on the hand. 'Never too late for you, shweetheart,' I said in my best Bogart. That got a tiny smile out of her.

We sat there in the silence, each thinking our own thoughts. The newsreader had said the cause of the softness had been discovered: A virus, a freak mutation that disrupted the calcium matrix of bones.

Yeah. Sure. That's what they said last year when the first cases cropped up in Boston. A virus. But they never isolated the virus, and the softness spread all over the world. So they began searching for 'a subtle and elusive environmental toxin.' They never pinned that one down either.

Now we were back to a virus again. Who cared? It didn't matter. Judy and I had beat it. Whether we had formed the right antibodies or the right antitoxin was just a stupid academic question. The process had been arrested in us. Sure, it had done some damage, but it wasn't doing any more, and that was the important thing. We'd never be the same, but we were going to live!

'But that man,' Judy said, nodding toward the TV. 'He said they were looking for people in whom the disease had started and then stopped. That's us, Dad. They said they need to examine people like us so they can find out how to fight it, maybe develop a serum against it. We should–'

'Judy-Judy-Judy!' I said in Cary Grantese to hide my annoyance. How many times did I have to go over this? 'We've been through all this before. I told you: It's too late for them. Too late for everybody but us immunes.'

I didn't want to discuss it – Judy didn't understand about those kinds of people, how you can't deal with them.

'I want you to take me down there,' she said in the tone she used when she wanted to be stubborn. 'If you don't want to help, okay. But *I* do.'

'No!' I said that louder than I wanted to and she flinched. More softly: 'I know those people. I worked all those years in the Health Department. They'd turn us into lab specimens. They'll suck us dry and use our immunity to try and save themselves.'

'But I want to help *some*body! I don't want us to be the last two people on earth!'

She began to cry again.

Judy was frustrated. I could understand that. She was unable to leave the apartment by herself and probably saw me at times as a dictator who had her at his mercy. And she was frightened, probably more frightened than I could imagine. She was only eighteen and everyone she had ever known in her life – including her mother – was dead.

I hoisted myself into the chair next to her and put my arm around her shoulders. She was the only person in the world who mattered to me. That had been true even before the softness began.

'We're not alone. Take George, for example. And I'm sure there are plenty of other immunes around, hiding like us. When the weather warms up, we'll find each other and start everything over new. But until then, we can't allow the bloodsuckers to drain off whatever it is we've got that protects us.'

She nodded without saying anything. I wondered if she was agreeing with me or just trying to shut me up.

'Let's eat,' I said with a gusto I didn't really feel.

'Not hungry.'

'Got to keep up your strength. We'll have soup. How's that sound?'

She smiled weakly. 'Okay… soup.'

I forgot and almost tried to stand up. Old habits die hard. My lower legs were hanging over the edge of the chair like a pair of sand-filled dancer's tights. I could twitch the muscles and see them ripple under the skin, but a muscle is pretty useless unless it's attached to a bone, and the bones down there were gone.

I slipped off my chair to what was left of my knees and shuffled over to the stove. The feel of those limp and useless leg muscles squishing under me was repulsive but I was getting used to it.

It hit the kids and old people first, supposedly because their bones were a little soft to begin with, then moved on to the rest of us, starting at the bottom and working its way up – sort of like a Horatio Alger success story. At least that's the way it worked in most people. There were exceptions, of course, like that newscaster. I had followed true to form: My left lower leg collapsed at the end of last month; my right went a few days later. It wasn't a terrible shock. My feet had already gone soft so I knew the legs were next. Besides, I'd heard the sound.

The sound comes in the night when all is quiet. It starts a day or two before a bone goes. A soft sound, like someone gently crinkling cellophane inside your head. No one else can hear it. Only you. I think it comes from the bone itself – from millions of tiny fractures slowly interconnecting into a mosaic that eventually causes the bone to dissolve into mush. Like an on-rushing train far far away can be heard if you press your ear to the track, so the sound of each microfracture transmits from bone to bone until it reaches your middle ear.

I haven't heard the sound in almost four weeks. I thought I did a couple of times and broke out in a cold, shaking sweat, but no more of my bones have gone. Neither have Judy's. The average case goes from normal person to lump of jelly in three to four weeks. Sometimes it takes longer, but there's always a steady progression. Nothing more has happened to me or Judy since last month.

Somehow, someway, we're immune.

With my lower legs dragging behind me, I got to the counter of the kitchenette and kneed my way up the stepstool to where I could reach things. I filled a pot with water – at least the pressure was still up – and set it on the sterno stove. With gas and electricity long gone, sterno was a lifesaver.

While waiting for the water to boil I went to the window and looked out. The late afternoon March sky was full of dark gray clouds streaking to the east. Nothing moving on West Street one floor below but a few windblown leaves from God-knows-where. I glanced across at the windows of George's apartment, looking for movement but finding none, then back down to the street below.

I hadn't seen anybody but George on the street for ages, hadn't seen or smelled smoke in well over two months. The last fires must have finally burned themselves out. The riots were one direct result of the viral theory. Half the city went up in the big riot last fall – half the city and an awful lot of people. Seems someone got the bright idea that if all the people going soft were put out of their misery and their bodies burned, the plague could be stopped, at least here in Manhattan. The few cops left couldn't stop the mobs. In fact a lot of the city's ex-cops had been *in* the mobs! Judy and I lost our apartment when our building went up. Luckily we hadn't any signs of softness then. We got away with our lives and little else.

'Water's boiling, Dad,' Judy said from across the room.

I turned and went back to the stove, not saying anything, still thinking about how fast our nice rent-stabilized apartment house had burned, taking everything we had with it.

Everything was gone… furniture and futures… gone. All my plans. Gone. Here I stood – if you could call it that – a man with a college education, a B.S. in biology, a secure city job, and what was left? No job. Hell – no *city!* I'd had it all planned for my dancer. She was going to make it *so* big. I'd hang onto my city job with all those civil service idiots in the Department of Health, putting up with their sniping and their backstabbing and their lousy office politics so I could keep all the fringe benefits and foot the bill while Judy pursued the dance. She was going to have it *all*! Now what? All her talent, all her potential… where was it going?

Going soft…

I poured the dry contents of the Lipton envelope into the boiling water and soon the odor of chicken noodle soup filled the room.

Which meant we'd have company soon.

I dragged the stepstool over to the door. Already I could hear their claws begin to scrape against the outer surface of the door, their tiny teeth begin to gnaw at its edges. I climbed up and peered through the hole I'd made last month at what had then been eye-level.

There they were. The landing was full of them. Gray and brown and dirty, with glinty little eyes and naked tails. Revulsion rippled down my skin. I watched their growing numbers every day now, every time I cooked something, but still hadn't got used to them.

So I did Cagney for them: 'Yooou diirty raaats!' and turned to wink at Judy on the far side of the fold-out bed. Her expression remained grim.

Rats. They were taking over the city. They seemed to be immune to the softness and were traveling in packs that got bigger and bolder with each passing day. Which was why I'd chosen this building for us: Each apartment was boxed in with pre-stressed concrete block. No rats in the walls here.

I waited for the inevitable. Soon it happened:

A number of them squealed, screeched, and thrashed as the crowding pushed them at each other's throats, and then there was bedlam out there. I didn't bother to watch any more. I saw it every day. The pack jumped on the wounded ones. Never failed. They were so hungry they'd eat anything, even each other. And while they were fighting among themselves they'd leave us in peace with our soup.

Soon I had the card table between us and we were sipping the yellow broth and those tiny noodles. I did a lot of *mmm-good*ing but got no response from Judy. Her eyes were fixed on the walkie-talkie on the end table.

'How come we haven't heard from him?'

Good question – one that had been bothering me for a couple of days now. Where *was* George? Usually he stopped by every other day or so to see if there was anything we needed. And if he didn't stop by, he'd call us on the walkie-talkie. We had an arrangement between us that we'd both turn on our headsets every day at six p.m. just in case we needed to be in touch. I'd been calling over to George's place across the street at six o'clock sharp for three days running now with no result.

'He's probably wandering around the city seeing what he can pick up. He's a resourceful guy. Probably came back with something we can really use but haven't thought of.'

Judy didn't flash me the anticipated smile. Instead, she frowned. 'What if he went down to the research center?'

'I'm sure he didn't,' I told her. 'He's a trusting soul, but he's not a fool.'

I kept my eyes down as I spoke. I'm not a good liar. And that very question had been nagging at my gut. What if George had been stupid enough to present himself to the researchers? If he had, he was through. They'd never let him go and we'd never see him again.

For George wasn't an immune like us. He was different. Judy and I had caught the virus – or toxin – and defeated it. We were left with terrible scars from the battle but we had survived. We *acquired* our immunity through battle with the softness agent. George was special – he had remained untouched. He'd exposed himself to infected people for months as he helped everyone he could, and was still hard all over. Not so much as a little toe had gone soft on him. Which meant – to me at least – that George had been *born* with some sort of immunity to the softness.

Wouldn't those researchers love to get their needles and scalpels into *him*!

I wondered if they had. It was possible George might have been picked up and brought down to the research center against his will. He told me once that he'd seen official-looking vans and cars prowling the streets, driven by guys wearing gas masks or the like. But that had been months ago and he hadn't reported anything like it since. Certainly no cars had been on this street in recent memory. I warned him time and again about roaming around in the daylight but he always laughed good-naturedly and said nobody'd ever catch him – he was too fast.

What if he'd run into someone faster?

There was only one thing to do.

'I'm going to take a stroll over to George's just to see if he's okay.'

Judy gasped. 'No, Dad! You can't! It's too far!'

'Only across the street.'

'But your legs –'

'– are only half gone.'

I'd met George shortly after the last riot. I had two hard legs then. I'd come looking for a sturdier building than the one we'd been burned out of. He helped us move in here.

I was suspicious at first, I admit that. I mean, I kept asking myself, *What does this guy want?* Turned out he only wanted to be friends. And so friends we became. He was soon the only other man I trusted in this whole world. And that being the case, I wanted a gun – for protection against all those other men I didn't trust. George told me he had stolen a bunch during the early lootings. I traded him some sterno and batteries for a .38 and a pump-action 12-gauge shotgun with ammo for both. I promptly sawed off the barrel of the shotgun. If the need arose, I could clear a room real fast with that baby.

So it was the shotgun I reached for now. No need to fool with it – I kept its chamber empty and its magazine loaded with #5 shells. I laid it on the floor and reached into the rag bag by the door and began tying old undershirts around my knees. Maybe I shouldn't call them knees; with the lower legs and caps gone, 'knee' hardly seems appropriate, but it'll have to serve.

From there it was a look through the peep hole to make sure the hall was clear, a blown kiss to Judy, then a shuffle into the hall. I was extra wary at first, ranging the landing up and down, looking for rats. But there weren't any in sight. I slung the shotgun around my neck, letting it hang in front as I started down the stairs one by one on hands and butt, knees first, each flabby lower leg dragging alongside its respective thigh.

Two flights down to the lobby, then up on my padded knees to the swinging door, a hard push through and I was out on the street.

Silence.

We kept our windows tightly closed against the cold and so I hadn't noticed the change. Now it hit me like a slap in the face. As a lifelong New Yorker I'd never heard – or *not* heard – the city like this. Even when there'd been nothing doing on your street, you could always hear that dull roar pulsing from the sky and the pavement and the walls of the buildings. It was the life sound of the city, the beating of its heart, the whisper of its breath, the susurrant rush of blood through its capillaries.

It had stopped.

The shiver that ran over me was not just the result of the sharp edge of the March wind. The street was deserted. A plague had been through here, but there were no contorted bodies strewn about. You didn't fall down and die on the spot with the softness. No, that would be too kind. You died by inches, by bone lengths, in back rooms, trapped, unable to make it to the street. No public displays of morbidity. Just solitary deaths of quiet desperation.

In a secret way I was glad everyone was gone – nobody around to see me tooling across the sidewalk on my rag-wrapped knees like some skid row geek.

The city looked different from down here. You never realize how cracked the sidewalks are, how *dirty*, when you have legs to stand on. The buildings, their windows glaring red with the setting sun that had poked through the clouds over New Jersey, looked half again as tall as they had when I was a taller man.

I shuffled to the street and caught myself looking both ways before sliding off the curb. I smiled at the thought of getting run down by a truck on my first trip in over a month across a street that probably hadn't seen the underside of a car since December.

Despite the absurdity of it, I hurried across, and felt relief when I finally reached the far curb. Pulling open the damn doors to George's apartment building was a chore, but I slipped through both of them and into the lobby. George's bike – a light frame Italian model ten-speeder – was there. I didn't like that. George took that bike everywhere. Of course he could have found a car and some gas and gone sightseeing and not told me, but still the sight of that bike standing there made me uneasy.

I shuffled by the silent bank of elevators, watching my longing expression reflected in their silent, immobile chrome doors as I passed. The fire door to the stairwell was a heavy one, but I squeezed through and started up the steps – backwards. Maybe there was a better way, but I hadn't found it. It was all in the arms: Sit on the bottom step, get your arms back, palms down on the step above, lever yourself up. Repeat this ten times and you've done a flight of stairs. Two flights per floor. Thank the Lord or Whatever that George had decided he preferred a second floor apartment to a penthouse after the final power failure.

It was a good thing I was going up backwards. I might never have seen the rats if I'd been faced around the other way.

Just one appeared at first. Alone, it was almost cute with its twitching whiskers and its head bobbing up and down as it sniffed the air at the bottom of the flight. Then two more joined it, then another half dozen. Soon they were a brown wave, undulating up the steps toward me. I hesitated for an instant, horrified and fascinated by their numbers and all their little black eyes sweeping toward me, then I jolted myself into action. I swung the scatter gun around, pumped a shell into the chamber, and let them have a blast. Dimly through the reverberating roar of the shotgun I heard a chorus of squeals and saw flashes of flying crimson blossoms, then I was ducking my face into my arms to protect my eyes from the ricocheting shot. I should have realized the danger of shooting in a cinder-block stairwell like this. Not that it would have changed things – I still had to protect myself – but I should have anticipated the ricochets.

The rats did what I'd hoped they'd do – jumped on the dead and near-dead of their number and forgot about me. I let the gun hang in front of me again and continued up the stairs to George's floor.

He didn't answer his bell but the door was unlocked. I'd warned him about that in the past but he'd only laughed in that carefree way of his. 'Who's gonna pop in?' he'd say. Probably no one. But that didn't keep me from locking mine, even though George was the only one who knew where I lived. I wondered if that meant I didn't really trust George.

I put the question aside and pushed the door open.

It stank inside. And it was empty as far as I could see. But there was this sound, this wheezing, coming from one of the bedrooms. Calling his name and announcing my own so I wouldn't get my head blown off, I closed the door behind me – locked it – and followed the sound. I found George.

And retched.

George was a blob of flesh in the middle of his bed. Everything but some ribs, some of his facial bones, and the back of his skull had gone soft on him.

I stood there on my knees in shock, wondering how this could have happened. George was *immune*! He'd laughed at the softness! He'd been walking around as good as new just last week. And now…

His lips were dry and cracked and blue – he couldn't speak, couldn't swallow, could barely breathe. And his eyes… they seemed to be just floating there in a quivering pool of flesh, begging me… darting to his left again and again… begging me…

For what?

I looked to his left and saw the guns. He had a suitcase full of them by the bedroom door. All kinds. I picked up a heavy-looking revolver – an S&W .357 – and glanced at him. He closed his eyes and I thought he smiled.

I almost dropped the pistol when I realized what he wanted.

'No, George!'

He opened his eyes again. They began to fill with tears.

'George – I can't!'

Something like a sob bubbled past his lips. And his eyes… his pleading eyes…

I stood there a long time in the stink of his bedroom, listening to him wheeze, feeling the sweat collect between my palm and the pistol grip. I knew I couldn't do it. Not George, the big, friendly, good-natured slob I'd been depending on.

Suddenly, I felt my pity begin to evaporate as a flare of irrational anger began to rise. I *had* been depending on George now that my legs were half gone, and here he'd gone soft on me. The bitter disappointment fueled the anger. I knew it wasn't right, but I couldn't help hating George just then for letting me down.

'Damn you, George!'

I raised the pistol and pointed it where I thought his brain should be. I turned my head away and pulled the trigger. Twice. The pistol jumped in my hand. The sound was deafening in the confines of the bedroom.

Then all was quiet except for the ringing in my ears. George wasn't wheezing anymore. I didn't look around. I didn't have to see. I have a good imagination.

I fled that apartment as fast as my ruined legs would carry me.

But I couldn't escape the vision of George and how he looked before I shot him. It haunted me every inch of the way home, down the now empty stairs where only a few tufts of dirty brown fur were left to indicate that rats had been swarming there, out into the dusk and across the street and up more stairs to home.

George… how could it be? He was immune!

Or was he? Maybe the softness had followed a different course in George, slowly building up in his system until every bone in his body was riddled with it and he went soft all at once. *God,* what a noise he must have heard when all those bones went in one shot! That was why he hadn't been able to call or answer the walkie-talkie.

But what if it had been something else? What if the virus theory was right and George was the victim of a more virulent mutation? The thought made me sick with dread. Because if that were true, it meant Judy would eventually end up like George. And I was going to have to do for her what I'd done for George.

But what of me, then? Who was going to end it for *me*? I didn't know if I had the guts to shoot myself. And what if my hands went soft before I had the chance?

I didn't want to think about it, but it wouldn't go away. I couldn't remember ever being so frightened. I almost considered going down to Rockefeller Center and presenting Judy and myself to the leechers, but killed that idea real quick. Never. I'm no jerk. I'm college educated. A degree in biology! I know what they'd do to us!

Inside, Judy had wheeled her chair over to the door and was waiting for me. I couldn't let her know.

'Not there,' I told her before she could ask, and I busied myself with putting the shotgun away so I wouldn't have to look her straight in the eyes.

'Where could he be?' Her voice was tight.

'I wish I knew. Maybe he went down to Rockefeller Center. If he did, it's the last we'll ever see of him.'

'I can't believe that.'

'Then tell me where else he can be.'

She was silent.

I did Warner Oland's Chan: 'Numbah One Dawtah is finally at loss for words. Peace reigns at last.'

I could see that I failed to amuse, so I decided a change of subject was in order.

'I'm tired,' I said. It was the truth. The trip across the street had been exhausting.

'Me, too.' She yawned.

'Want to get some sleep?' I knew she did. I was just staying a step or two ahead of her so she wouldn't have to ask to be put to bed. She was a dancer, a fine, proud artist. Judy would never have to ask anyone to put her to bed. Not while I was around. As long as I was able I would spare her the indignity of dragging herself along the floor.

I gathered Judy up in my arms. The whole lower half of her body was soft; her legs hung over my left arm like weighted drapes. It was all I could do to keep from crying when I felt them so limp and formless. My dancer... you should have seen her in *Swan Lake*. Her legs had been so strong, so sleekly muscular, like her mother's...

I took her to the bathroom and left her in there. Which left me alone with my daymares. What if there really was a mutation of the softness and my dancer began leaving me again, slowly, inch by inch. What was I going to do when she was gone? My wife was gone. My folks were gone. What few friends I'd ever had were gone. Judy was the only attachment I had left. Without her I'd break loose from everything and just float off into space. I needed her...

When she was finished in the bathroom I carried her out and arranged her on the bed. I tucked her in and kissed her goodnight.

Out in the living room I slipped under the covers of the fold-out bed and tried to sleep. It was useless. The fear wouldn't leave me alone. I fought it, telling myself that George was a freak case, that Judy and I had licked the softness. We were *immune* and we'd *stay* immune. Let everyone else turn into puddles of Jell-O, I wasn't going to let them suck us dry to save themselves. We were on our way to inheriting the earth, Judy and I, and we didn't even have to be meek about it.

But still sleep refused to come. So I lay there in the growing darkness in the center of the silent city and listened... listened as I did every night... as I knew I would listen for the rest of my life... listened for that sound... that cellophane crinkling sound...

BLOODCHILD

Octavia E. Butler

Octavia Butler (1947–2006) was an American writer who became the first science fiction writer ever to receive the MacArthur Foundation Genius Grant. At the time, Butler was also one of the only African American women in the science fiction field. In 2010, she was inducted into the Science Fiction Hall of Fame. Butler's novels include *Kindred* (1979) and *Parable of the Sower* (1993). 'Bloodchild' (1984) is her most famous story, winning both the Hugo and the Nebula Award for best novelette. Although 'Bloodchild' might be the best example of weird science fiction by Butler, she often included horrific elements in her work. Butler wrote the story as a way of overcoming her fear of bot flies.

My last night of childhood began with a visit home. T'Gatoi's sister had given us two sterile eggs. T'Gatoi gave one to my mother, brother, and sisters. She insisted that I eat the other one alone. It didn't matter. There was still enough to leave everyone feeling good. Almost everyone. My mother wouldn't take any. She sat, watching everyone drifting and dreaming without her. Most of the time she watched me.

I lay against T'Gatoi's long, velvet underside, sipping from my egg now and then, wondering why my mother denied herself such a harmless pleasure. Less of her hair would be gray if she indulged now and then. The eggs prolonged life, prolonged vigor. My father, who had never refused one in his life, had lived more than twice as long as he should have. And toward the end of his life, when he should have been slowing down, he had married my mother and fathered four children.

But my mother seemed content to age before she had to. I saw her turn away as several of T'Gatoi's limbs secured me closer. T'Gatoi liked our body heat and took advantage of it whenever she could. When I was little and at home more, my mother used to try to tell me how to behave with T'Gatoi – how to be respectful and always obedient because T'Gatoi was the Tlic government official in charge of the Preserve, and thus the most important of her kind to deal directly with Terrans. It was an honor, my mother said, that such a person had chosen to come into the family. My mother was at her most formal and severe when she was lying.

I had no idea why she was lying, or even what she was lying about. It was an honor to have T'Gatoi in the family, but it was hardly a novelty. T'Gatoi and my mother had been friends all my mother's life, and T'Gatoi was not interested in being honored in the house she considered her second home. She simply came in, climbed onto one of her special couches, and called me over to keep her warm. It was impossible to be formal with her while lying against her and hearing her complain as usual that I was too skinny.

'You're better,' she said this time, probing me with six or seven of her limbs. 'You're gaining weight finally. Thinness is dangerous.' The probing changed subtly, became a series of caresses.

'He's still too thin,' my mother said sharply.

T'Gatoi lifted her head and perhaps a meter of her body off the couch as though she were sitting up. She looked at my mother, and my mother, her face lined and old looking, turned away.

'Lien, I would like you to have what's left of Gan's egg.'

'The eggs are for the children,' my mother said.

'They are for the family. Please take it.'

Unwillingly obedient, my mother took it from me and put it to her mouth. There were only a few drops left in the now-shrunken, elastic shell, but she squeezed them out, swallowed them, and after a few moments some of the lines of tension began to smooth from her face.

'It's good,' she whispered. 'Sometimes I forget how good it is.'

'You should take more,' T'Gatoi said. 'Why are you in such a hurry to be old?'

My mother said nothing.

'I like being able to come here,' T'Gatoi said. 'This place is a refuge because of you, yet you won't take care of yourself.'

T'Gatoi was hounded on the outside. Her people wanted more of us made available. Only she and her political faction stood between us and the hordes who did not understand why there was a Preserve – why any Terran could not be courted, paid, drafted, in some way made available to them. Or they did understand, but in their desperation, they did not care. She parceled us out to the desperate and sold us to the rich and powerful for their political support. Thus, we were necessities, status symbols, and an independent people. She oversaw the joining of families, putting an end to the final remnants of the earlier system of breaking up Terran families to suit impatient Tlic. I had lived outside with her. I had seen the desperate eagerness in the way some people looked at me. It was a little frightening to know that only she stood between us and that desperation that could so easily swallow us. My mother would look at her sometimes and say to me, 'Take care of her.' And I would remember that she too had been outside, had seen.

Now T'Gatoi used four of her limbs to push me away from her onto the floor. 'Go on, Gan,' she said. 'Sit down there with your sisters and enjoy not being sober. You had most of the egg. Lien, come warm me.'

'Nothing can buy him from me.' Sober, she would not have permitted herself to refer to such things.

'Nothing,' T'Gatoi agreed, humoring her.

'Did you think I would sell him for eggs? For long life? My son?'

'Not for anything,' T'Gatoi said, stroking my mother's shoulders, toying with her long, graying hair.

I would like to have touched my mother, shared that moment with her. She would take my hand if I touched her now. Freed by the egg and the sting, she would smile and perhaps say things long held in. But tomorrow, she would remember all this as a humiliation. I did not want to be part of a remembered humiliation. Best just be still and know she loved me under all the duty and pride and pain.

'Xuan Hoa, take off her shoes,' T'Gatoi said. 'In a little while I'll sting her again and she can sleep.'

My older sister obeyed, swaying drunkenly as she stood up. When she had finished, she sat down beside me and took my hand. We had always been a unit, she and I.

My mother put the back of her head against T'Gatoi's underside and tried from that impossible angle to look up into the broad, round face. 'You're going to sting me again?'

'Yes, Lien.'

'I'll sleep until tomorrow noon.'

'Good. You need it. When did you sleep last?'

My mother made a wordless sound of annoyance. 'I should have stepped on you when you were small enough,' she muttered.

It was an old joke between them. They had grown up together, sort of, though T'Gatoi had not, in my mother's lifetime, been small enough for any Terran to step on. She was nearly three times my mother's present age, yet would still be young when my mother died of age. But T'Gatoi and my mother had met as T'Gatoi was coming into a period of rapid development – a kind of Tlic adolescence. My mother was only a child, but for a while they developed at the same rate and had no better friends than each other.

T'Gatoi had even introduced my mother to the man who became my father. My parents, pleased with each other in spite of their different ages, married as T'Gatoi was going into her family's business – politics. She and my mother saw each other less. But sometime before my older sister was born, my mother promised T'Gatoi one of her children. She would have to give one of us to someone, and she preferred T'Gatoi to some stranger.

Years passed. T'Gatoi traveled and increased her influence. The Preserve was hers by the time she came back to my mother to collect what she probably saw as her just reward for her hard work. My older sister took an instant liking to her and wanted to be chosen, but my mother was just coming to term with me and T'Gatoi liked the idea of choosing an infant and watching and taking part in all the phases of development. I'm told I was first caged within T'Gatoi's many limbs only three minutes after my birth. A few days later, I was given my first taste of egg. I tell Terrans that when they ask whether I was ever afraid of her. And I tell it to Tlic when T'Gatoi suggests a young Terran child for them and they, anxious and ignorant, demand an adolescent. Even my brother who had somehow grown up to fear and distrust the Tlic could probably have gone smoothly into one of their families if he had been adopted early enough. Sometimes, I think for his sake he should have been. I looked at him, stretched out on the floor across the room, his eyes open, but glazed as he dreamed his egg dream. No matter what he felt toward the Tlic, he always demanded his share of egg.

'Lien, can you stand up?' T'Gatoi asked suddenly.

'Stand?' my mother said. 'I thought I was going to sleep.'

'Later. Something sounds wrong outside.' The cage was abruptly gone.

'What?'

'Up, Lien!'

My mother recognized her tone and got up just in time to avoid being dumped on the floor. T'Gatoi whipped her three meters of body off her couch, toward the door, and out at full speed. She had bones – ribs, a long spine, a skull, four sets of limb bones per segment. But when she moved that way, twisting, hurling herself into controlled falls, landing running, she seemed not only boneless, but aquatic – something swimming through the air as though it were water. I loved watching her move.

I left my sister and started to follow her out the door, though I wasn't very steady on my own feet. It would have been better to sit and dream, better yet to find a girl and share a waking dream with her. Back when the Tlic saw us as not much more than convenient, big, warm-blooded animals, they would pen several of us together, male and female, and feed us only eggs. That way they could be sure of getting another generation of us no matter how we tried to hold out. We were lucky that didn't go on long. A few generations of it and we would have *been* little more than convenient, big animals.

'Hold the door open, Gan,' T'Gatoi said. 'And tell the family to stay back.'

'What is it?' I asked.

'N'Tlic.'

I shrank back against the door. 'Here? Alone?'

'He was trying to reach a call box, I suppose.' She carried the man past me, unconscious, folded like a coat over some of her limbs. He looked young – my brother's age perhaps – and he was thinner than he should have been. What T'Gatoi would have called dangerously thin.

'Gan, go to the call box,' she said. She put the man on the floor and began stripping off his clothing.

I did not move.

After a moment, she looked up at me, her sudden stillness a sign of deep impatience.

'Send Qui,' I told her. 'I'll stay here. Maybe I can help.'

She let her limbs begin to move again, lifting the man and pulling his shirt over his head. 'You don't want to see this,' she said. 'It will be hard. I can't help this man the way his Tlic could.'

'I know. But send Qui. He won't want to be of any help here. I'm at least willing to try.'

She looked at my brother – older, bigger, stronger, certainly more able to help her here. He was sitting up now, braced against the wall, staring at the man on the floor with undisguised fear and revulsion. Even she could see that he would be useless.

'Qui, go!' she said

He didn't argue. He stood up, swayed briefly, then steadied, frightened sober.

'This man's name is Bram Lomas,' she told him, reading from the man's armband. I fingered my own armband in sympathy. 'He needs T'Khotgif Teh. Do you hear?'

'Bram Lomas, T'Khotgif Teh,' my brother said. 'I'm going.' He edged around Lomas and ran out the door.

Lomas began to regain consciousness. He only moaned at first and clutched spasmodically at a pair of T'Gatoi's limbs. My younger sister, finally awake from her egg dream, came close to look at him, until my mother pulled her back.

T'Gatoi removed the man's shoes, then his pants, all the while leaving him two of her limbs to grip. Except for the final few, all her limbs were equally dexterous. 'I want no argument from you this time, Gan,' she said.

I straightened. 'What shall I do?'

'Go out and slaughter an animal that is at least half your size.'

'Slaughter? But I've never–'

She knocked me across the room. Her tail was an efficient weapon whether she exposed the sting or not.

I got up, feeling stupid for having ignored her warning, and went into the kitchen. Maybe I could kill something with a knife or an ax. My mother raised a few Terran animals for the table and several thousand local ones for their fur. T'Gatoi would probably prefer something local. An achti, perhaps. Some of those were the right size, though they had about three times as many teeth as I did and a real love of using them. My mother, Hoa, and Qui could kill them with knives. I had never killed one at all, had never slaughtered any animal. I had spent most of my time with T'Gatoi while my brother and sisters were learning the family business. T'Gatoi had been right. I should have been the one to go to the call box. At least I could do that.

I went to the corner cabinet where my mother kept her large house and garden tools. At the back of the cabinet there was a pipe that carried off waste water from the kitchen – except that it didn't anymore. My father had rerouted the waste water below before I was born. Now the pipe could be turned so that one half slid around the other and a rifle could be stored inside. This wasn't our only gun, but it was our most easily accessible one. I would have to use it to shoot one of the biggest of the achti. Then T'Gatoi would probably confiscate it. Firearms were illegal in the Preserve. There had been incidents right after the Preserve was established – Terrans shooting Tlic, shooting N'Tlic. This was before the Joining of families began, before everyone had a personal stake in keeping the peace. No one had shot a Tlic in my lifetime or my mother's, but the law still stood – for our protection, we were told. There were stories of whole Terran families wiped out in reprisal back during the assassinations.

I went out to the cages and shot the biggest achti I could find. It was a handsome breeding male, and my mother would not be pleased to see me bring it in. But it was the right size, and I was in a hurry.

I put the achti's long, warm body over my shoulder – glad that some of the weight I'd gained was muscle – and took it to the kitchen. There, I put the gun back in its hiding place. If T'Gatoi noticed the achti's wounds and demanded the gun, I would give it to her. Otherwise, let it stay where my father wanted it.

I turned to take the achti to her, then hesitated. For several seconds, I stood in front of the closed door wondering why I was suddenly afraid. I knew what was going to happen. I hadn't seen it before but T'Gatoi had shown me diagrams and drawings. She had made sure I knew the truth as soon as I was old enough to understand it.

Yet I did not want to go into that room. I wasted a little time choosing a knife from the carved, wooden box in which my mother kept them. T'Gatoi might want one, I told myself, for the tough, heavily furred hide of the achti.

'Gan!' T'Gatoi called, her voice harsh with urgency.

I swallowed. I had not imagined a single moving of the feet could be so difficult. I realized I was trembling and that shamed me. Shame impelled me through the door.

I put the achti down near T'Gatoi and saw that Lomas was unconscious again. She, Lomas, and I were alone in the room – my mother and sisters probably sent out so they would not have to watch. I envied them.

But my mother came back into the room as T'Gatoi seized the achti. Ignoring the knife I offered her, she extended claws from several of her limbs and slit the achti from throat to anus. She looked at me, her yellow eyes intent. 'Hold this man's shoulders, Gan.'

I stared at Lomas in panic, realizing that I did not want to touch him, let alone hold him. This would not be like shooting an animal. Not as quick, not as merciful, and, I hoped, not as final, but there was nothing I wanted less than to be part of it.

My mother came forward. 'Gan, you hold his right side,' she said. 'I'll hold his left.' And if he came to, he would throw her off without realizing he had done it. She was a tiny woman. She often wondered aloud how she had produced, as she said, such 'huge' children.

'Never mind,' I told her, taking the man's shoulders. 'I'll do it.' She hovered nearby.

'Don't worry,' I said. 'I won't shame you. You don't have to stay and watch.'

She looked at me uncertainly, then touched my face in a rare caress. Finally, she went back to her bedroom.

T'Gatoi lowered her head in relief. 'Thank you, Gan,' she said with courtesy more Terran than Tlic. 'That one… she is always finding new ways for me to make her suffer.'

Lomas began to groan and make choked sounds. I had hoped he would stay unconscious. T'Gatoi put her face near his so that he focused on her.

'I've stung you as much as I dare for now,' she told him. 'When this is over, I'll sting you to sleep and you won't hurt anymore.'

'Please,' the man begged. 'Wait…'

'There's no more time, Bram. I'll sting you as soon as it's over. When T'Khotgif arrives she'll give you eggs to help you heal. It will be over soon.'

'T'Khotgif!' the man shouted, straining against my hands.

'Soon, Bram.' T'Gatoi glanced at me, then placed a claw against his abdomen slightly to the right of the middle, just below the left rib. There was movement on the right side – tiny, seemingly random pulsations moving his brown flesh, creating a concavity here, a convexity there, over and until I could see the rhythm of it and knew where the next pulse would be.

Lomas's entire body stiffened under T'Gatoi's claw, though she merely rested it against him as she wound the rear section of her body around his legs. He might break my grip, but he would not break hers. He wept helplessly as she used his pants to tie his hands, then pushed his hands above his head so that I could kneel on the cloth between them and pin them in place. She rolled up his shirt and gave it to him to bite down on.

And she opened him.

His body convulsed with the first cut. He almost tore himself away from me. The sound he made… I had never heard such sounds come from anything human. T'Gatoi seemed to pay no attention as she lengthened and deepened the cut, now and then pausing to lick away blood. His blood vessels contracted, reacting to the chemistry of her saliva, and the bleeding slowed.

I felt as though I were helping her torture him, helping her consume him. I knew I would vomit soon, didn't know why I hadn't already. I couldn't possibly last until she was finished.

She found the first grub. It was fat and deep red with his blood – both inside and out. It had already eaten its own egg case but apparently had not yet begun to eat its host. At this stage, it would eat any flesh except its mother's. Let alone, it would have gone on excreting the poisons that had both sickened and alerted Lomas. Eventually it would have begun to eat. By the time it ate its way out of Lomas's flesh, Lomas would be dead or dying – and unable to take revenge on the thing that was killing him. There was always a grace period between the time the host sickened and the time the grubs began to eat him.

T'Gatoi picked up the writhing grub carefully and looked at it, somehow ignoring the terrible groans of the man.

Abruptly, the man lost consciousness.

'Good,' T'Gatoi looked down at him. 'I wish you Terrans could do that at will.' She felt nothing. And the thing she held...

It was limbless and boneless at this stage, perhaps fifteen centimeters long and two thick, blind and slimy with blood. It was like a large worm. T'Gatoi put it into the belly of the achti, and it began at once to burrow. It would stay there and eat as long as there was anything to eat.

Probing through Lomas's flesh, she found two more, one of them smaller and more vigorous. 'A male!' she said happily. He would be dead before I would. He would be through his metamorphosis and screwing everything that would hold still before his sisters even had limbs. He was the only one to make a serious effort to bite T'Gatoi as she placed him in the achti.

Paler worms oozed to visibility in Lomas's flesh. I closed my eyes. It was worse than finding something dead, rotting, and filled with tiny animal grubs. And it was far worse than any drawing or diagram.

'Ah, there are more,' T'Gatoi said, plucking out two long, thick grubs. 'You may have to kill another animal, Gan. Everything lives inside you Terrans.'

I had been told all my life that this was a good and necessary thing Tlic and Terran did together – a kind of birth. I had believed it until now. I knew birth was painful and bloody, no matter what. But this was something else, something worse. And I wasn't ready to see it. Maybe I never would be. Yet I couldn't not see it. Closing my eyes didn't help.

T'Gatoi found a grub still eating its egg case. The remains of the case were still wired into a blood vessel by their own little tube or hook or whatever. That was the way the grubs were anchored and the way they fed. They took only blood until they were ready to emerge. Then they ate their stretched, elastic egg cases. Then they ate their hosts.

T'Gatoi bit away the egg case, licked away the blood. Did she like the taste? Did childhood habits die hard – or not die at all?

The whole procedure was wrong, alien. I wouldn't have thought anything about her could seem alien to me.

'One more, I think,' she said. 'Perhaps two. A good family. In a host animal these days, we would be happy to find one or two alive.' She glanced at me. 'Go outside, Gan, and empty your stomach. Go now while the man is unconscious.'

I staggered out, barely made it. Beneath the tree just beyond the front door, I vomited until there was nothing left to bring up. Finally, I stood shaking, tears streaming down my face. I did not know why I was crying, but I could not stop. I went further from the house to avoid being seen. Every time I closed my eyes I saw red worms crawling over redder human flesh.

There was a car coming toward the house. Since Terrans were forbidden motorized vehicles except for certain farm equipment, I knew this must be Lomas's Tlic with Qui and perhaps a Terran doctor. I wiped my face on my shirt, struggled for control.

'Gan,' Qui called as the car stopped. 'What happened?' He crawled out of the low, round, Tlic-convenient car door. Another Terran crawled out the other side and went into the house without speaking to me. The doctor. With his help and a few eggs, Lomas might make it.

'T'Khotgif Teh?' I said.

The Tlic driver surged out of her car, reared up half her length before me. She was paler and smaller than T'Gatoi – probably born from the body of an animal. Tlic from Terran bodies were always larger as well as more numerous.

'Six young,' I told her. 'Maybe seven, all alive. At least one male.'

'Lomas?' she said harshly. I liked her for the question and the concern in her voice when she asked it. The last coherent thing he had said was her name.

'He's alive,' I said.

She surged away to the house without another word.

'She's been sick,' my brother said, watching her go. 'When I called, I could hear people telling her she wasn't well enough to go out even for this.'

I said nothing. I had extended courtesy to the Tlic. Now I didn't want to talk to anyone. I hoped he would go in – out of curiosity if nothing else.

'Finally found out more than you wanted to know, eh?'

I looked at him.

'Don't give me one of *her* looks,' he said. 'You're not her. You're just her property.'

One of her looks. Had I picked up even an ability to imitate her expressions?

'What'd you do, puke?' He sniffed the air. 'So now you know what you're in for.'

I walked away from him. He and I had been close when we were kids. He would let me follow him around when I was home, and sometimes T'Gatoi would let me bring him along when she took me into the city. But something had happened when he reached adolescence. I never knew what. He began keeping out of T'Gatoi's way. Then he began running away – until he realized there was no 'away'. Not in the Preserve. Certainly not outside. After that he concentrated on getting his share of every egg that came into the house and on looking out for me in a way that made me all but hate him – a way that clearly said, as long as I was all right, he was safe from the Tlic.

'How was it, really?' he demanded, following me.

'I killed an achti. The young ate it.'

'You didn't run out of the house and puke because they ate an achti.'

'I had… never seen a person cut open before.' That was true, and enough for him to know. I couldn't talk about the other. Not with him.

'Oh,' he said. He glanced at me as though he wanted to say more, but he kept quiet.

We walked, not really headed anywhere. Toward the back, toward the cages, toward the fields.

'Did he say anything?' Qui asked. 'Lomas, I mean.'

Who else would he mean? 'He said T'Khotgif.'

Qui shuddered. 'If she had done that to me, she'd be the last person I'd call for.'

'You'd call for her. Her sting would ease your pain without killing the grubs in you.'

'You think I'd care if they died?'

No. Of course he wouldn't. Would I?

'Shit!' He drew a deep breath. 'I've seen what they do. You think this thing with Lomas was bad? It was nothing.'

I didn't argue. He didn't know what he was talking about.

'*I saw them eat a man*,' he said.

I turned to face him. 'You're lying!'

'I saw them eat a man.' He paused. 'It was when I was little. I had been to the Hartmund house and I was on my way home. Halfway here, I saw a man and a Tlic and the man was N'Tlic. The ground was hilly. I was able to hide from them and watch. The Tlic wouldn't open the man because she had nothing to feed the grubs. The man couldn't go any further and there were no houses around. He was in so much pain, he told her to kill him. He begged her to kill him. Finally, she did. She cut his throat. One swipe of one claw. I saw the grubs eat their way out, then burrow in again, still eating.'

His words made me see Lomas's flesh again, parasitized, crawling. 'Why didn't you tell me that?' I whispered.

He looked startled as though he'd forgotten I was listening. 'I don't know.'

'You started to run away not long after that, didn't you?'

'Yeah. Stupid. Running inside the Preserve. Running in a cage.'

I shook my head, said what I should have said to him long ago. 'She wouldn't take you, Qui. You don't have to worry.'

'She would… if anything happened to you.'

'No. She'd take Xuan Hoa. Hoa… wants it.' She wouldn't if she had stayed to watch Lomas.

'They don't take women,' he said with contempt.

'They do sometimes.' I glanced at him. Actually, they prefer women. You should be around them when they talk among themselves. They say women have more body fat to protect the grubs. But they usually take men to leave the women free to bear their own young.'

'To provide the next generation of host animals,' he said, switching from contempt to bitterness.

'It's more than that!' I countered. Was it?

'If it were going to happen to me, I'd want to believe it was more, too.

'It is more!' I felt like a kid. Stupid argument.

'Did you think so while T'Gatoi was picking worms out of that guy's guts?'

'It's not supposed to happen that way.'

'Sure it is. You weren't supposed to see it, that's all. And his Tlic was supposed to do it. She could sting him unconscious and the operation wouldn't have been as painful. But she'd still open him, pick out the grubs, and if she missed even one, it would poison him and eat him from the inside out.'

There was actually a time when my mother told me to show respect for Qui because he was my older brother. I walked away, hating him. In his way, he was gloating. He was safe and I wasn't. I could have hit him, but I didn't think I would be able to stand it when he refused to hit back, when he looked at me with contempt and pity.

He wouldn't let me get away. Longer legged, he swung ahead of me and made me feel as though I were following him.

'I'm sorry,' he said.

I strode on, sick and furious.

'Look, it probably won't be that bad with you. T'Gatoi likes you. She'll be careful.'

I turned back toward the house, almost running from him.

'Has she done it to you yet?' he asked, keeping up easily. 'I mean, you're about the right age for implantation. Has she–'

I hit him. I didn't know I was going to do it, but I think I meant to kill him. If he hadn't been bigger and stronger, I think I would have.

He tried to hold me off, but in the end, had to defend himself. He only hit me a couple of times. That was plenty. I don't remember going down, but when I came to, he was gone. It was worth the pain to be rid of him.

I got up and walked slowly toward the house. The back was dark. No one was in the kitchen. My mother and sisters were sleeping in their bedrooms – or pretending to.

Once I was in the kitchen, I could hear voices – Tlic and Terran from the next room. I couldn't make out what they were saying – didn't want to make it out.

I sat down at my mother's table, waiting for quiet. The table was smooth and worn, heavy and well crafted. My father had made it for her just before he died. I remembered hanging around underfoot when he built it. He didn't mind. Now I sat leaning on it, missing him. I could have talked to him. He had done it three times in his long life. Three clutches of eggs, three times being opened up and sewed up. How had he done it? How did anyone do it?

I got up, took the rifle from its hiding place, and sat down again with it. It needed cleaning, oiling.

All I did was load it.

'Gan?'

She made a lot of little clicking sounds when she walked on bare floor, each limb clicking in succession as it touched down. Waves of little clicks.

She came to the table, raised the front half of her body above it, and surged onto it. Sometimes she moved so smoothly she seemed to flow like water itself She coiled herself into a small hill in the middle of the table and looked at me.

'That was bad,' she said softly. 'You should not have seen it. It need not be that way.'

'I know.'

'T'Khotgif – Ch'Khotgif now – she will die of her disease. She will not live to raise her children. But her sister will provide for them, and for Bram Lomas.' Sterile sister. One fertile female in every lot. One to keep the family going. That sister owed Lomas more than she could ever repay.

'He'll live then?'

'Yes.'

'I wonder if he would do it again.'

'No one would ask him to do that again.'

I looked into the yellow eyes, wondering how much I saw and understood there, and how much I only imagined. 'No one ever asks us,' I said. 'You never asked me.'

She moved her head slightly. 'What's the matter with your face?'

'Nothing. Nothing important.' Human eyes probably wouldn't have noticed the swelling in the darkness. The only light was from one of the moons, shining through a window across the room.

'Did you use the rifle to shoot the achti?'

'Yes.'

'And do you mean to use it to shoot me?'

I stared at her, outlined in the moonlight – coiled, graceful body. 'What does Terran blood taste like to you?'

She said nothing.

'What are you?' I whispered. 'What are we to you?'

She lay still, rested her head on her topmost coil. 'You know me as no other does,' she said softly. 'You must decide.'

'That's what happened to my face,' I told her.

'What?'

'Qui goaded me into deciding to do something. It didn't turn out very well.' I moved the gun slightly, brought the barrel up diagonally under my own chin. 'At least it was a decision I made.'

'As this will be.'

'Ask me, Gatoi.'

'For my children's lives?'

She would say something like that. She knew how to manipulate people, Terran and Tlic. But not this time.

'I don't want to be a host animal,' I said. 'Not even yours.'

It took her a long time to answer. 'We use almost no host animals these days,' she said. 'You know that.'

'You use us.'

'We do. We wait long years for you and teach you and join our families to yours.' She moved restlessly. 'You know you aren't animals to us.'

I stared at her, saying nothing.

'The animals we once used began killing most of our eggs after implantation long before your ancestors arrived,' she said softly. 'You know these things, Gan. Because your people arrived, we are relearning what it means to be a healthy, thriving people. And your ancestors, fleeing from their homeworld, from their own kind who would have killed or enslaved them – they survived because of us. We saw them as people and gave them the Preserve when they still tried to kill us as worms.'

At the word 'worms,' I jumped. I couldn't help it, and she couldn't help noticing it.

'I see,' she said quietly. 'Would you really rather die than bear my young, Gan?'

I didn't answer.

'Shall I go to Xuan Hoa?'

'Yes!' Hoa wanted it. Let her have it. She hadn't had to watch Lomas. She'd be proud… Not terrified.

T'Gatoi flowed off the table onto the floor, startling me almost too much.

'I'll sleep in Hoa's room tonight,' she said. 'And sometime tonight or in the morning, I'll tell her.'

This was going too fast. My sister Hoa had had almost as much to do with raising me as my mother. I was still close to her – not like Qui. She could want T'Gatoi and still love me.

'Wait! Gatoi!'

She looked back, then raised nearly half her length off the floor and turned to face me. 'These are adult things, Gan. This is my life, my family!'

'But she's… my sister.'

'I have done what you demanded. I have asked you!'

'But–'

'It will be easier for Hoa. She has always expected to carry other lives inside her.'

Human lives. Human young who should someday drink at her breasts, not at her veins.

I shook my head. 'Don't do it to her, Gatoi.' I was not Qui. It seemed I could become him, though, with no effort at all. I could make Xuan Hoa my shield. Would it be easier to know that red worms were growing in her flesh instead of mine?

'Don't do it to Hoa,' I repeated.

She stared at me, utterly still.

I looked away, then back at her. 'Do it to me.'

I lowered the gun from my throat and she leaned forward to take it.

'No,' I told her.

'It's the law,' she said.

'Leave it for the family. One of them might use it to save my life someday.'

She grasped the rifle barrel, but I wouldn't let go. I was pulled into a standing position over her.

'Leave it here!' I repeated. 'If we're not your animals, if these are adult things, accept the risk. There is risk, Gatoi, in dealing with a partner.'

It was clearly hard for her to let go of the rifle. A shudder went through her and she made a hissing sound of distress. It occurred to me that she was afraid. She was old enough to have seen what guns could do to people. Now her young and this gun would be together in the same house. She did not know about the other guns. In this dispute, they did not matter.

'I will implant the first egg tonight,' she said as I put the gun away. 'Do you hear, Gan?'

Why else had I been given a whole egg to eat while the rest of the family was left to share one?

Why else had my mother kept looking at me as though I were going away from her, going where she could not follow? Did T'Gatoi imagine I hadn't known?

'I hear.'

'Now!' I let her push me out of the kitchen, then walked ahead of her toward my bedroom. The sudden urgency in her voice sounded real. 'You would have done it to Hoa tonight!' I accused.

'I must do it to someone tonight.'

I stopped in spite of her urgency and stood in her way. 'Don't you care who?'

She flowed around me and into my bedroom. I found her waiting on the couch we shared. There was nothing in Hoa's room that she could have used. She would have done it to Hoa on the floor. The thought of her doing it to Hoa at all disturbed me in a different way now, and I was suddenly angry.

Yet I undressed and lay down beside her. I knew what to do, what to expect. I had been told all my life. I felt the familiar sting, narcotic, mildly pleasant. Then the blind probing of her ovipositor. The puncture was painless, easy. So easy going in. She undulated slowly against me, her muscles forcing the egg from her body into mine. I held on to a pair of her limbs until I remembered Lomas holding her that way. Then I let go, moved inadvertently, and hurt her. She gave a low cry of pain and I expected to be caged at once within her limbs. When I wasn't, I held on to her again, feeling oddly ashamed.

'I'm sorry,' I whispered.

She rubbed my shoulders with four of her limbs.

'Do you care?' I asked. 'Do you care that it's me?'

She did not answer for some time. Finally, 'You were the one making the choices tonight, Gan. I made mine long ago.'

'Would you have gone to Hoa?'

'Yes. How could I put my children into the care of one who hates them?'

'It wasn't… hate.'

'I know what it was.'

'I was afraid.'

Silence.

'I still am.' I could admit it to her here, now.

'But you came to me… to save Hoa.'

'Yes.' I leaned my forehead against her. She was cool velvet, deceptively soft. 'And to keep you for myself,' I said. It was so. I didn't understand it, but it was so.

She made a soft hum of contentment. 'I couldn't believe I had made such a mistake with you,' she said. 'I chose you. I believed you had grown to choose me.'

'I had, but…'

'Lomas.'

'Yes.'

'I had never known a Terran to see a birth and take it well. Qui has seen one, hasn't he?'

'Yes.'

'Terrans should be protected from seeing.'

I didn't like the sound of that – and I doubted that it was possible. 'Not protected,' I said. 'Shown. Shown when we're young kids, and shown more than once. Gatoi, no Terran ever sees a birth that goes right. All we see is N'Tlic – pain and terror and maybe death.'

She looked down at me. 'It is a private thing. It has always been a private thing.'

Her tone kept me from insisting – that and the knowledge that if she changed her mind, I might be the first public example. But I had planted the thought in her mind. Chances were it would grow, and eventually, she would experiment.

'You won't see it again,' she said. 'I don't want you thinking any more about shooting me.'

The small amount of fluid that came into me with her egg relaxed me as completely as a sterile egg would have, so that I could remember the rifle in my hands and my feelings of fear and revulsion, anger and despair. I could remember the feelings without reviving them. I could talk about them.

'I wouldn't have shot you,' I said. 'Not you.' She had been taken from my father's flesh when he was my age.

'You could have,' she insisted.

'Not you.' She stood between us and her own people, protecting, interweaving.

'Would you have destroyed yourself?'

I moved carefully, uncomfortable. 'I could have done that. I nearly did. That's Qui's 'away.' I wonder if he knows.'

'What?'

I did not answer.

'You will live now.'

'Yes.' *Take care of her*, my mother used to say. Yes.

'I'm healthy and young,' she said. 'I won't leave you as Lomas was left – alone, N'Tlic. I'll take care of you.'

IN THE HILLS, THE CITIES

Clive Barker

Clive Barker (1952–) is an English writer best known for his work in both fantasy and horror fiction. His first interests were the theater and painting, but he burst onto the publishing scene in the mid-1980s with The Books of Blood. The stories published in these volumes permanently changed the landscape of weird fiction. They were visceral; modern; went beyond the scare into richer, deeper territory; and often featured transgressive body horror. 'In the Hills, the Cities' (1984) is a classic from this period, continuing this anthology's theme of 'weird ritual.' Barker has since written many novels and other works, and his fiction has been adapted into motion pictures, notably the Hellraiser series.

It wasn't until the first week of the Yugoslavian trip that Mick discovered what a political bigot he'd chosen as a lover. Certainly, he'd been warned. One of the queens at the Baths had told him Judd was to the Right of Attila the Hun, but the man had been one of Judd's ex-affairs, and Mick had presumed there was more spite than perception in the character assassination.

If only he'd listened. Then he wouldn't be driving along an interminable road in a Volkswagen that suddenly seemed the size of a coffin, listening to Judd's views on Soviet expansionism. Jesus, he was so boring. He didn't converse, he lectured, and endlessly. In Italy the sermon had been on the way the Communists had exploited the peasant vote. Now, in Yugoslavia, Judd had really warmed to this theme, and Mick was just about ready to take a hammer to his self-opinionated head.

It wasn't that he disagreed with everything Judd said. Some of the arguments (the ones Mick understood) seemed quite sensible. But then, what did he know? He was a dance teacher. Judd was a journalist, a professional pundit. He felt, like most journalists Mick had encountered, that he was obliged to have an opinion on everything under the sun. Especially politics; that was the best trough to wallow in. You could get your snout, eyes, head and front hooves in that mess of muck and have a fine old time splashing around. It was an inexhaustible subject to devour, a swill with a little of everything in it, because everything, according to Judd, was political. The arts were political. Sex was political. Religion, commerce, gardening, eating, drinking and farting – all political.

Jesus, it was mind-blowingly boring; killingly, love-deadeningly boring.

Worse still, Judd didn't seem to notice how bored Mick had become, or if he noticed, he didn't care. He just rambled on, his arguments getting windier and windier, his sentences lengthening with every mile they drove.

Judd, Mick had decided, was a selfish bastard, and as soon as their honeymoon was over he'd part with the guy.

It was not until their trip, that endless, motiveless caravan through the graveyards of mid-European culture, that Judd realized what a political lightweight he had in Mick. The guy showed precious little interest in the economics or the politics of the countries they passed through. He registered indifference to the full facts behind the Italian situation, and yawned, yes, yawned when he tried (and failed) to debate the Russian threat to world peace. He had to face the bitter truth: Mick was a queen; there was no other word for him; all right, perhaps he didn't mince or wear jewelry to excess, but he was a queen nevertheless, happy to wallow in a dreamworld of early Renaissance frescoes and Yugoslavian icons. The complexities, the contradictions, even the agonies that made those cultures blossom and wither were just tiresome to him. His mind was no deeper than his looks; he was a well-groomed nobody.

Some honeymoon.

The road south from Belgrade to Novi Pazar was, by Yugoslavian standards, a good one. There were fewer potholes than on many of the roads they'd travelled, and it was relatively straight. The town of Novi Pazar lay in the valley of the River Raska, south of the city named after the river. It wasn't an area particularly popular with the tourists. Despite the good road it was still inaccessible, and lacked sophisticated amenities; but Mick was determined to see the monastery at Sopocani, to the west of the town, and after some bitter argument, he'd won.

The journey had proved uninspiring. On either side of the road the cultivated fields looked parched and dusty. The summer had been unusually hot, and droughts were affecting many of the villages. Crops had failed, and livestock had been prematurely slaughtered to prevent them dying of malnutrition. There was a defeated look about the few faces they glimpsed at the roadside. Even the children had dour expressions; brows as heavy as the stale heat that hung over the valley.

Now, with the cards on the table after a row at Belgrade, they drove in silence most of the time; but the straight road, like most straight roads, invited dispute. When the driving was easy, the mind rooted for something to keep it engaged. What better than a fight?

'Why the hell do you want to see this damn monastery?' Judd demanded.

It was an unmistakable invitation.

'We've come all this way... ' Mick tried to keep the tone conversational. He wasn't in the mood for an argument.

'More fucking Virgins, is it?'

Keeping his voice as even as he could, Mick picked up the *Guide* and read aloud from it: '...there, some of the greatest works of Serbian painting can still be seen and enjoyed, including what many commentators agree to be the enduring masterpiece of the Raska school: *The Dormition of the Virgin*.'

Silence.

Then Judd: 'I'm up to here with churches.'

'It's a masterpiece.'

'They're all masterpieces according to that bloody book.'

Mick felt his control slipping.

'Two and a half hours at most–'

'I told you, I don't want to see another church; the smell of the places makes me sick. Stale incense, old sweat and lies...'

'It's a short detour; then we can get back on to the road and you can give me another lecture on farming subsidies in the Sandzak.'

'I'm just trying to get some decent conversation going instead of this endless tripe about Serbian fucking masterpieces–

'Stop the car!'

'What?'

'Stop the car!'

Judd pulled the Volkswagen onto the side of the road. Mick got out.

The road was hot, but there was a slight breeze. He took a deep breath, and wandered into the middle of the road. Empty of traffic and of pedestrians in both directions. In every direction, empty. The hills shimmered in the heat off the fields. There were wild poppies growing in the ditches. Mick crossed the road, squatted on his haunches and picked one.

Behind him he heard the VW's door slam.

'What did you stop us for?' Judd said. His voice was edgy, still hoping for that argument, begging for it.

Mick stood up, playing with the poppy. It was close to seeding, late in the season. The petals fell from the receptacle as soon as he touched them, little splashes of red fluttering down on to the grey tarmac.

'I asked you a question,' Judd said again.

Mick looked around. Judd was standing along the far side of the car, his brows a knitted line of burgeoning anger. But handsome; oh yes; a face that made women weep with frustration that he was gay. A heavy black moustache (perfectly trimmed) and eyes you could watch forever, and never see the same light in them twice. Why in God's name, thought Mick, does a man as fine as that have to be such an insensitive little shit?

Judd returned the look of contemptuous appraisal, staring at the pouting pretty boy across the road. It made him want to puke, seeing the little act Mick was performing for his benefit. It might just have been plausible in a sixteen-year-old virgin. In a twenty-five-year-old, it lacked credibility.

Mick dropped the flower, and untucked his T-shirt from his jeans. A tight stomach, then a slim, smooth chest were revealed as he pulled it off. His hair was ruffled when his head reappeared, and his face wore a broad grin. Judd looked at the torso. Neat, not too muscular. An appendix scar peering over his faded jeans. A gold chain, small but catching the sun, dipped in the hollow of his throat. Without meaning to, he returned Mick's grin, and a kind of peace was made between them.

Mick was unbuckling his belt.

'Want to fuck?' he said, the grin not faltering.

'It's no use,' came an answer, though not to that question.

'What isn't?'

'We're not compatible.'

'Want a bet?'

Now he was unzipped, and turning away towards the wheat field that bordered the road.

Judd watched as Mick cut a swathe through the swaying sea, his back the color of the grain, so that he was almost camouflaged by it. It was a dangerous game, screwing in the open air – this wasn't San Francisco, or even Hampstead Heath. Nervously, Judd glanced along the road. Still empty in both directions. And Mick was turning, deep in the field, turning and smiling and waving like a swimmer buoyed up in a golden surf. What the hell… there was nobody to see, nobody to know. Just the hills, liquid in the heat-haze, their forested backs bent to the business of the earth, and a lost dog, sitting at the edge of the road, waiting for some lost master.

Judd followed Mick's path through the wheat, unbuttoning his shirt as he walked. Field mice ran ahead of him, scurrying through the stalks as the giant came their way, his feet like thunder. Judd saw their panic, and smiled. He meant no harm to them, but then how were they to know that? Maybe he'd put out a hundred lives, mice, beetles, worms, before he reached the spot where Mick was lying, stark bollock naked, on a bed of trampled grain, still grinning.

It was good love they made, good, strong love, equal in pleasure for both; there was a precision to their passion, sensing the moment when effortless delight became urgent, when desire became necessity. They locked together, limb around limb, tongue around tongue, in a knot only orgasm could untie, their backs alternately scorched and scratched as they rolled around exchanging blows and kisses. In the thick of it, creaming together, they heard the phut-phut-phut of a tractor passing by; but they were past caring.

They made their way back to the Volkswagen with body-threshed wheat in their hair and their ears, in their socks and between their toes. Their grins had been replaced with easy smiles: the truce, if not permanent, would last a few hours at least.

The car was baking hot, and they had to open all the windows and doors to let the breeze cool it before they started towards Novi Pazar. It was four o'clock, and there was still an hour's driving ahead.

As they got into the car Mick said, 'We'll forget the monastery, eh?'

Judd gaped.

'I thought–'

'I couldn't bear another fucking Virgin–'

They laughed lightly together, then kissed, tasting each other and themselves, a mingling of saliva, and the aftertaste of salt semen.

The following day was bright, but not particularly warm. No blue skies: just an even layer of white cloud. The morning air was sharp in the lining of the nostrils, like ether, or peppermint.

Vaslav Jelovsek watched the pigeons in the

main square of Popolac courting death as they skipped and fluttered ahead of the vehicles that were buzzing around. Some about military business, some civilian. An air of sober intention barely suppressed the excitement he felt on this day, an excitement he knew was shared by every man, woman and child in Popolac. Shared by the pigeons too for all he knew. Maybe that was why they played under the wheels with such dexterity, knowing that on this day of days no harm could come to them.

He scanned the sky again, that same white sky he'd been peering at since dawn. The cloud-layer was low; not ideal for the celebrations. A phrase passed through his mind, an English phrase he'd heard from a friend, 'to have your head in the clouds.' It meant, he gathered, to be lost in a reverie, in a white, sightless dream. That, he thought wryly, was all the West knew about clouds, that they stood for dreams. It took a vision they lacked to make a truth out of that casual turn of phrase. Here, in these secret hills, wouldn't they create a spectacular reality from those idle words? A living proverb.

A head in the clouds.

Already the first contingent was assembling in the square. There were one or two absentees owing to illness, but the auxiliaries were ready and waiting to take their places. Such eagerness! Such wide smiles when an auxiliary heard his or her name and number called and was taken out of line to join the limb that was already taking shape. On every side, miracles of organization. Everyone with a job to do and a place to go. There was no shouting or pushing: indeed, voices were scarcely raised above an eager whisper. He watched in admiration as the work of positioning and buckling and roping went on.

It was going to be a long and arduous day. Vaslav had been in the square since an hour before dawn, drinking coffee from imported plastic cups, discussing the half-hourly meteorological reports coming in from Pristina and Mitrovica, and watching the starless sky as the grey light of morning crept across it. Now he was drinking his sixth coffee of the day, and it was still barely seven o'clock. Across the square Metzinger looked as tired and as anxious as Vaslav felt.

They'd watched the dawn seep out of the east together. Metzinger and he. But now they had separated, forgetting previous companionship, and would not speak until the contest was over. After all Metzinger was from Podujevo. He had his own city to support in the coming battle. Tomorrow they'd exchange tales of their adventures, but for today they must behave as if they didn't know each other, not even to exchange a smile. For today they had to be utterly partisan, caring only for the victory of their own city over the opposition.

Now the first leg of Popolac was erected, to the mutual satisfaction of Metzinger and Vaslav. All the safety checks had been meticulously made, and the leg left the square, its shadow falling hugely across the face of the Town Hall.

Vaslav sipped his sweet, sweet coffee and allowed himself a little grunt of satisfaction. Such days, such days. Days filled with glory, with snapping flags and high, stomach-turning sights, enough to last a man a lifetime. It was a golden foretaste of Heaven.

Let America have its simple pleasures, its cartoon mice, its candy-coated castles, its cults and its technologies, he wanted none of it. The greatest wonder of the world was here, hidden in the hills.

Ah, such days.

In the main square of Podujevo the scene was no less animated, and no less inspiring. Perhaps there was a muted sense of sadness underlying this year's celebration, but that was understandable. Nita Obrenovic, Podujevo's loved and respected organizer, was no longer living. The previous winter had claimed her at the age of ninety-four, leaving the city bereft of her fierce opinions and her fiercer proportions. For sixty years Nita had worked with the citizens of Podujevo, always planning for the next contest and improving on the designs, her energies spent on making the next creation more ambitious and more lifelike than the last.

Now she was dead, and sorely missed. There was no disorganization in the streets without her, the people were far too disciplined for that, but they were already falling behind schedule, and it was almost seven-twenty-five. Nita's daughter had taken over in her mother's stead, but she lacked

Nita's power to galvanize the people into action. She was, in a word, too gentle for the job at hand. It required a leader who was part prophet and part ringmaster, to coax and bully and inspire the citizens into their places. Maybe, after two or three decades, and with a few more contests under her belt, Nita Obrenovic's daughter would make the grade. But for today Podujevo was behindhand; safety-checks were being overlooked; nervous looks replaced the confidence of earlier years.

Nevertheless, at six minutes before eight the first limb of Podujevo made its way out of the city to the assembly point, to wait for its fellow.

By that time the flanks were already lashed together in Popolac, and armed contingents were awaiting orders in the Town Square.

Mick woke promptly at seven, though there was no alarm clock in their simply furnished room at the Hotel Beograd. He lay in his bed and listened to Judd's regular breathing from the twin bed across the room. A dull morning light whimpered through the thin curtains, not encouraging an early departure. After a few minutes' staring at the cracked paintwork on the ceiling, and a while longer at the crudely carved crucifix on the opposite wall, Mick got up and went to the window. It was a dull day, as he had guessed. The sky was overcast, and the roofs of Novi Pazar were grey and featureless in the flat morning light. But beyond the roofs, to the east, he could see the hills. There was sun there. He could see shafts of light catching the blue-green of the forest, inviting a visit to their slopes.

Today maybe they would go south to Kosovska Mitrovica. There was a market there, wasn't there, and a museum? And they could drive down the valley of the Ibar, following the road beside the river, where the hills rose wild and shining on either side. The hills, yes; today he decided they would see the hills.

It was eight-fifteen.

By nine the main bodies of Popolac and Podujevo were substantially assembled. In their allotted districts the limbs of both cities were ready and waiting to join their expectant torsos.

Vaslav Jelovsek capped his gloved hands over his eyes and surveyed the sky. The cloud-base had risen in the last hour, no doubt of it, and there were breaks in the clouds to the west; even, on occasion, a few glimpses of the sun. It wouldn't be a perfect day for the contest perhaps, but certainly adequate.

Mick and Judd breakfasted late on hemendeks – roughly translated as ham and eggs – and several cups of good black coffee. It was brightening up, even in Novi Pazar, and their ambitions were set high. Kosovska Mitrovica by lunchtime, and maybe a visit to the hill-castle of Zvecan in the afternoon.

About nine-thirty they motored out of Novi Pazar and took the Srbovac road south to the Ibar valley. Not a good road, but the bumps and potholes couldn't spoil the new day.

The road was empty, except for the occasional pedestrian; and in place of the maize and corn fields they'd passed on the previous day the road was flanked by undulating hills, whose sides were thickly and darkly forested. Apart from a few birds, they saw no wildlife. Even their infrequent travelling companions petered out altogether after a few miles, and the occasional farmhouse they drove by appeared locked and shuttered up. Black pigs ran unattended in the yard, with no child to feed them. Washing snapped and billowed on a sagging line, with no washer-woman in sight.

At first this solitary journey through the hills was refreshing in its lack of human contact, but as the morning drew on, an uneasiness grew on them.

'Shouldn't we have seen a signpost to Mitrovica, Mick?'

He peered at the map.

'Maybe...'

'– we've taken the wrong road.'

'If there'd been a sign, I'd have seen it. I think we should try and get off this road, bear south a bit more – meet the valley closer to Mitrovica than we'd planned.'

'How do we get off this bloody road?'

'There've been a couple of turnings...'

'Dirt-tracks.'

'Well it's either that or going on the way we are.'

Judd pursed his lips.

'Cigarette?' he asked.

'Finished them miles back.'

In front of them, the hills formed an impenetrable line. There was no sign of life ahead; no frail wisp of chimney smoke, no sound of voice or vehicle.

'All right,' said Judd, 'we take the next turning. Anything's better than this.'

They drove on. The road was deteriorating rapidly, the potholes becoming craters, the hummocks feeling like bodies beneath the wheels.

Then:

'There!'

A turning: a palpable turning. Not a major road, certainly. In fact barely the dirt-track Judd had described the other roads as being, but it was an escape from the endless perspective of the road they were trapped on.

'This is becoming a bloody safari,' said Judd as the VW began to bump and grind its way along the doleful little track.

'Where's your sense of adventure?'

'I forgot to pack it.'

They were beginning to climb now, as the track wound its way up into the hills. The forest closed over them, blotting out the sky, so a shifting patchwork of light and shadow scooted over the bonnet as they drove. There was birdsong suddenly, vacuous and optimistic, and a smell of new pine and undug earth. A fox crossed the track, up ahead, and watched a long moment as the car grumbled up towards it. Then, with the leisurely stride of a fearless prince, it sauntered away into the trees.

Wherever they were going, Mick thought, this was better than the road they'd left. Soon maybe they'd stop, and walk a while, to find a promontory from which they could see the valley, even Novi Pazar, nestled behind them.

The two men were still an hour's drive from Popolac when the head of the contingent at last marched out of the Town Square and took up its position with the main body.

This last exit left the city completely deserted. Not even the sick or the old were neglected on this day; no one was to be denied the spectacle and the triumph of the contest. Every single citizen, however young or infirm, the blind, the crippled, babes in arms, pregnant women – all made their way up from their proud city to the stamping ground. It was the law that they should attend: but it needed no enforcing. No citizen of either city would have missed the chance to see that sight – to experience the thrill of that contest.

The confrontation had to be total, city against city. This was the way it had always been.

So the cities went up into the hills. By noon they were gathered, the citizens of Popolac and Podujevo, in the secret well of the hills, hidden from civilized eyes, to do ancient and ceremonial battle.

Tens of thousands of hearts beat faster. Tens of thousands of bodies stretched and strained and sweated as the twin cities took their positions. The shadows of the bodies darkened tracts of land the size of small towns; the weight of their feet trampled the grass to a green milk; their movement killed animals, crushed bushes and threw down trees. The earth literally reverberated with their passage, the hills echoing with the booming din of their steps.

In the towering body of Podujevo, a few technical hitches were becoming apparent. A slight flaw in the knitting of the left flank had resulted in a weakness there: and there were consequent problems in the swivelling mechanism of the hips. It was stiffer than it should be, and the movements were not smooth. As a result there was considerable strain being put upon that region of the city. It was being dealt with bravely; after all, the contest was intended to press the contestants to their limits. But breaking point was closer than anyone would have dared to admit. The citizens were not as resilient as they had been in previous contests. A bad decade for crops had produced bodies less well-nourished, spines less supple, wills less resolute. The badly knitted flank might not have caused an accident in itself, but further weakened by the frailty of the competitors it set a scene for death on an unprecedented scale.

They stopped the car.

'Hear that?'

Mick shook his head. His hearing hadn't been

good since he was an adolescent. Too many rock shows had blown his eardrums to hell.

Judd got out of the car.

The birds were quieter now. The noise he'd heard as they drove came again. It wasn't simply a noise: it was almost a motion in the earth, a roar that seemed seated in the substance of the hills.

Thunder, was it?

No, too rhythmical. It came again, through the soles of the feet –

Boom.

Mick heard it this time. He leaned out of the car window.

'It's up ahead somewhere. I hear it now.'

Judd nodded.

Boom.

The earth-thunder sounded again.

'What the hell is it?' said Mick.

'Whatever it is, I want to see it–'

Judd got back into the Volkswagen, smiling.

'Sounds almost like guns,' he said, starting the car. 'Big guns.'

Through his Russian-made binoculars Vaslav Jelovsek watched the starting-official raise his pistol. He saw the feather of white smoke rise from the barrel, and a second later heard the sound of the shot across the valley.

The contest had begun.

He looked up at twin towers of Popolac and Podujevo. Heads in the clouds – well almost. They practically stretched to touch the sky. It was an awesome sight, a breath-stopping, sleep-stabbing sight. Two cities swaying and writhing and preparing to take their first steps towards each other in this ritual battle.

Of the two, Podujevo seemed the less stable. There was a slight hesitation as the city raised its left leg to begin its march. Nothing serious, just a little difficulty in coordinating hip and thigh muscles. A couple of steps and the city would find its rhythm; a couple more and its inhabitants would be moving as one creature, one perfect giant set to match its grace and power against its mirror-image.

The gunshot had sent flurries of birds up from the trees that banked the hidden valley. They rose up in celebration of the great contest, chattering their excitement as they swooped over the stamping-ground.

'Did you hear a shot?' asked Judd.

Mick nodded.

'Military exercises…?' Judd's smile had broadened. He could see the headlines already – exclusive reports of secret maneuvers in the depths of the Yugoslavian countryside. Russian tanks perhaps, tactical exercises being held out of the West's prying sight. With luck, he would be the carrier of this news.

Boom.

Boom.

There were birds in the air. The thunder was louder now.

It did sound like guns.

'It's over the next ridge…' said Judd.

'I don't think we should go any further.'

'I have to see.'

'I don't. We're not supposed to be here.'

'I don't see any signs.'

'They'll cart us away; deport us – I don't know – I just think–'

Boom.

'I've got to see.'

The words were scarcely out of his mouth when the screaming started.

Podujevo was screaming: a death-cry. Someone buried in the weak flank had died of the strain, and had begun a chain of decay in the system. One man loosed his neighbor and that neighbor loosed his, spreading a cancer of chaos through the body of the city. The coherence of the towering structure deteriorated with terrifying rapidity as the failure of one part of the anatomy put unendurable pressure on the other.

The masterpiece that the good citizens of Podujevo had constructed of their own flesh and blood tottered and then – a dynamited skyscraper, it began to fall.

The broken flank spewed citizens like a slashed artery spitting blood. Then, with a graceful sloth that made the agonies of the citizens all the more horrible, it bowed towards the earth, all its limbs dissembling as it fell.

The huge head, that had brushed the clouds so recently, was flung back on its thick neck. Ten thousand mouths spoke a single scream for its vast mouth, a wordless, infinitely pitiable appeal to the sky. A howl of loss, a howl of anticipation, a howl of puzzlement. How, that scream demanded, could the day of days end like this, in a welter of falling bodies?

'Did you hear that?'

It was unmistakably human, though almost deafeningly loud. Judd's stomach convulsed. He looked across at Mick, who was as white as a sheet.

Judd stopped the car.

'No,' said Mick.

'Listen – for Christ's sake–'

The din of dying moans, appeals and imprecations flooded the air. It was very close. 'We've got to go on now,' Mick implored.

Judd shook his head. He was prepared for some military spectacle – all the Russian army massed over the next hill – but that noise in his ears was the noise of human flesh – too human for words. It reminded him of his childhood imaginings of Hell; the endless, unspeakable torments his mother had threatened him with if he failed to embrace Christ. It was a terror he'd forgotten for twenty years. But suddenly, here it was again, freshfaced. Maybe the pit itself gaped just over the next horizon, with his mother standing at its lip, inviting him to taste its punishments.

'If you won't drive, I will.'

Mick got out of the car and crossed in front of it, glancing up the track as he did so. There was a moment's hesitation, no more than a moment's, when his eyes flickered with disbelief, before he turned towards the windscreen, his face even paler than it had been previously and said: 'Jesus Christ...' in a voice that was thick with suppressed nausea.

His lover was still sitting behind the wheel, his head in his hands, trying to blot out memories.

'Judd...'

Judd looked up, slowly. Mick was staring at him like a wildman, his face shining with a sudden, icy sweat. Judd looked past him. A few meters ahead the track had mysteriously darkened, as a tide edged towards the car, a thick, deep tide of blood. Judd's reason twisted and turned to make any other sense of the sight than that inevitable conclusion. But there was no saner explanation. It was blood, in unendurable abundance, blood without end –

And now, in the breeze, there was the flavor of freshly opened carcasses: the smell out of the depths of the human body, part sweet, part savory.

Mick stumbled back to the passenger's side of the VW and fumbled weakly at the handle. The door opened suddenly and he lurched inside, his eyes glazed.

'Back up,' he said.

Judd reached for the ignition. The tide of blood was already sloshing against the front wheels. Ahead, the world had been painted red.

'Drive, for fuck's sake, drive!'

Judd was making no attempt to start the car.

'We must look,' he said, without conviction, 'we have to.'

'We don't have to do anything,' said Mick, 'but get the hell out of here. It's not our business...'

'Plane crash–'

'There's no smoke.'

'Those are human voices.'

Mick's instinct was to leave well enough alone. He could read about the tragedy in a newspaper – he could see the pictures tomorrow when they were grey and grainy. Today it was too fresh, too unpredictable –

Anything could be at the end of that track, bleeding –

'We must–'

Judd started the car, while beside him Mick began to moan quietly. The VW began to edge forward, nosing through the river of blood, its wheels spinning in the queasy, foaming tide.

'No,' said Mick, very quietly, 'please, no...'

'We must,' was Judd's reply. 'We must. We must.'

Only a few yards away the surviving city of Popolac was recovering from its first convulsions. It stared, with a thousand eyes, at the ruins of its ritual enemy, now spread in a tangle of rope and bodies over the impacted ground, shattered forever. Popolac staggered back from the sight, its vast legs flattening the forest that bounded the stamping-ground, its arms flailing the air. But it kept its balance, even as a common insanity, woken by the horror at its feet, surged through its sinews and curdled its brain. The order went out: the body thrashed and twisted and turned from the grisly carpet of Podujevo, and fled into the hills.

As it headed into oblivion, its towering form passed between the car and the sun, throwing its cold shadow over the bloody road. Mick saw nothing through his tears, and Judd, his eyes narrowed against the sight he feared seeing around the next bend, only dimly registered that something had blotted the light for a minute. A cloud, perhaps. A flock of birds. Had he looked up at that moment, just stolen a glance out towards the northeast, he would have seen Popolac's head, the vast, swarming head of a maddened city, disappearing below his line of vision, as it marched into the hills. He would have known that this territory was beyond his comprehension; and that there was no healing to be done in this corner of Hell. But he didn't see the city, and he and Mick's last turning-point had passed. From now on, like Popolac and its dead twin, they were lost to sanity, and to all hope of life.

They rounded the bend, and the ruins of Podujevo came into sight.

Their domesticated imaginations had never conceived of a sight so unspeakably brutal.

Perhaps in the battlefields of Europe as many corpses had been heaped together: but had so many of them been women and children, locked together with the corpses of men? There had been piles of dead as high, but ever so many so recently abundant with life? There had been cities laid waste as quickly, but ever an entire city lost to the simple dictate of gravity?

It was a sight beyond sickness. In the face of it the mind slowed to a snail's pace, the forces of reason picked over the evidence with meticulous hands, searching for a flaw in it, a place where it could say:

This is not happening. This is a dream of death, not death itself.

But reason could find no weakness in the wall. This was true. It was death indeed.

Podujevo had fallen.

Thirty-eight thousand, seven hundred and sixty-five citizens were spread on the ground, or rather flung in ungainly, seeping piles. Those who had not died of the fall, or of suffocation, were dying. There would be no survivors from that city except that bundle of onlookers that had traipsed out of their homes to watch the contest. Those few Podujevians, the crippled, the sick, the ancient few, were now staring, like Mick and Judd, at the carnage, trying not to believe.

Judd was first out of the car. The ground beneath his suedes was sticky with coagulating gore. He surveyed the carnage. There was no wreckage: no sign of a plane crash, no fire, no smell of fuel. Just tens of thousands of fresh bodies, all either naked or dressed in an identical grey serge, men, women and children alike. Some of them, he could see, wore leather harnesses, tightly buckled around their upper chests, and snaking out from these contraptions were lengths of rope, miles and miles of it. The closer he looked, the more he saw of the extraordinary system of knots and lashings that still held the bodies together. For some reason these people had been tied together, side by side. Some were yoked on their neighbors' shoulders, straddling them like boys playing at horseback riding. Others were locked arm in arm, knitted together with threads of rope in a wall of muscle and bone. Yet others were trussed in a ball, with their heads tucked between their knees. All were in some way connected up with their fellows, tied together as though in some insane collective bondage game.

Another shot.

Mick looked up.

Across the field a solitary man, dressed in a drab overcoat, was walking amongst the bodies with a revolver, dispatching the dying. It was a pitifully inadequate act of mercy, but he went on nevertheless, choosing the suffering children first. Emptying the revolver, filling it again, emptying it, filling it, emptying it –

Mick let go.

He yelled at the top of his voice over the moans of the injured.

'What is this?'

The man looked up from his appalling duty, his face as deadgrey as his coat.

'Uh?' he grunted, frowning at the two interlopers through his thick spectacles.

'What's happened here?' Mick shouted across at him. It felt good to shout, it felt good to sound angry at the man. Maybe he was to blame. It would be a fine thing, just to have someone to blame.

'Tell us –' Mick said. He could hear the tears throbbing in his voice. 'Tell us, for God's sake. Explain.'

Grey-coat shook his head. He didn't understand a word this young idiot was saying. It was English he spoke, but that's all he knew. Mick began to walk towards him, feeling all the time the eyes of the dead on him. Eyes like black, shining gems set in broken faces: eyes looking at him upside down, on heads severed from their seating. Eyes in heads that had solid howls for voices. Eyes in heads beyond howls, beyond breath.

Thousands of eyes.

He reached Grey-coat, whose gun was almost empty. He had taken off his spectacles and thrown them aside. He too was weeping, little jerks ran through his big, ungainly body.

At Mick's feet, somebody was reaching for him. He didn't want to look, but the hand touched his shoe and he had no choice but to see its owner. A young man, lying like a flesh swastika, every joint smashed. A child lay under him, her bloody legs poking out like two pink sticks.

He wanted the man's revolver, to stop the hand from touching him. Better still he wanted a machine-gun, a flame-thrower, anything to wipe the agony away.

As he looked up from the broken body, Mick saw Grey-coat raise the revolver.

'Judd–' he said, but as the word left his lips the muzzle of the revolver was slipped into Grey-coat's mouth and the trigger was pulled.

Grey-coat had saved the last bullet for himself. The back of his head opened like a dropped egg, the shell of his skull flying off. His body went limp and sank to the ground, the revolver still between his lips.

'We must–' began Mick, saying the words to nobody. 'We must...'

What was the imperative? In this situation, what *must* they do?

'We must–'

Judd was behind him.

'Help–' he said to Mick.

'Yes. We must get help. We must–'

'Go.'

Go! That was what they must do. On any pretext, for any fragile, cowardly reason, they must go. Get out of the battlefield, get out of the reach of a dying hand with a wound in place of a body.

'We have to tell the authorities. Find a town. Get help –'

'Priests,' said Mick. 'They need priests.'

It was absurd, to think of giving the Last Rites to so many people. It would take an army of priests, a water cannon filled with holy water, a loudspeaker to pronounce the benedictions.

They turned away, together, from the horror, and wrapped their arms around each other, then picked their way through the carnage to the car.

It was occupied.

Vaslav Jelovsek was sitting behind the wheel, and trying to start the Volkswagen. He turned the ignition key once. Twice. Third time the engine caught and the wheels spun in the crimson mud as he put her into reverse and backed down the track. Vaslav saw the Englishmen running towards the car, cursing him. There was no help for it – he didn't want to steal the vehicle, but he had work to do. He had been a referee, he had been responsible for the contest, and the safety of the contestants. One of the heroic cities had already fallen. He must do everything in his power to prevent Popolac from following its twin. He must chase Popolac, and reason with it. Talk it down out of its terrors with quiet words and promises. If he failed there would be another disaster the equal of the one in front of him, and his conscience was already broken enough.

Mick was still chasing the VW, shouting at Jelovsek. The thief took no notice, concentrating on maneuvering the car back down the narrow, slippery track. Mick was losing the chase rapidly. The car had begun to pick up speed. Furious, but without the breath to speak his fury, Mick stood in the road, hands on his knees, heaving and sobbing.

'Bastard!' said Judd.

Mick looked down the track. Their car had already disappeared.

'Fucker couldn't even drive properly.'

'We have… we have… to catch… up… ' said Mick through gulps of breath.

'How?'

'On foot… '

'We haven't even got a map… it's in the car.'

'Jesus… Christ… Almighty.'

They walked down the track together, away from the field.

After a few meters the tide of blood began to peter out. Just a few congealing rivulets dribbled on towards the main road. Mick and Judd followed the bloody tiremarks to the junction.

The Srbovac road was empty in both directions. The tiremarks showed a left turn. 'He's gone deeper into the hills,' said Judd, staring along the lovely road towards the blue-green distance. 'He's out of his mind!'

'Do we go back the way we came?'

'It'll take us all night on foot.'

'We'll hop a lift.'

Judd shook his head: his face was slack and his look lost. 'Don't you see, Mick, they all knew this was happening. The people in the farms – they got the hell out while those people went crazy up there. There'll be no cars along this road, I'll lay you anything – except maybe a couple of shit-dumb tourists like us – and no tourist would stop for the likes of us.'

He was right. They looked like butchers – splattered with blood. Their faces were shining with grease, their eyes maddened.

'We'll have to walk,' said Judd, 'the way he went.'

He pointed along the road. The hills were darker now; the sun had suddenly gone out on their slopes.

Mick shrugged. Either way he could see they had a night on the road ahead of them. But he wanted to walk somewhere – anywhere – as long as he put distance between him and the dead.

In Popolac a kind of peace reigned. Instead of a frenzy of panic, there was a numbness, a sheep-like acceptance of the world as it was. Locked in their positions, strapped, roped and harnessed to each other in a living system that allowed for no single voice to be louder than any other, nor any back to labor less than its neighbor's, they let an insane consensus replace the tranquil voice of reason. They were convulsed into one mind, one thought, one ambition. They became, in the space of a few moments, the single-minded giant whose image they had so brilliantly re-created. The illusion of petty individuality was swept away in an irresistible tide of collective feeling – not a mob's passion, but a telepathic surge that dissolved the voices of thousands into one irresistible command.

And the voice said: Go!

The voice said: take this horrible sight away, where I need never see it again.

Popolac turned away into the hills, its legs taking strides half a mile long. Each man, woman and child in that seething tower was sightless. They saw only through the eyes of the city. They were thoughtless, but to think the city's thoughts. And they believed themselves deathless, in their lumbering, relentless strength. Vast and mad and deathless.

Two miles along the road Mick and Judd smelt petrol in the air, and a little further along they came upon the VW. It had overturned in the reed-clogged drainage ditch at the side of the road. It had not caught fire.

The driver's door was open, and the body of Vaslav Jelovsek had tumbled out. His face was calm in unconsciousness. There seemed to be no sign of injury, except for a small cut or two on his sober face. They gently pulled the thief out of the wreckage and up out of the filth of the ditch on to the road. He moaned a little as they fussed about him, rolling Mick's sweater up to pillow his head and removing the man's jacket and tie.

Quite suddenly, he opened his eyes.

He stared at them both.

'Are you all right?' Mick asked.

The man said nothing for a moment. He seemed not to understand.

Then:

'English?' he said. His accent was thick, but the question was quite clear.

'Yes.'

'I heard your voices. English.'

He frowned and winced.

'Are you in pain?' said Judd.

The man seemed to find this amusing.

'Am I in pain?' he repeated, his face screwed up in a mixture of agony and delight.

'I shall die,' he said, through gritted teeth.

'No,' said Mick. 'You're all right–'

The man shook his head, his authority absolute.

'I shall die,' he said again, the voice full of determination, 'I want to die.'

Judd crouched closer to him. His voice was weaker by the moment.

'Tell us what to do,' he said. The man had closed his eyes. Judd shook him awake, roughly.

'Tell us,' he said again, his show of compassion rapidly disappearing. 'Tell us what this is all about.'

'About?' said the man, his eyes still closed. 'It was a fall, that's all. Just a fall ... '

'What fell?'

'The city. Podujevo. My city.'

'What did it fall from?'

'Itself, of course.'

The man was explaining nothing; just answering one riddle with another.

'Where were you going?' Mick inquired, trying to sound as unaggressive as possible.

'After Popolac,' said the man.

'Popolac?' said Judd.

Mick began to see some sense in the story.

'Popolac is another city. Like Podujevo. Twin cities. They're on the map–'

'Where's the city now?' said Judd.

Vaslav Jelovsek seemed to choose to tell the truth. There was a moment when he hovered between dying with a riddle on his lips, and living long enough to unburden his story. What did it matter if the tale was told now? There could never be another contest: all that was over.

'They came to fight,' he said, his voice now very soft, 'Popolac and Podujevo. They come every ten years –'

'Fight?' said Judd. 'You mean all those people were slaughtered?'

Vaslav shook his head.

'No, no. They fell. I told you.'

'Well how do they fight?' Mick said.

'Go into the hills,' was the only reply.

Vaslav opened his eyes a little. The faces that loomed over him were exhausted and sick. They had suffered, these innocents. They deserved some explanation.

'As giants,' he said. 'They fought as giants. They made a body out of their bodies, do you understand? The frame, the muscles, the bone, the eyes, nose, teeth all made of men and women.'

'He's delirious,' said Judd.

'You go into the hills,' the man repeated. 'See for yourselves how true it is.'

'Even supposing–' Mick began.

Vaslav interrupted him, eager to be finished. 'They were good at the game of giants. It took many centuries of practice: every ten years making the figure larger and larger. One always ambitious to be larger than the other. Ropes to tie them all together, flawlessly. Sinews ... ligaments ... There was food in its belly ... there were pipes from the loins, to take away the waste. The best-sighted sat in the eye-sockets, the best voiced in the mouth and throat. You wouldn't believe the engineering of it.'

'I don't,' said Judd, and stood up.

'It is the body of the state,' said Vaslav, so softly his voice was barely above a whisper, 'it is the shape of our lives.'

There was a silence. Small clouds passed over the road, soundlessly shedding their mass to the air.

'It was a miracle,' he said. It was as if he realized the true enormity of the fact for the first time. 'It was a miracle.'

It was enough. Yes. It was quite enough.

His mouth closed, the words said, and he died.

Mick felt this death more acutely than the thousands they had fled from; or rather this death was the key to unlock the anguish he felt for them all.

Whether the man had chosen to tell a fantastic lie as he died, or whether this story was in some way true, Mick felt useless in the face of it. His imagination was too narrow to encompass the idea. His brain ached with the thought of it, and his compassion cracked under the weight of misery he felt.

They stood on the road, while the clouds scudded by, their vague, grey shadows passing over them towards the enigmatic hills.

It was twilight.

Popolac could stride no further. It felt exhaustion in every muscle. Here and there in its huge anatomy deaths had occurred; but there was no grieving in the city for its deceased cells. If the dead were in the interior, the corpses were allowed to hang from their harnesses. If they formed the skin of the city they were unbuckled from their positions and released, to plunge into the forest below.

The giant was not capable of pity. It had no ambition but to continue until it ceased.

As the sun slunk out of sight Popolac rested, sitting on a small hillock, nursing its huge head in its huge hands.

The stars were coming out, with their familiar caution. Night was approaching, mercifully bandaging up the wounds of the day, blinding eyes that had seen too much.

Popolac rose to its feet again, and began to move, step by booming step. It would not be long surely, before fatigue overcame it: before it could lie down in the tomb of some lost valley and die.

But for a space yet it must walk on, each step more agonizingly slow than the last, while the night bloomed black around its head.

Mick wanted to bury the car thief, somewhere on the edge of the forest. Judd, however, pointed out that burying a body might seem, in tomorrow's saner light, a little suspicious. And besides, wasn't it absurd to concern themselves with one corpse when there were literally thousands of them lying a few miles from where they stood?

The body was left to lie, therefore, and the car to sink deeper into the ditch.

They began to walk again.

It was cold, and colder by the moment, and they were hungry. But the few houses they passed were all deserted, locked and shuttered, every one.

'What did he mean?' said Mick, as they stood looking at another locked door.

'He was talking metaphor–'

'All that stuff about giants?'

'It was some Trotskyist tripe–' Judd insisted.

'I don't think so.'

'I know so. It was his deathbed speech, he'd probably been preparing for years.'

'I don't think so,' Mick said again, and began walking back towards the road.

'Oh, how's that?' Judd was at his back.

'He wasn't towing some party line.'

'Are you saying you think there's some giant around here someplace? For God's sake!'

Mick turned to Judd. His face was difficult to see in the twilight. But his voice was sober with belief.

'Yes. I think he was telling the truth.'

'That's absurd. That's ridiculous. No.'

Judd hated Mick that moment. Hated his naïveté, his passion to believe any half-witted story if it had a whiff of romance about it. And this? This was the worst, the most preposterous...

'No,' he said again. 'No. No. No.'

The sky was porcelain smooth, and the outline of the hills black as pitch.

'I'm fucking freezing,' said Mick out of the ink. 'Are you staying here or walking with me?'

Judd shouted: 'We're not going to find anything this way.'

'Well it's a long way back.'

'We're just going deeper into the hills.'

'Do what you like – I'm walking.'

His footsteps receded: the dark encased him.

After a minute, Judd followed.

The night was cloudless and bitter. They walked on, their collars up against the chill, their feet swollen in their shoes. Above them the whole sky had become a parade of stars. A triumph of spilled light, from which the eye could make as many patterns as it had patience for. After a while, they slung their tired arms around each other, for comfort and warmth.

About eleven o'clock, they saw the glow of a window in the distance.

The woman at the door of the stone cottage didn't smile, but she understood their condition, and let them in. There seemed to be no purpose in trying to explain to either the woman or her crippled husband what they had seen. The cottage had no telephone, and there was no sign of a vehicle, so even had they found some way to express themselves, nothing could be done.

With mimes and face-pullings they explained that they were hungry and exhausted. They tried further to explain that they were lost, cursing themselves for leaving their phrasebook in the VW. She didn't seem to understand very much of what they said, but sat them down beside a blazing fire and put a pan of food on the stove to heat.

They ate thick unsalted pea soup and eggs, and occasionally smiled their thanks at the woman. Her husband sat beside the fire, making no attempt to talk, or even to look at the visitors.

The food was good. It buoyed their spirits.

They would sleep until morning and then begin the long trek back. By dawn the bodies in the field would be being quantified, identified, parcelled up and dispatched to their families. The air would be full of reassuring noises, cancelling out the moans that still rang in their ears. There would be helicopters, lorry loads of men organizing the clearing-up operations. All the rites and paraphernalia of a civilized disaster.

And in a while, it would be palatable. It would become part of their history: a tragedy, of course, but one they could explain, classify and learn to live with. All would be well, yes, all would be well. Come morning.

The sleep of sheer fatigue came on them suddenly. They lay where they had fallen, still sitting at the table, their heads on their crossed arms. A litter of empty bowls and bread crusts surrounded them.

They knew nothing. Dreamt nothing. Felt nothing.

Then the thunder began. In the earth, in the deep earth, a rhythmical tread, as of a titan, that came, by degrees, closer and closer.

The woman woke her husband. She blew out the lamp and went to the door. The night sky was luminous with stars: the hills black on every side.

The thunder still sounded: a full half-minute between every boom, but louder now. And louder with every new step.

They stood at the door together, husband and wife, and listened to the night-hills echo back and forth with the sound. There was no lightning to accompany the thunder.

Just the boom–

Boom–

Boom–

It made the ground shake: it threw dust down from the door-lintel, and rattled the window-latches.

Boom–

Boom–

They didn't know what approached, but whatever shape it took, and whatever it intended, there seemed no sense in running from it. Where they stood, in the pitiful shelter of their cottage, was as safe as any nook of the forest. How could they choose, out of a hundred thousand trees, which would be standing when the thunder had passed? Better to wait: and watch.

The wife's eyes were not good, and she doubted what she saw when the blackness of the hill changed shape and reared up to block the stars. But her husband had seen it too: the unimaginably huge head, vaster in the deceiving darkness, looming up and up, dwarfing the hills themselves with ambition.

He fell to his knees, babbling a prayer, his arthritic legs twisted beneath him.

His wife screamed: no words she knew could keep this monster at bay – no prayer, no plea, had power over it.

In the cottage, Mick woke and his outstretched arm, twitching with a sudden cramp, wiped the plate and the lamp off the table.

They smashed. Judd woke.

The screaming outside had stopped. The woman had disappeared from the doorway into the forest. Any tree, any tree at all, was better than this sight. Her husband still let a string of prayers dribble from his slack mouth, as the great leg of the giant rose to take another step–

Boom–

The cottage shook. Plates danced and smashed off the dresser. A clay pipe rolled from the mantelpiece and shattered in the ashes of the hearth.

The lovers knew the noise that sounded in their substance: that earth-thunder.

Mick reached for Judd, and took him by the

shoulder.

'You see,' he said, his teeth blue-grey in the darkness of the cottage. 'See? See?'

There was a kind of hysteria bubbling behind his words. He ran to the door, stumbling over a chair in the dark. Cursing and bruised he staggered out into the night–

Boom–

The thunder was deafening. This time it broke all the windows in the cottage. In the bedroom one of the roof-joists cracked and flung debris downstairs.

Judd joined his lover at the door. The old man was now face down on the ground, his sick and swollen fingers curled, his begging lips pressed to the damp soil.

Mick was looking up, towards the sky. Judd followed his gaze.

There was a place that showed no stars. It was a darkness in the shape of a man, a vast, broad human frame, a colossus that soared up to meet heaven. It was not quite a perfect giant. Its outline was not tidy; it seethed and swarmed.

He seemed broader too, this giant, than any real man. His legs were abnormally thick and stumpy, and his arms were not long. The hands, as they clenched and unclenched, seemed oddly jointed and over-delicate for its torso.

Then it raised one huge, flat foot and placed it on the earth, taking a stride towards them. Boom –

The step brought the roof collapsing in on the cottage. Everything that the car-thief had said was true. Popolac was a city and a giant; and it had gone into the hills...

Now their eyes were becoming accustomed to the night light. They could see in ever more horrible detail the way this monster was constructed. It was a masterpiece of human engineering: a man made entirely of men. Or rather, a sexless giant, made of men and women and children. All the citizens of Popolac writhed and strained in the body of this flesh-knitted giant, their muscles stretched to breaking point, their bones close to snapping.

They could see how the architects of Popolac had subtly altered the proportions of the human body; how the thing had been made squatter to lower its center of gravity; how its legs had been made elephantine to bear the weight of the torso; how the head was sunk low on to the wide shoulders, so that the problems of a weak neck had been minimized.

Despite these malformations, it was horribly lifelike. The bodies that were bound together to make its surface were naked but for their harnesses, so that its surface glistened in the starlight, like one vast human torso. Even the muscles were well copied, though simplified. They could see the way the roped bodies pushed and pulled against each other in solid cords of flesh and bone. They could see the intertwined people that made up the body: the backs like turtles packed together to offer the sweep of the pectorals; the lashed and knotted acrobats at the joints of the arms and the legs alike; rolling and unwinding to articulate the city.

But surely the most amazing sight of all was the face.

Cheeks of bodies; cavernous eye-sockets in which heads stared, five bound together for each eyeball; a broad, flat nose and a mouth that opened and closed, as the muscles of the jaw bunched and hollowed rhythmically. And from that mouth, lined with teeth of bald children, the voice of the giant, now only a weak copy of its former powers, spoke a single note of idiot music.

Popolac walked and Popolac sang.

Was there ever a sight in Europe the equal of it? They watched, Mick and Judd, as it took another step towards them.

The old man had wet his pants. Blubbering and begging, he dragged himself away from the ruined cottage into the surrounding trees, dragging his dead legs after him.

The Englishmen remained where they stood, watching the spectacle as it approached. Neither dread nor horror touched them now, just an awe that rooted them to the spot. They knew this was a sight they could never hope to see again; this was the apex – after this there was only common experience. Better to stay then, though every step brought death nearer, better to stay and see the sight while it was still there to be seen. And if it killed them, this monster, then at least they would have glimpsed a miracle, known this terrible majesty for a brief moment. It seemed a fair exchange.

Popolac was within two steps of the cottage. They could see the complexities of its structure quite clearly. The faces of the citizens were becoming detailed: white, sweat-wet, and content in their weariness. Some hung dead from their harnesses, their legs swinging back and forth like the hanged. Others, children particularly, had ceased to obey their training, and had relaxed their positions, so that the form of the body was degenerating, beginning to seethe with the boils of rebellious cells.

Yet it still walked, each step an incalculable effort of coordination and strength.

Boom–

The step that trod the cottage came sooner than they thought.

Mick saw the leg raised; saw the faces of the people in the shin and ankle and foot – they were as big as he was now – all huge men chosen to take the full weight of this great creation. Many were dead. The bottom of the foot, he could see, was a jigsaw of crushed and bloody bodies, pressed to death under the weight of their fellow citizens.

The foot descended with a roar.

In a matter of seconds the cottage was reduced to splinters and dust.

Popolac blotted the sky utterly. It was, for a moment, the whole world, heaven and earth, its presence filled the senses to overflowing. At this proximity one look could not encompass it, the eye had to range backwards and forwards over its mass to take it all in, and even then the mind refused to accept the whole truth.

A whirling fragment of stone, flung off from the cottage as it collapsed, struck Judd full in the face. In his head he heard the killing stroke like a ball hitting a wall: a play-yard death. No pain: no remorse. Out like a light, a tiny, insignificant light; his death-cry lost in the pandemonium, his body hidden in the smoke and darkness. Mick neither saw nor heard Judd die.

He was too busy staring at the foot as it settled for a moment in the ruins of the cottage, while the other leg mustered the will to move.

Mick took his chance. Howling like a banshee, he ran towards the leg, longing to embrace the monster. He stumbled in the wreckage, and stood again, bloodied, to reach for the foot before it was lifted and he was left behind. There was a clamor of agonized breath as the message came to the foot that it must move; Mick saw the muscles of the shin bunch and marry as the leg began to lift. He made one last lunge at the limb as it began to leave the ground, snatching a harness or a rope, or human hair, or flesh itself – anything to catch this passing miracle and be part of it. Better to go with it wherever it was going, serve it in its purpose, whatever that might be; better to die with it than live without it.

He caught the foot, and found a safe purchase on its ankle. Screaming his sheer ecstasy at his success he felt the great leg raised, and glanced down through the swirling dust to the spot where he had stood, already receding as the limb climbed.

The earth was gone from beneath him. He was a hitchhiker with a god: the mere life he had left was nothing to him now, or ever. He would live with this thing, yes, he would live with it – seeing it and seeing it and eating it with his eyes until he died of sheer gluttony.

He screamed and howled and swung on the ropes, drinking up his triumph. Below, far below, he glimpsed Judd's body, curled up pale on the dark ground, irretrievable. Love and life and sanity were gone, gone like the memory of his name, or his sex, or his ambition.

It all meant nothing. Nothing at all.

Boom–

Boom–

Popolac walked, the noise of its steps receding to the east. People walked, the hum of its voice lost in the night.

After a day, birds came, foxes came, flies, butterflies, wasps came. Judd moved, Judd shifted, Judd gave birth. In his belly maggots warmed themselves, in a vixen's den the good flesh of his thigh was fought over. After that, it was quick. The bones yellowing, the bones crumbling: soon, an empty space which he had once filled with breath and opinions.

Darkness, light, darkness, light. He interrupted neither with his name.

TAINARON: MAIL FROM ANOTHER CITY

Leena Krohn

TRANSLATED INTO ENGLISH BY HILDA HAWKINS

Leena Krohn (1947–) is one of the most respected Finnish writers of her generation. In her large body of work for adults and children, Krohn deals with issues related to the boundary between reality and illusion, artificial intelligence, and issues of morality and conscience. Her short novel *Tainaron: Mail From Another City*, reprinted herein, was nominated for a World Fantasy Award and International Horror Guild Award in 2005. *Tainaron* shares some affinities with the work of Kafka, while being utterly original. Each section of the novel illuminates the next, with the weird element serving both as strange adventure and parallel to the real world. It is one of the most important works of post-World War II dark fantasy.

THE MEADOW AND THE HONEY PATTERN

THE FIRST LETTER

How could I forget the spring when we walked in the University's botanical gardens; for there is such a park here in Tainaron, too, large and carefully tended. If you saw it you would be astonished, for it contains many plants that no one at home knows; even a species that flowers underground.

But most of all I like the meadow attached to the gardens, where only wild flowers grow: cornflower, cotton thistle, toadflax, spiked speedwell. But you would be wrong if you supposed them to be ordinary flowers of the field. No, they are some kind of hybrid, supernaturally large. Many of the knapweeds are as tall as a man, and their corollas are as broad as a human face; but I have also seen flowers into which one can step as if into a sunny bower.

It gives me pleasure to imagine that I might one day take you there, beneath the thistles. Their lovely corymbs are veiled by a downy web, which floats high above like the crowns of trees on a beach promenade.

You would enjoy a visit to the meadow, for in Tainaron it is summer and one can look at the flowers face to face. They are as open as the day itself and the hieroglyphs of the honey-patterns are precise and clear. We gaze at them, but they gaze only at the sun, which they resemble. It is so difficult to believe, in the warmth of the day's heart – just as difficult as before the face of children – that the colour and light of which they are made are matter, and that some time, soon, this very night, their dazzle will be extinguished and will no longer be visible.

Much happens in the meadow; it is a stage for fervent activity and a theatre of war. But everything serves just one purpose: immortality. The insects who are pursuing their own interests there do not know that they are at the same time fulfilling the flowers' hidden desires, any more than the flowers understand that to the insects, whom they consider their slaves, they are life and livelihood. Thus the selfishness of each individual works, in the meadow, for the happiness of all.

But it is not only the ordinary hover-flies and sawflies that come to the meadow of the botanical gardens to amuse themselves: the idle cityfolk spend their free moments here, whiling away their time in a way that is undeniably strange to us.

'Admiral! Admiral!' I heard Longhorn shout delightedly one Sunday, when once again we were wandering along the paths that criss-cross the meadow.

I looked around me past the flower-stalks – some of them were as strong as the trunks of young birch trees – but I could not see whom Longhorn had been talking to until he pointed to the corolla of an orchid-like flower. On its brilliantly red, slightly mottled lips there sat – or rather, skipped about on the spot – someone who seemed very anxious and very happy.

This Tainaronian waved all his legs at Longhorn, and began to whine earnestly: 'This way, ladies and gentlemen, please don't be shy!'

I must admit that his behaviour bewildered me, for he went on with his unsteady dance, bouncing from one petal to another and from time to time rubbing his backside against it. All of a sudden he dropped limply flat on his face and seemed to chew enthusiastically on the fine, downy fluff that straggled around the base of the lip. Well, we were in a public place, and I turned my face away from such debauchery.

But Longhorn peeped at my face and began to smile; and that only made me more angry.

'What a puritan!' he said. 'You disapprove of lonely people's most innocent and cheapest weekend amusements? They make love to the flowers and the flowers make them drunk; they go from flower to flower and at the same time pollinate them; is that not beneficial to the entire meadow, the entire city?'

At that very moment Longhorn's friend leaned over toward us from the broad, generously curving lip of the orchid, which swayed and rocked violently beneath him. Now I could see that he was stained from head to foot with sticky pollen, and when I looked upward, shading my eyes from the sun, a sweet droplet trickled from his long, fumbling proboscis and on to my lips. I licked it away; it was not unpleasant, but at the same time I remembered some lines I had read long ago.

Appeased, I would have liked to have recited them at once to Longhorn, but his friend was now speaking incessantly.

'My dear friends,' the Admiral stammered, 'I wager you have never seen nectaries like these, aaaah, follow me, quickly, I know the way...'

And with that he disappeared into the depths of the huge corolla, so that I could make out only one of his hind legs, wriggling deep in the quivering cavity.

'No,' I said finally, 'I will not go in there.'

'Well then,' said Longhorn amicably, 'let us continue on our way. Perhaps I may introduce you some other time. Let us continue now, and see whether the meadowsweet has flowered.'

As we wandered beneath the flowers, I knew their desire and their thirst, knew that what was visible of them, all their finery, was merely a stepping-stone for their seed. And I could not stop myself from teasing Longhorn by reciting the lines that the foolish Admiral had just recalled to my mind:

For what are anthers worth or petals
Or halo-rings? Mockeries, shadows
Of the heart of the flower, the central flame!

He seemed absent-minded as he listened, and finally he interrupted me.

'Can't you hear?'

Quite right, I thought I could distinguish a desperate howling that came from the south, from the other side of the field. This was what Longhorn had been listening for, throughout my recitation.

We had turned in the right direction, for we did not have far to go before we heard an anxious voice panting, 'I'm here, here!', and we saw, once more, a flower as big as a room, this time a glowing ultramarine, where a little mannikin was struggling, apparently stuck in its funnel-like stigma.

'Well, well,' said Longhorn, glumly, 'this is just what I expected. This is a vincetoxicum, a fly-trap.'

And he directed his words to the ensnared creature: 'You are not the first to have met this fate.'

And Longhorn climbed nimbly into the sparkling blue corolla, leaning on the axils of the stem. Without delay and briskly he grasped the victim beneath the arms. Hup! – and at the same moment there was a hissing sound like silk tearing, the corolla sagged downward, and both the helper and the flower's prisoner rolled on to the lawn.

But before I could reach them under the broken herb, both had risen to their feet and were brushing pollen off themselves, so that the air was dusty with a glittering haze.

'But you are limping,' said Longhorn sternly to the shy creature he had saved.

'Just a little accident,' said the luckless one, glancing at the ravaged plant as if a sudden attack could still be expected. 'There was some kind of trap in there....'

'Never trust a flower,' Longhorn advised. 'Next time, think where you put your head.'

I do not believe that the flower's victim intended ever to return to the meadow. He was already limping off under equally treacherous plants, and had forgotten to say thank you. Longhorn linked arms with me, and I was grateful, for I felt I needed support, as if it had been me who had suffered in the prison of the vincetoxicum.

The meadow murmured around us as I thought, and its scents began to make both of us feel faint. We walked under a clouds of meadowsweet – they were indeed in full flower – but at that moment I would rather have been walking on regular, hard, reliable paving stones.

But before me there constantly rose new eddies, glowing with light, strange, incomprehensible in their silence. I saw the silky glimmer of the flowers, their wings and carinas, I saw their dull down and their purple lustre and their seeds, which a gust of wind hurled from their tight capsules. Ouch! one of them hit my cheek, hurting me; it was as big as a cartridge, while others popped as they opened so that I jumped into the air. I heard thuds as nutlets fell from their open hulls, and sulphur-yellow spurs and swollen lips barred my way. My neck was tickled by the fleecy tips of bracts, bristles and seed-down, and the searing colours forced their way in through my pupils, however much they tried to shrink, and into my nostrils, palate, ears the cries of the honey-pattern and thousands of impudent scents.

'No, we do not know them,' I said to Longhorn, and he inclined his head silently.

Across the ground, which hid all the roots, the cold of the approaching evening began to move. While the sun still blazed on those large faces, which were now closing, I had not doubted or asked. But as soon as the first pale portent of withering rose toward the sky and we turned toward the city, all I knew with certainty was that I had was as lost as I had been before.

The Hum of the Wheel

THE SECOND LETTER

At night I awoke to a rattling and a ringing from the kitchenette. I am sure you know that Tainaron is located in a volcanic zone. Scientists claim that we have already arrived in a period when a large eruption is to be expected, so fateful that it may mark the destruction of the entire city.

So what? Do not suppose that it effects the lives of the Tainaronians. The shudders of the night are forgotten, and in the dazzle of morning, in the market-place through which I often take a short cut, a honeyed haze glows in the fruit baskets, and the paving beneath my feet is eternal once more.

And in the evening I look at the enormous Ferris wheel, whose circumference, centre and radii are marked out with thousands of points of light, like stars. Ferris wheel, wheel of fortune....

Sometimes my gaze fastens itself to its spinning and I seem to hear, until sleep comes, the constant humming of the wheel, which is the voice of Tainaron itself.

I do not believe that I have ever seen so many ages and so many gods at the same time as in

Tainaron. Where else but Tainaron can the eye encounter, in a single glance, the vanishing spires of cathedrals, the liquid gold of the cupolas of minarets and the pure capitals of a Doric temple? Here they rise, side by side and yet incomparable, each of them alone.

But in many buildings here there is something ill-proportioned, something that is almost ridiculous and makes one think of theatrical scenery. Where does that impression come from? The decoration of the friezes of the palace of supreme justice is ridiculously ornate, while essential parapets and canopies have been omitted from the chamber of commerce. And sometimes, when I begin to grow tired on my walks, I feel dizzy in streets and at crossroads, for the buildings look as if they are leaning and moving in the wind....

Yesterday I walked through an arcade, airy and light, stepping on paving laid by a master, and my gaze caressed the resilient columns, the glittering mosaics of the window recesses. The arcade came to an end, I crossed the square – and got a slap in the face. Before me there swaggered a concrete wall raised on elephants' feet, a featureless, gloomy variation of the colonnade I had just left, insulting and crushingly heavy. But it, too, is part of Tainaron, like the piece of ancient stone wall at the eastern edge of the city, in whose crevices a sand martin nests.

Do you know, I am sometimes startled when, from amid the throng, a snout-like face sways toward me, above which nimble antennae, supple as lashes, or when, in a café, a waiter approaches my table, his mandibles protruding just like those of a dragonfly-grub. And yesterday in the tram, a creature sat down next to me, his form recalling that of a leaf; he looked so light that I could have blown him away into the air like a dry weed.

I have met someone who supplies a special thread for the needs of the whole of Tainaron. It is so fine, so durable and so elastic that no industrially produced thread can bear comparison. He secretes it from the rear of his body, as much as 150 metres in 24 hours. The glittering filament, finer than a hair, is far less than a denier in thickness. When a ray of sunlight struck it at the window at which I was examining it, I saw the thread blaze with all the colours of the spectrum.

I should like a dress made only of this thread; a garment lighter, more festive or more beautiful I could not imagine.

But it is a childish dream: I shall never have such a dress. For the filament is so sticky that it would stick to my body like a corrosive glue.

So what is this thread used for? Do not ask me; I do not know, and I do not wish to know.

Shimmer

THE THIRD LETTER

And then the lights of evening are lit, with hundreds of reflections in water and eyes and windows. You know, don't you, that there are creatures who light up their vicinity with the glow of their own organs or parts of the body: fireflies in the gardens of the south, the glow-worm on its blade of grass and the creatures who live in moats, who carry lamps on their monstrous foreheads. Colder still is the vast lustre of rotten wood covered in honey fungus....

But here in Tainaron, too, there are those who, at evening, draw glances because they secrete a fine veil of light and at times, when they become agitated, glimmer and flash. I gaze at them with admiration as they hurry past me in the street – always quickly, with almost dancing steps. They emerge from their houses only at evening, and I have no idea what they do until then, the livelong day – perhaps they merely sleep.

I have never seen any of them alone; they move in flocks and free groupings as if participating in some kind of formation dancing in the squares. But if it rains or if there is a fresh breeze, the sparklers go out like candles and disappear beneath the roofs. Difficulties and a severe climate, tiring work and unexpected upheavals are not for their sort. Whenever I see them I find myself thinking that there must be a party somewhere and that lots of fun is to be expected. They look so cheerful and carefree, and their rose-pink or yellowish glow would embellish any ballroom.

In the middle of the city there is a stairway around which Tainaronians gather in the evenings to converse or merely to watch one another. It is here that the most colourful, the strangest, the most elegant, the richest and the most tattered of all meet, on these broad steps, worn over many centuries. The Fireflies, too – is that not a good name for these little shimmerers? – are seen here as soon as darkness falls, as long as the weather is calm and warm.

I feel melancholy when I look at them, but I have never tried to approach them. I do not even believe that they speak any of the city's official languages; I do not know whether they speak at all. They are as graceful as down, as fine and light as the first flush of youth that no one has ever lived.

Recently I have betaken myself on many evenings to the steps to rejoice in their glimmer. They do not notice me, but when they pass – dance! – past me and past the beggars and past the pomp of the blue-belted knight, hope quivers and the spirit of spring gusts around them as freshly as if nothing had ever yet been lost forever.

But I must tell you, too, that when, yesterday morning, I crossed the square on the way to a certain side-street, I saw in the ditch a dusty rag, with a few pitying backs bowed over it. I passed it by without stopping, but when, at the corner of the street, I stopped to look, I saw it being lifted from the ground and carried away. It was only then that I understood that I had seen one of the sparklers, but this time quite alone. It was no longer glimmering, even palely; it was just a small, dark mass. The spark of joy, the gleam of life itself, had been extinguished.

Wherever, whenever I happen to witness its destruction, bitter pain, seemingly incurable, weakens my sight and eats away from me, too, the small days of life.

But tonight in the city the Fireflies were on the move once more, as many in number as flocks of birds in spring, more joyful and glimmering more strongly than ever before.

Their Mother's Tears

THE FOURTH LETTER

There are strange houses in one of the suburbs. They are like goblets, very narrow and high, and to a certain extent they recall piles of ashes; but their reddish walls are as strong as concrete. In them live a countless mass of inhabitants, small but very industrious folk, who are in constant motion. They all resemble each other so closely that I should never learn to recognise any of them. One, however, is an exception.

It is already a long time since I asked Longhorn whether, one day, he would take me to one of those houses. 'Why do they interest you?' he asked. 'Their architecture is so extraordinary,' I said. 'Perhaps you know someone there? Perhaps I could go there with you sometime?'

'If you wish,' said Longhorn; but he did not look particularly keen.

Yesterday, at last, Longhorn took me to one of those dwellings. At the entrance was a doorman with whom he exchanged a few words and who set off to accompany me. 'We shall meet this evening,' shouted Longhorn, and disappeared into the gaudy bustle of Tainaron.

I was led along dim and intricate corridors that opened on halls, warehouses and living spaces of different sizes. Past me rushed large numbers of people; all of them seemed to be in a hurry and in the midst of important tasks. But I was taken to the innermost room of the house, at whose door stood more guards. There was no window in the room, but it was nevertheless almost unbearably bright, although I could not see the source of the light.

I certainly realised that there were other people in the room, but I could see only one. She was immeasurably larger than all the others, monumental, all the more so because she stayed in one place, unmoving. Her dimensions were enormous: her egg-shaped head grazed the roof of the vault and, in its half recumbent position, her breadth extended from the doorway to the back of the room. As I stepped inside and stood by the wall (there was hardly room anywhere else), there came from her mouth a creaking sound which I interpreted as a welcome.

'Show respect for the queen,' hissed my guide, and knelt down. Unaccustomed to such gestures, I felt embarrassed, but I followed his example.

Some time passed before any attention was paid to me. By the walls of the room, around the queen, rushed creatures whose task was evidently to satisfy all her needs. I soon realised that they were necessary, for the queen was so formless that she herself could hardly take a step. And I concluded that she could not possibly have gone out through the door; she must live and die within these walls, without ever seeing even a flicker of sun. Her plight horrified me, and I wanted to leave the glowing cave quickly.

At that moment the creaking voice startled me. I realised that the queen had turned her head a little so that she was now staring at me languidly, at the same time sipping a milky fluid from a goblet held under her infinitesimal jaw.

The straw fell from her lip, and new croaks followed. With difficulty, I made out the following words: 'I know what you're thinking, you little smidgeon.'

'I'm sorry,' I stammered, and vexation made me flushed.

'You think, don't you, that I am some kind of individual, a person, admit it!'

As she went on speaking, her voice grew deeper, and it was as if it began to buzz. It was a most extraordinary voice, for it seemed to be made up of the murmur of hundreds of voices.

'Yes, indeed, I mean. . . .' I grew completely confused for a moment and sat down on my heels, as kneeling on the hard floor was too tiring.

'Quite so, of course,' I said rapidly, completely puzzled.

'Didn't I guess?' she said, and burst into laughter, which sometimes boomed, sometimes tinkled in the corridors so infectiously that in the end all the inhabitants of the building seemed to be joining in, and the entire house was laughing at my simplicity.

Suddenly complete silence followed, and she said, pointing at me with her long proboscis, 'So tell me, who am I?'

Before I could even think of an answer to this question, I realised at last what was happening in the back part of the room, which was filled with the queen's great rear body. I had, in fact, been aware all the while that something was being done incessantly, but the nature of that activity hit me like a thunderbolt. Bundles had been carried past me, but it was only at the third or fourth that I looked more closely and saw: they were new-born babies.

The queen was giving birth! She was giving birth incessantly. And just as I realised that, I seemed to hear from all around me the din of a hammer, commands, the chirrup of a saw, and everywhere there hovered the stench of building mortar. I realised that more and more storeys were being added to the house, and that it was reaching ever higher into the serenity of the sea of air. The sounds of construction reached me even from deep under the ground, and in my mind's eye I could see corridors branching beneath the paving stones like roots, greedily growing from day to day. The tribe was increasing; the house was being extended. The city was growing.

'You are the mother of them all, your majesty,' I replied, humbly.

'But what is a mother?' she squealed, and suddenly her voice rose to a piercing height, as one of her antennae lashed through the air above my head like a whip.

I retreated and pressed myself to the wall, although I understood that she would not be able to come any nearer.

'She from whom everything flows is not a someone,' the queen hissed through her wide jaws, like a snake. I gazed at her, bewitched.

'You came to see me, admit it!' she growled, more deeply than I dared think. 'But you will be disappointed! You are already disappointed! Admit it!'

'No, not in the least,' I protested, anxiously.

'But there is no me here; look around you and understand that! And here, here in particular, there is less of me than anywhere. You think I fill this room. Wrong! Quite wrong! For I am the great hole out of which the city grows. I am the road everyone must travel! I am the salty sea from which everyone emerges, helpless, wet, wrinkled. . . .'

Her voice chided me warmly, like a great ocean swell. As she spoke, she glanced languidly behind her, at her formless, mountainous rear, from whose depths her latest offspring were being helped into the brightness of the lamps. They were all born silently, as if they were dead.

But suddenly I saw something gush from her eyes; it splashed on to the floor and the walls and wetted all my clothes.

She was no longer looking at me, and I rose and left the room, wet with the queen's tears.

The Burden

THE FIFTH LETTER

I have not told you that I am already living at my second address here in Tainaron. There were some difficulties with my first apartment, so vague that I have not written about them earlier, but at the same time serious enough to force me to move.

For my first week I lived in a northern suburb, in a building which must once have been plastered in pale green, but had since fallen badly into decay. The plaster had split off in great flakes, and the spaces they left behind them brought to mind faces and patterns seen long ago. At first, nevertheless, I liked both the house and the apartment a great deal: a room and small kitchen on the first floor, with a window opening on to a short, peaceful street.

Then, one night, I woke up. It was perhaps my third or fourth night. My upstairs neighbours were making a noise, and it was this which had woken me. Someone was moving a heavy piece of furniture – that is what it sounded like, at least – dragging it back and forth across the floor above my ceiling. I looked at the clock: it was a little past one. For some time I lay awake, waiting for the noise to end, but when the din went on I got up, angry and tired, to look for something with which to knock on the ceiling. I could not find anything; I had not yet bought even a broom for the apartment.

I opened the door that led to the stairway and listened: it seemed to me that the whole house must have woken up. But the noise was much fainter in the stairwell, and no one else had got up to wonder what it was. The calm light of the street-lamp drew a beautiful ornament in the cracked marble of the wall of the stairway.

I lay down once more and stared at the ceiling. It looked at me as if it were shaking under the heavy thumps that went on, one after another. I thought I had lain there for a long time, I thought it was already morning, when the noise suddenly ceased and it was as if everything was abruptly interrupted. When I glanced at the clock, I realised that it had all lasted for less than an hour.

The following night as I went to bed, I had already forgotten the matter. But my sleep was interrupted again by precisely the same kind of sound as on the previous night, and at exactly the same time. I tried to remain calm, and took up a book. I even leafed through it (it was the flora you gave me long ago), but the incessant knocking prevented me from understanding anything. The hands of the clock moved as if some nocturnal force were hindering them, but when they finally reached two, peace returned as suddenly as it had been broken.

The next day, I saw the upstairs resident in a small neighbourhood shop opposite our house. She was a fragile old spinster with astonishingly thin limbs, who supported herself with a slender stick with an elegantly turned head – it represented a creature with a beak and horns. The lady was known well in the shop and was served with respect. In the midst of her purchases she turned to me and asked, in a surprisingly strong, trumpet-like voice, 'Well, how do you find us?'

I had not in the least expected that she would know who I was. My landlord had only once pointed her out to me, through the window, when I was signing the rental agreement.

'That old lady lives above you,' was all he had said, and I had glanced at my neighbour in passing from my first-floor perspective.

'I am Pumilio,' the old lady said now, and now it was my turn to introduce myself; but I am sure that I was unable entirely to banish the quiver of suspicion from my face as she continued, immediately: 'Have you settled in to your new apartment?'

As she asked the question, quickly and animatedly, I thought her gaze held real curiosity, quite out of proportion to the formality of the question.

I hesitated, but managed to say: 'Thank you, it is a comfortable apartment. But at night I find it difficult to sleep.'

I took fright at my own boldness, and watched her closely.

'Really? Just fancy, and you are still so young. I am already quite old, as you see, but I sleep well. Quite well!' she repeated, examining me through her wide, motionless pupils.

I did not know what to think. She left the shop before me, leaning on her beautiful stick, and proceeding with some difficulty. But on the threshold she turned: 'Tonight I am sure you will be able to sleep.'

And she smiled, her mouth closed.

I hoped it was some kind of promise. I fell asleep quickly and, it may be said, in good faith, but my sleep was interrupted again in the same way and at the same time as on the previous two nights. Exhaustion and rage pounded at my forehead, but now I listened to the sounds from the floor above more closely than before. In particular, I tried to make out the tapping of Miss Pumilio's stick on the floor, for it seemed to me that it would be very difficult, if not impossible, for her to move without support. But all I could hear was heavy thumps and dragging sounds, and in addition I could see clearly in the light of the reading-lamp that the ceiling-lamp, a glass ball, was rocking slowly in its mount.

It began to seem incredible to me that Miss Pumilio, who was old, frail and, what is more, an invalid, could be capable, night after night, of the kinds of trials of strength that the noisy events upstairs would seem to presuppose. But above all I asked myself: why would she do anything like that? What reasons could force her to move furniture around in the middle of the night?

I could think of only two reasons, and both of them were linked with fear. First: Miss Pumilio feared something so strongly that, every night, she built a barricade in front of her door, using her heaviest furniture. Did that seem likely? Not really, because things were dragged above my head in a number of different directions – remember this – and besides, the mornings, when she would have had to have taken down her fortifications, were silent. Second: Miss Pumilio wanted me to be afraid, perhaps because, for one reason or another, she wanted me to move out.

On the fourth night, as soon as I awoke – and it happened a few dozen seconds before the noise began (and this time I was absolutely certain it would happen again) – I was extraordinarily afraid. It was as if the consuming fear that I had imagined Miss Pumilio felt (or that she wished me to feel) had, that night, been transferred to me. Most repugnant of all to me was that the noises always began at the very same stroke of the clock. I remember saying to myself, many times: 'But it is unnatural! It is unnatural!'

This time, however, I did not get out of bed, and the most difficult thing of all for me would have been to try to do anything to stop the noise. I would not have gone upstairs for any price, or rung Miss Pumilio's doorbell and enquired what the matter was and whether she could not do whatever she was doing at some more civilised hour.

Why was it is so impossible for me? I will tell you at once: because my mind was afflicted by a suspicion that was difficult to dismiss. You see, I suspected that if I really did go upstairs, if I really did ring Miss Pumilio's doorbell and say the words I intended to say to her, she would look at me with the dim eyes of a sleeper who has just been wakened from slumber and would not understand at all, at all, what I was talking about and what had given me the right to dare deprive her of her much-needed sleep.

And in fact this was the ultimate reason that cast me into despair and why I never examined the origin of the noise any more closely.

From time to time I saw Miss Pumilio in our street or in the little neighbourhood shop. She always greeted me amicably, but no longer made conversation with me. But sometimes when I had passed her on the street, it seemed to me as if she turned to look after me, and as if her bluish mosaic eyes glowed with a feeling or thought that I did not understand. But it could also be the case that she was looking through me, and was not even thinking about me.

At night, I stayed awake. And to keep up my courage. I repeated to myself: 'It's nothing! Nothing! I just don't happen to understand what is behind this, but I am sure it is something quite insignificant and ordinary. I am sure I would laugh if I found out what it is, and laugh heartily.'

But above my head the rumbling continued like a very localised storm, and along the creaking floorboards was pushed and pulled something that was heavy and recalcitrant and immense, something so formless that it resembled human life. At last came night and, staring at the shaking ceiling, I felt the foundations and the cellar of the house respond to the thundering sound from above. I fled those two sledge-hammers, of which one was the earth itself, to the open air, and have never returned to that address.

The Seventeenth Spring

THE SIXTH LETTER

In Tainaron, many things are different from at home. The first things that occur to me are eyes. For with many of the people here, you see, they grow so large that they take up as much as one third of their faces. Whether that makes their sight more accurate, I do not know, but I presume they see their surroundings to some extent differently from us. And, moreover, their organs of sight are made up of countless cones, and in the sunlight their lens-surfaces glitter like rainbows. At first I was troubled when I had to converse with such a person, for I could never be sure whether he was looking at me or past me. It no longer worries me. It is true that there are also people whose eyes are as small as points, but then there are many of them, in the forehead, at the ends of the antennae, even on the back.

Like their eyes, Tainaronians may have a number of pairs of hands and feet, too, but it does not seem to me that they run any faster than we do, or get more done in their lives. Some of them, it is true, have a jumping fork under their bellies, which they can, whenever necessary, release like a lever and thus hurl themselves forward, sometimes by dozens of metres.

The hustling forest of antennae and pedipalpi in the streets at rush-hour is certainly an extraordinary sight for people like us, but most difficult of all is to accustom oneself to a certain other phenomenon that marks the life of the majority of the inhabitants here in the city. This phenomenon is metamorphosis; and for me, at least, it is so strange, to my very marrow, that even to think about it makes me feel uncomfortable. For, you see, the people here live two or many consecutive lives, which may have nothing in common, although one follows from the last in a way that is incomprehensible to me.

We, too, change, but gradually. We are used to a certain continuity, and most of us have a character that remains more or less constant. It is different here. It remains a mystery to me what the real connection is between two consecutive lives. How can a person who changes so completely still say he is in any sense the same as before? How can he continue? How can he remember?

Here you can bump into a stranger, and he will come up to you like an old acquaintance and begin to remember some past amusing coincidence that you apparently experienced together. When you ask, 'When?', he laughs and answers: 'When I was someone else.'

But perhaps you will never discover with whom you have the honour of conversing, for they often change comprehensively and completely, both their appearance and their way of life.

There are also those who withdraw into total seclusion for as much as seventeen years. They live in tiny rooms, no more than boxes; they do not see anyone, do not go anywhere, and hardly eat. But whether they sleep or wake there, they are continually changing and forsaking the form they had before.

Seventeen years! And when, finally, the seventeenth spring arrives, they stop out of their hermit caves into full sunlight. And there begins their only summer, for in the autumn they die; but all summer long they celebrate all the more. What a life! Do you understand it?

But sometimes I feel a little envious: to be able to curl up in a pupal cell without hoping for dreams, knowing that one spring one will step before the eyes of the world, new, refreshed, free from the past…

Farewell once more; my head is heavy and I believe a thunderstorm is brewing. I ponder the reasons why you do not reply, and there are many. Are you dead? Have you moved? The city where you lived has perhaps disappeared from the face of the earth? And can I trust the mail of Tainaron; who knows on what back-garden compost-heap my letters are languishing? Or you stand on your doormat turning my letter over in your hands; turning it over and then putting it aside unopened, on top of the pile of newspapers and advertisements that grows and grows in the dusty corner.

Burning on the Mountain

THE SEVENTH LETTER

Behind the hillock where the amusement park of Tainaron is built rises another hillock, dim with distance. From time to time, at midnight moments, I have seen a fire blazing on its highest peak, small but very bright.

How I loved to look at it once. I thought about campfires and guitars, shared meals and hikers resting and telling stories after the exertions of the road. But later I began to suspect that it was perhaps not, after all, a campfire, but some kind of beacon, for it always lit so high up and it can be seen so far away in every direction; particularly, however, down in the city of Tainaron.

Some days ago I happened to mention the fire on the mountain to Longhorn, and I immediately felt embarrassed, for my question made his face grow harsh and severe. I had hardly ever seen such an expression on his calm face.

'Do not look at it; it is not for you,' he enjoined me quickly. 'When the time of the new moon comes, draw the curtains and go to sleep.'

The time of the new moon… Longhorn was right. I had last seen the fire about a month earlier, and that night there had been a new moon. The earth had cast a long shadow, and perhaps it was for that reason that the fire blazed so large and solitary. And had not two cycles of the moon passed since the earlier blaze?

Even though Longhorn had grown so uncommunicative-looking, I made so bold as to ask: 'Tell me: who lights those bonfires?'

'They are no bonfires,' he said, and his voice did not grow any milder. 'They are not intended to delight the eye, and their ashes are not used for baking root vegetables.'

'What are they, then?' I asked, and I realised my voice had dropped to a whisper.

'Burnt offerings, sacrifices. They are sacrifices,' he replied.

I felt I had known before I asked.

'Who is sacrificed?' I asked. In admiring the blaze, had I not noted a light smell hovering over the city?

'Why do you keep asking?' Longhorn cried, growing angry. 'They set fire to themselves.'

But I could not stop; I went on, stubbornly: 'But who are they? What do they want?'

Longhorn had turned his back to me and was pretending to examine my books. The conversation seemed repugnant in the extreme to him, and I was ashamed of my own tactlessness. Nevertheless, I felt that if I could solve the mystery of the fire I would also understand why some people chose destruction as if it were a privilege.

But Longhorn shrugged his back-armour wearily.

'What do they want, you ask. They are sectarian delusions. To redeem Tainaron, I suppose that is what they want. That the Tainaronians should live differently from how they do. That they should wake up from their sleep; that is what they say. Mad!'

And he shook his fists at the mist-clad mountain that bowed over the city. 'How many innocent souls will they yet take with them to the pyre?'

Yesterday it was new moon once more. Early in the evening, I had done exactly as Longhorn had instructed me: I had drawn the curtains across my windows. But after I had gone to bed I could not sleep, and it seemed to me that a red colour was shining through the curtains.

Then I got up, went on to the balcony and immediately saw the balefire, high on the mountain in the darkness of the new moon. None of the lights of Tainaron – not its neon colours, not the lights of its Ferris wheel – burned as brightly as the fire on the mountain. There it blazed, attracting the gazes of the city-dwellers as a lamp attracts moths. Even from miles away it was dazzling, and made my face glow.

Last night was calm, and the sacrifice burned evenly. It was a candle on the table, the night's focus and its terrible purifier. Who was he who was burning with such a high and unwavering flame? What did he believe he knew that no one in the valley of Tainaron knew, which was more than life, more than his own boiling tears and his scalding eyes? Was it as clearly visible to him as the fire on the mountain was to me? To me, lingering on the balcony; to me, who could not take my eyes off the fire, was no justification to him, no expiation, no comfort.

And I had gazed on the blaze as if it were a midnight flower, rejoicing!

No, as long as the sacrifice burned, I could not go to sleep, could not concentrate on anything. I stood on the balcony until he, whoever he was, had turned from fire into embers and from embers into ashes.

Will there ever be a new moon when there is no need to light a fire high on the hill?

Their Innumerable Dwellings

THE EIGHT LETTER

Tainaron is full of voices of a kind I have not heard anywhere else. Here I have come to realise that there is no clear dividing line between music and language. For the citizens, you see, secrete their voices from themselves which can be interpreted sometimes as speech, sometimes as music. I do not mean they sing; that is, at least, not very common here. Neither do they play instruments of any kind; instead, their voices are created with the help of muscles, glands and guts or chitin armature.

Their voices may well up from a surprising depth, as if from leagues away, so that it is no wonder that they are often so difficult to locate. For, you see, the Tainaronians' way of life is a very curious one. You will perhaps not have heard that they often have a number of dwellings, but not only in the way that we have city apartments and summer villas. No: the people here are able to live in many dwellings at the same time, as in a nest of boxes. Some of them carry their innermost apartment, a one-roomed flat which fits their dimensions like a glove, with them everywhere. But this has the drawback that one cannot always make sense of what they say, for it echoes and reverberates from the walls of their private apartments. It is also vexing to me that I cannot always tell where the dwelling ends and its inhabitant begins.

Poor things, who never come among people without this innermost shield. It reflects the terrible vulnerability of their lives. Their little home may be made of the most diverse ingredients: grains of sand, bark, straw, clay, leaves... But it protects them better than others are protected by armour, from every direction, and it is a direct continuation of themselves, much more so than clothes are to you or me. But if it is taken away from them, they die – perhaps simply of shame, perhaps because their skins are too soft for the outside air, or because they do not have any skin at all.

Who would be so cruel as to tear from them this last shield! Oh, I have heard that such things, too, happen here in Tainaron; I have been startled by the moans of death-throes in the deeps of the night.

But I have my own theory concerning why this happens. For, you see, those who constantly drag their houses with them remain unknown to other people. One can gain only a brief glimpse of them, if that; they are always in hiding.

And then there are those who cannot bear such a situation, those who wish to see everything face to face and to reveal, open, show the whole world the nakedness of things... Now and then the temptation becomes overwhelming to them, and they split open the house of some poor unfortunate. I awake to shrieking, sigh and turn over – and soon fall asleep again.

Like Burying Beetles

THE NINTH LETTER

You do not reply. It is something that stays in my mind almost incessantly. The reasons for this silence are perhaps independent of you; or then again not. But I continue writing – that freedom I do allow myself – and I believe, I trust – well, no more of that!

There is much here that reminds me of former things, particularly of the city in which we once lived, close to each other. For example, a particular office window brings to mind another shop window on the far side of the green and white Oceanos.

I walked past it almost every day, but I never stopped in front of it, because it was always the same. Behind the glass hung a skilfully draped blue curtain; in front of it were set a stone urn and a wreath of flowers tied with a white silk ribbon.

There is such a shop in Tainaron, too, but its windows display not urns but small, very beautiful boxes. One day I went inside with Longhorn, who continues to guide me patiently from day to day in this city.

Someone had died, someone who I heard only now had been alive and who had known Longhorn, perhaps well, so that it was his task now to care for the funeral arrangements. I followed Longhorn because I had often, passing by, looked at those small boxes, and I wanted to examine them more closely.

The shop was empty as we stepped inside, but on the shelves that ran along the walls I saw more boxes, of all shapes, some smaller even than matchboxes, and the largest the size of books. They were covered in multicoloured fine fabrics, or painted or engraved with mark and symbols whose meaning I did not understand. What astonished me the most was their smallness. Among the Tainaronians, it is true, there are some very small races, but even for the smallest baby these boxes were far too small.

'Are these urns?' I asked Longhorn, who was examining brochures at the counter. 'Are they used for dead people's ashes?'

'Ashes? No, there is no crematorium here,' he said. 'They are used for a single organ, often an eye or an antenna. But sometimes the family may chose part of a wing, a part with a beautiful pattern.'

I fingered one of the boxes. It was as delicate and pretty as a confectionery box, and lined in white silk. I remembered that I had once, as a child, received just such a box, in which there had been sweeties. It had been Easter morning, and I had just been allowed to get out of bed for the first time after a bout of bronchitis. I am still seeking the purity, the silken whiteness and the colours of the metallic foil of that convalescent morning, its pussy-willows, its feather-tufts, in the world.

'What happens to the rest of the body?' I asked, wrapped in my thoughts, but Longhorn did not reply, for out of the back room, at that moment, stepped the funeral director, a very imposing man. Most noticeable about him was, however, not his size, but his colours: they were as bright as the complicated patterns of the boxes. His chest ranged from green to lemon, while the knobs of his antennae were as yellow as clementines. He bowed elegantly, and was surrounded by a cloud of scent which I recognised only after a moment: it was undoubtedly musk.

He became absorbed, with Longhorn, in a conversation conducted in low voices, in conclusion of which one of the boxes was chosen from the shelf, round and grass-green, with sky-blue crescent moons.

When the funeral director turned to tap at the cash register, I went up to Longhorn and asked once more: 'What happens to the rest of the body?'

I was a little startled at Longhorn's look, for it betrayed irritation, from which I understood immediately that my question was unseemly. All the same, I waited for his answer.

'Do you really want to know?' he asked.

'Why not? I am interested in everything,' I said with some hauteur, and when he continued in silence, I asked again, with real curiosity, 'Is there something secret about it, then?'

'Very well,' said Longhorn, somewhat coolly. Suddenly he stepped up to the funeral director and whispered a couple of words to him, pointing in my direction.

The funeral director looked at me strangely, from head to foot, bowed once more in his cultivated way, and asked me to follow him. I looked interrogatively at Longhorn, and he growled: 'Go on, I'll stay here.'

The funeral director had already reached the back room and was waiting for me, silent but smiling. He opened a door leading to a badly lit stairway, which smelt of cellars and fish; or that is what I thought then. The funeral director gestured for me to walk in front of him, but when I shook my head he stepped past me into the gloom. My curiosity had now completely disappeared, but I followed the strange figure lower and lower down the steep and uneven stairs, regretting my frivolous wish for information. The deeper we went, the more uncomfortable I felt, above all because of the increasingly strong smell. Finally I stopped, intending to return to ground level without delay, but as it turned out the funeral director was now behind me, so close that his yellow chest was nearly touching my back and his musky vapours mixed with still odder scents. I continued my descent unhappily, for one way or another the man was pushing me forward, gently enough, it is true, but so firmly that it was no longer impossible for me to retreat.

'The fish is rotten,' I thought, but the smell of decay had already grown to a stench that filled my lungs with nausea. I scarcely realised that we had arrived in a great vault, and that it was filled with an extraordinary bustling.

I could no longer see my guide anywhere. I felt faint, and pressed my back against the damp stone wall. I already realised that I had been brought into a sepulchre. Before me on the earthen floor lay carcasses without number, but about them was such a ceaseless bustle that at times it looked as if there were still some degree of life in them. Around me moved dozens of creatures that were reminiscent in their appearance of the funeral director, but whose clothing was – if possible – still more brilliant. The more closely I examined them and their work, the more they reminded me of the toil of burying beetles.

I had descended into the Hades of Tainaron. I had asked: 'What happens to the bodies?' and the answer to my question was now before my eyes. One of the most prosaic and indispensable of the functions of the city of Tainaron was carried out here, shielded from the gaze of passers-by; but as I looked at their toil, my horror gave way and made space for impartial examination, even respect.

I spoke of Hades and a sepulchre, but in reality the space in which I found myself served the opposite purpose: it was a dining room and a nursery. Those who toiled here were not merely workers; they were also, above all, mothers. Now I could see that around every larger form flocked a swarm of smaller creatures, its offspring. As they did the work that had to be done for life in this city to be at all possible, these workers were at the same time feeding their heirs; and if the way in which they did it was not to my taste, where would I find more convincing proof of the never-broken alliance between destruction and florescence, birth and death?

So: there was a carcass, of which one could no longer detect who or what it had been when it was alive, so decomposed were its features. But I no longer felt sick, although I saw one of the mothers poking about in its pile of dross. For that was where the mother sought nourishment for her heirs, her snout buried in the stinking carcass, and look! there glistened a dark droplet, which one of the little ones drank, and after a moment the second received its share, and the third; no one was forgotten.

And here, then, was their work: to distil pure nectar from such filth, to extract from the slimy liquid of death health, strength and new life. How could I ever complain about what took place in the Hades of Tainaron. Truly, it is a laboratory compared to which even the greatest achievements of the alchemists are put to shame; but all that is done there is what the earth achieves every year when it builds a new spring from and on what rotted and died in the autumn.

'Have you seen enough?' someone asked behind me. I turned and saw Longhorn, who was standing at the mouth of the corridor, looking at me in a troubled way. I do not know whether his expression was caused merely by the stench, which my own nose hardly sensed any longer, or whether it was real grief. For his friend had just died, and I had hardly spared a thought for his feelings. But when our eyes met, I, too, felt the bite of suffering.

The kindness of his eyes! How had I never noticed it before. And they were so dazzlingly black, so wise and alive… But in fact I have seen just such a gaze before, and more than once. I have seen it – do not be shocked – in your eyes, too, different as they are. I have encountered it – or seen it pass me by – among acquaintances and strangers, at parties, in department stores, in my own home, in trains, on stations and in lecture-halls, shops and cafés; in summer, in the great lime trees in the park, where cast-iron benches have been placed for the citizens; and I am sure that at unguarded moments it has also resided in my own eyes.

That it ever disappears! It was the impossible, and unbearable, thing that, as I turned to look behind me and met Longhorn's eyes, was relentless in us both, and the strange meal we were following as onlookers offered no solution.

The soundless glitter of immense treasures – That it could be extinguished and sink into the cold mass of raw material as if it had not been anything more than the moisture of lachrymal fluid on the surface of the cornea...

'Come away,' said Longhorn, with unexpected softness, and we left Hades without looking at each other again.

The Charioteer

THE TENTH LETTER

I have received a card from my home country. Yes, it was not from you; we know that. The bronze statue on the card is two thousand four hundred years old, but he whom the card shows is a mere youth. His forehead is encircled by an ornamental ribbon, and his hair curls, lightly gilded, over his ears. He holds a pair of reins in his hands, and his eyes are dark stones, glittering, mysterious and surprised.

But what life and riches shine from them! It is hard for me to believe that what I see is merely coloured light reflected from stone. What a coincidence that it arrived just as I had sent you my last letter! For, don't you see, he has the same gaze, the one I was talking about, which hurts me, which I recognise everywhere.

But this young man is astonished at something; even his mouth is astonished, already ajar and about to open. I am sure I am not mistaken in remembering that I once saw a similar expression on the face of someone who was dying; all the tubes had been disengaged, and his eyes were wide open. The same concentration marks both their faces and forces both of them forward in an invisible race.

Why is it that it is in the form of this young man's face that I should most like to remember the face of humankind...

Tracks in the Dust

THE ELEVENTH LETTER

Have I told you that Tainaron has a prince? As a foreigner, I was unexpectedly offered the opportunity to attend his reception. I asked Longhorn for advice as to how I should dress for the occasion and what behaviour was expected. I felt his answer was vacuous, and did not help me one bit.

'You can go in whatever you like,' he said. 'You can ask whatever you want.'

And then he added: 'It's not important, after all.'

'Not important?' I was astonished. 'Do you just go there as you are, straight off the street, and say whatever comes to mind to the prince?'

But he did not give me any more clues, and I went there by myself, in my best dress of course, but distinctly nervous.

The prince lives in the middle of the city, in his palace, which is surrounded by a moat. The drawbridge was down, and there were no guards to be seen. People were going in and out, and no one paid any attention to me. I had been given a piece of paper, a promissory note which I tried to proffer to some of the passersby whom I guessed to be members of the palace staff, but no one wanted to accept it; everyone just waved their hands vaguely: 'It's not necessary.'

'Where does the prince hold his reception?' I asked three different times, and it was only on the third occasion that I was directed to the right place; but no one bothered to come with me as a guide, and the corridors along which I walked were empty. Through doors that had been left open I saw various different rooms: tambours, halls and stairwells, new colonnaded corridors and courtyards where landscape gardens had been built with pavilions, artificial lakes and bridges.

The prince received visitors in the tower at the heart of the palace, in the donjon. I saw him from a distance from the dim passageway on whose stone floor my shoes tapped alarmingly noisily.

The door to his reception room was wide open, and I could not see anyone else in the vicinity.

The salon was oval in shape and small. At its centre was a single chair, on which the prince sat.

The room was very high, in fact as high as the tower, so that the prince looked as if he were sitting at the bottom of a well.

I stopped before stepping across the threshold, for I did not know how I should approach him. He sat motionless, but seemed to be looking me straight in the eye. He was very old and frail. The way in which the light fell around him and on to his domed head from the upper windows made the vision desolate and melancholy.

I think I stood there for a long time, anxiously, but just as it began to seem to me that the prince was sleeping with his eyes open, his forelimb rose in an encouraging gesture, slowly and ceremoniously. I stepped into the room.

'Your highness,' I began, 'I have come...'

'Yes, yes,' he interrupted me before I had time to begin. 'It's perfectly clear. You can ask whatever you want.'

I had prepared many kinds of questions concerning both domestic and foreign policies, trade links and tax reform, but at the moment they all fell out of my head.

'May I ask, may I ask,' I mumbled, 'how you are?'

This was, of course, completely inappropriate, I understood that myself. But I could not get anything else out of my mouth, and I looked at him, dumbly, waiting for him to rise and announce that the audience was over.

Strangely enough, he seemed on the contrary to be engrossed by my question, as if it were completely apt for that time and place.

'As to my health, I have nothing to complain about,' he said, in such a low voice that I had to lean forward to hear. 'But I am worried about my ears. There is a murmuring in them all the time. Or else a ringing, of a little silver bell.'

And he suddenly shook his head, so that the fluffy blue collar that surrounded his neck hissed and rustled.

'And then there are the nights, they are definitely too big. They have grown larger and larger since the princess left, and the princess left thirty years ago, in her prime. You will not believe how small they were when she was still here. This small!'

He stretched out two of the downy pincers of his forelimb for me to see: they were almost touching. I looked at them with polite interest and nodded.

The prince leaned backward in his chair and spoke now more audibly, as if with greater warmth: 'When the princess had died, I often went into the city incognito, in strange armour. I stood by the bridge and did not let anyone by without inspecting him or her thoroughly from head to feet. But I never saw the princess again, for I should have known her in any disguise, even if she had been through the most comprehensive of metamorphoses, that you may believe. For the images of shared secrets had remained in the princess's eyes, and they, at last, would have revealed her immediately, but in the uninterrupted flow of oncomers there flowed only the loam of strange memories...'

And the prince's voice fell. I suspected that the audience should have ended long ago, and it tired me to stand before him as the only hearer of his ancient yearning. No one came to fetch me away, and in the palace there was a soundlessness as if there were no one else there.

'Do you know why we have been forgotten?' the prince whispered unexpectedly, and his choice of words surprised me: why that 'we', it was not really right in this situation, and why did he lower his voice in such a familiar way?

'Because it is all the same to them,' the prince whispered, 'what I do now, where I go or what I say, everything is permitted now. Do you understand?'

'No, I do not believe it, your highness,' I said hesitantly, but his forelimb crooked and beckoned me closer.

I bent obediently toward him and came so close that I thought I heard the little silver bell he had mentioned, as well as the scent of some bitter herb. Then he whispered into my ear: 'In reality, I am no longer the prince.'

He drew away to see the effect of his words on me. I can say that they did not really have any effect. I was convinced he was speaking the truth. Only thus did the emptiness and indifference which I had encountered in the palace – and earlier – make sense.

'I see you believe that I...,' the prince said heavily. 'But do not worry, that is not the case, not in the least. Know this: times change, but each is only one time of many. So what; it can be changed, like a change of clothes. Today I still sit in my palace. But often I ring my bell for a long while and no one comes. My shirt still bears the arms of Tainaron, but the wine which is brought to me is no longer of the same quality as before. So what. For tomorrow I shall be in exile, or my body will lie in that landscape garden on the little wooden bridge and the national guard will have pierced it with newly sharpened bayonets.'

Now he finally rose to his feet – I had been expecting it for a long time – and I realised, with relief, that the audience was over. I bowed respectfully, and when I turned, I saw only my own footprints in the heavy dust that completely covered the stone floor of the donjon.

Their solitude proved to me with complete clarity that no one had visited the room for ages, and that the prince himself had not left it.

He was a lost cause.

THE DAY OF THE GREAT MOGUL

THE TWELFTH LETTER

I do not know why I pick up my pen again. No longer because I might expect return mail. But I would like to tell someone that something strange has happened, some curious, unpleasant changes, and I have no idea what has caused them. Perhaps it is temporary, and my life will return to how it was before. Perhaps, too, the days that were like prizes, long ago, will return.

I have not travelled anywhere, but this city is now different. The change does not please me. When I look out, I see that it is as if it has been unclothed. The most important thing is absent; the thing that once, just a moment ago, made me strong and happy. I look at the ground, I look at the sky, and everywhere is the same absence, in the eyes that crowd the streets and the department stores as if they were seeking their lost pupils in the windows and sales counters. If I were to send you photographs of Tainaron before and Tainaron now, you would say no difference is visible, and perhaps it is so; but nevertheless I know that everything is decisively different.

If the sounds of the city were to be muted for a moment, I could hear a secretly crumbling sound as if a trickle of sand were falling from the side of a sandpit. And the vital force, which I believed to be inexhaustible, runs and runs somewhere where no one can use it.

Is this is what is known as growing old? Do I see it everywhere, although it exists only inside myself? And what once was happiness around me, was it too a mere reflection? But in that case how can I know anything of what Tainaron is, what it is like?

Today the book I open describes the great mogul Aurangzeb, who was a cruel tyrant. Fifteen of his elephants fell into a cleft on a mountain road, and on the back of one of them was his favourite wife.

'Remarkable,' writes the great mogul, 'empty-handed I came into this world, and now, as I leave it, I drag with me an enormous caravan of sins… My sorrow mortifies me. Farewell, farewell, farewell.'

I force myself to get up and open the door and step out into the street. I have decided to eat, but from the window table of the café the passers-by look as if they are dragging burdens which are invisible but nevertheless heavy. The liquid glimmers in my cup, and soon I shall have to swallow it. I look at it as if it were the goblet of today.

Under the marble table my legs wait, motionless, symmetrical, side by side. I do not know whether I have ever sensed their existence as such. They are alive, and all at once I am scorched by hot pity. My legs, my poor legs! Modest, sturdy and resilient, my own pillars, you too will wither!

Small days, small days. The woman who, in the tramcar, takes a comb from her handbag and, pulling it through her stiff hair, complains: 'The comb doesn't work, no. The concrete eats the hair so.'

A friend who sways toward me, his coat open, shaking his fingers. There was a time when he ran from table to table, his face flushed, to proclaim that his dogma was the youth of the world. What he says now is something quite different, quite different, but I do not listen; I mourn. The youth of the world!

How we secrete words around us, so that the eye of reality may not see us! In vain! So hopelessly thin and tattered a veil does not hide anything, and we writhe in the brightness of destiny. No shield, no armour, and neither will flesh ever return to the word.

And when I pass by the statue of the Great Sleeper, around it billows a tired song:

Sweet is my sleep, but more to be mere stone,
so long as ruin and dishonour reign;
to bear nought, to feel nought, is my great gain;
then wake me not, speak in an undertone!

My poor friend! I saw his finger fall and he wavered across the frosty wasteland and shut himself up in the fortress of the telephone kiosk in the square.

It happened there, not here in Tainaron, for these are different statues, but the days are as small everywhere and their shape is that of a funnel.

I wonder if you too have noticed: there are moments when you do not wish to wish and then you look inward and what is it that you see? An endless sequence of wishes, infinitely many yous, and all of the yous are threaded on to the tough thread of memory, and in the end you yourself are no more than that thinnest of thin threads, and it quivers, tensed…

But today I walked past a chirping flock of sparrows and it fell silent as a wave of nausea swept across me and suddenly the earth gave way beneath my feet and I remembered once more that beneath Tainaron is nothing but a crust, as insubstantial as one night's ice.

Proof Copy

THE THIRTEENTH LETTER

The rapist panted in my pursuit, reducing the distance between us with horrifying speed. Then I remembered that what I was seeing was a dream and that I therefore had an opportunity: with all my strength, I forced my feet to leave the ground, and as the murderer's filthy paw fumbled for my ankle, it slipped beyond his grasp and past the highest branches.

My unbelief had saved me, but the poor creature who believes that everything is true is the victim of his dreams.

Today I remembered that many years – many grace-filled years ago, I should say, for that is what they have been – we were walking up a street between two churches, and you said: 'The soul is what is visible.' Do you remember?

When I happened to look in the mirror a moment ago, you said it, from a long way off, but as clearly as you did then. I seldom look in the mirror, but always there is someone there who gives me my eyes. And the root of my nose is bluish; a line has inscribed itself at the corner of my mouth like a drypoint groove. But this is no proof copy, and the acid of everyday life corrodes, prepares that which is the soul.

Once you said, moaning: 'I would love you even if you were someone else.'

You are crazy! How the word reassured me, how calm it made me.

But yesterday morning I stood in front of a large department store where I planned to go and buy clothes, and the sun had just risen behind the roofs of Tainaron. I came to a halt because I happened to glance at my legs, for no particular reason; and from them grew two shadow-trees, and both of us were whole, I and the other.

Oh, I have something wider than a prairie, wider than Oceanos. I do not know where to put it, to whom to present it. I cannot show it; I cannot use it. It is too wide for this city; one life is too small for it. No one needs it, but today it has me flying and singing.

Sand

THE FOURTEENTH LETTER

The new day dawned low and cloudy. In my melancholy, I set out for a walk – alone – for Longhorn, after all, has his work, of which I know almost nothing; but I assume it is some kind of business activity.

I wanted to see something I had not seen before, and for that reason I set out toward the eastern part of the city, although I well remembered that Longhorn had urged me to stay away from those parts. When I asked why, he merely said that it was not safe to go there alone.

But it was midday, after all, and I was walking along a broad esplanade bordered on both sides by high poplars which were still green. Looked at from a distance, they recall the crowns of some other tree, standing on their bases. I walked past the theatre, on whose eaves snouty caryatids slumber; that building has a particular charm. I came to a cross-street full of expensive specialist shops and pretty little cafés. I myself have often sat at their clean tables, but now I did not stop. I was in a hurry, as if on my way to some agreed meeting.

Now I came to streets which were unfamiliar. I could no longer see business plaques or inventively decorated shop windows. The buildings became more closed, dilapidated and lower. I sank into melancholy, and for a while I went on hardly glancing around me, but the unevenness of the gravel under my heels startled me. Now I realised that the streets in this part of the city were not paved, or even asphalted. They were deeply rutted, in an almost unpassable condition, but neither did there seem to be any kind of traffic any longer in these parts. Pavements, too, had been left unbuilt, and between the buildings there meandered indistinct lanes. After a few steps I was forced to ask myself: were they buildings? For is it not the case that the buildings in which we live and our friends live have straight and solid walls? Are their roofs not covered in slates or tin and are their windows not made of glass?

As I walked, I remembered entrances and heavy front doors whose handles were of brass, gutters that drummed in the rain, and chimneys and chimney-pipes which, seen from an attic window, looked like solitary people. And behind the window panes? There should have been the glimmer of white curtains, eyes, cats and the dim perspectives of the life of strange rooms…

But there was nothing of the sort to be seen. The habitations past which I walked were lacking in all the characteristics of proper dwellings. First of all, there were no straight lines. Everything curved and twisted, meandered without direction, without clear corners. The dwellings rose from the earth, earth-coloured, made of clay and loam. They had indefinitely shaped openings in place of windows and doors. Where were the columns and capitals which one could admire in almost every square in the centre of the city? Where was the rosy golden glow of the cupolas, and the window recesses with their rich mosaic patterns? The wall-niche and the sandstone shapes that beckoned to them? The slender roof-groins and the pointed arches? The pilastered galleries and the atriums with their flowering trees?

I realised that there were two Tainarons, or perhaps even more, who knows… This was a Tainaron lacking in everything that is called culture, everything which joy and hope, prosperity and ambition, can build and embellish on Earth.

I cannot say I liked it.

I walked faster than before. My intention was now to traverse this obscure and peripheral part of the city as quickly as possible and spend a moment at the sandy beach of which I had heard. After that I decided to return to the centre of the city via the northern causeway, although it is long and dull.

The light increased, and from somewhere the shimmer of water was reflected over the nests, cells and systems of caves that were hollowed out of the sand and the rock. From in front of me I heard an incessant rustling and scouring, as if the earth were being swept with a large brush; but there was nothing to be seen. A couple of times I heard, from behind a stony hillock, the sound of dragging and something buzzing; I was certain that a lizard or reptile was hiding among the stones. I saw a couple of passers-by; they were small and fragile, dragonfly-like creatures. The last dwellings I passed were just low mounds and holes. They would offer shelter only to the most insignificant and modest beings, and they soon sank and merged into the fine, golden sand, which was certainly beautiful to look at, although it made my steps heavy and insinuated its way into my shoes and even into my mouth, making me thirsty.

Nevertheless, I decided to walk a few steps further, although I had already admitted to myself that my trip was not exactly fun. The sand spread before me in gently swelling dunes. I could no longer see any signs of the city around me. The sand radiated the same simple severity as the snowfields at home, the allure of inviolability, dreams and emptiness.

As I gazed at one particular sandbank, its shape reminded me of a sledging slope which, long ago, rose in the courtyard of my childhood home. I began to be very tired, and I felt like sprawling for a moment in its softness. Suddenly I was so sleepy that my thoughts became confused: what if I freeze?

I took a couple of steps toward the ridge, and at the same time my attention fastened on some insignificant protuberances that were at first hardly distinguishable from the surrounding sandy plain. When I went nearer, I saw earthworks of various sizes, all of them in the form of circles, forming concentric rings. At their centre was a conical pit, symmetrical and apparently purposebuilt, for wind or water could not possibly have built such exact forms. Those hollows reminded me of something... Long ago, I must have seen something similar; but it was quite painful that I could not bring to mind where it had happened.

Behind the sandbank I saw yet another earthwork, larger than all the others. I climbed up to its ridge and the sand immediately began to move under my feet. Small avalanches fell down the walls of the pit here and there, soundless falls and swifter torrents, making a rustling sound as if a woman in evening dress were rushing, complete with train, through a thicket.

It was not until a moment later that I noticed that there was a hole deeper in the pit. At first it looked infinitesimally small, but that could not be the case, for in fact I was still so far from it that it could well be wider than the circumference of my head. It looked immeasurably deep. The grains of sand that were displaced by the heels of my shoes as soon as I moved in the slightest fell over its fragile edges. I stood where I was – insofar as there was a definite place to stand, for something was continually happening on the ridge of the earthworks, so I did not have a firm foothold – yes, I stood where I was, and I could not take my eyes off that round hole. At first I felt that the movement I thought I noticed came from the shadow of my eyelashes, for my eyelids were fluttering. Then I saw it quite clearly, without any doubt: something was moving in the hole, very deep beneath the sand; and then the walls of the pit, too, began to undulate.

At that moment I believe I executed a very strange and, in relation to my strength, supernatural leap, for my foothold was finally giving way and I felt myself slipping with the sand toward the grave-dark hole.

On no account did I climb; I made a half-vault backward, for the next moment I found myself behind the earthwork, looking at the panicles of a tussock of grass, which moved lightly at the level of my eyes. I turned my head so that I now saw nothing but sand: dim quartz granules, deep red grains of granite, crushed snail shells. The clouds had dispersed; the sun shone on the shadowless sand. I felt as if I had never looked at anything so closely, because the gold of a particular vein of mica shone into my pupil, red as the embers of a fire.

I had thrown myself on the sand through the sheer weakness of fear, for I had been able to glimpse how some kind of point, a claw covered in fur or prickles, or perhaps a tooth, had flitted past the edge of the hole, but had immediately disappeared back into the darkness.

Later I got up and my feet took me back, but I do not remember the road; and it is of no importance. I have not yet met Longhorn, and I have no intention of telling him what happened today.

At this moment I could be hollow, as empty as the ants from which ant-lion grubs suck the innards and vital fluids. In writing this, I am a little ashamed, as if I wanted to disturb you by telling you this; but it is true, after all.

I examine my nails and the skin on the backs of my hands closely, knowing that they could be among the fragile and dry skins that are thrown over the ridge of the earthworks and which crumble to dust and disappear among the sand.

But the wind! It rises and distributes both dust and sand over the towers of Tainaron, and the dunes shift once more some distance toward the interior. From a high hillock a grating sound is heard, and I see the Ferris wheel spinning in the wind, but guess that its cogwheels, too, are now grinding sand from the shore. When I think about the buzzing, the sea of air that undulates around the antennae and the towers and which sets the papers in the gutter dancing, I am no longer at all afraid. Its reinvigorating breath passes through personal happiness and unhappiness, and they are no more than a couple of steps in the great dance.

But have I not just returned from a beach where I have no memory of water? Was it really the case that I did not even glance northward, across the expanse of Oceanos, but that the waves and details of the sand swallowed all my attention, just as they will one day cover the city of Tainaron? The skuas must have shrieked then, too, and the waves roared, but I, absentminded, saw nothing but the sand and the claw....

White Noise

THE FIFTEENTH LETTER

Sometimes, when I find myself in the street's densest throng, I am surrounded by such a confusion of voices that I feel like covering my ears with my hands. Someone croaks; someone else drums; from a third passer-by come snapping sounds that combine to make a kind of monotonous music. And what about the strange bellowing or shrill cries that from time to time pierce the spaces between the houses and rebound from one wall to the other? I understand them as little as I understand the screaming of birds, the silence of fish.

The state of confusion in which I often move in this city makes me remember and long for something. I remember the radio, whose place was on a low rosewood shelf in the bay window. I often sat on the floor in front of the radio for quite long times and listened.

But that happened only when I was able to be alone in the room. When the other children came to listen to the radio, I found other things to do, for I did not care for storytime, or for quizzes or sports commentaries. Why, then, did I dawdle, turning the knobs of the radio for so long that my mother often lost her temper and told me to stop?

Beside the radio there grew, in a large earthenware pot, a crown of thorns, and as I listened I liked to finger its sturdy prickles; they were shiny and amazingly sharp, as hard as bone.

'That's nothing but noise,' said my older brother, stepping into the room. 'Let me try.'

And he bent over the receiver and adjusted the vertical pointer to a station that broadcast music or sports commentaries or news.

'Is this what you wanted to listen to?' my brother asked, and out of politeness toward my brother, or rather in order to be left in peace the more quickly, I answered: 'Yes, this is it.'

But as soon as my brother had gone, I turned back to the dimly glowing pointer board and ran the red line through all the cities of Europe. I heard them murmur and sing, but their invitation did not move me. Although I did not understand their distant languages, I knew that they said the same things as in our own language, and at that time I doubted whether that could be used to say anything really important.

For precisely that reason, I did not pause at any of the big cities, but adjusted the pointer to the empty space between the radio stations, where no one was sending anything. To these regions, which were as deserted and roadless as the spaces between stars, I returned again and again. As I wandered through their integrity, I felt the happiness of an explorer, and I was bewitched by the ceaseless humming that rose like vapour from their nameless seas. It was secreted from the receiver as a radiation of the same strength, almost unchanging in wavelength, which brought to mind honey and the homes of thousands of bumblebees. It swayed before me like a curtain, like dancing dust; it was ceaseless happening, but nothing changed in it.

So I wandered through the forest, peaceful and alone. The language I listened to was so full of meaning that once I even felt my intestines pausing in their work in order to understand better. If I had been asked then, 'But what does it mean?', I should not have replied. For I could not have said anything but: 'It means everything,' and even to my own ears such an answer would have seemed senseless.

But that was precisely how it was. The roar that lured me was the chimera of all languages and all voices.

Once I heard the same storm rising elsewhere. I had a fever, and I was standing in line in the school playground. Faintness made me black out and dizziness thrust me to the ground. But I did not feel myself hit the gravel, for in my eyes and my blood there rose, roaring, such a plenitude and suction of voices that I dived into it headfirst as if into the sea, and there, too, 'everything' lived.

But from time to time as I listened to the noise of the radio, I could distinguish individual voices and call them to me. I did not always succeed, but sometimes all I needed to do was listen, and a whisper or a note would detach itself from the density of the cloud of voices and float in the foreground. But nothing I heard was unambiguous, so that often I wanted to tear the roaring aside as if it were a stage-curtain. But that, of course, was impossible: the voices were born and lived only in the fog, and if it lifted, 'everything' disappeared immediately into a deathly silence.

But one day I could hear the seagulls shrieking above the reef, and on another the trains dashed forward. It happened very far away, and I admit I was a little afraid.

Everything floated and changed; something was always happening. I could exert only the tiniest influence on what was born and died behind the calm fabric that covered the radio loudspeaker. Some events were terrible: cities destroyed by earthquakes, assassinations, collapsing stars. One eruption sparked another, the echo of ceaseless explosions never seemed to weaken. It was as if one were hearing, from afar, the birth of matter itself.

Then my fingers reached out once more for the spine of the cactus and tightly pressed its sharpest point, in extent warmer than a nail, living, steady.

Once I remembered, in front of the receiver, that I had a heart: that whatever I did, that heart beat and beat, ceaselessly. And as if in answer, through the tempest, I heard the beats of another heart, dull, even and self-assured. Then I found myself looking at the fabric that hid the loudspeaker behind it, but it did not sigh like my own chest; it did not even quiver.

Or I remembered the name I had once been given, and at the same time I was called by that name, but from a place so far off that I could never have reached there, even if I had set off immediately.

And when the dishes clattered in the kitchen, I was already sitting at table like the others.

The Mimic

THE SIXTEENTH LETTER

In Tainaron I have a balcony where I sometimes sit and bask when the sun shines and I have no reason to go into the city. For you it is autumn, but for us it is still high summer.

Yesterday the dazzle closed my eyelids and set fiery landsca pes rolling beneath them. There was a book on my lap, but I did not turn its pages. Here in the courtyard grows a great tree whose name I do not know, and the blaze of the sun was extinguished only when it was snared by the branches.

Look! At that moment I saw below me a group of stones. They were largish cobblestones, grey ones, dappled and reddish ones, granite or possibly gneiss. The centre of the courtyard was paved with them, and they were beautiful stones; but that was not why I was looking at them. It seemed to me that new stones had been brought to the courtyard and that some kind of a hillock had been built, which had certainly not been there before.

Just as this little riddle was beginning to trouble me, Longhorn stepped on to my balcony.

'Look under the tree,' I said to him. 'Do you understand why a hill like that has been built there?'

He looked, and began to smile – if the slow withdrawal of his jaws to the side of his face can be called a smile – I never get used to it.

'Perhaps you find it amusing,' I said, a little irritated, 'that all sorts of obstacles are built on the thoroughfares; I myself can see no sense in it.'

When I glanced at the pile of stones again, I was downhearted, for I thought it began to look like a small grave.

'Do not worry,' said Longhorn reassuringly, resting his light forelimb on my shoulder. 'I see you do not yet know the Mimic. If you wish, I will introduce him to you.'

'Who is he?' I asked, and my mood was cheerless, even though the day was bright and autumn was still far off.

'It is him you are looking at,' Longhorn said amiably.

I did not blink, but nevertheless something happened in my eyes, for now I could see that what was in the courtyard in the shade of the tree was no pile of stones but a living creature, motionless, whose back was covered in a reddish-grey, lumpy carapace.

I wanted to ask something, but Longhorn made a gesture with his hand. He has, you see, a habit of moving wonderfully gracefully and elegantly, and his movement silenced me indisputably.

'Now look,' he ordered, and there was no longer anything or anyone in the shade of the tree. But a round knoll had appeared on the strip of lawn beside the wall, and it, too, was as green as new grass.

'Is it...?' I began.

'Yes, he is quick,' Longhorn acceded.

'I do not understand,' I complained. 'Is he someone, then? Who is he?'

'My dear,' Longhorn said, and looked at me, waving the extensions of his antennae, 'do you believe that the Mimic could have a personality? Today he is one thing, tomorrow another. Wherever he is, that is what he is – stone a moment ago, now the summer's grass. Who knows what form he will take tomorrow. But come, let us go; I shall introduce you to one another.'

'No,' I said, feeling an obscure rage. 'I do not wish to. I have no intention of making the acquaintance of such a person. It certainly takes all sorts...'

'Really,' said Longhorn, without showing any kind of sympathy, in fact teasingly. 'So you want everyone to be someone. You want what someone is at the beginning to be what he is at the end.'

'But surely! There has to be some kind of continuity!' I shouted. 'Development, naturally, but at the same time – loyalty!'

I attempted to continue, but I could already feel my irritation slipping away into the summer day that embraced Tainaron from all directions. Soon I was feeling the desire to protect the unknown creature.

'In a sense I understand him,' I said with some considerable forebearance. 'He is seeking his own form.'

'Is that so?' said Longhorn, and we both leaned over the rail and looked downward. There was no longer any kind of hummock in the courtyard, but beside the large tree stood another tree, but much smaller and sturdier.

'Does he know we are here?' I asked. 'Does he do it for us, or for his own amusement?'

'It is his work,' said Longhorn, but I do not know if he was serious.

'Why are you laughing?' asked Longhorn in turn.

'How I love this city!' I said. 'Perhaps I shall stay here for ever.' (What on earth made me say it?)

'Yes, stay here forever,' Longhorn said, but his voice darkened to such a depth that I forgot the Mimic and turned toward him in astonishment.

The Great Window

THE SEVENTEENTH LETTER

It was evening once, and I was a child, out in the street. All the lights were on, street lamps, shop windows, car headlights; and I was standing in front of a toy shop. You know the shop; it is still there, in the centre of town, and you must have passed it many times, or perhaps you have even been inside it in the days before Christmas.

That window! It was lit with prodigal brightness, and along the glass flowed glistening drops; a rainstorm had just passed over the city and everything was clean, never before seen. In front of the dolls, cars, balls and games, immediately behind the glass, a large selection of marbles had been set out in the shape of the petals of a flower. Some of them were transparent, others brightly coloured, others as white as milk.

I had never owned any marbles, and their glow captivated me; I admired them for a long time, but all of a sudden, from far away and without warning, the terrible knowledge slid between them and me – that one day my mother would die.

When this pain hit me, I was looking at a particularly beautiful shimmering blue marble, and something happened: it changed. Its colour did not vary, its size was the same as before, and it remained steady in its place; but all the same it was quite different from before. Something had fallen away from it, something which only a moment ago had made it desirable, the most important thing of all. The marble was no longer of value; it was merely junk, and there was no longer anything in the entire shop window to interest me. It was as if stage spotlights had been extinguished in the middle of a performance and a curtain had been drawn from earth to heavens in front of all the magnificence, a curtain whose name was VOID.

Even the street in which I stood was now a strange street in a strange city; but I went on standing in the same place. A vague desire for knowledge forced me to make an experiment. I wanted to see whether I could make the marble change back to what it was before. Gazing at it unwaveringly, I began to struggle to disperse the thickness of night which, unseen, dominated everything I looked at.

I did not believe the darkness, I said, it is not true; and soon it was indeed not true; it paled and lifted like a night-mist. And the marble glowed before me, lovely as ever.

But then I understood that the plenty of the shop window, all the jewels of its treasure trove, were only a tiny foretaste of what life would bring me with both hands – no, a hundred hands! a thousand!

And I have never left that shop window. I stand and stand, I look and look at how it shines, and goes dark, and shines again. There is night and there is day, and I see both hell and heaven through the same window.

The Work of the Surveyor

THE EIGHTEENTH LETTER

Today I have looked through my window at the work of the City Surveyor. I have already watched him in another part of the city, fulfilling his professional responsibilities, and now, this morning, he has reached our street. He measures the lengths and widths of streets, the diameters of squares and the heights of buildings. I do not know why he measures them, but I suppose the information he produces is stored in an archive somewhere and that interested parties can consult them there.

His territory is rather large and he is very hardworking, but he has only one measuring device: his own body. It is a long, green body, and he uses it extremely skilfully; I have previously had the opportunity to admire such agility only in the performances of acrobats. Sometimes his body forms a large loop; the next moment it has stretched out again to a long, straight stretch and he has covered quite a distance along the street. He also has no trouble in climbing vertical brick walls, right up to the eaves, and he does not seem to suffer from vertigo of any kind.

As I came from the shop and took a short cut through the park, I saw the Surveyor eating his lunch on a bench. On his head was the white cap worn by city officials, decorated with spiral patterns. I asked if I might sit with him for a moment, and he willingly made space.

'Would you like some?' he asked, opening his lunch box. But I had already eaten, and refused, with thanks. There was something I wished to ask him.

'Do you find your work interesting?' I asked, for something to say.

'Extremely,' he replied, munching his sandwich. Behind us, in the playground, the children of Tainaron, screaming, were playing the games played by all the children in the world: running away, being had, and then exchanging prisoner for persecutor.

'Have you been doing it for long?'

'Ever since I reached my full height,' the Surveyor replied, pouring a steaming, sweet-smelling drink from his thermos flask into his cup.

Bells rang out from the cathedral, the children left the playground and disappeared into the shade of the trees. It was already almost noon, and the siesta was beginning. I could not see any movement anywhere, and heard only the booming of the bells. It felt as if life were standing still, resting and reviving like the Surveyor.

Through the incessant ringing, I heard his even voice: 'My father did the same work, and his father and his grandfather and his grandfather's father. A new City Surveyor is chosen from each generation; now it is I.'

And he added something which I did not hear, for the power of the bells swelled to numb the ears.

I bent over toward him and his flat face neared my mouth. Now I could hear what he said:

'I am the measure of all things.'

But he did not say it haughtily, merely stated it, brushing the crumbs from his chest.

'But this part of the city is old,' I thought aloud. 'Was it not surveyed many generations ago? What could there be to measure here?'

He looked at me in disbelief. 'What is there to measure?' he asked. 'It was a different time then. A different time, and different measuring devices. I and my grandfather are not at all the same size, as you may have thought.'

He took a large piece of fruit from his bag, sinking his many rows of healthy teeth into it. I no longer knew what to say, and felt a fool.

When the Surveyor had sucked the stem clean and dropped it into a rubbish bin decorated with the city arms, he rose decisively and felt it his duty to remark: 'Back to work!'

He, the measure of all things, hurried energetically to fulfil the demands of his job, growing smaller and smaller on the park path, and a straight, clear furrow was left in its raked sand. He went as official representatives of the people go, or as those who know that everything has its measure, and more – what and who he himself is.

And, following the Surveyor's example, time too moved on; a dry leaf fell before me on to the dust and it was the first leaf of autumn. The season had changed.

The bells had stopped echoing, but the city radiated its own sound, like a busy bumble-bee. The brightly coloured Ferris wheel of the Tainaron funfair, which was motionless for a moment at midday, started to spin once more. I saw it from the bench on which I was sitting, alone; it can be seen down in the harbour and in all the squares and markets, so high has it been set up, in the constant wind.

The Bystander

THE NINETEENTH LETTER

This morning as I woke up, in bed, I was overcome by a prurient restlessness whose reasons I could not immediately divine. For a long time I sat on my bed and listened. Although it was already late in the morning, the city was silent, as if not a single citizen had yet woken up, although it was a weekday and an ordinary working week.

I dressed myself in yesterday's clothes and, without eating my breakfast, went down to the street, seeking Longhorn's company.

But before I could open the front door a surprising sight opened up through the round window of the stairwell: the pavement in front of the building was full of backs, side by side, broad and narrow, long and sturdy; but all were united by stillness, the same direction and position.

All at once I thought of a picture which I had once seen, perhaps in a book, perhaps in a museum; I cannot remember. Perhaps you too have seen it? The crowd in the picture had a common object of interest, which was not visible; it was outside the edge of the picture, perhaps in reality too. But more than the invisible event and its observers, my attention was drawn to a man in the background of the picture who was looking in the opposite direction to all the others. Do you remember him too?

When I then stepped out on to the outside step – and I can tell you that I did it hesitantly, almost unwillingly – I can confirm that a fair number of people were standing in front of the opposite block, too, but that there too silence prevailed. I do not think I have yet mentioned that the boulevard on which I now live runs from east to west. When, this morning, I eyed it from my front door, it looked as if the entire city had gathered along this long, wide street and had been standing there silently – that was my impression – perhaps from the middle of the night onward. The din that, with such numbers of people, generally rises like puffs of smoke, is impressive, but the rage or joy of the crowd could not have dumbfounded me as completely as its silence.

Since autumn is already approaching here, the sun was hanging, at this time in the morning, fairly low at the eastern end of the street, but as far as I could see every single citizen was staring in the opposite direction, at the point in the distance where the boulevard shrinks to a small yellow flower: where the linden trees stand in their autumn glory.

The street was empty. I have often examined its surface, skilfully patterned in stone, but now, as it spread, deserted, before me, when not a single walker was crossing it and no vehicle was rolling along it, I hardly noticed its unique beauty. In the pure dawn of the new day the tramway rails sparkled as if they were made of silver.

Then it occurred to me that perhaps some national day was being celebrated in the city, and that the boulevard was closed to traffic for a great festival parade. It might be that we should soon see the prince himself – if he is still alive – driving past us, perhaps acknowledging us with a slender hand… Or were we expecting a state visit to the city? Would a procession of closed carriages glide past us, taking noble guests to a luncheon reception at the city hall?

But I was soon forced to abandon such thoughts. For nothing about the appearance of the Tainaronians suggested great festivities. There were no bunches of flowers, no balloons or masks. Not a single child was blowing the kind of whistle which, whining shrilly, unwinds from a roll to a long staff, and no one was flying a miniature Tainaron flag, a white pennant printed with a spiral (or perhaps a nautilus; I have never been quite sure which).

Yes, they went on standing silently, and the eastern sun infused the strong heat of copper into their back-armour.

Despite the disapproving glances which were cast at me, I pushed right through to the front row and found myself balancing on a narrow kerbstone of the pavement.

Beside me stood a gleaming black shape that reminded me of a diver. I knocked echoingly on his polished surface and said: 'Excuse me, but please would you tell me what day today is?'

He glanced at me, disturbed, and after making the rapid and sullen reply, 'The nineteenth,' he turned back at once toward the west.

I was none the wiser, but I had only myself to blame – the timing and phrasing of my question had been badly chosen.

Then, my dear, there was a sudden gust of wind, and the Tainaronians suddenly began to crowd around me, so that I had to stand with one foot in the gutter. That did not matter, since I had managed to secure a lookout spot for myself. For something was now happening at the point where the boulevard dived into a dusky tunnel under the linden trees. From that direction, some kind of procession was approaching, something very long and pale; but however much I screwed up my eyes I could not make out any details.

It progressed slowly, and our moments stretched with it, but inch by inch it approached our building; and the better I could make it out, the more astonished I was.

What a parade it was! I could see no glittering carriages or brass bands. Quite the reverse: as it approached, the silence deepened still further, for on the broad boulevard of Tainaron silence combined with silence; the silence of the procession merged with the stillness of the crowd. No flags or streamers, no songs, shots or slogans. But neither did this procession have any of the solemn brilliance of a funeral cortège; not a single flower or wreath gave it colour, and there were no candle flames to flutter and smoke.

When the head of the endlessly long ribbon, which took up almost the entire width of the street, reached us, new battalions rolled forth far away from under the trees. Battalions, I call them, but even today I still do not know whether these were in any sense military. I shall now try to describe to you what I saw before me this morning.

The procession was so uniform that it recalled a snake, but in fact it was made up of countless individuals. Its speed was leisurely, so that I had plenty of time to examine the beginning, which broadened like a reptile's head and which – apparently like the entire procession – was covered by a transparent, slightly shiny membrane, like an elastic cellophane bag. Inside this membrane, in rows and fronts, marched small creatures; as far as I could see from where I stood they were like grubs, almost colourless and about as thick as my middle finger, but a little longer. I shuddered slightly as I watched them as one shivers when one comes inside from the cold.

The procession was made up of two or even three layers: those below carried the surface layer, which moved more slowly than the lower layer along a living carpet. I think what happened was that when those on top reached the head of the procession, they joined the bottom layer and, in turn, carried the others. It was impossible to estimate the number of members of the procession, but I should imagine that it was a question of millions rather than hundreds of thousands of individuals.

As I gazed at the torrent that surged before me, I remembered that a few nights previously I had dreamed a dream in which this same street had become a river. Now I was, of course, tempted to see it as a prophetic dream, although I do not habitually do that.

I tell you, I would like to understand the nature of the silence with which the city greeted the march-past of this mass. Was it respect? fear? menace? Now, when I remember our morning, I am inclined to think that it included all those emotions, plus something else, which I shall never understand, for I am in the end a stranger here.

I – like the others who stood around me – saw at the same time that a small figure had appeared in the middle of the roadway, some kind of weevil, which stared dispiritedly at the approaching flattish serpent's head. There was nothing that was open to interpretation about its motionlessness: it was pure terror and catalepsy. The great head, which glistened unctuously in the sun, by now shining from high above, and which was made up – as I have already said – of hundreds of smaller heads, drew ineluctably nearer to the point on the cobblestones where the poor creature stood. At that petrified moment it did not even occur to me that I could have dashed into the roadway and dragged the creature to safety. For my part, I was convinced that the weevil would become food for that living rope; or, if not, that it would at least be an unwilling part of that strange procession.

But what happened was this: when the slowly undulating river reached the creature – which looked as if it was benumbed into a hypnosis-like state – its head split in two and left a space for the weevil without even brushing its unbudging form.

There was a sigh – it was unanimous – and the front part of the snake merged once more, but in the middle of the broad flow the little creature stood like an island, while the masses that seethed around it flowed, glistening, onward.

I do not know whether you will find this description strange. Have you ever, on your travels, encountered anything comparable? You have told me so little about the time when we did not yet know each other…

For my part, I am still bewildered by my morning experience. I do not know how long I stood on the spot, one foot on the pavement, the other in the gutter, as new battalions, divisions, regiments, rolled past us. I should like to say, too, that (with the exception of the case of the weevil) nothing about the procession suggested that anyone in it might have seen or noticed us, that we, the citizens of Tainaron (I am, after all, in a sense one of them) existed in any way for them, let alone that this great march was organised with us in mind.

If you were to ask, I would answer that I do not know. No, I really have not been able to find out what it was and why it went through Tainaron, where it came from and whether it had a destination. It could be that it was searching for something; it could be that it was fleeing something. If the others know something, if you receive any information about this matter, then tell me; do not hide anything!

When the tail of the procession, so thin that its tip was formed of just a few individuals – and they themselves were unusually slender and transparent – had finally slipped out of sight beyond the square where the boulevard terminates to the east, the crowds dispersed incredibly quickly. I looked around me and stood there, alone on the kerbstone, and the sun was at its highest. Everything bustled around me as before; the shops opened again and vehicles rolled both eastward and westward. Some dashed to banks and offices and secret assignations and others to meetings or to prepare the day's dinner. But in the middle of the street – as far as the eye could see, in either direction – ran a moist, slimy trail.

This afternoon, when I walked across the boulevard, I could no longer see it. It had dried up and was covered in the same sand and dust that dances before winter in each of the streets of Tainaron.

King Milinda's Question

THE TWENTIETH LETTER

My immediate neighbour, on the same floor, is an extraordinarily old person; much older than the prince. Some people claim he is already over one hundred and fifty years old, while others, like Longhorn, say that he is only one hundred and twenty-five or one hundred and thirty. But everyone who sees his frailty understands that he has lived past his own time, and it is incomprehensible and even cruel that he must continue living here in the city of Tainaron.

He has a servant – or perhaps he is one of his descendants – who takes him out every morning. He is dry and light and has shrunk so small that he is carried in a kind of bag or sack. The bag is set in the sun on a park bench and its sides are turned down a little so that the old man can take the air and look at the flowers and the passers-by. There he is left, and after a couple of hours he is taken home again. In his bag he looks, with his thin limbs, like nothing but a bunch of straw, as dry as kindling.

Do you think there is a place where people do not grow old? I wonder if I ever met an inhabitant of such a country when I was quite young? And will he met me again when my age is as great as that of the old man in the sack?

What a shock he will get. 'My dear friend,' he will stammer. 'What dreadful thing has happened? Who has treated you so badly? Where is your thick hair? Why do you walk so slowly and with such a stoop? Tell me who is to blame, and I shall make him answer for his deeds.'

Childish, ignorant person! Let him go back to where he came from!

I have seen a vision that came from the sack. It looked just as if there were a mirror in it. And the straw rose to give a sign; it beckoned to me. And so of course I went, I went and sat down next to the sack, which was very humble considering that one hundred and fifty years fitted inside.

The sack's voice was so weak and hoarse that I could not immediately understand it. The sack asked where I was from, and said that it had not been born in Tainaron either. And I had only sat there for a moment when I realised that the bag contained someone alive and remembering. And when I had sat there for another moment, I knew that he was not old. Old age was merely his disguise, as childhood had once been. I knew it as I once knew that a certain very small creature was right when she shrieked: 'I am not a child! I am not a child!' I knew it because I had not been a child myself, either; I knew it because I shall never be old. I knew it because I had heard King Milinda's question: 'Was he who was born the same as he who died?' and heard the answer, which was not yes or no.

And now the park's trees waved the shadows of their fluttering over my years and over the years of my companion, leaves that were still fastened to their branches, but were already yellow and would soon be dead, detached, absent.

I asked what had been most difficult in life, and the bag answered: 'The fact that everything recurs and must always return and that the same questions are asked again and again.'

But before I could ask more of the same questions, the servant or descendant approached us with purposeful strides. Lightly he lifted his burden – its years were feathers to him – and, grinding the gravel under his feet, took him back home.

I had got hot and, forgetting the old man in a moment, strolled slowly toward the harbour. There I saw the same white ship that once brought me to Tainaron; but why, I cannot remember.

Not Enough

THE TWENTY-FIRST LETTER

How are you? How are things with you? That you are so implacable in your silence makes you gradually become more like gods or the dead. Such is your metamorphosis; and it is not entirely repugnant to me.

For let me tell you what has happened to me. What has happened to me is that people are no longer enough. They are not enough, be they ever so great or beautiful or wise or complicated.

They are not enough, even if their antennae were to stretch further than radar beams and their clothes were to be stronger than armour.

For that reason I confess that everything I say

contains the unspoken hope that it is linked with all my actions as well as to the moments when I just sit and look. Ardent hope! Incorrigible hope! That gods and the dead might hear. That gods and the dead might see. That gods and the dead might know...

But there is only one who can make them hear their song. But he was one who became truly unhappy and was torn to pieces.

Last night I returned to you after long years, from such a distance and over many obstacles. Barricades and brushwood fences, barbed wire obstacles and piles of stones rose up in my path. Craters, chasms and stinking trenches opened up before my feet. But my speed was so dizzying that I flew over peaks and depths and sped along the bright, frozen channel that led straight to your door.

The bell rings through the house, through the darkness of the winter's day, and you open the door, the same as before. How happy we are! How we embrace each other!

But at once I notice how absent-minded you are. You are expecting something completely different; yes, I am right: you listen over my head, which is pressed against your chest. And now I, too, hear footsteps approaching below in the stairwell.

Then the light of a living flame spreads across your face as you ask: 'Are they coming here? Are they close? Are they not familiar footsteps?'

But I do not reply, and you would not hear what I said. Your arms have already loosened around me, and I have returned on the same road along which, just now, I sped toward you, trembling with anticipation.

Dayma

THE TWENTY-SECOND LETTER

Yesterday I wished to try, for my morning drink, the Tainaronians' favourite sweet, foaming dayma or daime, which is drunk through a straw. They like it so much that they drink it at every possible opportunity, cold or hot, and in addition to dayma they have dozens of other names for it. I have heard it said that in large quantities it has curious effects and that some may see strange and even improper things after drinking it.

For my part, I did not notice any such effects. But everything I see here is strange, even without drinking a drop of dayma.

I remembered a particularly pleasant little cake shop on the side of a canal where Longhorn took me soon after I arrived in Tainaron for the first time. I also wanted to try those particularly crisp herb pastries, as light as wafers, which smell of smoke and which I believe are not made anywhere else but in that bakery. My desire was so strong that my mouth watered and I had to swallow when the memory of the little pastries spread on to my tongue.

To my disappointment, I could no longer find the cross-street of the ring boulevard on which the café was located. I thought I was following the correct route; I turned at the same street corner as before, and carried on along the side of the canal, but soon I found myself in quite unknown quarters. There were unfinished buildings and enormous industrial shells from which the sound of turbines and the fumes of combustion engines rose into the air. The people there also looked completely different, poorer and smaller than the Tainaronians who had sat on the terrace of my favourite café. At last I found a glum coffee bar where badly foamed dayma was served in thick handleless cups and where the bread was dense and heavy.

'I should like to have a map of Tainaron,' I said yesterday to Longhorn. 'It would be much easier to wander here alone, and you would not always have the bother of being my guide. I could not find a single map in the department store. Could you perhaps find a map somewhere? Would it be possible?'

'Unfortunately it is impossible,' he answered.

'Why impossible? Have all the maps sold out?'

'That is not why,' he said. 'No comprehensive map of Tainaron has ever been made.'

'What? No proper map has been made? But that is very strange,' I said, dissatisfied and astonished.

'It is not at all strange,' Longhorn said abruptly. 'It would be sheer impossibility to draw up such a map, a completely senseless project.'

'Why so?' I asked, increasingly irritated. 'To me a kingdom which has no map is not a real kingdom but barbary, chaos, mere confusion.'

'You still know very little about Tainaron,' he said quietly. 'We too have our laws, but they are different from yours.'

I felt a little abashed, but that did not wipe away all my irritability.

'A map cannot be made,' he continued, 'because Tainaron is constantly changing.'

'All cities change,' I said.

'None as fast as Tainaron,' Longhorn replied. 'For what Tainaron was yesterday it is no longer today. No one can have a grasp of Tainaron as a whole. Every map would lead its user astray.'

'All cities must have maps, at least of some kind,' I continued to argue.

Longhorn sighed and looked at me kindly, but a little wearily.

'Come!' he said, and took me gently by the arm. 'Let's go!'

'Where to?' I asked.

'We are going to the observation tower,' Longhorn said. 'To make you understand.'

The observation tower was built on the same hill as the funfair. I had not noticed it until now, for the movement of the Ferris wheel had taken up all my attention. We had to climb for an agonisingly long time up the narrow wooden stairs which circled the outer wall of the tower like a creeper. I do not like such high places, and I felt as if the wind were rocking the frail construction. We climbed and climbed. As we circled the steps, the Ferris wheel, too, kept returning before my eyes; its carriages, now empty, shook and swayed, and its movement made my dizzy. We climbed, and I regretted that I had taken up Longhorn's offer.

Midway, I said to Longhorn: 'Now I cannot climb any farther. Let us stay here. We can see enough from here.'

But Longhorn's ears were deaf, and he continued his astonishingly agile clambering. At times he seemed to glide upward – but of course he did have more pairs of legs than I. He did not even glance behind him, and I had to follow him. I went on climbing.

At last! We were standing on the upper platform, but I had grown dizzy and did not immediately go right up to the rail. My eyes were sore from the wind and sunshine which, up here, seemed blindingly bright. I tried to breathe slowly; I swallowed and fastened my eyes on the fibres of the platform's planks. I had decided that I would not complain any more; for I suspected that Longhorn now considered me spoilt and bad company and by no means did I wish him to tire of acting as my guide.

But I could not help hoping that Longhorn would put one of his narrow, long upper limbs around my shoulders. He appeared not to have noticed my uncertain state, but was gazing absorbedly and – so it seemed to me – with eyes moist with pride the panorama that opened up before us. He began to hum a wordless song which I had never heard before, and its monotonous melody and the peaceful wave-forms of the timber fibres restored my balance.

I gathered my courage and looked downwards. We had been climbing for a long time, but I was still astonished that we were so excessively high up. I shaded my eyes and saw, in the dizzying depths, the plain of Tainaron, patterned with the shadows of frantically scurrying clouds. I also realised that the tower must be a little skew, for the horizon was clearly slanted. Directly below us was the little funfair, today deserted, with its gaudily coloured tents. Even the highest carriages of the Ferris wheel were far below us. Far away glass and steel glittered, bronze and gold glimmered, when a shimmering ray lit up the windows of a skyscraper or the cupolas of churches. This was Tainaron, his city, theirs – never mine.

But it was an astonishing city! Longhorn's pride was understandable. I had never understood how enormous Tainaron was. I saw the cone-like areas which I had once visited, only to be dampened by the queen's tears, I saw the prince's palace park with its paths and pagodas, and in the east the endless, muddled skeins of the slums.

We were so high up that from below all that could be heard was the occasional shriek, isolated, a shriller cry than the rest, and mysterious clinking sounds which I had also heard at night and whose origin I had never been able to trace. It sounded as if someone were tapping a glass with a silver spoon in order to make a speech. A little farther up, and everything would have been completely silent.

'Here is everything I have,' Longhorn said. 'You, too.'

The shining belt of Oceanos with its stripes of foam encircled us on all sides. A haze hid the horizon to the south, but to the north a high, silver-glowing cloud formation was visible, so motionless, in contrast to the clouds that slipped over Tainaron, that it looked like a metal sculpture. Its shape was like that of a human torso.

'Is there a storm brewing?' I asked.

'It is not a storm,' he said. 'Worse. It is winter. Although it will be a long time before it reaches us. But when it is here, I pity those who have not already gone to sleep!'

I already felt cold now, in full sunlight. We looked in silence at the majestic shape of snow and ice. To me it still did not look as if it were changing shape or approaching Tainaron.

'Perhaps it will not come this time, after all,' I said to Longhorn, half in earnest, and hopeful. 'Perhaps it will stay up there in the north.'

'What a child it is,' Longhorn said in an aside, as if there had been a third person with us on the platform. Then he continued, turning to me once more: 'I did not bring you here only to look at the coming of winter. Do you see?'

Longhorn gestured toward the northern edge of the city, below the winter, where there swelled a cluster of dwellings of different heights and shapes. It must have been because of my sore eyes that their outlines looked so indefinite. As we looked, it seemed strangely as if some of them were in motion.

'What is happening there?' I asked.

'Changes,' he said.

That was indeed how it looked. Clouds of dust spread on the plain – and in a moment all that could be seen where the crenellations of towers and blocks had meandered were mere ruins. But there had been no sound of any explosion.

'That part of the city no longer exists,' he said calmly.

'Not an earthquake, surely?' I asked fearfully, although I could not yet feel any tremors.

'No, they are merely demolishing the former Tainaron,' Longhorn said.

Longhorn raised his finger and pointed westward. And there, too, I saw demolition work, destruction, collapse, landslides. But almost at the same time, in place of the former constructions, new forms began to appear, softly curving mall complexes, flights of stairs that still ended in air, solitary spiral towers and colonnades which progressed meanderingly toward the empty shore.

'But...' I began.

'Shh,' Longhorn said. 'Look over there.'

I looked. There, where a straight boulevard had run a moment ago, narrow paths now wandered. Their network branched over a larger and larger area before my very eyes.

'And this goes on all the time, incessantly,' he said. 'Tainaron is not a place, as you perhaps think. It is an event which no one measures. It is no use anyone trying to make maps. It would be a waste of time and effort. Do you understand now?'

I could not deny that I understood that Tainaron lived in the same way as many of its inhabitants; it too was a creature that was shaped by irresistible forces. Now I also understood that I should never again taste those smoke-scented wafers which I had wanted so much this morning. And yet I understood very little.

'I am thirsty,' I said to Longhorn, longing once more for the foam of dayma.

The Dangler

THE TWENTY-THIRD LETTER

I really must say that many of the inhabitants of Tainaron have the most extraordinary habits, at least to the eyes of one who has come from so far away. Quite close to here, in the same block, lives a gentleman, tall and thin, who is in the habit of hanging upside-down from his balcony for a number of hours every day. This strange position does not seem to interest passers-by in the least, but when I passed under him for the first time I was so startled that I immediately thought of running for help. I thought, you see, that there had been an accident and that the man was clinging to the wrought-iron decorations of the balcony with his feet. Longhorn, who was beside me, remarked coolly that he had selected his pose through his own free choice and that I would be wise not to interfere so eagerly in other people's lives. I admit that I was offended by his remark, but recently I have begun meekly to take his advice.

I see the man most days, and whenever I walk under his balcony I greet him, even though he never responds. In fact, I think he is either asleep or meditating. In his chosen state he is so limp and floating that he recalls a garment that a washerwoman has hung out to dry. With incomparable calm he suspends his head above the busy street without stirring, even when the fire brigade drives under him, sirens wailing. He always looks the same: a bright, even gaudy, green, so that one can make him out from the broad steps of the bank at the end of the state like a living leaf against a red brick wall...

Does he dream as he hangs there, sometimes suspended from just one limb, but nevertheless apparently completely relaxed? I believe that is exactly how it is. I know from my own experience the difference between the immobility of fear and the immobility of the hunter, but this is neither. I believe he dreams, dreams swiftly, passionately and incessantly, dreams with death-defying intensity without sacrificing even a jot of consciousness to the struggles of everyday waking life. I believe he must long ago have become convinced that all action is unnecessary, or even dangerous.

There are days when I think that this gentleman is admirable and his way of spending moments of his life most enviable. On such days I, too, would like to concentrate on sweet communion with my private visions as headlong and with the same kind of mental calm as he. But do not imagine that it would be possible. In the evenings, even if I shut my window tightly, turn out my lamp and fill my ears with cotton-wool, this city teems before me, still more restless and colourful than in full daylight. Then I should like to get up and got to see whether the green gentleman is still hanging head-first from his balcony. I should like to climb up there myself and position my limbs just like his. Then, with my blood flooding my head, all of Tainaron would begin to dissolve into the mists and I, too, should begin a dream, endless and leaf-green...

But if, in the morning, my nocturnal experiences return to mind, if I have idled through agonising labyrinths, I know that I would not wish to spend my life in the city of dreams. If, on such a morning, I pass under the Dangler's balcony, I am more inclined to pity him than to admire him.

Then I know that in my dreams I can never capture the same sun-glow and that the air that I breathe can never, there, flow as freshly in my cells, and I can never see so sharply or so far; and I believe once more that what is true can be seen by everyone, everyone.

The Guardian of the Oddfellows

THE TWENTY-FOURTH LETTER

I admire her; I call her the Queen Bee. But Longhorn has another name for him, the name of an already forgotten saint: The Guardian of the Oddfellows. And indeed that is the nature of the Queen Bee: she cares tenderly for those whom many here in Tainaron consider strange and to be avoided: street singers, beggars and ladies of joy, people who are cracked in various ways or lost in their own drug-worlds.

All sorts of people visit the Queen Bee, both by day and by night. The light is always on in her house and the door is always swinging – to and fro, for it is a double-hinged door of the kind that one sometimes finds in obscure cafés. There is no threshold or latch, and the hubbub and singing from the Queen Bee's house can be heard distinctly a couple of blocks off.

There is room for everyone, although her house is not large. No, it is very, very medium in size and as modest in its external appearance as countless other houses outskirts of the city.

But sometimes, although the house is full of people, it is very quiet, and then the neighbours say that the Guardian of the Oddfellows is holding a Great Day of Remembrance once again.

'Whose memory are they celebrating?' I asked Longhorn, and it became clear that it was not a question of any particular dead person. The matter is as follows: the Queen Bee gathers memories;

she lives off memories, and it is perhaps only on account of memories that she receives so many people of so many different kinds. But she is not satisfied with any old memory; no, she can use only happy, sweet memories that sparkle with happiness, and if anyone were to try to offer her something cold and gloomy I think she would drive them mercilessly from her house.

Longhorn said that everyone who needs it receives both a meal and a bed for the night at the Queen Bee's house, but on certain days of the month everyone must bring her at least one happy memory in payment. That is the rent she demands, and there is no haggling.

On that day the Queen Bee spreads a white cloth on the table and lights dozens of candles so that it looks as if Christmas has come. But the table is not set, for on the Great Day of Remembrance no food is offered, only memories.

'But they really do satisfy your appetite,' says the Queen Bee, and all her drunks and madmen and beggars agree, as they must in order to be able next day to partake of a proper meal.

'Can I, too, participate in the Great Day of Remembrance some time?' I asked Longhorn.

'Everyone can,' he said, 'but not everyone wants to. And remember to take a really happy memory with you.'

'Oh, I have plenty of them,' I said light-heartedly, and when the next Great Day of Remembrance dawned I was sitting in the Queen Bee's house side by side with her Oddfellows.

I had already heard a few things about my table companions, so I sat a fair distance away from the Pickpocket (as if I had something valuable with me!) and even farther (although I felt ashamed of myself) from a black and spotted creature whom all the people of Tainaron dreaded, and who was called the Disease Carrier. But as I glanced around me, the Queen Bee's Oddfellows did not look to me any stranger than the people of Tainaron in general, and it was my turn to feel embarrassed when I realised what curious and even suspicious glances were being directed at my own person. I, too, was now one of the Oddfellows, perhaps the most obvious of the entire company in my foreignness. I, who have always believed I can merge into almost any crowd, who have always believed I can examine others while myself staying in the background, was now experiencing what it was like to be the object of the Tainaronians' attention.

But the Queen Bee was sitting opposite me and, once I had recovered from the confusion, I could at least gaze at her as much as I liked, her motherly form and her tight, tiger-striped dress, and her tousled, dark face, lit by the hazy glow of her seeing tubes.

'Let us begin!' shouted the Queen Bee in her resonant bass, which brought to mind the buzzing of a sunny meadow. 'Psammotettix, you are the first.'

I turned and saw that with this handsomely reverberant name she was addressing a greying, modest and clumsy-looking gentleman who had, since the beginning of the session, been mumbling incessantly to himself. I suppose he was repeating the memory he had chosen so that he would not forget it at the decisive moment.

With extraordinary speed, Psammotettix began a long story of which I understood scarcely a word, for it was interrupted – perhaps for effect – by a remarkable smacking and croaking noise which, at points of emphasis – so I supposed – became a rough croaking. The few words I could understand, because Psammotettix repeated them a number of times, were 'foam' and 'bubble'; but that was all.

On the other hand, the other participants in the Remembrance Festival followed Psammotettix's performance with interest, and when it was over they showed their approval in an extraordinarily wide range of ways: by clicking the chitin plates of their backs together, drumming, glowing, changing their colour or clapping their limbs together.

The Queen Bee raised a little hammer or club which gleamed gold in the candlelight, knocked it on the table and said: 'Accepted!', at the same time turning toward the Pickpocket, motioning him to start with a gesture of her hand.

'Once I went abroad,' the Pickpocket began hurriedly in a small voice, obviously nervous. The other Oddfellows interrupted him, howling:

'Not true! Not true!'

Then the hammer fell again, the others fell silent, and the Pickpocket began: 'Once in a foreign country, in a big city, my job took me to a certain department store. It was the eve of a great festival, and the people were swarming about, announcements and music flooded from the loudspeakers and the shoppers' attention was taken up with the brilliant displays and the shouts of the product demonstrators. The conditions were perfect, one could say, and for that reason that day was perhaps the most productive of my entire career.'

At this point the Pickpocket paused; grumbling began to be heard around the table and I saw the Queen Bee purse her lips.

'I cannot accept this,' she was beginning, but the Pickpocket shouted hurriedly, 'I have not finished, that is not all. You see, just as the department store was closing and I was already leaving with my swag, a fine lady swept past me with a bag on her shoulder, decorated with pearls. My practised eye noticed immediately that its silver lock only seemed to be closed and in a second I had caught up with the lady. I did this (and he waved a sharp nail in the air), the bag opened soundlessly, and in my own pocket there was – so I thought – a fine wad of the country's currency. But (and the Pickpocket raised a limp, demanding silence, for the guests had begun to babble once more) what did I see when I examined my trophy more closely? The notes were merely thin piles of paper, quite empty all except one. On it was written, on it was written…'

And here the Pickpocket's voice fell and he began to writhe on his chair, looking beseechingly at the Queen Bee.

'Carry on,' she said, nodding approvingly, but this did not seem to calm the Pickpocket.

'No, I can't, not with all these people listening,' he managed to mutter, gesturing at the other guests.

'He has forgotten his memory!' came a shout, and another: 'That's not a happy memory at all!'

'Come here,' ordered the Queen Bee. 'Whisper it in my ear. I shall consider the matter.'

And the Pickpocket went up to the Queen Bee and whispered a couple of words into her ear.

I tried to prick up my ears, but I was far too far away, and I regretted my choice of place, for I desperately wanted to know what could have been written on the paper that could turn the Pickpocket's disappointment into a happy memory.

'Accepted!' acceded the Queen Bee, and to my horror she turned to look at me, and the lenses of her seeing tubes glittered with strange colours.

Then something unexpected happened to me: my past disappeared. It sank among millions of other pasts, so that I could no longer distinguish a single one of my own memories, happy or sad, from among the swarm of countless memories.

It was as if walls and fences had fallen, as if dams – very necessary – had burst, and in the floodwater there floated long-forgotten fragments of conversations that I had happened to overhear, remarks from novels and films and a vortex of human faces and destinies which sped past me like bubbles in a surging wake.

Through it I could, however, see the unwavering face of the Queen Bee, which was still waiting in front of me, majestic and demanding, a trace of dissatisfaction already apparent in her expression. Desperately I grabbed one of the memories that spun around me and, extraordinarily enough, I knew its origin: it was a survey from a weekly magazine whose readers were asked to remember star moments from their lives. Praying mentally that it would be good enough for the Queen Bee and that my deception would not be noticed, I began:

'This happened ten years ago. My lover was massaging my face. Then, suddenly, I was seized by a sensation of lightness. Before my eyes a door opened, and behind it was a lighted room. Such a light room I have never seen, before or since. I went into the room. I have never felt as good as I did then.'

That was all. But as I set the sentences of the little interview one after another, from memory, which now worked with the accuracy of a photograph, I realised that it was no deception. What had happened had happened, all of it, to me, and I remembered the smell of my lover's fingers and the fact that it had been the first cool, high day after a long summer.

And, dumbfounded by the superabundance of my life, I fell silent, and waited for the rap of the golden gavel.

'Accepted,' the bass of the Queen Bee rang out, and I saw a veiled smile spread over her face as if something inexpressibly sweet had just dripped on to her palate. In such a way my memory, too, although stolen, was added to her collection, to the great store of honey which was the basis of her economy, to the honeycombs from which she drew her happiness and her hospitality and which no thief would ever empty.

The Cloaked Moth

THE TWENTY-FIFTH LETTER

Do you remember the entomologist who thought he saw a cloaked moth on the ground? He was delighted, and picked it up, only to realise that it was no more than a piece of rotten wood. Then, of course, he threw it away in disappointment.

I wonder why – already preparing to leave – he nevertheless crouched to seek once more the piece of branch he had thrown away. But how diligently and closely he had to examine it before he saw: it was a cloaked moth after all.

Tonight the earth carries the city steadily on its shoulders. Even the heavens are motionless, and the buildings have long roots. I confess: I have countless times been forced to return and fetch home what I have abandoned and thrown away as worthless. Other colours glimmer from beneath the camouflage coat, and who knows which of them is right.

When I open the curtain, I see a half-darkened street, and nothing is happening there, but in the emptiness which is not now fractured by steps the restlessness of the first step and the exhaustion of the last combine.

Tonight I see in the half-light as if it were broad daylight; I see so far and so clearly that I can make you out too, cloaked moth.

The Gate of Evening

THE TWENTY-SIXTH LETTER

Yesterday Longhorn and I visited the city museum. I wandered rather absent-mindedly through the echoing halls and corridors, which were full of the utensils of times gone by, tools, clothes and furniture. A flood of dates and names of kings flowed from Longhorn's mouth – his memory is astonishing – but hardly a detail lodged itself in my memory, although it would have been an opportunity to learn a great deal about Tainaron's past.

Weary, I happened to stop in front of a glass case where only one object was on display: a cap of some kind. It was deep black, but magnificently embroidered with stars, moons and suns. Gold and silver thread glittered as if the head-dress had just been sewn, but from the label fixed to the case I read that it was many hundreds of years old. In the centre of the cap – or perhaps it was a calotte – was a small hole.

'What kind of cap is that and why is there a hole in it?' I asked Longhorn, finally interested in what I saw.

'It is called the Gate of Evening,' Longhorn answered, delighted at the interest I showed, and immediately eager to give me all his information. 'In the old days, when Tainaronians grew old and frail and it was time for them to depart, one of their heirs brought them a cap like that. The dying person put it on their head, and it eased their last moments.'

'How on earth?' I asked.

'Because the hole is a gate, and it showed them the direction in which they were to go and so they did not stray from the right road.'

In the next room, too, there was something that aroused my interest: a row of masks. They were not demonic masks of the kind one often sees in folk museums; they were not grimacing or cruelly decorated or spattered with blood. I saw quite ordinary faces of the citizens of Tainaron staring peacefully out of point or compound eyes, antennae gently outstretched. One could see hundreds of such faces as one walked in the city; and that was what was most extraordinary about the masks.

'What are these used for?' I asked Longhorn.

'Ah,' he said thoughtfully. 'There was a time when a peculiar festival was held in Tainaron at the time of the autumn equinox, the day when day and night are equally long. These festivals gave employment to an entire profession: mask-makers. For the revellers had three kinds of mask: the first represented their faces as they were when they were quite young, the second showed their faces as they were at the midpoint of life, and the third mask as they would be when they were very old. They used the first mask in the morning, the second at midday and the third from evening to midnight.

'So at some time of the day their mask was like their own face?' I understood. The custom seemed very strange to me.

'Yes, it was the day of the equinox,' Longhorn said. 'It spanned a whole life.'

'And when were the masks taken off?' I asked.

'The masks were taken off at midnight,' he replied. 'They had fasted all day, but then they were allowed to eat and drink. There was everything in profusion, and beggars, too, were permitted to come to any table they wished.'

It was late at night by the time I returned from the city, and the vault of the sky was as black as the calotte which I had admired during the day. But behind the reflections of the city I could sense the promises of other lights, perhaps as deceptive as they. Here, too, their distance is as flabbergasting and strange as on the harbour pier where once, pierced by them, we lingered.

But I shall need no other gate of evening.

The Umbellifiers

THE TWENTY-SEVENTH LETTER

We grow cold and look inward, for the frost has breathed on us and the city is making ready for a long hibernation. The season is over and the city people withdraw to their homes, doors are locked, conversation decreases. In the streets there are fewer and fewer people and vehicles, and all of them have particular destinations.

In many shop windows I have already seen a careless scribbled notice announcing that the shop will next open in the spring. Only one in three or four street lamps are lighted in the evenings, and later – so I have been told – only squares and crossroads will be lit.

Tourists are scarcely to be seen any longer. Who would be amused, after all, by touring a cold, dark city.

It is sad, sad. I think the lights of Tainaron should shine now that the sun is seen only seldom, more plentiful and colourful than before, but instead the city becomes dimmer and more impoverished.

Life stops in a thin crust of ice like frozen water and in the eyes of the few passers-by there is only the glimmer of the need for well-earned rest, but I am restless and wish to live. I wish to come and go, I wish to do something with these hands I see before me on the table so pale and helpless; I wish to debate important questions and eat and clink glasses.

Too late! Longhorn, if I mention my wishes to him, merely shakes his head and reassures me: 'In the spring! When the winter has gone.'

And I see, of course I see exhaustion in his black jewel-eyes, I see that he himself would already prefer to withdraw to his home and stays on his feet only because I am here and in a way his guest. Always, before I meet him, I intend to say: 'Go, do go, you do not have to stay awake for my sake; I shall manage very well here.' But the words stick in my throat, for I know I shall be lost when he is gone.

And one cannot even see the fireflies here any longer; they have completely disappeared from the streets, and that, more than anything else, shows what hard times await us. Even the house of the Queen Bee looks bolted, and I cannot imagine where all the Oddfellows have scattered.

But today when I went past the house's battened-down shutters, I saw a little light coming out of one of the cracks. I got up on tiptoe and peered inside, but I did not see the Queen Bee. But the empty room was filled with a warm, rosy glow whose source is in the honeycombs of memory.

Perhaps its warmth will suffice for the Queen Bee, however long and hard the winter. The Dangler's balcony, too, is empty, and the street below it, one of Tainaron's busiest thoroughfares, cuts through the city, empty and clean. Just occasionally a hawkmoth or two rushes past me in its late refitting. Elsewhere it is quiet, but in my head clatter the melancholy words: chippings and clay! Chippings and clay!

The spring tide is over, and Oceanos is murmuring its winter story. It is unlikely that I shall ever again come to gaze longingly over its swelling waters.

If now it were to happen that a letter were to drop on to my doormat, I know what it would say. You would write: 'Why do you not go away?'

I can hear you say it, rather coldly and a little didactically, as if you were offering me something on a plate, but looking away at the same time. And I admit that I have heard those words before; I have asked myself the same question. And perhaps, if someone were to say the word, I would go. I taste the word in my mouth; how fresh and pure it tastes.

I had my reasons for coming to Tainaron; I am sure they were important reasons, but I have nevertheless forgotten what they were.

'Come!' What if I were to say that to you? It would be in vain, quite in vain, for all I could show you would be the wintry stalks of the umbellifers in the meadow at the Botanical Gardens.

Upright like them, I remain in this land of sleepers.

Date As Postmark

THE TWENTY-EIGHT LETTER

Today I opened the door, and before me rose the Rhinoceros beetle, as gloomy and simple as a mountain. He is a friend of Longhorn, but I have only met him in passing before.

'Come inside,' I asked, but he went on standing on the spot, swaying, and I could not fathom what he wanted.

'Have you seen Longhorn recently?' I asked at length, for I had not seen Longhorn for many days.

'It was Longhorn who sent me here,' he responded, and fell silent once more.

'And how is he?' I asked, becoming a little impatient.

'He told me to come here and ask if there is anything I can do for you,' the Rhinoceros Beetle managed to say, swaying in ever greater circles. I think he must weigh more than one hundred kilograms.

'Thank you, but I do not need anything,' I said in astonishment. 'But where is Longhorn himself?'

'I thought you already knew,' said the Rhinoceros Beetle, suddenly standing still.

'I do not know anything,' I said, fearing the worst. 'Has something happened to Longhorn?'

I felt like shaking the Rhinoceros Beetle, who remained motionless, but he was too wide. I thought I understood.

'Ah, he is already asleep,' I said, and was very offended. It was not polite to retire for the winter without even saying goodnight.

'He is in his pupal cell,' said the Rhinoceros Beetle, becoming even more massive than before.

This information came as a shock to me. For the sake of the Rhinoceros Beetle, I managed, with difficulty, to restrain myself, for I would have liked to have cursed him: 'Damned longhorn beetle! How dare you!'

The Rhinoceros Beetle left, but I went on standing in the doorway. I should never meet Longhorn again; not the Longhorn who had for so long been my patient guide in this strange city. If he were to return and step before me, I did not know who or what he would then be, or even when it would happen, for everything here has its own time and particular moment, unknown to others.

I should never again be able to turn to him, but when he nevertheless stepped before me, into the place where the Rhinoceros Beetle had just been standing, stood there and began to grow as the dead grow.

Then I saw that I had never known him and that I had never even wanted to know him. And as he grew, he became thinner and more indistinct; his form slipped into the darkness of the stairwell and he no longer had shape or mass.

But his eyes, his eyes remained, and his gaze, which is as black and piercing as it ever was, and as impenetrable. And when I look into the darkness of his eyes they gradually begin to sparkle like double stars, like the planets on which the sun shines and on which there are seas and continents, roads, valleys and waterfalls and great forests where many can live and sing.

Then I went inside and closed the door, a little less sad. For it was, after all, now clear that although I had lived beside him from the beginning to the end, not just one life but two or three,

I would never have learned to know him. His outline, which I had once drawn around him, in order to be able to show him and name him, had now disappeared. It liberated the great stranger who was a much realer Longhorn than the person I once knew, small and separate.

Such is my farewell to Longhorn today, date as postmark, in the city of Tainaron.

Passing Bells

THE TWENTY-NINTH LETTER

What a rumbling! Over all of Tainaron it spread, echoing from wall to wall, shaking the windowpanes and resonating in my own chest. When I pressed my fingers against the table, I could even feel the sound of the ore bells in my fingertips. And my toes, the soles of my feet, my elbows heard it, for the floor, all the soil of Tainaron quivered and resounded.

The prince had died, and now in all the churches, cathedrals and temples of the city, the many of them that there were, passing bells were being rung. They roared from morning to night as if to restore to the deceased the respect which no one had accorded to him before his death.

'What happened to the prince?' I asked the Rhinoceros Beetle. For the cause of his death had not been divulged on the news.

'Him? He just died,' the Rhinoceros Beetle answered, turning his slow gaze upon me. 'It was high time. He was an old man.'

'But was it not almost too fitting a time?'

I had seen, in the heart tower, what I had seen: the thin, expectant form of the prince, huddled on a simple chair which had been set in the middle of the floor without the company of adjutants or even the most lowly guardsman. His cloak was surrounded, like another cloak, by the aura of his fast approaching end. And it was not a natural end.

'Did it not happen very suddenly?'

'No more suddenly than anything else,' the Rhinoceros Beetle growled, even more dully than usual.

Slow-blooded, simple-minded creature! How could Longhorn ever have imagined that the Rhinoceros Beetle could have replaced him as my guide to Tainaron?

'I should like to know what will happen next,' I said.

'Now power will change hands,' the Rhinoceros Beetle said.

'Yes, of course,' I said impatiently. I knew that, of course, but I wanted to find out what it would mean in practice and what kind of leadership Tainaron would now receive. But as I looked at the Rhinoceros Beetle I realised that it was not worth pursuing the subject. I could already see that nothing could have interested him less.

At that moment he glanced at me askance, and behind the membrane that covered his black eyes there flashed something – like amusement. Was the Rhinoceros Beetle really capable of being amused by something? For a moment I felt I might have been mistaken in regard to him, as if his dullness might veil completely different characteristics which he hid for who knew what reason. I tried to find the light again, but his gaze extinguished, as normal. Perhaps the fleeting impression was caused merely by the lighting or by my own state of mind.

'Will you go to a memorial service in one of the temples? What religion do you belong to?' I found myself asking, for I wished to change the subject, which had proved fruitless.

'Each in turn,' he said. 'Naturally.'

'Each in turn? Surely that is not possible,' I said, stunned. And 'naturally' – surely that was too much.

'Why not?' he said, chewing something in his massive jaws. 'One must be impartial. At the moment I belong to the temple of the highest knowledge. Next month I shall move to – oh, I do not think I can remember the name of the parish.'

'But if where you are now has the highest knowledge, why is it worth moving to another parish?'

He did not answer, but chewed and swallowed some tough and gluey substance which from time to time stuck his jaws together. I could still hear the ringing of the passing bells, from both far and high, both low and from quite close by.

'Do you recognise the bells of your own temple?' I asked.

'I think they are the ones that are clattering quite close by,' he said. 'Or else those where you can hear a double ring between the low strokes. No, listen, I think after all that they are those slower ones from farther east, that always ring three and one, three and one,' he said.

I listened in vain. I could not distinguish the bells from each other; all I could hear was a roaring in which they were all mixed up. These Tainaronians! I do not suppose I shall ever learn to understand them. I am beginning to be weary of my long visit; yes, now I am weary.

The Rhinoceros Beetle has gone, but the prince's passing bells are still booming. And why should I not admit that today I am plagued by home-sickness. I am sick with home-sickness. But Oceanos is freezing for the winter, and not a single ship will leave the harbour before spring.

The tall trees of my home courtyard are now tossing in the grip of a storm. The slanting brightness of autumn falls into my room. I see the room's books and pictures and carefully chosen things; I remember its calm and its secret joy. It was at just this time of year, before winter, long ago, that you came into my room.

You came into my room as the morning dawned, and I did not know whether I slept or woke. I did not stir, but you, you squeezed your hard, salt-weathered lips silently to my throat, where the pulse beats, and then they pressed my temples and moved, hot, over my eyelids, until finally you felt for my mouth and opened it with your own lips. Then I tasted your taste, the taste of your thirst, and I answered, and answered, and moaned.

The Pupal Cell of My Home

THE THIRTIETH LETTER

How long I searched for a home back then. Before me furnished and cold rooms opened, broken rental agreements fell, houses with destruction orders collapsed, and the endless queues of housing offices wound in long roads without issue.

Now all that is in the past. In the room in which I now live I have everything I need, and more: if I step on to my balcony, I see the white pennants and golden cupolas of Tainaron, the cloud-girt mountains and the blue heart-waters of Oceanos.

Nevertheless, I have now started to prepare a new dwelling for myself, just in case. Yes, it is almost ready for me to move in, my little pupal cell; it can no longer be unsuccessful. It has the fresh smell of mud and algae and reeds, for I have gathered almost all the materials myself from the beach where I once almost found myself in the jaws of death. I have done it all with my own hands, and when I look inside I am satisfied. It is just my size, like a well-fitting garment which does not pull anywhere. It is small on the outside but spacious inside, just as a good dwelling-place should be.

It is dark there. When I peer in through its only opening which, when the occasion arises, I shall close from inside, I am overcome by irresistible sleepiness. I do not believe that the lack of space will trouble me, for once I reach it it will be as wide as the night.

The mail will go on being delivered for some time, so I have heard, but the city now seems dead. More and more people are withdrawing for their winter rest, some of them – like Longhorn and, before long, I myself too – will be away for much longer. I spoke of sleeping just now, but of course we shall not merely be resting, but changing. Will I know how? Will it be hard work? Will it bring pain or pleasure or will it mean the disappearance, too, of all regrets?

Some change imperceptibly, little by little, others quickly and once and for all, but everyone changes, and for that reason it is in vain to ask whose fate is the best.

My entire room stinks like an estuary! There was something I still had to tell you, but the smell of the sludge dulls my thoughts. I shall remember it once more when it is spring, and that will come soon, soon, the seventeenth, and all around will sparkle – droplets! and I shall rise; and we shall see again…

lace around the cuffs, which Bird-hands wore to fly around the room while the old woman exclaimed upon the beauty of the creature.

Another time, the welfare machine brought an old leather boot, and forced Hogfoot Right to wear it, making the foot clump around the room while the old woman sniggered at such a humorous sight. The welfare machine carefully watched her heartbeat monitor at times like these, intently observant for any variation in its pace and strength.

It was a very happy time for the old woman.

Until, one night, it all went wrong.

A terrible noise woke the old woman. It was the sound of crashing furniture and struggling bodies. A glass ornament smashed against a wall, spraying her legs with fragments. There was a life-and-death struggle going on somewhere in the room. A standard lamp fell across a table and shattered the ceramic stem. The old woman was too frightened to even turn on the light. She was sure that an android had entered her apartment: a rogue machine whose brain had suffered a malfunction and was on the rampage. All she could do was quietly guide her bed-chair to the corner of the room and stay there until the ruckus was over.

The fighting, she was sure, was between her pets and the intruder, and since there was little she could do she had to await the outcome without interfering.

Finally, after a long while, there was silence, and she ordered the light switch on. The scene that met her eyes was horrific. In the centre of the room were Bird-hands and Hogfoot Right, obviously squaring up to one another. Around them, bleeding, broken, and bruised, were the other pets. Moth-ears had been torn and crushed and was obviously dead. Snake-arm had been pierced by a long ceramic splinter which protruded from its head. It, too, was deathly still. Basil was black with bruises, having been beaten, fatally it seemed.

The old woman had not the slightest doubt that Hogfoot Right had gone berserk. There was no sign of any android intruder, and Hogfoot Right looked as though he were now about to attack Bird-hands.

The two combatants fell upon one another. There was a frenzied scrambling and clawing. The old woman began yelling like crazy for Bird-hands, telling her to dig her claws in, while the seemingly mad hog was butting her round and round the walls with its heel-hard head.

It was a vicious battle.

Furniture was scattered this way and that, and twice the old woman had to move her bed-chair to get out of their path as they rolled across the floor, locked in a tight ball. Once, she thought Hogfoot had had enough, as he backed away into a corner, but again he went forward, just when Bird-hands was trying to recover.

Finally, Bird-hands picked him up by the hindquarters and flung him at the exposed end of the standard lamp. It was bristling with live contacts. With a bouncing arc of his body he twisted in agony as the shock went through him. He lay broken and still, across the sputtering wires.

Bird-hands fluttered to the middle of the room.

'Well done,' cried the old woman. 'Well fought.'

Bird-hands just sat there, her thumb-head turned towards the window, through which the dawn was just beginning to emerge. Then suddenly the creature launched herself into the air and began throwing her body at the glass panes in a seemingly desperate attempt to smash her way through, like a wild bird that is trapped in a closed room.

Then the old woman understood. It had not been Hogfoot Right, but Bird-hands. She had seen the martins cutting through the blue sky outside and she wanted to be free too. She wanted to be out amongst those of her own kind. Maybe she had run amok amongst the others because they refused or were unable to understand her desire for escape? Perhaps she had tried to get them to open the window – something only the old woman could do with a brain command – only to find they could not help her? Anyway, she had killed them all. Even little Moth-ears. And Hogfoot Right, the bad-tempered one, had given her the toughest opposition of all.

Poor Hogfoot, misjudged right to the end.

Now Bird-hands sat on the ledge, her nails dripping with blood. She seemed to be waiting for the old woman to open the window, which could only be done by direct order. There came, in the silence, the sound of real birds chirruping outside, and Bird-hands, displaying restlessness. The old woman, still in a state of shock, refused to respond.

Bird-hands carefully wiped the gore from her fingerwings on one of the curtains. By this time the old woman had recovered a little but she had much of the stubbornness of her erstwhile right foot and she made it obvious that she was not going to comply.

Finally, Bird-hands flew to the ledge and settled on the old woman's neck. The creature began to stroke the withered throat sensuously, hoping perhaps to persuade her mistress to do what she wished. The woman sat rigidly still, grimfaced. Gradually the stroking became firmer. At the last, the fingerwings tightened and squeezed, slowly but effectively. There were a few minutes during which the old woman convulsed. Then the body went slack.

Bird-hands, after a long while, released her grip and fluttered down to the floor. She crabbed her way amongst the dead animals, inspecting them for signs of life. Then she came to Hogfoot Right, lying across the electrified strands of the light socket. Bird-hands observed her victim with seeming dispassion. She inched forward, close to the hog's head, looking down.

Suddenly there was a jerk from Hogfoot Right, as his head flashed out and his jaws clamped on a little finger. A brilliant shower of blue-white sparks rained around the pair, and then the stillness in the room was complete.

Later, the welfare machine came to call and surveyed the scene with mechanical surprise. It made a careful note of all of the damage and recorded a verdict of suicide. Just as it was about to leave, it sensed some vibrations coming from somewhere in the room. One of the creatures had stirred. Suddenly something snapped at its metal leg and then went careering through the open doorway and along the corridor.

SHADES

Lucius Shepard

Lucius Shepard (1947–) is an award-winning American writer whose fiction often contains an element of supernatural horror and reflects personal experience from his extensive travels overseas. Briefly associated with the cyberpunk movement, Shepard quickly established himself as *sui generis* with novels such as *Life During Wartime* (1987) and *The Scalehunter's Beautiful Daughter* (1988). More recently, novels such as *Viator* (2005) have confirmed Shepard's status as one of his generation's best writers of weird fiction. Long stories have been Shepard's particular strength, collected in, among others, *The Jaguar Hunter* (1987), *Trujillo* (2004), and *The Best of Lucius Shepard* (2008). 'Shades' is a unque and unflinchingly weird ghost story that also serves as a commentary on the devastation of war.

This little gook cadre with a pitted complexion drove me through the heart of Saigon – I couldn't relate to it as Ho Chi Minh City – and checked me into the Hotel Heroes of Tet, a place that must have been quietly elegant and very French back in the days when philosophy was discussed over Cointreau rather than practiced in the streets, but now was filled with cheap production-line furniture and tinted photographs of Uncle Ho. Glaring at me, the cadre suggested I would be advised to keep to my room until I left for Cam Le; to annoy him I strolled into the bar, where a couple of Americans – reporters, their table laden with notebooks and tape cassettes – were drinking shots from a bottle of George Dickel. 'How's it goin'?' I said, ambling over. 'Name's Tom Puleo. I'm doin' a piece on Stoner for *Esquire*.'

The bigger of them – chubby, red-faced guy about my age, maybe thirty-five, thirty-six – returned a fishy stare; but the younger one, who was thin and tanned and weaselly handsome, perked up and said, 'Hey, you're the guy was in Stoner's outfit, right?' I admitted it, and the chubby guy changed his attitude. He put on a welcome-to-the-lodge smile, stuck out a hand, and introduced himself as Ed Fierman, *Chicago Sun-Times*. His pal, he said, was Ken Witcover, CNN.

They tried to draw me out about Stoner, but I told them maybe later, that I wanted to unwind from the airplane ride, and we proceeded to do damage to the whiskey. By the time we'd sucked down three drinks, Fierman and I were into some heavy reminiscence. Turned out he had covered the war during my tour and knew my old top. Witcover was cherry in Vietnam, so he just tried to look wise and to laugh in the right spots. It got pretty drunk at that table. A security cadre – fortyish, cadaverous gook in yellow fatigues – sat nearby, cocking an ear toward us, and we pretended to be engaged in subversive activity, whispering and drawing maps on napkins. But it was Stoner who was really on all our minds, and Fierman – the drunkest of us – finally broached the subject, saying, 'A machine that traps ghosts! It's just like the gooks to come up with something that goddamn worthless!'

Witcover shushed him, glancing nervously at the security cadre, but Fierman was beyond caution. 'They could a done humanity a service,' he said, chuckling. 'Turned alla Russians into women or something. But, nah! The gooks get behind worthlessness. They may claim to be Marxists, but at heart they still wanna be inscrutable.'

'So,' said Witcover to me, ignoring Fierman, 'when you gonna fill us in on Stoner?'

I didn't care much for Witcover. It wasn't anything personal; I simply wasn't fond of his breed: compulsively neat (pencils lined up, name inscribed on every possession), edgy, on the make. I disliked him the way some people dislike yappy little dogs. But I couldn't argue with his desire to change the subject. 'He was a good soldier,' I said.

Fierman let out a mulish guffaw. 'Now that,' he said, 'that's what I call in-depth analysis.'

Witcover snickered.

'Tell you the truth' – I scowled at him, freighting my words with malice – 'I hated the son of a bitch. He had this young-professor air, this way of lookin' at you as if you were an interestin' specimen. And he came across pure phony. Y'know, the kind who's always talkin' like a black dude, sayin' "right on" and shit, and sayin' it all wrong.'

'Doesn't seem much reason for hating him,' said Witcover, and by his injured tone, I judged I had touched a nerve. Most likely he had once entertained soul-brother pretensions.

'Maybe not. Maybe if I'd met him back home, I'd have passed him off as a creep and gone about my business. But in combat situations, you don't have the energy to maintain that sort of neutrality. It's easier to hate. And anyway, Stoner could be a genuine pain in the ass.'

'How's that?' Fierman asked, getting interested.

'It was never anything unforgivable; he just never let up with it. Like one time a bunch of us were in this guy Gurney's hooch, and he was tellin' 'bout this badass he'd known in Detroit. The cops had been chasin' this guy across the rooftops, and he'd missed a jump. Fell seven floors and emptied his gun at the cops on the way down. Reaction was typical. Guys sayin' "Wow" and tryin' to think of a story to top it. But Stoner he nods sagely and says, "Yeah, there's a lot of that goin' around." As if this was a syndrome to which he's devoted years of study. But you knew he didn't have a clue, that he was too upscale to have met anybody like Gurney's badass.' I had a slug of whiskey. ' "There's a lot of that goin' around" was a totally inept comment. All it did was to bring everyone down from a nice buzz and make us aware of the shithole where we lived.'

Witcover looked puzzled, but Fierman made a noise that seemed to imply comprehension. 'How'd he die?' he asked. 'The handout says he was KIA, but it doesn't say what kind of action.'

'The fuckup kind,' I said. I didn't want to tell them. The closer I came to seeing Stoner, the leerier I got about the topic. Until this business had begun, I thought I'd buried all the death-tripping weirdness of Vietnam; now Stoner had unearthed it and I was having dreams again and I hated him for that worse than I ever had in life. What was I supposed to do? Feel sorry for him? Maybe ghosts didn't have bad dreams. Maybe it was terrific being a ghost, like with Casper... Anyway, I did tell them. How we had entered Cam Le, what was left of the patrol. How we had lined up the villagers, interrogated them, hit them, and God knows we might have killed them – we were freaked, bone-weary, an atrocity waiting to happen – if Stoner hadn't distracted us. He'd been wandering around, poking at stuff with his rifle, and then, with this ferocious expression on his face, he'd fired into one of the huts. The hut had been empty, but there must have been explosives hidden inside, because after a few rounds the whole damn thing had blown and taken Stoner with it.

Talking about him soured me on company, and shortly afterward I broke it off with Fierman and Witcover, and walked out into the city. The security cadre tagged along, his hand resting on the butt of his sidearm. I had a real load on and barely noticed my surroundings. The only salient points of difference between Saigon today and fifteen years before were the ubiquitous representations of Uncle Ho that covered the façades of many of the buildings, and the absence of motor scooters: the traffic consisted mainly of bicycles. I went a dozen blocks or so and stopped at a sidewalk café beneath sun-browned tamarinds, where I paid two dong for food tickets, my first experience with what the Communists called 'goods exchange' – a system they hoped would undermine the concept of monetary trade; I handed the tickets to the waitress, and she gave me a bottle of beer and a dish of fried peanuts. The security cadre, who had taken a table opposite mine, seemed no more impressed with the system than was I; he chided the waitress for her slowness and acted perturbed by the complexity accruing to his order of tea and cakes.

I sat and sipped and stared, thoughtless and unfocused. The bicyclists zipping past were bright blurs with jingling bells, and the light was that heavy leaded-gold light that occurs when a tropical sun has broken free of an overcast. Smells of charcoal, fish sauce, grease. The heat squeezed sweat from my every pore. I was brought back to alertness by angry voices. The security cadre was arguing with the waitress, insisting that the recorded music be turned on, and she was explaining that there weren't enough customers to warrant turning it on. He began to offer formal 'constructive criticism,' making clear that he considered her refusal both a breach of party ethics and the code of honorable service. About then, I realized I had begun to cry. Not sobs, just tears leaking. The tears had nothing to do with the argument or the depersonalized ugliness it signaled. I believe that the heat and the light and the smells had seeped into me, triggering a recognition of an awful familiarity that my mind had thus far rejected. I wiped my face and tried to suck it up before anyone could notice my emotionality; but a teenage boy on a bicycle slowed and gazed at me with an amused expression. To show my contempt, I spat on the sidewalk. Almost instantly, I felt much better.

Early the next day, thirty of us – all journalists – were bussed north to Cam Le. Mist still wreathed the paddies, the light had a yellowish green cast, and along the road women in black dresses were waiting for a southbound bus, with rumpled sacks of produce like sleepy brown animals at their feet. I sat beside Fierman, who, being as hung over as I was, made no effort at conversation; however, Witcover – sitting across the aisle – peppered me with inane questions until I told him to leave me alone. Just before we turned onto the dirt road that led to Cam Le, an information cadre boarded the bus and for the duration proceeded to fill us in on everything we already knew. Stuff about the machine, how its fields were generated, and so forth. Technical jargon gives me a pain, and I tried hard not to listen. But then he got off onto a tack that caught my interest. 'Since the machine has been in operation,' he said, 'the apparition seems to have grown more vital.'

'What's that mean?' I asked, waving my hand to attract his attention. 'Is he coming back to life?'

My colleagues laughed.

The cadre pondered this. 'It simply means that his effect has become more observable,' he said at last. And beyond that he would not specify.

Cam Le had been evacuated, its population shifted to temporary housing three miles east. The village itself was nothing like the place I had entered fifteen years before. Gone were the thatched huts, and in their stead were about two dozen small houses of concrete block painted a quarantine yellow, with banana trees set between them. All this encircled by thick jungle. Standing on the far side of the road from the group of houses was the long tin-roofed building that contained the machine. Two soldiers were lounging in front of it, and as the bus pulled up, they snapped to attention; a clutch of officers came out the door, followed by a portly white-haired gook: Phan Thnah Tuu, the machine's inventor. I disembarked and studied him while he shook hands with the other journalists; it wasn't every day that I met someone who claimed to be both Marxist and mystic, and had gone more than the required mile in establishing the validity of each. His hair was as fine as corn silk, a fat black mole punctuated one cheek, and his benign smile was unflagging, seeming a fixture of some deeply held good opinion attaching to everything he saw. Maybe, I thought, Fierman was right. In-fucking-scrutable.

'Ah,' he said, coming up, enveloping me in a cloud of perfumy cologne. 'Mr. Puleo. I hope this won't be painful for you.'

'Really,' I said. 'You hope that, do you?'

'I beg your pardon,' he said, taken aback.

'It's okay.' I grinned. 'You're forgiven.'

An unsmiling major led him away to press more

flesh, and he glanced back at me, perplexed. I was mildly ashamed of having fucked with him, but unlike Cassius Clay, I had plenty against them Viet Congs. Besides, my wiseass front was helping to stave off the yips.

After a brief welcome-to-the-wonderful-wacky-world-of-the-Commietechno-paradise speech given by the major, Tuu delivered an oration upon the nature of ghosts, worthy of mention only in that it rehashed every crackpot notion I'd ever heard: apparently Stoner hadn't yielded much in the way of hard data. He then warned us to keep our distance from the village. The fields would not harm us; they were currently in operation, undetectable to our senses and needing but a slight manipulation to 'focus' Stoner. But if we were to pass inside the fields, it was possible that Stoner himself might be able to cause us injury. With that, Tim bowed and reentered the building.

We stood facing the village, which – with its red dirt and yellow houses and green banana leaves – looked elementary and innocent under the leaden sky. Some of my colleagues whispered together, others checked their cameras. I felt numb and shaky, prepared to turn away quickly, much the way I once had felt when forced to identify the body of a chance acquaintance at a police morgue. Several minutes after Tuu had left us, there was a disturbance in the air at the center of the village. Similar to heat haze, but the ripples were slower. And then, with the suddenness of a slide shunted into a projector, Stoner appeared.

I think I had been expecting something bloody and ghoulish, or perhaps a gauzy insubstantial form; but he looked no different than he had on the day he died. Haggard; wearing sweat-stained fatigues; his face half-obscured by a week's growth of stubble. On his helmet were painted the words *Didi Mao* ('Fuck Off' in Vietnamese), and I could make out the yellowing photograph of his girl that he'd taped to his rifle stock. He didn't act startled by our presence; on the contrary, his attitude was nonchalant. He shouldered his rifle, tipped back his helmet, and sauntered toward us. He seemed to be recessed into the backdrop: it was as if reality were two-dimensional and he was a cutout held behind it to give the illusion of depth. At least that's how it was one moment. The next, he would appear to be set forward of the backdrop like a pop-up figure in a fancy greeting card. Watching him shift between these modes was unsettling... more than unsettling. My heart hammered, my mouth was cottony. I bumped into someone and realized that I had been backing away, that I was making a scratchy noise deep in my throat. Stoner's eyes, those eyes that had looked dead even in life, pupils about .45 caliber and hardly any iris showing, they were locked onto mine and the pressure of his stare was like two black bolts punching through into my skull.

'Puleo,' he said.

I couldn't hear him, but I saw his lips shape the name. With a mixture of longing and hopelessness harrowing his features, he kept on repeating it. And then I noticed something else. The closer he drew to me, the more in focus he became. It wasn't just a matter of the shortening distance; his stubble and sweat stains, the frays in his fatigues, his worry lines – all these were sharpening the way details become fixed in a developing photograph. But none of that disturbed me half as much as did the fact of a dead man calling my name. I couldn't handle that. I began to hyperventilate, to get dizzy, and I believe I might have blacked out; but before that could happen, Stoner reached the edge of the fields, the barrier beyond which he could not pass.

Had I had more mental distance from the event, I might have enjoyed the sound-and-light that ensued: it was spectacular. The instant Stoner hit the end of his tether, there was an earsplitting shriek of the kind metal emits under immense stress; it seemed to issue from the air, the trees, the earth, as if some ironclad physical constant had been breached. Stoner was frozen midstep, his mouth open, and opaque lightnings were forking away from him, taking on a violet tinge as they vanished, their passage illuminating the curvature of the fields. I heard a scream and assumed it must be Stoner. But somebody grabbed me, shook me, and I understood that I was the one screaming, screaming with throat-tearing abandon because his eyes were boring into me and I could have sworn that his thoughts, his sensations, were flowing to me along the track of his vision. I knew what he was feeling: not pain, not desperation, but emptiness. An emptiness made unbearable by his proximity to life, to fullness. It was the worst thing I'd ever felt, worse than grief and bullet wounds, and it had to be worse than dying – dying, you see, had an end, whereas this went on and on, and every time you thought you had adapted to it, it grew worse yet. I wanted it to stop. That was all I wanted. Ever. Just for it to stop.

Then, with the same abruptness that he had appeared, Stoner winked out of existence and the feeling of emptiness faded.

People pressed in, asking questions. I shouldered them aside and walked off a few paces. My hands were shaking, my eyes weepy. I stared at the ground. It looked blurred, an undifferentiated smear of green with a brown clot in the middle: this gradually resolved into grass and my left shoe. Ants were crawling over the laces, poking their heads into the eyelets. The sight was strengthening, a reassurance of the ordinary.

'Hey, man.' Witcover hove up beside me. 'You okay?' He rested a hand on my shoulder. I kept my eyes on the ants, saying nothing. If it had been anyone else, I might have responded to his solicitude; but I knew he was only sucking up to me, hoping to score some human interest for his satellite report. I glanced at him. He was wearing a pair of mirrored sunglasses, and that consolidated my anger. Why is it, I ask you, that every measly little wimp in the universe thinks he can put on a pair of mirrored sunglasses and instantly acquire magical hipness and cool, rather than – as is the case – looking like an asshole with reflecting eyes?

'Fuck off,' I told him in a tone that implied dire consequences were I not humored. He started to talk back, but thought better of it and stalked off. I returned to watching the ants; they were caravanning up inside my trousers and onto my calf. I would become a legend among them: The Human Who Stood Still for Biting.

From behind me came the sound of peremptory gook voices, angry American voices. I paid them no heed, content with my insect pals and the comforting state of thoughtlessness that watching them induced. A minute or so later, someone else moved up beside me and stood without speaking. I recognized Tuu's cologne and looked up. 'Mr. Puleo,' he said. 'I'd like to offer you an exclusive on this story.' Over his shoulder, I saw my colleagues staring at us through the windows of the bus, as wistful and forlorn as kids who have been denied Disneyland: they, like me, knew that big bucks were to be had from exploiting Stoner's plight.

'Why?' I asked.

'We want your help in conducting an experiment.'

I waited for him to continue.

'Did you notice,' he said, 'that after Stoner identified you, his image grew sharper?'

I nodded.

'We're interested in observing the two of you in close proximity. His reaction to you was unique.'

'You mean go in there?' I pointed to the village. 'You said it was dangerous.'

'Other subjects have entered the fields and shown no ill effects. But Stoner was not as intrigued by them as he was with you.' Tuu brushed a lock of hair back from his forehead. 'We have no idea of Stoner's capabilities, Mr. Puleo. It *is* a risk. But since you served in the Army, I assume you are accustomed to risk.'

I let him try to persuade me – the longer I held out, the stronger my bargaining position – but I had already decided to accept the offer. Though I wasn't eager to feel that emptiness again, I had convinced myself that it had been a product of nerves and an overactive imagination; now that I had confronted Stoner, I believed I would be able to control my reactions. Tim said that he would have the others driven back to Saigon, but I balked at that. I was not sufficiently secure to savor the prospect of being alone among the gooks, and I told Tuu I wanted Fierman and Witcover to stay. Why Witcover? At the time I might have said it was because he and Fierman were the only two of my colleagues whom I knew; but in retrospect, I think I may have anticipated the need for a whipping boy.

We were quartered in a house at the eastern edge of the village, one that the fields did not enclose. Three cots were set up inside, along with a table and chairs; the yellow walls were brocaded with mildew, and weeds grew sideways from chinks in the concrete blocks. Light was provided by an oil lamp that – as darkness fell – sent an inconstant glow lapping over the walls, making it appear that the room was filled with dirty orange water.

After dinner Fierman produced a bottle of whiskey – his briefcase contained three more – and a deck of cards, and we sat down to while away the evening. The one game we all knew was Hearts, and we each played according to the dictates of our personalities. Fierman became quickly drunk and attempted to Shoot the Moon on every hand, no matter how bad his cards; he seemed to be asking fate to pity a fool. I paid little attention to the game, my ears tuned to the night sounds, half expecting to hear the sputter of small-arms fire, the rumor of some ghostly engagement; it was by dint of luck alone that I maintained second place. Witcover played conservatively, building his score through our mistakes, and though we were only betting a nickel a point, to watch him sweat out every trick you would have thought a fortune hung in the balance; he chortled over our pitiful fuckups, rolling his eyes and shaking his head in delight, and whistled as he totaled up his winnings. The self-importance he derived from winning fouled the atmosphere, and the room acquired the staleness of a cell where we had been incarcerated for years. Finally, after a particularly childish display of glee, I pushed back my chair and stood.

'Where you going?' asked Witcover. 'Let's play.'

'No, thanks,' I said.

'Christ!' He picked up the discards and muttered something about sore losers.

'It's not that,' I told him. 'I'm worried if you win another hand, you're gonna come all over the fuckin' table. I don't wanna watch.'

Fierman snorted laughter.

Witcover shot me an aggrieved look. 'What's with you, man? You been on my case ever since the hotel.'

I shrugged and headed for the door.

'Asshole,' he said half under his breath.

'What?' An angry flush numbed my face as I turned back.

He tried to project an expression of manly belligerence, but his eyes darted from side to side.

'Asshole?' I said. 'Is that right?' I took a step toward him.

Fierman scrambled up, knocking over his chair, and began pushing me away. 'C'mon,' he said. 'It's not worth it. Chill out.' His boozy sincerity acted to diminish my anger, and I let him urge me out the door.

The night was moonless, with a few stars showing low on the horizon; the spiky crowns of the palms ringing the village were silhouettes pinned onto a lesser blackness. It was so humid, it felt like you could spoon in the air. I crossed the dirt road, found a patch of grass near the tin-roofed building, and sat down. The door to the building was cracked, spilling a diagonal of white radiance onto the ground, and I had the notion that there was no machine inside, only a mystic boil of whiteness emanating from Tuu's silky hair. A couple of soldiers walked past and nodded to me; they paused a few feet farther along to light cigarettes, which proceeded to brighten and fade with the regularity of tiny beacons.

Crickets sawed, frogs chirred, and listening to them, smelling the odor of sweet rot from the jungle, I thought about a similar night when I'd been stationed at Phnoc Vinh, about a party we'd had with a company of artillery. There had been a barbecue pit and iced beer and our CO had given special permission for whores to come on the base. It had been a great party; in fact, those days at Phnoc Vinh had been the best time of the war for me. The artillery company had had this terrific cook, and on movie nights he'd make doughnuts. Jesus, I'd loved those doughnuts! They'd tasted like home, like peace. I'd kick back and munch a doughnut and watch the bullshit movie, and it was almost like being in my own living room, watching the tube. Trouble was, Phnoc Vinh had softened me up, and after three weeks, when we'd been airlifted to Quan Loi, which was constantly under mortar and rocket fire, I'd nearly gotten my ass blown off.

Footsteps behind me. Startled, I turned and saw what looked to be a disembodied white shirt floating toward me. I came to one knee, convinced for the moment that some other ghost had been lured to the machine; but a second later a complete figure emerged from the dark: Tuu. Without a word, he sat cross-legged beside me. He was smoking a cigarette… or so I thought until I caught a whiff of marijuana. He took a deep drag, the coal illuminating his placid features, and offered me the joint. I hesitated, not wanting to be pals; but tempted by the smell, I accepted it, biting back a smartass remark about Marxist permissiveness. It was good shit. I could feel the smoke twisting through me, finding out all my hollow places. I handed it back, but he made a gesture of warding it off, and after a brief silence he said, 'What do you think about all this, Mr. Puleo?'

'About Stoner?'

'Yes.'

'I think' – I jetted smoke from my nostrils – 'it's crap that you've got him penned up in that astral tiger cage.'

'Had this discovery been made in the United States,' he said, 'the circumstances would be no different. Humane considerations – if, indeed, they apply – would have low priority.'

'Maybe,' I said. 'It's still crap.'

'Why? Do you believe Stoner is unhappy?'

'Don't you?' I had another hit. It was very good shit. The ground seemed to have a pulse. 'Ghosts are by nature unhappy.'

'Then you know what a ghost is?'

'Not hardly. But I figure unhappy's part of it.' The roach was getting too hot; I took a final hit and flipped it away. 'How 'bout you? You believe that garbage you preached this mornin'?'

His laugh was soft and cultivated. 'That was a press release. However, my actual opinion is neither less absurd-sounding nor more verifiable.'

'And what's that?'

He plucked a blade of grass, twiddled it. 'I believe a ghost is a quality that dies in a man long before he experiences physical death. Something that has grown acclimated to death and thus survives the body. It might be love or an ambition. An element of character… Anything.' He regarded me with his lips pursed. 'I have such a ghost within me. As do you, Mr. Puleo. My ghost senses yours.'

The theory was as harebrained as his others, but I wasn't able to deny it. I knew he was partly right, that a moral filament had snapped inside me during the war and since that time I had lacked the ingredient necessary to the development of a generous soul. Now it seemed that I could feel that lack as a restless presence straining against my flesh. The sawing of the crickets intensified, and I had a rush of paranoia, wondering if Tuu was fucking with my head. Then, moods shifting at the chemical mercies of the dope, my paranoia eroded and Tuu snapped into focus for me… or at least his ghost did. He had, I recalled, written poetry prior to the war, and I thought I saw the features of that lost poet melting up from his face: a dreamy fellow given to watching petals fall and contemplating the moon's reflection. I closed my eyes, trying to get a grip. This was the best dope I'd ever smoked. Commie Pink, pure buds of the revolution.

'Are you worried about tomorrow?' Tuu asked.

'Should I be?'

'I can only tell you what I did before – no one has been harmed.'

'What happened during those other experiments?' I asked.

'Very little, really. Stoner approached each subject, spoke to them. Then he lost interest and wandered off.'

'Spoke to them? Could they hear him?'

'Faintly. However, considering his reaction to you, I wouldn't be surprised if you could hear him quite well.'

I wasn't thrilled by that prospect. Having to look at Stoner was bad enough. I thought about the eerie shit he might say: admonitory pronouncements, sad questions, windy vowels gusting from his strange depths. Tuu said something and had to repeat it to snap me out of my reverie. He asked how it felt to be back in Vietnam, and without forethought, I said it wasn't a problem.

'And the first time you were here,' he said, an edge to his voice. 'Was that a problem?'

'What are you gettin' at?'

'I noticed in your records that you were awarded a Silver Star.'

'Yeah?'

'You must have been a good soldier. I wondered if you might not have found a calling in war.'

'If you're askin' what I think about the war,'

I said, getting pissed, 'I don't make judgments about it. It was a torment for me, nothing more. Its geopolitical consequences, cultural effects, they're irrelevant to me… maybe they're ultimately irrelevant. Though I doubt you'd agree.'

'We may agree more than you suspect.' He sighed pensively. 'For both of us, apparently, the war was a passion. In your case, an agonizing one. In mine, while there was also agony, it was essentially a love affair with revolution, with the idea of revolution. And as with all great passions, what was most alluring was not the object of passion but the new depth of my own feelings. Thus I was blind to the realities underlying it. Now' – he waved at the sky, the trees – 'now I inhabit those realities and I am not as much in love as once I was. Yet no matter how extreme my disillusionment, the passion continues. I want it to continue. I need the significance with which it imbues my past actions.' He studied me. 'Isn't that how it is for you? You say war was a torment, but don't you find those days empowering?'

Just as when he had offered me the joint, I realized that I didn't want this sort of peaceful intimacy with him; I preferred him to be my inscrutable enemy. Maybe he was right, maybe – like him – I needed this passion to continue in order to give significance to my past. Whatever, I felt vulnerable to him, to my perception of his humanity. 'Good night,' I said, getting to my feet. My ass was numb from sitting and soaked with dew.

He gazed up at me, unreadable, and fingered something from his shirt pocket. Another joint. He lit up, exhaling a billow of smoke. 'Good night,' he said coldly.

The next morning – sunny, cloudless – I staked myself out on the red dirt of Cam Le to wait for Stoner. Nervous, I paced back and forth until the air began to ripple and he materialized less than thirty feet away. He walked slowly toward me, his rifle dangling; a drop of sweat carved a cold groove across my rib cage. 'Puleo,' he said, and this time I heard him. His voice was faint, but it shook me.

Looking into his blown-out pupils, I was reminded of a day not long before he had died. We had been hunkered down together after a firefight, and our eyes had met, had locked as if sealed by a vacuum: like two senile old men, incapable of any communication aside from a recognition of the other's vacancy. As I remembered this, it hit home to me that though he hadn't been a friend, he was my brother-in-arms, and that as such, I owed him more than journalistic interest.

'Stoner!' I hadn't intended to shout, but in that outcry was a wealth of repressed emotion, of regret and guilt and anguish at not being able to help him elude the fate by which he had been overtaken.

He stopped short; for an instant the hopelessness drained from his face. His image was undergoing that uncanny sharpening of focus: sweat beads popping from his brow, a scab appearing on his chin. The lines of strain around his mouth and eyes were etched deep, filled in with grime, like cracks in his tan.

Tides of emotion were washing over me, and irrational though it seemed, I knew that some of these emotions – the fierce hunger for life in particular – were Stoner's. I believe we had made some sort of connection, and all our thoughts were in flux between us. He moved toward me again. My hands trembled, my knees buckled, and I had to sit down, overwhelmed not by fear but by the combination of his familiarity and utter strangeness. 'Jesus, Stoner,' I said. 'Jesus.'

He stood gazing dully down at me. 'My sending,' he said, his voice louder and with a pronounced resonance. 'Did you get it?'

A chill articulated my spine, but I forced myself to ignore it. 'Sending?' I said.

'Yesterday,' he said, 'I sent you what I was feeling. What it's like for me here.'

'How?' I asked, recalling the feeling of emptiness. 'How'd you do that?'

'It's easy, Puleo,' he said. 'All you have to do is die, and thoughts… dreams, they'll flake off you like old paint. But believe me, it's hardly adequate compensation.' He sat beside me, resting the rifle across his knees. This was no ordinary sequence of movements. His outline wavered, and his limbs appeared to drift apart: I might have been watching the collapse of a lifelike statue through a volume of disturbed water. It took all my self-control to keep from flinging myself away. His image steadied, and he stared at me. 'Last person I was this close to ran like hell,' he said. 'You always were a tough motherfucker, Puleo. I used to envy you that.'

If I hadn't believed before that he was Stoner, the way he spoke the word *motherfucker* would have cinched it for me: it had the stiffness of a practiced vernacular, a mode of expression that he hadn't mastered. This and his pathetic manner made him seem less menacing. 'You were tough, too,' I said glibly.

'I tried to be,' he said. 'I tried to copy you guys. But it was an act, a veneer. And when we hit Cam Le, the veneer cracked.'

'You remember…' I broke off because it didn't feel right, my asking him questions; the idea of translating his blood and bones into a best-seller was no longer acceptable.

'Dying?' His lips thinned. 'Oh, yeah. Every detail. You guys were hassling the villagers, and I thought, Christ, they're going to kill them. I didn't want to be involved, and… I was so tired, you know, so tired in my head, and I figured if I walked off a little ways, I wouldn't be part of it. I'd be innocent. So I did. I moved a ways off, and the wails, the shouts, they weren't real anymore. Then I came to this hut. I'd lost track of what was happening by that time. In my mind I was sure you'd already started shooting, and I said to myself, I'll show them I'm doing my bit, put a few rounds into this hut. Maybe' – his Adam's apple worked – 'maybe they'll think I killed somebody. Maybe that'll satisfy them.'

I looked down at the dirt, troubled by what I now understood to be my complicity in his death, and troubled also by a new understanding of the events surrounding the death. I realized that if anyone else had gotten himself blown up, the rest of us would have flipped out and likely have wasted the villagers. But since it had been Stoner, the explosion had had almost a calming effect: Cam Le had rid us of a nuisance.

Stoner reached out his hand to me. I was too mesmerized by the gesture, which left afterimages in the air, to recoil from it, and I watched horrified as his fingers gripped my upper arm, pressing wrinkles in my shirtsleeve. His touch was light and transmitted a dry coolness, and with it came a sensation of weakness. By all appearances, it was a normal hand, yet I kept expecting it to become translucent and merge with my flesh.

'It's going to be okay,' said Stoner.

His tone, though bemused, was confident, and I thought I detected a change in his face, but I couldn't put my finger on what the change was. 'Why's it gonna be okay?' I asked, my voice more frail and ghostly-sounding than his. 'It doesn't seem okay to me.'

'Because you're part of my process, my circuitry. Understand?'

'No,' I said. I had identified what had changed about him. Whereas a few moments before he had looked real, now he looked more than real, ultra-real; his features had acquired the kind of gloss found in air-brushed photographs, and for a split second his eyes were cored with points of glitter as if reflecting a camera flash… except these points were bluish white, not red. There was a coarseness to his face that hadn't been previously evident, and in contrast to my earlier perception of him, he now struck me as dangerous, malevolent.

He squinted and cocked his head. 'What's wrong, man? You scared of me?' He gave an amused sniff. 'Hang in there, Puleo. Tough guy like you, you'll make an adjustment.' My feeling of weakness had intensified: it was as if blood or some even more vital essence were trickling out of me. 'Come on, Puleo,' he said mockingly. 'Ask me some questions? That's what you're here for, isn't it? I mean this must be the goddamn scoop of the century. Good News From Beyond the Grave! Of course' – he pitched his voice low and sepulchral – 'the news isn't all that good.'

Those glittering cores resurfaced in his pupils, and I wanted to wrench free; but I felt helpless, wholly in his thrall.

'You see,' he went on, 'when I appeared in the village, when I walked around and' – he chuckled – 'haunted the place, those times were like sleepwalking. I barely knew what was happening. But the rest of the time, I was somewhere else. Somewhere really fucking weird.'

My weakness was bordering on vertigo, but I mustered my strength and croaked, 'Where?'

'The Land of Shades,' he said. 'That's what I call

it, anyway. You wouldn't like it, Puleo. It wouldn't fit your idea of order.'

The lights burned in his eyes, winking bright, and – as if in correspondence to their brightness – my dizziness increased. 'Tell me about it,' I said, trying to take my mind off the discomfort.

'I'd be delighted!' He grinned nastily. 'But not now. It's too complicated. Tonight, man. I'll send you a dream tonight. A bad dream. That'll satisfy your curiosity.'

My head was spinning, my stomach abubble with nausea. 'Lemme go, Stoner,' I said.

'Isn't this good for you, man? It's very good for me.' With a flick of his hand, he released my wrist.

I braced myself to keep from falling over, drew a deep breath, and gradually my strength returned. Stoner's eyes continued to burn, and his features maintained their coarsened appearance. The difference between the way he looked now and the lost soul I had first seen was like that between night and day, and I began to wonder whether or not his touching me and my resultant weakness had anything to do with the transformation. 'Part of your process,' I said. 'Does that…'

He looked me straight in the eyes, and I had the impression he was cautioning me to silence. It was more than a caution: a wordless command, a sending. 'Let me explain something,' he said. 'A ghost is merely a stage of growth. He walks because he grows strong by walking. The more he walks, the less he's bound to the world. When he's strong enough' – he made a planing gesture with his hand – 'he goes away.'

He seemed to be expecting a response. 'Where's he go?' I asked.

'Where he belongs,' he said. 'And if he's prevented from walking, from growing strong, he's doomed.'

'You mean he'll die?'

'Or worse.'

'And there's no other way out for him?'

'No.'

He was lying – I was sure of it. Somehow I posed for him a way out of Cam Le. 'Well… so,' I said, flustered, uncertain of what to do and at the same time pleased with the prospect of conspiring against Tuu.

'Just sit with me awhile,' he said, easing his left foot forward to touch my right ankle.

Once again I experienced weakness, and over the next seven or eight hours, he would alternately move his foot away, allowing me to recover, and then bring it back into contact with me. I'm not certain what was happening. One logic dictates that since I had been peripherally involved in his death – 'part of his process' – he was therefore able to draw strength from me. Likely as not, this was the case. Yet I've never been convinced that ordinary logic applied to our circumstance: it may be that we were governed by an arcane rationality to which we both were blind. Though his outward aspect did not appear to undergo further changes, his strength became tangible, a cold radiation that pulsed with the steadiness of an icy heart. I came to feel that the image I was seeing was the tip of an iceberg, the perceptible extremity of a huge power cell that existed mainly in dimensions beyond the range of mortal vision. I tried to give the impression of an interview to our observers by continuing to ask questions; but Stoner sat with his head down, his face hidden, and gave terse, disinterested replies.

The sun declined to the tops of the palms, the yellow paint of the houses took on a tawny hue, and – drained by the day-long alternation of weakness and recovery – I told Stoner I needed to rest. 'Tomorrow,' he said without looking up. 'Come back tomorrow.'

'All right.' I had no doubt that Tuu would be eager to go on with the experiment. I stood and turned to leave; but then another question, a pertinent one, occurred to me. 'If a ghost is a stage of growth,' I said, 'what's he grow into?'

He lifted his head, and I staggered back, terrified. His eyes were ablaze, even the whites winking with cold fire, as if nuggets of phosphorus were embedded in his skull.

'Tomorrow,' he said again.

During the debriefing that followed, I developed a bad case of the shakes and experienced a number of other, equally unpleasant, reactions; the places where Stoner had touched me seemed to have retained a chill, and the thought of that dead hand leeching me of energy was in retrospect thoroughly repellent. A good many of Tuu's subordinates, alarmed by Stoner's transformation, lobbied to break off the experiment. I did my best to soothe them, but I wasn't at all sure I wanted to return to the village. I couldn't tell whether Tuu noticed either my trepidation or the fact that I was being less than candid; he was too busy bringing his subordinates in line to question me in depth.

That night, when Fierman broke out his whiskey, I swilled it down as if it were an antidote to poison. To put it bluntly, I got shit-faced. Both Fierman and Witcover seemed warm human beings, old buddies, and our filthy yellow room with its flickering lamp took on the coziness of a cottage and hearth. The first stage of my drunk was maudlin, filled with self-recriminations over my past treatment of Stoner: I vowed not to shrink from helping him. The second stage… Well, once I caught Fierman gazing at me askance and registered that my behavior was verging on the manic. Laughing hysterically, talking like a speed freak. We talked about everything except Stoner, and I suppose it was inevitable that the conversation work itself around to the war and its aftermath. Dimly, I heard myself pontificating on a variety of related subjects. At one point Fierman asked what I thought of the Vietnam Memorial, and I told him I had mixed emotions.

'Why?' he asked.

'I go to the Memorial, man,' I said, standing up from the table where we had all been sitting. 'And I cry. You can't help but cryin', 'cause that' – I hunted for an appropriate image – 'that black dividin' line between nowheres, that says it just right 'bout the war. It feels good to cry, to go public with grief and take your place with all the vets of the truly outstandin' wars.' I swayed, righted myself. 'But the Memorial, the Unknown, the parades… basically they're bullshit.' I started to wander around the room, realized that I had forgotten why I had stood and leaned against the wall.

'How you mean?' asked Witcover, who was nearly as drunk as I was.

'Man,' I said, 'it's a shuck! I mean ten goddamn years go by, and alla sudden there's this blast of media warmth and government-sponsored emotion. "Welcome home, guys," ever'body's sayin'. "We're sorry we treated you so bad. Next time it's gonna be different. You wait and see."' I went back to the table and braced myself on it with both hands, staring blearily at Witcover: his tan looked blotchy. 'Hear that, man? "Next time." That's all it is. Nobody really gives a shit 'bout the vets. They're just pavin' the way for the next time.'

'I don't know,' said Witcover. 'Seems to–'

'Right!' I spanked the table with the flat of my hand. 'You don't know. You don't know shit 'bout it, so shut the fuck up!'

'Be cool,' advised Fierman. 'Man's entitled to his 'pinion.'

I looked at him, saw a flushed, fat face with bloodshot eyes and a stupid reproving frown. 'Fuck you,' I said. 'And fuck his 'pinion.' I turned back to Witcover. 'Whaddya think, man? That there's this genuine breath of conscience sweepin' the land? Open your goddamn eyes! You been to the movies lately? Jesus Christ! Courageous grunts strikin' fear into the heart of the Red Menace! Miraculous one-man missions to save our honor. Huh! Honor!' I took a long pull from the bottle. 'Those movies, they make war seem like a mystical opportunity. Well, man, when I was here it wasn't quite that way, y'know. It was leeches, fungus, the shits. It was searchin' in the weeds for your buddy's arm. It was lookin' into the snaky eyes of some whore you were bangin' and feelin' weird shit crawl along your spine and expectin' her head to do a Linda Blair three-sixty spin.' I slumped into a chair and leaned close to Witcover. 'It was Mordor, man. Stephen King-land. Horror. And now, now I look around at all these movies and monuments and crap, and it makes me wanna fuckin' puke to see what a noble hell it's turnin' out to be!'

I felt pleased with myself, having said this, and I leaned back, basking in a righteous glow. But Witcover was unimpressed. His face cinched into a scowl, and he said in a tight voice, 'You're startin' to really piss me off, y'know.'

'Yeah?' I said, and grinned. 'How 'bout that?'

'Yeah, all you war-torn creeps, you think you got papers sayin' you can make an ass outta yourself and everybody else gotta say, "Oh, you poor fucker! Give us more of your tortured wisdom!"'

Fierman muffled a laugh, and – rankled – I said, 'That so?'

Witcover hunched his shoulders as if preparing for an off-tackle plunge. 'I been listenin' to you guys for years, and you're alla goddamn same. You think you're owed something 'cause you got ground around in the political mill. Shit! I been in Salvador, Nicaragua, Afghanistan. Compared to those people, you didn't go through diddley. But you use what happened as an excuse for fuckin' up your lives … or for being assholes. Like you, man.' He affected a macho-sounding bass voice. ' "I been in a war. I am an expert on reality." You don't know how ridiculous you are.'

'Am I?' I was shaking again, but with adrenaline not fear, and I knew I was going to hit Witcover. He didn't know it – he was smirking, his eyes flicking toward Fierman, seeking approval – and that in itself was a sufficient reason to hit him, purely for educational purposes: I had, you see, reached the level of drunkenness at which an amoral man such as myself understands his whimsies to be moral imperatives. But the real reason, the one that had begun to rumble inside me, was Stoner. All my fear, all my reactions thus far, had merely been tremors signaling an imminent explosion, and now, thinking about him nearby, old horrors were stirred up, and I saw myself walking in a napalmed ville rife with dead VC, crispy critters, and beside me this weird little guy named Fellowes who claimed he could read the future from their scorched remains and would point at a hexagram-like structure of charred bone and gristle and say, 'That there means a bad moon on Wednesday,' and claimed, too, that he could read the past from the blood of head wounds, and then I was leaning over this Canadian nurse, beautiful blonde girl, disemboweled by a mine and somehow still alive, her organs dark and wet and pulsing, and somebody giggling, whispering about what he'd like to do, and then another scene that was whirled away so quickly, I could only make out the color of blood, and Witcover said something else, and a dead man was stretching out his hand to me and …

I nailed Witcover, and he flew sideways off the chair and rolled on the floor. I got to my feet, and Fierman grabbed me, trying to wrestle me away; but that was unnecessary, because all my craziness had been dissipated. 'I'm okay now,' I said, slurring the words, pushing him aside. He threw a looping punch that glanced off my neck, not even staggering me. Then Witcover yelled. He had pulled himself erect and was weaving toward me; an egg-shaped lump was swelling on his cheekbone. I laughed – he looked so puffed up with rage – and started for the door. As I went through it, he hit me on the back of the head. The blow stunned me a bit, but I was more amused than hurt; his fist had made a funny bonk sound on my skull, and that set me to laughing harder.

I stumbled between the houses, bouncing off walls, reeling out of control, and heard shouts … Vietnamese shouts. By the time I had regained my balance, I had reached the center of the village. The moon was almost full, pale yellow, its craters showing: a pitted eye in the black air. It kept shrinking and expanding, and – as it seemed to lurch farther off – I realized I had fallen and was lying flat on my back. More shouts. They sounded distant, a world away, and the moon had begun to spiral, to dwindle, like water being sucked down a drain. Jesus, I remember thinking just before I passed out, Jesus, how'd I get so drunk?

I'd forgotten Stoner's promise to tell me about the Land of Shades, but apparently he had not, for that night I had a dream in which I was Stoner. It was not that I thought I was him: I *was* him, prone to all his twitches, all his moods. I was walking in a pitch-dark void, possessed by a great hunger. Once this hunger might have been characterized as a yearning for the life I had lost, but it had been transformed into a lust for the life I might someday attain if I proved equal to the tests with which I was presented. That was all I knew of the land of Shades – that it was a testing ground, less a place than a sequence of events. It was up to me to gain strength from the tests, to ease my hunger as best I could. I was ruled by this hunger, and it was my only wish to ease it.

Soon I spotted an island of brightness floating in the dark, and as I drew near, the brightness resolved into an old French plantation house fronted by tamarinds and rubber trees; sections of white stucco wall and a verandah and a red tile roof were visible between the trunks. Patterns of soft radiance overlaid the grounds, yet there were neither stars nor moon nor any source of light I could discern. I was not alarmed by this – such discrepancies were typical of the Land of Shades.

When I reached the trees I paused, steeling myself for whatever lay ahead. Breezes sprang up to stir the leaves, and a sizzling chorus of crickets faded in from nowhere as if a recording of sensory detail had been switched on. Alert to every shift of shadow, I moved cautiously through the trees and up the verandah steps. Broken roof tiles crunched beneath my feet. Beside the door stood a bottomed-out cane chair; the rooms, however, were devoid of furnishings, the floors dusty, the whitewash flaking from the walls. The house appeared to be deserted, but I knew I was not alone. There was a hush in the air, the sort that arises from a secretive presence. Even had I failed to notice this, I could scarcely have missed the scent of perfume. I had never tested against a woman before, and, excited by the prospect, I was tempted to run through the house and ferret her out. But this would have been foolhardy, and I continued at a measured pace.

At the center of the house lay a courtyard, a rectangular space choked with waist-high growths of jungle plants, dominated by a stone fountain in the shape of a stylized orchid. The woman was leaning against the fountain, and despite the grayish-green half-light – a light that seemed to arise from the plants – I could see she was beautiful. Slim and honey-colored, with falls of black hair spilling over the shoulders of her *ao dai*. She did not move or speak, but the casualness of her pose was an invitation. I felt drawn to her, and as I pushed through the foliage, the fleshy leaves clung to my thighs and groin, touches that seemed designed to provoke arousal. I stopped an arm's length away and studied her. Her features were of a feline delicacy, and in the fullness of her lower lip, the petulant set of her mouth, I detected a trace of French breeding. She stared at me with palpable sexual interest. It had not occurred to me that the confrontation might take place on a sexual level, yet now I was certain this would be the case. I had to restrain myself from initiating the contact: there are rigorous formalities that must be observed prior to each test. And besides, I wanted to savor the experience.

'I am Tuyet,' she said in a voice that seemed to combine the qualities of smoke and music.

'Stoner,' I said.

The names hung in the air like the echoes of two gongs.

She lifted her hand as if to touch me, but lowered it: she, too, was practicing restraint. 'I was a prostitute,' she said. 'My home was Lai Khe, but I was an outcast. I worked the water points along Highway Thirteen.'

It was conceivable, I thought, that I may have known her. While I had been laid up in An Loc, I'd frequented those water points: bomb craters that had been turned into miniature lakes by the rains and served as filling stations for the water trucks attached to the First Infantry. Every morning the whores and their mama sans would drive out to the water points in three-wheeled motorcycle trucks; with them would be vendors selling combs and pushbutton knives and rubbers that came wrapped in gold foil, making them look like those disks of chocolate you can buy in the States. Most of these girls were more friendly than the city girls, and knowing that Tuyet had been one of them caused me to feel an affinity with her.

She went on to tell me that she had gone into the jungle with an American soldier and had been killed by a sniper. I told her my story in brief and then asked what she had learned of the Land of Shades. This is the most rigorous formality: I had never met anyone with whom I had failed to exchange information.

'Once,' Tuyet said, 'I met an old man, a Cao Dai medium from Black Virgin Mountain, who told me he had been to a place where a pillar of whirling light and dust joined earth to sky. Voices spoke from the pillar, sometimes many at once, and from them he understood that all wars are merely reflections of a deeper struggle, of a demon breaking free. The demon freed by our war, he said, was very strong, very dangerous. We the dead had been recruited to wage war against him.'

I had been told a similar story by an NLF captain,

and once, while crawling through a tunnel system, I myself had heard voices speaking from a skull half buried in the earth. But I had been too frightened to stay and listen. I related all this to Tuyet, and her response was to trail her fingers across my arm. My restraint, too, had frayed. I dragged her down into the thick foliage. It was as if we had been submerged in a sea of green light and fleshy stalks, as if the plantation house had vanished and we were adrift in an infinite vegetable depth where gravity had been replaced by some buoyant principle. I tore at her clothes, she at mine. Her *ao dai* shredded like crepe, and my fatigues came away in ribbons that dangled from her hooked fingers. Greedy for her, I pressed my mouth to her breasts. Her nipples looked black in contrast to her skin, and it seemed I could taste their blackness, tart and sour. Our breathing was hoarse, urgent, and the only other sound was the soft mulching of the leaves. With surprising strength, she pushed me onto my back and straddled my hips, guiding me inside her, sinking down until her buttocks were grinding against my thighs.

Her head flung back, she lifted and lowered herself. The leaves and stalks churned and intertwined around us as if they, too, were copulating. For a few moments my hunger was assuaged, but soon I noticed that the harder I thrust, the more fiercely she plunged, the less intense the sensations became. Though she gripped me tightly, the friction seemed to have been reduced. Frustrated, I dug my fingers into her plump hips and battered at her, trying to drive myself deeper. Then I squeezed one of her breasts and felt a searing pain to my palm. I snatched back my hand and saw that her nipple, both nipples, were twisting, elongating; I realized that they had been transformed into the heads of two black centipedes, and the artful movements of her internal muscles... they were too artful, too disconnectedly in motion. An instant later I felt that same searing pain in my cock and knew I was screwing myself into a nest of creatures like those protruding from her breasts. All her skin was rippling, reflecting the humping of thousands of centipedes beneath.

The pain was enormous, so much so that I thought my entire body must be glowing with it. But I did not dare fail this test, and I continued pumping into her, thrusting harder than ever. The leaves thrashed, the stalks thrashed as in a gale, and the green light grew livid. Tuyet began to scream – God knows what manner of pain I was causing her – and her screams completed a perverse circuit within me. I found I could channel my own pain into those shrill sounds. Still joined to her, I rolled atop her, clamped her wrists together, and pinned them above her head. Her screams rang louder, inspiring me to greater efforts yet. Despite the centipedes tipping her breasts, or perhaps because of them, because of the grotesque juxtaposition of the sensual and the horrid, her beauty seemed to have been enhanced, and my mastery over her actually provided me a modicum of pleasure.

The light began to whiten, and looking off, I saw that we were being borne by an invisible current through – as I had imagined – an infinite depth of stalks and leaves. The stalks that lashed around us thickened far below into huge pale trunks with circular ribbing. I could not make out where they met the earth – if, indeed, they did – and they appeared to rise an equal height above. The light brightened further, casting the distant stalks in silhouette, and I realized we were drifting toward the source of the whiteness, beyond which would lie another test, another confrontation. I glanced at Tuyet. Her skin no longer displayed that obscene rippling, her nipples had reverted to normal. Pain was evolving into pleasure, but I knew it would be shortlived, and I tried to resist the current, to hold on to pain, because even pain was preferable to the hunger I would soon experience. Tuyet clawed my back, and I felt the first dissolute rush of my orgasm. The current was irresistible. It flowed through my blood, my cells. It was part of me, or rather I was part of it. I let it move me, bringing me to completion.

Gradually the whipping of the stalks subsided to a pliant swaying motion. They parted for us, and we drifted through their interstices as serenely as a barge carved to resemble a coupling of two naked figures. I found I could not disengage from Tuyet, that the current enforced our union, and resigned to this, I gazed around, marveling at the vastness of this vegetable labyrinth and the strangeness of our fates. Beams of white light shined through the stalks, the brightness growing so profound that I thought I heard in it a roaring; and as my consciousness frayed, I saw myself reflected in Tuyet's eyes – a ragged dark creature wholly unlike my own self-image – and wondered for the thousandth time who had placed us in this world, who had placed these worlds in us.

Other dreams followed, but they were ordinary, the dreams of an ordinarily anxious, ordinarily drunken man, and it was the memory of this first dream that dominated my waking moments. I didn't want to wake because – along with a headache and other symptoms of hangover – I felt incredibly weak, incapable of standing and facing the world. Muzzy-headed, I ignored the reddish light prying under my eyelids and tried to remember more of the dream. Despite Stoner's attempts to appear streetwise, despite the changes I had observed in him, he had been at heart an innocent and it was difficult to accept that the oddly formal, brutally sexual protagonist of the dream had been in any way akin to him. Maybe, I thought, recalling Tuu's theory of ghosts, maybe that was the quality that had died in Stoner: his innocence. I began once again to suffer guilt feelings over my hatred of him, and, preferring a hangover to that, I propped myself on one elbow and opened my eyes.

I doubt more than a second or two passed before I sprang to my feet, hangover forgotten, electrified with fear; but in that brief span the reason for my weakness was made plain. Stoner was sitting close to where I had been lying, his hand outstretched to touch me, head down… exactly as he had sat the previous day. Aside from his pose, however, very little about him was the same.

The scene was of such complexity that now, thinking back on it, it strikes me as implausible that I could have noticed its every detail; yet I suppose that its power was equal to its complexity and thus I did not so much see it as it was imprinted on my eyes. Dawn was a crimson smear fanning across the lower sky, and the palms stood out blackly against it, their fronds twitching in the breeze like spiders impaled on pins. The ruddy light gave the rutted dirt of the street the look of a trough full of congealed blood. Stoner was motionless – that is to say, he didn't move his limbs, his head, or shift his position; but his image was pulsing, swelling to half again its normal size and then deflating, all with the rhythm of steady breathing. As he expanded, the cold white fire blazing from his eyes would spread in cracks that veined his entire form; as he contracted, the cracks would disappear and for a moment he would be – except for his eyes – the familiar figure I had known. It seemed that his outward appearance – his fatigues and helmet, his skin – was a shell from which some glowing inner man was attempting to break free. Grains of dust were whirling up from the ground beside him, more and more all the time: a miniature cyclone wherein he sat calm and ultimately distracted, the likeness of a warrior monk whose meditations had borne fruit.

Shouts behind me. I turned and saw Fierman, Tuu, Witcover, and various of the gooks standing at the edge of the village. Tuu beckoned to me, and I wanted to comply, to run, but I wasn't sure I had the strength. And, too, I didn't think Stoner would let me. His power surged around me, a cold windy voltage that whipped my clothes and set static charges crackling in my hair. 'Turn it off!' I shouted, pointing at the tin-roofed building. They shook their heads, shouting in return. '… can't,' I heard, and something about '… feedback.'

Then Stoner spoke. 'Puleo,' he said. His voice wasn't loud, but it was all-encompassing. I seemed to be inside it, balanced on a tongue of red dirt, within a throat of sky and jungle and yellow stone. I turned back to him. Looked into his eyes… fell into them, into a world of cold brilliance where a thousand fiery forms were materialized and dispersed every second, forms both of such beauty and hideousness that their effect on me, their beholder, was identical, a confusion of terror and exaltation. Whatever they were, the forms of Stoner's spirit, his potentials, or even of his thoughts, they were in their momentary life more vital and consequential than I could ever hope to be. Compelled by them, I walked over to him. I must have been afraid – I could feel wetness on my thighs and realized that my bladder had emptied – but he so dominated me that I knew only the need to obey. He did not stand, yet with each expansion his image would loom up before my eyes and I would stare into that dead face seamed by rivulets of molten diamond, its expression losing coherence, features splitting apart. Then he would shrink, leaving me gazing dumbly down at the top of his helmet. Dust stung my eyelids, my cheeks.

'What–' I began, intending to ask what he wanted; but before I could finish, he seized my wrist. Ice flowed up my arm, shocking my heart, and I heard myself… not screaming. No, this was the sound life makes leaving the body, like the squealing of gas released from a balloon that's half pinched shut.

Within seconds, drained of strength, I slumped to the ground, my vision reduced to a darkening fog. If he had maintained his hold much longer, I'm sure I would have died… and I was resigned to the idea. I had no weapon with which to fight him. But then I realized that the cold had receded from my limbs. Dazed, I looked around, and when I spotted him, I tried to stand, to run. Neither my arms nor legs would support me, and – desperate – I flopped on the red dirt, trying to crawl to safety; but after that initial burst of panic, the gland that governed my reactions must have overloaded, because I stopped crawling, rolled onto my back and stayed put, feeling stunned, weak, transfixed by what I saw. Yet not in the least afraid.

Stoner's inner man, now twice human-size, had broken free and was standing at the center of the village, some twenty feet off a bipedal silhouette through which it seemed you could look forever into a dimension of fire and crystal, like a hole burned in the fabric of the world. His movements were slow, tentative, as if he hadn't quite adapted to his new form, and penetrating him, arcing through the air from the tin-roofed building, their substance flowing toward him, were what appeared to be thousands of translucent wires, the structures of the fields. As I watched, they began to glow with Stoner's blue-white-diamond color, their substance to reverse its flow and pour back toward the building, and to emit a bass hum. Dents popped in the tin roof, the walls bulged inward, and with a grinding noise, a narrow fissure forked open in the earth beside it. The glowing wires grew brighter and brighter, and the building started to crumple, never collapsing, but – as if giant hands were pushing at it from every direction – compacting with terrible slowness until it had been squashed to perhaps a quarter of its original height. The hum died away. A fire broke out in the wreckage, pale flames leaping high and winnowing into black smoke.

Somebody clutched my shoulder, hands hauled me to my feet. It was Tuu and one of his soldiers. Their faces were knitted by lines of concern, and that concern rekindled my fear. I clawed at them, full of gratitude, and let them hustle me away. We took our places among the other observers, the smoking building at our backs, all gazing at the yellow houses and the burning giant in their midst.

The air around Stoner had become murky, turbulent, and this turbulence spread to obscure the center of the village. He stood unmoving, while small dust devils kicked up at his heels and went zipping about like a god's zany pets. One of the houses caved in with a *whump*, and pieces of yellow concrete began to lift from the ruins, to float toward Stoner; drawing near him, they acquired some of his brightness, glowing in their own right, and then vanished into the turbulence. Another house imploded, and the same process was initiated. The fact that all this was happening in dead silence – except for the caving in of the houses – made it seem even more eerie and menacing than if there had been sound.

The turbulence eddied faster and faster, thickening, and at last a strange vista faded in from the dark air, taking its place the way the picture melts up from the screen of an old television set. Four or five minutes must have passed before it became completely clear, and then it seemed sharper and more in focus than did the jungle and the houses, more even than the blazing figure who had summoned it: an acre-sized patch of hell or heaven or something in between, shining through the dilapidated structures and shabby colors of the ordinary, paling them. Beyond Stoner lay a vast forested plain dotted with fires…or maybe they weren't fires but some less chaotic form of energy, for though they gave off smoke, the flames maintained rigorous stylized shapes, showing like red fountains and poinsettias and other shapes yet against the poisonous green of the trees. Smoke hung like a gray pall over the plain and now and again beams of radiance – all so complexly figured, they appeared to be pillars of crystal – would shoot up from the forest into the grayness and resolve into a burst of light; and at the far limit of the plain, beyond a string of ragged hills, the dark sky would intermittently flash reddish orange as if great batteries of artillery were homing in upon some target there.

I had thought that Stoner would set forth at once into this other world, but instead he backed a step away and I felt despair for him, fear that he wouldn't seize his opportunity to escape. It may seem odd that I still thought of him as Stoner, and it may be that prior to that moment I had forgotten his human past; but now, sensing his trepidation, I understood that what enlivened this awesome figure was some scrap of soul belonging to the man-child I once had known. Silently, I urged him on. Yet he continued to hesitate.

It wasn't until someone tried to pull me back that I realized I was moving toward Stoner. I shook off whoever it was, walked to the edge of the village, and called Stoner's name. I didn't really expect him to acknowledge me, and I'm not clear as to what my motivations were: maybe it was just that since I had come this far with him I didn't want my efforts wasted. But I think it was something more, some old loyalty resurrected, one I had denied while he was alive.

'Get outta here!' I shouted. 'Go on! Get out!'

He turned that blind, fiery face toward me and despite its featurelessness, I could read therein the record of his solitude, his fears concerning its resolution. It was, I knew, a final sending. I sensed again his emptiness, but it wasn't so harrowing and hopeless as before; in it there was a measure of determination, of purpose, and, too, a kind of… I'm tempted to say gratitude, but in truth it was more a simple acknowledgment, like the wave of a hand given by one workman to another after the completion of a difficult task.

'Go.' I said it softly, the way you'd speak when urging a child to take his first step, and Stoner walked away.

For a few moments, though his legs moved, he didn't appear to be making any headway; his figure remained undiminished by distance. There was a tension in the air, an almost impalpable disturbance that quickly evolved into a heated pulse. One of the banana trees burst into flames, its leaves shriveling; a second tree ignited, a third, and soon all those trees close to the demarcation of that other world were burning like green ceremonial candles. The heat intensified, and the veils of dust that blew toward me carried a stinging residue of that heat; the sky for hundreds of feet above rippled as with the effects of an immense conflagration.

I stumbled back, tripped, and fell heavily. When I recovered I saw that Stoner was receding, that the world into which he was traveling was receding with him, or rather seeming to fold, to bisect and collapse around him: it looked as if that plain dotted with fires were painted on a curtain, and as he pushed forward, the fabric was drawn with him, its painted distances becoming foreshortened, its perspectives exaggerated and surreal, molding into a tunnel that conformed to his shape. His figure shrank to half its previous size, and then – some limit reached, some barrier penetrated – the heat died away, its dissipation accompanied by a seething hiss, and Stoner's white fire began to shine brighter and brighter, his form eroding in brightness. I had to shield my eyes, then shut them; but even so, I could see the soundless explosion that followed through my lids, and for several minutes I could make out its vague afterimage. A blast of wind pressed me flat, hot at first, but blowing colder and colder, setting my teeth to chattering. At last this subsided, and on opening my eyes I found that Stoner had vanished, and where the plain had been now lay a wreckage of yellow stone and seared banana trees, ringed by a few undamaged houses on the perimeter.

The only sound was the crackle of flames from the tin-roofed building. Moments later, however, I heard a patter of applause. I looked behind me: the gooks were all applauding Tuu, who was smiling and bowing like the author of a successful play. I was shocked at their reaction. How could they be concerned with accolades? Hadn't they been dazzled, as I had, their humanity diminished by the mystery and power of Stoner's metamorphosis? I went over to them, and drawing near, I overheard an officer congratulate Tuu on 'another triumph.' It took me a while to register the significance of those words, and when I did I pushed through the group and confronted Tuu.

'"Another triumph"?' I said.

He met my eyes, imperturbable. 'I wasn't aware you spoke our language, Mr. Puleo.'

'You've done this before,' I said, getting angry. 'Haven't you?'

'Twice before.' He tapped a cigarette from a pack of Marlboros; an officer rushed to light it. 'But never with an American spirit.'

'You coulda killed me!' I shouted, lunging for him. Two soldiers came between us, menacing me with their rifles.

Tuu blew out a plume of smoke that seemed to give visible evidence of his self-satisfaction. 'I told you it was a risk,' he said. 'Does it matter that I knew the extent of the risk and you did not? You were in no greater danger because of that. We were prepared to take steps if the situation warranted.'

'Don't bullshit me! You couldn't have done nothin' with Stoner!'

He let a smile nick the corners of his mouth.

'You had no right,' I said. 'You–'

Tuu's face hardened. 'We had no right to mislead you? Please, Mr. Puleo. Between our peoples, deception is a tradition.'

I fumed, wanting to get at him. Frustrated, I slugged my thigh with my fist, spun on my heel, and walked off. The two soldiers caught up with me and blocked my path. Furious, I swatted at their rifles; they disengaged their safeties and aimed at my stomach.

'If you wish to be alone,' Tuu called, 'I have no objection to you taking a walk. We have tests to complete. But please keep to the road. A car will come for you.'

Before the soldiers could step aside, I pushed past them.

'Keep to the road, Mr. Puleo!' In Tuu's voice was more than a touch of amusement. 'If you recall, we're quite adept at tracking.'

Anger was good for me; it kept my mind off what I had seen. I wasn't ready to deal with Stoner's evolution. I wanted to consider things in simple terms: a man I had hated had died to the world a second time and I had played a part in his release, a part in which I had no reason to take pride or bear shame, because I had been manipulated every step of the way. I was so full of anger, I must have done the first mile in under fifteen minutes, the next in not much more. By then the sun had risen above the treeline and I had worked up a sweat. Insects buzzed; monkeys screamed. I slowed my pace and turned my head from side to side as I went, as if I were walking point again. I had the idea my own ghost was walking with me, shifting around inside and burning to get out on its own.

After an hour or so I came to the temporary housing that had been erected for the populace of Cam Le: thatched huts; scrawny dogs slinking and chickens pecking; orange peels, palm litter, and piles of shit in the streets. Some old men smoking pipes by a cookfire blinked at me. Three girls carrying plastic jugs giggled, ran off behind a hut, and peeked back around the corner.

Vietnam.

I thought about the way I'd used to sneer the word. 'Nam, I'd say. Viet-fucking-nam! Now it was spoken proudly, printed in Twentieth Century-Fox monolithic capitals, brazen with hype. Perhaps between those two extremes was a mode of expression that captured the ordinary reality of the place, the poverty and peacefulness of this village; but if so, it wasn't accessible to me.

Some of the villagers were coming out of their doors to have a look at the stranger. I wondered if any of them recognized me. Maybe, I thought, chuckling madly, maybe if I bashed a couple on the head and screamed 'Number Ten VC!' maybe then they'd remember. I suddenly felt tired and empty, and I sat down by the road to wait. I was so distracted, I didn't notice at first that a number of flies had mistaken me for a new and bigger piece of shit and were orbiting me, crawling over my knuckles. I flicked them away, watched them spiral off and land on other parts of my body. I got into controlling their patterns of flight, seeing if I could make them all congregate on my left hand, which I kept still. Weird shudders began passing through my chest, and the vacuum inside my head filled with memories of Stoner, his bizarre dream, his terrible Valhalla. I tried to banish them, but they stuck there, replaying themselves over and over. I couldn't order them, couldn't derive any satisfaction from them. Like the passage of a comet, Stoner's escape from Cam Le had been a trivial cosmic event, causing momentary awe and providing a few more worthless clues to the nature of the absolute, but offering no human solutions. Nothing consequential had changed for me: I was as fucked up as ever, as hard-core disoriented. The buzzing sunlight grew hotter and hotter; the flies' dance quickened in the rippling air.

At long last a dusty car with a gook corporal at the wheel pulled up beside me. Fierman and Witcover were in back, and Witcover's eye was discolored, swollen shut. I went around to the passenger side, opened the front door, and heard behind me a spit-filled explosive sound. Turning, I saw that a kid of about eight or nine had jumped out of hiding to ambush me. He had a dirt-smeared belly that popped from the waist of his ragged shorts, and he was aiming a toy rifle made of sticks. He shot me again, jiggling the gun to simulate automatic fire. Little monster with slit black eyes. Staring daggers at me, thinking I'd killed his daddy. He probably would have loved it if I had keeled over, clutching my chest; but I wasn't in the mood. I pointed my finger, cocked the thumb, and shot him down like a dog.

He stared meanly and fired a third time: this was serious business, and he wanted me to die. 'Row-nal Ray-gun,' he said, and pretended to spit.

I just laughed and climbed into the car. The gook corporal engaged the gears, and we sped off into a boil of dust and light, as if – like Stoner – we were passing through a metaphysical barrier between worlds. My head bounced against the back of the seat, and with each impact I felt that my thoughts were clearing, that a poisonous sediment was being jolted loose and flushed from my bloodstream. Thick silence welled from the rear of the car, and not wanting to ride with hostiles all the way to Saigon, I turned to Witcover and apologized for having hit him. Pressure had done it to me, I told him. That, and bad memories of a bad time. His features tightened into a sour knot and he looked out the window, wholly unforgiving. But I refused to allow his response to disturb me – let him have his petty hate, his grudge, for whatever good it would do him – and I turned away to face the violent green sweep of the jungle, the great troubled rush of the world ahead, with a heart that seemed lighter by an ounce of anger, by one bitterness removed. To the end of that passion, at least, I had become reconciled.

THE FUNCTION OF DREAM SLEEP

Harlan Ellison®

Harlan Ellison (1934–) is an iconic writer called 'one of the great living American short story writers' by *The Washington Post*. His career has spanned over fifty years and he has won more awards for his work than any other living speculative fiction writer, with seventy-five books and over seventeen-thousand short stories, novellas, screenplays, teleplays, essays, and a wide range of criticism covering literature, film, television, and print media. He was editor and anthologist for two ground-breaking science fiction anthologies, *Dangerous Visions* and *Again, Dangerous Visions*. Although several classic earlier stories might have fit this anthology, 1988's 'The Function of Dream Sleep' best exemplifies Harlan Ellison's contributions to the weird tale.

McGrath awoke suddenly, just in time to see a huge mouth filled with small, sharp teeth closing in his side. In an instant it was gone, even as he shook himself awake.

Had he not been staring at the flesh, at the moment his eyes opened from sleep, he would have missed the faintest pink line of closure that remained only another heartbeat, then faded and was gone, leaving no indication the mouth had ever existed; a second – secret – mouth hiding in his skin.

At first he was sure he had wakened from a particularly nasty dream. But the memory of the thing that had escaped from within him, through the mouth, was a real memory – not a wisp of fading nightmare. He had *felt* the chilly passage of something rushing out of him. Like cold air from a leaking balloon. Like a chill down a hallway from a window left open in a distant room. And he had *seen* the mouth. It lay across the ribs vertically, just below his left nipple, running down to the bulge of fat parallel to his navel. Down his left side there had been a lipless mouth filled with teeth; and it had been open to permit a breeze of something to leave his body.

McGrath sat up on the bed. He was shaking. The Tensor lamp was still on, the paperback novel tented open on the sheet beside him, his body naked and perspiring in the August heat. The Tensor had been aimed directly at his side, bathing his flesh with light, when he had unexpectedly opened his eyes; and in that waking moment he had surprised his body in the act of opening its secret mouth.

He couldn't stop the trembling, and when the phone rang he had to steel himself to lift the receiver.

'Hello,' he heard himself say, in someone else's voice.

'Lonny,' said Victor Kayley's widow, 'I'm sorry to disturb you at this hour...'

'It's okay,' he said. Victor had died the day before yesterday. Sally relied on him for the arrangements, and hours of solace he didn't begrudge. Years before, Sally and he... then she drifted toward Victor, who had been McGrath's oldest, closest... they were drawn to each other more and more sweetly till... and finally, McGrath had taken them both to dinner at the old Steuben Tavern on West 47th, that dear old Steuben Tavern with its dark wood booths and sensational schnitzel, now gone, torn down and gone like so much else that was… and he had made them sit side by side in the booth across from him, and he took their hands in his… I love you both so much, he had said… I see the way you move when you're around each other… you're both my dearest friends, you put light in my world… and he laid their hands together under his, and he grinned at them for their nervousness…

'Are you all right; you sound so, I don't know, so *strained*?' Her voice was wide awake. But concerned.

'I'm, yeah, I'm okay. I just had the weirdest, I was dozing, fell asleep reading, and I had this, this *weird*– ' He trailed off. Then went back at it, more sternly: 'I'm okay. It was a scary dream.'

There was, then, a long measure of silence between them. Only the open line, with the sound of ions decaying.

'Are *you* okay?' he said, thinking of the funeral service day after tomorrow. She had asked him to select the casket. The anodized pink aluminum 'unit' they had tried to get him to go for, doing a bait-and-switch, had nauseated him. McGrath had settled on a simple copper casket, shrugging away suggestions by the Bereavement Counselor in the Casket Selection Parlor that 'consideration and thoughtfulness for the departed' might better be served by the Monaco, a 'Duraseal metal unit with Sea Mist Polished Finish, interior richly lined in 600 Aqua Supreme Cheney velvet, magnificently quilted and shirred, with matching jumbo bolster and coverlet.'

'I couldn't sleep,' she said. 'I was watching television, and they had a thing about the echidna, the Australian anteater, you know… ?' He made a sound that indicated he knew. 'And Vic never got over the trip we took to the Flinders Range in '82, and he just loved the Australian animals, and I turned in the bed to see him smiling…'

She began to cry.

He could feel his throat closing. He knew. The turning to tell your best friend something you'd just seen together, to get the reinforcement, the input, the expression on his face. And there was no face. There was emptiness in that place. He knew. He'd turned to Victor three dozen times in the past two days. Turned, to confront emptiness. Oh, he knew, all right.

'Sally,' he murmured. 'Sally, I know; I know.'

She pulled herself together, snuffled herself unclogged and cleared her throat. 'It's okay. I'm fine. It was just a second there…'

'Try to get some sleep. We have to do stuff tomorrow.'

'Of course,' she said, sounding really quite all right. 'I'll go back to bed. I'm sorry.' He told her to shut up, if you couldn't call a friend at that hour to talk about the echidna, who the hell *could* you call?

'Jerry Falwell,' she said. 'If I have to annoy someone at three in the morning, better it should be a shit like him.' They laughed quickly and emptily, she said good night and told him he had been much loved by both of them, he said I know that, and they hung up.

Lonny McGrath lay there, the paperback still tented at his side, the Tensor still warming his flesh, the sheets still soggy from the humidity, and he stared at the far wall of the bedroom on whose surface, like the surface of his skin, there lay no evidence whatever of secret mouths filled with teeth.

'I can't get it out of my mind.'

Dr. Jess ran her fingers down his side, looked closer. 'Well, it *is* red; but that's more chafing than anything out of Stephen King.'

'It's red because I keep rubbing it. I'm getting obsessive about it. And don't make fun, Jess. I can't get it out of my mind.'

She sighed and raked a hand back through her thick auburn hair. 'Sorry.' She got up and walked to the window in the examination room. Then, as an afterthought, she said, 'You can get dressed.' She stared out the window as McGrath hopped off the physical therapy table, nearly catching his heel on the retractable step. He partially folded the stiff paper gown that had covered his lap, and laid it on the padded seat. As he pulled up his undershorts, Dr. Jess turned and stared at him. He thought for the hundredth time that his initial fears, years before, at being examined by a female physician, had been foolish. His friend looked at him with concern, but without the *look* that passed between men and women. 'How long has it been since Victor died?'

'Three months, almost.'

'And Emily?'

'Six months.'

'And Steve and Melanie's son?'

'Oh, Christ, Jess!'

She pursed her lips. 'Look, Lonny, I'm not a psychotherapist, but even I can see that the death of all these friends is getting to you. Maybe you don't even see it, but you used the right word: obsessive. *Nobody* can sustain so much pain, over so brief a period, the loss of so many loved ones, without going into a spiral.'

'What did the X-rays show?'

'I told you.'

'But there might've been *some*thing. Some lesion, or inflammation; an irregularity in the dermis… *some*thing!'

'Lonny. Come *on*. I've never lied to you. You looked at them with me, did *you* see anything?' He sighed deeply, shook his head. She spread her hands as if to say, well, there you are, I can't make something sick where nothing sick exists. 'I can work on your soft prostate, and I can give you a shot of cortisone in the ball joint where that cop worked you over; but I can't treat something out of a penny dreadful novel that doesn't leave any trace.'

'You think I need a shrink?'

She turned back to the window. 'This is your third visit, Lonny. You're my pal, kiddo, but I think you need to get counseling of a different sort.'

McGrath knotted his tie and drew it up, spreading the wings of his shirt collar with his little fingers. She didn't turn around. 'I'm worried about you, Lonny. You ought to be married.'

'I *was* married. You're not talking wife, anyway. You're talking keeper.' She didn't turn. He pulled on his jacket, and waited. Finally, with his hand on the doorknob, he said, 'Maybe you're right. I've never been a melancholy sort, but all this… so many, in so short a time… maybe you're right.'

He opened the door. She looked out the window. 'We'll talk.' He started out, and without turning, she said, 'There won't be a charge for this visit.'

He smiled thinly, not at all happily. But she didn't see it. There is *always* a charge, of one kind or another.

He called Tommy and begged off from work. Tommy went into a snit. 'I'm up to my ass, Lonny,' he said, affecting his Dowager Empress tone. 'This is Black goddam Friday! The Eroica! That Fahrenheit woman, Farrenstock, whatever the hell it is…'

'Fahnestock,' Lonny said, smiling for the first time in days. 'I thought we'd seen the last of her when you suggested she look into the possibility of a leper sitting on her face.'

Tommy sighed. 'The grotesque bitch is simply a glutton. I swear to God she must be into bondage; the worse I treat her, the more often she comes in.'

'What'd she bring this time?'

'Another half dozen of those tacky petit-point things. I can barely bring myself to look at them. Bleeding martyrs and scenes of culturally depressed areas in, I suppose, Iowa or Indiana. Illinois, Idaho, I don't know: one of those places that begins with an I, teeming with people who bowl.'

Lonny always wound up framing Mrs. Fahnestock's gaucheries. Tommy always took one look, then went upstairs in back of the framing shop to lie down for a while. McGrath had asked the matron once, what she did with all of them. She replied that she gave them as gifts. Tommy, when he heard, fell to his knees and prayed to a God in which he did not believe that the woman would never hold him in enough esteem to feel he deserved such a gift. But she spent, oh my, how she spent.

'Let me guess,' McGrath said. 'She wants them blocked so tightly you could bounce a dime off them, with a fabric liner, a basic pearl matte, and the black lacquer frame from Chapin Molding. Right?'

'Yes, of course, right. Which is *another* reason your slacker behavior is particularly distressing. The truck from Chapin just dropped off a hundred feet of the oval top walnut molding. It's got to be unpacked, the footage measured, and put away. You *can't* take the day off.'

'Tommy, don't whip the guilt on me. I'm a goy, remember?'

'If it weren't for guilt, the *goyim* would have wiped us out three thousand years ago. It's more effective than a Star Wars defense system.' He puffed air through his lips for a moment, measuring how much he would *actually* be inconvenienced by his assistant's absence. 'Monday morning? Early?'

McGrath said, 'I'll be there no later than eight o'clock. I'll do the petit-points first.'

'All right. And by the way, you sound awful. D'you know the worst part about being an Atheist?'

Lonny smiled. Tommy would feel it was a closed bargain if he could pass on one of his horrendous jokes. 'No, what's the worst part about being an Atheist?'

'You've got no one to talk to when you're fucking.'

Lonny roared, silently. There was no need to give him the satisfaction. But Tommy knew. He couldn't see him, but Lonny knew he was grinning broadly at the other end of the line. 'So long, Tommy. See you Monday.'

He racked the receiver in the phone booth and looked across Pico Boulevard at the office building. He had lived in Los Angeles for eleven years, since he and Victor and Sally had fled New York, and he still couldn't get used to the golden patina that lay over the days here. Except when it rained, at which times the inclemency seemed so alien he had visions of giant mushrooms sprouting from the sidewalks. The office building was unimpressive, just three storeys high and brick; but a late afternoon shadow lay across its face, and it recalled for him the eighteen frontal views of the Rouen Cathedral that Monet had painted during the winter months of 1892 and 1893: the same façade, following the light from early morning till sunset. He had seen the Monet exhibition at MOMA. Then he remembered with whom he had taken in that exhibition, and he felt again the passage of chill leaving his body through that secret mouth. He stepped out of the booth and just wanted to go somewhere and cry. *Stop it!* he said inside. *Knock it off.* He swiped at the corner of his eye, and crossed the street. He passed through the shadow that cut the sidewalk.

Inside the tiny lobby he consulted the glass-paneled wall register. Mostly, the building housed dentists and philatelists, as best he could tell. But against the ribbed black panel he read the little white plastic letters that had been darted in to include THE REM GROUP 306. He walked up the stairs.

To find 306, he had to make a choice: go left or go right. There were no office location arrows on the wall. He went to the right, and was pleased. As the numbers went down, he began to hear someone speaking rather loudly. 'Sleep is of several kinds. Dream sleep, or rapid eye movement sleep – what we call REM sleep, and thus the name of our group – is predominantly found in mammals who bring forth living young, rather than eggs. Some birds and reptiles, as well.'

McGrath stood outside the glass-paneled door to 306, and he listened. *Viviparous mammals,* he thought. He could now discern that the speaker was a woman; and her use of 'living young, rather than eggs' instead of *viviparous* convinced him she was addressing one or more laypersons. *The echidna,* he thought. *A familiar viviparous mammal.*

'We now believe dreams originate in the brain's neocortex. Dreams have been used to attempt to foretell the future. Freud used dreams to explore the unconscious mind. Jung thought dreams formed a bridge of communication between the conscious and the unconscious.' *It wasn't a dream,* McGrath thought. *I was awake. I know the difference.*

The woman was saying, '... those who try to make dreams work for them, to create poetry, to solve problems; and it's generally thought that dreams aid in consolidating memories. How many of you believe that if you can only *remember* the dream when you waken, that you will understand something very important, or regain some special memory you've lost?'

How many of you. McGrath now understood that the dream therapy group was in session. Late on a Friday afternoon? It would have to be women in their thirties, forties.

He opened the door, to see if he was correct.

With their hands in the air, indicating they believed the capturing of a dream on awakening would bring back an old memory, all six of the women in the room, not one of them older than forty, turned to stare at McGrath as he entered. He closed the door behind him, and said, 'I don't agree. I think we dream to forget. And sometimes it doesn't work.'

He was looking at the woman standing in front of the six hand-raised members of the group. She stared back at him for a long moment, and all six heads turned back to her. Their hands were frozen in the air. The woman who had been speaking settled back till she was perched on the edge of her desk.

'Mr. McGrath?'

'Yes. I'm sorry I'm late. It's been a day.'

She smiled quickly, totally in command, putting him at ease. 'I'm Anna Picket. Tricia said you'd probably be along today. Please grab a chair.'

McGrath nodded and took a folding chair from the three remaining against the wall. He unfolded it and set it at the far left of the semicircle. The six well-tended, expensively coifed heads remained turned toward him as, one by one, the hands came down.

He wasn't at all sure letting his ex-wife call this Anna Picket, to get him into the group, had been such a good idea. They had remained friends after the divorce, and he trusted her judgment. Though he had never availed himself of her services after they'd separated and she had gone for her degree at UCLA, he'd been assured that Tricia was as good a family counseling therapist as one could find in Southern California. He had been shocked when she'd suggested a dream group. But he'd come: he had walked through the area most of the early part of the day, trying to decide if he wanted to do this, share what he'd experienced with total strangers; walked through the area stopping in at this shop and that boutique, having some gelato and shaking his head at how this neighborhood had been 'gentrified,' how it had changed so radically, how all the wonderful little tradesmen who had flourished here had been driven out by geysering rents; walked through the area growing more and more despondent at how nothing lasted, how joy was drained away shop by shop, neighborhood by neighborhood, person by...

Until one was left alone.

Standing on an empty plain. The dark wind blowing from the horizon. Cold, empty dark: with the knowledge that a pit of eternal loneliness lay just over that horizon, and that the frightening wind that blew up out of the pit would never cease. That one would stand there, all alone, on the empty plain, as one after another of the ones you loved were erased in a second.

Had walked through the area, all day, and finally had called Tommy, and finally had allowed Tricia's wisdom to lead him, and here he sat, in a folding straight-back chair, asking a total stranger to repeat what she had just said.

'I asked why you didn't agree with the group, that remembering dreams is a good thing?' She arched an eyebrow, and tilted her head.

McGrath felt uncomfortable for a moment. He blushed. It was something that had always caused him embarrassment. 'Well,' he said slowly, 'I don't want to seem like a smart aleck, one of those people who reads some popularized bit of science and then comes on like an authority...'

She smiled at his consternation, the flush of his cheeks. 'Please, Mr. McGrath, that's quite all right. Where dreams are concerned, we're *all* journeyists. What did you read?'

'The Crick-Mitchison theory. The paper on "unlearning". I don't know, it just seemed, well, *reasonable* to me.'

One of the women asked what that was.

Anna Picket said, 'Dr. Sir Francis Crick, you'll know of him because he won the Nobel Prize for his work with DNA; and Graeme Mitchison, he's a highly respected brain researcher at Cambridge. Their experiments in the early 1980s. They postulate that we dream to forget, not to remember.'

'The best way I understood it,' McGrath said, 'was using the analogy of cleaning out an office building at night, after all the workers are gone. Outdated reports are trashed, computer dump sheets are shredded, old memos tossed with the refuse. Every night our brains get cleaned during the one to two hours of REM sleep. The dreams pick up after us every day, sweep out the unnecessary, untrue, or just plain silly memories that could keep us from storing the important memories, or might keep us from rational thinking when we're awake. *Remembering* the dreams would be counter-productive, since the brain is trying to unlearn all that crap so we function better.'

Anna Picket smiled. 'You were sent from heaven, Mr. McGrath. I was going precisely to that theory when you came in. You've saved me a great deal of explanation.'

One of the six women said, 'Then you don't *want* us to write down our dreams and bring them in for discussion? I even put a tape recorder by the bed. For instance, I had a dream just last night in which my bicycle...'

He sat through the entire session, listening to things that infuriated him. They were so self-indulgent, making of the most minor inconveniences in their lives, mountains impossible to conquer. They were so different from the women he knew. They seemed to be antiquated creatures from some primitive time, confused by changing times and the demand on them to be utterly responsible for their existence. They seemed to want succor, to be told that there were greater forces at work in their world; powers and pressures and even conspiracies that existed solely to keep them nervous, uncomfortable, and helpless. Five of the six were divorcées, and only one of the five had a full-time job: selling real estate. The sixth was the daughter of an organized crime figure. McGrath felt no link with them. He didn't need a group therapy session. His life was as full as he wanted it to be... except that he was now always scared, and lost, and constantly depressed. Perhaps Dr. Jess was dead on target. Perhaps he *did* need a shrink.

He was certain he did not need Anna Picket and her well-tailored ladies whose greatest *real* anguish was making sure they got home in time to turn on the sprinklers.

When the session ended, he started toward the door without saying anything to the Picket woman. She was surrounded by the six. But she gently edged them aside and called to him, 'Mr. McGrath, would you wait a moment? I'd like to speak to you.' He took his hand off the doorknob, and went back to his chair. He bit the soft flesh of his inner cheek, annoyed.

She blew them off like dandelion fluff, far more quickly than McGrath thought possible, and did it without their taking it as rejection. In less than five minutes he was alone in the office with the dream therapist.

She closed the door behind the Mafia Princess and locked it. For a deranged moment he thought... but it passed, and the look on her face was concern, not lust. He started to rise. She laid a palm against the air, stopping him. He sank back onto the folding chair.

Then Anna Picket came to him and said, 'For McGrath hath murdered sleep.' He stared up at her as she put her left hand behind his head, cupping the nape with fingers extending up under his hair along the curve of the skull. 'Don't be nervous, this'll be all right,' she said, laying her right hand with the palm against his left cheek, the spread thumb and index finger bracketing an eye he tried mightily not to blink. Her thumb lay alongside his nose, the tip curving onto the bridge. The forefinger lay across the bony eye-ridge.

She pursed her lips, then sighed deeply. In a moment her body twitched with an involuntary rictus, and she gasped, as if she had had the wind knocked out of her. McGrath couldn't move. He could feel the strength of her hands cradling his head, and the tremors of – he wanted to say – *passion* slamming through her. Not the passion of strong amorous feeling, but passion in the sense of being acted upon by something external, something alien to one's nature.

The trembling in her grew more pronounced, and McGrath had the sense that power was being drained out of him, pouring into her, that it had reached saturation level and was leaking back along the system into him, but changed, more dangerous. But why dangerous? She was spasming now, her eyes closed, her head thrown back and to the side, her thick mass of hair swaying and bobbing as she jerked, a human double-circuit high-voltage tower about to overload.

She moaned softly, in pain, without the slightest trace of subliminal pleasure, and he could see she was biting her lower lip so fiercely that blood was beginning to coat her mouth. When the pain he saw in her face became more than he could bear, he reached up quickly and took her hands away with difficulty; breaking the circuit.

Anna Picket's legs went out and she keeled toward him. He tried to brace himself, but she hit him with full dead weight, and they went crashing to the floor entangled in the metal folding chair.

Frightened, thinking insanely *what if someone comes in and sees us like this, they'd think I was molesting her*, and in the next instant thinking with relief *she locked the door*, and in the next instant his fear was transmogrified into concern for her. He rolled out from under her trembling body, taking the chair with him, wrapped around one ankle. He shook off the chair, and got to his knees. Her eyes were half-closed, the lids flickering so rapidly she might have been in the line of strobe lights.

He hauled her around, settling her semi-upright with her head in his lap. He brushed the hair from her face, and shook her ever so lightly, because he had no water, and had no moist wash-cloth. Her breathing slowed, her chest heaved not quite so spastically, and her hand, flung away from her body, began to flex the fingers.

'Ms. Picket,' he whispered, 'can you talk? Are you all right? Is there some medicine you need… in your desk?'

She opened her eyes, then, and looked up at him. She tasted the blood on her lips and continued breathing raggedly, as though she had run a great distance. And finally she said, 'I could feel it in you when you walked in.'

He tried to ask what it was she had felt, what it was in him that had so unhinged her, but she reached in with the flexing hand and touched his forearm.

'You'll have to come with me.'

'Where?'

'To meet the *real* REM Group.'

And she began to cry. He knew immediately that she was weeping for him, and he murmured that he would come with her. She tried to smile reassurance, but there was still too much pain in her. They stayed that way for a time, and then they left the office building together.

They were impaired, every one of them in the sprawling ranch-style house in Hidden Hills. One was blind, another had only one hand. A third looked as if she had been in a terrible fire and had lost half her face, and another propelled herself through the house on a small wheeled platform with restraining bars to keep her from falling off.

They had taken the San Diego Freeway to the Ventura, and had driven west on 101 to the Calabasas exit. Climbing, then dropping behind the hills, they had turned up a side road that became a dirt road that became a horse path, Lonny driving Anna Picket's '85 Le Sabre.

The house lay within a bowl, completely concealed, even from the dirt road below. The horse trail passed behind low hills covered with mesquite and coast live oak, and abruptly became a perfectly surfaced blacktop. Like the roads Hearst had had cut in the hills leading up to San Simeon, concealing access to the Castle from the Coast Highway above Cambria, the blacktop had been poured on spiral rising cuts laid on a reverse bias.

Unless sought from the air, the enormous ranch house and its outbuildings and grounds would be unknown even to the most adventurous picnicker. 'How much of this acreage do you own?' McGrath asked, circling down the inside of the bowl.

'All this,' she said, waving an arm across the empty hills, 'almost to the edge of Ventura County.'

She had recovered completely, but had said very little during the hour and a half trip, even during the heaviest weekend traffic on the 101 Freeway crawling like a million-wheeled worm through the San Fernando Valley out of Los Angeles. 'Not a lot of casual drop-ins I should imagine,' he replied.

She looked at him across the front seat, fully for the first time since leaving Santa Monica. 'I hope you'll have faith in me, trust me just a while longer,' she said.

He paid strict attention to the driving.

He had been cramped within the Buick by a kind of dull fear that strangely reminded him of how he had always felt on Christmas Eve, as a child, lying in bed, afraid of, yet anxious for, the sleep that permitted Santa Claus to come.

In that house below lay something that knew of secret mouths and ancient winds from within. Had he not trusted her, he would have slammed the brake pedal and leaped from the car and not stopped running till he had reached the freeway.

And once inside the house, seeing all of them, so ruined and tragic, he was helpless to do anything but allow her to lead him to a large sitting-room, where a circle of comfortable over-stuffed chairs formed a pattern that made the fear more overwhelming.

They came, then, in twos and threes, the legless woman on the rolling cart propelling herself into the center of the ring. He sat there and watched them come, and his heart seemed to press against his chest. McGrath, as a young man, had gone to a Judy Garland film festival at the Thalia in New York. One of the revived movies had been *A Child Is Waiting*, a nonsinging role for Judy, a film about retarded children. Sally had had to help him out of the theater only halfway through. He could not see through his tears. His capacity for bearing the anguish of the crippled, particularly children, was less than that of most people. He brought himself up short: why had he thought of that afternoon at the Thalia now? These weren't children. They were adults. All of them. Every woman in the house was at least as old as he, surely older. Why had he been thinking of them as children?

Anna Picket took the chair beside him, and looked around the circle. One chair was empty. 'Catherine?' she asked.

The blind woman said, 'She died on Sunday.'

Anna closed her eyes and sank back into the chair. 'God be with her, and her pain ended.'

They sat quietly for a time, until the woman on the cart looked up at McGrath, smiled a very kind smile, and said, 'What is your name, young man?'

'Lonny,' McGrath said. He watched as she rolled herself to his feet and put a hand on his knee. He felt warmth flow through him, and his fear melted. But it only lasted for a moment, as she trembled and moaned softly; as Anna Picket had done in the office. Anna quickly rose and drew her away from McGrath. There were tears in the cart-woman's eyes.

A woman with gray hair and involuntary head tremors, indicative of Parkinson's, leaned forward and said, 'Lonny, tell us.'

He started to say *tell you what?* but she held up a finger and said the same thing again.

So he told them. As best he could. Putting words to feelings that always sounded melodramatic; words that were wholly inadequate for the tidal wave of sorrow that held him down in darkness. 'I miss them, oh God how I miss them,' he said, twisting his hands. 'I've never been like this. My mother died, and I was lost, I was miserable, yes there was a feeling my heart would break, because I loved her. But I could *handle* it. I could comfort my father and my sister, I had it in me to do that. But these last two years... one after another... so many who were close to me... pieces of my past, my life... friends I'd shared times with, and now those times are gone, they slip away as I try to think of them. I, I just don't know *what to do*.'

And he spoke of the mouth. The teeth. The closing of that mouth. The wind that had escaped from inside him.

'Did you ever sleepwalk, as a child?' a woman with a clubfoot asked. He said: yes, but only once. Tell us, they said.

'It was nothing. I was a little boy, maybe ten or eleven. My father found me standing in the hall-way outside my bedroom, at the head of the stairs. I was asleep, and I was looking at the wall. I said, "I don't see it here anywhere." My father told me I'd said that; the next morning he told me. He took me back to bed. That was the only time, as best I know.'

The women murmured around the circle to each other. Then the woman with Parkinson's said, 'No, I don't think that's anything.' Then she stood up, and came to him. She laid a hand on his fore-head and said, 'Go to sleep, Lonny.'

And he blinked once, and suddenly sat bolt upright. But it wasn't an instant, it had been much longer. He had been asleep. For a long while. He knew it was so instantly, because it was now dark outside the house, and the women looked as if they had been savaged by living jungles. The blind woman was bleeding from her eyes and ears; the woman on the cart had fallen over, lay unconscious at his feet; in the chair where the fire victim had sat, there was now only a charred outline of a human being, still faintly smoking.

McGrath leaped to his feet. He looked about wildly. He didn't know what to do to help them.

Beside him, Anna Picket lay slumped across the bolster arm of the chair, her body twisted and blood once again speckling her lips.

Then he realized: the woman who had touched him, the woman with Parkinson's, was gone.

They began to whimper, and several of them moved, their hands idly touching the air. A woman who had no nose tried to rise, slipped and fell. He rushed to her, helped her back into the chair, and he realized she was missing fingers on both hands. Leprosy… *no*! Hansen's disease, that's what it's called. She was coming to, and she whispered to him, 'There… Teresa… help her…' and he looked where she was pointing, at a woman as pale as crystal, her hair a glowing white, her eyes colorless. 'She… has… lupus…' the woman without a nose whispered.

McGrath went to Teresa. She looked up at him with fear and was barely able to say, 'Can you… please… take me to a dark place…?'

He lifted her in his arms. She weighed nothing. He let her direct him up the stairs to the second floor, to the third bedroom off the main corridor. He opened the door; inside it was musty and unlit. He could barely make out the shape of a bed. He carried her over and placed her gently on the puffy down comforter. She reached up and touched his hand. 'Thank you.' She spoke haltingly, having trouble breathing. 'We, we didn't expect anything… like that…'

McGrath was frantic. He didn't know what had happened, didn't know what he had done to them. He felt awful, felt responsible, *but he didn't know what he had done!*

'Go back to them,' she whispered. 'Help them.'

'Where is the woman who touched me…?'

He heard her sobbing. 'She's gone. Lurene is gone. It wasn't your fault. We didn't expect anything… like… that.'

He rushed back downstairs.

They were helping one another. Anna Picket had brought water, and bottles of medicine, and wet cloths. They were helping one another. The healthier ones limping and crawling to the ones still unconscious or groaning in pain. And he smelled the fried metal scent of ozone in the air. There was a charred patch on the ceiling above the chair where the burned woman had been sitting.

He tried to help Anna Picket, but when she realized it was McGrath, she slapped his hand away. Then she gasped, and her hand flew to her mouth, and she began to cry again, and reached out to apologize. 'Oh, my God, I'm so *sorry*! It wasn't your fault. You couldn't know… not even Lurene knew.' She swabbed at her eyes, and laid a hand on his chest. 'Go outside. Please. I'll be there in a moment.'

A wide streak of dove-gray now bolted through her tangled hair. It had not been there before the instant of his sleep.

He went outside and stood under the stars. It was night, but it had not been night before Lurene had touched him. He stared up at the cold points of light, and the sense of irreparable loss overwhelmed him. He wanted to sink to his knees, letting his life ebb into the ground, freeing him from this misery that would not let him breathe. He thought of Victor, and the casket being cranked down into the earth, as Sally clung to him, murmuring words he could not understand, and hitting him again and again on the chest; not hard, but without measure, without meaning, with nothing but simple human misery. He thought of Alan, dying in a Hollywood apartment from AIDS, tended by his mother and sister who were, themselves, hysterical and constantly praying, asking Jesus to help them; dying in that apartment with the two roommates who had been sharing the rent, keeping to themselves, eating off paper plates for fear of contracting the plague, trying to figure out if they could get a lawyer to force Alan's removal; dying in that miserable apartment because the Kaiser Hospital had found a way around his coverage, and had forced him into 'home care.' He thought of Emily, lying dead beside her bed, having just dressed for dinner with her daughter, being struck by the grand mal seizure and her heart exploding, lying there for a day, dressed for a dinner she would never eat, with a daughter she would never again see. He thought of Mike, trying to smile from the hospital bed, and forgetting from moment to moment who Lonny was, as the tumor consumed his brain. He thought of Ted seeking shamans and homeopathists, running full tilt till he was cut down. He thought of Roy, all alone now that DeeDee was gone: half a unit, a severed dream, an incomplete conversation. He stood there with his head in his hands, rocking back and forth, trying to ease the pain.

When Anna Picket touched him, he started violently, a small cry of desolation razoring into the darkness.

'What *happened* in there?' he demanded. 'Who *are* you people? What did I do to you? Please, oh please I'm asking you, tell me *what's going on*!'

'We absorb.'

'I don't know what– '

'We take illness. We've always been with you. As far back as we can know. We have always had that capacity, to assume the illness. There aren't many of us, but we're everywhere. We absorb. We try to help. As Jesus wrapped himself in the leper's garments, as he touched the lame and the blind, and they were healed. I don't know where it comes from, some sort of intense empathy. But... we do it... we absorb.'

'And with me... what was that in there... ?'

'We didn't know. We thought it was just the heartache. We've encountered it before. That was why Tricia suggested you come to the Group.'

'My wife... is Tricia one of you? Can she... take on the... does she absorb? I lived with her, I never– '

Anna was shaking her head. 'No, Tricia has no idea what we are. She's never been here. Very few people have been so needing that I've brought them here. But she's a fine therapist, and we've helped a few of her patients. She thought you...' She paused. 'She still cares for you. She felt your pain, and thought the Group might be able to help. She doesn't even know of the *real* REM Group.'

He grabbed her by the shoulders, intense now. '*What happened in there?*'

She bit her lip and closed her eyes tightly against the memory. 'It was as you said. The mouth. We'd never seen that before. It, it *opened*. And then... and then...'

He shook her. '*What!?!*'

She wailed against the memory. The sound slammed against him and against the hills and against the cold points of the stars. 'Mouths. In each of us! Opened. And the wind, it, it just, it just *hissed* out of us, each of us. And the pain we held, no, that *they* held – I'm just their contact for the world, they can't go anywhere, so I go and shop and bring and do – the pain *they* absorbed, it, it took some of them. Lurene and Margid... Teresa won't live... I know...'

McGrath was raving now. His head was about to burst. He shook her as she cried and moaned, demanding, 'What's happening to us, how could I do such an awfulness to you, why is this being done to me, to *us*, why *now*, what's going wrong, please, you've got to tell me, you've got to *help* me, we've got to *do* something–'

And they hugged each other, clinging tightly to the only thing that promised support: each other. The sky wheeled above them, and the ground seemed to fall away. But they kept their balance, and finally she pushed him to arm's length and looked closely at his face and said, 'I don't know. I *do not* know. This isn't like anything we've experienced before. Not even Alvarez or Ariès know about this. A wind, a terrible wind, something alive, leaving the body.'

'*Help me!*'

'I *can't* help you! No one can help you, I don't think *anyone* can help you. Not even Le Braz...'

He clutched at the name. 'Le Braz! Who's Le Braz?'

'No, you don't want to see Le Braz. Please, listen to me, try to go off where it's quiet, and lonely, and try to handle it yourself, that's the only way!'

'Tell me who Le Braz is!'

She slapped him. 'You're not hearing me. If *we* can't do for you, then no one can. Le Braz is beyond anything we know, he can't be trusted, he does things that are outside, that are awful, I think. I don't really know. I went to him once, years ago, it's not something you want to – '

I don't care, he said. I don't care about any of it now. I have to rid myself of this. It's too terrible to live with. I see their faces. They're calling and I can't answer them. They plead with me to say something to them. I don't know what to say. I can't sleep. And when I sleep I dream of them. I can't live like this, because this isn't living. So tell me how to find Le Braz. I don't care, to Hell with the whole thing, I just don't give a damn, so *tell me*!

She slapped him again. Much harder. And again. And he took it. And finally she told him.

He had been an abortionist. In the days before it was legal, he had been the last hope for hundreds of women. Once, long before, he had been a surgeon. But they had taken that away from him. So he did what he could do. In the days when women went to small rooms with long tables, or to coat hangers, he had helped. He had charged two hundred dollars, just to keep up with supplies. In those days of secret thousands in brown paper bags stored in clothes closets, two hundred dollars was as if he had done the work for free. And they had put him in prison. But when he came out, he went back at it.

Anna Picket told McGrath that there had been other…

… work. Other experiments. She had said the word *experiments*, with a tone in her voice that made McGrath shudder. And she had said again, 'For McGrath hath murdered sleep,' and he asked her if he could take her car, and she said yes, and he had driven back to the 101 Freeway and headed north toward Santa Barbara, where Anna Picket said Le Braz now lived, and had lived for years, in total seclusion.

It was difficult locating his estate. The only gas station open in Santa Barbara at that hour did not carry maps. It had been years since free maps had been a courtesy of gas stations. Like so many other small courtesies in McGrath's world that had been spirited away before he could lodge a complaint. But there was no complaint department, in any case.

So he went to the Hotel Miramar, and the night clerk was a woman in her sixties who knew every street in Santa Barbara and knew very well the location of the Le Braz 'place.' She looked at McGrath as if he had asked her the location of the local abattoir. But she gave him explicit directions, and he thanked her, and she didn't say you're welcome, and he left. It was just lightening in the east as dawn approached.

By the time he found the private drive that climbed through heavy woods to the high-fenced estate, it was fully light. Sun poured across the channel and made the foliage seem Rain Forest lush. He looked back over his shoulder as he stepped out of the Le Sabre, and the Santa Monica Channel was silver and rippled and utterly oblivious to shadows left behind from the night.

He walked to the gate, and pressed the button on the intercom system. He waited, and pressed it again. Then a voice – he could not tell if it was male or female, young or old – cracked, 'Who is it?'

'I've come from Anna Picket and the REM Group.' He paused a moment, and when the silence persisted, he added, 'The *real* REM Group. Women in a house in Hidden Hills.'

The voice said, 'Who are you? What's your name?'

'It doesn't matter. You don't know me. McGrath, my name is McGrath. I came a long way to see Le Braz.'

'About what?'

'Open the gate and you'll know.'

'We don't have visitors.'

'I saw… there was a… I woke up suddenly, there was a, a kind of *mouth* in my body… a wind passed…'

There was a whirring sound, and the iron gate began to withdraw into the brick wall. McGrath rushed back to the car and started the engine. As the gate opened completely, he decked the accelerator and leaped through, even as the gate began without hesitation to close.

He drove up the winding drive through the Rain Forest, and when he came out at the top, the large, fieldstone mansion sat there, hidden from all sides by tall stands of trees and thick foliage. He pulled up on the crushed rock drive, and sat for a moment staring at the leaded windows that looked down emptily. It was cool here, and dusky, even though it was burgeoning day. He got out and went to the carved oak door. He was reaching for the knocker when the door was opened. By a ruined thing.

McGrath couldn't help himself. He gasped and fell back, his hands coming up in front of him as if to ward off any approach by the barely human being that stood in the entranceway.

It was horribly pink where it was not burned. At first McGrath thought it was a woman, that was his quick impression; but then he could not discern its sex, it might have been male. It had certainly been tortured in flames. The head was without hair, almost without skin that was not charred black. There seemed to be too many bends and joints in the arms. The sense that it was female came from the floor-length wide skirt it wore. He was spared the sight of the lower body, but he could tell there was considerable bulk there, a bulk that seemed to move gelatinously, as if neither human torso nor human legs lay within the circle of fabric.

And the creature stared at him from one milky eye, and one eye so pure and blue that his heart ached with the beauty of it. As features between the eyes and the chin that became part of the chest, without discernible neck, there were only charred knobs and bumps, and a lipless mouth blacker than the surrounding flesh. 'Come inside,' the doorkeeper said.

McGrath hesitated.

'Or go away,' it said.

Lonny McGrath drew a deep breath and passed through. The doorkeeper moved aside only a trifle. They touched: blackened hip, back of a normal hand.

Closed and double-bolted, the passage out was now denied McGrath. He followed the asexual creature through a long, high-ceilinged foyer to a closed, heavily paneled door to the right of a spiral staircase that led to the floor above. The thing, either man or woman, indicated he should enter. Then it shambled away, toward the rear of the mansion.

McGrath stood a moment, then turned the ornate L-shaped door handle, and entered. The heavy drapes were drawn against the morning light, but in the outlaw beams that latticed the room here and there, he saw an old man sitting in a high-backed chair, a lap robe concealing his legs. He stepped inside the library, for library it had to be: floor to ceiling bookcases, spilling their contents in teetering stacks all around the floor. Music swirled through the room. Classical music; McGrath didn't recognize it.

'Dr. Le Braz?' he said. The old man did not move. His head lay sunk on his chest. His eyes were closed. McGrath moved closer. The music swelled toward a crescendo, something symphonic. Now he was only three steps from the old man, and he called the name Le Braz again.

The eyes opened, and the leonine head rose. He stared at McGrath unblinkingly. The music came to an end. Silence filled the library.

The old man smiled sadly. And all ominousness left the space between them. It was a sweet smile. He inclined his head toward a stool beside the wingback. McGrath tried to give back a small smile, and took the seat offered.

'It is my hope that you are not here to solicit my endorsement for some new pharmacological product,' the old man said.

'Are you Dr. Le Braz?'

'It is I who was, once, known by that name, yes.'

'You have to help me.'

Le Braz looked at him. There had been such a depth of ocean in the words McGrath had spoken, such a descent into stony caverns that all casualness was instantly denied. 'Help you?'

'Yes. Please. I can't bear what I'm feeling. I've been through so much, seen so much these last months, I...'

'Help you?' the old man said again, whispering the phrase as if it had been rendered in a lost language. 'I cannot even help myself... how can I possibly help you, young man?'

McGrath told him. Everything.

At some point the blackened creature entered the room, but McGrath was unaware of its presence till he had completed his story. Then, from behind him, he heard it say, 'You are a remarkable person. Not one living person in a million has ever seen the Thanatos mouth. Not one in a hundred million has felt the passage of the soul. Not one in the memory of the human race has been so tormented that he thought it was real, and not a dream.'

McGrath stared at the creature. It came lumbering across the room and stood just behind the old man's chair, not touching him. The old man sighed, and closed his eyes.

The creature said, 'This was Josef Le Braz, who lived and worked and cared for his fellow man, and woman. He saved lives, and he married out of love, and he pledged himself to leave the world slightly better for his passage. And his wife died, and he fell into a well of melancholy such as no man had ever suffered. And one night he woke, feeling a chill, but he did not see the Thanatos mouth. All he knew was that he missed his wife so terribly that he wanted to end his life.'

McGrath sat silently. He had no idea what this meant, this history of the desolate figure under the lap robe. But he waited, because if no help lay here in this house, of all houses secret and open in the world, then he knew that the next step for him was to buy a gun and to disperse the gray mist under which he lived.

Le Braz looked up. He drew in a deep breath and turned his eyes to McGrath. 'I went to the machine,' he said. 'I sought the aid of the circuit and the chip. I was cold, and could never stop crying. I missed her so, it was unbearable.'

The creature came around the wingback and stood over McGrath. 'He brought her back from the Other Side.'

McGrath's eyes widened. He understood.

The room was silent, building to a crescendo. He tried to get off the low stool, but he couldn't move. The creature stared down at him with its one gorgeous blue eye and its one unseeing milky marble. 'He deprived her of peace. Now she must live on, in this half-life.

'This is Josef Le Braz, and he cannot support his guilt.'

The old man was crying now. McGrath thought if one more tear was shed in the world he would say to hell with it and go for the gun. 'Do you understand?' the old man said softly.

'Do you take the point?' the creature said.

McGrath's hands came up, open and empty. 'The mouth… the wind…'

'The function of dream sleep,' the creature said, 'is to permit us to live. To flense the mind of that which dismays us. Otherwise, how could we bear the sorrow? The memories are their legacy, the parts of themselves left with us when they depart. But they are not whole, they are joys crying to be reunited with the one to whom they belong. You have seen the Thanatos mouth, you have felt a loved one departing. It should have freed you.'

McGrath shook his head slowly, slowly. No, it didn't free me, it enslaved me, it torments me. No, slowly, no. I cannot bear it.

'Then you do not yet take the point, do you?'

The creature touched the old man's sunken cheek with a charred twig that had been a hand. The old man tried to look up with affection, but his head would not come around. 'You must let it go, all of it,' Le Braz said. 'There is no other answer. Let it go… let *them* go. Give them back the parts they need to be whole on the Other Side, and let them in the name of kindness have the peace to which they are entitled.'

'Let the mouth open,' the creature said. 'We cannot abide here. Let the wind of the soul pass through, and take the emptiness as release.' And she said, 'Let me tell you what it's like on the Other Side. Perhaps it will help.'

McGrath laid a hand on his side. It hurt terribly, as of legions battering for release on a locked door.

He retraced his steps. He went back through previous days as if he were sleepwalking. *I don't see it here anywhere.*

He stayed at the ranch-style house in Hidden Hills, and helped Anna Picket as best he could. She drove him back to the city, and he picked up his car from the street in front of the office building on Pico. He put the three parking tickets in the glove compartment. That was work for the living. He went back to his apartment, and he took off his clothes, and he bathed. He lay naked on the bed where it had all started, and he tried to sleep. There were dreams. Dreams of smiling faces, and dreams of children he had known. Dreams of kindness, and dreams of hands that had held him.

And sometime during the long night a breeze blew.

But he never felt it.

And when he awoke, it was cooler in the world than it had been for a very long time; and when he cried for them, he was, at last, able to say goodbye.

A man is what he does with his attention.
John Ciardi

WORLDS THAT FLOURISH

Ben Okri

Ben Okri (1959–) is an iconic Nigerian writer who often experiments with new literary forms, styles, genres, and traditions. Although he began his career as a realist dealing with postcolonial themes, Okri soon delved into what has been called, for lack of a better term, a form of 'African magic realism'. Myths from the Yoruba culture have been particularly prominent in his subsequent work, including in his masterpiece, the Booker Prize winner *The Famished Road* (1991). Okri himself emphasizes that the surreal or fantastical elements in his work coexist with the real (and urban) world in his fiction. Luminous and strange, 'Worlds that Flourish' (1988) is a wonderful contemporary evocation of an encounter with the weird.

I was at work one day when a man came up to me and asked me my name. For some reason I couldn't tell it to him immediately and he didn't wait for me to get around to it before he turned and walked away. At lunch-time I went to the bukka to eat. When I got back to my desk someone came and told me that half the workers in the department had been sacked. I was one of them.

I had not been working long in the department and I left the job without bitterness. I packed my things that day and sorted out the money that was owed me. I got into my battered little car and drove home. When I arrived I parked my car three streets from where I lived, because the roads were bad. As I walked home the sight of tenements and zinc huts made me dizzy. Swirls of dust came at me from the untarred roads. Everything shimmered like mirages in an omnipotent heat.

Later in the evening I went out to buy some cooked food. On my way back a neighbour came to me and said:

'How are you?'

'Fine,' I said.

'Are you sure you are fine?'

'Yes. Why do you ask?'

'Well,' said the neighbour, 'it's because you go around as if you don't have any eyes.'

'What do you mean?'

'Since your wife died you've stopped using your eyes. Haven't you noticed that most of the compound people are gone?'

'Gone where?'

'Run away. To safety.'

'Why?'

'Don't ask me.'

'Why haven't you gone?'

'I'm happy here.'

'So am I,' I said, smiling. I went to my room.

Barely two hours after the conversation with my neighbour there was a knock on my door. I opened it and three men pushed their way in. Two of them carried machetes and the third had a gun. They weren't nasty or brutal. They merely asked me to sit quietly on the bed and invited me to watch them if I wanted. I watched them as they cleaned my room of my important possessions and took what money they could find. They chatted to me about how bad the roads were and how terrible the government was and how there were so many checkpoints around. While they chatted they bundled my things into a heap and carried them out to their lorry as though they were merely helping me to move. When they finished the man with the gun said:

'This is what we call scientific robbery. If you so much as cough after we've gone I will shoot out your eyes, you hear?'

I nodded. He left with a smile. A moment later I heard their lorry driving off down the untarred road. I rushed out and they were gone. I came back to my room to decide what next to do. I couldn't inform the police immediately because the nearest station was miles away and even if I did I couldn't really expect them to do anything. I sat on the bed and tried to convince myself that I was quite fortunate to still have the car and some money in the bank. But as it turned out I wasn't even allowed to feel fortunate. Not long after the thieves had left there was another knock on my door. I got up to open it when five soldiers with machine-guns stepped into the room. Apparently the thieves had been unable to get away. They were stopped at a checkpoint and to save their own necks they told the soldiers that I was their accomplice. Without ceremony, and with a great deal of roughness, the soldiers dragged me to their jeep. Visions of being executed as an armed robber at the beach filled me with vertigo. I told the soldiers that *I* was the one who was robbed but the soldiers began to beat me because it seemed to them I was trying to insult their intelligence with such a transparent lie. As they took me away, with their guns prodding my back, my neighbour came out of his room. When he saw the soldiers with me he said:

'I told you that you don't have eyes.'

Then he went to one of the soldiers and, to my astonishment, said:

'Mr Soldier, I hope you treat him as he deserves. I always thought something was wrong with his head.'

The soldiers took us to the nearest police station and we were all locked in the same cell. The real thieves, who seemed to find it all amusing, kept smiling at me. At night the soldiers came and beat us up with whips when we refused to confess anything. Then in the morning some policemen took us outside and made us strip naked and commanded us to face the street. The people that went past looked at us and hurried on. I shouted of my innocence and the policemen told me to shut up. We stayed out facing the whole world in our nakedness for most of the day. The children laughed at us. The women studied us. Photographers came and flashed their cameras in our eyes. When night fell a policeman came and offered me the opportunity to bribe my way out of trouble. I burned all over and my eyes were clogged with dust. I told him I had to go to the bank first. The thieves paid their dues and were freed. I stayed in a cell crammed with men screaming all night. In the morning one of the soldiers accompanied me to the bank. I drew out some money and paid my dues. I went home and slept for the rest of that day.

In the morning I went to have a shower. Going through the compound I was struck by the absence of communal noises. No music came from the rooms. No children cried. There were no married couples arguing and shouting behind red curtains. There were chickens and rats in the backyard. My neighbour came out of the toilet and smiled when he saw me.

'So they have released you,' he said, regretfully.

'You are a wicked man,' I shouted.

'People don't go out anymore,' he said, coolly ignoring me. 'It's very quiet. I like it this way.'

'Why were you so wicked to me?'

'I don't trust people who don't have eyes.'

'I might have been executed.'

'Are you better than those who have been?'

I stared at him in disbelief. He went and washed his hands at the pump and dried them against his trousers. He pushed past me and went to his room. A moment later I saw him going out.

I still felt sleepy even after my shower. I went to my room and got dressed. Then I went to the front of the compound. I sat on a bench and looked at the street. The churches around were not having their usual prayers and songs over loudspeakers. The muezzin was silent. The street was deserted. There were no signs of panic. The stalls still had their display of goods and the shops were open, but there was no one around. There were a lot of birds in the air, circling the aerials. Somewhere in the distance a radio had been left on. Across the street a goat wandered around the roots of a tree. The cocks didn't crow. After a while all I heard inside me was a confused droning, my incomprehension. Something had been creeping on us all along and now that the street was empty I couldn't even see what it was. I sat outside, fighting the mosquitoes, till it became dark. Then it dawned on me that something had happened to time. I seemed to be sitting in an empty space without history. The wind wasn't cooling. And then suddenly all the lights went out. It was as if the spirit of the world had finally died. The black-out lasted a long time.

For many days I wandered about in the darkness of the city. I drove around in the day looking for jobs. Everywhere I went workers were being sacked in great numbers. There were no strikes. Sometimes I listened to the Head of State's broadcasts on the radio. He spoke about austerity, about tightening the national belt, and about a great future. He sounded very lonely, as though he were talking in a vast and empty room. After his broadcasts music was played. The music sounded also as if it were played in an empty space.

In the evenings I went around looking for friends. They had gone and no explanations or forwarding addresses were given. When I went to their compounds I was surprised at how things had changed. The decay of the compounds seemed to have accelerated. Doors were left open. Cobwebs hung over the compound fronts. Outside the house of a friend I saw a boy staring at me with frightened eyes. When I started to ask him of the whereabouts of my friend, he got up and ran. I went back to my car and drove around the city, looking for people that I knew. Then I really began to notice things. There were people scattered in places of the city. There seemed no panic on their faces. It began to occur to me that the world was emptying out. When I took a closer look at the people a strange thought came to me: they seemed like sleep-walkers. I stopped the car and went amongst them to get a closer look, to talk with them, and find out exactly what was happening. (The radios and newspapers had long stopped giving information.) I went out into the street and approached a woman who was frying yams at the roadside. She looked at me with burning, suspicious eyes.

'What is happening to the country?' I asked her.

'Nothing is happening.'

'Where has everyone gone?'

'No one has gone anywhere. Why are you asking me? Go and ask someone else.'

As I turned to go the fire flared up, illuminating her face. And on her face I saw a sloping handwriting. On her forehead and on her cheeks there were words. Then I noticed that her hands were also covered in handwriting. I drew closer to read the words, but she began screaming. I heard the iron-clad boots of soldiers running down the streets towards us. I hurried to my car and drove off.

As I went home I noticed that a lot of the people in the streets had handwriting on their faces. I couldn't understand why I hadn't noticed it before. And then I was suddenly overcome with the notion that my neighbour had words on his face. I drove home hurriedly.

It was dark by the time I arrived. I couldn't risk having the car three streets away, so I parked it outside the compound. I think it was with that act of caution that the thought of fleeing first occurred to me. The birds had increased over our street. The radio was still on somewhere in the distance. Its battery was getting weaker. The wind whistled through the compounds. Stray dogs roamed down the street. I sat outside and waited for my neighbour. When he didn't come back for a long time I went and knocked on his door. There was no reply. I went to my room and ate, and then I went and sat outside again. I listened to the radio dying. I listened to the thin military voices. The night got darker and still my neighbour didn't return. I listened to the wind straining the branches of the trees. Stray cats eyed me in the dark. I went to my room and I slept that night with the feeling that something was breaking on my consciousness. When I woke up in the morning I noticed that the Head of State's lonely face kept slipping into my mind. I had a shower and ate and went and knocked on my neighbour's door. He still hadn't got back.

I prepared to go out but thunder sounded in the sky. By the afternoon it had started to rain. The street swelled with water. The gutters overran. The rain poured into the open doors of the rooms and fell on the stalls with their undisturbed display of goods and beat down on the clothes that had been left hanging. The wind blew very hard and shook our roof. The branches of a tree strained and then cracked. From afar I could see smoke above the houses. The rain poured down unceasingly for two days. My neighbour still didn't return. The water went up to the bumper of my car. The rain finally extinguished the distant radio. The Head of State made desperate broadcasts about cleaning the national stables. I sat in my room, imprisoned by the rain. I listened to the water endlessly falling. My roof began to leak. I heard a cat wailing above the steady din. Sometimes the rain accelerated in its fall, and managed to obliterate both time and memory. It soon seemed as if it had always been raining. With the city empty of people, I began to hear broadcasts in the rain. And then in the evening of the second day, a realization came upon me. I went to the window, my ears reverberating with persistently dripping water, and looked out. That was when I discovered I had temporarily lost the names of things.

I stayed indoors till the rain stopped. Then I stayed in another day, to enable the water to sink into the swollen earth. I went and tried my neighbour's door several times and then I went into his room. Nothing had been disturbed, but he seemed to have altogether vanished. On the fourth day I ventured down our street and witnessed the proliferation of disasters. Trees had fallen. Houses had crumbled before the force of the wind and rain. Dead cats floated in the gutters. There were no birds in the air. I went back to my room. My head jostled with signs. I got out my box and stuffed it full of my papers and clothes. I packed all my food into the back of the car. I left my door open. I tried my neighbour's room for the final time. I got into my car and set out on a journey without a destination through the vast, uncultivated country.

It wasn't easy getting out of the city. There were so many roadblocks and soldiers were all over the place. They stopped me and searched the car. At every one of the roadblocks the soldiers commented on the food I had at the back. They asked where I was going. I told them I was going to visit my mother who was ill in the village. Then they would ask if I thought that people were hungry. When I said no, the soldiers would take some of my food and wave me on. By the time I cleared through the last roadblock I had very little food left. But that wasn't what worried me. What made me anxious, as I drove through the forests, was that the car kept giving me trouble. It would stall and I had to sit at the wheel and wait for the engine to cool. When it did start, and move, it did so erratically. The car would suddenly, it seemed, start driving me. It picked up speed, and slowed down, of its own inscrutable volition.

I drove for a long time down the winding forest roads. I managed to cross a wooden bridge that had been partly devastated by rain. For long periods of time I heard only the purring sound of the car. Sometimes it seemed as if I were driving on one spot. The road and the forests didn't seem to change. I crossed the same partly devastated bridge several times. I got tired of driving without seeming to be moving. I stopped and locked all the doors and got some sleep.

I felt better when I woke up. I was driving for a while when I felt that I had broken the sameness of the journey. Mountain ranges, plateaus of ambergris rocks, and precipices, appeared all around me. I passed a clay-coloured anthill. I slowed down for a pack of hyenas to cross the road. I came to a petrol shack. The door was open. There were dirty barrels of petrol and diesel oil in the front yard. I stopped the car and parked. I passed the greasy hand-pump and knocked on the door. An old man came out. He had a pair of grey braces over a black shirt and he wore filthy khaki trousers. He was barefoot.

'You're the first person I've seen for a long time,' he said.

I asked him to fill the tank. He didn't say anything to me as he did so. I changed the water in the radiator. He didn't have any brake fluid. I sat on a bench and listened to the insects of the forest while he slowly and painstakingly looked the car over and tuned the engine.

'How do you manage to live here?'

'I manage. I like it.'

I paid him. As I was getting into the car the old man said:

'Don't go that way. I haven't seen any vehicles coming back. Stay where you can be happy.'

I nodded, smiling. I shut the door and started the car. As I moved away I waved at him. He didn't wave back. He stared at the car motionlessly. I drove on into the forest.

Further along I ran over a goat that had been crossing the road. I felt the wheels bump over its body and I stopped. The goat jerked on the tarmac. When I came out of the car I heard violent noises and saw people emerging from the forest and rushing towards me. The men had machetes and the women held long pieces of firewood. I ran back to the car, but when I started it the engine only whined. The people pounced on the car and smashed the bodywork with their machetes and firewood. They broke the windows and several hands reached for my face. The car started, suddenly, and I sped off with a few hands still grasping for my eyes. I swerved both ways and people fell off and I drove on without looking back. Afterwards I saw blood and bits of flesh on the jagged, broken windows.

And then it was as if the rain that had fallen in the city began to catch up with me, intensified. The forest reverberated with thunder. Lightning struck in the trees. The leaves were blown into frenzies by the relentless wind. The car kept swerving and sometimes it was as if the wind was blowing the car on, lifting it at the back. Sometimes I did not feel that the wheels were on the road. I drove on air. I drove on through the torrential rain. There were trees swaying and leaves flapping everywhere. And then there was water pouring on the trees everywhere. Now and again someone would emerge, soaking, from the forest and would run across the road and wave for me to stop. I did not stop for anybody, or for any reason. I drove on in demented concentration. Soon my eyes got tired. I was thrashed by the rain and all I could see was the windscreen and the forests distorted in the rain. I found it difficult to blink and when I did I felt the blankness pulling me into sleep. I would wake up to find myself veering off the road. I managed to sleep while driving.

When night came thickly over the forest I couldn't separate the darkness from the rain. Occasionally I saw a flash behind me which I thought belonged to a car. I adjusted the mirror and in the crack of a second I saw my face. Thunder broke and exploded in front of me. A moment later there was a forked, incandescent flash which lit up the handwriting on my face. I negotiated a bend and heard a deafening crash in the forest. Something shattered my windscreen and I drove wide-eyed into the darkness. Insects flew into my face. Wind, rain, and bits of glass momentarily blinded me. Then I saw that a tree had fallen across the road ahead of me. The car spun into the vortex of leaves and branches. And then there was stillness. For a long moment it was completely dark. I couldn't hear, see, or feel anything. And then I heard the whirring engine and the insistent din of insects and rain.

I tried to move, but couldn't: I felt I had become entangled in the car. I heard magnified grating noises. I was covered in crumbly earth which seemed alive and which stung me. Something settled inside me and I extricated myself from the front seat effortlessly. When I was out of the wreckage I saw that the car had run into a large anthill. There were ants everywhere. I pushed on through the rain. I couldn't find the road. I went on into the forest. I passed rocks flowering with lichen. I moved under the endless lattice of branches. Thorns of the forest cut into me. I didn't bleed.

I came to a river. When I swam across I noticed it was flowing in a direction opposite to how it seemed. As I came out on the other bank the water dried instantly on me. I went on through the undergrowth till I came to a village. At the entrance there were two palm trees growing upside down. I went between the trees and saw a man sitting on a chair outside a hut. When the man saw me his face lit up. He ululated suddenly and talking drums sounded at distances in the village. The man got up and rushed to me and embraced me:

'We've been waiting for you,' he said.

'What do you mean?'

'We've been waiting for you.'

'That can't be true.'

The man looked quite offended at my remark, but he said:

'I have been sitting outside this hut for three months. Waiting for you. I'm happy that you've made it. Come, the people of the village are expecting you.'

He led the way.

'Why?'

'You'll find out.'

I followed him silently. As we went on into the village, I noticed that there was a woman following us. Whenever I looked back she hid behind the trees and bushes.

'We've been cleaning up the village for your arrival,' the man said.

We passed a skyscraper that reflected the sunlight like blinding glass sheets.

'That's where the meeting will take place.'

The huts looked solid and clean with their white ochred walls. The iroko and baobab trees were neatly spaced. The bushes were lush. The air was scented with flamingo flowers.

We arrived at the village square when it occurred to me that the place was vaguely familiar. It was a very orderly and clean place. And then suddenly I realized that I couldn't see. I didn't hear the man leading me anymore. I heard singing and dancing all around. I panicked and started shouting. The dancing and singing stopped. I stood for a long time, casting about in the menacing silence. After a while, when I quietened down, I heard light footsteps coming towards me.

'Help me,' I said.

Then a woman, who smelt of cloves, in a sweet voice, said:

'Be quiet and follow me.'

I followed her till we came to a place that smelt of bark. She opened a door and we went in. She pulled up a stool for me. I could have been sitting on solid air for all I knew, but the woman's presence reassured me. I heard her moving about the place. She set down food for me. I ate. She set down drinks and I drank. Then she said:

'This will be your new home.'

Then I heard the door shut. I soon fell asleep.

When I woke up I felt things coming out of my ears. Things were crawling all over me. I stood up and called out. The door opened and the woman came in and led me to the place where I had a wash. After I had eaten, she sat near me and said:

'We heard you were coming. It took a long time.'

'How did you hear?'

'You will find out.'

'Why have you all been waiting for me?'

She was silent. Then she laughed and said:

'Didn't you know we have been waiting for you?'

'No.'

'Didn't you know you were coming here?'

'No. But why?'

'To take your place in the assembly.'

'What assembly?'

'We kept postponing the meeting because you hadn't arrived.'

I grew weary of asking questions.

'The people of the village have been anxious,' she said.

'When is this meeting taking place?'

'Two days' time.'

'Why not today?'

'The elders thought you needed time to rest and get used to the village. It's an important meeting.'

'What is the meeting about?'

'You are tired. Get some sleep. If you need me call.'

Then I heard the door open and shut again.

In the village everything had a voice and everything spoke at me. Sounds and voices assaulted me and my ears began to ache. Then slowly my sight returned. At first it was like seeing through milk. When my vision cleared, the voices stopped. Then I saw the village as I had not seen it before.

I went out of the place I was staying and walked around in bewilderment. Some of the people of the village had their feet facing backwards. I was amazed that they could walk. Some people came out of tree-trunks. Some had wings, but they couldn't fly. After a while I got used to the strangeness of the people. I ceased to really notice their three legs and elongated necks. What I couldn't get used to were the huts and houses that were walled round with mirrors on the outside. I didn't see myself reflected in them as I went past. Some people walked into the mirrors and disappeared. I couldn't walk into them.

After some time of moving around, I couldn't find my way back to where I stayed. I went about the village listening for the voice of the woman who had been taking care of me. I stopped at a communal water-pump and a woman came up to me and said:

'What are you doing here?'

'I'm lost.'

'I'll take you back.'

I followed her.

'So you can see now?' she asked, turning her head right round to me as she walked.

'Yes.'

And then I had the distinct and absurd feeling that I knew her. She was a robust figure, with a face of jagged and familiar beauty. She wore a single flowerprint wrapper and was barefoot. Her skin was covered in native chalk. Her eyes radiated a strange light which dazzled like a green mirror.

'Who are you?'

She didn't answer my question. When we got to an obeche tree she opened a door on the trunk. Inside I saw a perfect interior, neat and compact and warm.

'I'm not going in there,' I said.

She turned her head towards me, her face was expressionless.

'But this has been your new home,' she said.

'It can't be. It's too small.'

She laughed almost affectionately.

'When you come in you will find it is large enough.'

It was very spacious when I went in. I sat down on the wooden bed. She served me food in a half calabash. The rice seemed to move on the plate like several white maggots. I could have sworn it was covered in spider's webs. But it tasted sweet and was satisfying. The cup from which I was supposed to drink bled on the outside. After she had cleared the food from the table, I pretended to be asleep. Before she left I heard her say:

'Sleep well and regain your strength. The meeting is taking place tonight.'

I sat up.

'Who are you?' I asked.

She shut the door gently behind her.

I waited for some time before I got up and left the tree. I was intent on fleeing, but I didn't want to betray it. As I wandered round the village looking for the way out, I heard people dancing, I heard some disputing the village principles, I heard others reciting a long list of names, and I heard beautiful voices telling stories behind the trees. But I could not see any of the people.

And then as I passed a hut, from which came the high-pitched laughter of shy young girls, I noticed that a one-eyed goat was staring at me intently. I hurried on. Dogs and chickens gazed at me. I experienced the weird sensation that people were staring at me through the eyes of the animals. I passed the village shrine. In front of it there was the mighty statue of a god with big holes for eyes. I was convinced the god was spying on me.

I wandered for a long time looking for the exit. I heard disembodied voices saying that the big meeting would soon begin. The lights hadn't changed. I came to a frangipani tree full of white birds. Beyond the tree was the village square and beyond the square was the entrance. I pushed on till I came to the hut. Sitting on the chair outside the hut was a man who had three eyes on his face. He kept staring at me and I was forced to greet him.

'Don't greet me,' he said.

He went on staring at me, as though he expected me to recognize him. His three eyes puzzled and disorientated me. But when I concentrated on the two normal eyes I suddenly did recognize him. He was my vanished neighbour.

'What are you doing here?' I asked.

'What do you think?'

'I don't know.'

'A soldier shot me.'

'Shot you?' I asked, surprised.

'Yes.'

'Why?'

'To kill me. What are you doing here?'

'Me?'

'Yes.'

'I don't know.'

He laughed.

'They will tell you at the meeting.'

'What is the meeting about?'

'Life and death.'

'What life, what death?'

He laughed again, but more explosively. There was something about his mouth, the way his eyes moved, that gradually made things clear to me. I backed away in terror.

'You better not try and escape,' he said maliciously.

That was all I needed. I ran towards the entrance and things got scrambled up as I ran. And then I found that I was moving not forwards, but backwards. I passed the white ochred huts and the blinding skyscraper. I heard the high-pitched scream of a woman. Talking drums sounded in frenzies. When I stopped and ran backwards, I found I was actually running forwards. Then I saw the woman who had screamed, and for the first time I recognized her as my dead wife. She tore after me in great distress. Men and women and disembodied voices came after me with their wings that didn't help them fly and their feet which were turned backwards. I fled past the trees that were upside down and the cornfields outside the village entrance. The cornplumes were golden and beautiful. The people of the village pursued me all the way to the boundary.

I crossed the river. Birds came at me from the forest. I ran for a long time without stopping till I came to my car that had smashed through the branches of the tree and devastated the anthill. I am not sure what happened next but when I came to I found myself in the wreckage of the car. I was covered with ants and they bit me mercilessly. The twisted wreck of metal seemed to have grown on me and I could feel my blood drying on the seat. There were cuts and broken glass on my face. I spent a very long time struggling to get out of the car. When I did I felt about as wrecked as the car and my body felt like it had already died. I staggered through the forest. I ate lemon grass leaves. As I pushed my way through the forest I became aware that I could see spirits. It was morning before I could find the main road. After a while of stumbling down the road I saw a car coming towards me. I stuck out my hand and waved furiously and was surprised when the car stopped. There was a young man at the wheel. He wound down his side window and I said:

'Don't go that way. Find where you can be happy.'

But the young man looked me over, nodded, and drove straight on. I watched the car till it had disappeared. Then I trudged on with the hope of reaching the old man's shack before I died.

THE BOY IN THE TREE

Elizabeth Hand

Elizabeth Hand (1957–) is an American writer of cross-genre fiction who grew up in New York State. She has won the World Fantasy award, the James Tiptree Jr. Award, Nebula Award, and Shirley Jackson Award for novels and short fiction. Hand has long had an interest in outsider artists, and even her mainstream novel *Generation Loss* (2007) deals with that subject matter. As for the story reprinted herein, a unique blend of the supernatural and science fiction, it has its inspiration in real life: 'I had my own encounter with the numinous in... 1974, when I had an epiphanic vision of a Dionsyian figure I named The Boy in the Tree'. The result is a tale both disturbing and beautiful.

What if in your dream you dreamed, and what if in your dream you went to heaven and there plucked a strange and beautiful flower, and what if when you woke you had the flower in your hand?

– Samuel Taylor Coleridge

Our heart stops.

A moment I float beneath her, a starry shadow. Distant canyons where spectral lightning flashes: neurons firing as I tap into the heart of the poet, the dark core where desire and horror fuse and Morgan turns ever and again to stare out a bus window. The darkness clears. I taste for an instant the metal bile that signals the beginning of therapy, and then I'm gone.

I'm sitting on the autobus, the last seat where you can catch the bumps on the crumbling highway if you're going fast enough. Through the open windows a rush of Easter air tangles my hair. Later I will smell apple blossom in my auburn braids. Now I smell sour milk where Ronnie Abrams spilled his ration yesterday.

'Move over, Yates!' Ronnie caroms off the seat opposite, rams his leg into mine and flies back to pound his brother. From the front the driver yells 'Shut up!', vainly trying to silence forty-odd singing children.

On top of Old Smoky
All covered with blood
I shot my poor teacher
With a forty-four slug...

Ronnie grins at me, eyes glinting, then pops me right on the chin with a spitball. I stick my fingers in my ears and huddle closer to the window.

Met her at the door
With my trusty forty-four
Now she don't teach no more...

The autobus pulls into town and slows, stops behind a military truck. I press my face against the cracked window, shoving my glasses until lens kisses glass and I can see clearly to the street below. A young woman is standing on the curb holding a baby wrapped in a dirty pink blanket. At her ankles wriggles a dog, an emaciated puppy with whiptail and ears flopping as he nips at her bare feet. I tap at the window, trying to get the dog to look at me. In front of the bus two men in uniform clamber from the truck and start arguing. The woman screws up her face and says something to the men, moving her lips so that I know she's mad. The dog lunges at her ankles again and she kicks it gently, so that it dances along the curb. The soldiers glance at her, see the autobus waiting, and climb back into the truck. I hear the whoosh of releasing brakes. The autobus lurches forward and my glasses bang into the window. The rear wheels grind up onto the curb.

The dog barks and leaps onto the woman. Apple blossoms drift from a tree behind her as she draws her arms up alarmed, and, as I settle my glasses onto my nose and stare, drops the baby beneath the wheels of the bus.

Retching, I strive to pull Morgan away, turn her head from the window. A fine spray etches bright petals on the glass and her plastic lenses. My neck aches as I try to turn toward the inside of the autobus and efface forever that silent rain. But I cannot move. She is too strong. She will not look away.

I am clawing at the restraining ropes. A technician pulls the wires from my head while inches away Morgan Yates screams. I hear the hiss and soft pump of velvet thoughts into her periaqueductual gray area. The link is severed.

I sat up as they wheeled her into the next room. Morgan's screams abruptly stilled as the endorphins kicked in and her head flopped to one side of the gurney. For an instant the technician turned and stared at me as he slid Morgan through the door. He would not catch my eyes.

None of them will.

Through the glass panel I watched Emma Harrow hurry from another lab. She bent over Morgan and gently pulled the wires from between white braids still rusted with coppery streaks. Beside her the technicians looked worried. Other doctors slipped from adjoining rooms and blocked my view, all with strained faces.

When I was sure they'd forgotten me I dug out a cigarette and lit up. I tapped the ashes into my shoe and blew smoke into a ventilation shaft. I knew Morgan wouldn't make it. I could often tell, but even Dr. Harrow didn't listen to me this time. Morgan Yates was too important: one of the few living writers whose readers included both rebels and Ascendants.

'She will crack,' I told Dr. Harrow after reading Morgan's profile. Seven *poetry* collections published by the Ascendants. Recurrent nightmares revolving around a childhood trauma in the military creche; sadistic sexual behavior and a pathological fear of dogs. Nothing extraordinary there. But I knew she wouldn't make it.

'How do you know?'

I shrugged. 'She's too strong.'

Dr. Harrow stared at me, pinching her lower lip. She wasn't afraid of my eyes. 'What if it works?' she mused. 'She says she hasn't written in three years, because of this.'

I yawned. 'Maybe it will work. But she won't let me take it away. She won't let anyone take it.'

I was right. If Dr. Harrow hadn't been so anxious about the chance to reclaim one of the damned and her own reputation, she'd have known, too. Psychotics, autists, artists of the lesser rank: these could be altered by empatherapy. I'd siphoned off their sicknesses and night terrors, inhaled phobias like giddy ethers that set me giggling for days afterward. But the big ones, those whose madnesses were as carefully cultivated as the brain chemicals that allowed myself and others like me to tap into them: they were immune. They clung to their madnesses with the fever of true addiction. Even the dangers inherent to empatherapy weren't enough: they *couldn't* let go.

Dr. Harrow glanced up from the next room and frowned when she saw my cigarette. I stubbed it out in my shoe and slid my foot back in, wincing at the prick of heat beneath my sole.

She slipped out of the emergency room. Sighing, she leaned against the glass and looked at me.

'Was it bad, Wendy?'

I picked a fleck of tobacco from my lip. 'Pretty bad.' I had a rush recalling Morgan wailing as she stood at the window. For a moment I had to shut my eyes, riding that wave until my heart slowed and I looked up grinning into Dr. Harrow's compressed smile.

'Pretty good, you mean.' Her tight mouth never showed the disdain or revulsion of the others.

Only a little dismay, some sick pride perhaps in the beautiful thing she'd soldered together from an autistic girl and several ounces of precious glittering chemicals. 'Well,' she sighed, and walked to her desk. 'You can start on this.' She tossed me a blank report and returned to the emergency lab. I settled back on my cot and stared at the sheet.

PATIENT NAME: Wendy Wanders

In front of me the pages blurred. Shuddering I gripped the edge of my chair. Nausea exploded inside me, a fiery pressure building inside my head until I bowed to crack my forehead against the table edge, again and again, stammering my name until with a shout a technician ran to me and slapped an ampule to my neck. I couldn't bear the sight of my own name: Dr. Harrow usually filled in the charts for me and provided the sedatives, as she had a special lab all in gray for the empath who couldn't bear colors and wore black goggles outside; as she had the neural bath ready for another whose amnesia after a session left her unable to talk or stand or control her bowels. The technician stood above me until the drug took effect. I breathed deeply and stared at the wall, then reported on my unsuccessful session with the poet.

That evening I walked to the riverside. A trio of security sculls silently plied the river. At my feet water striders gracelessly mimicked them. I caught a handful of the insects and dropped them on the crumbling macadam at the water's edge, watched them jerk and twitch with crippled stepladder legs as they fought the hard skin of gravel and sand. Then I turned and wandered along the river walk, past rotting oak benches and the ruins of glass buildings, watching the sun sink through argent thunderheads.

A single remaining restaurant ziggurat towered above the walk. Wooden benches gave way to airy filigrees of iron, and at one of these tables I saw someone from the Human Engineering Laboratory.

'Anna or Andrew?' I called. By the time I was close enough for her to hear I knew it was Anna this time, peacock feathers and long blue macaw quills studding the soft raised nodes on her shaven temples.

'Wendy.' She gestured dreamily at a confectionery chair. 'Sit.'

I settled beside her, tweaking a cobalt plume, and wished I'd worn the fiery cock-of-the-rock quills I'd bought last spring. Anna was stunning, always: eyes brilliant with octine, small breasts tight against her tuxedo shirt. She was the only one of the other empties I spoke much with, although she beat me at faro and Andrew had once broken my tooth in an amphetamine rage. A saucer scattered with broken candicaine straws sat before her. Beside it a fluted parfait glass held several unbroken pipettes. I did one and settled back grinning.

'You had that woman today,' Anna hissed into my ear. Her rasping voice made me shiver with delight. 'The poet. I think I'm furious.'

Smiling, I shrugged. 'Luck of the draw.'

'How was she?' She blinked and I watched golden dust powder the air between us. 'Was she good, Wendy?' She stroked my thigh and I giggled.

'Great. She was great.' I lowered my eyes and squinted until the table disappeared into the steel rim of an autobus seat.

'Let me see.' Her whisper the sigh of air brakes. 'Wendy–'

The rush was too good to stop. I let her pull me forward until my forehead grazed hers and I felt the cold sting of electrolytic fluid where she strung the wire. I tasted brass: then bile and summer air and exhaust–

Too fast. I jerked my head up, choking as I inadvertently yanked the connector from Anna. She stared at me with huge blank eyes.

'Ch-c-c–' she gasped, spittle flying into the parfait glass. I swore and pushed the straws away, popped the wire and held her face close to mine.

'Ahhh–' Anna nodded suddenly. Her eyes focused and she drew back. 'Wendy. Good stuff.' She licked her lips, tongue a little loose from the hit so that she drooled. I grimaced.

'More, Wendy…'

'Not now.' I grabbed two more straws and cracked one. 'I have a follow-up with her tomorrow morning. I have to go.'

She nodded. I flicked the wire into her lap along with the vial of fluid and a napkin. 'Wipe your mouth, Anna. I'll tell Harrow I saw you so she won't worry.'

'Goodbye, Wendy.' She snapped a pocket open and the stuff disappeared. A server arrived as I left, its crooked wheels grating against the broken concrete as it listed toward the table. I glimpsed myself reflected in its blank black face, and hurried from the patio as behind me Anna ordered more straws.

I recall nothing before Dr. Harrow. The drugs they gave me – massive overdoses for a three-year-old – burned those memories as well as scorching every neural branch that might have helped me climb to feel the sun as other people do. But the drugs stopped the thrashing, the headbanging, the screaming. And slowly, other drugs rived through my tangled axons and forged new pathways. A few months and I could see again. A few more and my fingers moved. The wires that had stilled my screams eventually made me scream once more, and, finally, exploded a neural dam so that a year later I began to speak. By then the research money was pouring through other conduits, scarcely less complex than my own, and leading as well to the knot of electrodes in my brain.

In the early stages of her work, shortly after she took me from the military crèche, Dr. Harrow attempted a series of neuro-electrical implants between the two of us. It was an unsuccessful effort to reverse the damage done by the biochemicals. Seven children died before the minimum dosage was determined – enough to change the neural pattern behind autistic behavior, not enough to allow the patient to develop her own emotional responses to subsequent internal or external stimuli. I still have scars from the implants: fleshy nodes like tiny ears trying to sprout from my temples.

At first we lived well. As more empaths were developed and more military funding channeled for research, we lived extravagantly well. Dr. Harrow believed that exposure to sensation might eventually pattern true emotions in her affectively neutered charges. So we moved from the Human Engineering Laboratory's chilly fortress to the vast abandoned Linden Glory estate outside the old City.

Neurologists moved into the paneled bedrooms. Psycho-botanists tilled the ragged formal gardens and developed new strains of oleander within bell-shaped greenhouses. Empties moved into bungalows where valets and chefs once slept.

Lawrence Linden had been a patron of the arts: autographed copies of Joyce and Stein and the lost Crowley manuscripts graced the Linden Glory libraries. We had a minor Botticelli and many Raphaels; the famed pre-Columbian collection; antiquarian coins and shelves of fine and rare Egyptian glass. From the Victorian music room with its Whistler panels echoed the peacock screams of empties and patients engaged in therapy.

Always I remained Dr. Harrow's pet: an exquisite monster capable of miming every human emotion and even feeling many of them via the therapy I make possible. Every evening doctors administer syringes and capsules and tiny tabs that adhere to my temples like burdock pods, releasing chemicals directly into my corpus striatum. And every morning I wake from someone else's dreams.

Morgan sat in the gazebo when I arrived for our meeting, her hair pulled beneath a biretta of frayed indigo velvet. She had already eaten but servers had yet to clear her plate. I picked up the remains of a brioche and nibbled its sugary crust.

'None of you have any manners, do you?' She smiled, but her eyes were red and cloudy with hatred. 'They told me that during orientation.'

I ran my tongue over a sweet nugget in a molar and nodded. 'That's right.'

'You can't feel anything or learn anything unless it's slipped into your breakfast coffee.'

'I can't drink coffee.' I glanced around the Orphic Garden for a server. 'You're early.'

'I had trouble sleeping.'

I nodded and finished the brioche.

'I had trouble sleeping because I had no dreams.' She leaned across the table and repeated herself in a hiss. 'I had no dreams. I carried that memory around with me for sixty years and last night I had no dreams.'

Yawning I rubbed the back of my head, adjusting a quill. 'You still have all your memories. Dr. Harrow said you wanted to end the nightmares. I am surprised we were successful.'

'You were not successful.' She towered above me when she stood, the table tilting toward her as she clutched its edge. 'Monster.'

'Sacred monster. I thought you liked sacred monsters.' I grinned, pleased that I'd bothered to read her chart.

'Bitch. How dare you laugh at me. Whore – you're all whores and thieves.' She stepped toward me, her heel catching between the mosaic stones. 'No more of me – You'll steal no more of me–'

I drew back a little, blinking in the emerald light as I felt the first adrenaline pulse. 'You shouldn't be alone,' I murmured. 'Does Dr. Harrow know?'

She blocked the sun so that it exploded around the biretta's peaks in resplendent ribbons. 'Dr. Harrow will know,' she whispered, and drawing a swivel from her pocket she shot herself through the eye.

I knocked my chair over as I stumbled to her, knelt and caught the running blood and her last memory as I bowed to touch my tongue to her severed thoughts.

A window smeared with garnet light that ruddles across my hands. Burning wax in a small blue glass. A laughing dog; then darkness.

They hid me under guise of protecting me from the shock. I gave a sworn statement to the military and acknowledged in the HEL mortuary that the long body with the blackened face had indeed shared her breakfast brioche with me that morning. I glimpsed Dr. Harrow, white and taut as a thread as Dr. Leslie and the other HEL brass cornered her outside the Emergency Room. Then the aide Justice hurried me into the west wing, past the pre-Columbian collection and the ivory stair to an ancient Victorian elevator, clanking and lugubrious as a stage dragon.

'Dr. Harrow suggested that you might like the Home Room,' Justice remarked with a cough, sidling two steps away to the corner of the elevator. The brass door folded into a lattice of leaves and pigeons that expanded into peacocks. 'She's having your things sent up now. Anything else you need, please let her know.' He cleared his throat, staring straight ahead as we climbed through orchid-haunted clerestories and chambers where the oneironauts snored and tossed through their days. At the fourth floor the elevator ground to a stop. He tugged at the door until it opened and waited for me to pass into the hallway.

'I have never been in the Home Room,' I remarked, following him.

'I think that's why she thought you'd like it.' He glanced into an ornate mirror as we walked. I saw in his eyes a quiver of pity before he looked away. 'Down here.'

A wide hallway flanked by leaded windows overlooking the empties' cottages ended in an arch crowded with gilt satyrs.

'This is the Home Room,' murmured Justice. To the right a heavy oaken door hung open. Inside saffron-robed technicians strung cable. I made a face and tapped the door. It swung inward and struck a bundle of cable leading to the bank of monitors being installed next to a huge bed. I paced to the window and gazed down at the roof of my cottage. Around me the technicians scurried to finish, glancing at me sideways with anxious eyes. I ignored them and sat on the windowsill. There was no screen. A hawkmoth buzzed past my chin and I thought that I could hang hummingbird feeders from here and so, perhaps, lure them within reach of capture. Anna had a bandeau she had woven of hummingbird feathers which I much admired. The hawkmoth settled on a BEAM monitor beside the bed. The technicians packed to leave.

'Could you lie here for a moment, miss, while I test this?' The technician dropped a handful of cables behind the headboard. I nodded and stretched upon the bed, pummeling a pillow as he placed the wires upon my brow and temples. I turned sideways to watch the old BEAM monitor, the hawkmoth's wings forming a feline mask across the flickering map of my thoughts.

'Aggression, bliss, charity,' droned the technician, flicking the moth from the dusty screen. 'Desire, envy, fear,' I sighed and turned from the monitor while he adjusted dials. Finally he slipped the wires from me and left. Justice lingered a moment longer.

'You can go now,' I said flatly, and tossed the pillow against the headboard.

He stood by the door, uncomfortable, and finally said, 'Dr. Harrow wants me to be certain you check your prescriptions. Note she has increased your dosage of acetlethylene.'

I slid across the bed to where a tiny refrigerator had been hung for my medications. I pulled it open and saw the familiar battery of vials and bottles. As a child first under Dr. Harrow's care I had imagined them a city, saw the long cylinders and amber vials as battlements and turrets to be explored and climbed. Now I lived among those chilly buttresses, my only worship within bright cathedrals.

'Two hundred milligrams,' I said obediently, and replaced the bottle. 'Thank you very very much.' As I giggled he left the room.

I took the slender filaments that had tapped into my store of memories and braided them together, then slid the plait beneath a pillow and leaned back. A bed like a pirate ship, carved posts like riven masts spiring to the high ceiling. I had never seen a pirate ship, but once I tapped a boy who jerked off to images of red flags and heaving seas and wailing women. I recalled that now and untangled a single wire, placed it on my temple and masturbated until I saw the warning flare on the screen, the sanguine flash and flame across my pixilated brain. Then I went to sleep.

Faint tapping at the door woke me a short while later.

'Andrew,' I yawned, pointing to the crumpled sea of bed-clothes. 'Come in.'

He shut the door softly and slid beneath the sheets beside me. 'You're not supposed to have visitors, you now.'

'I'm not?' I stretched and curled my toes around his finger.

'No. Dr. Leslie was here all day, Anna said he's taking us back.'

'Me, too?'

He nodded, hugging a bolster. 'All of us. Forever.' He smiled, and the twilight made his face as beautiful as Anna's. 'I saw Dr. Harrow cry after he left.'

'How did you get here?' I sat up and played with his hair: long and silky except where the nodes bulged and the hair had never grown back. He wore Anna's bandeau, and I tugged it gently from his head.

'Back stairs. No one ever uses them. That way.' He pointed lazily with his foot toward a darkening corner. His voice rose plaintively. 'You shared that poet with Anna. You should've saved her.'

I shrugged. 'You weren't there.' The bandeau fit loosely over my forehead. When I tightened it tiny emerald feathers frosted my hand like the scales of moths. 'Would Anna give me this, do you think?'

Andrew pulled himself onto his elbows and stroked my breast with one hand. 'I'll give it to you, if you share.'

'There's not enough left to share,' I whined, and pulled away. In the mirror I caught myself in the bandeau. The stippled green feathers made my hair look a deeper auburn, like the poet's. I pulled a few dark curls through the feathers and pursed my lips. 'If you give this to me …'

Already he was reaching for the wires. 'Locked?' I breathed, glancing at the door.

'Shh …'

Afterward I gave him one of my new pills. There hadn't been much of Morgan left and I feared his disappointment would evoke Anna, who'd demand her bandeau back.

'Why can't I have visitors?'

I had switched off the lights. Andrew sat on the windowsill, luring lacewings with a silver cigarette lighter. Bats chased the insects to within inches of his face, veering away as he laughed and pretended to snatch at them. 'Dr. Harrow said there may be a psychic inquest. To see if you're accountable.'

'So?' I'd done one before, when a schizoid six-year-old hanged herself on a grosgrain ribbon after therapy with me. ' "I can't be responsible. I'm not responsible." ' We laughed: it was the classic empath defense.

'Dr. Harrow wants to see you herself.'

I kicked the sheets to the floor and turned

down the empty BEAM, to see the lacewings better. 'How do you know all this?'

A quick *fizz* as a moth singed itself. Andrew frowned and turned down the lighter flame. 'Anna told me,' he replied, and suddenly was gone.

I swore and tried to rearrange my curls so the bandeau wouldn't show. From the windowsill Anna stared blankly at the lighter for a moment, then groped in her pockets until she found a cigarette. She glanced coolly past me to the mirror, pulling a strand of hair forward until it fell framing her cheekbone. 'Who gave you that?' she asked as she blew smoke out the window.

I turned away. 'You know who,' I replied petulantly. 'I'm not supposed to have visitors.'

'Oh, you can keep it,' she said airily.

'Really?' I clapped in delight.

'I'll just make another.' She finished her cigarette, tossed it in an amber arc out the window. 'I better go down now. Which way's out?'

I pointed where Andrew had indicated, drawing her close to me to kiss her tongue as she left.

'Thank you, Anna,' I whispered to her at the door. 'I think I love this bandeau.'

'I think I loved it, too,' Anna nodded, and slipped away.

Dr. Harrow invited me to lunch with her in the Peach Tree Court the next afternoon. Justice appeared at my door and waited while I put on jeweled dark spectacles and a velvet biretta like Morgan Yates's.

'Very nice, Wendy,' he commented, amused. I smiled. When I wore the black glasses he was not afraid to look me in the face.

'I don't want the others to see my bandeau. Anna will steal it back,' I explained, lifting the hat so he could see the feathered riband beneath.

He laughed at that. I don't hear the aides laugh very often: when I was small, their voices frightened me. I thanked him as he held the door and followed him outside.

We passed the Orphic Garden. Servers had snaked hoses through the circle of lindens and were cleaning the mosaic stones. I peered curiously through the hedge as we walked down the pathway but the blood seemed to be all gone.

Once we were in the shade of the Peach Tree Walk I removed my glasses. Justice quickly averted his eyes.

'Do you think these peaches are ripe?' I wondered, twitching one from a branch as I passed beneath it.

'I doubt it.' Justice sighed, wincing as I bit into a small pink orb like a swollen eye. 'They'll make you sick, Wendy.'

Grinning, I swallowed my bite, then dropped the fruit. The little path dipped and rounded a corner hedged with forsythia. Three steps further and the path branched: right to the *trompe l'oeil* Glass Fountain, left to the Peach Tree Court, where Dr. Harrow waited in the Little Pagoda.

'Thank you, Justice.' Dr. Harrow rose and shook his hand. On several low tables lunch had already been laid for two. Justice stepped to a lacquered tray and sorted out my medication bottles, then stood and bowed before leaving.

Sunlight streamed through the bamboo frets above us as Dr. Harrow took my hand and drew me toward her.

'The new dosage. You remembered to take it?'

'Yes.' I removed my hat and dropped it. 'Anna gave me this bandeau.'

'It's lovely.' She knelt before one of the tables and motioned for me to do the same. Her face was puffy, her eyes slitted. I wondered if she would cry for me as she had for Andrew yesterday. 'Have you had breakfast?'

We ate goujonettes of hake with fennel and an aspic of lamb's blood. Dr. Harrow drank champagne and permitted me a sip – horrible, like thrashing water. Afterward a rusted, remodeled garden server removed our plates and brought me a chocolate wafer, which I slipped into my pocket to trade with Anna later, for news.

'You slept well,' Dr. Harrow stated. 'What did you dream?'

'I dreamed about Melisande's dog.'

Dr. Harrow stroked her chin, then adjusted her pince-nez to see me better. 'Not Morgan's dog?'

'No.' Melisande had been a girl my own age with a history of tormenting and sexually molesting animals. 'A small white dog. Like this.' I pushed my nose until it squashed against my face.

Dr. Harrow smiled ruefully. 'Well, good, because *I* dreamed about Morgan's dog.' She shook her head when I started to question her. 'Not really; a manner of speaking. I mean I didn't get much sleep.' She sighed and tilted her flute so it refracted golden diamonds. 'I made a very terrible error of judgment with Morgan Yates. I shouldn't have let you do it.'

'I knew what would happen,' I said matter-of-factly.

Dr. Harrow looked at her glass, then at me. 'Yes. Well, a number of people are wondering about that, Wendy.'

'She would not look away from the window.'

'No. They're wondering how you know when the therapy will succeed and when it won't. They're wondering whether the therapist is effecting her failures as well as her cures.'

'I'm not responsible. I can't be responsible.'

She placed the champagne flute very carefully on the lacquer table and took my hand. She squeezed it so tightly that I knew she wanted it to hurt. 'That is what's the matter, Wendy. If you are responsible – if empaths *can* be responsible – you can be executed for murder. We can all be held accountable for your failures. And if not...' She leaned back without releasing my hand, so that I had to edge nearer to her across the table. 'If not, HEL wants you back.'

I flounced back against the floor. 'Andrew told me.'

She rolled her eyes. 'Not you personally. Not necessarily. Anna, yes: they created Anna, they'll claim her first. But the others–' She traced a wave in the air, ended it with a finger pointing at me. 'And you... If they can trace what you do, find the bioprint and synthesize it...' Her finger touched the end of my nose, pressed it until I giggled. 'Just like Melisande's dog, Wendy.

'Odolf Leslie was here yesterday. He wants you for observation. He wants this–' She pressed both hands to her forehead and then waved them toward the sky, the fruit-laden trees and sloping lawns of Linden Glory. 'All this, Wendy. They will have me declared incompetent and our research a disaster, and then they'll move in.'

A server poured me more mineral water. 'Is he a nice doctor?'

For a moment I thought she'd upset the table, as Morgan had done in the Orphic Garden, Then, 'I don't know, Wendy. Perhaps he is.' She sighed, and motioned the server to bring another cold split.

'They'll take Anna first,' she said a few minutes later, almost to herself. Then, as if recalling me sitting across from her, she added, 'For espionage. They'll induce multiple personalities and train them when they're very young. Ideal terrorists.'

I drank my water and stared at the latticed roof of the pagoda, imagining Andrew and Anna without me. I took the chocolate wafer from my pocket and began to nibble it.

The server rolled back with a sweating silver bucket and opened another split for Dr. Harrow. She sipped it, watching me through narrowed gray eyes. 'Wendy,' she said at last. 'There's going to be an inquest. A military inquest. But before that, one more patient.' She reached beneath the table to her portfolio and removed a slender packet. 'This is the profile. I'd like you to read it.'

I took the file. Dr. Harrow poured the rest of her champagne and finished it, tilting her head to the server as she stood.

'I have a two o'clock meeting with Dr. Leslie. Why don't you meet me again for dinner tonight and we'll discuss this?'

'Where?'

She tapped her lower lip. 'The Peacock Room. At seven.' She bowed slightly and passed out of sight among the trees.

I waited until she disappeared, then gestured for the server. 'More chocolate, please,' I ordered, and waited until it returned with a chilled marble plate holding three wafers. I nibbled one, staring idly at the faux vellum cover of the profile with its engraved motto:

HUMAN ENGINEERING LABORATORY
PAULO MAIORA CANAMUS

' "Let us raise a somewhat loftier strain," ' Andrew had translated it for me once. 'Virgil. But it should be *deus ex machina*,' he added slyly.

God from the machine.

I licked melting chocolate from my fingers and began to read, skimming through the charts and anamnesis that followed. On the last sheet I read:

Client requests therapy in order to determine nature and cause of these obsessive nightmares.

Beneath this was Dr. Harrow's scrawled signature and the HEL stamp. I ate the last wafer, then mimed to the server that I was finished.

We dined alone in the Peacock Room. After setting our tiny table the servers disappeared, dismissed by Dr. Harrow's brusque gesture. A plateful of durians stood as our centerpiece, the spiky green globes piled atop a translucent porcelain tray. Dr. Harrow split one neatly for me, the round fruit oozing pale custard and a putrescent odor. She grimaced, then took a demure spoonful of the pulp and tasted it for me.

'Lovely,' she murmured, and handed me the spoon.

We ate in silence for several minutes beneath the flickering gaslit chandeliers.

'Did you read the profile I gave you?' Dr. Harrow asked at last, with studied casualness.

'Mmmm-mmm,' I grunted.

'And... ?'

'She will not make it.' I lofted another durian from the tray.

Dr. Harrow dipped her chin ever so slightly before asking, 'Why, Wendy?'

'I don't know.' This durian was not quite ripe. I winced and pushed it from my plate.

'Can't you give me any idea of what makes you feel that?'

'Nothing. I can't feel anything.' I took another fruit.

'Well, then, what makes you think she wouldn't be a good analysand?'

'I don't know. I just–' I sucked on my spoon, thinking. 'It's like when I see my name – the way everything starts to shiver and I get sick. But I don't throw up.'

Dr. Harrow tilted her head thoughtfully. 'Like a seizure. Well.' She smiled and spooned another mouthful.

I finished the last durian and glanced around impatiently. 'When will I meet her?'

'You already have.'

I kicked my chair. 'When?'

'Fourteen years ago, when you first came to HEL.'

'Why don't I remember her?'

'You do, Wendy.' She lifted her durian and took the last drop of custard upon her tongue. 'It's me.'

'Surprised?' Dr. Harrow grinned and raised the flamboyant sleeves of her embroidered haik.

'It's beautiful,' I said, fingering the flowing cuffs enviously.

She smiled and turned to the NET beside my bed. 'I'm the patient this morning. Are you ready?'

I nodded. Earlier she had wheeled in her own cot, and now sat on it readying her monitors. I settled on my bed and waited for her to finish. She finally turned to me and applied electrolytic fluid to the nodes on my temples, placed other wires upon my head and cheekbones before doing the same to herself.

'You have no technicians assisting you?' I asked.

She shook her head but made no reply as she adjusted her screens and, finally, settled onto her cot. I lay back against the pillow and shut my eyes.

The last thing I heard was the click of the adaptor freeing the current, and a gentle exhalation that might have been a sigh.

'Here we stand...'
'Here we stand...'
'Here we lie...'
'Here we lie...'
'Eye to hand and heart to head,
'Deep in the dark with the dead.*'*

It is spring, and not dark at all, but I repeat the incantation as Aidan gravely sprinkles apple blossoms upon my head. In the branches beneath us a bluejay shrieks at our bulldog, Molly, as she whines and scratches hopefully at her basket.

'Can't we bring her up?' I peer over the edge

of the rickety platform and Molly sneezes in excitement.

'Shhh!' Aidan commands, squeezing his eyes shut as he concentrates. After a moment he squints and reaches for his crumpled sweater. Several bay leaves filched from the kitchen crumble over me and I blink so the debris doesn't get in my eyes.

'I hate this junk in my hair,' I grumble. 'Next time I make the spells.'

'You can't.' Loftily Aidan stands on tiptoe and strips another branch of blossoms, sniffing them dramatically before tossing them in a flurry of pink and white. 'We need a virgin.'

'So?' I jerk on the rope leading to Molly's basket. 'You're a virgin. Next time we use you.'

Aidan stares at me, brows furrowed. 'That won't count,' he says at last. 'Say it again, Emma.'

'Here we stand…'

Every day of Easter break we come here: an overgrown apple orchard within the woods, uncultivated for a hundred years. Stone walls tumbled by time mark the gray boundaries of a colonial farm. Blackberry vines choke the rocks with breeze-blown petals. Our father showed us this place. Long ago he built the treehouse, its wood lichen-green now and wormed with holes. Rusted nails snag my knees when we climb: all that remains of other platforms and the crow's-nest at treetop.

I finish the incantation and kneel, calling to Molly to climb in her basket. When my twin yells I announce imperiously, 'The virgin needs her faithful consort. Get *in*, Molly.'

He demurs and helps to pull her up. Molly is trembling when we heave her onto the platform. As always, she remains huddled in her basket.

'She's sitting on the sandwiches,' I remark matter-of-factly. Aidan shoves Molly aside hastily and retrieves two squashed bags. 'I call we break for lunch.'

We eat in thoughtful silence. We never discuss the failure of the spells, although each afternoon Aidan hides in his secret place behind the wing chair in the den and pores through more brittle volumes. Sometimes I can feel them working – the air is so calm, the wind dies unexpectedly, and for a moment the woods glow so bright, so deep, their shadows still and green; and it is there: the secret to be revealed, the magic to unfold, the story to begin. Aidan flushes above me and his eyes shine, he raises his arms and –

And nothing. It is gone. A moment too long or too soon, I never know – but we have lost it again. For an instant Aidan's eyes gray with tears. Then the breeze rises, Molly yawns and snuffles, and once more we put aside the spells for lunch and other games.

That night I toss in my bed, finally throwing my pillow against the bookcase. From the open window stream the chimes of peepers in the swamp, their plangent song broidered with the trills of toads and leopard frogs. As I churn feverishly through the sheets it comes again, and I lie still: like a star's sigh, the shiver and promise of a door opening somewhere just out of reach. I hold my breath, waiting: will it close again?

But no. The curtains billow and I slip from my bed, bare feet curling upon the cold planked floor as I race silently to the window.

He is in the meadow at wood's edge, alone, hair misty with starlight, his pajamas spectral blue in the dark. As I watch he raises his arms to the sky, and though I am too far to hear, I whisper the words with him, my heart thumping counterpoint to our invocation. Then he is quiet, and stands alert, waiting.

I can no longer hear the peepers. The wind has risen, and the thrash of the beech trees at the edge of the forest drowns all other sounds. I can feel his heart now, beating within my own, and see the shadows with his eyes.

In the lower branches of the willow tree, the lone willow that feeds upon a hidden spring beside the sloping lawn, there is a boy. His eyes are green and lucent as tourmaline, and silvery moths are drawn to them. His hands clutch the slender willow-wands: strong hands, so pale that I trace the blood beneath, and see the muscles strung like young strong vines. As I watch he bends so that his head dips beneath a branch, new leaves tangling fair hair, and then slowly he uncurls one hand and, smiling, beckons my brother toward him.

The wind rises. Beneath his bare feet the dewy grass darkens as Aidan runs faster and faster, until he seems almost to be skimming across the lawn. And there, where the willow starts to shadow the starlit slope and the boy in the tree leans to take his hand, I tackle my brother and bring him crashing and swearing to earth.

For a moment he stares at me uncomprehending. Then he yells and slaps me, hits me harder until, remembering, he shoves me away and stumbles to his feet.

There is nothing there. The willow trembles, but only the wind shakes the new leaves. From the marsh the ringing chorus rises, swells, bursts as the peepers stir in the saw grass. In the old house yellow light stains an upstairs window and our father's voice calls out sleepily, then with concern, and finally bellows as he leans from the casement to spot us below. Aidan glances at the house and back again at the willow, and then he turns to me despairingly. Before I can say anything he punches me and runs, weeping, back to the house.

A gentler withdrawal than I'm accustomed to. For several minutes I lay with closed eyes, breathing gently as I tried to hold onto the scents of apple blossom and dew-washed grass. But they faded, along with the dreamy net of tree and stars. I sat up groggily, wires still taped to my head, and faced Dr. Harrow already recording her limbic system response from the NET.

'Thank you, Wendy,' she said brusquely without looking up. I glanced at the BEAM monitor, where the shaded image of my brain lingered, the last flash of activity staining the temporal lobe bright turquoise.

'I never saw that color there before,' I remarked as I leaned to examine it, when suddenly an unfocused wave of nausea choked me. I gagged and staggered against the bed, tearing at the wires.

Eyes: brilliant green lanced with cyanogen, unblinking as twin chrysolites. A wash of light: leaves stirring the surface of a still pool. They continued to stare through the shadows, heedless of the play of sun and moon, days and years and decades. The electrodes dangled from my fist as I stared at the blank screen, the single dancing line bisecting the NET monitor. The eyes in my head did not move, did not blink, did not disappear. They stared relentlessly from the shadows until the darkness itself swelled and was absorbed by their feral gaze. They saw me.

Not Dr. Harrow; not Aidan; not Morgan or Melisande or the others I'd absorbed in therapy.

Me.

I stumbled from the monitor to the window, dragging the wires behind me, heedless of Dr. Harrow's stunned expression. Grunting I shook my head like a dog, finally gripped the windowsill and slammed my head against the oaken frame, over and over and over, until Dr. Harrow tore me away. Still I saw them: unblinking glaucous eyes, tumbling into darkness as Dr. Harrow pumped the sedatives into my arm.

Much later I woke to see Dr. Harrow staring at me from the far end of the room. She watched me for a moment, and then walked slowly to the bed.

'What was it, Wendy?' she asked, smoothing her robe as she sat beside me. 'Your name?'

I shook my head. 'I don't know,' I stammered, biting the tip of my thumb. Then I twisted to stare at her and asked, 'Who was the boy?'

Her voice caught for an instant before she answered. 'My brother Aidan. My twin.'

'No – The other – The boy in the tree.'

This time she held her breath a long moment, then let it out in a sigh. 'I don't know,' she murmured. 'But you remember him?'

I nodded. 'Now. I can see him now. If I–' And I shut my eyes and drifted before snapping back. 'Like that. He comes to me on his own. Without me recalling him. Like–' I flexed my fingers helplessly. 'Like a dream, only I'm awake now.'

Slowly Dr. Harrow shook her head and reached to take my hand. 'That's how he found Aidan, too, the last time,' she said. 'And me. And now you.' For an instant something like hope flared in her eyes, but faded as she bowed her head. 'I think, Wendy...' She spoke with measured calm. 'I think we should keep this to ourselves right now. And tomorrow, perhaps, we'll try again.'

He sees me.

I woke with a garbled scream, arms flailing, to my dark room bathed in the ambient glow of monitors. I stumbled to the window, knelt with my forehead against the cool oak sill and blinked against tears that welled unbidden from my burning eyes. There I fell asleep with my head pillowed upon my arms, and woke next morning to Dr. Harrow's knock upon my door.

'Emma,' he whispers at the transom window. 'Let me in.'

The quilts piled on me muffle his voice. He calls again, louder, until I groan and sit up in bed, rubbing my eyes and glaring at the top of his head peeking through the narrow glass.

From the bottom of the door echoes faint scratching, Molly's whine. A thump. More scratching: Aidan crouched outside the room, growling through choked laughter. I drape a quilt around me like a toga and lean forward to unlatch the door.

Molly flops onto the floor, snorting when she bumps her nose and then drooling apologetically. Behind her stumbles Aidan, shivering in his worn kimono with its tattered sleeves and belt stolen from one of my old dresses. I giggle uncontrollably, and gesture for him to shut the door before Father hears us in his room below.

'It's fucking freezing in this place,' Aidan exclaims, pinning me to the bed and pulling the quilts over our heads. 'Oh, come on, dog.' Grunting, he hauls her up beside us. 'My room is like Antarctica. Tierra del Fuego. The Bering Strait.' He punctuates his words with kisses, elbowing Molly as she tries to slobber our faces. I squirm away and straighten my nightshirt.

'Hush. You'll wake Papa.'

Aidan rolls his eyes and stretches against the wall. 'Spare me.' Through the rents in his kimono I can see his skin, dusky in the moonlight. No one has skin like Aidan's, except for me: not white but the palest gray, almost blue, and fine and smooth as an eggshell. People stare at us in the street, especially at Aidan; at school girls stop talking when he passes, and fix me with narrowed eyes and lips pursed to mouth a question never asked.

Aidan yawns remorselessly as a cat. Aidan is the beauty: Aidan whose gray eyes flicker green whereas mine muddy to blue in sunlight; Aidan whose long legs wrap around me and shame my own, scraped and bruised from an unfortunate bout with Papa's razor.

'Molly. Here.' He grabs her into his lap, groaning at her weight, and pulls me as well, until we huddle in the middle of the bed. Our heads knock and he points with his chin to the mirror.

' "*Did you never see the picture of We Three?*" ' he warbles. Then, shoving Molly to the floor, he takes my shoulders and pulls the quilt from me.

My father had a daughter loved a man
As it might be perhaps, were I a woman,
I should your lordship.

He recites softly, in his own voice: not the deeper drone he affected when we had been paired in the play that Christmas. I start to slide from bed but he holds me tighter, twisting me to face him until our foreheads touch and I know that the mirror behind us reflects a moon-lapped Rorschach and, at our feet, our snuffling mournful fool.

' "*But died thy sister of her love, my boy?*" ' I whisper later, my lips brushing his neck where the hair, unfashionably long, waves to form a perfect S.

I am all the daughters of my father's house,
And all the brothers, too; and yet I know not.

He kisses me. Later he whispers nonsense, my name, rhyming words from our made-up language; a long and heated silence.

Afterward he sleeps, but I lie long awake, stroking his hair and watching the rise and fall of his slender chest. In the coldest hour he awakens and stares at me, eyes wide and black, and turning on his side moans, then begins to cry as though his heart will break. I clench my teeth and stare at the ceiling, trying not to blink, trying not to hear or feel him next to me, his pale gray skin, his eyes: my beautiful brother in the dark.

After this session Dr. Harrow let me sleep until early afternoon. The rush of summer rain against the high casements finally woke me, and I lay in bed staring up at a long fine crack that traversed the ceiling. To me it looked like the arm of some ghastly tree overtaking the room. It finally drove me downstairs. I ambled down the long glass-roofed corridor that led to the pre-Columbian annex. I paused to pluck a hibiscus blossom from a terra-cotta vase and arranged it behind one ear. Then I went on, until I reached the ancient elevator with its folding arabesques.

The second floor was off limits to empaths, but Anna had memorized a dead patient's release code and she and I occasionally crept up here to tap sleeping researchers. No medical personnel patrolled the rooms. Servers checked the monitors and recorded all responses. At the end of each twelve-hour shift doctors would flit in and out of the bedrooms, unhooking oneironauts and helping them stumble to other rooms where they could fall into yet another, though dreamless, sleep. I tapped the pirated code into the first security unit I saw, waiting for it to read my retina imprint and finally grant the access code that slid open the false paneled wall.

Here stretched the sleep labs: chambers swathed in yellowed challis and moth-eaten linens, huge canopied beds where masked oneironauts turned and sighed as their monitors clicked in draped alcoves. The oneironauts' skin shone glassy white; beneath the masks their eyes were bruised a tender green from enforced somnolence. I held my breath as long as I could: the air seethed with dreams. I hurried down the hall to a room with door ajar and an arched window columned with white drapes. A woman I did not recognize sprawled across a cherry four-poster, her demure lace gown at odds with the rakish mask covering her eyes. I slipped inside, locking the door behind me. Then I turned to the bed.

The research subject's hair formed a dark filigree against the disheveled linen sheets. I bowed to kiss her on the mouth, waiting to be certain she would not awake. Then I dipped my tongue between her lips and drew back, closing my eyes to unravel strands of desire and clouded abandon, pixie fancies. All faded in a moment: dreams, after all, are dreams. I reached to remove the wires connecting her to the monitors, adjusted the settings and hooked her into the NET. I did the same for myself with extra wires, relaying through the BEAM to the transmitter. I smoothed the sheets, lay beside her and closed my eyes.

A gray plain shot with sunlight. Clouds mist the air with a scent of rain and seawater. In the distance I hear waves. Turning I can see a line of small trees, contorted like crippled children at ocean's edge. We walk there, the oneironaut's will bending so easily to mine that I scarcely sense her: she is another salt-scattered breeze.

The trees draw nearer. I stare at them until they shift, stark lichened branches blurring into limbs bowed with green and gentle leaves. Another moment and we are beneath their heavy welcoming boughs.

I place my hand against the rough bark and stare into the heart of the greenery. Within the emerald shadows something stirs. Sunlit shards of leaf and twig align themselves into hands. Shadows shift to form a pair of slanted beryl eyes. There: crouched among the boughs like a dappled cat, his curls crowned with a ring of leaves, his lips parted to show small white teeth. He smiles at me.

Before he draws me any closer I withdraw, snapping the wires from my face. The tree shivers into white sheets and the shrouded body of the woman beside me.

My pounding heart slowed as I drew myself up on my elbows to watch her, carefully peeling the mask from her face. Beneath lids mapped with fine blue veins her eyes roll, tracking something unseen. Suddenly they steady. Her mouth relaxes into a smile, then into an expression of such blissful rapture that without thinking I kiss her and taste a burst of ecstatic, halycon joy.

And reel back as she suddenly claws at my chest, her mouth twisted to shout; but no sound comes. Bliss explodes into terror. Her eyes open and she stares, not at me but at something that looms before her. Her eyes grow wide and horrified, the pupils dilating as she grabs at my face, tears the hibiscus blossom from my hair and chokes a garbled scream, a shout I muffle with a pillow.

I whirled and reset the monitors, switched the NET's settings and fled out the door. In the hallway I hesitated and looked back. The woman pummeled the air before her blindly; she had not seen me. I turned and ran until I reached the doctors' stairway leading to the floors below, and slipped away unseen.

Downstairs all was silent. Servers creaked past bringing tea trays to doctors in their quarters. I hurried to the conservatory, where I inquired after the aide named Justice. The server directed me to a chamber where Justice stood recording the results of an evoked potential scan.

'Wendy!' Surprise melted into disquiet. 'What are you doing here?'

I shut the door and stepped to the window, tugging the heavy velvet drapes until they fell and the chamber darkened. 'I want you to scan me,' I whispered.

He shook his head. 'What? Why–' I grabbed his hand as he tried to turn up the lights and he nodded slowly, then dimmed the screen he had been working on. 'Where is Dr. Harrow?'

'I want you to do it.' I tightened my grip. 'I think I have entered a fugue state.'

He smiled, shaking his head. 'That's impossible, Wendy. You'd have no way of knowing it. You'd be catatonic, or –' He shrugged, then glanced uneasily at the door. 'What's going on? You know I'm not certified to do that alone.'

'But you know how,' I wheedled, stroking his hand. 'You are a student of their arts, you can do it as easily as Dr. Harrow.' Smiling, I leaned forward until my forehead rested against his, and kissed him tentatively on the mouth. His expression changed to fear as he trembled and tried to move away. Sexual contact between staff and experimental personnel was forbidden and punishable by execution of the medics in question; empaths were believed incapable of initiating such contact. I grinned more broadly and pinned both of his hands to the table, until he nodded and motioned with his head toward the PET unit.

'Sit down,' he croaked. I latched the door, then sat in the wing-back chair beside the bank of monitors.

In a few minutes I heard the dull hum of the scanners as he improvised the link for my reading. I waited until my brain's familiar patterns emerged on the screen.

'See?' Relief brightened his voice, and he tilted the monitor so that I could see it more clearly. 'All normal. Maybe she got your dosage wrong. Perhaps Dr. Silverthorn can suggest a–'

His words trickled into silence. I shut my eyes and drew up the image of the tree, beryl eyes and outstretched hand, then opened my eyes to see the PET scan showing intrusive activity in my temporal lobe: brain waves evident of an emergent secondary personality.

'That's impossible,' Justice breathed. 'You have no MPs, no independent emotions – What the hell is that?' He traced the patterns with an unsteady hand, then turned to stare at me. 'What did you do, Wendy?' he whispered.

I shook my head, crouching into the chair's corner, and carefully removed the wires. The last image shimmered on the screen like a cerebral ghost. 'Take them,' I said flatly, holding out the wires. 'Don't tell anyone.'

He let me pass without a word. Only when my hand grasped the doorknob did he touch me briefly on the shoulder.

'Where did it come from?' he faltered. 'What is it, Wendy?'

I stared past him at the monitor with its pulsing shadows. 'Not me,' I whispered at last. 'The boy in the tree.'

They found the sleep researcher at shift-change that evening, hanging by the swag that had decorated her canopied bed. Anna told me about it at dinner.

'Her monitors registered an emergent MP.' She licked her lips unconsciously, like a kitten. 'Do you think we could get into the morgue?'

I yawned and shook my head. 'Are you crazy?'

Anna giggled and rubbed my neck. 'Isn't everybody?'

Several aides entered the dining room, scanning warily before they started tapping empties on the shoulder and gesturing to the door. I looked up to see Justice, his face white and pinched as he stood behind me.

'You're to go to your chambers,' he announced. 'Dr. Harrow says you are not to talk to anyone.' He swallowed and avoided my eyes, then abruptly stared directly at me for the first time. 'I told her that I hadn't seen you yet but would make certain you knew.'

I nodded quickly and looked away. In a moment he was gone, and I started upstairs.

'I saw Dr. Leslie before,' Anna commented before she walked outside toward her cottage. 'He smiled at me and waved.' She hesitated, biting her lip thoughtfully. 'Maybe he will play with me this time,' she announced before turning down the rain-spattered path.

Dr. Harrow stood at the high window in the Home Room when I arrived. In her hand she held a drooping hibiscus flower.

'Shut the door,' she ordered. I did so. 'Now lock it and sit down.'

She had broken the hibiscus. Her fingers looked bruised from its stain: jaundiced yellow, ulcerous purple. As I stared she flung the flower into my lap.

'They know it was you,' she announced. 'They matched your retina print with the masterfile. How could you have thought you'd get away with it?' She sank onto the bed, her eyes dull with fatigue.

The rain had hung back for several hours, a heavy iron veil. Now it hammered the windows again, its steady tattoo punctuated by the rattle of hailstones.

'I did not mean to kill her,' I murmured. I smoothed my robe, flicking the broken blossom onto the floor.

She ground the hibiscus beneath her heel, took it and threw it out the window. 'Her face,' she said: as if replying to a question. 'Like my brother Aidan's.'

I stared at her blankly.

'When I found him,' she went on, turning to me with glittering eyes. 'On the tree.'

I shook my head. 'I don't know what you're talking about, Dr. Harrow.'

Her lips tightened against her teeth when she faced me. A drop of blood welled against her lower lip. I longed to lean forward to taste it, but did not dare. 'She was right, you know. You steal our dreams…'

'That's impossible.' I crossed my arms, shivering a little from the damp breeze. I hesitated. 'You told me that is impossible. Unscientific. Unprofessional thinking.'

She smiled, and ran her tongue over her lip to lick away the blood. 'Unprofessional? This has all been very unprofessional, Wendy. Didn't you know that?'

'The tenets of the Nuremberg Act state that a scientist should not perform any research upon a subject which she would not undergo herself.'

Dr. Harrow shook her head, ran a hand through damp hair. 'Is that what you thought it was? Research?'

I shrugged. 'I – I don't know. The boy – Your twin?'

'Aidan…' She spread her fingers against the bed's coverlet, flexed a finger that bore a simple silver ring. 'They found out. Teachers. Our father. About us. Do you understand?'

A flicker of the feeling she had evoked in bed with her brother returned, and I slitted my eyes, tracing it. 'Yes,' I whispered. 'I think so.'

'It is –' She fumbled for a phrase. 'Like what is forbidden here, between empaths and staff. They separated us. Aidan… They sent him away, to another kind of – school. Tested him.'

She stood and paced to the window, leaned with a hand upon each side so that the rain lashed about her, then turned back to me with her face streaming: whether with rain or tears I could not tell. 'Something happened that night…' Shaking her head furiously she pounded the wall with flattened palms. 'He was never the same. He had terrible dreams, he couldn't bear to sleep alone– That was how it started–

'And then he came home, for the holidays… Good Friday. He would not come to Mass with us. Papa was furious; but Aidan wouldn't leave his room. And when we returned, I looked for him, he wasn't there, not in his room, not anywhere…

'I found him. He had –' Her voice broke and she stared past me to the wall beyond. 'Apple blossom in his hair. And his face –'

I thought she would weep; but her expression twisted so that almost I could imagine she laughed to recall it.

'Like hers…'

She drew nearer, until her eyes were very close

to mine. I sniffed and moved to the edge of the bed warily: she had dosed herself with hyoscine derived from the herbarium. Now her words slurred as she spoke, spittle a fine hail about her face.

'Do you know what happens now, Wendy?' In the rain-streaked light she glowed faintly. 'Dr. Leslie was here tonight. They have canceled our term of research. We're all terminated. A purge. Tomorrow they take over.'

She made a clicking noise with her tongue. 'And you, Wendy. And Anna, and all the others. Toys. *Weapons*.' She swayed slightly as she leaned toward me. 'You especially. They'll find him, you know. Dig him up and use him.'

'Who?' I asked. Now sweat pearled where the rain had dried on her forehead. I clutched a bolster as she stretched a hand to graze my temples, and shivered.

'My brother,' she murmured.

'No, Dr. Harrow. The other – who is the other?'

Smiling she drew me toward her, the bolster pressing against her thigh as she reached for the NET's rig, flicking rain from the colored wires.

'Let's find out.'

I cried out at her clumsy hookup. A spot of blood welled from her temple and I protectively touched my own face, drew away a finger gelled with the fluid she had smeared carelessly from ear to jaw. Then, before I could lie down, she made the switch and I cried out at the dizzy vistas erupting behind my eyes.

Aniline lightning. Faculae stream from synapse to synapse as ptyalin floods my mouth and my head rears instinctively to smash against the headboard. She has not tied me down. The hyoscine lashes into me like a fiery bile and I open my mouth to scream. In the instant before it begins I taste something faint and caustic in the back of her throat and struggle to free myself from her arms. Then I'm gone.

Before me looms a willow tree shivering in a breeze frigid with the shadow of the northern mountains. Sap oozes from a raw flat yellow scar on the trunk above my head where, two days before, my father had sawed the damaged limb free. It had broken from the weight; when I found him he lay pillowed by a crush of twigs and young leaves and scattered bark, the blossoms in his hair alone unmarked by the fall. Now I stand on tiptoe and stroke the splintery wound, bring my finger to my lips and kiss it. I shut my eyes, because they burn so. No tears left to shed; only this terrible dry throbbing, as though my eyes have been etched with sand. The sobs begin again, suddenly. The wrenching weight in my chest drags me to my knees until I crouch before the tree, bow until my forehead brushes grass trampled by grieving family. I groan and try to think of words, imprecations, a curse to rend the light and living from my world so abruptly strangled and still. But I can only moan. My mouth opens upon dirt and shattered granite. My nails claw at the ground as though to wrest from it something besides stony roots and scurrying earwigs. The earth swallows my voice as I force myself to my knees and, sobbing, raise my head to the tree.

It is enough; he has heard me. Through the shroud of new leaves he peers with lambent eyes. April's first apple blossoms weave a snowy cloud about his brow. His eyes are huge, the palest, purest green in the cold morning sun. They stare at me unblinking; harsh and bright and implacable as moonlight, as languidly he extends his hand toward mine.

I stagger to my feet, clots of dirt falling from my palms. From the north the wind rises and rattles the willow branches. Behind me a door rattles as well, as my father leans out to call me back to the house. At the sound I start to turn, to break the reverie that binds me to this place, this tree stirred by a tainted wind riven from a bleak and noiseless shore.

And then I stop, where in memory I have stopped a thousand times; and turn back to the tree, and for the first time I meet his eyes.

He is waiting, as he has always waited; as he will always wait. At my neck the wind gnaws cold as bitter iron, stirring the collar of my blouse so that already the chill creeps down my chest, to nuzzle there at my breasts and burrow between them. I nod my head, very slightly, and glance back at the house.

All the colors have fled the world. For the first

time I see it clearly: the gray skin taut against granite hills and grassless haughs; the horizon livid with clouds like a rising barrow; the hollow bones and nerveless hands drowned beneath black waters lapping at the edge of a charred orchard. The rest is fled and I see the true world now, the sleeping world as it wakes, as it rears from the ruins and whispers in the wind at my cheeks, this is what awaits you; this and nothing more, the lie is revealed and now you are waking and the time has come, come to me, come to me…

In the ghastly light only his eyes glow, and it is to them that I turn, it is into those hands white and cold and welcome that I slip my own, it is to him that I have come, not weeping, no not ever again, not laughing, but still and steady and cold as the earth beneath my feet, the gray earth that feeds the roots and limbs and shuddering leaves of the tree…

And then pain rips through me, a flood of fire searing my mouth and ears, raging so that I stagger from the bed as tree and sky and earth tilt and shiver like images in black water. Gagging I reach into my own throat, trying to dislodge the capsule Emma Harrow has bitten; try to breath through the fumes that strip the skin from my gums. I open my mouth to scream but the fire churns through throat and chest, boils until my eyes run and stain the sky crimson.

And then I fall; the wires rip from my skull. Beside me on the floor Dr. Harrow thrashed, eyes staring wildly at the ceiling, her mouth rigid as she retched and blood spurted from her bitten tongue. I recoiled from the scent of bitter almond she exhaled; then watched as she suddenly grew still. Quickly I knelt, tilting her head away so that half of the broken capsule rolled onto the floor at my feet. I waited a moment, then bowed my head until my lips parted around her broken jaw and my tongue stretched gingerly to lap at the blood cupped in her cheek.

In the tree the boy laughs. A bowed branch shivers, and then, slowly, rises from the ground. Another boy dangles there, his long hair tangled in dark strands around a leather belt. I see him lift his head and, as the world rushes away in a blur of red and black, he smiles at me.

A cloud of frankincense. Seven stars limned against a dormer window. A boy with a bulldog puppy; and she is dead.

I cannot leave my room now. Beside me a screen dances with colored lights that refract and explode in brilliant parhelions when I dream. But I am not alone now, ever…

I see him waiting in the corner, laughing as his green eyes slip between the branches and the bars of my window, until the sunlight changes and he is lost to view once more, among the dappled and chattering leaves.

FAMILY

Joyce Carol Oates

Joyce Carol Oates (1938–) is an American author who has published over fifty novels, as well as many volumes of short stories, poetry, and nonfiction. Her novel *them* (1969) won the National Book Award, and her novels *Black Water* (1992), *What I Lived For* (1994), and *Blonde* (2000) were nominated for the Pulitzer Prize. In addition to portraying compelling, complex characters, Oates excels at writing stories with a New Gothic or weird sensibility, many of them terrifying or disturbing. 'Family' (1989) is a tale of weird science fiction horror and strange ritual that reads like the love-child of Shirley Jackson and China Miéville.

The days were brief and attenuated and the season appeared to be fixed – neither summer nor winter, spring nor fall. A thermal haze of inexpressible sweetness, though bearing tiny bits of grit or mica, had eased into the Valley from the industrial region to the north and there were nights when the sun set at the western horizon as if it were sinking through a porous red mass, and there were days when a hard-glaring moon like bone remained fixed in a single position, prominent in the sky. Above the patchwork of excavated land bordering our property – all of which had formerly been our property in Grandfather's time: thousands of acres of wheat, corn, oats, and open grazing land – a curious trembling rainbow sometimes defined itself, its colors shifting even as you stared, shades of blue, blue-green, blue-purple, orange, orange-red, orange-yellow, a translucent yellow that dissolved into mere moisture as the thermal breeze stirred, warm as an exhaled breath. And if you had run to tell others of the rainbow it was likely to be gone when they came. 'Liar,' my older brothers and sisters said, 'don't say such things if you don't mean them!' Father said, frowning, 'Don't say such things at all if you aren't certain they will be true for others, not simply for yourself.'

This begins in the time of family celebration – after Father succeeded in selling all but a few of the acres of land surrounding our house, his inheritance from Grandfather, and he and Mother were giddy as children with relief at having escaped the luckless fate of certain of our neighbors in the Valley, rancher-rivals of Grandfather's and their descendants, who had sold off their property years ago, before the market had begun to realize its full potential. (*Full potential* were words that Father often uttered, rolling the words about in his mouth like round, smooth stones whose taste absorbed him.) Now they were landless, and their investments were shaky and they had made their homes in cities of increasing inhospitality, where no country people could endure to live for long. They had virtually prostituted themselves, Father said, sighing, and smiling – and for so little! It was a saying of Grandfather's that a curse would befall anyone in the Valley who gloated over a neighbor's misfortune, but as Father said, it was damned difficult not to feel superior in this instance. And Mother vehemently agreed.

Our house was made of stone, stucco, and clapboard; the newer wings, designed by a big-city architect, had a good deal of glass, and looked out into the Valley, where on good days we could see for many miles while on humid hazy days we could see barely beyond the fence that marked the edge of our property. Father, however, preferred the roof: In his white, light-woolen three-piece suit, white fedora cocked back on his head, for luck, he spent many of his waking hours on the highest peak of the highest roof of the house, observing, through binoculars, the amazing progress of construction in the Valley – for overnight, it seemed, there appeared roads, expressways, sewers, drainage pipes, 'planned' communities with such names as Whispering Glades, Murmuring Oaks, Pheasant Run, Deer Willow, all of them walled to keep out intruders, and, yet more astonishing, towerlike buildings of aluminum and glass and steel and brick, buildings whose windows shone and winked like mirrors, splendid in sunshine like pillars of flame; such beauty where once there had been mere earth and sky, it caught at your throat like a great bird's talons, taking your breath away. 'The ways of beauty are as a honeycomb,' Father told us, and none of us could determine, staring at his slow-moving lips, whether the truth he spoke was a happy truth or not, whether even it was truth.

So mesmerized was Father by the transformation of the Valley, perceived with dreamlike acuity through the twin lenses of his binoculars, the poor man often forgot where he was; failed to come down for dinner, or for bed; and if Mother, thinking to indulge him, or hurt by his indifference to her, did not send one of the servants to summon him, he was likely to spend the entire night on the roof... and in the morning, smiling sheepishly, he would explain that he'd fallen asleep, or, conversely, that he had been troubled by having seen things for which he could not account – shadows the size of longhorns moving beyond our twelve-foot barbed-wire fence, and mysterious winking lights fifty miles away in the foothills. Mother dismissed the shadows as optical illusions caused by father's overwrought constitution, or the ghosts of old, long-since-slaughtered livestock; the lights, she said, were surely from the private airport at Furnace Creek – had Father forgotten already that he'd sold a large parcel of land for a small airport there? 'These lights more resemble fires,' Father said stubbornly. 'And they were in the foothills, not in the plain.'

There were times then of power failures, and financial losses, and Father was forced to give up nearly all of our servants, but he retained his rooftop vigil, white-clad, powerful lenses to his eyes, for he perceived himself as a witness and thought, should he live to a ripe old age, as Grandfather had (Grandfather was in his ninety-ninth year when he died, and then in a fall from a wasp-stung horse), he would be a chronicler of our time, like Thucydides of his, for 'Is there a world struggling to be born, or only struggle?'

Because of numerous dislocations in the Valley, of which we learned by degrees, the abandonment of houses, farms, livestock, even pets, it happened that packs of dogs began to roam about looking for food, particularly by night, poor starveling creatures that were becoming a nuisance in the region and should be, as authorities urged, shot down on sight – these dogs being not feral by birth of course but formerly domesticated terriers, setters, cocker spaniels, German shepherds, Labrador retrievers, even the larger and coarser breed of poodle – and it was the cause of some friction between Mother and Father that, despite his presence on the roof at all hours of the day and night, Father failed nonetheless to see a band of dogs dig beneath our fence and silently make their way to the dairy barn, where with terrifying efficiency they tore out the throats – and surely this could not have been in silence! – of our last six holsteins, and our last two she-goats, preparatory to devouring the poor creatures; nor did Father notice anything out of the ordinary on the night that two homeless derelicts, formerly farmhands of ours, impaled themselves on the fence (which was electrically charged, though in compliance with County Farm and Home Office regulations) and were found, dead, in the morning. (It was Kit, our sixteen-year-old, who found them, and the sight of the men, he said, tore his heart – so skinny, gray, grizzled, he scarcely recognized them. And the crows had been at them early.)

Following this episode Father journeyed to the state capital, with the purpose of taking out a loan, and reestablishing, as he called it, old ties with his politician friends, and Mother joined him a few days later for a greatly needed change of scene, as she said – 'Not that I don't love you all, and the farm, but I need to breathe other air for a while' – leaving us under the care of Mrs. Hoyt our housekeeper and our eldest sister, Cory. The decision to leave us at this time was not a judicious one: Mother had forgotten that Mrs. Hoyt was in poor health, or perhaps she had decided not to care; and she seemed ignorant of the fact that Cory, for all the innocence of her marigold eyes and melodic voice, was desperately in love with one of the National Guardsmen who patrolled the Valley in jeeps, authorized to shoot wild dogs and, upon certain occasions, vandals, would-be arsonists, and squatters who were deemed a threat to the public well-being. And when Mother returned, unaccompanied by Father, after what seemed to us a very long absence (two weeks? two months?) it was with shocking news: She and Father had, after heart-searching deliberation, decided that, for the good of all concerned, they must separate – they must officially dissolve the marriage bond. Mother's voice wavered as she spoke but fierce little pinpoints of light shone in her eyes. We children were so taken by surprise we could not speak at first. Separate! Dissolve! For the good of all! We stood staring and mute; not even Cory, Kit, and Dale, not even Lona, who was the most impulsive of us, found words with which to protest; the youngest children began whimpering helplessly, soon joined by the rest – and by our few remaining servants; and Mrs. Hoyt, whose features were already bloated by illness. Mother said, 'Don't! Please! I can hardly bear the pain myself!' She then played a video of Father's farewell to the family, which drew fresh tears… for there, suddenly framed on our television screen, where we had never seen his image before, and could not in our wildest fancies have imagined it, was Father, somberly dressed, his hair in thin steely bands combed wetly across the dome of his skull, and his eyes puffy, an unnatural sheen to his face as if it had been scoured hard. He sat stiffly erect in a chair with a high ornately carved back; his fingers were gripping the arms so tightly the blood had drained from his knuckles; his words were slow, halting, and faint, like the progress of a gut-shot deer across a field, but unmistakably his: *Dear children your mother and I after thirty years of marriage… very happy marriage have decided to… have decided to… have decided to…* One of the low-flying helicopters belonging to the National Guardsmen soared past the house, making the television screen shudder, but the sound seemed to be garbled in any case, as if the tape had been clumsily cut and spliced; there were miniature lightning flashes; and Father's clear face turned liquid, melting horizontally, his eyes long and narrow as slugs and his mouth distended like a drowning man's; and all we could hear were sounds, not words, resembling *Help me* or *I am innocent* or *I love you dear children* – and then the screen was dead.

That afternoon Mother introduced us to the man who was to be Father's successor in the household, and to his three children, who were to be our new brothers and sister, and we shook hands shyly, in a state of mutual shock, and regarded one another with wide staring eyes. Our new Father! Our new brothers and sister! As Mother explained patiently her new husband was no *step*father but a genuine *father;* which meant that we were to call him 'Father' at all times, and even, in our most private innermost thoughts, we were to think of him as 'Father': for otherwise he would be very hurt, and very displeased. And so too with Einar and Erastus, our new brothers (not *step*brothers), and Fifi, our new sister (not *step*sister).

Our new Father stood before us beaming, a man of our former Father's approximate age but heavier and more robust than that Father, with an unusually large head, the cranium particularly developed, and small shrewd quick-darting eyes beneath brows of bone. He wore a fashionably tailored suit so dark as to resemble an undertaker's, and sported a red carnation in his lapel; his black shoes shone so splendidly they might have been phosphorescent. 'Hello Father,' we murmured, hardly daring to raise our eyes to his. 'Hello Father.' 'Hello…' The man's jaws were elongated, the lower jaw a good inch longer than the upper, so that a wet malevolent ridge of teeth was revealed; and, as often happened in those days, a single thought shot like lightning among us children, from one to the other to the other to the other, each of us smiling guiltily as it struck us; *Crocodile!* Only little Jori burst into tears when the thought passed into her head and after an embarrassed moment our new Father stooped to pick her up in his arms and comfort her... and some of us could virtually see how the memory of our former Father passed from her, as cruelly as if it had been hosed out of her skull. She was three years old then, and not accountable for her behavior.

New Father's children were tall, big-boned, solemn, with a greenish peevish cast to their skin, like many city children; the boys had inherited their father's large head and protruding crocodile jaws but the girl, Fifi, seventeen years old, was eye-catching in her beauty, with hair as mutinous as Cory's, and wide-set brown eyes in which something wolfish glimmered.

That evening certain of the boys – Dale, Kit, and Hewett – gathered close around Fifi, telling her wild tales of the Valley, how we had to protect ourselves with rifles and shotguns from trespassers, and how there was a resurgence of rats and other rodents on the farm, as a consequence of so much excavation in the countryside, and these tales, silly as they were, and exaggerated, made the girl shudder and giggle and lean toward the boys as if she were in need of their protection. And when Dale hurried off to get Fifi a goblet of ice water – at her request – she took the glass from his fingers and lifted it prissily to the light to examine its contents, asking, 'Is this water *pure?* Is it safe to *drink?*' It was true, our water was sometimes strangely effervescent, and tasted of rust; after a heavy rainfall there were likely to be tiny red wriggly things in it, like animated tails; so we had learned not to examine it too closely, and as our initial attacks of nausea, diarrhea, and faint-headedness had more or less subsided, we rarely thought of it any longer but tried to be grateful, as Mrs. Hoyt used to urge us, that we had any drinking water at all. So it was offensive to us to see Fifi make such a face, handing the goblet of water back to Dale, and asking him how anyone in his right mind could drink such – spilth. Dale said angrily, 'How? This is *how!*' and drank the water down in a single thirsty gulp. And he and his new sister stood staring at each other, each of them trembling with passion.

As Cory observed smiling, yet with a trace of resentment or envy, 'It looks as if "new sister" has made a conquest!'

'But what will she do,' I couldn't help asking, ' – if she can't drink our water?'

'She'll drink it,' Cory said grimly. 'And she'll find it delicious, like the rest of us.' Which, of course, turned out very quickly to be true.

Cory's confinement came in a time of ever-increasing confusion... when there were frequent power failures in the Valley, and all foods except tinned goods were scarce, and the price of ammunition doubled, and quadrupled; and the sky by both day and night was criss-crossed by the contrails of unmarked bombers in a design both eerie and beautiful, like the web of a gigantic spider. By this time construction in most parts of the Valley had been halted, temporarily or indefinitely: Part-completed houses and high-rise office buildings punctuated the landscape; some were mere concrete foundations upon which girders had been erected, like exposed bone. The lovely 'Mirror Tower' – as we children called it: It must have had a real name – was a two-hundred-story patchwork of interlocking slots of reflecting glass with a pale turquoise tint, and where its elegant surface had once mirrored scenes of sparkling beauty there was now, from day to day, virtually nothing: a sky like soiled cotton batting, smoldering slag heaps, fantastic burdocks and thistles grown to the height of trees. Traffic had dwindled to a half-dozen diesel trucks per day hauling their massive cargo (much of it diseased livestock bound for northern slaughterhouses) and a very few passenger cars. There were cloverleafs that coiled endlessly upon themselves and elevated highways that broke off in midair, thus as authorities warned travelers you were in danger, if you ventured into the countryside, of being attacked by roaming gangs – but the rumor was that the most dangerous men were rogue Guardsmen who wore their uniforms inside out and preyed upon the very people they were paid to protect. None of the family left the compound without being well armed and of course the younger children no longer left at all. All schools, public and private, were temporarily shut down.

The most luxurious of the model communities, known to us as The Wheel – its original name was forgotten: Whispering Glades? Deer Willow? – had suffered so extreme a financial collapse that most of its services were said to be suspended, and many of its tenants had fled back to the cities from which they'd fled to the Valley. (The community was called The Wheel because its condominiums, office buildings, shops, schools, hospitals, and crematoria were arranged in spokes radiating outward from a single axis; and were protected at their twenty-mile circumference not by a visible wall, which the Japanese architect who had designed it had declared a vulgar and outmoded concept, but by a force field of electricity of lethal voltage.) Though the airport at Furnace Creek was officially closed, we often saw small aircraft taking off and landing there in the night, heard the insectlike whine of their engines and spied their winking red lights, and one night when the sun hung paralyzed at the horizon for several hours and visibility was poor though shot with a duplicitous sharpened clarity there was an airplane crash in a slag-heap area that had once been a grazing pasture for our cows, and some of the older boys insisted upon going out to investigate… returning with sober, stricken faces, and little to say of the sights they had seen except they wished they had not seen them. Miles away in the foothills were mysterious encampments, some of them mere camps, in which people lived and slept on the ground, others deliberately if crudely erected villages like those once displayed in museums as being the habitations of Native American peoples… the names of these 'peoples' long since forgotten. These were rumored to be unauthorized settlements of city dwellers who had fled their cities at the time of the general urban collapse, as well as former ranchers and their descendants, and various wanderers and evicted persons, criminals, the mentally ill, and victims of contagious diseases... all of these officially designated outlaw parties who were subject to harsh treatment by the Guardsmen, for the region was now under martial law, and only within compounds maintained by government-registered property owners and heads of families were civil rights, to a degree, still operative. Eagerly, we scanned the Valley for signs of life, passing among us a pair of binoculars like forbidden treasure whose original owner we could not recall – though Cory believed this person, an adult male, had lived with us before Father's time, and had been good to us. But not even Cory could remember his name. Cory's baby was born shortly after the funerals of two of the younger children, who had died of violent flulike illnesses, and of Uncle Darrah, who had died of shotgun wounds while driving his pick-up truck in the Valley; but this, we were assured by Mother and Father, was mere coincidence, and not to be taken as a sign. One by one we were led into the attic room set aside for Cory to stare in astonishment at the puppy-sized, red-faced, squalling, yet so wonderfully alive creature… with its large oval soft-looking head, its wizened angry features, its unblemished skin. Mother had found a cradle in the storage barn for the baby, a white wicker antique dating back to the previous century, perhaps a cradle she herself had used though she could not remember it, nor could any of us, her children, recall having slept in it; a piece of furniture too good for Cory's 'bastard child,' as Mother tearfully called it. (Though allowing that the infant's parentage was no fault of its own.) Fit punishment, Mother said, that Cory's breasts yielded milk so grudgingly, and what milk they did yield was frequently threaded with blood, fit punishment for her daughter's 'sluttish' behavior… but the family's luck held and one day the older boys returned from a hunting expedition with a dairy cow... a beautiful black-and-white marbled animal very like the kind, years ago, or was it only months ago, we ourselves had owned. The cow supplied us with sweet, fresh, reasonably pure milk, thus saving Cory's bastard infant's life, as Mother said – 'for whatever that life is worth.'

Though she was occupied with household tasks, and often with emergency situations, Mother seemed obsessed with ferreting out the identity of Cory's infant's father; Cory's secret lover, as Mother called him with a bitter twist of her lips. Yet it seemed to give her a prideful sort of pleasure that her eldest daughter had not only had a secret lover at one time in her life (the baby being irrefutable proof of this) but had one still – despite the fact that no lover had stepped forward to claim the baby, or the baby's mother; and that Cory, once the prettiest of the girls, was now disfigured by skin rashes covering most of her body. And since her pregnancy her lower body remained bloated while her upper body had become emaciated. Mother herself was frequently ill, with flaming rashes, respiratory illnesses, intestinal upsets, bone aches, uncertain vision; like most of us she was plagued with ticks – the smallest species of deer tick, which could burrow into the skin, particularly into the scalp, unnoticed, there to do its damage, and after weeks drop off, to be found on the floor, swollen with blood, black, shiny, about the size and apparent texture of a watermelon seed, deceptive to the eye. By degrees Mother had shrunk to a height of about four feet eight inches, very unlike the statuesque beauty of certain old photographs; with stark white matted hair, and pale silvery gray eyes as keen and suspicious as ever, and a voice so hard, harsh, brassy, and penetrating, a shout from her had the power to paralyze any of us where we stood... though we knew or believed ourselves safely hidden from her by a wall, or more than a single wall. Even the eldest of her sons, Kit, Hewett, Dale, tall ragged-bearded men who absented themselves from the compound for days at a stretch, were intimidated by Mother's authority, and, like poor Cory, shrank in guilty submission before her. Again and again Mother interrogated Cory, 'Who is your secret lover? Why are you so ashamed of him?' and Cory insisted she did not know who her lover was, or could not remember – 'Even if I see his face sometimes, in my sleep, I can't remember his name. Or who he was. Or who he claimed to be.'

Yet Mother continued her investigation, risking Father's displeasure in so ruthlessly questioning all males with whom she came into contact, not excluding Cory's cousins and uncles and even Cory's own brothers! – even those ravaged men and boys who made their homes, so to speak, in the drainage pipes beyond the compound, and whose services the family sometimes enlisted in times of emergency. But no one confessed; no one acknowledged Cory's baby as his. And one day when Cory lay ill upstairs in her attic room and I was entrusted with caring for the baby, feeding it from a bottle, in the kitchen, Mother came into the room with a look of such determination I felt terror for the baby, and hugged it to my bosom, and Mother said, 'Give me the bastard, girl,' and I said, 'No Mother, don't make me,' and Mother said, 'Are you disobeying me? *Give me the bastard,*' and I said, backing away, 'No Mother, Cory's baby belongs to Cory, and it isn't a bastard.' Mother advanced upon me, furious; her eyes whitely rimmed and her fingers – well, what talons they had become! – outstretched; her mouth twisting, working, distending itself – and I saw that in the midst of her passion she was forgetting what she meant to do, and that this might save Cory's baby. For often in those days when the family had little to eat except worm-riddled apples from the old orchard, and stunted blackened potatoes, and such wild game (or wildlife) as the boys could hunt down, we often forgot what we were doing in the very act of doing it; and in the midst of speaking we might forget the words we meant to speak, for instance *water, rainbow, grief, love, filth, God, deer tick*... and Father, who had become somber-minded with the onset of age, worried above all that as a family we might one day lose all sense of ourselves as a family should we forget, collectively, and in the same moment, the sacred word *family.*

And indeed Mother was forgetting. And indeed within the space of less than thirty seconds she had forgotten. She stared at the living thing, the quivering palpitating creature in my arms, with its soft flat shallow face, its tiny recessed eyes, its mere holes for nostrils, above all its small pursed mouth set like a manta ray's in its shallow face, and could not, simply could not, recall the word *baby*; or *infant*; or *Cory's bastard.* And shortly afterward there was a commotion of some kind outside, apparently rather close to the compound gate, and a sound of gunfire, familiar enough yet always jarring when unexpected, and Mother hurried out to investigate. And Cory's baby continued to suck hungrily at the bottle's frayed rubber nipple and all was safe for the time being.

But Cory, poor Cory, died a few days later: Early one morning Lona discovered her in her attic bed, her eyes opened wide and her pale mouth contorted, the bedclothes soaked in blood... and when in horror Lona drew the sheet away she saw that Cory's breasts had been partly devoured, and her chest cavity exposed; she must have been attacked in the night by rats, and had been too weak or too terrified to call for help. Yet her baby was sleeping only a few feet away in its antique cradle, untouched, sunk to that most profound and enviable level of sleep at which organic matter seems about to pass over again into the inorganic. The household rats with their glittering amaranthine eyes and stiff hairless tails had spared it! – had missed it entirely!

Lona snatched up the baby and ran screaming downstairs for help; and so fierce was she in possession she could scarcely be forced to surrender the sleepy infant to the rest of us: Her fingers had to be pried open. In a dazed gloating voice she said, 'It is my baby. It is Lona's baby now.' Father sharply rebuked her: 'It is the family's baby now.'

And Fifi too had a baby; or, rather, writhed and screamed in agony for a day and a night, before giving birth to a piteous undersized creature that lived for only a few minutes. Poor sister! – in the weeks that followed only our musical evenings, at which she excelled, gave her solace. If Dale tried to touch her, let alone comfort her, she shrank from him in repugnance. Nor would she allow Father or any male to come near. Sometimes she crawled into my bed and hugged me in her cold bone-thin arms. 'What I like best,' she whispered 'is the black waves that splash over us, at night.' And my heart was so swollen with emotion, I could not say no, or Oh yes.

For suddenly we had taken up music. In the evenings by kerosene lamp. In the worst, the most nightmarish of times. We played such musical instruments as fell into our hands discovered here and there in the house, or by way of strangers at our gate desperate to barter anything in their possession for food. Kit took up the violin doubtfully at first and then with growing joy, for, it seemed, he had musical talent! – practicing for hours on the beautiful though badly scarified old violin that had once belonged to Grandfather (so we surmised: One of Grandfather's portraits showed him as a child of eleven or twelve posed with the identical violin, then luminously gleaming, tucked under his chin); Jori took up the piccolo, which she shared with Vega; Hewett took up the drums, Dale the cymbals, Einar the oboe, Fifi the piano... and the rest of us sang, sang our hearts out, our collective voices sometimes frail as straws through which a rough careless wind blew but at other times, and always unpredictably, so harmonious, so strong, so commanding, our hearts beat hard in unquestioning love of one another and of any fate that might befall us. We sang after Mother's death and we sang when a feculent wind blew from the Valley day after day bearing the odor of decomposing flesh and we sang, though our noses and throats filled with smoke, when fires raged in the dry woodland areas to the west, and then too a relentless wind blew upon us barricaded in our stone house atop a high hill, winds from several directions they seemed, intent upon seeking us out, carrying sparks to our sanctuary, destroying us in a paroxysm of fire as others, human and beast, were being destroyed shrieking in pain and terror... and how else for us to endure such odors, such sights, such sounds than to take up our instruments and play them, and sing, and sing and sing and sing until our throats were raw, how else.

Yet it became a time of joy and even feasting, since the cow was dying in any case and might as well be quickly slaughtered, when Father brought his new wife home to meet us: New Mother some of us called her, or Young Mother, and Old Mother that fierce stooped wild-eyed old woman was forgotten, the strangeness of her death lingering only in whispers for had she like Cory died of household rats? Had she like Erastus grown pimples, then boils, then tumors over her entire body, swelling bulbs of flesh that drained away life? had she drowned in the cistern, had she died of thirst and malnutrition locked away in a distant room of the house, had she died of infection, of heartbreak, of her own rage, of Father's steely fingers closing about her neck... or had she not died at all but simply passed into oblivion, as the black waves splashed over her, and Young Mother stepped forward smiling to take her place...? Young Mother was stout and hearty-faced, plumply pretty about the eyes and cheeks, her color a rich earthen hue, her breasts capacious as large balloons filled to bursting with liquid, and she gave off a hot intoxicating smell of nutmeg, and small slippery flames darted when in a luxury of sighing, yawning, and stretching, she lifted with beringed hands the heavy mass of red-russet hair that hung between her shoulder blades, and fixed upon us her warm moist unblinking dark gaze. 'Mother!' we cried, even the eldest of us, 'Oh Mother!' begging would she hug us, would she fold us in those plump arms, press our faces against that bosom, each of us, all of us, weeping, in her arms, against her bosom, there. Cory's baby was not maturing as it was believed babies should, nor had it been named since we could not determine whether it was male or female, or both, or neither; and this household vexation Young Mother addressed herself to at once. No matter Lona's jealous love of the baby, Young Mother declared herself 'practical-minded': For why otherwise had Father brought her to this household but to reform it and give hope? She could not comprehend, she said, how and why an extra mouth, and in this case not only a useless but perhaps even a dangerous mouth, could be tolerated in a time of near famine, in violation of certain government edicts as she understood them. 'Drastic remedies in drastic times,' Young Mother said. Lona said, 'I will give it my food. I will protect it with my life.' And Young Mother simply repeated, smiling, her warm brown eyes easing like a caress over us all, 'Drastic remedies in drastic times.' There were those of us who loved Cory's baby and felt an unreasoned joy in its very existence, for it *was* flesh of our flesh, it *was* the future of the family; yet there were others, among them not only the males, who seemed fearful of it, keeping their distance when it was fed or bathed and averting their eyes when it crawled into a room to nudge its head or mouth against a foot, an ankle, a leg. Though it had not matured in the usual way, Cory's baby was considerably heavier than it had been at birth, and weighed now about forty pounds; but it was soft as a slug is soft, or an oyster; with an oyster's shape; seemingly boneless; the hue of bread dough, and hairless. As its small eyes lacked an iris, being entirely white, it was believed to be blind; its nose was but a rudimentary pair of nostrils, mere holes in the center of its face; its fishlike mouth was deceptive in that it seemed to possess its own intelligence, being ideally formed, not for human speech, but for seizing, sucking, and chewing. Though it had at best only a cartilaginous skeleton, it did boast two fully formed rows of tiny needle-sharp teeth, which it was not shy of using, particularly when ravenous for food; and it was often ravenous. At such times it groped its way around the house by instinct, sniffing and quivering, and if by chance it was drawn by the heat of your blood to your bed it would burrow against you beneath the covers, and nudge, and nuzzle, and begin like any nursing infant to suck, virtually any part of the body though preferring of course a female's breasts... and if not stopped in time it would bite, and chew, and *eat*... in all the brute innocence of appetite. So some of us surmised, though Lona angrily denied it, that Cory had not died of rat bites after all but of having been attacked and partly devoured by her own baby. (In this, Lona was duplicitous: taking care never to undress in Mother's presence for fear that Mother's sharp eye would take in the numerous wounds on her breasts, belly, and thighs.)

As the family had a custom of debating issues, in order that all divergent opinions might be honored, for instance should we pay the exorbitant price a cow or a she-goat now commanded, or should the boys be empowered to acquire one of these beasts however they could, for instance should we make an attempt to feed starving men, women, and children who gathered outside our fence, even if it was with food unfit for the family's own consumption – so naturally the issue of Cory's baby was taken up too, and threatened to split the family into two warring sides. For her part Mother argued persuasively that the baby was worthless, repulsive, and might one day be dangerous – not guessing that it had already proved dangerous, indeed; and for her part Lona argued persuasively that the baby, 'Lona's baby,' as she persisted in calling it, was a living human being, a member of the family, one of *us*. Mother said hotly, 'It is not one of *us*, girl, if by *us* you mean a family that includes *me*,' and Lona said with equal heat, 'It is one of *us* because it predates any family that includes *you*.'

So each of us argued in turn, and emotions ran high, and it was a curious phenomenon that many of us changed our minds repeatedly, now swayed by Mother's reasoning, and now by Lona's; now by Father, who spoke on behalf of Mother, or by Hewett, who spoke on behalf of Lona; or by Father, whose milky eyes gave him an air of patrician distinction and fair-mindedness, who spoke on behalf of Lona! The issue raged, and subsided, and raged again, and Mother dared not put her power to the vote for fear that Lona would prevail against her. Father acknowledged that however we felt about the baby it was our flesh and blood presumably, and embodied for us the great insoluble mystery of life… 'its soul bounded by its skull and its destiny no more problematic than the thin tubes that connect its mouth and its anus. Who are we to judge!'

Yet Mother had her way, as slyboots Mother was always to have her way… one morning soliciting the help of several of us, who were sworn to secrecy, and delighted to be her handmaidens, in a simple scheme: Lona being asleep in Cory's old bed, Mother led the baby out of the house by holding a piece of bread soaked in chicken blood just in front of its nostrils, led it crawling with surprising swiftness across the hard-packed earth, to one of the barns, and, inside, led it to a dark corner where she lifted it, grunting, and lowered it carefully into an old rain barrel empty except for a wriggling mass of half-grown baby rats that squealed in great excitement at being disturbed, or at the smell of the blood-soaked bread which Mother dropped on them. We then nailed a cover in place; and, as Mother said, her color warmly flushed and her breath coming fast, 'There – it is entirely out of our hands.'

And then one day it was spring. And Kit led a she-goat proudly into the kitchen, her bags primed with milk, swollen pink dugs leaking milk! How grateful we were, those of us who were with child, after the privations of so long a season, during which certain words had slipped from our memories, for instance *she-goat,* and *milk,* and as we realized, *rainbow,* for the rainbow too appeared, or reappeared, shimmering and translucent across the Valley. In the fire-ravaged plain was a sea of fresh green shoots and in the sky enormous dimpled clouds and that night we gathered around Fifi at the piano to play our instruments and sing. Father had passed away but Mother had remarried: a husky horseman whose white teeth flashed in his beard, and whose rowdy pinches meant love and good cheer, not hurt. We were so happy we debated turning the calendar ahead to the New Year. We were so happy we debated abolishing the calendar entirely and declaring it the year 1, and beginning Time anew.

HIS MOUTH WILL TASTE OF WORMWOOD

Poppy Z. Brite

Poppy Z. Brite (1967–) is an American author who initially achieved success during the 'new gothic' boom after publishing several critically acclaimed novels. However, Brite's work always contained more influence from Decadent-era French and English writers than the contemporary horror scene. 'His Mouth Will Taste of Wormwood' (1990) is a direct but original nod to those writers; Brite's strain of the weird is extravagantly and unrepentantly sensual. The writer is also influenced by the city of New Orleans, and has published a series of contemporary novels focused on the New Orleans restaurant world. Much of Brite's work features bisexual and gay characters, and her fiction from the 1990s must be considered ground-breaking for this reason also.

'To the treasures and the pleasures of the grave,' said my friend Louis, and raised his goblet of absinthe to me in drunken benediction.

'To the funeral lilies,' I replied, 'and to the calm pale bones.' I drank deeply from my own glass. The absinthe cauterized my throat with its flavor, part pepper, part licorice, part rot. It had been one of our greatest finds: more than fifty bottles of the now-outlawed liqueur, sealed up in a New Orleans family tomb. Transporting them was a nuisance, but once we had learned to enjoy the taste of wormwood, our continued drunkenness was ensured for a long, long time. We had taken the skull of the crypt's patriarch, too, and it now resided in a velvet-lined enclave in our museum.

Louis and I, you see, were dreamers of a dark and restless sort. We met in our second year of college and quickly found that we shared one vital trait: both of us were dissatisfied with everything. We drank straight whiskey and declared it too weak. We took strange drugs, but the visions they brought us were of emptiness, mindlessness, slow decay. The books we read were dull; the artists who sold their colorful drawings on the street were mere hacks in our eyes; the music we heard was never loud enough, never harsh enough to stir us. We were truly jaded, we told one another. For all the impression the world made upon us, our eyes might have been dead black holes in our heads.

For a time we thought our salvation lay in the sorcery wrought by music. We studied recordings of weird nameless dissonances, attended performances of obscure bands at ill-lit filthy clubs. But music did not save us. For a time we distracted ourselves with carnality. We explored the damp alien territory between the legs of any girl who would have us, sometimes separately, sometimes both of us in bed together with one girl or more. We bound their wrists and ankles with black lace, we lubricated and penetrated their every orifice, we shamed them with their own pleasures. I recall a mauve-haired beauty, Felicia, who was brought to wild sobbing orgasm by the rough tongue of a stray dog we trapped. We watched her from across the room, drug-dazed and unstirred.

When we had exhausted the possibilities of women we sought those of our own sex, craving the androgynous curve of a boy's cheekbone, the molten flood of ejaculation invading our mouths. Eventually we turned to one another, seeking the thresholds of pain and ecstasy no one else had been able to help us attain. Louis asked me to grow my nails long and file them into needle-sharp points. When I raked them down his back, tiny beads of blood welled up in the angry tracks they left. He loved to lie still, pretending to submit to me, as I licked the salty blood away. Afterward he would push me down and attack me with his mouth, his tongue seeming to sear a trail of liquid fire into my skin.

But sex did not save us either. We shut ourselves in our room and saw no one for days on end. At last we withdrew to the seclusion of Louis's ancestral home near Baton Rouge. Both his parents were dead – a suicide pact, Louis hinted, or perhaps a suicide and a murder. Louis, the only child, retained the family home and fortune. Built on the edge of a vast swamp, the plantation house loomed sepulchrally out of the gloom that surrounded it always, even in the middle of a summer afternoon. Oaks of primordial hugeness grew in a canopy over the house, their branches like black arms fraught with Spanish moss. The moss was everywhere, reminding me of brittle gray hair, stirring wraithlike in the dank breeze from the swamp. I had the impression that, left too long unchecked, the moss might begin to grow from the ornate window-frames and fluted columns of the house itself.

The place was deserted save for us. The air was heady with the luminous scent of magnolias and the fetor of swamp gas. At night we sat on the veranda and sipped bottles of wine from the family cellar, gazing through an increasingly alcoholic mist at the will-o'-the-wisps that beckoned far off in the swamp. Obsessively we talked of new thrills and how we might get them. Louis's wit sparkled liveliest when he was bored, and on the night he first mentioned grave robbing, I laughed. I could not imagine that he was serious.

'What would we do with a bunch of dried-up old remains? Grind them to make a voodoo potion? I preferred your idea of increasing our tolerance to various poisons.'

Louis's sharp face snapped toward me. His eyes were painfully sensitive to light, so that even in this gloaming he wore tinted glasses and it was impossible to see his expression. He kept his fair hair clipped very short, so that it stood up in crazy tufts when he raked a nervous hand through it. 'No, Howard. Think of it: our own collection of death. A catalogue of pain, of human frailty – all for us. Set against a backdrop of tranquil loveliness. Think what it would be to walk through such a place, meditating, reflecting upon your own ephemeral essence. Think of making love in a charnel-house! We have only to assemble the parts – they will create a whole into which we may fall.'

(Louis enjoyed speaking in cryptic puns; anagrams and palindromes, too, and any sort of puzzle appealed to him. I wonder whether that was not the root of his determination to look into the fathomless eye of death and master it. Perhaps he saw the mortality of the flesh as a gigantic jigsaw or crossword which, if he fitted all the parts into place, he might solve and thus defeat. Louis would have loved to live forever, though he would never have known what to do with all his time.)

He soon produced his hashish pipe to sweeten the taste of the wine, and we spoke no more of grave robbing that night. But the thought preyed upon me in the languorous weeks to come. The smell of a freshly opened grave, I thought, must in its way be as intoxicating as the perfume of the swamp or a girl's most intimate sweat. Could we truly assemble a collection of the grave's treasures that would be lovely to look upon, that would soothe our fevered souls?

The caresses of Louis's tongue grew languid. Sometimes, instead of nestling with me between the black satin sheets of our bed, he would sleep on a torn blanket in one of the underground rooms. These had originally been built for indeterminate but always intriguing purposes – abolitionist meetings had taken place there, Louis told me, and a weekend of free love, and an earnest but wildly incompetent Black Mass replete with a vestal virgin and phallic candles.

These rooms were where our museum would be set up. At last I came to agree with Louis that only the plundering of graves might cure us of the most stifling ennui we had yet suffered. I could not bear to watch his tormented sleep, the pallor of his hollow cheeks, the delicate bruise-like darkening of the skin beneath his flickering eyes. Besides, the notion of grave robbing had begun to entice me. In ultimate corruption, might we not find the path to ultimate salvation?

Our first grisly prize was the head of Louis's mother, rotten as a pumpkin forgotten on the vine, half-shattered by two bullets from an antique Civil War revolver. We took it from the family crypt by the light of a full moon. The will-o'-the-wisps glowed weakly, like dying beacons on some unattainable shore, as we crept back to the manse. I dragged pick and shovel behind me; Louis carried the putrescent trophy tucked beneath his arm. After we had descended into the museum, I lit three candles scented with the russet spices of autumn (the season when Louis's parents had died) while Louis placed the head in the alcove we had prepared for it. I thought I detected a certain tenderness in his manner. 'May she give us the family blessing,' he murmured, absently wiping on the lapel of his jacket a few shreds of pulpy flesh that had adhered to his fingers.

We spent a happy time refurbishing the museum, polishing the inlaid precious metals of the wall fixtures, brushing away the dust that frosted the velvet designs of the wallpaper, alternately burning incense and charring bits of cloth we had saturated with our blood, in order to give the rooms the odor we desired – a charnel perfume strong enough to drive us to frenzy. We travelled far in our collections, but always we returned home with crates full of things no man had ever been meant to possess. We heard of a girl with violet eyes who had died in some distant town; not seven days later we had those eyes in an ornate cut-glass jar, pickled in formaldehyde. We scraped bone dust and nitre from the bottoms of ancient coffins; we stole the barely withered heads and hands of children fresh in their graves, with their soft little fingers and their lips like flower petals. We had baubles and precious heirlooms, vermiculated prayerbooks and shrouds encrusted with mold. I had not taken seriously Louis's talk of making love in a charnel-house – but neither had I reckoned on the pleasure he could inflict with a femur dipped in rose-scented oil.

Upon the night I speak of – the night we drank our toast to the grave and its riches – we had just acquired our finest prize yet. Later in the evening we planned a celebratory debauch at a nightclub in the city. We had returned from our most recent travels not with the usual assortment of sacks and crates, but with only one small box carefully wrapped and tucked into Louis's breast pocket.

The box contained an object whose existence we had only speculated upon previously. From certain half-articulate mutterings of an old blind man plied with cheap liquor in a French Quarter bar, we traced rumors of a certain fetish or charm to a Negro graveyard in the southern bayou country. The fetish was said to be a thing of eerie beauty, capable of luring any lover to one's bed, hexing any enemy to a sick and painful death, and (this, I think, was what intrigued Louis the most) turning back tenfold on anyone who used it with less than the touch of a master.

A heavy mist hung low over the graveyard when we arrived there, lapping at our ankles, pooling around the markers of wood and stone, abruptly melting away in patches to reveal a gnarled root or a patch of blackened grass, then closing back in. By the light of a waning moon we made our way along a path overgrown with rioting weeds. The graves were decorated with elaborate mosaics of broken glass, coins, bottlecaps, oyster shells lacquered silver and gold. Some mounds were outlined by empty bottles shoved neck-downward into the earth. I saw a lone plaster saint whose features had been worn away by years of wind and rain. I kicked half-buried rusty cans that had once held flowers; now they held only bare brittle stems and pestilent rainwater, or nothing at all. Only the scent of wild spider lilies pervaded the night.

The earth in one corner of the graveyard seemed blacker than the rest. The grave we sought was marked only by a crude cross of charred and twisted wood. We were skilled at the art of violating the dead; soon we had the coffin uncovered. The boards were warped by years of burial in wet, foul earth. Louis pried up the lid with his spade and, by the moon's meager and watery light, we gazed upon what lay within.

Of the inhabitant we knew almost nothing. Some said a hideously disfigured old conjure woman lay buried here. Some said she was a young girl with a face as lovely and cold as moonlight on water, and a soul crueler than Fate itself. Some claimed the body was not a woman's at all, but that of a white voodoo priest who had ruled the bayou. He had features of a cool, unearthly beauty, they said, and a stock of fetishes and potions which he would hand out with the kindest blessing… or the direst curse. This was the story Louis and I liked best; the sorcerer's capriciousness appealed to us, and the fact that he was beautiful.

No trace of beauty remained to the thing in the coffin – at least not the sort of beauty that a healthy eye might cherish. Louis and I loved the translucent parchment skin stretched tight over long bones that seemed to have been carved from ivory. The delicate brittle hands folded across the sunken chest, the soft black caverns of the eyes, the colorless strands of hair that still clung to the fine white dome of the skull – to us these things were the poetry of death.

Louis played his flashlight over the withered cords of the neck. There, on a silver chain gone black with age, was the object we had come seeking. No crude wax doll or bit of dried root was this. Louis and I gazed at each other, moved by the beauty of the thing; then, as if in a dream, he reached to grasp it. This was our rightful night's prize, our plunder from a sorcerer's grave.

'How does it look?' Louis asked as we were dressing.

I never had to think about my clothes. On an evening such as this, when we were dressing to go out, I would choose the same garments I might wear for a night's digging in the graveyard – black, unornamented black, with only the whiteness of my face and hands showing against the backdrop of night. On a particularly festive occasion, such as this, I might smudge a bit of kohl round my eyes. The absence of color made me nearly invisible: if I walked with my shoulders hunched and my chin tucked down, no one except Louis would see me.

'Don't slouch so, Howard,' said Louis irritably as I ducked past the mirror. 'Turn around and look at me. Aren't I fine in my sorcerer's jewelry?'

Even when Louis wore black, he did it to be noticed. Tonight he was resplendent in narrow-legged trousers of purple paisley silk and a silvery jacket that seemed to turn all light iridescent. He had taken our prize out of its box and fastened it around his throat. As I came closer to look at it, I caught Louis's scent: rich and rather meaty, like blood kept too long in a stoppered bottle.

Against the sculpted hollow of Louis's throat, the thing on its chain seemed more strangely beautiful than ever. Have I neglected to describe the magical object, the voodoo fetish from the churned earth of the grave? I will never forget it. A polished sliver of bone (or a tooth, but what fang could have been so long, so sleekly honed, and still have somehow retained the look of a *human tooth?*) bound by a strip of copper. Set into the metal, a single ruby sparkled like a drop of gore against the verdigris. Etched in exquisite miniature upon the sliver of bone, and darkened by the rubbing in of some black-red substance, was an elaborate veve – one of the symbols used by voodooists to invoke their pantheon of terrible gods. Whoever was buried in that lonely bayou grave, he had been no mere dabbler in swamp magic. Every cross and swirl of the veve was reproduced to perfection. I thought the thing still retained a trace of the grave's scent – a dark odor like potatoes long spoiled. Each grave has its own peculiar scent, just as each living body does.

'Are you certain you should wear it?' I asked.

'It will go into the museum tomorrow,' he said, 'with a scarlet candle burning eternally before it. Tonight its powers are mine.'

The nightclub was in a part of the city that looked as if it had been gutted from the inside out by a righteous tongue of fire. The street was lit only by occasional scribbles of neon high overhead, advertisements for cheap hotels and all-night bars. Dark eyes stared at us from the crevices and pathways between buildings, disappearing only when Louis's hand crept toward the inner pocket of his jacket. He carried a small stiletto there, and knew how to use it for more than pleasure.

We slipped through a door at the end of an alley and descended the narrow staircase into the club. The lurid glow of a blue bulb flooded the stairs, making Louis's face look sunken and dead behind his tinted glasses. Feedback blasted us as we came in, and above it, a screaming battle of guitars. The inside of the club was a patchwork of flickering light and darkness. Graffiti covered the walls and the ceiling like a tangle of barbed wire come alive. I saw bands' insignia and jeering death's-heads, crucifixes bejewelled with broken glass and black obscenities writhing in the stroboscopic light.

Louis brought me a drink from the bar. I sipped it slowly, still drunk on absinthe. Since the music was too loud for conversation, I studied the club-goers around us. A quiet bunch, they were, staring fixedly at the stage as if they had been drugged (and no doubt many of them had – I remembered visiting a club one night on a dose of hallucinogenic mushrooms, watching in fascination as the guitar strings seemed to drip soft viscera onto the stage). Younger than Louis and myself, most of them were, and queerly beautiful in their thrift shop rags, their leather and fishnet and cheap costume jewelry, their pale faces and painted hair. Perhaps we would take one of them home with us tonight. We had done so before. 'The delicious guttersnipes,' Louis called them. A particularly beautiful face, starkly boned and androgynous, flickered at the edge of my vision. When I looked, it was gone.

I went into the restroom. A pair of boys stood at a single urinal, talking animatedly. I stood at the sink rinsing my hands, watching the boys in the mirror and trying to overhear their conversation. A hairline fracture in the glass seemed to pull the taller boy's eyes askew. 'Casper and Alyssa found her tonight,' he said. 'In some old warehouse by the river. I heard her skin was *gray*, man. And sort of withered, like something had sucked out most of the meat.'

'Far out,' said the other boy. His black-rimmed lips barely moved.

'She was only fifteen, you know?' said the tall boy as he zipped his ragged trousers.

'She was a cunt anyway.'

They turned away from the urinal and started talking about the band – Ritual Sacrifice, I gathered, whose name was scrawled on the walls of the club. As they went out, the boys glanced at the mirror and the tall one's eyes met mine for an instant. Nose like a haughty Indian chief's, eyelids smudged with black and silver. Louis would approve, I thought – but the night was young, and there were many drinks left to be had.

When the band took a break we visited the bar again. Louis edged in beside a thin dark-haired boy who was barechested except for a piece of torn lace tied about his throat. When he turned, I knew his was the androgynous and striking face I had glimpsed before. His beauty was almost feral, but overlaid with a cool elegance like a veneer of sanity hiding madness. His ivory skin stretched over cheekbones like razors; his eyes were hectic pools of darkness.

'I like your amulet,' he said to Louis. 'It's very unusual.'

'I have another one like it at home,' Louis told him.

'Really? I'd like to see them both together.' The boy paused to let Louis order our vodka gimlets, then said, 'I thought there was only one.'

Louis's back straightened like a string of beads being pulled taut. Behind his glasses, I knew, his pupils would have shrunk to pinpoints: the light pained him more when he was nervous. But no tremor in his voice betrayed him when he said, 'What do you know about it?'

The boy shrugged. On his bony shoulders, the movement was insouciant and drop-dead graceful. 'It's voodoo,' he said. 'I know what voodoo is. Do you?'

The implication stung, but Louis only bared his teeth the slightest bit; it might have been a smile. 'I am *conversant* in all types of magic,' he said, 'at least.'

The boy moved closer to Louis, so that their hips were almost touching, and lifted the amulet between thumb and forefinger. I thought I saw one long nail brush Louis's throat, but I could not be sure. 'I could tell you the meaning of this veve,' he said, 'if you were certain you wished to know.'

'It symbolizes power,' Louis said. 'All the power of my soul.' His voice was cold, but I saw his tongue dart out to moisten his lips. He was beginning to dislike this boy, and also to desire him.

'No,' said the boy so softly that I barely caught his words. He sounded almost sad. 'This cross in the center is inverted, you see, and the line encircling it represents a serpent. A thing like this can trap your soul. Instead of being rewarded with eternal life … you might be doomed to it.'

'Doomed to eternal life?' Louis permitted himself a small cold smile. 'Whatever do you mean?'

'The band is starting again. Find me after the show and I'll tell you. We can have a drink … and you can tell me all you know about voodoo.' The boy threw back his head and laughed. Only then did I notice that one of his upper canine teeth was missing.

The next part of the evening remains a blur of moonlight and neon, ice cubes and blue swirling smoke and sweet drunkenness. The boy drank glass after glass of absinthe with us, seeming to relish the bitter taste. None of our other guests had liked the liqueur. 'Where did you get it?' he asked. Louis was silent for a long moment before he said, 'It was sent over from France.' Except for its single black gap, the boy's smile would have been as perfect as the sharp-edged crescent moon.

'Another drink?' said Louis, refilling both our glasses.

When I next came to clarity, I was in the boy's arms. I could not make out the words he was whispering; they might have been an incantation, if magic may be sung to pleasure's music. A pair of hands cupped my face, guiding my lips over the boy's pale parchment skin. They might have been Louis's hands. I knew nothing except this boy, the fragile movement of the bones beneath the skin, the taste of his spit bitter with wormwood.

I do not remember when he finally turned away from me and began lavishing his love upon Louis. I wish I could have watched, could have seen the lust bleeding into Louis's eyes, the pleasure wracking his body. For, as it turned out, the boy loved Louis so much more thoroughly than ever he loved me.

When I awoke, the bass thump of my pulse echoing through my skull blotted out all other sensations. Gradually, though, I became aware of tangled silk sheets, of hot sunlight on my face. Not until I came fully awake did I see the thing I had cradled like a lover all through the night.

For an instant two realities shifted in uneasy juxtaposition and almost merged. I was in Louis's bed; I recognized the feel of the sheets, their odor of silk and sweat. But this thing I held – this was surely one of the fragile mummies we had dragged out of their graves, the things we dissected for our museum. It took me only a moment, though, to recognize the familiar ruined features – the sharp chin, the high elegant brow. Something had desiccated Louis, had drained him of every drop of his moisture, his vitality. His skin crackled and flaked away beneath my fingers. His hair stuck to my lips, dry and colorless. The amulet, which had still been around his throat in bed last night, was gone.

The boy had left no trace – or so I thought until I saw a nearly transparent thing at the foot of the bed. It was like a quantity of spiderweb, or a damp and insubstantial veil. I picked it up and shook it out, but could not see its features until I held it up to the window. The thing was vaguely human-shaped, with empty limbs trailing off into nearly invisible tatters. As the thing wafted and billowed, I saw part of a face in it – the sharp curve left by a cheekbone, the hole where an eye had been – as if a face were imprinted upon gauze.

I carried Louis's brittle shell of a corpse down into the museum. Laying him before his mother's niche, I left a stick of incense burning in his folded hands and a pillow of black silk cradling the papery dry bulb of his skull. He would have wished it thus.

The boy has not come to me again, though I leave the window open every night. I have been back to the club, where I stand sipping vodka and watching the crowd. I have seen many beauties, many strange wasted faces, but not the one I seek. I think I know where I will find him. Perhaps he still desires me – I must know.

I will go again to the lonely graveyard in the bayou. Once more – alone, this time – I will find the unmarked grave and plant my spade in its black earth. When I open the coffin – I know it, I am sure of it! – I will find not the mouldering thing we beheld before, but the calm beauty of replenished youth. The youth he drank from Louis. His face will be a scrimshaw mask of tranquility. The amulet – I know it; I am sure of it – will be around his neck.

Dying: the final shock of pain or nothingness that is the price we pay for everything. Could it not be the sweetest thrill, the only salvation we can attain … the only true moment of self-knowledge? The dark pools of his eyes will open, still and deep enough to drown in. He will hold out his arms to me, inviting me to lie down with him in his rich wormy bed.

With the first kiss his mouth will taste of wormwood. After that it will taste only of me – of my blood, my life, siphoning out of my body and into his. I will feel the sensations Louis felt: the shrivelling of my tissues, the drying-up of all my vital juices. I care not. The treasures and the pleasures of the grave? They are his hands, his lips, his tongue.

THE END OF THE GARDEN

Michal Ajvaz

TRANSLATED INTO ENGLISH BY JAMES NAUGHTON

Michal Ajvaz (1949–) is a Czech novelist, poet and translator. Born into an exiled Russian family, Ajvaz studied Czech studies and aesthetics at Charles University in Prague. He did not begin publishing fiction until 1989, probably due to the political repression in the Czech Republic (then Czechoslovakia) during the 1970s and 1980s. His novel *Prázdné ulice* (2004) was awarded the prestigious Jaroslav Seifert Prize for literary achievement (2005). English-language translations include the critically acclaimed *The Other City* (2009) and *The Golden Age* (2010). Ajvaz comes by the 'weirdness' in his fiction through dark humor and absurdity, as in 'The End of the Garden' (1991).

As I am passing, I hear a pathetic call for help from a ground-floor window. I clamber up to the sill and jump into the room; I find myself in a room with heavy dark furniture, with tassel-edged covers, with mountains of variegated little cushions, with a darkened painting of the Bay of Naples on the wall. Behind the great double bed something or other is wrestling on the ground, you can year puffing, groaning and blows. I rush over to the fight and see: a young woman in a black evening dress with narrow shoulder-straps and a plunging back is struggling with a lizard! It is evidently a huge monitor lizard (*Varanus komodoensis*), which lives on the island of Komodo in Indonesia and reaches a length of as much as three metres. Zoologists reckon that these lizards were able to reach such a length on Komodo due to the fact that on this island they had no natural enemies. I jump on the lizard like Saint George, I grab it by the floppy wrinkled skin under the neck and heave it about. While I am shaking it, the lamenting call for help continues to be heard. Suddenly I realise, it is not the woman calling for help, but the lizard! I let the beast go, sit down on the threadbare carpet and awkwardly observe the struggle. It really looks as if the woman is the assailant and the lizard the assaulted. If he didn't have any enemies on Komodo, I said to myself, here it is evidently otherwise. The lizard would clearly have done better to remain in Indonesia. He would have saved not only himself from a nasty situation but also me: for I was unable to decide how to behave; on the one hand the lizard was obviously the victim of an attack, on the other it seemed morally unacceptable for me to side with a lizard in this fight between a lizard and a human being. Hegel reproaches Kant for the merely formal and abstractly universal quality of his categorical imperative, which makes it unable to guide us sufficiently in concrete situations. 'Act in such a way that the principle of your behaviour may become a universal maxim': should this universal maxim rather be 'help those under attack' or 'help women who are struggling with monitor lizards'? Kant says: 'In your conduct let a human being be always the aim, not the means.' What of the lizard, can he be a means? On this subject the Critique of Practical Reason has absolutely nothing to say; as far as I know, in the whole of this extensive work there is not a single mention of monitor lizards.

Kant is of course partly excused by the fact that, as is generally known, he never left Konigsberg (though he speculated whether after our death we would inhabit other heavenly spheres), so that he quite certainly never encountered a Komodo lizard; on the other hand, however, he might surely have devoted at least a couple of lines to a creature as remarkable as the three-metre-long monitor lizard. Maybe this lizard is now pursuing him across the endless empty plains of some other star.

(Here, I think, lies the misfortune of philosophy: always we encounter on our travels some exceptional freak to which the philosophical rules are found to be non-applicable. Which are right – the freaks or the philosophical principles? I once had a lecture on this problem in a lift, inlaid with amber. On the one hand we are somewhat loath to dispose of the whole thing merely by saying 'so much worse for the freaks,' on the other we are also reluctant to accept that the whole of our fine system of thought be dependent on some ugly old freak. At the same time we fail to grasp the relativity of the concept of 'freakishness' – if there were no human beings with their evaluating criteria, there would be no 'freakishness' either – also we ignore the vicious circle of reasoning to which we fall victim: freakish for us is that which falls outside our own sense of order, but simultaneously we proclaim that this breaching of our own sense of order proves nothing against its truth value, since after all we are simply dealing with a freak.)

So I followed this struggle, full of feelings of confusion and ambivalence, until finally I tapped the woman strangling the fretful lizard on the shoulder and said in an uncertain voice: 'Please leave the lizard alone,' and when that did nothing, I added: 'He's a rare creature from Indonesia, everywhere else these lizards are only tiny.' Eventually the woman let the lizard go, he shambled off, head drooping into the farthest corner of the room, where he huddled up against a glass-fronted cabinet with shelves displaying china dogs and sea shells and began to sob loudly. The woman slowly got up from the floor, straightened her dress and looked at me severely. She had wavy black hair and an extraordinarily lovely, sharply sculptured face with an aquiline nose, her eyes were so vivaciously painted in various hues of turquoise, purple and green that it looked as if an exotic butterfly with outspread wings were perched on the top of her nose.

She went up to a glass-fronted bookcase holding neatly arranged rows of adventure novels by Alexandre Dumas pere and Paul Feval, printed sometime at the turn of last century. She turned the key in the lock, and the doors opened with a gentle creak. She reached confidently inside, pulled out a thick old book with gilt edging, covered in dust, and handed it to me. With astonishment I read my own name on the cover, set in a rounded *fin-de-siecle* typeface interlaced with tendrils of plant decoration which swirled across the entire binding in inextricably tangled swathes; below was the book's title: *At the End of the Garden*. I have never written a book in my life, although I have always wanted to be a writer, because I would enjoy working on a book in the mornings – I used to imagine it would be something between *Phenomenology of Mind, The Three Musketeers* and *Les Chants de Maldoror* (nothing funny in that!) – and in the afternoons I'd sit in a café, sip sweet coffee and watch the faces of the passers-by in the street through the glass like fish in an aquarium. Now I gazed in surprise at the book whose binding held my name. Do demons execute for us works we have dreamt of and never created? Do our hidden literary projects ripen in the dark depths of other people's libraries? Are the books we regard as our own creations only copies of texts engraved on glass sheets and deposited in a library situated in a labyrinth of malachite passageways beneath the city? In any case it seems that someone carries out unfulfilled tasks for us. I recalled how a musician friend once whispered to me in a pub about hearing beneath the surface of an evening pond in a desolate landscape the symphony he had resolved to write when he was studying at the conservatory, but of which he had only composed a few bars.

I opened the book, the work of a demon, and began to leaf through it. But wherever I opened the pages, though I saw the printed text, the letters immediately began to turn pale and vanish like ancient frescoes from the catacombs, exposed to fresh air, I only managed to glimpse a couple of words on each page; together they made up a mysterious sentence, oddly beautiful in its absurdity. It spoke of great railway-station halls, river embankments of marble, and the glass-fronted veranda of a mountain lodge. Beneath the melted text there remained only yellowed, melancholy fragrant paper, a few brown marks, only occasionally an isolated letter was left on the page or the fragment of a word.

But the pictures did not vanish. When the whole text had evaporated, I started to inspect them at last. I liked them, because they reminded me of the naïve wash illustrations from the books of Karl May which I read in my childhood when I was ill, lying by myself at home in an empty flat. All the pictures showed a monitor lizard in some situation or other, displaying him as a perfect scoundrel without a single jot of honour in all his long body. Here with lascivious paws he assails an innocent girl as she prepared in her translucent night-dress to lie down in her virginal bed, here we see him on top of the pyramid of Cheops, disguised as a bedouin, knocking over with his rifle butt a gentleman in a light-coloured colonial suit, who loses his balance and hurtles into the terrible abyss, his tropical helmet has fallen off his head – in the picture it hangs in the air a foot or two above the top of the pyramid. Another illustration is especially fine: we see a gloomy dark underground cavern, flooded with water, gushing in a great current out of the mouth of some pipe projecting from the wall. To the pillar supporting the vault an elegant mustachioed young man and a nice young girl are tied with a strong rope (the girl is maybe the same as the one in the picture of the bedroom); the water has reached up to their waists. The monitor lizard is standing over them at the top of the stairs, opening the door, through which rays of daylight penetrate, and turning his head towards the unfortunates. The text beneath this picture lasted a bit longer, so I managed to read all of it. It said: 'I am sorry, my dear Count, that we shall not have occasion to finish our interesting debate on Kant's moral. philosophy, begun during those unforgettable days in the gardens of El Amarna,' said the lizard with a devilish leer on his horrid face – p.427.

When I had finished looking through the illustrations, I glanced in surprise at the monitor lizard, huddled in the corner. He had covered his face with his paws, as though he were terribly ashamed, and tried to secrete himself right into the hollow between the display cabinet and the wall. He now surely regretted that his ancestors had attained such a length in Komodo. The woman took the book from my hand and placed it on a low round table, covered with a crocheted cloth. She looked at me frowningly and shook her head rebukingly. Although she was younger than I, she now looked like a school teacher. I began to feel ashamed too, I felt like crawling behind the cabinet after the lizard. Will this school teacher not complain to my parents that I make friends with lizards, that I am incapable of carrying out the categorical imperative in spite of going on about Kant all the time in Prague's Mala Strana restaurants, that I haven't written the book I was set to do as homework, that instead of working on this I spent my time aimlessly walking along past garden walls and fences, that my brain has produced nothing but incompletely crystallised thoughts, still half just the scents of places and inconsequential rhythms?

Now the monitor lizard got up and, still squinting timidly at the woman in the black dress, he opened a case lying on the cabinet. He took out of it a viola d'amore and tucked it under his lower jaw, after first pushing aside the obstructing flap of skin. He caught the bow in his other claw and started playing a waltz. Into the quavering sounds of the strings he mingled his unabated wailing lament, sometimes reminiscent of the whining of a dog. I went up to the woman, bowed slowly and grandly to her and took her round the waist. We started to dance, clumsily we circled the leather armchairs and lamps on long metal standards. The room echoed to the melancholy notes of the viola and the lizard's whimpering and whining.

But in his playing the lizard evidently forgot his pain, the music engrossed him more and more, the whining gradually ceased and the notes of the viola became louder, more emphatic and joyous, the melody became ever more boisterous and aggressive. He rose from his corner and, with the viola under his chin, he approached us, playing like the first fiddler at a gypsy ball after midnight, he whooped and thumped the beat with his tail on the floor. His boisterous smile gradually changed into a devilish leer. A change also came over the woman. Her face was no longer that of a school teacher, rather the face of a terrified little girl, she gazed in horror at the grinning monster and pressed herself timidly against me. I stroked her hair soothingly. Don't be afraid, I'm here with you, I won't let the lizard eat you up. She whispered to me: 'I love you very much, if we manage to escape the claws of this terrible beast, we'll go off together somewhere where no such horrid lizards live, there must be such a place, not long ago three-metre-long lizards were only to be found on Komodo, and now they're everywhere; when I ride in the metro, they're sitting opposite me, dozing, I have to spend the whole journey looking at their thick faces, at work they've made a lizard my new boss, he keeps coming up and pawing my shoulders when I'm typing, he makes lewd suggestions…' The lizard stood close beside us, his jaw hanging open, with ghastly teeth flashing, he played a wild Hungarian tune, he stamped his foot till the walls shook and cracks appeared in them, like branching roots, and he whooped loudly. But the tension fell away from me too, I wasn't afraid of the lizard's teeth, I no longer felt the need to give an account of myself, to apologise for not fulfilling my task, I knew now that no such task existed, there was only the quietly flowing river of being with its currents and scents, the unknown and the unenvisaged that ripens within the flow.

The lizard broke off the tune in mid-bar, shoved me, till I flew into the corner, and chucked the viola d'amore after me – that clearly meant it was my turn to play. Then he clutched the woman in his embrace and started dancing a strange lizard's tango with her. I was furious, but the fall had taken my breath away, so I wasn't able to get up at once and jump on the lizard. The woman was half-dead with fear, the lizard dragged her round the room like a rag puppet, croaking a wordless song and leaning over her hapless body in eccentric figures. During one of these they fell on the carpet and with lascivious huffing the lizard started to assault the woman, sticking his maw into her neckline. I recovered myself, with a leap and a bound I went over and with the viola I hit the lizard on the head with all my strength.

When the musical instrument shattered on the lizard's skull, a terrific bang was heard and the walls surrounding us collapsed. When the dust settled, I saw we were on wide plain, covered with yellow grass and low desiccated bushes. On one side of the distant horizon the plain descended to a harbour town, whose houses from a distance looked like little stones scattered round the curving bay. The only building on the empty plain was the National Museum. It stood some way off, the same size as in Prague, but all made of glass, through the glass walls you could see, flapping its mighty wings as it flew down the empty corridors, an Andean condor. The lizard staggered to its feet, clasping his head with both paws. He started to feel scared again and hid behind me, so that the woman wouldn't see him. My courage also left me. The woman got up, shaking with fury, and angrily hissing: 'You haven't heard the last of this!' I decided to back off, pushing the lizard in the rear, as he clung to my shirt and wept. But the woman let us alone, she went off towards the glass building; we could hear her muttering to herself: 'You'll pay for this, you blithering idiots' and 'It won't do you a bit of good, being a protected species, and the other little sod's also got it coming to him.' Up the glass ramp, past the glass statues she went, reached the main doorway and entered. She could be seen going up the glass staircase, walking slowly along the corridors, the condor slowly wheeling round her, occasionally brushing a wing against her hair. Should I go after her? I was attracted by the cold glass and the condor's sharp beak. Meanwhile the monitor lizard bit its teeth into some rope tied to the end of the bed. He turned his head and gave me a doggy look. I smiled sadly and lay down on the pale quilt. The lizard slowly walked off with the rope in his mouth the rope went taut and the bed started to move, it began bumping off along the plain. I lay on my back staring at the bright sky, sometimes I heard the cracking of a dry bush. After a while the lizard began to croon a little song, I didn't understand it too well, I only caught the words:

At the end of the garden
in thorn thicket's land
treasures are harboured
of Arabian sand.

You behold jewels' spark
from silvery shrines
when up with the lark
you creep there betimes.

Towards evening we found ourselves on the edge of the harbour town. The lizard kept pulling with all his strength. First I rode through an estate of luxury villas whose walls shone white through the darkening foliage of their gardens. Then the bed rolled along the asphalt of broad and practically empty streets, where the red rays of the setting sun, penetrating through gaps between the houses, lit up large letters on facades of bare brick and struck sharp blinding flashes which bounced off the chrome of cars which passed us from time to time. Finally we plunged into the winding lanes of the old harbour quarter, which were sometimes so narrow that the bed grated on the walls; then the lizard always turned round, patiently pushed the bed back and took another route. I was moving along in close proximity to men and women sitting at tables in front of little pubs; they shook hands with me, without having to get up from their seats, and shouted something at me in an unknown tongue. A little black bird jumped up on the bed, rode for a while and then flew off. People stood up, patted the lizard on the shoulder like a horse, someone brought a jug and tried to make the lizard drink some wine, by sticking his head into the jug. The lizard fended them all off benevolently with his paw and went on calmly pulling his load. Soon the harbour appeared at the end of one of the lanes. The red sun on the horizon was already touching the surface of the sea; the harbour was empty, only a few children were chasing a ball across the wide asphalt expanse, their shadows flitted across the distant facades of lengthy administrative buildings, reddened in the light of the setting sun. At the other end of the harbour cranes were unloading goods from a large white ship.

The lizard halted only on reaching the pier. A chill blew in from the sea. Yachts bobbed on the waves and scraped gently, the water splashed and there was a smell of rotting. The lizard curled up on the ground in a ball and slept. I felt sleepy too, what luck, not having to rush about an unfamiliar town looking for a room for the night in unwelcoming hotels. I buried myself in the quilt. When I shut my eyes I could hear the quiet voices of abandoned boats, the splashing of waves, the distant call of children.

(Sea, harbour piers, large letters on facades, worn-through plush of hotel armchair backs, lights in drinks, marbles, smells of corridors, an unfamiliar animal walking in the gestures of hands, from unrepeatable and unnecessary encounters which we forget, yet whose poison ripens in the blood, there may perhaps be born a future home, unlooked-for asylum.)

In the morning the lizard climbed on to the bed. I grasped the rope in my hands and started slowly pulling the bed in the direction of Prague. I think some other animals jumped on to the bed on the way, because it got heavier and heavier, apart from that behind my back the hooting and yelling of several voices resounded and sounds of wild struggles. But I didn't look back, I pulled the bed along empty highways, the mist rolling over them.

THE DARK

Karen Joy Fowler

Karen Joy Fowler (1950–) is an American writer who has written science fiction, fantasy novels and stories that tend to work by way of ambiguity, misdirection, and deep characterization. Although she is best-known for her *New York Times* bestseller *The Jane Austen Book Club* (2004), also made into a movie, novels such as *Sarah Canary* (1991), *The Sweetheart Season* (1996), and *Sister Noon* (2001) cemented her reputation as a writer of the first rank. Story collections include *Artificial Things* (1986), *Black Glass* (1997), and *What I Didn't See* (2010). Although Fowler rarely writes stories that could be called horror or weird, 'The Dark' is a powerful and topical exception.

In the summer of 1954, Anna and Richard Becker disappeared from Yosemite National Park along with Paul Becker, their three-year-old son. Their campsite was intact; two paper plates with half-eaten frankfurters remained on the picnic table, and a third frankfurter was in the trash. The rangers took several black-and-white photographs of the meal, which, when blown up to eight by ten, as part of the investigation, showed clearly the words *love bites*, carved into the wooden picnic table many years ago. There appeared to be some fresh scratches as well; the expert witness at the trial attributed them, with no great assurance, to raccoon.

The Beckers' car was still backed into the campsite, a green De Soto with a spare key under the right bumper and half a tank of gas. Inside the tent, two sleeping bags had been zipped together marital style and laid on a large tarp. A smaller flannel bag was spread over an inflated pool raft. Toiletries included three toothbrushes; Ipana toothpaste, squeezed in the middle; Ivory soap; three washcloths; and one towel. The newspapers discreetly made no mention of Anna's diaphragm, which remained powdered with talc, inside its pink shell, or of the fact that Paul apparently still took a bottle to bed with him.

Their nearest neighbor had seen nothing. He had been in his hammock, he said, listening to the game. Of course, the reception in Yosemite was lousy. At home he had a shortwave set; he said he had once pulled in Dover, clear as a bell. 'You had to really concentrate to hear the game,' he told the rangers. 'You could've dropped the bomb. I wouldn't have noticed.'

Anna Becker's mother, Edna, received a postcard postmarked a day earlier. 'Seen the firefall,' it said simply. 'Home Wednesday. Love.' Edna identified the bottle. 'Oh yes, that's Paul's bokkie,' she told the police. She dissolved into tears. 'He never goes anywhere without it,' she said.

In the spring of 1960, Mark Cooper and Manuel Rodriguez went on a fishing expedition in Yosemite. They set up a base camp in Tuolumne Meadows and went off to pursue steelhead. They were gone from camp approximately six hours, leaving their food and a six-pack of beer zipped inside their backpacks zipped inside their tent. When they returned, both beer and food were gone. Canine footprints circled the tent, but a small and mysterious handprint remained on the tent flap. 'Raccoon,' said the rangers who hadn't seen it. The tent and packs were undamaged. Whatever had taken the food had worked the zippers. 'Has to be raccoon.'

The last time Manuel had gone backpacking, he'd suspended his pack from a tree to protect it. A deer had stopped to investigate, and when Manuel shouted to warn it off the deer hooked the pack over its antlers in a panic, tearing the pack loose from the branch and carrying it away. Pack and antlers were so entangled, Manuel imagined the deer must have worn his provisions and clean shirts until antler-shedding season. He reported that incident to the rangers, too, but what could anyone do? He was reminded of it, guiltily, every time he read *Thidwick, the Big-Hearted Moose* to his four-year-old son.

Manuel and Mark arrived home three days early. Manuel's wife said she'd been expecting him.

She emptied his pack. 'Where's the can opener?' she asked.

'It's there somewhere,' said Manuel.

'It's not,' she said.

'Check the shirt pocket.'

'It's not here.' Manuel's wife held the pack upside down and shook it. Dead leaves fell out. 'How were you going to drink the beer?' she asked.

In August of 1962, Caroline Crosby, a teenager from Palo Alto, accompanied her family on a forced march from Tuolumne Meadows to Vogelsang. She carried fourteen pounds in a pack with an aluminum frame – and her father said it was the lightest pack on the market, and she should be able to carry one-third her weight, so fourteen pounds was nothing, but her pack stabbed her continuously in one coin-sized spot just below her right shoulder, and it still hurt the next morning. Her boots left a blister on her right heel, and her pack straps had rubbed. Her father had bought her a mummy bag with no zipper so as to minimize its weight; it was stiflingly hot, and she sweated all night. She missed an overnight at Ann Watson's house, where Ann showed them her sister's Mark Eden bust developer, and her sister retaliated by freezing all their bras behind the twin-pops. She missed *The Beverly Hillbillies*.

Caroline's father had quit smoking just for the duration of the trip, so as to spare himself the weight of cigarettes, and made continual comments about Nature, which were laudatory in content and increasingly abusive in tone. Caroline's mother kept telling her to smile.

In the morning her father mixed half a cup of stream water into a packet of powdered eggs and cooked them over a Coleman stove. 'Damn fine breakfast,' he told Caroline intimidatingly as she stared in horror at her plate. 'Out here in God's own country. What else could you ask for?' He turned to Caroline's mother, who was still trying to get a pot of water to come to a boil. 'Where's the goddamn coffee?' he asked. He went to the stream to brush his teeth with a toothbrush he had sawed the handle from in order to save the weight. Her mother told her to please make a little effort to be cheerful and not spoil the trip for everyone.

One week later she was in Letterman Hospital in San Francisco. The diagnosis was septicemic plague.

Which is finally where I come into the story. My name is Keith Harmon B.A. in history with a special emphasis on epidemics. I probably know as much as anyone about the plague of Athens. Typhus. Tarantism. Tsutsugamushi fever. It's an odder historical specialty than it ought to be. More battles have been decided by disease than by generals – and if you don't believe me, take a closer look at the Crusades or the fall of the Roman Empire or Napoleon's Russian campaign.

My M.A. is in public administration. Vietnam veteran, too, but in 1962 I worked for the state of California as part of the plague-monitoring team. When Letterman's reported a plague victim, Sacramento sent me down to talk to her.

Caroline had been moved to a private room. 'You're going to be fine,' I told her. Of course, she was. We still lose people to the pneumonic plague, but the slower form is easily cured. The only tricky part is making the diagnosis.

'I don't feel well. I don't like the food,' she said. She pointed out Letterman's Tuesday menu. 'Hawaiian Delight. You know what that is? Green Jell-O with a canned pineapple ring on top. What's delightful about that?' She was feverish and lethargic. Her hair lay limply about her head, and she kept tangling it in her fingers as she talked. 'I'm missing a lot of school.' Impossible to tell if this last was a complaint or a boast. She raised her bed to a sitting position and spent most of the rest of the interview looking out the window, making it clear that a view of the Letterman parking lot was more arresting than a conversation with an old man like me. She seemed younger than fifteen. Of course, everyone in a hospital bed feels young. Helpless. 'Will you ask them to let me wash and set my hair?'

I pulled a chair over to the bed. 'I need to know if you've been anywhere unusual recently. We know about Yosemite. Anywhere else. Hiking out around the airport, for instance.' The plague is endemic in the San Bruno Mountains by the San Francisco Airport. That particular species of flea doesn't bite humans, though. Or so we'd always thought. 'It's kind of a romantic spot for some teenagers, isn't it?'

I've seen some withering adolescent stares in my time, but this one was practiced. I still remember it. I may be sick, it said, but at least I'm not an idiot. 'Out by the airport?' she said. 'Oh, right. Real romantic. The radio playing and those 727s overhead. Give me a break.'

'Let's talk about Yosemite, then.'

She softened a little. 'In Palo Alto we go to the water temple,' she informed me. 'And, no, I haven't been there, either. My parents *made* me go to Yosemite. And now I've got bubonic plague.' Her tone was one of satisfaction. 'I think it was the powdered eggs. They *made* me eat them. I've been sick ever since.'

'Did you see any unusual wildlife there? Did you play with any squirrels?'

'Oh, right,' she said. 'I always play with squirrels. Birds sit on my fingers.' She resumed the stare. 'My parents didn't tell you what I saw?'

'No,' I said.

'Figures.' Caroline combed her fingers through her hair. 'If I had a brush, I could at least rat it. Will you ask the doctors to bring me a brush?'

'What did you see, Caroline?'

'Nothing. According to my parents. No big deal.' She looked out at the parking lot. 'I saw a boy.'

She wouldn't look at me, but she finished her story. I heard about the mummy bag and the overnight party she missed. I heard about the eggs. Apparently, the altercation over breakfast had escalated, culminating in Caroline's refusal to accompany her parents on a brisk hike to Ireland Lake. She stayed behind, lying on top of her sleeping bag and reading the part of *Green Mansions* where Abel eats a fine meal of anteater flesh. 'After the breakfast I had, my mouth was watering,' she told me. Something made her look up suddenly from her book. She said it wasn't a sound. She said it was a silence.

A naked boy dipped his hands into the stream and licked the water from his fingers. His fingernails curled toward his palms like claws. 'Hey,' Caroline told me she told him. She could see his penis and everything. The boy gave her a quick look and then backed away into the trees. She went back to her book.

She described him to her family when they returned. 'Real dirty,' she said. 'Real hairy.'

'You have a very superior attitude,' her mother noted. 'It's going to get you in trouble someday.'

'Fine,' said Caroline, feeling superior. 'Don't believe me.' She made a vow never to tell her parents anything again. 'And I never will,' she told me. 'Not if I have to eat powdered eggs until I die.'

At this time there started a plague. It appeared not in one part of the world only, not in one race of men only, and not in any particular season; but it spread over the entire earth, and afflicted all without mercy of both sexes and of every age. It began in Egypt, at Pelusium; thence it spread to Alexandria and to the rest of Egypt; then went to Palestine, and from there over the whole world...

In the second year, in the spring, it reached Byzantium and began in the following manner: To many there appeared phantoms in human form. Those who were so encountered, were struck by a blow from the phantom, and so contracted the disease. Others locked themselves into their houses. But then the phantoms appeared to them in dreams, or they heard voices that told them that they had been selected for death.

This comes from Procopius's account of the first pandemic. A.D. 541, *De Bello Persico*, chapter XXII. It's the only explanation I can give you for why

Caroline's story made me so uneasy, why I chose not to mention it to anyone. I thought she'd had a fever dream, but thinking this didn't settle me any. I talked to her parents briefly and then went back to Sacramento to write my report.

We have no way of calculating the deaths in the first pandemic. Gibbon says that during three months, five to ten thousand people died daily in Constantinople, and many Eastern cities were completely abandoned.

The second pandemic began in 1346. It was the darkest time the planet has known. A third of the world died. The Jews were blamed, and, throughout Europe, pogroms occurred wherever sufficient health remained for the activity. When murdering Jews provided no alleviation, a committee of doctors at the University of Paris concluded the plague was the result of an unfortunate conjunction of Saturn, Jupiter, and Mars.

The third pandemic occurred in Europe during the fifteenth to eighteenth centuries. The fourth began in China in 1855. It reached Hong Kong in 1894, where Alexandre Yersin of the Institut Pasteur at last identified the responsible bacilli. By 1898 the disease had killed six million people in India. Dr. Paul-Louis Simond, also working for the Institut Pasteur, but stationed in Bombay, finally identified fleas as the primary carriers. 'On June 2, 1898, I was overwhelmed,' he wrote. 'I had just unveiled a secret which had tormented man for so long.'

His discoveries went unnoticed for another decade or so. On June 27, 1899, the disease came to San Francisco. The governor of California, acting in protection of business interests, made it a felony to publicize the presence of the plague. People died instead of *syphilitic septicemia*. Because of this deception, thirteen of the Western states are still designated plague areas.

The state team went into the high country in early October. Think of us as soldiers. One of the great mysteries of history is why the plague finally disappeared. The rats are still here. The fleas are still here. The disease is still here; it shows up in isolated cases like Caroline's. Only the epidemic is missing. We're in the middle of the fourth assault. The enemy is elusive. The war is unwinnable. We remain vigilant.

The Vogelsang Camp had already been closed for the winter. No snow yet, but the days were chilly and the nights below freezing. If the plague was present, it wasn't really going to be a problem until spring. We amused ourselves, poking sticks into warm burrows looking for dead rodents. We set out some traps. Not many. You don't want to decrease the rodent population. Deprive the fleas of their natural hosts, and they just look for replacements. They just bring the war home.

We picked up a few bodies, but no positives. We could have dusted the place anyway as a precaution. *Silent Spring* came out in 1962, but I hadn't read it.

I saw the coyote on the fourth day. She came out of a hole on the bank of Lewis Creek and stood for a minute with her nose in the air. She was grayed with age around her muzzle, possibly a bit arthritic. She shook out one hind leg. She shook out the other. Then, right as I watched, Caroline's boy climbed out of the burrow after the coyote.

I couldn't see the boy's face. There was too much hair in the way. But his body was hairless, and even though his movements were peculiar and inhuman, I never thought that he was anything but a boy. Twelve years old or maybe thirteen, I thought, although small for thirteen. Wild as a wolf, obviously. Raised by coyotes maybe. But clearly human. Circumcised, if anyone is interested.

I didn't move. I forgot about Procopius and stepped into the *National Enquirer* instead. Marilyn was in my den. Elvis was in my rinse cycle. It was my lucky day. I was amusing myself when I should have been awed. It was a stupid mistake. I wish now that I'd been someone different.

The boy yawned and closed his eyes, then shook himself awake and followed the coyote along the creek and out of sight. I went back to camp. The next morning we surrounded the hole and netted them coming out. This is the moment it stopped being such a lark. This is an uncomfortable memory. The coyote was terrified, and we let her go. The boy was terrified, and we kept him. He scratched us and bit and snarled. He cut me, and I thought it was one of his nails, but he turned out to be holding a can opener. He was covered with fleas, fifty or sixty of them visible at a time, which jumped from him to us, and they all bit, too. It was like being attacked by a cloud. We sprayed the burrow and the boy and ourselves, but we'd all been bitten by then. We took an immediate blood sample. The boy screamed and rolled his eyes all the way through it. The reading was negative. By the time we all calmed down, the boy really didn't like us.

Clint and I tied him up, and we took turns carrying him down to Tuolumne. His odor was somewhere between dog and boy, and worse than both. We tried to clean him up in the showers at the ranger station. Clint and I both had to strip to do this, so God knows what he must have thought we were about. He reacted to the touch of water as if it burned. There was no way to shampoo his hair, and no one with the strength to cut it. So we settled for washing his face and hands, put our clothes back on, gave him a sweater that he dropped by the drain, put him in the backseat of my Rambler, and drove to Sacramento. He cried most of the way, and when we went around curves he allowed his body to be flung unresisting from one side of the car to the other, occasionally knocking his head against the door handle with a loud, painful sound.

I bought him a ham sandwich when we stopped for gas in Modesto, but he wouldn't eat it. He was a nice-looking kid, had a normal face, freckled, with blue eyes, brown hair, and if he'd had a haircut you could have imagined him in some Sears catalog modeling raincoats.

One of life's little ironies. It was October 14. We rescue a wild boy from isolation and deprivation and winter in the mountains. We bring him civilization and human contact. We bring him straight into the Cuban Missile Crisis.

Maybe that's why you don't remember reading about him in the paper. We turned him over to the state of California, which had other things on its mind.

The state put him in Mercy Hospital and assigned maybe a hundred doctors to the case. I was sent back to Yosemite to continue looking for fleas. The next time I saw the boy, about a week had passed. He'd been cleaned up, of course. Scoured of parasites, inside and out. Measured. He was just over four feet tall and weighed seventy-five pounds. His head was all but shaved so as not to interfere with the various neurological tests, which had turned out normal and were being redone. He had been observed rocking in a seated position, left to right and back to front, mouth closed, chin up, eyes staring at nothing. Occasionally he had small spasms, convulsive movements, which suggested abnormalities in the nervous system. His teeth needed extensive work. He was sleeping under his bed. He wouldn't touch his Hawaiian Delight. He liked us even less than before.

About this time I had a brief conversation with a doctor whose name I didn't notice. I was never able to find him again. Red-haired doctor with glasses. Maybe thirty, thirty-two years old. 'He's got some unusual musculature,' this red-haired doctor told me. 'Quite singular. Especially the development of the legs. He's shown us some really surprising capabilities.' The boy started to howl, an unpleasant, inhuman sound that started in his throat and ended in yours. It was so unhappy. It made me so unhappy to hear it. I never followed up on what the doctor had said.

I felt peculiar about the boy, responsible for him. He had such a *boyish* face. I visited several times, and I took him little presents, a Dodgers baseball cap and an illustrated *Goldilocks and the Three Bears* with the words printed big. Pretty silly, I suppose, but what would you have gotten? I drove to Fresno and asked Manuel Rodriguez if he could identify the can opener. 'Not with any assurance,' he said. I talked personally to Sergeant Redburn, the man from Missing Persons. When he told me about the Beckers, I went to the state library and read the newspaper articles for myself. Sergeant Redburn thought the boy might be just about the same age as Paul Becker, and I thought so, too. And I know the sergeant went to talk to Anna Becker's mother about it, because he told me she was going to come and try to identify the boy.

By now it's November. Suddenly I get a call sending me back to Yosemite. In Sacramento they claim the team has reported a positive, but when I arrive in Yosemite, the whole team denies it. Fleas are astounding creatures. They can be frozen for a year or more and then revived to full activity. But November in the mountains is a stupid time to be out looking for them. It's already snowed once, and it snows again, so that I can't get my team back out. We spend three weeks in the ranger station at Vogelsang huddled around our camp stoves while they air-drop supplies to us. And when I get back, a doctor I've never seen before, a Dr. Frank Li, tells me the boy, who was not Paul Becker, died suddenly of a seizure while he slept. I have to work hard to put away the sense that it was my fault, that I should have left the boy where he belonged.

And then I hear Sergeant Redburn has jumped off the Golden Gate Bridge.

Non Gratum Anus Rodentum. Not worth a rat's ass. This was the unofficial motto of the tunnel rats. We're leaping ahead here. Now it's 1967. Vietnam. Does the name Cu Chi mean anything to you? If not, why not? The district of Cu Chi is the most bombed, shelled, gassed, strafed, defoliated, and destroyed piece of earth in the history of warfare. And beneath Cu Chi runs the most complex part of a network of tunnels that connects Saigon all the way to the Cambodian border.

I want you to imagine, for a moment, a battle fought entirely in the dark. Imagine that you are in a hole that is too hot and too small. You cannot stand up; you must move on your hands and knees by touch and hearing alone through a terrain you can't see toward an enemy you can't see. At any moment you might trip a mine, put your hand on a snake, put your face on a decaying corpse. You know people who have done all three of these things. At any moment the air you breathe might turn to gas, the tunnel become so small you can't get back out; you could fall into a well of water and drown; you could be buried alive. If you are lucky, you will put your knife into an enemy you may never see before he puts his knife into you. In Cu Chi the Vietnamese and the Americans created, inch by inch, body part by body part, an entirely new type of warfare.

Among the Vietnamese who survived are soldiers who lived in the tiny underground tunnels without surfacing for five solid years. Their eyesight was permanently damaged. They suffered constant malnutrition, felt lucky when they could eat spoiled rice and rats. Self-deprivation was their weapon; they used it to force the soldiers of the most technically advanced army in the world to face them with knives, one on one, underground, in the dark.

On the American side, the tunnel rats were all volunteers. You can't force a man to do what he cannot do. Most Americans hyperventilated, had attacks of claustrophobia, were too big. The tunnel rats could be no bigger than the Vietnamese, or they wouldn't fit through the tunnels. Most of the tunnel rats were Hispanics and Puerto Ricans. They stopped wearing after-shave so the Vietcong wouldn't smell them. They stopped chewing gum, smoking, and eating candy because it impaired their ability to sense the enemy. They had to develop the sonar of bats. They had, in their own words, to become animals. What they did in the tunnels, they said, was unnatural.

In 1967 I was attached to the 521st Medical Detachment. I was an old man by Vietnamese standards, but then, I hadn't come to fight in the Vietnam War. Remember that the fourth pandemic began in China. Just before he died, Chinese poet Shih Tao-nan wrote:

> *Few days following the death of the rats,*
> *Men pass away like falling walls.*

Between 1965 and 1970, 24,848 cases of the plague were reported in Vietnam.

War is the perfect breeding ground for disease. They always go together, the trinity: war, disease, and cruelty. Disease was my war. I'd been sent to Vietnam to keep my war from interfering with everybody else's war.

In March we received by special courier a package containing three dead rats. The rats had been found – already dead, but leashed – inside a tunnel in Hau Nghia province. Also found – but not sent to us – were a syringe, a phial containing yellow fluid, and several cages. I did the test myself. One of the dead rats carried the plague.

There has been speculation that the Vietcong

were trying to use plague rats as weapons. It's also possible they were merely testing the rats prior to eating them themselves. In the end, it makes little difference. The plague was there in the tunnels whether the Vietcong used it or not.

I set up a tent outside Cu Chi town to give boosters to the tunnel rats. One of the men I inoculated was David Rivera. 'David has been into the tunnels so many times, he's a legend,' his companions told me.

'Yeah,' said David. 'Right. Me and Victor.'

'Victor Charlie?' I said. I was just making conversation. I could see David, whatever his record in the tunnels, was afraid of the needle. He held out one stiff arm. I was trying to get him to relax.

'No. Not hardly. Victor is the one.' He took his shot, put his shirt back on, gave up his place to the next man in line.

'Victor can see in the dark,' the next man told me.

'Victor Charlie?' I asked again.

'No,' the man said impatiently.

'You want to know about Victor?' David said. 'Let me tell you about Victor. Victor's the one who comes when someone goes down and doesn't come back out.'

'Victor can go faster on his hands and knees than most men can run,' the other man said. I pressed cotton on his arm after I withdrew the needle; he got up from the table. A third man sat down and took off his shirt.

David still stood next to me. 'I go into this tunnel. I'm not too scared, because I think it's cold; I'm not *feeling* anybody else there, and I'm maybe a quarter of a mile in, on my hands and knees, when I can almost see a hole in front of me, blacker than anything else in the tunnel, which is all black, you know. So I go into the hole, feeling my way, and I have this funny sense like I'm not moving into the hole; the hole is moving over to me. I put out my hands, and the ground moves under them.'

'Shit,' said the third man. I didn't know if it was David's story or the shot. A fourth man sat down.

'I risk a light, and the whole tunnel is covered with spiders, covered like wallpaper, only worse, two or three bodies thick,' David said. 'I'm sitting on them, and the spiders are already inside my pants and inside my shirt and covering my arms – and it's fucking Vietnam, you know; I don't even know if they're poisonous or not. Don't care, really, because I'm going to die just from having them on me. I can feel them moving toward my face. So I start to scream, and then this little guy comes and pulls me back out a ways, and then he sits for maybe half an hour, calm as can be, picking spiders off me. When I decide to live after all, I go back out. I tell everybody. "That was Victor," they say. "Had to be Victor." '

'I know a guy says Victor pulled him from a hole,' the fourth soldier said. 'He falls through a false floor down maybe twelve straight feet into this tiny little trap with straight walls all around and no way up, and Victor comes down after him. *Jumps* back out, holding the guy in his arms. Twelve feet; the guy swears it.'

'Tiny little guy,' said David. 'Even for V.C., this guy'd be tiny.'

'He just looks tiny,' the second soldier said. 'I know a guy saw Victor buried under more than a ton of dirt. Victor just digs his way out again. No broken bones, no nothing.'

Inexcusably slow, and I'd been told twice, but I had just figured out that Victor wasn't short for V.C. 'I'd better inoculate this Victor,' I said. 'You think you could send him in?'

The men stared at me. 'You don't get it, do you?' said David.

'Victor don't report,' the fourth man says.

'No C.O.,' says the third man. 'No unit.'

'He's got the uniform,' the second man tells me. 'So we don't know if he's special forces of some sort or if he's AWOL down in the tunnels.'

'Victor lives in the tunnels,' said David. 'Nobody up top has ever seen him.'

I tried to talk to one of the doctors about it. 'Tunnel vision,' he told me. 'We get a lot of that. Forget it.'

In May we got a report of more rats – some leashed, some in cages – in a tunnel near Ah Nhon Tay village in the Ho Bo Woods. But no one wanted to go in and get them, because these rats were alive. And somebody got the idea this was my job, and somebody else agreed. They would clear the tunnel of V.C. first, they promised me. So I volunteered.

Let me tell you about rats. Maybe they're not responsible for the plague, but they're still destructive to every kind of life-form and beneficial to none. They eat anything that lets them. They breed during all seasons. They kill their own kind; they can do it singly, but they can also organize and attack in hordes. The brown rat is currently embroiled in a war of extinction against the black rat. Most animals behave better than that.

I'm not afraid of rats. I read somewhere that about the turn of the century, a man in western Illinois heard a rustling in his fields one night. He got out of bed and went to the back door, and behind his house he saw a great mass of rats that stretched all the way to the horizon. I suppose this would have frightened me. All those naked tails in the moonlight. But I thought I could handle a few rats in cages, no problem.

It wasn't hard to locate them. I was on my hands and knees, but using a flashlight. I thought there might be some loose rats, too, and that I ought to look at least; and I'd also heard that there was an abandoned V.C. hospital in the tunnel that I was curious about. So I left the cages and poked around in the tunnels a bit; and when I'd had enough, I started back to get the rats, and I hit a water trap. There hadn't been a water trap before, so I knew I must have taken a wrong turn. I went back a bit, took another turn, and then another, and hit the water trap again. By now I was starting to panic. I couldn't find anything I'd ever seen before except the damn water. I went back again, farther without turning, took a turn, hit the trap.

I must have tried seven, eight times. I no longer thought the tunnel was cold. I thought the V.C. had closed the door on my original route so that I wouldn't find it again. I thought they were watching every move I made, pretty easy with me waving my flashlight about. I switched it off. I could hear them in the dark, their eyelids closing and opening, their hands tightening on their knives. I was sweating, head to toe, like I was ill, like I had the mysterious English sweating sickness or the *Suette des Picards.*

And I knew that to get back to the entrance, I had to go into the water. I sat and thought that through, and when I finished, I wasn't the same man I'd been when I began the thought.

It would have been bad to have to crawl back through the tunnels with no light. To go into the water with no light, not knowing how much water there was, not knowing if one lungful of air would be enough or if there were underwater turns so you might get lost before you found air again, was something you'd have to be crazy to do. I had to do it, so I had to be crazy first. It wasn't as hard as you might think. It took me only a minute.

I filled my lungs as full as I could. Emptied them once. Filled them again and dove in. Someone grabbed me by the ankle and hauled me back out. It frightened me so much I swallowed water, so I came up coughing and kicking. The hand released me at once, and I lay there for a bit, dripping water and still sweating, too, feeling the part of the tunnel that was directly below my body turn to mud, while I tried to convince myself that no one was touching me.

Then I was crazy enough to turn my light on. Far down the tunnel, just within range of the light, knelt a little kid dressed in the uniform of the rats. I tried to get closer to him. He moved away, just the same amount I had moved, always just in the light. I followed him down one tunnel, around a turn, down another. Outside, the sun rose and set. We crawled for days. My right knee began to bleed.

'Talk to me,' I asked him. He didn't.

Finally he stood up ahead of me. I could see the rat cages, and I knew where the entrance was behind him. And then he was gone. I tried to follow with my flashlight, but he'd jumped or something. He was just gone.

'Victor,' Rat Six told me when I finally came out. 'Goddamn Victor.'

Maybe so. If Victor was the same little boy I put a net over in the high country in Yosemite.

When I came out, they told me less than three hours had passed. I didn't believe them. I told them about Victor. Most of them didn't believe me. Nobody outside the tunnels believed in Victor. 'We just sent home one of the rats,' a doctor told me. 'He emptied his whole gun into a tunnel. Claimed there were V.C. all around him, but that he got them. He shot every one. Only, when we went down to clean it up, there were no bodies. All his bullets were found in the walls.

'Tunnel vision. Everyone sees things. It's the dark. Your eyes no longer impose any limit on the things you can see.'

I didn't listen. I made demands right up the chain of command for records: recruitment, AWOLs, special projects. I wanted to talk to everyone who'd ever seen Victor. I wrote Clint to see what he remembered of the drive back from Yosemite. I wrote a thousand letters to Mercy Hospital, telling them I'd uncovered their little game. I demanded to speak with the red-haired doctor with glasses whose name I never knew. I wrote the Curry Company and suggested they conduct a private investigation into the supposed suicide of Sergeant Redburn. I asked the CIA what they had done with Paul's parents. That part was paranoid. I was so unstrung I thought they'd killed his parents and given him to the coyote to raise him up for the tunnel wars. When I calmed down, I knew the CIA would never be so farsighted. I knew they'd just gotten lucky. I didn't know what happened to the parents; still don't.

There were so many crazy people in Vietnam, it could take them a long time to notice a new one, but I made a lot of noise. A team of three doctors talked to me for a total of seven hours. Then they said I was suffering from delayed guilt over the death of my little dog-boy, and that it surfaced, along with every other weak link in my personality, in the stress and the darkness of the tunnels. They sent me home. I missed the moon landing, because I was having a nice little time in a hospital of my own.

When I was finally and truly released, I went looking for Caroline Crosby. The Crosbys still lived in Palo Alto, but Caroline did not. She'd started college at Berkeley, but then she'd dropped out. Her parents hadn't seen her for several months.

Her mother took me through their beautiful house and showed me Caroline's old room. She had a canopy bed and her own bathroom. There was a mirror with old pictures of some boy on it. A throw rug with roses. There was a lot of pink. 'We drive through the Haight every weekend,' Caroline's mother said. 'Just looking.' She was pale and controlled. 'If you should see her, would you tell her to call?'

I would not. I made one attempt to return one little boy to his family, and look what happened. Either Sergeant Redburn jumped from the Golden Gate Bridge in the middle of his investigation or he didn't. Either Paul Becker died in Mercy Hospital or he was picked up by the military to be their special weapon in a special war.

I've thought about it now for a couple of decades, and I've decided that, at least for Paul, once he'd escaped from the military, things didn't work out so badly. He must have felt more at home in the tunnels under Cu Chi than he had under the bed in Mercy Hospital.

There is a darkness inside us all that is animal. Against some things – untreated or untreatable disease, for example, or old age – the darkness is all we are. Either we are strong enough animals or we are not. Such things pare everything that is not animal away from us. As animals we have a physical value, but in moral terms we are neither good nor bad. Morality begins on the way back from the darkness.

The first two plagues were largely believed to be a punishment for man's sinfulness. 'So many died,' wrote Agnolo di Tura the Fat, who buried all five of his own children himself, 'that all believed that it was the end of the world.' This being the case, you'd imagine the cessation of the plague must have been accompanied by outbreaks of charity and godliness. The truth was just the opposite. In 1349, in Erfurt, Germany, of the three thousand Jewish residents there, not one survived. This is a single instance of a barbarism so marked and so pervasive, it can be understood only as a form of mass insanity.

Here is what Procopius said: *And after the plague had ceased, there was so much depravity and general licentiousness, that it seemed as though the disease had left only the most wicked.*

When men are turned into animals, it's hard for them to find their way back to themselves. When children are turned into animals, there's no self to find. There's never been a feral child who found his way out of the dark. Maybe there's never been a feral child who wanted to.

You don't believe I saw Paul in the tunnels at all. You think I'm crazy or, charitably, that I was crazy then, just for a little while. Maybe you think the CIA would never have killed a policeman or tried to use a little child in a black war, even though the CIA has done everything else you've ever been told and refused to believe.

That's okay. I like your version just fine. Because if I made him up, and all the tunnel rats who ever saw him made him up, then he belongs to us, he marks us. Our vision, our Procopian phantom in the tunnels. Victor to take care of us in the dark.

Caroline came home without me. I read her wedding announcement in the paper more than twenty years ago. She married a Stanford chemist. There was a picture of her in her parents' backyard with gardenias in her hair. She was twenty-five years old. She looked happy. I never did go talk to her.

So here's a story for you, Caroline:

A small German town was much plagued by rats who ate the crops and the chickens, the ducks, the cloth and the seeds. Finally the citizens called in an exterminator. He was the best; he trapped and poisoned the rats. Within a month he had deprived the fleas of most of their hosts.

The fleas then bit the children of the town instead. Hundreds of children were taken with a strange dancing and raving disease. Their parents tried to control them, tried to keep them safe in their beds, but the moment their mothers' backs were turned, the children ran into the streets and danced. The town was Erfurt. The year was 1237.

Most of the children danced themselves to death. But not all. A few of them recovered and lived to be grown-ups. They married and worked and had their own children. They lived reasonable and productive lives.

The only thing is that they still twitch sometimes. Just now and then. They can't help it.

Stop me, Caroline, if you've heard this story before.

ANGELS IN LOVE

Kathe Koja

Kathe Koja (1960–) is an American writer who first emerged as a novelist during the US horror boom of the early 1990s. Kafkaesque, transgressive novels such as *The Cipher* (1991), *Bad Brains* (1992), *Skin* (1993), and *Strange Angels* (1994) established her as one of weird fiction's most innovative practitioners. Story collaborations with science fiction writer Barry Malzberg broadened her oeuvre, and as Koja moved into the realm of young adult novels her work continued to evade easy categorization. In 2010 her first historical novel, *Under the Poppy*, was published, with the sequel to follow in 2012. As 'Angels in Love' (1991) demonstrates, Koja's version of the weird is both claustrophobic and luminous, continually questioning the nature of reality.

LIKE WINGS. Rapturous as the muted screams, lush the beating of air through chipboard walls, luscious like sex and oh, my, far more forbidden: whatever it was, Lurleen *knew* it was wrong.

Knew it from the shrieks, gagged and that was no pillow, no sir no way, she herself was familiar with the gasp of muffled sex and this was definitely not it. And not – really – kinky, or not in any way she knew of, and with a half-shy swagger Lurleen could admit she had acquaintance of a few. Kiss me here. Let's see some teeth. Harder.

The sounds, arpeggio of groans, that basso almost-unheard thump, thump, rhythmic as a headboard or a set of baritone springs but that wasn't it either. Subsonic; felt by the bones. Lying there listening her own bones tingled, skin rippled light with goosebumps, speculation: who made those strange strange sounds? Someone with a taste for the rough stuff, maybe, someone who liked the doughy strop of flesh. Someone strong. An old boyfriend had used to say she fucked like an angel, she never understood the phrase till now. Her hands, deliberate stroll southward, shimmy of familiar fingers on as-familiar flesh; her own groans in counterpoint to the ones through the walls.

Waking heavy in the morning, green toothpaste spit and trying to brush her hair at the same time, late again. 'You're late,' Roger would say when she walked in, and she would flip fast through her catalog of excuses, which hadn't he heard lately? and try to give him something to get her by, thinking all the while of last night's tingle, puzzling again its ultimate source. It was kind of a sexy game to Lurleen, that puzzling; it gave her something to do at work.

Music store. No kind of music she liked but sometimes it wasn't too bad, and the store itself had a kind of smell that she enjoyed, like a library smell, like something educational was going on. Sheet music, music stands, Roger fussy with customers, turning the stereo on loud and saying stuff like, 'But have you heard Spivakov's Bach? Really quite good,' like he had probably heard Bach's Bach and could have suggested a few improvements. Right.

Today she felt, was, dopey and sluggish, simple transactions done twice and twice wrong; Roger was pissed, glowered as she slumped through the day. At quitting time he made a point of pointedly disappearing, not saying goodnight; sighing, she had to find him, hide and seek through the racks, he was a stickler for what he called the pleasantries: Goodnight, Lurleen. Goodnight, Roger. Every day.

Finally: hunched behind the order counter, flipping through the day's mail like he hadn't read it nine times already. Lurleen leaned tippy-toe over, flathanded on the cracking gray laminate: 'Goodnight, Roger.'

Chilly nod, like he'd just caught her trying to palm something: 'Goodnight, Lurleen.' Waited till she was almost out the door to say, 'Lurleen?'

Stopped, impatient keys in hand. 'What?'

'We open at ten o'clock. Every day.'

Asshole. 'See you tomorrow,' not banging the door, giving herself points for it. Outside her skin warmed, like butter, spread velvet all over, he always kept the fucking store too cold. Like the music'd melt or something if he turned it up past freezing. Rolling all her windows down, singing to the Top 40 station. Stopped at the party store for cigarettes and to flirt with the clerk, old guy just about as ugly as Roger but round where Roger was slack, furry where Roger was not.

'You headin' out tonight?' sliding the cigarettes across the counter, grinning at her tits. 'Have some fun?'

'Oh, I always manage to have fun,' over the shoulder smile as she headed for the door, Roger liked to stare at her tits too, she was positive, she just hadn't caught him at it yet. Asshole probably went home and jerked off, dreaming about her bouncing around to Bach. And she laughed, a little: who'd been flying solo last night, huh? But that was different.

In the dark, blind witness to the nightly ravishment, Lurleen, closed eyes, busy hands filling in the blanks, timing herself to the thump and stutter of the rapture beyond the walls. Longer tonight, ecstatic harmony of gulping cries, and after the crescendo wail, soundtrack to her own orgasm, she slept: to dream of flesh like iron, of rising whole, and drenched, and shiny-bright; shock-heavy with a pleasure poisonously rare. Woke just in time to see that she'd slept through the clock. Again.

In the hallway, pausing – already late, so what if she was later – before the door next door. Identical in nondescription to every other down the grimy hall, there was no way to tell by looking just what kind of fun went on there every night. Lurleen, tapping ignition key to lips, thoughtful sideways stare. Imagining, all the reluctant way to work, what sort of exotica, what moist brutalities were practiced there, what kinds of kinks indulged. Wriggling a little, skirt riding up and the cracked vinyl edges of the too-hot seat pressing voluptuously sharp into the damp flesh of her thighs.

It came to her that she had never really seen that next-door neighbor of hers. Maybe they'd bumped into each other, exchanged laundry-room hellos, but for the life of her Lurleen could not recall. She wasn't even sure if it was just one person or a couple. They sure were a couple at night, though, weren't they just.

The day spent avoiding Roger's gaze, colder than the store and just as constant, more than one smart remark about time clocks. Stopping for cigarettes, she picked up a six-pack too, clandestine sips at red lights, rehearsing queenly answers she would never give. It was so hot outside it felt good, brought a warm slow trickle of sweat down the plane of her temple, the hotter spot between her breasts.

She was going out tonight, that was for sure, she owed herself something for the just-past bitch of a day. Walking up the two flights a thought nudged her, firm and brisk to get past the beer. She leaned to sight up the stairwell, heart a trifle nervous, quick and jangly in her chest. Well. No time like the present, was there, to scratch a little itch? I'll just say hi, she thought, walking quicker now. I'll say, Hi, I'm your next-door neighbor, I just stopped by to say hello.

Fourth can in hand, smart tattoo on the door before she could change her mind. Wondering who would open, what they would look like. What they would smell like – Lurleen was a great believer in smells. If they would ask her in, and what she might say, knowing she would say yes and a smile past the thick spot in her throat, and she smiled at that, too, it wasn't that big a deal, was it?

Maybe it was.

Nothing. Silence inside so she knocked again, louder, humming to herself and oh boy here we go: winded swing of the door and 'Hi,' before it was all the way open. 'Hi, I'm Lurleen, your neighbor?'

Tall, her first thought. And skinny. Not model-skinny, just chicken bones, short blonde hair, Giants T-shirt over a flat chest. Anne, the girl said her name was, and past her curved shoulders Lurleen could see a flat as cramped and dingy as her own, a little emptier, maybe, a little less ripe, but nothing special. Purely ordinary. Like Anne herself: no exotic bruising, no secret sheen. Just stood there in the doorway playing with the end of her baggy T-shirt, flipping it as she talked and that thin-lipped smile that said Are you ready to leave yet? Just one big disappointment, but Lurleen didn't show it, kept up her own smile through the strain of the stillborn chatter until she was back inside her own place, sucking up the last of her beer.

'Well,' through a closed-mouth ladylike burp. 'Well.'

How could someone so dull have such a wild sex life? Be better off meeting the boyfriend, he had to be the real show. Fucking angel. Lurleen's giggles lasted through the rest of the beer, her long cool shower and half-hour's worth of mousse and primp. When she left for the bar Anne's flat was silent still, not even the requisite TV drone. From the parking lot the lifeless drift of her curtains, beige to Lurleen's red, was all there was to see.

At the bar she met a couple of guys, nice ones, she couldn't quite remember which was Jeff and which was Tony, but they kept her dancing, and drinking, and that was nice, too. After last call she swiveled off her seat, sweet and smiled and said she was sorry but she had an hour to make the airport to pick up her husband, and even as she said it she had to wonder why; it was one of them she'd planned on picking up, and never mind that she couldn't remember who was who, names didn't exactly matter at that time of night, words didn't matter past Who's got the rubber. But still she left alone.

Coming home, off-center slew into her parking space, radio up way too loud, singing and her voice a bray in the cut-engine quiet; she almost slipped going up the stairs. Shushing herself as she poured a glass of milk, her invariable after binge cure-all. Lifting the glass she caught from the damp skin of her forearm an aftershave scent, mixed with the male smell of Tony. Jeff? It didn't matter, such a pretty boy.

But not as pretty as the boy next door.

And, her thought seeming eerily a signal, she heard the preliminary noises, shifting warm through the wall as if they stroked her: Anne's breathy wordless voice, that rush of sound, half-sinister whirlwind pavane. Pressed against the wall itself, her bare-skinned sweat a warm adhesive, Lurleen stood, mouth open and eyes shut, working her thin imagination as Anne, presumably, worked her thin body, both – all three – ending in vortex, whirlpool, mouthing that dwindling symphony of screams, Lurleen herself louder than she'd ever been, with any man. Loud enough that they could, maybe, hear her through the walls.

Slumped, damp, she could not quite admit it, say to herself You want them to hear you. You want him to hear you, whoever he is. You want what Anne's getting, better than any bar pickup, better than anything you ever had. Glamorous and dirty. And scary. And hot.

By the next night she was ready, had turned her bed to face the wall lengthwise: willing herself, forcing herself like an unseen deliberate splinter in their shared and coupling flesh – she would be part of this. She had never had anything like what went on there, never anything good. She would have this if she had to knock down the wall to get it. Fingers splayed against her flesh, heels digging hard into the sheets and letting go, crying out, hear me. Hear me.

Exhausted at work, but on time, she couldn't take any of Roger's bitching now, not when she had to think. Make a plan. Anne, she was a sorry-looking bitch, no competition once the boyfriend got a good look at Lurleen. The trick was to get him to look. To see. See what he'd been hearing, night after night. Of course it wouldn't be all that easy, if Anne had any brains she would want to keep her boyfriend and Lurleen far far apart. Lurleen decided she would have to take it slow and smart, be smart, not exactly her strong point but she could be slick, she knew what she wanted.

She began to stalk Anne, never thinking of it in so many words but as sure and surely cautious as any predator. Waiting, lingering in the hallway after work, for Anne to come home from whatever unfathomable job she did all day. Never stopping to talk, just a smile, pleasant make-believe. She made it her business to do her laundry when Anne did hers; at the first whoosh and stagger of the old machine Lurleen was there, quarters in hand; her clothes had never been so clean; she had to see. Any jockey shorts, bikini underwear, jockstraps, what? She meant to take one if she could, steal it before, before it was clean. Smell it. You can tell a lot about a man, Lurleen believed, from the smell of his skin, not his aftershave or whatever but the pure smell of his body. Until his body was beneath hers it was the best she could do. She pawed through the laundry basket, poked around in the washer: nothing. Just Anne's Priss-Miss blouses, baggy slacks, cheap bras, and just about everything beige. Balked angry toss of the clothing, stepped on it to push it back into the basket. Maybe he liked Anne because she was so beige, so... nothing? Could a man want a woman to be nothing? Just a space to fill? Lurleen had known plenty of guys who liked their women dumb, it made them feel better, but anyway Anne didn't seem dumb. Just empty.

And still, night after night the same, bed against the wall, Lurleen could be determined, Lurleen could work for what she wanted. Drained every morning, the sting of tender skin in the shower, even Roger noticed her red eyes.

'Not moonlighting, are you,' but she saw he knew it was no question, half-gaze through those tired eyes and she even, for a moment, considered telling him, considered saying I want the boy next door, Roger, I want him real bad. I want him so much I even jerk off so he can hear me, so he can know how he turns me on. I want him so much I don't know what to do.

She wasn't getting anywhere. Drumming slow one finger against the order counter, staring right past some guy bumbling on about some opera or something, she wasn't getting anywhere and it was wearing her out. No time for anything else, bars, guys, whatever, there wasn't any other guy she wanted. Anne's smiles growing smaller, tighter, her gaze more pinched, was she catching on? Tired from sitting in the hallway, once or twice another neighbor had caught her at it, loitering tense and unseeing until the tap-tap-tap on her shoulder, Hey are you OK? 'Fine,' harsh involuntary blush, 'just looking for an earring.' Right. Tired from staking out the parking lot, hot breeze through the window; she didn't even know what kind of car he drove. Tired to death and still no glimpse of him, proud author of the sounds, it was killing her to listen but she couldn't stop. She didn't want to stop.

And then that night, mid-jerk, mid-groan, they stopped. The sounds. Ceased completely but not to complete silence, a waiting sound, a whisper. Whispering through the walls, such a willing sound.

She yanked on a T-shirt, ends tickling her bare ass as she ran, hit on the door with small quick fists, 'Anne? Are you OK?' never thinking how stupid she might look if the door opened, never considered what excuse she might give. I didn't hear anything so I thought you might be in trouble. Right. So what. Bang bang on the door.

'Anne?'

The whisper, against the door itself. Hearing it Lurleen shivered, convulsive twitch like a tic of the flesh, all down her body and she pressed against the door, listening with all her might. 'Anne,' but quietly, feeling the heat from her body, the windy rush of her heart. Waiting. 'Anne,' more quietly still, less than a murmuring breath, 'let me in.'

Abruptly, spooking her back a step: the sounds, hot, intensity trebled but wrong somehow, guttural, staggering where they should flow, a smell almost like garbage but she didn't care, once the first scare had passed she pressed harder into the door, as if by pure want she could break it down, she would get in, she would. T-shirt stuck, sweating like she'd run a mile. I'm sick of just listening. The hall was so hot. Sweat on her forehead, running into her eyes like leaking tears. The doorknob in her slick fingers.

It turned. Simple as that.

In the end so quick and easy and it seemed

almost that she could not breathe, could not get enough air to move but she moved all right, oh yes, stepped right inside into the semidarkness, a fake hurricane lamp broken beside the bed but there was light enough, enough to see by.

Like angels in love, mating in the cold graceful rapture of thin air. Hovering above the bed, at least a yard or maybe more, no wonder she never heard springs, instead the groaned complaint of the walls itself as his thrusting brushed them, on his back the enormous strange construction that kept them airborne, as careless as if it had grown there amongst the pebbled bumps and tiny iridescent fins. His body beautiful, and huge, not like a man's but so real it seemed to suck up all the space in the room, big elementary muscles and he was using them all. Anne, bent like a coat hanger, it hurt to see the angle of her back, her eyes wide and empty and some stuff coming out of her mouth like spoiled black jelly but it was too late, Lurleen had sent the door swinging backwards to close with a final catch, and in its sound his gaze swiveling to touch hers: the cold regard of a nova, the summoning glance of a star.

Her mouth as open as Anne's as she approached the vast brutality of his embrace, room enough for two there, oh my yes. Fierce relentless encroachment promising no pleasure but the pleasure of pain. Not an angel, never had been. Or maybe once, long, a long long time ago.

THE ICE MAN

Haruki Murakami

TRANSLATED INTO ENGLISH BY PHILIP GABRIEL

Haruki Murakami (1949–) is an iconic Japanese writer whose novels, short stories, and works of nonfiction have garnered him significant critical acclaim and numerous awards, including the Franz Kafka Prize and the World Fantasy Award for his novel *Kafka on the Shore* (2005). *The Guardian* praised him as 'one of the world's greatest living novelists' for his works and achievements. 'I write *weird* stories,' Murakami told *Salon* in 1997. 'I don't know why I like weirdness so much. Myself, I'm a very realistic person.' Based on a dream his wife had, Murakami's 'The Ice Man' (1991) is a prime example of the weirdness in his fiction, which usually comes intertwined with the surreal or quietly absurd.

My husband's an Ice Man.

The first time I met him was at a hotel at a ski resort. It's hard to imagine a more appropriate place to meet an Ice Man. He was in the lobby of the hotel, noisy and crowded with hordes of young people, seated in a corner as far as possible from the fireplace, quietly absorbed in a book. It was nearly noon, but the clear, cold morning light seemed to shine on him alone. '*That's an Ice Man*,' one of my friends whispered. At the time I had no idea what sort of person an Ice Man was, and my friend couldn't help me out. All she knew was that he was the sort of person who went by the name of Ice Man. 'They must call him that because he's made out of ice,' she added, a serious look on her face. As serious as if the topic wasn't an Ice Man but a ghost, or someone with a contagious disease.

The Ice Man looked young, though that was offset by the white strands, like patches of leftover snow, mixed in among his stiff, wiry head of hair. He was tall, his cheeks were sharply chiseled, like frozen crags, his fingers covered with frost that looked like it would never, ever melt. Other than this, he looked perfectly normal. He wasn't handsome, exactly, though some would find him quite appealing. There was something about him that pierced right through you. Especially his eyes, and that silent, transparent look that gleamed like an icicle on a winter's morning – the sole glint of life in an otherwise provisional body. I stood there for a while, gazing at the Ice Man from across the lobby. He was absorbed in his book, never once moving or looking up, as if trying to convince himself that he was utterly alone.

The next afternoon he was in the same spot, as before, reading his book. When I went to the dining room for lunch, and when I came back with my friends from skiing in the evening, he was always there, seated in the same chair, the same look in his eyes as he scanned the pages of the same book as before. And the next day was exactly the same. Dawn to dusk found him seated alone, quietly reading, for all the world like part of the frozen winter scene outside.

On the afternoon of the fourth day, I made up

an excuse and didn't join everyone on the slopes. Instead, I stayed behind in the hotel, wandering around the lobby. With everyone out skiing, the lobby was like an abandoned city. The air there was sticky and hot, filled with a strangely depressing odor – the smell of snow that had clung to the soles of people's boots and had slowly melted in front of the fireplace. I gazed out the windows, leafed through a newspaper. Finally I worked up my courage, went over to the Ice Man, and spoke to him. I'm pretty shy, and hardly ever strike up a conversation with a stranger, but I couldn't help myself. I *had* to talk to him. This was my last night in the hotel and if I let this chance pass I probably would never have another.

You're not skiing? I asked, trying to sound casual. The Ice Man slowly raised his head, looking like he was carefully listening to the wind blowing far away. He gazed intently at me and then quietly shook his head. I don't ski, he said. I'm fine just reading and looking out at the snow. His words floated up in the air, a white comic-book bubble of dialogue, every word visible before me. He gently wiped away some of the frost from his fingers.

I had no idea what to say next. I blushed and stood there, rooted to the spot. The Ice Man gazed into my eyes and gave what looked like a faint smile. Or was it? Had he really smiled? Maybe I was just imagining it. Would you like to sit down? he said. I know you're curious about me, so let's talk for a while. You want to know what an Ice Man is like, right? He chuckled. It's all right, he added. There's nothing to be afraid of. You're not going to catch a cold just talking to me.

We sat on a sofa in a corner of the lobby, hesitantly talking as we watched the swirling snow outside. I ordered a cup of hot cocoa, but the Ice Man didn't drink anything. He was just as shy as I was. On top of which, we had little in common to talk about. We talked about the weather at first, then the hotel. Did you come here alone? I asked him. I did, he responded. Do you like skiing? he asked. Not particularly, I replied. Some of my girlfriends dragged me here. I can barely ski. I was dying to find out more about what an Ice Man was all about. Was he really made out of ice? What did he eat? Where did he live in the summer? Did he have a family? Those sorts of questions. Unfortunately, the Ice Man didn't talk about himself at all, and I didn't dare ask the questions that whirled around in my head. I figured he didn't feel like talking about those things.

Instead he talked about me, who I am. It's hard to believe, but he knew everything there was to know about me. Who was in my family, my age, interests, my health, what school I was attending, my friends. He knew it all. Even things I'd long forgotten, he knew everything about.

I don't get it, I blushed. I felt like I had been stripped naked in front of people. How do you know so much about me? I asked. Are you a mind reader?

No, the Ice Man said, I can't read minds. I just know these things. Like I'm looking deep into a clear block of ice. When I gaze at you like this, I can see everything about you.

Can you see my future? I asked.

No, not the future, he replied blankly, slowly shaking his head. I'm not interested in the future. I have no concept of the future. Ice contains no future, just the past, sealed away. As if they're alive, everything in the world is sealed up inside, clear and distinct. Ice can preserve all kinds of things that way – cleanly, clearly. That's the essence of ice, the role it plays.

I'm glad, I replied, and smiled. I was relieved – there was no way I wanted to hear about my future.

We got together a few times after we returned to Tokyo, eventually dating every weekend. We didn't go on typical dates, to see movies, or spend time in coffee shops. We didn't even go out to eat. The Ice Man hardly ever ate. Instead we'd spend time on a park bench, side by side, talking. We discussed all kinds of subjects, yet not once did the Ice Man talk about himself. Why is this? I asked one day. Why don't you ever talk about yourself? I want to know more about you – where you were born, what kind of parents you had, how you came to be an Ice Man. The Ice Man gazed at me for a while, then slowly shook his head. I don't know the answer to those things, he responded quietly and decisively, exhaling his hard white breath. I have no past. I know the past of everything else, and preserve it. But I have no past myself. I have no idea where I was born. I don't know what my parents looked like, or whether I even had any. I don't know how old I am, or if I even have an age.

The Ice Man was as isolated and alone as an iceberg floating in the darkness.

I fell deeply in love with him, and he came to love me, the present me, apart from any past or future. And I came to love the Ice Man for who he is now, apart from any past or future. It was a wonderful thing. We began to talk about getting married. I had just turned twenty, and the Ice Man was the first person I'd ever truly loved. What loving him really meant was, at the time, beyond me. But that would have been true even if it hadn't been the Ice Man I was in love with then.

My mother and older sister were totally opposed to our marriage. You're too young to get married, they argued. You don't know the man's background – even where or when he was born. How are we supposed to explain that to our relatives? And listen, they went on, he's an Ice Man, so what happens if he melts? You don't seem to understand this, but when you get married you take on certain responsibilities. How can an Ice Man possibly fulfill his duties as a husband?

Their fears were groundless, however. The Ice Man wasn't really made out of ice. He was just as cold as ice. So even if it got hot, he wasn't about to melt. He was cold, all right, but this wasn't the kind of cold that was going to rob someone else of his body heat.

So we got married. No one celebrated our wedding. No one – not my friends, or relatives, or my family – was happy about us getting married. We didn't even have a wedding ceremony. The Ice Man didn't have a family register, so even a civil ceremony was out. The two of us simply decided that we were married. We bought a small cake and ate it, just the two of us. That was our ceremony. We rented a small apartment, and the Ice Man took a job at a refrigerated meat warehouse. The cold never bothered him, of course, and he never got tired, no matter how hard he worked. He never even ate very much. So his boss really liked him, and paid him more than any of his fellow employees. We lived a quiet life, just the two of us, not bothered by anyone else, not troubling anybody.

When we made love, I always pictured a solitary, silent clump of ice off somewhere. Hard ice, as hard as it could possibly be, the largest chunk of ice in the entire world. It was somewhere far away, though the Ice Man must know where that chunk of ice is. What he did was convey a memory of that ice. The first few times we made love, I was confused, but soon I grew used to it. I grew to love it when he took me in his arms. As always, he never said a word about himself, not even why he became an Ice Man, and I never asked him. The two of us simply held each other in the darkness, sharing that enormous ice, inside of which the world's past, millions of years' worth, was preserved.

Our married life was fine. We loved each other, and everyone left us alone. People found it hard at first to get used to the Ice Man, but after a while they started to talk with him. An Ice Man's not so different from anybody else, they concluded. But deep down, I knew they didn't accept him, and they didn't accept me for having married him. We're different people from *them*, they concluded, and the gulf separating them and us will never be filled.

We tried but failed to have a baby, perhaps because of a genetic difference between humans and Ice Men that made having children difficult. Without a baby to keep me busy, I found I had a lot of spare time on my hands. I'd straighten up the house in the morning, but after that had nothing to keep me busy. I didn't have any friends to talk to or go out with, and I didn't know anybody in the neighborhood. My mother and sister were still angry with me over marrying an Ice Man, and refused to get in touch. I was the family black sheep they were embarrassed about. There was no one to talk to, even over the phone. While the Ice Man was working in the warehouse, I stayed alone at home, reading or listening to music. I was a bit of a homebody anyway, and didn't mind being by myself all that much. Still, I was young, and couldn't put up with such a monotonous routine for long. Boredom didn't bother me as much as the sheer repetitiveness of each day. I started to see myself as nothing more than a repetitive shadow within that daily routine.

So, one day I suggested to my husband that we take a trip somewhere to break up the routine. A trip? the Ice Man asked, his eyes narrowing. Why would you want to go on a trip? You're not happy the way we are, just the two of us?

No, that's not it, I replied. I'm perfectly happy. We get along fine. It's just that I'm bored. I'd like to go someplace far away, see things I've never seen before, experience something new. Do you know what I mean? And besides, we never went on a honeymoon. We have enough saved up, plus you have plenty of vacation time. It would be nice to take a leisurely vacation for once.

The Ice Man let out a deep, nearly freezing sigh, which crystallized audibly in the air, then brought his long, frost-covered fingers together on his lap. Well, he said, if you really want to go on a trip that much, I don't see why not. I don't think traveling is all that great, but I'll do whatever it takes to make you happy, go wherever you want. I've worked hard at the warehouse and should be able to take some time off. It shouldn't be a problem. But where would you like to go?

How about the South Pole? I said. I picked the South Pole because I was sure the Ice Man would be interested in going there. And, truth be told, I'd always wanted to go see it. To see the aurora, and the penguins. I had this wonderful mental picture of myself in a hooded parka underneath the aurora, playing with the penguins.

The Ice Man looked deep into my eyes, unblinking. His look was like a sharply pointed icicle piercing deep into my brain. He was silent for a while, thinking, then with a twinkle in his voice he said, All right. If you'd really like to go to the South Pole then let's do it. You're sure that's where you want to go?

I nodded.

I can take a long vacation in a couple of weeks, he said. You should be able to get everything ready for the trip in the meantime. That's all right with you?

I couldn't respond. His icicle stare had frozen my brain and I couldn't think.

As the days passed, though, I started to regret bringing up the idea to my husband of a trip to the South Pole. I'm not sure why. It's like ever since I mentioned the name 'South Pole' he changed. His eyes grew more piercing and icicle-like than ever, his breath whiter, his fingers covered with an increasing amount of frost. He was quieter than before, and more stubborn. And he was no longer eating, which had me worried. Five days before we were set to depart I decided I had to say something. Let's not go to the South Pole after all, I said to him. It's too cold, and might not be good for us. It'd be better to go to some ordinary place – Europe or Spain or somewhere. We could drink some wine, eat some paella, watch a bullfight or two. But my husband ignored me. He had this faraway look for a while, then turned to me and looked deep into my eyes. His stare went so deep I felt like my body was about to vanish right then and there. No, my husband the Ice Man said flatly, Spain doesn't interest me. I'm sorry, but it's just too hot and dusty. And the food's too spicy. And I already bought our tickets to the South Pole, and a fur coat and fur-lined boots for you. We can't let those go to waste. We can't just back out now.

To tell you the truth, I was frightened. If we went to the South Pole, I felt sure something terrible was going to happen to us. I had the same awful dream night after night. I'm walking somewhere when I fall into a deep hole. Nobody finds me and I freeze solid. I'm frozen inside the ice, gazing up at the sky. I'm conscious but can't even move a finger. It's such a weird feeling. With each passing moment I'm becoming part of the past. There is no future for me, just the past steadily accumulating. Everybody is watching this happening to me. They're watching the past, watching as I slip further and further away.

Then I wake up and find the Ice Man sleeping beside me. He makes no sound as he sleeps, like something frozen and dead. I love him, though. I start to cry, my tears wetting his cheeks. He awakens and holds me close. I had an awful dream, I tell him. In the darkness he slowly shakes his head. It was only a dream, he says. Dreams come from the past, not from the future. Dreams shouldn't control you – you should control *them*.

You're right, I say – but I'm not at all certain.

So we ended up taking a plane to the South Pole. I couldn't find a reason to call off our trip.

The pilots and stewardesses in our plane barely said a word the whole way. I was hoping to enjoy the scenery as we flew, but the clouds were so thick I couldn't see a thing. Before long, the windows were covered with a thick film of ice. All this time, my husband just quietly read a book. I felt none of the usual excitement and happiness you feel as you set out on a trip, merely the feeling that we were fulfilling what we'd set out to do.

As we walked down the ramp and first set foot at the South Pole, I could feel my husband's whole body tremble. It all happened in the blink of an eye, in half an instant, and his expression didn't change a jot, so no one else noticed. But I didn't miss it. Something inside him sent a quiet yet intense jolt through him. I stared at his face. He stood there, looked up at the sky, then at his hands, and then let out a deep breath. He looked over at me and smiled. So this is where you wanted to come? he asked. That's right, I replied.

I knew the South Pole was going to be a lonely place, but it turned out to be lonelier than anything I could have imagined. Hardly anyone lived there. There was just one small featureless town, with one equally featureless hotel. The South Pole isn't much of a tourist destination. There weren't even any penguins, not to mention any aurora. Occasionally I'd stop passersby and ask where the penguins were, but they'd merely shake their head. They couldn't understand my words, so I'd end up sketching a penguin on a piece of paper to show them, but all I got was the same response – a silent shake of the head. I felt so alone. Step outside the town and all you saw was ice. No trees, no flowers, rivers, or ponds. Ice and nothing but – a frozen wasteland as far as the eye could see.

My husband, on the other hand, with his white breath, frosty fingers, and faraway look in his icicle eyes, strode tirelessly here and there. It wasn't long before he learned the language and spoke with the locals in hard, icy tones. They talked for hours, intense looks on their faces, but I didn't have a clue what they could be talking about. My husband was entranced by the whole place. Something about it appealed to him. It upset me at first, and I felt like I was left behind, betrayed and abandoned.

Finally, though, in the midst of this silent, icy world, all strength drained out of me, ebbing away bit by bit. Even, in the end, the strength to feel upset by my situation. My emotional compass had vanished. I lost all sense of direction, of time, of the sense of who I was. I don't know when it began, or when it ended, but before I knew it I was locked away, alone and numb in the endless winter of that world of ice. Even after I'd lost almost all sensation, I still knew this: *The husband here at the South Pole is not the husband I used to know.* I couldn't say how he'd changed, exactly, for he still was always thoughtful, always had kind words for me. And I knew he sincerely meant the things he said. But I also knew that the Ice Man before me now was not the Ice Man I'd first met at the ski resort. But who was I going to complain to? All the South Pole people liked him a lot, and they couldn't understand a word I said. With white breath and frosty faces they talked, joked around, and sang songs in that distinctively spirited language of theirs. I stayed shut up in my hotel room gazing out at the gray skies that wouldn't clear for months, struggling to learn the complicated grammar of the South Pole language, something I knew I'd never master.

There weren't any more airplanes at the airport. After the plane that carried us here departed no more landed. By this time the runway was buried beneath a hard sheet of ice. Just like my heart.

Winter's come, my husband said. A long, long winter. No planes will come, no ships either. Everything's frozen solid, he said. All we can do is wait for spring.

It was three months after we'd come to the South Pole that I realized I was pregnant. And I knew one thing: that the baby I was going to give birth to would be a tiny Ice Man. My womb had frozen over, a thin sheet of ice mixed in with my amniotic fluid. I could feel that chill deep inside my belly. And I knew this, too: my child would have the same icicle eyes as his father, the same frost-covered fingers. And I knew one more thing: our new little family would never step outside the South Pole again. The outrageous weight of the eternal past had grabbed us and wasn't about to let go. We'd never be able to shake free.

My heart is just about gone now. The warmth

I used to have has retreated somewhere far away. Sometimes I even forget that warmth ever existed. I'm still able to cry, though. I'm completely alone, in the coldest, loneliest place in the world. When I cry, my husband kisses my cheeks, turning my tears to ice. He peels off those frozen tears and puts them on his tongue. You know I love you, he says. And I know it's true. The Ice Man does love me. But the wind blows his frozen words further and further into the past. And I cry some more, icy tears welling up endlessly in our frozen little home in the far-off South Pole.

REPLACEMENTS

Lisa Tuttle

Lisa Tuttle (1952–) is an American writer of fantastical fiction who lives in Scotland. An early member of the Turkey City Writer's Workshop, she won the 1974 John W. Campbell Award for Best New Writer in Science Fiction. Her first novel came out in 1980 and was co-written with George R. R. Martin. Since then, Tuttle has published more than a dozen novels, including *Lost Futures* (1992), *Mad House* (1998), and *The Mysteries* (2005). Collections include *A Nest of Nightmares* (1985) and *My Pathology* (2001). The chilling and atmospheric 'The Replacements' (1992) is a weird classic, often reprinted, including in the Joyce Carol Oates-edited *American Gothic Tales*.

Walking through gray north London to the tube station, feeling guilty that he hadn't let Jenny drive him to work and yet relieved to have escaped another pointless argument, Stuart Holder glanced down at a pavement covered in a leaf-fall of fast-food cartons and white paper bags and saw, amid the dog turds, beer cans, and dead cigarettes, something horrible.

It was about the size of a cat, naked-looking, with leathery, hairless skin and thin, spiky limbs that seemed too frail to support the bulbous, ill-proportioned body. The face, with tiny bright eyes and a wet slit of a mouth, was like an evil monkey's. It saw him and moved in a crippled, spasmodic way. Reaching up, it made a clotted, strangled noise. The sound touched a nerve, like metal between the teeth, and the sight of it, mewling and choking and scrabbling, scaly claws flexing and wriggling, made him feel sick and terrified. He had no phobias, he found insects fascinating, not frightening, and regularly removed, unharmed, the spiders, wasps, and mayflies which made Jenny squeal or shudder helplessly.

But this was different. This wasn't some rare species of wingless bat escaped from a zoo, it wasn't something he would find pictured in any reference book. It was something that should not exist, a mistake, something alien. It did not belong in his world.

A little snarl escaped him and he took a step forward and brought his foot down hard.

The small, shrill scream lanced through him as he crushed it beneath his shoe and ground it into the road.

Afterward, as he scraped the sole of his shoe against the curb to clean it, nausea overwhelmed him. He leaned over and vomited helplessly into a red-and-white-striped box of chicken bones and crumpled paper.

He straightened up, shaking, and wiped his mouth again and again with his pocket handkerchief. He wondered if anyone had seen, and had a furtive look around. Cars passed at a steady crawl. Across the road a cluster of schoolgirls dawdled near a man smoking in front of a newsagent's, but on this side of the road the fried chicken franchise and bathroom suppliers had yet to open for the day and the nearest pedestrians were more than a hundred yards away.

Until that moment, Stuart had never killed anything in his life. Mosquitoes and flies of course, other insects probably, a nest of hornets once, that was all. He had never liked the idea of hunting, never lived in the country. He remembered his father putting out poisoned bait for rats, and he remembered shying bricks at those same vermin on a bit of waste ground where he had played as a boy. But rats weren't like other animals; they elicited no sympathy. Some things had to be killed if they would not be driven away.

He made himself look to make sure the thing was not still alive. Nothing should be left to suffer. But his heel had crushed the thing's face out of recognition, and it was unmistakably dead. He felt a cool tide of relief and satisfaction, followed at once, as he walked away, by a nagging uncertainty, the imminence of guilt. Was he right to have killed it, to have acted on violent, irrational impulse? He didn't even know what it was. It might have been somebody's pet.

He went hot and cold with shame and self-disgust. At the corner he stopped with five or six others waiting to cross the road and because he didn't want to look at them he looked down.

And there it was, alive again.

He stifled a scream. No, of course it was not the same one, but another. His leg twitched; he felt frantic with the desire to kill it, and the terror of his desire. The thin wet mouth was moving as if it wanted to speak.

As the crossing-signal began its nagging blare he tore his eyes away from the creature squirming at his feet. Everyone else had started to cross the street, their eyes, like their thoughts, directed ahead. All except one. A woman in a smart business suit was standing still on the pavement, looking down, a sick fascination on her face.

As he looked at her looking at it, the idea crossed his mind that he should kill it for her, as a chivalric, protective act. But she wouldn't see it that way. She would be repulsed by his violence. He didn't want her to think he was a monster. He didn't want to be the monster who had exulted in the crunch of fragile bones, the flesh and viscera merging pulpily beneath his shoe.

He forced himself to look away, to cross the road, to spare the alien life. But he wondered, as he did so, if he had been right to spare it.

Stuart Holder worked as an editor for a publishing company with offices an easy walk from St. Paul's. Jenny had worked there, too, as a secretary, when they met five years ago. Now, though, she had quite a senior position with another publishing house, south of the river, and recently they had given her a car. He had been supportive of her ambitions, supportive of her learning to drive, and proud of her on all fronts when she succeeded, yet he was aware, although he never spoke of it, that something about her success made him uneasy. One small, niggling, insecure part of himself was afraid that one day she would realize she didn't need him anymore. That was why he picked at her, and second-guessed her decisions when she was behind the wheel and he was in the passenger seat. He recognized this as he walked briskly through more crowded streets toward his office, and he told himself he would do better. He would have to. If anything drove them apart it was more likely to be his behavior than her career. He wished he had accepted her offer of a ride today. Better any amount of petty irritation between husband and wife than to be haunted by the memory of that tiny face, distorted in the death he had inflicted. Entering the building, he surreptitiously scraped the sole of his shoe against the carpet.

Upstairs two editors and one of the publicity girls were in a huddle around his secretary's desk; they turned on him the guilty-defensive faces of women who have been discussing secrets men aren't supposed to know.

He felt his own defensiveness rising to meet theirs as he smiled. 'Can I get any of you chaps a cup of coffee?'

'I'm sorry, Stuart, did you want . . . ?' As the others faded away, his secretary removed a stiff white paper bag with the NEXT logo, printed on it from her desktop.

'Joke, Frankie, joke.' He always got his own coffee because he liked the excuse to wander, and he was always having to reassure her that she was not failing in her secretarial duties. He wondered if Next sold sexy underwear, decided it would be unkind to tease her further.

He felt a strong urge to call Jenny and tell her what had happened, although he knew he wouldn't be able to explain, especially not over the phone. Just hearing her voice, the sound of sanity, would be a comfort, but he restrained himself until just after noon, when he made the call he made every day.

Her secretary told him she was in a meeting. 'Tell her Stuart rang,' he said, knowing she would call him back as always.

But that day she didn't. Finally, at five minutes to five, Stuart rang his wife's office and was told she had left for the day.

It was unthinkable for Jenny to leave work early, as unthinkable as for her not to return his call. He wondered if she was ill. Although he usually stayed in the office until well after six, now he shoved a manuscript in his briefcase and went out to brave the rush hour.

He wondered if she was mad at him. But Jenny didn't sulk. If she was angry she said so. They didn't lie or play those sorts of games with each other, pretending not to be in, 'forgetting' to return calls.

As he emerged from his local underground station Stuart felt apprehensive. His eyes scanned the pavement and the gutters, and once or twice the flutter of paper made him jump, but of the creatures he had seen that morning there were no signs. The body of the one he had killed was gone, perhaps eaten by a passing dog, perhaps returned to whatever strange dimension had spawned it. He noticed, before he turned off the high street, that other pedestrians were also taking a keener than usual interest in the pavement and the edge of the road, and that made him feel vindicated somehow.

London traffic being what it was, he was home before Jenny. While he waited for the sound of her key in the lock he made himself a cup of tea, cursed, poured it down the sink, and had a stiff whiskey instead. He had just finished it and was feeling much better when he heard the street door open.

'Oh!' The look on her face reminded him unpleasantly of those women in the office this morning, making him feel like an intruder in his own place. Now Jenny smiled, but it was too late. 'I didn't expect you to be here so early.'

'Nor me. I tried to call you, but they said you'd left already. I wondered if you were feeling all right.'

'I'm fine!'

'You look fine.' The familiar sight of her melted away his irritation. He loved the way she looked: her slender, boyish figure, her close-cropped, curly hair, her pale complexion and bright blue eyes.

Her cheeks now had a slight hectic flush. She caught her bottom lip between her teeth and gave him an assessing look before coming straight out with it. 'How would you feel about keeping a pet?'

Stuart felt a horrible conviction that she was not talking about a dog or a cat. He wondered if it was the whiskey on an empty stomach which made him feel dizzy.

'It was under my car. If I hadn't happened to notice something moving down there I could have run over it.' She lifted her shoulders in a delicate shudder.

'Oh, God, Jenny, you haven't brought it home!'

She looked indignant. 'Well, of course I did! I couldn't just leave it in the street – somebody else might have run it over.'

Or stepped on it, he thought, realizing now that he could never tell Jenny what he had done. That made him feel even worse, but maybe he was wrong. Maybe it was just a cat she'd rescued. 'What is it?'

She gave a strange, excited laugh. 'I don't know. Something very rare, I think. Here, look.' She slipped the large, woven bag off her shoulder, opening it, holding it out to him. 'Look. Isn't it the sweetest thing?'

How could two people who were so close, so alike in so many ways, see something so differently? He only wanted to kill it, even now, while she had obviously fallen in love. He kept his face carefully neutral although he couldn't help flinching from her description. *'Sweet?'*

It gave him a pang to see how she pulled back, holding the bag protectively close as she said, 'Well, I know it's not pretty, but so what? I thought it was horrible, too, at first sight....' Her face clouded, as if she found her first impression difficult to remember, or to credit, and her voice faltered a little. 'But then, then I realized how *helpless* it was. It needed me. It can't help how it looks. Anyway, doesn't it kind of remind you of the Psammead?'

'The what?'

'Psammead. You know, *The Five Children and It?*'

He recognized the title but her passion for old-fashioned children's books was something he didn't share. He shook his head impatiently. 'That thing didn't come out of a book, Jen. You found it in the street and you don't know what it is or where it came from. It could be dangerous, it could be diseased.'

'Dangerous,' she said in a withering tone.

'You don't know.'

'I've been with him all day and he hasn't hurt me, or anybody else at the office, he's perfectly happy being held, and he likes being scratched behind the ears.'

He did not miss the pronoun shift. 'It might have rabies.'

'Don't be silly.'

'Don't *you* be silly; it's not exactly native, is it? It might be carrying all sorts of foul parasites from South America or Africa or wherever.'

'Now you're being racist. I'm not going to listen to you. *And* you've been drinking.' She flounced out of the room.

If he'd been holding his glass still he might have thrown it. He closed his eyes and concentrated on breathing in and out slowly. This was worse than any argument they'd ever had, the only crucial disagreement of their marriage. Jenny had stronger views about many things than he did, so her wishes usually prevailed. He didn't mind that. But this was different. He wasn't having that creature in his home. He had to make her agree.

Necessity cooled his blood. He had his temper under control when his wife returned. 'I'm sorry,' he said, although she was the one who should have apologized. Still looking prickly, she shrugged and would not meet his eyes. 'Want to go out to dinner tonight?'

She shook her head. 'I'd rather not. I've got some work to do.'

'Can I get you something to drink? I'm only one whiskey ahead of you, honest.'

Her shoulders relaxed. 'I'm sorry. Low blow. Yeah, pour me one. And one for yourself.' She sat down on the couch, her bag by her feet. Leaning over, reaching inside, she cooed, 'Who's my little sweetheart, then?'

Normally he would have taken a seat beside her. Now, though, he eyed the pale, misshapen bundle on her lap and, after handing her a glass, retreated across the room. 'Don't get mad, but isn't having a pet one of those things we discuss and agree on beforehand?'

He saw the tension come back into her shoulders, but she went on stroking the thing, keeping herself calm. 'Normally, yes. But this is special. I didn't plan it. It happened, and now I've got a responsibility to him. Or her.' She giggled. 'We don't even know what sex you are, do we, my precious?'

He said carefully, 'I can see that you had to do something when you found it, but keeping it might not be the best thing.'

'I'm not going to put it out in the street.'

'No, no, but... don't you think it would make sense to let a professional have a look at it? Take it to a vet, get it checked out... maybe it needs shots or something.'

She gave him a withering look and for a moment he faltered, but then he rallied. 'Come on, Jenny, be reasonable! You can't just drag some strange animal in off the street and keep it, just like that. You don't even know what it eats.'

'I gave it some fruit at lunch. It ate that. Well, it sucked out the juice. I don't think it can chew.'

'But you don't know, do you? Maybe the fruit juice was just an aperitif, maybe it needs half its weight in live insects every day, or a couple of small, live mammals. Do you really think you could cope with feeding it mice or rabbits fresh from the pet shop every week?'

'Oh, Stuart.'

'Well? Will you just take it to a vet? Make sure it's healthy? Will you do that much?'

'And then I can keep it? If the vet says there's nothing wrong with it, and it doesn't need to eat anything too impossible?'

'Then we can talk about it. Hey, don't pout at me; I'm not your father, I'm not telling you what to do. We're partners, and partners don't make unilateral decisions about things that affect them both; partners discuss things and reach compromises and...'

'There can't be any compromise about this.'

He felt as if she'd doused him with ice water. 'What?'

'Either I win and I keep him or you win and I give him up. Where's the compromise?'

This was why wars were fought, thought Stuart, but he didn't say it. He was the picture of sweet reason, explaining as if he meant it, 'The compromise is that we each try to see the other person's point. You get the animal checked out, make sure it's healthy and I, I'll keep an open mind about having a pet, and see if I might start liking… him. Does he have a name yet?'

Her eyes flickered. 'No… we can choose one later, together. If we keep him.'

He still felt cold and, although he could think of no reason for it, he was certain she was lying to him.

In bed that night as he groped for sleep Stuart kept seeing the tiny, hideous face of the thing screaming as his foot came down on it. That moment of blind, killing rage was not like him. He couldn't deny he had done it, or how he had felt, but now, as Jenny slept innocently beside him, as the creature she had rescued, a twin to his victim, crouched alive in the bathroom, he tried to remember it differently.

In fantasy, he stopped his foot, he controlled his rage and, staring at the memory of the alien animal, he struggled to see past his anger and his fear, to see through those fiercer masculine emotions and find his way to Jenny's feminine pity. Maybe his intuition had been wrong and hers was right. Maybe, if he had waited a little longer, instead of lashing out, he would have seen how unnecessary his fear was.

Poor little thing, poor little thing. It's helpless, it needs me, it's harmless so I won't harm it.

Slowly, in imagination, he worked toward that feeling, *her* feeling, and then, suddenly, he was there, through the anger, through the fear, through the hate to . . . not love, he couldn't say that, but compassion. Glowing and warm, compassion filled his heart and flooded his veins, melting the ice there and washing him out into the sea of sleep, and dreams where Jenny smiled and loved him and there was no space between them for misunderstanding.

He woke in the middle of the night with a desperate urge to pee. He was out of bed in the dark hallway when he remembered what was waiting in the bathroom. He couldn't go back to bed with the need unsatisfied, but he stood outside the bathroom door, hand hovering over the light switch on this side, afraid to turn it on, open the door, go in.

It wasn't, he realized, that he was afraid of a creature no bigger than a football and less likely to hurt him; rather, he was afraid that he might hurt it. It was a stronger variant of that reckless vertigo he had felt sometimes in high places, the fear, not of falling, but of throwing oneself off, of losing control and giving in to self-destructive urges. He didn't *want* to kill the thing – had his own feelings not undergone a sea change, Jenny's love for it would have been enough to stop him – but something, some dark urge stronger than himself, might make him.

Finally he went down to the end of the hall and outside to the weedy, muddy little area which passed for the communal front garden and in which the rubbish bins, of necessity, were kept, and, shivering in his thin cotton pajamas in the damp, chilly air, he watered the sickly forsythia, or whatever it was, that Jenny had planted so optimistically last winter.

When he went back inside, more uncomfortable than when he had gone out, he saw the light was on in the bathroom, and as he approached the half-open door, he heard Jenny's voice, low and soothing. 'There, there. Nobody's going to hurt you, I promise. You're safe here. Go to sleep now. Go to sleep.'

He went past without pausing, knowing he would be viewed as an intruder, and got back into bed. He fell asleep, lulled by the meaningless murmur of her voice, still waiting for her to join him.

Stuart was not used to doubting Jenny, but when she told him she had visited a veterinarian who had given her new pet a clean bill of health, he did not believe her.

In a neutral tone he asked, 'Did he say what kind of animal it was?'

'He didn't know.'

'He didn't know what it was, but he was sure it was perfectly healthy.'

'God, Stuart, what do you want? It's obvious to everybody but you that my little friend is healthy and happy. What do you want, a birth certificate?'

He looked at her 'friend,' held close against her side, looking squashed and miserable. 'What do you mean, "everybody"?'

She shrugged. 'Everybody at work. They're all jealous as anything.' She planted a kiss on the thing's pointy head. Then she looked at him, and he realized that she had not kissed him, as she usually did, when he came in. She'd been clutching that thing the whole time. 'I'm going to keep him,' she said quietly. 'If you don't like it, then...' Her pause seemed to pile up in solid, transparent blocks between them. 'Then, I'm sorry, but that's how it is.'

So much for an equal relationship, he thought. So much for sharing. Mortally wounded, he decided to pretend it hadn't happened.

'Want to go out for Indian tonight?'

She shook her head, turning away. 'I want to stay in. There's something on telly. You go on. You could bring me something back, if you wouldn't mind. A spinach bahjee and a couple of nans would do me.'

'And what about... something for your little friend?'

She smiled a private smile. 'He's all right. I've fed him already.'

Then she raised her eyes to his and acknowledged his effort. 'Thanks.'

He went out and got take-away for them both, and stopped at the off-license for the Mexican beer Jenny favored. A radio in the off-license was playing a sentimental song about love that Stuart remembered from his earliest childhood: his mother used to sing it. He was shocked to realize he had tears in his eyes.

That night Jenny made up the sofa bed in the spare room, explaining, 'He can't stay in the bathroom; it's just not satisfactory, you know it's not.'

'He needs the bed?'

'I do. He's confused, everything is new and different, I'm the one thing he can count on. I have to stay with him. He needs me.'

'He needs you? What about me?'

'Oh, Stuart,' she said impatiently. 'You're a grown man. You can sleep by yourself for a night or two.'

'And that thing can't?'

'Don't call him a thing.'

'What am I supposed to call it? Look, you're not its mother – it doesn't need you as much as you'd like to think. It was perfectly all right in the bathroom last night – it'll be fine in here on its own.'

'Oh? And what do you know about it? You'd like to kill him, wouldn't you? Admit it.'

'No,' he said, terrified that she had guessed the truth. If she knew how he had killed one of those things she would never forgive him. 'It's not true, I don't – I couldn't hurt it any more than I could hurt you.'

Her face softened. She believed him. It didn't matter how he felt about the creature. Hurting it, knowing how she felt, would be like committing an act of violence against her, and they both knew he wouldn't do that. 'Just for a few nights, Stuart. Just until he settles in.'

He had to accept that. All he could do was hang on, hope that she still loved him and that this wouldn't be forever.

The days passed. Jenny no longer offered to drive him to work. When he asked her, she said it was out of her way and with traffic so bad a detour would make her late. She said it was silly to take him the short distance to the station, especially as there was nowhere she could safely stop to let him out, and anyway, the walk would do him good. They were all good reasons, which he had used in the old days himself, but her excuses struck him painfully when he remembered how eager she had once been for his company, how ready to make any detour for his sake. Her new pet accompanied her everywhere, even to work, snug in the little nest she had made for it in a woven carrier bag.

'Of course things are different now. But I haven't stopped loving you,' she said when he tried to talk to her about the breakdown of their marriage. 'It's not like I've found another man. This is something completely different. It doesn't threaten you; you're still my husband.'

But it was obvious to him that a husband was no

longer something she particularly valued. He began to have fantasies about killing it. Not, this time, in a blind rage, but as part of a carefully thought-out plan. He might poison it, or spirit it away somehow and pretend it had run away. Once it was gone he hoped Jenny would forget it and be his again.

But he never had a chance. Jenny was quite obsessive about the thing, as if it were too valuable to be left unguarded for a single minute. Even when she took a bath, or went to the toilet, the creature was with her, behind the locked door of the bathroom. When he offered to look after it for her for a few minutes she just smiled, as if the idea was manifestly ridiculous, and he didn't dare insist.

So he went to work, and went out for drinks with colleagues, and spent what time he could with Jenny, although they were never alone. He didn't argue with her, although he wasn't above trying to move her to pity if he could. He made seemingly casual comments designed to convince her of his change of heart so that eventually, weeks or months from now, she would trust him and leave the creature with him – and then, later, perhaps, they could put their marriage back together.

One afternoon, after an extended lunch break, Stuart returned to the office to find one of the senior editors crouched on the floor beside his secretary's empty desk, whispering and chuckling to herself.

He cleared his throat nervously. 'Linda?'

She lurched back on her heels and got up awkwardly. She blushed and ducked her head as she turned, looking very unlike her usual high-powered self. 'Oh, uh, Stuart, I was just –'

Frankie came in with a pile of photocopying. 'Uh-huh,' she said loudly.

Linda's face got even redder. 'Just going,' she mumbled, and fled.

Before he could ask, Stuart saw the creature, another crippled bat-without-wings, on the floor beside the open bottom drawer of Frankie's desk. It looked up at him, opened its slit of a mouth and gave a sad little hiss. Around one matchstick-thin leg it wore a fine golden chain which was fastened at the other end to the drawer.

'Some people would steal anything that's not chained down,' said Frankie darkly. 'People you wouldn't suspect.'

He stared at her, letting her see his disapproval, his annoyance, disgust, even. 'Animals in the office aren't part of the contract, Frankie.'

'It's not an animal.'

'What is it, then?'

'I don't know. You tell me.'

'It doesn't matter what it is, you can't have it here.'

'I can't leave it at home.'

'Why not?'

She turned away from him, busying herself with her stacks of paper. 'I can't leave it alone. It might get hurt. It might escape.'

'Chance would be a fine thing.'

She shot him a look, and he was certain she knew he wasn't talking about *her* pet. He said, 'What does your boyfriend think about it?'

'I don't have a boyfriend.' She sounded angry but then, abruptly, the anger dissipated, and she smirked. 'I don't have to have one, do I?'

'You can't have that animal here. Whatever it is. You'll have to take it home.'

She raised her fuzzy eyebrows. 'Right now?'

He was tempted to say yes, but thought of the manuscripts that wouldn't be sent out, the letters that wouldn't be typed, the delays and confusions, and he sighed. 'Just don't bring it back again. All right?'

'Yowza.'

He felt very tired. He could tell her what to do but she would no more obey than would his wife. She would bring it back the next day and keep bringing it back, maybe keeping it hidden, maybe not, until he either gave in or was forced into firing her. He went into his office, closed the door, and put his head down on his desk.

That evening he walked in on his wife feeding the creature with her blood.

It was immediately obvious that it was that way round. The creature might be a vampire – it obviously was – but his wife was no helpless victim. She was wide awake and in control, holding the creature firmly, letting it feed from a vein in her arm.

She flinched as if anticipating a shout, but he couldn't speak. He watched what was happening without attempting to interfere and gradually she relaxed again, as if he wasn't there.

When the creature, sated, fell off, she kept it cradled on her lap and reached with her other hand for the surgical spirit and cotton wool on the table, moistened a piece of cotton wool and tamped it to the tiny wound. Then, finally, she met her husband's eyes.

'He has to eat,' she said reasonably. 'He can't chew. He needs blood. Not very much, but...'

'And he needs it from you? You can't...?'

'I can't hold down some poor scared rabbit or dog for him, no.' She made a shuddering face. 'Well, really, think about it. You know how squeamish I am. This is so much easier. It doesn't hurt.'

It hurts me, he thought, but couldn't say it. 'Jenny...'

'Oh, don't start,' she said crossly. 'I'm not going to get any disease from it, and he doesn't take enough to make any difference. Actually, I like it. We both do.'

'Jenny, please don't. Please. For me. Give it up.'

'No.' She held the scraggy, ugly thing close and gazed at Stuart like a dispassionate executioner. 'I'm sorry, Stuart, I really am, but this is nonnegotiable. If you can't accept that you'd better leave.'

This was the showdown he had been avoiding, the end of it all. He tried to rally his arguments and then he realized he had none. She had said it. She had made her choice, and it was nonnegotiable. And he realized, looking at her now, that, although she reminded him of the woman he loved, he didn't want to live with what she had become.

He could have refused to leave. After all, he had done nothing wrong. Why should he give up his home, this flat which was half his? But he could not force Jenny out onto the streets with nowhere to go; he still felt responsible for her.

'I'll pack a bag, and make a few phone calls,' he said quietly. He knew someone from work who was looking for a lodger, and if all else failed, his brother had a spare room. Already, in his thoughts, he had left.

He ended up, once they'd sorted out their finances and formally separated, in a flat just off the Holloway Road, near Archway. It was not too far to walk if Jenny cared to visit, which she never did. Sometimes he called on her, but it was painful to feel himself an unwelcome visitor in the home they once had shared.

He never had to fire Frankie; she handed in her notice a week later, telling him she'd been offered an editorial job at The Women's Press. He wondered if pets in the office were part of the contract over there.

He never learned if the creatures had names. He never knew where they had come from, or how many there were. Had they fallen only in Islington? (Frankie had a flat somewhere off Upper Street.) He never saw anything on the news about them, or read any official confirmation of their existence, but he was aware of occasional oblique references to them in other contexts, occasional glimpses.

One evening, coming home on the tube, he found himself looking at the woman sitting opposite. She was about his own age, probably in her early thirties, with strawberry-blond hair, greenish eyes, and an almost translucent complexion. She was strikingly dressed in high, soft-leather boots, a long black woolen skirt, and an enveloping cashmere cloak of cranberry red. High on the cloak, below and to the right of the fastening at the neck, was a simple, gold circle brooch. Attached to it he noticed a very fine golden chain which vanished inside the cloak, like the end of a watch fob.

He looked at it idly, certain he had seen something like it before, on other women, knowing it reminded him of something. The train arrived at Archway, and as he rose to leave the train, so did the attractive woman. Her stride matched his. They might well leave the station together. He tried to think of something to say to her, some pretext for striking up a conversation. He was, after all, a single man again now, and she might be a single woman. He had forgotten how single people in London contrived to meet.

He looked at her again, sidelong, hoping she would turn her head and look at him. With one slender hand she toyed with her gold chain. Her cloak fell open slightly as she walked, and he caught a glimpse of the creature she carried beneath it, close to her body, attached by a slender golden chain.

He stopped walking and let her get away from him. He had to rest for a little while before he felt able to climb the stairs to the street.

By then he was wondering if he had really seen what he thought he had seen. The glimpse had been so brief. But he had been deeply shaken by what he saw or imagined, and he turned the wrong way outside the station. When he finally realized, he was at the corner of Jenny's road, which had once also been his. Rather than retrace his steps, he decided to take the turning and walk past her house.

Lights were on in the front room, the curtains drawn against the early winter dark. His footsteps slowed as he drew nearer. He felt such a longing to be inside, back home, belonging. He wondered if she would be pleased at all to see him. He wondered if she ever felt lonely, as he did.

Then he saw the tiny, dark figure between the curtains and the window. It was spread-eagled against the glass, scrabbling uselessly; inside, longing to be out.

As he stared, feeling its pain as his own, the curtains swayed and opened slightly as a human figure moved between them. He saw the woman reach out and pull the creature away from the glass, back into the warm, lighted room with her, and the curtains fell again, shutting him out.

THE DIANE ARBUS SUICIDE PORTFOLIO

Marc Laidlaw

Marc Laidlaw (1960–) is an eclectic American writer of science fiction and horror whose long career has included a stint in the cyberpunk movement and significant contributions to the popular Half-Life video game series. Laidlaw first started publishing idiosyncratic, hard-to-define short fiction in the late 1970s, but is perhaps best known for writing *Dad's Nuke* (1985) and *The 37th Mandala* (1996), which won the International Horror Guild Award. 'The Diane Arbus Suicide Portfolio' (1993) is one of a series of stories by Laidlaw with photographic themes. Laidlaw had 'always loved Arbus's photography' and was inspired by her sad but gripping biography. The story uses the weird as an entrypoint to appreciating Arbus's work.

'You'll like this,' said Schaeffer as he let Brovnik into the apartment. 'She was a photographer.'

Brovnik chuckled unhappily till the smell hit him; it fit right in with the buzzing of flies. The other cops' hard shoes clapped on the uncarpeted boards of the hall; their voices echoed in the cluttered flat. Brovnik walked slowly, as if in a sweltering museum. Dozens of unmounted photographs were thumbtacked to the walls, curled by the July humidity. Schaeffer went into the bathroom with everyone else. Brovnik wasn't in any hurry to learn the cause of the splashing he heard. He bent close to a picture of a white girl standing against a canvas tent, her head thrown back, arms spread wide, the hilt of a sword and part of the blade poking out of her gullet. The other pictures were just as freakish. He liked them.

'Come on, Bravo!'

He walked into the small tiled bathroom. Too many cops in it, and a humid jungle reek, tainted with carrion. Water dripped from the mirror.

'Give him some room, guys.'

The body slumped in the tub, mostly submerged, short-cropped thick brown hair matted on the surface like seagrass exposed at low tide. She was fully dressed. One arm floated, propped on a knee, the hand looking swollen and peeled. The water was murky pink. Streamers of red, like those little crepe-paper flowers you get in Chinatown; drop a clamshell in water so it slowly opens and a tissue flower unfurls. The room was too small and muggy. He clutched his camera gratefully to his face, confining vision to one small window on a distorted tunnel with suicide at the far end. Her other arm hung over one side of the tub, skin sucked in between the tendons. He nearly stepped in blood as he walked around to get a better angle. It was tacky, two days old, kept from hardening by humidity.

When he finished, the others came back in. He stood in the living room, smoking, agitated. Why? Because she was a photographer? He looked over more of the woman's prints. Dwarfs, giants, freaks, a man covered with tattoos. Wonder what kind of mind she'd had, to take pictures like this.

A few photos lay spread out on the couch, as if she'd been looking them over while the water was running. He didn't want to disturb them, but the one on top disturbed him. The last thing she'd seen? A picture of Death standing in a freshly mown field; Death as a woman in a Halloween skull, clutching a white sheet around her. Hell, she'd gone rattling around with a head full of death, hunting it with her camera. He couldn't understand a mind like that. With his job, it was different. He was a cop first, a photographer second, though these days he didn't do much of anything but photography and lab administration.

Schaeffer came up next to him, pointing at a picture of a shirtless Latin midget in a hat sitting on a bed with a bottle on the nightstand next to him. Schaeffer nudged him.

'What do you think, she slept with that dwarf to get his picture?'

'You're sick,' Brovnik said.

'Me? She's the one in the bath.'

'Bravo, hey,' came a call from the bathroom. 'You drop something in here?'

He walked back toward the bathroom, trying to see no more of the interior than he had to. Morrissey came out with a crumpled yellow foil film packet.

'Messy, messy,' he said.

'Fuck you, Morrissey. I'm shooting 35 – that's a 120 wrapper.'

'Where'd you pick that up from?' Schaeffer said.

Morrissey suddenly looked pale and stupid. 'It was under the tub. I – I remember right where.'

'You fucking idiot.' Schaeffer raised a hand as if to strike him. 'She was a photographer, too.'

Morrissey scurried backward into the bathroom, Schaeffer right behind him. Brovnik looked around the room at all the prints; most were square, two-and-a-quarter format, would have been shot on 120 roll film. Nice big negatives, real sharp. He had this little Pentax, light and quick, good enough for police work though it always felt too small in his hands.

He looked around the room for her camera while Schaeffer bawled out Morrissey, and finally found it in an open case behind the couch. He shivered when he saw she had a Pentax too.

How did rumors get started? How did they leak? Brovnik could never figure those things out. On the strength of a foil wrapper, the tabloids were claiming that the lady had somehow managed to photograph her own suicide. The press had called all day asking if the police planned to release the photographs. Denying their existence didn't help. If the department said it didn't have the photographs, the reporters asked who did. Who'd been in her apartment to take the shots? Did they have any leads?

Leads on a suicide? He had to laugh.

Brovnik was surprised that there had been any interest at all in the woman's death. He'd never thought of photography as 'art.' But apparently she was 'known,' and all this was just making her knowner. He wondered if she'd ever have guessed that sliding into a warm bath and opening her wrists would prove to be such a canny career move. Whatever her reasons, she hadn't wanted to flub the attempt; what was left of her blood had been rich in barbiturates.

Reading the papers, he learned a few things himself. Her name was – had been – Diane Arbus. She'd had a few shows, some critical success, though mainly she'd made her living as a fashion photographer. Hard to imagine how a mind like hers would portray glamorous models… wrap them in funeral shrouds, black veils?

In the lab, he looked over his own photographs with a more critical eye. The glaring flash had burned out the water in most of the shots, hiding the lines of her sunken body; hard to avoid that. He remembered how harsh the flash effects had been in her photographs. Deliberate? It must have been. She'd worked to get an effect like the one he came up with accidentally. That made him feel better about his pictures. She might've liked police work. Her interest in freaks and death and all that crap… reality. It would've been more than just a job to her. And how happy he'd be photographing gorgeous models all day instead of bloodbaths, car crashes, double homicides. God, give him an opportunity like that and he wouldn't waste it on dwarves.

Seeing things afresh, he felt inspired to go through some of his backfiles. Torso murders, decapitations, stabbings, mob killings. Not half bad, most of them. He kind of liked the grainy effects, the harsh lighting that sent deep shadows sprawling like duplicate corpses. Weegee had gotten famous with pictures like these. Not too surprising, really. People fed on this stuff. Consider the popularity of public executions.

A secretary opened the door and told him there was a call for him. No name. She put it through to the lab phone.

'Good evening, Inspector Brovnik. I understand you took some photographs of Diane Arbus in her bath.' A woman's voice, small, raspy and hoarse. 'I wonder if you'd be interested in a trade.'

'Who is this?'

'Just a friend.'

'Whose friend?'

'I took the other set.'

Brovnik didn't speak for a moment.

'Are you still there, Inspector? Or getting this call traced?'

'That was your 120 wrapper?'

'I photographed Diane's suicide. Twelve frames. The whole thing. Everything except the aftermath, really, and you took those. I'd like good copies if I can get them, to make my set complete.'

'And what about your set? Do I get a look at those?'

'As I said, we could arrange a trade.'

'You know, the investigation on a suicide is fairly straightforward. You telling me that someone else was involved, suddenly things start to look more complicated. You're asking for trouble.'

'She killed herself, Inspector Brovnik. She didn't have an accomplice.'

'What about you? You stood back and snapped off a dozen shots while your so-called friend bled to death?'

'Understand, she didn't want her death to be for nothing. She wanted those pictures taken.'

'And what'd she think she would do with them?'

'I can't answer that.'

'Look, I can't make this kind of deal, Miss–'

'You don't need my name. And if you involve anyone else, then you won't hear from me again. I got in touch with you because you're a photographer. I thought there might be some understanding between us.'

'Understanding?'

'Consider that I'm Diane's agent in this matter, Inspector. There has to be an element of trust. As an artist, you should be able to make the necessary intuitive leap.'

'Who said I was an artist?'

'You photographed Diane in death. Your eye has been changed… touched. I'm very interested in seeing your work.'

'This is crazy.'

'All right, so you need to think about it. I'll get back to you soon. I don't care who knows about the pictures once we've made our trade, but until then, you must act alone or it's all off. I'm eager for those pictures but I won't risk exposure. Diane wouldn't want that.'

'How can you be so sure what she'd want? I mean, look what she wanted for herself.'

'She was very hard on herself. Goodbye, Inspector.'

'Wait–'

But she didn't wait. After that, he had to live with his impatience for another week.

He didn't mention the call to anyone, contrary to his plans. He printed a duplicate set of the suicide photos, taking more care in the darkroom than ever before. He managed to burn some detail into the glare of flash on the bath water, enough so that he could see one of her hands with the fingers gently splayed beneath the surface, as if bathed in mercury. He worked long past his regular hours. Her curled prints were always tacked up in his memory, examples of an ideal he'd never known to strive for until now. He found himself working to extract subtle qualities of mood and tone from the negatives, fluttering his fingers beneath the enlarger lens, controlling contrast with split-bath developers – things he'd never bothered with before, except when making bad negatives into acceptable prints. Gradually he found the glossy bright snaps of death becoming utterly strange to him, unlike his other photographs which became more commonplace as he worked them over. These were beautiful, like paintings done in silver; morbid but alive in the way only photographs are alive. Finally he stood back from his handiwork and shook his head in disbelief, because he had made her poor drowned corpse immortal.

It was an awful responsibility. That night, late, the phone rang and he came awake to the reek of sulfur. It was on his hands and made his eyes sting when he wiped away tears. What had he been dreaming?

'It's me,' said the raspy little voice, and that was when he realized why it sounded so odd. It was a dwarf voice; gruff with age and tribulation, not squeaky but still small. This was one of Arbus's weird women.

'So it is,' he said. 'But it's the middle of the night.'

'I thought you'd be more likely to come alone that way.'

'What, now?'

'Have you got a pencil?'

He thought of telling her he didn't have the prints with him, but he found himself grabbing a pen and pad instead. He wrote down an address and agreed to meet her in half an hour. He was backing his car out of the driveway when he came fully awake and wondered what the fuck he was doing. Was this police procedure? He decided this didn't have anything to do with the department. This was for the sake of something else – call it moonlighting, like his work in the darkroom. He had to have something in his life besides a job, didn't he? Like Arbus, who'd shot models for a living and in her spare time went looking for freaks. Maybe she needed that, after overdosing on glamour all day. Maybe in his case, after the brutal repetitive ugliness of his day-today – dead junkies and hold-up victims who were a bit too slow (or low) with the cash – he needed something a little fantastic, something beautiful, like that silver glow he'd glimpsed on the surface of Arbus's bath, like the first rays of a silver sun about to rise, a hint of imminent revelation. He saw clues to that light hanging over the marble crypts of Brooklyn which spread away beneath him as he took the bridge; it was more explicit on the waters of the East River, increasingly lovely and plentiful as crushed jewels scattered over the black tombs of the Manhattan skyline. Then he drove down into the tunnel where the glare of fluorescents rubbed his eyes raw, dispelling all magic except for the sense of humid evil evoked by the sight of so much seeping greenish tile lining the tunnel walls. In his mind, water continued to drip from a mirror long after blood had ceased dripping from her dangling arm.

The address the dwarf gave him wasn't really an address. There were buildings on either side of it, in an alley, but the number itself did not exist. All he saw was a low wall of old brick topped by a spiked wrought-iron fence; an iron gate opened in the midst of it. Might have been a vacant lot behind that wall, anything. Shattered windows looked down from three sides, as if the rendezvous were nothing but the bottom of an airshaft choked with trash, castoffs. Not official business, no, but he was glad for his .38 and flashlight as he pushed through the gate into a cemetery.

He'd never seen the place before, not in years of patrolling the city on foot and in cars. He must have driven past – even down – this alley a hundred times and never noticed the wall and gate. As expected, it was full of trash; the old marble and granite headstones were shattered, chipped, vandalized, discolored. His shoes crunched through a fine covering of broken glass; it was like walking on the Coney Island shore, even down to the smell of urine. He flicked his flashlight over carved angels with brutalized faces and seared wings. Stubs of crosses with the arms snapped off appeared to give the finger to the living. Every beam he aimed into the tumble of graves sent off a hundred harsh new shadows. He couldn't be sure where he'd looked and where he hadn't.

He wiped off the lid of a relatively clean crypt and settled down to wait. With the flashlight off, his eyes adjusted quickly to the dark. His cigarette made the only human movement. So where was she? A dwarf could sneak around in here easier than a full-grown woman – but it would be hard to come soundlessly in all this glass. He laid the envelope of prints on the stone beside him and smoked three cigarettes before a shadow came out of nowhere. He jumped down from his seat and instantly lost sight of her among the stones.

'Who's there?' he said.

She came forward again. 'No names, Inspector. Of course, I already know yours.'

As he'd guessed, she was small as a child, her face a gray blur of blended shadows. He knew she wouldn't appreciate any light leaping on her.

Her hand darted out to the tombstone surface and stole away the envelope holding his prints. She slid them into her hand and made a frantic gesture for his flashlight. She turned away from him, crouched over and laid the prints on the ground. Shielding the light with her body, she switched it on.

He heard her gasp, then further sounds of pleasure. He tried to make out details he might use later to recognize her under other circumstances, but her silhouette was as empty as a doorway into a starless sky, with only little wisps of reflected light peeking through her spiky hair like bursts of solar flares. He grew impatient listening to her. She sounded like a starving animal wolfing down a huge meal.

'All right,' he said finally, 'you've seen enough.' As he stepped toward her, she shut off the light and jumped back. The prints lay on the ground between them like a dozen stray windows into a glossier world. He had the feeling that if he stepped on one he might fall into it – fall into that bathtub full of radiant blood. He could almost see the glare of the flash shining from the time-frozen surface. Even in black and white, it had a reddish tint.

'Come on, you said a trade. Let's have your dozen.'

She didn't move. He could tell she was measuring him, reading his character in a way he'd never experienced before, eating him up with the dark sunken pits in her face. He made a grab for his flashlight, wanting superstitiously to shine a beam into those hollows and fill them in with eyes.

She backed away, being small enough that an edge of crypt shadow neatly swallowed half of her. Another stupid move and the rest would disappear. Without the light he felt more helpless than if she'd taken his gun. He held his ground, stooping to gather his prints.

'I showed you mine,' he said, trying to keep the edge out of his voice. 'You're the one who talked about trust.'

'Mine didn't come out,' she said.

'What do you mean?'

'I mean the roll was fogged, all twelve negs burned black, pure white prints. Nothing on them. I thought I could bring them with me, but it didn't work.'

'Wait a minute. You telling me there's no trade?' Now he was pissed, and ready to make a grab at her. She was little, she could elude him. He'd have to be fast. 'Well fuck I'm giving you my prints.'

'I saw them, that's enough. They came out good. You're a fine photographer. I can tell how much work you put into them. And I… appreciate that.'

That was it for Brovnik. Her whole story of being an accomplice, nothing but a lie to get a look at private records. This was suddenly more than personal; he would make it official, too.

He hurled the prints at her. They curled off in twelve different arcs, like a blossom opening around him as he leapt to cut her off.

She gasped, spinning away, and found herself trapped in a corner where a tall family mausoleum backed up against the brick of the surrounding buildings, below a high row of broken windows. Nowhere for her to go.

He stooped for the flashlight, which she'd dropped. 'All right, lady,' he said, and switched it on.

The light caught her for a glancing instant, and that was all it took – all he got for his pains and for his memories. He saw that her skin was shimmery black, her short-cropped hair silvery gray, and the very centers of her eyes, brilliant white. Then she shrank to nothing and disappeared, like a little woman-shaped balloon deflating instantaneously to the size of a speck of lichen on the marble tomb, then even smaller, gone. The beam hit nothing but the chipped brick wall and a slab of marble with some cryptic gang hieroglyphs streaking the side.

He backed up, swinging the beam to and fro, up and down, looking for the crack she'd slid away through, the secret door that had opened to swallow her up, the rabbit hole, anything. Nothing. None of those things would explain what he'd seen, anyway.

In the time he'd had to look at her, really look – and it was an almost subliminal impression – he'd seen that she wasn't any dwarf. She had none of the characteristic squashed features, no stubby fingers or any of that. For her size, she was perfectly proportioned – like a normal grown woman who had shrunk in the wash. This remained true as she vanished: All proportions stayed constant as if she were zooming backward down a tunnel with her eyes fixed on his, until she blinked out. The last thing he remembered was her faintly wounded look, and her color… that shifting silvery black like nothing he'd ever seen in a person – though tantalizingly familiar.

Brovnik hunted through the cemetery till the sun came up, but he didn't find anything except his twelve dented, scratched prints. He shoved them in a crypt to rot and hurried back to his car. In the strong morning sunlight it was just barely possible to not think of her consciously. But somewhere inside, his mind kept going over the details; the cop inside him wouldn't quit.

It was his day off. After a few hours spent futilely trying to sleep, he went into the lab, fished out the negatives of the Arbus suicide, and studied them on the lightboard. The hair looked similar to what he'd seen in the flashlight beam – an odd shiny gray, cropped short. The skin was the same shade of silvery black that no negro's skin had ever been. But that didn't mean it was her. The face might have proved something, but he was spared the sight of her piercing white pupils staring out of his negatives because she'd slid face down in the tub. Still, when he looked at the spiky hair, he felt a chill he hoped wasn't wholly based on recognition.

The next few days passed with excruciating slowness as he waited for the sense of shock to move through his system and into the past so he could get on with a life of ordinary things. He had time off coming to him, and he took it. He went to the Catskills with an Instamatic camera and took color snaps of waterfalls and old bridges and empty inner tubes bobbing down the Esopus River. He didn't take any pictures of people. He met a woman in a restaurant bar who spent the night at his cabin; in the morning she was gone but he felt reassured because she had vanished in the usual way, while his eyes were closed. When he got back to the city after a week, he thought he'd put it all behind him; he thought he was refreshed.

His first night back on duty, a man shot his wife through the temples, cut the throats of his two-, three-, and four-year-olds, strangled the family Doberman (not necessarily in that order), and sentenced himself to life as a vegetable by badly misjudging the trajectory of his final bullet. The photography posed a number of technical problems for Brovnik, due to the cramped conditions, but he was working them out in a cool professional way when he happened to look through the open window onto the dark fire escape and saw the four of them standing there. Five, if you counted the dog. A tall silvery white woman, three little ones, and a four-legged mass of silver mist. Silvery white, with sharp white pupils, all looking at him as if he owed them something. It didn't make sense to him at first (and this was how his mind worked, hooked on little bits of logic he hoped might help him understand the larger problem) that they should all be silvery white, when the shrinking woman in the cemetery had been so inky black.

'What the fuck are you doing, Bravo? There's no pulse in that arm.' He looked down in horror and saw that he had been posing a limp arm – adjusting the dead to make a better picture.

He backed off and drew the camera defensively to his eye, aiming it at the mother's splattered skull. For the first time he noticed that she was black. The children were black as well. So was the Doberman. All black.

Lowering the camera, he saw five white negatives watching him.

What did she do to me? he wondered.

'Bravo? What is it?'

He didn't answer the other cops. He knew he wouldn't ever be able to answer their questions. He forced his way to the window and showed his camera to the watchers outside, let them witness him opening the back and exposing the film. He yanked out a yard of it, unspooling the celluloid, letting it go ribboning into the night with all the latent images burned out, never to be seen, sparing them his camera's bite of immortality.

As the woman in the graves had done, they shrank away to nothing. Five new stars burned briefly in the night, a bit too low to top the horizon, then blinked out.

'Brovnik, what the fuck is wrong?' Heavy steps came toward him.

'I have to get out,' he said, stepping through the window. Questioning cries followed him all the way down the fire escape to the street, where he walked away quickly from the lights of the squad cars, his camera tugging like a bloodhound on the trail of everything that had ever eluded him.

THE COUNTRY DOCTOR

Steven Utley

Steven Utley (1948–) is an American writer of science fiction and fantasy. Early on, Utley belonged to what would become the famous Turkey City Writers' Workshop, which also included Bruce Sterling and Lisa Tuttle (the latter also included in this volume). A Nebula Award finalist, Utley has frequently appeared in *Asimov's Science Fiction, The Magazine of Fantasy & Science Fiction,* and *Analog.* He is best known for his Silurian Tales, which chronicle the misadventures of a group of scientists sent back to the Paleozoic era. Collections include *Beasts of Love* (2005). 'The Country Doctor' is a bit of a departure for Utley, despite its archaeological bent: a creepy weird tale reminiscent of the work of Michael Shea.

Gardner was drowning, and strangers were laying hands on the bones of my forebears. I felt obligated to see that liberties weren't taken with my grandmother, my great-grandmother, and other good, God-fearing ladies, so I put the business on auto pilot and made the drive as if on auto pilot myself.

I viewed the visit as a familial duty, not a sentimental journey. I hadn't been back to Gardner in twenty-five years. I'd always told myself that, with my grandparents dead and their house taken over by obscure cousins-removed, there was nothing to come back for. Soon there would be nothing to come back to. The dam was completed, the waters were rising. Gardner was drowning.

Once in the town, however, I couldn't simply drive to the cemetery. It wouldn't have taken two minutes. Wherever you were in a place the size of Gardner, you weren't far from anywhere else, and now, especially, everything was smaller and closer together than it had seemed when I was a kid. But I found that I had to drive down my grandparents' old street, had to stop in front of what had been their house. I sat with the motor running and stared disconsolately. Throughout my childhood, though I moved wherever the military took my father, my grandparents' house, a big, warm clapboard pile, had remained the center of the world, the universe – home. My earliest memories were of being in that house, surrounded by relatives, loved, safe. Now it sat waiting for the water. My grandfather had been a carpenter, among other things; I could see his shed in back. There had been a vegetable patch back there, too. My grandmother had shelled a lot of peas and snapped a lot of beans from it.

The other houses on the block had once been features of a familiar landscape. Now, curtainless windows gave most of them a look of stupid surprise. One was carefully boarded up, as if the owners fully intended to return. The house next to it looked agape and miserable. Paint hung from it in strips. The owners must have stopped bothering with upkeep when they heard about the dam; finally, they'd just walked away. All but one of the lawns on the block were overgrown. A handful of people still remained, the die-hard element, determined to hold out until the water lapped over their doorsteps, and to keep their yards looking nice in the meantime.

It was three blocks to the cemetery, long blocks for someone dragging an orthopedic shoe. Nevertheless, I told myself. Nevertheless. I turned off the motor, got out of the car. The sun was at its zenith. There was no wind. A male chorus of cicadae sang of love's delights to prospective mates. The day felt and sounded exactly like all the summer days I'd spent in Gardner in my childhood. I put my hands in my pockets and started walking, slowly, stunned by the force of the memories crowding in on me. I remembered how my grandmother used to sit in a metal porch chair and, as she put it, have herself a little talk with Jesus while she snapped those beans. Sometimes she sang gospel songs. She only ever sang the melodies, but I had been to enough revival meetings to know the words to whatever she sang. Sometimes, hearing her, I'd stop my playing and sing the words while she hummed. . . .

My eyes began to sting. Gardner was drowning.

Around the corner had lived Blanche, who was my grandmother's age and whose relation to me was, then and now, unclear. Someone lived there still – a green station wagon with a dinged-up fender sat in the driveway, and there were curtains in the windows – but Blanche herself was long dead, killed in an automobile accident. I'd liked her a lot. One summer, she had given me the empty coffee can in which I buried my grandmother's dead parakeet Petey. I knew exactly where I'd scooped out Petey's grave and wondered what I might find if I were to open it now. Nothing, probably – at most, a few crumbling shards of coffee-can rust. Tiny little bones dissolve in no time. On the next block was the crumbling brick shell of Cobb's Corner Market, where I'd sometimes spent my entire weekly stipend, twenty-five cents, on comic books and a Coke. Dime comic books and nickel soft drinks – it had been that long ago, and it was all about to pass forever from sight and memory.

Drowning, drowning. . . .

More vehicles were parked by the cemetery than there were in the whole town. I saw many opened graves – it could have been the day after Resurrection Day. At least a dozen people wearing old clothes were working among the headstones. I knew in a very broad way what these archeologists were supposed to be doing here, and I did see individuals sifting dirt through screens or duck-walking around exhumed coffins with tape measures in their hands, but what I mostly saw looked like just a lot of hot, dirty shovel work with nothing scientific about it.

I came upon two youngish men at the end of the first row of graves. On the ground between them was a new coffin. Its lid was open, and I saw that it was empty. One of the men nodded a hello at me.

'How's it going?' I said.

'Well,' he said, 'it is going.'

I gestured vaguely around. 'These're all my relatives.'

They looked at me as if I'd caught them doing something naughty.

'Well,' said the one who'd spoken before, 'we're taking real good care of everyone. Mister–'

'Riddle.'

The second man pointed away and said, 'Most of the Riddle family's still located over on that side.'

'Yes,' I said, 'I know.' I did know; it was all coming back; I could have found the Riddles blindfolded, and the Riches and the Bassetts, too. I had seen both of my maternal grandfather's parents buried here, then his wife, finally his own self. The first Riches and Bassetts had been laid to rest here in the 1850s; Riddles came along after the war, when a lot of ruined Southerners were moving around and resettling. Relatively speaking, the concentration of Riddles wasn't great – Riddles, it once was explained to me, tended to die young and tended also to have wanderlust. My father had been orphaned when he was barely into his teens, and members of his line had come to rest in odd places throughout the South, the West, and as far away as the Coral Sea. The first graveside service I'd attended in the Gardner cemetery was for a young cousin of mine, Kermit, who one summer day had succumbed to the fascination of a fallen power line. The last one was for my grandfather.

I nodded at the new coffin. 'Who's this for?'

'Whoever,' one of the men said. 'We try to keep everything together, even the box somebody was buried in. Some of these old graves, though, you find a few splinters of wood and some rusty nails, nothing you could still call a coffin.'

'Is Doctor Taylor here?'

'He's somewhere around here.' He looked about and nodded off toward the south end of the cemetery. 'I think he's over that way.'

'Thank you.' The two men seemed glad to see me walk on. When I was a child, I'd sometimes been sent to spend the summer with my grandparents. My grandmother and great-grandmother had visited this cemetery often. Between them they must have known seven out of every ten people buried here. They always brought flowers, and usually they brought me. They'd move among the graves, place the flowers, murmur secrets to the dead or prayers to Jesus, murmur genealogy to me, life histories, accounts of untimely, often horrific, deaths – most of their anecdotes were imbued with pain and tragedy. Sometimes I was interested and listened. Sometimes I was bored, drowsy from the heat, and instead listened to the cicadae. The sound of those summers was one long insect song, cicadae and honey-bees by day, crickets and mosquitoes by night, punctuated by gospel-piano chords, hands clapping time, voices singing, 'I'm gonna have a little talk with Jesus, I'm qonna tell Him all about my trouble. . . .'

It kept coming back, coming back.

It came back as I passed Dr. Sweeny's headstone, which lay in the grass by the edge of the driveway. Nearby, a man wearing a faded plaid shirt was excavating the grave with a shovel. As headstones in this cemetery went, Dr. Sweeny's was pretty fancy, with some decorative cuts and a longer inscription than most.

> Dr. Chester Sweeny
> d. June 30, 1900
> Erected in respectful memory
> by those he tended
> these 30 years

Dr. Sweeny was the only doctor, the only Sweeny, and the only non-relative buried in the cemetery. I had been filled with dismay and disbelief the first time I saw his name on that stone. Until that moment, I'd thought that doctors were immune to sickness and exempt from death. Mammaw, I said to my great-grandmother, whom I'd been trailing past the rows, what kind of a doctor dies, Mammaw? 'Honey,' she told me, 'doctors die just like everybody else. Everybody's got to die. That's why the important thing in life's to be baptized in Jesus's name, so you'll go to heaven when you die.' But why, I demanded, do people have to die? She didn't answer, just looked at the stone, and after what was probably only seconds but must have seemed like a whole minute or a full hour to an impatient child, she said, 'Old Doc Sweeny. I went to his funeral. I was a girl then. I was nearly as young then as you are now.' She was in her sixties when she told me this; naturally, I couldn't think of her as a girl or imagine that she had ever been nearly as young as anybody. 'I remember because everybody in the whole valley come for it, and then's when I met your Pappaw for the first time. He didn't want nothing to do with me then, but later, well, I changed his mind. But that day everybody come to pay respects to old Doc Sweeny.' Was he as old as you, Mammaw? 'Doc Sweeny was as old as Methuselah. Why, my momma, that was your great-great-gran'maw Vannie Bassett, wasn't even born when he come here. My own daddy made the box to bury him in and druv it here in his wagon, and a man over to Dawson give this stone. Doc Sweeny was just as poor as everybody else and didn't have no money set aside. Seems like there never was so good a one as him again. He druv his buggy all over, day or night, rain or shine. Not like these doctors we got now. Poor as he was, too, he always had some candy and play-pretties for us littlens in his pockets. I remember him visiting my momma when she was sick, and when he was leaving, he give me a piece of peppermint candy and said, My child, my child. And I was a sassy thing then, just like you, didn't have no more manners'n a pig. Instead of thanking him for the candy, I just said, I ain't neither your child,' and she had laughed delightedly at the memory of her own devilishness.

Thereafter, throughout the remaining summers of my childhood, Dr. Sweeny occupied a place in my mind as special as the one he occupied in the cemetery. I soon got over his being a dead doctor, but I remained impressed by his anomalous presence in what was effectively an outsized family plot. It suggested to me that he must have been, somehow, one of us. Even now, he had power to fascinate me. Gazing down at his stone, I found myself wondering exactly what he must have done, besides giving candy and cheap toys to children, to so endear himself. Mostly just be there, I guessed, when folks needed a sympathetic ear and a few sugar pills. Doctors in Sweeny's day had done more nursing than actual doctoring. Much of the nursing was ineffectual, and most of the doctoring was downright savage. There was no Food and Drug Administration to look over a physician's shoulder as he dosed people with God only knew what. Maybe this particular country doctor had won his neighbors' trust and respect simply by not killing inordinate numbers of patients.

I tore myself away, moved on, and found Dr. Taylor and a woman squatting in shade at the end of a row. He was strongly built, balding, with a sunburnt face. She had long, reddish-brown hair tied back in a ponytail and was covered with freckles everywhere that I could see. A map of the graveyard was spread on the ground between them, with numbers and other marks scribbled all over it. None of the graves at this end of the row had been opened yet. I noticed four narrow, squarish stones set into the ground at the feet of two graves identified by a common headstone as those of John Hellman Rich and Julia Anne Rich.

'Doctor Taylor,' I said.

Both of them looked up, and I could tell from his expression that he didn't recognize me. We had met only briefly, weeks before.

'Doug Riddle,' I said.

'Mister Riddle!' He stood quickly, brushed dirt off his hands, started to offer to shake, pulled back suddenly. 'I don't know if you want to shake hands with me. I've been rooting around in graves all day.' He seemed genuinely flustered. He turned to the woman, who had risen with him. 'Gertie, this is Doug Riddle. My associate, Gertrude Latham.'

'I'm very pleased to meet you,' she said. She seemed as ill at ease as he. She had a wonderful accent, German come through the heart of the Deep South.

'Finding out what you came to find out?' I said.

Taylor made an attempt at a smile. 'In this line of work, you never know what you'll find out.'

'Some people,' I said, meaning mainly my irrepressible Uncle G. A., 'called this place Gardner Gardens.'

They looked uncertain, as if unsure they'd heard me right. He ventured to say, 'Oh?'

'The planting ground,' I said, then shrugged. 'Small-town black humor.'

'Ah. Yes.' Taylor smiled again, more feebly than before, and tried to make up the difference by adding a chuckle, with results that embarrassed everyone. My own smile began to hurt my mouth.

Gertrude Latham went for a save. She nodded toward Julia Anne Rich's grave and said, 'That headstone tells us a great deal about this young woman's life. Do you know anything about her?'

I glanced at the dates on the stone. Julia Anne Rich had died, age twenty-two, before the turn of the century, when my great-grandparents were children. 'I remember the name,' I said, 'from when I used to come here as a kid. I thought Julia Anne was a nice name –' I gave Latham an apologetic look '– for a girl's name. But I don't know anything about her in particular.'

Latham nodded at the grave again. 'Those are her babies there by her feet. Judging from the dates, she lost four of them in a row. The last one may have killed her.'

If this was archeology, I wasn't impressed. I felt sure I could have deduced as much from the information on the stones. Childbirth in the nineteenth century was perilous.

I said, 'There're more babies and mothers buried here than anything else. Lots of children's graves, too. Children used to die of everything. After World War Two, though, hardly anyone except old people got buried here. All the young people went into the service or moved to Evansville to work in the P-forty-seven factory. And they just never came back.'

The two archeologists were staring at me. There was something like admiration in Taylor's expression. I felt a sheepish sort of pleasure and could not help smiling as he asked me, 'Are you Gardner's official historian?'

I shook my head. 'But there was a time when I must've known the name on every last one of these headstones. I got to be a whiz at subtraction from figuring out by the dates how old people were when they died. And in the forties people did start going away and not coming back. My father went into the service and stayed in. And somebody in the family did go build P-forty-sevens, too. There were framed prints of the things hanging in a spare bedroom at my grandparents' house for years. Official prints, with the Republic Aircraft logo.'

'Mister Riddle,' Taylor said, 'we could use your knowledge to interpret this site. I'd appreciate it if you'd consider letting us interview you sometime.'

'You'd be what's known in anthropology as an informant,' said Latham.

Informant didn't have the ring to it that official historian did, but I was flattered all the same. There's little to compare with having people hang on everything you say. Anyway, I told myself, maybe Gardner was too small for a full-fledged historian. Nothing had ever happened here – nothing that mattered to anybody besides Riddles, Riches, and Bassetts, harvest time, tent meetings, weddings, funerals, somebody's barn being raised or burning down. No one famous had ever come from Gardner, or to it, for that matter. And it struck me then, with unexpected and shaming clarity, that I'd never made the effort to bring my own children or grandchildren to this place, that I should have been murmuring genealogy and tragic personal histories to them all their young lives, teaching them about family and the continuity of life. I should have been telling them, 'Every one of your ancestors lived and suffered and sometimes all but swam up waterfalls like salmon to make sure you'd be here today and the family would continue and the thread be unbroken. They were brave and wonderful people, and if you don't believe it, just look here at your great-aunt, your great-something Julia Anne, who lost four babies one right after another, which isn't even a record, and it must've seemed to her like the worst thing in the world to lose the first one but then she carried three more, suffered crushing loss every time, died a probably painful and possibly protracted death trying to deliver the last one –' And, 'Doug,' my wife would've said by then, 'Dad,' my daughter would've said by now, each with that same disapproving furrow between her eyebrows. I do get carried away at times.

I blinked the thoughts away and looked at the two scientists. 'So,' I said, 'what're you finding out?'

Latham said, 'We never really know what we've found until we've finished an excavation and, uh, put all the pieces of the puzzle together.'

'Is there a puzzle here?'

She essayed a smile. It was the best smile any of us had managed thus far. 'There's always a puzzle.'

'And you always find a solution?'

Her smile got even better. 'This is what you'd call quick and dirty archeology. We have to excavate by shovel, get as much information out as we can, as fast as we can, and move on. We don't have a lot of time. All we can do is figure out what the person was buried with and measure the bones. And we try to look for evidence of disease that would show up in the skeletal material.'

'Is there evidence of a lot of disease?'

Everything suddenly felt awkward again. I could tell by the look she gave Taylor that she regretted her last statement.

I looked over my shoulder and saw Roy Rich's grave right where I'd left it decades before. 'Here's a puzzle for you,' I said. 'What does this stone tell you about Roy Rich's life?'

Latham glanced at it. 'He died at age fifteen.'

'He was lucky to live that long,' I said. 'Or maybe not so lucky. I remember Roy. He was deformed. Not "differently abled," not even "physically handicapped." Deformed. His sister Betty, too.' I pointed to Betty's headstone, next to his. 'She died at age twelve. Those two had everything in the world wrong with them. I guess you'll see for yourself when you open the coffins.'

The two scientists were silent. It was very hot, and sweat gleamed on Taylor's pate and beaded on Latham's forehead and upper lip. I felt slimy inside my clothing. The cicadae would not shut up.

At last, Taylor said, stiffly. 'We'll write a report when we finish the excavation. If you like, I'll send you a copy.'

'I'm sure it'd be much too technical for me. Tell me something about my ancestors that I can go home and tell my wife.'

Taylor looked about as unhappy as any human being I'd seen lately. Latham looked as if she were trying to wish somebody away – me, of course. The more ill at ease they became, the pushier I felt. Maybe it was the gene for devilishness, handed down from Mammaw.

'It doesn't necessarily have to be something nice,' I said, 'if that's what's holding you back. Nothing you tell me can be any more horrible than some of the things Granny and Mammaw told me.' I looked over the rows. A truck pulled away from the gate, bearing some of my dead away to strange soil. 'Doctor Taylor, when we met last month, you said this ground's full of history, and this was a one-time-only chance to get at it.'

'Yes,' he said, slowly – warily, I thought. 'Yes, I did say that.'

'This is the last time I'll ever see this place. Living or dead, everyone's being scattered. I know it's true I'll be able to visit my relatives' new graves over in Dawson, but they'll be, they'll seem out of place over there. This is where my grandparents and great-grandparents were buried. This little spot in the road was their home. It was my home, too, for a while. Next year, it'll all be gone, the whole valley'll be under water. It'll be like Gardner never existed. So please indulge me. I'm not going to gum up the works for you, I really don't want to be in your way or bother you a lot, but I need… I need to carry away everything from here that I can this time.'

'We try,' Taylor said, 'we try very hard to be careful of the feelings of living relatives of the people we exhume. It's been my experience that relatives shouldn't, well, watch. And that despite what they say, they don't really want to know everything.'

'Look. There're a few chicken thieves buried here. There's even supposed to be a horse thief. And one of my cousins stabbed her husband with a big sharp kitchen knife when he beat up on the kids. He isn't buried here, but the point is, I don't have many illusions about my family. I'll try not to be shocked by anything you tell me.'

He manifestly wasn't convinced. 'It's not illusions I'm talking about. I'm talking more along the lines of –' he couldn't look at me now, so he compelled me not to look at him by pointing down at his map of the cemetery – 'grislier facts. Most people don't find it pleasant to contemplate, ah, physical abnormality.'

Pleasant or no, I almost said, I contemplate it with every step. I could've gone on, mentioned my children's and grandchildren's congenital problems, too. I did say, 'I'm not squeamish, either.'

He gave me an okay-but-I-warned-you look. 'There's evidence of pretty high incidences of birth defects, of bone disorders. Many of them are kind of gruesome and unusual.'

If he was expecting me to flinch, he was disappointed. If I was supposed to react strongly in any way, I failed. The only reaction I noticed in myself was some kind of inward shrug, meaning, approximately. Sure, of course, so what? In a community like Gardner, with no medical facilities and not even a resident doctor since Dr. Sweeny, there had been no avoiding the raw proof that flesh is weak, treacherous stuff. The maimed, the hideously diseased, and the genetic misfires had at all times been at least semi-present and semi-visible.

I said, 'Unusual how?'

He exhaled a soft, exasperated sound and said to Latham, 'Gertie, would you please take Mister Riddle over to where Dan and Greg are working and … show him.'

She almost managed to conceal her distress at finding herself appointed tour-guide. Anger flashed in her blue eyes, but she answered, 'Sure, Bob.'

We walked past the rows. Up ahead, I could see two men kneeling beside an open grave.

'Doctor Taylor,' I said, 'seems to think I'm made of glass.'

'Please try to understand. Working in recent graveyards is about the least pleasant job there is in archeology. It's very sensitive and very stressful, actually.'

One of the archeologists kneeling by the grave was writing in a notebook. The other poked at the contents of a coffin, yellow bones, disintegrating remnants of a dress. They smiled when they saw Latham, went blank when they saw me.

Introductions were made: the man with the notebook was Greg, the one doing the poking, Dan. They received the news that I was a relative without cheering.

Latham looked down at the bones and said, 'Is this one of the – is this one?'

'Yep,' said Dan.

'Would you please show Mister Riddle what you've got here?'

Both of the men regarded me doubtfully for a second, and then Dan said, 'Okay. Well, sir. Know anything about human anatomy?'

'Not much more than the foot bone's connected to the ankle bone.' I hadn't intended to call anyone's attention to my mismatched shoes, but Dan was the least-stiff person I'd met so far. He just nodded and turned to the bones and began speaking very easily. It was refreshing.

'I won't make this technical,' he said, 'and I'll skip the small stuff. Um, the long bones in your hand, how long'd you say they are?'

I glanced at the back of my hand. 'Three, four inches.'

'Close enough.' He directed my attention to the remains inside the coffin and pointed out an array of bones as long as cigars. 'These are the same bones, and there're the fingers. As you can see, it's a pretty extraordinarily oversized hand.'

It was almost an understatement. Whoever the dead girl or woman was – I looked for the name, but glare on the stone obscured it – she must have looked as if she had an oar up her sleeve.

'Typically,' Dan went on, 'congenital problems left the door open for all sorts of other problems. She must've been in pain her whole life. She was about eighteen or twenty when she died. Most of the others've been much younger.'

'There're really a lot of skeletons like this one?'

'Yep.' He watched me carefully now. 'Awful lot of 'em.'

'Enough to make you wonder,' said the other man, Greg, 'if the local drinking water isn't spiked with uranium dust or thalidomide or something.'

Latham shot him a thoroughly dismayed look. Greg cleared his throat and examined a page in his notebook very, very carefully.

'Actually,' I said, 'my family's probably just dangerously inbred.'

Latham and the two men seemed not to know how to take that remark. I let them twist in the wind, stared down at the tormented bones, thought, Roy Rich, Betty... I had sometimes glimpsed them through the half-open doors of their back bedrooms when my grandmother visited their mother and hauled me along. My cousin Dorsey would nowadays be called 'learning-disabled.' Aunt Jean was 'movement-impaired.' Several of her lower vertebrae were fused together; walking, standing, even sitting, all were torture for her. Once, I eavesdropped fascinatedly on a morbid conversation about her back and hip and knee problems and strange calcium spurs the doctor didn't know what to make of. Once, I was appointed to help her down the aisle at a revival meeting, at a pace glacial and excruciating even for me. The valley resounded with preaching on hot summer nights, and every household brought forth its lame, afflicted, dying, and sent them forward to be healed by faith. Summer after summer, I saw the lines of pain deepen around my aunt's mouth. I saw the microcephalic and the acromegalic, saw the man whose body appeared to be collapsing telescope-fashion, the man with the tumor that sat on the side of his neck like a second head, the woman with calves like some pachyderm's, the girl who was one great angry strawberry mark, saw it all and became inured to it. Faith never healed anyone, but no one ever lost faith. DNA had let us down, but Jesus would yet lift us up.

I was jarred out of this reverie as Dr. Taylor strode up in a hurry. He had a frown on his face and appeared not to notice me. 'Gertie,' he said, 'Rita's got something we better take a look at.'

He turned without waiting to see if she followed. She hurried after him, and after a moment's hesitation I went lugging after her. Two men and a woman with her nose painted white stood over a warped coffin. One of the men held the lid like a surfboard. We looked down, and Latham said, 'My God,' mah Gott.

Lying in the coffin was the apparently preserved body of an elderly man in a dirty funeral suit. Lying in the grass by the edge of the driveway was Dr. Chester Sweeny's headstone. I heard a roaring in my head.

The white-nosed woman, Rita, couldn't contain herself. She said, 'It's not a cadaver!'

Latham asked, 'What do you mean?'

'I'm saying this isn't a dead, embalmed body here! It's not a body at all!'

Rita pointed to the side of the elderly man's face. I peered and saw some sort of crease or seam under the jawline. It had come loose beneath one ear, and a flap of skin, if it was skin, was turned down there, exposing smooth white bone, if it was bone.

'Check it out,' said Rita, and used her thumb to push up an eyelid and show us a startlingly realistic fake eye set in a grimy socket. Then she pinched the loose flap of skin between her thumb and forefinger and pulled. It came off easily, exposing a bony tri-lobed bulb with openings that couldn't have been for eyes or any other familiar organ. Where the jaw ought to have been was a complicated prosthetic jaw complete with upper and lower rows of teeth and a fake tongue.

Nobody spoke for at least half a minute.

Latham looked at Rita and then at Taylor, whose frown deepened when he saw me. I said, 'What,' and then, 'Why did, why would someone bury this,' and couldn't think of a suitable noun.

I had to settle for gesturing.

'Prosthetics,' Rita said. 'The whole thing's goddamn prosthetics. Feel it,' and first Taylor, then Latham, and finally I knelt beside the coffin. I touched the right cheek. It felt gritty but… I pulled my hand away quickly.

Rita looked about wildly and said, 'Now what is that stuff?'

Latham said, 'It feels like,' and stopped and shook her head perplexedly.

'Fleshlike,' murmured Taylor, barely audibly.

Rita nodded vehemently. 'So what kind of stuff is it, Bob?'

'I don't know. Some plastic, I don't know.'

'This grave was dug and filled in nineteen hundred,' Rita said, 'and no one touched it until it was opened today. I know because Gil and I opened it ourselves, and we'd've known if it'd been disturbed. This thing was in the ground ever since it was put in the ground, back when nobody, nobody, could make plastic like this. '

'Rita,' Latham said, 'just calm down and–'

'Calm down? Gertie, nobody can make goddamn plastic like this now!'

Everybody was quiet again for a time. I looked around a circle of red sweaty faces. Taylor said to Rita, in a strangled voice, 'What's under the clothes?'

Rita carefully opened the coat and the shirt, exposing a dirty but otherwise normal-looking human torso. It was an old man's torso, flabby, loose-skinned, fish-belly white. Wiry hair grew in tufts around the nipples and furred the skin. Rita touched the belly gingerly, pinched up a fold, and, wide-eyed, peeled it right off like skin off a hard-boiled egg. The inner surface had many small fittings and trailed strands of wire as fine as spider web. Within the exposed cavity, where a ribcage ought to have been, was a structure like a curved piece of painted iron lawn furniture.

Someone muttered, 'What in the hell–' Maybe it was me, though I am not a swearing man.

Rita started to touch the structure, but her hand trembled, and she pulled it back. She looked around, gray-faced, and said, 'Too weird for me. Bob. Just too goddamn weird. I'm sorry.'

Taylor touched the bulb carefully, then the chest structure.

'Doctor,' I said, 'what're we looking at?'

'Well, obviously, some kind of articulated skeleton, but–'

'Is it, is this more – what, some birth defect, bone disease, what?' I was panting now, my heart was bursting out of my chest.

Taylor worried his lower lip with his teeth. 'No disease in the world twists ribs into latticework. Whatever this thing is, it looks like it was supposed to grow this way. I don't even think it's bone. It feels almost like… I don't know. Coral.'

'Coral?'

'Something.'

'Jesus, Jesus Christ,' and I pushed myself up. Latham looked after me and asked if I was all right; I barely heard her.

The roaring in my head was louder now, and I staggered away, ran as only lame men run, disjointedly, agonizedly, until I found myself standing shaking before my grandparents' common headstone. I sat down on the ground between their graves to let my breathing slow and my heart stop racing, stared at the stone, tried to draw some comfort, some something, from the inscription. Beloved in memory, Ralph Riddle, Mary Riddle. All I could think of, however, was furry pale plastic skin draped from Rita's fingers, the bony white bulb inside the headpiece, the false tongue in the false mouth.

'Are you all right. Mister Riddle?'

I started. Gertrude Latham had followed me and was hovering concernedly.

'Just an anxiety attack.' I punctuated the remark with a bark of mirthless laughter. 'I'll be back in a moment.' She choked on a reply to that, so I said it for her. 'You think I shouldn't go back?'

She all but wrung her hands.

'If you people are playing practical jokes–'

'We would never, ever, play jokes!'

'Somebody's up to something here! If this is some kind of, of stunt, you, Taylor, the historical commission, none of you will ever see the end of trouble. I can promise you that.'

'What do you think we'd possibly gain from a stunt?' she demanded hotly.

'Money, publicity, I don't know.'

'There's no money in archeology, Mister Riddle,' she said, biting off the words. 'Certainly not in this kind of archeology! You think we do this to get rich, to be on television?'

I was about to snap back, but then I saw that she was really angry, too, as angry as I was, maybe angrier. I got a hold on myself and said, in as reasonable a voice as I could manage, 'What is that thing?'

'It's not a joke!'

'Well, it's something, and it doesn't belong. If it's not a joke and not a box full of junk and not human – and it sure isn't human, or any animal, vegetable, mineral I've ever seen or heard about–'

'I'm sure there's a logical explanation,' she said, obviously not convinced herself. 'We'll be able to find out more when we get the… remains to the lab.'

'Yeah? And how long will that take?'

'We'll have to get all kinds of permission. It's going to be very complicated. Anything you could tell us about this Doctor Sweeny could be very important.'

'Doc Sweeny,' I said, and had to pause to clear my throat loudly. My voice was lined with wet sand. 'Doc Sweeny was the only doctor here for thirty years. My great-grandmother was at his funeral. She told me once the whole valley showed up to pay last respects. I don't know any more than what she told me and what's on his stone. He came here after the War Between the States. He died at the turn of the century.'

She didn't say anything for several seconds. Then: 'Where did he come from?'

'How would I know? Who knows if he ever said?'

'All right,' she said, 'then why did he come here?'

'Everybody's got to go somewhere.'

'But why here? We're not talking about your standard-issue nineteenth-century country doctor. We're talking about… God, I don't know what we're talking about. A guy with plastic skin, latticework for ribs. A skull like, like–'

She couldn't find the right word, if there was a right word, and the sentence hung unfinished in the air between us until I said, 'A skull like something. And a face like nothing. Those bones back there are the bones of a–'

'A Martian, for all anybody knows.' She was embarrassed to have said that, and I was embarrassed to have heard her say it. I couldn't look at her again for several seconds, until I heard her suck in a breath like a sob and say, 'Whatever he was, nobody caught on to him in thirty years. Thirty years! What was he doing here all that time?'

'Driving around the countryside in his buggy. Dispensing solicitude, advice, and placebos.'

'No, what was he really doing? Gardner's small, isolated, even backward.'

I could only nod. The roads hadn't been paved until the 1920s. There hadn't been plumbing and electricity in all the homes until the 1950s.

'There's no money to be made here,' she went on, 'and never has been.'

I nodded again.

'So why,' she began, and hesitated.

'Maybe he was stranded. Maybe the place just suited him.'

She appeared to mull that over for a moment, then nodded. 'Who'd've bothered, who'd've been able, to check anybody's background in a place like this in eighteen seventy? Why else except that a doctor, someone claiming to be a doctor and willing to settle here, would've seemed like a godsend? He could've given them anything he wanted to give them and called it medicine.'

I heard the roaring in my head again. I thought of my grandmother, breaking snap beans and humming. Are you washed in the blood? I murmured, 'Or candy.'

'What?'

The roaring in my head rose in pitch and blended into the incessant twirring of the cicadae. I thought suddenly that I knew the words to that song – it was a song of the need to obey the biological imperative; Keep your genetic material in circulation, the chorus went – and I suddenly felt cold and feverish.

I said, 'What if,' and then on second thought knew I could never go on and say what if Doc Sweeny had come to small, isolated, manageable Gardner from God knew where and become one of its citizens in order to become one with its citizens and had been accepted by them though the flesh of their children ever after twisted itself into knots trying to reject the alien matter he somehow had bequeathed to them, and those children, those who survived, had gone out into the world to pass along that same alien stuff to their children in turn, and –

So I said no more, only lurched past Gertrude Latham, and if she called after me, I didn't hear her. I wanted to be away from her and away from here, in my car, speeding away homeward with the radio turned way up and wind roaring past the open window. The waters could not close over Gardner soon enough to suit me. I didn't stop moving until I was through the cemetery gate, and then only because I put my bad foot in a shallow hole hidden in the grass and went down on one knee. The stab of pain in my leg and hip was so intense that I believed for a moment I was going to black out. Gasping, I dug my fingers into the earth, gripped it desperately. Maybe I was going to be sick anyway.

LAST RITES AND RESURRECTIONS

Martin Simpson

Martin Simpson (1962–) is an American writer who has won the British Fantasy Award and serves as the Director of the University of Florida's Reading & Writing Center. Ann VanderMeer published his first story, 'Last Rites and Resurrections' (1994), in her magazine *The Silver Web*. 'Last Rites' is a powerful meditation on loss that uses a naturalistic approach to the weird common to horror fiction from the 1990s. It subsequently became the title story of *The Third Alternative*'s first best-of anthology. The inspiration for the story came from Simpson's daily drive while an assistant professor. 'I began to get depressed by the amount of roadkill. Morose meditations led me to imagine the last thoughts of the animals.'

Every morning I drive the same route I drove when I still had to work. I take State Road 40 through the Ocala National Forest, forty miles from Barberville to just this side of Ocala. The road has two lanes, with a passing lane every five or six miles, first for the east bound traffic, then for the west. Each time I come to a passing lane, I pull into the slow lane and let everyone go by. I'm always on the lookout for dead animals.

The first dead animal's voice I ever heard came from a brown and white basset hound with a broken neck. He was lying in the grass beside the westbound lane in Astor, and I only noticed him because I had stopped behind a school bus that was picking up a couple of kids. The dog looked like Barney, my neighbor's basset when I was growing up on Lincoln Street in a small town in Illinois. The resemblance made my throat tighten; how long had it been since I'd thought about that neighbor, or his brown and white dog? When the bus's red lights stopped flashing and it moaned into first gear, I pulled my BMW off the road instead of following.

The dog lay on its side, his head lolling back at an impossible angle, one ear chastely flopped across his head, shielding his dead right eye from the sun that was just beginning to burn through the morning fog. I knelt beside him and patted his side. He wasn't bloated. He didn't smell. There was nothing wrong with him except for his neck, and it looked as if he might get up if I twisted his body and arranged his head just right.

I couldn't put him in the BMW; I had chosen the leather interior package, and who knows the mysteries of a basset hound's first few postmortem hours? It had to be the trunk.

I carried him carefully. As I leaned over the empty trunk I heard his voice. It wasn't an audible voice – the dog's mouth didn't move or anything – but it was English. It said, 'A motorcycle hit me twenty minutes ago. My legs are short and I never get along much faster than a trot; I meant to stay in the grass beside the road, but I guess I didn't. The motorcycle had a shield on to protect the rider from the wind, and the bottom of that shield hit me just beneath my ears. My body went numb right away, and I wish I had stayed in the grass beside the road.'

I stood cradling him over the dark gape of the trunk, but he wouldn't say anything else. Finally I gently lowered him in beside the spare tire. A muffled sound like gravel in a twisting sock came from inside his neck when I pulled back the arm that had been supporting his head.

I drove back toward Barberville, thinking: *This is it, Chris is taking his toll.*

When my son Chris was twelve years old, he knew more about chemotherapy and bone marrow and white blood counts than any twelve year old should. The doctors had diagnosed him just before he turned eleven. Very rare form, they said. Not responsive to traditional treatments, they said. Give me everything you've got, Chris said.

God, he was a beautiful kid.

Shortly after his twelfth birthday we all knew. So I quit my job and Sarah took three months off, and we took Chris all around the states, everywhere he'd wanted to go: DC, Denver, San Francisco. We went skiing in Aspen, walked through a stand of redwoods in Washington state, and visited Mark Twain's home in Hartford, Connecticut. The Museum of Modern Art in Chicago, the Alamo, the Liberty Bell, and the beach in San Diego all bored him. He loved Sea World, Pike's Peak, the view from the Sears tower in Chicago, and the arch in St Louis.

Before we could make it to New York City, Chris started fading. We brought him home, and in ten days he was gone. We buried him six weeks before the broken-necked dog spoke to me in gruff, phlegmy English.

As I drove back towards home with a dead dog in my trunk, I thought my grief had finally undone me. I'm not particularly good at expressing emotion. I had only cried a few times since Chris's death, but every night I went to bed with a heavy, brittle feeling in my chest, and every morning it was there waiting for me when I got up. Every day, on my way to work, I would ask myself: *How long will this last? How long can I stand it?*

And now, here was an answer. I fully expected to hear more voices on the trip home. The moss that hangs in grey clumps from trees alongside the road might whisper my name. The garage door opener, clinging to my visor just above and in front of my left ear, might tell me where to drive next. The sly windshield wipers might softly counsel suicide.

But I heard no voices on my way home.

I live alone in a small house with a back yard that slopes down to a small lake. Sarah and I had been in the process of splitting up when Chris was diagnosed. The funeral was the last time we had seen each other.

I got a shovel from the dusty-quiet garage and buried the basset in the back yard, in the shade of my magnolia tree.

Eight days went by before the next dead animal spoke to me. I heard it at the exact moment I saw it, a huddled mass in the opposite lane, yearning to breathe, period.

'A station wagon hit me,' it said, 'and my intestines blew out my asshole.'

The words came slower than the basset's had, and they were carefully enunciated.

I pulled over shakily, and when no cars were coming I pulled across the road and parked in the grass. It was a cat, grey and thick-necked, an unfixed male. Its intestines were where it said they were. It didn't have anything else to say.

I buried it beside the basset under the magnolia. The intestines had made transport and burial difficult and unpleasant. Since then I keep a plastic tarp in any vehicle I drive, and I never travel without a pair of long rubber gloves.

I am not the type to hear dead animals' voices in my head. Which is to say, I'm not crazy. I don't fit the profile of someone who is susceptible to the allure of the superstitions and mass-market voodoo of marginalised humanity. I've never bought a magazine in a supermarket checkout line, and I never read the horoscope, even for 'fun'. I don't believe in ouija boards, seances or tarot cards; I've never had my palm read; I've never even made a wish before I blow out the candles on a birthday cake. I don't believe that aliens live and walk among us. I do believe in God, but I manage to ignore Him until some disaster hits. Even then I am held in the grip of a cowardly self-consciousness, and I can't bring myself to pray with any fervor.

And yet.

Over the last four months I've buried nearly thirty members of the animal kingdom under my magnolia, and every one of them spoke a few well-chosen words to me, post-demise and pre-burial. I've interred a half-dozen cats, eight dogs, four raccoons (two couples, united in death just feet apart), three squirrels, and two armadillos.

I saw a man pulling a deer around toward the back of his pickup once. I stopped, suspicious that he had somehow hit the animal on purpose, not sure what I would do if he had. But the deer set my mind at ease.

'He couldn't help it,' said the deer, a medium-sized male with an unimpressive rack. 'I was running through the woods and I got carried away. I know better than to leap without looking, especially near a road. But I can feel God in me when I leap; I was meant for it. This man tried to miss me, and my feeling is: better to have leapt and lost…'

The deer wasn't the only dead animal with a sense of humor. Although two armadillos don't constitute a large enough sample from which to generalize about a whole species, I'd have to say the armadillo has a healthy, good-humored sense of the absurdity of its position in the world.

'Look at me,' the first one I found said. 'I'm basically a dinosaur, unchanged for millions of years. I should be sharing the road with a 1993 Saturn? That car has a micro-computer that controls its electrical systems; I've got *scales,* for God's sake. It's not easy being an anachronism.'

The second armadillo I found was severely mangled, a condition made more horrible by the animal's already naked, pink-and-grey vulnerability. I had to carry it by its tough rope of a tail; parts of it seeped and sagged all the way to my new truck.

'My only natural defense is to curl up into an armored ball and outwait my opponent,' the armadillo said. 'Not too effective against steel-belted radials.'

I never did go back to work full time after my last trip with Chris. I was a financial planner with one partner in our own small but reasonably prosperous practice. Two small business clients, a total of forty-five employees, plus a handful of couples that had been referred to us. I did a little of everything: set up IRAs, mutual funds, individual deferred comp packages, some tax planning. Sarah is a mid-level administrator and RN in an Ocala hospital, and we did okay. I put everything I could away, invested in the stock market. IBM in the mid-70s, Apple in the early 80s, small bio-medical research companies in the late 80s, tobacco stocks all the time.

When Chris was diagnosed I decided I didn't need to work anymore. When I finally came back, I kept a handful of clients whom I like and cut back to two mornings a week in a small office in Ocala. After the funeral and Sarah's departure, we went through a very adult divorce. Sold the house, didn't fight over money; we both have enough. I bought this medium-sized lot on the lake, with the little house on it, and Sarah bought a modest two-bedroom near her hospital.

After I buried the grey male cat in the sandy soil beneath my magnolia, next to the broken-necked basset, I sold my BMW and got a three year old Ford pickup. I put the tarp and rubber gloves in the back and began making a trip down State Road 40 once every morning and once every evening, just before sunset.

Sometimes as I'm driving I hear an animal but can't see it. I always pull over and search, but often I don't find it. In the course of one such search I realized that I could identify each species by voice. Some animals sound like you would expect them to sound, if you expected them to talk: dead dogs speak quickly and with tangled syntax that often produces circular sentences, while deceased cats are slower and more careful, measuring out the meticulous pronunciations of a Latin teacher. Squirrels communicate in staccato snippets that sound vaguely like Vietnamese to my ears. The posthumous speech of two other species I also associate with foreign language accents: the wry humor of armadillos comes wrapped in the harsh back-of-the-throat consonants of German, while clever raccoons trade in the nasal delicacy of French.

When I feel the occasional desire to go back to work full time, I entertain the notion of becoming either a medical examiner or a detective. My avocation has given me the appropriate mindset for either occupation. In the hieroglyphic carnage of State Road 40 I see patterns; the visceral geometry of each individual metal-vs-flesh collision tells a story that I can read with increasing acumen.

Single direct hits leave one dark blotch on the pavement, attached by fragile vapor trails of blood that stretch to where the body comes to rest after its short and final migration. More often there is multiple contact: a rear wheel finishes what a front wheel started, or the impact against a front fender ricochets the hapless beast against one of the dark humps and sinews of an undercarriage.

The worst accident scenes feature bizarre zigzag patterns that indicate a poor creature's careening path from one vehicle to another, sometimes from an unforgiving westbound chassis into an indifferent eastbound grillwork. After this sort of accident, the animal invariably confesses its confusion to me. 'Everything happened so fast,' it will tell me. 'I lost my balance and couldn't get it back.'

The 'best' scenes result from glancing blows, which most often produce quick and relatively painless broken necks. In many of these cases the victim literally does not know what hit it, and the bodies invariably have an attitude of peaceful drowsiness about them.

In a way, I feel better about my life now than I ever have. When I worked full time I was good at what I did, and I had a good relationship with most of my clients. But I had so little time for anything beyond 'maintenance': work, sleep, minimal conversation with Sarah and Chris. A forty-hour work week is a grotesque invention, if you think about it. That's just too much time. That much work insulates you from the rhythms of nature. I never soaked in the birth of a day at dawn or its death at dusk; I never sensed the slow turning of the seasons in the air. The birth, growth and death – of plants, of pets, of my own son – these things I never really noticed.

I probably spent more time with Chris than most fathers spend with their kids. We went to Disney World and the beach, saw some spring training games in St Pete, had supper together as a family at least three or four nights a week. I loved him fiercely from the moment he was born, but that feeling always struck me as biological, instinctive. Later, as his personality developed, I found him likeable; in his innocence he found me wise. Even after Sarah and I began to grow apart she said I was great with him. The night after he died she told me she felt he never loved her as much as he did me. We were sitting across from each other at the kitchen table when she said this, the overhead light cruelly exposing the lines on her forehead and her dark-circled eyes. I'll never forget the misery in her voice; I have no idea if she was right.

The dead animals I talk with show no signs of self-reproach, and very little concern for the mates and offspring they leave behind. Mostly they tell me the stories of their deaths. Sometimes an animal will spend its last energy regaling me with descriptions of the things it loved most on earth. One squirrel rivalled Wordsworth with her posthumous paeon to a kind of small nut that she favoured. Her sensual description – the tender cream of its waxy interior, the ripe brown smoothness of its outer shell, the delicate cap that sheltered its rounded top – was mesmerizing. The aesthetic alienness of a tin can, stripped of its wrapping and missing its top, elicited the fascinated admiration of one raccoon.

I used to be troubled by the gore that I see on State Road 40, but it doesn't bother me anymore. Partly, I suspect, because the mind can adjust to most any situation after enough repeated exposure; ask a paramedic, or a trauma surgeon in an emergency room, or a mortician. But part of my newfound ability to face the bloody wreckage left by violent collisions comes from the animals' own nonchalance. Not a single animal has ever dwelt in self-pity or compulsively bemoaned its mortal wounds to me. In fact, they demonstrate a remarkable equanimity about the physical processes their bodies undergo after death as well. Sometimes I come across their bodies shortly after they die, but most often I don't arrive until after at least the first few flies and worms have begun their humble ministrations. I have never heard an animal begrudge those scavengers their due. After four months on State Road 40, what doesn't bother my dead charges usually doesn't bother me.

The one exception was when I came upon an orange female tabby just before sunset a quarter mile east of the St John's river. I pulled over immediately, but it took me ten minutes to find her. She had been hit in the hindquarters, but crawled into the deep grass beside a fence post before giving up the ghost, or whatever it is animals give up when they die.

'This will be hard on you,' she warned me as I bent over her and stared at her distended abdomen. 'Two males and three females,' she said. 'I would have delivered them in eight days, but a van hit my legs and now there's no hope for them. One of the females wouldn't have made it anyway, but the others were fine.'

I knelt beside her and felt the tiny waves and ripples from inside her. 'Maybe it's not too late for all of them,' I said, wondering where a caesarean incision would be made on a cat.

'A mother knows these things,' she said in a very tired voice. 'This will be hard on you.' She said no more.

The first kitten died just as I laid the mother on the cold corrugations of my truck's bed. It started mewling the moment it died – too young, I suppose, to have the power of speech.

My house is less than nine miles from the St John's river, but by the time I got home a chorus of pitiful mewling filled my head. Five small dead voices. After a moment there were only four, then three. By the time I had dug a small sandy hollow – outside the shady reach of the magnolia's furthest limb now – the last voice had died away. The tabby had been right. It had been hard on me.

That night I awoke from a nightmare listening to the echoes of five pre-verbal voices. I put on some clothes and walked into the back yard. The sounds and smells of two in the morning always fill me with the hoarded privilege of sweet secrecy, and I started to walk down to the lake. As I passed the magnolia, I sensed a stirring. I knew without looking that small eyes were opening, small limbs being stretched.

I kept walking, afraid that if I stopped, or turned, or squinted into the shadows, the spell would be broken. I heard behind and around me the soft rustling of many paws, padded and rough, three- and four-toed. At the water's edge I headed east. I dared my first look at my spectral companions after I had moved halfway around the lake. A raccoon trundled along on the ribbon of packed sand to my left. To my right five kittens trailed on unsteady legs behind their mother.

I made a complete circle around the lake that night, and when I got back into my bed, the tightness in my chest was gone for the first time since Chris died.

Tonight I pulled into my driveway with a bloated cocker spaniel in the back of the truck to find Sarah's car parked there. She got up from where she had been sitting on the porch and walked over to meet me as I got out of the truck. She smelled the dog and stopped a couple of yards away.

'What is that?'

I shut the door and walked back toward the bed. 'Dead dog. Found him a couple of miles down 40.'

'Why did you bring him here?' she asked, up on her toes to get a glimpse of the body.

'You won't want to see this,' I said. She turned away quickly when I lifted him and started for the corner of the house. 'Why don't you go inside while I take care of this? I'll be in in just a minute.'

Digging is easy in sandy North Florida, and in ten minutes I stepped into the kitchen and took a drink of the ice water Sarah had poured for me. I went into the bathroom and washed my face and arms, and returned to the chair across the kitchen table from my ex-wife.

'How many are there?' she finally asked. She was looking out the sliding glass door toward the magnolia tree.

'More than twenty,' I said. I didn't know what else to say.

'Why?' she said.

'It makes me feel good.' She stared at me. 'It seems like they deserve better than to just lie beside the road and rot.'

I watched her while she thought about that, and I considered what a fragile thing a marriage is. It's as easily killed as any of those animals in the back yard. She sat across from me and I couldn't begin to tell her a true answer to her question. What would she think if I said that the animals talked to me after they died? If I said that I was their caretaker, their bereaved, their final confessor?

After some reflection, Sarah let the subject drop. She started to talk about what had brought her here. She said she had needed to be alone for a while after the funeral, to sort things out. She talked about being mad at Chris for dying, about blaming me, and about sleeping too much. She talked about getting a prescription for Valium from her doctor, about numbly going through the motions at work, and about loneliness.

As she talked I found that I still loved her, and that I had missed her. Some clinical part of my mind took note of the details of her face and body, instantly familiar again, but I felt no sexual attraction to her. I suppose that my administration of the last rites so often in the previous months imbued me with something of the priest's mortification of the flesh. In the absence of physical desire, though, I still found myself wanting Sarah back.

Soon she tentatively raised the subject of our marriage. She started to leave long pauses in her sentences, which I started to fill. We gradually realized that we both wanted to try again, but neither of us knew how. The wounds and grievances of a severed marriage rose up and silenced us. My mind was full, but I was mute. I expected her to leave.

But she said something about Chris, and I said something I remembered him doing, and before I knew it she was crying. Soon talk and memories and tears poured out of both of us and filled my small house on the lake.

After three hours of this a strange formality settled over both of us, and we both knew it was enough for tonight.

'I should be going,' she said, getting up. 'I have to be in at eight tomorrow.'

'Okay.' I followed her to the door, and we both felt stiff and self-conscious. I knew then that Chris was still between us, and that he would be for some time.

She found her keys and we stepped out onto the front porch. She looked at her car, and then down at her keys, and then back up at me. I kissed her, but the kiss didn't kill the awkwardness, and she stepped off the porch.

'I'll see you again soon?' she asked.

'I hope so,' I said.

She got into her car, and then leaned back out. 'I'll be extra careful to watch for animals crossing the road.'

'Please,' I said.

The car retreated down my driveway, and she gave me a little wave. After she was on the road and out of sight I stood on the porch and listened to the receding sounds of her car. Finally there were only the sounds of the breeze and the night. I stepped back into my house.

A garden of dead animals blooms in my back yard. Some nights when I'm walking around the lake, they just show up. I never know when it's going to happen. At first I thought maybe it happened the same time of the month. Moon phases or something. But that wasn't it. Then I thought maybe it had something to do with the weather, but that couldn't be, because sometimes they materialize after dry days and cloudless sunsets, and sometimes after rain and low skies. I only know it's happening again once I'm walking in the back yard and find myself surrounded by them. They pad all around me on soft feet, and each retains its personality. The squirrels maintain their small, nervous movements, the dogs their manic sociability, the raccoon its oddly masked guilelessness, the armadillo its impervious dignity. The cats stalk and pounce, and deep in their throats they softly hum their rightness with, and in, the world.

On such nights I walk among them and do not willingly go back indoors, St Francis in the final stages of mourning. I think Sarah's coming back, but I will still walk around the lake on nights when I can't sleep.

One night, I hope, when I am walking with them, we'll be joined by another.

Will he look in my eyes, in that quiet, crowded yard, and wonder at his presence there, and know me?

THE OCEAN AND ALL ITS DEVICES

William Browning Spencer

William Browning Spencer (1946–) is an award-winning American writer living in Austin, Texas. His weird tales often contain an undercurrent of dark humor while novels like 1995's quirky *Résumé With Monsters* and *Zod Wallop* seem both *sui generis* and steeped in the history of strange fiction. In 2005, his short story 'Pep Talk' was turned into a short film for Project Greenlight and premiered at the Santa Fe Film Festival in December 2006. 'The Ocean and All of Its Devices' (1994), about a strange family secret at an off-season hotel, is typical of Spencer's work: effortless, understated, at times terrifying, and nicely updating the weird tales tradition.

Left to its own enormouas devices the sea
in timeless reverie conceives of life
being itself the world in pantomime.
Lloyd Frankenberg, *The Sea*

The hotel's owner and manager, George Hume, sat on the edge of his bed and smoked a cigarette. 'The Franklins arrived today,' he said.

'Regular as clockwork,' his wife said.

George nodded. 'Eight years now. And why? Why ever do they come?'

George Hume's wife, an ample woman with soft, motherly features, sighed. 'They seem to get no pleasure from it, that's for certain. Might as well be a funeral they come for.'

The Franklins always arrived in late fall, when the beaches were cold and empty and the ocean, under dark skies, reclaimed its terrible majesty. The hotel was almost deserted at this time of year, and George had suggested closing early for the winter. Mrs. Hume had said, 'The Franklins will be coming, dear.'

So what? George might have said. Let them find other accommodations this year. But he didn't say that. They were sort of a tradition, the Franklins, and in a world so fraught with change, one just naturally protected the rare, enduring pattern.

They were a reserved family who came to this quiet hotel in North Carolina like refugees seeking safe harbor. George couldn't close early and send the Franklins off to some inferior establishment. Lord, they might wind up at The Cove with its garish lagoon pool and gaudy tropical lounge. That wouldn't suit them at all.

The Franklins (husband, younger wife, and pale, delicate-featured daughter) would dress rather formally and sit in the small opened section of the dining room – the rest of the room shrouded in dust covers while Jack, the hotel's aging waiter and handyman, would stand off to one side with a bleak, stoic expression.

Over the years George had come to know many of his regular guests well. But the Franklins had always remained aloof and enigmatic. Mr. Greg Franklin was a man in his mid or late forties, a handsome man, tall – over six feet – with precise, slow gestures and an oddly uninflected voice, as though he were reading from some internal script that failed to interest him. His much younger wife was stunning, her hair massed in brown ringlets, her eyes large and luminous and containing something like fear in their depths. She spoke rarely, and then in a whisper, preferring to let her husband talk.

Their child, Melissa, was a dark-haired girl – twelve or thirteen now, George guessed – a girl as pale as the moon's reflection in a rain barrel. Always dressed impeccably, she was as quiet as her mother, and George had the distinct impression, although he could not remember being told this by anyone, that she was sickly, that some traumatic infant's illness had almost killed her and so accounted for her methodical, wounded economy of motion.

George ushered the Franklins from his mind. It was late. He extinguished his cigarette and walked over to the window. Rain blew against the glass, and lightning would occasionally illuminate the white-capped waves.

'Is Nancy still coming?' Nancy, their daughter and only child, was a senior at Duke University. She had called the week before saying she might come and hang out for a week or two.

'As far as I know,' Mrs. Hume said. 'You know how she is. Everything on a whim. That's your side of the family, George.'

George turned away from the window and grinned. 'Well, I can't accuse your family of ever acting impulsively – although it would do them a world of good. Your family packs a suitcase to go to the grocery store.'

'And your side steals a car and goes to California without a toothbrush or a prayer.'

This was an old, well-worked routine, and they indulged it as they readied for bed. Then George turned off the light and the darkness brought silence.

It was still raining in the morning when George Hume woke. The violence of last night's thunderstorm had been replaced by a slow, business-like drizzle. Looking out the window, George saw the Franklins walking on the beach under black umbrellas. They were a cheerless sight. All three of them wore dark raincoats, and they might have been fugitives from some old Bergman film, inevitably tragic, moving slowly across a stark landscape.

When most families went to the beach, it was a more lively affair.

George turned away from the window and went into the bathroom to shave. As he lathered his face, he heard the boom of a radio, rock music blaring from the adjoining room, and he assumed, correctly, that his twenty-one-year-old daughter Nancy had arrived as planned.

Nancy had not come alone. 'This is Steve,' she said when her father sat down at the breakfast table.

Steve was a very young man – the young were getting younger – with a wide-eyed, waxy expression and a blond mustache that looked like it could be wiped off with a damp cloth.

Steve stood up and said how glad he was to meet Nancy's father. He shook George's hand enthusiastically, as though they had just struck a lucrative deal.

'Steve's in law school,' Mrs. Hume said, with a proprietary delight that her husband found grating.

Nancy was complaining. She had, her father thought, always been a querulous girl, at odds with the way the world was.

'I can't believe it,' she was saying. 'The whole mall is closed. The only – and I mean only – thing around here that is open is that cheesy little drugstore, and nobody actually buys anything in there. I know that, because I recognize stuff from when I was six. Is this some holiday I don't know about or what?'

'Honey, it's the off season. You know everything closes when the tourists leave.'

'Not the for-Christ-sakes mall!' Nancy said. 'I can't believe it.' Nancy frowned. 'This must be what Russia is like,' she said, closing one eye as smoke from her cigarette slid up her cheek.

George Hume watched his daughter gulp coffee. She was not a person who needed stimulants. She wore an ancient gray sweater and sweatpants. Her blonde hair was chopped short and ragged and kept in a state of disarray by the constant furrowing of nervous fingers. She was, her father thought, a pretty girl in disguise.

That night, George discovered that he could remember nothing of the spy novel he was reading, had forgotten, in fact, the hero's name. It was as though he had stumbled into a cocktail party in the wrong neighborhood, all strangers to him, the gossip meaningless.

He put the book on the nightstand, leaned back on the pillow, and said. 'This is her senior year. Doesn't she have classes to attend?'

His wife said nothing.

He sighed. 'I suppose they are staying in the same room.'

'Dear, I don't know,' Mrs. Hume said. 'I expect it is none of our business.'

'If it is not our business who stays in our hotel, then who in the name of hell's business is it?'

Mrs. Hume rubbed her husband's neck. 'Don't excite yourself, dear. You know what I mean. Nancy is a grown-up, you know.'

George did not respond to this and Mrs. Hume, changing the subject, said, 'I saw Mrs. Franklin and her daughter out walking on the beach again today. I don't know where Mr. Franklin was. It was pouring, and there they were, mother and daughter. You know...' Mrs. Hume paused. 'It's like they were waiting for something to come out of the sea. Like a vigil they were keeping. I've thought it before, but the notion was particularly strong today. I looked out past them, and there seemed no separation between the sea and the sky, just a black wall of water.' Mrs. Hume looked at herself in the dresser's mirror, as though her reflection might clarify matters. 'I've lived by the ocean all my life, and I've just taken it for granted, George. Suddenly it gave me the shivers. Just for a moment. I thought, Lord, how big it is, lying there cold and black, like some creature that has slept at your feet so long you never expect it to wake, have forgotten that it might be brutal, even vicious.'

'It's all this rain,' her husband said, hugging her and drawing her to him. 'It can make a person think some black thoughts.'

George left off worrying about his daughter and her young man's living arrangements, and in the morning, when Nancy and Steve appeared for breakfast, George didn't broach the subject – not even to himself.

Later that morning, he watched them drive off in Steve's shiny sports car – rich parents, lawyers themselves? – bound for Wilmington and shopping malls that were open.

The rain had stopped, but dark, massed clouds over the ocean suggested that this was a momentary respite. As George studied the beach, the Franklins came into view. They marched directly toward him, up and over the dunes, moving in a soldierly, clipped fashion. Mrs. Franklin was holding her daughter's hand and moving at a brisk pace, almost a run, while her husband faltered behind, his gait hesitant, as though uncertain of the wisdom of catching up.

Mrs. Franklin reached the steps and marched up them, her child tottering in tow, her boot heels sounding hollowly on the wood planks. George nodded, and she passed without speaking, seemed not to see him. In any event, George Hume would have been unable to speak. He was accustomed to the passive, demure countenance of this self-possessed woman, and the expression on her face, a wild distorting emotion, shocked and confounded him. It was an unreadable emotion, but its intensity was extraordinary and unsettling.

George had not recovered from the almost physical assault of Mrs. Franklin's emotional state, when her husband came up the stairs, nodded curtly, muttered something, and hastened after his wife.

George Hume looked after the retreating figures. Mr. Greg Franklin's face had been a mask of cold civility, none of his wife's passion written there, but the man's appearance was disturbing in its own way. Mr. Franklin had been soaking wet, his hair plastered to his skull, his overcoat dripping, the reek of salt water enfolding him like a shroud.

George walked on down the steps and out to the beach. The ocean was always some consolation, a quieting influence, but today it seemed hostile.

The sand was still wet from the recent rains and the footprints of the Franklins were all that marred the smooth expanse. George saw that the Franklins had walked down the beach along the edge of the tide and returned at a greater distance from the water. He set out in the wake of their footprints, soon lost to his own thoughts. He thought about his daughter, his wild Nancy, who had always been boy-crazy. At least this one didn't have a safety-pin through his ear or play in a rock band. *So lighten up*, George advised himself.

He stopped. The tracks had stopped. Here is where the Franklins turned and headed back to the hotel, walking higher up the beach, closer to the weedy debris-laden dunes.

But it was not the ending of the trail that stopped George's own progress down the beach. In fact, he had forgotten that he was absently following the Franklin's spore.

It was the litter of dead fish that stopped him. They were scattered at his feet in the tide. Small ghost crabs had already found the corpses and were laying their claims.

There might have been a hundred bodies. It was difficult to say, for not one of the bodies was whole. They had been hacked into many pieces, diced by some impossibly sharp blade that severed a head cleanly, flicked off a tail or dorsal fin. Here a scaled torso still danced in the sand, there a pale eye regarded the sky.

Crouching in the sand, George examined the bodies. He stood up, finally, as the first large drops of rain plunged from the sky. No doubt some fishermen had called it a day, tossed their scissored bait and gone home.

That this explanation did not satisfy George Hume was the result of a general sense of unease. *Too much rain.*

It rained sullenly and steadily for two days during which time George saw little of his daughter and her boyfriend. Nancy apparently had the young man on a strict regime of shopping, tourist attractions, and movies, and she was undaunted by the weather.

The Franklins kept inside, appearing briefly in the dining room for bodily sustenance and then retreating again to their rooms. And whatever did they do there? Did they play solitaire? Did they watch old reruns on TV?

On the third day, the sun came out, brazen, acting as though it had never been gone, but the air was colder. The Franklins, silhouetted like black crows on a barren field, resumed their shoreline treks.

Nancy and Steve rose early and were gone from the house before George arrived at the breakfast table. George spent the day endeavoring to satisfy the IRS's notion of a small businessman's obligations, and he was in a foul mood by dinner time.

After dinner, he tried to read, this time choosing a much-touted novel that proved to be about troubled youth. He was asleep within fifteen minutes of opening the book and awoke in an overstuffed armchair. The room was chilly, and his wife had tucked a quilt around his legs before abandoning him for bed. In the morning she would, he was certain, assure him that she had tried to rouse him before retiring, but he had no recollection of such an attempt.

'Half a bottle of wine might have something to do with that,' she would say.

He would deny the charge.

The advantage of being married a long time was that one could argue without the necessity of the other's actual, physical presence.

He smiled at this thought and pushed himself out of the chair, feeling groggy, head full of prickly flannel. He looked out the window. It was raining again – to the accompaniment of thunder and explosive, strobe-like lightning. The sports car was gone. The kids weren't home yet. Fine. Fine. None of my business.

Climbing the stairs, George paused. Something dark lay on the carpeted step, and as he bent over it, leaning forward, his mind sorted and discarded the possibilities: cat, wig, bird's nest, giant dust bunny. Touch and a strong olfactory cue identified the stuff: seaweed. Raising his head, he saw that two more clumps of the wet, rubbery plant lay on ascending steps, and gathering them – with no sense of revulsion for he was used to the ocean's disordered presence – he carried the weed up to his room and dumped it in the bathroom's wastebasket.

He scrubbed his hands in the sink, washing away the salty, stagnant reek, left the bathroom and crawled into bed beside his sleeping wife. He fell asleep immediately and was awakened later in the night with a suffocating sense of dread, a sure knowledge that an intruder had entered the room.

The intruder proved to be an odor, a powerful stench of decomposing fish, rotting vegetation and salt water. He climbed out of bed, coughing.

The source of this odor was instantly apparent and he swept up the wastebasket, preparing to gather the seaweed and flush it down the toilet.

The seaweed had melted into a black liquid, bubbles forming on its surface, a dark, gelatinous muck, simmering like heated tar. As George stared at the mess, a bubble burst, and the noxious gas it unleashed dazed him, sent him reeling backward with an inexplicable vision of some monstrous, shadowy form, silhouetted against green, mottled water.

George pitched himself forward, gathered the wastebasket in his arms, and fled the room. In the hall he wrenched open a window and hurled the wastebasket and its contents into the rain.

He stood then, gasping, the rain savage and cold on his face, his undershirt soaked, and he stood that way, clutching the window sill, until he was sure he would not faint.

Returning to bed, he found his wife still sleeping soundly and he knew, immediately, that he would say nothing in the morning, that the sense of suffocation, of fear, would seem unreal, its source irrational. Already the moment of panic was losing its reality, fading into the realm of nightmare.

The next day the rain stopped again and this time the sun was not routed. The police arrived on the third day of clear weather.

Mrs. Hume had opened the door, and she shouted up to her husband, who stood on the landing. 'It's about Mr. Franklin.'

Mrs. Franklin came out of her room then, and George Hume thought he saw the child behind her, through the open door. The girl, Melissa, was lying on the bed behind her mother and just for a moment it seemed that there was a spreading shadow under her, as though the bedclothes were soaked with dark water. Then the door closed as Mrs. Franklin came into the hall and George identified the expression he had last seen in her eyes for it was there again: fear, a racing engine of fear, gears stripped, the accelerator flat to the floor.

And Mrs. Franklin screamed, screamed and came falling to her knees and screamed again, prescient in her grief, and collapsed as George rushed toward her and two police officers and a paramedic, a woman, came bounding up the stairs.

Mr. Franklin had drowned. A fisherman had discovered the body. Mr. Franklin had been fully dressed, lying on his back with his eyes open. His wallet – and seven hundred dollars in cash and a host of credit cards – was still in his back pocket, and a business card identified him as vice president of marketing for a software firm in Fairfax, Virginia. The police had telephoned Franklin's firm in Virginia and so learned that he was on vacation. The secretary had the hotel's number.

After the ambulance left with Mrs. Franklin, they sat in silence until the police officer cleared his throat and said, 'She seemed to be expecting something like this.'

The words dropped into a silence.

Nancy and Steve and Mrs. Hume were seated on one of the lobby's sofas. George Hume came out of the office in the wake of the other policeman who paused at the door and spoke. 'We'd appreciate it if you could come down and identify the body. Just a formality, but it's not a job for his wife, not in the state she's in.' He coughed, shook his head. 'Or the state he's in, for that matter. Body got tore up some in the water, and, well, I still find it hard to believe that he was alive just yesterday. I would have guessed he'd been in the water two weeks minimum – the deterioration, you know.'

George Hume shook his head as though he did know and agreed to accompany the officer back into town.

George took a long look, longer than he wanted to, but the body wouldn't let him go, made mute, undeniable demands.

Yes, this was Mr. Greg Franklin. Yes, this would make eight years that he and his wife and his child had come to the hotel. No, no nothing out of the ordinary

George interrupted himself. 'The tattoos…' he said.

'Didn't know about the tattoos, I take it?' the officer said.

George shook his head. 'No.' The etched blue lines that laced the dead man's arms and chest were somehow more frightening than the damage the sea had done. Frightening because… because the reserved Mr. Franklin, businessman and stolid husband, did not look like someone who would illuminate his flesh with arcane symbols, pentagrams and ornate fish, their scales numbered according to some runic logic, and spidery, incomprehensible glyphs.

'Guess Franklin wasn't inclined to wear a bathing suit.'

'No.'

'Well, we are interested in those tattoos. I guess his wife knew about them. Hell, maybe she has some of her own.'

'Have you spoken to her?'

'Not yet. Called the hospital. They say she's sleeping. It can wait till morning.'

An officer drove George back to the hotel, and his wife greeted him at the door.

'She's sleeping,' Mrs. Hume said.

'Who?'

'Melissa.'

For a moment, George drew a blank, and then he nodded. 'What are we going to do with her?'

'Why, keep her,' his wife said. 'Until her mother is out of the hospital.'

'Maybe there are relatives,' George said, but he knew, saying it, that the Franklins were self-contained, a single unit, a closed universe.

His wife confirmed this. No one could be located, in any event.

'Melissa may not be aware that her father is dead,' Mrs. Hume said. 'The child is, I believe, a stranger girl than we ever realized. Here we were thinking she was just a quiet thing, well behaved. I think there is something wrong with her mind. I can't seem to talk to her, and what she says makes no sense. I've called Dr. Gowers, and he has agreed to see her. You remember Dr. Gowers, don't you? We sent Nancy to him when she was going through that bad time at thirteen.'

George remembered child psychiatrist Gowers as a bearded man with a swollen nose and thousands of small wrinkles around his eyes. He had seemed a very kind but somehow sad man, a little like Santa Claus if Santa Claus had suffered some disillusioning experience, an unpleasant divorce or other personal setback, perhaps.

Nancy came into the room as her mother finished speaking. 'Steve and I can take Melissa,' Nancy said.

'Well, that's very good of you, dear,' her mother said. 'I've already made an appointment for tomorrow morning at ten. I'm sure Dr. Gowers will be delighted to see you again.'

'I'll go too,' George said. He couldn't explain it but he was suddenly afraid.

The next morning when George came down to breakfast, Melissa was already seated at the table and Nancy was combing the child's hair.

'She isn't going to church,' George said, surprised at the growl in his voice.

'This is what she wanted to wear,' Nancy said. 'And it looks very nice, I think.'

Melissa was dressed in the sort of outfit a young girl might wear on Easter Sunday: a navy blue dress with white trim, white knee socks, black, shiny shoes. She had even donned pale blue gloves. Her black hair had been brushed to a satin sheen and her pale face seemed just-scrubbed, with the scent of soap lingering over her. A shiny black purse sat next to her plate of eggs and toast.

'You look very pretty,' George Hume said.

Melissa nodded, a sharp snap of the head, and said, 'I am an angel.'

Nancy laughed and hugged the child. George raised his eyebrows. 'No false modesty here,' he said. At least she could talk.

On the drive into town, Steve sat in the passenger seat while George drove. Nancy and Melissa sat in the back seat. Nancy spoke to the child in a slow, reassuring murmur.

Steve said nothing, sitting with his hands in his lap, looking out the window. *Might not be much in a crisis*, George thought. *A rich man's child.*

Steve stayed in the waiting room while the receptionist ushered Melissa and Nancy and George into Dr. Gowers' office. The psychiatrist seemed much as George remembered him, a silver-maned, benign old gent, exuding an air of competence. He asked them to sit on the sofa.

The child perched primly on the sofa, her little black purse cradled in her lap. She was flanked by George and Nancy.

Dr. Gowers knelt down in front of her. 'Well, Melissa. Is it all right if I call you Melissa?'

'Yes sir. That's what everyone calls me.'

'Well, Melissa, I'm glad you could come and see me today. I'm Dr. Gowers.'

'Yes sir.'

'I'm sorry about what happened to your father,' he said, looking in her eyes.

'Yes sir,' Melissa said. She leaned forward and touched her shoe.

'Do you know what happened to your father?' Dr. Gowers asked.

Melissa nodded her head and continued to study her shoes.

'What happened to your father?' Dr. Gowers asked.

'The machines got him,' Melissa said. She looked up at the doctor. 'The real machines,' she added. 'The ocean ones.'

'Your father drowned,' Dr. Gowers said.

Melissa nodded. 'Yes sir.' Slowly the little girl got up and began wandering around the room. She walked past a large saltwater aquarium next to a teak bookcase.

George thought the child must have bumped against the aquarium stand – although she hardly seemed close enough – because water spilled from the tank as she passed. She was humming. It was a bright, musical little tune, and he had heard it before, a children's song, perhaps? The words? Something like *by the sea, by the sea.*

The girl walked and gestured with a liquid motion that was oddly sophisticated, suggesting the calculated body language of an older and sexually self-assured woman.

'Melissa, would you come and sit down again so we can talk? I want to ask you some questions, and that is hard to do if you are walking around the room.'

'Yes sir,' Melissa said, returning to the sofa and resettling between George and his daughter. Melissa retrieved her purse and placed it on her lap again.

She looked down at the purse and up again. She smiled with a child's cunning. Then, very slowly, she opened the purse and showed it to Dr. Gowers.

'Yes?' he said, raising an eyebrow.

'There's nothing in it,' Melissa said. 'It's empty.' She giggled.

'Well yes, it is empty,' Dr. Gowers said, returning the child's smile. 'Why is that?'

Melissa snapped the purse closed. 'Because my real purse isn't here. It's in the real place, where I keep my things.'

'And where is that, Melissa?'

Melissa smiled and said, 'You know, silly.'

When the session ended, George phoned his wife.

'I don't know,' he said. 'I guess it went fine. I don't know. I've had no experience of this sort of thing. What about Mrs. Franklin?'

Mrs. Franklin was still in the hospital. She wanted to leave, but the hospital was reluctant to let her. She was still in shock, very disoriented. She seemed, indeed, to think that it was her daughter who had drowned.

'Did you talk to her?' George asked.

'Well yes, just briefly, but as I say, she made very little sense, got very excited when it became clear I wasn't going to fetch her if her doctor wanted her to remain there.'

'Can you remember anything she said?'

'Well, it was very jumbled, really. Something about a bad bargain. Something about, that Greek word, you know "hubris".'

'Hewbris?'

'Oh, back in school, you know, George. Hubris. A willful sort of pride that angers the gods. I'm sure you learned it in school yourself.'

'You are not making any sense,' he said, suddenly exasperated – and frightened.

'Well,' his wife said, 'you don't have to shout. Of course I don't make any sense. I am trying to repeat what Mrs. Franklin said, and that poor woman made no sense at all. I tried to reassure her that Melissa was fine and she screamed. She said Melissa was not fine at all and that I was a fool. Now you are shouting me, too.'

George apologized, said he had to be going, and hung up.

On the drive back from Dr. Gowers' office, Nancy sat in the back seat with Melissa. The child seemed unusually excited: her pale forehead was beaded with sweat, and she watched the ocean with great intensity.

'Did you like Dr. Gowers?' Nancy asked. 'He liked you. He wants to see you again, you know.'

Melissa nodded. 'He is a nice one.' She frowned. 'But he doesn't understand the real words either. No one here does.'

George glanced over his shoulder at the girl. *You are an odd ducky*, he thought.

A large, midday sun brightened the air and made the ocean glitter as though scaled. They were in a stretch of sand dunes and sea oats and high, wind-driven waves and, except for an occasional lumbering trailer truck, they seemed alone in this world of sleek, eternal forms.

Then Melissa began to cough. The coughing increased in volume, developed a quick, hysterical note.

'Pull over!' Nancy shouted, clutching the child.

George swung the car off the highway and hit the brakes. Gravel pinged against metal, the car fishtailed and lurched to a stop. George was out of the car instantly, in time to catch his daughter and the child in her arms as they came hurtling from the back seat. Melissa's face was red and her small chest heaved. Nancy had her arms around the girl's chest. 'Melissa!' Nancy was shouting. 'Melissa!'

Nancy jerked the child upwards and back. Melissa's body convulsed. Her breathing was labored, a broken whistle fluttering in her throat.

She shuddered and began to vomit. A hot, green odor, the smell of stagnant tidal pools, assaulted George. Nancy knelt beside Melissa, wiping the child's wet hair from her forehead. 'It's gonna be okay, honey,' she said. 'You got something stuck in your throat. It's all right now. You're all right.'

The child jumped up and ran down the beach.

'Melissa!' Nancy screamed, scrambling to her feet and pursuing the girl. George ran after them, fear hissing in him like some power line down in a storm, writhing and spewing sparks.

In her blue dress and knee socks – shoes left behind on the beach now – Melissa splashed into the ocean, arms pumping.

Out of the corner of his eye, George saw Steve come into view. He raced past George, past Nancy, moving with a frenzied pinwheeling of arms. 'I got her, I got her, I got her,' he chanted.

Don't, George thought. *Please don't.*

The beach was littered with debris, old, ocean-polished bottles, driftwood, seaweed, shattered conch shells. It was a rough ocean, still reverberating to the recent storm.

Steve had almost reached Melissa. George could see him reach out to clutch her shoulder.

Then something rose up in the water. It towered over man and child, and as the ocean fell away from it, it revealed smooth surfaces that glittered and writhed. The world was bathed with light, and George saw it plain. And yet, he could not later recall much detail. It was as though his mind refused entry to this monstrous thing, substituting other images – maggots winking from the eye sockets of some dead animal, flesh growing on a ruined structure of rusted metal – and while, in memory, those images were horrible enough and would not let him sleep, another part of his mind shrank from the knowledge that he had confronted something more hideous and ancient than his reason could acknowledge.

What happened next, happened in an instant. Steve staggered backwards and Melissa turned and ran sideways to the waves.

A greater wave, detached from the logic of the rolling ocean, sped over Steve, engulfing him, and he was gone, while Melissa continued to splash through the tide, now turning and running shoreward. The beast-thing was gone, and the old pattern of waves reasserted itself. Then Steve resurfaced, and with a lurch of understanding, as though the unnatural wave had struck at George's mind and left him dazed, he watched the head bob in the water, roll sickeningly, bounce on the crest of a second wave, and disappear.

Melissa lay face down on the wet sand, and Nancy raced to her, grabbed her up in her arms, and turned to her father.

'Where's Steve?' she shouted over the crash of the surf.

You didn't see then, George thought. *Thank God.*

'Where's Steve?' she shouted again.

George came up to his daughter and embraced her. His touch triggered racking sobs, and he held her tighter, the child Melissa between them.

And what if the boy's head rolls to our feet on the crest of the next wave? George thought, and the thought moved him to action. 'Let's get Melissa back to the car,' he said, taking the child from his daughter's arms.

It was a painful march back to the car, and George was convinced that at any moment either or both of his charges would bolt. He reached the car and helped his daughter into the back seat. She was shaking violently.

'Hold Melissa,' he said, passing the child to her. 'Don't let her go, Nancy.'

George pulled away from them and closed the car door. He turned then, refusing to look at the ocean as he did so. He looked down, stared for a moment at what was undoubtedly a wet clump of matted seaweed, and knew, with irrational certainty, that Melissa had choked on this same seaweed, had knelt here on the ground and painfully coughed it up.

He told the police that Melissa had run into the waves and that Steve had pursued her and drowned. This was all he could tell them – someday he hoped he would truly believe that it was all there was to tell. Thank God his daughter had not seen. And he realized then, with shame, that it was not even his daughter's feelings that were foremost in his mind but rather the relief, the immense relief, of knowing that what he had seen was not going to be corroborated and that with time and effort, he might really believe it was an illusion, the moment's horror, the tricks light plays with water.

He took the police back to where it had happened. But he would not go down to the tide. He waited in the police car while they walked along the beach.

If they returned with Steve's head, what would he say? *Oh yes, a big wave decapitated Steve. Didn't I mention that? Well, I meant to.*

But they found nothing.

Back at the hotel, George sat at the kitchen table and drank a beer. He was not a drinker, but it seemed to help. 'Where's Nancy?' he asked.

'Upstairs,' Mrs. Hume said. 'She's sleeping with the child. She wouldn't let me take Melissa. I tried to take the child and I thought… I thought my own daughter was going to attack me, hit me. Did she think I would hurt Melissa? What did she think?'

George studied his beer, shook his head sadly to indicate the absence of all conjecture.

Mrs. Hume dried her hands on the dish towel and, ducking her head, removed her apron. 'Romner Psychiatric called. A Doctor Melrose.'

George looked up. 'Is he releasing Mrs. Franklin?' *Please come and get your daughter,* George thought. *I have a daughter of my own.* Oh how he wanted to see the last of them.

'Not just yet. No. But he wanted to know about the family's visits every year. Dr. Melrose thought there might have been something different about that first year. He feels there is some sort of trauma associated with it.'

George Hume shrugged. 'Nothing out of the ordinary as I recall.'

Mrs. Hume put a hand to her cheek. 'Oh, but it was different. Don't you remember, George? They came earlier, with all the crowds, and they left abruptly. They had paid for two weeks, but they were gone on the third day. I remember being surprised when they returned the next year – and I thought then that it must have been the crowds they hated and that's why they came so late from then on.'

'Well…' Her husband closed his eyes. 'I can't say that I actually remember the first time.'

His wife shook her head. 'What can I expect from a man who can't remember his own wedding anniversary? That Melissa was just a tot back then, a little mite in a red bathing suit. Now that I think of it, she hasn't worn a bathing suit since.'

Before going to bed, George stopped at the door to his daughter's room. He pushed the door open carefully and peered in. She slept as she always slept, sprawled on her back, mouth open. She had always fallen asleep abruptly, in disarray, gunned down by the sandman. Tonight she was aided by the doctor's sedatives. The child Melissa snuggled next to her, and for one brief moment the small form seemed sinister and parasitic, as though attached to his daughter, drawing sustenance there.

'Come to bed,' his wife said, and George joined her under the covers.

'It's just that she wants to protect the girl,' George said. 'All she has, you know. She's just seen her boyfriend drown, and this… I think it gives her purpose.'

Mrs. Hume understood that this was in answer to the earlier question and she nodded her head. 'Yes, I know dear. But is it healthy? I've a bad feeling about it.'

'I know,' George said.

The shrill ringing of the phone woke him. 'Who is it?' his wife was asking as he fumbled in the dark for the receiver.

The night ward clerk was calling from Romner Psychiatric. She apologized for calling at such a late hour, but there might be cause for concern. Better safe than sorry, etc. Mrs. Franklin had apparently – well, had definitely – left the hospital. Should she return to the hotel, the hospital should be notified immediately.

George Hume thanked her, hung up the phone, and got out of bed. He pulled on his trousers, tugged a sweatshirt over his head.

'Where are you going?' his wife called after him.

'I won't be but a minute,' he said, closing the door behind him.

The floor was cold, the boards groaning under his bare feet. Slowly, with a certainty born of dread, expecting the empty bed, expecting the worst, he pushed open the door.

Nancy lay sleeping soundly.

The child was gone. Nancy lay as though still sheltering that small, mysterious form.

George pulled his head back and closed the door. He turned and hurried down the hall. He stopped on the stairs, willed his heart to silence, slowed his breathing. 'Melissa,' he whispered. No answer.

He ran down the stairs. The front doors were wide open. He ran out into the moonlight and down to the beach.

The beach itself was empty and chill; an unrelenting wind blew in from the ocean. The moon shone overhead as though carved from milky ice.

He saw them then, standing far out on the pier, mother and daughter, black shadows against the moon-gray clouds that bloomed on the horizon.

Dear God, George thought. *What does she intend to do?*

'Melissa!' George shouted, and began to run.

He was out of breath when he reached them. Mother and daughter regarded him coolly, having turned to watch his progress down the pier.

'Melissa,' George gasped. 'Are you all right?'

Melissa was wearing a pink nightgown and holding her mother's hand. It was her mother who spoke: 'We are beyond your concern. Mr. Hume. My husband is dead, and without him the contract cannot be renewed.'

Mrs. Franklin's eyes were lit with some extraordinary emotion and the wind, rougher and threatening to unbalance them all, made her hair quiver like a dark flame.

'You have your own daughter, Mr. Hume. That is a fine and wonderful thing. You have never watched your daughter die, watched her fade to utter stillness, dying on her back in the sand, sand on her lips, her eyelids; children are so untidy, even dying. It is an unholy and terrible thing to witness.'

The pier groaned and a loud crack heralded a sudden tilting of the world. George fell to his knees. A long sliver of wood entered the palm of his hand, and he tried to keep from pitching forward.

Mrs. Franklin, still standing, shouted over the wind. 'We came here every year to renew the bargain. Oh, it is not a good bargain. Our daughter is never with us entirely. But you would know, any parent would know, that love will take whatever it can scavenge, any small compromise. Anything less utter and awful than the grave.'

There were tears running down Mrs. Franklin's face now, silver tracks. 'This year I was greedy. I wanted Melissa back, all of her. And I thought, I am her mother. I have the first claim to her. So I demanded – demanded – that my husband set it all to rights. "Tell them we have come here for the last year," I said. And my husband allowed his love for me to override his reason. He did as I asked.'

Melissa, who seemed oblivious to her mother's voice, turned away and spoke into the darkness of the waters. Her words were in no language George Hume had ever heard, and they were greeted with a loud, rasping bellow that thrummed in the wood planks of the pier.

Then came the sound of wood splintering, and the pier abruptly tilted. George's hands gathered more spiky wooden needles as he slid forward. He heard himself scream, but the sound was torn away by the renewed force of the wind and a hideous roaring that accompanied the gale.

Looking up, George saw Melissa kneeling at the edge of the pier. Her mother was gone.

'Melissa!' George screamed, stumbling forward. 'Don't move.'

But the child was standing up, wobbling, her nightgown flapping behind her.

George leapt forward, caught the child, felt a momentary flare of hope, and then they both were hurtling forward and the pier was gone.

They plummeted toward the ocean, through a blackness defined by an inhuman sound, a sound that must have been the first sound God heard when He woke at the dawn of eternity.

And even as he fell, George felt the child wiggle in his arms. His arms encircled Melissa's waist, felt bare flesh. Had he looked skyward, he would have seen the nightgown, a pink ghost shape, sailing toward the moon.

But George Hume's eyes saw, instead, the waiting ocean and under it, a shape, a moving network of cold, uncanny machinery, and whether it was a living thing of immense size, or a city, or a machine, was irrelevant. He knew only that it was ancient beyond any land-born thing.

Still clutching the child he collided with the hard, cold back of the sea.

George Hume had been raised in close proximity to the ocean. He had learned to swim almost as soon as he had learned to walk. The cold might kill him, would almost certainly kill him if he did not reach shore quickly – but that he did. During the swim toward shore he lost Melissa and in that moment he understood not to turn back, not to seek the child.

He could not tell anyone how he knew a change had been irretrievably wrought and that there was no returning the girl to land. It was not something you could communicate – any more than you could communicate the dreadful ancient quality of the machinery under the sea.

Nonetheless, George knew the moment Melissa was lost to him. It was a precise and memorable moment. It was the moment the child had wriggled, with strange new, sinewy strength, flicked her tail and slid effortlessly from his grasp.

THE DELICATE

Jeffrey Ford

Jeffrey Ford (1955–) is an American writer whose fiction combines elements of traditional fantasy or magic realism with surrealism and horror. He studied with the novelist John Gardner at Binghamton University and he currently teaches at Brookdale Community College in New Jersey. His work has received and been nominated for many awards, including the World Fantasy Award, the International Horror Guild Award, the Edgar Allen Poe Award, the Hugo Award, and the Nebula Award. Although his fiction comes at the weird sideways, some of his stories, like 'The Delicate' (1994), enter weird territory with complete abandon. It's a short, sharp shock of the grotesque.

The Delicate is pale, limbs pipe-cleaner thin, with a head as shiny hard as beetle-back. Violent, in utero skull tectonics have led to a precipice of brow, a compression of matter past the point of truth. His eyes are crow eyes, and his ear holes winding tunnels to nowhere.

He comes in the latter days of afternoon, through blowing snow, dressed in black, while Schubert's 'Eighth' plays magically in the background. He comes to suck the breath out of passing fancies and to treat the infirm of mind, the particularly annoying, to a long sleep.

'In order to take the waters,' as he explains it, he comes to a resort town on the edge of reason. Beyond it, the wilderness stretches north to the frozen pole. God has never drawn breath there – the domain of bat-winged demons whose skin is the ringed wood of oak trees. These creatures fly out of the forest at night to snatch up children, their little legs kicking to the moon. To live in Absentia is to live with a soul that is liquid lead.

Perhaps it is the manner in which he holds his cigarette or maybe his distinguished apparel that immediately ingratiates him to both the guests and staff of the Hotel Providence. At his request, they call him Harding Jarvis and marvel at his grace and facility with foreign language. Though his face is more a cow skull than a thing of flesh, no one seems to notice except the woman who cleans his rooms. She knows him by his aroma – roses over bad meat. When he knows she knows, he wheezes into his wine glass.

No matter who Carlotta confesses her fears to, they brush her off, saying, 'Herr Jarvis? Not possible. My dear, you are disturbed.' She makes it a point never to enter his rooms when they are occupied. *Sleep to her is death,* say the toothpicks holding open her eyes. She lasts only three days before she sits down and closes them. To sleep is warm and beautiful, but the chair she sits in is at the foot of Herr Jarvis's bed. There is so much dirt on the floor – four ounces of fly meat on every windowsill.

He returns unexpectedly from an afternoon of playing whist with Madame Fesh of the colorful muff, Barlin the local logomancer, and Meme Haspin, taxidermist to the landed gentry, and discovers Carlotta asleep in the chair. With little pomp and less circumstance, he sucks the life out of her. The process is long and painful, and he doesn't spare her a minute of it. After hanging her withered corpse, like a wrinkled garment bag of flesh, on a peg in the closet, he sits down to smoke his clay pipe. Before long, he moves to the writing desk, where he takes up his pen and records the essence of the maid he has just ingested. The first phrase to crawl out onto paper is, 'Insouciance is the engine of regret,' and from there it is a smooth plunge into lyrical facility.

At first he thought it was the crab soufflé he had had for lunch, but then realized, too late, that something in Carlotta's blood was causing a strange transformation in him. With a popping of bone, a stretch of incisors, a whisper growth of fur and the shrinking of skin, he stoops to become a dog. His last oath is excremental before his words give way to growling.

The inhabitants of Absentia mention to each other the clever little hound that now wanders the streets looking for scraps. One boy tells how he heard it cry human, and the men who mine Mount Alfarabi are amused when the beast tries to have its way with a lady's shinbone outside the beer hall. Meanwhile, everybody who is anybody is seeking out Harding Jarvis for a ride in the car, a game of tennis, a cocktail party.

Pharsalus, the hunter, comes in from the wilderness with furs to sell and wild turkey feathers in his hat. With the money he makes, he goes directly to the beer hall and drinks many mugs. He tells those he hasn't seen in three seasons about the demon he shot and about the beautiful paradise surrounded by hundreds of miles of ice. For proof of the demon, he displays a pair of gnarled horns which he pulled like teeth, with a pair of pliers, from the forehead of the creature. As for paradise, he offers only a shrug.

The days of Night fall while Pharsalus is drinking. When he steps out of the beer hall, there is a brisk wind and winter chill. He stares up at the ice-bright stars and remembers tracking white apes at twilight. They moved like ghosts among the giant pines. They died with a cough of steam and a trickle of blood.

When his memory clears, Pharsalus notices a dog sitting in the street in front of him. Because the first hours of Night each year give him a desire to speak to something other than only the earth and wind, he decides to adopt the mutt as a hunting dog. Using scraps of dried caribou, he lures his new companion out of town and into the uncharted wilderness.

Night in the forest is either stone silence and falling snow or the sound of something dying. Demons fly out of the trees without warning, and Pharsalus is always ready with his gun. When they jump him from behind, he uses his long, curved knife and engages them in hand-to-hand combat. The dog helps in the kill. As the demons' mauled bodies expire at his feet, he questions them about the path to the Earthly Paradise. Some of the dying offer clues, but most go quietly, their barbed tails thrashing the snow. Pharsalus writes whatever they tell him in a little notebook and then pulls their horns out with a pair of pliers.

In spring, the hunter and dog traverse a pass that leads over the mountains. The sudden return of the days of Morning brings light that blinds. In those mountains there exist hundreds of small caves formed long ago in the Ice Age. Each year, he hunts them for snapping yellow back and artifacts left behind by the ancients who had once inhabited them.

In one cave, the hunter discovers the frozen corpse of a man, sitting on a large stone at a table hewn from rock. Icicles hang from the man's nose and frost glazes his eyes. From the worm-eaten journal laying open in front of the dead man, Pharsalus learns of his father's search for him. The hunter puts his arms around the dog and cries.

In one entry in his father's journal, the old man describes his love affair with a woman who lives at the bottom of a lake. Her skin is blue and her hair so long it turns into sea grass and trailing vines. He descends from his mountain perch every night to meet her on the shore of her lake.

They sit beneath a tall dune, the wind blowing around them. Above, stars smash into stars. He tells her how fifteen years earlier he left home to search for his son who had become a hunter in the wilderness. As he kisses her, he hears the immensity of paradise singing across the water to him.

Pharsalus dreams every night of the only beast he has any desire to hunt. It is a creature he has never actually seen, with many jumbled attributes – scales, fur, talons, fangs, feathers beneath and around the hide and hair. Every night it comes vividly to him and fills him with longing to hunt it. In the dream, he always hears it flying. There is a struggle and it bites him, like a snake, in the heel. He always awakens wondering if the bird part is rooster. But since he has gotten the dog, it has become more and more difficult to envision the dream kill.

In their wandering, the hunter and companion stumble upon a beautiful garden locked in ice. At the last second the Delicate steps out of the sloughed skin of the mutt to take the hunter by the throat. Lips meet lips and breath begins leaving, begins arriving. When the hunter is blind in one eye and his left rib cage shattered by the internal pressure, he summons those years of the kill and thrusts his hunting knife into the thorax of the Delicate. Streams of agony intermingle and separate out into fields of bright color. With a simple cracking noise the monster pushes a bony finger through the hunter's chest and turns off his heart.

But the Delicate is dying from his wound. He stumbles through the wilderness clutching his oozing side with a slim, sharp hand. He kneels and prays to heaven but nothing happens. The memories of other lifetimes swirl in his memory with an anguished forgetting of paradise. He cries for the loss of his delicate form, his exo-skeleton now a crystal meteor. If only he could change into a dog, he thinks, as life leaves him in a cascade of steam. With little conviction, he sucks it back up as it goes. In no time, he's good as new.

Back in the town of Absentia, in the very room of the Hotel Providence where he took Carlotta, he's now taking them two at a time. The empty husks of life pile up like fresh-cut bales of tobacco in his closet. Men catch their wives sneaking to his door. Wives catch their husbands at some shadowy rendezvous with him, and he takes them both as quick as you please. He takes the contessa from behind as she leans over to adjust her corset. Her piles of hair almost save her, but, in the end, she is as easy to draw the life out of as is Master Cley, or the mayor, or Madam Silwort, or the Grossdig Twins.

Someone notices the population of the town dwindling at an alarming rate and wires for the government to send troops, before the Delicate can snip the telegraph line with his incisors. When the army arrives and surrounds the town, he is huffing, as if taking snuff, the last few morsels of Mrs. Fleacox. He realizes too late that she has long since gone bad as a soft melon even though she keeps right on talking till the end. Her pointless words infect him with *flexis midocarsis,* and he slowly begins to disintegrate. In his final hour, he stands upon the balcony of the mayor's house, staring out over the wilderness, playing the violin until his fingers turn to salt and the instrument falls to the floor.

The soldiers break into Absentia, machine guns blurting out death, air cover dropping flames as if the clouds were on fire. They find the Delicate – a sorry, prodigious pile of cigarette ash. Mrs. Fleacox is lost between life and death, and they call for a specialist to administer the needle to the base of her spine. They collect the creature into a plastic bag and freeze-dry him. His remains are taken to Spire City in the Sunbelt where they are stored for the edification of future generations. The funding never comes through to study the crumbs of the Delicate, so he lies in a bag on a shelf and waits.

THE MAN IN THE BLACK SUIT

Stephen King

Stephen King (1947–) is one of the most influential post-World War II American writers of horror and weird fiction. His books have sold over three hundred and fifty million copies. Early classics that established King's reputation include *Salem's Lot* (1975), *The Shining* (1977), *The Stand* (1978), and *The Dark Tower: The Gunslinger* (1982). King has noted Richard Matheson, H .P. Lovecraft, and Shirley Jackson as among his many influences. He received the Medal of Distinguished Contribution to American Letters from the National Book Foundation in 2003. Other awards include the Hugo Award, O. Henry Award, and World Fantasy Award. 'The Man in the Black Suit' is a beautifully written and terrifying tale of an encounter with the weird.

I am now a very old man and this is something which happened to me when I was very young – only nine years old. It was 1914, the summer after my brother Dan died in the west field and three years before America got into World War I. I've never told anyone about what happened at the fork in the stream that day, and I never will... at least not with my mouth. I've decided to write it down, though, in this book which I will leave on the table beside my bed. I can't write long, because my hands shake so these days and I have next to no strength, but I don't think it will take long.

Later, someone may find what I have written. That seems likely to me, as it is pretty much human nature to look in a book marked DIARY after its owner has passed along. So yes – my words will probably be read. A better question is whether or not anyone will believe them. Almost certainly not, but that doesn't matter. It's not belief I'm interested in but freedom. Writing can give that, I've found. For twenty years I wrote a column called 'Long Ago and Far Away' for the Castle Rock *Call*, and I know that sometimes it works that way – what you write down sometimes leaves you forever, like old photographs left in the bright sun, fading to nothing but white.

I pray for that sort of release.

A man in his nineties should be well past the terrors of childhood, but as my infirmities slowly creep up on me, like waves licking closer and closer to some indifferently built castle of sand, that terrible face grows clearer and clearer in my mind's eye. It glows like a dark star in the constellations of my childhood. What I might have done yesterday, who I might have seen here in my room at the nursing home, what I might have said to them or they to me... those things are gone, but the face of the man in the black suit grows ever clearer, ever closer, and I remember every word he said. I don't want to think of him but I can't help it, and sometimes at night my old heart beats so hard and so fast I think it will tear itself right clear of my chest. So I uncap my fountain pen and force my trembling old hand to write this pointless anecdote in the diary one of my great-grandchildren – I can't remember her name for sure, at least not right now, but I know it starts with an S – gave to me last Christmas, and which I have never written in until now. Now I will write in it. I will write the story of how I met the man in the black suit on the bank of Castle Stream one afternoon in the summer of 1914.

The town of Motton was a different world in those days – more different than I could ever tell you. That was a world without airplanes droning overhead, a world almost without cars and trucks, a world where the skies were not cut into lanes and slices by overhead power lines.

There was not a single paved road in the whole town, and the business district consisted of nothing but Corson's General Store, Thut's Livery & Hardware, the Methodist Church at Christ's Corner, the school, the town hall, and Harry's Restaurant half a mile down from there, which my mother called, with unfailing disdain, 'the liquor house.'

Mostly, though, the difference was in how people lived – how apart they were.

I'm not sure people born after the middle of the twentieth century could quite credit that, although they might say they could, to be polite to old folks like me. There were no phones in western Maine back then, for one thing. The first one wouldn't be installed for another five years, and by the time there was one in our house, I was nineteen and going to college at the University of Maine in Orono.

But that is only the root of the thing. There was no doctor closer than Casco, and no more than a dozen houses in what you would call town. There were no neighborhoods (I'm not even sure we knew the word, although we had a verb – *neighboring* – that described church functions and barn dances), and open fields were the exception rather than the rule. Out of town the houses were farms that stood far apart from each other, and from December until middle March we mostly hunkered down in the little pockets of stove warmth we called families. We hunkered and listened to the wind in the chimney and hoped no one would get sick or break a leg or get a headful of bad ideas, like the farmer over in Castle Rock who had chopped up his wife and kids three winters before and then said in court that the ghosts made him do it. In those days before the Great War, most of Motton was woods and bog, dark long places full of moose and mosquitoes, snakes and secrets. In those days there were ghosts everywhere.

This thing I'm telling about happened on a Saturday. My father gave me a whole list of chores to do, including some that would have been Dan's, if he'd still been alive. He was my only brother, and he'd died of being stung by a bee. A year had gone by, and still my mother wouldn't hear that. She said it was something else, *had* to have been, that no one ever died of being stung by a bee. When Mama Sweet, the oldest lady in the Methodist Ladies' Aid, tried to tell her – at the church supper the previous winter, this was – that the same thing had happened to her favorite uncle back in '73, my mother clapped her hands over her ears, got up, and walked out of the church basement. She'd never been back since, either, and nothing my father could say to her would change her mind. She claimed she was done with church, and that if she ever had to see Helen Robichaud again (that was Mama Sweet's real name), she would slap her eyes out. She wouldn't be able to help herself, she said.

That day, Dad wanted me to lug wood for the cookstove, weed the beans and the cukes, pitch hay out of the loft, get two jugs of water to put in the cold pantry, and scrape as much old paint off the cellar bulkhead as I could. Then, he said, I could go fishing, if I didn't mind going by myself – he had to go over and see Bill Eversham about some cows. I said I sure didn't mind going by myself, and my Dad smiled like that didn't surprise him so very much. He'd given me a bamboo pole the week before – not because it was my birthday or anything, but just because he liked to give me things, sometimes – and I was wild to try it in Castle Stream, which was by far the troutiest brook I'd ever fished.

'But don't you go too far in the woods,' he told me. 'Not beyond where it splits.'

'No, sir.'

'Promise me.'

'Yessir, I promise.'

'Now promise your mother.'

We were standing on the back stoop; I had been bound for the springhouse with the water jugs when my Dad stopped me. Now he turned me around to face my mother, who was standing at the marble counter in a flood of strong morning sunshine falling through the double windows over the sink. There was a curl of hair lying across the side of her forehead and touching her eyebrow – you see how well I remember it all? The bright light turned that little curl to filaments of gold and made me want to run to her and put my arms around her. In that instant I saw her as a woman, saw her as my father must have seen her. She was wearing a housedress with little red roses all over it, I remember, and she was kneading bread. Candy Bill, our little black Scottie dog, was standing alertly beside her feet, looking up, waiting for anything that might drop. My mother was looking at me.

'I promise,' I said.

She smiled, but it was the worried kind of smile she always seemed to make since my father brought Dan back from the west field in his arms. My father had come sobbing and bare-chested. He had taken off his shirt and draped it over Dan's face, which had swelled and turned color. *My boy!* he had been crying. *Oh, look at my boy! Jesus, look at my boy!* I remember that as if it had been yesterday.

It was the only time I ever heard my Dad take the Savior's name in vain.

'What do you promise, Gary?' she asked.

'Promise not to go no further than where it forks, ma'am.'

'*Any* further.'

'Any.'

She gave me a patient look, saying nothing as her hands went on working in the dough, which now had a smooth, silky look.

'I promise not to go any further than where it forks, ma'am.'

'Thank you, Gary,' she said. 'And try to remember that grammar is for the world as well as for school.'

'Yes, ma'am.'

Candy Bill followed me as I did my chores, and sat between my feet as I bolted my lunch, looking up at me with the same attentiveness he had shown my mother while she was kneading her bread, but when I got my new bamboo pole and my old, splintery creel and started out of the dooryard, he stopped and only stood in the dust by an old roll of snowfence, watching. I called him but he wouldn't come. He yapped a time or two, as if telling me to come back, but that was all.

'Stay, then,' I said, trying to sound as if I didn't care. I did, though, at least a little. Candy Bill *always* went fishing with me.

My mother came to the door and looked out at me with her left hand held up to shade her eyes. I can see her that way still, and it's like looking at a photograph of someone who later became unhappy, or died suddenly. 'You mind your Dad now, Gary!'

'Yes, ma'am, I will.'

She waved. I waved, too. Then I turned my back on her and walked away.

The sun beat down on my neck, hard and hot, for the first quarter-mile or so, but then I entered the woods, where double shadow fell over the road and it was cool and fir-smelling and you could hear the wind hissing through the deep needled groves. I walked with my pole on my shoulder like boys did back then, holding my creel in my other hand like a valise or a salesman's sample-case.

About two miles into the woods along a road which was really nothing but a double rut with a grassy strip growing up the center hump, I began to hear the hurried, eager gossip of Castle Stream. I thought of trout with bright speckled backs and pure white bellies, and my heart went up in my chest.

The stream flowed under a little wooden bridge, and the banks leading down to the water were steep and brushy. I worked my way down carefully, holding on where I could and digging my heels in. I went down out of summer and back into mid-spring, or so it felt. The cool rose gently off the water, and a green smell like moss. When I got to the edge of the water I only stood there for a little while, breathing deep of that mossy smell and watching the dragonflies circle and the skitterbugs skate. Then, farther down, I saw a trout leap at a butterfly – a good big brookie, maybe fourteen inches long – and remembered I hadn't come here just to sightsee.

I walked along the bank, following the current,

and wet my line for the first time with the bridge still in sight upstream. Something jerked the tip of my pole down a time or two and ate half my worm, but he was too sly for my nine-year-old hands – or maybe just not hungry enough to be careless – so I went on.

I stopped at two or three other places before I got to the place where Castle Stream forks, going southwest into Castle Rock and southeast into Kashwakamak Township, and at one of them I caught the biggest trout I have ever caught in my life, a beauty that measured nineteen inches from tip to tail on the little ruler I kept in my creel. That was a monster of a brook trout, even for those days.

If I had accepted this as gift enough for one day and gone back, I would not be writing now (and this is going to turn out longer than I thought it would, I see that already), but I didn't. Instead I saw to my catch right then and there as my father had shown me – cleaning it, placing it on dry grass at the bottom of the creel, then laying damp grass on top of it – and went on. I did not, at age nine, think that catching a nineteen-inch brook trout was particularly remarkable, although I do remember being amazed that my line had not broken when I, netless as well as artless, had hauled it out and swung it toward me in a clumsy tail-flapping arc.

Ten minutes later, I came to the place where the stream split in those days (it is long gone now; there is a settlement of duplex homes where Castle Stream once went its course, and a district grammar school as well, and if there is a stream it goes in darkness), dividing around a huge gray rock nearly the size of our outhouse.

There was a pleasant flat space here, grassy and soft, overlooking what my Dad and I called South Branch. I squatted on my heels, dropped my line into the water, and almost immediately snagged a fine rainbow trout. He wasn't the size of my brookie – only a foot or so – but a good fish, just the same. I had it cleaned out before the gills had stopped flexing, stored it in my creel, and dropped my line back into the water.

This time there was no immediate bite so I leaned back, looking up at the blue stripe of sky I could see along the stream's course. Clouds floated by, west to east, and I tried to think what they looked like. I saw a unicorn, then a rooster, then a dog that looked a little like Candy Bill. I was looking for the next one when I drowsed off. Or maybe slept. I don't know for sure. All I know is that a tug on my line so strong it almost pulled the bamboo pole out of my hand was what brought me back into the afternoon. I sat up, clutched the pole, and suddenly became aware that something was sitting on the tip of my nose. I crossed my eyes and saw a bee. My heart seemed to fall dead in my chest, and for a horrible second I was sure I was going to wet my pants.

The tug on my line came again, stronger this time, but although I maintained my grip on the end of the pole so it wouldn't be pulled into the stream and perhaps carried away (I think I even had the presence of mind to snub the line with my forefinger), I made no effort to pull in my catch. All of my horrified attention was fixed on the fat black-and-yellow thing that was using my nose as a rest-stop.

I slowly poked out my lower lip and blew upward. The bee ruffled a little but kept its place. I blew again and it ruffled again... but this time it also seemed to shift impatiently, and I didn't dare blow anymore, for fear it would lose its temper completely and give me a shot. It was too close for me to focus on what it was doing, but it was easy to imagine it ramming its stinger into one of my nostrils and shooting its poison up toward my eyes. And my brain.

A terrible idea came to me: that this was the very bee which had killed my brother. I knew it wasn't true, and not only because honey-bees probably didn't live longer than a single year (except maybe for the queens; about them I was not so sure). It couldn't be true because bees died when they stung, and even at nine I knew it. Their stingers were barbed, and when they tried to fly away after doing the deed, they tore themselves apart. Still, the idea stayed. This was a special bee, a devil-bee, and it had come back to finish the other of Albion and Loretta's two boys.

And here is something else: I had been stung by bees before, and although the stings had swelled more than is perhaps usual (I can't really say for sure), I had never died of them. That was only for my brother, a terrible trap which had been laid for him in his very making, a trap which I had somehow escaped. But as I crossed my eyes until they hurt in an effort to focus on the bee, logic did not exist. It was the *bee* that existed, only that, the bee that had killed my brother, killed him so bad that my father had slipped down the straps of his overalls so he could take off his shirt and cover Dan's swelled, engorged face. Even in the depths of his grief he had done that, because he didn't want his wife to see what had become of her firstborn. Now the bee had returned, and now it would kill me. It would kill me and I would die in convulsions on the bank, flopping just as a brookie flops after you take the hook out of its mouth.

As I sat there trembling on the edge of panic – of simply bolting to my feet and then bolting anywhere – there came a report from behind me. It was as sharp and peremptory as a pistol-shot, but I knew it wasn't a pistol-shot; it was someone clapping his hands. One single clap. At the moment it came, the bee tumbled off my nose and fell into my lap. It lay there on my pants with its legs sticking up and its stinger a threatless black thread against the old scuffed brown of the corduroy. It was dead as a doornail, I saw that at once. At the same moment, the pole gave another tug – the hardest yet – and I almost lost it again.

I grabbed it with both hands and gave it a big stupid yank that would have made my father clutch his head with both hands, if he had been there to see it.

A rainbow trout, a good bit larger than the one I had already caught, rose out of the water in a wet, writhing flash, spraying fine drops of water from its filament of tail – it looked like one of those romanticized fishing pictures they used to put on the covers of men's magazines like *True* and *Man's Adventure* back in the forties and fifties. At that moment hauling in a big one was about the last thing on my mind, however, and when the line snapped and the fish fell back into the stream, I barely noticed. I looked over my shoulder to see who had clapped. A man was standing above me, at the edge of the trees. His face was very long and pale. His black hair was combed tight against his skull and parted with rigorous care on the left side of his narrow head.

He was very tall. He was wearing a black three-piece suit, and I knew right away that he was not a human being, because his eyes were the orangey-red of flames in a woodstove. I don't just mean the irises, because he *had* no irises, and no pupils, and certainly no whites. His eyes were completely orange – an orange that shifted and flickered. And it's really too late not to say exactly what I mean, isn't it? He was on fire inside, and his eyes were like the little isinglass portholes you sometimes see in stove doors.

My bladder let go, and the scuffed brown the dead bee was lying on went a darker brown. I was hardly aware of what had happened, and I couldn't take my eyes off the man standing on top of the bank and looking down at me, the man who had walked out of thirty miles of trackless western Maine woods in a fine black suit and narrow shoes of gleaming leather. I could see the watch-chain looped across his vest glittering in the summer sunshine. There was not so much as a single pine-needle on him. And he was smiling at me.

'Why, it's a fisherboy!' he cried in a mellow, pleasing voice. 'Imagine that! Are we well-met, fisherboy?'

'Hello, sir,' I said. The voice that came out of me did not tremble, but it didn't sound like my voice, either. It sounded older. Like Dan's voice, maybe. Or my father's, even. And all I could think was that maybe he would let me go if I pretended not to see what he was. If I pretended I didn't see there were flames glowing and dancing where his eyes should have been.

'I've saved you a nasty sting, perhaps,' he said, and then, to my horror, he came down the bank to where I sat with a dead bee in my wet lap and a bamboo fishing pole in my nerveless hands. His slick soled city shoes should have slipped on the low, grassy weeds which dressed the steep bank, but they didn't; nor did they leave tracks behind, I saw. Where his feet had touched – or seemed to touch – there was not a single broken twig, crushed leaf, or trampled shoeshape.

Even before he reached me, I recognized the aroma baking up from the skin under the suit – the

No, I tried to say, *please, no*, but no sound came out. He meant to do it, I saw. He really meant to do it.

'I'm just so *hungry*,' he said, both petulant and teasing. 'And you won't want to live without your precious mommy, anyhow, take my word for it. Because your father's the sort of man who'll have to have some warm hole to stick it in, believe me, and if you're the only one available, you're the one who'll have to serve. I'll save you all that discomfort and unpleasantness. Also, you'll go to Heaven, think of that. Murdered souls always go to Heaven. So we'll both be serving God this afternoon, Gary. Isn't that nice?'

He reached for me again with his long, pale hands, and without thinking what I was doing, I flipped open the top of my creel, pawed all the way down to the bottom, and brought out the monster brookie I'd caught earlier – the one I should have been satisfied with. I held it out to him blindly, my fingers in the red slit of its belly from which I had removed its insides as the man in the black suit had threatened to remove mine. The fish's glazed eye stared dreamily at me, the gold ring around the black center reminding me of my mother's wedding ring. And in that moment I saw her lying in her coffin with the sun shining off the wedding band and knew it was true – she had been stung by a bee, she had drowned in the warm, bread-smelling kitchen air, and Candy Bill had licked her dying tears from her swollen cheeks.

'Big fish!' the man in the black suit cried in a guttural, greedy voice. 'Oh, *biiig fiiish*!'

He snatched it away from me and crammed it into a mouth that opened wider than any human mouth ever could. Many years later, when I was sixty-five (I know it was sixty-five because that was the summer I retired from teaching), I went to the New England Aquarium and finally saw a shark. The mouth of the man in the black suit was like that shark's mouth when it opened, only his gullet was blazing red, the same color as his awful eyes, and I felt heat bake out of it and into my face, the way you feel a sudden wave of heat come pushing out of a fireplace when a dry piece of wood catches alight. And I didn't imagine that heat, either, I know I didn't, because just before he slid the head of my nineteen-inch brook trout between his gaping jaws, I saw the scales along the sides of the fish rise up and begin to curl like bits of paper floating over an open incinerator. He slid the fish in like a man in a travelling show swallowing a sword. He didn't chew, and his blazing eyes bulged out, as if in effort. The fish went in and went in, his throat bulged as it slid down his gullet, and now he began to cry tears of his own...except his tears were blood, scarlet and thick. I think it was the sight of those bloody tears that gave me my body back. I don't know why that should have been, but I think it was. I bolted to my feet like a jack released from its box, turned with my bamboo pole still in one hand, and fled up the bank, bending over and tearing tough bunches of weeds out with my free hand in an effort to get up the slope more quickly.

He made a strangled, furious noise – the sound of any man with his mouth too full – and I looked back just as I got to the top. He was coming after me, the back of his suit-coat flapping and his thin gold watch-chain flashing and winking in the sun. The tail of the fish was still protruding from his mouth and I could smell the rest of it, roasting in the oven of his throat. He reached for me, groping with his talons, and I fled along the top of the bank.

After a hundred yards or so I found my voice and went to screaming – screaming in fear, of course, but also screaming in grief for my beautiful dead mother.

He was coming along after me. I could hear snapping branches and whipping bushes, but I didn't look back again. I lowered my head, slitted my eyes against the bushes and low-hanging branches along the stream's bank, and ran as fast as I could. And at every step I expected to feel his hands descending on my shoulders pulling me back into a final hot hug.

That didn't happen. Some unknown length of time later – it couldn't have been longer than five or ten minutes, I suppose, but it seemed like forever – I saw the bridge through layerings of leaves and firs. Still screaming, but breathlessly now, sounding like a teakettle which has almost boiled dry, I reached this second, steeper bank and charged up to it.

Halfway to the top I slipped to my knees, looked over my shoulder, and saw the man in the black suit almost at my heels, his white face pulled into a convulsion of fury and greed. His cheeks were splattered with his bloody tears and his shark's mouth hung open like a hinge.

'*Fisherboy*!' he snarled, and started up the bank after me, grasping at my foot with one long hand. I tore free, turned, and threw my fishing pole at him.

He batted it down easily, but it tangled his feet up somehow and he went to his knees. I didn't wait to see anymore; I turned and bolted to the top of the slope.

I almost slipped at the very top, but managed to grab one of the support struts running beneath the bridge and save myself.

'You can't get away, fisherboy!' he cried from behind me. He sounded furious, but he also sounded as if he were laughing. 'It takes more than a mouthful of trout to fill *me* up!'

'Leave me alone!' I screamed back at him. I grabbed the bridge's railing and threw myself over it in a clumsy somersault, filling my hands with splinters and bumping my head so hard on the boards when I came down that I saw stars. I rolled over onto my belly and began crawling. I lurched to my feet just before I got to the end of the bridge, stumbled once, found my rhythm, and then began to run. I ran as only nine-year-old boys can run, which is like the wind. It felt as if my feet only touched the ground with every third or fourth stride, and for all I know, that may be true. I ran straight up the righthand wheelrut in the road, ran until my temples pounded and my eyes pulsed in their sockets, ran until I had a hot stitch in my left side from the bottom of my ribs to my armpit, ran until I could taste blood and something like metal-shavings in the back of my throat.

When I couldn't run anymore I stumbled to a stop and looked back over my shoulder, puffing and blowing like a windbroke horse. I was convinced I would see him standing right there behind me in his natty black suit, the watch-chain a glittering loop across his vest and not a hair out of place.

But he was gone. The road stretching back toward Castle Stream between the darkly massed pines and spruces was empty. And yet I sensed him somewhere near in those woods, watching me with his grassfire eyes, smelling of burnt matches and roasted fish. I turned and began walking as fast as I could, limping a little – I'd pulled muscles in both legs, and when I got out of bed the next morning I was so sore I could barely walk. I didn't notice those things then, though.

I just kept looking over my shoulder, needing again and again to verify that the road behind me was still empty. It was, each time I looked, but those backward glances seemed to increase my fear rather than lessening it. The firs looked darker, massier, and I kept imagining what lay behind the trees which marched beside the road – long, tangled corridors of forest, leg-breaking deadfalls, ravines where anything might live. Until that Saturday in 1914, I had thought that bears were the worst thing the forest could hold.

Now I knew better.

A mile or so further up the road, just beyond the place where it came out of the woods and joined the Geegan Flat Road, I saw my father walking toward me and whistling 'The Old Oaken Bucket.' He was carrying his own rod, the one with the fancy spinning reel from Monkey Ward. In his other hand he had his creel, the one with the ribbon my mother had woven through the handle back when Dan was still alive. DEDICATED TO JESUS, that ribbon said. I had been walking but when I saw him I started to run again, screaming *Dad! Dad! Dad!* at the top of my lungs and staggering from side to side on my tired, sprung legs like a drunken sailor. The expression of surprise on his face when he recognized me might have been comical under other circumstances, but not under these.

He dropped his rod and creel into the road without so much as a downward glance at them and ran to me. It was the fastest I ever saw my Dad run in his life; when we came together it was a wonder the impact didn't knock us both senseless, and I struck my face on his belt-buckle hard enough to start a little nosebleed. I didn't notice that until later, though. Right then I only reached out my arms and clutched him as hard as I could. I held on and rubbed my hot face back and forth against his belly, covering his old blue workshirt with blood and tears and snot.

'Gary, what is it? What happened? Are you all right?'

'Ma's dead!' I sobbed. 'I met a man in the woods and he told me! Ma's dead! She got stung by a bee and it swelled her all up just like what happened to Dan, and she's dead! She's on the kitchen floor and Candy Bill… licked the t-t-tears… off her… off her…'

Face was the last word I had to say, but by then my chest was hitching so bad I couldn't get it out. My tears were flowing again, and my Dad's startled, frightened face had blurred into three overlapping images. I began to howl – not like a little kid who's skun his knee but like a dog that's seen something bad by moonlight – and my father pressed my head against his hard flat stomach again.

I slipped out from under his hand, though, and looked back over my shoulder. I wanted to make sure the man in the black suit wasn't coming. There was no sign of him; the road winding back into the woods was completely empty. I promised myself I would never go back down that road again, not ever, no matter what, and I suppose now God's greatest blessing to His creatures below is that they can't see the future. It might have broken my mind if I had known I *would* be going back down that road, and not two hours later. For that moment, though, I was only relieved to see we were still alone. Then I thought of my mother – my beautiful dead mother – and laid my face back against my father's stomach and bawled some more.

'Gary, listen to me,' he said a moment or two later. I went on bawling. He gave me a little longer to do that, then reached down and lifted my chin so he could look into my face and I could look into his.

'Your Mom's fine,' he said.

I could only look at him with tears streaming down my cheeks. I didn't believe him.

'I don't know who told you different, or what kind of dirty dog would want to put a scare like that into a little boy, but I swear to God your mother's fine.'

'But… but he said…'

'I don't care *what* he said. I got back from Eversham's earlier than I expected – he doesn't want to sell any cows, it's all just talk – and decided I had time to catch up with you. I got my pole and my creel and your mother made us a couple of jelly fold-overs. Her new bread. Still warm. So she was fine half an hour ago, Gary, and there's nobody knows any different that's come from this direction, I guarantee you. Not in just half an hour's time.' He looked over my shoulder. 'Who was this man? And where was he? I'm going to find him and thrash him within an inch of his life.'

I thought a thousand things in just two seconds – that's what it seemed like, anyway – but the last thing I thought was the most powerful: if my Dad met up with the man in the black suit, I didn't think my Dad would be the one to do the thrashing. Or the walking away. I kept remembering those long white fingers, and the talons at the ends of them.

'Gary?'

'I don't know that I remember,' I said.

'Were you where the stream splits? The big rock?'

I could never lie to my father when he asked a direct question – not to save his life or mine. 'Yes, but don't go down there.' I seized his arm with both hands and tugged it hard. 'Please don't. He was a scary man.' Inspiration struck like an illuminating lightning-bolt. 'I think he had a gun.'

He looked at me thoughtfully. 'Maybe there wasn't a man,' he said, lifting his voice a little on the last word and turning it into something that was almost but not quite a question. 'Maybe you fell asleep while you were fishing, son, and had a bad dream. Like the ones you had about Danny last winter.'

I *had* had a lot of bad dreams about Dan last winter, dreams where I would open the door to our closet or to the dark, fruity interior of the cider shed and see him standing there and looking at me out of his purple strangulated face; from many of these dreams I had awakened screaming, and awakened my parents, as well. I had fallen asleep on the bank of the stream for a little while, too – dozed off, anyway – but I hadn't dreamed and I was sure I had awakened just before the man in the black suit clapped the bee dead, sending it tumbling off my nose and into my lap. I hadn't dreamed him the way I had dreamed Dan, I was quite sure of that, although my meeting with him had already attained a dreamlike quality in my mind, as I suppose supernatural occurrences always must. But if my Dad thought that the man had only existed in my own head, that might be better. Better for him.

'It might have been, I guess,' I said.

'Well, we ought to go back and find your rod and your creel.' He actually started in that direction, and I had to tug frantically at his arm to stop him again, and turn him back toward me.

'Later,' I said. 'Please, Dad? I want to see Mother. I've got to see her with my own eyes.'

He thought that over, then nodded. 'Yes, I suppose you do. We'll go home first, and get your rod and creel later.'

So we walked back to the farm together, my father with his fishpole propped on his shoulder just like one of my friends, me carrying his creel, both of us eating folded-over slices of my mother's bread smeared with blackcurrant jam.

'Did you catch anything?' he asked as we came in sight of the barn.

'Yes, sir,' I said. 'A rainbow. Pretty good-sized.' And a brookie that was a lot bigger, I thought but didn't say. *Biggest one I ever saw, to tell the truth, but I don't have that one to show you, Dad. I gave that one to the man in the black suit, so he wouldn't eat me. And it worked... but just barely.*

'That's all? Nothing else?'

'After I caught it I fell asleep.' This was not really an answer, but not really a lie, either.

'Lucky you didn't lose your pole. You didn't, did you, Gary?'

'No, sir,' I said, very reluctantly. Lying about that would do no good even if I'd been able to think up a whopper – not if he was set on going back to get my creel anyway, and I could see by his face that he was.

Up ahead, Candy Bill came racing out of the back door, barking his shrill bark and wagging his whole rear end back and forth the way Scotties do when they're excited. I couldn't wait any longer; hope and anxiety bubbled up in my throat like foam. I broke away from my father and ran to the house, still lugging his creel and still convinced, in my heart of hearts, that I was going to find my mother dead on the kitchen floor with her face swelled and purple like Dan's had been when my father carried him in from the west field, crying and calling the name of Jesus.

But she was standing at the counter, just as well and fine as when I had left her, humming a song as she shelled peas into a bowl. She looked around at me, first in surprise and then in fright as she took in my wide eyes and pale cheeks.

'Gary, what is it? What's the matter?'

I didn't answer, only ran to her and covered her with kisses. At some point my father came in and said, 'Don't worry, Lo – he's all right. He just had one of his bad dreams, down there by the brook.'

'Pray God it's the last of them,' she said, and hugged me tighter while Candy Bill danced around our feet, barking his shrill bark.

'You don't have to come with me if you don't want to, Gary,' my father said, although he had already made it clear that he thought I should – that I should go back, that I should face my fear, as I suppose folks would say nowadays. That's very well for fearful things that are make-believe, but two hours hadn't done much to change my conviction that the man in the black suit had been real. I wouldn't be able to convince my father of that, though. I don't think there was a nine-year-old that ever lived who would have been able to convince his father he'd seen the Devil come walking out of the woods in a black suit.

'I'll come,' I said. I had walked out of the house to join him before he left, mustering all my courage in order to get my feet moving, and now we were standing by the chopping-block in the side yard, not far from the woodpile.

'What you got behind your back?' he asked.

I brought it out slowly. I would go with him, and I would hope the man in the black suit with the arrow-straight part down the left side of his head was gone...but if he wasn't, I wanted to be prepared. As prepared as I could be, anyway. I had the family Bible in the hand I had brought out from behind my back. I'd set out just to bring my New Testament, which I had won for memorizing the most psalms in the Thursday night Youth Fellowship competition (I managed eight, although most of them except the Twenty-third had floated out of my mind in a week's time), but the little red Testament didn't seem like enough when you were maybe going to face the Devil himself, not even when the words of Jesus were marked out in red ink.

My father looked at the old Bible, swelled with family documents and pictures, and I thought he'd tell me to put it back, but he didn't. A look of mixed grief and sympathy crossed his face, and he nodded. 'All right,' he said. 'Does your mother know you took that?'

'No, sir.'

He nodded again. 'Then we'll hope she doesn't spot it gone before we get back. Come on. And don't drop it.'

Half an hour or so later, the two of us stood on the bank looking down at the place where Castle Stream forked, and at the flat place where I'd had my encounter with the man with the red-orange eyes. I had my bamboo rod in my hand – I'd picked it up below the bridge – and my creel lay down below, on the flat place. Its wicker top was flipped back. We stood looking down, my father and I, for a long time, and neither of us said anything.

Opal! Diamond! Sapphire! Jade! I smell Gary's lemonade! That had been his unpleasant little poem, and once he had recited it, he had thrown himself on his back, laughing like a child who has just discovered he has enough courage to say bathroom words like shit or piss. The flat place down there was as green and lush as any place in Maine that the sun can get to in early July...except where the stranger had lain. There the grass was dead and yellow in the shape of a man.

I looked down and saw I was holding our lumpy old family Bible straight out in front of me with both thumbs pressing so hard on the cover that they were white. It was the way Mama Sweet's husband Norville held a willow-fork when he was trying to dowse somebody a well.

'Stay here,' my father said at last, and skidded sideways down the bank, digging his shoes into the rich soft soil and holding his arms out for balance. I stood where I was, holding the Bible stiffly out at the ends of my arms like a willow-fork, my heart thumping wildly. I don't know if I had a sense of being watched that time or not; I was too scared to have a sense of anything, except for a sense of wanting to be far away from that place and those woods.

My Dad bent down, sniffed at where the grass was dead, and grimaced. I knew what he was smelling: something like burnt matches. Then he grabbed my creel and came on back up the bank, hurrying. He snagged one fast look over his shoulder to make sure nothing was coming along behind. Nothing was. When he handed me the creel, the lid was still hanging back on its cunning little leather hinges. I looked inside and saw nothing but two handfuls of grass.

'Thought you said you caught a rainbow,' my father said, 'but maybe you dreamed that, too.'

Something in his voice stung me. 'No, sir,' I said. 'I caught one.'

'Well, it sure as hell didn't flop out, not if it was gutted and cleaned. And you wouldn't put a catch into your fisherbox without doing that, would you, Gary? I taught you better than that.'

'Yes, sir, you did, but–'

'So if you didn't dream catching it and if it was dead in the box, something must have come along and eaten it,' my father said, and then he grabbed another quick glance over his shoulder, eyes wide, as if he had heard something move in the woods. I wasn't exactly surprised to see drops of sweat standing out on his forehead like big, clear jewels. 'Come on,' he said. 'Let's get the hell out of here.'

I was for that, and we went back along the bank to the bridge, walking quick without speaking. When we got there, my Dad dropped to one knee and examined the place where we'd found my rod. There was another patch of dead grass there, and the lady's slipper was all brown and curled in on itself, as if a blast of heat had charred it. While my father did this, I looked in my empty creel. 'He must have gone back and eaten my other fish, too,' I said.

My father looked up at me. '*Other* fish!'

'Yes, sir. I didn't tell you, but I caught a brookie, too. A big one. He was awful hungry, that fella.' I wanted to say more, and the words trembled just behind my lips, but in the end I didn't.

We climbed up to the bridge and helped one another over the railing. My father took my creel, looked into it, then went to the railing and threw it over.

I came up beside him in time to see it splash down and float away like a boat, riding lower and lower in the stream as the water poured in between the wicker weavings.

'It smelled bad,' my father said, but he didn't look at me when he said it, and his voice sounded oddly defensive. It was the only time I ever heard him speak just that way.

'Yes, sir.'

'We'll tell your mother we couldn't find it. If she asks. If she doesn't ask, we won't tell her anything.'

'No, sir, we won't.'

And she didn't and we didn't and that's the way it was.

That day in the woods is eighty-one years gone, and for many of the years in between I have never even thought of it... not awake, at least. Like any other man or woman who ever lived, I can't say about my dreams, not for sure. But now I'm old, and I dream awake, it seems. My infirmities have crept up like waves which will soon take a child's abandoned sand castle, and my memories have also crept up, making me think of some old rhyme that went, in part, 'Just leave them alone/And they'll come home/Wagging their tails behind them.' I remember meals I ate, games I played, girls I kissed in the school cloakroom when we played Post Office, boys I chummed with, the first drink I ever took, the first cigarette I ever smoked (cornshuck behind Dicky Hammer's pig-shed, and I threw up). Yet of all the memories, the one of the man in the black suit is the strongest, and glows with its own spectral, haunted light. He was real, he was the Devil, and that day I was either his errand or his luck. I feel more and more strongly that escaping him was my luck – *just* luck, and not the intercession of the God I have worshipped and sung hymns to all my life.

As I lie here in my nursing-home room, and in the ruined sand castle that is my body, I tell myself that I need not fear the Devil – that I have lived a good, kindly life, and I need not fear the Devil. Sometimes I remind myself that it was I, not my father, who finally coaxed my mother back to church later on that summer.

In the dark, however, these thoughts have no power to ease or comfort. In the dark comes a voice which whispers that the nine-year-old boy I was had done nothing for which he might legitimately fear the devil either...and yet the Devil came. And in the dark I sometimes hear that voice drop even lower, into ranges which are inhuman. *Big fish!* it whispers in tones of hushed greed, and all the truths of the moral world fall to ruin before its hunger. *Biiig fiiish!*

The Devil came to me once, long ago; suppose he were to come again now? I am too old to run now; I can't even get to the bathroom and back without my walker. I have no fine large brook trout with which to propitiate him, either, even for a moment or two; I am old and my creel is empty. Suppose he were to come back and find me so?

And suppose he is still hungry?

THE SNOW PAVILION

Angela Carter

Angela Carter (1940–1992) was an English writer of fantastical fiction ranked tenth by *The Times* in 2008 on their list of 'The 50 greatest British writers since 1945'. Always a maverick, Carter filtered a love for weird fiction, folktales, and surrealists like Leonora Carrington through a feminist lens to create abidingly unique stories and novels that rank amongst the best of the twentieth century. Carter's classics include *The Infernal Desire Machines of Doctor Hoffman* (1972) and *Nights at the Circus* (1984), along with several iconic story collections, especially *Fireworks* (1974) and *The Bloody Chamber* (1979). 'The Snow Pavilion' (1995) is a later story and perhaps the most evocative expression of the weird in her short fiction.

The motor stalled in the middle of a snowy landscape, lodged in a rut, wouldn't budge an inch. How I swore! I'd planned to be snug in front of a roaring fire, by now, a single malt on the mahogany wine-table (a connoisseur's piece) beside me, the five courses of Melissa's dinner savourously aromatising the kitchen; to complete the décor, a labrador retriever's head laid on my knee as trustingly as if I were indeed a country gentleman and lolled by rights among the chintz. After dinner, before I read our customary pre-coital poetry aloud to her, my elegant and accomplished mistress, also a connoisseur's piece, might play the piano for her part-time pasha while I sipped black, acrid coffee from her precious little cups.

Melissa was rich, beautiful and rather older than I. The servants slipped me looks of sly complicity; no matter how carefully I rumpled my sheets, they knew when a bed hadn't been slept in. The master of the house had a pied-à-terre in London when the House was sitting and the House was sitting tight. I'd met him only once, at the same dinner party where I'd met her – he'd been off-hand with me, gruff. I was young and handsome and full of promise; my relations with husbands rarely prospered. Wives were quite amother matter. Women, as Mayakovosky justly opined, are very partial to poets.

And now her glamorous motor car had broken down in the snow. I'd borrowed it for a trip to Oxford, ostensibly to buy books, utilising, with my instinctual cunning, the weather as an excuse. Last night, the old woman had been shaking her mattress with a vengeance – such snow! When I woke up the bedroom was full of luminous snow light, catching in the coils of Melissa's honey-coloured hair, and I'd experienced, once again, but, this time, almost uncontrollably, the sense of claustrophobia that sometimes afflicted me when I was with her.

I'd said, let's read some snowy poetry together, after dinner tonight, Melissa, a tribute of white verses to the iconography of the weather. Any excuse, no matter how far fetched, to get her out of the house – too much luxury on an empty stomach, that was the trouble. Always the same eyes too big for his belly, as grandma used to say; grandma spotted the trait when this little fellow lisped and toddled and pissed the bed before he knew what luxury was, even. Cultural indigestion, I tell you, the gripe in the bowels of your spirit. How can I get out of here, away from her subtly flawed antique mirrors, her French perfume decanted into eighteenth-century crystal bottles, her inscrutably smirking ancestresses in their gilt, oval frames? And her dolls, worst of all, her blasted dolls.

Those dolls that had never have been played with, her fine collection of antique women, part of the apparatus of Melissa's charm, her piquant originality that lay well on the safe side of quaint. A dozen or so of the finest lived in her bedroom in a glass-fronted, satinwood cabinet lavishly equipped with such toyland artefacts and miniature sofas and teeny-tiny grand pianos. They had heads made of moulded porcelain, each dimple and bee-stung underlip sculpted with loving care. Their wigs and over-lifelike eyelashes were made of real hair. She told me their eyes had been manufactured by the same craftsman in glass who made those terribly precious paperweights filled with magic snowstorms. Whenever I woke up in Melissa's bed, the first thing I saw were a dozen pairs of shining eyes that seemed to gleam wetly, as if in lacrimonious accusation of my presence there, for the dolls, like Melissa, were perfect ladies and I, in my upwardly social mobile nakedness – a nakedness that was, indeed, the essential battledress for such storm-troopers as I! – patently no gentleman.

After three days of that kind of style, I badly needed to sit in a public bar, drink coarse pints of bitter, swap double entendres with the barmaid; but I could hardly tell milady that. Instead, I must use my vocation to justify my day off. Lend me the car, Melissa, so that I can drive to Oxford and buy a book of snowy verses, since there's no such book in the house. And I'd made my purchase and managed to fit in my bread, cheese and badinage as well. A good day. Then, almost home again and here I was, stuck fast.

The fields were all brim-full of snow and the dark sky of late afternoon already swollen and discoloured with the next fall. Flocks of crows wheeled endlessly upon the invisible carousels of the upper air, occasionally emitting a rusty caw. A glance beneath the bonnet showed me only that I did not know what was wrong and must get out to trudge along a lane where the mauve shadows told me snow and the night would arrive together. My breath smoked. I wound Melissa's husband's muffler round my neck and dug my fists into his sheepskin pockets; his borrowed coat kept me snug and warm, although the cold made the nerves in my forehead hum with a thin, high sound like that of the wind in telephone wires.

The leafless trees, the hillside quilted by intersections of dry-stone walling – all had been subdued to monochrome by the severity of last night's blizzard. Snow clogged every sound but that of the ironic punctuation of the crows. No sign of another presence; the pastoral cows were all locked up in the steaming byre, Colin Clout and Hobbinol sucked their pipes by the fireside in pastoral domesticity. Who would be outside, today, when he could be warm and dry, inside.

Too white. It is too white, out. Silence and whiteness at such a pitch of twinned intensity you know what it must be like to live in a country where snow is not a charming, since infrequent, visitor that puts its cold garlands on the trees so prettily we think they are playing at blossoming. (What an aptly fragile simile, with its Botticellian nuance. I congratulated myself.) No. Today is as cold as the killing cold of the perpetually white countries; today's atrocious candour is that of those white freckles that are the stigmata of frostbite.

My sensibility, the exquisite sensibility of a minor poet, tingled and crisped at the sight of so much whiteness.

I was certain that soon I'd come to a village where I could telephone Melissa; then she would send the village taxi for me. But the snow-fields now glimmered spectrally in an ever-thickening light and still there was no sign of life about me in the whole, white world but for the helmeted crows creaking down towards their nests.

Then I came to a pair of wrought-iron gates standing open on a drive. There must be some mansion or other at the end of the drive that would offer me shelter and, if they were half as rich as they ought to be, to live in such style, then they would certainly know Melissa and might even have me driven back to her by their own chauffeur in a warm car that would smell deliciously of new leather. I was sure they must be rich, the country side was lousy with the rich; hadn't I flattened a brace of pheasants on my way to Oxford? Encouraged, I turned in between the gate-posts, on which snarled iron gryphons sporting circumcision caps of snow.

The drive wound through an elm copse where the upper limbs of the bare trees were clogged with beastly lice of old crows' nests. I could tell that nobody had come this way since the snow fell, for only rabbit slots and the cuneiform prints of birds marked surfaces already crisping with frost. The drive took me uphill. My shoes and trouser bottoms were already wet through; it grew darker, colder and the old woman must have given her mattress a tentative shake or two, again, for a few more flakes drifted down and caught on my eyelashes so I first saw that house through a dazzle as of unshed tears, although, I assure you, I was out of the habit of crying.

I had reached the brow of a hill. Before me, in a hollow, magically surrounded by a snowy formal garden, lay a jewel of a mansion in a voluptuous style of English renaissance and every one of its windows blazed with light. I imagined myself describing it to Melissa – 'a vista like visible Debussy'. Enchanting. But, though lights streamed out in every direction, all was silent except for the crackling of the frosty trees. Lights and frost; in the winter sky above me, stars were coming out. Especially for my cultured patroness, I made an elision of the stars in the mansion of the heavens and the lights of the great house. So who was it, this snowy afternoon, who'd bagged a triad of fine images for her? Why, her clever boy! How pleased she'd be. And now I could declare the image factory closed for the day and get on with the real business of living, the experience of which that lovely house seemed to promise me in such abundance.

Yet, since the place was so well lit, the front door at the top of the serpentine staircase left open as for expected guests, why were there still no traces of arrivals or departures in the snow on which my footprints extended backwards to the lane and Melissa's abandoned car? And no figures to be glimpsed through any window, nor sound of life at all?

The vast empty hall serenely dominated by an immense chandelier, the faceted pendants of which chinked faintly in the currents of warm air and stippled with shifting, prismatic shadows walls wreathed in white stucco. This chandelier intimidated me, like too grand a butler but, all the same, I found the bellpull and tugged it. Somewhere inside a full-mouthed bell tolled; its reverberations set the chandelier a-tinkle but even when everything settled down again, nobody came.

I hauled again on the bellpull; still no reply, but a sudden wind blew a flurry of snow or sleet around me into the hall. The chandelier rocked musically in the draught. Behind me, outside, the air was full of the taste of snow – the storm was about to begin again. Nothing for it but to step bravely over the indifferent threshold and stamp my feet on the doormat with enough *éclat* to announce my arrival to the entire ground floor.

It was by far the most magnificent house I'd ever seen, and warm, so warm my frozen fingers throbbed. Yet all was white inside as the night outside, white walls, white paint, white drapes and a faint perfume everywhere, as though many rich women in beautiful dresses had drifted through the hall on their way to drinks before dinner, leaving behind them their spoor of musk and civet. The very air, here, mimicked the caress of their naked arms, intimate, voluptuous, rare.

My nostrils flared and quivered. I should have liked to have made love to every one of those lovely beings whose presence here was most poignant in her absence; it was a house built and furnished only for pleasure, for the indulgence of the flesh, for elegant concupiscence. I felt like Mignon in the land of the lemon trees; this is the place where I would like to live. I screwed up sufficient wincing courage to shout out: 'Anyone at home?' But only the chandelier tinkled in reply.

Then, a sudden creak behind me; I spun round to see the door swing to on its hinges with a soft, inexorable click. At that, the chandelier above me seemed to titter uncontrollably, as if with glee to see me locked in.

It is the wind, only the wind. Try to believe it is only the wind that blew the door shut behind you, keep a strong hold on that imagination of yours. Stop that shaking, all at once uneasy; walk slowly to the door, don't look nervous. It is the wind. Or else – perhaps – a trick of the owners, a practical joke. I grasped the notion gratefully. I knew the rich loved practical jokes.

But as soon as I realised it must be a practical joke, I knew I was not alone in the house because its apparent emptiness was all part of the joke. Then I exchanged one kind of unease for another. I became terribly self-conscious. Now I must watch my step; whatever happened, I must look as if I knew how to play the game in which I found myself. I tried the door but I was locked firmly in, of course. In spite of myself, I felt a faint panic, stifled it ... No, you are *not* at their mercy.

The hall remained perfectly empty. Closed doors on either side of me; the staircase swept up to an empty landing. Am I to meet my hosts in embarrassment and humiliation, will they all come bouncing – 'boo!' – out of hidey holes in the panelling, from behind sweeping curtains to make fun of me? A huge mirror behind an extravagant arrangement of arum lilies showed me a poor poet not altogether convincingly rigged out in borrowed country squire's gear. I thought, how pinched and pale my face looks; a face that's eaten too much bread and margarine in its time. Come, now, liven up! You left bread and margarine behind you long ago, at grandma's house. Now you are a house-guest of the Lady Melissa. Your car has just broken down in the lane; you are looking for assistance.

Then, to my relief but also my increased disquiet, I saw a face behind my own, reflected, like mine, in the mirror. She must have known I could spy her, peeking at me behind my back. It was a pale, soft, pretty face, streaming blonde hair, and it sprang out quite suddenly from the reflections of the backs of the lilies. But when I turned, she – young, tricksy, fleet of foot – was gone already, though I could have sworn I heard a carillon of giggles, unless my sharp, startled movement had disturbed the chandelier, again.

This fleeting apparition let me know for sure I was observed. ('How amusing, a game of hide-and-seek. All the same, do you think, perhaps, the chauffeur could ...') With the sullen knowledge of myself as appointed clown, I opened the first door I came to on the ground floor, expecting to discover my tittering audience awaiting me.

It was perfectly empty.

A white on white reception room, all bleached, all pale, sidetables of glass and chrome, artefacts of white lacquer, upholstery of thick, white velvet. Company was expected; there were decanters, bowls of ice, dishes of nuts and olives. I was tempted to swallow a cut-glass tumbler full of something-or-other, to snatch a handful of salted almonds – I was parched and starving, only that pub sandwich since breakfast. But it would never do to be caught in the act by the fair-haired girl I'd glimpsed in the hall. Look, she's left her doll behind her, forgotten in the deep cushioning of an armchair.

How the rich indulge their children! Not a doll so much as a little work of art; the cash register at the back of my mind rang up twenty guineas at the sight of this floppy Pierrot with his skull-cap, his white satin pyjamas with the black buttons down the front, all complete, and that authentic pout of comic sadness on his fine china face. *Mon ami Pierrot*, poor old fellow, limp limbs a-dangle, all anguished sensibility and no moral fibre. I know how you feel. But, as I exchanged my glance of pitying complicity with him, there came a sharp, melodious twang like a note from an imperious tuning fork, from beyond the half-open double doors. After a startled moment, I sprang into the dining room, summoned.

I had never seen anything like that dining room, except at the movies – not even at the dinner where I'd met Melissa. Fifteen covers laid out on a tongue-shaped spit of glass; but I hardly had time to take in the splendour of the fine china, the lead crystal, because the door into the hall still swung on its hinges and I knew I had missed her by seconds. So the daughter of the house is indeed playing 'catch' with me; and where has she got to, now?

Soft, softly on the white carpets; I leave deep prints behind me but do not make a sound. And still no sign of life, only the pale shadows of the candles; yet, somehow, everywhere a sense of hushed expectancy, as of the night before Christmas.

Then I heard a patter of running footsteps. But these footsteps came from a part of the house where no carpets muffled them, somewhere high above me. As I poised, ears a-twitch, there came from upstairs or downstairs, or milady's chamber, a spring of thin, high laughter agitating the chandeliers; then the sound of many, many running feet overhead. For a moment, the whole house seemed to tremble with unseen movement; then, just as suddenly, all was silent again.

I resolutely set myself to search the upper rooms.

All these rooms were quite empty. But my always nascent paranoia, now tingling at the tip of every nerve, assured me they had all been vacated the very moment I entered them. Every now and then, as I made my increasingly grim-faced tour of the house, I heard bursts of all kinds of delicious merriments but never from the room next to the one in which I stood. These voices started and stopped as if switched on and off and, of course, were part and parcel of the joke; this joke was, my unease. In what, by its size and luxury, must have been the master bedroom, the polar bearskin rug thrown over the bed was warm and rumpled as if someone had just been lying there and now hid, perhaps, in the ivorine wardrobe, enjoying my perplexity. And I could have wrecked their fun if only – if only! – I had the courage to fling open the pale doors and catch my reluctant hosts crouching, as I thought, among the couture. But I did not dare do that.

The staircarpets gave way to scrubbed boards and still I had not seen anything living except the possibility of a face in the mirror, although the entire house was full of evidence of life. These upper floors were dimly lit, only single lights in holders at intervals along the walls, but one door was standing open and light spilled out onto the passage, like an invitation.

A good fire glowed in a neat little range where nightclothes were warming on the brass fender. I felt a sudden, sharp pang of disappointment to find her trail lead me to the nursery; I had been duped of all the fleshly adventures the house had promised me and that, damn them, must be part of the joke, too. All the same, if I indulged the fancy of the child I'd seen in the mirror, perhaps I might engage the fancy of her mother, who must be still young enough to enjoy the caress of a bearskin bedstead; and not, I'd be bound, inimical to poetry, either.

This mother, who had condemned even the nursery to whiteness, white walls, white painted furniture, white rug, white curtains, all chic as hell. Even the child had been made a slave to fashion. Yet, though the nursery itself had succumbed to the interior designer's snowdrift that had engulfed the entire house, its inhabitants had not. I'd never seen so many dolls before, not even in Melissa's cabinet, and all quite exquisite, as if they'd just come from the shop, although some of them must be older than I was. How Melissa would have loved them!

Dolls sat on shelves with their legs stuck out before them, dolls spilled from toychests. Fine ladies in taffeta bustles and French hats, babies in every gradation of cuteness. A limp-limbed, golden-haired creature in pink satin sprawled as if in sensual abandon on the rug in front of the fire. A wonderfully elaborate lady in a kitsch Victorian pelisse of maroon silk, with brown hair under a feather straw bonnet, lay in an armchair by the fire with as proprietorial an air as if the room belonged to her. A delicious lass in a purple velvet riding habit occupied the saddle of the wonderful albino rocking horse.

Now at last I was surrounded by beautiful women and they were dumb repositories of all the lively colours that had been exiled from the place, vivid as a hot-house, but none of them existed, all were mute, were fictions and that multitude of glass eyes, like tears congealed in time, made me feel very lonely.

Outside, the snow flurried against the windows; the storm had begun in earnest. Inside, there was still one threshold left to cross. I guessed she would be there, waiting for me, whoever she was, although I hesitated, if only momentarily, before the door that lead to the night nursery, as if unseen gryphons might guard it.

Faint glow of a night light on the mantelpiece; a dim tranquillity, here, where the air is full of the warm, pale smells of childhood, of clean hair, of soap, of talcum powder, the incenses of her sanctuary. And the moment I entered the night nursery, I could hear her transparent breathing; she had hardly hidden herself at all, not even pulled the covers of her white-enamelled crib around her. I had taken the game seriously but she, its instigator, had not; she had fallen fast asleep in the middle of it, her eyelids buttoned down, her long, blonde, patrician hair streaming over the pillow.

She wore a white, fragile, lace smock and her long, white stockings were fine as the smoky breath of a winter's morning. She had kicked off her white kid sandals. This little hunter, this little quarry, lay curled up with her thumb wedged, baby-like, in her mouth.

The wind yowled in the chimney and snow pelted the window. The curtains were not yet drawn so I closed them for her and at once the room denied tempest, so I could have thought I had been snug all my life. Weariness came over me; I sank down in the basketwork chair by her bed. I was loath to leave the company of the only living thing I'd found in the mansion and even if Nanny brusquely stormed in to interrogate me, I reassured myself that she must know how fond her little charge was of hide-and-seek indeed, must have been in complicity with the game, to let me wander about the nursery suite in this unconventional fashion. And if Mummy came in, now, for goodnight kisses? Well so much the better; I should be discovered demonstrating the tenderness of a poet at the cradle of a child.

If nobody came? I would endure the anticlimax; I'd just take the weight off my feet for a while, and then slip out. Yet I must admit I felt a touch of disappointment as time passed and I was forced reluctantly to abandon all hope of an invitation to dinner. They'd forgotten all about me! Careless even of their own games, they had left off playing in the middle of the chase, just as the child had done, and retired into the immutable privacy of the rich. I promised myself that at least I'd help myself to half a tumbler of good whisky on my way out, to see me warmly back to the lane and the stark trudge home.

The child stirred in her sleep and muttered indecipherably. Her fists clenched and unclenched. Her cheeks were delicately flushed a pale, luminous pink. Such skin – the fine texture of childhood, the incomparable down of skin that has never gone out in the cold. The more I watched beside her, the frailer she looked, the more transparent. I had never, in my life before, watched beside a sleeping child. The milky smell of innocence and sentiment suffused the night nursery.

I had anticipated, I suppose, some sort of gratified lust from this game of hide-and-seek through the mansion if not the satisfaction of lust of the flesh, then that of lust of the spirit, of vanity; but the more I mimicked tenderness towards the sleeper, the more tender I became. Oh, my shabby-sordid life! I thought. How she, in her untouchable sleep, judges me.

Yet she was not a peaceful sleeper. She twitched like a dog dreaming of rabbits and sometimes she moaned. She snuffled constantly and then, quite loudly, coughed. The cough rumbled in her narrow chest for a long time and it struck me that the child, so pale and sleeping with such racked exhaustion, was a sick child. A sick, spoiled little girl who ruled the household with a whim, and yet, poor little tyrant, went unloved; they must have been glad she had dropped off to sleep, so they could abandon the game she had forced them to play. She had fairy-tale, flaxen hair and eyelids so delicate the eyes beneath them almost showed glowing through; and if, indeed, it had been she who secreted all the grumbling grown-ups in their wardrobes and bathrooms and wound me through the house on an invisible spool towards her, well, I could scarcely begrudge her her fun. And her game had been as much with those grown-ups as it had been with me; hadn't she tidied them all away as if they'd been dolls she'd stowed in the huge toychest of this exquisite house?

When I thought of that, I went so far in forgiveness as to stroke her eggshell cheek with my finger. Her skin was soft as plumage of snow and sensitive as that of the princess in the story of the princess and the pea; when I touched her, she stirred. She shrugged away from my touch, muttering, and rolled over uneasily. As she did so, a gleaming bundle slithered from between her covers on to the floor, banging its china head on the scrubbed linoleum.

She must have tiptoed down to collect her forgotten doll while I went prowling about the bedrooms. Here he was again, her Pierrot in his shining white pyjamas, her little friend. Perhaps her only friend. I bent to pick him up from the floor for her and, as I did so, something caught the light and glittered at the corner of his huge, tragic, glass eye. A sequin? A brilliant? The moon is your country, old chap; perhaps they've put stars in your eyes for you.

I looked more closely.

It was wet.

It was a tear.

Then I felt a succinct blow on the back of my neck, so sudden, so powerful, so unexpected that I felt only a vague astonishment as I pitched forward on my face into a black vanishment.

When I opened my eyes, I saw a troubled absence of light around me; when I tried to move, a dozen little daggers serrated me. It was terribly cold and I was lying on, yes, marble, as if I was already dead, and I was trapped inside a little hill of broken glass inside the wet carapace of Melissa's husband's sheepskin coat that was sodden with melting snow.

After a few, careful, agonising twitches, I thought it best to stay quite still in this dank, lightless hall where the snow drove in through an open door whose outline I could dimly see against the white night outside. Slow as a dream, the door shifted back and forth on rusty hinges with a raucous, mechanical, monotonous caw, like that of crows.

I tried to piece together what had happened to me. I guessed I lay on the floor of the hall of the house I could have sworn I'd just explored, though I could see very little of its interior in the ghostly light – but all must once have been painted white, though now sadly and obscenely scribbled over by rude village boys with paint and chalks. The despoiled pallor reflected itself in a cracked mirror of immense size on the wall.

Perhaps I had been trapped by the fall of a chandelier. Certainly, I had been caught in the half-shattered glass viscera of the chandelier that I thought I'd just seen multiplying its reflections in another hall than the one in which I lay and every bone in my body ached and throbbed. If time had loosened the chandelier from its moorings in the flaking plaster above me, the chandelier might very well have come tumbling down on me as I sheltered from the storm that howled and gibbered around the house but then it might have killed me and I knew by my throbbing bruises that I was still alive. But had I not just walked through this very hall when it was warm and perfumed and suave with money? Or had I not.

Then I was pierced by a beam of light that struck cold green fire from the prisms around me. The invisible behind the flashlight addressed me unceremoniously in a cracked, old woman's voice, a crone's voice. Who be you? What be you up to?

Trapped in the splintered glass, the splintered light, I told her how my car had broken down in the snow and I had come here for assistance. This alibi now seemed to me a very feeble one.

I could not see the old woman at all, could not even make out her vague shape behind the light, but I told her I was staying with the Lady Melissa, to impress her old country crone's snobbery. She exclaimed and muttered when she heard Melissa's name; when she spoke again, her manner was almost excessively conciliatory. She has to be careful, poor old woman, all alone in the house; thieves come for lead from the roof and young couples up to no good come and so on and on. But, if I am the Lady Melissa's guest, then she is sure it is perfectly all right for me to shelter here. No, there is no telephone. I must wait here till the storm dies down. The new snow will have blocked the lane by now – we are quite cut off! she says; and titters.

I must follow her carefully, walk this way; she gives me a hand out of the mess, so much broken glass... take care. What a crash, when the chandelier came down! You'd have thought the world had come to an end. Come with her, she has her rooms; she is quite cosy, sir, with a roaring fire. (What weather, eh?)

She led me solicitously out of the glass trap and took me past our phantoms moving like deep sea fish in the choked depths of the mirror; up the stairs we went, through the ruins of the house I thought I had explored in my waking faint or system of linked hallucinations, snow induced, or, perhaps, induced by a mild concussion. For I am shaky and a little nauseous; I grasp the banisters too tight.

The doors shudder on their hinges. I glimpse rooms with the furniture spookily shrouded in white sheets but the beam of her torch does not linger on anything; her carpet slippers go flipperty-flopperty, flipperty-flopperty, she is an intrepid negotiator of the shadows. And still I cannot see her clearly, although I hear the rustle of her dress and smell her musty, frowsty, second-hand clothes store, typical crone smell, like grandma's smell, smell of my childhood women.

She has, of course, ensconced herself in the nursery. And how I gasped, in my mild fever, to see so many dolls had set up camp in this decay!

Dolls everywhere higgledy-piggledy, dolls thrust down the sides of chairs, dolls spilled out of tea chests, dolls propped up on the mantelpiece with blank, battered faces. Had she gathered all the dolls of all the departed daughters of the house here, around her, for company? The dolls stared at me dumbly from glass eyes that might hold in suspension the magic snow-storm that trapped me here; I felt I was the cynosure of all their blind eyes.

And have I indeed met any of these now moth-gnawed creatures in this room before? When I first fainted in the hall, did I fall back in time to encounter on a white beach of years ago this young lady, whose heavy head drops forward on her bosom since her limp body has lost too much sawdust to continue to support it? The struts of her satin crinoline, stove in like a broken umbrella. Her blousy neighbour's dark red silk dress has faded to a thin pink but she has not lost her parasol because it had been sewn to her hand and her straw bonnet with the draggled feathers still hangs by a few threads from the brunette wig now awry on a china scalp.

And I almost tripped over a poor corpse on the floor in a purplish jacket of balding velvet, her worn, wax face raddled with age, only a few strands left of all that honey-coloured hair…

Yet if any of the denizens of that imaginary nursery were visiting this one, slipped out of my dream through a warp of the imagination, then I couldn't recognise them, thank God, among the dolls half loved to death and now scattered about a room whose present owner had consecrated it to a geriatric cosiness. Nevertheless, I felt a certain sense of disquiet, not so much fear as foreboding; but I was too preoccupied with my physical discomfort, my horrid aches, pains and scratches, to pay much attention to a prickling of the nerves.

And in the old woman's room, all was as comforting as a glowing fire, a steaming kettle could make it, even if eldritchly illuminated by a candle stuck in its own grease on to the mantelpiece. The very homeliness of the room went some way towards restoring my battered spirits and the crone made me very welcome, bustled me out of the sheepskin coat with almost as much solicitude as if she knew who it belonged to, set me down in an armchair. In its red plush death-throes, this armchair looked nothing like those bleached, remembered splendours; I told myself the snow had got into my eyes and brain. The old woman crouched down to take off my wet shoes for me; poured me thick, rich tea from her ever-ready pot; cut me a slice of dark gingerbread that she kept in an old biscuit tin with a picture of kittens on the lid. No spook or phantom could have had a hand in the making of that sagging, treacly, indigestible goody! I felt better, already; outside, the blizzard might rage but I was safe and warm, inside, even if in the company of an authentic crone.

For such she undeniably was, bent almost to a hoop with age, salt and pepper hair skewered up on top of her head with tortoiseshell pins, a face so eroded with wrinkles it was hard to tell whether she was smiling or not. She and her quarters had not seen soap and water for a long time and the lingering, sour, rank odour of uncaredforness faintly repelled me but the tea went down like blood. And don't you remember the slops and old clothes smell of grandma's kitchen? Colin Clout's come home again, with a vengeance.

She poured tea for herself and perched on top of the pile of old newspapers and discarded clothing that cushioned her own chair at the other side of the fire, to sip from her cup and chatter about the violence of the weather whilst I went on thawing myself out, eyeing – nervously, I must admit – the dolls propped on every flat surface, the roomful of bedizened raggle-taggles.

When she saw me looking at the dolls, she said: 'I see you're admiring my beauties.' Meanwhile, snow drove against the curtainless window-panes like furious birds and blasts echoed through the house. The old woman thrust her empty cup away in the grate, all at once moved as if by a sudden sense of purpose; I saw I must pay in kind for my kind reception, I must give her a piece of undivided attention. She scooped up an armful of dolls and began to introduce them to me one by one. Dotty. Quite dotty, poor old thing.

The Hon. Frances Brambell had one eye out and her bell-shaped, satin skirt had collapsed but she must have been a pretty acquisition to the toy cupboard in her day; time, however, has its revenges, the three divorces, the voluntary exile in Morocco, the hashish, the gigolos, the slow erosion of her beauty... how it made the old woman chuckle! But how enchanting the girl had looked when she was presented, the ostrich feathers nodding above her curls! I looked from the old woman to the doll and back again; now the crone was animated, a thick track of spittle descended her chin. With an ironic laugh, she tossed the Hon. Frances Brambell to one side; the china head bounced off the wall and her limbs jerked a little before she lay still on the floor.

Seraphine, Duchess of Pyke, wore faded maroon silk and what had once been a feathered hat. She hailed, initially, from Paris and still possessed a certain style, even in her old age, although the Duchess had been by no means a model of propriety and, even if she carried off her acquired rank to the manner born, there is no more perfect a lady than one who is no better than she should be, suggested the old woman. In a paroxysm of wheezing laughter, she cast the Duchess and her pretensions on top of the Hon. Frances Brambell and told me now I must meet Lady Lucy, ah! she would be a marchioness when she inherited but had been infected with moth in her most sensitive parts and grown emaciated, in spite of her pretty velvet riding habit. She always wore purple, the colour of passion. The sins of the fathers, insinuated this gossipy harridan, a congenital affliction... the future held in store for the poor girl only clinics, sanatoria, a wheel-chair, dementia, premature death.

Each doll's murky history was unfolded to me; the old woman picked them up and dismissed them with such confident authority I soon realised she knew all the little girls whose names she'd given to the dolls intimately. She must have been the nanny here, I thought; and stayed on after the family all left the sinking ship, after her last charge, that little daughter who might, might she not? have looked just like my imaginary blonde heiress, ran off with a virile but uncouth chauffeur, or, perhaps, the black saxophonist in the dance band of an ocean liner. And the retainer inherited the desuetude. In the old days, she must have wiped their pretty noses for them, cut their bread and butter into piano keys for them... all the little girls must once have played in this very nursery, come for tea with the young mistress, gone out riding on ponies, grown up to come to dances in wonderful dresses, stayed over for house parties, golf by day, affairs of the heart by night. Had my Melissa, herself, danced here, perhaps, in her unimaginable adolescence?

I thought of all the beautiful women with round, bare shoulders discreet as pearls going in to dinner in dresses as brilliant as the hot-house flowers that surrounded them, handsomely set off by the dinner-jackets of their partners, though they would have been far more finely accessorised by me – women who had once filled the whole house with that ineffable perfume of sex and luxury that drew me greedily to Melissa's bed. And time, now, frosting those lovely faces, the years falling on their head like snow.

The wind howled, the logs hissed in the grate. The crone began to yawn and so did I. I can easily curl up in this armchair beside the fire; I'm half asleep already – please don't trouble yourself. But, no; I must have the bed, she said.

You shall sleep in the bed.

And, with that, cackled furiously, jolting me from my bitter-sweet reverie. Her rheumy eyes flashed; I was stricken with the ghastly notion she wanted to sacrifice me to some aged lust of hers as the price of my night's lodging but I said: 'Oh,

I can't possibly take your bed, please no!' But her only reply was to cackle again.

When she rose to her feet, she looked far taller than she had been, she towered over me. Now, mysteriously, she resumed her old authority; her word was law in the nursery. She grasped my wrist in a hold like lockjaw and dragged me, weakly protesting, to the door that I knew, with a shock of perfect recognition, led to the night nursery.

I was cruelly precipitated back into the heart of my dream.

Beyond the door, on the threshold of which I stumbled, all was as it had been before, as if the night nursery were the changeless, unvaryingly eye of the storm and its whiteness that of a place beyond the spectrum of colours. The same scent of washed hair, the dim tranquillity of the night light. The white-enamelled crib, with its dreaming occupant. The storm crooned a lullaby; the little heiress of the snow pavilion had eyelids like carved alabaster that hold the light in a luminous cup, but she was a flawed jewel, this one, a shattered replica, a drawing that has been scribbled over, and, for the first time in all that night, I felt a pure fear.

The old woman softly approached her charge, and plucked an object, some floppy, cloth thing, from between the covers, where it had lain in the child's pale arms. And this object she, cackling again with obscure glee, handed to me as ceremoniously as if it were a present from a Christmas tree. I jumped when I touched Pierrot, as if there were an electric charge in his satin pyjamas.

He was still crying. Fascinated, fearful, I touched the shining teardrop pendant on his cheek and licked my finger. Salt. Another tear welled up from the glass eye to replace the one I had stolen, then another, and another. Until the eyelids quivered and closed. I had seen his face before, a face that had eaten too much bread and margarine in its time. A magic snow-storm blinded my eyes; I wept, too.

Tell Melissa the image factory is bankrupt, grandma.

Diffuse, ironic benediction of the night light. The sleeping child extended her warm, sticky hand to grasp mine; in a terror of consolation, I took her in my arms, in spite of her impetigo, her lice, her stench of wet sheets.

THE MEAT GARDEN

Craig Padawer

Craig Padawer (1961–) is an American fiction writer whose work has appeared in *Conjunctions, Fiction International,* and *After Yesterday's Crash: The Avant-Pop Anthology*. He received his master's degree in fiction writing from Brown University. 'The Meat Garden' (1996) comes to the weird from the surreal, creating a snapshot of a war both familiar and dislocatingly strange. According to Padawer, the story had its inspiration in both the Iraq War and 'the notion of a body at war with itself... [the tumor] that would inevitably bloom into my father's death was growing essentially in his mind. It was transforming him in every possible way – not just physically, but mentally. I still find that notion simultaneously terrifying and somehow absurdly beautiful.'

They humped it over metal hills and down through tortured valleys of scrap and smoking slag. For two days, Pilorus had been bitching about how he was swelling inside his suit. His tongue grew so thick that the grunts couldn't understand what he was saying anymore – but it didn't matter: they'd been hearing it for days. By late afternoon he was having trouble breathing, lagging badly behind the column so that Wally had to keep falling back to push him along. That night, in their trench, while he tried to eat a can of peaches, something broke inside his throat. And then the thing happened to his hands. It was awful and beautiful and later Wally would feel guilty at the way he'd just sat there, watching in fascination as Pilorus went through those hard changes. The hardest changes Wally had ever seen, until the Consolidation came along and rewrote the rules.

Toward the end, his head burst in a blizzard of seeds that hung in the lamplight and drifted slowly to the ground like a tiny division of poison paratroopers. Only then did Wally reach for his mask and scuttle out of the trench.

The platoon took friendly fire from behind and was harassed along its flanks by rogue Vegan units that had skipped over to Mack through some warp in ideology or the mysterious exigencies of politics. They wore their body armor even after the deep heat had set in, and on certain blistering noons Wally thought he could smell himself cooking inside the government steel. A crack leafhead sniper could thread a seed through a seam in an armadillo suit with all the accuracy of a seamstress, but a grunt would pay any price for the illusion of safety. And so they sweated it. In some sectors the air was so thick with pod shrapnel and spore that they had to wear pollen masks. And they took weird casualties there.

It was a problem of sensation. If it sometimes took minutes to realize you'd just lost your leg to a Mechanical Mary, it could take days before you knew that a Vegan round was germinating inside you, and weeks before your body began to blossom into death. Seed flak passed into you like a bullet fired in a dream, soft and bloodless – you couldn't tell an entry from a mosquito bite; and there were artillery spores so small they could enter the flesh without leaving any wound at all. In the absence of any pain by which to forecast his death, every grunt imagined he was dying at any given moment.

Mack fire, when it came, was almost a relief. A clock rocket with its shrapnel of escapements and flaming numerals provided instant blood, bones, burning hair. The ringing alarm let you know your time was up as the blast blew the memories out of your meat like a bad odor. And a television bomb would instantly blind you with its eruption of images as its icons burned through your flesh and imprinted themselves on your bones in tiny hieroglyphs that recounted the brief history of the body's destruction. There was no ambiguity to such wounds. You were either hit or whole, and you knew which pretty quickly.

But a Vegan wound was a covert wound. Once planted in flesh, the round put out roots and tendrils. It drank the blood out of the body and began to feed on the meat until its branches grew inside the victim's skin like a second set of bones and the body burst into flower. Sometimes you could see a grunt's face freeze with the knowledge. But most of the time it just arrived, like some sudden agonizing spring, some personal season of devastation. The body ripened with that secret penetration and then almost overnight the wounds opened and the limbs went rigid. A grunt's first reaction always seemed to be a sort of admiration for the beauty of his own destruction. Wally watched guys look on in fascination as their fingertips burst and the first buds unfolded from their bones.

Vegan ammunition took root in the rubble and the grunts came down out of molten metal hills into steaming basins of greenery where birds clotted the trees and shrieked above their tents at night. They ran spider wire out on the perimeter and laid down trip flares and mirror mines designed to kill the enemy with his own image. Mack anti-floral units operating in their sector hauled spare bladders filled with Blue Elixir and shrivel spray: Intel reports said they could defoliate a Vegan ammo dump in twenty minutes, but what the grunts knew was that the stench could melt your eyes. The enemy was doing such a thorough job that HQ decided to can their crop dusters. Anyway, Mack was just relocating the vegetation: the next barrage would fall two clicks north or east and begin to sprout in a matter of hours. From the air, the sector looked like a scorched grunt undergoing hair restoration. Acres of scrap and dust patched with horticulture. Jungle rose and fell overnight. Their maps were meaningless. And each temporary forest was an ambush waiting to happen.

One night in some nameless cube of greenery not marked on their maps, Wally crawled out of his tent to squat in the rain and he watched through the hole in his poncho as a scissor of lightning clipped through the canopy and suddenly revealed the jungle to be a vast impersonation of vegetable artillery, bark boots and moss fatigues. He was crawling back in a panic when the first zook whistled through the leaves and exploded against the backdrop of trees with a heavy *splurt.* He screamed ambush but something had happened to his ears and he couldn't hear himself. Tracers flashed through the canopy and the grunts were spilling out of their tents with defoliant grenades and half-assembled flame guns. As Wally scrambled in, Reno tossed him a piece and he found himself crouched in a nest of vines firing a music gun that he'd lifted off a dead Mack a week before. Wherever he aimed, the notes blew holes in the rain and trees exploded in flaming arpeggios. He spotted a sniper clothed in leaves beneath the slow fall of a phosphor flare, and when he pulled the trigger, music erupted from the barrel and entered the verdant figure in the form of a vicious dance that bent his bones into clefs and fiddled off his flesh in melodic intervals as his body disintegrated into music and the meat's melody multiplied into the cacophony of death.

Seed flak shredded the leaves overhead and ricocheted off the trees. Grunts were caught without their armor and the rain fed their wounds. The darkness was filled with cries and moans. Men were laying fire down into the feet of the trees, and in some small corner of the night a figure burned inside its uniform of leaves. The air smelled of phosphor and blossoms. The grunts called in for arty, for air, but nobody was sure of their coordinates. And then someone yelled for them to back it out of there before the leafheads sewed them in. The Cav was coming. They began to withdraw, leaving their gear behind and hauling only as much ammo as they could strap to their backs. But when they hit the perimeter, they got caught up in their own wire and had to cut their way out with heat knives while the vegheads routed them with seed flak and compost pellets. In the panic, Tibs tripped one of their own mirror mines and what it did to his image in that instant made his face break like glass.

When the wire finally fell, the grunts broke from the treeline and regrouped, hauling what wounded they could. Stimpfel and Weeps set up a chatter gun on a nearby hilltop and kept the veegs pinned to the horticulture until the Cav came in and laid down dispersion foam. Grunts were stripping down in the rain and frantically running flashlights over their bodies, searching for anything that looked like seed entry. They radioed for medevac and set up triage behind a hill of blistered tin out of which the half-melted corpses of Macks erupted like an expedition of puppets frozen in a glacier.

Wally was tearing open packets of herbicide with his teeth and handing them to Slice. Cecum had taken two rounds of high-speed seed in his gut before being hit by a nitrogen pellet, and the wound was blooming fast. His right arm burst and the medic lopped it off to stop the spread. But the fertilizer was feeding the seeds now and the bullets wrapped their roots around his bones, burrowing into everything inside Cecum that was soft and vital. They'd kept him standing to cut down on the ground surface, and now his boots had broken open and his feet had taken root.

'That's cool,' Slice kept saying, 'that's what we want.'

Air support thundered over their heads and the rain fell and grunts were screaming to be pruned, and in the middle of all the shit coming down on them, somebody was singing. At first Wally thought it was a music gun, but then he recognized Vomer's voice. He was crooning a weepy ballad about a woman who fashions a tiny man out of chicken to remind her of her lover gone away to war; she lets the little man build a house for himself inside her vagina, and when one day the lover returns she is forced to choose between responsibility and desire.

Whatever was growing inside Cecum had made him rigid, and he stood there in the downpour with his arms forking out along the horizon as if he'd been crucified to the rain. 'I'm fucked. Oh man, look at me, I'm fucked,' he wailed until his screams turned to leaves and his eyes burst into blossoms, and Slice told Wally all they could do now was pack him for flight.

A lone leafhead was still sniping at them with a compost gun and some grunts had gathered around the chatter rifle and were taking bets on who could pop him.

'Dumb fucker,' Stevo laughed, his voice edging into hysteria. 'Who's he think he's gonna hit with that fert? Cecum here's already a fuckin' forest. And I know *I* didn't catch any seed.'

'Yeah,' Vomer grinned, 'how d'you know that?'

'I just fuckin' *know,* asshole.'

Dustoff finally showed, dropping down through the rain in a swarm of lights and wind. They clipped Cecum's roots, sprayed him down with liquid starch and wrapped him in wet burlap like a tree about to be shipped through the mail. Then they strapped him to a chopper and scrambled out from under the blades.

The Cav dropped in a team of Root Rangers with ugly hardware, and after the greenery had been leveled the grunts went in behind them to mop up. They unzippered the trees and found the roasted corpses of leafheads curled like fetuses inside their wooden wombs.

The veegs must have had a Mack advisor attached to their unit because the grunts found a Wooden Colonel lying scorched in that burnt wreckage of trees. It sat in the mud with its legs broken beneath it and its wooden head swollen with rain. The mouth tried to speak but all that came out was a clicking sound and the grunts stood around draped in their ponchos like great dark birds, joking nervously while Litz radioed back for orders. The Mack's chestpan was cracked and someone reached in there with a stick and tickled the pink flaps of flesh dangling through the breach in the steel. The thing coughed feebly and puked up a bit of pulp wrapped in threads of radiator sputum.

'Hey, don't fuck with that thing, man.'

Litz crouched in the mud, his ears plugged into the ether. 'They want us to break him down,' he said.

'Shit.' Vomer spat into the rain. 'Fuckin' spooks.'

The Mack wasn't dead yet, so they stapled it to the dirt, and as they worked it watched them through lenses clouded with lymph. They ran a wire into him and when they opened his seams with a heat knife and a portable saw they found a live pigeon in there, its body woven through with wires. Vomer clipped the fibers, then held the bird by its wings and beat it against a tree until it looked like a feathered mojo bag leaking gruel. The apertures of the Mack's eyes clicked closed. 'You're set,' someone said. Reno hit it twice with an air chisel and its head broke open. Vomer checked it out for triggers and when nothing showed they fished out the map cylinder with a wire, cataloged it and sent it back to Intel in a sealed pouch. Then they cut the lenses out, crouched in the smoldering mud and drew cards for them.

Fuck protocol. They'd lost seven men.

That autumn, Mack shelled the city and fire roosted above the buildings like some new form of weather. Toward the end of October a team of wooden guerrillas with wires and rubber fingers commandeered one of the radio stations and Emma saw an old woman and her chauffeur killed in their car by a boobytrapped song. Their heads seemed to swell with music and then burst against the glass, and when the cops finally cut through the hood, clipped the battery cables and opened the car the interior looked like one of those canvasses she'd seen before the war in uptown galleries specializing in Impact Painting. At night, despite repeated protests from the Vegan ambassador, defol trucks rumbled down the avenues, watering the asphalt with herbicide. Come morning the air had a thin bitter smell and the trees sewn to their cubes of dirt stood dark and crooked against the dawn. The panic was on. Everyone was holding their money or shifting it out of the city in preparation for flight, and of necessity the skin industry seemed to pass overnight into a division of the War Department. The premier flesh houses were occupied by noncom officers and spooks from Intel, while the rest of the waterfront was overrun with grunts on three-day passes. Of the civilian clientele, only a few hardcore fatalists still haunted The Hairy Clam, Merkle's Rubber Womb or the black and blue bar of The Iron Tongue, where the whores had to unzipper their faces to suck you.

Emma's girls were skittish. The blare of a car horn sent them bolting from their beds, and every Friday at noon, when the carting company came through, the crash of the dumpster out back brought them up out of their sleep still dripping dreams and togaed in sheets damp with business and fear. They would pull on their pollen masks and clot the hallways like trapped crickets, chittering, goggle-eyed and anonymous, and no amount of Darvon could coax them back to sleep.

She had the house on Albacore Street by then. Her maids swept throat clamps and bits of metal out of the beds in the morning. At night, tracers stitched the northern sky with messages too brief to read, as if the war were some subliminal advertisement for a product no one could name. When the peace talks collapsed in early November, Emma shifted her money into an offshore account, had her windows painted with anti-flak lacquer and installed an escape ladder in her third-floor bedroom. At Hippolyta's urging she increased the brothel's security budget and rented a goon from one of the waterfront temp agencies in order to beef up the door during business hours. They kept a riot gun, a pair of pruning shears, a spray rifle full of Blue Elixir and two canisters of silence foam behind the bar. But the threats were myriad; there were only so many precautions Emma could take and inevitably the changes brought by the war left her confused and depressed. All these attempts to reduce risk, to make the city safe, to quantify it, were like trying to capture fire inside a paper box. The war could not be reduced to something logical. Her clientele had changed drastically, their desires mystified her, and for the first time since she had opened her own house Emma was scared. On her afternoon rounds of the rooms she came across ominous objects deposited in ashtrays and toilets. Three teeth wrapped in leaves. Dried vegetable ligaments. A pair of paper ears. A knackle of wet seeds webbed in pulp and hair. And once, in one of the third-floor bathrooms, something small and dark unfurling in the water at the bottom of the bowl, bleeding color.

City Hall ferried grunts in from the zone on fuck junkets for R&R. They arrived at the bordello's check-in desk like travelers disembarking from a dream. Eyes baked into a glaze. Skin ravaged by de-fol. Divots of hair scooped from their scalps by parasites, fear and fert burns. They wore necklaces of detonator cable strung with wooden tongues, lung sprockets and scrimshawed stalks of bone. They kept love letters, dried Yap paws, and puppets of cloth and bundled leaves tucked inside their helmet liners to shelter their heads from stray pieces of sky. Some had their nostrils pierced with firing pins; others wore keechee pouches stapled to their tongues and stuffed with curative seeds, twigs and Vegan prayers tattooed on scraps of rind. One grunt had a trained clock spider that lived inside his nose and roamed his face on a thin leash that was anchored to his ear; in a fit of nostalgia he'd removed the spider's trigger and now it was just a gimmick ticking in his head. Others converted to Carnism, swore off flesh and wore the anal effigies that the monks shipped to the front by the crateful... and still, come R&R, they shuffled into the madam's kitchen in embarrassment, asking for jars of vinegar in which to soak their effigies while they fucked her girls.

One night an Aluminum Terrorist slipped through a checkpoint on the northern border with forged documents and a paper face. He took a table at The Golden Triangle, then went into the bathroom, where he opened his own seams with a heat knife and assembled a music gun from the pieces he'd concealed inside his body. He came out firing staccatos and fugues. The diners were caught with their food in the air. The music funneled into their ears and traveled down their bones, tearing holes in their bodies as it sought some point of exit. In some cases, it erupted from the victims' mouths in a bloody song, bursting their tongues and blowing out their teeth, sparing the vital organs. As they lay bleeding, music pouring out of them, the wounded tried to plug their ears with napkins or bits of food. A desperate few pierced their eardrums with toothpicks and chopsticks then cowered beneath their tables as the mechanical assassin moved through the nightclub, until finally one of Ho's sumos, his ears sealed with wonton skins, managed to draw his pocket cannon and blow a hole in the Mack's chestpan. Mucus and motor lymph spurted from the wound and the killer's paper clothes began to dissolve as the fluids saturated them. By the time the cops, the AT boys and the spooks from Intel arrived, the sumos had stomped him flat as a cookie sheet. A pair of trigger specialists had to lift him with a spatula and tongs, while the AT crew sprayed everything down with silence foam. They brought in bunting and sound tarpaulins to muffle the lingering music, and they wrapped the wounded in soundproof blankets to keep them from contaminating the medical crews.

The following evening G.A.S.M. convened an emergency meeting. By the time Emma arrived everyone was talking about the latest attack. Earlier that day, a typewriter bomb had exploded at a blackmarket skin house over on Eel Street, sending words raining through the cardboard walls of the boudoirs and tattooing copies of the Machinist's 'Twelve Terms' on the bodies of whores and patrons alike. Forty pieces of merch ruined. Their bodies had been obliterated by language, all traces of their sexuality buried beneath a storm of words. There was something horrific about the sight of those who had survived a typewriter attack. Their faces scarred with text, as if they had become hostages to some awful advertisement. A few of the victims took to working the streets around the library where bibliophiles sometimes paid them to satisfy their fantasies amid the desolate hush of the reading rooms and the deserted stacks where the only witnesses to this erotic pantomime of the blank body and its printed partner were other words.

Everyone was wearing muscle. Ho arrived dressed in a live suit of sumos, a fat jigsaw of killers tailored into a sort of double-breasted kung-fu affair replete with epaulets of braided hair and a shirt that seemed to have been woven out of eyes. Rumors were rampant. The enemy, someone said, had launched a major offensive to coincide with the spring thaw. The situation was so dire that Morrison Carney himself was expected to attend that evening's meeting. Everyone was a wreck. Galena had doubled up on her vitamin enemas and confessed to Emma that she was undergoing sneeze therapy to deal with her anxiety. And even Merkle seemed to have developed a nervous leak. His cheeks were slack and stitched with fine wrinkles. His clothes hung on him, and the inflation specialist he traveled with was checking his air pressure every ten minutes.

Just as Vito Vesuvius gaveled the meeting to order, there was a commotion out in the lobby. The doors of the assembly spilled open and Morrison Carney rode down the velvet aisle of the chamber trailing his mute entourage of accountants, Carnite monks and tailored killers, and driving before him the ancient doorkeeper like some gaudy defector from an army of circus monkeys in his blood-colored uniform with its ridiculous panoply of sashes and honorary medals from apocryphal orders and secret societies for the preservation of pleasure: golden penises, ribbons, lace garters, and tiny velvet vaginas embroidered with jewels. Carney's mechanical chair came to rest at the foot of the speaker's podium.

The tycoon was accompanied by a pair of Mouths, one of whom served as his interpreter. The first Mouth carried a pair of ivory chopsticks in his pocket – talking sticks, which he used specifically for the purpose of communicating with the Carnites.

Carney nodded, cheeks puckered as he gummed the stone fetish in his mouth. A couple of Emma's clients were Carnite buffs, and she'd heard it said that the mannequin in his mouth had no face. That the old man's own effigy was the Thirteenth Aspect, CARNEY ABSENT, and that each of his effigies was carved by a blind monk and delivered to the tycoon's mansion in an opaque hingeless box of hardened water so that no one but Carney would ever set eyes on it.

The two monks walked up and down the aisles with carved lumen trays tweezered between their Edgar sticks. Piled upon the trays were tiny stone effigies of Morrison Carney affixed with rubber gaskets.

'Mr. Carney must ask you to please seal your ears,' said the first Mouth. He was wearing razor-tipped Teflon espadrilles and a tie made of water. As one of the trays passed before him he chose two stones and gently screwed them into his ears. When he lifted his arms, Emma could see the dark lump of the holster fastened to his upper torso like a nylon leech.

The second Mouth was blind and his ears had been sewn shut. Someone had sawn off his fingers and his hands looked like two canoe paddles. Sockets sealed with scars.

When everyone's ears were safely sealed, the monks unmuzzled the blind one's mouth and Emma saw his lips move. Across the room, the prisoner suddenly stiffened in its skin of burlap and blue plastic, and then something inside it softened, some secret wire went slack, and the Mack collapsed in a heap on the floor of the assembly.

For a moment nobody moved. Then Carney nodded hungrily. The monks placed the harness back on the blind Mouth's head and tightened the jaw screws. The one in the Teflon espadrilles removed the effigies from his ears and gestured for the pimps to do the same. The lumen platters were passed around and for a moment the only noise in the hall was the sound of the small stones clattering against the trays of hardened light. Emma watched as Carney's monks approached the fallen figure and rolled it over on its back. One began cutting into its chest with a water knife, while the other inserted his sticks into the wound, pried back the edges and removed a dark object: a hardened bird. Emma heard Merkle gasp beside her and for a moment she thought one of the ear effigies had pierced his latex and he'd sprung a leak. But then she heard his sibilant lisp – he seemed to be speaking from somewhere inside her hair, murmuring his astonishment.

The extracted bird looked like a statue carved out of bread and the monk waved it in the air as if it were a trophy.

Vito climbed down from his chair and pushed his way through the wall of owners to where the Mouth stood beside Carney and the leashed leathermouth. The Mouth cocked his head toward the monks and gestured with one of his talking sticks.

'Go touch it,' he told Vito. 'Don't be afraid. Yes, yes,' he nodded, 'it's all right, touch it! You'll find it's quite dead.'

Vito snatched the ivory stick out of the Mouth's hand and cautiously approached the monks. One of them lifted the hardened bird in his Edgar sticks and Vesuvius stopped in his tracks.

'A little moral support would be nice,' he hissed over his shoulder.

There was a mechanical chorus of clicks as muscle and management alike, reaching into their suits and purses, hitching up their skirts to get at thigh holsters, produced a small arsenal of weapons and cocked them at the object tweezered in the monk's sticks.

Vito poked at the bird with the talking stick. Tapped on it. Then, satisfied, tossed the stick aside and took the bird from the monk. He hefted it in his hands, lifted it over his head and hurled it at the floor, where it shattered into clumps and fine brown powder. He crouched. 'Fuckin' clay.'

'The principle is simple,' explained the Mouth. 'The Word turns clay into flesh. But when spoken in reverse, the Word will render flesh into clay.'

Morrison Carney's thin sticks quivered like two wires nailed into the wooden knots of his hands.

Checkpoint… checkpoint… checkpoint… dull ribbon of road and sentries. Another spring of endless mud has been launched… drenched trenches, flooded lines, scarecrows blooming along the washed-out routes. Couriers to the front carry the Word sealed inside leather mouths. Steel arabesques of wire, a bleeding pigeon flutters in its cage of concertina. The grunts toss canned crackers at it and watch the bird slice itself to ribbons trying to eat.

Addendums to the Battle Manual have been issued: procedures for handling the Word, for implanting the leather mouths inside the routed faces and hollowed heads of captured Macks and recoding their map cylinders so that they return to their platoons and speak the poison.

The courier eats his canned pears in the rain, the forked fruit round and luminous, as if the Army had sealed the pale asses of infants in syrup and tin. He dreams of his wife back in the city, the child growing inside her. When he returns it will be with a new fear of her flesh and what it harbors. There are barrages aimed at the city. She could be swelling with anything – some seed other than his own.

Weeks of mud and broken throats. A crude surgery beneath sandbag ceilings with screws and water saws and stale coffee at noon under the tarpaulin roof of the officer's bar. Rain stuttering against the empty de-fol drums. Mold bearding the wooden faces of the Macks behind their veil of razor wire. The courier combs the shell with soundsticks. Ties off wires. Drills holes in the aluminum skin to administer anesthesia. The leather mouth unsewn and every ear stoppered in case of a malfunction.

The courier's ears are raw from the plugs. He rubs ointment on them. Snatches sleep as the jeep rumbles through scorched hamlets and villes… troop movements that the recon readers mistake for a proliferation of the local horticulture… a charred carcass stapled to a tree – a small dog or a child with a tail. He's read the Intel reports but the information is always sketchy: Mack moving through animalist villes, burning coops and hooches; children barking down the roads, slaughtered in ditches and sprinkled down with lime and Rot Powder.

He wakes mid-journey to find his travel pillow smeared black with blood.

Early May, LZ Zero. The courier is holed up in a cardboard room under a pale canopy of seed netting. He's got a case of canned fruit, a pound of reconstituted coffee that he traded for his last pair of dry socks, and a jar of squink he pulled from the reeking wreckage of a Vegan distillery near Hill 186. He's been waiting two days for a transport to come through, to carry him back cityside. He only sees the sun to pee. He's still carrying one leather mouthpiece in his pouch. Couldn't make the delivery. When he got to 186, the hill wasn't there. Gone. Just a burnt pan of dust and stubble weed.

He sleeps and his wife creeps into his dreams with her swollen belly and a tongue of leaves. He wakes into a neon blizzard of fruit flies, burns a bug chip and nurses the bottle. When a whore convoy rolls in at dusk he picks a girl and pays her in chocolate and cigarettes. Out in front of the Media bunker the network vampires in their plastic helmets and high-end eyewear roast pods the size of dogs on elaborate rotisseries. The whores disembark in their combat boots and their cardboard lingerie, their skin brittle with anti-seed sealant. Behind the latrine, the garbage ditch is peppered with disposable vinegar bottles and packets of powdered douche.

That June the platoon crawled into LZ Bravo for debriefing and resupply. Two nights in, Wally was called to the Colonel's bunker. The old man poured thimblefuls of squink from a canteen. The Lieutenant was there with a courier from Intel, and the spook proceeded to give Wally a lecture on the Word. The lecture was like one of those declassified documents that the censors have gone over with a blackout marker.

'I don't get it,' Wally said.

'You're not supposed to,' the courier told him. 'This is a weapon. You're a grunt. Your job is to listen and do what you're told. I have other deliveries to make, so we don't have very much time. All you have to know is that the Word is a sound-based weapon, like a music gun. If your ears aren't properly plugged, it will be the last thing you ever hear.'

It came sealed inside a leather mouth which they affixed to Wally's face with wires and straps. 'The flap fits under the tongue,' the courier explained to the Lieutenant and the Colonel. 'Your people should always wear ear protection when they install this.' Wally panicked and started to struggle when they put it on him. Tasted blood or metal or maybe the Word itself, he couldn't tell which. The Lieutenant put a hand on his shoulder, told him to cut it out and sit still. The Colonel grunted and turned away with a look of disdain, but whether it was intended for the weapon or its wearer Wally couldn't tell.

They strapped him to the chair and brought him something in a cage. A mute yap child dressed in rind with long ears and a pink hairless tail. It cowered in its wire box nervously gnawing the tip of its tail. The courier sealed Wally's ears, unlatched the mouth and nodded to him. Wally opened his jaws and felt the Word being launched from its leather harness. A moment later, the spook leaned forward, latched the mouth shut and removed it from Wally's face. A subtle change seemed to have occurred in the room, but Wally couldn't put his finger on what it was.

'I'll be damned,' the Colonel muttered. The squink had turned to dust in his glass. And now Wally noticed that the yap had turned an ashen color inside its box of wires. The courier produced a water knife and cut the cage apart. The yap remained motionless.

'If you don't mind, Colonel… your sidearm.'

The old man unbuckled his holster and handed his weapon over in a trance. The courier gently tapped the child on the head with the butt of the revolver and the creature crumbled.

The Lieutenant let out a long whistle and crouched on the floor of the bunker, dipping his fingers in the dust and sniffing them.

A week later they kicked north into Yellow Sector, warding off the firefall with voodoo and canned music and rain puppets that the grunts had pinned with prayers and tucked inside their helmet liners. They carried the Word with them, loaded inside its leather mouth and sealed in a lock-box lined with silencing foam, ready to be taken out and affixed to Wally's face at the first sign of enemy movement. It took two keys to open the box (Wally wore one on his tag wire and the Lieutenant carried the other) and the lid was rigged with a trip charge so that if the locks weren't turned in the proper sequence chances were pretty good that Wally and the Lieutenant wouldn't be going home for Christmas.

All that spring and into the summer they humped it through burning hamlets and animalist villes, forcing Mack out into open ground and killing him with language. The new weapon was thorough and unspectacular. It was a stillness that came in the form of a secret sound, hardening the air, turning animals into coal. The grunts left behind them a trail of dead rivers and great sections of sky that had hardened and fallen to ground like broken blue windshields. Whole fields lay frozen into gray dust. They moved from town to town in mute procession with Wally hoisted on a pole, the automatic mouth strapped to his face and loaded with language ... the sound sweeping before them through the long, silent summer and into autumn, until winter arrived to impose its armistice of snow, the war a white page on which the enemy stood hardened in postures of flight: an alphabet of frozen gestures in which Wally searched vainly for some semblance of meaning.

THE STIFF AND THE STILE

Stepan Chapman

Stepan Chapman (1951–) is a visionary American writer of speculative fiction best known for the Philip K. Dick Award-winning novel *The Troika* (1997). His first published story was selected for *Analog* by John W. Campbell with other early fiction in the Damon Knight-edited *Orbit* anthologies. Over the past three decades, Chapman has primarily been published in US literary magazines. Collections include *Danger Music* (1997) and *Dossier* (2001). Chapman is best thought of as the bastard love-child of Mark Twain, Leonora Carrington, and Philip K. Dick. His underrated tales often take the form of fables or cautionary *contes cruels* and combine absurdism with the horrific – as in 'The Stiff and the Stile' (1997).

In the vast desert known as Oregon, during the peak years of the Bovine Brain Rot, a poor old woman lived all by herself, in a hovel in a graveyard. Her tin roof shed the worst of the acid rain, and she was glad to have the graveyard's thick stone wall between her and the half-starved cutthroats that roved the road. The old woman lived by her wits, venturing by night into the ruins of Portland to steal garbage from the dumpsters there.

One summer afternoon she hobbled into town with a purse full of coins and a shopping basket. She'd resolved to purchase a bit of fresh meat for her larder – a string of worm sausages perhaps, or a nice roast of dog.

She dickered with a one-legged butcher for over an hour and bought herself an elderly male corpse. The cadaver was a plague victim but in those days no one could afford to be choosy. The butcher thumped the corpse soundly on its skull with a mallet before winding it in butcher's paper. It wasn't completely dead yet, which proved the freshness of the meat.

The old woman grabbed the stiff's ankles and dragged it out of town along the muddy turnpike that led to her cozy graveyard. As twilight fell, she'd got as far as the graveyard wall. Built into the wall was a narrow gap, which served as a stile for foot traffic but kept out the mad cows.

The corpse had submitted gracefully to being dragged through the mud, but at the stile it turned contrary and feigned rigor mortise. Whichever way the old woman turned it, however she shoved it or kicked it or rearranged its limbs, the stiff refused to go through the stile. The old woman had no intention of spending all night on the open road. She shouted angrily at the corpse.

'Stiff, Stiff, go through the stile! Elseways I shan't get home tonight!' But the stiff just stuck out its chin and stared at her rudely. Some people don't know what's good for them.

The old woman called to the graveyard's ditch rat. 'Rat, Rat, bite this Stiff! It won't go through the stile, and I shan't get home tonight!' The rat crept out of the weeds, sniffed the corpse, then scurried off again, sniggering nastily.

The old woman hid the stiff beneath some brambles and started back toward Portland to seek assistance. She came to a dumpster which was the home of a mutant trash goblin.

'Goblin, Goblin, strangle Rat! Rat won't bite Stiff. Stiff won't go through the stile, and I shan't get home by dark!' The unsanitary goblin lifted its pointy head to listen, then smirked and slipped back into the refuse. The old woman resumed her search for help.

She hobbled to the industrial district, to a derelict radio factory where the Buzz Saw That Frightened Itself was hiding from the police. (The saw was a runaway lumber mill from a local timber yard. On its first day on the job, it had slaughtered a nest of baby sparrows, and its mind had snapped. Now it led the life of a hermit, wanted by its owners, shunned by other power tools, and torturing itself every night with an industrial grinder.)

'Saw, Saw, gore Goblin! Goblin won't strangle Rat. Rat won't bite Stiff. The Stiff won't go through the stile, and I can't go home!' The saw only cowered into a corner and whimpered. The old woman turned away in disgust.

She shifted a manhole cover and climbed down a shaft into the sewer system. She made her way to the cesspit where The Giant Poisoned Lamprey lived, coiled below a churning morass of filth that glowed with a yellow light and belched brown vapors. (In her youth, the lamprey had sucked some nuclear waste out of a steel barrel, and afterwards she'd never been the same.)

'Lamprey, Lamprey, poison Saw! Saw won't gore Goblin. Goblin won't strangle Rat. Rat won't bite Stiff. The Stiff won't go through the stile, and I can't get home to my miserable hovel!' The lamprey only smiled in her long wet whiskers, down in the spongy grungy scum, and passed bubbles of noxious gas from her nether regions. The old woman retreated, holding her nose.

She found the one-legged butcher. All her troubles were his fault, in a sense. He'd sold her spoiled meat. She expected meat to show more cooperation. She yanked at his bloody sleeve and pleaded her case.

'Butcher, Butcher, carve Lamprey! Lamprey won't poison Saw. Saw won't gore Goblin. Goblin won't strangle Rat. Rat won't bite Stiff. The Stiff won't go through the stile, and I'm *stressed out*!' The butcher shook his bald head. He had enough work to do in a day.

The old woman located the butcher's armored delivery van, which was parked near the Burnside Bridge. She whispered into its air manifold. 'Van, Van, maim Butcher! Butcher won't carve Lamprey. Lamprey won't poison Saw. Saw won't gore Goblin. Goblin won't strangle Rat. Rat won't bite Stiff. The Stiff won't go through the stile, and I'm *messed up* behind it!' The van made no reply, but only pointed a rifle at the old woman.

Walking dejectedly past the Burnside underpass, the old woman noticed a gang of bad-ass fleas in leather jackets who were viciously mugging a punk shrimp who had his shell dyed green and safety pins in his feelers. The fleas stole the rubber condoms from the shrimp's pockets and ate them right out of the foil packets, for they were bad-ass recombinant rubber-eating fleas. The old woman fell on her knees before the gang of fleas. She saw them as her last hope.

'Fleas, Fleas, chew on Van! Van won't maim Butcher. Butcher won't carve Lamprey. Lamprey won't poison Saw. Saw won't gore Goblin. Goblin won't strangle Rat. Rat won't bite Stiff. Stiff won't go through the stile, and I shan't get home tonight!'

The fleas were always hungry for automobile tires, so...

The fleas began to chew on the van. The van began to maim the butcher. The butcher began to carve the lamprey. The lamprey began to poison the saw. The saw began to gore the goblin. The goblin began to strangle the rat. The rat began to bite the stiff. And the stiff, naturally enough, shrank from the rat's short sharp teeth and scrambled through the stile into the graveyard.

The old woman hit it with a brick and boiled its head for her supper.

A happy ending. (For the old woman, if not for the corpse.)

YELLOW AND RED

Tanith Lee

Tanith Lee (1947–) is a highly respected English writer of science fiction, horror, and fantasy, with over seventy novels and hundreds of short stories to her credit. She has been a regular contributor over many years to *Weird Tales* magazine. She has won the World Fantasy Award, the British Fantasy Award, and the Nebula Award multiple times. Along with Daphne du Maurier, Lee has established herself as one of the pre-eminent writers coming to the weird from Gothic fiction. 'Yellow and Red' (1998) contains several of the Lee trademarks: atmosphere, a sensual style, and a creeping sense of dread. It also seems to riff off of M. R. James's classic 'Casting the Runes'.

From the Diary of Gordon Martyce:

9th September 195–: 7:00 p.m.

Coming down to the old house was at first interesting, and then depressing. The train journey was tedious and slow, and after the second hour, over and again, I began to wish I had not undertaken this. But that would be foolish. The house, by the quirkiness of my Uncle's will, is now mine. One day I may even live in it, although for now my job, which I value, and my flat, which I like, keep me in London. Of course, Lucy is terribly interested in the idea of an old place in the country. I could see her eyes, lit by her second gin, gleam with visions of chintz curtains, china on the mantlepiece, an old, dark, loudly ticking cloak. But it is not that sort of house – I knew that even then, never having seen inside it in my life. As for Lucy, I am never sure. She has stuck to me for five years, and so I have not quite given up on the notion of one day having a wife, perhaps a family. Quite a pretty woman, quite vivacious in her way, which sometimes, I confess, tires me a little. Well, if it comes to that, she can do what she wants with the house. It is gloomy enough as it stands.

Beyond the train, the trees were putting on their September garments, brown and red and yellow, but soon a drizzle began which blotted up detail. It was raining more earnestly when I reached the station and got out. I had only one small bag, the essentials for a stay of a couple of nights. That was good, for there was no transport of any kind.

I walked to the village, and there was given a cup of tea, the keys, and a lift the last mile and a half.

Johnson, the agent, let me off on the drive. He had offered to take me round, but I said this was not necessary. There is a woman, Mrs Gold, who comes in every day, and I was told, she would have put things ready for me – I trusted this was true.

The rain eased as I walked along the last curve of the drive. Presently I saw the house, and recognized it from a photograph I had observed often enough in my Father's study. A two-storey building, with green shutters. Big oaks stood around it that had done the walls some damage, and introduced damp. I supposed they could be cut down. Above, was my Grandfather's weather-vane, which I had never been able, properly, to make out in the photograph, but which my Father told me was in the shape of some Oriental animal deity. Even now, it remained a mystery to me, between the leaves of the oaks and the moving, leaden sky.

I got up the steps, and opened the front door,

and stepped into the big dark hall. The trees oppress this house, that is certain, and the old stained glass of the hall windows change the light to mulberry and spinach. However, I saw through into the sitting room, and a fire had been laid, and wood put ready. A touch on a switch reassured me that the electricity still worked. On the table near the door I found Mrs Gold's rather poorly spelled note. But she had done everything one could expect, even to leaving me a cold supper of ham and salad, apple pie and cheese. She would be in tomorrow at eleven. I need have no fears.

I looked round. I am not fearful by nature. I always do my best, and am seldom in a position to dread very much. A childhood visit to the dentist, perhaps, for an especially painful filling – something of that apprehension seized me. But it was the nasty dark light in the hall. My Uncle died in this house not three months ago. Before him, he had lost his family, his wife and sister, and two sons. Before them another generation had perished. As Shakespeare points out, it is common for people to die.

Going through into the sitting room, I have put a match to the fire. This has improved things. On a sideboard stands a tray with brandy, whisky and soda. Though it is early for me, I shall pour myself a small measure. I gather the boiler is at work, and I can count on a hot bath. I do not want a chill.

10th September: 2:00 p.m.

The house is a mausoleum. Lucy be blowed, I think I shall sell it. Last night was dreadful. Creaks and groans of woodwork, an eldritch wind at the windows and down the chimneys. I read until nearly two a.m. Then at three I was woken by a persistent owl hooting in the garden trees. I am not a country person. I longed for my warm city flat and the vague roar of traffic.

However, this morning early I went over the place thoroughly, from attic to cellar. There are a great many rooms, more than I should ever want, and the heating would be prohibitive. It is very old fashioned, those thick, bottle-green and oxblood curtains favoured by our grandfathers – evidently by mine, and my Uncle William, too – enormous cliffs of furniture, and endless curios, some of them I expect very valuable, from the East – Egypt, India and China. I am not particularly partial to any of this sort of thing. I find the house uncomfortable, both physically – it is cold and damp – and aesthetically.

At about eleven thirty, the not very punctual Mrs Gold arrived. I was not surprised. Women are generally unreliable. I have learnt this from Lucy. Nevertheless, I commended Mrs Gold on keeping the house clean, which she has more or less done, and on the supper left for me yesterday. She is a large woman, constructed like a figurehead, with severe grey hair. She began, of course, at once to tell me all about my Uncle, and what she knows of my Grandfather before him. She is, naturally, as her class nearly always are, fascinated by details of all the deaths. It was with some difficulty that I got her to resume her work. Going into the library, I then took down some boxes of photographs, and began to go through them, more to pass the time than anything else. The agent is coming tomorrow, to discuss things, or I would have tried to get home today.

The photographs, most of which have dates and names written on the back, are generally displeasing, many the dull, antique kind where everyone stands like a waxwork, as the primitive camera performs its task. My grandfather was a formidable old boy, with bushy whiskers, in several scenes out in some foreign landscape, clutching his gun, or his spade, for he had been involved in one or two famous excavations, in the East. Here he had taken his own photographs, some of which had appeared in prominent journals of the day. These, obviously, were not among the general portraits, nor was I especially interested to look them out. My father had been wont to tell me, at length, how Grandfather Martyce had taken the very first photograph inside some remarkable ancient tomb. I had found this, I am afraid, extremely boring, then, and scarcely less so now. I have, too, forgotten the location. Lucy has often commented that I am not a romantic. I am glad to say I am not.

Eventually Mrs Gold finished her ministrations, and I went down to learn her wages, which were modest enough. She had put into the oven for me, besides, a substantial hot-pot.

'Your Uncle was very fond of those, I must say,' she announced. 'He relied on me, once the old cook had retired. Mrs Martyce was often ill, you understand, Miss Martyce too. I had a free hand.'

I said something gallant about her cooking. She ignored this.

'It was a great worry,' she said, 'to see them waste away. First the boys, and then the sister and the wife. Your Uncle was the last to go. He was very strong, fought it off, so to speak. The doctors couldn't find anything wrong with him. But it was the same as with the ladies, and the children.'

I privately thought that no doubt a reliance on elderly country doctors was to blame here, but I nodded lugubriously, and was apparently anticipated.

'Your Grandfather now,' persisted this tragic choric Mrs Gold, glowering on me in the stone kitchen, the pans partly gleaming at her back from her somewhat hard work upon them, 'he was the same, but they put it down to some foreign affliction, bad water, those dirty heathen foods. You understand, Mr Martyce – your Uncle, Mr William Martyce, was only in the house a year before he first fell ill. And before that, never a day's indisposion.' I noted that, not only did she employ words she could not, probably, spell, but that she was also able to invent them.

'It seems an unfortunate house,' I said. She appeared to wish me to.

'That's as may be. The cook was never out of sorts, nor any of the maids, while they had them. And I've never had a day in bed, excepting my parturiton.' I assumed she meant childbirth, and kept a stern face. Mrs Gold was certainly most serious. She said, 'If I was you, sir, I'd put this house up for sale.'

'That might be an idea,' I said.

'Not that I want to cause you misgivings.'

'Not at all. But it will be too big for me, I'm sure.'

When she had gone, I ate the beef sandwiches she had left me, and was grateful her meals were more cheerful than her talk, although I have jotted down here her two interesting words, to make Lucy laugh.

10th September: 6:00 p.m.

I do not like this house. No, I am not being superstitious. I believe there is not a fanciful bone in my body. But it depresses me utterly. The furnishings, the darkness, the chilliness, which lighting all the fires I reasonably can – in the sitting room, dining room, my bedroom, the library – cannot dispel. And the things which so many would find intriguing – old letters in bundles, in horrible brown, ornate, indecipherable writing – caskets of incenses and peculiar amulets – such items fill me with aversion. I want my orderly room with its small fire that warms every inch, my sensible plain chairs, the newspaper, and a good, down-to-earth detective novel.

I have already taken to drink – a whisky at lunch, and now another before dinner – and even this went awry. I am not a man who spills things. I have a sound eye and a steady hand. However, sitting over the fire in the library, crouching, should I say, with pure ice at my back, I was looking again at some of the more recent photographs. These comprised a picture of my Uncle and his sons on the lawn before the house, and some oddments of him, pruning a small tree, standing with a group I took to be the local vicar and various worthies of the nearby village. In these scenes, my Uncle is about forty, and again about fifty. He looks hale enough, but I had already gathered from the delightful Gold that he was, even then, frequently laid low.

Finally I put the pictures down on the side table, and rested my whisky, half full, beside them. I then stood up to reach for my tobacco. I have often seen Lucy have little accidents like this. Women are inclined to be clumsy, I find, something to do with their physique, probably. In brief, I knocked the table, the whisky glass skidded over it, and upset its contents in four sploshes, one on each of the photographs.

I gave a curse, I regret to say, and set to mopping up with my handkerchief. The pictures seemed no worse for the libation, and so I went downstairs to refill my glass. Having looked in on the hot-pot, I decided to give it another half hour, and came back reluctantly upstairs, meaning to try to find some book I could read – my own volume was finished during the early hours this morning. There was not much doing in this line, but at last I found some essays on prominent men, and this would have to serve. Returning to the fire in haste, I there found that each of the photographs on which the alcohol had spilled was blotched with an erratic burn. I must say, I had no notion malt whisky could inflict such a wound, but there, I am not a photographer.

This annoyed me. Although I have no interest in the photographs particularly, I know my Father would have had one, and for his sake, I would not have desecrated them. I am not a Vandal. I feel foolishly ashamed of myself.

I began to think then about my Father and my Uncle William, of how they had lost touch with each other, and how, oddly, we had never been on a visit to this house. One assumes there had come to be a rift between the two men. There was a marked difference in age. Even so, I recall my Father speaking of my Uncle as the former neared his end. 'Poor William,' he said. 'What could I do?' I had not wanted to press him, his heart was giving out.

Irritated, uneasy and out of sorts, I have pushed the damaged photographs together, and come down again, to eat of Mrs Gold's bounty.

10th September: 10:30 p.m.

Something very odd. How to put this down... Well, I had better be as scientific as I can. I had forgotten my book, and, deciding on an early bed, since I am feeling rather fatigued – the country air, no doubt – I came up to the library to collect the volume. It lay on the table, and going to pick it up, I saw again the spoiled photographs.

While I had been downstairs dining, something had gone on. The stains had changed, rather they had taken on a colour, deep swirls of raw red and sickly yellow. This was particularly unpleasant on the black and white surface of the original scenes. I examined each photograph in turn, and all four were now disfigured in this way. I had already resolved that it was no use crying over spilt milk, or whisky, to be more precise, and was about to put them down again, when something else arrested my attention.

Of course, I am aware that random arrangements or marks can take on apparently coherent forms – the 'faces' that one occasionally makes out in the trunks of old trees, for example, or the famous Rorschach inkblot test. Yes, the random may form the seemingly concrete, and mean very little, save in the realms of imagination and psychiatry.

However. However – where the whisky had burned the photographs, a shape had been formed, now very definite, and filled in by rich, bilious colour. Not in fact a shape that I could recognize – yet, yet it was consistent, for in each of the four pictures, it was almost exactly the same. And it was – it is – a horrible shape. Most decidedly that. I do not like it. There is something repulsive, odious, about it. I suppose that is because it is like some sort of *creature* – and yet a creature that can hardly, I would think, exist.

Then, I am being rather silly. I had better describe what I see. What is the matter with me?

There, I have had another whisky – I shall certainly have a thick head in the morning! – and I will write this down with a steady hand.

The thing that the whisky has burnt out in the photographs is, in each one, identical, allowing for certain differences of – what I shall have to call – posture, and size. It has the head of a sort of frog, but this is horned, with two flat horns – or possibly ears – that slant out from its head sideways. The body is bulbous at the front, and it has two arms or forelegs, which end in paws, resembling those of a large cat. The body ends not in legs, but in a tail like that of a slug. This is all bad enough, but in the visage or head are always two red dots, that give the impression of eyes.

It is a beastly thing. I fear I cannot convey how vile, nor what a turn it has given me.

The varying size of the – what shall I call it? – apparition? – is another matter. I can only conclude the whisky fell in a smaller drop here, a larger there. Although that is not what I recollect quite. It seemed to me my drink had spread in roughly equal splashes on each photograph. But there.

In these two, where my Uncle William prunes the tree, the thing is quite small. But here, where he is in conversation with the vicar and the worthies, it is larger. And here, where William is standing with his sons, the thing is at its largest.

It is so curiously placed in this view, that it seems to recline at William's very feet, spacing its paws for balance. In relation to the man and boys, it is the equivalent of a medium-sized dog. I cannot escape the illusion that it has not grown bigger, but – got nearer. That way madness lies.

If there were a telephone here, I would put a call through to Saunders, or Eric Smith, even to Lucy. But there is no telephone. Perhaps, a good thing. What would I say?

I know I am behaving in an irrational and idiotic manner. I must pull myself together.

I have put the photographs back on the table and turned them face down. I shall go up and take a couple of aspirins. Obviously, in months to come, I will reread these entries and laugh at them.

11th September: 11:00 a.m.

Johnson, the agent, arrived efficiently at ten, and we perfunctorily discussed my plans. I had no hesitation in telling him that I would probably wish to put the house up for sale. I passed a restless night, mostly lying listening to the grim silence of this place. I would have been glad for the creaking of the boards I had heard on my first night, even for the boisterous owl. But both failed me. Everything seemed locked in the cupboard of the darkness, and now and then, like a child, I sighed or moved about, to make some sound.

I got a little sleep for an hour or so after dawn, and came down bleary-eyed but resolved. I had put myself into a foolish state over those confounded burns on the photographs. Perhaps this is the price for allowing myself to become a middle-aged bachelor. No matter. I am going back to London this evening. Back to traffic and fog and lights, and human company if I wish it. I must take myself in hand. I do not want to become one of those querulous neurasthenic fools one reads of. Good God, I have gone through a World War, and although luck put me out of the way of most of the action, I was ready enough to do my part. Is some childish horror going to undo me now?

As he was leaving, Johnson recommended that I seek out the vicar. 'If you want to know anything about your Uncle's tenancy here, that is.'

'Oh, yes. A Reverend Dale, I believe.'

'That's right. He's getting on, but pretty spry. A wise old bird.'

I said that I might not have the time, but thanked Johnson all the same. What, after all, did I want to know? My Grandfather's forays in the East did not interest me, and all the rest seemed decline, disease, and death. Charming points of conversation – besides, the bubbling Mrs Gold had already rejoiced me with enough of all that.

'Incidentally, Johnson,' I said, as I saw him to the door, 'I suppose there is some use of photography in your business.'

'There is,' he agreed.

'I wonder if you've ever heard of – alcohol making a burn on a photograph?'

'Well, I never have,' he said. He thought deeply. 'It might, perhaps. But not anything pure, I wouldn't have thought.'

'Whisky,' I said.

'From a still, maybe. Not the stuff in a bottle. Why do you ask?'

'Oh, something a friend told me of.'

Johnson shrugged and laughed. 'A waste of a good beverage,' he said.

When he was gone, I made a decision. It was because I had begun to feel angry.

Mrs Gold was not to come today until three, but she had left me another cold plate. This I tried to eat, but did not really fancy it, although I had had no breakfast.

Eventually I took the largest soup tureen I could find from the kitchen, and the whisky decanter, and went up to the library. The quickest way to be rid of my 'monster' was to carry out an experiment. It was quite simple. I would place a selection of photographs in the tureen and pour over them enough whisky to cover them entirely. Either nothing would happen to them, or they would burn – burn all over into yellow and red. And that would be that. No random marks, no possible coincidences of shape. No doubt the pictures that I spoiled underwent some flaw in their reproduction, or there was some weakness in the material on which they were printed. I was confident, to the point of belligerence, that by this means I should be free of the horror I had unwittingly unleashed. As for ruining more photographs, if I did so, there comes a point where one must put oneself first.

I set the tureen down on the big table in the library. Outside, the birds were singing. There was a view of the lawn, and the big oaks, golden and crimson in the dying of the leaves. It is a sunny day.

I took three photographs from the box more or less at random, a scene of my Uncle and his son by the little summer house, the two boys playing some game under the trees when they were small. To this selection I added one of the former casualties, the photograph of my Uncle pruning the tree. One thing I had made sure of, the three new scenes were of different dates, and had therefore been processed on other paper.

Dropping the four into the bowl, I poured in a generous measure of the whisky. A waste, as Johnson had said.

I have come away to write this, leaving a proper space of time, and now I am going back to look. There will be nothing, I believe, or complete obliteration. I am already beginning to feel I have made an idiot of myself. Perhaps I will tear out these pages.

11th September: 6:00 p.m.

The walk down to the village, just under a mile and a half, took me longer than it should have. I arrived feeling quite done up, and went into the little pub, which had some quaint name I forget, and had a brandy and soda.

Across the green was the vicarage, a picturesque building of grey stone, and behind it the Norman church, probably of interest to those with an historical concern. When I got to the vicarage door, and knocked, a homely fat woman came and let me in, all smiles, to the vicar's den. It was a nice, masculine place, redolent of pipe smoke, with a big dog lying on the hearth, who wagged his tail at me politely.

The Reverend Dale greeted me, and called for tea, which the fat nymph presently brought with a plate of her own shortbread. This tasted very good, although I am afraid I could eat no more than a bite.

The vicar let me settle myself, and we talked about ordinary things, the autumn, elements of the country round about, and of London. At last, leaning forward, the old man peered at me through his glasses.

'Are you quite well, Mr Martyce?'

'Perfectly. Just a trifle tired. I haven't slept well at the house.'

He looked long at me and said, 'I'm afraid people often don't.'

I took a deep breath. 'In what way?' I asked.

'Your family, Mr Martyce, has been inclined to insomnia there. The domestics have never complained. Indeed, I never heard a servant from there that had anything but praise for the house and the family. Mrs Allen, the former cook, retired only when she was seventy-six and could no longer manage. She was loath to go.'

'But my family – there has been a deal of illness.'

'Yes, I'm afraid that is so. Your Grandfather – he was before my time, of course. And his wife. Your father was long from home, and his brother, Mr William, was sent out into the world at twenty... before there was any – problem at the house. The two brothers did not at first choose to come back. And your father, I think, not at all. He lived to a good age?'

'He was nearly eighty. There was quite a gap between him and William – my Grandfather's travels.'

'Eighty – yes, that's splendid. But poor William did not do so well. He was, as you know, only sixty-two when he succumbed. His wife was a mere fifty, and your Aunt in her forties. But, in later life, she had never been well.'

I tried a laugh. It sounded hollow. 'That house doesn't seem very healthy for the Martyces.'

Reverend Dale looked grave. 'It does not.'

'And what explanation do you have for that, sir?'

'I fear that, although I am a man of God, and might be expected to incline to esoteric conclusions, I have none.'

I said, flatly, 'Do you think there is a malevolent ghost?'

'I am not supposed to believe in ghosts,' said the Reverend Dale. 'However, I can't quite rid myself of a belief in – *influences*.'

A cold tremor passed up my back. I deduce I may have gone pale, for the vicar got up and went over to his cabinet, from which he produced some brandy. A glass of this he gave me – I really must put a stop to all this profligate drinking! I confess I downed it.

'You must understand,' he said, 'I'm speaking not as a man of the cloth, but simply – as a witness. I've seen very clearly that, in the Martyce family, those who spend much or all of their time at the house, sicken. Some are more susceptible, they fail more swiftly. Some are stronger, and hold at bay or temporarily throw off the malaise, at first. Your Grandfather lived into his nineties, yet from his sixties he had hardly a day without severe illness. Perhaps, in a man of advancing years, that is not uncommon. And yet, before this time, he was one of the fittest men on record, apparently he put the local youth, who are hardy, to shame. Again, some who aren't strong, also linger in a pathetic, sickly state – your Aunt was one of these. She succumbed only in her adult years, but then her life was a burden for her. One wondered how she bore with it. Even she, at length...' he sighed. 'Her end was a release, I am inclined to think. A satisfactory cause of death meanwhile has never been established. In your Grandfather's case, necessarily it was put down to old age. As with his wife, since she died in her sixties. In the cases of others, death must be questionable. Or unreasonable. As with your Uncle's two sons. They were fourteen and nineteen years.'

'I assumed some childish malady –'

'Not at all. Clemens was their doctor, then. I will reveal, he confided in me somewhat. He was baffled. The same symptoms – inertia, low pulse, some vertigo, headache, an inclination not to eat. But no fever, no malignancy, no defect. You will perhaps know, William's health was poor enough to keep him out of the War. He was utterly refused.'

I said, briskly, 'Well, I'm leaving tonight.'

'I am glad to hear that you are.'

'But, I had intended to put the house up for sale –'

'I think you need have no qualms, Mr Martyce. Remember, no one who has lived there, who is not a member of your family, has ever been ill. If anything, the reverse.'

'A family curse,' I said. I meant to sound humorous and ironic. I did not succeed.

The Reverend Dale looked down upon his serviceable desk.

'I shall tell you something, Mr Martyce. You are, evidently, a sensible man. I can't guarantee my words, I'm afraid. The previous incumbent of the parish passed them on to me. But he was vicar in your Grandfather's time. It seems your Grandfather, always a regular churchgoer when at home, asked for an interview. This was about three years after his final return from the East. He was getting on in years, and had recently had a debilitating bout of illness, but recovered, and no one was in any apprehension for him, at that time.' The vicar paused.

'Go on,' I said.

'Your Grandfather it seems posed a question. He had heard, he said, of a belief among primitive peoples, that when a camera is used to take a photograph, the soul is caught inside the machine.'

'I've heard of this,' I said. 'There is a lack of education among savages.'

'Quite. But it appears your Grandfather asked my predecessor if he thought that such a thing were truly possible.'

I sat in silence. I felt cold, and wanted another brandy, but instead I sipped my tepid tea.

'What did he say, your predecessor?'

'Naturally, that he did not credit such an idea.'

'To which my Grandfather said what?'

'It seems he wondered if, rather than catch a human soul, a camera might sometimes snare... something else. Something not human or corporeal. Some sort of spirit.'

Before the eye of my mind, there passed the memory of how my Grandfather had photographed so many exotic things. And of the pictures taken inside the ancient and remarkable tomb. I am not given to fancies. I do not think it *was* a fancy. Like a detective, I strove to solve this puzzle.

I stood up before I had meant to, I did not mean to be rude.

The old man also rose, and the dog. Both looked at me kindly, yes, I would swear, even the dumb animal had an expression of compassion.

'Excuse me,' I said, 'I have to hurry to be sure of my train.'

'You're not returning to the house?' said the Reverend Dale.

'No. It's all locked up. The cleaning lady has

been and gone. I promised her she'd be kept on until any new tenants take over. They must make their own arrangements.'

'I think you have been very wise,' said the vicar.

He himself showed me to the door of the stone house. 'It's a lovely afternoon,' he said. 'You look rather exhausted. That cottage there, with the green door. Peter will drive you to the station. Just give him something towards the petrol.'

I shook his hand, and like some callow youth, felt near to tears.

In future I must take more exercise. It is not like me to be so flabby. Thank God, Peter was amenable.

I have written all this down in the train. It has not been easy, with the jolting, and once I leaned back and fell fast asleep. I am better for that. I want to make an end of it here, and so return into London and my life, clear of it.

No, I cannot say I know what has gone on. When I put the four photographs into the tureen and poured in the whisky, I thought myself, frankly, an imbecile.

I had left them for perhaps twenty minutes, possibly a fraction longer. I approached the table with no sense of apprehension. Rather, I felt stupid.

Looking in, I saw at once, but the brain needs sometimes an interim to catch up with the quirkiness of the eye. So I experienced a numbing, ghastly dread, but even so I took out the photographs one by one, and laid them on the newspaper I had left ready.

The original had not altered. That is, the photograph, already damaged, of my Uncle by the tree. It had not changed, nor the mark, the yellow and red mark, that had the shape of a horned creature with forelegs and the hind body of a giant slug. There it still was, quite near to him but yet not close. There it was with its blind red dots of eyes, brilliant on the black and white surface of that simple scene.

The other three images are quickly described, and I should like to be quick. The whisky had affected them all only in one place. And in that place, always a different one, exactly similarly. The demon was there. The same. Absolute.

Where the two boys are playing as children, it is some way off, among the trees. It is coiled there, as if resting, watching them, like a pet cat.

In the photograph of William and his wife and sister – my Aunt – the thing is much nearer, lying in the grass at their feet – again, again, like some awful pet.

But it is the last picture, the most recent picture of my Uncle William's younger son, it is *that* one – They are standing by the summer house. The boy is about thirteen, and the date on the back, that the whisky has blurred, gives evidence that this is so.

They do not look so very unhappy. Only formal, straight and stone still. That is probably the very worst thing. They should be in turmoil – and the boy – the boy should be writhing, flailing, screaming –

The demon is close as can be. It has hold of the boy's leg. *It is climbing up him.* Its tail is coiled about his knee – Oh God, its head is lying on his thigh. The head has tilted. It gazes up at him. It has wrapped him in its grip. He does not – *he does not know.*

I shall write no more now. I do not want to open this diary again. The lights of London will be coming soon, out of the autumn dusk. Smells of smoke, cooking, and unhygenic humanity. Thank God. Thank God I have got away. Thank God. Thank God.

From a letter by Lucy Wright to her friend J.B.:

1st November 195-:
Your letter did cheer me up a bit, though I cried a bit after. Yes, I'd love to come for a visit, and it would help to get my mind off – this. Then, I feel guilty. But what can I do? I was totally in the dark. I didn't know. He never confided in me. I don't understand.

I'd always known Gordon was a bit of an old stick-in-the-mud. But he was kind and hardworking, and I did hope he'd get round to popping the question one day. No one else has made any offers. And of course, he was well-off. Not that that was my main reason. But, well, I've never been rich, and it would be nice, not to worry all the time, where the rent's coming from, or if you can afford a new pair of nylons.

The funny thing was, when he came back from that house of his uncle's in the country (and strangely he wouldn't discuss that at all), he couldn't see enough of me. We were out every night, like a couple of twenty-year-olds. The pictures, concerts, even dinners in a lovely little restaurant up West. And he made a real fuss of me. He even bought me roses. I thought, this is it. He's going to ask me now. And I thought, I can change him, get him to brighten up a bit. But then – well it was a funny thing that happened. It was really silly and – nasty. Peculiar.

It was my birthday – that was the time he gave me the roses – and one of my cousins, Bunty, well she sent me a really lovely present. It was a little camera. What do you expect – I wanted to use it. And one night when Gordon and I were in that nice restaurant, I was showing him the camera, and the manager, who knows Gordon, came up and said, 'Let me take a picture of you, Mr Martyce, and your young lady.' Well I was a bit giggly – we'd had some lovely wine – and I was all for it, but Gordon got really funny. No, I mean he got really angry, sort of well – frightened, red in the face – but the manager just laughed, and he took the photograph anyway, with me very nervous and Gordon all hard and angry and scared. The manager said Gordon would have to be less camera-shy, for the wedding.

I thought, Gordon's angry because he feels he's being forced to think about that, about getting married. And he doesn't want to. And that depressed me, because things had seemed to be going so well. So it ended up a miserable evening. And he took me home. And – well. That was the last time I saw him. I mean, the last time I *saw* him. Because I don't count the funeral. How can I? They had to close the coffin. Anyway. He was dead then. I'm sorry. Look, a tear's fallen in the ink. What a silly girl. Crying over a man that didn't even want me.

Of course, I did speak to him just once more, on the telephone. He rang me up about a week after the dinner, and he said he was going to collect the films – the photographs, you see. And I was glad he'd rung me, so I said yes. I was a bit embarrassed, because the rest of the film was all of my family, dad and mum, and Alice and the babies, and it was the first time I'd taken any photographs, and I was sure they'd be bad.

But then I didn't hear again, and the next thing was, the policeman coming round in the afternoon, just as I was trying to get money in that rotten meter that's so stiff. My washing was everywhere – it was Saturday – but he didn't look. He helped me with the meter and then he put me in a chair, and he told me. Gordon had gone out on the Northern Line and – well, you know. He'd fallen under a train. Well they said, he'd thrown himself under. People had seen him do it. But how can I believe that? I mean, Gordon. It must be a mistake. But then, where was he going? He doesn't have any relatives, and no friends out that way. Didn't have. Well.

But I was so glad to get your kind letter. You see, I went round to Gordon's flat this afternoon, they let me, because there were a few things of mine there, a couple of books I tried to get Gordon to read – I don't think he did – and some gloves I'd left, little things – oh, and a casserole dish I'd bought him. It was a nice one. I thought I'd better have it, now.

And on the table in his room, there were the photographs. The police had obviously been there, because things were a bit disturbed, not the way Gordon would have left them. But the odd thing was, these photographs were lying on a newspaper, and they'd stuck to it, so they must have got wet. And – there was a strong smell of whisky, as if he'd spilled some. Maybe he had. He'd been drinking more lately, more than I'd known him do. I remember he said something strange – something about using a spirit to show a spirit. But he was always too clever for me.

Any way, I did look at the photographs, and I wondered if I could take them home, but I wasn't sure, so I didn't, though I can't see that they'll be any help to the police or anyone. Actually, I hadn't done too badly for a beginner. The ones of the babies are really nice, though I'd made Alice look a bit fat, and she wouldn't like that. The last one was the one the manager at the restaurant took of Gordon and me, and it was really a pity. I admit, it made me cry a bit. Because, it would have been nice to have a picture of him and me together, something to remember him by. It wasn't just that we looked really daft – me all grinning and silly, and Gordon so puffed up and upset. No, there was this horrible big red and yellowish mark on the picture – I suppose something went wrong when it was taken, perhaps some light got in, or something, that can happen, can't it?

The funny thing is, I can't explain this, but there was something – something really awful about this mark. It sounds crazy and you'll think I'm a proper dope. You know what an imagination I've got. You see, it looked to me like a funny sort of animal – a sort of snake thing, with hands – and a face. And the oddest part of all, it was in just this place that it looked as if it was sitting square on Gordon's shoulders, with its tail coming down his collar, and its arm-things round his throat, and its face pressed close to his, as if it loved him and would never let go.

THE SPECIALIST'S HAT

Kelly Link

Kelly Link (1969–) is an influential American writer of hard-to-classify short fiction that has been described as fantasy, slipstream, or magic realism. Link has published three collections: *Stranger Things Happen* (2001), *Magic for Beginners* (2005), and *Pretty Monsters* (2008). Her stories have won the Nebula, Hugo, and World Fantasy Awards. Although not known as a writer of 'weird tales' per se, most of Link's stories tend to be grounded in an underlying darkness. The story reprinted here, 'The Specialist's Hat' (1998), creeps up on the reader, slowly trading a sense of innocence for one of terror. The story is technically as perfect as Shirley Jackson's 'The Summer People' and showcases the effortless complexity of Link's fiction.

'When you're Dead,' Samantha says, 'you don't have to brush your teeth…"

'When you're Dead,' Claire says, 'you live in a box, and it's always dark, but you're not ever afraid.'

Claire and Samantha are identical twins. Their combined age is twenty years, four months, and six days. Claire is better at being Dead than Samantha.

The babysitter yawns, covering up her mouth with a long white hand. 'I said to brush your teeth and that it's time for bed,' she says. She sits crosslegged on the flowered bedspread between them. She has been teaching them a card game called Pounce, which involves three decks of cards, one for each of them. Samantha's deck is missing the Jack of Spades and the Two of Hearts, and Claire keeps on cheating. The babysitter wins anyway. There are still flecks of dried shaving cream and toilet paper on her arms. It is hard to tell how old she is – at first they thought she must be a grownup, but now she hardly looks older than them. Samantha has forgotten the babysitter's name.

Claire's face is stubborn. 'When you're Dead,' she says, 'you stay up all night long.'

'When you're Dead,' the babysitter snaps, 'it's always very cold and damp, and you have to be very, very quiet or else the Specialist will get you.'

'This house is haunted,' Claire says.

'I know it is,' the babysitter says. 'I used to live here.'

Something is creeping up the stairs,
Something is standing outside the door,
Something is sobbing, sobbing in the dark;
Something is sighing across the floor.

Claire and Samantha are spending the summer with their father, in the house called Eight Chimneys. Their mother is dead. She has been dead for exactly 282 days.

Their father is writing a history of Eight Chimneys and of the poet Charles Cheatham Rash, who lived here at the turn of the century, and who ran away to sea when he was thirteen, and returned when he was thirty-eight. He married, fathered a child, wrote three volumes of bad, obscure poetry, and an even worse and more obscure novel, *The One Who Is Watching Me Through the Window*, before disappearing again in 1907, this time for good. Samantha and Claire's father says that some of the poetry is actually quite readable and at least the novel isn't very long.

When Samantha asked him why he was writing about Rash, he replied that no one else had, and why didn't she and Samantha go play outside. When she pointed out that she was Samantha, he just scowled and said how could he be expected to tell them apart when they both wore blue jeans and flannel shirts, and why couldn't one of them dress all in green and the other in pink?

Claire and Samantha prefer to play inside. Eight Chimneys is as big as a castle, but dustier and darker than Samantha imagines a castle would be. There are more sofas, more china shepherdesses with chipped fingers, fewer suits of armor. No moat.

The house is open to the public, and, during the day, people – families – driving along the Blue Ridge Parkway will stop to tour the grounds and the first story; the third story belongs to Claire and Samantha. Sometimes they play explorers, and sometimes they follow the caretaker as he gives tours to visitors. After a few weeks, they have memorized his lecture, and they mouth it along with him. They help him sell postcards and copies of Rash's poetry to the tourist families who come into the little gift shop.

When the mothers smile at them and say how sweet they are, they stare back and don't say anything at all. The dim light in the house makes the mothers look pale and flickery and tired. They leave Eight Chimneys, mothers and families, looking not quite as real as they did before they paid their admissions, and of course Claire and Samantha will never see them again, so maybe they aren't real. Better to stay inside the house, they want to tell the families, and if you must leave, then go straight to your cars.

The caretaker says the woods aren't safe.

Their father stays in the library on the second story all morning, typing, and in the afternoon he takes long walks. He takes his pocket recorder along with him and a hip flask of Gentleman Jack, but not Samantha and Claire.

The caretaker of Eight Chimneys is Mr. Coeslak. His left leg is noticeably shorter than his right. He wears one stacked heel. Short black hairs grow out of his ears and his nostrils and there is no hair at all on top of his head, but he's given Samantha and Claire permission to explore the whole of the house. It was Mr. Coeslak who told them that there are copperheads in the woods, and that the house is haunted. He says they are all, ghosts and snakes, a pretty badtempered lot, and Samantha and Claire should stick to the marked trails, and stay out of the attic.

Mr. Coeslak can tell the twins apart, even if their father can't; Claire's eyes are grey, like a cat's fur, he says, but Samantha's are *gray*, like the ocean when it has been raining.

Samantha and Claire went walking in the woods on the second day that they were at Eight Chimneys. They saw something. Samantha thought it was a woman, but Claire said it was a snake. The staircase that goes up to the attic has been locked. They peeked through the keyhole, but it was too dark to see anything.

And so he had a wife, and they say she was real pretty. There was another man who wanted to go with her, and first she wouldn't, because she was afraid of her husband, and then she did. Her husband found out, and they say he killed a snake and got some of this snake's blood and put it in some whiskey and gave it to her. He had learned this from an island man who had been on a ship with him. And in about six months snakes created in her and they got between her meat and the skin. And they say you could just see them running up and down her legs. They say she was just hollow to the top of her body, and it kept on like that till she died. Now my daddy said he saw it.

– An Oral History of Eight Chimneys

Eight Chimneys is over two hundred years old. It is named for the eight chimneys that are each big enough that Samantha and Claire can both fit in one fireplace. The chimneys are red brick, and on each floor there are eight fireplaces, making a total of twenty-four. Samantha imagines the chimney stacks stretching like stout red tree trunks, all the way up through the slate roof of the house. Beside each fireplace is a heavy black firedog, and a set of wrought iron pokers shaped like snakes. Claire and Samantha pretend to duel with the snake-pokers before the fireplace in their bedroom on the third floor. Wind rises up the back of the chimney. When they stick their faces in, they can feel the air rushing damply upwards, like a river. The flue smells old and sooty and wet, like stones from a river.

Their bedroom was once the nursery. They sleep together in a poster bed which resembles a ship with four masts. It smells of mothballs, and Claire kicks in her sleep. Charles Cheatham Rash slept here when he was a little boy, and also his daughter. She disappeared when her father did. It might have been gambling debts. They may have moved to New Orleans. She was fourteen years old, Mr. Coeslak said. What was her name, Claire asked. What happened to her mother, Samantha wanted to know. Mr. Coeslak closed his eyes in an almost wink. Mrs. Rash had died the year before her husband and daughter disappeared, he said, of a mysterious wasting disease. He can't remember the name of the poor little girl, he said.

Eight Chimneys has exactly one hundred windows, all still with the original wavery panes of handblown glass. With so many windows, Samantha thinks, Eight Chimneys should always be full of light, but instead the trees press close against the house, so that the rooms on the first and second story – even the third-story rooms – are green and dim, as if Samantha and Claire are living deep under the sea. This is the light that makes the tourists into ghosts. In the morning, and again towards evening, a fog settles in around the house. Sometimes it is grey like Claire's eyes, and sometimes it is gray, like Samantha's eyes.

I met a woman in the wood,
Her lips were two red snakes.
She smiled at me, her eyes were lewd
And burning like a fire.

A few nights ago, the wind was sighing in the nursery chimney. Their father had already tucked them in and turned off the light. Claire dared Samantha to stick her head into the fireplace, in the dark, and so she did. The cold wet air licked at her face and it almost sounded like voices talking low, muttering. She couldn't quite make out what they were saying.

Their father has mostly ignored Claire and Samantha since they arrived at Eight Chimneys. He never mentions their mother. One evening they heard him shouting in the library, and when they came downstairs, there was a large sticky stain on the desk, where a glass of whiskey had been knocked over. It was looking at me, he said, through the window. It had orange eyes.

Samantha and Claire refrained from pointing out that the library is on the second story.

At night, their father's breath has been sweet from drinking, and he is spending more and more time in the woods, and less in the library. At dinner, usually hot dogs and baked beans from a can, which they eat off of paper plates in the first-floor dining room, beneath the Austrian chandelier (which has exactly 632 leaded crystals shaped like teardrops), their father recites the poetry of Charles Cheatham Rash, which neither Samantha nor Claire cares for.

He has been reading the ship diaries that Rash kept, and he says that he has discovered proof in them that Rash's most famous poem, 'The Specialist's Hat,' is not a poem at all, and in any case, Rash didn't write it. It is something that one of the men on the whaler used to say, to conjure up a whale. Rash simply copied it down and stuck an end on it and said it was his.

The man was from Mulatuppu, which is a place neither Samantha nor Claire has ever heard of. Their father says that the man was supposed to be some sort of magician, but he drowned shortly before Rash came back to Eight Chimneys. Their father says that the other sailors wanted to throw the magician's chest overboard, but Rash persuaded them to let him keep it until he could be put ashore, with the chest, off the coast of North Carolina.

The specialist's hat makes a noise like an agouti;
The specialist's hat makes a noise like a collared peccary;
The specialist's hat makes a noise like a white-lipped peccary;
The specialist's hat makes a noise like a tapir;
The specialist's hat makes a noise like a rabbit;

The specialist's hat makes a noise like a squirrel;
The specialist's hat makes a noise like a curassow;
The specialist's hat moans like a whale in the water;
The specialist's hat moans like the wind in my wife's hair;
The specialist's hat makes a noise like a snake;
I have hung the hat of the specialist upon my wall.

The reason that Claire and Samantha have a babysitter is that their father met a woman in the woods. He is going to see her tonight, and they are going to have a picnic supper and look at the stars. This is the time of year when the Perseids can be seen, falling across the sky on clear nights. Their father said that he has been walking with the woman every afternoon. She is a distant relation of Rash and besides, he said, he needs a night off and some grownup conversation.

Mr. Coeslak won't stay in the house after dark, but he agreed to find someone to look after Samantha and Claire. Then their father couldn't find Mr. Coeslak, but the babysitter showed up precisely at seven o'clock. The babysitter, whose name neither twin quite caught, wears a blue cotton dress with short floaty sleeves. Both Samantha and Claire think she is pretty in an old-fashioned sort of way.

They were in the library with their father, looking up Mulatuppu in the red leather atlas, when she arrived. She didn't knock on the front door, she simply walked in and then up the stairs, as if she knew where to find them.

Their father kissed them goodbye, a hasty smack, told them to be good and he would take them into town on the weekend to see the Disney film. They went to the window to watch as he walked into the woods. Already it was getting dark and there were fireflies, tiny yellow-hot sparks in the air. When their father had entirely disappeared into the trees, they turned around and stared at the babysitter instead. She raised one eyebrow. 'Well,' she said. 'What sort of games do you like to play?'

Widdershins around the chimneys,
Once, twice, again.
The spokes click like a clock on the bicycle;
They tick down the days of the life of a man.

First they played Go Fish, and then they played Crazy Eights, and then they made the babysitter into a mummy by putting shaving cream from their father's bathroom on her arms and legs, and wrapping her in toilet paper. She is the best babysitter they have ever had.

At nine-thirty, she tried to put them to bed. Neither Claire nor Samantha wanted to go to bed, so they began to play the Dead game. The Dead game is a let's pretend that they have been playing every day for 274 days now, but never in front of their father or any other adult. When they are Dead, they are allowed to do anything they want to. They can even fly by jumping off the nursery bed, and just waving their arms. Someday this will work, if they practice hard enough.

The Dead game has three rules.

One. Numbers are significant. The twins keep a list of important numbers in a green address book that belonged to their mother. Mr. Coeslak's tour has been a good source of significant amounts and tallies: they are writing a tragical history of numbers.

Two. The twins don't play the Dead game in front of grownups. They have been summing up the babysitter, and have decided that she doesn't count. They tell her the rules.

Three is the best and most important rule. When you are Dead, you don't have to be afraid of anything. Samantha and Claire aren't sure who the Specialist is, but they aren't afraid of him.

To become Dead, they hold their breath while counting to thirty-five, which is as high as their mother got, not counting a few days.

'You never lived here,' Claire says. 'Mr. Coeslak lives here.'

'Not at night,' says the babysitter. 'This was my bedroom when I was little.'

'Really?' Samantha says. Claire says, 'Prove it.'

The babysitter gives Samantha and Claire a look, as if she is measuring them: how old, how smart, how brave, how tall. Then she nods. The wind is in the flue, and in the dim nursery light they can see the milky strands of fog seeping out of the fireplace. 'Go stand in the chimney,' she instructs them. 'Stick your hand as far up as you can, and there is a little hole on the left side, with a key in it.'

Samantha looks at Claire, who says, 'Go ahead.' Claire is fifteen minutes and some few uncounted seconds older than Samantha, and therefore gets to tell Samantha what to do. Samantha remembers the muttering voices and then reminds herself that she is Dead. She goes over to the fireplace and ducks inside.

When Samantha stands up in the chimney, she can only see the very edge of the room. She can see the fringe of the mothy blue rug, and one bed leg, and beside it, Claire's foot, swinging back and forth like a metronome. Claire's shoelace has come undone and there is a Band-Aid on her ankle. It all looks very pleasant and peaceful from inside the chimney, like a dream, and for a moment she almost wishes she didn't have to be Dead. But it's safer, really.

She sticks her left hand up as far as she can reach, trailing it along the crumbly wall, until she feels an indentation. She thinks about spiders and severed fingers, and rusty razorblades, and then she reaches inside. She keeps her eyes lowered, focused on the corner of the room and Claire's twitchy foot.

Inside the hole, there is a tiny cold key, its teeth facing outward. She pulls it out, and ducks back into the room. 'She wasn't lying,' she tells Claire.

'Of course I wasn't lying,' the babysitter says. 'When you're Dead, you're not allowed to tell lies.'

'Unless you want to,' Claire says.

Dreary and dreadful beats the sea at the shore.
Ghastly and dripping is the mist at the door.
The clock in the hall is chiming one, two, three, four.
The morning comes not, no, never, no more.

Samantha and Claire have gone to camp for three weeks every summer since they were seven. This year their father didn't ask them if they wanted to go back and, after discussing it, they decided that it was just as well. They didn't want to have to explain to all their friends how they were half-orphans now. They are used to being envied, because they are identical twins. They don't want to be pitiful.

It has not even been a year, but Samantha realizes that she is forgetting what her mother looked like. Not her mother's face so much as the way she smelled, which was something like dry hay, and something like Chanel No. 5, and like something else too. She can't remember whether her mother had gray eyes, like her, or grey eyes, like Claire. She doesn't dream about her mother anymore, but she does dream about Prince Charming, a bay whom she once rode in the horse show at her camp. In the dream, Prince Charming did not smell like a horse at all. He smelled like Chanel No. 5. When she is Dead, she can have all the horses she wants, and they all smell like Chanel No. 5.

'Where does the key go to?' Samantha says.

The babysitter holds out her hand. 'To the attic. You don't really need it, but taking the stairs is easier than the chimney. At least the first time.'

'Aren't you going to make us go to bed?' Claire says.

The babysitter ignores Claire. 'My father used to lock me in the attic when I was little, but I didn't mind. There was a bicycle up there and I used to ride it around and around the chimneys until my mother let me out again. Do you know how to ride a bicycle?'

'Of course,' Claire says.

'If you ride fast enough, the Specialist can't catch you.'

'What's the Specialist?' Samantha says. Bicycles are okay, but horses can go faster.

'The Specialist wears a hat,' says the babysitter. 'The hat makes noises.'

She doesn't say anything else.

When you're dead, the grass is greener
Over your grave. The wind is keener.
Your eyes sink in, your flesh decays. You
Grow accustomed to slowness; expect delays.

The attic is somehow bigger and lonelier than Samantha and Claire thought it would be. The babysitter's key opens the locked door at the end of the hallway, revealing a narrow set of stairs. She waves them ahead and upwards.

It isn't as dark in the attic as they had imagined. The oaks that block the light and make the first three stories so dim and green and mysterious during the day, don't reach all the way up. Extravagant moonlight, dusty and pale, streams in the angled dormer windows. It lights the length of the attic, which is wide enough to hold a softball game in, and lined with trunks where Samantha imagines people could sit, could be hiding and watching. The ceiling slopes down, impaled upon the eight thickwaisted chimney stacks. The chimneys seem too alive, somehow, to be contained in this empty, neglected place; they thrust almost angrily through the roof and attic floor. In the moonlight they look like they are breathing. 'They're so beautiful,' she says.

'Which chimney is the nursery chimney?' Claire says.

The babysitter points to the nearest righthand stack. 'That one,' she says. 'It runs up through the ballroom on the first floor, the library, the nursery.'

Hanging from a nail on the nursery chimney is a long black object. It looks lumpy and heavy, as if it were full of things. The babysitter takes it down, twirls it on her finger. There are holes in the black thing and it whistles mournfully as she spins it. 'The Specialist's hat,' she says.

'That doesn't look like a hat,' says Claire. 'It doesn't look like anything at all.' She goes to look through the boxes and trunks that are stacked against the far wall.

'It's a special hat,' the babysitter says. 'It's not supposed to look like anything. But it can sound like anything you can imagine. My father made it.'

'Our father writes books,' Samantha says.

'My father did too.' The babysitter hangs the hat back on the nail. It curls blackly against the chimney. Samantha stares at it. It nickers at her. 'He was a bad poet, but he was worse at magic.'

Last summer, Samantha wished more than anything that she could have a horse. She thought she would have given up anything for one – even being a twin was not as good as having a horse. She still doesn't have a horse, but she doesn't have a mother either, and she can't help wondering if it's her fault. The hat nickers again, or maybe it is the wind in the chimney.

'What happened to him?' Claire asks.

'After he made the hat, the Specialist came and took him away. I hid in the nursery chimney while it was looking for him, and it didn't find me.'

'Weren't you scared?'

There is a clattering, shivering, clicking noise. Claire has found the babysitter's bike and is dragging it towards them by the handlebars. The babysitter shrugs. 'Rule number three,' she says.

Claire snatches the hat off the nail. 'I'm the Specialist!' she says, putting the hat on her head. It falls over her eyes, the floppy shapeless brim sewn with little asymmetrical buttons that flash and catch at the moonlight like teeth. Samantha looks again and sees that they are teeth. Without counting, she suddenly knows that there are exactly fifty-two teeth on the hat, and that they are the teeth of agoutis, of curassows, of white-lipped peccaries, and of the wife of Charles Cheatham Rash. The chimneys are moaning, and Claire's voice booms hollowly beneath the hat. 'Run away, or I'll catch you and eat you!'

Samantha and the babysitter run away, laughing as Claire mounts the rusty, noisy bicycle and pedals madly after them. She rings the bicycle bell as she rides, and the Specialist's hat bobs up and down on her head. It spits like a cat. The bell is shrill and thin, and the bike wails and shrieks. It leans first towards the right and then to the left. Claire's knobby knees stick out on either side like makeshift counterweights.

Claire weaves in and out between the chimneys, chasing Samantha and the babysitter. Samantha is slow, turning to look behind. As Claire approaches, she keeps one hand on the handlebars and stretches the other hand out towards Samantha. Just as she is about to grab Samantha, the babysitter turns back and plucks the hat off Claire's head.

'Shit!' the babysitter says, and drops it. There is a drop of blood forming on the fleshy part of the babysitter's hand, black in the moonlight, where the Specialist's hat has bitten her.

Claire dismounts, giggling. Samantha watches as the Specialist's hat rolls away. It picks up speed, veering across the attic floor, and disappears, thumping down the stairs. 'Go get it,' Claire says. 'You can be the Specialist this time.'

'No,' the babysitter says, sucking at her palm. 'It's time for bed.'

When they go down the stairs, there is no sign of the Specialist's hat. They brush their teeth, climb into the ship-bed, and pull the covers up to their necks. The babysitter sits between their feet. 'When you're Dead,' Samantha says, 'do you still get tired and have to go to sleep? Do you have dreams?'

'When you're Dead,' the babysitter says, 'everything's a lot easier. You don't have to do anything that you don't want to. You don't have to have a name, you don't have to remember. You don't even have to breathe.'

She shows them exactly what she means.

When she has time to think about it (and now she has all the time in the world to think), Samantha realizes with a small pang that she is now stuck indefinitely between ten and eleven years old, stuck with Claire and the babysitter. She considers this. The number 10 is pleasing and round, like a beach ball, but all in all, it hasn't been an easy year. She wonders what 11 would have been like. Sharper, like needles maybe. She has chosen to be Dead, instead. She hopes that she's made the right decision. She wonders if her mother would have decided to be Dead, instead of dead, if she could have.

Last year they were learning fractions in school, when her mother died. Fractions remind Samantha of herds of wild horses, piebalds and pintos and palominos. There are so many of them, and they are, well, fractious and unruly. Just when you think you have one under control, it throws up its head and tosses you off. Claire's favorite number is 4, which she says is a tall, skinny boy. Samantha doesn't care for boys that much. She likes numbers. Take the number 8 for instance, which can be more than one thing at once. Looked at one way, 8 looks like a bent woman with curvy hair. But if you lay it down on its side, it looks like a snake curled with its tail in its mouth. This is sort of like the difference between being Dead and being dead. Maybe when Samantha is tired of one, she will try the other.

On the lawn, under the oak trees, she hears someone calling her name. Samantha climbs out of bed and goes to the nursery window. She looks out through the wavy glass. It's Mr. Coeslak. 'Samantha, Claire!' he calls up to her. 'Are you all right? Is your father there?' Samantha can almost see the moonlight shining through him. 'They're always locking me in the tool room. Goddamn spooky things,' he says. 'Are you there, Samantha? Claire? Girls?'

The babysitter comes and stands beside Samantha. The babysitter puts her finger to her lip. Claire's eyes glitter at them from the dark bed. Samantha doesn't say anything, but she waves at Mr. Coeslak. The babysitter waves too. Maybe he can see them waving, because after a little while he stops shouting and goes away. 'Be careful,' the babysitter says. '*He'll* be coming soon. It will be coming soon.'

She takes Samantha's hand, and leads her back to the bed, where Claire is waiting. They sit and wait. Time passes, but they don't get tired, they don't get any older.

Who's there?
Just air.

The front door opens on the first floor, and Samantha, Claire, and the babysitter can hear someone creeping, creeping up the stairs. 'Be quiet,' the babysitter says. 'It's the Specialist.'

Samantha and Claire are quiet. The nursery is dark and the wind crackles like a fire in the fireplace.

'Claire, Samantha, Samantha, Claire?' The Specialist's voice is blurry and wet. It sounds like their father's voice, but that's because the hat can imitate any noise, any voice. 'Are you still awake?'

'Quick,' the babysitter says. 'It's time to go up to the attic and hide.'

Claire and Samantha slip out from under the covers and dress quickly and silently. They follow her. Without speech, without breathing, she pulls them into the safety of the chimney. It is too dark to see, but they understand the babysitter perfectly when she mouths the word, *Up.* She goes first, so they can see where the finger-holds are, the bricks that jut out for their feet. Then Claire. Samantha watches her sister's foot ascend like smoke, the shoelace still untied.

'Claire? Samantha? Goddammit, you're scaring me. Where are you?' The Specialist is standing just outside the half-open door. 'Samantha? I think I've been bitten by something. I think I've been bitten by a goddamn snake.' Samantha hesitates for only a second. Then she is climbing up, up, up the nursery chimney.

A REDRESS FOR ANDROMEDA

Caitlín R. Kiernan

Caitlín R. Kiernan (1964–) is an American author who has steadily moved beyond a reputation as an heir to the legacy of H. P. Lovecraft and Southern Gothic literature, to become one of the most original and audacious weird writers of her generation. In addition to her many award-winning novels and stories, Kiernan has written scientific papers that reflect her love of herpetology and paleontology, also reflected in her fiction. Perhaps more than any other writer of the past thirty years, Kiernan places the reader somewhere alien and inhabits points of view that seem both luminous and edgy. 'A Redress for Andromeda' (2000) is a perfect example of Kiernan's ability to portray the uncanny in original and terrifying ways.

Where the land ends and the unsleeping, omnivorous Pacific has chewed the edge of the continent ragged, the old house sits alone in the tall grass, waiting for Tara. She parks the rented car at the edge of the sandy dirt road and gets out, staring towards the house and the sea, breathing the salt and the night, the moonlight and all the wine- and apple-crisp October smells. The wind whips the grass, whips it into tall waves and fleeting troughs the way it whips the sea, and Tara watches the house as the house watches her. Mutual curiosity or wary misgiving, one or the other or both, and she decides to leave the car here and walk the rest of the way.

There are a few other cars, parked much closer to the house, though not as many as she expected, and the porch is burning down in a mad conflagration of jack-o'-lanterns, a hundred candle-lit eyes and mouths and nostrils, or at least that's how it looks to her. Walking along the sandy road as it curves towards the ocean and the high gabled house with its turrets and lightning rods, that's how it looks; the house besieged by all those carved and flaming pumpkins, and she takes her time, walking slowly, listening to the wind and the sea slamming itself against the headland. The wind is colder than Tara thought it would be, and all she's wearing is a white dress, one of her simple shirtwaist dresses fashionable forty or forty-five years ago, a dress her mother might have worn when she was a girl; the white dress with its sensible cuffs and collars, and black espadrilles on her feet, shoes as plain as the dress because Darren said to keep it simple. *It isn't a masquerade,* he told her. *Nothing like that at all. Just be yourself.* But she wishes she'd remembered her coat. It's lying on the passenger seat of the rental car. She thinks about going back for it, and then decides she can stand the chill as far as the front door.

Tara knows a little of this house's history, but only what Darren has told her about it. She knows it's called the Dandridge House, because the man who built it in 1890 was named Machen Dandridge. Back in the sixties it was one of those places that hippies and occultists liked to haunt, someplace remote enough that nobody would notice if you sacrificed a farm animal now and then. Darren told her ghost stories, too, since a house like this has to have a few ghost stories, but she took two Xanax on the drive up from Monterey, and the stories have all run together in her head.

It's not much farther before a narrow, sandy trail turns off the sandy road. There's a rusty mailbox on a post that's fallen over, and no one's bothered to set it right again. Tara follows the trail towards the wide, pumpkin-crowded porch that seems to wrap itself all the way around the house. Her shoes are already full of sand, sand getting in between her toes, and she stops and looks back towards her car, all alone at the edge of the road. The car seems far, far away.

There's a black-haired woman sitting on the porch steps, smoking a cigarette and watching her. When Tara smiles the woman returns the smile.

'You must be Tara,' the woman says and holds out her hand. 'Darren told us that you'd be late. I thought someone should wait out here for you. A friendly face in the wilderness, you know.'

Tara says thank you and shakes the woman's hand. This close, the jack-o'-lanterns seem to have grown even brighter. They hurt her eyes after so many miles of night. She squints at them and nods to the woman on the steps of the house.

'You didn't have any trouble finding us?' the woman asks.

'No,' Tara says. 'No trouble at all. Darren gives good directions.'

'Well, it's not as if there's much of anything else out here,' the woman says. She releases Tara's hand and glances past all the jack-o'-lanterns towards the cliffs and the sea. 'You just keep going until there's nowhere left to go, and here it is.'

'Who carved all these?' Tara asks. 'There must be a hundred of them.' She points at one of the jack-o-lanterns, and the woman on the steps smiles again and takes another drag off her brown cigarette, exhaling smoke that smells like cloves and cinnamon.

'One hundred and eleven, actually,' she says. 'They're like birthday candles. One for every year since the house was built. We've been carving them for a week.'

'Oh,' Tara says, because she doesn't know what else to say. 'I see.'

'You should go on inside,' the woman tells her. 'They'll be waiting. It's getting late,' and Tara says nice to meet you, we'll talk some more later, something polite and obligatory like that. She steps past the smoking woman, towards the front door, past and between the grinning and grimacing and frowning pumpkin faces.

'Yes, she's the one that I was telling you about last week,' Darren is saying to them all, 'the marine biologist.' He laughs, and Tara shakes someone else's hand. It's getting hard to keep them straight, all these pale people in their impeccable black clothing. She feels like a pigeon dropped into a flock of crows. Sure, it's not a masquerade, *not* a costume party, but she could have at least had the good sense to wear black. A tall, painfully thin woman with a thick French accent touches the back of Tara's hand. The woman's nails are lacquered the red-brown color of kelp, and her smile is as gentle as was the woman's out on the porch.

'It's always so nice to see a new face,' the French woman says. 'Especially when it's such a fine and splendid face.' The woman kisses the back of Tara's hand, and then Darren's introducing her to a short, fat man wearing an ascot the color of a stormy summer sky.

'Ah,' he says, and shakes Tara's hand so forcefully it hurts. 'A scientist. That's grand. We've had so few scientists, you know.' She isn't sure if his accent is Scots or Irish, but it's heavy, like his wide, jowly face.

'We've had *medical* doctors, yes,' the fat man continues. 'Lots and lots of medical doctors. Once we had a neurologist, even. But I've never thought doctors were quite the same thing. As scientists, I mean. Doctors aren't really much more than glorified mechanics, are they?'

'I never really thought of it that way,' Tara says, which isn't exactly true. She manages to slip free of the fat man's endless, crushing handshake without seeming rude, then glances towards Darren, hoping that he can read the discomfort, the unease, in her eyes.

'If you'll all please excuse us for a moment,' he says, so she knows that he's seen, that he understands, and he puts one of his long arms around her shoulders. 'I need to steal her away for just a few minutes.' There's a splash of soft, knowing laughter from the little crowd of people.

He leads her from the front parlor into what might once have been a dining room, and Tara's beginning to realize how very empty the house is. The way it looked from the outside, she expected the place to be full of antiques, perhaps neglected antiques gone just a bit shabby, a threadbare and discrepant mix of Edwardian and Victorian. But still, she thought that it would be furnished. These rooms are almost empty, not even carpets on the floors or drapes on the tall windows; the velvet wallpaper is faded and torn in places, hanging down in strips here and there, like a reptile shedding its skin. And there's no electricity, as far as she can tell, just candles and old-fashioned gaslight fixtures on the walls, warm and flickering light held inside frosted crystal flowers.

'They can be somewhat intimidating at first, I know that,' Darren says. 'It's a pretty close-knit group. I should have warned you.' But she shakes her head, smiles and tells him no, it's fine, it's not a problem.

'They're probably as anxious about your being here,' he says, 'as you are about meeting them.' He rubs his hands together in a nervous sort of way, and glances back towards the crows milling about in the parlor, whispering among themselves. *Are they talking about me?* Tara wonders. *Are they asking each other questions about me?*

'I trust you didn't have any trouble finding the house?' Darren asks. 'It's pretty far off the beaten track. We had someone get lost once.'

'No,' she replies. 'Finding the house was easy. With all those jack-o-lanterns, it's almost like a lighthouse.' And she thinks that's probably exactly what it would look like to a ship passing in the night, to fishermen or a tanker passing on their way north or south, an unblinking lighthouse perched high on the craggy shore.

'The pumpkins. That's one of the traditions,' Darren says, brushing his long black bangs away from his face. It's not exactly a handsome face, something more honest than handsome. She thinks maybe that's one of the reasons she finds him attractive.

'One of the traditions? Are there many others?'

'A few. I hope all this isn't freaking you out.'

'No, it isn't,' she replies, and turns her head towards a window, towards the moonlight shining in clean through the glass, shining white off the sea. 'Not at all. It's all very dignified, I think. Not like Halloween in the city. All the noisy drunks and drag queens, those gaudy parades. I like this much better than that. I wish you'd told me to wear black, though,' and he laughs at her then.

'I don't think it's funny,' she says, frowning slightly, still watching the moon riding on the waves, and he puts a hand on her arm. 'I must stick out like a sore thumb.'

'A bit of contrast isn't a bad thing,' Darren says, and she turns away from the window, turning back to him, his high cheekbones and high forehead, his long aquiline nose and eyes that are neither blue nor green.

'I think you need a drink,' he says, and Tara nods and smiles for him.

'I think maybe I need two or three.'

'That can be arranged,' he tells her, then leads Tara back towards the crows. A few of them turn their heads to see, dark eyes watching her, and she half expects them to spread wide black wings and fly away.

'They'll ask you questions,' and now Darren's almost whispering, hushed words meant for her and no one else. 'But don't ever feel like you have to tell them anything you don't *want* to tell them. They don't mean to be pushy, Tara. They're just impatient, that's all.' She starts to ask what he means by that exactly, *impatient*, but then she and Darren are already in the parlor again. The small and murmuring crowd opens momentarily, parting long enough to take them in, and then it closes eagerly around them.

The evening proceeds, and an hour or so later, she's looking on as members of a string quartet carefully return their sleek instruments to black violin and viola and cello cases, cases lined in aubergine and lavender velvet. They played Bach and Chopin, and there was only one piece she didn't recognize.

'It really isn't very fair of you, Mr. Quince,' someone says. Tara turns around and sees that it's the dapper fat man with the blue-gray ascot, the man who's either Irish or Scottish. 'The way you're keeping her all to yourself like this,' he says, and he glances coyly past her to Darren. The fat man smiles and rubs at his short salt-and-pepper beard.

'I'm sorry. I wasn't aware,' Darren says, and he looks at Tara, then, checking to be sure she's okay before leaving her in the man's company.

'Oh, I think we'll be fine,' she says, and Darren nods once before disappearing into the crowd.

'I am Peterson,' the man says, 'Ahmed Peterson.' He kisses the back of her hand the same way that the tall French woman did earlier. There's the same peculiar formality about him, about all of them, manners that ought to come across as affected, but don't somehow. He has a walking stick topped with a silver dolphin.

'Quince tells us that you're a marine biologist,' he says, releasing her hand and standing very straight, but he's still a few inches shorter than Tara.

'An ichthyologist, actually. I do some work at the aquarium in Monterey and teach at Cal State. That's where I met Darren.'

'How very marvelous,' Peterson beams. 'You know, my dear, I once came across an oarfish, a great, long, spiny thing, stranded on the shingle at Lyme Regis. The fellow I was with thought sure we'd found ourselves a sea serpent.'

'I actually saw an oarfish alive,' Tara says, 'off the coast of Oregon about ten years ago, when I was still a grad student.' She's finally starting to relax, beginning to feel less like an outsider. This is familiar ground, swapping fish stories with the fat man. 'We estimated it at almost twenty feet.'

'Ah, well, mine was smaller,' he says, sounding a little disappointed. Then, suddenly, there's a jolting, reverberating *crash*, and Tara turns to see that one of the women is holding up a small brass gong.

'Oh my,' the fat man says. 'Is it really that late already? I lost track,' and then Darren's standing next to her again.

'What's happening?' she asks.

'You'll see,' he replies, taking her hand and slipping something cold and metallic into her palm, a coin or a token.

'What's this?'

'Just hang onto it,' he replies. 'Don't lose it. You'll need it later.'

So, it's a game, she thinks. *Yes, it must be some sort of party game.*

And now everyone is starting to leave the parlor. She lets Darren lead her, and they follow the others, filing along a narrow hallway to a locked door near the very back of the house. Behind the door are stairs winding down and down and down, steps that seem to have been cut directly into the native rock, and damp stone walls rise up around them. Some of the guests have candles or oil lanterns. Tara slips once, and Darren catches her. He leans close and whispers in her ear, and his breath is very faintly sour.

'Watch your step,' he says. 'It's not much farther, but you wouldn't want to fall.' There are cool gusts of salty air rising up from below, not the sort of air she'd expect from a cellar at all; cool air against her skin, but air tainted by an oily, fishy odor, a low tide sort of a smell, bladderwrack and dying starfish trapped in stagnant tidal pools.

'Where the hell are we going?' she asks him, not bothering to whisper, and a woman with a conch shell tattooed on her forehead turns around and looks at her with a guarded hint of disapproval, and then she turns away again.

'You'll see,' Darren whispers. 'In a moment you'll see.' And Tara realizes that there's something besides the salty darkness and the light from the candles and lanterns, a softer chartreuse glow coming from somewhere below, yellow-green light that gets a little brighter with every step she takes towards the bottom of the stairway.

And now, if Darren were to ask again whether or not she was getting freaked out, now she might say yes. Now, she might even tell him she really should be going, that it's late, and she needs to get back to the city. She could say that she has papers to grade or a test to write for her oceanography class, anything that sounds plausible enough to get her out of the house and onto the pumpkin-littered porch, back down the trail to her rented car. She imagines her relief at being free of the house. There would be stars overhead, instead of stone. But he doesn't ask again, so she keeps quiet. The chartreuse light grows brighter and brighter, and in a few more minutes they've come to the bottom.

'No one ever understands at first,' Darren says. He has one hand gripped just a little too tightly around her left wrist, and Tara's about to tell him that it hurts, about to ask him to let go, when she sees the pool and forgets about everything else.

There's a sort of a boardwalk at the bottom of the stairs, a short path of warped planks and rails and pilings gone driftwood soft from the perpetually damp air, from the spray and seawater lapping restlessly at the wood. The strange light is coming from the water, from the wide pool that entirely fills the cavern at the foot of the stairs, coruscating light that rises in dancing fairy shafts to play across the uneven ceiling of the chamber. Tara's stopped moving, and people are having to step around her, all the impatient crows grown quiet and beginning to take their places on the boardwalk, no sound now but the hollow clock, clock, clock of their shoes on the planks and the waves splashing against the pier and the limestone walls of the sea cave.

It's like they've all done this thing a hundred, hundred times before, and she looks to Darren for an explanation, for a wink or a smile to tell her this really is just some odd Halloween game. However, his blue-green eyes are fixed on the far end of the boardwalk, and he doesn't seem to notice.

'Take me back now,' she says. 'I don't want to see this,' but if he's heard her it doesn't show on his face, his long, angular face reflecting the light from the pool. He has the awed and joyous expression of someone witnessing a miracle. The sort of expression that Hollywood always gives a Joan of Arc or a Bernadette, the eyes of someone who's seen God, she thinks, and then Tara looks towards the end of the boardwalk again. The crowd parts on cue, stepping aside so that she can see the rocks jutting up from the middle of the pool, from whatever depths there are beneath her feet, those stones stacked one upon the other as precarious as jackstraws. The rocks and the thing that's chained there, and in a moment she knows that it's seen her, as well.

'When I was five,' she says, 'when I was five, I found a sea turtle dead on the beach near Santa Cruz.' She opens her hand again to stare at the coin that Darren gave her upstairs.

'No, dear,' Ahmed Peterson says. 'It was an oarfish. Don't you remember?' and she shakes her head, because it wasn't an oarfish that time. That time it was a turtle, and the maggots and the gulls had eaten away its eyes.

'You must be mistaken,' the fat man says again, and her coin glints and glimmers in the yellow-green light, glinting purest moonlight silver in her palm. She doesn't want to give it away, as all the others have already done. It may be the only thing still tethering her to the world, and she doesn't want to drop it into the water and watch as it spirals down to nowhere, that see-saw spiral descent towards the blazing deep, and she quickly closes her hand again. She makes a tight fist. The fat man huffs and grumbles, and she looks up at the moon instead of the pool.

'You may not have lived much under the sea,' he says.

'No, I haven't,' Tara confesses. 'I haven't.'

'Perhaps you were never even introduced to a lobster,' he says.

She thinks about that for a moment, about brown claws boiled orange and jointed crustacean legs on china plates.

'I once tasted –' but then she stops herself, because she's almost certain having eaten lobster is something she shouldn't admit. 'No, never,' Tara whispers, instead.

And the sea slams itself against the cliffs below the house, the angry sea, the cheated sea that wants to drown all the land again. Darren is lying in the tall grass, and Tara can hear a train far away in the night, its steam-throat whistle and steel-razor wheels, rolling from *there* to *there*, and she traces a line in the dark with the tip of one index finger, horizon to horizon, sea to sky, stitching with her finger.

'She keeps the balance,' Darren says, and Tara knows he's talking about the woman on the rocks in the cave below the house. The thing that was a woman once. 'She stands between the worlds,' he says. 'She watches all the gates.'

'Did she have a choice?' Tara asks him, and now he's pulling her down into the grass, the sea of grass washed beneath a harvest moon. He smells like fresh hay and pumpkin flesh, nutmeg and candy corn.

'Do saints ever have choices?'

And Tara's trying to remember, if they ever do, when Ahmed and the woman with the conch-shell tattoo lean in close and whisper the names of deep-sea things in her ears, a rushed and bathypelagic litany of fish and jellies, squid and the translucent larvae of shrimp and crabs.

Saccopharynx, Stylephorus, Pelagothuria, Asteronyx.

'Not so *fast*,' she says. 'Not so fast, *please*.'

Caulophyrne, Lasiognathus, Sqaulogadus, Abyssobrotula.

'You can really have no notion, how delightful it will be,' sings Ahmed Peterson, and then the tattooed woman finishes for him. 'When they take us up and throw us, with the lobsters, out to sea.'

It's easier to shut her eyes and lie in Darren's arms, hidden by the merciful, undulating grass, easier than listening, easier than *hearing*. 'The jack-o'-lanterns,' he says again, because she asked him why the need for all the jack-o'-lanterns. 'You said it yourself, Tara. Remember? A lighthouse. One night a year, they rise, and we want them to know we're watching.'

'Beneath the waters of the sea, Are lobsters thick as thick can be – They love to dance with you and me. My own and gentle Salmon.'

'It hurts her,' Tara says, watching the woman on the rocks, the lady of spines and scales and the squirming podia sprouting from her distended belly.

'Drop the coin, Tara,' Darren murmurs, and, somehow, his voice manages to be urgent, but not impatient. 'Drop the coin into the pool. It helps her hold the line.'

Drop the coin, the coin, the candy in a plastic pumpkin grinning basket.

'The reason is,' says the Gryphon, who was a moment before the woman with the conch on her forehead, 'that they *would* go with the lobsters to the dance. So they got thrown out to sea. So they had to fall a long, long way.'

And the Mock Turtle – who was previously Ahmed Peterson – glares at the Gryphon. 'I never went to him,' he huffs. 'He taught Laughing and Grief, they used to say.'

'Someone got lost,' Darren whispers. 'We had to have another. The number is fixed,' and the black-salt breeze blows unseen through the concealing grass. She can't hear the train any longer. And the moon stares down at them with its single swollen jaundiced eye, searching and dragging the ocean against the rocks.

It will find me soon, and what then?

'Drop the coin, Tara. There's not much time left. It's almost midnight,' and the woman on the rocks strains against her shackles, the rusted chains that hold her there, and cold corroded iron bites into her pulpy cheese-white skin. The crimson tentacles between her alabaster thighs, the barnacles that have encrusted her legs, and her lips move without making a sound.

'They're rising, Tara,' Darren says, and he sounds scared and stares down into the glowing water, the abyss below the boardwalk, the pool that's so much deeper than any ocean has ever been. And there is movement down there, she can see that, the coils and lashing fins. The woman on the rock makes a sound like a dying whale.

'There is another shore, you know, upon the other side.'

'*Now*, goddamn it,' Darren says, and the coin slips so easily through her fingers.

'Will you, won't you, will you, won't you, will you join the dance…'

She watches it sink, taking a living part of her down with it, drowning some speck of her soul. Because it isn't only the woman on the rock that holds back the sea; it's all of them, the crows, and now she's burned as black as the rest, scorched feathers and strangled hearts, falling from the sun into the greedy maelstrom.

And the moon can see her now.

'I *told* them you were strong,' Darren whispers, proud of her, and he wipes the tears from her face. The crows are dancing on the boardwalk, circling them, clomp clomp clomp, while the woman on the rock slips silently away into a stinging anemone-choked crevice on her island.

'Will you, won't you, will you, won't you, won't you join the dance?'

Tara wakes up shivering, lying in the grass beneath a wide gray sky spitting cold raindrops down at her, the wind and the roar of the breakers in her ears. She lies there for a few more minutes, remembering what she can about the night before. She has no recollection of making her way back up the stairs from the sea cave, from the phosphorescent pool below the house. No memory of leaving the house, either, but here she is, staring up at the leaden sky and the faint glow where the sun is hiding itself safe behind the clouds.

Someone's left her purse nearby, Darren or some other thoughtful crow, and she reaches for it, sitting up in the wet grass, staring back towards the house. Those walls and shuttered windows, the spires and gables, no less severe for this wounded daylight; more so, perhaps. The house wears the bitter face of anything that has to keep such secrets in its bowels, that has to hide the world's shame beneath its floors. The house is dark, all the other cars have gone, and there's no sign of the one hundred and eleven jack-o'-lanterns.

She stands and looks out to sea for a moment, watching a handful of white birds buffeted by the gales and whitecaps. *Next year*, she thinks, next year she'll be here a week before Halloween to help carve the lighthouse faces, and next year she'll know to dress in black. She'll know to drop the silver coin quickly and turn quickly away.

One of the gulls dives suddenly and pulls something dark and wriggling from the seething, storm-tossed ocean. Tara looks away, wiping the rain from her eyes, rain that could be tears, and wet bits of grass from her skirt. And then she begins the walk that will carry her past the house and down the sandy road to her car.

THE GOD OF DARK LAUGHTER

Michael Chabon

Michael Chabon (1963–) is a celebrated American writer who has written in several different genres, although best-known for novels of mainstream realism with elements of fantasy. His novels include *Wonder Boys* (1995), *The Amazing Adventures of Kavalier & Clay* (2000) and the alternative history mystery *The Yiddish Policemen's Union* (2007). Chabon has won the Pulitzer Prize for fiction, the Hugo Award, Sidewise Award, and the Nebula Award. A fan of the weird tale, Chabon has written several stories in that mode including 'The God of Dark Laughter,' which contains references to Lovecraft and a nod to the work of Edgar Allan Poe. The story was first published in 2001 in the *New Yorker*.

Thirteen days after the Entwhistle-Ealing Bros. circus left Ashtown, beating a long retreat toward its winter headquarters in Peru, Indiana, two boys out hunting squirrels in the woods along Portwine Road stumbled on a body that was dressed in a mad suit of purple and orange velour. They found it at the end of a muddy strip of gravel that began, five miles to the west, as Yuggogheny County Road 22A. Another half mile farther to the east and it would have been left to my colleagues over in Fayette County to puzzle out the question of who had shot the man and skinned his head from chin to crown and clavicle to clavicle, taking ears, eyelids, lips, and scalp in a single grisly flap, like the cupped husk of a peeled orange. My name is Edward D. Satterlee, and for the last twelve years I have faithfully served Yuggogheny County as its district attorney, in cases that have all too often run to the outrageous and bizarre. I make the following report in no confidence that it, or I, will be believed, and beg the reader to consider this, at least in part, my letter of resignation.

The boys who found the body were themselves fresh from several hours' worth of bloody amusement with long knives and dead squirrels, and at first the investigating officers took them for the perpetrators of the crime. There was blood on the boys' cuffs, their shirttails, and the bills of their gray twill caps. But the county detectives and I quickly moved beyond Joey Matuszak and Frankie Corro. For all their familiarity with gristle and sinew and the bright-purple discovered interior of a body, the boys had come into the station looking pale and bewildered, and we found ample evidence at the crime scene of their having lost the contents of their stomachs when confronted with the corpse.

Now, I have every intention of setting down the facts of this case as I understand and experienced them, without fear of the reader's doubting them (or my own sanity), but I see no point in mentioning any further *anatomical* details of the crime, except to say that our coroner, Dr. Sauer, though he labored at the problem with a sad fervor, was hard put to establish conclusively that the victim had been dead before his killer went to work on him with a very long, very sharp knife.

The dead man, as I have already mentioned, was attired in a curious suit – the trousers and jacket of threadbare purple velour, the waistcoat bright orange, the whole thing patched with outsized squares of fabric cut from a variety of loudly clashing plaids. It was on account of the patches, along with the victim's cracked and split-soled shoes and a certain undeniable shabbiness in the stuff of the suit, that the primary detective – a man not apt to see deeper than the outermost wrapper of the world (we do not attract, I must confess, the finest police talent in this doleful little corner of western Pennsylvania) – had already figured the victim for a vagrant, albeit one with extraordinarily big feet.

'Those cannot possibly be his real shoes, Ganz, you idiot,' I gently suggested. The call, patched through to my boarding house from that gruesome clearing in the woods, had interrupted my supper, which by a grim coincidence had been a Brunswick stew (the specialty of my Virginia-born landlady) of pork and *squirrel*. 'They're supposed to make you laugh.'

'They *are* pretty funny,' said Ganz. 'Come to think of it.' Detective John Ganz was a large-boned fellow, upholstered in a layer of ruddy flesh. He breathed through his mouth, and walked with a tall man's defeated stoop, and five times a day he took out his comb and ritually plastered his thinning blond hair to the top of his head with a dime-size dab of Tres Flores.

When I arrived at the clearing, having abandoned my solitary dinner, I found the corpse lying just as the young hunters had come upon it, supine, arms thrown up and to either side of the flayed face in a startled attitude that fuelled the hopes of poor Dr. Sauer that the victim's death by gunshot had preceded his mutilation. Ganz or one of the other investigators had kindly thrown a chamois cloth over the vandalized head. I took enough of a peek beneath it to provide me with everything that I or the reader could possibly need to know about the condition of the head – I will never forget the sight of that monstrous, fleshless grin – and to remark the dead man's unusual choice of cravat. It was a giant, floppy bow tie, white with orange and purple polka dots.

'Damn you, Ganz,' I said, though I was not in truth addressing the poor fellow, who, I knew, would not be able to answer my question anytime soon. 'What's a dead clown doing in my woods?'

We found no wallet on the corpse, nor any kind of identifying objects. My men, along with the better part of the Ashtown Police Department, went over and over the woods east of town, hourly widening the radius of their search. That day, when not attending to my other duties (I was then in the process of breaking up the Dushnyk cigarette-smuggling ring), I managed to work my way back along a chain of inferences to the Entwhistle-Ealing Bros. Circus, which, as I eventually recalled, had recently stayed on the eastern outskirts of Ashtown, at the fringe of the woods where the body was found.

The following day, I succeeded in reaching the circus's general manager, a man named Onheuser, at their winter headquarters in Peru. He informed me over the phone that the company had left Pennsylvania and was now en route to Peru, and I asked him if he had received any reports from the road manager of a clown's having suddenly gone missing.

'Missing?' he said. I wished that I could see his face, for I thought I heard the flatted note of something false in his tone. Perhaps he was merely nervous about talking to a county district attorney. The Entwhistle-Ealing Bros. Circus was a mangy affair, by all accounts, and probably no stranger to pursuit by officers of the court. 'Why, I don't believe so, no.'

I explained to him that a man who gave every indication of having once been a circus clown had turned up dead in a pinewood outside Ashtown, Pennsylvania.

'Oh, no,' Onheuser said. 'I truly hope he wasn't one of mine, Mr. Satterlee.'

'Is it possible you might have left one of your clowns behind, Mr. Onheuser?'

'Clowns are special people,' Onheuser replied, sounding a touch on the defensive. 'They love their work, but sometimes it can get to be a little, well, too much for them.' It developed that Mr. Onheuser had, in his younger days, performed as a clown, under the name of Mr. Wingo, in the circus of which he was now the general manager. 'It's not unusual for a clown to drop out for a little while, cool his heels, you know, in some town where he can get a few months of well-earned rest. It isn't *common,* I wouldn't say, but it's not unusual. I will wire my road manager – they're in Canton, Ohio – and see what I can find out.'

I gathered, reading between the lines, that clowns were high-strung types, and not above going off on the occasional bender. This poor fellow had probably jumped ship here two weeks ago, holing up somewhere with a case of rye, only to run afoul of a very nasty person, possibly one who harbored no great love of clowns. In fact, I had an odd feeling, nothing more than a hunch, really, that the ordinary citizens of Ashtown and its environs were safe, even though the killer was still at large. Once more, I picked up a slip of paper that I had tucked into my desk blotter that morning. It was something that Dr. Sauer had clipped from his files and passed along to me. *Coulrophobia: morbid, irrational fear of or aversion to clowns.*

'Er, listen, Mr. Satterlee,' Onheuser went on. 'I hope you won't mind my asking. That is, I hope it's not a, well, a confidential police matter, or something of the sort. But I know that when I do get through to them, out in Canton, they're going to want to know.'

I guessed, somehow, what he was about to ask me. I could hear the prickling fear behind his curiosity, the note of dread in his voice. I waited him out.

'Did they – was there any – how did he die?'

'He was shot,' I said, for the moment supplying only the least interesting part of the answer, tugging on that loose thread of fear. 'In the head.'

'And there was... forgive me. No... no harm done? To the body? Other than the gunshot wound, I mean to say.'

'Well, yes, his head *was* rather savagely mutilated,' I said brightly. 'Is that what you mean to say?'

'Ah! No, no, I don't –'

'The killer or killers removed all the skin from the cranium. It was very skillfully done. Now, suppose you tell me what you know about it.'

There was another pause, and a stream of agitated electrons burbled along between us.

'I don't know anything, Mr. District Attorney. I'm sorry. I really must go now. I'll wire you when I have some –'

The line went dead. He was so keen to hang up on me that he could not even wait to finish his sentence. I got up and went to the shelf where, in recent months, I had taken to keeping a bottle of whiskey tucked behind my bust of Daniel Webster. Carrying the bottle and a dusty glass back to my desk, I sat down and tried to reconcile myself to the thought that I was confronted – not, alas, for the first time in my tenure as chief law-enforcement officer of Yuggogheny County – with a crime whose explanation was going to involve not the usual amalgam of stupidity, meanness, and singularly poor judgment but the incalculable intentions of a being who was genuinely evil. What disheartened me was not that I viewed a crime committed out of the promptings of an evil nature as inherently less liable to solution than the misdeeds of the foolish, the unlucky, or the habitually cruel. On the contrary, evil often expresses itself through refreshingly discernible patterns, through schedules and syllogisms. But the presence of evil, once scented, tends to bring out all that is most irrational and uncontrollable in the public imagination. It is a catalyst for pea-brained theories, gimcrack scholarship, and the credulous cosmologies of hysteria.

At that moment, there was a knock on the door to my office, and Detective Ganz came in. At one time I would have tried to hide the glass of whiskey, behind the typewriter or the photo of my wife and son, but now it did not seem to be worth the effort. I was not fooling anyone. Ganz took note of the glass in my hand with a raised eyebrow and a schoolmarmish pursing of his lips.

'Well?' I said. There had been a brief period, following my son's death and the subsequent suicide of my dear wife, Mary, when I had indulged the pitying regard of my staff. I now found that I regretted having shown such weakness. 'What is it, then? Has something turned up?'

'A cave,' Ganz said. 'The poor bastard was living in a cave.'

The range of low hills and hollows separating lower Yuggogheny from Fayette County is rotten with caves. For many years, when I was a boy, a man named Colonel Earnshawe operated penny tours of the iridescent organ pipes and jagged stone teeth of Neighborsburg Caverns, before they collapsed in the mysterious earthquake of 1919, killing the Colonel and his sister Irene, and putting to rest many strange rumors about that eccentric old pair. My childhood friends and I, ranging in the woods, would from time to time come upon the root-choked mouth of a cave exhaling its cool plutonic breath, and dare one another to leave the sunshine and enter that world of shadow – that entrance, as it always seemed to me, to the legendary past itself, where the bones of Indians and Frenchmen might lie moldering. It was in one of these anterooms of buried history that the beam of a flashlight, wielded by a deputy sheriff from Plunkettsburg, had struck the silvery lip of a can of pork and beans. Calling to his companions, the deputy plunged through a curtain of spiderweb and found himself in the parlor, bedroom, and kitchen of the dead man. There were some cans of chili and hash, a Primus stove, a lantern, a bedroll, a mess kit, and an old Colt revolver, Army issue, loaded and apparently not fired for some time. And there were also books – a Scout guide to roughing it, a collected Blake, and a couple of odd texts, elderly and tattered: one in German called 'Über das Finstere Lachen,' by a man named Friedrich von Junzt, which appeared to be religious or philosophical in nature, and one a small volume bound in black leather and printed in no alphabet known to me, the letters sinuous and furred with wild diacritical marks.

'Pretty heavy reading for a clown,' Ganz said.

'It's not all rubber chickens and hosing each other down with seltzer bottles, Jack.'

'Oh, no?'

'No, sir. Clowns have unsuspected depths.'

'I'm starting to get that impression, sir.'

Propped against the straightest wall of the cave, just beside the lantern, there was a large mirror, still bearing the bent clasps and sheared bolts that had once, I inferred, held it to the wall of a filling-station men's room. At its foot was the item that had earlier confirmed to Detective Ganz – and now confirmed to me as I went to inspect it – the recent habitation of the cave by a painted circus clown: a large, padlocked wooden makeup kit, of heavy and rather elaborate construction. I directed Ganz to send for a Pittsburgh criminalist who had served us with discretion in the horrific Primm case, reminding him that nothing must be touched until this Mr. Espy and his black bag of dusts and luminous powders arrived.

The air in the cave had a sharp, briny tinge; beneath it there was a stale animal musk that reminded me, absurdly, of the smell inside a circus tent.

'Why was he living in a cave?' I said to Ganz. 'We have a perfectly nice hotel in town.'

'Maybe he was broke.'

'Or maybe he thought that a hotel was the first place they would look for him.'

Ganz looked confused, and a little annoyed, as if he thought I were being deliberately mysterious.

'*Who* was looking for him?'

'I don't know, Detective. Maybe no one. I'm just thinking out loud.'

Impatience marred Ganz's fair, bland features. He could tell that I was in the grip of a hunch, and hunches were always among the first considerations ruled out by the procedural practices of Detective John Ganz. My hunches had, admittedly, an uneven record. In the Primm business, one had very nearly got both Ganz and me killed. As for the wayward hunch about my mother's old crony Thaddeus Craven and the strength of his will to quit drinking – I suppose I shall regret indulging that one for the rest of my life.

'If you'll excuse me, Jack...' I said. 'I'm having a bit of a hard time with the stench in here.'

'I was thinking he might have been keeping a pig.' Ganz inclined his head to one side and gave an empirical sniff. 'It smells like pig to me.'

I covered my mouth and hurried outside into the cool, dank pinewood. I gathered in great lungfuls of air. The nausea passed, and I filled my pipe, walking up and down outside the mouth of the cave and trying to connect this new discovery to my talk with the circus man, Onheuser. Clearly, he had suspected that this clown might have met with a grisly end. Not only that, he had known that his fellow circus people would fear the very same thing – as if there were some coulrophobic madman with a knife who was as much a part of circus lore as the prohibition on whistling in the dressing room or on looking over your shoulder when you marched in the circus parade.

I got my pipe lit, and wandered down into the woods, toward the clearing where the boys had stumbled over the dead man, following a rough trail that the police had found. Really, it was not a trail so much as an impromptu alley of broken saplings and trampled ground that wound a convoluted course down the hill from the cave to the clearing. It appeared to have been blazed a few days before by the victim and his pursuer; near the bottom, where the trees gave way to open sky, there were grooves of plowed earth that corresponded neatly with encrustations on the heels of the clown's giant brogues. The killer must have caught the clown at the edge of the clearing, and then dragged him along by the hair, or by the collar of his shirt, for the last twenty-five yards, leaving this furrowed record of the panicked, slipping flight of the clown. The presumed killer's footprints were everywhere in evidence, and appeared to have been made by a pair of long and pointed boots. But the really puzzling thing was a third set of prints, which Ganz had noticed and mentioned to me, scattered here and there along the cold black mud of the path. They seemed to have been made by a barefoot child of eight or nine years. And damned, as Ganz had concluded his report to me, if that barefoot child did not appear to have been dancing!

I came into the clearing, a little short of breath, and stood listening to the wind in the pines and the distant rumble of the state highway, until my pipe went out. It was a cool afternoon, but the sky had been blue all day and the woods were peaceful and fragrant. Nevertheless, I was conscious of a mounting sense of disquiet as I stood over the bed of sodden leaves where the body had been found. I did not then, nor do I now, believe in ghosts, but as the sun dipped down behind the tops of the trees, lengthening the long shadows encompassing me, I became aware of an irresistible feeling that somebody was watching me. After a moment, the feeling intensified, and localized, as it were so I was certain that to see who it was I need only turn around. Bravely – meaning not that I am a brave man but that I behaved as if I were – I took my matches from my jacket pocket and relit my pipe. Then I turned. I knew that when I glanced behind me I would not see Jack Ganz or one of the other policemen standing there; any of them would have said something to me by now. No, it was either going to be nothing at all or something that I could not even allow myself to imagine.

It was, in fact, a baboon, crouching on its hind legs in the middle of the trail, regarding me with close-set orange eyes, one hand cupped at its side. It had great puffed whiskers and a long canine snout. There was something in the barrel chest and the muttonchop sideburns that led me to conclude, correctly, as it turned out, that the specimen was male. For all his majestic bulk, the old fellow presented a rather sad spectacle. His fur was matted and caked with mud, and a sticky coating of pine needles clung to his feet. The expression in his eyes was unsettlingly forlorn, almost pleading, I would have said, and in his mute gaze I imagined I detected a hint of outraged dignity. This might, of course, have been due to the hat he was wearing. It was conical, particolored with orange and purple lozenges, and ornamented at the tip with a bright-orange pompom. Tied under his chin with a length of black ribbon, it hung from the side of his head at a humorous angle. I myself might have been tempted to kill the man who had tied it to my head.

'Was it you?' I said, thinking of Poe's story of the rampaging orang swinging a razor in a Parisian apartment. Had that story had any basis in fact? Could the dead clown have been killed by the pet or sidekick with whom, as the mystery of the animal smell in the cave now resolved itself, he had shared his fugitive existence?

The baboon declined to answer my question. After a moment, though, he raised his long crooked left arm and gestured vaguely toward his belly. The import of this message was unmistakable, and thus I had the answer to my question – if he could not open a can of franks and beans, he would not have been able to perform that awful surgery on his owner or partner.

'All right, old boy,' I said. 'Let's get you something to eat.' I took a step toward him, watching for signs that he might bolt or, worse, throw himself at me. But he sat, looking miserable, clenching something in his right paw. I crossed the distance between us. His rancid-hair smell was unbearable. 'You need a bath, don't you?' I spoke, by reflex, as if I were talking to somebody's tired old dog. 'Were you and your friend in the habit of bathing together? Were you there when it happened, old boy? Any idea who did it?'

The animal gazed up at me, its eyes kindled with that luminous and sagacious sorrow that lends to the faces of apes and mandrills an air of cousinly reproach, as if we humans have betrayed the principles of our kind. Tentatively, I reached out to him with one hand. He grasped my fingers in his dry leather paw, and then the next instant he had leapt bodily into my arms, like a child seeking solace. The garbage-and-skunk stench of him burned my nose. I gagged and stumbled backward as the baboon scrambled to wrap his arms and legs around me. I must have cried out; a moment later a pair of iron lids seemed to slam against my skull, and the animal went slack, sliding, with a horrible, human sigh of disappointment, to the ground at my feet.

Ganz and two Ashtown policemen came running over and dragged the dead baboon away from me.

'He wasn't – he was just –' I was too outraged to form a coherent expression of my anger. 'You could have hit *me!*'

Ganz closed the animal's eyes, and laid its arms out at its sides. The right paw was still clenched in a shaggy fist. Ganz, not without some difficulty, managed to pry it open. He uttered an unprintable oath.

In the baboon's palm lay a human finger. Ganz and I looked at each other, wordlessly confirming that the dead clown had been in possession of a full complement of digits.

'See that Espy gets that finger,' I said. 'Maybe we can find out whose it was.'

'It's a woman's,' Ganz said. 'Look at that nail.'

I took it from him, holding it by the chewed and bloody end so as not to dislodge any evidence that might be trapped under the long nail. Though rigid, it was strangely warm, perhaps from having spent a few days in the vengeful grip of the animal who had claimed it from his master's murderer. It appeared to be an index finger, with a manicured, pointed nail nearly three-quarters of an inch long. I shook my head.

'It isn't painted,' I said. 'Not even varnished. How many women wear their nails like that?'

'Maybe the paint rubbed off,' one of the policemen suggested.

'Maybe,' I said. I knelt on the ground beside the body of the baboon. There was, I noted, a wound on the back of his neck, long and deep and crusted over with dirt and dried blood. I now saw him in my mind's eye, dancing like a barefoot child around the murderer and the victim as they struggled down the path to the clearing. It would take a powerful man to fight such an animal off. 'I can't believe you killed our only witness, Detective Ganz. The poor bastard was just giving me a hug.'

This information seemed to amuse Ganz nearly as much as it puzzled him.

'He was a monkey, sir,' Ganz said. 'I doubt he –'

'He could make signs, you fool! He told me he was *hungry*.'

Ganz blinked, trying, I supposed, to append to his personal operations manual this evidence of the potential usefulness of circus apes to police inquiries.

'If I had a dozen baboons like that one on my staff,' I said, 'I would never have to leave the office.'

That evening, before going home, I stopped by the evidence room in the High Street annex and signed out the two books that had been found in the cave that morning. As I walked back into the corridor, I thought I detected an odd odor – odd, at any rate, for that dull expanse of linoleum and buzzing fluorescent tubes – of the sea: a sharp, salty, briny smell. I decided that it must be some new disinfectant being used by the custodian, but it reminded me of the smell of blood from the specimen bags and sealed containers in the evidence room. I turned the lock on the room's door and slipped the books, in their waxy protective envelopes, into my briefcase, and walked down High Street to Dennistoun Road, where the public library was. It stayed open late on Wednesday nights, and I would need a German–English dictionary if my college German and I were going to get anywhere with Herr von Junzt.

The librarian, Lucy Brand, returned my greeting with the circumspect air of one who hopes to be rewarded for her forbearance with a wealth of juicy tidbits. Word of the murder, denuded of most of the relevant details, had made the Ashtown *Ambler* yesterday morning, and though I had cautioned the unlucky young squirrel hunters against talking about the case, already conjectures, misprisions, and outright lies had begun wildly to coalesce; I knew the temper of my home town well enough to realize that if I did not close this case soon things might get out of hand. Ashtown, as the events surrounding the appearance of the so-called Green Man, in 1932, amply demonstrated, has a lamentable tendency toward municipal panic.

Having secured a copy of Köhler's Dictionary of the English and German Languages, I went, on an impulse, to the card catalogue and looked up von Junzt, Friedrich. There was no card for any work by this author – hardly surprising, perhaps, in a small-town library like ours. I returned to the reference shelf, and consulted an encyclopedia of philosophical biography and comparable volumes of philologic reference, but found no entry for any von Junzt – a diplomate, by the testimony of his title page, of the University of Tübingen and of the Sorbonne. It seemed that von Junzt had been dismissed, or expunged, from the dusty memory of his discipline.

It was as I was closing the Encyclopedia of Archaeo-Anthropological Research that a name suddenly leapt out at me, catching my eye just before the pages slammed together. It was a word that I had noticed in von Junzt's book: 'Urartu.' I barely managed to slip the edge of my thumb into the encyclopedia to mark the place; half a second later and the reference might have been lost to me. As it turned out, the name of von Junzt itself was also contained – sealed up – in the sarcophagus of this entry, a long and tedious one devoted to the work of an Oxford man by the name of St. Dennis T. R. Gladfellow, 'a noted scholar,' as the entry had it, 'in the field of inquiry into the beliefs of the ancient, largely unknown peoples referred to conjecturally today as proto-Urartians.' The reference lay buried in a column dense with comparisons among various bits of obsidian and broken bronze:

G.'s analysis of the meaning of such ceremonial blades admittedly was aided by the earlier discoveries of Friedrich von Junzt, at the site of the former Temple of Yrrh, in north central Armenia, among them certain sacrificial artifacts pertaining to the worship of the proto-Urartian deity Yê-Heh, rather grandly (though regrettably without credible evidence) styled 'the god of dark or mocking laughter' by the German, a notorious adventurer and fake whose work, nevertheless, in this instance, has managed to prove useful to science.

The prospect of spending the evening in the company of Herr von Junzt began to seem even less appealing. One of the most tedious human beings I have ever known was my own mother, who, early in my childhood, fell under the spell of Madame Blavatsky and her followers and proceeded to weary my youth and deplete my patrimony with her devotion to that indigestible caseation of balderdash and lies. Mother drew a number of local simpletons into her orbit, among them poor old drunken Thaddeus Craven, and burnt them up as thoroughly as the earth's atmosphere consumes asteroids. The most satisfying episodes of my career have been those which afforded me the opportunity to prosecute charlatans and frauds and those who preyed on the credulous; I did not now relish the thought of sitting at home with such a man all evening, in particular one who spoke only German.

Nevertheless, I could not ignore the undeniable novelty of a murdered circus clown who was familiar with scholarship – however spurious or misguided – concerning the religious beliefs of proto-Urartians. I carried the Köhler's over to the counter, where Lucy Brand waited eagerly for me to spill some small ration of beans. When I offered nothing for her delectation, she finally spoke.

'Was he a German?' she said, showing unaccustomed boldness, it seemed to me.

'Was *who* a German, my dear Miss Brand?'

'The victim.' She lowered her voice to a textbook librarian's whisper, though there was no one in the building but old Bob Spherakis, asleep and snoring in the periodicals room over a copy of *Grit*.

'I – I don't know,' I said, taken aback by the simplicity of her inference, or rather by its having escaped me. 'I suppose he may have been, yes.'

She slid the book across the counter toward me.

'There was another one of them in here this afternoon,' she said. 'At least, I think he was a German. A Jew, come to think of it. Somehow he managed to find the only book in Hebrew we have in our collection. It's one of the books old Mr. Vorzeichen donated when he died. A prayer book, I think it is. Tiny little thing. Black leather.'

This information ought to have struck a chord in my memory, of course, but it did not. I settled my hat on my head, bid Miss Brand good night, and walked slowly home, with the dictionary under my arm, and, in my briefcase, von Junzt's stout tome and the little black-leather volume filled with sinuous mysterious script.

I will not tax the reader with an account of my struggles with Köhler's dictionary and the thorny bramble of von Junzt's overheated German prose. Suffice to say that it took me the better part of the evening to make my way through the introduction. It was well past midnight by the time I arrived at the first chapter, and nearing two o'clock before I had amassed the information that I will now pass along to the reader, with no endorsement beyond the testimony of these pages, nor any hope of its being believed.

It was a blustery night; I sat in the study on the top floor of my old house's round tower, listening to the windows rattle in their casements, as if a gang of intruders were seeking a way in. In this high room, in 1885, it was said, Howard Ash, the last living descendant of our town's founder, General Hannaniah Ash, had sealed the blank note of his life and dispatched himself, with postage due, to his Creator. A fugitive draft blew from time to time across my desk and stirred the pages of the dictionary by my left hand. I felt, as I read, as if the whole world were asleep – benighted, ignorant, and dreaming – while I had been left to man the crow's nest, standing lonely vigil in the teeth of a storm that was blowing in from a tropic of dread.

According to the scholar or charlatan Friedrich von Junzt, the regions around what is now northern Armenia had spawned, along with an entire cosmology, two competing cults of incalculable antiquity, which survived to the present day: that of Yê-Heh, the God of Dark Laughter, and that of Ai, the God of Unbearable and Ubiquitous Sorrow. The Yê-Hehists viewed the universe as a cosmic hoax, perpetrated by the father-god Yrrh for unknowable purposes: a place of calamity and cruel irony so overwhelming that the only possible response was a malevolent laughter like that, presumably, of Yrrh himself. The laughing followers of baboon-headed Yê-Heh created a sacred burlesque, mentioned by Pausanias and by one of the travellers in Plutarch's dialogue 'On the Passing of the Oracles,' to express their mockery of life, death, and all human aspirations. The rite involved the flaying of a human head, severed from the shoulders of one who had died in battle or in the course of some other supposedly exalted endeavor. The clown-priest would don the bloodless mask and then dance, making a public travesty of the noble dead. Through generations of inbreeding, the worshippers of Yê-Heh had evolved into a virtual subspecies of humanity, characterized by distended grins and skin as white as chalk. Von Junzt even claimed that the tradition of painted circus clowns derived from the clumsy imitation, by noninitiates, of these ancient kooks.

The 'immemorial foes' of the baboon boys, as the reader may have surmised, were the followers of Ai, the God Who Mourns. These gloomy fanatics saw the world as no less horrifying and cruel than did their archenemies, but their response to the whole mess was a more or less permanent wailing. Over the long millennia since the heyday of ancient Urartu, the Aiites had developed a complicated physical discipline, a sort of jujitsu or calisthenics of murder, which they chiefly employed in a ruthless hunt of followers of Yê-Heh. For they believed that Yrrh, the Absent One, the Silent Devisor who, an eternity ago, tossed the cosmos over his shoulder like a sheet of fish wrap and wandered away leaving not a clue as to his intentions, would not return to explain the meaning of his inexplicable and tragic creation until the progeny of Yê-Heh, along with all copies of the Yê-Hehist sacred book, 'Khndzut Dzul,' or 'The Unfathomable Ruse,' had been expunged from the face of the earth. Only then would Yrrh return from his primeval hiatus – 'bringing what new horror or redemption,' as the German intoned, 'none can say.'

All this struck me as a gamier variety of the same loony, Zoroastrian plonk that my mother had spent her life decanting, and I might have been inclined to set the whole business aside and leave the case to be swept under the administrative rug by Jack Ganz had it not been for the words with which Herr von Junzt concluded the second chapter of his tedious work:

While the Yê-Hehist gospel of cynicism and ridicule has, quite obviously, spread around the world, the cult itself has largely died out, in part through the predations of foes and in part through chronic health problems brought about by inbreeding. Today [von Junzt's book carried a date of 1849] it is reported that there may be fewer than 150 of the Yê-Hehists left in the world. They have survived, for the most part, by taking on work in travelling circuses. While their existence is known to ordinary members of the circus world, their secret has, by and large, been kept. And in the sideshows they have gone to ground, awaiting the tread outside the wagon, the shadow on the tent-flap, the cruel knife that will, in a mockery of their own long-abandoned ritual of mockery, deprive them of the lily-white flesh of their skulls.

Here I put down the book, my hands trembling from fatigue, and took up the other one, printed in an unknown tongue. 'The Unfathomable Ruse'? I hardly thought so; I was inclined to give as little credit as I reasonably could to Herr von Junzt's account. More than likely the small black volume was some inspirational text in the mother tongue of the dead man, a translation of the Gospels, perhaps. And yet I must confess that there were a few tangential points in von Junzt's account that caused me some misgiving.

There was a scrape then just outside my window, as if a finger with a very long nail were being drawn almost lovingly along the glass. But the finger turned out to be one of the branches of a fine old horse-chestnut tree that stood outside the tower, scratching at the window in the wind. I was relieved and humiliated. Time to go to bed, I said to myself. Before I turned in, I went to the shelf and moved to one side the bust of Galen that I had inherited from my father, a country doctor. I took a quick snort of good Tennessee whiskey, a taste for which I had also inherited from the old man. Thus emboldened, I went over to the desk and picked up the books. To be frank, I would have preferred to leave them there – I would have preferred to burn them, to be really frank – but I felt that it was my duty to keep them about me while they were under my watch. So I slept with the books beneath my pillow, in their wax envelopes, and I had the worst dream of my life.

It was one of those dreams where you are a fly on the wall, a phantom bystander, disembodied, unable to speak or intervene. In it, I was treated to the spectacle of a man whose young son was going to die. The man lived in a corner of the world where, from time to time, evil seemed to bubble up from the rusty red earth like a black combustible compound of ancient things long dead. And yet, year after year, this man met each new outburst of horror, true to his code, with nothing but law books, statutes, and county ordinances, as if sheltering with only a sheet of newspaper those he had sworn to protect, insisting that the steaming black geyser pouring down on them was nothing but a light spring rain. That vision started me laughing, but the cream of the jest came when, seized by a spasm of forgiveness toward his late, mad mother, the man decided not to prosecute one of her old paramours, a rummy by the name of Craven, for driving under the influence. Shortly thereafter, Craven steered his old Hudson Terraplane the wrong way down a one-way street, where it encountered, with appropriate cartoon sound effects, an oncoming bicycle ridden by the man's heedless, darling, wildly pedalling son. That was the funniest thing of all, funnier than the amusing ironies of the man's profession, than his furtive drinking and his wordless, solitary suppers, funnier even than his having been widowed by suicide: the joke of a father's outliving his boy. It was so funny that, watching this ridiculous man in my dream, I could not catch my breath for laughing. I laughed so hard that my eyes popped from their sockets, and my smile stretched until it broke my aching jaw. I laughed until the husk of my head burst like a pod and fell away, and my skull and brains went floating off into the sky, white dandelion fluff, a cloud of fairy parasols.

Around four o'clock in the morning, I woke and was conscious of someone in the room with me. There was an unmistakable tang of the sea in the air. My eyesight is poor and it took me a while to make him out in the darkness, though he was standing just beside my bed, with his long thin arm snaked under my pillow, creeping around. I lay perfectly still, aware of the tips of this slender shadow's fingernails and the scrape of his scaly knuckles, as he rifled the contents of my head and absconded with them through the bedroom window, which was somehow also the mouth of the Neighborsburg Caverns, with tiny old Colonel Earnshaw taking tickets in the booth.

I awakened now in truth, and reached immediately under the pillow. The books were still there. I returned them to the evidence room at eight o'clock this morning. At nine, there was a call from Dolores and Victor Abbott, at their motor lodge out on the Plunkettsburg Pike. A guest had made an abrupt departure, leaving a mess. I got into a car with Ganz and we drove out to get a look. The Ashtown police were already there, going over the buildings and grounds of the Vista Dolores Lodge. The bathroom wastebasket of Room 201 was overflowing with blood-soaked bandages. There was evidence that the guest had been keeping some kind of live bird in the room; one of the neighboring guests reported that it had sounded like a crow. And over the whole room there hung a salt smell that I recognized immediately, a smell that some compared to the smell of the ocean, and others to that of blood. When the pillow, wringing wet, was sent up to Pittsburgh for analysis by Mr. Espy, it was found to have been saturated with human tears.

When I returned from court, late this afternoon, there was a message from Dr. Sauer. He had completed his postmortem and wondered if I would drop by. I took the bottle from behind Daniel Webster and headed on down to the county morgue.

'He was already dead, the poor son of a biscuit eater,' Dr. Sauer said, looking less morose than he had the last time we spoke. Sauer was a gaunt old Methodist who avoided strong language but never, so long as I had known him, strong drink. I poured us each a tumbler, and then a second. 'It took me a while to establish it because there was something about the fellow that I was missing.'

'What was that?'

'Well, I'm reasonably sure that he was a hemophiliac. So my reckoning time of death by coagulation of the blood was all thrown off.'

'Hemophilia,' I said.

'Yes,' Dr. Sauer said. 'It is associated sometimes with inbreeding, as in the case of royal families of Europe.'

Inbreeding. We stood there for a while, looking at the sad bulk of the dead man under the sheet.

'I also found a tattoo,' Dr. Sauer added. 'The head of a grinning baboon. On his left forearm. Oh, and one other thing. He suffered from some kind of vitiligo. There are white patches on his nape and throat.'

Let the record show that the contents of the victim's makeup kit, when it was inventoried, included cold cream, rouge, red greasepaint, a powder puff, some brushes, cotton swabs, and five cans of foundation in a tint the label described as 'Olive Male.' There was no trace, however, of the white greasepaint with which clowns daub their grinning faces.

Here I conclude my report, and with it my tenure as district attorney for this blighted and unfortunate county. I have staked my career – my life itself – on the things I could see, on the stories I could credit, and on the eventual vindication, when the book was closed, of the reasonable and skeptical approach. In the face of twenty-five years of bloodshed, mayhem, criminality, and the universal human pastime of ruination, I have clung fiercely to Occam's razor, seeking always to keep my solutions unadorned and free of conjecture, and never to resort to conspiracy or any kind of prosecutorial woolgathering. My mother, whenever she was confronted by calamity or personal sorrow, invoked cosmic emanations, invisible empires, ancient prophecies, and intrigues; it has been the business of my life to reject such folderol and seek the simpler explanation. But we were fools, she and I, arrant blockheads, each of us blind to or heedless of the readiest explanation: that the world is an ungettable joke, and our human need to explain its wonders and horrors, our appalling genius for devising such explanations, is nothing more than the rim shot that accompanies the punch line.

I do not know if that nameless clown was the last, but in any case, with such pursuers, there can be few of his kind left. And if there is any truth in the grim doctrine of those hunters, then the return of our father Yrrh, with his inscrutable intentions, cannot be far off. But I fear that, in spite of their efforts over the last ten thousand years, the followers of Ai are going to be gravely disappointed when, at the end of all we know and everything we have ever lost or imagined, the rafters of the world are shaken by a single, a terrible guffaw.

DETAILS

China Miéville

China Miéville (1972–) is an influential English writer known for revitalizing weird fiction, and remains the leading figure in the New Weird movement. He has won the World Fantasy Award and multiple Arthur C. Clarke awards, among others. Miéville's early novels – including *Perdido Street Station* (2001) and *The Scar* (2002) – fused the weird with body transformation, Marxist politics, secondary world settings, and a bold, often pulpy style. Later novels like *The City and the City* (2009) and *Embassytown* (2011) feature a more stripped-down style without sacrificing the visionary quality of the weird. Stories like 'Details' (2002) show that he had delicacy of touch early in his career, as well as an encyclopedic knowledge of weird fiction.

When the boy upstairs got hold of a pellet gun and fired snips of potato at passing cars, I took a turn. I was part of everything. I wasn't an outsider. But I wouldn't join in when my friends went to the yellow house to scribble on the bricks and listen at the windows. One girl teased me about it, but everyone else told her to shut up. They defended me, even though they didn't understand why I wouldn't come.

I don't remember a time before I visited the yellow house for my mother.

On Wednesday mornings at about nine o'clock I would open the front door of the decrepit building with a key from the bunch my mother had given me. Inside was a hall and two doors, one broken and leading to splintering stairs. I would unlock the other and enter the dark flat. The corridor was unlit and smelled of old, wet air. I never walked even two steps down that hallway. Rot and shadows merged, and it looked as if the passage disappeared a few yards from me. The door to Mrs. Miller's room was right in front of me. I would lean forward and knock.

Quite often there were signs that someone else had been there recently. Scuffed dust and bits of litter. Sometimes I was not alone. There were two other children I sometimes saw slipping in or out of the house. There were a handful of adults who visited Mrs. Miller.

I might find one or another of them in the hallway outside the door to her flat, or even in the flat itself, slouching in the crumbling dark hallway. They would be slumped over or reading some cheap-looking book or swearing loudly as they waited.

There was a young Asian woman who wore a lot of makeup and smoked obsessively. She ignored me totally. There were two drunks who came sometimes. One would greet me boisterously and incomprehensibly, raising his arms as if he wanted to hug me into his stinking, stinking jumper. I would grin and wave nervously, walk past him. The other seemed alternately melancholic and angry. Occasionally I'd meet him by the door to Mrs. Miller's room, swearing in a strong cockney accent. I remember the first time I saw him, he was standing there, his red face contorted, slurring and moaning loudly.

'Come on, you old slag,' he wailed, 'you sodding old *slag*. Come on, please, you cow.'

His words scared me but his tone was wheedling, and I realized I could hear her voice, Mrs. Miller's voice, from inside the room, answering him back. She did not sound frightened or angry.

I hung back, not sure what to do, and she kept speaking, and eventually the drunken man shambled miserably away. And then I could continue as usual.

I asked my mother once if I could have any of Mrs. Miller's food. She laughed very hard and shook her head. In all the Wednesdays of bringing the food over, I never even dipped my finger in to suck it.

My mum spent an hour every Tuesday night making the stuff up. She dissolved a bit of gelatin or cornflour with some milk, threw in a load of sugar or flavorings, and crushed a clutch of vitamin pills into the mess. She stirred it until it thickened and let it set in a plain white plastic bowl. In the morning it would be a kind of strong-smelling custard that my mother put a dishcloth over and gave me, along with a list of any questions or requests for Mrs. Miller and sometimes a plastic bucket full of white paint.

So I would stand in front of Mrs. Miller's door, knocking, with a bowl at my feet. I'd hear a shifting and then her voice from close by the door.

'Hello,' she would call, and then say my name a couple of times. 'Have you my breakfast? Are you ready?'

I would creep up close to the door and hold the food ready. I would tell her I was.

Mrs. Miller would slowly count to three. On three, the door suddenly swung open a snatch, just a foot or two, and I thrust my bowl into the gap. She grabbed it and slammed the door quickly in my face.

I couldn't see very much inside the room. The door was open for less than a second. My strongest impression was of the whiteness of the walls. Mrs. Miller's sleeves were white, too, and made of plastic. I never got much of a glimpse at her face, but what I saw was unmemorable. A middle-aged woman's eager face.

If I had a bucket full of paint, we would run through the routine again. Then I would sit cross-legged in front of her door and listen to her eat.

'How's your mother' she would shout. At that I'd unfold my mother's careful queries. She's okay, I'd say, she's fine. She says she has some questions for you.

I'd read my mother's strange questions in my careful childish monotone, and Mrs. Miller would pause and make interested sounds, and clear her throat and think out loud. Sometimes she took ages to come to an answer, and sometimes it would be almost immediate.

'Tell your mother she can't tell if a man's good or bad from that,' she'd say; 'Tell her to remember the problems she had with your father.' Or: 'Yes, she can take the heart of it out. Only she has to paint it with the special oil I told her about.' 'Tell your mother seven. But only four of them concern her and three of them used to be dead.'

'I can't help her with that,' she told me once, quietly. 'Tell her to go to a doctor, quickly.' And my mother did, and she got well again.

'What do you not want to be when you grow up?' Mrs. Miller asked me one day.

That morning when I had come to the house the sad cockney vagrant had been banging on the door of her room again, the keys to the flat flailing in his hand.

'He's begging you, you old tart, please, you owe him, he's so bloody angry,' he was shouting, 'only it ain't you gets the sharp end, is it? *Please*, you cow, you sodding cow, I'm on me knees...'

'My door knows you, man,' Mrs. Miller declared from within. 'It knows you and so do I, you know it won't open to you. I didn't take out my eyes and I'm not giving in now. Go home.'

I waited nervously as the man gathered himself and staggered away, and then, looking behind me, I knocked on the door and announced myself. It was after I'd given her the food that she asked her question.

'What do you not want to be when you grow up?'

If I had been a few years older her inversion of the cliché would have annoyed me. It would have seemed mannered and contrived. But I was only a young child, and I was quite delighted.

I don't want to be a lawyer, I told her carefully. I spoke out of loyalty to my mother, who periodically received crisp letters that made her cry or smoke fiercely, and swear at lawyers, bloody smartarse lawyers.

Mrs. Miller was delighted.

'Good boy!' she snorted. 'We know all about lawyers. Bastards, right? With the small print. Never be tricked by the small print! It's right there in front of you, *right there in front of you*, and you can't even *see* it and then suddenly it *makes you notice it!* And I tell you, once you've seen it it's got you!' She laughed excitedly. 'Don't let the small print get you. I'll tell you a secret.' I waited quietly, and my head slipped nearer the door.

'The devil's in the details!' She laughed again. 'You ask your mother if that's not true. The devil is in the details!'

I'd wait the twenty minutes or so until Mrs. Miller had finished eating, and then we'd reverse our previous procedure and she'd quickly hand me out an empty bowl. I would return home with the empty container and tell my mother the various answers to her various questions. Usually she would nod and make notes. Occasionally she would cry.

After I told Mrs. Miller that I did not want to be a lawyer she started asking me to read to her. She made me tell my mother, and told me to bring a newspaper or one of a number of books. My mother nodded at the message and packed me a sandwich the next Wednesday, along with the *Mirror*. She told me to be polite and do what Mrs. Miller asked, and that she'd see me in the afternoon.

I wasn't afraid. Mrs. Miller had never treated me badly from behind her door. I was resigned and only a little bit nervous.

Mrs. Miller made me read stories to her from specific pages that she shouted out. She made me recite them again and again, very carefully. Afterward she would talk to me. Usually she started with a joke about lawyers, and about small print.

'There's three ways not to see what you don't want to,' she told me. 'One is the coward's way and too damned painful. The other is to close your eyes forever which is the same as the first, when it comes to it. The third is the hardest and the best: You have to make sure *only the things you can afford to see* come before you.'

One morning when I arrived the stylish Asian woman was whispering fiercely through the wood of the door, and I could hear Mrs. Miller responding with shouts of amused disapproval. Eventually the young woman swept past me, leaving me cowed by her perfume.

Mrs. Miller was laughing, and she was talkative when she had eaten.

'She's heading for trouble, messing with the wrong family! You have to be careful with all of them,' she told me. 'Every single *one* of them on that other side of things is a tricksy bastard who'll kill you as soon as *look* at you, given half a chance.

'There's the gnarly throat-tripped one... and there's old hasty, who I think had best remain nameless,' she said wryly. 'All old bastards, all of them. You *can't trust them* at all, that's what I say. I should know, eh? Shouldn't I?' She laughed. 'Trust me, trust me on this: It's too easy to get on the wrong side of them.

'What's it like out today?' she asked me. I told her that it was cloudy.

'You want to be careful with that,' she said. 'All sorts of faces in the clouds, aren't there? Can't help noticing, can you?' She was whispering now. 'Do me a favor when you go home to your mum: Don't look up, there's a boy. Don't look up at all.'

When I left her, however, the day had changed. The sky was hot, and quite blue.

The two drunk men were squabbling in the front hall and I edged past them to her door. They continued bickering in a depressing, garbled murmur throughout my visit.

'D'you know, I can't even really remember what it was all *about*, now!' Mrs. Miller said when I had finished reading to her. 'I can't remember! That's a terrible thing. But you don't forget the basics. The exact question escapes me, and to be honest I think maybe I was just being *nosy* or *showing off*...

I can't say I'm proud of it but it could have been that. It could. But whatever the question, it was all about a way of seeing an answer.

'There's a way of looking that lets you read things. If you look at a pattern of tar on a wall, or a crumbling mound of brick or somesuch… there's a way of unpicking it. And if you know how, you can trace it and read it out and see the things hidden *right there in front of you*, the things you've been seeing but not noticing, all along. But you have to learn how.' She laughed. It was a high-pitched, unpleasant sound. 'Someone has to teach you. So you have to make certain friends.

'But you can't make friends without making enemies.

'You have to open it all up for you to see inside. You have to make what you see into a window, and you see what you want through it. You make what you see a sort of *door*.'

She was silent for a long time. Then: 'Is it cloudy again?' she asked suddenly. She went on before I answered.

'If you look up, you look into the clouds for long enough and you'll see a face. Or in a tree. Look in a tree, look in the branches and soon you'll see them just so, and there's a face or a running man, or a bat or whatever. You'll see it all suddenly, a picture in the pattern of the branches, and you won't have *chosen* to see it. And you can't *unsee* it.

'That's what you have to learn to do, to read the details like that and see what's what and learn things. But you've to be damn careful. You've to be careful not to disturb anything.' Her voice was absolutely cold, and I was suddenly very frightened.

'Open up that window, you'd better be damn careful that what's in the details doesn't look back and see you.'

The next time I went, the maudlin drunk was there again wailing obscenities at her through the door. She shouted at me to come back later, that she didn't need her food right now. She sounded resigned and irritated, and she went back to scolding her visitor before I had backed out of earshot.

He was screaming at her that she'd gone too far, that she'd pissed about too long, that things were coming to a head, that there was going to be hell to pay, that she couldn't avoid it forever, that it was her own fault.

When I came back he was asleep, snoring loudly, curled up a few feet into the mildewing passage. Mrs. Miller took her food and ate it quickly, returned it without speaking.

When I returned the following week, she began to whisper to me as soon as I knocked on the door, hissing urgently as she opened it briefly and grabbed the bowl.

'It was an accident, you know,' she said, as if responding to something I'd said. 'I mean of *course* you know in *theory* that anything might happen, you get *warned*, don't you? But oh my… oh my *God* it took the breath out of me and made me cold to realize what had happened.'

I waited. I could not leave, because she had not returned the bowl. She had not said I could go. She spoke again, very slowly.

'It was a new day.' Her voice was distant and breathy. 'Can you even imagine? Can you see what I was ready to do? I was poised… to change… to see everything that's hidden. The best place to hide a book is in a library. The best place to hide secret things is there, in the visible angles, in our view, in plain sight.

'I had studied and sought, and learnt, finally, to see. It was time to learn truths.

'I opened my eyes fully, for the first time.

'I had chosen an old wall. I was looking for the answer to some question that I told you I can't even *remember* now, but the question wasn't the main thing. That was the opening of my eyes.

'I stared at the whole mass of the bricks. I took another glance, relaxed my sight. At first I couldn't stop seeing the bricks as bricks, the divisions as layers of cement, but after a time they became pure vision. And as the whole broke down into lines and shapes and shades, I held my breath as I began to see.

'Alternatives appeared to me. Messages written in the pockmarks. Insinuations in the forms. Secrets unraveling. It was bliss.

'And then without warning my heart went tight, as I saw something. I made sense of the pattern.

'It was a mess of cracks and lines and crumbling cement, and as I looked at it, I saw a pattern in the wall.

'I saw a clutch of lines that looked just like something... terrible... something old and predatory and utterly terrible... staring right back at me.

'And then I saw it move.'

'You have to understand me,' she said. '*Nothing changed.* See? All the time I was looking I saw the wall. But that first moment, it was like when you see a face in the cloud. I just *noticed* in the pattern in the brick, I just *noticed* something, looking at me. Something angry.

'And then in the very next moment, I just... I just *noticed* another load of lines – cracks that had always been there, you understand? Patterns in broken brick that I'd seen only a second before – that looked exactly like that same thing, a little closer to me. And in the next moment a third picture in the brick, a picture of the thing closer still.

'Reaching for me.'

'I broke free then,' she whispered. 'I ran away from there in terror, with my hands in front of my eyes and I was *screaming*. I ran and ran.

'And when I stopped and opened my eyes again, I had to run to the edges of a park, and I took my hands slowly down and dared to look behind me, and saw that there was nothing coming from the alley where I'd been. So I turned to the little snatch of scrub and grass and trees.

'And I saw the thing again.'

Mrs. Miller's voice was stretched out as if she was dreaming. My mouth was open and I huddled closer to the door.

'I saw it in the leaves,' she said forlornly. 'As I turned I saw the leaves in such a way... just a *chance conjuncture*, you understand? I noticed a pattern. I *couldn't not*. You don't choose whether to see faces in the clouds. I saw the monstrous thing again and it still reached for me, and I shrieked and all the mothers and fathers and children in the park turned and gazed at me, and I turned my eyes from that tree and whirled on my feet to face a little family in my way.

'And the thing was there in the same pose,' she whispered in misery. 'I saw it in the outlines of the father's coat and the spokes of the baby's pushchair, and the tangles of the mother's hair. It was just another mess of lines, you see? But you *don't choose what you notice*. And I couldn't help but notice *just the right lines* out of the whole, just the lines out of all the lines there, just the ones to see the thing again, a little closer, looking at me.

'And I turned and saw it closer still in the clouds, and I turned again and it was clutching for me in the rippling weeds in the pond, and as I closed my eyes I swear I felt something touch my dress.

'You understand me? You understand?'

I didn't know if I understood or not. Of course now I know that I did not.

'It lives in the details,' she said bleakly. 'It travels in that... in that perception. It moves through those chance meetings of lines. Maybe you glimpse it sometimes when you stare at clouds, and then maybe it might catch a glimpse of you, too.

'But it saw me *full* on. It's jealous of... of its place, and there I was peering through without permission, like a nosy neighbor through a hole in the fence. I know what it is. I know what happened.

'It lurks before us, in the everyday. It's the boss of *all the things* hidden in plain sight. Terrible things, they are. Appalling things. Just almost in reach. Brazen and invisible.

'It caught my glances. It can move through whatever I see.

'For most people it's just chance, isn't it? What shapes they see in a tangle of wire. There's a thousand pictures there, and when you look, some of them just appear. But now... the thing in the lines chooses the pictures for me. It can thrust itself forward. It makes me see it. It's found its way through. To me. Through what I see. *I opened a door into my perception*.'

She sounded frozen with terror. I was not equipped for that kind of adult fear, and my mouth worked silently for something to say.

'That was a long, long journey home. Every time I peeked through the cracks in my fingers, I saw that thing crawling for me.

'It waited ready to pounce, and when I opened my eyes even a crack I opened the door again. I saw the back of a woman's jumper and in the detail of the fabric the thing leapt for me. I glimpsed a yard of broken paving and I noticed just the lines that showed me the thing... *baying*.

'I had to shut my eyes quick.

'I *groped* my way home.

'And then I taped my eyes shut and I tried to think about things.'

There was silence for a time.

'See, there was always the easy way, that scared me rotten, because I was never one for blood and pain,' she said suddenly, and her voice was harder. 'I held the scissors in front of my eyes a couple of times, but even bandaged blind as I was I couldn't bear it. I suppose I could've gone to a doctor. I can pull strings, I could pull in a few favors, have them do the job without pain.

'But you know I never... really... reckoned... that's what I'd do,' she said thoughtfully. 'What if you found a way to close the door? Eh? And you'd already put out your eyes? You'd feel such a *fool*, wouldn't you?

'And as you know it wouldn't be good enough to wear pads and eyepatches and all. I tried. You catch glimpses. You see the glimmers of light and maybe a few of your own hairs, and that's *the doorway right there*, when the hairs cross in the corner of your eye so that if you notice just a few of them in just the right way... they look like something coming for you. That's a doorway.

'It's... unbearable... having sight, but trapping it like that.

'I'm not giving up. See...' Her voice lowered, and she spoke conspiratorially. '*I still think I can close the door*. I learnt to see. I can unlearn. I'm looking for ways. I want to see a wall as... as bricks again. Nothing more. That's why you read for me,' she said. '*Research*. Can't look at it myself of course, too many edges and lines and so on on a printed page, so you do it for me. And you're a good boy to do it.'

I've thought about what she said many times, and still it makes no sense to me. The books I read to Mrs. Miller were school textbooks, old and dull village histories, the occasional romantic novel. I think that she must have been talking of some of her other visitors, who perhaps read her more esoteric stuff than I did. Either that, or the information she sought was buried very cleverly in the banal prose I faltered through.

'In the meantime, there's another way of surviving,' she said slyly. 'Leave the eyes where they are, but *don't give them any details*.

'That... thing can force me to notice its shape, but only in what's there. That's how it travels. You imagine if I saw a field of wheat. Doesn't even bear *thinking* about! A million million little bloody *edges*, a million lines. You could make pictures of damn *anything* out of them, couldn't you? It wouldn't take any effort at *all* for the thing to make me notice it. The damn *lurker*. Or in a gravel drive or, or a building site, or a lawn...

'But I can outsmart it.' The note of cunning in her voice made her sound deranged. 'Keep it away till I work out how to close it off.

'I had to prepare this blind, with the wrappings around my head. Took me a while, but here I am now. Safe. I'm safe in my little cold room. I keep the walls *flat white*. I covered the windows and painted them, too. I made my cloak out of plastic, so's I can't catch a glimpse of cotton weave or anything when I wake up.

'I keep my place nice and... simple. When it was all done, I unwrapped the bandages from my head, and I blinked slowly... and I was alright. Clean walls, no cracks, no features. I don't look at my hands often or for long. Too many creases. Your mother makes me a good healthy soup looks like cream, so if I accidentally look in the bowl, there's no broccoli or rice or tangled up spaghetti to make *lines and edges*.

'I open and shut the door so damned quick because I can only afford a moment. *That thing is ready to pounce*. It wouldn't take a second for it to leap up at me out of the sight of your hair or your books or whatever.'

Her voice ebbed out. I waited a minute for her to resume, but she did not do so. Eventually I knocked nervously on the door and called her name. There was no answer. I put my ear to the door. I could hear her crying, quietly.

I went home without the bowl. My mother pursed her lips a little but said nothing. I didn't tell her any of what Mrs. Miller had said. I was troubled and totally confused.

The next time I delivered Mrs. Miller's food, in a new container, she whispered harshly to me: 'It preys on my eyes, all the *white*. Nothing to see. Can't look out the window, can't read, can't gaze at my nails. Preys on my mind.

'Not even my memories are left,' she said in misery. 'It's colonizing them. I remember things... happy times... and the thing's waiting in the texture of my dress, or in the crumbs of my birthday cake. I didn't notice it then. But I can see it now. My memories aren't mine anymore. Not even my imaginings. Last night I thought about going to the seaside, and then the thing was there in the foam on the waves.'

She spoke very little the next few times I visited her. I read the chapters she demanded and she grunted curtly in her response. She ate quickly.

Her other visitors were there more often now, as the spring came in. I saw them in new combinations and situations: the glamorous young woman arguing with the friendly drunk; the old man sobbing at the far end of the hall. The aggressive man was often there, cajoling and moaning, and occasionally talking conversationally through the door, being answered like an equal. Other times he screamed at her as usual.

I arrived on a chilly day to find the drunken cockney man sleeping a few feet from the door, snoring gutturally. I gave Mrs. Miller her food and then sat on my coat and read to her from a women's magazine as she ate.

When she had finished her food I waited with my arms outstretched, ready to snatch the bowl from her. I remember that I was very uneasy, that I sensed something wrong. I was looking around me anxiously, but everything seemed normal. I looked down at my coat and the crumpled magazine, at the man who still sprawled comatose in the hall.

As I heard Mrs. Miller's hands on the door, I realized what had changed. The drunken man was not snoring. He was holding his breath.

For a tiny moment I thought he had died, but I could see his body trembling, and my eyes began to open wide and I stretched my mouth to scream a warning, but the door had already begun to swing in its tight, quick arc, and before I could even exhale the stinking man pushed himself up faster than I would have thought him capable and bore down on me with bloodshot eyes.

I managed to keen as he reached me, and the door faltered for an instant, as Mrs. Miller heard my voice. But the man grabbed hold of me in a terrifying, heavy fug of alcohol. He reached down and snatched my coat from the floor, tugged at the jumper I had tied around my waist with his other hand, and hurled me hard at the door.

It flew open, smacking Mrs. Miller aside. I was screaming and crying. My eyes hurt at the sudden burst of cold white light from all the walls. I saw Mrs. Miller rubbing her head in the corner, struggling to her senses. The staggering, drunken man hurled my checked coat and my patterned jumper in front of her, reached down and snatched my feet, tugged me out of the room in an agony of splinters. I wailed snottily with fear.

Behind me, Mrs. Miller began to scream and curse, but I could not hear her well because the man had clutched me to him and pulled my head to his chest. I fought and cried and felt myself lurch as he leaned forward and slammed the door closed.

He held it shut.

When I fought myself free of him I heard him shouting.

'I told you, you slapper,' he wailed unhappily. 'I bloody told you, you silly old whore. I warned you it was time...' Behind his voice I could hear shrieks of misery and terror from the room. Both of them kept shouting and crying and screaming, and the floorboards pounded, and the door shook, and I heard something else as well.

As if the notes of all the different noises in the house fell into a chance meeting, and sounded like more than dissonance. The shouts and bangs and cries of fear combined in a sudden audible illusion like another presence.

Like a snarling voice. A lingering, hungry exhalation.

I ran then, screaming and terrified, my skin freezing in my T-shirt. I was sobbing and retching with fear, little bleats bursting from me. I stumbled home and was sick in my mother's room, and kept crying and crying as she grabbed hold of me and I tried to tell her what had happened, until I was drowsy and confused and I fell into silence.

My mother said nothing about Mrs. Miller. The next Wednesday we got up early and went to the zoo, the two of us, and at the time I would usually be knocking on Mrs. Miller's door I was laughing at camels. The Wednesday after that I was taken to see a film, and the one after that my mother stayed in bed and sent me to fetch cigarettes and bread from the local shop, and I made our breakfast and ate it in her room.

My friends could tell that something had changed in the yellow house, but they did not speak to me about it, and it quickly became uninteresting to them.

I saw the Asian woman once more, smoking with her friends in the park several weeks later, and to my amazement she nodded to me and came over, interrupted her companions' conversation.

'Are you alright?' she asked me peremptorily. 'How are you doing?'

I nodded shyly back and told her that I was fine, thank you, and how was she?

She nodded and walked away.

I never saw the drunken, violent man again.

There were people I could probably have gone to to understand more about what had happened to Mrs. Miller. There was a story that I could chase, if I wanted to. People I had never seen before came to my house and spoke quietly to my mother, and looked at me with what I suppose was pity or concern. I could have asked them. But I was thinking more and more about my own life. I didn't want to know Mrs. Miller's details.

I went back to the yellow house once, nearly a year after that awful morning. It was winter. I remembered the last time I spoke to Mrs. Miller and I felt so much older it was almost giddying. It seemed such a vastly long time ago.

I crept up to the house one evening, trying the keys I still had, which to my surprise worked. The hallway was freezing, dark, and stinking more strongly than ever. I hesitated, then pushed open Mrs. Miller's door.

It opened easily, without a sound. The occasional muffled noise from the street seemed so distant it was like a memory. I entered.

She had covered the windows very carefully, and still no light made its way through from outside. It was extremely dark. I waited until I could see better in the ambient glow from the outside hallway.

I was alone.

My old coat and jumper lay spread-eagled in the corner of the room. I shivered to see them, went over, and fingered them softly. They were damp and mildewing, covered in wet dust.

The white paint was crumbling off the wall in scabs. It looked as if it had been left untended for several years. I could not believe the extent of the decay.

I turned slowly around and gazed at each wall in turn. I took in the chaotic, intricate patterns of crumbling paint and damp plaster. They looked like maps, like a rocky landscape.

I looked for a long time at the wall farthest from my jacket. I was very cold. After a long time I saw a shape in the ruined paint. I moved closer with a dumb curiosity far stronger than any fear.

In the crumbling texture of the wall was a spreading anatomy of cracks that – seen from a certain angle, caught just right in the scraps of light – looked in outline something like a woman. As I stared at it, it took shape, and I stopped noticing the extraneous lines, and focused without effort or decision on the relevant ones. I saw a woman looking out at me.

I could make out the suggestion of her face. The patch of rot that constituted it made it look as if she was screaming.

One of her arms was flung back away from her body, which seemed to strain against it, as if she was being pulled away by her hand, and was fighting to escape, and was failing. At the end of her crack-arm, in the space where her captor would be, the paint had fallen away in a great slab, uncovering a huge patch of wet, stained, textured cement.

And in that dark infinity of markings, I could make out any shape I wanted.

THE GENIUS OF ASSASSINS: THREE DREAMS OF MURDER IN THE FIRST PERSON

Michael Cisco

Michael Cisco (1970–) is an American writer best known for his first novel, *The Divinity Student* (1999), which was published by Ann VanderMeer's Buzzcity Press and won the International Horror Guild Award in 1999. Since then, Cisco has published *The Tyrant* (2003), *The San Veneficio Canon* (2005), *The Traitor* (2007), *The Narrator* (2010), and *The Great Lover* (2011). Taken together, these books represent the greatest oeuvre of any late-twentieth/early-twenty-first century writer of weird fiction – all the more remarkable because of the difficulty of sustaining the visionary quality of such narratives over the novel length. 'The Genius of Assassins' (2002) is a harrowing and hallucinogenic story that ventures far beyond most writers' comfort zone but is typical of Cisco's work.

Foreword

From the brambles of a murderer's eyes the gaze of the genius of assassins falls on you: a sooty-winged owl with a blanched, dead mask of livid unfeathered skin. The eyes are sacs of blood that glow with a cold red flame, with a dagger in between – it wants to share its savage idiocy with you. It's small; it hides itself easily in those brambles, and stares. Small though it is, when it draws near, the shade of its outspread wings, shedding their heavy dust, is broad enough to blot out a mind completely, and all too briefly. Wide-eyed unblinking it descends out of darkness on silent pinions, and snatches away its quarry with a movement too swift to follow. A face turns into a livid mask and a body is galvanically transformed. With an inconsequential-looking gesture the knife makes a little opening somewhere and the appalled life gushes out; the mask shifts from the murderer's softening features to the victim's stiffening face. The victim's body undergoes its own transformation: it cools, darkens, sours, stinks, by turns slack and rigid. The murderer is gone; the genius is hidden; a raw new person flees in panic, flees his gory hands.

The genius of assassins has no words, but it will address you in a gust of fright. You will know that you are not alone, in a park, or on a subway platform, or at home. Its cry is your mute astonishment at the miracle of violence. Its wings are the murderer's hands outspread; the hands are organs with the fundamental power to stop organs forever. The killer's hands will conduct orchestral, organized life through a brief lapse, and into lasting stillness. The same hands that flap on the obscure walls of caves, and whose fingertips are inked in the glare of police stations, mark time by erasing life; flutter and shed soot around the icy, fanatic mask of their genius.

The Paradise of Murderers

I'm a lonely so-and-so without much in his day to do, I don't enjoy reading, I don't even like standing still when I eat. Boring or not the streets want to feel the tramp of my foot up and down; I like to be obliging. I step out of doors in the morning when all the bells are ringing, and I stop in at my door as best I can when my head is heavy. Now and then I will stop sing dance and drink with this or that so-and-so, but I come and go and it makes no difference. I can sit up with statues or pigeons and trees in the park, headstones and piles of fruit and zoo animals and newspaper bundles and cops.

Now I take the tram across the Plague Bridge to the Old Island where the streets are lean and full of matted trash – smelly houses, children scatter like pigeons as I come up with a stone head full of matted newspaper fruits zoo cops and piles of animal bundles; drifting past my face the white branches, a park filled with statues of trees. Under the boughs, in the lanes, gutters cough and drains chatter, under the eaves, in the shade of the front porch a woman offers me a drink, shapeless grey dress sweat-patched in the chest hanging off her skinny frame. She's friendly because I am a neat-looking clean pressed young man. We drink together happily like two old failures. The ice rings the sides of the glasses like cowbell clappers and when I go I am sober but tired, my head droops in waves of crows and cobbled rows warped where the streets have been disrupted.

Here's a stoop, and a front door to lean against that falls in as I lean – here's me, on the floor looking up at yellow-brown water stains on a plaster ceiling. Someone is behind me, behind the crown of my head, lying on voluminous mattresses; fat, sad face slick with perspiration peers curiously at me.

'You startled me!'

Piercingly sad voice, thin and high.

I apologize as I pull myself up and right my head; my tumble has shocked me awake. The curtains are all drawn, thin material covered in big brown and yellow blossoms. Bed, table beside the bed, filmy wallpaper. Thin sweet smell like a candy mist – 'You all right mister?'

'I'm very ill – are you hurt? Perhaps you would like to sit a moment?'

I sit by the bed – 'Do you want the door closed?'

'No, I think the air feels good.'

He looks wanly out the door. I don't suppose he's been through it lately. He pours himself a glass of water from the pitcher on the bedside table – 'There's a glass for you if you like,' he points to the kitchen counter across the room.

'No thank you.'

He leans his head back on a soaking pillow and gazes at the rectangle of sunset in the door, the children flashing by – 'You think about death much?'

'All the time.'

'Ever kill anything?'

There are certain times when I just need to be alone – I've always been like that. I'm not unreasonable about it, but I hate being spied on. When I was a boy, I was pacing up and down once in my room, thinking I was alone, talking to myself and acting out a little scene – then I see our cat is there, watching me from beneath the bed. Incensed by his eyes I went after him, eventually I caught him – I put his head on the windowsill and crushed his throat with the window. His feet flapped a few times against the wall and the sill; then he died.

A few weeks later, I was lying in bed trying to sleep, when I heard a voice in the hall, speaking muffled words. I opened my door just a crack. I could see the cat sitting in the shadows by the attic door. It was glaring fixedly off into the distance, and this sight, and the nearly inaudible words that sounded from its red regularly throbbing mouth, comforted me against my will, so that everything dark in me drained away, and I went to bed calmly, like a zombie.

'That's really something,' he says, and dabs his throat with a napkin. 'I never heard about anything like that before.'

He adjusts himself in the bed uncomfortably, and whimpers as he moves. For a moment he lies still, breathing fast because he's in pain, and he looks up at the stained ceiling still in pain, his eyes look out from pain. When he catches his breath, he asks or tells me, 'That house – you don't live in that house anymore, do you?'

'No.' I look at him for a while. 'I have a place on the mainland.'

'What do you do?' He asks distracted, his eyes ticking in their sockets, as though there was some escape for them. When I don't say anything he turns his head to me a moment. 'I didn't mean to pry.'

'I don't care. I don't do anything, I'm a zero.'

'I don't think anyone is really a zero,' he says softly, looks at me with concern.

'Well, that's all right, I'm a zero, and I don't even care anymore. I don't care about me, and I don't think about tomorrow, or anything. I know tomorrow isn't thinking about *me*.'

'No family or anything, huh?'

'No, no, not that care, nobody here. I go wherever, I do whatever – what do they care – nothing.' I just smile, shrug. 'I'm one of those people, when I die they're going to find out that I'm dead because some neighbor was investigating a smell.'

'I wish I could die.'

'Well, I suppose you *could*.'

'*No*,' his eyes are ocean-indigo, dark and bright at once. They hold on to me, as though he were clutching my lapels. 'That's part of my sickness.'

'I never heard of it,' I say, blank.

He looks down at his pudgy hands, toys with the dingy quilt. 'I wasn't born here, either – I miss my family. They're unable to visit me here, unfortunately… How did you end up here?'

'I had to go somewhere. I grew up, I stopped dreaming, I went out into the world, I tried work, I tried women, and – well, well, well…' I'm just smiling, talking in a quiet voice. 'And now it's just me and the drinks… I can't even make it as a drunk, I drink, I puke, but I don't get drunk.'

He leans forward, suddenly avid, and touches my knee, looking up through his thin eyebrows at me. 'I see now – you're not a doer, you're an *un-doer*. That's what you are, see? Everybody is something – everybody *has to be something*.' He speaks it vicious as the curse it is, glancing bitterly away for a moment. Then, leaning back, he holds me with his gaze. 'I know something you can un-do.'

When he doesn't go on, I shrug.

'Someone like you, you could do me a big favor. I mean you could really help me a lot.' He holds out his hands, indicating himself. 'I'm all knotted up, see? That's my sickness. I'm bound up in a knot – I *am* the knot,' he adds vehemently, '– and it's torture for me.'

'You want me to – *un-do* you?'

His eyes glistening, he nods, his head resting on the backboard.

'How?'

'If you kill a man – would you do that?'

'Sure, sure, yeah – I mean, I could do that.'

'Really? You could, really?'

'Sure.'

'Any man at all, it doesn't matter. If you go outside the city here, there are a lot of farms and roadside places, people do all kinds of things alone out there – I'm sure you could find somebody.'

'OK, sure.'

He opens a carved wooden case on the nightstand and pulls out a shining stylus, long and thin. 'When he's dead, write the circle on the ground with his blood – use this.' He hands me the stylus. It's cool, it's actually cold, with a film of condensation on it. 'You'll have to find a flat spot.'

'Thanks.' I put the stylus in my breast pocket.

'Please hurry – do it today, please.'

'Yeah, I'll do it today. I mean, I'll try – I'll go now.'

'Do you want any water?'

'No, thanks – I'll just get going.'

There are a number of thin metal plinth-bridges, that connect the island on this side with the mainland. From there, it's only a brief walk to the edge of town, where there's a chain-link fence mounded over with ivy. The suburbs for which these roads were laid out never happened; the ancient farms crumble under their eaves and sagging roofs, flopped out on their overgrown lots, now plotted on an incongruous grid of dirt roads sighing dust. I start at the nearest corner of the grid and round off square by square. The day is warm. Everything is warm and tilted and eternal and infinite, I'll walk these rounds of unbuilt blocks forever with the white sun spreading its hot grey mane there above my left shoulder, my shoes scuff blonde furry ground tufted with leaves of paralyzed grass that are flames the emerald color of lime flesh.

Now here's an A-frame farmhouse with chickens clucking in the yard. I see a woman and two little ones far away, bobbing in the waist-high corn, heading in the direction of town. I walk unevenly up the dirt path, wobbling a little on my ankles. As I come around the woodpile toward the porch a man appears and starts at the sight of me. I see his face and so I cut it – there is a hatchet there on the pile and I take it up. I swing once overhand and chop into his face through the center, pull it out with a yank of my wrist. It goes in easily and my arm is not strained. He bends, and I catch him once again backhanded through the cheekbones making a cross. He falls on the ground, his tongue hanging from his mouth. He mumbles in his blood. I straddle him but I'm facing the wrong way so I turn straddling him standing. He does not die until I strike him twice again over the head with the back of the hatchet. I drop the hatchet, and pick him up, carry him a few feet to a bare spot of ground where a moment ago the chickens were scratching. The blood seeps out from his hair with a quiet sound like a guitar being gently strummed, flows on the ground. I take out the stylus and stop –

I don't know what I'm doing –

'Yes you do!'

I begin crooning words I don't know. I draw the circle in his black blood, which slips out from his head in laps. I write around the borders of the circle in unfamiliar letters.

'Yes that's right – that's right – don't stop!'

The aching song wavers from my tense mouth, filled with longing, in waves that roll my body back and forth as though I stand waist deep in surf. The language isn't mine but the words yearn in my throat – here come branches, bare and sooty, up around me, and the chiming of tiny bells – I run down a waist-high groove cut in the ground, lined with stones, black wire boughs steeple their fingers just above my head, my hands make scoops in the air, right then left then right again, before my chest as I run making the world streak – now I am out in the open on pale green grass so soft it turns to powder as I tread on it, my cuffs are wet with dew and slap my ankles, I only run faster still. Here are rolling hills, copses and a high caer above the salt flats and tidal flats and inky bogs and iridescent brown bogs – emerging from the bogs are great plumed anemonoids, their gelatin arms waving rapturously singing in every part. These are nurtured on human sacrifices: lovingly the tendrils snatch the victim up into the screening white branches, which are swiftly streaked with red... the cries of the victims are audible for hours, and the trees sing blithely, their leaves flickering in the breeze like shining coins.

Their path will cross my own – that line of men, running arm in arm, in white shirts and black trousers, black bow ties and white aprons. Their hair glistens pomaded sleek and fragrant on their heads, their legs swing perfectly synchronized; these men dressed as waiters are my fellow killers, my blood brothers. The line swings away from me. Our paths won't cross after all. I'm breathing too hard to shout after them. I've never seen such speed. Their scissoring legs seem to kick them weightless over the ground like ballet dancers, and even where the ground is uneven their coordination never breaks. My heart bangs against my ribs. Any moment the flutter at my side will flare and stitch my lung, my throat thickens – they're only a few feet before me now! Still in my ears though not from my throat the yearning voice pleads and sighs its song, if I could speak I would beg them not to leave me behind – I can almost reach to the shoulder of the rightmost runner – now it's happening, I'm coming up alongside, I can see the looped arm held out to me by the rightmost runner, and as I slip my arm through it I slot into step with them, my apron pressed flat against me, my shoulders jerking up and down as I run, my legs flying, my head thrown back I can feel the cool tracks of my tears stream back from my eyes into my pomaded hair – the voice is singing now still but its yearning sound is joyful to me now – we fly so fast and faster still always faster, but effortlessly, speeding up the slope of the high caer, toward the spot where the slope is broken off in midair high above the sweet rocks and creamy surf.

In voluminous sighs the fat man smiles beatifically and spreads his hands. His body comes apart into silver wires and bells, swells like a great, white tree.

The Whitest Teeth

When I was a boy, my friend Kajetan and I lived in the same U-shaped apartment building, with a common area within the loop of the U. This common area was a lumpy mattress of lawn that never completely dried out. Even in the summertime, it was dank and shady, an assembly of clumps of grass and big sinuous puddles.

Our families lived opposite each other. All the apartments were the same, porcelain floors in the bathrooms, kitchens, hallways, and in the other rooms a dingy chitin of pressed ivory shavings, suspended in a crinkly sheath of yellowing resin, had been laid down. The same, fantastically heavy burgundy curtains, with thick, burdensome golden fringes, hung over every window, shutting out all trace of daylight. Kajetan and I would meet in front of his door every morning and walk to the Lycée together; we attended different classes, but we always ate lunch together. He was a quiet, fawning boy; he never had a teacher who didn't instantly love him. No one in the school was as fair as Kajetan. His hair, his flesh, except for his lips, were all white, and he had a blazing, retiring smile, like the dazzle of daylight on drifted snow.

That day, the day I am thinking of, I had been gloating over some dirty postcards that I had found somewhere. I pored over the grey bodies, the black eyes and lips, the dark islands and white prominences, filled with riddles, all bordered with dark burgundy red, and gold braid. I was too young to be aroused by these images, but I was aflame with curiosity about them. After devouring a card with my eyes, I would hand it to Kajetan, who kneeled beside me in the mud. We studied together in silence. Here were all my postcards, the grey, supine, obliging or oblivious bodies, scattered on the muddy ground. I was reaching to gather them up when I felt something cool on my upper lip. I looked down, and saw drops of my blood falling into one of the puddles. The drops bloomed when they struck the water, making little billows of fine red threads. Two more drops, big ones, fell, and sank to the bottom. They hovered there, conspiring together in the depths, without dissolving. I crushed my nostril shut and tilted my head back. After a few minutes, I stopped pressing on my nostril, and it opened slowly, tearing through the membrane of candied blood that had congealed over it. The bleeding had stopped. Kajetan had noticed my problem, looked at the last couple of postcards, then put them aside and sat with his hands in his lap, his eyes on the ground.

He'd had a nightmare, he said after a few minutes – a horrible, frog-like man with a huge, round, smiling face, hiding in the reeds by a pond, or a pool. This man hadn't threatened him at all – he had only smiled, with closed lips. He had attacked Kajetan with the sight of this wide, wide smile.

'You won't have nightmares any more when you grow up.' I solemnly believed this.

He looked at me levelly, and said softly, 'When I grow up, I'm going to kill you.' His smile slowly came out then, like the sun in a winter cloud.

In my memory, the sentence stretches, and seems to be said a hundred times not quite at once. That sentence has its own particular, special moment in time, which lasts until now.

Kajetan made me this promise, but he was not the one who would go on to take life. That might have been his calling, but he failed to answer, and I was chosen instead.

I was the energetic one. Kajetan was lazy. He spent his time with me because I always had some project in the works. After his sister's health collapsed, and his parents separated, he moved away, and thereafter I saw him only in my dreams, sliding into the shadows of an arched doorway in a stone wall… which the rain had marked with grey-brown stains… his white head gleaming in the dusky light… fluorescing, like a will-o-the-wisp, as he floated into the dark.

That wall and doorway, I soon discovered, belong to the estate by the sea; a palace of gnarled stone surrounded by black pines and beech trees. The gloom of the place drew me strongly; on the grounds, the sound of the surf is audible, but the sea is not visible. The underbrush here is thick and elastic, the leaves made rubbery by the salt wind, and difficult to penetrate. One follows the sound of the waves, and eventually the soil becomes sandy and thin, the vegetation more sparse, and then the dunes and the horizon appear together. The house looms above the level of the beach on a slanted promontory of rock, its shuttered windows refusing to open on the sea. I have the impression the place is in probate, some sort of protracted dispute; it is empty and neglected. Only occasional trespassers from town make use of it. I secretly oblige the owners, whoever they are, by killing these trespassers.

The first time, I was kneeling in a clump of ferns, watching a man. He was sitting on a stone beneath a tree. He'd taken his rucksack from his back and set it beside him, eaten his lunch and now was smoking, leaning back against the trunk. A hiker, apparently. He finished his smoke, crushing the butt out under a rock, and knelt, tying his bootlaces. I leapt on him then, weightless, the sound of the wind and surf very loud, his grunt of surprise very far away. I rolled on top of him and drove my fists into his face – his hands outflung made a sort of thicket between me and his face – I swatted at him with a rock, he tried to wrestle it from me, all the while yelping bits of sentences at me – I released the rock, took up another and swiftly smashed his head with it. I sunk my fingers into his cheeks and eyes bent forward and pulled his face in half with my hands – his body bucked and thrashed under me, his arms flailing. Finally I strangled him, staring and dripping perspiration down into the torn flesh, and exposed bone, of his face.

Satisfied, I assembled his meagre possessions and dragged him down the beach to the water. Launching his body from the rocks, I could be assured the current would accept him. This sea, sky, woods, house, were all my accomplices. Kajetan's face dwindling in shadowy passageways, his flickering smile flashed white in the instant before shades filled his features altogether.

The second time, a woman was taking photographs on the beach. I hid in the rocks and jumped her from behind. There were many deep tidal pools here between the boulders. I seized her by the hair and pushed her head into the water. I straightened my arm – she clawed at me, kicked back at me, but her angle was all wrong. After a few moments she went limp – a ruse. I did not budge. A few more seconds of frantic activity, shreds of water dashing in all directions, and then nothing but the rumble of the waves.

Drowning is one of the better ways to kill someone, provided circumstances allow for it. At its edges, the estate dwindles into flat, sallow land, grey soil, grey sky, a handful of scarred, defiant trees, and a handful of farms. Black clouds turned the dim, watery light of that day a brownish-green color. A stand of dead trees, pinched off by an arm of sand from the body of the woods that surround the house. The trees enclose a little depression in the ground where rain water collects to form a broad, shallow pond of iridescent brown. A dirt road runs by the stand. A few heavy branches bristling with grey, wiry sticks had blown down and dammed the wind's flow of dead leaves and bits of bracken. The road was blocked. I found a farmer clearing the debris out of the way and offered to help – seamed, lean face, slow, patiently moving body. I clubbed him over the head with a rock when his back was turned and dragged him, surprisingly light and thin, to the pond. I knelt on his back and held his head down. He was unable to struggle. His body seemed heavy and tired. He seemed to lie beneath me resigned, his face mired in black, stagnant mud and thick brown water. Everything was quiet. Despite his weakness, I remained kneeling a long time – every now and then thinking I felt a sort of inner tick beneath my knees. This farmer was like a plant himself – I had to dig his life out of him by its roots to keep it from growing back, and it took a long time. Kneeling there, my gaze was drawn out across the pond toward the house and the grounds, and further to the sea. Although I was drowning a man, I felt as peaceful as a stone. After a long time, I rose and he drifted out from the bank. I almost left him floating face down in brown water, brown light.

I caught a woman from behind with my necktie, stood motionless as a statue while she clawed at her throat, twisted this way and that. I turned my head to see our shadows together on the stone wall. They looked strange. When her knees buckled I straddled her, her body lying flat on its stomach, her head dangling from her neck, which I held above the ground with the tie. She had been strolling the grounds hand in hand with a man. I had watched them draw near the house, and took hasty advantage of his leaving her alone a moment. When he returned, he found her at once and knelt slowly beside her with his bearded mouth open. I stepped from the hiding place, the doorway I had seen in my dream. He looked mutely up at me, and I struck him in the face with an axe. The single blow killed him. I am strong, the axe swung light as a reed in my hand. The red dew of his blood congealed on her icy cheeks like studs of cinnamon candy.

In my dreams I see again the enigmatic seeds of his teeth. I rise in the morning, my curtained room is dark. My employer will send a car for me. I must deliver some records to our office in the adjacent town.

I return on foot. When the pavement gives way to rutted clay I realize I've been on the wrong road for several miles. After a moment's reckoning I decide I'm better off going on than back. I'm heading in the right direction, by a more rambling route. After half a mile more the road dwindles to a broad level path bordered by rattling humps of ivy, and tall grass. The breeze flourishes into a steady, nervous wind. The sky is dense, silver and black; the humid air is thick with captive rain. I can hear surf. I'm approaching the sea.

There before me is a wide ribbon of black trees, and peaked slate rooftops above the trees, black against the sky as dried blood. I have been here so many times, I remember them all, but I have no memories to compare with this; I have no memories of coming or going. Why do I only now realize this? Rain patters all around. I walk with a little difficulty through the tall grass into the shade of the trees. As I cross the boundary, some fraction of the daylight is absorbed by the air. Colorless shade rises from the ground.

The path runs by the wall, toward a paved terrace surrounded by overgrown planters. Over the sound of the rain, which still forms in distinct drops, instead of a seamless hush, and the remote surf, I hear violent splashing. In the middle of the terrace, I know, there is a rectangular, lichen-encrusted pool, now drained. When I once lifted the tarp that covered it, I saw only the crumpled brown remains of dead water lilies smeared against the bottom. The terrace is ringed with empty pedestals upon which some classical figures once had stood – I come up behind one of these, to which there still adheres a single broken, heavily veined foot, flexed in mid-step, in time to see a figure recoil into the bushes opposite me. A young woman lies flat on the pavement, her head bobs in the agitated blue water of the pool – who refilled it? – her arms up hands floating half netted in the black tendrils of her hair.

I step forward, looking at her in confusion. Someone else works here?

I hear a step behind me and feel a light hand on my shoulder, and sudden pain – my heart gulps, flails… dizzy, my body weighted, I turn a little as the hand is removed from my shoulder. Something is pulled from my back. The world lists and slides away, the picture I see sets back into my mind slowly – lean Kajetan, tall, hands diffident behind his back, his face fluoresced in a white smile. White and red. The pavement buffets me. Now I am floating, the wind in my hair, not on my face.

Water clicks at intervals in my ear, the water is red and white. My hands rise nerveless to the surface. The water convulses once, the body beside me launches forward curling limp down into the water trailing long lacy sleeves of bubbles, and a plume of her blood like thick smoke rises and envelopes me. Long sleeves of red reach languidly for the bottom, and cross long white sleeves of bubbles.

Now I can see only the featureless, blue depths.

His memories remove their disguises and show themselves for what they are. His dreams file past, smiling, showing their teeth – I am trying to keep hold of them… of one at least, only leave me one.

None of them are mine.

… the water grows calmer and calmer, and soon will be completely still.

… the motion it lends me will abandon me,

and I will lie completely still.

... my face is dead, my harmless teeth smiling bitterly. Yes ... yes, of course.

My Father's Friends

This is theatre critic Simon Klai – here is his wife Doriandra, these are their two sons: Louy and Leonard. Simon is acerbic, impatient, acute, aloof. He loves his family as if from on high.

First Exhibit:

Simon on his way to the newspaper office to present his copy. Double breasted suit, silk tie, hat, overcoat ... walking stick, soft leather briefcase with two buckled straps. It is early morning. The streets are still fairly empty. His breath mists in the air. Alert, leaning forward, walking briskly although he is not late, he watches the pavement pass under his feet ... darts glances this way and that. The sun is still low and cold in the sky. Crossing a bridge, Simon's steps come slower; he is looking at the sun. He stops, his eyes on the sun. He does not lean on the bridge's stone rail; he is rigid, shoulders back, briefcase at the end of his arm, his stick held firmly in his right hand at about a forty-five degree angle to the street. A car whirs by, misses him only by inches – he does not move. He is staring at the sun as though he'd never seen it before.

Second Exhibit:

Later the same day: Simon is sitting on a bench with his head back. After a few hours he rises stiffly and crosses the park, walking slowly, a little unevenly. Presently he raises his head – he is on a narrow side street that curves away to the left. Just ahead, a hotel signboard hangs over the street; white façade, billowing urns of flowers. The lobby is small, filled with dusky golden light and a carpet smell. Simon takes a suite on the uppermost floor; in shirtsleeves and stockings he orders a bottle sent up from the bar. He tips the girl lavishly. In the days to come, despite his straitened condition, he will stop ordering bottles; sortie out to the stores and back, instead.

On the tenth day, he checks out. Home is only a few blocks away. He lets himself in during the middle of the day, when the boys are at school and Doriandra is rehearsing. Lying on the bed, the pillows smell of her hair. When she returns, he will present her with an uncannily reasonable excuse for his absence.

Third Exhibit:

It is a cloudy morning. Simon reaches for his umbrella, taking its handle with two fingers, then his head twists on his neck slightly as though a thought had very forcibly occurred to him, and he instead takes his heavy walking stick. As he steps down the stairs he inspects the stick, peels the india rubber tip from the end and tosses it back into the umbrella stand.

On the street: the inaugurating first drops of rain patter on his shoulders. Cause and effect – he heads for the awning of a bakery along with several other adjacent pedestrians. Halfway there he stops, and then continues past the bakery through empty streets, keeping to the lee of the buildings so as to stay dry – into an area of a few blocks in size currently under renovation after a fire – burnt shells, new lumber, frames and bricks, tools lie in the street. Striding against the rain all at once he stops, turns a little indecisively to the right, looking around as though trying to sight a sound, then slips into the gaping front door of a partially rebuilt house. Once under its roof, he shakes the rain from his hat and coat. He stands, seems to wait, in what once was the entry way – smell of plaster dust and fresh paint. Now he quietly climbs the stairs to the second floor apartment, which opens out to the right. The kitchen – a white box, fifteen feet square, two windows without glass admit the sound of the rain. A boy about eight or nine looks up at him, rain dropping from his clothes. Simon walks toward the boy.

'I was trying to get out of the rain.'

He seems to think Simon is a contractor, or a security man. Simon's stick flashes up and cracks down over the boy's head. The boy crouches without quite falling down and veers randomly toward the wall opposite the door. Simon raises the stick again, then his head jerks and he alters his grip, taking the stick in both hands and driving the end into the boy's stomach. A purple stain spreads from the boy's solar plexus and he falls on his side holding himself. Simon straddles the boy and churns the stick up and down on him with all his weight. There are two softly audible snapping sounds. Now the boy is limp, breath rattling. Simon turns him on his back with his toe, drops to his knees on the boy's chest, and presses his stick across the boy's throat. The eyes are still sluggishly moving. There is still a remnant of fear, surprise, imploring, on the boy's face. Simon's face is attentive, impassive. He looks like a dentist bending over a patient. The boy fumbles the stick weakly, then his limp hands fall away.

Now the boy's face is dark. Simon slips from the house. It is dusk; the rain has stopped; the uninhabited street is dark. Simon tosses his stick over a fence into a vacant lot as he walks briskly home. Drops of the boy's blood seep into the dry grass.

Fourth Exhibit:
Autumnal gloom in the park of dead trees: mercurial light fades against a sky of deepening indigo. Simon passes the brick kiosk which houses the public bathrooms – he abruptly stops, and walks back to the kiosk.

Behind the kiosk, there is a square of bare pavement hidden from public view by the overgrown iron fence that rings the park. A gun lies in the center of this area. It is loaded and fits in his coat pocket easily.

Fifth Exhibit:
A month later. The gun lies between a double row of books on Simon's shelves. He keeps it in a cloth sack so that the powder won't be smelled. The smell is strongest of course immediately after use.

Doriandra has taken Leonard to visit her cousin. Simon is alone in the house with Louy, who has a cold. It's night; Louy is asleep. Simon is reading – now he sets the book down, goes to the bookshelf, leaves the house.

Two hours later he returns. He goes to the bookshelf.

Louy is still asleep. Simon has crept into his room and sits on the edge of his bed, watching Louy sleep. He leans forward extremely slowly, and carefully takes Louy's head in his hands. His thumbs drop down onto Louy's eyelids with smooth, hydraulic control. Slow and gentle his thumbs roll the lids up, exposing the dreaming eyes. Simon leans forward, pouring his gaze into Louy's eyes.

Louy stirs, starts panting. His body twitches. He groans with a stifled voice that sounds as though it came from far away, from beneath the earth. Simon is curved over him, unblinking eyes' gaze fastened on the boy's dreaming eyes. Louy is screaming softly, his voice is trapped down inside him.

Now Louy screams. He struggles with his father, awake, screwing his eyes shut, the screams siren out of him bigger than the room. Simon seizes Louy by the shoulders and shakes him violently, without saying a word. Louy's head whips back and forth, back and forth, back and forth. Simon shakes him shakes him – Louy goes limp, his head flips forward his chin striking his chest with a wet smack then is wrenched backward thumping against the pillow or the backboard. Simon shakes him, his arms pump mechanically in and out – in and out – in and out.

Sixth Exhibit:
A series of newspaper headlines – cholera has broken out here, here, and here. And now here, and now here. Growing concern – it's an epidemic. A state of emergency is declared, cars spill out of the city, jam up on stone bridges, uniformed men check documents and direct traffic.

Leonard sits in the back seat of his cousin's car. His mother, Doriandra, and his cousin are carrying Louy down the front steps to the street. Louy is lean, feeble… dull eyes, slack mouth, nerveless limbs dangling. Tenderly they seat him next to Leonard, resting his head on Leonard's lap. Cousin gets into the driver's seat, the car bobbing under him like a raft. Doriandra walks around the car to the front passenger seat… hard, metallic eyes.

This car will take them out to their cousin's place in the country, where they will be safe from the plague.

… Newspapers… they filter in now and then… and on the radio – stories of riots… chaos…

Seventh Exhibit:
Hands in his coat pockets, Simon moves powerfully down the street. Now and then groups of youths rush past – cold gusts of wind bring chaotic noise of a window breaking here, a dreamlike police whistle far away.

Suddenly alone in the street, Simon turns into an alley which intersects another at a right angle, a T. Two boys and a girl eating old bread, he shoots the one on the left. The boy crumples, his head striking the pavement with a sharp, hollow noise. The girl springs to her feet and runs down the right arm of the T, and the other boy stands up staring at his dead friend with his mouth open. Arm straight Simon aims at him and shoots him in the stomach. The boy's body folds forward at the waist and he falls on his head face down. His legs slide back gradually, his bottom in the air.

The right arm of the T opens into a small enclosed lot – the girl rounds the corner of the building to the right as he fires his gun. The bullet tugs at her right heel, blows off the heel strap of her shoe – it drops on a tuft of grass – she disappears behind the corner.

The lot is framed by the solid, continuous wall of the armory running the length of the block, on his left. To Simon's right, the building whose corner she had turned; and before him, the rear of an L-shaped hotel… heaps of rubbish, trash cans, mattresses, a stove. Two escapes: she might run straight ahead, or to the right.

Simon turns to the right – with his left eye he detects a patch of red earth by the stove. There is another red spot, there between the two garbage cans by the armory wall, the other way out. The girl hops from her hiding place. Simon's arm flies automatically out and up level. He shoots her in the head, the girl plops onto the ground, a wide tear in her head above the ear. The bullet strikes the wall and shears off a flake of brick. It spins through the reverberating air like a wobbling top, and hits the grass with a muffled thump.

Simon trots past the girl's folded body, down the alley. He is heading for the street when like a marionette his body jerkily twists to the left and he slips instead through a back door hanging off its hinges. A moment later curious heads are craning, peering down the alley… mouths are rounding, they see a heavy bundle there, lying bisected by watery sunlight. They see it is a dead girl. As they rush to her side, Simon emerges calmly from the front door of the building into which he had so awkwardly retreated, walking with unremarkable haste. He raises his left arm and pulls the sleeve away from his watch; his eyes, shaded by the brim of his hat, hawkishly scan the street.

Poster on the corner: 'Is it working?'

Eighth Exhibit:
Months and months of plague. Bullets disappear from their red and black boxes in Simon's bureau drawer.

Ninth Exhibit:
Simon is caught in a riot. It starts with a puff of alarm, and suddenly everyone is squalling in all directions. Simon moves diagonally through the racing figures, toward the shelter of deserted, burnt-out buildings. Police swarm the streets with keening whistles – Simon trips on the pavement – his gun slides from his pocket across the pavement. The police have seen him, his gun – two or three charge at him. Under the regime of the epidemic there is no due process, the police do as they please – now their eyes have fastened on him.

Simon dashes into the building, throws shut the door. The lock still works. He sets the chain – recoils as fists thump and bang against the wood. He flings a half-demolished wardrobe and a heavy table in front of the door. He can't block the windows, but he can lock the hall doors. He checks the back door; it's painted over, jammed shut; there's nothing he can open it with. Upstairs the fire escape is on the front of the building. On the roof – it's too far to jump across to the neighboring house. He tries, peering over the edge, but panic fear he can't overcome drives him back, nearly paralyzed. Half to himself he is saying 'I *can't!* I *can't do it!* I need something *else!*' Crashing from downstairs, wood tearing and splintering.

He goes to the center of the roof, staring at a door that will burst open soon. Simon draws himself up, staring, his mouth set. He tightens into himself, his features crush together. He melts into air… vanishes across renovated buildings, alleys, sterile apartments… bullet spins cold in the sky… continuous wall of heads for the sharp, hollow noise… Louy is still asleep… the other boy watching a white box disappear from the sun, staring at his friend Louy sleep… the boy takes Louy's head in rain… his thumbs drop nine… two burnt shells, rain dropping from his stick… Simon leans forward, pouring in the dead trees… between two garbage cans he opens his gaze into Louy's eyes… from her hiding place – the riots – the girl sees she is suddenly alone… billowing urns shoot her in the head, hat and coat… the bullet tugs her to the right street… Simon turns into a wall of the kiosk of flowers… the lobby is the girl, filled with a wide tear in her head above what was the entry way… her shoe drops on a right fence that rings golden light… flake of brick sailing… two boys… the park lying in the carpet smell…

There is nothing strange about me but my happiness. The only difficulty I have ever given anyone has been to contain someway my dangerous happiness, which makes me thoughtless. My exuberance breaks things, breaks me. It marches me up to people and elicits from me declarations of love, if only to give me the satisfaction of disappointment, to know that I am in love. I am forever building up this edifice of love and happiness, which would get to be as big as the world, or bigger, if it weren't for the storms, eruptions, convulsions, that tear it all down again. When any of it comes down, it all comes down. Although these catastrophic failures deeply wound me, still I am grateful for the opportunity to rebuild, and to renew my trust with the world. I do everything on the scale of the world, as the only thing commensurate to my happiness.

Only by understanding my father's life will you understand my death. I will have to adopt a conversational manner, for the moment, to tell you these everyday things. For most of my childhood, my father worked as a theatre critic. His articles were widely read and his opinions seriously received. I never understood exactly what he did, or why he was so inattentive to us. Over time, he withdrew from us. For reasons I would learn later, he once disappeared altogether for about ten days. We were told he had been depressed; he had thought some time alone would do him good, so he had taken a room at a hotel. I wanted to offer some comfort to him, if he was suffering – he seemed to sense my feeling, and headed it off by adopting an especially frosty manner with me. My mother was mystified by his changes, and her uncertainty unnerved me. While I lacked confidence in my own judgement, it seemed to me my father sullenly avoided us all, stayed away from home.

I made friends easily, but I always lost them. My exuberance, my complicated games only exasperated and taxed them. Most of the time I kept company with my older brother Louy, whom I very little resembled; while I was nervous, enthusiastic, busy, thoughtless, Louy was ghostly and quiet. He had a gentle, warm little voice like a candle flame, and wet, red lips. He almost always seemed preoccupied and far away, but then he would astonish me with a near-clairvoyant observation about someone or something we had seen: and I would realize again that he missed nothing.

A few days after Louy's thirteenth birthday, my mother took me away to visit with her sister for a few days, leaving him alone with my father. When we came back – what had happened to Louy? We found him catatonic in his bed, apparently unable to speak or move. I remember the slack mouth, the frightening dullness of his eyes. A new awkwardness had insinuated itself into his body somehow – he even lay awkwardly in his bed. My mother frantically chafed his hands, his arms, caressed his face, implored him to speak. I was sent to fetch our downstairs neighbor the doctor. He examined Louy carefully and took my mother aside. I never knew what he told her.

Louy was condemned to lie inert for the rest of his life; thin, frail, he could barely speak. His eyes would sometimes become glassy and seem to flicker under his heavy lids, but this was not the light of intelligence they formerly had had. While I am sure she could not have known what had happened, my mother angrily blamed Louy's condition on my father, and they separated almost immediately. I seldom saw my father after that; we did not visit together, and my mother never spoke of him.

When the epidemic broke out the following year, my mother took Louy and me out to the country, to stay with her cousins. We were there for eight months, during which time we never heard from my father. Upon our return to the city, we learned that he had disappeared shortly after the state of emergency was declared. Officers of the health department had already declared him dead, 'succumbed to the disease.' The epidemic had maddened the city. Hundreds of people had vanished without a trace in riots or clandestine violence, and the police had done as they pleased with the rest. In the depths of the epidemic, heaps of unidentified bodies were burned or buried in vast pits every day – so my father's case was not apparently unusual.

I remember hiding from my friends behind our school's small library once. I picked up a branch from the dry grass at the edge of the gravel path, but as I raised it I saw that it was a charred bone, nearly as long as my arm. For days after that, I wondered if it had been my father's.

The contents of his apartment were boxed and piled away by my grandfather, upon whose death it fell to me to sort them out. My father's clothes and books were almost entirely ruined by seeping water and mold, but I salvaged what I could – I had always been curious about my father. Under a blanket I found one of my father's jackets, which, at the time the boxes were packed, had been used as a sort of makeshift bag. His watches, shaving kit, and a few other things had been bundled up inside – a notebook among them. In it, I found many brief sentences like these:

'7 September, three boys.'

'20 September, two boys, very nice.'

'21 September, nothing today, an admonition.'

'29 September, two boys, a girl today, very nice.'

'2 October, necessarily three boys. Last one caused some trouble.'

'10 October, nothing – reprisal.'

'13 October, one boy – misfire, strangle – very memorable expression.'

Interleaved among these tallying sentences were terse notes:

'I have still the habit of writing – they say your habit of writing is the manufacture of self-incriminating evidence / your habit of writing is a sign of bad conscience / you are to wean yourself of your habit of writing'

'With the epidemic, everything is possible.'

The earliest entry was dated just before his ten-day disappearance:

'the low sun white and cold, and full of worms. Then a fan of white, gelatinous rays, transparent tubes whose ends mouth the earth. A flat, white opening in the sky, whose light silvered the air, dotted with their shadows. They are the larvae of the sun and will become themselves stars.'

I had seen this light around my father – vividly I see it now, cold and white, as he sits in his shirt-sleeves, the long cuffs bent back, writing; heavy ropes of smoke coil around him. His creased face is drawn, inert, his writing hand palpitates like a bug on the paper.

'My brain shining in the dark like a planet, streaked with long, glistening white clouds that I came to see were worms, beneath the meniscus of brain fluid a translucent sheet under which they tossed and turned. Some lay and some reclined on the tissue, like opulent ladies on perfumed sofas; their puckered heads swayed gently.'

These were compulsory sacrifices, as I came to understand. There was no quid pro quo, there was no deal or anything like that with the larvae. They addressed him from time to time, directly or by means of fugitive bits of graffiti, or slogans on posters – 'do not open door' – 'dead or alive?' – 'focus!'

'I realized what it was necessary to do.'

He attacked children only because they were easier to kill. The first time he was taken by surprise, guided by the larvae to a house under renovation, a child taking refuge from the rain. 'Do not swing – you waste energy that way. Thrust.' – 'Don't do it halfway,' the larvae said. And after – 'Sloppy.'

'They led me to the gun.'

'It is difficult to talk to you,' the larvae said, 'you understand so little.'

'Rain falls, scattering its rings across the puddles – and each death is a drop that makes the mass quiver and thrill, and each drop lends vital force to what would otherwise be an inert, passive, shrinking thing, a body of stillborn larvae.'

'Don't forget what you owe the larvae of thought,' the larvae would say. 'Don't forget your solar responsibilities.'

On Louy's thirteenth birthday, the larvae said: 'He should be old enough now to help you.' In his room – 'Open his eyes. Show him dreams.' Hopeless – he refuses to understand. 'Shut him up. Shut him up.'

'The alley flashed at me, the gun tingled... you see how the larvae protect me. "Look at the time."'

'I don't feel the murders – would I feel them more if I cut them open and rooted in their entrails, perhaps while they still throb with life, before they lose consciousness? I am told "It is not necessary to feel it, only to see to it."'

'Glancing up now at the radiator I know I would do it even if it were as abstract and numb a matter as turning that knob – in a windowless closet deep in basements I see three little bodies, heads in a row, weak and dazed from hunger and thirst lying on a metal grill bunk – as I turn the knob the dim, orange-brown light fades and goes out, and the little chamber swiftly fills with a flavorless gas which will lead these children so deep into the mazes of sleep that they will never find their way out again.

'"This is not a matter of gratification, it is a matter of generating numbers."

'The gun is a magic instrument, converting children to numbers.'

'I know I am now able to will myself out of existence. They have shown me, and told me to extinguish myself if I am threatened with capture. I will not hesitate to do as they ask, not because I feel that my actions are wrong, and that, by them, I have merited my death, but because the situation will then no longer be under my control, or it will be teetering on the brink, about to slip out of my grasp; and by disappearing, I will seal it and keep it – control – perfect forever.'

I remember the disembodied, unreal feeling I had as I finished reading. His words sank through and past me, and drained out of me.

I read his words, and the larvae hatched in my mind.

(what or how did the larvae appear to me... such questions can only waste our time together. In the water I see the lights trail their long beards that are emaciated gold and silver flames withered to compass needles whose points sway before my feet, everything turns into everything else... For my father they were voices. To me they are shafts of glowing, orating red and gold sunlight walking up and down inside my head) –

Every week I visit Louy at the hotel de santé. He lies always in a white iron bed in a vast half-deserted ward, whose booming silence solidifies now and then into a moan or a flicker of nurse's feet, rustle of stiff sheets. I sit beside the bed. Late afternoon light sifts into the room, tall orange projections on the wall, and deep shadows. Louy is lying on his left side, an ungainly body of long bones under the sheet, his head tilted up toward me – a constant tremor wags it from side to side. His rumpled face, the red arch of his lip, and his long wet teeth, wet breaths; the eyes never waver from my face, although there is no expression – his wounded mind no longer has the strength to find its way out to me. I only want to be with him. He grew up like this; his face has aged seventeen years unmarked. In all that time, he has had only one never-ending experience.

I sit and he lies. A few beds down the ward, a nurse changes the dressing on an injured arm. She takes a roll of fresh linen bandage from a tray on the nightstand, which she has moved away from the wall, out toward the aisle. When I next look up, the nurse is cutting the bandage from the roll – she sets the roll on the tray, and lays the scissors next to the roll. The blades of the scissors are acutely pointed, and, as she had placed them casually on the tray, not quite in alignment. They are tilted up on the linen roll. Those two blades gleam white like mirrors against the shadows of the room. The two very sharp blades are fixed together, they cross each other and are bolted together, cut toward each other. As it drops low in the sky, the sun's light becomes redder and redder. Tall panels of red light slide down the walls. The two blades of the scissors are two red blazes, I can see the sun reflected in the blade whose polished side faces me. Their brilliance occludes the ward, the nurse, the beds. I see instead another room, with bare walls, no furniture, dead leaves, newspaper – a hallway in front of me. The windows are boarded up. I stand in the room with my shoulders back and my chin up, my arms a little less than fully outstretched. My right hand holds something wet and light; looking I see I am holding the red scissors. My left hand is further down than my right; very gradually I notice it throbs and moves on its own. My left hand is clutching tightly at something, the fingers are aching. I look down at my left hand – it grips the right shoulder of a small boy with a gaping red throat, his struggles communicate up my arm along nerves finely laced around my heart – a hot electric web, hot and fine. I am breathing hard, a feeling is swelling up in me – I can't stand the imploring, suffering look on the boy's appalling white face, but it is too beautiful, I have to look at him because I love him, and I pity him, this strange boy I've never met, and I need to be close to him and share with him, and this is the only way we can be friends. The boy steadily weakens, but still tugs at my hand. I look down again – I am in the ward, my brother wrings my hand, gazing up into my face. With an imploring look, he rocks back and forth hoisting his upper lip, desperately trying to form words without a voice, with disobedient muscles. My heart glows incandescent through my breast, the little boy's legs fold under him, I drop the scissors and pick him up, press him to me, so he won't feel alone. His warm blood seeps through my shirt, I smell his hair, the soap he washed his face with. Louy yanks at my left hand, his eyes push at mine. I place my right hand over his, and clasp it firmly. As the sunlight fades from the scissors on the tray, the boy in my mind drops to the floor, without a sound. Louy's head falls back on the pillow, with a long despairing sob. A pang of intense love stabs me. I smooth his hair and wipe his face, his eyes, with my handkerchief. The nurse stands at the foot of the bed, telling me softly that visiting hours are over.

'Rest now,' I say to him.

Now I am walking. I pass an open alleyway – I turn back, go into the alley. It forms a T. I follow the right branch of the T into a little courtyard. This brick is scarred – a round, puckered spot, where my father's bullet struck it, after passing through the brains of a nameless little girl. Crouching down I put my eye on the level of the spot, looking back toward the courtyard. I see the girl frozen in midstep, one arm forward one arm back, one leg forward one leg back, terror on the blurred features; and beyond her stands my father in his coat and hat, the gun up level at the end of his arm, obscuring his face.

I go back to my apartment. I climb the stairs and turn right, into my kitchen. Though the room is dark, a knife blazes with reflected sunlight in the sink. From my kitchen window I can see the people in the street blazing, each one with his or her own spotlight. I take off my clothes and go to bed.

I dream this:

A brilliant, empty beach – a broad round ramp of yellow land slopes down between shaggy, high cliffs. Even in the dream the light dazzles me; I have an impression of squinting. Sky like blue mercury, sun's light spawns a billion flakes on the water's indigo blades. Hundreds of gulls hurtle round in long-winged circles funneling down to my remains lying on my back half in tall grass, my head on the sand toward the sea, one arm up by my right ear the other down in the grass thick as the comforter under which I lie asleep. I lie there and some way I observe too from nearby. Very calm and happy, and now and then trembling with the proximity of an overflowing happiness. I see the beautiful purple water roil on the blonde sand, the gleaming prints of pale lime foam that it leaves, takes back, redeposits, the exuberance of the cartwheeling wind. My face is also blue and green, in places livid, and it sways gently with the tugging of the gulls, who seem to sprout from my body. The cavity is completely torn open, the gulls hop on the exposed edges of my ribs and thrust their heads down, root vehemently and then strut away with shreds of my flesh in their beaks. My arms are wide open for them; my remains are kind, accommodating. One of them plucks the glasses from my face and stalks off with them.

The tide comes in. Water sluices from the dimples that were my eyes, and froths at my slack grin. My head nods and sways tenderly; the busy, shining water laves it in renewed bliss. It won't be long before I look up to see the pale belly of the waves.

A friend of my mother's telephoned me the next morning, to tell me that, during the night, Louy had somehow gotten out of his bed and stabbed himself with a pair of scissors. A nurse found his body as the sun was rising.

I ride the subways until well past midnight. The Plaza stop is one of the largest stations, with four levels. My train stops at the lowermost platform – in time it would return the way it came, but I leave the cars and find my way up the stairs. The third level has many passages, radiating from a large domed chamber with a cement floor and wooden, high-backed benches. At this hour, it is empty. I cross to my stairway and start to climb. Footsteps draw my attention – lean middle-aged man in a hat and grey raincoat behind me, changing trains. I look at him, and the breath courses in my nostrils, my heart glows, my heavy body lifts, I fall, I fly out from the stairway as he passes swinging my knife, he is knocked aside the point of the knife glancing across his chest, cutting his coat, his shirt, but a shallow cut – he swipes at my face with his walking stick, I'm off balance, I stagger into a garbage can and follow it to the floor. I hear his feet slapping the concrete, his shouts of alarm. I'm on my knees, dazed, I touch my head, a little blood. I laugh – this is wonderful! I pick up the knife again and run after him – he took one of the passageways. I pick up my knees and run as fast as I can – I'm running! I *am* running. I run, laugh, pounce, slash, eruption of frightened blood, brilliant pain of this unknown man I love, who runs from me, his heart pumping the dying blood in my veins.

I am light, as spirit. I hear his footsteps. Turning a corner, I see his feet flashing up stairs, I switch my knife to my pocket and dart my hand through the railing catching at his left ankle. He wheels and flops on his back and to one side, seizing the opposite railing and catching himself. I come round the bottom of the stairs and he kicks me in the chest – his kick kicks another laugh out of me and I throw myself forward, the knife again in my hand. He shoves me backwards and I slash uselessly at the air. He throws his briefcase at me and I fall back on the steps, buffeted aside as weightless as a balloon. He turns to run to the other end of the platform, the other staircase, I can hear his heavy breath, smell his aftershave, he is beautiful, angry, afraid, his outrage is beautiful – I lunge at him and he knocks me down again, turns to run. I twist on the ground and whip out with my knife, slicing across the back of his left knee, through the gabardine slacks into the joint. He cries out and falls clutching his leg, kicking the other defiantly at me wonderful, blood running over his fingers where he clutches his knee, I hear the drops striking the dirty tiles. I crawl toward him nearly rising – he avoids me – surprising me with his speed, he rolls under a bench – I vault the back of the bench and land on the seat – he scrabbles on the ground, on his back, staring up at me – I pounce on him – my knee comes down on his left bicep, pinning it to the ground, I straddle his ribcage – his free hand claws at my face but I batter it aside, I put the point of my knife beneath his chin near his left ear, hold the handle with the left hand I put the palm of my right against the butt of the handle and drive the blade up into his head.

I see but don't feel the blood on my hands, it is the same temperature as my skin – he gulps and struggles. Now his struggles are only spasms. I change my grip on the knife, taking the handle in both hands I lean down on it, like the handle of a paper cutter, pushing the blade down through his neck. Now I know it's finished. He is still, his face has gone out. I look down gratefully at him. I leave him the knife.

No one sees me climb the stairs. I can feel the night air pouring down the last flight. I float up into the black panel at the top of the steps, and now I'm in the dark, cool night air. I run down the steep streets, my momentum building, I peel off my coat, my tie, my shirt, my belt, I stagger and fall, tumble on the damp ground dragging off my shoes, my stockings and pants, all my clothes, and now without them I am hurtling down the streets, my legs kick up behind me, the ground skates by, my legs take yards and yards at a stride, my arms turn in the air, the breeze cooler and cooler over my skin, my sticky hands. The city opens on all sides of me like a drawn curtain and I see the vast blue darkness of the ocean, the boards of the pier thud under my feet, the pier ends, I launch myself into space…

... and now everything is foam, and now cold shocking green water. In my mind I can see a line connecting me to the horizon, and this is my course. I will swim until the sinews in my shoulders crack and my lungs tire and wilt in me, and my eyes and lashes are pearly with salt, the black heaven joyous above me, the happy green abyss below me. I tell you these things so that you may understand them, and by understanding them, you may pierce the veil into the secret of my crime. You will understand. You will know joy. You will be nothing. You will be me.

FEEDERS AND EATERS

Neil Gaiman

Neil Gaiman (1960–) is an iconic and hugely popular bestselling English writer living in America. He has written across multiple genres and media, including fiction, graphic novels, and film. Gaiman has won many awards, including the Hugo Award, Nebula Award, Locus Award, Newbery Medal and the Carnegie Medal in Literature. The majority of his fiction tends to fall into categories related to general fantasy, urban fantasy, contemporary horror, and mythology. However, a story like 'Feeders and Eaters' reveals an even darker, weirder side to Gaiman's muse and is reminiscent of the approach in Jeffrey Ford's 'The Beautiful Gelreesh' (2003), H. F. Arnold's 'The Night Wire' (1926), and Ramsey Campbell's 'The Brood' (1980).

This is a true story, pretty much. As far as that goes, and whatever good it does anybody.

It was late one night, and I was cold, in a city where I had no right to be. Not at that time of night, anyway. I won't tell you which city. I'd missed my last train, and I wasn't sleepy, so I prowled the streets around the station until I found an all-night café. Somewhere warm to sit.

You know the kind of place; you've been there: café's name on a Pepsi sign above a dirty plate-glass window, dried egg residue between the tines of all their forks. I wasn't hungry, but I bought a slice of toast and a mug of greasy tea, so they'd leave me alone.

There were a couple of other people in there, sitting alone at their tables, derelicts and insomniacs huddled over their empty plates, dirty coats and donkey jackets buttoned up to the neck.

I was walking back from the counter with my tray when somebody said, 'Hey.' It was a man's voice. 'You,' the voice said, and I knew he was talking to me, not to the room. 'I know you. Come here. Sit over here.'

I ignored it. You don't want to get involved, not with anyone you'd run into in a place like that.

Then he said my name, and I turned and looked at him. When someone knows your name, you don't have any option.

'Don't you know me?' he asked. I shook my head. I didn't know anyone who looked like that. You don't forget something like that. 'It's me,' he said, his voice a pleading whisper. 'Eddie Barrow. Come on, mate. You know me.'

And when he said his name I did know him, more or less. I mean, I knew Eddie Barrow. We had worked on a building site together, ten years back, during my only real flirtation with manual work.

Eddie Barrow was tall, and heavily muscled, with a movie star smile and lazy good looks. He was ex-police. Sometimes he'd tell me stories, true tales of fitting-up and doing-over, of punishment and crime. He had left the force after some trouble between him and one of the top brass. He said it was the Chief Superintendent's wife forced him to leave. Eddie was always getting into trouble with women. They really liked him, women.

When we were working together on the building site they'd hunt him down, give him sandwiches, little presents, whatever. He never seemed to *do* anything to make them like him; they just liked him. I used to watch him to see how he did it, but it didn't seem to be anything he did. Eventually, I decided it was just the way he was: big, strong, not very bright, and terribly, terribly good-looking.

But that was ten years ago.

The man sitting at the Formica table wasn't good-looking. His eyes were dull and rimmed with red, and they stared down at the tabletop without hope. His skin was gray. He was too thin, obscenely thin. I could see his scalp through his filthy hair. I said, 'What happened to you?'

'How d'you mean?'

'You look a bit rough,' I said, although he looked worse than rough; he looked dead. Eddie Barrow had been a big guy. Now he'd collapsed in on himself. All bones and flaking skin.

'Yeah,' he said. Or maybe 'Yeah?' I couldn't tell. Then, resigned, flatly, 'Happens to us all in the end.'

He gestured with his left hand, pointed at the seat opposite him. His right arm hung stiffly at his side, his right hand safe in the pocket of his coat.

Eddie's table was by the window, where anyone could see you walking past. Not somewhere I'd sit by choice, not if it was up to me. But it was too late now. I sat down facing him and I sipped my tea. I didn't say anything, which could have been a mistake. Small talk might have kept his demons at a distance. But I cradled my mug and said nothing. So I suppose he must have thought that I wanted to know more, that I cared. I didn't care. I had enough problems of my own. I didn't want to know about his struggle with whatever it was that had brought him to this state – drink, or drugs, or disease – but he started to talk, in a gray voice, and I listened.

'I came here a few years back, when they were building the bypass. Stuck around after, the way you do. Got a room in an old place around the back of Prince Regent's Street. Room in the attic. It was a family house, really. They only rented out the top floor, so there were just the two boarders, me and Miss Corvier. We were both up in the attic, but in separate rooms, next door to each other. I'd hear her moving about. And there was a cat. It was the family cat, but it came upstairs to say hello, every now and again, which was more than the family ever did.

'I always had my meals with the family, but Miss Corvier, she didn't ever come down for meals, so it was a week before I met her. She was coming out of the upstairs lavvy. She looked so old. Wrinkled face, like an old, old monkey. But long hair, down to her waist, like a young girl.

'It's funny, with old people, you don't think they feel things like we do. I mean, here's her, old enough to be my granny and…' He stopped. Licked his lips with a gray tongue. 'Anyway… I came up to the room one night and there's a brown paper bag of mushrooms outside my door on the ground. It was a present, I knew that straight off. A present for me. Not normal mushrooms, though. So I knocked on her door.

'I says, are these for me?

'Picked them meself, Mister Barrow, she says.

'They aren't like toadstools or anything? I asked. Y'know, poisonous? Or funny mushrooms?

'She just laughs. Cackles even. They're for eating, she says. They're fine. Shaggy inkcaps, they are. Eat them soon now. They go off quick. They're best fried up with a little butter and garlic.

'I say, are you having some, too?

'She says, no. She says, I used to be a proper one for mushrooms, but not anymore, not with my stomach. But they're lovely. Nothing better than a young shaggy inkcap mushroom. It's astonishing the things that people don't eat. All the things around them that people could eat, if only they knew it.

'I said thanks, and went back into my half of the attic. They'd done the conversion a few years before, nice job really. I put the mushrooms down by the sink. After a few days they dissolved into black stuff, like ink, and I had to put the whole mess into a plastic bag and throw it away.

'I'm on my way downstairs with the plastic bag, and I run into her on the stairs, she says, Hullo, Mister B.

'I say, Hello, Miss Corvier.

'Call me Effie, she says. How were the mushrooms?

'Very nice, thank you, I said. They were lovely.

'She'd leave me other things after that, little presents, flowers in old milk-bottles, things like that, then nothing. I was a bit relieved when the presents suddenly stopped.

'So I'm down at dinner with the family, the lad at the poly, he was home for the holidays. It was August. Really hot. And someone says they hadn't seen her for about a week, and could I look in on her. I said I didn't mind.

'So I did. The door wasn't locked. She was in bed. She had a thin sheet over her, but you could see she was naked under the sheet. Not that I was trying to see anything, it'd be like looking at your gran in the altogether. This old lady. But she looked so pleased to see me.

'Do you need a doctor? I says.

'She shakes her head. I'm not ill, she says. I'm hungry. That's all.

'Are you sure, I say, because I can call someone, it's not a bother. They'll come out for old people.

'She says, Edward? I don't want to be a burden on anyone, but I'm so hungry.

'Right. I'll get you something to eat, I said. Something easy on your tummy, I says. That's when she surprises me. She looks embarrassed. Then she says, very quietly, *Meat*. It's got to be fresh meat, and raw. I won't let anyone else cook for me. Meat. Please, Edward.

'Not a problem I says, and I go downstairs. I thought for a moment about nicking it from the cat's bowl, but of course I didn't. It was like, I knew she wanted it, so I had to do it. I had no choice. I went down to Safeways, and I bought her a packet of best ground sirloin.

'The cat smelled it. Followed me up the stairs. I said, you get down, puss. It's not for you, I said. It's for Miss Corvier and she's not feeling well, and she's going to need it for her supper, and the thing mewed at me as if it hadn't been fed in a week, which I knew wasn't true because its bowl was still half full. Stupid, that cat was.

'I knock on her door, she says Come in. She's still in the bed, and I give her the pack of meat, and she says, Thank you, Edward, you've got a good heart. And she starts to tear off the plastic wrap, there in the bed. There's a puddle of brown blood under the plastic tray, and it drips onto her sheet, but she doesn't notice. Makes me shiver.

'I'm going out the door, and I can already hear her starting to eat with her fingers, cramming the raw mince into her mouth. And she hadn't got out of bed.

'But the next day she's up and about, and from there on she's in and out at all hours, in spite of her age, and I think there you are. They say red meat's bad for you, but it did her the world of good. And raw, well, it's just steak tartare, isn't it? You ever eaten raw meat?'

The question came as a surprise. I said, 'Me?'

Eddie looked at me with his dead eyes, and he said, 'Nobody else at this table.'

'Yes. A little. When I was a small boy – four, five years old – my grandmother would take me to the butcher's with her, and he'd give me slices of raw liver, and I'd just eat them, there in the shop, like that. And everyone would laugh.'

I hadn't thought of that in twenty years. But it was true.

I still like my liver rare, and sometimes, if I'm cooking and if nobody else is around, I'll cut a thin slice of raw liver before I season it, and I'll eat it, relishing the texture and the naked, iron taste.

'Not me,' he said. 'I liked my meat properly cooked. So the next thing that happened was Thompson went missing.'

'Thompson?'

'The cat. Somebody said there used to be two of them, and they called them Thompson and Thompson. I don't know why. Stupid, giving them both the same name. The first one was squashed by a lorry.' He pushed at a small mound of sugar on the Formica top with a fingertip. His left hand, still. I was beginning to wonder whether he had a right arm. Maybe the sleeve was empty. Not that it was any of my business. Nobody gets through life without losing a few things on the way.

I was trying to think of some way of telling him I didn't have any money, just in case he was going to ask me for something when he got to the end of his story. I didn't have any money: just a train ticket and enough pennies for the bus ticket home.

'I was never much of a one for cats,' he said suddenly. 'Not really. I liked dogs. Big, faithful things.

You knew where you were with a dog. Not cats. Go off for days on end, you don't see them. When I was a lad, we had a cat, it was called Ginger. There was a family down the street, they had a cat they called Marmalade. Turned out it was the same cat, getting fed by all of us. Well, I mean. Sneaky little buggers. You can't trust them.

'That was why I didn't think anything when Thompson went away. The family was worried. Not me. I knew it'd come back. They always do.

'Anyway, a few nights later, I heard it. I was trying to sleep, and I couldn't. It was the middle of the night, and I heard this mewing. Going on, and on, and on. It wasn't loud, but when you can't sleep these things just get on your nerves. I thought maybe it was stuck up in the rafters, or out on the roof outside. Wherever it was, there wasn't any point in trying to sleep through it. I knew that. So I got up, and I got dressed, even put my boots on in case I was going to be climbing out onto the roof, and I went looking for the cat.

'I went out in the corridor. It was coming from Miss Corvier's room on the other side of the attic. I knocked on her door, but no one answered. Tried the door. It wasn't locked. So I went in. I thought maybe that the cat was stuck somewhere. Or hurt. I don't know. I just wanted to help, really.

'Miss Corvier wasn't there. I mean, you know sometimes if there's anyone in a room, and that room was empty. Except there's something on the floor in the corner going *Mrie, Mrie*... And I turned on the light to see what it was.'

He stopped then for almost a minute, the fingers of his left hand picking at the black goo that had crusted around the neck of the ketchup bottle. It was shaped like a large tomato. Then he said, 'What I didn't understand was how it could still be alive. I mean, it was. And from the chest up, it was alive, and breathing, and fur and everything. But its back legs, its rib cage. Like a chicken carcass. Just bones. And what are they called, sinews? And, it lifted its head, and it looked at me.

'It may have been a cat, but I knew what it wanted. It was in its eyes. I mean.' He stopped. 'Well, I just knew. I'd never seen eyes like that. You would have known what it wanted, all it wanted, if you'd seen those eyes. I did what it wanted. You'd have to be a monster not to.'

'What did you do?'

'I used my boots.' Pause. 'There wasn't much blood. Not really. I just stamped, and stamped on its head, until there wasn't really anything much left that looked like anything. If you'd seen it looking at you like that, you would have done what I did.'

I didn't say anything.

'And then I heard someone coming up the stairs to the attic, and I thought I ought to do something, I mean, it didn't look good, I don't know what it must have looked like really, but I just stood there, feeling stupid, with a stinking mess on my boots, and when the door opens, it's Miss Corvier.

'And she sees it all. She looks at me. And she says, You killed him. I can hear something funny in her voice, and for a moment I don't know what it is, and then she comes closer, and I realize that she's crying.

'That's something about old people, when they cry like children, you don't know where to look, do you? And she says, He was all I had to keep me going, and you killed him. After all I've done, she says, making it so the meat stays fresh, so the life stays on. After all I've done.

'I'm an old woman, she says. I need my meat.

'I didn't know what to say.

'She's wiping her eyes with her hand. I don't want to be a burden on anybody, she says. She's crying now. And she's looking at me. She says, I never wanted to be a burden. She says, that was my meat. Now, she says, who's going to feed me now?'

He stopped, rested his gray face in his left hand, as if he was tired. Tired of talking to me, tired of the story, tired of life. Then he shook his head and looked at me and said, 'If you'd seen that cat, you would have done what I did. Anyone would have done.'

He raised his head then, for the first time in his story, looked me in the eyes. I thought I saw an appeal for help in his eyes, something he was too proud to say aloud.

Here it comes, I thought. This is where he asks me for money.

Somebody outside tapped on the window

of the café. It wasn't a loud tapping, but Eddie jumped. He said, 'I have to go now. That means I have to go.'

I just nodded. He got up from the table. He was still a tall man, which almost surprised me: he'd collapsed in on himself in so many other ways. He pushed the table away as he got up, and as he got up he took his right hand out of his coat pocket. For balance, I suppose. I don't know.

Maybe he wanted me to see it. But if he wanted me to see it, why did he keep it in his pocket the whole time? No, I don't think he wanted me to see it. I think it was an accident.

He wasn't wearing a shirt or a jumper under his coat, so I could see his arm, and his wrist. Nothing wrong with either of them. He had a normal wrist. It was only when you looked below the wrist that you saw most of the flesh had been picked from the bones, chewed like chicken wings, leaving only dried morsels of meat, scraps and crumbs, and little else. He only had three fingers left, and most of a thumb. I suppose the other finger bones must have just fallen right off, with no skin or flesh to hold them on.

That was what I saw. Only for a moment, then he put his hand back in his pocket and pushed out of the door into the chilly night.

I watched him then, through the dirty plate-glass of the café window.

It was funny. From everything he'd said, I'd imagined Miss Corvier to be an old woman. But the woman waiting for him, outside, on the pavement, couldn't have been much over thirty. She had long, long hair, though. The kind of hair you can sit on, as they say, although that always sounds faintly like a line from a dirty joke. She looked a bit like a hippy, I suppose. Sort of pretty, in a hungry kind of way.

She took his arm and looked up into his eyes, and they walked away out of the café's light for all the world like a couple of teenagers who were just beginning to realize that they were in love.

I went back up to the counter and bought another cup of tea and a couple of packets of crisps to see me through until the morning, and I sat and thought about the expression on his face when he'd looked at me that last time.

On the milk train back to the big city I sat opposite a woman carrying a baby. It was floating in formaldehyde, in a heavy glass container. She needed to sell it, rather urgently, and although I was extremely tired we talked about her reasons for selling it, and about other things, for the rest of the journey.

THE CAGE

Jeff VanderMeer

Jeff VanderMeer (1968–) is an American writer and editor sometimes associated with the New Weird because of his surreal, grotesque fictions set in the fantasy city of Ambergris. A World Fantasy Award-winner, VanderMeer has also been a finalist for the Hugo, Nebula, Shirley Jackson, and Philip K. Dick awards. Spanning a period of five hundred years, the Ambergris Cycle consists of *City of Saints & Madmen* (2001), *Shriek: An Afterword* (2006), and *Finch* (2009). Short story collections include *Secret Life* (2004) and *The Third Bear* (2010). His major influences include Vladimir Nabokov and Angela Carter. The creepy and luminous 'The Cage', reprinted from *City of Saints*, chronicles the dangerous impulse to deliberately seek out the weird.

The hall contained the following items, some of which were later catalogued on faded yellow sheets constrained by blue lines and anointed with mildew:

– 24 moving boxes, stacked three high. Atop the boxes stood

– 1 stuffed black swan with banded blood-red legs, its marble eyes plucked, the empty sockets a shock of outrushing cotton (or was it fungus?), the bird merely a scout for the

– 5,325 specimens from far-off lands placed on shelves that ran along the four walls and into the adjoining corridors, lit with what he could later only describe as a dark light: it illuminated but did not lift the gloom. Iridescent thrush corpses, the exhausted remains of tattered jellyfish floating in amber bottles, tiny mammals with bright eyes that hinted at the memory of catastrophe, their bodies frozen in brittle poses. The stink of chemicals, a whiff of blood, and

– 1 phonograph, in perfect condition, wedged beside the jagged black teeth of 11 broken records and

– 8 framed daguerreotypes of the family that had lived in the mansion. On vacation in the Southern Isles. Posed in front of a hedge. Blissful on the front porch. His favorite picture showed a boy of seven or eight sticking his tongue out, face animated by indecipherable delight. The frame was cracked, a smudge of blood in the lower left corner. Phonograph, records, and daguerreotypes stood atop

– 1 long oak table covered by a dark green cloth that could not conceal the upward thrust that had splintered the surface of the wood. Around the table stood

– 8 oak chairs, silver lion paws sheathing their legs. The chairs dated to back before the reign of Trillian the Great Banker, the first true ruler of Ambergris. He could not help but wince noting the abuse to which the chairs had been subjected, or fail to notice

– 1 grandfather clock, its blood-spattered glass face cracked, the hands frozen at a point just before midnight, a faint repressed ticking coming from somewhere within its gears, as if the hands sought to move once again, and beneath the clock

– 1 embroidered rug, clearly woven in the north, near the city of Morrow, perhaps even by one of his own ancestors. It depicted the arrival of Morrow cavalry in Ambergris at the time of the mass disappearances known as the Silence, the horses and riders bathed in a halo of blood that might, in another light, be seen as part of the tapestry. Although no light could conceal

– 1 bookcase, lacquered, stacks with books wounded, ravaged, as if something had torn through the spines. Beside the bookcase

– 1 solicitor, dressed all in black. The solicitor wore a cloth mask over his nose and mouth. It was a popular fashion, for those who believed in the dangers of the 'Invisible World' newly mapped by the Kalif's scientists. Nervous and fatigued, the solicitor, eyes blinking rapidly over the top of the mask, stood next to

– 1 pale, slender woman in a white dress. Her hooded eyes never blinked, the ethereal quality of her gaze weaving cobwebs into the distance. Her hands had recently been hacked off, the end of the bloody bandage that hid her left nub held by

– 1 pale gaunt boy with wide, twitchy eyes. At the end of his other arm dangled a small blue-green suitcase, his grasp as fragile as his mother's gaze. His legs trembled in his ashgrey trousers. He stared at

– 1 metal cage, three feet tall and in shape similar to the squat mortar shells that the Kalif's troops had only the year before rained down upon Ambergris during the ill-fated Occupation. An emerald green cover hid its bars from view. The boy's gaze, which required him to twist neck and shoulder to the right while also raising his head to look up and behind, drew the attention of

– 1 exporter-importer, Robert Hoegbotton, 35 years old: neither thin nor fat, neither handsome nor ugly. He wore a drab grey suit he hoped displayed neither imagination nor lack of it. He too wore a cloth mask over his (small) nose and (wide, sardonic) mouth, although not for the same reasons as the solicitor. Hoegbotton considered the mask a weakness, an inconvenience, a superstition. His gaze followed that of the boy up to the high perch, an alcove set halfway up the wall where the cage sat on a window ledge. Rivulets of rain seethed against the window's thick green glass. It was the season of downpours in Ambergris. The rain would not let up for days on end, the skies blue-green-grey with moisture. Fruiting bodies would rise in all the hidden corners of the city. Nothing in the bruised sky would reveal whether it was morning, noon, or dusk. It was an atmosphere well suited to the city's subterranean inhabitants, the gray caps, who in recent years came and went like the ebb and flow of a tide – now underground, now above ground, as if in a perpetual migration between light and dark – appearing suddenly and unwanted, only to disappear just as quickly. As they had here.

Nothing could make one safe. Witnessing the great spasm among the rich of buying houses without basements, or with stone floors, Hoegbotton had been tempted to branch out into real estate, but who knew how long the frenzy would last? No one had yet proven that such a measure, or any measure, helped. The random nature of the events had instilled a certain fatalism. Most of the city's inhabitants had no choice but to go about their business, hoping they would not be next.

The solicitor was talking and had been for what seemed to Hoegbotton like a rather long time.

'That black swan, for example, is in bad condition,' Hoegbotton said, just to slow the solicitor's relentless chatter.

The solicitor wiped his beaded forehead with a handkerchief tinged a pale green.

'The bird? The *bird*,' the solicitor said, 'is in superb condition. Missing eyes, yes. Yes, this is true. But,' he gestured at the walls, 'surely you see the richness of Daffed's collection.'

Thomas Daffed. The last in a long line of driven zoologists. Daffed's wife and son stood beside the solicitor, the remnants of a family of six.

Hoegbotton frowned. 'It's a fine collection, very fine' – and he meant it; he admired a man who could so single-mindedly, perhaps obsessively, acquire such a diverse yet unified assortment of *things* – 'but my average customer needs a pot or an umbrella or a stove. I stock the odd curio from time to time, but a collection of this size?' Hoegbotton shrugged the famous shrug of indifference, perfected over years of haggling, that disguised a more predatory sentiment.

The solicitor stared at Hoegbotton as if he did

not believe him. 'What's your offer? What will you take?'

'I'm still calculating that figure.'

The solicitor stood uncomfortably close to Hoegbotton, his breath sour and thick, a great smudge of a man. He was sweating profusely. A greenish pallor had begun to infiltrate his skin. 'You might consider a little *haste*. Should I call Slattery or Ungdom instead?' As if in the grip of a new, perhaps deadly emotion, his voice seemed more distorted than the mask, which puffed in and out from the violence of his speech.

Hoegbotton took a step back from the ferocity of the solicitor's distress. The names of his chief rivals had made a little vein in his left eyelid pulse in and out. Especially Ungdom – towering John Ungdom, he of the wide belly, steeped in alcohol and pork lard.

'Call for them, then,' he said, staring the solicitor down.

Neither Slattery nor Ungdom would come. Despite being ruthless, their devotion to their job was incomplete, insufficient, inadequate. Hoegbotton imagined them both taken up into the rain and torn to pieces by the wind. As they deserved, for the simple damning fact of their fear.

The solicitor's gaze bored into his cheek for a long moment. Then with a sigh of defeat the foul presence was gone. The solicitor slumped into one of the chairs, loosening his collar with all the urgency of a suffocating man.

'I'm sorry for your loss – all of your losses,' Hoegbotton said, turning to the mother and child who stood in mute acceptance of their fate. 'I promise I won't keep you much longer.' He meant the words sincerely, but knew his intent was meaningless to them in that moment.

The solicitor made a noise between a groan and a choke that Hoegbotton did not bother to catalog. His thoughts had returned to the merchandise: rug, clock, bookcase, phonograph, table, desk. What price might they accept?

Even then, Hoegbotton might not have included the cage in his calculations if the boy's stare had not kept flickering wildly toward it and back down again, stuttering like Hoegbotton's own over the remnants of a success that had become utter failure. For of all the outlandish things in the room – the boy's own mother to be counted among them – the boy seemed most agitated by the cage, an object that had no more been created to harm him than the green suitcase that hung from his arm.

'Tell me about the cage,' Hoegbotton said suddenly, surprising himself. 'The cage up there' – he pointed – 'is it for sale, too?'

The boy stiffened, stared at the floor. Outside, his father, brother, and two sisters were being burned as a precaution, the bodies too mutilated to have withstood a viewing anyway.

A reflexive sadness ran through Hoegbotton, even as he noted the delicacy of the silver engravings on the legs of a nearby chair and the authentic maker's mark stitched onto the cushioned seat.

He smiled at the boy, whose gaze remained directed at the floor. 'Don't you know you're safe now?' The words sounded ludicrous.

The woman turned to look at Hoegbotton. Her eyes were black as an abyss; they did not blink and reflected nothing. He felt for a moment balanced precariously between the son's alarm and the mother's regard.

'The cage was always open,' the woman said, her voice gravelly, something stuck in her throat. 'We had a bird. We always let it fly around. It was a pretty bird. It flew high through the rooms. It – No one could find the bird. After.' The terrible pressure of the word *after* appeared to be too much for her and she fell back into her silence.

'We've never had a cage,' the boy said, the dark green suitcase swaying. 'We've never had a bird. They left it here. They left it.'

A kind of rapturous chill ran through Hoegbotton. The sleepy gaze of a pig embryo floating in a jar caught his eye. Opportunity or disaster? The value of an artifact *they* had left behind might be considerable. The risks, however, might be more than considerable. This was the third time in the last nine months that he had been called to a house visited by the gray caps. Each of the previous times, he had escaped unharmed. In fact, he had come to believe that late arrivals like himself, who took precautions and knew their history, were impervious to any side effects.

Yet even he had experienced moments of discomfort, as when, at the last house, he had walked down a white hallway to the room where the merchandise awaited him and found a series of dark smudges and trails and tracks of blood. Halfway there, he had spied a dark object, shaped like a piece of dried fruit, glistening from the floor. Puzzled, he had stood there for a moment, only to recoil when he realized it was a human ear.

This time, according to the messenger Hoegbotton paid to keep him apprised of potential opportunities, the solicitor had arrived in the early afternoon to find the bodies and survivors. Arms and legs had been stuck into the walls between specimen jars, arranged in intricate poses that displayed a perverse sense of humor.

A tingling sensation crept into Hoegbotton's fingertips. A price had materialized in his mind. The silence became more absolute. All around, dead things watched one another, saw everything but remembered nothing.

'Two thousand – for everything.'

The solicitor sighed, almost crumpled in on himself. The woman blinked rapidly, as if puzzled, and then stared at Hoegbotton with a hatred more real for being so distant. All the former protests of the solicitor, even the boy's fear, were nothing next to that look. The red at the end of her arms had become paler, as if the white bandages had begun to heal her.

He heard himself say, 'Three thousand. If you include the cage.' And it was true, he realized – he wanted the cage.

The solicitor, trying to mask some small personal distress now, giggled and said, 'Done. But you must retrieve it yourself. I'm not well.'

A sour smell had entered the room.

On the ladder, Hoegbotton experienced a moment of vertigo. The world spun, then righted itself as he continued to the top. He peered onto the windowsill.

Something stared at him from beside the cage.

A horrible 'uhh!' sound came from his mouth, and he recoiled, almost lost his balance as he flailed at empty air, managed to fall back against the ladder...and only then realized that what he had seen were just the missing marble eyes of the swan. Placed there by some prankster, or... ? He caught his breath, tried to swallow the unease that pressed down on his shoulders, his tongue, his eyelids.

The cage stood to the right of the ladder and he was acutely conscious of having to lock his legs onto the ladder's sides as he slowly leaned toward the cage.

Below, the solicitor and the boy were speaking, but their voices seemed dulled and distant. He hesitated. What might be in the cage? What horrible thing far worse than a human ear? The odd idea struck him that he would pull the cord to reveal Thomas Daffed's severed head. He could see the bars beneath the cloth, though. Whatever lived inside the cage would remain inside the cage. Now that it was his property, his acquisition, he refused to suffer the same failure of nerve as a Slattery or an Ungdom.

The cover of the cage, which in the dim light appeared to be sprinkled with a luminous green dust, opened like a curtain. With a sharp yank on the drawstring, Hoegbotton drew aside the cover – and flinched, again nearly fell, a sensation of displaced air flowing across his face, as if something moved within.

But the cage was empty. He stood there for an instant, breathing heavily, staring into the cage. Nothing. It contained nothing. Relief came burrowing out of his bones, followed by disappointment. Empty. Except for some straw lining the bottom of the cage and, dangling near the back, almost as an afterthought, a perch that swayed back and forth, the movement no doubt caused by the speed with which he had drawn back the cover. A latched door extended the full three feet from the base to the top of the cage and could be slid back on special grooves. Stained green, the metal bars featured detail-work as fine as he had ever seen – intricate flowers and vines with sinister little figures peering out of a background rich with mushrooms. He could sell it for four or five thousand with the right sales pitch.

Hoegbotton looked down through a murk somehow encouraged by the few lamps.

'It's empty,' he shouted down. 'The cage is empty. But I'll take it.'

An unintelligible answer floated up. As his sight adjusted to the scene below, the distant solicitor in his chair, the other two still standing, he thought for a horrible second that they were melting. The boy seemed melded to his suitcase, the green of it inseparable from the white of the attached arm. The woman's nubs were impossibly white, as if she had grown new bones. The solicitor was just a splash of green.

When he stood on solid ground again, facing them, he could not control his shaking.

All around, on the arms of the chairs, on the table, atop the bookcase, white mushrooms had risen on slender stalks, their gills tinged red.

'I'll have the papers to you tomorrow, after I've catalogued all of the items,' he said. No, he wouldn't. He knew that now.

The solicitor just sat in his chair and giggled uncontrollably.

'It was nice to meet you,' Hoegbotton said, unwilling to let any of them out of his sight as he backed slowly across the room to the door that led to the next room and the room after that and then, hopefully, the outside, by which time he would be running.

'Yes, yes, yes, yes,' the solicitor said, and giggled again, his face as green and wrinkly as lizard skin.

The woman's stubs had sprouted white tendrils of fungus that lazily wound their way around the dried blood and obscured it. Her eyes were slowly filling with white.

Hoegbotton bumped into the damaged table and almost fell. He edged toward the door, groping behind him for the knob. 'I will see you again, soon, and under better… under better…' He could not finish his sentence.

The boy's arms were dark green, fuzzy and indistinct, as if he were a still-life made of points of paint on a canvas. His suitcase, once blue, had turned a blackish green, for the fungi had engulfed it much as ivy had engulfed the eastern wall of the mansion. All the terrible knowledge of his condition shone through the boy's eyes and yet still he held his mother's arm as the white tendrils wound round both their limbs in an ever more permanent embrace.

Hoegbotton later believed he would have stood at the door forever, hand on the knob, the solicitor's giggle a low whine in the background, if not for what happened next.

The broken clock groaned and finally struck midnight. The shuddering stroke reverberated through the thousands of jars of preserved animals. The solicitor looked up in sudden terror and, with a soft popping sound, exploded into a lightly falling rain of emerald spores that drifted to the floor with as slow and tranquil a grace as the seeds of a dandelion.

Outside, Hoegbotton tore off his mask, knelt, and threw up beside the fountain that guarded the path back to Albumuth Boulevard. Behind him, across a square of dark green grass, watched over by the current ruler's grim-looking soldiers: the bodies of Daffed, his daughters, his other son, smoldering grey and black. The charred smell mixed with mildew and the rain that stippled his back. His arms and legs trembled with an enervating weakness. His mouth felt hot and dry. For a long time, he sat in the same position, watching pinpricks break his reflection in the fountain. He shivered as the water shivered.

He had never come this close before. Either they had died long before he arrived or long after he left. The solicitor's liquid giggle trickled through his ears, along with the soft pop of the spores. He shuddered, relaxed, shuddered again.

When his assistant Alan Bristlewing questioned, as he often did, the wisdom of taking on such hazardous work, Hoegbotton would smile and change the subject. He could not choose between two conflicting impulses: the upwelling of excitement at pursuit of a mystery and the desire to flee Ambergris and return to Morrow, the city of his birth. As each new episode receded into memory, his nerve returned, somehow stronger.

The boy's arm, fused to his suitcase.

Holding onto the lichen-flecked stone lip of the pool, Hoegbotton plunged his head into the smooth water. The chill shocked him. It prickled his skin, cut through the numbness to burn the inside of his nose. He reared up, and a sob escaped him, and another, and then a third that bent him over the water again. The back of his neck was suddenly cool. When he pulled away, he looked down at his reflection – and the mask he had made to hide his emotions was gone. He was himself again.

The cage stood beside him, slick with rain. Hoegbotton had gripped its handle so hard during his escape – from every corner, Daffed's infernal collection of dead things staring innocently at him – that he had been branded where the skin had not been rubbed off his palm. He bore the mark of the handle: a filigree of unfamiliar symbols from behind which strange eyes peered out. In the fading light, with the rain falling harder, the fungi appeared to have been washed off the cover of the cage. Perversely, this fact disappointed him. With each new encounter, he had come to expect further revelations.

Hoegbotton stood up. Across the courtyard, the unfortunate soldiers assigned to the bodies had begun to nail boards across the doors and windows of the mansion. One look at his face as he had staggered to safety had told them everything. No doubt they would have boarded him in too, if not for his continual bribes and uncanny ability (in their view) to avoid contamination.

No one pulled the shades open to protest being trapped inside. No one banged on the door, begging to be let out. They had already begun their journey.

Hoegbotton wiped his mouth with his handkerchief. In truth, all he had done was steal a cage. Depending on what hysteria-induced rules the city's leaders had adopted this fortnight, the mansion grounds might be cordoned off or the mansion itself put to the torch and the merchandise he had 'acquired' go unnoted except in his ledger of 'Potential Acquisitions Lost.'

The woman's blank gaze.

Blinking away the rain, Hoegbotton let out a deep breath, stuffed his mask in a pocket, wrapped the cloth around his injured hand, and picked up the cage. He would have to hurry to beat the curfew, a measure he *did* approve of. Ambergris at night the past few weeks, made difficult by the constant rain, had played host to an unnerving amount of debauchery. Days of wholesome trade and other industrious activity became the mirror opposite after dusk, as if the gray caps' presence had had other effects. Orgies had been reported in abandoned churches. Grotesque and lewd water puppet shows were staged down by the docks. Weekly, the merchant quarter held midnight auctions of paintings that could only be termed obscene.

The clock struck midnight.

The cage made him list to the side as he started walking up the path to the main road. Whenever he stopped to switch the cage from his left to his right hand and back again, the weight never seemed the same, at first heavier than he remembered it, and then lighter.

Hoegbotton's wife Rebecca was already asleep when he walked up the seven flights of stairs and entered their apartment. She had turned off the lamps because it gave her the advantage in case of an intruder. The faint scent of lilacs and honeysuckle told him the flower vendor from the floor above them had been by.

A dim half-light shone through from the living room to his left as he set down the cage, took off his shoes and socks, and hung his raincoat on the coat rack. Directly ahead lay the dining room, with its mold-encrusted window, the purple sheen burning darkly as the rain fed it. He had checked the fungal guard just a week ago and found no leakage, but he made a mental note to check it again in the morning.

Hoegbotton found a towel in the hall closet and used it to dry his face, his hair, and then the outside of the cage. Again picking up its uncomfortable weight, he tiptoed into the living room, the rug beneath his feet thick but cold. A series of dark shapes greeted him, most of them items from his store: Lamps and side tables, a couch, a long low coffee table, a bookcase, a grandfather clock. Beyond them lay the balcony, long lost to fungi and locked up as a result.

The fey light almost transformed the living room's contents into the priceless artifacts he had told her they were. He had chosen them not for their value but for their texture, their smell, and for the sounds they made when moved or sat upon or opened. Little of it appealed visually, but she delighted in what he had chosen and it meant he could store the most important merchandise at the shop, where it was more secure.

Hoegbotton set the cage down on the living room table. The palms of his hands were hot and raw from carrying it. He took off the rest of his clothes and laid them on the arm of the couch.

The light came from the bedroom, which lay beyond the living room. He walked into the bedroom and turned to the left, the closed window above the bed reflecting back the iridescent light that came from her and her alone. Rebecca lay on her back, the sheets draped across her body, exposing the long, black, vaguely tear-shaped scar on her left thigh. He ran his gaze over it lustfully.

Hoegbotton walked around to the right side and eased himself into the bed. He moved up beside her and pressed himself against the darkness of the scar. An image of the woman from the mansion flashed through his mind.

Rebecca turned in her sleep and put an arm across his chest as he moved onto his back. Her hand, warm and soft, was as delicate as the starfish that glided through the shallows down by the docks. It looked so small against his chest.

The light came from her open eyes, although he could tell she was asleep. It was a silvery glow awash with faint phosphorescent sparks of blue, green, and red: shivers and hiccups of splintered light, as if a half-dozen tiny lightning storms had welled up in her gaze. What rich worlds did she dream of? And, for the thousandth time: What did the light mean? He had met her on a business trip to Stockton, after the fungal infection that had resulted in the blindness, the odd light, the scar. He had never known her whole.

A joyful sorrow rose within him as he watched the light emanating from her. They had argued about having children just the day before. Every word he had thrown at her in anger had hurt him so deeply that finally he had been wordless, and all he could do was stare at her. Looking at her now, her face unguarded, her body next to his, he could not help loving her for the scar, the eyes, even if it meant he wished her to be this way.

2

The next morning, Hoegbotton woke to the fading image of the woman's bloody bandages and the sounds of Rebecca making breakfast. She knew the apartment better than he did – knew its surfaces, its edges, the exact number of steps from table to chair to doorway – and she liked to make meals in a kitchen that had become more familiar to her than it could ever be to him. Yet she also asked him to bring back more furniture for the living room and bedroom or rearrange existing furniture. She became bored otherwise. 'I want an unexplored country. I want a hint of the unknown,' she said once, and Hoegbotton agreed with that sentiment – up to a point.

There were things Hoegbotton wished would stay unknown. On the mantel opposite the bed, for example, lay those of his grandmother's possessions that his relatives in Morrow had sent to him: a pin, a series of portraits of family members, a set of spoons, a poorly copied family history. A letter from his sister Emily had accompanied the heirlooms, describing his grandmother's last days, which had not been without pain, perhaps deservedly so. But even Hoegbotton had recoiled from the ghoulishness with which Emily had described her wasting away. He had not gone to the funeral. He had not even brought himself to tell Rebecca about the death, six weeks before. All she knew of it was the crinkling of the envelope as he had smoothed out the letter to read it, that he'd brought a pin and spoon home from the store. Telling her would have meant explaining why he hadn't gone to the funeral.

The smell of bacon and eggs spurred him into a bathrobe, and a bleary-eyed stumble through the living room to the kitchen. A dead sort of almost-sunlight – pale and lukewarm – suffused the kitchen window through the purple mold and thin veins of green. A watermark of the city appeared on the glass: wavery spires, forlorn flags, the indistinct shapes of other apartment buildings.

Rebecca stood in the kitchen, spatula in hand, framed by the dour light. Her black hair was brightly dark. Her dress, a green-and-blue sweep of fabric, fit her loosely. She was intent on the skillet in front of her, gaze unblinking, mouth pursed.

As he wrapped his arms around Rebecca, a sense of guilt made him frown. He had come so *close* last night, almost as close as the boy, the woman. Was that as close as he could get without . . . ? The question had haunted him throughout his quest. A sudden depth of emotion arose from nowhere, and he found that his eyes were wet.

Rebecca snuggled into his embrace and turned toward him. Her eyes looked almost normal during the day. Flecks of phosphorescence shot lazily across the pupils.

'Did you sleep well?' she asked. 'You came home so late.'

'I slept. I'm sorry I was late. It was a difficult job this time.' When he had to lie to her, even his thoughts became very still.

'Profitable?' Her elbow nudged him as she turned the eggs over with the spatula.

'Not very.'

'Really? Why not?'

He stiffened. If she'd been there, would Rebecca have realized the mansion had become a deathtrap? Would she have smelled the blood, tasted the fear? He served as her eyes, but would he deprive her anything by not describing its horrors in every detail?

'Well . . .' he began. He shut his eyes. *The sick gaze of the solicitor flickering over the scene of his own death*. Even as he held Rebecca, he could feel a distance opening up between them.

'You don't need to shut your eyes to see,' she said, pulling out of his embrace.

'How did you know?' He knew what she would say.

'I heard you close them.' She smiled with grim satisfaction.

'It was sad,' he said, sitting down at the kitchen table. 'Nothing terrible. Just sad. The wife had lost her husband and had to sell the estate. She had a boy with her who kept holding on to a little suitcase.' *The remnants of the solicitor floating to the ground, curling up like confetti. The boy's stare fluttering between him and the cage.* 'I felt sorry for them. They had some nice heirlooms, but most of it was already promised to Slattery and Ungdom. I didn't get much. They had a nice rug from Morrow, from before the Silence. Nice detail of Morrow cavalry coming to our rescue. I would have liked to have bought it.'

She carefully slid the eggs and bacon onto a plate and brought it to the table.

'Thank you,' he said. She had burned the bacon. The eggs were too dry. He never mentioned it. She needed these little sleights of hand, these illusions of illumination. It was edible.

'Mrs. Bloodgood took me down to the Morhaim Museum yesterday,' she said. 'Many of their artifacts are on open display. The textures were amazing. And the flower vendor visited, as you may have guessed.'

Rebecca's father, Paul, was the curator for a small museum in her home town of Stockton. Her father liked to joke that Hoegbotton was just the temporary caretaker for items that would eventually find their way to him, while Hoegbotton had always thought museums hoarded that which should be available on the open market. Rebecca had been her father's assistant until the disease stole her sight. Now Hoegbotton sometimes took her down to his store to help him sort and catalog new acquisitions.

'I did notice the flowers,' he said. 'I'm glad the museum was worth it.'

For some reason, his hand shook as he ate his eggs. He put his fork down.

'Isn't it good?' she asked.

'It's very good,' he said. 'I just need water.'

He got up and walked to the sink. The faucet had been put in five weeks ago, after a two-year wait. Before, they had gotten jugs of water from a well down in the valley. He watched with satisfaction as the faucet spluttered and his glass gradually filled up.

'It's a nice bird or whatever,' she said from behind him.

'Bird.' The glass clinked against the edge of the sink as he momentarily lost his grip.

'Or lizard. Or whatever it is. What is it?'

He turned, leaned against the sink. 'What are you talking about?'

'That cage you brought home with you.'

A vague fear crept up his spine. Was she joking? 'There's nothing in the cage. It's empty.'

Rebecca laughed, a pleasant, liquid sound.

'That's funny, because your empty cage was rattling earlier. At first, it scared me. Something was moving around in there. I couldn't tell if it was a bird or a lizard or I would have reached through the bars and touched it.'

'But you didn't.'

'No.'

'There's nothing in the cage.'

Her face underwent a subtle change and he knew she thought he doubted her on something at which she was expert: the interpretation of sound.

He couldn't stay quiet for long. She couldn't read his face without touching it, but he suspected she knew the difference between types of silence.

He laughed. 'I'm joking. It's a lizard – but it bites. So you were wise not to touch it.'

Suspicion tightened her features. Then she relaxed and smiled at him. She reached out, felt for his plate with her left hand, and stole a piece of his bacon. 'I knew it was a lizard!'

He longed to go into the living room where the cage stood atop the table. But he couldn't, not just yet.

'It's quiet in here,' he said softly, already expecting the reply.

'No it's not. It's not quiet at all. It's loud.'

The left corner of his mouth curled up as he replied by rote: 'What do you hear?'

Her smile widened. 'Well, first, there's your voice, my love – a nice, deep baritone. Then there's Hobson downstairs, playing a phonograph as low as he can to avoid disturbing the Potaks, who are at this moment in an argument about something so petty I will not give you the details, while to the side, just below them' – her eyes narrowed – 'I believe the Smythes are also making bacon. Above us, old man Clox is pacing and pacing with his cane, muttering about money. On his balcony, there's a sparrow chirping, which makes me realize now that the animal in your cage must be a lizard, because it sounds like something clicking and clucking, not chirping – unless you've got a chicken in there?'

'No, no – it's a lizard.' Now he had, for a second time, admitted aloud that *something* might indeed be in the cage.

'What kind of lizard?'

'It's a Saphant Fire Lizard from the Southern Isles,' he said. 'It only ever grows in cages, which it makes itself by chewing up dirt, changing it into metal, and regurgitating it. It can only eat animals that can't see it.'

She laughed in appreciation and got up and hugged him. The feel of her, the smell of her hair, made him forget his fear. 'It's a good story, but I don't believe you. I do know this, though – you are going to be late to work.'

Once on the ground floor, where he did not think it would make a difference if Rebecca heard, Hoegbotton set down the cage. The awkwardness of carrying it, uneven and swaying, down the spiral staircase had unnerved him further. He was sweating under his rain coat. His breath came hard and fast. The musty quality of the lobby, the traces of tiny rust mushrooms that had spread along the floor like mouse tracks, the mottled green-orange mold on the windows in the front door, did not put him at ease.

Someone had left a worn umbrella leaning against the front door. He grabbed it and turned back to stare at the cage. Was this the moment that Ungdom and Slattery's ill-wishes caught up with him? He drove the umbrella tip between the bars. The cover gave a little, creasing, and then regained its former shape as he withdrew the umbrella.

Nothing came leaping out at him.

He tried again. No response.

'Is something in there?' he asked. The cage did not reply.

Umbrella held like a sword in front of him, Hoegbotton shoved the cover aside – and leapt back.

The cage was still empty. The perch swung back and forth madly from the violence with which he had pulled aside the cover. The woman had said, 'The cage was always open.' The boy had said, 'We never had a cage.' The solicitor had never offered an opinion. The swinging perch, the emptiness of the cage, depressed him. He could not say why.

He drew the cover back across the cage, felt someone's gaze at his back, and whirled around to find their landlady, the emaciated Mrs. Willis, glaring at him from the stairway. He had a sudden vision of how strange he must look to her.

Mrs. Willis said, in a clipped tone that admitted no humor, 'I don't know *exactly* what you're doing, but *whatever* you're doing I don't believe Miss Constance from the third floor would like that you are doing it *with her umbrella*.'

'Robert Hoegbotton & Sons: Quality Importers of Fine New & Used Items From Home & Abroad' was situated on Albumuth Boulevard, halfway between the docks and the residential sections that descended into a valley ever in danger of flooding. It took up the first floor of a solid two-story wooden building owned by a monk in the Religious Quarter. The sign exhibited optimism; there were no sons. Not yet. The time was not right, the situation too uncertain, no matter what Rebecca might say. Always in the back of his mind, spurring him on: his brother Richard's threat to swoop down with the rest of the Hoegbotton clan to save the family name should he fail. But fail at what? The missives Richard sent from Morrow every few months were masterpieces of vague and rambling aggression, to which he rarely replied.

The display window, protected from the rain by an awning, held a battered mauve couch, an opulent, gold-leaf-covered chair (nicked by Hoegbotton, along with several other treasures, during the panicked withdrawal of the Kalif's troops), a phonograph, a large red vase, an undistinguished-looking saddle, and Alan Bristlewing, his assistant.

Bristlewing knelt inside the display, carefully placing records in the stand beside the phonograph. He had already wiped the outside of the window clean of fungi that had accumulated the night before. A sour smell emanated from these remnants, but the rain would wash it all away in an hour or two.

Hoegbotton plunged on through the open door, ignoring Bristlewing's wave and banging the cage against the frame despite his best efforts. A few button-shaped mushrooms, a fiery red, fell to the floor.

Bristlewing framed by the window display was a scruffy, short, animated man with a perpetual laconic grin, outfitted with some antiques of his own, courtesy of a sidewalk dentist. He smelled of cigar smoke and often disappeared for days on end. Rumors of debaucheries with prostitutes and week-long fishing trips down the River Moth buzzed around Bristlewing without settling on him. Hoegbotton could not afford to hire more dependable help.

'Morning,' Bristlewing said, on one knee looking up at him.

'Good morning,' Hoegbotton replied. 'Any customers last night?'

'None with any money.' Bristlewing's grin vanished as he saw the cage. 'Oh. I see you went to another one.' He stood and put one hand out to take the cage from Hoegbotton.

'Don't touch it!' The surge of anger surprised Hoegbotton and froze Bristlewing in mid-grasp. Hoegbotton struggled for control, managed to follow up with, 'I'll put it in the back, thanks very much.'

Bristlewing raised one eyebrow, pulling back his hand with exaggerated slowness. 'Suit yourself.'

With an effort Hoegbotton asked, 'Are the inventory books up-to-date?'

'Course they're current,' Bristlewing said, turning stiffly away.

By design, the way to Hoegbotton's makeshift office was blocked by a maze of items, from which rose a collective must-metal-rotted-dusty smell that he loved fiercely. This smell, of an authentic and pure antiquity, validated his selections as surely as any papers or certificates. That customers tripped and lost their bearings as they wandered the arbitrary footpaths mattered little to Hoegbotton. The received family wisdom said that thus hemmed in the customer had no choice but to buy something from the stacks of chairs, umbrellas, watches, pens, fishing rods, clothes, enameled boxes, plaster casts of lizards, elegant mirrors of glass and copper, reading glasses, Truffidian religious icons, boards for playing dice made of oliphaunt ivory, porcelain water jugs, globes of the world, model ships, old medals, sword canes, musical clocks, and other ephemera from past lives or distant places. And, in seeking out a perfectly ordinary set of dinner plates, a customer might have an even more intimate encounter, be forced, for example, to face the flared nostrils and questing tongue of a Skamoo erotic mask. An overwhelming sense of the secret history of these objects could sometimes send him into a trance.

At the back, Hoegbotton's work space had been colonized by a similar morass of riches. His former desk lay beneath a stack of oversized and ancient books, folders full of invoices, a gigantic fire-glazed pot, several telescopes he'd been unable to unload, and a collection of metal and wooden frogs he'd acquired impulsively. Shoved in around the edges, personal keepsakes: a favorite pen, a shell he had found while on vacation in the Southern Isles when he was six, and daguerreotypes of family: Rebecca, his brother Stephen (lost to the family now, having signed up for Morrow's army on a monstrous but historically common whim), and his mother Gertrude standing on the lawn of someone else's mansion in Morrow.

Beyond the besieged desk, against the back wall, stood two doors. The first led to a private bathroom, recently installed, much to Bristlewing's delight. Hoegbotton headed for the second door, which was very old, wormholed, and studded with odd metal symbols that Hoegbotton had filched from an abandoned shrine in the Religious Quarter.

He could hear Bristlewing worrying at some artifact behind a row of old bookcases stacked high with cracked flowerpots, so he pulled the key out of his pants pocket, unlocked the door and went inside. Why should it matter if Bristlewing saw him go in? And yet it did.

The door shut silently behind him and he was alone, except for the cage. The light that cast its yellowing glare upon the room came from an old-fashioned oil lamp nailed into the room's far wall.

Nothing, at first glance, distinguished the room from any other room. It contained a tired-looking dining table around which stood four worn chairs. To one side, plates, cups, bowls, and utensils sat atop a cabinet with a mirror that served as a backboard. The mirror was veined with a purplish fungus that had managed to infiltrate the minute fractures in the glass. He had worried that the city's enforcers might confiscate the mirror on one of their weekly inspections of his store, but they had ignored it, perhaps recognizing the age of the mirror and the way mold had itself begun to grow over the fungus.

In addition to three inventory ledgers, the table held three place settings. Across the middle of the table lay a parchment, so old that it looked as if it might disintegrate into dust at the slightest touch. A bottle of port, half-full, stood at the far end of the table.

This was his new office, having been driven there by his own acquisitions. Hoegbotton set the cage down beside the table. His hand stung from where the imprint of the handle had branded itself onto his skin.

Bound in red leather, the ledger books were imported from Morrow. The off-white pages were tissue paper thin to accommodate as many sheets as possible. The three ledgers represented the inventory for the past three months. Thirty others, as massive and unwieldy, had been wrapped in a blanket and carefully hidden beneath the floorboards in his office. (Two separate notebooks to record unfortunate but necessary dealings with Ungdom and Slattery, suitably yellow and brown, had been tossed into an unlocked drawer of his abandoned desk.)

Yesterday had been slow – only five items sold, two of them phonograph records. He frowned when he read Bristlewing's description of the buyers as 'Short lady with walking stick. Did not give a name.' and 'Man looked sick. Took forever to make up his mind. Bought one record after all that time.' Bristlewing did not respect the system. By contrast, a typical Hoegbotton-penned buyer entry read like an investigative report: 'Miss Glissandra Bustel, 4232 East Munrale Street, late 40s. Grey-silver hair. Startling blue eyes. Wore an expensive green dress but cheap black shoes, scuffed. She insisted on calling me "Mr. Hoegbotton." She examined a very expensive Occidental vase and commented favorably on a bone hairpin, a pearl snuffbox, and a watch once worn by a prominent Truffidian priest. However, she only bought the hairpin.'

If Bristlewing disliked the detail required by

Hoegbotton for the ledgers, he disliked the room itself even more. After carefully cataloguing its contents upon their arrival three years before, Hoegbotton had asked Bristlewing a question.

'Do you know what this is?'

'Old musty room. No air.'

'No. It's not an old musty room with no air.'

'Fooled me,' Bristlewing had said and, scowling, left him there.

3

But Bristlewing was wrong – dead wrong. Bristlewing did not understand the first thing about the room. How could he? And how could Hoegbotton explain that the room was perhaps the most important room in the world, that he often found himself inside it even while walking around the city, at home reading to his wife, or buying fruit and eggs from the farmers' market? That, in his mind, the room and the cage were one and the same?

The history of the room went back to the Silence itself. His great-great-grandfather, Samuel Hoegbotton, had been the first Hoegbotton to move to Ambergris, much against the wishes of the rest of his extended family, including his twenty-year-old son, John, who stayed in Morrow.

For a man who had uprooted his wife and daughter from all that was familiar to take up residence in an unknown, sometimes cruel, city, Samuel Hoegbotton became remarkably successful, establishing three stores down by the docks. It seemed only a matter of time before more of the Hoegbotton clan moved down to Ambergris.

However, this was not to be. One day, Samuel Hoegbotton, his wife, and his daughter disappeared, just three of the many thousands of souls who vanished from Ambergris during the episode known as the Silence – leaving behind empty buildings, empty courtyards, empty houses, and both dread and emptiness in the lives of those left behind. With no clues as to what had happened or how. It was now one hundred years since the Silence, and people could be forgiven their loss of memory, for wanting to ignore the horror in the idea that the gray caps might have been the cause. Everyone still thought it, but few said it. What could not be proven should not be given voice. Should be forgotten.

Hoegbotton remembered one line in particular from John's diary: *'I cannot believe my father has really disappeared. It is possible he could have come to harm, but to simply* disappear*? Along with my mother and sister? I keep thinking that they will return one day and explain what happened to me. It is too difficult to live with, otherwise. It is a wound that never heals.'*

Sitting in his mother's bedroom with the diary open before him, the young Robert Hoegbotton had felt a chill across the back of his neck. What had happened to Samuel Hoegbotton? He had spent many summer afternoons in the attic, surrounded by antiquities, trying to find out. He combed through old letters Samuel had sent home before his disappearance. He visited the family archive. He wrote to relatives in other cities.

His mother merely disapproved of such inquiries; his grandmother actively taunted him. 'Yes, waste your life with that nonsense,' she would say from the huge throne of an ancient king they'd bought on the cheap, which seemed to best suit her rock-hard old bones. 'You won't get any farther than your father, or his father before him. The lot of you aren't smart enough to cook an egg properly.' He could not talk to his father about it; that cold and distant figure was rarely home. But he had them both to thank for something at least: he prided himself on rarely sharing his opinions with anyone. Appearing to be a blank slate stood him in good stead in his business.

With his sister, the young Hoegbotton continued his investigations behind his grandmother's back, would act out scenarios with the house as the backdrop. They would ask the maids questions to fill gaps in their knowledge and thus uncovered the meaning of words like 'gray cap.' On his thirteenth birthday, he helped himself to an old sketch in his grandmother's upstairs bedroom that showed the apartment's living room – Samuel Hoegbotton surrounded by smiling relatives on a visit. Then, with a profound and uncomplicated sense of happiness, listened from downstairs to her shrieks of displeasure upon finding it missing. But for his sister all of this was just relief of a temporary boredom, and he was soon so busy learning the family business that the mystery faded from his thoughts.

By the age of twenty, he decided to leave Morrow and travel to Ambergris, surprised to see his grandmother crying as he left. No Hoegbotton had set foot in Ambergris for ninety years and it was precisely for this reason that he chose the city, or so he told himself. In Morrow, under the predatory eye of Richard, he had felt as if none of his plans would ever be successful. In Ambergris, he started out poor but independent, operating a sidewalk stall that sold fruit and broadsheets. At odd times – at an auction, looking at jewelry that reminded him of something his mother might wear; sneaking around Ungdom's store examining all that merchandise, so much richer than what he could acquire at the time – thoughts of the Silence wormed their way into his head.

The day after he signed the lease on his own store, Hoegbotton visited Samuel's apartment. He had the address from some of the man's letters. The building lay in a warren of derelict structures that rose from the side of the valley to the east of the Merchant Quarter. It took Hoegbotton an hour to find it, the carriage ride followed by progress on foot. He knew he was close when he had to climb over a wooden fence with a sign on it that read 'Off Limits By Order of the Ruling Council.' The sky was overcast, the sunlight weak yet bright, and he walked through the tenements feeling ethereal, dislocated. Here and there, he found walls where bones had been mixed with the mortar and he knew by these signs that such places had been turned into graveyards.

When he finally stood in front of the apartment – on the ground level of a three-story building – he wondered if he should turn around and go home. The exterior was boarded up, fire-scorched and splotched with brown-yellow fungi. The facing rows of buildings formed a corridor of light, at the end of which a stray dog sniffed at the ground, picking up a scent. He could see its ribs even from so far away. Somewhere, a child began to cry, the sound thin, attenuated, automatic. The sound was so unexpected, almost horrifying, that he thought it must not be a baby at all, but something mimicking a baby, hoping to lure him closer.

After a few more moments, he reached a decision and took a crowbar from his pack. Ten minutes later, he had pried up the boards and the door stood revealed, a pale 'X' running across the dark wood. He realized he was breathing in shallow gasps. No one could help him if he opened the door and needed help, but he still wanted whatever was inside the apartment. It could be anything, even the end of his life, and yet anticipation surged through him, and he didn't know why.

Hoegbotton pulled the door open and stepped inside, crowbar held like a weapon.

It took a moment for his eyes to adjust to the darkness. The air was stale. Windows to the right and left of the hallway, although boarded up, let in enough light to make patches of dust on the floor shine like colonies of tiny, subdued fireflies. The hallway was perversely ordinary. In the even more dimly lit living room, Hoegbotton could make out that some vagrant had long ago set up digs and abandoned them. A sofa had been overturned and a blanket used as a roof for a makeshift tent. Dog droppings were more recent. A rabbit carcass, withered but caked with dried blood, might have been as fresh as the week before. The wallpaper had collapsed into a mumbling senility of fragments and strips. Paintings lay in tumbled flight against the floor. A faint, bitter smell rose from the room – a sourness that revealed hidden negotiations between wood and fungi. Hoegbotton relaxed. The gray caps had not been in the apartment for a long time. He let the crowbar dangle in his hand.

Hoegbotton entered the dining room. Brittle pages of newsprint lay across the dining room table, held in place by a bottle of port with a glass beside it. Infiltrated by cobwebs, by dust, by mottled fragments of wood, the table also held plates and place settings. The stale air had preserved the contents of the plates in a mummified state. Three plates. Three pieces of ossified chicken, accompanied by a green smear of some vegetable long since dried out. Samuel Hoegbotton. His wife Sarah. His daughter Jane. All three chairs, worm-eaten and rickety, were pulled out slightly from the table. A fourth chair lay off to the side, smashed into fragments by time or violence.

Hoegbotton stared at the chairs for a long time. Had they been moved at all in the last century? How could anyone know? Unfolded napkins lay on the seats of two of the chairs. The third – that of the person who would have been reading the newspaper – had not been used, nor had the silverware for that setting. The silverware of the other two was positioned peculiarly. On the right side, the fork lay at an angle near the plate, as if thrown there. Something dark and withered had been skewered by the fork's tines. Did it match an irregularity in the dry flesh of the chicken upon the matching plate? The knife was missing entirely. On the left side of the table, the fork was still stuck into its piece of chicken, the knife sawing into the flesh beside it.

A prickly, cold sensation spread across Hoegbotton's skin. Had the family been eating and simply… disappeared… in mid-meal? The fork. The knife. The chairs. The broadsheet. The meals uneaten, half-eaten. The bottle of port. The mystery gnawed at him even as it became ever more impenetrable. Nothing he and his sister had imagined could account for it.

Taking out his pocketknife, Hoegbotton leaned over the table. He carefully pulled aside one leaf of the broadsheet to reveal the date: the very day of the Silence. The date transfixed him. He pulled out the chair where surely Samuel Hoegbotton must have sat, reading his papers, and slowly slid into it. Looked down the table to where his daughter and wife would have been sitting. Continued to read the paper with its articles on the turmoil at the docks, preparing for the windfall due with the return of the fishing fleet; a brief message on blasphemy from a priest; the crossword puzzle. A sudden shift, a dislocation, a puzzled look from his wife, and he had stared up from his paper in that last moment to see… what?

Hoegbotton stared across the table again, focused on the bottle of port. The glass was half-full. He leaned forward, examined the glass. The liquid inside had dried into sludge over time. A faint imprint of tiny lips could be seen on the edge of the glass. The cork was tightly wedged into the mouth of the bottle. A further mystery. When had the port been poured?

Beyond the bottle, the fork with the skewered meat came into focus. It did not, from this angle, look as if it came from the piece of chicken on the plate – *and the plate was nailed to the table.*

He pulled back, as much from a thought that had suddenly occurred to him as from the strangeness of the fork, the plate. A dim glint from the floor beside the chair caught his eye. Samuel Hoegbotton's glasses. Twisted into a shape that resembled a circle attached to a line and two 'u' shapes on either end. As he stared at the glasses, the questions overwhelmed him, until he was not just sitting in Samuel Hoegbotton's chair, but in the chairs of thousands of souls, looking out into darkness, trying to see what they had seen, to know what they came to know.

The thing that might have been a baby was still screaming as Hoegbotton stumbled outside, gasping. He ran over bits of brick and rubble. He ran through the long weeds. He ran past the buildings with mortar made from bones. He scrambled over the fence that said he should not have been there. When he did stop, gasping for breath, having reached the familiar cobblestones of Albumuth, the pressure in his temples remained, the stray thought lodged in his head like a virus.

What had Samuel Hoegbotton seen? And was it necessary to *disappear* to have seen it?

After that visit, even the abandoned rooms of the Silence lost their hold on Hoegbotton. He would go in with the workmen and find old, dimly lit spaces from which whatever had briefly imbued them with a ghastly intensity had long since departed. He stopped acquiring artifacts from such places, although in a sense, it was too late. Ungdom, Slattery, and their ilk had already begun to slander him, spreading rumors about his intent and his sanity. Then, finally, the breakthrough: a series of atrocities at one mansion after the other, bringing him closer than ever before.

That was the hundred-year-old trail that had led him to this point, now, in that room – moved at great expense – staring at a cage that might or might not contain an answer.

4

That night, he made love to Rebecca. Her scar gleamed by the light from her eyes, which, at the height of her rapture, blazed so brightly that the bedroom seemed transported from night to day. As he reached release, the light registered as an ecstatic shudder that penetrated his skin, his bones, his heart. She called out his name and ran her hands down his back, across his face, her eyes sparking with pleasure. At such moments, when the strangeness of her seeped through into him, he would suffer a sudden panic, as if he was losing himself, as if he no longer knew his own name. He would sit up, as now, all the muscles in his back rigid.

She knew him well enough not to ask what was wrong, but, sleep besotted, the light from her eyes dimming to a satisfied glow, said, simply, 'I love you.'

'Your eyes are full of fireflies,' he replied.

She laughed, but he meant it: entire cities, entire worlds, pulsed inside those eyes, hinting at an existence beyond the mundane.

Something in her gaze reminded him suddenly of the woman with the missing hands and he looked away, toward the window that, though closed, let in the persistent sound of rain. Beside the window, his grandmother's possessions still lay in shadows on the mantel.

The next day, as he sat in Samuel Hoegbotton's room writing out invoices for the week's exports – Saphant carnival masks, rare eelwood furniture, necklaces from Nicea, all destined for Morrow – he noticed something odd. He drew his breath in sharply. He pushed his chair back and stood up.

There, growing at a right angle from the green cloth that covered the cage, was a fragile, milk-white fruiting body on a long stem, the gills tinged red. It was identical to the mushrooms that had appeared in Daffed's mansion. He cast about for a weapon, his gaze fixed on the cage. There was nothing but the bottle of port. Beyond the cage, the fungus that had infiltrated the cracks of the mirror appeared to have darkened and thickened.

Irrationally, he decided he had to remove the cage from the room. *The room had schemed with the cage to produce the mushroom.* Picking up a napkin, he wound it around the handle of the cage, which felt hot, and carried it out of the room, to his desk.

He stared across the store, trying to locate Bristlewing through the clutter. His assistant stood in a far corner helping an elderly gentleman decide on a chair. Hoegbotton could just see the back of Bristlewing's head, nodding at something the potential customer had said, both of them obscured by a column of school desks.

Slowly, as if the mushroom were watching him, Hoegbotton slid his hand over to the top drawer of his desk, pulled it open and took out a silver letter opener. Holding it in front of him, he approached the cage. Images of the woman and her son flickered in his mind. He couldn't keep his hand still. He hesitated. A vision of the mushroom multiplying into two, three, four came to him. Hoegbotton leaned over his desk, chopped the mushroom off the side of the cage. It fell onto his desk, leaving behind only a small, circular white spot on the green cover, as innocent as a bird dropping.

Hoegbotton pulled his handkerchief out of his breast pocket and squashed the mushroom in its folds, careful not to touch any part of it. He stuffed the handkerchief into the wastebasket at his side. Then he fished out the handkerchief, decided against it and placed the handkerchief back into the wastebasket. Fished it out again.

Hoegbotton realized that both Bristlewing and his customer were now standing a few feet away, staring at him. He froze, then smiled.

'My dear Bristlewing,' he said. 'What can I help you with?'

Bristlewing gave him a disgusted look. 'Mr. Sporlender here was interested in a writing desk, for his son. We've a good, solid chair but, rather horrendously, nothing appropriate in a desk. Anything in storage?'

Hoegbotton smiled, intensely aware of the dead mushroom in his hand. The irritation caused by the handle of the cage flared up, pulsing across his palm. 'Yes, actually, Mr. Sporlender, if you would come back tomorrow, I believe we might have something to show you.' Just so long as he left the shop.

Hoegbotton nudged Bristlewing out of the way

and guided the man toward the door, babbling about the rain, about the importance of a writing desk, about anything at all, while Bristlewing's stare burned into the back of his head. Hoegbotton had never been more impatient to reach the rain-scoured street. When it came, it was like a wave – of light, of fresh air. It hit him with such force that he gasped, drawing a sharp look from Mr. Sporlender.

As they stood there, on the cusp of the street, the door at Hoegbotton's back, the man stared at him through narrowed eyes. 'Really, Mr. Hoegbotton – should I come back tomorrow? Would you truly advise that?'

Hoegbotton stared down at his hand, which was about to rebel and throw the handkerchief and mushroom as far away as possible. Some of the early afternoon passersby already stared curiously at the two of them.

'It's up to you, really. We might have a desk in storage…'

Sporlender sneered. 'I saw what you put in the handkerchief. I know what it is.'

'Well in that case,' Hoegbotton said, 'why don't you take it with you, instead of a desk,' and held the handkerchief out toward the man.

'Keep that away from me,' Sporlender said and hurried off down the street, concentrating on putting as much distance between them as possible.

It was of no consequence to Hoegbotton in that moment. Ignoring the stares of those around him and feeling strangely lightheaded, he started off in the opposite direction, past sidewalk vendors, a thin stream of pedestrians, and an even thinner stream of carts and carriages, which the rain rendered in smudges and humid smells. Only after three or four blocks, soaked to the skin, did he feel comfortable tossing the handkerchief and its contents into a public trashcan. He already had an image in his head of soldiers searching his store for traces of the wrong kind of mushroom.

A man was throwing up into the gutter. A woman was yelling at her husband. Two Dogghe tribesmen hunched against the closed doors of a bank, their distinctive green spiraled hats pulled down low over their weathered faces. The sky was a uniform grey. The rain was unending, as common as the very air. He couldn't even feel it anymore. Everywhere, in the cracks of the sidewalk, in the minute spaces between bricks in shop fronts, new fungi was growing. He wondered if anything he did mattered.

He wondered if Sporlender would tell anyone.

Back at the store, Bristlewing was grumpily moving some boxes around. He spared Hoegbotton only a quick glance – watchful, wary. Hoegbotton brushed by him and headed for the bathroom, where he scrubbed his hands red before coming out again to examine the cage. It looked just as he had left it. The green cover was unblemished but for the white spot. There had been no proliferation of mushrooms in his absence. This was good. This meant he had done the right thing. (Why, then, was it so hard to draw breath? Why so difficult to stop shaking?)

He sat down behind the desk, staring at the cage. The inside of his mouth felt dry and thick. Nothing happened without a reason. The mushroom had not appeared by coincidence. This he could not believe. How could he?

Against his instincts, he reached over to the cage and pulled the cover aside, the green giving way to the finely etched metal bars, the shadows of the bars letting the light slide around them so that he saw the perch, gently swinging, and, below it, a pale white hand. Slender and delicate. The end a mass of dried blood. He became utterly still. A vision overtook him: that he was Samuel Hoegbotton, staring across the dining room table at the cage, which was the last thing he would ever see. The hand, he had no doubt, was from Daffed's wife. What would it take to make it go away?

But then his mind registered a much more important detail, one that made him bite down hard on his lower lip to stop from screaming. The cage door was open, slid to the side as neatly as the cover. He sat there, motionless, staring, for several seconds. Throughout the store, he could hear the myriad clocks ticking forward. No mask could help him now. The hand. The open cage. The fey brightness of the bars. A *rippling* at the edges of his vision.

Somewhere, Hoegbotton found the nerve. He reached out and slid the door back into position with both hands, worked the latch shut – just as he felt a sudden weight on the other side, rushing up to meet him. It brushed against his fingers and chilled them. He drew back with a gasp. The door rattled once, twice, fell still. The perch began to swing violently back and forth as if something had pushed up against it. Then it too fell still. Suddenly.

He could not breathe. He could not call out for help. His heart was beating so fast, he thought it might burst. This was not how he had imagined it. This was not how he had imagined it.

Something invisible picked up the hand and forced it through the bars. The hand fell onto his blotter, rocked once, twice, and was still.

It took five or six tries, his fingers nimble as blocks of wood, but he managed to find the cord to the cover and slide it back into position.

Then he sat there for a long time, staring at the green cover of the cage. Nothing happened. Nothing bad. The sense of weight on the other side of the bars had vanished with the drawing of the veil. The hand that lay on his blotter did not seem real. It looked like alabaster. It looked like wax. It was a candle without a wick. It was a piece of a statue.

An hour could have passed, or a minute, before he found a paper bag, nudged the hand into it using the letter opener, and folded the bag shut.

Bristlewing appeared in his field of vision some time later.

'Bristlewing,' Hoegbotton said. 'I'm glad. You're here.'

'Eh?'

'You see this cage?' Tight, tight control, imprisoning his own thoughts.

'Yes.'

'I need you to take it to Ungdom.'

'Ungdom?' Bristlewing's face brightened. He clearly thought this was a joke.

'Yes. To Ungdom. Tell him that I send it with my compliments. That I offer it as a token of renewed friendship.' Somewhere inside, he was laughing at Ungdom's future discomfort. Somewhere inside, he was screaming for help.

Bristlewing snorted. 'Is it wise?'

Hoegbotton stared up at him, as if through a haze of smoke. 'Wise? No. It isn't *wise*. But I would like you to do it anyway.'

Bristlewing waited for a moment, as if there might be something more, but there was nothing more. He walked forward, picked up the cage. As Bristlewing bent over the cage, Hoegbotton thought he saw a patch of green at the base of his assistant's neck, under his left ear. Was Bristlewing already infected? Was Bristlewing the threat?

'Another thing. Take the rest of the week off. Once you've delivered the cage to Ungdom.' If his assistant was going to dissolve into spores, let him do it elsewhere. Hoegbotton suppressed a giggle of hysteria, felt a sudden kinship with the dead solicitor.

Suspicious, Bristlewing frowned. 'And if I want to work?'

'It's a vacation. A vacation. I've never given you one. I'll pay you for the time.'

'All right,' Bristlewing said. Now the look he gave Hoegbotton was, to Hoegbotton's eye, very close to pity. 'I'll give the cage to Ungdom and take the week off.'

'That's what I said.'

'Right. Bye then.'

'Goodbye.'

As Bristlewing negotiated the tiny flotsam-lined pathway, Hoegbotton could not help but notice that his assistant seemed to list to one side, as if the cage had grown unaccountably heavy.

Five minutes after Bristlewing had left, Hoegbotton closed up the shop for the day. It only took seven tries for him to lock the door behind him.

5

When he arrived at the apartment, Hoegbotton told Rebecca he was home early because he had learned of his grandmother's death. She seemed to interpret his shakes and shudders, the trembling of his voice, the way he needed to touch her, as consistent with his grief. They ate dinner in silence, her hand in his hand.

'You should talk to me,' she said afterwards and he catalogued all the symptoms of fear as if they were the symptoms of loss, of grief. Everywhere he turned, the woman from the mansion confronted him, her gaze now angry, now mournful. Her wounds bled copiously down her dress but she did nothing to staunch the flow.

They went to bed early and Rebecca held him until he found a path toward sleep. But sleep held images to torment him. In his dreams, he walked through Samuel Hoegbotton's apartment until he reached a long, white hallway he had never seen before. At the opposite end of the hallway, he could see the woman and the boy from the mansion, surrounded by great wealth, antiques fit for a god winking at him in their burnished multitudes. He was walking across a carpet of small, severed hands to reach them. This fact revolted him, but he could not stop walking: the promise of what lay ahead was too great. Even when he began to see his head, his arms, his own legs, crudely soldered to the walls using his own blood, he could not stop his progress toward the end of the hallway. The hands were cold and soft and pleading.

But despite the dreams, Hoegbotton woke the next morning feeling energetic and calm. The cage was gone. He had another chance. He did not feel the need to follow in Samuel Hoegbotton's footsteps. Even the imprint on his hand throbbed less painfully. The rain clattering down made him happy for obscure, childhood reasons – memories of sneaking out into thunderstorms to play under the dark clouds, of taking to the water on a rare fishing trip with his father while drops sprinkled the dark, languid surface of the River Moth.

At breakfast, he even told Rebecca that perhaps he had been wrong and they should have a child. Rebecca hugged him, and told him they should wait to talk about it until after he had recovered from his grandmother's death. When she did not ask him about the funeral arrangements, he wondered if she knew he had lied to her. On his way out the door, he held her close and kissed her. Her lips tasted of honey from the toast. Her eyes were, as ever, a mystery.

Once at work, Bristlewing blissfully absent, Hoegbotton searched the store for any sign of mushrooms. Donning long gloves and a mask, he spent most of his time in the old dining room, scuffing his knees to examine the underside of the table, cleaning every surface. The fungus embedded in the mirror had lost its appearance of renewed vigor. Nevertheless, he took an old toothbrush and knife and spent half an hour gleefully scraping it away.

Then, divesting himself of mask and gloves, he went through the same routines with his ledgers as in the past, this time reading the entries aloud since Bristlewing was not there to frown at him for doing so. Fragments of disturbing images fluttered in his mind like caged birds, but he ignored them, bending himself to his routine that he might allow himself no other thoughts.

By noon, the rain had turned to light hail, discouraging many erstwhile customers. Those who did enter the store alighted like crows fleeing bad weather, shaking their raincoat-and-umbrella wings and unlikely to buy anything.

By one o'clock, he had made very little. It didn't matter. It was almost liberating. He was beginning to think he had escaped great danger. Nor did he believe that Sporlender had told anyone.

But at two o'clock, his spirits still high, Hoegbotton received a shock when a grim-faced member of the city's security forces entered the store. The man was in full protective gear from head to foot, a grey mask covering his entire face except for his eyes. What could they know? It wasn't time for an inspection. Had Sporlender talked after all? Hoegbotton scratched at his wounded palm.

'How can I help you?' he asked.

The man stared at him for a moment, then said, 'I'm looking for a purse for my mother's birthday.'

Hoegbotton burst out laughing and had to convince the man it was not directed at him.

No one entered the store for half an hour after the man left. Hoegbotton had worked himself into a fever pitch of calm by the time a messenger arrived around three o'clock: a boy on a bicycle, pinched and drawn, wearing dirty clothes, who knocked at the door and waited for Hoegbotton to arrive before letting an envelope flutter to the welcome mat outside the door. The boy pulled his bicycle back to the sidewalk and pedaled away, ringing his bell.

Hoegbotton, softly singing to himself, leaned down to pick up the envelope. He opened it. The letter inside read, in a spidery scrawl:

Thank you, Robert, for your very fine gift, but your bird has flown away home. I couldn't keep such a treasure. My regards to your wife. – John Ungdom.

Hoegbotton stared at the note, chuckling at the sarcasm. Read it again, a frown closing his lips. *Flown away home.* Read it a third time, his stomach filling with stones. *My regards to your wife.*

He dropped the note, flung on his raincoat, and, not bothering to lock the store behind him, ran out onto the street, into the blinding rain. He headed up Albumuth Boulevard, through the Bureaucratic Quarter, toward home. He felt as if he were running in place. Every pedestrian hindered him. Every horse and cart blocked his path. As the rain came down harder, it beat a rhythmic message into Hoegbotton's shoulders. The raindrops sounded like the tapping claws of something demonic. Through the haze, the dull shapes of buildings became landmarks to anchor his staggering progress. Passersby stared at him as if he were crazy.

By the time he reached the apartment building lobby, his sides ached and he was drenched in sweat. He had fallen repeatedly on the slick pavement and bloodied his hands. He took the stairs three at a time, ran down the hallway to the apartment shouting 'Rebecca!'

The apartment door was ajar. He tried to catch his breath, bending over as he slowly pushed the door open. A line of white mushrooms ran through the hallway, low to the ground, their gills stained red. Where his hand held the door, fungus touched his fingers. He recoiled, straightened up.

'Rebecca?' he said, staring into the kitchen. *No one.* The inside of the kitchen window was covered in purple fungus. A cane lay next to the coat rack, a gift from his father. He took it and walked into the apartment, picking his way between the white mushrooms as he pulled the edge of his raincoat up over his mouth. The doorway to the living room was directly to his left. He could hear nothing, as if his head were stuffed with cloth. Slowly, he peered around the doorway.

The living room was aglow with fungi, white and purple, green and yellow. Shelves of fungi jutted from the walls. Bottle-shaped mushrooms, a deep burgundy, wavering like balloons, were anchored to the floor. Hoegbotton's palm burned fiercely. Now he was in the dream, not before.

The cage stood on the coffee table, the cover drawn aside, the door open. Next to the cage lay another alabaster hand. This did not surprise him. It hardly registered. For, beyond the table, the doors to the balcony had been thrown wide open. Rebecca stood on the balcony, in the rain, her hair slick and bright, her eyes dim. Strewn around her, as if in tribute, the strange growths that had long ago claimed the balcony: orange strands whipping in the winds, transparent bulbs that stood rigid, mosaic patterns of gold-green mold imprinted on the balcony's corroded railing. Beyond: the dark grey shadows of the city, dotted with smudges of light.

Rebecca was looking down at... nothing... her hands held out before her as if trying to touch something.

'Rebecca!' he shouted. Or thought he shouted. His mouth was tight and dry. He began to walk across the living room, the mushrooms pulling against his shoes, his pants, the air alive with spores. He blinked, sneezed, stopped just short of the balcony. Rebecca had still not looked up. Rain splattered against his boots.

'Rebecca,' he said, afraid that she would not hear him, that the distance between them was somehow too great. 'Come away from there. It isn't safe.' She was shivering. He could see her shivering.

Rebecca turned toward him and smiled. 'Isn't safe? You did this yourself, didn't you? Opened the balcony for me before you left this morning?' She frowned. 'But then I was puzzled. You had the cage sent back even though Mrs. Willis said we couldn't keep pets.'

'I didn't open the balcony. I didn't send back the cage.' His boots were tinged green. His shoulders ached.

'Well, someone brought it here – and I opened it. I was bored. The flower vendor was supposed to come and take me to the market, but he didn't.'

'Rebecca, come away from the balcony.' His

words were dull, unconvincing, even to himself. A lethargy had begun to envelop his body.

'I wish I knew what it was,' she said. 'You said it was a lizard. But it isn't. Can you see it? It's right here – in front of me.'

He started to say no, he couldn't see it, but then he realized he could see it. He was gasping from the sight of it. He was choking from the sight of it. Blood trickled down his chin where he had bitten into his lip. All the courage he had built up for Rebecca's sake melted away.

'Come here, Rebecca,' he managed to say.

'Yes. Okay,' she said in a small voice, as if his tone had finally gotten to her.

Tripping over fungi, she walked into the apartment. He met her at the coffee table, drew her against him, whispered into her ear, 'You need to get out of here, Rebecca. I need you to go downstairs. Find Mrs. Willis. Have her send for enforcers.' Her hair was wet against his face. He stroked it gently.

'You're scaring me,' she whispered back, arms thrown around him. 'Come with me.'

'I will, Rebecca. Rebecca, I will. In just a minute. But now, I need you to leave.' He was trembling from the horror of the thought that he might never say her name again and relief, because now he knew why he loved her.

Then her weight was gone as she moved past him to the door and, perversely, his burden returned to him.

The thing had not moved from the balcony. It was not truly invisible but camouflaged itself by perfectly matching its background. The bars of a cage. The spaces between the bars. A perch. He could only glimpse it now because it could not adjust quickly enough to the raindrops that fell upon it.

Hoegbotton walked out onto the balcony. The rain felt good on his face. His legs were numb so he lowered himself into an old rotting chair that they had never bothered to take off the balcony. While the thing watched, he sat there, staring between the bars of the railing out into the city. The rain trickled through his hair. He tried not to look at his hands, which were tinged green. He tried to laugh, but it came out as a rasping gurgle. The thought came to him that he must still be back in the mansion with the woman and the boy, that he had never really left, because, honestly, how could you escape such horror? How could anyone escape something like that?

The thing padded up to him on its quiet feet and sang to him. Because it no longer mattered, Hoegbotton turned to look at it. He choked back a sob. He had not expected this. It was beautiful. Its single eye, so like Rebecca's eyes, shone with an unearthly light, phosphorescent flashes darting across it. Its mirror skin shimmered with the rain. Its mouth, full of knives, smiled in a way that did not mean the same thing as a human smile. This was as close as he could get, he knew now, staring into that beautiful eye. This was as close. Maybe there was something else, something beyond. Maybe there was a knowledge still more secret than this knowledge, but he would never experience it.

The thing held out a clawed hand and, after a time, Hoegbotton took it in his own.

THE BEAUTIFUL GELREESH

Jeffrey Ford

Jeffrey Ford (1955–) is a highly respected US writer from New Jersey whose story 'The Delicate' appeared earlier in this volume. In his best work, Ford makes the familiar unfamiliar, leading the reader into new territory. Ford is known for highly personal, beautifully told stories that reflect both genre and literary influences. But 'The Beautiful Gelreesh' (2003), which first appeared in Jeff VanderMeer's anthology *Album Zutique #1*, primarily reflects the strange as filtered through a Decadent sensibility. It's a cruel and pointed tale that is matter-of-fact in that cruelty, and would have fit well within the certain Belgian traditions of the weird.

His facial fur was a swirling wonder of blond and blue with highlights the deep orange of a November sun. It covered every inch of his brow and cheeks, the blunt ridge of his nose, even his eyelids. When beset by a bout of overwhelming sympathy, he would twirl the thicket of longer strands that sprouted from the center of his forehead. His bright silver eyes emitted invisible beams that penetrated the most guarded demeanors of his patients and shed light upon the condition of their souls. Discovering the essence of an individual, the Gelreesh would sit quietly, staring, tapping the black enamel nails of his hirsute hands together in an incantatory rhythm that would regulate the heartbeat of his visitor to that of his own blood muscle.

'And when, may I ask, did you perceive the first inklings of your despair?' he would say with a sudden whimper.

Once his question was posed, the subject was no longer distracted by the charm of his prominent incisors. He would lick his lips once, twice, three times, with diminishing speed, adjusting the initiate's respiration and brain pulse. Then the loveliness of his pointed ears, the grace of his silk fashions would melt away, and his lucky interlocutor would have no choice but to tell the truth, even if in her heart of hearts she believed herself to be lying.

'When my father left us,' might be the answer.

'Let us walk, my dear,' the Gelreesh would suggest.

The woman or man or child, as the case might be, would put a hand into the warm hand of the heart's physician. He would lead them through his antechamber into the hallway and out through a back entrance of his house. To walk with the Gelreesh, matching his languorous stride, was to partake in a slow, stately procession. His gentle direction would guide one down the garden path to the hole in the crumbling brick and mortar wall netted with ivy. Before leaving the confines of the wild garden, he might pluck a lily to be handed to his troubled charge.

The path through the woods snaked in great loops around stands of oak and maple. Although the garden appeared to be at the height of summer life, this adjacent stretch of forest, leading toward the sea, was forever trapped in autumn. Here, just above the murmur of the wind and just below the rustle of red and yellow leaves, the Gelreesh would methodically pose his questions designed to fan the flames of his companion's anguish. With each troubled answer, he would respond with phrases he was certain would keep that melancholic heart drenched in a black sweat. 'Horrible,' he would say in the whine of a dog dreaming. 'My dear, that's ghastly.' 'How can you go on?' 'If I were you I would be weeping,' was one that never failed to turn the trick.

When the tears would begin to flow, he'd reach into the pocket of his loose-fitting jacket of paisley design for a handkerchief stitched in vermillion, bearing the symbol of a broken heart. Handing it to his patient, he would again continue walking and the gentle interrogation would resume.

An hour might pass, even two, but there was no rush. There were so many questions to be asked and answered. Upon finally reaching the edge of the cliff that gave a view outward of the boundless ocean, the Gelreesh would release the hand of his subject and say with tender conviction, 'And so, you see, this ocean must be for you a representation of the overwhelming, intractable dilemma that gnaws at your heart. You know without my telling you that there is really only one solution. You must move toward peace, to a better place.'

'Yes, yes, thank you,' would come the response followed by a fresh torrent of tears. The handkerchief would be employed, and then the Gelreesh would kindly ask for it back.

'The future lies ahead of you and the troubled past bites at your heels, my child.'

Three steps forward and the prescription would be filled. A short flight of freedom, a moment of calm for the tortured soul, and then endless rest on the rocks below surrounded by the rib cages and skulls of fellow travelers once pursued by grief and now cured.

The marvelous creature would pause and dab a tear or two from the corners of his own eyes before undressing. Then, naked but for the spiral pattern of his body's fur, he would walk ten paces to the east where he kept a long rope tied at one end to the base of a mighty oak growing at the very edge of the cliff. His descent could only be described as acrobatic, pointing to a history with the circus. When finally down among the rocks, he would find the corpse of the new immigrant to the country without care and tidily devour every trace of flesh.

Later, in the confines of his office, he would compose a letter in turquoise ink on yellow paper, assuring the loved ones of his most recent patient that she or he, seeking the solace of a warm sun and crystal sea, had booked passage for a two-year vacation on the island of Valshavar – a paradisiacal atoll strung like a bead on the necklace of the equator. *Let not the price of this journey trouble your minds, for I, understanding the exemplary nature of the individual in question, have decided to pay all expenses for their escape from torment. In a year or two, when next you meet them, they will appear younger, and in their laughter you will feel the warmth of the tropical sun. With their touch, your own problems will vanish as if conjured away by island magic.* This missive would then be rolled like a scroll, tied fast with a length of green ribbon, and given into the talon of a great horned owl to be delivered.

And so it was that the Gelreesh operated, from continent to continent, dispensing his exquisite pity and relieving his patients of their unnecessary mortal coils. When suspicion arose to the point where doubt began to negate his beauty in the eyes of the populace, then, by dark of night, he would flee on all fours, accompanied by the owl, deep into the deepest forest, never to be seen again in that locale. The pile of bones he'd leave behind was undeniable proof of his treachery, but the victims' families preferred to think of their loved ones stretched out beneath a palm frond canopy on the pink beach of Valshavar, being fed peeled grapes by a monkey valet. This daydream in the face of horror would deflate all attempts at organizing a search party to hunt him down.

Although he would invariably move on, setting up a practice in a new locale rich in heavy hearts and haunted minds, something of him would remain behind in the form of a question, namely, 'What was The Beautiful Gelreesh?' Granted, there were no end of accounts of his illusory form – everything from that of a dashing cavalry officer with waxed mustache to the refined blond impertinence of a symphony conductor. He reminded one young woman whom he had danced with at a certain town soiree as being a blend of her father, her boss, and her older brother. In fact, when notes were later compared, no two could agree on the precise details of his splendor.

He was finally captured during one of his escapes, found with his leg in a fox trap only a mile from the village he had last bestowed his pity upon. This beast in pain could not fully concentrate on creating the illusion of loveliness, and the incredulous chicken farmer who discovered him writhing in the bite of the steel jaws witnessed him shifting back and forth between suave charm and gnashing horror. The poor farmer was certain he had snared the devil. A special investigator was sent to handle the case. Blind and somewhat autistic, the famous detective, Gal de Gui, methodically put the entire legacy together as if it was a child's jigsaw puzzle. Of course, in the moments of interrogation by de Gui, the Gelreesh tried to catch him up with a glamorous illusion. The detective responded to this deception with a yawn. The creature later told his prison guards that de Gui's soul was blank as a white wall and perfect. De Gui's final comment on the Gelreesh was, 'Put down some newspaper and give him a bone. Here is the classic case of man's best friend.'

It was when the Gelreesh related his own life story to the court, eliciting pity from a people who previously desired his, that he allowed himself to appear as the hominid-canine entity that had always lurked behind his illusion. As the tears filled the eyes of the jury, his handsome visage wavered like a desert mirage and then lifted away to reveal fur and fangs. No longer were his words the mellifluous susurrations of the sympathetic therapist, but now came through as growling dog-talk in a spray of spittle. Even the huge owl that sat on his shoulder in the witness stand shrunk and darkened to become a grackle.

As he told it, he had been born to an aristocratic family, the name of which everyone present would have known, but he would not mention it for fear of bringing reprisals down upon them for his actions. Because of his frightening aspect at birth, his father accused his mother of bestiality. The venerable patriarch made plans to do away with his wife, but she saved him the trouble by poisoning herself with small sips of opium and an arsenic pastry of her own recipe. The strange child was named Rameau after a distant relation on the mother's side, and sent to live in a newly constructed barn on the outskirts of the family estate. At the same time that the father ordered the local clergy to try to exorcise the beast out of him, there was a standing order for the caretaker to feed him nothing but raw meat. As the Gelreesh had said on the witness stand, 'My father spent little time thinking about me, but when he did, the fact of my existence twisted his thinking so that it labored pointlessly at cross-purposes.'

The family priest taught the young Rameau how to speak and read, so that the strange child could learn the Bible. Through this knowledge of language he was soon able to understand the holy man's philosophy, which, in brief, was that the world was a ball of shit adrift in a sea of sin and the sooner one passed to heaven the better. As the Gelreesh confessed, he took these lessons to heart, and so later in life when he helped free his patients' souls from excremental bondage, he felt he was actually doing them a great favor. It was from that bald and jowly man of God that the creature became acquainted with the power of pity.

On the other hand, the caretaker who daily brought the beef was a man of the world. He was very old and had traveled far and wide. This kindly aged vagabond would tell the young Rameau stories of far-off places – islands at the equator and tundra crowded with migrating elk. One day, he told the boy about a fellow he had met in a far-off kingdom that sat along the old Silk Road to China. This remarkable fellow, Ibn Sadi was his name, had the power of persuasion. With subtle movements of his body, certain tricks of respiration in accordance with that of his audience, he could make himself invisible or appear as a beautiful woman. It was an illusion, of course, but to the viewer it seemed as real as the day. 'What was his secret?' asked Rameau. The old man leaned in close to the boy's cage and whispered, 'Listen to the rhythm of life and, when you look, do not accept but project. Feel what the other is feeling and make what they have felt what you feel. Speak only their own desire to them in a calm, soft voice, and they will see you as beautiful as they wish themselves to be.'

The Gelreesh had time, days on end, to mull over his formula for control. He worked at it and tried different variations, until one day he was able to look into the soul of the priest and discover what it was – a mouse nibbling a wedge of wooden cheese. Soon after, he devised the technique of clicking together his fingernails in order to send out a hypnotic pulse, and with this welded the power of pity to the devices of the adept from the kingdom along the old Silk Road. Imagine the innate intelligence of this boy they considered a beast. A week following, he had escaped. For some reason, the priest had opened the cage, and, for his trouble, was found by the caretaker to have been ushered into the next and better world minus the baggage of his flesh.

The jury heard the story of the Gelreesh's wanderings and the perfection of his art, how he changed his name to that of a certain brand of Mediterranean cigarettes he had enjoyed. 'I wanted to help the emotionally wounded,' he had said to his accusers, and all grew sympathetic, but when they vented their grief for his solitary life and saw his true form, they unanimously voted for his execution. Just prior to accepting, against his will, the thirty bullets from the rifles of the firing squad marksmen, the Gelreesh performed a spectacular display of metamorphosis, becoming, in turn, each of his executioners. Before the captain of the guard could shout the order for the deadly volley, the beautiful one became, again, himself, shouted, 'I feel your pain,' and begged for all in attendance to participate in devouring him completely once he was dead. This final plea went unheeded. His corpse was left to the dogs and carrion birds. His bones were later gathered and sent to the Museum of Natural Science in the city of Nethit. The grackle was released into the wild.

Once he had been disposed of and the truth had been circulated, it seemed that everyone on all continents wanted to claim some attachment to the Gelreesh. For a five-year period there was no international figure more popular. My god, the stories told about him: women claimed to have had his children, men claimed they were him or his brother or at least the son of the caretaker who gave him his first clues to the protocol of persuasion. Children played Gelreesh, and the lucky tyke who got to be his namesake retained for the day ultimate power in the game. An entire branch of psychotherapy had sprung up called Non-Consumptive Gelreeshia, meaning that the therapists swamped their patients with pity but had designs not on the consumption of their flesh, merely their bank accounts. There were studies written about him, novels and plays and an epic poem entitled *Monster of Pity*. The phenomenon of his popularity had given rise to a philosophical reevaluation of *Beauty*.

Gelreesh mania died out in the year of the great comet, for here was something even more spectacular for people to turn their attention to. With the promise of the end of the world, mankind had learned to pity itself. Fortunately or unfortunately, however one might see it, this spinning ball of shit, this paradisiacal Valshavar of planets, was spared for another millennium in which more startling forms of anomalous humanity might spring up and lend perspective to the mundane herd.

And now, ages hence, recent news from Nethit concerning the Gelreesh. Two years ago, an enterprising graduate student from Nethit University, having been told the legends of the beautiful one when he was a child, went in search through the basement of the museum to try to uncover the box containing the creature's remains. The catacombs that lay beneath the imposing structure are vast. The records kept as to what had been stored where have been eaten by an unusual mite that was believed to have been introduced into the environs of the museum by a mummy brought back from a glacier at the top of the world. Apparently, this termitic flea species awoke in the underground warmth and discovered its taste for paper, so that now the ledgers are filled with sheets of lace, more hole than text.

Still, the conscientious young man continued to search for over a year. His desire was to study the physiological form of this legend. Eventually, after months of exhaustive searching, he came upon a crate marked with grease pencil: *Gelreesh*. Upon prying open the box, he found inside a collection of bones wrapped in a tattered garment of maroon silk. There was also a handkerchief bearing the stitched symbol of a broken heart. When he uncovered the bones, he was shocked to find the skeleton of a very large bird instead of a mutant human. A professor of his from the university determined upon inspection that these were indeed the remains of a great horned owl.

THE TOWN MANAGER

Thomas Ligotti

Thomas Ligotti (1953–) is an iconic American writer of weird short fiction whose *oeuvre* has been as ground-breaking as, if not always as well-acknowledged as, that of Edgar Allan Poe, Franz Kafka, and H. P. Lovecraft. His first collection, *Songs of a Dead Dreamer* (1986), is an outright classic in the field. His subsequent compilation, *The Nightmare Factory* (1996), won both the Bram Stoker Award and the British Fantasy Award. The influence of workplace experiences infused Ligotti's fiction with fresh energy, resulting in the masterpiece *My Work Is Not Yet Done* (2002). 'The Town Manager' (2003) showcases Ligotti in his mature phase. The underlying dark sense of humor is more prevalent in his fiction generally than is acknowledged by most critics.

One gray morning not long before the onset of winter, some troubling news swiftly travelled among us: the town manager was not in his office and seemed nowhere to be found. We allowed this situation, or apparent situation, to remain tentative for as long as we could. This was simply how we had handled such developments in the past.

It was Carnes, the man who operated the trolley which ran up and down Main Street, who initially recognized the possibility that the town manager was no longer with us. He was the first one who noticed, as he was walking from his house at one end of town to the trolley station at the other end, that the dim lamp which had always remained switched on inside the town manager's office was now off.

Of course, it was not beyond all credibility that the light bulb in the lamp that stood in the corner of the town manager's desk had simply burned out or that there had been a short circuit in the electrical system of the small office on Main Street. There might even have been a more extensive power failure that also affected the rooms above the office, where the town manager resided since he had first arrived among us to assume his duties. Certainly we all knew the town manager as someone who was in no way vigilant regarding the state of either his public office or his private living quarters.

Consequently, those of us in the crowd that had gathered outside the town manager's office, and his home, considered both the theory of an expired light bulb and that of an electrical short circuit at some length. Yet all the while, our agitation only increased. Carnes was the one whose anxiety over this matter was the most severe, for the present state of affairs had afflicted him longer than anyone else, if only by a few minutes. As I have already indicated, this was not the first time that we had been faced with such a development. So when Carnes finally called for action, the rest of us soon abandoned our refuge in the theoretical. 'It's time to do something,' said the trolley driver. 'We have to know.'

Ritter, who ran the local hardware store, jimmied open the door to the town manager's office, and several of us were soon searching around inside. The place was fairly neat, if only by virtue of being practically unfurnished. There was simply a chair, a desk, and the lamp on top of the desk. The rest of it was just empty floor space and bare walls. Even the drawers of the desk, as some of the more curious members of our search party discovered, were all empty. Ritter was checking the wall socket into which the lamp's cord was plugged, and someone else was inspecting the fuse box at the back of the office. But these were merely stall tactics. No one wanted to reach under the lamp shade and click the switch to find out whether the bulb had merely burned out or, more ominously, if that place had been given over to darkness by design. The latter action, as all of us were aware, signaled that the tenure of any given town manager was no longer in effect.

At one time, our nexus of public services and functions was a traditional town hall rising up at the south end of Main Street. Rather than a small lamp clinging to the edge of a time-worn desk, that impressive structure was outfitted with a great chandelier. This dazzling fixture served as a beacon assuring us that the town's chief official was still with us. When the town hall fell into decay and finally had to be abandoned, other buildings gave out their illumination – from the upper floors of the old opera house (also vacated in the course of time) to the present storefront office that more recently had served as the center of the town's civic administration. But there always came a day when, without notice to anyone in the town, the light went out.

'He's not upstairs,' Carnes yelled down to us from the town manager's private rooms. At that precise moment, I had taken it upon myself to try the light switch. The bulb lit up, and everyone in the room went mute. After a time, somebody – to this day I cannot recall who it was – stated in a resigned voice, 'He has left us.'

Those were the words that passed through the crowd outside the town manager's office ... until everyone knew the truth. No one even speculated that this development might have been caused by mischief or a mistake. The only conclusion was that the old town manager was no longer in control and that a new appointment would be made, if in fact this had not already been done.

Nonetheless, we still had to go through the motions. Throughout the rest of that gray morning and into the afternoon, a search was conducted. Over the course of my life, these searches were performed with increasingly greater speed and efficiency whenever one town manager turned up missing as the prelude to the installation of another. The buildings and houses comprising our town were now far fewer than in my childhood and youth. Whole sections that had once been districts of prolific activity had been transformed by a remarkable corrosion into empty lots where only a few bricks and some broken glass indicated that anything besides weeds and desiccated earth had ever existed there. During my years of youthful ambition, I had determined that one day I would have a house in a grand neighborhood known as The Hill. This area was still known as such, a designation bitterly retained even though the real estate in question – now a rough and empty stretch of ground – no longer rose to a higher elevation than the land surrounding it.

After satisfying ourselves that the town manager was nowhere to be found within the town, we moved out into the countryside. Just as we were going through the motions when we searched inside the town limits, we continued going through the motions as we tramped through the landscape beyond them. As previously stated, the time of year was close to the onset of winter, and there were only a few bare trees to obstruct our view in any direction as we wandered over the hardening earth. We kept our eyes open, but we could not pretend to be meticulous searchers.

In the past, no town manager had ever been found, either alive or dead, once he had gone missing and the light in his office had been turned off. Our only concern was to act in such a way that would allow us to report to the new town manager, when he appeared, that we had made an effort to discover the whereabouts of his predecessor. Yet this ritual seemed to matter less and less to each successive town manager, the most recent of whom barely acknowledged our attempts to locate the dead or living body of the previous administrator. 'What?' he said after he finally emerged from dozing behind the desk in his office.

'We did the best we could,' repeated one of us who had led the search, which on that occasion had taken place in early spring. 'It stormed the entire time,' said another.

After hearing our report, the town manager merely replied, 'Oh, I see. Yes, well done.' Then he dismissed us and returned to his nap.

'Why do we even bother?' said Leeman the barber when were outside the town manager's office. 'We never find anything.'

I referred him and the others to the section of the town charter, a brief document to be sure, that required 'a fair search of the town and its environs' whenever a town manager went missing. This was part of an arrangement that had been made by the founders and that had been upheld throughout succeeding generations. Unfortunately, nothing in the records that had come to be stored in the new opera house, and were subsequently lost to the same fire that destroyed this shoddily constructed building some years before, had ever overtly stated with whom this arrangement had been made. (The town charter itself was now only a few poorly phrased notes assembled from recollections and lore, although the specifics of this rudimentary document were seldom disputed.) At the time, no doubt, the founders had taken what seemed the best course for the survival and prosperity of the town, and they forged an arrangement that committed their descendants to this same course. There was nothing extraordinary about such actions and agreements.

'But that was years ago,' said Leeman on that rainy spring afternoon. 'I for one think that it's time to find out just who we're dealing with.'

Others agreed with him. I myself did not disagree. Nonetheless, we never did manage to broach the subject with the old town manager. But as we walked across the countryside on that day so close to the onset of winter, we talked among ourselves and vowed that we would pose certain questions to the new town manager, who usually arrived not long after the disappearance or abdication of the previous administrator, sometimes on the very same day.

The first matter we wished to take up was the reason we were required to conduct a futile search for missing town managers. Some of us believed that these searches were merely a way of distracting us, so that the new town manager could take office before anyone had a chance to observe by what means he arrived or from what direction he came. Others were of the opinion that these expeditions did in fact serve some purpose, although what that may have been was beyond our understanding. Either way, we were all agreed that it was time for the town – that is, what there was left of it – to enter a new and more enlightened era in its history. However, by the time we reached the ruined farmhouse, all our resolutions dissolved into the grayness in which that day had been enveloped.

Traditionally, the ruined farmhouse, along with the wooden shed that stood nearby it, marked the point at which we ended our search and returned to town. It was now close to sundown, which would give us just enough time to be back in our homes before dark once we had made a perfunctory inspection of the farmhouse and its shed. But we never made it that far. This time we kept our distance from that farmhouse, which was no more than a jagged and tilting outline against the gray sky, as well as from the shed, a narrow structure of thin wooden planks that someone had hammered together long ago. There was something written across those weathered boards, markings that none of us had ever seen before. They were scored into the wood, as if with a sharp blade. Some of the letters were either missing or unreadable in the places where they were gouged into planks that had separated from one another. Carnes the trolley man was standing at my side.

'Does that say what I think it says,' he said to me, almost in a whisper.

'I think so.'

'And the light inside?'

'Like smoldering embers,' I said concerning the reddish glow that was shining through the wooden slats of the shed.

Having recognized the arrival of the new town manager – from whatever direction and by whatever means he may have come – we all turned away and walked silently toward town, pacing slowly through the gray countryside that day by day was being seized by the coming winter.

Despite what we had come across during our search, we soon reconciled ourselves to it, or at least had reached a point where we no longer openly expressed our anxiety. Did it really matter if, rather than occupying a building on Main Street with a sign that read 'Town Manager' over the door, the one who now held this position chose to occupy a shed whose rotting wooden planks had roughly the same words inscribed upon them with a sharp blade? Things had always been moving in that direction. At one time the town manager conducted business from a suite of offices in the town hall and lived in a fine house in The Hill district of town. Now this official would be working out of a weather-beaten shed next to a ruined farmhouse. Nothing remained the same for very long. Change was the very essence of our lives.

My own situation was typical. As previously mentioned, I had ambitions of owning a residence in The Hill district. For a time I operated a delivery business that almost certainly would have led to my attaining this goal. However, by the time the old town manager arrived, I was sweeping the floors at Leeman's barbershop and taking whatever odd jobs came along. In any case, my drive to build up a successful delivery business was all but extinguished once The Hill district had eroded away to nothing.

Perhaps the general decline in the conditions of the town, as well as the circumstances of its residents, could be attributed to poor officiating on the part of our town managers, who in many ways seemed to be less and less able in their duties as one succeeded the other over the years. Whatever apprehensions we had about the new town manager, it could not be said that the old town manager was a model administer. For some time before his term came to an end, he spent the whole of each working day asleep behind his desk.

On the other hand, every town manager could be credited with introducing some element of change, some official project of one kind or another, that was difficult to condemn as wholly detrimental. Even if the new opera house had never been anything but a shoddily constructed firetrap, it nonetheless represented an effort at civic rehabilitation, or seemed to be such. For his part, the old manager was responsible for the trolley which ran up and down Main Street. In the early days of his administration, he brought in workers from outside the town to construct this monument to his spirit of innovation. Not that there had ever been a great outcry for such a conveyance in our town, which could easily be traversed from one end to the other either on foot or by bicycle without causing the least exertion to those of us who were in reasonably good health. Nevertheless, once the trolley had been built, most of us rode the thing at one time or another, if only for the novelty of it. Some people, for whatever reason, made regular use of this new means of transportation and even seemed to depend on it to carry them the distance of only a few blocks. If nothing else, the trolley provided Carnes with regular employment, which he had not formerly enjoyed.

In brief, we had always managed to adapt to the ways of each town manager who had been sent to us. The difficult part was waiting for new administrators to reveal the nature of their plans for the town and then adjusting ourselves to whatever form they might take. This was the system in which we had functioned for generations. This was the order of things into which we had been born and to which we had committed ourselves by compliance. The risk of opposing this order, of plunging into the unknown, was simply too much for us to contemplate for very long. But we did not foresee, despite having witnessed the spectacle of the shed beside the ruined farmhouse, that the town was about to enter a radically new epoch in its history.

The first directive from the new town manager was communicated to us by a torn piece of paper that came skipping down the sidewalk of Main Street one day and was picked up by an old woman, who showed it to the rest of us. The paper was made from a pulpy stock and was brownish in color. The writing on the paper looked as if it had been made with charred wood and resembled the same hand that had written those words across the old boards of the town manager's shed. The message was this: DUSTROY TROLY.

While the literal sense of these words was apparent enough, we were reluctant to act upon a demand that was so obscure in its point and purpose. It was not unprecedented for a new town manager to obliterate some structure or symbol that marked the administration of the one who had come before him, so that the way might be cleared for him to erect a defining structure or symbol of his own, or simply to efface any prominent sign of the previous order and thereby display the presence of a new one. But usually some reason was offered, some excuse was made, for taking this action. This obviously was not the case with the town manager's instruction to destroy the trolley. So we decided to do nothing until we received some enhancement regarding this matter. Ritter suggested that we might consider composing a note of our own to request further instructions. This note could be left outside the door of the town manager's shed. Not surprisingly, there were no volunteers for this mission. And until we received a more detailed notice, the trolley would remain intact.

The following morning the trolley came tooting down Main Street for its first run of the day. However, it made no stops for those waiting along the sidewalk. 'Look at this,' Leeman said to me as he stared out the front window of his barbershop. Then he went outside. I set my broom against a wall and joined him. Others were already standing on the street, watching the trolley until it finally came to rest at the other end of town. 'There was no one at the switch,' said Leeman, an observation that a number of persons echoed. When it seemed that the trolley was not going to make a return trip, several of us walked down the street to investigate. When we entered the vehicle, we found the naked body of Carnes the trolley driver lying on the floor. He had been severely mutilated and was dead. Burned into his chest were the words: DUSTROY TROLY.

We spent the next few days doing exactly that. We also pulled up the tracks that ran the length of the town and tore down the electrical system that had powered the trolley. Just as we were completing these labors, someone spotted another piece of that torn, brownish paper. It was being pushed about by the wind in the sky above us, jerking about like a kite. Eventually it descended into our midst. Standing in a circle around the piece of paper, we read the scrawled words of the message. 'GUD,' it said. 'NXT YUR JBS WULL CHNG.'

Not only did our jobs change, but so did the entire face of the town. Once again, workmen came from outside with orders to perform various kinds of construction, demolition, and decoration that began along Main Street and ultimately extended into the outlying neighborhoods. We had been instructed by the usual means not to interfere with them. Throughout the deep gray winter, they worked on the interiors of the town's buildings. With the coming of spring, they finished off the exteriors and were gone. What they left behind them was a place that did not resemble a town as much as it did a carnival funhouse. And those of us who lived there functioned as sideshow freaks once we had been notified, by the usual method, of exactly how our jobs had changed.

For example, Ritter's Hardware had been emptied of its traditional merchandise and restructured as an elaborate maze of lavatories. Upon entering the front door you immediately found yourself standing between a toilet and a sink. Built into one of the walls of this small room was another door that opened upon another lavatory that was somewhat larger in dimensions. This room had two doors that led to further lavatories, some of which could be reached only by ascending a spiral staircase or walking down a long, narrow corridor. Each lavatory differed somewhat in size and decor. None of the lavatories was functional. The exterior of Ritter's Hardware was a given a new façade constructed of large stone blocks and a pair of fake towers standing on either side of the building and rising some distance above it. A sign above the front door designated the former hardware store as 'Comfort Castle.' Ritter's new job was to sit in a chair on the sidewalk outside his former place of business wearing a simple uniform with the word 'Attendant' displayed in sewn lettering below the left shoulder.

Leeman the barber was even less fortunate in the new career that had been assigned to him. His shop, renamed 'Baby Town,' had been refurbished into a gigantic playpen. Amid stuffed animals and an array of toys, Leeman was required to languish in infants' clothing sized for an adult.

All of the businesses along Main Street had been transformed in some manner, although their tone was not always as whimsical as Ritter's Comfort Castle or Leeman's Baby Town. A number of the buildings appeared simply as abandoned storefronts ... until one explored the interior and discovered that the back room was actually a miniature movie theater where foreign cartoons were projected upon a bare wall or that hidden in the basement was an art gallery filled entirely with paintings and sketches of questionable taste. Sometimes these abandoned storefronts were precisely what they appeared to be, except you would find yourself locked inside once the door had closed, forcing you to exit out the back.

Behind the stores of Main Street was a world of alleys where it was perpetually night, an effect created by tunnel-like arcades enclosing this vast area. Dim lamps were strategically placed so that no stretch of alley was entirely in darkness as you wandered between high wooden fences or brick walls. Many of the alleys ended up in someone's kitchen or living room, allowing an escape back into the town. Some of them kept growing more and more narrow until no further progress was possible and every step leading to this point needed to be retraced. Other alleys gradually altered as one walked along their length, eventually presenting a complete change of scene from that of a small town to one of a big city where screams and sirens could be heard in the distance, although these sounds were only recordings piped in through hidden speakers. It was in just such a vicinity, where painted theatrical backdrops of tall tenement buildings with zig-zagging fire escapes rose up on every side, that I worked at my own new job.

At the terminus of an obscure alley where steam was pumped through the holes of a false sewer grating, I had been stationed in a kiosk where I sold soup in paper cups. To be more accurate, it was not actually soup that I was given to sell but something more like boullion. Behind the counter that fronted my kiosk there was a thin mattress on the floor where I could sleep at night, or whenever I felt like sleeping, since it seemed unlikely that any customers would venture through that labyrinth of alleys so that I might serve them. I subsisted on my own boullion and the water I used to concoct this desolate repast. It seemed to me that the new town manager would finally succeed in the task which his predecessors had but lazily pursued over the years: that of thoroughly bleeding the town of the few resources that had been left to it. I could not have been more wrong in this assessment.

Within a matter of weeks, I had a steady stream of customers lined up outside my boullion concession who were willing to pay an outrageous price for my watery, yellowish liquid. These were not my fellow citizens but people from outside. I noticed that nearly all of them carried folded brochures which either extruded from their pockets or were grasped in their hands. One of these was left behind on the counter that fronted my kiosk, and I read it as soon as business slowed down. The cover of the brochure bore the words 'Have a Fun Time in Funny Town.' Inside were several captioned photographs of the various 'attractions' that our town had to offer to the curious tourist. I was in awe of the town manager's scheme. Not only had this faceless person taken our last penny to finance the most extensive construction project the town had ever seen, from which there was no doubt a considerable amount of kickback involved, but this ingenious boondoggle had additionally brought an unprecedented flood of revenue into our town.

Yet the only one who truly prospered was the town manager. Daily, sometimes hourly, collections were made at each of the town's attractions and concessions. These were carried out by solemn-faced strangers who were visibly armed with an array of weapons. In addition, I noticed that spies had been integrated among the tourists, just to insure that none of us withheld more than a meager allotment of the profits that derived from the town's new enterprise. Nonetheless, whereas we had once had reason to expect nothing less than total impoverishment under the governance of the town manager, it now appeared that we would at least survive.

One day, however, the crowds of tourists began to thin out. In short order, the town's new business dwindled to nothing. The solemn-faced men no longer bothered to make their collections, and we began to fear the worst. Hesitantly, we started to emerge from our places and gathered together on Main Street under a sagging banner that read 'Welcome to Funny Town.'

'I think that's it,' said Ritter, who was still wearing his bathroom attendant's uniform.

'Only one way to be sure,' said Leeman, now back in adult clothes.

Once again we tramped out to the countryside under a gray sky some weeks before the onset of winter. It was approaching dusk, and long before we reached the town manager's shed we could see that no reddish light glowed inside. Nevertheless, we searched the shed. Then we searched the farmhouse. There was no town manager. There was no money. There was nothing.

When the rest of them turned away and began to head back to town, I stayed behind. Another town manager would arrive before long, and I did not wish to see what form the new administration would take. This was the way it had always been – one town manager succeeding another, each of them exhibiting signs of greater degeneracy, as if they were festering away into who knows what. And there was no telling where it would all end. How many others would come and go, taking with them more and more of the place where I had been born and was beginning to grow old? I thought about how different that place had been when I was a child. I thought about my youthful dream of having a home in The Hill district. I thought about my old delivery business.

Then I walked in the opposite direction from the town. I walked until I came to a road. And I walked down that road until I came to another town. I passed through many towns, as well as large cities, doing clean-up work and odd jobs to keep myself going. All of them were managed according to the same principles as my old home town, although I came upon none that had reached such an advanced stage of degeneracy. I had fled that place in hopes of finding another that had been founded upon different principles and operated under a different order. But there was no such place, or none that I could find. It seemed the only course of action left to me was to make an end of it.

Not long after realizing the aforementioned facts of my existence, I was sitting at the counter of a crummy little coffee shop. It was late at night, and I was eating soup. I was also thinking about how I might make an end of it. The coffee shop may have been in a small town or a large city. Now that I think of it, the place stood beneath a highway overpass, so it must have been the latter. The only other customer in the place was a well-dressed man sitting at the other end of the counter. He was drinking a cup of coffee and, I noted, directing a sidelong glance at me every so often. I turned my head toward him and gave him a protracted stare. He smiled and asked if he could join me at my end of the counter.

'You can do whatever you like. I'm leaving.'

'Not just yet,' he said as sat down at the counter stool next to mine. 'What business are you in?'

'None in particular. Why?'

'I don't know. You just seem like someone who knows his way around. You've been some places, am I right?'

'I suppose so,' I said.

'I thought as much. Look, I'm not just interested in chit-chat here. I work on commission finding people like you. And I think you've got what it takes.'

'For what?' I asked.

'Town management,' he replied.

I finished off the last few spoonfuls of my soup. I wiped my mouth with a paper napkin. 'Tell me more,' I said.

It was either that or make an end of it.

THE BROTHERHOOD OF MUTILATION

Brian Evenson

Brian Evenson (1966–) is an influential writer of dark fiction that often seems surreal or Kafkaesque. He is also a translator of French literature and the Chair of the Literary Arts Program at Brown University, as well as a senior editor of the *Conjunctions* literary journal published by Bard College. Evenson's critically acclaimed story collections include *The Wavering Knife* (2004) and *Fugue State* (2009). Strange or absurd happenings occur with frequency in his fiction, and nothing could be odder than the events that occur in 'The Brotherhood of Mutilation' (2003), later expanded into the novel *Last Days* (2009). The novella is a modern classic of weird ritual, mixed with noir and horror.

And if thy right eye offend thee, pluck it out, and cast it from thee… And if thy right hand offend thee, cut it off and cast it from thee…

Matthew 5:29–30

It was only later that he realized the reason they had called him, but by then it was too late for the information to do him any good. At the time, all the two men had told him on the telephone was that they'd seen his picture in the paper, read about his infiltration and so-called heroism and how, even when faced with the man with the cleaver – or *the gentleman with the cleaver* as they chose to call him – he hadn't flinched, hadn't given a thing away. Was it true, they wanted to know, that he hadn't flinched? That he had simply watched the man raise the cleaver and bring it down, his hand suddenly becoming a separate, moribund creature?

He didn't bother to answer. He only sat holding the telephone receiver against his face with his remaining hand and looking at the stump that marked the end of the other arm. The shiny, slightly puckered termination of flesh, flaked and angry at its extreme.

'Who is this?' he finally asked.

The men on the other end of the telephone laughed. 'This is opportunity knocking,' one of them said, the one with the deeper voice. 'Do you want to be trapped behind a desk the rest of your life, Mr. Kline?'

The other voice, the one with a lisp, kept asking questions. Was it true, it wanted to know, that after he had removed his belt with his remaining hand and tightened it as a tourniquet around the stump, he then stood up, turned on one of the burners on the stovetop, and cauterized the wound himself?

'Maybe,' Kline said.

'Maybe to what?' asked Low Voice.

'I have it on authority that you did,' said Lisp. 'Was it electric or gas? I would think electric would be better. But then again it would take a while for electric to warm up.'

'It was a hotplate,' said Kline.

'A hotplate?' said Low Voice. 'Good Lord, a hotplate?'

'So, electric?' asked Lisp.

'I didn't have anything else,' said Kline. 'There was only a hotplate.'

'And then, once cauterized, you turned around and shot him through the eye,' said Lisp. 'Left-handed no less.'

'Maybe,' said Kline. 'But that wasn't in the papers. Who told you that?'

'I have it on authority,' said Lisp. 'That's all.'

'Look,' said Kline. 'What's this all about?'

'Opportunity, Mr. Kline,' said Low Voice. 'I told you already.'

'There's a plane ticket waiting under your name at the airport.'

'Why?' asked Kline.

'Why?' asked Lisp. 'Because we admire you, Mr. Kline.'

'And we'd like your help.'

'What sort of help?'

'We must have *you*, Mr. Kline. Nobody else will do,' said Low Voice.

'No?' said Kline. 'Why should I trust you? And who are you exactly?'

Lisp laughed. 'Mr. Kline, surely by now you realize that you can't trust anyone. But why not take a chance?'

There was no reason to go. It was not a question, as Low Voice had suggested, of either a desk job or their offer, whatever their offer happened to be. The pension he had received was enough to live on. Plus, right after he had lost his hand and cauterized the wound himself and then shot the so-called gentleman with the cleaver through the eye, he had taken the liberty, in recompense for the loss of his hand, of helping himself to a briefcase containing several hundred thousand dollars. This he saw as a profoundly moral act in a kind of moral, biblical, old testament sense: an eye for a hand, and a bag of money thrown in. The fact that the eye had had a brain and a skull behind it was incidental.

So, in short, there was no reason to accept the invitation. Better to stay put, have a lifelike prosthetic made to fit over the stump or, at the very least, wear and learn how to use the hooks that had been given him. Perfect a game of one-handed golf. Purchase a drawerful of prosthetics for all occasions. Buy some cigars. All of life was open to him, he told himself. Opportunity could knock all it liked.

And besides, he was having trouble getting out of bed. Not that he was depressed, but it was hard to get out of bed especially when he remembered that the first thing he'd be doing was trying to brush his teeth left-handed. So, instead, he spent more and more time rubbing the end of his stump, or simply staring at it. It seemed, the termination of it, at once a part of him and not at all part of him, fascinating. Sometimes he still reached for things with his missing hand. Most days he couldn't even put on the hooks. And if he couldn't bring himself to strap on the hooks, how could he be expected to leave the house? And if he didn't leave the house, how could he be expected to go to the airport, let alone pick up the ticket, let alone board a plane?

Things will get better, he told his stump. *Someday we'll leave the house. Things are bound to improve.*

A week after the first call, they called back.

'You missed it,' said Lisp. 'You missed the flight.'

'Is it because of fear?' asked Low Voice. 'Are you afraid of flying?'

'How can you say that to him?' Lisp asked Low Voice. 'A man who cauterizes his own stump isn't going to let a little something like that get to him, is he?'

'So he missed the flight,' said Low Voice. 'He didn't allow for enough time. Got held up at security, maybe.'

'Yes,' said Lisp. 'That's sure to be it.'

They both fell silent. Kline kept the receiver pressed against his ear.

'Well?' asked Lisp.

'Well what?' asked Kline.

'What happened?' asked Lisp.

'I didn't go.'

'He didn't go,' said Low Voice.

'We know that,' said Lisp. 'We know you didn't go, otherwise you'd be here. If you'd gone we wouldn't be calling you there.'

'No,' said Kline.

The phone was silent again. Kline listened to it, staring at the veiled window.

'So?' said Low Voice.

'So what?'

'Goddammit,' said Lisp. 'Do we have to go through this again?'

'Look,' said Kline. 'I don't even know who you are.'

'We already told you who we are,' said Lisp.

'We're opportunity,' said Low Voice. 'And we're knocking.'

'I'm going to hang up,' said Kline.

'He's hanging up,' said Low Voice, his voice sounded worn out and exhausted.

'Wait!' said Lisp. 'No!'

'Nothing personal,' said Kline. 'I'm just not your man.'

Almost as soon as he hung up, the telephone began ringing again. He let it ring. He stood up and walked around the apartment, from room to room. There were four rooms, if you counted the bathroom as a room. In every one he could hear the telephone clearly. It kept ringing.

In the end, he picked up the receiver. 'What?' he said.

'But you *are* our man,' said Lisp, his voice desperate. 'We're just like you.'

'There's the ticket –' said Low Voice.

'– no ticket,' said Kline. 'No opportunity. I'm not your man.'

'Do you think we are acquaintances of the man with the the hatchet?' asked Lisp.

'Cleaver,' said Low Voice.

'We are not acquaintances of the man with the hatchet,' Lisp said. 'We're just like you.'

'And what am I like, exactly?' said Kline.

'Come and see,' said Low Voice. 'Why not come and see?'

'If we wanted to kill you,' Lisp said. 'You'd be dead by now.' It was odd, thought Kline, to be threatened by a man with a lisp.

'Please, Mr. Kline,' said Low Voice.

'We don't want to kill you,' said Lisp. 'Ergo, you're still alive.'

'Aren't you even a little curious, Mr. Kline?' asked Low Voice.

'No,' said Kline. And hung up the telephone.

When the telephone began to ring again, he unplugged it from the wall. Rolling the cord up around it, he packed it away in the closet.

He walked around the house. He would have to go out, he realized, in a day or two, to buy food. He went into the bathroom and took, from the table beside the bed, a notepad and a pen. Going into the kitchen he opened all the doors of the cabinets, the refrigerator, the freezer, and sat thinking.

Eggs, he thought.

Eggs, he wrote, though doing it with his left hand it came out looking like *Esgs*.

My left hand doesn't want eggs, he thought. It wants *esgs*.

He kept writing, his left hand mutilating each word slightly. *What do yo think of that?* he asked his stump. And then wondered if he was speaking to his stump or to his missing hand. Did it matter? he wondered. He wondered what had become of his hand. Probably it had stayed on the table where it had been cut off. Probably it had still been there when the police arrived and had been taken away to be frozen and marked as an exhibit. It was probably still frozen somewhere.

Esgs it is, he thought. And *dread*. And maybe a glass or two of *nelk*.

He stared at the notepad, stopped staring only when he heard water dripping out of the defrosting freezer. He was not sure how much time had passed.

He got up and closed the freezer and fridge, and then stood waiting, listening for the motor to kick in.

A few days went by. His electric razor broke, emitting only a low hum when he plugged it in. He stopped shaving. The food mostly ran out. *I need to get some food*, he thought, but instead drank a glass of sour milk.

He lay in the bed, holding the milk-ghosted glass with one hand, balanced on his chest. He could get up, he thought. He could get out of bed and get up and get out of the house. *I need to get some food,* he thought, and then thought, *later.* There would always be time to get food later. *Esges* and *dread.* At some point he realized that the glass he had thought he was holding he was holding with his missing hand. The glass was balanced on his chest, the stump stationed beside it, a blunt animal. He was not quite sure how the glass had got there.

He was not going out, he realized hours later. The milk still ringing the bottom of the glass had dried into a white sheet and had begun to crack. Perhaps it was days later. He had missed his chance, he realized, and now what little will he had had slipped away and it was too late.

He closed his eyes. When he opened them it was dark outside, so he closed them again.

When he opened them, a pale daylight was leaking into the room through the curtains. Beside him, sitting on kitchen chairs they had dragged into the bedroom, were two men. They were bundled in heavy coats and gloves and scarves despite the warmth of the room.

'Hello, hello,' said the first, his voice bass.

'We knocked,' said the other. His upper lip was mostly missing, a ragged scar in its place; it looked as if the lip had been cut into with a pair of pinking shears. 'We knocked and knocked, but nobody answered. So we let ourselves in. It was locked,' he said, 'but we knew you didn't mean the lock for us.'

When Kline didn't say anything, the one with the torn lip said, 'You remember us? The telephone?' The man lisped on the *us.*

'The telephone,' said Kline, his voice raspy.

The torn-lipped man raised his eyebrows and looked at his companion. 'He's pretending not to remember,' he said.

'Of course you remember,' said the one with the bass voice. 'Opportunity knocking? All that?'

'Ah,' said Kline. 'I'm afraid so.'

'Look at you,' said Torn-Lip. 'Do you want to die in bed?'

'You don't want to die in bed,' said Low Voice.

'We're here to save you,' said Torn-Lip.

'I don't want to be saved,' said Kline.

'He doesn't want to be saved,' said Low Voice.

'Sure he does,' said Torn-Lip. 'He just doesn't know it yet.'

'But I –'

'– Mr. Kline,' said Torn-Lip, 'we have given you every opportunity to be reasonable. Why didn't you take advantage of either of the tickets we left for you?'

'I don't need your ticket,' said Kline.

'When was the last time you ate?' asked Low Voice.

Torn-Lip reached out and prodded Kline's face with a gloved finger. 'Clearly, you are your own worst enemy, Mr. Kline.'

'Depression,' said Low Voice. 'Lassitude, ennui. I so diagnose.'

'Look,' said Kline, struggling to lift himself up a little in the bed. 'I'm going to have to ask you to leave.'

'He sits,' said Torn-Lip.

'Or nearly so. Who says the man doesn't have any fight left to him?'

'That's the spirit,' said Torn-Lip. 'That's the man who can have his hand cut off and not flinch.'

'Come away with us, Mr. Kline.'

'No,' said Kline.

'What can we say to convince you?'

'Nothing,' said Kline.

'Well, then,' said Torn-Lip. 'Perhaps there are means other than words.'

Kline watched as the man grasped one of his gloved hands with the other. He twisted the hand about and levered it downward and the hand came free. Kline felt his stump tingle. The other man, he saw, was doing the same thing. They pulled back their sleeves to show him the bare exposed lumps of flesh in which their forearms terminated.

'You see,' said Torn-Lip, 'just like you.'

'Come with us,' said the other.

'But,' said Kline. 'I don't –'

'He thinks we're asking,' said Torn-Lip, leaning in over the bed, his damaged mouth livid. 'We're not asking. We're telling.'

II

Before he knew it, their hands were screwed back on and they had him out of the bed and were dragging him down the emergency stairwell.

'Wait,' he said. 'My claw.'

'Your claw?'

'For my hand.'

You don't need it, they claimed, and kept pulling him down the stairs.

'Where are you taking me?' he asked.

'He wants to know where we're taking him, Ramse,' said Low Voice.

'To the car,' said Torn-Lip – said Ramse – grunting the words. They came to a landing and Kline felt his own body sway to one side and then steady itself. Ramse was beside him, his head sticking out from under Kline's arm, his torn lips tight. 'Tell him we're going to the car,' Ramse said.

'We're going to the car,' said Low Voice, and Kline looked over to find Low Voice's head under the other arm.

'But,' he said.

'Enough questions,' said Ramse. 'Just try to move your feet. If you have them, may as well use them.'

He looked down and could not see feet, only legs. There was a whispery sound, but it wasn't until they left the landing and started down the next set of stairs and the sound changed to a thumping that he realized it was his own feet dragging. He tried to get them underneath him, but the two men were moving too quickly and all he could do was to nearly trip them all down the stairs.

'Never mind, never mind,' said Ramse. We're almost there.' And indeed, Kline realized, they were pushing through the fire exit door and into full sunlight. There was a car there, long and black with tinted windows. They hustled him into the back of it.

Ramse got in on the driver's side, Low Voice on the other. There was something wrong with the steering wheel, Kline noticed, as if a cup holder had been welded into it. Low Voice opened the glove box, awkwardly groped a candy bar out of it with his artificial hand, passed it back to Kline.

'Eat this,' he said. 'It'll help focus you.'

Kline heard the locks snap down. He took the candy bar, began to strip the wrapper off it. It was almost more than he could manage. In the front, the two men were shucking their coats and hats, piling them on the seat between them. He watched Ramse snap off his artificial hand, glove and all, and drop it atop the pile. Low Voice did the same.

'That's better,' Low Voice said.

Kline ate a little of the candy bar. It was chocolate, something crispy inside it. He chewed. Ramse, he realized, was holding his remaining hand up, toward the other man.

'Gous?' he asked.

'What?' the man said. 'Yes, right,' Gous said. 'Sorry.'

With his single hand he reached out and took Ramse's remaining hand and twisted it. Kline watched the hand circle about and break free. Ramse rubbed his two stumps against each other. Gous reached out and took hold of Ramse's ear, tore it off. It came free, leaving a gaping unwhelked hole behind.

'There,' said Ramse. 'That's better.' He looked at Kline in the rearview mirror, lifted up both stumps. 'Like you,' he said, smiling. 'Only more so.'

They drove, the city slowly dissolving around them and breaking up into fields and trees. Gous kept rummaging in the glove box, passing back food. There was another candy bar, a plastic bag of broken pretzels, a tin of sardines. Kline took a little of each, left what remained on the seat beside him. He was beginning to feel a little more alert. Outside, the sun was high; even through the tinted glass it looked hot outside. They turned right and went up a ramp and entered the freeway, the car quickly gaining speed.

'Where are we?' Kline asked.

'Here we go,' said Gous, ignoring him.

'Smooth sailing from here on out,' said Ramse. 'For a while anyway.'

'But,' said Kline. 'Where, I don't –'

'Mr. Kline,' said Gous. 'Please sit back and enjoy the ride.'

'What else?' asked Kline.

'What else?' said Gous.

'What do you mean what else?' asked Ramse.

'What else comes off?'

'Besides the hands and the ear?' said Ramse. 'Some toes,' he said, 'but they're already off. Three gone from one foot, two from the other.'

'What happened?' asked Kline.

'What do you mean *what happened,* Mr. Kline? Nothing *happened.*'

'We don't do accidents,' said Gous. 'Accidents and acts of God don't mean a thing, unless they're followed later by acts of will. Pretzel?' he asked.

'Your own case was hotly debated,' said Ramse. 'Some wanted to classify it as accident.'

'But it was no accident,' said Gous.

'No,' said Ramse. 'Others argued, successfully, that it was no accident but instead an act of will. But then the question came *An act of will on whose part?* On the part of the gentleman with the hatchet, surely, no denying that, but responsibility can hardly rest solely with him, can it now, Mr. Kline?' He turned a little around as he said it, pivoting his missing ear toward Kline. 'All you had to do was tell him one thing, Mr. Kline, just a lie, and you would have kept your hand. But you didn't say a thing. A matter of will, Mr. Kline. Your will to lose the hand far outweighed your will to retain it.'

Outside the highway had narrowed to a two lane road, cutting through dry scraggled woods, the road's shoulder heaped in dust.

'What about you?' Kline asked Gous.

'Me?' said Gous, blushing. 'Just the hand,' he said. 'I'm still new.'

'Have to start somewhere,' said Ramse. 'We brought him along because the powers that be thought you might be more comfortable with someone like you.'

'He's not like me.'

'You have one amputation, he has one amputation,' said Ramse. 'Yours is a hand, his is a hand. In that sense, he's like you. When you start to look closer, well…'

'I used anesthetic,' said Gous.

'You, Mr. Kline, did not use anesthetic. You weren't given that option.'

'It's frowned upon,' said Gous, 'but not forbidden.'

'And more or less expected for the first several amputations,' said Ramse. 'It makes you exceptional, Mr. Kline.'

Kline looked at the seat next to him, the open tin of sardines, the filets shining in their oil.

'I'm exceptional as well,' said Ramse. 'I've never been anesthetized.'

'He's an inspiration to us all,' said Gous.

'But that you cauterized your wound yourself, Mr. Kline,' said Ramse. 'That makes you truly exceptional.'

'I'd like to get out of the car now,' said Kline softly.

'Don't be ridiculous, Mr. Kline,' said Gous, grinning. 'We're in the middle of nowhere.'

'I could count the number of people who self-cauterize on one finger of one hand,' said Ramse.

'If he had a hand,' said Gous.

'If I had a hand,' said Ramse.

They drove for a while in silence. Kline stayed as still as he could in the back seat. The sun had slid some little way down the horizon. After a while it vanished. The tin of sardines had slid down the seat and were now at an angle, their oil leaking slowly out. He straightened the tin, then rubbed his fingers dry on the floor carpeting. It was hard not to stare at Ramse's missing ear. He looked down at his own stump, looked at Gous' stump balanced on the seat's back. The two stumps were actually quite different, he thought. The end of Gous' was puckered. His own had been puckered and scarred from the makeshift cauterization; after the fact, a doctor had cut a little higher and smoothed it off, planed it. Outside, the trees, already sparse, seemed to vanish almost entirely, perhaps partly because of the gathering darkness but also the landscape was changing. Ramse pushed one of his stumps into the panel and turned on the headlights.

'Eight,' said Ramse, gesturing his head slightly backwards.

'Eight?' asked Kline. 'Eight what?'

'Amputations,' said Ramse. Kline watched the back of his head. 'Of course that doesn't mean a thing,' he said. 'Could be just eight toes, all done under anesthetic, the big toes left for balance. That should hardly qualify for an eight,' he said.

Gous nodded next to him. He held up his stump, looked over the back. 'This counts as a one,' he said. 'But I could have left the hand and cut off all the fingers and I'd be a four. Five if you took the thumb.'

They were waiting for Kline to say something. 'That hardly seems fair,' he offered.

'But which is more of a shock?' asked Ramse. 'A man losing his fingers or a man losing his hand?'

Kline didn't know if he was expected to answer.

'I'd like to get out of the car,' he said.

'So there are eights,' said Ramse, 'and then there are eights.' They came to a curve. Kline watched Ramse post the other hand on the steering wheel for balance, turning the wheel with his cupped stump. 'Personally I prefer a system of minor and major amputations, according to which I'd be a 2/3.

'I prefer by weight,' said Gous. 'Weigh the lopped off organ, I say.'

'But you see,' said Ramse, 'bled or unbled? And doesn't that give a certain advantage to the corpulent?'

'You develop standards,' said Gous. 'Penalties and handicaps.'

'Why do you need me?' asked Kline.

'Excuse me?' asked Ramse.

'He wants to know why we need him,' said Gous.

'That's easy,' said Ramse. 'A crime has been committed.'

'Why me?' asked Kline.

'You have a certain amount of experience in investigation,' said Gous.

'Not investigation exactly, but infiltration,' said Ramse.

'And you don't flinch, Mr. Kline,' said Gous.

'No, he doesn't flinch.'

'But –' said Kline.

'You'll be briefed,' said Ramse. 'You'll be told what to do.'

'But the police –'

'No police,' said Ramse. 'It was hard enough to get the others to agree on you.'

'If it hadn't been for the hand,' said Gous.

'If it hadn't been for the hand,' said Ramse, 'you wouldn't be here. But you're one of us, like it or not.'

III

He woke up when the car stopped before a set of metal gates. It was fully dark outside.

'Almost there,' said Ramse from the front.

The gate opened a little and a small man stepped out, turning pale and white in the overbright halogen glow of the headlights. The man came over to the driver's door. Kline could see he was missing an eye, one closed lid seeming flat and deflated. He was wearing a uniform. Ramse rolled down the window, and the man peered into the car.

'Mr. Ramse,' said the guard. 'And Mr. Gous. Who's in the back?'

'That would be Mr. Kline,' said Ramse. 'Hold up your arm, Mr. Kline,' said Ramse.

Kline lifted his hand.

'No, the other one,' said Ramse.

He lifted the stumped arm and the guard nodded. 'A one?' he asked.

'Right,' said Ramse. 'But self-cauterized.'

The guard whistled. He made his way away from the window and back to the gates, which he drew open wide just enough for the car to pass through. Through the rear window, Kline watched him draw it shut after them.

'Welcome home, Mr. Kline,' said Ramse.

Kline didn't say anything.

They passed a row of houses, turned down a smaller road where the houses were a little more spread out, then down a third smaller tree-lined alley that dead ended in front of a small, two story building. Ramse stopped the car. The three of them climbed out.

'You'll be staying here, Mr. Kline,' said Ramse. 'First floor, second door to the left once you go through the entrance.

'There's probably an hour or two of night left,' he said. 'We'll see you in the morning. For now, why don't you try to get some sleep?'

When he went in, he couldn't figure out how to turn the hall light on so, instead, wandered down the dark hall dragging his hand along the wall, feeling for doorways. His fingers stuttered past one. He lifted his fingers from the wall and brought them near his face. They smelled of dust. He went on until he came to another doorframe, fumbled around for the handle.

Inside, he found a switch. It was a small windowless room, containing a narrow single bed with a thin, ratty blanket. In one corner was a metal cabinet. The floor was linoleum, a streaked blue. The light, he saw, was a naked bulb, hanging from the center of the ceiling. The walls' paint was cracking.

Welcome home, he thought.

He closed the door. There was no lock on it. He opened the cabinet. It was full of stacks of calendars, each month featuring a woman in various states of undress, smiling furiously. He looked at the first picture for some time before realizing the girl was missing one of her thumbs. With each month, the losses became more obvious and more numerous, March losing a breast, July missing both breasts, a hand, and a forearm. The December girl was little more than a torso, her breasts shaved off, wearing nothing but a thin white cloth banner from one shoulder to the opposite hip, reading *Miss Less is More.*

He put the calendar back and closed the cabinet. Turning off the light he lay in the bed, but kept seeing *Miss Less is More*'s face contorted with joy. There was Ramse's face too, his mutilated ear just above the car seatback angling itself toward him. His own stump was tingling. He got up and turned on the light, tried to sleep with it on.

He dreamt that he was sitting at the table again, the gentleman with the cleaver standing before him, cleaver coming down. Only in his dream he wasn't just the man losing his hand but also the man with the cleaver. He watched himself bring the cleaver down and the hand come free and the fingers pulse. The sheared plane of his wrist grew pale and then suddenly puffed, blood pulsing out. He stripped off his belt with his remaining hand and tightened it quickly around his arm until the bleeding slowed and mostly stopped. He watched himself do it, holding the cleaver in his hand. Then he watched himself, pale, holding the belt tight, go to the stove and turn it on, wait for the coils of the burner to smoke and begin to glow. He put his stump down and heard it sizzle and smelt the burnt flesh, and when he lifted the stump away it was smoking. Bits of flesh and blood were stuck to the burner and smouldering.

Then then, with his left hand, face livid with pain, he took out his gun and, left-handed, shot himself through the eye. It was a hell of a thing to watch, a hell of a thing to feel. And as soon as it was over it started again, and kept starting until he forced himself awake.

Gous and Ramse were in the room, the first standing at the open cabinet looking through the calendar, rubbing at his crotch with his stump, the second standing near the bed, looking at Kline.

'Rise and shine,' said Ramse.

Kline sat on the edge of the bed, pulling his pants on awkwardly with stump and arm. Ramse watched. Only when he was done did he say,

'There's new clothes for you.'

'Where?' asked Kline.

'Gous has them,' said Ramse. 'Gous?' he said, louder.

'What?' said Gous, turning stiffly away from the calendar, face red with shame or heat, or perhaps both.

'Clothes, Gous,' said Ramse.

'Oh, right,' said Gous, and picking up a pile of clothing near his feet, threw it to Kline.

Kline stripped out of the clothes he had just put on as Ramse watched. The new clothing consisted of a pair of gray slacks, a white shirt, a red clip-on tie. The buttons weren't easy one-handed, particularly since the shirt was freshly starched, but after the first three it got easier. He tried to leave the tie on the bed, but Ramse stopped him.

'Put it on,' he said.

'Why?'

'I'm wearing one, Gous is wearing one,' said Ramse. And indeed, Kline had failed to notice, their outfits were the same as his: white shirts, gray slacks, red clip-on tie. He found himself wondering how Ramse had managed to put on his shirt by himself. Perhaps he hadn't.

'Look,' said Ramse, once they were out the door and walking down the drive. 'Things are done in certain way here. We hope you'll try to respect that.'

'All right,' said Kline.

'The other thing,' said Ramse. 'The investigation.'

'He's taking you to Borchert,' said Gous.

'I'm taking you to Borchert,' said Ramse. 'He'll tell you about the investigation.'

'Who's Borchert?'

'It's not who's Borchert,' said Ramse, 'but what he is. And what he is is a twelve.'

'A twelve?'

'That's right,' said Gous, then rattled off in a schoolboy's voice, 'Leg, toe, toe, toe, toe, toe, left arm, finger, finger, ear, eye, ear.'

'A twelve,' said Ramse. 'Of course that includes a lot of digits, but when you add in two lopped limps, it's impressive.'

'He's second in command,' said Gous. 'After Aline.'

'I see,' said Kline. 'What's the investigation about?'

'We don't know,' said Gous.

'Borchert will tell you,' said Ramse.

'You don't know?' asked Kline.

'I know a little. I should know more,' said Ramse wistfully. 'I'm an eight. There's no reason to keep me in the dark. Gous is another story.'

'I'm just a one,' admitted Gous.

'He's just a one,' said Ramse, smiling. 'At least for now.'

'I'm a one too,' said Kline.

'That's right,' said Gous to Ramse. 'He's a one but he's going to find out.'

'He's an exception,' said Ramse. 'He's the exception that proves the rule.'

'Why?' asked Kline. They came to a small path cutting away from the road, paved with crushed white shells. Ramse and Gous stepped onto it, Kline followed.

'Yes, why?' asked Gous.

'How the hell should I know,' asked Ramse. 'I'm an eight. They don't always tell me very much. Maybe because he's a self-cauterizer.'

'Listen,' said Kline. 'I'll see Borchert and talk to him, but that's it. I'm not interested in staying.'

'Borchert can be very persuasive,' said Ramse.

'Don't insult Borchert,' said Gous. 'Be polite to him, listen to him, don't talk back.'

'He's a twelve,' said Ramse. 'Plus his leg's amputated at the hip. That's commitment for you, eh?'

He stayed awake for the operation,' said Gous.

'But he had anesthetic,' said Ramse.

'Still,' said Gous.

'What about cauterization?' asked Kline.

'The cauterization?' asked Gous. 'Don't know. Ramse, was he anesthetized for that too?'

'Don't know,' said Ramse. 'Probably. In any case, he didn't self-cauterize.'

'Almost nobody does,' said Gous.

'Really nobody but you,' said Ramse.

The path moved back into trees, descending into a sort of depression. Kline saw, affixed to an old oak, a security camera. Then the path took a sharp curve and started uphill again. It widened into a tree-lined avenue, at the end of which was what looked like an old manor house, or a boarding school, made of gray stone. Kline counted six sets of windows in rows three tall.

They came to the gate, Kline listening to the shells crunching beneath his feet. A guard came out from behind a pillar of the house and stood on the opposite side of the gate, watching them with a single eye.

'What is wanted?' he asked, his hands folded.

'Cut it out,' said Ramse. 'This isn't ceremonial. We're here to see Borchert.'

'Borchert?' said the guard. 'What is wanted?'

'Cut it out,' said Ramse. 'This is Kline.'

'Kline?' said the guard, unfolding his arms to reveal hands shorn of all but a thumb, a forefinger, and a middle finger. He took hold of the key and fitted it to the lock. 'Why didn't you say so?' the guard said. 'Let him enter.'

'Are all the guards missing an eye?' asked Kline.

'Yes,' Gous said happily. 'All of them.'

'They made a pact,' said Ramse, knocking on the door. 'It's a subsect. Whatever else they're missing they cut out the eye once they're initiated. Borchert started down that path,' said Ramse. 'He was a guard initiate, and then gave it up. What his connection to the guards is now isn't quite clear, is mysterious. That's why he's second in command, not first.'

'And the eye's not all,' said Gous.

'No?' said Kline.

'Let's just say that a guard can hit all the high notes and none of the low ones.'

'Well,' said Ramse, 'nobody knows about that for certain except the guards. And they don't discuss it.'

The door was opened by another guard who asked again *What is wanted?* This time Ramse brought his heels together and rattled off what to Kline seemed clearly a memorized, ritual response. *Having been faithful in all things, we come to see he who is even more faithful than we.*

'That is correct,' said the guard. 'And what are the three of you?'

'Two ones,' said Gous. 'And an eight.'

'Which is the eight?'

'I am,' said Ramse.

'You may enter,' said the guard. 'The others may not.'

'But we're here with Kline,' said Ramse. We're bringing Kline to Borchert.'

'Kline?' said the guard. 'We've been waiting for him. He can come in, too, the other one will have to wait outside.'

Kline felt something on his shoulder and looked back to see Gous' stump lying there. 'A pleasure, Mr. Kline,' Gous said. 'Don't forget me.'

'I won't,' said Kline, confused.

The guard ushered them through the door and into a bare, white hall. Before the door closed Kline looked behind him to see Gous on the other side, tilting his head trying to see in. This guard, Kline saw, had only one hand, all the fingers on it shaved away except for thumb and the bottom half of the forefinger.

The guard led them down the white hall, to a door at the end of it, knocked three times.

'You're lucky,' said Ramse.

'Lucky?'

'To come in,' said Ramse. 'Normally a one wouldn't be allowed. There had to be a special dispensation.'

'I don't feel lucky,' said Kline. The guard turned around and looked at him, hard, then turned away, rapped thrice more.

'Don't say that,' whispered Ramse. 'You don't know how hard it was to convince them to bring you.'

The door came open, another guard pushing his face out. Ramse and Kline watched their guard push his face in and whisper to the other. They whispered back and forth a few times then the other guard nodded, opened the door.

'Go ahead,' said the first guard. 'Go through.'

They passed through the door, the other guard shutting it behind them. Behind was a stairwell. The guard led them up it to the third floor, led them down a hall, past three doors, stopped to knock on a fourth. When a muffled voice answered from behind, he opened it, ushered them in.

The room was large, Spartan in furnishing: a bed sitting low to the floor, a low desk, a small bookshelf, a reclining chair. In the latter sat a man wearing a bathrobe. He was missing an arm and a leg, his robe cut away and left open at shoulder and hip to reveal the planed surfaces, hardly stumps at all. The other arm and leg were intact, though the hand was missing all but two of its fingers, the foot all but the big toe. Both ears, too, had been cut off, leaving only a hole and a shiny patch of flesh on either side of the head. One eyelid was open, revealing a piercing eye, the other closed but deflated, the eye under it clearly absent.

'Ah,' said the man. 'Mr. Kline, I presume. I had assumed you had refused our invitation several weeks ago.'

'It seems not,' said Kline.

'He's delighted to be here,' said Ramse, quickly. 'It's a true pleasure for him, as well as for me, sir, to be granted audience with –'

'– I wonder,' said Borchert, raising his voice. 'Mr. Ramse, isn't it?'

'Yes,' said Ramse, 'I'm –'

'I wonder, Mr. Ramse, if you'd mind waiting outside. Mr. Kline and I have private matters to discuss.'

'Oh,' said Ramse, looking crestfallen. 'Yes, of course.'

'An eight,' said Borchert, once Ramse was gone, 'though you wouldn't know it to look at him. What does he mean wearing shoes in here? Where are his manners?'

'Do you want me to take my shoes off?'

'Are you missing any toes?'

'No,' said Kline.

'There's no point then, is there?' said Borchert. 'But come a little closer and show me your stump.'

Kline went closer. He held his missing hand out; Borchert took it deftly between his remaining fingers and thumb and pulled it forward until it was only inches from his face, his eye dilating.

'Yes, nicely done,' said Borchert. 'Quite profession. But I'd thought you were a self-cauterizer?'

'I was,' said Kline. 'It was redone afterwards.'

'What a shame,' said Borchert, smiling thinly.

'Still, a good start nonetheless.' He let go of Kline's hand, readjusted himself in his chair. 'You're welcome to sit down,' he said. 'Unfortunately I'm in the only chair. Do feel free to help yourself to the floor.'

Kline looked about him, finally settling to the floor, posting his stump against it and bringing the rest of his body down.

'There,' said Borchert. 'That's better now, isn't it. I suppose you're wondering why you're here.'

'The investigation,' said Kline.

'The investigation,' said Borchert. 'That's right. You want the details.'

'No,' said Kline.

'No?'

'I'm wondering how I can arrange to leave.'

'Leave me?' said Borchert. 'You find me offensive somehow?'

'Leave this whole place.'

'But why, Mr. Kline?' said Borchert, smiling. 'This is paradise.'

Kline did not say anything.

Borchert let his smile fade slowly, artificially. 'I was against bringing you,' he said. 'I don't mind telling you. *No outsiders* has always been my policy, and no recruiting. But some of the others were impressed by this story of self-cauterization. Perhaps it's nothing more than a story, Mr. Kline?'

'No,' said Kline. It's true.'

'But why, Mr. Kline? Surely you could have easily applied a tourniquet and called a doctor?'

'Then I wouldn't have been able to kill the man who cut my hand off.'

'The so-called gentleman with the cleaver,' said Borchert, nodding. 'But surely you could have killed the fellow later?'

'No,' said Kline. 'It was either him or me, right then. I cauterized the arm to distract him. He couldn't quite take in what I was doing, which game me a certain advantage. Otherwise, he would have shot me.'

'Yet you could take it in, Mr. Kline, even though it was your own arm. And afterwards your remaining hand was steady enough to shoot him through the eye. You were a God for a moment, even if you didn't realize it. I suspect you tapped into something without knowing it, Mr. Kline. An ecstacy. I almost begin to suspect we have something to learn from you.'

'I wouldn't think so,' said Kline.

'Modest, too,' said Borchert. 'You know what you've done to our community? You've started something, Mr. Kline. Everybody is talking about self-cauterization. The creed is threatening to transform. Schism. No self-cauterizers yet, but it's only a matter of time, and then smoothly cut surfaces,' he said, gesturing at his missing arm and leg, 'are likely to give way to hard-puckered and rippled stumps, ugly and dappled. A little bit rough trade, no? I can't say it's to my taste, Mr. Kline, but perhaps I'm becoming antiquated.'

'Perhaps,' said Kline.

Borchert looked at him sharply. 'I doubt it,' he said. 'In any case, Mr. Kline, despite my personal objections to you, now that you are here, I can't afford to let you go. Too much is at stake. I send you out of here without an investigation and we'll have schism.'

'I'm not staying,' said Kline.

'You leave and I'll have to kill you,' said Borchert. 'For the good of the faith. Nothing personal.'

Kline looked at his hand, then looked at Borchert.

'Wouldn't you like to at least hear about it, Mr. Kline? Before deciding if it's worth dying for?'

'All right,' said Kline. 'Why not?'

'A crime has been committed. You are not to discuss the specific details of this crime with anyone with less than ten amputations. Do I make myself clear?'

'Yes,' said Kline.

'And in any case, Mr. Kline, I expect you to be discreet. This is a somewhat precarious society. The only one who knows the full extent of this crime is myself and, in a moment, yourself.'

Kline just nodded.

'In short, we've had a murder,' said Borchert.

'A murder,' said Kline. 'Murder's not exactly my speciality.'

'No,' said Borchert. 'But you're all we have.'

'May I ask who was murdered?'

'A man called Aline,' said Borchert. 'He organized this community, this brotherhood. A prophet, a visionary. Both arms lopped off at the shoulder, legs gone, penis severed, ears removed, eyes removed, tongue cut partly out, teeth removed, lips peeled away, nipples sliced off, buttocks gone. Anything that could be removed removed. A true visonary. Murdered.'

'How was he murdered?'

'Someone broke open his sternum, chopped his heart out.'

'Do you have any idea who –'

'– no,' said Borchert. 'And we'd like the heart back if possible.'

'Why do you need the heart back?'

Borchert smiled. 'Mr. Kline,' he said. 'We're a brotherhood. This is a religion. His heart means something to us.'

Kline shrugged.

'I don't expect you to understand,' said Borchert. 'You're an outsider. But perhaps you'll understand one day.' He moved awkwardly in his chiar. 'By the way,' he said, 'what became of your own hand?'

'I don't know,' said Kline.

'You don't know,' said Borchert. 'Imagine that. Colonel Pierre Souvestre's leg was buried in a full blown state funeral when he lost it in 1917. Your hand, on the other hand, is probably rotting in a pile of garbage somewhere.'

Kline stood up. 'When can I see the body?' he asked.

Borchert sighed. 'I've told you everything you need to know about it,' he said. 'There's no need to to see the body.'

'You don't have the body anymore?'

'No,' said Borchert. 'It's not that.'

'Then what?'

'His body is sacred to us,' said Borchert. 'Even without the heart.'

'Are there any witnesses?'

'You're not to approach anyone with more than ten amputations without an invitation.'

Kline looked about the room. 'That makes the investigation a little difficult.'

'I'm sure you'll manage,' Borchert said.

'Can I at least see the room?'

'Yes,' said Borchert, slowly. 'I suppose we could manage that.'

'So I'm to investigate a murder without seeing a body and without being able to interview witnesses or suspects?'

'Don't exaggerate, Mr. Kline. Just don't break in on anyone unannounced. Talk to me and I'll make arrangements.'

Turning, Kline made for the door.

'Oh, and one more thing, Mr. Kline,' said Borchert.

'What's that?' asked Kline.

Borchert held up one of his two remaining fingers. 'As an act of good faith,' he said, 'to show you I have nothing against self-cauterization, that I'm an open-minded man, I'd like your help removing the upper joint of this.'

'You want me to cut it off.'

'Just the top joint,' Borchert said. 'Little more than a symbolic gesture, a pact if you will. You'll find a cleaver in the top drawer,' he said, gesturing to the back of the room with a flick of his head. 'There's a stove there as well, Mr. Kline, built into the counter, which I'll ask you to turn on.'

Kline looked at him, looked into the back of the room, shrugged. 'Why not?' he asked.

Opening the drawer, he removed the cleaver. He placed it on the counter, resting it on a butcher's block, the wood of which was laced with dozens of thin crosshatched marks. He went back to Borchert, and dragged his chair back, set it flush against the counter.

'You don't know what an honor this is for you,' said Borchert. 'It's quite a gesture of intimacy. Almost anyone here would kill for it. A shame it's wasted on you.'

'I'll take your word for it,' said Kline.

He took Borchert by the wrist and placed the hand on the butcher's block. He folded the index finger back into Borchert's palm, leaving the remaining finger, the middle finger, angled down against the butcher's block. The burner had warmed now and was glowing red, smoking slightly. He rested his stump just above Borchert's knuckle and held the finger steady, pushed it down slightly so that he first joint was firmly against the wood.

'Just the first joint?' he asked.

Borchert smiled. 'For now,' he said.

He lifted the cleaver and brought it down hard and fast, as had been done to him, to his hand. The blade was sharp; there was almost no resistance as it went through the joint, perhaps a slight snap as it chopped through bone. The finger's nail and the flesh and bone just below it sat on one side of the blade, the rest of the finger on the other. Borchert's face, he saw, had gone pale.

'Well done,' said Borchert, his voice strained. 'Now, Mr. Kline, if you would see your way clear of releasing my hand…'

Looking down, Kline realized that his stump was pushing down on Borchert's hand so hard that Borchert couldn't move. Blood was sputtering a little out of the finger's end, weakly. He lifted his stump and Borchert moved his finger away from the blade slightly and blood came puddling up now against the blade. He watched Borchert swing the hand about and, stretching his arm, bring it down onto the burner coil.

The flesh hissed, the blood hissing too, the air quickly filling with a smell that seemed to Kline like the smell of his own burning flesh. *Now,* he thought, *it is time for Borchert to pick up the gun and shoot me through the eye.* When Borchert took his finger away, Kline could still hear it hissing a little. And then Borchert turned to face him, his face wreathed in ecstacy, his eye dilated wide.

IV

He was allowed to go back to his room and rest. He seemed to be the only one occupying the house, despite there being a half dozen other rooms. Gous brought him a tray of food at lunchtime, and Gous sat at the small table with him, querying him gently about what Borchert had said, while he ate. Kline didn't answer.

'Of course I understand,' said Gous. 'There's an order to these things. A one can't be told much.'

'Where's Ramse?' asked Kline.

Gous shrugged. 'Ramse was needed elsewhere,' he said. 'We're not glued at the hip.'

Kline nodded, cutting into his meat, pork he thought, with his knife, keeping the plate from sliding with his stump. He put down the knife, picked up the fork, speared the meat.

'Do you know Aline?' he asked, once he had finished chewing.

'Aline?' asked Gous. 'Everbody knows Aline. Not personally, maybe, but we know him. He's the prophet. He's the great one.'

'Gous,' said Kline. 'Don't take this the wrong way, but how did you get involved in all this?'

'In all what?'

'All this,' said Kline, gesturing with his stump. 'This whole place.' He reached out and took hold of Gous's stump. 'In this,' he said.

'Ramse,' said Gous. 'He got me started.'

'He came up to you and said, "Why don't you hack that off?"'

'It's not something I'm supposed to talk about,' said Gous. 'Not with outsiders.'

'Am I an outsider, Gous?'

'Well,' said Gous. 'Yes and no.'

'Here I am,' said Kline. 'I'm right here, just like you.'

'True,' said Gous.

'I've talked with Borchert,' said Kline. 'Have you talked with Borchert?'

'No,' said Gous.

'Well, then?'

Gous held his head with his hand. 'I'm not supposed to talk about it,' he said.

'It's a secret,' said Kline.

'Not secret, sacred,' said Gous. He looked straight at Kline. 'When you have the call, you'll know,' he said.

'Maybe I've already had the call.'

'Maybe,' said Gous. 'It's not for me to say.'

He spent the day thinking. Aline was dead, the cult in crisis. What he was being called upon to do was to investigate, discoverer the murderer, and thus redeem the cult, allow it to go on. Was that right? Yet, according to Borchert he would not be allowed to see the body, would have to ask permission to interview anyone, would be monitored every step of the way. Was he really there to investigate at all, or was he simply Borchert's concession to someone else?

Near dark Ramse arrived, a basket full of food

slung over one of his arms.

'Well, well,' he said. 'Had a good day?'

'Fair,' said Kline. He opened the basket, dished up the food. There were two plates, so he gave some to Ramse as well.

'Borchert's quite a fellow, no?'

'Yes, quite.'

'They don't make them better than that,' said Ramse. 'And a twelve too, to boot.'

'Thirteen,' said Kline. He began eating. Ramse, he noticed, wasn't touching his food.

'Thirteen?' asked Ramse, looking stricken. 'What do you mean?'

'He had me cut off something.'

'Leg, toe, toe, toe, toe, toe, left arm, finger, finger, ear, eye, ear. What else?'

'Finger,' said Kline.

'The whole finger?'

'Just the first joint,' said Kline.

'That hardly counts as a thirteen,' said Ramse, looking relieved.

'You're not eating,' said Kline.

'No,' said Ramse.

'You already ate?'

'I don't have any hands,' said Ramse. 'You'll have to feed me when you're done.'

Kline nodded, began to eat more quickly. When he was done, he pulled Ramse's plate closer, dipped his spoon in, lifted the spoon to Ramse's mouth.

'Do you have a picture of Aline?' he asked.

Ramse shook his head. 'No pictures,' he said. 'The man's a prophet.'

'That doesn't mean you can't have a picture.'

'We're not Catholics,' said Ramse between mouthfuls. 'Or Mormons. Besides, we're concentrating on his absence, not his presence, on what he's severed rather than what remains.'

Kline nodded. He kept shovelling food onto the spoon, lifting it into Ramse's mouth. *Not even the presence of an absence,* he thought, *but absence as absence proper. It shouldn't be called a twelve, but a minus twelve.*

'Ramse,' said Kline, once the food was gone. 'How did you get involved?'

'Involved,' asked Ramse. 'I'm an eight, aren't I? They can't withhold everything from me.'

'Not in the investigation,' said Kline. 'In the cult.'

Ramse stared at him. 'First of all, it's not a cult,' he said. 'Second, I can't tell you.'

'That's what Gous said.'

Ramse smiled. 'Why do you want to know?'

'I don't know,' said Kline. 'Curious, I suppose.'

'Just curious?'

'I don't know,' said Kline. He sat running the edge of his stump along the grain of the table.

'What did Borchert have to say?' Ramse asked.

'A great guy, Borchert.'

'You shouldn't make fun.'

'Who says I'm making fun? He told me not to talk about it.'

'I'm an eight, aren't I? You can talk to me. You don't have to keep a secret from me.'

Kline shook his head, smiled. 'It's not secret, it's sacred,' he said.

'You shouldn't make fun,' Ramse said again. 'You should tolerate other people's religious beliefs. Besides, I already know a few things about it.'

'Oh?' said Kline. 'Why don't you tell me what you know?'

'Tit for tat,' said Ramse. He slashed his stump bluntly past his face. 'My lips are sealed,' he said. 'Besides, I've come on an errand. I'm supposed to conduct you to the scene of the crime.'

The crime scene was in the same building that Borchert had been in. Ramse tried to follow him up but the guard instead locked Ramse outside on the porch, led Kline up alone.

'What do you know about this?' Kline asked.

'About what?' the guard asked.

'About the crime.'

'What crime?'

'The murder.'

'What murder?'

Kline stopped asking. On the third floor they passed the first and second doors, stopped at the third. The guard gestured to it.

'I'll wait here,' he said.

'You don't care to come in?' asked Kline.

The guard said nothing. 'Whose room is this?' asked Kline. The guard said nothing. 'Aline's room?' asked Kline. The guard still said nothing.

'You're not allowed to come in?'

'I'll be waiting,' said the guard. 'Right here.'

Kline sighed. Opening the door, he went in.

Inside, the room looked much like Borchert's room: a simple bed, a chair, a bare floor, little more. On the floor near the bed was a large irregular bloodstain, perhaps three times the size of Kline's head. The wall nearby was spattered with blood as well. Someone had drawn a figure in chalk on the floor, though it took Kline a moment to realize that was what it was. It looked like a simple blotch at first, but in a moment he realized what he was seeing was the outline of an armless and legless torso.

'Good Christ,' he said.

He got down on his knees and looked more closely at the chalk figure. It must have been drawn wrong, for the head didn't fit snugly into the pool of dried blood that had spread out of it. He got up, brushed off his knees, went over to look at the nearest wall. Blood was fanned all along it but in no regular pattern, as if spattered from eight or ten different blows. No blood on the other walls. It was as if the killer had struck the limbless torso once and then had hauled it a few feet away to strike it again, and so on. Surely a man missing his arms and legs wouldn't be able to move far while being stabbed, no?

He had stared at the wall for quite some time before it struck him that something else was wrong. He didn't have to bend over to see the spatter. He knelt down again beside the chalk torso and measured it roughly with his arm. It was slightly shorter than the arm itself. The spatter should be quite a bit lower on the wall.

Maybe, he thought, Aline had been in chair. But the only chair in the room had no bloodstains on it. Maybe, he thought, whoever killed Aline did so while holding him in their arms, perhaps dancing or spinning as he stabbed. He could imagine the limbless torso stiff, rigid, struggling.

But that didn't strike him as quite right either. True, he had been trained to infiltrate; true, his experience with crime scenes was far less than most of his former colleagues. Perhaps the killer had struck upward each time, as if carrying a golf swing through? Perhaps that would account for the odd spatter and the decreased amount of blood on the lower part of the wall?

But why? he wondered. Why strike that way at all?

And what was the instrument? From the way the spatter was slung he would have guessed a knife, some kind of blade. Without seeing a photograph of the body it was difficult to be sure. It hardly seemed likely that one would attempt to use a knife as if it were a golf club. Something was wrong.

He regarded the chalk torso, the way the blood had pooled uncovincingly out of the chalk head. It had been drawn wrong somehow. He reached out to touch the surface of the pool of dried blood. It looked almost lacquered. It was slick in some places, cracking on the surface in others, darker and thicker in the center. The light from the ceiling shined off it in a kind of busted nimbus, the shape not unlike that of a broken jaw.

What could blood tell? he wondered. Where blood was could tell a lot. Could blood itself tell nothing?

He got out his keys and dug at the blood in the center of the stain. The top 1/4' layer cracked away in bits, but underneath it merely separated. Right near the floor the blood was almost moist, like a dough.

How long had it been? he wondered. They had started calling him several weeks ago. At least that; it could have been longer: he had been in no shape at the time to say how much time had passed. Aline, then, must have been dead for at least three weeks, perhaps more than a month. There was no way blood would stay moist for that long. It would either dry out completely or it would begin to rot and stink. And why were there no flies?

He went out into the hall. The guard was waiting, standing as stiffly as he had been when Kline had gone into the room.

'Nobody was killed in that room,' said Kline

'I don't know what you're talking about,' said the guard.

'Whose room is it?'

The guard just looked at him.

'I need to see Borchert,' said Kline. 'Right now.'

'The room, Mr. Kline?' said Borchert absently. 'What room is that exactly?' He held his mutilated finger between them and scrutinized it, his eyes flashing back and forth between it and Kline. 'Nice work, don't you think, Mr. Kline?'

The fingertip was pale and puffy, streaked dark at the end, a sort of red collar just below the cut.

'It's infected,' said Kline.

'Nonsense,' said Borchert. 'What you see is simply the body sealing itself off.'

'About the room –'

'– I can see the appeal of self-cauterization, Mr. Kline,' said Borchert. 'Ugly, true, but you really do have something there. Less clinical. A return to natural religion, so to speak.'

'I don't have anything,' said Kline. 'This has nothing to do with me.'

'Oh, but it does, Mr. Kline. You may be an unintentional avatar, but you are an avatar nonetheless.'

'Look,' said Kline. 'I'm done with this. I'm leaving.'

'So sorry, Mr. Kline,' said Borchert. 'But we've talked about this. If you try to leave, you'll be killed. Now what was this about the room?'

Kline shook his head. 'Nobody was killed in that room.'

'What room?'

'The murder room.'

'Oh,' said Borchert. 'I see.' He used his arm to raise himself out of the chair and onto his remaining leg and then stood there, half gone. He stood tilted slightly in the direction of his absent limbs, as if crimped at the side, for balance. 'How can you be so sure, Mr. Kline?'

'Everything is wrong,' said Kline. 'The blood spatter pattern is irregular, the positioning of the body isn't right in regard to blood flow –

'– but surely, Mr. Kline, irregular doesn't mean falsified. Perhaps it's simply an unusual circumstance.'

'Perhaps,' said Kline. 'But there's something wrong with the blood.'

'The blood?'

'It isn't completely dry.'

'But surely –'

'– It's been artificially dried. A fan or a hair dryer or something. But it's still damp underneath. It couldn't possibly belong to the body of a man killed several weeks ago.'

Borchert looked at him thoughtfully, a long moment, slowly hopped his way around so he could slide back into the chair.

'Well?' said Kline.

'So it's a reconstruction,' said Borchert. 'So what?'

'So what?' said Kline. 'How can I be expected to solve a crime by looking at a reconstruction of it?'

'Mr. Kline, surely you're enough of an armchair philosopher to realize that everything is a reconstruction of something else? Reality is a desperate and evasive creature.'

'Am I being asked to solve the crime or the reconstruction of the crime?'

'The crime,' said Borchert. 'The reconstruction,' he said, gesturing to himself with his thumb and his one and two thirds fingers, 'c'est moi.'

'I can't get anywhere without real evidence.'

'I have perfect faith in you, Mr. Kline.'

'At least let me talk to a few people who might know something.'

'Somewhat tricky,' said Borchert, 'but, ever the optimist, I'm convinced something can be arranged.'

Shaking his head, Kline went toward the door. Once there he turned, saw Borchert smiling in his chair behind him. When he smiled, Kline realized that all his bottom teeth had been removed.

'This is going well, don't you think?' said Borchert, speaking loudly, perhaps for the sake of the guard. 'Thank you, dear friend, for stopping by.'

V

Ramse showed up a few days later with a tape recorder balanced on his forearms. He put it on the table near Kline.

'What's this for?' asked Kline.

'It's a tape recorder,' said Ramse. 'For taping things. Borchert asked me to bring it.'

'What does he want me to do with it?'

'It's for the interviews,' said Ramse. 'For the crime.'

Kline nodded. He poured himself a glass of milk, drank it slowly as Ramse watched.

'Anything else you need?' Kline asked.

'No,' said Ramse. 'Just that.'

Kline nodded. 'Right,' he said. 'Where's Gous?'

'He's getting ready for the party.'

'The party?'

'Didn't he send you an invitation?'

'No.'

Ramse furrowed his brow. 'An oversight,' he said. 'He'd want you to come. I'm sure he wants you to come. Will you?'

Kline shrugged. 'Why not?' he said.

'It's settled then,' said Ramse. 'I'll pick you up at eight.'

Kline nodded, looked absently at his watch. Until the accident, he had worn his watch on his right arm, but now if he wore it there it threatened to slide off the stump.

Across the table, Ramse cleared his throat.

'You're still here?' asked Kline.

'Shall I wait outside or would you rather I came back later?' asked Ramse.

'For the party?'

'You don't understand,' claimed Ramse. 'I'm supposed to take the tape back.'

'But I haven't conducted any interviews yet.'

'That's what the tape's for.'

'Right,' said Kline. 'To tape the interviews.'

'No,' said Ramse. 'To tape the questions.'

'To tape the questions?'

Ramse nodded. 'These people,' he said. 'They're all ten or above. You're a one. You can't see them in person.'

'But I see Borchert.'

'Borchert's the exception,' said Ramse. 'You see him when someone above a ten has to be seen. If you were a three or a four some might condescend to see you, but they won't see a one. Not even a self-cauterizer.'

'Jesus,' said Kline. 'That's ridiculous.'

'I've been instructed by Borchert not to listen to the questions,' said Ramse. 'I'm only an eight. I don't need to know everything. I'm to take the tape back to Borchert once you've finished recording. Would you like me to wait in the hall or would you prefer I come back later?'

He sat staring at the tape recorder. It was ridiculous, he knew. Perhaps Ramse was right, it was only a question of proper behavior, no ones among the tens, but why in that case even bring him in at all? Why not solve their own murder?

He went and opened the door. Ramse was there, waiting, leaning against the wall. Kline closed the door again.

What were his options? One, he could refuse to send the tape back. Borchert would hardly allow that. He would be punished in some way, he was certain. And it would only prolong the amount of time he would have to spend in the compound. Two, he could send back a blank tape. Same problem: it bought him a little time, but time for what? Three, he could send back a series of questions. That had the advantage of moving things forward, or at least of moving them in some direction.

He sighed. He went to the table and pressed the record button:

One, State your name and your relation to the deceased.

Two, Where were you on the night Aline was murdered?

Three, Do you know of anyone who might want Aline dead for any reason?

Four, Did you see the body? If so, please describe in detail what you saw.

Five, Are you absolutely certain that Aline's death wasn't a suicide?

Six, Did you kill Aline?

It was ridiculous, but at least it was a start. They would tell him nothing, he was almost sure. He turned the tape off.

Ramse showed up at eight o'clock sharp, wearing a tuxedo that had been modified to better reveal his amputations, no shoes, no socks. He had, slung over one arm, a plastic dry cleaner's bag containing another tuxedo, which he handed to Kline.

'Try this on,' he said.

Kline did. It was a little loose but generally fit quite well, the right sleeve cut back slightly to reveal his stump.

They walked across the gravel lot before the house, following the road towards the gate, turning down a footpath after about a hundred meters. At the end was a gravel circle, a bar to the left, a neon one-legged woman on the sign. A well-lit lodge structure was to the right, which was where they went.

A one-handed man was standing at the open door, smiling. Kline could hear music blaring from the door behind him.

'Hello, Ramse,' the man said affably. 'This the guy?'

'This is him, John,' said Ramse. 'In the flesh.'

They both laughed at that for some reason. The man held out his remaining hand, his right. 'Put it there,' he said, which Kline tried, left-handed, very awkwardly, to do.

'Self-cauterizer, huh?' asked John. 'People have been talking. There's a buzz going.'

'Don't embarrass him, John,' said Ramse. Ushering Kline before him, he made his way in.

Inside, the room was filled with several dozen men in tuxedos, all amputees. Streamers descended without pattern from the ceiling, brushing against men's shoulders, dipping into their drinks. Ramse took him to the bar and Kline got a drink and stood next to Ramse nursing it, giving Ramse sips of it from time to time. The men were mostly ones or twos as far as Kline could tell in the dim light, though there were fours and fives as well and one person that Kline thought might be a seven or eight – the room was dark and in motion so it was hard to tell how many toes the man was actually missing. Then suddenly Gous was beside him, rubbing his shoulder with his stump.

'How nice of you to come,' he said to Kline, smiling. He was dressed different than the others. He was wearing a tuxedo, but one sleeve of it had been wrapped in plastic, and a line had been drawn in permanent marker between his middle and fourth finger, angling across his palm to terminate at the palm's edge just before the wrist. 'Ramse didn't know if you'd come,' he said, 'but I was sure you would.' He turned to Ramse. 'Stretter didn't come, the bastard.'

'I'm sure he meant to,' said Ramse. 'Something must have come up.'

'No,' said Gous. 'He never meant to. I came for him three times, but now that he's a five, he's too good for me.'

'Surely he can't mean it personally,' said Ramse. 'It's just some sort of mistake.'

But Gous was already turning away, shaking his head. Kline watched Ramse go after him. He took a sip of his drink, looked around, then began to walk slowly around the room. There were no women, he quickly realized, nothing but men, everyone in their thirties and forties, nobody either very young or very old.

The back of the room wasn't a solid wall at all but a divider, a series of linked panels that, he saw, looking more closely, slid along a metal track in the floor. The two central panels each had a handle and a latch holding them together.

'Would you like to have a look?' asked a voice behind him.

'Where are all the women?' asked Kline, turning. Behind him was John.

'Aren't any here,' said John, smiling. 'There are a few over in the bar, but otherwise none. This is a brotherhood, after all.'

Kline nodded, looked about him.

'So, you want a preview?' asked John.

Kline shrugged.

'I don't think anyone would mind,' John said. 'They've all seen it before anyway.'

He put his drink down on the floor, used his hand to turn one of the latches. The panel disengaged and slid open an inch. He rolled it along the track until there was enough space for Kline to slide through.

'Go on,' he said, stooping for his drink. 'I'll wait out here.'

Kline slid through, careful not to spill his drink. On the other side, the remainder of the hall was dark and bare and sober except for a rolling metal table draped in white cloth. A smaller square table, also draped in cloth, was beside it. A large domed light was over them. It was the only light in the room, the dome functioning like a spotlight.

He smelled the smoke before he saw the man step out of the darkness and move toward him. The man was wearing scrubs, had his cloth surgical mask pulled down around his neck so he could smoke a cigarette. When he lifted the cigarette to his lips, Kline could see he was missing a finger.

'Is it time?' he asked. And then, seeing the drink in Kline's hand, 'Are you bringing that for me?'

Kline handed him the drink, and without a word left.

'Well,' said John. 'What do you think? First rate set-up, no?'

'Where's Ramse?' asked Kline.

'Ramse?' said John. 'I don't know,' he said. 'Maybe over there?'

Kline started across the hall, moving from cluster to cluster until he found Ramse speaking to a man in a chair whose legs had been cut off at the knee.

'I need to talk to you,' he said.

'All right,' said Ramse, excusing himself from the legless man. 'What's the trouble?'

'Jesus,' said Kline. 'What kind of party is this?'

'It's Gous' party,' said Ramse. 'His three. Where's your drink? Do you need another drink?'

'What the hell does that mean?'

'Isn't it obvious?' said Ramse. He looked at Kline, eyes wide, then shook his head. 'I forget you don't know us very well,' he said. 'It's an amputation party.'

'An amputation party.'

'Like a coming out,' said Ramse. 'Gous is giving up two fingers. He's gathered his friends around him for the occasion. He's going from a one to a three.'

'Jesus,' said Kline. 'I have to leave.'

He tried to make for the door but Ramse was pressing his forearm to his chest. 'You can't leave,' hissed Ramse, 'not now that you've come. It'd break Gous' heart.'

'But,' said Kline. 'I don't believe in any of this. I can't stay here.'

'It's not that you don't believe,' said Ramse. 'It's just that you don't have the call yet.'

'No,' said Kline. 'It's that I don't believe.'

'I don't care what you believe,' said Ramse. 'Just do this for Gous. He admires you. What has he ever done to you to deserve this?'

'What has he ever done to deserve losing his fingers?'

'He doesn't see it that way,' said Ramse. 'He's had the call. This for him is an act of faith. You don't have to believe in it, but you can still respect him.'

'I have to go,' said Kline, pushing against his arm.

'No,' said Ramse. 'Please, just for Gous. Have compassion. Please.'

By the time the amputation took place, Kline had had a few drinks, had drunk enough in fact that he had trouble making his eyes focus. To see reasonably well, he had to cover one eye with his stump. Eventually Ramse, just before the amputation, coaxed the drink out of his hand, coaxed him now through the open partition and into the half-room beyond.

He stood on the edge of the lit circle, swaying slightly, Ramse beside him, Ramse's forearm tucked under his arm. In the center was the doctor, his mask up now. He had stripped the cloth off the small metal cart to reveal an array of tools that seemed half to be medical instruments, half to be from the knifeblock of a gourmet chef. *Jesus*, Kline thought.

Gous came into the circle, smiling, while the tuxedo-dressed gentleman clapped gently. Two gentlemen were called forward as witnesses, each of them placing a stump under one of Gous' arms. He leaned over the large table, placed his hand on it, palm up. The doctor took a hypodermic off the table and slid its needle into Kline's hand. His fingers twitched. Or rather *Gous'* fingers, Kline realized; it was not his own hand, he could not start to think of it as his own hand. The four of them – the doctor, Gous, the two witnesses – stood as if in tableau, motionless in a way that Kline found unbearable, only the doctor moving from time to time to regard his watch. At last he took a metal probe from the small metal cart and pushed at the hand.

Gous watched him, then nodded slightly. The two witnesses braced themselves behind him. The doctor switched on a cauterizer. After a moment, Kline could smell the way it oxidized the air. The doctor let his fingers run over the instruments, then took up the cauterizer with one hand. What looked like a stylized and carefully balanced cleaver was in the other. He approached the table, lined the cleaver along the line Gous had drawn on his hand, and then raised it, brought it swiftly down.

Kline saw Gous' eyelids flutter, then the rest of

his body faltered and was supported and caught by the witnesses behind him. All around, the men began to clap quietly, and blood began to spurt from the wound. Kline closed his eyes, felt himself begin to lean to one side, but Ramse caught him, held him upright. He could hear the buzz of the cauterizer and a moment later began to smell burning flesh.

'Hey,' whispered Ramse. 'Are you all right?' All around them, men were beginning to move.

'Just a little drunk,' said Kline, opening his eyes. Gous was there before him, having his hand bandaged.

'That wasn't so bad, was it?' asked Ramse. 'Gous certainly didn't think so. Not so bad, eh?'

'I don't know,' Kline said. 'I want to go home.'

'The night's still young,' said Ramse. 'We're only getting started.'

The rest of the night was a blur to him. At some point he lost his tuxedo jacket; at another point, he found the next day, someone had smeared a swath of blood across his forehead. At one point he could hear Ramse telling everyone not to give him another drink and then he was outside, vomiting onto the gravel, Ramse seeming to be trying at once to hold him up and to knock him over. Then they were stumbling across the gravel courtyard, Kline covering one of his eyes so he could see, and into the bar where he was drinking not whiskey but first coffee and then water. It was not exactly a bar either, but more like a club. They were sitting in armchairs, a small coffee table before them, pointed toward a stage, and Kline realized the curtain was opening.

The stage was bare at first, lit by a reddish spotlight, and then a woman came out onto it swaddled from knees to neck in boas.

'Watch this,' said Ramse, his words slurring even more than usual. 'She's really something.'

A strip show, thought Kline. He had seen a strip show before, more than once, had seen several in fact with the man who had since come to be known as the gentleman with the cleaver, the man who was dead now. He didn't care about them one way or the other. He watched the woman lose one boa after another while Ramse whistled. She would let a boa trail first and then finally let it flop all the way off and then kick it to one side of the stage. And then finally she was done, stripped naked, blurred in the red light, not particularly attractive.

He waited for the curtain to go down but the curtain did not go down. He turned to Ramse but found him still staring rapt at the girl, and so he himself turned back to her and watched as, with a flick of the wrist, she cracked off her hand.

A dim howl went up through the house and Kline heard, scattered through the chairs, a dull thumping, the sound of stumps beating against one another. She made her way toward one side of the stage, spinning slightly, and then snapped the stump of her arm against her remaining hand and Kline saw three fingers wobble loose and slough away. The crowd roared. He tried to stand up but Ramse had his hand on his shoulder and was shouting in his ear: *Just wait, the best is yet to come.*

And then the woman sashayed across the stage and reached up with her remaining finger and thumb to tear free her ear. She spun it around a few times before tossing it out into the audience. Kline saw a group of men rise up in a dark mass trying somehow, with what hands they had left between them, to catch it. And then she turned away, turned her back to them, and when she turned back her artificial breasts had been pulled away to hang like an apron around her belly, revealing two shiny flat patches where they had been. She spread her legs and squatted and Kline imagined her legs were beginning to separate, to split up. *Jesus, God,* he thought, and tried to stand, and felt Ramse trying to hold him down, and felt the blood rush to his head. He staggered forward and into the small table, hot coffee sloshing all over his legs, and looked up to see the woman on the stage gouging her fingers beneath one side of her face, but mercifully, before she had torn it away, he had fallen and did not, despite Ramse's urging, get up again.

VI

It was late in the afternoon before he could bring himself to get up again, his head still spinning. He went into the bathroom and drank cup after cup of water and then turned on the water, stood under

'I need to see them,' Kline said. 'Rules or no.'

'And you want me to make the necessary arrangements. You're certain of it?'

'Yes,' said Kline.

Borchert sighed. 'So be it,' he said. 'I'll make the necessary arrangements, Mr. Kline. You'll see them tomorrow.'

'I want to see them today.'

'Not today, tomorrow. Don't push your luck.'

Kline nodded, stood to go. His body was sore, bruised.

'Would you mind wiping your blood off the floor before you go, Mr. Kline?' asked Borchert, rising from the chair to stand perfectly balanced on his remaining leg. 'And Mr. Kline,' he said, 'Now you have a history of violence. I advise you to be careful.'

Late evening, Gous arrived with a half-empty bottle of Scotch cradled in the crook of his elbow, Scotch which was, according to him, *compliments of Borchert.*

'How kind of him,' said Kline, flatly.

'Why he should care after your escapade this afternoon is beyond me,' said Gous.

'Maybe that's why I only get half a bottle.'

Gous nodded. 'Do you have glasses?' he asked.

'No.'

'I guess Borchert didn't think you rated glasses,' said Gous. He fumbled awkwardly at the lid with his bandaged hand. 'I'm going to have to ask you to open it,' he said.

'How's your hand?' asked Kline.

'Nice of you to ask,' said Gous. 'Recovering nicely, thank you,' he said, lifting the bandaged lump in the air. 'I'm supposed to keep it elevated. And I shouldn't drink too much,' he said. 'Alcohol thins the blood and all that.'

Kline screwed the cap off the bottle and drank. It was good Scotch, or at least good enough. He took another mouthful then pushed the bottle over to Gous, who, using his forearms like chopsticks, managed to get it to his mouth. He almost upset the bottle putting it back on the table.

'What made you change your mind?' he asked.

'My mind?' asked Kline.

'About amputation.'

'Who said I changed my mind?' Lifting the bottle, he took another drink.

'Why would Borchert have sent over a bottle otherwise? Did you get a call?'

'I don't know what you're talking about.'

Gous nodded. 'It's nobody's business but your own,' he said.

Kline reached for the bottle, watched the stump at the end of his arm knock against it, nearly knock it over. 'Nobody's business but my own,' he said, aloud, his voice sounding quite distant.

'That's right,' Gous said. 'That's what *I* said.'

Kline could see on the end of his arm, the ghost of his hand, pale and transparent, sprouting oddly from the stump. 'That's right,' he heard himself say. He flexed his missing fingers, saw them move. They had cut off his hand but the ghost of his hand was still there. Perhaps this was what was meant by a call? Perhaps Borchert, shorn of most of his limbs, saw the ghosts of what was missing: vanished limbs grown uncarnate, pure.

He looked up. There was Gous, across the table from him, his eyes drooping, half-closed, his face mostly gone in shadow. Kline tried to reach for the bottle but couldn't find it.

'Where was I?' he asked.

He saw Gous' eyelids wince, come all the way open. 'We should get you into bed,' Gous said. 'While I still can.'

'It isn't Scotch,' said Kline, to where Gous had been, but Gous wasn't there anymore. It took him some time to realize that Gous was there beside him, looming above him, trying to get him out of the chair. And then, without knowing how, he was standing, Gous beside him, and they were gliding slowly through the room.

'No,' said Gous, slowly. 'It *is* Scotch. But that's not all it is.'

Fuck, thought Kline. 'I thought you were my friend,' he said, and felt himself falling. And then he was on the bed, sprawled, Gous sitting beside him looking down at him.

'I am your friend,' Gous said. 'I drank with you, didn't I?'

Kline tried to nod but nothing happened. He could see the wrappings around Gous' hand staining with blood.

'Besides,' said Gous, 'friendship is one thing, God another.'

'Scoot over,' Gous said. Kline was not sure how much time had passed. 'There's enough room on that bed for two.'

Gous' cheek on the pillow, just next to his own eye, was the last thing he would remember until, hours later, he awoke, alone, to the sight of his bandaged foot, the bandages already steeped with blood. Even then it was not until he felt the dressings with his remaining hand that he realized that three of his toes had been removed.

VII

'This is what you wanted,' said Borchert after Kline had forced his shoe over his bandaged foot and limped over to his room. It had been difficult to walk without the toes, hard to keep his balance and very painful. By the time he had reached the building his shoe was saturated with blood. The guard, perhaps the same guard as the day before, had regarded him with one eye and said *What is wanted?* In answer he had merely lifted his bloody shoe slightly. The guard, without another word, let him pass, as did the guard behind the door. And now here he was, upstairs, across from Borchert, in Borchert's room, being told that he had gotten what he wanted.

'You should be careful about what you ask for,' said Borchert.

'I didn't ask for anything.'

'You asked,' said Borchert, 'to interview certain people in person. I told you I would make arrangements. I have made them. I took the fewest number of toes possible,' he said. 'Even now, for them to see you is to stretch the rules a little. A four, normally… but it isn't unheard of.'

'I want to leave,' said Kline.

'Of course you do,' said Borchert cheerily. 'But I believed we've already discussed that. It's not possible.'

'Why are you doing this?'

'What am I doing exactly?' asked Borchert. 'I've made you a four. I've done you a favor.'

'I don't see it that way.'

'Perhaps someday you will.'

'I doubt it.'

Borchert looked at him seriously. 'I doubt it too,' he said. 'Look,' he said, 'at your missing hand.'

'When can I leave?' asked Kline.

'When all this is done.'

'When will that be?'

Borchert shrugged. 'That depends on you,' he said. He lifted his remaining hand, pointed his crippled middle digit at Kline. 'Now, if I'm not mistaken, you have interviews to conduct.'

He was taken down a floor and then down the hall to another door, behind which was one of the interviewees, an eleven, his legs hacked off at the knees, his fingers and one thumb all shaved down nearly to knuckle. He recognized his voice as the third on the tape: Andreissen. Before he would speak with Kline Andreissen demanded to see the missing toes, suggesting that Kline should not *hide his light under a bushel.*

Kline sat and loosened his shoe and slowly worked it off, blood dripping from it to puddle on the floor. He dropped the shoe onto the floor and began unwrapping the sodden dressing. Andreissen came nimbly out of his chair and, like an ape, propelled himself across the floor on his knuckles and the stumps of his knees. His eyes were lucid and shining, and when Kline got the wrapping off to reveal his mangled foot Andreissen came very close indeed. Kline could hardly bear to look at the foot, the place where the toes had been cauterized but now cracked and seeping a flux of blood and pus.

'I thought you self-cauterized,' said Andreissen. 'Part of the reason I agreed to this was because I wanted to see what self-cauterization looked like.'

'I didn't do this,' said Kline.

'You shouldn't be walking on it,' he said. 'Doesn't it hurt?'

'Of course it hurts.'

Andreissen nodded. He knuckled his way back across the floor, clambered back into the chair. 'As I told Borchert,' he said, once properly situated, 'I'm here to help. I'm all for law and order.'

'Good for you,' said Kline.

'But, honestly, I said all there was to say on the tape.'

Kline nodded. He dragged his foot along the floor, watching the thin lines of blood run. 'It's about the tape,' he said. 'That's what I came about.'

'Oh?'

'There's something wrong with the tape,' said Kline. 'I need to figure out what.'

'The tape didn't work?'

'Something like that,' said Kline. 'So I'm just going to ask the questions again, all right?'

'Why don't you talk to Borchert?' he asked. 'Why don't you ask him?'

'First question,' said Kline. 'State your name and your relation to the deceased.'

'Technically that's not a question.'

'Please answer,' said Kline.

'I believe you already know my name,' he said. 'It's Andreissen.'

'Thank you,' said Kline. 'What was your relation to the deceased?'

'The deceased?' said Andreissen. 'I thought you were sticking to the original questions.'

'That is one of the original questions.'

'No it isn't.'

'It's not?' said Kline.

'What's this talk of the deceased? There is no deceased.'

'Aline.'

'What about Aline?'

'He's the deceased.'

'Aline?' Andreissen shook his head, laughed. 'You're pulling my leg.'

'Aline's dead.'

'It's impossible,' said Andreissen.

'Why do you think I'm here?'

'I saw him just yesterday,' said Andreissen. 'He seemed very much alive to me.'

'You're lying,' said Kline.

'I swear to you,' said Andreissen. 'On my missing legs.'

Kline stood, limped around the room.

'Can you stop that?' said Andreissen. 'You're getting blood everywhere.'

'What were the questions you were asked? On the tape, what were the questions.'

'Me? About the robbery of course.'

'What robbery?'

Andreissen narrowed his eyes. 'What is this all about? Do you think I did it? I didn't do it.'

'Do what?'

'The robbery.'

'What robbery?'

'Christ,' said Andreissen. 'What sort of game are you playing?'

'Where's Aline's room? Down the hall?'

'No,' said Andreissen. 'Up a level. Last door. Why?'

'I was told it was on that floor, but the third door.'

'What is this?' asked Andreissen. He posted his palms against the chair's arms, pulled himself up to stand in the chair's seat on his stumps. 'I didn't agree to this. Borchert didn't say anything abou this. I want you to leave.'

'Fine,' said Kline. 'I'm leaving.'

He went out into the hall. The guard was gone. He went to the stairs but instead of going down went up and down to the end of the hall. A guard was standing in front of the last door. He watched Kline nervously.

'This is Aline's room?' Kline asked.

The guard made no gesture, said nothing.

'Mind if I see for myself?' asked Kline, and reached for the doorknob.

The guard struck him once with the edge of his palm, fast, in the throat. He couldn't breathe. He stumbled back, his hand to his throat, still unable to breathe, and then made a conscious decision to stumble forward instead, throwing himself against the door. The handle was locked. The guard hit him again, in the side of the temple, and he slid down along the door, and then the guard was pulling him back into the middle of the hall, massaging his throat, trying to get him to breathe.

'Well,' said Borchert. 'Mr. Kline. Always a pleasant surprise. You should be more careful. You should have a little more respect.'

'Aline's not dead,' said Kline, still rubbing his throat.

'Of course he is,' said Borchert. 'Whatever gave you that idea?'

'Andreissen.'

'Why would he say that?' asked Borchert.

'He said I was here to investigate a robbery.'

'No, no,' said Borchert. 'Aline's dead. You're here for Aline.'

'Who's dead?'

'It's that you're only a four,' said Borchert. 'He's not telling you the truth because of that.'

'You're lying.'

'Maybe we should remove another toe,' said Borchert. 'Or maybe two more. Then we'll see if Andreissen tells you the truth.'

'No,' said Kline. 'No more toes.'

'All right, then,' said Borchert. 'Perhaps one of the others will be a little more forthcoming.'

'No more interviews.'

'All right,' said Borchert. 'You're the investigator. You should do what feels right.'

Using his remaining foot, Borchert pushed the chair slowly along the floor until he was back by the counter. Slowly he managed to open the cabinet above it and to tug down first one glass and then another. And then, more precariously, a bottle of Scotch. He took off the cap with his mouth. He moved the glasses to the edge of the counter and, pinning the bottle between his arm and his body, poured.

'Drink?' he asked.

'Absolutely not,' said Kline.

'Oh come on,' said Borchert. 'It's Scotch, plain and simple. Nothing but Scotch.'

'No,' said Kline.

'Suit yourself,' said Borchert. He pinched the glass' rim between his thumb and remaining half-finger, lifted it to his lips, drank. 'So,' he said. 'Made any progress, have we?'

'On what?'

'On finding Aline's killer.'

'My guess is that Aline is still very much alive.'

'Please, Mr. Kline. Let's have no more such talk.'

'Show me the body.'

Borchert shook his head. 'I can't allow you to see the body. At the very least you'd have to lose a few more toes.'

'This is absurd.'

'Be that as it may, Mr. Kline,' said Borchert, taking a large swallow. 'Be that as it may.'

Later that evening he wandered out of his room and down the hall and into the gravel yard in front of the building. He stood looking up at the stars, his foot aching with pain, feeling slightly feverish. He did not understand, he thought, what it was he had gotten himself into, nor for that matter how he had gotten himself into it. But the more important question was, now that he was in, how to get out.

He walked out to the main road, turned, limped toward the main gates. A man was dead, murdered, or perhaps very much alive. Borchert was playing with him, and perhaps the others were as well. The night was cool, cloudless. Where was this place? He turned and looked back, saw the building he was staying in, the only light being that of his own room. Why was nobody else in the building? Had there been anyone living in the building but him since his arrival? Where did Gous and Ramse sleep?

At the main gate at the edge of the compound, the guard stepped out of the shadows and flicked on his flashlight, shining the beam into Kline's eyes.

'What is wanted?' he asked.

'It's Kline,' Kline said, squinting his eyes.

'Right,' said the guard. 'We met the first night. A one. Self-cauterizer. Right hand, right?'

'Yes,' said Kline. 'Now a four.'

'A four?' said the guard. 'That was quick. What else?'

'A few toes,' he said. 'Nothing much.'

The guard moved the flashbeam down, shined it on Kline's feet. Kline could see the man now, a dim shape just behind the flashlight.

'I need to leave,' said Kline. 'Please open the gate.'

'I'm sorry,' said the guard. 'I can't do that.'

'My work here is finished,' said Kline.

'I have my orders, I'm afraid,' said the guard.

Kline took a step forward. The guard brought the light up and into his eyes. Kline took another step and heard a rustling and a click and the guard quickly flashed the light back on himself to reveal a sort of metal prosthetic slipped over his stump, a gun barrel at the end of it.

'I thought prosthetics were frowned upon,' said Kline.

'We don't like to use them,' said the guard. 'But

when we have to, we do.'

'Say I climb the fence somewhere.'

'You're welcome to try. My guess is we'd catch you eventually.'

Kline nodded, turned to leave.

'Very nice to see you, Mr. Kline,' said the guard. 'If you have any more questions, don't hesitate to ask.'

He found Gous and Ramse in the bar, already drunk, Ramse in particular, who was drinking whiskey through a straw. Gous kept saying he had to go easy, that it thinned the blood, and then taking another drink. They cheered when they caught sight of Kline, clapped him on the back with their stumps.

'Drink?' asked Ramse.

Kline nodded. Ramse called the bartender over. 'A drink for my friend here,' he said.

'The self-cauterizer.'

'Word gets around,' said Ramse.

'Say,' said Gous, his voice slurred and too slow. 'When do the women come out?'

'Ten,' said the bartender. 'I told you already. Ten.'

'Drink?' Ramse asked Kline.

'He's already getting me a drink,' said Kline.

'Hell,' said Ramse. 'I wanted to get you a drink.'

'You did,' said Kline.

'What?' asked Ramse. 'What?'

'Never mind,' said Kline.

'Just so you know,' said Ramse. 'I'm buying the next one.'

Kline smiled.

'So,' said Gous, hunched over his drink. 'How's the investigation?'

'It's not.'

'No?' said Gous. 'Thash too bad.'

'Do you want to hear about it?' asked Kline.

'About what?' asked Ramse.

'The investigation,' said Kline. The bartender put the drink on the counter before him and he took it up in his left hand and drank from it.

'Oh, no,' said Ramse. 'You can't tell Gous anything.'

'Why not?' asked Gous. 'Why not?'

'Gous is a one,' said Ramse. 'We can't bring a one in.'

'I was a one,' said Kline. 'They brought me in.'

'I'm not a one,' said Gous, lifting up his hand. 'Not any more.'

'Still,' said Ramse. 'You're not much. You're what you are and we love you for it, but you're not much.'

'It's all right, Ramse,' said Kline. 'Trust me.'

'I just don't think –'

'– Ramse,' said Kline. 'Trust me and listen.'

Ramse opened his mouth, then closed it again.

'Aline is dead,' Kline said.

'Aline is dead?' said Ramse, his voice rising.

'Is that possible?' said Gous. 'How is that possible?'

'Or not,' said Kline. 'Maybe not.'

'Well,' said Gous. 'Which is it?'

'What did you say about Aline?' asked the bartender.

'Nothing,' said Kline.

'Oh, God,' said Ramse, shaking his head. 'Dear God.'

'Aline is either dead or not dead,' said Gous to the bartender.

'Be quiet, Gous,' said Kline.

'Well, which is he?' asked the bartender. 'Dead or not dead? There's a big difference, you know.'

'That,' said Gous, stabbing the air with his stump. 'Is what I intend to find out.'

'You don't think there's a big difference?' asked Ramse.

'Ramse,' said Kline. 'Look at me. Why am I here? What am I investigating?'

'What?' said Ramse. 'Smuggling.'

'Smuggling?' Gous, Kline noticed, was watching them more intently.

'Somebody smuggled out pictures.'

'What sorts of pictures?'

'Sex pictures,' said Ramse. 'Of people missing limbs. Somebody stealing them and selling them without the proceeds benefitting the community.'

'That,' said Kline, 'in your opinion, is why I am here?'

Ramse nodded.

'No,' said Kline. 'I'm here because of Aline.'

'Who's either dead or not dead.'

'Exactly,' said Kline.

'There's a big difference,' said Gous. 'That's

what we intend to find out.'

'What?' said Ramse.

'That,' said Gous.

'What?' said Ramse, looking around. 'What's going on?'

'Exactly,' said Kline. 'That's what I want to know.'

VIII

There were two possibilities, he thought, as he was escorted on his way to visit Borchert the next morning, a hungover Ramse on one side of him, a hungover Gous on the other side. He was coming at Borchert's request. *Possibility one, Aline is dead. Possibility two, Aline is alive.* Perhaps Ramse was right, perhaps he really did know something and the reason he, Kline, was here was because of smuggling or theft. But if it was smuggling, why hadn't he been told? Why had Borchert told him he was investigating a murder? Certainly, considering what Kline's speciality had been before, it seemed more logical that they would recruit him to investigate a smuggling operation.

Perhaps Borchert himself had a vested interest, had reasons to stop the smuggling from being investigated.

But even so, why declare Aline dead? Why suggest there is a murder to be investigated? Why not simply suggest something a little more benign?

And here he was, standing alone in front of Borchert, with Gous and Ramse abandoned at the gate, the one-armed, one-legged man looking grimly at him from his chair.

'I thought we had an agreement,' Borchert was saying.

'What agreement?'

'I asked you not to speak about the case with those who didn't need to know. Instead, you've been spreading rumors.'

'Look,' said Kline. 'I don't know what I'm doing here. What exactly am I investigating?'

'Aline's death.'

'I don't believe Aline is dead.'

'No,' said Borchert. 'You've made that quite clear.'

'What about the smuggling?'

'The smuggling,' said Borchert. 'A cover story. Something we agreed to tell people like Ramse.'

'And Andreissen?'

'We talked about that,' said Borchert. 'I give my solemn word that if you simply have one or two more amputations, Andreissen will change his story. Why didn't you speak to any of the others? Perhaps one of them would tell you the truth.'

'You're lying.'

Borchert sighed. 'Well,' he said. 'I was hoping it wouldn't come to this, but you're a stubborn bastard and have your own particular way of conducting business. You'd be better off if you were willing to take some things on faith, but *Thou woulds't doubt*, as Jesus said, and for the doubting there's nothing but what you can touch.' He turned his head, gestured with his chin to the counter behind. 'There's a gun there,' he said. 'In the drawer. No bullets in it, but the guard outside Aline's door doesn't need to know that. If you need to go see for yourself, go see for yourself. I wouldn't advise it, but neither will I prevent you.'

Kline took the gun and left. He could see, as soon as he opened the door to the hall, the guard in front of what he had been told by Andreissen was Aline's door. Was it the door Borchert expected him to go to as well? he wondered. Or was he being told to visit the room where Borchert had led him before, the faked crime scene?

'Is this the door to Aline's room?' Kline asked the guard.

The guard did not reply. Kline realized the man's lone eye was directed downward, fixed on his hand, and then Kline remembered the gun. He lifted his hand, pointed the gun at the man's head.

'Please open the door,' he said.

The guard shook his head.

'I'll kill you,' said Kline.

'Then kill me.'

Kline hit the guard hard in the face with his stump, then raked the pistol across his jaw. The guard took two awkward steps, wavering into the door, and Kline struck him with the pistol, just behind the ear. The man went down in a heap.

The door was unlocked. He opened it and went in, locking it behind him.

Inside, it was dark. He felt around on the wall to either side of the door for a switch, only found one after his eyes had adjusted enough to see it, low on the wall, at knee level.

The room was as simple as Borchert's. A counter and a small kitchen in the back of the room. A single chair, this one with a sort of net webbing draped over it. A bed, in this case, three feet long, flush to the floor, pushed against one wall.

In the bed, a mutilated head rode on the pillow, the rest of the body covered by a blanket. He knelt down beside it. The eyes had been dug out, the lids cut off as well. The ears had been shorn away to leave two whirls of slick pink flesh. The nose, too, was gone, leaving a dark gaping hole. The lips seemed to have been gnawed mostly away, perhaps by the teeth that now loomed through their gap.

As he watched, the flesh on the face shivered and the head turned slightly, the missing eyes seeming to bore into his own eyes. He broke the gaze and then, grabbing the blanket, tugged it off the body.

Underneath was only a torso, all limbs gone, nipples cut away, penis severed. He sat watching the chest rise and fall, air whistling between the teeth. There was something wrong with the way the body lay, he realized, and he pushed it over onto the side a little, enough to see that the buttocks had been shaved away.

The mouth said something urgently but he couldn't understand what because most of the tongue was gone. He let go of the body. He looked away, let himself slip from his knees to lie on the floor. Behind him, he could hear someone pounding at the door. He stayed there, staring up at the ceiling, listening to Aline babble, until they came and dragged him away.

'So,' said Borchert, 'now you've seen for yourself.' He was standing using a cane, precariously grounded in his palm to support himself. Kline was in the chair now, Borchert's chair, having been brought there by the guards after they had dragged him by the feet out of Aline's room and down the stairs, his head bumping against each step.

'What's wrong with you?' asked Borchert. 'You look feverish.'

'Aline's alive,' said Kline.

'Of course he's alive,' said Borchert. 'I must apologize for lying, Mr. Kline, but trust I had my reasons.'

'Why?'

'Why, Mr Kline?' Borchert turned, moved closer by hopping slightly. 'You want to know?'

'Yes.'

Borchert smiled. 'Knowledge is the most valuable of commodities,' he said. 'Shall we trade? I'll trade you knowledge for a limb.'

'What?'

'You heard me,' said Borchert. 'Knowledge for a limb. You choose the limb. Or even just a hand or foot. That should be enough.'

'No,' said Kline.

'That's you're problem,' said Borchert. 'You don't want to know badly enough.'

'I want to know,' said Kline.

'Truth or flesh,' said Borchert. 'Which is more important?'

Kline didn't answer.

'Or say just a digit,' said Borchert. 'A single finger or toe. What does a finger or toe matter? You've already lost eight digits. What difference would one more make?'

Kline stood up, made for the door. He could hear Borchert behind him, chuckling.

'The offer stands, Mr. Kline,' he said. 'Come back any time.'

He lay in bed, thinking. With the light off he kept seeing Aline's mutilated face, the head riding up on the pillow, blankets tucked just below the chin. Eventually he got up and turned the light on.

His foot ached. It was still weeping blood and fluid where the toes had been, and the foot itself was oddly dark, seemed swollen. He put it on a pillow, kept it elevated, which seemed to help a little.

What was the truth? he wondered. How important was it to know? And once he knew, what then?

He looked at his stump. He could still, sometimes, feel the hand there. And, when Borchert had drugged him, he had been able to see it as well, half-present, like a ghost. He tried to will himself to see it again, could not.

Maybe there was someone who could give

him something for his foot, he thought, an anti-inflammatory or perhaps something more, before the foot became too swollen, too painful, to walk on. He would take that, and then stay in bed, waiting for the toes to heal.

Why? he wondered, again seeing Aline's face despite the light still being on. Why had Borchert lied to him? What did he have to gain by pretending Aline was dead when he was actually alive?

He kept turning the question around in his head.

And when, at last, he came up with an answer, he realized he was in very great trouble indeed.

IX

The guard at the gate didn't want to admit him when he arrived, but Kline told him he was coming for an amputation, that Borchert had invited him to return. The guard consulted his fellow behind the door and then waited with Kline at the gate in the dark while the latter guard went upstairs to consult Borchert.

'It's very late,' said the guard.

'He'll see me,' said Kline. 'He told me to come.'

And, indeed, when the other guard returned he was admitted.

He went with the other guard, up the stairs, to Borchert's room. The guard knocked. When Borchert called back, he opened the door, allowed Kline to enter alone.

'Well,' said Borchert. 'Truth is important to you after all, Mr. Kline.'

He was sitting in his chair, a gun in his hand gripped awkwardly with his remaining fingers. 'Please stay right there, Mr. Kline,' he said.

'It's not loaded,' said Kline.

'No?' said Borchert. 'What makes you think that?'

'The gun you gave me wasn't,' said Kline.

'No, it wasn't,' said Borchert, 'but wasn't that perhaps because I was giving it to you?'

Kline didn't answer.

'Care to tell me what you know?' asked Borchert.

'You're planning to kill Aline,' said Kline.

'And?'

'And planning to make it look like I killed him.'

'You've been most obliging in that regard,' said Borchert. 'You've acted your role nicely. A documented penchant for violence. A certain obsession with Aline, dead or alive. You're only wrong in one particular, that being that I've already killed Aline.'

'When?'

'Not long after you last left. For a limbless man he put up quite a fight.'

'Why?'

'Ah,' said Borchert. 'Mr. Kline, I doubt if I can make you understand.'

'Try me.'

'*Try me*, Mr. Kline? How colloquial of you. It was a matter of belief. Aline and I disagreed on certain particulars, questions of belief. Either he or I had to be done away with for the good of the faith in a way that would leave the survivor blameless. Otherwise there would have been a schism. Naturally, I, in my position, preferred that he be done away with rather than I.'

'You were enemies.'

'Not at all. Each of us admired the other. It was simply an expedient political move, Mr. Kline. It had to be done.'

'Why me?'

'Why you, Mr. Kline? Simply because you were there, and because God had touched you with his grace, had chosen you by removing your hand. You'll of course be rewarded in heaven for your role in all this. Whether you'll be rewarded in this life, though, is entirely another matter.'

'Perhaps I should go,' said Kline.

'A good question, Mr. Kline. Do I kill you or do I let you go? Hmmm? What do you think, Mr. Kline? Shall I let you go? Shall we flip a coin?'

Kline did not answer.

'No coin?' asked Borchert. 'Do you care to express an opinion?'

'I'd like to go,' said Kline.

'Of course you would,' said Borchert. 'And so you shall. Today shall be a day for mercy, not justice. Perhaps, with a little luck, you'll even be able to make it out the gate and past the guards to the so-called freedom of the outside world.'

Kline turned toward the door.

'But then again,' he heard from behind him,

'surely justice must temper mercy, Mr. Kline. Am I right? So perhaps you'd care to leave a little something we can remember you by.'

Kline stood still. And then, without turning around, he reached slowly for the door handle.

'I wouldn't do that if I were you,' said Borchert. 'I hate to shoot a man in the back.'

Kline stopped, turned to face him.

'What do you want?' he asked.

'You know exactly what I want,' said Borchert, his eye steady. 'Flesh for knowledge.'

'No,' said Kline.

'You told the guard you'd come up here for an amputation,' said Borchert. 'There's a cleaver on the counter. The same cleaver you used on my finger. Where the hand is gone, the arm shall follow. Otherwise I shoot you. It makes honestly no difference to me, Mr. Kline. You've accomplished your purpose. Technically, you're no longer needed.'

Kline started slowly for the back of the room. Borchert watched him go, pushing at the floor with his foot to turn his chair around.

There was a cleaver there, embedded in the butcher's block.

'Go ahead, Mr. Kline. 'Take it by the cronge and tug it free.'

He took the cleaver. 'What's to stop me from killing you?' he asked.

'Do you really know how to throw a cleaver, Mr. Kline? Where does one learn such skills? Some sort of Vo-Tec? Can you imagine you'd be able to hit me, let alone hit me so that the blade itself will stick? And even if you did, I imagine I'd be able to squeeze off a shot beforehand –'

'– assuming the gun is loaded.'

'Assuming the gun is loaded,' agreed Borchert affably. 'A shot that would bring the guards running and that would get you killed. So, Mr. Kline, you'd be trading the possibility of killing me for your own life. Is that really what you want to do? No? Now be a good boy and cut off your arm.'

He turned on the burner in the countertop, waited for it to heat up. The cleaver seemed sharp enough, though he realized it might have some difficulty cutting through bone. If he hit the joint just right it probably wouldn't matter, though he shouldn't forget he was cutting left-handed; did he have sufficient force in his left hand to cut all the way through in a single blow?

He lined the cleaver along the crease of his elbow, found the flesh to run from one end of the blade to the other. He would have to hit it exactly right.

In his mind's eye, the cleaver is already coming swiftly down, beginning to bite through skin and flesh and bone. He will be washed over with pain and will stagger, but before going down he must remember to thrust the new end of his arm against the burner to cauterize it, so that he doesn't bleed to death. And then, if he is still standing, he may manage to stagger from the room and down the stairs and eventually out of the compound altogether, where, limping, feverish, in pain, he will make his way out into the lone and dreary world.

And this, he realizes, is only the best possible outcome. In all probability it will be much worse. The hatchet will strike wrong and he will have to strike a second time. He will wooze and fall before cauterizing the wound and then lie on the floor bleeding to death from the wound. The guards will catch him at the gate and kill him. Or even worse, all will go well, the arm coming smoothly off, but Borchert, smiling, will say 'Very good, Mr. Kline. But why stop there? What shall we cut off next?'

He raises the cleaver high. His whole life is waiting for him. He only needs to bring the cleaver down for it to begin.

THE WHITE HANDS

Mark Samuels

Mark Samuels (1967–) is an English writer of weird fiction in the tradition of Arthur Machen and H. P. Lovecraft. Many of his short stories map the outlines of a shadowy modern London that hides a dark and terrifying secret. Samuel's first collection, *The White Hands* (2003) was shortlisted for the British Fantasy Award, along with the title story, reprinted herein. His first long novella, *The Face of Twilight,* was published by PS Publishing in 2005 and a new collection published in 2010. 'The White Hands' is that rarest of weird tales: a self-referential piece, steeped in knowledge of the genre, that succeeds in being scary and original rather than simply a sly in-joke.

You may remember Alfred Muswell, whom devotees of the weird tale will know as the author of numerous articles on the subject of literary ghost stories. He died in obscurity just over a year ago.

Muswell had been an Oxford don for a time, but left the cloisters of the University after an academic scandal. A former student (now a journalist) wrote of him in a privately published memoir:

Muswell attempted single-handedly to alter the academic criteria of excellence in literature. He sought to eradicate what he termed the 'tyranny of materialism and realism' from his teaching. He would loom over us in his black robes at lectures and tutorials, tearing prescribed and classic books to shreds with his gloved hands, urging us to read instead work by the likes of Sheridan Le Fanu, Vernon Lee, M.R. James and Lilith Blake. Muswell was a familiar sight amongst the squares and courtyards of the colleges at night and would stalk abroad like some bookish revenant. He had a very plump face and a pair of circular spectacles. His eyes peered into the darkness with an indefinable expression that could be somewhat disturbing.

You will recall that Muswell's eccentric theories about literature enjoyed a brief but notorious vogue in the 1950s. In a series of essays in the short-lived American fantasy magazine *The Necrophile,* he championed the supernatural tale. This was at a time when other academics and critics were turning away from the genre in disgust, following the illiterate excesses of pulp magazines such as *Weird Tales.* Muswell argued that the anthropocentric concerns of realism had the effect of stifling the much more profound study of infinity. Contemplation of the infinite, he contended, was the faculty that separated man from beast. Realism, in his view, was the literature of the prosaic. It was the quest for the hidden mysteries, he contended, which formed the proper subject of all great literature. Muswell also believed that literature, in its highest form, should unravel the secrets of life and death. This latter concept was never fully explained by him but he hinted that its attainment would involve some actual alteration in the structure of reality itself. This, perhaps inevitably, led to him being dismissed in academic circles as a foolish mystic.

After his quiet expulsion from Oxford, Muswell retreated to the lofty heights of Highgate. From here, the London village that had harboured Samuel Taylor Coleridge during the final phase of his struggle against opium addiction, Muswell continued his literary crusade. A series of photographs reproduced in the fourth issue of *The Necrophile* show Muswell wandering through the leafy streets of Highgate clad in his black three-piece suit, cigarette jammed between lips, plump and be-spectacled. In one of his gloved hands is a book of ghost stories by the writer he most admired, Lilith Blake. This Victorian author is perhaps best known for her collection of short stories, *The Reunion and Others*. Then, as now, fabulously rare, this book was printed in an edition of only one hundred copies. Amongst the cognoscenti, it has acquired legendary status. Muswell was undoubtedly the greatest authority on her life and works. He alone possessed the little that remained of her extant correspondence, as well as diaries, photographs and other personal effects.

In moving to Highgate, Muswell was perhaps most influenced by the fact that Blake had been resident in the village for all of the twenty-two years of her brief life. Her mortal remains were interred in the old West Cemetery in Swains Lane.

I first met Alfred Muswell after writing a letter to him requesting information about Lilith Blake for an article I was planning on supernatural writers of the late-nineteenth and early-twentieth centuries. After an exchange of correspondence he suggested that we should meet one afternoon in the reading room of the Highgate Literary and Scientific Institution. From there he would escort me to his rooms, which, apparently, were difficult to find without help, being hidden in the maze of narrow brick passageways beyond Pond Square.

It was a very cold, clear winter afternoon when I alighted at the Underground station in Highgate and made my way up Southwood Lane towards its village. Snow had fallen since the night before and the lane was almost deserted. Only the sound of my footsteps crunching in the brittle snow broke the silence. When I reached the village I paused for a while to take in my surroundings. The Georgian houses were cloaked in white and glittered in the freezing sunshine. A sharp wind blew chilly gusts across the sagging roofs and chimney pots. One or two residents, clad in greatcoats and well muffled, plodded warily along.

I accosted one of these pedestrians and was directed by him towards the Institute. This was a whitewashed structure, two floors high, facing the square on the corner of Swains Lane. I could see the glow of a coal fire within and a plump man reading in an easy chair through one of the ground floor windows. It was Alfred Muswell.

After dusting the snowflakes from my clothes, I made my way inside and introduced myself to him. He struggled out of his chair, stood upright like a hermit crab quitting its shell, and threw out a gloved hand for me to grasp. He was dressed in his habitual black suit, a cigarette drooping from his bottom lip. His eyes peered at me intensely from behind those round glasses. His hair had thinned and grown white since the photographs in *The Necrophile*. The loss of hair was mainly around the crown, giving him a somewhat monkish appearance.

I hung up my duffel coat and scarf and sat down in the chair facing him.

'We can sit here undisturbed for a few more minutes at least,' he said, 'the other members are in the library attending some lecture about that charlatan, James Joyce.'

I nodded as if in agreement, but my attention was fixed on Muswell's leather gloves. He seemed always to wear them. He had worn a similar pair in *The Necrophile* photographs. I noticed the apparent emaciation of the hands and long fingers that the gloves concealed. His right hand fidgeted constantly with his cigarette while the fingers of his left coiled and uncoiled repeatedly. It was almost as if he were uncomfortable with the appendages.

'I'm very pleased to talk with a fellow devotee of Lilith Blake's tales,' he said, in his odd, strained voice.

'Oh, I wouldn't describe myself as a devotee. Her work is striking, of course, but my own preferences are for Blackwood and Machen. Blake seems to me to lack balance. Her world is one of unremitting gloom and decay.'

Muswell snorted at my comment. He exhaled a great breath of cigarette smoke in my direction and said:

'Unremitting gloom and decay? Rather say that she makes desolation glorious! I believe that De Quincey once wrote "Holy was the grave. Saintly its darkness. Pure its corruption."

Words that describe Lilith Blake's work perfectly. Machen indeed! That red-faced old coot with his deluded Anglo-Catholic rubbish! The man was a drunken clown obsessed by sin. And Blackwood? Pantheistic rot that belongs to the Stone Age. The man wrote mainly for money and he wrote too much. No, no. Believe me, if you want the truth beyond the frontier of appearances it is to Lilith Blake you must turn. She never compromises. Her stories are infinitely more than mere accounts of supernatural phenomena ... '

His voice had reached a peak of shrillness and it was all I could do not to squirm in my chair. Then he seemed to regain his composure and drew a handkerchief across his brow.

'You must excuse me. I have allowed my convictions to ruin my manners. I so seldom engage in debate these days that when I do I become over-excited.' He allowed himself to calm down and was about to speak again when a side door opened and a group of people bustled into the room. They were chatting about the Joyce lecture that had evidently just finished. Muswell got to his feet and made for his hat and overcoat. I followed him.

Outside, in the cold afternoon air, he looked back over his shoulder and crumpled up his face in a gesture of disgust.

'How I detest those fools,' he intoned.

We trudged through the snow, across the square and into a series of passageways. Tall buildings with dusty windows pressed upon us from both sides and, after a number of twists and turns, we reached the building that contained Muswell's rooms. They were in the basement and we walked down some well-worn steps outside, leaving the daylight above us.

He opened the front door and I followed him inside.

Muswell flicked on the light switch and a single bulb suspended from the ceiling and reaching halfway towards the bare floor revealed the meagre room. On each of the walls were long bookcases stuffed with volumes. There was an armchair and footstool in one corner along with a small, circular table on which a pile of books teetered precariously. A dangerous-looking Calor gas fire stood in the opposite corner. Muswell brought another chair (with a canvas back and seat) from an adjoining room and invited me to sit down. Soon afterwards he hauled a large trunk from the same room. It was extremely old and bore the monogram 'L.B.' on its side. He unlocked the trunk with some ceremony, and then sat down, lighting yet another cigarette, his eyes fixed on my face.

I took a notebook from my pocket and, drawing sheaves of manuscripts from the trunk, began to scan them. It seemed dark stuff, and rather strange, but just what I needed for the article. And there was a mountain of it to get through. Muswell, meanwhile, made a melancholy remark, apropos of nothing, the significance of which I did not appreciate until much later.

'Loneliness,' he said, 'can drive a man into mental regions of extreme strangeness.'

I nodded absently. I had found a small box and, on opening it, my excitement mounted. It contained a sepia-coloured photographic portrait of Lilith Blake, dated 1890. It was the first I had seen of her, and must have been taken just before her death. Her beauty was quite astonishing.

Muswell leaned forward. He seemed to be watching my reaction with redoubled interest.

Lilith Blake's raven-black and luxuriant hair curled down to her shoulders. Her face was oval, finished with a small pointed chin. The eyes, wide-apart and piercing, seemed to gaze across the vastness of the time which separated us. Her throat was long and pale, her forehead rounded and stray curls of hair framed the temples. The fleshy lips were slightly parted and her small, sharp teeth gleamed whitely. Around her neck hung a string of pearls and she wore a jet-black, velvet dress. The most delicate and lovely white hands I had ever seen were folded across her bosom. Although the alabaster skin of her face and neck was extremely pale, her hands were paler. They were whiter than the purest snow. It was as if daylight had never touched them. The length of her graceful fingers astonished me.

I must have sat there for some time in silent contemplation of that intoxicating image. Muswell, becoming impatient, finally broke my reverie in a most violent and unnecessary manner. He snatched the photograph from me and held it in the air while he spoke, his voice rising to a feverish pitch:

'Here is the hopeless despair of one haunted by the night. One who had gone down willingly into the grave with a black ecstasy in her heart instead of fear!'

I could only sit there in stunned silence. To me, Muswell seemed close to a complete nervous breakdown.

Later, Muswell must have helped me to sort through the various papers in the trunk. I remember little of the detail. I do know that by the time I finally left his rooms and found my way back to the square through the snow, I had realised that my research into Blake's work would be of the utmost importance to my academic career. Muswell had treasure in his keeping, a literary gold mine, and, given the right handling, it could make my name.

After that, my days were not my own. Try as I might, I could not expunge the vision of Blake from my mind. Her face haunted my thoughts, beckoning me onwards in my quest to discover the true meaning of her work. The correspondence between Muswell and myself grew voluminous as I sought to arrange a time when I would be enabled to draw further on his collection. For a while he seemed to distrust my mounting interest, but at last he accepted my enthusiasm as genuine. He welcomed me as a kindred spirit. By a happy chance, I even managed to rent a room in his building.

And so, during the course of the winter months, I shut myself away with Muswell, poring over Blake's letters and personal effects. I cannot deny that the handling of those things began to feel almost sacrilegious. But as I read the letters, diaries and notebooks I could see that Muswell had spoken only the truth when he described Blake as supreme in the field of supernatural literature.

He would scuttle around his library like a spider, climbing stepladders and hauling out volumes from the shelves, passing them down through the gloomy space to me. He would mark certain passages that he believed furthered a greater understanding of Blake's life and work. Outside, the frequent snow-showers filled the gap between his basement window and the pavement above with icy whiteness. My research was progressing well; my notebook filling up with useful quotations and annotations, but somehow I felt that I was failing to reach the essence of Lilith; the most potent aspect of her vision was eluding my understanding. It was becoming agonising to be so close to her, and yet to feel that her most secret and beautiful mysteries were buried from my view.

'I believe,' Muswell once said, 'that mental isolation is the essence of weird fiction. Isolation when confronted with disease, with madness, with horror and with death. These are the reverberations of the infinity that torments us. It is Blake who delineates these echoes of doom for us. She alone exposes our inescapable, blind stumbling towards eternal annihilation. She alone shows our souls screaming in the darkness with none to heed our cries. Ironic, isn't it, that such a beautiful young woman should possess an imagination so dark and riddled with nightmare?'

Muswell took a deep drag of his cigarette, and, in contemplating his words, seemed to gaze through everything into a limitless void.

Sometimes, when Muswell was away, I would have the collection to myself. Blake's personal letters became as sacred relics to me. Her framed photograph attained a special significance, and I was often unable to prevent myself from running my fingers around the outline of her lovely face.

As time passed, and my research into Lilith Blake's oeuvre began to yield ever more fascinating results, I felt that I was now ready to posthumously afford her the attention that she so richly deserved. Whereas previously I had planned to merely include references to her work in my lengthy article on supernatural fiction during the late-nineteenth and early-twentieth centuries, I now realised that she had to be accorded a complete critical book of her own, such was the importance of the literary legacy I had stumbled across by associating with Muswell. It seemed obvious to me that the man had little real idea of the prime importance of the materials in his possession and that his reclusive lifestyle had led him to regard anything relating to this dead and beautiful creature as his own personal property. His understanding was hopelessly confused by the unsubstantiated assertion that he made of the importance of the 'work behind the works', which I took to mean some obscure mystical interpretation he had formulated from his own muddled, ageing brain.

One afternoon he came across me working on my proposed book and took an apparent polite interest in my writing, but mingled in with that interest was an infuriating sarcasm. I voiced my contention that Blake deserved a much higher place in the literary pantheon. The only reasonable explanation for the failure of her work to achieve this was, I had discovered, the almost total lack of contemporary interest in it. I could trace neither extant reviews of *The Reunion and Others* in any of the literary journals nor mention of her in society columns of the time. At this statement he actually laughed out loud. Holding one of his cigarettes between those thin, gloved fingers he waved it in the air dismissively, and said:

'I should have thought that you would have found the silence surrounding her person and work suggestive, as I did. Do not mistake silence for indifference. Any imbecile might make that erroneous conclusion and indeed many have done so in the past. Lilith Blake was no Count Stenbock, merely awaiting rediscovery. She was *deliberately* not mentioned; her work was specifically excluded from consideration. How much do you think was paid simply to ensure she had a fitting tomb in Highgate Cemetery?! But pray continue, tell me more of your article and I shall try to take into consideration your youthful naiveté.'

As I continued to expand on my theories I saw clearly that he began to smirk in a most offensive fashion. Why, it was as if he were humouring me! My face flushed and I stood up, my back rigid with tension. I was close to breaking point and could not tolerate this old fool's patronising attitude any longer. Muswell took a step backwards and bowed, rather ornately, in some idiotic gentlemanly gesture. But as he did so, he almost lost his footing, as if a bout of dizziness had overcome him. I was momentarily startled by the action and he took the opportunity to make his exit. But before he did so he uttered some departing words:

'If you knew what I know, my friend, and perhaps you soon will, then you would find this literary criticism as horribly amusing as I do. But I am extremely tired and will leave you to your work.'

It seemed obvious to me at that point that Muswell was simply not fit to act as the trustee for Lilith Blake's estate. Moreover, his theatrics and lack of appreciation for my insights indicated progressive mental deterioration. I would somehow have to wrest control over the estate from his enfeebled grasp, for the sake of Blake's reputation.

The opportunity came more quickly than I could have dared hope.

One evening in February Muswell returned from one of his infrequent appointments looking particularly exhausted. I had noticed the creeping fatigue in his movements for a number of weeks. In addition to an almost constant sense of distraction he had also lost a considerable amount of weight. His subsequent confession did not, in any case, come as a shock.

'The game is up for me,' he said, 'I am wasting away. The doctor says I will not last much longer. I am glad that the moment of my assignation with Blake draws near. You must ensure that I am buried with her.'

Muswell contemplated me from across the room, the light of the dim electric bulb reflected off the lenses of his spectacles, veiling the eyes behind. He continued:

'There are secrets which I have hidden from you, but I will reveal them now. I have come to learn that there are those who, though dead, lie in their coffins beyond the grip of decay. The power of eternal visions preserves them: there they lie, softly dead and dreaming. Lilith Blake is one of these and I shall be another. You will be our guardian in this world. You will ensure that our bodies are not disturbed. Once dead, we must not be awakened from the eternal dream. It is for the protection of Lilith and myself that I have allowed you to share in my thoughts and her literary legacy. Everything will make sense once you have read her final works.'

He climbed up the steepest stepladder to the twilight of the room's ceiling and took a metal box from the top of one of the bookcases. He unlocked it and drew an old writing book bound in crumpled black leather from within. The title page was written in Lilith Blake's distinctive longhand style. I could see that it bore the title *The White Hands and Other Tales*.

'This volume,' he said, handing it to me, 'contains the final stories. They establish the truth of all that I have told you. The book must now be published. I want to be vindicated after I die. This book will prove, in the most shocking way, the supremacy of the horror tale over all other forms of literature. As I intimated to you once before, these stories are not accounts of supernatural phenomena but supernatural phenomena in themselves.

'Understand this: Blake was dead when these stories were conceived. But she still dreams and transmitted these images from her tomb to me so that I might transcribe them for her. When you read them you will know that I am not insane. All will become clear to you. You will understand how, at the point of death, the eternal dream is begun. It allows dissolution of the body to be held at bay for as long as one continues the dreaming.'

I realised that Muswell's illness had deeply affected his mind. In order to bring him back to some awareness of reality I said:

'You say that Blake telepathically dictated the stories and you transcribed them? Then how is it that the handwriting is hers and not your own?'

Muswell smiled painfully, paused, and then, for the first and last time, took off his gloves. The hands were Lilith Blake's, the same pale, attenuated forms I recognised from her photograph.

'I asked for a sign that I was not mad,' said Muswell, 'and it was given to me.'

Four weeks later Muswell died.

The doctor's certificate listed the cause of death as heart failure. I had been careful, and as he was already ill, there was little reason for the authorities to suspect anything.

Frankly, I had never countenanced the idea of fulfilling any of Muswell's requests and I arranged for his body to be cremated and interred at Marylebone and St. Pancras Cemetery, amongst a plain of small, indistinguishable graves and headstones. He would not rest at Highgate Cemetery alongside Lilith Blake.

The ceremony was a simple one and beside myself there were no other mourners in attendance. Muswell's expulsion from Oxford had ensured that his old colleagues were wary of keeping in touch with him and there were no surviving members of his family who chose to pay their last respects. The urn containing his ashes was interred in an unmarked plot and the priest who presided over the affair muttered his way through the rites in a mechanical, indifferent fashion. As the ceremony concluded and I made my way across that dull sepulchral plain, under a grey and miserable sky, I had a sense of finality. Muswell was gone forever and had found that oblivion he seemed so anxious to avoid.

It was a few days later that I made my first visit to Lilith Blake's vault. She had been interred in the old West section of Highgate Cemetery and I was unable to gain access alone. There were only official tours of the place available and I attended one, but afterwards I paid the guide to conduct me privately to Blake's vault. We had to negotiate our way through a tangle of overgrown pathways and crumbling gravestones. The vault was located in a near inaccessible portion of the hillside cemetery and as we proceeded through the undergrowth, with thick brambles catching on our trousers, the guide told me that he had only once before visited this vault. This was in the company of another man whose description led me to conclude had been Muswell himself. The guide mentioned that this particular area was a source of some curiosity to the various guides, volunteers and conservationists who worked here. Although wildlife flourished in other parts of the cemetery, here it was conspicuous by its absence. Even the birds seemed to avoid the place.

I remember distinctly that the sun had just set and that we reached the tomb in the twilight. The sycamores around us only added to the gloom. Then I caught sight of an arched roof covered with ivy just ahead, and the guide told me that we had reached our destination. As we approached it and the structure came fully into view I felt a mounting sense of anticipation. Some of the masonry had crumbled away but it was still an impressive example of High Victorian Gothic architecture. The corners of its square exterior were adorned with towers and each side boasted a miniature portico. On one of the sides, almost obliterated by neglect and decay, was a memorial stone, bearing the epitaph:

LILITH BLAKE. BORN 25 DECEMBER 1874. DIED 1 NOVEMBER 1896.

'It is getting late,' the guide whispered to me, 'we must get back.'

I saw his face in the gloom and he had a restless expression. His words had broken in on the strange silence that enveloped the area. I nodded absently, but made my way around to the front of the vault and the rusty trellis gates blocking the entrance to a stairway that led down to her coffin. Peering through the gates I could see the flight of stairs, covered by lichen, but darkness obscured its lower depths. The guide was at my elbow now and tugging my jacket sleeve.

'Come on, come on,' he moaned, 'I could get in real trouble for doing this.'

There was something down there. I had the unnerving sensation that I was, in turn, being scrutinised by some presence in that perpetual darkness. It was almost as if it were trying to communicate with me, and images began to form in my mind, flashes of distorted scenes, of corpses that did not rot, of dreams that things no longer human might dream.

Then the guide got a grip of my arm and began forcibly dragging me away. I stumbled along with him as if in a trance, but the hallucinations seemed to fade the further away we got from the vault and by the time we reached the main gate, I had regained my mental faculties. Thereafter the guide refused any request that I made for him to again take me to the vault and my attempts to persuade his colleagues were met with the same response. In the end I was no longer even granted access to the cemetery on official tours. I later learned that my connection with Muswell had been discovered and that he had caused much trouble to the cemetery authorities in the past with his demands for unsupervised access. On one occasion there were even threats of legal action for trespassing.

As indicated, Muswell had informed me that I was to be his literary executor and thus his collection of Blakeiana was left in my control. I also gained possession of his rooms. So I turned again to the study of Blake's work, hoping therein to further my understanding of the enigma that had taken control of my life. I had still to read *The White Hands and Other Tales* and had been put off doing so by Muswell's insistence that this would enlighten me. I still held to the view that his mystical interpretation was fallacious and the thought that this book might be what he actually claimed it to be was almost detestable to me. I wanted desperately to believe that Muswell had written the book himself, rather than as a conduit for Blake. And yet, even if I dismissed the fact of his peculiar hands, so like Blake's own, even if I put that down to some self-inflicted mutilation due to his long-disordered mental state, not to mention the book's comparatively recent age, still there remained the experience at the vault to undermine my certainty. And so it was to *The White Hands and Other Tales* I turned, hoping there to determine matters once and for all.

I had only managed to read the title story. Frankly, the book was too hideous for anyone but a lunatic to read in its entirety. The tale was like an incantation. The further one progressed the more incomprehensible and sinister the words became. They were sometimes reversed and increasingly obscene. The words in that book conjured visions of eternal desolation. The little that I had read had already damaged my own mind. I became obsessed with the idea of her lying in her coffin, dreaming and waiting for me to liberate her.

During the nights of sleeplessness her voice would call across the dark. When I was able to sleep strange dreams came to me. I would be walking among pale shades in an overgrown and crumbling necropolis. The moonlight seemed abnormally bright and even filtered down to the catacombs where I would follow the shrouded form of Lilith Blake. The world of the dead seemed to be replacing my own.

For weeks, I drew down the blinds in Muswell's library, shutting out the daylight, lost in my speculations.

As time passed I began to wonder just why Muswell had been so insistent that he must be interred with Blake at all costs? My experiences at her vault and the strange hallucinations that I had suffered; might they not have been authentic after all? Could it be that Muswell had actually divined some other mode of existence beyond death, which I too had gleaned only dimly? I did not reach this conclusion lightly. I had explored many avenues of philosophical enquiry before coming back again and again to the conclusion that I might have to rely on Muswell's own interpretation. The critical book on Blake that I proposed to write floundered lost in its own limitations. For, incredible as it seemed, the only explanation that lay before me was that the corpse itself did harbour some form of unnatural sentience, and that close contact with it brought final understanding of the mystery.

I sought to solve a riddle beyond life and death yet feared the answer. The image that held the solution to the enigma that tormented me was the corpse of Lilith Blake. I had to see it in the flesh.

I decided that I would arrange for the body to be exhumed and brought to me here in Muswell's – *my* – rooms. It took me weeks to make the necessary contacts and raise the money required. How difficult it can be to get something done, even something so seemingly simple! How tedious the search for the sordid haunts of the necessary types, the hints dropped in endless conversations with untrustworthy strangers in dirty public houses. How venal, how mercenary is the world at large. During the nights of sleeplessness Lilith Blake's voice would sometimes seem to call to me across the darkness. When I was able to sleep I encountered beautiful dreams, where I would be walking among pale shades in an overgrown and crumbling necropolis. The moonlight seemed abnormally bright and even filtered down to the catacombs where I would find Lilith's shrouded form.

At last terms were agreed. Two labourers were hired to undertake the job, and on the appointed night I waited in my rooms. Outside, the rain was falling heavily and in my mind's eye, as I sat anxiously in the armchair smoking cigarette after cigarette, I saw the deed done; the two simpletons, clad in their raincoats and with crowbars and pickaxes, climbing over the high wall which ran along Swains Lane, stumbling through the storm and the overgrown grounds past stone angels and ruined monuments, down worn steps to the circular avenue, deep in the earth, but open to the mottled grey-and-black sky. Wet leaves must have choked the passageways. I could see the rain sweeping over the hillside cemetery as they levered open the door to her vault, their coats floundering in the wind. The memory of Lilith Blake's face rose before me through the hours that passed. I seemed to see it in every object that caught my gaze. I had left the blind up and watched the rain beating at the window above me, the water streaming down the small Georgian panes. I began to feel like an outcast of the universe.

As I waited, I thought I saw a pair of eyes staring back at me in the clock on the mantelpiece. I thought too that I saw two huge and thin white spiders crawling across the books on the shelves.

At last there were three loud knocks on the door and I came to in my chair, my heart pounding in my chest. I opened the door to the still-pouring rain, and there at last, shadowy in the night, were my two graverobbers. They were smiling unpleasantly, their hair plastered down over their worm-white faces. I pulled the wad of bank notes from my pocket and stuffed them into the nearest one's grasp.

They lugged the coffin inside and set it down in the middle of the room.

And then they left me alone with the thing. For a while, the sodden coffin dripped silently onto the rug, the dark pools forming at its foot spreading slowly outwards, sinking gradually into the worn and faded pile. Although its wooden boards were decrepit and disfigured with dank patches of greenish mould, the lid remained securely battened down by a phalanx of rusty nails. I had prepared for this moment carefully; I had all the tools I needed ready in the adjoining room, but something, a sudden sense of foreboding, made me hesitate foolishly. At last, with a massive effort of will, I fetched the claw hammer and chisel, and knelt beside the coffin. Once I had prised the lid upwards and then down again, leaving the rusted nail-tops proud, I drew them out one by one. It seemed to take forever – levering each one up and out and dropping it onto the slowly growing pile at my feet. My lips were dry and I could barely grip the tools in my slippery hands. The shadows of the rain still trickling down the window were thrown over the room and across the coffin by the orange glow of the street lamp outside.

Very slowly, I lifted the lid.

Resting in the coffin was a figure clothed in a muslin shroud that was discoloured with age. Those long hands and attenuated fingers were folded across its bosom. Lilith Blake's raven-black hair seemed to have grown whilst she had slept in the vault and it reached down to her waist. Her head was lost in shadow, so I bent closer to examine it. There was no trace of decay in the features, which were of those in the photograph and yet it now had a horrible aspect, quite unlike that decomposition I might have anticipated. The skin was puffy and white, resembling paint applied on a tailor's dummy. Those fleshy lips that so attracted me in the photograph were now repulsive. They were lustreless and drew back from her yellowed, sharp little teeth. The eyes were closed and even the lashes seemed longer, as if they too had grown, and they reminded me of the limbs of a spider. As I gazed at the face and fought back my repulsion, I had again the sensation that I had experienced at the vault.

Consciousness seemed to mingle with dreams. The two states were becoming one and I saw visions of some hellish ecstasy. At first I again glimpsed corpses that did not rot, as if a million graves had been opened, illuminated by the phosphoric radiance of suspended decay. But these gave way to wilder nightmares that I could glimpse only dimly, as if through a billowing vapour; nightmares that to see clearly would result in my mind being destroyed. And I could not help being reminded of the notion that what we term sanity is only a measure of success in concealing underlying madness.

Then I came back to myself and saw Lilith Blake appearing to awaken. As she slowly opened her eyes, the spell was broken, and I looked into them with mounting horror. They were blank and repugnant, no longer belonging in a human face; the eyes of a thing that had seen sights no living creature could see. Then one of her hands reached up and her long fingers clutched feebly against my throat as if trying to scratch, or perhaps caress, me.

With the touch of those clammy hands I managed to summon up enough self-control to close the lid and begin replacing the coffin nails, fighting against the impulses that were driving me to gaze again upon the awakened apparition. Then, during a lull in the rain, I burned the coffin and its deathly contents in the back yard. As I watched the fire build I thought that I heard a shrieking, like a curse being invoked in the sinister and incomprehensible language of Blake's tale. But the noise was soon lost in the roar of the flames.

It was only after many days that I discovered that the touch of Lilith Blake's long white fingers had produced marks that, once visible, remained permanently impressed upon my throat.

I travelled abroad for some months afterwards, seeking southern climes bathed in warm sunshine and blessed with short nights. But my thoughts gradually returned to *The White Hands and Other Tales*. I wondered if it might be possible to achieve control over it, to read it in its entirety and use it to attain my goal. Finally, its lure proved decisive. I convinced myself that I had already borne the darkest horrors, that this would have proved a meet preparation for its mysteries, however obscenely they were clothed. And so, returning once more to Highgate, I began the task of transcribing and interpreting the occult language of the book, delving far into its deep mysteries. Surely I could mould the dreams to my own will and overcome the nightmare. Once achieved, I would dwell forever, in Paradise…

Text of a letter written by John Harrington whilst under confinement in Maudsley Psychiatric Hospital:

My dearest wife Lilith,

I do not know why you have not written or come to see me.

The gentlemen looking after me here are

very kind but will not allow any mirrors. I know there is something awful about my face. Everyone is scared to look at it.

They have taken your book away. They say it is gibberish. But I know all the secrets now.

Sometimes I laugh and laugh.

But I like the white hands that crawl around my bed at night like two spiders. They laugh with me.

Please write or come.

With all my heart,

John.

FLAT DIANE

Daniel Abraham

Daniel Abraham (1969–) is an American author who lives in Albuquerque, New Mexico. His first short story, 'Mixing Rebecca', was published by Ann VanderMeer in *The Silver Web* in 1996. Since then his short stories have appeared in numerous publications and anthologies. The disturbing novelette 'Flat Diane' (2004) reprinted here was nominated for the Nebula Award and won the International Horror Guild Award in 2005. Abraham has also been nominated for the Hugo Award and the World Fantasy Award. He is primarily known for his fantasy series such as the *Long Price Quartet,* which features a world where poets use magic in a struggle for power. However, his early short fiction made powerful use of surrealism and horror.

His hands didn't tremble as he traced his daughter. She lay on the kitchen floor, pressing her back against the long, wide, white paper he'd brought, her small movements translated into soft scratching sounds where the cut end tried to curl down into the floor. His pen moved along the horizons of her body – here, where her wrist widened, and then each finger; down her side; rounding the ball of her feet like the passage around the Cape of Good Hope; up to where her wide shorts made it clear this wasn't a work of pornography; then back down the other leg and around. When he came to her spilling hair, he traced its silhouette rather than remain strictly against her skin. He wanted it to look like her, and Diane had thick, curly, gorgeous hair just like her mother had.

'Just almost done, sweetie,' he said when she started to shift and fidget. She quieted until the pen tip touched the point where it had started, the circle closed. As he sat back, she jumped up to see. The shape was imperfect – the legs ended in awkward Thalidomide bulbs, the hair obscured the long oval face, the lines of the tile were clear where the pen had jumped.

Still.

'Okay,' Ian said. 'Now let's just put this on here, and then … '

'I want to write it,' Diane said.

Diane was eight, and penmanship was new to her and a thing of pride. Ian reached up to the table, took down a wooden ruler with a sharp metal edge, and drew lines for his daughter to follow. He handed her the pen and she hunched over.

'Okay, sweetie. Write this. Ready?'

She nodded, her hair spilling into her face. She pushed it away impatiently, a gesture of her mother's. Candice, who pushed a lot of things away impatiently.

'Hi,' Ian said, slowly, giving his daughter time to follow. 'I'm Flat Diane. My real girl, Diane Bursen, sent me out to travel for her. I can't write because I'm only paper. Would you please send her a picture of us, so she can see where I am and what adventures (Ian stopped here to spell the word out) I'm having?'

Ian had to draw more lines on the other side of Flat Diane for the mailing address, but Diane waited and then filled that out too, only forgetting the zip code.

Together, they rolled Flat Diane thin and put her in a mailing tube, capped the end with a white plastic lid and sealed it with tape.

'Can we send Flat Diane to see Mommy?'

He could feel his reaction at the corners of his mouth. Diane's face fell even before he spoke, her lower lip out, her brown eyes hard. Ian stroked her hair.

'We will, sweetheart. Just as soon as she's ready to let us know where we can mail things to her, we will.'

Diane jerked away, stomped off to the living room and turned on the TV, sulking. Ian addressed the package to his mother in Scotland, since it seemed unlikely that either of them would be able to afford a transatlantic vacation anytime soon. When the evening news came on with its roster of rapes and killings, he turned off the set, escorted his protesting daughter through her evening rituals, tucked her into bed and then went to his room and lay sleepless until after midnight.

The photograph shows his mother, smiling. Her face is broader than he remembered it, the hair a uniform grey but not yet white. She holds Flat Diane up, and behind them the half-remembered streets of Glasgow.

There is writing on the back in blue pen and a familiar hand:

Flat Diane arrived yesterday. I'm taking her to my favorite teahouse this afternoon. It was designed by Charles Rennie Mackintosh – one of the best architects ever to come out of Glasgow, and the scones are lovely. Tomorrow, we are going to work together. My love to Ian and the real Diane.

Mother Bursen.

Diane was elated, and Ian was both pleased that the plan was working and saddened to realize how rare his daughter's elation had become. She had insisted that the picture go with her to school, and while she promised that she would care for it, Ian was anxious for it. It was precious, irreplaceable, and therefore fragile.

After work, he went to collect her from her friend Kit's house, anxiety for the picture still in the back of his mind.

'Today,' Kit's father Tohiro reported as they drank their ritual cup of coffee, 'everything was Scotland. How the people talk in Scotland. How the tea is made in Scotland. Whether you have to share tables at restaurants in Scotland. Diane has become the expert in everything.'

'It's my mother. She sent a picture.'

'I saw. She told us about the ... what? The drawing? Flat Diane? It's a good idea.'

'It gives her something to look forward to. And I wanted her to know how many people there are looking out for her. I haven't much family in the States. And with her mother gone ...'

A cascade of thumps announced the girls as they came down the stairs. Diane stalked into the kitchen, her brows furrowed, hair curled around her head like a stormcloud. She went to her father, arms extended in demand, and he lifted her familiar weight to his lap.

'I want to go home now,' she said. 'Kit's a butthead.'

Ian grimaced an apology. Tohiro smiled – amused, weary – and sipped his coffee.

'Okay, sweetie. Go get your coat, okay?'

'I don't want my coat.'

'Diane.'

His tone was warning enough. She got down and, looking over her shoulder once in anger at the betrayal of insisting on her coat, vanished again. Ian sighed.

'She's just tired,' Tohiro said. 'Kit's the same way.'

They drove home through a rising fog. Though it made Ian nervous, driving when he couldn't quite make out what was coming, Diane only chattered on, stringing together the events of her day with *and* after *and* after *and.* No matter if no two facts led one to another – they were what she had to say, and he listened half from weariness and half from love.

An accident of timers turned the lights on just as they pulled into the driveway, as if someone were there to greet them. There was nothing in the mailbox from Flat Diane. Or from Candice.

'Daddy?'

Ian snapped to, as if coming awake. Diane held the screen door open, frowning at him impatiently. He couldn't say how long she'd been there, how long he'd fallen into dim reverie.

'Sorry, sweetie,' he said, pulling keys from his pocket. 'Just got lost in the fog a minute.'

Diane turned, looking out at the risen grey. His daughter narrowed her eyes, looking out into nothing.

'I like the fog,' she said, delivering the pronouncement with the weight of law. 'It smells like Scotland.'

And for a moment, it did.

The photograph isn't really a photograph but a color printout from an old printer, the ink shinier than the paper it stains. On it Flat Diane is unfurled between a smiling couple. The man is thick, wide-lipped, greying at the temple. He wears a yellow polo shirt and makes a thumbs-up with the hand that isn't supporting Flat Diane. The woman is smaller, thinner. Her smile is pinched. She only looks like her brother Ian around the eyes and in the tilt of her nose.

Behind them is a simple living room, the light buttery yellow and somehow dirty.

The bottom of the page carries a message typed as part of the same document:

Dear Ian and Diane,

Flat Diane is here with us in Dallas. She's just in time for Valentine's day. She's coming out to our special dinner with us tonight at Carmine's Bistro – Italian food. Yum!

Hope everything's good with you. See you soon. Much love.

Aunt Harriet and Uncle Bobby.

In two weeks, Diane would be nine. It was a foreign thought. So little time seemed to have passed since her last birthday until he realized that Candice hadn't quite left then. This, now, was his first birthday as both of her parents. He had demanded the day off, and his manager had acquiesced. He had arranged with the school to take her out for the day. A movie, a day with him, and a party that night with all her friends. Kit's parents Anna and Tohiro were helping to drive them all.

He knew he was overcompensating. He hoped it would be enough, and not only for her. There was a loneliness in him that also had to be appeased. Over the course of months, the traces of his wife – still his wife, still only separated – had begun to erode. The last of her special toothpaste used up; the pillows no longer smelling of her hair; the foods that only she ate spoiled and thrown away. In their place were the toys Diane didn't put away, the homework left half-done on the table, the sugared breakfast cereals too sweet for Ian to enjoy except as candy.

But Diane's things were all part his – hers to enjoy, and his to shepherd. Nothing had to be put away unless he said it did, nothing had to be finished unless he insisted, nothing was too sweet, too empty, too bad for you to be dinner except that Ian – big bad unreasonable mean Daddy – said no. Daddy who, after all, couldn't even keep a wife.

It was Friday, and Kit was sleeping over. The girls were in the back – in Diane's room – playing video games. Ian sat on the couch with a beer sweating itself slick in his hand while a news magazine show told of a child drowned in the bathtub by his mother. The place smelled of order-out pizza and the toy perfume from the beauty salon toys that Kit brought over; costume jewelry spread out on the carpet, glittering and abandoned.

Ian's thoughts were pleasantly vague – the dim interest in the tragedy playing out on the television, the nagging knowledge that he would have to pretend to make the girls go to sleep soon (they would stay up anyway), the usual pleasure of a week's work ended. Kit's shriek bolted him half across the house before his mind quite understood what the sound had been.

In the bedroom, the tableau. Kit sat inelegantly on the floor, her hand to her cheek, her nose bloody. The controllers for the game box splayed out, black plastic tentacles abandoned on the carpet; the electric music still looping. And Diane, her hand still in a fist, but her eyes wide and horrified.

'What in Christ's name is going on in here?' Ian demanded.

'Sh … she hit me,' Kit began, her voice rising as the tears began. 'I didn't do anything and she just hit me.'

'Diane?'

His daughter blinked and her gaze flickered at her friend, as if looking for support. And then her own eyes filled.

'It was my turn,' Diane said, defensively.

'So you hit her?'

'I was mad.'

'I'm going *home*!' Kit howled and bolted for the bathroom. Ian paused for a half second, then scowled and went after the girl leaving Diane behind. Kit was in the bathroom, trying to staunch the blood with her hand. Ian helped her, sitting her on the toilet with her head tipped back, a wad of tissue pressed to her lip. The bleeding wasn't bad; it stopped quickly. There was no blood on the girl's clothes. When he was sure it wouldn't start again, he wetted a washcloth and wiped Kit's face gently, the blood pinking the terrycloth.

Diane haunted the doorway, her dark eyes profound with confusion and regret.

'I want to go home,' Kit said when he had finished. Her small mouth was pressed thin. Ian felt his heart bind. If Diane lost Kit, he'd loose Tohiro and Anna. It was a fleeting thought, and he was ashamed of it the moment it struck him.

'Of course,' he said. 'I'll take you there. But first I think Diane owes you an apology.'

Diane was weeping openly, the tears gathering on her chin. Kit turned to her, and Ian crossed his arms.

'I didn't mean to,' Diane said. 'It's just that when people get mad, they hit each other sometimes.'

'Diane, what are you thinking? Where did you get an idea like that?'

'Uncle Bobby does, when he's mad. He hits Aunt Harriet all the time.'

Ian felt his lips press thin.

'Really. And have you seen him hit her? Diane, have you seen Bobby hit anyone, ever?'

Diane frowned, thinking, trying to remember something. The failure emptied her.

'No.'

'Did anyone tell you a story about Bobby hitting Harriet?'

Again the pause, and confusion deep as stone.

'No.'

'And?'

Diane stared at him, her mouth half open, her eyes lost.

'I think the words we're looking for are "I'm sorry,"' Ian said. It was the way his father would have said it.

'I'm sorry, Kitty. I'm sorry. I thought . . .' and Diane shook her head, held out her hands, palms up in a shrug that broke his heart. 'I'm sorry, Kitty. I won't do it again ever, I swear. Don't go home, okay?'

Kit, sullen, scowled at the white and blue tile at her feet.

'Please?' Diane said. He could hear in the softness of her voice how much the word had cost. He paused, hoping that Kit would relent, that she would simply take the blow and accept it, that she would believe that Diane would never do it again.

''Kay,' Kit said. Ian's relief was palpable, and he saw it in Diane. His daughter ran over grabbed her friend's hand, pulled her out, back to the room. Ian looked in on them. Diane was showering Kit with affection, flattering her shamelessly, letting her play as many times as she cared to. Diane was showing her belly. And it worked. Kit came back from the edge, and they were best friends again.

He put them both to bed, making them promise unconvincingly not to stay up talking, then went through the house, checking that the doors and windows were all locked, turning off the lights. He ended in the living room, in the overstuffed chair he'd brought from his home when he and Candice first became lovers. The cushions knew the shape of his back. Sitting under a single lamp that was the only light in the house, he closed his eyes for a moment and drank in silence. The book he was reading – a police procedural set in New Orleans – lay closed on his knee. His body was too tired to rest yet, his mind spun too fast by Diane and his isolation and the endless stretch of working at his desk. When he finally did open his book, the story of grotesque murder and alluring voodoo queens was a relief.

Diane walked in on bare feet just as he was preparing to dog-ear the page, check the girls, and crawl into bed. She crossed the room, walking past the pool of light and receding for a moment into the darkness before coming back to him. In her hand was the scrapbook he'd set aside for Flat

Diane. Without speaking, she crawled onto his lap, opened the book with a creak of plastic and cheap glued spine, and took out the page they'd just gotten. His sister, her husband. The meaty hand and sausage-thick thumb. His sister's pinched smile. The filthy light.

'I don't want this one in here,' Diane said, handing it to him. Her voice was small, frightened. 'I don't like Uncle Bobby.'

'Okay, sweetie,' he said, taking it from her.

She leaned against him now, her arms pressed into her chest, her knees drawn up. He put his arms around her and rocked gently until they were both near to sleep.

It was the moment, looking back, that he would say he understood what Flat Diane had become.

There are over a dozen photographs in the book now, but this latest addition commands its own page. In it, Candice is sitting at a simple wooden table. Her hair is pulled back in a ponytail that even where it is bound is thick as her forearm. Her eyes slant down at the corners, but her skin is the same tone as Diane's, the oval face clearly the product of the same blood. There is a spider fern hanging above her. The impression is of melancholy and calm and tremendous intimacy. It is not clear who operated the camera.

Flat Diane is in the chair beside her, folded as if she were sitting with her mother. A small, cartoon heart has been added to the paper, though it is not clear by whom.

The real Diane has outstripped her shadow – taller, thinner, more awkward about the knees and elbows. This silhouette is already the artifact of a girl who has moved on, but this is not obvious from the picture. In the scrapbook, the only sign of change is a bend on one corner of Flat Diane's wide paper, a design drawn in the white space over the outlined left shoulder, and the lock of white hair across Candice's forehead.

The letter reads:

Diane –

Flat Diane arrived yesterday. I have to tell you she makes me miss you. You can see she's here with me in my apartment.

I love you very much, Diane. I know that it can't seem like it right now, but please believe me when I say it's true. There is no one in the world more important to me than you are. And I hope that, when your father and I have worked out the paths our souls need to take, we can be together again. Whatever happens, I will always be your mother.

It is signed Candice Calvino, her maiden name.

The other letter is not in the scrapbook. It reads:

Ian –

Christ, Ian, I really don't know what to say. I thought that I could just sit down and write this to you rationally, but I am just so goddam pissed off, I'm not sure that's possible.

This stunt is exactly the kind of emotional extortion that made it impossible for me to stay near you. What were you thinking? That you could hold her up, maybe wave her around like a flag, and make me come trotting back – we could just stay together for the children's sake? Our daughter should be more than just the easiest tool for you to get in a dig at me. How could you do this to her?

If you wanted to make me feel guilty or shamed or selfish, well nice job, Ian. You did.

Never use her like this again. If it isn't beneath you, it goddam well should be.

C.

The hallway outside the school's administrative offices had white stucco walls, linoleum flooring worn by millions of footsteps from thousands of students, harsh fluorescent lighting. An old clock – white face yellow with age – reported twenty minutes before the noon bell would ring, the press of small bodies filling the halls like spring tadpoles. When Ian walked in, straightening his tie, swallowing his dread, his footsteps echoed.

The secretary smiled professionally when he gave her his name, and led him to a smaller room in the back. The placard on the door – white letters on false woodgrain – said that the principal's name was Claude Bruchelli. The secretary knocked once, opened the door, and stepped aside to let Ian pass through a cloud of her cloying perfume and into the office.

The principal rose, stretching out a hand, establishing for Diane that the grownups were together, that they had special rules of respect and courtesy. It was the sort of thing Ian remembered with resentment from when he'd been her age, but he shook the man's hand all the same.

'Thanks for coming, Mr. Bursen. I know it's hard to just leave work like this. But we have a problem.'

Diane, sitting on a hardbacked chair, stared at her feet. The way she drummed her heels lightly against the chair legs told him that this was not resentment, but remorse. Ian cleared his throat.

'All right,' he said. 'What's she done?'

'Mr. Bursen, we have some very strict guidelines from the city about fighting.'

'Another fight?'

The principal nodded gravely. It had been at morning recess. Her friend Kit had been adamant that the other girl had started it, but the teacher who had seen it all reported otherwise. No, there had been no injuries beyond a few scratches. This was, however the third time, which meant a mandatory three-day suspension.

Diane, stone-faced, seemed to be staring at a banner on the wall that blared 'We Aim For Excellence! We Expect The Best Of You!'

'All right,' Ian said. 'I can get her homework for her and she can do it at home.'

The principal nodded, but didn't speak. He looked at Ian from under furrowed brows.

'Mr. Bursen, I have to follow the guidelines. And they're good as far as they go, but Diane's anger problems aren't going to go away. I wish you'd reconsider letting Mrs. Birch…'

'No. I'm sorry, no. I've had a certain amount of counseling myself, one time and another. It doesn't do any good to force a child into it.'

'Perhaps Diane would choose to,' the principal said as if she wasn't there, as if her dark, hard eyes weren't fixed on his wall. Ian shrugged.

'Well, what of it, Diane? Care to see Mrs. Birch?' He'd meant to say it gently, but the tone when it left his mouth sounded more of sarcasm. Diane shook her head. Ian met the principal's gaze.

All the way back home, Diane pressed herself against the car door, keeping as far from Ian as she could. He didn't try to speak, not until he knew which words were in him. Instead, he ran through all the people he could think of who might be able or willing to look after Diane for the duration of her exile.

When, that night, he finally spoke, he did it poorly. They were eating dinner – chicken soup and peanut butter sandwiches. He hadn't spoken, she had sulked. Between them the house had been a bent twig, tension ready to snap.

'I can't afford to take three days off work,' he said. 'They'll fire me.'

Diane shrugged, a movement she inherited from him. Her father, who shrugged a lot of feelings away.

'Di, can you at least tell me what this is all about? Fighting at school. It isn't like you, is it?'

'Lisa started it. She called me a nerd.'

'And so you hit her?'

Diane nodded and took a bite of her sandwich. Ian felt the blood rushing into his face.

'Jesus Christ, Di. You can't do this! What… I don't know what you're thinking! I am holding on to this house by a thread. I am working every day for you, and you are being a little brat! I don't deserve this from you, you know that?'

The bowl sailed across the room, soup arcing out behind it. It shattered where it landed. Diane's bowl. Ian went silent. She stood on her chair, making small grunting noises as she tore the sandwich and squeezed the bread and butter into paste.

'You never listen to me! You always take everyone else's side!'

'Diane…'

'When?' she screamed. 'Exactly when in all this do I start to matter?'

It was her mother's voice, her mother's tone and vocabulary. Ian's chest ached suddenly, and the thought came unbidden *What has Candice said in front of that drawing?* Diane turned and bolted from the room.

When the shards of their dinner were disposed of, the salt of soup and sweet of sandwich buried alike in the disposal, Ian went to her. In the dark of her room, Diane was curled on her bed. He sat beside her and stroked her hair.

'I didn't do anything wrong,' she said, her

voice thick with tears. She didn't mean fighting or throwing soup bowls. She meant that she had done nothing to deserve her mother's absence.

'I know, sweetie. I know you didn't.'

'I want to see Mrs. Birch.'

He felt his hand falter, forced it to keep touching her, keep reassuring her that he was there, that they were a family, that all would be well.

'If you want, sweetie,' he said. 'We can do that if you want.'

He felt her nod. That night, trying to sleep, he thought of every mean-spirited thing he'd ever said to Diane, of every slight and disappointment and failure that he'd added to her burden. Candice's letter – the private one she'd sent to him – rang in his mind. Diane would be confessing all his sins to someone he'd never met, who would be taking confidences from his daughter that he might never know.

For all the weeks and months that he'd silently prayed for someone to help, someone to shoulder part of the burden of Diane's soul, the granting tasted bitter. His fears were unfounded.

The time came, and Mrs. Birch – a thick woman with a pocked face and gentle voice – became a character in Diane's tales of her days. He waited with a sense of dread, but no recriminations came back to him from the school, no letters condemning him as a man and a father. In fact, over the weeks, Diane seemed to become more herself. The routine of fight and reconciliation with Kit, the occasional missive from Flat Diane's latest hosts, the complaints about schoolwork and clothes and how little money he had to spend on her all came almost back to normal. Once, he saw what might have been anger when Diane saw a photograph of her mother. After that he noticed that she had stopped asking when Mommy was coming home. He couldn't have said, if asked, whether the sorrow, the sense of triumph, or the guilt over that sense was the strongest of his reactions.

Everything was fine until the night in February when she woke up screaming and didn't stop.

The picture is cheap – the color balance is off, giving the man's face an unnatural yellow tint. He is in his later twenties, perhaps his early thirties, the presentiment of jowls already plucking the flesh of his jaws. His hair is short and pale. His eyes are blue.

In the picture, Flat Diane has been taped around a wide pillar, her arms and legs bending back out of sight. A long black cloth wraps across where the eyes might be, had Ian drawn them in; a blindfold.

The man who Ian doesn't know, has never met, is caressing a drawn-in breast. His tongue protrudes from his viciously grinning mouth, its tip flickering distance from the silhouette's thigh. He looks not like Satan, but like someone who wishes that he were, someone trying very hard to be.

The writing on the back of the photograph is block letters, written in blue felt-tip.

It reads: Flat Diane has gone astray.

A new photograph comes every week. Some might be amusing to another person, most make him want to retch.

The best trick Hell has to play against its inmates is to whisper to them that this – this now – is the bottom. Nothing can be worse than this. And then to pull the floor away.

'I'm sorry,' Ian said, refusing to understand. 'I didn't catch that.'

Mrs. Birch leaned back, her wide, pitted face tired and impassive. She laced her hands on her desk. The hiss of the heating system was the only sound while she brought herself to break the news again. This time, she took a less direct approach.

'Diane has always had an anger problem. There's no good time to lose your mother, but this stage of development is particularly bad. And I think that accounts for a lot of her long-term behaviors. The fighting, the acting out in class, but these *new* issues...'

'Child protective services?' Ian said, able at last to repeat the counselor's statement and plumb the next depth of hell. 'You called child protective services?'

'The kind of sudden change we've seen in her – the nightmares, the anxiety attacks... She's in fifth grade, Mr. Bursen. No kid in fifth grade should be having anxiety attacks. When she went to the doctor, you and he and two nurses together couldn't get her to undress, and you say she never had a problem with it before. That kind of sudden change means trauma. Nothing *does* that but trauma.'

Ian closed his eyes, the heel of his palm pressed to brow, rubbing deeply. His body shook, but it seemed unconnected to his terrible clarity of mind, like the tremors were something being done to him.

'The Buspar seems to be helping,' he said. An idiot change of subject, and not at all to the point, but Mrs. Birch shifted in her chair and went there with him.

'There are a lot of anti-anxiety drugs,' she agreed. 'Some of them may help. But only with the symptoms, not the problem. And the trauma, whatever it is... it may be something ongoing.'

'Christ.'

'She's graduating in a few weeks here. Next year's middle school, and I won't be able to see her any more. With CPS, you'll have a caseworker, someone who isn't going to change every time she switches schools. And who knows? Maybe the investigation will help. I'm sorry. About all of this. I really am. But it's the right thing.'

Now it was Ian's turn to go silent, to gather himself. Speaking the words was like standing at the edge of a cliff.

'You think I'm fucking my kid.'

'No,' Mrs. Birch said in the voice of a woman for whom this territory was not new. 'But I think somebody is.'

Diane waited for him in the outer office, looking smaller than she was, folded in on herself. He forced himself to look at her as she was, and not as he wanted her to be. She forced a smile and raised a hand, sarcastic and sad. Ian knelt at her feet and took her hand, but Diane would not meet his gaze. Mrs. Birch was a presence he felt behind him, but didn't see.

'Sweetie,' he said.

Diane didn't look up. He reached out to stroke her hair, but hesitated, pulled back. It was that fear that touching his child would be interpreted as sex that brought home how much they had lost.

'It's going to be okay, sweetie,' he said, and Diane nodded, though she didn't believe it. When he stood, she scooped up her book bag and went out with him. In the hallway, with Mrs. Birch still haunting the door to the office, Diane reached up and put her hand in his. It was a thin victory, hardly any comfort at all.

The clouds were close, smelling of rain. He drove home slowly, the sense of disconnection, of unreality, growing as the familiar streets passed by. Diane sat alert but silent until they were almost home.

'Are they going to make me live with Mom?'

A pang of fear so sharp it was hard to differentiate from nausea struck him, but he kept his voice calm. He couldn't let her think they might lose each other.

'Make you? No, sweet. There's going to be someone from the state who's going to want to talk to you, but that's all.'

'Okay.'

'They're going to ask you questions,' he continued, the words leaking from him like air from a pricked balloon. 'You just need to tell them the truth. Even if you get embarrassed or someone told you that you shouldn't tell them something, you should tell them the truth.'

'Okay.'

He pulled into the driveway, their house – Christ, the mortgage payment was a week late already; he had to remember to mail the check tomorrow – looming in the twilight. The lawn was the spare, pale green of spring.

'You should tell me the truth too,' he said, amazed by how sane he sounded, how reasonable. 'Sweetie? Is there anyone who's doing things to you? Things you don't like?'

'Like am I getting molested?'

Amazing too how old she had become. He killed the engine. There had to be some way to ask gently, some approach to this where he could still treat her like a child, still protect her innocence. He didn't know it, couldn't find it. The rich scent of spring was an insult.

'Are you?' he asked.

Diane's eyes focused on the middle distance, her face a mask of concentration. Slowly, she shook her head, but her hands plucked at the seat, popping the cloth upholstery in wordless distress.

'If something were happening, Di, you could tell me. There wouldn't be anything to be afraid of.'

'It's not so bad during the day,' she said. 'It's

at night. It's like I know things… there's things I know and things I can almost remember. But they didn't happen.'

'You're sure they didn't?'

A hesitation, but a nod – firm and certain.

'The doctor's going to want to examine you,' he said.

'I don't want him to.'

'Would it be better with a different doctor?'

'No.'

'What if it was a woman? Would that make it easier?'

Diane frowned out the window of the car.

'Maybe,' she said softly. Then, 'I don't want to be crazy.'

'You're not, sweet. You're not crazy. No more than I am.'

They ate dinner together, talking about other things, laughing even. A thin varnish of normalcy that Ian felt his daughter clinging to as desperately as he was. Afterwards, Kit called, and Diane retreated to gossip in privacy while Ian cleaned the dishes. He read her to sleep, watching her chest from the corner of his eye until her breath was steady and deep and calm. He left a night light glowing, a habit she'd returned to recently.

He sat in the kitchen and slowly, his hands shaking, laid out the pictures of Flat Diane – the ones recently arrived, the ones he hadn't shown her. He shuffled them, rearranged them, spread them out like tarot.

It had been stupid, sending out their real address. Ian saw that now, and twisted the thought to better feel the pain of it. What if this mad fucker had tracked down Diane because Ian had as good as sent out directions to her… ?

But no, he didn't believe that. Or that Tohiro or one of her teachers or some evil pizza delivery man had targeted her. The photographs were too much a coincidence, the timing too precise.

He recalled vividly his art history teacher back at university, back at home in Scotland. The old man had told each of them to bring in a picture of a person they loved – mother, father, brother, lover, pet. And then, he'd told them to gouge out the eyes. The shocked silence was the first moment of his lecture on the power of image, the power of art. These were dumb bits of paper, but each of them that touched pen-tip to a beloved eye knew – did not believe, but *knew* – that the pictures were connected with the people they represented.

Ian had sent his daughter's soul voyaging. He hadn't even considered the risks. It was worse than sending only their address; he might as well have delivered her, trussed and helpless. And now…

And now Flat Diane had gone astray.

With a boning knife, he cut out the blond man's blue eyes, but he felt the effort's emptiness. Nothing so poetic for him. Instead, he took the envelopes to his study, turned on his computer, and scanned in the bastard's face. When it was saved, he dropped it into email and then got on the phone.

'Hello?' Candice said from a thousand miles away. Her voice was uncertain – wondering, he supposed, who would be calling her so late at night.

'It's Ian. Check your email.'

The pause would have been strained if he'd cared more. If this had still been about the two of them and what they'd had and lost and why. Only it wasn't and the hesitation at the far end of the line only made him impatient.

'Ian, what's this about?'

'Flat Diane, actually. I've had a letter for her. Several. I need to know who the man is in the pictures.'

Another pause, but this one different. Ian could hear it in the way she breathed. Intimacy can lead to this, he supposed. Teach you how to read a woman by her breath on the far end of a phone line.

'You already know,' he said. 'Don't you.'

'My computer's in another room. I can call you back.'

'I'll wait,' he said.

She was back within five minutes, the hard plastic fumbling as she picked the handset back up giving way to her voice.

'I'm sorry, Ian,' she said. 'This is my fault. His name is Stan Leckey. He… he was a neighbor of mine when I came out here. A friend.'

'A lover?'

'No, Ian. Just a friend. But… he started saying things that made me… We had a falling out. I got a restraining order. He moved away eight or nine months ago.'

'He was the one who took the picture of you, wasn't he? The picture of you and Flat Diane.'

'Yes.'

Ian considered the envelope that had contained the latest atrocity. The postmark was from Seattle. Stan Lecky in Seattle. And a photo of him, no less. Certainly it couldn't be so hard with all that to find an address.

'She hasn't seen that, has she?' Candice asked. He didn't know how best to answer.

Ian slept in on Saturday, pretending that the dead black sleep and the hung-over exhaustion of his body was related somehow to luxury. It had been years since he'd been able to sleep past six a.m. He had Diane to feed and dress and shuffle off to school. He had his commute. His body learned its rhythms, and then it held to them. But Saturday, Ian rose at ten.

Diane was already on the couch, a bowl of cereal in her lap, her eyes clouded. Her skin seemed paler, framed by the darkness of her hair. Bags under her eyes like bruises. Ian recalled Victorian death pictures – photographs of the dead kept as mementos, or perhaps to hold a bit of the soul that had fled. He made himself toast and tea, and sat beside his daughter.

On the TV, girls three or four years older than Diane were talking animatedly about their boyfriends. They wore tight jeans and midriff tops, and no one thought it odd. No one wondered whether this was the path of wisdom. He found himself wondering what Diane made of it, but didn't ask. There were more pressing issues.

'How'd you sleep?' he asked.

'Okay.'

'More nightmares?'

She shrugged, her gaze fixed on the screen. Ian nodded, accepting the tacit yes. He finished his toast, washed down the last of his tea, smacked his lips.

'I have to go out for a little while. Errands.'

'Want me to come too?'

'No, you stay here. I won't be long.'

Diane looked away and down. It made his heart ache to see it. Part of that was knowing that he'd once again failed to protect her from some little pain, and part a presentiment of the longer absence she would have to endure. He leaned over and kissed the crown of her head where the bones hadn't been closed the first time he'd held her.

'I'll be right back, kiddo,' he murmured, and she smiled wanly, accepting his half-apology. And yet, by the time he had his keys, she was lost again in the television, gone into her own world as if he had never been there.

Tohiro was sitting in his driveway, a lawnmower partially disassembled before him. He nodded as Ian came up the path, but neither rose nor turned back to his work. Ian squatted beside him.

'I don't know why I think I can do this,' Tohiro said. 'Every time I start, it's like I don't remember how poorly it went the time before. And by the time it comes back to me, it's too late, the thing's already in pieces.'

'Hard. I do the same thing myself.'

Tohiro nodded.

'I need a favor,' Ian said. 'I have to go away for a bit. Diane's mother and I… there are some things we need to discuss. I might be away for week, perhaps. Perhaps less. I was wondering if…'

It choked him. Asking for help had never been a strong suit, nor lying. The two together were almost more than he could manage. Tohiro frowned and leaned forward, picking up a small, grease-covered bit of machinery and dropping it thoughtfully into a can of gasoline.

'Are you sure that's wise?' Tohiro asked. 'The timing might look…'

He knew then. Diane had told Kit, and Kit her parents; nothing could be more natural.

'I don't have the option,' Ian said.

'This is about what's happening to Diane?'

'Yes.'

Ian's knees were starting to ache a bit, but he didn't move, nor did Tohiro. The moment stretched, then:

'It might be better if Kit invited her,' Tohiro said. 'If it were a treat – a week-long slumber party – it could mask the sting.'

'Do you think she would?'

'For Diane? Kit would learn to fly if Diane asked her. Girls.'

'I'd appreciate it. More than I can say.'

'You are putting a certain faith in me.'

Tohiro met his gaze, expression almost challenging.

'It isn't you,' Ian said, softly. 'I'm fairly sure I know who it is.'

'I see.'

Ian shrugged, aware as he did so that it was a mirror of his daughter's, and that Tohirio would understand its eloquence as Ian had understood Diane's.

'I'll let you know when it's going to happen,' Ian said. 'I can't go before the CPS home visit, but it won't be long after that. And if you ever need the same of me, only say so.'

The man shifted under Ian's words, uneased. Dark eyes looked up at him and then away. Tohiro stuck fingers into the gasoline, pulling out the shining metal that the fuel had cleaned.

'That brings up something. Ian… Anna and I would rather not have Kit stay over with Diane. I know it isn't you, that you wouldn't… but the stakes are high, and I can't afford being wrong.'

Ian rocked back. A too-wide rictus grin forced its way onto his face – he could feel the skin pulling.

'I'm sorry, Ian, it's just…'

'It's the right thing,' he forced out, ignoring the anger and shock, pushing it down. 'If I thought for a minute that it was you… or even if I only weren't certain, then…'

Ian opened his hands, fingers spread; the gesture a suggestion of open possibility, a euphemism for violence. It was something they both understood. Men protected their children. Men like the two of them, at least.

Ian pulled himself up, his knees creaking. Kit, in the window, caught sight of him and waved. She was lighter than Diane, but not as pretty, Ian thought.

'I'll call later,' Ian said.

'Do. I'll talk with Kit. We'll arrange things. But, Ian? Diane needs you.'

'I know she does. I don't want to leave her. Especially now, I just…'

'I didn't mean don't go,' Tohiro said. 'I meant don't get caught.'

The home visit was less than he expected. Two women in casual businesswear appeared at the appointed hour. One took Diane away, the other asked him profoundly personal questions – Why had his wife left him? Had he been in therapy? Did he have a police record? Could he describe his relationship with his daughter? Only the last of these pushed him to tears. The woman was sympathetic, but unmoved; a citizen of a nation of tears from innocent and guilty alike.

She arranged a time and place for Diane to see a doctor – a woman doctor and Ian hadn't even had to ask. He promised that Diane would be there, and she explained the legal ramifications if she were not. The other woman appeared with Diane at her side. Diane's face was grey with exhaustion. Ian shook their hands, thanked them explicitly for coming, implicitly for not taking his child from him.

When they had gone, Diane went out to the back steps, looking out over a yard gone to seed – long grass and weeds. Her head rested in her hands. Ian sat beside her.

'Not so bad, was it?' he asked.

'She asked me a lot of questions,' Diane said. 'I don't know if I answered them all right.'

'Did you tell her the truth?'

'I think so.'

'Only think?'

Diane's brow furrowed as she looked at the horizon. Her shoulders hunched forward.

'She asks if things happened. And sometimes I think they did, but then I can't remember. After a while I start getting scared.'

'It's like you're living a life you don't know about,' Ian said, and she nodded. He put an arm around her shoulders, and she leaned in to him, trembling and starting to cry. Her sobs wracked her thin body like vomiting. Ian, holding her, wept.

'I'm not okay, Daddy,' she wailed to his breast. 'I'm not okay. I'm not okay.'

'You will be, sweetie. You will.'

The picture is cropped. In the original, things had been happening as unnatural to paper as they would be to a child. In this version, only the man's chest above the nipples, his shoulders, his face, his smug expression. These are all the details that matter. In this photograph, he could be anyone, doing anything. It is a headshot, something to put down on a bar or store counter, the sort of photograph that seems to fit perfectly with the phrase 'I'm looking for someone; maybe you've seen him.'

The original photo has obscenities and suggestions written on it. There is no writing on this copy, no note to accompany it. Nothing that will tie it back to Ian, should the police find it and not him.

He had driven to Seattle – a two-day trip – in a day and a half. Flying would have been faster, but he'd taken his pistol out of storage. Driving with a handgun was easy; flying impossible or, if not impossible, not worth doing.

He arrived in the city late at night and called Diane from a payphone using a card he'd bought with cash. She was fine. School was boring. Kit was a butthead. Her voice was almost normal – if he knew her less, he might have mistaken it. He was her father, though, and he knew what she sounded like when things were okay and when she only wanted them to be. They didn't talk about the nightmares. He told her he loved her, and she evaded, embarrassed. With the handset back in its cradle, the gun in his jacket pocket pulling the fabric down like a hand on his shoulder, Ian stood in the rain, the cool near-mist soaking him. In time, he gathered himself together enough to find a hotel and a bed to lie in while his flesh hummed from exhaustion and the road.

Finding Lecky took all the next day and part of the night, but he did it. The morning sun gave the lie to the city's grey reputation – clouds of perfect white stretched, thinned, vanished, reformed against a perfect blue sky. Nature ignoring Ian's desperation. The kids spare changing on the street corners avoided his gaze.

It was early, the morning rush hour still a half hour from starting. Ian didn't want the beast to go off to work, didn't want to spend a day waiting for the confrontation. He wanted it over now.

The house was in a bad part of town, but the lawn was trim, the windows clean. Moss stained the concrete walk, and the morning paper lay on the step, wrapped in dewey plastic. Ian picked it up, shaking the drops from it, and then rang the doorbell. His breath was shaking. The door opened and the beast appeared, a cup of coffee in one hand.

There was no glimmer of recognition, no particular sense of confusion or unease. Here, Ian thought, was a man with a clear conscience. A man who had done no wrong.

'I need to talk to you,' Ian said, handing the man his newspaper.

'I'm sorry. Do I know you?'

'No. But we have business in common. We have people in common, I think. May I come in?'

The man frowned down at Ian and put down the paper.

'I'm sorry,' the beast said, smiling as he stepped back, preparing to close the door. 'I have to get to work here, and really I don't want whatever you're selling. Thanks, though.'

'I've come for Flat Diane.'

The man's expression shifted – surprise, chagrin, anger all in the course of a single breath. Ian clamped his hand on the butt of his pistol, his finger resting against the trigger.

'Don't pretend you don't know what I'm talking about,' Ian said. 'I have the pictures.'

The beast shook his head, defensive and dismissive at the same time.

'Okay,' the man said. 'Okay, look, so it was a bad joke. All right. I mean, it's not like anyone got hurt, right?'

'What do you know about it?'

Something in Ian's voice caught his attention. Pale blue eyes fixed on him, the first hint of fear behind them. Ian didn't soften. His heart was tripping over like he'd been running, but his head felt very calm.

'No one got hurt,' the man said. 'It's just paper. So maybe it was a little crude. It was just a joke, right? You're, like, Diane's dad? Look, I'm sorry if that was a little upsetting, but…'

'I saw what you did to her.'

'To who?' The eyes were showing their fear, their confusion.

'My daughter.'

'I never *touched* your daughter.'

'No?'

It was a joy, stripping his certainty away, seeing the smug, leering face confused and frightened. Ian leaned in.

'Tell you what. Give me Flat Diane,' he said, 'and I might let you live.'

The panic in the pale eyes was joyous, but even in his victory, Ian felt the hint that it was too much; he'd gone too far.

'Sure,' the beast said, nodding. 'No, really, sure. Come on, I'll...'

And he tried to slam the door. Ian had known it was coming, was ready for it. His foot blocked the closing door and he pulled the gun from his pocket. The beast jumped back, lost his balance, toppled. The coffee fanned out behind him and splashed on the hardwood floor as Ian kicked the door closed behind him.

The beast was blinking, confused. His hands were raised, not in surrender, but protection, as if his fingers might deflect a bullet. A radio was playing – morning show chatter. Ian smelled bacon grease on the air.

'Please,' the beast said. 'Look, it's going to be okay, guy. Just no guns. All right? No guns.'

'Where is she?'

'Who?'

'Flat Diane!' Ian yelled, pleased to see the beast flinch.

'It's not here anymore. Seriously. Seriously, it's gone. Joke over. Honestly.'

'I don't believe you.'

'Look, it's a long story. There were some things that happened and it just made sense to get rid of it, you know? Let it go. It was only supposed to be a joke. You know Candice...'

Ian shook his head. He felt strange; his mind was thick as cotton and yet perfectly lucid.

'I'm not leaving without her,' he said.

'It's not *here*!' the beast shouted, his face flushed red. He rolled over, suddenly facing the back of the house. Running. With a feeling like reaching out to tap the fleeing man's shoulder, Ian raised the gun and fired. The back of the beast's head bloomed like a rose, and he fell.

Oh Jesus, Ian thought. And then, a moment later, *I couldn't have made that shot if I'd tried.*

He walked forward, pistol trained on the unmoving shape, but there was no need. The beast was dead. He'd killed him. Ian stood silently, watching the pool of blood seep across the floor. There was less than he'd thought. The morning show announcers laughed at something. Outside, a semi drove by, rattling the windows. Ian put the gun in his pocket, ignoring the heat.

He hadn't touched anything, not with his hands. There were no fingerprints. But he didn't have Flat Diane. He had to search the place. He had to hurry. Perhaps the beast kept plastic gloves. The kind you use for housework.

He searched the bedroom, the bath. The kitchen where half an egg was growing cold and solid on its plate. And then the room in the back. The room from the pictures. He went though everything – the stacks of pornography, the camera equipment. He didn't look away, no matter how vile the things he found. Rape porn. Children being used. Other things. Worse. But not his daughter.

He sat on the edge of the bathtub, head in his hands, when the voice came. The house was a shambles. Flat Diane wasn't there, or if she was, she was too well hidden. He didn't know what to do. The doorbell chimed innocently and a faint voice came.

'Stan?' it said. A woman's voice. 'Stan, are you in there? It's Margie.'

Ian stood and walked. He didn't run. He stepped over the corpse, calmly out the back door, stuffing the rubber gloves into his pockets as he went. There was an alleyway, and he opened the gate and stepped out into it. He didn't run. If he ran, they'd know he was running from something. And Diane needed him, didn't she. Needed him not to get caught.

Ian didn't stop to retrieve his things from the hotel; he walked to his car, slipped behind the wheel, drove. Twenty minutes east of Klamath Falls, he pulled to the side, walked to a tree, and leaning against it vomited until he wept.

'I didn't mean to,' he said through his horror. 'Christ, I didn't mean to.'

He hadn't called Diane from his room. He hadn't given anyone his name. He'd even found a hotel that took cash. Of course he'd fucking meant to.

'I didn't mean to,' he said.

He slept that night at a rest stop, bent uncomfortably across the back seat. In his dreams, he saw the moment again and again; felt the pistol jump;

heard the body strike wood. The pistol jumped; the body struck the floor. The pale head, round as an egg, cracked open. The man fled, heels kicking back behind him; the pistol jumped.

Morning was sick. A pale sun in an empty sky. Ian stretched out the vicious kinks in his back, washed his face in the restroom sink, and drove until nightfall.

He hadn't found Flat Diane, but he couldn't go back for her – not now. Maybe later, when things cooled down. But by then she could have been thrown away or burned or cut to pieces. And he couldn't guess what might happen to Diane when her shadow was destroyed – freedom or death or something entirely else. He didn't want to think about it. The worst was over, though. The worst had to be over, or else he didn't think he could keep breathing.

Tohiro and Anna's house glowed in the twilight, windows bright and cheerful and warm and normal. He watched them from the street, his back knotted from driving, the car ticking as it cooled. Tohiro passed by the picture window, his expression calm, distant and slightly amused. Anna was in the kitchen, the back of her head moving as her hands worked at something; washing, cutting, wringing – there was no way to tell. Somewhere in there, Kit and Diane played the games they always did. The pistol jumped; the body fell. Ian started the car, steadied his hands on the wheel, then killed the engine and got out.

Tohiro's eyebrows rose a fraction and a half-smile graced his mouth when he opened the door.

'Welcome back,' Tohiro said, stepping back to let him in. 'We weren't expecting you until tomorrow. Things went better than you thought?'

'Things went faster.'

Curiosity plucked at the corners of Tohiro's eyes. Ian gazed into the house, willing away the questions that begged to be asked. Tohiro closed the door.

'You look ...' he began.

Ian waited. *Like shit.* Or maybe *pounded.* The silence stretched and he glanced over. Tohiro's face was a soft melancholy. Ian nodded, barely moving, half asking him to finish, half daring him.

'You look older.'

'Yeah, well. You know. Time.'

A shriek and the drumming of bare feet and Diane had leapt into his arms. His spine protested the weight. Ian held her carefully, like something precious. Then, as if she'd suddenly remembered that they weren't alone, she drew back, tried to make it all seem casual.

'Hey,' she said.

'Hey. You been good?'

Diane shrugged – an I *guess* gesture.

'We were just about to have supper,' Tohiro said. 'If you'd like to join us?'

Ian looked at Diane. Her face was impassive, blank, but at the edges there were the touches invisible to anyone else, anyone who didn't know her as he did.

'I think I'd rather just roll on home,' Ian said. 'That good by you, sweetie?'

'Sure,' she said, upbeat enough that he knew it had been her fondest wish. He let her ride him to the car, piggyback.

That night, they both suffered nightmares. It struck Ian, as he calmed Diane from hers and waited for his own to fade, that there would be more nights like this; screams from her or from him, then warm milk and nightlights and empty talk that gave the evil some time to fade. That if they were *lucky* there would be many more. Nothing more would happen to Flat Diane; justice would not come to call for him. It was the best he could hope for.

'It's okay,' he whispered to her as she began to drowse. Curled into her blanket, her breath came deeper, more regular. 'It's over. It's over, sweetie. It's all right.'

He didn't add that just being over didn't mean it hadn't changed everything forever, or that some things don't stop just because they've ended. Or that a girl set voyaging takes her own chances, and no father's love – however profound – can ever call her back. Those weren't the sorts of things you said when all you had to offer your child were comfort and hope.

SINGING MY SISTER DOWN

Margo Lanagan

Margo Lanagan (1960–) is an Australian writer primarily known for her dark fantasy short stories, some of which are influenced by folktale. Although Lanagan has been a published author since 1990, she first came to the attention of readers outside of her own country with the collection *Black Juice* (2004), for which she won a World Fantasy Award and a Michael L. Printz Honor Award. Subsequently, Lanagan has become perhaps the most critically acclaimed contemporary Australian fantasist, and her novel *Tender Morsels* (2008) also won a World Fantasy Award. New work includes the novel *Watered Silk* (2011) and the story collection *Yellowcake* (2011). The horrifying 'Singing My Sister Down' (2005) is Lanagan's most anthologized story and continues the thread of 'weird ritual' stories in this volume.

We all went down to the tar-pit, with mats to spread our weight.

Ikky was standing on the bank, her hands in a metal twin-loop behind her. She'd stopped sulking; now she looked, more, stare-y and puzzled.

Chief Barnarndra pointed to the pit. 'Out you go then, girl. You must walk on out there to the middle and stand. When you picked a spot, your people can join you.'

So Ik stepped out, very ordinary. She walked out. I thought – hoped, even – she might walk right across and into the thorns the other side; at the same time, I knew she wouldn't do that.

She walked the way you walk on the tar, except without the arms balancing. She nearly fell from a stumble once, but Mumma hulloo'd to her, and she straightened and walked upright out to the very middle, where she slowed and stopped.

Mumma didn't look to the chief, but all us kids and the rest did. 'Right, then,' he said.

Mumma stepped out as if she'd just herself that moment happened to decide to. We went after her – only us, Ik's family, which was like us being punished, too, everyone watching us walk out to that girl who was our shame.

In the winter you come to the pit to warm your feet in the tar. You stand long enough to sink as far as your ankles – the littler you are, the longer you can stand. You soak the heat in for as long as the tar doesn't close over your feet and grip, and it's as good as warmed boots wrapping your feet. But in summer, like this day, you keep away from the tar, because it makes the air hotter and you mind about the stink.

But today we had to go out, and everyone had to see us go.

Ikky was tall, but she was thin and light from all the worry and prison; she was going to take a long time about sinking. We got our mats down, all the food parcels and ice-baskets and instruments and such spread out evenly on the broad planks Dash and Felly had carried out.

'You start, Dash,' said Mumma, and Dash got up and put his drum-ette to his hip and began with 'Fork-Tail Trio', and it did feel a bit like a party. It stirred Ikky awake from her hung-headed shame;

she lifted up and even laughed, and I saw her hips move in the last chorus, side to side.

Then Mumma got out one of the ice-baskets, which was already black on the bottom from meltwater.

Ikky gasped. 'Ha! What! Crab! Where'd that come from?'

'Never you mind, sweet-thing.' Mumma lifted some meat to Ikky's mouth, and rubbed some of the crush-ice into her hair.

'Oh, Mumma!' Ik said with her mouth full.

'May as well have the best of this world while you're here,' said Mumma. She stood there and fed Ikky like a baby, like a pet guinea-bird.

'I thought Auntie Mai would come,' said Ik.

'Auntie Mai, she's useless,' said Dash. 'She's sitting at home with her handkerchief.'

'I wouldn't've cared, her crying,' said Ik. 'I would've thought she'd say goodbye to me.'

'Her heart's too hurt,' said Mumma. 'You frightened her. And she's such a straight lady – she sees shame where some of us just see people. Here, inside the big claw, that's the sweetest meat.'

'Ooh, *yes*! Is anyone else feasting with me?'

'No, darlin', this is your day only. Well, okay, I'll give some to this little sad-eyes here, huh? Felly never had crab but the once. Is it yum? Ooh, it's yum! Look at him!'

Next she called me to do my flute – the flashiest, hardest music I knew. And Ik listened; Ik who usually screamed at me to stop pushing spikes into her brain, she watched my fingers on the flute-holes and my sweating face and my straining, bowing body and, for the first time, I didn't feel like just the nuisance-brother. I played well, out of the surprise of her not minding. I couldn't've played better. I heard everyone else being surprised, too, at the end of those tunes that they must've known, too well from all my practising.

I sat down, very hungry. Mumma passed me the water-cup and a damp-roll.

'I'm stuck now,' said Ik, and it was true – the tar had her by the feet, closed in a gleaming line like that pair of zipper-slippers I saw once in the shoemaster's vitrine.

'Oh yeah, well and truly stuck,' said Mumma. 'But then, you knew when you picked up that axe-handle you were sticking yourself.'

'I did know.'

'No coming unstuck from this one. You could've let that handle lie.'

That was some serious teasing.

'No, I couldn't, Mumma, and *you* know.'

'I do, baby chicken. I always knew you'd be too angry, once the wedding-glitter rubbed off your skin. It was a good party, though, wasn't it?' And they laughed at each other, Mumma having to steady Ikky or her ankles would've snapped over. And when their laughter started going strange Mumma said, 'Well, *this* party's going to be almost as good, 'cause it's got children. And look what else!' And she reached for the next ice-basket.

And so the whole long day went, in treats and songs, in ice and stink and joke-stories and gossip and party-pieces. On the banks, people came and went, and the chief sat in his chair and was fanned and fed, and the family of Ikky's husband sat around the chief, being served, too, all in purple-cloth with flashing edging, very prideful.

She went down so slowly.

'Isn't it hot?' Felly asked her.

'It's like a big warm hug up my legs,' said Ik. 'Come here and give me a hug, little stick-arms, and let me check. Oof, yes, it's just like that, only lower down.'

'You're coming down to me,' said Fel, pleased.

'Yeah, soon I'll be able to bite your ankles like you bite mine.'

Around midafternoon, Ikky couldn't move her arms any more and had a panic, just quiet, not so the bank-people would've noticed.

'What'm I going to do, Mumma?' she said. 'When it comes up over my face? When it closes my nose?'

'Don't you worry. You won't be awake for that.' And Mumma cooled her hands in the ice, dried them on her dress, and rubbed them over Ik's shoulders, down Ik's arms to where the tar had locked her wrists.

'You'd better not give me any teas, or herbs, or anything,' said Ik. 'They'll get you, too, if you help me. They'll come out to make sure.'

Mumma put her hands over Felly's ears. 'Tristem gave me a gun,' she whispered.

Ikky's eyes went wide. 'But you can't! Everyone'll hear!'

'It's got a thing on it, quietens it. I can slip it in a tar-wrinkle, get you in the head when your head is part sunk, fold back the wrinkle, tell 'em your heart stopped, the tar pressed it stopped.'

Felly shook his head free. Ikky was looking at Mumma, quietening. There was only the sound of Dash tearing bread with his teeth, and the breeze whistling in the thorn-galls away over on the shore. I was watching Mumma and Ikky closely – I'd wondered about that last part, too. But now this girl up to her waist in the pit didn't even look like our Ikky. Her face was changing like a cloud, or like a masque-lizard's colours; you don't see them move but they *become* something else, then something else again.

'No,' she said, still looking at Mumma. 'You won't do that. You won't have to.' Her face had a smile on it that touched off one on Mumma's, too, so that they were both quiet, smiling at something in each other that I couldn't see.

And then their eyes ran over and they were crying *and* smiling, and then Mumma was kneeling on the wood, her arms around Ikky, and Ikky was ugly against her shoulder, crying in a way that we couldn't interrupt them.

That was when I realised how many people were watching, when they set up a big, spooky ooolooling and stamping on the banks, to see Mumma grieve.

'Fo!' I said to Dash, to stop the hair creeping around on my head from that noise. 'There never was such a crowd when Chep's daddy went down.'

'Ah, but he was old and crazy,' said Dash through a mouthful of bread, 'and only killed other olds and crazies.'

'Are those fish-people? And look at the yellowcloths – they're from up among the caves, all that way!'

'Well, it's nearly Langasday, too,' said Dash. 'Lots of people on the move, just happening by.'

'Maybe. Is that an honour, or a greater shame?'

Dash shrugged. 'This whole thing is upended. Who would have a party in the tar, and with family going down?'

'It's what Mumma wanted.'

'Better than having her and Ik be like this *all day*.' Dash's hand slipped into the nearest ice-basket and brought out a crumb of gilded macaroon. He ate it as if he had a perfect right.

Everything went slippery in my mind, after that. We were being watched so hard! Even though it was quiet out here, the pothering wind brought crowd-mumble and scraps of music and smoke our way, so often that we couldn't be private and ourselves. Besides, there was Ikky with the sun on her face, but the rest of her from the rib-peaks down gloved in tar, never to see sun again. Time seemed to just have *gone*, in big clumps, or all the day was happening at once or something, I was wondering so hard about what was to come, I was watching so hard the differences from our normal days. I wished I had more time to think, before she went right down; my mind was going breathless, trying to get all its thinking done.

But evening came and Ik was a head and shoulders, singing along with us in the lamplight, all the old songs – 'A Flower for You', 'Hen and Chicken Bay', 'Walking the Tracks with Beejum Singh', 'Dollarberries'. She sang all Felly's little-kid songs that normally she'd sneer at; she got Dash to teach her his new one, 'The Careless Wanderer', with the tricky chorus. She made us work on that one like she was trying to stop us noticing the monster bonfires around the shore, the other singing, of fishing songs and forest songs, the stomp and clatter of dancing in the gathering darkness. But they were there, however well we sang, and no other singing in our lives had had all this going on behind it.

When the tar began to tip Ik's chin up, Mumma sent me for the wreath. 'Mai will have brought it, over by the chief's chair.'

I got up and started across the tar, and it was as if I cast magic ahead of me, silence-making magic, for as I walked – and it was good to be walking, not sitting – musics petered out, and laughter stopped, and dancers stood still, and there were eyes at me, all along the dark banks, strange eyes and familiar both.

The wreath showed up in the crowd ahead, a

big, pale ring trailing spirals of whisper-vine, the beautifullest thing. I climbed up the low bank there, and the ground felt hard and cold after a day on the squishy tar. My ankles shivered as I took the wreath from Mai. It was heavy; it was fat with heavenly scents.

'You'll have to carry those,' I said to Mai, as someone handed her the other garlands. 'You should come out, anyway. Ik wants you there.'

She shook her head. 'She's cloven my heart in two with that axe of hers.'

'What, so you'll chop hers as well, this last hour?'

We glared at each other in the bonfire light, all loaded down with the fine, pale flowers.

'I never heard this boy speak with a voice before, Mai,' said someone behind her.

'He's very sure,' said someone else. 'This is Ikky's Last Things we're talking about, Mai. If she wants you to be one of them...'

'She shouldn't have shamed us, then,' Mai said, but weakly.

'You going to look back on this and think yourself a po-face,' said the first someone.

'But it's like –' May sagged and clicked her tongue. 'She should have *cared* what she did to this family,' she said with her last fight. 'It's more than just herself.'

'Take the flowers, Mai. Don't make the boy do this twice over. Time is short.'

'Yeah, *everybody's* time is short,' said the first someone.

Mai stood, pulling her mouth to one side.

I turned and propped the top of the wreath on my forehead, so that I was like a little boy-bride, trailing a head of flowers down my back to the ground. I set off over the tar, leaving the magic silence in the crowd. There was only the rub and squeak of flower stalks in my ears; in my eyes, instead of the flourishes of bonfires, there were only the lamps in a ring around Mumma, Felly, Dash, and Ikky's head. Mumma was kneeling bonty-up on the wood, talking to Ikky; in the time it had taken me to get the wreath, Ikky's head had been locked still.

'Oh, the baby,' Mai whimpered behind me. 'The little darling.'

Bit late for darling-ing now, I almost said. I felt cross and frightened and too grown-up for Mai's silliness.

'Here, Ik, we'll make you beautiful now,' said Mumma, laying the wreath around Ik's head. 'We'll come out here to these flowers when you're gone, and know you're here.'

'They'll die pretty quick – I've seen it.' Ik's voice was getting squashed, coming out through closed jaws. 'The heat wilts 'em.'

'They'll always look beautiful to you,' said Mumma. 'You'll carry down this beautiful wreath, and your family singing.'

I trailed the vines out from the wreath like flares from the edge of the sun.

'Is that Mai?' said Ik. Mai looked up, startled, from laying the garlands between the vines. 'Show me the extras, Mai.'

Mai held up a garland. 'Aren't they good? Trumpets from Low Swamp, Auntie Patti's whisper-vine, and star-weed to bind. You never thought ordinary old stars could look so good, I'll bet.'

'I never did.'

It was all set out right, now. It went in the order: head, half-ring of lamps behind (so as not to glare in her eyes), wreath, half-ring of garlands behind, leaving space in front of her for us.

'Okay, we're going to sing you down now,' said Mumma. 'Everybody get in and say a proper goodbye.' And she knelt inside the wreath a moment herself, murmured something in Ikky's ear and kissed her on the forehead.

We kids all went one by one. Felly got clingy and made Ikky cry; Dash dashed in and planted a quick kiss while she was still upset and would hardly have noticed him; Mumma gave me a cloth and I crouched down and wiped Ik's eyes and nose – and then could not speak to her bare, blinking face.

'You're getting good at that flute,' she said.

But this isn't about me, Ik. This is *not at all* about me.

'Will you come out here some time, and play over me, when no one else's around?'

I nodded. Then I had to say some words, of some kind, I knew. I wouldn't get away without speaking. 'If you want.'

'I want, okay? Now give me a kiss.'

I gave her a kid's kiss, on the mouth. Last time I kissed her, it was carefully on the cheek as she was leaving for her wedding. Some of her glitter had come off on my lips. Now I patted her hair and backed away over the wreath.

Mai came in last. 'Fairy doll,' I heard her say sobbingly. 'Only-one.'

And Ik. 'It's all right, Auntie. It'll be over so soon, you'll see. And I want to hear your voice nice and strong in the singing.'

We readied ourselves, Felly in Mumma's lap, then Dash, then me next to Mai. I tried to stay attentive to Mumma, so Mai wouldn't mess me up with her weeping. It was quiet except for the distant flubber and snap of the bonfires.

We started up, all the ordinary evening songs for putting babies to sleep, for farewelling, for soothing broke-hearted people – all the ones everyone knew so well that they'd long ago made rude versions and joke-songs of them. We sang them plain, following Mumma's lead; we sang them straight, into Ikky's glistening eyes, as the tar climbed her chin. We stood tall, so as to see her, and she us, as her face became the sunken centre of that giant flower, the wreath. Dash's little drum held us together and kept us singing, as Ik's eyes rolled and she struggled for breath against the pressing tar, as the chief and the husband's family came and stood across from us, shifting from foot to foot, with torches raised to watch her sink away.

Mai began to crumble and falter beside me as the tar closed in on Ik's face, a slow, sticky, rolling oval. I sang good and strong – I didn't want to hear any last whimper, any stopped breath. I took Mai's arm and tried to hold her together that way, but she only swayed worse, and wept louder. I listened for Mumma under the noise, pressed my eyes shut and made my voice follow hers. By the time I'd steadied myself that way, Ik's eyes were closing.

Through our singing, I thought I heard her cry for Mumma; I tried not to, yet my ears went on hearing. *This will happen only the once – you can't do it over again if ever you feel like remembering.* And Mumma went to her, and I could not tell whether Ik was crying and babbling, or whether it was a trick of our voices, or whether the people on the banks of the tar had started up again. I watched Mumma, because Mumma knew what to do; she knew to lie there on the matting, and dip her cloth in the last water with the little fading fish-scales of ice in it, and squeeze the cloth out and cool the shrinking face in the hole.

And the voice of Ik must have been ours or others' voices, because the hole Mumma was dampening with her cloth was, by her hand movements, only the size of a brassboy now. And by a certain shake of her shoulders I could tell: Mumma knew it was all right to be weeping now, now that Ik was surely gone, was just a nose or just a mouth with the breath crushed out of it, just an eye seeing nothing. And very suddenly it was too much – the flowers nodding in the lamplight, our own sister hanging in tar, going slowly, slowly down like Vanderberg's truck that time, like Jappity's cabin with the old man still inside it, or any old villain or scofflaw of around these parts, and I had a big sicking-up of tears, and they tell me I made an awful noise that frightened everybody right up to the chief, and that the husband's parents thought I was a very ill-brought-up boy for upsetting them instead of allowing them to serenely and superiorly watch justice be done for their lost son.

I don't remember a lot about that part. I came back to myself walking dully across the tar between Mai and Mumma, hand-in-hand, carrying nothing, when I had come out here laden, when we had all had to help. *We must have eaten everything,* I thought. *But what about the mats and pans and planks?* Then I hear a screeking clanking behind me, which was Dash hoisting up too heavy a load of pots.

And Mumma was talking, wearily, as if she'd been going on a long time, and soothingly, which was like a beautiful guide-rope out of my sickness, which my brain was following hand over hand. *It's what they do to people, what they have to do, and all you can do about it is watch out who you go loving, right? Make sure it's not someone who'll rouse that killing-anger in you, if you've got that rage, if you're like our Ik –*

Then the bank came up high in front of us,

topped with grass that was white in Mumma's lamp's light. Beyond it were all the eyes, and attached to the eyes the bodies, flat and black against bonfire or starry sky. They shuffled aside for us.

I knew we had to leave Ik behind, and I didn't make a fuss, not now. I had done my fussing, all at once; I had blown myself to bits out on the tar, and now several monstrous things, several gaping mouths of truth, were rattling pieces of me around their teeth. I would be all right, if Mai stayed quiet, if Mumma kept murmuring, if both their hands held me as we passed through this forest of people, these flitting firefly eyes.

They got me up the bank, Mumma and Auntie; I paused and they stumped up and then lifted me, and I walked up the impossible slope like a demon, horizontal for a moment and then stiffly over the top–

–and into my Mumma, whose arms were ready. She couldn't've carried me out on the tar. We'd both have sunk, with me grown so big now. But here on the hard ground she took me up, too big as I was for it. And, too big as I was, I held myself onto her, crossing my feet around her back, my arms behind her neck. And she carried me like Jappity's wife used to carry Jappity's idiot son, and I felt just like that boy, as if the thoughts that were all right for everyone else weren't coming now, and never would come, to me. As if all I could do was watch, but not ever know anything, not ever understand. I pushed my face into Mumma's warm neck; I sealed my eyes shut against her skin; I let her strong warm arms carry me away in the dark.

THE PEOPLE ON THE ISLAND

T. M. Wright

T. M. Wright (1968–) is an American horror writer whose first novel, *Strange Seed* (1978), was nominated for a World Fantasy Award. More than a dozen novels have appeared since, including *The Playground* (1982), *Carlisle Street* (1983), *The Island* (1988), *The Place* (1989), *The School* (1990), *Boundaries* (1990), *The Last Vampire* (1991), and *Little Boy Lost* (1992). Wright's short fiction has appeared in *Twilight Zone* magazine and many others. His seventh novel, *A Manhattan Ghost Story* (1984), has had fourteen foreign editions. The disturbing and surreal 'The People on the Island' (2005) is an unusual tale that at times evokes Shirley Jackson while placing its characters fully within the weird.

This winter morning, when we crossed over the dune, we saw a man lying face down in a shallow tide pool half a dozen yards from us. A gull waddled about agitatedly near him and squawked now and then.

'Oh God,' Elizabeth said, and stopped walking, as I had. She put her hand to her mouth, said again, 'Oh God,' and added, after a moment, 'Another.'

I love such winter walks on the beach. Even before we came to the island, I found them bracing. I claimed to the skeptical that they made me 'feel alive.'

The man in the half-frozen tide pool wore a black suit, and his shoulder-length hair also was black, as were his shoes. He wore several playfully grotesque rings on his right hand. One was purple, another green.

Elizabeth asked, 'Do you think he drowned?' She looked questioningly at me, then at the man, again.

I answered, 'Who's to say?'

She looked at me again and frowned a bit. '*He* would. If he could.'

Over lunch, we discussed the morning. Our discovery of the black-suited man was, of course, at the forefront of our conversation.

'I'm sick of these people,' Elizabeth said, and sipped her tea. She was having a chocolate scone with the tea, but had not yet touched it. 'Where do they come from?'

'I think we should go and look at him, again,' I said.

Elizabeth broke off a small piece of her scone and popped it delicately into her mouth. She is a very courteous woman. Very aware of etiquette. 'Go and look at him again,' she echoed as she chewed.

'Yes,' I said. 'But more closely this time.'

She glanced sadly toward the window, which overlooks the water.

I said, 'Perhaps we should even… turn him onto his back.'

She looked at me, brow furrowed, as if she were troubled. She looks at me like that quite a lot lately.

'Perhaps we really should do that,' I said. 'Turn him onto his back. Look at his face. It's possible we know him, Elizabeth.'

'I don't think so,' she said. 'We know none of these people.'

'But you're so wrong,' I said. 'We know them

only too well. They're simply what they are. They are organs, flesh, hair. And blood as thick as pudding. How can they be any more or less than that?'

'I don't understand you,' Elizabeth said. 'I don't think I ever have.'

I nodded. 'Maybe that's for the good.'

She shook her head. 'You only think it is, George.'

'And what of the woman in the parlor?'

Elizabeth sighed. 'She'll keep. Every one of these people will keep.'

'Yes,' I said. 'It's amazing, isn't it?' I smiled a little. 'They keep so damned well.'

Elizabeth awoke screaming early the following morning. I took her hard into my arms, gave her kisses and whispered assurances that 'everything is all right,' until at last she became calm, and she said, 'How long is this going to continue, George? How long do we have to endure it?'

I shook my head and held her more tightly. 'My love,' I told her, 'our needs and our dreams can be demons. I've learned that much, here, at least. But our demons will bring us so much, if we let them, if only we can hear and understand their song.'

This house is small, comfortable and easy to clean, a plus when the wind is fierce, as it usually is, and the fine sand insinuates itself through every crack and crevice. Winters are the best time for that, and this winter has been no exception. Often, it seems as if the wind blows in four directions at once, and the house shivers, shrieks, and complains. But although the house is small, it's quite sturdy, and I have never worried about being tossed into the elements late one evening, or of coming back from one of our winter walks to find the house not where I'd left it.

Elizabeth says she's waiting impatiently for the first snowfall. She says it brightens the landscape, reflects sunlight (should we ever have it), masks the grotesque. I tell her there's no reason to mask the grotesque; I tell her it can be beautiful. She merely shakes her head and scowls.

The black-haired man in the black suit was missing from the tide pool. I assumed several possibilities – he had been carried off by the tide itself, carrion eaters had quickly dispatched his remains, others on the island had spirited him away. That last possibility is remote, however. As far as I've been able to ascertain, there are no others living on this island. I've circumnavigated it several times (quite time consuming), and, except for a few scrubby trees, and the poor excuse for a lawn I try to maintain around the house, there's an almost complete lack of flora; animal life is restricted to a few gulls and herons (they seem confused, somehow, even a bit logy; I can't imagine why), and an animal I've only heard, but have never seen. I believe it's a stray dog.

The woman in the parlor in the other house is perched on an exercise bike. She has both hands tightly on the handlebars and both feet on the pedals. She's wearing bright red nail polish, and she's leaning forward slightly, in the position a bike rider would use. Her head is up a bit, her gaze forward, her eyes open halfway. They're robin's-egg blue. Her hair is blond, straight, long, and stunning. She's wearing a gray, loose-fitting exercise suit with the words 'Find Out For Yourself' emblazoned across the chest in green, art deco-style letters.

I believe her name is Jane. Elizabeth is skeptical about this: 'It could be anything,' she said. 'It could be Barbara, or Helen, or Jacqueline.'

'No,' I said. 'I believe it's Jane.'

Elizabeth gave me a puzzled look. 'She doesn't look like a Jane to me. Where do you get these ideas, anyway? Why assign names to these people at all?'

'Because it amuses me,' I said. 'They amuse me.'

She scowled.

We went to visit Jane this afternoon. It has been three days since our last visit, and she was precisely as we had left her. The parlor was cold, as was the entire house, I assume, since it's not heated, and there was even a little frost on the backs of Jane's hands, on her forehead, and on her eyes. I gestured to indicate the frost, because I found it almost decorative.

'Look there,' I said. 'Look at the frost.' I smiled.

'It's sad,' Elizabeth said.

'I don't think so,' I said. 'I think it becomes her.'

'Good Lord,' Elizabeth whispered.

She doesn't like to visit Jane. She likes visiting none of those who exist here. But she most dislikes visiting Jane because, she says, Jane looks angry. 'It's in her eyes,' Elizabeth said. 'And in the line of her mouth.'

I agreed, and added, 'But I can't imagine that she would have any reason to be angry. She is, after all, beyond anger.'

'And everything else, as well,' Elizabeth said.

'My point exactly. Don't you see? Isn't it obvious?'

'Nothing's obvious,' Elizabeth snapped. 'Nothing's obvious!' she repeated. 'And *that's* the whole point, isn't it?'

She's right. That is the whole point. Nothing's obvious. Is the wind actually fierce and cold? Is the landscape actually barren? Is there a stray dog loose somewhere on the island? And what is Jane doing on the exercise bike in the parlor of the other house? Who put her there? And why? And what of the others? Henry, Joanna, and the rest. They're fascinating. Complexity to simplicity to eternity in one effortless outflow of breath. Past and soul, needs and lusts and longing gone forever in a moment without oxygen. And perhaps their purpose is simply to be fascinating, grotesque, and predictable. Like chess pieces. Pets. Stories told around a campfire.

But there are some givens. My fingers actually do have ink on them from the leaky fountain pen I'm using. Elizabeth's hair has indeed begun to turn gray since we've come here. And I'm positive this is winter, positive about the wind and the barrenness of the landscape. Positive that the grandfather's clock in Jane's parlor predictably strikes the hour and the quarter hour. Positive there's a purpose to my presence on this island. Positive it is an island. That it sits in an ocean. That the ocean churns and throws whitecaps at sandy beaches which – I'm positive – are eroding rapidly. Positive no one walks these beaches except Elizabeth and I, a few logy herons and gulls, and a creature that barks hoarsely at a distance. Positive this landscape has as much to do with heaven as it has to do with hell. The others in that other house may have once believed in their immortality, and so they have it now, in a way. Caught forever in the positions of life – eating, taking a bath, arranging shoes, feeding an absent cat, making love, becoming old, drowning. I am not surprised that there are no ghosts on this island. The others in that other house, and on the island in various places, are stationery ghosts we may touch, if we wish. But Elizabeth says that the touch of death is miserable, that it stinks. I disagree, of course. I tell her that death is as necessary to us as a beating heart.

Elizabeth and I have stopped having sex. She no longer parades around naked in front of me, nor I in front of her. It's something we used to revel in, something we found exciting and necessary – after a shower, or just before bed, or simply as an enticement. But we don't do it, anymore, though I believe desperately that I want it for us both. We don't know why we've abandoned our nakedness – at least I don't know why.

We don't prepare meals for one another, either. Various pasta dishes were our favorite, and I had become something of a pastry chef. But we don't prepare meals for one another, anymore. We hardly eat, anymore, and hardly ever together. We eat when we're hungry, and I think that neither of us finds any pleasure in it, though we have all the food we need, and the little kitchen is delightful and well-equipped.

It strikes me that Elizabeth and I are necessarily together here, on this island and in this house, and necessarily drifting apart. She is drifting off to a world that's more confusing, complex and gaudy – in a Technicolor way – than I like. And though I hate to do it, I think I have no choice but to let her go there.

'How do they arrive?' Elizabeth asked.

'By boat, I imagine,' I answered.

She turned her head toward me, and, in the half-light, I could see her frown. Prior to coming here, her frowns were elegantly expressive of much more than I had come to expect from any frown; but here, they're merely expressive of sadness and confusion. 'You mean they pilot a boat to this island – they get in a boat and, start the engine, and … '

'Of course that's not what I mean,' I answered, regretting my abruptness.

We were lying in bed, comforter and blanket pulled up to our necks. The air in the room was cold, good for sleeping. 'I meant that they're brought here.'

'By who?'

I shrugged. 'By elves,' I said, and grinned.

She said nothing.

'Did you hear me?' I said.

'Large elves,' she said. I tried, unsuccessfully, to hear a tone of amusement in her voice.

'Elves with grunt and grit and muscle,' I said. What a fascinating and grotesque idea, I thought. Elves piloting boats filled with the dead. Elves unloading the dead on my island and arranging them in various positions of life. It was an idea I could embrace, and which made me warm.

'We would hear such elves,' Elizabeth said. 'We would hear their boats.'

'Above that wind?' I asked.

She said nothing.

The others who've been put here do not argue or cajole or laugh or make meaningless conversation, though one might expect from looking at them that argument or cajoling, laughter or meaningless talk could well be their intention, had they any intentions left. But they are at the mercy of the wind's intentions, now, the intentions of the winter, the intentions of those – unseen – who move them about, from place to place, and from attitude to attitude. I have never seen this being done, but I'm sure that it is done.

Jane is no longer perched on her exercise bike. I don't know where she is; Elizabeth says she's reluctant to look elsewhere in that big house in fear we'll find still others in the attitudes of life. We believe, however, that Jane is indeed in the house because we can see what appear to be drag marks in the thin layer of sand throughout the house's first floor. The drag marks stop halfway up the flight of stairs that's off the parlor, where the layer of sand ends. So we assume that Jane is on the second or third floor of the house. We have no idea why she's been moved.

Tonight, the creature that barks hoarsely, and which I assume, perhaps incorrectly, to be a dog, seemed closer than it has on previous nights.

I have never seen the sunrise, here. From time to time, on our walks, I see a diffuse patch of light through the overcast and I assume it's the sun – it can be nothing else. I've seen a sunset or two, but these are dull events which possess nothing of the brilliance of sunsets in other places. The sky does not turn to fire, the pale and fragile blue at the horizon does not become a delicate, short-lived rosé. No pale and fragile blue exists here, only a horizon the color of lead, which, in its own way, is quite remarkable.

I went to the other house without Elizabeth and found Jane lying on her back in a four-poster bed on the house's third floor. She was wearing her gray exercise outfit, and her hands were clasped over her stomach, legs straight. Her sneakers were on the floor beside the bed. Her socks had been put neatly into the sneakers.

One of the room's tall, thin windows was open wide, so the room was very cold.

Jane's faded blue eyes were open wide, too, as if someone had forced them open. Her look of anger seemed to have passed. This confused me, and made *me* angry. It passed quickly.

'Whose world is this?' Elizabeth asked.

'It's not a world,' I answered. 'It's an island.'

'That's the same thing as a world.' She sounded petulant. It's a tone I used to find amusing – as if she had momentarily become a small girl; it reminded me of our first few years together, when we were young children, before we started noticing, in earnest, that we were different sexes.

Her petulance, now, is merely annoying. Like her frown.

I think I would find even her laughter annoying, if she laughed anymore.

I wish she were someone else.

'What are we going to *do* with them?' Elizabeth asked.

I shrugged. 'What *can* we do with them?' I

shook my head a little. 'I'm not even sure we're *supposed* to do anything with them.' I grinned. 'We can arrange them,' I said.

'Arrange them?' She seemed astonished by the idea.

'Sure. We can make them be… what we want them to be. We can make them smile. We can make them look attentive and interested.'

'That's pathetic, George. They're not dolls. They're not marionettes.'

'What are they, then?'

We were on one of our walks, which have grown less and less frequent because there are so few areas on this island, now, that are unsullied by the others propped up in their various positions of life. I find it very disconcerting to come across one of them – even those with whom I'm familiar; perhaps because they are, as well, so grotesquely *un*familiar as their positions change from day to day and week to week. I maintained to Elizabeth that the others should, at least, remain predictable. If they are in an attitude of repose, then that is as they should remain. If they are in some other attitude – an attitude of life, as I call it – then that is as they should remain, as well. They have no choice.

Elizabeth had no idea what I was talking about. I think, at times, that she does not appreciate the situation we have here as much as I. I believe that she sees it as a burden.

Sometimes I wish that she were somewhere else.

We've spotted the black-haired man in the black suit, though at a short distance. He was seated in a high-backed wooden chair on a dune overlooking the ocean. He was facing away from us, though we knew it was the same man we'd discovered two weeks earlier. When we saw him, we both stopped walking and Elizabeth whispered an obscenity. We were perhaps 50 yards from the man and the brisk wind was blowing his black hair about.

'He's watching,' Elizabeth said, then added, 'or waiting.'

'How could he be watching anything? Or, for that matter, waiting for anything?' I asked.

'Why not?' she said. 'Why couldn't he, or any of them, be watching? And waiting?'

'They've nothing to watch, and nothing to wait for,' I said.

'They have everything to wait for,' she said. 'How do we know they don't? How do we know anything about them? We don't even know their names.'

'You're being argumentative,' I said.

'No, I'm being realistic,' she said.

'And you're being confrontational, too,' I said.

She shook her head. 'No,' she whispered, then nodded at the black-haired man. 'He is.' She paused. 'They all are.'

I managed a brief and unsatisfying glimpse of the creature we supposed was a dog. It awakened Elizabeth and me early in the morning, when the sky had begun to lighten. It sounded as if it were very close to the house, perhaps on the little patch of scrubby lawn that I have tried hard to maintain. I could hear a slight warble in its hoarse bark, as if it were attempting song.

'Listen to that,' Elizabeth said. 'Listen to that,' she repeated. 'It's awful.'

I looked at her, saw the pale oval of her face in the semi-darkness. 'I don't think it's awful,' I said.

'It's grisly,' she said. 'It's awful,' she repeated. 'This entire island is awful. These people all around us are awful. They're sickening and awful, George! Look at them!'

'I have.'

'Not in any meaningful way. You've looked at them as if they're merely… lawn ornaments.'

'I haven't!'

'But you have. I know you have. You always have.'

'Always? We haven't been here that long.'

'Haven't we?'

'It only feels that way, Elizabeth.'

'We've been here since we were children. I know it.'

The creature near the house barked again. Its warble was longer this time, more pronounced, as if it really were attempting song.

Then what passes here for morning came, and when I went to the window, I saw the creature moving off, toward the center of the island. It was larger than a large dog, though it was vaguely the shape of a dog. I saw only its dark silhouette against the gray light, as it moved away from me. When I study it again, with the eye of memory, I don't believe that it was a dog, however. I believe that it was human, or something trying to be human, or something which may have once been human. I said as much to Elizabeth, while I stood at the window and she lay in bed.

She laughed. It was a joyless noise. 'You live for drama,' she said. She grimaced. 'More precisely, you live for the drama of death. I think you always have.'

I didn't like her laugh. I liked her grimace even less. It made me quite angry. I could feel it in my hands and arms; I could feel it in my ears and my mouth. 'Damn you!' I whispered.

She turned over, as if to go back to sleep. I was certain she hadn't heard me.

One of the others is a woman I call Joanne. She's young, pretty, and she wears a black bikini, which fits her well. She sits upright in a two-seat wooden rowboat that has the words 'The Arrangement' painted poorly in black on the port bow. Joanne has red hair and green eyes and, unlike so many of the others, she looks happy. I could be wrong, but I'm almost sure there's the ghost of a smile on her broad, red mouth. She has her hands on the rowboat's oars, which are at right angles to the rowboat, in the sand – which is where the rowboats sits, at the bottom of a dune about a half mile from the house Elizabeth and I share.

Sometimes I speak to Joanne, as I do to many of the others, though I've never shared this fact with Elizabeth. 'Hello, Joanne,' I say. 'Beautiful name – Joanne. I've never known anyone with that name, except you.' She never responds, of course. I think that I would jump out of my shoes if she did.

Her skin has a pale blue cast. All of the others on the island have that same cast, even Elizabeth, when the gray light catches her correctly. Sometimes I think that it's simply the quality of light which causes this cast, if – were the sun to appear – it would cause many changes, not just in the cast of skin. Perhaps the winds would cease. Perhaps the air would grow warm. Perhaps rain would come. And perhaps, when all of these things happened, the others here would begin the slow but inexorable processes which would take them from me, and back to the earth, forever.

I'd miss them. Elizabeth may have been right; in some strange way, I may think of them as ornaments. As bric-a-brac, perhaps. Knickknacks. It's a grisly idea. But it's entertaining.

What does one do with a missing wife? More correctly, what *can* one do with a missing wife? Encounter her living ghost on the stairway? Conjure up memories at bedtime? Prepare tea and scones and leave them on the table always?

But then, I don't know what I want to do with her, or what I'd do with her if I found her, or if she found me, or if we came across one another on the island, or in that other house.

Of course I've looked everywhere. I'm sure that I've found her footprints in the dunes, and it occurs to me that she may have simply walked into the ocean, sick to death of the life that has been provided her here, on this grotesque and lovely island. But I've found no evidence of footprints on the ocean side of the dunes, which suggests little, because such footprints would last only half a day or so in this wind.

I've called to her, too. But, again, the wind covers much, and I'm all-but certain she cannot hear me.

I think, however, that she has never heard me. She has her gaudy, Technicolor world. And I have my world. So I've lost little.

The creature which once may have been human warbled beneath the bedroom window before daylight. There was no hint, in the sound it made, of the bark which heralded its first appearances. Only that warble, which is so close to song, and which is almost soothing in its strange atonality, as if – like so many; like myself – it is simply trying hard to find its place in a universe that is a friend to no one. And so it warbles off key, in various keys, trying to find the tone which resonates in its miserable gut and heart in the air and earth around it.

I went to the window and peered down at the creature. I couldn't see its face. I saw a rough texture to the darkness, nothing more. But I believe it was peering back at me. I believe that its eyes, which may have been green, or blue-green, or blue, locked on mine, and that when I spoke to it, it spoke back, though I heard nothing except its atonal warbling.

I am arranging the others as I feel they should have been arranged when I came to this island. I am arranging them as they no doubt want to be arranged, as *I* would want to be arranged were I in their shoes. But it is no small chore to arrange them. I'm as old or older than any of them, and they offer me no help whatsoever. Of course, I know that they're beyond helping themselves, or helping me, but when one sees arms, and legs looking fit, and strong backs, one naturally hopes for help.

The arrangement I found for Joanne was simple enough. I sent her off in her rowboat. I pushed the thing out as far as I could into the choppy ocean, perhaps fifty yards, and I let the currents grab her. In no time, she was gone.

And I put the black-haired man back in the tide pool. Face down.

And I've put Jane back on her exercise bike, though she seems angry again.

And I've put a young man named Henry on his back on a blanket, on a dune near the ocean. I've covered his midsection with a towel. He used to be taking a bath in one of the bathrooms in the other house. He used to have one arm up, so he could use a scrub brush (absent) on his back. I didn't like this. His genitals were huge, all too apparent, blue and ugly.

And one I've named Rebecca is writing her first novel here in the dining room of my little house. She's using an old Remington Rand Noiseless typewriter. Her fingers are poised above the keys, her head is lowered slightly over the platen, and she's reading what she's written – which is absolutely nothing, to date, and which will remain nothing forever. Rebecca used to be washing dishes at the other house.

I've seen Elizabeth as a silhouette against the horizon, at dusk. I'm sure it was Elizabeth. It could have been no one else. She has a distinctive figure. An hourglass figure. And she walks slowly, gracefully. I saw her from my bedroom window. She was a hundred yards away, walking toward the ocean, over a dune. I called to her, 'Elizabeth, what are you doing?'

Then sunlight grabbed her and, in a moment, both she and the sunlight were gone.

It is the first sunlight I've seen here.

I must admit that it scares me.

The others do not stay as I've arranged them. As if they have minds to command them, and hands that grasp, and legs that can make them walk, they have all gone off into other arrangements – the black-suited man is again in his high-backed chair on the dune, and Jane is now washing dishes at the other house, and the man named Henry is fishing, rod and reel poised, and Joanne is sunbathing under a gray sky, and Rebecca is standing just outside the house with an artist's brush in hand, as if at an easel.

This makes me very angry, very angry. I can feel it in my ears and behind my eyes. These people are at the mercy of the wind's intentions, the winter's intentions, *my* intentions. They are beyond their own intentions. They have no memories, no needs, no wants, no lusts. They are organs, flesh, hair, and blood as thick as pudding. They are bric-a-brac, adornments; they serve the ambulatory, they serve *me*.

The sun made a brief appearance today. It changed the wind and changed the temperature. It is changing the others, too. It's corrupting them, however slightly. The pale blue cast of their skin is becoming blemished by small irregular patches of white, and green. This is most apparent in those who remain outside.

I pray for cold, and wind, and cloud.

Quite early this morning, I awoke suddenly, without knowing why, made my way downstairs, and saw that the front door was open, that Elizabeth was standing on the front porch looking in at me. I saw her face well, despite the darkness. I think it was illuminated from above by light coming out my bedroom window.

I said, 'Elizabeth.' It wasn't a question. I was merely mouthing her name.

She closed her eyes briefly and sighed.

'Elizabeth,' I said, 'I'm very lonely here. I'm very lonely here. Come inside.'

She shook her head slightly, as if the gesture gave her sorrow.

I was half a room away; I did not move toward her.

Eventually, she turned and walked off.

The sun's brief appearances have grown less and less brief. It rises each day, and it sets. And the others have become corruptible. Skin sloughs off. Breasts wrinkle. Eyes descend.

This makes me very angry. I can feel it everywhere.

And all the while, Elizabeth watches – from a distance, on the dunes, at the windows, too. But never here, inside my little house.

I cried to her, this morning, about loneliness, again. I felt foolish and vulnerable, but I babbled and blubbered at her nonetheless, until she simply wasn't there anymore.

She could not hear me.

She has never heard me.

So I've lost little.

But how can I be lonely, now, with the others all about, arranged so prettily in the positions of life, and protected, here – inside this little house – from the lingering and awful sunlight?

I keep them away from the windows, where the sunlight insinuates itself and causes skin and hands and noses and eyes and necks to decay.

I speak to them. They do not speak back, or change their attitudes of life. I think I would jump out of my shoes if they did.

It's a bit close here, now, in this small house. I have barely room to sit in my chair. Elbows and breasts and thighs, knees and feet and chins and hair are arrayed around me like shadows at dusk.

I don't turn to the windows anymore. The sunlight is there. And I know Elizabeth is there, too, looking in at me, doubtless with pity, always with pity. And the creature which may have once been human is at a different window – one shaded from sunlight – and it is warbling its atonal song. That song is constant, now. As the wind was. It's a beautiful song, one I know I've always heard, even in childhood, and one which I think I understand, at last.

THE FOREST

Laird Barron

Laird Barron (1970–) is an American writer, much of whose critically acclaimed work falls within the horror, noir, and dark fantasy genres. In his fiction, the influence of Lovecraft and Lucius Shepard has been subsumed by his own themes and concerns, creating such potent and original modern takes on the weird tale as 'The Forest' (2007). Barron spent his early years in Alaska and moved to Washington in 1994, where he became a certified strength trainer and earned a third degree brown belt in Professor Bradley J. Steiner's Jen Do Tao system. He has received multiple Shirley Jackson awards for his fiction.

After the drive had grown long and monotonous, Partridge shut his eyes and the woman was waiting. She wore a cold white mask similar to the mask Bengali woodcutters donned when they ventured into the mangrove forests along the coast. The tigers of the forest were stealthy. The tigers hated to be watched; they preferred to sneak up on prey from behind, so natives wore the masks on the backs of their heads as they gathered wood. Sometimes this kept the tigers from dragging them away.

The woman in the cold white mask reached into a wooden box. She lifted a tarantula from the box and held it to her breast like a black carnation. The contrast was as magnificent as a stark Monet if Monet had painted watercolors of emaciated patricians and their pet spiders.

Partridge sat on his high, wooden chair and whimpered in animal terror. In the daydream, he was always very young and powerless. The woman tilted her head. She came near and extended the tarantula in her long, gray hand. 'For you,' she said. Sometimes she carried herself more like Father and said in a voice of gravel, 'Here is the end of fear.' Sometimes the tarantula was a hissing cockroach of prehistoric girth, or a horned beetle. Sometimes it was a strange, dark flower. Sometimes it was an embryo uncurling to form a miniature adult human that grinned a monkey's hateful grin.

The woman offered him a black phone. The woman said, 'Come say goodbye and good luck. Come quick!' Except the woman did not speak. Toshi's breathless voice bled through the receiver. The woman in the cold white mask brightened then dimmed like a dying coal or a piece of metal coiling into itself.

Partridge opened his eyes and rested his brow against window glass. He was alone with the driver. The bus trawled through a night forest. Black trees dripped with fog. The narrow black road crumbled from decades of neglect. Sometimes poor houses and fences stood among the weeds and the ferns and mutely suggested many more were lost in the dark. Wilderness had arisen to reclaim its possessions.

Royals hunted in woods like these. He snapped on the overhead lamp and then opened his briefcase. *Stags, wild boar, witches. Convicts.* The briefcase was nearly empty. He had tossed in some traveler's checks, a paperback novel and his address book. No cell phone, although he left a note for his lawyer and a recorded message at Kyla's place in Malibu warning them it might be a few days, perhaps a week, that there probably was not even phone service where he was going. Carry on, carry on. He had hopped a redeye jet to Boston and once there eschewed the convenience of renting a car or hiring a chauffeur and limo. He chose instead the relative anonymity of mass transit. The appeal of traveling incognito overwhelmed his normally staid sensibilities. Here was the first adventure he had undertaken in ages. The solitude presented an opportunity to compose his thoughts – his excuses, more likely.

He'd cheerfully abandoned the usual host of unresolved items and potential brushfires that went with the territory – a possible trip to the Andes if a certain Famous Director's film got green-lighted and if the Famous Director's drunken assertion to assorted executive producers and hangers-on over barbecued ribs and flaming daiquiris at the Monarch Grille that Richard Jefferson Partridge was the only man for the job meant a blessed thing. There were several smaller opportunities, namely an L.A. documentary about a powerhouse high school basketball team that recently graced the cover of *Sports Illustrated*, unless the documentary guy, a Cannes Film Festival sweetheart, decided to try to bring down the Governor of California instead, as he had threatened to do time and again, a pet crusade of his with the elections coming that fall, and then the director would surely use his politically savvy compatriot, the cinematographer from France. He'd also been approached regarding a proposed documentary about prisoners and guards at San Quentin. Certainly there were other, lesser engagements he'd lost track of, these doubtless scribbled on memo pads in his home office.

He knew he should hire a reliable secretary. He promised himself to do just that every year. It was hard. He missed Jean. She'd had a lazy eye and a droll wit; made bad coffee and kept sand-filled frogs and fake petunias on her desk. Jean left him for Universal Studios and then slammed into a reef in Maui learning to surf with her new boss. The idea of writing the want-ad, of sorting the applications and conducting the interviews and finally letting the new person, the stranger, sit where Jean had sat and handle his papers, summoned a mosquito's thrum in the bones behind Partridge's ear.

These details would surely keep despite what hysterics might come in the meanwhile. Better, much better, not to endure the buzzing and whining and the imprecations and demands that he return at once on pain of immediate career death, over a dicey relay. He had not packed a camera, either. He was on vacation. His mind would store what his eye could catch and that was all.

The light was poor. Partridge held the address book close to his face. He had scribbled the directions from margin to margin and drawn a crude map with arrows and lopsided boxes and jotted the initials of the principles: Dr. Toshi Ryoko; Dr. Howard Campbell; Beasley; and Nadine. Of course, Nadine – she snapped her fingers and here he came at a loyal trot. There were no mileposts on the road to confirm the impression that his destination was near. The weight in his belly sufficed. It was a fat stone grown from a pebble.

Partridge's instincts did not fail him. A few minutes before dawn, the forest receded and they entered Warrenburgh. Warrenburgh was a loveless hamlet of crabbed New England shop fronts and angular plank and shingle houses with tall, thin doors and oily windows. Streetlights glowed along Main Street with black gaps like a broken pearl necklace. The street itself was buckled and rutted by poorly tarred cracks that caused sections to cohere uneasily as interleaved ice floes. The sea loomed near and heavy and palpable beneath a layer of rolling gloom.

Partridge did not like what little he glimpsed of the surroundings. Long ago, his friend Toshi had resided in New Mexico and Southern California, did his best work in Polynesia and the jungles of Central America. The doctor was a creature of warmth and light. *Rolling Stone* had characterized him as 'a rock star among zoologists' and as the 'Jacques Cousteau of the jungle', the kind of man who hired mercenaries to guard him, performers to entertain his sun-drenched villa, and filmmakers to document his exploits. This temperate landscape, so cool and provincial, so removed from Partridge's experience of all things Toshi, seemed to herald a host of unwelcome revelations.

Beasley, longstanding attendant of the eccentric researcher, waited at the station. 'Rich! At least you don't look like the big asshole *Variety* says you are.' He nodded soberly and scooped Partridge up for a brief hug in his powerful arms. This was like being embraced by an earth mover. Beasley had played Australian rules football for a while after he left the Army and before he came to work for Toshi. His nose was squashed and his ears were cauliflowers. He was magnetic and striking as any character actor, nonetheless. 'Hey, let me get that.' He set Partridge aside and grabbed the luggage the driver had dragged from the innards of the bus. He hoisted the suitcases into the bed of a '56 Ford farm truck. The truck was museum quality. It was fire engine red with a dinky American flag on the antenna.

They rumbled inland. Rusty light gradually exposed counterchange shelves of empty fields and canted telephone poles strung together with thick, dipping old-fashioned cables. Ducks pelted from a hollow in the road. The ducks spread themselves in a wavering pattern against the sky.

'Been shooting?' Partridge indicated the .20 gauge softly clattering in the rack behind their heads.

'When T isn't looking. Yeah, I roam the marshes a bit. You?'

'No.'

'Yah?'

'Not in ages. Things get in the way. Life, you know?'

'Oh, well, we'll go out one day this week. Bag a mallard or two. Raise the dust.'

Partridge stared at the moving scenery. Toshi was disinterested in hunting and thought it generally a waste of energy. Nadine detested the sport without reserve. He tasted brackish water, metallic from the canteen. The odor of gun oil and cigarette smoke was strong in the cab. The smell reminded him of hip waders, muddy clay banks and gnats in their biting millions among the reeds. 'Okay. Thanks.'

'Forget it, man.'

They drove in silence until Beasley hooked left onto a dirt road that followed a ridge of brambles and oak trees. On the passenger side overgrown pastures dwindled into moiling vapors. The road was secured by a heavy iron gate with the usual complement of grimy warning signs. Beasley climbed out and unlocked the gate and swung it aside. Partridge realized that somehow this was the same ruggedly charismatic Beasley, plus a streak of gray in the beard and minus the spring-loaded tension and the whiskey musk. Beasley at peace was an enigma. Maybe he had quit the bottle for good this time around. The thought was not as comforting as it should have been. If this elemental truth – Beasley the chronic drunk, the lovable, but damaged brute – had ceased to hold, then what else lurked in the wings?

When they had begun to jounce along the washboard lane, Partridge said, 'Did T get sick? Somebody – I think Frank Ledbetter – told me T had some heart problems. Angina.'

'Frankie… I haven't seen him since forever. He still working for Boeing?'

'Lockheed-Martin.'

'Yah? Good ol' L&M. Well, no business like war business,' Beasley said. 'The old boy's fine. Sure, things were in the shitter for a bit after New Guinea, but we all got over it. Water down the sluice.' Again, the knowing, sidelong glance. 'Don't worry so much. He misses you. Everybody does, man.'

Toshi's farm was more of a compound lumped in the torso of a great, irregular field. The road terminated in a hard pack lot bordered by a sprawl of sheds and shacks, gutted chicken coops and labyrinthine hog pens fallen to ruin. The main house, a Queen Anne, dominated. The house was a full three stories of spires, gables, spinning iron weathercocks and acres of slate tiles. A monster of a house, yet somehow hunched upon itself. It was brooding and squat and low as a brick and timber mausoleum. The detached garage seemed new. So too the tarp and plastic-sheeted nurseries, the electric fence that partitioned the back forty into quadrants and the military drab shortwave antenna array crowning the A-frame barn. No private security forces were in evidence, no British mercenaries with submachine guns on shoulder slings, nor packs of sleek, bullet-headed attack dogs cruising the property. The golden age had obviously passed into twilight.

'Behold the Moorehead Estate,' Beasley said

as he parked by slamming the brakes so the truck skidded sideways and its tires sent up a geyser of dirt. 'Howard and Toshi bought it from the county about fifteen years ago – guess the original family died out, changed their names, whatever. Been here in one form or another since 1762. The original burned to the foundation in 1886, which is roughly when the town – Orren Towne, 'bout two miles west of here – dried up and blew away. As you can see, they made some progress fixing this place since then.'

Partridge whistled as he eyed the setup. 'Really, ah, cozy.'

There were other cars scattered in the lot: a Bentley; a Nixon-era Cadillac; an archaic Land Rover that might have done a tour in the Sahara; a couple of battered pickup trucks and an Army surplus jeep. These told Partridge a thing or two, but not enough to surmise the number of guests or the nature of Toshi's interest in them. He had spotted the tail rotor of a helicopter poking from behind the barn.

Partridge did not recognize any of the half-a-dozen grizzled men loitering near the bunkhouse. Those would be the roustabouts and the techs. The men passed around steaming thermoses of coffee. They pretended not to watch him and Beasley unload the luggage.

'For God's sake, boy, why didn't you catch a plane?' Toshi called down from a perilously decrepit veranda. He was wiry and sallow and vitally ancient. He dressed in a bland short sleeve button up shirt a couple of neck sizes too large and his ever present gypsy kerchief. He leaned way over the precarious railing and smoked a cigarette. His cigarettes were invariably Russian and came in tin boxes blazoned with hyperbolic full color logos and garbled English mottos and blurbs such as, 'Prince of Peace! and 'Yankee Flavor!'

'The Lear's in the shop.' Partridge waved and headed for the porch.

'You don't drive, either, eh?' Toshi flicked his hand impatiently. 'Come on, then. Beasley – the Garden Room, please.'

Beasley escorted Partridge through the gloomy maze of cramped halls and groaning stairs. Everything was dark: from the cryptic hangings and oil paintings of Mooreheads long returned to dust, to the shiny walnut planks that squeaked and shifted everywhere underfoot.

Partridge was presented a key by the new housekeeper, Mrs. Grant. She was a brusque woman of formidable brawn and comport; perhaps Beasley's mother in another life. Beasley informed him that 'new' was a relative term as she had been in Campbell's employ for the better portion of a decade. She had made the voyage from Orange County and brought along three maids and a gardener/handyman who was also her current lover.

The Garden Room was on the second floor of the east wing and carefully isolated from the more heavily trafficked byways. It was a modest, L-shaped room with a low, harshly textured ceiling, a coffin wardrobe carved from the heart of some extinct tree, a matching dresser and a diminutive brass bed that sagged ominously. The portrait of a solemn girl in a garden hat was centered amidst otherwise negative space across from the bed. Vases of fresh cut flowers were arranged on the window sills. Someone had plugged in a rose-scented air freshener to subdue the abiding taint of wet plaster and rotting wood; mostly in vain. French doors let out to a balcony overlooking tumbledown stone walls of a lost garden and then a plain of waist-high grass gone the shade of wicker. The grass flowed into foothills. The foothills formed an indistinct line in the blue mist.

'Home away from home, eh?' Beasley said. He wrung his hands, out of place as a bear in the confined quarters. 'Let's see if those bastards left us any crumbs.'

Howard Campbell and Toshi were standing around the bottom of the stairs with a couple of other elder statesmen types – one, a bluff, aristocratic fellow with handlebar mustaches and fat hands, reclined in a hydraulic wheelchair. The second man was also a specimen of genteel extract, but clean-shaven and decked in a linen suit that had doubtless been the height of ballroom fashion during Truman's watch. This fellow leaned heavily upon an ornate blackthorn cane. He occasionally pressed an oxygen mask over his mouth and nose and snuffled deeply. Both men stank of medicinal alcohol and shoe polish. A pair of bodyguards hovered nearby. The guards were physically powerful men in tight suit-jackets. Their nicked up faces wore the perpetual scowls of peasant trustees.

Toshi lectured about a so-called supercolony of ants that stretched six thousand kilometers from the mountains of Northern Italy down along the coasts of France and into Spain. According to the reports, this was the largest ant colony on record; a piece of entomological history in the making. He halted his oration to lackadaisically introduce the Eastern gentlemen as Mr. Jackson Phillips and Mr. Carrey Montague and then jabbed Campbell in the ribs, saying, 'What'd I tell you? Rich is as suave as an Italian prince. Thank God I don't have a daughter for him to knock up.' To Partridge he said, 'Now go eat before cook throws it to the pigs. Go, go!' Campbell, the tallest and gravest of the congregation, gave Partridge a subtle wink. Meanwhile, the man in the wheelchair raised his voice to demand an explanation for why his valuable time was being wasted on an ant seminar. He had not come to listen to a dissertation and Toshi damned-well knew better… Partridge did not catch the rest because Beasley ushered him into the kitchen whilst surreptitiously flicking Mr. Jackson Phillips the bird.

The cook was an impeccable Hungarian named Gertz, whom Campbell had lured, or possibly blackmailed, away from a popular restaurant in Santa Monica. In any event, Gertz knew his business.

Partridge slumped on a wooden stool at the kitchen counter. He worked his way through what Gertz apologetically called 'leftovers.' These included sourdough waffles and strawberries, whipped eggs, biscuits, sliced apples, honey dew melon and chilled milk. The coffee was a hand ground Columbian blend strong enough to peel paint. Beasley slapped him on the shoulder and said something about chores.

Partridge was sipping his second mug of coffee, liberally dosed with cream and sugar, when Nadine sat down close to him. Nadine shone darkly and smelled of fresh cut hayricks and sweet, highly polished leather. She leaned in tight and plucked the teaspoon from his abruptly nerveless fingers. She licked the teaspoon and dropped it on the saucer and she did not smile at all. She looked at him with metallic eyes that held nothing but a prediction of snow.

'And… action,' Nadine said in a soft, yet resonant voice that could have placed her center stage on Broadway had she ever desired to dwell in the Apple and ride her soap and water sex appeal to the bank and back. She spoke without a trace of humor, which was a worthless gauge to ascertain her mood anyhow, she being a classical Stoic. Her mouth was full and lovely and inches from Partridge's own. She did not wear lipstick.

'You're pissed,' Partridge said. He felt slightly dizzy. He was conscious of his sticky fingers and the seeds in his teeth.

'Lucky guess.'

'I'm a Scientologist, Grade Two. We get ESP at G-2. No luck involved.'

'Oh, they got you, too. Pity. Inevitable, but still a pity.'

'I'm kidding.'

'What… even the cultists don't want you?'

'I'm sure they want my money.'

Nadine tilted her head slightly. 'I owe the Beez twenty bucks, speaking of. Know why?'

'No,' Partridge said. 'Wait. You said I wouldn't show–'

'–because you're a busy man–'

'That's the absolute truth. I'm busier than a one-armed paper hanger.'

'I'm sure. Anyway, I said you'd duck us once again. A big movie deal, fucking a B-list starlet in the South of France. It'd be something.'

'–and then Beasley said something on the order of–'

'Hell yeah, my boy will be here!–'

'–come hell or high water!'

'Pretty much, yeah. He believes in you.'

Partridge tried not to squirm even as her pitiless gaze bore into him. 'Well, it was close. I cancelled some things. Broke an engagement or two.'

'Mmm. It's okay, Rich. You've been promising yourself a vacation, haven't you? This makes a handy excuse; do a little R&R, get some *you* time in for a change. It's for your mental health. Bet you can write it off.'

'Since this is going so well… How's Coop?' He had noticed she was not wearing the ring. Handsome hubby Dan Cooper was doubtless a sore subject, he being the hapless CEO of an obscure defense contractor that got caught up in a Federal dragnet. He would not be racing his classic Jaguar along hairpin coastal highways for the next five to seven years, even assuming time off for good behavior. Poor Coop was another victim of Nadine's gothic curse. 'Condolences, naturally. If I didn't send a card… '

'He *loves* Federal prison. It's a country club, really. How's that bitch you introduced me to? I forget her name.'

'Rachel.'

'Yep, that's it. The makeup lady. She pancaked Thurman like a corpse on that flick you shot for Coppola.'

'Ha, yeah. She's around. We're friends.'

'Always nice to have friends.'

Partridge forced a smile. 'I'm seeing someone else.'

'Kyla Sherwood – the Peroxide Puppet. Tabloids know all, my dear.'

'But it's not serious.'

'News to her, hey?'

He was boiling alive in his Aspen-chic sweater and charcoal slacks. Sweat trickled down his neck and the hairs on his thighs prickled and chorused their disquiet. He wondered if that was a massive pimple pinching the flesh between his eyes. That was where he had always gotten the worst of them in high school. His face swelled so majestically people thought he had broken his nose playing softball. What could he say with this unbearable pressure building in his lungs? Their history had grown to epic dimensions. The kitchen was too small to contain such a thing. He said, 'Toshi said it was important. That I come to this… what? Party? Reunion? Whatever it is. God knows I love a mystery.'

Nadine stared the stare that gave away nothing. She finally glanced at her watch and stood. She leaned over him so that her hot breath brushed his ear. 'Mmm. Look at the time. Lovely seeing you, Rich. Maybe later we can do lunch.'

He watched her walk away. As his pulse slowed and his breathing loosened, he waited for his erection to subside and tried to pinpoint what it was that nagged him, what it was that tripped the machinery beneath the liquid surface of his guilt-crazed, testosterone-glutted brain. Nadine had always reminded him of a duskier, more ferocious Bettie Page. She was thinner now; her prominent cheekbones, the fragile symmetry of her scapulae through the open-back blouse, registered with him as he sat recovering his wits with the numb intensity of a soldier who had just clambered from a trench following a mortar barrage.

Gertz slunk out of hiding and poured more coffee into Partridge's cup. He dumped in some Schnapps from a hip flask. 'Hang in there, my friend,' he said drolly.

'I just got my head beaten in,' Partridge said.

'Round one,' Gertz said. He took a hefty pull from the flask. 'Pace yourself, champ.'

Partridge wandered the grounds until he found Toshi in D-Lab. Toshi was surveying a breeding colony of cockroaches: *Pariplenata americana*, he proclaimed them with a mixture of pride and annoyance. The lab was actually a big tool shed with the windows painted over. Industrial-sized aquariums occupied most of the floor space. The air had acquired a peculiar, spicy odor reminiscent of hazelnuts and fermented bananas. The chamber was illuminated by infrared lamps. Partridge could not observe much activity within the aquariums unless he stood next to the glass. That was not going to happen. He contented himself to lurk at Toshi's elbow while a pair of men in coveralls and rubber gloves performed maintenance on an empty pen. The men scraped substrate into garbage bags and hosed the container and applied copious swathes of petroleum jelly to the rim where the mesh lid attached. Cockroaches were escape artists extraordinaire, according to Toshi.

'Most folks are trying to figure the best pesticide to squirt on these little fellas. Here you are a cockroach rancher,' Partridge said.

'Cockroaches… I care nothing for cockroaches. This is scarcely more than a side effect, the obligatory nod to cladistics, if you will. Cockroaches… beetles… there are superficial similarities. These animals crawl and burrow, they predate us humans by hundreds of millions of years. But… beetles are infinitely more interesting. The naturalist's best friend. Museums and taxidermists love them, you see. Great for cleaning skeletal structures, antlers and the like.'

'Nature's efficiency experts. What's the latest venture?'

'A-Lab – I will show you.' Toshi became slightly animated. He straightened his crunched shoulders to gesticulate. His hand glimmered like a glow tube at a rock concert. 'I keep a dozen colonies of dermestid beetles in operation. Have to house them in glass or stainless steel – they nibble through anything.'

This house of creepy-crawlies was not good for Partridge's nerves. He thought of the chair and the woman and her tarantula. He was sickly aware that if he closed his eyes at that very moment the stranger would remove the mask and reveal Nadine's face. Thinking of Nadine's face and its feverish luminescence, he said, 'She's dying.'

Toshi shrugged. 'Johns-Hopkins… my friends at Fred Hutch… nobody can do anything. This is the very bad stuff; very quick.'

'How long has she got.' The floor threatened to slide from under Partridge's feet. Cockroaches milled in their shavings and hidey holes; their tick-tack impacts burrowed under his skin.

'Not long. Probably three or four months.'

'Okay.' Partridge tasted breakfast returned as acid in his mouth.

The technicians finished their task and began sweeping. Toshi gave some orders. He said to Partridge, 'Let's go see the beetles.'

A-Lab was identical to D-Lab except for the wave of charnel rot that met Partridge as he entered. The dermestid colonies were housed in corrugated metal canisters. Toshi raised the lid to show Partridge how industriously a particular group of larvae were stripping the greasy flesh of a small mixed breed dog. Clean white bone peeked through coagulated muscle fibers and patches of coarse, blond fur.

Partridge managed to stagger the fifteen or so feet and vomit into a plastic sink. Toshi shut the lid and nodded wisely. 'Some fresh air, then.'

Toshi conducted a perfunctory tour, complete with a wheezing narrative regarding matters coleopteran and teuthological, the latter being one of his comrade Howard Campbell's manifold specialties. Campbell had held since the early 70s that One Day Soon the snail cone or some species of jellyfish was going to revolutionize neurology. Partridge nodded politely and dwelt on his erupting misery. His stomach felt as if a brawler had used it for a speed bag. He trembled and dripped with cold sweats.

Then, as they ambled along a fence holding back the wasteland beyond the barn, he spotted a cluster of three satellite dishes. The dishes' antennas were angled downward at a sizable oblong depression like aardvark snouts poised to siphon musty earth. These were lightweight models, each no more than four meters across and positioned as to be hidden from casual view from the main house. Their trapezoidal shapes didn't jibe with photos Partridge had seen of similar devices. These objects gleamed the yellow-gray gleam of rotting teeth. His skin crawled as he studied them and the area of crushed soil. The depression was over a foot deep and shaped not unlike a kiddy wading pool. This presence in the field was incongruous and somehow sinister. He immediately regretted discarding his trusty Canon. He stopped and pointed. 'What are those?'

'Radio telescopes, obviously.'

'Yeah, what kind of metal is that? Don't they work better if you point them at the sky?'

'The sky. Ah, well, perhaps later. You note the unique design, eh? Campbell and I… invented them. Basically.'

'Really? Interesting segue from entomological investigation, doc.'

'See what happens when you roll in the mud with NASA? The notion of first contact is so glamorous, it begins to rub off. Worse than drugs. I'm in recovery.'

Partridge stared at the radio dishes. 'UFOs and whatnot, huh. You stargazer, you. When did you get into that field?' It bemused him how Toshi Ryoko hop-scotched from discipline to discipline with a breezy facility that unnerved even the mavericks among his colleagues.

'I most assuredly haven't migrated to that field – however, I will admit to grazing as the occasion warrants. The dishes are a link in the chain. We've got miles of conductive coil buried around here. All part of a comprehensive surveillance plexus. We monitor everything that crawls, swims or flies. Howard and I have become enamored of astrobiology, crypto zoology, the occulted world. Do you recall when we closed shop in California? That was roughly concomitant with our lamentably over-publicized misadventures in New Guinea.'

'Umm.' Partridge had heard that Campbell and Toshi disappeared into the back country for three weeks after they lost a dozen porters and two graduate students in a river accident. Maybe alcohol and drugs were involved. There was an investigation and all charges were waived. The students' families had sued and sued, of course. Partridge knew he should have called to offer moral support. Unfortunately, associating with Toshi in that time of crisis might have been an unwise career move and he let it slide. *But nothing slides forever, does it?*

'New Guinea wasn't really a disaster. Indeed, it served to crystallize the focus of our research, to open new doors…'

Partridge was not thrilled to discuss New Guinea. 'Intriguing. I'm glad you're going great guns. It's over my head, but I'm glad. Sincerely.' Several crows described broad, looping circles near the unwholesome machines. Near, but not too near.

'Ah, but that's not important. I imagine I shall die before any of this work comes to fruition.' Toshi smiled fondly and evasively. He gave Partridge an avuncular pat on the arm. 'You're here for Nadine's grand farewell. She will leave the farm after the weekend. Everything is settled. You see now why I called. '

Partridge was not convinced. Nadine seemed to resent his presence – she'd always been hot and cold when it came to him. What did Toshi want him to do? 'Absolutely,' he said.

They walked back to the house and sat on the porch in rocking chairs. Gertz brought them a pitcher of iced tea and frosted glasses on trays. Campbell emerged in his trademark double-breasted steel-blue suit and horn rim glasses. For the better part of three decades he had played the mild, urbane foil to Toshi's megalomaniacal iconoclast. In private, Campbell was easily the dominant of the pair. He leaned against a post and held out his hand until Toshi passed him a smoldering cigarette. 'I'm glad you know,' he said, fastening his murky eyes on Partridge. 'I didn't have the nerve to tell you myself.'

Partridge felt raw, exhausted, and bruised. He changed the subject. 'So… those guys in the suits. Montague and Phillips. How do you know them? Financiers, I presume?'

'Patrons,' Campbell said. 'As you can see, we've scaled back the operation. It's difficult to run things off the cuff.' Lolling against the post, a peculiar hybrid of William Burroughs and Walter Cronkite, he radiated folksy charm that mostly diluted underlying hints of decadence. This charm often won the hearts of flabby dilettante crones looking for a cause to champion. 'Fortunately, there are always interested parties with deep pockets.'

Partridge chuckled to cover his unease. His stomach was getting worse. 'Toshi promised to get me up to speed on your latest and greatest contribution to the world of science. Or do I want to know?'

'You showed him the telescopes? Anything else?' Campbell glanced to Toshi and arched his brow.

Toshi's grin was equal portions condescension and mania. He rubbed his spindly hands together like a spider combing its pedipalps. 'Howard… I haven't, he hasn't been to the site. He has visited with our pets, however. Mind your shoes if you fancy them, by the way.'

'Toshi has developed a knack for beetles,' Campbell said. 'I don't know what he sees in them, frankly. Boring, boring. Pardon the pun – I'm stone knackered on Dewar's. My bloody joints are positively gigantic in this climate. Oh – have you seen reports of the impending Yellow Disaster? China will have the whole of Asia Minor deforested in the next decade. I imagine you haven't – you don't film horror movies, right? At least not reality horror.' He laughed as if to say, You realize I'm kidding, don't you, lad? *We're all friends here.* 'Mankind is definitely eating himself out of house and home. The beetles and cockroaches are in the direct line of succession.'

'Scary,' Partridge said. He waited doggedly for the punch line. Although, free association was another grace note of Campbell's and Toshi's. The punch line might not even exist. Give them thirty seconds and they would be nattering about engineering E. coli to perform microscopic stupid pet tricks or how much they missed those good old Bangkok whores.

Toshi lighted another cigarette and waved it carelessly. 'The boy probably hasn't the foggiest notion as to the utility of our naturalistic endeavors. Look, after dinner, we'll give a demonstration. We'll hold a séance.'

'Oh, horseshit, Toshi!' Campbell scowled fearsomely. This was always a remarkable transformation for those not accustomed to his moods. 'Considering the circumstances, that's extremely tasteless.'

'Not to mention premature,' Partridge said through a grim smile. He rose, upsetting his drink in a clatter of softened ice cubes and limpid orange rinds and strode from the porch. He averted his face. He was not certain if Campbell called after him because of the blood beating in his ears. Toshi did clearly say, 'Let him go, let him be, Howard... She'll talk to him...'

He stumbled to his room and crashed into his too-short bed and fell unconscious.

Partridge owed much of his success to Toshi. Even that debt might not have been sufficient to justify the New England odyssey. The real reason, the motive force under the hood of Partridge's lamentable midlife crisis, and the magnetic compulsion to heed that bizarre late-night call, was certainly his sense of unfinished business with Nadine. Arguably, he had Toshi to thank for that, too.

Toshi Ryoko immigrated to Britain, and later the U.S., from Okinawa in the latter '60s. This occurred a few years after he had begun to attract attention from the international scientific community for his brilliant work in behavioral ecology and prior to his stratospheric rise to popular fame due to daredevil eccentricities and an Academy Award nominated documentary of his harrowing expedition into the depths of a Bengali wildlife preserve. The name of the preserve loosely translated into English as 'The Forest that Eats Men.' Partridge had been the twenty-three year old cinematographer brought aboard at the last possible moment to photograph the expedition. No more qualified person could be found on the ridiculously short notice that Toshi announced for departure. The director/producer was none other than Toshi himself. It was his first and last film. There were, of course, myriad subsequent independent features, newspaper and radio accounts – the major slicks covered Toshi's controversial exploits, but he lost interest in filmmaking after the initial hubbub and eventually faded from the public eye. Possibly his increasing affiliation with clandestine U.S. government projects was to blame. The cause was immaterial. Toshi's fascinations were mercurial and stardom proved incidental to his mission of untangling the enigmas of evolutionary origins and ultimate destination.

Partridge profited greatly from that tumultuous voyage into the watery hell of man eating tigers and killer bees. He emerged from the crucible as a legend fully formed. His genesis was as Minerva's, that warrior-daughter sprung whole from Jupiter's aching skull. All the great directors wanted him. His name was gold – it was nothing but Beluga caviar and box seats at the Rose Bowl, a string of 'where are they now' actresses on his arm, an executive membership in the Ferrari Club and posh homes in Malibu and Ireland. Someday they would hang his portrait in the American Society of Cinematography archives and blazon his star on Hollywood Boulevard.

There was just one glitch in his happily-ever-after: Nadine. Nadine Thompson was the whip smart Stanford physiologist who had gone along for the ride to Bangladesh as Toshi's chief disciple.

She was not Hollywood sultry, yet the camera found her to be eerily riveting in a way that was simultaneously erotic and repellant. The audience never saw a *scientist* when the camera tracked Nadine across the rancid deck of that river barge. They saw a woman-child – ripe, lithe and lethally carnal.

She was doomed. Jobs came and went. Some were comparative plums, yes. None of them led to prominence indicative of her formal education and nascent talent. None of them opened the way to the marquee projects, postings or commissions. She eventually settled for a staff position at a museum in Buffalo. An eighty-seven minute film shot on super-sixteen millimeter consigned her to professional purgatory. Maybe a touch of that taint had rubbed off on Partridge. Nadine was the youthful excess that Hollywood could not supply, despite its excess of youth, the one he still longed for during the long, blank Malibu nights. He carried a load of guilt about the whole affair as well.

Occasionally, in the strange, hollow years after the hoopla, the groundswell of acclaim and infamy, she would corner Partridge in a remote getaway bungalow, or a honeymoon seaside cottage, for a weekend of gin and bitters and savage lovemaking. In the languorous aftermath, she often confided how his magic Panaflex had destroyed her career. She would forever be 'the woman in that movie.' She was branded a real life scream queen and the sex pot with the so-so face and magnificent ass.

Nadine was right, as usual. 'The Forest that Eats Men' never let go once it sank its teeth.

He dreamed of poling a raft on a warm, muddy river. Mangroves hemmed them in corridors of convoluted blacks and greens. Creepers and vines strung the winding waterway. Pale sunlight sifted down through the screen of vegetation; a dim, smoky light full of shadows and shifting clouds of gnats and mosquitoes. Birds warbled and screeched. He crouched in the stern of the raft and stared at the person directly before him. That person's wooden mask with its dead eyes and wooden smile gaped at him, fitted as it was to the back of the man's head. The wooden mouth whispered, 'You forgot your mask.' Partridge reached back and found, with burgeoning horror, that his skull was indeed naked and defenseless.

'They're coming. They're coming.' The mask grinned soullessly.

He inhaled to scream and jerked awake, twisted in the sheets and sweating. Red light poured through the thin curtains. Nadine sat in the shadows at the foot of his bed. Her hair was loose and her skin reflected the ruddy light. He thought of the goddess Kali shrunk to mortal dimensions.

'You don't sleep well either, huh,' she said.

'Nope. Not since Bangladesh.'

'That long. Huh.'

He propped himself on his elbow and studied her. 'I've been considering my options lately. I'm thinking it might be time to hang up my spurs. Go live in the Bahamas.'

She said, 'You're too young to go.' That was her mocking tone.

'You too.'

She didn't say anything for a while. Then, 'Rich, you ever get the feeling you're being watched?'

'Like when you snuck in here while I was sleeping? Funny you should mention it...'

'Rich.'

He saw that she was serious. 'Sometimes, yeah.'

'Well you are. Always. I want you to keep that in mind.'

'Okay. Will it help?'

'Good question.'

The room darkened, bit by bit. He said, 'You think you would've made it back to the barge?' He couldn't distance himself from her cry as she flailed overboard and hit the water like a stone. There were crocodiles everywhere. No one moved. The whole crew was frozen in that moment between disbelief and action. He had shoved the camera at, who? Beasley. He had done that and then gone in and gotten her. Blood warm water, brown with mud. He did not remember much of the rest. The camera caught it all.

'No,' she said. 'Not even close.'

He climbed over the bed and hugged her. She was warm. He pressed his face into her hair. Her hair trapped the faint, cloying odor of sickness. 'I'm so fucking sorry,' he said.

She didn't say anything. She rubbed his shoulder.

That night was quiet at the Moorehead Estate. There was a subdued dinner and afterward some drinks. Everybody chatted about the good old days. The real ones and the imaginary ones too. Phillips and Montague disappeared early on and took their men-at-arms with them. Nadine sat aloof. She held onto a hardback – one of Toshi's long out of print treatises on insect behavior and ecological patterns. Partridge could tell she was only pretending to look at it.

Later, after lights out, Partridge roused from a dream of drowning in something that wasn't quite water. His name was whispered from the foot of the bed. He fumbled upright in the smothering dark. 'Nadine?' He clicked on the lamp and saw he was alone.

It rained in the morning. Toshi was undeterred. He put on a slicker and took a drive in the Land Rover to move the radio telescopes and other equipment into more remote fields. A truckload of the burly, grim laborers followed. The technicians trudged about their daily routine, indifferent to the weather. Campbell disappeared with Phillips and Montague. Nadine remained in her room. Partridge spent the morning playing poker with Beasley and Gertz on the rear porch. They drank whiskey – coffee for Beasley – and watched water drip from the eaves and thunderheads roll across the horizon trailing occasional whip-cracks of lightning. Then it stopped raining and the sun transformed the landscape into a mass of illuminated rust and glass.

Partridge went for a long walk around the property to clear his head and savor the clean air. The sun was melting toward the horizon when Beasley found him dozing in the shade of an oak. It was a huge tree with yellowing leaves and exposed roots. The roots crawled with pill bugs. Between yawns Partridge observed the insects go about their tiny business.

'C'mon. You gotta see the ghost town before it gets dark,' Beasley said. Partridge didn't bother to protest. Nadine waited in the jeep. She wore tortoise shell sunglasses and a red scarf in her hair. He decided she looked better in a scarf than Toshi ever had, no question. Partridge opened his mouth and Beasley gave him a friendly shove into the front passenger seat.

'Sulk, sulk, sulk!' Nadine laughed at him. 'In the garden, eating worms?'

'Close enough,' Partridge said and hung on as Beasley gunned the jeep through a break in the fence line and zoomed along an overgrown track that was invisible until they were right on top of it. The farm became a picture on a stamp and then they passed through a belt of paper birches and red maples. They crossed a ramshackle bridge that spanned an ebon stream and drove into a clearing. Beasley ground gears until they gained the crown of a long, tabletop hill. He killed the engine and coasted to a halt amid tangled grass and wildflowers and said, 'Orren Towne. Died circa 1890s.'

Below their vantage, remnants of a village occupied the banks of a shallow valley. If Orren Towne was dead its death was the living kind. A score of saltbox houses and the brooding hulk of a Second Empire church waited somberly. Petrified roofs were dappled by the shadows of moving clouds. Facades were brim with the ephemeral light of the magic hour. Beasley's walkie-talkie crackled and he stepped aside to answer the call.

Nadine walked part way down the slope and stretched her arms. Her muscles stood forth in cords of sinew and gristle. She looked over her shoulder at Partridge. Her smile was alien. 'Don't you wish you'd brought your camera?'

The brain is a camera. What Partridge really wished was that he had gone to his room and slept. His emotions were on the verge of running amok. The animal fear from his daydreams had sneaked up again. He smelled the musk of his own adrenaline and sweat. *The brain is a camera and once it sees what it sees there's no taking it back.* He noticed another of Toshi's bizarre radio dishes perched on a bluff. The antenna was focused upon the deserted buildings. 'I don't like this place,' he said. But she kept walking and he trailed along. It was cooler among the houses. The earth was trampled into concrete and veined with minerals. Nothing organic grew and no birds sang. The subtly deformed structures were encased in a transparent resin that lent the town the aspect of a waxworks. He thought it might be shellac.

Shadows fell across Partridge's path. Open doorways and sugar spun windows fronted darkness. These doors and windows were as unwelcoming as the throats of ancient wells, the mouths of caves. He breathed heavily. 'How did Toshi do this? *Why* did he do this?'

Nadine laughed and took his hand playfully. Hers was dry and too warm, like a leather wallet left in direct sunlight. 'Toshi only discovered it. Do you seriously think he and Howard are capable of devising something this extraordinary?'

'No.'

'Quite a few people spent their lives in this valley. Decent farming and hunting in these parts. The Mooreheads owned about everything. They owned a brewery and a mill down the road, near their estate. All those busy little worker bees going about their jobs, going to church on Sunday. I'm sure it was a classic Hallmark. Then it got cold. One of those long winters that never ends. Nothing wanted to grow and the game disappeared. The house burned. Sad for the Mooreheads. Sadder for the people who depended on them. The family circled its wagons to rebuild the mansion, but the community never fully recovered. Orren Towne was here today, gone tomorrow. At least that's the story we hear told by the old timers at the Mad Rooster over cribbage and a pint of stout.' Nadine stood in the shade of the church, gazing up, up at the crucifix. 'This is how it will all be someday. Empty buildings. Empty skies. The grass will come and eat everything we ever made. The waters will swallow it. It puts my situation into perspective, lemme tell you.'

'These buildings should've fallen down. Somebody's gone through a lot of trouble to keep this like – '

'A museum. Yeah, somebody has. This isn't the only place it's been done, either.'

'Places like this? Where?' Partridge said. He edged closer to the bright center of the village square.

'I don't know. They're all over if you know what to look for.'

'Nadine, maybe … Jesus!' He jerked his head to peer at a doorway. The darkness inside the house seemed fuller and more complete. 'Are there people here?' His mind jumped to an image of the masks that the natives wore to ward off tigers. He swallowed hard.

'Just us chickens, love.'

A stiff breeze rushed from the northwest and whipped the outlying grass. Early autumn leaves skated across the glassy rooftops and swirled in barren yards. Leaves fell dead and dry. Night was coming hard.

'I'm twitchy – jet lag, probably. What do those weird-looking rigs do?' He pointed at the dish on the hill. 'Toshi said they're radio telescopes he invented.'

'He said he invented them? Oh my. I dearly love that man, but sometimes he's such an asshole.'

'Yeah. How do they work?'

Nadine shrugged. 'They read frequencies on the electromagnetic spectrum.'

'Radio signals from underground. Why does that sound totally backwards to me?'

'I didn't say anything about radio signals.'

'Then what did you say?'

'When we get back, ask Toshi about the node.'

'What are you talking about?' Partridge's attention was divided between her and the beautifully grotesque houses and the blackness inside them.

'You'll see. Get him to show you the node. That'll clear some of this stuff up, pronto.'

Beasley called to them. He and the jeep were a merged silhouette against the failing sky. He swung his arm overhead until Nadine yelled that they would start back in a minute. She removed her shades and met Partridge's eyes. 'You okay, Rich?' She refused to relinquish her grip on his hand.

'You're asking me?'

She gave him another of her inscrutable looks. She reached up and pushed an unkempt lock from his forehead. 'I'm not mad, in case you're still wondering. I wanted you to see me off. Not like there're anymore weekend rendezvous in the stars for us.'

'That's no way to talk,' he said.

'Just sayin'.' She dropped his hand and walked away. In a moment he followed. By the time they made the summit, darkness had covered the valley.

Beasley had to use the headlights to find the way home.

Gertz served prawns for dinner. They ate at the long mahogany table in the formal dining room. Jackson Phillips begged off due to an urgent matter in the city. Beasley packed him and one of the muscle bound bodyguards into the helicopter and flew away. That left six: Toshi; Campbell; Nadine; Carrey Montague and the other bodyguard, and Partridge. The men wore suits and ties. Nadine wore a cream-colored silk chiffon evening gown. There were candles and elaborate floral arrangements and dusty bottles of wine from the Moorehead cellar and magnums of top dollar French champagne from a Boston importer who catered to those with exclusive tastes and affiliations. Toshi proposed a toast and said a few words in Japanese and then the assembly began to eat and drink.

Somewhere in the middle of the third or fourth course, Partridge realized he was cataclysmically drunk. They kept setting them up and he kept knocking them down. Toshi or Campbell frequently clapped his back and clinked his glass and shouted, '*Sic itur ad astra!*' and another round would magically appear. His head was swollen and empty as an echo chamber. The winking silverware and sloshing wineglasses, the bared teeth and hearty laughter came to him from a sea shell. He caught Nadine watching him from across the table, her eyes cool, her mouth set inscrutably. He poured more liquor down his throat to break their moment of recognition, and when he checked again she'd left the table, her untouched meal, and sailed from the room.

Dinner blurred into a collage of sense and chaos, of light and dark, and he gripped his glass and blinked dumbly against the shattering flare of the low slung chandelier and laughed uproariously. Without transition, dinner was concluded and the men had repaired to the den to relax over snifters of Hennessy. They lounged in wing-backed leather chairs and upon opulent leather divans. Partridge admired the vaulted ceiling, the library of towering lacquered oak bookcases and the impressive collection of antique British rifles and British cavalry sabers cached in rearing cabinets of chocolate wood and softly warped glass. Everything was so huge and shiny and far away. When the cigar and pipe smoke hung thick and the men's cheeks were glazed and rosy as the cheeks of Russian dolls, he managed, 'I'm supposed to ask you about the node.'

Campbell smiled a broad and genial smile. 'The node, yes. The node, of course, is the very reason Mr. Phillips and Mr. Montague have come to pay their respects. They hope to buy their way into Heaven.'

'He's right, he's right,' Mr. Carrey Montague said with an air of merry indulgence. 'Jack had his shot. Didn't he though. Couldn't hack it and off he flew.'

'I was getting to this,' Toshi said. 'In a roundabout fashion.'

'Exceedingly so,' Campbell said.

'Didn't want to frighten him. It's a delicate matter.'

'Yes,' Campbell said dryly. He puffed on his pipe and his eyes were red around the edges and in the center of his pupils.

'Shall I? Or do you want a go?' Toshi shrugged his indifference.

'The node is a communication device,' Campbell said through a mouthful of smoke. 'Crude, really. Danforth Moorehead, the Moorehead patriarch, developed the current model. Ahem, the schematic was delivered to him and he effected the necessary modifications, at any rate. Admittedly, it's superior to the primitive methods – scrying, séances, psychedelic drugs, that nonsense. Not to mention some of the more gruesome customs we've observed in the provincial regions. Compared to that, the node is state of the art. It is a reservoir that filters and translates frequency imaging captured by our clever, clever radio telescopes. It permits us to exchange information with our… neighbors.'

Partridge dimly perceived that the others were watching him with something like fascination. Their eyes glittered through the haze. 'With who? I don't–'

'Our neighbors,' Campbell said.

'Oh, the things they show you.' Carrey

Montague sucked on his oxygen mask until he resembled a ghoul.

Partridge swung his head to look from face to face. The men were drunk. The men seethed with restrained glee. No one appeared to be joking. 'Well, go on then,' he said dreamily. His face was made of plaster. Black spots revolved before him like ashen snowflakes.

'I told you, Richard. Mankind can't go on like this.'

'Like what?'

Toshi chuckled. 'Assuming we don't obliterate ourselves, or that a meteorite doesn't smack us back to the Cambrian, if not the Cryptozoic, this planet will succumb to the exhaustion of Sol. First the mammals, then the reptiles, right down the line until all that's left of any complexity are the arthropods: beetles and cockroaches and their oceanic cousins, practically speaking. Evolution is a circle – we're sliding back to that endless sea of protoplasmic goop.'

'I'm betting on the nuclear holocaust,' Campbell said.

Partridge slopped more brandy into his mouth. He was far beyond tasting it. 'Mmm hmm,' he said intelligently and cast about for a place to inconspicuously ditch his glass.

'NASA and its holy grail – First Contact, the quest for intelligent life in the universe... all hogwash, all lies.' Toshi gently took the snifter away and handed him a fresh drink in a ceramic mug. This was not brandy; it was rich and dark as honey in moonlight. 'Private stock, my boy. Drink up!' Partridge drank and his eyes flooded and he choked a little. Toshi nodded in satisfaction. 'We know now what we've always suspected. Man is completely and utterly alone in a sea of dust and smoke. Alone and inevitably slipping into extinction.'

'Not quite alone,' Campbell said. 'There are an estimated five to eight million species of insects as of yet unknown and unclassified. Hell of a lot of insects, hmm? But why stop at bugs? Only a damned fool would suppose that was anything but the tip of the iceberg. When the time of Man comes to an end their time will begin. And be certain this is not an invasion or a hostile occupation. We'll be dead as Dodos a goodly period before they emerge to claim the surface. They won't rule forever. The planet will eventually become cold and inhospitable to any mortal organism. But trust that their rule will make the reign of the terrible lizards seem a flicker of an eyelash.'

'You're talking about cockroaches,' Partridge said in triumph. 'Fucking cockroaches.' That was too amusing and so he snorted on his pungent liquor and had a coughing fit.

'No, we are not,' Campbell said.

'We aren't talking about spiders or beetles, either,' Toshi said. He gave Partridge's knee an earnest squeeze. 'To even compare them with the citizens of the *Great Kingdom*... I shudder. However, if I were to make that comparison, I'd say this intelligence is the Ur-progenitor of those insects scrabbling in the muck. The mother race of idiot stepchildren.'

Campbell knelt before him so they were eye to eye. The older man's face was radiant and distant as the moon. 'This is a momentous discovery. We've established contact. Not us, actually. It's been going on forever. We are the latest... emissaries, if you will. Trustees to the grandest secret of them all.'

'Hoo boy. You guys. You fucking guys. Is Nadine in on this?'

'Best that you see firsthand. Would you like that, Rich?'

'Uhmm-wha?' Partridge did not know what he wanted except that he wanted the carousel to stop.

Campbell and Toshi stood. They took his arms and the next thing he knew they were outside in the humid country night with darkness all around. He tried to walk, but his legs wouldn't cooperate much. They half dragged him to a dim metal door and there was a lamp bulb spinning in space and then steep, winding concrete stairs and cracked concrete walls ribbed with mold. They went down and down and a strong, earthy smell overcame Partridge's senses. People spoke to him in rumbling nonsense phrases. Someone ruffled his hair and laughed. His vision fractured. He glimpsed hands and feet, a piece of jaw illumed by a quivering fluorescent glow. When the hands stopped supporting him, he slid to his knees. He had the impression of kneeling in a cellar. Water dripped and a pale overhead lamp hummed like a wasp in a jar. From the corner of his eye he got the sense of table legs and cables and he smelled an acrid smell like cleaning solvents. He thought it might be a laboratory.

– Crawl forward just a bit.

It was strange whatever lay before him. Something curved, spiral-shaped and darkly wet. A horn, a giant conch shell, it was impossible to be certain. There was an opening, as the *external os* of a cervix, large enough to accommodate him in all his lanky height. Inside it was moist and muffled and black.

– There's a lad. Curl up inside. Don't fight. There, there. That's my boy. Won't be long. Not long. Don't be afraid. This is only a window, not a doorway.

Then nothing and nothing and nothing; only his heart, his breathing and a whispery static thrum that might've been the electromagnetic current tracing its circuit through his nerves.

Nothingness grew very dense.

Partridge tried to shriek when water, or something thicker than water flowed over his head and into his sinuses and throat. Low static built in his ears and the abject blackness was replaced by flashes of white imagery. He fell from an impossible height. He saw only high velocity jump-cuts of the world and each caromed from him and into the gulf almost instantly. Fire and blood and moving tides of unleashed water. Bones of men and women and cities. Dead, mummified cities gone so long without inhabitants they had become cold and brittle and smooth as mighty forests of stone. There loomed over everything a silence that held to its sterile bosom countless screams and the sibilant chafe of swirling dust. Nadine stood naked as ebony in the heart of a ruined square. She wore a white mask, but he knew her with the immediacy of a nightmare. She lifted her mask and looked at him. She smiled and raised her hand. Men and women emerged from the broken skyscrapers and collapsed bunkers. They were naked and pallid and smiling. In the distance the sun heaved up, slow and red. Its deathly light cascaded upon the lines and curves of cyclopean structures. These were colossal, inhuman edifices of fossil bone and obsidian and anthracite that glittered not unlike behemoth carapaces. He thrashed and fell and fell and drowned.

Nadine said in his ear, *Come down. We love you.*

The cellar floor was cool upon his cheek. He was paralyzed and choking. The men spoke to him in soothing voices. Someone pressed a damp cloth to his brow.

– Take it easy, son. The first ride or two is a bitch and a half. Get his head.

Partridge groaned as gravity crushed him into the moldy concrete.

Someone murmured to him.

– They are interested in preserving aspects of our culture. Thus Orren Towne and places, hidden places most white men will never tread. Of course, it's a multifaceted project. Preserving artifacts, buildings, that's hardly enough to satisfy such an advanced intellect…

Partridge tired to speak. His jaw worked spastically. No sound emerged. The concrete went soft and everyone fell silent at once.

Partridge stirred and sat up. He tried to piece together how he ended up on the back porch sprawled in a wooden folding chair. He was still in his suit and it was damp and clung to him the way clothes do after they have been slept in. The world teetered on the cusp of night. Parts of the sky were orange as fire and other parts were covered by purple-tinted rain clouds like a pall of cannon smoke. Partridge's hair stood in gummy spikes. His mouth was swollen and cottony. He had drooled in his long sleep. His body was stiff as an old plank.

Beasley came out of the house and handed him a glass of seltzer water. 'Can't hold your liquor anymore?'

Partridge took the glass in both hands and drank greedily. 'Oh, you're back. Must've been a hell of a party,' he said at last. He had slept for at least sixteen hours according to his watch. His memory was a smooth and frictionless void.

'Yeah,' Beasley said. 'You okay?'

Partridge was not sure. 'Uh,' he said. He rolled his head to survey the twilight vista. 'Beasley.'

'Yeah?'

'All this.' Partridge swept his hand to encompass the swamped gardens and the decrepit outbuildings. 'They're letting it fall down. Nobody left from the old days.'

'You and me. And Nadine.'

'And when we're gone?'

'We're all gonna be gone sooner or later. The docs ... they just do what they can. There's nothing else, pal.' Beasley gave him a searching look. He shook his shaggy head and chuckled. 'Don't get morbid on me, Hollywood. Been a good run if you ask me. Hell, we may get a few more years before the plug gets pulled.'

'Is Montague still here?'

'Why do you ask?'

'I heard someone yelling, cursing. Earlier, while I slept.'

'Huh. Yeah, there was a little fight. The old fella didn't get his golden ticket. He wasn't wanted. Few are. He shipped out. Won't be coming back.'

'I guess not. What was he after?'

'Same thing as everybody else, I suppose. People think Toshi is the Devil, that he can give them their heart's desire if they sign on the dotted line. It ain't so simple.'

Partridge had a wry chuckle at that. 'Damned right it's not simple, partner. I'm still selling my soul to Tinsel Town. No such luck as to unload the whole shebang at once.' Partridge shook with a sudden chill. His memory shucked and jittered; it spun off the reel in his brain and he could not gather it fast enough to make sense of what he had seen in the disjointed frames. 'Lord, I hate the country. Always have. I really should get out of here, soon.'

'My advice – when you get on that bus, don't look back,' Beasley said. 'And keep your light on at night. You done with that?'

'Um-hmm.' He could not summon the energy to say more right then. The strength and the will had run out of him. He put his hand over his eyes and tried to concentrate.

Beasley took the empty glass and went back into the house. Darkness came and the yard lamps sizzled to life. Moths fluttered near his face, battened at the windows and Partridge wondered why that panicked him, why his heart surged and his fingernails dug into the arm rests. In the misty fields the drone of night insects began.

He eventually heaved to his feet and went inside and walked the dim, ugly corridors for an interminable period. He stumbled aimlessly as if he were yet drunk. His thoughts buzzed and muttered and were incoherent. He found Toshi and Campbell crouched in the den like grave robbers over a stack of shrunken, musty ledgers with hand sewn covers and other stacks of photographic plates like the kind shot from the air or a doctor's X ray machine. The den was tomb-dark except for a single flimsy desk lamp. He swayed in the doorway, clinging to the jam as if he were in a cabin on a ship. He said, 'Where is Nadine?'

The old men glanced up from their documents and squinted at him. Toshi shook his head and sucked his teeth. Campbell pointed at the ceiling. 'She's in her room. Packing. It's Sunday night,' he said. 'You should go see her.'

'She has to leave,' Toshi said.

Partridge turned and left. He made his way up the great central staircase and tried a number of doors that let into dusty rooms with painters cloth draping the furniture. Light leaked from the jamb of one door and he went in without knocking.

'I've been waiting,' Nadine said. Her room was smaller and more feminine than the Garden Room. She sat lotus on a poster bed. She wore a simple yellow sun dress and her hair in a knot. Her face was dented with exhaustion. 'I got scared you might not come to say goodbye.'

Partridge did not see any suitcases. A mostly empty bottle of pain medication sat on the night stand beside her wedding ring and a silver locket she had inherited from her great grandmother. He picked up the locket and let it spill through his fingers, back and forth between his hands.

'It's very late,' she said. Her voice was not tired like her face. Her voice was steady and full of conviction. 'Take me for a walk.'

'Where?' He said.

'In the fields. One more walk in the fields.'

He was afraid as he had been afraid when the moths came over him and against the windows. He was afraid as he had been when he pulled her from the water all those years ago and then lay in his hammock bunk dreaming and dreaming of the crocodiles and the bottomless depths warm as the recesses of his own body and she had shuddered against him, entwined with him and inextricably linked with him. He did not wish to leave the house, not at night. He said, 'Sure. If you want to.'

She climbed from the bed and took his hand. They walked down the stairs and through the quiet house. They left the house and the spectral yard and walked through a gate into the field and then farther into heavier and heavier shadows.

Partridge let Nadine lead. He stepped gingerly. He was mostly night blind and his head ached. Wet grass rubbed his thighs. He was soaked right away. A chipped edge of the ivory moon bit through the moving clouds. There were a few stars. They came to a shallow depression where the grass had been trampled or had sunk beneath the surface. Something in his memory twitched and a terrible cold knot formed in his stomach. He whined in his throat, uncomprehendingly, like a dog.

She hesitated in the depression and pulled her pale dress over her head. She tossed the dress away and stood naked and half hidden in the fog and darkness. He did not need to see her, he had memorized everything. She slipped into the circle of his arms and he embraced her without thinking. She leaned up and kissed him. Her mouth was dry and hot. 'Come on,' she muttered against his lips. 'Come on.' Her hands were sinewy as talons and very strong. She grasped his hair and drew him against her and they slowly folded into the moist earth. The soft earth was disfigured with their writhing and a deep, resonant vibration traveled through it and into them where it yammered through their blood and bones. She kissed him fiercely, viciously, and locked her thighs over his hips and squeezed until he gasped and kissed her back. She did not relinquish her fistful of his hair and she did not close her eyes. He stared into them and saw a ghost of a girl he knew and his own gaunt reflection which he did not know at all. They were sinking.

Nadine stopped sucking at him and turned her head against the black dirt and toward the high, shivering grass. There was no breeze and the night lay dead and still. The grass sighed and muffled an approaching sound that struck Partridge as the thrum of fluorescent lights or high voltage current through a wire or, as it came swiftly closer, the clatter of pebbles rolling over slate. Nadine tightened her grip and looked at him with a sublime combination of glassy terror and exultation. She said, 'Rich–'

The grass shook violently beneath a vast, invisible hand and a tide of chirring and burring and click-clacking blackness poured into the depression from far flung expanses of lost pasture and haunted wilderness, from the moist abyssal womb that opens beneath everything, everywhere. The cacophony was a murderous tectonic snarl out of Pandemonium, Gehenna and Hell; the slaughterhouse gnash and whicker and serrated wail of legion bloodthirsty drills and meat-hungry saw teeth. The ebony breaker crashed over them and buried them and swallowed their screams before their screams began.

After the blackness ebbed and receded and was finally gone, it became quiet. At last the frogs tentatively groaned and the crickets warmed by degrees to their songs of loneliness and sorrow. The moon slipped into the moat around the Earth.

He rose alone, black on black, from the muck and walked back in shambling steps to the house.

Partridge sat rigid and upright at the scarred table in the blue-gray gloom of the kitchen. Through the one grimy window above the sink, the predawn sky glowed the hue of gun metal. His eyes glistened and caught that feeble light and held it fast like the eyes of a carp in its market bed of ice. His black face dripped onto his white shirt which was also black. His black hands lay motionless on the table. He stank of copper and urine and shit. Water leaked in fat drops from the stainless steel gooseneck tap. A grandfather clock ticked and tocked from the hall and counted down the seconds of the revolutions of the Earth. The house settled and groaned fitfully, a guilty pensioner caught fast in dreams.

Toshi materialized in the crooked shadows near the stove. His face was masked by the shadows. He said in a low, hoarse voice that suggested a quantity of alcohol and tears, 'Occasionally one of us, a volunteer, is permitted to cross over, to relinquish his or her flesh to the appetites of the colony and exist among them in a state of pure consciousness. That's how it's always been. These volunteers become the interpreters, the facilitators of communication between our species. They become undying repositories of our civilization... a civilization that shall become ancient history one day very soon.'

Partridge said nothing.

Toshi said in his hoarse, mournful voice, 'She'll never truly die. She'll be with them until this place is a frozen graveyard orbiting a cinder. It is an honor. Yet she waited. She wanted to say goodbye in person.'

Partridge said nothing. The sun floated to the black rim of the horizon. The sun hung crimson and boiling and a shaft of bloody light passed through the window and bathed his hand.

'Oh!' Toshi said and his mouth was invisible, but his eyes were bright and wet in the gathering light. 'Can you imagine gazing upon constellations a hundred million years from this dawn? Can you imagine the wonder of gazing upon those constellations from a hundred million eyes? Oh, imagine it, my boy...'

Partridge stood and went wordlessly, ponderously, to the window and lingered there a moment, his mud-caked face afire with the bloody radiance of a dying star. He drank in the slumbering fields, the distant fog-wreathed forests, as if he might never look upon any of it again. He reached up and pulled the shade down tight against the sill and it was dark.

THE HIDE

Liz Williams

Liz Williams (1965–) is an English writer of science fiction and fantasy whose first two novels, *The Ghost Sister* (2001) and *Empire of Bones* (2002), were nominated for the Philip K. Dick Award. She is the daughter of a conjurer and a gothic novelist and has a Ph.D. in science from Cambridge. From the mid-nineties until 2000, she lived and worked in Kazakhstan. Her short fiction has appeared in *Asimov's Science Fiction, Interzone, Strange Horizons, Realms of Fantasy, The Third Alternative* and many others. The beautifully written weird tale 'The Hide' (2007) conveys a sense of place and of modern unease reminiscent of M. John Harrison or Ramsey Campbell but with Williams' own unique perspective and style.

The birds were white as they flew over the marsh, across the reedbeds and the frosted meres, but as they drew level with the hide their shade changed, from white to black. I saw their crimson eyes, sparks in the cloudy dark, as they disappeared into the storm. Richard and I crouched in the hide and waited.

'Jude, can you see her? Can you see?' Richard whispered.

But all I could see was darkness, and the distant storm.

People lived here once. A very long time ago, when this land was called the Summer Country: named not for cowslip meadows or hazy warmth, but because it only appeared in summer, when the waters had retreated towards the Severn Estuary and the marshes were dry enough to be negotiated on foot. During all other times of year, this land – gleaming wet marshes, dense beds of dull golden reeds, and groves of alder and unpollarded willow – was the haunt only of ducks and herons, and the small people who lived along the causeways and in the lake villages.

Richard and my sister Clare and I had followed the Sweet Track the summer before, when the heat hung heavily over the water meadows, with the damselflies zooming through the kingcups that grew along the margins of the dug-out peat beds. The Track, discovered years before by an academic named Sweet, is an old road, one of the oldest in the country. I was researching it, and studying Sweet's own research, at the Moors Centre, lying right in the middle of Sedgemoor.

Hard to imagine winter, in those dreaming meadows. But I knew that come September the fog would start drifting in from the Bristol Channel, smelling of salt mud and sea, hiding first the whale-humps of islands, then the arch of Brent Knoll, then the flat lands all the way to the Tor with its tower. After that would come flood and then frost, and the long, dim, damp winter.

I'd been there for six months, but Clare was living in Manchester then, working as a fundraiser for some big arts project, and this was her first visit to the area. Her New Age soul was enchanted by it all, by the faux-Arthuriana of Glastonbury and the rather more real claims of Cadbury, by the startling caverns of the Mendips and the flat lands between, where the lake villages had once stood. She and Richard had apparently met through some university bird-watching society – though I'd never known Clare to be interested in birds before. She was more enthusiastic about it in summer, perhaps, out in the wilds with a couple of bottles of beer and a blanket, and that's how we discovered the hide.

I hadn't realised it was there, although I'd been to the bird reserve a couple of times before. I must have walked right past it, but it was Clare who spotted it, as we walked along the track with the remains of a picnic in a rucksack.

'Richie! Jude! There's a causeway, in the reeds. Can we go and look?'

Moments later, she was gone. I remember feeling an odd moment of panic, as though she'd performed some unnatural conjuring trick. Then her voice came from among the russet tassels nodding several inches above our heads. 'Look at this! This is so cool!'

The causeway was built of slats placed on piles, close together and easy to walk on, with the addition of a handrail, which the original Lake Village structures would not have had. Quite contemporary and not all that old, judging from the scrubbed pallor of the wood. I'd have told her all this, but I'd grown too used to the rather glazed expression that came over Clare's face whenever I talked about my work. We'd both had our noses in books as kids, but they hadn't been the same ones. She liked the myths. She was less interested in fact.

At first, I couldn't see where the causeway led. A dogleg in the middle took it out of eyesight, deep into the reeds. Clare and Richard vanished around the bend. I stood for a moment, just before the turn. The reeds swallowed sound. Distant traffic and the lowing of cattle were cut off, and the sudden rattle of a coot in the rushes made me jump. When I turned the corner, I saw that the little causeway ended in a long low structure, also raised on pilings, but with a tarpaulin roof and a laminated National Trust information sheet tacked to the wall by the door. There was nothing ancient about this place; it was not even a reconstruction like the round houses at the Bronze Age information centre some miles away. It was a bird-watching hide.

As I came close to the door, I found something on the boards: a small black wing, very soft and dense. I didn't recognise the bird: this wasn't the right kind of terrain for blackbirds. Perhaps something – kestrel, maybe – had dropped it. It was clearly a recent kill; there was still a bloody fragment of meat on the bone, an electric red against the dull background of the planks. I picked it up and put it on the flat surface of the railing, not quite knowing why, as if it was a child's glove for which the owner might shortly return.

Inside, the hide was dark and still, stifling in the afternoon heat and filled with the limey odour of bird droppings. When my eyes adjusted, I saw that the floor was white with them. I looked up, but the rafters were empty. Swifts, perhaps, but I couldn't see any round hummocks of nests and they'd be in residence at this time of the year.

'Richard?' Clare's voice cut through the gloom. 'Come and see!'

I went around the corner of the central notice board. Clare and Richard were standing shoulder to shoulder and I stifled an old familiar sensation. I allowed myself to wonder what would have happened if Richard had met me first – but I knew from experience that it wouldn't have made any difference.

When she saw me, Clare raised the hatch that faced out over the other side of the marsh, and fastened it with a wooden peg.

'Look.'

There was a heron among the reeds, a common enough bird in this area but still alien, predatory, as startling as a pterodactyl in its blue and grey plumage. It was stalking through the shallow water at the edge of one of the reedbeds and as we stared, breathless, the long beak stabbed downwards and came up with a fish. Silver caught the light. The heron flipped it up and swallowed, then was gone into the reeds in search of new prey.

We kept looking for a moment, hoping it would come back. Then Clare said, 'What are those?'

There were three of them, gliding over the crest of the reedbeds. They had long necks, long beaks, but at first I thought they must be gulls because their wings caught a shaft of sunlight, gleaming white as they turned. Then they veered again and I saw that their wings were shadow-black, a strange trick of the light. Cormorants, perhaps. They were common along the coast and you frequently found them inland, sharing prey with the herons. They were flying west, towards the estuary.

We watched them go and then, as if some decision had been made, we filed out of the hide like obedient schoolchildren, into the hot day, and back along the track. Clare said she wanted to go back into Glastonbury and see some of the shops. She wanted to buy a crystal, or something. I just wanted a cup of tea. We headed back to where Richard had left the battered 2CV.

The car park had been empty when we'd arrived, but now there were a few more vehicles in it. One of them was a van, painted in rough red and green stripes, a homemade hippie job. As we approached the car park, a young man came around the side: typical of travellers in this part of the world, dreadlocks, mud-coloured clothes, a joint held between two fingers. A dog skulked at his heels, a black and tan thing with heavy jowls and a surly look. But the young man was affable enough.

'Nice afternoon,' he said. 'Been out to the bird sanctuary?'

'Yes, just for a stroll. We saw a few things.'

'You want to wait for evening. All the starlings come then – like a cloud. Thousands of 'em. This place is known for it.'

'Starlings?' Clare asked. 'Maybe we'll come back. We found the hide.'

'Did you, now?' the young man said. He took a drag on the joint; sultry smoke coiled into the warm air. I thought there was a fractional sharpening of his interest, but perhaps it was only the dope. 'See anything?'

'A heron,' I said. He nodded, interest waning, until I added, 'And some cormorants.'

'You saw those?' He was staring at Clare, not me, half amused, half something else, an expression I could not identify. But that he was looking at her at all irritated me. 'Black or white?'

'Black,' I said, not understanding. 'You don't get white ones, I thought.'

'Sometimes you do.' The young man spoke with assurance and I didn't know all that much about birds. I wasn't prepared to argue the toss. 'How many?'

'Three. There were three of them.'

'Okay. Well. Let's hope you don't see them again.' I was about to ask him what he meant but he turned away, clicking his fingers at the dog, which was wandering. Richard opened the car and we drove into Glastonbury, where Richard and I spent the rest of the afternoon in one of the little cafés around the market cross while Clare shopped. If I thought about the bird sanctuary at all, then or in the days that followed, it was simply as a fading memory of a half-pleasant, half-painful afternoon. I did not think about the cormorants at all.

For the next few months, I was busy with research in the Centre and elsewhere. Richard and Clare went back up north and I tried not to wonder when I'd see Richard again. I knew I'd never be able to tell her how I'd started to feel about him, and I didn't want to. There was something behind the New Age stuff in her, something competitive and deep, something sisterly, and not in a right-on feminist way. Anyway, it was too embarrassing to talk about and God knows it wasn't as if it hadn't happened before. Perhaps she knew what was going through my head, all the same. I told myself that she seemed happy with Richard and I should be happy for them, and could not be. There should be a natural end to it, now they had returned to the north.

But when I next saw them, and summer itself was over, I found that things weren't as I'd thought.

I'd been to a conference at Lancaster, stopping off at Clare's on the way back. But when I got to her place, she wasn't there. Instead, I found Richard.

She'd been moody ever since they came back, Richard told me, over a glass of wine in a nearby bar. It was October now. At first he'd put it down to anxiety over the coming months, the time when the success or failure of Clare's fundraising bid was going to be decided. She was snappy and short-tempered, which was new to Richard if not to me, and he'd deemed it wiser to leave her alone to get on with her work. At first, he thought this approach was a success: she was heading off to the office every morning, but three weeks or so later he had run into a colleague of Clare's, who asked how she was, given that she was on sick leave.

'I didn't want to ask her about it,' Richard told me. He took a sip of his drink. 'But it freaked me out. I thought – I thought she'd found someone else, but, you know, sick leave, it's not just sneaking off for an hour or two.'

'Is there someone else?' I felt a cold growing elation at what he was about to say and I hated myself.

'No. I don't know. She said there wasn't, but I – I didn't believe her. I told her I did, then when she went out the next morning, I followed her. She went straight to the canal and sat on the bank. For the rest of the day, as far as I could see. I went to a pub for lunch, even, and when I came back, she was still there.'

'Maybe she reckoned you'd follow her, and she thought she might as well lead you on.'

'Maybe.' He looked dubious. 'I suppose I wouldn't have blamed her.'

'Funny place to sit, the Ship Canal. It's not exactly Hawaii.'

Richard looked suddenly defeated. I nearly reached out to him but stopped myself in time. 'It's a shithole, Jude. They keep saying they cleaned it up for that sports bid, but it's still a murky, dirty drain. What appeal could it possibly have?'

Unless you were thinking of chucking yourself into it, I thought, but did not say, and I hated myself a little more. There was something gruesome about the idea of my sister sitting by the side of that grim channel of water, staring into grey scummy nothing, contemplating what?

'Did you follow her again?' I asked.

'A couple of times. She went back to the canal once, and then the next time she just wandered around. This was a few days ago.'

'Do you think she's having some kind of breakdown?'

'I don't know. She's been worried about her work, thinks they screwed up on the funding bid, didn't have enough of the required elements. I tried talking about it last night and she said she thought she needed a break. I was wondering if she could come down to you for a few days. I know it's not exactly the weather for it, but it's not the weather for perching on the side of the bloody Ship Canal, either.'

All I could see in his face was concern. I had the sense of a trap, closing. I bit back what I had so nearly told him and felt something brush my clenched hands under the table, something soft, like feathers.

'Of course she can come,' I said.

Having her in the house was odd and awkward, even more so because Clare exhibited none of the signs of anxiety or depression that I'd been expecting. That made me think that the main problem lay with Richard and that, of course, gave me hope. But I told myself that I was being stupid. Clare and I went out to dinner at the local pub on the night she arrived, and when we got back to the house I bolted up to bed before we really had a chance to talk, not that we were likely to. She'd never been in the habit of opening up, after all.

I went to sleep quickly, but in the middle of the night, something woke me up. I sat up in bed, clutching at the covers. There was no one in the room, but it smelled dank, like marsh water. Worrying about damp-proofing and winter, I went back to sleep.

In the morning, Clare was gone. I sat at the kitchen table, worrying and wondering if she'd gone off like some marsh spirit, wandering the Levels in the morning mist. Twenty minutes after I'd drunk my second cup of tea, she was back, looking rosy-cheeked and cheerful, and announced that she'd been for a walk down the lane and had met a nice horse in a field. The canal-haunting woman whom Richard had described seemed to have flown like the mist itself, upwards into the sunlit air.

I had to go to the Centre that morning, so Clare said she'd come with me. I spent the next couple of hours going through records, while Clare – I learned at lunch – had passed the morning in looking through the information section, learning about the Lake Villagers.

'I'm surprised how much is known about them,' she said, over soup and bread in the Centre's café.

'Well, peat preserves things. If the structure's there, then you can build up guesstimates from that. I'll have to show you some of the computer reconstructions: I've got some on CD back at home.'

'It's fascinating,' Clare said. 'Like a world built on water.'

I stiffened, anticipating canal revelations, but all she said was, 'It must have been bloody cold in the winter.'

It wasn't exactly warm that afternoon. We went into Glastonbury for a cup of tea and there was a distinct sense of the year beginning to wind down, a faded quality to the light, a bite on the wind's breath.

'I keep thinking of that afternoon we spent down here,' Clare said in the café. She was looking down at the table, playing with her teaspoon. 'Do you remember? Everything golden and grey, and the birds in the reeds.'

'That was the day we saw the cormorants.'

'I've dreamed of them, you know.' She spoke with a sudden rush, as if confessing something forbidden. 'They keep changing. Sometimes they're black and sometimes they're white.'

'Things stick in your mind,' I said. 'When I was a kid, we went to Tenby for a holiday – there's a fortress on a rock, just beyond the bay, and I still dream about that sometimes.'

She nodded, but she looked slightly disappointed, as though she had been expecting me to say something else and I'd let her down. We did not discuss when she might be going back.

Next day, I went to the museum, but Clare did not come with me: she said she wanted to sleep in. Still nervy about signs of depression, I didn't attempt to dissuade her. When I got back to the house about mid-afternoon and found a note saying that she'd gone out for a walk, I wasn't worried.

But she didn't come back.

It was dark by six and I was starting to get seriously freaked out. I tried her mobile and got her answering service, left messages. I got the car out and drove into Glastonbury, wondering whether she'd gone into town. But I did not see her along the road, and she wasn't in any of the pubs. I drove back, hoping to find her at home, but the house was as dark and silent as I'd left it.

I didn't want to ring Richard, but if it turned out that something had happened to Clare, I wouldn't have been able to face myself. His landline rang and rang; I tried his own mobile and that, too, was switched off. I left more messages, tried to decide whether it was too early to call the police and then decided that I'd rather look like an idiot than risk Clare's life. It was cold outside, with the stars hanging heavy and burning over the low black land.

The police took me seriously, though with a certain weariness, but said there was little they could do. If Clare continued to be missing, then they'd initiate a search, but until then, all they could do was keep an eye out and wait. The implication was that I should do the same.

When the doorbell rang, all my foolishness came crashing in on me. She had got lost and forgotten her key, that was all. I threw the front door open.

'Clare, I'm so–' But it wasn't Clare. It was Richard.

He didn't seem to know anything about my phone messages. He said that he was there because he had had a dream. He was dishevelled, a bit stare-eyed, and he smelled dank, the sort of smell you might acquire on too close an acquaintance with the greasy waters of the Ship Canal. Both this, and the account of his dream, were completely out of character: the only thing that made me listen to him at all, rather than insisting on rest and a bath, was the fact that he knew Clare was missing.

My mind, wandering in areas that I did not understand, started to invoke further paranoia. This was all some weird game, either involving me or, worse still, directed at me. They had set it up between them, it was all planned. But then Richard started to tell me about the dream itself.

'She was walking in a dark place. She was lost, and there was a storm, but no rain. I knew that it was cold, and then I saw that she was out on the mere. You know, where we went for a walk? Where we saw the hide? And the hide was in the dream, too – I knew that if she could get to it, she'd be okay, we could pull her back. But then I saw the birds.'

'The birds?' But I already knew which ones he meant.

'The cormorants, or whatever they were. Long necks, sharp beaks. They were white when I first saw them and as they flew towards her, they changed to black. Then it started to snow and the snow was black, too, like little beads of jet, and it covered her, she stood still like a statue and when I touched her, I realised she had turned to peat and she crumbled into the water.'

There was a long silence after he recounted his dream, but it was just a nightmare, nothing more. Wasn't it? Richard was staring ahead into the heart of the fire as if trying to conjure its warmth back into his bones. He said, 'She's out there, Jude, and we have to find her. We have to bring her back.'

His eyes were burning and he looked thinner since I had last seen him, as if he'd aged in the past few days. I did not know what to make of his dream, but it was easier to leap up and go out, knowing that I'd already contacted the police and could do no more if we stayed home. Knowing that action was always easier than just sitting, with the unspoken accusation ringing in my head: it was under my care that Clare had become lost.

'Let's go, then,' I said.

October had borrowed a night; when we stepped outside it felt more like the middle of January, a raw moonless landscape with the mist breathing off the ditches. A bone-coldness, seeping in even through my Barbour jacket and fisherman's sweater. I thought of Clare staring into a canal for hours at a time, and I grew colder still.

We took the car out to the bird sanctuary, driving slowly with the window down so that Richard would spot her on the road, if she should come that way. But we passed no one on the road and once we had turned into the track that led to the bird sanctuary car park, the night closed in, a clammy dark with the stars swallowed by cloud and the reedbeds swimming out of the mist.

Richard was out of the car even before I'd switched the engine off, walking quickly towards the hide. I had to run to catch up with him and he did not turn to see whether I was with him or not. He was looking straight ahead, like someone possessed.

We reached the hide. As we did so, a breeze sprang up, but it didn't seem to make any difference to the mist. I thrust my hands further into my pockets and found something brittle and sticky in there. I pulled out the black bird's wing that I'd found on the way to the hide, the last time we'd come. I remembered leaving it on the rail. There was no smell, but the bloody flesh had not clotted, it was still moist, and cold as ice. I was so revolted that I nearly dropped it, but then I heard Richard's voice, calling my name, and I stuffed the thing back into my pocket and ran along the walkway.

He was standing in the entrance to the hide, clutching both sides of the doorframe. His face was suffused with a kind of strange joy. He said, 'Jude! It's okay. She's here.'

'What? Is she all right?' I had visions of Clare collapsed, huddled against the wall in a disorientated daze, but when I pushed past him into the hide, limp with sudden relief, no one was there.

'Richard, where is she?'

'She's there,' he said. He gave me an odd look, as if I was behaving like an idiot. He pointed to the shuttered window of the hide. The shutters were raised, angling out onto the reedbeds. It was pitch black in here, apart from the tiny light of my torch: I couldn't believe that he'd managed to see anything.

Then I looked through the shutter, and saw for myself.

There were more than three birds. This time, there was a flock, perhaps twenty or more, flying from east to west. I saw a smear of pale light in the east, like the grey minutes before dawn, and on the western horizon, just above the reeds, a thin red line in the sky with the storm clouds rising above it. The birds were straggling, and the ones in the east were white, but as they passed the hide, I saw the darkness melt over them, changing them to black.

Richard whispered, 'Jude, can you see her? Can you see?'

The reedbeds were the same, but nothing else. There was a kind of house opposite the hide, a hut on stilts. It stood in a patch of reeds, but I saw, as you see in dreams, that they were black, with crimson tips that looked like ragged bulbs of flesh. Clare stood on the balustrade that surrounded it. I leaned out, shouting.

'Clare! Clare, can you hear me?'

A shutter rattled, from across the water. A black oblong opened at Clare's shoulder, and something looked out of it. I saw myself looking at my own face, but it was changed: I looked older, lined, bitter. Across the water I saw myself raise something and wave it in mockery: something black and dripping, like the blood-drenched wing of a bird. Then the face changed and was no longer mine, was no longer anything human.

There was a splash. I looked down, and Richard was in the water, ploughing through the reeds towards the opposite hut.

'Richard! Don't go, come back!' I might as well have been whispering. As the last of the birds reached the hide and changed, I saw Clare bend over the rail and reach down a hand to pull Richard up. The bird in the sky changed to black. I saw its reflection, shining white in the water below, the light breaking the water up into a thousand dazzling splinters and the hide, the fleshy reeds, the gleam on both sides of the sky, everything was gone. I was alone, and it was night, and it was cold.

I would like to say that after I made my way home in a daze, I woke up the next day to find it had all been a dream. But Richard's rucksack was there to remind me, and Clare's belongings, and a message from the police to ask me to let them know if she appeared. She did not. There was a hunt, and they dragged the waters of the bird sanctuary. I went with them, although the place terrified me. They found nothing. They asked me a lot of questions, but I did not get the sense that I was under suspicion. The case made the papers, and after a while, the authorities and the media lost interest.

I had dreams, too. They were always the same: two dark birds, flying west. I thought a lot about the bird sanctuary, about the kind of place it might be. I thought of the people of the Summer Country, living in the liminal lands between sea and pasture, summer and winter, life and death. The area around Glastonbury was known to be the land of the dead, the Celtic lord of the dead dwelling beneath the Tor. I did not know if this was what I had seen, some kind of ancient conjured hell, filled with spirits that I, with my imperfect human sight, could only see as birds. But I gradually came to think that it was simpler than that: that just as we had gone to the hide to spy upon the life of birds, so something somewhere else had also set up a hide, to watch us, and when the time was right, to take.

DUST ENFORCER

Reza Negarestani

Reza Negarestani (1977–) is an Iranian writer and philosopher who has worked in different areas of contemporary philosophy, speculative thought, and politics. These studies inform his stories, which tend to use the shell of nonfiction forms in a Borgesian way, often as a delivery system for the weird. His most recent book is *Cyclonopedia: Complicity with Anonymous Materials* (2008), which is at once a horror fiction, an atlas of demonology, a political samizdat, and a philosophic grimoire. Perhaps the most innovative and audacious weird text of the decade, the book fuses Lovecraftian horror and Middle Eastern history with occult war machines and the US 'war on terror.' 'The Dust Enforcer' is a chapter from *Cyclonopedia*.

Pazuzu, the Sumero-Assyrian demon of epidemics (the southwestern desert wind) is an occultural operative of the xero-informatic Abomination or Dust (= 100 = NO GOD), and possibly the most awe-inspiring cultist of Tellurian Dustism in ancient Mesopotamia. For wind is truly the high acolyte of dust, as well as being the dust-enforcer. In his *Notes on Reliquology*, Parsani put forward Pazuzu as a schematic diagram of the middle-eastern population and its peculiarities.

Pazuzu specializes in scavenging the stratified Earth and its biosphere in the form of dust, which then is uplinked to alien currents flowing in the universe. These combinations of dryness and wetness are carried back to earth to disseminate disease. According to the Assyrian axis of Evil-against-Evil, Pazuzu the demon feeds on dust, which is qabbalistically equal to No God (=100). Pazuzu scavenges the surface biosphere of earth as dust clouds or inorganic bacterial relics; then conducting them to xenochemical hydro-currents, or what in ancient Greece was called cosmic wetness (hydrochemical singularities). This is why Pazuzu is associated with the emergence of plagues. Pazuzu then carries the plagues back to the surface biosphere in the guise of dust-soups, arid floods, messy rains, unheard-of epidemics and xero-informatic communications which usually manifest in the form of demonic possession (*The Exorcist*). This process of dust-scavenging and plague-engineering takes the form of an accelerating non-Aristotelian spiral or cycle when the terrestrial hygiene industry incrementally spreads more anti-pest agents and over-produces defense mechanisms (to ward off plagues) which once again are scavenged by Pazuzu's pest-industry. In this sense, the accelerated rate of resistance ironically intensifies the emergence of plagues and dust-floods, speeding the journey of plagues back to the surface biosphere. When it comes to recollecting all that exists as dust, there is no need to be fastidious.

The horror of Pazuzu is usually embodied as a winged bipedal human-like beast with talons instead of feet and a head concretized through an almost fleshless dog- or lion-skull. The long reptilian penis of Pazuzu (a pest-seeding machine or a disseminator, according to glossaries of epidemiology) is a later pestilential modification to its body, which strangely has two pairs of wings instead of one, as if two wings are not adequate for its missions. Pazuzu is also visualized with the right hand upward and the left hand downward, heralding the Pest-Cycle of dust whose axis is a double-flight (Pazuzu's tetra-winged body) or a ferocious interdimensional 'line of flight' (Deleuze and Guattari) from the Earth to without, and from without to the Earth: the tactical line of the xero-informatic Abomination (dust) and the traffic zone of its bacterial data. Pazuzu exhibits several morphological anomalies and peculiarities which separate him from other Akkadian, Babylonian and Assyrian demons. According to the first excavated Bronze statue of Pazuzu (Iraq, post-Paleolithic era, 800-600 BC) these morphological features include:

- Extremely thin legs bearing an unusually skinny torso. Chest bones are clearly visible as if it suffers anorexia or fatigue; a body struck by famine and carrying its ailing flesh with difficulty. Its wasting body narrates the cyclical desert famine of the Middle East, accompanied by vast locust-swarms (as vehicles of desolation) and other pestilential omens. If the body of Beelzebub (*ba'al zebub*) insinuates a legion of flies, with their perverse collective enthusiasm to come together over a fresh deliquescing carrion or a yellowish lump of excrement, Pazuzu's anthropo-insectoid body bears the black humor of all bodies it overruns, strips naked of flesh, all the bodies chewed and peeled off by a sky-blackening swarm of locusts, by the hurtling body of Pazuzu, dehydrated and reduced to a twisted spectre of bone and wrinkled skin. Make yourself many, like the locust! Make yourself many, like the swarming locusts!
- Four wings instead of two: The wings seem to be feathered (later statuettes confirm this hypothesis: the feathers become visible as remiges, the powerful flight feathers which provide the main propulsive force during the powered flight of the rapax bird) and emphasize a demonic lust for flying, for speed and migration. Such wings engineer a flight corresponding to desert whirlwinds, dust devils and other meteorological phenomena of deserts which are believed to have been created by Anzu, the beast of flight, who stole the tablet of destiny and eventually was slain by Ninurta. The Sumero-Akkadian epic of Ninurta portrays Anzu as the forerunner of later flying demons, the engineer of demonic flight and of beasts with feathered wings which are linked to cyclogenesis, sonic havoc, spiraling storms across deserts and dust devils. These four wings render the demon a perfect vehicle for carrying pestilential particles (*Namtar*) and delivering them to their destination without delay, always promptly on time.
- A snake-headed penis, a pest-fertilizing machine which confirms Pazuzu's kinship with Humbaba (*Khombabos*, the guardian of cedar forests and the city of gods, who was defeated and killed by Gilgamesh and Enkidu). Humbaba has the same reptilian phallus and is believed to be the son or brother of Pazuzu. Both Humbaba and Pazuzu are able to reflect a prognosticated future of each individual: Humbaba's labyrinthine face (with unicursal human entrails as the beard) recalls the early art of *Haruspicy* (divination using the liver or entrails) in ancient Mesopotamian cultures, later developed by the Etruscans. Pazuzu as the demon of the south-west wind is associated with *Rammalie* (an Arabic word for communication with other worlds and aeons through patterns on pebbles and desert sand). His roaring flight introduces rhythmic ripples as crypto-vermiform parasites upon dunes which cumulate transiently as short-term inorganic memories of desert winds; then, ripples and other intermittent patterns can be deciphered as runic alphabets of epidemic journeys and plague-propagations aerated by desert winds and narrated on sand. Abdul Al-Hazred as an adept *rammal* (sand-sorcerer) probably wrote *Al Azif* through the dust-infested language of Pazuzu, who constantly enriches its howls with pest-spores in order to expand the hallucinatory space of progressive arid diseases.

- A dignatary's beard, bringing Pazuzu into the fold of Evil-against-Evil and making of him an apotropaic character. Pazuzu, like other demons who belong to the axis of Evil-against-Evil (for example Ugallu), can simultaneously spread terminal plagues and cure certain maladies. According to the Assyrian Axis of Evil-against-Evil, every human is constantly a puppet of demons, suspended from the labyrinth of their strings. During illnesses, witch doctors attempt to repel hostile demons from the patient and summon a protector-demon to possess the sick person. Pazuzu is among the chosen demons, one who could even pass the last guardian Lamassu or the Repellent of Evil: a Pazuzu-demon guards the niche in the bathroom of Ashurbanipal's palace at Nineveh, Iraq.
- An almost fleshless head that cannot be distinguished clearly, Pazuzu's head diagrams the metamorphosis of three carnivorous animals frequently appearing in the Babylonian / Assyrian pandemonium: the rabid dog, the *Shogal* (jackal) and the *Kaftaar* (hyena). Ibn Hamedani, in his book *Aja'ib Nameh* (*The Book of Marvels*), calls Kaftaar 'a terrible beast'. The hyena, from an afro-asiatic lineage, is possibly the most cursed, obscene and lewd animal in Mesopotamian folklore. Ibn Hamedani tells horrifying stories about this desert-beast who has sex with its prey while devouring it. The Hyena emits high-pitched cacophonic cries of mirth, enough to drive a lone desert traveler mad. Rabid dogs are the spawns of *Abzu* (Abyss), and the *Shoghal* or jackal connects Pazuzu to the Egyptian Anubis and the dead.

The face is of limited relevance for a rigorous archeological investigation into the demonic. Even the most distorted, disfigured and grotesque faces cannot be identified as evidence of a demon (xeno-agent) – that is to say, (de) faciality cannot be a constitutive element in diagramming a demon (especially in the period from the rise of Mesopotamian civilizations to the end of antiquity and the early Middle Ages). All

PAZUZU-DEMON

UGALLU-DEMON

radical xeno-demons have a diagrammatic seal of their own; they are always delineated by anomalous cartographies or diagrams based on which their bodies, positions, and arrangement of their appendages (organs?) are presented, built and (re)composed. Or else they are identified by their coming in pairs (one a recognizable entity and the other an obscure twin of the familiar entity; examples include the Phoenician and Etruscanian demons). The most well-known demonograms are as follows:

- The right hand upward, and the left hand downward suggests a swash-backwash model of epidemics; it is the seal of pest enforcers.
- Outstretched hands, one pointing east and one pointing west – solar demons. The Romans borrowed the same diagrammatic

position from Babylonians for their crucifixions. This demonogram later influenced the religious iconography of Mithraism and then Christianity, the most prominent examples being, of course, the iconographic portraits of the crucified Jesus.

- Bodily organs (appendages) connected to each other by curves and circles which construct a closed or sealed labyrinthine convolution.
- Smaller wings attached to the main wings, or possession of more wings than are necessary for flying and migration.
- Horns forming spirals (in contrast to general belief, horns are not satanic agents) or horns pointing to each other which signify arch-demons.
- Legs open, far apart so as to draw a triangle, also known as the three-dotted profanity, which is among the most significant diagrams of unlocalizable or betraying demons.

The demonogram of Pazuzu (the right hand upward, and the left hand downward) is the unique ABYZmal cartography of disease; it signifies the rotation of The Wheel of Pestilence. This demonogram confirms that Pazuzu (like Ugallu) belongs to the legion of plague-dissipating demons. Demonograms demonstrate the abstract distribution of demons; they are plans for demonic mobilization – mobilization in a military sense.

> *They believe Mesopotamia and the whole Middle East is overclouded by some kind of fog of war which is peculiar to the near and middle-eastern regions of Asia. That you must practice blindness, must dry out your lungs and return to dust in order to coalesce with the reeking pit of the Middle East. The inhabitants of a village near Tell-Kuyunjik, which is believed to be the ancient site of Nineveh, told us that this arid fog is the haze of Pazuzu, the searing mushroom cloud of Middle East. To live in dust requires a certain degree of demonism which western people deem too much for humans. Jackson West does not think the Middle East is a geopolitical region, he thinks that the Middle East is alive. Not metaphorically; it is alive in a real sense, waiting to let loose its sentience. 'It is alive but it doesn't need to survive, because it has a life of its own' – this was the last thing West told me before reconnoitring Mosul with his sons to locate that Iranian oil smuggler and that guy Omar who claims to have the diaries of Ibn Maimum, the Persian occult-saboteur, guerilla expert and conspiracist who assisted the Al-Fatemid to overthrow the Caliphate regime in Egypt.*
>
> 1st Lt. Ali Osa, US 1st Battalion,
> 41st Infantry Regiment
> Tell-Kuyunjik: Nineveh 36° 24′ N 43° 08′ E

Excursus VI (Xeno-agents and the Assyrian Axis of Evil-against-Evil)

The human defense mechanism is the most consistent entity on this planet; its self-fertilizing paranoia is capable of grasping and identifying every contact only in terms of a potential incursion. When this paranoid consistency (or consistency of paranoia, since paranoia, ironically, tends to be consistent) attains autonomy, it becomes ruthlessly schizoid by passively opening itself to unknown threats from the Outside or xeno-agents. The anthropomorphic security system is a Pandora's Box of unrecorded diseases, emerging from the consistent resistance of the system to outside invasions on the one hand, and the consistently escalating invasion on the other hand. In this sense, the human security system is a projection of the intensity of the conflict between the xeno-agent (demon) and the system that registers new indefinable plagues mapped at the outer limits of the demon and the system.

Unlike Martin Bergman's still profoundly religious demonology – which insists that a demon should be exorcised not to save the possessed but to assist the demon to escape from the 'mammal meat' – according to the Assyrian Axis of Evil-against-Evil, the demon infects a person to extract a wide array of pest-insurgencies from the security system not by possessing it (in the sense of seizing a property from the monopoly of the Divine – for example, the human as belonging to God), but by turning the Divine and its secured properties into intermediate parasites (pimps) for incoming diseases. In the Assyrian politics of demonism, the Divine and its world are turned into a pest-feeding farm. Their resistance and blind oppositions are encouraged because each instance of resistance harbors more incursions from the Outside. Pests, xeno-excitations, cosmic diseases kick in when capacity is reached and the security system of the anthropomorphic agency starts to crack and waste, consequently trying to survive at all costs which in turn causes a wider array of pestilential activities. In this panorama, survival and security reinforcement (as opposed to the dying system) 'turns on' the demon to no end. Modern criminology refuses to acknowledge the presence of demons, in the same way that secular disbelief condemns the inanity of a demon possessing a helpless human: if demons exist and are that powerful then why would they possess a wretched anthropian? Such an objection misunderstands the mechanisms involved in the communication between xeno-agents and the human security system. For demons maintain their outsideness precisely through a power of overkilling (sheer exteriority of a force), inflicting more power than is needed just to unlock a gate. Demons simply crack open the prey. The overkilling power effectuates an openness outside the system's capacity to afford it. Once openness cannot be afforded by the system's capacity, it turns into an instance of butchery rather than an act of emancipation characterized by human 'access' to the outside. Overkill is a spectacle staged on the fundamental incapacity of the system to cope with the outside. Through overkill, the xeno-agent performs its demonic spectacle and effectuates its exteriority which the system cannot afford. The exteriority of the demon cannot be captured by the desire of the system for openness, and for this reason such exteriority overkills (butchers open) the system. To possess a strong man is certainly enough to flaunt the demon's power, but all the better if the possessed is a child or old woman, to signify the outsideness of the demon through which overkilling power is generated.

On the Assyrian Axis of Evil-against-Evil, the demon does not seek to dismantle (anthropomorphic) identity; instead it tries to make identity a gate for summoning new demons from the furious clashes between xeno-particles and the resisting system. Beyond the borders of identity lies the indifferent realm of unconditional (absolute) madness, or that which can never be schizoid, since schizophrenia germinates on the wasted remains of boundary, territory and capacity. Schizophrenia needs a minimum degree of organization and system to spread, to be mobilized, to transform into agitations and to interlock with xeno-excitations and demons. Schizophrenia is engineered through the synergetic oppositions between xeno-excitations (demonic particles of the Outside graspable as uncontrollable intensities) and the forces of the boundary; it is restlessly mobilized through attacks and counter-attacks, one attack from xeno-particles, two or more counter-attacks from the system. The furious resistance is exponentially intensified and progressively overrun by xeno-agents until meltdown, the becoming-GAS of all particles.

Schiz-fluxes only flow on differentiated zones, meaning that there must be at least two opposite sides – identity and its nemeses. Since the rise of Foucauldian psychoanalysis, the only image of a schizo represented in pop-culture is the external image of madness, that of an inconceivable, semi-paralyzed madman lurching in the manner of an intoxicated spider. The schizo can be found everywhere except in madness. Schizophrenia comes with delirium (*Jnun*), the passion for terminal disease (which presupposes health), war-torn realms of organic survival, attacks and increasing counter-attacks diagrammatically narrating their tireless, attritional engagement on a draco-spiral which sometimes melts, sometimes evaporates, burns incompletely and blurs into particles instead of dissolving into nothingness. Everything excitingly schizoid, capable of attracting the merciless invasion of xeno-particles and igniting criminal excitations, happens on the borders of identity and its regimes which balefully put up their resistance against any malicious force. In order to draw schizo-lines of communication from the Outside, a rigorous course for dismantling identity is necessary, yet any serious attempt for total eradication of identity intrinsically excludes the space of xeno-excitations and ends up in autistic nihilism.

In the Middle East, the Arabic word *Jin* (or *Jinn*) refers to a race created by Allah prior to the creation of humans, made of fire and thus capable of shape-shifting (unlike the human, which was created from dust and water, the bacterial mess of dust-soups). In the Quran and in Islamic demonology – unlike in Christianity – *Shaytan* (Satan) is not a fallen angel but the first Jinn (Man's nemesis) created by Allah. According to the Quran, angels have no Will; as a result, they have no ability to disobey or choose. However, Jinns, with their unfathomable intelligence, can choose their paths; they have the Will to disobey or obey, be loyal or be a traitor (*Khazoola*). A Jinn or Djinn is male, the female side of this race is called Jnun (in plural form), a polysemous word which also means delirium, maddening love and terminal schizophrenia (corrosive tidal waves of xeno-excitations).

In Persian mythology, Jnun are descended from Jeh or Jahi, the first anti-creationist agent engineered by Ahriman's own body, the daughter of Ahriman who awakened her father from ten thousand years of slumber to spawn a pest-legion. Jahi is the first woman whose mission was to undo the entire pro-creationist project of Ahura Mazda. In Arabic folklore, Jnun are daughters of Lilith. Rûb-al-Khâlie, the dreadful desert where Abdul Al-Hazred settled for ten years, was inhabited by Jnun – not Jinn – which operate as female gates to the Outside. Al-Hazred must have communicated with the female side of the Outside (i.e. Jnun) in writing his nocturnally encrypted *Necronomicon*, a *chef d'œuvre* on cosmodromic blasphemy and on the realism of openness.

Jnun possess men, yet they do not occupy or colonize their hosts. Instead they lay open male hosts to the Outside, an openness in the sense of being laid, cracked, butchered open (as in the case of the Moroccan jinniya, Aisha Qandisha, or Aiesheh Ghediseh, who is also called 'the Opener'). Possessed by Jnun, Abdul Al-Hazred found this path the only reliable polytics to communicate with the cosmodrome of the Outside demarcated in the Numogram as the region of Djynxx or more precisely, XX-djinns. The path to Djynxx or the region of XX-djinns is mapped as becoming-woman via Jnun who, according to Arabic and Farsi folklore, narrate untold stories for the one who is opened and devoured by them. Lilith tells travelers forbidden stories before opening and devouring them. In this sense, Jnun (mapped as the region Djynxx in the Numogram) is a direct link to the cosmic blasphemy and the female current of the Outside. The reason that Lovecraft frequently calls Al-Hazred the 'mad' poet or the 'mad' Arab is that communicating with Jnun, as the female gates (vulvo-cosmic singularities) to the Outside, has one inevitable consequence – radical delirium. In Arabic and Farsi the word Jnun also means delirium, maddening love, terminal madness as the result of being laid open by the female cutting-edge of the Outside. However, Jnun is not compatible with the western definition of Madness. It cannot be translated properly, but suffice to say that it is mainly comprised of three elements and is developed through their compositions: Possession, Love and utter Openness. Abdul Al-Hazrad is a *majnun*, a man laid open by Jnun and at the same time, a majnun man, a madman (majnun) who immediately reminds us of the melancholic tale of *Leyili and Majnun*, their love story which converges in madness, openness, and a delirious love – the Forbidden.

Aisha Qandisha or Aisha Qadisha or Ghediseh is one of the most popular and fearsome Jinniya (female Jinn) in Moroccan folklore. Beliefs and rituals for Aisha have continued into the twenty-first century. She is both a hunter and a healer, sometimes appearing as a beautiful (irresistibly seductive) woman and sometimes as a Hag. When she possesses a man, she does not take over the new host, but opens the man to a storm of incoming Jnun and Jinns, demons and sorcerous particles of all kinds; making the man a traffic zone of sweeping cosmodromic data. This is why she is feared. And she never leaves – she always resides in the man to guarantee his total openness, which is not always pleasant. According to the Moroccans, the only way to feel comfortable with Aisha (the new mistress / lover) is by participating with her, feeding her, exciting her through passionate and barbaric music rites with cacosonic rhythms.

THE FAMILIARS

Micaela Morrissette

Micaela Morrissette (1979–) is an American writer who, thus far, specializes in short fiction, fueled by Decadent, fantastical, and weird sensibilities. She is a senior editor for the US literary magazine *Conjunctions* and a fiction reviewer for *Jacket* and *Rain Taxi*. The recipient of a Pushcart Prize, Morrissette has published fiction in *Conjunctions, Weird Tales, Best American Fantasy,* and *The Year's Best Fantasy and Horror*, among others. On the basis of just a handful of tales, she is one of the best of the next generation of weird writers. Displaying the full range of her talents, 'The Familiars' (2009) takes an almost Bradbury-esque idea and revitalizes it to chilling effect.

The boy and his mother wake late in the swampy summer mornings and sit on the edge of the porch drinking their first glass of water and spooning out their wedges of melon and picking the dead heads off poppies with their toes. They brush their teeth side by side at the kitchen sink and sometimes the mother lathers the boy's cheeks with almond soap and pretends to shave him with a butter knife, chattering in an arch accent that aspires to cockney. They fill the wheelbarrow with the boy's stuffed animals and matchbox cars and his wand for blowing bubbles and his kazoo and tambourine and truck down to the pond where the boy lies in the hammock, holding his toys in the air and swooping them up and down and crooning to them, and the mother reads paperbacks in the deep low wicker rocker, pushing the hammock gently back and forth with her foot.

For lunch there is French bread spread with soft cheese and served with purple pickled eggs and Jordan almonds. They picnic under the sycamore on one of the boy's old bed sheets, patterned with smiling clouds and pastel rainbows, too childish for him now, and suck the candy shells from the nuts, and see who can flick an ant the farthest. The sheet smells as the boy used to, hot heavy cream, slightly soured, and powdered sugar, and cough syrup, black cherry.

They put on their cleanest clothes and drift through the heat down the dirt road to town, the mother pale beneath a black umbrella and the boy's head swimming in a man-sized baseball cap. They check at the post office for their bills and catalogues and postcards of the town which the mother has sent to the boy on the sly, and they buy a wheel of licorice or a birch beer or a small wooden crate of sour clementines. They also buy a backpack, or some tennis shoes, or a lunch box, for the boy's first day of school, which is nearly upon them. With two pennies they wish in the fountain, and they walk home, carefully matching their steps to the footprints they made on the first leg of their journey.

They plant mason jars in the garden to steep their sun tea, and they blow trumpeting squeals on blades of grass. They play a game that is both tic-tac-toe and hopscotch with chalk and stones on the cement walkway, and the mother turns the hose on the boy and washes off the chalk and dust and sweat while he shrills and capers. For dinner there are drumsticks, sticky and burnt, off the old gas grill, or hotdogs charred on sticks at the fire pit. Then cold red wine with seltzer water for the mother, and warm milk with vanilla and sugar for the boy, in the swooning, exhausted armchairs of the living room, with the white gauze curtains swelling at every breath of breeze.

The mother reads to the boy in bed, adventure stories about islands or magic pools or noble lovers or gallant orphans, or the boy tells ghost stories to the mother, in which crushed faces press against the glass of windows, or trees grown over graves sigh and weep and rustle their leaves. The mother sleeps on one side of an enormous mattress, under an avalanche of pillows, and in another room the boy sleeps in a red wooden bed and his legs and arms tumble over the sides.

It's dawn and the boy has woken early when the friend appears. It unfurls from under the bed. Its features have not quite coalesced. Its skin rises up like a blush. The mouth, full of rapid shadows, comes painfully. As the boy watches, its teeth emerge and its eyes take on their hues. It's both gawky and graceful and the boy is touched by the tentativeness of its existence. Its limbs fold out with small tremblings. The boy moves over in the bed and the friend huddles gratefully into the warm depression he leaves. The boy knows not to touch the friend as it is born. Shyly, the boy indicates that the friend is welcome.

The friend begins right away to tell secrets. Some of them are astounding, and the boy giggles in nervous exhilaration. Some of them the boy already knew without knowing it. The wonderful thing is that the boy has secrets too, and the friend is fascinated, and they whisper under the covers until the mother pokes her head around the door, stirring honey into the first glass of their new batch of sun tea for the boy's good morning. The friend is under the bed so quickly that the boy has no time to feel alarm. But when the mother asks, was he talking to himself, the boy responds without hesitation that he was talking to his invisible friend. His mother smiles and asks what's his friend's name, and since the boy doesn't know, he says it's a secret.

His mother smiles and looks proud in a forlorn sort of way and brushes back his hair with her fingers and he feels the happy little pokes and tickles of his friend through the mattress, approving him, and all three are happy, and he drinks his sun tea with the honey not quite dissolved, coating his tongue and staying sweet there for some minutes. The damp smell that attends the friend, a stain of its birth, is clogging the air of the room, but the mother says nothing and the boy thinks that perhaps the friend is invisible after all.

That day it rains and the boy and his friend play in the attic. There is a trunk full of clothes and dust and the boy's friend dresses up as the princess and the boy as the minstrel without any money, or the boy dresses up as a monster of the air and the friend as a monster of the deep, or the boy dresses up as a man of the future and the friend holds over his face a helmet that carries the boy through time and space. The rain assaults the roof of the attic. They have stores of crackers and dried fruit and they plant flashlights all over the floor, the beams gaping up at the rafters. There is a box of paper houses that unfold: castles, a Hindu temple, a Victorian country-home. They set these up and populate the rooms with colored plastic figurines from sets of jungle beasts, dinosaurs, and the Wild West.

The Christmas tree is stored in the attic, still tangled in its lights. The boy and his friend creep in under the lowest fronds, curling themselves around the base, and turn the beams of their flashlights out through the strings of dead bulbs to make them glow.

Between the panes of the windows are cemeteries of moth wings and wasp heads and fly legs. The attic swells into the rain.

They find a punchbowl roped in cobwebs and fill it with water and stare in to see the silk awake. They turn off all the flashlights and haunt each other in the dark with sobs and screeches. They roast marshmallows with a butane lighter. The boy recites the alphabet backwards. The friend dances.

By nightfall the sky has cleared and the mother takes the boy out onto the slanting roof of the house and they lie on their backs on the shingles and she shows him the constellations. The dippers, the hunter, the seven sisters, the two bears. The mother tells the boy how the stars are immense balls of flame millions of miles away, and how many of them may already have been dead for hundreds of thousands of years.

Hidden behind the stack of the chimney, the friend laughs in derision and reaches out its hand and rubs the pattern off the sky. Then it draws new figures: the claw, the widow, the thief, the cocoon. The planet shudders and rocks and the boy loses his grip and skids down the plane of the roof until the mother catches his hand and pulls him to safety. She bundles him into her arms and totes him down the attic stair, soothing and scolding and breathless, while he cranes his neck to peer behind him at the lights scattering across the dark like startled starlings.

The boy and his friend play in the garden, under the sun. They play in the garden, which is on the edge of the wood, and the trees shade it, many games. They play pick-up sticks, checkers, hide-and-go-seek, and things, and the sun enacts changes in their skin and hair and eyes. They play in the garden, and smile. They smile and smile and smile and smile and smile.

The boy's mother puts an extra cookie on the plate for the friend, but the boy says the friend doesn't eat. She brings an extra pillow for the bed, but the boy says the friend doesn't sleep. What does it do all night then, she asks the boy, doesn't it get bored? Plays in my dreams, the boy tells her.

The boy and his friend make shadow puppets in the afternoon. The boy curtains the windows and holds his hands in front of the lamp and does a bird, a rabbit, a hunchback, a spider. The friend opens the curtains and crouches on the windowsill, a black silhouette against the sun. The sun pulses and shivers in the sky and the outline of the friend flickers and wavers at the edges. Its body makes an ocean wave, a spouting volcano, a hurricane, a shape-changing cloud: giraffe, dragon, whale. The boy crows and claps his hands. The friend grows huge in the window and blots out the light, making the night sky. It spreads its limbs so no sliver of sunlight peeks through and it makes the bottomless well.

The boy's mother sits on the edge of the tub and the steam clings to her; she is composed of droplets. At bath time the friend disappears, the boy says; it hates water. The mother runs the hot when the boy complains that the bath is cooling. She shampoos the boy's golden hair with the tips of her fingers. She rubs the puffs and cracks of deep pruning on his hands. When he announces that the bath is over, she starts a splashing war to make him forget.

The boy has a duck for the bath, and to play with the duck, an inflatable bear, and to amuse the bear, little pills that pop open into sponges, and to collect the sponges, a net with butterfly shapes sewn into the webbing, and to transport the net, a battleship that sprays water through its nose, and to fight the battleship, a tin rocket that rusts in the water, and the mother cuts her hand on the crumbling metal and the blood makes a blossom in the bath. The boy leaps up and shouts out that his friend is calling and he runs shivering and half drowned out of the bathroom.

The mother stays behind and bandages her hand into an enormous white paw. When she tucks the boy in that night, she brandishes the paw and growls and tickles his stomach. But he says the friend can smell the rusty blood and he insists that she leave, and she does and wonders if the boy is weary of her or protecting her from his imaginary friend, and she sits for an hour in the window seat in her bedroom, watching trees and clouds move across the reflection of her face in the pane.

The boy and his friend camp out in the treehouse. They make believe there's a siege and they're starving to death. They make believe there's a war and they're hidden in a priest's hole. They make believe it's a nuclear winter and they're trapped in a fallout shelter. They make believe they're princes locked in a dungeon by the king's wicked councillor. They make believe they're hermits fasting in a mountain cave. They make believe they're stowaways in the hold of a galleon. They make believe they're magicians tied up in a chest. They make believe they're scientists in a sunken bathysphere. They make believe they've been swallowed by a giant and explore the vast cavern of his stomach. They make believe they're in a spaceship warping through black holes. They make believe they're shrunken to the size of tiny bugs, stuck in a raindrop falling to earth. Sometimes they climb through the trapdoor out into the treetop and sit astride the sturdy limbs and pretend they're galloping on white stallions in a thundering herd of wild black horses.

Sometimes they close their eyes and pretend to be blind and they feel each other's faces and the boy is careful not to hurt the friend. Sometimes the friend grooms the boy, picking the bark and sap from his hair and licking the pollen dust from his face. Sometimes the boy curls up in the lap of the friend and the friend asks him questions. What animal would you like to be? What food would you eat if you could only eat one? How would you choose to die? What is your greatest fear? What superpower would be the best? If you could save the world by sacrificing one life, would you do it? What was your first word? What is your earliest memory?

The mother calls the boy into her bedroom and shows him the photographs she has spilled out over the white froth of tumbled linens. The scent of the soap washed into the sheets has always reminded the boy of snow, but tonight it stings his cringing nose, astringent.

She shows the boy pictures in dull umbers and maroons, long-ago film, of the boy's parents before he was born. This is his mother, distracted in an itchy sweater, in a cabin on her honeymoon, lamplight the color of cooking oil shining and blurring on her face. Her hair is shorter and it looks rough and blunt and prickly. Her smile is unfamiliar. Here is his father, forehead buried in a dark navy watchman's cap, chin and nose smothered in a charcoal turtleneck, marking off a pale strip of skin out of which black eyes gape, the inverse of the bandit's eye mask.

Now pictures of the boy as a baby, with a fat lolling neck and a glazed expression, bulbous and gaping in a matted blue towel, or seemingly deserted in a flat field on a gray day. The photos get glossier and brighter as they go on. Last year on the ferry, noses and eyelids smashed flat by the wind. This past winter, roasting potatoes in foil in the fireplace here, the lighting off, their hands red and their faces smeared across the exposure. The boy and the mother on the boy's birthday at the zoo. A leather-chested gorilla with blood in its eyes stands behind them as they pose, the spit spray of its roar fouling the glass wall of the enclosure. The boy squirms on the bed, bored and truculent.

In the night the boy and the friend sneak back into the mother's bedroom and steal the box of photographs. They draw the friend into the pictures: sometimes a black zigzag of shadow at the corner of the frame behind the mother, sometimes a silvery trail the friend makes with the point of a needle, a shape hovering between the boy and the lens. With crayons, the boy draws the friend's scales and the stripes of its fur onto the face of his father, and the friend shades its own eyes within the eyes of the gorilla.

When the mother finds the pictures in the morning she cries and screams at the boy, and he takes off, kicking the ground, the corners of his mouth wrenching down despite himself, and runs to the wood, and begs the friend to take him inside, behind the tree line, and the friend does, and comforts him.

The boy and the mother make up and on Sunday they bake cookies for breakfast. They have a collection of cookie cutters and they bake pigs and crescent moons and hearts and maple leaves, royal crowns and saxophones and lighthouses and bumblebees. They sprinkle jimmies on the tops, or push in currants with their thumbs. Shivery with sugar, they bustle into town and the mother, rapid and excitable, buys suspenders and striped shoelaces for the boy's first day of school, and a set of stencils, and stickers that smell of chocolate, bubble gum, peanut butter, and green apple. On the way home she asks casually how the friend will keep busy when the boy is at school all day. It will come with me, says the boy, startled, and the mother, kind and vague, shakes her head with her eyes set on the distance.

When they reach the house, the boy tears through the rooms, but the friend is nowhere to be found. At last the boy discovers it in the basement, huddled beneath the stairs, tearing apart a daddy longlegs. I won't go! promises the boy, and any other supplication he can think of. By and by, he's able to coax the friend upstairs, where it scuttles into the boy's bedroom and under his bed. It stays there through the evening and all night, and in the morning the mother sees the boy's face is puffed and flushed as if he's been stung, and his eyes have a queer translucence.

The mother invites the boy and the friend to dance. She pushes the armchairs and ottomans to the outskirts of the living room and sweeps the floor, making an odd pile of broken dried leaves, frayed and twisted threads of gold and purple, small slivers of glass, dust clumps woven in spheres like tumbleweeds, and wasps, curled in on themselves like fetuses, their antennae shattered.

The mother wears an ivory slip and black opera gloves and, on a long chain, a cameo that chills her through the thin silk of her slip. The boy comes down in his small black suit, which still fits him perfectly. He hasn't grown. The mother rummages in the spare room for a man's dove-gray fedora, which engulfs the boy's ears and slips backward, the brim chafing his neck. Baby's breath is wedged in the band.

The boy informs the mother solemnly that the friend has sent its regrets. The mother, stymied, asks if he and she might go together to press the invitation, but the boy fuddles the needle onto the record and extends his hand without answering. The boy and the mother waltz awkwardly. Where did you learn to dance? says the mother, I thought I would have to teach you. My friend taught me, says the boy, are you jealous? The mother stares at him. No, she says, that's not it. The needle staggers into a gouge in the record. Oh, dear, the mother says, what a shame. My friend loves this song, says the boy. He puts his arms up trustingly, as if to be carried, high above his head, and his fingers curl around where the shoulders of the friend might be. They sweep about the room, the friend a confident lead, the boy swooning gracefully in its embrace. The mother forms an encouraging smile. I'll get some refreshments, she says, champagne with ginger ale, and lemon ices. Switch off the lights when you go, says the boy, still revolving. The mother hesitates, flicks the switch, and mounts the stairs. Sometime in the night the music skids to a halt.

She knows it's beautiful. She knows what kind of skin it has – blue-veined, with a thick translucence like shellfish, bruising easily in a kind of panic. She knows because it's obvious.

She knows, because her son has told her, in a voice with a reverential, primal hush, like the silence of dim morning air at ease on still water, that his friend has a wonderful facility of climbing in the trees and running in the tallest, most whipping, stinging grass. She knows that a heartbeat will slow to the rhythm of its voice. She knows its eyes are colors from another spectrum. She knows the fine golden down that covers its limbs; she just knows.

She knows the ravishable tenderness of its throat. She knows the coils of its ears can provoke a dangerous hypnosis if regarded too long. She knows the razor sharpness of its elbows and the woozy perfume of its breath.

She knows that the rays of the sun are addicted to its body and that it drinks in the moonlight with upturned mouth. She's never seen it, but she knows. She doesn't know the secrets it shares, the memories it hides, the fears it cherishes, or why it is vying for her son.

Past the tree line, just within the wood, is the skeleton of a burned-down barn, and brambles of blackberries and bushes of lady's slippers have gentled the ruins. Past the barn, a deer trail leads through a claustrophobia of clawing saplings and lashing briars, until the wood opens, and the floor is a miniature forest of tiny trees of climacium moss. Long gray vines sway from the canopy; the branches over which they're looped are lost in leaves and in the clouds of spores and insects that laze overhead. The boy grabs a vine and swings. He whoops once, then swoops silently between the trunks on the endless arc of his pendulum. The friend tugs the vine to a halt and brushes the boy's face in apology. Hurry, it says.

They trudge out of the forest of moss and down a short bank graceful with ferns and irises and ending in a stream that cuts through the wood. Waterfleas flash in the current and the boy sees the velvety puffs of silt where crawfish have shot back under rocks with fear of him. Before the water, the friend pants in terror, so the boy tucks it in his pocket and hops carefully across the rocks to the opposite bank. The leaves of the wood rustle and sunshine shakes down in a brief warm muddy rain. Beyond the stream is the dank overhang of the cliff, under which round stones mark out a ring in the mud. There are some curls of burned metal, mildewed spent shells from a shotgun, and bones chewed by an animal. The friend breathes deeply here, and traces its hand against the soot smoked on the rock ceiling, and a silver skin oozes down to blind its eye. Up the back of the cliff they go, grabbing at tree trunks and clawing the dirt to ascend the incline. Then suddenly they've plunged to the top and the summer has fallen away.

The ground is covered with black and brown leaves, and the wind has shaken the treetops gray. There's a gravestone, white with chips of mica, and with a carving of an arum lily garbled and shallowed by weather, and violets growing all around. All already ready, says the friend. The boy sighs. Let's run away, he says. The friend is silent. I'm hungry, says the boy. You're never hungry now, says the friend, and that's true. The boy shrugs. The friend ruminates, and chews a sprig of poison ivy. Suddenly its hot hiss snakes out and its tongue is in the boy's ear. Poisoned you! cries the friend. The boy screams his laughter and he's running through the wood yelling, I'll find the antidote, and the friend strolls after him, smiling.

The boy and the mother sit Indian style on the boy's bed and play Cat's Cradle. The boy threads his fingers through the string to make the Cradle. The mother slips her hands into the maze. Pinching the taut cord, she whisks the boy's fingers free, and makes the Soldier's Bed. The boy snatches at the intersections, and pulls them through themselves, and the Candles shine in his hands. The mother reaches over awkwardly, and twists the string. Its bite tightens around the boy, and his skin swells and reddens. With a wrench of her wrist, she constructs the Manger between them. The boy's tiny fingers go darting among the knots. Before she knows it, he's imprisoned in Diamonds. We won! exults the mother. The boy smiles at her. His eyes are prisms for the day's light. She sees that there's something he holds in his mouth, gleaming dark and wet. A candy, a tongue, a morsel of mercury.

The mother reaches slowly for the bowl of water that stands by her son's painting set, on the night table, dips her hand in it, and with a panicked lunge, she flicks the liquid on the boy. It wrenches back on the bed with a jolt and a high-pitched moan. Her hand flies to her throat. She squeezes her eyes closed. Hey! protests the boy. What are you doing? Then he lurches for the bowl and begins to flick her back, in messy muddy splashes. The mother quavers and laughs in great gulps. The paint water soaks into the blankets, patterning her legs and hands with blurred designs, mottled markings, scaly smudges in brownish red and brownish blue and brownish green.

She lets the boy spill out the whole bowl, and although she changes the linens and blots the bed with towels to soak up the moisture, he still makes her flip the whole mattress before bedtime, so that the friend can nest there with no fear of the wet.

The boy discovers the friend hidden away in the fortress that sprawls across the living room, layer upon layer of sheets and wool blankets and towels and clothes slung between armchairs. The friend is prone, half sunk into the floor, disappearing into the wood like a ship slowly submerging below the skin of the sea. The boy throws his arms about the friend and covers it with chafing kisses. The friend coughs faintly but its eyes flash into brightness, burning the boy where the friend's gaze falls on him. What's wrong? the boy whispers fiercely. What's happened? You haven't gone, croaks the friend, you're here. I'm here, says the boy, of course I'm here.

The friend and the boy stand up and spin themselves in circles. Even when the dizziness has passed the boy can't remember what's where in the room outside the fortress. The french doors, the fireplace, the grandfather clock have all lost their places. The friend draws three doors for the boy. Where do they lead? says the friend.

The boy thinks hard. The first door, he says, a garden full of delicious fruit that feels pain when you bite it. Your turn. The friend considers. It says, the second door: a world in the center of the earth where you're turned inside out. You walk backward, talk backward, and see backward. Third door? The boy imagines. Third door, he says, somebody else. You can live in their body, but they control all your movements and your thoughts. The friend laughs. Pick a door, it says. The boy spins and spins until he doesn't remember which door is which. He opens one and falls out into darkness.

In the yard, in her bathing suit and sunglasses, the mother sits rigid in the blare of the sun. Little worms of perspiration nose their way out of her skin and trail across her upper lip. Beside her is a glass of ice water; she picks it up to watch the blades of grass, pale with the cold of the glass, rise shakily from their crushing. Glossy crows settle over the lawn. She lies down but finds she can't endure the crawling of the grass across the back of her neck. A dragonfly comes crashing toward her face and she gasps. A gnat executes stiff seizures in the cold of the ice water. Her fingernails ache from the dirt packed beneath them. She puffs at a dying dandelion to make a wish, and the seeds blow back and stick to her lips and tongue. She plucks at the petals of a daisy, then beheads the whole thing summarily with a jerk of her thumb. *Mama had a baby and its head popped off*! she sings.

The boy is staring at the lion and he doesn't dare to move. The boy is in the big blue armchair in the living room, with the lamp in the shape of a dancing lady spilling light from the table beside him, but the lion only a few feet away is in darkness, a darkness that grows thicker and thinner, so the boy keeps losing sight of the lion, though neither of them is moving.

Into the boy's dream comes the friend, and the boy feels relief like the sudden release of a waterfall that's been dammed up, and with his eyes he signals the presence of the lion to the friend. The friend stays very still, and the darkness blows like wind over its face, and the boy loses and finds the friend's features for hours. At last the boy comes to wonder, in a rush of urgency, why the friend doesn't slay the lion. Kill it! whispers the boy. Please, kill it! The friend makes a sign and the boy sees that he himself is holding a long dagger. Me? I can't, pleads the boy. Please, kill it. The friend gestures to the boy to make use of the dagger. The boy stares aghast at the lion. Its eyes are mournful like the eyes of the boy's dog that had died, but there's a low growl coming from it like the moans of the tomcats that fight in the yard at night. The boy doesn't move. The lion climbs painfully to its feet and pads over to the boy and lies down beside him. Wondering and trembling, the boy places his hand on the lion's head. The friend spins around, claps its hands, and screams, and the lion's jaws hurtle open and its roar is pounding the boy like blows, and his terror is gagging his throat.

He comes awake with the friend beside him in bed, laughing and fanning the boy's face. That was a close one! says the friend, twinkling. What were you thinking? You almost got us killed, it giggles, and cuddles. The boy falls back into sleep, with his eyes screwed tight shut against dreams, and his skin smelling sour with dried crust of sweat.

The mother goes in the gloaming to the grave in the wood. She sits. Moths smack against her flashlight and are snarled in her hair. After some time, she climbs back down the cliff and wades into the stream, flinching at the bite of the water on her skin. She drops a ring, a small plastic figurine, and a gray fedora into the water. She makes three wishes. With her toe she buries the ring and the toy in the mud, and she watches the floating fedora tear against some bracken on the bank and be devoured by shadows. On the way home she bats in a fury against the thorns that snag her clothes and beat her legs.

She sits on the porch. The screaming of the mosquitoes, an incessant and furious anguish, is overwhelming; it seems to the mother that all the darkness of the lawn might be a black cloud of suffering insects; but nothing bites her. There's a damp smell and she feels her skin crawling, flinching away from her bones. Behind her, the screen door slaps against the jamb in the windless, ponderous night, and the mother stays very still, only slightly stiffening her back.

Before dawn she goes into the boy's room and lifts his body from the bed. She bears him cautiously out of the house to the car, and tucks him into the back seat. His clothes are already folded on the passenger seat. In the minute between the starting of the car and rolling out of their driveway, the mother's alarm grows so fierce that her vision is blurred. Once they gain the public road, it's vanished, and she's calm and deadened. She drives to the school and she parks.

When the sun comes up and the doors groan open and the flag struggles up into the pale air above her, she's ready. By the time the buses come marching in disciplined formation up the drive, he's awake. He doesn't seem alarmed by his abduction; just sleepy and bewildered and quiescent. They get his overalls on and his velcro firmly strapped. He observes the patterns described by the hundreds of small milling bodies with grave interest. She holds onto his hand as far as the classroom door. For some time she sits in the car and watches, but nothing comes or goes until she does.

Alone in the house, the friend trickles from room to room, carried by a draught that floats past the curtains, through the walls, and around the doors. The molecules of the air bruise the friend's body and it suffers this.

In her car, driving, the mother thinks of the friend with shaken pity, and in his classroom the boy draws a picture with a blank face and long arms like tangled ropes and a sky full of dashes like rain falling like arrows or like shooting stars.

The friend drifts into a cobweb and clings there till its weight rends the strands and it resumes its meandering course. Where it drags along the floor, dust gathers on its skin, smothering the pores. The eyes of the friend empty and its mouth consumes itself. At last, with a sigh, it disperses.

At the end of the day, the mother watches to see that thc boy files out with the others, and then in her car she shoots out ahead of the schoolbus to be ready to greet him when he jumps down the steps to disembark at the end of their drive. He's glowing like a new penny and he navigates the yard in a series of bounds. He has a collage for the fridge, of black horses pasted on a picture of a coral reef, and he has a caterpillar made of pipe cleaners. The mother and the boy nestle the caterpillar in the grass at the base of the sycamore to protect the treehouse.

There are mimeographed lists from the teacher, of Things to Buy and Things to Do, and the boy has won a ribbon for thinking of the most words beginning with A. At lunchtime the other children had raised an outcry over the boy's purple pickled egg, and the mother promises that tomorrow he will have a white-bread sandwich cut in triangles and an apple with a leaf still on the stem. For recess they learned to jump rope while singing songs and afterward the teacher read a story that the boy had never heard, about a child who flies on the back of the wind. The boy runs about the house, visiting the attic and the basement and the bathroom, as if to see how different they've become. He told a girl in his class about the pond and the girl didn't believe that he has one and the mother says that the girl can come and see for herself, with some other of the boy's classmates, if he would like.

During dinner the boy bounces up and down, upsetting the jar of cucumber salad. He runs out twice to make sure that he has everything in his backpack that he'll need at school the next day, and three times to check that the caterpillar is still in place, guarding the treehouse. He doesn't mention the friend, and his eyes are the color that the mother remembers.

By bedtime the boy is exhausted and the mother tucks him in and sings *mairzy doats and dozy doats and liddle lamzy divey* and he accompanies her in a contented blur of humming that spins around the edge of the tune. When she turns out the light and clicks closed the door he's already quite asleep.

He wakes not because of the volume of the breathing in the room or because of its horrible wet crackling and sucking, but because of the heat the breath gives off, a heat like an anvil, which crushes him into the bed. The windows are fogged over and the moon leaks through the droplets on the glass in weak smears of sickly light, like the ghosts of murdered stars.

He knows his waking has been noticed, for whatever it is is now holding its breath. He can hear the interminable, deliberate creak of the floorboards where something is shifting its weight under the bed with infinite caution and cunning. Then a terrible quiet. The boy quakes and his spasmodic gasp is like a slap cracking across the silent face of the darkness. The longest pause. At last the bed begins to joggle teasingly and then to rock violently so he can barely keep from sliding off. Every time his hand or foot slips over the side of the mattress he sobs with terror and feels the humid wind where something has just missed its snatch at him. The earthquake in the bed is because the thing is shaking with laughter. Whatever is under the bed is laughing.

Then the laughter stops, and the smell comes up, dank and congealed, and he can feel the putrefying odor worming inside his pyjamas and bloating his skin with its stink, and the monster stretches itself. The room tilts as the monster ripples its spine, voluptuous; and the flayed leather of its body rustles and sucks as it moves, and it unfurls from under the bed, he sees its arm creep out, as if on a thousand little millipedal feet, right there before him, in the same air that's burning and lashing against his own starting eyeballs, and the nails of the thing shred whatever faint moonlight has crept through the steam in the room, and the boy knows, he knows, its head is coming out next, and he hears the cut and the thrust and the singing of its teeth as they emerge, smiling and smiling and smiling.

THE LION'S DEN

Steve Duffy

Steve Duffy (1963–) is a contemporary British writer who has lived in Norfolk and London, but is currently living and working on the North Wales coast. He is a recipient of the International Horror Guild Award for the story 'The Rag-and-Bone Men' and has published two short story collections, *Tragic Life Stories* and *The Moment of Panic*. Duffy's work has appeared in several of Datlow and Windling's The Year's Best Fantasy and Horror anthologies. 'In the Lion's Den' (2009) is one of those most difficult of weird fictions to write: a tale in which references to modern technology add to, rather than detract from, the rising sense of unease.

It's so familiar now, that grainy digital footage of the lions' den. We've rerun it a hundred times, picked over it obsessively, advanced it frame by fuzzy frame. I'm sure all the experts, the psychologists, the security consultants that were brought in to analyse the clip (but who failed entirely in their glib attempts to explain it all away), feel in some way that they themselves experienced the whole thing. It's easy to forget that only a few people actually witnessed the incident first-hand, that Thursday afternoon in the late autumn of the last year of the old century. I was one of them. My colleagues and I saw it all first-hand. It gave us the edge on all the rest; we saw and heard and felt things no camera could catch, let alone one being operated by an overexcited amateur. But even we remain at a loss to explain exactly what happened…

Perhaps we're all trying too hard. Most people have written it off long since as fundamentally inexplicable – just one of those things. The boy was mad, they said, to do what he did: simple as that. But since when has madness been synonymous with simplicity? Granted, the incident was simple enough, on the face of it. Maybe it was precisely that simplicity which for some of us made the whole thing impossible, even then, to dismiss. The zoo sits amongst quiet leafy suburbs, out where the city begins to lose interest in itself. Built in the 1960s, its enclosures are adequate – at a pinch – to the animals' needs, in terms of size and layout. Iron railings and concrete moats surround modest expanses of grassy slope and pruned-back leafless trees. An artificial river runs through the grounds, with an observation barge that sails on the hour, every hour; there are nocturamas for the insects, aviaries for the birds. On a day like that November day, a dull grey weekday nipped with the coming of winter, there will be only a handful of visitors. And I remember there were no school parties of screaming preteens, no coachloads of the elderly: only a handful of people wandering the broad tarmac paths between the enclosures, consulting their guides, adjusting the lenses on their cameras as the animals blinked listlessly back at them through the bars.

In the observation tower above the main block is the surveillance post, with its panoramic view across the whole of the compound. Further out, beyond the perimeter walls, the rooftops of a thousand bungalows, chimney-tops and satellite dishes peeking through the screens of quick-growing *leylandii*; beyond these, raw winter ground-mist on the plain, and the grey smudge of the distant city tower blocks. The view always depresses me, during my shifts in the tower. Maybe anyone who spends long enough around cages, whether as captive or keeper, will sooner or later feel the need for liberty, for transcendence; will at the very least catch himself gazing beyond the bars, meditating on the interconnected concepts of inside-outside. Reminding us where our duties lie, the CCTV cameras flick monotonously through their cycles of the main perimeter, pen to pen, avenue to avenue. Up in the God-seat we follow the sequence, indiscriminately surveilling animal and human, spectacle and spectator.

As familiar as some of the animals are the regulars, those people who visit the zoo so frequently as to become instantly recognisable to the security staff. We have nicknames for them, and in some instances their photos pinned up on the corkboard, with cautionary Post-It notes attached. It's our job to watch them and decide whether their interest in this or that animal goes beyond innocent curiosity; the endless enthralment of seeing a creature in its cage.

Inevitably, you see, a zoo will attract certain types of people, over and above its core visitor group. These range from the mostly harmless – the lonely and inadequate, the homeless, the community-care brigade – through to the more problematic types, the obsessives, the neurotics, and in extreme instances the dangerously, even suicidally unhinged. With the former, our job consists mostly of moving them on at closing time, rousing them if they try to sleep in the dark musty tunnels of the nocturama or the vivarium, making sure they don't present a nuisance to the staff or to other zoo users. With the latter, it can be very different.

Most identify with a particular animal, usually to the exclusion of all others. Often, it'll be monkeys, of which we have several species, or the great apes. They stand gripping the bars, watching as the simians dangle from their tyre swings or munch their way phlegmatically through buckets of bruised fruit. Occasionally, one will try to make contact: a hand will be thrust through the bars, and we need to be sure nothing is being passed that might be harmful, intentionally or otherwise. We took off one such woman a notepad and pencil; perhaps she expected the ape to communicate with her in some way or another, to provide some signifying rebus of his existence. On the pad she'd drawn herself, to a high degree of anatomical detail, in the pose of Leonardo's Universal Man. Above the self-portrait she'd scrawled the words *look monkey*. In the enclosure the ape sighed, settled back into his flaccid hairy old-man's pelt, scratched at his fleas with melancholy acceptance. Who knows? Perhaps he felt resentful that we'd confiscated the pad and pencil, denied him even this meagre opportunity for self-affirmation. They say an ape in the Paris zoo, given paintbrush and paper, once made a painting of the bars of his cage. But that's another matter entirely. We're keepers, first and foremost, not art critics. Before anything, it's our job to keep the animals out of harm's way.

Some people, you see, come armed with more than pencils. We've confiscated knives from people, air-rifles; apples with razor-blades stuck inside them, more than once. Out-and-out mutilators are pretty uncommon, thank god, but all zoo staff are perpetually on their guard against them. Why would anyone do a thing like that? It's well known that sadism presents early in life as a predilection for harming animals, but I've wondered sometimes: might there be a weird sort of jealousy mixed up with it too?

Consider for a moment the lot of your average zoo animal. They need no affirmation, know no doubt; existentially, they've got it cracked. Even without the identifying plaque in front of its enclosure, an ape is still an ape, unchallengeable in the fact of its apehood. No insecurity, no inadequacy to speak of outside the basic social dynamics of the group: the ranking ladder, who gets to mate with which females, who's in charge and who's not. And what have these sad sacks of humans got, the ones who mock and throw stones? Not even a plaque in front of their enclosure. Perhaps it's easier being a caged monkey then a caged man? But even so, it'd still be a pretty weak excuse. Just because an ape may have the existential edge on you is no reason to feed it a sandwich full of rat poison. We're always on the lookout for these suspect types, the vagrant ones, the loiterers, the sunken-eyed prowlers round cages and pens.

That day – that day and a thousand others, before and since – I was up in the God-seat, cycling through the CCTV feeds around the site. It was late in the afternoon; another two hours and we'd be closed. It hadn't been a particularly busy day, and there were fewer than thirty people spread out across the whole expanse of the zoo. A minibus-full of teenagers with Down's syndrome from a nearby sheltered-housing group; half-a-dozen students from the local college of art with folders and easels; two or three elderly couples; and a handful of unclassifiable adults. The kids were well-behaved enough for me not to worry about them getting up on top of walls or climbing fences, and the pensioners looked about ready to call it a day. I was concentrating on picking out the loners, the singletons.

And that's how I came to notice him on the CCTV: the boy, standing alongside the wall of the lion compound. He seemed young, not much older than a teenager, and at first I took him for one of the art students. But he had no sketchpad, no portfolio. As I looked, two or three of the students went past, and none of them acknowledged him, nor he them. I activated the manual override on the camera controls, and zoomed in on the boy.

He was facing slightly away from the camera, so I tried another angle from a different side of the compound. That didn't give me enough of a close-up. Back on the original camera, all I could make out was his clothing. He was wearing jeans and a camouflage jacket, and his sunbleached hair was hacked into a spiky straggling brush. *Come on, sonny,* I found myself muttering, *show yourself.* Obligingly he half-turned, and for the first time I got a look at his face.

Stubble, a scrappy sort of beard; but it's been a while now since stubble signified anything. He might have been sleeping rough, or he might have been a fashion model. It cut both ways. He was gaunt-looking, hollow-cheeked, but reasonably clean. His behaviour didn't strike me as particularly furtive, which went in his favour, but neither did he seem like one of those people who stand by the cage long enough to watch the animals do their tricks, then wander off in search of the cafeteria and the gift shop. I was sufficiently interested to keep the live camera on him, while at the same time spooling back through the last half-hour of lion-enclosure footage on the auxiliary monitor.

There he was. He'd hardly moved in all that time: as I glanced from the main monitor to the auxiliary, only the time-stamp on the latter showed up the difference. I was going to call it down on the walkie-talkie to one of the guards on the ground, but we were a man short that day anyway, so I decided to have a look myself. I handed over the control system to my colleague Graham Morris, told him where I was going and why, and picked up an on-charge walkie-talkie from the rack. I did briefly look at the firearms cabinet, where the guns and tranquilliser darts were kept, but decided against it. No sense in alarming anyone.

Clanking down the metal steps from the surveillance post I had three or four possibilities in mind concerning our mystery visitor, assuming that he wasn't some innocent sightseer who just happened to have a thing for lions. One, believe it or not, was drugs. I know it sounds ridiculous, not to say sick in the extreme, but we've had that problem in the past. A few years back one of our chimpanzees was slipped a dose of LSD, we think inside an apple. She went into an extended psychotic fugue, kept slamming her head into the bars till the vets had to put her down. That was radical by any standards: not particularly common, granted, but I hated to think what a tripping lion might do before we managed to sedate it.

Another (and you shouldn't get the wrong idea about this) was sex. Now I don't mean to suggest I thought the boy was going to try anything directly with a lion – though it's happened with most of the smaller mammals in the past, and at sea zoos practically all the time with porpoises and dolphins, so I'm told. There are all sorts of ways to get your jollies, and we've dragged our fair share of flashers and masturbators away from the railings, before and since. What all *that's* about I don't pretend to know, except that sex is at the bottom of so much, one way or another. When something goes wrong inside, then it's as likely to show up in a sexual context first as it is any other way, I suppose. But a lion… surely a lion would be a daunting enough proposition to make most people think twice?

Of course there was the animal-rights angle, which from what I'd seen on the CCTV seemed a distinct possibility. The boy did have that look of the zealot about him, I thought, as I swiped my smartcard through the security lock on the way out of the staff compound; a definite whiff of high ideals and crazy dreams. But then the timing was all wrong for an attempted release. Animal-rights activists tend (for obvious reasons) to hit a zoo at night, but since we'd beefed up our perimeter security with trip alarms and night vision, the Animal Liberation Front might find it a more tempting option to hide in the light, so to speak. Or it might not be a jailbreak, but a demonstration of some kind – though to whom he was planning to demonstrate, in an all but empty zoo, I couldn't quite imagine.

As I crossed the main piazza there was still another possibility in the back of my mind, grimmer than the others, probably the one which was worrying me the most. Every day someone out there comes to the end of his tether, decides he can't carry on any more, and starts looking for a really good method to end it all. How do you do it? Let me count the ways.

Pills: they make you vomit, before they do anything else. Plus, if you underestimate the dose you're apt to end up alive still, but hooked up in perpetuity to a dialysis machine, with maybe a really incapacitating stroke or two to boot. Gas stinks, and you need the nerve to stay put until the anoxia kicks in. Rope's tricky: if the drop's too short you'll choke slowly, and if it's too long, you'll decapitate yourself. Neither one of those outcomes is for the squeamish. Heights: well, lots of people have problems with heights at the best of times, and it's among the messiest and most traumatic of scenarios for the relicts, the discards, those you leave behind, the ones who have to identify you afterwards. Knives sting, and even the deepest cut can clot once you've passed out. Guns: would you believe the number of people who've held a firearm to their heads, pulled the trigger – and missed? Not missed entirely, of course; just missed enough to make sure they'll spend the rest of their lives in an IC ward being fed intravenously and turned each day to have their bedsores dressed. If they're lucky. Death's fraught with mistakes, and given the options, you might well decide it makes perfect sense to go down to the zoo, wait till it's not too busy and then let yourself down into the lions' den. Leave it to the experts, so to speak.

I'm not joking. The act has a sort of logic to it. The big cats are swift enough killers, as we've seen on a thousand wildlife documentaries, brief savage scuffles on the dusty Serengeti, and there is something about the act… I don't want to give the wrong impression here, but something almost approaching dignity. Some quality of fitness and distinction that's lacking in those other methods I've mentioned. Something gladiatorial, almost: a willingness to look death straight in the face. To look into its eyes, to feel its reeking carnivore's breath on your cheek…

But it's hell for us keepers. Once a big cat has tasted manflesh, it can never again be trusted. The line has been crossed: you know it, the beast knows it too, and you have to scrutinise every facet of its behavioural patterns around humans thereafter. If it shows the slightest deviation, there's only one thing for it. Hesitate, and you're lost. That's not a thing you'll hear for public consumption from the zoo authorities – they're far more likely to dole out the usual platitudes, there's no such thing as a maneater, there are only wild animals, doing what wild animals do, and our duty of care remains unchanged, blah blah – but believe me. In practice, the days of any such beast are numbered. As a keeper, someone who puts himself on the line with these creatures each day, you'd have to be either stupidly trusting, or just plain stupid, not to be aware of the situation, and ready to act upon it if necessary. I quickened my step almost unconsciously, skirting the artificial knoll where the baboons swarmed and barked to approach the lion enclosure from behind and slightly above where the boy had been standing.

There it was, a moated expanse of drab suburban veldt across the river; and there was the boy. I got out my field glasses and gave him the once-over. So far as I could tell, he seemed not to have moved. By now I wasn't thinking sex: half-an-hour is just too long for a compulsive masturbator to stay still, really. As far as animal rights went, he didn't appear to have either the equipment or the back-up for anything I could imagine a protestor would want to do. Violence was still at the back of my mind, as was self-destruction. I watched him through the glasses as he watched the lions, and the time wore on, another five, ten minutes. It was late in the afternoon now, and starting to get cold. You could smell the frost lying in wait behind autumn's mud and woodsmoke, and the first wisps of ground-mist were starting to rise along the riverbank. Before long Graham's voice would come over the tannoy, *the park is closing in twenty minutes, please make your way towards the main exit…*

Would the boy make his move before then? And what would it be? Above me the light sensors tripped in, and the bright white floods lit up along the broad avenues. Reflexively the boy looked up, then around him, as if startled out of his reverie. I decided it was time to go in closer. Casually, trying my best not to look like a policeman, I began to stroll down towards the lion enclosure, a couple of hundred yards off down the path.

I'd just reached the footbridge over the river when it all started to go off. The shrubs along the riverbank blocked my view of the compound for a moment. All I could see was a couple of the art students, pointing and shouting. I quickened my pace to jog on to the bridge, then broke into a flat-out run when I saw what was happening by the compound.

The boy was standing on the waist-high concrete wall, hauling himself up the railings. I shouted *no*, fumbled my walkie-talkie clear of its clip and gave the all-channel alert as I ran. We were going to need the tranquilliser darts, and quickly; or else medical support at best.

He was over the railings now, sliding out of sight down the concrete ramp into the moat. One of the students, a girl, was hanging over the wall, arms outstretched and yelling to him, but he took no notice.

I reached the compound just as he hit the bottom of the moat. All of us by the outer wall were shouting now, but I don't know whether he heard a thing. If he did, he showed no sign of responding. Instead, he straightened up from his crouch, and began to climb the opposite side.

Two or three other people had come over by now, drawn by the commotion. One of them owned a hand-held camcorder, and was filming continuously throughout what happened next. Looking at the film, this is what you see:

Jerks and blurs, then a wobbly balance as the autofocus kicks in. The boy has reached the top of the inner wall: he stands on the concrete lip a while before letting himself down into the compound proper. Nothing is hurried about him, nothing hesitant; he glances from side to side, almost expectantly: *where are they?*

They were there all right. Five in the pride: two males, one little more than a cub; three females, one of them pregnant. All of them in good condition, fit and active, a functioning pack. They have names, which we use when we have to in order to distinguish them, but I don't honestly see any point in naming a wild thing. It's a false sort of domesticity: it encourages you to project human motivations, human emotions on what's basically a natural born killer, pure and simple. Calling it 'Simba' doesn't change its essential nature, or turn it into something out of Disney. It doesn't make it any more knowable, nor is it something you can shout out in times of crisis, like a dog's name. All any lion does that matters much can really be summed up under the most basic of headings. It eats, it sleeps, it procreates. Given the opportunity, it stalks and kills. And these lions weren't sleeping any more. All around the compound they were waking up and beginning to take notice, and they were getting ready to stalk.

You can see on the video; first one, then another comes into view, at the periphery of the screen. The big male, watching; and the most inquisitive of the females. The camera jumps around a lot – it's being operated by Mrs Nora Bowen, sixty-three years old and growing more agitated by the minute – but you can make out the lions well enough. Three, four, five, here they all come. And the boy, stepping away from the retaining wall.

The condenser microphone on the camera is mostly picking up Mrs Bowen, whose alarm and concern is immediately evident, and Mr Bowen, who is alternately trying to get his wife to give him the camera and offering her technical instruction. Above their broad Lancashire accents you can just make out the sound of a man shouting in the distance. That's me.

I was at the lip of the moat, scrambling over: no time to get around to the proper entrance on the far side of the compound. Stay still, I was yelling; don't panic. (I suspect that whenever we tell someone not to panic, we're always partly talking to ourselves: I know I was.) Sliding inelegantly down the concrete, I lost sight of what was going on in the compound.

On the video, you can see what I was missing. Not much. Slowly and deliberately, the boy walks out into the middle of the flat grassy area, then stops. The lions are surrounding him in a rough semicircle. No escape.

Scrambling to the top of the inner moat wall – it's half the height of the outer, six feet as opposed to twelve – I knelt on the rim and took stock of the situation as best I could. I was now much closer to the boy, yards closer than Mrs Bowen with her video camera. On the tape you can just about hear me calling – not yelling any more, I was too close to yell, it would have spooked the lions – calling to him to start walking backwards in my direction. Up on the wall, I could hear him. He was talking, but I couldn't understand anything that he said.

It wasn't any language I'd heard before. Thinking back now, it still sounds like the strangest mixture of sounds; but I can say with a degree of certainty that whatever it was, it wasn't gibberish. Peter Whelan, the first keeper to answer my emergency summons, thinks the boy was just making noises to mimic an animal, chatter and meaningless babble. The thing is, though, he hardly heard any of it, arriving as he did at the critical point in time when things began to get confused. I had a decent chance to listen to it, and it sounded to me structured, as if it carried significance and meaning.

What did the lions make of it? That's just another imponderable. They held their ground against the intrusion on to their territory, shifted their forepaws a little and gazed stonily at the intruder. The big male roared once, as if in warning, and some of the others were already growling, their heads low and watchful.

Slowly, still speaking to the lions in that same fluently hypnotic way, the boy began to undo the buttons on his jacket. He slipped it off, dropped it to one side, and then started on his shirt. Hello, here we go, I thought, glancing round distractedly for back-up: we've got an exhibitionist. For some reason, it was vitally important that the lions see his dangly bits. Stupid little sod. What is it with people, I asked myself helplessly. Couldn't they recognise a bad idea when they had one? Now it was up to me to stop him, or to pick up the bits when it was all over. 'Get back here,' I hissed. 'Start walking backwards.' I wonder if he even heard me.

He was taking his trousers off: I'd already spotted his desert boots, discarded at the bottom of the moat. In a few seconds he was naked under the floodlights, exposed to the pitiless scrutiny of the lions.

Beneath the panic that had impelled me across the moat I began to feel a deeper, more fundamental fear. *This isn't going to turn out well,* I told myself, wincing at the puniness of his skinny white body as he turned slightly, first one way, then the other, as if acknowledging each beast in turn. *This is going to be bad.* I'd never seen lions attacking a human before, not under these circumstances. I was fairly sure that was exactly what I was going to be seeing, any time now.

Again I glanced round for back-up. I could see Peter Whelan running at top speed over the brow of the hill near the baboon enclosure. He had a gun. I thought we were probably going to need it. I was horribly, miserably scared, because I could see already how this was going to end – the two of us, on the ground, trying to frighten off the lions, but there were only two of us, and there were five of them…

With a grunt Peter hit the bottom of the moat and scrambled up the other side to where I was. 'Slowly,' I warned him, hoisting him up alongside me. 'Quiet. Don't get them any more wound up.'

Though out of breath from his sprint, Peter understood the need for quiet. 'Bloody hell, Jim,' he panted, 'this is a bad 'un.'

'Went over a couple of minutes ago,' I whispered back. 'Then he got his kit off. What have you got?'

'Tranks,' he said, unslinging his rifle, 'and an airhorn.' They run on compressed air, and sometimes come in useful for frightening a beast off. 'Manoj is bringing the rest of the stuff.'

'Right,' I said. 'I'm trying to get him to come back this way, but he isn't listening.'

'What's he doing with his clothes off?' Peter frowned. 'He's not trying it on, is he?'

'Not as yet,' I told him. 'Anyway, he doesn't seem that excited, does he?' This may seem not just distasteful, but irrelevant, but at least a hard-on would have been indicative of some sort of motive. As it was, another explainable scenario had gone out of the window, and we were still none the wiser as to his intentions.

'Actually, I wasn't looking, meself,' whispered Peter, glancing over his shoulder. 'Here's Manoj coming now.'

Just then several things happened in quick succession. The boy's soft babbling had been gradually increasing in volume; now, it was loud enough to be picked up by the Bowens' camcorder mike. The tape's been played for a linguist from the nearby university: he said it didn't belong to any of the language groups he knew about, but was intrigued enough to request a copy of the tape. We had to tell him no. Too many outsiders have already seen it, and we don't want it ending up on the internet for the delectation of the clicktrance classes.

For a moment the boy's shouting distracted me from the arrival of Manoj, who'd just reached the other side of the moat, where the Bowens were. On the video you can see me glancing towards the camera, making first a shush gesture, then a hurry-up. Then, I turn back to the enclosure. On the audio, you can hear the boy, ranting away at the top of his voice, and the big male roaring. A moment of clarity on the tape catches him to perfection, head thrown back, no more than fifteen yards away from the boy.

'Give me the airhorn,' I told Peter. 'Take aim.'

Peter raised the rifle to his shoulder. 'Which one?' he said. 'The big bastard?'

'Your call,' I said. Under normal hunting circumstances, the females make the kill, but these circumstances were about as far from normal as you could imagine. It's the male's pleasure to ring-fence the pride from intruders, so my money was on the noisy alpha. But I had a nasty feeling that when one went, they'd all join in, and there was no way Peter could reload that fast. Maybe if he took the big fella first...

The boy was screaming himself hoarse by now; no trace of panic, but a commanding, almost exhortative tone, like a hellfire preacher at the climax of his sermon. He started jumping up and down, pumping his fists and stamping on the bare soil – that wasn't too preacherly a sight, I grant you, not in his state of undress. The lions surrounding him in their semicircle snarled and twitched their tails. My finger twitched on the trigger of the airhorn.

'Why doesn't he bloody shut it?' hissed Peter. '*Oy!*' Loud enough for the boy to hear him, under normal circumstances. Loud enough for the lions to react too, I thought. But none of them seemed to hear us, neither man nor beasts. They were too wrapped up in each other. We were fast approaching the moment of truth.

The next three things happened almost simultaneously. First, Manoj came clambering up the retaining wall of the moat, and we had to give him a hand, loaded down as he was with rifle and ammo – all live rounds, no tranquillizers.

Second, there was movement in the compound behind us. All of us – Peter, Manoj, and myself – looked up just in time to catch it. There was the boy, shrieking one last commandment to the evening sky, his breath condensing in the winter chill. And there were the lions, galvanised into life, up off their haunches and running at him. All five of them, all at once.

Peter tried to take the alpha male. He missed – we found the dart later, stuck into the ground. Manoj was just fumbling his rifle to his shoulder. I was blowing the airhorn in short sharp blasts, then just one long continuous hoot, feeling totally useless. Beside me, Manoj managed to get one shot off – again, a miss, which saved him a great deal of trouble later on – and then they were too close to the boy, practically on him already.

Then, in a sudden sparking fall of brilliance, all the floodlights round the compound shorted and went out.

To this day, we don't know the reason for that. The timing was too spot-on for it to have been coincidental, yet what could have caused it? On the video, everything goes dark, exaggeratedly so, darker than the time of day would strictly warrant, and then there's one brief explosion of light that floods out the whole screen. That's Mr Bowen, alongside his wife, who's just remembered he has another camera, for stills. He presses the shutter release more or less by reflex, and the automatic flash kicks in.

Looking at his picture, you can see Peter and Manoj and me, up on the inner wall of the moat; I'm turning round to see why the lights have gone out. That's why I caught the flash full-on, which in turn is why I was functionally sightless for the next ten seconds or so. It's hard to make out anything inside the compound with the naked eye. Mr Bowen's built-in flash was only good over a few yards, up close at parties, and it couldn't cut through the insidious dusk which had been gathering all the time, unnoticed under the floodlights. A digitally enhanced version of the photo brings out a little more detail: a blurred, indistinct heap, at just about the spot on which the boy was standing. They were all upon him.

Up on the wall, we could hear snarling and snapping and the thud of bodies on tight-packed soil, but we couldn't see anything of the boy. None of us could: I was squinting blind after taking the brunt of Mr Bowen's flash, and the other two were still trying to adjust their vision after the floodlights went out. They both saw the lions fall upon him, and then he was lost beneath their colliding bodies, trapped under a rugby scrum of hot fur and strapping muscle. It wasn't until three or four minutes later, when the rest of the backup arrived with lanterns and a big mobile lighting rig we used for night photography, that we were able to get a proper look inside the compound. When we did, two things were immediately apparent.

The first thing was that the lions had dispersed back to their various areas of the compound. Our searching beams picked them up under trees, behind brush cover; we saw them snarl, bare their teeth at the intrusive shafts of light.

The other thing was more of an absence. Throughout all the compound, there was no trace whatsoever of the boy, alive or dead.

Not a sign. Later, back in the surveillance post, we ran all the CCTV from all over the zoo, and you never see him leave. It was probably because I spent more time than any of the others poring over the monitors that I came to realise something else, something equally weird; you never see him arrive. You see him going from compound to compound, on the way to the lions, but you never see him at the gate or outside, in the car park. No vehicle was left unaccounted for, and he hadn't been on any of the coaches. I'd thought he was one of the art students. He wasn't.

All of this was after we'd searched the lion compound, thoroughly, all six of us. We closed down the zoo, got everybody out (after securing the video from Mr & Mrs Bowen), and we went through the whole compound, twice – once, quickly, by electric light, in the company of three extremely nervous policemen, and then a proper fingertip search the next morning. The lions were edgy throughout, irritable and jittery. They didn't like it any more than we did, and they needed watching. I don't think any of us had ever felt more vulnerable in the presence of the big cats than we did that evening, so soon after witnessing the beginning of a mauling incident.

But in a mauling incident you expect blood, and a carcass, and there was none – not even on the clothes. The compound was clean. There were some gnawed cow bones from the lions' last feed-time, and that was all. Nothing to suggest fresh predation. Nothing to suggest anybody had even been in there, except for the little pile of torn and tattered (but still unbloodied) clothing where the attack had taken place. We even went through their scat for the best part of a week, sifting the piles of acrid reeking carnivore stool for bone and tissue fragments. I suppose that was as good a way as any of demonstrating exactly where we were with the whole investigation. We just didn't have a clue.

So, back to the video evidence; back to the

CCTV, and Mr Bowen's photo. Long hours scouring the tapes, till we pieced together a narrative of the incident. The trouble was, it turned out to be one of those modern narratives, the open-ended kind where you're supposed to decide for yourself what the hell happened in the end. Art-house cinema of the most infuriating kind, with no climax, no release.

There's the boy, standing by the moat, climbing the wall. Here I come, just too late to stop him. There he is in the compound, stripped off and preaching his incomprehensible sermon to the lions. And then bang, out go the lights and all hell breaks loose. What I've told you is all we know, including the stuff you don't see on the video, my own impressions and sensations. And I defy you to make any more sense of it than we were able to at the time.

We were closed the next day and the Saturday as well, partly to do a proper search of the entire zoo, partly because we wanted to assess the behaviour of the lions. The search turned up nothing – I may as well tell you that straight away. As to the lions and their behaviour, that was a different matter, and a more troubling one. I'm not a qualified animal behaviourist, like Manoj; I am a zookeeper, though, which I think qualifies me as a high-ranking amateur. I know how big cats act: I know the rules of engagement, how to approach them, what signs to look out for. I know when to stand my ground, and when to run. It's hard-earned knowledge, and you come to rely on it. There are circumstances in which it's necessary to your survival, and you wouldn't want to get it wrong. And that Friday morning, when I was walking the lion compound with the other keepers, I felt something was wrong, even though we were doing everything right.

It would be stupid and incorrect to say that we never get nervous. A little nervousness around the carnivores is no bad thing, it stops you getting sloppy and keeps you alert. But that's fear of a known thing, a possibility comprehended. This was different. This was the feeling of not knowing what to be scared of. I felt – talking over things later we all felt – that there *were* signs out there, but we were missing them. Crucial signals, impacting directly on our safety and well-being, that we weren't picking up on because we couldn't recognise them. And even if we managed to spot them after all, would we understand them? I don't know. I felt as if the rules had been changed, and nobody had told us.

After a while it became actively unsettling, and I was very glad to get out. I remember the sky above the compound was black with starlings, one of those preposterously big flocks with thousands of birds wheeling and plummeting in perfect formation. Their hoarse raucous squawks filled the air as we left the enclosure. The lions padded back out of the holding area and congregated in the middle of the grassed area, watching us go. The male roared, once. Up on the hill, the baboons started up a racket of their own as if in answer. From all across the site, each animal seemed to join in the chorus. None of us keepers could think of anything to say.

And so the incident fizzled out. We'd managed to keep it out of the press, so there was no grief from that quarter. A local paper ran a brief story on an inside page the next day, but none of the nationals ever picked it up, nor the TV, which was just as well. I suppose some soap star broke up with her footballer boyfriend, or perhaps it was just the millennial ballyhoo waiting round the corner. The police kept an open case file on the incident, but seemed happy enough to drop it as soon as they could. There wasn't a lot in it for them, really. No missing person in the outside world to match up with our missing person inside the bars, if you see what I mean. I think they were treating it as petty trespass at best: no-one hurt and no victim, no real harm done, and no repercussions for anyone. And so the zoo settled back into its hibernatory winter peace and tranquillity… only not quite.

The first incident came just after New Year. This time, it's safe to say absolutely no-one was watching. I wasn't on duty that day, but I got the phone call around nine a.m. – could I come in straight away? It was urgent.

Up in the surveillance post that morning had been Graham. At the start of his shift, he'd been checking through the CCTV, going from compound to compound and along the avenues between. Everything was quiet. It was a dull rainy morning, and all the beasts were sheltering. Then, as the next camera clicked in, he got a shock. There was a lion loose outside the compound.

Unlike the previous incident, there's no permanent record of this. The system was in the middle of a refit, and no tape exists of what Graham saw that morning. However, he describes it consistently and straightforwardly, and his word is good enough for me. He saw a lion – a big male, but not *our* big male – out of the enclosure, padding up the path that led past the baboon enclosure.

As Graham caught sight of it, the lion looked up in the direction of the camera. As if it had seen him too, he said; as if the surveillance apparatus worked both ways. For a moment they looked at each other – 'well, that was what it felt like,' says Graham, somewhat embarrassedly. He's not a particularly imaginative man, so I don't believe that was a later embellishment of the truth. If he said it at all, it would have been because that was the impression he got. So they stared at one another, man and beast. After a long second or two the lion moved swiftly, out of shot and into the cover of some nearby bushes.

A dangerous animal out of its compound is automatically a grade-A emergency. Thankfully, the main gates wouldn't be open for another hour-and-a-half, but all timetables had gone out of the window now, of course. Immediately, Graham was on the walkie-talkies and the tannoy, ascertaining the whereabouts of every staff member. Once everyone was accounted for, he called the police. Next, he rang around all the other off-shift keepers, me included.

I arrived not long after the police. I showed them my accreditation (which mostly consisted of my uniform), and managed to attach myself to the first team to enter the park. I think they were glad to have me there. Though they looked every inch the television SWAT team with their flak jackets and SLRs, I could tell they were as nervous as hell. Overhead the helicopter was clattering in a circle around the perimeter. At least it drove the starlings away.

We were getting ready to enter through the main gates when the mobile phone of the co-ordinating officer rang. He answered it, listened briefly, and looked up. 'Panic over,' he said, unmistakable relief all over his rain-wet face. 'It's back in its cage.'

What had happened was, Graham had been checking the lion enclosure all the while, trying to ascertain which animal had got out. It might well have made a difference, since each beast has its own personality. Some can be easily cowed, and some are more prone to confrontation than others. The rain made things difficult. The pride were sheltering in and around the den, and it wasn't until Graham actually got in the Land Rover and went to check, that he was able to report back. Two males, three females, all present and correct.

We still searched the entire zoo, of course, although the search took place in an altogether more laid-back spirit than would otherwise have been the case. Unfortunately, the laid-backness didn't last, and before long we got the distinct impression that the police were a bit fed up with us. Bringing them all the way out to the suburbs on these false alarms – couldn't we run our own zoo properly, or what? They didn't exactly accuse us of wasting their time, but they came very close.

Graham took some flak, from zoo management as well as police, for sounding the alarm. I thought this was not just unfair but deeply, dangerously ignorant. What was he supposed to do? There was an animal outside its enclosure and running loose: a big predator, the biggest we had. All the protocols were in place for such an incident, and he'd had no choice but to follow them to the letter. Ah, but obviously you didn't check, they told him. Wouldn't it have been better if you'd checked? To which he could only point out, I did check, to the best of my ability – and besides, I saw what I saw. A lion, loose outside the compound. And then they would look at him, you know, in that *oh, really?* way, and Graham would have to bite his lip and try not to lose his temper.

Once the police had got back in their vans and cleared off, the rest of us keepers checked out the lion enclosure. There was no sign of an obvious breach of security. We looked in the bottom of the moat for scat, which you'd expect to find if one of the animals had been down there even temporarily. Twelve feet of more-or-less sheer concrete would be a formidable obstacle, after all. Nothing down there. No breaches of the fence around the back of the compound, either, so we were left with a variant on the same question that had troubled us the last time. How did it get out? And, come to that, how did it get back in again?

It had me beat. I believed Graham: how could I not? I trusted him absolutely. And for the next week I found myself lingering round the lion compound, just watching them, trying to work it out. That's how I saw their behaviour patterns had definitely changed. It hadn't just been a nervous reaction, that first morning after we lost the boy. You could see a real difference, if you knew what to look for. It wasn't the behaviour of beasts in a cage – nor, come to that, of uncaged beasts. It was something none of us had seen.

I asked Manoj, with his academic background in behavioural study, and he agreed. 'It's not standard pack behaviour,' he said, 'it doesn't fit the captivity model, or any other model I've ever heard of. Over and above that –' he began, and stopped.

'It's bloody creepy,' I finished, and he frowned at me. I don't think that was supposed to be part of the behavioural lexicon.

We didn't know it yet, but our troubles with the lions were only beginning. In the weeks and months that followed Graham's sighting, lions were spotted outside their compound on no less that five occasions – three times on CCTV, twice by keepers on foot. Concerning the former, we have tape of one such sighting. You can just about make out the unmistakable shape of the predator, moving through bushes around the edge of the zebra enclosure. This was the strangest of all, the one that completely defied all explanation. To be where it was when it was caught on camera, the lion would've had to escape its own compound, negotiate the moat and the twelve-foot wall and all that, pass – on a normal working day, with upwards of a hundred people on site – along the main thoroughfare of the zoo, and scale a ten-foot fence with spikes at the top. And it would have had to have done it all again, in reverse, to get back in the lions' den with the rest of its mates by the time Manoj and I arrived on the scene with our tranquilliser rifles. Because, as usual, we counted five lions in the compound by the time we got there.

On the tape, the zebras don't even seem to see the lion. There's no alarm, they don't go charging away to the far side of the compound. But as soon as they saw Manoj and me, they couldn't move fast enough. One glance, and they were gone, off in a snorting, cantering rumble of hooves, leaving only a pile or two of steaming crap on the trampled grass. This was something we were getting used to by now. Even the friendliest beasts, the apes and the elephants, were starting to shy away from us, if not become actively hostile. This was odd – downright worrying, even – but it wasn't our biggest problem that spring.

The biggest problem was that we'd effectively lost any measure of control with regard to security in the most dangerous area of the whole zoo. Once you discounted (as you obviously had to) the notion that there was a stray lion, not a member of our pride, loose and roaming around the zoo, then you were left with the unpalatable fact that if one of ours did get out, then we'd have no way of distinguishing it from the phantom animal we were seeing on the CCTV. All our security compromised, in the worst possible way.

What were we supposed to do? Keep calling the police out on wild goose chases? We'd be like the boy who cried 'wolf' once too often. Sooner or later, they wouldn't bother turning out; and who was to say that wouldn't be just the occasion they were needed? As a compromise measure, the management hired new guards – not experienced keepers, just untrained muscle from Group 4, really nothing more than glorified bouncers. They were supposed to patrol the avenues and walkways, with orders to call in anything out of the ordinary straight away. They were no use whatsoever; we might as well have saved our money. In fact, they were the proximate cause of our key fatality.

This was in April, an unseasonably hot spell towards the end of the month. I always used to like going about the grounds in springtime, the smells and sounds of nature reawakening from its winter hiatus, the blossom on the trees, the contentment of every animal at the return of sun and warmth.

For the space of a week or so, I felt better walking my beat than I had since the turn of the year. It helped take my mind off things: not only the business with the lions, but now a problem with the new guards.

One or two of them had been seen behaving inappropriately round the animals. They'd been caught on CCTV hanging over the moats and throwing sweets, sometimes sticks and stones, cans of Coke, even. Some were actually taunting the animals through the bars of their cages. Stupid, loutish behaviour, the sort of thing we'd eject a member of the public for. By April, there was a significant undercurrent of hostility between the full-time staff and the temporaries. We were hardly even talking to each other, let alone co-operating fully and closely, as per the plan. That might have helped avoid the tragedy… but then again, didn't they bring it on themselves? Don't we all, in the last analysis?

It was late in the afternoon again, but the day had been warm and the sky was still filled with light. The last of the visitors had just left, and we'd locked down the outer compound. Peter and I were doing one last walk-through, checking there were no stragglers left behind, getting ready to put everything to bed. Usually this was my favourite time of day, in my favourite season. Under normal circumstances, I would have been relishing this stroll around the grounds. As it was, I was unaccountably nervous. Peter says he felt it too, and as I mentioned before, he's not an overly imaginative man.

There was something in the air – I think the animals sensed it too, because all over the site they were skittish, restless, unusually noisy. The gemsboks, when we passed by the antelope enclosure, were actually butting the fences. I got on the walkie-talkie to Manoj, up in the surveillance post, to get his opinion.

'I'll have a look,' he said. 'Stay on while I just get this … ah, you bloody thing. I hate these gadgets.' I knew what he'd be doing: clicking through the various camera angles from the CCTV around the zoo till he got one that showed the antelopes. It sounded as if he was having a few technical problems. 'Why don't they make these things – *oh, shit.*' Over the course of two words his entire tone changed. 'Sam. Peter. You copy?'

'Yeah.'

'Incident in progress, north side of the baboon enclosure. Two of the new guards, attack under way. Get over there right now. Stay on the line.'

Again, it's captured on tape, but again there's a complication. Because it was spring, the blossom was out on the cherry trees that line the main avenue through the zoo. The blossom restricted the view of the baboon enclosure as seen from one of the CCTV cameras – the one, as luck would have it, through which Manoj was watching the developing incident. What he'd seen was this:

Two of the hired guards, standing by the wire mesh of the fence, making fun of the baboons. The leader of the troop, a powerful adult chacma, was practically in their faces, the other side of the chain-link. He was a grumpy, muscular specimen, a natural boss and something of a bully to boot. He wasn't above stamping his authority on the group, usually by means of his teeth. Manoj told me once something he'd read about the species in an old and extremely politically incorrect text, something along the lines of: 'A full-grown chacma is more than a match for two good dogs.' This one, Manoj thought, would probably be more than a match for two stupid security men.

As he'd watched, one of the guards had actually jumped on to the fence and started rattling it, shaking it on its stanchions in imitation of a monkey, or so it looks on the tape. The other one had moved slightly to one side, obscured by the blossom of one of the nearby cherry trees. Like the other one, he was far too close to the fence.

Watching the tape, all you get is that there's some kind of commotion. The blossom stops you from seeing exactly what's happening, but you can see the reaction of the other guard. He drops down from the fence, and runs over to help his mate. You can also see the rest of the baboons stop hooting and grimacing, and watch. Just watch.

'That's the weird bit,' Manoj said to me afterwards, the first time we looked through the VT together. 'See the troop leader there?'

'He isn't doing anything,' I said.

'Exactly.' Manoj looked at me. 'He's ceded authority to another animal.'

I was confused. 'Another member of the troop?'

'Not a chance,' Manoj said decisively. 'This boy? Never.'

But it's true: you can see him standing back with the others, just watching, like us. After what seems like ages, but according to the timestamp on the tape is just over ten seconds, the guard falls back from the fence and into camera shot again.

Even on the tape you can see he's very badly messed up. The paramedics tried to save one of his eyes, I believe, but it was too late probably from the start. Most of the rest of his face he left inside the compound. Inside the cage, the baboons leap and cavort in a frenzy of excitement.

The other guard, who's dragged his wounded mate away from the fence and back on to the tarmac path, now lays him on the ground. Quite forgivably, he turns away for a moment to be sick before fumbling for his walkie-talkie. Then, something he sees away behind the cherry trees makes him stop what he's doing. He freezes for a second, and then he's off and running, disappearing out of shot.

God knows what he was running *from*, but he was heading towards us. We were on the far side of the zoo, sprinting flat out towards the baboon enclosure. Under normal circumstances we'd have met up near by the main block, and who knows? Things might have gone very differently for him – for all of us. As it was, he never got that far.

We could hear noise from all over the zoo by now: attack cries, hoarse belligerent roars and squawks and hoots that ranged across the whole spectrum of aggression. On bits and scraps of tape that follow the guard's progress along the main avenue, you can piece together what's happening. Each enclosure that he passes is filled with shrieking animals, pressed close to bars and fences. More than once the proximity of these malevolent creatures cause him to shy away, take evasive action. The chimps clinging to their chain-link fence scream and hurl excrement at him, and he trips and stumbles, but he's up on his feet and running again within a second.

He looks as if he's scared out of his wits. It would have been something to see what it was, back by the baboon enclosure, that put the fear of God up him that way. When he draws level with the elephants, lined up by the edge of their enclosure and trumpeting ferociously, it's their sheer bulk, I think, that sends him veering off in a different direction, off the main avenue and on to on of the side paths. This is the way to the nocturama, a tunnel sunk below ground level, home of the night creatures.

Manoj saw him sprinting down the brick-lined cutting that leads to the entrance to the tunnel. There's no CCTV inside there: it's too dark in the normal course of events. There's red-light illumination that lets you see the exhibits, but that's all. Only in an emergency are the normal bulbs switched on, from a switch-box by the entrance. And only later, long after it was of any practical use to us, did we remember that fact.

We were still running. From where we were, on the slightly higher ground, we could see the guard disappear into the cutting. What on earth was he doing down there? Thumbing the walkie-talkie switch I panted, 'Manoj?'

'Here.'

'Why's he gone down the tunnel?'

'I don't know. *Wait* –' Manoj sounded rattled.

'What?'

'Did you see that? What's he doing with his clothes off?'

'What? Where?'

'... Never mind,' directed Manoj. 'The man that needs your help is over by the baboon compound. Leave that other now. Let him run around the place stark naked if he likes.'

'But –'

But nothing. Already it was too late. From down in the nocturama we could hear the screams. The other guard had run into trouble.

Without thinking I changed course, ran down the slope towards the other entrance to the tunnel. Behind me Peter was arguing with Manoj on the walkie-talkie, but I only had ears for the screaming.

Please God, I was thinking as I ran, *for fuck's sake, no more bother. Just keep a lid on it until we can get these idiots out of here.* I don't know who I was praying to, if that was a prayer. It's not a thing I do. It must have been the screaming that got to me.

It came echoing out of the open-ended tunnel, so piercing and intense that as I drew level with the entrance I actually came to a stop, trying to remember what exactly we kept down there. Insects, bats, moths... nothing dangerous that I could bring to mind. Perhaps the bloke just had a thing about the dark, I told myself. Maybe he just got the fear. But I knew it was worse than that; every shred of instinct told me so. Fifteen years' experience in zoos, maybe. I suspect it was more like two million years' worth of evolutionary impulse.

The screaming stopped abruptly as I reached the head of the steps down into the tunnel. I thought I heard the sound of something running – I was going to say, footsteps, but it's as well to be exact. Something running, down in the dark.

I took one step down, and then another, then found myself unable to go any further. Coming up from that tunnel mouth was a stink like nothing I'd come across in all the years I'd spent around animals. I can hardly describe it, except to say that it reached deep into the ancestral parts of the brain, the centres of instinct and fear. It was stale and cloacal and rotten; it was the smell of must and decay, spoiled meat and sour animal piss. Rising through it like a basenote was the overpowering stink of blood.

Gagging at the stench, I took another few steps down into the tunnel. Peter caught up with me then, and it was easier with him there. We advanced down to the bottom of the steps, and into the nocturama. That stupid little prayer was running through my head still, like a mantra.

It was musty and mildewed and dripping down there. Green slime coated the plastic windows of the exhibits, and there was nowhere near enough light. We walked on into the dark, past moths measuring out the dimensions of their prisons, past fireflies flashing unintelligible signals. On the other side of the tunnel, the chiroptera: avid famished bats that swooped through the lightless recesses and clustered on the dead boughs of artificial trees. Predators and prey in the natural scheme of things. Now, they merely pressed closer to the glass and watched as we advanced.

On we went around the corner, where the stink was mounting. I'd slowed now to something less than walking pace. Had we been going any faster, we'd have fallen over it. It was hard to see in the semidark, but we could make out the shape clearly enough. A man, lying on his back. The red lightbulbs in the animal recesses made the blood seem almost transparent at first. Then Peter focused his flashlight, and we saw what was left of him; which was not a lot. Down in that sewer-smelling tunnel, trapped in such a narrow space with a thing like that... I wonder can you imagine how awful it was? Along the walls, the watching worm-lizards pressed greedily against the windows, tongues darting in and out of their cruel slits of mouths. And everywhere now, through all the length of the tunnel, the fierce reek of blood.

That was really the last straw, so far as the zoo was concerned. One guard dead in the tunnel, horribly mauled by some as yet unidentified predator. Another with the front half of his face chewed off: by a baboon, it was officially decided, though some responsible authorities, Manoj amongst them, begged to differ. These latter pointed out certain aspects of bite radius and attack pattern, and at the back of Manoj's mind – though it never really came up at the inquest – was the behaviour pattern of the other baboons in the enclosure, the temporary submissiveness of the troop leader.

Either way, we were doomed. The local council had been treating us like pariahs for god knows how long, even before the incident. We had animal-rights protestors crawling all over us at the best of times. Now, one man was dead and another maimed for life, and driven half crazy into the bargain. Wouldn't you be? It wasn't our fault, was all we could say in our defence: not that that cut any ice with the police. There was a full investigation, conducted of course in the hot moralistic glow of the media spotlight. That was hardly the best sort of publicity, as I'm sure you can imagine.

We were closed all through the Easter holidays, one of our busiest times, and then to cap it all the Health & Safety Directorate weighed in with their report. They delivered a damning assessment of our operation: among other things, they said the safety of the zoo was thoroughly and irretrievably compromised, that our security measures were demonstrably inadequate, and that we seemed to have no effective control over the movements of the animals, up to and including the most dangerous of the predators. In short, they had no option but to withdraw our public safety certificate, effective immediately.

That was it. In very short order, the council swung the axe, the board of directors resigned, and we were finished. Arrangements were made to flog off the assets and rehouse the animals in zoos around the country. Then the bulldozers would move in, the land would be sold for redevelopment, and a line would be drawn under the whole unfortunate affair. Which brings me more or less up to where we are right now.

These last few weeks and months before the closure have been the strangest of all. We run a skeleton staff – no need for security any more, not without visitors, no need to walk the compound more than once or twice a day. That's our excuse, anyway. The plain and simple fact is, we're scared now. The Health & Safety people were right, to that extent: we *have* lost our grip. Ever since the accident we've effectively lost track of how many animals there are in any given enclosure, at any given time. The most basic rule of zoo security has been breached, utterly and irrevocably it seems. Once darkness falls, animals are loose and roaming across the compound, and they run in strange new packs. It's no longer unusual to see big cats in with ungulates, or birds flocking across species. You'd expect a bloodbath every night, but it never happens.

By the same token, there have been no more attacks on humans since the killing of the guard, but still you can imagine how we feel. It's far from unusual for a keeper on the ground to see something on the path, ahead of him or behind him, towards the hours of dusk, or when mist and rain affect the visibility. At night, we basically cede control of the zoo; we have no choice. It's shameful – we can hardly look at each other sometimes – but it's also an oddly liberating thing to admit it. Peter feels the same way, Graham, even Manoj. After all we've seen, we can't be around these animals for long without getting the creeps.

You feel it at feeding times and during routine medical procedures. Even walking past the enclosures you sense it. A subtle, yet decisive change in the balance of our interaction; a shift in power. Though we're at least nominally free, able to leave at the end of our shifts and drive home to our empty houses in the suburbs, it's hard not to feel claustrophobic, imprisoned. The bars are there to protect us. Have we really come to depend on them so much? It's as if the beasts are the free ones, not us, not any more. As if some inconceivable insight has emancipated them, raised their consciousness to a level no one thought they'd ever reach. Those are Manoj's words, not mine. When he said it to me, just the other day, I asked him what he meant, and he threw up his hands in the air. 'I don't know. I sound like a bloody swami, don't I?'

'You do, a bit,' I said. We were up in the Godseat, watching the closed-circuit.

'Well, look at them,' he said, indicating the lions on the monitor. 'I'm keeping all the tapes, you know. I'm thinking of going back to university, doing my post-grad. I can use them for my thesis.'

'Which will be?'

'I haven't got a title for it yet,' he admitted. 'This. All of this. How they've changed.'

'That'll take some working-out,' I said.

He nodded glumly. 'Tell me about it,' he sighed. It was as if the change came as a personal affront to him. 'Breakdown of the old pack structures. Atypical response patterns in the presence of keepers and other humans. Complete lack of interspecies aggression. It's not natural.'

'That can't be a permanent behavioural shift, though?' I wasn't having that. 'We're not talking about the holy-rollers here, are we? And the lion shall lie down with the lamb?' As I said it, I remembered that evening by the lions' den. I'd thought the boy was a sacrificial lamb of his own appointing, another deluded Daniel driven crazy by too much Sunday school and animal-rights sermonising. Now, I didn't know what to think.

'I'm not sure it is a permanent shift, not in that sense, anyway. But suppose it isn't?' Manoj leaned back from the monitor, ran his hands through his thick black hair. 'That's almost worse, if you think about it.'

'How so?'

'Okay. We observe behavioural patterns in animals, which are the result of millions of years of evolutionary adaptation. Over the last three months, our animals here have demonstrated profound behavioural alterations, across all species, across all hierarchical relationships. Now, we either assume this change is a non-volitional response to external stimuli – that is, they used to behave *this* way, and now they behave *that* way, because there's something in the water, or they all had the same sort of brainstorm, or whatever – or else...'

'Or else?'

Manoj looked as if he was chewing a wasp. 'Or else what we're seeing here is a volitional behaviour shift.'

'You mean – they *decided* to do it?'

'They chose, yes. That would be the other alternative.' I could see Manoj liked this option even less. 'According to that scenario, what we're seeing here would be interpreted as possibly the first recorded instance of altruistic co-operation *across species* towards a common, mutually desirable goal – though what that might be, I have no idea. How could I? Now that sort of conceptualisation would require a level of self-awareness...' He broke off, lost in his own thoughts.

A movement on screen caught my eye. 'Hang on – look there, at the lions. How many are there in those bushes?'

Manoj waved a hand in dismissal. 'Don't bother,' he said resignedly. 'You can't keep track these days. Five, six. Who knows?'

It was true. It was a wilderness in there. Once, it had been a jungle, cut into manageable chunks and fenced in with steel and glass. We used to stand by the windows and listen to the racket, the bellows of frustration, the mournful shrieks and howls. What this new thing is... it's hard to say. More than anything, it feels like the calm before the storm.

We're aware of the consequences, even if we can't fully understand them. Soon, these animals with their strange new behaviours, their disconcerting calm and uncanny self-possession, will be crated up and shipped to a dozen zoos across Europe. What happens if they replicate these new memes in their new surroundings? What if they pass them on?

Over and above that, there's a world beyond the bars. The starlings flock each night in ever-growing numbers above the compound, roosting in the trees as the animals below stare unblinkingly upwards, as if towards the stars, the old bestiary of myths and legends in the sky. Maybe the ancient fables don't hold water any more. Maybe a change has come upon us, and nothing's safe in its cage.

LITTLE LAMBS

Stephen Graham Jones

Stephen Graham Jones (1972–) is an American writer of both stories and novels. His most recent books are *It Came from Del Rio* (2010) and *The Ones That Got Away* (2010). Jones has been a finalist for the Shirley Jackson Award and Black Quill Award, as well as a winner of the Texas Institute of Letters Award and a National Endowment for the Arts Fellow in fiction. His short fiction has appeared in *Cemetery Dance, Asimov's Science Fiction Magazine, Weird Tales,* and multiple best-of-the-year compilations. 'Little Lambs' (2009) is a perfect example of Jones at his chilling and slightly experimental best, evoking, as the story does, both weird classics and more avant garde work from the likes of Mark Danielewski.

We're not supposed to walk through the structure, but for eight years we've been watching it from sixty-two feet away, too. Watching it on so many monitors and at so many wavelengths that sometimes you just want to step outside the bunker, see it with your eyes. Just to be sure it's real, that it's still there.

For reasons of security, our watch only rotates among us four.

The crewcuts we had when first assigned to monitor the structure, they're grown out long and shaggy like our beards. Our BDUs are folded in our lockers. The last inspection was thirteen months ago. We look Wyoming now. Like we know the winter, like the sound of frozen grass breaking under our boots, we don't hear it with our ears anymore, but feel it instead, in the base of our jaws.

Our eyes have gone hollow with longing, too, but we don't blame Wyoming for that. It's more like people with that kind of vacant, yearning stare, they're always drifting to Wyoming. The way the open lands undulate, writhe almost, it's a cadence that feels right to us. After a while, you feel the swells of grass in your chest, I mean. And the sudden drops. And your face doesn't change expression because of it.

The structure seems to fit out here too, like it's always been here.

There are no fences or warning signs around it.

The four acres it occupies is Bureau of Land Management land. In the distance we've seen antelope and sheep and, once, two bull elk, walking with their chins in the air, as if their swept-back racks were unbearably heavy. Two winters ago one of the sheep wandered in from the snow. It was wearing a diaper, because a rancher had pulled it into his trailer with him, to keep it alive.

I opened the first door of the bunker for it, but then Hendrikson took my forearm in his hand, shook his head no, maybe saved us all.

We don't know what's a trick, what's not.

The sheep finally walked away from the door, became a heat signature on our thermal monitor, a yellow-tinged splotch wending into the structure. But standing in the structure is no protection from winter.

What the structure is is rebar and iron girders and I-beams and chain-link. It looks like an unfinished project, like the funding fell through and now it's been abandoned, left to rust back into the earth.

This is why nobody stops.

How long we've been here is ninety-six months.

My daughter Sheila, she's about that old now. When my wife called to report her first steps, there were approximately fourteen relays between her voice and my ear.

I walked out into the night after that, no jacket.

The structure was a skeletal silhouette against the bright sky.

Since we started monitoring it, it's moved north-northeast exactly six and one-eighths inches. It doesn't displace the soil as it goes. In its track, the grass stands as if it's always been there.

On every spectrum we know to look at it with, it appears to be just what it is: iron and steel, the metal guts of a prison built in West Virginia in 1918.

The reason we're here is that, eight and a half years ago, that prison collapsed and killed all seventy-eight prisoners and guards sleeping inside it. The concrete walls just crumbled down on them, as if there was nothing supporting them anymore. Because there wasn't. It had been dreamed away.

Three months later, four Casper men were brought up on charges of killing their friend.

When they were arrested, they were in a bar. Only one of them was drinking. The other three were just sitting there, holding drinks as if they know they were supposed to be drinking them, but the ice or the glass or the alcohol, it all had all just become too heavy.

Their testimony was that they were collecting scrap metal from some old place on BLM land, and their friend, an ex-lumberjack named Manny, he kept walking down all the halls trying to get an echo or something, and then he just suddenly wasn't there anymore.

Without a body to support foul play, or any kind of motive, or history of malice, the four men were never convicted. Instead, four different men were assigned to watch a structure that nobody remembered, that wasn't registered at the county courthouse, and didn't show up on satellite photos as recent as four months before. The structure that would turn out to have the same floorplan as that West Virginia prison.

What Hendrikson thinks is that what the lumberjack did was turn just the right series of corners, like cracking a code, and that the next time he looked up, it was to a chunk of concrete falling down onto him. A whole ceiling of concrete.

Maybe.

The first time I placed my naked palm to one of the I-beams of the structure, I was crying.

Later I would watch a recording of myself in infrared, touching the I-beam.

On the recording, of course, there's no sound.

What I was saying, though, was *please.*

Some nights Ben forgets he's sleeping, and sits at the controls, his fingers running over the board.

Used to, we'd wake him, try to make him understand, but now we know he just recalibrates a lens or two then goes back to bed. And it's usually a lens that needs recalibrating.

For a while, Hendrikson had me believing I was doing that too, but then I tied my feet together with knotted-together socks one night, proved him wrong. Unless of course I retied them in my sleep as well.

Our commanding officer, Russell, he's tried to kill himself forty-two times now. We know all the ways to bring him back.

Because of Sheila, I've never tried to kill myself.

I think of that sheep in a diaper more than I should, though.

We don't know if it ever left the structure or not. Maybe, just on dumb animal luck, it stumbled onto that series of halls that the lumberjack did, and went to someplace warmer.

The next morning, anyway, the structure was unchanged.

And it's a lie that I've never tried to kill myself, of course. I just did all that before coming here. It's out of my system now.

The joke we still say is what we were originally told: that this would be a temporary assignment. That relief's being trained as we speak.

My wife's name is Joella, and Maryann, and

Wanda. Her face mixes with all the other girls I've known.

She's living with a guy off-base now.

She says she's sorry.

The one time I tried to run away, Hendrikson tracked me on satellite until I collapsed, and then he walked out with a sled and pulled me back, took my shift.

When I asked him why, he said it was because I was the life of the party, man, and then slapped me on the upper arm, cupped my shoulder in his large hand.

The northern lights with the naked eye are a curtain of light.

Your lips can turn blue, watching them, so that if you smiled, it would hurt. But smiling wouldn't be enough, either.

One of the ways Russell tried to kill himself was climbing as high as he could up the structure, and jumping off.

We nursed him back to health. Ben even gave him two pints of his own blood.

The structure moves so slowly you can only see its progress on paper.

It neither speeds up nor slows down.

If you get Hendrikson drunk enough, he'll explain it to you, the structure. How what happened was, one night some prisoner, probably a new one, he laid in bed all day just thinking about getting out. That that occupied his whole and complete mind. But he wasn't thinking rocket packs and helicopters or any of that. What that prisoner wanted to do was walk out. And, for that to happen, the prison would have to fall down around him.

Meaning, after he fell asleep, he somehow wished the prison gone.

Only he wasn't strong enough, or wasn't particular enough in his wish, or didn't word it right, or – and this is what I think – only metal of a certain age can be physically transported in a dream like that.

Of course this prisoner, what he really did that night was kill himself.

When Hendrikson tells this story, Russell leans forward on his cot and stares at him with his face turned half away.

Of the four of us, I'm the only one with a child.

The reason for this is Sheila was born after I was assigned here, to a woman who was only my girlfriend of two weeks then. She's my wife now, yeah – we were married on the telephone, and by mail, because the government wouldn't pay for her healthcare any other way – but I don't know that she's ever used my name.

The pictures of Sheila, though.

I can tell which is which by how they feel.

The time Ben tried to run away, he was sleeping, so it doesn't count, I don't think, though he insists it does.

We got in a fight over this. It broke my nose.

Afterwards, we didn't talk for weeks, until, finally, just to prove himself right, he ran off into a blizzard.

Where I found him was curled up behind a shrub that was a sieve for the wind.

I held him to me until he was warm.

The northern lights on infrared are nothing. According to Russell, who saw them from the top of the structure, they're not what they seem to be, the lights, but he won't tell us anymore than that, even with vodka in him.

It doesn't matter, though. For the lights not to be what they seem to be they would have to be seeming to be something in the first place.

Ben knows I walk through the structure for twenty minutes each night, but if I pretend to be asleep then he doesn't say anything to me about it.

Whether he tells the others or documents it in the log, I don't know.

The only thing we know for sure about the structure is that if you bolt a lightning rod to it, if you bolt *two hundred* lightning rods all over it, so it bristles, still, when the lightning finally comes months later, it'll strike our antenna instead, which is four meters lower.

This gives us faith that our watch is worthwhile.

Snow coats the structure like it coats everything in Wyoming, though. And – we're not supposed to know this either – you can cut it with a torch, just like regular steel. The gas and smoke that rose from it as we were cutting, we saved it in an upside down jar, and were going to keep it forever until Russell tried to kill himself one night by breathing it in all at once.

It didn't do anything to him.

It's embarrassing to try to kill yourself and have it not work out, I think. But it's good to not be dead too.

Whatever part of our rations we don't finish, Russell always eats.

Whether he came from a large family or grew up poor or both, or whether this is another, longer suicide attempt, we don't know, and don't ask.

If you could somehow live off light, cut it up on your plate and fork it in, that's what I would want to do, I think. Not because it would taste good or be filling, but because a little girl, watching her father do that, she wouldn't say anything, would just watch, her eyes wide with wonder, and she would never forget it for however long she'd live. Which would maybe be forever.

What I don't tell Hendrikson, even though it's regulation too, and we've made promises besides, is that a few nights ago, walking through the structure during my shift, I saw a shape walking ahead of me. Not if I looked straight on, but he was there.

It was the lumberjack.

When I stopped walking, he looked back.

The way I knew he was real was that he wasn't holding a double-edged axe, like all the lumberjacks from my childhood did.

He wasn't lost, either.

'Tad,' he called back to me.

That's my name.

I looked away and he was gone.

He's not on any of the recordings, either. I checked.

What Ben thought I was doing, stopping like that in the hall, I don't know.

I did cry that night though, for some reason. Finally Hendrikson came over to my bunk and laid down beside me and touched my shoulder like he does, and then that made me cry more and harder.

It's nothing unusual in the bunker, though, crying like that.

You just have to ride it out.

That night I didn't dream of the sheep in the diaper, but I wanted to. I don't know if that counts or not.

If you look at the structure long enough, you lose a kind of perspective and it just becomes a tangle of rust-colored lines. They don't move or anything, and it's all in your head anyway, but – it's like if you say a word enough times, it starts to lose meaning. And then, the next time somebody says it just in normal conversation, you'll get a dull jolt, like you've got a funny story associated with that word, but then you won't be able to remember it and people will just think you've maybe had enough to drink already.

That's how it is with the structure. You get drunk on it. And then you laugh a little, because, for the four of you, it still is what it always was: a prison.

But then you think maybe it's more, too.

And you don't tell anybody, even your best friend.

And it's winter of course, but this is Wyoming, too. Even when it's not winter, it's winter.

Whatever you're planning, though – you're afraid to even say it in your head, because somebody might steal it – Russell messes it up by making everybody get their gear on and do the drill he made up. All it is is walking up and down the halls of the path of rocks we've laid out to the north of the structure. They perfectly mirror, down to the inch, the floorplan of the structure. To the east, in more rocks, is the slightly smaller floorplan of the second floor. To the south, the single room of the third floor – the watchtower, Russell calls it. He's the only one who can stand there.

We didn't use the land west of the structure because Russell's superstitious.

And, though the rocks are tall, still, we have to dig them out until our mittens are crusted with ice.

What Russell thinks is the same thing he always thinks: that he's cracked the code, figured it out.

So what we do is tie strings between two of us, while the third watches the structure and Russell directs.

The idea is that when we unlock whatever's here, there'll be some glimmer or something in the real structure.

Russell's theory is that whatever happened,

it wasn't because of the structure, but because of whatever pattern that one inmate walked the day before the prison fell down on him.

By the time we're done, our eyelashes are frozen stalks, our beards slush.

In the kitchen, Russell tries to stab his wrist with a dull fork, but his blood is sluggish, his skin over it calloused, tired.

Hendrikson says if we don't make him clean it up himself, he'll never learn.

We don't write any of this down in the log.

My daughter is almost nine. I say this out loud to Ben one night, but he's sleepwalking, sleep-*monitor*ing, so I don't think it really registers. But then he says her name back to me in his toneless voice.

I stand, watching him adjust a dial, and, because it's either hit him in the back of the head or walk away, I walk away.

If you make your hand into a fist and blow into the tunnel of your palm, you can calm down from almost anything. It doesn't matter what your other hand's doing. It could be playing piano or cooking bacon or any of a hundred other things.

What I finally decide is that Ben saying my daughter's name like that, it means something. There are no accidents in the bunker. Not after nearly nine years.

Instead of just leaving Hendrikson without saying anything, I walk by his bunk to tell him bye while he's sleeping, but see that he's pulled the covers up from his feet. What's under them, tucked up against his wall, are powdery-white bricks, like the kind you build a fireplace from.

I stare at them and stare at them.

In the pictures we have of the old prison, before it crumbled, it's made of these exact same bricks.

What this means, God.

Is the structure growing back?

Are all the men going to still be inside, sleeping, or will they be dead?

But – Hendrikson.

What I think is that whatever bricks the structure's been able to call across the void to itself, he's been sneaking them back to his bunk.

Because he doesn't want our watch to be over?

Because he's afraid of the structure ever getting complete?

I lean against the wall by his bunk. I'm sweating.

In the bathroom, I towel it all off, keep nodding to myself, about what I'm not sure.

Ben tells me nighty-night as I shuffle past his chair. Like every other night, I don't say anything, just keep moving, a moth with no wings.

In the snow and the wind I just stand for a long time, my fingertips shoved up into my armpits, my breath swirling away to wrap around the planet.

The night I saw the lumberjack, I remember all the turns I made. It's something you learn to do, something you learn to do without really meaning to.

And I know that Ben's watching me, and know that he knows I know he's watching me, so I try to just stare straight ahead, not shake my head *no* or anything.

And then I duck into the wind, walk ahead to the structure, and step through the east-facing cell I started in that one night, and, and the trick is, I think, the way I remember it anyway, is that I'm mopping, and that I keep looking back to see my trail of wetness, and that's how I remember.

Two hours later, he's standing there at his end of the hall, the lumberjack. Manny.

My jaw is trembling, my heart in my throat.

Where I don't belong, I know, is Wyoming.

All he's doing is staring at me, too. To see each other, we have to look sideways, not straight on, like we're each suspicious.

For him, I think, it's still the night he came to salvage metal.

What I am, then, is an authority, the owner of the structure maybe, who saw flashlights bobbing through all this scrap metal.

I don't know where the prisoners are, or the guards. Or West Virginia.

What I do know is that I've left my coat by Hendrikson's bunk. Or in the bathroom.

The way I know this is that Manny approaches, keeping close to one side of the hall, which is as open to the wind as any other part, that he approaches and offers me the second of the two flannel shirts he's wearing.

I take it, wrap it around my shoulders without pushing my hands through the sleeves, and Manny nods to me, smiles with one side of his face.

According to our training, the shirt I'm wearing isn't a shirt, but an artifact to be catalogued, processed, dissected.

But it's warm, from him.

I close my eyes to him in thanks, and then, when he's shuffling away, looking for his echo, waiting for his voice to come back to him, I get him to turn around somehow. Not with my voice, I don't think, though my mouth's open. But it doesn't matter. What does is that he waits for me to make my way closer, still pushing the idea of the mop, and then takes what I give him, holding it tight by the corner, against the wind: a picture of Sheila.

For a long time he studies it, then looks up to me, and then, behind him, there's a brick along the edge of the hall where there's never been a brick before.

I only notice this because I've been trained to.

'Yours?' he says, holding the picture up, and I nod, say that she looks like her mother, that her mother's a real beauty, and then I look behind me to the idea of the trail of wetness, just so I don't get lost in here like he has.

When I come back around, he's gone.

What this looks like to Ben, I have no idea, and don't care either. We don't make eye contact as I pass his station anyway. At the kitchen table, Russell has all of our pills, antibiotics and vitamins and mood-regulators, lined up in the floorplan of the structure. What he's doing is taking them one by one, as if he's walking through. Since the last two times, though, they're filled with confectioner's sugar. He'll get a cavity, maybe.

I don't make eye contact with him either, just feel my way to my bunk, lean over Hendrikson to put this next brick with all his.

'Yours,' I whisper, almost smiling, and he stirs, feeling me over him, but doesn't wake, and, truly, I don't know how long we can go on like this. But I don't know what else we could be doing, either.

SAVING THE GLEEFUL HORSE

K. J. Bishop

K. J. Bishop (1972–) is an Australian writer and artist. In 2004, her neo-Decadent fantasy novel *The Etched City* was nominated for a World Fantasy Award and she won the William L. Crawford Award, the Ditmar Award for Best Novel, and the Ditmar Award for Best New Talent. Her work has appeared in several publications including *Leviathan 4*, *Fantasy* magazine, and *Subterranean* magazine. Most infamously, her novella 'Maldoror Abroad' appeared in *Album Zutique*; the story riffed on the original *Les Chants de Maldoror* (1869) by Isidore Lucien Ducasse under the pen name 'Comte de Lautréamont'. Her tale 'Saving the Gleeful Horse' (2010) shares affinities with Decadent modes of writing, including the Alfred Kubin excerpt that opened *The Weird*.

Children are cruel. No one who has lived in the world need ask for proof of that. So it is nothing for them to beat a living creature – a rare, marvellous creature at that – to death. They do so in order to seize the treasure inside it, but one sees the pleasure they take in this assassination of life, even before the plunder starts. Their laughter bounces from yard-wall to yard-wall and their eyes shine darkly as they beat the animal, which has done nothing to them, with wooden sticks and swords, until holes open in its body and the prizes – caramels, toys, game money printed with pictures of wrestlers and cartoon characters – rain down into their hands.

I am Molimus. I live under the bridge where the day-boats go from wet and wooden Bracklow to the foot of the sweeping stone stair going up the hill to Firmitas and the military school.

I am called Molimus the Great by some here in Bracklow, in recognition of my height and strength. My shirt is made of four men's shirts sewn together, and an eight-pound cheese wheel fits in the palm of my hand. By profession I trade in flotsam, which I catch under the bridge in these great hands of mine and sell at the Pauper's Forum up by Shindy Estate.

Because of this occupation, which keeps me under the bridge watching the water from morning until late at night, I oftentimes see the dead animals. If the husks are not burnt, people toss them into the river. I see them on holidays, especially, when the slaughtered numbers are high, but they are killed all year round.

To look at them! Never did dreams supply such a zoo of little spotted and striped horses and chequered gazelles, sky-blue lions, dawn-pink bears, gallant golden beetles, chivalrous silver anteaters! I have even seen elephants amongst them, and star-shaped beasts that must have come from the carved waves of the sea before they were captured and hung up to be put to death.

To see their poor empty bodies makes me cry into the water – sometimes so much that I think the tears of Molimus could turn the river salty.

I can't even salvage them for trading. The bodies last for very little time after they have yielded up the ghost. The husks are as diaphanous as cellophane, and any part submerged below the water dissolves like bread in soup.

I had never thought to see a live one that wasn't already hanging in a yard, soon to die. But that is what happened. It was an October night, a while after sundown, when the day-boats were back at their moorings and the water was full of the dark medicinal colour of an overcast sky. I saw the head of a little horse, banded in red, blue, white and gold like the flag of some merry knight, tossing on the river waves – another dead victim of a party, I assumed, until I came to see the striped legs that were churning the water.

Despite his predicament there was nothing frightful about his looks, as I saw when his head turned towards me. Far from showing panic, he gave me a game sort of grin and rolled his eye as if to say, 'It's the world! What can you do?'

It was a simple thing to reach out and carry him into my little hut of boards and bark, where I wrapped him in a blanket and set him in front of the oil stove to get dry and warm.

I had saved a life and that life therefore became my responsibility. I did all I could to nurse the little striped horse, who I named the Gleeful Horse, but I could see my efforts coming to nothing. He was as full of holes as a sieve and his legs were twisted. I bound his wounds with clean rags and tried to feed him, but he had no appetite, despite his steady good cheer.

It became clear to me that I would have to take the bus out to Barrage Cross to get help from near there. I went in the early morning and carried the Gleeful Horse in a string bag. He seemed to enjoy the sight of the green market gardens of Shindy Back through the windows of the bus, and as we drove through the chalk hills that roll away behind the gardens his fiddle-shaped nostrils and his round hindquarters twitched, as if in his own mind he was galloping about out there on the world's green grass.

From the Barrage Cross shops I walked out of the village, into the trees, and down the little grey weedy paths through the birch and buckthorn, going by the way that leads to the Garth of the Aorist: where trunk and branch turn, by and rumly by, into pillar and vault, and the path passes into the shade of stone arcades forming a four-sided cloister around a garth choked high with enormous brambles.

As you must, I walked around the cloister with the sun a certain number of times, then against the sun another number, then with the sun again, so that the brambles withdrew underground, all the thorny bundles coming apart and slithering below in one rush as if a giant in the earth had them on a rope (the effect on the eye is striking). After this, where all was a wild saw-toothed muddle just a moment or two ago, in another moment the lawn of trefoil and clover grew, which grows no matter the season – as dainty a green spread as you could wish for a picnic or a wedding. Upon the grass, as settled as a hen in the middle of the sweet-smelling lawn, there appeared the dwelling that appears: a round, rose-bosomed hut of dry-stone, having a chimney at the rear and one doorless doorway at the front, facing the coming visitor across the green court.

Entering this shelter, half house, half dovecote, as it were, with the Gleeful Horse in the string bag under my arm, I tugged my cap to the White Ma'at, the last Ma'at.

Whoever first painted the omen-card where she is shown as a figure seated with legs crosswise in front of a painted hearth must have seen her, or been advised by someone who had; at any rate, I have never found her arranged other than in this way when I come to her house.

The White Ma'at: a woman, or a woman-shaped thing, built in a long and heavy way, with a tall forehead like a white wall and a knotty blue vein labouring up it. What lies on the other side is a great store of irregular, wonderful knowledge; a cellar provisioned with all the vintages of magic. What she doesn't see through her milky cataracts would fit in a baby's sock.

She already knows about the Gleeful Horse.

'That is a treasure animal,' she says, even before I've finished pulling him out of the bag. He has no fear of her; he gives even the White Ma'at his qualmless grin. Nor does he mind that she doesn't grin back. When she taps on his bandaged belly with a sharp knuckle he only rolls his eye and winks at me. He makes no fuss even when the

Ma'at prises his mouth open and squints inside. Her parsnip-white fingers find something under his tongue. A toy – a plastic ring with a false emerald. She shows it to me and puts it back.

'When all their treasure is gone, they die,' she says simply.

My poor horse, having to hang onto that uncomfortable lump. I suppose that if he swallowed it, it might fall out one of the holes in his side when the bandages I put on come loose, as they not infrequently do.

I take him from the White Ma'at and sit with him in my lap, expecting her to offer me a healing charm or a recipe for physick. But instead, she tells me:

'You mustn't blame the children. They don't see that this is a living thing, Molimus.'

'They do see,' I say in reply, uncomfortably, for it isn't really safe to argue with the White Ma'at. 'And they enjoy turning it into a dead thing.'

'Molimus,' she starts, and I know she is going to defend them, and I can't fathom why – 'Molimus, you have a foot in both worlds. And in one world this animal has life, and you see it, and I see it, but in the other world it has no life, it is a thing. You see more than most persons, true, but that's damning with faint praise. Your eyes have a picture of cruelty on the inside. You see that picture clearly, and because of it, see other things unclearly.'

I think of what I might say and choose silence. When I think of how that picture came to be there on the inside of my eyes, I am certain beyond any possibility of error that children know what is alive, and moreover that they are disposed to do harm with this knowledge. I'm surprised that the Ma'at doesn't know.

But in any case, I don't see what this has to do with my horse and his needs.

Then, rare for her, she asks a question: 'Why do you want to save that thing?'

I feel like answering that I didn't come all this way to talk to a town matron with ordinary vulgar ideas. I wish I could hide the thought, but she says, 'What do I care about your dull thoughts, Molimus?' Her hands fall at her sides after she speaks. The unstrung gesture is not one that should belong to her. She isn't like herself at all today, so that I dare to ask:

'Is anything wrong, Ma'at?'

There's nothing to like about the distracted way she pinches at the folds of her clothing, as if the white wool were full of seeds and burrs, nor the way her jaw goes around like a cow's chewing cud. Thankfully, both motions cease and she retires her hands to her sides again – they look better hanging than twitching.

There's no reason why the Ma'at shouldn't be tired, of course. She was old a long time ago, and her life has certainly had its ups and downs. But it's too much to believe that she is actually infirm in either body or mind. Or that she is changing. The world changes. The White Ma'at doesn't.

'The White Ma'at doesn't,' she echoes me aloud. I can't tell whether she is agreeing or mocking me.

I try to think of nothing, while her eyes move back and forth under the cataracts, probably following the movements of figures she sees in her head.

It comes to me that she would surely have dismissed me by now if she didn't have any magic for the Gleeful Horse. So perhaps she wants to bargain, after all, and has a peculiar way of saying so today.

The White Ma'at is a great one for bargaining. When she was young, as they tell it in Bracklow and Shindy, she lost a battle that she shouldn't have lost. Rather than blame herself she blamed her armies and cursed those of her loyal men who were left alive. She cast a spell that pushed them into the chalk hills like raisins in a pudding, so that they all died in the white dark.

After that she slept, and was captured whilst asleep. She was to have been hung and burnt, but she escaped – by means of a bargain with Prince November himself. That's why she never leaves her house in the midst of the cloister. Prince November keeps her there. He knows she'd escape from him forever if he let her wander even as far as to the paths in the birch wood, never mind to the bus stop at Barrage Cross. Gossip says he drinks knowledge from the vein on her forehead at night and uses it for his business in the world.

The White Ma'at says she doesn't care about my dull thoughts. But if I had some thoughts that glimmered a little? Perhaps she wants payment or part-payment in that coin. She is getting fretful, it may be, like a bored child, sick of her boxed-in life, and wants to hear a wonder-tale. I would rather believe that than believe she has changed, or is changing.

But how to give wonder to a creature like her?

'Well, White Ma'at,' I begin at last, 'as for why I want to save him, it's like this …'

From the seed of the name I gave him there grows a tale of happiness and delight that was lost to the world even before the long-ago age when the Ma'ats ruled from their halls where Shindy Estate is now. The gist is that my Gleeful Horse will bring this happiness back to us.

Or the beginning of the tale grows, anyway, issuing from me like a run of notes from a whistle. I use my best words – words and devices of speech I have heard during my life and remembered for their decorative and noble effects but have never had occasion to use aloud.

My efforts sound very handsome to me – so handsome that they even sound truthful.

But before I am much past the beginning, the White Ma'at snaps 'Enough!' so sharply that I jump. In the glare of her cataracts, my story lies dead. If it had been a treasure animal it would have been not beaten with wooden weapons but dispatched in an instant with one swing of a real sword.

I want to cry out that this is not a game. It's all I can do to bite my tongue. I can't make myself not think of putting my huge hands around the neck of the White-Ma'at and shutting her throat for her. Of course, if I tried something so mad, she might drum me into the ground like the biggest raisin of all. I feel sick, not for my sake but for the sake of my horse, whose winking eye shows how little he understands.

But the White Ma'at only twitches her lips, as if she were amused at last.

'Let's not tell the end of the story,' she says, and her voice is calm. And she, then: 'You must fill that sorry thing with treasures again, Molimus.' I don't like her calling him a sorry thing. But I hearken to what she tells me, now that she is speaking about the Gleeful Horse.

'You don't know at all why you want to save it. But I know on your behalf. The future will work through you, Molimus. Who would have imagined that? Replenish his treasures – you have your work, Molimus the Great. Replenish them abundantly.'

'And how shall I do that?' I ask gruffly. Her insults and sneering tone have rubbed me up the wrong way, and I can't hide it – but I think she was telling the truth that she doesn't care about my thoughts, even if they're disrespectful. 'Should I buy caramels and trinkets and feed them to him?'

'No,' she answers to my words. 'The world inside him is yet another world. You can't see it, Molimus. These things, these nothings that fall out of a treasure animal, are altogether different when they're inside him. In the world inside him, they are more like stars. It is elements – starlike pieces – of this sort that you must gather and feed to him. He has one left, as you saw. One is not enough.'

I feel a qualm, as if conspiracy sits there with us. The Ma'at sounds more like herself again, but I am suddenly ill with a spasm that feels like shame. I can't say whether this is the reasonable compunction that belongs properly to the healthy conscience of a man, or an imaginative, fanciful shame. Whatever it is, here in the Garth of the Aorist it has the shape of a real, solid thing stuck in my gullet, making me gag around it. My tongue feels it as it comes up with a mouthful of bile. It is annular, with an embellishment on one side: a sort of ornamented sphincter. I spit the plastic ring out onto the floor, where its stones of pure false red blink sleepily in the weak sun that has placed one foot through the opening in the wall.

The White Ma'at picks it up and makes it vanish between her fingers like a street magician doing a coin trick.

'Was that a starlike piece?' I ask.

She says no, it wasn't, but it was something I should feel better for having got out of me.

And waits, until I ask where I should find them.

Within every living thing is a starlike piece. Those within human beings are bright, and those within children are the brightest of all. As people age, the starlike parts grow dim as though with distance, except in the cases of certain geniuses and half-wits. At first I didn't understand how children can be so cruel and their starlike parts so bright, but the White Ma'at, who told me these things when she gave me the Wine of Smoke, said that she knew nothing of stars being kind, only of their being powerful.

She asked me three times if I really wished to drink the Wine of Smoke.

The Wine of Smoke was acquired by her, hundreds of years ago, from a man who combined the talents of wizard and vintner, who had come to the Garth of the Aorist to bargain with her. She intended to use it to escape from the confinement that Prince November had forced on her. But even after drinking a draft and becoming smoke, she found that she still could not penetrate past the cloister. The White Ma'at spent more than a century in sorcerous meditation of the most strenuous kind to turn her body back to flesh.

For someone who is not a sorcerer there is no such possibility of return. And the gift of death is lost. If one who had drunk the Wine of Smoke were captured and, for example, shut within a bottle and the bottle sent deep into the earth, he would be stuck in that bind until the end of time. This, said the White Ma'at, is the penalty I should expect to suffer if I ever break our agreement.

As if I would ever break it – for all is well with the Gleeful Horse. He greets me leaping and grinning when I return home in the early mornings. Even before I get back, I hear him whinny merrily when he smells me coming through the fog on the river.

I think he has forgotten that he was ever hurt. There's no rancour or fear in him, nothing timorous or furtive. He breathes in the starry motes – they look like sun-kissed thistledown – through his fiddle-shaped nostrils. He capers all around the bridge and the docks, rolling his eyes and winking, brave as a flag, friend to cats and dogs, and that is as it should be. I only wish I could pet him; but in the afternoons I lead him by my scent to Shindy Park, and the old ladies who feed the ducks there make a great fuss of him.

The starlike pieces don't last very long – this being because they aren't his own, the White Ma'at taught me – so I must keep putting them inside him, as she told me to do. For each one that I give to him, I must take another to give to her.

Over in Firmitas they shut all their gilded and vermilion windows at night, and in Bracklow and Shindy they hang up charms next to fireplaces. On both sides of the river they talk in whispers about the smoke that sticks to the life of children and pulls it away. The ones the smoke touches sicken and die quickly. Before they die they change, becoming like wax paper figures. You could light candles in them and they would be child-shaped lanterns. Because they become hollow, like treasure animals, the sick ones are euphemistically called Treasure Children.

Bracklow wonders where Molimus the Great has gone, but I'm still around, in the smoke of chimneys and bus exhausts, and in the engine smoke of the day boats ferrying the folk who work as maids and porters in Firmitas. I believe I know what the White Ma'at does with her share of the starlike pieces, for I've seen Prince November in his tin-shingled carriage out on the chalk hills more than once, with his retinue in dun and black, driving toward the birch wood. He and she have come to a new agreement, I think, whereby she is paying off her debts.

The vein on her forehead has become a lode of white gold: often swollen, but sometimes flat, so that the gossip about Prince November drinking from her has gained more currency amongst those who go to see her. But not so many do these days. Unthinkable as it is, she has changed. She is nearly always queer now. I never know whether she will be distracted or depressed or silly when I come with the lovely motes for her to inhale. She wears the ring I coughed up, and when she's in her whimsical mood she steals admiring looks at it, as if it were a real ruby on her finger.

I would not have believed it possible, but since the emptying sickness has been in the world the old game of murdering treasure animals has fallen out of favour. Ball games and swap cards are popular now, and pageant games.

In the pageants, a character called Grinning Horse has for some time been a playground hero.

He is the one who saves children by breathing in the smoke before it can reach them. He is also the one who, by the laws of the games, is the bold opponent of a certain Prince No-Never, and his old nurse, the Wheat Mate, and defeats them (as he defeats policemen, schoolmasters, and other vile enemies – often in rough and bloody ways, children being what they are). For months, I could make no pretence to having an explanation for this, but eventually I began to hear things. It seems that the Treasure Children themselves started the invention of Grinning Horse, Prince No-Never and the Wheat Mate. If what I have heard is true, the Treasure Children dream of these characters after the smoke visits them, and they say the smoke gives them the dreams in exchange for their lives. The dreams, and the part played by the smoke, they confide about to friends and siblings before they are seized by the silence that comes with the hollowing effect of the illness, and the accounts are reinforced by others who fall sick.

I remember the White Ma'at's words concerning the future, and how my never-finished tale of the Gleeful Horse sounded true when I tried to tell it.

So perhaps it will all be just as I imagined.

AFTERWEIRD: THE EFFICACY OF A WORM-EATEN DICTIONARY

China Miéville

How should we conduct investigations? We need access to the innards of whatever we would understand, but if we take a scalpel to their skins we change them, and the only thing we end up investigating then is something open and bleeding – as in very different grotesque ways both Heym's and Shea's dissection stories here make clear. Faced with objects whose terms and natures are not self-evident what we need is some variant of diaphanisation, that enzymatic process that makes transparent the flesh, makes the body a window. This is true of our heuristic terms and functions as much as of the objects they are intended to illumine. It's as true of

our microscope-machines

(those were not here a moment ago, were they?) as of the microbes we stare at through them. We should wish, in other words, not only to examine history – cultural, literary, whatever – through some filter, but to turn our gaze on that filter itself. This book you hold is a collection of 'The Weird'? Which is what, please? How to proceed?

Etymology as a making-transparent. Word-history is one of the most common

little doors-in-the-tree(-or-wall)

scholars start by opening. 'This is a study of "Blah" or "Blahist" study', a book announces. 'The dictionary tells us that the root of the word "Blah"…' Etc. So: the Weird. Running a rough plough through

the archaeology

of language brings up 'Wyrd', that Anglo-Saxonism of knotting cause and effect, as cats-cradle intricate and splendid as any Sutton Hoo buckle: Fate, Destiny. Sometimes even Doom. Personified in *those* women on *that* blasted heath, the implication is of a tug at some

slub

in the life-weft, the snarl of interweaving, the ineluctable. 'Wyrd', as the great Old English poem 'The Wanderer' insists, 'bið ful aræd!' Fate is inexorable. Sometimes cruel, desserts wrought not always according to our own morality, but part of something utter and *total*. The Wyrd is perhaps not holy, but it is whole-y.

Thus Wyrd-armed we go back to the Weird, in this book in your hands, and in the world itself. We sensitise ourselves to certain moments. Those that we experience not merely as odd, or strange, or surprising, but as *weird*. We shove a

fate-shaped key

at the Weird keyhole (or pry at the Weird

doorframe with a fate-shaped jimmy

). Beyond, testing our hypothesis, we find among other artefacts: the presences of Blackwood and Morrissette's 'Familiars', Krohn's insects, the family-monsters of Butler's 'Bloodchild', oneiric patchworks of biology and impossibility; the baleful spooks of modernity, in 'Smoke Ghost' that have, spuriously efficient as the industry they haunt, bypassed the necessity of dying or living in the first place; the uneasy almost-recognition of the punishments in Lanagan's 'Singing My Sister Down'; the fungal universe of Bernanos; the displacements of Leman's 'Window' and Jones' 'Little Lambs'; vividly present unplaces ('The Shadowy Street'; 'The Night Wire'); unclearly suggestive fables (Chapman and Bhêly-Quenum); opaque punishments (Kafka and Sansom); lessons and items of all kinds. Bearing the meaning we've learnt, our

weapon

pilfered from the Anglo-Saxon wordhoard, we go to war against incomprehension. 'Weird is Wyrd,' we say, and see how this clarifies.

And after a long time trying to apply that as insight we nod and stop and consider again and must finally ask: What if etymology is fucking useless?

What if it's worse than useless?

What if thinking through the prehistory of the term 'Weird' is utterly counterproductive? If the shift that occurred some time in the 19th Century is not an evolution of meaning but a cleft, a repudiation, a revolution, a violence, a break? If Weird is the ungrateful

feral child

of Wyrd, raised by Modernity's wolves? And what if this semiotic abandonment means no Oedipal drama, no tedious lullaby of reconciliation or loss or mutual learning but instead an unexpectedly clear, debate-ending statement about the heritability of meme-content: that there is none at fucking all. That the Weird is not a new iteration of fatefulness, but its rebuke, a contingency, a newness that shreds the sealed totality its parental theme pretended existed. The fact of the Weird is the fact that the worldweave is ripped and unfinished. Moth-eaten, ill-made. And that through the little tears, from behind the ragged

edges

, things are looking at us.

The Weird is neither holy nor whole-y. It is hole-y.

Like flies in rot, frogs in the rich mud of the Nile, like mice in spoiled grain, the things that watch – Outer Monstrosities, Great Old Ones, as Hodgson and Lovecraft had it – were spontaneously generated. Larvae budding in the fruit of the world-loom. Modernity weaves a moth-eaten cloth, and it is the final instars of those bad eaters that watch us through rifts their maggoty baby selves made.

Weird is anti-Wyrd. A subtraction of the D (always a weak letter, prone to replacement), and its usurpation by M. Weird ≠ Wyrd. Weird = Wyrm. This is the vermiformalist fact of the matter.

The dwellers in holes are not punishments. That they watch us is as random as a rip, the shape of threadbareness. That is the Weird: that we are watched from holes.

You feel eyes on you. Weird is an affect. We know it when we feel it. It's constrained neither by 'level' of culture – there is pulp here, and there is 'haute' literature, by Bruno Schulz, Tagore, Leonora Carrington – nor by nationality, nor subject matter. Certainly there are monsters but there is emotion and character and monsterless places too. Supernature is strong, but by no means the only transmitter of that alien unease.

It is not uncanny – we might post-facto decode whatever metaphor we make of it, but its interior is less repressed than unrecognised. The Weird is not the un- but the abcanny.

This canon changes. Its edges are as protean, its membranes as permeable and oozing as the breaching biology of Lovecraft's Dunwich Horror. We interpret it, of course: our minds are meaning-factories. But the ground below them is hole-y. There are cracks and chaos, meaningquakes. The metaphors we walk on are

scree

.

In this book is a Weird Canon. It is not exactly yours – how could it be? We don't fray the world quite the same, and different things watch each of us. Nor is it quite mine. But we recognize it, and recognize the ways we don't recognize it. The same book, read twice, in different frames of mind, might be once quotidian, unthreatening, and the next time – was it our own urgent fingers that snagged those threads? – frayed. Weird.

Weird travels with us, each reader a Typhoid Mary in every library. It passes from us into pages, infects healthy fiction (pretend for a moment there might be any such thing). A virus of holes, a burrowing infestation, an infestation of burrowingness itself, that births its own pestilential hole-dweller.

There's a slip again.

Pick ourselves up, try to regain footing. Where are we? The world is a many-shelved library. The shovel-handed Things of Johnson's 'Far Below', dholes, conqueror worms, cloth-maggots, bookworms. Burrowers have various names. They chew through books, and leave their exudations, that spoor of anxiety. We have all felt that tacky residue.

We're tempted to hunt

Patient Zero

. Is there a culprit in this library? Which book was first sick? (Of course they're all in terrible health.)

Turn to Margaret Irwin's 'The Book'. Ultimately it alleges malevolent orders, a struggle not to succumb, a heroic assertion of familial piety. Such nostrums are resilient, and do no real harm. But that is far the least, the weakest weird of this most weird Weird Tale. An extensive postscript. The story's pinnacle is its magnificent vision of the viral Weird, a bad sensibility breaching the cover-membranes of books, spreading the disease dis-ease. So that, slowly, the shelf of abutting volumes become nasty stories.

Like the proto-postmodern rewriting of *Don Quixote* brilliantly formulated by Borges's Pierre Menard, which changes Cervantes' passages solely by considering them in new contexts, Irwin's Book alters no specific 'words' of the texts it abuts. But it corrupts them. The protagonist, reading them after they have sat too near the Book, finds in Dickens 'revolting pleasure in cruelty', in Stevenson 'sickly attraction to brutality', in Charlotte Bronte 'a raving, craving maenad'.

All books alter the books that are (read) near them. Here, it is the unease, the strange, the alien malevolent, in its alterity, its Weird, that spreads. That contingent and unwyrdly, that wyrms its way throughout the library.

Thus the canon grows like mould, mildew-damp, eldritch, its vectors vermiform, gnaw-claiming even works that we had thought sedate, a subterranean countertradition, an abcanny that has nothing to do with memory and everything to do with the unsuspected. Burrowers cause the scree slippage of solid ground.

This collection is not (just) an act of canon. It does not, nor could it, enshrine one set of texts. Without motion – of crawling and wriggling kind – there is no Weird. All canons are tombs, yes, but this collection is a post-elegy, wearing

an *eaten* shroud

– a long-dead rag for the dead. But this is Weird, and as Lovecraft insisted, 'That is not dead which can eternal lie / and with strange aeons even death may die'. The answer to that riddle is simple. What can be the vector of the hole-y unholy post-life life but the worm?

These are strange aeons. These texts, dead and/or not, burrow, and we cannot predict everything they will infect or eat their path through. But certainly your brain, and they will eat the books you read from today on, too. That is how the Weird recruits.

This is a worm farm. These stories are worms.

ACKNOWLEDGMENTS

Any project this ambitious and with this wide a scope depends on the help of many people. For key translations, advice and negotiations we must profusely thank Gio Clairval; without her efforts this anthology would be much the poorer. Thanks, too, for largesse and special ops, to Edward Duff, Jonathan K. Stephens, Armando Corridore and Konrad Walewski.

In addition to advice from our editor, Nicolas Cheetham, we had access to invaluable resources in the form of prior anthologies that helped shape *The Weird*. Our thanks in particular to the following editors, many of whom also provided advice, resources, or other valuable information: David Hartwell, Kathryn Cramer, Ellen Datlow, Marvin Kaye, Kirby McCauley, S.T. Joshi, Jessica Amanda Salmonson, Ramsey Campbell, J.N. Williamson, Leonard Wolf, Peter Crowther, William J. Tyler, Robert Weinberg, John Betancourt, Dennis Etchison, Stefan R. Dziemianowicz, Martin H. Greenberg, Richard Dalby, Jonathan Strahan, Peter Straub, Bradford Morrow and Alberto Manguel. Special thanks to Ray Russell at Tartarus Press for massive amounts of help well beyond the call of duty, Jerad Walters at Centipede Press for access to rare materials, and to William Schafer at Subterranean Press for several key story suggestions – all of you are class acts. Thanks to Dedalus and Atlas Press for access to the most decadent permutations of the weird. Thanks also to Anil Menon, Jaya Bhattacharji, Alan Swirsky, Nick Wood, Matthew Cheney, Eric Schaller, and Larry Nolen for various contributions to the effort. Thanks to Liz Gorinsky, our editor at Tor, and everyone at Tor who worked on this project.

Our appreciation for recommendations from many dozens of other people, too many to list individually, but thank you for your help. Further thanks to *all* of the publishers, estates, agents and writers who made this book possible. Heart-felt thanks to Becci Sharpe at Corvus for tracking down certain permissions, and to the Corvus team: Nicolas Cheetham, Mathilda Imlah, Nicole Muir and Sachna Hanspal.

Thanks to Bruegger's Bagels, Hopkins Eatery and Monks for keeping us fed and sane. Finally, thanks to our families and friends for putting up with us while we worked on this project (and neglected them) – it devoured our lives for several months.

For more information on weird fiction, especially the works in this anthology, visit www.weirdfictionreview.com.

EXTENDED COPYRIGHTS

Daniel Abraham: 'Flat Diane' by Daniel Abraham, copyright © 2004 by Daniel Abraham. Originally published in *The Magazine of Fantasy and Science Fiction*, October/November 2004. Reprinted by permission of the author.

Robert Aickman: 'The Hospice' by Robert Aickman, copyright © 1975 The Estate of Robert Aickman. Originally published in *Cold Hand In Mine: Eight Strange Stories*. Reprinted by permission of the author's estate.

Michal Ajvaz: 'The End of the Garden' by Michal Ajvaz, copyright © 1991. Originally published in *Návrat Starého Varana*. Translation by James Naughton copyright © 1994. Reprinted by permission of the author and translator.

Ryūnosuke Akutagawa: 'The Hell Screen' by Ryūnosuke Akutagawa. Originally published in *Osaka Mainichi* (1918). Translation by Morinaka Akira, copyright © 2011. Published by permission of the translator.

H. F. Arnold: 'The Night Wire' by H. F. Arnold. Originally published in the Sept. 1926 issue of *Weird Tales*.

Clive Barker: 'In the Hills, The Cities' by Clive Barker, copyright © 1984, 1988, 1998 by Clive Barker. Originally published in 1984 in *The First Books Of Blood*. Reprinted by permission of the author and Sphere, an imprint of Little, Brown Book Group.

Laird Barron: 'The Forest' by Laird Barron, copyright © 2007. Originally published in *Inferno: New Tales of Terror and the Supernatural*, 2007, edited by Ellen Datlow. Reprinted by permission of the author.

Eric Basso: 'The Beak Doctor' by Eric Basso, copyright © 1976. Originally published in *The Chicago Review*, 1977. Reprinted by permission of the author.

Charles Beaumont: 'The Howling Man' by Charles Beaumont, copyright © 1959 by the Greenleaf Publishing Company, renewed 1987 by Christopher Beaumont. Originally published in *Rogue Magazine*, November 1959. Reprinted by permission of Don Congdon Associates.

Michel Bernanos: 'The Other Side of the Mountain' by Michel Bernanos, copyright © 1967. Originally published in book form in French by Jean-Jacques Pauvert under the title *La Montagne Morte de la Vie* in 1967. This new translation by Gio Clairval, copyright © 2011. Published by permission of the translator and the author's estate.

Olympe Bhêly-Quénum: 'A Child in the Bush of Ghosts' by Olympe Bhêly-Quénum, copyright © 1949. Originally published in *Liaison d'un été*. Reprinted by permission of the author.

K. J. Bishop: 'Saving the Gleeful Horse' by K.J. Bishop, copyright © 2009. Originally published in *Fantasy Magazine*, 2010. Reprinted by permission of the author.

Jerome Bixby: 'It's a *Good* Life' by Jerome Bixby. Originally published in *Star Science Fiction Stories No. 2*, 1953.

Algernon Blackwood: 'The Willows' by Algernon Blackwood. Originally published in *The Listener and Other Stories* (1907).

Robert Bloch: 'The Hungry House' by Robert Bloch, copyright © 1951. Originally published in *Imagination*. Reprinted by permission of the author's estate.

Jorge Luis Borges: 'The Aleph' by Jorge Luis Borges, copyright © 1945. From *Collected Fictions* by Jorge Luis Borges, translated by Andrew Hurley, copyright © 1998 by Maria Kodama; translation copyright © 1998 by Penguin Putnam Inc. Originally published in the Argentine journal *Sur*, 1945. Reprinted by permission of Andrew Hurley, Viking Penguin, a division of Penguin Group (USA), Inc, The Wylie Agency LLC, and Penguin Canada.

Ray Bradbury: 'The Crowd' by Ray Bradbury, copyright © 1943, renewed 1970 by Ray Bradbury. Originally published in *Weird Tales*, March 1943. Reprinted by permission of Don Congdon Associates.

Poppy Z. Brite: 'His Mouth Will Taste of Wormwood' by Poppy Z. Brite, copyright © 1990. Originally published in *Borderlands* 1, 1990, edited by Tom Monteleone. Reprinted by permission of the author.

Octavia Butler: 'Bloodchild' by Octavia Butler, copyright © 1984, 1995 by Octavia Butler. Originally published in *Isaac Asimov's Science Fiction Magazine*, June 1984. Reprinted in *Bloodchild And Other Stories*, 1995. Reprinted by permission of Seven Stories Press.

Dino Buzzati: 'The Colomber' by Dino Buzzati, copyright © 1966. Originally published in Italian by Arnoldo Mondadori Editore. This new translation by Gio Clairval, copyright © 2011. Published by permission of the translator and the author's estate.

Ramsey Campbell: 'The Brood' by Ramsey Campbell, copyright © 1980. Originally published in *Dark Forces*, 1980, edited by Kirby McCauley. Reprinted by permission of the author.

Leonora Carrington: 'White Rabbits' by Leonora Carrington, copyright © 1941. Originally published in *View* no. 9–10, New York 1941–1942. First published in book form in *The Seventh Horse* by Leonora Carrington, 1988. Reprinted by permission of Flammarion, Paris.

Angela Carter: 'The Snow Pavilion' by Angela Carter, copyright © 1995 Angela Carter. Originally published in *Burning Your Boats*. Reprinted by permission of the author's estate, c/o Rogers, Coleridge & White Ltd.

Michael Chabon: 'The God of Dark Laughter' by Michael Chabon, copyright © 2001. Originally published in the *New Yorker*, April 2001. Reprinted by arrangement with Mary Evans Inc.

Stepan Chapman: 'The Stiff and the Stile' by Stepan Chapman, copyright © 1997. Originally published in *Xero Magazine* no. 1–4, 1997. Reprinted by permission of the author.

Michael Cisco: 'The Genius of Assassins' by Michael Cisco, copyright © 2002. Originally published in *Leviathan 3*, 2002, edited by Forrest Aguirre and Jeff VanderMeer. Reprinted by permission of the author.

Julio Cortázar: 'Axolotl' by Julio Cortázar, copyright © 1956. Originally published in *Final del juego* by Los Presentes, México. This new translation by Gio Clairval, copyright © 2011. Published by permission of the translator and the author's estate.

F. Marion Crawford: 'The Screaming Skull' by F. Marion Crawford. Originally published in *Collier's Magazine*, July 1908. First collected in *Uncanny Tales* (UK) and *Wandering Ghosts* (US) 1911.

Daphne du Maurier: 'Don't Look Now' by Daphne du Maurier, copyright © 1971. Originally published in *Not After Midnight*, Gollancz, (UK) and *Don't Look Now and Other Stories*, Doubleday, (US). Reprinted by permission of the author's estate.

Steve Duffy: 'The Lion's Den' by Steve Duffy, copyright © 2009. Originally published in *Cern Zoo: Nemonymous 9*, 2009. Reprinted by permission of the author.

Lord Dunsany: 'How Nuth Would Have Practiced His Art' by Lord Dunsany. Originally published in *The Book of Wonder*, 1912.

Harlan Ellison: 'The Function of Dream Sleep' by Harlan Ellison, copyright © 1988 by The Kilimanjaro Corporation. Reprinted by arrangement with, and permission of, the Author and the Author's agent, Richard Curtis Associates, Inc., New York. All rights reserved. Harlan Ellison® is a registered trademark of The Kilimanjaro Corporation.

Dennis Etchison: 'It Only Comes Out at Night' by Dennis Etchison, copyright © 1976 by Kirby McCauley, © 1982 by Dennis Etchison. Originally published in *Frights*, edited by Kirby McCauley. Reprinted by permission of the author.

Brian Evenson: 'The Brotherhood of Mutilation' by Brian Evenson, copyright © 2003. Originally published as a chapbook by Earthling Press, 2003. Reprinted by permission of the author.

Hanns Heinz Ewers: 'The Spider' by Hanns Heinz Ewers. Originally published in 1915.

Jeffrey Ford: 'The Delicate' by Jeffrey Ford, copyright © 1994, 2002. Revised from its original publication in *Space and Time*, no. 83, 1994 and reprinted in *The Fantasy Writer's Assistant and Other Stories*, Golden Gryphon, 2002. Reprinted by permission of the author.

Jeffrey Ford: 'The Beautiful Gelreesh' by Jeffrey Ford, copyright © 2003. Originally published in *Album Zutique #1*, edited by Jeff VanderMeer. Reprinted by permission of the author.

Karen Joy Fowler: 'The Dark' by Karen Joy Fowler, copyright © 1991. Originally published in *The Magazine of Fantasy and Science Fiction*. Reprinted by permission of the author.

Neil Gaiman: 'Feeders and Eaters' by Neil Gaiman, copyright © 1990, 2002. Originally published as a comic book in *Revolver Horror Special*. First published in this form in *Keep Out the Night*, edited by Stephen Jones. Reprinted by permission of the author.

William Gibson & John Shirley: 'The Belonging Kind' by William Gibson & John Shirley, copyright © 1981. Originally published in *Shadows 4*, 1981, edited by Charles L. Grant. Reprinted by permission of the authors.

Stefan Grabiński: 'The White Weyrak' by Stefan Grabiński, translated by Miroslaw Lipinski, copyright © 1994. Originally published in *Slowo Polskie*, 1921. Reprinted by permission of the translator.

Elizabeth Hand: 'The Boy in the Tree' by Elizabeth Hand, copyright © 1989. Originally published in *Full Spectrum 2*, edited by Lou Aronica, Patrick LoBrutto, Shawna McCarthy, and Amy Stout. Reprinted by permission of the author.

M. John Harrison: 'Engaro' by M. John Harrison, copyright © 1981. Originally published in *Winter Tales 27*. Reprinted by permission of the author.

M. John Harrison: 'The New Rays' by M. John Harrison, copyright © 1982. Originally published in *Interzone 1*. Reprinted by permission of the author.

Georg Heym: 'The Dissection' by Georg Heym. Originally published in *Der Dieb. Ein Novellenbuch*, 1913. This new translation by Gio Clairval, copyright © 2011. Published by permission of the translator.

Margaret Irwin: 'The Book' by Margaret Irwin, copyright © 1930. Originally published in *The London Mercury*. Reprinted by permission of PFD (www.pfd.co.co.uk) on behalf of the Estate of Margaret Irwin.

Shirley Jackson: 'The Summer People' by Shirley Jackson, copyright © 1948, 1952, 1960 by Shirley Jackson. Originally published in *Come Along With Me*. Reprinted by permission of the author's estate and Viking Penguin, a division of Penguin Group (USA), Inc.

M.R. James: 'Casting the Runes' by M.R. James. Originally published in *More Ghost Stories of an Antiquary*, 1911.

Robert Barbour Johnson: 'Far Below' by Robert Barbour Johnson. Originally published in *Weird Tales*, 1939.

Stephen Graham Jones: 'Little Lambs' by Stephen Graham Jones, copyright © 2009. Originally published in *Iron Horse Literary Review*. Reprinted by permission of the author.

Craig Padawer: 'The Meat Garden' by Craig Padawer, copyright © 1996. Originally published in *Conjunctions 26: Sticks and Stones*. Reprinted by permission of the author.

Mervyn Peake: 'Same Time, Same Place' by Mervyn Peake, copyright © 1963. Originally published in *Science Fantasy*, 1963, Vol. 20 # 60. Reprinted by permission of PFD (www.pfd.co.uk) on behalf of the Estate of Mervyn Peake.

Jean Ray: 'The *Mainz Psalter*' by Jean Ray. Originally published as 'Le Psautier de Mayence' in *Le Bien Public*, 6 May, 1930. From *Ghouls In My Grave*, translated by Lowell Bair, copyright © 1965 by the Berkeley Publishing Corporation. Reprinted by permission of Berkeley Publishing Group, a division of Penguin Group (USA) Inc.

Jean Ray: 'The Shadowy Street' by Jean Ray. Originally published as 'La Ruelle Ténébreuse' in *La Croisière des Ombres*, 1931. From *Ghouls In My Grave*, translated by Lowell Bair, copyright © 1965 by the Berkeley Publishing Corporation. Reprinted by permission of Berkeley Publishing Group, a division of Penguin Group (USA) Inc.

Mercè Rodoreda: 'The Salamander' by Mercè Rodoreda, copyright © 1967. Originally published as part of the collection *La meva Cristina i alters contes, Barcelona: Edicions 62*. Translation by Martha Tennent, copyright © 2008 from *The Review of Contemporary Fiction: New Catalan Fiction*, Spring 2008, Vol. XXCVIII, No. 1: 15-22. Copyright © Institut d.Estudis Catalans. Reprinted by permission of the translator and the author's estate.

Joanna Russ: 'The Little Dirty Girl' by Joanna Russ, copyright © 1982. Originally published in *Elsewhere*, Volume 2, ed. Terri Windling and Mark Alan Arnold, Ace, 1982. Reprinted by permission of the author's agent.

Saki: 'Sredna Vashtar' by Saki. Originally published in *The Chronicles of Clovis*, 1910.

Hagiwara Sakutarō: 'The Town of Cats' by Hagiwara Sakutarō, copyright © 2008 University of Hawai'i Press . Originally published in Japanese (*Nekomachi)*, 1935. Published in English in *Modanizumu,* 2008. Translated by Jeffrey Angles. Reprinted by permission of the University of Hawai'i Press.

Mark Samuels: 'The White Hands' by Mark Samuels, copyright © 2003. Originally published in *The White Hands and Other Weird Tales*. Reprinted by permission of the author.

William Sansom: 'The Long Sheet' by William Sansom, copyright © 1944. Originally published in *Something Terrible, Something Lovely*. Reprinted by permission of the author's estate.

William Sansom: 'A Woman Seldom Found' by William Sansom, copyright © 1956. Originally published in *A Contest of Ladies*. Reprinted by permission of the author's estate.

Bruno Schulz: 'The Sanatorium Under the Sign of the Hourglass' by Bruno Schulz, copyright © 1967. Originally published as part of the volume *Sanatorium pod Klepsydra* © 1937. Reprinted by permission of the author's estate and Walker & Co.

Claude Seignolle: 'The Ghoulbird' by Claude Seignolle, copyright © 1967. Originally published as 'Hupeur' in the collection *Les Chevaux de la nuit et autres récits cruels,* published by Marabout–Gérard. This new translation by Gio Clairval, copyright © 2011. Reprinted by permission of the translator and the author.

Michael Shea: 'The Autopsy' by Michael Shea, copyright © 1979. Originally published in *The Magazine of Fantasy and Science Fiction,* Dec 1980. Reprinted by permission of the author.

Lucius Shepard: 'Shades' by Lucius Shepard, copyright © 1987. Originally published in *In The Field Of Fire,* edited by Jeanne Van Buren Dann and Jack Dann. Reprinted by permission of the author.

Martin Simpson: 'Last Rites and Resurrections' by Martin Simpson, copyright © 1994. Originally published in *The Silver Web #11.* Reprinted by permission of the author.

Clark Ashton Smith: 'Genius Loci' by Clark Ashton Smith. Originally published in *Weird Tales,* June 1933.

William Browning Spencer: 'The Ocean and All Its Devices' by William Browning Spencer, copyright © 1994. Originally published in *Borderlands 4,* edited by Thomas F. Monteleone and Elizabeth E. Monteleone. Reprinted by permission of the author.

Margaret St. Clair: 'The Man Who Sold Rope to the Gnoles' by Margaret St. Clair, copyright © 1951, 1979. Originally published in *The Magazine of Fantasy & Science Fiction,* October 1951. Reprinted by permission of the author's estate.

Francis Stevens: 'Unseen – Unfeared' by Gertrude Barrows Bennett. Originally published in *People's Favorite Magazine,* 10 February, 1919.

Rabindranath Tagore: 'The Hungry Stones' by Rabindranath Tagore. From *The Hungry Stones and Other Stories,* 1916.

James Tiptree, Jr.: 'The Psychologist Who Wouldn't Do Awful Things to Rats' by James Tiptree, Jr., copyright © 1976, 2004. Originally published in *New Dimensions 6,* edited by Robert Silverberg. Reprinted by permission of the author's estate and the estate's agents, The Virginia Kidd Agency.

Lisa Tuttle: 'Replacements' by Lisa Tuttle, copyright © 1992. Originally published in *Metahorror,* edited by Dennis Etchison. Reprinted by permission of the author.

Amos Tutuola: Excerpt from *The Palm Wine Drinkard* by Amos Tutuola, copyright © 1952. Originally published in *The Palm Wine Drinkard,* Faber and Faber. Reprinted by permission of Faber and Faber and the author's estate.

Luigi Ugolini: 'The Vegetable Man' by Luigi Ugolini, copyright © 1917. Originally published in *Giornale Illustrato dei Viaggi e delle Avventure di Terra e di Mare,* Italy, 1 July, 1917. This first English translation copyright © 2011 by Brendan and Anna Connell. Published by permission of the translators.

Steven Utley: 'The Country Doctor' by Steven Utley, copyright © 1993. Originally published in *Isaac Asimov's Science Fiction Magazine,* October 1993. Reprinted by permission of the author.